A SON OF
THE CIRCUS

A SON OF THE CIRCUS

John Irving

BLOOMSBURY

First published in Great Britain 1994

Copyright © 1994 by Garp Enterprises, Ltd

The moral right of the author has been asserted

Bloomsbury Publishing plc, 2 Soho Square, London W1V 5DE

A CIP catalogue record for this book
is available from the British Library

10 9 8 7 6 5 4 3 2 1

ISBN 0 7475 1763 0

Printed in Great Britain by Clays Ltd, St Ives plc

AUTHOR'S NOTES

This novel isn't about India. I don't know India. I was there only once, for less than a month. When I was there, I was struck by the country's foreignness; it remains obdurately foreign to me. But long before I went to India, I began to imagine a man who has been born there and has moved away; I imagined a character who keeps coming back again and again. He's compelled to keep returning; yet, with each return trip, his sense of India's foreignness only deepens. India remains unyieldingly foreign, even to him.

My Indian friends said, "Make him an Indian—definitely an Indian but *not* an Indian." They told me that everywhere he goes—including where he lives, outside India—should also strike him as foreign; the point is, he's always the foreigner. "You just have to get the details right," they said.

I went to India at the request of Martin Bell and his wife, Mary Ellen Mark. Martin and Mary Ellen asked me to write a screenplay for them, about the child performers in an Indian circus. I've been working on that screenplay and this novel, simultaneously, for more than four years; as of this writing, I'm revising the screenplay, which is also titled *A Son of the Circus*, although it isn't the same story as the novel. Probably I'll continue to rewrite the screenplay until the film is produced—*if* the film is produced. Martin and Mary Ellen took me to India; in a sense, they began *A Son of the Circus.*

I also owe a great deal to those Indian friends who were with me in Bombay in January of 1990—I'm thinking of Ananda Jaisingh, particularly—and to those members of the Great Royal Circus who gave me so much of their time when I was living with the circus in Junagadh. Most of all, I'm indebted to four Indian friends who've read and reread the manuscript; their efforts to overcome my ignorance and a multitude of errors made my writing possible. I want to acknowledge them by name; their importance to *A Son of the Circus* is immeasurable.

My thanks to Dayanita Singh in New Delhi; to Farrokh Chothia in Bombay; to Dr. Abraham Verghese in El Paso, Texas; and to Rita Mathur in Toronto. I would also like to thank my friend Michael Ondaatje, who introduced me to Rohinton Mistry—it was Rohinton who introduced me to Rita. And my friend James Salter has been extremely tolerant and good-humored in allowing me to make mischievous use of several passages from his elegant novel *A Sport and a Pastime.* Thanks, Jim.

As always, I have other writers to thank: my friend Peter Matthiessen, who read the earliest draft and wisely suggested surgery; my friends David Calicchio, Craig Nova, Gail Godwin and Ron Hansen (not to mention his twin brother, Rob) also suffered through earlier drafts. And I'm indebted to Ved Mehta for his advice, through correspondence.

As usual, I have more than one doctor to thank, too. For his careful reading of the penultimate draft, my thanks to Dr. Martin Schwartz in Toronto. In addition, I'm grateful to Dr. Sherwin Nuland in Hamden, Connecticut, and to Dr. Burton Berson in New York; they provided me with the clinical studies of achondroplasia.

The generosity of June Callwood, and of John Flannery—the director of nursing at Casey House in Toronto—is also much appreciated. And over the four years I've been writing *A Son of the Circus,* the work of three assistants has been outstanding: Heather Cochran, Alison Rivers and Allan Reeder. But there's only one reader who's read, or heard aloud, every draft of this story: my wife, Janet. For, literally, the thousands of pages she's endured—not to mention her tolerance of enforced travel—I thank her, with all my love.

Lastly, I want to express my affection for my editor, Harvey Ginsberg, who officially retired before I handed him the 1,094-page manuscript; retired or not, Harvey edited me.

I repeat: I don't "know" India, and *A Son of the Circus* isn't "about"

India. It is, however, a novel set in India—a story about an Indian (but *not* an Indian), for whom India will always remain an unknown and unknowable country. If I've managed to get the details right, my Indian friends deserve the credit.

—J. I.

For Salman

CONTENTS

4. THE OLD DAYS

5. THE VERMIN

6. THE FIRST ONE OUT

7. DR. DARUWALLA HIDES IN HIS BEDROOM

8. TOO MANY MESSAGES

9. SECOND HONEYMOON

10. CROSSED PATHS

11. THE DILDO

12. THE RATS

13. NOT A DREAM

14. TWENTY YEARS

15. DHAR'S TWIN

16. MR. GARG'S GIRL

17. STRANGE CUSTOMS

18. A STORY SET IN MOTION BY THE VIRGIN MARY

19. OUR LADY OF VICTORIES

A SON OF
THE CIRCUS

1. THE CROW
ON THE CEILING FAN

Blood from Dwarfs

Usually, the dwarfs kept bringing him back—back to the circus *and* back to India. The doctor was familiar with the feeling of leaving Bombay "for the last time"; almost every time he left India, he vowed that he'd never come back. Then the years would pass—as a rule, not more than four or five—and once again he'd be taking the long flight from Toronto. That he was born in Bombay was *not* the reason; at least this was what the doctor claimed. Both his mother and father were dead; his sister lived in London, his brother in Zürich. The doctor's wife was Austrian, and their children and grandchildren lived in England and in Canada; none of them wanted to live in India—they rarely visited the country—nor had a single one of them been born there. But the doctor was fated to go back to Bombay; he would keep returning again and again—if not forever, at least for as long as there were dwarfs in the circus.

Achondroplastic dwarfs comprise the majority of circus clowns in India; they are the so-called circus midgets, but they're not midgets—they're dwarfs. Achondroplasia is the most common type of short-limbed dwarfism. An achondroplastic dwarf can be born of normal parents, but the dwarf's children have a 50 percent chance of being dwarfs. This type of dwarfism is most often the result of a rare genetic event, a spontaneous mutation, which then becomes a dominant characteristic in the dwarf's children. No one has discovered a genetic marker for this characteristic—and none of the best minds in genetics are bothering to search for such a marker.

Quite possibly, only Dr. Farrokh Daruwalla had the far-fetched idea of finding a genetic marker for this type of dwarfism. By the passion of such a wishful discovery, the doctor was driven to gather samples of dwarf blood. The whimsy of his idea was plain: his dwarf-blood project was of no orthopedic interest, and he was an orthopedic surgeon; genetics was only one of his hobbies. Yet, although Farrokh's visits to Bombay were infrequent and the duration of his stay was always short, no one in India had ever drawn blood from so many dwarfs; no one had bled as many dwarfs as Dr. Daruwalla had bled. In those Indian circuses that passed through Bombay, or in such circuses as frequented the smaller towns in Gujarat and Maharashtra, it was with affection that Farrokh was called "the vampire."

This is not to suggest that a physician in Dr. Daruwalla's field in India wouldn't stumble across a fair number of dwarfs; they suffer from chronic orthopedic problems—aching knees and ankles, not to mention low back pain. Their symptoms are progressive, according to their age and weight; as dwarfs grow older and heavier, their pain gradually radiates into the buttocks, posterior thighs and calves.

At the Hospital for Sick Children in Toronto, Dr. Daruwalla saw very few dwarfs; however, at the Hospital for Crippled Children in Bombay—where, from time to time, upon his return visits, Farrokh enjoyed the title of Honorary Consultant Surgeon—the doctor examined many dwarf patients. But these dwarfs, although they would provide Dr. Daruwalla with their family histories, would not readily give him their blood. It would have been unethical of him to draw the dwarfs' blood against their will; the majority of orthopedic ailments afflicting achondroplastic dwarfs don't necessitate testing their blood. Therefore, it was only fair that Farrokh would explain the scientific nature of his research project and that he would *ask* these dwarfs for their blood. Almost always, the dwarfs said no.

A case in point was Dr. Daruwalla's closest dwarf acquaintance in Bombay; in the vernacular of friendship, Farrokh and Vinod went back a long way, for the dwarf was the doctor's most visceral connection to the circus—Vinod was the first dwarf whom Dr. Daruwalla had asked for blood. They had met in the examining room of the doctor's office at the Hospital for Crippled Children; their conversation coincided with the religious holiday of Diwali, which had brought the Great Blue Nile

Circus to Bombay for an engagement at Cross Maidan. A dwarf clown (Vinod) and his normal wife (Deepa) had brought their dwarf son (Shivaji) to the hospital to have the child's ears examined. Vinod had never imagined that the Hospital for Crippled Children concerned itself with *ears*—ears weren't a common area of orthopedic complaint—but the dwarf correctly assumed that all dwarfs were cripples.

Yet the doctor could never persuade Vinod to believe in the genetic reasons for either his or his son's dwarfism. That Vinod came from normal parents and was nonetheless a dwarf was not in Vinod's view the result of a mutation. The dwarf believed his mother's story: that, the morning after she conceived, she looked out the window and the first living thing she saw was a dwarf. That Vinod's wife, Deepa, was a normal woman—"almost beautiful," by Vinod's description—didn't prevent Vinod's son, Shivaji, from being a dwarf. However, in Vinod's view, this was *not* the result of a dominant gene, but rather the misfortune of Deepa forgetting what Vinod had told her. The morning after Deepa conceived, the first living thing she looked at was Vinod, and *that* was why Shivaji was also a dwarf. Vinod had told Deepa not to look at him in the morning, but she forgot.

That Deepa was "almost beautiful" (or at least a normal woman), and yet she was married to a dwarf—this was the result of her having no dowry. She'd been sold to the Great Blue Nile Circus by her mother. And since Deepa was still very much a novice trapeze artist, she earned almost no money at all. "Only a dwarf would be marrying her," Vinod said.

As for their child, Shivaji, recurrent and chronic middle-ear infections are common among achondroplastic dwarfs until the age of 8 or 10; if untreated, such infections often lead to significant hearing loss. Vinod himself was half deaf. But it simply wasn't possible for Farrokh to educate Vinod on this matter, or on other matters pertaining to the genetics of his and Shivaji's type of dwarfism; his so-called trident hands, for example—the stubby fingers were characteristically splayed. Dr. Daruwalla also noted the dwarf's short, broad feet and the flexed position of his elbows, which could never be fully extended; the doctor tried to make Vinod admit that, like his son's, his fingertips reached only to his hips, his abdomen protruded and—even lying on his back—the dwarf exhibited the typical forward curvature of the spine. This lumbar lordosis and a tilted pelvis explain why all dwarfs waddle.

"Dwarfs are just naturally waddling," Vinod replied. He was religiously stubborn and utterly unwilling to part with as much as a single

Vacutainer of his blood. There he sat on the examining table, shaking his head at Dr. Daruwalla's theories of dwarfism.

Vinod's head, like the heads of all achondroplastic dwarfs, was exceedingly large. His face failed to convey a visible intelligence, unless a bulging forehead could be attributed to brain power; the midface, again typical of achondroplasia, was recessed. The cheeks and the bridge of the nose were flattened, although the tip of the nose was fleshy and upturned; the jaw protruded to such a degree that Vinod's chin was prominent; and while his thrusting head did not communicate the greatest common sense, Vinod's overall manner proclaimed a personality of great determination. His aggressive appearance was further enhanced by a trait common among achondroplastic dwarfs: because their tubular bones are shortened, their muscle mass is concentrated, creating an impression of considerable strength. In Vinod's case, a life of tumbling and other acrobatics had given him especially well delineated shoulder muscles; his forearms and his biceps bulged. He was a veteran circus clown, but he looked like a miniature thug. Farrokh was a little afraid of him.

"And just what are you wanting with my blood?" the dwarf clown asked the doctor.

"I'm looking for that secret thing which made you a dwarf," Dr. Daruwalla replied.

"Being a dwarf is no secret!" Vinod argued.

"I'm looking for something in your blood that, if I find it, will help other people not to give birth to dwarfs," the doctor explained.

"Why are you wanting to put an end to dwarfs?" the dwarf asked.

"It doesn't hurt to give blood," Dr. Daruwalla reasoned. "The needle doesn't hurt."

"All needles are hurting," Vinod said.

"So you're afraid of needles?" Farrokh asked the dwarf.

"I am just needing my blood right now," Vinod answered.

The almost-beautiful Deepa wouldn't permit the doctor to prick her dwarf child with a needle, either, although both Deepa and Vinod suggested that the Great Blue Nile Circus, which was in Bombay for another week, was full of other dwarfs who might give Dr. Daruwalla *their* blood. Vinod said he'd be happy to introduce the doctor to the Blue Nile's clowns. Furthermore, Vinod advised the doctor to bribe the clowns with alcohol and tobacco, and it was at Vinod's prompting that Farrokh revised his stated reason for wanting the dwarfs' blood. "Tell them you are using their blood to give strength to a dying dwarf," Vinod suggested.

This was the way the dwarf-blood project began. It had been 15 years ago when Dr. Daruwalla drove to the circus grounds at Cross Maidan. He brought his needles, his plastic needle holders, his glass vials (or Vacutainers). To bribe the dwarfs, he brought two cases of Kingfisher lager and two cartons of Marlboro cigarettes; according to Vinod, the latter were popular among his fellow clowns because of the dwarfs' high regard for the Marlboro Man. As it turned out, Farrokh should have left the beer at home. In the stillness of the early-evening heat, the Great Blue Nile's clowns drank too many Kingfishers; two dwarfs fainted while the doctor was drawing their blood, which provided further evidence for Vinod that he should retain every drop of his own.

Even poor Deepa guzzled a Kingfisher; shortly before her performance, she complained of a slight dizziness, which was exacerbated when she hung by her knees from the high trapeze. Deepa then tried swinging in a sitting position, but the heat had risen to the top of the tent and the dwarf's wife felt that her head was trapped in the hottest possible air. She felt only a little better when she gripped the bar in both hands and swung herself with more and more force; hers was the simplest exchange for an aerialist to master, but she still hadn't learned how to let the catcher grab her wrists before she tried to grab his. Deepa simply would release the bar when her body was parallel to the ground; then she'd throw back her head so that her shoulders dropped below the level of her feet, and the catcher would catch hold of her by her ankles. Ideally, when the catcher caught her, Deepa's head was approximately 50 feet above the safety net, but the dwarf's wife was a beginner and she let go of the trapeze before her body was fully extended. The catcher had to lunge for her; he was able to grab only one of her feet, and he caught her at an unfortunate angle. Deepa screamed so loudly when her hip was dislocated that the catcher thought the best thing he could do for her was to drop her into the safety net, which he did. Dr. Daruwalla had never seen a more awkward fall.

A small, dark girl from rural Maharashtra, Deepa might have been 18 but she looked 16 to the doctor; her dwarf son, Shivaji, was not quite two. Her mother had sold her to the Great Blue Nile when Deepa was 11 or 12—at an age when her mother might also have been tempted to sell her to a brothel. Deepa knew she was lucky to have been sold to a circus. She was so thin that the Blue Nile had at first tried to train her as a contortionist—a so-called boneless girl, a plastic lady. But as Deepa grew older, she became too inflexible to be "boneless." Even Vinod was of the opinion that Deepa was too old when she began her training as a flyer; most trapeze artists learn to fly when they're children.

The dwarf's wife was, if not almost beautiful, at least pretty from a certain distance; her forehead was pockmarked and she bore the stigmata of rickets . . . frontal bossing, rachitic rosary. (It's called a "rosary" because at every junction of rib and cartilage there's a marblelike protuberance, like a bead.) Deepa was so small-breasted that her chest was nearly as flat as a boy's; however, her hips were womanly, and it was partly the way the safety net sagged with her weight that made her appear to be lying facedown in the net while her pelvis was tilted *up*—toward the empty, swinging trapeze.

From the way she'd fallen and was lying in the safety net, Farrokh felt almost certain that the problem was Deepa's hip, not her neck or back. But until someone could keep her from flopping around in the net, the doctor didn't dare go to her. Vinod had instantly crawled into the net. Now Farrokh told him to clamp Deepa's head between his knees and hold her shoulders with his hands. Only when the dwarf securely held her—only when Deepa couldn't move her neck or her back, or even rotate her shoulders—did Dr. Daruwalla dare to enter the net.

In the time it had taken Vinod to crawl into the net with her, and all the time that the dwarf held his wife's head tightly between his knees— while Dr. Daruwalla crawled into the sagging net and made his slow, awkward way toward them—the net never stopped swaying and the empty trapeze that dangled above them moved out of rhythm with the net.

Farrokh had never been in a safety net before. He was a nonathlete who was (even 15 years ago) noticeably plump, and his climb into the trapeze artists' net was a monumental struggle, aided only by his gratitude for his first samples of dwarf blood. As Dr. Daruwalla proceeded on all fours across the dipping, swaying net to where poor Deepa lay in her dwarf husband's clutches, the doctor most resembled a fat, tentative mouse traversing a vast spiderweb.

Farrokh's unreasonable fear of being pitched out of the net at least distracted him from the murmuring of the circus audience; they were impatient for the rescue process to hurry up. That the loudspeaker had introduced him to the restless crowd did nothing to prepare Dr. Daruwalla for the arduousness of his adventure. "Here is coming the doctor!" the ringmaster had declared over the loudspeaker, in a melodramatic effort to hold the crowd. But what a long time it took the doctor to reach the fallen flyer! Furthermore, Farrokh's weight caused the net to dip nearer the ground; he was like an ungainly lover approaching his prey in a soft bed that sags in the middle.

Then, suddenly, the net sagged so steeply that Dr. Daruwalla was thrown off balance; clumsily, he fell forward. The plump physician thrust his fingers through the holes in the net; since he'd already removed his sandals before climbing into the net, he tried to insert his toes (like claws) through the holes in the net, too. But in spite of this effort to slow his own momentum, which was now of a pace to at last be of interest to the bored audience, gravity prevailed. Dr. Daruwalla pitched headfirst into the sequined belly of Deepa's tight singlet.

Deepa's neck and back were undamaged—the doctor had correctly diagnosed her injury from his view of her fall. Her hip was dislocated; it hurt her when Farrokh fell upon her abdomen. The doctor's forehead was scratched by the pink and fire-engine-red sequins that formed a star over Deepa's pelvis, and the bridge of Dr. Daruwalla's nose ground to a sharp halt against her pubis.

Under vastly different circumstances, their collision might have been sexually thrilling, but not to a woman with a dislocated hip (and with her head clamped tightly between a dwarf's knees). For Dr. Daruwalla— the fallen flyer's pain and her screams notwithstanding—this encounter with Deepa's pubic bone would be recorded as his single extramarital experience. Farrokh would never forget it.

Here he'd been called out of the audience to aid a dwarf's wife in distress. And then, in full view of the unimpressed crowd, the doctor had ended up with his face jammed into the injured woman's crotch. Was it any wonder he couldn't forget her, or the mixed sensations that she'd caused him?

Even today, so many years later, Farrokh felt flushed with embarrassment and titillation, for his memory of the trapeze artist's taut belly still excited him. Where his cheek had come to rest against her inner thigh, Farrokh could still feel how her tights were soaked with sweat. All the time he heard Deepa screaming in pain (as the doctor clumsily struggled to move his weight off her), he also heard the cartilage in his nose cracking, for Deepa's pubis was as hard as an ankle or an elbow. And when Dr. Daruwalla breathed in her dangerous aroma, he thought he'd at last identified the smell of sex, which struck him as an earthy commingling of death and flowers.

It was there, in the swaying safety net, that Vinod first accused him.

"All this is happening because you are wanting blood from dwarfs," the dwarf said.

The Doctor Dwells on
Lady Duckworth's Breasts

In 15 years, the Indian customs authorities had detained Dr. Daruwalla only twice; both times, the disposable hypodermic needles—about a hundred of them—had caught their attention. It had been necessary for the doctor to explain the difference between syringes, which are used to give injections, and Vacutainers, which are used to draw blood; in the Vacutainer system, neither the glass vials nor the plastic needle holders are equipped with plungers. The doctor wasn't carrying syringes, for putting drugs in; he was carrying Vacutainers, for taking blood out.

"Whose blood is being taken out?" the customs man had asked.

Even the answer to that question had been easier to explain than the problem that currently presented itself to the doctor.

The current problem was, Dr. Daruwalla had upsetting news for the famous actor with the unlikely name of Inspector Dhar. Not sure of the degree to which Dhar would be distressed, the doctor was impelled by cowardice; he planned to give the movie star the bad news in a public place. Inspector Dhar's poise in public was renowned; Farrokh felt he could rely on the actor to keep his composure. Not everyone in Bombay would have thought of a private club as a public place, but Dr. Daruwalla believed that the choice was both private and public enough for the crisis at hand.

That morning, when Dr. Daruwalla had arrived at the Duckworth Sports Club, he had thought it was unremarkable to see a vulture high in the sky above the golf course; he didn't consider the bird of death as an omen attached to the unwelcome news he carried. The club was in Mahalaxmi, not far from Malabar Hill; everyone in Bombay knew why vultures were attracted to Malabar Hill. When a corpse was placed in the Towers of Silence, the vultures—from as far as 30 miles outside Bombay—could scent the ripening remains.

Farrokh was familiar with Doongarwadi. The so-called Towers of Silence are seven huge cairns on Malabar Hill where the Parsis lay out the naked cadavers of their dead to be picked clean by the carrion eaters. As a Parsi, Dr. Daruwalla was descended from Persian Zoroastrians who had come to India in the seventh and eighth centuries to escape Muslim persecution. Farrokh's father, however, was such a virulent, acerbic atheist that the doctor had never been a practicing Zoroastrian. And Farrokh's conversion to Christianity would doubtless have killed his godless father, except that his father was already dead; the doctor didn't convert until he was almost 40.

Because Dr. Daruwalla was a Christian, his own mortal body would never be exposed in the Towers of Silence; but despite his father's inflammatory atheism, Farrokh respected the habits of his fellow Parsis and practicing Zoroastrians—and he *expected* to see vultures flying to and from Ridge Road. Nor was the doctor surprised that the particular vulture above the Duckworth golf course appeared in no hurry to arrive at the Towers of Silence; the area was entangled with vines, and not even other Parsis, unless they were dead, were welcome at the burial wells.

In general, Dr. Daruwalla wished the vultures well. The limestone cairns contributed to the swift decomposition of even the larger bones, and those parts of Parsis that stayed intact were washed away in the monsoon season. In regard to disposing of the dead, in the doctor's opinion, the Parsis had found an admirable solution.

As for the living, Dr. Daruwalla had this morning, as on most mornings, been up early. His first surgeries at the Hospital for Crippled Children, where he continued to enjoy the title of Honorary Consultant Surgeon, included one operation for clubfoot and another for wryneck; the latter is an infrequent operation nowadays, and it was not the sort of surgery that reflected Farrokh's main interest in practicing orthopedics, albeit intermittently, in Bombay. Dr. Daruwalla was interested in bone and joint infections. In India, such infections typically follow a motor-vehicle accident and a compound fracture; the fracture is exposed to the air because the skin is broken, and five weeks after the injury, pus is bubbling from a sinus (a puckered opening) in the wound. These infections are chronic because the bone is dead, and dead bone behaves like a foreign body. Dead bone is called sequestrum; in Bombay, Farrokh's fellow orthopedists liked to call him "Dead Bone" Daruwalla—those who knew him best called him "Dwarf Blood" Daruwalla, too. Teasing aside, infected bones and joints were not another hobby—they were Farrokh's field.

In Canada, it often seemed to the doctor that his orthopedic practice involved almost as many sports injuries as birth defects or spasmodic contractions. In Toronto, Dr. Daruwalla still specialized in orthopedics for children, but he felt more essentially needed—hence more exhilarated—in Bombay. In India, it was common to see orthopedic patients with little handkerchiefs tied around their legs; the handkerchiefs covered sinus tracts, which drained small amounts of pus—for years. In Bombay, there was also more willingness among patients *and* surgeons to accept amputations and the quick fitting of a simple prosthesis; such solutions were unacceptable in Toronto, where Dr. Daruwalla was known for a new technique in microvascular surgery.

In India, without removal of the dead bone, there was no cure; often there was too much dead bone to remove—to take it out would compromise the ability of the limb to bear weight. But in Canada, with the aid of prolonged intravenous antibiotics, Farrokh could combine dead-bone removal with a plastic procedure—a muscle and its blood supply are brought into the infected area. Dr. Daruwalla couldn't duplicate such procedures in Bombay, unless he limited his practice to very rich people in hospitals like Jaslok. At the Hospital for Crippled Children, the doctor resorted to the quick restoration of a limb's function; this often amounted to an amputation and a prosthesis in place of a cure. To Dr. Daruwalla, a sinus tract draining pus wasn't the worst thing; in India, he let the pus drain.

And in keeping with the enthusiasm characteristic of converts to Christianity—the doctor was a confirmed Anglican who was both suspicious and in awe of Catholics—Dr. Daruwalla was also exhilarated by the Christmas season, which in Bombay isn't as garishly festooned with commercial enterprise as it has become in Christian countries. This particular Christmas was cautiously joyous for the doctor: he'd attended a Catholic Mass on Christmas Eve *and* an Anglican service on Christmas Day. He was a holiday churchgoer, if hardly a regular one; yet his double churchgoing was an inexplicable overdose—Farrokh's wife was worried about him.

The doctor's wife was Viennese, the former Julia Zilk—no relation to the city mayor of that name. The former *Fräulein* Zilk came from an aristocratic and imperious family of Roman Catholics. During the Daruwalla family's short, infrequent visits to Bombay, the Daruwalla children had attended Jesuit schools; however, this wasn't because the children were brought up as Catholics—it was only the result of Farrokh maintaining "family connections" with these schools, which were otherwise difficult to get into. The Daruwalla children were confirmed Anglicans; they'd received Anglican schooling in Toronto.

But despite Farrokh's preference for a Protestant faith, he'd been pleased to entertain his few Jesuit acquaintances on Boxing Day; they were much livelier conversationalists than the Anglicans he knew in Bombay. Christmas itself was a glad tiding, surely; it was a season that produced in the doctor an effusion of goodwill. In the spirit of Christmas, Farrokh could almost forget that the effects of his 20-year-old conversion to Christianity were weakening.

And Dr. Daruwalla didn't give a second thought to the vulture high above the golf course at the Duckworth Club. The only cloud on the doctor's horizon was how to tell Inspector Dhar the upsetting news. These were not glad tidings for Dhar. But until this unforeseen bad news, it hadn't been that bad a week.

It was the week between Christmas and New Year's. The weather in Bombay was uncommonly cool and dry. The active membership of the Duckworth Sports Club had reached 6,000; considering that there was a 22-year waiting list for new members, this number had been rather gradually achieved. That morning, there was a meeting of the Membership Committee, of which the distinguished Dr. Daruwalla was guest chairman, to determine whether member number 6,000 should receive any special notification of his extraordinary status. The suggestions ranged from a plaque in the snooker room (where there were sizable gaps among the trophies), to a small reception in the Ladies' Garden (where the usual bloom of the bougainvillea was diminished by an undiagnosed blight), to a simple typewritten memo thumbtacked alongside the list of Temporarily Elected Members.

Farrokh had often objected to the title of this list, which was posted in a locked glass case in the foyer of the Duckworth Club. He complained that "temporarily elected" meant merely nominated—they weren't elected at all—but this term had been the accepted usage since the club had been founded 130 years ago. A spider crouched beside the short column of names; it had crouched there for so long, it was presumed dead—or perhaps the spider was also seeking permanent membership. This was Dr. Daruwalla's joke, but the joke was old; it was rumored to have been repeated by all 6,000 members.

It was midmorning, and the committeemen were drinking Thums Up cola and Gold Spot orange soda in the card room when Dr. Daruwalla suggested that the matter be dropped.

"Stopped?" said Mr. Dua, who was deaf in one ear from a tennis injury, never to be forgotten: his doubles partner had double-faulted and flung his racquet. Since he was only "temporarily elected" at the time, this shocking display of bad temper had put an end to the partner's quest for permanent membership.

"I move," Dr. Daruwalla now shouted, "that member number six thousand *not* be notified!" The motion was quickly seconded and passed; not even so much as a typewritten memo would announce the event. Dr. Sorabjee, Farrokh's colleague at the Hospital for Crippled Children, said facetiously that the decision was among the wisest ever made by the Membership Committee. In truth, Dr. Daruwalla thought, no one wanted to risk disturbing the spider.

In the card room, the committeemen sat in silence, satisfied with the conclusion of their business; the ceiling fans only slightly ruffled the trim decks of cards that stood perfectly in place at the appropriate tables, which were topped with tightly stretched green felt. A waiter, removing an empty Thums Up bottle from the table where the committeemen sat, paused to straighten one errant deck of cards before leaving the room, although only the top two cards of the deck had been edged out of alignment by the nearest ceiling fan.

That was when Mr. Bannerjee walked into the card room, looking for his golfing opponent, Mr. Lal. Old Mr. Lal was late for their regular nine holes, and Mr. Bannerjee told the committee the amusing results of their competition together the day before. Mr. Lal had lost a one-stroke lead in a spectacular blunder on the ninth hole: he'd chipped a shot entirely over the green and into a profusion of the blighted bougainvillea, where he'd hacked away in misery and in vain.

Rather than return to the clubhouse, Mr. Lal had shaken Mr. Bannerjee's hand and marched in a fury to the bougainvillea; there Mr. Bannerjee had left him. Mr. Lal was intent on practicing how to escape from this trap should he ever blunder into it again. Petals were flying when Mr. Bannerjee parted from his friend; that evening, the gardener (the head mali, no less) was dismayed to observe the damage to the vines and to the flowers. But old Mr. Lal was among the more venerable of the Duckworth's members—if he insisted on learning how to escape the bougainvillea, no one would be so bold as to prevent him. And now Mr. Lal was late. Dr. Daruwalla suggested to Mr. Bannerjee that quite possibly his opponent was still practicing, and that he should search for him in the ruined bougainvillea.

Thus the committee meeting disbanded in characteristic and desultory laughter. Mr. Bannerjee went seeking Mr. Lal in the men's dressing room; Dr. Sorabjee went off to the hospital for office calls; Mr. Dua, whose deafness somehow suited his retirement from the percussiveness of the tire business, wandered into the snooker room to have a crack at some innocent balls, which he would barely hear. Others stayed where they were, turning to the ready decks of cards, or else they found comfort in the cool leather chairs in the reading room, where they ordered Kingfisher lagers or London Diet beers. It was getting on toward late morning, but it was generally thought to be too early for gin and tonics or adding a shot of rum to the Thums Up colas.

In the men's dressing room and the clubhouse bar, the younger members and actual athletes were returning from their sets of tennis or their badminton or their squash. For the most part, they were tea drinkers at this time of the morning. Those returning from the golf course heartily complained about the mess of flower petals that by now had drifted over the ninth green. (These golfers wrongly assumed that the bougainvillea blight had taken a new and nasty turn.) Mr. Bannerjee told his story several more times; each time, the efforts of Mr. Lal to defeat the bougainvillea were described in more reckless and damaging terms. A generous good humor pervaded the clubhouse and the dressing room. Mr. Bannerjee didn't seem to mind that it was now too late in the morning to play golf.

The unexpected cool weather could not change the habits of the Duckworthians; they were used to playing their golf and tennis before 11:00 in the morning or after 4:00 in the afternoon. During the midday hours, the members drank or lunched or simply sat under the ceiling fans or in the deep shade of the Ladies' Garden, which was never exclusively used by (or especially full of) ladies—not nowadays. Yet the garden's name was unchanged from purdah times, when the seclusion of women from the sight of men or strangers was practiced by some Muslims and Hindus. Farrokh found this odd, for the founding members of the Duckworth Sports Club were the British, who were still welcome there and even comprised a small proportion of the membership. To Dr. Daruwalla's knowledge, the British had never practiced purdah. The Duckworth's founders had intended the club for any and all citizens of Bombay, provided that they'd distinguished themselves in community leadership. As Farrokh and the other members of the Membership Committee would attest, the definition of "community leadership" could be argued for the length of the monsoon, and beyond.

By tradition, the chairman of the Duckworth Club was the governor of Maharashtra; yet Lord Duckworth himself, for whom the club was named, had never been governor. Lord D. (as he was called) had long sought the office, but the eccentricities of his wife were too notorious. Lady Duckworth was afflicted with exhibitionism in general—and with the astonishing wild habit of exposing her breasts in particular. Although this affliction endeared both Lord *and* Lady Duckworth to many members of the club, it was a gesture thought lacking in gubernatorial merit.

Dr. Daruwalla stood in the penetrating cool of the empty dance hall, viewing—as he often did—the splendid and abundant trophies and the spellbinding old photographs of Members Past. Farrokh enjoyed such controlled sightings of his father, and of his grandfather, and of the countless avuncular gentlemen among his father's and grandfather's friends. He imagined that he could remember every man who'd ever laid a hand on his shoulder or touched the top of his head. Dr. Daruwalla's familiarity with these photographs belied the fact that the doctor himself had spent very few of his 59 years in India. When he was visiting Bombay, Dr. Daruwalla was sensitive to anyone or anything that reminded him of how little he knew or understood the country of his birthplace. The more time he spent in the haven of the Duckworth Club, the more the doctor could sustain the illusion that he was comfortable being in India.

At home, in Toronto, where he'd spent most of his adult life, the doctor enjoyed the reputation—especially among Indians who'd never been to India, or who'd never gone back—of being a genuine "old India hand"; he was even considered quite brave. After all, it was every few years that Farrokh returned to his native land under what were presumed to be primitive conditions—practicing medicine in a country of such claustrophobic overpopulation. And where were the amenities that could live up to a Canadian standard of comfort?

Weren't there water shortages and bread strikes, and the rationing of oil or rice, not to mention food adulteration and those gas cylinders that always ran out of gas in the midst of a dinner party? And one often heard about the shoddy construction of buildings, the falling plaster and so on. But only rarely did Dr. Daruwalla return to India during the monsoon months, which were the most "primitive" in Bombay. Furthermore, to his fellow Torontonians, Farrokh tended to downplay the fact that he never stayed in India for long.

In Toronto, the doctor spoke of his childhood (as a Bombayite) as if it had been both more colorful and more authentically Indian than it truly had been. Educated by the Jesuits, Dr. Daruwalla had attended St. Ignatius School in Mazagaon; for recreation, he'd enjoyed the privileges of organized sports and dances at the Duckworth Club. When he reached university age, he was sent to Austria; even his eight years in Vienna, where he completed medical school, were tame and controlled—he'd lived the whole time with his elder brother.

But in the Duckworth's dance hall, in the sacred presence of those portraits of Members Past, Dr. Daruwalla could momentarily imagine that he truly came from somewhere, and that he belonged somewhere. Increasingly, as he approached 60, the doctor acknowledged (only to himself) that in Toronto he often *acted* far more Indian than he was; he could instantly acquire a Hindi accent, or drop it, depending on the company he kept. Only a fellow Parsi would know that English had been his veritable mother tongue, and that the doctor would have learned his Hindi in school. During Farrokh's visits to India, he was similarly ashamed of himself for how completely European or North American he pretended to be. In Bombay, his Hindi accent disappeared; one had only to hear the doctor's English to be convinced that he'd been totally assimilated in Canada. In truth, it was only when he was surrounded by the old photographs in the dance hall of the Duckworth Club that Dr. Daruwalla felt at home.

Of Lady Duckworth, Dr. Daruwalla had only heard her story. In each of her stunning photographs, her breasts were properly if not modestly covered. Yes, a highly elevated and sizable bosom could be detected in her pictures, even when Lady Duckworth was well advanced in years; and yes, her habit of exposing herself supposedly increased as she grew older—her breasts were reported to be well formed (and well worth revealing) into her seventies.

She'd been 75 when she revealed herself in the club's circular driveway to a horde of young people arriving for the Sons and Daughters of Members' Ball. This incident resulted in a multivehicle collision that was reputed to bear responsibility for the enlargement of the speed bumps, which were implanted the entire length of the access road. In Farrokh's opinion, the Duckworth Club was permanently fixed at the speed indicated by those signs posted at both ends of the drive: DEAD SLOW. But this, for the most part, contented him; the admonition to go dead slow didn't strike Dr. Daruwalla as an imposition, although the doctor did regret not being alive for at least one glimpse of Lady Duckworth's long-ago breasts. The club couldn't have been dead slow in her day.

As he had sighed aloud in the empty dance hall perhaps a hundred times, Dr. Daruwalla sighed again and softly said to himself, "Those were the good old days." But it was only a joke; he didn't really mean it. Those "good old days" were as unknowable to him as Canada—his cold, adopted country—or as the India he only pretended to be comfortable in. Furthermore, Farrokh never spoke or sighed loudly enough to be heard by anyone else.

In the vast, cool hall, he listened: he could hear the waiters and the busboys in the dining room, setting the tables for lunch; he could hear the clicks and thumps of the snooker balls and the flat, authoritative snap of a card turned faceup on a table. And although it was now past 11:00, two die-hards were still playing tennis; by the soft, slowly paced *pops* of the ball, Dr. Daruwalla concluded that it wasn't a very spirited match.

It was unmistakably the head gardener's truck that sped along the access road, hitting each of the speed bumps with abandon; there followed the resounding clatter of hoes and rakes and spades, and then an abstract cursing—the head mali was a moron.

There was a photograph that Farrokh was particularly fond of, and he looked intently at it; then he closed his eyes so that he might see the picture better. In Lord Duckworth's expression there was much charity and tolerance and patience; yet there was something stupefied in his faraway gaze, as if he'd only recently recognized and accepted his own futility. Although Lord Duckworth was broad-shouldered and had a deep chest and he firmly held a sword, there was also a kind of gentle idiot's resignation at the turned-down corners of his eyes and the drooping ends of his mustache. He was perpetually *almost* the governor of Maharashtra, but never the governor. And the hand that he placed around Lady Duckworth's girlish waist was clearly a hand that touched her without weight, that held her without strength—if it held her at all.

Lord D. committed suicide on New Year's Eve, precisely at the turn of the century. For many more years Lady Duckworth would reveal her breasts, but it was agreed that, as a widow, although she exposed herself more often, she did so halfheartedly. Cynics said that had she lived, and continued to show India her gifts, Lady D. might have thwarted Independence.

In the photograph that so appealed to Dr. Daruwalla, Lady Duckworth's chin was tilted down, her eyes mischievously gazing up, as if she'd just been caught peering into her own thrilling cleavage and had instantly looked away. Her bosom was a broad, strong shelf supporting her pretty face. Even fully clothed, there was something unrestrained about the woman; her arms hung straight down at her sides, but her fingers were spread wide apart—with her palms presented to the camera, as if for crucifixion—and a wild strand of her allegedly blond hair, which was otherwise held high off her graceful neck, was childishly twisted and coiled like a snake around one of the world's perfect little ears.

In future years, her hair turned from blond to gray without losing its thick body or its deep luster; her breasts, despite being so often and so long exposed, never sagged. Dr. Daruwalla was a happily married man; however, he would have admitted—even to his dear wife—that he was in love with Lady Duckworth, for he'd fallen in love with her photographs *and* with her story when he was a child.

But it could have a lugubrious effect on the doctor—if he spent too much time in the dance hall, reviewing the photographs of Members Past. Most of the Members Past were deceased; as the circus people said of their dead, they had fallen without a net. (Of the living, the expression was reversed. Whenever Dr. Daruwalla inquired after Vinod's health—the doctor never failed to ask about the dwarf's wife, too—Vinod would always reply, "We are still falling in the net.")

Of Lady Duckworth—at least, from her photographs—Farrokh would say that her breasts were still falling in the net; possibly they were immortal.

Mr. Lal Has Missed the Net

And then, suddenly, a small and seemingly unimportant incident distracted Dr. Daruwalla from his entrancement with Lady Duckworth's bosom. The doctor would need to be in touch with his subconscious to remember this, for it was only a slight disturbance from the dining room that drew his attention. A crow, with something shiny seized in its beak, had swept in from the open veranda and had landed rakishly on the broad, oar-shaped blade of one of the ceiling fans. The bird precariously tilted the fan, but it continued to ride the blade around and around, shitting in a consistently circular form—on the floor, on a portion of one tablecloth and on a salad plate, just missing a fork. A waiter flapped a napkin and the crow took flight again, raucously cawing as it escaped through the veranda and rose above the golf course that stood shimmering in the noon sun. Whatever had been in its beak was gone, perhaps swallowed. First the waiters and busboys rushed to change the befouled tablecloth and place setting, although it was still early for lunch; then a sweeper was summoned to mop the floor.

Owing to his early-morning surgeries, Dr. Daruwalla lunched earlier

than most Duckworthians. Farrokh's appointment for lunch with Inspector Dhar was at half past noon. The doctor strolled into the Ladies'
Garden, where he located a break in the dense bower that afforded him
a view of the expanse of sky above the golf course; there he seated
himself in a rose-colored wicker chair. His little pot belly seemed to get
his attention, especially when he sat down; Farrokh ordered a London
Diet beer, although he wanted a Kingfisher lager.

To Dr. Daruwalla's surprise, he saw a vulture (possibly the same
vulture) above the golf course again; the bird was lower in the sky, as
if it was *not* en route to or from the Towers of Silence but as if it was
descending. Knowing how ferociously the Parsis defended their burial
rites, it amused Farrokh to imagine that they might be offended by any
distraction caused to any vulture. Perhaps a horse had dropped dead on
the Mahalaxmi race course; maybe a dog had been killed in Tardeo or
a body had washed ashore at Haji Ali's Tomb. Whatever the reason, here
was one vulture that was not performing the sacred chore at the Towers
of Silence.

Dr. Daruwalla looked at his watch. He expected his luncheon companion at any moment; he sipped his London Diet beer, trying to
pretend it was a Kingfisher lager—he was imagining that he was slim
again. (Farrokh had never been slim.) While he watched the vulture
carve its descending spirals, another vulture joined it, and then another;
this gave him an unexpected chill. Farrokh quite forgot to prepare
himself for the news he had to deliver to Inspector Dhar—not that there
was any good way to do it. The doctor grew so entranced by the birds
that he didn't notice the typically smooth, eerily graceful arrival of his
handsome younger friend.

Putting his hand on Dr. Daruwalla's shoulder, Dhar said, "Someone's
dead out there, Farrokh—who is it?" This caused a new waiter—the
same waiter who'd driven the crow off the ceiling fan—to mishandle a
soup tureen and a ladle. The waiter had recognized Inspector Dhar;
what shocked him was to hear the movie star speak English without a
trace of a Hindi accent. The resounding clatter seemed to herald Mr.
Bannerjee's sudden arrival in the Ladies' Garden, where he seized both
Dr. Daruwalla and Inspector Dhar by an arm.

"The vultures are landing on the ninth green!" he cried. "I think it's
poor Mr. Lal! He must have *died* in the bougainvillea!"

Dr. Daruwalla whispered in Inspector Dhar's ear. The younger man's
expression never changed as Farrokh said, "This is *your* line of work,
Inspector." Typical of the doctor, this was a joke; yet without hesitation

Inspector Dhar led them across the fairways. They could see a dozen of the leathery birds flapping and hopping in their ungainly fashion, dirtying the ninth green; their long necks rose above and then probed into the bougainvillea, their hooked beaks brightly spattered with gore.

Mr. Bannerjee wouldn't step on the green, and the smell of putrefaction that clung to the vultures took Dr. Daruwalla by surprise; he stopped, overcome, near the flag at the ninth hole. But Inspector Dhar parted the stinking birds as he kicked his way, straight ahead, into the bougainvillea. The vultures rose all around him. My God, thought Farrokh, he looks like he's a *real* police inspector—he's just an actor, but he doesn't know it!

The waiter who'd saved the ceiling fan from the crow, and had wrestled with the soup tureen and ladle with less success, also followed the excited Duckworthians a short distance onto the golf course, but he turned back to the dining room when he saw Inspector Dhar scatter the vultures. The waiter was among that multitude of fans who had seen every Inspector Dhar movie (he'd seen two or three of them a half-dozen times); therefore, he could safely be characterized as a young man who was enthralled by cheap violence and criminal bloodshed, not to mention enamored of Bombay's most lurid element—the city's sleaziest underscum, which was so lavishly depicted in all the Inspector Dhar movies. But when the waiter saw the flock of vultures that the famous actor had put to flight, the reality of an actual corpse in the vicinity of the ninth green greatly upset him. He retreated to the club, where his presence had been missed by the elderly disapproving steward, Mr. Sethna, who owed his job to Farrokh's late father.

"Inspector Dhar has found a *real* body this time!" the waiter said to the old steward.

Mr. Sethna said, "Your station today is in the Ladies' Garden. Kindly remain at your station!"

Old Mr. Sethna disapproved of Inspector Dhar movies. He was exceptionally disapproving in general, a quality regarded as enhancing to his position as steward at the Duckworth Club, where he routinely behaved as if he were empowered with the authority of the club secretary. Mr. Sethna had ruled the dining room and the Ladies' Garden with his disapproving frowns longer than Inspector Dhar had been a member—although Mr. Sethna hadn't always been steward for the Duckworthians. He'd previously been steward at the Ripon Club, a club that only Parsis join, and a club unsullied by sports of any kind; the Ripon Club existed for the purpose of good food and good conversation, period. Dr.

Daruwalla was also a member there. The Ripon *and* the Duckworth suited Farrokh's diverse nature: as a Parsi *and* a Christian, a Bombayite *and* a Torontonian, an orthopedic surgeon *and* a dwarf-blood collector, Dr. Daruwalla could never have been satisfied by just one club.

As for Mr. Sethna, who was descended from a not-so-old-money family of Parsis, the Ripon Club had suited him better than the Duckworth; however, circumstances that had brought out his highly disapproving nature had led to his dismissal there. His "highly disapproving nature" had already led Mr. Sethna to lose his not-so-old money, and the steward's money had been exceedingly difficult to lose. It was money from the Raj, British money, but Mr. Sethna had so disapproved of it that he'd most cunningly and deliberately pissed it all away. He'd endured more than a normal lifetime at the Mahalaxmi race course; and all he'd retained from his betting years was a memory of the tattoo of the horses' hooves, which he expertly drummed on his silver serving tray with his long fingers.

Mr. Sethna was distantly related to the Guzdars, an old-money family of Parsis who'd kept their money; they'd been shipbuilders for the British Navy. Alas, it happened that a young Ripon Club member had offended Mr. Sethna's extended-family sensibilities; the stern steward had overheard compromising mention of the virtue of a Guzdar young lady—a cousin, many times removed. Because of the vulgar wit that amused these younger, nonreligious Parsis, there'd also been compromising mention of the cosmic intertwinement between Spenta Mainyu (the Zoroastrian spirit of good) and Angra Mainyu (the spirit of evil). In the case of Mr. Sethna's Guzdar cousin, the spirit of *sex* was said to be winning her favors.

The young dandy who was doing this verbal damage wore a wig, a vanity of which Mr. Sethna also disapproved. Therefore, Mr. Sethna poured hot tea on top of the gentleman's head, causing him to leap to his feet and literally snatch himself bald in the presence of his surprised luncheon companions.

Mr. Sethna's actions, although considered most honorable among many old-money and new-money Parsis, were judged as unsuitable behavior for a steward; "violent aggression with hot tea" were the stated grounds for Mr. Sethna's dismissal. But the steward received the highest recommendation imaginable from Dr. Daruwalla's father; it was on the strength of the elder Daruwalla's praise that Mr. Sethna was instantly hired at the Duckworth Club. Farrokh's father viewed the tea episode as an act of heroism: the impugned Guzdar young lady was above reproach; Mr. Sethna had been correct in defending the mistreated girl's virtue. The steward was such a fanatical Zoroastrian that Farrokh's fiercely opinionated father had described Mr. Sethna as a Parsi who carried all of Persia on his shoulders.

To everyone who'd suffered his disapproving frowns in the Duckworth Club dining room or in the Ladies' Garden, old Mr. Sethna looked like a steward who would gladly pour hot tea on *anyone's* head. He was tall and exceedingly lean, as if he generally disapproved of eating, and he had a hooked, disdainful nose, as if he also disapproved of how everything smelled. And the old steward was so fair-skinned— most Parsis are fairer-skinned than most Indians—that Mr. Sethna was presumed to be racially disapproving, too.

At present, Mr. Sethna looked disapprovingly at the commotion that engulfed the golf course. His lips were thin and tightly closed, and he had the narrow, jutting, tufted chin of a goat. He disapproved of sports, and most avowedly disliked the mixing of sporting activities with the more dignified pursuits of dining and sharp debate.

The golf course was in riot: half-dressed men came running from the locker room—as if their sporting attire (when they were fully clothed) weren't distasteful enough. As a Parsi, Mr. Sethna had a high regard for justice; he thought there was something immoral about a death, which was so enduringly serious, occurring on a golf course, which was so disturbingly trivial. As a true believer whose naked body would one day lie in the Towers of Silence, the old steward found the presence of so many vultures profoundly moving; he preferred, therefore, to ignore them and to concentrate his attention and his scorn on the human turmoil. The moronic head mali had been summoned; he stupidly drove his rattling truck across the golf course, gouging up the grass that the assistant malis had recently groomed with the roller.

Mr. Sethna couldn't see Inspector Dhar, who was deep in the bougainvillea, but he had no doubt that the crude movie star was in the thick of this crisis; the steward sighed in disapproval at the very idea of Inspector Dhar.

Then there came a high-pitched ringing of a fork against a water glass—a vulgar means by which to summon a waiter. Mr. Sethna turned to the offending table and realized that *he*, not the waiter, was being summoned by the second Mrs. Dogar. She was called the beautiful Mrs. Dogar to her face and the second Mrs. Dogar behind her back. Mr. Sethna didn't find her especially beautiful, and he most adamantly disapproved of second marriages.

Furthermore, it was generally admitted among the members of the club that Mrs. Dogar's beauty was coarse in nature and had faded over time. No amount of *Mr.* Dogar's money could improve his new wife's garish tastes. No degree of physical fitness, which the second Mrs. Dogar was reputed to worship to excess, could conceal from even the most casual observer that she was at least 42. To Mr. Sethna's critical eye, she was already pushing (if not past) 50; he also thought she was much too tall. And there was many a golf-loving Duckworthian who took offense at her outspoken, insensitive opinion that golf was insufficient exercise for anyone in pursuit of good health.

This day, Mrs. Dogar was lunching alone—a habit of which Mr. Sethna also disapproved. At a proper club, the steward believed, women wouldn't be allowed to eat alone.

The marriage was still new enough that Mr. Dogar often joined his wife for lunch; the marriage was also old enough that Mr. Dogar felt free to cancel these luncheon dates, should some matter of more important business intervene. And lately he'd taken to canceling at the last minute, which left his wife no time to make plans of her own. Mr. Sethna had observed that being left alone made the new Mrs. Dogar restless and cross.

On the other hand, the steward had also observed a certain tension between the newlyweds when they dined together; Mrs. Dogar was inclined to speak sharply to her husband, who was considerably older than she was. Mr. Sethna supposed this was a penalty to be expected, for he especially disapproved of men who married younger women. But the steward thought it best to put himself at the aggressive wife's disposal lest she shatter her water glass with another blow from her fork; the fork itself looked surprisingly small in her large, sinewy hand.

"My dear Mr. Sethna," said the second Mrs. Dogar.

Mr. Sethna answered: "How may I be of service to the beautiful Mrs. Dogar?"

"You may tell me what all the fuss is about," Mrs. Dogar replied.

Mr. Sethna spoke as deliberately as he would pour hot tea. "It is most assuredly nothing to upset yourself about," the old Parsi said. "It is merely a dead golfer."

2. THE UPSETTING NEWS

Still Tingling

Thirty years ago, there were more than 50 circuses of some merit in India; today there aren't more than 15 that are any good. Many of them are named the Great This or the Great That. Among Dr. Daruwalla's favorites were the Great Bombay, the Jumbo, the Great Golden, the Gemini, the Great Rayman, the Famous, the Great Oriental and the Raj Kamal; of them all, Farrokh felt most fond of the Great Royal Circus. Before Independence, it was called simply the Royal; in 1947 it became the "Great." It began as a two-pole tent; in '47 the Great Royal added two more poles. But it was the owner who'd made such a positive impression on Farrokh. Because Pratap Walawalkar was such a well-traveled man, he seemed the most sophisticated of the circus owners to Dr. Daruwalla; or else Farrokh's fondness for Pratap Walawalkar was simply because the Great Royal's owner never teased the doctor about his interest in dwarf blood.

In the 1960's, the Great Royal traveled everywhere. Business was bad in Egypt, best in Iran; business was good in Beirut and Singapore, Pratap Walawalkar said—and of all the countries where the circus traveled, Bali was the most beautiful. Travel was too expensive now. With a half-dozen elephants and two dozen big cats, not to mention a dozen horses and almost a dozen chimpanzees, the Great Royal rarely traveled outside the states of Maharashtra and Gujarat. With uncounted cockatoos and parrots, and dozens of dogs (not to mention 150 people, including almost a dozen dwarfs), the Great Royal never left India.

This was the real history of a real circus, but Dr. Daruwalla had committed these details to that quality of memory which most of us reserve for our childhoods. Farrokh's childhood had failed to make much of an impression on him; he vastly preferred the history and the memorabilia he'd absorbed as a behind-the-scenes observer of the circus. He remembered Pratap Walawalkar saying in an offhand manner: "Ethiopian lions have brown manes, but they're just like other lions—they won't listen to you if you don't call them by their right names." Farrokh had retained this morsel of information as if it were part of a beloved bedtime story.

In the early mornings, en route to his surgeries (even in Canada), the doctor often recalled the big basins steaming over the gas rings in the cook's tent. In one pot was the water for tea, but in two of the basins the cook was heating milk; the first milk that came to a boil wasn't for tea—it was to make oatmeal for the chimpanzees. As for tea, the chimps didn't like it hot; they liked their tea tepid. Farrokh also remembered the extra flatbread; it was for the elephants—they enjoyed roti. And the tigers took vitamins, which turned their milk pink. As an orthopedic surgeon, Dr. Daruwalla could make no medical use of these cherished details; nevertheless, he'd breathed them in as if they were his own background.

Dr. Daruwalla's wife wore wonderful jewelry, some of which had belonged to his mother; none of it was at all memorable to the doctor, who (however) could describe in the most exact detail a tiger-claw necklace that belonged to Pratap Singh, the ringmaster and wild-animal trainer for the Great Royal Circus—a man much admired by Farrokh. Pratap Singh had once shared his remedy for dizziness with the doctor: a potion of red chili and burned human hair. For asthma, the ringmaster recommended a clove soaked in tiger urine; you allow the clove to dry, then you grind it up and inhale the powder. Moreover, the animal trainer warned the doctor, you should never swallow a tiger's whiskers; swallowing tiger whiskers will kill you.

Had Farrokh read of these remedies in some crackpot's column in *The Times of India*, he'd have written a scathing letter for publication in the Opinion section. In the name of real medicine, Dr. Daruwalla would have denounced such "holistic folly," which was his phrase of choice whenever he addressed the issue of so-called unscientific or magical thinking. But the source of the human-hair-and-red-chili recipe, as well as of the tiger-urine cure (not to mention the tiger-whiskers warning), was the great Pratap Singh. In Dr. Daruwalla's view, the ringmaster and wild-animal trainer was undeniably a man who knew his business.

This kind of lore, and blood from dwarfs, enhanced Farrokh's abiding feeling that, as a result of flopping around in a safety net and falling on a poor dwarf's wife, he had become an adopted son of the circus. For Farrokh, the honor of clumsily coming to Deepa's rescue was lasting. Whenever *any* circus was performing in Bombay, Dr. Daruwalla could be found in a front-row seat; he could also be detected mingling with the acrobats and the animal trainers—most of all, he enjoyed observing the practice sessions and the tent life. These intimate views from the wing of the main tent, these close-ups of the troupe tents and the cages—they were the privileges that made Farrokh feel he'd been adopted. At times, he wished he were a *real* son of the circus; instead, Farrokh supposed, he was merely a guest of honor. Nevertheless, this wasn't a fleeting honor—not to him.

Ironically, Dr. Daruwalla's children and grandchildren were unimpressed by the Indian circuses. These two generations had been born and raised in London or Toronto; they'd not only seen bigger and fancier circuses—they'd seen cleaner. The doctor was disappointed that his children and grandchildren were so dirt-obsessed; they considered the tent life of the acrobats and the animal trainers to be shabby, even "underprivileged." Although the dirt floors of the tents were swept several times daily, Dr. Daruwalla's children and grandchildren believed that the tents were filthy.

To the doctor, however, the circus was an orderly, well-kept oasis surrounded by a world of disease and chaos. His children and grandchildren saw the dwarf clowns as merely grotesque; in the circus, they existed solely to be laughed at. But Farrokh felt that the dwarf clowns were appreciated—maybe even loved, not to mention gainfully employed. The doctor's children and grandchildren thought that the risks taken by the child performers were especially "harsh"; yet Farrokh felt that these acrobatic children were the lucky ones—they'd been rescued.

Dr. Daruwalla knew that the majority of these child acrobats were (like Deepa) sold to the circus by their parents, who'd been unable to support them; others were orphans—they'd been truly adopted. If they hadn't been performing in the circus, where they were well fed and protected, they'd have been begging. They would be the street children you saw doing handstands and other stunts for a few rupees in Bombay, or in the smaller towns throughout Gujarat and Maharashtra, where even the Great Royal Circus more frequently performed—these days, fewer circuses came to Bombay. During Diwali and the winter holidays, there were still two or three circuses performing in or around the city, but TV and the videocassette recorder had hurt the circus business; too many people rented movies and stayed at home.

To hear the Daruwalla children and grandchildren discuss it, the child acrobats who were sold to the circus were long-suffering child laborers in a high-risk profession; their hardworking, no-escape existence was tantamount to slavery. Untrained children were paid nothing for six months; thereafter, they started with a salary of 3 rupees a day—only 90 rupees a month, less than 4 dollars! But Dr. Daruwalla argued that safe food and a safe place to sleep were better than nothing; what these children were given was a chance.

Circus people boiled their water and their milk. They bought and cooked their own food; they dug and cleaned their own latrines. And a well-trained acrobat was often paid 500 or 600 rupees a month, even if it was only 25 dollars. Granted, although the Great Royal took good care of its children, Farrokh couldn't say with certainty that the child performers were as well treated in *all* the Indian circuses; the performances in several of these circuses were so abject—not to mention unskilled and careless—that the doctor surmised that the tent life in such places was shabbier, too.

Life was surely shabby in the Great Blue Nile; indeed, among the Great This and Great That circuses of India, the Great Blue Nile was the shabbiest—or at least the least great. Deepa would agree. A former child contortionist, the dwarf's wife, reincarnated as a trapeze artist, was lacking both in polish and in common sense; it wasn't merely the beer that had made her let go of the bar too soon.

Deepa's injuries were complicated but not severe; in addition to the dislocation of her hip joint, she'd suffered a tear in the transverse ligament. Not only would Dr. Daruwalla brand Deepa's hip with a memorable scar, but, in prepping the area, he would be confronted by the irrefutable blackness of Deepa's pubic hair; this would be a dark reminder of the disturbing contact between her pubis and the bridge of his nose.

Farrokh's nose was still tingling when he helped Deepa be admitted to the hospital; out of guilt, he'd left the circus grounds with her. But the admitting process had barely begun when the doctor was summoned by one of the hospital secretaries; there'd been a phone call for him while he was en route from the Blue Nile.

"Do you know any clowns?" the secretary asked him.

"Well, as a matter of fact, yes," Farrokh admitted.

"*Dwarf* clowns?" asked the secretary.

"Yes—several! I just met them," the doctor added. Farrokh was too ashamed to admit that he'd also just bled them.

"Apparently, one of them has been injured at that circus at Cross Maidan," the secretary said.

"Not Vinod!" Dr. Daruwalla exclaimed.

"Yes, that's him," she said. "That's why they want you back at the circus."

"What happened to Vinod?" Dr. Daruwalla asked the somewhat disdainful secretary; she was one of many medical secretaries who embraced sarcasm.

"I couldn't ascertain the clown's condition from a phone message," she replied. "The description was hysterical. I gather he was trampled by elephants or shot from a cannon, or both. And now that this dwarf lies dying, he is declaring *you* to be his doctor."

And so to the circus grounds at Cross Maidan did Dr. Daruwalla go. All the way back to the deeply flawed performance of the Great Blue Nile, the doctor's nose tingled.

For 15 years, merely remembering the dwarf's wife would activate Farrokh's nose. And now, the fact that Mr. Lal had fallen without a net (for the body on the golf course was indeed dead)—even this evidence of death reminded Dr. Daruwalla that Deepa had survived her fall *and* her unwelcome and painful contact with the clumsy doctor.

The Famous Twin

Upon Inspector Dhar's intrusion, the vultures had risen but they'd not departed. Dr. Daruwalla knew that the carrion eaters still floated overhead because their putrescence lingered in the air and their shadows drifted back and forth across the ninth green and the bougainvillea, where Dhar—a mere movie-star detective—knelt beside poor Mr. Lal.

"Don't touch the body!" Dr. Daruwalla said.

"I know," the veteran actor replied coldly.

Oh, he's not in a good mood, Farrokh thought; it would be unwise to tell him the upsetting news now. The doctor doubted that Dhar's mood would *ever* be good enough to make him magnanimous upon receiving such news—and who could blame him? An overwhelming sense of unfairness lay at the heart of it, for Dhar was an identical twin who'd been separated from his brother at birth. Although Dhar had been told the story of his birth, Dhar's twin knew nothing of the story; Dhar's twin didn't even know he was a twin. And now Dhar's twin was coming to Bombay.

Dr. Daruwalla had always believed that nothing good could come from such deception. Although Dhar had accepted the willful arbitrariness of the situation, a certain aloofness had been the cost; he was a man who, as far as Farrokh knew, withheld affection and resolutely withstood any display of affection from others. Who could blame him? the doctor thought. Dhar had accepted the existence of a mother and father and identical twin brother he'd never seen; Dhar had abided by that tiresome adage, which is still popularly evoked—to let sleeping dogs lie. But now: this most upsetting news was surely in that category of another tiresome adage which is still popularly evoked—this was the last straw.

In Dr. Daruwalla's opinion, Dhar's mother had always been too selfish for motherhood; and 40 years after the accident of conception, the woman was demonstrating her selfishness again. That she'd arbitrarily decided to take one twin and abandon the other was sufficient selfishness for a normal lifetime; that she'd chosen to protect herself from her husband's potentially harsh opinion of her by keeping from him the fact that there'd *ever been* a twin was selfishness of a heightened, even of a monstrous, kind; and that she'd so sheltered the twin whom she'd kept from any knowledge of his identical brother was yet again as selfish as it was deeply insensitive to the feelings of the twin she'd left behind . . . the twin who knew everything.

Well, the doctor thought, Dhar knew everything except that his twin was coming to Bombay and that his mother had begged Dr. Daruwalla to be sure that the twins didn't meet!

In such circumstances Dr. Daruwalla felt briefly grateful for the distraction of old Mr. Lal's apparent heart attack. Except when eating, Farrokh embraced procrastination as one greets an unexpected virtue. The belch of exhaust from the head gardener's truck blew a wave of flower petals from the wrecked bougainvillea over Dr. Daruwalla's feet; he stared in surprise at his light-brown toes in his dark-brown sandals, which were almost buried in the vivid pink petals.

That was when the head mali, who'd left the truck running, sidled over to the ninth green and stood smirking beside Dr. Daruwalla. The mali was clearly more excited by the sight of Inspector Dhar in action than he appeared to be disturbed by the death of poor Mr. Lal. With a nod toward the scene unfolding in the bougainvillea, the gardener whispered to Farrokh, "It looks just like a movie!" This observation quickly returned Dr. Daruwalla to the crisis at hand, namely the impossibility of shielding Dhar's twin from the existence of his famous brother, who, even in a city of movie stars, was indubitably the most recognizable star in Bombay.

Even if the famous actor agreed to keep himself in hiding, his identical twin brother would constantly be mistaken for Inspector Dhar. Dr. Daruwalla admired the mental toughness of the Jesuits, but the twin—who was what the Jesuits call a scholastic (in training to be a priest)—would have to be more than mentally tough in order to endure a recurring mistaken identity of this magnitude. And from what Farrokh had been told of Dhar's twin, self-confidence was not high on the man's listed features. After all, who is almost 40 and only "in training" to be a priest? the doctor wondered. Given Bombay's feelings for Dhar, Dhar's Jesuit twin might be killed! Despite his conversion to Christianity, Dr. Daruwalla had little faith in the powers of a presumably naïve American missionary to survive—or even comprehend—the depth of resentment that Bombay harbored for Inspector Dhar.

For example, it was common in Bombay to deface all the advertisements for all the Inspector Dhar movies. Only on the higher-placed hoardings—those larger-than-life billboards that were everywhere in the city—was the giant likeness of Inspector Dhar's cruel, handsome face spared the abundant filth that was flung at it from street level. But even above human reach, the familiar face of the detested antihero couldn't escape creative defilement from Bombay's most expressive birds. The crows and the fork-tailed kites appeared to be drawn, as to a target, to the dark, piercing eyes—and to that sneer which the famous actor had perfected. All over town, Dhar's movie-poster face was spotted with bird shit. But even his many detractors admitted that Inspector Dhar achieved a kind of perfection with his sneer. It was the look of a lover who was leaving you, while thoroughly relishing your misery. All of Bombay felt the sting of it.

The rest of the world, even most of the rest of India, didn't suffer the sneer with which Inspector Dhar constantly looked down upon Bombay. The box-office success of the Inspector Dhar movies was inexplicably limited to Maharashtra and stood in violent contradiction to how unanimously Dhar himself was loathed; not only the character, but also the actor who brought him to life, was one of those luminaries in popular culture whom the public loves to hate. As for the actor who took responsibility for the role, he appeared to so enjoy the passionate hostility he inspired that he undertook no other roles; he used no other name—he had *become* Inspector Dhar. It was even the name on his passport.

It was the name on his *Indian* passport, which was a fake. India doesn't permit dual citizenship. Dr. Daruwalla knew that Dhar had a Swiss passport, which was genuine; he was a Swiss citizen. In truth, the crafty actor had a Swiss *life*, for which he would always be grateful to Farrokh. The success of the Inspector Dhar movies was based, at least in part, on how closely Dhar had guarded his privacy, and how well hidden he'd kept his past. No amount of public scrutiny, which was considerable, could unearth more biographical information on the mystery man than he permitted—and, like his movies, Dhar's autobiography was highly far-fetched and contrived, wholly lacking in credible detail. That Inspector Dhar had invented himself, and that he appeared to have got away with his preposterous and unexaminable fiction, was surely a contributing reason for the virulence with which he was despised.

But the fury of the film press only fed Dhar's stardom. Since he refused to give these gossip journalists the facts, they wrote completely fabricated stories about him; Dhar being Dhar, this suited him perfectly—lies merely served to heighten his mystery and the general hysteria he inspired. Inspector Dhar movies were so popular, Dhar must have had fans, probably a multitude of admirers; but the film audience swore that they despised him. Dhar's indifference to his audience was also a reason to hate him. The actor himself suggested that even his fans were largely motivated to watch his films because they longed to see him fail; their faithful attendance, even if they hoped to witness a flop, assured Dhar of one hit after another. In the Bombay cinema, demigods were common; hero worship was the norm. What was uncommon was that Inspector Dhar was loathed but that he was nonetheless a star.

As for twins separated at birth, the irony was that this is an extremely popular theme with Hindi screenwriters. Such a separation frequently happens at the hospital—or during a storm, or in a railway accident. Typically, one twin takes a virtuous path while the other wallows in evil. Usually, there is some key that links them—maybe a torn two-rupee note (each twin keeps a half). And often, at the moment they are about to kill each other, the telltale half of the two-rupee note flutters out from one twin's pocket. Thus reunited, the twins vent their always-justifiable anger on a *real* villain, an inconceivable scoundrel (conveniently introduced to the audience at an earlier stage in the preposterous story).

How Bombay hated Inspector Dhar! But Dhar was a *real* twin, *truly* separated at birth, and Dhar's actual story was more unbelievable than any story concocted in the imagination of a Hindi screenwriter. Moreover, almost no one in Bombay, or in all of Maharashtra, knew Dhar's true story.

The Doctor as Closet Screenwriter

On the ninth green, with the pink petals of the bougainvillea caressing his feet, Dr. Daruwalla could detect the hatred that the moronic head mali felt for Inspector Dhar. The lout still lurked at Farrokh's side, clearly relishing the irony that Dhar, who only pretended to be a police inspector, found himself playing the role in close proximity to an actual corpse. Dr. Daruwalla then remembered his own first response to the awareness that poor Mr. Lal had fallen prey to vultures; he recalled how he'd relished the irony, too! What had he whispered to Dhar? "This is *your* line of work, Inspector." Farrokh was mortified that he'd said this.

If Dr. Daruwalla felt vaguely guilty that he knew very little about either his native or his adopted country, and if his self-confidence was a mild casualty of his general out-of-itness in both Bombay and Toronto, the doctor was *more* clearly and acutely agonized by anything in himself that identified him with the lowly masses—the poor slob on the street, the mere commoner: in short, his fellow man. If it embarrassed him to be a passive resident of both Canada and India, which was a passivity born of insufficient knowledge and experience, it shamed him hugely to catch himself thinking like anyone else. He may have been alienated but he was also a snob. And here, in the presence of death itself, Dr. Daruwalla was humiliated by his apparent lack of originality—namely, he discovered he was on the same wavelength as an entirely stupid and disagreeable gardener.

The doctor was so ashamed that he briefly turned his attention to Mr. Lal's grief-stricken golfing partner, Mr. Bannerjee, who'd approached no closer than a spot within reach of the number-nine flag, which hung limply from the slender pole stuck in the cup.

Then Dhar spoke quite suddenly, and with more curiosity than surprise. "There's quite a lot of blood by one ear," he said.

"I suppose the vultures were pecking at him for some time," Dr. Daruwalla replied. He wouldn't venture any nearer himself—after all, he was an orthopedist, not a medical examiner.

"But it doesn't look like that," said Inspector Dhar.

"Oh, stop playing the part of a policeman!" Farrokh said impatiently.

Dhar gave him a stern, reproachful look, which the doctor believed he absolutely deserved. He sheepishly scuffed his feet in the flowers, but several bright petals of the bougainvillea were caught between his toes. He was embarrassed by the visible cruelty on the head mali's eager face; he felt ashamed of himself for not attending to the living, for quite clearly Mr. Bannerjee was suffering all alone—there was nothing the doctor could do for Mr. Lal. To poor Mr. Bannerjee, Dr. Daruwalla must have seemed indifferent to the body! And of the upsetting news that he couldn't yet bring himself to impart to his dear younger friend, Farrokh felt afraid.

Oh, the injustice that such unwelcome news should be *my* burden! Dr. Daruwalla thought—momentarily forgetting the greater unfairness to Dhar. For hadn't the poor actor already contended with quite enough? Dhar had not only kept his sanity, which nothing less than the fierce maintenance of his privacy could ensure; he'd honored Dr. Daruwalla's privacy, too, for Dhar knew that the doctor had written the screenplays for all the Inspector Dhar movies—Dhar knew that Farrokh had created the very character whom Dhar was now condemned to be.

It was supposed to be a gift, Dr. Daruwalla remembered; he'd so loved the younger man, as he would his own son—he'd expressly written the part *just for him*. Now, to avoid the reproachful look that Dhar gave him, Farrokh knelt down and picked the petals of bougainvillea from between his toes.

Oh, dear boy, what have I gotten you into? Dr. Daruwalla thought. Although Dhar was almost 40, he was still a boy to Dr. Daruwalla. The doctor had not only invented the character of the controversial police inspector, he'd not only created the movies that inspired madness throughout Maharashtra; he'd also fabricated the absurd autobiography that the famous actor attempted to pass off to the public as the story of his life. Quite understandably, the public didn't buy it. Farrokh knew that the public wouldn't have bought Dhar's true story, either.

Inspector Dhar's fictional autobiography manifested a fondness for shock value and sentiment that was remindful of his films. He claimed to have been born out of wedlock; he said his mother was an American—currently a has-been Hollywood movie star—and his father was an actual Bombay police inspector, long since retired. Forty years ago (Inspector Dhar was 39), the Hollywood mother had been shooting a film in Bombay. The police inspector responsible for the star's security had fallen in love with her; their trysting place had been the Taj Mahal Hotel. When the movie star knew she was pregnant, she struck a deal with the inspector.

At the time Dhar was born, the lifetime support of an Indian police inspector seemed no more prohibitive an expense to the Hollywood star than her habit of adding coconut oil to her bath, or so the story went. A baby, especially out of wedlock, and with an Indian father, would have compromised her career. According to Dhar, his mother had paid the police inspector to take full responsibility for the child. Enough money was involved so that the inspector could retire; he clearly passed on his intimate knowledge of police business, including the bribes, to his son. In his movies, Inspector Dhar was always above being bribed. All the *real* police inspectors in Bombay said that, if they knew who Dhar's father was, they would kill him. All the real policemen made it clear that they would enjoy killing Inspector Dhar, too.

To Dr. Daruwalla's shame, it was a story full of holes, beginning with the unknown movie. More movies are made in Bombay than in Hollywood. But in 1949, no American films were made in Maharashtra—at least none that were ever released. And, suspiciously, there were no records of the policemen assigned to foreign film sets for security, although copious records exist in other years, suggesting that the accounts for 1949 were liberated from the files, doubtless by means of a bribe. But why? As for the so-called has-been Hollywood star, if she was an American in Bombay making a movie, she would have been *considered* a Hollywood star—even if she was an unknown actress, and a terrible actress, and even if the movie had never been released.

Inspector Dhar had claimed, at best, indifference regarding her identity. It was said that Dhar had never been to the United States. Although his English was reported to be perfect, even accentless, he said that he preferred to speak Hindi and that he dated only Indian women.

Dhar had confessed, at worst, a mild contempt for his mother, whoever she was. And he professed a fierce and abiding loyalty to his father, which was marked by Dhar's resolute vow to keep his father's identity secret. It was rumored that they met only in Europe!

It must be said, in Dr. Daruwalla's defense, that the improbable nature of his fiction was at least based on reality. The fault rested with the unexplained gaps in the story. Inspector Dhar made his first movie in his early twenties, but where was he as a child? In Bombay, such a handsome man wouldn't have gone unnoticed as a boy, especially as a teenager; furthermore, his skin was simply too fair—only in Europe or in North America would he have been called dark-skinned. He had such dark-brown hair that it was almost black, and such charcoal-gray eyes that they were almost black, too; but if he actually had an Indian father, there wasn't a discernible trace of even a fair-skinned Indian in the son.

Everyone said that possibly the mother was a blue-eyed blonde, and all that the police inspector could contribute to the child was a racially neutralizing effect and a fervor for homicide cases. Nevertheless, all of Bombay complained that the box-office star of its Hindi movie madness *looked* to all the world like a 100 percent North American or European. There was no credible explanation for his all-white appearance, which fueled the rumor that Dhar was the child of Farrokh's brother, who'd married an Austrian; and since it was well known that Farrokh was married to this European's sister, it was also rumored that Dhar was the doctor's child.

The doctor expressed boredom for the notion, in spite of the fact that there were many living Duckworthians who could remember Dr. Daruwalla's father in the company of an ephemeral, fair-skinned boy who was only an occasional summer visitor. And this suspiciously all-white boy was reputed to be the senior Daruwalla's grandson! But the best way to answer these charges, Farrokh knew, was not to answer them beyond the bluntest denial.

It's well known that many Indians think fair skin is beautiful; in addition, Dhar was ruggedly handsome. However, it was considered perverse of Inspector Dhar that he refused to speak English in public, or spoke it with an obviously exaggerated Hindi accent. It was rumored that he spoke accentless English in private, but how would anyone know? Inspector Dhar granted only a limited number of interviews, which were restricted to questions regarding his "art"; he insisted that his personal life was a forbidden topic. (Dhar's "personal life" was the only topic of possible interest to anyone.) When cornered by the film press at a nightclub, at a restaurant, at a photo session in connection with the release of a new Inspector Dhar movie, the actor would apply his famous sneer. It didn't matter what question he was asked; either he answered facetiously or, regardless of the question, he would say in Hindi, or in English with his phony accent, "I have never been to the United States. I have no interest in my mother. If I have babies, they will be Indian babies. They are the most clever."

And Dhar could return and outlast anyone's stare; he could also manipulate the eye of any camera. Alarmingly, he possessed an increasingly bulky strength. Until he was in his mid-thirties, his muscles had been well defined, his stomach flat. Whether it was middle age, or whether Dhar had yielded to the usual bodily measurements for success among Bombay's matinee idols—or whether it was his love of weight lifting in tandem with his professed capacity for beer—the actor's stoutness threatened to overtake his reputation as a tough guy. (In Bombay, he was perceived as a well-fed tough guy.) His critics liked to call him Beer Belly, but not to his face; after all, Dhar wasn't in bad shape for a guy who was almost 40.

As for Dr. Daruwalla's screenplays, they deviated from the usual masala mixture of the Hindi cinema. Farrokh's scripts were both corny and tawdry, but the vulgarity was decidedly Western—the hero's own nastiness was extolled as a virtue (Dhar was routinely nastier than most villains)—and the peculiar sentimentality bordered on undergraduate existentialism (Dhar was beyond loneliness in that he appeared to enjoy being alienated from everyone). There were token gestures to the Hindi cinema, which Dr. Daruwalla viewed with the mocking irony of an outsider: gods frequently descended from the heavens (usually to provide Inspector Dhar with inside information), and all the villains were demonic (if ineffectual). Villainy, in general, was represented by criminals and the majority of the police force; sexual conquest was reserved for Inspector Dhar, whose heroism operated both within and above the law. As for the women who provided the sexual conquests, Dhar remained largely indifferent to them, which was suspiciously European.

There was music of the standard Hindi combination: choruses of girls oohing and aahing to the clamor of guitars, tablas, violins and vinas. And Inspector Dhar himself, despite his ingrained cynicism, would occasionally lip-sync a song. Although he lip-synced well, the lyrics are not worth repeating—he would snarl such poetry as, "Baby, I guarantee it, you're gonna find me gratifying!" Such songs, in the Hindi cinema, are in Hindi, but this was another instance of how the Inspector Dhar films were deliberately scripted against the grain. Dhar's songs were in English, with his deplorable Hindi accent; even his theme song, which was sung by an all-girl chorus and repeated at least twice in every Inspector Dhar movie, was in English. It, too, was loathed; it was also a hit. Although he'd written it, it made Dr. Daruwalla cringe to hear it.

> So you say Inspector Dhar is
> a mere mortal—

so you say, so you say!
He looks like a god to us!

So you say this is
a little rain shower—
so you say, so you say!
It looks like the monsoon to us!

If Dhar was a good lip-syncer, he also demonstrated no enthusiasm for the much-maligned art. One critic had dubbed him "Lazy Lips." Another critic complained that nothing energized Dhar—he lacked enthusiasm for everything. As an actor, Dhar had mass appeal—possibly because he seemed constantly depressed, as if sordidness were a magnet to him, and his eventual triumph over evil were a perpetual curse. Therefore, a certain wistfulness was ascribed to every victim whom Inspector Dhar sought to rescue or avenge; a graphic violence attended Dhar's punishment of each and every evildoer.

As for sex, satire prevailed. In place of lovemaking, old newsreel footage of a rocking train would be substituted; ejaculation was characterized by listless waves breaking on shore. Furthermore, and in compliance with the rules of censorship in India, nudity, which was *not* permitted, was replaced by wetness; there was much fondling (fully clothed) in the rain, as if Inspector Dhar solved crimes only during the monsoon season. The occasional nipple could be glimpsed, or at least imagined, under a fully soaked sari; this was more titillating than erotic.

Social relevance and ideology were similarly muted, if not altogether absent. (Both in Toronto *and* in Bombay, these latter instincts were similarly undeveloped in Dr. Daruwalla.) Beyond the commonplace observation that the police were thoroughly corrupted by a system based on bribery, there was little preaching. Scenes of violent but maudlin death, followed by scenes of tearful mourning, were more important than messages intended to inspire a national conscience.

The character of Inspector Dhar was brutally vindictive; he was also utterly incorruptible—except sexually. Women were easily and simplistically identified as good or bad; yet Dhar permitted himself the greatest liberties with both—indeed, with all. Well, with *almost* all. He wouldn't indulge a Western woman, and in every Inspector Dhar movie there was always at least one Western, ultra-white woman who craved a sexual adventure with Inspector Dhar; that he faithfully and cruelly spurned her was his signature, his trademark, and the part of his films that made

Indian women and young girls adore him. Whether this aspect of Dhar's character reflected his feelings for his mother or gave fictional evidence of his stated intentions to sire only Indian babies—well, who knew? Who really knew anything about Inspector Dhar? Hated by all men, loved by all women (who *said* that they hated him).

Even the Indian women who'd dated him were uniform in the zeal they demonstrated in protection of his privacy. They would say, "He's not at all like he is in his movies." (No examples were ever forthcoming.) They would say, "He's very old-fashioned, a real gentleman." (No examples were ever asked for.) "He's very modest, really—and very quiet," they would say.

Everyone could believe he was "quiet"; there were suspicions that he never spoke an unscripted line—these were happy, mindless contradictions of the rumor regarding his accentless English. No one believed anything, or else they believed everything they'd ever heard. That he had two wives—one in Europe. That he had a dozen children—none he would acknowledge, all of them illegitimate. That he actually lived in Los Angeles, in his vile mother's house!

In the face of all rumors, and in keeping with the violent contrasts created by the extreme popularity of his movies and the extreme animosity toward him that was inspired by his sneer, Dhar himself remained inscrutable. No small amount of sarcasm was detectable in his sneer; no other thick-set, middle-aged man could possibly have seemed so self-possessed.

Dhar endorsed only one charity; so totally and convincingly did he solicit the public's support of his personal crusade that he had achieved a philanthropic status as high as any among the several benefactors of Bombay. He made television commercials for the Hospital for Crippled Children. The advertisements were made at Dhar's own expense and they were devastatingly effective. (Dr. Daruwalla was the author of these commercials as well.)

On the TV, Inspector Dhar faces the camera in medium close-up, wearing a loose-fitting white shirt—a collarless or mandarin-style kurta—and he holds his practiced sneer only as long as he imagines it takes to get the viewer's full attention. Then he says, "You may love to hate me—I make a lot of money and I don't give any of it to anyone, except to these children." There then follows a series of shots of Dhar among the crippled children at the orthopedic hospital: a deformed little girl crawls toward Inspector Dhar, who holds out his hands to her; Inspector Dhar is surrounded by staring children in wheelchairs; Inspector Dhar lifts a little boy from a swirling whirlpool bath and carries him to a clean white table, where two nurses assemble the child's leg braces for him—the boy's legs aren't as big around as his arms.

Regardless, Inspector Dhar was still hated; on occasion, he was even attacked. Local bullies wanted to see if he was as tough and practiced in the martial arts as the police inspector he portrayed; apparently, he was. He would respond to any and all verbal abuse with a queerly restrained version of his sneer. It made him appear mildly drunk. But if physically threatened, he wouldn't hesitate to retaliate in kind; once, assaulted by a man with a chair, Dhar struck back with a table. He was reputed to be as dangerous as his screen persona. He'd occasionally broken other people's bones; perhaps from his understanding of ortho-pedics, he'd caused serious injuries to the joints of his assailants. He was capable of real damage. But Dhar didn't pick fights, he simply won them.

His trashy films were hastily made, his publicity appearances mini-mal; the rumor was, he spent next to no time in Bombay. His chauffeur was an unfriendly dwarf, a former circus clown whom the film-gossip press had confidently labeled a thug. (Vinod was proud of this allega-tion.) And except for the plentiful number of Indian women who'd dated him, Dhar wasn't known to have any friends. His most public acquaint-ance—with an infrequent visitor to Bombay, an Honorary Consultant Surgeon at the Hospital for Crippled Children who was the hospital's usual spokesman for its foreign fund-raising efforts—was accepted as a longstanding relationship that had withstood invasions from the media. Dr. Daruwalla—a distinguished Canadian physician and family man, and a son of the former chief of staff of Bombay's Hospital for Crippled Children (the late Dr. Lowji Daruwalla)—was witheringly brief to the press. When asked about his relationship to and with Inspector Dhar, Dr. Daruwalla would say, "I'm a doctor, not a gossip." Besides, the younger and the elder man were seen together only at the Duckworth Club. The media weren't welcome there, and among the members of the club, eavesdropping (except by the old Parsi steward) was generally deplored.

There was, however, much speculation about how Inspector Dhar could conceivably have become a member of the Duckworth Club. Movie stars weren't welcome there, either. And given the 22-year wait-ing list and the fact that the actor became a member when he was only 26, Dhar must have applied for membership when he was four! Or someone had applied for him. Furthermore, it had *not* been sufficiently demonstrated to many Duckworthians that Inspector Dhar had distin-guished himself in "community leadership"; some members pointed to

his efforts for the Hospital for Crippled Children, but others argued that
Inspector Dhar's movies were destructive to all of Bombay. Quite understandably, there was no suppressing the rumors or the complaints
that circulated through the old club on this subject.

Dr. Daruwalla Is Stricken with Self-doubt

There was also no suppressing the exciting news about the dead golfer
in the bougainvillea near the ninth green. True to his fictional character,
Inspector Dhar himself had located the body. Doubtless the press would
expect Dhar to solve the crime. It didn't appear there had been a crime,
although there was talk among the Duckworthians that Mr. Lal's excesses on the golf course were of a criminal nature, and surely his
exertions in the wrecked bougainvillea hadn't served the old gentleman
well. The vultures had spoiled a clear impression, but it seemed that Mr.
Lal had been the victim of his own chip shot. His lifelong opponent, Mr.
Bannerjee, told Dr. Daruwalla that he felt as if he'd murdered his friend.
    "He always fell apart at the ninth hole!" Mr. Bannerjee exclaimed. "I
never should have teased him about it!"
    Dr. Daruwalla was thinking that he'd often teased Mr. Lal along
similar lines; it had been irresistible to tease Mr. Lal in regard to the zeal
with which he played a game for which he manifested minimal talent.
But now that he appeared to have died at the game, Mr. Lal's enthusiasm
for golf seemed less funny than before.
    Farrokh found himself sensing some faint analogy between his cre-
ation of Inspector Dhar and Mr. Lal's golf game, and this unwanted
connection came to him as the result of a sudden, unpleasant odor. It
wasn't as strong an impression as the stench of a man defecating at close
quarters, but instead the smell was at once more familiar and more
removed—sun-rotted garbage, perhaps, or clogged drains. Farrokh
thought of potted flowers and human urine.
    Far-fetched or not, the nature of the comparison between Mr. Lal's
lethal golf habit and Dr. Daruwalla's screenwriting was simply this: the
Inspector Dhar movies were judged to be of no artistic merit whatsoever, but the labors that the doctor performed to write these screenplays
were intense; the nature of Inspector Dhar's character was crude to most
viewers, and outrageously offensive to many, but the doctor had created
Dhar out of the purest love; and Farrokh's fragile self-esteem rested as
much on his sense of himself as a closet writer as it did on his established

reputation as a surgeon, even if he was only a *screen*writer and, worse, even though he was perceived to be such a shameless hack—such a whore for the money—that he wouldn't even lend his name to his creations. Understandably, since the actor who played Inspector Dhar had himself become (in the public eye) the very character he portrayed, the authorship of the screenplays was ascribed to Dhar. What gave Farrokh so much pleasure was the actual writing of the screenplays themselves; yet, despite his own enjoyment of the craft, the results were ridiculed and hated.

Recently, in the light of certain death threats that Inspector Dhar had received, Dr. Daruwalla had even considered retiring; the doctor had meant to sound out the actor in regard to this notion. If I stop, Farrokh wondered, what will Dhar do? If I stop, what will *I* do? he'd also wondered, for he'd long suspected that Dhar wouldn't be opposed to the idea of getting out of the business of being Dhar—especially now. To suffer the verbal abuse of *The Times of India* was one thing; death threats were something altogether different.

And now this unlikely association to Mr. Lal's golf game, this un-veiled reek of sun-rotted garbage, this ancient smell from a clogged drain—or had someone been peeing in the bougainvillea? These thoughts were most unwelcome. Dr. Daruwalla suddenly saw himself as the poor, doomed Mr. Lal; he thought he was as bad but as compulsive a writer as Mr. Lal had been a golfer. For example, he'd not only written another screenplay; they'd already finished the final cut of the picture. Coincidentally, the new movie would be released shortly before or after the arrival in Bombay of Dhar's twin. Dhar himself was just hanging around—he was under contract for a very limited number of interviews and photo opportunities to publicize the new release. (This forced intimacy with the film press could never be limited enough to suit Dhar.) Also, there was every reason to believe that the new film might make as much trouble as the last. And so the time to stop is *now*, thought Dr. Daruwalla, before I begin another one!

But how could he stop? It was something he loved. And how could he hope to improve? Farrokh was doing the best that he could; like poor Mr. Lal, he was hopelessly returning to the ninth green. Each time, the flowers would fly but the golf ball would remain more or less unrespon-sive; each time, he would be knee-deep in the blighted bougainvillea, slashing wildly at the little white ball. Then, one day, the vultures would be overhead and descending.

There was just one choice: either hit the ball and *not* the flowers, or stop the game. Dr. Daruwalla understood this, yet he couldn't decide—no more than he could bring himself to tell Inspector Dhar the upsetting news. After all, the doctor thought, how can I hope to be any better than my proven abilities? And how can I stop it, when "it" is merely what I do?

It soothed him to think of the circus. Like a child who's proud to recite the names of Santa's reindeer or the Seven Dwarfs, Farrokh tested himself by remembering the names of the Great Royal's lions: Ram, Raja, Wazir, Mother, Diamond, Shanker, Crown, Max, Hondo, Highness, Lillie Mol, Leo and Tex. And then there were the cubs: Sita, Gita, Julie, Devi, Bheem and Lucy. The lions were most dangerous between their first and second feedings of meat. The meat made their paws slippery; while they paced in their cages, in expectation of their second serving, they often slipped and fell down, or they slid sideways into the bars. After their second feeding, they calmed down and licked the grease off their paws. With lions, you could count on certain things. They were always themselves. Lions didn't try to be what they couldn't be, the way Dr. Daruwalla kept trying to be a writer—the way I keep trying to be an Indian! he thought.

And in 15 years, he'd not found a genetic marker for achondroplastic dwarfism, nor had anyone encouraged him to look. But he kept trying. The doctor's dwarf-blood project wasn't dead; he wouldn't let it die—not yet.

Because an Elephant Stepped on a Seesaw

By the time Dr. Daruwalla was in his late fifties, the exuberant details of the doctor's conversion to Christianity were entirely absent from his conversation; it was as if he were slowly becoming unconverted. But 15 years ago—as the doctor drove to the circus grounds at Cross Maidan to assess what damage had been done to the dwarf—Farrokh's faith was still new enough that he'd already imparted the miraculous particulars of his belief to Vinod. If the dwarf was truly dying, the doctor was at least slightly comforted by his memory of their religious discussion—for Vinod was a deeply religious man. In the coming years, Farrokh's faith would comfort him less deeply, and he would one day flee from *any* religious discourse with Vinod. Over time, the dwarf would strike the doctor as a giant zealot.

But while the doctor was en route to discover whatever disaster had befallen the dwarf at the Great Blue Nile, he found it heartening to dwell on the dwarf's expressed excitement over the parallels between Vinod's version of Hinduism and Dr. Daruwalla's Christianity.

"We are having a kind of Trinity, too!" the dwarf had exclaimed.

"Brahma, Shiva, Vishnu—is that what you mean?" the doctor asked.

"All creation is being in the hands of three gods," Vinod said. "First is Brahma, the God of Creation—there is only one temple in all of India to him! Second is Vishnu, the God of Preservation or Existence. And third is Shiva, the God of Change."

"Change?" Farrokh asked. "I thought Shiva was the Destroyer—the God of Destruction."

"Why is everyone saying this?" the dwarf exclaimed. "All creation is being cyclic—there is no finality. I am liking it better to think of Shiva as the God of Change. Sometimes death is change, too."

"I see," Dr. Daruwalla replied. "That's a positive way of looking at it."

"This is our Trinity," the dwarf went on. "Creation, Preservation, Change."

"I guess I don't understand the *female* forms," Farrokh boldly admitted.

"The power of the gods is being represented by the females," Vinod explained. "Durga is the female form of Shiva—she is the Goddess of Death and Destruction."

"But you just said Shiva was the God of Change," the doctor interjected.

"His *female* form, Durga, is the Goddess of Death and Destruction," the dwarf repeated.

"I see," Dr. Daruwalla responded; it seemed best to say so.

"Durga is looking after me—I am praying to her," Vinod added.

"The Goddess of Death and Destruction is looking after you?" Farrokh inquired.

"She is always protecting me," the dwarf insisted.

"I see," Dr. Daruwalla said; he guessed that being protected by the Goddess of Death and Destruction had a kind of karmic ring to it.

Finally, Farrokh found Vinod lying in the dirt under the bleachers; it appeared that the dwarf had fallen through the wooden planks, from perhaps the fourth or fifth row of seats. The roustabouts had cleared the crowd from only a small section of the audience area, below which Vinod lay, unmoving. But how and why the dwarf had landed there wasn't immediately clear. Was there a clown act that required audience participation?

On the far side of the ring, a desultory gathering of dwarf clowns was bravely trying to keep the crowd's attention; it was the familiar Farting Clown act—through a hole in the seat of his colorful pants, one dwarf kept "farting" talcum powder on the other dwarfs. They didn't appear to be weakened or otherwise the worse for giving the doctor a Vacutainer of their blood, which Vinod had shamelessly entreated them to do; just as shamelessly, Dr. Daruwalla had lied to them—exactly as Vinod had advised him. The dwarfs' blood would be used to give strength to a dying dwarf; Vinod had even compounded this fiction by telling his fellow clowns that he'd already been bled to the doctor's satisfaction.

This time, mercifully, the ringmaster's voice on the loudspeaker had not heralded the doctor's arrival. Since Vinod lay under the bleacher seats, most of the crowd couldn't see him. Farrokh knelt in the dirt, which was littered with the audience's leavings: greasy paper cones, soft-drink bottles, peanut shells and discarded betel-nut pieces. On the underside of the bleachers, Farrokh could see the white stripes of lime paste that streaked the wooden planks; the paan users had wiped their fingers under their seats.

"I think I am not ending up here," Vinod whispered to the doctor. "I think I am not dying—just changing."

"Try not to move," Dr. Daruwalla replied. "Just tell me where you're hurting."

"I am not moving. I am not hurting," the dwarf answered. "I am just not feeling my backside."

Quite in character for a man of faith, the dwarf lay stoically suffering with his trident hands crossed upon his chest. He complained later that no one had dared to approach him, except a vendor—a channa-walla with his tray of nuts around his neck. Vinod had told the vendor about the numbness in his backside; hence the ringmaster assumed that the dwarf had broken his neck or his back. Vinod thought that someone should at least have talked to him or listened to the story of his life; someone should have held his head or offered him water until the stretcher bearers in their dirty-white dhotis came for him.

"This is Shiva—this is being his business," the dwarf told Dr. Daruwalla. "This is change—not death, I think. If Durga is doing this, then okay—I am dying. But I think I am merely changing."

"Let's hope so," Dr. Daruwalla replied; he made Vinod grip his fingers. Then the doctor touched the backs of Vinod's legs.

"I am feeling you only a little," the dwarf responded.

"I'm touching you only a little," Farrokh explained.

"This is meaning I am not dying," said the dwarf. "This is merely the gods advising me."

"What are they telling you?" the doctor asked.

"They are saying I am ready to leave the circus," Vinod answered. "At least *this* circus."

Slowly, the faces from the Great Blue Nile gathered around them. The ringmaster, the boneless girls and the plastic ladies—even the lion tamer, who toyed with his whip. But the doctor wouldn't allow the stretcher bearers to move the dwarf until someone explained how Vinod had been injured. Vinod believed that only the other dwarfs could describe the accident properly; for this reason, the Farting Clown act had to be halted. By now the act had deteriorated in the usual fashion: the offending dwarf was farting talcum powder into the front-row seats. Since the front row of the audience was chiefly populated with children, the farting was considered no great offense. However, the crowd was already dispersing; the Farting Clown act was never funny for very long. The Great Blue Nile had exhausted its entire repertoire in a half-successful effort to keep the audience seated until the doctor arrived.

Now the gathering clowns confessed to the doctor that Vinod had been injured in other acts, before. Once he'd fallen off a horse; once he'd been chased and bitten by a chimpanzee. Once, when the Blue Nile had a female bear, the bear had butted Vinod into a bucket of diluted shaving lather; this was a scripted part of the act, but the bear had butted Vinod too hard—he'd had his breath knocked out, and (as a consequence) the dwarf had then inhaled and swallowed the soapy water. Vinod's fellow clowns had also seen him hurt in the Cricket-Playing Elephants act. Apparently, to the degree that Dr. Daruwalla could understand the stunt at all, one elephant was the bowler and a second elephant was the batsman; it held and swung the bat with its trunk. Vinod was the cricket ball. It *hurt* to be bowled by one elephant and batted by another, even though the bat was made of rubber.

As Farrokh would learn later, the Great Royal Circus never put *their* dwarf clowns at such risk, but this was the Great Blue Nile. The terrible teeterboard accident, which was responsible for Vinod's pained position under the bleacher seats, was simply another elephant act of ill repute. The acts in an Indian circus are called "items"; in terms of accuracy, the

Elephant on a Teeterboard item wasn't as precise as the Cricket-Playing Elephants but it was a favorite with children, who were more familiar with a seesaw or a teeter-totter than with cricket.

In the Elephant on a Teeterboard item, Vinod acted the part of a crabby clown, a spoilsport who wouldn't play with his fellow dwarfs on the seesaw. Whenever they balanced the teeter-totter, Vinod jumped on one end and knocked them all off. Then he sat on the teeterboard with his back to them. One by one, they crept onto the other end of the board, until Vinod was up in the air; whereupon, he turned around and slid down the board into the other dwarfs, knocking them all off again. It was thus established for the audience that Vinod was guilty of antisocial behavior. His fellow dwarfs left him sitting on one end of the seesaw, with his back to them, while they fetched an elephant.

The only part of this act that is of possible interest to grownups is the demonstration that elephants can count—at least as high as three. The dwarfs tried to coax the elephant to stamp on the raised end of the teeterboard while Vinod was sitting on the other end, but the elephant was taught to delay stamping on the teeterboard until the third time. The first two times that the elephant raised its huge foot above the teeterboard, it *didn't* stamp on the board; twice, at the last second, it flapped its ears and turned away. The idea was planted with the audience that the elephant wouldn't really do it. The third time, when the elephant stamped down on the seesaw and Vinod was propelled into the air, the crowd was properly surprised.

Vinod was supposed to be launched upward into the rolled nets that were lowered only for the trapeze performance. He would cling to the underside of this netting like a bat, screaming at his fellow dwarfs to get him down. Naturally, they couldn't reach him without the help of the elephant, of which Vinod was demonstrably afraid. Typical circus slapstick; yet it was important that the teeterboard was aimed *exactly* at the rolled-up safety nets. That fateful night his life changed, Vinod realized (as he sat on the seesaw) that the teeterboard was pointed into the audience.

This could be blamed on the Kingfisher lager; such big bottles of beer had an unsteadying effect on dwarfs. Dr. Daruwalla would never again bribe dwarfs with beer. Sadly, the seesaw was pointed in the wrong direction *and* Vinod had neglected to count the number of times that the elephant had raised its foot, which the dwarf had previously managed to do without seeing the elephant; Vinod always counted the times the elephant raised its foot by the gasps of anticipation in the audience. Of course, Vinod could have turned his head and looked at the elephant to see where the beast's great foot was. But Vinod held himself accountable for certain standards: if he'd turned to look at the elephant, it would have spoiled the act completely.

As it happened, Vinod was flung into the fourth row of seats. He remembered hoping that he wouldn't land on any children, but he needn't have worried; the audience scattered before he arrived. He struck the empty wooden bleachers and fell through the space between the planks.

Created by spontaneous mutation, an achondroplastic dwarf lives in pain; his knees ache, his elbows ache—not to mention that they won't extend. His ankles ache and his back aches, too—not to mention the degenerative arthritis. Of course there are worse types of dwarfism: pseudoachondroplastic dwarfs suffer so-called windswept deformities— bowleg on one limb, knock-knee on the other. Dr. Daruwalla had seen dwarfs who couldn't walk at all. Even so, given the pain that Vinod was accustomed to, the dwarf didn't mind that his backside was numb; it was possibly the best that the dwarf had felt in years—in spite of being catapulted 40 feet by an elephant and landing on his coccyx on a wooden plank.

Thus did the injured dwarf become Dr. Daruwalla's patient. Vinod had suffered a slight fracture in the apex of his coccyx, and he'd bruised the tendon of his external sphincter muscle, which is attached to this apex; in short, he'd quite literally busted his ass. Vinod had also torn some of the sacrosciatic ligaments, which are attached to the narrow borders of the coccyx. The numbness of his backside, which soon abated—thence Vinod would return to the world of his routine aches and pains—was possibly the result of some pressure on one or more of the sacral nerves. His recovery would be complete, although slower than Deepa's; yet Vinod insisted he'd been permanently disabled. What he meant was he'd lost his nerve.

Future flight experiments with the clowns of the Great Blue Nile would have to be conducted without Vinod's participation—or so the dwarf claimed. If Shiva was the God of Change, and not merely the Destroyer, perhaps the change that Lord Shiva intended for Vinod was actually a career move. But the veteran clown would always be a dwarf, and Vinod struck Farrokh as lacking the qualifications for a job outside the circus.

Vinod and his wife were recovering from their respective surgeries when the Great Blue Nile completed its term of engagement in Bombay. While both Deepa and her dwarf husband were hospitalized, Dr. Daruwalla and his wife took care of Shivaji; after all, someone had to look after the dwarf child—and the doctor still held himself accountable for the Kingfisher. It had been some years since the Daruwallas had struggled to manage a two-year-old, and they'd never before tried to manage a *dwarf* two-year-old, but this period of convalescence proved fruitful for Vinod.

The dwarf was a compulsive list maker, and he enjoyed showing his lists to Dr. Daruwalla. There was quite a long list of Vinod's acquired circus skills, and a sadly shorter list of the dwarf's other accomplishments. On the shorter list, Dr. Daruwalla saw it written that the dwarf could drive a car. Farrokh felt certain that Vinod was lying; after all, hadn't Vinod proposed that very lie which the doctor had used to bleed the dwarfs of the Great Blue Nile?

"What sort of car can you drive, Vinod?" the doctor asked the recuperating dwarf. "How can your feet reach the pedals?"

It was to another word on the short list that Vinod proudly pointed. The word was "mechanics"; Farrokh had at first ignored it—he'd skipped straight to "car driving." Dr. Daruwalla assumed that "mechanics" meant fixing unicycles or other toys of the circus, but Vinod had dabbled in auto mechanics *and* in unicycles; the dwarf had actually designed and installed hand controls for a car. Naturally, this was inspired by a dwarf item for the Great Blue Nile: ten clowns climb out of one small car. But first a dwarf had to be able to drive the car; that dwarf had been Vinod. The hand controls had been complicated, Vinod confessed. ("Lots of experiments are failing," Vinod said philosophically.) The driving, the dwarf said, had been relatively easy.

"You can drive a car," Dr. Daruwalla said, as if to himself.

"Both fast and slow!" Vinod exclaimed.

"The car must have an automatic transmission," Farrokh reasoned.

"No clutching—just braking and speeding," the dwarf explained.

"There are *two* hand controls?" the doctor inquired.

"Who is needing more than two?" the dwarf asked.

"So . . . when you slow down or speed up, you must have just *one* hand on the steering wheel," Farrokh inferred.

"Who is needing both hands for steering?" Vinod replied.

"You can drive a car," Dr. Daruwalla repeated.

Somehow, this seemed harder to believe than the Elephant on a Teeterboard or the Cricket-Playing Elephants—for Farrokh could imagine no other life for Vinod. The doctor believed that the dwarf was doomed to be a clown for the Great Blue Nile forever.

"I am teaching Deepa to do car driving, too," Vinod added.

"But Deepa doesn't need hand controls," Farrokh observed.

The dwarf shrugged. "At the Blue Nile, we are naturally driving the same car," he explained.

Thus, it was there—in the dwarf's ward in the Hospital for Crippled Children—that a future hero of "car driving" was first introduced to Dr. Daruwalla. Farrokh simply couldn't imagine that, 15 years later, a veritable limousine legend would have been born in Bombay. Not that Vinod would immediately escape the circus; all legends take time. Not that Deepa, the dwarf's wife, would in the end entirely escape the circus. Not that Shivaji, the dwarf's son, would ever dream of escaping it. But all this was truly happening because Dr. Farrokh Daruwalla wanted blood from dwarfs.

3. THE REAL POLICEMAN

Mrs. Dogar Reminds Farrokh of Someone Else

For 15 years, Dr. Daruwalla would indulge himself with his memory of Deepa in the safety net. Of course this is an exaggeration, of that kind which caused the doctor to often reflect on his surprise at Vinod becoming a veritable limousine legend in Bombay; in the heyday of the dwarf's success at car driving, Vinod could never be credited with chauffeuring a *limo*, much less owning a limousine company. At best, Vinod owned a half-dozen cars; none of them was a Mercedes—including the two that the dwarf drove, with hand controls.

What Vinod would briefly manage to achieve was a modest profit in the private-taxi business, or "luxury taxis" as they're called in Bombay. Vinod's cars were never luxurious—nor could the dwarf have managed private ownership of these thoroughly secondhand vehicles without accepting a loan from Dr. Daruwalla. If the dwarf was even fleetingly a legend, neither the number nor the quality of Vinod's automobiles was the reason—they were *not* limousines. The dwarf's legendary status owed its existence to Vinod's famous client, the aforementioned actor with the improbable name of Inspector Dhar. At most, Dhar lived part-time in Bombay.

And poor Vinod could never completely sever his ties to the circus.

Shivaji, the dwarf's dwarf son, was now a teenager; as such, he suffered from strong and contrary opinions. Had Vinod continued to be an active clown in the Great Blue Nile, Shivaji would doubtless have rejected the circus; the contentious boy would probably have chosen to drive a taxi in Bombay—purely out of hatred for the very idea of being a *comic* dwarf. But since his father had made such an effort to establish a taxi business, and since Vinod had struggled to free himself from the dangerous daily grind of the Great Blue Nile, Shivaji was determined to become a clown. Therefore, Deepa often traveled with her son; and while the Blue Nile was performing throughout Gujarat and Maharashtra, Vinod devoted himself to the car-driving business in Bombay.

For 15 years, the dwarf had been unable to teach his wife how to drive. Since her fall, Deepa had given up the trapeze, but the Blue Nile paid her to train the child contortionists; while Shivaji developed his skills as a clown, his mother put the plastic ladies through their boneless items. When the dwarf succumbed to missing his wife and son, he'd go back to the Blue Nile. There Vinod eschewed the riskier acts in the dwarf-clown repertoire, contenting himself with instructing the younger dwarfs, his own son among them. But whether clowns are shot off seesaws by elephants, or chased by chimps, or butted by bears, there's only so much for them to learn. Beyond the demanding drills, which require practice—how to dismount the collapsing unicycle, and so forth—only makeup, timing and falling can be taught. At the Great Blue Nile, it seemed to Vinod that there was mainly falling.

In his absence from Bombay, Vinod's taxi enterprise would suffer and the dwarf would feel compelled to return to the city. Since Dr. Daruwalla was only periodically in India, the doctor couldn't always keep track of where Vinod was; as if trapped in a ceaseless clown item, the dwarf was constantly moving.

What was also constant was Farrokh's habit of letting his mind wander to that long-ago night when he had bashed his nose on Deepa's pubic bone. Not that this was the only circus image that the doctor's mind would wander to; those scratchy sequins on Deepa's tight singlet, not to mention the conflicting scents of Deepa's earthy aroma—these were understandably the most vivid circus images in Farrokh's memory. And at no time did Dr. Daruwalla daydream so vividly about the circus as he did when anything unpleasant was pending.

Currently, Farrokh found himself reflecting that, for 15 years, Vinod had steadfastly refused to give the doctor a single Vacutainer of blood. Dr. Daruwalla had drawn the blood from almost every active dwarf clown, in almost every active circus in Gujarat and Maharashtra, but the doctor hadn't drawn a drop from Vinod. As angry as this fact made him, Farrokh preferred to reflect on it rather than to concern himself with the more pressing problem, which was suddenly at hand.

Dr. Daruwalla was a coward. That Mr. Lal had fallen on the golf course, without a net, was no reason not to tell Inspector Dhar the upsetting news. Quite simply, the doctor didn't dare tell Dhar.

It was characteristic of Dr. Daruwalla to tell belabored jokes, especially when he'd made a disquieting self-discovery. Inspector Dhar was characteristically silent—"characteristically," depending on which rumors you believed. Dhar knew that Farrokh had been fond of Mr. Lal, and that the doctor's strident sense of humor was most often engaged when he sought to distract himself from any unhappiness. At the Duckworth Club, Dhar spent most of lunch listening to Dr. Daruwalla go on and on about this new offense to the Parsis: how the recent Parsi dead had been overlooked by the vultures attending to Mr. Lal on the golf course. Farrokh found a forced humor in imagining the more fervent Zoroastrians who'd be up in arms about the interference caused to the vulture community by the dead golfer. Dr. Daruwalla thought they should ask Mr. Sethna if *he* was offended; throughout lunch the old steward had managed to look most offended, although the source of the particular offense appeared to be the second Mrs. Dogar. It was clear that Mr. Sethna disapproved of her, whatever her intentions.

She'd deliberately positioned herself at her table so that she could stare at Inspector Dhar, who never once returned her gaze. Dr. Daruwalla assumed it was just another case of an immodest woman seeking Dhar's attention—in vain, the doctor knew. He wished he could prepare the second Mrs. Dogar for how rejected she would soon feel from the actor's obliviousness to her. For a while, she'd even pushed her chair away from the table so that her fetching navel was beautifully framed by the bold colors of her sari; her navel was pointed at Dhar like a single and very determined eye. Although Mrs. Dogar's advances appeared to go unnoticed by Inspector Dhar, Dr. Daruwalla found it most difficult not to look at her.

In the doctor's view, her behavior was shameless for a married, middle-aged lady—Dr. Daruwalla calculated that she was in her early fifties. Yet Farrokh found the second Mrs. Dogar attractive, in a threatening kind of way. He couldn't locate exactly what it was that attracted him to the woman, whose arms were long and unflatteringly muscular, and whose lean, hard face was handsome and challenging in an almost masculine way. To be sure, her bosom was shapely (if not full) and her bottom was high and firm—especially for a woman her age—and there was no question that her long waist and aforementioned navel were enhancing contributions to the pleasurable impression she made in a sari. But she was too tall, her shoulders were too pronounced and her hands appeared absurdly large and restless; she picked up her silverware and toyed with it as if she were a bored child.

Furthermore, Farrokh had caught a glimpse of Mrs. Dogar's feet—actually, just one of her feet, which was bare. She must have kicked her shoes off under her table, but all that Dr. Daruwalla saw was a flash of her gnarled foot; a thin gold chain hung loosely around her surprisingly thick ankle and a wide gold ring gripped one of her clawlike toes.

Perhaps what attracted the doctor to Mrs. Dogar was how she reminded him of someone else, but he couldn't think of who it might be. A long-ago movie star, he suspected. Then, as a doctor whose patients were children, he realized that he might have known the new Mrs. Dogar as a child; why this would make the woman attractive to him was yet another, exasperating unknown. Moreover, the second Mrs. Dogar seemed not more than six or seven years younger than Dr. Daruwalla; virtually, they'd been children together.

Dhar caught the doctor by surprise when he said, "If you could see yourself looking at that woman, Farrokh, I think you'd be embarrassed." When he was embarrassed, the doctor had an annoying habit of abruptly changing the subject.

"And you! You should have seen *yourself!*" Dr. Daruwalla said to Inspector Dhar. "You looked like a bloody police inspector—I mean, you looked like the real bloody thing!"

It irritated Dhar when Dr. Daruwalla spoke such absurdly unnatural English; it wasn't even the English with a singsong Hindi lilt, which was also unnatural for Dr. Daruwalla. This was worse; it was something wholly fake—the affected British flavor of that particularly Indian English, the inflections of which were common among young college graduates working as food-and-beverage consultants at the Taj, or as production managers for Britannia Biscuits. Dhar knew that this unsuitable accent was Farrokh's self-consciousness talking—he was so out of it in Bombay.

Quietly, but in accentless English, Inspector Dhar spoke to his excited companion. "Which rumor about me are we encouraging today? Should I shout at you in Hindi? Or is this a good day for English as a second language?"

Dhar's sardonic tone and expression hurt Dr. Daruwalla, notwith-standing that these mannerisms were trademarks of the fictional charac-ter Dr. Daruwalla had created and that all of Bombay had come to loathe. Although the secret screenwriter had grown morally uncertain of his creation, this doubt was not discernible in the unreserved fondness that the doctor felt for the younger man; in public or in private, it was Dr. Daruwalla's love for Dhar that showed.

The taunting quality of Dhar's remarks, not to mention the sting of Dhar's delivery, wounded Dr. Daruwalla; even so, he regarded the slightly spoiled handsomeness of the actor with great tenderness. Dhar allowed his sneer to soften into a smile. With an affection that alarmed the nearest and ever-observant waiter—the same poor fellow whose daily course had coincided with the shitting crow and with the trouble-some tureen and ladle—the doctor reached out and clasped the younger man's hand.

In plain English, Dr. Daruwalla whispered, "I'm really just so sorry—I mean, I feel so sorry for you, my dear boy," he said.

"Don't," Inspector Dhar whispered back. His smile faded and his sneer returned; he freed his hand from the elder man's grip.

Tell him now! Dr. Daruwalla told himself, but he didn't dare—he didn't know where to begin.

They were sitting quietly with their tea and some sweets when the *real* policeman approached their table. They'd already been interrogated by the duty officer from the Tardeo Police Station, an Inspector Some-body—not very impressive. The inspector had arrived with a team of subinspectors and constables in two Jeeps—hardly necessary for a golf-ing death, Dr. Daruwalla had felt. The Tardeo inspector had been unctuous but condescending to Inspector Dhar and servile to Farrokh.

"I am hoping you are excusing me, Doctor," the duty officer had begun; his English was a strain. "I am being most sorry I am taking *your* time, saar," the inspector added to Inspector Dhar. Dhar responded in Hindi.

"You are not examining the body, Doctor?" the policeman asked; he persisted with his English.

"Certainly not," Dr. Daruwalla replied.

"You are never touching the body, saar?" the duty officer asked the famous actor.

"I are never touching it," Dhar answered in English—in a flawless imitation of the policeman's Hindi accent.

Upon departing, the duty officer's heavy brogues had scraped a little too loudly on the stone floor of the Duckworth Club's dining room; thus had the policeman's exit drawn Mr. Sethna's predictable disapproval. Doubtless the old steward had also disapproved of the condition of the duty officer's uniform; his khaki shirt was soiled by the thali the inspector must have encountered for lunch—a generous portion of dhal was slopped on his breast pocket, and a brightly colored stain (the obvious orange-yellow of turmeric) lit up the messy policeman's drab collar.

But the second policeman, who now approached their table in the Ladies' Garden, was no mere inspector; this man was of a higher rank—and of a noticeably elevated neatness. At the very least, he looked like a deputy commissioner. From Farrokh's research—for the Inspector Dhar screenplays were scrupulously researched, if not aesthetically pleasing—the screenwriter was certain that they were about to be confronted by a deputy commissioner from Crime Branch Headquarters at Crawford Market.

"All this for *golf?*" whispered Inspector Dhar, but not so loudly that the approaching detective could hear him.

Not a Wise Choice of People to Offend

As the most recent Inspector Dhar movie had pointed out, the official salary of a Bombay police inspector is only 2,500 to 3,000 rupees a month—roughly 100 dollars. In order to secure a more lucrative posting, in an area of heavy crime, an inspector would need to bribe an administrative officer. For a payment in the vicinity of 75,000 to 200,000 rupees (but generally for less than 7,000 dollars), an inspector might secure a posting that would earn him from 300,000 to 400,000 rupees a year (usually not more than 15,000 dollars). One issue posed by the new Inspector Dhar movie concerned just *how* an inspector making only 3,000 rupees a month could get his hands on the 100,000 rupees that were necessary for the bribe. In the movie, an especially hypocritical and corrupt police inspector accomplishes this by doubling as a pimp and a landlord for a eunuch-transvestite brothel on Falkland Road.

In the pinched smile of the second policeman who approached Dr. Daruwalla and Inspector Dhar at their table, there could be discerned the unanimous outrage of the Bombay police force. The prostitute community was no less offended; the prostitutes had greater cause for anger. The most recent movie, *Inspector Dhar and the Cage-Girl Killer,* seemed to be responsible for putting the lowliest of Bombay's prostitutes—the so-called cage girls—in particular peril. Because of the movie, about a serial killer who murders cage girls and draws an inappropriately mirthful elephant on their naked bellies, a *real* murderer appeared to have stolen the idea. Now *real* prostitutes were being killed and decorated in this cartoonish fashion; the actual murders were unsolved. In the red-light district, on Falkland Road and Grant Road —and throughout the multitude of brothels in the many lanes of Kamathipura—the hardworking whores had expressed a *real* desire to kill Inspector Dhar.

The feeling for vengeance toward Dhar was especially strong among the eunuch-transvestite prostitutes. In the movie, a eunuch-transvestite prostitute turns out to be the serial cartoonist and killer. This was offensive to eunuch-transvestites, for by no means were all of them prostitutes—nor were they ever known to be serial killers. They are an accepted third gender in India; they are called "hijras"—an Urdu word of masculine gender meaning "hermaphrodite." But hijras are not born hermaphrodites; they are emasculated—hence "eunuch" is the truer word for them. They are also a cult; devotees of the Mother Goddess Bahuchara Mata, they achieve their powers—either to bless or to curse—by being neither male nor female. Traditionally, hijras earn their living by begging; they also perform songs and dances at weddings and festivals—most of all, they give their blessings at births (of male infants, especially). And hijras dress as women—hence the term "eunuch-transvestite" comes closest to what they are.

The mannerisms of hijras are ultra-feminine but coarse; they flirt outrageously, and they display themselves with sexually overt gestures—inappropriate for women in India. Beyond their castration and their female dress, they do little to otherwise feminize themselves; most hijras eschew the use of estrogens, and some of them pluck their facial hair so indifferently, it's not uncommon to see them with several days' growth of beard. Should hijras find themselves abused or harassed, or should they encounter those Indians who've been seduced by Western values and who therefore don't believe in the hijras' "sacred" powers to bless and curse, hijras will be so bold as to lift their dresses and rudely expose their mutilated genitals.

Dr. Daruwalla, in creating his screenplay for *Inspector Dhar and the Cage-Girl Killer,* never intended to offend the hijras—there are more than 5,000 in Bombay alone. But, as a surgeon, Farrokh found their method of emasculation truly barbarous. Both castration and sex-change operations are illegal in India, but a hijra's "operation"—they use the English word—is performed by other hijras. The patient stares at a portrait of the Mother Goddess Bahuchara Mata; he is advised to bite his own hair, for there's no anesthetic, although the patient is sedated with alcohol or opium. The surgeon (who is not a surgeon) ties a string around the penis and the testicles in order to get a clean cut—for it is with one cut that both the testicles and the penis are removed. The patient is allowed to bleed freely; it's believed that maleness is a kind of poison, purged by bleeding. No stitches are made; the large, raw area is cauterized with hot oil. As the wound begins to heal, the urethra is kept open by repeated probing. The resultant puckered scar resembles a vagina.

Hijras are no mere cross-dressers; their contempt for simple transvestites (whose male parts are intact) is profound. These fake hijras are called "zenanas." Every world has its hierarchy. Within the prostitute community, hijras command a higher price than real women, but it was unclear to Dr. Daruwalla why this was so. There was considerable debate as to whether hijra prostitutes were homosexuals, although it was certain that many of their male customers used them in that way; and among hijra teenagers, even before their emasculation, studies indicated frequent homosexual activity. But Farrokh suspected that many Indian men favored the hijra prostitutes because the hijras were more like women than women; they were certainly bolder than any Indian woman—and with their almost-a-vagina, who knew what they could imitate?

If hijras themselves were homosexually oriented, why would they emasculate themselves? It seemed probable to the doctor that, although there were many customers in the hijra brothels who were homosexuals, not every customer went there for anal intercourse. Whatever one thought or said about hijras, they *were* a third gender—they were simply (or not so simply) another sex. What was also true was that, in Bombay, fewer and fewer hijras were able to support themselves by conferring blessings or by begging; more and more of them were becoming prostitutes.

But why had Farrokh chosen a hijra to be the serial killer and cartoonist in the most recent Inspector Dhar movie? Now that a real killer was imitating the behavior of the fictional character—the police would say only that the real killer's drawing was "an obvious variation on the movie theme"—Dr. Daruwalla had *really* gotten Inspector Dhar in trouble. This particular film had inspired something worse than hatred, for the hijra prostitutes not only approved of killing Dhar—they wanted to maim him first.

"They want to cut off your cock and balls, dear boy," Farrokh had warned his favorite young man. "You must be careful how you get around town!"

With a sarcasm that was consistent with his famous role, Dhar had replied in his most deadpan manner: "You're telling me." (It was something he said at least once in all his movies.)

In contrast to the lurid agitation caused by the most recent Inspector Dhar movie, the appearance of a real policeman among the proper Duckworthians seemed dull. Surely the hijra prostitutes hadn't murdered Mr. Lal! There'd been no indication that the body had been sexually mutilated, nor was there a possibility that even a demented hijra could have mistaken the old man for Inspector Dhar. Dhar never played golf.

A Real Detective at Work

Detective Patel, as Dr. Daruwalla had guessed, was a deputy commissioner of police—D.C.P. Patel, officially. The detective was from Crime Branch Headquarters at Crawford Market—*not* from the nearby Tardeo Police Station, as Farrokh had also correctly surmised—because certain evidence, discovered during the examination of Mr. Lal's body, had elevated the old golfer's death to a category of interest that was special to the deputy commissioner.

What such a category of interest could be wasn't immediately clear to Dr. Daruwalla or to Inspector Dhar, nor was Deputy Commissioner Patel inclined to clarify the matter promptly.

"You must forgive me, Doctor—please do excuse me, Mr. Dhar," the detective said; he was in his forties, a pleasant-looking man whose formerly delicate, sharp-boned face had slightly given way to his jowls. His alert eyes and the deliberate cadence of the deputy commissioner's speech indicated that he was a careful man. "Which one of you was the very first to find the body?" the detective asked.

Dr. Daruwalla could rarely resist making a joke. "I believe the very first to find the body was a vulture," the doctor said.

"Oh, quite so!" said the deputy commissioner, smiling tolerantly. Then Detective Patel sat down, uninvited, at their table—in the chair nearer Inspector Dhar. "*After* the vultures," the policeman said to the actor, "I believe *you* were the next to find the body."

"I didn't move it or even touch it," Dhar said, anticipating the question; it was a question *he* usually asked—in his movies.

"Oh, very good, thank you," said D.C.P. Patel, turning his attention to Dr. Daruwalla. "And *you*, most naturally, examined the body, Doctor?" he asked.

"I most naturally did *not* examine it," Dr. Daruwalla replied. "I'm an orthopedist, not a pathologist. I merely observed that Mr. Lal was dead."

"Oh, quite so!" Patel said. "But did you give any thought to the cause of death?"

"Golf," said Dr. Daruwalla; he'd never played the game but he detested it at a distance. Dhar smiled. "In Mr. Lal's case," the doctor continued, "I suppose you might say he was killed by an excessive desire to improve. He most probably had high blood pressure, too—a man his age shouldn't repeatedly lose his temper in the hot sun."

"But our weather is really quite cool," the deputy commissioner said.

As if he'd been thinking about it for an extended time, Inspector Dhar said, "The body didn't smell. The vultures stank, but not the body."

Detective Patel appeared to be surprised and favorably impressed by this report, but all he said was, "Precisely."

Dr. Daruwalla spoke with impatience: "My dear Deputy Commissioner, why don't you begin by telling us what you know?"

"Oh, that's absolutely not our way," the deputy commissioner cordially replied. "Is it?" he asked Inspector Dhar.

"No, it isn't," Dhar agreed. "Just when do you estimate the time of death?" he asked the detective.

"Oh, what a very good question!" Patel remarked. "We estimate this morning—not even two hours before you found the body!"

Dr. Daruwalla considered this. While Mr. Bannerjee had been searching the clubhouse for his opponent and old friend, Mr. Lal had strolled to the ninth green and the bougainvillea beyond, once more to practice a good escape from his nemesis of the day before. Mr. Lal had *not* been late for his appointed game; if anything, poor Mr. Lal had been a little too early—at least, too eager.

"But there wouldn't have been vultures so soon," Dr. Daruwalla said. "There would have been no scent."

"Not unless there was quite a lot of blood, or an open wound . . . and in this sun," Inspector Dhar said. He'd learned much from his movies, even though they were very bad movies; even D.C.P. Patel was beginning to appreciate that.

"Quite so," the detective said. "There *was* quite a lot of blood."

"There was a lot of blood by the time we *found* him!" said Dr. Daruwalla, who still didn't understand. "Especially around his eyes and mouth—I just assumed that the vultures had begun."

"Vultures start pecking where there's already blood, and at the naturally wet places," said Detective Patel. His English was unusually good for a policeman, even for a deputy commissioner, Dr. Daruwalla thought.

The doctor was sensitive about his Hindi; he was aware that Dhar spoke the language more comfortably than he did. This was a slight embarrassment for Dr. Daruwalla, who wrote all of Dhar's movie dialogue and his voice-over in English. The translation into Hindi was done by Dhar; those phrases that particularly appealed to him—there weren't many—the actor left in English. And here was a not-so-common policeman indulging in the one-upmanship of speaking English to the renowned *Canadian;* it was what Dr. Daruwalla called "the Canadian treatment"—when a Bombayite wouldn't even try to speak Hindi or Marathi to him. Although almost everyone spoke English at the Duckworth Club, Farrokh was thinking of something witty to say to Detective Patel in Hindi, but Dhar (in his accentless English) spoke first. Only then did the doctor realize that Dhar had not once used his showbusiness Hindi accent with the deputy commissioner.

"There was quite a lot of blood by one ear," the actor said, as if he'd never stopped wondering about it.

"Very good—there absolutely was!" said the encouraging detective. "Mr. Lal was struck behind one ear, and also once in the temple—probably after he fell."

"Struck by *what?*" Dr. Daruwalla asked.

"By *what*, we know—it was his putter!" said Detective Patel. "By *whom*, we don't know."

In the 130-year history of the Duckworth Sports Club—through all the perils of Independence and those many diverting occasions that could have led to violence (for example, those wild times when the inflammatory Lady Duckworth bared her breasts)—there had never been a murder! Dr. Daruwalla thought of how he would phrase this news to the Membership Committee.

It was characteristic of Farrokh not to consider his esteemed late father as the actual first murder victim in the 130-year history of Duckworthians in Bombay. The chief reason for this oversight was that Farrokh tried very hard not to think about his father's murder at all, but a secondary reason was surely that the doctor didn't want his father's violent death to cloud his otherwise sunny feelings for the Duckworth Club, which has already been described as the only place (other than the circus) where Dr. Daruwalla felt at home.

Besides, Dr. Daruwalla's father wasn't murdered *at* the Duckworth Club. The car that he was driving exploded in Tardeo, not in Mahalaxmi, although these are neighboring districts. But it was generally admitted, even among Duckworthians, that the car bomb was probably installed while the senior Daruwalla's car was parked in the Duckworth Club parking lot. Duckworthians were quick to point out that the only other person who was killed had no relationship to the club; the poor woman wasn't even an employee. She was a construction worker, and she was said to be carrying a straw basket full of rocks on her head when the flying right-front fender of the senior Daruwalla's car decapitated her.

But this was old news. The first Duckworthian to be murdered on the actual property of the Duckworth Club was Mr. Lal.

"Mr. Lal," explained Detective Patel, "was engaged in swinging what I believe they call a 'mashie,' or is it a 'wedgie'—what *do* they call the club you hit a chip shot with?" Neither Dr. Daruwalla nor Inspector Dhar was a golfer; a mashie *or* a wedgie sounded close enough to the real and stupid thing to them. "Well, it doesn't matter," the detective said. "Mr. Lal was holding one club when he was struck from behind with another—his own putter! We found it and his golf bag in the bougainvillea."

Inspector Dhar had assumed a familiar film pose, or else he was merely thinking; he lifted his face as his fingers lightly stroked his chin, which enhanced his sneer. What he said was something that Dr. Daruwalla and Deputy Commissioner Patel had heard him say many times before; he said it in every movie.

"Forgive me for sounding most theoretical," Dhar said. This favorite bit of dialogue was of that kind which Dhar preferred to deliver in English, although he'd delivered the line on more than one occasion in Hindi, too. "It seems," Dhar said, "that the killer didn't care especially *who* his victim was. Mr. Lal was not scheduled to meet anyone in the bougainvillea at the ninth green. It was an accident that he was there— the killer couldn't have known."

"Very good," said D.C.P. Patel. "Please go on."

"Since the killer didn't seem to care who he killed," Inspector Dhar said, "perhaps it was intended only that the victim be one of *us*."

"Do you mean one of the *members?*" cried Dr. Daruwalla. "Do you mean a *Duckworthian?*"

"It's just a theory," said Inspector Dhar. Again, this was an echo; it was something he said in every movie.

"There is some evidence to support your theory, Mr. Dhar," Detective Patel said almost casually. The deputy commissioner removed his sunglasses from the breast pocket of his crisp white shirt, which showed not a trace of evidence of his latest meal; he probed deeper into the pocket and extracted a folded square of plastic wrapping, large enough to cover a wedge of tomato or a slice of onion. From the plastic he unwrapped a two-rupee note that had previously been rolled into a typewriter, for typed on the serial-number side of the bill, in capital letters, was this warning: MORE MEMBERS DIE IF DHAR REMAINS A MEMBER.

"Forgive me, Mr. Dhar, if I ask you the obvious," said Detective Patel.

"Yes, I have enemies," Dhar said, without waiting for the question. "Yes, there are people who'd like to kill me."

"But *everyone* would like to kill him!" cried Dr. Daruwalla. Then he touched the younger man's hand. "Sorry," he added.

Deputy Commissioner Patel returned the two-rupee note to his pocket. As he put on his sunglasses, the detective's pencil-thin mustache suggested to Dr. Daruwalla a punctiliousness in shaving that the doctor had abandoned in his twenties. Such a mustache, etched both below the nose and above the lip, requires a younger man's steady hand. At his age, the deputy commissioner must have had to prop his elbow fast against the mirror, for shaving of this kind could only be accomplished by removing the razor blade from the razor and holding the blade *just so.* A time-consuming vanity for a man in his forties, Farrokh imagined; or maybe someone else shaved the deputy commissioner—possibly a younger woman, with an untrembling hand.

"In summary," the detective was saying to Dhar, "I don't suppose you know who *all* your enemies are." He didn't wait for an answer. "I suppose we could start with *all* the prostitutes—not just the hijras—and most policemen."

"I would start with the hijras," Farrokh broke in; he was thinking like a screenwriter again.

"I wouldn't," said Detective Patel. "What do the hijras care if Dhar is or isn't a member of this club? What they want is his penis and his testicles."

"You're telling me," said Inspector Dhar.

"I very much doubt that the murderer is a member of this club," said Dr. Daruwalla.

"Don't rule that out," Dhar said.

"I won't," said Detective Patel. He gave both Dr. Daruwalla and Inspector Dhar his card. "If *you* call me," he said to Dhar, "you better call me at home—I wouldn't leave any messages at Crime Branch Headquarters. You know all about how we policemen can't be trusted."

"Yes," the actor said. "I know."

"Excuse me, Detective Patel," said Dr. Daruwalla. "Where did you find the two-rupee note?"

"It was folded in Mr. Lal's mouth," the detective said.

When the deputy commissioner had departed, the two friends sat listening to the late-afternoon sounds. They were so absorbed in their listening that they didn't notice the prolonged departure of the second Mrs. Dogar. She left her table, then she stopped to look over her shoulder at the unresponsive Inspector Dhar, then she walked only a little farther before she stopped and looked again, then she looked *again*.

Watching her, Mr. Sethna concluded that she was insane. Mr. Sethna observed every stage of the second Mrs. Dogar's most complicated exit from the Ladies' Garden and the dining room, but Inspector Dhar didn't appear to see the woman at all. It interested the old steward that Mrs. Dogar had stared so exclusively at Dhar; not once had her gaze shifted to Dr. Daruwalla, and never to the policeman—but then, Detective Patel had kept his back to her.

Mr. Sethna also watched the deputy commissioner make a phone call from the booth in the foyer. The detective was momentarily distracted by Mrs. Dogar's agitated condition; as the woman marched to the driveway and ordered the parking-lot attendant to fetch her car, the policeman appeared to make note of her attractiveness, her haste and her expression of something like rage. Perhaps the deputy commissioner was considering whether or not this woman looked like someone who'd recently clubbed an old man to death; in truth, thought Mr. Sethna, the second Mrs. Dogar looked as if she *wanted* to murder someone. But Detective Patel paid only passing attention to Mrs. Dogar; he seemed more interested in his phone call.

The apparent topic of conversation was so domestic that it surpassed even the interest of Mr. Sethna, who eavesdropped only long enough to assure himself that D.C.P. Patel was not engaged in police business. Mr. Sethna was certain that the policeman was talking to his wife.

"No, sweetie," said the detective, who then listened patiently to the

receiver before he said, "No, I would have told you, sweetie." Then he
listened again. "Yes, of course I promise, sweetie," he finally said. For a
while, the deputy commissioner shut his eyes while he listened to the
receiver; in observing him, Mr. Sethna felt extremely self-satisfied that
he'd never married. "But I *haven't* dismissed your theories!" Detective
Patel suddenly said into the phone. "No, of course I'm not angry," he
added with resignation. "I'm sorry if I *sounded* angry, sweetie."

Not even as veteran a snoop as Mr. Sethna could stand another word;
he decided to permit the policeman to continue his conversation in
privacy. It was only a mild surprise to Mr. Sethna that D.C.P. Patel
spoke English to his own wife. The old steward concluded that this was
why the detective's English was above average—practice. But at what
a demeaning cost! Mr. Sethna returned to that part of the dining room
nearest the Ladies' Garden, and to his lengthy observation of Dr. Daruwalla and Inspector Dhar. They were still absorbed in the late-afternoon
sounds. They weren't much fun to observe, but at least they weren't
married to each other.

The tennis balls were back in action, and someone was snoring in the
reading room; the busboys, making their typical clatter, had cleared
every dining table but the table where the doctor and the actor sat with
their cold tea. (Detective Patel had polished off all the sweets.) The
sounds of the Duckworth Club spoke distinctly for themselves: the sharp
shuffling of a fresh deck of cards, the crisp contact of the snooker balls,
the steady sweeping out of the dance hall—it was swept at the same time
every afternoon, although there were rarely dances on weeknights.
There was also a ceaseless insanity to the patter and squeak of the shoes
on the polished hardwood of the badminton court; compared to the
frenzy of this activity, the dull whacking of the shuttlecock sounded like
someone killing flies.

Dr. Daruwalla believed that this wasn't a good moment to give Inspector Dhar more bad news. The murder and the unusual death threat
were quite enough for one afternoon. "Perhaps you should come home
for supper," Dr. Daruwalla said to his friend.

"Yes, I'd like that, Farrokh," Dhar said. Normally, he might have said
something snide about Dr. Daruwalla's use of the word "supper." Dhar
disliked too loose a use of the word; in the actor's fussy opinion, the
word should be reserved for either a light meal in the early evening or
for an after-the-theater repast. In Dhar's opinion, North Americans
tended to use the word as if it were interchangeable with dinner; Farrokh felt that supper *was* interchangeable with dinner.

There was something fatherly in his voice to Dhar when Dr. Daruwalla adopted a critical tone. He said to the actor, "It's quite out of character for you to sound off in such accentless English to a total stranger."

"Policemen aren't exactly strangers to me," Dhar said. "They talk to each other but they never talk to the press."

"Oh, I forgot you knew everything about police business!" Farrokh said sarcastically. But Inspector Dhar was back in character; he was good at keeping quiet. Dr. Daruwalla regretted what he'd said. He'd wanted to say, Oh, dear boy, you may not be the hero of *this* story! Now he wanted to say, Dear boy, there *are* people who love you—*I* love you. You surely must know I do!

But instead, Dr. Daruwalla said, "As guest chairman of the Membership Committee, I feel I must inform the committeemen of this threat to the other members. We'll vote on it, but I feel there will be strong opinion that the other members should know."

"Of course they should know," said Inspector Dhar. "And I should *not* remain a member," he said.

It was unthinkable to Dr. Daruwalla that an extortionist and a murderer could so swiftly and concretely disrupt the most cherished aspect of the character of the Duckworth Club, which (in his view) was a deep, almost remote sense of privacy, as if Duckworthians were afforded the luxury of not actually living in Bombay.

"Dear boy," said the doctor, "what will you do?"

Dhar's answer shouldn't have surprised Dr. Daruwalla as forcefully as it did; the doctor had heard the response many times, in every Inspector Dhar movie. After all, Farrokh had *written* the response. "What will I do?" Dhar asked himself aloud. "Find out who it is and get them."

"Don't speak to me in character!" Dr. Daruwalla said sharply. "You're not in a movie now!"

"I'm always in a movie," Dhar snapped. "I was *born* in a movie! Then I was almost immediately put into another movie, wasn't I?"

Since Dr. Daruwalla and his wife thought they were the only people in Bombay who knew exactly where the younger man had come from and everything about who he was, it was the doctor's turn to keep quiet. In our hearts, Dr. Daruwalla thought, there must abide some pity for those people who have always felt themselves to be separate from even their most familiar surroundings, those people who either *are* foreigners or who suffer a singular point of view that makes them *feel* as if they're foreigners—even in their native lands. In our hearts, Farrokh knew, there also abides a certain suspicion that such people *need* to feel set apart from their society. But people who initiate their loneliness are no less lonely than those who are suddenly surprised by loneliness, nor are they undeserving of our pity—Dr. Daruwalla felt certain of that. However, the doctor was unsure if he'd been thinking of Dhar or of himself.

Then Farrokh realized he was alone at the table; Dhar had departed as eerily as he'd arrived. The glint of Mr. Sethna's silver serving tray caught Dr. Daruwalla's eye, reminding him of that shiny something which the crow had held so briefly in its beak.

The old steward reacted to Dr. Daruwalla's recognition as if summoned. "I'll have a Kingfisher, please," the doctor said.

How the Doctor's Mind Will Wander

The late-afternoon light cast longer and longer shadows in the Ladies' Garden, and Dr. Daruwalla gloomily observed that the bright pink of the bougainvillea had turned a darker shade; it seemed to him that the flowers had a blood-red hue, although this was an exaggeration—quite characteristic of the creator of Inspector Dhar. In reality, the bougainvillea was as pink (*and* as white) as before.

Later, Mr. Sethna grew alarmed that the doctor hadn't touched his favorite beer.

"Is there something wrong?" the old steward asked, his long finger indicating the Kingfisher lager.

"No, no—it's not the beer!" Farrokh said; he took a swallow that gave him little comfort. "The beer is fine," he said.

Old Mr. Sethna nodded as if he knew everything that was troubling Dr. Daruwalla; Mr. Sethna presumed to know such things routinely.

"I know, I know," muttered the old Parsi. "The old days are gone— it's not like the old days."

Insipid truths were an area of Mr. Sethna's expertise that Dr. Daruwalla found most irritating. The next thing you know, Farrokh thought, the tedious old fool will tell me that I'm not my esteemed late father. Truly, the steward seemed on the verge of making another observation when an unpleasant sound came from the dining room; it reached Mr. Sethna and Dr. Daruwalla in the Ladies' Garden with the crass, attention-getting quality of a man cracking his knuckles.

Mr. Sethna went to investigate. Without moving from his chair, Farrokh already knew what was making the sound. It was the ceiling fan, the one the crow had landed on and used as a shitting platform. Perhaps the crow had bent the blade of the fan, or else the bird had knocked a screw loose; maybe the fan was operated by ball bearings running in a groove, and one of these was out of position, or if there was a ball-and-socket joint, it needed grease. The ceiling fan appeared to catch on something; it clicked as it turned. It faltered; it almost stopped but it kept turning. With each revolution, there was a snapping sound, as if the mechanism were about to grind to a halt.

Mr. Sethna stood under the fan, staring stupidly up at it. He probably doesn't remember the shitting crow, Dr. Daruwalla thought. The doctor was readying himself to take charge of the situation when the unpleasant noise simply stopped. The ceiling fan turned freely, as before. Mr. Sethna looked all around, as if he weren't sure how he'd arrived at this spot in the dining room. Then the steward's gaze fixed upon the Ladies' Garden, where Farrokh was still sitting. He's not the man his father was, the old Parsi thought.

4. THE OLD DAYS

The Bully

Dr. Lowji Daruwalla took a personal interest in the crippling conditions affecting children. As a child, he'd developed tuberculosis of the spine. Although he recovered sufficiently to become India's most famous pioneer in orthopedic surgery, he always said it was his own experience with spinal deformity—the fatigue and the pain imposed on him—that made his commitment to the care of cripples so steadfast and long-enduring. "A personal injustice is stronger motivation than any instinct for philanthropy," Lowji said. He tended to speak in statements. As an adult, he would forever be recognized by the telltale gibbousness of Pott's disease. All his life, Lowji was as humpbacked as a small, upright camel.

Is it any wonder that his son Farrokh felt inferior to such a commitment? He would enter his father's field, but only as a follower; he would continue to pay his respects to India, but he'd always feel he was a mere visitor. Education and travel can be humbling; the younger Dr. Daruwalla took naturally to feelings of intellectual inferiority. Possibly Farrokh too simplistically attributed his alienation to the one conviction in his life that was as paralyzing as his conversion to Christianity: that he was utterly without a sense of place, that he was a man without a country, that there was nowhere he could go where he felt he belonged—except the circus and the Duckworth Club.

But what can be said about a man who keeps his needs and his obsessions largely to himself? When a man expresses what he's afraid of, his fears and longings undergo revision in the telling and retelling—friends and family have their own ways of altering the material—and soon the so-called fears and longings become almost comfortable with overuse. But Dr. Daruwalla held his feelings inside himself. Not even his wife knew how out of it the doctor felt in Bombay—and how could she, if he wouldn't tell her? Since Julia was Viennese, however little Dr. Daruwalla knew about India, he knew more than she did. And "at home" in Toronto, Farrokh allowed Julia to be the authority; she was the boss there. This was an easy privilege for the doctor to extend to his wife because she believed that *he* was in charge in Bombay. For so many years now, he'd got away with this.

Of course his wife knew about the screenplays—but only that he wrote them, not what he truly felt about them. Farrokh was careful to speak lightly of them to Julia. He was quite good at mocking them; after all, they were a joke to everyone else—it was easy for Farrokh to convince his wife that the Inspector Dhar movies were just a joke to him. More important, Julia knew how much Dhar (the dear boy) meant to him. So what if she had no idea how much the screenplays meant to Farrokh, too? And so these things, because they were so deeply concealed, were more important to Dr. Daruwalla than they should have been.

As for Farrokh's not belonging, surely the same could never be said of his father. Old Lowji liked to complain about India, and the nature of his complaints was often puerile. His medical colleagues chided him for his intrepid criticism of India; it was fortunate for his patients, they said, that his surgical procedures were more careful—and more accurate. But if Lowji was off-the-wall about his own country, at least it *was* his own country, Farrokh thought.

A founder of the Hospital for Crippled Children in Bombay and the chairman of India's first Infantile Paralysis Commission, the senior Daruwalla published monographs on polio and various bone diseases that were the best of his day. A master surgeon, he perfected procedures for the correction of deformities, such as clubfoot, spinal curvature and wryneck. A superb linguist, he read the work of Little in English, of Stromeyer in German, of Guerin and Bouvier in French. An outspoken atheist, Lowji Daruwalla nevertheless persuaded the Jesuits to establish clinics, both in Bombay and in Poona, for the study and treatment of scoliosis, paralysis due to birth injuries, and poliomyelitis. It was largely Muslim money that he secured to pay for a visiting roentgenologist at the Hospital for Crippled Children; it was wealthy Hindus he hit on for the research and treatment programs he initiated for arthritis. Lowji even wrote a sympathy letter to U.S. President Franklin D. Roosevelt, an Episcopalian, mentioning the number of Indians who suffered from the president's condition; he received a polite reply and a personal check.

Lowji made a name for himself in the short-lived movement called Disaster Medicine, especially during the demonstrations prior to Independence and the bloody rioting before and after the Partition. To this day, volunteer workers in Disaster Medicine attempt to revive the movement by quoting his much-advertised advice. "In order of importance, look for dramatic amputations and severe extremity injuries before treating fractures or lacerations. Best to leave all head injuries to the experts, if there are any." Any experts, he meant—there were always head injuries. (Privately, he referred to the failed movement as Riot Medicine—"something India will always be in need of," old Lowji said.)

He was the first in India to respond to the revolutionary change in thinking about the origin of low back pain, for which he said the credit belonged to Harvard's Joseph Seaton Barr. Admittedly, Farrokh's esteemed father was better remembered at the Duckworth Sports Club for his ice treatments of tennis elbow and his habit, when drinking, of denouncing the waiters for their deplorable posture. ("Look at me! I have a hump, and I'm still standing up straighter than you!") In reverence of the great Dr. Lowji Daruwalla, rigidity of the spine was a habit ferociously maintained by the old Parsi steward Mr. Sethna.

Why, then, did the younger Dr. Daruwalla *not* revere his late father? It wasn't because Farrokh was the second-born son and the youngest of Lowji's three children; he'd never felt slighted. Farrokh's elder brother, Jamshed, who'd led Farrokh to Vienna and now practiced child psychiatry in Zürich, had also led Farrokh to the idea of a European wife. But old Lowji never opposed mixed marriages—not on principle, surely, and not in the case of Jamshed's Viennese bride, whose younger sister married Farrokh. Julia became old Lowji's favorite in-law; he preferred her company even to the London otologist who married Farrokh's sister—and Lowji Daruwalla was an unabashed Anglophile. After Independence, Lowji admired and clung to whatever Englishness endured in India.

But the source of Farrokh's lack of reverence for his famous father wasn't old Lowji's "Englishness," either. His many years in Canada had made a moderate Anglophile out of the younger Dr. Daruwalla. (Granted, Englishness in Canada is quite different from in India—not politically tainted, always socially acceptable; many Canadians like the British.)

And that old Lowji was outspoken in his loathing for Mohandas K. Gandhi did not upset Farrokh in the slightest. At dinner parties, especially with non-Indians in Toronto, the younger Daruwalla was quite pleased at the surprise he could instantly evoke by quoting his late father on the late Mahatma.

"He was a bloody charka-spinning, loin-clothed pandit!" the senior Daruwalla had complained. "He dragged his religion into his political activism—then he turned his political activism into a religion." And the old man was unafraid of expressing his views *in* India—and not only in the safety of the Duckworth Club. "Bloody Hindus . . . bloody Sikhs . . . bloody Muslims," he would say. "And bloody Parsis, too!" he would add, if the more fervent of the Zoroastrian faith pressed him for some display of Parsi loyalty. "Bloody Catholics," he would murmur on those rare occasions when he appeared at St. Ignatius—only to attend those dreadful school plays in which his own sons took small parts.

Old Lowji declared that dharma was "sheer complacency—nothing but a justification for nondoing." He said that caste and the upholding of untouchability was "nothing but the perpetual worship of shit—if you worship shit, most naturally you must declare it the duty of certain people to take the shit away!" Absurdly, Lowji presumed he was permitted to make such irreverent utterances because the evidence of his dedication to crippled children was unparalleled.

He railed that India was without an ideology. "Religion and nationalism are our feeble substitutes for constructive ideas," he pronounced. "Meditation is as destructive to the individual as caste, for what is it but a way of diminishing the self? Indians follow groups instead of their own ideas: we subscribe to rituals and taboos instead of establishing goals for social change—for the improvement of our society. Move the bowels before breakfast, not after! Who cares? Make the woman wear a veil! Why bother? Meanwhile, we have no rules against filth, against chaos!"

In such a sensitive country, brashness is frankly stupid. In retrospect, the younger Dr. Daruwalla realized that his father was a car bomb waiting to happen. No one—not even a doctor devoted to crippled children—can go around saying that "karma is the bullshit that keeps

India a backward country." The idea that one's present life, however horrible, is the acceptable payment for one's life in the past may fairly be said to be a rationale for doing nothing conducive to self-improvement, but it's surely best *not* to call such a belief "bullshit." Even as a Parsi, and as a convert to Christianity—and although Farrokh was never a Hindu—the younger Dr. Daruwalla saw that his father's overstatements were unwise.

But if old Lowji was dead set against Hindus, he was equally offensive in speaking of Muslims—"Everyone should send a Muslim a roast pig for Christmas!"—and his prescriptions for the Church of Rome were dire indeed. He said that every last Catholic should be driven from Goa, or, preferably, publicly executed in remembrance of the persecutions and burnings at the stake that they themselves had performed. He proposed that "the disgusting cruelty depicted on the crucifix shouldn't be allowed in India"—he meant the mere sight of Christ on the cross, which he called "a kind of Western pornography." Furthermore, he declared that all Protestants were closet Calvinists—and that Calvin was a closet Hindu! Lowji meant by this that he loathed anything resembling the acceptance of human wretchedness—not to mention a belief in divine predestination, which Lowji called "Christian dharma." He was fond of quoting Martin Luther, who had said: "What wrong can there be in telling a downright good lie for a good cause and for the advancement of the Christian Church?" By this Lowji meant that he believed in free will, and in so-called good works, *and* in "no damn God at all."

As for the car bomb, there was an old rumor at the Duckworth Club that it had been the brainchild of a Hindu-Muslim-Christian conspiracy—perhaps the first cooperative effort of its kind—but the younger Dr. Daruwalla knew that even the Parsis, who were rarely violent, couldn't be ruled out as contributing assassins. Although old Lowji was a Parsi, he was as mocking of the true believers of the Zoroastrian faith as he was of *any* true believers. Somehow, only Mr. Sethna had escaped his contempt, and Lowji stood alone in Mr. Sethna's esteem; he was the only atheist who'd never suffered the zealous steward's undying scorn. Perhaps it was the hot-tea incident that bound them together and overcame even their religious differences.

To the end, it was the concept of dharma that Lowji could least leave alone. "If you're born in a latrine, it's better to die in the latrine than to aspire to a better-smelling station in life! Now I ask you: Is that not nonsense?" But Farrokh felt that his father was crazy—or that, outside the field of orthopedic surgery, the old humpback simply didn't know what he was talking about. Even beggars aspired to improve, didn't they? One can imagine how the calm of the Duckworth Club was often shattered by old Lowji declaring to everyone—even the waiters with bad posture—that caste prejudice was the root of all evil in India, although most Duckworthians privately shared this view.

What Farrokh most resented about his father was how the contentious old athiest had robbed him of a religion *and* a country. More than intellectually spoiling the concept of a nation for his children, because of his unrestrained hatred of nationalism, Dr. Lowji Daruwalla had driven his children away from Bombay. For the sake of their education and refinement, he'd sent his only daughter to London and his two sons to Vienna; then he had the gall to be disappointed with all three of them for not choosing to live in India.

"Immigrants are immigrants all their lives!" Lowji Daruwalla had declared. It was just another of his pronouncements, but this one had a lasting sting.

Austrian Interlude

Farrokh had arrived in Austria in July of 1947 to prepare for his undergraduate studies at the University of Vienna; hence he missed Independence. (Later he thought he'd simply not been at home when it counted; thereafter, he supposed, he was never "at home.") What a time to be an Indian in India! Instead, young Farrokh Daruwalla was acquainting himself with his favorite dessert, *Sachertorte mit Schlag,* and making himself known to the other residents of the Pension Amerling on the Prinz Eugene Strasse, which was in the Soviet sector of occupation. In those days, Vienna was divided in four. The Americans and British grabbed the choicest residential districts, and the French took the best shopping areas. The Russians were realistic: they settled themselves in the outlying working-class precincts, where all the industry was, and they crouched around the Inner City, near the embassies and government buildings.

As for the Pension Amerling, its tall windows, with the rusted-iron flower boxes and yellowing curtains, overlooked the war rubble on the Prinz Eugene Strasse and faced the chestnut trees of the Belvedere Gardens. From his third-story bedroom window, young Farrokh could see that the stone wall between the upper and the lower Belvedere

term "wog"—at least the correct racial slur—was used. Doubtless it would have unnerved him to have been mistaken for a Hungarian Gypsy *twice*. And by his bold interference, young Daruwalla had saved the Allied Council from committing an embarrassing error; it was, therefore, never entered into the official minutes that a witness to *Fräulein* Hellein's rape and murder and decapitation had mistaken the victim for a giraffe. On top of everything else that the deceased had suffered, she was spared this further outrage.

But when young Farrokh Daruwalla returned to India in the fall of 1955, this episode was as much a part of history as he felt himself to be; he didn't come home a confident young man. Granted, he had not spent the entire eight years outside of India, but a brief visit in the middle of his undergraduate studies (in the summer of 1949) hardly prepared him for the confusion he would encounter six years later—when he came "home" to an India that would forever make him feel like a foreigner.

He was used to feeling like a foreigner; Vienna had prepared him for that. And his several pleasant visits to London to see his sister were marred by his one trip to London that coincided with his father's invitation to address the Royal College of Surgeons—a great honor. It was the obsession of Indians, and of former British colonies in general, to become Fellows of the Royal College of Surgeons—old Lowji was extremely proud of his "F," as it was called. The "F" would mean less to the younger Dr. Daruwalla, who would also become an F.R.C.S.—of Canada. But on the occasion of Farrokh attending his father's lecture in London, old Lowji chose to pay tribute to the American founder of the British Orthopedic Association—the celebrated Dr. Robert Bayley Osgood, one of the few Americans to captivate this British institution—and it was during Lowji's speech (which would go on to emphasize the problems of infantile paralysis in India) that young Farrokh overheard a most disparaging remark. It would keep him from ever considering a life in London.

"What monkeys they are," said a florid orthopedist to a fellow Brit. "They are the most presumptuous imitators. They observe us for all of five minutes, then they think they can do it, too."

Young Farrokh sat paralyzed in a room of men fascinated by the diseases of bones and joints; he couldn't move, he couldn't speak. This wasn't a simple matter of mistaking a prostitute for a giraffe. His own medical studies had just begun; he wasn't sure if he understood what the "it" referred to. Farrokh was so unsure of himself, he first supposed that the "it" was something medical—some actual knowledge—but before his father's speech had ended, Farrokh understood. "It" was only Englishness, "it" was merely *being them*. Even in a gathering of what his father boastfully called "fellow professionals," the "it" was all they'd noticed—simply what of their Englishness had been successfully or unsuccessfully copied. And for the remainder of old Lowji's exploration of infantile paralysis, young Farrokh was ashamed that he saw his ambitious father as the British saw him: a smug ape who'd succeeded in imitating *them*. It was the first time Farrokh realized how it was possible to love Englishness and yet loathe the British.

And so, before he ruled out India as a country where he could live, he'd already ruled out England. It was the summer of '49, during an at-home stay in Bombay, when young Farrokh Daruwalla suffered the experience that would (for him) rule out living in the United States, too. It was the same summer that another of his father's more embarrassing weaknesses was revealed to him. Farrokh discounted the continuous discomfort of his father's spinal deformity; this was not in the category of a weakness of any kind—on the contrary, Lowji's hump was a source of inspiration. But now, in addition to Lowji's overstatements of a political and religious nature, the senior Daruwalla unveiled a taste for romantic movies. Farrokh was already familiar with his father's unbridled passion for *Waterloo Bridge;* tears sprang to his father's eyes at the mere mention of Vivien Leigh, and no concept in storytelling struck old Lowji with such tragic force as those twists of fate that could cause a woman, both good and pure, to fall to the lowly rank of prostitute.

But in the summer of '49, young Farrokh was quite unprepared to find his father so infatuated with the commonplace hysteria of a film-in-progress. To make matters worse, it was a Hollywood film—of no special distinction beyond that endless capacity for compromise which was the principal gift of the film's participants. Farrokh was appalled to witness his father's slavishness before everyone who was even marginally involved.

One shouldn't be surprised that Lowji was vulnerable to movie people, or that the presumed glamour of postwar Hollywood was magnified by its considerable distance from Bombay. These particular lowlifes who'd invaded Maharashtra for the purpose of moviemaking had sizably damaged reputations—even in Hollywood, where shame is seldom suffered for long—but how could the senior Daruwalla have known this? Like many physicians the world over, Lowji imagined that he could have been a great writer—if medicine hadn't attracted him first—and he further deluded himself that a second career opportunity lay ahead of him, perhaps in his retirement. He supposed that, with more time on his hands, it would take no great effort to write a novel—and surely less to write a screenplay. Although the latter assumption is quite true, even the effort of a screenplay would prove too great for old Lowji; it was never necessarily the power of his imagination that gave him great technique and foresight as a surgeon.

Sadly, a natural arrogance often attends the ability to heal and cure. Renowned in Bombay—even recognized abroad for his accomplishments in India—Dr. Lowji Daruwalla nevertheless craved intimate contact with the so-called creative process. In the summer of 1949, with his highly principled younger son as a witness, the senior Daruwalla got what he desired.

Inexplicable Hairlessness

Often when a man of vision and character falls among the unscrupulous cowards of mediocrity, there is an intermediary, a petty villain in the guise of a matchmaker—one skilled in currying favor for small but gratifying gain. In this instance, she was a Malabar Hill lady of imposing wealth and only slightly less imposing presence; although she wouldn't have categorized herself as a maiden aunt, she played this role in the lives of her undeserving nephews—the two scoundrel sons of her impoverished brother. She'd also suffered the tragic history of having been jilted by the same man on two different wedding days, a condition that prompted Dr. Lowji Daruwalla to privately refer to her as "the Miss Havisham of Bombay—times two."

Her name was Promila Rai, and prior to her insidious role of introducing Lowji to the movie vermin, her communications with the Daruwalla family had been merely rude. She'd once sought the senior Daruwalla's advice regarding the inexplicable hairlessness of the younger of her loathsome two nephews—an odd boy named Rahul Rai. At the time of the doctor's examination, which Lowji had at first resisted conducting on the grounds that he was an orthopedist, Rahul was only 8 or 10. The doctor found nothing "inexplicable" about his hairlessness. The absence of body hair wasn't that unusual; the lad had bushy eyebrows and a thick head of hair. Yet Miss Promila Rai found old Lowji's analysis lacking. "Well, after all, you're only a *joint* doctor," she said dismissively, to the orthopedist's considerable irritation.

But now Rahul Rai was 12 or 13, and the hairlessness of his mahogany skin was more apparent. Farrokh Daruwalla, who was 19 in the summer of '49, had never liked the boy; he was an oily brat of a disquieting sexual ambiguity—possibly influenced by his elder brother, Subodh, a dancer and occasional actor in the emerging Hindi film scene. Subodh was better known for his flamboyant homosexuality than for his theatrical talents.

For Farrokh to return from Vienna to find his father on friendly terms with Promila Rai and her sexually suspect nephews—well, one can imagine. In his undergraduate years, young Farrokh had developed intellectual and literary pretensions that were easily offended by the Hollywood scum who'd ingratiated themselves with his vulnerable, albeit famous, father.

Quite simply, Promila Rai had wanted her actor-nephew Subodh to have a role in the movie; she also had wanted the prepubescent Rahul to be employed as a plaything of this court of creativity. The hairless boy's apparently unformed sexuality made him the little darling of the Californians; they found him an able interpreter and an eager errand boy. And what had the Hollywood types wanted from Promila Rai in exchange for making creative use of her nephews? They wanted access to a private club—to the Duckworth Sports Club, which was highly recommended even in their lowlife circles—and they wanted a doctor, someone to look after their ailments. In truth, it was their terror of all the *possible* ailments of India that needed looking after, for in the beginning there was nothing in the slightest that was ailing them.

It was a shock to young Farrokh to come home to this unlikely degradation of his father; his mother was mortified by his father's choice of such crude companions and by what she considered to be his father's shameless manipulation by Promila Rai. By giving this American movie rabble unlimited access to the club, old Lowji (who was chairman of the Rules Committee) had bent a sacred law of the Duckworthians. Previously, guests of members were permitted in the club only if they arrived *and remained with* a member, but the senior Daruwalla was so infatuated with his newfound friends that he'd extended special privileges to them. Moreover, the screenwriter, from whom Lowji believed he had the most to learn, was unwanted on the set; this sensitive artist and outcast had become a virtual resident of the Duckworth Club—and a constant source of bickering between Farrokh's parents.

It's often embarrassing to discover the marital cuteness that exists among couples whose social importance is esteemed. Farrokh's mother, Meher, was renowned for flirting with his father in public. Because there was nothing coarse in her overtures to her husband, Meher Daruwalla was recognized among Duckworthians as an exceptionally devoted wife; therefore, she'd attracted all the more attention at the Duckworth Club when she *stopped* flirting with Lowji. It was plain to everyone that Meher was feuding with Lowji instead. To young Farrokh's shame, the whole Duckworth Club was put on edge by this obvious tension in the venerable Daruwalla marriage.

A sizable part of Farrokh's summer agenda was to prepare his parents for the romance that was developing for their two sons with the fabulous Zilk sisters—"the Vienna Woods girls," as Jamshed called them. It struck Farrokh that the state of his parents' marriage might make an unfavorable climate for a discussion of romance of any kind—not to mention his parents' possible reluctance to accept the idea of their only sons marrying Viennese Roman Catholics.

It was typical of Jamshed's successful manipulation of his younger brother that Farrokh had been selected to return home for the summer in order to broach this subject. Farrokh was less intellectually challenging to Lowji; he was also the baby of the family, and therefore he appeared to be loved with the least reservation. And Farrokh's intentions to follow his father in orthopedics doubtless pleased the old man and made Farrokh a more welcome bearer of conceivably unwelcome tidings than Jamshed would have been. The latter's interest in psychiatry, which old Lowji spoke of as "an inexact science"—he meant in comparison with orthopedic surgery—had already driven a wedge between the father and his elder son.

In any case, Farrokh saw that it would be poor timing for him to introduce the topic of the *Fräuleins* Josefine and Julia Zilk; his praise of their loveliness and virtues would have to wait. The story of their courageous widowed mother and her efforts to educate her daughters would have to wait, too. The dreadful American movie was consuming Farrokh's helpless parents. Even the young man's intellectual pursuits failed to capture his father's attention.

For example, when Farrokh admitted that he shared Jamshed's passion for Freud, his father expressed alarm that Farrokh's devotion to the more exact science of orthopedic surgery was waning. It was certainly the wrong idea to attempt to reassure his father on this point by quoting at length from Freud's "General Remarks on Hysterical Attacks"; the concept that "the hysterical fit is an equivalent to coitus" wasn't welcome information to old Lowji. Furthermore, Farrokh's father absolutely rejected the notion of the hysterical symptom corresponding to a

form of sexual gratification. In regard to so-called multiple sexual identification—as in the case of the patient who attempted to rip off her dress
with one hand (this was said to be her *man's* hand) while at the same time
she desperately clutched her dress to her body (with her *woman's*
hand)—old Lowji Daruwalla was outraged by the concept.

"Is this the result of a European education?" he cried. "To attach any
meaning whatsoever to what a woman is thinking when she takes off her
clothes—this is true madness!"

The senior Daruwalla wouldn't listen to a sentence with Freud's
name in it. That his father should reject Freud was further evidence to
Farrokh of the tyrant's intellectual rigidity and his old-fashioned beliefs.
As an intended put-down of Freud, Lowji paraphrased an aphorism of
the great Canadian physician Sir William Osler. A bedside clinician
extraordinaire and a gifted essayist, Osler was a favorite of Farrokh's,
too. It was outrageous of Lowji to use Sir William to refute Freud; the
old blunderbuss referred to the well-known Osler admonition that
warns against studying medicine without textbooks—for this is akin to
going to sea without a chart. Farrokh argued that this was a half-
understanding of Osler and less than half an understanding of Freud, for
hadn't Sir William also warned that to study medicine without studying
patients was not to go to sea at all? Freud, after all, had studied patients.
But Lowji was unbudgeable.

Farrokh was disgusted with his father. The young man had left home
as a mere 17-year-old; at last he was a worldly and well read 19. Far from
being a paragon of brilliance and nobility, old Lowji now looked like a
buffoon. In a rash moment, Farrokh gave his father a book to read. It was
Graham Greene's *The Power and the Glory*, a modern novel—at least it
was "modern" to Lowji. It was also a religious novel, which was (in
Lowji's case) akin to holding the cape before the bull. Farrokh presented
the novel to his father with the added temptation that the book had
given considerable offense to the Church of Rome. This was a clever bit
of baiting, and the old man was especially excited to learn that the book
had been denounced by French bishops. For reasons Lowji never bothered to explain, he didn't like the French. For reasons he explained
entirely too often, Lowji thought *all* religions were "monsters."

It was surely idealistic of young Farrokh to imagine that he could
draw his fierce, old-fashioned father into his recently acquired European
sensibilities—especially by as simple a device as a favorite novel.
Naïvely, Farrokh hoped that a shared appreciation of Graham Greene
might lead to a discussion of the enlightened Zilk sisters, who, although

Roman Catholics, did not share the consternation caused the Church of Rome by *The Power and the Glory*. And this discussion might lead to the matter of who these liberal-thinking Zilk sisters might be, and so on and so forth.

But old Lowji despised the novel. He denounced it as morally contra-dictory—in his own words, "a big confusion of good and evil." In the first place, Lowji argued, the lieutenant who puts the priest to death is portrayed as a man of integrity—a man of high ideals. The priest, on the other hand, is utterly corrupted—a lecher, a drunk, an absent father to his illegitimate daughter.

"The man *should* have been put to death!" the senior Daruwalla exclaimed. "Only not necessarily because he was a priest!"

Farrokh was bitterly disappointed by this pig-headed reaction to a novel he so loved that he'd already read it a half-dozen times. He deliberately provoked his father by telling him that his denouncement of the book was remarkably similar to the line of attack taken by the Church of Rome.

And so the summer and the monsoon of 1949 began.

Stuck in the Past

Here come the characters who comprise the movie vermin, the Holly-wood scum, the film slime—the aforementioned "unscrupulous cowards of mediocrity." Fortunately, they are minor characters, yet so distasteful that their introduction has been delayed as long as possible. Besides, the past has already made an unwelcome intrusion into this narrative; the younger Dr. Daruwalla, who's no stranger to unwanted and lengthy intrusions from the past, has all this time been sitting in the Ladies' Garden of the Duckworth Club. The past has descended upon him with such lugubrious weight that he hasn't touched his Kingfisher lager, which has grown undrinkably warm.

The doctor knows he should at least get up from the table and call his wife. Julia should be told right away about poor Mr. Lal and the threat to their beloved Dhar: MORE MEMBERS DIE IF DHAR REMAINS A MEMBER. Farrokh should also forewarn her that Dhar is coming home for supper, not to mention that the doctor owes his wife some explanation regarding his cowardice; she will surely think him a coward for not telling Dhar the upsetting news—for Dr. Daruwalla knows that, any day now, Dhar's twin is expected in Bombay. Yet he can't even drink his beer or rise from his chair; it's as if he were the second bludgeoned victim of the putter that cracked the skull of poor Mr. Lal.

And all this time, Mr. Sethna has been watching him. Mr. Sethna is worried about the doctor—he's never seen him not finish a Kingfisher before. The busboys are whispering; they must change the tablecloths in the Ladies' Garden. The tablecloths for dinner, which are a saffron color, are quite different from the luncheon tablecloths, which are more of a vermillion hue. But Mr. Sethna won't allow them to disturb Dr. Daruwalla. He's not the man his father was, Mr. Sethna knows, but Mr. Sethna's loyalty to Lowji is unquestionably extended beyond the grave—not only to Lowji's children but even to that mysterious fair-skinned boy whom Mr. Sethna heard Lowji call "my grandchild" on more than one occasion.

Such is Mr. Sethna's loyalty to the Daruwalla name that he won't tolerate the gossip in the kitchen. There is, for example, an elderly cook who swears that this so-called grandchild is the very same all-white actor who parades before them as Inspector Dhar. Although Mr. Sethna privately may believe this, he violently maintains that this couldn't be true. If the younger Dr. Daruwalla claims that Dhar is neither his nephew nor his son—which he *has* claimed—this is good enough for Mr. Sethna. He declares emphatically to the kitchen staff, and to all the waiters and the busboys, too: "That boy we saw with old Lowji was someone else."

And now a half-dozen busboys glide into the failing light in the Ladies' Garden, Mr. Sethna silently directing them with his piercing eyes and with hand signals. There are only a few saucers and an ashtray, together with the vase of flowers and the warm beer, on Dr. Daruwalla's table. Each busboy knows his assignment: one takes the ashtray and another removes the tablecloth, precisely following the exact second when Mr. Sethna plucks up the neglected beer. There are three busboys who, between them, exchange the vermillion tablecloth for the saffron; then the same flower vase and a different ashtray are returned to the table. Dr. Daruwalla doesn't notice, at first, that Mr. Sethna has substituted a cold Kingfisher for the warm one.

It's only after they've departed that Dr. Daruwalla appears to appreciate how the dusk has softened the brightness of both the pink and the white bougainvillea in the Ladies' Garden, and how his brimming glass of Kingfisher is freshly beaded with condensation; the glass itself is so wet and cool, it seems to draw his hand. The beer is so cold and biting, he takes a long, grateful swallow—and then another and another. He drinks until the glass is empty, but still he stays at the table in the Ladies' Garden, as if he's waiting for someone—even though he knows his wife is expecting him at home.

For a while, the doctor forgets to refill his glass; then he refills it. It's a 21-ounce bottle—entirely too much beer for dwarfs, Farrokh remembers. Then a look crosses his face, of the kind one hopes will pass quickly. But the look remains, fixed and distant, and as bitter as the aftertaste of the beer. Mr. Sethna recognizes this look; he knows at once that the past has reclaimed Dr. Daruwalla, and by the bitterness of the doctor's expression, Mr. Sethna thinks he knows *which* past. It's those *movie* people, Mr. Sethna knows. They've come back again.

5. THE VERMIN

Learning the Movie Business

The director, Gordon Hathaway, would meet his end on the Santa Monica Freeway, but in the summer of '49 he was riding the fading success of a private-investigator movie. Perversely, it had inflamed his long-dormant desire to make what movie people call a "quality" picture. This picture wouldn't be it. Although the director would manage to shoot the film, overcoming considerable adversity, the movie would never be released. Having had his fling with "quality," Hathaway would return with a modest vengeance, and more modest success, to the so-called P.I. genre. In the 1960's, he would make the downward move to television, where he awaited the unnoticed conclusion of his career.

Few aspects of Gordon Hathaway's personality were unique. He called all actors and actresses by their first names, including the ones he'd never met, which was the case with most of them, and he wetly kissed on both cheeks both the men and women he was saying adieu to, which included those he'd met for only the first or second time. He would marry four times, in each marriage goatishly siring children who would revile him before they were teenagers. In each account, Gordon would be unsurprisingly cast as the villain, while the four respective mothers (his ex-wives) emerged as highly compromised yet sainted. Hathaway said he'd had the misfortune to sire only daughters.

Sons, he claimed, would have taken *his* side—to quote him, "At least one out of four fuckin' times."

As for his dress, he was a marginal eccentric; as he aged—and as he more peaceably embraced a directorial career of complete compromise—he grew more outlandish in his attire, as if his clothes had become his foremost creative act. Sometimes he wore a woman's blouse, open to the waist, and he arranged his hair in a long white ponytail, which became his trademark; in his many films and TV crime dramas, there could be found no such identifying features. And all the while, he decried the "suits"—which was his word for the producers—"the fuckin' three-piece mentalities," who, Hathaway said, had "a fuckin' stranglehold on all the talent in Hollywood."

This was an odd accusation, in that Gordon Hathaway had spent a long and modestly profitable career in close cahoots with these same "suits." Producers, in truth, *loved* him. But none of these details is original, or even memorable.

In Bombay, however, the first truly distinctive element of Gordon Hathaway's character was brought to light: namely, he was so frightened of the food in India—and so hysterically conscious of those diseases that, he was certain, would destroy his intestinal tract—that he ate nothing but room-service food, which he personally washed in his bathtub. The Taj Mahal Hotel was not unused to such habits among the foreign, but by this extremely selective diet Hathaway had severely constipated himself and suffered from hemorrhoids.

In addition, the hot, damp weather of Bombay had excited his chronic proneness to fungal infections. Hathaway stuck cotton balls between his toes—he had the most persistent case of athlete's foot that Dr. Lowji Daruwalla had ever seen—and a fungus as unstoppable as bread mold had invaded his ears. Old Lowji believed that the director was capable of producing his own mushrooms. Gordon Hathaway's ears itched to the point of madness, and he was so deaf from both the fungus and the fungicidal ear drops—not to mention the cotton balls that he stuck in his ears—that his communication on the film set was comedic with misunderstanding.

As for the ear drops, they were a solution of gentian violet, an indelible purple dye. Therefore, the collars and shoulders of Hathaway's shirts were dotted with violet stains, for the cotton balls frequently fell out of his ears—or else Hathaway, in his frustration at being deaf, plucked out the cotton balls himself. The director was a born litterer; everywhere he went, the world was colorfully marked by his violet ear-cottons. Sometimes the purple solution streaked Hathaway's face, giving him the appearance of someone who'd been deliberately painted; he looked like a member of a religious cult, or of an unknown tribe. Gordon Hathaway's fingertips were similarly stained with gentian violet; he was always poking his fingers in his ears.

But Lowji was nevertheless impressed by the fabled artistic temperament of the first (and only) Hollywood director he'd ever met. The senior Daruwalla told Meher (she told Farrokh) that it was "charming" how Hathaway had blamed his hemorrhoids and his fungus *neither* on his bathtub diet *nor* on the Bombay climate. Instead, the director faulted "the fuckin' stress" of the compromising relationship he was compelled to conduct with the film's philistine producer, a much defamed "suit," who (coincidentally) was married to Gordon's ambitious sister.

"That cunt of misery!" Gordon would often exclaim. Failing originality in all his cinematic pursuits, Gordon Hathaway was nevertheless rumored to be the first to coin this vulgar phrase. "Fuckin' ahead of my time" was a way he often spoke of himself; in this coarse instance, he may have been correct.

It was a great source of frustration to Meher and Farrokh to hear Lowji defend the grossness of Gordon Hathaway on grounds of the man's "artistic temperament." It was never clear if the philistine producer's success in exerting certain pressures on Gordon was because of Gordon's desire to please the suit himself, or whether the true force of the exertion emanated from Gordon's sister—the so-called C. of M. herself. It was never clear who had whom "by the balls," as Gordon put it; it was unclear who "jerked" whose "wire," as he otherwise put it.

As an admitted newcomer to the creative process, Lowji was undeterred by such talk; he sought to draw out of Gordon Hathaway the presumed aesthetic principles that guided the director through the frenzy with which this particular movie was being made. Even a novice could sense the hectic pace at which the film was being shot; even Lowji's untested artistic sensibilities could detect the aura of tension with which the screenplay underwent revision every evening in the dining room of the Duckworth Club.

"I trust my fuckin' instinct for storytellin', pal," Gordon Hathaway confided to the senior Daruwalla, who was in such earnest search of a retirement career. "That's the fuckin' key."

How it shamed Farrokh and his poor mother: to observe, throughout dinner, that Lowji was taking notes.

As for the screenwriter, whose shared dream of a "quality" picture

was nightly and disastrously changing before his eyes, he was an alcoholic whose bar bill at the Duckworth Club threatened to exceed the
Daruwalla family's resources; it was a tab that pinched even the seemingly bottomless purse of the well-heeled Promila Rai. His name was
Danny Mills, and he'd started out with a story about a married couple
who come to India because the wife is dying of cancer; they'd promised
themselves that they would go to India "one day." It was originally
titled, with the utmost sincerity, *One Day We'll Go to India;* then Gordon
Hathaway retitled it *One Day We'll Go to India, Darling.* That small change
initiated a major revision of the story, and sank Danny Mills all the
deeper into his alcoholic gloom.

It was actually a step up for Danny Mills—to have begun this screenplay from scratch. It was, if only in the beginning, his original story. He'd
started out as the lowliest of studio contract writers; his first job, at
Universal, was for 100 dollars a week, and all he did was tamper with
existing scripts. Danny Mills still had more screen credits for "additional
dialogue" than for "co-script," and his solo screenplay credits (there
were only two) were for flops—utter bombs. At the moment, he prided
himself for being an "independent," which is to say he was under no
studio contract; however, this was because the studios thought he was
unreliable, not only for his drinking but for his reputation as a loner.
Danny wasn't content to be a team player, and he became especially
cantankerous in the cases of those screenplays that had already engaged
the creative genius of a half-dozen or more writers. Although it clearly
depressed Danny to revise on demand, which he was doing as a result
of the nightly whims of Gordon Hathaway, it was entirely rare for
Danny to be working on a story that had at least originated with him.
For this reason, Gordon Hathaway thought that Danny shouldn't complain.

It wasn't as if Danny had contributed a word to *The Big Sleep* or even
Cobra Woman, and he'd had nothing to do with *Woman of the Year* or even
Hot Cargo; he'd written neither *Rope* nor *Gaslight*—he hadn't added so
much as a comma to *Son of Dracula,* or taken one away from *Frisco
Sal*—and although for a while he'd been identified as the uncredited
screenwriter for *When Strangers Marry,* this proved to be false. In Hollywood, he simply hadn't been playing in the big leagues; the general
feeling was that "additional dialogue" was the very zenith of his ability,
and so he came to Bombay with more experience in fixing other people's
messes than with creating his own. Doubtless it hurt Danny that Gordon
Hathaway didn't refer to him as "the writer" at all. Gordon called Danny

Mills "the fixer," but in truth there was more that needed fixing in *One Day We'll Go to India, Darling* after Hathaway started changing it.

Danny had envisioned the movie as a love story with a twist; the "twist" was the wife dying. In the original screenplay, the couple—in her dying days—succumb to the fakery of a snake guru; they are rescued from this charlatan and his gang of demonic snake-worshipers by a *true* guru. Instead of pretending to cure the wife, the true guru teaches her how to die with dignity. According to the philistine producer, or else to his wife—Gordon Hathaway's interfering C. of M. sister—this last part was lacking in both action and suspense.

"Despite how happy the wife is, she still fuckin' dies, doesn't she?" Gordon said.

Therefore, against the slightly better instincts of Danny Mills, Gordon Hathaway altered the story. Gordon believed that the snake guru wasn't villainous enough; hence the snake-worshipers were revised. The snake guru actually abducts the wife from the Taj and keeps her a prisoner in his harem of drugged women, while he instructs them in a method of meditation that concludes with having sex—either with the snakes or with him. This is an ashram of evil, surely. The distraught husband, in the company of a Jesuit missionary—a none-too-subtle replacement for the true guru—tracks the wife down and saves her from a fate presumed worse than her anticipated death by cancer. It is Christianity that the dying wife embraces at the end, and—no surprise!—she doesn't die after all.

Gordon Hathaway explained it to a surprised Lowji Daruwalla: "The cancer just sort of goes away—it just fuckin' dries up and goes away. That happens sometimes, doesn't it?"

"Well, it doesn't exactly 'dry up,' but there are cases of remission," the senior Dr. Daruwalla answered uncertainly, while Farrokh and Meher suffered enormous embarrassment for him.

"What's that?" Gordon Hathaway asked. He knew what a remission was; he just hadn't heard the doctor because his ears were crammed full of fungus and gentian violet and cotton balls.

"Yes! Sometimes a cancer can just sort of go away!" old Lowji shouted.

"Yeah, that's what I thought—I knew that!" Gordon Hathaway said.

In his embarrassment for his father, Farrokh sought to turn the conversation toward India itself. Surely the gravity of the Partition and Independence—when a million Hindus and Muslims were killed, and 12 million became refugees—interested the foreigners a *little*.

"Listen, kid," Gordon Hathaway said, "when you're makin' a fuckin' movie, nothin' else interests you." There was hearty consent to this at the dinner table; Farrokh felt that even the silence of his usually opinionated father served to rebuke him. Only Danny Mills appeared to be interested in the subject of local color; Danny also appeared to be drunk.

Although Danny Mills considered religion and politics as tedious forms of "local color," Danny was nevertheless disappointed that *One Day We'll Go to India, Darling* had very little to do with India. Danny had already suggested that the climate of religious violence in the days of the Partition might at least make a brief appearance in the background of the story.

"Politics is just fuckin' exposition," Gordon Hathaway had said, dismissing the idea. "I'd end up cutting the shit out of it later."

In response to the present debate between the director and Farrokh, Danny Mills once more expressed his desire that the movie reflect at least a *hint* of Muslim-Hindu tensions, but Gordon Hathaway bluntly challenged Farrokh to tell him just one "sore point" between Muslims and Hindus that wouldn't be boring on film. And since this was the year that Hindus had snuck into the Mosque of Babar with idols of their god-prince Rama, Farrokh imagined that he knew a good story. The Hindus had claimed that the site of the mosque was the birthplace of Rama, but the placing of Hindu idols in an historic mosque wasn't well received by Muslims—they hate idols of any kind. Muslims don't believe in representations of God, not to mention lots of gods, while Hindus pray to idols (*and* to lots of gods) all the time. To avoid more Hindu-Muslim bloodshed, the state had locked up the Mosque of Babar. "Perhaps they should have removed the idols of Rama first," Farrokh explained. Muslims were enraged that these Hindu idols were occupying their mosque. Hindus not only wanted the idols to remain—they wanted to build a temple to Rama at the site.

At this point, Gordon Hathaway interrupted Farrokh's story to express anew his dislike of exposition. "You'll never write for the movies, kid," Gordon said. "You wanna write for the movies, you gotta get to the point quicker than this."

"I don't think we can use it," said Danny Mills thoughtfully, "but I thought it was a nice story."

"Thank you," Farrokh said.

Poor Meher, the oft-neglected *Mrs.* Daruwalla, was sufficiently provoked to change the subject. She offered a comment on the pleasure of a sudden evening breeze. She noted the rustling of a neem tree in the Ladies' Garden. Meher would have elaborated on the merits of the neem tree, but she saw that the foreigners' interest—which was never great—had already waned.

Gordon Hathaway was holding the violet-colored cotton balls he'd taken from his ears, shaking them in the closed palm of one hand, like dice. "What's a fuckin' *neem* tree?" he asked, as if the tree itself had annoyed him.

"They're all around town," said Danny Mills. "They're a tropical kind of tree, I think."

"I'm sure you've seen them," Farrokh said to the director.

"Listen, kid," said Gordon Hathaway, "when you're makin' a movie, you don't have time to look at the fuckin' trees."

It must have hurt Meher to see by her husband's expression that Lowji had found this remark most sage. Meanwhile, Gordon Hathaway indicated that the conversation was over by turning his attention to a pretty, underage girl at an adjacent table. This left Farrokh with a view of the director's arrogant profile, and an especially alarming glimpse of the deep and permanent purple of Hathaway's inner ear. The ear was actually a rainbow of colors, from raw red to violet, as unsuitably iridescent as the face of a mandrill baboon.

Later, after the colorful director had returned to the Taj—presumably to wash more food in his bathtub before retiring to bed—Farrokh was forced to observe his father fawning over the drunken Danny Mills.

"It must be difficult to revise a screenplay under these conditions," Lowji ventured.

"You mean at night? Over food? After I've been drinking?" Danny asked.

"I mean so spur-of-the-moment," Lowji said. "It would seem more prudent to shoot the story you've already written."

"Yes, it would," poor Danny agreed. "But they never do it that way."

"They like the spontaneity, I suppose," Lowji said.

"They don't think the writing is very important," said Danny Mills.

"They *don't*?" Lowji exclaimed.

"They never do," Danny told him. Poor Lowji had never considered the unimportance of the writer of a movie. Even Farrokh looked with compassion on Danny Mills, who was an affectionate, sentimental man with a gentle manner and a face that women liked—until they knew him better. Then they either disliked his central weakness or exploited it. Alcohol was certainly a problem for him, but his drinking was more a symptom of his failure than a cause of it. He was always out of money and, as a consequence, he rarely finished a piece of writing and sold it from any position of strength; usually, he would sell only an idea for a piece of writing, or a piece of writing that was very much a fragment—a story barely in progress—and as a result he lost all control of the outcome of whatever the piece of writing was.

He'd never finished a novel, although he'd begun several; when he needed money, he would put the novel aside and write a screenplay—selling the screenplay before he finished it. That was always the pattern. By the time he went back to the novel, he had enough distance from it to see how bad it was.

But Farrokh couldn't dislike Danny the way he disliked Gordon Hathaway; Farrokh could see that Danny liked Lowji, too. Danny also made an effort to protect Farrokh's father from further embarrassing himself.

"Here's the way it is," Danny told Lowji. He swirled the melting ice in the bottom of his glass; in the kilnlike heat before the monsoon, the ice melted quickly—but never as quickly as Danny drank the gin. "You're screwed if you sell something before you finish it," Danny Mills told the senior Daruwalla. "Never even *show* anybody what you're writing until you finish it. Just do the work. When you know it's good, show it to someone who's made a movie you like."

"Like a director, you mean?" asked Lowji, who was still writing everything down.

"Definitely a director," said Danny Mills. "I don't mean a studio."

"And so you show it to someone you like, a director, and *then* you get paid?" asked the senior Daruwalla.

"No," said Danny Mills. "You take *no* money until the whole deal is in place. The minute you take any money, you're screwed."

"But when *do* you take the money?" Lowji asked.

"When they've signed the actors you want, when they've signed the director—*and* given him the final cut of the picture. When everyone likes the screenplay so much, you know they wouldn't dare change a word of it—and if you doubt this, demand final script approval. Then be prepared to walk away."

"This is what you do?" Lowji asked.

"Not me," Danny said. "I take the money up front, as much as I can get. Then they screw me."

"But who does it the way you suggest?" Lowji asked; he was so confused, he'd stopped writing.

"Nobody I know," said Danny Mills. "Everyone I know gets screwed."

"So you didn't go to Gordon Hathaway—you didn't choose him?" Lowji asked.

"Only a studio would choose Gordon," Danny said.

He had that uncommon smoothness of skin which appears so confounding on the faces of some alcoholics; it was as if Danny's baby-faced complexion were the direct result of the pickling process—as if the growth of his beard were as arrested as his speech. Danny looked like he needed to shave only once a week, although he was almost 35.

"I'll tell you about Gordon," Danny said. "It was Gordon's idea to expand the role of the snake guru in the story—Gordon's idea of the epitome of evil is an ashram with snakes. I'll tell you about Gordon," Danny Mills went on, when neither Lowji nor Farrokh had interrupted him. "Gordon's never *met* a guru, with or without snakes. Gordon's never *seen* an ashram, not even in California."

"It would be easy to arrange a meeting with a guru," Lowji said. "It would be easy to visit an ashram."

"I'm sure you know what Gordon would say to that idea," said Danny Mills, but the drunken screenwriter was looking at Farrokh.

Farrokh attempted the best imitation of Gordon Hathaway that he could manage. "I'm makin' a fuckin' movie," Farrokh said. "Do I got the time to meet a fuckin' guru or go to a fuckin' ashram when I'm in the middle of makin' a fuckin' movie?"

"Smart boy," said Danny Mills. It was to old Lowji that Danny confided: "Your son understands the movie business."

Although Danny Mills appeared to be a destroyed man, it was hard not to like him, Farrokh thought. Then he looked down in his beer and saw the two vivid violet cotton balls from Gordon Hathaway's ears. How did they end up in my beer? Farrokh wondered. He needed to use a parfait spoon to extract them, dripping, from his beer glass. He put Gordon Hathaway's soggy ear-cottons on a tea saucer, wondering how long they'd been soaking in his beer—and how much beer he'd drunk while Gordon Hathaway's ear-cottons were sponging up the beer at the bottom of his glass. Danny Mills was laughing so hard, he couldn't speak. Lowji could see what his critical son was thinking.

"Don't be ridiculous, Farrokh!" his father told him. "Surely it was an accident." This made Danny Mills laugh harder and harder, drawing Mr. Sethna to their table—where the steward stared in disapproval at the tea saucer containing the beer-soaked, still-purple cotton balls. Farrokh's remaining beer was purple, too. Mr. Sethna was thinking that it was at least fortunate that *Mrs.* Daruwalla had already gone home for the evening.

Farrokh helped his father arrange Danny Mills in the back seat of the car. Danny would be sound asleep before they'd traveled the length of the driveway of the Duckworth Club, or at least by the time they'd left Mahalaxmi. The screenwriter was always asleep by that time, if he didn't go home earlier; when they dropped him at the Taj, Farrokh's father would tip one of the tall Sikh doormen, who would transport Danny to his room on a luggage cart.

This night—Farrokh in the passenger seat, his father driving, and Danny Mills asleep in the back seat—they had just entered Tardeo when his father said, "In your nearly constant expression, you might be wise not to display such obvious distaste for these people. I know you think you're very sophisticated—and that they are vermin, beneath your contempt—but I'll tell you what is most *un*sophisticated, and that is to wear your feelings so frankly on your face."

Farrokh would remember this, for he took the sting of such a rebuke very much to heart, while at the same time he sat silently seething in anger at his father, who wasn't as entirely stupid as his young son had presumed him to be. Farrokh would remember this, too, because the car was exactly at that location in Tardeo where, 20 years later, his father would be blown to smithereens.

"You should listen to these people, Farrokh," his father was telling him. "It isn't necessary for them to be your moral equals in order for you to learn something from them."

Farrokh would remember the irony, too. Although this was his father's idea, Farrokh would be the one who actually learned something from the wretched foreigners; he'd be the one who took Danny's advice.

But Had He Learned Anything Worth Knowing?

Farrokh wasn't 19 now; he was 59. It was already past dusk at the Duckworth Club, but the doctor still sat slumped in his chair in the Ladies' Garden. The younger Dr. Daruwalla wore an expression generally associated with failure; although he'd maintained absolute control of his Inspector Dhar screenplays—Farrokh was always granted "final

script approval"—what did it matter? Everything he'd written was crap.
The irony was, he'd been very successful writing movies that were no
better than *One Day We'll Go to India, Darling.*

Dr. Daruwalla wondered if other screenwriters who'd written crap
nevertheless dreamed, as he did, of writing a "quality" picture. In Farrokh's case, his quality story always began in the same way; he just
couldn't get past the beginning.

There was an opening shot of Victoria Terminus, the Gothic station
with its stained-glass windows, its friezes, its flying buttresses, its ornate
dome with the watchful gargoyles—in Farrokh's opinion, it was the
heart of Bombay. Inside the echoing station were a half-million com-
muters and the ever-arriving migrants; these latter travelers had brought
everything with them, from their children to their chickens.

Outside the huge depot was the vast display of produce in Crawford
Market, not to mention the pet stalls, where you could buy parrots or
piranhas or monkeys. And among the porters and the vendors, the
beggars and the newcomers and the pickpockets, the camera (somehow)
would single out his hero, although he was just a child and crippled.
What *other* hero would an orthopedic surgeon imagine? And with the
magical simultaneity that movies can occasionally manage, the boy's
face (a close-up) would let us know that *his* story had been chosen—
among millions—while at that exact moment the boy's voice-over
would tell us his name.

Farrokh was overly fond of the old-fashioned technique of voice-
over; he'd used it to excess in every Inspector Dhar movie. There's one
that begins with the camera following a pretty young woman through
Crawford Market. She's anxious, as if she knows she's being followed,
and this causes her to topple a heaped-up pile of pineapples at a fruit
stand, which makes her run; *this* causes her to slip on the rotting compost
underfoot, which makes her bump into a pet stall, where a vicious
cockatoo pecks her hand. That's when we see Inspector Dhar. As the
young woman runs on, Dhar calmly follows her. He pauses by the stand
of exotic birds only long enough to give the cockatoo a cuff with the
back of his hand.

His voice-over says, "It was the third time I'd tailed her, but she was
still crazy enough to think she could shake me."

Dhar pauses again as the pretty girl, in her haste, collides with a
heaped-up pile of mangoes. Dhar is enough of a gentleman to wait for
the vendor to clear a path through the fallen fruit, but the next time he

catches up with the woman, she's dead. A bullet hole is smack between her wide-open eyes, which Dhar politely closes for her.

His voice-over says, "It's a pity I wasn't the only one tailing her. She had trouble shaking someone else, too."

From his view of the younger Dr. Daruwalla in the Ladies' Garden, old Mr. Sethna was sure he knew the source of the hatred he saw in the doctor's eyes; the steward thought he knew the particular, long-ago vermin that the doctor was thinking of. But Mr. Sethna was unfamiliar with self-doubt and self-loathing. The old Parsi would never have imagined that Dr. Daruwalla was thinking about himself.

Farrokh was taking himself to task for leaving that crippled boy at Victoria Terminus, where he'd arrived; so many Bombay stories began at Victoria Terminus, but Dr. Daruwalla had been unable to imagine *any* story for that abandoned child. The doctor was still wondering what could happen to the boy *after* he came to Bombay. Anything and everything could happen, Farrokh knew; instead, the screenwriter had settled for Inspector Dhar, whose tough-guy talk was as unoriginal as the rest of him.

Dr. Daruwalla tried to save himself by thinking of a story with the innocence and purity of his favorite acts from the Great Royal Circus, but Farrokh couldn't imagine a story as good as even the simplest of the so-called items that he loved. He couldn't even think of a story as good as the daily routine of the circus. There were no wasted efforts in the course of the long day, which began with tea at 6:00 in the morning. The child performers and other acrobats did their strength and flexibility exercises and practiced their new items until 9:00 or 10:00, when they ate a light breakfast and cleaned their tents; in the rising heat, they sewed sequins on their costumes or they attended to other, almost motionless chores. There was no animal training from midmorning on; it was too hot for the big cats, and the horses and the elephants stirred up too much dust.

Through the middle of the day, the tigers and lions lolled in their cages with their tails and paws and even their ears sticking out between the bars, as if they hoped that these extremities might attract a breeze; only their tails moved, among an orchestra of flies. The horses remained standing—it was cooler than lying down—and two boys took turns dusting the elephants with a torn cloth sack that had once held onions or potatoes. Another boy watered the floor of the main tent with a hose; in the midday heat, this didn't dampen the dust for long. The overall torpor affected even the chimpanzees, who stopped swinging from their cages; they still screamed occasionally—and they jumped up and down, as always. But if a dog so much as whined, not to mention barked, someone kicked it.

At noon, the animal trainers and the acrobats ate a big lunch; then they slept until midafternoon—their first performance always began after 3:00. The heat was still stultifying, and the motes of dust rose and sparkled like stars in the sunlight, which slanted through the vents in the main tent; in these harsh slashes of light, the dust appeared to swarm as intensely as the flies. In the breaks between their musical numbers, the band members passed a wet rag with which they wiped their brass instruments and, more often, their heads.

There was usually a sparse audience in attendance at the 3:30 performance. They were an odd mix of people too old for a full day's work and preschool children; in both cases, their alertness to the performances of the acrobats and the animals was below average, as if their limited powers of concentration were further impaired by the lingering heat and dust. Over the years, Dr. Daruwalla had never sensed that the 3:30 performance itself was ever a diminished effort; the acrobats and the animal trainers, and even the animals, were as steady as they had to be. It was the audience that was a little off.

For this reason, Farrokh preferred the early-evening performance. Whole families came—young workingmen and -women, and children who were old enough to pay attention—and the scant, dying sunlight seemed distant, even gentle; the dust motes weren't visible. It was the time of the evening when the flies appeared to have departed with the glare, and it was still too early for the mosquitoes. For the 6:30 performance, the place was always packed.

The first item was the Plastic Lady, a "boneless" girl named Laxmi (the Goddess of Wealth). She was a beautiful contortionist—no sign of rickets. Laxmi was only 14, but the sharp definition of the bones in her face made her seem older. She wore a bright-orange bikini with yellow and red sequins that glittered in the strobe light; she looked like a fish with its scales reflecting a light that shone from underwater. It was dark enough in the main tent so that the changing colors of the stroboscope were effective, but enough of the late sunlight still illuminated the tent so that you could make out the faces of the children in the audience. Dr. Daruwalla thought that whoever said circuses were for children was only half right; the circus was also for grownups who enjoyed seeing children so enthralled.

Why can't I do that? the doctor wondered, thinking about the simple brilliance of the boneless girl named Laxmi—thinking of the crippled boy abandoned in Victoria Terminus, where Dr. Daruwalla's imagination had stalled as soon as it had begun. Instead of creating something as pure and riveting as the circus, he'd turned his mind to mayhem and murder—personified by Inspector Dhar.

What old Mr. Sethna mistook in Dr. Daruwalla's miserable expression was simply the doctor's deep disappointment with himself. With a sympathetic nod to the doctor, who sat forlornly in the Ladies' Garden, the Parsi steward allowed himself a rare moment of familiarity with a passing waiter.

"I'm glad *I'm* not the rat he's thinking of," Mr. Sethna said.

Not the Curry

Of course there was more wrong with *One Day We'll Go to India, Darling* than Danny Mills's alcoholism or his unsubtle plagiarism of *Dark Victory*; much more was amiss than Gordon Hathaway's crass alterations of Danny's "original" screenplay, or the director's attendant hemorrhoids and fungus. To make matters worse, the actress who was playing the dying but saved wife was that talentless beauty and denizen of the gossip columns Veronica Rose. Her friends and colleagues called her Vera, but she was born in Brooklyn with the name Hermione Rosen and she was Gordon Hathaway's niece (the C. of M.'s daughter). Small world, Farrokh would learn.

The producer, Harold Rosen, would one day find his daughter as tiresomely tasteless as the rest of the world judged her to be upon the merest introduction; however, Harold was as easily bullied by his wife (the C. of M. sister of Gordon Hathaway) as Gordon was. Harold was operating on his wife's assumption that Hermione Rosen, by her transformation to Veronica Rose, would one day be a star. Vera's lack of talent and intelligence would prove too great an obstacle for such a goal—this in tandem with a compulsion to expose her breasts that even Lady Duckworth would have scorned.

But at the Duckworth Club in the summer of '49, a rumor was in circulation that Vera was soon to have a huge success. Concerning Hollywood, what did Bombay know? That Vera had been cast in the role of the dying but saved wife was all that Lowji Daruwalla knew. It would take a while for Farrokh to find out that Danny Mills had objected to Vera having the part—until she seduced him and made him imagine that he was in love with her. Then he trotted at her heels like a dog. Danny believed it was the intense pressure of the role that had cooled Vera's brief ardor for him—Vera had her own room at the Taj, and she'd refused to sleep with Danny since the commencement of principal photography—but, in truth, she was having an obvious affair with her leading man. It wasn't obvious to Danny, who usually drank himself to sleep and got up late.

As for the leading man, he was a bisexual named Neville Eden. Neville was an uprooted Englishman and a properly trained actor, if not exactly brimming with natural ability, but his move to Los Angeles had turned sour when a certain predictability in the parts he was offered grew clear to him. He'd become too easy to cast as any number of stereotypical Brits. There was the Brit-twit role—the kind of instant Brit whom more rowdy and less educated Americans deplore—and then there was the sophisticated English gentleman who becomes the love interest of an impressionable American girl before she realizes her mistake and chooses the more substantial (if duller) American male. There was also the role of the visiting British cousin—sometimes this was a war buddy—who would comically display his inability to ride a horse, or to drive a car on the right-hand side of the road, or to successfully engage in fisticuffs in low bars. In all these roles, Neville felt he was supplying moronic reassurance to an audience that equated manliness with qualities only to be found in American men. This discovery tended to irritate him; doubtless it also fueled what he called his "homosexual self."

About *One Day We'll Go to India, Darling* Neville was philosophic: at least it was a leading role, and the part wasn't quite in the vein of the dimly perceived British types he was usually asked to portray—after all, in this story he was a happily married Englishman with a dying American wife. But even for Neville Eden the loser combination of Danny Mills, Gordon Hathaway and Veronica Rose was a trifle daunting. Neville knew from past experience that contact with a compromised script, a second-rate director and a floozy for a co-star tended to make him churlish. And Neville cared nothing for Vera, who was beginning to imagine that she was in love with him; yet he found fornicating with her altogether more inspiring, and amusing, than *acting* with her—and he was mightily bored.

He was also married, which Vera knew; it caused her great anguish, or at least virulent insomnia. Of course she did *not* know that Neville was bisexual; this revelation was often the means by which Neville broke off such passing affairs. He'd found it instantly effective—to tell whichever floozy it was that she was the first *woman* to capture his heart and his attention to such a degree, but that his homosexual self was simply stronger than both of them. That usually worked; that got rid of them, in a hurry. All but the wife.

As for Gordon Hathaway, he had his hands full; his hemorrhoids and his fungus were trifling in comparison to the certain catastrophe he was facing. Veronica Rose wanted Danny Mills to go home so she could lavish even more obvious attention on Neville Eden. Gordon Hathaway complied with Vera's request only to the degree that he forbade Danny's presence on the set. The writer's presence, Gordon claimed, "fuckin' confused" the cast. But Gordon could hardly comply with his niece's request to send Danny home; he needed Danny every night, to revise the ever-changing script. Understandably, Danny Mills wanted to reinstate his original script, which Neville Eden had agreed was better than the picture they were making. Danny thought Neville was a good chap, though it would have destroyed him to learn that Neville was fornicating with Vera. Vera, above all, dearly desired to *sleep*, and Dr. Lowji Daruwalla was alarmed by the sleeping pills she requested; yet he was such a fool for movies—he found her "charming," too.

His son Farrokh wasn't exactly charmed by Veronica Rose; neither was he altogether immune to her attractions. Soon a conflict of emotions engulfed the tender 19-year-old. Vera was clearly a coarse young woman, which is not without allure to 19-year-olds, especially when the woman in question is intriguingly older—Vera was 25. Furthermore, while he knew nothing of the random pleasure Vera took in exposing her breasts, Farrokh found that the actress bore a remarkable resemblance to the old photographs he so relished of Lady Duckworth.

It had been an evening in the empty dance hall when not even that depth of stone and the constant stirring of the ceiling fans could cool the stifling and humid night air, which had entered the Duckworth Club as heavily as a fog from the Arabian Sea. Even atheists, like Lowji, were praying for the monsoon rains. After dinner, Farrokh had escorted Vera from the table to the dance hall, not to dance with her but to show her Lady Duckworth's photographs.

"There is someone you resemble," the young man told the actress. "Please come and see." Then he'd smiled at his mother, Meher, who didn't appear to be very happily entertained by the surly arrogance of Neville Eden, who sat to her left, or by the drunken Danny Mills, who sat to her right with his head upon his folded arms, which rested in his plate.

"Yeah!" Gordon Hathaway said to his niece. "You oughta see the pictures of this broad, Vera. She showed her tits to everybody, too!" By this word "too," Farrokh should have been forewarned, but he supposed Gordon meant only that Lady Duckworth exposed herself "in addition to" her other traits.

Veronica Rose wore a sleeveless muslin dress that clung to her back where she'd sweated against her chair; her bare upper arms caused excruciating offense to the Duckworthians, and especially to the recently acquired Parsi steward, Mr. Sethna, who thought that for a woman to bare her upper arms in public was a violation of scandalous proportion—the slut might as well show her breasts, too!

When Vera saw Lady Duckworth's pictures, she was flattered; she lifted her damp blond hair off the back of her slender wet neck and she turned to young Farrokh, who felt an erotic flush at the sight of a rivulet of sweat that coursed from Vera's near armpit. "Maybe I oughta wear my hair like hers," Vera said; then she let her hair fall back in place. As Farrokh followed her to the dining room, he couldn't help but notice—through the drenched back of her dress—that she wore no bra.

"So how'd ya like the fuckin' exhibitionist?" her uncle asked her upon her return to the table.

Vera unbuttoned the front of her white muslin dress, showing her breasts to them all—Dr. Lowji Daruwalla and Mrs. Daruwalla, too. And the Lals, dining with the Bannerjees at a nearby table, certainly saw Veronica Rose's breasts very clearly. And Mr. Sethna, so recently dismissed from the Ripon Club for attacking a crass member there with hot tea—Mr. Sethna clutched his silver serving tray, as if he thought of striking the Hollywood wench dead with it.

"Well, whatta ya think?" Vera asked her audience. "I don't know if she was an exhibitionist—I think she was just too fuckin' *hot!*" She added that she wanted to return to the Taj, where at least there was a sea breeze. In truth, she looked forward to feeding the rats that gathered at the water's edge beneath the Gateway of India; the rats were unafraid of people, and Vera enjoyed teasing them with expensive table scraps—the way some people enjoy feeding ducks or pigeons. Thereafter, she would go to Neville's room and straddle him until his cock was sore.

But in the morning, in addition to suffering the tribulation of her insomnia, Vera was sick; she was sick every morning for a week before she consulted Dr. Lowji Daruwalla, who, even though he was an ortho-pedist, had no trouble ascertaining that the actress was pregnant.

"Shit," Vera said. "I thought it was the fuckin' curry."

But no; it was just the fucking. Either Danny Mills or Neville Eden was the father. Vera hoped it was Neville, because he was better-looking. She also theorized that alcoholism like Danny's was genetic.

"Christ, it *must* be Neville!" said Vera Rose. "Danny's so pickled, I think he's sterile."

Dr. Lowji Daruwalla was understandably taken aback by the crude-ness of the lovely movie star, who wasn't really a movie star and who was suddenly terrified that her uncle, the director, would discover that she was pregnant and fire her from the picture. Old Lowji pointed out to Miss Rose that she had fewer than three weeks remaining on the shooting schedule; she wouldn't begin to *look* pregnant for another three months or more.

Miss Rose then became obsessed with the question of whether or not Neville Eden would leave his wife and marry her. Dr. Lowji Daruwalla thought not, but he chose to soften the blow with an indirect remark.

"I believe that Mr. Danny Mills would marry you," the senior Daru-walla offered tactfully, but this truth only depressed Veronica Rose, who commenced to weep. As for weeping, it wasn't as commonplace at the Hospital for Crippled Children as one might suppose. Dr. Lowji Daru-walla led the sobbing actress out of his office and through the waiting room, which was full of injured and crippled and deformed children; they all looked pityingly upon the crying fair-haired lady, imagining that she'd just received some awful news regarding a child of her own. In a sense, she had.

A Slum Is Born

At first, the news that Vera was pregnant didn't spread far. Lowji told Meher, and Meher told Farrokh. No one else knew, and a special effort was made to keep this news from Lowji's South Indian secretary, a brilliant young man from Madras. His name was Ranjit and he, too, had high hopes of becoming a screenwriter. Ranjit was only a few years older than Farrokh, his spoken English was impeccable, but thus far his writ-ing had been limited to the excellent case histories of the senior Dr. Daruwalla's patients that he composed, and to his lengthy memos to

Lowji concerning what recent articles he'd read in the doctor's orthopedic journals. These memos were written not to gain favor with old Lowji but as a means of giving the busy doctor some shorthand information regarding what he might like to read himself.

Although he came from a Hindu family of strictly vegetarian Brahmins, Ranjit had told Lowji—in his job interview—that he was wholly without religion and that he considered caste as "largely a means to hold everyone down." Lowji had hired the young man in an instant.

But that had been five years ago. Although Ranjit totally pleased the senior Daruwalla as a secretary and Lowji had made every effort to further brainwash the young man in an atheistic direction, Ranjit was finding it exceedingly difficult to attract a prospective bride—or, more important, a prospective father-in-law—by the matrimonial advertisements he regularly submitted to *The Times of India*. He wouldn't advertise that he was a Brahmin and a strict vegetarian, and although these things might not have mattered to him, they were of great concern to prospective fathers-in-law; it was usually the fathers-in-law, not the would-be brides, who responded to the advertisements—if anyone responded.

And now there was bickering between old Lowji and Ranjit because Ranjit had given in. His most recent advertisement in *The Times of India* had drawn over 100 responses; this was because he'd presented himself as someone who cared about caste and followed a strict vegetarian diet. After all, he told Lowji, he'd been made to observe these things as a child and they hadn't killed him. "If it helps me to get married," Ranjit said, "sporting a fresh puja mark, so to speak, will not kill me now."

Lowji was crushed by this traitorousness; he'd considered Ranjit like a third son, and a cohort in atheism. Furthermore, the interviews (with over 100 prospective fathers-in-law) were having a deleterious influence on Ranjit's efficiency; he was exhausted all the time, and no wonder—his mind was reeling with comparisons among 100 future wives.

But even in this state of mind, Ranjit was very attentive to the office visit of the Hollywood film goddess Veronica Rose. And since it was Ranjit's job to formally compose old Lowji's scribbles into a proper Orthopedic Report, the young man was surprised—after Vera's teary departure—to see that Lowji had scrawled no more than "joint problem" in the sex symbol's file. It was highly unusual for the senior Daruwalla to escort any of his patients home, particularly following a mere office visit—and especially when there were other patients waiting to see him. Furthermore, old Dr. Daruwalla had called his *own* home and told his wife that he was bringing Miss Rose *there*. All this for a joint problem? Ranjit thought it was most irregular.

Fortunately, the rigorous interviews that were the result of his highly successful matrimonial ads didn't allow Ranjit much time or energy for speculation on Vera's "joint problem." His interest was provoked no further than to ask the senior Daruwalla what *sort* of joint problem the actress was suffering; Ranjit wasn't used to typing up an incomplete Orthopedic Report.

"Well, actually," Lowji said, "I have referred her to another physician."

"*Not* a joint problem then?" Ranjit inquired. All he cared about was correctly typing the report.

"Possibly gynecological," Lowji answered warily.

"What sort of joint problem did she *think* she had?" Ranjit asked in surprise.

"Her knees," Lowji said vaguely, with a dismissive wave of his hand. "But I judged this to be psychosomatic."

"The gynecological problem is psychosomatic, too?" Ranjit inquired. He foresaw difficult typing ahead.

"Possibly," Lowji said.

"What *sort* of gynecological problem is it?" Ranjit persisted. At his age, and with his ambition to be a screenwriter, he was thinking that the problem was venereal.

"Itching," said the senior Daruwalla—and to halt the inquisition at this juncture, he wisely added, "Vaginal itching." No young man, he knew, cared to contemplate this. The matter was closed. Ranjit's Orthopedic Report on Veronica Rose was the closest he would ever come to writing a screenplay (many years later, the younger Dr. Daruwalla would read this report with consistent pleasure—whenever he desired to make some contact with the old days).

The patient is confused by her knees. She imagines that she has no vaginal itching, which indeed she has, while at the same time she feels some pain in her knees, which in fact she does not have. Most naturally, a gynecologist is recommended.

And *what* a gynecologist was selected for the task! Few patients would ever claim that their confidence soared when they placed themselves in the hands of the ancient, accident-prone Dr. Tata. Lowji chose him because he was so senile, he was certain to be discreet; his powers of memory were too depleted for gossip. Sadly, the selection of Dr. Tata was lacking in obstetrical merit.

At least Lowji had the good sense to entrust his wife with the psychological care of Veronica Rose. Meher tucked the pregnant bombshell into a guest bed in the Daruwalla family mansion on old Ridge Road. Meher treated Vera like a little girl who'd just suffered a tonsillectomy. Although doubtless soothing, this mothering wouldn't solve Vera's problem; nor was Vera much comforted by Meher's claim that, in her own case, she hadn't really remembered the agony and the gore of childbirth. Over time, Meher told the knocked-up actress, only the positive parts of the experience stood out in her mind.

To Lowji, Meher was less optimistic. "Here is a bizarre and thankless situation that you have gotten us into," she informed her husband. Then the situation worsened.

The next day, Gordon Hathaway called the senior Dr. Daruwalla from the slum set with the bothersome news that Veronica Rose had collapsed between takes. Actually, that was not what had happened. Vera's so-called collapse had had nothing whatsoever to do with her unwanted pregnancy; she'd simply fainted because a cow had licked her and then sneezed on her. Not that this wasn't disturbing to Vera, but the incident—like so many day-to-day occurrences in an actual slum—had been poorly observed and fervently misinterpreted by the horde of onlookers who reported the confused event.

Farrokh couldn't remember if the rudiments for a real slum existed in the area of Sophia Zuber Road in the summer of '49; he recalled only that there was both a Muslim and a Hindu population in that vicinity, for it wasn't far from where he'd attended school—at St. Ignatius in Mazagaon. Probably, some kind of slum was already there. And certainly today there is a slum of good size and modest respectability on Sophia Zuber Road.

It's fair to say that Gordon Hathaway's movie set at least contributed to what now passes for acceptable housing in the slum on Sophia Zuber Road, for it was there that the slum set was hastily constructed. Naturally, among those hired as extras—to act the part of the slum residents—were actual citizens of Bombay who were looking for an actual slum to move into. And once they'd moved in, they objected to these movie people, who were constantly invading their privacy. Rather quickly, it had become *their* slum.

Also, there was the matter of the latrine. An army of movie-crew coolies—thugs with entrenching tools—had dug the latrine. But one cannot create a new place to shit without expecting people to shit there. A universal code of defecation applies: if some people are shitting somewhere, others will shit there, too. This is only fair. Defecation in India is endlessly creative. Here was a new latrine; quickly it wasn't new. And one mustn't forget the intense heat before the monsoon breaks, and the ensuing floods that attend the onset of the monsoon; these factors, in addition to the sudden plenitude of human excrement, doubtless exacerbated Vera's morning sickness—not to mention her proneness to fainting on that particular day when she was both licked and sneezed on by a cow.

Gordon Hathaway and the film crew were shooting the scene where the abductors of the dying wife (Vera) are carrying her through the slum en route to the ashram of the snake guru. This is the moment when the idealistic Jesuit missionary, who just happens to be performing various labors of selflessness in the slum, sees the beautiful and unmistakably blond woman whisked along Sophia Zuber Road by a band of ruffians unsuitable for her company. There later follows the distraught husband (Neville) and a stereotypically stupid policeman who has clumsily lost the trail. This is the first meeting between the husband and the Jesuit, but it was *not* the first meeting between Neville and the arrogant Indian actor Subodh Rai, who played the missionary with inappropriately secular handsomeness and cunning.

Meanwhile, many of the new slum's residents had been forced to move out of "their" slum in order for Gordon Hathaway to shoot this scene. Many more future residents of this new slum were crowding around, desirous to move in. Had any of these onlookers *not* been so transfixed by Veronica Rose, Neville and Subodh could have been observed flirting with each other off-camera; they were playfully pinching and tickling each other when Vera unaccountably found herself face-to-face with the cow.

Cows, Vera had heard, were holy—although not to the majority of beef-eating bystanders, who were Muslims—but Vera was so shocked to see *this* cow, first standing in her path and then approaching her, that she took rather a long time to determine what course of action she should choose. By then, the cow's moist breath was detectable in her cleavage; since she'd been abducted from the Taj (in the movie) in her nightgown, Vera's cleavage was quite considerable and exposed. The cow was garlanded with flowers; brightly colored beads were strung on thongs tied around its ears. Neither the cow nor Vera seemed to know what to make of this confrontation, although Vera was certain that she didn't want to cause some religious offense by being in the least aggressive toward the cow.

"Oh, what pretty flowers!" she remarked. "Oh, what a *nice* cow!" she said to it. (Veronica Rose's repertoire of friendly, inoffensive responses was exceedingly small.) She didn't think she should throw her arms around the cow's neck and kiss its long, sad face; she wasn't sure if she should touch the cow at all. But the cow made the first move. It was simply on its way somewhere, and suddenly a film crew in general and a silly woman in particular stood in its way; therefore, it stepped slowly forward—it trod on Vera's bare foot. Since she'd just been abducted (in the movie), her foot was bare.

Even in great pain, Vera had such a fear of religious zealotry that she didn't dare scream in the cow's face, the wet muzzle of which was now pressed against her chest. Not only because of the humid weather but also because of her fear and pain, Vera was soaked with sweat; whether it was merely the salt on her fair skin, or her inviting fragrance—for doubtless Vera smelled vastly better than the other residents of Sophia Zuber Road—the cow at this moment licked her. Both the length and feel of the cow's tongue was a new experience for Vera, who fainted when the cow violently sneezed in her face. Then the cow bent over her and licked her chest and shoulders.

Thereafter, no one saw clearly what happened. There was demonstrable consternation for Miss Rose's welfare, and some rioting by those onlookers who were outraged by what they'd seen; the rioters themselves were uncertain of what they'd seen. Only Vera would later conclude that the rioters had rioted on behalf of a sacred cow. Neville Eden and Subodh Rai vaguely wondered if Vera had fainted in response to their observed sexual interest in each other.

By the time the Daruwallas found their way to the van, which served as Miss Rose's makeup room and a first-aid station, the Muslim owner of a bidi shop had spread the word all along Sophia Zuber Road that a blond American movie star, naked to her waist, had licked a cow and thereby caused widespread rioting among the sensitive Hindu population. Such mischief was unnecessary; riots didn't need reasons. If there was a reason for this one, it was probably that too many people wanted to move into the movie-set slum and they were impatient that they had to wait for the movie; they wanted to start living there immediately. But Vera, of course, would always imagine that everything had happened because of her and the cow.

It was into the midst of this bedlam that the Daruwalla family arrived to rescue the indelicately pregnant Miss Rose. Her state of mind hadn't been improved by the cow, but the senior Dr. Daruwalla could conclude only that Vera had a bruised and swollen right foot—and that she was still pregnant. "If Neville won't have me, I'll put the baby up for adoption," Vera said. "But *you've* got to arrange it all here," she told Lowji and Meher and Farrokh. She felt certain that her "American audience" wouldn't sympathize with her for a child born out of wedlock; more to the point, her uncle wouldn't use her in another picture (if he knew); worse, Danny Mills, out of a drunk's special sentimentality, would insist on adopting the baby himself (if *he* knew). "This has gotta be strictly between us!" Miss Rose told the helpless Daruwallas. "Find me some fuckin' rich people who want a white baby!"

The interior of the van was a virtual sauna; the Daruwallas wondered if Vera was suffering from dehydration. Admittedly, Lowji and Meher felt unfamiliar with the moral logic of Westerners; they turned to their European-educated son for some guidance on this subject. But even to Farrokh it seemed an odd, questionable gift—to present India with *another* baby. Young Farrokh politely suggested that a baby might be more welcome for adoption in Europe or America, but Miss Rose sought secrecy at all cost—as if, morally, whatever she did in India, and whomever she left behind here, would somehow remain unrecorded, or at least never be counted against her.

"You could have an abortion," the senior Dr. Daruwalla suggested.

"Don't you *dare* mention that word to me," said Veronica Rose. "I'm not that kind of person—I was brought up with certain moral values!"

While the Daruwallas puzzled over Vera's "moral values," the van was rocked violently from side to side by a rowdy mob of men and boys. Lipstick and eyeliner rolled off the shelves of the van—and powders, and moisturizers, and rouge. A jar of sterile water crashed, and one of alcohol; Farrokh caught a falling box of gauze pads, and another of Band-Aids, as his father made his way to the sliding panel door. Veronica Rose screamed so loudly that she didn't hear what old Lowji shouted to the men outside; nor did she hear the sound of the several beatings, as various thugs among the film-crew coolies fell upon the mob with the entrenching tools they'd used to dig the not-so-new latrine. Miss Rose lay on her back, clutching the sides of her trembling cot, as small, colorful jars of this and that dropped harmlessly on her.

"Oh, I *hate* this country!" she yelled.

"It is merely a passing riot," Meher assured her.

"I *hate* it, I *hate* it, I *hate* it!" Vera cried. "It is the most *awful* country in the world—I simply *hate* it!"

It occurred to young Farrokh to ask the actress *why*, then, she would ever want to leave her own baby here in Bombay, but he felt he was too ignorant of the cultural differences between Miss Rose and himself to be critical. Farrokh wished to remain forever ignorant of the differences between these movie people and himself. At 19, young men are given to moral generalizations of a sweeping kind. To hold the rest of the United States responsible for the behavior of the former Hermione Rosen was a tad severe; nevertheless, Farrokh felt himself edging away from a future residence in the United States.

In short, Veronica Rose made Farrokh feel physically ill. Surely the woman should take *some* responsibility for her own pregnancy. And she'd tarnished Farrokh's sacred memory of Lady Duckworth's exhibitionism! In legend, Lady Duckworth's self-exposure had seemed elegant but not greatly tempting. In Farrokh's mind, Lady Duckworth's breasts were only a symbolic display. But, forever after, Farrokh was left with the more tangible memory of Vera's raw tits—they were such a sincerely carnal offering.

The Camphor Man

With all this trash in his past, it's little wonder that Farrokh was *still* sitting at his table in the darkening Ladies' Garden of the Duckworth Club. In the time it had taken the younger Dr. Daruwalla to recall such a past, Mr. Sethna had provided him with another cold Kingfisher. Farrokh hadn't touched his new beer. The faraway look in Dr. Daruwalla's eyes was almost as distant as that gaze of death which the doctor had recently seen in the eyes of Mr. Lal, although (it's already been said) the vultures had spoiled a clear impression.

At the Great Royal Circus, about an hour before the early-evening performance, a stooped man carrying a burning brazier would walk along the avenue of troupe tents; live coals were glowing in the brazier, and the aromatic camphor smoke drifted into the tents of the acrobats and the animal trainers. The camphor man would pause by each tent to be sure that enough smoke wafted inside. In addition to the medicinal properties attributed to camphor—it was often used as a counter-irritant for infections and in the treatment of itching—the smoke was of superstitious importance to the circus performers. They believed that inhaling camphor smoke protected them from the evil eye and the dangers of their profession—animal attacks, falling.

When Mr. Sethna saw Dr. Daruwalla close his eyes and throw back his head and draw a deep breath of the flowery air in the Ladies' Garden, the old Parsi steward mistook the reason. Mr. Sethna wrongly assumed that Farrokh had felt an evening breeze and therefore was enjoying a sudden infusion of the scent from the surrounding bougainvillea. But Dr. Daruwalla was sniffing for the camphor man, as if the doctor's memories of the past were in need of both a disinfectant and a blessing.

6. THE FIRST ONE OUT

Separated at Birth

As for Vera, young Farrokh wouldn't be a witness to the woman's worst behavior; he would be back in school in Vienna when Veronica Rose gave birth to twins and elected to leave one of them in the city she hated—she took the other one home with her. This was a shocking decision, but Farrokh wasn't surprised; Vera was a spur-of-the-moment sort of woman, and Farrokh had observed the monsoon months of her pregnancy—he knew the kind of insensitivity that she was capable of. In Bombay, the monsoon rains begin in mid-June and last until September. To most Bombayites, the rains are a relief from the heat, despite the blocked drains. It was only July when the shooting of the terrible film was finished and the movie rabble left Bombay—alas, leaving poor Vera behind for the remainder of the monsoon and beyond.

It was for "soul-searching" that she told them all she was staying. Neville Eden didn't care whether she was staying or going; he'd taken Subodh Rai to Italy—a pasta diet, Neville told young Farrokh with relish, improved one's stamina for the rigors of buggery. Gordon Hathaway was attempting to edit *One Day We'll Go to India, Darling* in Los Angeles; despite changing its title to *The Dying Wife*, no amount or convolution of editing could save the picture. Every day, Gordon cursed his family for burdening him with a niece as willful and untalented as Vera.

Danny Mills was drying out in a private sanitarium in Laguna Beach, California; the sanitarium was slightly ahead of its time—it favored vigorous calisthenics in tandem with a grapefruit-and-avocado diet. Danny was also being sued by a limousine company, because Harold Rosen the producer was no longer paying for Danny's so-called business trips. (When Danny couldn't stand it another second in the sanitarium, he'd call a limo to drive him to L.A. and wait for him while he consumed a hearty beef-oriented dinner and two or three bottles of a good red wine; then the limo would return him to Laguna Beach, where Danny would arrive sated but with his tongue the shape and color of a raw chicken liver. Whenever he was drying out, it was red wine he craved above all else.) Danny wrote to Vera daily—staggeringly claustrophobic love letters, some of them running 20 typed pages. The gist of these letters was always the same and quite simple to understand: that Danny would "change" if Vera would marry him.

Vera, meanwhile, had made her plans, presuming the complete cooperation of the Daruwallas. She would move into hiding, with Dr. Lowji and his family, until the child was born. The prenatal care and delivery would be the responsibility of the senile friend of the senior Dr. Daruwalla, the ancient and accident-prone Dr. Tata. It was unusual for Dr. Tata to make house calls, but he agreed, given his friendship with the Daruwallas and his understanding of the extreme sensitivity ascribed to the hypochondriac movie star. This was just as well, Meher said, because Veronica Rose would *not* have responded confidently to the peculiar sign with large lettering that was posted outside Dr. Tata's office building.

DR TATA'S BEST,

MOST FAMOUS CLINIC

FOR GYNECOLOGICAL &

MATERNITY NEEDS

It was surely wise to spare Vera the knowledge that Dr. Tata found it necessary to advertise his services as "best" and "most famous," for Vera would doubtless conclude that Dr. Tata suffered from insecurity. And so Dr. Tata made frequent house calls to the esteemed Daruwalla residence on Ridge Road; because Dr. Tata was far too old to drive a car safely, his arrivals and departures were usually marked by the presence of taxis in the Daruwallas' driveway—except for one time when Farrokh observed Dr. Tata stumbling into the driveway from the back seat of a private car. This wouldn't have been of special interest to the young man except that the car was driven by Promila Rai; beside her in the passenger seat was her allegedly hairless nephew, Rahul—the very boy whose sexual ambiguity so discomforted Farrokh.

This loomed as a violation of that secrecy which all the Daruwallas sought for Vera and her pending child; but Promila and her unnerving nephew drove off as soon as Dr. Tata was deposited in the driveway, and Dr. Tata told Lowji that he was sure he'd thrown Promila "off the trail." He'd told her he was making a house call to see Meher. Meher was offended that a woman as loathsome to her as Promila Rai would be presuming all sorts of female plumbing problems of an intimate nature. It was long after Dr. Tata had departed that Meher's irritation subsided and she thought to ask Lowji and Farrokh what Promila and Rahul Rai were doing with old Dr. Tata in the first place. Lowji pondered the question as if for the first time.

"I suppose she was concluding an office visit and he asked her for a ride," Farrokh informed his mother.

"She is a woman past childbearing years," Meher delightedly pointed out. "If she was concluding an office visit, it would have been for something gynecological. For such a visit, why would she take her nephew?"

Lowji said, "Perhaps it was the *nephew's* office visit—probably it has something to do with the hairlessness business!"

"I know Promila Rai," Meher said. "She won't believe for one minute that Dr. Tata was house-calling to see *me*."

And then, one evening, following a function where there'd been interminable speeches at the Duckworth Club, Promila Rai approached Dr. Lowji Daruwalla and said to him, "I know all about the blond baby—I will take it."

The senior Dr. Daruwalla cautiously said, "What baby?" Then he added, "There's no certainty it will be blond!"

"Of course it will," said Promila Rai. "I know these things. At least it will be fair-skinned."

Lowji considered that the child might indeed be fair-skinned; however, both Danny Mills and Neville Eden had very dark hair, and the doctor sincerely doubted the baby would be as blond as Veronica Rose.

Meher was opposed, on principle, to Promila Rai being an adoptive mother. In the first place, Promila was in her fifties—not only a spinster but an evil, spurned woman.

"She's a bitter, resentful witch," Meher said. "She'd be an *awful* mother!"

"She must have a dozen servants," Lowji replied, but Meher accused him of forgetting how offended he'd once been by Promila Rai.

As a Malabar Hill resident, Promila had led a protest campaign against the Towers of Silence. She'd offended the entire Parsi community, even old Lowji. Promila had claimed that the vultures were certain to drop body parts in various residents' gardens, or on their terraces. Promila even alleged that she'd spotted a bit of a finger floating in her balcony birdbath. Dr. Lowji Daruwalla had written an angry letter explaining to Promila that vultures didn't fly around with the fingers or toes of corpses in their beaks; vultures consumed what they wanted on the ground—anyone who knew anything about vultures knew that.

"And now you want Promila Rai to be a *mother!*" Meher exclaimed.

"It isn't that I *want* her to be a mother," the senior Dr. Daruwalla said. "However, there isn't exactly a lineup of wealthy matrons seeking to adopt an American movie star's unwanted child!"

"Furthermore," Meher said, "Promila Rai is a man-hater. What if that poor baby is a boy?"

Lowji didn't dare tell Meher what Promila had already said to him. Promila was not only certain that the baby would be blond, she was also quite sure it would be a girl.

"I know these things," Promila had told him. "You're only a doctor—and one for joints, not babies!"

The senior Dr. Daruwalla didn't suggest that Veronica Rose and Promila Rai discuss their transaction with each other; instead, he did everything he could to keep them from such a discussion—they didn't seem to have much interest in each other, anyway. It mattered to Vera only that Promila was rich, or so it appeared. It mattered most of all to Promila that Vera was healthy. Promila had a sizable fear of drugs; it was drugs, she was certain, that had poisoned her fiancé's brain and caused him to change his mind about marrying her—twice. After all, had he been drug-free and clear-headed, why wouldn't he have married her—at least once?

Lowji could assure Promila that Vera was drug-free. Now that Neville and Danny had left Bombay and Vera wasn't trying to be an actress every day, she didn't need the sleeping pills; in fact, she slept most of the time.

Almost anyone could see where this was going; it was a pity that Lowji couldn't. His own wife thought him criminal even to consider putting a newborn baby into the hands of Promila Rai; Promila would doubtless reject the child if it was male, or even slightly dark-haired. And then Lowji heard the worst news, from old Dr. Tata—namely, that Veronica Rose wasn't a true blonde.

"I've seen where you haven't seen," old Dr. Tata told him. "She has *black* hair, very black—maybe the blackest hair I've ever seen. Even in India!"

Farrokh felt he could imagine the conclusion to this melodrama. The child would be a boy with black hair; Promila Rai wouldn't want him, and Meher wouldn't want Promila to have him, anyway. Therefore, the Daruwallas would end up adopting Vera's baby. What Farrokh failed to imagine was that Veronica Rose wasn't entirely as artless as she'd appeared; Vera had already chosen the Daruwallas as her baby's adoptive parents. Upon the child's birth, Vera had planned to stage a breakdown; the reason she'd appeared so indifferent to discussions with Promila was that Vera had decided she'd reject *any* would-be adoptive parent—not only Promila. She'd guessed that the Daruwallas were suckers when it came to children, and she'd not guessed wrong.

What no one had imagined was that there wouldn't be just one dark-haired baby boy, there would be *two*—identical twin boys with the most gorgeous, almond-shaped faces and jet-black hair! Promila Rai wouldn't want them, and not only because they were dark-haired boys; she would claim that any woman who had twins was clearly taking drugs.

But the most unexpected turn of events would be engineered by the persistent love letters of Danny Mills to Veronica Rose, and by the death of Neville Eden—the victim of a car crash in Italy, an accident that also ended the flamboyant life of Subodh Rai. Until the news of the car crash, Vera had been illogically hoping that Neville might come back to her; now she determined that the fatal accident was divine retribution for Neville's preferring Subodh to her. She would carry this thought still further in her elder years, believing that AIDS was God's well-intentioned effort to restore a natural order to the universe; like many morons, Vera would believe the scourge was a godsend plague in judgment of homosexuals. This was remarkable thinking, really, for a woman who wasn't imaginative enough to believe in God.

It had been clear to Vera that if Neville ever would have wanted her, he wouldn't have wanted her cluttered up with a baby. But upon Neville's abrupt departure, Vera turned her thoughts to Danny. Would Danny *still* want to marry her if she brought him home a little surprise? Vera was sure he would.

"Darling," Vera wrote to Danny. "I've not wanted to test how much you love me, but all this while I've been carrying *our* child." (Her months with Lowji and Meher had markedly improved Vera's English.) Naturally, when she first saw the twins, Vera immediately pronounced them to be Neville's; in her view, they were far too pretty to be Danny's.

Danny Mills, for his odd part, hadn't considered having a child before. He was descended from weary but pleasant parents who'd had too many children before Danny had been born and who'd treated Danny with cordial indifference bordering on neglect. Danny wrote cautiously to his beloved Vera that he was thrilled she was carrying *their* child; a child was a fine idea—he hoped only that she didn't desire to start a whole family.

Twins are "a whole family" unto themselves, as any fool knows, and thus the dilemma would sort itself out in the predictable fashion: Vera would take one home and the Daruwallas would keep the other. Simply put, Vera didn't want to overwhelm Danny's limited enthusiasm for fatherhood.

Among the host of surprises awaiting Lowji, not the least would be the advice given to him by his senile friend Dr. Tata: "When it comes to twins, put your money on the first one out." The senior Dr. Daruwalla was shocked, but being an orthopedist, not an obstetrician, he sought to comply with Dr. Tata's recommendation. However, such excitement and confusion attended the birth of the twins that none of the nurses kept track of which one came out first; old Dr. Tata himself couldn't remember.

In this respect was Dr. Tata said to be "accident-prone": he blamed the unprofessionalism of the house calls for his failure to hear the two heartbeats whenever he put his stethoscope to Vera's big belly; he said that in his office, under appropriate conditions, he would surely have heard the two hearts. As it was—whether it was the music that Meher played or the constant sounds of housecleaning by the several servants—old Dr. Tata simply assumed that Vera's baby had an unusually strong and active heartbeat. On more than one occasion, he said, "Your baby has just been exercising, I think."

"I could have told you that," Vera always replied.

And so it wasn't until she was in labor that the monitoring of the fetal heartbeats told the tale. "What a lucky lady!" Dr. Tata told Vera Rose. "You have not one but two!"

A Knack for Offending People

In the summer of '49, when the monsoon rains drenched Bombay, the aforementioned melodrama lay, heavy and unseen, in young Farrokh Daruwalla's future—like a fog so far out in the Indian Ocean, it hadn't yet reached the Arabian Sea. He would be back in Vienna, where he and Jamshed were continuing their lengthy and proper courtship of the Zilk sisters, when he heard the news.

"Not one but two!" And Vera took only one with her.

To Farrokh and Jamshed, their parents were already elderly. Even Lowji and Meher might have agreed that the most vigorous of their child-raising abilities were behind them; they'd do their best with the little boy, but after Jamshed married Josefine Zilk, it made sense for the younger couple to take over the responsibility. Theirs was a mixed marriage, anyway; and Zürich, where they would settle, was an international city—a dark-haired boy of strictly white parentage would easily fit in. By then he knew Hindi in addition to English; in Zürich he would learn German, although Jamshed and Josefine would start him in an English-speaking school. After a time, the senior Daruwallas became like grandparents to the boy; from the beginning, Lowji had legally adopted him.

And after Jamshed and Josefine had children of their own—and there came that inevitable passage through adolescence, wherein the orphaned twin expressed a disgruntled alienation from them all—it was only natural that Farrokh would emerge as a kind of big brother to the boy. The 20-year difference between them made Farrokh something of another father to the child, too. By then, Farrokh was married to the former Julia Zilk, and they'd started a family of their own. Wherever he went, the adopted boy appeared to belong, but Farrokh and Julia were his favorites.

One shouldn't feel sorry for Vera's abandoned child. He was always part of a large family, even if there was something dislocating in the geographical upheavals in the young man's life—between Toronto, Zürich and Bombay—and even if, at an early age, there could be detected in him a certain detachment. And later there was in his language—in his German, in his English, in his Hindi—something decidedly odd, if not exactly a speech impediment. He spoke very slowly, as if he were composing a written sentence, complete with punctuation, in his mind's eye. If he had an accent, it was nothing traceable; it was more a matter of his enunciation, which was so very deliberate, as if he were in the habit of speaking to children, or addressing crowds.

And the issue that naturally intrigued them all, which was whether he was the offspring of Neville Eden or of Danny Mills, would not be easily decided. In the medical records of *One Day We'll Go to India, Darling*—which are, to this day, the only enduring records that the film was ever made—it was clearly noted that Neville and Danny were of the same common blood group, and the very same type that the twins would share.

Various Daruwallas argued that *their* twin was too good-looking, and too disinclined toward strong drink, to be a conceivable creation of Danny's. Furthermore, the boy showed little interest in reading, much less in writing—he didn't even keep a diary—whereas he was quite a gifted and highly disciplined young actor, even in grammar school. (This pointed the finger at the late Neville.) But, of course, the Daruwallas knew very little about the *other* twin. If one is determined to feel sorry for either of these twins, perhaps one should indulge such a feeling for the child Vera kept.

As for the little boy who was abandoned in India, his first days were marked by the necessity of giving him a name. He would be a Daruwalla, but in concession to his all-white appearance, it was agreed he should have an English first name. The family concurred that his name should be John, which was the Christian name of none other than Lord Duckworth himself; even Lowji conceded that the Duckworth Club was the source of the responsibility he bore for Veronica Rose's cast-off child. Needless to say, no one would have been so stupid as to name a boy *Duckworth* Daruwalla. *John* Daruwalla, on the other hand, had a friendly Anglo-Indian ring.

Everyone could more or less pronounce this name. Indians are familiar with the letter *J*; even German-speaking Swiss don't badly maul the name John, although they tend to Frenchify the name as "Jean." Daruwalla is as phonetic as most names come, although German-speaking Swiss pronounce the *W* as *V*, hence the young man was known in Zürich as Jean Daruvalla; this was close enough. His Swiss passport was issued in the name of John Daruwalla—plain but distinctive.

Not for 39 years did there awaken in Farrokh that first stirring of the creative process, which old Lowji would never experience. Now, nearly 40 years after the birth of Vera's twins, Farrokh found himself wishing that he'd never experienced the creative process, either. For it was by the interference of Farrokh's imagination that little John Daruwalla had become Inspector Dhar, the man Bombay most loved to hate—and Bombay was a city of many passionate hatreds.

Farrokh had conceived Inspector Dhar in the spirit of satire—of *quality* satire. Why were there so many easily offended people? Why had they reacted to Inspector Dhar so humorlessly? Had they no appreciation for comedy? Only now, when he was almost 60, did it occur to Farrokh that he was his father's son in this respect: he'd uncovered a natural talent for pissing people off. If Lowji had long been perceived as an assassination-in-progress, why had Farrokh been blind to this possible result in the case of Inspector Dhar? And he'd thought he was being so careful!

He'd written that first screenplay slowly and with great attention to detail. This was the surgeon in him; he hadn't learned such carefulness or authenticity from Danny Mills, and certainly not from his attendance at those three-hour spectacles in the shabby downtown cinema palaces of Bombay—those art-deco ruins where the air-conditioning was always "undergoing repair" and the urine frequently overflowed the lavatories.

More than the movies, he'd watched the audience eating their snacks. In the 1950's and '60's, the masala recipe was working—not only in Bombay but throughout South and Southeast Asia and the Middle East, and even in the Soviet Union. There was music mixed with murder, sob stories intercut with slapstick, mayhem in tandem with the most maudlin sentimentality—and, above all, the satisfying violence that occurs whenever the forces of good confront and punish the forces of evil. There were gods, too; they helped the heroes. But Dr. Daruwalla didn't believe in the usual gods; when he started writing, he'd just recently become a convert to Christianity. To that Hindi hodgepodge which was the Bombay cinema, the doctor added his tough-guy voice-over and Dhar's antiheroic sneer. Farrokh would wisely leave his newfound Christianity out of the picture.

He'd followed Danny Mills's recommendations to the letter. He selected a director he liked. Balraj Gupta was a young man with a less heavy hand than most—he had an almost self-mocking manner—and more important, he was not such a well-known director that Dr. Daruwalla couldn't bully him a little. The deal was as Danny Mills had said a deal should be, including the doctor's choice of the young, unknown actor who would play Inspector Dhar. John Daruwalla was 22.

Farrokh's first effort to pass off the young man as an Anglo-Indian wasn't at all convincing to Balraj Gupta. "He looks like some kind of

European to me," the director complained, "but his Hindi is the real thing, I guess." And after the success of the first Inspector Dhar movie, Balraj Gupta would never dream of interfering with the orthopedist (from Canada!) who'd given Bombay its most hated antihero.

The first movie was called *Inspector Dhar and the Hanging Mali*. This was more than 20 years after a *real* gardener had been found hanging from a neem tree on old Ridge Road in Malabar Hill, a posh part of town for anyone to be hanged in. The mali was a Muslim who'd just been dismissed from tending the gardens of several Malabar Hill residents; he'd been accused of stealing, but the charge had never been proven and there were those who claimed that the real-life gardener had been fired because of his extremist views. The mali was said to be furious about the closing of the Mosque of Babar.

Although Farrokh fictionalized the mali's story 20 years after the little-known facts of the case, *Inspector Dhar and the Hanging Mali* wasn't viewed as a period piece. For one thing, the 16th-century Babri mosque was still in dispute. The Hindus still wanted their idols to remain in the mosque in honor of the birthplace of Rama. The Muslims still wanted the idols removed. In the late 1960's, very much in keeping with the language of that time, the Muslims said they wanted to "liberate" the Mosque of Babar—whereas it was the birthplace of Rama that the Hindus said *they* wanted to liberate.

In the movie, Inspector Dhar sought to keep the peace. And, of course, this was impossible. The essence of an Inspector Dhar movie was that violence could be relied upon to erupt around him. Among the earliest of the victims was Inspector Dhar's wife! Yes, he was married in the first movie, albeit briefly; the car-bomb death of his wife apparently justified his sexual licentiousness for the rest of the movie—and for all the other Inspector Dhar movies to come. And everyone was supposed to believe that this all-white Dhar was a Hindu. He's seen lighting his wife's cremation fire; he's seen wearing the traditional dhoti, with his head traditionally shaved. All during the course of the first movie, his hair is growing back. Other women rub the stubble, as if in the most profound respect for his late wife. His status as a widower gains him great sympathy and lots of women—a very Western idea, and very offensive.

To begin with, both Hindus and Muslims were offended. Widowers were offended, not to mention widows and gardeners. And from the very first Inspector Dhar movie, policemen were offended. The misfortune of the real-life hanging mali had never been explained. The crime—that is, if it *was* a crime, if the gardener hadn't hanged himself—was never solved.

In the movie, the audience is offered three versions of the hanging, each one a perfect solution. Thus the unfortunate mali is hanged three times, and each hanging offended some group. Muslims were angry that Muslim fanatics were blamed for hanging the gardener. Hindus were outraged that Hindu fundamentalists were blamed for hanging the gardener; and Sikhs were incensed that Sikh extremists were blamed for hanging the gardener, as a means of setting Muslims and Hindus against each other. The Sikhs were also offended because every time there's a taxi in the movie, it's driven wildly and aggressively by someone who's perceived to be a crazed Sikh.

But the film was terribly *funny*! Dr. Daruwalla had thought.

In the darkness of the Ladies' Garden, Farrokh reconsidered. *Inspector Dhar and the Hanging Mali* might have been terribly funny to *Canadians*, he imagined—with the notable exception of Canadian gardeners. But Canadians had never seen the film, except those former Bombayites who lived in Toronto; they'd watched all the Inspector Dhar movies on videocassettes, and even *they* were offended. Inspector Dhar himself had never found his films especially funny. And when Dr. Daruwalla had questioned Balraj Gupta concerning the comic (or at least satiric) nature of the Inspector Dhar movies, the director had responded in a most offhand manner. "They make lots of lakhs!" the director had said. "Now *that's* funny!"

But it was no longer funny to Farrokh.

What if Mrs. Dogar Was a Hijra?

In the first darkness of the evening, the Duckworthians with small children had begun to occupy the tables in the Ladies' Garden. The children enjoyed eating outdoors, but not even their enthusiastic high-pitched voices disturbed Farrokh's journey into the past. Mr. Sethna disapproved of all small children—he especially disapproved of eating with them—but he nevertheless considered it his duty to oversee Dr. Daruwalla's state of mind in the Ladies' Garden.

Mr. Sethna had seen Dhar leave with the dwarf, but when Vinod returned to the Duckworth Club—the steward assumed that the nasty-looking midget was simply making his taxi available to Dr. Daruwalla, too—the dwarf hadn't waddled in and out of the foyer, as usual; Vinod had gone into the Sports Shop, where the dwarf was on friendly terms with the ball boys and the racquet stringers. Vinod had become their favorite scavenger. Mr. Sethna disapproved of scavenging *and* of dwarfs; the steward thought dwarfs were disgusting. As for the ball boys and the racquet stringers, they thought Vinod was cute.

If the film press was at first being facetious when they referred to Vinod as "Inspector Dhar's dwarf bodyguard"—they also called the dwarf "Dhar's thug chauffeur"—Vinod took his reputation seriously. The dwarf was always well armed, and his weapons of choice were both legal and easily concealed in his taxi. Vinod collected squash-racquet handles from the racquet stringers at the Duckworth Sports Shop. When a racquet head was broken, a stringer sawed the head off and sanded down the stump until it was smooth; the remaining squash-racquet handle was of the right length and weight for a dwarf, and the wood was very hard. Vinod wanted only wooden racquet handles, which were becoming scarce. But the dwarf hoarded them; and the way he used them, he rarely broke one. He would jab or strike with only one racquet handle—he would go for the balls or the knees, or both—while he held the other handle out of reach. Invariably, the man under attack would grab hold of the offending racquet handle; thereupon Vinod would bring the other handle down on the man's wrist.

It had been an unbeatable tactic. Invite the man to grab one racquet handle, then break his wrist with the other handle. The hell with a man's head—Vinod often couldn't reach a man's head, anyway. A broken wrist usually stopped a fight; if a fool wanted to keep fighting, he would be fighting with one hand against two squash-racquet handles. If the film press had turned the dwarf into a bodyguard and a thug, Vinod didn't mind. He was genuinely protective of Inspector Dhar.

Mr. Sethna disapproved of such violence, *and* of the Sport Shop racquet stringers who happily provided Vinod with his arsenal of squash-racquet handles. The ball boys also gave the dwarf dozens of discarded tennis balls. In the car-driving business, as Vinod described it, there was a lot of "just waiting" in his car. The former clown and acrobat liked to keep busy. By squeezing the dead tennis balls, Vinod strengthened his hands; the dwarf also claimed that this exercise relieved his arthritis, although Dr. Daruwalla believed that aspirin was probably a more reliable source of relief.

It had occurred to Mr. Sethna that Dr. Daruwalla's longstanding relationship with Vinod was probably the reason the doctor didn't drive a car; it had been years since Farrokh had even owned a car in Bombay. The dwarf's reputation as Dhar's driver tended to obscure, for most observers, the fact that Vinod also drove for Dr. Daruwalla. It spooked Mr. Sethna how the doctor and the dwarf seemed so aware of each other—even as the dwarf loaded up his car with squash-racquet handles and old tennis balls, even as the doctor went on sitting in the Ladies' Garden. It was as if Farrokh always knew that Vinod was available—as if the dwarf were waiting only for him. Well, either for him or for Dhar.

It now occurred to Mr. Sethna that Dr. Daruwalla was intending to occupy his luncheon table through the dinner hours; perhaps the doctor was expecting dinner guests and had decided it was the simplest way to hold the table. But when the old steward inquired of Dr. Daruwalla about the number of place settings, Mr. Sethna was informed that the doctor was going home for "supper." Promptly, as if he'd been awakened from a dream, Farrokh got up to leave.

Mr. Sethna observed and overheard him calling his wife from the telephone in the foyer.

"Nein, Liebchen," said Dr. Daruwalla. "I have *not* told him—there wasn't a good moment to tell him." Then Mr. Sethna listened to Dr. Daruwalla on the subject of the murder of Mr. Lal. So it *is* a murder! Mr. Sethna thought. Bonked by his own putter! And when he heard the part about the two-rupee note in Mr. Lal's mouth, and specifically the intriguing threat that was connected to Inspector Dhar—MORE MEMBERS DIE IF DHAR REMAINS A MEMBER—Mr. Sethna felt that his eavesdropping efforts had been rewarded, at least for this day.

Then something mildly remarkable happened. Dr. Daruwalla hung up the phone and turned into the foyer without first looking where he was going, and who should he run smack into but the second Mrs. Dogar. The doctor bumped into her so hard, Mr. Sethna was excited by the possibility that the vulgar woman would be knocked down. But instead it was Farrokh who fell. More astonishing, upon the collision, Mrs. Dogar was shoved backward into *Mr.* Dogar—and *he* fell down, too. What a fool for marrying such a younger, stronger woman! Mr. Sethna thought. Then there was the usual bowing and apologizing, and everyone assured everyone else that he or she was absolutely fine. Sometimes the absurdities of good manners, which were demonstrated in such profusion at the Duckworth Club, gave Mr. Sethna gas.

Thus, finally, Farrokh escaped from the old steward's overseeing eye. But while he waited for Vinod to fetch the car, Dr. Daruwalla—unobserved by Mr. Sethna—touched the sore spot in his ribs, where there would surely be a bruise, and he marveled at the hardness and sturdiness of the second Mrs. Dogar. It was like running into a stone wall!

It crossed the doctor's mind that Mrs. Dogar was sufficiently masculine to be a hijra—not a hijra prostitute, of course, but just an *ordinary* eunuch-transvestite. In which case Mrs. Dogar might not have been eyeballing Inspector Dhar for the purpose of seducing him; instead, she might have had it in her mind to *castrate* him!

Farrokh felt ashamed of himself for thinking like a screenwriter again. How many Kingfishers have I had? he wondered; it relieved him to hold the beer accountable for his far-fetched fantasizing. In truth, he knew nothing about Mrs. Dogar—where she'd come from—but hijras occupied such a marginal position in Indian society; the doctor was aware that most of them came from the lower classes. Whoever she was, the second Mrs. Dogar was an upper-class woman. And *Mr.* Dogar—although he was a foolish old fart, in Farrokh's opinion—was a Malabar Hill man; he came from old money, and lots of it. Nor was Mr. Dogar *such* a fool that he wouldn't know the difference between a vagina and a burn scar from the famous hijra hot-oil treatment.

While he waited for Vinod, Dr. Daruwalla watched the second Mrs. Dogar help Mr. Dogar into their car. She towered over the poor parking-lot attendant, who sheepishly opened the driver's-side door for her. Farrokh was unsurprised to see that Mrs. Dogar was the driver in the family. He'd heard all about her fitness training, which he knew included weight lifting and other unfeminine pursuits. Perhaps she takes testosterone, too, the doctor imagined, for the second Mrs. Dogar looked as if her sex hormones were raging—her *male* sex hormones, Dr. Daruwalla speculated. He'd heard that such women sometimes develop a clitoris as large as a finger, as long as a young boy's penis!

When either too much Kingfisher *or* his run-amuck imagination caused Dr. Daruwalla to speculate in this fashion, the doctor was grateful that he was merely an orthopedic surgeon. He truly didn't want to know too much about these other things. Yet Farrokh had to force himself from further contemplation, for he found that he was wondering what would be worse: that the second Mrs. Dogar sought to emasculate Inspector Dhar, or that she was in amorous pursuit of the handsome actor—*and* that she possessed a clitoris of an altogether unseemly size.

Dr. Daruwalla was in such a transfixed state of mind, he didn't notice that Vinod had one-handedly wheeled into the circular driveway of the Duckworth Club and was, with his other hand, belatedly applying the brakes. The dwarf nearly ran the doctor down. At least this served to take Dr. Daruwalla's mind off the second Mrs. Dogar. If only for the moment, Farrokh forgot her.

Load Cycle

The better of the dwarf's two taxis—of those two that were equipped with hand controls—was in the shop. "The carburetor is being revised," Vinod explained. Since Dr. Daruwalla had no idea how one accomplished a carburetor revision, he didn't press the dwarf for details. They departed the Duckworth Club in Vinod's decaying Ambassador, which was the off-white color of a pearl—like graying teeth, Farrokh reflected. Also, its hand control for acceleration was inclined to stick.

Nevertheless, Dr. Daruwalla abruptly asked the dwarf to drive him past his father's former house on old Ridge Road, Malabar Hill; this was doubtless because Farrokh had his father and Malabar Hill on his mind. Farrokh and Jamshed had sold the house shortly after their father's murder—when Meher had decided to live out the rest of her life in the company of her children and her grandchildren, all of whom had already chosen *not* to live in India. Dr. Daruwalla's mother would die in Toronto, in the doctor's guest bedroom. Meher's death, in her sleep— when it had snowed all night—was as peaceful as the bombing of old Lowji had been violent.

It wasn't the first time Farrokh had asked Vinod to drive by his old Malabar Hill home. From the moving taxi, the house was barely visible. The former Daruwalla family estate reminded the doctor of how tangential his contact with the country of his birthplace had become, for Farrokh was a foreigner on Malabar Hill. Dr. Daruwalla lived, like a visitor, in one of those ugly apartment buildings on Marine Drive; he had the same view of the Arabian Sea as could be found from a dozen similar places. He'd paid 60 lakhs (about 250,000 dollars) for a flat of less than 1,200 square feet, and he hardly lived there at all—he visited India so rarely. He was ashamed that, the rest of the time, he didn't rent it out. But Farrokh knew he would have been a fool to do so; the tenancy laws in Bombay favor the tenants. If Dr. Daruwalla had tenants, he'd never get them out. Besides, from the Inspector Dhar movies, the doctor had made so many lakhs that he supposed he should spend some of them in Bombay. Through the marvels of a Swiss bank account and the guile of a cunning money-dealer, Dhar had been successful in getting a sizable portion of their earnings out of India. Dr. Daruwalla also felt ashamed of that.

Vinod seemed to sense when Dr. Daruwalla was vulnerable to charity. It was his own charitable enterprise that the dwarf was thinking of; Vinod was routinely shameless in seeking the doctor's support of his most fervent cause.

Vinod and Deepa had taken it upon themselves to rescue various urchins from the slums of Bombay; in short, they recruited street kids for the circus. They sought the more acrobatic beggars—demonstrably well coordinated children—and Vinod made every effort to steer these talented waifs toward circuses of more merit than the Great Blue Nile. Deepa was particularly devoted to saving child prostitutes, or would-be child prostitutes; rarely were these girls suitable circus material. To Dr. Daruwalla's knowledge, the only circus that had stooped to adopt any of Vinod and Deepa's discoveries was the less-than-great Blue Nile.

To Farrokh's considerable discomfort, many of these girls were Mr. Garg's discoveries—that is, long before Vinod and Deepa had found them. Mr. Garg was the owner and manager of the Wetness Cabaret, where a kind of concealed grossness was the norm. Strip joints, not to mention sex shows, aren't permitted in Bombay—at least not to the degree of explicitness that exists in Europe and in North America. In India, there's no nudity, whereas "wetness"—meaning wet, clinging, almost transparent clothing—is much in evidence, and sexually sugges-tive gestures are the mainstay of so-called exotic dancers in such seedy entertainment spots as Mr. Garg's. Among such spots, even including the Bombay Eros Palace, the Wetness Cabaret was the worst; yet the dwarf and his wife insisted to Dr. Daruwalla that Mr. Garg was the Good Samaritan of Kamathipura. In the many lanes of brothels that were there, and throughout the red-light district on Falkland Road and on Grant Road, the Wetness Cabaret was a haven.

It was only a haven compared to a brothel, Farrokh supposed. Whether one called Garg's girls strippers or "exotic dancers," most of them weren't whores. But many of them were runaways from the Kama-thipura brothels, or from the brothels on Falkland Road and on Grant Road. In the brothels, the virginity of these girls had been only briefly prized—until the madam supposed they were old enough, or until there was a high enough offer. But when many of these girls ran away to Mr. Garg, they were much too young for what the Wetness Cabaret offered;

ironically, they were old enough for prostitution but far too young to be exotic dancers.

According to Vinod, most men who wanted to *look* at women wanted the women to look like women; apparently, these weren't the same men who wanted to have sex with underage girls—and even those men, Vinod claimed, didn't necessarily want to *look* at those young girls. Therefore, Mr. Garg couldn't use them at the Wetness Cabaret, although Farrokh fantasized that Mr. Garg *had* used them in some private, unmentionable way.

Dr. Daruwalla's Dickensian theory was that Mr. Garg was perverse *because of* his physical appearance. The man gave Farrokh the creeps. Mr. Garg had made an astonishingly vivid impression on Dr. Daruwalla, considering that they had met only once; Vinod had introduced them. The enterprising dwarf was also Garg's driver.

Mr. Garg was tall and of military erectness, but with the sort of sallow complexion that Farrokh associated with a lack of exposure to daylight. The skin on Garg's face had an unhealthy, waxy sheen, and it was unusually taut, like the skin of a corpse. Further enhancing Mr. Garg's cadaverlike appearance was an unnatural slackness to his mouth; his lips were always parted, like the lips of someone who'd fallen asleep in a seated position, and his eye sockets were dark and bloated, as if full of stagnant blood. Worse, Mr. Garg's eyes were as yellow and opaque as a lion's—and as unreadable, Dr. Daruwalla thought. Worst of all was the burn scar. Acid had been flung in Mr. Garg's face, which he'd managed to turn to the side; the acid had shriveled one ear and burned a swath along his jawline and down the side of his throat, where the raw pink smear disappeared under the collar of his shirt. Not even Vinod knew who'd thrown the acid, or why.

All Mr. Garg's girls needed from Dr. Daruwalla was the trusted physician's assurance to the circuses that these girls were in the pink of health. But what could Farrokh say about the health of those girls from the brothels? Some of them were *born* in brothels; certain indications of congenital syphilis were easy to spot. And nowadays, the doctor couldn't recommend them to a circus without having them tested for AIDS; few circuses—not even the Great Blue Nile—would take a girl if she was HIV-positive. Most of them carried something venereal; at the very least, the girls always had to be de-wormed. So few of them were ever taken, even by the Great Blue Nile.

When the girls were rejected by the circus, what became of them?

("We are being good by trying," Vinod would answer.) Did Mr. Garg sell them back to a brothel, or did he wait for them to grow old enough to be Wetness Cabaret material? It appalled Farrokh that, by the standards of Kamathipura, Mr. Garg was considered a benevolent presence; yet Dr. Daruwalla knew of no evidence against Mr. Garg—at least nothing beyond the common knowledge that he bribed the police, who only occasionally raided the Wetness Cabaret.

The doctor had once imagined Mr. Garg as a character in an Inspector Dhar movie; in a first draft of *Inspector Dhar and the Cage-Girl Killer*, Dr. Daruwalla had written a cameo role for Mr. Garg—he was a child molester named Acid Man. Then Farrokh had thought better of it. Mr. Garg was too well known in Bombay. It might have become a legal matter, and there'd been the added risk of insulting Vinod and Deepa, which Dr. Daruwalla would never do. If Garg was no Good Samaritan, the doctor nevertheless believed that the dwarf and his wife were the real thing—they were saints to these children, or they tried to be. They were, as Vinod had said, "being good by trying."

Vinod's off-white Ambassador was approaching Marine Drive when the doctor gave in to the dwarf's nagging. "All right, all right—I'll examine her," Dr. Daruwalla told Vinod. "Who is she this time, and what's her story?"

"She is being a virgin," the dwarf explained. "Deepa is saying that she is already an almost boneless girl—a future plastic lady!"

"Who is saying she's a virgin?" the doctor asked.

"She is saying so," Vinod said. "Garg is telling Deepa that the girl is running away from a brothel before anyone is touching her."

"So *Garg* is saying she's a virgin?" Farrokh asked Vinod.

"Maybe almost a virgin—maybe close," the dwarf replied. "I am thinking she used to be a dwarf, too," Vinod added. "Or maybe she is being part-dwarf. I am almost thinking so."

"That's not possible, Vinod," said Dr. Daruwalla.

As the dwarf shrugged, the Ambassador surged into a rotary; the roundabout turn caused several tennis balls to roll across Farrokh's feet, and the doctor heard the clunking of squash-racquet handles from under Vinod's elevated seat. The dwarf had explained to Dr. Daruwalla that the handles of badminton racquets were too flimsy—they broke—and the handles of tennis racquets were too heavy to swing with sufficient quickness. The squash-racquet handles were just right.

Only because he already knew where it was, Farrokh could faintly make out the odd billboard that floated on the boat moored offshore in the Arabian Sea; the hoarding bobbed on the water. TIKTOK TISSUES were being advertised again tonight.

And tonight, and every night, the metal signs on the lampposts promised a good ride on APOLLO TYRES. The rush-hour traffic along Marine Drive had long ago subsided, and the doctor could tell by the lights from his own apartment that Dhar had already arrived; the balcony was lit up and Julia never sat on the balcony alone. They'd probably watched the sunset together, the doctor thought; he was aware, too, that the sun had set a long time ago. They'll both be mad at me, Farrokh decided.

The doctor told Vinod that he'd examine the "almost boneless" girl in the morning—the almost-a-virgin, Dr. Daruwalla almost said. The half-dwarf or former dwarf, the doctor imagined. Mr. Garg's girl! he thought grimly.

In the stark lobby of his apartment building, Farrokh felt for a moment that he could have been anywhere in the modern world. But when the elevator door opened, he was greeted by a familiar sign, which he detested.

SERVANTS ARE NOT ALLOWED

TO USE THE LIFT

UNLESS ACCOMPANIED BY CHILDREN

The sign assaulted him with a numbing sense of inadequacy. It was a part of the pecking order of Indian life—not only the acceptance of discrimination, which was worldwide, but the deification of it, which Lowji Daruwalla had believed was so infuriatingly Indian, even though much of it was inherited from the Raj.

Farrokh had tried to convince the Residents' Society to remove the offensive sign, but the rules about servants were inflexible. Dr. Daruwalla was the only resident of the building who wasn't in favor of forcing servants to use the stairs. Also, the Residents' Society discounted Farrokh's opinion on the grounds that he was a Non-Resident Indian— "NRI" was the doctor's official government category. If this dispute about the use of the lift was the kind of issue that old Lowji would have got himself killed over, the younger Dr. Daruwalla self-deprecatingly viewed his failure with the Residents' Society as typical of his political ineffectualness and his general out-of-itness.

As he got off the elevator, he said to himself, I'm not a functioning Indian. The other day, someone at the Duckworth Club had been outraged that a political candidate in New Delhi was conducting a campaign "strictly on the cow issue"; Dr. Daruwalla had been unable to contribute an opinion because he was unsure what the cow issue *was*. He was aware of the rise of groups to protect cows, and he supposed they were a part of the Hindu-revivalist wave, like those Hindu-chauvinist holy men proclaiming themselves to be reincarnations of the gods themselves—and demanding to be worshiped as gods, too. He knew that there was *still* Hindu-Muslim rioting over the Mosque of Babar—the underlying subject of his first Inspector Dhar movie, which he'd found so funny at the time. Now thousands of bricks had been consecrated and stamped SHRI RAMA, which means "respected Rama," and the foundation for a temple to Rama had been laid less than 200 feet from the Babri mosque. Not even Dr. Daruwalla imagined that the outcome of the 40-year feud over the Mosque of Babar would be "funny."

Here he was again, with his pathetic sense of *not belonging*. He knew that there were Sikh extremists, but he didn't know one personally. At the Duckworth Club, he was on the friendliest terms with Mr. Bakshi—a Sikh novelist, and a great conversationalist on the subject of American movie classics—yet they'd never discussed Sikh terrorists. And Farrokh knew about the Shiv Sena and the Dalit Panthers and the Tamil Tigers, but he knew nothing *personally*. There were more than 600 million Hindus in India; there were 100 million Muslims, and millions of Sikhs and Christians, too. There were probably not even 80,000 Parsis, Farrokh thought. But in his own small part of India—in his ugly apartment building on Marine Drive—all these contentious millions were reduced in the doctor's mind to what he called the elevator issue. Concerning the stupid lift, all these warring factions concurred: they disagreed only with *him*. Make the servants climb the stairs.

Farrokh had recently read about a man who was murdered because his mustache gave "caste offense"; apparently, the mustache was waxed to curl up—it should have drooped down. Dr. Daruwalla decided: Inspector Dhar should leave India and never come back. And *I* should leave India and never come back, too! he thought. For *so what* if he helped a few crippled children in Bombay? What business did he have even imagining "funny" movies about a country like this? He wasn't a writer. And what business did he have taking blood from dwarfs? He wasn't a geneticist, either.

Thus, with a characteristic loss of self-confidence, Dr. Daruwalla entered his apartment to face the music he was certain he would hear. He'd been late in telling his beloved wife that he'd invited his beloved

John Daruwalla for the evening meal, and the doctor had kept them both waiting. Also, he'd lacked the courage to tell Inspector Dhar the upsetting news.

Farrokh felt he was trapped in a circus act of his own creation, an annoying pattern of procrastination that he couldn't break out of. He was reminded of an item in the Great Royal Circus; at first he'd found it a charming sort of madness, but now he thought it might drive him crazy if he ever saw it again. It conveyed such a meaningless but relentless insanity, and the accompanying music was so repetitious; in Dr. Daruwalla's mind, the act stood for the lunatic monotony that weighed on everyone's life from time to time. The item was called Load Cycle, and it was a case of simplicity carried to idiotic extremes.

There were two bicycles, each one pedaled by a very solid, strong-looking woman. The pair followed each other around the ring. They were joined by other plump, dark-skinned women, who found a variety of means by which to mount the moving bicycles. Some of the women perched on little posts that extended from the hubs of the front and back wheels; some mounted the handlebars and wobbled precariously there—others teetered on the rear fenders. And regardless of how many women mounted the bicycles, the two strong-looking women kept pedaling. Then little girls appeared; they climbed on the shoulders and stood on the heads of the other women—including the laboring, sturdy pedalers—until two struggling *pyramids* of women were clinging to these two bicycles, which never stopped circling the ring.

The music was of a sustained madness equal to one fragment of the cancan, repeated and repeated, and all the dark-skinned women—both the fat, older women *and* the little girls—wore too much face powder, which gave them a minstrel-like aura of unreality. They also wore pale-purple tutus, and they smiled and smiled and smiled as they tottered around and around and around the ring. The last time the doctor had seen a performance of this item, he'd thought it would never end.

Perhaps there's a Load Cycle in everyone's life, thought Dr. Daruwalla. As he paused at the door of his apartment, Farrokh felt he'd been enduring a Load Cycle sort of day. Dr. Daruwalla could imagine the cancan music starting up again, as if he were about to be greeted by a dozen dark-skinned girls in pale-purple tutus—all of them white-faced and moving to the insane, incessant rhythm.

7. DR. DARUWALLA HIDES IN HIS BEDROOM

Now the Elephants Will Be Angry

But the past is a labyrinth. Where's the way out? In the front hall of his apartment, where there were no dark-skinned, white-faced women in tutus, the doctor was halted by the clear but distant sound of his wife's voice. It reached him all the way from the balcony, where Julia was indulging Inspector Dhar with his favorite view of Marine Drive. On occasion, Dhar slept on that balcony, either when he stayed so late that he preferred to spend the night, or else when he'd just arrived in Bombay and needed to reacquaint himself with the city's smell.

Dhar swore this was the secret to his successful, almost instant adjustment to India. He could arrive from Europe, straight from Switzerland's fresh air—tainted, in Zürich, with restaurant fumes and diesel exhaust, with burning coal and hints of sewer gas—but after just two or three days in Bombay, Dhar claimed, he was unbothered by the smog, or by the two or three million small fires for cooking food in the slums, or by the sweet rot of garbage, or even by the excremental horror of the four or five million who squatted at the curb or at the water's edge of the surrounding sea. For in a city of nine million, surely the shit of half of these was evident in the Bombay air. It took Dr. Daruwalla two or three weeks to adjust to that permeating odor.

In the front hall, where the prevailing smell was of mildew, the doctor quietly removed his sandals; he deposited his briefcase and his old dark-brown doctor's bag. He noted that the umbrellas in the umbrella stand were dusty with disuse; it had been three months since the end of the monsoon rains. Even from the closed kitchen he could detect the mutton and the dhal—so that's what we're having, again, he thought—but the aroma of the evening meal couldn't distract Dr. Daruwalla from the powerful nostalgia of his wife speaking German, which she always spoke whenever she and Dhar were alone.

Farrokh stood and listened to the Austrian rhythms of Julia's German—always the *ish* sound, never the *ick*—and in his mind's eye he could see her when she was 18 or 19, when he'd courted her in her mother's old yellow-walled house in Grinzing. It was a house cluttered with Biedermeier culture. There was a bust of Franz Grillparzer by the coat tree in the foyer. The work of a portraitist obsessively committed to children's innocent expressions dominated the tea room, which was crowded with more cutesiness in the form of porcelain birds and silver antelopes. Farrokh remembered the afternoon he'd made a nervous, sweeping gesture with the sugar bowl—he broke a painted-glass lamp shade.

There were two clocks in the room. One of them played a fragment of a waltz by Lanner on the half hour and a slightly longer fragment of a Strauss waltz on the hour; the second clock paid similar token acknowledgments to Beethoven and Schubert—understandably, it was set a full minute behind the other. Farrokh remembered that, while Julia and her mother cleaned up the mess he'd made of the lamp shade, first the Strauss and then the Schubert played.

Whenever he recalled their many afternoon teas together, he could visualize his wife as a teenager. She was always dressed in a fashion Lady Duckworth would have admired. Julia wore a cream-colored blouse with flounced sleeves and a high, ruffled collar. They spoke German because her mother's English wasn't as good as theirs. Nowadays, Farrokh and Julia spoke German only occasionally. It was still their love-making language, or what they spoke in the dark. It was the language in which Julia had told him, "I find you very attractive." After two years of courting her, he'd nevertheless felt this was forward of her; he'd been speechless. He was struggling with how to phrase the question—whether or not she was troubled by his darker color—when she'd added, "Especially your skin. The picture of your skin against my skin is very attractive." (*Das Bild*—"the picture.")

When people say that German or any other language is romantic, Dr.

Daruwalla thought, all they really mean is that they've enjoyed a past in the language. There was even a certain intimacy in listening to Julia speak German to Dhar, whom she always called John D. This was the servants' name for him, which Julia had adopted, much as she and Dr. Daruwalla had "adopted" the servants.

They were a feeble old couple, Nalin and Swaroop—Dr. Daruwalla's children and John D. had always called her Roopa—but they'd outlived Lowji and Meher, whom they'd first served. It was a form of semiretirement to work for Farrokh and Julia; they were so infrequently in Bombay. The rest of the time, Nalin and Roopa were caretakers for the flat. If Dr. Daruwalla sold the apartment, where could the old couple go? He'd agreed with Julia that they would try to sell the place, but only after the old servants died. Even if Farrokh kept returning to India, he was rarely in Bombay so long that he couldn't afford to stay in a decent hotel. Once, when one of the doctor's Canadian colleagues had teased him for being so conservative about things, Julia had remarked, "Farrokh isn't conservative—he's absolutely extravagant. He maintains an apartment in Bombay so that his parents' former servants will have a place to live!"

Just then the doctor overheard Julia say something about the Queen's Necklace, which was the local name for the string of lights along Marine Drive. This name originated when the lamplights were white; the smog lights were yellow now. Julia was saying that yellow wasn't a proper color for the necklace of a queen.

What a European she is! Dr. Daruwalla thought. He had the greatest affection for the way she'd managed to adapt to their life in Canada and to their sporadic visits to India without ever losing her old-world sensibility, which remained as distinctive in her voice as in her habit of "dressing" for dinner—even in Bombay. It wasn't the content of Julia's speech that Dr. Daruwalla was listening to—he wasn't eavesdropping. It was only to hear the sound of her German, her soft accent in combination with such exact phrasing. But he realized that if Julia was talking about the Queen's Necklace, she couldn't possibly have told Dhar the upsetting news; the doctor's heart sank because he realized how much he'd been hoping that his wife would have told the dear boy.

Then John D. spoke. If it soothed Farrokh to hear Julia's German, it disturbed him to hear German from Inspector Dhar. In German, the doctor could barely recognize the John D. he knew, and it disquieted Dr. Daruwalla to hear how much more energetically Dhar spoke in German than he spoke in English. This emphasized to Dr. Daruwalla the distance that had grown between them. But Dhar's university education had been in Zürich; he'd spent most of his life in Switzerland. And his serious (if not widely recognized) work as an actor in the theater, at the Schauspielhaus Zürich, was something that John Daruwalla took more pride in than he appeared to take in the commercial success of his role as Inspector Dhar. Why wouldn't his German be perfect?

There was also not the slightest edge of sarcasm in Dhar's voice when he spoke to Julia. Farrokh recognized a longstanding jealousy. John D. is more affectionate to Julia than he is to me, Dr. Daruwalla thought. And after all I've done for him! There was a fatherly bitterness to this idea, and it shamed him.

He slipped quietly into the kitchen, where the racket of the apparently never-ending preparation of the evening meal kept him from hearing the actor's well-trained voice. Besides, Farrokh had at first (and falsely) assumed that Dhar was merely contributing to the conversation about the Queen's Necklace. Then Dr. Daruwalla had heard the sudden mention of his own name—it was that old story about "the time Farrokh took me to watch the elephants in the sea." The doctor hadn't wanted to hear more, because he was afraid of the detectable tone of complaint he heard emerging in John D.'s memory. The dear boy was recalling that time he'd been frightened during the festival of Ganesh Chaturthi; it seemed that half the city had flocked to Chowpatty Beach, where they'd immersed their idols of the elephant-headed god, Ganesh. Farrokh hadn't prepared the child for the orgiastic frenzy of the crowd—not to mention the size of the elephant heads, many of which were larger than the heads of real elephants. Farrokh remembered the outing as the first and only time he'd seen John D. become hysterical. The dear boy was crying, "They're drowning the elephants! Now the elephants will be angry!"

And to think that Farrokh had criticized old Lowji for keeping the boy so sheltered. "If you take him only to the Duckworth Club," Farrokh had told his father, "what's he ever going to know about India?" What a hypocrite I've turned out to be! Dr. Daruwalla thought, for he knew of no one in Bombay who'd hidden from India as successfully as he'd concealed himself at the Duckworth Club—for years.

He'd taken an eight-year-old to Chowpatty Beach to watch a mob; there were hundreds of thousands dunking their idols of the elephant-headed god in the sea. What had he thought the child would make of this? It wasn't the time to explain the British ban on "gathering," their infuriating anti-assembly strictures; the hysterical eight-year-old was too young to appreciate this symbolic demonstration for freedom of expression. Farrokh tried to carry the crying boy against the grain of the crowd, but more and more the giant idols of Lord Ganesha were pressed against them; they were herded back to the sea. "It's just a celebration," he'd whispered in the child's ear. "It's not a riot." In his arms, Farrokh felt the little boy trembling. Thus had the doctor realized the full weight of his ignorance, not only of India but of the fragility of children.

Now he wondered if John D. was telling Julia, "This is my first memory of Farrokh." And I'm *still* getting the dear boy in trouble! Dr. Daruwalla thought.

The doctor distracted himself by poking his nose into the big pot of dhal. Roopa had long ago added the mutton, and she reminded him that he was late by remarking how fortunate it was that mutton usually defied overcooking. "The rice has dried out," she added sadly.

Old Nalin, ever the optimist, tried to make Dr. Daruwalla feel better. In his fragmentary English, Nalin said, "But plenty of beer!"

Dr. Daruwalla felt guilty that there was always so much beer around; the doctor's capacity for beer alarmed him, and Dhar's fondness for the brew seemed limitless. Since Nalin and Roopa did the shopping, the thought of the old couple struggling with those heavy bottles also made Dr. Daruwalla feel guilty. And there was the elevator issue: because they were servants, Nalin and Roopa weren't permitted to ride in the lift. Even with all those beer bottles, the elderly servants trudged up the stairs.

"And plenty of messages!" Nalin told the doctor. The old man was very fond of the new answering machine. Julia had insisted on it because Nalin and Roopa were terrible at taking messages; they couldn't transcribe a phone number or spell anyone's name. When the machine answered, the old man was thrilled to listen to it because he was absolved of any responsibility for the messages.

Farrokh took a beer with him. The apartment seemed so small. In Toronto, the Daruwallas owned a huge house. In Bombay, the doctor had to sneak through the living room, which was also the dining room, in order to get to the bedroom and the bathroom. But Dhar and Julia were still talking on the balcony; they didn't see him. John D. was reciting the most famous part of the story; it always made Julia laugh.

"They're drowning the elephants!" John D. was crying. "Now the elephants will be angry!" Dr. Daruwalla never thought that this sounded quite right in German.

If I run a bath, Farrokh speculated, they'll hear it and know I'm home.

I'll have a quick wash in the sink instead, the doctor thought. He spread out a clean white shirt on the bed. He chose an uncharacteristically loud necktie with a bright-green parrot on it; it was an old Christmas present from John D.—not a tie that the doctor would ever wear in public. Farrokh was unaware how the tie would at least enliven his navy-blue suit. These were absurd clothes for Bombay, especially when dining at home, but Julia was Julia.

After he'd washed, the doctor took a quick look at his answering machine; the message light was flickering. He didn't bother to count the number of messages. Don't listen to them now, he warned himself. Yet the spirit of procrastination was deeply ingrained in him; to join in John D. and Julia's conversation would lead to the inevitable confrontation concerning John D.'s twin. As Farrokh was deliberating, he saw the bundle of mail on his writing desk. Dhar must have gone out to the film studio and collected the fan mail, which was mostly hate mail.

It had long been their understanding that Dr. Daruwalla deserved the task of opening and reading the mail. Although the letters were addressed to Inspector Dhar, the content of these letters only rarely concerned Dhar's acting or lip-syncing skills; instead, the letters were invariably about the creation of Dhar's character or about a particular script. Because it was presumed that Dhar was the author of the screenplays, and thus the creator of his own character, the author himself was the source of the letter writers' principal outrage; their attacks were leveled at the man who'd made it all up.

Before the death threats, especially before the real-life murders of actual prostitutes, Dr. Daruwalla had been in no great hurry to read his mail. But the serial killings of the cage girls had become so publicly acknowledged as imitations of the movie murders that Inspector Dhar's mail had taken a turn for the worse. And in the light of Mr. Lal's murder, Dr. Daruwalla felt compelled to search the mail for threats of any kind. He looked at the sizable bundle of new letters and wondered if, under these circumstances, he should ask Dhar and Julia to help him read through them. As if their evening together didn't promise to be difficult enough! Maybe later, Farrokh thought—if the conversation comes around to it.

But, as he dressed, the doctor couldn't ignore the insistent flickering of the message light on his answering machine. Well, he needn't take the time to call anyone back, he thought, as he knotted his tie. Surely it wouldn't hurt to hear what these messages were about—he could just jot them down and return the calls later. And so Farrokh searched for a pad of paper and a pen, which wasn't easy to do without being heard, because the tiny bedroom was crammed full of the fragile, tinkling Victoriana he'd inherited from Lowji's mansion on Ridge Road. Although he'd taken only what he couldn't bear to auction, even his writing desk was crowded with the bric-a-brac of his childhood, not to mention the photographs of his three daughters; they were married, and therefore Dr. Daruwalla's writing desk also exhibited their wedding pictures—and the pictures of his several grandchildren. Then there were his favorite photographs of John D.—downhill-skiing at Wengen and at Klosters, cross-country skiing in Pontresina and hiking in Zermatt—and several framed playbills from the Schauspielhaus Zürich, with John Daruwalla in both supporting and leading roles. He was Jean in Strindberg's *Fräulein Julie*, he was Christopher Mahon in John Millington Synge's *Ein wahrer Held*, he was Achilles in Heinrich von Kleist's *Penthesilea*, he was Fernando in Goethe's *Stella*, he was Ivan in Chekhov's *Onkel Vanja*, he was Antonio in Shakespeare's *Der Kaufmann von Venedig*—once he'd been Bassanio. Shakespeare in German sounded so foreign to Farrokh. It depressed the doctor that he'd lost touch with the language of his romantic years.

At last he found a pen. Then he spotted a pad of paper under the silver statuette of Ganesh as a baby; the little elephant-headed god was sitting on the lap of his human mother, Parvati—a cute pose. Unfortunately, the grotesque reaction to *Inspector Dhar and the Cage-Girl Killer* had sickened Farrokh with elephants. This was unfair, for Ganesh was merely elephant-headed; the god had four human arms with human hands, and two human feet. Also, Lord Ganesha sported only one whole tusk—although sometimes the god held his broken tusk in one of his four hands.

Ganesh truly bore no resemblance to the drawing of that inappropriately mirthful elephant which, in the most recent Inspector Dhar film, was the signature of a serial killer—that unsuitable cartoon which the movie murderer drew on the bellies of slain prostitutes. That elephant was no god. Besides, *that* elephant had both tusks intact. Even so, Dr. Daruwalla was off elephants—in any form. The doctor wished he'd asked Deputy Commissioner Patel about those drawings that the *real* murderer was making, for the police had said no more to the press than that the artwork of the real-life killer and serial cartoonist was "an obvious variation on the movie theme." What did that mean?

The question deeply disturbed Dr. Daruwalla, who shuddered to recall the origin of his idea for the cartoon-drawing killer; the source of the doctor's inspiration had been nothing less than an *actual* drawing on the belly of an *actual* murder victim. Twenty years ago, Dr. Daruwalla had been the examining physician at the scene of a crime that was never solved. Now the police were claiming that a killer-cartoonist had stolen the mocking elephant from a movie, but the screenwriter knew where the original idea had come from. Farrokh had stolen it from a murderer—maybe from the *same* murderer. Wouldn't the killer know that the most recent Inspector Dhar movie was imitating *him?*

I'm over my head, as usual, Dr. Daruwalla decided. He also decided that he should give this information to Detective Patel—in case, somehow, the deputy commissioner didn't already know it. But how would Patel already know it? Farrokh wondered. Second-guessing himself was the doctor's second nature. At the Duckworth Club, Dr. Daruwalla had been impressed by the composure of the deputy commissioner; moreover, the doctor couldn't rid himself of the impression that Detective Patel had been hiding something.

Farrokh interrupted these unwelcome thoughts as quickly as they'd come to him. Sitting next to his answering machine, he turned the volume down before he pushed the button. Still in hiding, the secret screenwriter listened to the messages.

The First-Floor Dogs

Upon hearing Ranjit's complaining voice, Dr. Daruwalla instantly regretted his decision to forsake even one minute of Dhar and Julia's company for as much as one phone message. A few years older than the doctor, Ranjit had nevertheless maintained both unsuitable expectations and youthful indignation; the former involved his ongoing matrimonial advertisements, which Dr. Daruwalla found inappropriate for a medical secretary in his sixties. Ranjit's "youthful indignation" was most apparent in his responses to those women who, upon meeting him, turned him down. Naturally, Ranjit hadn't all this time been conducting nonstop matrimonial advertisements, dating back to his earliest employment as old Lowji's secretary. After exhaustive interviews, Ranjit had been successfully married—and long enough before Lowji's death so that the senior Dr. Daruwalla had once more enjoyed the secretary's prematrimonial industriousness.

But Ranjit's wife had recently died, and he was only a few years away from retirement. He still worked for the surgical associates at the Hospital for Crippled Children, and he always served as Farrokh's secretary whenever the Canadian was an Honorary Consultant Surgeon in Bombay. And Ranjit had decided that the time for remarrying was ripe. He thought he should do it without delay, for it made him sound younger to describe himself as a working medical secretary than to confess he was retired; just to be sure, in his more recent matrimonial advertisements, he'd attempted to capitalize on both his position *and* his pending retirement, citing that he was "rewardingly employed" *and* "anticipating a v. active, early retirement."

It was things like "v. active" that Dr. Daruwalla found unseemly about Ranjit's present matrimonials, and the fact that Ranjit was a shameless liar. Because of a standard policy at *The Times of India*—the advertising brides and grooms eschewed revealing their names, preferring the confidentiality of a number—it was possible for Ranjit to publish a half-dozen ads in the same Sunday's matrimonial pages. Ranjit had discovered it was popular to claim that caste was "no bar," while it was also still popular to declare himself a Hindu Brahmin—"caste-conscious and religion-minded, matching horoscopes a must." Therefore, Ranjit advertised several versions of himself simultaneously. He told Farrokh that he was seeking the very best wife, with or without caste-consciousness or religion. Why not give himself the benefit of meeting everyone who was available?

Dr. Daruwalla was embarrassed that he'd been inexorably drawn into the world of Ranjit's matrimonials. Every Sunday, Farrokh and Julia read through the marriage advertisements in *The Times of India*. It was a contest, to see which of them could identify all of Ranjit's ads. But Ranjit's phone message was not of a matrimonial nature. Once again, the aging secretary had called to complain about "the dwarf's wife." This was Ranjit's condemning reference to Deepa, for whom he harbored a forbidding disapproval—the kind that only Mr. Sethna might have shared. Dr. Daruwalla wondered if medical secretaries were universally cruel and dismissive to anyone seeking a doctor's attention. Was such hostility engendered only by a heartfelt desire to protect all doctors from wasting their time?

To be fair to Ranjit, Deepa was exceptionally aggressive in wasting Dr. Daruwalla's time. She'd called to make a morning appointment for the runaway child prostitute—even before Vinod had persuaded the doctor to examine this new addition to Mr. Garg's stable of street girls. Ranjit described the patient as "someone allegedly without bones," for Deepa had doubtless used her circus terminology ("boneless") with him.

Ranjit was communicating his scorn for the vocabulary of the dwarf's wife. From Deepa's description, the child prostitute might have been made of pure plastic—"another medical marvel, and no doubt a virgin," Ranjit concluded his sardonic message.

The next message was an old one, from Vinod. The dwarf must have called while Farrokh was still sitting in the Ladies' Garden at the Duckworth Club. The message was really for Inspector Dhar.

"Our favorite inspector is telling me he is sleeping on your balcony tonight," the dwarf began. "If he is changing his mind, I am just cruising—just killing time, you know. If the inspector is wanting me, he is already knowing the doormen at the Taj and at the Oberoi—for message-leaving, I am meaning. I am having a late-night picking-up at the Wetness Cabaret," Vinod admitted, "but this is being while you are sleeping. In the morning, I am picking up you, as usual. By the way, I am reading a magazine with *me* in it!" the dwarf concluded.

The only magazines that Vinod read were movie magazines, where he could occasionally glimpse himself in the celebrity snapshots opening the door of one of his Ambassadors for Inspector Dhar. There on the door would be the red circle with the *T* in it (for taxi) and the name of the dwarf's company, which was often partially obscured.

VINOD'S BLUE

NILE, LTD.

As opposed to "great," Farrokh presumed.

Dhar was the only movie star who rode in Vinod's cars; and the dwarf relished his occasional appearances with his "favorite inspector" in the film-gossip magazines. Vinod was enduringly hopeful that other movie stars would follow Dhar's lead, but Dimple Kapadia and Jaya Prada and Pooja Bedi and Pooja Bhatt—not to mention Chunky Pandey and Sunny Deol, or Madhuri Dixit and Moon Moon Sen, to name only a few—had all declined to ride in the dwarf's "luxury" taxis. Possibly they thought it would damage their reputations to be seen with Dhar's thug.

As for the "cruising" back and forth between the Oberoi and the Taj, these were Vinod's favorite territories for moonlighting. The dwarf was recognized and well treated by the doormen because whenever Dhar was in Bombay, the actor stayed at the Oberoi *and* at the Taj. By maintaining a suite at both hotels, Dhar was assured of good service; as long as the Oberoi and the Taj knew they were in competition with each other, they outdid themselves to give Dhar the utmost privacy. The house detectives were harsh with autograph seekers or other celebrity hounds; at the reception desk of either hotel, if you didn't know the given code name, which kept changing, you were told that the movie star was not a guest.

By "killing time," Vinod meant he was picking up extra money. The dwarf was good at spotting hapless tourists in the lobbies of both hotels; he would offer to drive the foreigners to a good restaurant, or wherever they wanted to go. Vinod was also gifted at recognizing those tourists who'd had harrowing taxi experiences and were therefore vulnerable to the temptations of his "luxury" service.

Dr. Daruwalla understood that the dwarf could hardly have supported himself by driving only the doctor and Dhar around. Mr. Garg was a more regular customer. Farrokh was also familiar with the dwarf's habit of "message-leaving," for Vinod had taken advantage of Inspector Dhar's celebrity status with the doormen at the Oberoi and at the Taj. It may have been awkward, but it was Vinod's only means of putting himself "on call." There were no cellular phones in Bombay; car phones were unknown—a decided inconvenience in the private-taxi business, which Vinod complained about periodically. There were radio pagers, or "beepers," but the dwarf wouldn't use them. "I am preferring to be holding out," Vinod maintained, by which he meant he was waiting for the day when cellular phones would upgrade his car-driving enterprise.

Therefore, if Farrokh or John D. wanted the dwarf, they left a message for him with the doormen at the Taj and the Oberoi. But there was another reason for Vinod to call. Vinod didn't like showing up at Dr. Daruwalla's apartment building unannounced; there was no phone in the lobby, and Vinod refused to see himself as a "servant"—he refused to climb the stairs. When it came to climbing stairs, his dwarfism was a handicap. Dr. Daruwalla had protested, on Vinod's behalf, to the Residents' Society. At first, Farrokh had argued that the dwarf was a cripple—cripples shouldn't be forced to use the stairs. The Residents' Society had argued that cripples shouldn't be servants. Dr. Daruwalla had countered that Vinod was an independent businessman; the dwarf was nobody's servant. After all, Vinod owned a private-taxi company. A chauffeur was a servant, the Residents' Society said.

Regardless of the absurd ruling, Farrokh had told Vinod that if he ever had to come to the Daruwallas' sixth-floor flat, he was to take the restricted residents' elevator. But whenever Vinod stood in the lobby and waited for the elevator—regardless of the lateness of the hour—his presence would be detected by the first-floor dogs. The first-floor flats harbored a disproportionate number of dogs; and although the doctor was disinclined to believe Vinod's interpretation—that all dogs hated all dwarfs—he could offer no scientifically acceptable reason why all the first-floor dogs should suddenly awake and commence their frenzied barking whenever Vinod was waiting for the forbidden lift.

And so it was tediously necessary for Vinod to arrange an exact time for picking up Farrokh or John D. so that the dwarf could wait in the Ambassador at the curb—or in the nearby alley—and not enter the lobby of the apartment building at all. Besides, it sorely tested the delicate ecosystem of the apartment building to have Vinod attract the late-night, furious attention of the first-floor dogs; and Farrokh was already in hot water with the Residents' Society—his dissent to their opinion on the elevator issue had offended the building's other residents.

Since the doctor was the son of an acknowledged great man—and a famously assassinated great man, too—there was other fuel for resenting Dr. Daruwalla. That he lived abroad and could still afford to have his apartment occupied by his servants—often, for years without a single visit—had certainly made him unpopular, if not openly despised.

That the dogs appeared guilty of discrimination against dwarfs wasn't the sole reason that Dr. Daruwalla disliked them. Their insane barking disturbed the doctor because of its total irrationality; *any* irrationality reminded Farrokh of everything he failed to comprehend about India.

Only that morning he'd stood on his balcony and overheard his fifth-floor neighbor, Dr. Malik Abdul Aziz—a model "Servant of the Almighty"—praying on the balcony below him. When Dhar slept on the balcony, he often commented to Farrokh on how soothing it was to wake up to the prayers of Dr. Aziz.

"Praise be to Allah, Lord of Creation"—that much Dr. Daruwalla had understood. And later there was something about "the straight path." It was a very pure prayer—Farrokh had liked it, and he'd long admired Dr. Aziz for his unswerving faith—but Dr. Daruwalla's thoughts had veered sharply away from religion, in the direction of politics, because he was reminded of the aggressive billboards he'd seen around the city. The messages on such hoardings were essentially hostile; they merely purported to be religious.

ISLAM IS THE ONE PATH
TO HUMANITY FOR ALL

And that wasn't as bad as those Shiv Sena slogans, which were all over Bombay. (MAHARASHTRA FOR MAHARASHTRIANS. Or, SAY IT WITH PRIDE: I'M A HINDU.)

Something evil had corrupted the purity of prayer. Something as dignified and private as Dr. Aziz, with his prayer rug rolled out on his own balcony, had been compromised by proselytizing, had been distorted by politics. And if this madness had a sound, Farrokh knew, it would be the sound of irrationally barking dogs.

Inoperable

In the apartment building, Dr. Daruwalla and Dr. Aziz were the most consistent early risers; surgeries for both—Dr. Aziz was a urologist. If he prays every morning, so should I, Farrokh thought. Politely, that morning, he had waited for the Muslim to finish. There followed the shuffling sound of Dr. Aziz's slippers as he rolled up his prayer rug while Dr. Daruwalla leafed through his *Book of Common Prayer;* Farrokh was looking for something appropriate, or at least familiar. He was ashamed that his ardor for Christianity seemed to be receding into the past, or had his faith entirely retreated? After all, it had been only a minor sort of miracle that had converted him; perhaps Farrokh needed another small miracle to inspire him now. He realized that most Christians were faithful without the incentive of any miracle, and this realization instantly interfered with his search for a prayer. As a Christian, too, he'd lately begun to wonder if he was a fake.

In Toronto, Farrokh was an unassimilated Canadian—*and* an Indian who avoided the Indian community. In Bombay, the doctor was constantly confronted with how little he knew India—and how unlike an Indian he thought himself to be. In truth, Dr. Daruwalla was an orthopedist and a Duckworthian, and—in both cases—he was merely a member of two private clubs. Even his conversion to Christianity felt false; he was merely a holiday churchgoer, Christmas and Easter—he couldn't remember when he'd last partaken of the innermost pleasure of prayer.

Although it was quite a mouthful—and it was the whole story of what he was supposed to believe, in a nutshell—Dr. Daruwalla had begun his experiment in prayer with the so-called Apostles' Creed, the standard Confession of the Faith. " 'I believe in God the Father Almighty, Maker of heaven and earth . . .'" Farrokh recited breathlessly, but the capital letters were a distraction to him; he stopped.

Later, as he had stepped into the elevator, Dr. Daruwalla reflected on how easily his mood for prayer had been lost. He resolved that he would compliment Dr. Aziz on his highly disciplined faith at the first opportunity. But when Dr. Aziz stepped into the elevator at the fifth floor, Farrokh was completely flustered. He scarcely managed to say, "Good morning, Doctor—you're looking well!"

"Why, thank you—so are you, Doctor!" said Dr. Aziz, looking somewhat sly and conspiratorial. When the elevator door closed and they were alone together, Dr. Aziz said, "Have you heard about Dr. Dev?"

Farrokh wondered, *Which* Dr. Dev? There was a Dr. Dev who was a cardiologist, there was another Dev who was an anesthesiologist—there are a bunch of Devs, he thought. Even Dr. Aziz was known in the medical community as Urology Aziz, which was the only sensible way to distinguish him from a half-dozen other Dr. Azizes.

"Dr. Dev?" Dr. Daruwalla asked cautiously.

"Gastroenterology Dev," said Urology Aziz.

"Oh, yes, *that* Dr. Dev," Farrokh said.

"But have you heard?" asked Dr. Aziz. "He has AIDS—he caught it from a patient. And I don't mean from sexual contact."

"From *examining* a patient?" Dr. Daruwalla said.

"From a colonoscopy, I believe," said Dr. Aziz. "She was a prostitute."

"From a colonoscopy . . . but *how?*" Dr. Daruwalla asked.

"At least forty percent of the prostitutes must be infected with the virus," Dr. Aziz said. "Among my patients, the ones who see prostitutes test HIV-positive twenty percent of the time!"

"But from a colonoscopy. I don't understand *how,*" Farrokh insisted, but Dr. Aziz was too excited to listen.

"I have patients telling *me*—a urologist—that they have cured themselves of AIDS by drinking their own urine!" Dr. Aziz said.

"Ah, yes, urine therapy," said Dr. Daruwalla. "Very popular, but—"

"But *here* is the problem!" cried Dr. Aziz. He pulled a folded piece of paper from his pocket; some words were scrawled on the paper in longhand. "Do you know what the *Kama Sutra* says?" Dr. Aziz asked Farrokh. Here was a Muslim asking a Parsi (and a convert to Christianity) about a Hindu collection of aphorisms concerning sexual exploits— some would say "love." Dr. Daruwalla thought it wise to be careful; he said nothing.

As for urine therapy, it was also wise to say nothing. Moraji Desai, the former prime minister, was a practitioner of urine therapy—and wasn't there something called the Water of Life Foundation? Best to say nothing about that, too, Farrokh concluded. Besides, Urology Aziz wanted to read something from the *Kama Sutra*. It would be best to listen.

"Among the *many* situations where adultery is allowed," Dr. Aziz said, "just listen to *this:* 'When such clandestine relations are safe and a sure method of earning money.' " Dr. Aziz refolded the often-folded piece of paper and returned this evidence to his pocket. "Well, do you see?" he said.

"What do you mean?" Farrokh asked.

"Well, that's the problem—obviously!" Dr. Aziz said.

Farrokh was still trying to figure out how Dr. Dev had caught AIDS while performing a colonoscopy; meanwhile, Dr. Aziz had concluded that AIDS among prostitutes was caused directly by the bad advice given in the *Kama Sutra*. (Farrokh doubted that most prostitutes could read.) This was another example of the first-floor dogs—they were barking again. Dr. Daruwalla smiled nervously all the way to the entrance to the alley, where Urology Aziz had parked his car.

There'd been some brief confusion, because Vinod's Ambassador had momentarily blocked the alley, but Dr. Aziz was soon on his way. Farrokh had waited in the alley for the dwarf to turn his car around. It was a close, narrow alley—briny-smelling, because of the proximity of the sea, and as warm and steamy as a blocked drain. The alley was a haven for the beggars who frequented the small seaside hotels along Marine Drive. Dr. Daruwalla supposed that these beggars were especially interested in the Arab clientele; they were reputed to give more money. But the beggar who suddenly emerged from the alley wasn't one of these.

He was a badly limping boy who could occasionally be seen standing on his head at Chowpatty Beach. The doctor knew that this wasn't a trick of sufficient promise for Vinod and Deepa to offer the urchin a home at the circus. The boy had slept on the beach—his hair was caked with sand—and the first sunlight had driven him into the alley for a few more hours' sleep. The two automobiles, arriving and departing, had probably attracted his attention. When Vinod backed the Ambassador into the alley, the beggar blocked the doctor's way to the car. The boy stood with both arms extended, palms up; there was a veil of mucous over his eyes and a whitish paste marked the corners of his mouth.

The eyes of the orthopedic surgeon were drawn to the boy's limp. The beggar's right foot was rigidly locked in a right-angle position, as

if the foot and ankle were permanently fused—a deformity called ankylosis, which was familiar to Dr. Daruwalla from the common congenital
condition of clubfoot. Yet both the foot and ankle were unusually
flattened—a crush injury, the doctor guessed—and the boy bore his
weight on his heel alone. Also, the bad foot was considerably smaller
than the good one; this led the doctor to imagine that the injury had
damaged the epiphyseal plates, which is the region in bones where
growth takes place. It wasn't only that the boy's foot had fused with his
ankle; his foot had also stopped growing. Farrokh felt certain that the
boy was inoperable.

Just then, Vinod opened the driver's-side door. The beggar was wary
of the dwarf, but Vinod wasn't brandishing his squash-racquet handles.
The dwarf was nevertheless determined to open the rear door for Dr.
Daruwalla, who observed that the beggar was taller but frailer than
Vinod—Vinod simply pushed the boy out of the way. Farrokh saw the
beggar stumble; his mashed foot was as stiff as a hammer. Once inside
the Ambassador, the doctor lowered the window only enough so that the
boy could hear him.

"Maaf karo," Dr. Daruwalla said gently. It was what he always said to
beggars: "Forgive me."

The boy spoke English. "I *don't* forgive you," he said.

Also in English, Farrokh said what was on his mind: "What happened
to your foot?"

"An elephant stepped on it," the cripple replied.

That would explain it, the doctor thought, but he didn't believe the
story; beggars were liars.

"Was it being a circus elephant?" Vinod inquired.

"It was just an elephant stepping off a train," the boy told the dwarf.
"I was a baby, and my father left me lying on the station platform—he
was in a bidi shop."

"You were stepped on by an elephant while your father was buying
cigarettes?" Farrokh asked. This certainly sounded like a tall tale, but
the cripple listlessly nodded. "So I suppose your name is Ganesh—after
the elephant god," Dr. Daruwalla asked the boy. Without appearing to
notice the doctor's sarcasm, the cripple nodded again.

"It was the wrong name for me," the boy replied.

Apparently, Vinod believed the beggar. "He is being a doctor," the
dwarf said, pointing to Farrokh. "He is fixing you, maybe," Vinod added,
pointing to the boy. But the beggar was already limping away from the
car.

"You can't fix what elephants do," Ganesh said.

The doctor didn't believe he could fix what the elephant had done, either. "Maaf karo," Dr. Daruwalla repeated. Neither stopping nor bothering to look back, the cripple made no further response to Farrokh's favorite expression.

Then the dwarf drove Dr. Daruwalla to the hospital, where one surgery for clubfoot and another for wryneck awaited him. Farrokh tried to distract himself by daydreaming about a back operation—a laminectomy with fusion. Then Dr. Daruwalla dreamed of something more ambitious—the placement of Harrington rods for a severe vertebral infection, with vertebral collapse. But even in prepping his surgeries for the clubfoot and the wryneck, the doctor would keep thinking about how he might fix the beggar's foot.

Farrokh could cut through the fibrous tissue and the contracted, shrunken tendons—there were plastic procedures to elongate tendons—but the problem with such a crush injury was the bony fusion; Dr. Daruwalla would have to saw through bone. By damaging the vascular bundles around the foot, he could compromise the blood supply; the result might be gangrene. Of course there was always amputation and the fitting of a prosthesis, but the boy would probably refuse such an operation. In fact, Farrokh knew, his own father would have refused to perform such an operation; as a surgeon, Lowji had lived by the old adage *primum non nocere*—above all, do no harm.

Forget the boy, Farrokh had thought. Thus he'd performed the clubfoot and the wryneck and, thereafter, he'd faced the Membership Committee at the Duckworth Club, where he had also lunched with Inspector Dhar, a lunch much disturbed by the death of Mr. Lal and the discomfort that D.C.P. Patel had caused them. (Dr. Daruwalla had had a busy day.)

And now, as he listened to the phone messages on his answering machine, Farrokh was trying to imagine the precise moment in the bougainvillea by the ninth green when Mr. Lal had been struck down. Perhaps when Dr. Daruwalla was in surgery; possibly before, when he'd encountered Dr. Aziz on the elevator, or one of the times when he'd said "Maaf karo" to the crippled beggar whose English was unbelievably good.

Doubtless the boy was one of those enterprising beggars who sold himself as a guide to foreign tourists. Cripples were the best hustlers, Farrokh knew. Many of them had maimed themselves; some of them had been purposefully injured by their parents—for being crippled improved their opportunities as beggars. These thoughts of mutilation, especially of self-inflicted wounds, led the doctor to thinking about the hijras again. Then his thoughts returned to the golf-course murder.

In retrospect, what astonished Dr. Daruwalla was how anyone could have gotten close enough to Mr. Lal to strike the old golfer with his own putter. For how could you sneak up on a man who was flailing away in the flowers? His body would have been twisting from side to side, and bending over to fuss with the stupid ball. And where would his golf bag have been? Not far away. How could anyone approach Mr. Lal's golf bag, take out the putter and then hit Mr. Lal—all when Mr. Lal wasn't looking? It wouldn't work in a movie, Farrokh knew—not even in an Inspector Dhar movie.

That was when the doctor realized that Mr. Lal's murderer had to have been someone Mr. Lal knew, and if the murderer had been another golfer—presumably with his own bag of clubs—why would he have needed to use Mr. Lal's putter? But what a nongolfer could have been doing in the vicinity of the ninth green—and still not have aroused Mr. Lal's suspicions—was at least for the moment quite beyond the imaginative powers of Inspector Dhar's creator.

Farrokh wondered what sort of dogs were barking in the killer's head. Angry dogs, Dr. Daruwalla supposed, for in the murderer's mind there was such a terrifying irrationality; the mind of Dr. Aziz would appear reasonable in comparison. But then Farrokh's speculations on this subject were interrupted by the third phone message. The doctor's answering machine was truly relentless.

"Goodness!" cried the unidentified voice. It was a voice of such lunatic exuberance, Dr. Daruwalla presumed it was no one he knew.

8. TOO MANY MESSAGES

For Once, the Jesuits Don't Know Everything

At first Farrokh failed to recognize the hysterical enthusiasm that characterized the voice of the ever-optimistic Father Cecil, who was 72 and therefore easily panicked by the challenge to speak clearly and calmly to an answering machine. Father Cecil was the senior priest at St. Ignatius, an Indian Jesuit of unrelenting good cheer; as such, he stood in startling juxtaposition to the Father Rector—Father Julian—who was 68 years old and English and one of those intellectual Jesuits with a caustic disposition. Father Julian was so sarcastic that he was an instant source of renewing Dr. Daruwalla's combined awe and suspicion of Catholics. But the message was from Father Cecil—therefore free of facetiousness. "Goodness!" Father Cecil began, as if offering a general description of the world he saw all around him.

What now? thought Dr. Daruwalla. Because he was among the distinguished alumni of St. Ignatius School, Farrokh was frequently asked to give inspirational speeches to the students; in previous years, he'd also addressed the Young Women's Christian Association. He'd once been an almost active member of the Catholic and Anglican Community for Christian Unity and the so-called Hope Alive Committee. But such activities failed to interest him anymore. Dr. Daruwalla sincerely hoped that Father Cecil wasn't calling him with a repeat request for the doctor to relate *again* the stirring experience of his conversion.

After all, despite Dr. Daruwalla's past commitment to Catholic and Anglican unity, he was an Anglican; he felt uncomfortable in the presence of a certain overzealous, albeit small, percentage of the faithful followers of St. Ignatius Church. Farrokh had declined a recent invitation to speak at the Catholic Charismatic Information Centre; the suggested topic had been "The Charismatic Renewal in India." The doctor had replied that his own *small* experience—the entirely quiet, *little* miracle of his conversion—didn't compare to ecstatic religious experiences (speaking in tongues and spontaneous healing, and so forth). "But a miracle is a miracle!" Father Cecil had said. To Farrokh's surprise, Father Julian had taken the doctor's side.

"I quite agree with Dr. Daruwalla," Father Julian had said. "His experience hardly qualifies as a miracle at all."

Dr. Daruwalla had been miffed. He was quite willing to portray his conversion experience as a low-key kind of miracle; he was always humble when relating the story. There were no marks on his body that even remotely resembled the wounds on the crucified body of Christ. His was no stigmata story. He wasn't one of those nonstop bleeders! But for the Father Rector to dismiss his experience as hardly qualifying as a miracle *at all* . . . well, this sorely vexed Dr. Daruwalla. The insult fueled Farrokh's insecurities and prejudices in regard to the superior education of the Jesuits. They were not only holier than thou, they were more *knowing* than thou! But the message was about Dhar's twin, not about the doctor's conversion.

Of course! Dhar's twin was the first American missionary in the highly esteemed 125-year history of St. Ignatius; neither the church nor the school had been blessed with an American missionary before. Dhar's twin was what the Jesuits call a scholastic, which Dr. Daruwalla already understood to mean that he'd endured much religious and philosophic study and that he'd taken his simple vows. However, the doctor knew, Dhar's twin was still a few years away from being ordained as a priest. This was a period of soul-searching, Dr. Daruwalla supposed—the final test of those simple vows.

The vows themselves gave Farrokh the shivers. Poverty, chastity, obedience—they weren't so "simple." It was hard to imagine the progeny of a Hollywood screenwriter like Danny Mills opting for poverty; it was harder still to conceive of the offspring of Veronica Rose choosing chastity. And regarding the tricky Jesuitical ramifications of obedience,

Dr. Daruwalla knew that he himself didn't know nearly enough. What he also suspected was that, should one of those crafty Jesuits try to explain "obedience" to him, the explanation itself would be a marvel of equivocation—of oversubtle reasoning—and, in the end, Farrokh would have no clearer understanding of a vow of obedience than he'd had before. In Dr. Daruwalla's estimation, the Jesuits were intellectually crafty and sly. And this was hardest of all for the doctor to imagine: that a child of Danny Mills and Veronica Rose could be intellectually crafty and sly. Even Dhar, who'd had a decent European education, was no intellectual.

But then Dr. Daruwalla reminded himself that Dhar and his twin could also be the genetic creation of Neville Eden. Neville had always struck Farrokh as crafty and sly. What a puzzle! Just what was a man who was almost 40 *doing* by becoming—or trying to become—a priest? What failures had led him to this? Farrokh assumed that only blunders or disillusionments could lead a man to vows of such a radically repressive nature.

Now here was Father Cecil saying that "young Martin" had mentioned, in a letter, that Dr. Daruwalla was "an old friend of the family." So his name was Martin—Martin Mills. Farrokh remembered that, in *her* letter to him, Vera had already told him this. And "young Martin" wasn't so young, Dr. Daruwalla knew—except to Father Cecil, who was 72. But the gist of Father Cecil's phone message caught Dr. Daruwalla by surprise.

"Do you know exactly when he's coming?" Father Cecil asked.

What does he mean—do *I* know? Farrokh thought. Why doesn't *he* know? But neither Father Julian nor Father Cecil could remember exactly when Martin Mills was arriving; they blamed Brother Gabriel for losing the American's letter.

Brother Gabriel had come to Bombay and St. Ignatius after the Spanish Civil War; he'd been on the Communist side, and his first contribution to St. Ignatius had been to collect the Russian and Byzantine icons for which the mission chapel and its icon-collection room were famous. Brother Gabriel was also in charge of the mail.

When Farrokh was 10 or 12 and a student at St. Ignatius, Brother Gabriel would have been 26 or 28; Dr. Daruwalla remembered that Brother Gabriel was at that time still struggling to learn Hindi and Marathi, and that his English was melodious, with a Spanish accent. The doctor recalled a short, sturdy man in a black cassock, exhorting an army of sweepers to raise more and more clouds of dust from the stone floors.

Farrokh also remembered that Brother Gabriel was in charge of the other servants, and the garden, and the kitchen, *and* the linen room—in addition to the mail. But the icons were his passion. He was a friendly, vigorous man, neither an intellectual· nor a priest, and Dr. Daruwalla calculated that, today, Brother Gabriel would be around 75. No wonder he's losing letters, Farrokh thought.

So no one knew exactly when Dhar's twin would arrive! Father Cecil added that the American's teaching duties would commence almost immediately. St. Ignatius didn't recognize the week between Christmas and New Year's as a holiday; only Christmas Day and New Year's Day were school vacations, an annoyance that Farrokh remembered from his own school days. The doctor guessed that the school was still sensitive to the charge made by many non-Christian parents that Christmas was overemphasized.

It was possible, Father Cecil opined, that young Martin would make contact with Dr. Daruwalla before he contacted anyone at St. Ignatius. Or perhaps the doctor had already heard from the American? *Already heard?* thought Dr. Daruwalla, in a panic.

Here was Dhar's twin—due to arrive any day now—and Dhar still didn't know! And the naïve American would arrive at Sahar Airport at 2:00 or 3:00 in the morning; that was when all the flights from Europe and North America arrived. (Dr. Daruwalla presumed that *all* Americans coming to India were "naïve.") At that dreadfully early hour, St. Ignatius would quite literally be closed—like a castle, like an army barracks, like the compound or the cloister that it was. If the priests and brothers didn't know exactly when Martin Mills was arriving, no one would leave any lights on or any doors open for him—no one would meet his plane. And so the bewildered missionary might come directly to Dr. Daruwalla; he might simply show up on the doctor's doorstep at 3:00 or 4:00 in the morning. (Dr. Daruwalla presumed that *all* missionaries coming to India were "bewildered.")

Farrokh couldn't remember what he'd written to Vera. Had he given the horrid woman his home address or the address of the Hospital for Crippled Children? Fittingly, she'd written to him in care of the Duckworth Club. Of Bombay, of all of India, it was possibly only the Duckworth Club that Vera remembered. (Doubtless she'd repressed the cow.)

Damn other people's messes! Dr. Daruwalla was muttering aloud. He was a surgeon; as such, he was an extremely neat and tidy man. The sheer sloppiness of human relationships appalled him, especially those relationships to which he felt he'd brought a special responsibility and care. Brother-sister, brother-brother, child-parent, parent-child. What was the matter with human beings, that they made such a shambles out of these basic relationships?

Dr. Daruwalla didn't want to hide Dhar from his twin. He didn't want to hurt Danny—with the cruel evidence of what his wife had done, and how she'd lied—but he felt he was largely protecting Vera by helping her to keep her lie intact. As for Dhar, he was so disgusted by everything he'd heard about his mother, he'd stopped being curious about her when he was in his twenties; he'd never expressed a desire to know her—not even to meet her. Admittedly, his curiosity about his father had persisted into his thirties, but Dhar had lately seemed resigned to the fact that he would never know him. Perhaps the proper word was "hardened," not "resigned."

At 39, John D. had simply grown accustomed to not knowing his mother and father. But who wouldn't want to know, or at least meet, his own twin? Why not simply introduce the fool missionary to his twin? the doctor asked himself. "Martin, this is your brother—you'd better get used to the idea." (Dr. Daruwalla presumed that all missionaries were, in one way or another, fools.) Telling the truth to Dhar's twin would serve Vera right, Farrokh thought. It might even prevent Martin Mills from doing anything as confining as becoming a priest. It was most definitely the Anglican in Dr. Daruwalla that stopped short of the very idea of chastity, which seemed utterly confining to him.

Farrokh remembered what his contentious father had had to say about chastity. Lowji had considered the subject in the light of Gandhi's experience. The Mahatma had been married at 13; he was 37 when he took a vow of sexual abstinence. "By my calculations," Lowji had said, "this amounts to twenty-four years of sex. Many people don't have that many years of sex in their entire lifetime. So the Mahatma chose sexual abstinence after twenty-four years of sexual activity. He was a bloody womanizer flanked by a bunch of Mary Magdalens!"

As with all his father's pronouncements, that voice of steadfast authority rang down through the years, for old Lowji proclaimed everything in the same strident, inflammatory tones; he mocked, he defamed, he provoked, he advised. Whether he was giving good advice (usually of a medical nature) or speaking out of the most dire prejudice—or expressing the most eccentric, simplistic opinion—Lowji had the tone of voice of a self-declared expert. To everyone, and in consideration of all subjects, he used the same famous tone of voice with which he'd made a name for himself in the days of Independence and during the

Partition, when he'd so authoritatively addressed the issue of Disaster Medicine. ("In order of importance, look for dramatic amputations and severe extremity injuries before treating fractures or lacerations. Best to leave all head injuries to the experts, if there are any.") It was a pity that such sensible advice was wasted on a movement that didn't last, although the present volunteers in the field still spoke of Disaster Medicine as a worthy cause.

Upon that memory, Dr. Farrokh Daruwalla attempted to extricate himself from the past. He forced himself to view the melodrama of Dhar's twin as the particular crisis at hand. With refreshing and unusual clarity, the doctor decided that it should be Dhar's decision whether or not poor Martin Mills should know that he had a twin brother. Martin Mills wasn't the twin the doctor knew and loved. It should be a matter of what the doctor's beloved John D. wanted: to know his brother or not to know him. And to hell with Danny and Vera, and whatever mess they might have made of their lives—especially to hell with Vera. She would be 65, Farrokh realized, and Danny was almost 10 years older; they were both old enough to face the music like grownups.

But Dr. Daruwalla's reasoning was entirely swept away by the next phone message, alongside which everything to do with Dhar and his twin assumed the lesser stature of gossip, of mere trivia.

"Patel here," said the voice, which instantly impressed Farrokh with a moral detachment he'd never known. Anesthesiology Patel? Radiology Patel? It was a Gujarati name—there weren't all that many Patels in Bombay. And then, with a sensation of sudden coldness—almost as cold as the voice on his answering machine—Farrokh knew who it was. It was Deputy Commissioner Patel, the *real* policeman. He must be the only Gujarati on the Bombay police force, Farrokh thought, for surely the local police were mostly Maharashtrians.

"Doctor," the detective said, "there is quite a different subject we must discuss—*not* in Dhar's presence, please. I want to speak with you alone." The hanging up of the phone was as abrupt as the message.

Had he not been so agitated by the call, Dr. Daruwalla might have prided himself for his insight as a screenwriter, for he'd always given Inspector Dhar a similar succinctness when speaking on the telephone—especially to answering machines. But the screenwriter took no pride in the accuracy of his characterization; instead, Farrokh was overcome with curiosity regarding what the "different subject" that Detective Patel wished to discuss *was,* not to mention why this subject couldn't be discussed in front of Dhar. At the same time, Dr. Daruwalla absolutely dreaded the deputy commissioner's presumed knowledge of crime.

Was there another clue to Mr. Lal's murder, or another threat to Dhar? Or was this "different subject" the cage-girl killings—the real-life murders of those prostitutes, not the movie version?

But the doctor had no time to contemplate the mystery. With the *next* phone message, Dr. Daruwalla was once more ensnared by the past.

The Same Old Scare; a Brand-New Threat

It was an old message, one he'd been hearing for 20 years. He'd received these calls in Toronto and in Bombay, both at his home and at his office. He'd tried having the calls traced, but without success; they were made from public phones—from post offices, hotel lobbies, airports, hospitals. And regardless of how familiar Farrokh was with the content of these calls, the hatred that inspired them never failed to engage his complete attention.

The voice, full of cruel mockery, began by quoting old Lowji's advice to the Disaster Medicine volunteers—" '. . . look for dramatic amputations and severe extremity injuries,' " the voice began. And then, interrupting itself, the voice said, "When it comes to 'dramatic amputations'—your father's head was off, completely *off* ! I saw it sitting on the passenger seat before the flames engulfed the car. And when it comes to 'severe extremity injuries'—his hands couldn't let go of the steering wheel, even though his fingers were on fire! I saw the burned hairs on the backs of his hands, before the crowd formed and I had to slip away. And your father said it was 'best to leave all head injuries to the experts'—when it comes to 'head injuries,' *I'm* the expert! I did it. I blew his head off. I watched him burn. And I'm telling you, he deserved it. Your whole family deserves it."

It was the same old scare—he'd been hearing it for 20 years—but it never affected Dr. Daruwalla any less. He sat shivering in his bedroom as he'd sat shivering about a hundred times before. His sister, in London, had never received these calls. Farrokh assumed that she was spared only because the caller didn't know her married name. His brother, Jamshed, had received these calls in Zürich. The calls to both brothers had been recorded on various answering machines and on several tapes made by the police. Once, in Zürich, the Daruwalla brothers and their wives had listened to one of these recordings over and over again. No one recognized the voice of the caller, but to Farrokh's and Jamshed's surprise, their wives were convinced that the caller was a woman. The brothers had always thought the voice was unmistakably a man's. As sisters, Julia and Josefine were adamant in regard to the mystical correctness of anything they agreed about. The caller was a woman—they were sure.

The dispute was still raging when John D. arrived at Jamshed and Josefine's apartment for dinner. Everyone insisted that Inspector Dhar should settle the argument. After all, an actor has a trained voice and acute powers for studying and imitating the voices of others. John D. listened to the recording only once.

"It's a man trying to sound like a woman," he said.

Dr. Daruwalla was outraged—not so much by the opinion, which the doctor found simply outlandish, but by the infuriating authority with which John D. had spoken. It was the actor speaking, the doctor was certain—the actor in his role as detective. That was where the arrogant, self-assured manner came from—from *fiction*!

Everyone had objected to Dhar's conclusion, and so the actor had rewound the tape; he'd listened to it again—actually, two more times. Then suddenly the mannerisms that Dr. Daruwalla associated with Inspector Dhar vanished; it was a serious, apologetic John D. who spoke to them.

"I'm sorry—I was wrong," John D. said. "It's a woman trying to sound like a man."

Because this assessment was spoken with a different kind of confidence and not at all as Inspector Dhar would have delivered the line, Dr. Daruwalla said, "Rewind it. Play it again." This time they'd all agreed with John D. It was a woman, and she was trying to sound like a man. It was no one whose voice they'd ever heard before—they'd all agreed to that, too. Her English was almost perfect—very British. She had only a trace of a Hindi accent.

"I did it. I blew his head off. I watched him burn. And I'm telling you, he deserved it. Your whole family deserves it," the woman had said for 20 years, probably more than 100 times. But who was she? Where did her hatred come from? And had she really done it?

Her hatred might be even stronger if she'd *not* done it. But then why take credit for doing it? the doctor wondered. How could anyone have hated Lowji *that* much? Farrokh knew that his father had said much to offend everybody, but, to Farrokh's knowledge, his father hadn't *person-ally* wronged anyone. It was easy, in India, to assume that the source of any violence was either political outrage or religious offense. When someone as prominent and outspoken as Lowji was blown up by a car bomb, it was automatic to label the killing an assassination. But Farrokh had to wonder if his father might have inspired a more personal anger, and if his killing hadn't been just a plain old murder.

It was hard for Farrokh to imagine anyone, especially a woman, with a private grievance against his father. Then he thought of the deeply personal loathing that Mr. Lal's murderer must feel for Inspector Dhar. (MORE MEMBERS DIE IF DHAR REMAINS A MEMBER.) And it occurred to Dr. Daruwalla that perhaps they were all being hasty to assume it was Dhar's movie persona that had inspired such a venomous anger. Had Dr. Daruwalla's dear boy—his beloved John D.—got himself into some *private* trouble? Was this a case of a personal relationship that had soured into a murderous hatred? Dr. Daruwalla felt ashamed of himself that he'd inquired so little about Dhar's personal life. He feared he'd given John D. the impression that he was indifferent to the younger man's private affairs.

Certainly, John D. was chaste when he was in Bombay; at least he *said* he was. There were the public appearances with starlets—the ever-available cinema bimbos—but such couplings were choreographed to create the desired scandal, which both parties would later deny. These weren't "relationships"—they were "publicity."

The Inspector Dhar movies thrived on giving offense—in India, a risky enterprise. Yet the senselessness of murdering Mr. Lal indicated a hatred more vicious than anything Dr. Daruwalla could detect in the usual reactions to Dhar. As if on cue, as if prompted by the mere thought of giving or taking *offense,* the next phone message was from the director of all the Inspector Dhar movies. Balraj Gupta had been pestering Dr. Daruwalla about the extremely touchy subject of *when* to release the new Inspector Dhar movie. Because of the prostitute killings and the general disfavor incurred by *Inspector Dhar and the Cage-Girl Killer,* Gupta had delayed its opening and he was increasingly impatient.

Dr. Daruwalla had privately decided that he never wanted the new Inspector Dhar film to be seen, but he knew that the movie *would be* released; he couldn't stop it. Nor could he appeal to Balraj Gupta's deficient instincts for social responsibility much longer; such maladroit feelings as Gupta might have had for the real-life murdered prostitutes were short-lived.

"Gupta here!" the director said. "Look at it this way. The new one will cause *new* offense. Whoever is killing the cage girls might give it up and kill someone else! We give the public something new to make them wild and crazy—we'll be doing the prostitutes a favor!" Balraj Gupta possessed the logic of a politician; the doctor had no doubt that the new Inspector Dhar movie would make a different group of moviegoers "wild and crazy."

It was called *Inspector Dhar and the Towers of Silence;* the title alone would be offensive to the entire Parsi community, because the Towers of Silence were the burial wells for the Parsi dead. There were always naked corpses of Parsis in the Towers of Silence, which was why Dr. Daruwalla had first supposed that *they* were the attraction to the first vulture he'd seen above the golf course at the Duckworth Club. The Parsis were understandably protective of their Towers of Silence; as a Parsi, Dr. Daruwalla knew this very well. Yet in the new Inspector Dhar movie, someone is murdering Western hippies and depositing *their* bodies in the Towers of Silence. Many Indians readily took offense at European and American hippies when they were *alive.* Doongarwadi is an accepted part of Bombay culture. At the very least, the Parsis would be disgusted. And all Bombayites would reject the premise of the film as absurd. No one can get near the Towers of Silence—not even other Parsis! (Not unless they're dead.) But of course, Dr. Daruwalla thought proudly, that was what was neat and tricky about the film—*how* the bodies are deposited there, and *how* the intrepid Inspector Dhar figures this out.

With resignation, Dr. Daruwalla knew that he couldn't stall the release of *Inspector Dhar and the Towers of Silence* much longer; he could, however, fast-forward through Balraj Gupta's remaining arguments for releasing the film immediately. Besides, the doctor enjoyed the high-speed distortion of Balraj Gupta's voice far more than he appreciated the real thing.

While the doctor was being playful, he came to the last message on his answering machine. The caller was a woman. At first Farrokh supposed it was no one he knew. "Is that the doctor?" she asked. It was a voice long past exhaustion, of someone who was terminally depressed. She spoke as if her mouth were too wide open, as if her lower jaw were permanently dropped. There was a deadpan, don't-give-a-damn quality to her voice, and her accent was plain and flat—North American, surely, but Dr. Daruwalla (who was good at accents) guessed more specifically that she was from the American Midwest or the Canadian prairies. Omaha or Sioux City, Regina or Saskatoon.

"Is that the doctor?" she asked. "I know who you really are, I know what you really do," the woman went on. "Tell the deputy commissioner—the *real* policeman. Tell him who you are. Tell him what you do." The hang-up was a little out of control, as if she'd meant to slam the phone into its cradle but, in her restrained anger, had missed the mark.

Farrokh sat trembling in his bedroom. From the dining room of his apartment, he could now hear Roopa laying out their supper on the glass-topped table. She would any minute announce to Dhar and Julia that the doctor was home and that their extraordinarily late meal was finally served. Julia would wonder why he'd snuck into the bedroom like a thief. In truth, Farrokh felt like a thief—but one unsure of what he'd stolen, and from whom.

Dr. Daruwalla rewound the tape and replayed the last message. This was a brand-new threat; and because he was concentrating so hard upon the meaning of the call, the doctor almost missed the most important clue, which was the caller. Farrokh had always known that *someone* would discover him as Inspector Dhar's creator; that part of the message was not unexpected. But why was this any business of the *real* policeman? Why did someone think that Deputy Commissioner Patel should know?

"I know who you really are, I know what you really do." But so what? the screenwriter thought. "Tell him who you are. Tell him what you do." But why? Farrokh wondered. Then, by accident, the doctor found himself listening repeatedly to the woman's opening line, the part he'd almost missed. "Is that the doctor?" He played it again and again, until his hands were shaking so badly that he rewound the tape all the way into Balraj Gupta's list of reasons for releasing the new Inspector Dhar film now.

"Is that the doctor?"

Dr. Daruwalla's heart had never seemed to stand so still before. It can't be *her*! he thought. But it *was* her—Farrokh was sure of it. After all these years—it *couldn't* be! But of course, he realized, if it was her, she would know; with an intelligent guess, she could have figured it out.

That was when his wife burst into the bedroom. "Farrokh!" Julia said. "I never knew you were home!"

But I'm not "home," the doctor thought; I'm in a very, very foreign country.

"Liebchen," he said softly to his wife. Whenever he used the German endearment, Julia knew he was feeling tender—or else he was in trouble.

"What is it, *Liebchen?*" she asked him. He held out his hand and she went to him; she sat close enough beside him to feel that he was shivering. She put her arms around him.

"Please listen to this," Farrokh said to her. *"Bitte."*

The first time Julia listened, Farrokh could see by her face that she was making *his* mistake; she was concentrating too hard on the content of the message.

"Never mind what she says," said Dr. Daruwalla. "Think about who she is."

It was the third time before Farrokh saw Julia's expression change.

"It's *her*, isn't it?" he asked his wife.

"But this is a much older woman," Julia said quickly.

"It's been twenty years, Julia!" Dr. Daruwalla said. "She *would be* a much older woman now! She *is* a much older woman!"

They listened together a few more times. At last Julia said, "Yes, I think it *is* her, but what's her connection with what's happening now?"

In the cold bedroom—in his funereal navy-blue suit, which was comically offset by the bright-green parrot on his necktie—Dr. Daruwalla was afraid that he knew what the connection was.

The Skywalk

The past surrounded him like faces in a crowd. Among them, there was one he knew, but whose face was it? As always, something from the Great Royal Circus offered itself as a beacon. The ringmaster, Pratap Singh, was married to a lovely woman named Sumitra—everyone called her Sumi. She was in her thirties, possibly her forties; and she not only played the role of mother to many of the child performers, she was also a gifted acrobat. Sumi performed in the item called Double-Wheel Cycle, a bicycle act, with her sister-in-law Suman. Suman was Pratap's unmarried, adopted sister; she must have been in her late twenties, possibly her thirties, when Dr. Daruwalla last saw her—a petite and muscular beauty, and the best acrobat in Pratap's troupe. Her name meant "rose flower"—or was it "scent of the rose flower," or merely the scent of flowers in general? Farrokh had never actually known, no more than he knew the story concerning *when* Suman had been adopted, or by whom.

It didn't matter. Suman and Sumi's bicycle duet was much loved. They could ride their bicycles backward, or lie down on them and pedal them with their hands; they could ride them on one wheel, like unicycles, or pedal them while sitting on the handlebars. Perhaps it was a special softness in Farrokh that he took such pleasure from seeing two pretty women do something so graceful together. But Suman was the star, and her Skywalk item was the best act in the Great Royal Circus.

Pratap Singh had taught Suman how to "skywalk" after he'd seen it performed on television; Farrokh supposed that the act had originated with one of the European circuses. (The ringmaster couldn't resist training everyone, not just the lions.) He'd installed a ladderlike device on the roof of the family troupe tent; the rungs of the ladder were loops of rope and the ladder was bracketed to extend horizontally across the tent roof. Suman hung upside down with her feet in the loops. She swung herself back and forth, the loops chafing the tops of her feet, which she kept rigid—at right angles to her ankles. When she'd gathered the necessary momentum, she "walked" upside down—from one end of the ladder to the other—simply by stepping her feet in and out of the loops as she swung. When she practiced this across the roof of the family troupe tent, her head was only inches above the dirt floor. Pratap Singh stood next to her, to catch her if she fell.

But when Suman performed the Skywalk from the top of the main tent, she was 80 feet from the dirt floor and she refused to use a net. If Pratap Singh had tried to catch her—*if* Suman fell—they both would have been killed. If the ringmaster threw his body under her, trying to guess where she'd land, Pratap might break Suman's fall; then only he would be killed.

There were 18 loops in the ladder. The audience silently counted Suman's steps. But Suman never counted her steps; it was better, she said, to "just walk." Pratap told her it wasn't a good idea to look down. Between the top of the tent and the faraway floor, there were only the upside-down faces of the audience, staring back at her—waiting for her to fall.

That was what the past was like, thought Dr. Daruwalla—all those swaying, upside-down faces. It wasn't a good idea to look at them, he knew.

9. SECOND HONEYMOON

Before His Conversion,
Farrokh Mocks the Faithful

Twenty years ago, when he was drawn to Goa by his epicurean nostalgia for pork—scarce in the rest of India, but a staple of Goan cuisine—Dr. Daruwalla was converted to Christianity by the big toe of his right foot. He spoke of his religious conversion with the sincerest humility. That the doctor had recently visited the miraculously preserved mummy of St. Francis Xavier was *not* the cause of his conversion; previous to his personal experience with divine intervention, Dr. Daruwalla had even mocked the saint's relics, which were kept under glass in the Basilica de Bom Jesus in Old Goa.

Farrokh supposed that he'd made fun of the missionary's remains because he enjoyed teasing his wife about her religion, although Julia was never a practicing Catholic and she often expressed how it pleased her to have left the Roman trappings of her childhood in Vienna. Nevertheless, prior to their marriage, Farrokh had submitted to some tedious religious instruction from a Viennese priest. The doctor had understood that he was demonstrating a kind of theological passivity only to satisfy Julia's mother; but—again, to tease Julia—Farrokh insisted on referring to the ring-blessing ceremony as the "ring-washing ritual," and he pretended to be more offended by this Catholic charade than he was. In truth, he'd enjoyed telling the priest that, although he was unbaptized and had never been a practicing Zoroastrian, he nonetheless had always believed in "something"; at the time, he'd believed in nothing at all. And he'd calmly lied to both the priest and Julia's mother—that he had no objections to his children being baptized and raised as Roman Catholics. He and Julia had privately agreed that this was a worthwhile, if not entirely innocent deception—again, to put Julia's mother at ease.

It hadn't hurt his daughters to have them baptized, Farrokh supposed. When Julia's mother was still alive, and only when she'd visited the Daruwallas and their children in Toronto, or when the Daruwallas had visited her in Vienna, it had never been too painful to attend Mass. Farrokh and Julia had told their little girls that they were making their grandmother happy. This was an acceptable, even an honorable, tradition in the history of Christian churchgoing: to go through the motions of worship as a favor to a family member who appeared to be that most intractable personage, a true believer. No one had objected to this occasional enactment of a faith that was frankly quite foreign to them all, maybe even to Julia's mother. Farrokh sometimes wondered if *she* had been going through the motions of worship only to please *them*.

It was exactly as the Daruwallas had anticipated: when Julia's mother died, the family's intermittent Catholicism more than lapsed—their churchgoing virtually stopped. In retrospect, Dr. Daruwalla concluded that his daughters had been preconditioned to accept that *all* religion was nothing more than going through the motions of worship to make someone else happy. It had been to please the doctor, after his conversion, that his daughters were administered the sacrament of marriage and other rites and ceremonies according to the Anglican Church of Canada. Maybe this was why Father Julian was so dismissive of the miracle by which Farrokh had been converted to Christianity. In the Father Rector's opinion, it must have been only a minor miracle, if the experience managed merely to make Dr. Daruwalla an Anglican. In other words, it hadn't been enough of a miracle to make the doctor a Roman Catholic.

It was a good time to go to Goa, Farrokh had thought. "The trip is a kind of second honeymoon for Julia," he'd told his father.

"What kind of honeymoon is it when you take the children?" Lowji had asked; he and Meher resented that their three granddaughters weren't being left with them. Farrokh knew that the girls, who were 11, 13, and 15, would not have stood for being left behind; the reputation of the Goa beaches was far more exciting to them than the prospect of staying with their grandparents. And the girls were determinedly committed to this vacation because John D. was going to be there. No other babysitter could command such authority over them; they were decidedly in love with their adopted elder brother.

In June of 1969, John D. was 19, and—especially to Dr. Daruwalla's daughters—an extremely handsome European. Julia and Farrokh certainly admired the beautiful boy, but less for his good looks than for his tolerant disposition toward their children; not every 19-year-old boy could stomach so much giddy affection from three underage girls, but John D. was patient, even charming, with them. And having been schooled in Switzerland, John D. would probably be undaunted by the freaks who overran Goa—or so Farrokh had thought. In 1969, the European and American hippies were called "freaks"—especially in India.

"This is some second honeymoon, my dear," old Lowji had said to Julia. "He is taking you and the children to the dirty beaches where the freaks debauch themselves, and it is all because of his love of *pork!*"

With this blessing did the younger Daruwallas depart for the former Portuguese enclave. Farrokh told Julia and John D. and his indifferent daughters that the churches and cathedrals of Goa were among the gaudier landmarks of Indian Christendom. Dr. Daruwalla was a connoisseur of Goan architecture: monumentality and massiveness he enjoyed; excessiveness, which was also reflected in the doctor's diet, he found thrilling.

He preferred the Cathedral of St. Catherine da Se and the façade of the Franciscan Church to the unimpressive Church of the Miraculous Cross, but his overall preference for the Basilica de Bom Jesus wasn't rooted in his architectural snobbery; rather, he was wildly amused by the silliness of the pilgrims—even Hindus!—who flocked to the basilica to view the mummified remains of St. Francis.

It is suspected, especially among non-Christians in India, that St. Francis Xavier contributed more to the Christianization of Goa *after* his death than the Jesuit had managed—in his short stay of only a few months—while he was alive. He died and was buried on an island off the Cantonese coast; but when he suffered the further indignity of disinterment, it was discovered that he'd hardly decomposed at all. The miracle of his intact body was shipped back to Goa, where his remarkable remains drew crowds of frenzied pilgrims. Farrokh's favorite part of the story concerned a woman who, with the worshipful intensity of the most devout, bit off a toe of the splendid corpse. Xavier would lose more of himself, too: the Vatican required that his right arm be shipped to Rome, without which evidence St. Francis's canonization might never have occurred.

How Dr. Daruwalla loved this story! How hungrily he viewed the shriveled relic, which was richly swaddled in vestments and brandished a staff of gold; the staff itself was encrusted with emeralds. The doctor assumed that the saint was kept under glass and elevated on a gabled monument in order to discourage other pilgrims from demonstrating their devotion with more zealous biting. Chuckling to himself while remaining outwardly most respectful, Dr. Daruwalla had surveyed the mausoleum with restrained glee. All around him, even on the casket, were numerous depictions of Xavier's missionary heroics; but none of the saint's adventures—not to mention the surrounding silver, or the crystal, or the alabaster, or the jasper, or even the purple marble—was as impressive to Farrokh as St. Francis's gobbled toe.

"Now *that's* what I call a miracle!" the doctor would say. "To have seen that might even have made a Christian out of *me!*"

When he was in a less playful temper, Farrokh harangued Julia with tales of the Holy Inquisition in Goa, for the missionary zeal that followed the Portuguese was marked by conversions under threat of death, confiscation of Hindu property and the burning of Hindu temples—not to mention the burning of heretics and grandly staged acts of faith. How it would have pleased old Lowji to hear his son carrying on in this irreverent fashion. As for Julia, she found it irritating that Farrokh so resembled his father in this respect. When it came to baiting anyone who was even remotely religious, Julia was superstitious and opposed.

"I don't mock your lack of belief," the doctor's wife told him. "Don't blame me for the Inquisition or laugh about St. Francis's poor toe."

The Doctor Is Turned On

Farrokh and Julia rarely argued with any venom, but they enjoyed teasing each other. An exaggerated, dramatic banter, which they weren't inclined to suppress in public places, made the couple appear quarrelsome to the usual eavesdroppers—hotel staff, waiters or the sad couple with nothing to say to each other at an adjacent table. In those days, in the '60's, when the Daruwallas traveled *en famille,* the girlish hysteria of their daughters added to the general rumpus. Therefore, when they undertook their outing in June of '69, the Daruwallas declined several invitations to lodge themselves in some of the better villas in Old Goa.

Because they were such a loud mob, and because Dr. Daruwalla enjoyed eating at all times of the day and night, they thought it wiser and more diplomatic—at least until the children were older—*not* to stay in another family's mansion, with all the breakable Portuguese pottery and the polished rosewood furniture. Instead, the Daruwallas occupied one of those beach hotels that even then had seen better days, but could neither be destroyed by the children nor offended by Dr. Daruwalla's unceasing appetite. The spirited teasing between Farrokh and Julia was entirely overlooked by the ragged staff and the world-weary clientele of the Hotel Bardez, where the food was plentiful and fresh if not altogether appetizing, and where the rooms were almost clean. After all, it was the beach that mattered.

The Bardez had been recommended to Dr. Daruwalla by one of the younger members of the Duckworth Club. The doctor wished he could remember exactly who had praised the hotel, and why, but only snippets of the recommendation had remained in his memory. The guests were mostly Europeans, and Farrokh had thought that this would appeal to Julia and put young John D. at ease. Julia had teased her husband regarding the concept of putting John D. "at ease"; it was absurd, she pointed out, to imagine that the young man could be more at ease than he already was. As for the European clientele, they weren't the sort of people Julia would ever want to know; they were trashy, even by John D.'s standards. In his university days in Zürich, John D. was probably as morally relaxed as other young men—or so Dr. Daruwalla supposed.

As for the Daruwalla contingent, John D. certainly stood out among them; he was as serenely composed, as ethereally calm, as the Daruwalla daughters were frenetic. The daughters were fascinated by the more unlikable European guests at the Hotel Bardez, although they clung to John D.; he was their protector whenever the young women or the young men, both in their string bikinis, would come too close. In truth, it appeared that these young women *and* young men approached the Daruwalla family solely to have a better view of John D., whose sublime beauty surpassed that of other young men in general and other 19-year-olds in particular.

Even Farrokh tended to gape at John D., although he knew from Jamshed and Josefine that only the dramatic arts interested the young man and that, especially for these thespian pursuits, he seemed inappropriately shy. But to *see* the boy, Farrokh thought, belied all the worries he'd heard expressed by his brother and sister-in-law. It was Julia who first said that John D. looked like a movie star; she said she meant by this that you were drawn to watch him even when he appeared to be doing nothing or thinking of nothing. In addition, his wife pointed out to Dr. Daruwalla, John D. projected an indeterminate age. When he was closely shaven, his skin was so perfectly smooth that he seemed much younger than 19—almost prepubescent. But when he allowed his beard to grow, even only as much as one day's stubble, he became a grown man—at least in his late twenties—and he looked savvy and cocksure and dangerous.

"This is what you mean by a movie star?" Farrokh asked his wife.

"This is what's attractive to women," Julia said frankly. "That boy is a man *and* a boy."

But for the first few days of his vacation, Dr. Daruwalla was too distracted to think about John D.'s potential as a movie star. Julia had made Farrokh nervous about the Duckworthian source of the recommendation for the Hotel Bardez. It was amusing to observe the European trash and the interesting Goans, but what if other *Duckworthians* were guests of the Hotel Bardez? It would be as if they'd never left Bombay, Julia said.

And so the doctor nervously examined the Hotel Bardez for stray Duckworthians, fearing that the Sorabjees would mysteriously materialize in the café-restaurant, or the Bannerjees would float ashore from out of the Arabian Sea, or the Lals would leap out and surprise him from behind the areca palms. Meanwhile, all Farrokh wanted was the peace of mind to reflect on his growing impulse to be more creative.

Dr. Daruwalla was disappointed that he was no longer the reader he'd once been. Watching movies was easier; he felt he'd been seduced by the sheer laziness of absorbing images on film. He was proud that he'd at least held himself above the masala movies—those junk films of the Bombay cinema, those Hindi hodgepodges of song and violence. But Farrokh was enthralled by any sleazy offering from Europe or America in the hard-boiled-detective genre; it was all-white, tough-guy trash that attracted him.

The doctor's taste in films was in sharp contrast to what his wife liked to read. For this particular holiday Julia had brought along the autobiography of Anthony Trollope, which Farrokh was not looking forward to hearing. Julia enjoyed reading aloud to him from passages of a book she found especially well written or amusing or moving, but Farrokh's prejudice against Dickens extended to Trollope, whose novels he'd never finished and whose autobiography he couldn't imagine even beginning. Julia generally preferred to read fiction, but Farrokh supposed that the autobiography of a novelist almost qualified as fiction—surely novelists wouldn't resist the impulse to make up their autobiographies.

And this led the doctor to daydreaming further on the matter of his underdeveloped creativity. Since he'd virtually stopped being a reader, he wondered if he shouldn't try his hand at writing. An autobiography, however, was the domain of the already famous—unless, Farrokh mused, the subject had led a thrilling life. Since the doctor was neither famous nor had he, in his opinion, led a life of much excitement, he believed that an autobiography was not for him. Nevertheless, he thought, he would glance at the Trollope—when Julia wasn't looking, and only to see if it might provide him with any inspiration. He doubted that it would.

Unfortunately, his wife's only other reading material was a novel that had caused Farrokh some alarm. When Julia wasn't looking, he'd already glanced at it, and the subject seemed to be relentlessly, obsessively sexual; in addition, the author was totally unknown to Dr. Daruwalla, which intimidated him as profoundly as the novel's explicit erotica. It was one of those very skillful novels, exquisitely written in limpid prose—Farrokh knew that much—and this intimidated him, too.

Dr. Daruwalla began all novels irritably and with impatience. Julia read slowly, as if she were tasting the words, but Farrokh plunged restlessly ahead, gathering a list of petty grievances against the author until he happened on *something* that persuaded him the novel was worthwhile—or until he encountered some perceived blunder or an entrenched boredom, either of which would cause him to read not one more word. Whenever Farrokh had decided against a novel, he would then berate Julia for the apparent pleasure she was taking from the book. His wife was a reader of broad interests, and she finished almost everything she started; her voraciousness intimidated Dr. Daruwalla, too.

So here he was, on his second honeymoon—a term he'd used much too loosely, because he'd not so much as flirted with his wife since they'd arrived in Goa—and he was fearfully on the lookout for Duckworthians, whose dreaded appearance threatened to ruin his holiday altogether. To make matters worse, he'd found himself greatly upset—but also sexually aroused—by the novel his wife was reading. At least he *thought* she was reading it; maybe she hadn't begun. If she was reading it, she'd not read any of it aloud to him, and given the calm but intense depiction of act after sexual act, surely Julia would be too embarrassed to read such passages aloud to him. Or would it be *me* who'd be embarrassed? he wondered.

The novel was so compelling that his covert glances at it were insufficient satisfaction; he'd begun concealing it in a newspaper or a magazine and sneaking off to a hammock with it. Julia didn't appear to miss it; perhaps she was reading the Trollope.

The first image that captured Farrokh's attention was only a couple of pages into the first chapter. The narrator was riding on a train in France. "Across from me the girl has fallen asleep. She has a narrow mouth, cast down at the corners, weighted there by the sourness of knowledge." Immediately, Dr. Daruwalla felt that this was good stuff, but he also surmised that the story would end unhappily. It had never occurred to the doctor that a stumbling block between himself and most serious literature was that he disliked unhappy endings. Farrokh had forgotten that, as a younger reader, he'd once preferred unhappy endings.

It wasn't until the fifth chapter that Dr. Daruwalla became disturbed by the first-person narrator's frankly voyeuristic qualities, for these same qualities strongly brought out the doctor's own troubling voyeurism. "When she walks, she leaves me weak. A hobbled, feminine step. Full hips. Small waist." Faithfully, as always, Farrokh thought of Julia. "There's a glint of white slip where her sweater parts slightly at the bosom. My eyes keep going there in quick, helpless glances." Does Julia *like* this kind of thing? Farrokh wondered. And then, in the eighth chapter, the novel took a turn that made Dr. Daruwalla miserable with envy and desire. Some second honeymoon! he thought. "Her back is towards him. In a single move she pulls off her sweater and then, reaching behind herself in that elbow-awkward way, unfastens her brassiere. Slowly he turns her around."

Dr. Daruwalla was suspicious of the narrator, this first person who is obsessed with every detail of the sexual explorations of a young American abroad and a French girl from the country—an 18-year-old Anne-Marie. Farrokh didn't understand that without the narrator's discomforting presence, the reader couldn't experience the envy and desire of the perpetual onlooker, which was precisely what haunted Farrokh and impelled him to read on and on. "The next morning they do it again. Grey light, it's very early. Her breath is bad."

That was when Dr. Daruwalla knew that one of the lovers was going to die; her bad breath was an unpleasant hint of mortality. He wanted to stop reading but he couldn't. He decided that he disliked the young

American—he was supported by his father, he didn't even have a job—but his heart ached for the French girl, whose innocence was being lost. The doctor didn't know that he was supposed to feel these things. The book was beyond him.

Because his medical practice was an exercise of almost pure goodness, he was ill prepared for the real world. Mostly he saw malformations and deformities and injuries to children; he tried to restore their little joints to their intended perfection. The real world had no purpose as clear as that.

I'll read just one more chapter, Dr. Daruwalla thought. He'd already read nine. At the inland edge of the beach, he lay in the midday heat in a hammock under the dead-still fronds of the areca and coconut palms. The smell of coconut and fish and salt was occasionally laced with the smell of hashish, drifting along the beach. Where the beach touched the tropical-green mass of tangled vegetation, a sugarcane stall competed for a small triangle of shade with a wagon selling mango milkshakes. The melting ice had wet the sand.

The Daruwallas had commandeered a fleet of rooms—an entire floor of the Hotel Bardez—and there was a generous outdoor balcony, although the balcony was outfitted with only one sleeping hammock and young John D. had claimed it. Dr. Daruwalla felt so comfortable in the beach hammock that he resolved he would persuade John D. to allow him to sleep in the balcony hammock for at least one night; after all, John D. had a bed in his own room, and Farrokh and Julia could stand to be separated overnight—by which the doctor meant that he and his wife weren't inclined to make love as often as every night, or even as often as twice a week. Some second honeymoon! Farrokh thought again. He sighed.

He should have left the tenth chapter for another time, but suddenly he was reading again; like any good novel, it kept lulling him into an almost tranquil state of awareness before it jolted him—it caught him completely by surprise. "Then hurriedly, as an afterthought, he takes off his clothes and slips in beside her. An act which threatens us all. The town is silent around them. On the milk-white faces of the clock the hands, in unison, jerk to new positions. The trains are running on time. Along the empty streets, yellow headlights of a car occasionally pass and bells mark the hours, the quarters, the halves. With a touch like flowers, she is gently tracing the base of his cock, driven by now all the way into her, touching his balls, and beginning to writhe slowly beneath him in a sort of obedient rebellion while in his own dream he rises a little and defines the moist rim of her cunt with his finger, and as he does, he comes like a bull. They remain close for a long time, still without talking. It is these exchanges which cement them, that is the terrible thing. These atrocities induce them towards love."

It wasn't even the end of the chapter, but Dr. Daruwalla had to stop reading. He was shocked; and he had an erection, which he concealed with the book, allowing it to cover his crotch like a tent. All of a sudden, in the midst of such lucid prose, of such terse elegance, there were a "cock" and "balls" and even a "cunt" (with a "moist rim")—and these acts that the lovers performed were "atrocities." Farrokh shut his eyes. Had Julia read *this* part? He was usually indifferent to his wife's pleasure in the passages she read aloud to him; she enjoyed discussing how certain passages affected her—they rarely had *any* effect on Farrokh. Dr. Daruwalla felt a surprising need to discuss the effect of *this* passage with his wife, and the thought of discussing such a thing with Julia inspired the doctor's erection; he felt his hard-on touching the astonishing book.

The Doctor Encounters a Sex-Change-in-Progress

When he opened his eyes, the doctor wondered if he'd died and had awakened in what the Christians call hell, for standing beside his hammock and peering down at him were two Duckworthians who were no favorites of his.

"Are you reading that book, or are you just using it to put you to sleep?" asked Promila Rai. Beside her was her sole surviving nephew, that loathsome and formerly hairless boy Rahul Rai. But something was wrong with Rahul, the doctor noticed. Rahul appeared to be a woman now. At least he had a woman's breasts; certainly, he wasn't a boy.

Understandably, Dr. Daruwalla was speechless.

"Are you still asleep?" Promila Rai asked him. She tilted her head so that she could read the novel's title and the author's name, while Farrokh tightly held the book in its tentlike position above his erection, which he naturally preferred *not* to reveal to Promila—or to her terrifying nephew-with-breasts.

Aggressively, Promila read the title aloud. "*A Sport and a Pastime.* I've never heard of it," she said.

"It's very good," Farrokh assured her.

Suspiciously, Promila read the author's name aloud. "James Salter. Who is he?" she asked.

"Someone wonderful," Farrokh replied.

"Well, what's it about?" Promila asked him impatiently.

"France," the doctor said. "The real France." It was an expression he remembered from the novel.

Already Promila was bored with him, Dr. Daruwalla realized. It had been some years since he'd last seen her; Farrokh's mother, Meher, had reported on the frequency of Promila's trips abroad, and the incomplete results of her cosmetic surgery. Looking up at Promila from his hammock, the doctor could recognize (under her eyes) the unnatural tightness of her latest face lift; yet she needed more tightening elsewhere. She was strikingly ugly, like a rare kind of poultry with an excess of wattles at her throat. It wasn't astonishing to Farrokh that the same man had left her at the altar twice; what astonished him was that the same man would have dared to come as close to Promila a second time—for she seemed, as old Lowji put it, "a Miss Havisham times two" in more than one way. Not only had she been jilted twice, but she seemed twice as vindictive, and twice as dangerous, and—to judge by her ominous nephew-with-breasts—twice as covert.

"You remember Rahul," Promila said to Farrokh, and, to be certain that she commanded the doctor's full attention, she tapped her long, veiny fingers on the spine of the book, which still concealed Farrokh's cowering erection. When he looked up at Rahul, Dr. Daruwalla felt his hard-on wither.

"Yes, of course—Rahul!" the doctor said. Farrokh had heard the rumors, but he'd imagined nothing more outrageous than that Rahul had embraced his late brother's flamboyant homosexuality, possibly in homage to Subodh's memory. It had been that terrible monsoon of '49 when Neville Eden had deliberately shocked Farrokh by telling him that he was taking Subodh Rai to Italy because a pasta diet improved one's stamina for the rigors of buggery. Then they'd both died in that car crash. Dr. Daruwalla supposed that young Rahul had taken it rather hard, but not *this* hard!

"Rahul has undergone a little sex change," said Promila Rai, with a vulgarity that was generally accepted as the utmost in sophistication by the out of it and the insecure.

Rahul corrected his aunt in a voice that reflected conflicting hormonal surges. "I'm still undergoing it, Auntie," he remarked. "I'm not quite *complete*," he said pointedly to Dr. Daruwalla.

"I see," the doctor replied, but he didn't see—he couldn't conceive of the changes Rahul had undergone, not to mention what was required to make Rahul "complete." The breasts were fairly small but firm and very nicely shaped; the lips were fuller and softer than Farrokh remembered them, and the makeup around the eyes was enhancing without tending to excess. If Rahul had been 12 or 13 in '49—and no more than 8 or 10 when Lowji had examined him for what his aunt had called his inexplicable hairlessness—Rahul was now 32 or 33, Farrokh figured. From his back, in the hammock, the doctor's view of Rahul was cut off just below the waist, which was as slender and pliant as a young girl's.

It was clear to the doctor that estrogens were in use, and to judge these by Rahul's breasts and flawless skin, the estrogens had been a noteworthy success; the effects on Rahul's voice were at best still in progress, because the voice had both male and female resonances in rich confusion. Had Rahul been castrated? Did one dare ask? He looked more womanly than most hijras. And why would he have had his penis removed if he intended to be "complete," for didn't that mean a fully fashioned vagina, and wasn't this vagina surgically constructed from the penis turned inside out? I'm just an orthopedist, Dr. Daruwalla thought gratefully. All the doctor asked Rahul was, "Are you changing your name, too?"

Boldly, even flirtatiously, Rahul smiled down at Farrokh; once again, the male and the female were at war within Rahul's voice. "Not until I'm the real thing," Rahul answered.

"I see," the doctor replied; he made an effort to return Rahul's smile, or at least to imply tolerance. Once more Promila startled Farrokh by drumming her fingers on the spine of his tightly held book.

"Is the whole family here?" Promila asked. She made "the whole family" sound like a grotesque element, like an entire population that was out of control.

"Yes," Dr. Daruwalla answered.

"And that beautiful boy is here, too, I hope—I want Rahul to see him!" Promila said.

"He must be eighteen—no, nineteen," Rahul said dreamily.

"Yes, nineteen," the doctor said stiffly.

"Don't anyone point him out to me," Rahul said. "I want to see if I can pick him out of the crowd." Upon this remark, Rahul turned from the hammock and moved away across the beach. Dr. Daruwalla thought that the angle of Rahul's departure was deliberate—to give the doctor, from his hammock, the best possible view of Rahul's womanly hips.

Rahul's buttocks were also shown to good advantage in a snug sarong, and the tight-fitting halter top was similarly enhancing to Rahul's breasts. Still, Farrokh critically observed, the hands were too large, the shoulders too broad, the upper arms too muscular . . . the feet were too long, the ankles too sturdy. Rahul was neither perfect nor complete.

"Isn't she delicious?" Promila whispered in the doctor's ear. She leaned over him in the hammock and Farrokh felt the heavy silver pendant, the main piece of her necklace, thump against his chest. So Rahul was already a full-fledged "she" in Promila's mind.

"She seems so . . . womanly," Dr. Daruwalla said to the proud aunt.

"She *is* womanly!" replied Promila Rai.

"Well . . . yes," the doctor said. He felt trapped in the hammock, with Promila suspended above him like some bird of prey—some *poultry* of prey. Promila's scent was permeating—a blend of sandalwood and embalming fluid, something oniony but also like moss. Dr. Daruwalla made an effort not to gag. He felt Promila pulling the novel by James Salter away from him, but he grasped the book in both hands.

"If this is such a wonderful book," she said doubtingly, "I hope you'll lend it to me."

"I think Meher's reading it next," he said, but he didn't mean Meher, his mother; he'd meant to say Julia, his wife.

"Is Meher here, too?" Promila asked quickly.

"No—I meant Julia," Farrokh said sheepishly. By Promila's sneer, he could tell she was judging him, as if his sexual life were so dull that he'd confused his mother with his wife—and before he was 40! Farrokh felt ashamed, but he was also angry. What had initially upset him about *A Sport and a Pastime* was now enthralling to him; he felt highly stimulated, but not in that guilty way of pornography. This was something so refined *and* erotic, he wanted to share it with Julia. Quite simply, and wonderfully, the novel had made him feel young again.

Dr. Daruwalla saw Rahul and Promila as sexually aberrant beings. They'd ruined his mood; they'd overshadowed something that was sexy and sincerely written, because they were so unnatural—so perverse. Farrokh supposed he should go warn Julia that Promila Rai and her nephew-with-breasts were on the prowl. The Daruwallas might have to give their underage daughters some explanation about what wasn't quite right with Rahul. Farrokh decided he would tell John D., in any case. The doctor hadn't liked how Rahul had been so eager to pick John D. "out of the crowd."

Promila had doubtless impressed her nephew-with-breasts with her own opinion—that John D. was entirely too beautiful to be the child of Danny Mills. Dr. Daruwalla thought that Rahul had gone looking for John D. because the would-be transsexual hoped to glimpse something of Neville Eden in the doctor's dear boy!

Promila had turned away from his hammock, as if she were scanning the beach for the "delicious" Rahul; Dr. Daruwalla took this occasion to stare at the back of her neck. He regretted it, for staring back at him among the discolored wrinkles was a tumorous growth with melanoid characteristics; the doctor couldn't bring himself to advise Promila that she should have a doctor look at this. It wasn't a job for an orthopedist, anyway, and Farrokh remembered how unkindly Promila had responded to Lowji's dismissal of Rahul's hairlessness. Thinking of Rahul, Dr. Daruwalla wondered if his father's diagnosis might have been hasty; possibly the hairlessness had been an early signal that something sexual needed rectifying in Rahul.

He struggled to recall the unanswered question concerning Dr. Tata. He remembered that day when Promila and Rahul had delivered the old fool to the Daruwalla estate: there'd been some speculation regarding what either Promila or Rahul would have been seeing Dr. Tata for. It was unlikely that DR TATA'S BEST, MOST FAMOUS CLINIC FOR GYNECOLOGI-CAL & MATERNITY NEEDS could have been treating Promila, who would never have risked her precious parts to a physician reputed to be worse than ordinary. It was Lowji who'd suggested that it might have been Rahul who was Dr. Tata's patient. "Something to do with the hairlessness business," the senior Daruwalla had said, hadn't he?

Now old Dr. Tata was dead. In keeping with the more low-key times, his son, who was also an obstetrician and gynecologist, had deleted the "best, most famous" from the clinic's name—although, as a physician, the son was reputed to be as far below ordinary as his father; within the Bombay medical community he was consistently referred to as "Tata Two." Nevertheless, maybe Tata Two had kept his father's records. Farrokh thought it might be interesting to know more about Rahul's hairlessness.

It amused Dr. Daruwalla to imagine that Promila and Rahul had been so single-minded about getting Rahul a sex change that they might have assumed a gynecological surgeon was the correct doctor to ask. You don't ask the physician who's familiar with the parts you *want*, but rather the doctor who knows and understands the parts you *have*! A urological surgeon would be required. Dr. Daruwalla presumed there would have to be a psychiatric evaluation, too; surely no responsible physician would perform a complete sex-change operation on demand.

Then Farrokh remembered that sex-change operations were illegal in India, although this hardly prevented the hijras from castrating themselves; emasculation appeared to be the caste duty of the hijras. Apparently, Rahul suffered from no such burden of "duty"; Rahul's choice seemed to be motivated by something else—not to be the isolated third gender of a eunuch-transvestite, but to be "complete." An actual woman—this was what Rahul wanted to be, Dr. Daruwalla imagined.

"I suppose it was young Sidhwa who recommended the Hotel Bardez to you," Promila coolly said to the doctor, which forced Dr. Daruwalla to remember the unlikely source of his information. Sidhwa was a young man whose tastes struck Farrokh as entirely too trendy, but in the case of the Hotel Bardez, Sidhwa had spoken with unbridled enthusiasm—and at length.

"Yes, it was Sidhwa," the doctor replied. "I suppose he told you, too."

Promila Rai peered down at Dr. Daruwalla in his hammock. There was in her expression a condescension of a cold, reptilian nature; there wasn't even a flicker of pity in her gaze, but only that which passes for eagerness in a lizard's eyes as it singles out a fly.

"I told *him*," Promila told Farrokh. "The Bardez is *my* hotel. I've been coming here for years."

Oh, what a choice I've made! thought Dr. Daruwalla. But Promila was through with him, at least for the moment. She simply wandered away, not standing on a single ceremony that could even faintly be associated with common politeness, although she'd certainly been exposed to good manners and she could apply such etiquette in excess whenever she chose.

So that was the bad news that he had for Julia, Farrokh thought: two detestable Duckworthians had arrived at the Hotel Bardez, which turned out to be one of their personal favorites. But the good news was *A Sport and a Pastime* by James Salter, for Farrokh was 39 and it had been a long time since a book had so possessed his mind and body.

Dr. Daruwalla desired his wife—as suddenly, as disturbingly, as unashamedly as he'd ever desired her—and he marveled at the power of Mr. Salter's prose to do that: both to be aesthetically pleasing *and* to give him far more than a simple hard-on. The novel seemed like a heroic act of seduction; it had enlivened all of the doctor's senses.

He felt how the beach sand was cooling; at midday it had so burned underfoot that he could cross it only with his sandals on, but now he comfortably walked barefoot in the sand—it seemed an ideal temperature. He vowed to get up very early one morning so that he could also experience the sand at its coldest, but he would forget his vow. Nevertheless, these were the stirrings within him of a second honeymoon, for sure. I shall write a letter to Mr. James Salter, he resolved. The rest of his life, Dr. Daruwalla would regret his neglecting to write that letter, but on this day in June—in 1969, on Baga Beach in Goa—the doctor briefly felt like a new man. Farrokh was only one day away from meeting the stranger whose voice on his answering machine 20 years later still commanded the authority to fill him with dread.

"Is that him? Is that the doctor?" she would ask. When Farrokh had first heard those questions, he had no idea of the world he was about to enter.

10. CROSSED PATHS

Testing for Syphilis

At the Hotel Bardez, the front-desk staff told Dr. Daruwalla that the young woman had limped down the beach, all the way from a hippie enclave at Anjuna; she was checking the hotels for a doctor. "Any doctor?" she'd asked. They were proud of themselves for sending her away, but they warned the doctor that they were sure she'd be back; she wouldn't find anyone to care for her foot at Calangute Beach, and if she made it as far as Aguada, she'd be turned away. Because of how she looked, someone might call the police.

Farrokh desired to uphold the Parsi reputation for fairness and social justice; certainly he sought to help the crippled and the maimed—a girl with a limp was at least in a category of patients the orthopedist felt familiar with. It wasn't as if his services were sought for the purpose of making Rahul Rai complete. Yet Farrokh couldn't be angry with the staff at the Hotel Bardez. It was out of respect for Dr. Daruwalla's privacy that they'd sent the limping woman away; they'd meant only to protect him, although doubtless they took a degree of pleasure in abusing an apparent freak. Among the Goans, especially as the 1960's were ending, there was a felt resentment of the European and American hippies who roamed the beaches; the hippies weren't big spenders—some of them even stole—and they were perceived as an undesirable element by the wealthier Western and Indian tourists whom the Goans wished to attract. And so, without condemning their behavior, Dr. Daruwalla politely informed the staff at the Hotel Bardez that he wished to examine the lame hippie should she return.

The doctor's decision seemed especially disappointing to the aged tea-server who shuffled back and forth between the Hotel Bardez and the various encampments of thatch-roofed shelters; these four-poled structures, stuck in the sand and roofed with the dried fronds of coconut palms, dotted the beach. The tea-server had several times approached Dr. Daruwalla in his hammock under the palms, and it was largely out of diagnostic interest that Farrokh had observed the old man so closely. His name was Ali Ahmed; he said he was only 60 years old, although he looked 80, and he exhibited a few of the more easily recognizable and colorful physical signs of congenital syphilis. Upon his first tea service, the doctor had spotted Ali Ahmed's "Hutchinson's teeth"—the unmistakable peg-shaped incisors. The tea-server's deafness, in addition to the characteristic clouding of the cornea, had confirmed Dr. Daruwalla's diagnosis.

Farrokh was chiefly interested in positioning Ali Ahmed in such a way that the tea-server faced the morning sun. Dr. Daruwalla was trying to spot a fourth symptom, a rarity in congenital syphilis—the Argyll Robertson pupil is much more common in syphilis acquired later in life—and the doctor had cleverly thought of a way to examine the old man without his knowledge.

From his hammock, where he received his tea, Farrokh faced the Arabian Sea. Inland, at his back, the morning sun was a hazy glare above the village; from that direction, wafting over the beach, there emanated an aroma of fermented coconuts. Looking into the cloudy eyes of Ali Ahmed, Farrokh asked with feigned innocence, "What's that smell, Ali, and where's it coming from?" To be sure he'd be heard, Farrokh had to raise his voice.

The tea-server was at the time focused on handing the doctor a glass of tea; his pupils were constricted to accommodate the object nearby— namely, the tea glass. But when the doctor asked him from whence the powerful odor came, Ali Ahmed looked in the direction of the village; his pupils dilated (to accommodate the distant tops of the coconut and areca palms), but even as his face was lifted to the harsh sunlight his pupils did *not* constrict in reaction to the glare. It was the classic Argyll Robertson pupil, Dr. Daruwalla decided.

Farrokh recalled his favorite professor of infectious diseases, *Herr*

Doktor Fritz Meitner; Dr. Meitner was fond of telling his medical students that the best way to remember the behavior of the Argyll Robertson pupil was to think of a prostitute: she accommodates, but doesn't react. It was an all-male class; they all had laughed, but Farrokh had felt uncertain of his laughter. He'd never been with a prostitute, although they were popular in both Vienna and Bombay.

"Feni," the tea-server said, to explain the smell. But Dr. Daruwalla already knew the answer, just as he knew that the pupils of some syphilitics don't respond to light.

A Literary Seduction Scene

In the village—or perhaps the source of the smell was as far away as Panjim—they were distilling coconuts for the local brew called feni; the heavy, sickly-sweet fumes of the liquor drifted over the few tourists and families on holiday at Baga Beach.

Dr. Daruwalla and his family were already favorites with the staff of the small hotel, and they were passionately welcomed in the little lean-to restaurant and taverna that the Daruwallas frequented on the beachfront. The doctor was a big tipper, his wife was a classical beauty of a European tradition (as opposed to the seedy, hippie trash), his daughters were vibrantly bright and pretty—they were still of the innocent school—and the striking John D. was mesmerizing to Indians and foreigners alike. It was only to those rare families as likable as the Daruwallas that the staff of the Hotel Bardez apologized for the smell of the feni.

In those days, in the premonsoon months of May and June, both knowledgeable foreigners and Indians avoided the Goa beaches; it was too hot. It was, however, when the Goans who lived away from Goa came home to visit their families and friends. The children were through with school. The shrimp and lobster and fish were plentiful, and the mangoes were at their peak. (Dr. Daruwalla was enamored of mangoes.) In keeping with the holiday spirit and in order to placate all the Christians, the Catholic Church provided an abundance of feast days; although he wasn't yet religious, the doctor had nothing against a banquet or two.

The Catholics were no longer the majority in Goa—the migrant iron miners who'd arrived early in this century were Hindus—but Farrokh, like his father, persisted in the belief that "the Romans" still overran the place. The Portuguese influence endured in the monumental architecture that Dr. Daruwalla adored; it could distinctly be tasted in the cuisine that the doctor relished. And among the names of the boats of the Christian fisherman, "Christ the King" was quite common. Bumper stickers, of both the comic and proselytizing variety, were a new if not widespread fad in Bombay; the doctor joked that the names of the boats of the Christian fishermen were *Goan* bumper stickers. Julia was no more amused by this than by Farrokh's constant ridicule of St. Francis's violated remains.

"I don't know how anyone can justify canonization," Dr. Daruwalla reflected to John D., largely because Julia wouldn't listen to her husband but also because the young man had studied some theology in university. In Zürich, it would have been Protestant theology, Farrokh assumed. "Just imagine it!" Farrokh lectured to the young man. "A violent woman swallows Xavier's toe, and they cut off his arm and send it to Rome!"

John D. smiled silently over his breakfast. The Daruwalla daughters smiled helplessly at John D. When he looked at his wife, Farrokh was surprised that she was looking straight back at him—she was smiling, too. Clearly, she'd not been listening to a word he was saying. The doctor blushed. Julia's smile wasn't in the least cynical; on the contrary, his wife's expression was so sincerely amorous, Farrokh felt certain that she was determined to remind him of their pleasure the night before— even in front of John D. and the children! And judging from their night together, and the visible randiness of his wife's thoughts on the morning after, their holiday had become a second honeymoon after all.

Reading in bed would never seem innocent again, the doctor thought, although everything had begun quite innocently. His wife had been reading the Trollope, and Farrokh hadn't been reading at all; he'd been trying to get up the nerve to read *A Sport and a Pastime* in front of Julia. Instead, he lay on his back with his fingers intertwined upon his rumbling belly—an excess of pork, or else the dinner conversation had upset him. Over dinner, he'd tried to explain to his family his need to be more creative, his desire to write something, but his daughters had paid no attention to him and Julia had misunderstood him; she'd suggested a medical-advice column—if not for *The Times of India,* then for *The Globe and Mail.* John D. had advised Farrokh to keep a diary; the young man said he'd kept one once, and he'd enjoyed it—then a girlfriend had stolen it and he'd gotten out of the habit. At that point, the conversation entirely deteriorated because the Daruwalla daughters had pestered John D. about the number of girlfriends the young man had *had*.

After all, it was the tail end of the '60's; even innocent young girls *talked* as if they were sexually knowledgeable. It disturbed Farrokh that his daughters were clearly asking John D. to tell them the number of young women he'd slept with. Typical of John D., and to Dr. Daruwalla's great relief, the young man had skillfully and charmingly ducked the question. But the matter of the doctor's unfulfilled creativity had been dismissed or ignored.

The subject, however, hadn't eluded Julia. In bed after dinner, propped up with a stack of pillows—while Farrokh lay flat upon his back—his wife had assaulted him with the Trollope.

"Listen to this, *Liebchen*," Julia said. " 'Early in life, at the age of fifteen, I commenced the dangerous habit of keeping a journal, and this I maintained for ten years. The volumes remained in my possession, unregarded—never looked at—till 1870, when I examined them, and, with many blushes, destroyed them. They convicted me of folly, ignorance, indiscretion, idleness, extravagance, and conceit. But they had habituated me to the rapid use of pen and ink, and taught me how to express myself with facility.' "

"I don't want or need to keep a *journal*," Farrokh said abruptly. "And I already know how to express myself *with facility*."

"There's no need to be defensive," Julia told him. "I just thought you'd be interested in the subject."

"I want to *create* something," Dr. Daruwalla announced. "I'm not interested in recording the mundane details of my life."

"I wasn't aware that our life was altogether mundane," Julia said.

The doctor, realizing his error, said, "Certainly it's not. I meant only that I prefer to try my hand at something imaginative—I want to *imagine* something."

"Do you mean fiction?" his wife asked.

"Yes," Farrokh said. "Ideally, I should like to write a novel, but I don't suppose I could write a very good one."

"Well, there are all kinds of novels," Julia said helpfully.

Thus emboldened, Dr. Daruwalla withdrew James Salter's *A Sport and a Pastime* from its hiding place, which was under the newspaper on the floor beside the bed. He brought forth the novel carefully, as if it were a potentially dangerous weapon, which it was.

"For example," Farrokh said, "I don't suppose I could ever write a novel as good as this one."

Julia glanced at the Salter quickly before returning her eyes to the Trollope. "No, I wouldn't think so," she said.

Aha! the doctor thought. So she *has* read it! But he asked with forced indifference, "Have you read the Salter?"

"Oh, yes," his wife said, not taking her eyes off the Trollope. "I brought it along to *re*read it, actually."

It was hard for Farrokh to remain casual, but he tried. "So you *liked* it, I presume?" he inquired.

"Oh, yes—very much," Julia answered. After a weighty pause, she asked him, "And you?"

"I find it rather good," the doctor confessed. "I suppose," he added, "some readers might be shocked, or offended, by certain parts."

"Oh, yes," Julia agreed. Then she closed the Trollope and looked at him. "Which parts are you thinking of?"

It hadn't happened quite as he'd imagined it, but this was what he wanted. Since Julia had most of the pillows, he rolled over on his stomach and propped himself up on his elbows. He began with a somewhat cautious passage. " 'He pauses at last,' " Farrokh read aloud. " 'He leans over to admire her, she does not see him. Hair covers her cheek. Her skin seems very white. He kisses her side and then, without force, as one stirs a favorite mare, begins again. She comes to life with a soft, exhausted sound, like someone saved from drowning.' "

Julia also rolled over on her stomach, gathering the pillows to her breasts. "It's hard to imagine anyone being shocked or offended by *that* part," she said.

Dr. Daruwalla cleared his throat. The ceiling fan was stirring the down on the back of Julia's neck; her thick hair had fallen forward, hiding her eyes from his view. When he held his breath, he could hear her breathing. " 'She cannot be satisfied,' " he read on, while Julia buried her face in her arms. " 'She will not let him alone. She removes her clothes and calls to him. Once that night and twice the next morning he complies and in the darkness between lies awake, the lights of Dijon faint on the ceiling, the boulevards still. It's a bitter night. Flats of rain are passing. Heavy drops ring in the gutter outside their window, but they are in a dovecote, they are pigeons beneath the eaves. The rain is falling all around them. Deep in feathers, breathing softly, they lie. His sperm swims slowly inside her, oozing out between her legs.' "

"Yes, that's better," Julia said. When he looked at her, he saw she'd turned her face to look at him; the yellow, unsteady light from the kerosene lamps wasn't as ghostly pale as the moonlight he'd seen on her face on their *first* honeymoon, but even this tarnished light conveyed her willingness to trust him. Their wedding night, in the Austrian winter, was in one of those snowy Alpine towns, and their train from Vienna had arrived almost too late for them to be admitted to the *Gasthof,* despite their reservation. It must have been 2:00 in the morning by the time they'd undressed and bathed and got into the feather bed, which was as white as the mountains of snow that reflected the moonlight—it was a timeless glowing—in their window.

But on their *second* honeymoon, Dr. Daruwalla came dangerously close to ruining the mood when he offered a faint criticism of the Salter. "I'm not sure how accurate it is to suggest that sperm swim 'slowly,' " he said, "and technically, I suppose, it's *semen,* not sperm, that would be oozing out between her legs."

"For God's sake, Farrokh," his wife said. "Give me the book."

She had no difficulty locating the passage she was looking for, although the book was unmarked. Farrokh lay on his side and watched her while she read aloud to him. " 'She is so wet by the time he has the pillows under her gleaming stomach that he goes right into her in one long, delicious move. They begin slowly. When he is close to coming he pulls his prick out and lets it cool. Then he starts again, guiding it with one hand, feeding it in like a line. She begins to roll her hips, to cry out. It's like ministering to a lunatic. Finally he takes it out again. As he waits, tranquil, deliberate, his eye keeps falling on lubricants—her face cream, bottles in the *armoire.* They distract him. Their presence seems frightening, like evidence. They begin once more and this time do not stop until she cries out and he feels himself come in long, trembling runs, the head of his prick touching bone, it seems.' "

Julia handed the book back to him. "Your turn," she said then. She also lay on her side, watching him, but as he began to read to her, she shut her eyes; he saw her face on the pillow almost exactly as he'd seen it that morning in the Alps. St. Anton—that was the place—and he'd awakened to the sound of the skiers' boots tramping on the hard-packed snow; it seemed that an army of skiers was marching through the town to the ski lift. Only Julia and he were *not* there to ski. They were there to *fuck,* Farrokh thought, watching his wife's sleeping face. And that was how they'd spent the week, making brief forays into the snowy paths of the town and then hurrying back to their feather bed. In the evenings, they'd had no less appetite for the hearty food than the skiers had. Watching Julia as he read to her, Farrokh remembered every day and night in St. Anton.

" 'He is thinking of the waiters in the casino, the audience at the cinema, the dark hotels as she lies on her stomach and with the ease of sitting down at a well-laid table, but no more than that, he introduces himself. They lie on their sides. He tries not to move. There are only the little, invisible twitches, like a nibbling of fish.' "

Julia opened her eyes as Farrokh searched for another passage. "Don't stop," she told him.

Then Dr. Daruwalla found what he was looking for—a rather short and simple part. " 'Her breasts are hard,' " he read to his wife. " 'Her cunt is sopping.' " The doctor paused. "I suppose there'd be some readers who'd be shocked or offended by that," he added.

"Not me," his wife told him. He closed the book and returned it to the newspaper on the floor. When he rolled back to Julia, she'd arranged the pillows under her hips and lay waiting for him. He touched her breasts first.

"*Your* breasts are hard," he said to her.

"They are *not,*" she told him. "My breasts are old and soft."

"I like soft better," he said.

After she kissed him, she said, "My cunt is sopping."

"It *isn't!*" he said instinctively, but when she took his hand and made him touch her, he realized she wasn't lying.

In the morning, the sunlight passed through the narrow slats of the blinds and stood out in horizontal bars across the bare coffee-colored wall. The newspaper on the floor was stirred by a small lizard, a gecko—only its snout protruded from between the pages—and when Dr. Daruwalla reached to pick up *A Sport and a Pastime,* the gecko darted under the bed. *Sopping!* the doctor thought to himself. He opened the book quietly, thinking his wife was still asleep.

"Keep reading—aloud," Julia murmured.

Lunch Is Followed by Depression

It was with a renewed sexual confidence that Farrokh faced the situation of the morning. Rahul Rai had struck up a conversation with John D., and although—even by the doctor's standards—Rahul looked fetching in "her" bikini, the small *lump* of evidence in the bikini's bottom half provided Dr. Daruwalla with sufficient reason to rescue John D. from a potential confrontation. While Julia sat on the beach with the Daruwalla daughters, the doctor and John D. strolled in a manly and confiding fashion along the water's edge.

"There's something you should know about Rahul," Farrokh began.

"What's her name?" John D. asked.

"*His* name is Rahul," Farrokh explained. "If you were to look under *his* panties, I'm almost certain you would find a penis and a pair of balls—rather small, in both cases." They continued walking along the shoreline, with John D. appearing to pay obsessive attention to the smooth, sand-rubbed stones and the rounded, broken bits of shells.

Finally, John D. said, "The breasts look real."

"Definitely induced—hormonally induced," Dr. Daruwalla said. The doctor described how estrogens worked . . . the development of breasts, of hips; how the penis shrank to the size of a little boy's. The testes were so reduced they resembled vulva. The penis was so shrunken it resembled an enlarged clitoris. The doctor explained as much as he knew about a *complete* sex-change operation, too.

"Far out," John D. remarked. They discussed whether Rahul would be more interested in men or women. Since he *wanted* to be a woman, Dr. Daruwalla deduced that Rahul was sexually interested in men. "It's hard to tell," John D. suggested; indeed, when they returned to where the Daruwalla daughters were encamped under a thatch-roofed shelter, there was Rahul Rai in conversation with Julia!

Julia said later, "I think it's young men who interest him, although I suppose a young woman would do."

Would *do?* Dr. Daruwalla thought. Promila had confided to Farrokh that this was a bad time for "poor Rahul." Apparently, they'd not traveled from Bombay together, but Promila had met her nephew at the Bardez; he'd been alone in the area for more than a week. He had "hippie friends," Promila said—somewhere near Anjuna—but things hadn't worked out as Rahul had hoped. Farrokh didn't desire to know more, but Promila offered her speculations anyway.

"I presume that sexually confusing things must have happened," she told Dr. Daruwalla.

"Yes, I suppose," the doctor said. Normally, all of this would have upset Farrokh greatly, but something from his sexual triumphs with Julia had carried over into the following day. Despite everything that was "sexually confusing" about Rahul, which was sexually disturbing to

Dr. Daruwalla, not even the doctor's appetite was affected, although the heat was fierce.

It was unmercifully hot at midday, and there was no perceptible breeze. Along the shoreline, the fronds of the areca and coconut palms were as motionless as the grand old cashew and mango trees farther inland in the dead-still villages and towns. Not even the passing of a three-wheeled rickshaw with a damaged muffler could rouse a single dog to bark. Were it not for the heavy presence of the distilling feni, Dr. Daruwalla would have guessed that the air wasn't moving at all.

But the heat didn't dampen the doctor's enthusiasm for his lunch. He started with an oyster guisado and steamed prawns in a yogurt-mustard sauce; then he tried the vindaloo fish, the gravy for which was so piquant that his upper lip felt numb and he instantly perspired. He drank an ice-cold ginger feni with his meal—actually, he had two—and for dessert he ordered the bebinca. His wife was easily satisfied with a xacuti, which she shared with the girls; it was a fiery curry made almost soothing with coconut milk, cloves and nutmeg. The daughters also tried a frozen mango dessert; Dr. Daruwalla had a taste, but nothing could abate the burning sensation in his mouth. As a remedy, he ordered a cold beer. Then he criticized Julia for allowing the girls to drink so much sugarcane juice.

"In this heat, too much sugar will make them sick," Farrokh told his wife.

"Listen to who's talking!" Julia said.

Farrokh sulked. The beer was an unfamiliar brand, which he would never remember. He would recall, however, the part of the label that said LIQUOR RUINS COUNTRY, FAMILY AND LIFE.

But as much as Dr. Daruwalla was a man of unstoppable appetites, his plumpness had never been—nor would it become—displeasing to the eye. He was a fairly small man—his smallness was most apparent in the delicacy of his hands and in the neat, well-formed features of his face, which was round, boyish and friendly—and his arms and legs were thin and wiry; his bum was small, too. Even his little pot belly merely served to emphasize his smallness, his neatness, his tidiness. He liked a small, well-trimmed beard, for he also liked to shave; his throat and the sides of his face were usually clean-shaven. When he wore a mustache, it, too, was neat and small. His skin wasn't much browner than an almond shell; his hair was black—it would soon turn gray. He would never be bald; his hair was thick, with a slight wave, and he left it long on top, although he kept it cut short on the back of his neck and above his ears, which were also small and lay perfectly flat against his head. His eyes were such a dark-brown color that they looked almost black, and because his face was so small, his eyes seemed large—maybe they *were* large. If so, only his eyes reflected his appetites. And only in comparison to John D. would someone *not* have thought of Dr. Daruwalla as handsome—*small, but handsome*. He was not a fat man, but a plump one—a little, pot-bellied man.

While the doctor struggled to digest his meal, it might have crossed his mind that the others had behaved more sensibly. John D., as if demonstrating the self-discipline and dietary restraint that future movie stars would be wise to imitate, eschewed eating in the midday heat. He chose this time of day to take long walks on the beach; he swam intermittently and lazily—only to cool off. From his languid attitude, it was hard to tell if he walked the beach in order to look at the assembled young women or to afford them the luxury of looking at him.

In the torpid aftermath of his lunch, Dr. Daruwalla barely noticed that Rahul Rai was nowhere to be seen. Farrokh was frankly relieved that the would-be transsexual wasn't pursuing John D.; and Promila Rai had accompanied John D. for only a short distance along the water's edge, as if the young man had immediately discouraged her by declaring his intentions to walk to the next village, or to the village after that. Wearing an absurdly wide-brimmed hat—as if it weren't already too late to protect her cancerous skin—Promila had returned, alone, to the spot of shade allotted by her thatch-roofed shelter, and there she appeared to embalm herself with a variety of oils and chemicals.

Under their own array of thatch-roofed shelters, the Daruwalla daughters applied different oils and chemicals to their vastly younger and superior bodies; then they ventured among the intrepid sunbathers—mostly Europeans, and relatively few of them at this time of year. The Daruwalla girls were forbidden to follow John D. on his midday hikes; both Julia and Farrokh felt that the young man deserved this period of time to be free of them.

But the most sensibly behaved person at midday was always the doctor's wife. Julia retired to the relative cool of their second-floor rooms. There was a shaded balcony with John D.'s sleeping hammock and a cot; the balcony was a good place to read or nap.

It was clearly nap time for Dr. Daruwalla, who doubted he could manage the climb to the second floor of the hotel. From the taverna, he could see the balcony attached to his rooms, and he looked longingly in that direction. He thought the hammock would be nice, and he considered that he would try sleeping there tonight; if the mosquito netting was good, he'd be very comfortable, and all night he'd hear the Arabian Sea. The longer he allowed John D. to sleep there, the more firmly the young man would presume it was *his* place to sleep. But Farrokh's renewed sexual interest in Julia gave him pause in regard to his sleeping-hammock plan; there were passages of *A Sport and a Pastime* he'd not yet discussed with his wife.

Dr. Daruwalla wished he knew what else Mr. James Salter had written. However, as exhilarating as this unexpected stimulation to his marriage had been, Farrokh felt slightly depressed. Mr. Salter's writing was so far above anything Dr. Daruwalla could hope to imagine—much less hope to achieve—and the doctor had guessed right: one of the lovers dies, strongly implying that a love of such overpowering passion never lasts. Moreover, the novel concluded in a tone of voice that was almost physically painful to Dr. Daruwalla. In the end, Farrokh felt that the very life he led with Julia—the life he cherished—was being mocked. Or was it?

Of the French girl—Anne-Marie, the surviving lover—there is only this final offering: "She is married. I suppose there are children. They walk together on Sundays, the sunlight falling upon them. They visit friends, talk, go home in the evening, deep in the life we all agree is so greatly to be desired." Wasn't there an underlying cruelty to this? Because such a life *is* "greatly to be desired," isn't it? Dr. Daruwalla thought. And how could anyone expect the married life to compete with the burning intensity of a love affair?

What disturbed the doctor was that the end of the novel made him feel ignorant, or at least inexperienced. And what was more humiliating, Farrokh felt certain, was that Julia could probably explain the ending to him in such a way that he'd understand it. It was all a matter of tone of voice; perhaps the author had intended irony, but not sarcasm. Mr. Salter's use of language was crystalline; if something was unclear, the fuzzy-headedness surely should be attributed to the reader.

But more than technical virtuosity separated Dr. Daruwalla from Mr. James Salter, or from any other accomplished novelist. Mr. Salter and his peers wrote from a vision; they were convinced about something, and it was at least partly the passion of these writers' convictions that gave their novels such value. Dr. Daruwalla was convinced only that he would like to be more creative, that he would like to make something up. There were a lot of novelists like that, and Farrokh didn't care to embarrass himself by being one of them. He concluded that a more shameless form of entertainment suited him; if he couldn't write novels, maybe he could write screenplays. After all, movies weren't as serious as novels; certainly, they weren't as long. Dr. Daruwalla presumed that his lack of a "vision" wouldn't hamper his success in the screenplay form.

But his conclusion depressed him. In the search for something to occupy his untapped creativity, the doctor had already accepted a compromise—before he'd even begun! This thought moved him to consider consoling himself with his wife's affections. But gazing again to the distant balcony didn't bring the doctor any closer to Julia, and Dr. Daruwalla doubted that imbibing feni and beer was a wise prelude to an amorous adventure—especially in such abiding heat. Something Mr. Salter had written appeared to shimmer over Dr. Daruwalla in the midday inferno: "The more clearly one sees this world, the more one is obliged to pretend it does not exist." There is a growing list of things I don't know, the doctor thought.

He didn't know, for example, the name of the thick vine that had crawled upward from the ground to embrace both the second- and the third-floor balconies of the Hotel Bardez. The vine was put to active use by the small striped squirrels that scurried over it; at night, the geckos raced up and down the vine with far greater speed and agility than any squirrel. When the sun shone against this wall of the hotel, the smallest, palest-pink flowers opened up along the vine, but Dr. Daruwalla didn't know that these flowers were not what attracted the finches to the vine. Finches are seed eaters, but Dr. Daruwalla didn't know this, nor did the doctor know that the green parrot perching on the vine had feet with two toes pointing forward and two backward. These were the details he missed, and they contributed to the growing list of things he didn't know. This was the kind of Everyman he was—a little lost, a little misinformed (or uninformed), almost everywhere he ever was. Yet, even overfed, the doctor was undeniably attractive. Not every Everyman is attractive.

A Dirty Hippie

Dr. Daruwalla grew so drowsy at the littered table, one of the Bardez servant boys suggested he move into a new hammock that was strung in the shade of the areca and coconut palms. Complaining to the boy that he feared the hammock was too near the main beach and he'd be bothered by sand fleas, the doctor nevertheless tested the hammock; Farrokh wasn't sure it would support his weight. But the hammock held. For the moment, the doctor detected no sand fleas. Therefore, he was obliged to give the boy a tip.

This boy, Punkaj, seemed employed solely for the purpose of tipping, for the messages that he delivered to the Hotel Bardez and the adjacent lean-to restaurant and taverna were usually of his own invention and wholly unnecessary. For example, Punkaj asked Dr. Daruwalla if he should run to the hotel and tell "the Mrs. Doctor" that the doctor was napping in a hammock near the beach. Dr. Daruwalla said no. But in a short while, Punkaj was back beside the hammock. He reported: "The Mrs. Doctor is reading what I think is a book."

"Go away, Punkaj," said Dr. Daruwalla, but he tipped the worthless boy nonetheless. Then the doctor lay wondering if his wife was reading the Trollope or rereading the Salter.

Considering the size of his lunch, Farrokh was fortunate that he was able to sleep at all. The strenuousness of his digestive system made a sound sleep impossible, but throughout the grumbling and rumbling of his stomach—and the occasional hiccup or belch—the doctor fitfully dozed and dreamed, and woke up all of a sudden to wonder if his daughters were drowned or suffering from sunstroke or sexual attack. Then he dozed off again.

As Farrokh fell in and out of sleep, the imagined details of Rahul Rai's complete sex change appeared and disappeared in his mind's eye, drifting in and out of consciousness like the fumes from the distilling feni. This exotic aberration clashed with Farrokh's fairly ordinary ideals: his belief in the purity of his daughters, his fidelity to his wife. Only slightly less common was Dr. Daruwalla's vision of John D., which was simply the doctor's desire to see the young man rise above the sordid circumstances of his birth and abandonment. And if I could only play a part in *that*, Dr. Daruwalla dreamed, I might one day be as creative as Mr. James Salter.

But John D.'s only visible qualities were of a fleeting and superficial nature; he was arrestingly handsome, and he was so steadfastly self-confident that his poise concealed his lack of other qualities—sadly, the doctor presumed that John D. lacked other qualities. In this belief, Farrokh was aware that he relied too heavily on his brother's estimation and his sister-in-law's confirmation, for both Jamshed and Josefine were chronically worried that the boy had no future. He was "uninvolved" with his studies, they said. But couldn't this be an early indication of thespian detachment?

Yes, why not? John D. could be a movie star! Dr. Daruwalla decided, forgetting that this notion had originated with his wife. It suddenly seemed to the doctor that John D. was *destined* to be a movie star, or else he would be nothing. It was Farrokh's first realization that a hint of despair can start the creative juices flowing. And it must have been these juices, in combination with the more scientifically supported juices of digestion, that got the doctor's imagination going.

But, just then, a belch so alarming he failed to recognize it as his own awakened Dr. Daruwalla from these imaginings; he shifted in his hammock in order to confirm that his daughters had not been violated by either the forces of nature or the hand of man. Then he fell asleep with his mouth open, the splayed fingers of one hand lolling in the sand.

Dreamlessly, the noonday passed. The beach began to cool. A slight breeze rose; it softly gave sway to the hammock where Dr. Daruwalla lay digesting. Something had left a sour taste in his mouth—the doctor suspected the vindaloo fish or the beer—and he felt flatulent. Farrokh opened his eyes slightly to see if anyone was near his hammock—in which case it would be impolite for him to fart—and there was that pest Punkaj, the worthless servant boy.

"She come back," Punkaj said.

"Go away, Punkaj," said Dr. Daruwalla.

"She looking for you—that hippie with her bad foot," the boy said. He pronounced the word "heepee," so that Dr. Daruwalla, in his digestive daze, still didn't understand.

"Go away, Punkaj!" the doctor repeated. Then he saw the young woman limping toward him.

"Is that him? Is that the doctor?" she asked Punkaj.

"You wait there! *I* ask doctor first!" the boy said to her. At a glance, she could have been 18 or 25, but she was a big-boned young woman, broad-shouldered and heavy-breasted and thick through her hips. She also had thick ankles and very strong-looking hands, and she lifted the boy off the ground—holding him by the front of his shirt—and threw him on his back in the sand.

"Go fuck yourself," she told him. Punkaj picked himself up and ran toward the hotel. Farrokh swung his legs unsteadily out of the hammock and faced her. When he stood up, he was surprised at how much the late-afternoon breeze had cooled the sand; he was also surprised that the young woman was so much taller than he was. He quickly bent down to put on his sandals; that was when he saw she was barefoot—and that one foot was nearly twice the size of the other. While the doctor was still down on one knee, the young woman rotated her swollen foot and showed him the filthy, inflamed sole.

"I stepped on some glass," she said slowly. "I thought I picked it all out, but I guess not."

He took her foot in his hand and felt her lean heavily on his shoulder for balance. There were several small lacerations, all closed and red and puckered with infection, and on the ball of her foot was a fiery swelling the size of an egg; in its center was an inch-long, oozing gash that was scabbed over.

Dr. Daruwalla looked up at her, but she wasn't looking down at him; she was gazing off somewhere, and the doctor was shocked not only by her stature but by her solidity as well. She had a full, womanly figure and a peasant muscularity; her dirty, unshaven legs were ragged with golden hair, and her cut-off blue jeans were slightly torn at the crotch seam, through which poked an outrageous tuft of her golden pubic hair. She wore a black, sleeveless T-shirt with a silver skull-and-crossbones insignia, and her loose, low-slung breasts hung over Farrokh like a warning. When he stood up and looked into her face, he saw she couldn't have been older than 18. She had full, round, freckled cheeks, and her lips were badly sun-blistered. She had a child's little nose, also sun-burned, and almost-white blond hair, which was matted and tangled and discolored by the suntan oil she'd used to try to protect her face.

Her eyes were startling to Dr. Daruwalla, not only for their pale, ice-blue color but because they reminded him of the eyes of an animal that wasn't quite awake—not fully alert. As soon as she noticed he was looking at her, her pupils constricted and fixed hard upon him—also like an animal's. Now she was wary; all her instincts were suddenly engaged. The doctor couldn't return the intensity of her gaze; he looked away from her.

"I think I need some antibiotics," the young woman said.

"Yes, you have an infection," Dr. Daruwalla said. "I have to lance that swelling. There's something in there—it has to come out." She had a pretty good infection going; the doctor had also noticed the lymphangitic streaking.

The young woman shrugged; and when she moved her shoulders only that slightly, Farrokh caught the scent of her. It wasn't just an acrid armpit odor; there was also something like the tang of urine in the way she smelled, and there was a heavy, ripe smell—faintly rotten or decayed.

"It is essential for you to be clean before I cut into you," Dr. Daruwalla said. He was staring at the young woman's hands; there appeared to be dried blood caked under her nails. Once more the young woman shrugged, and Dr. Daruwalla took a step back from her.

"So . . . where do you want to do it?" she asked, looking around.

At the taverna, the bartender was watching them. In the lean-to restaurant, only one of the tables was occupied. There were three men drinking feni; even these impaired feni drinkers were watching the girl.

"There's a bathtub in our hotel," the doctor said. "My wife will help you."

"I know how to take a bath," the young woman told him.

Farrokh was thinking that she couldn't have walked very far on that foot. As she hobbled between the taverna and the hotel, her limp was pronounced; she leaned hard on the rail as they climbed the stairs to the rooms.

"You didn't walk all the way from Anjuna, did you?" he asked her.

"I'm from Iowa," she answered. For a moment, Dr. Daruwalla didn't understand—he was trying to think of an "Iowa" in Goa. Then he laughed, but she didn't.

"I meant, where are you staying in Goa?" he asked her.

"I'm not staying," she told him. "I'm taking the ferry to Bombay—as soon as I can walk."

"But where did you cut your foot?" he asked.

"On some glass," she said. "It was sort of near Anjuna."

This conversation, and watching her climb the stairs, exhausted Dr. Daruwalla. He preceded the girl into his rooms; he wanted to alert Julia that he'd found a patient on the beach, or that she'd found him.

Farrokh and Julia waited on the balcony while the young woman took a bath. They waited quite a long time, staring—with little comment—at the girl's battered canvas rucksack, which she'd left with them on the balcony. Apparently, she wasn't considering a change of clothes, or else the clothes in the rucksack were dirtier than the clothes she wore, although this was hard to imagine. Odd cloth badges were sewn to the rucksack—the insignia of the times, Dr. Daruwalla supposed. He recognized the peace symbol, the pastel flowers, Bugs Bunny, a U.S. flag with the face of a pig superimposed on it, and another silver skull and crossbones. He didn't recognize the black-and-yellow cartoon bird with the menacing expression; he doubted it was a version of the American eagle. There was no way the doctor could have been familiar with Herky the Hawk, the wrathful symbol of athletic teams from the University of Iowa. Looking more closely, Farrokh read the words under the black-and-yellow bird: GO, HAWKEYES!

"She must belong to some sort of strange club," the doctor said to his wife. In response, Julia sighed. It was the way she feigned indifference; Julia was still somewhat in shock at the sight of the huge young woman, not to mention the great clumps of blond hair the girl had grown in her armpits.

In the bathroom, the girl filled and emptied the tub twice. The first time was to shave her legs, but not her underarms—she valued the hair in her armpits as an indication of her rebellion; she thought of it and her pubic hair as her "fur." She used Dr. Daruwalla's razor; she thought about stealing it, but then she remembered she'd left her rucksack out on the balcony. The memory distracted her; she shrugged, and put the razor back where she'd found it. As she settled into the second tub of water, she fell instantly asleep—she was so exhausted—but she woke up as soon as her mouth dipped below the water. She soaped herself, she shampooed her hair, she rinsed. Then she emptied the tub and drew a *third* bath, letting the water rise around her.

What puzzled her about the murders was that she couldn't locate in herself the slightest feeling of remorse. The murders weren't her fault—whether or not they might be judged her unwitting responsibility. She refused to feel guilty, because there was absolutely nothing she could have done to save the victims. She thought only vaguely about the fact that she hadn't tried to prevent the murders. After all, she decided, she was also a victim and, as such, a kind of eternal absolution appeared to hover over her, as detectable as the steam ascending from her bathwater.

She groaned; the water was as hot as she could stand it. She was amazed at the scum on the surface of the water. It was her third bath, but the dirt was still coming out of her.

11. THE DILDO

Behind Every Journey Is a Reason

It was her parents' fault, she decided. Her name was Nancy, she came
from an Iowa pig-farming family of German descent and she'd been a
good girl all through high school in a small Iowa town; then she'd gone
to the university in Iowa City. Because she was so blond and bosomy,
she'd been a popular candidate for the cheerleading squad, although she
lacked the requisite personality and wasn't chosen; still, it was her
contact with the cheerleaders that led her to meet so many football
players. There was a lot of partying, which Nancy was unfamiliar with,
and she'd not only slept with a boy for the first time; she'd slept with her
first black person, her first Hawaiian person, and the first person she'd
ever known who came from New England—he was from somewhere in
Maine, or maybe it was Massachusetts.

She flunked out of the University of Iowa at the end of her first
semester; when she went home to the small town she'd grown up in, she
was pregnant. She thought she was still a good girl, to the degree that
she submitted to her parents' recommendation without questioning it:
she would have the baby, put it up for adoption and get a job. She went
to work at the local hardware store, in feed-and-grain supply, while she
was still carrying the child; soon she began to doubt the wisdom of her

parents' recommendation—men her father's age began propositioning her, *while* she was pregnant.

She delivered the child in Texas, where the orphanage physician never let her see it—the nurses never even let her know which sex it was—and when she came home, her parents sat her down and told her that they hoped she'd learned her "lesson"; they hoped she would "behave." Her mother said she prayed that some decent man in the town would be "forgiving" enough to marry her, one day. Her father said that God had been "lenient" with her; he implied that God was disinclined toward leniency twice.

For a while, Nancy tried to comply, but so many men of the town attempted to seduce her—they assumed she'd be easy—and so many women were worse; they assumed she was already sleeping with everyone. This punitive experience had a strange effect on her; it didn't make her revile the football players who'd contributed to her downfall—oddly, what she loathed most was her own innocence. She refused to believe she was immoral. What degraded her was to feel stupid. And with this feeling came an anger she was unfamiliar with—it felt foreign; yet this anger was as much a part of her as the fetus she'd carried for so long but had never seen.

She applied for a passport. When it came, she robbed the hardware store—feed-and-grain, especially—of every cent she could steal. She knew that her family originally came from Germany; she thought she should go there. The cheapest flight (from Chicago) was to Frankfurt; but if Iowa City had been too sophisticated for her, Nancy was unprepared for the enterprising young Germans who frequented the area of the Hauptbahnhof and the Kaiserstrasse, where almost immediately she met a tall, dark drug dealer named Dieter. He was enduringly small-time.

The first thrilling, albeit petty, crime he introduced her to involved her posing as a prostitute on those nasty side streets off the Kaiserstrasse—the ones named after the German rivers. She'd ask for so much money that only the wealthiest, stupidest tourist or businessman would follow her to a shabby room on the Elbestrasse or the Moselstrasse; Dieter would be waiting there. Nancy made the man pay her before she unlocked the door of the room; once they were inside, Dieter would pretend to surprise her—grabbing her roughly and throwing her on the bed, abusing her for her faithlessness and her dishonesty, threatening to kill her while the man who'd paid for her services invariably fled. Not one of the men ever tried to help her. Nancy enjoyed taking advantage of their lust, and there was something gratifying about their uniform cowardice. In her mind, she was repaying those men who'd made her feel so miserable in feed-and-grain supply.

It was Dieter's theory that all Germans were sexually ashamed of themselves. That was why he preferred India; it was both a spiritual and a sensual country. What he meant was that, for very little, you could buy anything there. He meant women and young girls, in addition to the bhang and the ganja, but he told her only about the quality of the hashish—what he would pay for it there, and what he would get for it back in Germany. He didn't tell her the whole plan—specifically, that her American passport and her farm-girl looks were the means by which he would get the stuff through German customs. Nancy was also the means by which he'd planned to get the Deutsche marks through Indian customs. (It was marks he took to India; it was hashish he brought back.) Dieter had made the trip with American girls before; he'd also used Canadian girls—their passports aroused even less suspicion.

With both nationalities, Dieter followed a simple procedure: he never flew on the same plane with them; he made sure they'd arrived and passed through customs before he boarded a plane for Bombay. He always told them he wanted them to recover from the jet lag in a comfortable room at the Taj, because, when he got there, they'd be doing some "serious business"; he meant they'd be staying in less conspicuous lodgings, and he knew that the bus ride from Bombay to Goa could be disagreeable. Dieter could buy what he wanted in Bombay; but, inevitably, he'd be persuaded—usually by the friend of a friend—to do his buying in Goa. The hash was more expensive there, because the European and American hippies bought up the stuff like bottled water, but the quality was more reliable. It was the quality that fetched a good price in Frankfurt.

As for the trip back to Germany, Dieter would precede the designated young woman by a day; if she were ever delayed in German customs, Dieter would take this as a sign that he shouldn't meet her. But Dieter had a system, and not one of his young women had ever been caught—at either end.

Dieter's women were outfitted with the kind of well-worn travel guides and paperback novels that suggested earnestness in the extreme. The travel guides were dog-eared and scribbled in to draw the attention of customs officials to those areas of cultural or historical importance so keenly boring that they attracted only graduate students in the field. As for the paperback novels, by Hermann Hesse or Lawrence Durrell, they were fairly standard indications of their readers' proclivities for the mystical and poetic; these latter tendencies were dismissed by customs officials as the habitual concerns of young women who'd never been motivated by money. Without a profit motive, surely drug trafficking could be of no interest to them.

However, these young women were not above suspicion as occasional drug users; their personal effects were thoroughly searched for a modest stash. Not once had a shred of evidence been found. Dieter was undeniably clever; a large amount of the stuff was always successfully secreted in a dog-proof container of unflinchingly crass but basic ingenuity.

In retrospect, poor Nancy would agree that the enslavement of sexual corruption empowered all of Dieter's other abilities. In the relative safety of the Daruwallas' bathtub at the Hotel Bardez, Nancy supposed that she'd gone along with Dieter strictly because of the sex. Her football players had been friendly oafs, and most of the time she'd been drunk on beer. With Dieter, she smoked just the right amount of hashish or marijuana—Dieter was no oaf. He had the gaunt good looks of a young man who'd recently recovered from a life-threatening illness; had he not been murdered, he doubtless would have become one of those men who progress through a number of increasingly young and naïve women, his sexual appetite growing confused with his desire to introduce the innocent to a series of successively degrading experiences. For as soon as he gave Nancy some courage in her sexual potential, he undermined what slight self-esteem she had; he made her doubt herself and hate herself in ways she'd never thought possible.

In the beginning, Dieter had simply asked her, "What is the first sexual experience that you had some confidence in?" And when she didn't answer him—because she was thinking to herself that masturbation was the *only* sexual experience that she had *any* confidence in—he suddenly said, "Masturbation, right?"

"Yes," Nancy said quietly. He was very gentle with her. At first, they'd just talked about it.

"Everyone is different," Dieter said philosophically. "You just have to learn what your own best way is."

Then he told her some stories to relax her. One time, as an adolescent, he'd actually stolen a pair of panties from the lingerie drawer of his best friend's mother. "When they lost whatever scent they had, I put them back in her drawer and stole a fresh pair," he told Nancy. "The thing about masturbation was that I was always afraid I'd be caught. I knew a girl who could make it work only when she was standing up."

Nancy told him, "I have to be lying down."

This conversation itself was more intimate than anything she'd known. It seemed so natural, how he'd led her to show him how she masturbated. She would lie rigidly on her back with her left hand clenching her left buttock; she wouldn't actually touch the spot (it never worked when she did). Instead, she'd rub herself just above the spot with three fingers of her right hand—her thumb and pinky finger spread like wings. She turned her face to the side and Dieter would lie beside her, kissing her, until she needed to turn away from him to breathe. When she finished, he entered her; at that point, she was always aroused.

One time, when she'd finished, he said, "Roll over on your stomach. Just wait right there. I have a surprise for you." When he came back to their bed, he snuggled beside her, kissing her again and again—deep kisses, with his tongue—while he moved one hand underneath her until he could touch her with his fingers, exactly as she'd touched herself. The first time, she never saw the dildo.

Slowly, with the other hand, he began to work the device into her; at first she pressed herself down into his fingers, as if to get away from it, but later she lifted herself up to meet the dildo. It was very big but he never hurt her with it, and when she was so excited that she had to stop kissing him—she had to scream—he took the dildo out of her and entered her himself, from behind and with the fingers of his hand still touching her and touching her. (Compared to the dildo, Dieter was a little disappointing.)

Her parents had once warned Nancy that "experimenting with sex" could make her crazy, but the madness that Dieter had incited didn't seem to be a dangerous madness. Still, it wasn't the best reason to go to India.

A Memorable Arrival

There'd been some trouble with her visa, and she was worried if she'd had the right shots; because the names were in German, she hadn't understood all the inoculations. She was sure she was taking too many antimalarial pills, but Dieter couldn't tell her how many to take; he seemed indifferent to disease. He was more concerned that an Indian customs official would confiscate the dildo—but only if Nancy took pains to conceal it, he said. Dieter insisted that she carry it casually— with her toilet articles, in her carry-on bag. But the thing was enormous. Worse, it was of a frightening pink, mock-flesh color, and the tip, which was modeled on a circumcised penis, had a bluish tinge—like a cock left out in the cold, Nancy thought. And where the fake foreskin was rolled, there seemed to linger a residue of the lubricating jelly, which could never quite be wiped away.

Nancy put the thing in an old white athletic sock—the long kind, meant to be worn above the calf. She prayed that the Indian customs officials would ascribe to the dildo some unmentionable medicinal pur- pose—anything other than that most obvious purpose for which it was intended. Understandably, she wanted Dieter to take it with *him*, on *his* plane, but he pointed out to her that the customs officials would then conclude he was a homosexual; homosexuals, she should know, were routinely abused at every country's port of entry. Dieter also told Nancy that the excessive illegal Deutsche marks were traveling with him, on his plane, and that the reason he didn't want her flying with him was that he didn't want her to be incriminated if he was caught.

Soaking herself in the bathtub at the Hotel Bardez, Nancy wondered why she'd believed him; with hindsight, such errors of judgment are plain to see. Nancy reflected that it hadn't been difficult for Dieter to convince her to bring the dildo to Bombay. It hadn't been the first time that a dildo gained such easy access to India, but what a lot of trouble this particular instrument inspired.

Nancy had never been to the East; she was introduced to it at the Bombay airport, at about 2:00 in the morning. She'd not seen men so diminished, so damaged and so transformed by turmoil, by din and by wasteful energy; their ceaseless motion and their aggressive curiosity reminded her of scurrying rats. And so many of them were barefoot. She tried to concentrate on the customs inspector, who was attended by two policemen; they weren't barefoot. But the policemen—a couple of con- stables in blue shirts and wide blue shorts—were wearing the most absurd leg warmers she'd ever seen, especially in such hot weather. And she'd never seen Nehru caps on cops before.

In Frankfurt, Dieter had arranged for Nancy to be examined—in regard to the proper size for a diaphragm—but when the doctor had discovered she'd had a baby, he'd outfitted her with an intrauterine device instead. She hadn't wanted one. When the customs inspector was examining her toiletries and one of the overseeing policemen opened a jar of her moisturizer and scooped out a gob of the cream with his finger, which the other policeman then sniffed, Nancy was grateful that there was no diaphragm or spermicidal ointment for them to play with. The constables couldn't see or touch or smell her IUD.

But of course there was the dildo, which lay untouched in the long athletic sock while the policemen and the customs inspector pawed through the clothes in her rucksack and emptied her carry-on bag, which was really just an oversized imitation-leather purse. One of the policemen picked up the battered paperback copy of Lawrence Durrell's *Clea*, the fourth novel of the Alexandria Quartet, of which Dieter had read only the first, *Justine*. Nancy hadn't read any of them; but the novel was dog-eared where the last reader had presumably stopped reading, and it was at this marked page that the constable opened the book, his eyes quickly finding that passage which Dieter had underlined in pencil for just such an occasion. In truth, this copy of *Clea* had made the trip to India and the return trip to Germany with two of Dieter's other women, neither of whom had read the novel or even the passage Dieter had marked. He'd chosen the particular passage because it would doubtless identify the reader to any international customs authority as a harmless fool.

The policeman was so stymied by the passage that he handed the book to his fellow constable, who looked stricken, as if he'd been asked to crack an indecipherable code; he, too, passed the book on. It was the customs inspector who finally read the passage. Nancy watched the clumsy, involuntary movement of the man's lips, as if he were isolating olive pits. Gradually the words, or something like the words, emerged aloud; they frankly seemed incomprehensible to Nancy. She couldn't imagine what the customs inspector and the constables made of them.

" 'The whole quarter lay drowsing in the umbrageous violet of approaching nightfall,' " the customs inspector read. " 'A sky of palpitating velours which was cut into by the stark flare of a thousand electric light bulbs. It lay over Tatwig Street, that night, like a velvet rind.' " The customs inspector stopped reading, looking like a man who'd just eaten something odd. One of the policemen stared angrily at the book, as if he felt compelled to confiscate it or destroy it on the spot, but the other constable was as distracted as a bored child; he picked up the dildo in the athletic sock and unsheathed the giant penis as one would unsheathe a sword. The sock drooped limply in the policeman's left hand while his right hand grasped the great cock at its root, at the rock-hard pair of makeshift balls.

Suddenly seeing what he held, the policeman quickly extended the dildo to his fellow constable, who took hold of the instrument by the rolled foreskin before he recognized the exaggerated male member, which he instantly handed to the customs inspector. Still holding *Clea* in his left hand, the customs inspector seized the dildo at the scrotum; then he dropped the novel and snatched the sock from the first, gaping policeman. But the impressive penis was more difficult to sheathe than to unsheathe, and in his haste the customs inspector inserted the instrument the wrong way. Thus were the balls jammed into the heel of the sock, where they made an awkward lump—they didn't fit—and the bluish tip of the thing (the circumcised head) protruded loosely from the open end of the sock. The hole at the end of the enormous cock appeared to stare out at the constables and the customs inspector like the proverbial evil eye.

"Where you stay?" one of the policemen asked Nancy. He was furiously wiping his hand on his leg warmers—a trace of the lubricating jelly, perhaps.

"Always carry your own bag," the other constable advised her.

"Agree to a price with the taxi-walla before you get in the car," the first policeman said.

The customs inspector wouldn't look at her. She'd expected something worse; surely the dildo would provoke leering—at least rude or suggestive laughter, she'd thought. But she was in the land of the lingam—or so she imagined. Wasn't the phallic symbol worshiped here? Nancy thought she'd read that the penis was a symbol of Lord Shiva. Maybe what Nancy carried in her purse was as realistic (albeit exaggerated) a lingam as these men had ever seen. Maybe she'd made an unholy use of such a symbol—was that why these men wanted nothing to do with her? But the constables and the customs inspector weren't thinking of lingams or Lord Shiva; they were simply appalled at the portable penis.

Poor Nancy was left to find her own way out of the airport and into the shrill cries of the taxi-wallas. An unending lineup of taxis extended into the infernal blackness of this outlying district of Bombay; except for the oasis, which was the airport, there were no lights in Santa Cruz—there was no Sahar in 1969. It was then about 3:00 in the morning.

Nancy had to haggle with her taxi-walla over the fare into Bombay. After she arranged the prepaid trip, she still encountered some difficulty with her driver; he was a Tamil, apparently new to Bombay. He claimed to not understand Hindi or Marathi; it was in uncertain English that

Nancy heard him asking the other taxi-wallas for directions to the Taj.

"Lady, you don't want to go with him," one of the taxi-wallas told her, but she'd already paid and was sitting in the back seat of the taxi.

As they drove toward the city, the Tamil continued a lengthy debate with another Tamil driver who drove his taxi perilously close to theirs; for several miles, they drove like this—past the unlit slums in the predawn, immeasurable darkness, wherein the slum dwellers were distinguishable only by the smell of their excrement and their dead or dying fires. (What were they burning? Rubbish?) When the sidewalks on the outskirts of Bombay first appeared, still without electric light, the two Tamils raced side by side—even through the traffic circles, those wild roundabouts—their discourse progressing from an argument to a shouting match to threats, which sounded (even in Tamil) quite dire to Nancy.

The seemingly unconcerned passengers in the other Tamil's taxi were a well-dressed British couple in their forties. Nancy guessed they were also headed to the Taj, and that this coincidence lay at the heart of the dispute between the two Tamils. (Dieter had warned her of this common practice: two drivers with two separate fares, headed for the same place. Naturally, one of the drivers was attempting to persuade the other to carry both fares.)

At a traffic light, the two stopped taxis were suddenly surrounded by barking dogs—starving curs, all snapping at one another—and Nancy imagined that, if one jumped through the open window at her, she could club it with the dildo. This passing idea perhaps prepared her for what happened at the next intersection, where again the light was against them; while they waited this time, they were slowly approached by beggars instead of dogs. The shouting Tamils had attracted some of the sidewalk sleepers, whose mounded bodies under their light-colored clothing could be dimly seen to contrast with the darkened streets and buildings. First a man in a ragged, filthy dhoti stuck his arm in Nancy's window. Nancy noticed that the prim British couple—not in fear but out of sheer obstinacy—had closed their windows, despite the moist heat. Nancy thought she would suffocate if she closed hers.

Instead, she spoke sharply to her driver—to *go*! After all, the light had changed. But her Tamil and the other Tamil were too engrossed in their confrontation to obey the traffic signal. Her Tamil ignored her, and, to Nancy's further irritation, the other Tamil now coerced his British passengers into the street; he was beckoning to them that they must join Nancy in *her* cab, exactly as Dieter had foretold.

Nancy shouted at her driver, who turned to her and shrugged; she shouted out the window to the other Tamil, who shouted back at her. Nancy shouted to the British couple that they shouldn't allow themselves to be so taken advantage of; they should demand of their driver that he bring them to their prearranged, prepaid destination.

"Don't let the bastards screw you!" Nancy shouted. Then she realized that she was waving the dildo at them; to be sure, it was still in the sock and they didn't *know* it was a dildo; they could only suppose she was an hysterical young woman threatening them with a sock.

Nancy slid over in her seat. "Please get in," she said to the British couple, but when they opened the door, Nancy's driver protested. He even jerked the car a little forward. Nancy tapped him on his shoulder with the dildo—still in the sock. Her driver looked indifferent; his counterpart was already stuffing the British couple's luggage into the trunk as the twosome squeezed into the seat beside her.

Nancy was pressed against the window when a beggar woman pushed a baby in the window and held it in front of her face; the child was foul-smelling, unmoving, expressionless—it looked half dead. Nancy raised the dildo, but what could she do? Whom should she hit? Instead, she screamed at the woman, who indignantly withdrew the baby from the taxi. Maybe it wasn't even her baby, Nancy considered; possibly it was just a baby that people used for begging. Perhaps it wasn't even a real baby.

Ahead of them, two young men were supporting a drunken or a drugged companion. They paused in crossing the road, as if they weren't sure that the taxi had stopped. But the taxi was stopped, and Nancy was incensed that her driver and the other Tamil were *still* arguing. She leaned forward and brought the dildo down across the back of her driver's neck. That was when the sock flew off. The driver turned to face her. She struck him squarely on his nose with the huge cock in her hand.

"Drive on!" she shouted at the Tamil. Suitably impressed with the giant penis, he lurched the taxi forward—through the traffic light, which had turned red again. Fortunately, no other traffic was on the street. Unfortunately, the two young men and their slumped companion were directly in the taxi's path. At first, it seemed to Nancy that all three of them were hit. Later, she distinctly remembered that two of them had run away, although she couldn't say that she'd actually seen the impact; she must have closed her eyes.

While the Englishman helped the driver put the body in the front seat of the taxi, Nancy realized that the young man who'd been hit was the one who'd appeared to be drunk or drugged. It never occurred to her that the young man might already have been dead when the car hit him. But this was the subject of the Englishman's conversation with the Tamil driver: had the boy or young man been pushed into the path of the taxi deliberately, and was he even conscious before the taxi struck him?

"He *looked* dead," the Englishman kept saying.

"Yes, he is dying before!" the Tamil shouted. "*I* am not killing him!"

"Is he dead now?" Nancy asked quietly.

"Oh, definitely," the Englishman replied. Like the customs inspector, he wouldn't look at her, but the Englishman's wife was staring at Nancy, who still clutched the fierce dildo in her fist. Still not looking at her, the Englishman handed her the sock. She covered the weapon and returned it to her big purse.

"Is this your first visit to India?" the Englishwoman asked her, while the crazed Tamil drove them faster and faster through the streets now more and more blessed with electric light; the colorful mounds of the sidewalk sleepers were visible all around them. "In Bombay, half the population sleeps on the streets—but it's really quite safe here," the Englishwoman said. Nancy's pinched expression implied to the British couple that she was a newcomer to the city and its smells. Actually, it was the lingering smell of the baby that pinched Nancy's face—how something so small could reek with such force.

The body in the front seat made its deadness known. The young man's head lolled lifelessly, his shoulders impossibly slack. Whenever the Tamil braked or cornered, the body responded as heavily as a bag of sand. Nancy was grateful that she couldn't see the young man's face, which was making a dull sound against the windshield—his face rested flush against the glass—until the Tamil cornered again and then accelerated.

Still not looking at Nancy, the Englishman said, "Don't mind the body, dear." It seemed unclear whether he'd spoken to Nancy or to his wife.

"It doesn't bother me," his wife answered.

Over Marine Drive, a thick smog hung suspended, as warm as a woolen shroud; the Arabian Sea was veiled, but the Englishwoman pointed to where the sea should have been. "Out there is the ocean," she told Nancy, who began to gag. Overhead, on the lampposts, not even the advertisements were visible in the smog. The lights strung along Marine Drive weren't smog lights, then; they were white, not yellow.

In the careening taxi, the Englishman pointed out the window into the veil of smog. "This is the Queen's Necklace," he told Nancy. As the taxi raced on, he added—more to assure himself and his wife than to comfort Nancy—"Well, we're almost there."

"I'm going to throw up," Nancy said.

"If you don't *think* about being sick, dear, you won't *be* sick," the Englishwoman said.

The taxi departed Marine Drive for the narrower, winding streets; the three living passengers leaned in to the corners, and the dead boy in the front seat appeared to come alive. His head walloped the side window; he slid forward and his face glanced off the windshield, skidding him into the Tamil driver, who elbowed the body away. The young man's hands flew up to his face, as if he'd just remembered something important. Then, once again, the boy's body appeared to forget everything.

There were whistles, piercing sharp and loud: these were the sounds of the tall Sikh doormen who directed the traffic at the Taj, but Nancy was searching for some evidence of the police. Nearby, at the looming Gateway of India, Nancy thought she'd seen some sort of police activity; there were lights, the sound of hysterics, a sort of disturbance. At first, some beggar urchins were reputed to be the cause; the story was, they'd failed to beg a single rupee from a young Swedish couple who'd been photographing the Gateway of India with an ostentatious and professional use of bright-white lights and reflectors. Hence the urchins had urinated on the Gateway of India in an effort to spoil the picture, and when they'd failed to gain suitable attention from the foreigners—the Swedes allegedly found this demonstration symbolically interesting— the urchins then attempted to urinate on the photographic equipment, and that was the cause of the ruckus. But further investigation would reveal that the Swedes had paid the beggars to pee on the Gateway of India, which had little effect—the Gateway of India was already soiled. The urchins had never attempted to pee on the Swedes' photographic equipment; that would have been far too bold for them—they'd merely complained that they weren't paid enough for pissing on the Gateway of India. *That* was the true cause of the ruckus.

Meanwhile, the dead boy in the taxi had to wait. In the driveway of the Taj, the Tamil driver became hysterical; a dead man had been thrown into the path of his car—apparently, there was a dent. The British couple confided to a policeman that the Tamil had run a red light (upon being struck by a dildo). The policeman was the bewildered constable who'd finally freed himself from the crime of urination at the Gateway of India. It wasn't clear to Nancy if the British couple was blaming her for the accident, if it even had been an accident. After all, the Tamil and the Englishman agreed that the boy had looked dead before the taxi hit him. What was clear to Nancy was that the policeman didn't know what a "dildo" was.

"A penis—a rather large one," the Englishman explained to the constable.

"*She?*" the policeman asked, pointing to Nancy. "She is hitting the taxi-walla with a *what?*"

"You'll have to show him, dear," the Englishwoman told Nancy.

"I'm not showing him anything," Nancy said.

Our Friend, the Real Policeman

It took an hour before Nancy was free to register in the hotel. A half hour later—she'd just finished soaking in a hot bath—a second police-man came to her room. This one wasn't a constable—no blue shorts a yard wide, no silly leg warmers. This one wasn't another nerd in a Nehru cap; he wore an officer's cap with the Maharashtrian police insignia and a khaki shirt, long khaki pants, black shoes, a revolver. It was the duty officer from the Colaba Police Station, which has jurisdic-tion over the Taj. Without his jowls, but even then sporting that pencil-thin mustache—and 20 years before he would have occasion to question Dr. Daruwalla and Inspector Dhar at the Duckworth Club—the young Inspector Patel gave a good first impression of himself. A future deputy commissioner could be discerned in the young police-man's composure.

Inspector Patel was aggressive but courteous, and even in his twenties he was an intimidating detective in the way that he invited a certain misunderstanding of his questions. His manner persuaded you to believe that he already knew the answers to many of the questions he asked, although he usually didn't; thus he encouraged you to tell the truth by implying that he already knew it. And his method of questioning carried the added implication that, within your answers, Inspector Patel could discern your moral character.

In her current state, Nancy was vulnerable to such an uncommonly proper and pleasant-looking young man. To sympathize with Nancy's situation: Inspector Patel did not present himself as a person whom even a brazen or a supremely self-confident young woman would *choose* to show a dildo to. Also, it was about 5:00 in the morning. There may have been some eager early risers who were heralding the sunrise that—when viewed across the water, and perfectly framed in the arch of the Gateway of India—could still summon the vainglorious days of the British Raj, but poor Nancy wasn't among them. Besides, her only windows and the small balcony didn't afford her a view of the sea. Dieter had arranged for one of the cheaper rooms.

Below her, in the gray-brown light, was the usual gathering of beggars—child performers, for the most part. Those international travelers who were still staggered by jet lag would find these early-morning urchins their first contact with India in the light of day.

Nancy sat at the foot of her bed in her bathrobe. The inspector sat in the only chair not strewn with her clothes or her bags. They could both hear the emptying of Nancy's bath. Highly visible, as Dieter had advised, were the used-looking but unused guidebook and the unread novel by Lawrence Durrell.

It was not uncommon, the inspector told her, for someone to be murdered and then shoved in front of a moving car. In this case, what was unusual was that the hoax had been so obvious.

"Not to me," Nancy told him. She explained that she'd not seen the moment of impact; she'd thought all three of them were hit—probably because she'd shut her eyes.

The Englishwoman hadn't observed the moment of impact, either, Inspector Patel informed Nancy. "She was looking at you instead," the policeman explained.

"Oh, I see," Nancy said.

The Englishman was quite sure that a body—at least an unconscious body, if not a dead one—had been pushed into the path of the oncoming car. "But the taxi-walla doesn't know what he saw," said Inspector Patel. "The Tamil keeps changing his story." When Nancy continued to stare blankly at him, the policeman added, "The driver says he was distracted."

"By what?" Nancy asked, although she knew by what.

"By what you hit him with," Inspector Patel replied.

There was an uncomfortable pause while the policeman looked from chair to chair, surveying her emptied bags, the two books, her clothes. Nancy thought he must be at least five years older than she was, although he looked younger. His self-assurance made him seem disarmingly grown-up; yet he didn't exhibit the cocksure arrogance of cops. Inspector Patel didn't swagger; there was something in his controlled mannerisms that came from an absolute correctness of purpose. What struck Nancy as his pure goodness was riveting. And she thought he was a wonderful coffee-and-cream color; he had the blackest hair—and such a thin, perfectly edged mustache that Nancy wanted to touch it.

The overall nattiness of the young man stood in obvious contrast to that absence of vanity which is commonly associated with a happily married man. Here in the Taj, in the presence of such a buxom blonde in her bathrobe, Inspector Patel was obviously unmarried; he was as alert to the details of his appearance as he was to every inch of Nancy, and to the particular revelations of Nancy's room. She didn't realize he was looking for the dildo.

"May I see the thing you hit the taxi-walla with?" the inspector asked finally. God knows how the idiot Tamil had described it. Nancy went to get it from the bathroom, having decided to keep it with her toilet articles. God knows what the British couple had told the inspector. If the inspector had talked to them, they'd doubtless described her as a rude young woman brandishing an enormous cock.

Nancy gave the dildo to Inspector Patel, and again sat down at the foot of her bed. The young policeman politely handed the instrument back without looking at her.

"I'm sorry—it was necessary for me to see it," Inspector Patel said. "I was having some difficulty *imagining* it," he explained.

"Both drivers were paid their fares at the airport," Nancy told him. "I don't like to be cheated," she said.

"It's not the easiest country for a woman traveling alone," the inspector said. By the quick way he glanced at her, she understood this was a question.

"Friends are meeting me," Nancy told him. "I'm just waiting for them to call." (Dieter had advised her to say this; anyone assessing her student clothing and her cheap bags would know that she couldn't afford many nights at the Taj.)

"So will you be traveling with your friends or staying in Bombay?" the inspector asked her.

Nancy recognized her advantage. As long as she held the dildo, the young policeman would find it awkward to look in her eyes.

"I'll do what they do," she said indifferently. She held the penis in her lap; with the slightest movement of her wrist, she discovered, she could tap the circumcised head against her bare knee. But it was her bare feet that appeared to transfix Inspector Patel; perhaps it was their impossible whiteness, or else their improbable size—even bare, Nancy's feet were bigger than the inspector's little shoes.

Nancy stared at him without mercy. She enjoyed the prominent bones in his sharply featured face; it would have been impossible for her to look at his face and imagine it—even in 20 years—with jowls. She thought he had the blackest eyes and the longest eyelashes.

Still staring at Nancy's feet, Inspector Patel spoke forlornly: "I suppose there's no known phone number or an address where I could reach you."

Nancy felt she understood everything that attracted her to him. She'd certainly tried hard to lose her innocence in Iowa, but the football players hadn't touched it. She'd spoiled her real innocence in Germany, with Dieter, and now it was lost for good. But here was a man who was still innocent. She probably both frightened and attracted him—if he even knew it, Nancy thought.

"Do you want to see me again?" she asked him. She thought the question was ambiguous enough, but he stared at her feet—with both longing and horror, she imagined.

"But you couldn't identify the two other men, even if we found them," said Inspector Patel.

"I could identify the other taxi driver," Nancy said.

"We've already got him," the inspector told her.

Nancy stood up from the bed and carried the dildo to the bathroom. When she came back, Inspector Patel was at the window, watching the beggars. She didn't want to have any advantage over him anymore. Maybe she was imagining that the inspector had fallen hopelessly in love with her and that, if she shoved him on the bed and fell on top of him, he would worship her and be her slave forever. Maybe it wasn't even *him* she wanted; possibly it was only his obvious propriety, and only because she felt she'd given away her essential goodness and would never get it back.

Then it struck her that he was no longer interested in her feet; he kept glancing at her *hands*. Even though she'd put away the dildo, he wouldn't look in her eyes.

"Do you want to see me again?" Nancy repeated. There was no ambiguity to her question now. She stood closer to him than was necessary, but he ignored the question by pointing to the child performers far below them.

"Always the same stunts—they never change," Inspector Patel remarked. Nancy refused to look at the beggars; she continued to stare at Inspector Patel.

"You could give me your phone number," she said. "Then I could call you."

"But why would you?" the inspector asked her. He kept watching the beggars. Nancy turned away from him and stretched out on the bed. She lay on her stomach with the robe gathered tightly around her. She thought about her blond hair; she thought it must look nice, spread out on the pillows, but she didn't know if Inspector Patel was looking at her. She just knew that her voice would be muffled by the pillows, and that he'd have to come closer to the bed in order to hear her.

"What if I need you?" she asked him. "What if I get in some trouble and need the police?"

"That young man was strangled," Inspector Patel told her; by the sound of his voice, she knew he was near her.

Nancy kept her face buried in the pillows, but she reached out to the sides of the bed with her hands. She'd been thinking that she'd never learn anything about the dead boy—not even if the act of killing him had been wicked and full of hatred or merely inadvertent. Now she knew—the young man couldn't have been inadvertently strangled.

"*I* didn't strangle him," Nancy said.

"I know that," said Inspector Patel. When he touched her hand, she lay absolutely motionless; then his touch was gone. In a second, she heard him in the bathroom. It sounded as if he was running a bath.

"You have big hands," he called to her. She didn't move. "The boy was strangled by someone with small hands. Probably another boy, but maybe a woman."

"You suspected *me*," Nancy said; she couldn't tell if he'd heard her over the running bathwater. "I said, you suspected *me*—until you saw my hands," Nancy called to him.

He shut the water off. The tub couldn't be very full, Nancy thought.

"I suspect everybody," Inspector Patel said, "but I didn't really suspect you of strangling the boy."

Nancy was simply too curious; she got up from the bed and went to the bathroom. Inspector Patel was sitting on the edge of the tub, watching the dildo float around and around like a toy boat.

"Just as I thought—it floats," he said. Then he submerged it; he held it under the water for almost a full minute, never taking his eyes off it. "No bubbles," he said. "It floats because it's hollow," he told her. "But if it came apart—if you could open it—there would be bubbles. I thought it would come apart." He let the water out of the tub and wiped the dildo dry with a towel. "One of your friends called while you were registering," Inspector Patel told Nancy. "He didn't want to speak with you—he just wanted to know if you'd checked in." Nancy was blocking the bathroom door; the inspector paused for her to get out of his way. "Usually, this means that someone is interested to know if you've passed safely through customs. Therefore, I thought you were bringing something in. But you weren't, were you?"

"No," Nancy managed to say.

"Well, then, as I leave, I'll tell the hotel to give you your messages directly," the inspector said.

"Thank you," Nancy replied.

He'd already opened the door to the hall before he handed her his card. "*Do* call me if you get into any trouble," he told her. She chose to stare at the card; it was better than watching him leave. There were several printed phone numbers, one circled with a ballpoint pen, and his printed name and title.

VIJAY PATEL

POLICE INSPECTOR

COLABA STATION

Nancy didn't know how far from home Vijay Patel was. When his whole family had left Gujarat for Kenya, Vijay had come to Bombay. For a Gujarati to make any headway on a Maharashtrian police force was no small accomplishment; but the Gujarati Patels in Vijay's family were merchants—they wouldn't have been impressed. Vijay was as cut off from them—they were in business in Nairobi—as Nancy was from Iowa.

After she'd read and reread the policeman's card, Nancy went out to the balcony and watched the beggars for a while. The children were enterprising performers, and there was a monotony to their stunts that was soothing. Like most foreigners, she was easily impressed by the contortionists.

Occasionally, one of the guests would throw an orange to the child performers, or a banana; some threw coins. Nancy thought it was cruel the way a crippled boy, with one leg and a padded crutch, was always beaten by the other children when he attempted to hop and stagger ahead of them to the money or the fruit. She didn't realize that the cripple's role was choreographed; he was central to the dramatic action. He was also older than the other children, and he was their leader; in reality, he could beat up the other children—and, on occasion, had.

But the pathos was unfamiliar to Nancy and she looked for something to throw to him; all she could find was a 10-rupee note. This was too much money to give to a beggar, but she didn't know any better. She weighted the bill down with two bobby pins and stood on the balcony with the money held above her head until she caught the crippled boy's attention.

"Hey, lady!" he called. Some of the child performers paused in their handstands and their contortions, and Nancy sailed the 10-rupee note into the air; it rose briefly in an updraft before it floated down. The children ran back and forth, trying to be in the right place to catch it. The crippled boy appeared content to let one of the other children grab the money.

"No, it's for you—for *you!*" Nancy cried to him, but he ignored her. A tall girl, one of the contortionists, caught the 10-rupee note; she was so surprised at the amount, she didn't hand it over to the crippled boy quite quickly enough, and so he struck her in the small of her back with his crutch—a blow with sufficient force to knock her to her hands and knees. Then the cripple snatched up the money and hopped away from the girl, who had begun crying.

Nancy realized that she'd disrupted the usual drama; somehow *she* was at fault. As the beggars scattered, one of the tall Sikh doormen from the Taj approached the crying girl. He carried a long wooden pole with a gleaming brass hook on one end—it was a transom pole, for opening and closing the transom windows above the tall doors—and the doorman used this pole to lift the ragged skirt of the girl's torn and filthy dress. He deftly exposed her before she could snatch the skirt of her dress between her legs and cover herself. Then he poked the girl in the chest with the brass end of the pole, and when she tried to stand, he whacked her hard in the small of her back, exactly where the cripple had hit her with his crutch. The girl cried out. Then she scurried away from the Sikh on all fours. He was skillful in pursuing her—at herding her with sharp jabs and thrusts with the pole. Finally, she got to her feet and outran him.

The Sikh had a dark, spade-shaped beard flecked with silver, and he wore a dark-red turban; he shouldered the transom pole like a rifle, and he cast a cursory glance to Nancy on her balcony. She retreated into her room; she was sure he could see under her bathrobe and straight up her crotch—he was directly below her. But the balcony itself prevented such a view. Nancy imagined things.

Obviously, there were rules, she thought. The beggars could beg, but they couldn't cry; it was too early in the morning, and crying would wake the guests who were managing to sleep. Nancy instantly ordered the most American thing she could find on the room-service menu—scrambled eggs and toast—and when they brought her tray, she saw two sealed envelopes propped between the orange juice and the tea. Her heart jumped because she hoped they were declarations of undying love from Inspector Patel. But one was the message from Dieter that the inspector had intercepted; it said simply that Dieter had called. He was glad she'd arrived safely—he'd see her soon. And the other was a printed request from the hotel management, asking her to kindly refrain from throwing things out her window.

She was ravenous, and as soon as she'd finished eating, she was sleepy. She closed the curtains against the light of day and turned up the ceiling fan as fast as it would go. For a while she lay awake, thinking of Inspector Patel. She even toyed with the idea of Dieter being caught with the money as he tried to pass through customs. Nancy was still naïve enough to imagine that the Deutsche marks were coming into the country with Dieter. It hadn't even crossed her mind that she'd already brought the money in.

The Unwitting Courier

It seemed to her that she slept for days. It was dark when she woke. She would never know if it was the predawn darkness of the next day, or the predawn of the day after that. She awoke to some sort of commotion in the hall outside her room; someone was trying to get in, but she'd double-locked the door and there was a safety chain, too. She got out of bed. There, in the hall, was Dieter; he was surly to the porter, whom he sent away without a tip. Once inside the room, but only after he'd double-locked the door and hooked the safety chain in place, he turned to her and asked her where the dildo was. This wasn't exactly gallant of him, Nancy thought, but in her sleepiness she supposed it was merely his aggressive way of being amorous. She pointed to it in the bathroom.

Then she opened her robe and let it slip off her shoulders and fall at her feet; she stood in the bathroom doorway, expecting him to kiss her, or at least look at her. Dieter held the dildo over the sink; he appeared to be heating the unnatural head of the penis with his cigarette lighter. Nancy woke up in a hurry. She picked up her bathrobe and put it back on; she stepped away from the bathroom door, but she could still observe Dieter. He was careful not to let the flame blacken the dildo, and he concentrated the heat not at the tip but at the place where the fake foreskin was rolled. It then appeared to Nancy that he was slowly melting the dildo; she realized that there was a substance, like wax, dripping into the sink. Where the fake foreskin was rolled, there emerged a thin line, circumscribing the head. When Dieter had melted the wax seal, he ran the tip of the big penis under cold water and then grasped the circumcised head with a towel. He needed quite a lot of force to unscrew the dildo, which was as hollow as Inspector Patel had observed. The wax seal had prevented any air from escaping; there'd been no bubbles underwater. Inspector Patel had been half right; he'd looked in the right place, but not in the right way—a young policeman's error.

Inside the dildo, rolled very tightly, were thousands of Deutsche marks. For the return trip to Germany, quite a lot of high-quality hashish could be packed very tightly in such a big dildo; the wax seal would prevent the dogs at German customs from smelling the Indian hemp inside.

Nancy sat at the foot of the bed while Dieter removed a roll of marks from the dildo and spread the bills out flat in his hand. Then he zipped the marks into a money belt, which was around his waist under his shirt. He left several sizable rolls of marks in the dildo, which he reassembled; he screwed the tip on tight, but he didn't bother resealing it with wax. The line where the thing unscrewed was barely visible anyway; it was partially hidden by the fake foreskin. When Dieter had finished with this, his chief concern, he undressed and filled the bathtub. It wasn't until he settled into the tub that Nancy spoke to him.

"What would have happened to me if I'd been caught?" she asked him.

"But they wouldn't have caught you, babe," Dieter told her. He'd picked up the "babe" from watching American movies, he said.

"Couldn't you have *told* me?" Nancy asked him.

"Then you would have been nervous," Dieter said. "Then they *would* have caught you."

After his bath, he rolled a joint, which they smoked together; although Nancy thought she was being cautious, she got higher than she wanted to, and just a little disoriented. It was strong stuff; Dieter assured her that it was by no means the best stuff—it was just something he'd bought en route from the airport.

"I made a little detour," he told her. She was too stoned to ask him where he could have gone at 2:00 or 3:00 in the morning, and he didn't bother to tell her that he'd gone to a brothel in Kamathipura. He'd bought the stuff from the madam, and while he was at it he'd fucked a 13-year-old prostitute for only five rupees. He was told she was the only girl not with a customer at the time, and Dieter had fucked her standing up, in a kind of hall, because all the cots in all the cubicles were occupied—or so the madam had said.

After Dieter and Nancy smoked the joint, Dieter was able to encourage Nancy to masturbate; it seemed to her that it took a long time, and she couldn't remember him leaving the bed to get the dildo. Later, when he was asleep, she lay awake and thought for a while about the thousands of Deutsche marks that were inside the thing that had been inside her. She decided not to tell Dieter about the murdered boy or Inspector Patel. She got out of bed and made sure the card the inspector had given her was well concealed among her clothes. She didn't go back to bed; she was standing on the balcony at dawn when the first of the beggars arrived. After a while, the same child performers were perfectly in place, like figures painted by the daylight itself—even the crippled boy with his padded crutch. He waved to her. It was so early, he was careful not to call too loudly, but Nancy could hear him distinctly.

"Hey, lady!"

He made her cry. She went back inside the room and watched Dieter while he was sleeping. She thought again about the thousands of Deutsche marks; she wanted to throw them out the window to the child performers, but it frightened her to imagine what a terrible scene she might cause. She went into the bathroom and tried to unscrew the dildo to count how many marks were inside, but Dieter had screwed the thing too tightly together. This was probably deliberate, she realized; at last, she was learning.

She went through his clothes, looking for the money belt—she thought she could count how many marks were there—but she couldn't find it. She lifted the bedsheet and saw that Dieter was naked except for the money belt. It worried her that she couldn't remember falling asleep, nor could she remember Dieter getting out of bed to put the money belt on. She would have to be more careful, she thought. Nancy was beginning to appreciate the extent to which Dieter might be willing to use her; she worried that she'd developed a morbid curiosity about how far he would go.

Nancy found it calming to speculate about Inspector Patel. She indulged herself with the comforting notion that she could turn to the inspector if she needed him, if she was *really* in trouble. Although the morning was intensely bright, Nancy didn't close the curtains; in the light of day, it was easier for her to imagine that leaving Dieter was merely a matter of picking the right time. And if things get *too* bad, Nancy thought to herself, I can just pick up the phone and ask for Vijay Patel—Police Inspector, Colaba Station.

But Nancy had never been to the East. She didn't know where she was. She had no idea.

12. THE RATS

Four Baths

In Bombay, in his bedroom, where Dr. Daruwalla sat shivering in Julia's embrace, the unresolved nature of the majority of the doctor's phone messages depressed him: Ranjit's peevish complaints about the dwarf's wife; Deepa's expectations regarding the potential bonelessness of a child prostitute; Vinod's fear of the first-floor dogs; Father Cecil's consternation that none of the Jesuits at St. Ignatius knew exactly when Dhar's twin was arriving; and director Balraj Gupta's greedy desire to release the new Inspector Dhar movie in the midst of the murders inspired by the last Inspector Dhar movie. To be sure, there was the familiar voice of the woman who tried to sound like a man and who repeatedly relished the details of old Lowji's car bombing; this message wasn't lacking in resolution, but it was muted by excessive repetition. And Detective Patel's cool delivery of the news that he had a private matter to discuss didn't sound "unresolved" to the doctor; although Dr. Daruwalla may not have known what the message meant, the deputy commissioner seemed to have made up his mind about the matter. But all these things were only mildly depressing in comparison to Farrokh's memory of the big blonde with her bad foot.

"Liebchen," Julia whispered to her husband. "We shouldn't leave John D. alone. Think about the hippie another time."

Both to break him from his trance and as a physical reminder of her affection for him, Julia squeezed Farrokh. She simply hugged him, more or less in the area of his lower chest, or just above his little beer belly. It surprised her how her husband winced in pain. The sharp tweak in his side—it must have been a rib—instantly reminded Dr. Daruwalla of his collision with the second Mrs. Dogar in the foyer of the Duckworth Club. Farrokh then told Julia the story: how the vulgar woman's body was as hard as a stone wall.

"But you said you fell down," Julia told him. "I would guess it was your contact with the stone floor that caused your injury."

"No! It was that damn woman herself—her body is a rock!" Dr. Daruwalla said. "*Mr.* Dogar was knocked down, too! Only that crude woman was left standing."

"Well, she's supposed to be a fitness freak," Julia replied.

"She's a weight lifter!" Farrokh said. Then he remembered that the second Mrs. Dogar had reminded him of someone—definitely a long-ago movie star, he decided. He imagined that one night he would discover who it was on the videocassette recorder; both in Bombay and in Toronto, he had so many tapes of old movies that it was hard for him to remember how he'd lived before the VCR.

Farrokh sighed and his sore rib responded with a little twinge of pain.

"Let me rub some liniment on you, *Liebchen*," Julia said.

"Liniment is for muscles—it was my *rib* she hurt," the doctor complained.

Although Julia still favored the theory that the stone floor was the source of her husband's pain, she humored him. "Was it Mrs. Dogar's shoulder or her elbow that hit you?" she asked.

"You're going to think it's funny," Farrokh admitted to Julia, "but I swear I ran right into her bosom."

"Then it's no wonder she hurt you, *Liebchen*," Julia replied. It was Julia's opinion that the second Mrs. Dogar had no bosom to speak of.

Dr. Daruwalla could sense his wife's impatience on John D.'s behalf, but less for the fact that Inspector Dhar had been left alone than that the dear boy hadn't been forewarned of the pending arrival of his twin. Yet even this dilemma struck the doctor as trivial—as insubstantial as the second Mrs. Dogar's bosom—in comparison to the big blonde in the bathtub at the Hotel Bardez. Twenty years couldn't lessen the impact of what had happened to Dr. Daruwalla there, for it had changed him more than anything in his whole life had changed him, and the long-ago memory of it endured unfaded, although he'd never returned to Goa. All other beach resorts had been ruined for him by the unpleasant association.

Julia recognized her husband's expression. She could see how far away he was; she knew exactly *where* he was. Although she wanted to reassure John D. that the doctor would join them soon, it would have been heartless of her to leave her husband; dutifully, she remained seated beside him. Sometimes she thought she ought to tell him that it was his own curiosity that had got him into trouble. But this wasn't entirely a fair accusation; dutifully, she remained silent. Her own memory, although it didn't torture her with the same details that made the doctor miserable, was surprisingly vivid. She could still see Farrokh on the balcony of the Hotel Bardez, where he'd been as restless and bored as a little boy.

"What a long bath the hippie is taking!" the doctor had said to his wife.

"She looked like she needed a long bath, *Liebchen*," Julia had told him. That was when Farrokh pulled the hippie's rucksack closer to him and peered into the top of it; the top wouldn't quite close.

"Don't look at her things!" Julia told him.

"It's just a book," Farrokh said; he pulled the copy of *Clea* from the top of the rucksack. "I was just curious to know what she was reading."

"Put it back," Julia said.

"I *will*!" the doctor said, but he was reading the marked passage, the same bit about the "umbrageous violet" and the "velvet rind" that one customs official and two policemen had already found so spellbinding. "She has a poetic sensibility," Dr. Daruwalla said.

"I find that hard to believe," Julia told him. "Put it back!"

But putting the book back presented the doctor with a new difficulty: something was in the way.

"Stop groping through her things!" Julia said.

"The damn book doesn't fit," Farrokh said. "I'm *not* groping through her things." An overpowering mustiness embraced him from the depths of the rucksack, a stale exhalation. The hippie's clothing felt damp. As a married man with daughters, Dr. Daruwalla was particularly sensitive to an abundance of dirty underpants in *any* woman's laundry. A mangled bra clung to his wrist as he tried to extract his hand, and still the copy of *Clea* wouldn't lie flat at the top of the rucksack; something poked against the book. What the hell *is* this thing? the doctor wondered. Then Julia heard him gasp; she saw him spring away from the rucksack as if an animal had bitten his hand.

"What is it?" she cried.

"I don't know!" the doctor moaned. He staggered to the rail of the balcony, where he gripped the tangled branches of the clinging vine. Several bright-yellow finches with seeds falling from their beaks exploded from among the flowers, and a gecko sprang from the branch nearest the doctor's right hand; it wriggled into the open end of a drainpipe just as Dr. Daruwalla leaned over the balcony and vomited onto the patio below. Fortunately, no one was having afternoon tea there. There was only one of the hotel's sweepers, who'd fallen asleep in a curled position in the shade of a large potted plant. The doctor's falling vomit left the sweeper undisturbed.

"Liebchen!" Julia cried.

"I'm all right," Farrokh said. "It's nothing, really—it's just . . . lunch." Julia was staring at the hippie's rucksack as if she expected something to crawl out from under the copy of *Clea*.

"What was it—what did you see?" she asked Farrokh.

"I'm not sure," he said, but Julia was thoroughly exasperated with him.

"You don't know, you're not sure, it's nothing, really—it just made you throw up!" she said. She reached for the rucksack. "Well, if you don't tell me, I'll just see for myself."

"No, don't!" the doctor cried.

"Then tell me," Julia said.

"I saw a penis," Farrokh said.

Not even Julia could think of anything to say.

"I mean, it can't be a *real* penis," he continued. "I don't mean that it's someone's severed penis, or anything ghastly like that."

"What *do* you mean?" Julia asked him.

"I mean, it's a very lifelike, very graphic, very *large* male member— it's an enormous cock, with balls!" Dr. Daruwalla said.

"Do you mean a dildo?" Julia asked him. Farrokh was shocked that she knew the word; he barely knew it himself. A colleague in Toronto, a fellow surgeon, kept a collection of pornographic magazines in his hospital locker, and it was only in one of these that Dr. Daruwalla had ever seen a dildo; the advertisement hadn't been nearly as realistic as the terrifying thing in the hippie's rucksack.

"I think it *is* a dildo, yes," Farrokh said.

"Let me see," Julia said; she attempted to dodge past her husband to the rucksack.

"No, Julia! Please!" Farrokh cried.

"Well, *you* saw it—*I* want to see it," Julia said.

"I don't think you do," the doctor said.

"For God's sake, Farrokh," Julia said. He sheepishly stood aside; then he glanced nervously at the bathroom door, behind which the huge hippie was *still* bathing.

"Hurry up, Julia, and don't mess up her things," Dr. Daruwalla said.

"It's not as if everything has been neatly folded—*oh*, my goodness!" Julia said.

"Well, there it is—you've seen it. Now get away!" said Dr. Daruwalla, who was a little surprised that his wife had not recoiled in horror.

"Does it use batteries?" Julia asked; she was still looking at it.

"Batteries!" Farrokh cried. "For God's sake, Julia—please get away!" The concept of such a thing being battery-powered would haunt the doctor's dreams for 20 years. The idea certainly worsened the agony of waiting for the hippie to finish her bath.

Fearing that the freakish girl had drowned, Dr. Daruwalla timidly approached the bathroom door, through which he heard neither singing nor splashing; there wasn't a sign of bathtub life. But before he could knock on the door, the doctor was surprised by the uncanny powers of the bathing hippie; she seemed to sense that someone was near.

"Hello out there," the girl said laconically. "Would you bring me my rucksack? I forgot it."

Dr. Daruwalla fetched the rucksack; for its size, it was uncommonly heavy. Full of batteries, Farrokh supposed. He opened the bathroom door cautiously, and only partially—just enough to reach his hand with the rucksack inside the door. Steam, with a thousand, conflicting scents, engulfed him. The girl said, "Thanks. Just drop it." The doctor withdrew his hand and closed the door, wondering at the sound of metal as the rucksack struck the floor. Either a machete or a machine gun, Farrokh imagined; he didn't want to know.

Julia had arranged a sturdy table on the balcony and covered it with a clean white sheet. Even late in the day, there was better light for surgery outside than in the rooms. Dr. Daruwalla assembled his instruments and prepared the anesthetic.

In the bathroom, Nancy managed to reach her rucksack without getting out of the bathtub; she began a search for anything marginally cleaner than what she'd been wearing. It was a matter of exchanging one kind of dirt for another, but she wanted to wear a long-sleeved cotton blouse and a bra and long pants; she also wanted to wash the dildo, and—if she was strong enough—she wanted to unscrew the thing and count how much money was left. It was repellent to her to touch the cock, but she managed to withdraw it from the rucksack by pinching one of the balls between the thumb and index finger of her right hand; then she dropped the dildo into the bath, where (of course) it floated, the balls slightly submerged, the circumcised head raised—almost in the manner of a perplexed, solitary swimmer. Its single, evil eye was on her.

As for Dr. Daruwalla and his wife, their growing anxiety was in no way lessened by the unmistakable sounds of the bathtub being emptied and refilled. It was the hippie's *fourth* bath.

One can sympathize with Farrokh and Julia for their misunderstanding of the grunts and groans that Nancy made while she was struggling to unscrew the preposterous penis and determine the amount of Deutsche marks that it contained. After all, despite their rekindling of the sexual flame, the pleasure of which was partially owed to Mr. James Salter, the Daruwallas were sexually tame souls. Given the size of the intimidating instrument that they'd seen in the hippie's rucksack, and the sounds of physical exertion that passed from behind the bathroom door, it's forgivable that Farrokh and Julia allowed their imaginations to run away with them. How could the Daruwallas have known that Nancy's cries and curses of frustration were simply the result of her being unable to unscrew the dildo? And despite how far the Daruwallas allowed their imaginations to run, they never could have imagined what truly had happened to Nancy.

Four baths wouldn't wash away what had happened to her.

With Dieter

From the moment Dieter had moved them out of the Taj, everything for Nancy had gone from bad to worse. Their new lodgings were in a small place on Marine Drive, the Sea Green Guest House, which Nancy noticed was an off-white color—or maybe, in the smog, a kind of blue-gray. Dieter said he favored the place because it was popular with an Arab clientele, and Arabs were safe. Nancy didn't notice many Arabs, but she might not have spotted all of them, she supposed. She also didn't know what Dieter meant by "safe"—he meant only that the Arabs were indifferent to drug trafficking on such a small scale as his.

At the Sea Green Guest House, Nancy was introduced to one of the featured activities involved in buying high-quality narcotics—namely, waiting. Dieter made some phone calls; then they waited. According to

Dieter, the best deals came to you indirectly. No matter how hard you tried to make a direct deal, and to make it in Bombay, you always ended up in Goa, doing your business with the friend of a friend. And you always had to wait.

This time the friend of a friend was known to frequent the brothel area of Bombay, although the word on the street was that the guy had already gone to Goa; Dieter would have to find him there. The way you found him was, you rented a cottage on a certain beach; then you waited. You could ask for him, but even so you'd never find him; he always found you. This time his name was Rahul. It was always a common name and you never knew the last name—just Rahul. In the red-light district, they called him "Pretty."

"That's a funny thing to call a guy," Nancy observed.

"He's probably one of those chicks with dicks," Dieter said. This expression was new to Nancy; she doubted that Dieter had picked it up from watching American movies.

Dieter attempted to explain the transvestite scene to Nancy, but he'd never understood that the hijras were eunuchs—that they'd truly been emasculated. He'd confused the hijras with the zenanas—the unaltered transvestites. A hijra had once exposed himself to Dieter, but Dieter had mistaken the scar for a vagina—he'd thought the hijra was a real woman. As for the zenanas, the so-called chicks with dicks, Dieter also called them "little boys with breasts." Dieter said that they were all fags who took estrogens to make their tits bigger, but the estrogens also made their pricks get smaller and smaller until they looked like little boys.

Dieter tended to dwell on sexual things, and he used the halfhearted hope of finding Rahul in Bombay as an excuse to take Nancy to the red-light district. She didn't want to go; but Dieter seemed destined to act out the old dictum that there is at least a kind of certainty in degradation. Debasement is specific. There is something exact about sexual corruption that Dieter probably found comforting in comparison to the vagueness of looking for Rahul.

For Nancy, the wet heat and ripe smell of Bombay were only enhanced by close proximity to the cage girls on Falkland Road. "Aren't they amazing?" Dieter asked her. But why they were "amazing" eluded Nancy. On the ground floor of the old wooden buildings, there were cagelike rooms with beckoning girls inside them; above these cages, the buildings rose not more than four or five stories, with more girls on the windowsills—or else a curtain was drawn across a window to indicate that a prostitute was with a customer.

Nancy and Dieter drank tea at the Olympia on Falkland Road; it was an old, mirror-lined café frequented by the street prostitutes and their pimps, several of whom Dieter seemed to know. But these contacts either couldn't or wouldn't shed any light on the whereabouts of Rahul; they wouldn't even speak of Rahul—except to say that he belonged to the transvestite scene, which they wanted no part of.

"I told you he was one of those chicks with dicks," Dieter told Nancy. It was growing dark when they left the café, and the cage girls demonstrated a more aggressive interest in her as she and Dieter passed. Some of them lifted their skirts and made obscene gestures, some of them threw garbage at her, and sudden groups of men surrounded her on the street; Dieter, almost casually, drove them away from her. He seemed to find the attention amusing; the more vulgar the attention was, the more it amused Dieter.

Nancy had been too overwhelmed to question him, which she realized (as she sank deeper into Dr. Daruwalla's bathtub) was a pattern she had finally broken. She submerged the dildo, holding it against her stomach. Because the dildo had not been resealed with wax, there were bubbles. Afraid that the Deutsche marks might get wet, Nancy stopped toying with the instrument. Instead, she thought of the entrenching tool in her rucksack; the doctor had surely heard it clank against the floor.

Dieter had bought it at an army-surplus shop in Bombay. The tool was an olive-drab color; fully extended, it was a spade with a short, two-foot handle which could be folded by means of an iron hinge, and the blade of the spade could be turned at a right angle to the handle until it resembled a foot-long hoe. If Dieter were alive, he would be the first to agree that it could also be successfully employed as a tomahawk. He'd told Nancy that the entrenching tool might be useful in Goa, both for defense against the dacoits—bandits occasionally preyed upon the hippies there—and for digging the spontaneous latrine. Nancy now smiled ruefully as she reflected on the expanded features of the tool. Certainly, she'd found it adequate for digging Dieter's grave.

When she shut her eyes and sank deeper into the tub, she could still taste the sweet, smoky tea that they served at the Olympia; she could remember its dry, bitter aftertaste, too. With her eyes shut and the warm water holding her, she could remember her changing expression in the pitted mirrors of the café. The tea had made her feel lightheaded. She was unfamiliar with the red spittle from the betel chewing that was expectorated everywhere around them, and not even the Hindi film songs and the Qawwali on the jukebox in the Olympia had prepared her for the assault of noise along Falkland Road. A drunken man followed her and pulled her hair until Dieter knocked him down and kicked him.

"The better brothels are in the rooms above the cages," Dieter told her knowingly. A boy with a goatskin full of water collided with her; she was sure he'd meant to step on her foot. Someone pinched her breast, but she didn't see who it was—man, woman or child.

Dieter pulled her into a bidi shop, where they also sold stationery and silver trinkets and the small pipes for smoking ganja.

"Hey, ganja-man—Mistah bhang-walla!" the proprietor greeted Dieter. He smiled happily at Nancy as he pointed to Dieter. "He Mistah bhang-master—the very best ganja-walla!" the proprietor said appreciatively.

Nancy was fingering an unusual ballpoint pen; it was real silver, and *Made in India* was written in script lengthwise along the pen. The bottom part said *Made in*, the top part said *India;* the pen wouldn't close securely if the script wasn't perfectly aligned. She thought this was a stupid flaw. Also, when you wrote with the pen, the words were all wrong; *in Made India*, the pen said—and *in Made* was upside down. "Very best quality," the proprietor told her. "Made in England!"

"It says it's made in India," Nancy said.

"Yes—they make it in India, too!" the proprietor agreed.

"You're a shitty liar," Dieter told him, but he bought Nancy the pen.

Nancy was thinking she'd like to go somewhere cool and write postcards. In Iowa, wouldn't they be surprised to hear where she was? But, at the same time, she was thinking, They'll never hear from me again. Bombay both terrified and exhilarated her; it was so foreign and seemingly lawless that Nancy felt she could be anybody she wanted to be. It was the clean slate she was looking for, and in the back of her mind, with the persistence of something permanent, was that impossible goal of purity to which she'd been drawn in the person of Inspector Patel.

In the overly dramatic manner of many fallen young women, Nancy believed that only two roads remained open to her: she could keep on falling until she was indifferent to her own defilement, or else she could aspire to acts of social conscience so great and self-sacrificing that she could reclaim her innocence and redeem everything. In the world she'd descended to, there were only these choices: stay with Dieter or go to Inspector Patel. But what had *she* to give to Vijay Patel? Nancy feared it was nothing that the good policeman wanted.

Later, in the doorway of a transvestite brothel, a hijra exposed himself so boldly and suddenly that Nancy hadn't time to look away. Even

Dieter was forced to admit that there was no evidence of a penis—not even a little one. As to what was there, Nancy wasn't sure. Dieter concluded that Rahul might be one of these—"a kind of radical eunuch," he said.

Dieter's questions about Rahul were greeted with sullenness, if not hostility. The only hijra who permitted them to come inside his cage was a fussy middle-aged transvestite who sat before a mirror in growing disappointment with his wig. In the same tiny room, a younger hijra was feeding a watery gray milk to a newborn goat by means of a baby's bottle.

On the subject of Rahul, all the younger one would say was, "He is not being one of us." The older one said only that Rahul was in Goa. Neither of the hijras could be drawn into a discussion of Rahul's nickname. At the mere mention of "Pretty," the one who was feeding the goat abruptly pulled the baby bottle out of the goat's mouth; it made a *pop* and the goat bleated in surprise. The younger hijra pointed the baby bottle at Nancy and made a disparaging gesture. Nancy interpreted the bottle-pointing as an indication that she wasn't as pretty as Rahul. She was relieved that Dieter seemed disinclined to fight, although she could sense he was angry; he wasn't exactly gallant on her behalf, but at least he was angry.

Back on the street, to assure him she was philosophic about the insult of being ill compared to Rahul, Nancy said something that she hoped sounded tolerant in a live-and-let-live sort of way.

"Well, they weren't very nice," she observed, "but it was nice how they were taking care of the goat."

"Don't be a fool," Dieter told her. "Some people fuck girls, some people fuck eunuchs in drag—others fuck goats." This terrible thought made her anxious again; she knew she'd deceived herself if she'd believed she'd stopped falling.

In Kamathipura, there were other brothels. Outside a warren of small rooms, a fat woman in a magenta sari sat cross-legged on a rope bed supported by orange crates; either the woman or the bed swayed slightly. She was the madam for a higher class of prostitutes than one could find on Falkland Road or Grant Road. Naturally, Dieter didn't tell Nancy that this was the same brothel where he'd fucked the 13-year-old girl for only five rupees because they had to do it standing up.

It seemed to Nancy that Dieter knew the enormous madam, but she couldn't understand their conversation; two of the bolder prostitutes had come out of the brothel to stare at her close up.

A third girl, who was perhaps 12 or 13, was especially curious; she remembered Dieter from the night before. Nancy saw the blue tattoo on her upper arm, which Dieter later said was just the prostitute's name. It was impossible for Nancy to know if her body's other ornaments were of any religious significance or if they were merely decorative. Her bindi—the cosmetic dot on her forehead—was a saffron color edged with gold, and she wore a gold nose ring in her left nostril.

The girl's curiosity was a little too extreme for Nancy, who turned away—Dieter was still talking to the madam. Their conversation had grown heated; vagueness made Dieter angry, and *everyone* was vague about Rahul.

"You go to Goa," the fat madam had advised. "You say you looking for him. Then he find you." But Nancy could tell that Dieter preferred to be in more control of the situation.

She also knew what would happen next. Back at the Sea Green Guest House, Dieter was very desirous; anger frequently had this effect on him. First he made Nancy masturbate; then he used the dildo rather roughly on her. She was surprised she was even remotely excited. Afterward, Dieter was still angry. While they waited for an overnight bus to Goa, Nancy was beginning to imagine how she would leave him. The country was so intimidating, it was hard to see herself leaving him if there was no one else.

On the bus, they saw a small American girl; she was being bothered by some Indian men. Nancy spoke up: "Are you a coward, Dieter? Why don't you tell those guys to leave that girl alone? Why don't you ask that girl to sit with us?"

Nancy Gets Sick

Remembering when her relationship with Dieter took such a heralded turn, Nancy felt a renewal of self-confidence in the bathroom of the Hotel Bardez. So what if she couldn't unscrew the dildo? She would find someone with stronger hands, if not a pair of pliers. With that relaxing thought, she threw the dildo across the bathroom; it struck the blue-tiled wall and bounced back toward the bathtub. Thereupon Nancy pulled the plug, the drain gurgled loudly, and Dr. Daruwalla scurried away from his side of the bathroom door.

On the balcony, he told his wife, "I think she's finally finished. I believe she threw the cock against the wall—she threw something, anyway."

"It's a dildo," Julia said. "I wish you wouldn't call it a cock."

"Whatever it is, I believe she threw it," Farrokh said.

They listened to the tub; it went on gurgling. Below them, on the patio, the sweeper had awakened from his nap beneath the shade of the potted plant; they could hear him discussing the doctor's vomit with Punkaj, the servant boy. Punkaj's opinion was that the culprit was a dog.

It wasn't until Nancy stood in the tub to dry herself that the pain in her foot reminded her of why she'd come to where she was. She welcomed whatever small surgery was required to remove the glass; she was a young woman in a position to find a certain anticipated pain almost purifying.

"Are you a coward, Dieter?" Nancy whispered to herself, just to hear herself say it again; it had been so briefly gratifying.

The small girl on the bus, who was originally from Seattle, turned out to be an ashram groupie who'd traveled through the subcontinent, constantly changing her religion. She said she'd been thrown out of the Punjab for doing something insulting to the Sikhs, although she hadn't understood what it was she'd done. She wore a close-fitting, low-cut tank top; it was evident that she didn't wear a bra. She'd also acquired some silver bangles, which she wore on her wrists; she'd been told that the bangles had been part of someone's dowry. (They weren't the usual dowry material.)

Her name was Beth. She'd lost her fondness for Buddhism when a high-placed bodhisattva had tried to seduce her with chang; Nancy assumed this was something you smoked, but Dieter told her it was Tibetan rice beer, which reputedly made Westerners ill.

In Maharashtra, Beth said, she'd been to Poona, but only to express her contempt for her fellow Americans who were meditating at the Rajneesh ashram. She'd lost her fondness for what she called "California meditating," too. No "lousy export guru" was going to win her over.

Beth was taking a "scholarly approach" to Hinduism. She wasn't ready to study the Vedas—the ancient spiritual texts, the orthodox Hindu scriptures—under any kind of supervision; Beth would begin with her own interpretations of *The Upanishads*, which she was currently reading. She showed the small book of spiritual treatises to Nancy and Dieter; it was one of those thin volumes in which the Introduction and the Note on the Translations amounted to more pages than the text.

Beth didn't think it odd to pursue her study of Hinduism by journeying to Goa, which attracted more Christian pilgrims than any other kind; she admitted she was going for the beaches, and for the companionship of people like herself. Besides, soon the monsoon would be everywhere, and by then she'd be in Rajasthan; the lakes were lovely during the monsoon—she'd heard about an ashram on a lake. Meanwhile, she was grateful for the company; it was no fun being a woman on your own in India, Beth assured them.

Around her neck was a rawhide thong, from which dangled a polished vulva-shaped stone. Beth explained that this was her yoni, an object of veneration in Shiva temples. The phallic lingam, representing the penis of Lord Shiva, is placed in the vulvate yoni, representing the vagina of Shiva's wife, Parvati. Priests pour a libation over the two symbols; worshipers partake of a kind of communion in the runoff.

After this puzzling account of her unusual necklace, Beth was exhausted and curled up on the seat beside Nancy; she fell asleep with her head in Nancy's lap. Dieter also fell asleep, in the seat across the aisle, but not before saying to Nancy that he thought it would be great fun to show Beth the dildo. "Let her put *that* lingam in her stupid yoni," he said crudely. Nancy sat awake, hating him, as the bus moved through Maharashtra.

In the darkness, the most constant sound was the bus driver's tape recorder, which played only Qawwali; the recorder was turned to a low volume, and Nancy found the religious verses soothing. Of course she didn't know that they were Muslim verses, nor would she have cared. Beth's breathing was soft and regular against her thigh; Nancy thought about how long it had been since she'd had a friend—just a friend.

The dawn light in Goa was the color of sand. Nancy marveled at how childlike Beth appeared in her sleep; in both her small hands, the waif clutched the stone vagina as if this yoni were powerful enough to protect her from every evil on the subcontinent—even from Dieter and Nancy.

In Mapusa, they changed buses because their bus from Bombay went on to Panjim. They spent a long day in Calangute while Dieter did his business, which amounted to repeatedly harassing the patrons of the bus stop for any information related to Rahul. Along Baga Road, they also stopped at the bars, the hotels and the stalls for cold drinks; in all these places, Dieter spoke privately with someone while Beth and Nancy waited. Everyone claimed to have heard of Rahul, but no one had ever seen him.

Dieter had arranged for a cottage near the beach. There was only one bathroom, and the toilet and tub needed to be flushed and filled by hand with buckets from an outdoor well, but there were two big beds that looked pretty clean and a standing partition of wooden latticework—it was almost a wall, almost private. They had a propane hot plate for boiling water. A motionless ceiling fan had been installed in the optimistic faith that one day there would also be electricity; and although there were no screens, there were mosquito nets in fair repair on both beds. Outside, there was a cistern of fresh (if not clean) water; the water in the well, with which they flushed the toilet and in which they bathed, was slightly salty. By the cistern was a hut of palm leaves; if they kept the leaves wet, this hut was an adequate cooler for soda and juice and fresh fruit. Beth was disappointed that they were some distance from the beach. Although they could hear the Arabian Sea, especially at night, they had to tramp across an area of dead and rotting palm fronds before they could walk on the sand or even see the water.

Both these luxuries and inconveniences were wasted on Nancy; upon arrival, she was immediately sick. She vomited; she was so weak from diarrhea that Beth had to fetch the water to flush the toilet for her. Beth also filled the tub for Nancy's baths. Nancy had a fever with chills so violent and sweating so profuse that she stayed in bed all day and night, except when Beth stripped the sheets and gave them to the dhobi, who came for the laundry.

Dieter was disgusted with her; he went on about his business of looking for Rahul. Beth fixed her tea and brought her fresh bananas; when Nancy was stronger, Beth cooked her some rice. Because of the fever, Nancy tossed and turned all night and Dieter wouldn't sleep in the same bed with her. Beth slept in a small corner of the bed beside her; Dieter slept behind the latticework partition, alone. Nancy told herself that, when she was healthy, she would go to Rajasthan with Beth. She hoped Beth hadn't been revolted by her illness.

Then, one evening, Nancy woke up and felt a little better. She thought her fever was gone because she was so clear-headed; she thought she was past the vomiting and the diarrhea because she was ravenous. Dieter and Beth were out of the cottage; they'd gone to the disco in Calangute. There was a place called something stupid, like Coco Banana, where Dieter asked a lot of questions about Rahul. Dieter said it was cooler to go there with a girl than to look like a loser, which was apparently what you looked like when you went there alone.

There was nothing to eat in the cottage but bananas, and Nancy ate three; then she made herself some tea. After that, she went in and out, drawing water for a bath. She was surprised how tired she was after she'd carried the water, and with her fever gone, the bath felt chilly.

After her bath, she went outside to the palm-hut cooler and drank some bottled sugarcane juice, which she hoped wouldn't bring back her diarrhea. There was nothing to do but wait for Dieter and Beth to come back. She tried reading *The Upanishads,* but it had made more sense to her when she had a fever and Beth read it aloud. Besides, she had lit an oil lamp to read and there were suddenly a million mosquitoes. Also, she encountered an exasperating passage in "Katha Upanishad"; it repeated, as a refrain, an irritating sentence: "This in truth is That." She thought the phrase would drive her crazy if she read it one more time. She blew out the oil lamp and retreated under the mosquito net.

She brought the entrenching tool into the bed beside her because she was frightened to be alone in the cottage at night. There was not only the threat of bandits, of dacoit gangs; there was a gecko that lived behind the bathroom mirror—it often raced across the bathroom walls and ceiling while Nancy took her bath. She hadn't seen the gecko tonight. She wished she knew where it was.

When she'd been feverish, she'd wondered at the shadows cast by the strange gargoyles along the top of the latticework partition; then one night the gargoyles weren't there, and another night there'd been only one. Now that her fever was gone, she realized the "gargoyles" were in nearly constant motion—they were rats. They favored the vantage point that the partition gave them, to look down upon both beds. Nancy watched them until she fell asleep.

She was beginning to understand that she was a long way from Bombay, which was a long way from anywhere else. Not even young Vijay Patel—Police Inspector, Colaba Station—could help her here.

13. NOT A DREAM

A Beautiful Stranger

When Nancy's fever came back, the sweating didn't wake her but the chills did. She knew she was delirious because it was impossible that a beautiful woman in a sari could be sitting on the bed beside her, holding her hand. At 31 or 32, the woman was at the very peak of her beauty, and her subtle jasmine scent should have told Nancy that the beautiful woman was *not* the result of delirium. A woman with such a wonderful smell could never be dreamed. When the woman spoke, even Nancy had reason to doubt that she was any kind of hallucination at all.

"You're the one who's sick, aren't you?" the woman asked Nancy. "And they've left you all alone, haven't they?"

"Yes," Nancy whispered; she was shivering so hard, her teeth were chattering. Although she clutched the entrenching tool, she doubted she could summon the strength to lift it.

Then, as so often happens in dreams, there was no transition, no logic to the order of events, because the beautiful woman unwound her sari—she completely undressed. Even in the ghostly pallor of the moonlight, she was the color of tea; her limbs looked as smooth and hard as fine wood, like cherry. Her breasts were only slightly bigger than Beth's, but much more upright, and when she slipped past the mosquito net and into the bed beside Nancy, Nancy relinquished her grip on the entrenching tool and allowed the beautiful woman to hold her.

"They shouldn't leave you all alone, should they?" the woman asked Nancy.

"No," Nancy whispered; her teeth had stopped chattering, and her shivers subsided in the beautiful woman's strong arms. At first they lay face-to-face, the woman's firm breasts against Nancy's softer bosom, their legs entwined. Then Nancy rolled onto her other side and the woman pressed herself against Nancy's back; in this position, the woman's breasts touched Nancy's shoulder blades—the woman's breath stirred Nancy's hair. Nancy was impressed by the suppleness of the woman's long, slender waist—how it curved to accommodate Nancy's broad hips and her round bottom. And to Nancy's surprise, the woman's hands, which gently held Nancy's heavy breasts, were even bigger than Nancy's hands.

"This is better, isn't it?" the woman asked her.

"Yes," Nancy whispered, but her own voice sounded uncharacteristically hoarse and far away. An unshakable drowsiness attended the woman's embrace, or else this was a new stage in Nancy's fever, which signaled the beginning of a sleep deeper than dreams.

Nancy had never slept with a woman's breasts pressed against her back; she marveled at how soothing it was, and she wondered if this was what men felt when they fell asleep this way. Previously, Nancy *had* fallen asleep with that odd sensation of a man's inert and usually small penis brushing against her buttocks. It was upon this awareness, and on the edge of sleep, that Nancy was suddenly aware of an unusual situation, which was surely in the area of dream or delirium or both, because she felt—at the same time!—a woman's breasts pressed against her back *and* a man's sleepy penis curled against her buttocks. Another fever dream, Nancy decided.

"Won't they be surprised, when they get here?" the beautiful woman asked her, but Nancy's mind had drifted too far away for her to answer.

Nancy Is a Witness

When Nancy woke up, she lay alone in the moonlight, smelling the ganja and listening to Dieter and Beth; they were whispering on the other side of the partition. The rats on the latticework were so still that they appeared to be listening, too—or else the rats were stoned, because Dieter and Beth were smoking up a storm.

Nancy heard Dieter ask Beth, "What is the first sexual experience that you had some confidence in?" Nancy counted to herself in the silence; of course she knew what Beth was thinking. Then Dieter said, "Masturbation, right?"

Nancy heard Beth whisper, "Yes."

"Everyone is different," Dieter told Beth philosophically. "You just have to learn what your own best way is."

Nancy lay watching the rats while she listened to Dieter. He was successful in getting Beth to relax, although Beth did possess the decency to ask, if only once, "What about Nancy?"

"Nancy is asleep," Dieter said. "Nancy won't object."

"I have to be lying on my tummy," Beth told Dieter, whose grasp of English vernacular wasn't sound enough for him to understand "tummy."

Nancy heard Beth roll over. There was no sound for a while, and then there came a change in Beth's breathing, to which Dieter whispered some encouragement. There was the sound of messy kissing, and Beth panting, and then Beth uttered that special sound, which made the rats run along the top of the latticework partition and caused Nancy to reach for the entrenching tool with her big hands.

While Beth was still moaning, Dieter said to her, "Just wait right there. I have a surprise for you."

The surprise for Nancy was that the entrenching tool was gone; she was sure she'd brought it to bed with her. She wanted to crack Dieter in the shins with it, just to drop him to his knees so that she could tell him what she thought of him. She'd give Beth one more chance. As she groped under the mosquito net and along the floor beside the bed, looking for the entrenching tool, Nancy still hoped that she and Beth could go to Rajasthan together.

That was when her hand found the jasmine-scented sari that the beautiful woman in the dream had worn. Nancy pulled the sari into bed with her and breathed it in; the scent of it brought the beautiful woman back to her mind—the woman's unusually large, strong hands . . . the woman's unusually upright, firm breasts. Last came the memory of the woman's unusual penis, which had curled like a snail against Nancy's buttocks as Nancy drifted into sleep.

"Dieter?" Nancy tried to whisper, but her voice made no sound. It was exactly as they'd told Dieter in Bombay: you go to Goa *not* to find Rahul but to let Rahul find you. Dieter had been right about one thing: there *were* chicks with dicks. Rahul wasn't a hijra—he was a zenana, after all.

Nancy could hear Dieter in the bathroom, looking for the dildo in the semidarkness. She heard a bottle break against the stone floor. Dieter must have placed the bottle precariously on the edge of the tub; not much moonlight penetrated the bathroom, and he probably needed to search for the dildo with both hands. Briefly, Dieter cursed; he must have cursed in German because Nancy didn't catch the word.

Beth called out to Dieter—she'd obviously forgotten that Nancy was supposed to be sleeping. "Did you break your Coke, Dieter?" Beth called; her own question dissolved her into mindless giggles—Dieter was addicted to Coca-Cola.

"*Ssshhh!*" Dieter said from the bathroom.

"*Ssshhh!*" Beth repeated; she made a failed effort to stifle her laughter.

The next sound that Nancy heard was one she'd been fearing, but she'd been unable to find her voice—to warn Dieter that someone else was here. She heard what she was sure was the entrenching tool, the spade end, as it made full-force contact with what sounded like the base of Dieter's skull. A metallic after-ring followed the blow, but surprisingly little noise attended Dieter falling. Then there was the second sound of violent contact, almost as if a spade or a heavy shovel had been swung against the trunk of a tree. Nancy realized that Beth hadn't heard this because Beth was sucking on the ganja pipe as if the fire had died in the bowl and she was trying to revive it.

Nancy lay very still, holding the jasmine-scented sari in her arms. The spectral figure with the small, upright breasts and the little boy's penis passed close to Nancy's bed without a sound. It was no wonder that Rahul was called Pretty, Nancy thought.

"Beth!" Nancy tried to say, but once again her voice had abandoned her.

From the other side of the partition, a sudden light came through the latticework in patches; the shadows of the startled rats were cast upon the ceiling. Nancy could see through the latticing. Beth had completely opened the mosquito net in order to light an oil lamp; she was looking for more ganja for the pipe when the naked tea-colored body appeared beside her bed. Rahul's big hands held the entrenching tool with the handle nestled in the delicate curve of the small of his back, the spade end concealed between his shoulder blades.

"Hi," Rahul said to Beth.

"Hi. Who are you?" Beth said. Then Beth managed a gasp, which caused Nancy to stop looking through the space between the latticework. Nancy lay on her back with the jasmine-scented sari covering her face; she didn't want to look at the ceiling, either, because she knew that the shadows of the rats would be twitching there.

"Hey, like, what *are* you?" she heard Beth say. "Are you a boy or a girl?"

"I'm pretty, aren't I?" Rahul said.

"You sure are . . . different," Beth replied.

From the responding sound of the entrenching tool, Nancy guessed that Rahul was displeased to be called "different." Rahul's preferred nickname was "Pretty." Nancy pushed the jasmine-scented sari entirely off the bed and outside the mosquito net. She hoped it fell to the floor very close to where Rahul had left it. Then she lay with her eyes open, staring at the ceiling, where the shadows of the rats scurried back and forth; it was almost as if the second and third blows from the entrenching tool were a kind of starting signal for the rats.

Later, Nancy quietly rolled on her side so that she could peek through the latticing and watch what Rahul was doing; he appeared to be performing a kind of surgery on Beth's stomach, but Nancy soon realized that Rahul was drawing a picture on Beth's belly. Nancy shut her eyes and wished that her fever would come back; even though she wasn't feverish, she was so frightened that she began to shiver. It was the shivers that saved her. When Rahul came to her, Nancy's teeth were chattering as uncontrollably as before. Instantly, she felt his lack of sexual interest; he was mocking her, or merely curious.

"Is that bad old fever back again?" Rahul asked her.

"I keep dreaming," Nancy told him.

"Yes, of course you do, dear," Rahul said.

"I keep trying to sleep but I keep dreaming," Nancy said.

"Are they bad dreams?" Rahul asked her.

"Pretty bad," Nancy said.

"Do you want to tell me about them, dear?" Rahul asked her.

"I just want to sleep," Nancy told him. To her surprise, he let her. He parted the mosquito net and sat on the bed beside her; he rubbed her between her shoulder blades until the shivers went away and she could imitate the regular breathing of a deep sleep—she even parted her lips and tried to imagine that she was already dead. He kissed her once on the temple, and once on the tip of her nose. At last, she felt Rahul's weight leave the bed. She also felt the entrenching tool, when Rahul gently returned it to her hands. Although she never heard a door open or close, she knew Rahul was gone when she heard the rats racing recklessly through the cottage; they even scampered under the mosquito net and across her bed, as if they were secure in their belief that there were three dead people in the cottage instead of two. That was when Nancy knew it was safe to get up. If Rahul had still been there, the rats would have known.

In the predawn light, Nancy saw that Rahul had used the dhobi pen—and indelible dhobi ink—to decorate Beth's belly. The laundry-marking pen was a crude wooden handle with a simple, broad nib; the ink was black. Rahul had left the ink bottle and the dhobi pen on Nancy's pillow. Nancy recalled that she'd picked up the ink bottle and the dhobi pen before putting them both back on her bed; her fingerprints were also all over the handle of the entrenching tool.

She'd become ill so soon upon her arrival; yet it was Nancy's strong impression that this was a rustic sort of place. She doubted she'd have much success convincing the local police that a beautiful woman with a little boy's penis had murdered Dieter and Beth. And Rahul had been smart enough not to empty Dieter's money belt; he'd taken the money belt with him. There was no evidence of a robbery. Beth's jewelry was untouched, and there was even some money in Dieter's wallet; their passports weren't stolen. Nancy knew that most of the money was in the dildo, which she didn't even try to open because Dieter had bled on it and it was sticky to touch. She wiped it with a wet towel; then she packed it in the rucksack with her things.

She thought Inspector Patel would believe her, provided she could get back to Bombay without the local police finding her first. On the surface, Nancy thought, it would be judged a crime of passion—one of those triangular relationships that had turned a little twisted. And the drawing on Beth's belly gave the murders a hint of diabolism, or at least a flair for sarcasm. The elephant was surprisingly small and un-adorned—a frontal view. The head was wider than it was long, the eyes were unmatched and one was squinting—actually, one eye seemed puckered, Nancy thought. The trunk hung slack, pointing straight down; from the end of the trunk, the artist had drawn several broad lines in the shape of a fan—a childish indication that water sprayed from the elephant's trunk, as from a showerhead or from the nozzle of a hose. These lines extended into Beth's pubic hair. The entire drawing was the size of a small hand.

Then Nancy realized why the drawing was slightly off center, and why one eye seemed "puckered." One of the eyes was Beth's navel, outlined in dhobi ink; the other eye was an imperfect imitation of the navel. Because the navel had real depth, the eyes weren't the same; one eye appeared to be winking. Beth's navel was the winking eye. What further contributed to the elephant's mirthful or mocking expression was that one of its tusks drooped in the normal position; the opposing tusk was raised, almost as if an elephant could lift a tusk in the manner that a human being can cock an eyebrow. This was a small, ironical elephant—an elephant with an inappropriate sense of humor, to be sure.

The Getaway

Nancy dressed Beth's body in the tank top that Beth had been wearing when Nancy first met her; at least it covered the drawing. She left Beth's sacred yoni in place, at her throat, as if it might prove itself to be a more successful talisman in the next world than it had demonstrated itself to be in this.

The sun rose inland and a tan light filtered through the areca and coconut palms, leaving most of the beach in shade, which was a blessing for Nancy, who labored for over an hour with the entrenching tool; yet she managed to dig no better than a shallow pit near the tidemark for high tide. The pit was already half full of water when she dragged Dieter's body along the beach and rolled him into the hole. By the time she'd arranged Beth's body next to his, Nancy was aware of the blue crabs that she'd uncovered with her digging; they were scurrying to bury themselves again. She'd chosen an especially soft stretch of sand, the part of the beach that was nearest the cottage; now Nancy realized why the sand was soft. A tidal inlet cut through the beach and drained into the matted jungle; she'd dug too close to this inlet. Nancy knew the bodies wouldn't stay buried for long.

Worse, in her haste to clean up the broken glass in the bathroom, she'd stepped on the jagged heel of the Coca-Cola bottle; several pieces of glass had broken off in her foot. She was wrong to think she'd picked all the pieces out, but she was in a hurry. She'd bled so heavily on the bathroom mat, she was forced to roll it up and put it (with the broken glass) in the grave; she buried it, together with the rest of Dieter's and Beth's things, including Beth's silver bangles, which were much too small for Nancy, and Beth's beloved copy of *The Upanishads,* which Nancy had no interest in reading herself.

It had surprised Nancy that digging the grave was harder work than dragging Dieter's body to the beach; Dieter was tall, but he weighed less than she'd ever imagined. It crossed her mind that she could have left him anytime she'd wanted to; she could have picked him up and thrown him against a wall. She felt incredibly strong, but as soon as she'd filled the grave, she was exhausted.

A moment of panic nearly overcame Nancy when she discovered that she couldn't find the top half of the silver ballpoint pen that Dieter had given her—the pen with *Made in India* written lengthwise on it in script. The bottom part said *Made in,* the missing part said *India.* Nancy had already discovered the flaw in the pen's design: the pen wouldn't snap securely together if the script wasn't perfectly aligned; the top and the bottom were always getting separated. Nancy looked through the cottage for the missing top; she thought it unlikely that Rahul had taken it—it wasn't the part of the pen that you could write with. Nancy had the part that wrote, and so she kept it; because it was small, it would make its way to the bottom of her rucksack. At least it was real silver.

Nancy knew her fever had finally gone because she was smart enough to take Dieter's and Beth's passports; she also reminded herself that their bodies would be found soon. Whoever rented the cottage to Dieter had known there were three of them. She suspected that the police would assume she'd leave by bus from Calangute or by ferry from Panjim. Nancy's plan was remarkably clear-headed: she would place Dieter's and Beth's passports in a conspicuous place at the bus stand in Calangute, but she would take the ferry from Panjim to Bombay. That way, with any luck—and while she was on the ferry—the police would be looking for her in bus stations.

But Nancy would be the beneficiary of better luck than this. When the bodies were discovered, the landlord who rented the cottage to Dieter admitted that he'd seen Beth and Nancy only at a distance. Since Dieter was German, the landlord assumed the other two were Germans; also, he mistook Nancy for a man. After all, she was so big—especially beside Beth. The landlord would tell the police that they were looking for a German hippie male. When the passports were found in Calangute, the police realized that Beth had been an American; yet they persisted in their belief that the murderer was a German man, traveling by bus.

The grave wouldn't be discovered right away; the tide eroded the sand near the inlet only a little bit at a time. It would be unclear whether the carrion birds or the pye-dogs were the first to catch wind of something; by then, Nancy was gone.

She waited only for the sun to top the palm trees and flood the beach in white light; it took just a few minutes for the sun to dry the wet sand of the grave. With a palm frond, Nancy wiped smooth the stretch of beach leading to the jungle and the cottage; then she limped on her way. It was still early morning when she left Anjuna. She deemed she'd discovered an isolated pocket of eccentrics when she saw the nude sunbathers and swimmers who were almost a tradition in the area. She'd been sick—she didn't know.

The first day, her foot wasn't too bad, but she had to walk all over Calangute after she placed the passports. There was no doctor staying at Meena's or Varma's. Someone told her that an English-speaking doctor was staying at the Concha Hotel; when she got there, the doctor had checked out. At the Concha, they told her there was an English-speaking doctor in Baga at the Hotel Bardez. The next day, when she went there, they turned her away; by then, her foot was infected.

As she emerged from her endless baths in Dr. Daruwalla's tub, Nancy couldn't remember if the murders were two or three days old. She did, however, remember a glaring error in her judgment. She'd already told Dr. Daruwalla that she was taking the ferry to Bombay; that was decidedly unwise. When the doctor and his wife helped her onto the table on the balcony, they mistook her silence for anxiety regarding the small surgery, but Nancy was thinking of how to rectify her mistake. She hardly flinched at the anesthetic, and while Dr. Daruwalla probed for the broken glass, Nancy calmly said, "You know, I've changed my mind about Bombay. I'm going south instead. I'll take the bus from Calangute to Panjim, then I'll take the bus to Margao. I want to go to Mysore, where they make the incense—you know? Then I want to go to Kerala. What do you think of that?" she asked the doctor. She wanted him to remember her false itinerary.

"I think you must be a very ambitious traveler!" said Dr. Daruwalla. He extracted a surprisingly big, half-moon-shaped piece of glass from her foot; it was probably a piece from the thick heel of a Coke bottle, the doctor told her. He disinfected the smaller cuts once they were free of glass fragments. He packed the larger wound with iodophor gauze. Dr. Daruwalla also gave Nancy an antibiotic that he'd brought with him to Goa for his children. She'd have to see a doctor in a few days— sooner, if there was any redness around the wound or if she had a fever.

Nancy wasn't listening; she was worrying how she would pay him. She didn't think it would be proper to ask the doctor to unscrew the dildo; she also didn't think he looked strong enough. Farrokh, in his own way, was also distracted by his thoughts about the dildo.

"I can't pay you very much," Nancy told the doctor.

"I don't want you to pay me at all!" Dr. Daruwalla said. He gave her his card; it was just his habit.

Nancy read the card and said, "But I told you—I'm not going to Bombay."

"I know, but if you feel feverish or the infection worsens, you should call me—from wherever you are. Or if you see a doctor who can't understand you, have the doctor call me," Farrokh said.

"Thank you," Nancy told him.

"And don't walk on it any more than you have to," the doctor told her.

"I'll be on the *bus*," Nancy insisted.

As she was limping to the stairs, the doctor introduced her to John D. She was in no mood to meet such a handsome young man, and although he was very polite to her—he even offered to help her down the stairs—Nancy felt extremely vulnerable to his kind of European superiority. He showed not the slightest spark of sexual interest in her, and this hurt her more than her foot did. But she said good-bye to Dr. Daruwalla and allowed John D. to carry her downstairs; she knew she was heavy, but he looked strong. The desire to shock him grew overwhelming. Besides, she knew he was strong enough to unscrew the dildo.

"If it's not too much trouble," she said to him in the lobby of the hotel, "you could do me a big favor." She showed him the dildo without removing it from her rucksack. "The tip unscrews," she told him, watching his eyes. "But I'm just not strong enough." She continued to regard his face while he gripped the big cock in both hands; she would remember him because of how poised he was.

As soon as he loosened the tip, she stopped him.

"That's enough," she told him; she didn't want him to see the money. It disappointed her that he seemed unshockable, but she kept trying. She resolved she would look into his eyes until he had to look away. "I'm going to spare you," she said softly. "You don't want to know what's inside the thing."

She would remember him for his instinctive sneer, for John D. was an actor long before he was Inspector Dhar. She would remember that sneer, the same sneer with which Inspector Dhar would later incense all of Bombay. It was Nancy who had to look away from him; she would remember that, too.

She avoided the bus stand in Calangute; she would try to hitchhike to Panjim, even if it meant she had to walk—or defend herself with the entrenching tool. She hoped she still had a day or two before the bodies were found. But before she located the road to Panjim, she remembered the big piece of glass the doctor had removed from her foot. After showing it to her, he'd put it in an ashtray on a small table near the hammock; probably he would throw it away, she thought. But what if he heard about the broken glass in the hippie grave—it would soon be called the "hippie grave"—and what if he wondered if the piece of glass from her foot would match?

It was late at night when Nancy returned to the Hotel Bardez. The door to the lobby was locked, and the boy who slept on a rush mat in the lobby all night was still engaged in talking to the dog that spent every night with him; that was why the dog never heard Nancy when she climbed the vine to the Daruwallas' second-floor balcony. Her procaine injection had worn off and her foot throbbed; but Nancy could have screamed in pain and knocked over the furniture and still she would never have awakened Dr. Daruwalla.

The doctor's lunch has been described. It would be superfluous to provide similar detail regarding the doctor's dinner; suffice it to say that he substituted the vindaloo-style pork for the fish, and he further indulged in a pork stew called sorpotel, which features pig's liver and is abundantly flavored with vinegar. Yet it was the dried duckling with tamarind that dominated the aroma of his heavy breathing, and his snores were scented with sharp blasts of a raw red wine, which he would deeply regret in the morning. He should have stuck to the beer. Julia was grateful that Dr. Daruwalla had elected to sleep in the hammock on the balcony, where only the Arabian Sea—and the lizards and insects that in the night were legion—would be disturbed by the doctor's windy noises. Julia also desired a rest from the passions inspired by Mr. James Salter's artistry. For the moment, her private speculations concerning the departed hippie's dildo had cooled Julia's sexual ardor.

As for the insect and lizard life that clung to the mosquito net enclosing the cherubic doctor in his hammock, the gecko and mosquito world appeared to be charmed by both the doctor's music and his vapors. The doctor had bathed just before retiring, and his plump pale-brown body was everywhere dusted with Cuticura powder—from his neck to between his toes. His closely shaven throat and cheeks were refreshed with a powerful astringent redolent of lemons. He'd even shaved his mustache off, leaving only a little clump of a beard on his chin; he was almost as smooth-faced as a baby. Dr. Daruwalla was so clean and he smelled so wonderful that Nancy had the impression that only the mosquito net prevented the geckos and mosquitoes from devouring him.

At a level of sleep so deep it seemed to Farrokh that he had died and lay buried somewhere in China, the doctor dreamed that his most ardent admirers were digging up his body—to prove a point. The doctor wished they would leave him undisturbed, for he felt he was at peace; in truth, he'd passed out in the hammock in a stupor of overeating—not to mention the effect of the wine. To dream that he was prey to gravediggers was surely an indication of his overindulgence.

So what if my body is a miracle, he was dreaming—please just leave it alone!

Meanwhile, Nancy found what she was looking for; in the ashtray, where it had left only a spot of dried blood, lay the half-moon-shaped piece of glass. As she took it, she heard Dr. Daruwalla cry out, "Leave me in China!" The doctor thrashed his legs, and Nancy saw that one of his beautiful eggshell-brown feet had escaped the mosquito net and was protruding from the hammock—exposed to the terrors of the night. This disturbance sent the geckos darting in all directions and caused the mosquitoes to swarm.

Well, Nancy thought, the doctor had done her a favor, hadn't he? She stood stock-still until she was sure Dr. Daruwalla was sound asleep; she didn't want to wake him up, but it was hard for her to leave him when his gorgeous foot was prey to the elements. Nancy contemplated how she might safely return Farrokh's foot to the mosquito net, but her newfound good sense persuaded her not to risk it. She descended the vine from the balcony to the patio; this required the use of both her hands, and so she delicately held the piece of broken glass in her teeth—careful that it not cut her tongue or her lips. She was limping along the dark road to Calangute when she threw the glass away. It was lost in a dense grove of palms, where it disappeared without a sound—as unseen by any living human eye as Nancy's lost innocence.

The Wrong Toe

Nancy had been fortunate to leave the Hotel Bardez when she had. She never knew that Rahul was a guest there, nor did Rahul know that Nancy had been Dr. Daruwalla's patient. This was *extremely* lucky, because Rahul also climbed the vine to the Daruwallas' second-floor balcony—on that very same night. Nancy had come and gone; but when Rahul arrived on the balcony, Dr. Daruwalla's poor foot was still vulnerable to the nighttime predators.

Rahul himself had come as a predator. He'd learned from Dr. Daruwalla's innocent daughters that John D. usually slept in the hammock on the balcony. Rahul had come to the balcony to seduce John D. The sexually curious may find it interesting to speculate whether or not Rahul would have met with success in his attempted seduction of the beautiful young man, but John D. was spared this test because Dr. Daruwalla was sleeping in the hammock on this busy night.

In the darkness—not to mention that he was blinded by his overeagerness—Rahul was confused. The body asleep under the mosquito net was certainly of a desirable fragrance. Maybe it was the moonlight that played tricks with skin color. Possibly it was only the moonlight which gave Rahul the impression that John D. had grown a little clump of a beard. As for the toes of the doctor's exposed foot, they were tiny and hairless, and the foot itself was as small as a young girl's. Rahul found that the ball of the foot was endearingly fleshy and soft, and he thought that the sole of Dr. Daruwalla's foot was almost indecently pink—in contrast to the doctor's sleek, brown ankle.

Rahul knelt by the doctor's small foot; he stroked it with his large hand; he brushed his cheek against the doctor's freshly scented toes. Naturally, it would have startled him if Dr. Daruwalla had cried out, "But I don't *want* to be a miracle!"

The doctor was dreaming that he was Francis Xavier, dug up from his grave and taken against his will to the Basilica de Bom Jesus in Goa. More accurately, he was dreaming that he was Francis Xavier's miraculously preserved *body*, and things were about to be done to his body—also against his will. But despite the terror of what was happening to him, in his dream Farrokh couldn't give utterance to his fears; he was so heavily sedated with food and wine that he was forced to suffer in silence—even though he anticipated that a crazed pilgrim was about to eat his toe. After all, he knew the story.

Rahul ran his tongue along the sole of the doctor's fragrant foot, which tasted strongly of Cuticura powder and vaguely of garlic. Because Dr. Daruwalla's foot was the single part of him that was unprotected by the mosquito net, Rahul could manifest his powerful attraction to the delicious John D. only by enclosing what he presumed to be the big toe of John D.'s right foot in his warm mouth. Rahul then sucked on this toe with such force that Dr. Daruwalla moaned. Rahul at first fought against the desire to bite him, but he gave in to this urge and slowly sank his teeth into the squirming toe; then he once more resisted the compelling impulse to bite—then he weakened and bit down harder. It was torture for Rahul to stop himself from going too far—from swallowing Dr. Daruwalla, either whole or in pieces. When he at last released the doctor's foot, both Rahul *and* Dr. Daruwalla were gasping. In his dream, the doctor was certain that the obsessed woman had already done her damage; she'd bitten off the sacred relic of his toe, and now there was tragically less of his miraculous body than they had buried.

As Rahul undressed himself, Dr. Daruwalla withdrew his maimed foot from the dangerous world; he curled himself tightly into his hammock under the mosquito net, for in his dream he was fearing that the emissaries from the Vatican were approaching—to take his arm to Rome. As Farrokh struggled to give voice to his terror of amputation, Rahul attempted to penetrate the mysteries of the mosquito net.

Rahul thought it would be best if John D. awoke to find his face firmly between Rahul's breasts, for these latter creations were surely to be counted among Rahul's best features. But then, since Rahul thought that the young man appeared to have been aroused by the oddity of having his big toe sucked and bitten, perhaps a bolder approach would succeed. It was frustrating to Rahul that he could proceed with *no* approach until he solved the puzzle of entrance to the mosquito net, which was vexing. And it was at this complicated juncture in Rahul's attempted seduction that Farrokh finally found the voice to express his fears. Rahul, who recognized the doctor's voice, distinctly heard Dr. Daruwalla shout, "I don't *want* to be a saint! I *need* that arm—it's a very good arm!"

At this, the boy's dog in the lobby barked briefly; the boy once more began to talk to the animal. Rahul hated Dr. Daruwalla as fervently as he desired John D.; therefore, Rahul was appalled that he'd caressed the doctor's foot, and he was nauseated that he'd sucked and bitten the doctor's big toe. As he hurriedly dressed himself, Rahul was also embarrassed. The taste of Cuticura powder was bitter on his tongue as he climbed down the vine to the patio, where the dog in the lobby heard him spit; the dog barked again, and this time the boy unlocked the door to the lobby and peered anxiously at the misty beach.

The boy heard Dr. Daruwalla cry out from the balcony: "Cannibals! Catholic maniacs!" Even to an inexperienced Hindu boy, this seemed a fearful combination. Then the dog's barking exploded at the door to the lobby, where both the boy and the dog were surprised by the sudden appearance of Rahul.

"Don't lock me out," Rahul said. The boy let him in and gave him his room key. Rahul wore a loose-fitting skirt of a kind that's easy to put on and take off, and a bright-yellow halter top of a kind that drew the boy's awkward attention to Rahul's well-shaped breasts. There was a time when Rahul would have grabbed the boy's face in both hands and pulled him into his bosom; then he might have played with the boy's little prick, or else he might have kissed him, in which case Rahul would have stuck his tongue so far down the boy's throat that the boy would have gagged. But not now; Rahul wasn't in the mood.

He went upstairs to his room; he brushed his teeth until the taste of Dr. Daruwalla's Cuticura powder was gone. Then he undressed and lay down on his bed, where he could look at himself in the mirror. He wasn't in the mood to masturbate. He made some drawings, but nothing worked. Rahul was furious at Dr. Daruwalla for being in John D.'s hammock; it made him so angry that he couldn't even arouse himself. In the adjacent room, Aunt Promila was snoring.

Down in the lobby, the boy tried to calm the dog down. He thought it was peculiar that the dog was so agitated; usually, women had no effect on the dog. It was only men who made the dog's fur stand up, or made the dog walk around stiff-legged—sniffing everywhere the men had been. It puzzled the boy that the dog had reacted in this fashion to Rahul. The boy also needed to calm himself down; he'd reacted to Rahul's breasts in his own fashion; he was so aroused that he had a sizable erection—for a boy. And he knew perfectly well that the lobby of the Hotel Bardez was no place for him to indulge his fantasies. There was nothing the boy could do. He lay down on the rush mat, where he at last coaxed the dog to join him, and there he went on speaking to the dog as before.

Farrokh Is Converted

At dawn, on the road to Panjim, Nancy had the good fortune to arouse the sympathy of a motorcyclist who noticed her limp. It wasn't much of a motorcycle, but it would do; it was a 250 cc. Yezdi with red plastic tassles hanging from the handlebars, a black dot painted on the headlight, and a sari-guard mounted on the left-side rear wheel. Nancy was wearing jeans, and she simply straddled the seat behind the skinny teenaged driver. She locked her hands around the boy's waist without a word; she knew he couldn't drive fast enough to scare her.

The Yezdi was equipped with crash bars that protruded from the motorcycle in the manner of a full fairing. In Dr. Daruwalla's profession, these so-called crash bars were known as tibial-fracture bars; they were renowned for breaking the tibias of motorcyclists—all for the sake of not denting the gas tank.

Nancy's weight was at first disconcerting to the young driver; she had a dangerously wide effect on his cornering—he held his speed down. "Can't this thing go any faster?" she asked him. He half-understood her, or else her voice in his ear was thrilling; possibly it hadn't been her limp he'd noticed but the tightness of her jeans, or her blond hair—or even the swaying of her breasts, which the teenager felt pressing against his back. "That's better," Nancy told him, after he dared to speed up. Streaming from the handlebars, the red plastic tassles were whipped by the rushing wind; they appeared to beckon Nancy toward the steamer jetty and her chosen destiny in Bombay.

She'd embraced evil; she'd found it lacking. She was the sinner in search of the impossible salvation; she thought that only the uncorrupted and incorruptible policeman could restore her essential goodness. She had spotted something conflicted about Inspector Patel. She believed that he was virtuous and honorable, but also that she could seduce him; her logic was such that she thought of his virtue and his honor as transferable to her. Nancy's illusion was not uncommon—nor is it an illusion limited to women. It is an old belief: that several sexually wrong decisions can be remedied—even utterly erased—by one decision that is sexually right. No one should blame Nancy for trying.

As Nancy rode the Yezdi to the ferry, and to her fate, a dull but persistent pain in the big toe of his right foot awakened Dr. Daruwalla from a night of bedlam dreams and indigestion. He freed himself from the mosquito net and swung his legs from the hammock, but when he put only the slightest weight on his right foot, his big toe stabbed him with a sharp pain; for a second, he imagined he was still dreaming he was St. Francis's body. In the early light, which was a muted brown—not unlike the color of Dr. Daruwalla's skin—the doctor inspected his toe. The skin was unbroken, but deep bruises of a crimson and purple hue clearly indicated the bite marks. Dr. Daruwalla screamed.

"Julia! I've been bitten by a *ghost!*" the doctor cried. His wife came running.

"What is it, *Liebchen?*" she asked him.

"Look at my big toe!" the doctor demanded.

"Have you been biting yourself?" Julia asked him with unconcealed distaste.

"It's a *miracle!*" shouted Dr. Daruwalla. "It was the ghost of that crazy woman who bit St. Francis!" Farrokh shouted.

"Don't be a blasphemer," Julia cautioned him.

"I am being a *believer*—not a blasphemer!" the doctor cried. He ventured a step on his right foot, but the pain in his big toe was so wilting that he fell, screaming, to his knees.

"Hush or you'll wake up the children—you'll wake up everybody!" Julia scolded him.

"Praise the Lord," Farrokh whispered, crawling back to his hammock. "I believe, God—please don't torture me further!" He collapsed into the hammock, hugging both his arms around his chest. "What if they come for my arm?" he asked his wife.

Julia was disgusted with him. "I think it must be something you ate," she said. "Or else you've been dreaming about the dildo."

"I suppose *you've* been dreaming about it," Farrokh said sullenly. "Here I've suffered some sort of *conversion* and you're thinking about a big cock!"

"I'm thinking about how you're behaving in a peculiar fashion," Julia told him.

"But I've had some sort of religious *experience!*" Farrokh insisted.

"I don't see what's religious about it," Julia said.

"Look at my toe!" the doctor cried.

"Maybe you bit it in your sleep," his wife suggested.

"Julia!" Dr. Daruwalla said. "I thought you were already a Christian."

"Well, I don't go around yelling and moaning about it," Julia said.

John D. appeared on the balcony, never realizing that Dr. Daruwalla's religious experience was very nearly his own experience—of another kind.

"What's going on?" the young man asked.

"It's apparently unsafe to sleep on the balcony," Julia told him. "Something bit Farrokh—some kind of animal."

"Those are *human* teeth marks!" the doctor declared. John D. examined the bitten toe with his usual detachment.

"Maybe it was a monkey," he said.

Dr. Daruwalla curled himself into a ball in the hammock, deciding to give his wife and his favorite young man the silent treatment. Julia and John D. took their breakfast with the Daruwalla daughters on the patio below the balcony; at times they would raise their eyes and look up the vine in the direction where they presumed Farrokh lay sulking. They were wrong; he wasn't sulking—he was praying. Since the doctor was inexperienced at prayer, his praying resembled an interior monologue of a fairly standard confessional kind—especially that kind which is brought on by a bad hangover.

O God! prayed Dr. Daruwalla. *It isn't necessary to take my arm—the toe convinced me. I don't need any more convincing. You got me the first time, God.* The doctor paused. *Please leave the arm alone,* he added.

Later, from the lobby of the Hotel Bardez, the syphilitic tea-server thought he heard voices from the Daruwallas' second-floor balcony. Since Ali Ahmed was known to be almost entirely deaf, it was assumed that he probably always heard "voices." But Ali Ahmed had actually heard Dr. Daruwalla praying, for by midmorning the doctor was murmuring aloud and the pitch of his prayers was precisely in a register that the syphilitic tea-server could hear.

"I am heartily sorry if I have offended Thee, God!" Dr. Daruwalla murmured intensely. "Heartily sorry—very sorry, really! I never meant to mock anybody—I was only kidding," he confessed. "St. Francis— you, too—please forgive me!" An unusual number of dogs were barking, as if the pitch of the doctor's prayers were precisely in a register that the dogs could hear, too. "I am a surgeon, God," the doctor moaned. "I *need* my arm—*both* my arms!" Thus did Dr. Daruwalla refuse to leave the hammock of his miraculous conversion, while Julia and John D. spent the morning plotting how to prevent the doctor from spending another night on the balcony.

Later in the day, as his hangover abated, Farrokh regained a little of his self-confidence. He said to Julia that he thought it would be enough for him to become a Christian; he meant that perhaps it wasn't necessary for him to become a *Catholic*. Did Julia think that becoming a Protestant would be good enough? Maybe an Anglican would do. By now, Julia was quite frightened by the depth and color of the bite marks on her husband's toe; even though the skin was unbroken, she was afraid of rabies.

"Julia!" Farrokh complained. "Here I am worrying about my mortal soul, and you're worried about rabies!"

"Lots of monkeys have rabies," John D. offered.

"*What* monkeys?" Dr. Daruwalla shouted. "*I* don't see any monkeys here! Have *you* seen any monkeys?"

While they were arguing, they failed to notice Promila Rai and her nephew-with-breasts checking out of the hotel. They were going back to Bombay, but not tonight; Nancy was again fortunate—Rahul wouldn't be on *her* ferry. Promila knew that Rahul's holiday had been disappointing to him, and so she'd accepted an invitation for them both to spend the night at someone's villa in Old Goa; there would be a costume party, which Rahul might find amusing.

It hadn't been an entirely disappointing holiday for Rahul. His aunt was generous with her money, but she expected him to make his own contribution toward a much-discussed trip to London; Promila would help Rahul financially, but she wanted him to come up with *some* money of his own. There were several thousand Deutsche marks in Dieter's money belt, but Rahul had been expecting more—given the quality and the amount of hashish that Dieter had told everyone he wanted to buy. Of course, there *was* more, *much* more—in the dildo.

Promila thought that her nephew was interested in art school in London. She also knew he was seeking a *complete* sex change, and she knew such operations were expensive; given her loathing for men, Promila was delighted with her nephew's choice—to become her niece—but she was deluding herself if she thought that the strongest motivating factor behind Rahul's proposed move to London was "art school."

If the maid who cleaned Rahul's room had looked more carefully at the discarded drawings in the wastebasket, she could have told Promila that Rahul's talent with a pen was of a pornographic persuasion that most art schools would discourage. The self-portraits would have especially disturbed the maid, but all the discarded drawings were nothing but balled-up pieces of paper to her; she didn't trouble herself to examine them.

They were en route to the villa in Old Goa when Promila peered into Rahul's purse and saw Rahul's new, curious money clip; at least he was using it as a money clip—it was really nothing but the top half of a silver pen.

"My dear, you *are* eccentric!" Promila said. "Why don't you get a *real* money clip, if you like those things?"

"Well, Auntie," Rahul patiently explained, "I find that real money clips are too loose, unless you carry a great *wad* of money in them. What I like is to carry just a few small notes outside my wallet—something handy to pay for a taxi, or for tipping." He demonstrated that the top half of the silver pen possessed a very strong, tight clip—where it was meant to attach itself to a jacket pocket or a shirt pocket—and that this clip was perfect for holding just a few rupees. "Besides, it's real silver," Rahul added.

Promila held it in her veinous hand. "Why so it is, dear," she remarked. She read aloud the one word, in script, that was engraved on the top half of the pen: "*India*—isn't *that* quaint?"

"*I* certainly thought so," Rahul remarked, returning the eccentric item to his purse.

Meanwhile, as Dr. Daruwalla grew hungrier, he also grew more relaxed about his praying; he cautiously rekindled his sense of humor. After he'd eaten, Farrokh could almost joke about his conversion. "I wonder what next the Almighty will ask of me!" he said to Julia, who once more cautioned her husband about blasphemy.

What was next in store for Dr. Daruwalla would test his newfound faith in ways the doctor would find most disturbing. By the same means that Nancy had discovered the doctor's whereabouts, the police also discovered him. They'd found what everyone now called the "hippie grave" and they needed a doctor to hazard a guess concerning the cause of death of the grave's ghastly occupants. They'd gone looking for a doctor on holiday. A *local* doctor would talk too much about the crime; at least this was what the local police told Dr. Daruwalla.

"But I don't do autopsies!" Dr. Daruwalla protested; yet he went to Anjuna to view the remains.

It was generally supposed that the blue crabs were the reason the bodies spoiled for viewing; and if the salt water proved itself to be a modest preservative, it did little to veil the stench. Farrokh easily concluded that several blows to the head had done them both in, but the female's body was messier. Her forearms and the backs of her hands were battered, which suggested that she'd tried to defend herself; the male, clearly, had never known what hit him.

It was the elephant drawing that Farrokh would remember. The murdered girl's navel had been transformed to a winking eye; the opposing tusk had been flippantly raised, like the tipping of an imaginary hat. Short, childish lines indicated that the elephant's trunk was spraying—the "water" fanning over the dead girl's pubic hair. Such intended mockery would remain with Dr. Daruwalla for 20 years; the doctor would remember the little drawing too well.

When Farrokh saw the broken glass, he suffered only the slightest discomfort, and the feeling quickly passed. Back at the Hotel Bardez, he was unable to find the piece of glass he'd removed from the young woman's foot. And so what if the glass from the grave had matched? he thought. There were soda bottles everywhere. Besides, the police had already told him that the suspected murderer was a German male.

Farrokh thought that this theory suited the prejudices of the local police—namely, that only a hippie from Europe or North America could possibly perform a double slaying and then trivialize the murders with a cartoonish drawing. Ironically, these killings and that drawing stimulated Dr. Daruwalla's need to be more creative. He found himself fantasizing that *he* was a detective.

The doctor's success in the orthopedic field had given him certain commercial expectations; these considerations doubtless returned the doctor's imagination to that notion of himself as a screenwriter. No *one* movie could have satisfied Farrokh's suddenly insatiable creativity; nothing less than a series of movies, featuring the same detective, would do. Finally, that was how it happened. At the end of his holiday, on the ferry back to Bombay, Dr. Daruwalla invented Inspector Dhar.

Farrokh was watching how the young women on board the ferry couldn't take their eyes off the beautiful John D. Suddenly, the doctor could envision the hero that these young women imagined when they looked at a young man like that. The excitement that Mr. James Salter's example had inspired was already becoming a moment of the sexual past; it was becoming a part of the second honeymoon that Dr. Daruwalla was leaving behind. To the doctor, murder and corruption spoke louder than art. And besides, what a career John D. might have!

It would never have occurred to Farrokh that the young woman with the big dildo had seen the same murder victims he had seen. But 20 years later, even the movie version of that drawing on Beth's belly would ring a bell with Nancy. How could it be a coincidence that the victim's navel was the elephant's winking eye, or that the opposing tusk was raised? In the movie, no pubic hair was shown, but those childish lines indicated to Nancy that the elephant's trunk was still spraying— like a showerhead, or like the nozzle of a hose.

Nancy would also remember the beautiful, unshockable young man she'd been introduced to by Dr. Daruwalla. When she saw her first Inspector Dhar movie, Nancy would recall the first time she'd seen that knowing sneer. The future actor had been strong enough to carry her downstairs without apparent effort; the future movie star had been poised enough to unscrew the troublesome dildo without appearing to be appalled.

And all of this was what she meant when she left her uncompromising message on Dr. Daruwalla's answering machine. "I know who you really are, I know what you really do," Nancy had informed the doctor. "Tell the deputy commissioner—the *real* policeman. Tell him who you are.

Tell him what you do," Nancy had instructed the secret screenwriter, for she'd figured out who Inspector Dhar's creator was.

Nancy knew that no one could have imagined the movie version of that drawing on Beth's belly; Inspector Dhar's creator had to have seen what *she* had seen. And the handsome John D., who now passed himself off as Inspector Dhar—that young man would never have been invited to view the murder victims. That would have been the doctor's job. Therefore, Nancy knew that Dhar hadn't created himself; Inspector Dhar had also been the doctor's job.

Dr. Daruwalla was confused. He remembered introducing Nancy to John D., and how gallantly John D. had carried the heavy young woman downstairs. Had Nancy seen an Inspector Dhar movie, or all of them? Had she recognized the more mature John D.? Fine; but how had she made the imaginative leap that the doctor was Dhar's creator? And how could she know "the *real* policeman," as she called him? Dr. Daruwalla could only assume that she meant Deputy Commissioner Patel. Of course, the doctor didn't realize that Nancy had known Detective Patel for 20 years—not to mention that she was married to him.

The Doctor and His Patient Are Reunited

One might recall that Dr. Daruwalla had all this time been sitting in his bedroom in Bombay, where the doctor was alone again. Julia had at last left him sitting there; she'd gone to apologize to John D.—and to be sure that their supper was still warm enough to eat. Dr. Daruwalla knew it was an unprecedented rudeness to have kept his favorite young man waiting, but in the light of Nancy's phone message, the doctor felt compelled to speak to D.C.P. Patel. The subject that the deputy commissioner wished to discuss in private with Dr. Daruwalla was only a part of what prompted the doctor to make the call; of more interest to Farrokh was where Nancy was now and why she knew "the *real* policeman."

Given the hour, Dr. Daruwalla phoned Detective Patel at home. Farrokh was thinking that there were Patels all over Gujarat; there were many Patels in Africa, too. He knew both a hotel-chain Patel and a department-store Patel in Nairobi. He was thinking he knew only *one* Patel who was a policeman, when—as luck would have it—Nancy answered the phone. All she said was, "Hello," but the one word was sufficient for Farrokh to recognize her voice. Dr. Daruwalla was too confused to speak, but his silence was all the identification that Nancy needed.

"Is that the doctor?" she asked in her familiar fashion.

Dr. Daruwalla supposed it would be stupid of him to hang up, but for a moment he couldn't imagine what else to do. He knew from the surprising experience of his long and happy marriage to Julia that there was no understanding what drew or held people together. If the doctor had known that the relationship between Nancy and Detective Patel was deeply connected to the dildo, he would have admitted that his understanding of sexual attraction and compatibility was even less than he supposed. The doctor suspected some elements of interracial interest on the part of both parties—Farrokh and Julia had surely felt this. And in the curious case of Nancy and Deputy Commissioner Patel, Dr. Daruwalla also guessed that Nancy's bad-girl appearance possibly concealed a good-girl heart; the doctor could easily imagine that Nancy had *wanted* a cop. As for what had attracted the deputy commissioner to Nancy, Farrokh tended to overestimate the value of a light complexion; after all, he adored the fairness of Julia's skin, and Julia wasn't even a blonde. What the doctor's research for the Inspector Dhar movies had failed to uncover was a characteristic common to many policemen—a love of confession. Poor Vijay Patel was prone to enjoy the confessing of crimes, and Nancy had held nothing back. She'd begun by handing him the dildo.

"You were right," she'd told him. "It unscrews. Only it was sealed with wax. I didn't know it came apart. I didn't know what was in it. But look what I brought into the country," she said. As Inspector Patel counted the Deutsche marks, Nancy kept talking. "There was more," she said, "but Dieter spent some, and some of it was stolen." After a short pause, she added, "There were two murders, but just one drawing." Then she told him absolutely everything, beginning with the football players. People have fallen in love for stranger reasons.

Meanwhile, still waiting for the doctor's answer on the telephone, Nancy grew impatient. "Hello?" she said. "Is anyone there? *Is that the doctor?*" she repeated.

A born procrastinator, Dr. Daruwalla nevertheless knew that Nancy wouldn't be denied; still, he didn't like to be bullied. Countless stupid remarks came to the closet screenwriter's mind; they were smart-ass, tough-guy wisecracks—the usual voice-over from old Inspector Dhar movies. ("Bad things had happened—worse things were happening. The woman was worth it—after all, she might know something. It was time to put all the cards on the table.") After a career of such glibness, it was hard for Dr. Daruwalla to know what to say to Nancy. After 20 years, it was difficult to sound casual, but the doctor lamely tried.

"So—it's *you!*" he said.

On her end of the phone, Nancy just waited. It was as if she expected nothing less than a full confession. Farrokh felt he was being treated unfairly. Why should Nancy want to make him feel guilty? He should have known that Nancy's sense of humor wasn't easy to locate, but Dr. Daruwalla foolishly kept trying to find it.

"So—how's the foot?" he asked her. "All better?"

14. TWENTY YEARS

A Complete Woman, but
One Who Hates Women

The hollowness of the doctor's dumb joke contributed to an empty sound that the receiver made against his ear, for Nancy wasn't talking; her silence echoed, as if the phone call were transnational. Then Dr. Daruwalla heard Nancy say to someone else, "It's him." Her voice was indistinct, although her effort to cover the mouthpiece with her hand had been halfhearted. Farrokh couldn't have known how 20 years had stolen the enthusiasm from many of Nancy's efforts.

And yet, 20 years ago, she'd reintroduced herself to young Inspector Patel with admirable resolve, not only presenting the policeman with the dildo and the sordid particulars of Dieter's crimes, but strengthening her confession with her intention to change. Nancy said she sought a life of righting wrongs, and she declared the extent of her attraction to young Patel in such graphic terms that she gave the proper policeman pause. Also, as Nancy had anticipated, she managed to give the inspector pangs of the severest desire, which he wouldn't act upon, for he was both a highly professional detective and a gentleman—neither an oafish football player nor a jaded European. If the physical attraction that drew Nancy and Inspector Patel together was ever to be acted upon, Nancy knew that *she* would need to initiate the contact.

Although she trusted that, in the end, she would marry the idealistic detective, certain conditions beyond her control contributed to Nancy's delay of the matter. For example, there was the distress caused by the disappearance of Rahul. As a most recent and eager convert to the pursuit of justice, Nancy was deeply disappointed that Rahul could not be found. The allegedly murderous zenana, who'd only briefly achieved a legendary status in the brothel area of Bombay, had vanished from Falkland Road and Grant Road and Kamathipura. Also, Inspector Patel discovered that the transvestite known as Pretty had always been an outsider; the hijras hated him—the few who knew him—and his fellow zenanas hated him, too.

Rahul had sold his services for an uncommonly high price, but what he sold was merely his appearance; his good looks, which were the result of his outstanding femininity in juxtaposition to his dominating physical size and strength, made him an attractive showpiece for any transvestite brothel. Once a customer was lured into the brothel by Rahul's presence, the other zenanas—or the hijras—were the only transvestites who made themselves available for sexual contact. Hence there was to his nickname, Pretty, both an honest appraisal of his powers to attract and a disparagement of his character; for, by his refusal to do more than display himself, Rahul brandished a high-mindedness that insulted the transvestite prostitutes.

They could see he was indifferent to the offense he caused; he was also too big and strong and confident for them to threaten. The hijras hated him because he was a zenana; his fellow zenanas hated him because he'd told them he intended to make himself "complete." But *all* the transvestite prostitutes hated Rahul because he wasn't a prostitute.

There prevailed some nasty rumors about Rahul, although any evidence of these allegations eluded Inspector Patel. Some transvestite prostitutes claimed that Rahul frequented a female brothel in Kamathipura; it further outraged the transvestites to imagine that, when Rahul chose to advertise himself in *their* brothels on Falkland Road and Grant Road, he was in reality merely slumming. Also, there were ugly stories concerning how Rahul made use of the female prostitutes in Kamathipura; it was claimed that he never had sex with the girls but that he beat them. There was mention of a flexible rubber billy stick. If these rumors were true, the beaten girls would have nothing but raised red welts to show for their pain; such marks faded quickly and were thought to be insubstantial in comparison to broken bones or the deeper, darker discolorations of those bruises inflicted by a harder weapon. There was no legal recourse for the girls who might have suffered such beatings; whoever Rahul was, he was smart. Shortly after murdering Dieter and Beth, he was also out of the country.

Inspector Patel suspected that Rahul had left India. This was no consolation to Nancy; having chosen goodness over evil, she anticipated resolution. It was a pity that Nancy would wait 20 years for a simple but informative conversation with Dr. Daruwalla which would reveal to them both that they'd made acquaintance with the *same* Rahul. However, not even a detective as dogged as D.C.P. Patel could have been expected to guess that a sexually altered killer might have been found at the Duckworth Club. Moreover, for 15 years, Rahul would *not* have been found there—at least not very often. He was more frequently in London, where, after the lengthy and painful completion of his sex-change operation, he was able to give more of his energy and concentration to what he called his art. Alas . . . no excess of energy or concentration would much expand his talent or his range; the cartoon quality of his belly drawings persisted. His tendency toward sexually explicit caricature endured.

It was thematic with Rahul—an inappropriately mirthful elephant with one tusk raised, one eye winking, and water spraying from the end of its downward-pointing trunk. The size and shape of the victims' navels afforded the artist a considerable variety of winking eyes; the amount and color of the victims' pubic hair also varied. The water from the elephant's trunk was constant; the elephant sprayed, with seeming indifference, over all. Many of the murdered prostitutes had shaved their pubic hair; the elephant appeared not to notice, or not to care.

But it wasn't only that his imagination was sexually perverse, for within Rahul a veritable war was being waged over the true identity of his sexual self, which, to his astonishment, was not appreciably clarified by the successful completion of his long-awaited sex change. Now Rahul was to all appearances a woman; if he couldn't bear children, it had never been the desire to bear children that had compelled him to become a her. However, it was Rahul's illusion that a new sexual identity could provide a lasting peace of mind.

Rahul had loathed being a man. In the company of homosexuals, he'd never felt he was one of them, either. But he'd experienced little closeness with his fellow transvestites; in the company of hijras or zenanas, Rahul had felt both different and superior. It didn't occur to him that they were content to be what they were—Rahul had never been content. There's more than one way to be a third gender; but Rahul's uniqueness was inseparable from his viciousness, which extended even toward his fellow transvestites.

He detested the all-too-womanly gestures of most hijras and zenanas; he thought the mischief with which they dressed indicated an all-too-womanly frivolity. As for the traditional powers of the hijras to bless or to curse, Rahul had no belief that they possessed such powers; he believed they tended to parade themselves, either for the smug amusement of boring heterosexuals or for the titillation of more conventional homosexuals. In the homosexual community, at least there were those few—like Subodh, Rahul's late brother—who defiantly stood out; they advertised their sexual orientation *not* for the entertainment of the timid but in order to discomfort the intolerant. Yet Rahul imagined that even those homosexuals who were as bold as Subodh were vulnerable to how slavishly they sought the affections of other homosexuals. Rahul had hated how girlishly Subodh had allowed himself to be dominated by Neville Eden.

Rahul had imagined that it was only as a woman that *she* could dominate both women and men. He'd also imagined that being a woman would make him envy other women less, or not at all; he'd even thought that his desire to hurt and humiliate women would somehow *evanesce*. He was unprepared for how he would continue to hate them and desire to do them harm; prostitutes—and other women of what he presumed to be loose behavior—especially offended him, in part because of how lightly they regarded their sexual favors, and how they took for granted their sexual parts, which Rahul had been forced to acquire through such perseverance and pain.

Rahul had put himself through the rigors of what he believed was necessary to make him happy; yet he still raged. Like some (but fortunately few) *real* women, Rahul was contemptuous of those men who sought his attention, while at the same time he strongly desired those men who remained indifferent to his obvious beauty. And this was only half his problem; the other half was that his need to kill certain women was surprisingly (to him) unchanged. And after he'd strangled or bludgeoned them—he favored the latter form of execution—he couldn't resist creating his signature work of art upon their flaccid bellies; the soft stomach of a dead woman was Rahul's preferred medium, his canvas of choice.

Beth had been the first; killing Dieter was unmemorable to Rahul. But the spontaneity with which he'd struck down Beth and the utter unresponsiveness of her abdomen to the dhobi pen were stimulations so extreme that Rahul continued to yield to them.

In this sense was his tragedy compounded, for his sex change had not enabled him to view other women as companionable human beings. And because Rahul still hated women, he knew he'd failed to become a woman at all. Further isolating him, in London, was the fact that Rahul also loathed his fellow transsexuals. Before his operation, he'd suffered countless psychological interviews; obviously, they were superficial, for Rahul had managed to convey an utter lack of sexual anger. He'd observed that friendliness, which he interpreted as an impulse toward a cloying kind of sympathy, impressed the evaluating psychiatrist and the sex therapists.

There were meetings with other would-be transsexuals, both those applying for the operation and those in the more advanced phase of "training" for the postoperative women they would soon become. Complete transsexuals also attended these agonizing meetings. It was supposed to be encouraging to socialize with complete transsexuals, just to see what real women they were. This was nauseating to Rahul, who hated it when anyone dared to suggest that he or she was like him; Rahul knew that he wasn't "like" anyone.

It appalled him that these *complete* transsexuals even shared the names and phone numbers of former boyfriends. These were men, they said, who weren't at all repulsed by women "like us"—possibly these interesting men were even attracted by them. What a concept! Rahul thought. He wasn't becoming a woman in order to become a member of some transsexual *club;* if the operation was complete, no one would ever know that Rahul had not been born a woman.

But there was one who knew: Aunt Promila. She'd been such a supporter. Gradually, Rahul resented how she sought to control him. She would continue her most generous financial assistance to his life in London, but only if he promised not to forget her—only if he would come pay some attention to her from time to time. Rahul wasn't opposed to these periodic visits to Bombay; he was merely annoyed that his aunt manipulated how often and when he traveled to see her. And as she grew older, she grew more needy; shamelessly, and frequently, she referred to Rahul's elevated status in her will.

Even with Promila's considerable influence, it took Rahul longer to legalize his change of name than it had taken him to change his sex—in spite of the bribes. And although there were many other women's names that he preferred, it was politic of him to choose Promila, which greatly

pleased his aunt and assured him an indeed favorable position in her
much-mentioned will. Nevertheless, the new name on the new passport
left Rahul feeling incomplete. Perhaps he felt that he could never *be*
Promila Rai as long as his Aunt Promila was alive. Since Promila was
the only person on earth whom Rahul loved, it made him feel guilty that
he grew impatient with how long he had to wait for her to die.

Remembering Aunt Promila

He was five or six, or maybe only four; Rahul could never remember.
What he did recall was that he thought he was old enough to be going
to the men's room by himself. Aunt Promila took him to the ladies'
room—she took him with her into the toilet stall, too. He'd told her that
there were urinals in the men's room and that the men stood up to pee.
    "I know a better way to pee," she'd told him.
    At the Duckworth Club, the ladies' room suffered from an elephant
motif; in the men's room, the tiger-hunt decor was far less obtrusive. For
example, in the ladies' room toilet stalls, there was a pull-down platform
on the inside of the stall door. It was simply a shelf that folded flat against
the door when not in use. By means of a handle, the shelf could be pulled
down; on this platform, a lady could put her handbag—or whatever else
she took with her into the toilet stall. The handle was a ring that passed
like an earring through the base of an elephant's trunk.
    Promila would lift her skirt and pull down her panties; then she sat
on the toilet seat, and Rahul—who'd also pulled down his pants and his
underpants—would sit on her lap.
    "Pull down the elephant, dear," Aunt Promila would tell him, and
Rahul would lean forward until he could reach the ring through the
elephant's trunk. The elephant had no tusks; Rahul found the elephant
generally lacking in realism—for example, there was no opening at the
end of the elephant's trunk.
    First Promila peed, then Rahul. He sat on his aunt's lap, listening to
her. When she wiped herself, he could feel the back of her hand against
his bare bum. Then she would reach into his lap and point his little penis
down into the toilet. It was difficult for him to pee from her lap.
    "Don't miss," she'd whisper in his ear. "Are you being careful?" Rahul
tried to be careful. When he was finished, Aunt Promila wiped his penis
with some toilet paper. Then she felt his penis with her bare hand. "Let's
be sure you're dry, dear," Promila would say to him. She always held

him until his penis was stiff. "What a big boy you are," she'd whisper. When they were finished, they washed their hands together.

"The hot water is too hot—it will burn you," Aunt Promila would warn him. Together they stood at the wildly ornate sink. There was a single faucet in the form of an elephant's head. The water flowed through the elephant's trunk, emerging in a broad spray. You lifted one tusk for the hot water, the other tusk for the cold. "Just the cold water, dear," Aunt Promila told him. She let Rahul operate the faucet for both of them; he would raise and lower the tusk for cold water—just one tusk. "Always wash your hands, dear," Aunt Promila would say.

"Yes, Auntie," Rahul answered. He'd supposed his aunt's preference for cold water was a sign of her age; she must have remembered a time before there was hot water.

When he was older, maybe 8 or 9—he could have been 10—Promila sent him to see Dr. Lowji Daruwalla. She was concerned with what she called Rahul's inexplicable hairlessness—or so she told the doctor. In retrospect, Rahul realized that he'd disappointed his aunt—and on more than one occasion. Promila's disappointment, Rahul also realized, was sexual; his so-called hairlessness had little to do with it. But there was no way for Promila Rai to complain about the size or the short-lived stiffness of her nephew's penis—certainly not to Dr. Lowji Daruwalla! The question of whether or not Rahul was impotent would have to wait until Rahul was 12 or 13; at that time, the examining physician would be old Dr. Tata.

In retrospect, Rahul would realize that his aunt was chiefly interested in knowing whether he was impotent or merely impotent with *her*. Naturally, she'd not told Tata that she was having a repeatedly disappointing sexual experience with Rahul; she'd implied that Rahul himself was concerned because he'd failed to maintain an erection with a prostitute. Dr. Tata's response had been disappointing to Aunt Promila, too.

"Perhaps it was the prostitute," old Dr. Tata had replied.

Years later, when he thought of his Aunt Promila, Rahul would remember that. Perhaps it was the prostitute, he would think to himself; possibly he'd not been impotent after all. All things considered, now that Rahul was a woman, what did it really matter? He sincerely loved his Aunt Promila. As for washing his hands, the memory of the elephant with one tusk raised would never be lost on Rahul; but he preferred to wash his hands in hot water.

A Childless Couple Searches for Rahul

With hindsight, it is impressive how Deputy Commissioner Patel fathomed Rahul's attachment to family money—in India. The detective thought that a well-to-do relative might explain the killer's few but periodic visits to Bombay. For 15 years, the victims who were decorated with the winking elephant were prostitutes from the Kamathipura brothels or from the brothels on Grant Road and Falkland Road. Their murders occurred in groups of two or three, within two or three weeks' time, and then not again for nearly nine months or a year. There were no murders recorded in the hottest months, just before the monsoon, or during the monsoon itself; the murderer struck at a more comfortable time of the year. Only the first two murders, in Goa, were hot-weather murders.

Detective Patel could find no evidence of murders with elephant drawings in any other Indian city; this was why he had concluded that the killer lived abroad. It wasn't hard to uncover the relatively few murders of this nature in London; although these weren't restricted to the Indian community, the victims were always prostitutes or students—the latter, usually of an artistic inclination, were reputed to have lived in a bohemian or otherwise unconventional way. The more he studied the murderer, and the more deeply he loved Nancy, the more the deputy commissioner realized that Nancy was lucky to be alive.

But with the passage of time, Nancy less and less wore the countenance of a woman who felt herself to be lucky. The Deutsche marks in the dildo—such an excessive amount that, at first, both Nancy and young Inspector Patel had felt quite liberated—were the beginning of Nancy and Patel's feeling that they had been compromised. It made only the smallest dent in the sum for Nancy to send what she'd stolen from the hardware store to her parents. It was, she thought, the best way to erase the past, but her newfound crusade for justice interfered with the purity of her intention. The money was to repay the hardware store, but in sending it to her parents she couldn't resist naming those men (in feed-and-grain supply) who'd made her feel like dirt. If her parents wanted to repay the store after knowing what had happened to their daughter there, that would be *their* decision.

Thus she created a moral dilemma for her parents, which had quite the opposite effect from what Nancy desired. She had *not* erased the past; she'd brought it to life in her parents' eyes, and for almost 20 years (until they died), her parents faithfully described their ongoing torment in Iowa to her—all the while begging her to come "home" but refusing to come visit her. It was never clear to Nancy what they finally did with the money.

As for young Inspector Patel, it made a similarly small dent in the sum of Dieter's Deutsche marks for the previously uncorrupted policeman to engage in his first and last bribe. It was simply the usual and necessary sum required for promotion, for a more lucrative posting—and one must remember that Vijay Patel was not a Maharashtrian. For a Gujarati to make the move from an inspector at the Colaba Station to a deputy commissioner in Crime Branch Headquarters at Crawford Market required what is called greasing the wheel. But—over the years, and in combination with his failure to find Rahul—the bribe had etched itself into a part of the deputy commissioner's vulnerable self-esteem. It had been a reasonable expense, certainly not a lavish amount of money; and contrary to the infuriating fiction represented by the Inspector Dhar movies, there was no significant advancement within the Bombay police force without a *little* bribery.

And although Nancy and the detective were a love story, they were unhappy. It wasn't only that the sheer grimness of serving justice had grown to be a task, nor was it simply that Rahul had escaped unpunished. Both Mr. and Mrs. Patel assumed that a higher judgment had been made against them; for Nancy was infertile, and they'd spent nearly a decade learning the reason—and then another decade, first trying to adopt a child and finally deciding against adoption.

In the first decade of their efforts to conceive a child, both Nancy and young Patel—she called him Vijay—believed that they were being punished for dipping into the Deutsche marks. Nancy had entirely forgotten a brief period of physical discomfort upon her return to Bombay with the dildo. A slight burning in her urethra and the appearance in her underwear of an insignificant vaginal discharge had contributed to Nancy's delay in initiating a sexual relationship with Vijay Patel. The symptoms were mild, and they overlapped, to some degree, with cystitis (inflammation of the bladder) and urinary tract infection. She didn't want to imagine that Dieter had given her something venereal, although her memory of that brothel in Kamathipura, and how familiarly Dieter had spoken with the madam, gave Nancy good reason to be worried.

Moreover, at the time, she could plainly see that she and young Patel were falling in love with each other; she wasn't about to ask *him* to recommend a suitable physician. Instead, in that well-worn travel guide, which she still faithfully carried, was an on-the-road recipe for a douche; but she misread the proper proportion of vinegar and gave herself much worse burning than she began with. For a week, there was an even yellower stain in her underwear, which she ascribed to the unwise remedy of her homemade douche. As for the abdominal pain, it closely attended the onset of her period, which was unusually heavy; she had much cramping and even a little chill. She wondered if her body was trying to reject the IUD. And then she completely recovered; she only remembered this episode 10 years later. She was sitting with her husband in the office of a fancy private venereologist, and—with Vijay's help—she was filling out a detailed questionnaire; it was part of the infertility work.

What had happened was that Dieter had given her a dose of gonorrhea, which he'd caught from the 13-year-old prostitute he'd fucked standing up in the hall of that brothel in Kamathipura. It hadn't been true, as the madam had told him, that there were no available cubicles with mattresses or cots; instead, it was the young prostitute's request to have sex standing up, for her case of gonorrhea had advanced to the more uncomfortable symptoms of pelvic inflammatory disease. She was suffering from the so-called chandelier sign, where moving the cervix up and down elicits pain in the tubes and ovaries; in short, it hurt her to have a man's weight pounding on her belly. It was better for her when she stood up.

As for Dieter, he was a fastidious young German who gave himself a shot of penicillin before he left the brothel; a medical student among his friends had told him that this worked well to prevent incubating syphilis. The injection, however, did nothing to abort the penicillinase-producing *Neisseria gonorrhea*. No one had told him that these strains were endemic in the tropics. Besides, less than a week after his contact with the infected prostitute, Dieter was murdered; he'd begun to notice only the slightest symptoms.

And what relatively mild symptoms Nancy had experienced before her spontaneous healing and the scarring were the result of the inflammation spreading from her cervix to the lining of her uterus and her tubes. When the venereologist explained to Mr. and Mrs. Patel that this was the cause of Nancy's infertility, the distraught couple firmly believed that Dieter's nasty disease—even from the hippie grave—was final proof of the judgment against them. They should never have taken a pfennig of those dirty Deutsche marks in the dildo.

In their ensuing efforts to adopt a child, their experience was not uncommon. The better adoption agencies, which kept prenatal records as well as a history of the natural mother's health, were uncharitable on the issue of their "mixed" marriage; this wouldn't have deterred the Patels in the end, but it prolonged the process of humiliating interviews and the swamp of petty paperwork. In the interim, while they awaited approval, first Nancy and then Vijay expressed whatever slight doubts they both felt about the disappointment of adopting a child when they'd hoped to have one of their own. If they'd been able to adopt a child quickly, they would have begun to love it before their doubts could have mounted; but in the extended period of waiting, they lost their nerve. It wasn't that they believed they would have loved an adopted child insufficiently; it was that they believed the judgment against them would condemn the child to some unbearable fate.

They'd done something wrong. They were paying for it. They wouldn't ask a child to pay for it, too. And so the Patels accepted childlessness; after almost 15 years of expecting a child, this acceptance came to them at considerable cost. In the way they walked, in the detectable lethargy with which they raised their many cups and glasses of tea, they reflected their own consciousness of this resignation to their fate. About that time, Nancy went to work—first in one of the adoption agencies that had so rigorously interviewed her, then as a volunteer in an orphanage. It wasn't the sort of work she could sustain for very long—it made her think of the child she'd given up in Texas.

And, after 15 years or so, D.C.P. Patel began to believe that Rahul had come back to Bombay, this time to stay. The murders were now evenly spaced over the calendar year; in London, the killings had altogether stopped. What had happened was that Rahul's Aunt Promila had finally died, and her estate on old Ridge Road—not to mention the considerable allowance she'd bestowed upon her only *niece*—had passed into the hands of her namesake, the former Rahul. He had become Promila's heir, or—to be more anatomically correct—*she* had become Promila's *heiress*. And the *new* Promila had not long to wait for her acceptance at the Duckworth Club, where her aunt had faithfully made application for her niece's membership—even before she technically had a niece.

This niece was slow and deliberate about her entry into that society which the Duckworth Club would offer her; she was in no hurry to be seen. Some Duckworthians, upon meeting her, found her a touch crude—and almost all Duckworthians agreed that, although she must have been a great beauty in her prime, she was rather well advanced into that phase called middle age . . . especially for someone who'd never been married. That struck nearly everyone as odd, but before there was time for much talk about it, the *new* Promila Rai—with surprising swiftness, considering that hardly anyone really knew her—was engaged to be married. And to another Duckworthian, an elderly gentleman of such sizable wealth that *his* estate on old Ridge Road was rumored to put the late Promila's place to shame! It was no surprise that the wedding was held at the Duckworth Club, but it was too bad that the wedding took place at a time when Dr. Daruwalla was in Toronto, for he—or certainly Julia—might have recognized this *new* Promila who'd so successfully passed herself off as the *old* Promila's niece.

By the time the Daruwallas and Inspector Dhar were back in Bombay, the new Promila Rai was identified by her married name—actually by two names, one of which was never used to her face. Rahul, who'd become Promila, had lately become the beautiful Mrs. Dogar, as old Mr. Sethna usually addressed her.

Yes, *of course*—the former Rahul was none other than the second Mrs. Dogar, and each time Dr. Daruwalla felt the stab of pain in his ribs, where she'd collided with him in the foyer of the Duckworth Club, he mistakenly searched his forgetful mind for those now-faded film stars he saw over and over again on so many of his favorite videos. Farrokh would never find her there. Rahul wasn't hiding in the old movies.

The Police Know the Movie Is Innocent

Just when Deputy Commissioner Patel had decided that he would never find Rahul, there was released in Bombay another predictably dreadful Inspector Dhar film. The real policeman had no desire to be further insulted; but when he learned what *Inspector Dhar and the Cage-Girl Killer* was about, the deputy commissioner not only went to see the film—he took Nancy to see it with him the second time. There could be no doubt regarding the source of that elephant drawing. Nancy was sure she knew where that jaunty little elephant had come from. No *two* minds could imagine a dead woman's navel as a winking eye; even in the movie version, the elephant raised just one tusk—it was always the same tusk, too. And the water spraying from the elephant's trunk—who would think of such a thing? Nancy had wondered, for 20 years. A *child* might think of such a thing, the deputy commissioner had told her.

The police had never given out such details to the press; the police preferred to keep their business to themselves—they'd not even informed the public about the existence of such an artistic serial killer. People often killed prostitutes. Why invite the press to sensationalize the presence of a single fiend? So, in truth, the police—most especially Detective Patel—*knew* that these murders had long predated the release of such a fantasy as *Inspector Dhar and the Cage-Girl Killer.* The movie merely drew the public's attention to the real murders. The media assumed, wrongly, that the movie was to blame.

It had been Deputy Commissioner Patel's idea to allow the misunderstanding to pass; the deputy commissioner wanted to see if the movie might inspire some jealousy on the part of Rahul, for the detective was of the opinion that, if his wife recognized the source of the inspiration of Inspector Dhar's creator, so would the real murderer. The killing of Mr. Lal—especially the interesting two-rupee note in his mouth—indicated that the deputy commissioner had been right. Rahul must have seen the movie—assuming that *Rahul* wasn't the screenwriter.

What puzzled the detective was that the note said MORE MEMBERS DIE IF DHAR REMAINS A MEMBER. Since Nancy had been smart enough to figure out that only a doctor would have been shown Beth's decorated body, surely Rahul would know as well that it wasn't Dhar himself who'd seen one of Rahul's works of art; it could only be the doctor who was so frequently in Dhar's company.

The matter that Detective Patel wished to speak of with Dr. Daruwalla in private was simply this. The detective wanted the doctor to confirm Nancy's theories—that he was Dhar's true creator and had seen the drawing on Beth's belly. But the deputy commissioner also wanted to warn Dr. Daruwalla. MORE MEMBERS DIE . . . this could mean that the doctor might be Rahul's future target. Detective Patel and Nancy believed that Farrokh was a more likely target than Dhar himself.

On the telephone, such complicated news took time for the policeman to deliver and for the doctor to comprehend. And since Nancy had passed the telephone to her husband, that element of the real murderer being a transvestite, or even a thoroughly convincing *woman,* wasn't a part of Detective Patel's conversation with Farrokh. Unfortunately, the name Rahul was never mentioned. It was simply agreed that Dr. Daruwalla would come to Crime Branch Headquarters, where the deputy commissioner would show him photographs of the elephants drawn on the murdered women—this for the sake of mere confirmation—and that both Dhar and the doctor should exercise extreme caution. The real murderer had seemingly been provoked by *Inspector Dhar and the Cage-*

Girl Killer—if not exactly in the way that the public and many angry prostitutes believed.

A View of Two Marriages at a Vulnerable Hour

As soon as Dr. Daruwalla hung up the phone, he carried his agitation to the dinner table, where Roopa apologized for the utter deterioration of the mutton, which was her way of saying that this mushy meat in her beloved dhal was all the doctor's fault, which of course it was. Dhar then asked the doctor if he'd read the new hate mail—Farrokh had not. A pity, John D. said, because it might well be the last of the mail from those infuriated prostitutes. Balraj Gupta, the director, had informed John D. that the new Inspector Dhar movie (*Inspector Dhar and the Towers of Silence*) was being released tomorrow. After that, John D. said ironically, the hate mail would most likely be from all the offended Parsis.

"Tomorrow!" cried Dr. Daruwalla.

"Well, actually, after midnight tonight," Dhar said.

Dr. Daruwalla should have known. Whenever Balraj Gupta called him and asked to discuss with him something that the director wanted to do, it invariably meant that the director had already done it.

"But no more of this trivia!" Farrokh said to his wife and John D. The doctor took a deep breath; then he informed them of everything that Deputy Commissioner Patel had told him.

All Julia asked was, "How many murders has this killer managed—how many victims are there?"

"Sixty-nine," said Dr. Daruwalla. Julia's gasp was less surprising than John D.'s inappropriate calm.

"Does that count Mr. Lal?" Dhar asked.

"Mr. Lal makes seventy—*if* Mr. Lal is truly connected," Farrokh replied.

"Of course he's *connected*," said Inspector Dhar, which irritated Dr. Daruwalla in the usual way. Here was his fictional creation once again sounding like an authority; but what Farrokh failed to acknowledge was that Dhar was a good and well-trained actor. Dhar had faithfully studied the role and taken many components of the part into himself; instinctually, he'd become quite a good detective—Dr. Daruwalla had only made up the character. Dhar's character was an utter fiction to Farrokh, who could scarcely remember his research on various aspects of police work from screenplay to screenplay; Dhar, on the other hand, rarely forgot either these finer points or his less-than-original lines. As a screenwriter, Dr. Daruwalla was at best a gifted amateur, but Inspector Dhar was closer to the real thing than either Dhar or his creator knew.

"May I go with you to see the photographs?" Dhar asked his creator.

"I believe that the deputy commissioner wished me to see them privately," the doctor replied.

"I'd like to see them, Farrokh," John D. said.

"He should see them if he wants to!" Julia snapped.

"I'm not sure the police would agree," Dr. Daruwalla began to say, but Inspector Dhar gave a most familiar and dismissive wave of his hand, a perfect gesture of contempt. Farrokh felt his exhaustion draw close to him—like old friends and family gathering around his imagined sickbed.

When John D. retired to the balcony to sleep, Julia was quick to change the subject—even before Farrokh had managed to undress for bed.

"You didn't *tell* him!" she cried.

"Oh, please stop it about the damnable *twin* business!" he said to her. "What makes you think that's such a priority? Especially now!"

"I think that the arrival of his twin might be *more* of a priority to John D.," Julia remarked decisively. She left her husband alone in the bedroom while she used the bathroom. Then, after Farrokh had had his turn in the bathroom, he noted that Julia had already fallen asleep—or else she was pretending to be asleep.

At first he tried to sleep on his side, which was his usual preference, but in that position he was conscious of the soreness in his ribs; on his stomach, the pain was more evident. Flat on his back—where he struggled in vain to fall asleep, and where he was inclined to snore—he wracked his overexcited brain for the precise image of the movie actress he was sure he was reminded of when he'd shamelessly stared at the second Mrs. Dogar. Despite himself, he grew sleepy. The names of actresses came to and left his lips. He saw Neelam's full mouth, and Rekha's nice mouth, too; he thought of Sridevi's mischievous smile—and almost everything there was to think about Sonu Walia, too. Then he half-waked himself and thought, No, no . . . it's no one contemporary, and she's probably not even Indian. Jennifer Jones? he wondered. Ida Lupino? Rita Moreno? Dorothy Lamour! No, no . . . what was he thinking? It was someone whose beauty was much more cruel than the beauty of any of these. This insight nearly woke him. Had he awakened simultaneously with the reminder caused by the pain in his ribs, he might have got it. But although the hour was now late, it was still too soon for him to know.

There was more communication in the marriage bed of Mr. and Mrs. Patel at this very same late hour. Nancy was crying; her tears, as they often were, were a mix of misery and frustration. Deputy Commissioner Patel was trying, as he often did, to be comforting.

Nancy had suddenly remembered what had happened to her—maybe two weeks after the last of her symptoms of gonorrhea had disappeared. She'd broken out in a terrible rash, red and sore and with unbearable itching, and she'd assumed that this was a new phase of something venereal she'd caught from Dieter. Furthermore, there was no hiding *this* phase from her beloved policeman; young Inspector Patel had straightaway brought her to a doctor, who informed her that she'd been taking too many antimalarial pills—she was simply suffering from an allergic reaction. But how this had frightened her! And she only now remembered the goats.

For all these years, she'd thought about the goats in the brothels, but she'd not remembered how she'd first feared that it was something from the goats that had given her such a hideous rash and such uncontrollable itching. That had been her worst fear. For 20 years, when she'd thought about those brothels and the women who'd been murdered there, she'd forgotten the men Dieter had told her about—the terrible men who fucked goats. Maybe Dieter had fucked goats, too. No wonder she'd at least *tried* to forget this.

"But nobody is fucking those goats," Vijay just now informed her.

"What?" Nancy said.

"Well, I don't presume to know about the United States—or even about certain rural areas of India—but no one in Bombay is fucking goats," her husband assured her.

"What?" Nancy said. "Dieter *told* me that they fucked the goats."

"Well, it's not at all true," the detective said. "Those goats are pets. Of course some of them give milk. This is a bonus—for the children, I suppose. But they're pets, just pets."

"Oh, Vijay!" Nancy cried. He had to hold her. "Oh, Dieter *lied* to me!" she cried. "Oh, how he lied to me . . . all those years I *believed* it! Oh, that *fucker!*" The word was so sharply spoken, it caused a dog in the alley below them to stop rooting through the garbage and bark. Over their heads, the ceiling fan barely stirred the close air, which seemed always to smell of the perpetually blocked drains, and of the sea, which in their neighborhood was not especially clean or fresh-smelling. "Oh, it was another lie!" Nancy screamed. Vijay went on holding her, although to do so for long would make them both sweat. The air was unmoving where they lived.

The goats were just pets. Yet, for 20 years, what Dieter had told her had hurt her so badly; at times, it had made her physically sick. And the heat, and the sewer smell, and the fact that, whoever Rahul was, he was still getting away with it—all this Nancy had accepted, but in the fashion that she'd accepted her childlessness, which she'd accepted so slowly and only after what had felt to her like a lingering and merciless defeat.

What the Dwarf Sees

It was late. While Nancy cried herself to sleep and Dr. Daruwalla failed to realize that the second and beautiful Mrs. Dogar had reminded him of Rahul, Vinod was driving one of Mr. Garg's exotic dancers home from the Wetness Cabaret.

She was a middle-aged Maharashtrian with the English name of Muriel—not her real name but her exotic-dancing name—and she was upset because one of the patrons of the Wetness Cabaret had thrown an orange at her while she was dancing. The clientele of the Wetness Cabaret was vile, Muriel had decided. Even so, she rationalized, Mr. Garg was a gentleman. Garg had recognized that Muriel was upset by the episode with the orange; he'd personally engaged Vinod's "luxury" taxi to drive Muriel home.

Although Vinod had praised Mr. Garg's humanitarian efforts on behalf of runaway child prostitutes, the dwarf wouldn't have gone so far as to call Mr. Garg a gentleman; possibly Garg was more of a gentleman with middle-aged women. With younger girls, Vinod wasn't sure. The dwarf didn't entirely share Dr. Daruwalla's suspicions of Mr. Garg, but Vinod and Deepa had occasionally encountered a child prostitute who seemed in need of rescuing *from* Garg. Save this poor child, Mr. Garg seemed to be saying; save her from *me*, Garg might have meant.

It wouldn't have helped Vinod and Deepa's child-rescue operations to have Dr. Daruwalla treating Garg like a criminal. The new runaway, the boneless one—a potential plastic lady—was a case in point. Although she'd appeared to be more personally involved with Mr. Garg than she should have been, such implications wouldn't help her cause

with Dr. Daruwalla; the doctor had to pronounce her healthy or the
Great Blue Nile wouldn't take her.

Vinod now noted that the middle-aged woman with the exotic-
dancing name of Muriel had fallen asleep; she slept with a somewhat
sour expression, her mouth disagreeably open and her hands resting on
her fat breasts. The dwarf thought that it made more sense to throw an
orange at her than it did to watch her dance. But Vinod's humanitarian
instincts extended even to middle-aged strippers; he slowed down because the streets were bumpy, seeing no reason to wake the poor woman
before she was home. In her sleep, Muriel suddenly cringed. She was
ducking oranges, the dwarf imagined.

After Vinod dropped off Muriel, it was too late for him to go anywhere but back to the brothel area; the red-light district was the only
part of Bombay where people needed a taxi at 2:00 in the morning. Soon
the international travelers would be arriving at the Oberoi and the Taj,
but no one who'd just flown in from Europe or North America would
have the slightest inclination to cruise around the city.

Vinod thought he'd wait for the end of the last show at the Wetness
Cabaret; one of Mr. Garg's other exotic dancers might want a safe ride
home. It amazed Vinod that the Wetness Cabaret, the building itself,
was "home" to Mr. Garg; the dwarf couldn't imagine sleeping there. He
supposed there were rooms upstairs, above the slick bar and the sticky
tables and the sloping stage. Vinod shivered to think of the dimly lit bar,
the brightly lit stage, the darkened tables where the men sat—some of
them masturbating, although the dominant odor of the Wetness Cabaret
was one of urine. How could Garg sleep in such a place, even if he slept
above it?

But as distasteful as it was to Vinod—to cruise the brothel area, as if
he carried a potential customer in the Ambassador's back seat—the
dwarf had decided that he might as well stay awake. Vinod was fascinated by that hour when most of the brothels switched over; in Kamathipura, on Falkland Road and Grant Road, there came an hour of the
early morning when most of the brothels would accept only all-night
customers. In the dwarf's opinion, these were different and desperate
men. Who else would want to spend *all night* with a prostitute?

Vinod grew alert and edgy at this hour, as if—particularly in those
little lanes in Kamathipura—he might spot a man who wasn't entirely
human. When he got tired, the dwarf dozed in his car; his car was more
home to him than home, at least when Deepa was away at the circus.
And when he was bored, Vinod would cruise past the transvestite

brothels on Falkland Road and Grant Road. Vinod liked the hijras; they were so bold and so outrageous—they also seemed to like dwarfs. Possibly the hijras thought that *dwarfs* were outrageous.

Vinod was aware that some of the hijras *didn't* like him; they were the ones who knew that the dwarf was Inspector Dhar's driver—the ones who hated *Inspector Dhar and the Cage-Girl Killer*. Lately, Vinod had to be a little careful in the brothel area; the prostitute murders had made Dhar *and* Dhar's dwarf more than a little unpopular. Thus that hour when most of the brothels "switched over" made Vinod more alert and edgy than usual.

While he cruised, the dwarf was among the first to notice what had changed about Bombay; the change was being enacted before Vinod's very eyes. Gone was the movie poster of his most famous client, that larger-than-life image of Inspector Dhar which Vinod and all of Bombay had grown so used to—the huge hoardings, the overhead billboards that advertised *Inspector Dhar and the Cage-Girl Killer*. Dhar's handsome face, albeit bleeding slightly; the torn white shirt, open to expose Dhar's muscular chest; the pretty, ravaged young woman slung over Dhar's strong shoulder; and, always, the blue-gray semi-automatic pistol held in Dhar's hard right hand. In its place, everywhere in Bombay, was a brand-new poster. Vinod thought that only the semi-automatic was the same, although Inspector Dhar's sneer was remarkably familiar. *Inspector Dhar and the Towers of Silence:* this time, the young woman slung over Dhar's shoulder was noticeably dead—more noticeably, she was a Western hippie.

It was the only safe time to put the posters up; if people had been awake, they would doubtless have attacked the poster-wallas. The old posters in the brothel area had long ago been destroyed; tonight, perhaps, the prostitutes left the poster-wallas unharmed because the prostitutes were happy to see that *Inspector Dhar and the Cage-Girl Killer* was being replaced with a new offense—this time, to somebody else.

But, upon closer inspection, Vinod noted that not so much was different about the new poster as he'd first observed. The posture of the young woman over Dhar's shoulder was quite the same, alive or dead; and again, albeit from a slightly different spot, Inspector Dhar's cruel, handsome face was bleeding. The longer Vinod looked at the new poster, the more he found it to resemble the previous poster; it seemed to the dwarf that Dhar even wore the same torn shirt. This possibly explained why the dwarf had driven around Bombay for more than two hours before he'd noticed that a new Inspector Dhar film had been born into the world. Vinod couldn't wait to see it.

The unspeakable life of the red-light district teemed all around him—the bartering and the betrayals and the frightening, unseen beatings—or so the excited dwarf imagined. About the most hopeful thing that could be said is that throughout the brothel area of Bombay, no one—truly no one—was fucking a goat.

15. DHAR'S TWIN

Three Old Missionaries Fall Asleep

That week between Christmas and New Year's, when the first American missionary was due to arrive at St. Ignatius in Mazagaon, the Jesuit mission prepared a celebration in honor of 1990. St. Ignatius was a Bombay landmark; it would soon be 125 years old—in all these years, it had faithfully managed its holy and secular tasks without the assistance of an American. The management of St. Ignatius was a threesome of responsibility, and these three had been almost as successful as the Blessed Trinity. The Father Rector (Father Julian, who was 68 years old and English), the senior priest (Father Cecil, who was 72 and Indian), and Brother Gabriel (who was around 75 and had fled Spain after the Civil War) were a triumvirate of authority that was seldom questioned and never overruled; they were also unanimous in their opinion that St. Ignatius could continue to serve mankind and the heavenly kingdom without the aid of *any* American—yet one had been offered. To be sure, they would have preferred another Indian, or at least a European, but since these three wise men were of an average age of 71 years and eight months, they were attracted to one aspect of the "young" scholastic, as they called him. At 39, Martin Mills was no kid. Only Dr. Daruwalla would have judged "young" Martin to be unsuitably old for a man who was still in training to be a priest. That the so-called scholastic was almost 40 was at least mildly comforting to Father Julian and Father Cecil and Brother Gabriel, although they shared the conviction that the mission's 125th jubilee was diminished by their obligation to welcome the former Californian, who was allegedly fond of Hawaiian shirts.

They knew of this laughable eccentricity from the otherwise impressive dossier of Martin Mills, whose letters of recommendation were glowing. However, the Father Rector said that when it came to Americans, one must read between the lines. For example, Father Julian pointed out, Martin Mills had evidently eschewed his native California, although nowhere in his dossier did it say so. He'd been schooled elsewhere in the United States and had taken a teaching job in Boston, which was about as far away from California as one could get. Clearly, said Father Julian, this indicated that Martin Mills had come from a troubled family. Perhaps it was his own mother or father whom he'd "eschewed."

And along with young Martin's unexplained attraction to the garish, which Father Julian concluded was the root cause of the scholastic's reported fondness for Hawaiian shirts, there was mention in the dossier of Martin Mills's success with apostolic work—even as a novice, and especially with young people. Bombay's St. Ignatius was a good school, and Martin Mills was expected to be a good teacher; most of the students weren't Catholics—many weren't even Christians. "It won't do to have a crazed American proselyte-hunting among our pupils," the Father Rector warned, although there was no mention in the dossier of Martin Mills being either "crazed" or a proselyte-hunter.

The dossier did say that he'd undertaken a six-week pilgrimage as part of his novitiate, and that during this pilgrimage he'd spent no money—not a penny. He'd managed to find places to live and work in return for humanitarian services; these included soup kitchens for the homeless, hospitals for handicapped children, homes for the elderly, shelters for AIDS patients and a clinic for babies suffering from fetal alcohol syndrome—this was on a Native American reservation.

Brother Gabriel and Father Cecil were inclined to view Martin Mills's dossier in a positive light. Father Julian, on the other hand, quoted from Thomas à Kempis's *Imitation of Christ:* "Be rarely with young people and strangers." The Father Rector had read through Martin Mills's dossier as if it were a code to be deciphered. The task of teaching at St. Ignatius, and otherwise serving the mission, was a part of the typical three-year service in preparation for the priesthood; it was called regency, and it was followed by another three years of theological study. Ordination followed theology; Martin Mills would complete a fourth year of theological study after his ordination.

He'd completed the two-year Jesuit novitiate at St. Aloysius in Massachusetts, which Father Julian said was an extremist's choice because of the reputed harshness of its winters. This suggested a proneness to self-flagellation and other chastisements of the flesh—even an inclination to fasting, which the Jesuits discouraged; they encouraged fasting only in moderation. But, once again, the Father Rector seemed to be searching through Martin Mills's dossier for some hidden evidence of the scholastic's flawed character. Brother Gabriel and Father Cecil pointed out to Father Julian that Martin had joined the New England Province of the Society of Jesus while he was teaching in Boston. The province's novitiate was in Massachusetts; it was only natural for Martin Mills to have been a novice at St. Aloysius—it hadn't really been a "choice."

But why had he taught for 10 years in a dismal parochial school in Boston? His dossier didn't say that the school was "dismal"; however, it was admitted that the school was not accredited. Actually, it was a kind of reform school, where young criminals were encouraged to give up their delinquent behavior; as far as the Father Rector could tell, the means by which this was accomplished was theatrical. Martin Mills had directed *plays* wherein all the roles were acted by former felons and miscreants and thugs! In such an environment Martin Mills had first felt his vocation—namely, he'd felt Christ's presence and had been drawn to the priesthood. But why did it take 10 years? Father Julian questioned. After completing his novitiate, Martin Mills was sent to Boston College to study philosophy; that met with the Father Rector's approval. But then, in the midst of his regency, young Martin had requested a three-month "experiment" in India. Did this mean that the scholastic had suffered doubts about his vocation? Father Julian asked.

"Well, we'll soon see," Father Cecil said. "He seems perfectly all right to *me.*" Father Cecil had almost said that Martin Mills seemed perfectly "Loyola-like," but he'd thought better of it because he knew how the Father Rector distrusted those Jesuits who too consciously patterned their behavior on the life of St. Ignatius Loyola—the founder of the Jesuit order, the Society of Jesus.

Even a pilgrimage could be a fool's errand when undertaken by a fool. The *Spiritual Exercises* of St. Ignatius Loyola is a handbook for the retreat master, not for the retreatant; it was never intended to be published, much less memorized by would-be priests—not that Martin Mills's dossier suggested that the missionary had followed the *Spiritual Exercises* to such an excess. Once again, the Father Rector's suspicion of Martin Mills's extreme piety was intuitive. Father Julian suspected all Americans of an unflagging fanaticism, which the Father Rector believed was emboldened by a frightening reliance on self-education—or "reading on a deserted island," as Father Julian called an American education. Father Cecil, on the other hand, was a kindly man—of that school which said Martin Mills should be given a chance to prove himself.

The senior priest chided the Father Rector for his cynicism: "You don't know for a fact that our Martin wanted to be a novice at St. Aloysius because he *sought* the harshness of a New England winter." Father Cecil further implied that Father Julian was only guessing that Martin Mills had hoped to attend St. Aloysius as a form of penitential practice, to chastise his flesh. Indeed, Father Julian was wrong. Had he known the *real* reason why Martin Mills wanted St. Aloysius for his novitiate, the Father Rector *really* would have been worried, for Martin Mills had desired to be a novice at St. Aloysius solely because of his identification with St. Aloysius Gonzaga, that avid Italian whose chastity was so fervent that he refused to look upon his own mother after taking his permanent vows.

This was Martin Mills's favorite example of that "custody of the senses" which every Jesuit sought to attain. To Martin's thinking, there was much to admire in the very notion of never again seeing one's own mother. His mother, after all, was Veronica Rose, and to deny himself even a farewell glimpse of *her* would certainly be enhancing to his Jesuitical goal of keeping his voice, his body and his curiosity in check. Martin Mills was very much held in check, and both his pious intentions and the life that had fueled them were more fanatically shot through and through with zeal than Father Julian could have guessed.

And now Brother Gabriel—that 75-year-old icon collector—had lost the scholastic's letter. If they didn't know when the new missionary was arriving, how could they meet his plane?

"After all," Father Julian said, "it seems that our Martin *likes* challenges."

Father Cecil thought that this was cruel of the Father Rector. For Martin Mills to arrive in Bombay at that dead-of-night hour when the international flights landed in Sahar, and then to have to find his own way to the mission, which would be locked up and virtually impenetrable until the early-morning Mass . . . this was worse than any pilgrimage the missionary had previously undertaken.

"After all," Father Julian said with characteristic sarcasm, "St. Ignatius Loyola managed to find his way to Jerusalem. No one met *his* plane."

It was unfair, Father Cecil thought. And so he'd called Dr. Daruwalla to ask the doctor if he knew when Martin Mills was arriving. But the senior priest had reached only the doctor's answering machine, and Dr. Daruwalla hadn't returned his call. And so Father Cecil prayed for Martin Mills in general. In particular, Father Cecil prayed that the missionary would not have too traumatic a first encounter upon his arrival in Bombay.

Brother Gabriel also prayed for Martin Mills in general. In particular, Brother Gabriel prayed that he might yet find the scholastic's lost letter. But the letter was never found. Long before Dr. Daruwalla drifted into sleep, in the midst of his efforts to locate a movie star who resembled the second Mrs. Dogar, Brother Gabriel gave up looking for the letter and went to bed, where he also fell asleep. When Vinod drove Muriel home—it was while the dwarf and the exotic dancer were considering the vileness of the clientele at the Wetness Cabaret—Father Cecil stopped praying, and then he fell asleep, too. And shortly after Vinod noticed that *Inspector Dhar and the Towers of Silence* was about to be launched upon the sleeping city, Father Julian locked the cloister gate and the school-bus gate and the gate that admitted entrance to St. Ignatius Church. And shortly after that, the Father Rector was sound asleep as well.

Early Indications of Mistaken Identity

At approximately 2:00 in the morning—that very same hour when the poster-wallas were plastering the advertisements for the new Inspector Dhar movie all over Bombay, and when Vinod was cruising by the brothels in Kamathipura—the airplane carrying Dhar's twin landed safely in Sahar. Dhar himself was at that moment sleeping on Dr. Daruwalla's balcony.

However, the customs official who looked back and forth from the intense expression of the new missionary to the utterly bland passport photograph of Martin Mills was convinced that he stood face-to-face with Inspector Dhar. The Hawaiian shirt was a mild surprise, for the customs official couldn't imagine why Dhar would attempt to conceal himself as a tourist; similarly, shaving off the identifying Dhar mustache was a lame disguise—with the upper lip exposed, something of the inimitable Dhar sneer was even more pronounced.

It was a U.S. passport—*that* was clever! thought the customs official— but the passport admitted that this so-called Martin Mills had been born in Bombay. The customs official pointed to this evidence in the passport; then he winked at the missionary, as a way of indicating to Inspector Dhar that *this* customs official was nobody's fool.

Martin Mills was very tired; it had been a long flight, which he'd spent studying Hindi and otherwise informing himself of the particulars of "native behavior." He knew all about the salaam, for example, but the customs official had distinctly *winked* at him—he had not salaamed— and Martin Mills hadn't encountered any information regarding the wink in his reading about native behavior. The missionary didn't wish to be impolite; therefore, he winked back, and he salaamed a little, too, just to be sure.

The customs official was very pleased with himself. He'd seen the wink in a recent Charles Bronson movie, but he was uncertain if it would be a cool thing to do to Inspector Dhar; above all, in dealing with Dhar, the customs official wanted to be perceived as cool. Unlike most Bombayites and all policemen, the customs official *loved* Inspector Dhar movies. So far, no customs officials had been portrayed in the films; therefore, none had been offended. And prior to his service as a customs official, he'd been rejected for police work; therefore, the constant mock- ery of the police—the prevalence of bribe taking, which was basic to every Inspector Dhar movie—was adored by the customs official.

Nevertheless, it was most irregular for someone to be entering the country under a false identity, and the customs official wanted Dhar to know that he was hip to Dhar's disguise, while at the same time he would do nothing to interfere with the creative genius who stood before him. Besides, Dhar didn't look well. His color was poor—he was mostly pale and blotchy—and he appeared to have lost a lot of weight.

"Is this your first time in Bombay since your birth?" the customs official asked Martin Mills. Thereupon the official winked again and smiled.

Martin Mills smiled and winked back. "Yes," he said. "But I'm going to stay here for at least three months."

This was an absurdity to the customs official, but he insisted on being cool about it. He saw that the missionary's visa was "conditional"; it was possible to extend it for three months. The examination of the visa elicited more winking. It was also expected of the customs official that he look through the missionary's belongings. For a visit of three months, the scholastic had brought only a single suitcase, albeit a large and heavy one, and in his ungainly luggage were some surprises: the black shirts with the white detachable collars—for although Martin Mills wasn't an ordained priest, he was permitted to wear such clerical garb. There was also a wrinkled black suit and about a half-dozen more Hawaiian shirts, and then came the *culpa* beads and the foot-long whip with the braided cords, not to mention the leg iron that was worn around the thigh; the wire prongs pointed inward, toward the flesh. But the customs official remained calm; he just kept smiling and winking, despite his horror at these instruments of self-torture.

The Father Rector, Father Julian, would also have been horrified to see such antiquities of mortification as these; they were artifacts of an earlier time—even Father Cecil would have been horrified, or else much amused. Whips and leg irons had never been notable parts of the Jesuit "way of perfection." Even the *culpa* beads were an indication that Martin Mills might not have a true Jesuit vocation.

As for the customs official, the scholastic's books contributed further to the authenticity of Inspector Dhar's "disguise," which is what the customs official took all of this to be—an actor's elaborate props. Doubtless Dhar was preparing himself for yet another challenging role. This time he plays a *priest?* the customs official wondered. He looked over the books—all the while winking and smiling in ceaseless approval, while the baffled missionary kept winking and smiling back. There was the 1988 edition of the *Catholic Almanac* and many pamphlets of something called *Studies in the Spirituality of Jesuits;* there was a *Pocket Catholic Catechism* and a *Compact Dictionary of the Bible;* there was both a Bible and a Lectionary, and a thin book called *Sadhana: A Way to God* by Anthony de Mello, S.J.; there was *The Autobiography of St. Ignatius Loyola* and a copy of the *Spiritual Exercises*—there were many other books, too. Altogether, there were more books than there were Hawaiian shirts and clerical collars combined.

"And where will you be staying—for three months?" the customs official asked Martin Mills, whose left eye was growing tired from all the winking.

"At St. Ignatius in Mazagaon," the Jesuit replied.

"Oh, of course!" said the customs official. "I greatly admire your work!" he whispered. Then he gave the surprised Jesuit one more wink for the road.

A fellow Christian where one least expected to meet one! the new missionary thought.

All this winking would leave poor Martin Mills ill prepared for the "native behavior" of most Bombayites, who find winking an exceptionally aggressive, suggestive and rude thing to do. But thus did the scholastic pass through customs and into the shit-smelling night air—all the while expecting a friendly greeting from one of his brother Jesuits.

Where were they? the new missionary wondered. Delayed in traffic? Outside the airport there was much confusion; at the same time, there was little traffic. There were many standing taxis, all parked at the edge of an immense darkness, as if the airport were not huge and teeming (as Martin Mills had first thought), but a fragile wilderness outpost in a vast desert, where unseen fires were dying out and unseen squatters were defecating, without interruption, throughout the night.

Then, like flies, the taxi-wallas lighted on him; they pecked at his clothes, they tugged at his suitcase, which—although it was extremely heavy—he would not relinquish.

"No, thank you, I'm being met," he said. He realized that his Hindi had abandoned him, which was just as well; he spoke it very poorly, anyway. The weary missionary suspected himself of suffering from that paranoia which is commonplace to first-time travelers to the East, for he grew increasingly apprehensive of the way the taxi-wallas looked at him. Some were in utter awe; others appeared to want to kill him. They assumed he was Inspector Dhar, and although they flitted near to him like flies, and darted away from him like flies, they seemed entirely too dangerous for flies.

After an hour, Martin Mills was still standing there, warding off newly arrived flies; the old flies hovered at a distance, still watching him but not bothering to approach him again. The missionary was so tired, he got the idea that the taxi-wallas were of the hyena class of animal, and that they were waiting for him to exhibit a loss of vital signs before they swarmed over him en masse. A prayer fluttered to his lips, but he was too exhausted to utter it. He was thinking that the other missionaries were perhaps too old to have met his plane, for he'd been informed of their advanced ages. He also knew about the jubilee celebration that was pending; surely the proper recognition of 125 years of service to God and to humanity was more worthwhile than meeting a newcomer's plane. This was Martin Mills in a nutshell: he practiced self-deprecation to such a degree that it had become a vanity with him.

He shifted the suitcase from one hand to the other; he wouldn't allow it to rest on the pavement, not only because this sign of weakness would invite the lingering taxi-wallas to approach him but also because the weight of the suitcase was steadily becoming a welcome chastisement of his flesh. Martin Mills found a certain focus, a pleasing purpose, to the specificity of such pain. It was neither as exquisite nor as unending a pain as the leg iron when properly tightened around the thigh; it wasn't as sudden or breathtaking a pain as the whip on his bare back. Yet he greeted the pain of the suitcase warmly, and the suitcase itself bore a reminder of the ongoing task of Martin's formation, of his search for God's will and the strength of his self-denial. Inscribed in the old leather was the Latin *Nostris* ("Ours")—meaning *us Jesuits,* meaning "the Life" (as it was called) in the Society of Jesus.

The suitcase itself called to memory Martin's two years in the novitiate at St. Aloysius; his room had only a table, a straight-backed chair, a bed and a two-inch-high wooden kneeler. As his lips formed the word *Nostris,* he could summon to his memory the little bell that signaled *flagellatio;* he recalled the 30 days of his first silent retreat. He still took strength from these two years: pray, shave, work, be silent, study, pray. His was no fit of devotion but an orderly submission to rules: perpetual poverty, chastity, obedience. Obedience to a religious superior, yes; but, more important, obedience to a community life. Such rules made him feel free. Yet, on the matter of obedience, it haunted him that his previous superior had once criticized him on the grounds that Martin Mills seemed more suited to a monastic order—a *stricter* order, such as the Carthusians. Jesuits are meant to go out into the world; if not on our terms "worldly," they are also not monks.

"I am *not* a monk," Martin Mills said aloud. The nearby taxi-wallas understood this as a summons; once again, they swarmed around him.

"Avoid worldliness," Martin cautioned himself. He smiled tolerantly at the milling taxi-wallas. There had been an admonition in Latin above his bed at St. Aloysius; it was an indirect reminder that a man should make his own bed—*etiam si sacerdotes sint* ("even if they be priests"). Therefore, Martin Mills decided, he would get himself into Bombay.

The Wrong Taxi-Walla

Of the taxi-wallas, there was only one who looked strong enough to handle the suitcase. He was tall and bearded, with a swarthy complexion and an exceedingly sharp, aggressive thrust to his nose.

"St. Ignatius, Mazagaon," Martin said to this taxi-walla, who struck the missionary as a university student with a demanding night job—an admirable young man, probably paying his way through school.

With a savage glare, the young man took the suitcase and hurled it into his waiting taxi. All the taxi-wallas had been waiting for the Ambassador with the thug dwarf driver, for none of them had really believed that Inspector Dhar would stoop to use any other cab. There'd been many depictions of taxi-wallas in Inspector Dhar films; they were always portrayed as reckless and crazy.

The particular taxi-walla who'd seized the missionary's suitcase and now watched Martin Mills slide into the back seat was a violent-minded young man named Bahadur. He'd just been expelled from a hotel-management school for cheating on a food-services exam—he'd plagiarized the answer to a simple question about catering. ("Bahadur" means "brave.") He'd also just driven to the airport from Bombay and had seen the posters advertising *Inspector Dhar and the Towers of Silence*, which had greatly offended his loyal sensibilities. Although taxi driving wasn't his preferred profession, Bahadur was grateful to his present employer, Mr. Mirza. Mr. Mirza was a Parsi; doubtless *Inspector Dhar and the Towers of Silence* would be monstrously offensive to Mr. Mirza. Bahadur felt honor-bound to represent the feelings of his boss.

Not surprisingly, Bahadur had hated all the earlier Dhar films. Before the release of this new offense, Bahadur had been hoping that Inspector Dhar would be murdered by offended hijras or offended female prostitutes. Bahadur generally favored the notion of murdering famous people, for he found it offensive to *un*famous people that only very few people were famous. Moreover, he felt that driving a taxi was beneath him; he was doing it only to prove to a rich uncle that he was capable of "mingling with the masses." It was Bahadur's expectation that this uncle would soon send him off to another school. The present interim was unfortunate, but one could do worse than work for Mr. Mirza; like Vinod, Mr. Mirza operated a privately owned taxi company. Meanwhile, in his spare time, Bahadur was seeking to improve his English by concentrating on vulgar and profane expressions. Should he ever encounter a famous person, Bahadur wished to have such expressions on the tip of his tongue.

The reputations of famous people were entirely inflated, Bahadur knew. He'd heard stories of how tough Inspector Dhar was supposed to be, also that Dhar was a weight lifter! One look at the missionary's scrawny arms proved this to be a typical lie. Movie hype! Bahadur thought. He liked to drive by the film studios, hoping to give actresses a ride. But no one important ever chose his taxi, and at Asha Pictures—and at Rajkamal Studio and Famous Studio and Central Studio—he'd been accosted by the police for loitering. *Fuck* these film people! Bahadur thought.

"I suppose you know where St. Ignatius is," Martin Mills said nervously, once they were under way. "It's a Jesuit mission, a church, a school," he added, looking for some sign of recognition in the glare of the taxi-walla. When the scholastic saw that the young man was watching him in the rearview mirror, Martin did the friendly thing—at least he presumed it was the native-behavior thing to do. He winked.

That does it! Bahadur thought. Whether the wink was condescending, or whether it was the lewd invitation of a homosexual, Bahadur had made up his mind. Inspector Dhar should *not* be allowed to get away with the violent farce he made of Bombay life. In the middle of the night, Dhar wanted to go to St. Ignatius! What was he going to do there? Pray?

In addition to everything else that was fake about Inspector Dhar, Bahadur decided that the man was a fake Hindu, too. Inspector Dhar was a bleeding Christian!

"You're supposed to be a Hindu," Bahadur told the Jesuit.

Martin Mills was thrilled. His first religious confrontation in the missionary kingdom—his first Hindu! He knew they were the majority religion here.

"Well . . . well," Martin said cheerfully. "Men of all faiths must be brothers."

"Fuck your Jesus, and fuck you," Bahadur remarked coldly.

"Well . . . well," Martin said. Possibly there was a time to wink and a time *not* to wink, the new missionary thought.

Proselyte-Hunting Among the Prostitutes

Through the smoldering, reeking darkness, the taxi careened, but darkness had never intimidated Martin Mills. In crowds, he could be anxious, but the black of night did not menace him. Nor did it concern the missionary that he was in danger of some violence. He meditated on the unfulfilled dream of the Middle Ages, which was to win back Jerusalem for Christ. He contemplated that St. Ignatius Loyola's own pilgrimage to Jerusalem had been a journey fraught with endless dangers and accidents. Ignatius's attempted conquest of the Holy Land was a failure, for he was sent back; yet the saint's desire to rescue unsaved souls remained ardent. It was always the Ignatian purpose to conform to the will of God. It was no coincidence that, to this end, the *Spiritual Exercises* of St. Ignatius began with a vivid representation of hell in all its horror. The fear of God was purifying; it had long been so to Martin Mills. To see both the fires of hell and a union with God in mystical ecstasy, one needed only to follow the *Spiritual Exercises* and call upon "the eye of the imagination," for the missionary had no doubt that this was the clearest eye of all.

"Toil and will," Martin Mills said aloud. This was his creed.

"I said, *fuck* your Jesus, and *fuck you!*" the taxi-walla repeated.

"Bless you," Martin said. "Even you, and whatever you do to me, is God's will—though you know not what you do."

Most of all, Martin admired Ignatius Loyola's notable encounter with the Moor on a mule and their ensuing discussion of the Holy Virgin. The Moor said he could believe that Our Lady had conceived without a man, but he could *not* believe that she'd remained a virgin after giving birth. After the Moor rode on, young Ignatius thought that he should hurry after the Muslim and kill him. He felt obliged to defend Our Lady's honor. The defaming of the Virgin's postbirth vaginal condition was gross and unacceptable behavior. Ignatius, as always, sought God's will on the matter. Where the road parted, he let his own mule's reins go slack; if the animal followed the Moor, Ignatius would kill the infidel. But the mule chose the other road.

"And *fuck* your St. Ignatius!" the taxi-walla shouted.

"St. Ignatius is where I would like to go," Martin replied calmly. "But take me where you will." Where they went, the missionary believed, would be God's will. Martin Mills was just the passenger.

He thought of the late Father de Mello's renowned book *Christian Exercises in Eastern Form;* so many of these exercises had helped him in the past. For example, there was that exercise which concerned the "healing of hurtful memories." Whenever Martin Mills was troubled by the shame his parents had caused him, or by his seeming inability to love and forgive and honor his parents, he followed Father de Mello's exercise verbatim. "Return to some unpleasant event"; such events were never hard to recall, but the selection of *which* horror to revisit was always an arduous decision. "Now place yourself before Christ Crucified"—that always had a certain power. Even the depravities of Veronica Rose paled before such an agony; even the self-destruction of Danny Mills seemed a trifling pain. "Keep commuting between the unpleasant event and the scene of Jesus on the Cross"; for years, Martin Mills had engaged in such commuting. Father de Mello was a hero to him. He had been born in Bombay, and until his death was the director of the Sadhana Institute of Pastoral Counseling (near Poona); it had been Father de Mello who had inspired Martin Mills to come to India.

Now, as the embracing darkness gradually yielded to the lights of Bombay, the bodies of the sidewalk sleepers appeared in mounds. The moonlight glinted off Mahim Bay. Martin couldn't smell the horses as the taxi rocketed past the Mahalaxmi Race Course, but he could see the dark silhouette of Haji Ali's Tomb; the slender minarets stood out against the fish-scale glint of the Arabian Sea. Then the taxi veered away from the moonlit ocean, and the missionary saw the sleeping city come to life—if the eternal sexual activity of Kamathipura could fairly be called life. It wasn't a life that Martin Mills had ever known—it was nothing he'd ever imagined—and he prayed that his brief glimpse of the Muslim mausoleum wouldn't be the last holy edifice he'd see in his allotted time on this mortal earth.

He saw the brothels overflowing into the little lanes. He saw the sex-stoned faces of the men let loose from the Wetness Cabaret; the last show was over, and the men who couldn't yet bear to go home were wandering. And just when Martin Mills thought he'd encountered a greater evil than St. Ignatius Loyola had met on the streets of Rome, the taxi-walla jostled and edged his way into a darker hell. There were suddenly those prostitutes in human cages on Falkland Road.

"Won't the cage girls just love to get a look at *you!*" cried Bahadur, who saw himself as Inspector Dhar's designated persecutor.

Martin Mills remembered how Ignatius had raised money among rich people and founded an asylum for fallen women. It was in Rome where the saint had announced that he would sacrifice his life if he could prevent the sins of a single prostitute on a single night.

"Thank you for bringing me here," the missionary said to the taxi-walla, who screeched to a halt in front of a compelling display of eunuch-transvestites in their cages. Bahadur assumed that the hijra prostitutes were by far the angriest at Inspector Dhar. But, to the taxi-walla's surprise, Martin Mills cheerfully opened the rear door and stepped into Falkland Road with a look of eager anticipation. He took his heavy suitcase from the trunk; and when the taxi-walla hurled the money for the fare at the missionary's feet and spat on it—for the trip from the airport had been prepaid—Martin retrieved the wet money and handed it back to Bahadur.

"No, no—you've done your job. I am where I should be," the missionary said. A circle of pickpockets and street prostitutes with their pimps
were slowly surrounding the scholastic, but Bahadur wanted the hijras
to be certain to see their enemy, and so he pushed against the gathering
crowd.

"Dhar—Inspector *Dhar*! Dhar! Dhar!" the taxi-walla cried. But this
was entirely unnecessary, for the word that Dhar was on Falkland Road
had traveled ahead of the taxi-walla's cries. Martin Mills quite easily
made his own way through the crowd; the degraded women in those
cages were the ones he wished to address. (It never occurred to him, of
course, that they weren't really women.)

"Please, let me speak with you," the missionary said to a transvestite
in his cage. Most of the hijras were, at first, too stunned to attack the
hated actor. "Surely you must know of the diseases—nowadays, of the
certain death you are exposing yourselves to! But I tell you, if you want
to be saved, that is all you need—to *want* to be."

Two pickpockets and several pimps were fighting over the money
that Martin had tried to give back to the taxi-walla. Bahadur had already
been beaten to his knees, and several street prostitutes continued to kick
at him. But Martin Mills was oblivious to what was behind him. The
apparent women in the cages faced him, and it was only to them that he
spoke. "St. Ignatius," he said. "In Mazagaon? You must know it. I can
always be found there. You have only to come there."

It is intriguing to imagine how Father Julian and Father Cecil might
have responded to this generous invitation, for surely the mission's
125th jubilee would be a much more colorful celebration with the added
presence of several eunuch-transvestite prostitutes in search of salvation. Unfortunately, the Father Rector and the senior priest were not on
hand to witness Martin Mills's extraordinary proposition. Did Martin
suppose that if the prostitutes arrived at St. Ignatius during school hours,
the schoolchildren might benefit from the visible conversion of these
fallen women?

"If you feel but the slightest remorse, you must take this as a sign that
you can be saved," the scholastic told them.

It wasn't a hijra who struck the first blow, but one of the street
prostitutes; probably she was feeling ignored. She shoved Martin in the
small of his back and he stumbled forward on one knee; then the pimps
and pickpockets pulled his suitcase away from him—that was when the
hijras became involved. After all, Dhar had been speaking to *them;* they
didn't want their territory, or their vengeance, trespassed on—certainly

not by this common rabble off the street. The transvestite prostitutes easily beat away the street prostitutes and their pimps, and not even the pickpockets could escape with the heavy suitcase, which the hijras opened for themselves.

They wouldn't touch the wrinkled black suit and the black shirts or the clerical collars—these weren't their style—but the Hawaiian shirts were appealing to them, and they quickly took these. Then one of them stripped the shirt off Martin Mills, being careful not to tear it, and when the missionary was naked above his waist, one of the hijras discovered the whip with the braided cords, which was too tempting to ignore. With the first of the stinging lashes from the whip, Martin lay on his stomach; then he curled himself into a ball. He wouldn't cover his face, for it mattered too much to him that he clasped his hands together in prayer; thus he maintained the extreme conviction that even such a beating as this was *ad majorem Dei Gloriam* ("to the great glory of God").

The transvestite prostitutes were respectful of all the assembled evidence of education that was contained in the suitcase; even in their excitement to each take a turn with the whip, they wouldn't tear or wrinkle a page of a single book. The leg iron, however, was misinterpreted by them, as were the *culpa* beads; a transvestite prostitute tried to eat the beads before he threw them away. As for the leg iron, the hijras didn't know it went around the thigh—or else they simply thought it would be more suitable to attach the device around Inspector Dhar's neck, which they did. It wasn't too tight a fit, but the wire prongs had raked the missionary's face—the hijras were so impatient that they'd scraped the leg iron over their victim's head—and now the prongs dug into Martin's throat, which caused a multitude of minor cuts. The missionary's torso was striped with blood.

Gamely, he tried to stand. As he kept trying, he faced the whip. The transvestites stepped away from him, for he wasn't behaving as they'd expected. He didn't fight back; he didn't beg for his life, either. "It is you, and everything that happens to you, that I care for!" Martin Mills called to them. "Though you revile me, and I am nothing, I want only for you to save yourselves. I can show you how, but only if you let me."

The hijras passed the whip, but there was noticeably less enthusiasm among them. When one would hold it, he would quickly pass it on, without taking a whack. The raised red welts covered Martin's exposed flesh—they were especially startling on his face—and the blood from the wrongly placed leg iron streaked his chest. He protected not himself but his books! He closed the suitcase safely around these treasures of his learning, and *still* he beseeched the prostitutes to join him.

"Take me to Mazagaon," he said to them. "Take me to St. Ignatius, and you shall also be welcome there." To those few of them who understood what he said, the concept was preposterous. To their surprise, the man before them was a physical weakling, but his courage seemed unsurpassed; it wasn't the kind of toughness they'd anticipated. Suddenly, no one wanted to hurt him. They hated him; yet he made them feel ashamed.

But the street prostitutes and their pimps, and the pickpockets—they would have made short work of him, just as soon as the hijras left him. This was precisely when that familiar off-white Ambassador, which all night had cruised between Kamathipura and Grant Road and Falkland Road, cruised by them again. In the driver's-side window, soberly looking them over, was the driver they all thought of as Dhar's thug dwarf.

One can imagine Vinod's surprise upon seeing his famous client stripped of half his clothes and bloodied. The wretched villains had even shaved off Inspector Dhar's mustache! This was a humiliation beyond the obvious pain that the beloved movie star had suffered. And what ghastly instrument of torture had the filthy prostitutes fitted around the actor's neck? It looked like a dog's collar, only the spikes were on the inside. Furthermore, poor Dhar was as pale and scrawny as a cadaver. It looked like Vinod's famous client had lost 20 pounds!

A pimp with a big brass ring of keys scratched a key against the driver's-side door of the Ambassador—all the while meeting Vinod's eyes, straight on. He didn't see Vinod reach under his specially constructed car seat, where the dwarf driver kept a ready supply of squash-racquet handles. There was confusion regarding what happened next. Some claimed that the dwarf's taxi swerved and deliberately ran over the pimp's foot; others explained that the Ambassador jumped the curb and that it was the panicked crowd that pushed the pimp—either way, his foot was run over by the car. All agreed that Vinod was hard to see in the crowd; he was so much shorter than everyone else. His presence could be detected by the wary, however, for everywhere people were dropping from sight, clutching their knees or their wrists and writhing on the garbage-strewn pavement. Vinod swung the squash-racquet handles at a level equal to most people's knees. Their cries commingled with the cries of the cage girls on Falkland Road continuously hawking their wares.

When Martin Mills saw the grim face of the dwarf who was whacking his way toward him, the scholastic thought that his time had come. He repeated what Jesus said to Pilate [John 18:36], "My kingdom is not of this world." Then he turned to face the oncoming dwarf. "I forgive you," Martin said; he bowed his head, as if awaiting the executioner's blow. It didn't occur to him that if he *hadn't* bowed his head, Vinod never could have reached his head with the racquet handles.

But Vinod simply grabbed the missionary by the rear pocket of his pants and steered him to the taxi. When Martin was rescued—pinned under the weight of his suitcase in the back seat of the car—the scholastic foolishly struggled, albeit briefly, to return to Falkland Road.

"Wait!" he cried. "I want my whip—that's *my* whip!"

Vinod had already swung a racquet handle and cracked the wrist of the unfortunate hijra who was the last to hold the whip. The dwarf easily retrieved Martin Mills's mortification toy and handed it to him. "Bless you!" the scholastic said. The doors of the Ambassador slammed solidly around him; the sudden acceleration pressed him against the seat. "St. Ignatius," he told the brutal driver. Vinod thought that Dhar was praying, which was dismaying to the dwarf because he'd never thought of Dhar as a religious man.

At the intersection of Falkland Road and Grant Road, a boy who was a tea-server for one of the brothels threw a glass of tea at the passing taxi. Vinod just kept going, although his stubby fingers reached under the car seat to reassure himself that the squash-racquet handles were properly in place.

Before the taxi turned onto Marine Drive, Vinod stopped the car and lowered the rear windows; he knew how Dhar enjoyed the smell of the sea. "You sure are fooling me," Vinod said to his battered client. "I am thinking you are sleeping the whole night on Daruwalla's balcony!" But the missionary was asleep. In the rearview mirror, the sight of him took Vinod's breath away. It wasn't the lash marks on his swollen face, or even his bare, bloodied torso; it was the spiked leg iron around his neck, for the dwarf had seen the terrible depictions that the Christians worshiped—their gory versions of Christ on the Cross—and to Vinod it appeared that Inspector Dhar had undertaken the role of Christ. However, his crown of thorns had slipped; the cruel device gripped the famous actor by his throat.

All Together—in One Small Apartment

As for Dhar, the *real* Dhar, a smog the consistency and color of egg whites had rolled over Dr. Daruwalla's balcony, where the actor was still sleeping. Had he looked, he couldn't have seen through this soup—at least not six floors below him to the predawn sidewalk, where Vinod struggled with the movie star's semiconscious twin. Nor did Dhar hear the predictable eruption from the first-floor dogs. Vinod allowed the missionary to lean heavily on him, while the dwarf dragged the suitcase carrying Martin Mills's education across the lobby to the forbidden lift. A first-floor apartment owner, a member of the Residents' Society, got a glimpse of the thug driver and his mangled companion before the elevator door closed.

Martin Mills, even as mauled and mindless of his surroundings as he was, was surprised by the elevator and the modernity of the apartment building, for he knew that the mission school and its venerable church were 125 years old. The sound of savage dogs seemed out of place.

"St. Ignatius?" the missionary asked the Good Samaritan midget.

"You are not needing a saint—you are needing a doctor!" the dwarf told him.

"Actually, I *know* a doctor in Bombay. He's a friend of my mother and father—a certain Dr. Daruwalla," Martin Mills said.

Vinod was truly alarmed. The lashes from the whip and even the bleeding from the leg iron around the poor man's neck seemed superficial; but this incomprehensible muttering about Dr. Daruwalla was an indication to Vinod that the movie star was suffering from some sort of amnesia. A serious head injury, perhaps!

"Of *course* you are knowing Dr. Daruwalla!" Vinod shouted. "We are going to see Dr. Daruwalla!"

"Ah, so you know him, *too*?" said the astonished scholastic.

"Try to not be moving your head," the worried dwarf replied.

In a reference to the echoing dogs, which Vinod completely failed to grasp, Martin Mills said, "It sounds like a veterinarian's—I thought he was an orthopedist."

"Of *course* he is being an orthopedist!" Vinod cried. Standing on tiptoe, the dwarf tried to peer into Martin's ears, as if he were expecting to see some stray brain matter there. But Vinod wasn't tall enough.

Dr. Daruwalla woke to the distant orchestra of the dogs. From the sixth floor, their barks and howls were muted but nonetheless identifiable; the doctor had no doubt as to the cause of their cacophony.

"That damn dwarf!" he said aloud, to which Julia didn't respond; she was familiar with the many things her husband said in his sleep. But when Farrokh got out of bed and put on his robe, Julia was instantly awake.

"Is it Vinod again?" she asked him.

"I assume so," Dr. Daruwalla replied.

It was a little before 5:00 in the morning when the doctor crept past the closed sliding-glass doors that led to the balcony, which was completely enveloped in a mournful-looking mist. The smog had mingled with a dense sea fog. The doctor couldn't see Dhar's cot or the Tortoise mosquito coils with which the actor surrounded himself whenever he slept on the balcony. In the foyer, Farrokh seized a dusty umbrella; he was hoping to give Vinod a good scare. Then the doctor opened his apartment door. The dwarf and the missionary had just exited from the lift; when Dr. Daruwalla first saw Martin Mills, the doctor feared that Dhar had violently shaved off his mustache in the smog—thus inflicting on himself a multitude of razor cuts—and then, doubtless depressed, the much-reviled actor had jumped off the sixth-floor balcony.

As for the missionary, he was taken aback to see a man in a black kimono holding a black umbrella—an ominous image. But the umbrella was undaunting to Vinod, who slipped close to Dr. Daruwalla and whispered, "I am finding him preaching to transvestite prostitutes—the hijras are almost killing him!"

Farrokh knew who Martin Mills was as soon as the missionary spoke: "I believe you've met my mother and father—my name is Martin, Martin Mills."

"Please come in—I've been expecting you," Dr. Daruwalla said, taking the beaten man's arm.

"You *have?*" said Martin Mills.

"There is being brain damage!" Vinod whispered to the doctor, who supported the wobbly missionary into the bathroom, where he told Martin to strip. Then the doctor prepared an Epsom-salts bath. While the bath was filling, Farrokh got Julia out of bed and told her to get rid of Vinod.

"Who's taking a bath at this hour?" she asked her husband.

"It's John D.'s twin," Dr. Daruwalla said.

Free Will

Julia had managed to coax Vinod no farther than the foyer when the phone rang. She answered quickly. Vinod could hear the entire conversation because the man on the other end of the phone was screaming. It was Mr. Munim, the first-floor member of the Residents' Society.

"I saw him getting on the lift! He woke all the dogs! I saw him—your dwarf!" Mr. Munim shouted.

Julia said, "I beg your pardon—we don't own a dwarf."

"You don't fool me!" Mr. Munim hollered. "That movie star's dwarf—that's who I mean!"

"We don't own a movie star, either," Julia told him.

"You are violating a stated rule!" Mr. Munim screamed.

"I don't know what you mean—you must be out of your mind," Julia replied.

"The taxi-walla used the lift—that midget thug!" Mr. Munim cried.

"Don't make me call the police," Julia said; then she hung up.

"I am using the stairs, but they are making me limp—the whole six floors," Vinod said. Martyrdom strangely suited him, Julia thought, but she realized that Vinod was lingering in the foyer for a purpose. "There are being *five* umbrellas in your umbrella stand," the dwarf observed.

"Would you like to borrow one, Vinod?" Julia asked him.

"Only for helping me on the stairs," Vinod replied. "I am needing a cane." He'd left the squash-racquet handles in his taxi; were he to encounter either a first-floor dog or Mr. Munim, Vinod wanted a weapon. Therefore, he took an umbrella with him; Julia let him out the kitchen door, which led to the back stairs.

"Maybe you are never seeing me again," Vinod told her. As the dwarf peered down the stairwell, Julia noticed that he was slightly shorter than the umbrella that he'd chosen; Vinod had taken the biggest umbrella.

In the bathtub, Martin Mills looked as if he welcomed the stings from his raised red welts, and he never flinched while Dr. Daruwalla sponged off the multitude of minor wounds caused by the gruesome leg iron; the doctor thought that the missionary appeared to miss the leg iron after it had been removed, and Martin twice expressed concern that he'd left his whip in the heroic dwarf's car.

"Vinod will surely return it to you," Dr. Daruwalla said. The doctor was not as amazed by the missionary's story as the missionary himself was amazed; given the magnitude of the mistaken identity, Dr. Daruwalla was astonished that Martin Mills was still alive—not to mention that his wounds were minor. And the more the missionary babbled on and on about his experience, the less he bore any resemblance, in Farrokh's eyes, to his taciturn twin. Dhar didn't babble.

"Well, I mean I *knew* I wasn't among Christians," Martin Mills said, "but still I hardly expected the *violent* hostility toward Christianity that I encountered."

"Now, now—I wouldn't jump to *that* conclusion," Dr. Daruwalla cautioned the agitated scholastic. "There is some sensitivity, however, toward proselytizing . . . of any kind."

"Saving souls is *not* proselytizing," Martin Mills said defensively.

"Well, as you say, you were not exactly in Christian territory," Dr. Daruwalla replied.

"How many of those prostitutes are carrying the AIDS virus?" Martin asked.

"I'm an orthopedist," the doctor reminded the scholastic, "but people who know say forty percent—some say sixty."

"Either way," said Martin Mills, "that's Christian territory."

For the first time, Farrokh considered that the madman before him posed a threat to himself that might exceed the danger presented by his striking resemblance to Inspector Dhar.

"But I thought you were an English teacher," said Dr. Daruwalla. "As a former student of the place, I can assure you, St. Ignatius is first and foremost a *school.*" The doctor knew the Father Rector; Dr. Daruwalla could well anticipate that this was precisely what Father Julian would have to say about the matter of saving prostitutes' souls. But as Farrokh watched Martin step naked from the bath—whereupon, unmindful of his wounds, the missionary began to vigorously towel himself dry—the doctor further anticipated that the Father Rector and all the aged defenders of the faith at St. Ignatius would have a hard time convincing such a zealous scholastic as this that his duties were restricted to improving the English of the upper classes. For as he rubbed and rubbed the towel against his lash marks until his face and torso were striped as bright red as when the whip had only just struck him, Martin Mills was all the while thinking of a reply. Like the crafty Jesuit that he was, he began his answer with a question.

"Aren't you a Christian?" the missionary asked the doctor. "I believe my father said you were converted, but that you're not a Roman Catholic."

"Yes, that's true," Dr. Daruwalla replied cautiously. He gave Martin

Mills a clean pair of his best silk pajamas, but the scholastic preferred to stand naked.

"Are you familiar with the Calvinist, Jansenist position in regard to free will?" Martin asked Farrokh. "I'm greatly oversimplifying, but this was that dispute born of Luther and those Protestant divines of the Reformation—namely, the idea that we're doomed by original sin and can expect salvation only through divine grace. Luther denied that good works could contribute to our salvation. Calvin further denied that our faith could save us. According to Calvin, we are all predestined to be saved—or not. Do you believe that?"

By the way the logic of the Jesuit was leaning, Farrokh guessed that he should *not* believe that, and so he said, "No—not exactly."

"Well, good—then you're not a Jansenist," the scholastic said. "They were very discouraging—their doctrine of grace over that of free will was quite defeatist, really. They made us all feel that there was absolutely nothing we could do to be saved—in short, why bother with good works? And so what if we sin?"

"Are you still oversimplifying?" asked Dr. Daruwalla. The Jesuit regarded the doctor with sly respect; he also took this interruption as a useful time in which to put on the doctor's silk pajamas.

"If you're suggesting that it's almost impossible to reconcile the concept of free will with our belief in an omnipotent and omniscient God, I agree with you—it's difficult," Martin said. "The question of the relationship between human will and divine omnipotence . . . is that your question?"

Dr. Daruwalla guessed that this *should* be his question, and so he said, "Yes—something like that."

"Well, that really *is* an interesting question," the Jesuit said. "I just hate it when people try to reduce the spiritual world with purely mechanical theories—those behaviorists, for example. Who cares about Loeb's plant-lice theories or Pavlov's dog?" Dr. Daruwalla nodded, but he didn't dare speak; he'd never heard of plant lice. He'd heard of Pavlov's dog, of course; he could even recall what made the dog salivate and what the saliva meant.

"We must seem excessively strict to you—we Catholics to you Protestants, I mean," Martin said. Dr. Daruwalla shook his head. "Oh, yes we do!" the missionary said. "We are a theology of rewards and punishments, which are meted out in the life after death. Compared to you, we make much of sin. We Jesuits, however, tend to minimize those sins of thought."

"As opposed to those of deed," interjected Dr. Daruwalla, for although this was obvious and totally unnecessary to say, the doctor felt that only a fool would have nothing to say, and he'd been saying nothing.

"To us—to us Catholics, I mean—you Protestants appear, at times, to overemphasize the human propensity toward evil . . ." And here the missionary paused; but Dr. Daruwalla, unsure whether he should nod or shake his head, just stared stupidly at the bathwater spiraling down the drain, as if the water were his own thoughts, escaping him.

"Do you know Leibniz?" the Jesuit suddenly asked him.

"Well, in university . . . but that was years ago," the doctor said.

"The Leibniz assumption is that man's freedom was not taken from him by his fall, which makes Leibniz quite a friend of ours—of us Jesuits, I mean," Martin said. "There is some Leibniz I can never forget, such as, 'Although the impulse and the help come from God, they are at all times accompanied by a certain co-operation of man himself; if not, we could not say that we had acted'—but you agree, don't you?"

"Yes, of course," said Dr. Daruwalla.

"Well, you see, that's why I can't be *just* an English teacher," the Jesuit replied. "Naturally, I shall endeavor to improve the children's English—and to the most perfect degree possible. But, given that I am free to act—'although the impulse and the help come from God,' of course—I must do what I can, not only to save *my* soul but to rescue the souls of others."

"I see," said Dr. Daruwalla, who was also beginning to understand why the enraged transvestite prostitutes had failed to make much of a dent in the flesh *or* the indomitable will of Martin Mills.

Furthermore, the doctor found that he was standing in his own living room and watching Martin lie down on the couch, without the slightest recollection of having left the bathroom. That was when the missionary handed the leg iron to the doctor, who received the instrument reluctantly.

"I can see I will not be needing this here," the scholastic said. "There will be sufficient adversity without it. St. Ignatius Loyola also changed his mind in regard to these weapons of mortification."

"He did?" said Farrokh.

"I think he overused them—but only out of a positive abhorrence of his earlier sins," the Jesuit said. "In fact, in the later version of the *Spiritual Exercises,* St. Ignatius urges against such scourges of the flesh—he is also opposed to heavy fasting."

"So am I," said Dr. Daruwalla, who didn't know what to do with the cruel leg iron.

"Please throw it away," Martin said to him. "And perhaps you'd be so kind as to tell the dwarf to keep the whip—I don't want it."

Dr. Daruwalla knew all about Vinod's racquet handles; the prospect of what use the dwarf might make of the whip was chilling. Then the doctor noticed that Martin Mills had fallen asleep. With his fingers interlocked on his chest, and with an utterly beatific expression, the missionary resembled a martyr en route to the heavenly kingdom.

Farrokh brought Julia into the living room to see him. At first, she wouldn't approach past the glass-topped table—she viewed him as one might view a contaminated corpse—but the doctor encouraged her to take a closer look. The nearer Julia drew to Martin Mills, the more relaxed she became. It was as if—at least, when he was asleep—Martin had a pacifying effect on everyone around him. Eventually, Julia sat on the floor beside the couch. She would say later that he reminded her of John D. as a much younger, more carefree man, although Farrokh maintained that Martin Mills was simply the result of no weight lifting and no beer—meaning that he had no muscles but that he had no belly, either.

Without remembering when he sat down, the doctor found himself on the floor beside his wife. They were both sitting beside the couch, as if transfixed by the sleeping body, when Dhar came in from the balcony to have a shower and to brush his teeth; from Dhar's perspective, Farrokh and Julia appeared to be praying. Then the movie star saw the dead person—at least, the person looked dead to Dhar—and without taking too close a look, he said, "Who's that?"

Farrokh and Julia were shocked that John D. didn't immediately recognize his twin; after all, an actor is especially familiar with his own facial features—and under a variety of makeup, including the radical altering of his age—but Dhar had never seen such an expression on his own face. It's doubtful that Dhar's face ever reflected beatification, for not even in his sleep had Inspector Dhar imagined the happiness of heaven. Dhar had many expressions, but none of them was saintly.

Finally, the actor whispered, "Well, okay, I see *who* it is, but what's he doing here? Is he going to die?"

"He's trying to be a priest," Farrokh whispered.

"Jesus Christ!" John D. said. Either he should have whispered or else the particular name he spoke was one that Martin Mills was prone to hear; a smile of such immense gratitude crossed the missionary's sleeping face that Dhar and the Daruwallas felt suddenly ashamed. Without a word to one another, they tiptoed into the kitchen, as if they were unanimously embarrassed that they'd been spying on a sleeping man; what truly had disturbed them, and had made them feel as if they didn't belong where they were, was the utter contentment of a man momentarily at peace with his soul—although none of them could have identified what it was that so upset them.

"What's wrong with him?" Dhar asked.

"Nothing's wrong with him!" Dr. Daruwalla said; then he wondered why he'd said that about a man who'd been whipped and beaten while he was proselytizing among transvestite prostitutes. "I should have told you he was coming," the doctor added sheepishly, to which John D. merely rolled his eyes; his anger was often understated. Julia rolled her eyes, too.

"As far as I'm concerned," Farrokh said to John D., "it's entirely your decision as to whether or not you want to let him know that you exist. Although I don't know if *now* would be the right time to tell him."

"Forget about now," Dhar said. "Tell me what he's like."

Dr. Daruwalla could not utter the first word that came to his lips—the word was "crazy." On second thought, he almost said, Like *you*, except that *he* talks. But this was such a contradictory concept—the very idea of a Dhar who talked might be insulting to Dhar.

"I said, what's he like?" John D. repeated.

"I saw him only when he was asleep," Julia told John D. Both of them were staring at Farrokh, whose mind—on the matter of what Martin Mills was "like"—was truly blank. Not a single picture came to his mind, although the missionary had managed to argue with him, lecture to him and even educate him—and most of this had transpired while the zealot was naked.

"He's somewhat zealous," the doctor offered cautiously.

"Zealous?" said Dhar.

"*Liebchen,* is that all you can say?" Julia asked Farrokh. "I heard him talking and talking in the bathroom. He must have been saying *something!*"

"In the bathroom?" John D. asked.

"He's very determined," Farrokh blurted.

"I guess that would follow from being 'zealous,' " said Inspector Dhar; he was at his most sarcastic.

It was exasperating to Dr. Daruwalla that they expected him to be able to summarize the Jesuit's character on the basis of this one peculiar meeting.

The doctor didn't know the history of that other zealot—the greatest zealot of the 16th century, St. Ignatius Loyola—who had so inspired Martin Mills. When Ignatius died without ever having permitted a portrait of himself to be painted, the brothers of the order sought to have a portrait made of the dead man. A famous painter tried and failed. The disciples declared that the death mask, which was the work of an unknown, was also not the true face of the father of the Jesuits. Three other artists tried and failed to capture him, but they had only the death mask for their model. It was finally decided that God did not wish for Ignatius Loyola, His servant, to be painted. Dr. Daruwalla couldn't have known how greatly Martin Mills loved this story, but it doubtless would have pleased the new missionary to see how the doctor struggled to describe even such a fledgling servant of God as this mere scholastic. Farrokh felt the right word come to his lips, but then it escaped him.

"He's well educated," Farrokh managed to say. Both John D. and Julia groaned. "Well, damn it, he's *complicated!*" Dr. Daruwalla shouted. "It's too soon to know what he's like!"

"*Ssshhh!* You'll wake him up," Julia told Farrokh.

"If it's too soon to know what he's like," John D. said, "then it's too soon for me to know if I want to meet him."

Dr. Daruwalla was irritated; he felt that this was a typical Inspector Dhar thing to say.

Julia knew what her husband was thinking. "Hold your tongue," she told him. She made coffee for herself and John D.—for Farrokh, she made a pot of tea. Together, the Daruwallas watched their beloved movie star leave by the kitchen door. Dhar liked to use the back stairs so that he wouldn't be seen; the early morning—it wasn't quite 6:00—was one of the few times he could walk from Marine Drive to the Taj without being recognized and surrounded. At that hour, only the beggars would hassle him; they hassled everyone equally. It simply didn't matter to the beggars that he was Inspector Dhar; many beggars went to the cinema, but what did a movie star matter to them?

Standing Still: An Exercise

At exactly 6:00 in the morning, when Farrokh and Julia were sharing a bath together—she soaped his back, he soaped her breasts, but there was no more extensive hanky-panky than that—Martin Mills awoke to the soothing sounds of Dr. Aziz, the praying urologist. "Praise be to Allah, Lord of Creation"—Dr. Aziz's incantations to Allah drifted upward from his fifth-floor balcony and brought the new missionary instantly to his feet. Although he'd been asleep for less than an hour, the Jesuit felt as refreshed as a normal man who had slept the whole night through; thus invigorated, he bounded to Dr. Daruwalla's balcony, where he could oversee the morning ritual that Urology Aziz enacted on his prayer rug. From the vantage point of the Daruwallas' sixth-floor apartment, the view of Back Bay was stunning. Martin Mills could see Malabar Hill and Nariman Point; in the distance, a small city of people had already congregated on Chowpatty Beach. But the Jesuit had not come to Bombay for the view. He followed the prayers of Dr. Aziz with the keenest concentration. There was always something one could learn from the holiness of others.

Martin Mills did not take prayer for granted. He knew that prayer wasn't the same as thinking, nor was it an escape from thinking. It was never as simple as mere asking. Instead, it was the seeking of instruction; for to know God's will was Martin's heart's desire, and to attain such a state of perfection—a union with God in mystical ecstasy—required the patience of a corpse.

Watching Urology Aziz roll up his prayer rug, Martin Mills knew it was the perfect time for him to practice another exercise of Father de Mello's *Christian Exercises in Eastern Form*—namely, "stillness." Most people didn't appreciate how impossible it was to stand absolutely still; it could be painful, too, but Martin was good at it. He stood so still that, 10 minutes later, a passing fork-tailed kite almost landed on his head. It wasn't because the missionary so much as blinked that the bird suddenly veered away from him; the light that was reflected in the brightness of the missionary's eyes frightened the bird away.

Meanwhile, Dr. Daruwalla was tearing through his hate mail, wherein he found a troubling two-rupee note. The envelope was addressed to Inspector Dhar in care of the film studio; typed on the serial-number side of the money, in capital letters, was this warning: YOU'RE AS DEAD AS LAL. The doctor would show this to Deputy Commissioner Patel, of course, but Farrokh felt he didn't need the detective's confirmation in order to know that the typist was the same lunatic who'd typed the message on the money found in Mr. Lal's mouth.

Then Julia burst into the bedroom. She'd peeked into the living room to see if Martin Mills was still sleeping, but he wasn't on the couch. The sliding-glass doors to the balcony were open, but she'd not seen the missionary on the balcony—he was standing so still, she'd missed him. Dr. Daruwalla stuffed the two-rupee note into his pocket and rushed to the balcony.

By the time the doctor got there, the missionary had moved ahead to a new prayer tactic—this one being one of Father de Mello's exercises in the area of "body sensations" and "thought control." Martin would lift his right foot, move it forward, then put it down. As he did this, he would chant, "Lifting . . . lifting . . . lifting," and then (naturally) "Moving . . . moving . . . moving," and (finally) "Placing . . . placing . . . placing." In short, he was merely walking across the balcony, but with an exaggerated slowness—all the while exclaiming aloud his exact movements. To Dr. Daruwalla, Martin Mills resembled a patient in physical therapy—someone recovering from a recent stroke—for the missionary appeared to be teaching himself how to speak and walk at the same time, with only modest success.

Farrokh tiptoed back to the bedroom and Julia.

"Perhaps I've underestimated his injuries," the doctor said. "I'll have to take him to the office with me. At least for a while, it's best to keep an eye on him."

But when the Daruwallas cautiously approached the Jesuit, he was dressed in clerical garb. He was looking through his suitcase.

"They took only my *culpa* beads and my casual clothes," Martin remarked. "I'll have to buy some cheap local wear—it would be ostentatious to show up at St. Ignatius looking like this!" Whereupon he laughed and plucked at his startlingly white collar.

It certainly won't do to have him walking around Bombay like this, Dr. Daruwalla thought. What was required was the sort of clothing that would allow the madman somehow to fit in. Possibly I could arrange to shave his head, the doctor thought. Julia simply gaped at Martin Mills, but as soon as he began to relate (again!) the tale of his introduction to the city, he completely charmed her, and she became as alternately flirtatious and shy as a schoolgirl. For a man who'd taken a vow of chastity, the Jesuit was remarkably at ease with women—at least with an older woman, Dr. Daruwalla thought.

The complexities of the day ahead for Dr. Daruwalla were almost as frightening to the doctor as the thought of spending the next 12 hours in the missionary's discarded leg iron—or being followed around by Vinod, with the angry dwarf wielding the missionary's whip.

There was no time to lose. While Julia fixed a cup of coffee for

Martin, Farrokh glanced hurriedly at the library collected in the Jesuit's suitcase. Father de Mello's *Sadhana: A Way to God* drew a particularly covert look, for in it Farrokh found a dog-eared page and an assertively underlined sentence: "One of the biggest enemies to prayer is nervous tension." I guess that's why I can't do it, Dr. Daruwalla thought.

In the lobby, the doctor and the missionary didn't escape the notice of that first-floor member of the Residents' Society, the murderous Mr. Munim.

"So! There is your movie star! Where is your dwarf?" Mr. Munim shouted.

"Pay no attention to this man," Farrokh told Martin. "He's completely crazy."

"The dwarf is in the suitcase!" Mr. Munim cried. Thereupon he kicked the scholastic's suitcase, which was ill considered, because he was wearing only a floppy pair of the most insubstantial sandals; from the instant expression of pain on Mr. Munim's face, it was clear that he'd made contact with one of the more solid tomes in Martin Mills's library—maybe the *Compact Dictionary of the Bible*, which was compact but not soft.

"I assure you, sir, there is no dwarf in this suitcase," Martin Mills began to say, but Dr. Daruwalla pulled him on. The doctor was beginning to realize that it was the new missionary's most basic inclination to talk to anyone.

In the alley, they found Vinod asleep in the Ambassador; the dwarf had locked the car. Leaning against the driver's-side door was the exact "anyone" whom Dr. Daruwalla most feared, for the doctor imagined there was no one more inspiring of missionary zeal than a crippled child ... unless there'd been a child missing both arms and both legs. By the shine of excitement in the scholastic's eyes, Farrokh could tell that the boy with the mangled foot was sufficiently inspiring to Martin Mills.

Bird-Shit Boy

It was the beggar from the day before—the boy who stood on his head at Chowpatty Beach, the cripple who slept in the sand. The crushed right foot was once again an offense to the doctor's standard of surgical neatness, but Martin Mills was fatally drawn to the rheumy discharge about the beggar's eyes; to his missionary mind, it was as if the stricken child already clutched a crucifix. The scholastic only momentarily took his eyes off the boy—to glance heavenward—but that was long enough for the little beggar to fool Martin with the infamous Bombay bird-shit trick.

In Dr. Daruwalla's experience, it was a filthy trick, usually performed in the following fashion: while one hand pointed to the sky—to the nonexistent passing bird—the other hand of the little villain squirted your shoe or your pants. The instrument that applied the presumed "bird shit" was similar to a turkey baster, but any kind of bulb with a syringelike nozzle would suffice. The fluid it contained was some whitish stuff—often curdled milk or flour and water—but on your shoe or your pants, it appeared to be bird shit. When you looked down from the sky, having failed to see the bird, there was the shit—it had already hit you—and the sneaky little beggar was wiping it off your shoe or your pants with a handy rag. You then rewarded him with at least a rupee or two.

But in this instance Martin Mills didn't comprehend that a reward was expected. He'd looked in a heavenly direction without the boy needing to point; thereupon the beggar had drawn out the syringe and squirted the Jesuit's scuffed black shoe. The cripple was so quick on the draw and so smooth at concealing the syringe under his shirt that Dr. Daruwalla had seen neither the quick draw nor the shot—only the slick return to the shirt. Martin Mills believed that a bird had unceremoniously shat on his shoe, and that the tragically mutilated boy was wiping off this bird shit with the tattered leg of his baggy shorts. To the missionary, this maimed child was definitely heaven-sent.

With that in mind, there in the alley, the scholastic dropped to his knees, which wasn't the usual response that was made to the outstretched hand of the beggar. The boy was frightened by the missionary's embrace. "O God—thank you!" Martin Mills cried, while the cripple looked to Dr. Daruwalla for help. "This is your lucky day," the missionary told the greatly bewildered beggar. "That man is a *doctor*," Martin Mills told the lame boy. "That man can fix your foot."

"I can't fix his foot!" Dr. Daruwalla cried. "Don't tell him that!"

"Well, certainly you can make it look better than this!" Martin replied. The cripple crouched like a cornered animal, his eyes darting back and forth between the two men.

"It's not as if I haven't already thought of it," Farrokh said defensively. "But I'm sure I can't give him a foot that works. And what do you think a boy like this cares for the appearance of the thing? He'll still limp!"

"Wouldn't you like your foot to be *cleaner-looking?*" Martin Mills asked the cripple. "Wouldn't you like it to look less like a *hoe* or a *club?*" As he spoke, he cupped his hand near the bony fusion of ankle and foot, which the beggar awkwardly rested on the heel. Close up, the doctor could confirm his earlier suspicion: he would have to saw through bone. There would be little chance of success, a greater chance of risk.

"*Primum non nocere,*" Farrokh said to Martin Mills. "I presume you know Latin."

" 'Above all, do no harm,' " the Jesuit replied.

"He was stepped on by an elephant," Dr. Daruwalla explained. Then Farrokh remembered what the cripple had said. Dr. Daruwalla repeated this to the missionary, but the doctor looked at the boy when he spoke: "You can't fix what elephants do." The boy nodded, albeit cautiously.

"Do you have a mother or a father?" the Jesuit asked. The beggar shook his head. "Does anyone look after you?" Martin asked. The cripple shook his head again. Dr. Daruwalla knew it was impossible to understand how much the boy understood, but the doctor remembered that the boy's English was better than he was letting on—a clever boy.

"There's a gang of them at Chowpatty," the doctor said. "There's a kind of pecking order to their begging." But Martin Mills wasn't listening to him; although the zealot manifested a certain "modesty of the eyes," which was encouraged among the Jesuits, there was nonetheless an intensity to his gazing into the rheumy eyes of the crippled child. Dr. Daruwalla realized that the boy was mesmerized.

"But there *is* someone looking after you," the missionary said to the beggar. Slowly, the cripple nodded.

"Do you have any other clothes but these?" the missionary asked.

"No clothes," the boy instantly said. He was undersized, but hardened by the street life. Maybe he was 8, or 10.

"And how long has it been since you've had any food—since you've had a *lot* of food?" Martin asked him.

"Long time," the beggar said. At the most, he might have been 12.

"You can't do this, Martin," Farrokh said. "In Bombay, there are more boys like this than would fit into all of St. Ignatius. They wouldn't fit in the school or in the church or in the cloister—they wouldn't fit in the schoolyard, or in the parking lot! There are too many boys like this— you can't begin your first day here by *adopting* them!"

"Not 'them'—just this one," the missionary replied. "St. Ignatius said that he would sacrifice his life if he could prevent the sins of a single prostitute on a single night."

"Oh, I see," said Dr. Daruwalla. "I understand you've already *tried* that!"

"It's very simple, really," said Martin Mills. "I was going to buy clothes—I'll buy half as many for me, and the rest for him. I presume that I will eat something sometime later today. I'll eat half as much as I normally would have eaten . . ."

"And—don't tell me!—the rest is for *him,*" Dr. Daruwalla said angrily. "Oh, this is brilliant. I wonder why *I* didn't think of it years ago!"

"Everything is just a start," the Jesuit calmly replied. "Nothing is overwhelming if you take one step at a time." Then he stood up with the child in his arms, leaving his suitcase for Dr. Daruwalla to deal with. He walked with the boy, circling Vinod's taxi as the dwarf slept on and on. "Lifting . . . lifting . . . lifting," Martin Mills said. "Moving . . . moving . . . moving," he repeated. "Placing . . . placing . . . placing," the missionary said. The boy thought this was a game—he laughed.

"You see? He's happy," Martin Mills announced. "First the clothes, then the food, then—if not the foot—you can at least do something about his eyes, can't you?"

"I'm not an eye doctor," Dr. Daruwalla replied. "Eye diseases are common here. I could refer him to someone . . ."

"Well, that's a start, isn't it?" Martin said. "We're just going to get you *started,*" he told the cripple.

Dr. Daruwalla pounded on the driver's-side window, startling Vinod awake; the dwarf's stubby fingers were groping for his squash-racquet handles before he recognized the doctor. Vinod hurried to unlock the car. If, in the light of day, the dwarf saw that Martin Mills bore a less-than-exact resemblance to his famous twin, Vinod gave no indication of any suspicion. Not even the missionary's clerical collar appeared to faze the dwarf. If Dhar looked different to Vinod, the dwarf assumed this was the result of being beaten by transvestite whores. Furiously, Farrokh threw the fool's suitcase into the trunk.

There was no time to lose. The doctor realized that he had to get Martin Mills to St. Ignatius as soon as he could. Father Julian and the others would lock him up. Martin would have to obey them—after all, wasn't that what a vow of obedience meant? The doctor's advice to the Father Rector would be simple enough: keep Martin Mills in the mission, or keep him in school. *Don't* let him loose in the rest of Bombay! The chaos he could cause was inconceivable!

As Vinod backed the Ambassador out of the alley, Dr. Daruwalla saw that both the scholastic and the crippled child were smiling. That was when Farrokh thought of the word that had escaped him; it floated to his lips, in belated answer to John D.'s question regarding what Martin Mills was like. The word was "dangerous." The doctor couldn't stop himself from saying it.

"You know what you are?" Dr. Daruwalla asked the missionary. "You're *dangerous*."

"Thank you," the Jesuit said.

There was no further conversation until the dwarf was struggling to park the taxi on that busy stretch of Cross Maidan near the Bombay Gymkhana. Dr. Daruwalla was taking Martin Mills and the cripple to Fashion Street, where they could buy the cheapest cotton clothes—factory seconds, with small defects—when the doctor caught sight of the gob of fake bird shit that had hardened on the strap of his right sandal; Farrokh could feel that a bit of the stuff had also dried between his bare toes. The boy must have squirted Dr. Daruwalla while the doctor and the scholastic had been arguing, although the doctor supposed there was a slim possibility that the bird shit was authentic.

"What's your name?" the missionary asked the beggar.

"Ganesh," the boy replied.

"After the elephant-headed god—the most popular god in Maharashtra," Dr. Daruwalla explained to Martin Mills. It was the name of every other boy on Chowpatty Beach.

"Ganesh—may I call you Bird-Shit Boy?" Farrokh asked the beggar. But there was no reading the deep-black eyes that flashed in the cripple's feral face; either he didn't understand or he thought it was politic to remain silent—a clever boy.

"You certainly shouldn't call him Bird-Shit Boy!" the missionary protested.

"Ganesh?" said Dr. Daruwalla. "I think *you* are dangerous, too, Ganesh." The black eyes moved quickly to Martin Mills; then they fixed once again on Farrokh.

"Thank you," Ganesh said.

Vinod had the last word; unlike the missionary, the dwarf was not automatically moved to pity cripples.

"You, Bird-Shit Boy," Vinod said. "You are definitely being dangerous," the dwarf told him.

16. MR. GARG'S GIRL

A Little Something Venereal

Deepa had taken the night train to Bombay; she'd traveled from some-where in Gujarat—from wherever the Great Blue Nile was playing. She'd arranged to bring the runaway child prostitute to Dr. Daruwalla's office at the Hospital for Crippled Children, intending to shepherd the girl through her examination—it was the child's first doctor's visit. Deepa didn't expect there would be anything wrong; she planned to take the girl back to the Great Blue Nile with her. It was true that the child had run away from a brothel, but—according to Mr. Garg—she'd managed to run away when she was still a virgin. Dr. Daruwalla didn't think so.

Her name was Madhu, which means "honey." She had the floppy, oversized hands and feet and the disproportionately small body of a large-pawed puppy, of the kind one always assumes will become a big dog. But in Madhu's case this was a sign of malnutrition; her body had failed to develop in proportion to her hands and feet. Also, Madhu's head wasn't as large as it appeared at first glance. Her long, oval face was simply unmatched to her petite body. Her protuberant eyes were the tawny yellow of a lion's, but remote with distraction; her lips were full and womanly and entirely too grown-up for her unformed face, which was still the face of a child.

It was her child-woman appearance that must have been Madhu's particular appeal in the brothel she'd run away from; her undersized body reflected this disquieting ambivalence. She had no hips—that is, she had the hips of a boy—but her breasts, which were absurdly small, were nonetheless as fully formed and womanly as her compelling mouth. Although Garg had told Deepa that the child was prepubescent, Dr. Daruwalla guessed that Madhu had not yet had her period because she'd never had enough to eat and she was overworked; furthermore, it was not that the girl hadn't grown any underarm or pubic hair—someone had skillfully shaved her. Farrokh made Deepa feel the faint stubble that was growing in Madhu's armpits.

The doctor's memory of his accidental encounter with Deepa's pudenda surfaced at the oddest times. The sight of the dwarf's wife touching the hollow of the young girl's armpit gave Farrokh the shivers. It was the wiry strength of the former flyer's hand that the doctor remembered—how she'd grabbed his chin as he'd struggled to raise the bridge of his nose off her pubic bone, how she'd simply wrenched his head out of her crotch. And he was off balance, his forehead pressing into her belly and the scratchy sequins on her singlet, so that a good portion of his weight rested on her; yet Deepa had cranked on his chin with only one hand and had managed to lift him. Her hands were strong from the trapeze work. And now the sight of Deepa's sinewy hand in the girl's armpit was enough to make Farrokh turn away—not from the exposed girl but from Deepa.

Farrokh realized that probably there remained more innocence in Deepa than what innocence, if any, remained in Madhu; the dwarf's wife had never been a prostitute. The indifference with which Madhu had undressed for Dr. Daruwalla's cursory examination made the doctor feel that the girl was probably an *experienced* prostitute. Farrokh knew how awkwardly most children Madhu's age undressed. After all, it wasn't only that he was a doctor; he had daughters.

Madhu was silent; perhaps she didn't comprehend the reason for her physical exam, or else she was ashamed. When she covered her breasts and held her hand over her mouth, Madhu looked like an 8-year-old child. But Dr. Daruwalla believed that the girl was at least 13 or 14.

"I'm sure it was someone else who shaved her—she didn't shave herself," Farrokh told Deepa. From his research for *Inspector Dhar and the Cage-Girl Killer*, the doctor knew a few things about the brothels. In the brothels, virginity was a term of sale—not one of accuracy. Maybe in order to *look* like a virgin, one had to be shaved. The doctor knew that most of the older prostitutes were also shaved. Pubic hair, like underarm hair, was simply an invitation to lice.

The dwarf's wife was disappointed; she'd hoped that Dr. Daruwalla was going to be the first and last doctor whom Madhu would be required to see. Dr. Daruwalla didn't think so. He found Madhu disturbingly mature; not even to please Deepa could he give the girl a clean bill of health, not without first making Madhu see Gynecology Tata—Tata Two, as he was more commonly known.

Dr. Tata (the son) was not the best OB/GYN in Bombay, but—like his father before him—he saw any referral from any other physician immediately. It had long been Dr. Daruwalla's suspicion that these referrals were the heart of Tata Two's business. Farrokh doubted that many patients were inclined to see Tata Two twice. Despite removing the adjectival "best" and "most famous" from his clinic's description—it was now called DR TATA'S CLINIC FOR GYNECOLOGICAL & MATERNITY NEEDS—the clinic was the most steadfastly mediocre in the city. If one of his orthopedic patients had a problem of an OB/GYN nature, Dr. Daruwalla never would have referred her to Tata Two. But for a routine examination—for a simple certificate of health, or a standard venereal-disease screening—Tata Two would do, and Tata Two was fast.

He was remarkably fast in Madhu's case. While Vinod drove Deepa and Madhu to Dr. Tata's office, where Dr. Tata would keep them waiting only a short time, Farrokh attempted to restrain Martin Mills from playing too zealous a role in embracing that cause which the dwarf and his wife practiced like a religion. Having observed the scholastic's compassion for the elephant-footed beggar, Vinod had wasted little time in enlisting the famous Inspector Dhar's services. Unfortunately, it had been impossible to conceal from the missionary that the only *un*crippled child in Dr. Daruwalla's waiting room was, or had been, a child prostitute.

Even before Dr. Daruwalla could complete his examination of Madhu, the damage had been done: Martin Mills had been totally swayed by Vinod and Deepa's insane idea that every runaway from the brothels of Bombay could become an acrobat in the circus. To Martin, sending child prostitutes to the circus was a step en route to saving their souls. Farrokh feared what was coming next—that is, as soon as it occurred to Martin. It was only a matter of time before the missionary would decide that Ganesh, the elephant-footed boy, could save *his* little soul at the circus, too. Dr. Daruwalla knew there weren't enough circuses for all the children that the Jesuit believed he could rescue.

Then Dr. Tata called with the news about Madhu.

"Yes, she is certainly sexually active—too many previous partners to count!—and yes, she has a little something venereal," said Tata Two. "But, under the circumstances, it could be a lot worse."

"And you'll check if she's HIV-positive?" asked Dr. Daruwalla.

"We're checking—we'll let you know," Dr. Tata said.

"So what have you found?" Farrokh asked. "Is it gonorrhea?"

"No, but there's some inflammation of the cervix, and a slight discharge," Dr. Tata explained. "She doesn't complain of any urethritis—the inflammation in her urethra is so mild, it may go unnoticed. I'm guessing it's chlamydia. I'll put her on a course of tetracycline. But it's difficult to diagnose a chlamydial infection—as you know, chlamydiae are not visible under the microscope."

"Yes, yes," said Dr. Daruwalla impatiently; he *didn't* know this about chlamydiae, but he didn't care to know. He had been lectured to enough for one day, commencing with a rehashing of the Protestant Reformation and the Jesuitical approach to free will. All he wanted to know was if Madhu was sexually active. And might there be something venereal that he could pin on the acid-scarred Mr. Garg? *All* of Mr. Garg's previous discoveries had carried something venereal; the doctor would have loved to attribute the blame for this to Garg himself. Farrokh didn't believe that the cause of the sexually transmitted disease was always the brothel that the girl was running away from. Most of all—and the doctor couldn't have explained why—it was Deepa and Vinod's seemingly good opinion of Mr. Garg that Dr. Daruwalla wished he could change. Why didn't the dwarf and his wife see that Mr. Garg was egregiously slimy?

"So, if she's *not* HIV-positive, you'll call her clean?" Farrokh asked Tata Two.

"After the course of tetracycline, *and* provided no one lets her return to the brothel," Dr. Tata said.

And provided Deepa doesn't take the girl back to the Wetness Cabaret, or to Mr. Garg, Farrokh thought. Dr. Daruwalla understood that Deepa would need to return to the Great Blue Nile before the doctor knew the results of Madhu's HIV test. Vinod would have to look after Madhu and keep her away from Garg; the girl would be safe with the dwarf.

Meanwhile, the doctor could observe that the morally meddlesome nature of Martin Mills had been momentarily curbed; the missionary was enthralled by Farrokh's favorite circus photograph—the doctor always kept it on his office desk. It was a picture of Pratap Singh's adopted sister, Suman, the star of the Great Royal Circus. Suman was in her costume for the Peacock Dance; she stood in the wing of the main tent, helping two little girls into their peacock costumes. The peacocks were always played by little girls. Suman was putting on their peacock heads; she was tucking their hair under the blue-green feathers of the long peacock necks.

The Peacock Dance was performed in all the Indian circuses. (The peacock is the national bird of India.) In the Great Royal, Suman always played the legendary woman whose lover has been cast under a spell to make him forget her. In the moonlight, she dances with two peacocks; she wears bells on her ankles and wrists.

But what haunted Dr. Daruwalla about the Peacock Dance was neither Suman's beauty nor the little girls in their peacock costumes. Instead, it always seemed to him that the little girls (the peacocks) were about to die. The music for the dance was soft and eerie, and the lions were audible in the background. In the darkness outside the ring, the lions were being moved from their cages and into the holding tunnel, which was a long, tubular cage that led to the ring. The lions hated the holding tunnel. They fought among themselves because they were pressed too low to the ground; they could neither go back to their cages nor advance into the ring. Farrokh had always imagined that a lion would escape. When the peacock girls were finished with their dance and running back to their troupe tent—there in the dark avenue, the escaped lion would catch them and kill them.

After the Peacock Dance, the roustabouts set up the cage for the lions in the ring. To distract the audience from the tedious assembly of the cage and the setting up of the hoops of fire, a motorcycle act was performed in the open wing of the main tent. It was so insanely loud, no one would hear the peacock girls screaming if a lion was loose. The motorcycles raced in opposite directions inside a steel-mesh ball; this was called the Globe of Death, because *if* the motorcycles ever collided, it was possible that both riders could be killed. But Dr. Daruwalla imagined it was called the Globe of Death because the sound of the motorcycles concealed the fate of the peacock girls.

The first time he'd seen Suman, she was helping the little girls into their peacock costumes; she seemed to be a mother to them, although she had no children of her own. But it also seemed to Farrokh that

Suman was dressing the little girls for the last time. They would run out of the ring, the Globe of Death would begin and the escaped lion would already be waiting for them in the dark avenue of the troupe tents.

Maybe, if she wasn't HIV-positive, Madhu would become one of the peacock girls at the Great Blue Nile. Either way, whether she was HIV-positive or a peacock girl, Dr. Daruwalla thought that Madhu's chances were pretty slim. Garg's girls were always in need of more than a dose of tetracycline.

Martin Luther Is Put to Dubious Use

Martin Mills had insisted on observing Dr. Daruwalla at his doctor's chores, for the zealot had proclaimed—even before he saw a single one of Dr. Daruwalla's patients—that the doctor was performing "the Lord's work." After all, what activity was nearer to Jesus than healing crippled children? It was right up there with saving their little souls, Farrokh guessed. Dr. Daruwalla had allowed the missionary to follow him as closely as his own shadow, but only because he wanted to observe how the zealot was recovering from his beating. The doctor had alertly anticipated any indications that the scholastic might have suffered a serious head injury, but Martin Mills was ploddingly disproving this theory. Martin's particular madness seemed in no way trauma-related; rather, it appeared to be the result of blind conviction and a systematic education. Furthermore, after their experience on Fashion Street, Dr. Daruwalla didn't dare let Martin Mills wander freely in Bombay; yet the doctor hadn't found the time to deliver the madman to the presumed safety of St. Ignatius.

On Fashion Street, Martin Mills had been completely unaware of that giant likeness of Inspector Dhar which was freshly plastered above the stalls of the clothes bazaar. The missionary had noticed the other movie advertisement; side by side with *Inspector Dhar and the Towers of Silence* was a poster for *Death Wish*, with a sizable likeness of Charles Bronson.

"That looks like Charles Bronson!" the Jesuit had observed.

"That *is* Charles Bronson," Farrokh had informed him. But of himself, in the image of Inspector Dhar, the missionary saw no resemblance. The clothes vendors, however, looked upon the Jesuit with baleful eyes. One refused to sell him anything; the scholastic assumed that the merchant had nothing in the right size. Another screamed at Martin Mills that his appearance on Fashion Street was nothing but a film-publicity stunt.

This was probably because the missionary insisted on carrying the crippled beggar. The accusation had been made in Marathi, and the elephant-footed boy had enlivened the exchange by spitting on a rack of the merchant's clothes.

"Now, now—even though they revile you, simply smile," Martin Mills had told the crippled boy. "Show them charity." The Jesuit must have assumed it was Ganesh and his crushed foot that had caused the outburst.

It was a wonder they'd escaped from Fashion Street with their lives; Dr. Daruwalla had also managed to persuade Martin Mills to get his hair cut. It was short enough to begin with, but the doctor had said something about the weather growing hotter and hotter, and that in India many ascetics and holy men shaved their heads. The haircut that Farrokh had arranged—with one of those three-rupee curbside barbers who hang out at the end of the clothing stalls on Fashion Street—had been as close to a shaven head as possible. But even as a "skinhead," Martin Mills exhibited something of Inspector Dhar's aggressive quality. The resemblance went well beyond the propensity for the family sneer.

John D. had little to say; yet he was unstoppably opinionated—and when he was acting, he always knew his lines. Martin Mills, on the other hand, never shut up; but wasn't what Martin had to say also a recitation? Weren't they the lines of another kind of actor, the ceaseless intervening of a true believer? Weren't *both* twins unstoppably opinionated? Certainly they were both stubborn.

The doctor was fascinated that barely a majority of Bombayites appeared to recognize Inspector Dhar in Martin Mills; there were almost as many individuals who seemed to see no resemblance whatsoever. Vinod, who knew Dhar well, never doubted that Martin was Dhar. Deepa also knew Dhar, and she was indifferent to the movie star's fame; because she'd never seen an Inspector Dhar movie, the character meant nothing to her. When Deepa met the missionary in Dr. Daruwalla's waiting room, she instantly took Martin Mills for what he was: an American do-gooder. But this had long been her opinion of *Dhar.* If the dwarf's wife had never seen an Inspector Dhar movie, she had seen Dhar's TV appearance on behalf of the Hospital for Crippled Children. Dhar had always struck Deepa as a do-gooder *and* a non-Indian. On the other hand, Ranjit wasn't fooled. The medical secretary saw only the slightest resemblance to Dhar in the frail missionary. Ranjit didn't even suspect the two of being twins; his only comment, which he whispered to Dr. Daruwalla, was that he'd never known Dhar had a brother. Given

Martin Mills's ravaged condition, Ranjit assumed he was Dhar's *older* brother.

Dr. Daruwalla's first concern was to keep Martin Mills in the dark; once the doctor could get the missionary to St. Ignatius, Martin would be kept in perpetual darkness—or so the doctor hoped. Farrokh wanted it to be John D.'s decision whether to know his twin or not. But in the doctor's office, and in the waiting room, it had been awkward to keep Martin Mills separated from Vinod and Deepa. Short of telling the dwarf and his wife that the missionary was Dhar's twin, Dr. Daruwalla didn't know what to do or how to keep them apart.

It was upon Vinod's initiative that Madhu and Ganesh were introduced to each other, as if a 13-year-old child prostitute and a 10-year-old beggar who'd allegedly been stepped on by an elephant would instantly have worlds in common. To Dr. Daruwalla's surprise, the children appeared to hit it off. Madhu was excited to learn that the ugly problem with Ganesh's eyes—if not the ugly foot—might soon be corrected. Ganesh imagined that he could do very well for himself in the circus, too.

"With that foot?" Farrokh said. "What could you do in the circus with that foot?"

"Well, there are things he can do with his *arms*," Martin Mills replied. Dr. Daruwalla feared that the Jesuit had been schooled to refute any defeatist argument.

"Vinod," Farrokh said beseechingly. "Could the boy even be a roustabout with a limp like that? Do you see them letting him shovel the elephant shit? He could limp after the wheelbarrow, I suppose . . ."

"Clowns are limping," Vinod replied. "*I* am limping," the dwarf added.

"So you're saying that he can limp and be laughed at, like a clown," said Dr. Daruwalla.

"There's always working in the cook's tent," Vinod said stubbornly. "He could be kneading and rolling out the dough for the chapati. He could be chopping up the garlic and the onions for the dhal."

"But why would they take *him*, when there are countless boys with two good feet to do that?" Dr. Daruwalla asked. The doctor kept his eye on Bird-Shit Boy, knowing that his discouraging arguments might meet with the beggar's disapproval and a corresponding measure of bird shit.

"We could tell the circus that they had to take the two of them together!" Martin cried. "Madhu *and* Ganesh—we could say that they're brother and sister, that one looks after the other!"

"We could *lie*, in other words," said Dr. Daruwalla.

"For the good of these children, *I* could lie!" the missionary said.

"I'll bet you could!" Farrokh cried. He was frustrated that he couldn't remember his father's favorite condemnation of Martin Luther. What had old Lowji said about Luther's justification for lying? Farrokh wished he could surprise the scholastic with what he recalled as a fitting quotation, but it was Martin Mills who surprised him.

"You're a Protestant, aren't you?" the Jesuit asked the doctor. "You should be advised by what your old friend Luther said: 'What wrong can there be in telling a downright good lie for a good cause . . .' "

"Luther is *not* my old friend!" Dr. Daruwalla snapped. Martin Mills had left something out of the quotation, but Farrokh couldn't remember what it was. What was missing was the part about this downright good lie being not only for a good cause but also "for the advancement of the Christian Church." Farrokh knew he'd been fooled, but he lacked the necessary information to fight back; therefore, he chose to fight with Vinod instead.

"And I suppose you're telling me that Madhu here is another Pinky— is that it?" Farrokh asked the dwarf.

This was a sore point between them. Because Vinod and Deepa had been Great Blue Nile performers, they were sensitive to Dr. Daruwalla's preference for the performers of the Great Royal. There was a "Pinky" in the Great Royal Circus; she was a star. She'd been bought by the circus when she was only three or four. She'd been trained by Pratap Singh and his wife, Sumi. By the time Pinky was seven or eight, she could balance on her forehead at the top of a 10-foot-high bamboo pole; the pole was balanced on the forehead of a bigger girl, who stood on another girl's shoulders . . . the act was that kind of impossible thing. It was an item that called for a girl whose sense of balance was one in a million. Although Deepa and Vinod had never performed for the Great Royal Circus, they knew which circuses had high standards—at least higher than the standards at the Great Blue Nile. Yet Deepa brought the doctor these wrecked little whores from Kamathipura and proclaimed them circus material; at best, they were Great Blue Nile material.

"Can Madhu even stand on her head?" Farrokh asked Deepa. "Can she walk on her hands?"

The dwarf's wife suggested that the child could learn. After all, Deepa had been sold to the Great Blue Nile as a boneless girl, a future plastic lady; she had learned to be a trapeze artist, a flyer.

"But you fell," the doctor reminded Deepa.

"She is merely falling into a net!" Vinod exclaimed.

"There isn't always a net," Dr. Daruwalla said. "Did *you* land in a net, Vinod?" Farrokh asked the dwarf.

"I am being fortunate in other ways," Vinod replied. "Madhu won't be working with clowns—or with elephants," the dwarf added.

But Farrokh had the feeling that Madhu was clumsy; she *looked* clumsy—not to mention the dubious coordination of the limping garlic-and-onion chopper, Madhu's newly appointed brother. Farrokh felt certain that the elephant-footed boy would find another elephant to step on him. Dr. Daruwalla imagined that the Great Blue Nile might even conceive of a way to display the cripple's mashed foot; Ganesh would become a minor sideshow event—the elephant boy, they would call him.

That was when the missionary, on the evidence of less than one day's experience in Bombay, had said to Dr. Daruwalla, "Whatever the dangers in the circus, the circus will be better for them than their present situation—we know the alternatives to their being in the circus."

Vinod had remarked to Inspector Dhar that he was looking surprisingly well recovered from his nightmarish experience on Falkland Road. (Farrokh thought the missionary looked awful.) To keep the dwarf and the missionary from talking further to each other, which Dr. Daruwalla knew would be confusing to them both, the doctor pulled Vinod aside and informed him that he should humor Dhar—"and by no means contradict him"—because the dwarf had correctly diagnosed the movie star. There *had* been brain damage; it would be delicate to assess how much.

"Are you having to delouse him, too?" Vinod had whispered to Farrokh. The dwarf was referring to the reason for the scholastic's horrible haircut, but Dr. Daruwalla had solemnly agreed. Yes, there had been lice *and* brain damage.

"Those are being filthy prostitutes!" Vinod had exclaimed.

What a morning it had been already! Dr. Daruwalla thought. He'd finally gotten rid of Vinod and Deepa—by sending them with Madhu to Dr. Tata. Dr. Daruwalla had not expected Tata Two to send them back so soon. Farrokh barely had time to get rid of Martin Mills; the doctor wanted the scholastic out of the office and the waiting room before Vinod and Deepa and Madhu returned. What's more, Dr. Daruwalla wanted time to be alone; the deputy commissioner expected the doctor to come to Crime Branch Headquarters. Doubtless the doctor's viewing of the photographs of the murdered prostitutes would serve to undermine the collected optimism of the Jesuit, the dwarf and the dwarf's wife. But before Farrokh could slip away to Crawford Market, where he was meeting Deputy Commissioner Patel, it was necessary for the doctor to create an errand for Martin Mills; if only for an hour or two, the missionary was in need of a mission.

Another Warning

The elephant boy was a problem. Ganesh had behaved badly in the exercise yard, where many of the postoperative patients among the crippled children were engaged in their various physical-therapy assignments. Ganesh took this opportunity to squirt several of the more defenseless children with the bird-shit syringe; when Ranjit took the syringe away from the aggressive boy, Ganesh bit Dr. Daruwalla's faithful secretary on the hand. Ranjit was offended that he'd been bitten by a beggar; dealing with the unruly likes of the elephant-footed boy wasn't a suitable use of the medical secretary's training.

On a day that had barely begun, Dr. Daruwalla was already exhausted. Nevertheless, the doctor made quick and clever use of the biting episode. If Martin Mills was so sure that Bird-Shit Boy was capable of contributing to the daily chores of a circus, perhaps the missionary could be persuaded to take some responsibility for the little beggar. Martin Mills was eager to take responsibility for the elephant boy; the zealot would be likely to claim responsibility for a world of cripples, Farrokh imagined. Thereupon Dr. Daruwalla assigned Martin Mills the task of taking Ganesh to Parsi General Hospital; the doctor wanted the crippled beggar to be examined by Eye, Ear, Nose and Throat Jeejeebhoy—Double E-NT Jeejeebhoy, as he was called. Dr. Jeejeebhoy was an expert on the eye problems that were epidemic in India.

Although there was a rheumy discharge and Ganesh had said that his eyelids were gummed shut every morning, there wasn't that softness of the eyeballs that Dr. Daruwalla thought of as end-stage or "white" eyes; then the cornea is dull and opaque, and the patient is blind. Farrokh hoped that, whatever was wrong with Ganesh, it was in an early stage. Vinod had admitted that the circus wouldn't take a boy who was going blind—not even the Great Blue Nile.

But before Farrokh could hurry the elephant boy and the Jesuit on their way to Parsi General, which wasn't far, Martin Mills had spontaneously come to the aid of a woman in the waiting room. She was the mother of a crippled child; the missionary had dropped to his knees at her feet, which Farrokh found to be an irritating habit of the zealot. The woman was frightened by the gesture. Also, she wasn't in need of aid; she was *not* bleeding from her lips and gums, as the scholastic had declared—she was merely eating betel nut, which the Jesuit had never seen.

Dr. Daruwalla ushered Martin from the waiting room to his office, where the doctor believed that the missionary could do slightly less harm. Dr. Daruwalla insisted that Ganesh come with them, for the doctor was fearful that the dangerous beggar might bite someone else. Thereupon Farrokh calmly told Martin Mills what paan was—the local version of betel. The areca nut is wrapped in a betel leaf. Other common ingredients are rose syrup, aniseed, lime paste . . . but people put almost everything in the betel leaf, even cocaine. The veteran betel-nut eater has red-stained lips and teeth and gums. The woman the missionary had alarmed was *not* bleeding; she was merely eating paan.

Finally, Farrokh was able to free himself from Martin Mills. Dr. Daruwalla hoped that Double E-NT Jeejeebhoy would take forever to examine Ganesh's eyes.

By midmorning, the day's confusion had achieved a lunatic pace. It was already a day that brought to Farrokh's mind those white-faced, dark-skinned girls in their purple tutus; it was a Load Cycle kind of day, as if everyone in the doctor's office and waiting room were riding bicycles to cancan music. As if to emphasize this chaos, Ranjit walked into the office without knocking; the medical secretary had just read Dr. Daruwalla's mail. Although the envelope that Ranjit handed to Dr. Daruwalla was addressed to the doctor, *not* to Inspector Dhar, there was something familiar about the cold neutrality of the typescript; even before the doctor looked inside the envelope and saw the two-rupee note, he knew what he'd find. Farrokh was nevertheless stunned to read the message typed in capital letters on the serial-number side of the money. This time the warning said, YOU'RE AS DEAD AS DHAR.

Madhu Uses Her Tongue

There was a telephone call that added to the general confusion; in his distress, Ranjit made a mistake. The secretary thought the caller was Radiology Patel—it was a question regarding when Dr. Daruwalla would come to view the photographs. Ranjit assumed that the "photographs" were X rays, and he answered abruptly that the doctor was busy; either Ranjit or the doctor would call back with the answer. But after the secretary hung up, he realized that the caller hadn't been *Radiology* Patel. It had been Deputy Commissioner Patel, of course.

"There was a . . . Patel on the phone for you," Ranjit told Farrokh in an offhand fashion. "He wants to know when you're coming to see the photographs."

And now there were *two* two-rupee notes in Dr. Daruwalla's pocket; there was the warning to Dhar (YOU'RE AS DEAD AS LAL) and the warning to the doctor (YOU'RE AS DEAD AS DHAR). Farrokh felt certain that these threats would enhance the grimness of the photographs that the deputy commissioner wanted to show him.

Farrokh knew that John D., who was good at concealing his anger, was already angry with him for not forewarning the actor of the arrival of his bothersome twin. Dhar would be even angrier if Dr. Daruwalla saw the photographs of the elephants drawn on the murdered prostitutes without him, but the doctor thought it unwise to bring Dhar to Crime Branch Headquarters—nor would it be advisable to bring Martin Mills. The particular police station was near St. Xavier's College, another Jesuit institution; this one was coeducational—St. Ignatius admitted only boys. Martin Mills would doubtless attempt to persuade his fellow Jesuits to admit Madhu to their school in case she wasn't acceptable to the circus. The madman would probably insist that St. Xavier's offer scholarships to other available child prostitutes! The scholastic had already announced that he would approach the Father Rector of St. Ignatius on Ganesh's behalf. Dr. Daruwalla couldn't wait to hear Father Julian's response to the notion of St. Ignatius School attempting to educate a crippled beggar from Chowpatty Beach!

While the doctor was speculating in this fashion, and as he was hurrying to examine his remaining patients, Vinod and Deepa returned with Madhu and the tetracycline. Before he could abscond to the police station, Farrokh felt obliged to set a trap for Mr. Garg. The doctor told Deepa to tell Garg that Madhu was being treated for a sexually transmitted disease; that sounded vague enough. If Mr. Garg had diddled the child, he would need to call Dr. Daruwalla to find out *which* disease—in order to learn the prescribed cure.

"And tell him we're checking to see if she's HIV-positive," Farrokh said. *That* ought to make the bastard squirm, Dr. Daruwalla thought.

The doctor wanted Deepa and Vinod to understand that Madhu must be kept away from the Wetness Cabaret, and away from Garg. The dwarf would drive his wife to the train station—Deepa had to return to the Great Blue Nile—but Vinod had to keep Madhu with him.

"And, remember, she's *not* clean until she's taken all the tetracycline," the doctor told the dwarf.

"I am remembering," Vinod said.

Then the dwarf asked about Dhar. Where was he? Was he all right? And didn't Dhar need his faithful driver? Dr. Daruwalla explained to Vinod that Dhar was suffering from the common post-trauma delusion that he was someone else.

"Who is he being?" the dwarf inquired.

"A Jesuit missionary in training to be a priest," the doctor replied.

Vinod was instantly sympathetic to this delusion. The actor was even more brain-damaged than the dwarf had first suspected! The key to dealing with Dhar, the doctor explained, was to expect him to be one person one minute and another person the next. The dwarf gravely nodded his big head.

Then Deepa kissed the doctor good-bye. There always lingered on her lips the sticky sweetness of those lemon drops she liked. Any physical contact with the dwarf's wife made Dr. Daruwalla blush.

Farrokh could feel himself blush, but he'd never known if his blushes were visible. He knew he was dark-skinned for a Parsi, although he was fair-skinned in comparison to many other Indians—certainly, say, to a Goan or to a South Indian. In Canada, of course, the doctor was well aware that he was usually perceived as a man "of color," but when it came to blushing, he never knew whether or not he could blush undetected. Naturally, his embarrassment was communicated by other signals quite unrelated to his complexion and utterly unknown to him. For example, in the aftermath of Deepa's kiss, he averted his eyes but his lips remained parted, as if he'd forgotten something he was about to say. Thus he was caught all the more off guard when Madhu kissed him.

He wanted to believe that the child was merely imitating the dwarf's wife, but the girl's kiss was too lush and knowing—Deepa had *not* inserted her tongue. Farrokh felt Madhu's tongue flick his own tongue, dartingly. And the girl's breath was redolent of some dark spice—not lemon drops, possibly cardamom or clove. As Madhu withdrew from him, she flashed her first smile, and Dr. Daruwalla saw the blood-red edge to her teeth at the gum line. For Farrokh to realize that the child prostitute was a veteran betel-nut eater was only a mild surprise, even anticlimactic. The doctor presumed that an addiction to paan was the least of Madhu's problems.

A Meeting at Crime Branch Headquarters

The inappropriately lewd encounter with Madhu left Dr. Daruwalla in no mood to be tolerant of the photographic record of Rahul's artistry on the bellies of the murdered whores. The subject matter was no less limited than what the doctor had seen depicted on Beth's belly 20 years ago, nor had the intervening years imparted to the artist any measurable subtlety of style. The ever-mirthful elephant winked its eye and raised the opposite tusk. The water from the end of the elephant's trunk continued to spray the pubic hair—in many cases, the shaved pubic area—of the dead women. Not even the passing of so many years, not to mention the horror of so many murders, was sufficient to inspire Rahul beyond the first act of his imagination—namely, that the victim's navel was always the winking eye. The differences among the women's navels provided the only variety in the many photographs. Detective Patel remarked that both the drawings and the murders gave new meaning to that tired old phrase "a one-track mind." Dr. Daruwalla, who was too appalled to speak, could only nod that he agreed.

Farrokh showed the deputy commissioner the threatening two-rupee notes, but D.C.P. Patel was unsurprised; he'd been expecting more warnings. The deputy commissioner knew that the note in Mr. Lal's mouth had been just the beginning; no murderer the detective had ever known was content to threaten potential victims only once. Either killers didn't warn you or they repeatedly warned you. Yet, for 20 years, *this* killer hadn't given anyone a warning; only now, beginning with Mr. Lal, had there emerged a kind of vendetta against Inspector Dhar and Dr. Daruwalla. It seemed unlikely to the deputy commissioner that the sole motivation for this change in Rahul had been a stupid movie. Something about the Daruwalla-Dhar connection must have infuriated Rahul—both personally *and* for a long time. It was the deputy commissioner's suspicion that *Inspector Dhar and the Cage-Girl Killer* had simply exacerbated Rahul's longstanding hatred.

"Tell me—I'm just curious," said Detective Patel to Dr. Daruwalla. "Do you know any hijras—I mean *personally?*" But as soon as he saw that the doctor was thinking about the question—the doctor had been unable to answer spontaneously—the detective added, "In your movie, you made a hijra the murderer. Whatever gave you such an idea? I mean, in *my* experience, the hijras *I* know are reasonably gentle—they're mostly nice people. The hijra prostitutes may be bolder than the female prostitutes, yet I don't think of them as dangerous. But possibly you knew one—someone who wasn't very nice. I'm just curious."

"Well, *someone* had to be the murderer," Dr. Daruwalla said defensively. "It was nothing personal."

"Let me be more specific," said the deputy commissioner. It was a line that got Dr. Daruwalla's attention, because the doctor had often written that line for Inspector Dhar. "Did you ever know somebody with a woman's breasts and a boy's penis? It was a rather small penis, from all reports," the detective added. "I don't mean a hijra. I mean a zenana—a transvestite with a penis, but with breasts."

That was when Farrokh felt a flutter of pain in the area of his heart. It was his injured rib, trying to remind him of Rahul. The rib was crying out to him that Rahul was the second Mrs. Dogar, but the doctor mistook the pain for an actual signal from his heart. His heart said, *Rahul!* But Rahul's connection to Mrs. Dogar still eluded Dr. Daruwalla.

"Yes, or maybe—I mean, I knew a man who was trying to become a woman," Farrokh replied. "He'd obviously taken estrogens, maybe he'd even had surgical implants—he definitely had a woman's breasts. But whether he'd been castrated, or if he'd had other surgery, I don't know—I mean, I *presumed* he had a penis because he was interested in the *complete* operation . . . a total sex change."

"And did he have this operation?" the deputy commissioner asked.

"I wouldn't know," the doctor replied. "I haven't seen him, or her, for twenty years."

"That would be the right number of years, wouldn't it?" the detective asked. Again, Farrokh felt the twinge in his rib that he confused with his excited heart.

"He was hoping to go to London for the operation," Farrokh explained. "In those days, I believe it would have been very difficult to get a complete sex-change operation in India. They're still illegal here."

"I believe that our murderer also went to London," Patel informed the doctor. "Obviously, and only recently, he—or she—came back."

"The person I knew was interested in going to art school . . . in London," Farrokh said numbly. The photographs of the drawings on the bellies of the murdered prostitutes grew clearer in his mind, although the photographs lay facedown on the deputy commissioner's desk. It was Patel who picked one up and looked at it again.

"Not a very good art school would have taken him, I suspect," the detective said.

He never shut his office door, which opened on an outdoor balcony; there were a dozen such offices off this balcony, and it was the deputy commissioner's policy that no one ever closed a door—except in the monsoon rains, and then only when the wind was wrong. With the doors open, no one being interrogated could later claim that they'd been beaten. Also, the sound of the police secretaries typing their officers' reports was a sound that the deputy commissioner enjoyed; the cacophony of typewriters implied both industry and order. He knew that many of his fellow policemen were lazy and their secretaries were sloppy; the typed reports themselves were rarely as orderly as the clacking of the keys. On his desk, Deputy Commissioner Patel faced three reports in need of rewriting, and an additional report in greater need, but he pushed these four reports aside in order to spread out the photographs of the murdered whores' bellies. The elephant drawings were so familiar to him that they calmed him; he didn't want the doctor to sense his eagerness.

"And would this person that you knew have had a common sort of name, a name like Rahul?" the detective asked. It was a delivery worthy of the insincerity of Inspector Dhar.

"Rahul Rai," said Dr. Daruwalla; it was almost a whisper, but this didn't lessen the deputy commissioner's quickening pleasure.

"And would this Rahul Rai have been in Goa . . . perhaps visiting the beaches . . . at or about the time when the German and the American— those bodies you saw—were murdered?" Patel asked. The doctor was slumped in his chair as if bent by indigestion.

"At my hotel—at the Bardez," Farrokh replied. "He was staying with his aunt. And the thing is, if Rahul *is* in Bombay, he is certainly familiar with the Duckworth Club—his aunt was a member!"

"Was?" the detective said.

"She's dead," Dr. Daruwalla said. "I would presume that Rahul, he or she, inherited her fortune."

D.C.P. Patel touched the raised tusk of the elephant in one of the photographs; then he stacked the photos in a single neat pile. He'd always known there was family money in India, but the Duckworth Club connection was a surprise. What had misled him for 20 years was

Rahul's brief notoriety in the transvestite brothels on Falkland Road and Grant Road; these were hardly the usual haunts of a Duckworthian.

"Of course I know that you know my wife," the detective said. "I must put you together with her. She knows your Rahul, too, and it might help me to hear you compare notes—so to speak."

"We could have lunch at the club. Someone there might know more about Rahul," Farrokh suggested.

"Don't *you* ask any questions!" the deputy commissioner suddenly shouted. It offended Dr. Daruwalla to be yelled at, but the detective was quickly tactful, if not exactly mollifying. "We wouldn't want to warn Rahul, would we?" Patel said, as if he were speaking to a child.

The rising dust from the courtyard had coated the leaves of the neem trees; the rail of the balcony was also coated with dust. In the detective's office, the dull brass ceiling fan labored in an effort to push the motes of dust back out the open door. The darting shadows of fork-tailed kites occasionally moved across the deputy commissioner's desk. The one open eye of the topmost elephant in the stack of photos seemed to notice all these things, which the doctor knew he would never forget.

"Lunch *today?*" suggested the detective.

"Tomorrow is better for me," Dr. Daruwalla said. His pending obligation to deliver Martin Mills into the hands of the Jesuits at St. Ignatius was a welcome intrusion; he also needed to talk to Julia, and he wanted the time to tell Dhar—Dhar should be at the lunch with the wounded hippie. Farrokh knew that John D. had a superior memory, maybe even of Rahul.

"Tomorrow is fine," said the deputy commissioner, but his disappointment was evident. The words his wife had used to describe Rahul were constantly with him. Also with him was the size of Rahul's big hands, which had held his wife's big breasts; also, the erectness and the shapeliness of Rahul's breasts, which Nancy had felt against her back; also, the small, silky little boy's penis, which his wife had felt against her buttocks. Nancy had said he was condescending, mocking, teasing— certainly sophisticated, probably cruel.

Because Dr. Daruwalla had only begun the struggle to compose a written report on Rahul Rai, the detective couldn't quite leave him alone. "Give me one word for Rahul," Patel asked Farrokh. "The first word that comes to your mind—I'm just curious," the detective said.

"Arrogant," the doctor replied. After 20 years, it was visible on Detective Patel's face that this was unsatisfactory.

"Please try another," the detective said.

"Superior," said Dr. Daruwalla.

"You're getting closer," Patel replied.

"Rahul is a tease," Farrokh explained. "He condescends to you, he mocks you, he bullies you with a sort of self-satisfied sophistication. Like his late aunt, he uses his sophistication as a weapon. I think he is basically a cruel person." The doctor paused in his description because the detective had closed his eyes and sat smiling at his desk. All the while, Deputy Commissioner Patel articulated his fingers as if he were typing up another report, but his fingers weren't tapping the keys of his typewriter; the detective had once more spread out the photographs—they covered his desk—and he typed on the many heads of the mocking elephants, his fingers finding the navels of the murdered prostitutes . . . all those ceaselessly winking eyes.

Down the balcony, from another detective's office, a man was screaming that he was telling the truth, while a policeman calmly contradicted him with the almost harmonious repetition of the word "lies." From the courtyard kennel came a corresponding clamor—the police attack dogs.

After Dr. Daruwalla had completed his written report on Rahul, the doctor wandered onto the balcony to have a look at the dogs; they'd barked themselves out. The late-morning sun was now beating down on the courtyard; the police dogs, all Dobermans, were asleep in the only shady corner of their kennel, which was obscured from Farrokh's view by a clump of neem trees. On the balcony itself, however, was a small cage with a newspaper floor, and the doctor knelt to play with a Doberman pinscher puppy—a prisoner in a portable pen. The puppy wriggled and whined for Farrokh's attention. It thrust its sleek black muzzle through a square of the wire mesh; it licked the doctor's hand—its needle-sharp teeth nipped his fingers.

"Are you a good dog?" Farrokh asked the puppy. Its wild eyes were ringed with the rusty-brown markings of its breed, which is preferred for police work in Bombay because the Doberman's short hair is suitable for the hot weather. The dogs were large and powerful and fast; they had the terrier's jaws and tenacity, although they weren't quite as intelligent as German shepherds.

A subinspector, a junior officer, came out of an office where at least three typewriters were resounding, and this young, officious policeman spoke aggressively to Dr. Daruwalla . . . something to the effect that "spoiling" the Doberman puppy would make it untrainable for police business, something about not treating a future attack dog as a pet. Whenever anyone spoke Hindi this abruptly to the doctor, Farrokh felt frozen by his lack of fluency in the language.

"I'm sorry," Dr. Daruwalla said in English.

"No, don't *you* be sorry!" someone suddenly shouted. It was Deputy Commissioner Patel; he'd popped out of his office onto the balcony, where he stood clutching Farrokh's written statement in his hands. "Go on—play with the puppy all you want to!" the deputy commissioner shouted.

The junior policeman realized his error and quickly apologized to Dr. Daruwalla. "I'm sorry, saar," he said. But before the subinspector could slip back into his office and the safe din of the typewriters, he was barked at by Detective Patel, too.

"You *should* be sorry—speaking to *my* witness!" the deputy commissioner yelled.

So I am a "witness," Farrokh realized. He'd made a small fortune satirizing the police; now he knew he was in utter ignorance of even a matter as trivial as the pecking order among policemen.

"Go on—play with the puppy!" Patel repeated to the doctor, and so Farrokh once more turned his attention to the Doberman. Since the little dog had just dropped a surprisingly large turd on the newspaper floor of its cage, Dr. Daruwalla's attention was momentarily attracted to the turd. That was when he saw that the newspaper was today's edition of *The Times of India*, and that the Doberman's turd had fallen on the review of *Inspector Dhar and the Towers of Silence*. It was a bad review, of such a hostile nature that its surliness seemed enhanced by the smell of dog shit.

The turd prevented all but a partial reading of the review, which was just as well; Farrokh was angered enough. There was even a gratuitous swipe taken at Dhar's perceived weight problem. The reviewer asserted that Inspector Dhar sported too protrusive a beer belly to justify the film studio's claim that Dhar was the Charles Bronson of Bombay.

By the nearby flutter of pages, Dr. Daruwalla realized that the deputy commissioner had finished reading the doctor's statement. The detective also stood close enough to the puppy's cage to observe what Farrokh had been reading; Detective Patel was the one who had put the newspaper there.

"I'm afraid it's not a very good review," the deputy commissioner observed.

"They never are," Farrokh said. He followed Patel back to his office.

Dr. Daruwalla could feel that the detective wasn't altogether pleased by the doctor's written report.

"Sit down," Detective Patel said, but when the doctor moved to the chair he'd sat in before, the detective caught his arm and steered him around the desk. "No, no—you sit where *I* usually sit!" And so Farrokh seated himself in the deputy commissioner's chair. It was higher than the doctor's previous seat; the photographs of the murdered prostitutes were easier to see, or else harder to ignore. The doctor remembered the day at Chowpatty Beach when little John D. had been so frightened by the festival mob, by all the elephant heads being carried into the sea. "They're drowning the elephants!" the child had cried. "Now the elephants will be angry!"

In his written statement, Farrokh had said that he believed the hateful phone calls about his father's assassination had been from Rahul; after all, it was the voice of a woman trying to sound like a man, and this might suit whatever voice Rahul had ended up with. Twenty years ago, Rahul's voice had been a work-in-progress; it had been sexually undecided. But although Detective Patel found this speculation interesting, the detective was disturbed by Dr. Daruwalla's conclusion: that Rahul had been old Lowji's assassin. This was too imaginative—it was too big a leap. This was the kind of conjecture that marred the doctor's written report and made it, in the deputy commissioner's opinion, "amateurish."

"Your father was blown up by professionals," D.C.P. Patel informed Farrokh. "I was still an inspector at the Colaba Station—only the duty officer. The Tardeo Police Station answered that call. I wasn't allowed at the scene of the crime, and then the investigation was turned over to the government. But I know for a fact that Lowji Daruwalla was exploded by a team. For a while, I heard that they thought the head mali might have been involved."

"The Duckworth Club gardener?" cried Dr. Daruwalla; he'd always disliked the head mali, without knowing why.

"There was a different head mali then . . . you will remember," the detective said.

"Oh," Farrokh said. He was feeling more and more amateurish by the minute.

"Anyway, Rahul is possibly the one making the phone calls—that's as good a guess as any," Patel said. "But he's no car-bomb expert."

The doctor sat dismally still, looking at the photographic history of the murdered women. "But why would Rahul hate me—*or* Dhar?" Dr. Daruwalla asked.

"*That* is the question you don't answer, or even ask, in your written statement," said D.C.P. Patel. "Why, indeed?"

Thus were both men left with this unanswered question—Dr. Daruwalla as he took a taxi uptown to meet Martin Mills, and Detective Patel as he reclaimed his desk chair. There the deputy commissioner once more faced the winking elephants on the slack bellies of the brutalized women.

No Motive

The deputy commissioner reflected that the mystery of Rahul's hatred was probably unsolvable. There would be no end to the conjecture on this subject, which would remain unsatisfactorily answered, probably forever. The matter of what motivated Rahul's hatred would remain incomplete. What was truly implausible in all the Inspector Dhar films was that *all* the murderers' motives were plainly established; the reasons for this or that hatred, which would lead to this or that violence, were always clear. Detective Patel regretted that Rahul Rai wasn't in a movie.

In addition to Dr. Daruwalla's written statement, the detective had secured a letter from the doctor, for it hadn't escaped Patel's attention that Dr. Daruwalla was guest chairman of the Membership Committee at the Duckworth Club. On behalf of Deputy Commissioner Patel, the Duckworth Club was requested to release the names of its new members—"new" as of the last 20 years. The deputy commissioner sent a subinspector to the club with the letter of requisition; the subinspector was instructed not to leave the Duckworth Club without the list of names. Detective Patel doubted that he would need to peruse the names of all 6,000 members; with any luck, a recent membership to a relative of the late Promila Rai would be easy to spot. It was hard for the deputy commissioner to contain himself while he waited for the subinspector to bring him the list.

At his desk, Detective Patel sat among the dust motes that danced in the movement of the ceiling fan, which was silent not because it was truly noiseless, but because the constant orchestra of the secretaries' typewriters concealed the fan's faint whirs and ticks. At first, the deputy commissioner had been enthusiastic about the information he'd received from Dr. Daruwalla. The detective had never been this close to Rahul; now he thought it was inevitable that the killer would be apprehended—an arrest seemed imminent. Yet Detective Patel couldn't bring himself to share his enthusiasm with his wife; he would hate to see her disappointed if there remained something inconclusive. There was always something inconclusive, the detective knew.

"But why would Rahul hate me—*or* Dhar?" Dr. Daruwalla had asked. To the deputy commissioner, this question had been a typical inanity from the creator of Inspector Dhar; even so, the detective—the *real* detective—had encouraged the doctor to keep asking himself that same inane question.

Detective Patel had lived with the photographs for too long; that little elephant with its cocky tusk and its mischievous eyes had gotten to him, not to mention those murdered women with their unresponsive stomachs. There would never be a satisfactory motive for such hatred, the deputy commissioner believed. Rahul's *real* crime was that he didn't have sufficient justification for his actions. Something about Rahul would remain uncaptured; the horror about murders like his was that they were never sufficiently motivated. And so it seemed to Detective Patel that his wife was destined to be disappointed; he wouldn't call her because he didn't want to get her hopes up. As he might have guessed, Nancy called him.

"No, sweetie," the detective said.

From the adjacent office, the sound of typing ceased; then, from the next office, the typing also stopped—and so on, all along the balcony.

"No, I would have told you, sweetie," the deputy commissioner said.

For 20 years, Nancy had called him almost every day. She always asked him if he'd caught Beth's killer.

"Yes, of course I promise, sweetie," the detective said.

Below, in the courtyard, the big Dobermans were still asleep, and the police mechanic had mercifully stopped his infernal revving of the patrolmen's motorcycles. The tuning of these ancient engines was so constant, the dogs usually slept through it. But even this sound had ceased, as if the mechanic—in spite of his throttling up and throttling down—had managed to hear the typing stop. The motorcycle mechanic had joined the speechless typewriters.

"Yes, I showed the doctor the photographs," Patel told Nancy. "Yes, of course you were right, sweetie," the deputy commissioner told his wife.

There was a new sound in Detective Patel's office; the detective looked all around, trying to identify it. Gradually, he became aware of the absence of typing. Then he looked up at the revolving ceiling fan and realized that it was the fan's whirring and ticking that he heard. It was so quiet, he could hear the rusted iron wheels of the hot-lunch wagons that were pushed by hand along Dr. Dadabhai Navroji Road; the dabba-wallas were on their way to deliver hot lunches to the office workers uptown.

Deputy Commissioner Patel knew that his fellow policemen and their secretaries were listening to every word of his conversation, and so he whispered into the phone. "Sweetie," the detective said, "it is slightly better than you first believed. The doctor didn't merely see the bodies, the doctor also knows Rahul. Both Daruwalla and Dhar—they actually know who he is . . . or at least who he, or she, *was*." Patel paused, and then he whispered, "No, sweetie—they haven't *seen* him, or her . . . not for twenty years."

Then the detective once more listened to his wife—and to the ceiling fan, and to the grinding wheels of the dabba-wallas' faraway wagons.

When the deputy commissioner spoke again, it was an outburst, not a whisper. "But I *never* dismissed your theories!" he cried into the phone. Then there entered into his voice a familiar tone of resignation; it so pained his fellow policemen, who all admired him and could no more fathom the *motive* for the extreme love that Detective Patel felt for his wife than there was any fathoming the motivation for Rahul's extreme hatred. There was simply no determining where either a love or a hate like that came from, and this mystery compelled the officers and their secretaries to listen. All along the balcony, it overwhelmed them to hear the intensity of what appeared to them to be a groundless, irrational love.

"No, of course I'm not angry," Patel told Nancy. "I'm sorry if I *sounded* angry, sweetie." The detective sounded drained; the officers and their secretaries wished only that they could help him. They weren't eavesdropping for information related to those murdered prostitutes; they knew that the evidence of what had been done to those women was never farther away from the deputy commissioner than the top drawer of his desk. It was the pathetic sound of Detective Patel's love for his wretched wife that removed the hand of the motorcycle mechanic from the throttle.

In his office, Patel was painstakingly returning the photographs to his top drawer; he always returned them one by one, just as he reviewed them faithfully and in the exact order in which the crimes had been discovered. "I love you, *too*, sweetie," the detective said into the phone. He always waited for Nancy to hang up first. Then he slammed shut the top drawer of his desk and rushed to the balcony. He caught his fellow policemen and their secretaries by surprise; not one of them was fast enough to start typing before the deputy commissioner started shouting.

"Have you run out of things to describe?" he hollered. "Have your fingers all fallen off?" he screamed. "Are there no more murders? Is crime a thing of the past? Have you all gone on holiday? Have you nothing better to do than listen to *me*?"

The typing began again, although Detective Patel knew that most of these first words would be meaningless. Below him, in the courtyard, the Doberman pinschers started barking witlessly; he could see them lunging in their kennel. Also below him, the police mechanic had mounted the nearest motorcycle and was jumping again and again, but without success, on the kick starter. The engine made a dry, gasping sound, like the catching of a pawl against a ratchet wheel.

"Bleed the carburetor—there's too much air!" Patel shouted to the mechanic, who quickly fussed with the carburetor; his tireless leg continued to flail the kick starter. When the engine caught and the mechanic revved the throttle so loudly that the barking Dobermans were drowned out of hearing, the deputy commissioner returned to his office and sat at his desk with his eyes closed. Gradually, his head began to bob, as if he'd found a followable rhythm, if not a melody, among the staccato outbursts from the police secretaries' typewriters.

He'd not exactly neglected to tell Nancy that they would have lunch tomorrow at the Duckworth Club with Dr. Daruwalla—probably with Inspector Dhar, too. He'd purposefully withheld this information from his wife. He knew it would worry her, or bring her to tears—or at least cause her another long night of sleeplessness and helpless sorrowing. Nancy hated to go out in public. Moreover, she'd developed a pointless dislike of both Inspector Dhar's creator and Dhar himself. Detective Patel understood that his wife's dislike was no more logical than her blaming both men for failing to comprehend how savagely she'd been traumatized in Goa. With equal illogic, the detective anticipated, Nancy would be ashamed of herself in both Daruwalla and Dhar's company, for she couldn't bear the thought of encountering anyone who'd known her *then*.

He would tell her about lunch at the Duckworth Club in the morning, the detective thought; that way, his wife might have a fair night's sleep. Also, once he'd read over the names of the new members at the club, the deputy commissioner hoped he might know who Rahul was—or who he or she was pretending to be nowadays.

Patel's fellow policemen and their secretaries didn't relax until they heard the sound of his typewriter contributing its tedious music to their own. This was a welcome boredom, they knew, for with the flat clacking of the deputy commissioner's keys, Patel's colleagues were relieved to know that the deputy commissioner had returned to sanity—if not to peace of mind. It even comforted his junior officers to know that Patel was rewriting their own botched reports. They also knew they could expect that sometime in the afternoon Detective Patel would have their original reports back on their desks; the revised reports would be prefaced by a creative array of insults directed to their myriad inabilities—for none of them, in Detective Patel's opinion, knew how to write a proper report. And the secretaries would be taken to task for their typing errors. He was so disdainful of the secretaries, the deputy commissioner did his own typing.

Martin's Mother Makes Him Sick

Trachoma, which is one of the leading causes of blindness in the world, is easily treatable at its earliest phase—a chlamydial infection of the conjunctiva. In Ganesh's case, there was no scarring of the cornea. Double E-NT Jeejeebhoy had prescribed three weeks of tetracycline orally, together with a tetracycline ointment. Sometimes, multiple courses of treatment were needed, Dr. Jeejeebhoy had said; the elephant boy's weepy eyes would likely clear up.

"You see?" Martin Mills asked Dr. Daruwalla. "We've already done the boy some good. It wasn't hard, was it?"

It seemed disloyal of the doctor that they were riding in a taxi *not* driven by Vinod; it wasn't even a taxi from the dwarf's company. It also seemed dangerous, for the decrepit driver had warned them that he was unfamiliar with Bombay. Before they proceeded to the mission in Mazagaon, they dropped the beggar at Chowpatty Beach, where he said he wanted to go. Dr. Daruwalla couldn't resist saying to Martin Mills that the little cripple was doubtless eager to sell his Fashion Street clothes.

"You're so cynical," the scholastic said.

"He'll probably sell the tetracycline, too," Farrokh replied. "He'll probably be blind before he gets to see the circus."

As he escorted the missionary to St. Ignatius, Farrokh felt sufficiently overwhelmed to have reached the stage of making bitter resolutions to himself. Dr. Daruwalla had resolved that he would never write another

Inspector Dhar movie; the doctor had resolved that he would call a press conference, at which he would take the full blame for Dhar's creation upon himself.

Thus distracted, and always a nervous passenger in Bombay—even when Vinod was at the wheel, and the dwarf was a decent driver—Dr. Daruwalla was frightened to see that their taxi had nearly mowed down a pedestrian. The near-accident had no effect on Martin Mills's impromptu lecture on Jainism. "A pre-Buddhist offshoot of Hinduism," Martin declared. The Jains were absolutely pure, the missionary explained . . . not just no meat, but no eggs; kill nothing, not even flies; bathe every morning. He would love to meet a Jain, Martin said. Just that quickly was the chaos of the morning behind him, if not entirely forgotten.

Apropos of nothing, the missionary then moved on to the well-worn subject of Gandhi. Farrokh reflected on how he might derail this conversation; possibly the doctor could say he preferred the warrior Shivaji to Gandhi—none of this turn-the-other-cheek shit for Shivaji! But before the doctor could deflate so much as a sentence of the scholastic's zeal for Gandhi, Martin Mills once more changed the subject.

"Personally, I'm more interested in Shirdi Sai Baba," the missionary said.

"Ah, yes—the Jesus of Maharashtra," Farrokh replied facetiously. Sai Baba was a patron saint of many circus performers; the acrobats wore little Shirdi Sai Baba medallions around their necks—the Hindu equivalents of St. Christopher medals. There were Shirdi Sai Baba calendars hanging in the troupe tents of the Great Royal and the Great Blue Nile. The saint's shrine was in Maharashtra.

"The parallels to Jesus are understandable," Martin Mills began, "although Sai Baba was a teenager before he gained attention and he was an old man, in his eighties, when he died . . . I believe in 1918."

"From his pictures, I always thought he looked a little like Lee Marvin . . . the Lee Marvin of Maharashtra," Farrokh said.

"Lee Marvin! *Not* Shirdi Sai Baba . . ." the missionary protested.

And here, in an effort to interrupt the zealot's upcoming lecture on the parallels between Christianity and the cult of Sai Baba worship, the doctor launched into a description of the terrible teeterboard item that bore responsibility for Vinod's aerial assault of the surprised audience at the less-than-great Blue Nile Circus. Dr. Daruwalla made it clear that such careless elephant-stamping acts would likely be in store for the less-than-innocent Madhu and the elephant-footed Ganesh. But the doctor's calculated pessimism failed to bait the missionary into repeating his claim that the perils of the circus—of *any* circus—paled in comparison to the hardships facing a prostitute or a beggar in Bombay. As swiftly as he'd dropped Gandhi for Sai Baba, Martin Mills now abandoned the Jesus of Maharashtra, too.

The missionary's new and sudden interest was prompted by a billboard they were passing, an advertisement for Close-Up.

DO YOU MOUTHWASH WHEN YOU TOOTHPASTE?

"Look at that!" cried Martin Mills. Their taxi's startled driver barely avoided being broadsided by a Thums Up cola truck; it was as big and bright red as a fire engine. "English usage is *so* important," the scholastic declared. "What worries me about those children is that their English will deteriorate in the circus. Perhaps we could insist that someone in the circus tutor them!"

"How will speaking English serve them in the circus?" Farrokh asked. He knew it was nonsense to think that Madhu possessed enough English for her grasp of the language to "deteriorate." It was still a mystery to Dr. Daruwalla that the elephant boy's spoken English and his apparent understanding of the language were as good as they were; perhaps someone had already tutored him. Maybe the missionary would suggest that Ganesh tutor Madhu! But Martin Mills didn't wait for the doctor to elaborate on his thesis that English would never provide these children with any advantage—not in the circus.

"Speaking English serves anyone well," said the English teacher. "One day, English will be the language of the world."

"*Bad* English is already the language of the world," said Dr. Daruwalla despairingly. That the children might be mashed by elephants was not the missionary's concern, but the moron wished proper English usage on them!

Passing Dr. Vora's Gynecological and Maternity Hospital, Farrokh realized that their decrepit driver was lost; the wretch made a sudden turn and was almost sideswiped by a careening olive-drab van belonging to the Spastics' Society of India. Only a moment later—or so it seemed; it was longer—the doctor realized that his own sense of direction had deserted him, for they were passing the Times of India Building when Martin Mills announced, "We could give the children a subscription to *The Times of India* and have it sent to them at the circus. We'd have to insist that they give it at least an hour a day of their attention, of course."

"Of course . . ." said Dr. Daruwalla. The doctor thought he might faint with frustration, for their troubled driver had missed the turn he should have taken—there went Sir J. J. Road.

"I'm planning to read the newspaper myself, daily," the missionary went on. "When you're a foreigner, there's nothing like a local newspaper to orient you." The thought of anyone becoming oriented by *The Times of India* made Farrokh feel that a head-on collision with an approaching double-decker bus might be an improvement on the scholastic's continued conversation. Then, in the next instant, they'd plunged into Mazagaon—St. Ignatius was now very near—and the doctor, for no calculated reason, instructed their driver to take a slight detour through the slum on Sophia Zuber Road.

"A part of this slum was once a movie set," Dr. Daruwalla explained to Martin Mills. "It was in this very slum that your mother fainted when she was sneezed on, and then licked, by a cow. Of course, she was pregnant with you at the time—I suppose you've heard the story . . ."

"Please stop the car!" the missionary cried.

When their driver braked, but before the taxi came to a complete halt, Martin Mills opened the rear door and vomited into the moving street. Because nothing in a slum goes unseen, this episode attracted the attention of several slum dwellers, who began to jog beside the slowing car. Their frightened driver speeded up in order to get away from them.

"After your mother fainted, there was a riot," Farrokh continued. "Apparently, there was massive confusion concerning who licked whom . . . your mother or the cow."

"Please stop—*not* the car. Please don't mention my mother," Martin said.

"I'm sorry," said Dr. Daruwalla, who was secretly excited. At last Farrokh had found a subject that gave him the upper hand.

A Half-Dozen Cobras

It would be no less long a day for Deputy Commissioner Patel than it would be for Dr. Daruwalla, but the level of confusion in the detective's day would be slightly less overwhelming. The deputy commissioner easily revised the first botched report that awaited his attention—a suspected murder at the Suba Guest House. It turned out to be a suicide. The report had to be rewritten because the duty officer had misinterpreted the young man's suicide note as a clue left behind by the presumed murderer. Later, the victim's mother had identified her son's handwriting. The deputy commissioner could sympathize with the duty officer's mistake, for it wasn't much of a suicide note.

Had sex with a woman who smelled like meat. Not very pure.

As for the second report in need of rewriting, the deputy commissioner was less sympathetic with the subinspector who'd been summoned to the Alexandria Girls' English Institution. A young student had been discovered in the lavatory, presumably raped and murdered. But when the subinspector arrived at the school, he found the girl to be very much alive; she was totally recovered from her own murder and indignant at the suggestion that she'd been raped. It turned out she'd suffered her first period, and—withdrawing to the lavatory to look more closely at what was happening to her—she'd fainted at the sight of her own blood. There a hysterical teacher had found her, mistaking the blood as proof of the rape of a virgin. The teacher also assumed that the girl was dead.

The reason the report had to be rewritten was that the subinspector couldn't bring himself to mention that the poor girl had suffered her "period"; it was, he said upon interrogation, as morally impossible for him to write this word as it would be for him to write the word "menstruation," which (he added) was very nearly a morally impossible word for him even to say. And so the erroneously reported rape and murder was called, in writing, "a case of first female bleeding." Detective Patel needed to remind himself that his 20 years with Nancy had made it easy for him to recognize the tortured morality of many of his colleagues; he restrained himself from too harsh a judgment of the subinspector.

The third report that needed to be revised was Dhar-related; it had never been reported as a crime at all. There'd been a perplexing brouhaha on Falkland Road in the wee hours. Dhar's dwarf bodyguard—that cocky thug!—had beaten up a half-dozen hijras. Two were still hospitalized, and one of the four who'd been released was wearing a cast on a broken wrist. Two of the transvestite prostitutes had been persuaded not to press charges against Dhar's dwarf, whom the investigating officer referred to by the name many policemen used for Vinod: "the half-bodyguard." But the report was stupidly written because the part about Inspector Dhar being under attack, and Vinod coming to his rescue, was merely a footnote; there was no mention of what Dhar had been doing in the neighborhood in the first place—the report was too unfinished for submission.

The deputy commissioner made a note to inquire of Dhar what had possessed the actor to approach the hijra prostitutes. If the fool wanted to fuck a prostitute, surely an expensive call girl would be within his financial reach—and safer. The incident struck the detective as highly out of character for the circumspect celebrity. Wouldn't it be funny if Inspector Dhar was a homosexual? the deputy commissioner thought.

There was at least some humor in the deputy commissioner's day. The fourth report had come to Crime Branch Headquarters from the Tardeo Police Station. At least six snakes were loose near the Mahalaxmi temple, but there were no reported bitings—meaning, none yet. The duty officer from the Tardeo Station had taken photographs. Detective Patel recognized the broad expanse of stairs leading to the Mahalaxmi. At the top of the steps, where the temple loomed, there was a wide pavilion where the worshipers bought coconut and flowers for their offerings; this was also where the worshipers left their sandals and shoes. But, in the photos, the deputy commissioner could see that the stairs leading to the temple were dotted with stray sandals and shoes— indicating that a panicked crowd had only recently fled up or down the steps. In the aftermath of riots, the ground was always strewn with sandals and shoes; people had run right out of them or up the backs of other people's heels.

The temple steps were usually crowded; now they were deserted— the flower stalls and the coconut shops were empty of people, too. Everywhere there were only scattered sandals and shoes! At the bottom of the temple stairs, Detective Patel noted the tall woven baskets where the cobras were kept; the baskets were overturned, presumably empty. The snake charmers had fled with everyone else. But where had the cobras gone?

It must have been quite a scene, the deputy commissioner imagined. The worshipers running and screaming, the snakes slithering away. Detective Patel thought that most of the cobras belonging to snake charmers had no venom, although they could still bite.

The puzzle in the photographs was what was missing from the pictures. What had been the crime? Had one snake charmer thrown his cobra at another snake charmer? Had a tourist tripped over one of the cobra baskets? In one second the snakes were loose, in another second people were running out of their shoes. But what was the crime?

Deputy Commissioner Patel sent the snake report back to the Tardeo

Police Station. The escaped cobras were their problem. *Probably* the snakes were venomless; if they were snake charmers' snakes, at least they were tame. The detective knew that a half-dozen cobras in Mahalaxmi weren't half as dangerous as Rahul.

At the Mission, Farrokh Is Inspired

It was a surprisingly subdued missionary whom Farrokh delivered to the Jesuits at St. Ignatius. Inside the cloister, Martin Mills exhibited the obedience of a well-trained dog; the once-admired "modesty of the eyes" became a fixed feature of his face—he looked more like a monk than a Jesuit. The doctor couldn't have known that the Father Rector and Father Cecil and Brother Gabriel had been expecting a loud clown in a Hawaiian shirt; Dr. Daruwalla was disappointed at the almost reverential greeting the scholastic received. In his unpressed Fashion Street shirt—not to mention his haunted, scratched face and his concentration-camp haircut—the new missionary made a serious first impression.

Dr. Daruwalla unaccountably lingered at the mission. Farrokh supposed that he was hoping for an opportunity to warn Father Julian that Martin Mills was a madman; but the doctor was of a considerably mixed mind when it came to involving himself to a greater extent in the newcomer's future. Furthermore, Farrokh found that it was impossible to get the Father Rector alone. They'd arrived just after the schoolboys had finished lunch. Father Cecil and Brother Gabriel—with not fewer than a combined 145 years between them—insisted on struggling with the scholastic's suitcase, and this left Father Julian to conduct Martin's first tour of St. Ignatius. Dr. Daruwalla followed behind.

Since his own school days, Farrokh had spent only intermittent time at the place. He reviewed the examination scrolls in the entrance hall with a detached curiosity. The Indian Certificate of Secondary Education (I.C.S.E.) marked the completion of junior high school. In the Examination Certificate of 1973, St. Ignatius demonstrated its Spanish connection by commemorating the death of Picasso; this must have been Brother Gabriel's idea. A photograph of the artist was among the photos of that year's graduates, as if Picasso had also passed the requisite exam; and there were these few words: PICASSO PASSES AWAY. In 1975, the 300th anniversary of Shivaji's Coronation was commemorated; in '76, the Montreal Olympics was observed; in '77, the deaths of both Charlie

Chaplin and Elvis were mourned—they were also pictured among the graduates. This yearbook-minded sentimentality was intermixed with religious and nationalistic fervor. The centerpiece of the entrance hall was a larger-than-life statue of the Virgin Mary standing on the head of the serpent with the apple in its mouth, as if she thus circumvented or had altered the Old Testament. And over the entranceway itself were side-by-side portraits—one of the pope of the moment, the other of Nehru as a young man.

Haunted by nostalgia, but more strongly disturbed by a culture that had never become his, Farrokh felt himself losing his faint resolve. Why warn the Father Rector about Martin Mills? Why try to warn *any* of them? The whole place, perhaps owing its inspiration to St. Ignatius Loyola himself, spoke of survival—not to mention a humbling instinct for repentance. As for the Jesuits' success in Bombay and the rest of India, Farrokh assumed that the Indian stress on mother-worship gave the Catholics a certain advantage. The cult of the Virgin Mary was just more mother-worship, wasn't it? Even in an all-boys' school, the Holy Mother dominated the statuary.

Only a scattering of English names appeared on the examination scrolls, yet passable English was an admissions requirement and fluency in the language was expected of any St. Ignatius graduate; it was the classroom language throughout the school, and the only language posted in writing.

At the student canteen, in the courtyard, was a photograph of the junior school's most recent trip: there were the boys in their white shirts with navy-blue ties; they wore navy-blue shorts and kneesocks, too— and black shoes. The caption to this photo said: OUR JUNIORS, INC. OUR MIDGETS AND OUR SUB-MIDGETS. (Dr. Daruwalla disapproved of abbreviations.)

In the first-aid room, a boy with a stomach ache lay curled on a cot, above which was tacked a photo of the stereotypical sunset at Haji Ali's Tomb. The caption that accompanied this sunset was as egregious a non sequitur as any that had thus far been uttered by Martin Mills: YOU ONLY LIVE ONCE, BUT IF YOU LIVE RIGHT, ONCE IS ENOUGH.

Moving on to the music parlor, the doctor was struck by the tunelessness of the piano, which, in combination with the abrasive singing of the untalented music teacher, made it hard for Dr. Daruwalla to recognize even as oft-droned a dirge as "Swing Low, Sweet Chariot." She was an English teacher, a certain Miss Tanuja, and Farrokh overheard Father Julian explaining to Martin Mills that this time-honored method of teaching a language through song lyrics was still popular with the younger children. Since very few of the children were contributing more than mumbles to Miss Tanuja's braying voice, Farrokh doubted the Father Rector on this point; maybe the problem wasn't the method but Miss Tanuja.

She struck Dr. Daruwalla as one of those Indian women who remain uncontained by Western clothes, which Miss Tanuja was wearing with special gracelessness and folly. Perhaps the children couldn't sing "Swing Low, Sweet Chariot" because they were distracted by the riotous array of Miss Tanuja's ensemble; the doctor observed that even Martin Mills appeared to be distracted by her. Farrokh cruelly assumed that Miss Tanuja was desperate to marry. She was very round-faced and of a medium, milk-chocolate complexion, and she wore very sharply angled glasses—of the kind with upward-sweeping wing tips embedded with small, bright gems. Perhaps Miss Tanuja thought that these eyeglasses contrasted pleasingly with the smoothness and roundness of her face.

She had the plump, youthful figure of a high-school voluptuary, but she wore a dark skirt that hugged her hips too tightly and was the wrong length for her. Miss Tanuja was short and the dress chopped her legs off at midcalf, which gave Dr. Daruwalla the impression that her thick ankles were wrists and her fat little feet were hands. Her blouse had a reflecting luminosity of a blue-green nature, as if flecked with algae dredged from a pond; and although the woman's most pleasing quality was an overall curvaceousness, she'd chosen a bra that served her badly. From what little Dr. Daruwalla knew of bras, he judged it to be the old-fashioned pointy type—one of those rigidly constructed halters more suitable for protecting women from fencing injuries than for enhancing their natural shapeliness. And between Miss Tanuja's outrageously uplifted and sharply pointed breasts, there hung a crucifix, as if the Christ on Miss Tanuja's cross—in addition to his other agonies—were expected to endure the misery of bouncing on the teacher's ample but spear-headed bosoms.

"Miss Tanuja has been with us for many years," Father Julian whispered.

"I see," said Dr. Daruwalla, but Martin Mills merely stared.

Then they passed a classroom of smaller children in I-3. The kids were napping with their heads on their desks—either "midgets" or "sub-midgets," Farrokh guessed.

"Do you play the piano?" the Father Rector was asking the new missionary.

"I always wanted to learn," Martin said. Maybe the madman could practice the piano between bouts of orienting himself in *The Times of India*, Dr. Daruwalla thought.

And to change the subject from his lack of musical skills, the scholastic asked Father Julian about the sweepers, for there were everywhere about the mission an abundance of men and women who were sweeping—they also cleaned the toilets—and the missionary assumed that these sweepers were people from the untouchable castes.

The Father Rector used the words "bhangee" and "maitrani," but Martin Mills was a man with more of a mission than Father Julian supposed. Martin asked the Father Rector directly: "And do *their* children attend this school?" All of a sudden, Dr. Daruwalla liked him.

"Well, no—that wouldn't be suitable, you see," Father Julian was saying, but Farrokh was impressed by how gracefully Martin Mills interrupted the Father Rector. The scholastic simply breezed into a description of "rescuing" the crippled beggar and the child prostitute; it was Martin's one-step-at-a-time method, and the missionary virtually waltzed the Father Rector through the steps. First the circus—instead of begging, or the brothel. Then the mastery of the English language—"so civilizing as to be essential"—and *then* "the intelligent conversion"; Martin Mills also called this "the informed life in Christ."

A class of seniors, on recess, was enjoying a savage, silent dirt fight in the courtyard, but Dr. Daruwalla marveled how the Jesuits were undistracted by this minor violence; they spoke and listened with the concentration of lions stalking a kill.

"But surely, Martin, you wouldn't credit *yourself* with these children's conversion?" Father Julian said. "That is, should they eventually be converted."

"Well, no . . . what do you mean?" Martin asked.

"Only that I never know if *I* have converted anyone," the Father Rector replied. "And if these children were converted, how could you presume it happened because of you? Don't be too proud. If it happens, it was God. It wasn't you."

"Why, no—of course not!" said Martin Mills. "If it happens, it was God!"

Was this "obedience"? Dr. Daruwalla wondered.

When Father Julian led Martin to his cubicle, which Dr. Daruwalla imagined as a kind of prison cell with built-in instruments to chastise the flesh, the doctor continued to roam; he wanted to look at the sleeping children again, because that image of sleeping with his head on his desk was more appealing than anything else he could remember about attending St. Ignatius School—it had been so many years ago. But when he peered into I-3 again, a teacher he hadn't seen before regarded him sternly, as if his presence in the doorway would disturb the children. And this time the doctor noticed the exposed wiring for the fluorescent lights, which were off, and the exposed wiring for the ceiling fan, which was on. Suspended over the blackboard like a puppet on tangled, immobile strings was yet another statue of the Virgin Mary. From Farrokh's Canadian perspective, this particular Holy Mother was covered with frost, or a light snow; but it was only rising chalk dust from the blackboard that had settled on the statue.

Dr. Daruwalla amused himself by reading as many printed messages and announcements as he could find. There was a plea from the Social Concern Group—"to help less fortunate brothers and sisters." Prayers were offered for the Souls in Purgatory. There was the pleasing juxtaposition of the Minimax fire extinguisher that was mounted on the wall beside the statue of Christ with the sick child; in fire-extinguisher language, a short list of instructions was printed next to a page from a lined notebook on which a child's handwriting proclaimed, "Thanks to Infant Jesus and Our Lady of Perpetual Help." Farrokh felt somewhat more comforted by the presence of the fire extinguisher. The great stone mission had been erected in 1865; the fluorescent lights, the ceiling fans, the vast network of haphazard wiring—these had been added later. The doctor concluded that an electrical fire was entirely possible.

Farrokh tried to familiarize himself with all the meetings that a good Christian could go to. There was an announced Meeting of Liturgical Readers, and the Meeting of the Members of the Cross—"to make parish members more politically conscious." The present topic of proposed conversation in the Adult Catholic Education Program was "The Christian Today in the World of Non-Christian Religions." This month, the Hope Alive Center was conducted by Dr. Yusuf Merchant. Dr. Daruwalla wondered what "conducted by" meant. There was a Get to Know Each Other Party for the Altar Service Corps, which Farrokh suspected would be a grim gathering.

Under the archway of the second-floor balcony, the doctor was struck by the unfinished irregularity of the pieces of stained glass—as if the very notion of God were this fragmented, this incomplete. In the Icon Chapel, the doctor abruptly closed a hymnal upon encountering the hymn called "Bring Me Oil." Then he read the bookmark that he'd removed from the hymnal; the bookmark celebrated St. Ignatius's upcoming jubilee year—"a labour of love in building youth for 125 years." There was also the word "world-affirming"; Dr. Daruwalla had never had the slightest idea what this implied. Farrokh peeked into the hymnal again, but even the name of the thing offended him; it was called the "Song Book of the Charismatic Renewal in India"—he hadn't known that there *was* any charismatic renewal! And so he exchanged the hymnal for a prayer book, wherein he looked no further than the opening line of the first prayer: "Keep us, Lord, as the apple of Your eye."

Dr. Daruwalla then discovered the Holy Father's Intentions for 1990. For January, it was advised that the dialogue between the Catholic and Anglican communities continue in the quest for Christian unity. For February, prayers were offered for those Catholics who, in many parts of the world, suffered either verbal or physical persecution. For March, the parishioners were exhorted to give a more authentic witness for support of the needy—and fidelity to the poverty of the Gospels. Dr. Daruwalla couldn't read past March, for the phrase "poverty of the Gospels" stopped him. Farrokh felt surrounded by too much that was meaningless to him.

Even Brother Gabriel's fastidious collecting of icons meant little to the doctor, and the icon-collection room at St. Ignatius was famous in Bombay. To Farrokh, the depictions were lugubrious and obscure. There was a 16th-century Adoration of the Magi, of the Ukrainian School; there was a 15th-century Decapitation of John the Baptist, of the Central Northern School. In the Passing of Our Lord category, there was a Last Supper, a Crucifixion, a Deposition (the taking of Christ's body from the cross), an Entombment, a Resurrection and an Ascension; they were all icons from the 14th through the 18th centuries, and they varied among the Novgorod School, the Byzantine School, the Moscow School . . . and so on. There was one called the Dormition of the Virgin, and that did it for Dr. Daruwalla; the doctor didn't know what the Dormition was.

From the icons, the doctor roamed to the Father Rector's office, where something resembling a cribbage board was nailed to the closed door; by means of holes and pegs, Father Julian could indicate his whereabouts or availability—"back soon" or "do not disturb," "rec.

room" or "back late," "back for supper" or "out of Bombay." That was when Dr. Daruwalla considered that *he* should be "out of Bombay"; that he'd been born here didn't mean that he belonged here.

When he heard the bell signifying the end of school, Farrokh realized that it was already 3:00 in the afternoon. He stood on the second-floor balcony and watched the schoolboys racing through the dusty courtyard. Cars and buses were taking them away; either their mothers or their ayahs were coming to fetch them home. From the perspective of the balcony, Dr. Daruwalla determined that they were the fattest children he'd ever seen in India. This was uncharitable; not half the children at St. Ignatius were half as plump as Farrokh. Nevertheless, the doctor knew that he would no more interfere with the new missionary's zeal than he would choose to leap from the balcony and kill himself in front of these blameless children.

Farrokh also knew that almost no one of rank at the mission would mistake Martin Mills for Inspector Dhar. The Jesuits weren't known for their appreciation of so-called Bollywood, the trashy Hindi film scene; young women in soaking-wet saris weren't their thing. Superheroes and fiendish villains, violence and vulgarity, tawdriness and corniness—and the occasional descending god, intervening in pathetic, merely human affairs . . . Inspector Dhar was *not* famous at St. Ignatius. Among the schoolboys, however, more than one student of Martin Mills might note the resemblance. Inspector Dhar was popular with schoolboys.

Dr. Daruwalla still lingered; he had things to do, but he couldn't make himself leave. He didn't know that he was *writing;* it had never begun quite like this before. When the children were gone, he went inside St. Ignatius Church—but not to pray. A huge wheel of unlit candles hung above the center table, which resembled a refectory table only in its shape; in fact, it was a folding table of a household kind—better suited, say, for sorting laundry. The pulpit, to the right of this table (as Farrokh faced the altar), was equipped with an inappropriately shiny microphone; upon this pulpit a Lectionary lay open, from which the doctor assumed that the lector would be reading—possibly at the evening Mass. Dr. Daruwalla couldn't resist snooping. The Lectionary was open to the Second Epistle of Paul to the Corinthians.

"Therefore, since we have this ministry, as we have received mercy, we do not lose heart," wrote the converted one. [II Corinthians 4:1] Skipping ahead, the doctor read: "*We are* hard pressed on every side, yet not crushed; *we are* perplexed, but not in despair; persecuted, but not forsaken; struck down, but not destroyed—always carrying about in the body the dying of the Lord Jesus, that the life of Jesus may also be manifested in our body." [4:8–10]

Dr. Daruwalla felt small. He ventured into a pew in one of the side aisles—as if he wasn't significant enough, in his lack of faith, to sit in a center-aisle seat. His own conversion seemed trifling, and very far behind him; in his daily thoughts, he barely honored it—perhaps he *had* been bitten by a monkey, he concluded. He noted that the church was without an organ; another, probably tuneless piano stood to the left of the folding table—another inappropriately shiny microphone stood on it.

From far outside the church, the doctor was aware of the constantly passing mopeds—the snarling of their low-powered engines, the duck-like quacking of their infernal horns. The highly staged altarpiece drew the doctor's eye: there was Christ on the Cross and those two familiar women forlornly flanking him. Mother Mary and Mary Magdalen, Dr. Daruwalla presumed. The life-sized figures of the saints, all in stone, were mounted on the columns that defined the aisles; these massive pillars each supported a saint, and at the saints' feet were tilted oscillating fans—pointed down, in order to cool the congregation.

Blasphemously, Dr. Daruwalla noticed that one of the stone saints had worked herself loose from her pillar; a thick chain had been secured around the saint's neck, and this chain was attached to the pillar by a sizable steel grommet. The doctor wished he knew which saint she was; he thought that all the female saints too closely resembled the Virgin Mary—at least as statues. Whoever this saint was, she appeared to have been hung in effigy; but without the chain around her neck, she might have toppled into a pew. Dr. Daruwalla judged that the stone saint was big enough to kill a pew of worshipers.

Finally, Farrokh said his good-byes to Martin Mills and the other Jesuits. The scholastic suddenly begged to hear the details of Dr. Daruwalla's conversion. The doctor supposed that Father Julian had given Martin a cunning and sarcastic rendition of the story.

"Oh, it was nothing," Farrokh replied modestly. This probably concurred with the Father Rector's version.

"But I should love to hear about it!" Martin said.

"If you tell him yours, I'm sure he'll tell you *his*," Father Julian said to Farrokh.

"Maybe another time," Dr. Daruwalla said. Never had he so much desired to flee. He had to promise that he'd attend Martin's lecture at the YWCA, although he had no intentions of attending; he would rather die than attend. He'd heard quite enough lecturing from Martin Mills!

"It's the YWCA at Cooperage, you know," Father Cecil informed him. Since Dr. Daruwalla was sensitive to those Bombayites who assumed that he barely knew his way around the city, the doctor was snappish in his reply.

"I *know* where it is!" Farrokh said.

Then a little girl appeared, out of nowhere. She was crying because she'd come to St. Ignatius with her mother, to pick up her brother after school, and somehow they'd left without her. There'd been other children in the car. It wasn't a crisis, the Jesuits decided. The mother would realize what had happened and return to the school. It was merely necessary to comfort the child, and someone should call the mother so that she'd not drive recklessly in fear that her daughter was lost. But there was another problem: the little girl confided to them that she needed to pee. Brother Gabriel declared to Dr. Daruwalla that there was "no official peeing place for girls" at St. Ignatius.

"But where does Miss Tanuja pee?" Martin Mills asked.

Good for him! Dr. Daruwalla thought. He's going to drive them all crazy.

"And I saw several women among the sweepers," Martin added.

"There must be three or four women teachers, aren't there?" Dr. Daruwalla asked innocently.

Of *course* there was a peeing place for girls! These old men simply didn't know where it was.

"Someone could see if a men's room is unoccupied," Father Cecil suggested.

"Then one of us could guard the door," Father Julian advised.

When Farrokh finally left them all, they were still discussing this awkward necessity to bend the rules. The doctor presumed that the little girl still needed to pee.

Tetracycline

Dr. Daruwalla was on his way back to the Hospital for Crippled Children when he realized that he'd started another screenplay; he knew that this one would *not* be starring Inspector Dhar. In his mind's eye, he saw a beggar working the Arab hotels along Marine Drive; he saw the Queen's Necklace at night . . . that string of yellow smog lights . . . and he heard Julia saying that yellow wasn't the proper color for the necklace of a queen. For the first time, Farrokh felt that he understood the start of a story—the characters were set in motion by the fates that awaited them. Something of the authority of an ending was already contained in the beginning scene.

He was exhausted; he had much to talk about with Julia, and he had to talk to John D. Dr. Daruwalla and his wife were having an early dinner at the Ripon Club. Then the doctor had planned to write a first draft of a little speech he would be giving soon; he'd been invited to say something to the Society for the Rehabilitation of Crippled Children— they were such faithful sponsors of the hospital. But now he knew he would write all night—and not his speech. At last, he thought, he had a screenplay in him that justified the telling. In his mind's eye, he saw the characters arriving at Victoria Terminus, but this time he knew where they were going; he wondered if he'd ever been so excited.

The familiar figure in Dr. Daruwalla's waiting room distracted the doctor from the story he'd imagined; among the waiting children, the tall man indeed stood out. Even seated, his military erectness immediately captured Farrokh's attention. The taut sallow skin and the slack mouth; the lion-yellow eyes; the acid-shriveled ear and the raw pink smear that had burned a swath along his jawline and down the side of his throat, where it disappeared under the collar of Mr. Garg's shirt—all this captured Dr. Daruwalla's attention, too.

One look at the nervously wriggling fingers of Mr. Garg's locked hands confirmed Farrokh's suspicions. It was clear to the doctor that Garg was itching to know the specific nature of Madhu's "sexually transmitted disease"; Dr. Daruwalla felt only an empty triumph. To see Garg—guilty and ready to grovel, and reduced to waiting his turn among the crippled children—would be the full extent of the doctor's slight victory, for Dr. Daruwalla knew, even at this very moment, that something more than professional confidentiality would prevent him from disclosing Mr. Garg's guilt to Deepa and Vinod. Besides, how could the dwarf and his wife not already know that Garg diddled young girls? It may have been Garg's guilt that compelled him to allow Deepa and Vinod to attempt their circus rescues of so many of these children. Surely the dwarf and his wife already knew what Farrokh was only beginning to guess: that many of these little prostitutes would have preferred to stay with Mr. Garg. Like the circus, even the Great Blue Nile, maybe Garg was better than a brothel.

Mr. Garg stood and faced Farrokh. The eyes of every crippled child in Dr. Daruwalla's waiting room were fixed on the acid scar, but the doctor looked only at the whites of Garg's eyes, which were a jaundice-yellow—and at the deeper, tawny lion-yellow of Garg's irises, which offset his black pupils. Garg had the same eyes as Madhu. The doctor passingly wondered if they might be related.

"I was here first—before any of them," Mr. Garg whispered.

"I'll bet you were," said Dr. Daruwalla.

If it was guilt that had flickered in Garg's lion eyes, it seemed to be fading; a shy smile tightened his usually slack lips, and something conspiratorial crept into his voice. "So . . . I guess you know about Madhu and me," Mr. Garg said.

What can one say to such a man? Dr. Daruwalla thought. The doctor realized that Deepa and Vinod and even Martin Mills were right: let *every* girl-child be an acrobat in the circus, even in the Great Blue Nile—even if they fall and die. Let them be eaten by lions! For it was true that Madhu was both a child and a prostitute—worse, she was Mr. Garg's girl. There was truly nothing to say to such a man. Only a strictly professional question came to Dr. Daruwalla's mind, and he put it to Garg as bluntly as he could.

"Are you allergic to tetracycline?" the doctor asked him.

17. STRANGE CUSTOMS

Southern California

Because he had a history of suffering in unfamiliar bedrooms, Martin Mills lay awake in his cubicle at the mission of St. Ignatius. At first he followed the advice of St. Teresa of Avila—her favorite spiritual exercise, which allowed her to experience the love of Christ—but not even this remedy would permit the new missionary to fall asleep. The idea was to imagine that Christ saw you. *"Mira que te mira,"* St. Teresa said. "Notice him looking at you." But try as he might to notice such a thing, Martin Mills wasn't comforted; he couldn't sleep.

He loathed his memory of the many bedrooms that his awful mother and pathetic father had exposed him to. This was the result of Danny Mills overpaying for a house in Westwood, which was near the U.C.L.A. campus but which the family could rarely afford to live in; it was perpetually rented so that Danny and Vera could live off the rent. This also provided their decaying marriage with frequent opportunities for them not to live with each other. As a child, Martin Mills was always missing clothes and toys that had somehow become the temporary possessions of the tenants of the Westwood house, which he only vaguely could remember.

He remembered better the U.C.L.A. student who was his babysitter, for she used to drag him by his arm across Wilshire Boulevard at high speed, and usually not at the proper crosswalks. She had a boyfriend who ran around and around the U.C.L.A. track; she'd take Martin to the track and they'd watch the boyfriend run and run. She made Martin's fingers ache, she held his hand so tightly. If the traffic on Wilshire had forced an uncommonly hasty crossing of the boulevard, Martin's upper arm would throb.

Whenever Danny and Vera went out in the evening, Vera insisted that Martin sleep in the other twin bed in the babysitter's bedroom; the rest of her quarters consisted only of a tiny kitchenette—a kind of breakfast nook where a black-and-white television shared the small countertop with a toaster. Here the babysitter sat on one of two barstools, because there wasn't enough space for chairs and a table.

Often, when he lay in the bedroom with the babysitter, Martin Mills could hear her masturbating; because the room was sealed and permanently air-conditioned, more often he would wake up in the morning and detect that she *had* masturbated by the smell, which was on the fingers of her right hand when she stroked his face and told him it was time for him to get up and brush his teeth. Then she'd drive him to school, which she did in a manner of recklessness equivalent to her habit of dragging him across Wilshire Boulevard. There was an exit from the San Diego Freeway that seemed to draw out of the babysitter a dramatic catching of her breath, which reminded Martin Mills of the sound she made while masturbating; just before this exit, Martin would always close his eyes.

It was a good school, an accelerated program conducted by the Jesuits at Loyola Marymount University, which was a fair drive from West-wood. But although the traveling to school and back was hazardous, the fact that Martin Mills was first educated in facilities also used by university students seemed to have an austere effect on the boy. Befitting an experiment in early-childhood education—the program was discontinued after a few years—even the chairs were grownup-sized, and the classrooms were not festooned with children's crayon drawings or animals wearing the letters of the alphabet. In the men's room used by these gifted children, the smaller boys stood on a stool to pee—these were the days before there were urinals at wheelchair level for the handicapped. Thus, both at the towering urinals and in the undecorated classrooms, it was as if these special children had been granted the opportunity to skip over childhood. But if the classrooms and the urinals spoke of the seriousness of the business at hand, they also suffered from the anonymity and impersonality of the many bedrooms in young Martin's life.

Whenever the Westwood house was rented, Danny and Vera also lost the services of the U.C.L.A. babysitter. Then—from other, unfamiliar parts of town—Danny would be the designated driver who spirited Martin Mills to his accelerated education at Loyola Marymount. Driving with Danny was no less dangerous than the trip from and to Westwood with the U.C.L.A. babysitter. Danny would be hungover at the early-morning hour, if he wasn't still inebriated, and by the time Martin was ready to be picked up after school, Danny would have begun to drink again. As for Vera, she didn't drive. The former Hermione Rosen had never learned to drive, which is not unusual among people who pass their teenage years in Brooklyn or Manhattan. Her father, the producer Harold Rosen, had also never learned to drive; he was a frequent limousine-user, and once—for several months, when Danny Mills had lost his driver's license to a DWI conviction—Harold had sent a limo to take Martin Mills to school.

On the other hand, Vera's uncle, the director Gordon Hathaway, was a veteran speedster behind the wheel, and his penchant for speed in combination with his permanently purple ears (of varying deafness) would result in the periodic suspension of his driver's license. Gordon never yielded to fire trucks or ambulances or police cars; as for his own horn, since he couldn't hear it, he never used it, and he was utterly oblivious to the warning blasts that emanated from other vehicles. He would meet his Maker on the Santa Monica Freeway, where he rear-ended a station wagon full of surfers. Gordon was killed instantly by a surfboard; maybe it flew off the roof rack of the station wagon, or out of the open tailgate—either way, it came through Gordon's windshield. There were ensuing vehicular collisions spanning four lanes, in two directions, and involving eight automobiles and a motorcycle; only Gordon was killed. Surely the director had a second or two to see his death coming, but at his memorial service his renowned C. of M. sister, who was Harold Rosen's wife and Vera's mother, remarked that Gordon's deafness had at least spared him the *noise* of his own death, for it was generally agreed that the sounds of a nine-vehicle collision must have been considerable.

Nevertheless, Martin Mills survived the harrowing trips to his advanced schooling at Loyola Marymount; it was the bedrooms—their foreignness, their disorientation—that got to him. The quintessential sellout, Danny had rashly bought the Westwood house with the money he'd received for a three-screenplay deal; unfortunately, at the time he took the money the screenplays were unwritten—none would be produced. Then, as always, there were more deals based on unfinished work. Danny would have to rent Westwood. This depressed him; he drank to blur his self-disgust. This also led him to live in other people's houses; these were usually the houses of producers or directors or actors to whom Danny owed a finished screenplay. Since these philanthropic souls could stand neither the spectacle nor the company of the desperate writer, they would vacate their houses and run off to New York or Europe. Sometimes, Martin Mills learned later, Vera would run off with them.

Writing a script under such pressure was a process Danny Mills referred to as "ball-busting," which had long been a favorite expression of Gordon Hathaway's. As Martin Mills lay awake in his cubicle at St. Ignatius, the new missionary couldn't stop himself from remembering these houses belonging to strangers, who were always people in a position of power over his feckless father.

There'd been the house belonging to a director in Beverly Hills; it was on Franklin Canyon Drive, and Danny lost the privilege of living there because the driveway was so steep—that was how Danny put it. What happened was, he came home drunk; he left the director's car in neutral (with the brake off) and the garage door open, and the car rolled over a grapefruit tree and into the swimming pool. This wouldn't have been so damaging had Vera not been having an affair with the director's maid, who the next morning dove naked into the swimming pool and broke her jaw and collarbone against the submerged windshield of the car. This happened while Danny was calling the police to report that the car had been stolen. Naturally, the maid sued the director for having a car in his pool. The movie that Danny was writing at the time was never produced, which was not an infrequent conclusion to Danny busting his balls.

Martin Mills had liked that house, if not that maid. In retrospect, Martin regretted that his mother's sexual preference for young women had been passing; her appetite for young men was messier. As for Martin's particular bedroom in the house on Franklin Canyon Drive, it had seemed nicer than the rest. It was a corner room with enough natural ventilation that he could sleep without the air conditioner; that was why he'd heard the car sinking into the swimming pool—first the splash, then all the bubbles. But he'd not gotten out of bed to look because he assumed it was his drunken father; by the sound, Martin suspected that Danny was cavorting with about a dozen drunken men—

they were belching and farting underwater, he deduced. He had no idea
a *car* had been involved.

In the morning, up early (as always), Martin had been only mildly
surprised to see the car resting on the bottom of the deep end. Slowly
it occurred to him that his father might be trapped inside. Martin was
naked and crying when he ran downstairs to the swimming pool, where
he found the naked maid; she was drowning under the diving board.
Martin would never be credited with rescuing her. He picked up the
long pole with the net on one end, which was used for skimming frogs
and salamanders out of the water, and he extended this to the brown,
feral-looking little woman of Mexican descent, but she couldn't speak
(because her jaw was broken) and she couldn't lift herself out of the pool
(because her collarbone was broken, too). She held fast to the pole while
Martin towed her to the pool curb, and there she clung; she looked
beseechingly at Martin Mills, who covered his genitals with his hands.
From the depths of the pool, the sunken car emitted another bubble.

That was when Martin's mother exited the maid's bungalow, which
was next to the shed for pool toys. Wrapped in a towel, Vera saw Martin
standing naked by the deep end, but she failed to see her floundering
lover of the night before.

"Martin, you know what I think of skinny-dipping," Vera told the
boy. "Go put on your trunks before Maria sees you." Maria, of course,
was also skinny-dipping.

As for putting on his clothes, that was the moment when Martin Mills
identified one of his dislikes for his repeated use of someone else's
bedroom; *their* clothes were in the drawers—at best, the bottommost
drawers had been emptied for Martin—and *their* clothes hung lifelessly
but prepossessingly in the closets. Their old toys filled up a chest; their
baby pictures were on the walls. Sometimes their tennis trophies or
horse-riding ribbons were displayed. Often there were shrines to their
first dogs or cats, apparently deceased; this could be discerned by the
presence of a glass jar that contained a dog's toenail or a tuft from a cat's
tail. And when Martin would carry his little triumphs "home" from
school—his "A" papers and other evidence of his accelerated education—he wasn't allowed to display these on *their* walls.

Then, in Los Angeles, there'd been an actor's virtually unlived-in
house on South Lorraine—a huge, grandly conceived mansion with
many small, musty bedrooms all boasting blurry, enlarged photographs
of unknown children of a conspicuously similar age. It seemed to Martin

that the children who grew up there had died when they were six or eight, or that they'd uniformly become uninteresting subjects for photography upon reaching this approximate age; but there had simply been a divorce. In that house, time had stopped—Martin had hated it there—and Danny had at last outworn his welcome by falling asleep while smoking on the couch in front of the TV. The smoke alarm woke him, but he was drunk; he called the police instead of the fire department, and by the time that confusion was sorted out, the entire living room was consumed in flames. Danny took Martin to the pool, where he paddled about on an inflated raft in the form of Donald Duck—another relic of the permanently six- and eight-year-old children.

Danny waded back and forth in the shallow end of the pool, although he wore long trousers and a wrinkled dress shirt instead of a bathing suit, and he held the pages of his screenplay-in-progress against his chest; clearly, he didn't want the pages to get wet. Together, father and son watched the firefighters subduing the disaster.

The actor, who was almost famous and whose living room was ruined, came home much later—after the fire was out and the firemen had left. Danny and Martin Mills were still playing in the swimming pool.

"Let's wait up for Mommy, so you can tell her all about the fire," Danny had suggested.

"Where's Mommy?" Martin had asked.

"Out," Danny had replied. She was "out" with the actor. When Vera and the actor returned together, Martin imagined that his father was slightly pleased with the smoldering wreck he'd made of the living room. The screenplay wasn't going too well; it was to be an opportunity for the actor to do something "timely"—it was a story about a younger man with an older woman . . . "something bittersweet," the actor had suggested. Vera was hoping for the role of the older woman. But that screenplay was never made into a movie, either. Martin Mills was not sorry to leave those permanently six- and eight-year-old children on South Lorraine.

In his stark cubicle at St. Ignatius in Mazagaon, the missionary was now looking for his copy of the *Pocket Catholic Catechism;* he hoped that these essentials of his faith might rescue him from reliving every bedroom he'd ever slept in in California. But he couldn't find the reassuring little paperback; he presumed he'd left it on Dr. Daruwalla's glass-topped table—in fact, he had. Dr. Daruwalla had already put it to use. Farrokh had read up on Extreme Unction, the Sacrament of the Anointing of the Sick, for this fit rather neatly into the new screenplay that the doctor was dying to begin; he'd also skimmed a passage about the crucifixion—he thought that he might make some sly use of it. The doctor was feeling mischievous, and the earlier hours of the evening had seemed interminable to him because nothing mattered to him as much as beginning this suddenly important piece of writing. Had Martin Mills known that Dr. Daruwalla was about to re-create him as a character in a romantic comedy, the unfortunate missionary might have welcomed the distraction of remembering his itinerant childhood in Los Angeles.

There'd been another L.A. house, on Kings Road, and Martin had cautiously loved that one; it had a fish pond, and the producer-owner kept rare birds, which were unfortunately Danny's responsibility while he lived and wrote there. On the very first day, Martin had observed that the house had no screens. The rare birds weren't caged; they were chained to their perches. One evening, during a dinner party, a hawk flew inside the house—and then another hawk flew inside—and to the considerable alarm of the assembled dinner guests, the rare birds fell victims to these visiting birds of prey. While the rare birds were shrieking and dying, Danny was so drunk that he insisted on finishing his version of how he was evicted from his favorite beach-view duplex in Venice. It was a story that never failed to bring tears to Martin's eyes, because it concerned the death of his only dog. Meanwhile, the hawks swooped and killed; and the dinner guests—at first, just the women— put their heads under the dining-room table. Danny kept telling the story.

It had not yet occurred to young Martin that the declining fortunes of his father's screenwriting career would occasionally result in low-rent housing. Although this was a step down from freeloading in the generally well-to-do homes of directors and producers and almost-famous actors, the cheap rentals were at least free of other people's clothes and toys; in this sense, these rentals seemed a step *up* to Martin Mills. But not Venice. It had also not occurred to young Martin that Danny and Vera were simply waiting for their son to be old enough to send away to school. They presumed this would spare the child the continuing embarrassment of his parents' lives—their virtually separate existences, even within the confines of the same residence, their coping with Vera's affairs and with Danny's drinking. But Venice was too low-rent for Vera; she chose to spend the time in New York, while Danny was pounding the keys of a portable typewriter and dangerously driving Martin to and from Loyola Marymount. In Venice, they'd shared the ground-floor half of a shocking-pink duplex on the beach.

"It was the best place we ever lived, because it was so fucking real!" Danny explained to his cowering dinner guests. "Isn't that right, Marty?" But young Martin was silent; he was noticing the death agonies of a mynah—the bird was succumbing to a hawk, very near where the uneaten hors d'oeuvres still occupied a coffee table in the living room.

In truth, Martin thought, Venice had seemed rather *un*real to him. There were drugged hippies on South Venice Boulevard; Martin Mills was terrified of such an environment, but Danny touched and surprised him by giving him a dog for a pre-Christmas present. It was a beagle-sized mongrel from the pound—"Saved from death!" Danny said. He named it "Whiskey," because of its color and in spite of Martin's protests. This must have condemned the dog, to name it after booze.

Whiskey slept with Martin, and Martin was allowed to put his own things on the ocean-damp walls. When he came "home" from school, he waited until the lifeguards were off-duty before he took Whiskey walking on the beach, where for the first time he imagined he was the envy of those children who can always be found in public playgrounds—in this case, those children who stood in line to use the slide on Venice Beach. Surely they would have liked a dog of their own to walk on the sand.

For Christmas, Vera visited—albeit briefly. She refused to stay in Venice. She claimed a suite of rooms at a plain but clean hotel on Ocean Avenue in Santa Monica; there she ate a Christmas breakfast with Martin—the first of many lonely meals he would remember with his mother, whose principal measure of luxury was drawn from her qualified praise of room service. Veronica Rose repeatedly said that she would be happier living on reliable room service than in a house of her own—throw the towels on the floor, leave the dishes on the bed, that kind of thing. She gave young Martin a dog collar for Christmas, which profoundly moved him because he could remember no other instance of apparent collaboration between his mother and father; in this isolated case, Danny must have communicated with Vera—at least enough for Vera to know that Danny had given the boy a dog.

But on New Year's Eve, a roller skater (who lived in the turquoise duplex next door) fed the dog a big plate of marijuana lasagna. When Danny and Martin took Whiskey out for a walk after midnight, the stoned runt attacked a weight lifter's Rottweiler; Whiskey was killed by the first snap and shake.

The Rottweiler's owner was a contrite sort of muscle man wearing a tank top and a pair of gym shorts; Danny fetched a shovel, and the apologetic weight lifter dug an enormous grave in the vicinity of the children's slide. No one was permitted to bury a dead dog on Venice Beach; some civic-minded observer called the police. Martin was awakened by two cops very early on New Year's morning, when Danny was too hungover to assist him and there was no weight lifter available to help him dig the dead dog up. When Martin had finished stuffing Whiskey in a trash bag, one of the cops put the body in the trunk of the police car and the other cop, at the moment he handed Martin his fine, asked the boy where he went to school.

"I'm part of an accelerated educational program at Loyola Marymount," Martin Mills explained to the cop.

Not even this distinction would prevent the landlord from evicting Danny and Martin shortly thereafter, out of fear of further trouble with the police. By the time they left, Martin Mills had changed his mind about the place. Almost every day, he'd seen the weight lifter with his murderous Rottweiler; and—either entering or leaving the turquoise duplex next door—the roller skater with a fondness for marijuana lasagna was a daily presence, too. Once again, Martin wasn't sorry to go.

It was Danny who mindlessly loved the story. In the producer's house on Kings Road, Danny seemed to prolong the telling of the tale, almost as if the ongoing bird deaths were an enhancement to the suddenness of poor Whiskey's demise. "What a great fucking neighborhood that was!" Danny was shouting to his dinner guests. By now, all the men had put their heads under the table with the women. Both sexes were fearful that the swooping hawks would mistake them for rare birds.

"Daddy, there are *hawks* in the house!" Martin had cried. "Daddy— the *birds!*"

"This is Hollywood, Marty," Danny Mills had replied. "Don't worry about the birds—the birds don't matter. This is Hollywood. The *story* is all that matters."

That screenplay wasn't made into a movie, either; this was almost a refrain for Danny Mills. The bill for the rare, dead birds would reintroduce the Millses to more low-rent housing.

It was at this juncture in his memories that Martin Mills struggled to stop remembering; for if young Martin's familiarity with his father's shortcomings was well established *before* the boy was sent away to school, it was *after* he'd been sent away that his mother's moral unconcern became more apparent and struck young Martin as more odious than any weakness to be found in Danny.

Alone in his cubicle in Mazagaon, the new missionary now sought *any* means by which he might halt further memories of his mother. He thought of Father Joseph Moriarity, S.J.; he'd been young Martin's mentor at Loyola Marymount, and when Martin had been sent to Massachusetts—where he was *not* enrolled in Jesuit (or even in Catholic) schools—it had been Father Joe who'd answered the boy's religious questions, by mail. Martin Mills also thought of Brother Brennan and Brother LaBombard, his *coadjutores,* or "fellow workers," in his novice years at St. Aloysius. He even remembered Brother Flynn inquiring if nocturnal emissions were "allowed"—for was this not the impossible? Namely, sex without sin. Was it Father Toland or Father Feeney who'd implied that a nocturnal emission was in all likelihood an unconscious act of masturbation? Martin was certain that it was either Brother Monahan or Brother Dooley who'd inquired if the act of masturbation was still forbidden in the case of it being "unconscious."

"Yes, always," Father Gannon had said. Father Gannon was bonkers, of course. No priest in his right mind would call an involuntary nocturnal emission an act of masturbation; nothing unconscious is ever a sin, since "sin" implies freedom of choice. Father Gannon would one day be taken bodily from his classroom at St. Aloysius, for his ravings were considered to lend credence to those 19th-century antipapist tracts in which convents are depicted as brothels for priests.

But how Martin Mills had approved of Father Gannon's answer; *that* will separate the men from the boys, he'd thought. It was a rule he'd been able to live with—no nocturnal emissions, unconscious or otherwise. He never touched himself.

But Martin Mills knew that even his triumph over masturbation would lead him to thinking of his mother, and so he tried to think of something else—of *anything* else. He repeated 100 times the date of August 15, 1534; it was the day St. Ignatius Loyola, in a chapel in Paris, had taken the vow to go to Jerusalem. For 15 minutes, Martin Mills concentrated on the correct pronunciation of Montmartre. When this didn't work—when he found himself seeing the way his mother brushed her hair before she went to bed—Martin opened his Bible to Genesis, Chapter 19, for the Lord's destruction of Sodom and Gomorrah always calmed him, and within the story of God's wrath was also deftly planted that lesson in obedience which Martin Mills much admired. It was terribly human of Lot's wife ... that she should look back, even though the Lord had commanded all of them, "Do not look behind you ... ," but Lot's wife was nevertheless turned to a pillar of salt for her disobedience. As well she *should* have been, thought Martin Mills. But even his pleasure at the Lord's destruction of those cities that flaunted their depravities did not spare the missionary from his keenest memories of being sent away to school.

Turkey (Bird and Country)

Veronica Rose and Danny Mills had agreed that their academically gifted son should attend a New England prep school, but Vera didn't wait for young Martin to be of high-school age; in Vera's view, the boy was becoming too religious. As if it wasn't enough that the Jesuits were educating him, they'd managed to put it in the boy's head that he should attend Mass on Sunday and get himself to Confession, too. "What does *this* kid have to confess?" Vera would ask Danny. She meant that young Martin was far too well behaved for a normal boy. As for Mass, Vera said that it "screwed up" her weekends, and so Danny took him. A free Sunday morning was wasted on Danny, anyway; with hangovers like his, he might as well have been sitting and kneeling at a Mass.

They sent young Martin first to the Fessenden School in Massachusetts; it was strict but not religious, and Vera liked it because it was close to Boston. When she visited Martin, she could stay at the Ritz-Carlton and not in some dreary motel or a cutesy-quaint country inn. Martin started Fessenden in the sixth grade and would stay through the ninth grade, which was the school's final year; he didn't feel especially sorry for himself—there were even younger boarders at the school, although the majority of boarders were of the five-day variety, which meant that they went home every weekend. The seven-day boarders, like Martin, included many foreign students, or Americans whose families were in diplomatic service in unfriendly countries. Some of the foreign students, like Martin's roommate, were the children of diplomats in residence in Washington or New York.

Despite the roommate, for Martin Mills would rather have had a single room, young Martin enjoyed the crowded cubicle; he was allowed to put his own things on the walls, provided that this could be done without damage to the walls and that the subject matter was not obscene. Obscene subject matter wouldn't have tempted Martin Mills, but young Martin's roommate was tempted.

His name was Arif Koma, and he was from Turkey; his father was with the Turkish Consulate in New York. Arif stashed a calendar of women in bathing suits between his mattress and the bedsprings. Arif didn't offer to share his calendar with Martin, and the Turk usually waited until he thought Martin was asleep before he made masturbatory use of the 12 women. Often a full half hour after the required lights out, Martin would notice Arif's flashlight—the glow emerging from under the sheets and blanket—and the corresponding creak of Arif's bed-springs. Martin had looked at the calendar privately—when Arif was in the shower, or otherwise out of the cubicle—and it appeared (from the more abused pages) that Arif preferred March and August to the other women, although Martin couldn't fathom why. But Martin didn't observe the calendar in great detail, or for long; there was no door on the cubicle he shared with Arif—there was only a curtain—and should a faculty member have found him with the swimsuit calendar, the women (all 12 months of them) would have been confiscated. Martin would have considered this unfair to Arif.

It was less out of growing friendship than out of some silent, mutual respect that the two boys continued to be roommates into their final year at Fessenden. The school assumed that if you didn't complain about your roommate, you must like him. Furthermore, the boys had attended the same summer camp. In the spring of his first year at Fessenden, when Martin was sincerely missing his father and actually looking forward to what residential horrors he might encounter in the summer months, back in L.A., Vera had sent the boy a summer-camp brochure. This was where he was going; it was a matter that had already been decided—it wasn't a question—and as Martin leafed through the brochure, Arif looked at the pictures with him.

"I might as well go to that one, too," the Turk had told Martin. "I mean, I'll have to go *somewhere.*"

But there was another reason they stayed together; they were both unathletic, and neither was inclined to assert any physical superiority over the other. At a school like Fessenden, where sports were compulsory and the boys grew feverishly competitive, Arif and Martin could protect their lack of athletic interest only by remaining roommates. They joked to each other that Fessenden's most rabidly despised athletic rivals were schools named Fay and Fenn. They found it comic that these were other "F" schools, as if the letter *F* signified a conspiracy of athleticism—a "frenzy" of the competitive spirit. Having concurred on this observation, the two roommates devised a private way to indicate their contempt of Fessenden's obsessively athletic vigor; Arif and Martin resolved not only to remain unathletic—they would use an "F" word for all the things they found distasteful about the school.

To the dominant colors of the faculty dress shirts, which were a button-down variety of pinks and yellows, the boys would say "fashionable." Of an unattractive faculty wife, "far from fetching." To the school rule that the top button of the shirt must always be buttoned when wearing a tie, they would respond with "fastidious." Other favorites, for varying encounters with the faculty and their fellow students, included "faltering," "fascistic," "fatuous," "fawning," "featherbrained," "fecal," "fervid," "fiendish," "fishy," "flatulent," "fogyish," "forbidding," "foul," "fraudulent," "freakish," "frigid," "fulsome" and "fussy."

These one-word adjectival signals amused them; Martin and Arif became, like many roommates, a secret society. Naturally, this led other boys to call them "fags," "faggots," "fruits," "flits" and "fairies," but the only sexual activity that took place in their shared cubicle was Arif's regular masturbation. By the time they were ninth graders, they were given a room with a door. This inspired Arif to take fewer pains to conceal his flashlight.

With this memory, the 39-year-old missionary, who was alone and wide awake in his cubicle at St. Ignatius, realized that the subject of masturbation was insidious. In a desperate effort to distract himself from where he knew this subject would lead him—namely, to his mother— Martin Mills sat bolt upright on his cot, turned on his light and began to read at random in *The Times of India*. It wasn't even a recent issue of the newspaper; it was at least two weeks old and rolled into a tube, and it was kept under the cot, where it was handy for killing cockroaches and mosquitoes. But thus it happened that the new missionary began the first of the exercises with which he intended to orient himself in Bombay. A more important matter—that being whether there was anything in *The Times of India* that could defuse Martin's memory of his mother and her connection to the unwelcome theme of masturbation—would remain, for the moment, unresolved.

As Martin's luck would have it, his eyes fell first upon the matrimonials. He saw that a 32-year-old public-school teacher, in search of a bride, confessed to a "minor squint in one eye"; a government servant (with his own house) admitted to a "slight skewness in the legs," but he maintained that he was able to walk perfectly—he would also accept a handicapped spouse. Elsewhere, a "60-ish issueless widower of wheatish complexion" sought a "slim beautiful homely wheatish non-smoker teetotaller vegetarian under 40 with sharp features"; on the other hand, the widower tolerantly proclaimed, caste, language, state and education were "no bar" to him (this was one of Ranjit's ads, of course). A bride seeking a groom advertised herself as having "an attractive face with an Embroidery Diploma"; another "slim beautiful homely girl," who said she was planning to study computers, sought an independent young man who was "sufficiently educated not to have the usual hang-ups about fair complexion, caste and dowry."

About all that Martin Mills could conclude from these self-advertisements, and these desires, was that "homely" meant well suited for domestic life and that a "wheatish" complexion meant reasonably fair-skinned—probably a pale yellow-brown, like Dr. Daruwalla. Martin couldn't have guessed that the "60-ish issueless widower of wheatish complexion" was Ranjit; he'd met Ranjit, who was dark-skinned—definitely not "wheatish." To the missionary, any matrimonial advertisement—any expressed longing to be a couple—seemed merely desperate and sad. He got off his cot and lit another mosquito coil, not because he'd noticed any mosquitoes but because Brother Gabriel had lit the last coil for him and Martin wanted to light one for himself.

He wondered if his former roommate, Arif Koma, had had a "wheatish" complexion. No; Arif was darker than wheat, Martin thought, remembering how clear the Turk's complexion had been. In one's teenage years, a clear complexion was more remarkable than any color. In the ninth grade, Arif already needed to shave every day, which made his face appear much more mature than the faces of the other ninth graders; yet Arif was utterly boyish in his lack of body hair—his hairless chest, his smooth legs, his girlishly unhairy bum . . . such attributes as these connoted a feminine sleekness. Although they'd been roommates for three years, it wasn't until the ninth grade that Martin began to think of Arif as beautiful. Later, he would realize that even his earliest perception of Arif's beauty had been planted by Vera. "And how is your pretty roommate—that beautiful boy?" Martin's mother would ask him whenever she called.

It was customary in boarding schools for visiting parents to take their children out to dinner; often roommates were invited along. Understandably, Martin Mills's parents never visited him together; like a divorced couple, although they weren't divorced, Vera and Danny saw Martin separately. Danny usually took Martin and Arif to an inn in New Hampshire for the Thanksgiving holiday; Vera was more inclined to visits of a single night.

During the Thanksgiving break in their ninth-grade year, Arif and Martin were treated to the inn in New Hampshire with Danny *and* to a one-night visit with Vera—that being the Saturday night of the long weekend. Danny returned the boys to Boston, where Vera was waiting for them at the Ritz. She had arranged a two-bedroom suite. Her quarters were rather grand, with a king-sized bed and a sumptuous bathroom; the boys received a smaller bedroom, with two twin beds and an adjacent shower and toilet.

Martin had enjoyed the time at the inn in New Hampshire. There'd been a similar arrangement of rooms, but different; at the inn, Arif was given a bedroom and a bathroom of his own, while Danny had shared a room with twin beds with his son. For this enforced isolation, Danny was apologetic to Arif. "You get to have him as your roommate all the time," Danny explained to the Turk.

"Sure—I understand," Arif had said. After all, in Turkey, seniority was the basic criterion for relationships of superiority and deference. "I'm used to deference to seniority," Arif had added pleasantly.

Sadly, Danny drank too much; he fell almost instantly asleep and snored. Martin was disappointed that there'd been little conversation between them. But before Danny passed out, and as they both lay awake in the dark, the father had said to the son, "I hope you're happy. I hope you'll confide in me if you're ever *not* happy—or just tell me what you're thinking, in general." Before Martin could think of what to say, he'd heard his father's snores. Nevertheless, the boy had appreciated the thought. In the morning, to have witnessed Danny's affection and pride, one would have presumed that the father and son had talked intimately.

Then, in Boston on Saturday night, Vera wanted to stray no farther than the dining room at the Ritz; her heaven was a good hotel, and she was already in it. But the dress code in the Ritz dining room was even more severe than Fessenden's. The captain stopped them because Martin was wearing white athletic socks with his loafers. Vera said simply, "I was going to mention it, darling—now someone else has." She gave him the room key, to go change his socks, while she waited with Arif. Martin had to borrow a pair of Arif's calf-length black hose. The incident drew Vera's attention to how much more comfortably Arif wore "proper" clothes; she waited for Martin to rejoin them in the dining room before making her observation known.

"It must be your exposure to the diplomatic life," Martin's mother remarked to the Turk. "I suppose there are all sorts of dress-up occasions at the Turkish Embassy."

"The Turkish Consulate," Arif corrected her, as he had corrected her a dozen times.

"I'm frightfully uninterested in details," Vera told the boy. "I challenge you to make the difference between an embassy and a consulate interesting—I give you one minute."

This was embarrassing to Martin, for it seemed to him that his mother had only recently learned to talk this way. She'd been such a vulgar young woman, and she'd gained no further education since that trashy time of her life; yet, in the absence of acting jobs, she'd learned to imitate the language of the educated upper classes. Vera was clever enough to know that trashiness was less appealing in older women. As for the adverb "frightfully," and the prefatory phrase "I challenge you," Martin Mills was ashamed to know where Vera had acquired this particular foppery.

There was a pretentious Brit in Hollywood, just another would-be director who'd failed to get a film made; Danny had written the unsuccessful script. To console himself, the Brit had made a series of moisturizer commercials; they were aimed at the older woman who was making an effort to preserve her skin, and Vera had been the model.

Shamelessly, there was his mother in a revealing camisole, seated in front of a makeup mirror—the kind that was framed with bright balls of light. Superimposed, the titles read: VERONICA ROSE, HOLLYWOOD ACTRESS. (To Martin's knowledge, this commercial had been his mother's first acting job in years.)

"I'm frightfully opposed to dry skin," Vera is saying to the makeup mirror (and to the camera). "In this town, only the youthful last." The camera closes on the corners of her mouth; a pretty finger applies the moisturizing lotion. Are those the telltale lines of age we see? Something appears to pucker the skin of her upper lip where it meets the well-defined edge of her mouth, but then the lip is miraculously smooth again; possibly this is only our imagination. "I challenge you to tell me I'm getting old," the lips say. It was a trick with the camera, Martin Mills was sure. Before the close-up, that was his mother; yet those lips, up close, were unfamiliar to him—someone else's *younger* mouth, Martin guessed.

It was a favorite TV commercial among the ninth-grade boys at Fessenden; when they gathered to watch an occasional television show in one of the dorm masters' apartments, the boys were always ready to answer the question that the close-up lips posed: "I challenge you to tell me I'm getting old."

"You're *already* old!" the boys would shout. Only two of them knew that Veronica Rose the Hollywood actress was Martin's mother. Martin would never have identified her, and Arif Koma was a loyal roommate.

Arif always said, "She looks young enough to *me*."

So it was doubly embarrassing, in the Ritz dining room, when Martin's mother said to Arif, "I'm frightfully uninterested in details. I challenge you to make the difference between an embassy and a consulate interesting—I give you one minute." Martin knew that Arif must have known that the "frightfully" and the "I challenge you" had come from the moisturizer commercial.

In the roommates' secret language, Martin Mills suddenly said, "Frightfully." He thought Arif would understand; Martin was indicating that his own mother merited an "F" word. But Arif was taking Vera seriously.

"An embassy is entrusted with a mission to a government and is headed by an ambassador," the Turk explained. "A consulate is the official premises of a consul, who is simply an official appointed by the government of one country to look after its commercial interests and the welfare of its citizens in another country. My father is the consul general in New York—New York being a place of commercial importance. A consul general is a consular officer of the highest rank, in charge of lower-ranking consular agents."

"That took just thirty seconds," Martin Mills informed his mother, but Vera was paying no attention to the time.

"Tell me about Turkey," she said to Arif. "You have thirty seconds."

"Turkish is the mother tongue of more than ninety percent of the population, and we are more than ninety-nine percent Muslims." Here Arif Koma paused, for Vera had shivered—the word "Muslims" made her shiver every time. "Ethnically, we are a melting pot," the boy continued. "Turks may be blond and blue-eyed; we may be of Alpine stock—that is, round-headed with dark hair and dark eyes. We may be of Mediterranean stock, dark, but long-headed. We may be Mongoloid, with high cheekbones."

"What are you?" Vera interrupted.

"That was only twenty seconds," Martin pointed out, but it was as if he weren't there at the dinner table with them; just the two of them were talking.

"I'm mostly Mediterranean," Arif guessed. "But my cheekbones are a little Mongoloid."

"I don't think so," Vera told him. "And where do your eyelashes come from?"

"From my mother," Arif replied shyly.

"What a lucky mother," said Veronica Rose.

"Who's going to have what?" asked Martin Mills; he was the only one looking at the menu. "I think I'm going to have the turkey."

"You must have some strange customs," Vera said to Arif. "Tell me something strange—I mean, sexually."

"Marriage is permitted between close kin—under the incest rules of Islam," Arif answered.

"Something stranger," Vera demanded.

"Boys are circumcised at any age from about six to twelve," Arif said; his dark eyes were downcast, roaming the menu.

"How old were you?" Vera asked him.

"It's a public ceremony," the boy mumbled. "I was ten."

"So you must remember it very clearly," Vera said.

"I think I'll have the turkey, too," Arif said to Martin.

"What do you remember about it, Arif?" Vera asked him.

"How you behave during the operation reflects on your family's reputation," Arif replied, but as he spoke he looked at his roommate—not at his roommate's mother.

"And how did *you* behave?" Vera asked.

"I didn't cry—it would have dishonored my family," the boy told her. "I'll have the turkey," he repeated.

"Didn't you two have turkey two days ago?" Vera asked them. "Don't have the turkey *again*—how boring! Have something different!"

"Okay—I'll have the lobster," Arif replied.

"That's a good choice—I'll have the lobster, too," Vera said. "What are you having, Martin?"

"I'll take the turkey," said Martin Mills. The sudden strength of his own will surprised him; in the power of his will there was already something Jesuitical.

This particular recollection gave the missionary the strength to return his attention to *The Times of India*, wherein he read about a family of 14 who'd been burned alive; their house had been set on fire by a rival family. Martin Mills wondered what a "rival family" was; then he prayed for the 14 souls who'd been burned alive.

Brother Gabriel, who'd been awakened by roosting pigeons, could see the light shining under Martin's door. Another of Brother Gabriel's myriad responsibilities at St. Ignatius was to foil the pigeons in their efforts to roost at the mission; the old Spaniard could detect pigeons roosting in his sleep. The many columns of the second-floor outdoor balcony afforded the pigeons almost unlimited access to the overhanging cornices. One by one, Brother Gabriel had fenced in the cornices with wire. After he'd shooed away these particular pigeons, he left the step-ladder leaning against the column; that way, he would know which cornice to re-enclose with wire in the morning.

When Brother Gabriel passed by Martin Mills's cubicle again, on his way back to bed, the new missionary's light was *still* on. Pausing by the cubicle door, Brother Gabriel listened; he feared that "young" Martin might be ill. But to his surprise and eternal comfort, Brother Gabriel heard Martin Mills praying. Such late-night litanies suggested to Brother Gabriel that the new missionary was a man very strongly in God's clutches; yet the Spaniard was sure he'd misunderstood what he heard of the prayer. It must be the American accent, old Brother Gabriel thought, for although the tone of voice and the repetition was very much in the nature of a prayer, the words made no sense at all.

To remind himself of the power of his will, which surely was evidence of God's will within him, Martin Mills was repeating and repeating that long-ago proof of his inner courage. "I'll take the turkey," the missionary was saying. "I'll take the turkey," he said again. He knelt on the stone floor beside his cot, clutching the rolled-up copy of *The Times of India* in his hands.

A prostitute had tried to eat his *culpa* beads, then she'd thrown them away; a dwarf had his whip; he'd rashly told Dr. Daruwalla to dispose of his leg iron. It would take a while for the stone floor to hurt his knees, but Martin Mills would wait for the pain—worse, he would welcome it. "I'll take the turkey," he prayed. He saw so clearly how Arif Koma was unable to raise his dark eyes to meet Vera's fixed stare, which so steadily scrutinized the circumcised Turk.

"It must have been frightfully painful," Vera was saying. "And you honestly didn't cry?"

"It would have dishonored my family," Arif said again. Martin Mills could tell that his roommate was about to cry; he'd seen Arif cry before. Vera could tell, too.

"But it's all right to cry now," she was saying to the boy. Arif shook his head, but the tears were coming. Vera used her handkerchief to pat Arif's eyes. For a while, Arif completely covered his face with Vera's handkerchief; it was a strongly scented handkerchief, Martin Mills knew. His mother's scent could sometimes make him gag.

"I'll take the turkey, I'll take the turkey, I'll take the turkey," the missionary prayed. It was such a steady-sounding prayer, Brother Gabriel decided; oddly, it reminded him of the pigeons, maniacally roosting on the cornices.

Two Different Men, Both Wide Awake

It was a different issue of *The Times of India* that Dr. Daruwalla was reading—it was the current day's issue. If the sleeplessness of this night seemed full of the torments of hell for Martin Mills, Dr. Daruwalla was exhilarated to feel so wide awake. Farrokh was merely using *The Times of India*, which he hated, as a means to energize himself. Nothing enlivened him with such loathing as reading the review of a new Inspector Dhar film. USUAL INSPECTOR DHAR IDIOM, the headline said. Farrokh found this typically infuriating. The reviewer was the sort of cultural commissar who'd never stoop to say a single favorable word about *any* Inspector Dhar film. That dog turd which had prevented Dr. Daruwalla from more than a partial reading of this review had been a blessing; it was a form of foolish self-punishment for the doctor to read the entire thing. The first sentence was bad enough: "The problem with Inspector Dhar is his tenacious umbilical bindings with his first few creations." Farrokh felt that this sentence alone would provide him with the desired fury to write all night.

"Umbilical bindings!" Dr. Daruwalla cried aloud. Then he cautioned himself not to wake up Julia; she was already angry with him. He made further use of *The Times of India* by putting it under his typewriter; the newspaper would keep the typewriter from rattling against the glass-topped table. He had set up his writing materials in the dining room; his writing desk, which was in the bedroom, was out of the question at this late hour.

But he'd never tried to write in the dining room before. The glass-topped table was too low. It had never been a satisfactory dining-room table; it was more like a coffee table—to eat at it, one sat on cushions on the floor. Now, in an effort to make himself more comfortable, Farrokh tried sitting on *two* cushions; he rested his elbows on either side of the typewriter. As an orthopedist, Dr. Daruwalla was aware that this position was unwise for his back; also, it was distracting to peer through the glass-topped table at his own crossed legs and bare feet. For a while, the doctor was additionally distracted by what he thought was the unfairness of Julia's being angry with him.

Their dinner at the Ripon Club had been hasty and quarrelsome. It was a difficult day to summarize, and Julia was of the opinion that her husband was condensing too much interesting material in his recitation of the day; she was ready to speculate all night on the subject of Rahul

Rai as a serial killer. Moreover, she was perturbed with Farrokh that he thought her presence at the Duckworth Club lunch with Detective Patel and Nancy would be "inappropriate"; after all, John D. was going to be there.

"I'm asking him to be present because of his memory," Dr. Daruwalla had claimed.

"I suppose I don't have a memory," Julia had replied.

Even more frustrating was that Farrokh had not been successful in reaching John D. He'd left messages at both the Taj and the Oberoi concerning an important lunch at the Duckworth Club, but Dhar hadn't returned his calls; probably the actor was still miffed about the unannounced-twin business, not that he would deign to admit it.

As for the efforts now under way to send poor Madhu and the elephant-footed Ganesh to the Great Blue Nile Circus, Julia had questioned the wisdom of Farrokh involving himself in "such dramatic intervention," as she called it; she wondered why he'd never so directly undertaken the dubious rescue of maimed beggars and child prostitutes before. Dr. Daruwalla was irritated because he already suffered from similar misgivings. As for the screenplay that the doctor was dying to begin, Julia expressed further criticism: she was surprised that Farrokh could be so self-centered at such a time—implying that it was selfish of him to be thinking of his own writing when so much that was violent and traumatic was happening in the lives of others.

They'd even had a spat about what to listen to on the radio. Julia chose those channels with programs that made her sleepy; "song miscellany" and "regional light music" were her favorites. But Dr. Daruwalla became caught up in the last stages of an interview with some complaining writer who was incensed that there was "no follow-through" in India. "Everything is left incomplete!" the writer was complaining. "We get to the bottom of nothing!" he cried. "As soon as we poke our noses into something interesting, we take our noses away again!" The writer's anger interested Farrokh, but Julia flipped to a channel featuring "instrumental music"; by the time Dr. Daruwalla found the complaining writer again, the writer's anger was being directed at a news story he'd heard today. A rape and murder had been reported at the Alexandria Girls' English Institution. The account that the writer had heard went as follows: "There was no rape and no murder, as previously and erroneously reported, at the Alexandria Girls' English Institution today." This was the kind of thing that drove the writer crazy; Farrokh guessed it was what he meant by "no follow-through."

"It's truly ridiculous to listen to this!" Julia had said, and so he'd left her with her "instrumental music."

Now Dr. Daruwalla put all this behind him. He thought about limps—all the different kinds he'd seen. He wouldn't use Madhu's name; he would call the girl in his screenplay Pinky, because Pinky was a real star. He would also make the girl much younger than Madhu; that way, nothing sexual could threaten her—not in Dr. Daruwalla's story.

Ganesh was the right name for the boy, but in the movie the boy would be older than the girl. Farrokh would simply reverse the ages of the *real* children. He would give *his* Ganesh a bad limp, too, but not nearly so grotesquely crushed a foot as the real Ganesh had; it would be too hard to find a child actor with such a nasty deformity. And the children should have a mother, because the screenwriter had already planned how he would take their mother away. Storytelling was a ruthless business.

Briefly Dr. Daruwalla considered that he'd not only failed to understand the country of his origin; he'd also failed to love it. He realized he was about to invent an India he could both comprehend and love—a simplified version. But his self-doubt passed—as self-doubt must, in order to begin a story.

It was a story set in motion by the Virgin Mary, Farrokh believed. He meant the stone statue of the unnamed saint in St. Ignatius Church—the one that needed to be restrained with a chain and a steel grommet. She wasn't really the Blessed Mother, but she had nevertheless become the Virgin Mary to Dr. Daruwalla. He liked the phrase well enough to write it down—"a story set in motion by the Virgin Mary." It was a pity that it wouldn't work as a title. For a title, he would need to find something shorter; but the simple repetition of this phrase enabled him to begin. He wrote it down again, and then again—"a story set in motion by the Virgin Mary." Then he crossed out every trace of this phrase, so that not even he could read it. Instead, he said it aloud—repeatedly.

Thus, in the dead of night, while almost five million residents of Bombay were fast asleep on the sidewalks of the city, these two men were wide awake and mumbling. One spoke only to himself—"a story set in motion by the Virgin Mary"—and this allowed him to get started. The other spoke not only to himself but to God; understandably, his mumbles were a little louder. He was saying, "I'll take the turkey," and his repetitions—he hoped—would prevent him from being consumed by that past which everywhere surrounded him. It was the past that had given him his tenacious will, which he believed was the will of God within him; yet how he feared the past.

"I'll take the turkey," said Martin Mills. By now his knees were throbbing. "I'll take the turkey, I'll take the turkey, I'll take the turkey."

18. A STORY SET IN MOTION BY THE VIRGIN MARY

Limo Roulette

In the morning, Julia found Farrokh slumped over the glass-topped table as if he'd fallen asleep while looking through the glass at the big toe of his right foot. Julia knew this was the same toe that had been bitten by a monkey, for which the family had suffered some religious disruption; she was thankful that the effects of the monkey bite had been neither fanatical nor long-lasting, but to observe her husband in the apparent position of praying to this same toe was disconcerting.

Julia was relieved to see the pages of the screenplay-in-progress, which she realized had been the true object of Farrokh's scrutiny—not his toe. The typewriter had been pushed aside; the typed pages had many penciled corrections written on them, and the doctor still held the pencil in his right hand. It appeared to Julia that her husband's own writing had served him as a soporific. She assumed she was a witness to the genesis of yet another Inspector Dhar disaster, but she saw at a glance that Dhar was not the voice-over character; after reading the first five pages, she wondered if Dhar was even in the movie. How odd! she thought. Altogether, there were about 25 pages. She took them into the kitchen with her; there she made coffee for herself and tea for Farrokh.

The voice-over was that of a 12-year-old boy who'd been crippled by an elephant. Oh, no—it's *Ganesh*! Julia thought. She knew the beggar. Whenever she left the apartment building, he was there to follow her; she'd bought him many things, most of which he'd sold, but his unusually good English had charmed her. Unlike Dr. Daruwalla, Julia knew *why* Ganesh's English was so polished.

Once, when he'd been begging at the Taj, an English couple had spotted him; they were traveling with a shy, lonely boy a little younger than Ganesh, and the child had requested that they find him someone to play with. There was also a nanny in tow, and Ganesh had traveled with this family for over a month. They fed him and clothed him and kept him atypically clean—they had him examined by a doctor, to be sure he wasn't carrying any infectious diseases—just so he could be a playmate for their lonely child. The nanny taught Ganesh English during the several hours of every day that she was under orders to give language instruction to the English boy. And when it was time for the family to return to England, they simply left Ganesh where they'd found him—begging at the Taj. He quickly sold the unnecessary clothes. For a time, Ganesh said, he'd missed the nanny. The story had touched Julia. It also struck her as highly unlikely. But why would the beggar have made it up? Now here was her husband, putting the poor cripple in a movie!

And Farrokh had given Ganesh a sister, a six-year-old girl named Pinky; she was a gifted street acrobat, a sidewalk beggar who performed various tricks. This didn't fool Julia. Julia knew the real Pinky—she was a circus star. It was also obvious that another inspiration for the fictional Pinky was Madhu, Deepa and Vinod's newest child prostitute; in the movie, Farrokh had made Pinky totally innocent. These fictional children were also fortunate to have a mother. (Not for long.)

The mother is a sweeper at St. Ignatius, where the Jesuits have not only employed her—they've converted her. Her children are strict vegetarian Hindus; they're quite disgusted by their mother's conversion, but especially by the concept of Holy Communion. The idea that the wine really *is* Christ's blood, and the bread really *is* his body . . . well, understandably, this is nauseating to the little vegetarians.

It shocked Julia to see that her husband, as a writer, was such a shameless borrower, for she knew he'd robbed the memoir of a nun; it was a terrible story that had long amused him—and old Lowji before him. The nun was working hard to convert a tribe of former cannibals. She had a difficult time explaining the concept of the body and blood of Jesus in the Eucharist. Since there were many former cannibals in the tribe who could still remember eating human flesh, the theological notion of Holy Communion pushed a lot of buttons for them.

Julia saw that her husband was up to his usual blasphemies. But where was Inspector Dhar?

Julia half-expected to see Dhar come to the children's rescue, but the story went on without him. The mother is killed in St. Ignatius Church, while genuflecting. A statue of the Virgin Mary falls from a pedestal and crushes her; she is given Extreme Unction on the spot. Ganesh does not mourn her passing greatly. "At least she was happy," says his voice-over. "It is not every Christian who is fortunate enough to be instantly killed by the Blessed Virgin." If there was ever a time for Dhar to come to the rescue, now's the time, Julia thought. But Dhar didn't come.

Instead, the little beggars begin to play a game called "limo roulette." All the street children in Bombay know there are two special limousines that cruise the city. In one is a scout for the circus—a dwarf named Vinod, of course. The dwarf is a former circus clown; his job is looking for gifted acrobats. Pinky is so gifted, the crippled Ganesh believes that Vinod would let him go to the circus *with* Pinky—so that he could look after her. The problem is, there's another scout. He's a man who steals children for the freak circus. He's called Acid Man because he pours acid on your face. The acid is so disfiguring that your own family wouldn't recognize you. Only the circus for freaks will take care of you.

So Farrokh was after Mr. Garg again, Julia thought. What an appalling story! Even without Inspector Dhar, good and evil were once more plainly in position. Which scout would find the children first? Would it be the Good Samaritan dwarf, or would it be Acid Man?

The limos move around at night. We see a sleek car pass the children, who run after it. We see the brake lights flicker, but then the dark car drives on; other children are chasing after it. We see a limousine stopped at the curb, motor running; the children approach it cautiously. The driver's-side window opens a crack; we see the stubby fingers on the edge of the glass, like claws. When the window is rolled down, there is the dwarf's big head. This is the right limo—this is Vinod.

Or else it's the wrong limo. The back door opens, a kind of frost escapes; it's as if the car's air-conditioning is too cold—the car is like a freezer or a meat locker. Possibly the acid must be preserved at such a temperature; maybe Acid Man himself must be kept this cold, or else he'll rot.

Apparently, the poor children wouldn't be forced to play "limo roulette" if the Virgin Mary hadn't toppled off a pedestal and murdered their mother. What was her husband thinking? Julia wondered. She was used to reading Farrokh's first drafts, his raw beginnings. Normally, she felt she wasn't invading her husband's privacy; he always shared with her his work-in-progress. But Julia was worried that this screenplay was something he'd never share with her. There was something desperate about it. Probably it suffered from the potential disappointment of attempted art—a vulnerability that had certainly been lacking in the doctor's Inspector Dhar scripts. It occurred to Julia that Farrokh might care too much about this one.

It was this reasoning that led her to return the manuscript to its previous position on the glass-topped table, more or less between the typewriter and her husband's head. Farrokh was still asleep, although a smile of drooling-idiot proportions indicated that he was dreaming, and he emitted a nasal humming—an unfollowable tune. The awkward position of the doctor's head on the glass-topped table allowed him to imagine that he was a child again, napping at St. Ignatius School with his head on his desk in I-3.

Suddenly, Farrokh snorted in his sleep. Julia could tell that her husband was about to wake up, but she was startled when he woke up screaming. She thought he'd had a nightmare but it turned out to be a cramp in the arch of his right foot. He looked so disheveled, she was embarrassed for him. Then her anger with him returned . . . that he'd thought it "inappropriate" for her to attend the interesting lunch with the deputy commissioner and the limping hippie from 20 years ago. Worse, Farrokh drank his tea without mentioning his screenplay-in-progress; he even attempted to conceal the pages in his doctor's bag.

Julia remained aloof when he kissed her good-bye, but she stood in the open doorway of the apartment and watched him push the button for the lift. If the doctor was demonstrating the early symptoms of an artistic temperament, Julia thought she should nip such an ailment in the bud. She waited until the elevator door opened before she called to him.

"If that ever was a movie," Julia said, "Mr. Garg would sue you."

Dr. Daruwalla stood dumbfounded while the elevator door closed on his doctor's bag, and then opened; the door kept opening and closing on his bag as he stared indignantly at his wife. Julia blew him a kiss, just to make him cross. The elevator door grew more aggressive; Farrokh was forced to fight his way inside. He hadn't time to retort to Julia before the door closed and he was descending; he'd never successfully kept a secret from her. Besides, Julia was right: Garg *would* sue him! Dr. Daruwalla wondered if the creative process had eclipsed his common sense.

In the alley, another blow to his common sense awaited him. When Vinod opened the door of the Ambassador for him, the doctor saw the elephant-footed beggar asleep in the back seat. Madhu had chosen to sit up front, beside the dwarf driver. Except for the crusty exudation on his eyelashes, the sleeping boy looked angelic. His crushed foot was covered with one of the rags he carried for wiping off the fake bird shit; even in his sleep, Ganesh had managed to conceal his deformity. This wasn't a make-believe Ganesh, but a real boy; nevertheless, Farrokh found himself looking at the cripple as he might stand back and take pride in one of his fictional creations. The doctor was still thinking about his story; he was thinking that what would happen next to Ganesh was entirely a matter of the screenwriter's imagination. But the *real* beggar had found a benefactor; until the circus took him, the back seat of Vinod's Ambassador would do—it was already better than what he was used to.

"Good morning, Ganesh," the doctor said. The boy was instantly awake, as alert as a squirrel.

"What are we doing today?" the beggar asked.

"No more bird-shit tricks," the doctor said.

The beggar registered his understanding with a tight-lipped smile. "But what are we doing?" the boy repeated.

"We're going to my office," Dr. Daruwalla said. "We're waiting for some test results for Madhu, before we make our plans. And this morning you will be kind enough *not* to practice the bird-shit trick on those postoperative children in the exercise yard." The boy's black eyes kept darting with the movements of the traffic. The doctor could see Madhu's face reflected in the rearview mirror; she'd not responded—she'd not even glanced in the mirror at the mention of her name.

"What concerns me, about the *circus* . . ." Dr. Daruwalla said; he paused deliberately. The emphasis he'd given to the word had gained Ganesh's full attention, but not Madhu's.

"My arms are the best—very strong. I could ride a pony—no legs necessary with hands as strong as mine," Ganesh suggested. "I could do lots of tricks—hang by my arms from an elephant's trunk, maybe ride a lion."

"But what concerns me is that they won't *let* you do tricks—no tricks,"

Dr. Daruwalla replied. "They'll give you all the bad jobs, all the hard work. Scooping up the elephant shit, for example—not hanging from their trunks."

"I'll have to show them," Ganesh said. "But what do you do to the lions to make them stand on those little stools?"

"*Your* job would be to wash the lion piss off the stools," Farrokh told him.

"And what do you do with tigers?" Ganesh asked.

"What *you* would do with tigers is clean their cages—tiger shit!" said Dr. Daruwalla.

"I'll have to show them," the boy repeated. "Maybe something with their tails—tigers have long tails."

The dwarf entered the roundabout that the doctor hated. There were too many easily distracted drivers who stared at the sea and at the worshipers milling in the mudflats around Haji Ali's Tomb; the rotary was near Tardeo, where Farrokh's father had been blown to smithereens. Now, in the midst of this roundabout, the traffic swerved to avoid a lunatic cripple; a legless man in one of those makeshift wheelchairs powered by a hand crank was navigating the rotary against the flow of other vehicles. The doctor could follow Ganesh's roaming gaze; the boy's black eyes either ignored or avoided the wheelchair madman. The little beggar was probably still thinking about the tigers.

Dr. Daruwalla didn't know the exact ending of his screenplay; he had only a general idea of what would happen to *his* Pinky, to *his* Ganesh. Caught in the roundabout, the doctor realized that the fate of the real Ganesh—in addition to Madhu's fate—was out of his hands. But Farrokh felt responsible for beginning *their* stories, just as surely as he'd begun the story he was making up.

In the rearview mirror, Dr. Daruwalla could see that Madhu's lion-yellow eyes were following the movements of the legless maniac. Then the dwarf needed to brake sharply; he brought his taxi to a full stop in order to avoid the crazed cripple in the wrong-way wheelchair. The wheelchair sported a bumper sticker opposed to horn blowing.

PRACTICE THE VIRTUE OF PATIENCE

A battered oil truck loomed over the wheelchair lunatic; in a fury, the oil-truck driver repeatedly blew his horn. The great cylindrical body of the truck was covered with foot-high lettering the color of flame.

WORLD'S FIRST CHOICE
—GULF ENGINE OILS

The oil truck also sported a bumper sticker, which was almost illegible behind flecks of tar and splattered insects.

KEEP A FIRE EXTINGUISHER IN YOUR GLOVE COMPARTMENT

Dr. Daruwalla knew that Vinod didn't have one.

As if it wasn't irritating enough to be obstructing traffic, the cripple was begging among the stopped cars. The clumsy wheelchair bumped against the Ambassador's rear door. Farrokh was incensed when Ganesh rolled down the rear window, toward which the wheelchair madman extended his arm.

"Don't give that idiot anything!" the doctor cried, but Farrokh had underestimated the speed of Bird-Shit Boy. Dr. Daruwalla never saw the bird-shit syringe, only the look of surprise on the face of the crazed cripple in the wheelchair; he quickly withdrew his arm—his palm, his wrist, his whole forearm dripping bird shit. Vinod cheered.

"Got him," Ganesh said.

A passing paint truck nearly obliterated the wheelchair lunatic. Vinod cheered for the paint truck, too.

CELEBRATE WITH ASIAN PAINTS

When the paint truck was gone from view, the traffic moved again—the dwarf's taxi taking the lead. The doctor remembered the bumper sticker on Vinod's Ambassador.

HEY YOU WITH THE EVIL EYE,
MAY YOUR FACE TURN BLACK!

"I said no more bird-shit tricks, Ganesh," Farrokh told the boy. In the rearview mirror, Dr. Daruwalla could see Madhu watching him; when he met her eyes, she looked away. Through the open window, the air was hot and dry, but the pleasure of a moving car was new to the boy, if not to the child prostitute. Maybe nothing was new to her, the doctor feared. But for the beggar, if not for Madhu, this was the start of an adventure.

"Where *is* the circus?" Ganesh asked. "Is it far?"

Farrokh knew that the Great Blue Nile might be anywhere in Gujarat. The question that concerned Dr. Daruwalla was not *where* the circus was, but whether it would be safe.

Ahead, the traffic slowed again; probably pedestrians, Dr. Daruwalla thought—shoppers from the nearby chowk, crowding into the street. Then the doctor saw the body of a man in the gutter; his legs extended into the road. The traffic was squeezed into one lane because the oncoming drivers didn't want to drive over the dead man's feet or ankles. A crowd was quickly forming; soon there would be the usual chaos. For the moment, the only concession made to the dead man was that no one drove over him.

"Is the circus *far*?" Ganesh asked again.

"Yes, it's far—it's a world apart," said Dr. Daruwalla. "A world apart" was what he hoped for the boy, whose bright black eyes spotted the body in the road. Ganesh quickly looked away. The dwarf's taxi inched past the dead man; once more, Vinod moved ahead of the traffic.

"Did you see that?" Farrokh asked Ganesh.

"See what?" the cripple said.

"There is a man being dead," Vinod said.

"They are nonpersons," Ganesh replied. "You think you see them but they are not really being there."

O God, keep this boy from becoming a nonperson! Dr. Daruwalla thought. His fear surprised him; he couldn't bring himself to seek the cripple's hopeful face. In the rearview mirror, Madhu was watching the doctor again. Her indifference was chilling. It had been quite a while since Dr. Daruwalla had prayed, but he began.

India wasn't limo roulette. There were no good scouts or bad scouts for the circus; there was no freak circus, either. There were no right-limo, wrong-limo choices. For these children, the real roulette would begin after they got to the circus—*if* they got there. At the circus, no Good Samaritan dwarf could save them. At the Great Blue Nile, Acid Man—a comic-book villain—wasn't the danger.

Mother Mary

In the new missionary's cubicle, the last mosquito coil had burned out just before dawn. The mosquitoes had come with the early gray light and had departed with the first heat of the day—all but the mosquito that Martin Mills had mashed against the white wall above his cot. He'd killed it with the rolled-up issue of *The Times of India* after the mosquito was full of blood; the bloodstain on the wall was conspicuous and only a few inches below the crucifix that hung there, which gave Martin the gruesome impression that a sizable drop of Christ's blood had spotted the wall.

In his inexperience, Martin had lit the last mosquito coil too close to his cot. When his hand trailed on the floor, his fingers must have groped through the dead ashes. Then, in his brief and troubled sleep, he'd touched his face. This was the only explanation for the surprising view of himself that he saw in the pitted mirror above the sink; his face was dotted with fingerprints of ash, as if he'd meant to mock Ash Wednesday—or as if a ghost had passed through his cubicle and fingered him. The marks struck him as a sarcastic blessing, or else they made him look like an insincere penitent.

When he'd filled the sink and wet his face to shave, he held the razor in his right hand and reached for the small sliver of soap with his left. It was a jagged-shaped piece of such an iridescent blue-green color that it was reflected in the silver soap dish; it turned out to be a lizard, which leaped into his hair before he could touch it. The missionary was frightened to feel the reptile race across his scalp. The lizard launched itself from the top of Martin's head to the crucifix on the wall above the cot; then it jumped from Christ's face to the partially open slats of the window blind, through which the light from the low sun slanted across the floor of the cubicle.

Martin Mills had been startled; in an effort to brush the lizard out of his hair, he'd slashed his nose with the razor. An imperceptible breeze stirred the ashes from the mosquito coils, and the missionary watched himself bleed into the water in the sink. He'd long ago given up shaving lather; plain soap was good enough. In the absence of soap, he shaved himself in the cold, bloody water.

It was only 6:00 in the morning. Martin Mills had to survive another hour before Mass. He thought it would be a good idea to go to St. Ignatius Church early; if the church wasn't locked, he could sit quietly in one of the pews—that usually helped. But his stupid nose kept bleeding; he didn't want to bleed all over the church. He'd neglected to pack any handkerchiefs—he'd have to buy some—and so for now he chose a pair of black socks; although they were of a thin material, not very absorbent, at least they wouldn't show the bloodstains. He soaked the socks in fresh cold water in the sink; he wrung them out until they were merely damp. He balled up a sock in each hand and, first with one hand and then the other, he restlessly dabbed at the wound on his nose.

Someone watching Martin Mills dress himself might have suspected the missionary of being in a deep trance; a less kind observer might have concluded that the zealot was semiretarded, for he wouldn't put down the socks. The awkward pulling on of his trousers—when he tied his shoes, he held the socks in his teeth—and the buttoning of his short-sleeved shirt . . . these normally simple tasks were turned arduous, almost athletic; these clumsy feats were punctuated by the ceaseless dabbing at his nose. In the second buttonhole of his shirt, Martin Mills affixed a silver cross like a lapel pin, and together with this adornment he left a thumbprint of blood on his shirt, for the socks had already stained his hands.

St. Ignatius Church was unlocked. The Father Rector unlocked the church at 6:00 every morning, and so Martin Mills had a safe place to sit and wait for Mass. For a while, he watched the altar boys setting up the candles. He sat in a center-aisle pew, alternately praying and dabbing at his bleeding nose. He saw that the kneeling pad was hinged. Martin didn't like hinged kneelers because they reminded him of the Protestant school where Danny and Vera had sent him after Fessenden.

St. Luke's was an Episcopalian place; as such, in Martin's view, it was barely a religious school at all. The morning service was only a hymn and a prayer and a virtuous thought for the day, which was followed by a curiously secular benediction—hardly a blessing, but some sage advice about studying relentlessly and never plagiarizing. Sunday church attendance was required, but in St. Luke's Chapel the service was of such a *low* Episcopalian nature that no one knelt for prayers. Instead, the students slumped in their pews; probably they weren't sincere Episcopalians. And whenever Martin Mills would attempt to lower the hinged kneeling pad—so that he could properly kneel to pray—his fellow students in the pew would firmly hold the hinged kneeler in the upright, nonpraying position. They insisted on using the kneeling pad as a footrest. When Martin complained to the school's headmaster, the Reverend Rick Utley informed the underclassman that only *senior* Catholics and *senior* Jews were permitted to attend worship services in their churches and synagogues of choice; until Martin was a senior, St. Luke's would have to do—in other words, no kneeling.

In St. Ignatius Church, Martin Mills lowered the kneeling pad and knelt in prayer. In the pew was a rack that held the hymnals and prayer books; whenever Martin bled on the binding of the nearest hymnal, he dabbed at his nose with one sock and wiped the hymnal with the other.

He prayed for the strength to love his father, for merely pitying him seemed insufficient. Although Martin knew that the task of loving his mother was an insurmountable one, he prayed for the charity to forgive her. And he prayed for the soul of Arif Koma. Martin had long ago forgiven Arif, but every morning he prayed that the Holy Virgin would forgive Arif, too. The missionary always began this prayer in the same way.

"O Mother Mary, it was *my* fault!" Martin prayed. In a way, the new missionary's story had also been set in motion by the Virgin Mary—in the sense that Martin held her in higher esteem than he held his own mother. Had Vera been killed by a falling statue of the Blessed Virgin— especially if such good riddance had occurred when the zealot was of a tender, unformed age—Martin might never have become a Jesuit at all.

His nose was still bleeding. A drop of his blood dripped on the hymnal; once more the missionary dabbed at his wound. Arbitrarily, he decided *not* to wipe the song book; perhaps he thought that bloodstains would give the hymnal character. After all, it was a religion steeped in blood—Christ's blood and the blood of saints and martyrs. It would be glorious to be a martyr, Martin thought. He looked at his watch. In just half an hour, if he could make it, the missionary knew he would be saved by the Mass.

Is There a Gene for It, Whatever It Is?

In his stepped-up efforts to save Madhu from Mr. Garg, Dr. Daruwalla placed a phone call to Tata Two. But the OB/GYN's secretary told Farrokh that Dr. Tata was already in surgery. The poor patient, who-ever she was, Dr. Daruwalla thought. Farrokh wouldn't want a woman he knew to be subjected to the uncertain scalpel of Tata Two, for (fairly or unfairly) Farrokh assumed that the surgical procedures of the second Dr. Tata were second-rate, too. It was quickly apparent to Dr. Daruwalla that Tata Two's medical secretary lived up to the family reputation for mediocrity, because the doctor's simple request for the quickest possible results of Madhu's HIV test were met with suspicion and condescension. Dr. Tata's secretary had already identified himself, rather arrogantly, as *Mister* Subhash.

"You are wanting a rush job?" Mr. Subhash asked Dr. Daruwalla. "Are you being aware that you are paying more for it?"

"Of course!" Farrokh said.

"It is normally costing four hundred rupees," Mr. Subhash informed Dr. Daruwalla. "A rush job is costing you a thousand rupees. Or is the patient paying?"

"No, *I'm* paying. I want the quickest possible results," Farrokh replied.

"It is normally taking ten days or two weeks," Mr. Subhash explained. "It is most conveniently being done in *batches*. We are normally waiting until we are having forty specimens."

"But I don't want you to wait in this case," Dr. Daruwalla replied. "That's why I called—I know how it's normally done."

"If the ELISA is being positive, we are normally confirming the results by Western Blot. The ELISA is having a lot of false positives, you know," Mr. Subhash explained.

"I know," said Dr. Daruwalla. "If you get a positive ELISA, please send it on for a Western Blot."

"This is prolonging the turnaround time for a positive test," Mr. Subhash explained.

"Yes, I *know*," Dr. Daruwalla replied.

"If the test is being negative, you are having the results in two days," Mr. Subhash explained. "Naturally, if it is being positive . . ."

"Then it would take longer—I *know!*" Dr. Daruwalla cried. "Please just order the test immediately. That's why I called."

"Only Dr. Tata is ordering the testing," Mr. Subhash said. "But of course I am telling him what you are wanting."

"Thank you," Dr. Daruwalla replied.

"Is there anything else you are wanting?" Mr. Subhash asked.

There *had* been something else, but Farrokh had forgotten what it was that he'd meant to ask Tata Two. Doubtless it would come back to him.

"Please just ask Dr. Tata to call me," Farrokh replied.

"And what is being the subject you are wishing to discuss with Dr. Tata?" Mr. Subhash asked.

"It is a subject of discussion between *doctors*," Dr. Daruwalla said.

"I am telling him," Mr. Subhash said testily.

Dr. Daruwalla resolved that he would never again complain about the nincompoopish matrimonial activities of Ranjit. Ranjit was competent and he was polite. Moreover, Dr. Daruwalla's secretary had steadfastly maintained his enthusiasm for the doctor's dwarf-blood project. No one else had ever encouraged the doctor's genetic studies—least of all, the dwarfs. Dr. Daruwalla had to admit that even his own enthusiasm for the project was slipping.

The ELISA test for HIV was simple in comparison to Farrokh's genetic studies, for the latter had to be performed on cells (rather than on serum). Whole blood needed to be sent for the studies, and the unclotted blood had to be transported at room temperature. Blood specimens could cross international boundaries, although the paperwork was formidable; the specimens were usually shipped on dry ice, to preserve the proteins. But in the case of a genetic study, shipping dwarf blood from Bombay to Toronto was risky; it was likely that the cells would be killed before reaching Canada.

Dr. Daruwalla had solved this problem with the help of an Indian medical school in Bombay; the doctor let their research lab perform the studies and prepare the slides. The lab gave Farrokh finished sets of photographs of the chromosomes; it was easy to carry the photographs back to Toronto. But there the dwarf-blood project had stalled. Through a close friend and colleague—a fellow orthopedic surgeon at the Hospital for Sick Children in Toronto—Farrokh had been introduced to a geneticist at the university. Even this contact proved fruitless, for the geneticist maintained that there was no identifiable genetic marker for this type of dwarfism.

The geneticist at the University of Toronto was quite emphatic to Farrokh: it was far-fetched to imagine that he would find a genetic marker for this autosomal dominant trait—achondroplasia is transmitted by a single autosomal dominant gene. This was a type of dwarfism that resulted from a spontaneous mutation. In the case of a spontaneous mutation, unaffected parents of dwarf children have essentially no further risk of producing another dwarf child; the unaffected brothers and sisters of an achondroplastic dwarf are similarly not at risk—they won't necessarily produce dwarfs, either. The dwarfs themselves, on the other hand, are quite likely to pass the trait on to their children—half their children will be dwarfs. As for a genetic marker for this dominant characteristic, none could be found.

Dr. Daruwalla doubted that he knew enough about genetics to argue with a geneticist; the doctor simply continued to draw samples of the dwarfs' blood, and he kept bringing the photographs of the chromosomes back to Toronto. The U. of T. geneticist was discouraging but fairly friendly, if not sympathetic. He was also the boyfriend of Farrokh's friend and colleague at the Hospital for Sick Children—Sick Kids, they called the hospital in Toronto. Farrokh's friend and the geneticist were gay.

Dr. Gordon Macfarlane, who was the same age as Dr. Daruwalla, had joined the orthopedic group at the Hospital for Sick Children in the same year as Farrokh; their hospital offices were next door to each other. Since Farrokh hated to drive, he often rode back and forth to work with Macfarlane; they both lived in Forest Hill. Early on in their relationship, there'd been those comic occasions when Julia and Farrokh had tried to interest Mac in various single or divorced women. Eventually, the matter of Macfarlane's sexual orientation grew clear; in no time, Mac was bringing his boyfriend to dinner.

Dr. Duncan Frasier, the gay geneticist, was renowned for his research on the so-called (and elusive) gay chromosomes; Frasier was used to being teased about it. Biological studies of homosexuality generally irritate everybody. The debate as to whether homosexuality is present at birth or is a learned behavior is always inflamed with politics. Conservatives reject scientific suggestions that sexual orientation is biological; liberals anguish over the possible medical misuse of an identifiable genetic marker for homosexuality—should one be found. But Dr. Frasier's research had led him to a fairly cautious and reasonable conclusion. There were only two "natural" sexual orientations among humans—one in the majority, one in the minority. Nothing he'd studied about homosexuality, nor anything he'd personally experienced or had ever felt, could persuade Dr. Frasier that either homosexuality *or* heterosexuality was a matter of choice. Sexual orientation wasn't a "lifestyle."

"We are born with what we desire—whatever it is," Frasier liked to say.

Farrokh found it an interesting subject. But if the search for gay genes was so fascinating to Dr. Frasier, it discouraged Dr. Daruwalla that the gay geneticist would entertain no hope of finding a genetic marker for Vinod's dwarfism. Sometimes Dr. Daruwalla was guilty of thinking that Frasier had no personal interest in dwarfs, whereas gays got the geneticist's full attention. Nevertheless, Farrokh's friendship with Macfarlane was unshakable; soon Farrokh was admitting to his gay friend how he'd always disliked the word "gay" in its current, commonplace homosexual sense. To Farrokh's surprise, Mac had agreed; he said he wished that something as important to him as his homosexuality had a word of its own—a word that had no other meaning.

" 'Gay' is such a frivolous word," Macfarlane had said.

Dr. Daruwalla's dislike of the contemporary usage of the word was more a generational matter than a matter of prejudice—or so the doctor believed. It was a word his mother, Meher, had loved but overused. "We had a gay time," she would say. "What a gay evening we had—even your father was in a gay mood."

It disheartened Dr. Daruwalla to see this old-fashioned adjective—a synonym for "jolly" or "merry" or "frolicsome" or "blithe"—take on a much more serious meaning.

"Come to think of it, 'straight' isn't an original word, either," Farrokh had said.

Macfarlane laughed, but his longtime companion, Frasier, responded with a touch of bitterness. "What you're telling us, Farrokh, is that you accept gays when we're so quiet about it that we might as well still be in the closet—*and* provided that we don't dare call ourselves gay, which offends you. Isn't that what you're saying?" But this wasn't what Farrokh meant.

"I'm not criticizing your orientation," Dr. Daruwalla replied. "I just don't like the word for it."

There lingered an air of dismissiveness about Dr. Frasier; the rebuke reminded Dr. Daruwalla of the geneticist's dismissal of the notion that the doctor might find a genetic marker for the most common type of dwarfism.

The last time Dr. Daruwalla had brought Dr. Frasier the photographs of the dwarfs' chromosomes, the gay geneticist had been more dismissive than usual. "Those dwarfs must be bleeding to death, Farrokh," Frasier told him. "Why don't you leave the little buggers alone?"

"If *I* used the word 'bugger,' you would be offended," Farrokh said. But what did Dr. Daruwalla expect? Dwarf genes or gay genes, genetics was a touchy subject.

All this left Farrokh feeling full of contempt for his own lack of follow-through on his dwarf-blood project. Dr. Daruwalla didn't realize that his notion of "follow-through" (or lack thereof) had originated with the radio interview he'd briefly overheard the previous evening—that silliness with the complaining writer. But, at last, the doctor stopped brooding on the dwarf-blood subject.

Farrokh now made the morning's second phone call.

The Enigmatic Actor

It was early to call John D., but Dr. Daruwalla hadn't told him about Rahul; the doctor also wanted to stress the importance of John D.'s attending the lunch at the Duckworth Club with Detective Patel and Nancy. To Farrokh's surprise, it was an alert Inspector Dhar who answered the phone in his suite at the Taj.

"You sound awake!" Dr. Daruwalla said. "What are you doing?"

"I'm reading a play—actually, two plays," John D. replied. "What are *you* doing? Isn't it time you were cutting open someone's knee?"

This was the famous distant Dhar; the doctor felt he'd created this character, cold and sarcastic. Farrokh immediately launched into the news about Rahul—that he had a female identity these days; that, in all likelihood, the complete sex change had been accomplished. But John D. seemed barely interested. As for participating in the lunch at the Duckworth Club, not even the prospect of taking part in the capture of a serial murderer (or murderess) could engage the actor's enthusiasm.

"I have a lot of reading to do," John D. told Farrokh.

"But you can't read all day," the doctor said. "*What* reading?"

"I told you—two plays," said Inspector Dhar.

"Oh, you mean homework," Farrokh said. He assumed that John D. was studying his lines for his upcoming parts at the Schauspielhaus Zürich. The actor was thinking of Switzerland, of his day job, the doctor supposed. John D. was thinking of going home. After all, what was keeping him here? If, under the present threat, he gave up his membership at the Duckworth Club, what would he do with himself? Stay in his suite at the Taj, or at the Oberoi? Like Farrokh, John D. *lived* at the Duckworth Club when he was in Bombay.

"But now that the murderer is *known*, it's absurd to resign from the club!" Dr. Daruwalla cried. "Any day now, they're going to catch him!"

"Catch *her*," Inspector Dhar corrected the doctor.

"Well, him *or* her," Farrokh said impatiently. "The point is, the police know who they're looking for. There won't be any more killings."

"I suppose seventy *is* enough," John D. said. He was in a simply infuriating mood, Dr. Daruwalla thought.

"So, what are these plays?" Farrokh asked, in exasperation.

"I have only two leading roles this year," John D. replied. "In the spring, it's Osborne's *Der Entertainer*—I'm Billy Rice—and in the fall I'm Friedrich Hofreiter in Schnitzler's *Das weite Land*."

"I see," Farrokh said, but this was all foreign to him. He knew only that John Daruwalla was a respected professional as an actor, and that the Schauspielhaus Zürich was a sophisticated city theater with a reputation for performing both classical and modern plays. In Farrokh's opinion, they gave short shrift to slapstick; he wondered if there were more slapstick comedies performed at the Bernhard or at the Theater am Hechtplatz—he didn't really know Zürich.

The doctor knew only what his brother, Jamshed, had told him, and Jamshed was no veteran theatergoer—he went to see John D. In addition to Jamshed's possibly philistine opinions, there was what little information Farrokh could force out of the guarded Dhar. The doctor didn't know if two leading roles a year were enough, or if John D. had chosen only two such roles. The actor went on to say that he had smaller parts in something by Dürrenmatt and something by Brecht. A year ago, he'd made his directing debut—it was something by Max Frisch—and he'd played the eponymous Volpone in the Ben Jonson play. Next year, John D. had said, he hoped to direct Gorki's *Wassa Schelesnowa*.

It was a pity that everything had to be in German, Dr. Daruwalla thought.

Except for his outstanding success as Inspector Dhar, John D. had never acted in films; he never auditioned. Was he lacking in ambition? Dr. Daruwalla wondered, for it seemed a mistake for Dhar not to take advantage of his perfect English. Yet John D. said he detested England, and he refused to set foot in the United States; he ventured to Toronto only to visit Farrokh and Julia. The actor wouldn't even stray to Germany to audition for a film!

Many of the guest performers at the Schauspielhaus Zürich were German actors and actresses—Katharina Thalbach, for example. Jamshed had once told Farrokh that John D. had been romantically linked with the German actress, but John D. denied this. Dhar never appeared in a German theater, and (to Farrokh's knowledge) there was no one at the Schauspielhaus Zürich to whom the actor had ever been "romantically linked." Dhar was a friend of the famous Maria Becker, but not *romantically* a friend. Besides, Dr. Daruwalla guessed, Maria Becker would be a little too old for John D. And Jamshed had reported seeing John D. out to dinner at the Kronenhalle with Christiane Hörbiger, who was also famous—and closer to John D.'s age, the doctor speculated. But Dr. Daruwalla suspected that this sighting was no more significant than spotting John D. with any other of the regular performers at the Schauspielhaus. John D. was also friends with Fritz Schediwy and Peter Ehrlich and Peter Arens. Dhar was seen dining, on more than one occasion, with the pretty Eva Rieck. Jamshed also reported that he frequently saw John D. with the director Gerd Heinz—and as often with a local terror of the avant-garde, Matthias Frei.

John D., as an actor, eschewed the avant-garde; yet, apparently, he was on friendly terms with one of Zürich's elder statesmen of such theater. Matthias Frei was a director and occasional playwright, a kind of deliberately underground and incomprehensible fellow—or so Dr. Daruwalla believed. Frei was about the doctor's age, but he looked older, more rumpled; he was certainly wilder. Jamshed had told Farrokh that John D. even split the expense of renting a flat or a chalet in the mountains with Matthias Frei; one year they would rent something in the Grisons, another year they'd try the Bernese Oberland. Supposedly, it was agreeable for them to share a place because John D. preferred the mountains in the ski season and Matthias Frei liked the hiking in the summer; also, Dr. Daruwalla presumed, Frei's friends would be people of a different generation from John D.'s friends.

But, once again, Farrokh's view of the culture John D. inhabited was marginal. As for the actor's love life, there was no understanding his aloofness. He'd appeared to have a long relationship with someone in a publishing house—a publicist, or so Farrokh remembered her. She was an attractive, intelligent younger woman. They'd occasionally traveled together, but not to India; for Dhar, India was strictly business. They'd never lived together. And now, Farrokh was told, this publicist and John D. were "just good friends."

Julia surmised that John D. didn't want to have children, and that this would eventually turn most younger women away. But now, at 39, John D. might meet a woman his own age, or a little older—someone who would accept childlessness. Or, Julia had said, perhaps he'd meet a nice divorced woman who'd already had her children—someone whose children would be grownups. That would be ideal for John D., Julia had decided.

But Dr. Daruwalla didn't think so. Inspector Dhar had never exhibited a nesting instinct. The rentals in the mountains, a different one each year, utterly suited John D. Even in Zürich, he made a point of owning very little. His flat—which was within walking distance of the theater, the lake, the Limmat, the Kronenhalle—was also rented. He didn't want a car. He seemed proud of his framed playbills, and even an Inspector Dhar poster or two; in Zürich, Dr. Daruwalla supposed, these Hindi cinema advertisements were probably amusing to John D.'s friends. They could never have imagined that such craziness translated into a raving audience beyond the wildest dreams of the Schauspielhaus.

In Zürich, Jamshed had observed, John D. was infrequently recognized; he was hardly the best-known of the Schauspielhaus troupe. Not exactly a character actor, he was also no star. In restaurants around town, theatergoers might recognize him, but they wouldn't necessarily know his name. Only schoolchildren, after a comedy, would ask for his autograph; the children simply held out their playbills to anyone in the cast.

Jamshed said that Zürich had no money to give to the arts. There'd recently been a scandal because the city wanted to close down the Schauspielhaus Keller; this was the more avant-garde theater, for younger theatergoers. John D.'s friend Matthias Frei had made a big fuss. As far as Jamshed knew, the theater was always in need of money. Technical personnel hadn't been given an annual raise; if they quit, they weren't replaced. Farrokh and Jamshed speculated that John D.'s salary couldn't be very significant. But of course he didn't need the money; Inspector Dhar was rich. What did it matter to Dhar that the Schauspielhaus Zürich was inadequately subsidized by the city, by the banks, by private donations?

Julia also implied that the theater somewhat complacently rested on its illustrious history in the 1930's and '40's, when it was a refuge for people fleeing from Germany, not only Jews but Social Democrats and Communists—or anyone who'd spoken out against the Nazis and as a result either weren't permitted to work or were in danger. There'd been a time when a production of *Wilhelm Tell* was defiant, even revolutionary—a symbolic blow against the Nazis. Many Swiss had been afraid to get involved in the war, yet the Schauspielhaus Zürich had been courageous at a time when any performance of Goethe's *Faust* might have been the last. They'd also performed Sartre, and von Hofmannsthal, and a young Max Frisch. The Jewish refugee Kurt Hirschfeld had found a home there. But nowadays, Julia thought, there were many younger intellectuals who might find the Schauspielhaus rather staid. Dr. Daruwalla suspected that "staid" suited John D. What mattered to him was that in Zürich he was *not* Inspector Dhar.

When the Hindi movie star was asked where he lived, because it was obvious that he spent very little time in Bombay, Dhar always replied (with characteristic vagueness) that he lived in the Himalayas—"the abode of snow." But John D.'s abode of snow was in the Alps, and in the city on the lake. The doctor thought that Dhar was probably a Kashmiri name, but neither Dr. Daruwalla nor Inspector Dhar had ever been to the Himalayas.

Now, on the spur of the moment, the doctor decided to tell John D. his decision.

"I'm not writing another Inspector Dhar movie," Farrokh informed the actor. "I'm going to have a press conference and identify myself as

the man responsible for Inspector Dhar's creation. I want to call an end
to it, and let you off the hook—so to speak. If you don't mind," the
doctor added uncertainly.

"Of course I don't mind," John D. said. "But you should let the real
policeman find the real murderer—you don't want to interfere with
that."

"Well, I won't!" Dr. Daruwalla said defensively. "But if you'd only
come to lunch . . . I just thought you might remember something. You
have an eye for detail, you know."

"What sort of detail have you got in mind?" John D. asked.

"Well, anything you might remember about Rahul, or about that time
in Goa. I don't know, really—just *anything!*" Farrokh said.

"I remember the hippie," said Inspector Dhar. He began with his
memory of her weight; after all, he'd carried her down the stairs of the
Hotel Bardez and into the lobby. She was very solid. She'd looked into
his eyes the whole time, and there was her fragrance—he knew she'd
just had a bath.

Then, in the lobby, she'd said, "If it's not too much trouble, you could
do me a big favor." She'd showed him the dildo without removing it
from her rucksack; Dhar remembered its appalling size, and the head of
the thing pointing at him. "The tip unscrews," Nancy had told him; she
was still watching his eyes. "But I'm just not strong enough." It was
screwed together so tightly, he needed to grip the big cock in both
hands. And then she stopped him, as soon as he'd loosened the tip.
"That's enough," she told him. "I'm going to spare you," she said too
softly. "You don't want to know what's inside the thing."

It had been quite a challenge—to meet her eyes, to stare her down.
John D. had focused on the idea of the big dildo inside her; he believed
that she would see in his eyes what he was thinking. What he thought
he'd seen in Nancy's eyes was that she'd courted danger before—maybe
it had even thrilled her—but that she wasn't so sure about danger
anymore. Then she'd looked away.

"I can't imagine what's become of the hippie!" Dr. Daruwalla blurted
out suddenly. "It's inconceivable—a woman like that, with Deputy
Commissioner Patel!"

"Lunch *is* tempting, if only to see what she looks like . . . after twenty
years," said Inspector Dhar.

He's just acting, thought Dr. Daruwalla. Dhar didn't care what Nancy
looked like; something else was on the actor's mind.

"So . . . you'll come to lunch?" the doctor asked.

"Sure. Why not?" the actor said. But Dr. Daruwalla knew that John D. wasn't as indifferent as he seemed.

As for Inspector Dhar, he'd never intended to miss the lunch at the Duckworth Club, and he thought he would rather be murdered by Rahul than resign his membership under a threat so coarse that it had to be left in a dead man's mouth. It was not how Nancy looked that mattered to him; rather, he was an actor—a professional—and even 20 years ago he'd known that Nancy had been acting. She wasn't the young woman she'd pretended to be. Twenty years ago, even the young John D. could tell that Nancy had been terrified, that she'd been bluffing.

Now the actor wanted to see if Nancy was still bluffing, if she was still pretending. Maybe now, Dhar thought, Nancy had stopped acting; maybe now, after 20 years, she simply let her terror show.

Something Rather Odd

It was 6:45 in the morning when Nancy awoke in her husband's arms. Vijay was holding her the way she loved to be held; it was the best way for her to wake up, and she was astonished at what a good night's sleep she'd had. She felt Vijay's chest against her back; his delicate hands held her breasts, his breath slightly stirred her hair. Detective Patel's penis was quite stiff, and Nancy could feel its light but insistent pulse against the base of her spine. Nancy knew she was fortunate to have such a good husband, and such a kind one. She regretted how difficult she was to live with; Vijay took such pains to protect her. She began to move her hips against him; it was one of the ways he liked to make love to her—to enter her from behind while she was on her side. But the deputy commissioner didn't respond to the rolling motion of his wife's hips, although he truly worshiped her nakedness—her whiteness, her blondness, her voluptuousness. The policeman let go of Nancy's breasts, and simultaneously (with his retreating from her) she noticed that the bathroom door was open; they always went to sleep with the door closed. The bedroom smelled fresh, like soap; her husband had already had his morning shower. Nancy turned to face Vijay—she touched his wet hair. He couldn't meet her eyes.

"It's almost seven o'clock," the detective told her.

Detective Patel was normally out of bed before 6:00; he usually left for Crime Branch Headquarters before 7:00. But this morning he'd let her sleep; he'd showered and then he'd got back into bed beside her.

He'd merely been waiting for her to wake up, Nancy thought; yet he hadn't been waiting to have sex.

"What are you going to tell me?" Nancy asked him. "What have you *not* told me, Vijay?"

"It's really nothing—just a little lunch," Patel replied.

"Who's having lunch?" Nancy asked him.

"*We* are—at the Duckworth Club," the policeman told her.

"With the doctor, you mean," Nancy said.

"With the actor, too, I imagine," the detective said.

"Oh, Vijay. No . . . not Dhar!" she cried.

"I think Dhar will be there," Vijay told her. "They both know Rahul," he explained. It sounded crude to him, to put it the way he'd said it yesterday, to the doctor ("to compare notes"), and so he said, "It could be valuable, just to hear what all of you remember. There might be some detail that would help me . . ." His voice trailed off. He hated to see his wife so withdrawn. Then she was suddenly wracked with sobs.

"We're not *members* of the Duckworth Club!" Nancy cried.

"We've been invited—we're guests," Patel told her.

"But they'll *see* me, they'll think I'm horrible," Nancy moaned.

"They know you're my wife. They just want to help," the deputy commissioner replied.

"What if Rahul sees me?" Nancy asked him. She was always raising this question.

"Would you recognize Rahul?" Patel asked. The detective thought it was unlikely that any of them would recognize Rahul, but the question was spurious; Nancy wasn't in disguise.

"I don't think so, but maybe," Nancy said.

Deputy Commissioner Patel dressed himself and left her while she was still naked in the bedroom; Nancy was aimlessly searching through her clothes. The dilemma of what she should wear to the Duckworth Club was gradually overwhelming her. Vijay had told her that he would come home from the police station to drive her to the Duckworth Club; Nancy wouldn't have to get herself there. But the detective doubted that she'd heard him. He'd have to come home early, because he suspected she would still be naked in the bedroom; possibly she'd have progressed to trying on her clothes.

Sometimes (on her "good days") she wandered into the kitchen, which was the only room where the sun penetrated the apartment, and she would lie on the countertop in a long patch of sunlight; the sun came through the open window for only two hours of the morning, but it was enough to give her a sunburn if she didn't apply some protection to her skin. Once, she'd stretched herself out on the countertop, completely naked, and a woman from a neighboring flat had called the police. The caller had described Nancy as "obscene." After that, she'd always worn something, even if it was only one of Vijay's shirts. Sometimes she wore sunglasses, too, although she liked to have a nice tan and the sunglasses gave her "raccoon eyes," she said.

She never shopped for food, because she said the beggars assailed her. Nancy was a decent cook but Vijay did the shopping. They didn't believe in grocery lists; he brought home something that appealed to him and she would think of a way to prepare it. Once or twice a month, she went out to buy books. She preferred shopping curbside, along Churchgate and at the intersection of Mahatma Gandhi and Hornby roads. She liked secondhand books best, especially memoirs; her favorite was *A Combat Widow of the Raj*—a memoir that ended with a suicide note. She also bought a lot of remaindered American novels; for one of these novels, she rarely paid more than 15 rupees—sometimes as little as 5. She said that beggars didn't bother people who bought books.

Once or twice a week, Vijay took her out to dinner. Although they'd still not spent all of the dildo money, they thought they couldn't afford the hotel restaurants, which were the only places where Nancy could feel she was anonymous—among foreigners. Only once had they argued about it; Vijay had told her that he suspected she preferred the hotel restaurants because she could imagine that she was only a tourist, just passing through. He'd accused her of wishing that she didn't live in India—of wanting to be back in the States. She'd showed him. The next time they went to their regular restaurant—a Chinese place called Kamling, at Churchgate—Nancy had summoned the owner to their table. She'd asked the owner if he knew that her husband was a deputy commissioner; indeed, the Chinese gentleman knew this—Crime Branch Headquarters was nearby, just opposite Crawford Market.

"Well, then," Nancy wanted to know, "how come you never offer us a free meal?"

After that, they always ate there for free; they were treated splendidly, too. Nancy said that, with the money they'd saved, they could afford to go to one of the hotel restaurants—or at least to one of the hotel bars—but they rarely did so. On those few occasions, Nancy mercilessly criticized the food; she would also pick out the Americans and say hateful things about them.

"Don't you dare tell me that I want to go back to the States, Vijay," she said; she only had to say it once. The deputy commissioner never suggested it again, and Nancy could tell he was pleased; all of it had needed saying. This was how they lived, with a delicate passion—with something usually held back. They were so careful. Nancy felt it was unfair that a lunch at the Duckworth Club could completely undo her.

She put on one of the dresses that she knew she would never wear to the club; she didn't bother with underwear, because she supposed she would just keep changing it. Nancy went into the kitchen and made some tea for herself. Then she found her sunglasses and she stretched out on her back in the long patch of sunlight on the countertop. She'd forgotten to put any sunscreen on her face—it was hard to find sunscreen in Bombay—but she told herself that she would lie there for only an hour; in a half hour, she'd take the sunglasses off. She didn't want "raccoon eyes," but she wanted Dr. Daruwalla and Inspector Dhar to see that she was healthy, that she took care of herself.

Nancy wished the apartment had a view; she would have liked to see a sunrise or a sunset. (What were they saving the dildo money *for?*) Coming from Iowa, Nancy would have especially appreciated a view of the Arabian Sea, which was the view to the west. Instead, she stared out the open window; she could see other women in the windows of other apartments, but they were constantly in motion, too busy to notice her. One day, Nancy hoped she might spot the woman who'd called the police and told them that she was "obscene." But Nancy didn't know how she would ever recognize the anonymous caller.

This thought led her to wondering if she would recognize Rahul; it was of more concern to Nancy that Rahul might recognize *her.* What if she was alone, just buying a book, and Rahul saw her and knew who she was?

She lay on the countertop, staring at the sun until it was blocked by an adjacent building. Now I'll have raccoon eyes, she told herself, but another thought obsessed her: that she would one day be standing right next to Rahul and she wouldn't know who Rahul was; yet Rahul would know who she was. That was her fear.

Nancy removed the sunglasses but she remained motionless, on her back on the countertop. She was thinking about the curl to Inspector Dhar's lip. He had an almost perfect mouth, and she recalled how the curl to his lip had first struck her as friendly, even inviting; then she'd realized he was sneering at her.

Nancy knew she was attractive to men. In 20 years, she'd gained 15 pounds, but only a woman would have been troubled by the way she'd put on the weight. The 15 pounds had spread themselves over her generously; they hadn't all ended up in her face, or on the backs of her thighs. Nancy's face had always been round, but it was still firm; her breasts had always been good—now, for most men, they were better. Certainly, they were bigger. Her hips were a little fuller, her waist a little thicker; the exaggerated curvaceousness of her body lent to her overall figure a voluptuous definition. Her waist, however thickened, still went in; her breasts and her hips still stood out. She was about Dhar's age, not quite 40, but it was not only her blondness or the fairness of her skin that made her seem younger; it was her nervousness. She was as awkward as a teenager who believes everyone is staring at her. This was because she was convinced that Rahul was watching her, everywhere she went.

Unfortunately, in a crowd, or in a new place where people would look at her—and people tended to look at her, both men and women—Nancy became so self-conscious that she found it difficult to speak. She thought that people stared at her because she was grotesque; on her good days, she thought she was merely fat. And whenever she was around strangers, she would recall Dhar's sneer. She'd been a pretty girl then, but he hadn't noticed; she'd shown him a huge dildo, and she'd asked him (quite suggestively) to unscrew it for her. She'd added that she was sparing him . . . to not let him see what was inside the thing. Yet, in his sneer, there'd not been the smallest measure of attraction to her; Nancy believed that she'd disgusted him.

She wandered back into the bedroom, where she removed the unsuitable dress; once again, she stood naked. She was surprised at herself for wanting to look her best for Inspector Dhar; she thought she hated him. But the strangest conviction was compelling her to dress herself for him. She knew he wasn't a *real* inspector, but Nancy believed that Dhar had certain powers. Nancy believed that it would *not* be her beloved husband, Vijay Patel, who would catch the killer; nor would the funny doctor be the hero. There was no reason for it—none beyond the authority of an actor's sneer—but Nancy believed that Inspector Dhar would be Rahul's undoing.

But what exactly did Dhar like? He must like something rather odd, Nancy decided. A faint ridge of blond fuzz extended from her pubic hair to her navel, which was especially long and deep. When Nancy rubbed her belly with coconut oil, this blond streak of fur would darken slightly and become more noticeable. If she wore a sari, she could leave her navel bare. Maybe Dhar would like her furry navel. Nancy knew that Vijay liked it.

19. OUR LADY OF VICTORIES

Another Author in Search of an Ending

The second Mrs. Dogar also suspected Dhar of unconventional sexual interests. It was frustrating to the former Rahul that Inspector Dhar had not returned the recently married woman's attentions. And although both the disapproving Mr. Sethna and Dr. Daruwalla had observed the unrequited flirtations of Mrs. Dogar, neither gentleman had truly appreciated the seriousness of Mrs. Dogar's designs. The former Rahul did not suffer rejection lightly.

While Farrokh had been struggling to begin his first artistic screenplay, his first quality picture, the second Mrs. Dogar had also undertaken the first draft of a story-in-progress; she had hatched a plot. Last night at the Duckworth Club, the second Mrs. Dogar had loudly denounced her husband for having had too much to drink. Mr. Dogar had had no more than his usual one whiskey and two beers; he was surprised at his wife's accusations.

"This is *your* night to drive—this is *my* night to drink!" Mrs. Dogar had said.

She'd spoken distinctly, and deliberately in the presence of the ever-disapproving Mr. Sethna—one waiter and one busboy had overheard her, too—and she'd chosen to utter her criticism at a lull in the other conversations in the Ladies' Garden, where the grieving Bannerjees were the only Duckworthians still dining.

The Bannerjees had been having a late, sober dinner; the murder of Mr. Lal had upset Mrs. Bannerjee too much to cook, and her intermittent conversation with her husband had concerned what efforts they might make to comfort Mr. Lal's widow. The Bannerjees would never have guessed that the second Mrs. Dogar's rude outburst was as premeditated as her intentions to soon join Mrs. Lal in the state of widowhood. Rahul had married Mr. Dogar out of eagerness to become his widow.

Also deliberately, Mrs. Dogar had turned to Mr. Sethna and said, "My dear Mr. Sethna, would you kindly call us a taxi? My husband is in no condition to drive us home."

"Promila, *please* . . ." Mr. Dogar began to say.

"Give me your keys," Mrs. Dogar commanded him. "You can take a taxi with me or you can call your own taxi, but you're *not* driving a car."

Sheepishly, Mr. Dogar handed her his ring of keys.

"Now just *sit* here—don't get up and wander around," Mrs. Dogar told him. Mrs. Dogar herself stood up. "Wait for me," she ordered her husband—the rejected designated driver. When Mr. Dogar was alone, he glanced at the Bannerjees, who looked away; not even the waiter would look at the condemned drunk, and the busboy had slunk into the circular driveway to smoke a cigarette.

Rahul timed how long everything took. He—or, rather, *she* (if outward anatomy is the measure of a man or a woman)—walked into the men's room by the door from the foyer. She knew no one could be in the men's room, for none of the wait-staff were permitted to use it—except Mr. Sethna, who so disapproved of peeing with the hired help that he made uncontested use of the facilities marked FOR MEMBERS ONLY. The old steward was more in charge of the Duckworth Club than any member. But Mrs. Dogar knew that Mr. Sethna was busy calling a taxi.

Since she'd become a woman, Mrs. Dogar didn't regret not using the men's room at the Duckworth Club; its decor wasn't as pleasing to her as the ladies' room—Rahul loathed the men's room wallpaper. She found the tiger-hunting motif brutal and stupid.

She moved past the urinals, the toilet stalls, the sinks for shaving, and into the darkened locker room, which extended to the clubhouse and the clubhouse bar; these latter facilities were never in use at night, and Mrs. Dogar wanted to be sure that she could navigate their interiors in darkness. The big windows of frosted glass admitted the moonlight that reflected from the tennis courts and the swimming pool, which was presently under repair and not in service; it was an empty cement-lined hole with some construction debris in the deep end, and the members were already betting that it wouldn't be ready for use in the hotter months ahead.

Mrs. Dogar had sufficient moonlight to unlock the rear door to the clubhouse; she found the right key in less than a minute—then she relocked the door. This was just a test. She also found Mr. Dogar's locker and unlocked it; it took the smallest key on the ring, and Mrs. Dogar discovered that she could easily find this key by touch. She unlocked and relocked the locker by touch, too, although she could see everything in the moonlight; one night, she might not have the moon.

Rahul could quite clearly make out the shrine of old golf clubs displayed on the wall. These were the clubs of famous Golfers Past and of some living, less famous Duckworthians who had retired from active play. Mrs. Dogar needed to assure herself that these clubs could be easily removed from the wall. After all, it had been a while since Rahul had visited the men's locker room; she hadn't been there since she'd been a boy. When she'd handled a few of the clubs to her satisfaction, she went back into the men's room—after assuring herself that neither Mr. Sethna nor Mr. Bannerjee was using the facilities. She knew her husband wouldn't leave the table in the Ladies' Garden; he did what he was told.

When she could see (from the men's room) that there was no one in the foyer, she returned to the Ladies' Garden. She went directly to the Bannerjees' table—they weren't friends of the Dogars's—and she whispered to them, "I'm sorry for my outspokenness. But when he's like this, he's virtually a baby—he's so senile, he's not to be trusted. And not only in a car. One night, after dinner—he had all his clothes on—I stopped him just before he dove into the club pool."

"The *empty* pool?" said Mr. Bannerjee.

"I'm glad you understand," Mrs. Dogar replied. "That's what I'm talking about. If I don't treat him like a child, he'll hurt himself."

Then she went to her husband, leaving the Bannerjees with this impression of Mr. Dogar's senility and self-destructiveness—for her husband being found dead in the deep end of the club's empty pool was one of the possible outcomes for the first draft that the second Mrs. Dogar was hard at work on. She was merely foreshadowing, as any good storyteller does. She also knew that she should set up other options, and these alternative endings were already in her mind.

"I hate to treat you like this, darling, but just sit tight while I see about our cab," Mrs. Dogar told her husband. He was bewildered. Although his second wife was in her fifties, she was a young woman in comparison to what Mr. Dogar had been used to; the old gentleman was in his seventies—he'd been a widower for the last 10 years. He supposed these swings of mood were characteristic among younger women. He wondered if perhaps he *had* drunk too much. He *did* remember that his new wife had lost a brother to an automobile accident in Italy; he just couldn't recall if alcohol had been the cause of the wreck.

Now Rahul was off whispering to Mr. Sethna, who disapproved of women whispering to men—for whatever reason.

"My dear Mr. Sethna," the second Mrs. Dogar said. "I *do* hope you'll forgive my aggressive behavior, but he's simply not fit to wander about the club—much less drive a car. I'm sure he's the one who's been killing the flowers."

Mr. Sethna was shocked by this allegation, but he was also eager to believe it was true. Something or someone *was* killing the flowers. An undiagnosed blight had struck patches of the bougainvillea. The head mali was stymied. Here, at last, was an answer: Mr. Dogar had been pissing on the flowers!

"He's . . . incontinent?" Mr. Sethna inquired.

"Not at all," said Mrs. Dogar. "He's doing it deliberately."

"He wants to kill the flowers?" Mr. Sethna asked.

"I'm glad you understand," Mrs. Dogar replied. "Poor man." With a wave, she indicated the surrounding golf course. "Naturally, he wanders out there only after dark. Like a dog, he always goes to the same spots!"

"Territorial, I suppose," said Mr. Sethna.

"I'm glad you understand," Mrs. Dogar said. "Now, where's our cab?"

In the taxi, old Mr. Dogar looked as if he wasn't sure if he should apologize or complain. But, before he could decide, his younger wife once more surprised him.

"Oh, darling, never let me treat you like that again—at least not in public. I'm so ashamed!" she cried. "They'll think I bully you. You mustn't let me. If I *ever* tell you that you can't drive a car again, here's what you must do . . . are you listening, or are you too drunk?" Mrs. Dogar asked him.

"No . . . I mean *yes*, I'm listening," Mr. Dogar said. "No, I'm *not* too drunk," the old man assured her.

"You must *throw* the keys on the floor and make me pick them up, as if I were your servant," Mrs. Dogar told him.

"What?" he asked.

"Then tell me that you always carry an extra set of keys and that you'll drive the car home, when and if you choose. Then tell me to *go*—tell me you wouldn't drive me home if I *begged* you!" Mrs. Dogar cried.

"But, Promila, I would never..." Mr. Dogar began to say, but his wife cut him off.

"Just promise me one thing—never back down to me," she told him. Then she seized his face in her hands and kissed him on his mouth. "First, you should tell me to take a taxi—you just carry on sitting at the dinner table, as if you're smoldering with rage. Then you should go to the men's room and wash your face."

"Wash my face?" said Mr. Dogar with surprise.

"I can't stand the smell of food on your face, darling," Mrs. Dogar told her husband. "Just wash your face—soap and warm water. *Then* come home to me. I'll be waiting for you. That's how I want you to treat me. Only you must wash your face first. Promise me."

It had been years since Mr. Dogar had been so aroused, nor had he ever been so confused. It was difficult to understand a younger woman, he decided—yet surely worth it.

This was a pretty good first draft, Rahul felt certain. The next time, Mr. Dogar would do as he was told. He would be abusive to her and tell her to go. But she would take the taxi no farther than the access road to the Duckworth Club, or perhaps three quarters of the length of the driveway—just out of the reach of the overhead lamps. She'd tell the driver to wait for her because she'd forgotten her purse. Then she'd cross the first green of the golf course and enter the clubhouse through the rear door, which she would have previously unlocked. She'd take off her shoes and cross the dark locker room and wait there until she heard her husband washing his face. She'd either kill him with a single blow from one of the "retired" golf clubs in the locker room, or (if possible) kill him by lifting his head by his hair and smashing his skull against the sink. Her preference for the latter method was because she preferred the swimming-pool ending. She'd be careful to clean the sink; then Mrs. Dogar would drag her husband's body out the rear door of the clubhouse and dump him in the deep end of the empty pool. She wouldn't keep her taxi waiting long—at the most, 10 minutes.

But killing him with a golf club would certainly be easier. After she had clubbed her husband to death, she would put a two-rupee note in his mouth and stuff his body in his locker. The note, which Mrs. Dogar already carried in her purse, displayed a typed message on the serial-number side of the money.

... BECAUSE DHAR IS STILL A MEMBER

It was an intriguing decision—which ending Rahul would choose—for although she liked the appearance of the "accidental" death in the deep end of the pool, she also favored the attention-getting murder of another Duckworthian, especially if Inspector Dhar didn't give up his membership. The second Mrs. Dogar was quite sure that Dhar *wouldn't* resign, at least not without another killing to coax him into it.

The Way It Happened to Mr. Lal

It was an embarrassed and exhausted-looking Mr. Dogar who appeared at the Duckworth Club before 7:00 the next morning, looking every inch the portrait of a hangover. But it wasn't alcohol that had wrecked him. Mrs. Dogar had made violent love to him the previous night; she'd scarcely waited for the taxi to depart their driveway, or for Mr. Dogar to unlock the door—she'd given him back his keys. They were fortunate that the servants didn't mistake them for intruders, for Mrs. Dogar had pounced on her husband in the front hall; she'd torn the clothes off both of them while they were still on the first floor of the house. Then she'd made the old man run up the stairs after her, and she'd straddled him on the bedroom floor; she wouldn't let him crawl a few feet farther so that they could do it on the bed—nor had she once volunteered to relinquish the top position.

This was, of course, another first-draft possibility . . . that old Mr. Dogar would suffer a heart attack while Rahul was deliberately overexciting him. But the second Mrs. Dogar had resolved that she wouldn't wait as long as a year for this "natural" ending to occur. It was simply too boring. If it happened soon, fine. If not, there was always the golf-club, locker-room ending; in this version, it amused the second Mrs. Dogar to imagine how they might finally find the body.

She would report that her husband had not come home for the night. They would find his car in the Duckworth Club parking lot. The wait-staff would relate what had transpired after the Dogars had eaten their dinner; doubtless, Mr. Sethna would convey more intimate infor-

mation. It was possible that no one would think to look for Mr. Dogar
in his locker until the body began to stink.

But the swimming-pool version also intrigued Rahul. The Bannerjees
would confide to the authorities that such a dive in the pool was reputed
to be the old fool's inclination. Mrs. Dogar herself could always say, "I
told you so." For Rahul, the hard part about this version would be
maintaining a straight face. And the rumor that old Mr. Dogar was
pissing on the bougainvillea was already established.

When the ashamed Mr. Dogar appeared at the Duckworth Club to
claim his car, he spoke in apologetic tones to the disapproving Mr.
Sethna, to whom the very idea of urinating outdoors was repugnant.

"Did I seem especially drunk to you, Mr. Sethna?" Mr. Dogar asked
the venerable steward. "I'm really very sorry . . . if I behaved insensi-
tively."

"Nothing happened, really," Mr. Sethna replied coldly. He'd already
spoken to the head mali about the bougainvillea. The fool gardener
confirmed that there were only isolated patches of the blight. The dead
spots in the bougainvillea bordered the greens at the fifth and the ninth
holes; both these greens were out of sight of the Duckworth Club dining
room and the clubhouse—also, they couldn't be seen from the Ladies'
Garden. As for that bougainvillea which surrounded the Ladies' Garden,
there was only one dead patch and it was suspiciously in a spot that was
out of sight from any of the club's facilities. Mr. Sethna surmised that
this gave credence to Mrs. Dogar's urine theory—poor old Mr. Dogar
was peeing on the flowers!

It would never have occurred to the old steward that a *woman*—not
even as vulgar a member of the species as Mrs. Dogar—could be the
pissing culprit. But the killer was no amateur at foreshadowing. She'd
been systematically murdering the bougainvillea for months. One of
many things that the new Mrs. Dogar liked about wearing dresses was
that it was comfortable not to wear underwear. The only thing Rahul
missed about having a penis was how convenient it had been to pee
outdoors. But her penchant for pissing on certain out-of-the-way plots
of the bougainvillea was not whimsical. While in the pursuit of this odd
habit, Mrs. Dogar had been mindful of her larger work-in-progress.
Even before the unfortunate Mr. Lal had happened upon her while she
was squatting in the bougainvillea by the fatal ninth hole (which had
long been Mr. Lal's nemesis), Rahul had already made a plan.

In her purse, for weeks, she'd carried the two-rupee note with her first
typed message to the Duckworthians: MORE MEMBERS DIE IF DHAR RE-

MAINS A MEMBER. She'd always assumed that the easiest Duckworthian to murder would be someone who stumbled into her in one of her out-of-the-way peeing places. She'd thought it would happen at night—in the darkness. She'd imagined a younger member than Mr. Lal, probably someone who'd drunk too much beer and wandered out on the nighttime golf course—drawn by the same need that had drawn Mrs. Dogar there. She'd imagined a brief flirtation—they were the best kind.

"So! You had to pee, too? If you tell me what you like about doing it outdoors, I'll tell you *my* reasons!" Or maybe: "What *else* do you like to do outdoors?"

Mrs. Dogar had also imagined that she might indulge in a kiss and a little fondling; she liked fondling. Then she would kill him, whoever he was, and she'd stick the two-rupee note in his mouth. She'd never strangled a man; with her hand strength, she didn't doubt she could do it. She'd never much liked strangling women—not as much as she enjoyed the pure strength of a blow from a blunt instrument—but she was looking forward to strangling a man because she wanted to see if that old story was true . . . if men got erections and ejaculated when they were close to choking to death.

Disappointingly, old Mr. Lal had afforded Mrs. Dogar neither the opportunity for a brief flirtation nor the novelty of a strangulation. Rahul was so lazy, she rarely made breakfast for herself. Although he was officially retired, Mr. Dogar left early for his office, and Mrs. Dogar often indulged in an early-morning pee on the golf course—before even the most zealous golfers were on the fairways. Then she'd have her tea and some fruit in the Ladies' Garden and go to her health club to lift weights and skip rope. She'd been surprised by old Mr. Lal's early-morning assault on the bougainvillea at the ninth green.

Rahul had only just finished peeing; she rose up out of the flowers, and there was the old duffer plodding off the green and tripping through the vines. Mr. Lal was searching for a challenging spot in this jungle in which to deposit the stupid golf ball. When he looked up from the flowers, the second Mrs. Dogar was standing directly in front of him. She'd startled him so—for a moment, she thought it would be unnecessary to kill him. He clutched his chest and staggered away from her.

"Mrs. Dogar!" he cried. "What's happened to you? Has someone . . . *molested* you?" Thus he gave her the idea; after all, her dress was still hiked up to her hips. Clearly distraught, she wriggled her dress down. (She would change into a sari for lunch.)

"Oh, Mr. Lal! Thank God it's you!" she cried. "I've been . . . taken advantage of!" she told him.

"What a world, Mrs. Dogar! But how may I assist you? *Help!*" the old man shouted out.

"Oh no, please! I couldn't bear to see anyone else—I'm so ashamed!" she confided to him.

"But how may I help you, Mrs. Dogar?" Mr. Lal inquired.

"It's painful for me to walk," she confessed. "They hurt me."

"*They!*" the old man shouted.

"Perhaps if you would lend me one of your clubs . . . if I could just use it as a cane," Mrs. Dogar suggested. Mr. Lal was on the verge of handing her his nine iron, then changed his mind.

"The putter would be best!" he declared. Poor Mr. Lal was out of breath from the short trot to his golf bag and his stumbling return to her side through the tangled vines, the destroyed flowers. He was much shorter than Mrs. Dogar; she was able to put one of her big hands on his shoulder—the putter in her other hand. That way, she could see over the old man's head to the green and the fairway; no one was there.

"You could rest on the green while I fetch you a golf cart," Mr. Lal suggested.

"Yes, thank you—you go ahead," she told him. He tripped purposefully forward, but she was right behind him; before he reached the green, she had struck him senseless—she hit him just behind one ear. After he'd fallen, she bashed him directly in the temple that was turned toward her, but his eyes were already open and unmoving when she struck him the second time. Mrs. Dogar suspected he'd been killed by the first blow.

In her purse, she had no difficulty finding the two-rupee note. For 20 years, she'd clipped her small bills to the top half of that silver ballpoint pen which she'd stolen from the beach cottage in Goa. She even kept this silly memento well polished. The clip—the "pocket clasp," as her Aunt Promila had called it—continued to maintain the perfect tension on a small number of bills, and the polished silver made the top half of the pen easy to spot in her purse; she hated how small things could become lost in purses.

She'd inserted the two-rupee note in Mr. Lal's gaping mouth; to her surprise, when she closed his mouth, it opened again. She'd never tried to close a dead person's mouth before. She'd assumed that the body parts of the dead would be fairly controllable; that had certainly been her experience with manipulating limbs—sometimes an elbow or a knee had been in the way of her belly drawing, and she'd easily rearranged it.

The distracting detail of Mr. Lal's mouth was what caused her to be careless. She'd returned the remaining small notes to her purse, but *not* the top half of the well-traveled pen; it must have fallen in the bougainvillea. She hadn't been able to find it later, and there in the bougainvillea was the last place she recalled holding it in her hand. Mrs. Dogar assumed that the police were presently puzzling over it; with the widow Lal's help, they'd probably determined that the top half of the pen hadn't belonged to Mr. Lal. Mrs. Dogar speculated that the police might even conclude that no Duckworthian would be caught dead with such a pen; that it was made of real silver was somehow negated by the sheer tackiness of the engraved word, *India*. Rahul found tacky things amusing. It also amused Rahul to imagine how aimlessly the police must be tracking her, for Mrs. Dogar believed that the half-pen would be just another link in a chain of meaningless clues.

Some Small Tragedy

It was after Mr. Dogar had apologized to Mr. Sethna and retrieved his car from the Duckworth Club parking lot that the old steward received the phone call from Mrs. Dogar. "Is my husband still there? I suppose not. I'd meant to remind him of something to attend to—he's so forgetful."

"He was here, but he's gone," Mr. Sethna informed her.

"Did he remember to cancel our reservation for lunch? I suppose not. Anyway, we're *not* coming," Rahul told the steward. Mr. Sethna prided himself in his daily memorizing of the reservations for lunch and dinner; he knew that there'd been no reservation for the Dogars. But when he informed Mrs. Dogar of this fact, she surprised him. "Oh, the poor man!" she cried. "He forgot to cancel the reservation, but he was so drunk last night that he forgot to *make* the reservation in the first place. This would be comic if it weren't also so tragic, I suppose."

"I suppose . . ." Mr. Sethna replied, but Rahul could tell that she'd achieved her goal. One day Mr. Sethna would be an important witness to Mr. Dogar's utter frailty. Foreshadowing was simply necessary preparation. Rahul knew that Mr. Sethna would be unsurprised when Mr. Dogar became a victim—either of a murder in the locker room *or* of a swimming-pool mishap.

In some ways, this was the best part of a murder, Rahul believed. In the first draft of a work-in-progress, you had so many options—more options than you would end up with in the final act. It was only in the planning phase that you saw so many possibilities, so many variations on the outcome. In the end, it was always over too quickly; that is, if you cared about neatness, you couldn't prolong it.

"The poor man!" Mrs. Dogar repeated to Mr. Sethna. The poor man, indeed! Mr. Sethna thought. With a wife like Mrs. Dogar, Mr. Sethna presumed it might even be a comfort to already have one foot in the grave, so to speak.

The old steward had just hung up the phone when Dr. Daruwalla called the Duckworth Club to make a reservation. There would be four for lunch, the doctor informed Mr. Sethna; he hoped no one had already taken his favorite table in the Ladies' Garden. There was plenty of room, but Mr. Sethna disapproved of making a reservation for lunch on the morning of the same day; people shouldn't trust in plans that were so spur-of-the-moment.

"You're in luck—I've just had a cancellation," the steward told the doctor.

"May I have the table at noon?" Farrokh asked.

"One o'clock would be better," Mr. Sethna instructed him, for the steward also disapproved of the doctor's inclination to eat his lunch early. Mr. Sethna theorized that early lunch-eating contributed to the doctor's being overweight. It was most unsightly for *small* men to be overweight, Mr. Sethna thought.

Dr. Daruwalla had just hung up the phone when Dr. Tata returned his call. Farrokh remembered instantly what he'd wanted to ask Tata Two.

"Do you remember Rahul Rai and his Aunt Promila?" Farrokh asked.

"Doesn't everybody remember them?" Tata Two replied.

"But this is a professional question," Dr. Daruwalla said. "I believe your father examined Rahul when he was twelve or thirteen. That would have been in 1949. *My* father examined Rahul when he was only eight or ten. It was his Aunt Promila's request—the matter of his hairlessness was bothering her. My father dismissed it, but I believe Promila took Rahul to see your father. I was wondering if the alleged hairlessness was still the issue."

"Why would anyone see your father *or* mine about hairlessness?" asked Dr. Tata.

"A good question," Farrokh replied. "I believe that the real issue concerned Rahul's sexual identity. Possibly a sex change would have been requested."

"My father didn't do sex changes!" said Tata Two. "He was a gynecologist, an obstetrician . . ."

"I know what he was," said Dr. Daruwalla. "But he might have been asked to make a diagnosis . . . I'm speaking of Rahul's reproductive organs, whether there was anything peculiar about them that would have warranted a sex-change operation—at least in the boy's mind, or in his aunt's mind. If you've kept your father's records . . . I have *my* father's."

"Of course I've kept his records!" Dr. Tata cried. "Mr. Subhash can have them on my desk in two minutes. I'll call you back in five." So . . . even Tata Two called his medical secretary *Mister*; perhaps, like Ranjit, Mr. Subhash was a medical secretary who'd remained in the family. Dr. Daruwalla reflected that Mr. Subhash had sounded (on the phone) like a man in his eighties!

Ten minutes later, when Dr. Tata had not called him back, Farrokh also reflected on the presumed chaos of Tata Two's record keeping; apparently, old Dr. Tata's file on Rahul wasn't exactly at Mr. Subhash's fingertips. Or maybe it was the diagnosis of Rahul that gave Tata Two pause? Regardless, Farrokh told Ranjit that he would take no calls except one he was expecting from Dr. Tata.

Dr. Daruwalla had one office appointment before his much-anticipated lunch at the Duckworth Club, and he told Ranjit to cancel it. Dr. Desai, from London, was in town; in his spare time from his own surgical practice, Dr. Desai was a designer of artificial joints. He was a man with a theme; joint replacement was his only topic of conversation. This made it hard on Julia whenever Farrokh tried to converse with Dr. Desai at the Duckworth Club. It was easier to deal with Desai in the office. "Should the implant be fixated to the skeleton with bone cement or is biologic fixation the method of choice?" This was typical of Dr. Desai's initial conversation; it was what Dr. Desai said instead of, "How are your wife and kids?" For Dr. Daruwalla to cancel an office appointment with Dr. Desai was tantamount to his admitting a lack of interest in his chosen orthopedic field; but the doctor had his mind on his new screenplay—he wanted to write.

To this end, Farrokh sat on the opposite side of his desk, eliminating his usual view; the doctor found the exercise yard of the Hospital for Crippled Children distracting—the physical therapy for some of his postoperative patients was hard for him to ignore. Dr. Daruwalla was more enticed by a make-believe world than he was drawn to confront the world he lived in.

For the most part, Inspector Dhar's creator was unaware of the real-life dramas that teemed all around him. Poor Nancy, with her raccoon eyes, was dressing herself for Inspector Dhar. The famous actor, even offstage and off-camera, was still acting. Mr. Sethna, who so strongly disapproved of everything, had discovered (to his deep distaste) that human urine was killing the bougainvillea. And that wasn't the only murder-in-progress at the Duckworth Club, where Rahul was already envisioning herself as the widow Dogar. But Dr. Daruwalla was still untouched by these realities. Instead, for his inspiration, the doctor chose to stare at the circus photograph on his desk.

There was the beautiful Suman—Suman the skywalker. The last time Dr. Daruwalla had seen her, she'd been unmarried—a 29-year-old star acrobat, the idol of all the child acrobats in training. The screenwriter was presuming that Suman was 29, and that it was high time for her to be wed; she should be engaged in more practical activities than walking upside down across the roof of the main tent, 80 feet from the ground, with no net. A woman as wonderful as Suman should definitely be married, the screenwriter thought. Suman was an acrobat, not an actress. The screenwriter intended to give his circus characters very little re-sponsibility in the way of acting. The boy, Ganesh, would be an accom-plished actor, but his sister, Pinky, would be the *real* Pinky—from the Great Royal Circus. Pinky would perform as an acrobat; it wouldn't be necessary to have her talk. (Keep her dialogue to a minimum, the screenwriter thought.)

Farrokh was getting ahead of himself; he was already casting the movie. In his screenplay, he still had to get the children to the circus. That was when Dr. Daruwalla thought of the new missionary; in the screenplay, the doctor wouldn't call him Martin Mills—the name Mills was too boring. The screenwriter would call him simply "Mr. Martin." The Jesuit mission would take charge of these children because their mother was killed in St. Ignatius Church by an unsafe statue of the Holy Virgin; St. Ignatius would certainly bear some responsibility for that. And so the children would manage to be picked up by the *right* limou-sine, by Vinod; the so-called Good Samaritan dwarf would still need to get the Jesuits' permission to take the kids to the circus. Oh, this is brilliant! thought Dr. Daruwalla. That would be how Suman and Mr. Martin meet. The morally meddlesome missionary takes the children to the circus, and the fool falls in love with the skywalker!

Why not? The Jesuit would soon find Suman preferable to chastity. The fictional Mr. Martin would have to be a skilled actor, and the screenwriter would provide the character with a far more winning personality than that of Martin Mills. In the screenplay, the seduction of Mr. Martin would be an *un*conversion story. There was no small measure of mischief in the screenwriter's next idea: that John D. would play a perfect Mr. Martin. How happy he'd be—to not be Inspector Dhar!

What a screenplay this was going to be—what an improvement on reality! That was when Dr. Daruwalla realized that nothing was preventing him from putting himself in the movie. He wouldn't presume to make himself a hero—perhaps a minor character with admirable intentions would suffice. But how should he describe himself? Farrokh wondered. The screenwriter didn't know he was handsome, and to speak of himself as "highly intelligent" sounded defensive; also, in movies, you could only describe how one *appeared*.

There was no mirror in the doctor's office and so he saw himself as he often looked in the full-length mirror in the foyer of the Duckworth Club, which doubtless conveyed to Dr. Daruwalla a Duckworthian sense of himself as an elegant gentleman. Such a gentlemanly doctor could play a small but pivotal role in the screenplay, for the character of the do-gooder missionary would naturally be obsessed with the idea that Ganesh's limp could be fixed. Ideally, the character of Mr. Martin would bring the boy to be examined by none other than Dr. Daruwalla. The doctor would announce the hard truth: there were exercises that Ganesh could do—these would strengthen his legs, including the crippled leg—but the boy would always limp. (A few scenes of the crippled boy struggling bravely to perform these exercises would be excellent for audience sympathy, the screenwriter believed.)

Like Rahul, Dr. Daruwalla enjoyed this phase of storytelling—namely, plot. The thrill of exploring one's options! In the beginning, there were always so many.

But euphoria, in the case of murder *and* in the case of writing, is short-lived. Farrokh began to worry that his masterpiece had already been reduced to a romantic comedy. The two kids escape in the right limo; the circus is their salvation. Suman gives up skywalking to marry a missionary, who gives up being a missionary. Even Inspector Dhar's creator suspected that this ending was too happy. Surely something *bad* should happen, the screenwriter thought.

Thus the doctor sat pondering in his office at the Hospital for Crippled Children, with his back to the exercise yard. In such a setting, one might imagine that Dr. Daruwalla must have felt ashamed of himself for trying to imagine some small tragedy.

Not a Romantic Comedy

Contrary to Rahul's opinion, the police had *not* found the top half of the silver pen with *India* inscribed on it. Rahul's money clip had no longer been in the bougainvillea when the deputy commissioner had examined Mr. Lal's body. The silver was so shiny in the morning sun, it had caught a crow's sharp eyes. It was the half-pen that led the crow to discover the corpse. The crow had begun by pecking out one of Mr. Lal's eyes; the bird was busy at the open wound behind Mr. Lal's ear and at the wound at Mr. Lal's temple when the first of the vultures settled on the ninth green. The crow had stood its ground until more vultures came; after all, it had found the body first. And before taking flight, the crow had stolen the silver half-pen. Crows were always stealing shiny objects. That this crow had promptly lost its prize in the ceiling fan in the Duckworth Club dining room was not necessarily a comment on the bird's overall intelligence, but the blade of the fan (at that time of the morning) had moved in and out of the sunlight; the fan had also caught the crow's sharp eyes. It was a silly place for a crow to land, and a waiter had rudely shooed the shitting bird away.

As for the shiny object that the crow had held so tenaciously in its beak, it had been left where it occasionally disturbed the mechanism of the ceiling fan. Dr. Daruwalla had observed one such disturbance; the doctor had also observed the landing of the shitting crow upon the fan. And so the top half of the silver pen existed only in the crowded memory of Dr. Daruwalla, and the doctor had already forgotten that the second Mrs. Dogar had reminded him of someone else—an old movie star. Farrokh had also forgotten the pain of his collision with Mrs. Dogar in the foyer of the Duckworth Club. That shiny something, which first Nancy and then Rahul and then the crow had lost, might now be lost forever, for its discovery lay within the limited abilities of Dr. Daruwalla. Frankly, both the memory and the powers of observation of a closet screenwriter are not the best. One might more sensibly rely on the mechanism of the ceiling fan to spit out the half-pen and present it, as a miracle, to Detective Patel (or to Nancy).

An unlikely miracle of that coincidental kind was exactly what was needed to rescue Martin Mills, for the Mass had been celebrated too late to save the missionary from his worst memories. There were times when every church reminded Martin of Our Lady of Victories. When his mother was in Boston, Martin always went to Mass at Our Lady of Victories on Isabella Street; it was only an eight-minute walk from the Ritz. That Sunday morning of the long Thanksgiving weekend of his ninth-grade year, young Martin slipped out of the bedroom he shared with Arif Koma without waking the Turk up. In the living room of the two-bedroom suite at the hotel, Martin saw that the door to his mother's bedroom was ajar; this struck the boy as indicative of Vera's carelessness, and he was about to close the door—before he left the suite to go to Mass—when his mother spoke to him.

"Is that you, Martin?" Vera asked. "Come kiss me good-morning."

Dutifully, although he was loath to see his mother in the strongly scented disarray of her boudoir, Martin went to her. To his surprise, both Vera and her bed were unrumpled; he had the impression that his mother had already bathed and brushed her teeth and combed her hair. The sheets weren't in their usual knot of apparent bad dreams. Also, Vera's nightgown was a pretty, almost girlish thing; it was revealing of her dramatic bosom but not sluttishly revealing, as was often the case. Martin cautiously kissed her cheek.

"Off to church?" his mother asked him.

"To Mass—yes," Martin told her.

"Is Arif still sleeping?" Vera inquired.

"Yes, I think so," Martin replied. Arif's name on his mother's lips reminded Martin of the painful embarrassment of the night before. "I don't think you should ask Arif about such . . . personal things," Martin said suddenly.

"Personal? Do you mean *sexual?*" Vera asked her son. "Honestly, Martin, the poor boy has probably been *dying* to talk to someone about his terrible circumcision. Don't be such a prude!"

"I think Arif is a very private person," Martin said. "Also," he added stubbornly, "I think he might be a bit . . . disturbed."

Vera sat up in her bed with new interest. "*Sexually* disturbed?" she asked her son. "What gives you that idea?"

It didn't seem a betrayal, not at the time; Martin thought he was speaking to his mother in order to protect Arif. "He masturbates," Martin said quietly.

"Goodness, I should *hope* so!" Vera exclaimed. "I certainly hope that *you* do!"

Martin wouldn't take this bait, but he replied, "I mean that he masturbates a *lot*—almost every night."

"The poor boy!" Vera remarked. "But you sound so disapproving, Martin."

"I think it's . . . excessive," her son told her.

"*I* think masturbation is quite healthy for boys your age. Have you discussed masturbation with your father?" Vera asked him.

"Discussed" wasn't the right word. Martin had listened to Danny go on and on in reassuring tones in regard to all the desires Danny presumed that Martin was experiencing—how such desires were perfectly natural . . . that was Danny's theme.

"Yes," Martin told his mother. "Dad thinks masturbation is . . . normal."

"Well, there—you see?" Vera said sarcastically. "If your sainted father says it's normal, I suppose we should *all* be trying it!"

"I'll be late for Mass," Martin said.

"Run along, then," his mother replied. Martin was about to close the door to her bedroom behind him when his mother gave him a parting shot. "Personally, dear, I think masturbation would be better for you than Mass. And please leave the door open—I like it that way." Martin remembered to take the room key in case Arif was still sleeping when he came back from Mass—in case his mother was in the bathroom or talking on the telephone.

When Mass was over, he looked briefly at a window display of men's suits in a Brooks Brothers store; the mannequins wore Christmas-tree neckties, but Martin was struck by the smoothness of the mannequins' skin—it reminded him of Arif's perfect complexion. Except for his pausing at this window, Martin came straight back to the suite at the Ritz. When he unlocked the door, he was happy he'd brought the room key because he thought his mother was talking on the phone; it was a one-sided conversation—all Vera. But then the awful words themselves were clear to him.

"I'm going to make you squirt again," his mother was saying. "I absolutely know you can squirt again—I can feel you. You're going to squirt again *soon*—aren't you? Aren't you?" The door to his mother's bedroom was still open—a little wider open than the way she liked it—and Martin Mills could see her naked back, her naked hips and the crack in her shapely ass. She was riding Arif Koma, who lay wordlessly under her; Martin was grateful that he couldn't see his roommate's face.

He quietly let himself out of the suite as his mother continued to urge

Arif to squirt. On the short walk back to Isabella Street, Martin wondered if it had been his own revelation of Arif's penchant for masturbation that had given Vera the idea; probably his mother had already had the seduction in mind, but the masturbation story must have provided her with greater incentive.

Martin Mills had sat as stupefied in Our Lady of Victories Church as he'd sat waiting for the Mass at St. Ignatius. Brother Gabriel was worried about him. First the late-night prayers—"I'll take the turkey, I'll take the turkey"—and then, even after Mass was over, the missionary knelt on the kneeling pad as if he were waiting for the *next* Mass. That was exactly what he'd done in Our Lady of Victories on Isabella Street; he'd waited for the next Mass, as if one Mass hadn't been enough.

What also troubled Brother Gabriel were the bloodstains on the missionary's balled-up fists. Brother Gabriel couldn't have known about Martin's nose, for the wound had stopped bleeding and was almost entirely concealed by a small scab on one nostril; but Brother Gabriel wondered about the bloody socks that Martin Mills clutched in his hands. The blood had dried between his knuckles and under his nails, and Brother Gabriel feared that the source of the bleeding might have been the missionary's palms. That's all we need to make our jubilee year a success, Brother Gabriel thought—an outbreak of stigmata!

But later, when Martin attended the morning classes, he seemed back on track, so to speak; he was lively with the students, humble with the other teachers—although, as a teacher, he'd had more experience than many of the staff at St. Ignatius School. Watching the new scholastic interact with both the pupils and the staff, the Father Rector suspended his earlier anxieties that the American might be a crazed zealot. And Father Cecil found Martin Mills to be every bit as charming and dedicated as he'd hoped.

Brother Gabriel kept silent about the turkey prayer and the bloody socks; but he noted the haunted, faraway smile that occasionally stole over the scholastic's repertoire of otherwise earnest expressions. Martin seemed to be struck by some remembrance, possibly inspired by a face among the upper-school boys, as if the smooth, dark skin of one of the 15-year-olds had called to mind someone he'd once known . . . or so Brother Gabriel guessed. It was an innocent, friendly smile—almost too friendly, Brother Gabriel thought.

But Martin Mills was just remembering. Back in school, at Fessenden, after the long Thanksgiving weekend, he'd waited until the lights were out before saying what he wanted to say.

"Fucker," Martin quietly said.

"What's that?" Arif asked him.

"I said 'fucker,' as in motherfucker," Martin said.

"Is this a game?" Arif inquired after too long a pause.

"You know what I mean, you *motherfucker*," said Martin Mills.

After another long pause, Arif said, "She made me do it—sort of."

"You'll probably get a disease," Martin told his roommate. Martin didn't really mean it, nor would he have said it had it occurred to him that Arif might have fallen in love with Vera. He was surprised when Arif pounced on him in the dark and began to hit his face.

"Don't ever say that . . . about your mother!" the Turk cried. "Not about your mother! She's *beautiful*!"

Mr. Weems, the dorm master, broke up the fight; neither of the boys was hurt—neither of them knew how to fight. Mr. Weems was kindly; with rougher boys, he was entirely ineffectual. He was a music teacher, and—with hindsight, this is easy to say—most likely a homosexual, but no one thought of him that way (except a few of the brassier faculty wives, women of the type who thought that *any* unmarried man over 30 was a queer). Mr. Weems was well liked by the boys, despite his taking no part in the school's prevailing athleticism. In his report to the Discipline Committee, the dorm master would dismiss the altercation between Martin and Arif as a "spat." This unfortunate choice of a word would have grave consequences.

Later, when Arif Koma was diagnosed as suffering from gonorrhea—and when he wouldn't tell the school doctor where he might have acquired it—the suspicion fell on Martin Mills. That word "spat" connoted a lover's quarrel—at least to the more manly members of the Discipline Committee. Mr. Weems was instructed to ask the boys if they were homosexuals, if they'd been doing it. The dorm master was more sympathetic to the notion that Arif and Martin might be "doing it" than any of the faculty jocks would have been.

"If you boys are lovers, then you should see the doctor, too, Martin," Mr. Weems explained.

"Tell him!" Martin said to Arif.

"We're not lovers," Arif said.

"That's right—we're not lovers," Martin repeated. "But go on—tell him. I dare you," Martin said to Arif.

"Tell me what?" the dorm master asked.

"He hates his mother," Arif explained to Mr. Weems. Mr. Weems had met Vera; he could understand. "He's going to tell you that I got the disease from his mother—that's how much he hates her."

"He fucked my mother—or, rather, she fucked him," Martin told Mr. Weems.

"You see what I mean?" Arif Koma said.

At most private schools, the faculty is composed of truly saintly people and incompetent ogres. Martin and Arif were fortunate that their dorm master was a teacher of the saintly category; yet Mr. Weems was *so* well-meaning, he was perhaps more blind to depravity than a normal person.

"Please, Martin," the dorm master said. "A sexually transmitted disease, especially at an all-boys' school, is not something to lie about. Whatever your feelings are for your mother, what we hope to learn here is the truth—not to punish anyone, but only so that we may advise you. How can we instruct you, how can we tell you what we think you should do, if you won't tell us the truth?"

"My mother fucked him when she thought I was at Mass," Martin told Mr. Weems. Mr. Weems shut his eyes and smiled; he did this when he was counting, which he did to summon patience.

"I was trying to protect you, Martin," Arif Koma said, "but I can see it's no use."

"Boys, please . . . one of you is lying," the dorm master said.

"Okay—so we tell him," Arif said to Martin. "What do you say?"

"Okay," Martin replied. He knew that he liked Arif; for three years, Arif had been his only friend. If Arif wanted to say they'd been lovers, why not go along with it? There was no one else Martin Mills wanted to please as much as he wanted to please Arif. "Okay," Martin repeated.

"Okay *what?*" Mr. Weems asked.

"Okay, we're lovers," said Martin Mills.

"I don't know why he doesn't have the disease," Arif explained. "He *should* have it. Maybe he's immune."

"Are we going to get thrown out of school?" Martin asked the dorm master. He hoped so. It might teach his mother something, Martin thought; at 15, he still thought Vera was educable.

"All we did was *try* it," Arif said. "We didn't *like* it."

"We don't do it anymore," Martin added. This was the first and last time that he'd lied; it made him feel giddy—it was almost as if he were drunk.

"But one of you must have caught this disease from someone else,"

Mr. Weems reasoned. "I mean, it couldn't have *originated* here, with you
. . . not if each of you has had no other sexual contact."

Martin Mills knew that Arif Koma had been phoning Vera and that
she wouldn't talk to the Turk; Martin knew that Arif had written to
Vera, too—and that she'd not written the boy back. But it was only now
that Martin realized how far his friend would go to protect Vera. He
must have been absolutely gaga about her.

"I paid a prostitute. I caught this disease from a whore," Arif told Mr.
Weems.

"Where would you ever see a whore, Arif?" the dorm master asked.

"You don't know Boston?" Arif Koma asked him. "I stayed with
Martin and his mother at the Ritz. When they were asleep, I left the
hotel. I asked the doorman to get me a taxi. I asked the taxi driver to find
me a hooker. That's the way you do it in New York, too," Arif explained.
"Or at least that's the only way *I* know how to do it."

And so Arif Koma was booted from the Fessenden School for catching
a venereal disease from a whore. There was a statute in the school's book
of rules, something pertaining to morally reprehensible behavior with
women or girls being punishable by dismissal; under this rubric, the
Discipline Committee (despite Mr. Weems's protestations) expelled
Arif. It was judged that having sex with a prostitute was not a gray area
when it came to "morally reprehensible behavior with women or girls."

As for Martin, Mr. Weems also pleaded on his behalf. His homosexual
encounter was a single episode of sexual experimentation; the incident
should be forgotten. But the Discipline Committee insisted that Vera
and Danny should know. Vera's first response was to reiterate that
masturbation was preferable for boys Martin's age. All Martin said to his
mother—naturally, *not* in Danny's hearing—was, "Arif Koma has gonorrhea and so do you."

There was barely time to talk to Arif before he was sent home. The
last thing Martin said to the Turk was, "Don't hurt yourself trying to
protect my mother."

"But I also like your father," Arif explained. Once again, Vera had
gotten away with murder because no one wanted to hurt Danny.

Arif's suicide was the bigger shock. The note to Martin didn't arrive
in his Fessenden mailbox until two days after Arif had jumped out of the
10th-floor window of his parents' apartment on Park Avenue. *Dishonored
my family*—that was all the note said. Martin recalled that it was for the

purpose of *not* dishonoring his parents, or reflecting ill on his family's reputation, that Arif hadn't shed a tear at his own circumcision.

There was no blaming Vera for it. The first time she was alone with Martin, Vera said, "Don't try to tell me that it's *my* fault, dear. You told me he was disturbed—sexually disturbed. You said so yourself. Besides, you don't want to do anything that would hurt your father, do you?"

Actually, it had hurt Danny quite a bit to hear that his son had dabbled in a homosexual experience, even if it was only a single episode. Martin assured his father that he'd only tried it, and that he hadn't liked it. Still, Martin realized that this was the sole impression Danny had of his son's sexuality: he'd screwed his Turkish roommate when both boys were only 15 years old. It didn't occur to Martin Mills that the *truth* about his sexuality might have been even more painful for Danny— namely, that his son was a 39-year-old virgin who'd never even masturbated. Nor had it occurred to Martin that he might actually have been in love with Arif Koma; certainly this was more plausible, not to mention more justifiable, than Arif falling in love with Vera.

Now here was Dr. Daruwalla "inventing" a missionary called Mr. Martin. The screenwriter knew that he needed to provide motives for Mr. Martin's decision to become a priest; even in a movie, Farrokh felt that a vow of chastity required *some* explanation. Having met Vera, the screenwriter should have guessed that the *real* missionary's motives in taking a vow of chastity and becoming a priest were not made of the material usually found in a romantic comedy.

A Make-Believe Death; the Real Children

The screenwriter had the good sense to know he was stalling. The problem was, who was going to die? In real life, it was the doctor's hope that Madhu and Ganesh would be saved by the circus. In the screenplay, it simply wasn't realistic for both children to live happily ever after. The more believable story was that only one of them would be a survivor. Pinky was the acrobat, the star. The crippled Ganesh could hope for no role more important than that of a cook's helper—the circus's servant boy, the circus's sweeper. The circus would surely start him out at the bottom; he'd be scooping up the elephant shit and washing the lion piss off the stools. From such a shit-and-piss beginning, Ganesh would be fortunate to be promoted to the cook's tent; cooking food, or serving it, would represent a form of graduation—probably the best that the crippled boy could hope for. This was true for the real Ganesh *and* for the character in the screenplay—this was realism, Dr. Daruwalla believed.

It should be Pinky who dies, the screenwriter decided. The only reason that the circus accepted the crippled brother in the first place was that they wanted the talented sister; the brother was part of the deal. That was the premise of the story. But if Pinky was to die, why wouldn't the circus get rid of Ganesh? What use does the circus have for a cripple? Now this is a *better* story, Farrokh imagined. The burden of performance is suddenly shifted to the cripple; Ganesh must come up with something to do so that the circus will find him worth keeping. A boy without a limp can shovel the elephant shit faster.

But it was the bane of the screenwriter to always be rushing ahead of himself. Before he found something for Ganesh to do at the circus, wasn't it necessary to determine *how* Pinky would die? Well, she's an acrobat—she could always fall, the doctor prematurely decided. Maybe she's trying to learn Suman's Skywalk item and she simply falls. But, realistically, Pinky wouldn't be learning to skywalk from the roof of the main tent. At the Great Royal, Pratap Singh always taught the Skywalk from the roof of the family troupe tent; the rope rungs of the ladder weren't 80 feet in the air—the upside-down skywalker wasn't more than a foot or two above the ground. If Farrokh wanted to use the real Great Royal Circus, which he did—and if he wanted to use his actual favorite performers (Pinky and Suman and Pratap, principally)—then the screenwriter could *not* have a death attributed to carelessness or to some cheap accident. Farrokh meant only to praise the Great Royal and circus life—not to condemn them. No; Pinky's death couldn't be the responsibility of the circus—that wasn't the right story.

That was when Dr. Daruwalla thought of Mr. Garg, the real-life Acid Man. After all, Acid Man was already an established villain in the screenplay; why not use him? (The threat of a lawsuit seemed remote in these moments when sheer invention struck.) Acid Man could be so enthralled by Pinky's loveliness and ability, he simply can't bear her rising stardom—or that she's escaped disfigurement of his special kind. Having lost Pinky to the Great Royal, the fiend performs acts of sabotage at the circus. One of the lion cubs is burned with acid, or maybe one of the dwarf clowns. Poor Pinky is killed by a lion that escapes its cage because Acid Man has burned off the lock.

Great stuff! the screenwriter thought. The irony momentarily eluded Dr. Daruwalla: here he was, plotting the death of his fictional Pinky while at the same time he awaited the *real* results of Madhu's HIV test.

But Farrokh had once more got ahead of himself; he was trying to imagine what Ganesh could do to make himself irreplaceable to the circus. The boy is a lowly cripple, a mere beggar; he's clumsy, he'll always limp—the only stunt he can perform is the bird-shit trick. (The screenwriter made a hasty note to put the bird-shit trick in the screenplay; more comic relief was necessary, now that Pinky was going to be killed by a lion.)

At that moment, Ranjit put through the phone call from Dr. Tata. Farrokh's forward momentum, his entire train of thought, was interrupted. Farrokh was even more annoyed by the nature of Dr. Tata's information.

"Oh, dear—dear old Dad," said Tata Two. "I'm rather afraid he blew this one!"

It wouldn't have surprised Dr. Daruwalla to learn that the senior Dr. Tata had blown many a diagnosis; after all, the old fool had not known (until the delivery) that Vera was giving birth to twins. What is it *this* time? Farrokh was tempted to ask. But he more politely inquired, "So he *did* see Rahul?"

"You bet he did!" said Dr. Tata. "It must have been an exciting examination—Promila claimed that the boy had proved himself to be impotent in an alleged single episode with a prostitute! But I suspect the diagnosis was a bit premature."

"What *was* the diagnosis?" Dr. Daruwalla asked.

"Eunuchoidism!" cried Tata Two. "Nowadays, we would use the term hypogonadism. But, call it what you will, this is merely a symptom or syndrome with several possible causes. Rather like the syndrome of headache or dizziness . . ."

"Yes, yes," Dr. Daruwalla said impatiently. He could tell that Tata Two had been doing a little research, or perhaps he'd been talking to a better OB/GYN; most OB/GYNs tended to know more about this sort of thing than other doctors—because they were well versed in hormones, Farrokh supposed. "What conditions might cause you to suspect hypogonadism?" Dr. Daruwalla asked Tata Two.

"If I saw a boy or a man with long limbs and an arm span—when he stretches his arms out—that is two inches more than his height. Also, his pubis-to-floor height being greater than his pubis-to-crown height," Dr. Tata replied. He *must* be reading from a book, Dr. Daruwalla thought. "And if this boy or man also had absent secondary sexual characteristics . . ." Tata Two continued, ". . . you know—voice, muscular development, phallic development, extension of pubic hair up the belly in a diamond pattern . . ."

"But how could you assess such secondary sexual characteristics as being incomplete, unless the boy is over fifteen or so?" Dr. Daruwalla asked.

"Well, that's the problem—you really couldn't," said Tata Two.

"Rahul was only twelve or thirteen in 1949!" Farrokh cried. It was preposterous that Promila had pronounced the boy impotent because he hadn't been able to get an erection, or keep an erection, with a prostitute; it was more preposterous that old Dr. Tata had believed her!

"Well, that's what I mean by the diagnosis being a bit premature," Tata Two admitted. "The process of maturation begins at eleven or twelve . . . is heralded by the hardening of the testes and is usually completed within five years—although some things, like the growth of chest hair, may take another decade." With the word "heralded," Dr. Daruwalla was certain that Tata Two was reading from a book.

"In short, you mean that Rahul's puberty might simply have been delayed. It was entirely too soon to call him a kind of *eunuch!*" Farrokh cried.

"Well, now, to say 'eunuchoidism' isn't really calling someone 'a kind of eunuch,' " Dr. Tata explained.

"To a twelve- or thirteen-year-old boy, this diagnosis would have come at an impressionable age—wouldn't you agree?" asked Dr. Daruwalla.

"That's true," Tata Two replied. "It might be a more appropriate diagnosis in the case of an eighteen-year-old with a microphallus."

"Jesus Christ," said Dr. Daruwalla.

"Well, we must remember that all the Rais were rather strange," Dr. Tata reasoned.

"Just the sort of family to make the most out of a misdiagnosis," Dr. Daruwalla remarked.

"I wouldn't call it a 'misdiagnosis'—just a bit early to know for sure," Tata Two said defensively. It was understandable why Dr. Tata then wanted to change the subject. "Oh, I have an answer for you about the girl. Mr. Subhash told me you wanted a rush job." Actually, Mr. Subhash had told Dr. Daruwalla that the HIV test would take at least two days—more, if the first phase was positive. "Anyway, she's okay. The test was negative," Dr. Tata said.

"That was fast," Dr. Daruwalla replied. "This is the girl who's named Madhu? Her name is Madhu?"

"Yes, yes," said Dr. Tata; it was his turn to sound impatient. "I'm looking at the results! The name is Madhu. The test was negative. Mr. Subhash just put the file on my desk."

How *old* is Mr. Subhash? Dr. Daruwalla wanted to ask, but he was annoyed enough for one conversation; at least he could get the girl out of town. He thanked Tata Two, then hung up the phone. He wanted to go back to his screenplay, but first he called Ranjit into his office and asked the secretary to notify Mr. Garg that Madhu was *not* HIV-positive; the doctor himself didn't want to give Garg the satisfaction.

"That was fast," Ranjit said; but the screenplay was still occupying the majority of Dr. Daruwalla's thoughts. At the moment, he was giving more of his attention to *those* children than to the children in his charge.

The doctor did remember to ask Ranjit to contact the dwarf's wife; Deepa should be told that Madhu and Ganesh were coming to the circus—and that Dr. Daruwalla needed to know where (in all of Gujarat) the circus was. Farrokh should also have called the new missionary—to forewarn the Jesuit that they would be spending the weekend traveling to the circus with the children—but the screenplay beckoned to him; the fictional Mr. Martin was more compelling to Dr. Daruwalla than Martin Mills.

Unfortunately, the more vividly the screenwriter recalled and described the acts of the Great Royal Circus, the more he dreaded the disappointment he was certain he'd feel when he and Martin Mills delivered the *real* children to the Great Blue Nile.

20. THE BRIBE

Time to Slip Away

As for Martin Mills and how he compared to the fictional Mr. Martin, Farrokh felt only the slightest guilt; the screenwriter suspected he'd created a lightweight fool out of a heavyweight lunatic, but this was only the faintest suspicion. In the screenplay, the first time the missionary visits the children in the circus, he slips and falls in elephant shit. It hadn't yet crossed Dr. Daruwalla's mind that the *real* missionary had possibly stepped into a worse mess than elephant shit.

As for *Elephant Shit*, it wouldn't work as a title. Farrokh had written it in the margin of the page where the phrase first appeared, but now he crossed this out. A film of that title would be banned in India. Besides, who would want to go to a movie called *Elephant Shit?* People wouldn't bring their children, and it was a movie *for* children, Dr. Daruwalla hoped—if it was for anybody, he thought darkly. Thus did self-doubt, the screenwriter's old enemy, assail him; he seemed to welcome it as a friend.

The screenwriter baited himself with other bad-title possibilities. *Limo Roulette* was the arty choice. Farrokh worried that dwarfs the world over would be offended by the film, no matter what the title was. In his closet career as a screenwriter, Dr. Daruwalla had managed to offend almost everyone else. Rather than worry about offending dwarfs, the doctor took up the even smaller task of wondering which movie magazine would be the first to misunderstand and mock his efforts. The two he detested most were *Stardust* and *Cine Blitz*. He thought they were the most scandalous and libelous of the film-gossip press.

The mere thought of these media goons, this journalistic slime, set Farrokh to worrying about the press conference at which he intended to announce an end to Inspector Dhar. It occurred to Farrokh that if *he* called for a press conference, no one would attend; the screenwriter would have to ask Dhar to call for such a conference, and Dhar would have to be there—otherwise, it would look like a hoax. Worse, Dhar himself would have to do the talking; after all, he was the movie star. The trashy journalists would be less interested in Dr. Daruwalla's motives for perpetrating this fraud than in the reasons for Dhar's complicity. Why had Dhar gone along with the fiction that the actor was his own creator? As always, even at such a revealing press conference as Farrokh had imagined, Dhar would deliver the lines that the screenwriter had written.

The truth would simply be another acting job; moreover, the most important truth would never be told—that it was out of love for John D. that Dr. Daruwalla had invented Inspector Dhar. Such a truth would be wasted on the media sleaze. Farrokh knew that he wouldn't want to read what mockery would be made of such a love, especially in *Stardust* or *Cine Blitz*.

Dhar's last press conference had been deliberately conducted as a farce. Dhar had chosen the swimming pool at the Taj as the site, for he said he enjoyed the bewildered gaping of foreigners. The journalists were instantly irritated because they'd expected a more intimate environment. "Are you trying to emphasize that *you* are a foreigner, that you aren't really Indian at all?" That had been the first question; Dhar had responded by diving into the pool. He'd meant to splash the photographers; that had been no accident. He'd answered only what he wanted to and ignored the rest. It was an interview punctuated by Dhar repeatedly diving into the pool. The journalists said insulting things about him while he was underwater.

Farrokh presumed that John D. would be happy to be free of the role of Inspector Dhar; the actor had enough money, and he clearly preferred his Swiss life. Yet Dr. Daruwalla suspected that, deep down, Dhar had cherished the loathing he'd inspired among the media scum; earning the hatred of the cinema-gossip journalists might have been John D.'s best performance. With that in mind, Farrokh thought he knew what John D.

would prefer: no press conference, no announcement. "Let them won-der," Dhar would say—Dhar had often said.

There was another line that the screenwriter remembered; after all, he'd not only written it—it was repeated in every Inspector Dhar movie near the end of the story. There was always the temptation for Dhar to do something more—to seduce one more woman, to gun down one more villain—but Inspector Dhar knew when to stop. He knew when the action was over. Sometimes to a scheming bartender, sometimes to a fellow policeman of a generally dissatisfied nature, sometimes to a pretty woman who'd been waiting impatiently to make love to him, Inspector Dhar would say, "Time to slip away." Then he would.

In this case, facing the facts—that he wanted to call an end to Inspec-tor Dhar *and* that he wanted to finally leave Bombay—Farrokh knew what John D.'s advice would be. "Time to slip away," Inspector Dhar would say.

Bedbugs Ahead

In the old days, before the doctors' offices and the examining rooms of the Hospital for Crippled Children were air-conditioned, there'd been a ceiling fan over the desk where Dr. Daruwalla now sat thinking, and the window to the exercise yard was always open. Nowadays, with the window closed and the hum of the air-conditioning a reassuring con-stant, Farrokh was cut off from the sound of children crying in the exercise yard. When the doctor walked through the yard, or when he was called to observe the progress of one of his postoperative patients in physical therapy, the crying children did not greatly upset him. Farrokh associated some pain with recovery; a joint, after surgery—*especially* after surgery—had to be moved. But in addition to the cries of pain, there were the whines that children made in anticipation of their pain, and this piteous mewling affected the doctor strongly.

Farrokh turned and faced the closed window with its view of the exercise yard; from the soundless expressions of the children, the doctor could still discern the difference between those children who were in pain and those who were pitifully frightened of the pain they expected. Soundlessly, the therapists were coaxing the children to move; there was the recent hip replacement being told to stand up, there was the new knee being asked to step forward—and the first rotation of the new elbow. The landscape of the exercise yard was timeless to Dr. Daruwalla, who reflected that his ability to hear that which was soundless was the only measure of his humanity that he was certain of. Even with the air-conditioning on, even with the window closed, Dr. Daruwalla could hear the whimpering. Time to slip away, he thought.

He opened the window and leaned outside. The heat at midday was oppressive in the rising dust, although (for Bombay) the weather had remained relatively cool and dry. The cries of the children commingled with the car horns and the chainsaw clamor of the mopeds. Dr. Daruwalla breathed it all in. He squinted into the dusty glare. He gave the exercise yard an almost detached appraisal; it was a good-bye look. Then the doctor called Ranjit for his messages.

It was no surprise to Dr. Daruwalla that Deepa had already negotiated with the Great Blue Nile; the doctor hadn't expected the dwarf's wife to get a better deal. The circus would attempt to train the talented "sister." They would commit themselves to this effort for three months; they'd feed her, clothe her, shelter her and care for her crippled "brother." If Madhu could be trained, the Great Blue Nile would keep both children; if she was untrainable, the circus would let them go.

In Farrokh's screenplay, the Great Royal paid Pinky three rupees a day while they trained her; the fictional Ganesh worked without pay for his food and shelter. At the Great Blue Nile, Madhu's training was considered a privilege; she wouldn't be paid at all. And for a real boy with a crushed foot, it was enough of a privilege to be fed and sheltered; the real Ganesh would work, too. At the parents' expense—or, in the case of orphans, it was the obligation of the children's "sponsors"— Madhu and Ganesh would be brought to the site of the Great Blue Nile's present location. At this time, the circus was performing in Juna-gadh, a small city of about 100,000 people in Gujarat.

Junagadh! It would take a day to get there, another day to get back. They would have to fly to Rajkot and then endure a car ride of two or three hours to the smaller town; a driver from the circus would meet their plane—doubtless a reckless roustabout. But the train would be worse. Farrokh knew that Julia hated him to be away overnight, and in Junagadh there would probably be nowhere to stay but the Government Circuit House; lice were likely, bedbugs a certainty. There would be 48 hours of conversation with Martin Mills, and no time to keep writing the screenplay. It had also occurred to the screenwriter that the *real* Dr. Daruwalla was part of a parallel story-in-progress.

Raging Hormones

When Dr. Daruwalla phoned St. Ignatius School to alert the new missionary to their upcoming journey, the doctor wondered if his writing was prophetic. He'd already described the fictional Mr. Martin as "the most popular teacher at the school"; now here was Father Cecil telling the screenwriter that Martin Mills, on the evidence of his first morning of visiting the classrooms, had instantly made "a most popular impression." Young Martin, as Father Cecil still called him, had even persuaded the Father Rector to permit the teaching of Graham Greene to the upper-school boys; although controversial, Graham Greene was one of Martin Mills's Catholic heroes. "After all, the novelist popularized Catholic issues," Father Cecil said.

Farrokh, who considered himself an old fan of Graham Greene, asked suspiciously, "Catholic issues?"

"Suicide as a mortal sin, for example," Father Cecil replied. (Apparently, Father Julian was allowing Martin Mills to teach *The Heart of the Matter* to the upper school.) Dr. Daruwalla felt briefly uplifted; on the long trip to Junagadh and back, perhaps the doctor would be able to steer the missionary's conversation to Graham Greene. Who were some of the zealot's *other* heroes? the doctor wondered.

Farrokh hadn't had a good discussion of Graham Greene in quite a while. Julia and her literary friends were happier discussing more contemporary authors; they found it old-fashioned of Farrokh to prefer rereading those books he regarded as classics. Dr. Daruwalla was intimidated by Martin Mills's education, but possibly the doctor and the scholastic would discover a common ground in the novels of Graham Greene.

Dr. Daruwalla couldn't have known that the subject of suicide was of more interest to Martin Mills than the craft of Graham Greene as a writer. For a Catholic, suicide was a violation of God's dominion over human life. In the case of Arif Koma, Martin reasoned, the Muslim hadn't been in full possession of his faculties; falling in love with Vera surely suggested a loss of faculties, or a vastly different set of faculties altogether.

The denial of ecclesiastical burial was a horror to Martin Mills; however, the Church permitted suicides among those who'd lost their senses or were unaware that they were killing themselves. The missionary hoped that God would judge the Turk's suicide as an out-of-his-head kind. After all, Martin's mother had fucked the boy's brains out. How could Arif have made a sane decision after that?

But if Dr. Daruwalla would be unprepared for Martin Mills's Catholic interpretation of the doctor's much-admired author, Farrokh was also in the dark regarding the unwelcome disturbance that had shaken St. Ignatius School in the late morning, to which Father Cecil made incoherent references. The mission had been disrupted by an unruly intruder; the police had been forced to subdue the violent individual, whose violence Father Cecil attributed to "raging hormones."

Farrokh liked the phrase so much that he wrote it down.

"It was a transvestite prostitute, of all things," Father Cecil whispered into the phone.

"Why are you whispering?" Dr. Daruwalla asked.

"The Father Rector is still upset about the episode," Father Cecil confided to Farrokh. "Can you imagine? A *hijra* coming here—and during school hours!"

Dr. Daruwalla was amused at the presumed spectacle. "Perhaps he, or she, wanted to be better educated," the doctor suggested to Father Cecil.

"It claimed it had been invited," Father Cecil replied.

"*It!*" Dr. Daruwalla cried.

"Well, he or she—whatever it was, it was big and strong. A rampaging prostitute, a crazed cross-dresser!" Father Cecil whispered. "They give themselves hormones, don't they?"

"Not hijras," Dr. Daruwalla replied. "They don't take estrogens; they have their balls and their penises removed—with a single cut. The wound is then cauterized with hot oil. It resembles a vagina."

"Goodness—don't tell me!" Father Cecil said.

"Sometimes, but not usually, their breasts are surgically implanted," Dr. Daruwalla informed the priest.

"This one was implanted with *iron!*" Father Cecil said enthusiastically. "And young Martin was busy teaching. The Father Rector and I, and poor Brother Gabriel, had to deal with the creature by ourselves—until the police came."

"It sounds exciting," Farrokh remarked.

"Fortunately, none of the children saw it," Father Cecil said.

"Aren't transvestite prostitutes allowed to convert?" asked Dr. Daruwalla, who enjoyed teasing any priest.

"Raging hormones," Father Cecil repeated. "It must have just given itself an overdose."

"I told you—they don't usually take estrogens," the doctor said.

"This one was taking something," Father Cecil insisted.

"May I speak with Martin now?" Dr. Daruwalla asked. "Or is he still busy teaching?"

"He's eating his lunch with the midgets, or maybe he's with the submidgets today," Father Cecil replied.

It was almost time for the doctor's lunch at the Duckworth Club. Dr. Daruwalla left a message for Martin Mills, but Father Cecil struggled with the message to such a degree that the doctor knew he'd have to call again. "Just tell him I'll call him back," Farrokh finally said. "And tell him we're definitely going to the circus."

"Oh, won't that be fun!" Father Cecil said.

The Hawaiian Shirt

Detective Patel had wanted to compose himself before his lunch at the Duckworth Club; however, there was the interruption of this incident at St. Ignatius. It was merely a misdemeanor, but the episode had been brought to the deputy commissioner's attention because it fell into the category of Dhar-related crimes. The perpetrator was one of the transvestite prostitutes who'd been injured by Dhar's dwarf driver in the fracas on Falkland Road; it was the hijra whose wrist had been broken by a blow from one of Vinod's squash-racquet handles. The eunuch-transvestite had shown up at St. Ignatius, clubbing the old priests with his cast; his story was that Inspector Dhar had told all the transvestite prostitutes that they'd be welcome at the mission. Also, Dhar had told the hijras that they could always find him there.

"But it wasn't Dhar," the hijra told Detective Patel in Hindi. "It was someone being a Dhar imposter." It would have been laughable to Patel, to hear a transvestite complaining that someone else was an "imposter," if the detective had been in a laughing mood; instead, the deputy commissioner looked at the hijra with impatience and scorn. He was a tall, broad-shouldered, bony-faced hooker whose small breasts were showing because the top two buttons of his Hawaiian shirt were unbuttoned and the shirt was too loose for him; the looseness of his shirt and the tightness of his scarlet miniskirt were an absurd combination—hijra prostitutes usually wore saris. Also, they generally made more of an effort to be feminine than this one was making; his breasts (what the deputy commissioner could see of them) were shapely—in fact, they were very well formed—but there were whiskers on his chin and the noticeable shadow of a mustache on his upper lip. Possibly the hijra had thought that the colors of the Hawaiian shirt were feminine, not to mention the parrots and flowers; yet the shirt did little for his figure.

D.C.P. Patel continued the interrogation in Hindi. "Where'd you get that shirt?" the detective asked.

"Dhar was wearing it," the prostitute replied.

"Not likely," said the deputy commissioner.

"I told you he was being an imposter," the prostitute said.

"What sort of fool would pretend to be Dhar, and dare show his face on Falkland Road?" Patel asked.

"He looked like he didn't know he was Dhar," the hijra replied.

"Oh, I see," said Detective Patel. "He was an imposter but he didn't *know* he was an imposter." The hijra scratched his hooked nose with the cast on his wrist. Patel was bored with the interrogation; he kept the hijra sitting there only because the preposterous sight of him helped the detective to focus on Rahul. Of course Rahul would be 53 or 54 now, and she wouldn't stand out as someone who was making a half-assed effort to *look* like a woman.

It had occurred to the deputy commissioner that this might be one of the ways that Rahul managed to commit so many murders in the same area of Bombay. Rahul could enter a brothel as a man and leave looking like a hag; she could also leave looking like an attractive, middle-aged woman. And until this waste-of-time hijra had interrupted him, Patel had been enjoying a fairly profitable morning's work; the deputy commissioner's research on Rahul was progressing rather nicely. The list of new members at the Duckworth Club had been helpful.

"Did you ever hear of a zenana by the name of Rahul?" Patel asked the hijra.

"That old question," the transvestite said.

"Only she'd be a *real* woman now—the complete operation," the detective added. He knew there were some hijras who envied the very idea of a *complete* transsexual, but not most; most hijras were exactly what they wanted to be—they had no use for a fully fashioned vagina.

"If I knew of there being someone like that, I'd probably kill her," the hijra said good-naturedly. "For her *parts*," he added with a smile; he was just kidding, of course. Detective Patel knew more about Rahul than this hijra did; in the last 24 hours, the detective had learned more about Rahul than he'd known for 20 years.

"You may go now," said the deputy commissioner. "But leave the shirt. By your own admission, you stole it."

"But I have nothing else to wear!" the hijra cried.

"We'll find you something you can wear," the policeman said. "It just may not match your miniskirt."

When Detective Patel left Crime Branch Headquarters for his lunch at the Duckworth Club, he took a paper bag with him; in it was the Hawaiian shirt that belonged to Dhar's imposter. The deputy commissioner knew that not every question would or could be answered over one lunch, but the question posed by the Hawaiian shirt seemed a relatively simple one.

The Actor Guesses Right

"No," said Inspector Dhar. "I would never wear a shirt like that." He'd glanced quickly and indifferently into the bag, not bothering to draw out the shirt—not even touching the material.

"It has a California label," Detective Patel informed the actor.

"I've never been to California," Dhar replied.

The deputy commissioner put the paper bag under his chair; he seemed disappointed that the Hawaiian shirt had not served as an icebreaker to their conversation, which had halted once again. Poor Nancy hadn't spoken at all. Worse, she'd chosen to wear a sari, wound up in the navel-revealing fashion; the golden hairs that curled upward in a sleek line to her belly button were as worrisome to Mr. Sethna as the unsightly paper bag the policeman had placed under his chair. It was the kind of bag that a bomb would be in, the old steward thought. And how he disapproved of Western women in Indian attire! Furthermore, the fair skin of this particular woman's midriff clashed with her sunburned face. She must have been lying in the sun with tea saucers over her eyes, Mr. Sethna thought; any evidence of women lying on their backs disturbed him.

As for the ever-voyeuristic Dr. Daruwalla, his eyes were repeatedly drawn to Nancy's furry navel; since she'd pulled her chair snugly to their table in the Ladies' Garden, the doctor was restless because he could no longer see this marvel. Farrokh found himself glancing sideways at Nancy's raccoon eyes instead. The doctor made Nancy so nervous that she took her sunglasses out of her purse and put them on. She had the look of someone who was trying to gather herself together for a performance.

Inspector Dhar knew how to handle sunglasses. He simply stared into them with a satisfied expression on his face, which implied to Nancy that her sunglasses were no impediment to *his* vision—that he could see her clearly nonetheless. Dhar knew this would soon cause her to take the sunglasses off.

Oh, great—they're *both* acting! Dr. Daruwalla thought.

Mr. Sethna was disgusted with all of them. They were as socially graceless as teenagers. Not one of them had glanced at a menu; none of them had so much as raised an eyebrow to a waiter to suggest an aperitif, and they couldn't even talk to one another! Mr. Sethna was also full of indignation at the explanation that was now before him of why Detective Patel spoke such good English: the policeman's wife was a slatternly American! Needless to say, Mr. Sethna considered this a "mixed marriage," of which he strongly disapproved. And the old steward was no less outraged that Inspector Dhar should have brashly presented himself at the Duckworth Club so soon after the warning in the late Mr. Lal's mouth; the actor was recklessly endangering other Duckworthians! That Mr. Sethna had come by this information through the relentlessness and the practiced stealth of his eavesdropping didn't cause the old steward to consider that he might not know the whole story. To a man with Mr. Sethna's readiness to disapprove, a mere shred of information was sufficient to form a full opinion.

But of course Mr. Sethna had another reason to be outraged with Inspector Dhar. As a Parsi and a practicing Zoroastrian, the old steward had reacted predictably to the posters for the newest Inspector Dhar absurdity. Not since his days at the Ripon Club, and his famous decision to pour hot tea on the head of the man wearing the wig, had Mr. Sethna felt so aroused to righteous anger. He'd seen the work of the poster-wallas on his way home from the Duckworth Club, and he blamed *Inspector Dhar and the Towers of Silence* for giving him uncharacteristically lurid dreams.

He'd suffered a vision of a ghostly-white statue of Queen Victoria that resembled the one they took away from Victoria Terminus, but in his dream the statue was levitating; Queen Victoria was hovering about a foot off the floor of Mr. Sethna's beloved fire-temple, and all the Parsi faithful were bolting for the doorway. Were it not for the blasphemous cinema poster, Mr. Sethna believed he would never have had such a blasphemous dream. He'd promptly woken up and donned his prayer cap, but the prayer cap fell off when he suffered another dream. He was riding in the Parsi Panchayat Hearse to the Towers of Silence; although he was already a dead body, he could smell the rites attendant to his own

death—the scent of burning sandalwood. Suddenly the stink of putrefaction, which clung to the vultures' beaks and talons, was choking him;
he woke again. His prayer cap was on the floor, where he mistook it for
a waiting hunchbacked crow; pathetically, he'd tried to shoo the imagined crow away.

Dr. Daruwalla glanced only once at Mr. Sethna. From the steward's
withering stare, the doctor wondered if another hot-tea incident was
brewing. Mr. Sethna interpreted the doctor's glance as a summons.

"An aperitif before lunch, perhaps?" the steward asked the awkward
foursome. Since "aperitif" wasn't a word much used in Iowa—nor had
Nancy heard it from Dieter, nor was it ever spoken in her life with Vijay
Patel—she made no response to Mr. Sethna, who was looking directly
at her. (If anywhere, Nancy might have encountered the word in one or
another of the remaindered American novels she'd read, but she
wouldn't have known how to pronounce "aperitif" and she would have
assumed that the word was inessential to understanding the plot.)

"Would the lady enjoy something to drink before her lunch?" Mr.
Sethna asked, still looking at Nancy. No one at the table could hear what
she said, but the old steward understood that she'd whispered for a
Thums Up cola. The deputy commissioner ordered a Gold Spot orange
soda, Dr. Daruwalla asked for a London Diet beer and Dhar wanted a
Kingfisher.

"Well, this should be lively," Dr. Daruwalla joked. "Two teetotalers
and two beer drinkers!" This lead balloon lay on the table, which
inspired the doctor to discourse, at length, on the history of the lunch
menu.

It was Chinese Day at the Duckworth Club, the culinary low point
of the week. In the old days, there'd been a Chinese chef among
the kitchen staff, and Chinese Day had been an epicure's delight. But
the Chinese chef had left the club to open his own restaurant, and the
present-day collection of cooks could not concoct Chinese; yet, one day
a week, they tried.

"It's probably safest to stick with something vegetarian," Farrokh
recommended.

"By the time you saw the bodies," Nancy suddenly began, "I suppose
they were pretty bad."

"Yes—I'm afraid the crabs had found them," Dr. Daruwalla replied.

"But I guess the drawing was still clear, or you wouldn't have remembered it," Nancy said.

"Yes—indelible ink, I'm sure," said Dr. Daruwalla.

"It was a laundry-marking pen—a dhobi pen," Nancy told him, although she appeared to be looking at Dhar. With her sunglasses on, who knew where she was looking? "I buried them, you know," Nancy went on. "I didn't see them die, but I heard them. The sound of the spade," she added.

Dhar continued to stare at her, his lip not quite sneering. Nancy took her sunglasses off and returned them to her purse. Something she saw in her purse made her pause; she held her lower lip in her teeth for three or four seconds. Then she reached in her purse and brought out the bottom half of the silver ballpoint pen, which she'd carried with her, everywhere she'd gone, for 20 years.

"He stole the other half of this—he or she," Nancy said. She handed the half-pen to Dhar, who read the interrupted inscription.

" 'Made in' *where?*" Dhar asked her.

"India," said Nancy. "Rahul must have stolen it."

"Who would want the top half of a pen?" Farrokh asked Detective Patel.

"Not a writer," Dhar replied; he passed the half-pen to Dr. Daruwalla.

"It's real silver," the doctor observed.

"It needs to be polished," Nancy said. The deputy commissioner looked away; he knew his wife had polished the thing only last week. Dr. Daruwalla couldn't see any indication that the silver was dull or blackened; everything was shiny, even the inscription. When he handed the half-pen to Nancy, she didn't put it back in her purse; instead, she placed it alongside her knife and spoon—it was brighter than both. "I use an old toothbrush to polish the lettering," she said. Even Dhar looked away from her; that he couldn't meet her eyes gave her confidence. "In real life," Nancy said to the actor, "have you ever taken a bribe?" She saw the sneer she'd been looking for; she'd been expecting it.

"No, never," Dhar told her. Now Nancy had to look away from him; she looked straight at Dr. Daruwalla.

"How come you keep it a secret . . . that you write all his movies?" Nancy asked the doctor.

"I already have a career," Dr. Daruwalla replied. "The idea was to create a career for *him.*"

"Well, you sure did it," Nancy told Farrokh. Detective Patel reached for her left hand, which was on the table by her fork, but Nancy put her hand in her lap. Then she faced Dhar.

"And how do you like it? Your *career . . .*" Nancy asked the actor. He responded with his patterned shrug, which enhanced his sneer. Something both cruel and merry entered his eyes.

"I have a day job . . . another life," Dhar replied.

"Lucky you," Nancy told him.

"Sweetie," said the deputy commissioner; he reached into his wife's lap and took her hand. She seemed to go a little limp in the rattan chair. Even Mr. Sethna could hear her exhale; the old steward had heard almost everything else, too, and what he hadn't actually heard he'd fairly accurately surmised from reading their lips. Mr. Sethna was a good lip-reader, and for an elderly man he could move spryly around a conversation; a table for four posed few problems for him. It was easier to pick up conversation in the Ladies' Garden than in the main dining room, because only the bower of flowers was overhead; there were no ceiling fans.

From Mr. Sethna's point of view, it was already a much more interesting lunch than he'd anticipated. Dead bodies! A stolen part of a pen? And the most startling revelation—that Dr. Daruwalla was the actual author of that trash which had elevated Inspector Dhar to stardom! In a way, Mr. Sethna believed that he'd known it all along; the old steward had always sensed that Farrokh wasn't the man his father was.

Mr. Sethna glided in with the drinks; then he glided away. The venomous feelings that the old steward had felt for Dhar were now what Mr. Sethna was feeling for Dr. Daruwalla. A Parsi writing for the Hindi cinema! And making fun of other Parsis! How dare he? Mr. Sethna could barely restrain himself. In his mind, he could hear the sound that his silver serving tray would make off the crown of Dr. Daruwalla's head; it sounded like a gong. The steward had needed all his strength to resist the temptation to cover that appalling woman's fuzzy navel with her napkin, which was carelessly lumped in her lap. A belly button like hers should be clothed—if not banned! But Mr. Sethna quickly calmed himself, for he didn't want to miss what the real policeman was saying.

"I should like to hear the three of you describe what Rahul would look like today, assuming that Rahul is now a woman," said the deputy commissioner. "You first," Patel said to Dhar.

"Vanity and an overall sense of physical superiority would keep her looking younger than she is," Dhar began.

"But she would be fifty-three or fifty-four," Dr. Daruwalla interjected.

"You're next. Please let him finish," said Detective Patel.

"She wouldn't *look* fifty-three or fifty-four, except maybe very early in the morning," Dhar continued. "And she would be very fit. She has a predatory aura. She's a stalker—I mean sexually."

"I think she was quite hot for him when he was a boy!" Dr. Daruwalla remarked.

"Who *wasn't?*" Nancy asked bitterly. Only her husband looked at her.

"Please let him finish," Patel said patiently.

"She's also the sort of woman who enjoys making you want her, even if she intends to reject you," Dhar said. He made a point of looking at Nancy. "And I would assume that, like her late aunt, she has a caustic manner. She would always be ready to ridicule someone, or some idea—anything."

"Yes, yes," said Dr. Daruwalla impatiently, "but don't forget, she is also a *starer.*"

"Excuse me—a *what?*" asked Detective Patel.

"A family trait—she stares at everyone. Rahul is a compulsive *starer!*" Farrokh replied. "She does it because she's deliberately rude but also because she has a kind of uninhibited curiosity. That was her aunt, in spades! Rahul was brought up that way. No modesty whatsoever. Now she would be very feminine, I suppose, but not with her eyes. She is a *man* with her eyes—she's always looking you over and staring you down."

"Were you finished?" the deputy commissioner asked Dhar.

"I think so," the actor replied.

"I never saw her clearly," Nancy said suddenly. "There was no light, or the light was bad—only an oil lamp. I got just a peek at her, and I was sick—I had a fever." She toyed with the bottom half of the ballpoint pen on the table, turning it at a right angle to her knife and spoon, then lining it up again. "She smelled good, and she felt very silky—but strong," Nancy added.

"Talk about her *now*, not then," Patel said. "What would she be like now?"

"The thing is," Nancy said, "I think she feels like she can't control something in herself, like she just *needs* to do things. She can't stop herself. The things she wants are just too strong."

"What things?" asked the detective.

"You know. We've talked about it," Nancy told him.

"Tell *them*," her husband said.

"She's horny—I think she's horny all the time," Nancy told them.

"That's unusual for someone who's fifty-three or fifty-four," Dr. Daruwalla observed.

"That's just the feeling she gives you—believe me," Nancy said. "She's awfully horny."

"Does this remind you of someone you know?" the detective asked Inspector Dhar, but Dhar kept looking at Nancy; he didn't shrug. "Or *you*, Doctor—are you reminded of anyone?" the deputy commissioner asked Farrokh.

"Are you talking about someone we've actually met—as a woman?" Dr. Daruwalla asked the deputy commissioner.

"Precisely," said Detective Patel.

Dhar was still looking at Nancy when he spoke. "Mrs. Dogar," Dhar said. Farrokh put both his hands on his chest, exactly where the familiar pain in his ribs was suddenly sharp enough to take his breath away.

"Oh, very good—very *impressive*," said Detective Patel. He reached across the table and patted the back of Dhar's hand. "You wouldn't have made a bad policeman, even if you don't take bribes," the detective told the actor.

"Mrs. Dogar!" Dr. Daruwalla gasped. "I *knew* she reminded me of someone!"

"But there's something wrong, isn't there?" Dhar asked the deputy commissioner. "I mean, you haven't arrested her—have you?"

"Quite so," Patel said. "Something is wrong."

"I *told* you he'd know who it was," Nancy told her husband.

"Yes, sweetie," the detective said. "But it's not a crime for Rahul to be Mrs. Dogar."

"How did you find out?" Dr. Daruwalla asked the deputy commissioner. "Of course—the list of new members!"

"It was a good place to start," said Detective Patel. "The estate of Promila Rai was inherited by her niece, not her nephew."

"I never knew there was a niece," Farrokh said.

"There wasn't," Patel replied. "Rahul, her nephew, went to London. He came back as her niece. He even gave himself her name—Promila. It's perfectly legal to change your sex in England. It's perfectly legal to change your name—even in India."

"Rahul Rai married Mr. Dogar?" Farrokh asked.

"That was perfectly legal, too," the detective replied. "Don't you see, Doctor? The fact that you and Dhar could verify that Rahul was there in Goa, at the Hotel Bardez, does *not* confirm that Rahul was ever at the scene of the crime. And it would *not* be believable for Nancy to physically identify Mrs. Dogar as the Rahul of twenty years ago. As she told you, she hardly saw Rahul."

"Besides, he had a penis then," Nancy said.

"But, in all these killings, are there no fingerprints?" Farrokh asked.

"In the cases of the prostitutes, there are *hundreds* of fingerprints," D.C.P. Patel replied.

"What about the putter that killed Mr. Lal?" Dhar asked.

"Oh, very good!" the deputy commissioner said. "But the putter was wiped clean."

"Those drawings!" Dr. Daruwalla said. "Rahul always fancied himself an artist. Surely Mrs. Dogar must have some drawings around."

"That would be convenient," Patel replied. "But this very morning I sent someone to the Dogar house—to bribe the servants." The detective paused and looked directly at Dhar. "There *were* no drawings. There wasn't even a typewriter."

"There must be ten typewriters in this club," Dhar said. "The typed messages on the two-rupee notes—were they all typed on the same machine?"

"Oh, what a very good question," said Detective Patel. "So far, three messages—two different typewriters. Both in this club."

"Mrs. Dogar!" Dr. Daruwalla said again.

"Be quiet, please," the deputy commissioner said. He suddenly pointed to Mr. Sethna. The old steward attempted to hide his face with his silver serving tray, but Detective Patel was too fast for him. "What is that old snoop's name?" the detective asked Dr. Daruwalla.

"That's Mr. Sethna," Farrokh said.

"Please come here, Mr. Sethna," the deputy commissioner said. He didn't raise his voice or look in the steward's direction; when Mr. Sethna pretended that he hadn't heard, the detective said, "You heard me." Mr. Sethna did as he was told.

"Since you've been listening to us—Wednesday you listened to my telephone conversation with my wife—you will kindly give me your assistance," Detective Patel said.

"Yes, sir," Mr. Sethna said.

"Every time Mrs. Dogar is in this club, you call me," the deputy commissioner said. "Every reservation she makes, lunch or dinner, you let me know about it. Every little thing you know about her, I want to know, too—am I making myself clear?"

"Perfectly clear, sir," said Mr. Sethna. "She said her husband is peeing on the flowers and that one night he'll try to dive into the empty pool," Mr. Sethna babbled. "She said he's senile—and a drunk."

"You can tell me later," Detective Patel said. "I have just three questions. Then I want you to go far enough away from this table so that you don't hear another word."

"Yes, sir," Mr. Sethna said.

"On the morning of Mr. Lal's death ... I don't mean lunch, because I already know that she was here for lunch, but in the morning, well before lunch ... did you see Mrs. Dogar here? That's the first question," the deputy commissioner said.

"Yes, she was here for a bit of breakfast—very early," Mr. Sethna informed the detective. "She likes to walk on the golf course before the golfers are playing. Then she has a little fruit before she does her fitness training."

"Second question," Patel said. "Between breakfast and lunch, did she change what she was wearing?"

"Yes, sir," the old steward replied. "She was wearing a dress, rather wrinkled, at breakfast. For lunch she wore a sari."

"Third question," the deputy commissioner said. He handed Mr. Sethna his card—his telephone number at Crime Branch Headquarters and his home number. "Were her shoes wet? I mean, for breakfast."

"I didn't notice," Mr. Sethna admitted.

"Try to improve your noticing," Detective Patel told the old steward. "Now, go far away from this table—I mean it."

"Yes, sir," said Mr. Sethna, already doing what he did best—gliding away. Nor did the prying old steward approach the Ladies' Garden again during the foursome's solemn lunch. But even at a considerable distance, Mr. Sethna was able to observe that the woman with the fuzzy navel ate very little; her rude husband ate half her food and all his own. At a proper club, people would be forbidden to eat off one another's plates, Mr. Sethna thought. He went into the men's room and stood in front of the full-length mirror, in which he appeared to be trembling. He held the silver serving tray in one hand and pounded it against the heel of his other hand, but he felt little satisfaction from the sound it made—a muffled bonging. He *hated* policemen, the old steward decided.

Farrokh Remembers the Crow

In the Ladies' Garden, the early-afternoon sun had slanted past the apex of the bower and no longer touched the lunchers' heads; the rays of sunlight now penetrated the wall of flowers only in patches. The table-cloth was mottled by this intermittent light, and Dr. Daruwalla watched a tiny diamond of the sun—it was reflected in the bottom half of the ballpoint pen. The brilliantly white point of light shone in the doctor's eye as he pecked at his soggy stir-fry; the limp, dull-colored vegetables reminded him of the monsoon.

At that time of year, the Ladies' Garden would be strewn with torn petals of the bougainvillea, the skeletal vines still clinging to the bower—with the brown sky showing through and the rain coming through. All the wicker and rattan furniture would be heaped upon itself in the ballroom, for there were no balls in the monsoon season. The golfers would sit drinking in the clubhouse bar, forlornly staring out the streaked windows at the sodden fairways. Wild clumps of the dead garden would be blowing across the greens.

The food on Chinese Day always depressed Farrokh, but there was something about the winking sun that was reflected in the bottom half of the silver ballpoint pen, something that both caught and held the doctor's attention; something flickered in his memory. What was it? That reflected light, that shiny something . . . it was as small and lonely but as absolutely a presence as the far-off light of another airplane when you were flying across the miles of darkness over the Arabian Sea at night.

Farrokh stared into the dining room and at the open veranda, through which the shitting crow had flown. Dr. Daruwalla looked at the ceiling fan where the crow had landed; the doctor kept watching the fan, as if he were waiting for it to falter, or for the mechanism to catch on something—that shiny something which the shitting crow had held in its beak. Whatever it was, it was too big for the crow to have swallowed, Dr. Daruwalla thought. He took a wild guess.

"I know what it was," the doctor said aloud. No one else had been talking; the others just looked at him as he left the table in the Ladies' Garden and walked into the dining room, where he stood directly under the fan. Then he drew an unused chair away from the nearest table; but when he stood on it, he was still too short to reach over the top of the blades.

"Turn the fan off!" Dr. Daruwalla shouted to Mr. Sethna, who was no stranger to the doctor's eccentric behavior—and his father's before him. The old steward shut off the fan. Almost everyone in the dining room had stopped eating.

Dhar and Detective Patel rose from their table in the Ladies' Garden and approached Farrokh, but the doctor waved them away. "Neither of you is tall enough," he told them. "Only *she* is tall enough." The doctor was pointing at Nancy. He was also following the good advice that the deputy commissioner had given to Mr. Sethna. ("Try to improve your noticing.")

The fan slowed; the blades were unmoving by the time the three men helped Nancy to stand on the chair.

"Just reach over the top of the fan," the doctor instructed her. "Do you feel a groove?" Her full figure above them in the chair was quite striking as she reached into the mechanism.

"I feel something," she said.

"Walk your fingers around the groove," said Dr. Daruwalla.

"What am I looking for?" Nancy asked him.

"You're going to feel it," he told her. "I think it's the top half of your pen."

They had to hold her or she would have fallen, for her fingers found it almost the instant that the doctor warned her what it was.

"Try not to handle it—just hold it very lightly," the deputy commissioner said to his wife. She dropped it on the stone floor and the detective retrieved it with a napkin, holding it only by the pocket clasp.

" 'India,' " Patel said aloud, reading that inscription which had been separated from *Made in* for 20 years.

It was Dhar who lifted Nancy down from the chair. She felt heavier to him than she had 20 years before. She said she needed a moment to be alone with her husband; they stood whispering together in the Ladies' Garden, while Farrokh and John D. watched the fan start up again. Then the doctor and the actor went to join the detective and his wife, who'd returned to the table.

"Surely now you'll have Rahul's fingerprints," Dr. Daruwalla told the deputy commissioner.

"Probably," said Detective Patel. "When Mrs. Dogar comes to eat here, we'll have the steward save us her fork or her spoon—to compare. But her fingerprints on the top of the pen don't place her at the crime."

Dr. Daruwalla told them all about the crow. Clearly the crow had brought the pen from the bougainvillea at the ninth green. Crows are carrion eaters.

"But what would Rahul have been doing with the top of the pen—I mean *during* the murder of Mr. Lal?" Detective Patel asked.

In frustration, Dr. Daruwalla blurted out, "You make it sound as if you have to witness another murder—or do you expect Mrs. Dogar to offer you a full confession?"

"It's only necessary to make Mrs. Dogar think that we know more than we know," the deputy commissioner answered.

"That's easy," Dhar said suddenly. "You tell the murderer what the murderer *would* confess, if the murderer were confessing. The trick is, you've got to make the murderer think that you really *know* the murderer."

"Precisely," Patel said.

"Wasn't that in *Inspector Dhar and the Hanging Mali?*" Nancy asked the actor; she meant that it was Dr. Daruwalla's line.

"Very good," Dr. Daruwalla told her.

Detective Patel didn't pat the back of Dhar's hand; he tapped Dhar on one knuckle—just once, but sharply—with a dessert spoon. "Let's be serious," said the deputy commissioner. "I'm going to offer you a bribe—something you've always wanted."

"There's nothing I want," Dhar replied.

"I think there is," the detective told him. "I think you'd like to play a *real* policeman. I think you'd like to make a *real* arrest."

Dhar said nothing—he didn't even sneer.

"Do you think you're still attractive to Mrs. Dogar?" the detective asked him.

"Oh, absolutely—you should see how she looks him over!" cried Dr. Daruwalla.

"I'm asking *him*," said Detective Patel.

"Yes, I think she wants me," Dhar replied.

"Of course she does," Nancy said angrily.

"And if I told you how to approach her, do you think you could do it—I mean *exactly* as I tell you?" the detective asked Dhar.

"Oh, yes—you give him *any* line, he can deliver it!" cried Dr. Daruwalla.

"I'm asking *you*," the policeman said to Dhar. This time, the dessert spoon rapped his knuckle hard enough for Dhar to take his hand off the table.

"You want to set her up—is that it?" Dhar asked the deputy commissioner.

"Precisely," Patel said.

"And I just follow your instructions?" the actor asked him.

"That's it—*exactly*," said the deputy commissioner.

"You can do it!" Dr. Daruwalla declared to Dhar.

"That's not the question," Nancy said.

"The question is, do you *want* to do it?" Detective Patel asked Dhar. "I think you really want to."

"All right," Dhar said. "Okay. Yes, I want to."

For the first time in the course of the long lunch, Patel smiled. "I feel better, now that I've bribed you," the deputy commissioner told Dhar. "Do you see? That's all a bribe is, really—just something you want, in exchange for something else. It's no big deal, is it?"

"We'll see," Dhar said. When he looked at Nancy, she was looking at him.

"You're not sneering," Nancy said.

"Sweetie," said Detective Patel, taking her hand.

"I need to go to the ladies' room," she said. "You show me where it is," she said to Dhar. But before his wife or the actor could stand up, the deputy commissioner stopped them.

"Just a trivial matter, before you go," the detective said. "What is this nonsense about you and the dwarf brawling with prostitutes on Falkland Road—what is this nonsense about?" Detective Patel asked Dhar.

"That wasn't him," said Dr. Daruwalla quickly.

"So there's some truth to the rumor of a Dhar imposter?" the detective asked.

"Not an imposter—a twin," the doctor replied.

"You have a *twin?*" Nancy asked the actor.

"Identical," said Dhar.

"That's hard to believe," she said.

"They're not at all alike, but they're identical," Farrokh explained.

"It's not the best time for you to have a twin in Bombay," Detective Patel told the actor.

"Don't worry—the twin is totally out of it. A missionary!" Farrokh declared.

"God help us," Nancy said.

"Anyway, I'm taking the twin out of town for a couple of days—at least overnight," Dr. Daruwalla told them. The doctor started to explain about the children and the circus, but no one was interested.

"The ladies' room," Nancy said to Dhar. "Where is it?"

Dhar was about to take her arm when she walked past him untouched; he followed her to the foyer. Almost everyone in the dining room watched her walk—the woman who'd stood on a chair.

"It will be nice for you to get out of town for a couple of days," the deputy commissioner said to Dr. Daruwalla. Time to slip away, Farrokh was thinking; then he realized that even the moment of Nancy leaving the Ladies' Garden with Dhar had been planned.

"Was there something you wanted her to say to him, something only she could say—alone?" the doctor asked the detective.

"Oh, what a very good question," Patel replied. "You're learning, Doctor," the deputy commissioner added. "I'll bet you could write a better movie now."

A Three-Dollar Bill?

In the foyer, Nancy said to Dhar, "I've thought about you almost as much as I've thought about Rahul. Sometimes, you upset me more."

"I never intended to upset you," Dhar replied.

"What *have* you intended? What *do* you intend?" she asked him.

When he didn't answer her, Nancy asked him, "How did you like lifting me? You're always carrying me. Do I feel heavier to you?"

"We're both a little heavier than we were," Dhar answered cautiously.

"I weigh a ton, and you know it," Nancy told him. "But I'm not trash—I never was."

"I never thought you were trash," Dhar told her.

"You should never look at people the way you look at me," Nancy said. He did it again; there was his sneer. "That's what I mean," she told him. "I hate you for it—the way you make me feel. Later, after you're gone, it makes me keep thinking about you. I've thought about you for twenty years." She was about three inches taller than the actor; when she reached out suddenly and touched his upper lip, he stopped sneering. "That's better. Now say something," Nancy told him. But Dhar was thinking about the dildo—if she still had it. He couldn't think of what to say. "You know, you really should take some responsibility for the effect you have on people. Do you ever think about that?"

"I think about it all the time—I'm *supposed* to have an effect," Dhar said finally. "I'm an actor."

"You sure are," Nancy said. She could see him stop himself from shrugging; when he wasn't sneering, she liked his mouth more than she thought was possible. "Do you *want* me? Do you ever think about *that*?" she asked him. She saw him thinking about what to say, so she didn't wait. "You don't know how to read what *I* want, do you?" she asked him. "You're going to have to be better than this with Rahul. You can't tell me what I want to hear because you don't really know if I want you, do you? You're going to have to read Rahul better than you can read me," Nancy repeated.

"I can read you," Dhar told her. "I was just trying to be polite."

"I don't believe you—you don't convince me," Nancy said. "Bad acting," she added, but she believed him.

In the ladies' room, when she washed her hands in the sink, Nancy saw the absurd faucet—the water flowing from the single spigot, which was an elephant's trunk. Nancy adjusted the degree of hot and cold water, first with one tusk, then the other. Twenty years ago, at the Hotel Bardez, not even four baths had made her feel clean; now Nancy felt unclean again. She was at least relieved to see that there was no winking eye; that much Rahul had imagined, with the help of many murdered women's navels.

She'd also noticed the pull-down platform on the inside of the toilet-stall door; the handle that lowered the shelf was a ring through an elephant's trunk. Nancy reflected on the psychology that had compelled Rahul to select one elephant and reject the other.

When Nancy returned to the Ladies' Garden, she offered only a matter-of-fact comment on her discovery of what she believed to be the source of inspiration for Rahul's belly drawings. The deputy commissioner and the doctor rushed off to the ladies' room to see the telltale elephant for themselves; their opportunity to view the Victorian faucet was delayed until the last woman had vacated the ladies' room. Even from a considerable distance—from the far side of the dining room—Mr. Sethna was able to observe that Inspector Dhar and the woman with the obscene navel had nothing to say to each other, although they were left alone in the Ladies' Garden for an uncomfortable amount of time.

Later, in the car, Detective Patel spoke to Nancy—before they'd left the driveway of the Duckworth Club. "I have to go back to headquarters, but I'll take you home first," he told her.

"You should be more careful about what you ask me to do, Vijay," Nancy said.

"I'm sorry, sweetie," Patel replied. "But I wanted to know your opinion. Can I trust him?" The deputy commissioner saw that his wife was about to cry again.

"You can trust *me*!" Nancy cried.

"I *know* I can trust you, sweetie," Patel said. "But what about *him*? Do you think he can do it?"

"He'll do anything you tell him, if he knows what you want," Nancy answered.

"And you think Rahul will go for him?" her husband asked.

"Oh, yes," she said bitterly.

"Dhar is a pretty cool customer!" said the detective admiringly.

"Dhar is as queer as a three-dollar bill," Nancy told him.

Not being from Iowa, Detective Patel had some difficulty with the concept of how "queer" a three-dollar bill was—not to mention that, in Bombay, they call a bill a note. "You mean that he's gay—a homosexual?" her husband asked.

"No doubt about it. You can trust me," Nancy repeated. They were almost home before she spoke again. "A *very* cool customer," she added.

"I'm sorry, sweetie," said the deputy commissioner, because he saw that his wife couldn't stop crying.

"I *do* love you, Vijay," she managed to say.

"I love you, *too*, sweetie," the detective told her.

Just Some Old Attraction-Repulsion Kind of Thing

In the Ladies' Garden, the sun now slanted sideways through the latticework of the bower; the same shade of pinkness from the bougainvillea dappled the tablecloth, which Mr. Sethna had brushed free of crumbs. It seemed to the old steward that Dhar and Dr. Daruwalla would never leave the table. They'd long ago stopped talking about Rahul—or, rather, Mrs. Dogar. For the moment, they were both more interested in Nancy.

"But exactly what do you think is *wrong* with her?" Farrokh asked John D.

"It appears that the events of the last twenty years have had a strong effect on her," Dhar answered.

"Oh, elephant shit!" cried Dr. Daruwalla. "Can't you just once say what you're really feeling?"

"Okay," Dhar said. "It appears that she and her husband are a real couple . . . very much in love, and all of that."

"Yes, that does appear to be the main thing about them," the doctor agreed. But Farrokh realized that this observation didn't greatly interest him; after all, he was still very much in love with Julia and he'd been married longer than Detective Patel. "But what was happening between the two of you—between you and her?" the doctor asked Dhar.

"It was just some old attraction-repulsion kind of thing," John D. answered evasively.

"The next thing you'll tell me is that the world is round," Farrokh said, but the actor merely shrugged. Suddenly, it was not Rahul (or Mrs. Dogar) who frightened Dr. Daruwalla; it was *Dhar* the doctor was afraid of, and only because Dr. Daruwalla felt that he didn't really know Dhar—not even after all these years. As before—because he felt that something unpleasant was pending—Farrokh thought of the circus; yet when he mentioned again his upcoming journey to Junagadh, he saw that John D. still wasn't interested.

"You probably think it's doomed to fail—just another save-the-children project," said Dr. Daruwalla. "Like coins in a wishing well, like pebbles in the sea."

"It sounds as if *you* think it's doomed to fail," Dhar told him.

It was truly time to slip away, the doctor thought. Then Dr. Daruwalla spotted the Hawaiian shirt in the paper bag; Detective Patel had left the package under his chair. Both men were standing, ready to leave, when the doctor pulled the loud shirt out of the bag.

"Well, look at that. The deputy commissioner actually forgot something. How uncharacteristic," John D. remarked.

"I doubt that he forgot it. I think he wanted you to have it," Dr. Daruwalla said. Impulsively, the doctor held up the riotous display of parrots in palm trees; there were flowers, too—red and orange and yellow against a jungle of impossible green. Farrokh placed the shoulders of the shirt against Dhar's shoulders. "It's the right size for you," the doctor observed. "Are you sure you don't want it?"

"I have all the shirts I need," the actor told him. "Give it to my fucking twin."

21. ESCAPING MAHARASHTRA

Ready for Rabies

This time, Julia found him in the morning with his face pressing a pencil against the glass-topped table in the dining room. An ongoing title search was evident from Farrokh's last jottings. There was *Lion Piss* (crossed out, blessedly) and *Raging Hormones* (also crossed out, she was happy to see), but the one that appeared to have pleased the screen-writer before he fell asleep was circled. As a movie title, Julia had her doubts about it. It was *Limo Roulette*, which reminded Julia of one of those French films that defy common sense—even when one manages to read every word of the subtitles.

But this was far too busy a morning for Julia to take the time to read the new pages. She woke up Farrokh by blowing in his ear; while he was in the bathtub, she made his tea. She'd already packed his toilet articles and a change of clothes, and she'd teased her husband about his habit of taking with him a medical-emergency kit of an elaborately paranoid nature; after all, he was going to be away only one night.

But Dr. Daruwalla never traveled anywhere in India without bringing with him certain precautionary items: erythromycin, the preferred anti-biotic for bronchitis; Lomotil, for diarrhea. He even carried a kit of surgical instruments, including sutures and iodophor gauze—and both an antibiotic powder and an ointment. In the usual weather, infection thrived in the simplest wound. And the doctor would never travel without a sample selection of condoms, which he freely dispensed without invitation. Indian men were renowned for not using condoms. All Dr. Daruwalla had to do was meet a man who so much as joked about prostitutes; in the doctor's mind, this amounted to a confession. "Here— next time try one of these," Dr. Daruwalla would say.

The doctor also toted with him a half-dozen sterile disposable needles and syringes—just in case anyone needed any kind of shot. At a circus, people were always being bitten by dogs and monkeys. Someone had told Dr. Daruwalla that rabies was endemic among chimpanzees. For this trip, especially, Farrokh brought along three starter-doses of rabies vaccine, together with three 10mL vials of human rabies immune globu-lin. Both the vaccine and the immune globulin required refrigeration, but for a journey of less than 48 hours a thermos with ice would be sufficient.

"Are you expecting to be bitten by something?" Julia had asked him.

"I was thinking of the new missionary," Farrokh had replied; for he believed that, if *he* were a rabid chimpanzee at the Great Blue Nile, he would certainly be inclined to bite Martin Mills. Yet Julia knew that he'd packed enough vaccine and immune globulin to treat himself and the missionary and both children—just in case a rabid chimpanzee attacked them all.

Lucky Day

In the morning, the doctor longed to read and revise the new pages of his screenplay, but there was too much to do. The elephant boy had sold all the clothes that Martin Mills had bought for him on Fashion Street. Julia had anticipated this; she'd bought the ungrateful little wretch more clothes. It was a struggle to get Ganesh to take a bath—at first because he wanted to do nothing but ride in the elevator, and then because he'd never been in a building with a balcony overlooking Marine Drive; all he wanted to do was stare at the view. Ganesh also objected to wearing a sandal on his good foot, and even Julia doubted the wisdom of conceal-ing the mangled foot in a clean white sock; the sock wouldn't stay clean or white for long. As for the lone sandal, Ganesh complained that the strap across the top of his foot hurt him so much, he could scarcely walk.

When the doctor had kissed Julia good-bye, he steered the disgrun-tled boy to Vinod's waiting taxi; there, in the front seat beside the dwarf, was the sullen Madhu. She was irritated by Dr. Daruwalla's difficulty in understanding her languages. She had to try both Marathi and Hindi before the doctor understood that Madhu was displeased with the way Vinod had dressed her; Deepa had told the dwarf how to dress the girl.

"I'm not a child," the former child prostitute said, although it was clear that it had been Deepa's intention to make the little whore *look* like a child.

"The circus wants you to look like a child," Dr. Daruwalla told Madhu, but the girl pouted; nor did she respond to Ganesh in a sisterly fashion.

Madhu glanced briefly, and with disgust, at the boy's viscid eyes; there was a film of tetracycline ointment, which had been recently applied—it tended to give Ganesh's eyes a glazed quality. The boy would need to continue the medication for a week or more before his eyes looked normal. "I thought they were fixing your eyes," Madhu said cruelly; she spoke in Hindi. It had been Farrokh's impression, when he'd been alone with Madhu or alone with Ganesh, that both children endeavored to speak English; now that the kids were together, they lapsed into Hindi and Marathi. At best, the doctor spoke Hindi tentatively—and Marathi hardly at all.

"It's important that you behave like a brother and sister," Farrokh reminded them, but the cripple's mood was as sulky as Madhu's.

"If she were my sister, I'd beat her up," Ganesh said.

"Not with that foot, you wouldn't," Madhu told him.

"Now, now," said Dr. Daruwalla; he'd decided to speak English because he was almost certain that Madhu, as well as Ganesh, could understand him, and he presumed that in English he commanded more authority. "This is your lucky day," he told them.

"What's a lucky day?" Madhu asked the doctor.

"It doesn't mean anything," Ganesh said.

"It's just an expression," Dr. Daruwalla admitted, "but it does mean something. It means that today it is your good fortune to be leaving Bombay, to be going to the circus."

"So you mean that *we're* lucky—not the day," the elephant-footed boy replied.

"It's too soon to say if we're lucky," said the child prostitute.

On that note, they arrived at St. Ignatius, where the single-minded missionary had been waiting for them. Martin Mills climbed into the back seat of the Ambassador, an air of boundless enthusiasm surrounding him. "This is your lucky day!" the zealot announced to the children.

"We've been through that," said Dr. Daruwalla. It was only 7:30 on a Saturday morning.

Out of Place at the Taj

It was 8:30 when they arrived at the terminal for domestic flights in Santa Cruz, where they were told that their flight to Rajkot would be delayed until the end of the day.

"Indian Airlines!" Dr. Daruwalla exclaimed.

"At least they are admitting it," Vinod said.

Dr. Daruwalla decided that they could wait somewhere more comfortable than the Santa Cruz terminal. But before Farrokh could usher them all back inside the dwarf's taxi, Martin Mills had wandered off and bought the morning newspaper; on their way back to Bombay, in rush-hour traffic, the missionary treated them to snippets from *The Times of India.* It would be 10:30 before they arrived at the Taj. (It was Dr. Daruwalla's eccentric decision that they should wait for their flight to Rajkot in the lobby of the Taj Mahal Hotel.)

"Listen to this," Martin began. " 'Two brothers stabbed.... The police have arrested one assailant while two other accused are absconding on a scooter in a rash manner.' An unexpected use of the present tense, not to mention 'rash,' " the English teacher observed. "Not to mention 'absconding.' "

" 'Absconding' is a very popular word here," Farrokh explained.

"Sometimes it is the police who are absconding," Ganesh said.

"What did he say?" the missionary asked.

"When a crime happens, often the police abscond," Farrokh replied. "They're embarrassed that they couldn't prevent the crime, or that they can't catch the criminal, so they run away." But Dr. Daruwalla was thinking that this pattern of behavior didn't apply to Detective Patel. According to John D., the deputy commissioner intended to spend the day in the actor's suite at the Oberoi, rehearsing the best way to approach Rahul. It hurt Farrokh's feelings that he'd not been invited to participate, or that they hadn't offered to hold up the rehearsal until the screenwriter returned from the circus; after all, there would be dialogue to imagine and to compose, and although dialogue wasn't part of the doctor's day job, it was at least his other business.

"Let me be sure that I understand this," Martin Mills said. "Sometimes, when there's a crime, both the criminals *and* the police are 'absconding.' "

"Quite so," replied Dr. Daruwalla. He was unaware that he'd borrowed this expression from Detective Patel. The screenwriter was distracted by pride; he was thinking how clever he'd been, for he'd already made similar disrespectful use of *The Times of India* in his screenplay. (The fictional Mr. Martin is always reading something stupid aloud to the fictional children.)

Life imitates art, Farrokh was thinking, when Martin Mills announced, "Here's a refreshingly frank opinion." Martin had found the Opinion section of *The Times of India;* he was reading one of the letters. "Listen to this," the missionary said. " 'Our culture will have to be changed. It should start in primary schools by teaching boys not to urinate in the open.' "

"Catch them young, in other words," said Dr. Daruwalla.

Then Ganesh said something that made Madhu laugh.

"What did he say?" Martin asked Farrokh.

"He said there's no place to pee *except* in the open," Dr. Daruwalla replied.

Then Madhu said something that Ganesh clearly approved of.

"What did *she* say?" the missionary asked.

"She said she prefers to pee in parked cars—particularly at night," the doctor told him.

When they arrived at the Taj, Madhu's mouth was full of betel juice; the blood-red spittle overflowed the corners of her mouth.

"No betel chewing in the Taj," the doctor said. The girl spat the lurid mess on the front tire of Vinod's taxi; both the dwarf and the Sikh doorman observed, with disgust, how the stain extended into the circular driveway. "You won't be allowed any paan at the circus," the doctor reminded Madhu.

"We're not at the circus yet," said the sullen little whore.

The circular driveway was overcrowded with taxis and an array of expensive-looking vehicles. The elephant-footed boy said something to Madhu, who was amused.

"What did he say?" the missionary asked Dr. Daruwalla.

"He said there are lots of cars to pee in," the doctor replied. Then he overheard Madhu telling Ganesh that she'd been in a car like one of the expensive-looking cars before; it didn't sound like an empty boast, but Farrokh resisted the temptation to translate this information for the Jesuit. As much as Dr. Daruwalla enjoyed shocking Martin Mills, it seemed prurient to speculate on what a child prostitute had been doing in such an expensive-looking car.

"What did Madhu say?" Martin asked Farrokh.

"She said she would use the ladies' room, instead," Dr. Daruwalla lied.

"Good for you!" Martin told the girl. When she parted her lips to smile at him, her teeth were brightly smeared from the paan; it was as if her gums were bleeding. The doctor hoped that it was only his imagination that he saw something lewd in Madhu's smile. When they entered the lobby, Dr. Daruwalla didn't like the way the doorman followed Madhu with his eyes; the Sikh seemed to know that she wasn't the sort of girl who was permitted at the Taj. No matter how Deepa had told Vinod to dress her, Madhu didn't look like a child.

Ganesh was already shivering from the air-conditioning; the cripple looked anxious, as if he thought the Sikh doormen might throw him out. The Taj was no place for a beggar and a child prostitute, Dr. Daruwalla was thinking; it was a mistake to have brought them here.

"We'll just have some tea," Farrokh assured the children. "We'll keep checking on the plane," the doctor told the missionary. Like Madhu and Ganesh, Martin appeared overwhelmed by the opulence of the lobby. In the few minutes it took Dr. Daruwalla to arrange for special treatment from the assistant manager, some lesser official among the hotel staff had already asked the Jesuit and the children to leave. When that misunderstanding was cleared up, Vinod appeared in the lobby with the paper bag containing the Hawaiian shirt. The dwarf was dutifully observing, without comment, what he thought were Inspector Dhar's delusions—namely, that the famous actor was a Jesuit missionary in training to be a priest. Dr. Daruwalla had meant to give the Hawaiian shirt to Martin Mills, but the doctor had forgotten the bag in the dwarf's taxi. (Not just any taxi-walla would have been permitted in the lobby of the Taj, but Vinod was known as Inspector Dhar's driver.)

When Farrokh presented the Hawaiian shirt to Martin Mills, the missionary was excited.

"Oh, it's wonderful!" the zealot cried. "I used to have one just like it!"

"Actually, this is the one you used to have," Farrokh admitted.

"No, no," Martin whispered. "The shirt I used to have was stolen from me—one of those prostitutes took it."

"The prostitute gave it back," Dr. Daruwalla whispered.

"She *did*? Why, that's remarkable!" said Martin Mills. "Was she contrite?"

"*He*, not she," said Dr. Daruwalla. "No—he wasn't contrite, I think."

"What do you mean? *He . . .*" the missionary said.

"I mean that the prostitute was a *him*, not a her," the doctor told Martin Mills. "He was a eunuch-transvestite—all of them were men. Well, *sort of* men."

"What do you mean? *Sort of . . .*" the missionary said.

"They're called hijras—they've been emasculated," the doctor whispered. A typical surgeon, Dr. Daruwalla liked to describe the procedure in exact detail—including the cauterizing of the wound with hot oil, and not forgetting that part of the female anatomy which the puckered scar resembled when it healed.

When Martin Mills came back from the men's room, he was wearing the Hawaiian shirt, the brilliant colors of which were a contrast to his pallor. Farrokh assumed that the paper bag now contained the shirt that the missionary had been wearing, upon which poor Martin had been sick.

"It's a good thing that we're getting these children out of this city," the zealot gravely told the doctor, who once more happily entertained the notion that life was imitating art. Now, if only the fool would shut up so that the screenwriter could read over his new pages!

Dr. Daruwalla knew that they couldn't spend the whole day at the Taj. The children were already restless. Madhu might proposition stray guests at the hotel, and the elephant boy would probably steal something—those silver trinkets from the souvenir shop, the doctor supposed. Dr. Daruwalla didn't dare leave the children with Martin Mills while he phoned Ranjit to check his messages; he wasn't expecting any messages, anyway—nothing but emergencies happened on Saturday, and the doctor wasn't on call this weekend.

The girl's posture further upset Farrokh; Madhu more than slouched in the soft chair—she lolled. Her dress was hiked up nearly to her hips and she stared into the eyes of every man who passed. This certainly detracted from her looking like a child. Worse, Madhu seemed to be wearing perfume; she smelled a little like Deepa to Dr. Daruwalla. (Doubtless Vinod had allowed the girl some access to Deepa's things, and Madhu had liked the perfume that the dwarf's wife wore.) Also, the doctor believed that the air-conditioning at the Taj was too comfortable—in fact, it was too cold. At the Government Circuit House in Junagadh, where Dr. Daruwalla had arranged for them all to spend the night, there wouldn't be any air-conditioning—just ceiling fans—and in the circus, where the children would spend the following night (and every night thereafter), there would be only tents. No ceiling fans

. . . and probably the mosquito netting would be in disrepair. Every second they stayed in the lobby of the Taj, Dr. Daruwalla realized that he was making it harder for the children to adjust to the Great Blue Nile.

Then a most irksome thing happened. A messenger boy was paging Inspector Dhar. The method for paging at the Taj was rudimentary; some thought it quaint. The messenger tramped through the lobby with a chalkboard that dangled brass chimes, treating everyone in the lobby to an insistent dinging. The messenger boy, who thought that he'd recognized Inspector Dhar, stopped in front of Martin Mills and shook the board with its incessant chimes. Chalked on the board was MR DHAR.

"Wrong man," Dr. Daruwalla told the messenger boy, but the boy continued to shake the chimes. "Wrong man, you moron!" the doctor shouted. But the boy was no moron; he wouldn't leave without a tip. Once he got it, he strolled casually away, still chiming. Farrokh was furious.

"We're going now," he said abruptly.

"Going where?" Madhu asked him.

"To the circus?" asked Ganesh.

"No, not yet—we're just going somewhere else," the doctor informed them.

"Aren't we comfortable here?" the missionary asked.

"*Too* comfortable," Dr. Daruwalla replied.

"Actually, a tour of Bombay would be nice—for me," the scholastic said. "I realize the rest of you are familiar with the city, but possibly there's something you wouldn't mind showing me. Public gardens, perhaps. I also like marketplaces."

Not a great idea, Farrokh knew—to be dragging Dhar's twin through public places. Dr. Daruwalla was thinking that he could take them all to the Duckworth Club for lunch. It was certain that they wouldn't run into Dhar at the Taj, because John D. was rehearsing with Detective Patel at the Oberoi; it was therefore likely that they wouldn't run into John D. at the club, either. As for the outside chance that they might encounter Rahul, it didn't bother Dr. Daruwalla to contemplate having another look at the second Mrs. Dogar; the doctor would do nothing to arouse her suspicions. But it was too early to go to lunch at the Duckworth Club, and he had to phone for a reservation; without one, Mr. Sethna would be rude to them.

Too Loud for a Library

Back in the Ambassador, the doctor instructed Vinod to drive them to the Asiatic Society Library, opposite Horniman Circle; this was one of those oases in the teeming city—not unlike the Duckworth Club or St. Ignatius—where the doctor was hoping that Dhar's twin would be safe. Dr. Daruwalla was a member of the Asiatic Society Library; he'd often dozed in the cool, high-ceilinged reading rooms. The larger-than-life statues of literary geniuses had barely noticed the screenwriter's quiet ascending and descending of the magnificent staircase.

"I'm taking you to the grandest library in Bombay," Dr. Daruwalla told Martin Mills. "Almost a million books! Almost as many bibliophiles!"

Meanwhile, the doctor told Vinod to drive the children "around and around." He also told the dwarf that it was important not to let the kids out of the car. They liked riding in the Ambassador, anyway—the anonymity of cruising the city, the secrecy of staring at the passing world. Madhu and Ganesh were unfamiliar with taxi riding; they stared at everyone as if they themselves were invisible—as if the dwarf's crude Ambassador were equipped with one-way windows. Dr. Daruwalla wondered if this was because they knew they were safe with Vinod; they'd never been safe before.

The doctor had caught just a departing glimpse of the children's faces. At that moment, they'd looked frightened—frightened of what? It certainly wasn't that they feared they were being abandoned with a dwarf; they weren't afraid of Vinod. No; on their faces Farrokh had seen a greater anxiety—that the circus they were supposedly being delivered to was only a dream, that they would never get out of Bombay.

Escaping Maharashtra: it suddenly struck him as a better title than *Limo Roulette.* But maybe not, Farrokh thought.

"I'm quite fond of bibliophiles," Martin Mills was saying as they climbed the stairs. For the first time, Dr. Daruwalla was aware of how loudly the scholastic spoke; the zealot was too loud for a library.

"There are over eight hundred thousand volumes here," Farrokh whispered. "This includes ten thousand manuscripts!"

"I'm glad we're alone for a moment," the missionary said in a voice that rattled the wrought iron of the loggia.

"Ssshhh!" the doctor hissed. The marble statues frowned down upon them; 80 or 90 of the library staffers had long ago assumed the frowning

air of the statuary, and Dr. Daruwalla foresaw that the zealot with his booming voice would soon be rebuked by one of the slipper-clad, scolding types who scurried through the musty recesses of the Asiatic Society Library. To avoid a confrontation, the doctor steered the scholastic into a reading room with no one in it.

The ceiling fan had snagged the string that turned the fan on and off, and only the slight ticking of the string against the blades disturbed the silence of the moldering air. The dusty books sagged on the carved teak shelves; numbered cartons of manuscripts were stacked against the bookcases; wide-bottomed, leather-padded chairs surrounded an oval table that was strewn with pencils and pads of notepaper. Only one of these chairs was on castors; it was tilted, for it was four-legged and had only three castors—the missing castor, like a paperweight, held down one of the pads of notepaper.

The American zealot, as if compelled by his countrymen's irritating instinct to appear handy with all things, instantly undertook the task of repairing the broken chair. There were a half-dozen other chairs that the doctor and the missionary could have sat in, and Dr. Daruwalla suspected that the chair with the detached castor had probably maintained its disabled condition, untouched, for the last 10 or 20 years; perhaps the chair had been partially destroyed in celebration of Independence— more than 40 years ago! Yet here was this fool, determined to make it right. Is there no place in town I can take this idiot? Farrokh wondered. Before the doctor could stop the zealot, Martin Mills had upended the chair on the oval table, where it made a loud thump.

"Come on—you must tell me," the missionary said. "I'm dying to hear the story of your conversion. Naturally, the Father Rector has told me about it."

Naturally, Dr. Daruwalla thought; Father Julian had doubtless made the doctor come off as a deluded, false convert. Then, suddenly, to Farrokh's surprise, the missionary produced a knife! It was one of those Swiss Army knives that Dhar liked so much—a kind of toolbox unto itself. With something that resembled a leather-punch, the Jesuit was boring a hole into the leg of the chair. The rotting wood fell on the table.

"It just needs a new screw hole," Martin exclaimed. "I can't believe no one knew how to fix it."

"I suppose people just sat in the other chairs," Dr. Daruwalla suggested. While the scholastic wrestled with the chair leg, the nasty little tool on the knife suddenly snapped closed, neatly removing a hunk of Martin's index finger. The Jesuit bled profusely onto a pad of notepaper.

"Now, look, you've cut yourself . . ." Dr. Daruwalla began.

"It's nothing," the zealot said, but it was evident that the chair was beginning to make the man of God angry. "I want to hear your story. Come on. I know how it starts . . . you're in Goa, aren't you? You've just gone to visit the sainted remains of our Francis Xavier . . . what's left of him. And you go to sleep thinking of that pilgrim who bit off St. Francis's toe."

"I went to sleep thinking of nothing at all!" Farrokh insisted, his voice rising.

"*Ssshhh!* This is a library," the missionary reminded Dr. Daruwalla.

"I *know* it's a library!" the doctor cried—too loudly, for they weren't alone. At first unseen but now emerging from a pile of manuscripts was an old man who'd been sleeping in a corner chair; it was another chair on castors, for it wheeled their way. Its disagreeable rider, who'd been roused from the depths of whatever sleep his reading material had sunk him into, was wearing a Nehru jacket, which (like his hands) was gray from transmitted newsprint.

"*Ssshhh!*" the old reader said. Then he wheeled back into his corner of the room.

"Maybe we should find another place to discuss my conversion," Farrokh whispered to Martin Mills.

"I'm going to fix this chair," the Jesuit replied. Now bleeding onto the chair and the table *and* the pad of notepaper, Martin Mills jammed the rebellious castor into the inverted chair leg; with another dangerous-looking tool, a stubby screwdriver, he struggled to affix the castor to the chair. "So . . . you went to sleep . . . your mind an absolute blank, or so you're telling me. And then what?"

"I dreamt I was St. Francis's corpse . . ." Dr. Daruwalla began.

"Body dreams, very common," the zealot whispered.

"*Ssshhh!*" said the old man in the Nehru jacket, from the corner.

"I dreamt that the crazed pilgrim was biting off my toe!" Farrokh hissed.

"You *felt* this?" Martin asked.

"Of *course* I felt it!" hissed the doctor.

"But corpses don't feel, do they?" the scholastic said. "Oh, well . . . so you *felt* the bite, and then?"

"When I woke up, my toe was *throbbing.* I couldn't stand on that foot, much less walk! And there were bite marks—not broken skin, mind you, but actual teeth marks! Those marks were *real*! The *bite* was real!" Farrokh insisted.

"Of course it was real," the missionary said. "Something real bit you. What could it have been?"

"I was on a balcony—I was in the *air!*" Farrokh whispered hoarsely.

"Try to keep it down," the Jesuit whispered. "Are you telling me that this balcony was utterly unapproachable?"

"Through locked doors... where my wife and children were asleep..." Farrokh began.

"Ah, the *children!*" Martin Mills cried out. "How old were they?"

"I wasn't bitten by my own children!" Dr. Daruwalla hissed.

"Children *do* bite, from time to time—or as a prank," the missionary replied. "I've heard that children go through actual *biting ages*—when they're especially prone to bite."

"I suppose my wife could have been hungry, too," Farrokh said sarcastically.

"There were no trees around the balcony?" Martin Mills asked; he was now both bleeding and sweating over the stubborn chair.

"I see it coming," Dr. Daruwalla said. "Father Julian's monkey theory. Biting apes, swinging from vines—is that what you think?"

"The point is, you were *really* bitten, weren't you?" the Jesuit asked him. "People get so confused about miracles. The miracle wasn't that something bit you. The miracle is that you believe! Your *faith* is the miracle. It hardly matters that it was something . . . common that triggered it."

"What happened to my toe wasn't *common!*" the doctor cried.

The old reader in the Nehru jacket shot out of his corner on his chair on castors. *"Ssshhh!"* the old man hissed.

"Are you trying to read or trying to *sleep?*" the doctor shouted at the old gentleman.

"Come on—you're disturbing him. He was here first," Martin Mills told Dr. Daruwalla. "Look!" the scholastic said to the old man, as if the angry reader were a child. "See this chair? I've fixed it. Want to try it?" The missionary set the chair on all four castors and rolled it back and forth. The gentleman in the Nehru jacket eyed the zealot warily.

"He has his own chair, for God's sake," Farrokh said.

"Come on—give it a try!" the missionary urged the old reader.

"I have to find a telephone," Dr. Daruwalla pleaded with the zealot. "I should make a reservation for lunch. And we should stay with the children—they're probably bored." But, to his dismay, the doctor saw that Martin Mills was staring up at the ceiling fan; the tangled string had caught the handyman's eye.

"That string is annoying—if you're trying to read," the scholastic said. He climbed up on the oval table, which accepted his weight reluctantly.

"You'll break the table," the doctor warned him.

"I won't break the table—I'm thinking of fixing the fan," Martin Mills replied. Slowly and awkwardly, the Jesuit went from kneeling to standing.

"I can see what you're thinking—you're crazy!" Dr. Daruwalla said.

"Come on—you're just angry about your miracle," the missionary said. "I'm not trying to take your miracle away from you. I'm only trying to make you see the *real* miracle. It is simply that you believe—not the silly thing that made you believe. The biting was only a vehicle."

"The *biting* was the miracle!" Dr. Daruwalla cried.

"No, no—that's where you're wrong," Martin Mills managed to say, just before the table collapsed under him. Falling, he reached for—and fortunately missed—the fan. The gentleman in the Nehru jacket was the most astonished; when Martin Mills fell, the old reader was cautiously trying out the newly repaired chair. The collapse of the table and the missionary's cry of alarm sent the old man scrambling. The chair leg with the freshly bored hole rejected the castor. While both the old reader and the Jesuit lay on the floor, Dr. Daruwalla was left to calm down the outraged library staffer who'd shuffled into the reading room in his slippers.

"We were just leaving," Dr. Daruwalla told the librarian. "It's too noisy here to concentrate on anything at all!"

Sweating and bleeding and limping, the missionary followed Farrokh down the grand staircase, under the frowning statues. To relax himself, Dr. Daruwalla was chanting, "Life imitates art. Life imitates art."

"What's that you say?" asked Martin Mills.

"*Ssshhh!*" the doctor told him. "This is a library."

"Don't be angry about your miracle," the zealot said.

"It was long ago. I don't think I believe in anything anymore," Farrokh replied.

"Don't say that!" the missionary cried.

"*Ssshhh!*" Farrokh whispered to him.

"I know, I know," said Martin Mills. "This is a library."

It was almost noon. Outside, in the glaring sunlight, they stared into the street without seeing the taxi that was parked at the curb. Vinod had to walk up to them; the dwarf led them to the car as if they were blind.

Inside the Ambassador, the children were crying. They were sure that
the circus was a myth or a hoax.

"No, no—it's real," Dr. Daruwalla assured them. "We're going there,
we really are—it's just that the plane is delayed." But what did Madhu
or Ganesh know about airplanes? The doctor assumed that they'd never
flown; flying would be another terror for them. And when the children
saw that Martin Mills was bleeding, they were worried that there'd been
some violence. "Only to a chair," Farrokh said. He was angry at himself,
for in the confusion he'd forgotten to reserve his favorite table in the
Ladies' Garden. He knew that Mr. Sethna would find a way to abuse him
for this oversight.

A Misunderstanding at the Urinal

As punishment, Mr. Sethna had given the doctor's table to Mr. and Mrs.
Kohinoor and Mrs. Kohinoor's noisy, unmarried sister. The latter
woman was so shrill, not even the bower of flowers in the Ladies'
Garden could absorb her whinnies or brays. Probably on purpose, Mr.
Sethna had seated Dr. Daruwalla's party at a table in a neglected corner
of the garden, where the waiters either ignored you or failed to see you
from their stations in the dining room. A torn vine of the bougainvillea
hung down from the bower and brushed the back of Dr. Daruwalla's
neck like a claw. The good news was it wasn't Chinese Day. Madhu and
Ganesh ordered vegetarian kabobs; the vegetables were broiled or
grilled on skewers. It was a dish that children sometimes ate with their
fingers. While the doctor hoped that Madhu's and Ganesh's un-
familiarity with knives and forks would go unnoticed, Mr. Sethna speculated on whose children they were.

The old steward observed that the cripple had kicked his one sandal
off; the calluses on the sole of the boy's good foot were as thick as a
beggar's. The foot the elephant had stepped on was still concealed by the
sock, which was already gray-brown, and it didn't fool Mr. Sethna, who
could tell that the hidden foot was oddly flattened—the boy had limped
on his heel. On the ball of the bad foot, the sock was still mostly white.

As for the girl, the steward detected something lascivious in her
posture; furthermore, Mr. Sethna concluded that Madhu had never been
in a restaurant before—she stared too openly at the waiters. Dr. Daruwalla's grandchildren would have been better behaved than this; and

although Inspector Dhar had proclaimed to the press that he would sire only Indian babies, these children bore no resemblance to the famous actor.

As for the actor, he looked *awful*, Mr. Sethna thought. Possibly he'd forgotten to wear his makeup. Inspector Dhar looked pale and in need of sleep; his gaudy shirt was outrageous, there was blood on his pants and overnight his physique had deteriorated—he must be suffering from acute diarrhea, the old steward determined. How else does one manage to lose 15 or 20 pounds in a day? And had the actor's head been shaved by muggers, or was his hair falling out? On second thought, Mr. Sethna suspected that Dhar was the victim of a sexually transmitted disease. In a sick culture, where movie actors were revered as demigods, a lifestyle contagion was to be expected. That will bring the bastard down to earth, Mr. Sethna thought. Maybe Inspector Dhar has AIDS! The old steward was sorely tempted to place an anonymous phone call to *Stardust* or *Cine Blitz;* surely either of these film-gossip magazines would be intrigued by such a rumor.

"I wouldn't marry him if he owned the Queen's Necklace and he offered me *half!*" cried Mrs. Kohinoor's unmarried sister. "I wouldn't marry him if he gave me all of *London!*"

If you were *in* London, I could still hear you, thought Dr. Daruwalla. He picked at his pomfret; the fish at the Duckworth Club was unfailingly overcooked—Farrokh wondered why he'd ordered it. He envied how Martin Mills attacked his meat kabobs. The meat kept falling out of the flatbread; because Martin had stripped the skewers and tried to make a sandwich, the missionary's hands were covered with chopped onions. A dark-green flag of mint leaf was stuck between the zealot's upper front teeth. As a polite way of suggesting that the Jesuit take a look at himself in a mirror, Farrokh said, "You might want to use the men's room here, Martin. It's more comfortable than the facilities at the airport."

Throughout lunch, Dr. Daruwalla couldn't stop glancing at his watch, even though Vinod had called Indian Airlines repeatedly; the dwarf predicted a late-afternoon departure at the earliest. They were in no hurry. The doctor had called his office only to learn that there were no messages of any importance; there'd been just one call for him, and Ranjit had handled the matter competently. Mr. Garg had phoned for the mailing address, in Junagadh, of the Great Blue Nile Circus; Garg had told Ranjit that he wanted to send Madhu a letter. It was odd that Mr. Garg hadn't asked Vinod or Deepa for the address, for the doctor had obtained the address from the dwarf's wife. It was odder still how

Garg imagined that Madhu could read a letter, or even a postcard; Madhu couldn't read. But the doctor guessed that Mr. Garg was euphoric to learn that Madhu was *not* HIV-positive; maybe the creep wanted to send the poor child a thank-you note, or merely give her good-luck wishes.

Now, short of telling him that he wore a mint leaf on his front teeth, there seemed no way to compel Martin Mills to visit the men's room. The scholastic took the children to the card room; there he tried in vain to teach them crazy eights. Soon the cards were speckled with blood; the zealot's index finger was still bleeding. Rather than unearth his medical supplies from his suitcase, which was in the Ambassador—besides, the doctor had packed nothing as simple as a Band-Aid—Farrokh asked Mr. Sethna for a small bandage. The old steward delivered the Band-Aid to the card room with characteristic scorn and inappropriate ceremony; he presented the bandage to Martin Mills on the silver serving tray, which the steward extended at arm's length. Dr. Daruwalla took this occasion to tell the Jesuit, "You should probably wash that wound in the men's room—*before* you bandage it."

But Martin Mills washed and bandaged his finger without once looking in the mirror above the sink, or in the full-length mirror—except at some distance, and only to appraise his lost-and-found Hawaiian shirt. The missionary never spotted the mint leaf on his teeth. He did, however, notice a tissue dispenser near the flush handle for the urinal, and he noted further that every flush handle had a tissue dispenser in close proximity to it. These tissues, when used, were *not* carelessly deposited in the urinals; rather, there was a silver bucket at the end of the lineup of urinals, something like an ice bucket without ice, and the used tissues were deposited in it.

This system seemed exceedingly fastidious and ultra-hygienic to Martin Mills, who reflected that he'd never wiped his penis with a tissue before. The process of urinating was made to seem more important, certainly more solemn, by the expectation of wiping one's penis after the act. At least, this is what Martin Mills *assumed* the tissues were for. It troubled him that no other Duckworthians were urinating at any of the other urinals; therefore, he couldn't be *sure* of the purpose of the tissue dispensers. He was about to finish peeing as usual—that is, without wiping himself—when the unfriendly old steward who had presented the Jesuit with his Band-Aid entered the men's room. The silver serving tray was stuck in one armpit and rested against the forearm of the same arm, as if Mr. Sethna were carrying a rifle.

Because someone was watching him, Martin Mills thought he should use a tissue. He tried to wipe himself as if he always completed a responsible act of urination in this fashion; but he was so unfamiliar with the process, the tissue briefly caught on the end of his penis and then fell into the urinal. What was the protocol in the case of such a mishap? Martin wondered. The steward's beady eyes were fastened on the Jesuit. As if inspired, Martin Mills seized several fresh tissues, and with these held between his bandaged index finger and his thumb, he plucked the lost tissue from the urinal. With a flourish, he deposited the bunch of tissues in the silver bucket, which tilted suddenly, and almost toppled; the missionary had to steady it with both hands. Martin tried to smile reassuringly to Mr. Sethna, but he realized that because he'd grabbed the silver bucket with both hands, he'd neglected to return his penis to his pants. Maybe this was why the old steward looked away.

When Martin Mills had left the men's room, Mr. Sethna gave the missionary's urinal a wide berth; the steward peed as far away as possible from where the diseased actor had peed. It was definitely a sexually transmitted disease, Mr. Sethna thought. The steward had never witnessed such a grotesque example of urination. He couldn't imagine the medical necessity of dabbing one's penis every time one peed. The old steward didn't know for certain if there were other Duckworthians who made the same use of the tissue dispensers as Martin Mills had made. For years, Mr. Sethna had assumed that the tissues were for wiping one's *fingers*. And now, after he'd wiped his fingers, Mr. Sethna accurately deposited his tissue in the silver bucket, ruefully reflecting on the fate of Inspector Dhar. Once a demigod, now a terminal patient. For the first time since he'd poured hot tea on the head of that fop wearing the wig, the world struck Mr. Sethna as fair and just.

In the card room, while Martin Mills had been experimenting at the urinal, Dr. Daruwalla realized why the children had such difficulty in grasping crazy eights, or any other card game. No one had ever taught them their numbers; not only could they not read, they couldn't count. The doctor was holding up his fingers with the corresponding playing card—three fingers with the three of hearts—when Martin Mills returned from the men's room, still sporting the mint leaf on his front teeth.

Fear No Evil

Their plane to Rajkot took off at 5:10 in the afternoon, not quite eight hours after its scheduled departure. It was a tired-looking 737. The inscription on the fuselage was legible but faded.

FORTY YEARS OF FREEDOM

Dr. Daruwalla quickly calculated that the plane had first been put in service in India in 1987. Where it had flown before then was anybody's guess.

Their departure was further delayed by the need of the petty officials to confiscate Martin Mills's Swiss Army knife—a potential terrorist's tool. The pilot would carry the "weapon" in his pocket and hand it over to Martin in Rajkot.

"Well, I suppose I'll never see it again," the missionary said; he didn't say this stoically, but more like a martyr.

Farrokh wasted no time in teasing him. "It can't matter to you," the doctor told him. "You've taken a vow of poverty, haven't you?"

"I know what you think about my vows," Martin replied. "You think that, because I've accepted poverty, I must have no fondness for material things. This shirt, for example—my knife, my books. And you think that, because I've accepted chastity, I must be free of sexual desire. Well, I'll tell you: I resisted the commitment to become a priest not only because of how much I *did* like my few things, but also because I imagined I was in love. For ten years, I was smitten. I not only suffered from sexual desire; I'd embraced a sexual obsession. There was absolutely no getting this person out of my mind. Does this surprise you?"

"Yes, it does," Dr. Daruwalla admitted humbly. He was also afraid of what the lunatic might confess in front of the children, but Ganesh and Madhu were too enthralled with the airplane's preparations for takeoff to pay the slightest attention to the Jesuit's confession.

"I continued to teach at this wretched school—the students were delinquents, not scholars—and all because I had to test myself," Martin Mills told Dr. Daruwalla. "The object of my desire was there. Were I to leave, to run away, I would never have known if I had the strength to resist such a temptation. And so I stayed. I forced myself into the closest possible proximity to this person, only to see if I had the courage to withstand such an attraction. But I know what you think of priestly denial. You think that priests are people who simply don't feel these ordinary desires, or who feel them less strongly than you do."

"I'm not judging you!" said Dr. Daruwalla.

"Yes you are," Martin replied. "You think you know all about me."

"This person that you were in love with . . ." the doctor began.

"It was another teacher at the school," the missionary answered. "I was crippled by desire. But I kept the object of my desire *this* close to me!" And here the zealot held his hand in front of his face. "Eventually, the attraction lessened."

"Lessened?" Farrokh repeated.

"Either the attraction went away or I overcame it," said Martin Mills. "Finally, I won."

"What did you win?" Farrokh asked.

"Not freedom from desire," the would-be priest declared. "It is more like freedom from the fear of desire. Now I know I can resist it."

"But what about *her?"* Dr. Daruwalla asked.

"Her?" said Martin Mills.

"I mean, what were *her* feelings for *you?"* the doctor asked him. "Did she even know how you felt about her?"

"Him," the missionary replied. "It was a *he,* not a she. Does that surprise you?"

"Yes, it does," the doctor lied. What surprised him was how *un*surprised he was by the Jesuit's confession. The doctor was upset without understanding why; Farrokh felt greatly disturbed, without knowing the reason.

But the plane was taxiing, and even its lumbering movement on the runway was sufficient to panic Madhu; she'd been sitting across the aisle from Dr. Daruwalla and the missionary—now she wanted to move over and sit with the doctor. Ganesh was happily ensconced in the window seat. Awkwardly, Martin Mills changed places with Madhu; the Jesuit sat with the enraptured boy, and the child prostitute slipped into the aisle seat next to Farrokh.

"Don't be frightened," the doctor told her.

"I don't want to go to the circus," the girl said; she stared down the aisle, refusing to look out the windows. She wasn't alone in her inexperience; half the passengers appeared to be flying for the first time. One hand reached to adjust the flow of air; then 35 other hands were reaching. Despite the repeated announcement that carry-on baggage be stowed under the seats, the passengers insisted on piling their heavy bags on what the flight attendant kept calling the hat rack, although there were few hats on board. Perhaps the fault lay with the long delay, but there were many flies on board; they were treated with a vast indifference by the otherwise excited passengers. Someone was already vomiting, and they hadn't even taken off. At last, they took off.

The elephant boy believed *he* could fly. His animation appeared to be lifting the plane. The little beggar will ride a lion if they tell him to; he'll wrestle a tiger, Dr. Daruwalla thought. How suddenly the doctor felt afraid for the cripple! Ganesh would climb to the top of the tent—the full 80 feet. Probably in compensation for his useless foot, the boy's hands and arms were exceptionally strong. What instincts will protect him? the doctor wondered, while in his arms he felt Madhu tremble; she was moaning. In her slight bosom, the beating of her heart throbbed against Farrokh's chest.

"If we crash, do we burn or fly apart in little pieces?" the girl asked him, her mouth against his throat.

"We *won't* crash, Madhu," he told her.

"You don't know," she replied. "At the circus, I could be eaten by a wild animal or I could fall. And what if they can't train me or if they beat me?"

"Listen to me," said Dr. Daruwalla. He was a father again. He remembered his daughters—their nightmares, their scrapes and bruises and their worst days at school. Their awful first boyfriends, who were beyond redemption. But the consequences for the crying girl in his arms were greater. "Try to look at it this way," the doctor said. "You are *escaping.*" But he could say no more; he knew only what she was escaping—not what she was fleeing to. Out of the jaws of one kind of death, into the jaws of another . . . I hope not, was all the doctor thought.

"Something will get me," Madhu replied. With her hot, shallow breathing against his neck, Farrokh instantly knew why Martin Mills's admission of homosexual desire had distressed him. If Dhar's twin was fighting against his sexual inclination, what was John D. doing?

Dr. Duncan Frasier had convinced Dr. Daruwalla that homosexuality was more a matter of biology than of conditioning. Frasier had once told Farrokh that there was a 52 percent chance that the identical twin of a gay male would also be gay. Furthermore, Farrokh's friend and colleague Dr. Macfarlane had convinced him that homosexuality was immutable. ("If homosexuality is a learned behavior, how come it can't be *un*learned?" Mac had said.)

But what upset Dr. Daruwalla was *not* the doctor's sudden conviction that John D. must also be a homosexual; rather, it was all the years of

John D.'s aloofness and the remoteness of his Swiss life. Neville, not Danny, must have been the twins' father, after all! And what does it say about *me* that John D. wouldn't tell me? the doctor wondered.

Instinctively (as if *she* were his beloved John D.), Farrokh hugged the girl. Later, he supposed that Madhu only did as she'd been taught to do; she hugged him back, but in an inappropriately wriggling fashion. It shocked him; he pulled away from her when she began to kiss his throat.

"No, please . . ." he began to say.

Then the missionary spoke to him. Clearly, the elephant boy's delight with flying had delighted Martin Mills. "Look at him! I'll bet he'd try to walk on the wing, if we told him it was safe!" the zealot said.

"Yes, I'll bet he would," said Dr. Daruwalla, whose gaze never left Madhu's face. The fear and confusion of the child prostitute were a mirror of Farrokh's feelings.

"What do you want?" the girl whispered to him.

"No, it's not what you think . . . I want you to *escape*," the doctor told her. The concept meant nothing to her; she didn't respond. She continued to stare at him; in her eyes, trust still lingered with her confusion. At the blood-red edge of her lips, the unnatural redness once more overflowed her mouth; Madhu was eating paan again. Where she'd kissed Farrokh, his throat was marked with the lurid stain, as if a vampire had bitten him. He touched the mark and his fingertips came away with the color on them. The Jesuit saw him staring at his hand.

"Did you cut yourself?" Martin Mills asked.

"No, I'm fine," Dr. Daruwalla replied, but he wasn't. Farrokh was admitting to himself that he knew even less about desire than the would-be priest did.

Probably sensing his confusion, Madhu once more pressed herself against the doctor's chest. Once again, in a whisper, she asked him, "What do you want?" It horrified the doctor to realize that Madhu was asking him a sexual question.

"I want you to be a child, because you *are* a child," Farrokh told the girl. "Please, won't you try to be a child?" There was such an eagerness in Madhu's smile that, for a moment, the doctor believed the girl had understood him. Quite like a child, she walked her fingers over his thigh; then, unlike a child, Madhu pressed her small palm firmly on Dr. Daruwalla's penis. There'd been no groping for it; she'd known exactly where it was. Through the summer-weight material of his pants, the doctor felt the heat of Madhu's hand.

"I'll try what you want—anything you want," the child prostitute told him. Instantly, Dr. Daruwalla pulled her hand away.

"Stop that!" Farrokh cried.

"I want to sit with Ganesh," the girl told him. Farrokh let her change seats with Martin Mills.

"There's a matter I've been pondering," the missionary whispered to the doctor. "You said we had two rooms for the night. Only two?"

"I suppose we could get more . . ." the doctor began. His legs were shaking.

"No, no—that's not what I'm getting at," Martin said. "I mean, were you thinking the children would share one room, and we'd share the other?"

"Yes," Dr. Daruwalla replied. He couldn't stop his legs from shaking.

"But—well, I know you'll think this is silly, *but*—it would seem prudent to me to not allow them to sleep together. I mean, not in the same room," the missionary added. "After all, there is the matter of what we can only guess has been the girl's orientation."

"Her *what?*" the doctor asked. He could stop one leg from shaking, but not the other.

"Her sexual experience, I mean," said Martin Mills. "We must assume she's had some . . . sexual contact. What I mean is, what if Madhu is inclined to *seduce* Ganesh? Do you know what I mean?"

Dr. Daruwalla knew very well what Martin Mills meant. "You have a point," was all the doctor said in reply.

"Well, then, suppose the boy and I take one room, and you and Madhu take the other? You see, I don't think the Father Rector would approve of someone in my position sharing a room with the girl," Martin explained. "It might seem contradictory to my vows."

"Yes . . . your vows," Farrokh replied. Finally, his other leg stopped shaking.

"Do you think I'm being totally silly?" the Jesuit asked the doctor. "I suppose you think it's idiotic of me to suggest that Madhu might be so *inclined*—just because the poor child was . . . what she was." But Farrokh could feel that he still had an erection, and Madhu had touched him so briefly.

"No, I think you're wise to be a little worried about her . . . inclination," Dr. Daruwalla answered. He spoke slowly because he was trying to remember the popular psalm. "How does it go—the twenty-third psalm?" the doctor asked the scholastic. " 'Yea, though I walk through the valley of the shadow of death . . .' "

" 'I will fear no evil . . .' " said Martin Mills.

"Yes—that's it. 'I will fear no evil,' " Farrokh repeated.

Dr. Daruwalla assumed that the plane had left Maharashtra; he guessed they were already flying over Gujarat. Below them, the land was flat and dry-looking in the late-afternoon haze. The sky was as brown as the ground. *Limo Roulette* or *Escaping Maharashtra*—the screenwriter couldn't make up his mind between the two titles. Farrokh thought: It depends on what happens—it depends on how the story ends.

22. THE TEMPTATION OF DR. DARUWALLA

On the Road to Junagadh

At the airport in Rajkot, they were testing the loudspeaker system. It was a test without urgency, as if the loudspeaker were of no real importance—as if no one believed there could be an emergency.

"One, two, three, four, five," said a voice. "Five, four, three, two, one." Then the message was repeated. Maybe they *weren't* testing the loudspeaker system, thought Dr. Daruwalla; possibly they were testing their counting skills.

While the doctor and Martin Mills were gathering the bags, their pilot appeared and handed the Swiss Army knife to the missionary. At first Martin was embarrassed—he'd forgotten that he'd been forced to relinquish the weapon in Bombay. Then he was ashamed, for he'd assumed the pilot was a thief. While this demonstration of social awkwardness was unfolding, Madhu and Ganesh each ordered and drank two glasses of tea; Dr. Daruwalla was left to haggle with the chai vendor.

"We'll have to be stopping all the way to Junagadh, so you can pee," Farrokh told the children. Then they waited nearly an hour in Rajkot for their driver to arrive. All the while, the loudspeaker system went on counting up to five and down to one. It was an annoying airport, but Madhu and Ganesh had plenty of time to pee.

Their driver's name was Ramu. He was a roustabout who'd joined the

Great Blue Nile Circus in Maharashtra, and this was his second round trip between Junagadh and Rajkot today. He'd been on time to meet the plane in the morning; when he learned that the flight was delayed, he drove back to the circus in Junagadh—only because he liked to drive. It was nearly a three-hour trip one way, but Ramu proudly told them that he usually covered the distance in under two hours. They soon saw why.

Ramu drove a battered Land Rover, spattered with mud (or the dried blood of unlucky pedestrians and animals). He was a slight young man, perhaps 18 or 20, and he wore a baggy pair of shorts and a begrimed T-shirt. Most notably, Ramu drove barefoot. The padding had worn off the clutch and brake pedals—their smooth metal surfaces looked slippery—and the doubtlessly overused accelerator pedal had been replaced by a piece of wood; it looked as flimsy as a shingle, but Ramu never took his right foot off it. He preferred to operate both the clutch and the brake with his left foot, although the latter pedal received little attention.

Through Rajkot, they roared into the twilight. They passed a water tower, a women's hospital, a bus station, a bank, a fruit market, a statue of Gandhi, a telegraph office, a library, a cemetery, the Havmore Restaurant and the Hotel Intimate. When they raced through the bazaar area, Dr. Daruwalla couldn't look anymore. There were too many children—not to mention the elderly, who weren't as quick to get out of the way as the children; not to mention the bullock carts and the camel wagons, and the cows and donkeys and goats; not to mention the mopeds and the bicycles and the bicycle rickshaws and the three-wheeled rickshaws, and of course there were cars and trucks and buses, too. At the edge of town, off the side of the road, Farrokh was sure that he spotted a dead man—another "nonperson," as Ganesh would say—but at the speed they were traveling, there was no time for Dr. Daruwalla to ask Martin Mills to verify the shape of death with the frozen face that the doctor saw.

Once they were out of town, Ramu drove faster. The roustabout subscribed to the open-road school of driving. There were no rules about passing; in the lane of oncoming traffic, Ramu yielded only to those vehicles that were bigger. In Ramu's mind, the Land Rover was bigger than anything on the road—except for buses and a highly selective category of heavy-duty trucks. Dr. Daruwalla was grateful that Ganesh sat in the passenger seat; both the boy and Madhu had wanted that seat, but the doctor was afraid that Madhu would distract the driver—a high-speed seduction. So the girl sulked in the back with the doctor and the missionary while the elephant boy chatted nonstop with Ramu.

Ganesh had probably expected that the driver would speak only Gujarati; to discover that Ramu was a fellow Maharashtrian who spoke Marathi and Hindi inspired the beggar. Although Farrokh found their conversation difficult to follow, it seemed that Ganesh wanted to list all the possible circus-related activities that a cripple with one good foot might do. For his part, Ramu was discouraging; he preferred to talk about driving while demonstrating his violent technique of upshifting and downshifting (instead of using the brakes), assuring Ganesh that it would be impossible to match his skill as a driver without a functioning right foot.

To Ramu's credit, he didn't look at Ganesh when he talked; thankfully, the driver was transfixed by the developing madness on the road. Soon it would be dark; perhaps then the doctor could relax, for it would be better not to see one's own death approaching. After nightfall, there would be only the sudden nearness of a blaring horn and the blinding, onrushing headlights. Farrokh imagined the entanglement of bodies in the rolling Land Rover; a foot here, a hand there, the back of someone's head, a flailing elbow—and not knowing who was who, or in which direction the ground was, or the black sky (for the headlights would surely be shattered, and in one's hair there would be fragments of glass, as fine as sand). They would smell the gasoline; it would be soaking their clothes. At last, they would see the ball of flame.

"Distract me," Dr. Daruwalla said to Martin Mills. "Start talking. Tell me anything at all." The Jesuit, who'd spent his childhood on the Los Angeles freeways, seemed at ease in the careening Land Rover. The burned-out wrecks off the side of the road were of no interest to him—not even the occasional upside-down car that was still on fire—and the carnage of animals that dotted the highway interested him only when he couldn't identify their remains.

"What was that? Did you see that?" the missionary asked, his head whipping around.

"A dead bullock," answered Dr. Daruwalla. "Please talk to me, Martin."

"I know it was dead," said Martin Mills. "What's a bullock?"

"A castrated bull—a steer," Farrokh replied.

"There's another one!" the scholastic cried, his head turning again.

"No, that was a cow," the doctor said.

"I saw a camel earlier," Martin remarked. "Did you see the camel?"

"Yes, I saw it," Farrokh answered him. "Now tell me a story. It will be dark soon."

"A pity—there's so much to see!" said Martin Mills.

"*Distract* me, for God's sake!" Dr. Daruwalla cried. "I know you like to talk—tell me anything at all!"

"Well . . . what do you want me to tell you about?" the missionary asked. Farrokh wanted to kill him.

The girl had fallen asleep. They'd made her sit between them because they were afraid she'd lean against one of the rear doors; now she could lean only against them. Asleep, Madhu seemed as frail as a rag doll; they had to press against her and hold her shoulders to keep her from flopping around.

Her scented hair brushed against Dr. Daruwalla's throat at the open collar of his shirt; her hair smelled like clove. Then the Land Rover would swerve and Madhu would slump against the Jesuit, who took no notice of her. But Farrokh felt her hip against his. As the Land Rover again pulled out to pass, Madhu's shoulder ground against the doctor's ribs; her hand, which was limp, dragged across his thigh. Sometimes, when Farrokh could feel Madhu breathe, he held his breath. The doctor wasn't looking forward to the awkwardness of spending the night in the same room with her. It was not only from Ramu's reckless driving that Farrokh sought some distraction.

"Tell me about your mother," Dr. Daruwalla said to Martin Mills. "How *is* she?" In the failing but lingering light, the doctor could see the missionary's neck tighten; his eyes narrowed. "And your father—how's Danny doing?" the doctor added, but the damage had already been done. Farrokh could tell that Martin hadn't heard him the second time; the Jesuit was searching the past. The landscape of hideously slain animals flew by, but the zealot no longer noticed.

"All right, if that's what you want. I'm going to tell you a little story about my mother," said Martin Mills. Somehow, Dr. Daruwalla knew that the story wouldn't be "little." The missionary wasn't a minimalist; he favored description. In fact, Martin left out no detail; he told Farrokh absolutely everything he could remember. The exquisiteness of Arif Koma's complexion, the different odors of masturbation—not only Arif's, but also the smell that lingered on the U.C.L.A. babysitter's fingers.

Thus they hurtled through the darkened countryside and the dimly lit towns, where the reek of cooking and excrement assailed them—

together with the squabbling of chickens, the barking of dogs and the savage threats of the shouting, almost-runover pedestrians. Ramu apologized that his driver's-side window was missing; not only did the rushing night air grow cooler, but the back-seat passengers were struck by flying insects. Once, something the size of a hummingbird smacked against Martin's forehead; it must have stung, and for five minutes or more it lay buzzing and whirring on the floor before it died—whatever it was. But the missionary's story was unstoppable; nothing could deter him.

It took him all the way to Junagadh to finish. As they entered the brightly lit town, the streets were teeming; two crowds were surging against each other. A loudspeaker on a parked truck played circus music. One crowd was coming from the early-evening show, the other hurrying to line up for the show that was to start later on.

I should tell the poor bastard everything, Dr. Daruwalla was thinking. That he has a twin, that his mother was always a slut, that Neville Eden was probably his real father. Danny was too dumb to be the father; both John D. and Martin Mills were smart. Neville, although Farrokh had never liked him, had been smart. But Martin's story had struck Farrokh speechless. Moreover, the doctor believed that these revelations should be John D.'s decision. And although Dr. Daruwalla wanted to punish Vera in almost any way that he could, the one thing that Martin had said about Danny contributed further to the doctor's silence: "I love my father—I just wish I didn't pity him."

The rest of the story was all about Vera; Martin hadn't said another word about Danny. The doctor decided that it wasn't a good time for the Jesuit to hear that his probable father was a two-timing, bisexual shit named Neville Eden. This news would not help Martin to pity Danny any less.

Besides, they were almost at the circus. The elephant-footed boy was so excited, he was kneeling on the front seat and waving out the window at the mob. The circus music, which was blaring at them over the loudspeaker, had managed to wake up Madhu.

"Here's your new life," Dr. Daruwalla told the child prostitute. "Wake up and see it."

A Racist Chimpanzee

Although Ramu never stopped blowing the horn, the Land Rover barely crawled through the crowd. Several small boys clung to the door handles and the rear bumper, allowing themselves to be dragged along the road. Everyone stared into the back seat. Madhu was mistaken to be anxious; the crowd wasn't staring at her. It was Martin Mills who drew their attention; they were unused to white men. Junagadh wasn't a tourist town. The missionary's skin was as pale as dough in the glare from the streetlights. Because they were forced to move ahead so slowly, it grew hot in the car, but when Martin rolled his rear window down, people reached inside the Land Rover just to touch him.

Far ahead of them, a dwarf clown on stilts was leading the throng. It was even more congested at the circus because it was too early to let the crowd in; the Land Rover had to inch its way through the well-guarded gate. Once inside the compound, Dr. Daruwalla appreciated a familiar sensation: the circus was a cloister, a protected place; it was as exempt from the mayhem of Junagadh as St. Ignatius stood, like a fort, within the chaos of Bombay. The children would be safe here, provided that they gave the place a chance—provided that the circus gave *them* a chance.

But the first omen was inhospitable: Deepa didn't meet them; the dwarf's wife and son were sick—confined to their tent. And, almost immediately, Dr. Daruwalla could sense how the Great Blue Nile compared unfavorably to the Great Royal. There was no owner of the charm and dignity of Pratap Walawalkar; in fact, the owner of the Great Blue Nile was away. No dinner was waiting for them in the owner's tent, which they never saw. The ringmaster was a Bengali named Das; there was no food in Mr. Das's tent, and the sleeping cots were all in a row, as in a spartan barracks; a minimum of ornamentation was draped on the walls. The dirt floor was completely covered with rugs; bolts of brightly colored fabric, for costumes, were hung high in the apex of the tent, out of everyone's way, and the trappings of a temple were prominently displayed alongside the TV and the VCR.

A cot like all the others was identified as Madhu's; Mr. Das was putting her between two older girls, who (he said) would mind her. Mrs. Das, the ringmaster assured them, would "mind" Madhu, too. As for Mrs. Das, she didn't get off her cot to greet them. She sat sewing sequins on a costume, and only as they were leaving the tent did she speak to Madhu.

"I am meeting you tomorrow," she told the girl.

"What time shall we come in the morning?" Dr. Daruwalla asked, but Mrs. Das—who manifested something of the victimized severity of an unexpectedly divorced aunt—didn't answer him. Her head remained lowered, her eyes on her sewing.

"Don't come too early, because we'll be watching television," Mr. Das told the doctor.

Well, naturally . . . Dr. Daruwalla thought.

Ganesh's cot would be set up in the cook's tent, where Mr. Das escorted them—and where he left them. He said he had to prepare for the 9:30 show. The cook, whose name was Chandra, assumed that Ganesh had been sent to help him; Chandra began to identify his utensils to the cripple, who listened indifferently—Dr. Daruwalla knew that the boy wanted to see the lions.

"Kadhai," a wok. "Jhara," a slotted spoon. "Kisni," a coconut grater. From outside the cook's tent, in the darkness, they also listened to the regular coughs of the lions. The crowd still hadn't been admitted to the main tent but they were present in the darkness, like the lions, as a kind of background murmur.

Dr. Daruwalla didn't notice the mosquitoes until he began to eat. The doctor and the others ate standing up, off stainless-steel plates—curried potatoes and eggplant with too much cumin. Then they were offered a plate of raw vegetables—carrots and radishes, onions and tomatoes— which they washed down with warm orange soda. Good old Gold Spot. Gujarat was a dry state, because Gandhi was born there—the tedious teetotaler. Farrokh reflected that he would probably be awake all night. He'd been counting on beer to keep him away from his screenplay, to help him sleep. Then he remembered that he'd be sharing a room with Madhu; in that case, it would be best to stay awake all night and to *not* have any beer.

Throughout their hasty, unsatisfying meal, Chandra progressed to naming vegetables to Ganesh, as if the cook assumed the boy had lost his language in the same accident that had mangled his foot. ("Aloo," potato. "Chawli," a white pea. "Baingan," eggplant.) As for Madhu, she appeared neglected, and she was shivering. Surely she had a shawl or a sweater in her small bag, but all their bags were still in the Land Rover, which was parked God knew where; Ramu, their driver, was God knew where, too. Besides, it was almost time for the late show.

When they stepped into the avenue of troupe tents, they saw that the performers were already in costume; the elephants were being led down the aisle. In the wing of the main tent, the horses were standing in line. A roustabout had already saddled the first horse. Then a trainer prodded a big chimpanzee with a stick, launching the animal into what appeared to be a vertical leap of at least five feet. The horse had started forward, just a nervous step or two, when the chimpanzee landed on the saddle. There the chimp squatted on all fours; when the trainer touched the saddle with his stick, the chimpanzee performed a front flip on the horse's back—and then another.

The band was already on the platform stage above the arena, which was still filling with the crowd. The visitors would be in the way if they stood in the wing, but Mr. Das, the ringmaster, hadn't appeared; there was no one to show them to their seats. Martin Mills suggested that they find seats for themselves before the tent was full; Dr. Daruwalla resented such informality. While the doctor and the missionary were arguing about what to do, the chimp doing front flips on the horse grew distracted. Martin Mills was the distraction.

The chimpanzee was an old male named Gautam, because even as a baby he'd demonstrated a remarkable similarity to Buddha; he could sit in the same position and stare at the same thing for hours. As he'd aged, Gautam had extended his capacity for meditation to include certain repetitive exercises; the front flips on the horse's back were but one example. Gautam could repeat the move tirelessly; whether the horse was galloping or standing still, the chimpanzee always landed on the saddle. There was, however, a diminished enthusiasm to Gautam's front flips, and to his other activities as well. His trainer, Kunal, attributed Gautam's emotional decline to the big chimp's infatuation with Mira, a young female chimpanzee. Mira was new to the Great Blue Nile, and Gautam could be observed pining for her—often at inappropriate times.

If he saw Mira when he was doing front flips, Gautam would miss not only the saddle but the whole horse. Hence Mira rode a horse far back in the procession of animals that paraded around the main tent during the Grand Entry. It was only when Gautam was warming up in the wing that the old chimpanzee could spot Mira; she was kept near the elephants, because Gautam was afraid of elephants. At some trancelike distance in Gautam's mind, this view of Mira—as the big chimp waited for the curtains to open and the Grand Entry music to begin—satisfied him. He kept doing front flips, mechanically, almost as if the jumps were triggered by a mild electrical shock, at about five-second intervals. In the corner of Gautam's eye, Mira was a faraway presence; nevertheless, she was enough of a presence to soothe him.

Gautam became extremely unhappy if his view of Mira was blocked. Only Kunal was allowed to pass between the chimp and his view of

Mira. Kunal never stood anywhere near Gautam without a stick in his hand. Gautam was big for a chimp; according to Kunal, the ape weighed 145 pounds and was almost five feet tall.

Simply put, Martin Mills was standing in the wrong place at the wrong time. After the attack, Kunal speculated that Gautam might have imagined that the missionary was another male chimpanzee; not only had Martin blocked Gautam's view of Mira, but Gautam might have assumed that the missionary was seeking Mira's affection—for Mira was a very affectionate female, and her friendliness (to male chimpanzees) was something that regularly drove Gautam insane. As for *why* Gautam might have mistaken Martin Mills for an ape, Kunal suggested that the paleness of the scholastic's skin would surely have struck Gautam as unnatural for a human being. If Martin's skin color was a novelty to the people of Junagadh—who, after all, had gawked at him and pawed him over in the passing Land Rover—Martin's skin was only slightly less foreign to Gautam's experience. Since, to Gautam, Martin Mills didn't look like a human being, the ape probably thought that the missionary was a male chimpanzee.

It was with a logic of this kind that Gautam interrupted his front flips on the horse's back. The chimpanzee screamed once and bared his fangs; then he vaulted from the rump of the horse and over the back of another horse, landing on Martin's shoulders and chest and driving the missionary to his back on the ground. There Gautam sunk his teeth into the side of the surprised Jesuit's neck. Martin was fortunate to have protected his throat with his hand, but this meant that his hand was bitten, too. When it was over, there was a deep puncture wound in Martin's neck and a slash wound from the heel of his hand to the ball of his thumb; and a small piece of the missionary's right earlobe was missing. Gautam was too strong to be pulled off the struggling scholastic, but Kunal was able to beat the ape away with his stick. The whole time Mira was shrieking; it was hard to tell if her cries signified requited love or disapproval.

The discussion of whether the chimp attack had been racially motivated or sexually inspired, or both, continued throughout the late-evening show. Martin Mills refused to allow Dr. Daruwalla to attend to his wounds until the performance was concluded; the Jesuit insisted that the children would learn a valuable lesson from his stoicism, which the doctor regarded as a *stupid* stoicism of the show-must-go-on variety. Both Madhu and Ganesh were distracted by the missionary's missing earlobe and the other gory evidence of the savage biting that the zealot had suffered; Madhu hardly watched the circus at all. Farrokh, however, paid close attention. The doctor was content to let the missionary bleed. Dr. Daruwalla didn't want to miss the performance.

A Perfect Ending

The better acts had been borrowed from the Great Royal—in particular, an item called Bicycle Waltz, for which the band played "The Yellow Rose of Texas." A thin, muscular woman of an obvious sinewy strength performed the Skywalk at a fast, mechanical pace. The audience was unfrightened for her; even without a safety net, there was no palpable fear that she could fall. While Suman looked beautiful and vulnerable— as could be expected of a young woman hanging upside down at 80 feet—the skywalker at the Great Blue Nile resembled a middle-aged robot. Her name was Mrs. Bhagwan, and Farrokh recognized her as the knife thrower's assistant; she was also his wife.

In the knife-throwing item, Mrs. Bhagwan was spread-eagled on a wooden wheel; the wheel was painted as a target, with Mrs. Bhagwan's belly covering the bull's-eye. Throughout the act, the wheel revolved faster and faster, and Mr. Bhagwan hurled knives at his wife. When the wheel was stopped, the knives were stuck every which way in the wood; not even the crudest pattern could be discerned, except that there were no knives sticking in Mrs. Bhagwan's spread-eagled body.

Mr. Bhagwan's other specialty was the item called Elephant Passing, which almost every circus in India performs. Mr. Bhagwan lies in the arena, sandwiched between mattresses that are then covered with a plank; an elephant walks this plank, over Mr. Bhagwan's chest. Farrokh observed that this was the only act that *didn't* prompt Ganesh to say he could learn it, although being crippled wouldn't have interfered with the boy's ability to lie under a passing elephant.

Once, when Mr. Bhagwan had been stricken with acute diarrhea, Mrs. Bhagwan had replaced her husband in the Elephant Passing item. But the woman was too thin for Elephant Passing. There was a story that she'd bled internally for days and that, even after she'd recovered, she was never the same again; both her diet and her disposition had been ruined by the elephant.

Of Mrs. Bhagwan, Farrokh understood that her version of the Sky-walk and her passive contribution to the knife-throwing act were one and the same; it was less a skill she had learned, or even a drama to be enacted, than a mechanical submission to her fate. Her husband's errant knife or the fall from 80 feet—they were one and the same. Mrs. Bhagwan *was* a robot, Dr. Daruwalla believed. Possibly the Elephant Passing had done this to her.

Mr. Das confided this feeling to Farrokh. When the ringmaster briefly joined them in the audience—to apologize for Gautam's rude attack, and to add his own ideas to the doctor's and the Jesuit's speculations regarding the ape's racism and/or sexual jealousy—Mr. Das attributed Mrs. Bhagwan's lackluster performance to her elephant episode.

"But in other ways it's better since she's been married," Mr. Das admitted. Before Mrs. Bhagwan's marriage, she'd complained bitterly about her menstrual cycle—how hanging upside down when she was bleeding was unusually uncomfortable. "And before she was married, of course it wasn't proper for her to use a tampon," Mr. Das added.

"No, of course not," said Dr. Daruwalla, who was appalled.

When there were lulls in the acts, which there often were—or when the band was resting between items—they could hear the sounds of the chimp being beaten. Kunal was "disciplining" Gautam, Mr. Das explained. In some of the towns where the Great Blue Nile played, there might be other white males in the audience; they couldn't allow Gautam to think that white males were fair game.

"No, of course not," said Dr. Daruwalla. The big ape's screams and the sounds of Kunal's stick were carried to them in the still night air. When the band played, no matter how badly, the doctor and the missionary and the children were grateful.

If Gautam was rabid, the ape would die; better to beat him, in case he wasn't rabid and he lived—this was Kunal's philosophy. As for treating Martin Mills, Dr. Daruwalla knew it was wise to assume the chimp was rabid. But, for now, the children were laughing.

When one of the lions pissed violently on its stool and then stamped in the puddle, both Madhu and Ganesh laughed. Yet Farrokh felt obliged to remind the elephant boy that washing this same stool might be his first job.

There was a Peacock Dance, of course—two little girls played the peacocks, as always—and the screenwriter thought that his Pinky character should be in a peacock costume when the escaped lion kills her. Farrokh thought it would be best if the lion kills her because the lion thinks she *is* a peacock. More poignant that way ... more sympathy for the lion. Thus would the screenwriter act out his old presentiment— that the restless lions in the holding tunnel were restless because their act was next and the peacock girls were temptingly in sight. When Acid

Man applied his acid to the locked cage, the lion that got loose would be in an agitated, antipeacock mood. Poor Pinky!

There was an encore to the Skywalk item. Mrs. Bhagwan didn't climb all the way to the top of the tent to repeat the Skywalk, which had left the audience largely unimpressed the first time. She climbed to the top of the tent only to repeat her descent on the dental trapeze. It was the dental trapeze that the audience had liked; more specifically, it was Mrs. Bhagwan's *neck* that they had liked. She had an extremely muscular neck, overdeveloped from all her dental-trapezing, and when she descended—twirling, from the top of the tent, with the trapeze clamped tightly in her teeth—her neck muscles bulged, the spotlight turning from green to gold.

"I could do that," Ganesh whispered to Dr. Daruwalla. "I have a strong neck. And strong teeth," he added.

"And I suppose you could hang, and walk, upside down," the doctor replied. "You have to hold both feet rigid, at right angles—your ankles support all your weight." As soon as he spoke, Farrokh realized his error. The cripple's crushed foot was permanently fused at his ankle—a perfect right angle. It would be no problem for him to keep that foot in a rigid right-angle position.

There was an idiotic finale in progress in the ring—chimps and dwarf clowns riding mopeds. The lead chimp was dressed as a Gujarati milkman, which the local crowd loved. The elephant-footed boy was smiling serenely in the semidarkness.

"So it would be only my *good* foot that I would have to make stronger—is this what you are telling me?" the cripple asked.

"What I'm telling you, Ganesh, is that *your* job is with the lion piss and the elephant shit. And maybe, if you're lucky," Farrokh told the boy, "you'll get to work with the food."

Now the ponies and the elephants entered the ring, as in the beginning, and the band played loudly; it was impossible to hear Gautam being beaten. Not once had Madhu said, "I could do that"—not about a single act—but here was the elephant-footed boy, already imagining that he could learn to walk on the sky.

"Up there," Ganesh told Dr. Daruwalla, pointing to the top of the tent, "I wouldn't walk with a limp."

"Don't even think about it," the doctor said.

But the screenwriter couldn't stop thinking about it, for it would be the perfect ending to his movie. After the lion kills Pinky—and justice is done to Acid Man (perhaps acid could accidentally be spilled in the villain's crotch)—Ganesh knows that the circus won't keep him unless he can make a contribution. No one believes he can be a skywalker—Suman won't give the crippled boy lessons, and Pratap won't let him practice on the ladder in the troupe tent. There is nowhere he can learn to skywalk, except in the main tent; if he's going to try it, he must climb up to the real device and do the real thing—at 80 feet, with no net.

What a great scene! the screenwriter thought. The boy slips out of the cook's tent in the predawn light. There's no one in the main tent to see him climb the trapeze rope to the top. "If I fall, death happens," his voice-over says. "If no one sees you die, no one says any prayers for you." Good line! Dr. Daruwalla thought; he wondered if it was true.

The camera is 80 feet below the boy when he hangs upside down from the ladder; he holds the sides of the ladder with both hands as he puts his good foot and then his bad one into the first two loops. There are 18 loops of rope running the length of the ladder; the Skywalk requires 16 steps. "There is a moment when you must let go with your hands," Ganesh's voice-over says. "I do not know whose hands I am in then."

The boy lets go of the ladder with both hands; he hangs by his feet. (The trick is, you have to start swinging your body; it's the momentum you gather, from swinging, that allows you to step forward—one foot at a time, out of the first loop and into the next one, still swinging. Never stop the momentum . . . keep the forward motion constant.) "I think there is a moment when you must decide where you belong," the boy's voice-over says. Now the camera approaches him, from 80 feet away; the camera closes in on his feet. "At that moment, you are in no one's hands," the voice-over says. "At that moment, everyone walks on the sky."

From another angle, we see that the cook has discovered what Ganesh is doing; the cook stands very still, looking up—he's counting. Other performers have come into the tent—Pratap Singh, Suman, the dwarf clowns (one of them still brushing his teeth). They follow the crippled boy with their eyes; they're all counting—they all know how many steps there are in the Skywalk.

"Let other people do the counting," Ganesh's voice-over says. "What I tell myself is, I am just walking—I don't think *skywalking,* I think *just walking.* That's my little secret. Nobody else would be much impressed by the thought of just walking. Nobody else could concentrate very hard on that. But for me the thought of *just walking* is very special. What I tell myself is, I am walking without a limp."

Not bad, Dr. Daruwalla thought. And there should be a scene later, with the boy in full costume—a singlet sewn with blue-green sequins. As he descends on the dental trapeze, spinning in the spotlight, the gleaming sequins throw back the light. Ganesh should never quite touch the ground; instead, he descends into Pratap's waiting arms. Pratap lifts the boy up to the cheering crowd. Then Pratap runs out of the ring with Ganesh in his arms—because after a cripple has walked on the sky, no one should see him limp.

It could work, the screenwriter thought.

After the performance, they managed to find where Ramu had parked the Land Rover, but they couldn't find Ramu. The four of them required two rickshaws for the trip across town to the Government Circuit House; Madhu and Farrokh followed the rickshaw carrying Ganesh and Martin Mills. These were the three-wheeled rickshaws that Dr. Daruwalla hated; old Lowji had once declared that a three-wheeled rickshaw made as much sense as a moped towing a lawn chair. But Madhu and Ganesh were enjoying the ride. As their rickshaw bounced along, Madhu tightly gripped Farrokh's knee with one hand. It was a child's grip—not sexual groping, Dr. Daruwalla assured himself. With her other hand, Madhu waved to Ganesh. Looking at her, the doctor kept thinking: Maybe the girl will be all right—maybe she'll make it.

On the mud flaps of the rickshaw ahead of them, Farrokh saw the face of a movie star; he thought it might be a poor likeness of either Madhuri Dixit or Jaya Prada—in any case, it wasn't Inspector Dhar. In the cheap plastic window of the rickshaw, there was Ganesh's face—the *real* Ganesh, the screenwriter reminded himself. It was such a perfect ending, Farrokh was thinking—all the more remarkable because the *real* cripple had given him the idea.

In the window of the bouncing rickshaw, the boy's dark eyes were shining. The headlight from the following rickshaw kept crossing the cripple's smiling face. Given the distance between the two rickshaws and the fact that it was night, Dr. Daruwalla observed that the boy's eyes looked healthy; you couldn't see the slight discharge or the cloudiness from the tetracycline ointment. From such a partial view, you couldn't tell that Ganesh was crippled; he looked like a happy, normal boy.

How the doctor wished it were true.

The Night of 10,000 Steps

There was nothing to do about the missing piece of Martin's earlobe. Altogether, Dr. Daruwalla used two 10mL vials of the human rabies immune globulin; he injected a half-vial directly into each of the three wound areas—the earlobe, the neck, the hand—and he administered the remaining half-vial by a deep intramuscular injection in Martin's buttocks.

The hand was the worst—a slash wound, which the doctor packed with iodophor gauze. A bite should drain, and heal from the inside, so Dr. Daruwalla wouldn't stitch the wound—nor did the doctor offer anything for the pain. Dr. Daruwalla had observed that the missionary was enjoying his pain. However, the zealot's limited sense of humor didn't permit him to appreciate Dr. Daruwalla's joke—that the Jesuit appeared to suffer from "chimpanzee stigmata." The doctor also couldn't resist pointing out to Martin Mills that, on the evidence of the scholastic's wounds, whatever had bitten Farrokh (and converted him) in Goa was certainly *not* a chimp; such an ape would have consumed the whole toe—maybe half the foot.

"Still angry about your miracle, I see," Martin replied.

On that testy note, the two men said their good-nights. Farrokh didn't envy the Jesuit the task of calming Ganesh down, for the elephant boy was in no mood to sleep; the cripple couldn't wait for his first full day at the circus to begin. Madhu, on the other hand, seemed bored and listless, if not exactly sleepy.

Their rooms at the Government Circuit House were adjacent to each other on the third floor. Off Farrokh and Madhu's bedroom, two glass doors opened onto a small balcony covered with bird droppings. They had their own bathroom with a sink and a toilet, but no door; there was just a rug hung from a curtain rod—it didn't quite touch the floor. The toilet could be flushed only with a bucket, which was conveniently positioned under a faucet that dripped. There was also a shower, of sorts; an open-ended pipe, without a showerhead, poked out of the bathroom wall. There was no curtain for the shower, but there was a sloped floor leading to an open drain, which (upon closer inspection) appeared to be the temporary residence of a rat; Farrokh saw its tail disappearing down the hole. Very close to the drain was a diminished bar of soap, the edges nibbled.

In the bedroom, the two beds were too close together—and doubtless infested. Both mosquito nets were yellowed and stiff, and one was torn. The one window that opened had no screen, and little air was inclined to move through it. Dr. Daruwalla thought they might as well open the glass doors to the balcony, but Madhu said she was afraid that a monkey would come inside.

The ceiling fan had only two speeds: one was so slow that the fan had no effect at all, and the other was so fast that the mosquito nets were blown away from the beds. Even in the main tent at the circus, the night air had felt cool, but the third floor of the Government Circuit House was hot and airless. Madhu solved this problem by using the bathroom first; she wet a towel and wrung it out, and then she lay naked under the towel—on the better bed, the one with the untorn mosquito net. Madhu was small, but so was the towel; it scarcely covered her breasts and left her thighs exposed. A deliberate girl, the doctor thought.

Lying there, she said, "I'm still hungry. There was nothing sweet."

"You want a dessert?" Dr. Daruwalla asked.

"If it's sweet," she said.

The doctor carried the thermos with the rest of the rabies vaccine and the immune globulin down to the lobby; he hoped there was a refrigerator, for the thermos was already tepid. What if Gautam bit someone else tomorrow? Kunal had informed the doctor that the chimpanzee was "almost definitely" rabid. Rabid or not, the chimp shouldn't be beaten; in the doctor's opinion, only a second-rate circus beat its animals.

In the lobby, a Muslim boy was tending the desk, listening to the Qawwali on the radio; he appeared to be eating ice cream to the religious verses—his head nodding while he ate, the spoon conducting the air between the container and his mouth. But it wasn't ice cream, the boy told Dr. Daruwalla; he offered the doctor a spoon and invited him to take a taste. The texture differed from that of ice cream—a cardamom-scented, saffron-colored yogurt, sweetened with sugar. There was a refrigerator full of the stuff, and Farrokh took a container and spoon for Madhu. He left the vaccine and the immune globulin in the refrigerator, after assuring himself that the boy knew better than to eat it.

When the doctor returned to his room, Madhu had discarded the towel. He tried to give her the Gujarati dessert without looking at her; probably on purpose, she made it awkward for him to hand her the spoon and container—he was sure she was pretending that she didn't know where the mosquito net opened. She sat naked in bed, eating the sweetened yogurt and watching him while he arranged his writing materials.

There was an unsteady table, a thick candle affixed by wax to a dirty ashtray, a packet of matches alongside a mosquito coil. When Farrokh had spread out his pages and smoothed his hand over the pad of fresh paper, he lit the candle and the mosquito coil and turned off the overhead light. At high speed, the ceiling fan would have disturbed his work and Madhu's mosquito net, so the doctor kept the fan on low; although this was ineffectual, he hoped that the movement of the blade might make Madhu sleepy.

"What are you doing?" the child prostitute asked him.

"Writing," he told her.

"Read it to me," Madhu asked him.

"You wouldn't understand it," Farrokh replied.

"Are you going to be sleeping?" the girl asked.

"Maybe later," said Dr. Daruwalla.

He tried to block her out of his mind, but this was difficult. She kept watching him; the sound of her spoon in the container of yogurt was as regular as the drone of the fan. Her purposeful nakedness was oppressive, but not because he was actually tempted by her; it was more that the pure evil of having sex with her (the very *idea* of it) was suddenly his obsession. He didn't *want* to have sex with her—he felt only the most passing desire for her—but the sheer obviousness of her availability was numbing to his other senses. It struck him that an evil this pure, something so clearly wrong, wasn't often presented without consequence; the horror was that it seemed there could be no harmful result of sex between them. If he permitted her to seduce him, nothing would come of it—nothing beyond what he would remember and feel guilty for, forever.

The lucky girl was not HIV-positive; besides, he happened to be traveling in India, as usual—with condoms. And Madhu wasn't a girl who would ever tell anyone; she wasn't a talker. In her present situation, she might never have the occasion to tell anyone. It was not only the child's tarnished innocence that convinced him of the purity of this evil, like almost no other evil he'd ever imagined; it was also her strident amorality—whether this had been acquired in the brothel or, hideously, taught to her by Mr. Garg. Whatever one did to her, one wouldn't pay for it—not in this life, or only in the torments of one's soul. These were the darkest thoughts that Dr. Daruwalla had ever had, but he nevertheless thought his way through them; soon he was writing again.

By the movement of his pen (for she'd never stopped watching him), Madhu seemed to sense that she'd lost him. Also, her dessert was gone.

She got out of the bed and walked naked to him; she peered over his shoulder, as if she knew how to read what he was writing. The screenwriter could feel her hair against his cheek and neck.

"Read it to me—just that part," Madhu said. She leaned more firmly against him as she reached and touched the paper with her hand; she touched his last sentence. The cardamom-scented yogurt smelled sickly on her breath, and there was something like the smell of dead flowers—possibly the saffron.

The screenwriter read aloud to her: " 'Two stretcher bearers in white dhotis are running with the body of Acid Man, who is curled in a fetal position on the stretcher—his face glazed in pain, smoke still drifting from the area of his crotch.' "

Madhu made him read it again; then she said, "In *what* position?"

"Fetal," said Dr. Daruwalla. "Like a baby inside its mother."

"Who is Acid Man?" the child prostitute asked him.

"A man who's been scarred by acid—like Mr. Garg," Farrokh told her. At the mention of Garg's name, there wasn't even a flicker of recognition in the girl's face. The doctor refused to look at her naked body, although Madhu still clung to his shoulder; where she pressed against him, he felt himself begin to sweat.

"The smoke is coming from *what* area?" Madhu asked.

"From his crotch," the screenwriter replied.

"Where's that?" the child prostitute asked him.

"You know where that is, Madhu—go back to bed," he told her.

She raised one arm to show him her armpit. "The hair is growing back," she said. "You can feel it."

"I can see that it's growing back—I don't need to feel it," Farrokh replied.

"It's growing back everywhere," Madhu said.

"Go back to bed," the doctor told her.

He could tell from the change in her breathing; he knew the moment when she finally fell asleep. Then he thought it was safe to lie down on the other bed. Although he was exhausted, he'd not yet fallen asleep when he felt the first of the fleas or the bedbugs. They didn't seem to jump like fleas, and they were invisible; probably they were bedbugs. Evidently, Madhu was used to them—she hadn't noticed.

Farrokh decided that he would rather try to sleep among the bird droppings on the balcony; possibly it was cool enough outside so there wouldn't be any mosquitoes. But when the doctor stepped out on his balcony, there on the adjacent balcony was a wide-awake Martin Mills.

"There are a million things in my bed!" the missionary whispered.

"In mine, too," Farrokh replied.

"I don't know how the boy manages to sleep through all the biting and crawling!" the scholastic said.

"There are probably a million fewer things here than he's used to in Bombay," Dr. Daruwalla said.

The night sky was yielding to the dawn; soon the sky would be the same milky-tea color as the ground. Against such gray-brown tones, the white of the missionary's new bandages was startling—his mittened hand, his wrapped neck, his patched ear.

"You're quite a sight," the doctor told him.

"You should see yourself," the missionary replied. "Have you slept at all?"

Since the children were sleeping so soundly—and they'd only recently fallen asleep—the two men decided to take a tour of the town. After all, Mr. Das had warned them not to come to the circus too early, or else they'd interrupt the television watching. It being a Sunday, the doctor presumed that the televisions in all the troupe tents would be tuned to the *Mahabharata;* the popular Hindu epic had been broadcast every Sunday morning for more than a year—altogether, there were 93 episodes, each an hour long, and the great journey to the gates of heaven (where the epic ends) wouldn't be over until the coming summer. It was the world's most successful soap opera, depicting religion as heroic action; it was a legend with countless homilies, not to mention blindness and illegitimate births, battles and women-stealing. A record number of robberies had occurred during the broadcasts because the thieves knew that almost everyone in India would be glued to the TV. The missionary would be consumed with Christian envy, Dr. Daruwalla thought.

In the lobby, the Muslim boy was no longer eating to the Qawwali on the radio; the religious verses had put him to sleep. There was no need to wake him. In the driveway of the Government Circuit House, a half-dozen three-wheeled rickshaws were parked for the night; their drivers, all but one, were asleep in the passenger seats. The one driver who was awake was finishing his prayers when the doctor and the missionary hired his services. Through the sleeping town, they rode in the rickshaw; such peacefulness was improbable in Bombay.

By the Junagadh railroad station, they saw a yellow shack where several early risers were renting bicycles. They passed a coconut plantation. They saw a sign to the zoo, with a leopard on it. They passed a mosque, a hospital, the Hotel Relief, a vegetable market and an old fort; they saw two temples, two water tanks, some mango groves and what Dr. Daruwalla said was a baobab tree—Martin Mills said it wasn't. Their driver took them to a teak forest. This was the start of the climb up Girnar Hill, the driver told them; from this point on, they would have to proceed on foot. It was a 600-meter ascent up 10,000 stone steps; it would take them about two hours, their driver said.

"Why on earth does he think we want to climb ten thousand steps for two hours?" Martin asked Farrokh. But when the doctor explained that the hill was sacred to the Jains, the Jesuit wanted to climb it.

"It's just a bunch of temples!" Dr. Daruwalla cried. The place would probably be crawling with sadhus, practicing yoga. There would be unappetizing refreshment stalls and scavenging monkeys and the repugnant evidence of human feces along the way. (There would be eagles soaring overhead, their rickshaw driver informed them.)

There was no stopping the Jesuit from his holy climb; the doctor wondered if the arduous trek was a substitute for Mass. The climb took them barely an hour and a half, largely because the scholastic walked so fast. There were monkeys nearby, and these doubtless made the missionary walk faster; after his chimp experience, Martin was wary of ape-related animals—even small ones. They saw only one eagle. They passed several sadhus, who were climbing up the holy hill as the doctor and the Jesuit were walking down. It was too early for most of the refreshment stalls to be open; at one stall, they split an orange soda between them. The doctor had to agree that the marble temples near the summit were impressive, especially the largest and the oldest, which was a Jain temple from the 12th century.

By the time they descended, they were both panting, and Dr. Daruwalla remarked that his knees were killing him; no religion was worth 10,000 steps, Farrokh said. The occasional encounters with human feces had depressed him, and during the entire hike he'd worried that their driver would abandon them and they'd be forced to walk back to town. If Farrokh had tipped the driver too much before their climb, there would be no incentive for the driver to stay; if Farrokh had tipped him too little, the driver would be too insulted to wait for them.

"It will be a miracle if our driver hasn't absconded," Farrokh told Martin. But their driver was not only waiting for them; as they came upon him, they saw that the faithful man was cleaning his rickshaw.

"You really should restrict your use of this word 'miracle,'" the missionary said; his neck bandage was beginning to unravel because the hike had made him sweat.

It was time to wake the children and take them to the circus. It vexed Farrokh that Martin Mills had waited until now to say the obvious. The scholastic would say it only once. "Dear God," the Jesuit said, "I hope we're doing the right thing."

23. LEAVING THE CHILDREN

Not Charlton Heston

For weeks after the unusual foursome had departed from the Government Circuit House in Junagadh, the rabies vaccine and the vial of immune globulin, which Dr. Daruwalla had forgotten, remained in the lobby refrigerator. One night, the Muslim boy who regularly ate the saffron-colored yogurt remembered that the unclaimed package was the doctor's medicine; everyone was afraid to touch it, but someone mustered the courage and threw it out. As for the one sock and the lone left-footed sandal, which the elephant boy had intentionally left behind, these were donated to the town hospital, although it was improbable that anyone there could use them. At the circus, Ganesh knew, neither the sock nor the sandal would be of any value to him; they weren't necessary for a cook's helper, or for a skywalker.

The cripple was a barefoot boy when he limped into the ringmaster's troupe tent on Sunday morning; it was still before 10:00, and Mr. and Mrs. Das (and at least a dozen child acrobats) were sitting cross-legged on the rugs, watching the *Mahabharata* on TV. Despite their hike up Girnar Hill, the doctor and the missionary had brought the children to the circus too early. No one greeted them, which made Madhu instantly awkward; she bumped into a bigger girl, who still paid no attention to her. Mrs. Das, without taking her eyes from the television, waved both her arms—a confusing signal. Did she mean for them to go away or should they sit down? The ringmaster cleared up the matter. "Sit— anywhere!" Mr. Das commanded.

Ganesh and Madhu were immediately riveted to the TV; the serious- ness of the *Mahabharata* was obvious to them. Even beggars knew the Sunday-morning routine; they often watched the program through storefront windows. Sometimes people without televisions assembled quietly outside the open windows of those apartments where the TV was on; it didn't matter if they couldn't see the screen—they could still hear the battles and the singing. Child prostitutes, too, the doctor as- sumed, were familiar with the famous show. Only Martin Mills was perplexed by the visible reverence in the troupe tent; the zealot failed to recognize that everyone's attention had been captured by a religious epic.

"Is this a popular musical?" the Jesuit whispered to Dr. Daruwalla.

"It's the *Mahabharata*—be quiet!" Farrokh told him.

"The *Mahabharata* is on television?" the missionary cried. "The whole thing? It must be ten times as long as the Bible!"

"*Ssshhh!*" the doctor replied. Mrs. Das waved both her arms again.

There on the screen was Lord Krishna, "the dark one"—an avatar of Vishnu. The child acrobats gaped in awe; Ganesh and Madhu were transfixed. Mrs. Das rocked back and forth; she was quietly humming. Even the ringmaster hung on Krishna's every word. The sound of weeping was in the background of the scene; apparently Lord Krishna's speech was emotionally stirring.

"Who's that guy?" Martin whispered.

"Lord Krishna," whispered Dr. Daruwalla.

There went both of Mrs. Das's arms again, but the scholastic was too excited to keep quiet. Just before the show was over, the Jesuit whis- pered once more in the doctor's ear; the zealot felt compelled to say that Lord Krishna reminded him of Charlton Heston.

But Sunday morning at the circus was special for more reasons than the *Mahabharata*. It was the only morning in the week when the child acrobats didn't practice their acts, or learn new items, or even do their strength and flexibility exercises. They did do their chores; they would sweep and neaten their bed areas, and they swept and cleaned the tiny kitchen in the troupe tent. If there were sequins missing from their costumes, they would get out the old tea tins that were filled with sequins—one color per tin—and sew new sequins on their singlets.

Mrs. Das wasn't unfriendly as she introduced Madhu to these chores;

nor were the other girls in the troupe tent unwelcoming to Madhu. An older girl went through the costume trunks, pulling out the singlets that she thought might fit the child prostitute. Madhu was interested in the costumes; she was even eager to try them on.

Mrs. Das confided to Dr. Daruwalla that she was happy Madhu wasn't from Kerala. "Kerala girls want too much," said the ringmaster's wife. "They expect good food all the time, and coconut hair oil."

Mr. Das spoke to Dr. Daruwalla in hushed confidentiality; Kerala girls were reputed to be a hot lay, a virtue negated by the fact that these girls would attempt to unionize everyone. The circus was no place for a Communist-party revolt; the ringmaster concurred with his wife—it was a good thing Madhu wasn't a Kerala girl. This was as close as Mr. and Mrs. Das could come to sounding reassuring—by expressing a common prejudice against people from somewhere else.

The child acrobats were not unkind to Ganesh; they simply ignored him. Martin Mills in his bandages was more interesting to them; they'd all heard about the chimp attack—many of them had seen it. The elaborately bandaged wounds excited them, although they were disappointed that Dr. Daruwalla refused to unwrap the ear; they wanted to see what was missing.

"How much? This much?" one of the acrobats asked the missionary.

"Actually," Martin replied, "I didn't see how much was missing."

This conversation deteriorated into speculation about whether or not Gautam had swallowed the piece of earlobe. Dr. Daruwalla observed that none of the child acrobats appeared to notice how the missionary resembled Inspector Dhar, although Hindi films were a part of their world. Their interest was in the missing piece of Martin's earlobe, and whether or not the ape had eaten it.

"Chimps aren't meat eaters," said an older boy. "If Gautam swallowed it, he'd be sick this morning." Some of them, those who'd finished their chores, went to see if Gautam was sick; they insisted that the missionary come with them. Dr. Daruwalla realized that he shouldn't linger; it wouldn't do Madhu any good.

"I'll say good-bye now," the doctor told the child prostitute. "I hope that your new life is happy. Please be careful."

When she put her arms around his neck, Farrokh flinched; he thought she was going to kiss him, but he was mistaken. All she wanted to do was whisper in his ear. "Take me home," Madhu whispered. But what was "home"—what could she mean? the doctor wondered. Before he could ask her, she told him. "I want to be with Acid Man," she whispered. Just that simply, Madhu had adopted Dr. Daruwalla's name for Mr. Garg. All the screenwriter could do was take her arms from his neck and give her a worried look. Then the older girl distracted Madhu with a brightly sequined singlet—the front was red, the back orange—and Farrokh was able to slip away.

Chandra had built a bed for the elephant boy in a wing of the cook's tent; Ganesh would sleep surrounded by sacks of onions and rice—a wall of tea tins was the makeshift headboard for his bed. So that the boy wouldn't be homesick, the cook had given him a Maharashtrian calendar; there was Parvati with her elephant-headed son, Ganesh—Lord Ganesha, "the lord of hosts," the one-tusked deity.

It was hard for Farrokh to say good-bye. He asked the cook's permission to take a walk with the elephant-footed boy. They went to look at the lions and tigers, but it was well before meat-feeding time; the big cats were either asleep or cranky. Then the doctor and the cripple strolled in the avenue of troupe tents. A dwarf clown was washing his hair in a bucket, another was shaving; Farrokh was relieved that none of the clowns had tried to imitate Ganesh's limp, although Vinod had warned the boy that this was sure to happen. They paused at Mr. and Mrs. Bhagwan's tent; in front was a display of the knife thrower's knives— apparently it was knife-sharpening day for Mr. Bhagwan—and in the doorway Mrs. Bhagwan was unbraiding her long black hair, which reached nearly to her waist.

When the skywalker saw the cripple, she called him to her. Dr. Daruwalla followed shyly. Everyone who limps needs extra protection, Mrs. Bhagwan was telling the elephant boy; therefore, she wanted him to have a Shirdi Sai Baba medallion—Sai Baba, she said, was the patron saint of all people who were afraid of falling. "Now he won't be afraid," Mrs. Bhagwan explained to Dr. Daruwalla. She tied the trinket around the boy's neck; it was a very thin piece of silver on a rawhide thong. Watching her, the doctor could only marvel at how, as an unmarried woman, she'd once suffered the Skywalk while bleeding from her period—before it was proper for her to use a tampon. Now she mechanically submitted to the Skywalk, and to her husband's knives.

Although Mrs. Bhagwan wasn't pretty, her hair was shiny and beautiful; yet Ganesh wasn't looking at her hair—he was staring into her tent. Along the roof was the practice model for the Skywalk, the ladderlike device, complete with exactly 18 loops. Not even Mrs. Bhagwan could skywalk without practice. Also hanging from the roof of the troupe tent was a dental trapeze; it was as shiny as Mrs. Bhagwan's hair—the doctor imagined that it might still be wet from her mouth.

Mrs. Bhagwan saw where the boy was looking.

"He's got this foolish idea that he wants to be a skywalker," Farrokh explained.

Mrs. Bhagwan looked sternly at Ganesh. "That *is* a foolish idea," she said to the cripple. She took hold of her gift, the boy's Sai Baba medallion, and tugged it gently in her gnarled hand. Dr. Daruwalla realized that Mrs. Bhagwan's hands were as large and powerful-looking as a man's; the doctor was unpleasantly reminded of his last glimpse of the second Mrs. Dogar's hands—how they'd restlessly plucked at the tablecloth, how they'd looked like paws. "Not even Shirdi Sai Baba can save a skywalker from falling," Mrs. Bhagwan told Ganesh.

"What saves *you*, then?" the boy asked her.

The skywalker showed him her feet; they were bare under the long skirt of her sari, and they were oddly graceful, even delicate, in comparison to her hands. But the tops of her feet and the fronts of her ankles were so roughly chafed that the normal skin was gone; in its place was hardened scar tissue, wrinkled and cracked.

"Feel them," Mrs. Bhagwan told the boy. "You, too," she said to the doctor, who obeyed. He'd never touched the skin of an elephant or a rhino before; he'd only imagined their tough, leathery hides. The doctor couldn't help speculating that there must be an ointment or a lotion that Mrs. Bhagwan could put on her poor feet to help heal the cracks in her hardened skin; then it occurred to him that if the cracks were healed, her skin would be too callused to allow her to feel the loops chafing against her feet. If her cracked skin gave her pain, the pain was also her guide to knowing that her feet were securely in the loops—the right way. Without pain, Mrs. Bhagwan would have to rely on her sense of sight alone; when it came to putting her feet in the loops, two senses (pain *and* sight) were probably better than one.

Ganesh didn't appear to be discouraged by the look and feel of Mrs. Bhagwan's feet. His eyes were healing—they looked clearer every day—and in the cripple's alert face there was that radiance which reflected his unchanged belief in the future. He knew he could master the Skywalk. One foot was ready to begin; it was merely a matter of bringing the other foot along.

Jesus in the Parking Lot

Meanwhile, the missionary had provoked mayhem in the area of the chimp cages. Gautam was infuriated to see him—the bandages being even whiter than the scholastic's skin. On the other hand, the flirtatious Mira reached her long arms through the bars of her cage as if she were beseeching Martin for an embrace. Gautam responded by forcefully urinating in the missionary's direction. Martin believed he should remove himself from the chimpanzees' view rather than stand there and encourage their apery, but Kunal wanted the missionary to stay. It would be a valuable lesson to Gautam, Kunal reasoned: the more violently the ape reacted to the Jesuit's presence, the more Kunal beat the ape. To Martin's mind, the psychology of disciplining Gautam in this fashion seemed flawed; yet the Jesuit obeyed the trainer's instructions.

In Gautam's cage, there was an old tire; the tread was bald and the tire swung from a frayed rope. In his anger, Gautam hurled the tire against the bars of his cage; then he seized the tire and sank his teeth into the rubber. Kunal responded by reaching through the bars and jabbing Gautam with a bamboo pole. Mira rolled onto her back.

When Dr. Daruwalla finally found the missionary, Martin Mills was standing helplessly before this apish drama, looking as guilty and as compromised as a prisoner.

"For God's sake—why are you standing here?" the doctor asked him. "If you just walked away, all this would stop!"

"That's what *I* think," the Jesuit replied. "But the trainer told me to stay."

"Is he *your* trainer or the chimps' trainer?" Farrokh asked Martin.

Thus the missionary's good-byes to Ganesh were conducted with the racist ape's shrieks and howls in the background; it was hard to imagine this as a learning experience for Gautam. The two men followed Ramu to the Land Rover. The last cages they passed were those of the sleepy, disgruntled lions; the tigers looked equally listless and out of humor. The reckless driver ran his fingers along the bars of the big cats' cages; occasionally a paw (claws extended) flicked out, but Ramu confidently withdrew his hand in time.

"One more hour until meat-feeding time," Ramu sang to the lions and tigers. "One whole hour."

It was unfortunate that such a note of mockery, if not an underlying cruelty, described their departure from the Great Blue Nile. Dr. Daruwalla looked only once at the elephant boy's retreating figure. Ganesh was limping back to the cook's tent. In the cripple's unsteady gait, his right heel appeared to bear the weight of two or three boys; like a dewclaw on a dog or a cat, the ball of the boy's right foot (and his toes) never touched the ground. No wonder he wanted to walk on the sky.

As for Farrokh and Martin, their lives were once again in Ramu's hands. Their drive to the airport in Rajkot was in daylight. Both the highway's carnage and the Land Rover's near misses could be clearly seen. Once again, Dr. Daruwalla sought to be distracted from Ramu's driving, but the doctor found himself up front in the passenger seat this time, and there was no seat belt. Martin clung to the back of the front seat, his head over Farrokh's shoulder, which probably blocked whatever view Ramu might have had in the rearview mirror—not that Ramu would even glance at what might be coming up behind him, or that anything could be fast enough to be coming up from behind.

Because Junagadh was the jumping-off point for visits to the Gir Forest, which was the last habitat of the Asian lion, Ramu wanted to know if they'd seen the forest—they hadn't—and Martin Mills wanted to know what Ramu had said. This would be a long trip, the doctor imagined—Ramu speaking Marathi and Hindi, Farrokh struggling to translate. The missionary was sorry that they hadn't seen the Gir lions. Maybe when they returned to visit the children, they could see the forest. By then, the doctor suspected, the Great Blue Nile would be playing in another town. There were a few Asian lions in the town zoo, Ramu told them; they could have a quick look at the lions and still manage to catch their plane in Rajkot. But Farrokh wisely vetoed this idea; he knew that any delay in their departure from Junagadh would make Ramu drive to Rajkot all the faster.

Nor was a discussion of Graham Greene as distracting as Farrokh had hoped. The Jesuit's "Catholic interpretation" of *The Heart of the Matter* wasn't at all what the doctor was looking for; it was infuriating. Not even a novel as profoundly about faith as *The Power and the Glory* could or should be discussed in strictly "Catholic" terms, Dr. Daruwalla argued; the doctor quoted, from memory, that passage which he loved. " 'There is always one moment in childhood when the door opens and lets the future in.'

"Perhaps you'll tell me what is especially Catholic about that," the doctor challenged the scholastic, but Martin skillfully changed the subject.

"Let us pray that this door opens and lets the future in for our children at the circus," the Jesuit said. What a sneaky mind he had!

Farrokh didn't dare ask him anything more about his mother; not even Ramu's driving was as daunting as the possibility of another story about Vera. What Farrokh desired to hear was more about the homosexual inclinations of Dhar's twin; the doctor was chiefly curious to learn whether or not John D. was so inclined, but Dr. Daruwalla felt uncertain of how to inspire such a subject of conversation with John D.'s twin. However, it would be an easier subject to broach with Martin than with John D.

"You say you were in love with a man, and that your feelings for him finally *lessened*," the doctor began.

"That's correct," the scholastic said stiffly.

"But can you point to any moment or to any single episode that marked the end of your infatuation?" Farrokh asked. "Did anything happen—was there an incident that convinced you? What made you decide you could resist such an attraction and become a priest?" This was beating around the bush, Dr. Daruwalla knew, but the doctor had to begin somewhere.

"I saw how Christ existed for me. I saw that Jesus had never abandoned me," the zealot said.

"Do you mean you had a *vision?*" Farrokh asked.

"In a way," the Jesuit said mysteriously. "I was at a low point in my relationship with Jesus. And I'd reached a very cynical decision. There is no lack of resistance that is as great a giving-up as fatalism—I'm ashamed to say I was totally fatalistic."

"Did you actually see Christ or didn't you?" the doctor asked him.

"Actually, it was only a *statue* of Christ," the missionary admitted.

"You mean it was real?" Farrokh asked.

"Of course it was real—it was at the end of a parking lot, at the school where I taught. I used to see it every day—twice a day, in fact," Martin said. "It was just a white stone statue of Christ in a typical pose." And there, in the back seat of the speeding Land Rover, the zealot rotated both his palms toward heaven, apparently to demonstrate the pose of the supplicant.

"It sounds truly tasteless—Christ in a parking lot!" Dr. Daruwalla remarked.

"It wasn't very artistic," the Jesuit replied. "Occasionally, as I recall, the statue was vandalized."

"I can't imagine why," Farrokh muttered.

"Well, anyway, I had stayed at the school quite late one night—I was directing a school play, another musical . . . I can't remember which one. And this man who'd been such an obsession for me . . . he was also staying late. But his car wouldn't start—he had an awful car—and he asked me for a ride home."

"Uh-oh," said Dr. Daruwalla.

"My feelings for him had already lessened, as I've said, but I was still not immune to his attractiveness," the missionary admitted. "Here was such a sudden opportunity—the *availability* of him was painfully apparent. Do you know what I mean?"

Dr. Daruwalla, who was remembering his disturbing night with Madhu, said, "Yes—of course I know. What happened?"

"This is what I mean by how cynical I was," the scholastic said. "I was so totally fatalistic, I decided that if he made the slightest advance toward me, I would respond. I wouldn't initiate such an advance, but I knew I would respond."

"And did you? Did *he?*" the doctor asked.

"Then I couldn't find my car—it was a huge parking lot," Martin said. "But I remembered that I always tried to park near Christ . . ."

"The statue, you mean . . ." Farrokh interrupted.

"Yes, the statue, of course—I had parked right in front of it," the Jesuit explained. "When I finally found my car, it was so dark I couldn't see the statue, not even when I was sitting inside my car. But I knew exactly where Christ was. It was a funny moment. I was waiting for this man to touch me, but all the while I was looking into the darkness at that exact spot where Jesus was."

"Did the guy touch you?" Farrokh asked.

"I turned on the headlights before he had a chance," Martin Mills replied. "And there was Christ—he stood out very brightly in the headlights. He was exactly where I knew he would be."

"Where *else* would a statue be?" Dr. Daruwalla cried. "Do statues move around in your country?"

"You belittle the experience to focus on the statue," the Jesuit said. "The statue was just the vehicle. What I felt was the presence of God. I felt a oneness with Jesus, too—not with the statue. I felt I'd been shown what believing in Christ was like—for me. Even in the darkness—even as I sat expecting something horrible to happen to me—there was a certainty that he was there. Christ was there for me; he'd not abandoned me. I could still see him."

"I guess I'm not making the necessary leap," said Dr. Daruwalla. "I mean, your belief in Christ is one thing. But wanting to be a priest . . . how did you get from Jesus in the parking lot to wanting to be a priest?"

"Well, that's different," Martin confessed.

"That's the part I don't get," Farrokh replied. Then he said it: "And was that the end of all such desires? I mean, was your homosexuality ever again engaged . . . so to speak . . ."

"Homosexuality?" said the Jesuit. "That's not the point. I'm not a homosexual, nor am I a heterosexual. I am simply not a sexual entity— not anymore."

"Come on," the doctor said. "If you *were* to be sexually attracted, it would be a homosexual attraction, wouldn't it?"

"That's not a relevant question," the scholastic replied. "It isn't that I'm without sexual feelings, but I have resisted sexual attraction. I will have no problem continuing to resist it."

"But what you're resisting is a *homosexual* inclination, isn't it?" Farrokh asked. "I mean, let us speculate—you can speculate, can't you?"

"I don't speculate on the subject of my vows," the Jesuit said.

"But, please indulge me, if something happened—if for *any* reason you decided *not* to be a priest—then wouldn't you be a homosexual?" Dr. Daruwalla asked.

"Mercy! You are the most stubborn person!" Martin Mills cried out good-naturedly.

"*I* am stubborn?" the doctor shouted.

"I am neither a homosexual nor a heterosexual," the Jesuit calmly stated. "The terms don't necessarily apply to *inclinations,* or do they? I had a passing inclination."

"It has passed? Completely? Is that what you're saying?" Dr. Daruwalla asked.

"Mercy," Martin repeated.

"You become a person of no identifiable sexuality on the basis of an encounter with a statue in a parking lot; yet you deny the possibility that I was bitten by a ghost!" Dr. Daruwalla cried. "Am I following your reasoning correctly?"

"I don't believe in ghosts, per se," the Jesuit replied.

"But you believe you experienced a oneness with Jesus. You felt the presence of God—in a parking lot!" Farrokh shouted.

"I believe that our conversation—that is, if you continue to raise your voice—is a distraction to our driver," said Martin Mills. "Perhaps we should resume discussion of this subject after we've safely arrived at the airport."

They were still nearly an hour from Rajkot, with Ramu dodging death every few miles; then there would be the wait at the airport, not to mention a likely delay, and finally the flight itself. On a Sunday afternoon or evening, the taxi from Santa Cruz into Bombay could take another 45 minutes or an hour. Worse, it was a special Sunday; it was December 31, 1989, but neither the doctor nor the missionary knew it was New Year's Eve—or if they knew, they'd forgotten.

At St. Ignatius, the jubilee celebration was planned for New Year's Day, which Martin Mills had also forgotten, and the New Year's Eve party at the Duckworth Sports Club was a black-tie occasion of uncharacteristic merriment; there would be dancing to a live band and a splendid midnight supper—not to mention the unusual, once-a-year quality of the champagne. No Duckworthian in Bombay would willingly miss the New Year's Eve party.

John D. and Deputy Commissioner Patel were sure that Rahul would be there—Mr. Sethna had already informed them. They'd spent much of the day rehearsing what Inspector Dhar would say when he and the second Mrs. Dogar danced. Julia had pressed Farrokh's tuxedo, which needed a lengthy airing on the balcony to rid it of its mothball aroma. But both New Year's Eve and the Duckworth Club were far from Farrokh's mind. The doctor was focused on what remained of his journey to Rajkot, after which he still had to travel to Bombay. If Farrokh couldn't endure another minute of Martin's arguments, he had to initiate a different conversation.

"Perhaps we should change the subject," Dr. Daruwalla suggested. "And keep our voices down."

"As you wish. I promise to keep *mine* down," the missionary said with satisfaction.

Farrokh was at a loss to know what to talk about. He tried to think of a long personal story, something which would allow him to talk and talk, and which would render the missionary speechless—powerless to interrupt. The doctor could begin, "I know your twin"; that would lead to quite a long personal story. *That* would shut Martin Mills up! But, as before, Farrokh felt it wasn't his place to tell this story; that was John D.'s decision.

"Well, *I* can think of something to say," the scholastic said; he'd been politely waiting for Dr. Daruwalla to begin, but he hadn't waited long.

"Very well—go ahead," the doctor replied.

"I think that you shouldn't go witch-hunting for homosexuals," the Jesuit began. "Not *these* days. Not when there is understandable sensitivity toward anything remotely homophobic. What do you have against homosexuals, anyway?"

"I have *nothing* against homosexuals. I'm *not* homophobic," Dr. Daruwalla snapped. "And you haven't exactly changed the subject!"

"You're not exactly keeping your voice down," Martin said.

Little India

At the airport in Rajkot, the loudspeaker system had progressed to a new test; more advanced counting skills were being demonstrated. "Eleven, twenty-two, thirty-three, forty-four, fifty-five," said the tireless voice. There was no telling where this would lead; it hinted at infinity. The voice was without emotion; the counting was so mechanical that Dr. Daruwalla thought he might go mad. Instead of listening to the numbers or enduring the Jesuitical provocations of Martin Mills, Farrokh chose to tell a story. Although it was a true story—and, as the doctor would soon discover, painful to tell—it suffered from the disadvantage that the storyteller had never told it before; even true stories are improved by revision. But the doctor hoped that his tale would illustrate how the missionary's allegations of homophobia were false, for Dr. Daruwalla's favorite colleague in Toronto was a homosexual. Gordon Macfarlane was also Farrokh's best friend.

Unfortunately, the screenwriter began the story in the wrong place. Dr. Daruwalla should have started with his earliest acquaintance of Dr. Macfarlane, including how the two had concurred on the misuse of the word "gay"; that they'd generally agreed with the findings of Mac's boyfriend, the gay geneticist—regarding the biology of homosexuality—was also interesting. Had Dr. Daruwalla started with a discussion of this subject, he might not have prejudiced Martin Mills against him. But, at the airport in Rajkot, he'd made the mistake of inserting Dr. Macfarlane in the form of a flashback—as if Mac were only a minor character and not a friend who was often foremost on Farrokh's mind.

He'd begun with the wrong story, about the time he'd been abducted by a crazed cab driver, for Farrokh's training as a writer of action films had preconditioned him to begin any story with the most violent action he could imagine (or, in this case, remember). But to begin with an episode of racial abuse was misleading to the missionary, who concluded that Farrokh's friendship with Gordon Macfarlane was secondary to the doctor's outrage at his own mistreatment as an Indian in Toronto. This was inept storytelling, for Farrokh had meant only to convey how his mistreatment as an obvious immigrant of color in Canada had further solidified his friendship with a homosexual, who was no stranger to discrimination of another kind.

It was a Friday in the spring; many of Farrokh's colleagues left their offices early on Friday afternoons because they were cottagers, but the Daruwallas enjoyed their weekends in Toronto—their second home was in Bombay. Farrokh had had a cancellation; hence he was free to leave early—otherwise, he would have asked Macfarlane for a ride home or called a cab. Mac also spent his weekends in Toronto and kept late office hours on Friday.

Since it wasn't yet rush hour, Farrokh thought he'd walk for a while and then hail a taxi from the street, probably in front of the museum. For some years he'd avoided the subway; an uncomfortable racial incident had happened there. Oh, there'd been shouts from the occasional passing car—no one had ever called him a Parsi; in Toronto, few people knew what a Parsi was. What they called out was "Paki bastard!" or "Wog!" or "Babu!" or "Go home!" His pale-brown coloring and jet-black hair made it difficult for them; he wasn't as identifiable as many Indians. Sometimes they called him an Arab—twice he'd been called a Jew. It was his Persian ancestry; he could pass for a Middle Easterner. But whoever the shouters were, they knew he was foreign—racially different.

Once he'd even been called a Wop! At the time, he'd wondered what sort of idiot could mistake him for an Italian. Now he knew that it wasn't *what* he was that bothered the shouters; it was only that he wasn't one of them. But most often the theme of the slurs subscribed to that view of him which can only clumsily be expressed as "an immigrant of color." In Canada, it seemed, the prejudice against the *immigrant* composition of his features was as strong as whatever prejudice existed of the *of-color* kind.

He stopped taking the subway after an episode with three teenage boys. At first, they hadn't seemed so threatening—more mischievous. There was a hint of menace only because they sat so deliberately close to him; there were many other places for them to sit. One sat on either side of him, the third across the aisle. The boy to the doctor's left nudged his arm. "We've got a bet going," the boy said. "What *are* you?"

Dr. Daruwalla realized later that the only reason he'd found them unthreatening was that they wore their school blazers and ties. After the incident, he could have called their school; he never did.

"I said what *are* you?" the boy repeated. That was the first moment Farrokh felt threatened.

"I'm a doctor," Dr. Daruwalla replied.

The boys on either side of him looked decidedly hostile; it was the boy across the aisle who saved him. "My dad's a doctor," the boy stupidly remarked.

"Are you going to be a doctor, too?" Farrokh asked him.

The other two got up; they pulled the third boy along with them.

"Fuck you," the first boy said to Farrokh, but the doctor knew this was a harmless bomb—already defused.

He never took the subway again. But after his worst episode, the subway incident seemed mild. After his worst episode, Farrokh was so upset, he couldn't remember whether the taxi driver had pulled over before or after the intersection of University and Gerrard; either way, he'd just left the hospital and he was daydreaming. What was odd, he remembered, was that the driver already had a passenger, and that the passenger was riding in the front seat. The driver said, "Don't mind him. He's just a friend with nothing to do."

"I'm not a fare," the driver's friend said.

Later, Farrokh remembered only that it wasn't one of Metro's taxis or one of Beck's—the two companies he most often called. It was probably what they call a gypsy cab.

"I said where are you going?" the driver asked Dr. Daruwalla.

"Home," Farrokh replied. (It struck him as pointless to add that he'd intended to walk for a while. Here was a taxi. Why not take it?)

"Where's 'home'?" the friend in the front seat asked.

"Russell Hill Road, north of St. Clair—just north of Lonsdale," the doctor answered; he'd stopped walking—the taxi had stopped, too. "Actually, I was going to stop at the beer store—and then go home," Farrokh added.

"Get in, if you want," the driver said.

Dr. Daruwalla didn't feel anxious until he was settled in the back seat and the taxi began to move. The friend in the front seat belched once, sharply, and the driver laughed. The windshield visor in front of the driver's friend was pushed flat against the windshield, and the glove-compartment door was missing. Farrokh couldn't remember if these were the places where the driver's certification was posted—or was it usually on the Plexiglas divider between the front and back seats? (The

Plexiglas divider itself was unusual; in Toronto, most taxis didn't have these dividers.) Anyway, there was no visible driver's certification inside the cab, and the taxi was already moving too fast for Dr. Daruwalla to get out—maybe at a red light, the doctor thought. But there were no red lights for a while and the taxi ran the first red light it came to; that was when the driver's friend in the front seat turned around and faced Farrokh.

"So where's your *real* home?" the friend asked.

"Russell Hill Road," Dr. Daruwalla repeated.

"Before that, asshole," the driver said.

"I was born in Bombay, but I left India when I was a teenager. I'm a Canadian citizen," Farrokh said.

"Didn't I tell you?" the driver said to his friend.

"Let's take him home," the friend said.

The driver glanced in the rearview mirror and made a sudden U-turn. Farrokh was thrown against the door.

"We'll show you where your home is, babu," the driver said.

At no time could Dr. Daruwalla have escaped. When they crawled slowly ahead in the traffic, or when they were stopped at a red light, the doctor was too afraid to attempt it. They were moving fairly fast when the driver slammed on the brakes. The doctor's head bounced off the Plexiglas shield. Dr. Daruwalla was pressed back into the seat when the driver accelerated. Farrokh felt the tightness of the instant swelling; by the time he gently touched his puffy eyebrow, blood was already running into his eye. Four stitches, maybe six, the doctor's fingers told him.

The area of Little India is not extensive; it stretches along Gerrard from Coxwell to Hiawatha—some would say as far as Woodfield. Everyone would agree that by the time you get to Greenwood, Little India is over; and even in Little India, the Chinese community is interspersed. The taxi stopped in front of the Ahmad Grocers on Gerrard, at Coxwell; it was probably no coincidence that the grocer was diagonally across the street from the offices of the Canadian Ethnic Immigration Services— this was where the driver's friend dragged Farrokh out of the back seat. "You're home now—better stay here," the friend told Dr. Daruwalla.

"Better yet, babu—go back to Bombay," the driver added.

As the taxi pulled away, the doctor could see it clearly out of only one eye; he was so relieved to be free of the thugs that he paid scant attention to the identifying marks of the car. It was red—maybe red and white. If Farrokh saw any printed names or numbers, he wouldn't remember them.

Little India appeared to be mostly closed on Friday. Apparently, no one had seen the doctor roughly pulled out of the taxi; no one approached him, although he was dazed and bleeding—clearly disoriented. A small, pot-bellied man in a dark suit—his white shirt was ruined from the blood that flowed from his split eyebrow—he clutched his doctor's bag in one hand. He began to walk. On the sidewalk, dancing in the spring air, kaftans were hanging on a clothes rack. Later, Farrokh struggled to remember the names of the places. Pindi Embroidery? Nirma Fashions? There was another grocery with fresh fruits and vegetables—maybe the Singh Farm? At the United Church, there was a sign saying that the church also served as the Shri Ram Hindu Temple on Sunday evenings. At the corner of Craven and Gerrard, a restaurant claimed to be "Indian Cuisine Specialists." There was also the familiar advertisement for Kingfisher lager—INSTILLED WITH INNER STRENGTH. A poster, promising an ASIA SUPERSTARS NITE, displayed the usual faces: Dimple Kapadia, Sunny Deol, Jaya Prada—with music by Bappi Lahiri.

Dr. Daruwalla never came to Little India. In the storefront windows, the mannequins in their saris seemed to rebuke him. Farrokh saw few Indians in Toronto; he had no close Indian friends there. Parsi parents would bring him their sick children—on the evidence of his name in the telephone directory, Dr. Daruwalla supposed. Among the mannequins, a blonde in her sari struck Farrokh as sharing his own disorientation.

At Raja Jewellers, someone was staring out the window at him, probably noticing that the doctor was bleeding. There was a South Indian "Pure Vegetarian Restaurant" near Ashdale and Gerrard. At the Chaat Hut, they advertised "all kinds of kulfi, faluda and paan." At the Bombay Bhel, the sign said FOR TRUE AUTHENTIC GOL GUPPA . . . ALOO TIKKI . . . ETC. They served Thunderbolt beer, SUPER STRONG LAGER . . . THE SPIRIT OF EXCITEMENT. More saris were in a window at Hiawatha and Gerrard. And at the Shree Groceries, a pile of ginger root overflowed the store, extending onto the sidewalk. The doctor gazed at the India Theater . . . at the Silk Den.

At J. S. Addison Plumbing, at the corner of Woodfield and Gerrard, Farrokh saw a fabulous copper bathtub with ornate faucets; the handles were tiger heads, the tigers roaring—it was like the tub he'd bathed in as a boy on old Ridge Road, Malabar Hill. Dr. Daruwalla began to cry. Staring at the display of copper sinks and drains and other bathroom Victoriana, he was suddenly aware of a man's concerned face staring back at him. The man came out on the sidewalk.

"You've been hurt—may I help you?" the man asked; he wasn't an Indian.

"I'm a doctor," said Dr. Daruwalla. "Please just call me a taxi—I know where to go." He had the taxi take him back to the Hospital for Sick Children.

"You sure you want Sick Kids, mon?" the driver asked; he was a West Indian, a black man—very black. "You don't look like a sick kid to me."

"I'm a doctor," Farrokh said. "I work there."

"Who done that to you, mon?" the driver asked.

"Two guys who don't like people like me—or like you," the doctor told him.

"I know them—they everywhere, mon," the driver said.

Dr. Daruwalla was relieved that his secretary and his nurse had gone home. He kept a change of clothes in his office; after he was stitched up, he would throw the shirt away . . . he'd ask his secretary to have the suit dry-cleaned.

He examined the split wound on his eyebrow; using the mirror, he shaved around the gash. This was easy, but he was used to shaving in a mirror; then he contemplated the procaine injection and the sutures— to do these properly in the mirror was baffling to him, especially the sewing. Farrokh called Dr. Macfarlane's office and asked the secretary to have Mac stop by when he was ready to go home.

Farrokh first tried to tell Macfarlane that he'd hit his head in a taxi because of a reckless driver, the brakes throwing him forward into the Plexiglas divider. Although it was the truth, or only a lie of omission, his voice trailed off; his fear, the insult, his anger—these things were still reflected in his eyes.

"Who did this to you, Farrokh?" Mac asked.

Dr. Daruwalla told Dr. Macfarlane the whole story—beginning with the three teenagers on the subway and including the shouts from the passing cars. By the time Mac had stitched him up—it required five sutures to close the wound—Farrokh had used the expression "an immigrant of color" more times than he'd ever uttered it aloud before, even to Julia. He would never tell Julia about Little India, either; that Mac knew was comfort enough.

Dr. Macfarlane had his own stories. He'd never been beaten up, but he'd been threatened and intimidated. There were phone calls late at night; he'd changed his number three times. There were also phone calls to his office; two of his former secretaries had resigned, and one of his former nurses. Sometimes letters or notes were shoved under his office

door; perhaps these were from the parents of former patients, or from
his fellow doctors, or from other people who worked at Sick Kids.

Mac helped Farrokh rehearse how he would describe his "accident"
to Julia. It sounded more plausible if it wasn't the taxi driver's fault.
They decided that an idiot woman had pulled out from the curb without
looking; the driver had had no choice but to hit the brakes. (A blameless
woman driver had been blamed again.) As soon as he realized he was cut
and bleeding, Farrokh had asked the driver to take him back to the
hospital; fortunately, Macfarlane was still there and had stitched him up.
Just five sutures. His white shirt was a total loss, and he wouldn't know
about the suit until it came back from the cleaner's.

"Why not just tell Julia what happened?" Mac asked.

"She'll be disappointed in me—because I didn't do anything," Farrokh told him.

"I doubt that," Macfarlane said.

"*I'm* disappointed that I didn't do anything," Dr. Daruwalla admitted.

"That can't be helped," Mac said.

On the way home to Russell Hill Road, Farrokh asked Mac about his
work at the AIDS hospice—there was a good one in Toronto.

"I'm just a volunteer," Macfarlane explained.

"But you're a *doctor*," Dr. Daruwalla said. "I mean, it must be interesting there. But exactly what can an orthopedist do?"

"Nothing," Mac said. "I'm not a doctor there."

"But of course you're a doctor—you're a doctor anywhere!" Farrokh
cried. "There must be patients with bed sores. We know what to do with
bed sores. And what about pain control?" Dr. Daruwalla was thinking of
morphine, a wonderful drug; it disconnects the lungs from the brain.
Wouldn't many of the deaths in an AIDS hospice be respiratory deaths?
Wouldn't morphine be especially useful there? The respiratory distress
is unchanged, but the patient is unaware of it. "And what about muscular
wasting, from being bedridden?" Farrokh added. "Surely you could
instruct families in passive range-of-motion exercises, or dispense tennis
balls for the patients to squeeze . . ."

Dr. Macfarlane laughed. "The hospice has its own doctors. They're
AIDS doctors," Macfarlane said. "I'm absolutely not a doctor there.
That's something I like about it—I'm just a volunteer."

"What about the catheters?" Farrokh asked. "They must get blocked,
the skin tunnels get inflamed . . ." His voice fell away; he was wondering
if you could unplug them by flushing them with an anticoagulant, but
Macfarlane wouldn't let him finish the thought.

"I don't do anything medical there," Mac told him.

"Then what *do* you do?" Dr. Daruwalla asked.

"One night I did all the laundry," Macfarlane replied. "Another night I answered the phone."

"But anyone could do that!" Farrokh cried.

"Yes—any volunteer," Mac agreed.

"Listen. There's a seizure, a patient seizes from uncontrolled infection," Dr. Daruwalla began. "What do you do? Do you give intravenous Valium?"

"I call the doctor," Dr. Macfarlane said.

"You're kidding me!" said Dr. Daruwalla. "And what about the feeding tubes? They slip out. Then what? Do you have your own X ray facilities or do you have to take them to a hospital?"

"I call the doctor," Macfarlane repeated. "It's a hospice—they're not there to get well. One night I read aloud to someone who couldn't sleep. Lately, I've been writing letters for a man who wants to contact his family and his friends—he wants to say good-bye, but he never learned how to write."

"Incredible!" Dr. Daruwalla said.

"They come there to die, Farrokh. We try to help them control it. We can't help them like we're used to helping most of our patients," Macfarlane explained.

"So you just go there, you show up," Farrokh began. "You check in . . . tell someone you've arrived. Then what?"

"Usually a nurse tells me what to do," Mac said.

"A nurse tells the doctor what to do!" cried Dr. Daruwalla.

"Now you're getting it," Dr. Macfarlane told him.

There was his home on Russell Hill Road. It was a long way from Bombay; it was a long way from Little India, too.

"Honestly, if you want to know what *I* think," said Martin Mills, who'd interrupted Farrokh's story only a half-dozen times, "*I* think you must drive your poor friend Macfarlane crazy. Obviously, you like him, but on whose terms? On *your* terms—on your heterosexual doctor terms."

"But that's what I *am!*" Dr. Daruwalla shouted. "I'm a heterosexual doctor!" Several people in the Rajkot airport looked mildly surprised.

"Three thousand, eight hundred and ninety-four," the voice on the loudspeaker said.

"The point is, could you empathize with a *raving* gay man?" the missionary asked. "*Not* a doctor, and someone not even in the least sympathetic to *your* problems—someone who could care less about racism, or what happens to immigrants of color, as you say? You think you're not homophobic, but how much could you care about someone like that?"

"Why *should* I care about someone like that?" Farrokh screamed.

"That's my point about you. Do you see what I mean?" the missionary asked. "You're a typical homophobe."

"Three thousand, nine hundred and forty-nine," the voice on the loudspeaker droned.

"You can't even listen to a story," Dr. Daruwalla told the Jesuit.

"Mercy!" said Martin Mills.

They were delayed in boarding the plane because the authorities again confiscated the scholastic's dangerous Swiss Army knife.

"Couldn't you have remembered to pack the damn knife in your bag?" Dr. Daruwalla asked the scholastic.

"Given the mood you're in, I'd be foolish to answer questions of that kind," Martin replied. When they were finally on board the aircraft, Martin said, "Look. We're both worried about the children—I know that. But we've done the best we can for them."

"Short of adopting them," Dr. Daruwalla remarked.

"Well, we weren't in a position to do that, were we?" the Jesuit asked. "My point is, we've put them in a position where at least they can help themselves."

"Don't make me throw up," Farrokh said.

"They're safer in the circus than where they were," the zealot insisted. "In how many weeks or months would the boy have been blind? How long would it have taken the girl to contract some horrible disease—even the worst? Not to mention what she would have endured before that. Of *course* you're worried. So am I. But there's nothing more we can do."

"Is this fatalism I hear?" Farrokh asked.

"Mercy, no!" the missionary replied. "Those children are in God's hands—that's what I mean."

"I guess that's why I'm worried," Dr. Daruwalla replied.

"You weren't bitten by a monkey!" Martin Mills shouted.

"I *told* you I wasn't," Farrokh said.

"You must have been bitten by a snake—a *poisonous* snake," the missionary said. "Or else the Devil himself bit you."

After almost two hours of silence—their plane had landed and Vinod's taxi was navigating the Sunday traffic from Santa Cruz to

Bombay—Martin Mills thought of something to add. "Furthermore," the Jesuit said, "I get the feeling you're keeping something from me. It's as if you're always stopping yourself—you're always biting your tongue."

I'm not telling you *half*! the doctor almost hollered. But Farrokh bit his tongue again. In the slanting light of the late afternoon, the lurid movie posters displayed the confident image of Martin Mills's twin. Many of the posters for *Inspector Dhar and the Towers of Silence* were already defaced; yet through the tatters and the muck flung from the street, Dhar's sneer seemed to be assessing them.

In reality, John D. had been rehearsing a different role, for the seduction of the second Mrs. Dogar was out of Inspector Dhar's genre. Rahul wasn't the usual cinema bimbo. If Dr. Daruwalla had known who'd bitten him in his hammock at the Hotel Bardez, the doctor would have agreed with Martin Mills, for Farrokh truly had been bitten by the Devil himself . . . by the Devil *herself*, the second Mrs. Dogar would prefer.

As the dwarf's taxi came into Bombay, it was momentarily stalled near an Iranian restaurant—of a kind not quite in a class with Lucky New Moon or Light of Asia, Dr. Daruwalla was thinking. The doctor was hungry. Towering over the restaurant was a nearly destroyed Inspector Dhar poster; the movie star was ripped open from his cheek to his waist, but his sneer was undamaged. Beside the mutilated Dhar was a poster of Lord Ganesha; the elephant-headed deity might have been advertising an upcoming religious festival, but the traffic began to move before Farrokh could translate the announcement.

The god was short and fat, but surpassingly beautiful to his believers; Lord Ganesha's elephant face was as red as a China rose and he sported the lotus smile of a perpetual daydreamer. His four human arms swarmed with bees—doubtless attracted by the perfume of the ichor flowing in his godly veins—and his three all-seeing eyes looked down upon Bombay with a benevolence that challenged Dhar's sneer. Lord Ganesha's pot belly hung almost to his human feet; his toenails were as long and brightly painted as a woman's. In the sharply angled light, his one unbroken tusk gleamed.

"That elephant is everywhere!" exclaimed the Jesuit. "What happened to its other tusk?"

The myth that Farrokh had loved best as a child was that Lord Ganesha broke off his own tusk and threw it at the moon; the moon had mocked the elephant-headed god for his portliness and for being clumsy. Old Lowji had liked this story; he'd told it to Farrokh and

Jamshed when they were small boys. Only now did Dr. Daruwalla wonder if this was a real myth, or if it was only Lowji's myth; the old man wasn't above making up a myth of his own.

There were other myths; there was more than one story about Ganesh's birth, too. In a South Indian version, Parvati saw the sacred syllable "Om," and her mere glance transformed it into two coupling elephants, who gave birth to Lord Ganesha and then resumed the form of the sacred syllable. But in a darker version, which attests to the reputed sexual antagonism between Parvati and her husband, Lord Shiva, a considerable jealousy attended Shiva's feelings for Parvati's son, who—not unlike the baby Jesus—was never described as being born from Parvati in the "natural" manner.

In the darker myth, it was Shiva's evil eye that beheaded the newborn Ganesh, who wasn't born with an elephant's head. The only way the child could live was if someone else's head—someone facing north—was found and attached to the headless boy. What was found, after a great battle, was an unfortunate elephant, and in the violent course of the elephant's beheading, one tusk was broken.

But because he'd first heard it as a boy, Farrokh preferred the myth of the moon.

"Excuse me—did you hear me?" Martin asked the doctor. "I was inquiring what happened to that elephant's other tusk."

"He broke it himself," Dr. Daruwalla replied. "He got pissed off and threw it at the moon." In the rearview mirror, the dwarf gave the doctor the evil eye; a good Hindu, Vinod wasn't amused by Dr. Daruwalla's blasphemy. Surely Lord Ganesha was never "pissed off," which was strictly a mortal weakness.

The missionary's sigh was intended to convey his long-suffering patience with whatever vexatious mood the doctor was in. "There you go again," the Jesuit said. "Still keeping something from me."

24. THE DEVIL HERSELF

Getting Ready for Rahul

Although Deputy Commissioner Patel had insulted Mr. Sethna, the disapproving steward relished his new role as a police informant, for self-importance was Mr. Sethna's middle name; also, the deputy commissioner's stated objective of entrapping the second Mrs. Dogar greatly pleased the old Parsi. Nonetheless, Mr. Sethna faulted Detective Patel for not trusting him more completely; it irritated the steward that he was given his instructions without being informed of the overall plan. But the extent of the intrigue against Rahul was contingent on how Rahul responded to John D.'s sexual overtures. In rehearsing Inspector Dhar's seduction of Mrs. Dogar, both the real policeman and the actor were forced to consider more than one outcome. That was why they'd been waiting for Farrokh to come back from the circus; not only did they want the screenwriter to provide Dhar with some dialogue—Dhar also needed to know some alternative conversation, in case his first advances were rebuffed.

This was vastly more demanding dialogue than Dr. Daruwalla was accustomed to writing, for it was not just that he was required to anticipate the various responses that Rahul might make; the screenwriter also needed to guess what Mrs. Dogar might *like*—that is, sexually. Would she be more attracted to John D. if he was gentlemanly or if he was crude? For flirtation, did she favor the discreet approach or the explicit? A screenwriter could only suggest certain directions in which the dialogue might roam; Dhar could charm her, tease her, tempt her, shock her, but the particular approach that the actor chose would necessarily be a spontaneous decision. John D. had to rely on his instincts for what would work. After Dr. Daruwalla's most revealing conversations with Dhar's twin, the doctor could only wonder what John D.'s "instincts" were.

Farrokh wasn't prepared to find Detective Patel and Inspector Dhar waiting for him in his Marine Drive apartment. To begin with, Dr. Daruwalla wondered why they were so well dressed; he still didn't realize it was New Year's Eve—not until he saw what Julia was wearing. Then it puzzled him why everyone had dressed for New Year's Eve so early; no one ever showed up for the party at the Duckworth Club before 8:00 or 9:00.

But no one had wanted to waste time dressing when they could be rehearsing, and they couldn't properly rehearse Dhar's options for dialogue until *after* the screenwriter was home from the circus and had written the lines. Farrokh felt flattered—having first suffered the keenest disappointment for being left out of the process—but he was also overwhelmed; he'd been writing for the last three nights, and he feared he might be written-out. And he hated New Year's Eve; the night seemed to prey on his natural inclination toward nostalgia (especially at the Duckworth Club), although Julia did enjoy the dancing.

Dr. Daruwalla expressed his regret that there wasn't time to tell them what had happened at the circus; interesting things had transpired there. That was when John D. said something insensitive by stating that preparing himself for the seduction of the second Mrs. Dogar was "no circus"; those were the disparaging words he used—meaning that the doctor should save his silly circus stories for another, more frivolous time.

Detective Patel came to the point even more bluntly. The top half of the silver ballpoint pen had not only revealed Rahul's fingerprints; a speck of dried blood had been removed from the pocket clasp—it was human blood, of Mr. Lal's type. "May I remind you, Doctor," said the deputy commissioner, "it is still necessary to determine what Rahul would have been doing with the top half of the pen . . . *during* the murder of Mr. Lal."

"It's also necessary for Mrs. Dogar to admit that the top half of the pen is hers," John D. interrupted.

"Yes, thank you," Patel said, "but the top half of the pen isn't incriminating evidence—at least not by itself. What we really need to establish is that no one else could have made those drawings. I'm told that drawings like those are as identifiable as a signature, but it's necessary to induce Mrs. Dogar to *draw*."

"If there was a way for me to suggest to her that she should *show* me what it might be like . . . between us," Dhar told the screenwriter. "Maybe I could ask her to give me just a hint of what she preferred—I mean, sexually. Or I could ask her to tease me with something—I mean, something sexually explicit," the actor said.

"Yes, yes—I get the picture," Dr. Daruwalla said impatiently.

"And then there are the two-rupee notes," the real policeman said. "If Rahul is thinking of killing anyone else, perhaps there exist some notes with the appropriate warnings or messages already typed on the money."

"Surely *that* would be incriminating evidence, as you call it," Farrokh said.

"I would prefer all three—a connection to the top half of the pen, a drawing *and* something typed on the money," Patel replied. "That would be evidence enough."

"How fast do you want to go?" Farrokh asked. "In a seduction, there's usually the setting up—some kind of mutual sexual spark is ignited. Then there's the assignation—or at least a discussion of the trysting place, if not the actual tryst."

It was of small comfort to the screenwriter when Inspector Dhar said ambiguously, "I think I'd prefer to avoid the actual tryst, if it's possible—if things don't have to go that far."

"You *think*! You don't *know*?" Dr. Daruwalla cried.

"The point is, I need dialogue to cover every contingency," the actor said.

"Precisely," said Detective Patel.

"The deputy commissioner showed me the photographs of those drawings," John D. said; his voice dropped away. "There must also be private drawings—things she keeps secret." Again Farrokh was reminded of the boy who'd cried out, "They're drowning the elephants! Now the elephants will be angry!"

Julia went to help Nancy finish dressing. Nancy had brought a suitcase of her clothes to the Daruwallas', for she couldn't make up her mind about what to wear to the New Year's Eve party—not without Julia's help. The two women decided on something surprisingly demure; it was a gray sleeveless sheath with a mandarin collar, with which Nancy wore a simple string of pearls. Dr. Daruwalla recognized the necklace because it was Julia's. When the doctor retired to his bedroom and his bath, he brought a clipboard and a pad of lined paper with him; he also brought a bottle of beer. He was so tired, the hot bath and the cold beer made him instantly sleepy, but even with his eyes closed he was seeing the possible options for dialogue between John D. and the second Mrs. Dogar—or was he writing for Rahul and Inspector Dhar? That was a part of the problem; the screenwriter felt he didn't know the characters he was writing dialogue for.

Julia told Farrokh how Nancy had become so agitated—trying to decide what to wear—that the poor woman had worked herself into a sweat; she'd had to take a bath in the Daruwallas' tub, a concept that caused the screenwriter's mind to wander. There was a lingering scent in the bathroom—probably not a perfume or a bath oil but something unfamiliar, *not* Julia's—and the strangeness of it mingled with the doctor's memory of that time in Goa. The foremost issue to resolve, in order to initiate the opening line of Inspector Dhar's dialogue, was whether or not to have John D. know that Mrs. Dogar was Rahul. Shouldn't he tell her that he knew who she was—that he knew her former self—and shouldn't this be the first phase of the seduction? ("I always wanted you"—that kind of thing.)

The decision to have Nancy dress so demurely—she even wore her hair pulled up, off her neck—had sprung from Nancy's desire not to be recognized by Rahul. Although the deputy commissioner had repeatedly told his wife that he very much doubted Rahul would recognize her, Nancy's fear of being recognized persisted. The only time Rahul had seen her, Nancy had been naked and her hair was down. Now Nancy wanted her hair up; she'd told Julia that her choice of dress was "the opposite of naked."

But if the gray sheath was severe, there was no hiding the heavy womanliness of Nancy's hips and breasts; also, her heavy hair, which usually rested on her shoulders, was too thick and not quite long enough to be held neatly up and kept off her neck—especially if she danced. Strands of her hair would come loose; Nancy would soon look uncontained. The screenwriter decided that he wanted Nancy to dance with Dhar; after that, the possible scenes began to flow.

Farrokh put a towel around his waist and poked his head into the dining room, where Julia was serving some snacks; although it would be a long time before the midnight supper at the Duckworth Club, no one really wanted to eat. The doctor decided to send Dhar down to the alley, where the dwarf was waiting in the Ambassador. Dr. Daruwalla knew that Vinod was acquainted with many of the exotic dancers at the Wetness Cabaret; possibly there was one who owed the dwarf a favor.

"I want to get you a date," Farrokh told John D.

"With a stripper?" John D. asked.

"Tell Vinod the more tarted up she is, the better," the screenwriter replied. He guessed that New Year's Eve was an important night at the Wetness Cabaret; whoever the exotic dancer was, she'd have to leave the Duckworth Club early. That was fine with Farrokh; he wanted the woman to make something of a production over leaving before midnight. Whoever she was, the screenwriter knew that her choice of dress would be the opposite of demure—she certainly wouldn't look very Duckworthian. She'd be sure to get everyone's attention.

On such short notice, Vinod wouldn't have a wide range of choices; of the women at the Wetness Cabaret, the dwarf picked the one with the exotic-dancing name of Muriel. She'd impressed Vinod as being more sensitive than the other strippers. After all, someone in the audience had thrown an orange at her; such blatant disrespect had upset her. To be hired for a little dancing at the Duckworth Club—particularly, to be asked to dance with Inspector Dhar—would be quite a step up in the world for Muriel. Short notice or not, Vinod delivered the exotic dancer to the Daruwallas' apartment in a hurry.

When Dr. Daruwalla had finished dressing, there was barely time for John D. to rehearse the dialogue. Both Nancy and Muriel needed coaching, and Detective Patel had to get Mr. Sethna on the phone; the detective recited quite a long list of instructions to the steward, which doubtless left the old eavesdropper with a surfeit of disapproval. Vinod would drive Dhar and the exotic dancer to the Duckworth Club; Farrokh and Julia would follow with the Patels.

John D. managed to pull Dr. Daruwalla aside; the actor steered the screenwriter out on the balcony. When they were alone, Dhar said, "I've got a question regarding my character, Farrokh, for you seem to have given me some dialogue that is sexually ambiguous—at best."

"I was just trying to cover every contingency, as you would say," the screenwriter replied.

"But I gather that I'm supposed to be interested in Mrs. Dogar as a woman—that is, as a man would be interested in her," Dhar said. "While at the same time, I seem to be implying that I was once interested in Rahul as a man—that is, as a man is interested in another man."

"Yes," Farrokh said cautiously. "I'm trying to imply that you're sexually curious, and sexually aggressive—a bit of a bisexual, maybe . . ."

"Or even strictly a homosexual whose interest in Mrs. Dogar is, in part, because of how interested I *was* in Rahul," John D. interrupted. "Is that it?"

"Something like that," said Dr. Daruwalla. "I mean, we think Rahul was once attracted to you—we think Mrs. Dogar is *still* attracted to you. Beyond that, what do we really know?"

"But you've made my character a kind of sexual mystery," the actor complained. "You've made me *odd*. It's as if you're gambling that the weirder I am, the more Mrs. Dogar will go for me. Is that it?"

Actors are truly impossible, the screenwriter thought. What Dr. Daruwalla wanted to say was this: Your twin has experienced decidedly homosexual inclinations. Does this sound familiar to you? Instead, what Farrokh said was this: "I don't know how to shock a serial killer. I'm just trying to attract one."

"And I'm just asking you for a fix on my character," Inspector Dhar replied. "It's always easier when I know who I'm supposed to be."

There was the old Dhar, Dr. Daruwalla thought—sarcastic to the core. Farrokh was relieved to see that the movie star had regained his self-confidence.

That was when Nancy came out on the balcony. "I'm not interrupting anything, am I?" she asked, but she went straight to the railing and leaned on it; she didn't wait for an answer.

"No, no," Dr. Daruwalla mumbled.

"That's west, isn't it?" Nancy asked. She was pointing to the sunset.

"The sun usually sets in the west," Dhar said.

"And if you went west across the sea—from Bombay straight across the Arabian Sea—what would you come to?" Nancy asked. "Make it west and a little north," she added.

"Well," Dr. Daruwalla said cautiously. "West and a little north from here is the Gulf of Oman, then the Persian Gulf . . ."

"Then Saudi Arabia," Dhar interrupted.

"Keep going," Nancy told him. "Keep going west and a little north."

"That would take you across Jordan . . . into Israel, and into the Mediterranean," Farrokh said.

"Or across North Africa," said Inspector Dhar.

"Well, yes," Dr. Daruwalla said. "Across Egypt . . . what's after Egypt?" he asked John D.

"Libya, Tunisia, Algeria, Morocco," the actor replied. "You could pass through the Straits of Gibraltar, or touch the coast of Spain, if you like."

"Yes—that's the way I want to go," Nancy told him. "I touch the coast of Spain. Then what?"

"Then you're in the North Atlantic," Dr. Daruwalla said.

"Go west," Nancy said. "And a little north."

"New York?" Dr. Daruwalla guessed.

"I know the way from there," Nancy said suddenly. "From there I go straight west."

Both Dhar and Dr. Daruwalla didn't know what Nancy would come to next; they weren't familiar with the geography of the United States.

"Pennsylvania, Ohio, Indiana, Illinois," Nancy told them. "Maybe I'd have to go through New Jersey before I got to Pennsylvania."

"Where are you going?" Dr. Daruwalla asked.

"Home," Nancy answered. "Home to Iowa—Iowa comes after Illinois."

"Do you want to go home?" John D. asked her.

"Never," Nancy said. "I never want to go home."

The screenwriter saw that the zipper of the gray sheath dress was a straight line down her back; it clasped at the top of her high mandarin collar.

"If you wouldn't mind," Farrokh said to her, "perhaps you could have your husband unfasten the zipper of your dress. If it were unzipped just a little—down to somewhere between your shoulder blades—that would be better. When you're dancing, I mean," the doctor added.

"Wouldn't it be better if *I* unzipped it?" the actor asked. "I mean, when we're dancing?"

"Well, yes, that would be best," Dr. Daruwalla said.

Still looking west into the sunset, Nancy said, "Just don't unzip me too far. I don't care what the script says—if you unzip me too far, I'll let you know it."

"It's time," said Detective Patel. No one was sure how long he'd been on the balcony.

In departing, it was fortunate that none of them really looked at one another; their faces conveyed a certain dread of the event, like mourners preparing to attend the funeral of a child. The deputy commissioner was almost avuncular; he affectionately patted Dr. Daruwalla's shoulder, he warmly shook Inspector Dhar's hand, he held his troubled wife at her waist—his fingers familiarly spreading to the small of her back, where he knew she felt some occasional pain. It was his way of saying, I'm in charge—everything's going to be okay.

But there was that interminable period when they had to wait in the policeman's car; Vinod had taken Dhar and Muriel ahead. As the driver, the deputy commissioner sat up front with the screenwriter, who wanted Dhar and Muriel to be already dancing when the Daruwallas and their guests, the Patels, arrived. In the back seat, Julia sat with Nancy. The detective avoided his wife's eyes in the rearview mirror; Patel also tried not to grip the steering wheel too tightly—he didn't want any of them to see how nervous he was.

The passing headlights flowed like water along Marine Drive, and when the sun finally dipped into the Arabian Sea, the sea turned quickly from pink to purple to burgundy to black, like the phases of a bruise. The doctor said, "They must be dancing by now." The detective started the car, easing them into the flow of traffic.

In a misguided effort to sound positive, Dr. Daruwalla said, "Let's go get the bitch, let's put her away."

"Not tonight," Detective Patel said quietly. "We won't catch her tonight. Let's just hope she takes the bait."

"She'll take it," Nancy said from the back seat.

There was nothing the deputy commissioner wanted to say. He smiled. He hoped he looked confident. But the real policeman knew there was really no getting ready for Rahul.

Just Dancing

Mr. Sethna had to wonder what was going on; wonderment was not among the few expressions that the old Parsi favored. To anyone who observed the steward's sour, intolerant visage, Mr. Sethna was simply expressing his contempt for New Year's Eve; he thought the party at the Duckworth Club was superfluous. Pateti, the Parsi New Year, comes in the late summer or the early fall; it is followed a fortnight later by the anniversary of the prophet Zarathustra's birth. By the time of the New Year's Eve party at the Duckworth Club, Mr. Sethna had already cele-brated *his* New Year. As for the Duckworthian version of New Year's Eve, Mr. Sethna viewed it as a tradition for Anglophiles. It was also morbid that New Year's Eve at the Duckworth Club was doubly special to those many Duckworthians who enjoyed the party as an anniversary—this year it was the 90th anniversary—of Lord Duckworth's suicide.

The steward also thought that the events of the evening were foolishly ordered. Duckworthians, in general, were an older crowd, especially at this time of year; with a 22-year waiting list for membership, one would expect the members to be "older," but this was also the result of the younger Duckworthians being away at school—for the most part, in England. In the summer months, when the student generation was back in India, Duckworthians appeared to be younger. But now here were all these older people, who should be eating their dinners at a reasonable hour; they were expected to drink and dance until the midnight supper was served—an ass-backward order of events, Mr. Sethna believed. Feed them early and *then* let them dance—if they're able. The effects of too much champagne on empty stomachs were particularly deleterious to the elderly. Some couples lacked the stamina to last until the midnight supper. And wasn't the point of the silly evening—apparently, the only point—to last until midnight?

From the way he was dancing, Dhar couldn't last until midnight, Mr. Sethna presumed; yet the steward was impressed at how the actor had rebounded from his dreadful appearance of the day before. On Saturday, the diseased man had been ghostly pale and dabbing at his penis over the urinal—a sickening sight. Now here he was on Sunday night, tanned and looking positively beefy; he was dancing up a storm. Perhaps the actor's sexually transmitted disease was in remission, Mr. Sethna speculated, as Dhar continued to hurl Muriel around the dance floor. And where had the movie-star slime found a woman like that?

Once, there'd been a banner draped from the marquee of the Bombay Eros Palace, and the woman painted on that banner had looked like Muriel, Mr. Sethna remembered. (The woman had actually been Muriel, of course; the Wetness Cabaret was a step down from the Bombay Eros Palace.) Mr. Sethna had never seen a Duckworthian in such a costume as Muriel wore. The glitter of her turquoise sequins, her plunging neckline, her miniskirt at midthigh . . . her dress hugged her bum so tightly, Mr. Sethna expected that some of her sequins would pop off and litter the dance floor. Muriel had maintained the high, hard athletic bum of a dancer; and although she was certainly a few years older than Inspector Dhar, she looked as if she could both outdance and outsweat him. Their dancing lacked the element of courtship; they were brutally aggressive—astonishingly rough with each other—which implied to the disapproving steward that dancing was merely the public forum in which they lewdly hinted at the violence of their more private lovemaking.

Mr. Sethna also observed that everyone was watching them. By design, Mr. Sethna knew, they kept to that portion of the dance floor which was visible from the main dining room, forcing numerous couples to see them perform their gyrations. Nearest to this view of the ballroom was the table Mr. Sethna had reserved for Mr. and Mrs. Dogar; the steward had followed Detective Patel's instructions to the letter, taking care that the second Mrs. Dogar was shown to the chair that offered her the very best view of Dhar dancing.

From the Ladies' Garden, the Daruwallas' table looked in upon the main dining room; from where the doctor and the detective were seated, they could observe Mrs. Dogar but not the ballroom. It wasn't Dhar they wanted to see. Blessedly, the big blonde had hidden her unusual navel, Mr. Sethna observed; Nancy was dressed like the headmistress of a school—or a nanny, or a clergyman's wife—but the steward nevertheless detected her lawlessness, her penchant for unpredictable or inexplicable behavior. She sat with her back to Mrs. Dogar, staring into the gathering darkness beyond the trellis; at this hour, the bougainvillea had the luster of velvet. The exposed nape of Nancy's neck—the downy blond hair that looked so soft there—reminded Mr. Sethna of her furry navel.

The doctor's sleek tuxedo and black silk tie clashed with the deputy commissioner's badly wrinkled Nehru suit; Mr. Sethna determined that most Duckworthians were never in contact with that element of society which could recognize policemen by their clothes. The steward approved of Julia's gown, which was a proper gown—the long skirt almost brushing the floor, the long sleeves ruffled at the cuffs, the neckline not a mandarin choker but a decent distance above any discernible cleavage. Ah, the old days, Mr. Sethna mourned; as if anticipating his thoughts, the band responded with a slower number.

Dhar and Muriel, breathing hard, relaxed a little too languidly into each other's arms; she hung on his neck, his hand resting possessively on the hard beaded sequins at her hip. She appeared to be whispering to him—actually, she was just singing the words to the song, for Muriel knew every song that this band knew, and many more besides—while Inspector Dhar smiled knowingly at what she was saying. There was his sneer, which was almost a smirk—that look of disdain, which was at once decadent and bored. Actually, Dhar was amused by Muriel's accent; he thought the stripper was very funny. But what the second Mrs.

Dogar saw did not amuse her. She saw John D. dancing with a tart, a presumably loose woman—and one close to Mrs. Dogar's age. Women like that were so easy; surely Dhar could do better, Rahul thought.

On the dance floor, the staid Duckworthians who dared to dance—they'd been waiting for a slow number—kept their distance from Dhar and Muriel, who was clearly no lady. Mr. Sethna, the old eavesdropper and lip-reader *extraordinaire*, easily caught what Mr. Dogar said to his wife. "Has the actor brought an actual prostitute to the party? I must say she looks like a whore."

"I think she's a stripper," said Mrs. Dogar—Rahul had honed a sharp eye for such social details.

"Perhaps she's an actress," Mr. Dogar said.

"She's acting, but she's no actress," Mrs. Dogar replied.

From what Farrokh could see of Rahul, the transsexual had inherited the reptilian scrutiny of her Aunt Promila; it was as if, when she looked at you, she were seeing a different life form—certainly not a fellow human being.

"It's hard to tell from here," said Dr. Daruwalla. "I don't know if she's attracted to him or if she wants to kill him."

"Maybe with her," said the deputy commissioner, "the feeling is one and the same."

"Whatever else she feels, she's attracted," Nancy said. Her back was the only part of her that Rahul could see, if Rahul had been looking. But Rahul had eyes for John D. only.

When the band played a faster number, Dhar and Muriel grew even rougher with each other, as if invigorated by the slower interlude or by their closer contact. A few of the cheap sequins were torn from Muriel's dress; they glittered on the dance floor, reflecting the light from the ballroom chandelier—when Dhar or Muriel stepped on them, they crunched. A constant rivulet of sweat ran its course in Muriel's cleavage, and Dhar was bleeding slightly from a scratch on his wrist; the cuff of his white shirt was dotted with blood. Because of how tightly he held Muriel at her waist, a sequin had scratched him. He paid the scratch only passing attention, but Muriel took his wrist in her hands and covered the cut with her mouth. In this way, with his wrist to her lips, they kept dancing. Mr. Sethna had seen such things only in the movies. The steward didn't realize that this was what he was seeing: a screenplay by Farrokh Daruwalla, a movie starring Inspector Dhar.

When Muriel left the Duckworth Club, she made a fuss over her departure. She danced one last dance (another slow one) with her shawl

on; she downed a nearly full glass of champagne in the foyer. Then the
exotic dancer leaned on Vinod's head while the dwarf walked her to the
Ambassador.

"A to-do worthy of a slut," said Mr. Dogar. "I suppose she's going
back to the brothel."

But Rahul merely glanced at the time. The second Mrs. Dogar was
a close observer of Bombay's low life; she knew that the hour for the first
show at the Eros Palace was fast approaching, or maybe Dhar's tart
worked at the Wetness Cabaret—the first show there was 15 minutes
later.

When Dhar asked the Sorabjee daughter to dance, a new tension
could be felt throughout the main dining room and the Ladies' Garden.
Even with her back to the action, Nancy knew that something unscripted had happened.

"He's asked someone else to dance, hasn't he?" she said; her face and
the nape of her neck were flushed.

"Who's that young girl? She's not part of our plan!" said Detective
Patel.

"Trust him—he's a great improviser," the screenwriter said. "He
always understands who he is and what his role is. He knows what he's
doing."

Nancy was pinching a pearl on her necklace; her thumb and index
finger were white. "You bet he knows," she said. Julia turned around, but
she couldn't see the ballroom—only the look of loathing that was
unconcealed on Mrs. Dogar's face.

"It's little Amy Sorabjee—she must be back from school," Dr. Daruwalla informed his wife.

"She's only a teenager!" Julia cried.

"I think she's a little older," the real policeman replied.

"It's a brilliant move!" the screenwriter said. "Mrs. Dogar doesn't
know *what* to think!"

"I know how she feels," Nancy told him.

"It'll be all right, sweetie," the deputy commissioner told his wife.
When he took her hand, she pulled it away.

"Am I next?" Nancy asked. "Do I wait in line?"

Almost every face in the main dining room was turned toward the
ballroom. They watched the unstoppable sweating movie star with his
bulky shoulders and his beer belly; he was twirling little Amy Sorabjee
around as if she were no heavier than her clothes.

Although the Sorabjees and the Daruwallas were old friends, Dr. and

Mrs. Sorabjee had been surprised at Dhar's spur-of-the-moment invitation—and that Amy had accepted. She was a silly girl in her twenties, a former university student who hadn't merely come home for the holiday; she'd been withdrawn from school. Granted, Dhar wasn't mashing her; the actor was behaving like a proper gentleman—excessively charming, possibly, but the young lady seemed delighted. Theirs was a different kind of dancing from Dhar's performance with Muriel; the friskiness of the youthful girl was appealingly offset by the sure, smooth quality of the older man's gestures.

"Now he's seducing children!" Mr. Dogar announced to his wife. "He's going to dance his way through all the women—I'm sure he'll ask you, too, Promila!"

Mrs. Dogar was visibly upset. She excused herself for the ladies' room, where she was reminded of how she hated this aspect of being a woman—waiting to pee. There was too long a line; Rahul slipped through the foyer and into the closed and darkened administrative offices of the old club. There was enough moonlight for her to type by, and she rolled a two-rupee note into the typewriter that was nearest a window. On the money, the typed message was as spontaneous as her feelings at the moment.

A MEMBER NO MORE

This was a message meant for Dhar's mouth, and Mrs. Dogar slipped it into her purse where it could keep company with the message she'd already typed for her husband.

. . . BECAUSE DHAR IS STILL A MEMBER

It comforted Mrs. Dogar to have these two-rupee notes in place; she always felt better when she was prepared for every contingency. She slipped back through the foyer and into the ladies' room, where the line ahead of her wasn't so long. When Rahul returned to her table in the main dining room, Dhar was dancing with a new partner.

Mr. Sethna, who'd been happily monitoring the conversation between the Dogars, was thrilled to note Mr. Dogar's observation to his coarse wife: "Now Dhar's dancing with that hefty Anglo who came with the Daruwallas. I think she's the white half of a mixed marriage. Her husband looks like a pathetic civil servant."

But Mrs. Dogar was prevented from seeing the new dancers. Dhar had wheeled Nancy into the part of the ballroom that wasn't visible from the main dining room. Only intermittently did a glimpse of them appear. Earlier, Rahul had taken little notice of the big blonde. When Mrs. Dogar glanced at the Daruwallas' table, the Daruwallas were bent in conversation with the out-of-place "pathetic civil servant," as her husband had described him. Maybe he was a minor magistrate, Rahul guessed—or some controlling little guru who'd met his Western wife in an ashram.

Then Dhar and the heavy woman danced into view. Mrs. Dogar sensed the strength with which they gripped each other—the woman's broad hand held fast to Dhar's neck, and the biceps of his right arm was locked in her armpit (as if he were trying to lift her up). She was taller than he was; from the way she grasped his neck, it was impossible for Rahul to tell if Nancy was pulling Dhar's face into the side of her throat or if she was struggling to prevent him from nuzzling her. What was remarkable was that they were whispering fiercely to each other; neither one of them was listening, but they were talking urgently and at the same time. When they danced out of her sight again, Rahul couldn't stand it; Mrs. Dogar asked her husband to dance.

"He's got her! I told you he could do it," said Dr. Daruwalla.

"This is only the beginning," the deputy commissioner replied. "This is just the dancing."

Happy New Year

Fortunately for Mr. Dogar, it was a slow dance. His wife steered him past several faltering couples, who were disconcerted that Muriel's fallen sequins still crunched underfoot. Mrs. Dogar had Dhar and the big blonde in her sights.

"Is this in the script?" Nancy was whispering to the actor. "This isn't in the script, you bastard!"

"We're supposed to make something of a scene—like an old lovers' quarrel," Dhar whispered.

"You're embracing me!" Nancy told him.

"You're squeezing me back," he whispered.

"I wish I was killing you!" Nancy whispered.

"She's here," Dhar said softly. "She's following us."

With a pang, Rahul observed that the blond wench had gone limp in Dhar's arms—and she'd been resisting him; that had been obvious. Now it appeared to Mrs. Dogar that Dhar was supporting the heavy woman; the blonde might otherwise have fallen to the dance floor, so lifelessly was she draped on the actor. She'd thrown her arms over his shoulders and locked her hands behind his back; her face was buried in his neck—awkwardly, because she was taller. Rahul could see that Nancy was shaking her head while Dhar went on whispering to her. The blonde had that pleasing air of submission about her, as if she'd already given up; Rahul was reminded of the kind of woman who'd let you make love to her or let you kill her without a breath of complaint—like someone with a high fever, Rahul thought.

"Does she recognize me?" Nancy was whispering; she trembled, and then stumbled. Dhar had to hold her up with all his strength.

"She can't recognize you, she *doesn't* recognize you—she's just curious about what's between us," the actor replied.

"What *is* between us?" Nancy whispered. Where her hands were locked together, he felt her dig her knuckles into his spine.

"She's coming closer," Dhar warned Nancy. "She doesn't recognize you. She just wants to look. I'm going to do it now," he whispered.

"Do what?" Nancy asked; she'd forgotten—she was so frightened of Rahul.

"Unzip you," Dhar said.

"Not too far," Nancy told him.

The actor turned her suddenly; he had to stand on tiptoe to look over her shoulder, but he wanted to be sure that Mrs. Dogar saw his face. John D. looked straight at Rahul and smiled; he gave the killer a sly wink. Then he unzipped the back of Nancy's dress while Rahul watched. When he felt the clasp of Nancy's bra, he stopped; he spread his palm between her bare shoulder blades—she was sweating and he felt her shudder.

"Is she watching?" Nancy whispered. "I hate you," she added.

"She's right on top of us," Dhar whispered. "I'm going to go right at her. We're changing partners now."

"Zip me up first!" Nancy whispered. "Zip me up!"

With his right hand, John D. zipped Nancy up; with his left, he reached out and took the second Mrs. Dogar by the wrist—her arm was cool and dry, as sinewy as a strong rope.

"Let's switch partners for the next number!" said Inspector Dhar. But it was still the slow dance that played. Mr. Dogar staggered briefly; Nancy, who was relieved to be out of Dhar's arms, forcefully drew the old man to her chest. A lock of her hair had come undone; it hid her cheek. No one saw her tears, which might have been confused with her sweat.

"Hi," Nancy said. Before Mr. Dogar could respond, she palmed the back of his head; his cheek was pressed flat between her shoulder and her collarbone. Nancy moved the old man resolutely away from Dhar and Rahul; she wondered how long she had to wait until the band changed to a faster number.

What was left of the slow dance suited Dhar and Rahul. John D.'s eyes were level with a thin blue vein that ran the length of Mrs. Dogar's throat; something deep-black and polished, like onyx—a single stone, set in silver—rested in the perfect declivity where her throat met her sternum. Her dress, which was an emerald green, was cut low but it fit her breasts snugly; her hands were smooth and hard, her grip surprisingly light. She was light on her feet, too; no matter where John D. moved, she squared her shoulders to him—her eyes locked onto his eyes, as if she were reading the first page of a new book.

"That was rather crude—and clumsy, too," the second Mrs. Dogar said.

"I'm tired of trying to ignore you," the actor told her. "I'm sick of pretending that I don't know who you are . . . who you *were*," Dhar added, but her grip maintained its even, soft pressure—her body obediently followed his.

"Goodness, you *are* provincial!" Mrs. Dogar said. "Can't a man become a woman if she wants to?"

"It's certainly an exciting idea," said Inspector Dhar.

"You're not sneering, are you?" Mrs. Dogar asked him.

"Certainly not! I'm just remembering," the actor replied. "Twenty years ago, I couldn't get up the nerve to approach you—I didn't know how to begin."

"Twenty years ago, I wasn't *complete*," Rahul reminded him. "If you *had* approached me, what would you have done?"

"Frankly, I was too young to think of *doing*," Dhar replied. "I think I just wanted to *see* you!"

"I don't suppose that *seeing* me is all you have in mind today," Mrs. Dogar said.

"Certainly not!" said Inspector Dhar, but he couldn't muster the courage to squeeze her hand; she was everywhere so dry and cool and light of touch, but she was also very hard.

"Twenty years ago, I *tried* to approach you," Rahul admitted.

"It must have been too subtle for me—at least I missed it," John D. remarked.

"At the Bardez, I was told you slept in the hammock on the balcony," Rahul told him. "I went to you. The only part of you that was outside the mosquito net was your foot. I put your big toe in my mouth. I sucked it—actually, I bit you. But it wasn't you. It was Dr. Daruwalla. I was so disgusted, I never tried again."

This was not the conversation Dhar had expected. John D.'s options for dialogue didn't include a response to this interesting story, but while he was at a loss for words, the band saved him; they changed to a faster number. People were leaving the dance floor in droves, including Nancy with Mr. Dogar. Nancy led the old man to his table; he was almost breathless by the time she got him seated.

"Who are you, dear?" he managed to ask her.

"Mrs. Patel," Nancy replied.

"Ah," the old man said. "And your husband . . ." What Mr. Dogar meant was, *What does he do?* He wondered: *Which sort of civil-service employee is he?*

"My husband is Mr. Patel," Nancy told him; when she left him, she walked as carefully as possible to the Daruwallas' table.

"I don't think she recognized me," Nancy told them, "but I couldn't look at her. She looks the same, but ancient."

"Are they dancing?" Dr. Daruwalla asked. "Are they talking, too?"

"They're dancing *and* they're talking—that's all I know," Nancy told the screenwriter. "I couldn't look at her," she repeated.

"It's all right, sweetie," the deputy commissioner said. "You don't have to do anything more."

"I want to be there when you catch her, Vijay," Nancy told her husband.

"Well, we may not catch her in a place where you want to be," the detective replied.

"Please let me be there," Nancy said. "Am I zipped up?" she asked suddenly; she rotated her shoulders so that Julia could see her back.

"You're zipped up perfectly, dear," Julia told her.

Mr. Dogar, alone at his table, was gulping champagne and catching his breath, while Mr. Sethna plied him with hors d'oeuvres. Mrs. Dogar and Dhar were dancing in that part of the ballroom where Mr. Dogar couldn't see them.

"There was a time when I wanted you," Rahul was telling John D. "You were a beautiful boy."

"I still want you," Dhar told her.

"It seems you want everybody," Mrs. Dogar said. "Who's the strip-per?" she asked him. He had no dialogue for this.

"Just a stripper," Dhar answered.

"And who's the fat blonde?" Rahul asked him. This much Dr. Daru-walla had prepared him for.

"She's an old story," the actor replied. "Some people can't let go."

"You can have your choice of women—younger women, too," Mrs. Dogar told him. "What do you want with me?" This introduced a moment in the dialogue that the actor was afraid of; this required a quantum leap of faith in Farrokh's script. The actor had little confidence in his upcoming line.

"I need to know something," Dhar told Rahul. "Is your vagina really made from what used to be your penis?"

"Don't be crude," Mrs. Dogar said; then she started laughing.

"I wish there was another way to ask the question," John D. admitted. When she laughed more uncontrollably, her hands gripped him harder; he could feel the strength of her hands for the first time. "I suppose I could have been more indirect," Dhar continued, for her laughter en-couraged him. "I could have said, 'What sort of sensitivity do you have in that vagina of yours, anyway? I mean, does it feel sort of like a penis?'" The actor stopped; he couldn't make himself continue. The screenwriter's dialogue wasn't working—Farrokh was frequently hit-or-miss with dialogue.

Besides, Mrs. Dogar had stopped laughing. "So you're just curious—is that it?" she asked him. "You're attracted to the oddity of it."

Along the thin blue vein at Rahul's throat, there appeared a cloudy drop of sweat; it ran quickly between her taut breasts. John D. thought that they hadn't been dancing that hard. He hoped it was the right time. He took her around her waist with some force, and she followed his lead; when they crossed that part of the dance floor which made them visible to Mrs. Dogar's husband—and to Mr. Sethna—Dhar saw that the old steward had understood his signal. Mr. Sethna turned quickly from the dining room toward the foyer, and the actor again wheeled Mrs. Dogar into the more private part of the ballroom.

"I'm an actor," John D. told Rahul. "I can be anyone you want me to be—I can do absolutely anything you like. You just have to draw me a picture." (The actor winced; he had Farrokh to thank for that clunker, too.)

"What an eccentric presumption!" Mrs. Dogar said. "Draw you a picture of *what?*"

"Just give me an idea of what appeals to you. Then I can do it," Dhar told her.

"You said, 'Draw me a picture'—I heard you say it," Mrs. Dogar said.

"I meant, just tell me what you like—I mean sexually," the actor said.

"I know what you *mean,* but you said 'draw,' " Rahul replied coldly.

"Didn't you used to be an artist? Weren't you going to art school?" the actor asked. (What the hell is Mr. Sethna doing? Dhar was thinking. John D. was afraid that Rahul smelled a rat.)

"I didn't learn anything in art school," Mrs. Dogar told him.

In the utility closet, off the foyer, Mr. Sethna had discovered that he couldn't read the writing in the fuse box without his glasses, which he kept in a drawer in the kitchen. It took the steward a moment to decide whether or not to kill all the fuses.

"The old fool has probably electrocuted himself!" Dr. Daruwalla was saying to Detective Patel.

"Let's try to keep calm," the policeman said.

"If the lights don't go out, let Dhar improvise—if he's such a great improviser," Nancy said.

"I want you *not* as a curiosity," Dhar said suddenly to Mrs. Dogar. "I know you're strong, I think you're aggressive—I believe you can assert yourself." (It was the worst of Dr. Daruwalla's dialogue, the actor thought—it was sheer groping.) "I want you to tell me what you like. I want you to tell me what to do."

"I want you to submit to me," Rahul said.

"You can tie me up, if you want to," Dhar said agreeably.

"I mean more than that," Mrs. Dogar said. Then the ballroom and the entire first floor of the Duckworth Club were pitched into darkness. There was a communal gasp and a fumbling in the band; the number they were playing persisted through a few more toots and thumps. From the dining room came an artless clapping. Noises of chaos could be heard from the kitchen. Then the knives and forks and spoons began their impromptu music against the water glasses.

"Don't spill the champagne!" Mr. Bannerjee called out.

The girlish laughter probably came from Amy Sorabjee.

When John D. tried to kiss her in the darkness, Mrs. Dogar was too fast; his mouth was just touching hers when he felt her seize his lower lip in her teeth. While she held him thus, by the lip, her exaggerated breathing was heavy in his face; her cool, dry hands unzipped him and fondled him until he was hard. Dhar put his hands on her buttocks, which she instantly tightened. Still she clamped his lower lip between her teeth; her bite was hard enough to hurt him but not quite deep enough to make him bleed. As Mr. Sethna had been instructed, the lights flashed briefly on and then went out again; Mrs. Dogar let go of John D.—both with her teeth and with her hands. When he took his hands off her to zip up his fly, he lost her. When the lights came on, Dhar was no longer in contact with Mrs. Dogar.

"You want a picture? I'll show you a picture," Rahul said quietly. "I could have bitten your lip off."

"I have a suite at both the Oberoi and the Taj," the actor told her.

"No—I'll tell you where," Mrs. Dogar said. "I'll tell you at lunch."

"At lunch here?" Dhar asked her.

"Tomorrow," Rahul said. "I could have bitten your nose off, if I'd wanted to."

"Thank you for the dance," John D. said. As he turned to leave her, he was uncomfortably aware of his erection and the throbbing in his lower lip.

"Careful you don't knock over any chairs or tables," Mrs. Dogar said. "You're as big as an elephant." It was the word "elephant"—coming from Rahul—that most affected John D.'s walk. He crossed the dining room, still seeing the cloudy drop of her quickly disappearing sweat—still feeling her cool, dry hands. And the way she'd breathed into his open mouth when his lip was trapped . . . John D. suspected he would never forget that. He was thinking that the thin blue vein in her throat was so very still; it was as if she didn't have a pulse, or that she knew some way to suspend the normal beating of her heart.

When Dhar sat down at the table, Nancy couldn't look at him. Deputy Commissioner Patel didn't look at him, either, but that was because the policeman was more interested in watching Mr. and Mrs. Dogar. They were arguing—Mrs. Dogar wouldn't sit down, Mr. Dogar wouldn't stand up—and the detective noticed something extremely simple but peculiar about the two of them; they had almost exactly the same haircut. Mr. Dogar wore his wonderfully thick hair in a vain pompadour; it was cut short at the back of his neck, and it was tightly trimmed over his ears, but a surprisingly full and cocky wave of his hair was brushed high off his forehead—his hair was silver, with streaks of white. Mrs. Dogar's hair was black with streaks of silver (probably dyed), but her hairdo was the same as her husband's, albeit more stylish. It gave her a slightly Spanish appearance. A pompadour! Imagine that, thought Detective Patel. He saw that Mrs. Dogar had persuaded her husband to stand.

Mr. Sethna would later inform the deputy commissioner of what words passed between the Dogars, but the policeman could have guessed. Mrs. Dogar was complaining that her husband had already slurped too much champagne; she wouldn't tolerate a minute more of his drunkenness—she would have the servants fix them a midnight supper at home, where at least she would not be publicly embarrassed by Mr. Dogar's ill-considered behavior.

"They're leaving!" Dr. Daruwalla observed. "What happened? Did you agitate her?" the screenwriter asked the actor.

Dhar had a drink of champagne, which made his lip sting. The sweat was rolling down his face—after all, he'd been dancing all night—and his hands were noticeably shaky; they watched him exchange the champagne glass for his water glass. Even a sip of water caused him to wince. Nancy had had to force herself to look at him; now she couldn't look away.

The deputy commissioner was still thinking about the haircuts. The pompadour had a feminizing effect on old Mr. Dogar, but the same hairdo conveyed a mannishness to his wife. The detective concluded that Mrs. Dogar resembled a bullfighter; Detective Patel had never seen a bullfighter, of course.

Farrokh was dying to know which dialogue John D. had used. The sweating movie star was still fussing with his lip. The doctor observed that Dhar's lower lip was swollen; it had the increasingly purplish hue of a contusion. The doctor waved his arms for a waiter and asked for a tall glass of ice—just ice.

"So she kissed you," Nancy said.

"It was more like a bite," John D. replied.

"But what did you *say*?" Dr. Daruwalla cried.

"Did you arrange a meeting?" Detective Patel asked Dhar.

"Lunch here, tomorrow," the actor replied.

"Lunch!" the screenwriter said with disappointment.

"So you've made a start," the policeman said.

"Yes, I think so. It's something, anyway—I'm not sure what," Dhar remarked.

"So she *responded*?" Farrokh asked. He felt frustrated, for he wanted to hear the dialogue between them—word for word.

"Look at his lip!" Nancy told the doctor. "Of *course* she responded!"

"Did you ask her to draw you a picture?" Farrokh wanted to know.

"That part was scary—at least it got a little strange," Dhar said evasively. "But I think she's going to show me something."

"At *lunch*?" Dr. Daruwalla asked. John D. shrugged; he was clearly exasperated with all the questions.

"Let him talk, Farrokh. Stop putting words in his mouth," Julia told him.

"But he's *not* talking!" the doctor cried.

"She said she wanted me to submit to her," Dhar told the deputy commissioner.

"She wants to tie him up!" Farrokh shouted.

"She said she meant more than that," Dhar replied.

"What's 'more than that'?" Dr. Daruwalla asked.

The waiter brought the ice and John D. held a piece to his lip.

"Put the ice in your mouth and suck on it," the doctor told him, but John D. kept applying the ice in his own way.

"She bit me inside and out," was all he said.

"Did you get to the part about her sex-change operation?" the screenwriter asked.

"She thought that part was funny," John D. told them. "She laughed."

By now the indentations on the outside of Dhar's lower lip were easier to see, even in the candlelight in the Ladies' Garden; the teeth marks had left such deep bruises, the discolored lip was turning from a pale purple to a dark magenta, as if Mrs. Dogar's teeth had left a stain.

To her husband's surprise, Nancy helped herself to a second glass of champagne; Detective Patel had been mildly shocked that his wife had accepted the first glass. Now Nancy raised her glass, as if she were toasting everyone in the Ladies' Garden.

"Happy New Year," she said, but to no one in particular.

"Auld Lang Syne"

Finally, they served the midnight supper. Nancy picked at her food, which her husband eventually ate. John D. couldn't eat anything spicy because of his lip; he didn't tell them about the erection Mrs. Dogar had given him, or how—or about how she'd said he was as big as an elephant. Dhar decided he'd tell Detective Patel later, when they were alone.

When the policeman excused himself from the table, John D. followed him to the men's room and told him there.

"I didn't like the way she looked when she left here." That was all the detective would say.

Back at their table, Dr. Daruwalla told them that he had a plan to "introduce" the top half of the pen; Mr. Sethna was involved—it sounded complicated. John D. repeated that he hoped Rahul was going to make him a drawing.

"That would do it, wouldn't it?" Nancy asked her husband.

"That would help," the deputy commissioner said. He had a bad feeling. He once again excused himself from the table, this time to call Crime Branch Headquarters. He ordered a surveillance officer to watch the Dogars' house all night; if Mrs. Dogar left the house, he wanted the officer to follow her—and he wanted to be told if she left the house, whatever the hour.

In the men's room, Dhar had said that he'd never felt it was Rahul's intention to bite his lip off, nor even that taking his lip in her teeth was a deliberate decision—it wasn't something she'd done merely to scare him, either. The actor believed that Mrs. Dogar hadn't been able to stop herself; and all the while she'd held his lip, he'd felt that the transsexual was unable to let go.

"It wasn't that she *wanted* to bite me," Dhar had told the detective. "It was that she couldn't help it."

"Yes, I understand," the policeman had said; he'd resisted the temptation to add that only in the movies did every murderer have a clear motive.

Now, as he hung up the phone, a dreary song reached the deputy commissioner in the foyer. The band was playing "Auld Lang Syne"; the drunken Duckworthians were murdering the lyrics. Patel crossed the dining room with difficulty because so many of the maudlin members were leaving their tables and traipsing to the ballroom, singing as they staggered forth. There went Mr. Bannerjee, sandwiched between his wife and the widow Lal; he appeared to be manfully intent on dancing with them both. There went Dr. and Mrs. Sorabjee, leaving little Amy alone at their table.

When the detective returned to the Daruwallas' table, Nancy was nagging Dhar. "I'm sure that little girl is dying to dance with you again. And she's all alone. Why don't you ask her? Imagine how she feels. You started it," Nancy told him. She'd had three glasses of champagne, her husband calculated; this wasn't much, but she never drank—and she'd

eaten next to nothing. Dhar was managing not to sneer; he was trying
to ignore Nancy instead.

"Why don't you ask *me* to dance?" Julia asked John D. "I think
Farrokh has forgotten to ask me."

Without a word, Dhar led Julia to the ballroom; Amy Sorabjee
watched them all the way.

"I like your idea about the top half of the pen," Detective Patel told
Dr. Daruwalla.

The screenwriter was taken aback by this unexpected praise. "You
do?" Farrokh said. "The problem is, Mrs. Dogar's got to think that it's
been in her purse—that it's *always* been there."

"I agree that if Dhar can distract her, Mr. Sethna can plant the pen."
That was all the policeman would say.

"You *do?*" Dr. Daruwalla repeated.

"It would be nice if we found other things in her purse," the deputy
commissioner thought aloud.

"You mean the money with the typewritten warnings—or maybe
even a drawing," the doctor said.

"Precisely," Patel said.

"Well, I wish I could write *that!*" the screenwriter replied.

Suddenly Julia was back at the table; she'd lost John D. as a dance
partner when Amy Sorabjee had cut in.

"The shameless girl!" Dr. Daruwalla said.

"Come dance with me, *Liebchen*," Julia told him.

Then the Patels were alone at the table; in fact, they were alone in
the Ladies' Garden. In the main dining room, an unidentified man was
sleeping with his head on one of the dinner tables; everyone else was
dancing, or they were standing in the ballroom—apparently for the
morbid pleasure of singing "Auld Lang Syne." The waiters were beginning to scavenge the abandoned tables, but not a single waiter disturbed
Detective Patel and Nancy in the Ladies' Garden; Mr. Sethna had
instructed them to respect the couple's privacy.

Nancy's hair had come down, and she had trouble unfastening the
pearl necklace; her husband had to help her with the clasp.

"They're beautiful pearls, aren't they?" Nancy asked. "But if I don't
give them back to Mrs. Daruwalla now, I'll forget and wear them home.
They might get lost or stolen."

"I'll try to find you a necklace like this," Detective Patel told her.

"No, it's too expensive," Nancy said.

"You did a good job," her husband told her.

"We're going to catch her, aren't we, Vijay?" she asked him.

"Yes, we are, sweetie," he replied.

"She didn't recognize me!" Nancy cried.

"I told you she wouldn't, didn't I?" the detective said.

"She didn't even see me! She looked right through me—like I didn't exist! All these years, and she didn't even remember me," Nancy said.

The deputy commissioner held her hand. She rested her head on his shoulder; she felt so empty, she couldn't even cry.

"I'm sorry, Vijay, but I don't think I can dance. I just can't," Nancy said.

"That's all right, sweetie," her husband said. "I don't dance—remember?"

"He didn't have to unzip me—it was unnecessary," Nancy said.

"It was part of the overall effect," Patel replied.

"It was unnecessary," Nancy repeated. "And I didn't like the way he did it."

"The idea was, you weren't supposed to like it," the policeman told her.

"She must have tried to bite his whole lip off!" Nancy cried.

"I believe she barely managed to stop herself," the deputy commissioner said. This had the effect of releasing Nancy from her emptiness; at last, she was able to cry on her husband's shoulder. It seemed that the band would never stop playing the tiresome old song.

" 'We'll drink a cup of kindness yet . . .' " Mr. Bannerjee was shouting.

Mr. Sethna observed that Julia and Dr. Daruwalla were the most stately dancers on the floor. Dr. and Mrs. Sorabjee danced nervously; they didn't dare take their eyes off their daughter. Poor Amy had been brought home from England, where she hadn't been doing very well. Too much partying, her parents suspected—and, more disturbing, a reputed attraction to older men. At university, she was notoriously opposed to romances with her fellow students; rather, she'd thrown herself at one of her professors—a married chap. He'd not taken advantage of her, thank goodness. And now Dr. and Mrs. Sorabjee were tortured to see the young girl dancing with Dhar. From the frying pan to the fire! Mrs. Sorabjee thought. It was awkward for Mrs. Sorabjee, being a close friend of the Daruwallas' and therefore unable to express her opinion of Inspector Dhar.

"Do you know you're available in England—on videocassette?" Amy was telling the actor.

"*Am* I?" he said.

"Once we had a wine tasting and we rented you," Amy told him. "People who aren't from Bombay don't know what to make of you. The movies seem terribly odd to them."

"Yes," said Inspector Dhar. "To me, too," he added.

This made her laugh; she was an easy girl, he could tell—he felt a little sorry for her parents.

"All that music, mixed in with all the murders," Amy Sorabjee said.

"Don't forget the divine intervention," the actor remarked.

"Yes! And all the women—you *do* gather up a lot of women," Amy observed.

"Yes, I do," Dhar said.

" 'We'll drink a cup of kindness yet for the days of auld lang syne!' " the old dancers brayed; they sounded like donkeys.

"I like *Inspector Dhar and the Cage-Girl Killer* the best—it's the sexiest," said little Amy Sorabjee.

"I don't have a favorite," the actor confided to her; he guessed she was 22 or 23. He found her a pleasant distraction, but it irritated him that she kept staring at his lip.

"What happened to your lip?" she finally asked him in a whisper—her expression still girlish but sly, even conspiratorial.

"When the lights went out, I danced into a wall," Dhar told her.

"I think that horrid woman did it to you," Amy Sorabjee dared to say. "It looks like she bit you!"

John D. just kept dancing; the way his lip had swollen, it hurt to sneer.

"Everyone thinks she's a horrid woman, you know," Amy said; Dhar's silence had made her less sure of herself. "And who was that first woman you were with?" Amy asked him. "The one who left?"

"She's a stripper," said Inspector Dhar.

"Go on—not really!" Amy cried.

"Yes, really," John D. replied.

"And who is the blond lady?" Amy asked. "I thought she looked about to cry."

"She's a former friend," the actor answered; he was tired of the girl now. A young girl's idea of intimacy was getting answers to all her questions.

John D. was sure that Vinod would already be waiting outside; surely the dwarf had returned from taking Muriel to the Wetness Cabaret. Dhar wanted to go to bed, alone; he wanted to put more ice on his lip, and he wanted to apologize to Farrokh, too. It had been unkind of the actor to imply that preparing himself for the seduction of Mrs. Dogar was "no circus"; John D. knew what the circus meant to Dr. Daruwalla—the actor could have more charitably said that getting ready for Rahul was "no picnic." And now here was the insatiable Amy Sorabjee, trying to get him (and herself) into some unnecessary trouble. Time to slip away, the actor thought.

Just then, Amy took a quick look over Dhar's shoulder; she wanted to be exactly sure where her parents were. A doddering threesome had blocked Dr. and Mrs. Sorabjee from Amy's view—Mr. Bannerjee was struggling to dance with his wife and the widow Lal—and Amy seized this moment of privacy, for she knew she was only briefly free of her parents' scrutiny. She brushed her soft lips against John D.'s cheek; then she whispered overbreathlessly in the actor's ear. "I could kiss that lip and make it better!" she said.

John D., smoothly, just kept dancing. His unresponsiveness made Amy feel insecure, and so she whispered more plaintively—at least more matter-of-factly—"I prefer older men."

"*Do* you?" the movie star said. "Why, so do I," Inspector Dhar told the silly girl. "So do I!"

That got rid of her; it always worked. At last, Inspector Dhar could slip away.

25. JUBILEE DAY

No Monkey

It was January 1, 1990, a Monday. It was also Jubilee Day at St. Ignatius School in Mazagaon—the start of the mission's 126th year. Well-wishers were invited to a high tea, which amounted to a light supper in the early evening; this was scheduled to follow a special late-afternoon Mass. This was also the occasion that would formally serve to introduce Martin Mills to the Catholic community in Bombay; therefore, Father Julian and Father Cecil regretted that the scholastic had returned from the circus in such mutilated condition. The previous night, Martin had frightened Brother Gabriel, who mistook the mauled figure with his bloodstained and unraveling bandages for the wandering spirit of a previously persecuted Jesuit—some poor soul who'd been tortured and then put to death.

Earlier that same night, the zealot had prevailed upon Father Cecil to hear his confession. Father Cecil was so tired, he fell asleep before he could give Martin absolution. Typically, Martin's confession seemed unending—nor had Father Cecil caught the gist of it before he nodded off. It struck the old priest that Martin Mills was confessing nothing more serious than a lifelong disposition to complain.

Martin had begun by enumerating his several disappointments with himself, beginning with the period of his novitiate at St. Aloysius in

Massachusetts. Father Cecil tried to listen closely, for there was a tone of urgency in the scholastic's voice; yet young Martin's capacity for finding fault with himself was vast—the poor priest soon felt that his participation in Martin's confession was superfluous. For example, as a novice at St. Aloysius, Martin confessed, a significantly holy event had been entirely wasted on him; Martin had been unimpressed by the visit of the sacred arm of St. Francis Xavier to the Massachusetts novitiate. (Father Cecil didn't think this was so bad.)

The acolyte bearing the saint's severed arm was the famous Father Terry Finney, S.J.; Father Finney had selflessly undertaken the task of carrying the golden reliquary around the world. Martin confessed that, to him, the holy arm had been nothing but a skeletal limb under glass, like something partially eaten—like a leftover, Martin Mills had observed. Only now could the scholastic bear to confess having had such blasphemous thoughts. (By this time, Father Cecil was fast asleep.)

There was more; it troubled Martin that the issue of Divine Grace had taken him years to resolve to his satisfaction. And sometimes the scholastic felt he was merely making a conscious effort not to think about it. Old Father Cecil really should have heard this, for Martin Mills was dangerously full of doubt. The confession would eventually lead young Martin to his present disappointment with himself, which was the way he'd behaved on the trip to and from the circus.

The scholastic said he was guilty of loving the crippled boy more than he loved the child prostitute; his abhorrence of prostitution caused him to feel almost resigned to the girl's fate. And Dr. Daruwalla had provoked the Jesuit on the sensitive matter of homosexuality; Martin was sorry that he'd spoken to the doctor in an intellectually arrogant fashion. At this point, Father Cecil was sleeping so soundly, the poor priest never woke when he slumped forward in the confessional and his nose poked between the latticework where Martin Mills could see it.

When Martin saw the old priest's nose, he knew that Father Cecil was dead to the world. He didn't want to embarrass the poor man; however, it wasn't right to leave him sleeping in such an uncomfortable position. That was why the missionary crept away and went looking for Brother Gabriel; that was when poor Brother Gabriel mistook the wildly bandaged scholastic for a persecuted Christian from the past. After his fear had subsided, Brother Gabriel went to wake up Father Cecil, who thereafter suffered a sleepless night; the priest couldn't remember what Martin Mills had confessed, or whether or not he'd given the zealot absolution.

Martin slept blissfully. Even without absolution, it had felt good to say all those things against himself; tomorrow was soon enough for someone to hear his full confession—perhaps he'd ask Father Julian this time. Although Father Julian was scarier than Father Cecil, the Father Rector was also a bit younger. Thus, with his conscience clear and no bugs in his bed, Martin would sleep through the night. Full of doubt one minute, brimming with conviction the next, the missionary was a walking contradiction—he was dependably unreliable.

Nancy also slept through the night; one couldn't claim that she slept "blissfully," but at least she slept. Surely the champagne helped. She wouldn't hear the ringing of the phone, which Detective Patel answered in the kitchen. It was 4:00 on the morning of New Year's Day, and at first the deputy commissioner was relieved that the call was *not* from the surveillance officer who'd been assigned to watch the Dogars' house on old Ridge Road, Malabar Hill; it was a homicide report from the red-light district in Kamathipura—a prostitute had been murdered in one of the arguably better brothels. Ordinarily, no one would have awakened the deputy commissioner with such a report, but both the investigating officer and the medical examiner were certain that the crime was Dhar-related. Once again, there was the elephant drawing on the belly of the murdered whore, but there was also a fearsome new twist to this killing, which the caller was sure Detective Patel would want to see.

As for the surveillance officer, the subinspector who was watching the Dogars' house, he might as well have slept through the night, too. He swore that Mrs. Dogar had never left her house; only *Mr.* Dogar had left. The subinspector, whom the deputy commissioner would later reassign to something harmless, like answering letters of complaint, declared that he knew it was Mr. Dogar because of the old man's characteristic shuffle; also, the figure was stooped. Then there was the matter of the baggy suit, which was gray. It was a man's suit of an exceedingly loose fit—not what Mr. Dogar had worn to the New Year's Eve party at the Duckworth Club—and with it Mr. Dogar wore a white shirt, open at the throat. The old man climbed into a taxi at about 2:00 A.M.; he returned to his house, in another taxi, at 3:45 A.M. The surveillance officer (whom the deputy commissioner would also later demote from subinspector to constable) had smugly assumed that Mr. Dogar was visiting either a mistress or a prostitute.

Definitely a prostitute, thought Detective Patel. Unfortunately, it hadn't been *Mr.* Dogar.

The madam at the questionably better brothel in Kamathipura told the deputy commissioner that it was her brothel's policy to turn out the lights at 1:00 or 2:00 A.M., depending on the volume of customers or the lack thereof. After the lights were out, she accepted only all-night visitors; to spend the night with one of her girls, the madam charged from 100 rupees on up. The "old man" who'd arrived after 2:00 A.M., when the brothel was dark, had offered 300 rupees for the madam's smallest girl.

Detective Patel first thought the madam must have meant her *youngest* girl, but the madam said she was sure that the gentleman had requested her "smallest"; in any case, that's what he got. Asha was a very small, delicate girl—about 15, the madam declared. About 13, the deputy commissioner guessed.

Because the lights were out and there were no other girls in the hallway, no one but the madam and Asha saw the alleged old man—he wasn't *that* old, the madam believed. He wasn't at all stooped, either, the madam recalled, but (like the soon-to-be-demoted surveillance officer) she noted how loosely the suit fit him and that it was gray. "He" was very clean-shaven, except for a thin mustache—the latter was false, Detective Patel assumed—and an unusual hairdo . . . here the madam held her hands high above her forehead and said, "But it was cut short in the back, and over the ears."

"Yes, I know—a pompadour," Patel said. He knew that the hair would not have been silver, streaked with white, but he asked the question anyway.

"No, it was black, streaked with silver," the madam said.

And no one had seen the "old man" leave. The madam had been awakened by the presence of a nun. She'd heard what she thought was someone trying to open the door from the street; when she went to see, there was a nun outside the door—it must have been about 3:00 in the morning.

"Do you see a lot of nuns in this district at that hour?" the deputy commissioner asked her.

"Of course not!" the madam cried. She'd asked the nun what she wanted, and the nun had replied that she was searching for a Christian girl from Kerala; the madam responded that she had no Kerala Christians in her house.

"And what color was the nun's habit?" Patel asked, although he knew the answer would be "gray," which it was. It wasn't an unusual color for a habit of tropical weight, but it was also something that could have been fashioned from the same gray suit that Mrs. Dogar had worn when she

came to the brothel. The baggy suit had probably fitted over the habit;
then, in turn, the habit fit over the suit, or parts of the habit and the suit
were one and the same—at least the same fabric. The white shirt could
have various uses; maybe it was rolled, like a high collar, or else it could
cover the head, like a kind of cowl. The detective presumed that the
alleged nun didn't have a mustache. ("Of course not!" the madam declared.) And because the nun had covered her head, the madam
wouldn't have noticed the pompadour.

The only reason the madam had found the dead girl so soon was that
she'd been unable to fall back asleep; first, one of the all-night customers
was shouting, and then, when it was finally quiet, the madam had heard
the sound of water boiling, although it wasn't time for tea. In the dead
girl's cubicle, a pot of water had come to a boil on a heating coil; that
was how the madam discovered the body. Otherwise, it might have been
8:00 or 9:00 in the morning before the other prostitutes would have
noticed that tiny Asha wasn't up and about.

The deputy commissioner asked the madam about the sound of
someone trying to open the door from the street—the sound that had
awakened her. Wouldn't the door have made the same sound if it had
been opened from the *inside,* and then closed *behind* the departing nun?
The madam admitted that this would have made the same sound; in
short, if the madam hadn't heard the door, she never would have seen
the nun. And by the time Mrs. Dogar took a taxi home, she was no longer
a nun at all.

Detective Patel was exceedingly polite in asking the madam a most
obvious question: "Would you consider the idea that the not-so-old man
and the nun were in fact the same person?" The madam shrugged; she
doubted she could identify either of them. When the deputy commissioner pressed her on this point, all the madam would add was that she'd
been sleepy; both the not-so-old man and the nun had woken her up.

Nancy was still not awake when Detective Patel returned to his flat;
he'd already typed a scathing report, demoting the surveillance officer
and consigning him to the mailroom of Crime Branch Headquarters.
The deputy commissioner wanted to be home when his wife woke up;
he also didn't want to call Inspector Dhar and Dr. Daruwalla from the
police station. Detective Patel thought he'd let them all sleep a little
longer.

The deputy commissioner determined that Asha's neck had been
broken so cleanly for two reasons. One, she was small; two, she'd been
completely relaxed. Rahul must have coaxed her over onto her stomach,

as if to prepare her for sex in that position. But of course there'd been no sex. The deep fingerprint bruises in the prostitute's eye sockets—and on her throat, just below her jaw—suggested that Mrs. Dogar had grabbed Asha's face from behind; she'd wrenched the small girl's head back and to one side, until Asha's neck snapped.

Then Rahul had rolled Asha onto her back in order to make the drawing on her belly. Although the drawing was of the usual kind, it was of less than the usual quality; it suggested undue haste, which was strange—there was no urgency for Mrs. Dogar to leave the brothel. Yet something had compelled Rahul to hurry. As for the fearsome "new twist" to this killing, it sickened Detective Patel. The dead girl's lower lip was bitten clean through. Asha could not have been bitten so savagely while she was alive; her screams would have awakened the entire brothel. No; the bite had occurred after the murder and after the drawing. The minimal amount of bleeding indicated that Asha had been bitten after her heart had stopped. It was the idea of biting the girl that had made Mrs. Dogar hurry, the policeman thought. She couldn't wait to finish the drawing because Asha's lower lip was so tempting to her.

Even such slight bleeding had made a mess, which was uncharacteristic of Rahul. It must have been Mrs. Dogar who put the pot of water on the heating coil; her own face, at least her mouth, must have been marked with the prostitute's blood. When the water was warm, Rahul dipped some of the dead girl's clothes in the pot and used them to wash the blood off herself. Then she left—as a nun—forgetting that the heating coil was on. The boiling water had brought the madam. Although the nun had been a smart idea, this had otherwise been a sloppy job.

Nancy woke up about 8:00; she had a hangover, but Detective Patel didn't hesitate to tell her what had happened. He could hear her being sick in the bathroom; he called the actor first, then the screenwriter. He told Dhar about the lip, but not the doctor; with Dr. Daruwalla, the deputy commissioner wanted to emphasize the importance of a good script for Dhar's lunch with Mrs. Dogar. Patel told them both that he would have to arrest Rahul today; he hoped he had enough circumstantial evidence to arrest her. Whether or not he had enough evidence to *keep* her—that was another story. That was what he was counting on the actor and the screenwriter for: they had to make something happen over lunch.

Deputy Commissioner Patel was encouraged by one thing that the gullible surveillance officer had told him. After the disguised Mrs. Dogar had shuffled out of the taxi and into her house, the lights were turned on in a ground-floor room—not a bedroom—and these lights remained on well after daybreak. The deputy commissioner hoped that Rahul had been drawing.

As for Dr. Daruwalla, his first good night's sleep—for five nights, and counting—had been interrupted rather early. He had no surgeries scheduled for New Year's Day, and no office appointments, either; he'd been planning to sleep in. But upon hearing from Detective Patel, the screenwriter called John D. immediately. There was a lot to do before Dhar's lunch at the Duckworth Club; there would be much rehearsing—some of it would be awkward, because Mr. Sethna would have to be involved. The deputy commissioner had already notified the old steward.

It was from John D. that Farrokh heard about Asha's lower lip.

"Rahul must have been thinking of *you!*" Dr. Daruwalla cried.

"Well, we know she has a thing about biting," Dhar told the doctor. "In all likelihood, it started with *you.*"

"What do you mean?" Dr. Daruwalla asked, for John D. hadn't told him that Mrs. Dogar had confessed to gnawing on the doctor's toe.

"It all started with the big toe of your right foot, in Goa," John D. began. "That was Rahul who bit you. You were right all along—it was no monkey."

The Wrong Madhu

That Monday, well before meat-feeding time at the Great Blue Nile Circus in Junagadh, the elephant-footed boy would wake up to the steady coughs of the lions; their low roars rose and fell as regularly as breathing. It was a cold morning in that part of Gujarat. For the first time in his life, Ganesh could see his own breath; the huffs of breath from the lions were like blasts of steam escaping from their cages.

The Muslims delivered the meat in a wooden wagon, dotted with flies; the entire floor of the wagon was lifted from the cart and placed on the ground between the cook's tent and the big cats' cages—the raw beef was piled on this slab of rough wood, which was the approximate size of a double door. Even in the cold morning air, the flies hovered over the meat, which Chandra sorted. Sometimes there was mutton mixed in with the beef, and the cook wanted to rescue it; mutton was too expensive for lions and tigers.

The big cats were bellowing now; they could smell the meat, and some of them could see the cook separating the choicer pieces of mutton. If the elephant boy was frightened by how savagely the lions and tigers devoured the raw beef, Dr. Daruwalla would never learn of it; nor would the doctor ever know if the sight of the lions slipping in the meat grease upset the cripple. At the circus, it was one of the few things that always upset the doctor.

That same Monday, someone proposed to marry Madhu. The proposal, as was only proper, was first offered to Mr. and Mrs. Das; the ringmaster and his wife were surprised. Not only had they not begun to train the girl, but, because Madhu was untrained, she wasn't in evidence among the performers; yet the marriage proposal was offered by a gentleman who claimed to have been in the audience for the late-evening show on Sunday. Here he was, the following morning, professing his instant devotion!

The Bengali ringmaster and his wife had children of their own; their kids had rejected the circus life. But Mr. and Mrs. Das had trained many other children to be circus acrobats; they were kind to these adopted kids and especially protective of the girls. After all, when these girls were properly trained, they were of some value—not only to the circus. They had acquired a little glamour; they'd even earned some money, which they'd had no occasion to spend—hence the ringmaster and his wife were used to keeping dowries for them.

Mr. and Mrs. Das conscientiously advised the girls whether or not a marriage proposal was worthy of acceptance or negotiation, and they routinely gave up these adopted daughters—always to decent marriages, and often making their own contributions to the girls' dowries. In many cases, the ringmaster and his wife had grown so fond of these children that it broke their hearts to see them go. Almost all the girls would eventually leave the circus; the few who stayed became trainers.

Madhu was very young and totally unproven, and she had no dowry. Yet here was a gentleman of means, well dressed, clearly a city person— he owned property and managed an entertainment business in Bombay—and he was offering Madhu a marriage proposal that Mr. and Mrs. Das found extremely generous; he would take the poor girl *without* a dowry. Doubtless, in these premarital negotiations, there would have been some substantive discussion of the remuneration that the ringmaster and his wife deserved, for (who knows?) Madhu might have become a star of the Great Blue Nile. From Mr. and Mrs. Das's point of view, they were offered a sizable payment for a sullen girl who might never prove herself to be any kind of acrobat at all. It wasn't as if they were being asked to part with a young woman they'd grown fond of; they'd barely had time to talk with Madhu.

It may have crossed the Bengalis' minds to consult the doctor or the missionary; Mr. and Mrs. Das at least should have discussed the would-be marriage with Deepa, but the dwarf's wife was still sick. So what if Deepa was the one who'd spotted Madhu as a future boneless girl? The dwarf's wife was still confined to her tent. Moreover, the ringmaster held a grudge against Vinod. Mr. Das was envious of the dwarf's car-driving business; since Vinod had left the Great Blue Nile, the dwarf hadn't hesitated to exaggerate his success. And the ringmaster's wife felt herself to be vastly superior to the dwarf's wife; to consult with Deepa was beneath Mrs. Das—even if Deepa were healthy. Besides, Mrs. Das quickly persuaded her husband that Madhu's marriage proposal was a good deal. (It was certainly a good deal for them.)

If Madhu wasn't interested, they'd keep the silly child in the circus; but if the unworthy girl had the wisdom to recognize her good fortune, the ringmaster and his wife would let her go, with their blessings. As for the crippled brother, the gentleman from Bombay appeared to know nothing about him. Mr. and Mrs. Das felt some responsibility for the fact that the elephant-footed boy would be left on his own; they had considered it prudent to promise Dr. Daruwalla and Martin Mills that Ganesh would be given every chance to succeed. The ringmaster and his wife saw no reason to discuss Ganesh with Deepa; the cripple hadn't been a discovery of hers—she'd only claimed to discover the boneless girl. And what if the dwarf's wife had something contagious?

A phone call to the doctor or the missionary would have been an appreciated courtesy—if nothing more. But there were no telephones at the circus; a trip to either the post office or the telegraph office would have been required, and Madhu surprised the ringmaster and his wife by her immediate and unrestrained acceptance of the marriage proposal. She didn't feel that the gentleman was too old for her, as Mr. Das had feared; nor was Madhu repelled by the gentleman's physical appearance, which had been the primary concern of Mrs. Das. The ringmaster's wife was repulsed by the gentleman's disfiguring scar—some sort of burn, she supposed—but Madhu made no mention of it, nor did she otherwise seem to mind such a hideous flaw.

Probably sensing, in advance, Dr. Daruwalla's disapproval, the ringmaster would wisely send a telegram to Martin Mills; the missionary had struck Mr. and Mrs. Das as the more relaxed of the two—by which they meant the more accepting. Furthermore, the Jesuit had seemed slightly less concerned for Madhu's prospects—or else the doctor's concern had been more apparent. And because it was Jubilee Day at St. Ignatius, the school offices were closed; it would be Tuesday before anyone handed the telegram to Martin. Mr. Garg would already have brought his young wife back to the Wetness Cabaret.

Naturally, it was in the Bengali's best interests to make his telegram sound upbeat.

THAT GIRL MADHU / IT IS BEING HER LUCKY DAY / VERY ACCEPTABLE MATRIMONIAL MADE BY MIDDLE-AGED BUT MOST SUCCESSFUL BUSI-NESSMAN / IT IS WHAT SHE IS WANTING EVEN IF SHE ISN'T LOVING HIM EXACTLY AND IN SPITE OF HIS SCAR / MEANWHILE THE CRIPPLE IS BEING AFFORDED EVERY OPPORTUNITY OF WORKING HARD HERE / REST BEING ASSURED / DAS

By the time Dr. Daruwalla would hear the news, the doctor would be kicking himself; he should have known all along—for why else would Mr. Garg have asked Ranjit for the address of the Great Blue Nile? Surely Mr. Garg, like Dr. Daruwalla, knew that Madhu couldn't read; Acid Man had never intended to send the girl a letter. And when Ranjit gave Farrokh the message (that Garg had requested the circus's address), the faithful secretary failed to inform the doctor that Garg had also inquired *when* the doctor was returning from Junagadh. That same Sunday, when Dr. Daruwalla left the circus, Mr. Garg went there.

Farrokh wouldn't be persuaded by Vinod's notion—that Garg was so smitten by Madhu, he couldn't let her go. Maybe Mr. Garg had been unprepared for how much he would miss Madhu, the dwarf said. Deepa insisted on the importance of the fact that Acid Man had actually *married* Madhu; surely Garg had no intentions of sending the girl back to a brothel—not after he'd married her. The dwarf's wife would add that perhaps it *was* Madhu's "lucky day."

But this particular news wouldn't find its way to Dr. Daruwalla on Jubilee Day. This news would wait. Waiting with it was worse news. Ranjit would hear it first, and the medical secretary would elect to spare the doctor such bad tidings; they were unsuitable tidings for New Year's Day. But the busy office of Tata Two was in full operation on this holiday Monday—there were no holidays for Tata Two. It was Dr. Tata's ancient secretary, Mr. Subhash, who informed Ranjit of the problem. The two old secretaries conversed in the manner of hostile but toothless male dogs.

"I am having information for the doctor only," Mr. Subhash began, without bothering to identify himself.

"Then you'll have to wait until tomorrow," Ranjit informed the fool.

"This is Mr. Subhash, in Dr. Tata's office," the imperious secretary said.

"You'll still have to wait until tomorrow," Ranjit told him. "Dr. Daruwalla isn't here today."

"This is being important information—the doctor is definitely wanting to know it as soon as possible," Mr. Subhash said.

"Then tell me," Ranjit replied.

"Well . . . she is having it," Mr. Subhash announced dramatically.

"You've got to be clearer than that," Ranjit told him.

"That girl, Madhu—she is testing positive for HIV," Mr. Subhash said. Ranjit knew this contradicted the information he'd seen in Madhu's file; Tata Two had already told Dr. Daruwalla that Madhu's test was negative. If the girl was carrying the AIDS virus, Ranjit assumed that Dr. Daruwalla wouldn't have allowed her to go to the circus.

"The ELISA is being positive, and this is being confirmed by Western Blot," Mr. Subhash was saying.

"But Dr. Tata himself told Dr. Daruwalla that Madhu's test was *negative*," Ranjit said.

"That was definitely the wrong Madhu," old Mr. Subhash said dismissively. "*Your* Madhu is being HIV-positive."

"This is a serious mistake," Ranjit remarked.

"There is being no *mistake*," Mr. Subhash said indignantly. "This is merely a matter of there being two Madhus." But there was nothing "merely" about the matter.

Ranjit transcribed his phone conversation with Mr. Subhash into a neatly typed report, which he placed on Dr. Daruwalla's desk; from the existing evidence, the medical secretary concluded that Madhu and Mr. Garg might be sharing something a little more serious than chlamydia. What Ranjit couldn't have known was that Mr. Garg had gone to Junagadh and retrieved Madhu from the circus; probably Garg had made his plans to bring the girl back to Bombay only after he'd been told that Madhu was *not* HIV-positive—but maybe not. In the world of the Wetness Cabaret, and throughout the brothels in Kamathipura, a certain fatalism was the norm.

The news about the wrong Madhu would wait for Dr. Daruwalla, too. What was the point of hurrying evil tidings? After all, Ranjit believed that Madhu was still with the circus in Junagadh. As for Mr. Garg, Dr. Daruwalla's secretary wrongly assumed that Acid Man had never left Bombay. And when Martin Mills called Dr. Daruwalla's office, Ranjit saw no reason to inform the missionary that Madhu was carrying the AIDS virus. The zealot wanted his bandages changed; he'd been advised by the Father Rector that clean bandages would be more suitable for the Jubilee Day celebration. Ranjit told Martin that he'd have to call the doctor at home. Because Farrokh was hard at work—rehearsing for Rahul, with John D. and old Mr. Sethna—Julia took the message. She was surprised to hear that Dhar's twin had been bitten by a presumed-to-be-rabid chimpanzee. Martin was surprised, and his feelings were hurt, to hear that Dr. Daruwalla hadn't informed his wife of the painful episode.

Julia graciously accepted the Jesuit's invitation to the high tea in honor of Jubilee Day; she promised that she'd bring Farrokh to St. Ignatius before the start of the festivities so that the doctor would have plenty of time to change Martin's bandages. The scholastic thanked Julia, but when he hung up the phone, he felt overcome by the sheer foreignness of his situation. He'd been in India less than a week; suddenly, everything that was unfamiliar was exacting a toll.

To begin with, the zealot had been taken aback by Father Julian's response to his confession. The Father Rector had been impatient and argumentative; his absolution had been grudging and abrupt—and it had been hastily followed by Father Julian's insistence that Martin do something about his soiled and bloody bandages. But the priest and the scholastic had encountered a fundamental misunderstanding. At that point in his confession when Martin Mills had admitted to loving the crippled boy more than he could ever love the child prostitute, Father Julian had interrupted him and told him to be less concerned with his own capacity for love, by which the Father Rector meant that Martin should be *more* concerned with God's love and God's will—and that he should be more humble about his own, merely human role. Martin was a member of the Society of Jesus, and he should behave accordingly; he wasn't just another egocentric social worker—a do-gooder who was constantly evaluating, criticizing and congratulating himself.

"The fate of these children isn't in your hands," Father Julian told the scholastic, "nor will one of them suffer, more or less, because of *your* love for them—or your *lack* of love for them. Try to stop thinking so much about yourself. You're an instrument of God's will—you're not your own creation."

This not only struck the zealot as blunt; Martin Mills was confused. That the Father Rector saw the children as already consigned to their fate seemed remarkably Calvinistic for a Jesuit; Martin feared that Father Julian might also be suffering from the influence of Hinduism, for this notion of the children's "fate" had a karmic ring. And what was wrong with being a social worker? Hadn't St. Ignatius Loyola himself been a social worker of unflagging zeal? Or did the Father Rector mean only that Martin shouldn't take the fate of the circus children too *personally*? That the scholastic had intervened on the children's behalf did *not* mean he was responsible for every little thing that might happen to them.

It was in such a spiritual fog that Martin Mills took a walk in Mazagaon; he hadn't wandered far from the mission before he encountered that slum which Dr. Daruwalla had first shown to him—the former movie-set slum where his evil mother had fainted when she was stepped on and licked by a cow. Martin remembered that he'd vomited from the moving car.

At midmorning, on this busy Monday, the slum was teeming, but the missionary found that it was better to focus on such abjectness in a microcosmic fashion; rather than look up the length of Sophia Zuber Road for as far as he could see, Martin kept his eyes cast down—at his slowly moving feet. He never allowed his gaze to wander above ground level. Most of the slum dwellers were thus cut off at their ankles; he saw only the children's faces—naturally, the children were begging. He saw the paws and the inquiring noses of scavenging dogs. He saw a moped that had fallen or crashed in the gutter; a garland of marigolds was entwined on its handlebars, as if the moped were being prepared for cremation. He came upon a cow—a whole cow, not just the hooves, because the cow was lying down. It was hard to navigate around the cow. But when Martin Mills stopped walking, even though he'd been walking slowly, he found himself quickly surrounded; it should be stated clearly in every guidebook for tourists—never stand still in a slum.

The cow's long sad dignified face gazed up at him; its eyes were rimmed with flies. On the cow's tawny flank, a patch of the smooth hide was abraded—the raw spot was no bigger than a human fist, but it was encrusted with flies. This apparent abrasion was actually the entrance to a deep hole that had been made in the cow by a vehicle transporting a ship's mast; but Martin hadn't witnessed the collision, nor did the milling crowd permit him a comprehensive view of the cow's mortal wound.

Suddenly, the crowd parted; a procession was passing—all Martin saw was a lunatic mob of flower throwers. When the worshipers had filed by, the cow lay sprinkled with rose petals; some of the flowers were stuck to the wound, alongside the flies. One of the cow's long legs was extended, for the animal was lying on its side; the hoof almost reached the curb. There in the gutter, within inches of the hoof but entirely untouched, was (unmistakably) a human turd. Beyond the serenely undisturbed turd was a vendor's stall. They were selling something that looked purposeless to Martin Mills; it was a vivid scarlet powder, but the missionary doubted that it was a spice or anything edible. Some of it spilled into the gutter, where its dazzling red particles coated both the cow's hoof and the human turd.

That was Martin's microcosm of India: the mortally wounded animal, the religious ritual, the incessant flies, the unbelievably bright colors, the evidence of casual human shit—and of course the confusion of smells. The missionary had been forewarned: if he couldn't see beyond such abjectness, he would be of scant use to St. Ignatius—or to any mission in such a world. Shaken, the scholastic wondered if he had the stomach to be a priest. So vulnerable was his state of mind, Martin Mills was fortunate that the news about Madhu was still a day away.

Take Me Home

In the Ladies' Garden at the Duckworth Club, the noon sun shimmered above the bower. So dense was the bougainvillea, the sun shot through the flowers in pinholes; these beads of bright light dappled the table-cloths like sprinkled diamonds. Nancy passed her hands under the needle-thin rays. She was playing with the sun, trying to reflect its light in her wedding ring, when Detective Patel spoke to her. "You don't have to be here, sweetie," her husband said. "You can go home, you know."

"I want to be here," Nancy told him.

"I just want to warn you—don't expect this to be satisfying," the deputy commissioner said. "Somehow, even when you catch them, it's never quite satisfying."

Dr. Daruwalla, who kept looking at his watch, then remarked, "She's late."

"They're *both* late," Nancy said.

"Dhar is *supposed* to be late," the policeman reminded her.

Dhar was waiting in the kitchen. When the second Mrs. Dogar arrived, Mr. Sethna would observe the increasing degrees of her irritation; when the steward saw that she was clearly agitated, he would send Dhar to her table. Dr. Daruwalla was operating on the theory that agitation inspired Rahul to act rashly.

But when she arrived, they almost didn't recognize her. She was wearing what Western women familiarly call a little black dress; the skirt was short, with a slight flare, the waist very long and slimming. Mrs. Dogar's small, high breasts were displayed to good effect. If she'd worn a black-linen jacket, she would have looked almost businesslike, Dr. Daruwalla believed; without a jacket, the dress was more suitable for a cocktail party in Toronto. As if intended to offend Duckworthians, the dress was sleeveless, with spaghetti straps; the brawniness of Rahul's bare shoulders and upper arms, not to mention the breadth of her chest, hulked ostentatiously. She was too muscular for a dress like that, Farrokh decided; then it occurred to him that this was what she thought Dhar liked.

Yet Mrs. Dogar didn't move as if she were at all conscious that she was a woman of great strength or noticeable size. Her entry into the Duckworth Club dining room wasn't in the least aggressive. Her attitude was shy and girlish; rather than stride to her table, she allowed old Mr. Sethna to escort her on his arm—Dr. Daruwalla had never seen her this way. This wasn't a woman who would ever pick up a spoon or a fork and ring it against her water glass; this was an extremely feminine woman—she would rather starve at her table than cause herself any unflattering attention. She would sit smiling and waiting for Dhar until the club closed and someone sent her home. Apparently, Detective Patel was prepared for this change in her, because the deputy commissioner spoke quickly to the screenwriter; Mrs. Dogar had barely been seated at her table.

"Don't bother to keep her waiting," the policeman said. "She's a different woman today."

Farrokh summoned Mr. Sethna—to have John D. "arrive"—but all the while the deputy commissioner was watching what Mrs. Dogar did with her purse. It was a table for four, as the screenwriter had suggested; this had been Julia's idea. When there were only two people at a table for four, Julia said, a woman usually put her purse on one of the empty chairs—not on the floor—and Farrokh had wanted the purse on a chair.

"She put it on the floor, anyway," Detective Patel observed.

Dr. Daruwalla had been unable to prevent Julia from attending *this* lunch; now Julia said, "That's because she's not a real woman."

"Dhar will take care of it," the deputy commissioner said.

All Farrokh could think was that the change in Mrs. Dogar was terrifying.

"It was the murder, wasn't it?" the doctor asked the policeman. "I mean, the murder has totally calmed her—it's had a completely soothing effect on her, hasn't it?"

"It appears to have made her feel like a young girl," Patel replied.

"She must have a hard time feeling like a young girl," Nancy remarked. "What a lot to do—just to feel like a young girl."

Then Dhar was there, at Mrs. Dogar's table; he didn't kiss her. He approached her unseen, from behind, and he put both his hands on her bare shoulders; perhaps he leaned on her, because she appeared to stiffen, but he was only trying to kick her purse over. When he managed to do this, she picked her purse up and put it on an empty chair.

"We're forgetting to talk among ourselves," the deputy commissioner said. "We can't simply be staring at them and saying nothing."

"Please kill her, Vijay," Nancy said.

"I'm not carrying a gun, sweetie," the deputy commissioner lied.

"What will the law do to her?" Julia asked the policeman.

"Capital punishment exists in India," the detective said, "but the death penalty is rarely enacted."

"Death is by hanging," Dr. Daruwalla said.

"Yes, but there's no jury system in India," Patel said. "A single judge decides the prisoner's fate. Life imprisonment and hard labor are much more common than the death penalty. They won't hang her."

"You should kill her now," Nancy repeated.

They could see Mr. Sethna hovering around Mrs. Dogar's table like a nervous ghost. They couldn't see Dhar's left hand—it was under the table. Speculation was rife that his hand was on Rahul's thigh, or in her lap.

"Let's just keep talking," Patel told them cheerfully.

"Fuck you, fuck Rahul, fuck Dhar," Nancy told Patel. "Fuck you, too," she said to Farrokh. "Not you—I like you," she told Julia.

"Thank you, dear," Julia replied.

"Fuck, fuck, fuck," Nancy said.

"Your poor lip," Mrs. Dogar was saying to John D. This much Mr. Sethna understood; they would understand this much from the Ladies' Garden, too, because they saw Rahul touch Dhar's lower lip with her long index finger—it was just a brief, feather-light touch. Dhar's lower lip was a luminous navy blue.

"I hope you're not in a biting mood today," John D. told her.

"I'm in a very good mood today," Mrs. Dogar replied. "I want to know where you're going to take me, and what you're going to do to me," she said coquettishly. It was embarrassing how young and cute she seemed to think she was. Her lips were pursed, which exaggerated the deep wrinkles at the corners of her savage mouth; her smile was small and coy, as if she were blotting lipstick in a mirror. Although her makeup mostly concealed the mark, there was a tiny inflamed cut across the green-tinted eyelid of one of her eyes; it caused her to blink, as if the eye itself were sore. But it was only a small irritation, the tiniest scratch; it was all that the prostitute named Asha had been able to do to her—to flick back one hand, to poke at Rahul's eye—maybe a second or two before Rahul broke her neck.

"You've scratched your eye, haven't you?" Inspector Dhar observed, but he felt no stiffening in Mrs. Dogar's thighs; under the table, she gently pressed her thighs together on his hand.

"I must have been thinking of you in my sleep," she said dreamily. When she closed her eyes, her eyelids had the silver-green iridescence of a lizard; when she parted her lips, her long teeth were wet and shiny—her warm gums were the color of strong tea.

It made John D.'s lip throb to look at her, but he continued to press his palm against the inside of her thigh. He hated this part of the script. Dhar suddenly said, "Did you draw me a picture of what you want?" He felt the muscles in both her thighs grip his hand tightly—her mouth was also tightly closed—and her eyes opened wide and fixed on his lip.

"You can't expect me to show you *here*," Mrs. Dogar said.

"Just a peek," John D. begged her. "Otherwise, I'll be in too much of a hurry to eat."

Had he not been so easily offended by vulgarity, Mr. Sethna would have been in eavesdropper heaven; yet the steward was trembling with disapproval and responsibility. It struck the old Parsi as an awkward moment to bring them the menus, but he knew he needed to be near her purse.

"It's disgusting how much people eat—I loathe eating," Mrs. Dogar said. Dhar felt her thighs go slack; it was as if her concentration span were shorter than a child's—as if she were losing her sexual interest, and for no better reason than the merest mention of food.

"We don't have to eat at all—we haven't ordered," Dhar reminded her. "We could just go—now," he suggested, but even as he spoke he was prepared to hold her in her chair (if need be) with his left hand. The thought of being alone with her, in a suite at either the Oberoi or the Taj, would have frightened John D., except that he knew Detective Patel would never allow Rahul to leave the Duckworth Club. But Mrs. Dogar was almost strong enough to stand up, despite the downward pressure of Dhar's hand. "Just one picture," the actor pleaded with her. "Just show me something."

Rahul exhaled thinly through her nose. "I'm in too good a mood to be exasperated with you," she told him. "But you're a very naughty boy."

"Show me," Dhar said. In her thighs, he thought he felt those seemingly involuntary shivers that are visible on the flanks of a horse. When she turned to her purse, John D. raised his eyes to Mr. Sethna, but the old Parsi appeared to be suffering from stage fright; the steward clutched the menus in one hand, his silver serving tray in the other. How could the old fool upend Mrs. Dogar's purse if he didn't have a free hand? John D. wondered.

Rahul took the purse into her lap; Dhar could feel the bottom of it, for it briefly rested on his wrist. There was more than one drawing, and Mrs. Dogar appeared to hesitate before she withdrew all three; but she still didn't show him any of them. She held the drawings protectively in her right hand; with her left hand, she returned her purse to the empty chair—that was when Mr. Sethna sprang into erratic action. He dropped the serving tray; there was a resounding silvery clatter upon the dining room's stone floor. Then the steward stepped on the tray—he actually appeared to trip over it—and the menus flew from his hand into Mrs. Dogar's lap. Instinctively, she caught them, while the old Parsi staggered past her and collided with the all-important chair. There went her purse, upside down on the floor, but nothing spilled out of it until Mr. Sethna clumsily attempted to pick the purse up; then everything was everywhere. Of the three drawings, which Rahul had left unattended on the table, John D. could see only the one on top. It was enough.

The woman in the picture bore a striking resemblance to what Mrs. Dogar might have looked like as a young girl. Rahul had never exactly been a young girl, but this portrait reminded John D. of how she had looked in Goa 20 years ago. An elephant was mounting her, but this elephant had two trunks. The first trunk—it was in the usual place for an elephant's trunk—was deeply inside the young woman's mouth; in fact, it had emerged through the back of her head. The second trunk, which was the elephant's preposterous penis, had penetrated the woman's vagina; it was this trunk that had burst between the woman's shoulder blades. Approximately at the back of the woman's neck, John D. could see that the elephant's two trunks were touching each other; the actor could also see that the elephant was winking. Dhar would never see the other two drawings; he wouldn't want to. The movie star stepped quickly behind Mrs. Dogar's chair and pushed the fumbling Mr. Sethna out of the way.

"Allow me," Dhar said, bending to the spilled contents of her purse. Mrs. Dogar's mood had been so improved by her recent killing, she was remarkably unprovoked by the apparent accident.

"Oh, purses! They're *such* a nuisance!" Rahul said. Flirtatiously, she allowed her hand to touch the back of Inspector Dhar's neck. He was kneeling between her chair and the empty chair; he was gathering the contents of her purse, which he then put on the table. Quite casually, the actor pointed to the top half of the silver ballpoint pen, which he'd placed between a mirror and a jar of moisturizer.

"I don't see the bottom half of this," the actor said. "Maybe it's still in your purse." Then he handed her the purse, which was easily half full, and he pretended to look under the table for the bottom half of the silver ballpoint pen—that part which Nancy had kept so well polished these 20 years.

When John D. lifted his face to her, he was still kneeling; as such, his face was level with her small, well-shaped breasts. Mrs. Dogar was holding the top half of the pen. "A rupee for your thoughts," said Inspector Dhar; it was something he said in all his movies.

Rahul's lips were parted; she looked quizzically down at Dhar—her scratched eye blinking once, and then again. Her lips softly closed and she once more exhaled thinly through her nose, as if such controlled breathing helped her to think.

"I thought I'd lost this," Mrs. Dogar said slowly.

"It appears you've lost the other half," John D. replied; he stayed on his knees because he imagined that she liked looking down on him.

"This is the only half I ever had," Rahul explained.

Dhar stood up and walked behind her chair; he didn't want her to grab the drawings. When John D. returned to his seat, Rahul was staring at the half-pen.

"You might as well have lost *that* half," John D. told her. "You can't use it for anything."

"But you're wrong!" Mrs. Dogar cried. "It's really marvelous as a money clip."

"A money clip," the actor repeated.

"Look here," Rahul began. There was no money among the spilled contents of her purse, which John D. had spread on the table; she had to search in her purse. "The problem with money clips," Mrs. Dogar told him, "is that they're conceived for a big *wad* of money . . . the sort of wad of money that men are always flashing out of their pockets, you know."

"Yes, I know," said Inspector Dhar. He watched her fishing in her purse for some smaller bills. She pulled out a 10-rupee note, and two 5's, and when the actor saw the two 2-rupee notes with the unnatural typing on them, he raised his eyes to Mr. Sethna and the old steward began his hurried shuffle across the dining room to the Ladies' Garden.

"Look here," Rahul repeated. "When you have just a few small notes, which most women must carry—for tipping, for the odd beggar—this is the perfect money clip. It holds just a few notes, but quite snugly . . ." Her voice trailed away because she saw that Dhar had covered the drawings with his hand; he was sliding the three drawings across the tablecloth when Rahul reached out and grabbed his pinky finger, which she sharply lifted, breaking it. John D. still managed to pull the drawings into his lap. The pinky finger of his right hand pointed straight up, as if it grew out of the back of his hand; it was dislocated at the big knuckle joint. With his left hand, Dhar was able to protect the drawings from Mrs. Dogar's grasp. She was still struggling with him—she was trying to get the drawings away from him with her right hand—when Detective Patel hooked her neck in the crook of his elbow and pinned her left arm behind her chair.

"You're under arrest," the deputy commissioner told her.

"The top half of the pen is a money clip," said Inspector Dhar. "She uses it for small notes. When she put the note in Mr. Lal's mouth, the makeshift money clip must have fallen by the body—you know the rest. There's some typing on those two-rupee notes," Dhar told the real policeman.

"Read it to me," Patel said. Mrs. Dogar held herself very still; her free right hand, which had ceased struggling with John D. for the drawings, floated just above the tablecloth, as if she were about to give them all her blessing.

" 'A member no more,' " Dhar read aloud.

"That one was for you," the deputy commissioner told him.

" '. . . because Dhar is still a member,' " Dhar read.

"Who was that one for?" the policeman asked Rahul, but Mrs. Dogar was frozen in her chair, her hand still conducting an imaginary orchestra above the tablecloth; her eyes had never left Inspector Dhar. The top drawing had become wrinkled in the tussle, but John D. smoothed all three drawings against the tablecloth. He was careful not to look at them.

"You're quite an artist," the deputy commissioner told Rahul, but Mrs. Dogar just kept staring at Inspector Dhar.

Dr. Daruwalla regretted that he looked at the drawings; the second was worse than the first, and the third was the worst of all. He knew he would go to his grave still thinking of them. Julia alone had the sense to remain in the Ladies' Garden; she knew there was no good reason to come any closer. But Nancy must have felt compelled to confront the Devil herself; it would be uncomfortable for her later to recall the last words between Dhar and Rahul.

"I really wanted you—I wasn't kidding," Mrs. Dogar said to the actor.

To Dr. Daruwalla's surprise, John D. said to Mrs. Dogar, "I wasn't kidding, either."

It must have been hard for Nancy to feel that the focus of her victimization had shifted so far from herself; it still galled her that Rahul didn't remember who she was.

"I was in Goa," Nancy announced to the killer.

"Don't say anything, sweetie," her husband told her.

"Say anything you feel like saying, sweetie," Rahul said.

"I had a fever and you crawled into bed with me," Nancy said.

Mrs. Dogar appeared to be thoughtfully surprised. She stared at Nancy as she had previously stared at the top half of the pen, her recognition traveling over time. "Why, is it really *you*, dear?" Rahul asked Nancy. "But what on earth has happened to you?"

"You should have killed me when you had the chance," Nancy told her.

"You look already dead to me," Mrs. Dogar said.

"Please kill her, Vijay," Nancy said to her husband.

"I told you this wouldn't be very satisfying, sweetie." That was all the deputy commissioner would say to her.

When the uniformed constables and the subinspectors came, Detective Patel told them to put away their weapons. Rahul was not resisting arrest. The deep and unknown satisfactions of the previous night's murder seemed to radiate from Mrs. Dogar; she was no more violent on this New Year's Monday than whatever brief impulse had urged her to break John D.'s pinky finger. The serial killer's smile was serene.

Understandably, the deputy commissioner was worried about his wife. He told her he'd have to go directly to Crime Branch Headquarters, but surely she could get a ride home. Dhar's dwarf driver had already made his presence known; Vinod was prowling the foyer of the Duckworth Club. Detective Patel suggested that perhaps Dhar wouldn't mind taking Nancy home in his private taxi.

"Not a good idea." That was all Nancy would say to her husband.

Julia said that she and Dr. Daruwalla would bring Nancy home. Dhar offered to have Vinod drive Nancy home—just the dwarf, alone. That way, she wouldn't have to talk to anyone.

Nancy preferred this plan. "I'm safe around dwarfs," she said. "I like dwarfs."

When she'd gone with Vinod, Detective Patel asked Inspector Dhar how he liked being a real policeman. "It's better in the movies," the actor replied. "In the movies, things happen the way they should happen."

After the deputy commissioner had departed with Rahul, John D. let Dr. Daruwalla snap his pinky finger into place. "Just look away—look at Julia," the doctor recommended. Then he popped the dislocated finger back where it belonged. "We'll take an X ray tomorrow," Dr. Daruwalla said. "Maybe we'll splint it, but not until it's stopped swelling. For now, keep putting it in ice."

At the table in the Ladies' Garden, John D. responded to this advice by submersing his pinky in his water glass; most of the ice in the glass had melted, so Dr. Daruwalla summoned Mr. Sethna for more. Because the old Parsi seemed deeply disappointed that no one had congratulated him on his performance, Dhar said, "Mr. Sethna, that was really brilliant—how you fell over your own tray, for example. The distracting sound of the tray itself, your particularly purposeful but graceful awkwardness . . . truly brilliant."

"Thank you," Mr. Sethna replied. "I wasn't sure what to do with the menus."

"That was brilliant, too—the menus in her lap. Perfect!" said Inspector Dhar.

"Thank you," the steward repeated; he went away—he was so pleased with himself that he forgot to bring the ice.

No one had eaten any lunch. Dr. Daruwalla was the first to confess to a great hunger; Julia was so relieved that Mrs. Dogar was gone, she admitted to having a considerable appetite herself. John D. ate with them, although he seemed indifferent to the food.

Farrokh reminded Mr. Sethna that he'd forgotten to bring the ice, which the steward finally delivered to the table in a silver bowl; it was a bowl that was normally reserved for chilling tiger prawns, and the movie star stuck his swollen pinky finger in it with a vaguely mortified expression. Although the finger was still swelling, especially at the joint of the big knuckle, Dhar's pinky was not nearly as discolored as his lip.

The actor drank more beer than he usually permitted himself at midday, and his conversation was entirely concerned with when he would leave India. Certainly before the end of the month, he thought. He questioned whether or not he'd bother to do his fair share of publicity for *Inspector Dhar and the Towers of Silence;* now that the real-life version of the cage-girl killer was captured, Dhar commented that there might (for once) be some *favorable* publicity attached to his brief presence in Bombay. The more he mused out loud about it, the closer Dhar came to deciding that there was really nothing keeping him in India; from John D.'s point of view, the sooner he went back to Switzerland, the better.

The doctor remarked that he thought he and Julia would return to Canada earlier than they'd planned; Dr. Daruwalla also asserted that he couldn't imagine coming back to Bombay in the near future, and the longer one stayed away . . . well, the harder it would be to *ever* come back. Julia let them talk. She knew how men hated to feel overwhelmed; they were really such babies whenever they weren't in control of their surroundings—whenever they felt that they didn't belong where they were. Also, Julia had often heard Farrokh say that he was never coming back to India; she knew he always came back.

The late-afternoon sun was slanting sideways through the trellis in the Ladies' Garden; the light fell in long slashes across the tablecloth, where the most famous male movie star in Bombay entertained himself by flicking stray crumbs with his fork. The ice in the prawn bowl had melted. It was time for Dr. and Mrs. Daruwalla to make an appearance at the celebration at St. Ignatius; Julia had to remind the doctor that she'd promised Martin Mills an early arrival. Understandably, the scholastic wanted to wear clean bandages to the high-tea jubilee, his introduction to the Catholic community.

"Why does he need bandages?" John D. asked. "What's the matter with him now?"

"Your twin was bitten by a chimpanzee," Farrokh informed the actor. "Probably rabid."

There was certainly a lot of biting going around, Dhar thought, but the events of the day had sharply curtailed his inclination toward sarcasm. His finger throbbed and he knew his lip was ugly. Inspector Dhar didn't say a word.

When the Daruwallas left him sitting in the Ladies' Garden, the movie star closed his eyes; he looked asleep. Too much beer, the ever-watchful Mr. Sethna surmised; then the steward reminded himself of his conviction that Dhar was stricken with a sexually transmitted disease. The old Parsi revised his opinion—he determined that Dhar was suffering from both the beer *and* the disease—and he ordered the busboys to leave the actor undisturbed at his table in the Ladies' Garden. Mr. Sethna's disapproval of Dhar had softened considerably; the steward felt bloated with pride—to have had his small supporting role called "brilliant" and "perfect" by such a celebrity of the Hindi cinema!

But John D. wasn't asleep; he was trying to compose himself, which is an actor's nonstop job. He was thinking that it had been years since he'd felt the slightest sexual attraction to any woman; but Nancy had aroused him—it seemed to him that it was her anger he'd found so appealing—and for the second Mrs. Dogar John D. had felt an even more disturbing desire. With his eyes still closed, the actor tried to imagine his own face with an ironic expression—not quite a sneer. He was 39, an age when it was unseemly to have one's sexual identity shaken. He concluded that it hadn't been Mrs. Dogar who'd stimulated him; rather, he'd been reliving his attraction to the old Rahul—back in those Goa days when Rahul was still a sort of man. This thought comforted John D. Watching him, Mr. Sethna saw what he thought was a sneer on the sleeping movie star's face; then something soothing must have crossed the actor's mind, for the sneer softened to a smile. He's thinking of the old days, the steward imagined . . . before he contracted the presumed dread disease. But Inspector Dhar had amused himself with a radical idea.

Shit, I hope I'm not about to become interested in *women*! the actor thought. What a mess that would make of things.

At this same moment, Dr. Daruwalla was experiencing another kind of irony. His arrival at the mission of St. Ignatius marked his first occasion in Christian company since the doctor had discovered who'd bitten his big toe. Dr. Daruwalla's awareness that the source of his conversion to Christianity was the love bite of a transsexual serial killer had further diminished the doctor's already declining religious zeal; that the toe-biter had *not* been the ghost of the pilgrim who dismembered St. Francis Xavier was more than a little disappointing. It was also a vulnerable time for Father Julian to have greeted Farrokh as the Father Rector did. "Ah, Dr. Daruwalla, our esteemed alumnus! Have you had any miracles happen to you lately?"

Thus baited, the doctor couldn't resist rebandaging Martin in an eccentric fashion. Dr. Daruwalla padded the puncture wound in the scholastic's neck so that the bandage looked as if it were meant to conceal an enormous goiter. He then rebound the Jesuit's slashed hand in such a way that Martin had only partial use of his fingers. As for the half-eaten earlobe, the doctor was expansive with gauze and tape; he wrapped up the whole ear. The zealot could hear out of only one side of his head.

But the clean, bright bandages only served to heighten the new missionary's heroic appearance. Even Julia was impressed. And quickly the story circulated through the courtyard at dusk: the American missionary had just rescued two urchins from the streets of Bombay; he'd brought them to the relative safety of a circus, where a wild animal had attacked him. At the fringes of the high tea, where Dr. Daruwalla stood sulking, he overheard the story that Martin Mills had been mauled by a *lion;* it was only the scholastic's self-deprecating nature that made him say the biting had been done by a monkey.

It further depressed the doctor to see that the source of this fantasy was the piano-playing Miss Tanuja; she'd traded her wing-tipped eyeglasses for what appeared to be rose-tinted contact lenses, which lent to her eyes the glowing red bedazzlement of a laboratory rat. She still spilled recklessly beyond the confines of her Western clothes, a schoolgirl voluptuary wearing her elderly aunt's dress. And she still sported the spear-headed bra, which uplifted and thrust forth her breasts like the sharp spires of a fallen church. As before, the crucifix that dangled between Miss Tanuja's highly armed bosoms seemed to subject the dying Christ to a new agony—or such was Dr. Daruwalla's disillusionment with the religion he'd adopted when Rahul bit him.

Jubilee Day was definitely not the doctor's sort of celebration. He felt a vague loathing for such a hearty gathering of Christians in a non-Christian country; the atmosphere of religious complicity was uncomfortably claustrophobic. Julia found him engaged in standoffish if not openly antisocial behavior; he'd been reading the examination scrolls in the entrance hall and had wandered to that spot, at the foot of the courtyard stairs, where the statue of Christ with the sick child was mounted on the wall alongside the fire extinguisher. Julia knew why

Farrokh was loitering there; he was hoping that someone would speak to him and he could then comment on the irony of juxtaposing Jesus with a fire-fighting tool.

"I'm going to take you home," Julia warned him. Then she noticed how tired he looked, and how utterly out of place—how lost. Christianity had tricked him; India was no longer his country. When Julia kissed his cheek, she realized he'd been crying.

"Please *do* take me home," Farrokh told her.

26. GOOD-BYE, BOMBAY

Well, Then

Danny Mills died following a New Year's Eve party in New York. It was Tuesday, January 2, before Martin Mills and Dr. Daruwalla were notified. The delay was attributed to the time difference—New York is 10½ hours behind Bombay—but the real reason was that Vera hadn't spent New Year's Eve with Danny. Danny, who was almost 75, died alone. Vera, who was 65, didn't discover Danny's body until the evening of New Year's Day.

When Vera returned to their hotel, she wasn't fully recovered from a tryst with a rising star of a light-beer commercial—an unbefitting fling for a woman her age. She doubtless failed to note the irony that Danny had died with the DO NOT DISTURB sign hanging optimistically from their hotel-room door. The medical examiner concluded that Danny had choked on his own vomit, which was (like his blood) nearly 20 percent alcohol.

In her two telegrams, Vera cited no clinical evidence; yet she managed to convey Danny's inebriation to Martin in pejorative terms.

YOUR FATHER DIED DRUNK IN A NEW YORK HOTEL

This also communicated to her son the sordidness, not to mention the inconvenience; Vera was going to have to spend nearly all of that Tuesday shopping. Coming from California—their visit was intended to be short—neither Danny nor Vera had packed for an extended stay in the January climate.

Vera's telegram to Martin continued in a bitter vein.

BEING CATHOLIC, ALTHOUGH HARDLY A MODEL OF THE SPECIES, I'M
SURE DANNY WOULD HAVE WANTED YOU TO ARRANGE SOME SUITABLE
SERVICE OR LAST BIT OR WHATEVER IT'S CALLED

"Hardly a model of the species" was the sort of language Vera had learned from the moisturizer commercial of her son's long-ago and damaged youth.

The last dig was pure Vera—even in what passed for grief, she took a swipe at her son.

WILL OF COURSE UNDERSTAND COMPLETELY IF YOUR VOW OF POVERTY
MAKES IT IMPOSSIBLE FOR YOU TO ASSIST ME IN THIS MATTER / MOM

There followed only the name of the hotel in New York. Martin's "vow of poverty" notwithstanding, Vera wasn't offering to pay for his trip with *her* money.

Her telegram to Dr. Daruwalla was also pure Vera.

I FAIL TO IMAGINE HOW DANNY'S DEATH SHOULD ALTER YOUR DECISION
TO KEEP MARTIN FROM ANY KNOWLEDGE OF HIS TWIN

So suddenly it's *my* decision, Dr. Daruwalla thought.

PLEASE DON'T UPSET POOR MARTIN WITH MORE BAD NEWS

So now it's "poor Martin" who would be upset! Farrokh observed.

SINCE MARTIN HAS CHOSEN POVERTY FOR A PROFESSION, AND DANNY
HAS LEFT ME A WOMAN OF INSUFFICIENT MEANS, PERHAPS YOU'LL BE SO
KIND AS TO AID MARTIN WITH THE AIRFARE / OF COURSE IT'S DANNY
WHO WOULD HAVE WANTED HIM HERE / VERA

The only good news, which Dr. Daruwalla didn't know at the time, was that Danny Mills had left Vera a woman of even less means than she supposed. Danny had bequeathed what little he had to the Catholic Church—secure in the knowledge that if he'd given anything to Martin, that's what Martin would have done with the money. In the end, not even Vera would consider the amount worth fighting for.

In Bombay, the day after Jubilee Day was a big one for news. Danny's death and Vera's manipulations overlapped with Mr. Das's announcement that Madhu had left the Great Blue Nile with her new husband; both Martin Mills and Dr. Daruwalla had little doubt that Madhu's new husband was Mr. Garg. Farrokh was so sure of this that his brief telegram to the Bengali ringmaster was a statement, not a question.

YOU SAID THAT THE MAN WHO MARRIED MADHU HAD A SCAR / ACID, I PRESUME

Both the doctor and the missionary were outraged that Mr. and Mrs. Das had virtually sold Madhu to a man like Garg, but Martin urged Farrokh not to take the ringmaster to task. In the spirit of encouraging the Great Blue Nile to support the efforts of the elephant-footed cripple, Dr. Daruwalla concluded his telegram to Mr. Das in Junagadh on a tactful note.

I TRUST THAT THE BOY GANESH WILL BE WELL LOOKED AFTER

He didn't "trust"; he *hoped*.

In the light of Ranjit's message from Mr. Subhash (that Tata Two had given Dr. Daruwalla the HIV test results for the wrong Madhu), the doctor had sizably less hope for Madhu than for Ganesh. Ranjit's account of Mr. Subhash's offhand manner—the ancient secretary's virtual dismissal of the error—was infuriating, but even a proper apology from Dr. Tata wouldn't have lessened the fact that Madhu was HIV-positive. She didn't have AIDS yet; she was merely carrying the virus.

"How can you even think 'merely'?" cried Martin Mills, who seemed to be more devastated by Madhu's medical destiny than by the news of Danny's death; after all, Danny had been dying for years.

It was only midmorning; Martin had to interrupt their phone conversation in order to teach a class. Farrokh agreed to keep the missionary informed of the day's developments. The upper-school boys at St. Ignatius were about to receive a Catholic interpretation of Graham Greene's *The Heart of the Matter*, while Dr. Daruwalla attempted to find Madhu. But the doctor discovered that Garg's phone number was no longer in service; Mr. Garg was lying low. Vinod told Dr. Daruwalla that Deepa had already talked to Garg; according to the dwarf's wife, the owner of the Wetness Cabaret had complained about the doctor.

"Garg is thinking you are being too moral with him," the dwarf explained.

It was not morality that the doctor wanted to discuss with Madhu, or with Garg. The doctor's disapproval of Garg notwithstanding, Dr. Daruwalla wanted the opportunity to tell Madhu what it *meant* to be HIV-positive. Vinod implied that any opportunity for direct communication with Madhu was unpromising.

"It is working better another way," the dwarf suggested. "You are telling me. I am telling Deepa. She is telling Garg. Garg is telling the girl."

It was hard for Dr. Daruwalla to accept this as a "better" way, but the doctor was beginning to understand the essence of the dwarf's Good Samaritanism. Rescuing children from the brothels was simply what Vinod and Deepa did with their spare time; they would just keep doing it—needing to succeed at it might have diminished their efforts.

"Tell Garg he was misinformed," Dr. Daruwalla told Vinod. "Tell him Madhu is HIV-positive."

Interestingly, if Garg was uninfected, his odds were good; he probably wouldn't contract HIV from Madhu. (The nature of HIV transmission is such that it's not that easy for a woman to give it to a man.) Depressingly, if Garg *was* infected, Madhu had probably contracted it from him.

The dwarf must have sensed the doctor's depression; Vinod knew that a functioning Good Samaritan can't dwell on every little failure. "We are only showing them the net," Vinod tried to explain. "We are not being their wings."

"Their wings? *What* wings?" Farrokh asked.

"Not every girl is being able to fly," the dwarf said. "They are not all falling in the net."

It occurred to Dr. Daruwalla that he should impart this lesson to Martin Mills, but the scholastic was still in the process of watering down Graham Greene for the upper-school boys. Instead, the doctor called the deputy commissioner.

"Patel here," said the cold voice. The clatter of typewriters resounded in the background; rising, and then falling out of hearing, was the mindless revving of a motorcycle. Like punctuation to their phone conversation, there came and went the sharp barking of the Dobermans, complaining in the courtyard kennel. Dr. Daruwalla imagined that just out of his hearing a prisoner was professing his innocence, or else declaring that he'd spoken the truth. The doctor wondered if Rahul was there. What would she be wearing?

"I know this isn't exactly a crime-branch matter," Farrokh apologized in advance; then he told the deputy commissioner everything he knew about Madhu and Mr. Garg.

"Lots of pimps marry their best girls," Detective Patel informed the doctor. "Garg runs the Wetness Cabaret, but he's a pimp on the side."

"I just want a chance to tell her what to expect," said Dr. Daruwalla.

"She's another man's wife," Patel replied. "You want me to tell another man's wife that she has to talk to you?"

"Can't you *ask* her?" Farrokh asked.

"I can't believe I'm speaking to the creator of Inspector Dhar," the deputy commissioner said. "How does it go? It's one of my all-time favorites: 'The police don't *ask*—the police arrest, or the police harass.' Isn't that the line?"

"Yes, that's how it goes," Dr. Daruwalla confessed.

"So do you want me to harass her—and Garg, too?" the policeman asked. When the doctor didn't answer him, the deputy commissioner continued. "When Garg throws her out on the street, or when she runs away, then I can bring her in for questioning. *Then* you can talk to her. The problem is, if he throws her out or she runs away, I won't be able to find her. From what you say, she's too pretty and smart to be a street prostitute. She'll go to a brothel, and once she's in the brothel, she won't be out on the street. Someone will bring her food; the madam will buy her clothes."

"And when she gets sick?" the doctor asked.

"There are doctors who go to the brothels," Patel replied. "When she gets so sick that she can't be a prostitute, most madams would put her out on the street. But by then she'll be immune."

"What do you mean, 'immune'?" Dr. Daruwalla asked.

"When you're on the street and very sick, everyone leaves you alone. When nobody comes near you, you're immune," the policeman said.

"And then you could find her," Farrokh remarked.

"Then we *might* find her," Patel corrected him. "But by then it would hardly be necessary for you to tell her what to expect."

"So you're saying, 'Forget her.' Is that it?" the doctor asked.

"In your profession, you treat crippled children—isn't that right?" the deputy commissioner inquired.

"That's right," Dr. Daruwalla replied.

"Well, I don't know anything about your field," said Detective Patel, "but I would guess that your odds of success are slightly higher than in the red-light district."

"I get your point," Farrokh said. "And what are the odds that Rahul will hang?"

For a while, the policeman was silent. Only the typewriters responded to the question; they were the constant, occasionally interrupted by the revving motorcycle or the cacophony of Dobermans. "Do you hear the typewriters?" the deputy commissioner finally asked.

"Of course," Dr. Daruwalla answered.

"The report on Rahul will be very lengthy," Patel promised him. "But not even the sensational number of murders will impress the judge. I mean, just look at who most of the victims were—they weren't important."

"You mean they were prostitutes," said Dr. Daruwalla.

"Precisely," Patel replied. "We will need to develop another argument—namely, that Rahul must be confined with other women. Anatomically, she *is* a woman . . ."

"So the operation was complete," the doctor interrupted.

"So I'm told. Naturally, I didn't examine her myself," the deputy commissioner added.

"No, of course not . . ." Dr. Daruwalla said.

"What I mean is, Rahul cannot be imprisoned with men—Rahul is a woman," the detective said. "And solitary confinement is too expensive—impossible in cases of life imprisonment. And yet, if Rahul is confined with women prisoners, there's a problem. She's as strong as a man, and she has a history of killing women—you see my point?"

"So you're saying that she might receive the death penalty only because of how awkward it will be to imprison her with other women?" Farrokh asked.

"Precisely," Patel said. "That's our best argument. But I still don't believe she'll be hanged."

"Why not?" the doctor asked.

"Almost no one is hanged," the deputy commissioner replied. "With Rahul, they'll probably try hard labor and life imprisonment; then something will happen. Maybe she'll kill another prisoner."

"Or bite her," Dr. Daruwalla said.

"They won't hang her for biting," the policeman said. "But something will happen. Then they'll *have* to hang her."

"Naturally, this will take a long time," Farrokh guessed.

"Precisely," Patel said. "And it won't be very satisfying," the detective added.

That was a theme with the deputy commissioner, Dr. Daruwalla knew. It led the doctor to ask a different sort of question. "And what will *you* do—you and your wife?" Farrokh inquired.

"What do you mean?" said Detective Patel; for the first time, he sounded surprised.

"I mean, will you stay here—in Bombay, in India?" the doctor asked.

"Are you offering me a job?" the policeman replied.

Farrokh laughed. "Well, no," he admitted. "I was just curious if you were *staying*."

"But this is my country," the deputy commissioner told him. "*You're* the one who's not at home here."

This was awkward; first from Vinod and now from Detective Patel, the doctor had learned something. In both cases, the subject of the lesson was the acceptance of something unsatisfying.

"If you ever come to Canada," Farrokh blurted out, "I would be happy to be your host—to show you around."

It was the deputy commissioner's turn to laugh. "It's much more likely that I'll see you when you're back in Bombay," Patel said.

"I'm not coming back to Bombay," Dr. Daruwalla insisted. It wasn't the first time he'd spoken his thoughts so unequivocally on this subject.

Although Detective Patel politely accepted the statement, Dr. Daruwalla could tell that the deputy commissioner didn't believe him. "Well, then," Patel said. It was all there was to say. Not "Good-bye"; just "Well, then."

Not a Word

Martin Mills again confessed to Father Cecil, who this time managed to stay awake. The scholastic was guilty of jumping to conclusions; Martin interpreted Danny's death and his mother's request that he come to her assistance in New York as a sign. After all, Jesuits are relentless in seeking God's will, and Martin was an especially zealous example; the scholastic not only sought God's will, but he too often believed that he'd spontaneously intuited what it was. In this case, Martin confessed, his mother was still capable of making him feel guilty, for he was inclined to go to New York at her bidding; Martin also confessed that he didn't want to go. The conclusion Martin then jumped to was that this weakness—his inability to stand up to Vera—was an indication that he lacked the faith to become ordained. Worse, the child prostitute had not only forsaken the circus and returned to her life of sin, but she would almost certainly die of AIDS; what had befallen Madhu was an even darker sign, which Martin interpreted as a warning that he would be ineffectual as a priest.

"This is clearly meant to show me that I shall be unable to renew the grace received from God in ordination," Martin confessed to old Father Cecil, who wished that the Father Rector were hearing this; Father Julian would have put the presumptuous fool in his place. How impertinent—how utterly immodest—to be analyzing every moment of self-doubt as a sign from God! Whatever God's will was, Father Cecil was sure that Martin Mills had *not* been singled out to receive as much of it as he'd imagined.

Since he'd always been Martin's defender, Father Cecil surprised himself by saying, "If you doubt yourself so much, Martin, maybe you *shouldn't* be a priest."

"Oh, thank you, Father!" Martin said. It astonished Father Cecil to hear the now-*former* scholastic sound so relieved.

At the news of Martin's shocking decision—to leave the "Life," as it is called; not to be "One of Ours," as the Jesuits call themselves—the Father Rector was nonplussed but philosophic.

"India isn't for everybody," Father Julian remarked, preferring to give Martin's abrupt choice a secular interpretation. Blame it on Bombay, so to speak. Father Julian, after all, was English, and he credited himself with doubting the fitness of *American* missionaries; even on the slim evidence of Martin Mills's dossier, the Father Rector had expressed his reservations. Father Cecil, who was Indian, said he'd be sorry to see young Martin leave; the scholastic's energy as a teacher had been a welcome addition to St. Ignatius School.

Brother Gabriel, who quite liked and admired Martin, nevertheless remembered the bloody socks that the scholastic had been wringing in his hands—not to mention the "I'll take the turkey" prayer. The elderly Spaniard retreated, as he often did, to his icon-collection room; these countless images of suffering, which the Russian and Byzantine icons afforded Brother Gabriel, were at least traditional—thus reassuring. The Decapitation of John the Baptist, the Last Supper, the Deposition, which was the taking of Christ's body from the cross—even these terrible moments were preferable to that image of Martin Mills which poor old Brother Gabriel was doomed to remember: the crazed Californian with his bloody bandages awry, looking like the composite image of many murdered missionaries past. Perhaps it *was* God's will that Martin Mills should be summoned to New York.

"You're going to do *what?*" Dr. Daruwalla cried, for in the time it had taken the doctor to talk to Vinod and Detective Patel, Martin had not only given the St. Ignatius upper-school boys a Catholic interpretation of *The Heart of the Matter;* he had also "interpreted" God's will. According to Martin, God didn't want him to be a priest—God wanted him to go to New York!

"Let me see if I follow you," Farrokh said. "You've decided that Madhu's tragedy is your own personal failure. I know the feeling—we're both fools. And, in addition, you doubt the strength of your conviction to be ordained because you can still be manipulated by your mother, who's made a career out of manipulating everybody. So you're going to New York—just to prove her power over you—and also for Danny's sake, although Danny won't know if you go to New York or not. Or do you believe Danny will know?"

"That's a simplistic way to put it," Martin said. "I may lack the necessary will to be a priest, but I haven't entirely lost my faith."

"Your mother's a bitch," Dr. Daruwalla told him.

"That's a simplistic way to put it," Martin repeated. "Besides, I already know what she is."

How the doctor was tempted. *Tell* him—tell him *now!* Dr. Daruwalla thought.

"Naturally, I'll pay you back—I won't take the plane ticket as a gift," Martin Mills explained. "After all, my vow of poverty no longer applies. I do have the academic credentials to teach. I won't make a lot of money teaching, but certainly enough to pay you back—if you'll just give me a little time."

"It's not the money! I can afford to buy you a plane ticket—I can afford to buy you *twenty* plane tickets!" Farrokh cried. "But you're giving up your goal—that's what's so crazy about you. You're giving up, and for such stupid reasons!"

"It's not the reasons—it's my doubt," Martin said. "Just look at me. I'm thirty-nine. If I were going to be a priest, I should have already become one. No one who's still trying to 'find himself' at thirty-nine is very reliable."

You took the words right out of my mouth! Dr. Daruwalla thought, but all the doctor said was, "Don't worry about the ticket—I'll get you a ticket." He hated to see the fool look so defeated; Martin *was* a fool, but he was an idealistic fool. The idiot's idealism had grown on Dr. Daruwalla. And Martin was candid—unlike his twin! Ironically, the doctor felt he'd learned more about John D. from Martin Mills—in less than a week—than he'd learned from John D. in 39 years.

Dr. Daruwalla wondered if John D.'s remoteness, his not-thereness—his iconlike and opaque character—wasn't that part of him which was created *not* upon his birth but upon his becoming Inspector Dhar. Then the doctor reminded himself that John D. had been an actor before he became Inspector Dhar. If the identical twin of a gay male had a 52 percent chance of being gay, in what other ways did John D. and Martin Mills have a 52 percent chance of being alike? It occurred to Dr. Daruwalla that the twins had a 48 percent chance of being *un*alike, too; nevertheless, the doctor doubted that Danny Mills could be the twins' father. Moreover, Farrokh had grown too fond of Martin to continue to deceive him.

Tell him—tell him *now!* Farrokh told himself, but the words wouldn't come. Dr. Daruwalla could say only to himself what he wanted to say to Martin.

You *don't* have to deal with Danny's remains. Probably Neville Eden is your father, and Neville's remains were settled many years ago. You *don't* have to assist your mother, who's worse than a bitch. You *don't* know what she is, or all that she is. And there's someone you might like to know; you might even be of mutual assistance to each other. He could teach you how to relax—maybe even how to have some fun. You might teach him a little candor—maybe even how *not* to be an actor, at least not all the time.

But the doctor didn't say it. Not a word.

Dr. Daruwalla Decides

"So . . . he's a quitter," said Inspector Dhar, of his twin.

"He's confused, anyway," Dr. Daruwalla replied.

"A thirty-nine-year-old man shouldn't still be finding himself," John D. declared. The actor delivered the line with almost perfect indignation, never hinting that the matter of "finding himself" was at all familiar to him.

"I think you'd like him," Farrokh said cautiously.

"Well, you're the *writer,*" Dhar remarked with almost perfect ambiguity. Dr. Daruwalla wondered: Does he mean that the matter of whether or not they meet is in *my* hands? Or does he mean that only a writer would waste his time fantasizing that the twins *should* meet?

They were standing on the Daruwallas' balcony at sunset. The Arabian Sea was the faded purple of John D.'s slowly healing lower lip. The splint on his broken pinky finger provided the actor with an instrument for pointing; Dhar liked to point.

"Remember how Nancy responded to this view?" the actor asked, pointing west.

"All the way to Iowa," the doctor remarked.

"If you're never coming back to Bombay, Farrokh, you might give the deputy commissioner and Mrs. Patel this apartment." The line was delivered with almost perfect indifference. The screenwriter had to marvel at the hidden character he'd created; Dhar was almost perfectly mysterious. "I don't mean actually *give* it to them—the good detective would doubtless construe that as a bribe," Dhar went on. "But perhaps you could sell it to them for a ridiculous sum—a hundred rupees, for example. Of course you could stipulate that the Patels would have to maintain the servants—for as long as Nalin and Roopa are alive. I know you wouldn't want to turn them out on the street. As for the Residents' Society, I'm sure they wouldn't object to the Patels—every apartment dweller wants to have a policeman in the building." Dhar pointed his splint west again. "I believe this view would do Nancy some good," the actor added.

"I can see you've been thinking about this," Farrokh said.

"It's just an idea—*if* you're never coming back to Bombay," John D. replied. "I mean *really* never."

"Are *you* ever coming back?" Dr. Daruwalla asked him.

"Not in a million years," said Inspector Dhar.

"*That* old line!" Farrokh said fondly.

"You wrote it," John D. reminded him.

"You keep reminding me," the doctor said.

They stayed on the balcony until the Arabian Sea was the color of an overripe cherry, almost black. Julia had to clear the contents of John D.'s pockets off the glass-topped table in order for them to have their dinner. It was a habit that John D. had maintained from childhood. He would come into the house or the apartment, take off his coat and his shoes or sandals, and empty the contents of his pockets on the nearest table; this was more than a gesture to make himself feel at home, for the source lay with the Daruwallas' daughters. When they'd lived at home, they liked nothing better than wrestling with John D. He would lie on his back on the rug or the floor, or sometimes on the couch, and the younger girls would pounce on him; he never hurt them, just fended them off. And so Farrokh and Julia never chastised him for the contents of his pockets, which were messily in evidence on the tabletop of every house or apartment they'd ever lived in, although there were no children for John D. to wrestle with anymore. Keys, a wallet, sometimes a passport . . . and this evening, on the glass-topped table of the Daruwallas' Marine Drive apartment, a plane ticket.

"You're leaving Thursday?" Julia asked him.

"Thursday!" Dr. Daruwalla exclaimed. "That's the day after tomorrow!"

"Actually, I have to go to the airport Wednesday night—it's such an early-morning flight, you know," John D. said.

"That's tomorrow night!" Farrokh cried. The doctor took Dhar's wallet, keys and plane ticket from Julia and put them on the sideboard.

"Not there," Julia told him; she was serving one of their dinner dishes from the sideboard. Therefore, Dr. Daruwalla carried the contents of John D.'s pockets into the foyer and placed them on a low table by the door—that way, the doctor thought, John D. would be sure to see his things and not forget them when he left.

"Why should I stay longer?" John D. was asking Julia. "You're not staying much longer, are you?"

But Dr. Daruwalla lingered in the foyer; he had a look at Dhar's plane ticket. Swissair, nonstop to Zürich. Flight 197, departing Thursday at 1:45 A.M. It was first class, seat 4B. Dhar always chose an aisle seat. This was because he was a beer drinker; on a nine-hour flight, he got up to pee a lot—he didn't want to keep climbing over someone else.

That quickly—by the time Dr. Daruwalla had rejoined John D. and Julia, and even before he sat down to dinner—the doctor had made his decision; after all, as Dhar had told him, he was the writer. A writer could make things happen. They were twins; they didn't have to like each other, but they didn't have to be lonely.

Farrokh sat happily at his supper (as he insisted on calling it), smiling lovingly at John D. I'll teach you to be ambiguous with me! the doctor thought, but what Dr. Daruwalla said was, "Why *should* you stay any longer, indeed! Now's as good a time to go as any."

Both Julia and John D. looked at him as if he were having a seizure. "Well, I mean I'll miss you, of course—but I'll see you soon, one place or another. Canada or Switzerland . . . I'm looking forward to spending more time in the mountains."

"You *are?*" Julia asked him. Farrokh hated mountains. Inspector Dhar just stared.

"Yes, it's very healthy," the doctor replied. "All that Swiss ... air," he remarked absently; he was thinking of the airline of that name, and how he would buy a first-class ticket to Zürich for Martin Mills on Swissair 197, departing early Thursday morning. Seat 4A. Farrokh hoped that the ex-missionary would appreciate the window seat, *and* his interesting traveling companion.

They had a wonderful dinner, a lively time. Normally, when Dr. Daruwalla knew he was parting from John D., he was morose. But tonight the doctor felt euphoric.

"John D. has a terrific idea—about this apartment," Farrokh told his wife. Julia liked the idea very much; the three of them talked about it at length. Detective Patel was proud; so was Nancy. They would be sensitive if they felt the apartment was offered to them as charity; the trick would be to make them think they were doing the Daruwallas a favor by looking after and "maintaining" the old servants. The diners spoke admiringly of the deputy commissioner; they could have talked for hours about Nancy—she was certainly complex.

It was always easier, with John D., when the subject of conversation was someone else; it was himself, as a subject, that the actor avoided. And the diners were animated in their discussion of what the deputy com-missioner had confided to the doctor about Rahul ... the unlikelihood of her hanging.

Julia and John D. had rarely seen Farrokh so relaxed. The doctor spoke of his great desire to see more of his daughters and grandchildren, and he kept repeating that he wanted to see more of John D.—"in your Swiss life." The two men drank a lot of beer and sat up late on the balcony; they outlasted the traffic on Marine Drive. Julia sat up with them.

"You know, Farrokh, I *do* appreciate everything you've done for me," the actor said.

"It's been fun," the screenwriter replied. Farrokh fought back his tears—he was a sentimental man. He managed to feel quite happy, sitting there in the darkness. The smell of the Arabian Sea, the fumes of the city—even the constantly clogged drains and the persistence of human shit—rose almost comfortingly around them. Dr. Daruwalla insisted on drinking a toast to Danny Mills; Dhar politely drank to Danny's memory.

"He wasn't your father—I'm quite sure of that," Farrokh told John D.

"I'm quite sure of that, too," the actor replied.

"Why are you so happy, *Liebchen?*" Julia asked Farrokh.

"He's happy because he's leaving India and he's never coming back," Inspector Dhar answered; the line was delivered with almost perfect authority. This was mildly irritating to Farrokh, who suspected that leaving India and never coming back was an act of cowardice on his part. John D. was thinking of him, as he thought of his twin, as a quitter—*if* John D. truly believed that the doctor was never coming back.

"You'll see why I'm happy," Dr. Daruwalla told them. When he fell asleep on the balcony, John D. carried him to his bed.

"Look at him," Julia said. "He's smiling in his sleep."

There would be time to mourn Madhu another day. There would be time to worry about Ganesh, the elephant boy, too. And on his next birthday, the doctor would be 60. But right now Dr. Daruwalla was imagining the twins together on Swissair 197. Nine hours in the air should be sufficient for starting a relationship, the doctor thought.

Julia tried to read in bed, but Farrokh distracted her; he laughed out loud in his sleep. He must be drunk, she thought. Then she saw a frown cross his face. What a shame it was, Dr. Daruwalla was thinking; he wanted to be on the same plane with them—just to watch them, and to listen. Which seat is across the aisle from 4B? the doctor wondered. Seat 4J? Farrokh had taken that flight to Zürich many times. It was a 747; the seat across the aisle from 4B was 4J, he hoped.

"Four J," he told the flight attendant. Julia put down her book and stared at him.

"*Liebchen,*" she whispered, "either wake up or go to sleep." But her husband was once again smiling serenely. Dr. Daruwalla was where he wanted to be. It was early Thursday morning—1:45 A.M., to be exact—and Swissair 197 was taking off from Sahar. Across the aisle, the twins were staring at each other; neither of them could talk. It would take a little time for one of them to break the ice, but the doctor felt confident that they couldn't maintain their silence for the full nine hours. Although the actor had more interesting information, Farrokh bet that the ex-missionary would be the one to start blabbing. Martin Mills would blab all night, if John D. didn't start talking in self-defense.

Julia watched her sleeping husband touch his belly with his hands. Dr. Daruwalla was checking to be sure that his seat belt was correctly fastened; then he settled back, ready to enjoy the long flight.

Just Close Your Eyes

The next day was Wednesday. Dr. Daruwalla was watching the sunset from his balcony, this time with Dhar's twin. Martin was full of questions about his plane tickets. The screenwriter evaded these questions with the skill of someone who'd already imagined the possible dialogue.

"I fly to Zürich? That's strange—that's not the way I came," the ex-missionary remarked.

"I have connections with Swissair," Farrokh told him. "I'm a frequent flyer, so I get a special deal."

"Oh, I see. Well, I'm very grateful. I hear it's a marvelous airline," the former scholastic said. "These are first-class tickets!" Martin suddenly cried. "I can't repay you for first class!"

"I won't allow you to repay me," the doctor said. "I said I have connections—I get a special deal for first class. I won't let you repay me because the plane tickets cost me practically nothing."

"Oh, I see. I've never flown first class," the recent zealot said. Farrokh could tell that Martin was puzzling over the ticket for the connecting flight, from Zürich to New York. He would arrive in Zürich at 6:00 in the morning; his plane to New York didn't leave Zürich until 1:00 in the afternoon—a long layover, the onetime Jesuit was thinking . . . and there was something different about the New York ticket.

"That's an open ticket to New York," Farrokh said in an offhand manner. "It's a daily nonstop flight. You don't have to fly to New York on the day you arrive in Switzerland. You have a valid ticket for any day when there's an available seat in first class. I thought you might like to spend a day or two in Zürich—maybe the weekend. You'd be better rested when you got to New York."

"Well, that's awfully kind of you. But I'm not sure what I'd do in Zürich . . ." Martin was saying. Then he found the hotel voucher; it was with his plane tickets.

"Three nights at the Hotel zum Storchen—a decent hotel," Farrokh explained. "Your room overlooks the Limmat. You can walk in the old town, or to the lake. Have you ever been in Europe?"

"No, I haven't," said Martin Mills. He kept staring at the hotel voucher; it included his meals.

"Well, then," Dr. Daruwalla replied. Since the deputy commissioner had found this phrase so meaningful, the doctor thought he'd give it a try; it appeared to work on Martin Mills. Throughout dinner, the reformed Jesuit wasn't at all argumentative; he seemed subdued. Julia worried that it might have been the food, or that Dhar's unfortunate twin was ill, but Dr. Daruwalla had experienced failure before; the doctor knew what was bothering the ex-missionary.

John D. was wrong; his twin wasn't a quitter. Martin Mills had abandoned a quest, but he'd given up the priesthood when the priesthood was in sight—when it was easily obtainable. He'd not failed to be ordained; he'd been afraid of the kind of priest he might become. His decision to retreat, which had appeared to be so whimsical and sudden, had not come out of the blue; to Martin, his retreat must have seemed lifelong.

Because the security checks were so extensive, Martin Mills was required to be at Sahar two or three hours before his scheduled departure. Farrokh felt it would be unsafe to let him take a taxi with anyone but Vinod, and Vinod was unavailable; the dwarf was driving Dhar to the airport. Dr. Daruwalla hired an alleged luxury taxi from the fleet of Vinod's Blue Nile, Ltd. They were en route to Sahar when the doctor first realized how much he would miss the ex-missionary.

"I'm getting used to this," Martin said. They were passing a dead dog in the road, and Farrokh thought that Martin was commenting on his growing familiarity with slain animals. Martin explained that he meant he was getting used to leaving places in mild disgrace. "Oh, there's never anything scandalous—I'm never run out of town on a rail," he went on. "It's a sort of slinking away. I don't suppose I'm anything more than a passing embarrassment to those people who put their faith in me. I feel the same way about myself, really. There's never a crushing sense of disappointment, or of loss—it's more like a fleeting dishonor."

I'm going to miss this moron, Dr. Daruwalla thought, but what the doctor said was, "Do me a favor—just close your eyes."

"Is there something dead in the road?" Martin asked.

"Probably," the doctor replied. "But that's not the reason. Just close your eyes. Are they closed?"

"Yes, my eyes are closed," the former scholastic said. "What are you going to do?" he asked nervously.

"Just relax," Farrokh told him. "We're going to play a game."

"I don't like games!" Martin cried. He opened his eyes and looked wildly around.

"Close your eyes!" Dr. Daruwalla shouted. Although his vow of obedience was behind him, Martin obeyed. "I want you to imagine that parking lot with the Jesus statue," the doctor told him. "Can you see it?"

"Yes, of course," Martin Mills replied.

"Is Christ still there, in the parking lot?" Farrokh asked him. The fool opened his eyes.

"Well, I don't know about that—they were always expanding the capacity of the parking lot," Martin said. "There was always a lot of construction equipment around. They may have torn up that section of the lot—they might have had to move the statue . . ."

"That's not what I mean! Close your eyes!" Dr. Daruwalla cried. "What I mean is, in your *mind*, can you still see the damn statue? Jesus Christ in the dark parking lot—can you still *see* him?"

"Well, naturally—yes," Martin Mills admitted. He kept his eyes tightly closed, as if in pain; his mouth was shut, too, and his nose was wrinkled. They were passing a slum encampment lit only by rubbish fires, but the stench of human feces overpowered what they could smell of the burning trash. "Is that all?" Martin asked, eyes closed.

"Isn't that enough?" the doctor asked him. "For God's sake, open your eyes!"

Martin opened them. "Was that the game—the whole game?" he inquired.

"You saw Jesus Christ, didn't you? What more do you want?" Farrokh asked. "You must realize that it's possible to be a good Christian, as Christians are always saying, and at the same time *not* be a Catholic priest."

"Oh, is *that* what you mean?" said Martin Mills. "Well, certainly—I realize that!"

"I can't believe I'm going to miss you, but I really am," Dr. Daruwalla told him.

"I shall miss you, too, of course," Dhar's twin replied. "In particular, our little talks."

At the airport, there was the usual lineup for the security checks. After they'd said their good-byes (they actually embraced), Dr. Daruwalla continued to observe Martin from a distance. The doctor crossed a police barrier in order to keep watching him. It was hard to tell if his bandages drew everyone's attention or if it was his resemblance to Dhar, which leaped out at some observers and was utterly missed by others. The doctor had once again changed Martin's bandages; the neck wound was minimally covered with a gauze patch, and the mangled earlobe was left uncovered—it was ugly but largely healed. The hand was still mittened in gauze. To everyone who gawked at him, the chimpanzee's victim winked and smiled; it was a genuine smile, not Dhar's sneer, yet

Farrokh felt that the ex-missionary had never looked like such a dead ringer for Dhar. At the end of every Inspector Dhar movie, Dhar is walking away from the camera; in this case, Dr. Daruwalla was the camera. Farrokh felt greatly moved; he wondered if it was because Martin more and more reminded him of John D., or if it was because Martin himself had touched him.

John D. was nowhere to be seen. Dr. Daruwalla knew that the actor was always the first to board a plane—*any* plane—but the doctor kept looking for him. Aesthetically, Farrokh would have been disappointed if Inspector Dhar and Martin Mills met in the security lineup; the screenwriter wanted the twins to meet on the plane. Ideally, they should be sitting down, Dr. Daruwalla thought.

As he waited in line and then shuffled forward, and then waited again, Martin looked almost normal. There was something pathetic about his wearing the tropical-weight black suit over the Hawaiian shirt; he'd surely have to buy something warmer in Zürich, the expense of which had prompted Dr. Daruwalla to hand him several hundred Swiss francs—at the last minute, so that Martin had no time to refuse the money. And there was something barely noticeable but odd about his habit of closing his eyes while he waited in line. When the line stopped moving, Martin closed his eyes and smiled; then the line would inch forward, Martin with it, looking like a man refreshed. Farrokh knew what the fool was doing. Martin Mills was making sure that Jesus Christ was still in the parking lot.

Not even a mob of Indian workers returning from the Gulf could distract the former Jesuit from the latest of his spiritual exercises. The workers were what Farrokh's mother, Meher, used to call the Persia-returned crowd, but these workers weren't coming from Iran; they were returning from Kuwait—their two-in-ones or their three-in-ones were blasting. In addition to their boom boxes, they carried their foam mattresses; their plastic shoulder bags were bursting with whiskey bottles and wristwatches and assorted aftershaves and pocket calculators—some had even stolen the cutlery from the plane. Sometimes the workers went to Oman—or Qatar or Dubai. In Meher's day, the so-called Persia-returned crowd had brought back gold ingots in their hands—at least a sovereign or two. Nowadays, Farrokh guessed, they weren't bringing home much gold. Nevertheless, they got drunk on the plane. But even as he was jostled by the most unruly of these Persia-returned people, Martin Mills kept closing his eyes and smiling; as long as Jesus was still in that parking lot, all was right with Martin's world.

For his remaining days in Bombay, Dr. Daruwalla would regret that, when he closed *his* eyes, he saw no such reassuring vision; no Christ—not even a parking lot. He told Julia that he was suffering the sort of recurring dream that he hadn't had since he'd first left India for Austria; it was a common dream among adolescents, old Lowji had told him—for one reason or another, you find yourself naked in a public place. Long ago, Farrokh's opinionated father had offered an unlikely interpretation. "It's a new immigrant's dream," Lowji had declared. Maybe it was, Farrokh now believed. He'd left India many times before, but this was the first time he would leave his birthplace with the *certain* knowledge that he wasn't coming back; he'd never felt so sure.

For most of his adult life, he'd lived with the discomfort (especially in India) of feeling that he wasn't really Indian. Now how would he feel, living in Toronto with the discomfort of knowing that he'd never truly been assimilated there? Although he was a citizen of Canada, Dr. Daruwalla knew he was no Canadian; he would never feel "assimilated." Old Lowji's nasty remark would haunt Farrokh forever: "Immigrants are immigrants all their lives!" Once someone makes such a negative pronouncement, you might refute it but you never forget it; some ideas are so vividly planted, they become visible objects, actual things.

For example, a racial insult—not forgetting the accompanying loss of self-esteem. Or one of those more subtle Anglo-Saxon nuances, which frequently assailed Farrokh in Canada and made him feel that he was always standing at the periphery; this could be simply a sour glance—that familiar dour expression which attended the most commonplace exchange. The way they examined the signature on your credit card, as if it couldn't possibly comply with *your* signature; or when they gave you back your change, how their looks always lingered on the color of your upturned palm—it was a different color from the back of your hand. The difference was somehow greater than that difference which they took for granted—namely, between *their* palms and the backs of *their* hands. ("Immigrants are immigrants all their lives!")

The first time he saw Suman perform the Skywalk at the Great Royal Circus, Farrokh didn't believe she could fall; she looked perfect—she was so beautiful and her steps were so precise. Then, one time, he saw her standing in the wing of the main tent before her performance. He was surprised that she wasn't stretching her muscles. She wasn't even moving her feet; she stood completely still. Maybe she was concentrating, Dr. Daruwalla thought; he didn't want her to notice him looking at her—he didn't want to distract her.

When Suman turned to him, Farrokh realized that she really must have been concentrating because she didn't acknowledge him and she was always very polite; she looked right past him, or through him. The fresh puja mark on her forehead was smudged. It was the slightest flaw, but when Dr. Daruwalla saw the smudge, he instantly knew that Suman was mortal. From that moment, Farrokh believed she could fall. After that, he could never relax when he saw her skywalking—she seemed unbearably vulnerable. If someone ever were to tell him that Suman had fallen and died, Dr. Daruwalla would see her lying in the dirt with her puja mark smeared. ("Immigrants are immigrants all their lives" was this kind of smudge.)

It might have helped Dr. Daruwalla if he could have left Bombay as quickly as the twins had left. But retiring movie stars and ex-missionaries can leave town faster than doctors; surgeons have their operating schedules and their recovering patients. As for screenwriters, like other writers, they have their messy little details to attend to, too.

Farrokh knew he would never talk to Madhu; at best, he might communicate with her, or learn of her condition, through Vinod or Deepa. The doctor wished the child might have had the good luck to die in the circus; the death he'd created for his Pinky character—killed by a lion who mistakes her for a peacock—was a lot quicker than the one he imagined for Madhu.

Similarly, the screenwriter entertained little hope that the real Ganesh would succeed at the circus, at least not to the degree that the fictional Ganesh succeeds. There would be no skywalking for the elephant boy, which was a pity—it was such a perfect ending. If the real cripple became a successful cook's helper, that would be ample satisfaction for Farrokh. To this end, he wrote a friendly letter to Mr. and Mrs. Das at the Great Blue Nile; although the elephant-footed boy could never be trained as an acrobat, the doctor wanted the ringmaster and his wife to encourage Ganesh to be a good cook's helper. Dr. Daruwalla also wrote to Mr. and Mrs. Bhagwan—the knife thrower and his wife-assistant, the skywalker. Perhaps the skywalker would be so kind as to *gently* disabuse the elephant boy of his silly idea that he could perform the Skywalk. Possibly Mrs. Bhagwan could *show* Ganesh how hard it was to skywalk. She might let the cripple try it, using the model of that ladderlike device which hung from the roof of her own troupe tent; that would show him how impossible skywalking was—it would also be a safe exercise.

As for his screenplay, Farrokh had again titled it *Limo Roulette*; he came

back to this title because *Escaping Maharashtra* struck him as overopti-
mistic, if not wholly improbable. The screenplay had suffered from even
the briefest passage of time. The horror of Acid Man, the sensationalism
of the lion striking down the star of the circus (that innocent little girl)
... Farrokh feared that these elements echoed a Grand Guignol drama,
which he recognized as the essence of an Inspector Dhar story. Maybe
the screenwriter hadn't ventured as far from his old genre as he'd first
imagined.

Yet Farrokh disputed that opinion of himself which he'd read in so
many reviews—namely, that he was a deus-ex-machina writer, always
calling on the available gods (and other artificial devices) to bail himself
out of his plot. Real life itself was a deus-ex-machina *mess*! Dr. Daruwalla thought. Look at how he'd put Dhar and his twin together—
somebody had to do it! And hadn't he remembered that shiny something
which the shitting crow had held in its beak and then lost? It was a
deus-ex-machina *world*!

Still, the screenwriter was insecure. Before he left Bombay, Farrokh
thought he'd like to talk to Balraj Gupta, the director. *Limo Roulette* might
be only a small departure for the screenwriter, but Dr. Daruwalla
wanted Gupta's advice. Although Farrokh was certain that this wasn't a
Hindi cinema sort of film—a small circus was definitely not a likely
venue for Balraj Gupta—Gupta was the only director the screenwriter
knew.

Dr. Daruwalla should have known better than to talk to Balraj Gupta
about art—even flawed art. It didn't take long for Gupta to smell out the
"art" in the story; Farrokh never finished with his synopsis. "Did you say
a child *dies*?" Gupta interrupted him. "Do you bring it back to life?"

"No," Farrokh admitted.

"Can't a god save the child, or something?" Balraj Gupta asked.

"It's not that kind of film—that's what I'm trying to tell you," Farrokh
explained.

"Better give it to the Bengalis," Gupta advised. "If it's arty realism
that you're up to, better make it in Calcutta." When the screenwriter
didn't respond, Balraj Gupta said, "Maybe it's a *foreign* film. *Limo Roulette*—it sounds French!"

Farrokh thought of saying that the part of the missionary would be
a wonderful role for John D. And the screenwriter might have added that
Inspector Dhar, the actual star of the Hindi cinema, could have a dual
role; the mistaken-identity theme could be amusing. John D. could play
the missionary *and* he could make a cameo appearance as Dhar! But Dr.

Daruwalla knew what Balraj Gupta would say to *that* idea: "Let the critics mock him—he's a movie star. But movie stars shouldn't mock themselves." Farrokh had heard the director say it. Besides, if the Europeans or the Americans made *Limo Roulette*, they would never cast John D. as the missionary. Inspector Dhar meant nothing to Europeans or Americans; they would insist on casting one of *their* movie stars in that role.

Dr. Daruwalla was silent. He presumed that Balraj Gupta was angry with him for putting an end to the Inspector Dhar series; he already knew Gupta was angry with John D. because John D. had left town without doing much to promote *Inspector Dhar and the Towers of Silence*.

"I think you're angry with me," Farrokh began cautiously.

"Oh, no—not for a minute!" Gupta cried. "I never get angry with people who decide they're tired of making money. Such people are veritable emblems of humanity—don't you agree?"

"I *knew* you were angry with me," Dr. Daruwalla replied.

"Tell me about the love interest in your art film," Gupta demanded. "That will make you or break you, despite all this other foolishness. Dead children . . . why not show it to the South Indian socialists? *They* might like it!"

Dr. Daruwalla tried to talk about the love interest in the screenplay as if he believed in it. There was the American missionary, the would-be priest who falls in love with a beautiful circus acrobat; Suman was an actual acrobat, not an actress, the screenwriter explained.

"An acrobat!" cried Balraj Gupta. "Are you crazy? Have you seen their thighs? Women acrobats have terrifying thighs! And their thighs are magnified on film."

"I'm talking to the wrong person—I *must* be crazy," Farrokh replied. "Anyone who'd discuss a serious film with you is truly certifiable."

"The telltale word is 'serious,' " Balraj Gupta said. "I can see you've learned nothing from your success. Have you lost your bananas? Are you marbles?" the director shouted.

The screenwriter tried to correct the director's difficulties with English. "The phrases are, 'Have you lost your marbles?' and 'Are you bananas?'—I believe," Dr. Daruwalla told him.

"That's what I said!" Gupta shouted; like most directors, Balraj Gupta was always right. The doctor hung up the phone and packed his screenplay. *Limo Roulette* was the first thing Farrokh put in his suitcase; then he covered it with his Toronto clothes.

Just India

Vinod drove Dr. and Mrs. Daruwalla to the airport; the dwarf wept the whole way to Sahar, and Farrokh was afraid they'd have an accident. The thug driver had lost Inspector Dhar as a client; now, in addition to this tragedy, Vinod was losing his personal physician. It was shortly before midnight on a Monday evening; as if symbolic of Dhar's last film, the poster-wallas were already covering over some of the advertisements for *Inspector Dhar and the Towers of Silence.* The new posters weren't advertising a movie; they were proclamations of a different kind—celebratory announcements of Anti-Leprosy Day. That would be tomorrow, Tuesday, January 30. Julia and Farrokh would be leaving India on Anti-Leprosy Day at 2:50 A.M. on Air India 185. Bombay to Delhi, Delhi to London, London to Toronto (but you don't have to change planes). The Daruwallas would break up the long flight by staying a few nights in London.

In the intervening time since Dhar and his twin had departed for Switzerland, Dr. Daruwalla was disappointed to have heard so little from them. At first, Farrokh had worried that they were angry with him, or that their meeting had not gone well. Then a postcard came from the Upper Engadine: a cross-country skier, a *Langläufer,* is crossing a frozen white lake; the lake is rimmed with mountains, the sky cloudless and blue. The message, in John D.'s handwriting, was familiar to Farrokh because it was another of Inspector Dhar's repeated lines. In the movies, after the cool detective has slept with a new woman, something always interrupts them; they never have time to talk. Perhaps a gunfight breaks out, possibly a villain sets fire to their hotel (or their bed). In the ensuing and breathless action, Inspector Dhar and his lover have scarcely a moment to exchange pleasantries; they're usually fighting for their lives. But then there comes the inevitable break in the action—a brief pause before the grenade assault. The audience, already loathing him, is anticipating Dhar's signature remark to his lover. "By the way," he tells her, "thanks." That was John D.'s message on the postcard from the Upper Engadine.

By the way, thanks

Julia told Farrokh it was a touching message, because both twins had signed the postcard. She said it was what newlyweds did with Christmas cards and birthday greetings, but Dr. Daruwalla said (in his experience) it was what people did in doctors' offices when there was a group gift; the receptionist signed it, the secretaries signed it, the nurses signed it, the other surgeons signed it. What was so special or "touching" about that? John D. always signed his name as just plain "D." In unfamiliar handwriting, on the same postcard, was the name "Martin." So they were somewhere in the mountains. Farrokh hoped that John D. wasn't trying to teach his fool twin how to ski!

"At least they're together, and they appreciate it," Julia told him, but Farrokh wanted more. It almost killed him not to know every line of the dialogue between them.

When the Daruwallas arrived at the airport, Vinod weepingly handed the doctor a present. "Maybe you are never seeing me again," the dwarf said. As for the present, it was heavy and hard and rectangular; Vinod had wrapped it in newspapers. Through his sniffles, the dwarf managed to say that Farrokh was not to open the present until he was on the plane.

Later, the doctor would think that this was probably what terrorists said to unsuspecting passengers to whom they'd handed a bomb; just then the metal detector sounded, and Dr. Daruwalla was quickly surrounded by frightened men with guns. They asked him what was wrapped up in the newspapers. What could he tell them? A present from a dwarf? They made the doctor unwrap the newspapers while they stood at some distance; they looked less ready to shoot than to flee—to "abscond," as *The Times of India* would report the incident. But there was no incident.

Inside the newspapers was a brass plaque, a big brass sign; Dr. Daruwalla recognized it immediately. Vinod had removed the offensive message from the elevator of Farrokh's apartment building on Marine Drive.

SERVANTS ARE NOT ALLOWED

TO USE THE LIFT

UNLESS ACCOMPANIED BY CHILDREN

Julia told Farrokh that Vinod's gift was "touching," but although the security officers were relieved, they questioned the doctor about the source of the sign. They wanted to be sure that it hadn't been stolen from an historically protected building—that it was stolen from somewhere else didn't trouble them. Perhaps they didn't like the message any better than Farrokh and Vinod had liked it.

"A souvenir," Dr. Daruwalla assured them. To the doctor's surprise, the security officers let him keep the sign. It was cumbersome to carry it on board the plane, and even in first class the flight attendants were bitchy about stowing it out of everyone's way. First they made him unwrap it (again); then he was left with the unwanted newspapers.

"Remind me never to fly Air India," the doctor complained to his wife; he announced this loudly enough for the nearest flight attendant to hear him.

"I remind you every time," Julia replied, also loudly enough. To any fellow first-class passenger overhearing them, they might have seemed the epitome of a wealthy couple who commonly abuse those lesser people whose chore it is to wait on them. But this impression of the Daruwallas would be false; they were simply of a generation that reacted strongly to rudeness from anyone—they were well enough educated and old enough to be intolerant of intolerance. But what hadn't occurred to Farrokh or Julia was that perhaps the flight attendants were ill mannered about stowing the elevator sign *not* because of the inconvenience but because of the message; possibly the flight attendants were also incensed that servants weren't allowed to use the lift unless accompanied by children.

It was one of those little misunderstandings that no one would ever solve; it was a suitably sour note on which to leave one's country for the last time, Farrokh thought. Nor was he pleased by *The Times of India*, with which Vinod had wrapped the stolen sign. Of great prominence in the news lately was the report of food poisoning in East Delhi. Two children had died and eight others were hospitalized after they'd consumed some "stale" food from a garbage dump in the Shakurpur area. Dr. Daruwalla had been following this report with the keenest attention; he knew that the children hadn't died from eating "stale" food—the stupid newspaper meant "rotten" or "contaminated."

As far as Farrokh was concerned, the airplane couldn't take off fast enough. Like Dhar, the doctor preferred the aisle seat because he planned to drink beer and he would need to pee; Julia would sit by the window. It would be almost 10:00 in the morning, London time, before they landed in England. It would be dark all the way to Delhi. Literally, before he even left, the doctor thought he'd already seen the last of India.

Although Martin Mills might be tempted to say that it was God's will (that Dr. Daruwalla was saying good-bye to Bombay), the doctor wouldn't have agreed. It wasn't God's will; it was India, which wasn't for everybody—as Father Julian, unbeknownst to Dr. Daruwalla, had said. It was *not* God's will, Farrokh felt certain; it was just India, which was more than enough.

When Air India 185 lifted off the runway in Sahar, Dhar's thug taxi driver was again cruising the streets of Bombay; the dwarf was still crying—he was too upset to sleep. Vinod had returned to town too late to catch the last show at the Wetness Cabaret, where he'd been hoping to get a glimpse of Madhu; he'd have to look for her another night. It depressed the dwarf to keep cruising the red-light district, although it was a night like any night—Vinod might have found and saved a stray. At 3:00 A.M., the dwarf felt that the brothels resembled a failed circus. The ex-clown imagined the cages of lifeless animals—the rows of tents, full of exhausted and injured acrobats. He drove on.

It was almost 4:00 in the morning when Vinod parked the Ambassador in the alley alongside the Daruwallas' apartment building on Marine Drive. No one saw him slip into the building, but the dwarf roamed around the lobby, breathing heavily, until he had all the first-floor dogs barking. Then Vinod swaggered back to his taxi; he felt only mildly uplifted by the insults of the screaming residents, who'd earlier been disturbed by the report that their all-important elevator sign had been stolen.

Wherever the sad dwarf drove, the life of the city seemed to be eluding him; still, he wouldn't go home. In the predawn light, Vinod stopped the Ambassador to joke with a traffic policeman in Mazagaon.

"Where is the traffic being?" Vinod asked the constable. The policeman had his baton out, as if there were a crowd or a riot to direct. No one was anywhere around: not another car, not a single bicycle, not one pedestrian. Of the sidewalk sleepers, the few who were awake hadn't risen beyond a sitting position or from their knees. The constable recognized Dhar's thug driver—every policeman knew Vinod. The constable said there'd been a disturbance—a religious procession streaming out of Sophia Zuber Road—but Vinod had missed it. The abandoned traffic policeman said he'd be obliged to the dwarf if Vinod would drive him the length of Sophia Zuber Road, just to prove that there was no more trouble. And so, with the lonely constable in the car, Vinod cautiously proceeded through one of Bombay's better slums.

There wasn't much to see; more sidewalk sleepers were waking up, but the slum dwellers were still sleeping. At that part of Sophia Zuber Road where Martin Mills, almost a month ago, had encountered the mortally wounded cow, Vinod and the traffic policeman saw the tail end of a procession—a few sadhus chanting, the usual flower flingers. There was a huge clotted bloodstain in the gutter of the road, where the cow had finally died; the earlier disturbance, the religious procession, had been merely the removal of the dead cow's body. Some zealots had managed to keep the cow alive all this time.

This zeal was also not God's will, Dr. Daruwalla would have said; this doomed effort was also "just India," which was more than enough.

27. EPILOGUE

The Volunteer

On a Friday in May, more than two years after the Daruwallas had returned to Toronto from Bombay, Farrokh felt an urge to show Little India to his friend Macfarlane. They took Mac's car. It was their lunch hour, but the traffic on Gerrard was so congested, they soon realized they wouldn't have much time for lunch; they might barely have time to get to Little India and back to the hospital.

They'd been spending their lunch hour together for the past 18 months, ever since Macfarlane had tested HIV-positive; Mac's boy-friend—Dr. Duncan Frasier, the gay geneticist—had died of AIDS over a year ago. As for debating the merits of his dwarf-blood project, Farrokh had found no one to replace Frasier, and Mac hadn't found a new boyfriend.

The shorthand nature of the conversation between Dr. Daruwalla and Dr. Macfarlane, in regard to Mac's living with the AIDS virus, was a model of emotional restraint.

"How have you been doing?" Dr. Daruwalla would ask.

"Good," Dr. Macfarlane would reply. "I'm off AZT—switched to DDI. Didn't I tell you?"

"No—but why? Were your T cells dropping?"

"Kind of," Mac would say. "They dropped below two hundred. I was feeling like shit on AZT, so Schwartz decided to switch me to DDI. I feel better—I'm more energetic now. And I'm taking Bactrim prophylactically . . . to prevent PCP pneumonia."

"Oh," Farrokh would say.

"It isn't as bad as it sounds. I feel great," Mac would say. "If the DDI stops working, there's DDC and many more—I hope."

"I'm glad you feel that way," Farrokh would find himself saying.

"Meanwhile," Macfarlane would say, "I've got this little game going. I sit and visualize my healthy T cells—I picture them resisting the virus. I see my T cells shooting bullets at the virus, and the virus being cut down in a hail of gunfire—that's the idea, anyway."

"Is that Schwartz's idea?" Dr. Daruwalla would ask.

"No, it's *my* idea!"

"It sounds like Schwartz."

"And I go to my support group," Mac would add. "Support groups seem to be one of the things that correlate with long-term survival."

"Really," Farrokh would say.

"Really," Macfarlane would repeat. "And of course what they call taking charge of your illness—not being passive, and not necessarily accepting everything your doctor tells you."

"Poor Schwartz," Dr. Daruwalla would reply. "I'm glad *I'm* not your doctor."

"That makes two of us," Mac would say.

This was their two-minute drill; usually, they could cover the subject that quickly—at least they tried to. They liked to let their lunch hour be about other things: for example, Dr. Daruwalla's sudden desire to take Dr. Macfarlane to Little India.

It had been in May when the racist goons had driven Farrokh to Little India against his will; that had also been a Friday, a day when much of Little India had appeared to be closed—or were only the butcher shops closed? Dr. Daruwalla wondered if this was because the Friday prayers were faithfully attended by the local Muslims; it was one of those things he didn't know. Farrokh knew only that he wanted Macfarlane to see Little India, and he had this sudden feeling that he wanted all the conditions to be the same—the same weather, the same shops, the same mannequins (if not the same saris).

Doubtless, Dr. Daruwalla had been inspired by something he'd read in the newspapers, probably something about the Heritage Front. It greatly upset him to read about the Heritage Front—those neo-Nazi louts, that white supremacist scum. Since there were antihate laws in

Canada, Dr. Daruwalla wondered why groups like the Heritage Front were allowed to foment so much racist hatred.

Macfarlane had no difficulty finding a place to park; as before, Little India was fairly deserted—in this respect, it wasn't like India at all. Farrokh stopped walking in front of the Ahmad Grocers on Gerrard, at Coxwell; he pointed diagonally across the street to the boarded-up offices of the Canadian Ethnic Immigration Services—it looked closed for good, not just because it was Friday.

"This is where I was dragged out of the car," Dr. Daruwalla explained. They continued walking on Gerrard. Pindi Embroidery was gone, but a clothes rack of kaftans stood lifelessly on the sidewalk. "There was more wind the day I was here," Farrokh told Mac. "The kaftans were dancing in the wind."

At the corner of Rhodes and Gerrard, Nirma Fashions was still in business. They noted the Singh Farm, advertising fresh fruits and vegetables. They viewed the façade of the United Church, which also served as the Shri Ram Hindu Temple; the Reverend Lawrence Pushee, minister of the former, had chosen an interesting theme for the coming Sunday service. A Gandhi quotation forewarned the congregation: "There is enough for everyone's need but not enough for everyone's greed."

Not only the Canadian Ethnic Immigration Services, but also the Chinese were experiencing hard times; the Luck City Poultry Company was closed down. At the corner of Craven and Gerrard, the "Indian Cuisine Specialists," formerly the Nirala restaurant, were now calling themselves Hira Moti, and the familiar advertisement for Kingfisher lager promised that the beer was (as always) INSTILLED WITH INNER STRENGTH. A MEGASTARS poster advertised the arrival of Jeetendra and Bali of Patel Rap; Sapna Mukerjee was also performing.

"I walked along here, bleeding," Farrokh said to Mac. In the window of either Kala Kendar or Sonali's, the same blond mannequin was wearing a sari; she still looked out of place among the other mannequins. Dr. Daruwalla thought of Nancy.

They passed Satyam, "the store for the whole family"; they read an old announcement for the Miss Diwali competition. They walked up and down and across Gerrard, with no purpose. Farrokh kept repeating the names of the places. The Kohinoor supermarket, the Madras Durbar, the Apollo Video (promising ASIAN MOVIES), the India Theater— NOW PLAYING, TAMIL MOVIES! At the Chaat Hut, Farrokh explained to Mac what was meant by "all kinds of chaats." At the Bombay Bhel, they barely had time to eat their aloo tikki and drink their Thunderbolt beer.

Before they went back to the hospital, the doctors stopped at J. S. Addison Plumbing, at the corner of Woodfield. Dr. Daruwalla was looking for that splendid copper bathtub with the ornate faucets; the handles were tiger heads, the tigers roaring—it was exactly like the tub he'd bathed in as a boy on old Ridge Road, Malabar Hill. He'd had that bathtub on his mind ever since his last, unplanned visit to Little India. But the tub had been sold. What Farrokh found, instead, was another marvel of Victorian ornamentation. It was that same sink spout, with tusks for faucets, which had captured Rahul's imagination in the ladies' room of the Duckworth Club; it was that elephant-headed spigot, with the water spraying from the elephant's trunk. Farrokh touched the two tusks, one for hot water and the other for cold. Macfarlane thought it was ghastly, but Dr. Daruwalla didn't hesitate to buy it; it was the product of a recognizably British imagination, but it was made in India.

"Does it have a sentimental value?" Mac asked.

"Not exactly," Farrokh replied. Dr. Daruwalla wondered what he'd do with the ugly thing; he knew Julia would absolutely hate it.

"Those men who drove you here, and left you . . ." Mac suddenly said. "What about them?"

"Do you imagine that they bring other people here—like they brought you?"

"All the time," Farrokh said. "I imagine that they're bringing people here all the time."

Mac thought Farrokh looked mortally depressed and told him so.

How can I ever feel assimilated? Dr. Daruwalla wondered. "How am I supposed to feel like a Canadian?" Farrokh asked Mac.

Indeed, if one could believe the newspapers, there was a growing resistance to immigration; demographers were predicting a "racist backlash." The resistance to immigration *was* racist, Dr. Daruwalla believed; the doctor had become very sensitive to the phrase "visible minorities." He knew this didn't mean the Italians or the Germans or the Portuguese; they'd come to Canada in the 1950's. Until the last decade, by far the greatest proportion of immigrants came from Britain.

But not now; the new immigrants came from Hong Kong and China and India—half the immigrants who'd come to Canada in this decade were Asians. In Toronto, almost 40 percent of the population was immigrant—more than a million people.

Macfarlane suffered to see Farrokh so despondent. "Believe me, Farrokh," Mac said. "I know it's no circus to be an immigrant in this country, and although I trust that those thugs who dumped you in Little India have assaulted other immigrants in the city, I *don't* believe that they're transporting people all over town 'all the time,' as you say."

"Don't you mean it's *no picnic?* You said 'no circus,'" Farrokh told Mac.

"It's the same expression," Macfarlane replied.

"Do you know what my father said to me?" Dr. Daruwalla asked.

"Could it be, 'Immigrants are immigrants all their lives'?" Macfarlane inquired.

"Oh—I've already told you," Farrokh said.

"Too many times to count," Mac replied. "But I suppose you go around thinking of it all the time."

"All the time," Farrokh repeated. He felt grateful for what a good friend Mac was.

It had been Dr. Macfarlane who'd persuaded Dr. Daruwalla to volunteer his time at the AIDS hospice in Toronto; Duncan Frasier had died there. Farrokh had worked at the hospice for over a year. At first, he suspected his own motives, which he'd confessed to Mac; on Mac's advice, Farrokh had also discussed his special interest in the hospice with the director of nursing.

It had been awkward for Farrokh to tell a stranger the story of his relationship with John D.—how this young man, who was like an adopted son to Dr. Daruwalla, had always been a homosexual, but the doctor hadn't known it until John D. was almost 40; how, even now, when John D.'s sexual orientation was plainly clear, Farrokh and the not-so-young "young" man still didn't speak of the matter (at least not in depth). Dr. Daruwalla told Dr. Macfarlane *and* the hospice's director of nursing that he wanted to be involved with AIDS patients because he wanted to know more about the elusive John D. Farrokh admitted that he was terrified for John D.; that his beloved almost-like-a-son might die of AIDS was Farrokh's greatest fear. (Yes, he was afraid for Martin, too.)

Emotional restraint, which was repeatedly demonstrated in Dr. Daruwalla's friendship with Dr. Macfarlane—their understated conversation regarding the status of Macfarlane's HIV-positive condition was but one example—prevented Farrokh from admitting to his friend that he was also afraid of watching Mac die of AIDS. But it was perfectly well understood, by both doctors *and* by the hospice's director of nursing, that this was another motive underlying Farrokh's desire to familiarize himself with the functions of an AIDS hospice.

Dr. Daruwalla believed that the more naturally he could learn to behave in the presence of AIDS patients, not to mention gay men, the closer his relationship with John D. might become. They'd already grown closer together, ever since John D. had told Farrokh that he'd always been gay. Doubtless, Dr. Daruwalla's friendship with Dr. Macfarlane had helped. But what "father" can ever feel close enough to his "son"—that was the issue, wasn't it? Farrokh had asked Mac.

"Don't try to get *too* close to John D.," Macfarlane had advised. "Remember, you're not his father—and you're not gay."

It had been awkward—how Dr. Daruwalla had first tried to fit in at the hospice. As Mac had warned him, he had to learn that he wasn't *their* doctor—he was just a volunteer. He asked lots of doctor-type questions and generally drove the nurses crazy; taking orders from nurses was something Dr. Daruwalla had to get used to. It was an effort for him to limit his expertise to the issue of bed sores; he still couldn't be stopped from prescribing little exercises to combat the muscular wasting of the patients. He so freely dispensed tennis balls for squeezing that one of the nurses nicknamed him "Dr. Balls." After a while, the name pleased him.

He was good at taking care of the catheters, and he was capable of giving morphine injections when one of the hospice doctors or nurses asked him to. He grew familiar with the feeding tubes; he hated seeing the seizures. He hoped that he would never watch John D. die with fulminant diarrhea . . . with an uncontrolled infection . . . with a spiking fever.

"I hope not, too," Mac told him. "But if you're not prepared to watch *me* die, you'll be worthless to me when the time comes."

Dr. Daruwalla wanted to be prepared. Usually, his voluntary time was spent in ordinary chores. One night, he did the laundry, just as Macfarlane had proudly bragged about doing it years earlier—all the bed linens and the towels. He also read aloud to patients who couldn't read. He wrote letters for them, too.

One night, when Farrokh was working the switchboard, an angry woman called; she was indignant because she'd just learned that her only son was dying in the hospice and no one had officially informed her—not even her son. She was outraged, she said. She wanted to speak to someone in charge; she didn't ask to speak to her son.

Dr. Daruwalla supposed that, although he wasn't "in charge," the woman might as well speak to him; he knew the hospice and its rules well enough to advise her how to visit—when to come, how to show respect for privacy and so forth. But the woman wouldn't hear of it.

"*You're* not in charge!" she kept shouting. "I want to speak to a *doctor!*" she cried. "I want to talk to the *head* of the place!"

Dr. Daruwalla was about to tell her his full name, his profession, his age—even the number of his children and his grandchildren, if she liked. But before he could speak, she screamed at him. "Who *are* you, anyway? *What* are you?"

Dr. Daruwalla answered her with such conviction and pride that he surprised himself. "I'm a volunteer," the doctor said. The concept pleased him. Farrokh wondered if it felt as good to be assimilated as it did to be a volunteer.

The Bottommost Drawer

After Dr. Daruwalla left Bombay, there were other departures; in one case, there was a departure and a return. Suman, the skywalker par excellence, left the Great Royal Circus. She married a man in the milk business. Then, after various discussions with Pratap Walawalkar, the owner, Suman came back to the Great Royal, bringing her milk-business husband with her. Only recently, the doctor had heard that Suman's husband had become one of the managers of the Great Royal Circus, and that Suman was once again walking on the sky; she was still very much the star.

Farrokh also learned that Pratap Singh had quit the Great Royal; the ringmaster and wild-animal trainer had left with his wife, Sumi, and their troupe of child acrobats—the real Pinky among them—to join the New Grand Circus. Unlike the Pinky character in *Limo Roulette,* the real Pinky wasn't killed by a lion who mistook her for a peacock; the real Pinky was still performing, in one town after another. She would be 11 or 12, Farrokh guessed.

Dr. Daruwalla had heard that a girl named Ratna was performing the Skywalk at the New Grand; remarkably, Ratna could skywalk *backward!* The doctor was further informed that, by the time the New Grand Circus performed in Changanacheri, Pinky's name had been changed to Choti Rani, which means Little Queen. Possibly Pratap had chosen the new name not only because Choti Rani was suitably theatrical, but also because Pinky was so special to him; Pratap always said she was absolutely the best. Just plain Pinky was a little queen now.

As for Deepa and Shivaji, the dwarf's dwarf son, they had escaped the Great Blue Nile. Shivaji was very much Vinod's son, in respect to the dwarf's determination; as for Shivaji's talent, the young man was a better acrobat than his father—and, at worst, Vinod's equal as a clown. On the strength of Shivaji's abilities, he and his mother had moved to the Great Royal Circus, which was unquestionably a move up from the Great Blue Nile—and one that Deepa never could have made on the strength of her own *or* Vinod's talents. Farrokh had heard that the subtleties of Shivaji's Farting Clown act—not to mention the dwarf's signature item, which was called Elephant Dodging—put India's other farting clowns to shame.

The fate of those lesser performers who toiled for the Great Blue Nile was altogether less kind; there would be no escape for them. The elephant-footed boy had never been content to be a cook's helper; a higher aspiration afflicted him. The knife thrower's wife, Mrs. Bhagwan—the most mechanical of skywalkers—had failed to dissuade Ganesh from his delusions of athleticism. Despite falling many times from that model of the ladderlike device which hung from the roof of the Bhagwans' troupe tent, the cripple would never let go of the idea that he could learn to skywalk.

The perfect ending to Farrokh's screenplay is that the cripple learns to walk without a limp by walking on the sky; such an ending would *not* conclude the real Ganesh's story. The *real* Ganesh wouldn't rest until he'd tried the real thing. It was almost as Dr. Daruwalla had imagined it, almost as it was written. But it's unlikely that the real Ganesh was as eloquent; there would have been no voice-over. The elephant boy must have looked down at least once—enough to know that he shouldn't look down again. From the apex of the main tent, the ground was 80 feet below him. With his feet in the loops, it's doubtful that he even *thought* as poetically as Farrokh's fictional character.

("There is a moment when you must let go with your hands. At that moment, you are in no one's hands. At that moment, everyone walks on the sky.") Not likely—not a sentiment that would spontaneously leap to the mind of a cook's helper. The elephant-footed boy would probably have made the mistake of counting the loops, too. Whether counting or not counting, it's far-fetched to imagine him coaching himself across the ladder.

("What I tell myself is, I am walking without a limp.") That would be the day! Dr. Daruwalla thought. Judging from where they found the cripple's body, the real Ganesh fell when he was less than halfway across the top of the tent. There were 18 loops in the ladder; the Skywalk was 16 steps. It was Mrs. Bhagwan's expert opinion that the elephant boy had fallen after only four or five steps; he'd never managed more than four or five steps across the roof of *her* tent, the skywalker said.

This news came slowly to Toronto. Mr. and Mrs. Das conveyed their regrets, by letter, to Dr. Daruwalla; the letter was late—it was misaddressed. The ringmaster and his wife added that Mrs. Bhagwan blamed herself for the accident, but she also felt certain that the cripple could never have been taught to skywalk. Doubtless her distress distracted her. The next news from Mr. and Mrs. Das was that Mrs. Bhagwan had been cut by her knife-throwing husband as she lay spread-eagled on the revolving bull's-eye; it wasn't a serious wound, but she gave herself no time to heal. The following night, she fell from the Skywalk. She was only as far across the top of the tent as Ganesh had been, and she fell without a cry. Her husband said that she'd been having trouble with the fourth and fifth steps ever since the elephant boy had fallen.

Mr. Bhagwan wouldn't throw another knife, not even when they offered him a choice of targets, all of whom were small girls. The widower went into semiretirement, performing only the Elephant Passing item. There seemed to be some self-punishment about this elephant act—or so the ringmaster confided to Dr. Daruwalla. Mr. Bhagwan would lie down under the elephant—at first with fewer and fewer mattresses between his body and the elephant-walking plank, and between his body and the ground. Then he did it with no mattresses at all. There were internal injuries, the ringmaster and his wife implied. Mr. Bhagwan became ill; he was sent home. Later, Mr. and Mrs. Das heard that Mr. Bhagwan had died.

Then Dr. Daruwalla heard that they'd *all* become ill. There were no more letters from Mr. and Mrs. Das. The Great Blue Nile Circus had vanished. Their last place of performance was Poona, where the prevailing story about the Blue Nile was that they were brought down by a flood; it was a small flood, not a major disaster, except that the hygiene at the circus became lax. An unidentified disease killed several of the big cats, and bouts of diarrhea and gastroenteritis were rampant among the acrobats. Just that quickly, the Great Blue Nile was gone.

Had Gautam's death been a harbinger? The old chimpanzee had died of rabies not two weeks after he'd bitten Martin Mills; Kunal's efforts to discipline the ape by beating him had been wasted. But, among them all, Dr. Daruwalla mainly remembered Mrs. Bhagwan—her tough feet and her long black shiny hair.

The death of the elephant boy (a cripple no more) destroyed a small but important part of Farrokh. What happened to the real Ganesh had an immediate and diminishing effect on the screenwriter's already waning confidence in his powers of creation. The screenplay of *Limo Roulette* had suffered from comparisons to real life. In the end, the real Ganesh's remark rang truest. "You can't fix what elephants do," the cripple had said.

Like Mr. Bhagwan, who had retreated into Elephant Passing, which led to his death, the screenplay of *Limo Roulette* went into radical retirement. It occupied the bottommost drawer in Dr. Daruwalla's desk at home; he wouldn't keep a copy in his office at the hospital. If he were to die suddenly, he wouldn't have wanted anyone but Julia to discover the unproduced screenplay. The single copy was in a folder marked

PROPERTY OF INSPECTOR DHAR

for it was Farrokh's conviction that only John D. would one day know what to do with it.

Doubtless there would be compromises required in order for *Limo Roulette* to be produced; there were always compromises in the movie business. Someone would say that the voice-over was "emotionally distancing"—that was the fashionable opinion of voice-over. Someone would complain about the little girl being killed by the lion. (Couldn't Pinky be confined to a wheelchair, but happy, for the rest of the movie?) And despite what had happened to the real Ganesh, the screenwriter loved the ending as it was written; someone would want to tamper with that ending, which Dr. Daruwalla could never allow. The doctor knew that *Limo Roulette* would never be as perfect as it was in those days when he was writing it and he imagined that he was a better writer than he was.

It was a deep drawer for a mere 118 pages. As if to keep the abandoned screenplay company, Farrokh filled the drawer with photographs of chromosomes; ever since Duncan Frasier had died, Dr. Daruwalla's dwarf-blood project had passed beyond languishing—the doctor's enthusiasm for drawing blood from dwarfs was as dead as the gay geneticist. If anything or anyone were to tempt Dr. Daruwalla to return to India, this time the doctor couldn't claim that the dwarfs were bringing him back.

From time to time, Dr. Daruwalla would read that perfect ending to *Limo Roulette*—when the cripple walks on the sky—for only by this artificial means could the doctor keep the *real* Ganesh alive. The screenwriter loved that moment after the Skywalk when the boy is descending on the dental trapeze, spinning in the spotlight as the gleaming sequins on his singlet throw back the light. Farrokh loved how the cripple never touches the ground; how he descends into Pratap's waiting arms, and how Pratap holds the boy up to the cheering crowd. Then Pratap runs out of the ring with Ganesh in his arms, because after a cripple has walked on the sky, no one should see him limp. It could have worked, the screenwriter thought; it *should* have worked.

Dr. Daruwalla was 62; he was reasonably healthy. His weight was a small problem and he'd done little to rid his diet of admitted excesses, but the doctor nevertheless expected to live for another decade or two. John D. might well be in *his* sixties by the time *Limo Roulette* was put into the actor's hands. The former Inspector Dhar would know for whom the part of the missionary had been intended; the actor would also be relatively free of any personal attachments to the story or its characters. If certain compromises were necessary in order to produce *Limo Roulette*, John D. would be able to look at the screenplay objectively. Dr. Daruwalla had no doubt that the ex–Inspector Dhar would know what to do with the material.

But for now—for the rest of his life, Farrokh knew—the story belonged in the bottommost drawer.

Sort of Fading Now

Almost three years after he left Bombay, the retired screenwriter read about the destruction of the Mosque of Babar; the unending hostilities he'd once mocked in *Inspector Dhar and the Hanging Mali* had turned uglier still. Fanatical Hindus had destroyed the 16th-century Babri mosque; rioting had left more than 400 dead—Prime Minister Rao called for shooting rioters on sight, both in Bhopal and in Bombay. Hindu fundamentalists weren't pleased by Mr. Rao's promise to rebuild the mosque; these fanatics continued to claim that the mosque had been built on the birthplace of the Hindu god Rama—they'd already begun building a temple to Rama at the site of the destroyed mosque. The hostilities would go on and on, Dr. Daruwalla knew. The violence would endure; it was always what lasted longest.

And although Madhu would never be found, Detective Patel would keep inquiring for the girl; the child prostitute would be a woman now—if she was still managing to live with the AIDS virus, which was unlikely.

"If we crash, do we burn or fly apart in little pieces?" Madhu had asked Dr. Daruwalla. "Something will get me," she'd told the doctor. Farrokh couldn't stop imagining her. He was always envisioning Madhu with Mr. Garg; they were traveling together from Junagadh to Bombay, escaping the Great Blue Nile. Although it would have been considered highly disgraceful, they would probably have been touching each other, not even secretly—secure in the misinformation that all that was wrong with them was a case of chlamydia.

And almost as the deputy commissioner had predicted, the second Mrs. Dogar would be unable to resist the terrible temptations that presented themselves to her in her confinement with women. She bit off a fellow prisoner's nose. In the course of the subsequent and extremely hard labor to which Rahul was then subjected, she would rebel; it would be unnecessary to hang her, for she was beaten to death by her guards.

In another of life's little passages, Ranjit would both retire and re-marry. Dr. Daruwalla had never met the woman whose matrimonial advertisement in *The Times of India* finally snared his faithful medical secretary; however, the doctor had read the ad—Ranjit sent it to him. "An attractive woman of indeterminate age—innocently divorced, without issue—seeks a mature man, preferably a widower. Neatness and civility still count." Indeed, they do, the doctor thought. Julia joked that Ranjit had probably been attracted to the woman's punctuation.

Other couples came and went, but the nature of couples, like vio-lence, would endure. Even little Amy Sorabjee had married. (God help her husband.) And although Mrs. Bannerjee had died, Mr. Bannerjee wasn't a widower for long; he married the widow Lal. Of these unsavory couplings, of course, the unchanging Mr. Sethna steadfastly dis-approved.

However set in his ways, the old steward still ruled the Duckworth Club dining room and the Ladies' Garden with a possessiveness that was said to be enhanced by his newly acquired sense of himself as a promis-ing actor. Dr. Sorabjee wrote to Dr. Daruwalla that Mr. Sethna had been seen addressing himself in the men's-room mirror—long monologues of a thespian nature. And the old steward was observed to be slavishly devoted to Deputy Commissioner Patel, if not to the big blond wife who went everywhere with the esteemed detective. Apparently, the famous tea-pouring Parsi also fancied himself a promising policeman. Crime-branch investigation was no doubt perceived by Mr. Sethna as a height-ened form of eavesdropping.

Astonishingly, the old steward appeared to approve of something!

The unorthodoxy of the deputy commissioner and his American wife becoming members of the Duckworth Club didn't bother Mr. Sethna; it bothered many an orthodox Duckworthian. Clearly, the deputy commissioner hadn't waited 22 years for his membership; although Detective Patel satisfied the requirement for "community leadership," his instant acceptance at the club suggested that someone had bent the rules—someone had been looking for (and had found) a loophole. To many Duckworthians, the policeman's membership amounted to a miracle; it was also considered a scandal.

It was a *minor* miracle, in Detective Patel's opinion, that no one was ever bitten by the escaped cobras in Mahalaxmi, for (according to the deputy commissioner) those cobras had been "assimilated" into the life of Bombay without a single reported bite.

It wasn't even a minor miracle that the phone calls from the woman who tried to sound like a man continued—not only after Rahul's imprisonment, but also after her death. It strangely comforted Dr. Daruwalla to know that the caller had never been Rahul. Every time, as if reading from a script, the caller would leave nothing out. "Your father's head was off, completely *off*! I saw it sitting on the passenger seat before flames engulfed the car."

Farrokh had learned how to interrupt the unslackening voice. "I know—I know already," Dr. Daruwalla would say. "And his hands couldn't let go of the steering wheel, even though his fingers were on fire—is that what you're going to tell me? I've already heard it."

But the voice never relented. "I did it. I blew his head off. I watched him burn," said the woman who tried to sound like a man. "And I'm telling you, he deserved it. Your whole family deserves it."

"Oh, fuck you," Farrokh had learned to say, although he generally disliked such language.

Sometimes he would watch the video of *Inspector Dhar and the Cage-Girl Killer* (that was Farrokh's favorite) or *Inspector Dhar and the Towers of Silence,* which the former screenwriter believed was the most underrated of the Dhar films. But to his best friend, Mac, Farrokh would never confide that he'd written anything—not a word. Inspector Dhar was part of the doctor's past. John D. had almost completely let Dhar go. Dr. Daruwalla had to keep trying.

For three years, the twins had teased him; neither John D. nor Martin Mills would tell Dr. Daruwalla what had passed between them on their flight to Switzerland. While the doctor sought clarification, the twins deliberately confused him; they must have done it to exasperate him—

Farrokh was such a lot of fun when he was exasperated. The former Inspector Dhar's most irritating (and least believable) response was, "I don't remember." Martin Mills claimed to remember everything. But Martin never told the same story twice, and when John D. *did* admit to remembering something, the actor's version unfailingly contradicted the ex-missionary's.

"Let's try to begin at the beginning," Dr. Daruwalla would say. "I'm interested in that moment of recognition, the realization that you were face-to-face with your second self—so to speak."

"*I* boarded the plane first," both twins would tell him.

"I always do the same thing whenever I leave India," the retired Inspector Dhar insisted. "I find my seat and get my little complimentary toilet kit from the flight attendant. Then I go to the lavatory and shave off my mustache, while they're still boarding the plane."

This much was true. It was what John D. did to un-Dhar himself. This was an established fact, one of the few that Farrokh could cling to: both twins were mustacheless when they met.

"I was sitting in my seat when this man came out of the lavatory, and I thought I recognized him," Martin said.

"You were looking out the window," John D. declared. "You didn't turn to look at me until I'd sat down beside you and had spoken your name."

"You spoke his name?" Dr. Daruwalla always asked.

"Of course. I knew who he was instantly," the ex–Inspector Dhar would reply. "I thought to myself: Farrokh must imagine he's awfully clever—writing a script for everyone."

"He never spoke my name," Martin told the doctor. "I remember thinking that he was Satan, and that Satan had chosen to look like me, to take my own form—what a horror! I thought you were my dark side, my evil half."

"Your *smarter* half, you mean," John D. would invariably reply.

"He was just like the Devil. He was frighteningly arrogant," Martin told Farrokh.

"I simply told him that I knew who he was," John D. argued.

"You said nothing of the kind," Martin interjected. "You said, 'Fasten your fucking seat belt, pal, because are *you* ever in for a surprise!'"

"That sounds like what you'd say," Farrokh told the former Dhar.

"I couldn't get a word in edgewise," John D. complained. "Here I knew all about him, but *he* was the one who wouldn't stop talking. All the way to Zürich, he never shut up."

Dr. Daruwalla had to admit that this sounded like what Martin Mills would do.

"I kept thinking: This is Satan. I give up the idea of the priesthood and I meet the Devil—in first class! He had this constant sneer," Martin said. "It was a *Satanic* sneer—or so I thought."

"He started right out about Vera, our sainted mother," John D. related. "We were still crossing the Arabian Sea—utter darkness above and below us—when he got to the part about the roommate's suicide. I hadn't said a word!"

"That's not true—he kept interrupting me," Martin told Farrokh. "He kept asking me, 'Are you gay, or do you just not know it yet?' Honestly, I thought he was the rudest man I'd ever met!"

"Listen to me," the actor said. "You meet your twin brother on an airplane and you start right out with a list of everyone your mother's slept with. And you think *I'm* rude."

"You called me a 'quitter' before we'd even reached our cruising altitude," Martin said.

"But you must have started by telling him that you were his twin," Farrokh said to John D.

"He did nothing of the kind," said Martin Mills. "He said, 'You already know the bad news: your father died. Now here's the good news: he wasn't your father.' "

"You *didn't!*" Dr. Daruwalla said to John D.

"I can't remember," the actor would say.

"The word 'twin'—just tell me, who said it first?" the doctor asked.

"I asked the flight attendant if she saw any resemblance between us—*she* was the first to say the word 'twin,' " John D. replied.

"That's not exactly how it happened," Martin argued. "What he said to the flight attendant was, 'We were separated at birth. Try to guess which one of us has had the better time.' "

"He simply exhibited all the common symptoms of denial," John D. would respond. "He kept asking me if I had *proof* that we were related."

"He was utterly shameless," Martin told Farrokh. "He said, 'You can't deny that you've had at least one homosexual infatuation—there's your proof.' "

"That was bold of you," the doctor told John D. "Actually, there's only a fifty-two percent chance . . ."

"I knew he was gay the second I saw him," the retired movie star said.

"But when did you realize how much . . . else you had in common?"

Dr. Daruwalla asked. "When did you begin to recognize the traits you shared? When did your obvious similarities emerge?"

"Oh, long before we got to Zürich," Martin answered quickly.

"*What* similarities?" John D. asked.

"That's what I mean by arrogant—he's arrogant *and* rude," Martin told Farrokh.

"And when did you decide *not* to go to New York?" the doctor asked the ex-missionary. Dr. Daruwalla was especially interested in the part of the story where the twins told Vera off.

"We were working on our telegram to the bitch before we landed," John D. replied.

"But what did the telegram say?" Farrokh asked.

"I don't remember," John D. would always answer.

"Of *course* you remember!" cried Martin Mills. "You wrote it! He wouldn't let me write a word of the telegram," Martin told Dr. Daruwalla. "He said he was in the business of one-liners—he insisted on doing it himself."

"What *you* wanted to say to her wouldn't have fit in a telegram," John D. reminded his twin.

"What he said to her was unspeakably cruel. I couldn't believe how cruel he could be. And he didn't even know her!" Martin Mills told the doctor.

"He asked me to send the telegram. He had no second thoughts," John D. told Farrokh.

"But what was it that you said? What did the damn telegram *say?*" Dr. Daruwalla cried.

"It was unspeakably cruel," Martin repeated.

"She had it coming, and you know it," said the ex–Inspector Dhar.

Whatever the telegram said, Dr. Daruwalla knew that Vera didn't live very long after she received it. There was only her hysterical phone call to Farrokh, who was still in Bombay; Vera called the doctor's office and left a message with Ranjit.

"This is Veronica Rose—the actress," she told Dr. Daruwalla's secretary. Ranjit knew who she was; he would never forget typing the report on the problem Vera had with her knees, which turned out to be gynecological—"vaginal itching," Dr. Lowji Daruwalla had said.

"Tell the fucking doctor I know that he betrayed me!" Vera said to Ranjit.

"Is it your . . . knees again?" the old secretary had asked her.

Dr. Daruwalla never returned her call. Vera never made it back to California before she died; her death was related to the sleeping pills she regularly took, which she'd irregularly mixed with vodka.

Martin would stay in Europe. Switzerland suited him, he said. And the outings in the Alps—although the former scholastic had never been athletically inclined, these outings with John D. were wonderful for Martin Mills. He couldn't be taught to downhill-ski (he was too uncoordinated), but he liked cross-country skiing and hiking; he loved being with his brother. Even John D. admitted, albeit belatedly, that they loved being with each other.

The ex-missionary kept himself busy; he taught at City University (in the general-studies program) and at the American International School of Zürich—he was active at the Swiss Jesuit Centre, too. Occasionally, he would travel to other Jesuit institutions; there were youth centers and students' homes in Basel and Bern, and adult-education centers in Fribourg and Bad Schönbrunn—Martin Mills was doubtless effective as an inspirational speaker. Farrokh could only imagine that this meant more Christ-in-the-parking-lot sermonizing; the former zealot hadn't lost his energy for improving the attitudes of others.

As for John D., he continued in his craft; the journeyman actor was content with his roles at the Schauspielhaus Zürich. His friends were in the theater, or affiliated with the university, or with a publishing firm of excellent reputation—and of course he saw a great deal of Farrokh's brother, Jamshed, and Jamshed's wife (and Julia's sister), Josefine.

It was to this social circle that John D. would introduce his twin. An oddity at first—everyone is interested in a twins-separated-at-birth story—Martin made many friends in this community; in three years, the ex-missionary probably had more friends than the actor. In fact, Martin's first lover was an ex-boyfriend of John D.'s, which Dr. Daruwalla found strange; the twins made a joke of it—probably to exasperate him, the doctor thought.

As for lovers, Matthias Frei died; the onetime terror of the Zürich avant-garde had been John D.'s longstanding partner. It was Julia who informed Farrokh of this; she'd known for quite some time that John D. and Frei were a couple. "Frei didn't die of AIDS, did he?" the doctor asked his wife. She gave him the same sort of look that John D. would have given him; it was that smile from movie posters of faded memory, recalling the cutting sneer of Inspector Dhar.

"No, Frei didn't die of AIDS—he had a heart attack," Julia told her husband.

No one ever tells me anything! the doctor thought. It was just like that twinly conversation on Swissair 197, Bombay to Zürich, which would occupy a sizable part of Farrokh's imagination, largely because John D. and Martin Mills were so secretive about it.

"Now, listen to me, both of you," Dr. Daruwalla would tell the twins. "I'm *not* prying, I *do* respect your privacy—it's just that you know how much dialogue interests me. This feeling of closeness between you, for it's obvious to me that the two of you *are* close ... did it come from your very first meeting? It must have happened on the plane! There's surely something more between you than your mutual hatred of your late mother—or did the telegram to Vera really bring you together?"

"The telegram wasn't dialogue—I thought you were interested only in our *dialogue*," John D. replied.

"Such a telegram would never have occurred to *me*!" said Martin Mills.

"I couldn't get a word in edgewise," John D. repeated. "We didn't have any dialogue. Martin had one monologue after another."

"He's an actor, all right," Martin told Farrokh. "I know he can *create* a character, as they say, but I'm telling you I was convinced he was Satan—I mean the real thing."

"Nine hours is a long time to talk with anyone," John D. was fond of saying.

"The flight was nearly nine hours and fifteen minutes, to be more exact," Martin corrected him.

"The point is, I was dying to get off the plane," John D. told Dr. Daruwalla. "He kept telling me it was God's will that we met. I thought I was going to go mad. The only time I could get away from him was when I went to the lavatory."

"You practically *lived* in the lavatory! You drank so much beer. And it *was* God's will—you see that now, don't you?" Martin asked John D.

"It was *Farrokh's* will," John D. replied.

"You really *are* the Devil!" Martin told his twin.

"No, *both* of you are the Devil!" Dr. Daruwalla told them, although he would discover that he loved them—if never quite equally. He looked forward to seeing them, and to their letters or their calls. Martin wrote lengthy letters; John D. seldom wrote letters, but he called frequently. Sometimes, when he called, it was hard to know what he wanted. Occasionally, not often, it was hard to know *who* was calling—John D. or the old Inspector Dhar.

"Hi, it's *me*," he said to Farrokh one morning; he sounded smashed.

It would have been early afternoon in Zürich. John D. said he'd just had a foolish lunch; when the actor called his lunch or dinner "foolish," it usually meant that he'd had something stronger to drink than beer. Only two glasses of wine made him drunk.

"I hope you're not performing tonight!" Dr. Daruwalla said, regretting that he sounded like an overcritical father.

"It's my understudy's night to perform," the actor told him. Farrokh knew very little about the theater; he hadn't known that there were understudies at the Schauspielhaus—also, he was sure that John D. was currently playing a small supporting role.

"It's impressive that you have an understudy for such a little part," the doctor said cautiously.

"My 'understudy' is Martin," the twin confessed. "We thought we'd try it—just to see if anyone noticed."

Once again Farrokh sounded like an overcritical father. "You should be more protective of your career than that," Dr. Daruwalla chided John D. "Martin can be a clod! What if he can't act at all? He could completely embarrass you!"

"We've been practicing," said the old Inspector Dhar.

"And I suppose you've been posing as *him*," Farrokh remarked. "Lectures on Graham Greene, no doubt—Martin's favorite 'Catholic interpretation.' And a few inspirational speeches at those Jesuit centers—a Jesus in every parking lot, more than enough Christs to go around . . . that kind of thing."

"Yes," John D. admitted. "It's been fun."

"You should be ashamed—*both* of you!" Dr. Daruwalla cried.

"You put us together," John D. replied.

Nowadays, Farrokh knew, the twins were much more alike in their appearance. John D. had lost a little weight; Martin had put the pounds on—incredibly, the former Jesuit was going to a gym. They also cut their hair the same way. Having been separated for 39 years, the twins took being identical somewhat seriously.

Then there was that particularly transatlantic silence, with a rhythmic bleeping—a sound that seemed to count the time. And John D. remarked, "So . . . it's probably sunset there." When John D. said "there," he meant Bombay. Counting 10½ hours, Dr. Daruwalla figured that it would be more or less sunset. "I'll bet she's on the balcony, just watching," John D. went on. "What do you bet?" Dr. Daruwalla knew that the ex–Inspector Dhar was thinking of Nancy and her view to the west.

"I guess it's about that time," the doctor answered carefully.

"It's probably too early for the good policeman to be home," John D. continued. "She's all alone, but I'll bet she's on the balcony—just watching."

"Yes—probably," Dr. Daruwalla said.

"Want to bet?" John D. asked. "Why don't you call her and see if she's there? You can tell by how long it takes her to get to the phone."

"Why don't *you* call her?" Farrokh asked.

"I never call Nancy," John D. told him.

"She'd probably enjoy hearing from you," Farrokh lied.

"No, she wouldn't," John D. said. "But I'll bet you anything she's on the balcony. Go on and call her."

"*I* don't want to call her!" Dr. Daruwalla cried. "But I agree with you—she's probably on the balcony. So . . . you win the bet, or there's no bet. She's on the balcony. Just leave it at that." Where *else* would Nancy be? the doctor wondered; he was quite sure John D. was drunk.

"Please call her. Please do it for me, Farrokh," John D. said to him.

There wasn't much to it. Dr. Daruwalla called his former Marine Drive apartment. The phone rang and rang; it rang so long, the doctor almost hung up. Then Nancy picked up the phone. There was her defeated voice, expecting nothing. The doctor chatted aimlessly for a while; he pretended that the call was of no importance—just a whim. Vijay wasn't yet back from Crime Branch Headquarters, Nancy informed him. They would have dinner at the Duckworth Club, but a bit later than usual. She knew there'd been another bombing, but she didn't know the details.

"Is there a nice sunset?" Farrokh asked.

"Oh, yes . . . sort of fading now," Nancy told him.

"Well, I'll let you get back to it!" he told her a little too heartily. Then he called John D. and told him that she'd definitely been on the balcony; Farrokh repeated Nancy's remark about the sunset—"sort of fading now." The retired Inspector Dhar kept saying the line; he wouldn't stop practicing the phrase until Dr. Daruwalla assured him that he had it right—that he was saying it precisely as Nancy had said it. He really *is* a good actor, the former screenwriter thought; it was impressive how closely John D. could imitate the exact degree of deadness in Nancy's voice.

"Sort of fading now," John D. kept saying. "How's that?"

"That's it—you've got it," Farrokh told him.

"Sort of fading now," John D. repeated. "Is that better?"

"Yes, that's perfect," Dr. Daruwalla said.

"Sort of fading now," said the actor.

"Stop it," the ex-screenwriter said.

Allowed to Use the Lift at Last

As a former guest chairman of the Membership Committee, Dr. Daruwalla knew the rules of the Duckworth Club; the 22-year waiting list for applicants was inviolable. The death of a Duckworthian—for example, Mr. Dogar's fatal stroke, which followed fast upon the news that the second Mrs. Dogar had been beaten to death by her guards—did not necessarily speed up the process of membership. The Membership Committee never crassly viewed a fellow Duckworthian's death as a matter of making room. Not even the death of Mr. Dua would "make room" for a new member. And Mr. Dua was sorely missed; his deafness in one ear was legendary—the never-to-be-forgotten tennis injury, the senseless blow from the flung racket of his doubles partner (who'd double-faulted). Dead at last, poor Mr. Dua was deaf in both ears now; yet not one new membership came of it.

However, Farrokh knew that not even the rules of the Duckworth Club were safe from a single most interesting loophole. It was stated that upon the formal resignation of a Duckworthian, as distinct from a Duckworthian's demise, a new member could be spontaneously appointed to take the resigning member's place; such an appointment circumvented the normal process of nomination and election and the 22-year waiting list. Had this exception to the rules been overused, it doubtless would have been criticized and eliminated, but Duckworthians didn't resign. Even when they moved away from Bombay, they paid their dues and retained their membership; Duckworthians were Duckworthians forever.

Three years after he left India—"for good," or so he'd said—Dr. Daruwalla still faithfully paid his dues to the Duckworth Club; even in Toronto, the doctor read the club's monthly newsletter. But John D. did the unexpected, unheard-of, un-Duckworthian thing: he resigned his membership. Deputy Commissioner Patel was "spontaneously appointed" in the retired Inspector Dhar's stead. The former movie star was replaced by the real policeman, who (all agreed) had distinguished himself in "community leadership." If there were objections to the big blond wife who went everywhere with the esteemed detective, these objections were never too openly expressed, although Mr. Sethna was committed to remembering Nancy's furry navel and the day she'd stood on a chair and reached into the mechanism of the ceiling fan—not to mention the night she'd danced with Dhar and left the club in tears, or the day after, when she'd left the club in anger (with Dhar's dwarf).

Dr. Daruwalla would learn that Detective Patel and Nancy were controversial additions to the Duckworth Club. But the old club, the doctor knew, was just one more oasis—a place where Nancy might hope to contain herself, and where the deputy commissioner could indulge in a brief respite from the labors of his profession. This was how Farrokh preferred to think of the Patels—relaxing in the Ladies' Garden, watching a slower life go by than the life they'd lived. They deserved a break, didn't they? And although it had taken three years, the swimming pool was finally finished; in the hottest months, before the monsoon, the pool would be nice for Nancy.

It was never acknowledged that John D. had played the role of the Patels' benefactor or the part of Nancy's guardian angel. But not only had John D.'s resignation from the Duckworth Club provided a membership for the Patels; it had been John D.'s idea that the view from the Daruwallas' balcony would do Nancy some good. Without questioning the doctor's motives, the Patels had moved into the Marine Drive apartment—ostensibly to look after the aged servants.

In one of several flawlessly typed letters, Deputy Commissioner Patel wrote to Dr. Daruwalla that although the offensive elevator sign had not been replaced—that is, after it was stolen a *second* time—the Daruwallas' ancient servants nevertheless continued to struggle up and down the stairs. The old rules had penetrated Nalin and Roopa; the rules were permanently in place—they would outlive any sign. The servants themselves refused to ride in the lift; their tragic preconditioning couldn't be helped. The policeman expressed a deeper sympathy for the thief. The Residents' Society had assigned the task of catching the culprit to Detective Patel. The deputy commissioner confided to Dr. Daruwalla that he wasn't making much progress in solving the case, but that he suspected the *second* thief was Nancy—not Vinod.

As for the continued disruption to the building that was caused by the first-floor dogs, this always happened at an ungodly hour of the early morning. The first-floor residents claimed that the dogs were deliberately incited to bark by a familiar, violent-looking dwarf taxi driver—formerly a "chauffeur" for Dr. Daruwalla and the retired Inspector Dhar—but Detective Patel was inclined to lay the blame on various stray beggars off Chowpatty Beach. Even after a lock was fashioned for the lobby door, the dogs were occasionally driven insane, and the first-floor residents insisted that the dwarf had managed to gain unlawful entrance to the lobby; several of them said they'd seen an off-white Ambassador driving away. But these allegations were discounted by the deputy commissioner, for the first-floor dogs were barking in May of 1993—more than a month after those Bombay bombings that killed more than 200 people, Vinod among them.

The dogs were still barking, Detective Patel wrote to Dr. Daruwalla. It was Vinod's ghost who was disturbing them, Farrokh felt certain.

On the door of the downstairs bathroom in the Daruwallas' house on Russell Hill Road, there hung the sign that the dwarf had stolen for them. It was a big hit with their friends in Toronto.

SERVANTS ARE NOT ALLOWED
TO USE THE LIFT
UNLESS ACCOMPANIED BY CHILDREN

In retrospect, it seemed cruel that the ex-clown had survived the terrible teeterboard accident at the Great Blue Nile. It appeared that the gods had toyed with Vinod's fate—that he'd been launched by an elephant into the bleachers and had risen to a kind of local stardom in the private-taxi business seemed trivial. And that the dwarf had come to the rescue of Martin Mills, who'd fallen among those unusually violent prostitutes, seemed merely mock-heroic now. It struck Dr. Daruwalla as completely unfair that Vinod had been blown up in the bombing of the Air India building.

On the afternoon of March 12, 1993, a car bomb exploded on the exit ramp of the driveway, not far from the offices of the Bank of Oman. People were killed on the street; others were killed in the bank, which occupied that part of the Air India building nearest the site of the explosion. The Bank of Oman was demolished. Probably Vinod was waiting for a passenger who was doing business in the bank. The dwarf had been sitting at the wheel of his taxi, which was unfortunately parked next to the vehicle containing the car bomb. Only Deputy Commissioner Patel was capable of explaining why so many squash-racquet handles and old tennis balls were scattered all over the street.

There was a clock on the Air India hoarding, the billboard above the building; for two or three days after the bombing, the time was stuck at 2:48—strangely, Dr. Daruwalla would wonder if Vinod had noticed the time. The deputy commissioner implied that the dwarf had died instantly.

Patel reported that the pitiful assets of Vinod's Blue Nile, Ltd., would scarcely provide for the dwarf's wife and son; but Shivaji's success at the Great Royal Circus would take care of the young dwarf and his mother, and Deepa had earlier been left a sizable inheritance. To her surprise, she'd been more than mentioned in Mr. Garg's will. (Acid Man had died of AIDS within a year of the Daruwallas' departure from Bombay.) The holdings of the Wetness Cabaret had been huge in comparison to those of Vinod's Blue Nile, Ltd. The size of Deepa's share of the strip joint had been sufficient to close the cabaret down.

Exotic dancing had never meant actual stripping—real strip joints weren't allowed in Bombay. What passed for exotic dancing at the Wetness Cabaret had never amounted to more than strip*teasing.* The clientele, as Muriel had once observed, was truly vile, but the reason someone had thrown an orange at her was that the exotic dancer wouldn't take off her clothes. Muriel was a stripper who wouldn't strip, just as Garg had been a Good Samaritan who *wasn't* a Good Samaritan— or so Dr. Daruwalla supposed.

There was a photograph of Vinod that John D. had framed; the actor kept it on his desk in his Zürich apartment. It wasn't a picture of the dwarf in his car-driving days, when the former Inspector Dhar had known Vinod best; it was an old circus photo. It had always been John D.'s favorite photograph of Vinod. In the picture, the dwarf is wearing his clown costume; the baggy polka-dotted pants are so short, Vinod appears to be standing on his knees. He's wearing a tank top, a muscle shirt—with spiraling stripes, like the stripes on a barber's pole—and he's grinning at the camera, his smile enhanced by the larger smile that's painted on his face; the edges of his painted smile extend to the corners of the dwarf's bright eyes.

Standing directly beside Vinod, in profile to the camera, is an open-mouthed hippopotamus. What's shocking about the photograph is that the whole dwarf, standing up straight, would easily fit in the hippo's yawning mouth. The oddly opposed lower teeth are within Vinod's reach; the hippo's teeth are as long as the dwarf's arms. At the time, the little clown must have felt the heat from the hippo's mouth—the breath of rotting vegetables, the result of the lettuce that Vinod recalled feeding to the hippo, who swallowed the heads whole. "Like grapes," the dwarf had said.

Not even Deepa could remember how long ago the Great Blue Nile had had a hippo; by the time the dwarf's wife joined the circus, the hippopotamus had died. After the dwarf's death, John D. typed an epitaph for Vinod on the bottom of the hippo picture. Clearly, the epitaph was composed in memory of the forbidden elevator—that elite lift which the dwarf had never officially been allowed to use. *Presently accompanied by children,* the commemoration read.

It wasn't a bad epitaph, the retired screenwriter thought. Farrokh had acquired quite a collection of photographs of Vinod, most of which the dwarf had given him over the years. When Dr. Daruwalla wrote his condolences to Deepa, the doctor wanted to include a photo that he hoped the dwarf's wife and son would like. It was hard to select only one; the doctor had so many pictures of Vinod—many more were in his mind, of course.

While Farrokh was trying to find the perfect picture of Vinod to send to Deepa, the dwarf's wife wrote to him. It was just a postcard from Ahmedabad, where the Great Royal was performing, but the thought was what mattered to Dr. Daruwalla. Deepa had wanted the doctor to know that she and Shivaji were all right. "Still falling in the net," the dwarf's wife wrote.

That helped Farrokh find the photo he was looking for; it was a picture of Vinod in the dwarf's ward at the Hospital for Crippled Children. The dwarf is recovering from surgery, following the results of the Elephant on a Teeterboard item. This time, there's no clownish smile painted over Vinod's grin; the dwarf's natural smile is sufficient. In his stubby-fingered, trident hand, Vinod is clutching that list of his talents which featured car driving; the dwarf is holding his future in one hand. Dr. Daruwalla only vaguely remembered taking the picture.

Under the circumstances, Farrokh felt it was necessary for him to inscribe some endearment on the back of the photograph; Deepa wouldn't need to be reminded of the occasion of the photo—at the time, she'd been occupying a bed in the women's ward of the same hospital, recovering from the doctor's surgery on her hip. Inspired by John D.'s epitaph for Vinod, the doctor continued with the forbidden-elevator theme. *Allowed to use the lift at last,* the former screenwriter wrote, for although Vinod had missed the net, the dwarf had finally escaped the rules of the Residents' Society.

Not the Dwarfs

One day, how would Dr. Daruwalla be remembered? As a good doctor, of course; as a good husband, a good father—a good man, by all counts, though not a great writer. But whether he was walking on Bloor Street or stepping into a taxi on Avenue Road, almost no one seeing him would have thought twice about him; he was so seemingly assimilated. A well-dressed immigrant, perhaps; a nice, naturalized Canadian—maybe a well-to-do tourist. Although he was small, one could quibble about his weight; for a man in the late afternoon of his life, he would be wise to be thinner. Nevertheless, he was distinguished-looking.

Sometimes he seemed a little tired—chiefly in the area of his eyes— or else there was something faraway about his thoughts, which, for the most part, he kept to himself. No one could have fathomed what a life he'd led, for it was chiefly a life lived in his mind. Possibly what passed for his tiredness was nothing more than the cost of his considerable imagination, which had never found the outlet that it sought.

At the AIDS hospice, Farrokh would forever be remembered as Dr. Balls, but this was largely out of fondness. The one patient who'd *bounced* his tennis ball instead of squeezing it hadn't irritated the nurses or the other staff for very long. When a patient died, that patient's tennis ball would be returned to Dr. Daruwalla. The doctor had been only briefly bitten by religion; he wasn't religious anymore. Yet these tennis balls of former patients were almost holy objects to Farrokh.

At first, he would be at a loss with what to do with the old balls; he could never bring himself to throw them away, nor did he approve of giving them to new patients. Eventually, he disposed of them—but in an oddly ritualistic fashion. He buried them in Julia's herb garden, where dogs would occasionally dig them up. Dr. Daruwalla didn't mind that the dogs got to play with the tennis balls; the doctor found this a suitable conclusion to the life of these old balls—a pleasing cycle.

As for the damage to the herb garden, Julia put up with it; after all, it wasn't her husband's only eccentricity. She respected his rich and hidden interior life, which she thoroughly expected to yield a puzzling exterior; she knew Farrokh was an interior man. He had always been a daydreamer; now that he didn't write, he seemed to daydream a little more.

Once, Farrokh told Julia that he wondered if he was an avatar. In Hindu mythology, an avatar is a deity, descended to earth in an incarnate form or some manifest shape. Did Dr. Daruwalla really believe he was the incarnation of a god?

"*Which* god?" Julia asked him.

"I don't know," Farrokh humbly told her. Certainly he was no Lord Krishna, "the dark one"—an avatar of Vishnu. Just whom did he imagine he was an avatar *of*? The doctor was no more the incarnation of a god than he was a writer; he was, like most men, principally a dreamer.

It's best to picture him on a snowy evening, when darkness has fallen early in Toronto. Snow always made him melancholic, for it snowed all night the night his mother died. On snowy mornings, Farrokh would go sit in the guest bedroom where Meher had drifted away; some of her clothes were in the closet—something of her scent, which was the scent of a foreign country and its cooking, still lingered in her hanging saris.

But picture Dr. Daruwalla in the streetlight, standing directly under a lamppost in the falling snow. Picture him at the northeast corner of Lonsdale and Russell Hill Road; this Forest Hill intersection was familiar and comforting to Farrokh, not only because it was within a block of where he lived, but because, from this junction, he could view the route he'd taken those many days when he'd walked his children to school. In the opposite direction, there was Grace Church on-the-Hill ... where he'd passed a few reflective hours in the safety of his former faith. From this street corner, Dr. Daruwalla could also see the chapel and the Bishop Strachan School, where the doctor's daughters had ably demonstrated their intelligence; and Farrokh wasn't far from Upper Canada College, where his sons might have gone to school—if he'd had sons. But, the doctor reconsidered, he'd had *two* sons—counting John D. *and* the retired Inspector Dhar.

Farrokh tipped his face up to the falling snow; he felt the snow wet his eyelashes. Although Christmas was long past, Dr. Daruwalla was pleased to see that some of his neighbors' houses still displayed their yuletide ornamentation, which gave them unusual color and cheer. The snow falling in the streetlight gave the doctor such a pure-white, lonely feeling, Farrokh almost forgot why he was standing on this street corner on a winter evening. But he was waiting for his wife; the former Julia Zilk was due to pick him up. Julia was driving from one of her women's groups; she'd phoned and told Farrokh to wait at the corner. The Daruwallas were dining at a new restaurant not far from Harbourfront; Farrokh and Julia were a faithful audience for the authors' readings at Harbourfront.

As for the restaurant, Dr. Daruwalla would find it ordinary; also, they were eating too early for the doctor's taste. As for the authors' readings, Farrokh detested readings; so few writers knew how to read aloud. When you were reading a book to yourself, you could close the cover without shame and try something else, or watch a video, which the ex-screenwriter was more and more apt to do. His usual beer—and he often had wine with his dinner—made him too sleepy to read. At Harbourfront, he feared he'd start snoring in the audience and embarrass Julia; she loved the readings, which the doctor increasingly viewed as an endurance sport. Often, too many writers read in a single night, as if to make a public demonstration of Canada's esteemed subsidy of the arts; usually, there was an intermission, which was Dr. Daruwalla's principal reason for loathing the theater. And at the Harbourfront intermission, they'd be surrounded by Julia's well-read friends; her friends were more literary than Farrokh, and they knew it.

On this particular evening (Julia had warned him), there was an Indian author reading from his or her work; that always presented problems for Dr. Daruwalla. There was the palpable expectation that the doctor should "relate" to this author in some meaningful way, as if there were that recognizable "it" which the author would either get right or get wrong. In the case of an Indian writer, even Julia and her literary friends would defer to Farrokh's opinion; therefore, he would be pressed to *have* an opinion, *and* to state his views. Often, he had no views and would hide during the intermission; on occasion, to his shame, the retired screenwriter had hidden in the men's room.

Recently, quite a celebrated Parsi writer had read at Harbourfront; Dr. Daruwalla had the feeling that Julia and her friends expected the doctor to be aggressive enough to speak to the author, for Farrokh had read the justly acclaimed novel—he'd much admired it. The story concerned a small but sturdy pillar of a Parsi community in Bombay—a decent, compassionate family man was severely tested by the political corruption and deceit of that time when India and Pakistan were at war.

How could Julia and her friends imagine that Farrokh could talk with this author? What did Dr. Daruwalla know of a *real* Parsi community—either in Bombay or in Toronto? What "community" could the doctor presume to talk about?

Farrokh could only tell tales of the Duckworth Club—Lady Duckworth exposing herself, flashing her famous breasts. One didn't have to be a Duckworthian to have already heard that story, but what other stories did Dr. Daruwalla know? Only the doctor's own story, which was decidedly unsuitable for first acquaintances. Sex change and serial slaying; a conversion by love bite; the lost children who were *not* saved by the circus; Farrokh's father, blown to smithereens . . . and how could he talk about the twins to a total stranger?

It seemed to Dr. Daruwalla that his story was the opposite of universal; his story was simply strange—the doctor himself was singularly foreign. What Farrokh came in contact with, everywhere he went, was a perpetual foreignness—a reflection of that foreignness he carried with him, in the peculiarities of his heart. And so, in the falling snow, in Forest Hill, a Bombayite stood waiting for his Viennese wife to take him into downtown Toronto, where they would listen to an unknown Indian reader—perhaps a Sikh, possibly a Hindu, maybe a Muslim, or even another Parsi. It was likely that there would be other readers, too.

Across Russell Hill Road, the wet snow clung to the shoulders and hair of a mother and her small son; like Dr. Daruwalla, they stood under a lamppost, where the radiant streetlight brightened the snow and sharpened the features of their watchful faces—they appeared to be waiting for someone, too. The young boy seemed far less impatient than his mother. The child had his head tilted back, with his tongue stuck out to catch the falling snow, and he swung himself dreamily from his mother's arm—whereas she kept clutching at his hand, as if he were slipping from her grasp. She would occasionally jerk his arm to make him stop swinging, but this never worked for long, and nothing could compel the boy to withdraw his tongue; it remained sticking out, catching the snow.

As an orthopedist, Dr. Daruwalla disapproved of the way the mother jerked on her son's arm, which was totally relaxed—the boy was almost limp. The doctor feared for the child's elbow or his shoulder. But the mother had no intention of hurting her son; she was just impatient, and it was tedious for her—how the boy hung on her arm.

For a moment, Dr. Daruwalla smiled openly at this Madonna and Child; they were so clearly illuminated under their lamppost, the doctor should have known that they could see him standing under *his* lamppost—just as clearly. But Farrokh had forgotten where he was—not in India—and he'd overlooked the racial wariness he might provoke in the woman, who now regarded his unfamiliar face in the streetlight (and in the whiteness of the falling snow) as she might have regarded the sudden appearance of a large, unleashed dog. Why was this foreigner smiling at her?

The woman's obvious fear both offended and shamed Dr. Daruwalla; he quickly stopped smiling and looked away. Then the doctor realized that he was standing on the wrong corner of the intersection. Julia had plainly instructed him to stand on the north*west* corner of Lonsdale and Russell Hill Road, which was exactly where the mother and her son were standing. Farrokh knew that by crossing the street and standing beside them, he would probably create mayhem in the woman's mind— at best, extreme apprehension. At worst, she might scream for help; there would be accusations that could rouse the neighbors—conceivably, summon the police!

Therefore, Dr. Daruwalla crossed Russell Hill Road awkwardly, sidling head-down and furtively, which doubtless gave the woman all the more cause to suspect him of criminal behavior. Slinking across the street, Farrokh looked full of felonious intentions. He passed the woman and child quickly, scuttling by without a greeting—for a greeting, the doctor was sure, would startle the woman to such a degree that she might bolt into the traffic. (There *was* no traffic.) Dr. Daruwalla took up a position that was 10 yards away from where Julia was expecting to spot him. There the doctor stood, like a pervert getting up his nerve for a cowardly assault; he was aware that the streetlight barely reached to the curb where he waited.

The mother, who was of medium height and figure—and now thoroughly frightened—began to pace, dragging her small son with her. She was a well-dressed young woman in her twenties, but neither her attire nor her youth could conceal her struggle to combat her rising terror. From her expression, it was clear to Dr. Daruwalla that she believed she understood his heinous intentions. Under his seemingly tasteful topcoat, which was black wool with a black velvet collar and black velvet lapels, there surely lurked a naked man who was dying to expose himself to her and her child. The mother turned her trembling back on the doctor's reprehensible figure, but her small son had also noticed the stranger. The boy was unafraid—just curious. He kept tugging on his distraught mother's arm; with his little tongue still sticking straight out into the snow, the child couldn't take his eyes off the exotic foreigner.

Dr. Daruwalla tried to concentrate on the snow. Impulsively, the doctor stuck out his tongue; it was a reflex imitation of what he'd seen the small boy do—it hadn't occurred to Dr. Daruwalla to stick out his tongue for years. But now, in the falling snow, the young mother could see that the foreigner was radically deranged; his mouth lolled open, with his tongue sticking out, and his eyes blinked as the snowflakes fell on his lashes.

As for his eyelids, Farrokh felt they were heavy; to the casual observer, his eyelids were puffy—his age, his tiredness, the years of beer and wine. But to this young mother, in her growing panic, they must have struck her as the eyelids of the demonic East; slightly beyond illumination in the streetlight, Dr. Daruwalla's eyes appeared to be hooded—like a serpent's.

However, her son had no fear of the foreigner; their tongues in the snow seemed to connect them. The kinship of their extended tongues took immediate effect on the small boy. Farrokh's childish, unconscious gesture must have overridden the boy's natural reluctance to speak to strangers, for he suddenly broke free of his mother's grasp and ran with outstretched arms toward the astonished Indian.

The mother was too terrified to give clear utterance to her son's name. She managed only a gargling sound, a strangled gasp. She hesitated before stumbling after her son, as if her legs had turned to ice or stone. She was resigned to her fate; how well she knew what would happen next! The black topcoat would open as she approached the stranger, and she would be confronted with the male genitalia of the *truly* inscrutable East.

In order not to frighten her further, Dr. Daruwalla pretended not to notice that the child was running to him. He could imagine the mother thinking, Oh—these perverts are sly! Particularly those of us who are "of color," the doctor thought bitterly. This was precisely the situation that foreigners (especially those "of color") are taught to dread. Absolutely nothing was happening; yet the young woman was sure that she and her son teetered on the brink of a shocking, possibly even a scarring, episode.

Farrokh nearly cried out: Excuse me, pretty lady, but there is no episode here! He would have run away from the child, except that he suspected the boy could run faster; also, Julia was coming to pick him up, and there he would be—running away from a mother and her small son. That would be too absurd.

That was when the small boy touched him; it was a firm but gentle tug on his sleeve—then the miniature mittened hand grasped the doctor's gloved index finger and pulled. Dr. Daruwalla had no choice but to look down into the wide-eyed face that was peering up at him; the whiteness of the boy's cheeks was rose-tinted against the purer whiteness of the snow.

"Excuse me," the little gentleman said. "Where are you from?"

Well, that's the question, isn't it? thought Dr. Daruwalla. It was always the question. For his whole adult life, it was the question he usually answered with the literal truth, which in his heart felt like a lie.

"I'm from India," the doctor would say, but he didn't feel it; it didn't ring true. "I'm from Toronto," he sometimes said, but with more mischief than authority. Or else he would be clever. "I'm from Toronto, via Bombay," he would say. If he really wanted to be cute, he would answer, "I'm from Toronto, via Vienna and Bombay." He could go on, elaborating the lie—namely, that he was from *anywhere.*

He could always enhance the European qualities of his education, if he chose; he could create a spicy masala mixture for his childhood in Bombay, giving his accent that Hindi flavor; he could also kill the conversation with his merciless, deadpan Torontonian reserve. ("As you may know, there are many Indians in Toronto," he could say, when he felt like it.) Dr. Daruwalla could *seem* as comfortable with the places he'd lived as he was, truly, *un*comfortable.

But suddenly the boy's innocence demanded of the doctor a different kind of truth; in the child's face, Dr. Daruwalla could discern only frank curiosity—only the most genuine desire to know. It also moved the doctor that the boy had not let go of his index finger. Farrokh was aware that he had no time in which to formulate a witty answer or an ambiguous remark; the terrified mother would any second interrupt the moment, which would never return.

"Where are you from?" the child had asked him.

Dr. Daruwalla wished he knew; never had he so much wanted to tell the truth, and (more important) to feel that his response was as pure and natural as the currently falling snow. Bending close to the boy, so that the child could not mistake a word of his answer, and giving the boy's trusting hand a reflexive squeeze, the doctor spoke clearly in the sharp winter air.

"I'm from the circus," Farrokh said, without thinking—it was utterly spontaneous—but by the instant delight that was apparent in the child's broad smile and in his bright, admiring eyes, Dr. Daruwalla could tell that he'd answered the question correctly. What he saw in the boy's happy face was something he'd never felt before in his cold, adopted country. Such uncritical acceptance was the most satisfying pleasure that Dr. Daruwalla (or any immigrant of color) would ever know.

Then a car horn was blowing and the woman pulled her son away; the boy's father, the woman's husband—whoever he was—was helping them into his car. If Farrokh heard nothing of what the mother said, he would remember what the child told the man. "The circus is in town!"

the boy said. Then they drove away, leaving Dr. Daruwalla there; the doctor had the street corner to himself.

Julia was late. Farrokh fretted that they wouldn't have time to eat before the interminable Harbourfront readings. Then he needn't worry that he'd fall asleep and snore; instead, the audience and the unfortunate authors would be treated to his growling stomach.

The snow kept falling. No cars passed. In a distant window, the lights on a Christmas tree were blinking; Dr. Daruwalla tried to count the colors. The colored lights through the window glass were reminiscent of that light which is reflected in sequins—that glitter which is sewn into the singlets of the circus acrobats. Was there anything as wonderful as that reflected light? Farrokh wondered.

A car was passing; it threatened to break the spell that the doctor was under, for Dr. Daruwalla was halfway around the world from the corner of Lonsdale and Russell Hill Road. "Go home!" someone shouted to him from the window of the passing car.

It was an irony that the doctor didn't hear this, for he was in a position to inform the person that going home was easier said than done. More sounds, torn from the window of the moving car, were muffled by the snow—receding laughter, possibly a racial slur. But Dr. Daruwalla heard none of it. His eyes had risen from the Christmas tree in the window; at first he'd blinked at the falling snow, but then he allowed his eyes to close—the snow coolly covered his eyelids.

Farrokh saw the elephant-footed boy in his singlet with the blue-green sequins—as the little beggar was never dressed in real life. Farrokh saw Ganesh descending in the spotlight, twirling down—the cripple's teeth clamped tightly on the dental trapeze. This was the completion of another successful Skywalk, which in reality had never happened and never would. The *real* cripple was dead; it was only in the retired screenwriter's mind that Ganesh was a skywalker. Probably the movie would never be made. Yet, in his mind's eye, Farrokh saw the elephant boy walk without a limp across the sky. To Dr. Daruwalla, this existed; it was as real as the India the doctor thought he'd left behind. Now he saw that he was destined to see Bombay again. Farrokh knew there was no escaping Maharashtra, which was no circus.

That was when he knew he was going back—again and again, he would keep returning. It was India that kept bringing him back; this time, the dwarfs would have nothing to do with it. Farrokh knew this as distinctly as he could hear the applause for the skywalker. Dr. Daruwalla heard them clapping as the elephant boy descended on the dental trapeze; the doctor could hear them cheering for the cripple.

Julia, who'd stopped the car and was waiting for her distracted husband, honked the horn. But Dr. Daruwalla didn't hear her. Farrokh was listening to the applause—he was still at the circus.

ABOUT THE TYPE

The text of this book was set in Janson, a misnamed typeface designed in about 1690 by Nicholas Kis, a Hungarian in Amsterdam. In 1919 the matrices became the property of the Stempel Foundry in Frankfurt. It is an old-style book face of excellent clarity and sharpness. Janson serifs are concave and splayed; the contrast between thick and thin strokes is marked.

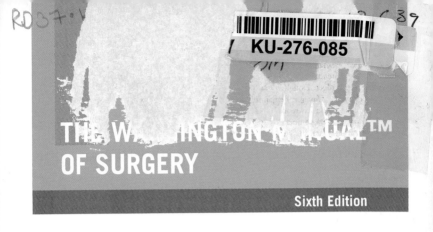

THE WASHINGTON MANUAL™
OF SURGERY

Sixth Edition

Department of Surgery
Washington University
School of Medicine
St. Louis, Missouri

Editors

Mary E. Klingensmith, MD

Abdulhameed Aziz, MD

Ankit Bharat, MD

Amy C. Fox, MD

Matthew R. Porembka, MD

Foreword by
Timothy J. Eberlein, MD
Bixby Professor and Chair of Surgery
Director, Siteman Cancer Center
Washington University
School of Medicine
St. Louis, Missouri

. Wolters Kluwer | Lippincott Williams & Wilkins
Health
Philadelphia · Baltimore · New York · London
Buenos Aires · Hong Kong · Sydney · Tokyo

Acquisitions Editor: Brian Brown
Product Manager: Brendan Huffman
Vendor Manager: Bridgett Dougherty
Senior Manufacturing Manager: Benjamin Rivera
Marketing Manager: Lisa Lawrence
Design Coordinator: Doug Smock
Production Service: Aptara, Inc.

© 2012 by LIPPINCOTT WILLIAMS & WILKINS, a WOLTERS KLUWER business
Two Commerce Square
2001 Market Street
Philadelphia, PA 19103 USA
LWW.com

Printed in China
Not authorised for Sale in North America or the Caribbean
CIP data available upon request

ISBN-13: 978-1-4511-7644-5

ISBN-10: 1-4511-7644-9

Care has been taken to confirm the accuracy of the information presented and to describe generally accepted practices. However, the authors, editors, and publisher are not responsible for errors or omissions or for any consequences from application of the information in this book and make no warranty, expressed or implied, with respect to the currency, completeness, or accuracy of the contents of the publication. Application of the information in a particular situation remains the professional responsibility of the practitioner.

The authors, editors, and publisher have exerted every effort to ensure that drug selection and dosage set forth in this text are in accordance with current recommendations and practice at the time of publication. However, in view of ongoing research, changes in government regulations, and the constant flow of information relating to drug therapy and drug reactions, the reader is urged to check the package insert for each drug for any change in indications and dosage and for added warnings and precautions. This is particularly important when the recommended agent is a new or infrequently employed drug.

Some drugs and medical devices presented in the publication have Food and Drug Administration (FDA) clearance for limited use in restricted research settings. It is the responsibility of the health care provider to ascertain the FDA status of each drug or device planned for use in their clinical practice.

To purchase additional copies of this book, call our customer service department at (800) 638-3030 or fax orders to (301) 223-2320. International customers should call (301) 223-2300.

Visit Lippincott Williams & Wilkins on the Internet: at LWW.com. Lippincott Williams & Wilkins customer service representatives are available from 8:30 am to 6 pm, EST.

10 9 8 7 6 5 4 3 2

CCS0212

Contributors

Christopher Anderson, MD
Associate Professor of Surgery
University of Mississippi Medical Center
Jackson, Mississippi

Michael Avidan, MBBCh
Professor of Anesthesiology and
*   Cardiothoracic Surgery*
Washington University School of Medicine
St. Louis, Missouri

Abdulhameed Aziz, MD
Resident in Surgery
Washington University School of Medicine
St. Louis, Missouri

Ankit Bharat, MD
Fellow in Cardiothoracic Surgery
Washington University School of Medicine
St. Louis, Missouri

Alejandro Bribiesco, MD
Resident in Surgery
Washington University School of Medicine
St. Louis, Missouri

L. Michael Brunt, MD
Professor of Surgery
Washington University School of Medicine
St. Louis, Missouri

Brian Bucher, MD
Resident in Surgery
Washington University School of Medicine
St. Louis, Missouri

Arnold Bullock, MD
Professor of Surgery
Washington University School of Medicine
St. Louis, Missouri

William Chapman, MD
Professor of Surgery
Washington University School of Medicine
St. Louis, Missouri

Michael Chicoine, MD
Associate Professor of Neurological Surgery
Washington University School of Medicine
St. Louis, Missouri

Kendra Conzen, MD
Resident in Surgery
Washington University School of Medicine
St. Louis, Missouri

Travis Crabtree, MD
Assistant Professor of Surgery
Washington University School of Medicine
St. Louis, Missouri

Ralph Damiano, MD
John M. Shoenberg Professor of Surgery
Washington University School of Medicine
St. Louis, Missouri

Charl De Wet, MD
Associate Professor of Anesthesiology and
*   Cardiothoracic Surgery*
Washington University School of Medicine
St. Louis, Missouri

Patrick Dillon, MD
Associate Professor of Surgery
Washington University School of Medicine
St. Louis, Missouri

Bernard DuBray, MD
Resident in Surgery
Washington University School of Medicine
St. Louis, Missouri

J. Christopher Eagon, MD
Associate Professor of Surgery
Washington University School of Medicine
St. Louis, Missouri

Oluwadamilola Fayanju, MD, MPHS
Resident in Surgery
Washington University School of Medicine
St. Louis, Missouri

Elizabeth Fialkowski, MD
Fellow in Pediatric Surgery
Washington University School of Medicine
St. Louis, Missouri

James Fleshman, MD
Professor of Surgery
Washington University School of Medicine
St. Louis, Missouri

Amy Fox, MD
Fellow in Endocrine Surgery
University of Michigan
Ann Arbor, Michigan

Bradley Freeman, MD
Professor of Surgery
Washington University School of Medicine
St. Louis, Missouri

Noopur Gangopadhyay, MD
Resident in Plastic and Reconstructive
  Surgery
Washington University School of Medicine
St. Louis, Missouri

Michael Gardner, MD
Assistant Professor of Orthopedic Surgery
Washington University School of Medicine
St. Louis, Missouri

Patrick Geraghty, MD
Associate Professor of Surgery and Radiology
Washington University School of Medicine
St. Louis, Missouri

Bruce Hall, MD, PhD, MBA
Professor of Surgery
Washington University School of Medicine
St. Louis, Missouri

Nicholas Hamilton, MD
Resident in Surgery
Washington University School of Medicine
St. Louis, Missouri

Bruce Haughey, MBChB, MS
Kimbrough Professor of Otolaryngology
Washington University School of Medicine
St. Louis, Missouri

William Hawkins, MD
Associate Professor of Surgery
Washington University School of Medicine
St. Louis, Missouri

Laureen Hill, MD
Professor of Anesthesiology and
  Cardiothoracic Surgery
Emory School of Medicine
Atlanta, Georgia

David Hoganson, MD
Resident in Surgery
Washington University School of Medicine
St. Louis, Missouri

Ashley Holder, MD
Resident in Surgery
Washington University School of Medicine
St. Louis, Missouri

Richard Hotchkiss, MD
Professor of Anesthesiology, Medicine, Surgery,
  Molecular Biology and Pharmacology
Washington University School of Medicine
St. Louis, Missouri

Steven Hunt, MD
Assistant Professor of Surgery
Washington University School of Medicine
St. Louis, Missouri

Samay Jain, MD
Resident in Urologic Surgery
Washington University School of Medicine
St. Louis, Missouri

Fabian Johnston, MD
Fellow in Surgical Oncology
Johns Hopkins School of Medicine
Baltimore, Maryland

Enjae Jung, MD
Resident in Surgery
Washington University School of Medicine
St. Louis, Missouri

Jason Keune, MD, MBA
Resident in Surgery
Washington University School of Medicine
St. Louis, Missouri

Alicia Kieninger, MD
Attending Surgeon
Saint Joseph's Mercy Health System
Oakland, Michigan

John Kirby, MD
Associate Professor of Surgery
Washington University School of Medicine
St. Louis, Missouri
Assistant Professor of Surgery
Washington University School of Medicine
St. Louis, Missouri

Mary E. Klingensmith, MD
Mary Culver Distinguished Professor of
 Surgery
Washington University School of Medicine
St. Louis, Missouri

Lindsay Kuroki, MD
Resident in Obstetrics and Gynecology
Washington University School of Medicine
St. Louis, Missouri

Anson Lee, MD
Resident in Surgery
Washington University School of Medicine
St. Louis, Missouri

Jeremy Leidenfrost, MD
Resident in Surgery
Washington University School of Medicine
St. Louis, Missouri

Jennifer Leinecke, MD
Resident in Surgery
Washington University School of Medicine
St. Louis, Missouri

David Linehan, MD
Professor of Surgery
Washington University School of Medicine
St. Louis, Missouri

Jeffrey Lowell, MD
Professor of Surgery and Pediatrics
Washington University School of Medicine
St. Louis, Missouri

Malcolm MacConamara, MD
Resident in Surgery
Washington University School of Medicine
St. Louis, Missouri

Susan Mackinnon, MD
Shoenberg Professor of Plastic and
 Reconstructive Surgery
Washington University School of Medicine
St. Louis, Missouri

Julie Margenthaler, MD
Associate Professor of Surgery
Washington University School of Medicine
St. Louis, Missouri

Brent Matthews, MD
Professor of Surgery
Washington University School of Medicine
St. Louis, Missouri

Kathleen Mckeon, MD
Resident in Orthopedic Surgery
Washington University School of Medicine
St. Louis, Missouri

Lora Melman, MD
Resident in Surgery
Washington University School of Medicine
St. Louis, Missouri

Bryan Meyers, MD, MPH
Patrick and Joy Williamson Professor of
 Surgery
Washington University School of Medicine
St. Louis, Missouri

Jonathan Mitchem, MD
Resident in Surgery
Washington University School of Medicine
St. Louis, Missouri

Jeffrey Moley, MD
Professor of Surgery
Washington University School of Medicine
St. Louis, Missouri

Susan Pitt, MD
Resident in Surgery
Washington University School of Medicine
St. Louis, Missouri

Matthew Porembka, MD
Resident in Surgery
Washington University School of Medicine
St. Louis, Missouri

Babafemi Pratt, MD
Resident in Surgery
Washington University School of Medicine
St. Louis, Missouri

Matthew Reynolds, MD
Resident in Neurological Surgery
Washington University School of Medicine
St. Louis, Missouri

T. Elizabeth Robertson, MD
Attending Surgeon
Saint Anthony's Medical Center
St. Louis, Missouri

Kathryn Rowland, MD
Resident in Surgery
Washington University School of Medicine
St. Louis, Missouri

Brian Rubin, MD
Professor of Surgery
Washington University School of Medicine
St. Louis, Missouri

Luis Sanchez, MD
Gregorio A. Sicard Professor of Surgery
Washington University School of Medicine
St. Louis, Missouri

Douglas Schuerer, MD
Associate Professor of Surgery
Washington University School of Medicine
St. Louis, Missouri

Sunitha Sequira, MD
Resident in Otolaryngology
Washington University School of Medicine
St. Louis, Missouri

Gergorio Sicard, MD
Eugene M. Bricker Professor of Surgery
Washington University School of Medicine
St. Louis, Missouri

Robert Southard, MD
Assistant Professor of Surgery
Washington University School of Medicine
St. Louis, Missouri

Lauren Steward, MD
Resident in Surgery
Washington University School of Medicine
St. Louis, Missouri

Steven Strasberg, MD
Pruett Professor of Surgery
Washington University School of Medicine
St. Louis, Missouri

William Symons, MD
Resident in Surgery
Washington University School of Medicine
St. Louis, Missouri

Marcus Tan, MD
Fellow in Surgical Oncology
Memorial Sloan-Kettering Cancer Center
New York, New York

Premal Thaker, MD, MS
Assistant Professor of Obstetrics and
  Gynecology
Washington University School of Medicine
St. Louis, Missouri

Amber Traugott, MD
Resident in Surgery
Washington University School of Medicine
St. Louis, Missouri

Thomas Tung, MD
Associate Professor of Surgery
Washington University School of Medicine
St. Louis, Missouri
Assistant Professor of Surgery
Washington University School of Medicine
St. Louis, Missouri

Isaiah Turnbull, MS
Resident in Surgery
Washington University School of Medicine
St. Louis, Missouri

Derek Wakeman, MD
Resident in Surgery
Washington University School of Medicine
St. Louis, Missouri

Foreword

Welcome to the sixth edition of *The Washington Manual^{TM} of Surgery.* The most important focus of our Department of Surgery is medical education of students, residents, fellows, and practicing surgeons. This commitment is no more evident than in the current edition of *The Washington Manual^{TM} of Surgery.*

The educational focus of our Department of Surgery has a rich tradition. The first full-time Head of the Department of Surgery at Washington University was Dr. Evarts A. Graham (1919–1951). Dr. Graham was a superb educator. Not only was he an outstanding technical surgeon but his insightful comments at conferences and ward rounds were well-known and appreciated by a generation of surgeons who learned at his elbow. Dr. Graham was a founding member of the American Board of Surgery and made many seminal contributions to the management of surgical patients. His work in the development of oral cholecystography actually helped establish the Mallinckrodt Institute of Radiology at Washington University. Dr. Graham was among the first to identify the epidemiological link of cigarette smoking to lung cancer and was instrumental in raising public health consciousness about the deleterious effect on health from cigarette smoke.

Dr. Carl Moyer (1951–1965) succeeded Dr. Graham. Dr. Moyer is still regarded as a legendary educator at Washington University. He was particularly known for his bedside teaching techniques, as well as for linking pathophysiology to patient care outcomes. Dr. Walter Ballinger (1967–1978) came from the Johns Hopkins University and incorporated the Halsted traditions of resident education. Dr. Ballinger introduced the importance of laboratory investigation and began to foster development of the surgeon/scientist in our department. Dr. Samuel A. Wells (1978–1997) is credited with establishing one of the most accomplished academic Departments of Surgery in the United States. Not only did he recruit world-class faculty but he increased the focus on research and patient care. Dr. Wells also placed a great emphasis on educating the future academic leaders of surgery.

As in previous editions, this sixth edition of *The Washington Manual^{TM} of Surgery* combines authorship of residents ably assisted by faculty coauthors and our senior editor, Dr. Mary Klingensmith, who is vice-chair for education in our department. This combination of resident and faculty participation has helped focus the chapters on issues that will be particularly helpful to the trainee in surgery. This new edition of the manual provides a complete list of updated references that will serve medical students, residents, and practicing surgeons who wish to delve more deeply into a particular topic. This manual does not attempt to extensively cover pathophysiology or history, but it presents brief and logical approaches to the management of patients with comprehensive surgical problems. In each of the chapters, the authors have attempted to provide the most up-to-date and important diagnostic and management information for a given topic. We have attempted to standardize each of the chapters so that the reader will be able to most easily obtain information regardless of subject matter.

The sixth edition has undergone a reorganization of chapters with an emphasis on clarity and consistency. As with the past edition, evidence-based medicine has been incorporated into each of the chapters, with updated information and references to reflect current knowledge and practice. All of the sections have been updated and rewritten to reflect the most current standards of practice in each topic. These updates have been carefully edited and integrated so that the volume of pages remains approximately the same. Our goal is to keep this volume concise, portable, and user-friendly.

I am truly indebted to Dr. Klingensmith for her passion for education and her specific devotion to this project. In addition, I am proud of the residents in the Department of Surgery at Washington University who have done such an outstanding job with their faculty members in this sixth edition. I hope that you will find *The Washington Manual*^{TM} *of Surgery* a reference you commonly utilize in the care of your patient with surgical disease.

Timothy J. Eberlein, MD
St. Louis, Missouri

Preface

As with the previous five editions, this sixth edition of *The Washington Manual*^{TM} *of Surgery* is designed to complement *The Washington Manual of Medical Therapeutics*. Written by resident and faculty members of the Department of Surgery, it presents a brief, rational approach to the management of patients with surgical problems. The text is directed to the reader at the level of the 2nd- or 3rd-year surgical resident, although surgical and nonsurgical attendings, medical students, physician assistants, nurse practitioners, and others who provide care for patients with surgical problems will find it of interest and assistance. The book provides a succinct discussion of surgical diseases, with algorithms for addressing problems based on the opinions of the physician authors. Although multiple approaches may be reasonable for some clinical situations, this manual attempts to present a single, effective approach for each. We have limited coverage of diagnosis and therapy; this is not an exhaustive surgical reference. Coverage of pathophysiology, the history of surgery, and extensive reference lists have been excluded from most areas.

This is the sixth edition of the manual; the first edition was published in 1997, followed by editions in 1999, 2002, 2005, and 2007. New to this volume is a chapter on "emergencies in surgical patients" as well as updated evidence-based medicine, with the latest information and treatment algorithms in each section. As with previous editions, this sixth edition includes updates on each topic as well as substantial new material.

This is a resident-prepared manual. Each chapter was updated and revised by a resident with assistance from a faculty coauthor. Editorial oversight for the manual was shared by four senior resident coeditors (Ankit Bharat, MD, Chapters 1, 3, 4, 7 to 9, 30, 31, and 38; Amy Fox, MD, Chapters 2, 21 to 25, 29, 32, 36, and 37; Abdulhameed Aziz, MD, Chapters 5, 6, 17 to 20, 26, 28, and 34; and Matthew Porembka, MD, Chapters 10 to 16, 27, 33, and 35). The tremendous effort of all involved—residents and faculty members and particularly the senior resident coeditors—is reflected in the quality and consistency of the chapters.

I am indebted to the former senior editor of this work, Gerard M. Doherty, MD, who developed and oversaw the first three editions, then handed over to me an exceptionally well-organized project. I am grateful for the continued tremendous support from Lippincott Williams & Wilkins, who have been supportive of the effort and have supplied dedicated assistance. Brian Brown has been tremendously helpful, and Brendan Huffman has been a terrific developmental editor, keeping me in line and on schedule.

Finally, I am grateful to have an outstanding mentor and friend in my department chair, Timothy J. Eberlein, MD. Dr. Eberlein has a very full professional life, overseeing both a productive department and a cancer center. Despite this, he continues to appreciate the individuals with whom he interacts. He is an inspiration for his friendship, leadership, and dedication.

M.E.K.

Contents

1

General and Perioperative Care of the Surgical Patient

Oluwadamilola M. Fayanju and Mary E. Klingensmith

I. PREOPERATIVE EVALUATION AND MANAGEMENT

A. **General Evaluation of the Surgical Patient.** The goals of preoperative evaluation are to (1) identify the patient's medical problems, (2) determine if further information is needed to characterize the patient's medical status, (3) establish if the patient's condition is medically optimized, and (4) confirm the appropriateness of the planned procedure.

1. **History and physical examination.** A thorough history and physical are essential in evaluating surgical patients. Key elements of the history should include preexisting medical conditions known to increase operative risk, such as ischemic heart disease, congestive heart failure (CHF), renal insufficiency, prior cerebrovascular accident (CVA), and diabetes mellitus. Prior operations, operative complications, medication allergies, and the patient's use of tobacco, alcohol, and/or drugs should also be noted.

2. **Routine diagnostic testing.** Minor surgical procedures and procedures on young, healthy patients often require minimal or no diagnostic testing. Table 1-1 lists routine preoperative diagnostic tests and reasons for their use. Inclusion or exclusion of these tests should be selected on a case-by-case basis with consideration of the probability that results will alter management.

3. **Preoperative medications.** In general, patients should continue their medications in the immediate preoperative period. Exceptions to this rule include diabetic medications (see Section I.B.6), anticoagulants (see Section I.B.8.a), and antiplatelet agents. The use of some medications such as statins and angiotensin-converting enzyme (ACE) inhibitors should be individualized. It is important to query patients regarding their use of over-the-counter and herbal medications.

B. **Specific Considerations in Preoperative Management**

1. **Cerebrovascular disease.** Perioperative stroke is an uncommon surgical complication, occurring in less than 1% of general patients and in 2% to 5% of cardiac surgical patients. The majority (>80%) of these events are postoperative, and they are most often caused by hypotension or cardiogenic emboli during atrial fibrillation. Acute surgical stress might cause focal signs from a previous stroke to recur, mimicking acute ischemia.

   a. **Risk factors** for perioperative stroke include previous CVA, age, hypertension, coronary artery disease (CAD), diabetes, and tobacco

1

TABLE 1-1	Routine Preoperative Testing
Test	**Comment**
Complete blood cell count	History of recent blood loss, sickle cell disease/thalassemia, bleeding disorder, thrombocytopenia, or liver disease/splenomegaly; all intermediate and major procedures (cases where EBL ≥500 mL is anticipated). Consider for patients with history of anemia, renal insufficiency, coronary artery disease, and recent chemotherapy.
Urinalysis	All implant cases.
Serum electrolytes, creatinine, and blood urea nitrogen	History of renal disease (can do point-of-care hemoglobin/hematocrit, K+, Na+ on day of surgery for patients on dialysis), diabetes mellitus, or hypertension; patients taking diuretics/digoxin/ACE inhibitors/ARBs. Creatinine should be obtained for all vascular surgery patients on day of surgery (unless prior result within 24 hours prior to operation).
Coagulation studies	History of bleeding disorder, liver disease, or excessive alcohol use; patients receiving anticoagulants (in particular, should check PT/INR on morning of surgery for patients instructed to discontinue warfarin); cardiothoracic, vascular, angiographic, and craniotomy procedures.
Biochemical and profiles (including liver enzymes)	History of liver disease/jaundice, biliary disease, bleeding disorder, or excessive alcohol use; cholecystectomy, cardiopulmonary bypass procedures. Consider in patients with pulmonary hypertension and right heart failure. Albumin is a strong predictor of perioperative morbidity and mortality and should be considered for major procedures.
Pregnancy testing	Menstruating women unable to assure (by history) that they are not pregnant or if >30 days have passed since last menstrual period; females <18 years of age.
Chest X-ray	Presence of acute cardiac or pulmonary symptoms. Patients undergoing cardiothoracic procedures should receive a CXR within 2 weeks of surgery; history of a chest CT within 2 weeks precludes the need for an additional CXR.

TABLE 1-1	Routine Preoperative Testing *(Continued)*
Test	**Comment**
Electrocardiogram	Within 12 weeks of surgery (or less if condition warrants) for patients with known heart disease; within 6 months prior to surgery for all patients >50 years of age.
Type and cross/type and screen	None if very low risk of blood loss; type and screen if risk of substantial blood loss is low to moderate; type and cross if moderate to high risk of substantial blood loss (greater than 500 mL).

ACE, angiotensin-converting enzyme; ARB, angiotensin receptor blocker; CXR, chest X-ray; EBL, estimated blood loss.

Adapted from the "Minimum Requirements for Preoperative Diagnostic Testing" issued by the Center for Preoperative Assessment & Planning (CPAP) with permission from Dr. Laureen Hill, Vice Chairperson of the Department of Anesthesiology, Washington University in St. Louis.

use. Known or suspected cerebrovascular disease requires special consideration.

   (1) **The asymptomatic carotid bruit** is relatively common, occurring in approximately 14% of surgical patients older than 55 years. However, fewer than 50% of bruits reflect hemodynamically significant disease. No increase in risk of stroke has been demonstrated during noncardiac surgery in the presence of an asymptomatic bruit.

   (2) **Patients with recent transient ischemic attacks (TIAs)** are at increased risk for perioperative stroke and should have preoperative neurologic evaluation [e.g., computed tomography (CT) of the head, echocardiography, carotid Doppler]. Patients with symptomatic carotid artery stenosis should have an endarterectomy or carotid stenting before elective surgery.

   (3) **Elective surgery for patients with a recent CVA** should be delayed for a minimum of 2 weeks, ideally for 6 weeks.

2. **Cardiovascular disease** is one of the leading causes of death after noncardiac surgery. Patients who experience a myocardial infarction (MI) after noncardiac surgery have a hospital mortality rate of 15% to 25% (*CMAJ*. 2005;173:627). A study of 4,315 patients older than 50 years between 1989 and 1994 undergoing nonemergent, noncardiac surgery with expected postoperative stays greater than 48 hours found that major perioperative cardiac events occur in 1.4% of the patients (*Circulation*. 1999;100:1043). Since more than 100 million adults worldwide undergo noncardiac surgery annually, approximately 500,000 to 900,000 patients each year experience perioperative cardiac

death, a nonfatal MI, or nonfatal cardiac arrest postoperatively. Risk stratification by the operating surgeon, anesthesiologist, and consulting internist is important.

a. **Risk factors.** The following risk factors have been associated with perioperative cardiac morbidity:

(1) **The patient's age** (>70 years) has been identified as an independent multivariate risk factor for cardiac morbidity.

(2) **Unstable angina** is defined as chest pain that does not correlate with the level of physical activity and, therefore, occurs at rest or with minimal physical exertion. Elective operation in patients with unstable angina is contraindicated and should be postponed pending further evaluation.

(3) **Recent MI** is a well-defined risk factor for cardiac morbidity. The risk of reinfarction is significant if an operation is performed within 6 months of an MI (11% to 16% at 3 to 6 months). This risk is still increased substantially after 6 months, in contrast to patients without a history of MI (4% to 5% vs. 0.13%).

(4) **Untreated CHF** is a predictor of perioperative cardiac morbidity. Consequently, these patients should be optimized before any operative procedures are performed.

(5) **Diabetes mellitus,** especially in those requiring insulin, is thought to confer additional independent risk for an adverse cardiac outcome.

(6) **Valvular heart disease.** Aortic stenosis is a significant risk factor and may confer a 14-fold increase in relative risk independent of the manifestations of CHF. Patients with unexplained symptoms of dyspnea on exertion, shortness of breath, chest pain, syncope, or an uncharacterized systolic ejection murmur should undergo further diagnostic evaluation before elective operation. All patients with valvular heart disease, even hemodynamically insignificant disease (excluding patients with only mitral valve prolapse and no murmur), should receive prophylactic antibiotics before any operation that can introduce bacteria into the bloodstream or any dental procedure to reduce the risk of infectious endocarditis (Table 1-2).

(7) **Arrhythmias and conduction defects.** Both supraventricular and ventricular arrhythmias have been identified as independent risk factors for perioperative coronary events. The existence of a preoperative arrhythmia should prompt a search for underlying cardiac or pulmonary disease.

(8) **Peripheral vascular disease (PVD).** Because of the high coexistence of CAD with PVD, a lower threshold for obtaining diagnostic testing is warranted.

(9) **Type of procedure.** Patients who are undergoing thoracic surgery, vascular surgery, or upper abdominal surgery are at higher risk for adverse cardiac outcomes. Other procedures considered high risk include emergent major operations,

TABLE 1-2	Antibiotic Prophylaxis of Bacterial Endocarditis for Adult Patients

Procedure	Situation	Regimen
Dental, oral, respiratory, esophageal	Standard	**Amoxicillin** 2 g PO 1 hr before procedure
	Unable to take PO	**Ampicillin** 2 g IM or IV 30 min before procedure
	Penicillin-allergic	**Clindamycin** 600 mg PO 1 hr before procedure; or **cephalexin**[a] or **cefadroxil**[a] 2 g PO 1 hr before procedure; or **clarithromycin** or **azithromycin** 500 mg PO 1 hr before procedure
	Penicillin-allergic and unable to take PO	**Clindamycin** 600 mg IV within 30 min before procedure or **cefazolin**[a] 1 g IV within 30 min before procedure
Gastrointestinal and genitourinary	High-risk patients	**Ampicillin** 2 g IM or IV, plus **gentamicin** 1.5 mg/kg (max 120 mg) within 30 min before procedure; 6 hr later, **ampicillin** 1 g IV/IM or **amoxicillin** 1 g PO
	High-risk, penicillin-allergic patients	**Vancomycin** 1 g IV plus **gentamicin** 1.5 mg/kg (max 120 mg) timed to finish within 30 min of starting procedure
	Moderate-risk patients	**Amoxicillin** 2 g PO 1 hr before procedure or **ampicillin** 2 g IM or IV 30 min before procedure
	Moderate-risk, penicillin allergic patients	**Vancomycin** 1 g IV timed to finish within 30 min of starting procedure

[a]Cephalosporins should not be used in patients with anaphylactic or urticarial reactions to penicillin.
IM, intravascular; IV, intravenous; PO, by mouth.

especially in the elderly, and prolonged procedures associated with large fluid shifts or significant blood loss.

(10) **Functional impairment.** Patients with a poor functional capacity have a significantly higher risk of experiencing a postoperative cardiac event. Poor function is an indication for more aggressive preoperative evaluation, whereas patients who exercise regularly generally have sufficient cardiac reserve to withstand stressful operations.

b. **Revised cardiac risk index.** See Table 1-3.

TABLE 1-3	Revised Cardiac Risk Index[a]
Risk factor	**Comment**
High-risk surgery	Intrathoracic, intraperitoneal, major vascular
Ischemic heart disease	History of myocardial infarction, positive exercise test, angina, nitrate therapy, electrocardiogram with abnormal Q waves
History of CHF	History of CHF, pulmonary edema, or paroxysmal nocturnal dyspnea, bilateral rales, S_3 gallop, chest X-ray showing pulmonary vascular redistribution
History of cerebrovascular disease	History of transient ischemic attack or stroke
Preoperative insulin therapy for diabetes	
Preoperative serum creatinine >2 mg/dL	

[a]Rates of major cardiac complication with 0, 1, 2, or 3 of these factors were 0.4%, 0.9%, 7.0%, and 11.0%, respectively.
CHF, congestive heart failure.
Adapted with permission from Lee TH, Marcantonio ER, Mangione CM, et al. Derivation and prospective validation of a simple index for prediction of cardiac risk of major noncardiac surgery. *Circulation* 1999;100:1043.

    c. Preoperative testing. Patients at intermediate risk for a perioperative myocardial event may require additional studies to determine if further therapy is needed to optimize their status.

       (1) A preoperative electrocardiogram (ECG) is warranted in intermediate- or high-risk patients with a history of recent chest pain scheduled for an intermediate- or high-risk procedure. In addition, our policy is to obtain an ECG on any patients with a cardiac history, concerning symptoms, or significant risk factors, especially diabetes and renal failure. A screening ECG is obtained on all patients over the age of 50 years.

       (2) Noninvasive testing. Patients who are identified to be at risk of a perioperative cardiovascular event by the revised cardiac risk index or who have other risk factors (e.g., PVD, unexplained chest pain, diabetes, and ECG abnormalities) should undergo further evaluation.

          (a) Exercise stress testing provides useful information for risk stratification. An inability to achieve even modest levels of exercise or the presence of exercise-induced ECG changes identifies patients at significant risk for an adverse outcome.

    (b) Dipyridamole thallium imaging has a very high negative predictive value of approximately 99% but a moderate positive predictive value ranging from 4% to 20%.

    (c) Dobutamine stress echocardiography is believed to provide similar adrenergic stimulus to perioperative stress. A meta-analysis of eight studies and 1,877 patients suggested a trend toward superior prognostic accuracy with dobutamine stress echocardiography compared to other tests, with a sensitivity of 85% and a specificity of 70% for predicting perioperative cardiac death or nonfatal MI in patients undergoing vascular surgery (*Heart.* 2003;89:1327).

(3) Invasive testing. Patients identified as high risk on noninvasive testing can be further evaluated with angiography. Patients with significant cardiac lesions should have definitive treatment [angioplasty or coronary artery bypass grafting (CABG)] prior to an elective surgical procedure.

d. Preoperative management

(1) Patients with pacemakers should have their pacemakers turned to the uninhibited mode (e.g., DOO) before surgery. In addition, a bipolar cautery should be used when possible in these patients. If unipolar cautery is necessary, the grounding pad should be placed away from the heart.

(2) Patients with internal defibrillators should have these devices turned off during surgery.

(3) Perioperative beta-blockade should be considered as part of a thorough evaluation of each patient's clinical and surgical risk. Preoperative evaluation should involve identification of active cardiac conditions that would require intensive management and may result in delay or cancelation of nonemergent operations. Over the past 15 years, there has been conflicting and poorly supported evidence regarding the efficacy of beta-blockers in reducing perioperative cardiac events. However, recent studies, including the PeriOperative ISchemic Evaluation (POISE) trial, suggest that beta-blockers reduce perioperative ischemia and may reduce the risk of MI and cardiovascular death in high-risk patients (*Lancet.* 2008;371:1839–1847; see Table 1-3 for revised cardiac risk index). However, in the case of beta-blocker-naïve patients, routine administration of higher-dose long-acting metoprolol on the day of surgery and without dose titration should be avoided as its use is associated with an overall increase in mortality. Ideally, in appropriate patients, beta-blockers should be started days to weeks before elective surgery. Preoperatively, each patient's dose should be titrated to achieve adequate heart rate control so that there is a greater likelihood of the patient's benefiting from beta-blockade while avoiding the risks of hypotension and bradycardia. Titrated rate control with beta-blockers should continue during and after the operation to maintain a heart rate between 60 and 80 beats per minute in the absence of hypotension, as this regimen has been demonstrated to be efficacious (*Circulation.* 2009;120:2123–2151).

(4) **Patients with recent angioplasty or stenting.** Over the past two decades, use of coronary angioplasty and stenting has increased dramatically. Several studies have shown a high incidence of cardiovascular complications when noncardiac surgery is performed shortly after coronary angioplasty or stenting. A study of 216 consecutive patients who underwent noncardiac surgery within 3 months of percutaneous coronary intervention demonstrated that significantly more adverse clinical events (acute MI, major bleeding, and death) occurred when noncardiac surgery was performed within 2 weeks of percutaneous coronary intervention (*Am J Cardiol.* 2006;97:1188). Current guidelines are to delay noncardiac surgery at least 6 weeks after coronary angioplasty or stenting.

3. **Pulmonary disease.** Preexisting lung disease confers a dramatically increased risk of perioperative pulmonary complications.
   a. **Preoperative evaluation and screening**
      (1) **Risk factors**
         (a) **Chronic obstructive pulmonary disease (COPD)** is by far the most important risk factor, increasing rates of pulmonary complications three- to fourfold.
         (b) **Smoking** is also a significant risk factor. Operative risk reduction has only been documented after 8 weeks of smoking cessation; however, there are physiologic benefits to stopping as little as 48 hours before surgery.
         (c) **Advanced age,** that is, older than 60 years.
         (d) **Obesity.** Body mass index (BMI) greater than 30 kg/m^2.
         (e) **Type of surgery.** Pulmonary complications occur at a much higher rate for thoracic and upper abdominal procedures.
         (f) **Acute respiratory infections.** Postoperative pulmonary complications occur at a much higher rate for patients with acute respiratory infections; therefore, elective operations should be postponed in these individuals.
         (g) **Functional status.** In the patient with pulmonary disease or a history of smoking, a detailed evaluation of the patient's ability to climb stairs, walk, and perform daily duties is vital to stratify risk. Clinical judgment has been shown to be of equal or greater value relative to pulmonary function testing for most patients.
      (2) **Physical examination** should be performed carefully, with attention paid to signs of lung disease (e.g., wheezing, prolonged expiratory–inspiratory ratio, clubbing, or use of accessory muscles of respiration).

(3) Diagnostic evaluation

    (a) Chest X-ray (CXR) should be done for acute symptoms related to pulmonary disease.

    (b) An **arterial blood gas (ABG)** should be considered in patients with a history of lung disease or smoking to provide a baseline for comparison with postoperative studies.

    (c) Preoperative pulmonary function testing is controversial and probably unnecessary in stable patients with previously characterized pulmonary disease undergoing nonthoracic procedures.

b. Preoperative prophylaxis and management

    (1) Pulmonary toilet. Increasing lung volume by the use of preoperative incentive spirometry is potentially effective in reducing pulmonary complications.

    (2) Antibiotics do not reduce pulmonary infectious complications in the absence of preoperative infection. Elective operations should be postponed in patients with respiratory infections. If emergent surgery is required, patients with acute pulmonary infections should receive intravenous (IV) antibiotic therapy.

    (3) Cessation of smoking. All patients should be encouraged to and assisted in smoking cessation before surgery.

    (4) Bronchodilators. In the patient with obstructive airway disease and evidence of a significant reactive component, bronchodilators may be required in the perioperative period. When possible, elective operation should be postponed in the patient who is actively wheezing.

4. Renal disease

a. Preoperative evaluation of patients with existing renal insufficiency

    (1) Risk factors

        (a) Additional underlying medical disease. A substantial percentage of patients who require chronic hemodialysis for chronic renal insufficiency (CRI) have diabetes or hypertension. The incidence of CAD is also substantially higher in these patients. Much of the perioperative morbidity and mortality arises from these coexisting illnesses.

        (b) Metabolic and physiologic derangements of CRI. A variety of abnormalities in normal physiology that occur as a result of CRI can affect operative outcome adversely; these include alterations in electrolyte concentrations, acid–base balance, platelet function, the cardiovascular system, and the immune system. Specifically, the most common abnormalities in the perioperative period include hyperkalemia, intravascular volume overload, and infectious complications.

        (c) Type of operative procedure. Minor procedures under local or regional anesthesia are usually well tolerated in patients with CRI; however, major procedures are associated with increased morbidity and mortality.

(2) **Evaluation**
  (a) **History.** It is important to ascertain the specific etiology of CRI because patients with hypertension or diabetes and CRI are at a substantially increased risk of perioperative morbidity and mortality. The timing of last dialysis, the amount of fluid removed, and the preoperative weight provide important information about the patient's expected volume status. In nonanuric patients, the amount of urine (s)he makes on a daily basis should also be documented.
  (b) **Physical examination** should be performed carefully to assess the volume status. Elevated jugular venous pulsations or crackles on lung examination can indicate intravascular volume overload.
  (c) **Diagnostic testing**
    (i) **Laboratory data.** Serum sodium, potassium, calcium, phosphorus, magnesium, and bicarbonate levels should be measured, as well as blood urea nitrogen (BUN) and creatinine levels. A complete blood cell count (CBC) should be obtained to evaluate for significant anemia or a low platelet level. Normal platelet numbers can mask platelet dysfunction in patients with chronic uremia.
    (ii) **Supplemental tests** such as noninvasive cardiac evaluation may be warranted in patients with CRI and other risk factors.

(3) **Management**
  (a) **Timing of dialysis.** Dialysis should be performed within 24 hours of the planned operative procedure.
  (b) **Intravascular volume status.** CAD is the most common cause of death in patients with CRI. Consequently, because of the high incidence of coexisting CAD, patients with CRI undergoing major operations may require invasive monitoring in the intraoperative and postoperative periods. Hypovolemia and volume overload are both poorly tolerated.

b. **Patients at risk for perioperative renal dysfunction.** The reported incidence of acute renal failure (ARF) after operations in patients without preexisting CRI ranges from 1.5% to 2.5% for cardiac surgical procedures to more than 10% for patients undergoing repair of supraceliac abdominal aortic aneurysms (AAAs).

(1) **Risk factors** for the development of ARF include elevated preoperative BUN or creatinine, CHF, advanced age, intraoperative hypotension, sepsis, aortic cross-clamping, and intravascular volume contraction. Additional risk factors include administration of nephrotoxic drugs, such as aminoglycosides, and the administration of radiocontrast agents.

(2) **Prevention**
  (a) **Intravascular volume expansion.** Adequate hydration is the most important preventive measure for reducing the

incidence of ARF because all mechanisms of renal failure are exacerbated by renal hypoperfusion caused by intravascular volume contraction.

(b) **Radiocontrast dye administration.** Patients undergoing radiocontrast dye studies have an increased incidence of postoperative renal failure. Fluid administration (1 to 2 L of isotonic saline) alone appears to confer protection against ARF. Additional measures for reducing the incidence of contrast dye–mediated ARF include the use of low-osmolality contrast agents, a bicarbonate drip, and oral *N*-acetylcysteine (600 mg orally two times a day on the day of and the day after contrast agent administration). A prospective, single-center, randomized trial conducted from 2002 to 2003 of 119 patients with stable serum creatinine levels of at least 1.1 mg/dL demonstrated that patients randomized to receive an infusion of sodium bicarbonate before and after IV contrast administration had a significantly lower rate of contrast-induced nephropathy than patients randomized to receive sodium chloride (13.5% vs. 1.7%) (*JAMA.* 2004;291:2376). A meta-analysis of 7 studies and 805 patients found that compared with preprocedural hydration alone, the administration of *N*-acetylcysteine and hydration significantly reduced the relative risk of contrast nephropathy by 56% in patients with CRI (*Lancet.* 2003;362:598). However, a follow-up meta-analysis of 13 randomized trials including 1,892 patients did not find conclusive evidence that *N*-acetylcysteine administration before coronary angiography in patients with impaired renal function reduced the incidence of contrast nephropathy (*Am J Heart.* 2006;151:140). *N*-acetylcysteine has minimal toxicity, and further studies are needed to define its exact role.

(c) **Other nephrotoxins**—including aminoglycoside antibiotics, nonsteroidal anti-inflammatory drugs (NSAIDs), and various anesthetic drugs—can predispose to renal failure and should be used judiciously in patients with other risk factors for the development of ARF.

5. **Infectious complications.** Infectious complications may arise in the surgical wound itself or in other organ systems. They may be initiated by changes in the physiologic state of the respiratory, genitourinary, or immune systems associated with surgery. It is impossible to overemphasize the importance of frequent hand washing or antiseptic foam use by all health care workers to prevent the spread of infection.

a. **Assessment of risk.** Risk factors for infectious complications after surgery can be grouped into procedure-specific and patient-specific risk factors.

(1) **Procedure-specific risk factors** include the type of operation, the degree of wound contamination (see Table 1-4), and the duration and urgency of the operation.

TABLE 1-4 Classification of Surgical Wounds

Wound Class	Definition	Examples of Typical Procedures	Wound Infection Rate (%)	Usual Organisms
Clean	Nontraumatic, elective surgery; no entry of GI, biliary, tracheobronchial, respiratory, or GU tracts	Wide local excision of breast mass	2	*Staphylococcus aureus*
Clean-contaminated	Respiratory, genitourinary, GI tract entered but minimal contamination	Gastrectomy, hysterectomy	<10	Related to the viscus entered
Contaminated	Open, fresh, traumatic wounds; uncontrolled spillage from an unprepared hollow viscus; minor break in sterile technique	Ruptured appendix; resection of unprepared bowel	20	Depends on underlying disease
Dirty	Open, traumatic, dirty wounds; traumatic perforated viscus; pus in the operative field	Intestinal fistula resection	28–70	Depends on underlying disease

GI, gastrointestinal.

(2) **Patient-specific risk factors** include age, diabetes, obesity, immunosuppression, malnutrition, preexisting infection, and other chronic illness.

b. **Prophylaxis**

(1) **Nonantimicrobial strategies** documented to decrease the risk of postoperative infection include strict sterile technique, maintaining normal body temperature, maintaining normal blood glucose levels, and hyperoxygenation.

(2) **Surgical wound infection.** Antibiotic prophylaxis has contributed to a reduction in superficial wound infection rates (see Table 1-5 for specific recommendations). To ensure the highest blood concentration of medication at the time the operation begins, antibiotic infusions should end immediately prior to, that is, within 0–60 minutes of, incision (Casabar E, Portell J. *The Tool Book: Drug Dosing and Treatment Guidelines, Barnes-Jewish Hospital.* 8th ed. St. Louis, MO: Department of Pharmacy, Barnes-Jewish Hospital; 2010). A prospective study of 2,847 patients undergoing elective clean or clean-contaminated surgical procedures in a community hospital demonstrated that prophylactic administration of antibiotics 2 hours before surgery significantly reduced the risk of postoperative wound infection to 1.4% compared to 3.3% and 3.8%, respectively, in patients who received antibiotics postoperatively and prior to 2 hours before surgery (*N Engl J Med.* 1992;326:281–286). Repeat doses should be administered according to the usual dosing protocol during prolonged procedures.

(3) **Preoperative skin antisepsis** also plays an important role in preventing postsurgical infection. A recent randomized-controlled trial demonstrated the superiority of prepping with chlorhexidine–alcohol scrub over prepping with povidone–iodine scrub and paint in decreasing rates of both superficial (4.2% vs. 8.6%) and deep (1% vs. 3%) incisional infections (*N Engl J Med.* 2010;362:18–26).

(4) **Respiratory infections.** Risk factors and measures for preventing pulmonary complications are discussed in Section I.B.3.

(5) **Genitourinary infections** may be caused by instrumentation of the urinary tract or placement of an indwelling urinary catheter. Preventive measures include sterile insertion of the catheter and removal of the catheter as soon as possible postoperatively. A prophylactic dose of antibiotics should be given after a difficult catheter insertion or if excessive manipulation of the urinary tract has occurred.

6. **Diabetes mellitus.** Diabetic patients experience significant stress during the perioperative period and are at an estimated 50% increased risk of morbidity and mortality versus nondiabetic patients. They experience more infectious complications and have impaired wound healing. Most importantly, vascular disease is common in diabetics, and silent CAD must always be considered. MI, often with an atypical presentation, is the leading cause of perioperative death among diabetic patients.

TABLE 1-5	Recommendations for Antibiotic Prophylaxis		
Nature of Operation	Likely Pathogens	Recommended Antibiotics	Adult Dose Before Surgery[a]
Cardiac: prosthetic valve and other procedures	Staphylococci, corynebacteria, enteric Gram-negative bacilli	Vancomycin and Cefazolin Vancomycin and Aztreonam[a]	1 g IV or 15 mg/kg IV 1–2 g IV 1 g IV or 15 mg/kg IV 1 g IV
Thoracic	Staphylococci	Cefazolin Vancomycin[a]	1–2 g IV 1 g IV or 15 mg/kg IV
Vascular: peripheral bypass or aortic surgery with prosthetic graft	Staphylococci, streptococci, enteric Gram-negative bacilli, clostridia	Cefazolin Vancomycin and Aztreonam[a]	1–2 g IV 1 g IV or 15 mg/kg IV 1 g IV
Orthopedic: total joint replacement or internal fixation of fractures	Staphylococci	Cefazolin Vancomycin[a]	1–2 g IV 1 g IV or 15 mg/kg IV
Gastrointestinal			
Upper GI and hepatobiliary	Enteric Gram-negative bacilli, enterococci, clostridia	Cefazolin Cefotetan Cefoxitin Clindamycin and Gentamicin[a] Ciprofloxacin and Metronidazole[a]	1–2 g IV 1–2 g IV 1–2 g IV 900 mg IV 1.5 mg/kg IV 400 mg IV 500 mg IV
Colorectal	Enteric Gram-negative bacilli, anaerobes, enterococci	Cefoxitin Cefotetan Ciprofloxacin and Metronidazole[a]	1–2 g IV 1–2 g IV 400 mg IV 500 mg IV
Appendectomy (no perforation)	Enteric Gram-negative bacilli, anaerobes, enterococci	Cefoxitin Cefotetan Ciprofloxacin and Metronidazole[a]	1–2 g IV 1–2 g IV 400 mg IV 500 mg IV

| TABLE 1-5 | Recommendations for Antibiotic Prophylaxis *(Continued)* | | |

Nature of Operation	Likely Pathogens	Recommended Antibiotics	Adult Dose Before Surgery[a]
Obstetrics/ gynecology	Enteric Gram-negative bacilli, anaerobes, group B streptococci, enterococci	Cefotetan	1–2 g IV
		Cefoxitin	1–2 g IV
		Cefazolin	1–2 g IV
		Clindamycin and	900 mg IV
		Gentamicin[a]	1.5 mg/kg IV

[a]Indicated for patients with penicillin/cephalosporin allergy.

IV, intravenous.

Source: Casabar E, Portell J. *The Tool Book: Drug Dosing and Treatment Guidelines, Barnes-Jewish Hospital.* 8th ed. St. Louis, MO: Department of Pharmacy, Barnes-Jewish Hospital; 2010.

  a. **Preoperative evaluation.** All diabetic patients should have their blood glucose checked on call to the operating room and during general anesthesia to prevent unrecognized hyperglycemia or hypoglycemia.
    (1) Patients with **diet-controlled diabetes mellitus** can be maintained safely without food or glucose infusion before surgery.
    (2) **Patients who are taking oral hypoglycemic agents** should discontinue these medications the evening before scheduled surgery. Patients who take long-acting agents such as chlorpropamide or glyburide should discontinue these medications 2 to 3 days before surgery.
    (3) **Patients who normally take insulin** require insulin and glucose preoperatively to prevent ketosis and catabolism. Patients undergoing major surgery should receive one half of their morning insulin dose and 5% dextrose intravenously at 100 to 125 mL/hour. Subsequent insulin administration by either subcutaneous (SC) sliding-scale or insulin infusion is guided by frequent (every 4 to 6 hours) blood glucose determinations. SC insulin pumps should be inactivated the morning of surgery.
7. **Adrenal insufficiency and steroid dependence**
  a. **Exogenous steroids** are used to treat a variety of diseases that are encountered in surgical patients. Perioperative management of these individuals requires knowledge of the dose amount and frequency for each type of steroid (long-acting vs. short-acting) as well as the length of preoperative treatment with exogenous steroids.
  b. **Perioperative stress-dose steroids** are indicated for patients undergoing major surgery who have received chronic steroid replacement or immunosuppressive steroid therapy within the preceding year.

c. **Dosage recommendations** for perioperative steroids reflect estimates of normal adrenal responses to major surgical stress. The normal adrenal gland produces 250 to 300 mg cortisol per day under maximal stress, peaking at 6 hours after stress commences and returning to baseline after 24 hours unless stress continues. A regimen of hydrocortisone sodium succinate (100 mg IV) on the evening before major surgery, at the beginning of surgery, and every 8 hours on the day of surgery approximates the normal adrenal stress response. Tapering is not necessary in uncomplicated cases. Patients who are undergoing minor surgery or diagnostic procedures usually do not require stress-dose steroids.

8. **Anticoagulation.** The most common indications for warfarin therapy are atrial fibrillation, venous thromboembolism (VTE), and mechanical heart valves. Mitigation of warfarin's anticoagulant effect occurs only after several days of cessation of the drug, and several days are required to reestablish the effect after warfarin is resumed. Recommendations for the management of anticoagulation in the perioperative period require weighing the risks of subtherapeutic anticoagulation (e.g., thromboembolic events) against the benefits (e.g., reduced incidence of perioperative bleeding).

a. **Preoperative anticoagulation.** It is generally considered safe to perform surgery when the international normalized ratio (INR) value is below 1.5. Patients whose INRs are maintained between 2.0 and 3.0 normally require withholding of the medication for 4 days preoperatively. For patients whose INRs are maintained at a value greater than 3.0, withholding medication for a longer period of time is necessary. The INR should be measured the day before surgery, if possible, to confirm that the anticoagulation is reversed. Alternate prophylaxis should be considered for the preoperative period when the INR is less than 2.0.

b. **Postoperative anticoagulation.** The anticoagulant effects of warfarin require several doses before therapeutic levels are reached. For this reason, in patients who can tolerate oral or nasogastric medications, warfarin therapy can be resumed on postoperative days 1 or 2. In patients with atrial fibrillation, mechanical heart valve, or VTE, those deemed to be at high risk for thromboembolism should be bridged with therapeutically dosed SC low molecular weight heparin (LMWH) or therapeutically dosed IV unfractionated heparin (UFH) until INR is therapeutic; moderate-risk patients can be bridged with therapeutically dosed SC LMWH, therapeutically dosed IV UFH, or prophylactically dosed SC LMWH. Low-risk patients do not need to be bridged to warfarin therapy (*Chest.* 2008;133(6, suppl):299S–339S; Table 1-6 in this chapter provides suggested risk stratification for likelihood of developing arterial or VTE). Despite these guidelines, however, the decision as to when and whether to anticoagulate postoperatively ultimately needs to be made after a collaborative risk–benefit analysis by a patient's surgeon and cardiologist or internist.

c. **Emergent procedures.** In urgent or emergent situations in which there is no time to reverse anticoagulation before surgery, plasma products must be administered. In addition, Factor VII can have immediate effects, whereas vitamin K will have observable effects within 8 hours.

II. POSTOPERATIVE CARE OF THE PATIENT. This section summarizes general considerations in all postoperative patients.

A. **Routine Postoperative Care**

1. **Intravenous fluids.** The intravascular volume of surgical patients is depleted by both insensible fluid losses and redistribution into the third space. As a general rule, patients should be maintained on IV fluids until they are tolerating oral intake. Extensive abdominal procedures require aggressive fluid resuscitation. Insensible fluid losses associated with an open abdomen can reach 500 to 1,000 mL/hour.

2. **Deep venous thrombosis prophylaxis.** Many postoperative patients are not immediately ambulatory. In these individuals, it is important to provide prophylactic therapy to reduce the risk of deep venous thrombosis (DVT) and pulmonary embolism (PE) (see Table 1-6). Prophylaxis should be started preoperatively in patients undergoing major procedures because venous stasis and relative hypercoagulability occur during the operation. The American College of Chest Physicians (ACCP) recommends the use of pharmacologic methods combined with the use of intermittent pneumatic compression devices in high-risk general surgery patients with multiple risk factors. Prophylaxis and management of patients with a history of DVT or PE are discussed in Chapter 20.

3. **Pulmonary toilet.** Pain and immobilization in the postoperative patient decrease the clearance of pulmonary secretions and the recruitment of alveoli. Patients with inadequate pulmonary toilet can develop fevers, hypoxemia, and pneumonia. Early mobilization, incentive spirometry, and cough and deep breathing exercises are indispensable to avoid these complications.

4. **Medications**

   a. **Antiemetics.** Postoperative nausea is common in patients after general anesthesia and in patients receiving narcotics.

   b. **Ulcer prophylaxis.** Patients with a history of peptic ulcer disease (PUD) should have some form of ulcer prophylaxis in the perioperative period with either acid-reducing agents or cytoprotective agents, such as sucralfate. Routine ulcer prophylaxis in patients without a history of PUD has only been of proven benefit in those with a coagulopathy or prolonged ventilator dependence.

   c. **Pain control.** Inadequate pain control can slow recovery or contribute to complications in postoperative patients. Individuals whose pain is poorly controlled are less likely to ambulate and take deep breaths and are more likely to be tachycardic.

TABLE 1-6	Levels of Thromboembolism Risk and Recommended Thromboprophylaxis in Hospital Patients		
Level of Risk		Approximate DVT Risk w/o Prophylaxis (%)	Suggested Thromboprophylaxis Options
Low	Minor surgery in mobile patients Medical patients who are fully mobile	<10	Early and "aggressive" ambulation
Moderate	Most general, open gynecologic or urologic surgery patients Medical patients who are on bed rest, "sick"	10–40	LMWH, unfractionated SC heparin BID or TID, fondaparinux
	Moderate VTE risk plus high bleeding risk		Mechanical thromboprophylaxis
High	THA, TKA, HFS Major trauma Spinal cord injury	40–80	LMWH, fondaparinux, warfarin (INR 2–3)
	High VTE risk plus high bleeding risk		Mechanical thromboprophylaxis

THA, total hip arthroplasty; TKA, total knee arthroplasty; HFS, hip fracture surgery; LMWH, low molecular weight heparin; VTE, venous thromboembolism; INR, international normalized ratio.
Adapted with permission from Geerts WH et al. *Prevention of Venous Thromboembolism: American College of Chest Physicians Evidence-Based Clinical Practice Guidelines.* 8th ed. *Chest* 2008;133:381S–453S.

    d. Antibiotics. Surgeon preferences often dictate the use of postoperative antibiotics in particular cases. Recommendations for specific procedures are given in Table 1-5. Antibiotic therapy for specific infectious etiologies is discussed in Section III.E.2.

  5. Laboratory tests. Postoperative laboratory tests should be individualized; however, the following considerations are important when planning laboratory evaluations:

    a. A **CBC** should be obtained in the immediate postoperative period and on subsequent postoperative days in any procedure in which significant blood loss occurred. If there is a concern for ongoing blood loss, serial hematocrits should be followed.

b. **Serum electrolytes, BUN, and creatinine** are important postoperatively in patients on nothing-by-mouth (NPO) status, with renal insufficiency, or who are receiving large volumes of IV fluids, total parenteral nutrition (TPN), or transfusions. In patients with large transfusion requirements, it is important to keep track of calcium and magnesium levels.

c. **Coagulation studies** are important in patients who have had insults to the liver or large transfusion requirements.

d. Daily **ECGs** and a series of three **troponin I** levels 8 hours apart are appropriate ways to monitor for myocardial ischemia in patients with significant cardiac risk factors.

e. **CXRs,** preferably in the PACU, are necessary after any procedure in which the thoracic cavity is entered or when central venous access is attempted. CXRs on subsequent postoperative days should be considered on an individual basis if significant pulmonary or cardiovascular disease is present.

III. COMPLICATIONS

A. **Neurologic Complications**

1. **Perioperative stroke**

   a. **Presentation.** Patients usually describe a rapid onset of focal loss of neurologic function (unilateral weakness or clumsiness, sensory loss, speech disorder, diplopia, or vertigo). Massive strokes can present with altered mental status.

   b. **Examination.** A thorough neurologic examination, in addition to vital signs, finger-stick glucose, and pulse oximetry, should be assessed.

   c. **Evaluation**

      (1) **Laboratory evaluation** should include a CBC, electrolytes, BUN, creatinine, and coagulation studies. An ECG should be done to rule out cardiac arrhythmia.

      (2) A **CT scan of the head** should be obtained urgently to rule out a hemorrhagic stroke.

      (3) **Further studies** including echocardiography, carotid and transcranial ultrasound, and magnetic resonance imaging (MRI) may be ordered in consultation with a neurologist.

2. **Treatment**

   a. **General supportive measures** include supplemental oxygen and IV fluid.

   b. **Aspirin** (325 mg orally) should be given immediately in ischemic stroke.

   c. **Thrombolysis** has been proven effective in improving outcomes from ischemic strokes; however, it is usually contraindicated in postoperative patients and should only be initiated in close consultation with a neurologist.

3. **Seizures.** Evaluation and treatment of postoperative seizures involve the same principles as those encountered in other settings. Most seizures in surgical patients without a history of seizure can be attributed

to metabolic derangements including electrolyte abnormalities (e.g., hyponatremia and hypocalcemia), hypoglycemia, sepsis, fever, and drugs (e.g., imipenem).

a. **Determine from patient history whether a true seizure was witnessed;** if so, note its type, characteristics (i.e., general vs. focal), and similarity to any previous seizures. New-onset seizures are worrisome and iatrogenic causes (e.g., medications) and CVA must be considered. A history of preoperative alcohol use may indicate withdrawal.

b. **Complete physical and neurologic examination** should focus on airway, oxygenation, and hemodynamics and then on any sequelae of seizure, including trauma, aspiration, or rhabdomyolysis. A focally abnormal neurologic examination, especially in the setting of a new-onset focal seizure, suggests a possible cerebrovascular event.

c. **Laboratory and diagnostic studies.** The immediate evaluation of a patient should consist of vital signs, a blood glucose determination, CBC, and serum chemistries, including calcium and magnesium. Serum levels of anticonvulsants should be measured in patients who normally take these medications. Patients with new-onset seizures who do not have identifiable metabolic or systemic causes warrant further evaluation with a head CT scan followed by a lumbar puncture.

d. **Treatment** of new-onset, single, nonrecurring seizures or recurrent generalized seizures with identifiable metabolic or systemic causes usually requires only correction of the underlying abnormality.

(1) **Recurrent generalized tonic–clonic seizures** require anticonvulsant therapy. A regimen beginning with a 15- to 20-mg/kg load of phenytoin, given parenterally in three divided doses, and followed by maintenance dosing of 5 mg/kg/day in three divided doses controls most seizures. Therapeutic serum levels are 10 to 20 mg/mL.

(2) **Status epilepticus,** defined as a seizure lasting more than 5 minutes or a series of multiple, continuous seizures without return to baseline mental status, is a medical emergency.

(a) **Monitor cardiopulmonary parameters and stabilize the patient's airway with a soft oral or nasal airway.** Endotracheal intubation might be required to protect the airway. Phenobarbital and benzodiazepines in combination severely depress the respiratory drive. IV access should be established immediately.

(b) **Administer parenteral anticonvulsants promptly.**

(i) **Lorazepam** (2 to 4 mg IV at a rate of 2 mg/min) should be administered to patients with generalized convulsions lasting longer than 5 minutes. Either lorazepam or fosphenytoin may be given intramuscularly in emergent situations if IV access has not yet been established. Results are usually seen within 10 minutes. A second parenteral anticonvulsant should be started concurrently, and a neurology consult should be obtained immediately (Casabar E, Portell J. *The Tool Book: Drug*

Dosing and Treatment Guidelines, Barnes-Jewish Hospital. 8th ed. St. Louis, MO: Department of Pharmacy, Barnes-Jewish Hospital; 2010).

(ii) **Fosphenytoin** (prescribed in phenytoin equivalents) administered parenterally is the first choice to supplement benzodiazepines in this setting.

(iii) **Phenobarbital** is a second-line agent and should be used when fosphenytoin is contraindicated (e.g., heart block) or ineffective. A loading dose of 20 mg/kg IV can be given at 100 mg/minute. Maintenance doses of 1 to 5 mg/kg/day intravenously or orally are required to achieve therapeutic plasma levels. Institution of a phenobarbital coma should be considered if status epilepticus continues.

4. **Delirium.** Delirium is fairly common in patients (especially the elderly) who undergo the stress of an operation. An underlying cause usually can be identified, and in most cases it involves medications or infection. Other causes include hypoxemia, electrolyte abnormalities, cardiac arrhythmias, MI, and stroke. Alcohol withdrawal, discussed in Section III.A.4, is another common cause of postoperative delirium.

   a. **Symptoms** include impaired memory, altered perception, and paranoia. Altered sleep patterns result in drowsiness during the day and wakefulness and agitation at night (i.e., sundowning). Disorientation and combativeness are common.

   b. **Management** begins with eliminating the possibility of an underlying physiologic or metabolic derangement. Heart rate, blood pressure (BP), temperature, and oxygen saturation should be assessed, and a thorough physical exam should be performed with attention to the possibility of infection. CBC and electrolytes should be obtained. Other testing, including ECG, ABG, urinalysis (UA), and CXR, is dictated by clinical suspicion. Medications should be reviewed carefully, with consideration directed toward anticholinergic agents, opiate analgesics, and antihistamines. If no underlying organic cause is identified, alteration in sleep patterns or sensory deprivation can be invoked, and haloperidol (1 to 5 mg orally or intramuscularly) can be prescribed. Often, family reassurance or transfer to a room with natural light is curative. Physical restraints might be necessary to prevent self-harm.

5. **Alcohol withdrawal** carries a significant risk of morbidity and mortality and requires a high level of vigilance.

   a. **Symptoms.** Minor withdrawal can begin 6 to 8 hours after cessation of alcohol intake and is characterized by anxiety, tremulousness, anorexia, and nausea. Signs include tachycardia, hypertension, and hyperreflexia. These signs and symptoms generally resolve within 24 to 48 hours. **Delirium tremens** typically occurs 72 to 96 hours or longer after cessation of alcohol intake and is characterized by disorientation, hallucinations, and autonomic lability that includes tachycardia, hypertension, fever, and profuse diaphoresis.

b. Treatment

(1) Benzodiazepines—such as chlordiazepoxide, 25 to 100 mg orally every 6 hours; oxazepam, 5 to 15 mg orally every 6 hours; or diazepam, 5 to 20 mg orally or IV every 6 hours— can be used as prophylaxis in alcoholics who have a history of withdrawal or to alleviate symptoms of minor withdrawal. Patients with delirium tremens should be given diazepam, 5 to 10 mg IV every 10 to 15 minutes, to control symptoms. Oversedation must be avoided through close monitoring. The dose of benzodiazepines should be reduced in patients with liver impairment. Moderate alcohol intake with meals can be a simple way to prevent and treat alcohol withdrawal.

(2) Clonidine, 0.1 mg orally four times a day, or atenolol, 50 to 100 mg orally every day, can be used to treat tachycardia or hypertension resulting from autonomic hyperactivity. Close hemodynamic monitoring is required during therapy.

(3) General medical care. Fluid and electrolyte abnormalities should be corrected, and fever should be treated with acetaminophen or cooling blankets as needed. Thiamine, 100 mg intramuscularly for 3 days followed by 100 mg orally every day, should be given to all suspected alcoholic patients to prevent development of Wernicke encephalopathy. Many chronic alcoholics have hypomagnesemia; if present, magnesium sulfate should be administered to patients with normal renal function. Folate should be given 1 mg intramuscularly or orally every day.

(4) Restraints should be used only when necessary to protect the patient from self-harm.

(5) Alcohol withdrawal seizures occur 12 to 48 hours after cessation of alcohol and are most often generalized tonic–clonic. They are usually brief and self-limited, although status epilepticus occurs in approximately 3% of cases. Benzodiazepines are most helpful in preventing recurrent seizures.

B. Cardiovascular Complications

1. Myocardial ischemia and infarction

a. The **presentation** of myocardial ischemia in the postoperative patient is often subtle. Frequently, perioperative MI is silent or presents with dyspnea, hypotension, or atypical pain.

b. In postoperative patients who present with chest pain, the **differential diagnosis** includes myocardial ischemia or infarction, PE, pneumonia, pericarditis, aortic dissection, and pneumothorax.

c. Evaluation

(1) Physical examination should be performed carefully to assess BP, heart rate, and organ and tissue perfusion. The lungs should be auscultated for signs of pulmonary edema and diminished or absent breath sounds unilaterally (concerning for pneumothorax). Auscultation of the heart can reveal a new murmur suggestive of ischemic mitral regurgitation or a pericardial friction rub suggestive of pericarditis.

(2) **Diagnostic testing**

   (a) An **ECG** is warranted in virtually all cases of postoperative chest pain, with comparison to prior tracings. Sinus tachycardia is one of the most common rhythms associated with myocardial ischemia.

   (b) **Laboratory data**

   (i) **Cardiac enzymes.** An elevated troponin I level is diagnostic of MI. A series of three samplings of troponin I 6–9 hours apart has a sensitivity and specificity of greater than 90% for detecting myocardial injury (*N Engl J Med.* 2009;361:868–877).

   (ii) **Routine serum chemistries and CBC.**

   (iii) **Oxygen saturation** should be determined via pulse oximetry, and supplemental oxygen should be administered. Significant hypoxia can be seen with MI, CHF, pneumonia, and PE.

   (c) **CXRs** should be obtained to evaluate for pneumothorax, infiltrate, or evidence of pulmonary edema.

   (d) **Further diagnostic evaluation** (e.g., echocardiography, coronary catheterization, ventilation–perfusion (V/Q) scintigraphy, or CT scan) should be pursued as indicated by the diagnostic workup.

(3) **Treatment**

   (a) **Telemetry** should be used in all patients with suspected myocardial ischemia.

   (b) **Oxygen therapy.** Arterial oxygen saturation should be kept greater than 90% with supplemental oxygen. Endotracheal intubation and mechanical ventilation are indicated for patients with respiratory fatigue, hypoxia that is refractory to supplemental oxygen therapy, and/or progressive hypercapnia.

   (c) **Pharmacologic therapy**

   (i) **Nitrates.** In the absence of hypotension (systolic BP <90 mm Hg), initial management of patients with chest pain of presumed cardiac origin includes the use of sublingual nitroglycerin (0.4 mg), which can be repeated every 5 minutes until pain resolves. Additionally, topical nitrate therapy (0.5 to 2 inches every 6 hours) can be instituted. Ongoing myocardial ischemia or infarction should be treated with IV nitroglycerin, starting with an infusion rate of 5 μg/minute and increased at 5-μg/minute increments until the chest pain is relieved or significant hypotension develops.

   (ii) **Beta-adrenergic receptor antagonists, that is, beta-blockers.** In the absence of significant contraindications (e.g., heart failure, bradycardia, heart block, or significant COPD), patients should be treated with IV beta-adrenergic receptor antagonists (e.g., metoprolol,

15 mg IV, in 5-mg doses every 5 minutes, followed by a 50- to 100-mg oral dose every 12 hours).

- **(iii) Morphine sulfate** (1 to 4 mg IV every hour) is also useful in the acute management of chest pain to decrease the sympathetic drive of an anxious patient.
- **(iv) Antiplatelet therapy** in the form of a nonenteric-coated aspirin (325 mg) can also be given if the patient is at low risk of perioperative bleeding.
- **(d) Other therapeutic measures.** Thrombolytic therapy, anticoagulation, or coronary catheterization should be considered on an individual basis in consultation with a cardiologist.

2. **Congestive heart failure**
    a. **Differential diagnosis** of shortness of breath or hypoxia in the peri-operative period includes CHF, pneumonia, atelectasis, PE, reactive airway disease (asthma, COPD exacerbation), and pneumothorax. These pulmonary conditions are discussed in Section III.C.
    b. **Evaluation**
        (1) **History.** CHF can occur immediately postoperatively as a result of excessive intraoperative administration of fluids or 24 to 48 hours postoperatively related to mobilization of fluids that are sequestered in the extracellular space. Myocardial ischemia or infarction can also result in CHF. Net fluid balance and weight for the preceding days should be assessed.
        (2) **Physical examination** should be directed toward signs and symptoms of fluid overload and myocardial ischemia.
        (3) **Diagnostic testing**
            (a) **Laboratory data.** Troponin I, B-type natriuretic peptide (BNP), ABG, CBC, electrolytes, and renal function tests should be obtained.
            (b) **Pulse oximetry.**
            (c) **ECG.**
            (d) **CXR.**
            (e) An **echocardiogram** is frequently indicated in patients with new CHF to evaluate valves, assess the contractility and dimensions of each cardiac chamber, and rule out tamponade.
            (f) Invasive measurement of cardiac output with a **pulmonary artery catheter** may be of use in assessing volume status.
    c. **Management of congestive heart failure**
        (1) **Supplemental oxygen** should be administered. Mechanical ventilation is indicated in patients with refractory hypoxemia.
        (2) **Diuretics.** Treatment should be initiated with furosemide (20 to 40 mg IV push), with doses up to 200 mg every 6 hours as necessary to achieve adequate diuresis. Furosemide drips can be effective in promoting diuresis. Fluid intake should be limited, and serum potassium should be monitored closely.
        (3) **Morphine** (1 to 4 mg IV pushed every hour)

(4) **Arterial vasodilators.** To reduce afterload and help the failing heart in the acute setting, sodium nitroprusside or ACE inhibitors can be used to lower the systolic BP to 90 to 100 mm Hg.

(5) **Inotropic agents.** Digoxin increases myocardial contractility and can be used to treat patients with mild failure. Patients with florid failure may need invasive monitoring and titration of drips if they do not respond to these measures. If there is a low cardiac index (<2.5 L/minute/m^2) with elevated filling pressures, inotropic agents are indicated. Therapy can be initiated with dobutamine (3 to 20 µg/kg/minute) to increase the cardiac index to a value near 3 L/minute/m^2. Milrinone is also a useful agent for refractory CHF. (A loading dose of 50 µg/kg is administered over 10 minutes, followed by a continuous infusion of 0.375 to 0.750 µg/kg/minute titrated for clinical response.) If hypotension is accompanied by low systemic vascular resistance, vasopressors may be useful (Table 1-7).

TABLE 1-7	Doses of Commonly Used Vasopressors		
Vasopressor	**Preparation**	**Infusion**	**Comments**
Dobutamine	250 mg/250 mL NS or D5 W	Start at 3 µg/kg/min and titrate up to 20 µg/kg/min based on clinical response	Beta-agonist
Dopamine	800 mg in 500 mL NS or D5 W	Start at 3 µg/kg/min and titrate to systolic BP	Beta-adrenergic effects dominate at lower infusion rates
Epinephrine	5 mg/500 mL NS or D5 W	1–4 µg/min and titrate to effect	Alpha and beta
Norepinephrine	8 mg in 500 mL D5 W	Start at 2 µg/min and titrate to systolic BP	Strong alpha-adrenergic agonist
Phenylephrine (Neo-Synephrine)	10 mg in 250 mL D5 W or NS	Start at 10 µg/min and titrate to systolic BP	May be ineffective in severe distributive shock

BP, blood pressure; D5 W, 5% dextrose in water; NS, normal saline.

C. **Pulmonary Complications**

1. The **differential diagnosis** of dyspnea includes atelectasis, lobar collapse, pneumonia, CHF, COPD, asthma exacerbation, pneumothorax, PE, and aspiration.

2. **Evaluation**

   a. **History.** Additional factors that help to differentiate disease entities include the presence of a fever, chest pain, and the time since surgery.

   b. **Physical examination** with attention to jugular venous distention, breath sounds (wheezing, crackles), symmetry, and respiratory effort.

   c. **Diagnostic testing**

      (1) **Laboratory.** CBC, chemistry profile, and pulse oximetry or ABG.

      (2) **ECGs** should be obtained for any patient older than 30 years with significant dyspnea or tachypnea to exclude myocardial ischemia and in any patient who is dyspneic in the setting of tachycardia.

      (3) **CXRs** are mandatory in all dyspneic patients.

      (4) **V/Q scan, spiral CT scan of the chest,** or **pulmonary angiogram** may be helpful.

3. **Management** of specific diagnoses

   a. **Atelectasis** commonly occurs in the first 36 hours after operation and typically presents with dyspnea and hypoxia. Therapy is aimed at reexpanding the collapsed alveoli. For most patients, deep breathing and coughing along with the use of incentive spirometry are adequate. Postoperative pain should be sufficiently controlled so that pulmonary mechanics are not significantly impaired. In patients with significant atelectasis or lobar collapse, chest physical therapy and nasotracheal suctioning might be required. In rare cases, bronchoscopy can aid in clearing mucus plugs that cannot be cleared using less invasive measures.

   b. **Pneumonia** is discussed in Section III.E.2.b.

   c. **Pulmonary embolism** is discussed in Section III.F.

   d. **Gastric aspiration** usually presents with acute dyspnea and fever. CXR might be normal initially but subsequently demonstrate a pattern of diffuse interstitial infiltrates. Therapy is supportive, and antibiotics are typically not given empirically.

   e. **Pneumothorax** is treated with tube thoracostomy. If tension pneumothorax is suspected, immediate needle decompression through the second intercostal space in the midclavicular line using a 14-gauge needle should precede controlled placement of a thoracostomy tube.

   f. **COPD and asthma exacerbations** present with dyspnea or tachypnea, wheezing, hypoxemia, and possibly hypercapnia. Acute therapy includes administration of supplemental oxygen and inhaled beta-adrenergic agonists (albuterol, 3.0 mL (2.5 mg) in 2 mL normal saline every 4 to 6 hours via nebulization). Beta-adrenergic agonists are indicated primarily for acute exacerbations rather than for long-term use. Anticholinergics such as ipratropium bromide metered-dose inhaler (Atrovent, 2 puffs every 4 to 6 hours) can also be used in the perioperative period, especially if the patient has significant pulmonary secretions. Patients with severe asthma or COPD may benefit from parenteral steroid therapy (methylprednisolone, 50 to 250 mg intravenously every 4 to 6 hours) as well as inhaled steroids (beclomethasone metered-dose inhaler, 2 puffs four times a day), but steroids require 6 to 12 hours to take effect.

D. Renal Complications
1. Acute renal failure
a. Causes.
The etiologies of postoperative renal insufficiency can be classified as prerenal, intrinsic renal, and postrenal (Table 1-8).
   (1) **Prerenal azotemia** results from decreased renal perfusion that might be secondary to hypotension, intravascular volume contraction, or decreased effective renal perfusion.
   (2) **Intrinsic renal** causes of ARF include drug-induced acute tubular necrosis, pigment-induced renal injury, radiocontrast dye administration, acute interstitial nephritis, and prolonged ischemia from suprarenal aortic cross-clamping.
   (3) **Postrenal causes** of ARF can result from obstruction of the ureters or bladder. Operations that involve dissection near the ureters, such as colectomy, colostomy closure, or total abdominal hysterectomy, have a higher incidence of ureteral injuries. In addition to ureteral injuries or obstruction, obstruction of the bladder from an enlarged prostate, narcotic use for management of postoperative pain, or an obstructed urinary catheter can contribute to postrenal ARF.
b. General evaluation
   (1) **History and physical examination**
   (2) **Laboratory evaluation**
      (a) **Urinalysis with microscopy and culture** (as indicated) can help to differentiate between etiologies of renal failure.
      (b) **Serum chemistries.**

TABLE 1-8	Laboratory Evaluation of Oliguria and Acute Renal Failure				
Category	FE_{Na}	U_{Osm}	RFI	U_{Cr}/P_{Cr}	U_{Na}
Prerenal	<1	>500	<1	>40	<20
Renal (acute tubular necrosis)	>1	<350	>1	<20	>40
Postrenal	>1	<50	>1	<20	>40

FE_{Na}, fractional excretion of sodium; RFI, renal failure index; U_{Cr}/P_{Cr}, urine–plasma creatinine ratio; U_{Na}, urine sodium; U_{Osm}, urine osmolality.

(c) **Urinary indices** help to classify ARF into prerenal, postrenal, or intrinsic renal categories (Table 1-8). Fractional excretion of sodium (FE_{Na}) can be calculated from

$$FE_{Na} = (U_{Na}/P_{Na})/(U_{Cr}/P_{cr}),$$

where U_{Na} is urine sodium, P_{Na} is plasma sodium, and U_{Cr}/P_{Cr} is urine–plasma creatinine ratio. The renal failure index (RFI) is $(U_{Na})(P_{Cr})/U_{Cr}$. These measurements must be obtained before diuretic administration.

(3) **Other diagnostic testing**

(a) **Renal ultrasonography** can be used to exclude obstructive uropathy, assess the chronicity of renal disease, and evaluate the renal vasculature with Doppler ultrasonography.

(b) **Radiologic studies** using IV contrast are contraindicated in patients with suspected ARF due to potential exacerbation of renal injury.

c. **Management of specific problems**

(1) **Oliguria** (<500 mL/day) in the postoperative period.

(a) **Evaluation.** The goal of this evaluation is to determine the patient's intravascular volume status and to differentiate the causes of oliguria. Cardiac echocardiography, central venous pressures, and pulmonary artery pressures can assist with the evaluation of volume status.

(b) **Management**

(i) **Prerenal.** In most surgical patients, oliguria is caused by hypovolemia. Initial management includes fluid challenges (e.g., normal saline boluses of 500 mL). Patients with adequate fluid resuscitation and CHF may benefit from invasive monitoring and optimization of cardiac function.

(ii) **Intrinsic renal.** Treat the underlying cause, if possible, and manage volume status.

(iii) **Postrenal.** Ureteral injuries or obstruction can be treated with percutaneous nephrostomy tubes and generally are managed in consultation with a urologist. Urinary retention and urethral obstruction can be managed by placement of a Foley catheter or, if necessary, a suprapubic catheter.

(2) **Elevated creatinine and ARF**

(a) **Evaluation.** The laboratory and diagnostic evaluation for patients with a rising creatinine is similar to the evaluation for patients with oliguria.

(b) **Management** includes careful attention to the intravascular volume status. The patient should be weighed daily, and intakes and outputs should be recorded carefully. Serum electrolytes should be monitored closely. The patient should be maintained in a euvolemic state. Hyperkalemia, metabolic acidosis, and hyperphosphatemia are common problems in patients with ARF and should be managed as discussed in Chapter 4. Medication doses should be adjusted appropriately and potassium removed from maintenance IV fluids.

    (i) Dialysis. Indications for dialysis include intravascular volume overload, hyperkalemia, severe metabolic acidosis, and complications of uremia (encephalopathy, pericarditis).

E. Infectious Complications

  1. Management of infection and fever

    a. Evaluation of fever should take into account the amount of time that has passed since the patient's most recent operation.

      (1) Intraoperative fever may be secondary to malignant hyperthermia, a transfusion reaction, or a preexisting infection.

        (a) Diagnosis and management of a transfusion reaction are discussed in Chapter 5.

        (b) Malignant hyperthermia is discussed in Chapter 3.

        (c) Preexisting infections should be treated with empiric IV antibiotics.

      (2) High fever (>39°C) in the first 24 hours is commonly the result of a streptococcal or clostridial wound infection, aspiration pneumonitis, or a preexisting infection.

        (a) Streptococcal wound infections present with severe local erythema and incisional pain. Penicillin G (2 million units IV every 6 hours) or ampicillin (1 to 2 g IV every 6 hours) is effective therapy. Patients with a **severe necrotizing clostridial infection** present with systemic toxemia, pain, and crepitus near the incision. Treatment includes emergent operative débridement and metronidazole (500 mg IV every 6 hours) or clindamycin (600 to 900 mg IV every 8 hours).

      (3) Fever that occurs more than 72 hours after surgery has a broad differential diagnosis, including pneumonia, urinary tract infection, thrombophlebitis, wound infection, intraabdominal abscess, and drug allergy.

    b. Diagnostic evaluation. The new onset of fever or leukocytosis without an obvious source of infection requires a thorough history and physical examination (including inspection of all wounds, tubes, and catheter sites) and selected laboratory tests.

    c. Specific laboratory tests

      (1) CBC.

      (2) Urinalysis.

      (3) CXR.

      (4) Gram stain/culture. Cultures of the blood, sputum, urine, and/or wound should be dictated by the clinical situation.

    d. Antibiotics. Empiric antibiotics can be initiated after collection of cultures, with therapy directed by clinical suspicion.

    e. Imaging studies such as ultrasound or CT should be chosen based on clinical context.

2. **Management of specific infectious etiologies**

   a. **Wound infection** is diagnosed by local erythema, swelling, pain, tenderness, and wound drainage. Fever and leukocytosis are usually present but may be absent in superficial wound infections. The primary treatment is to open the wound to allow drainage. The wound should be cultured. If the infection is contained in the superficial tissue layers, antibiotics are not required. In the case of a clean procedure that did not enter the bowel, the usual pathogens are staphylococcal and streptococcal species. If surrounding erythema is extensive, parenteral antibiotics should be initiated. Wound infections in the perineum or after bowel surgery are more likely to be caused by enteric pathogens and anaerobes. More aggressive infections with involvement of underlying fascia require emergent operative débridement and broad-spectrum IV antibiotics.

   b. **Respiratory infections.** Pneumonia is diagnosed by the presence of fever, leukocytosis, purulent sputum production, and an infiltrate on CXR. After Gram stain and culture of the sputum and blood is performed, empiric antibiotics can be started. Pneumonias that occur in postoperative patients should be treated as nosocomial infections. Patients requiring mechanical ventilation for longer than 48 hours are at risk for ventilator-associated pneumonia (VAP), which may require bronchoscopy for diagnosis.

   c. **Gastrointestinal infections** may present with fever, leukocytosis, and diarrhea. *Clostridium difficile* is a common cause of diarrhea in hospitalized patients, and there should be a low threshold for performing an assay for the *C. difficile* organism or toxin. Initial therapy includes fluid resuscitation and metronidazole (500 mg orally or IV every 6 to 8 hours) or vancomycin (250 to 500 mg orally every 6 hours).

   d. **Intraabdominal abscess or peritonitis** present with fever, leukocytosis, abdominal pain, and tenderness. If the patient has generalized peritonitis, emergency laparotomy is indicated. If the inflammation appears to be localized, a CT scan of the patient's abdomen and pelvis should be obtained. The primary management of an intraabdominal abscess is drainage. In many circumstances, this can be performed percutaneously with radiologic guidance. In other situations, operative débridement and drainage are required. Empiric antibiotic therapy should cover enteric pathogens and anaerobes.

   e. **Genitourinary infections.** After the urine is cultured, simple lower-tract infections can be managed with oral antibiotics. Ill patients or those with pyelonephritis require more aggressive therapy.

   f. **Prosthetic-device–related infections** may present with fever, leukocytosis, and systemic bacteremia. Infection of prosthetic valves may present with a new murmur. Management may require removal of the infected device and the use of long-term antibiotics.

   g. **Catheter-related infections** also are diagnosed by the presence of fever, leukocytosis, and systemic bacteremia. Local erythema and purulence may be present around central venous catheter insertion sites. Erythema, purulence, a tender thrombosed vein, or lymphangitis may be present near an infected peripheral IV line. Management includes removal of the catheter and IV antibiotic coverage.

h. Fascial or muscle infections may result from gross contamination of a surgical wound or from a previously infected wound. Fasciitis and deep-muscle infections can present with hemorrhagic bullae over the infected area, rapidly progressive edema with foul-smelling "dishwater" pus, erythema, pain, and/or crepitus. Fever, tachycardia, and ultimately cardiovascular collapse occur in rapid succession. Therapy includes emergent operative débridement, management of shock, and broad-spectrum antibiotics (including anaerobic coverage). Necrotizing fasciitis is a surgical emergency; death may result within a few hours of the development of symptoms.

i. Viral infections complicating operations are uncommon in immunocompetent patients.

j. Fungal infections (primarily with *Candida* species) occur most commonly after long-term antibiotic administration. In these patients, evaluation of persistent fever without an identified bacterial source should include several sets of routine and fungal blood cultures, removal of all IV catheters, and examination of the retina for *Candida endophthalmitis*. Therapy includes amphotericin B, fluconazole, or micafungin.

F. Deep Venous Thrombosis and Pulmonary Embolism

1. Diagnosis and treatment of DVT

a. Diagnosis

(1) Symptoms of DVT vary greatly, although classically they include pain and swelling of the affected extremity distal to the site of venous obstruction. Signs of DVT on physical examination may include edema, erythema, warmth, a palpable cord, or calf pain with dorsiflexion of the foot (Homan's sign). Physical examination alone is notoriously inaccurate in the diagnosis of DVT.

(2) Noninvasive studies of the venous system, most notably B-mode ultrasonography plus color Doppler (duplex scanning), have revolutionized the diagnosis and management of suspected DVT. Reported sensitivity and specificity of this test for the detection of proximal DVT are greater than 90% with nearly 100% positive predictive value. This modality is less reliable in the detection of infrapopliteal thrombi, and a negative study in symptomatic patients should be followed by repeat examination in 48 to 72 hours to evaluate for propagation of clot proximally. Patients in whom a negative study contrasts with a strong clinical suspicion may require contrast venography, the gold standard for diagnosis of DVT.

b. Treatment. See Chapter 20.

2. Diagnosis and treatment of PE

a. Diagnosis

(1) Symptoms of PE are neither sensitive nor specific. Mental status changes, dyspnea, pleuritic chest pain, and cough can occur, and hemoptysis is encountered occasionally. Signs of PE most commonly include tachypnea and tachycardia. Patients with massive PE may experience syncope or cardiovascular collapse. PE should be considered in any postoperative patient with unexplained dyspnea, hypoxia, tachycardia, or dysrhythmia.

(2) **Laboratory studies.** Initial evaluation of patients with suspected PE must include noninvasive assessment of arterial oxygen saturation, ECG, and CXR. Findings that are suggestive of PE include arterial oxygen desaturation, nonspecific ST-segment or T-wave changes on ECG, and atelectasis, parenchymal abnormalities, or pleural effusion on CXR. Such classic signs as $S_1Q_3T_3$ on ECG or a prominent central pulmonary artery with decreased pulmonary vascularity (Westermark's sign) on CXR are uncommon. ABG determination is a helpful adjunctive test; a decreased arterial oxygen tension (Pao_2) (<80 mm Hg), an elevated alveolar–arterial oxygen gradient, or a respiratory alkalosis may support clinical suspicion. Data that are obtained from these initial studies collectively may corroborate clinical suspicion but none of these alone is either sensitive or specific for PE. **D-Dimer** assays have a high negative predictive value; however, positive values, particularly in the setting of recent surgery, are less helpful because the postoperative period is one of many conditions that can cause an elevation of this test.

(3) **Imaging studies**

(a) **Spiral CT scan** is becoming the primary diagnostic modality for PE. The advantages of CT scans for PE include increased sensitivity, the ability to simultaneously evaluate other pulmonary and mediastinal abnormalities, greater after-hours availability, and the ability to obtain a CT venogram with the same dye load. This study subjects the patient to a contrast dye load and requires a large (18 g or higher) IV in the antecubital vein, but it is not invasive. There are still wide variations in technology and institutional expertise with this modality, with reported sensitivities ranging from 57% to 100% and specificity ranging from 78% to 100%.

(b) A **V/Q scan** that demonstrates one or more perfusion defects in the absence of matched ventilation defects is abnormal and may be interpreted as high, intermediate, or low probability for PE, depending on the type and degree of abnormality. V/Q scans alone are neither sensitive nor specific for PE, and their interpretation may be difficult in patients with preexisting lung disease, especially COPD. Nevertheless, high-probability scans are 90% predictive and suffice for diagnosis of PE. In the appropriate clinical setting, a high-probability V/Q scan should prompt treatment. Likewise, a normal scan virtually excludes PE (96%). Scans of intermediate probability require additional confirmatory tests.

(c) **Pulmonary angiography** is the reference standard for the diagnosis of PE, but it is an invasive test with some element of risk. This test is rapidly being supplanted by spiral CT for most circumstances. Its use should be reserved for (1) resolution of conflicting or inconclusive clinical and non-invasive data; (2) patients with high clinical suspicion for PE and extensive preexisting pulmonary disease in whom interpretation of V/Q scans is difficult without access to spiral CT; and (3) confirmation of clinical and noninvasive data in patients who are at high risk for anticoagulation or in unstable patients being considered for thrombolytic therapy, pulmonary embolectomy, or vena caval interruption.

(d) Treatment

(1) Supportive measures include administration of oxygen to correct hypoxemia and use of IV fluids to maintain BP. Hypotensive patients with high clinical suspicion of PE (i.e., high-risk patients, patients with acute right heart failure or right ventricular ischemia on ECG) require immediate transfer to an intensive care unit, where hemodynamic monitoring and vasoactive medications may be required.

(2) Anticoagulation with intravenous UFH or SC LMWH should be started immediately with a target activated partial thromboplastin time (PTT) of 50 to 80 seconds. Oral warfarin can be started concurrently while heparin is continued until a therapeutic PT is achieved. Anticoagulation should continue for 6 months unless risk factors persist or DVT recurs.

(3) Thrombolytic therapy is not indicated in the routine treatment of PE in surgical patients because the risk of hemorrhage in individuals with recent (<10 days) surgery outweighs the uncertain long-term benefits of this therapy. Surgical patients with shock secondary to angiographically proven massive PE that is refractory to anticoagulation should be considered for either transvenous embolectomy or open pulmonary embolectomy. These aggressive measures are rarely successful.

(4) Inferior vena caval filter placement is indicated when a contraindication to anticoagulation exists, a bleeding complication occurs while receiving anticoagulation, or a DVT or PE recurs during anticoagulation therapy.

G. Complications of Diabetes

1. Tight blood glucose control. A landmark prospective study of 1,548 patients who were admitted to a surgical intensive care unit on mechanical ventilation randomly assigned patients to tight control with intensive insulin therapy (blood glucose between 80 and 110 mg/dL) versus conventional control (blood glucose between 180 and 200 mg/dL and treatment only for levels >215 mg/dL). This study showed nearly a two-fold decrease in mortality in the tight-glucose-control group. Intensive insulin therapy also reduced overall in-hospital mortality, bloodstream infections, ARF, the median number of red blood cell transfusions, and critical illness polyneuropathy (*N Engl J Med.* 2001;345:1359).

2. **Diabetic ketoacidosis (DKA)** may occur in any diabetic patient who is sufficiently stressed by illness or surgery. DKA patients who require an operation should be provided every attempt at correction of metabolic abnormalities before surgery, although in cases such as gangrene, surgery may be essential for treatment of the underlying cause of DKA. DKA may occur without excessive elevation of the blood glucose. Management of this disorder should emphasize volume repletion, correction of acidosis and electrolyte abnormalities, and regulation of blood glucose with insulin infusion.

   a. **Laboratory tests** should include blood glucose, CBC, serum electrolytes, serum osmolarity, and ABG.

   b. **Restoration of intravascular volume** should be initiated with isotonic (0.9%) saline or lactated Ringer's solution without glucose. Patients without cardiac disease should receive 1 L or more of fluid per hour until objective evidence of normalization of intravascular volume is demonstrated by a urine output greater than 30 mL/hour and stabilization of hemodynamics. Invasive hemodynamic monitoring may be required to guide fluid replacement in some circumstances (i.e., CHF, MI, and renal failure). Maintenance fluids of 0.45% NaCl with potassium (20 to 40 mEq/L) can be instituted when intravascular volume has been restored. Dextrose should be added to fluids when the blood glucose is less than 400 mg/dL.

   c. **Correction of acidosis** with bicarbonate therapy is controversial but should be considered if the blood pH is less than 7.1 or shock is present. Two ampules (88 mEq $NaHCO_3$) of bicarbonate can be added to 0.45% NaCl and given during the initial resuscitation.

   d. **Potassium replacement** should be instituted immediately unless hyperkalemia with ECG changes exists. In nonoliguric patients, replacement should begin with 30 to 40 mEq/hour of KCl for serum potassium of less than 3; 20 to 30 mEq/hour of KCl for serum potassium of 3 to 4; and 10 to 20 mEq/hour of KCl for potassium of greater than 4 mEq/L.

   e. **Blood glucose** can be controlled with 10 units of insulin as an IV bolus followed by insulin infusion at 2 to 10 units per hour to a target range of 200 to 300 mg/dL. When the blood glucose falls below 400 mg/dL, 5% dextrose should be added to the IV fluids. Therapy is guided by hourly blood glucose determinations.

3. **Nonketotic hyperosmolar syndrome** is characterized by severe hyperglycemia and dehydration without ketoacidosis. This occurs most often in elderly noninsulin-dependent diabetes mellitus patients with renal impairment and may be precipitated by surgical illness or stress. Laboratory findings include blood glucose that exceeds 600 mg/dL and serum osmolarity of greater than 350 mOsm/L. Therapy is similar to that for DKA but with two notable exceptions: (1) Fluid requirements are often higher, and replacement should be with 0.45% saline; and (2) total insulin requirements are less.

H. Hypertension

1. **Definition.** Postoperative hypertension should be defined by the patient's preoperative BP. Patients with chronic hypertension have a shift in their cerebral autoregulatory system that may not allow for adequate cerebral perfusion at normotensive BPs. A reasonable goal of therapy for acute postoperative hypertension is within 10% of the patient's normal BP.

2. **Treatment.** Before using antihypertensive drugs in the treatment of postoperative hypertension, it is essential to diagnose and treat potentially correctable underlying causes, such as pain, hypoxemia, hypothermia, and acidosis. Acute hypertension can be managed with clonidine (0.1 mg orally every 6 hours), hydralazine (10 to 20 mg intravenously every 6 hours), labetalol (10 to 20 mg intravenously every 10 minutes, to a total dose of 300 mg), or a nitroprusside drip (0.25 to 8 µg/kg/minute intravenously). In situations in which the patient is unable to take oral medications and IV medications are not appropriate, nitroglycerin paste (0.5 to 2 inches every 6 hours) can be used.

IV. DOCUMENTATION. Optimal patient care requires not only appropriate management but also effective communication and documentation. Documentation is essential for communication among members of the health care team, risk management, and reimbursement. All documentation should include a date, time, legible signature, and contact information (such as phone or pager number) in case clarification is necessary.

A. Hospital Orders

1. **Admission orders** should detail every aspect of a patient's care. **ADCVAANDIML** is a simple mnemonic to help in organizing admission, postoperative, and transfer orders:

   a. **Admit.** Include nursing division, surgical service, attending physician, and admission status (in-patient vs. 23-hour observation).

   b. **Diagnosis.** The principal diagnosis and, if relevant, care path. Include the operation or procedure performed.

   c. **Condition.** Distinguish among stable, guarded, and critical.

   d. **Vitals.** Include the frequency with which vital signs should be obtained and special instructions for additional monitoring such as pulse oximetry and neurologic and vascular checks.

   e. **Allergies.** Include specific reactions if known.

   f. **Activity.** Include necessary supervision and weight-bearing status, if applicable. If mobilizing the patient, include specific instructions for ambulation. Patients on bedrest should be considered for DVT prophylaxis.

   g. **Nursing orders.** These may include dressing care, drain care, urine output monitoring, antiembolic stockings, and sequential compression devices. Include specific parameters for physician notification for abnormal results (such as low urine output or low BP). Daily weights, intake and output, pulmonary toilet (such as incentive spirometry), and regimens for turning patients should be addressed here. So should **ventilator settings,** if applicable. Include mode, rate, tidal volume or pressure support, positive end-expiratory pressure (PEEP), and oxygen percentage (FiO_2).

h. **Diet.** Include diet type (e.g., regular, American Diabetes Association, and renal) and consistency (e.g., clear liquids, full liquids, and pureed) as well as supervision instructions, if applicable. Patients are NPO after midnight if a procedure requiring sedation is planned for the following day.

i. **IV fluids.** Include fluid type, rate, and time interval.

j. **Medications.** Include home medications if appropriate. Reference to patient-controlled anesthesia forms should be made here. Indications for new medications should be provided. Include the dose, route, and frequency of each medication ordered.

k. **Laboratories.** All necessary laboratory and radiographic investigations should be listed here, as well as ECGs, cardiac diagnostic laboratory testing, pulmonary function tests, and other special procedures.

2. **Review orders with nursing staff.** All orders should be reviewed with the nursing staff, particularly any unusual orders or orders that must be expedited.

3. **STAT (immediate) orders** should be designated as such on the order form and brought to the attention of the nursing staff. This is especially true for orders for new medicines because the pharmacy must be notified and the medicine brought to the floor.

4. **Discharge orders**

a. **Discharge** should include location and condition. If a transfer to another institution is planned, copies of all medical records and a copy of current orders should be included.

b. **Activity limitations,** if applicable, should be included. Workplace or school documentation may also be necessary.

c. **Medicines.** Prescriptions for new medicines as well as detailed instructions are required.

d. **Follow-up.** Follow-up plans with the appropriate physicians should be clearly indicated, with contact information for their offices.

e. **Special.** Wound care, catheter care, physical therapy, home health care needs, or special studies should be described before discharge.

B. **Hospital Notes**

1. **History and physical examination.** The admission history and physical examination should be a complete record of the patient's history. Include past medical and surgical history, social history and family history, allergies, and home medications with doses and schedules. A complete review of systems should be documented. Outpatient records are often helpful and should be obtained if possible.

2. **Preoperative notes** summarize the results of pertinent laboratory tests and other investigations before one proceeds to the operating room (Table 1-9).

TABLE 1-9	Preoperative Note
Preoperative diagnosis
Procedure planned
Attending physician
Laboratory investigations
Electrocardiogram (if applicable)
Chest X-ray and other radiology (if applicable)
Informed consent
NPO (nothing by mouth) past midnight
Type and screen/cross (if applicable)

3. **Operative notes.** A brief operative note should be placed in the written medical record immediately following the operation, including the operative findings and the patient's condition at the conclusion of the procedure (Table 1-10). The surgeon should also complete a dictated operative note immediately after the operation. This dictated note should include specific operative indications, antibiotic administration, preparation and drape position, sponge and instrument count, and copy distribution.

4. **Postoperative check.** Several hours after an operation, a patient should be examined, with vital signs and urine output reviewed. Documentation in the medical record in the form of a SOAP (subjective-objective-assessment-plan) note should be included.

5. **Discharge summary.** A detailed account of a patient's hospitalization should be dictated at the time of discharge (Table 1-11). If a dictation confirmation number is provided, it should be recorded in the written medical record as the final note of the hospitalization. A discharge summary must accompany any patient who is being transferred to another institution.

V. INFORMED CONSENT

A. **Obtaining Informed Consent.** Recognition of patient autonomy dictates that physicians provide adequate information so that patients can make informed decisions regarding their medical care. Patients should understand the disease process, the natural course of the disease, the risks and benefits of the procedure under consideration, and potential alternative therapies.

TABLE 1-10	Brief Operative Note
Preoperative diagnosis	
Postoperative diagnosis	
Procedure performed	
Attending surgeon	
Assistant/resident surgeons	
Type of anesthesia	
Operative findings and complications	
Specimens removed	
Packs, drains, and catheters	
Estimated blood loss	
Urine output	
Fluids administered	
Blood products administered	
Antibiotics administered	
Documentation that "time-out" to verify correct patient, procedure, and site was performed	
Patient disposition and condition	

The most common and serious risks of the procedure as well as aspects of the patient's condition that might affect the outcome of a planned procedure or might place the patient at increased risk should all be discussed. Recovery time, including amount and expected duration of postoperative pain, hospitalization, and future functional status, should also be reviewed. The use of invasive monitoring devices, including arterial and pulmonary artery catheters, should be explained. These discussions should use terms that are readily understood by the patient. This is also an important opportunity for a physician to learn about the patient's wishes for aggressive treatment and acceptance of limitations to functional status.

TABLE 1-11	Discharge Summary (Dictated)
Your name, date, and time of dictation	
Patient name	
Patient registration number	
Attending physician	
Date of admission	
Date of discharge	
Principal diagnosis	
Secondary diagnosis	
Brief history and physical examination	
Laboratory/radiographic findings	
Hospital course	
List of procedures performed with dates	
Discharge instructions	
Discharge condition	
Copy distribution	

B. **Documentation of Informed Consent.** An informed consent form is completed and signed by the patient before any elective operative procedure. In addition to the generic consent form, informed consent discussions should be documented in the progress notes section of the medical record. These notes should document the salient features of the informed consent discussion and specifically document that the potential complications and outcomes were explained to the patient. The patient's refusal to undergo a procedure that has been recommended by the physician should be documented clearly in the chart. In certain situations, such as a medical emergency, it is impossible to obtain informed consent. Inability to obtain consent should be documented carefully in the medical record. Local medical bylaws generally have provisions for these types of situations and should be consulted on a case-by-case basis.

VI. ADVANCE DIRECTIVES. These are legal documents that allow patients to provide specific instructions for health care treatment in the event that the patient is unable to make or communicate these decisions personally. Advance directives commonly include standard living wills and durable powers of attorney for health care. With the growing realization that medical technology can prolong life considerably and sometimes even indefinitely beyond the point of significant or meaningful recovery, the importance of these issues is clear. Patients should be offered the opportunity to execute an advance directive on admission to the hospital.

A. **Living Wills.** Provide specific instructions for the withdrawal of medical treatment in the event that a patient is unable to make treatment decisions and is terminally ill. Living wills do not include withdrawal or withholding of any procedure to provide nutrition or hydration.

B. **Durable Powers of Attorney for Health Care.** These directives allow a patient to legally designate a surrogate or proxy to make health care decisions if the patient is unable to do so. Because of the difficulty of predicting the complexities of aggressive medical management, powers of attorney are often more helpful than living wills in making difficult treatment decisions.

C. **Implementation.** Advance directives are personal documents and therefore differ from patient to patient. These documents should be reviewed carefully before implementation. Advance directives are also legal documents, and they should be displayed prominently in the medical record. To be legally binding, the documents must be executed properly. If there is any question of validity, the risk management or legal staff of the hospital should be consulted. The most effective advance directives include specific instructions for health care decisions. Important issues to be addressed include the following:

1. **Intravenous fluids**
2. **Enteral and parenteral nutrition**
3. **Medicines**
4. **Inotropic support**
5. **Renal dialysis**
6. **Mechanical ventilation**
7. **Cardiopulmonary resuscitation**

D. **Conflicts.** Although advance directives can be helpful in the management of critically ill patients, their implementation often is difficult. Advance directives, by their nature, cannot provide for every medical situation. For this reason, it is important to communicate with the patient and family before the execution of an advance directive and with the family in the event that a patient becomes incapacitated. If no advance directive is available, the physician and family must consider carefully when life-prolonging medical treatments are no longer beneficial to the patient. In such a case, the state's interest in preserving life might conflict with the desires of the family and physician. If the family and physician do not agree, the hospital ethics committee or risk management staff should be consulted.

2 Nutrition

Bernard J. DuBray Jr and J. Chris Eagon

The human body is an engine designed to burn fuel in order to perform work. The fuels we utilize are called nutrients, which come in three flavors: **carbohydrates, lipids,** and **protein.** Oxidation releases potential energy stored in the chemical bonds of nutrients, which is then harnessed in the form of ATP. Our bodies use ATP as energy currency in order to perform everything from ion transport and biomolecular synthesis to locomotion.

Dietary nutrition supplies the nutrients that drive cellular metabolism. The chemical processes that maintain cellular viability consist of catabolic (breakdown) and anabolic (synthesis) reactions. Catabolism produces energy, whereas anabolism requires energy. While both processes occur concomitantly, our collective metabolism can be driven in either direction to balance our energy needs. Feeding drives synthesis and storage, whereas starvation promotes the mobilization of energy. In preparation to "fight or flight," physiological stressors also mobilize energy stores. Populations stressed by surgery are at a unique metabolic disadvantage since they are often nutritionally restricted perioperatively. A through understanding of metabolism and its influences is necessary to assess for nutritional adequacy in surgical patients.

NUTRIENT METABOLISM

I. **CARBOHYDRATES. Glucose** is the functional unit of carbohydrate metabolism. It is the body's primary energy source, providing 30% to 40% of calories in a typical diet. The brain and red blood cells rely almost exclusively on a steady supply of glucose to function. Whereas each gram of enteral carbohydrate provides **4 kcal** of energy, parenteral formulations are hydrated and thus provide only **3.4 kcal/g.**

A. **Glucose stores.** During fed states, hyperglycemia leads to insulin secretion, which promotes glycogen synthesis. About **12 hours** worth of glycogen is available in the **liver and skeletal muscles,** which can provide a steady supply of glucose in between meals. In times of starvation and stress, depleted glycogen stores cause the release of glucagon, which promotes hepatic gluconeogenesis from amino acids. If dietary carbohydrates are not resumed, glucagon promotes ketone body formation from lipids, which the brain can utilize. A minimum intake of 400 calories of carbohydrate per day minimizes protein breakdown, which can be given in maintenance intravenous (IV) fluids during times of nil per os (NPO).

B. **Carbohydrate digestion** is initiated by the action of salivary amylase, and absorption is generally completed within the first 1 to 1.5 m of small intestine. Salivary and pancreatic amylases cleave starches into oligosaccharides. Surface oligosaccharidases then hydrolyze and transport these molecules across the gastrointestinal (GI) tract mucosa. Diseases that result in generalized mucosal flattening (e.g., celiac sprue, Whipple disease, and hypogammaglobulinemia) may cause diminished uptake of carbohydrates because of resultant deficiencies in oligosaccharidases.

II. **LIPIDS. Fatty acids** are the functional units of lipid metabolism. They comprise 25% to 45% of calories in the typical diet. During starvation, lipids provide the majority of energy in the form of ketone bodies converted by the liver from long-chain fatty acids. Each gram of lipid provides **9 kcal** of energy.

A. **Lipid Storage.** Bound to a glycerol backbone, free fatty acids join to form triacylglycerols during fed states. **Triglycerides** are stored in adipocytes and can be mobilized in times of stress or starvation. Lipids are important energy sources for the heart, liver, and skeletal muscle. Lipolysis is stimulated by steroids, catecholamines, and glucagon. Insulin promotes synthesis and storage.

Roles of lipids. Whereas carbohydrates are used exclusively for fuel, lipids have additional functional and structural roles. In addition to energy storage, lipids **comprise membranes in cells,** serve as **signaling factors,** and are contained in certain **vitamins.**

B. **Digestion and absorption of lipids** is complex and utilizes nearly the entire GI tract. Coordination between **biliary and pancreatic secretions** as well as a functional jejunum and ileum are necessary. Fat in the duodenum stimulates cholecystokinin and secretin release, which leads to gallbladder contraction and pancreatic enzyme release, respectively. **Pancreatic secretions** contain a combination of lipase, cholesterol esterase, and phospholipase A_2. In the alkaline environment of the duodenum, lipase hydrolyzes triglycerides to one monoglyceride and two fatty acids. Bile salts emulsify fat into micelles, which facilitates absorption across the intestinal mucosal barrier by creating a hydrophilic outer coating. Bile salts are then reabsorbed in the terminal ileum to maintain the bile salt pool **(i.e., the enterohepatic circulation).** The liver is able to compensate for moderate intestinal bile salt losses by increased synthesis from cholesterol. Major ileal resection may lead to depletion of the bile salt pool and subsequent fat malabsorption. Clinical lipid deficiency results in a generalized scaling rash, poor wound healing, hepatic steatosis, and bone changes. This condition is usually a consequence of long-term fat-free parenteral nutrition, in which high glucose levels stimulate relative hyperinsulinemia, thus inhibiting lipolysis and preventing peripheral essential fatty acid liberation. This can be avoided by providing at least 3% of caloric intake as parenteral lipid.

III. **PROTEIN. Amino acids** are the functional units of protein metabolism. Whereas the body has energy reserves for carbohydrates and lipids, there are no stores of protein. All of the body's protein serves a functional purpose. Proteins are important for the biosynthesis of enzymes, structural molecules, and immunoglobulins. When energy needs are unmet by nutrition, muscle breakdown yields amino acids for hepatic gluconeogenesis, which can lead to wasting and deconditioning in severe circumstances. Each gram of protein can be converted into **4 kcal** of energy.

Daily protein requirements in the average healthy adult without excessive losses are approximately 0.8 g/kg body weight. In the United States, the

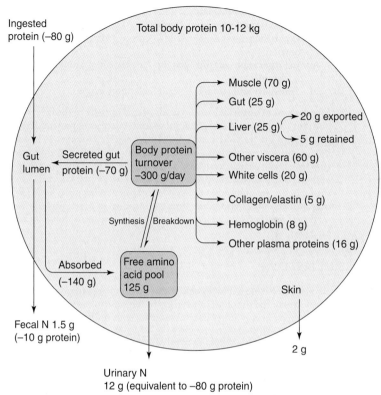

Figure 2-1. Distribution and utilization of total body protein. (Adapted from Mulholland MW, Lillemoe KD, Doherty GM, et al. Whole body protein metabolism in a normal 70 kg man. In: Greenfield LJ, Mulholland MW. *Greenfield's Surgery: Scientific Principles and Practice.* 5th ed., Philadelphia: Wolters Kluwer Health/Lippincott Williams & Wilkins; 2010:56.)

typical daily intake averages twice this amount. Requirements for patients with acute illness increase to 1.2 g/kg/day and up to 2.5 g/kg/day in severely physiologically stressed patients in the intensive care unit (Fig. 2-1).

A. **Digestion of proteins** yields dipeptides and single amino acids, which are actively absorbed. Gastric pepsin initiates the process of digestion. Pancreatic proteases, activated on exposure to enterokinase found throughout the duodenal mucosa, are the principal effectors of protein degradation. Once digested, almost 50% of protein absorption occurs in the duodenum, and complete protein absorption is achieved by the midjejunum. Protein absorption can effectively occur at every level of the small intestine; therefore, clinically significant protein malabsorption is relatively infrequent, even after extensive intestinal resection. The 20 amino acids are divided into essential and nonessential groups, depending on whether they can be synthesized *de novo* in the body.

1. **Major roles of amino acids** include the following:
   a. **Synthesis and recycling** of proteins.
   b. **Catabolic reactions,** resulting in energy generation and CO_2 production.
   c. **Incorporation of nitrogen** into nonessential amino acids and nucleotides.
   d. **Transport and storage** of small molecules and ions.

B. **Metabolism of absorbed amino acids** occurs initially in the liver where portions of amino acids are extracted to form circulating proteins. Excess amino acids can have their carbon skeletons oxidized for energy. In addition to dietary metabolism, existing structural protein is continuously recycled. Daily protein turnover is 250 to 300 g, or approximately 3% of total body protein. The primary site of turnover is the GI tract, where shed enterocytes and secreted digestive enzymes are regularly lost. Obligate nitrogen losses also occur from an inability to reuse nitrogen with 100% efficiency. Nitrogen loss of 10 to 15 g/day occurs through urinary excretion.

STRESS METABOLISM

Alterations in metabolism due to physiologic stress share similar patterns with simple starvation. Regardless of the stimulus, our conserved response to stress is the same—catabolic shifts mobilize energy stores in order to prepare us to "fight or flight."

A. **Simple Starvation.** After an overnight fast, liver glycogen is rapidly depleted as glucagon responds to falling serum glucose levels. Carbohydrate stores are exhausted after 24 hours. For the first few days during starvation, caloric needs are met by fat and protein degradation. Most of the protein is from breakdown of skeletal and visceral muscle, which is converted to glucose via hepatic gluconeogenesis. The brain preferentially uses this endogenously produced glucose, with the remainder consumed by red blood cells and leukocytes. Within approximately 10 days of starvation, the brain adapts and uses fat in the form of ketoacids as its fuel source. Produced by the liver from free fatty acids, the use of ketoacids has a protein-sparing effect.

B. **Physiologic stress.** The interaction of metabolic and endocrine responses that result from major operation, trauma, or sepsis can be divided into three phases.

1. **Catabolic phase.** After major injury, the metabolic demand is dramatically increased, as reflected in a significant rise in the urinary excretion of nitrogen (beyond that seen in simple starvation). Following a major surgical procedure, protein depletion inevitably occurs because patients are commonly prevented from eating in addition to having an elevated basal metabolic rate. The hormonal response of physiologic stress includes elevation in the serum levels of glucagon, glucocorticoids, and catecholamines and reduction in insulin.

2. The **early anabolic phase** is also called the *corticoid withdrawal phase* as the body shifts from catabolism to anabolism. The timing of this event

is variable, depending on the severity of stress, and ranges from several days to several weeks. The period of anabolism can last from a few weeks to a few months, depending on many factors, including the ability of the patient to obtain and use nutrients and the extent to which protein stores have been depleted. This phase is marked by a positive nitrogen balance, and there is a rapid and progressive gain in weight and muscular strength. The total amount of nitrogen gained is equivalent to the amount lost in the catabolic phase; however, the rate of repletion is much slower than the rapid rate of protein depletion after the original insult.

3. The **late anabolic phase** is the final period of recovery and may last from several weeks to months. Adipose stores are replenished gradually and nitrogen balance equilibrates. Weight gain is much slower during this period than in the early anabolic phase due to the higher caloric content of fat—the primary energy stores deposited during the early anabolic phase—as compared to protein.

NUTRITIONAL ASSESSMENT

Nutrition plays a vital and often underappreciated role in the recovery of patients from surgery. It is estimated that between 30% and 50% of hospitalized patients are malnourished. While most healthy patients can tolerate 7 days of starvation, subjects to major trauma, surgery, sepsis, or other critical illness require nutritional intervention earlier. Poor nutrition has deleterious effects on wound healing and immune function, which increases postoperative morbidity and mortality. Identification of those at risk for malnutrition is made through ongoing clinical assessments by vigilant clinicians.

I. TYPES OF MALNUTRITION

A. Overnutrition. Obesity as defined by body mass index >30

B. Undernutrition

1. Caloric
   a. **Marasmus** is characterized by inadequate protein *and* caloric intake, typically caused by illness-induced anorexia. It is a chronic nutritional deficiency marked by losses in weight, body fat, and skeletal muscle mass. Visceral protein stores remain normal, as do most lab indices.

2. Noncaloric
   a. **Kwashiorkor** is characterized by catabolic protein loss, resulting in **hypoalbuminemia** and generalized **edema.** This form of malnutrition develops with prolonged starvation or severe stress. Even in a well-nourished patient, a severe stress (e.g., major burn or prolonged sepsis) may rapidly lead to depletion of visceral protein stores and impairment in immune function.
   b. **Vitamins and trace elements.** In addition to the principle sources of energy, our metabolic machinery also requires various other substances in order to function efficiently. Vitamins are involved with

TABLE 2-1	Vitamins	

Vitamin	Function	Deficiency State
Fat Soluble		
A (Retinol)	Rhodopsin synthesis	Xerophthalmia, keratomalacia
D (Cholecalciferol)	Intestinal calcium absorption, bone remodeling	Rickets (children), osteomalacia (adults)
E (α-Tocopherol)	Antioxidant	Hemolytic anemia, neurologic damage
K (Naphthoquinone)	τ-Carboxylation of glutamate in clotting factors	Coagulopathy (deficiency in factors II, VII, IX, and XI)
Water Soluble		
B$_1$ (Thioamide)	Decarboxylation and aldehyde transfer reactions	Beriberi, neuropathy, fatigue, heart failure
B$_2$ (Riboflavin)	Oxidation-reduction reactions	Dermatitis, glossitis
B$_5$ (Niacin)	Oxidation-reduction reactions	Pellagra (dermatitis, diarrhea, dementia, death)
B$_6$ (Pyridoxal phosphate)	Transamination and decarboxylation reactions	Neuropathy, glossitis, anemia
B$_7$ (Biotin)	Carboxylation reactions	Dermatitis, alopecia
B$_9$ (Folate)	DNA synthesis	Megaloblastic anemia, glossitis
B$_{12}$ (Cyanocobalamin)	DNA synthesis, myelination	Megaloblastic anemia, Neuropathy
C (Ascorbic acid)	Hydroxylation of hormones, hydroxylation of proline in collagen synthesis, antioxidant	Scurvy

Adapted from Atluri P, Karakousis GC, Porrett PM, Kaiser LR. Vitamins. In: *The Surgical Review: An Integrated Basic Science and Clinical Science Study Guide.* 2nd ed. Philadelphia: Lippincott Williams & Wilkins; 2006:252.

wound healing and healthy immune function while many trace elements are important as cofactors and enzymatic catalysts. **These substances cannot be synthesized *de novo*** and therefore must be part of dietary intake. Deficiencies can have a multitude of detrimental effects (Tables 2-1 and 2-2).

TABLE 2-2	Minerals	
Trace Element	Function	Deficiency
Chromium	Promotes normal glucose utilization in combination with insulin	Glucose intolerance, peripheral neuropathy
Copper	Component of enzymes	Hypochromic microcytic anemia, neutropenia, bone demineralization, diarrhea
Fluorine	Essential for normal structure of bones and teeth	Caries
Iodine	Thyroid hormone production	Endemic goiter, hypothyroidism, myxedema, cretinism
Iron	Hemoglobin synthesis	Hypochromic microcytic anemia, glossitis, stomatitis
Manganese	Component of enzymes, essential for normal bone structure	Dermatitis, weight loss, nausea, vomiting, coagulopathy
Molybdenum	Component of enzymes	Neurologic abnormalities, night blindness
Selenium	Component of enzymes, antioxidant	Cardiomyopathy
Zinc	Component of enzymes involved in metabolism of lipids, proteins, carbohydrates, nucleic acids	Alopecia, hypogonadism, olfactory and gustatory dysfunction, impaired wound healing, acrodermatitis enteropathica, growth arrest

Adapted from Atluri P, Karakousis GC, Porrett PM, Kaiser LR. Trace elements. In: *The Surgical Review: An Integrated Basic Science and Clinical Science Study Guide.* 2nd ed. Philadelphia: Lippincott Williams & Wilkins; 2006:253.

II. CLINICAL ASSESSMENT

A. **History.** Every good clinical assessment should begin with a thorough history from the patient. Specific inquiries pertinent to nutritional status include recent history of weight fluctuation with attention as to the timing and intent.

Recent weight loss (5% in the last month or 10% over 6 months) or a current body weight of 80% to 85% (or less) of ideal body weight suggests significant malnutrition. Anorexia, nausea, vomiting, dysphagia, odynophagia, gastroesophageal reflux, or a history of generalized muscle weakness should prompt further evaluation. A complete history of current medications is essential to alert caretakers to potential underlying deficiencies as well as drug–nutrient interactions.

B. **Physical examination** may identify muscle wasting (especially thenar and temporal muscles), loose or flabby skin (indicating loss of subcutaneous fat), and peripheral edema and/or ascites (as a result of hypoproteinemia). Subtler findings of nutritional deficiency include skin rash, pallor, glossitis, gingival lesions, hair changes, hepatomegaly, neuropathy, and dementia (*The A.S.P.E.N. nutrition support practice manual,* 1998).

Adjuncts to physical examination:

Anthropometric measurements such as triceps skinfold thickness and midarm muscle circumference reflect body-fat stores and skeletal muscle mass, respectively. These values are standardized for gender and height and should be reported as a percentage of the predicted value. Along with body mass index, these values allow the clinician to assess the patient's visceral and somatic protein mass and fat reserve.

Creatinine-height index can be used to determine the degree of malnutrition. A 24-hour urinary creatinine excretion is measured and compared to normal standards. The creatinine height index is calculated using the following equation:

$$\text{CHI} = \frac{\text{Actual 24-hour creatinine excretion}}{\text{Predicted creatinine excretion}}.$$

Greater than 80% represents no to mild protein depletion, 60% to 80% represents moderate depletion, and less than 60% represents severe depletion.

C. **Laboratory tests** associated with nutrition are nonspecific indicators of the *degree of illness* rather than strict markers of nutrition. **Albumin, prealbumin, and transferrin** vary with the hepatic metabolic (decreased synthesis) and capillary leak (diluted serum levels) response to inflammation as well as the nutritional status (*J Am Diet Assoc.* 2004;104(8):1258–1264). Levels associated with illness are as follows:

1. **Serum albumin** of less than 3.5 g/dL (35 g/L) in a stable, hydrated patient; half-life is 14 to 20 days.

2. **Serum prealbumin** may be a more useful indicator of acute changes: 10 to 17 mg/dL corresponds to mild depletion, 5 to 10 mg/dL to moderate depletion, and less than 5 mg/dL to severe depletion; half-life is 2 to 3 days.

3. **Serum transferrin** of less than 200 mg/dL; half-life is 8 to 10 days.

III. ESTIMATION OF ENERGY NEEDS

A. **Basal energy expenditure** can be predicted by using the Harris-Benedict equation (in kilocalories per day):

> For **men** equals
> $66.4 + [13.7 \times \text{weight (kg)}] + [5 \times \text{height (cm)}] - [6.8 \times \text{age (years)}]$.
> For **women** equals
> $65.5 + [9.6 \times \text{weight (kg)}] + [1.7 \times \text{height (cm)}] - [4.7 \times \text{age (years)}]$.

These equations provide a reliable estimate of the energy requirements in approximately 80% of hospitalized patients. The actual caloric need is obtained by multiplying basal energy expenditure by specific stress factors (Table 2-3). Most stressed patients require 25 to 35 kcal/kg/day. In obese patients, these equations tend to overestimate caloric needs.

TABLE 2-3	Disease Stress Factors Used in Calculation of Total Energy Expenditure
Clinical Condition	**Stress Factor**
Starvation	0.80–1.00
Elective operation	1.00–1.10
Peritonitis or other infections	1.05–1.25
Adult respiratory distress syndrome or sepsis	1.30–1.35
Bone marrow transplant	1.20–1.30
Cardiopulmonary disease (noncomplicated)	0.80–1.00
Cardiopulmonary disease with dialysis or sepsis	1.20–1.30
Cardiopulmonary disease with major surgery	1.30–1.55
Acute renal failure	1.30
Liver failure	1.30–1.55
Liver transplant	1.20–1.50
Pancreatitis	1.30–1.80

Adapted from Shoppell JM, Hopkins B, Shronts EP. Nutrition screening and assessment. In: Gottschlich M, ed. *The Science and Practice of Nutrition Support: A Case Based Core Curriculum.* Dubuque, IA: Kendall/Hunt; 2001:107–140.

TABLE 2-4	Estimated Protein Requirements in Various Disease States

Clinical Condition	Protein Requirements (g/kg ideal body weight per day)
Healthy, nonstressed	0.80
Bone marrow transplant	1.40–1.50
Liver disease without encephalopathy	1.00–1.50
Liver disease with encephalopathy	0.50–0.75 (advance as tolerated)
Renal failure without dialysis	0.60–1.00
Renal failure with dialysis	1.00–1.30
Pregnancy	1.30–1.50
Simplified Estimates	
Mild metabolic stress (elective hospitalization)	1.00–1.10
Moderate metabolic stress (complicated postoperative care, infection)	1.20–1.40
Severe metabolic stress (major trauma, pancreatitis, sepsis)	1.50–2.50

Adapted from Nagel M. Nutrition screening: identifying patients at risk for malnutrition. *Nutr Clin Pract.* 1998;8:171–175.

B. **Estimates of protein requirements.** The appropriate calorie:nitrogen ratio is approximately 150:1 (calorie:protein ratio of 24:1), which increases to 300:1 to 400:1 in uremia. In the absence of severe renal or hepatic dysfunction, approximately **1.5 g protein per kilogram body weight** should be provided daily (Table 2-4).

Twenty-four-hour nitrogen balance is calculated by subtracting nitrogen loss from nitrogen intake. Nitrogen intake is the sum of nitrogen delivered from enteral and parenteral feedings. Nitrogen is lost through urine, fistula drainage, diarrhea, and so on. The usual approach is to measure the urine urea nitrogen concentration of a 24-hour urine collection and multiply by urine volume to estimate 24-hour urinary loss. Nitrogen loss equals $1.2 \times$ [24-hour urine urea nitrogen (g per day)] + 2 g per day as a correction factor to account for nitrogen losses in stool and skin exfoliation.

NUTRITION ADMINISTRATION

Surgical patients present a unique set of challenges to clinicians who must determine **when, how, and what** to feed them. Safe administration of an oral diet requires that the patient should have an intact chewing/swallowing mechanism along with a functioning alimentary tract. The timing, route, and type of nutrition are important considerations in surgical patients.

A. **Initial timing of administration.** Open abdominal surgery produces a **paralytic ileus** of variable length that alters the digestion and absorption of nutrients. Resolution, marked by the passage of flatus, occurs in most patients within 72 hours of surgery and is symptomatic of functional GI continuity. Traditionally, postoperative patients were maintained on dextrose-containing IV fluids and kept NPO for up to 7 days until evidence of bowel function returned. Several strategies have recently emerged to shorten postoperative ileus.

Strategies to hasten GI recovery following abdominal surgery:

1. **Laparoscopic surgery** is less traumatic and has been associated with shorter periods of ileus versus open approaches.

2. **Epidural analgesia** with an infusion of local anesthetic minimizes narcotic dependence on pain control and thus its adverse effects on gut motility (*Cleve Clin J Med.* 2009;76(11):641–648). In addition, thoracic epidurals are efficient at blocking many of the sympathetic reflex arcs that inhibit gut motility. Clinicians should be aware of the side effects of epidurals, which include hypotension and urinary retention.

3. **Selective use of nasogastric tubes** has been shown to decrease rates of pneumonia, fever, and atelectasis while hastening resumption of oral feeding (*Ann Surg.* 1995;221(5):469–476).

4. **Early enteral feeding** has been evaluated in a meta-analysis of 13 RCTs consisting of 1,173 patients undergoing GI surgery (*J Gastrointest Surg.* 2009;13(3):569–575). There were no significant differences in morbidity between groups fed within 24 hours and those fed after traditional return of bowel function.

> It is important to note that an ileus must be distinguished from more ominous conditions, such as an obstruction. A prolonged ileus may be the result of intra-abdominal pathology.

B. **Route of administration.** Oral administration of nutrition is the preferred route since it is the most physiologic and the least invasive. In patients with a functioning GI tract, several requirements must still be met, however, before initiating an oral diet.

1. **Mental alertness and orientation.** Patients who have altered mentation are at increased risk for aspiration and should not begin an oral nutrition regimen.

2. **Intact chewing/swallowing mechanism.** Patients who have had a stroke or undergone pharyngeal surgery may have difficulty swallowing. They may be candidates for modified oral diets, such as mechanical soft, or pureed.

C. **Diet selection**

1. **Transitional diets** minimize digestive stimulation and colonic residue while providing more calories than IV fluids alone in patients recovering from postoperative ileus. Advancement to the next stage should be predicated on frequent assessment of the patient's bowel function in the absence of nausea, vomiting, or distention (*Manual of Clinical Nutrition Management,* 2009).

Clear liquids provide fluids mostly in the form of sugar and water. Patients with evidence of bowel function or who have undergone laparoscopic surgery can be given clear liquids and expect between 700 and 1,000 additional kcal per day. Examples include most juices, coffee, and tea.

Full liquids are a bit more substantive and include foods that are liquid at body temperature, such as gels and frozen liquids. In addition, full liquids contain dairy products and would not be appropriate in patients who are lactose intolerant. Transition to full liquids is good for patients who have undergone head and neck surgery and thus may have some difficulty swallowing postoperatively. At goal, full liquids provide approximately 1,200 kcal and 40 g of protein per day (*Manual of Clinical Nutrition Management,* 2009).

Regular diet represents an unrestricted regimen that includes various foods designed to meet all caloric, protein, and elemental needs.

2. **Surgery-specific diets**
   a. **Postgastrectomy diet.** Procedures that reduce the reservoir capacity of the stomach can produce a "dumping syndrome" postoperatively. When undigested, hyperosmolar, food reaches the small bowel, massive fluid shifts lead to diaphoresis, abdominal cramping, and diarrhea. The postgastrectomy diet encourages small, frequent meals that minimize fluid intake and simple carbohydrates. Caloric needs are met mostly by protein and lipids (*Manual of Clinical Nutrition Management,* 2009).

Procedures that can cause dumping syndrome

Standard Whipple procedure
Partial/total gastrectomy/antrectomy
Esophagectomy
Pyloromyotomy

---

   b. **Postgastric bypass.** Patients who undergo bariatric surgery have unique postoperative nutritional needs as well as long-term goals of sustained weight loss.

   Postbariatric surgery transitional diets emphasize small meals without added sugar to avoid stretching the pouch and dumping syndrome, respectively. Patients progress from clear liquid to the regular bariatric diet in approximately 6 weeks. During this time, patients are taught to eat 3 to 5 small meals per day **slowly** over a period of 45 minutes in order to stay fuller longer. This pattern is preferred to "grazing" (small, frequent meals), which leads to higher caloric intake.

   Long-term nutritional goals promote healthy food choices that maintain weight loss while minimizing dyspepsia. Foods such as chicken, fish, fruit, vegetables, and salad are well tolerated by bariatric patients, whereas steak, rice, bread, soda, and ice cream are associated with dyspepsia and should be avoided.

   c. **Low-residue diet** is essentially a low-fiber diet (<10g/day) and is intended to delay transit, reduce residue, and allow bowel rest in times of colonic inflammation and/or irritation. Patients who benefit from a low-residue diet include those going through an acute phase of **IBD, diverticulitis, or regional enteritis** (*Manual of Clinical Nutrition Management,* 2009).

NUTRITIONAL SUPPORT

The need for nutritional support should be assessed continually in patients both preoperatively and postoperatively. Most elective surgical patients have adequate fuel reserves to withstand common catabolic stresses and partial starvation for up to 7 days and do not benefit from perioperative nutritional support (*Nutrition.* 2000;16(9):723–728). For these patients, IV fluids with appropriate electrolytes and a minimum of 100 g glucose daily (to minimize protein catabolism) is adequate. However, even well-nourished patients can quickly become malnourished following a major operation or trauma (*Curr Probl Surg.* 1995;32(10):833–917). Without nutritional intervention, these patients may suffer complications related to impaired immune function and poor wound healing from depleted visceral protein stores. Patients with a significant degree of preoperative malnutrition have less reserve, tolerate catabolic stress and starvation poorly, and are at higher risk for postoperative complications.

ROUTES OF NUTRITIONAL SUPPORT

A. **Enteral.** In general, the enteral route is preferred to the parenteral route. Enteral feeding is simple, physiologic, and relatively inexpensive. Enteral feeding maintains the GI tract cytoarchitecture and mucosal integrity (via trophic effects), absorptive function, and normal microbial flora. This results in less bacterial translocation and endotoxin release from the intestinal lumen into the bloodstream (*Nutrition.* 2000;16(7–8):606–611). Choice of appropriate feeding site, administration technique, formula, and equipment may circumvent these problems.

Enteral feedings are **indicated** for patients who have a functional GI tract but are unable to sustain an adequate oral diet.

Enteral feedings may be **contraindicated** in patients with an intestinal obstruction, ileus, GI bleeding, severe diarrhea, vomiting, enterocolitis, or a high-output enterocutaneous fistula.

---

1. **Feeding tubes.** Nasogastric, nasojejunal (e.g., Dobhoff), gastrostomy, and jejunal tubes are available for the administration of enteral feeds. Percutaneous gastrostomy tubes can be placed endoscopically or under fluoroscopy.

2. **Enteral feeding products.** Various commercially available enteral formulas are available. Standard solutions provide 1 kcal/mL; calorically concentrated solutions (>1 kcal/mL) are available for patients who require volume restriction. The available dietary formulations for enteral feedings can be divided into polymeric (blenderized and nutritionally complete commercial formulas), chemically defined formulas (elemental diets), and modular formulas (Table 2-5).

TABLE 2-5 Enteral Formulas

Product	Description	kcal/mL	mOsm	Protein g (% kcal)	Carbohydrates g (% kcal)	Fat g (% kcal)	H$_2$O (mL)	Na (mEq)	K (mEq)	Ca (mg)	PO$_4$ (mg)	Vitamin K (mg)
Standard												
Ensure	Lactose-free, low residue	1.06	470	37.2 (14)	145 (54.5)	37.2 (31.5)	845	36.8	40	530	530	43
Osmolite	Isotonic, lactose-free, low residue	1.06	300	37.2 (14)	145 (54.6)	38.5 (31.4)	841	27.6	25.9	530	530	43
Jevity	Isotonic, lactose-free, high dietary fiber (14.4 g/L), high nitrogen content	1.06	310	44.4 (16.7)	151.7 (53.3)	36.8 (30)	833	40.4	40	909	756	61
Glucerna	Lactose-free, low carbohydrates, high fiber (14.4 g/L)	1	375	41.8 (16.7)	93.7 (33.3)	55.7 (50)	873	40.3	40	703	703	57
Low Volume												
Ensure Plus	Lactose-free, low residue	1.5	690	54.9 (14.7)	200 (53.3)	53.3 (32)	769	45.9	49.7	704	704	57
Magnacal	Lactose-free, low residue	2	590	70 (14)	250 (50)	80 (34)	690	43.5	32	1,000	1,000	300
Low Volume, High Nitrogen												
Ensure Plus HN	Lactose-free, low residue	1.5	650	62.6 (16.7)	199.9 (53.3)	50 (30)	769	51.5	46.5	1,056	1,056	85
Perative	Lactose-free, low residue	1.3	425	66.6 (20.5)	177 (54.5)	37.3 (25)	789	45.2	44.3	867	867	70

Per 1,000 mL

Very High Nitrogen

Replete with Fiber	Lactose-free, high fiber (14 g/L)	1	300	62.5 (25)	113 (45)	34 (30)	840	21.7	40	1,000	1,000	80
Sustacal	Lactose-free, low residue	1.01	650	61 (24)	140 (55)	23 (21)	840	40	54	1,010	930	240
Elemental												
Vivonex TEN	Elemental, low fat, low residue	1	630	38.2 (15.3)	205.6 (82.2)	2.77 (2.5)	845	20	20	500	500	22.3
Pudding (per 5-oz serving)												
Ensure Pudding	Contains lactose		250	6.8	34.0	9.7		10.4	8.5	200	200	12
Modulars (analysis per tablespoon)												
Polycose Liquid	Glucose polymer		30		7.5							
ProMod	Protein supplement		17	3	0.4	0.4		0	1	15.6	15.6	
Microlipid	Fat supplement		67.5			7.5						
MCT Oil	MCT supplement		115.5			14						

MCT, medium-chain triglycerides.

3. **Enteral feeding protocols.** It is recommended to start with a full-strength formula at a slow rate, which is steadily advanced. This reduces the risk of microbial contamination and achieves goal intake earlier. Conservative initiation and advancement are recommended for patients who are critically ill, those who have not been fed for some time, and those receiving a high-osmolarity or calorie-dense formula.

   a. **Bolus feedings** are reserved for patients with nasogastric or gastrostomy feeding tubes. Feedings are administered by gravity, begin at 50 to 100 mL every 4 hours, and are increased in 50-mL increments until goal intake is reached (usually 240 to 360 mL every 4 hours). Tracheobronchial aspiration is a potentially serious complication because feedings are prepyloric. To reduce the risk of aspiration, the patient's head and body should be elevated to 30 to 45 degrees during feeding and for 1 to 2 hours after each feeding. The gastric residual volume should be measured before administration of the feeding bolus. If this volume is greater than 50% of the previous bolus, the next feeding should be held. The feeding tube should be flushed with approximately 30 mL of water after each use. Free water volume can be adjusted as needed to treat hypo- or hypernatremia.

   b. **Continuous infusion** administered by a pump is generally required for nasojejunal, gastrojejunal, or jejunal tubes. Feedings are initiated at 20 mL/hour and increased in 10- to 20-mL/hour increments every 4 to 6 hours until the desired goal is reached. The feeding tube should be flushed with approximately 30 mL of water every 4 hours. Feedings should be held or advancement should be slowed if abdominal distension or pain develops. For some patients, the entire day's feeding can be infused over 8 to 12 hours at night to allow the patient mobility free from the infusion pump during the day.

4. **Conversion to oral feeding.** When supplementation is no longer needed, an oral diet is resumed gradually. In an effort to stimulate appetite, enteral feeding can be modified by the following measures:

   a. **Providing fewer feedings.**

   b. **Holding daytime feedings.**

   c. **Decreasing the volume of feedings.** When oral intake provides approximately 75% of the required calories, tube feedings can be stopped.

5. **Complications**

   a. **Metabolic derangements.** Abnormalities in serum electrolytes, calcium, magnesium, and phosphorus can be minimized through vigilant monitoring. **Hypernatremia** may lead to the development of mental lethargy or obtundation. This is treated with the slow administration of free water by giving either dextrose 5% in water (D_5W) intravenously or additional water in the tube feedings. **Hyperglycemia** may occur in patients receiving tube feeds and is particularly common in preexisting diabetics or in the setting of sepsis. A sliding scale insulin protocol along with long-acting agents should be used to treat hyperglycemia in tube-fed patients.

b. **Clogging** can usually be prevented by careful routine flushing of the feeding tube. Instillation of carbonated soda, cranberry juice, or pancreatic enzyme replacement is sometimes useful for unclogging feeding tubes. Note the use of a 1 mL syringe with stopcock and IV tubing will generate a greater pressure than 60 mL GU syringe ($P = F/A$).

c. **Tracheobronchial aspiration** of tube feeds may occur with patients who are fed into the stomach or proximal small intestine and can lead to major morbidity. Patients at particular risk are those with central nervous system abnormalities and those who are sedated. Precautions include frequent assessment of gastric residuals as well as head of bed elevation.

d. **High gastric residuals** as a result of outlet obstruction, dysmotility, intestinal ileus, or bowel obstruction may limit the usefulness of nasogastric or gastrostomy feeding tubes. Treatment of this problem should be directed at the underlying cause. Gastroparesis frequently occurs in diabetic or head-injured patients. Promotility agents such as metoclopramide or erythromycin may aid in gastric emptying. If gastric retention prevents the administration of sufficient calories and intestinal ileus or obstruction can be excluded, a nasojejunal or jejunostomy feeding tube may be necessary.

e. **Diarrhea** occurs in 10% to 20% of patients; however, other causes of diarrhea (e.g., *Clostridium difficile* colitis) should be considered. Diarrhea may result from an overly rapid increase in the volume of hyperosmolar tube feedings, medications (e.g., metoclopramide), a high-fat diet, or the presence of components not tolerated by the patient (e.g., lactose). If other causes of diarrhea can be excluded, the volume or concentration of tube feedings should be decreased. If no improvement occurs, a different formula should be used. Antidiarrheal agents such as loperamide should be reserved for patients with severe diarrhea who have had infectious etiologies excluded.

B. **Parenteral nutrition** is indicated for patients who require nutritional support but cannot meet their needs through oral intake and for whom enteral feeding is contraindicated or not tolerated.

1. **Peripheral parenteral nutrition (PPN)** is administered through a peripheral IV catheter. The osmolarity of PPN solutions generally is limited to 1,000 mOsm (approximately 12% dextrose solution) to avoid phlebitis. Consequently, unacceptably large volumes (>2,500 mL) are necessary to meet the typical patient's nutritional requirements. Temporary nutritional supplementation with PPN may be useful in selected patients but is not typically indicated.

2. **Total parenteral nutrition (TPN)** provides complete nutritional support (*Surgery.* 1968;64(1):134–142). The solution, volume of administration, and additives are individualized on the basis of an assessment of the nutritional requirements.

a. **Access.** TPN solutions must be administered through a central venous catheter. A dedicated single-lumen catheter or a multilumen catheter can be used. Catheters should be replaced for unexplained fever or bacteremia.

b. TPN solutions are generally administered as a 3-in-1 admixture of protein, as amino acids (10%; 4 kcal/g); carbohydrate, as dextrose (70%; 3.4 kcal/g); and fat, as a lipid emulsion of soybean or safflower oil (20%; 9 kcal/g). Alternatively, the lipid emulsion can be administered as a separate IV "piggyback" infusion. Special solutions that contain low, intermediate, or high nitrogen concentrations as well as varying amounts of fat and carbohydrate are available for patients with diabetes, renal or pulmonary failure, or hepatic dysfunction.

Additives. Other elements can be added to the basic TPN solutions.

(1) Electrolytes (i.e., sodium, potassium, chloride, acetate, calcium, magnesium, phosphate) should be adjusted daily. The number of cations and anions must balance; this is achieved by altering the concentrations of chloride and acetate. The calcium:phosphate ratio must be monitored to prevent salt precipitation.

(2) Medications such as albumin, H_2-receptor antagonists, heparin, iron, dextran, insulin, and metoclopramide can be administered in TPN solutions. Regular insulin should initially be administered subcutaneously on the basis of the blood glucose level. After a stable insulin requirement has been established, insulin can then be administered via TPN solution—generally at two thirds the daily subcutaneous insulin dose.

(3) Vitamins and trace elements are added daily using a commercially prepared mixture (e.g., 10 mL MVI-12; 1 mL trace element-5: 1 mg copper, 12 µg chromium, 0.3 µg manganese, 60 µg selenium, and 5 mg zinc). Vitamin K is not included in most multivitamin mixtures and must be added separately (10 mg once a week).

C. **Administration of TPN** is most commonly a **continuous infusion.** A new 3-in-1 admixture bag of TPN is administered daily at a constant infusion rate over 24 hours. Additional maintenance IV fluids are unnecessary, and total infused volume should be kept constant while nutritional content is increased. Serum electrolytes should be obtained and TPN adjusted until the patient can be maintained on a stable regimen.

1. **Cyclic administration of TPN** solutions may be useful for selected patients, including (1) those who will be discharged from the hospital and subsequently receive home TPN, (2) those with limited IV access who require administration of other medications, and (3) those who are metabolically stable and desire a period during the day when they can be free of an infusion pump. Cyclic TPN is administered for 8 to 16 hours, most commonly at night. This should not be done until metabolic stability has been demonstrated for patients on standard, continuous TPN infusions.

D. **Discontinuation of TPN** should take place when the patient can satisfy 75% of his or her caloric and protein needs with oral intake or enteral feeding. The calories provided by TPN can be decreased in proportion to calories from the patient's increasing enteral intake. To discontinue TPN, the infusion rate should be halved for 1 hour, halved again the next hour, and then discontinued. Tapering in this manner prevents rebound hypoglycemia from hyperinsulinemia. It is not necessary to taper the rate if the patient demonstrates glycemic stability when TPN is abruptly discontinued (i.e., cycled TPN) or receives less than 1,000 kcal/day.

E. **Complications associated with TPN**

1. **Catheter-related complications** can be minimized by strict aseptic technique and routine catheter care (*Surg Clin North Am.* 1985; 65(4):835–865).

2. **Metabolic complications** include electrolyte abnormalities and glucose homeostasis. Strict maintenance of serum glucose level below 110 mg/dL improves mortality and reduces infectious complications in surgical intensive care unit patients (*N Engl J Med.* 2001;345(19):1359–1367).

   Cholestasis is another common metabolic complication of long-term parenteral nutrition. This is due to the lack of enteral stimulation for gallbladder contraction. Cholestatic liver disease may ultimately lead to biliary cirrhosis, which is treated with transplantation.

DISEASE-SPECIFIC NUTRITION

A. The increase in metabolic demands following **thermal injury** correlates with the extent of ungrafted body surface area. Providing analgesia and thermoneutral environments lowers the accelerated metabolic rate and helps to decrease catabolic protein loss until the surface can be grafted (*Compr Ther.* 1991;17(3):47–53).

B. **Diabetes** often complicates nutritional management. Hyperglycemia with glycosuria causes osmotic diuresis and loss of electrolytes in urine, whereas hypoglycemia can result in shock, seizures, or vascular instability. The goal in patients with diabetes is to maintain the serum glucose within the normal range. Adjustments in insulin dosing should be made with the understanding that insulin requirements will decrease as the patient recovers from the initial stress.

C. Patients with marginal pulmonary reserve who are ventilator dependent may be particularly **difficult to wean** (*JAMA.* 1980;243(14):1444–1447). Excessive carbohydrate administration increases CO_2 production, which is compensated by increasing minute ventilation. In patients with marginal reserve, increasing minute ventilation may lead to fatigue and difficulty weaning.

> The respiratory quotient (**RQ**) represents the balance between CO_2 production and O_2 consumption and is a general indicator of metabolism.
>
> $$RQ = \frac{\dot{V}_{CO_2}}{\dot{V}_{O_2}}.$$

D. Patients with **renal failure** can have excessive protein loss through dialysis, which may result in a negative nitrogen balance. These patients should be nutritionally replenished according to their calculated needs. Patients who receive peritoneal dialysis absorb approximately 80% of the dextrose in the dialysate fluid (assuming a normal serum glucose level).

E. Nutritional complications of **hepatic failure** include wasting of lean body mass, fluid retention, vitamin and trace metal deficiencies, anemia, and encephalopathy. Branched-chain amino acids (BCAA) are metabolized by skeletal muscle and may be helpful in limiting the severity of encephalopathy (*J Nutr.* 2006;136(1 suppl):295S–298S). The largest randomized controlled trial evaluating BCAA-enriched therapy including 646 cirrhotic patients showed a significant decrease in complication rates (progression of liver failure, development of liver cancer, rupture of esophageal varices) in patients receiving oral supplementation with BCAA (*Clin Gastroenterol Hepatol.* 2005;3(7):705–713).

F. **Cancer-related cachexia** is a syndrome of lean muscle wasting, peripheral insulin resistance, and increased lipolysis. More than two thirds of patients with cancer experience significant weight loss (*JPEN J Parenter Enteral Nutr.* 2002;26(5 suppl):S63–S71). Antineoplastic therapies, such as chemotherapy, radiation, or operative extirpation, can worsen malnutrition. While adding TPN improves weight, nitrogen balance, and biochemical markers, there is little support for a survival benefit. Megestrol acetate (Megace) improves food intake, fat gain, and patient mood but does not affect outcome.

G. **Short-bowel syndrome** occurs in patients with less than 180 cm of functional small bowel. Dietary management includes consuming frequent small meals, avoiding hyperosmolar foods, restricting fat intake, and limiting consumption of foods high in oxalate (precipitates nephrolithiasis). In addition to glutamine, recombinant human growth hormone (r-HGH) assists these patients in weaning from parenteral nutrition (*J Clin Gastroenterol.* 2006;(40 suppl 2):S99–S106). Definitive therapy involves either isolated intestinal or multivisceral (cases complicated by concomitant TPN-induced liver dysfunction) transplantation.

Life Support and Anesthesia

Jason D. Keune and Charl J. De Wet

3

LIFE SUPPORT

Sudden cardiac arrest continues to be a leading cause of death. The **time** from cardiopulmonary arrest to the initiation of **basic life support (BLS)** and **advanced cardiac life support (ACLS)** is critical to outcome. The following guidelines were developed by the American Heart Association (AHA) to standardize treatment for adults (*Circulation.* 2010; 122, Supplement). These guidelines were revised in 2010, and differ from those previously published.

LIFE SUPPORT AND CARDIOPULMONARY ARREST ALGORITHMS

I. **BLS.** The first three steps in the BLS algorithm are **recognition and activation,** early **cardiopulmonary resuscitation** (CPR) and rapid **defibrillation,** when appropriate:

A. **Determine unresponsiveness** by tapping the victim on the shoulder and shouting at the victim.

B. The **emergency response system** should be activated, whether in the community or in an institution with an emergency response system. A manual defibrillator or an automated external defibrillator (AED) should be obtained, if possible. If **two providers** are present, then one should proceed to CPR, and the other should perform these tasks.

C. Time to initiation of **CPR** is associated with higher likelihood of survival (*Circ Cardiovasc Qual Outcomes.* 2010;3:63–81); therefore, high-quality chest compressions should be initiated as early as possible. Providers should push **hard** and fast (since the resulting stroke volume is limited, maintenance of cardiac output relies on compression rate) and allow **complete recoil** of the chest.

D. **Rapid defibrillation** should be performed. If a manual defibrillator is used, then a shockable rhythm must be identified before proceeding with this step. If an AED is used, the device will identify a shockable rhythm and deliver a shock, if appropriate.

E. **Rescue breaths** should not be performed until after high-quality chest compressions have been initiated.

F. The **pulse check** has been removed from the algorithm for lay rescuers. Health-care providers should take no more than 10 seconds to detect a pulse.

G. The **AHA BLS algorithm for Health-care providers** is given in Figure 3-1.

Adult BLS Healthcare Providers

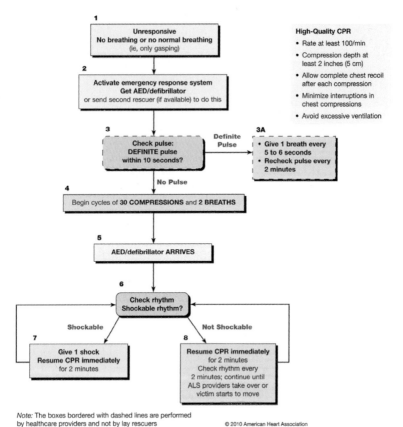

Figure 3-1. Adult basic life support algorithm, American Heart Association.

II. **ACLS.** Properly performed BLS is critical to the successful performance of ACLS, which is a team effort that depends on effective supervision by a team leader. The leader should ensure that the sequential actions of ACLS are expediently executed by the team.

A. **Sudden Cardiac Arrest**

1. **Airway**

   a. The provider should open the airway with a **head tilt-chin** lift maneuver.

   b. Airway adjuncts include **cricoid pressure, the oropharyngeal airway,** and **the nasopharyngeal airway.**

   c. The risks of the use of an **advanced airway** should be considered along with its benefits. The interruption in chest compressions that may be needed for airway placement should be minimized. Effective use of advanced airways is dependent on provider knowledge and practice. Care should be taken to ensure that airway placement and placement verification does not compromise high-quality CPR.

d. **Endotracheal intubation** remains the procedure of choice for the unconscious and/or apneic patient. When intubation is not possible, several alternative airway ventilation methods, such as the **Laryngeal Mask Airway** or the **Esophageal-Tracheal Combitube,** may provide more effective ventilation than a bag-mask apparatus.

e. **Continuous waveform capnography** and **clinical assessment** are recommended as the most reliable way to verify proper placement of an advanced airway.

2. **Breathing**
   a. When a **lone provider** is ventilating the patient, mouth-to-mouth or mouth-to-mask techniques are the most efficient.
   b. **Bag-mask ventilation** is an acceptable method of providing oxygenation and ventilation during CPR when two providers are present.
   c. If the patient is being ventilated with a **mask,** then one provider should open the airway and provide a tight seal between the mask and face, and the other should squeeze the bag. Two one-second breaths should be given during a brief pause after every 30 chest compressions.
   d. If an advanced airway has been placed, the provider should give one breath every 6 to 8 seconds without a pause in chest compressions.

3. **Circulation**
   a. In low blood flow states, **oxygen delivery** to the heart and brain is more dependent on blood flow than arterial oxygen content; therefore, an emphasis should be placed on **chest compressions** during the initial phase of resuscitation.

4. **Defibrillation**
   a. The only rhythms shown to increase survival to hospital discharge when defibrillated are **ventricular fibrillation** (VF) and **pulseless ventricular tachycardia** (VT).
   b. If a **biphasic defibrillator** is used, the initial shock should be delivered at the manufacturer's recommended dose. The provider may deliver a maximal dose if unsure as to the manufacturer's recommended initial dose. Subsequent energy doses should be equal to or greater than earlier doses.
   c. If a **monophasic defibrillator** is used, a 360-J initial shock should be delivered, with that dose being used for all subsequent shocks.

5. **Pulseless electrical activity (PEA) and asystole**
   a. If a rhythm check reveals an **organized, nonshockable rhythm,** a pulse check should be performed.
   b. If a pulse is detected, post–cardiac arrest care should be initiated.
   c. If a pulse is absent, or the rhythm is asystole, CPR should be resumed.

d. PEA is almost uniformly fatal unless an underlying cause can be identified and treated. Potentially reversible causes follow the acronym 6 H 5 T:

e. Hypovolemia, especially resulting from hemorrhage, is the most common cause of PEA.

f. Hypoxia.

g. Hypothermia.

h. Hydrogen ions (severe acidosis).

i. Hyperkalemia or **hypokalemia.**

j. Hypoglycemia.

k. Tablets/toxins.

l. Tension pneumothorax, evidenced by tracheal deviation and decreased ipsilateral breath sounds, should be treated by insertion of a large-bore angiocatheter (14-gauge) into the pleural space through the second intercostal space in the midclavicular line, followed by a thoracostomy tube.

m. Tamponade (pericardial) is treated by pericardiocentesis.

n. Thrombosis of coronary vessels (acute coronary syndromes).

o. Thrombosis of pulmonary vessels (pulmonary embolism).

6. Vasopressor use

a. Epinephrine (Adrenalin) has been shown, in retrospective analysis, to improve return of spontaneous circulation, when compared to no epinephrine for sustained VT and PEA/asystole. No difference in survival between treatment groups was seen (*Resuscitation.* 1995;29:195–201).

b. Epinephrine should be given intravenous/intraosseous (IV/IO) at a dose of 1 mg every 3 to 5 minutes during cardiac arrest.

c. If IV/IO access cannot be established, epinephrine can be given endotracheally at a dose of 2 to 2.5 mg.

d. Amiodarone (Pacerone, Cordarone) can be given for VF or pulseless VT unresponsive to CPR, defibrillation and vasopressor. The initial dose is 300 mg IV/IO. A second dose of 150 mg IV/IO can be given.

e. One dose of **vasopressin (Pitressin)** 40 units IV/IO may replace either the first or second dose of epinephrine.

7. The **AHA ACLS algorithm for adult cardiac arrest** is given in Figure 3-2.

B. Acute Symptomatic Arrhythmias. It is important to emphasize that electrocardiography (ECG) should be interpreted in the context of clinical assessment of the patient when evaluating acute symptomatic arrhythmias.

1. Bradycardia

a. Bradycardia is defined as heart rate less than 60 beats per minute.

b. The **symptoms** of unstable bradycardia include acutely altered mental status, angina, acute heart failure, hypotension, or shock that persists despite an adequate airway and breathing.

c. If unstable bradycardia is present, the primary treatment is **atropine** (at an initial dose of 0.5 mg IV. The dose can be repeated every 3 to 5 minutes to a maximum of 3 mg.

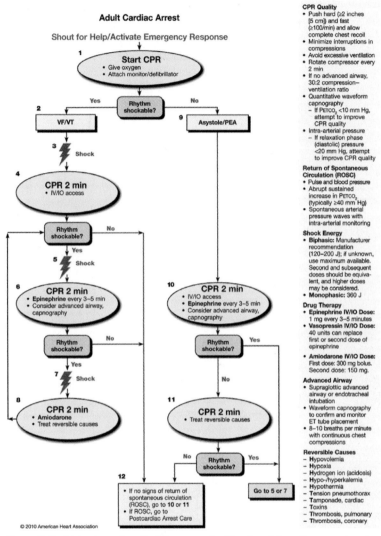

Figure 3-2. Adult advanced cardiac life support algorithm for adult cardiac arrest, American Heart Association.

    d. If atropine is not effective, then either dopamine or epinephrine infusion or transcutaneous pacing (TP) should be initiated.

        (1) Dopamine (Intropin) should be given at a dose of 2 to 10 mcg/kg/minute.

        (2) Epinephrine should be given at a dose of 0.02 to 0.3 mcg/kg/minute.

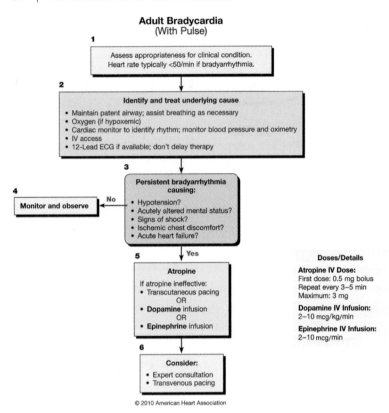

Figure 3-3. Adult bradycardia (with pulse) algorithm, American Heart Association.

        (3) TP is a temporizing measure that is painful in conscious patients. After initiation of TP, preparations for transvenous pacing should be made, and expert consultation should be sought.

    e. The **AHA ACLS bradycardia (with pulse) algorithm** is given in Figure 3-3.

  2. Tachycardia

    a. Tachycardia is defined as a heart rate greater than 100 beats per minute.

    b. The **symptoms** of unstable tachycardia include acutely altered mental status, angina, acute heart failure, hypotension or shock that persists despite an adequate airway and breathing.

    c. If unstable tachycardia is present, **synchronized cardioversion** should be performed, when indicated (see below).

        (1) If possible, IV access should be obtained and the patient should be sedated prior to proceeding. Cardioversion should not be delayed in the extremely unstable patient.

(2) Synchronized cardioversion is indicated for **unstable supraventricular tachycardia (SVT), unstable atrial fibrillation, unstable atrial flutter,** and **unstable monomorphic VT.**

(3) For cardioversion of **atrial fibrillation,** an initial biphasic energy dose of 120 to 200 J is recommended. The dose should be increased in a stepwise fashion if the initial shock fails.

(4) For cardioversion of **atrial flutter** or **SVT,** an initial biphasic energy dose of 50 to 100 J is recommended. The dose should be increased in a stepwise fashion if the initial shock fails.

(5) For cardioversion of **monomorphic VT,** an initial energy dose of 100 J is recommended. The dose can be increased in a stepwise fashion if the initial shock fails, but there is no evidence addressing this issue, and this recommendation is based on expert opinion alone.

(6) For **wide, irregular tachycardias,** unsynchronized defibrillation doses should be delivered.

d. **Sinus tachycardia** is usually caused by an underlying physiologic condition. Therapy should be directed at treatment of this underlying cause.

e. If the patient is **not hypotensive** and has a **narrow-complex SVT,** the following therapy should be attempted:

(1) A **vagal maneuver** (valsalva maneuver or carotid sinus massage) alone will terminate up to 25% of paroxysmal SVTs and should be performed first (not indicated if patient has significant carotid disease).

(2) If the vagal maneuver is unsuccessful, **adenosine** should be administered at a dose of **6 mg IV,** given by **rapid** IV push through a large vein, followed by a 20-mL flush.

(3) If the rhythm does not convert within 1 to 2 minutes, a dose of **12 mg IV** should be given using the same method.

(4) **Expert consultation** should be obtained.

f. If the patient is **stable,** an ECG should be obtained and the QRS complex evaluated to determine whether it is ≥0.12 seconds.

(1) If the QRS complex is ≥0.12 seconds (a **wide-complex tachycardia**), a determination should be made as to whether it is **regular** or **irregular.**

(2) If **regular,** the **wide-complex tachycardia** can be treated with **adenosine,** as above.

(3) If **irregular,** or **polymorphic,** adenosine should never be given, as it can precipitate degeneration to VF.

g. If the **regular, wide-complex tachycardia** is not terminated with adenosine, then antiarrhythmic infusion should be considered. A continuous ECG should be obtained as these drugs are given, to facilitate diagnosis.

(1) **Procainamide (Pronestyl, Procan, Procanbid)** can be administered at 20 to 50 mg/minute until either the rhythm is suppressed, hypotension ensues, QRS duration increases 50%, or the maximum dose is given (17 mg/kg). A maintenance dose is 1 to 4 mg/minute. Procainamide **should not be given** to patients prolonged QT or congestive heart failure.

(2) **Amiodarone** can be given at a dose of 150 mg IV over 10 minutes, with repeated dosing as needed to a maximum dose of 2.2 g IV per 24 hours. A maintenance infusion is 1 mg/minute over the first 6 hours.

(3) **Sotalol (Betapace)** can be given at a dose of 1.5 mg/kg over 5 minutes. Sotalol **should not be given** to patients with a prolonged QT interval.

(4) If one drug is not successful at termination of the rhythm, another drug should not be started without **expert consultation.**

h. If the wide-complex tachycardia is **irregular,** it is likely **atrial fibrillation** with aberrancy, **atrial fibrillation** using an accessory pathway, or **polymorphic VT/torsades de pointes.**

3. **Atrial fibrillation**
   a. Management of **atrial fibrillation** should center around control of the ventricular rate or conversion of the arrhythmia to sinus rhythm. **Cardioversion** should be attempted if unstable.
   b. Since patients with atrial fibrillation are at higher risk for **cardioembolic events** if the arrhythmia should persist for longer than **48 hours,** cardioversion or pharmacologic conversion should not be attempted in these patients, unless the patient is grossly unstable. It should be kept in mind that patients with atrial fibrillation of a shorter duration are not precluded from having such events. An alternative strategy in stable patients with atrial fibrillation persisting longer than 48 hours is to anticoagulate with heparin and perform transesophageal echocardiography to ensure absence of a left atrial thrombus prior to cardioversion.
   c. **Rate control** can be established in several ways.
      (1) **IV β-blockers** or **nondihydropyridine calcium channel blockers (e.g., diltiazem)** can be given for atrial fibrillation with rapid ventricular response.
      (2) **Amiodarone** or **digoxin (Digitek, Lanoxin, Lanoxicaps)** can be used for rate control in patients with congestive heart failure; however, providers should be mindful of the potential for rhythm conversion with the use of amiodarone.
   d. The AHA guidelines recommend expert consultation for **rhythm control** of atrial fibrillation.

4. **Polymorphic (irregular) VT/torsades de pointes**
   a. **Unstable polymorphic VT** should be treated with immediate defibrillation.
   b. If a long QT interval is observed during sinus rhythm, then the **irregular, wide-complex tachycardia** is likely **torsades de pointes.**
      (1) **Medications** known to prolong the QT interval should be stopped.
      (2) **Electrolyte imbalances** should be corrected.
      (3) **IV magnesium** can be given for torsades de pointes.
      (4) **Isoproterenol (Isuprel)** or **ventricular pacing** can be effective in terminating the arrhythmia associated with drug-induced QT prolongation.

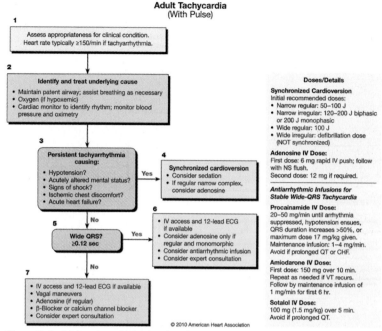

Figure 3-4. Adult tachycardia (with pulse) algorithm, American Heart Association.

    (5) If the arrhythmia is due to **familial long-QT syndrome, IV magnesium, pacing, and/or β-blockers** can be used. Isoproterenol should be avoided in this situation.

  c. If a long QT interval is not observed, then the **irregular, wide-complex tachycardia** may be VT due to myocardial ischemia.

    (1) **IV amiodarone** and **β-blockers** can be given to reduce the frequency of recurrence of this arrhythmia; however, efforts should be made to address revascularization.

  d. If **cardiac arrest** develops any time during the bradycardia or tachycardia algorithms, providers should implement the ACLS Cardiac Arrest Algorithm.

  e. **The AHA ACLS adult tachycardia (with pulse) algorithm** is given in Figure 3-4.

C. **Post–Cardiac Arrest Care**

  The initial goals of post–cardiac arrest care are as follows:

  1. To **optimize** cardiopulmonary function and vital organ perfusion.

  2. To **determine** the underlying cause of the arrest so as to prevent its recurrence.

  3. To **transfer** the patient to a setting in which acute coronary interventions, neurologic care, goal-directed critical care, and hypothermia are available.

Adult Immediate Postcardiac Arrest Care

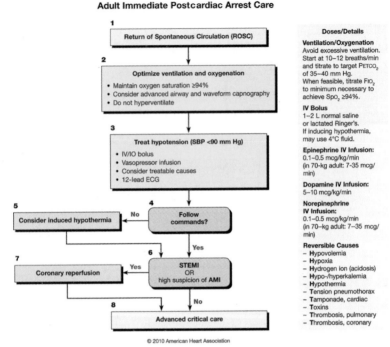

Figure 3-5. Adult post–cardiac arrest care algorithm, American Heart Association.

Subsequent goals include the following:

1. Control of **body temperature** to optimize neurologic recovery and overall survival
2. Treatment of **acute coronary syndromes**
3. Optimization of **mechanical ventilation**
4. Assessment of **prognosis**
5. **Provision** of rehabilitation services.

The **adult immediate post–cardiac arrest care algorithm** is given in Figure 3-5.

ANESTHESIA

Preparing the Patient

I. PATIENT PREPARATION FOR OPERATION

  A. Preoperative evaluation

    1. A **comprehensive preoperative evaluation** is critical to the safe administration of anesthetic care.

      a. A **complete history,** including medication usage and prior anesthetic usage, should be obtained.

    b. An **examination of airway,** vascular access, and other pertinent anatomy tailored to the anticipated operation should be undertaken.

2. In **patients without preexisting disease,** preoperative screening and testing are determined primarily by age.

    a. **Hemoglobin or hematocrit** may be the only test required in some healthy patients younger than 40 years.

    b. A **serum pregnancy test** should be obtained for female patients of childbearing age.

    c. A **screening chest X-ray and ECG** are obtained for patients who are 50 years or older, unless an indication is found from the history or physical examination, or both.

3. **Additional testing** may be required when clinically indicated.

    a. **Serum electrolytes** must be evaluated in patients with diabetes or renal insufficiency and in patients who are taking diuretics.

    b. **Coagulation studies** (prothrombin time, partial thromboplastin time, bleeding time) must be evaluated in patients who are receiving anticoagulation therapy or have a personal or family history that is suggestive of abnormal bleeding.

    c. **Additional testing or consultation** may be required in patients with evidence of severe coexisting disease, especially those with cardiac, pulmonary, or renal compromise.

4. Unstable or uncontrolled medical conditions, upper respiratory infections, and solid food ingestion within 6 hours of surgery are **indications to cancel or postpone elective surgery.**

5. **American Society of Anesthesiologists (ASA) criteria** (see Table 3-1)

TABLE 3-1	American Society of Anesthesiologists (ASA) Criteria
ASA Grade	**Description**
I	There is no organic, physiologic, biochemical, or psychiatric disturbance; the pathologic process for which the operation is to be performed is localized and is not a systemic disturbance.
II	Mild-to-moderate systemic disturbance caused by either the condition to be treated or other pathophysiologic processes
III	Severe systemic disturbance or disease for whatever cause, even though it may not be possible to define the degree of disability
IV	Indicative of the patient with severe systemic disorder that is already life-threatening and not always correctable by the operative procedure
V	The moribund patient who has little chance of survival but is submitted to operation in desperation

An E is added after a grade to indicate emergency surgery (e.g., IVE).

B. **Nothing by mouth (NPO) status**

1. For all patients, it is customary to abstain from any oral intake except for medications with sips of water for 8 hours before elective surgery. However, for adult patients who are not considered to be at increased risk for aspiration of gastric contents, the following **aspiration prophylaxis regimens** can be used.

   a. **Solid food** is permitted until 6 hours before surgery.

   b. **Clear liquids** (which do not include milk or juices containing pulp) are permitted until 2 hours before surgery (*Anesthesiology.* 1999;90:896).

2. **Patients with slowed or incomplete gastric emptying** (e.g., those who are morbidly obese, diabetic, or on narcotic therapy) **may require longer fasting periods and additional pretreatment with metoclopramide, histamine H_2-receptor antagonists, and/or oral sodium citrate.** Rapid-sequence induction should be considered in these patients. Maintenance IV fluids should be considered in NPO inpatients.

C. **Medications**

1. Patients can receive **benzodiazepines or narcotics** to alleviate preoperative anxiety and pain.

2. **Cardiovascular or other pertinent medications** usually are administered on the morning of surgery with small sips of water. Inpatients who normally receive scheduled insulin doses should instead be placed on sliding-scale insulin, with blood sugars checked frequently every 2 to 6 hours while NPO, depending on difficulty of their diabetic control. Outpatients should be instructed to take one-half to one-third of their regular insulin dose the morning of surgery and to check blood sugars frequently. **It is essential to avoid hypoglycemia.**

3. In general, antiplatelet medications such as **aspirin** or **clopidogrel** should be held 5 days prior to surgery unless otherwise specified.

D. **Obstructive sleep apnea (OSA)**

1. **Over the last few years,** OSA has been recognized as a significant source of perioperative morbidity and mortality in the United States. The American Society of Anesthesiology guidelines for the perioperative management of OSA are shown in Tables 3-2 and 3-3 (*Anesthesiology.* 2006,104:1081).

TYPES OF ANESTHESIA

I. **LOCAL ANESTHETICS** are categorized into two groups. **Esters (one i)** include tetracaine, procaine, cocaine, and chloroprocaine. **Amides (two i's)** include lidocaine, bupivacaine, ropivacaine, and mepivacaine. Characteristics of commonly used local anesthetic agents are summarized in Table 3-4.

A. **Mechanism of action**

1. **Local anesthetics** work by diffusing through the nerve plasma membrane and causing blockade of sodium channels. The nerve cell is unable to depolarize, and axonal conduction is inhibited.

| TABLE 3-2 | Identification and Assessment of Obstructive Sleep Apnea[a] |

A. Clinical signs and symptoms suggesting the possibility of OSA
  1. Predisposing physical characteristics
    a. BMI 55 kg/m^2 (95th percentile for age and gender)
    b. Neck circumference 17 in. (men) or 16 in. (women)
    c. Craniofacial abnormalities affecting the airway
    d. Anatomic nasal obstruction
    e. Tonsils nearly touching or touching in the midline
  2. History of apparent airway obstruction during sleep (two or more of the following are present; if patient lives alone or sleep is not observed by another person, then only one of the following needs to be present)
    a. Snoring (loud enough to be heard through closed door)
    b. Frequent snoring
    c. Observed pauses in breathing during sleep
    d. Awakens from sleep with choking sensation
    e. Frequent arousals from sleep
    f. Intermittent vocalization during sleep
    g. Parental report of restless sleep, difficulty breathing, or struggling respiratory efforts during sleep
  3. Somnolence (one or more of the following is present)
    a. Frequent somnolence or fatigue despite adequate "sleep"
    b. Falls asleep easily in a nonstimulating environment (e.g., watching TV, reading, riding in or driving a car, despite adequate "sleep")
    c. Parent or teacher comments that child appears sleepy during the day, is easily distracted, is overly aggressive, or has difficulty concentrating
    d. Child often difficult to arouse at usual awakening time

      If a patient has signs or symptoms in two or more of the foregoing categories, there is a significant probability that he or she has OSA. The severity of OSA may be determined by sleep study (see following tabulation). If a sleep study is not available, such patients should be treated as though they have moderate sleep apnea unless one or more of the foregoing signs or symptoms is severely abnormal (e.g., markedly increased BMI or neck circumference, respiratory pauses that are frightening to the observer, patient regularly falls asleep within minutes after being left unstimulated). In these cases, patients should be treated as though they have severe sleep apnea.
B. If a sleep study has been done, the results should be used to determine the perioperative anesthetic management of a patient. However, because sleep laboratories differ in their criteria for detecting episodes of apnea and hypopnea, the Task Force believes that the sleep laboratory's assessment (none, mild, moderate, or severe) should take precedence over the actual AHI (the number of episodes of sleep-disordered breathing per hour). If the overall severity is not indicated, it may be determined by using the following table.

(continued)

TABLE 3-2	Identification and Assessment of Obstructive Sleep Apnea*a* *(continued)*	
Severity of OSA	Adult AHI	Pediatric AHI
None	0–5	0
Mild OSA	6–20	1–5
Moderate OSA	21–40	6–10
Severe OSA	>40	>10

*a*Items in brackets refer to pediatric patients.
AHI, apnea-hypopnea index; BMI, body mass index; OSA, obstructive sleep apnea; TV, television.
With permission from Gross JB, Bachenberg KL, Benumof JL, et al. Practice guidelines for the perioperative management of patients with obstructive sleep apnea. *Anesthesiology.* 2006;104:1081–1093.

2. **Local tissue acidosis** (e.g., from infection) slows the onset and decreases the intensity of analgesia by causing local anesthetic molecules to become positively charged and less able to diffuse into the neuron.

B. Toxicity (dose dependent, except for allergic reactions)

1. **Central nervous system (CNS) toxicity**
   a. **Signs and symptoms** include mental status changes, dizziness, perioral numbness, a metallic taste, tinnitus, visual disturbances, and seizures. Seizures resulting from inadvertent intravascular injection usually last only minutes. Continuous infusion of local anesthetics may result in high plasma levels and prolonged seizures.
   b. **Treatment** involves airway support and ventilation with 100% oxygen, which should always be available. Prolonged seizures may require administration of benzodiazepines [midazolam (Versed), 1 to 5 mg intravenously; diazepam (Valium), 5 to 15 mg intravenously; or lorazepam (Ativan), 1 to 4 mg intravenously]. Intubation may be required to ensure adequate ventilation.

2. **Cardiovascular toxicity**
   a. **Signs and symptoms** range from decreased cardiac output to hypotension and cardiovascular collapse. Most local anesthetics cause CNS toxicity before cardiovascular toxicity. Bupivacaine (Marcaine) is an exception, and its intravascular injection can result in severe cardiac compromise.
   b. **Treatment** includes fluid resuscitation, administration of vasopressors, and CPR, if necessary.

3. **Hypersensitivity reactions,** although rare, have been described with **ester**-based local anesthetics and are attributed to the metabolite *p*-aminobenzoic acid. True amide-based local anesthetic anaphylactic reactions are questionable.

TABLE 3-3	Obstructive Sleep Apnea Scoring System	
		Points

A. Severity of sleep apnea based on sleep study (or clinical indicators if sleep study not available).
Point score – (0–3)[a,b]
Severity of OSA (Table 3-3)

	Points
None	0
Mild	1
Moderate	2
Severe	3

B. Invasiveness of surgery and anesthesia. Point score – (0–3)
Type of surgery and anesthesia

	Points
Superficial surgery under local or peripheral nerve block anesthesia without sedation	0
Superficial surgery with moderate sedation or general anesthesia	1
Peripheral surgery with spinal or epidural anesthesia (with no more than moderate sedation)	1
Peripheral surgery with general anesthesia	2
Airway surgery with moderate sedation	2
Major surgery, general anesthesia	3
Airway surgery, general anesthesia	3

C. Requirement for postoperative opioids. Point score – (0–3)
Opioid requirement

	Points
None	0
Low-dose oral opioids	1
High-dose oral opioids, parenteral, or neuraxial opioids	3

D. Estimation of perioperative risk. Overall score = score for A plus the greater of the score for either B or C. Point score – (0–6)[c]

Note: A scoring system similar to this table can be used to estimate whether a patient is at increased perioperative risk of complications from obstructive sleep apnea (OSA). This example, which has not been clinically validated, is meant only as a guide, and clinical judgment should be used to assess the risk of an individual patient.
[a]One point may be subtracted if a patient has been on continuous positive airway pressure (CPAP) or noninvasive positive-pressure ventilation (NIPPV) before surgery and will be using his or her appliance consistently during the postoperative period.
[b]One point should be added if a patient with mild or moderate OSA also has a resting arterial carbon dioxide tension (Pa_{CO_2}) >60 mm Hg.
[c]Patients with score of 4 may be at increased perioperative risk from OSA; patients with a score of 5 or 6 may be at significantly increased perioperative risk from OSA.
With permission from *Anesthesiology.* 2006;104:1081–1093.

    a. Signs and symptoms can range from urticaria to bronchospasm, hypotension, and anaphylactic shock.

    b. Treatment is similar to that for hypersensitivity reactions from other etiologies. Urticaria responds to diphenhydramine, 25 to 50 mg intravenously. Bronchospasm is treated with inhaled bronchodilators

TABLE 3-4	Local Anesthetics for Infiltration			
	Maximum Dose (mg/kg)		Length of Action (hr)	
Agent	**Plain**	**With Epinephrine**[a]	**Plain**	**With Epinephrine**[a]
Procaine	—	8	0.25–1	0.5–1.5
Lidocaine	5	7	0.5–1	2–6
Mepivacaine	5	7	0.75–1.5	2–6
Bupivacaine	2.5	3	2–4	3–7
Tetracaine	1.5		24	

[a]1:200,000.

(e.g., albuterol) and oxygen. Hypotension is treated with fluid resuscitation and vasopressors [e.g., phenylephrine hydrochloride (Neo-Synephrine)] or small incremental doses of epinephrine as required. Anaphylactic cardiovascular collapse should be treated with epinephrine, 0.5 to 1 mg, administered as an IV bolus.

C. **Epinephrine** (1:200,000, 5 µg/mL) is mixed with local anesthetic solutions to prolong the duration of neural blockade and reduce systemic drug absorption. Its use is **contraindicated** in areas where arterial spasm would lead to tissue necrosis (e.g., nose, ears, fingers, toes, and penis).

II. REGIONAL ANESTHESIA

A. **In the operating room**

1. **General considerations**

a. The **importance of preoperative communication between anesthesiologist and surgeon** cannot be overemphasized. The extent and duration of the procedure must be appreciated by the anesthesiologist so that the appropriate area and duration of anesthesia can be achieved. If the possibility of a prolonged or involved operative procedure is likely, a combined anesthetic technique (local/regional and general anesthesia), or general anesthetic only, may be more appropriate. Certain surgical positions are poorly tolerated by awake patients (e.g., steep Trendelenburg may cause respiratory compromise); in these instances, a general anesthetic is appropriate.

b. **Supplements to regional anesthesia.** No regional anesthetic technique is foolproof, and local infiltration by the surgeon may be required if there is an incomplete block. IV sedation using short-acting benzodiazepines, narcotics, barbiturates, or propofol can also be helpful. General anesthesia may be required when a regional technique provides inadequate analgesia.

    c. **NPO status.** Because any regional anesthetic may progress to a general anesthetic, NPO requirements for regional and general anesthetics are identical.

    d. **Monitoring requirements** are no different from those for general anesthesia. Heart rhythm, blood pressure (BP), and arterial oxygen saturation should be monitored regularly during regional or general anesthesia. Other monitoring may be indicated, depending on coexisting disease states.

2. Types of regional anesthesia

    a. **Spinal anesthesia** involves the injection of small volumes (low doses) of local anesthetic solution into the subarachnoid space at the level of the lumbar spine.

      (1) **Anatomy and placement** (Fig. 3-6)

        (a) With the use of sterile technique and after local anesthetic infiltration of the skin and subcutaneous tissues, a small (22- to 27-gauge) **spinal needle is passed between two adjacent lumbar spinous processes.** The needle is passed through the following structures: supraspinous ligament, interspinous ligament, ligamentum flavum, dura mater, and arachnoid mater. Cerebrospinal fluid (CSF) is aspirated, and the appropriate local anesthetic solution is injected.

      (2) **Level of analgesia**

        (a) **Multiple variables** affect the spread of analgesia. The **baricity** of the agent (solution density compared to that of CSF) and the position of the patient immediately after

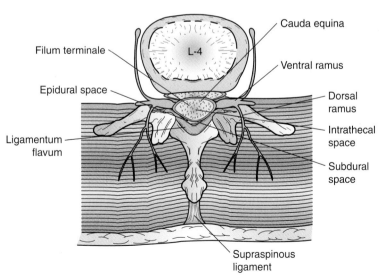

Figure 3-6. Anatomy for spinal and epidural anesthesia.

injection are major determinants of level. The **total dose injected** (increased dose results in higher spread) and the **total volume injected** (increased volume results in higher spread) are also important determinants of anesthetic level.

(b) **Older patients** tend to have greater spread of anesthesia by a few dermatomes, but clinical significance is variable.

(3) **Onset and duration of analgesia**

(a) The **specific characteristics of the local anesthetic** used and the **total dose injected** are the primary determinants of onset and duration of action. Epinephrine added to the solution increases the duration of analgesia.

(b) **The variability in length of analgesia** is significant, ranging from as little as 30 minutes [lidocaine (Xylocaine)] to up to 6 hours [tetracaine with epinephrine (Pontocaine, Dicaine)].

(4) **Complications**

(a) **Hypotension** may occur as a result of sympatholytic-induced vasodilation (decreased venous return to the heart followed by bradycardia). It may be more severe in hypovolemic patients or in those with preexisting cardiac dysfunction. Treatment includes volume resuscitation with crystalloid, vasopressors (epinephrine, 5 to 10 µg intravenously or phenylephrine hydrochloride, 50 to 100 µg intravenously), and positive inotropic and chronotropic drugs. It is advisable to administer 500 to 1,000 mL of crystalloid prior to spinal block to avoid hypotension due to spinal anesthesia. In refractory cases elevating the legs or placing the patient in Trendelenburg position may prevent cardiac arrest from decreased venous return to the heart. Under no circumstances should a hypotensive patient be placed in reverse Trendelenburg as this may lead to cardiac arrest.

(b) **High spinal blockade.** Inadvertently high levels of spinal blockade may result in hypotension (blocking dermatomes T1–4: preganglionic cardioaccelerator nerves), dyspnea (loss of chest proprioception or intercostal muscle function), or apnea (decreased medullary perfusion secondary to hypotension). Treatment consists of ventilatory support and/or intubation, fluid bolus, and chrono- and inotropic support of the heart. Once a high spinal block has occurred reversed, Trendelenburg position will be of no immediate benefit and is probably contraindicated since decreased venous return may lead to cardiac arrest.

(c) **Headache** after spinal anesthesia or diagnostic lumbar puncture is encountered with higher frequency in young or female patients. This is usually the result of leakage of CSF from the puncture site. A postural component is always present (i.e., symptoms worsened by sitting up or standing). The recent use of smaller-gauge spinal needles has reduced the frequency of this complication. Treatment includes oral or IV fluids, oral analgesics, and caffeinated beverages. Severe refractory headache may require placement of an epidural blood patch to prevent ongoing leakage of CSF.

   (d) **CNS infection** after spinal anesthesia, although extremely rare, may result in meningitis, epidural abscess, or arachnoiditis.

   (e) **Permanent nerve injury** is exceedingly rare and is seen with the same frequency as in general anesthesia.

   (f) **Urinary retention with bladder distention** occurs in patients with spinal anesthesia whose bladders are not drained by urethral catheters, which should remain in place until after the spinal anesthesia has been stopped and full sensation has returned.

(5) **Contraindications**

   (a) **Absolute contraindications** to spinal anesthesia are localized infection at the planned puncture site, increased intracranial pressure, generalized sepsis, coagulopathy, and lack of consent.

   (b) **Relative contraindications** include hypovolemia, preexisting CNS disease, chronic low back pain, platelet dysfunction, and preload-dependent valvular lesions such as aortic and mitral stenosis.

b. **Epidural anesthesia**

(1) **Anatomy and placement (Fig. 3-6)**

   (a) Inserting an epidural needle is similar to placing a spinal needle except that the **epidural needle is not advanced through the dura.** No CSF is obtained. The tip of the epidural needle lies in the epidural space between the ligamentum flavum posteriorly and the dura mater anteriorly. Local anesthetic solution can then be injected.

   (b) Either the **needle is removed** (single-shot method) or, more commonly, **a flexible catheter is passed through the needle** into the space and the needle is withdrawn over the catheter (continuous catheter technique). Local anesthetics or opioids can be infused as needed.

(2) **Level of analgesia**

   (a) Once injected into the epidural space, the local anesthetic solution diffuses through the dura and into the spinal nerve roots, usually resulting in a **bilateral dermatomal distribution of analgesia.**

   (b) The spread of nerve root blockade is primarily determined by the **volume** of injection and, to a lesser degree, by patient **position and age** and **area of placement.**

(3) **Onset and duration of analgesia**

   (a) **Epidural anesthesia develops more slowly than does spinal anesthesia** because the local anesthetic solution must diffuse farther. The rate of onset of sympathetic blockade and hypotension also is slowed, enabling more precise titration of hemodynamic therapy compared with spinal anesthesia.

   (b) The **dosing interval** depends on the agent used.

(4) Complications are similar to those encountered with spinal anesthesia.

   (a) Spinal headache may result from inadvertent perforation of the dura.

   (b) Epidural hematoma is rare and usually occurs with coexisting coagulopathy. Emergent laminectomy may be required to decompress the spinal cord and avoid permanent neurologic injury.

   (c) If a patient with an epidural catheter in place becomes **hypotensive,** stopping the infusion of anesthetic will often correct the BP. Alternatively a vasoconstrictor or chronotropic drug may be used to ameliorate the sympathetic blockade.

c. Combined spinal and epidural anesthesia

   (1) Anatomy and placement

   (a) A **small-gauge spinal needle** is placed through an epidural needle once the epidural space has been located. The dura is punctured only by the spinal needle, and placement is verified by CSF withdrawal. Subarachnoid local anesthetics or preservative-free opioids can then be administered via the spinal needle.

   (b) The **spinal needle** is withdrawn after the initial dosing, and an epidural catheter is threaded into the epidural space through the existing epidural needle.

   (2) Onset and duration. This procedure combines the quick onset of spinal analgesia with the continuous dosing advantages of epidural analgesia.

   (3) Complications are similar to those seen in spinal and epidural anesthesia.

d. Comparison of spinal or epidural anesthesia with general anesthesia. Although the incidence of thromboembolic complications and total blood loss is reduced in certain surgical procedures with spinal or epidural anesthesia, there is no evidence that long-term mortality is reduced compared with general anesthesia (*Br J Anaesth.* 1986;58:284; *Cochrane Database Syst Rev.* 2000;(4):CD000521).

e. Brachial plexus blockade. Injection of local anesthetic solution into the sheath surrounding the brachial plexus results in varying degrees of upper extremity blockade. This technique is indicated for any procedure involving the patient's shoulders, arms, or hands. Electrical nerve stimulation with/without ultrasound-guidance is now frequently used to aid in placement of these blocks. The approach taken depends on the distribution of blockade desired.

   (1) Axillary block. The needle is placed into the brachial plexus sheath from the axilla. Blockade above the patient's elbow is unreliable.

    (2) Supraclavicular blockade. The needle is directed caudally from behind the posterior border of the inner one-third of the clavicle. This technique reliably blocks the entire upper extremity, sparing the patient's shoulder. There is a risk of pneumothorax.

    (3) Interscalene blockade involves the cervical as well as brachial plexus and reliably blocks the patient's shoulder. There is a high incidence of phrenic nerve block, which increases the risk of pulmonary complications in patients with chronic obstructive pulmonary disease. This also serves as a contraindication to bilateral blockade.

  f. Cervical plexus blockade blocks the anterior divisions of C1 to C4 and is the anesthetic method of choice for carotid endarterectomy at many institutions. Inadvertent blockade of neighboring structures does occur.

    (1) Phrenic nerve blockade may result in transient diaphragmatic paralysis. Simultaneous bilateral cervical plexus blockade is therefore contraindicated.

    (2) Ipsilateral cervical sympathetic plexus blockade may result in Horner syndrome, producing transient ptosis, miosis, and facial anhidrosis.

B. Outside the operating room

  1. Intercostal nerve block is indicated after thoracotomy or before chest tube placement.

    a. Anatomy and placement (Fig. 3-7)

      (1) The **posterior axillary line is identified,** and with the use of sterile technique, a 23-gauge needle is placed perpendicular to the patient's skin until contact is made with his or her rib. The needle is then walked caudad off the patient's rib and advanced several millimeters. After negative aspiration, 5 mL of bupivacaine 0.25% to 0.50% with epinephrine (1:200,000) is injected.

      (2) Usually, **five interspaces** (including two above and two below the interspace of interest) are injected.

    b. Complications include pneumothorax and intravascular injection causing myocardial suppression and serious life-threatening arrhythmias. Bradycardia, asystole or heart block may result from inadvertent intravascular injection or rapid absorption of bupivacaine. Treatment should focus on hemodynamic support and with 20% intralipid. Injection into the nerve sheath with retrograde spread back to the spinal cord can produce a high spinal or epidural block.

  2. Digital block is indicated for minor procedures of the fingers.

    a. Anatomy and placement

      (1) From the **dorsal surface of the hand,** a 23-gauge needle is placed on either side of the metatarsal head and inserted until the increased resistance of the palmar connective tissue is felt. An injection of 1 to 2 mL of lidocaine 1% to 2% is made as the needle is withdrawn.

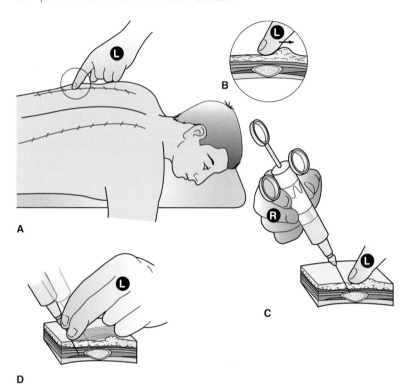

Figure 3-7. Anatomy and placement for intercostal nerve block. **(A)** The provider's hand closest to the patient's head (cephalic) first locates the target interspace and then **(B)** retracts the skin over the rib above. **(C)** The hand closest to the patient's feet (caudad) places the needle and attached syringe containing local anesthetic through the skin onto the rib at approximately a 30-degree angle, with the needle bevel directed cephalad. **(D)** The cephalic hand then grasps the needle while maintaining contact with the patient and allows the tension of the retracted skin to walk the needle off the inferior edge of the rib and advance 2 to 3 mm.

   (2) **Supplemental injection** of 0.5 to 1 mL of lidocaine 1% to 2% in the interdigital web on either side may be required.
  b. Epinephrine is contraindicated.
 C. Local infiltration
  1. In the operating room, the area of incision can be infiltrated before incision or at the conclusion of the operation. Evidence suggests that there is no difference in postoperative discomfort or analgesic use between pre- and postoperative infiltration with local anesthetic (*Arch Surg.* 1997;132(7):766–799). Bupivacaine is frequently used.
  2. Outside the operating room, local anesthetic infiltration may also be useful during wound débridement, central venous catheter placement, or repair of minor lacerations. The agent of choice is lidocaine 1% to

2% due to its quick onset and low toxicity. The area of interest should be injected liberally. Frequent aspiration helps to avoid intravascular injection. Injection should be repeated as necessary.

3. Local anesthetics containing **epinephrine** are **contraindicated** in areas where arterial spasm would lead to tissue necrosis (e.g., nose, ears, fingers, toes, and penis).

III. GENERAL ANESTHESIA. A balanced general anesthetic can provide hypnosis (unconsciousness), analgesia, amnesia, and skeletal muscle relaxation.

A. All patients who are undergoing general anesthesia require an appropriate **preoperative evaluation** and optimization of any coexisting medical problems (see "Preparing the Patient," Sections I.A.1 and I.A.2).

B. Monitoring. Basic monitoring requirements for general anesthesia are similar to those for regional anesthesia.

C. Induction of general anesthesia. IV agents are most widely used owing to rapid onset and ease of administration.

    1. Thiopental (Pentothal), a barbiturate (3 to 5 mg/kg intravenously), has a rapid onset and redistribution. However, there is often an associated decrease in cardiac output, BP, and cerebral blood flow. It should be used with caution in patients with hypotension or active coronary ischemia.

    2. Propofol (Diprivan), a phenol derivative (1 to 3 mg/kg intravenously), is used for both induction and maintenance of anesthesia. Onset of action is immediate. It has hemodynamic properties that are similar to those of thiopental but is associated with a low incidence of postoperative nausea and vomiting. The pharmacokinetics is not changed by chronic hepatic or renal failure. A water-soluble *prodrug* form, *fospropofol*, has recently been approved by the FDA. Fospropofol is rapidly broken down by the enzyme *alkaline phosphatase* to form propofol. This new formulation may not produce the pain at injection site that often occurs with the traditional form of the drug.

    3. Etomidate (Amidate), an imidazole derivative (0.3 mg/kg intravenously), has an onset of 30 to 60 seconds and has only mild direct hemodynamic depressant effects. Adrenal insufficiency may result from a single administration.

    4. Ketamine (Ketalar), a phencyclidine derivative (1 to 4 mg/kg intravenously), increases cardiac output and BP in patients who are not catecholamine depleted and provides dissociative anesthesia. It is also an excellent analgesic but raises intracranial pressure and is not used in patients with head trauma. The use of ketamine is limited owing to **emergence delirium** and nightmares and is often reserved for use in the pediatric population and has the advantage that it can be given **intramuscularly.**

D. Airway management. Ventilation during general anesthesia may be spontaneous, assisted, or controlled.

    1. Mask ventilation with spontaneous respiratory effort can be used during limited (usually peripheral) procedures that do not require neuromuscular relaxation. Because the airway is unprotected, this technique is contraindicated in patients at risk for aspiration.

2. **Endotracheal intubation** secures the airway, allows control of ventilation, and protects against aspiration. Although frequently performed orally with the laryngoscope, intubation can also be accomplished nasally and, in anatomically challenging patients, can be performed with the aid of a fiberoptic bronchoscope via oral or nasal routes. Newer video laryngoscopes may be helpful aids in difficult intubations.

3. The **Laryngeal Mask Airway (LMA)** is an alternative airway device used for anesthesia and airway support consisting of an inflatable silicone mask and rubber connecting tube. It is inserted blindly into the pharynx, forming a low-pressure seal around the laryngeal inlet and permitting gentle positive pressure ventilation. It is an appropriate airway choice when mask ventilation can be used but endotracheal intubation is not necessary. The use of LMA is contraindicated in nonfasted patients, morbidly obese patients, and patients with obstructive or abnormal lesions of the oropharynx.

E. **Neuromuscular blockade** facilitates tracheal intubation and is required for many surgical procedures. It provides the surgeon with improved working conditions and optimizes ventilatory support. Its use may increase the risk for intraoperative awareness and postoperative neuromuscular weakness. It should only be used when clinically indicated and normal neuromuscular function should be ascertained prior to extubation or stopping the anesthetic. Agents that produce neuromuscular blockade act on postsynaptic receptors in the neuromuscular junction to antagonize the effects of acetylcholine competitively. Agents are categorized as either depolarizing or nondepolarizing (Table 3-5).

1. **Succinylcholine (Anectine, Quelicin)** is a rapidly acting (60 seconds), rapidly metabolized [by plasma cholinesterase (a.k.a. pseudocholinesterase or butyrylcholinesterase)] depolarizing agent that allows return of neuromuscular function in 5 to 10 minutes. In certain patients, the normally mild hyperkalemic response that is almost immediate will be greatly exaggerated leading to cardiac arrest. Its use is therefore usually contraindicated in patients with severe burns, trauma, or paralysis or patients with other neuromuscular disorders or prolonged bedrest. In addition, it can cause increases in intraocular, intracranial, and gastric pressures. It is also contraindicated in those with a personal or family history of **malignant hyperthermia** – a rare but deadly complication (see Section H.1.). In patients with inherited pseudocholinesterase deficiency administration will result in prolonged neuromuscular blockade (up to 8 hours).

2. **Nondepolarizing muscle relaxants** can be divided into short-, intermediate-, and long-acting agents. Associated hemodynamic effects and elimination pathways vary.

a. **These agents are sometimes used in an intensive care setting** when paralysis is necessary for adequate ventilation of an intubated patient. Such patients must have adequate sedation and analgesia before and during paralysis. Duration of therapy should be as short as clinically feasible and dosage response should be monitored by train-of-four stimulus every 4 hours, with the goal being **at least**

TABLE 3-5   Agents Producing Neuromuscular Blockade

Agent	Initial Dose (mg/kg)	Duration (min)	Elimination	Associated Effects
Depolarizing				
Succinylcholine	1–1.5	3–5	Plasma cholinesterase	Fasciculations, increase or decrease in heart rate, transient hyperkalemia, known malignant hyperthermia trigger agent
Nondepolarizing				
Mivacurium	0.15	8–10	Plasma cholinesterase	Flushing, decrease in BP
Atracurium	0.2–0.4	20–35	Ester hydrolysis	Histamine release
Cisatracurium	0.1–0.2	20–35	Ester hydrolysis	—
Vecuronium	0.1–0.2	25–40	Primarily hepatic	—
Rocuronium	0.6–1.2	30	Primarily hepatic	—
d-Tubocurare	0.5–0.6	75–100	Primarily renal	Histamine release, decrease in BP
Pancuronium	0.04–0.1	45–90	Primarily renal	Increase in heart rate, mean arterial BP, and cardiac output
Doxacurium	0.05–0.08	90–180	Primarily renal	Decrease in BP

BP, blood pressure.

one out of four twitches. Corticosteroids, aminoglycosides, and long-term use of neuromuscular blockers potentiate the risk of a prolonged critical level of neuromyopathy.

  b. **Reversal of neuromuscular blockade** for patients who are receiving nondepolarizing muscle relaxants usually is performed before extubation to ensure full return of respiratory muscle function and protective airway reflexes. The diaphragm is less sensitive to muscle relaxants than are the muscles of the head and neck. A spontaneously ventilating patient **may be unable to protect the airway.** The definitive test for assessing the degree of remaining paralysis is to have the patient raise the head from the bed for 5 seconds or more. **Acetylcholinesterase inhibitors** (neostigmine, 0.06 to 0.07 mg/kg, and edrophonium, 0.1 mg/kg) act to increase the availability of acetylcholine at the neuromuscular junction, thereby reducing the binding frequency to the nicotinic receptors of the nondepolarizing muscle relaxant (competitive antagonism). Accumulation of acetylcholine also binds to muscarinic receptors. Muscarinic cholinergic side effects (bradycardia, bronchospasm, gastrointestinal hypermotility, excessive sweating and secretions, etc.) of these reversal drugs should always be prevented by combining these reversal agents with a muscarinic anticholinergic agent such as atropine or glycopyrrolate.

F. **Maintenance of anesthesia**

  1. The **goal of anesthesia** is to provide unconsciousness, amnesia, analgesia, and, usually, muscle relaxation. Balanced anesthesia involves the combined use of inhalational agents, narcotics, and muscle relaxants to attain this goal.

  2. **Inhalational agents**

     a. All inhalational agents provide varying degrees of unconsciousness, amnesia, and muscle relaxation.

     b. **Isoflurane (Forane)** has a relatively low rate of metabolism. It causes less cardiovascular depression than previously used agents. Newer agents are now commonly used. Sevoflurane (non-irritating – great for inhalational induction) and desflurane (more irritating to the airway, but less fat soluble and therefore faster clearance) are now much more commonly used.

     c. **Halothane (Fluothane)** use has decreased significantly. It has a rapid onset of action. Its use is excellent for asthmatics because of its bronchial smooth muscle-relaxing properties. However, it does sensitize the myocardium to catecholamines, increasing the rate of ventricular arrhythmias. Halothane should also be used with caution in patients with brain lesions because it is a potent vasodilator and can increase cerebral perfusion and intracranial pressure. It is rarely used in adult patients but is still used as an induction agent for pediatric patients because of the decreased irritating effects of halothane on the airway. Sevoflurane is now more commonly used in children for the same reason.

     d. **Nitrous oxide** by itself cannot provide surgical anesthesia. When combined with other inhalational agents, it reduces the required dose and subsequent side effects of the other agents. Nitrous oxide is extremely soluble and readily diffuses into any closed gas space, increasing its pressure. As a result, this agent should not be administered to patients with intestinal obstruction or suspected pneumothorax.

3. IV agents

   a. Narcotics can be administered continuously or intermittently. These agents provide superior analgesia but unreliable amnesia. Commonly used narcotics include fentanyl, sufentanil, alfentanil, remifentanil, morphine, and meperidine.

   b. Hypnotics, benzodiazepines, and propofol. Propofol infusion provides excellent hypnosis (unconsciousness) but insignificant analgesia and unreliable amnesia. It causes significant pain on injection and even small bolus doses may induce apnea in susceptible patients. The rapid dissipation of its effects and the low incidence of postoperative nausea have contributed to its widespread use in outpatient surgery. The maintenance dose is 0.1 to 0.2 mg/kg/minute. Lower-dose infusions can be used in the ICU setting. Prolonged infusions may cause hypertriglyceridemia.

   c. Ketamine by itself can provide total anesthesia. The associated emergence of delirium and nightmares limits its use. It provides excellent analgesia and is frequently used for burn patients requiring frequent dressing changes.

G. Recovery from general anesthesia. The goal at the conclusion of surgery is to provide a smooth, rapid return to consciousness, with stable hemodynamics and pulmonary function, protective airway reflexes, and continued analgesia.

   1. Preparation for emergence from anesthesia usually begins before surgical closure, and communication between the surgeon and anesthesiologist facilitates prompt emergence of the patient at the procedure's termination.

   2. Patients recover from the effects of sedation or general or regional anesthesia in the **postanesthesia care unit.** Once they are oriented, comfortable, hemodynamically stable, ventilating adequately, and without signs of anesthetic or surgical complications, they are discharged to the appropriate ward or to home.

H. Complications of general anesthesia

   1. Malignant hyperthermia is a hypermetabolic disorder of skeletal muscle that is characterized by intracellular hypercalcemia and rapid adenosine triphosphate consumption. This condition is initiated by exposure to one or more anesthetic-triggering agents, including desflurane, enflurane, halothane, isoflurane, sevoflurane, and succinylcholine. Its incidence is approximately 1 in 50,000 in adults and 1 in 15,000 in children. The Malignant Hyperthermia Association of the United States (MHAUS) may be called at anytime with questions: **1–800-MH-HYPER.**

   a. Signs and symptoms may occur in the operating room or more than 24 hours postoperatively and include tachycardia, tachypnea, hypertension, hypercapnia, hyperthermia, acidosis (metabolic with/without respiratory component), and skeletal muscle rigidity.

b. Treatment involves immediate administration of dantrolene (Dantrium, Dantamacrin) (1 mg/kg intravenously up to a cumulative dose of 10 mg/kg). This attenuates the rise in intracellular calcium. Repeat doses are given as needed if symptoms persist. Each vial commonly contains 20 mg of dantrolene and 3 g of mannitol and must be mixed with 50 mL of sterile water. Acidosis and hyperkalemia should be monitored and treated appropriately. Intensive care monitoring for 48 to 72 hours is indicated after an acute episode of malignant hyperthermia to evaluate for recurrence, acute tubular necrosis, pulmonary edema, and disseminated intravascular coagulation.

2. Laryngospasm

a. During emergence from anesthesia, noxious stimulation of the vocal cords can occur at light phases of anesthesia. In addition, blood or other oral secretions can irritate the larynx. As a result, the vocal cords may be brought into forceful apposition, and the flow of gas through the larynx may then be restricted or prevented completely. This alone may cause airway compromise or may lead to **negative-pressure pulmonary edema.**

b. Treatment involves the use of positive-pressure ventilation by mask to break the spasm. Such therapy usually is sufficient. Succinylcholine may be required in refractory cases to allow successful ventilation.

3. Nausea and vomiting

a. Cortical (pain, hypotension, hypoxia), **visceral** (gastric distention, visceral traction), **vestibular,** and **chemoreceptor trigger zone** (narcotics) afferent stimuli all can play a role in postoperative nausea and vomiting. The overall incidence is approximately 30%. It is more common in 11- to 14-year-old preadolescents, women, and obese patients. Narcotics, etomidate, inhalational gasses, and reversal agents such as neostigmine have also been implicated.

b. Treatment includes avoiding gastric distention during ventilation as well as administering agents such as prochlorperazine (Compazine), an antidopaminergic agent, 10 mg intravenously or orally every 4 to 6 hours as needed. Other useful agents include ondansetron (Zofran), 4 mg intravenously (dosing can be repeated every 6 to 8 hours if symptoms persist), or droperidol (Droleptan, Dridol) (0,625 mg IV). Droperidol is highly effective but may lead to sedation and the FDA has issued a black box warning because of possibility of prolonging the QT-interval and therefore the patient's ECG has to be monitored.

4. Urinary retention

a. Although very common with spinal anesthesia [see Section II.A.2.a(4)(f)], **urinary retention occurs in only 1% to 3% of cases involving general anesthesia.** It most commonly occurs after pelvic operations and in conjunction with benign prostatic hypertrophy.

   b. Treatment ranges from conservative (early ambulation, having patient sit or stand while attempting to micturate) to aggressive (bladder catheterization).

5. **Hypothermia**
   a. General anesthesia induction causes **peripheral vasodilation,** which leads to internal redistribution of heat, resulting in an increase in peripheral temperature at the expense of the core temperature. The core temperature then decreases in a linear manner until a plateau is reached. Such hypothermia is more pronounced in the elderly. Hypothermia may lead to cardiac arrhythmias and coagulopathy.
   b. Treatment should be preventative: the most effective being warming the operating room overnight or prior to the patient's arrival in the OR and minimizing unnecessary length and extent of exposure of the patient prior to draping. Other measures include passive warming during an operation by insulation of all exposed surfaces. In addition, active warming with forced-air convective warmers is effective, but care should be taken in using warmers with patients with vascular insufficiency (warmers should not be used on ischemic extremities).

6. **Nerve injury**
   a. Nerve palsies can occur secondary to improper positioning of the patient on the operating table or insufficient padding of dependent regions. Such palsies can be long lasting and debilitating.
   b. Prophylactic padding of sensitive regions and attention to **proper positioning** remain the most effective preventative therapies.

7. **Postanesthesia shaking/shivering**
   a. Meperidine (Demerol) and other narcotics (less effective) may relieve the clonic–tonic postanesthesia shivering, which occurs in up to two thirds of patients emerging from anesthesia. The clonic component from residual inhalational anesthetic is also triggered by hypothermia and accentuates the shivering. It has significant metabolic effects including acidosis and myocardial ischemia and may also be painful to the patient.

INTUBATION AND SEDATION

I. EMERGENT INTUBATION BY RAPID-SEQUENCE INDUCTION

A. Patients in respiratory distress outside the operating room may require intubation to ensure adequate oxygenation and ventilatory support. Whenever possible, an anesthesiologist should be alerted and present at the time of intubation to assist if necessary; however, intubation should not be unduly delayed while waiting for an anesthesiologist to arrive.

B. Airway support with 100% oxygen mask ventilation should be initiated before intubation. In the emergent setting or with the hemodynamically unstable patient, rapid-sequence induction of anesthesia with etomidate followed by succinylcholine may be preferred. Succinylcholine should be avoided in patients with severe burns, intracranial bleeds, and eye trauma. Intubation can then be performed via laryngoscopy using an endotracheal tube of appropriate size—in general, a size 8 tube for men and a size 7 tube for women. After inflation of the cuff, bilateral and equal breath sounds should be auscultated, end-tidal CO_2 and pulse oximetry measured, and a portable chest X-ray ordered to ensure proper placement. The patient should be continued on 100% oxygen until transfer to an intensive care setting.

II. SEDATION FOR PROCEDURES

A. Monitored anesthesia care

1. In monitored anesthesia care or local standby cases, **an anesthesiologist is present** to monitor and sedate the patient during the procedure. The surgeon is responsible for analgesia, which is accomplished with local infiltration or peripheral nerve blockade. Sedating or hypnotic medications (e.g., propofol) provide sedation only, and when given in conjunction with inadequate analgesia, they may result in a disinhibited, uncooperative patient.

2. **Monitoring is identical to that required for general or regional anesthesia.** Supplemental oxygen is provided by facemask or nasal cannula.

3. **NPO criteria** are identical to those for general or regional anesthesia.

4. **Considerable variation exists** regarding the response of patients to sedating medications, and protective airway reflexes may be diminished with even small doses.

B. Local procedures in the operating room

1. *Local* implies that **an anesthesiologist is not required** to monitor the patient or provide sedation. It still is advisable for the physician performing the procedure to monitor the ECG, arterial oxygen saturation, and BP even if sedation is not given.

2. **Painful stimuli** can increase vagal tone, resulting in bradycardia, hypotension, and hypoventilation.

C. Sedation outside the operating room

1. **Indications** are to relieve patient anxiety and avoid potentially detrimental hemodynamic sequelae during invasive procedures or diagnostic tests.

2. **Oxygen** should be supplied by nasal cannula or facemask when sedation is given. When benzodiazepines and narcotics are combined, even healthy patients breathing room air may become hypoxic.

3. **Monitoring** should include pulse oximetry, continuous ECG, and BP.

4. The end result should be a calm, easily arousable, cooperative patient. Oversedation may result in hypoventilation, airway obstruction, or disinhibition. Doses of commonly used sedatives are summarized in Table 3-6.

TABLE 3-6	Medications for Short-Term Sedation and Analgesia During Procedures		
Agent	**Route**	**Dose (as needed)**	**Comments**
Midazolam (Versed)	IV	0.5–1 mg q15 min	Benzodiazepines provide sedation only
Meperidine (Demerol)	IV	25–50 mg q10–15 min	Narcotics provide analgesia with unpredictable sedative effects
Fentanyl	IV	25–50 µg q5–10 min	Narcotics provide analgesia with unpredictable sedative effects
Propofol (Diprivan)	IV	10–20 mg over 3–5 min q10 min	May cause hypotension, especially with boluses

IV, intravenous; q, every.

5. **Side effects** that result from benzodiazepine administration include oversedation, respiratory depression, and depressed airway reflexes. Flumazenil (Romazicon), a benzodiazepine antagonist, can be used to reverse such effects. A dose of 0.2 mg intravenously should be administered and repeated every 60 seconds as required to a total dose of 1 mg. It can produce seizures and cardiac arrhythmias. Sedation can recur after 30 to 60 minutes, requiring repeated dosing.

POSTOPERATIVE MEDICATION AND COMPLICATIONS

I. **POSTOPERATIVE ANALGESIA** is provided to minimize patient discomfort and anxiety, attenuate the physiologic stress response to pain, enable optimal pulmonary toilet, and enable early ambulation. Analgesics can be administered by the oral, IV, or epidural route.

A. **IV route.** Many patients are unable to tolerate oral medications in the immediate postoperative period. For these patients, narcotics can be administered intravenously by several mechanisms.

1. **As needed (PRN)**
   a. **Narcotics**
      (1) The **intermittent administration of IV or intramuscular narcotics by nursing staff** has the disadvantage that the narcotics may be given too infrequently, too late, and in insufficient amounts to provide adequate pain control. This may be the only choice in patients who are functionally unable to operate a patient-controlled analgesia (PCA) device.

        (2) Morphine (Duramorph), 2 to 4 mg intravenously every 30 to 60 minutes, or **meperidine,** 50 to 100 mg intravenously every 30 to 60 minutes, should provide adequate analgesia for most patients. Orders should be written to withhold further injections for a respiratory rate of less than 12 breaths/minute or in cases of oversedation.

    b. Nonsteroidal anti-inflammatory drugs (NSAIDs)

        (1) Ketorolac (Toradol) is an NSAID that is available in oral and in injectable forms and is an effective adjunct to opioid therapy. The usual adult dose is 30 mg intramuscularly, followed by 15 to 30 mg every 6 hours for no longer than 48 hours.

        (2) Ketorolac shares the potential side effects of other NSAIDs and should be used cautiously in the elderly and in patients with a history of peptic ulcer disease, renal insufficiency, steroid use, or volume depletion.

  2. PCA

    a. With PCA, the patient has the ability to self-deliver analgesics within **preset safety parameters.** It is imperative to stress to family and friends that only the patient should administer the analgesic.

    b. Patients initially receive **morphine** (100 mg in 100 mL, with each dose delivering 1 mg), **hydromorphone (Dilaudid)** (50 mg in 100 mL, with each dose delivering 0.25 mg), or **meperidine** (1,000 mg in 100 mL, with each dose delivering 20 mg), with a maximum of one dose every 10 minutes. If this treatment provides inadequate pain control, the concentration of the drug can be increased and/or the lockout time period can be reduced.

  3. Continuous "basal" narcotic infusions are rarely used in the surgical population. Respiratory arrest can occur with the "buildup" of narcotic levels.

B. Epidural infusions are useful for treating postoperative pain caused by thoracotomy, extensive abdominal incisions, or orthopedic lower-extremity procedures. Narcotics, local anesthetics, or a mixture of the two can be infused continuously through catheters placed in the patient's lumbar or thoracic epidural space.

C. Oral agents. There are multiple oral agents and combination analgesics.

D. Side effects and complications

  1. Oversedation and respiratory depression

    a. Arousable, spontaneously breathing patients should be given supplemental oxygen and be monitored closely for signs of respiratory depression until mental status improves. Medications for pain or sedation should be decreased accordingly.

    b. Unarousable but spontaneously breathing patients should be treated with oxygen and naloxone (Narcan). One vial of naloxone (0.4 mg) should be diluted in a 10-mL syringe, and 1 mL (0.04 mg) should be administered every 30 to 60 seconds until the patient is arousable. Too much naloxone may result in severe pain and/or severe hypertension with possible pulmonary edema. Adequate ventilation should be confirmed by arterial blood gas measurement. Current opioid administration should be stopped and the regimen decreased. In addition to continuous-pulse oximetry, the patient should be monitored closely for potential recurrence of sedation as the effects of naloxone dissipate.

2. **Apnea**
   a. **Treatment** involves immediate supportive mask ventilation and possible intubation if no improvement in clinical status.
   b. **Naloxone,** 0.2 to 0.4 mg intravenously, should be considered. The same precautions need to be taken into account as mentioned above.

3. **Hypotension and bradycardia**
   a. **Local anesthetics administered via lumbar epidurals** decrease sympathetic tone to the abdominal viscera and lower extremities and greatly increase venous capacitance. Thoracic epidurals can additionally block the cardioaccelerator fibers, resulting in bradycardia.
   b. The **treatment** of choice for any of these situations (excluding bradycardia) is cessation of epidural infusion followed by volume resuscitation. Epinephrine can be used to raise BP acutely; 10 mg is diluted in 100 mL and given intravenously 1 mL at a time. If needed, this mixture can be infused intravenously starting at 15 mL/hour (25 μg/minute). Bradycardia can be treated with atropine, 0.4 to 1 mg intravenously, or glycopyrrolate (Robinul) given intravenously in 0.2-mg increments every 3 to 5 minutes as needed.

4. **Nausea and vomiting**
   a. **Naloxone** in small doses (0.04 to 0.1 mg intravenously as needed).
   b. **Prochlorperazine** (Compazine) 10 mg intravenously or orally every 4 to 6 hours.
   c. **Promethazine** (Phenergan) is a phenothiazine derivative that competitively blocks histamine H_1 receptors. Accidental intra-arterial injection can result in gangrene and there is therefore significant concerns regarding its use.
   d. **Ondansetron** (Zofran) 4 mg intravenously every 6 to 8 hours.
   e. **Metoclopramide** (Reglan) 10 mg intravenously every 6 to 8 hours. It should never be used as a first-line agent because of risk of extrapyramidal side effects.

5. **Pruritus**
   a. **Naloxone,** 0.04 to 0.1 mg intravenously, is effective.
   b. **Diphenhydramine (Benadryl),** 25 to 50 mg intravenously as needed, may provide symptomatic relief.

6. **Monoamine oxidase inhibitors** (e.g., isocarboxazid, phenelzine, and even hydralazine) may **interact adversely with** Phenylpiperidine derivative *Opioids* such as *Meperidine/(Pethidine), Tramadol, Methadone, Fentanyl.* This interaction may result in severe hemodynamic swings, respiratory depression, seizures, diaphoresis, hyperthermia, and coma. Meperidine has been most frequently implicated and should be avoided.

4

Fluid, Electrolyte, and Acid–Base Disorders

Ashley M. Holder and Richard S. Hotchkiss

DIAGNOSIS AND TREATMENT OF FLUID, ELECTROLYTE, AND ACID–BASE DISORDERS

I. DEFINITION OF BODY FLUID COMPARTMENTS. Water constitutes 50% to 70% of lean body weight. Total body water content is slightly higher in men, is most concentrated in skeletal muscle, and declines steadily with age. Total body water is divided into an intracellular fluid compartment and an extracellular fluid compartment, which consists of an intravascular compartment and an interstitial compartment, as illustrated in Figure 4-1. The extracellular and intracellular compartments have distinct electrolyte compositions. The principal extracellular cation is Na^+, and the principal extracellular anions are Cl^- and HCO_3^-. In contrast, the principal intracellular cations are K^+ and Mg^{2+}, and the principal intracellular anions are phosphates and negatively charged proteins.

II. OSMOLALITY AND TONICITY. *Osmolality* refers to the number of osmoles of solute particles per kilogram of water. Total osmolality is comprised of both effective and ineffective components. Effective osmoles cannot freely permeate cell membranes and are restricted to either the intracellular or extracellular fluid compartments. The asymmetric accumulation of effective osmoles in either extracellular fluid (e.g., Na^+, glucose, mannitol, and glycine) or intracellular fluid (e.g., K^+, amino acids, and organic acids) causes transcompartmental movement of water. Because the cell membrane is freely permeable to water, the osmolalities of the extracellular and intracellular compartments are equal. The effective osmolality of a solution is equivalent to its tonicity. Ineffective osmoles, in contrast, freely cross cell membranes and therefore are unable to affect the movement of water between compartments. Such ineffective solutes (e.g., urea, ethanol, and methanol) contribute to total osmolality but not to tonicity. *Tonicity,* not osmolality, is the physiologic parameter that the body attempts to regulate.

III. COMMON ELECTROLYTE DISORDERS

A. **Sodium**

1. **Physiology.** The normal individual consumes 3 to 5 g of NaCl (130 to 217 mmol Na^+) daily. Sodium balance is maintained primarily by the kidneys. Normal Na^+ concentration is 135 to 145 mmol/L (310 to 333 mg/dL). Potential sources of significant Na^+ loss include sweat,

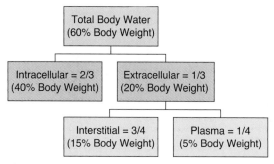

Figure 4-1. Body fluid compartments.

urine, and gastrointestinal secretions (Table 4-1). The Na^+ concentration largely determines the plasma osmolality (P_{osm}), which can be approximated by the following equation:

$$P_{osm}\left(mOsm\middle/L\right) = 2 \times serum \left[Na^+\left(\frac{mmol}{L}\right) + K^+\left(\frac{mmol}{L}\right)\right]$$

$$+ \frac{glucose\left(\frac{mg}{dL}\right)}{18} + \frac{BUN\left(\frac{mg}{dL}\right)}{2}.8,$$

where BUN is blood urea nitrogen. Normal P_{osm} is 290 to 310 mOsm/L. In general, hypotonicity and hypertonicity coincide with hyponatremia and hypernatremia, respectively. However, Na^+ concentration and total body water are controlled by independent mechanisms. As a consequence, hyponatremia or hypernatremia may occur in conjunction with hypovolemia, hypervolemia, or euvolemia.

2. **Hyponatremia**
   a. **Causes and diagnosis.** The diagnostic approach to hyponatremia is illustrated in Figure 4-2. Hyponatremia may occur in conjunction with hypertonicity, isotonicity, or hypotonicity. Consequently, it is necessary to measure the serum osmolality to evaluate patients with hyponatremia.
      (1) **Isotonic hyponatremia.** Hyperlipidemic and hyperproteinemic states result in an isotonic expansion of the circulating plasma volume and cause a decrease in serum Na^+ concentration, although total body Na^+ remains unchanged. The reduction in serum sodium (mmol/L) can be estimated by multiplying the measured plasma lipid concentration (mg/dL) by 0.002 or the increase in serum protein concentration above 8 g/dL by 0.25. Isotonic, sodium-free solutions of glucose, mannitol, and glycine are restricted initially to the extracellular fluid and may similarly result in transient hyponatremia [see Section III.A.2.c (5)].
      (2) **Hypertonic hyponatremia.** Hyperglycemia may result in a transient fluid shift from the intracellular to the extracellular compartment, thereby diluting serum Na^+ concentration.

TABLE 4-1	Composition of Gastrointestinal Secretions				
Source	Volume (mL/24 hr)[a]	Na⁺ (mmol/L)[b]	K⁺ (mmol/L)[b]	Cl⁻ (mmol/L)[b]	HCO₃ (mmol/L)[b]
Salivary	1,500 (500–2,000)	10 (2–10)	26 (20–30)	10 (8–18)	30
Stomach	1,500 (100–4,000)	60 (9–116)	10 (0–32)	130 (8–154)	0
Duodenum	(100–2,000)	140	5	80	0
Ileum	3,000	140 (80–150)	5 (2–8)	104 (43–137)	30
Colon	(100–9,000)	60	30	40	0
Pancreas	(100–800)	140 (113–185)	5 (3–7)	75 (54–95)	115
Bile	(50–800)	145 (131–164)	5 (312)	100 (89–180)	35

[a]Average volume (range).
[b]Average concentration (range).
Reprinted with permission from Faber MD, Schmidt RJ, Bear RA, et al. Management of fluid, electrolyte, and acid-base disorders in surgical patients. In: Narins RG, ed. *Clinical Disorders of Fluid and Electrolyte Metabolism.* New York: McGraw-Hill; 1994:1424.

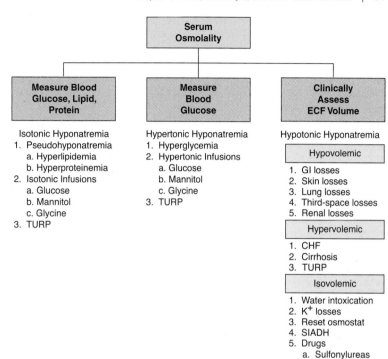

Figure 4-2. Diagnostic approach to hyponatremia. CHF, congestive heart failure; ECF, extracellular fluid; GI, gastrointestinal; SIADH, syndrome of inappropriate antidiuretic hormone secretion; TURP, transurethral resection of the prostate. (Adapted from Narins RG, Jones ER, Stom MC, et al. Diagnostic strategies in disorders of fluid, electrolyte, and acid–base homeostasis. *Am J Med.* 1982;72:496–520.)

The expected decrease in serum Na^+ is approximately 1.3 to 1.6 mmol/L (2.99 to 3.68 mg/dL) for each 100-mg/dL increase in blood glucose above 200 mg/dL. Rapid infusion of hypertonic solutions of glucose, mannitol, or glycine may have a similar effect on Na^+ concentration [see Section III.A.2.c (5)].

(3) **Hypotonic hyponatremia** is classified on the basis of extracellular fluid volume. Hypotonic hyponatremia generally develops as a consequence of the administration and retention of hypotonic fluids [e.g., dextrose 5% in water (D5 W) and 0.45% NaCl] and rarely from the loss of salt-containing fluids alone.

(a) **Hypovolemic hypotonic hyponatremia** in the surgical patient most commonly results from replacement of sodium-rich fluid losses (e.g., from the GI tract, skin, or lungs) with an insufficient volume of hypotonic fluid (e.g., D5 W and 0.45% NaCl).

(b) **Hypervolemic hypotonic hyponatremia.** The edematous states of congestive heart failure, liver disease, and nephrosis occur in conjunction with inadequate circulating blood volume. This serves as a stimulus for the renal retention of sodium and of water. Disproportionate accumulation of water results in hyponatremia.

(c) **Isovolemic hypotonic hyponatremia**

   (i) **Water intoxication** typically occurs in the patient who consumes large quantities of water and has mildly impaired renal function (primary polydipsia). Alternatively, it may be the result of the administration of large quantities of hypotonic fluid in the patient with generalized renal failure.

   (ii) **K^+ loss,** either from GI fluid loss or secondary to diuretics, may result in isovolemic hyponatremia due to cellular exchange of these cations.

   (iii) **Reset osmostat.** Normally, the serum "osmostat" is set at 285 mOsm/L. In some individuals, the osmostat is "reset" downward, thus maintaining a lower serum osmolality. Several chronic diseases (e.g., tuberculosis and cirrhosis) predispose to this condition. These patients respond normally to water loads with suppression of antidiuretic hormone (ADH) secretion and excretion of free water.

   (iv) **SIADH** (syndrome of inappropriate ADH) is characterized by low plasma osmolality (<280 mOsm/L), hyponatremia (<135 mmol/L), low urine output with concentrated urine (>100 mOsm/kg), elevated urine sodium (>20 mEq/L), and clinical euvolemia. The major causes of SIADH include pulmonary disorders (e.g., atelectasis, empyema, pneumothorax, and respiratory failure), central nervous system disorders (e.g., trauma, meningitis, tumors, and subarachnoid hemorrhage), drugs (e.g., cyclophosphamide, cisplatin, and nonsteroidal anti-inflammatory drugs), and ectopic ADH production (e.g., small-cell lung carcinoma).

(4) **Transurethral resection syndrome** refers to hyponatremia in conjunction with cardiovascular and neurologic manifestations, which infrequently follow transurethral resection of the prostate. This syndrome results from intraoperative absorption of significant amounts of irrigation fluid (e.g., glycine, sorbitol, or mannitol). Isotonic, hypotonic, or hypertonic hyponatremia may occur. Management of these patients may be complicated.

b. **Clinical manifestations.** Symptoms associated with hyponatremia are predominantly neurologic and result from hypoosmolality. A decrease in P_{osm} causes intracellular water influx, increased intracellular volume, and cerebral edema. Symptoms include lethargy, confusion, nausea, vomiting, seizures, and coma. The likelihood that symptoms will occur is related to the degree of hyponatremia and to the rapidity with which it develops. Chronic hyponatremia is often asymptomatic until the serum Na^+ concentration falls below 110 to 120 mEq/L (253 to 276 mg/dL). An acute drop in the serum Na^+ concentration to 120 to 130 mEq/L (276 to 299 mg/dL), conversely, may produce symptoms.

c. **Treatment**

(1) **Isotonic and hypertonic hyponatremia** correct with resolution of the underlying disorder.

(2) **Hypovolemic hyponatremia** can be managed with administration of 0.9% NaCl to correct volume deficits and replace ongoing losses.

(3) **Water intoxication** responds to fluid restriction (1,000 mL/day).

(4) For **SIADH,** water restriction (1,000 mL/day) should be attempted initially. The addition of a loop diuretic (furosemide) or an osmotic diuretic (mannitol) may be necessary in refractory cases.

(5) **Hypervolemic hyponatremia** may respond to water restriction (1,000 mL/day) to return Na^+ to greater than 130 mmol/L (299 mg/dL). In cases of severe congestive heart failure, optimizing cardiac performance may assist in Na^+ correction. If the edematous hyponatremic patient becomes symptomatic, plasma Na^+ can be increased to a safe level by the use of a loop diuretic (furosemide, 20 to 200 mg intravenously every 6 hours) while replacing urinary Na^+ losses with 3% NaCl. A reasonable approach is to replace approximately 25% of the hourly urine output with 3% NaCl. Hypertonic saline should not be administered to these patients without concomitant diuretic therapy. Administration of synthetic brain natriuretic peptide (BNP) is also useful therapeutically in the setting of acute heart failure because it inhibits Na^+ reabsorption at the cortical collecting duct and inhibits the action of vasopressin on water permeability at the inner medullary collecting duct.

(6) In the presence of symptoms or extreme hyponatremia [Na^+ <110 mmol/L (253 mg/dL)], hypertonic saline (3% NaCl) is indicated. Serum Na^+ should be corrected to approximately 120 mmol/L (276 mg/dL). The quantity of 3% NaCl that is required to increase serum Na^+ to 120 mmol/L (276 mg/dL) can be estimated by calculating the Na^+ deficit:

$$Na^+ \text{ deficit (mmol)} = 0.60 \times \text{lean body wt (kg)}$$
$$\times \left[120 - \text{measured } Na^+\left(\frac{mmol}{L} \right) \right]$$

(Each liter of 3% NaCl provides 513 mmol Na^+). The use of a loop diuretic (furosemide, 20 to 200 mg intravenously every 6 hours) may increase the effectiveness of 3% NaCl administration. Central pontine demyelination can occur in the setting of correction of hyponatremia. The risk factors for demyelination are controversial but appear to be related to the chronicity of hyponatremia (>48 hours) and the rate of correction. The serum Na^+ should be increased by no more than 12 mmol/L (27.6 mg/dL) in 24 hours of treatment [i.e., Na^+ <0.5 mmol (1.15 mg/dL)/hour]. For acute hyponatremia (<48 hours), the serum Na^+ may be corrected more rapidly [i.e., Na^+ = 1 to 2 mmol (2.3 to 4.6 mg/dL)/hour]. The patient's volume status should be carefully monitored over this time, and the serum Na^+ should be measured frequently (every 1 to 2 hours). Once the serum Na^+ concentration reaches 120 mmol/L (276 mg/dL) and symptoms have resolved, administration of hypertonic saline can be discontinued.

3. **Hypernatremia**
   a. **Diagnosis.** Hypernatremia is uniformly hypertonic and typically the result of water loss in excess of solute. Patients are categorized on the basis of their extracellular fluid volume status. The diagnostic approach to hypernatremia is illustrated in Figure 4-3.

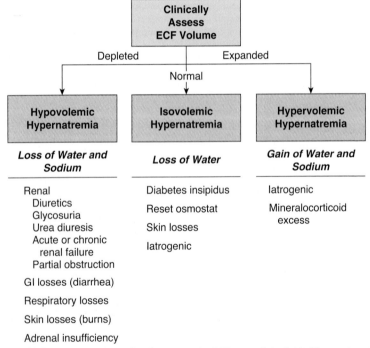

Figure 4-3. Diagnostic approach to hypernatremia. ECF, extracellular fluid; GI, gastrointestinal. (Adapted from Narins RG, Jones ER, Stom MC, et al. Diagnostic strategies in disorders of fluid, electrolyte, and acid-base homeostasis. *Am J Med.* 1982;72:496–520.)

(1) **Hypovolemic hypernatremia.** Any net loss of hypotonic body fluid results in extracellular volume depletion and hypernatremia. Common causes in the surgical patient include diuresis as well as GI, respiratory, and cutaneous (e.g., burns) fluid losses. Chronic renal failure and partial urinary tract obstruction also may cause hypovolemic hypernatremia.

(2) **Hypervolemic hypernatremia** in the surgical patient is most commonly iatrogenic and results from the parenteral administration of hypertonic solutions (e.g., $NaHCO_3$, saline, medications, and nutrition).

(3) **Isovolemic hypernatremia**

   (a) **Hypotonic losses.** Constant evaporative losses from the skin and respiratory tract, in addition to ongoing urinary free water losses, require the administration of approximately 750 mL of electrolyte-free water (e.g., D5 W) daily to parenterally maintained afebrile patients. Inappropriate replacement of these hypotonic losses with isotonic fluids is the most common cause of isovolemic hypernatremia in the hospitalized surgical patient.

   (b) **Diabetes insipidus** is characterized by polyuria and polydipsia in association with hypotonic urine (urine osmolality <200 mOsm/kg or a specific gravity of <1.005) and a high plasma osmolality (>287 mOsm/kg). *Central diabetes insipidus* (CDI) describes a defect in the hypothalamic secretion of ADH and is commonly seen after head trauma or hypophysectomy. CDI may also occur as a result of intracranial tumors, infections, vascular disorders (aneurysms), hypoxia, or medications (e.g., clonidine and phencyclidine). *Nephrogenic diabetes insipidus* (NDI) describes renal insensitivity to normally secreted ADH. NDI may be familial or drug induced (e.g., lithium, demeclocycline, methoxyflurane, and glyburide) or may occur as a result of hypokalemia, hypercalcemia, or intrinsic renal disease. If CDI and NDI are not distinguishable clinically, they can be differentiated by dehydration testing.

   (c) **Therapeutic.** Hypertonic saline may be administered for deliberate hypernatremia to control elevated intracranial pressure (ICP) and cerebral edema after head injury. Apart from osmotic properties, hypertonic saline also has hemodynamic, vasoregulatory, and immunomodulatory effects. Two prospective, randomized studies demonstrated the efficacy of using hypertonic saline to reduce ICP. A study of adult patients with brain injury in an intensive care unit (ICU) comparing a 7.5% saline/6% dextran solution (HSD) and a 20% mannitol solution showed that HSD lowered ICP more effectively and for a longer duration than did mannitol (*Crit Care Med.* 2005;33:196). Another study in children with severe head injury comparing hypertonic saline (Na^+ 268 mmol/L) with lactated

Ringer's solution (Na$^+$ 131 mmol/L) demonstrated that an increase in serum sodium concentration was correlated with a reduction in ICP and an elevation in cerebral perfusion pressure. The children receiving hypertonic saline had fewer complications and a shorter ICU stay than the children receiving lactated Ringer's solution (*Crit Care Med.* 1998;26:1265).

b. Clinical manifestations. Symptoms of hypernatremia that are related to the hyperosmolar state are primarily neurologic. These initially include lethargy, weakness, and irritability and may progress to fasciculations, seizures, coma, and irreversible neurologic damage.

c. Treatment

(1) **Water deficit** associated with hypernatremia can be estimated using the following equation where TBW = Total body weight:

$$\text{Water deficit (L)} = 0.60 \times \text{TBW(kg)} \times [(\text{serum Na}^\uparrow + (\text{mmol/L}))/140 - 1]$$

Rapid correction of hypernatremia can result in cerebral edema and permanent neurologic damage. Consequently, only one half of the water deficit should be corrected over the first 24 hours, with the remainder being corrected over the following 2 to 3 days. Serial Na$^+$ measurements are necessary to ensure that the rate of correction is adequate but not excessive. Oral fluid intake is acceptable for replacing water deficits. If oral intake is not possible, D5 W or D5 0.45% NaCl can be substituted. In addition to the actual water deficit, insensible losses and urinary output must be replaced.

(2) **Diabetes insipidus**

(a) **Central diabetes insipidus** can be treated with desmopressin acetate administered intranasally [0.1 to 0.4 mL (10 to 40 μg) daily] or subcutaneously or intravenously [0.5 to 1 mL (2 to 4 μg) daily].

(b) **Nephrogenic diabetes insipidus** treatment requires removal of any potentially offending drug and correction of electrolyte abnormalities. If these measures are ineffective, dietary sodium restriction in conjunction with a thiazide diuretic may be useful (hydrochlorothiazide, 50 to 100 mg/day orally).

B. Potassium

1. **Physiology.** K$^+$ is the major intracellular cation, with only 2% of total body K$^+$ located in the extracellular space. The normal serum concentration is 3.3 to 4.9 mmol/L (12.9 to 19.1 mg/dL). Approximately 50 to 100 mmol (195 to 390 mg/dL) K$^+$ is ingested and absorbed daily. Ninety percent of K$^+$ is renally excreted, with the remainder eliminated in stools.

2. **Hypokalemia**

a. **Causes.** K$^+$ depletion from inadequate intake alone is rare. Common causes of K$^+$ depletion in the surgical patient include GI losses (e.g., diarrhea, persistent vomiting, and nasogastric suctioning), renal losses (e.g., diuretics, fluid mobilization, and amphotericin B), and cutaneous losses (e.g., burns). Other causes of hypokalemia include acute intracellular K^+ uptake (associated with insulin excess, metabolic alkalosis, myocardial infarction, delirium tremens, hypothermia, and theophylline toxicity). Hypokalemia may also occur in the malnourished patient after initiation of total parenteral nutrition (refeeding syndrome), caused by the incorporation of K^+ into rapidly dividing cells.

b. **Clinical manifestations.** Mild hypokalemia [K^+ >3 mmol/L (11.7 mg/dL)] is generally asymptomatic. Symptoms occur with severe K^+ deficiency [K^+ <3 mmol/L (11.7 mg/dL)] and are primarily cardiovascular. Early electrocardiogram (ECG) manifestations include ectopy, T-wave depression, and prominent U waves. Severe depletion increases susceptibility to re-entrant arrhythmias.

c. **Treatment.** In mild hypokalemia, oral replacement is suitable. Typical daily therapy for the treatment of mild hypokalemia in the patient with intact renal function is 40 to 100 mmol (156 to 390 mg) KCl orally in single or divided doses. Parenteral therapy is indicated in the presence of severe depletion, significant symptoms, or oral intolerance. K^+ concentrations (administered as chloride, acetate, or phosphate) in peripherally administered intravenous fluids should not exceed 40 mmol/L (156 mg/dL), and the rate of administration should not exceed 20 mmol (78 mg)/hour. However, higher K^+ concentrations [60 to 80 mmol/L (234 to 312 mg/dL)] administered more rapidly (with cardiac monitoring) are indicated in cases of severe hypokalemia, for cardiac arrhythmias, and in the management of diabetic ketoacidosis. Administration of high K^+ concentrations via subclavian, jugular, or right atrial catheters should be avoided because local K^+ concentrations may be cardiotoxic. Hypomagnesemia frequently accompanies hypokalemia and generally must be corrected to replenish K^+ effectively.

3. **Hyperkalemia**

   a. **Causes and diagnosis.** Hyperkalemia may occur with normal or elevated stores of total body K^+. Pseudohyperkalemia is a laboratory abnormality that reflects K^+ release from leukocytes and platelets during coagulation. Spurious elevation in K^+ may result from hemolysis or phlebotomy from a strangulated arm. Abnormal redistribution of K^+ from the intracellular to the extracellular compartment may occur as a result of insulin deficiency, β-adrenergic receptor blockade, acute acidemia, rhabdomyolysis, cell lysis (after chemotherapy), digitalis intoxication, reperfusion of ischemic limbs, and succinylcholine administration.

   b. **Clinical manifestations.** Mild hyperkalemia [K^+ = 5 to 6 mmol/L (19.5 to 23.4 mg/dL)] is generally asymptomatic. Signs of significant hyperkalemia [K^+ >6.5 mmol/L (25.4 mg/dL)] are, most notably, ECG abnormalities: symmetric peaking of T waves, reduced P-wave voltage, and widening of the QRS complex. If untreated, severe hyperkalemia ultimately may cause a sinusoidal ECG pattern.

c. **Treatment**

(1) **Mild hyperkalemia** [K^+ = 5 to 6 mmol/L (19.5 to 23.4 mg/dL)] can be treated conservatively by the reduction in daily K^+ intake and, if needed, the addition of a loop diuretic (e.g., furosemide) to promote renal elimination. Any medication that is capable of impairing K^+ homeostasis (e.g., nonselective β-adrenergic antagonists, angiotensin-converting enzyme inhibitors, K^+-sparing diuretics, and nonsteroidal anti-inflammatory drugs) should be discontinued, if possible.

(2) **Severe hyperkalemia** [K^+ >6.5 mmol/L (25.4 mg/dL)]

(a) **Temporizing measures** produce shifts of potassium from the extracellular to the intracellular space.

(i) **$NaHCO_3$** [1 mmol/kg or 1 to 2 ampules (50 mL each) of 8.4% $NaHCO_3$] can be infused intravenously over a 3- to 5-minute period. This dose can be repeated after 10 to 15 minutes if ECG abnormalities persist.

(ii) **Dextrose** (0.5 g/kg body weight) infused with insulin (0.3 unit of regular insulin/g of dextrose) transiently lowers serum K^+ (the usual dose is 25 g dextrose, with 6 to 10 units of regular insulin given simultaneously as an intravenous bolus).

(iii) **Inhaled β-agonists** [e.g., albuterol sulfate, 2 to 4 mL of 0.5% solution (10 to 20 mg) delivered via nebulizer] have been shown to lower plasma K^+, with a duration of action of up to 2 hours. Although only modest increases in heart rate and blood pressure have been reported when the nebulized form of this drug is used, caution is warranted in patients with known or suspected cardiovascular disease.

(iv) **Calcium gluconate 10%** (5 to 10 mL intravenously over 2 minutes) should be administered to patients with profound ECG changes who are not receiving digitalis preparations. Calcium functions to stabilize the myocardium.

(b) **Therapeutic measures** to definitively decrease total body potassium by increasing potassium excretion:

(i) **Sodium polystyrene sulfonate** (Kayexalate), a Na^+-K^+ exchange resin, can be administered orally (20 to 50 g of the resin in 100 to 200 mL of 20% sorbitol every 4 hours) or rectally (as a retention enema, 50 g of the resin in 50 mL of 70% sorbitol added to 100 to 200 mL of water every 1 to 2 hours initially, followed by administration every 6 hours) to promote K^+ elimination. A decrease in serum K^+ level typically occurs 2 to 4 hours after administration.

(ii) **Hydration** with 0.9% NaCl in combination with a **loop diuretic** (e.g., furosemide, 20 to 100 mg intravenously) should be administered to patients with adequate renal function to promote renal K^+ excretion.

(iii) **Dialysis** is definitive therapy in severe, refractory, or life-threatening hyperkalemia.

C. **Calcium**

1. **Physiology.** Serum calcium (8.9 to 10.3 mg/dL or 2.23 to 2.57 mmol/L) exists in three forms: ionized (45%), protein bound (40%), and in a complex with freely diffusible compounds (15%). Only free ionized Ca^{2+} (4.6 to 5.1 mg/dL or 1.15 to 1.27 mmol/L) is physiologically active. Daily calcium intake ranges from 500 to 1,000 mg, with absorption varying considerably. Normal calcium metabolism is under the influence of parathyroid hormone (PTH) and vitamin D. PTH promotes calcium resorption from bone and reclamation of calcium from the glomerular filtrate. Vitamin D increases calcium absorption from the intestinal tract.

2. **Hypocalcemia**

   a. **Causes and diagnosis** Hypocalcemia most commonly occurs as a consequence of calcium sequestration or vitamin D deficiency. Calcium sequestration may occur in the setting of acute pancreatitis, rhabdomyolysis, or rapid administration of blood (citrate acting as a calcium chelator). Transient hypocalcemia may occur after total thyroidectomy, secondary to vascular compromise of the parathyroid glands, and after parathyroidectomy. In the latter case, serum Ca^{2+} reaches its lowest level within 48 to 72 hours after operation, returning to normal in 2 to 3 days. Hypocalcemia may occur in conjunction with Mg^{2+} depletion, which simultaneously impairs PTH secretion and function. Acute alkalemia (e.g., from rapid administration of parenteral bicarbonate or hyperventilation) may produce clinical hypocalcemia with a normal serum calcium concentration due to an abrupt decrease in the ionized fraction. Because 40% of serum calcium is bound to albumin, hypoalbuminemia may decrease total serum calcium significantly—a fall in serum albumin of 1 g/dL decreases serum calcium by approximately 0.8 mg/dL (0.2 mmol/L). Ionized Ca^{2+} is unaffected by albumin. As a consequence, the diagnosis of hypocalcemia should be based on ionized, not total serum, calcium.

   b. **Clinical manifestations.** Tetany is the major clinical finding and may be demonstrated by Chvostek's sign (facial muscle spasm elicited by tapping over the branches of the facial nerve). The patient may also complain of perioral numbness and tingling. In addition, hypocalcemia can be associated with QT-interval prolongation and ventricular arrhythmias.

   c. **Treatment**

      (1) **Parenteral therapy.** Asymptomatic patients, even those with moderate hypocalcemia (calcium 6 to 7 mg/dL or 1.5 to 1.75 mmol/L), do not require parenteral therapy. Symptoms such as overt tetany, laryngeal spasm, or seizures are indications for parenteral calcium. Approximately 200 mg of elemental calcium is needed to abort an attack of tetany. Initial therapy consists in the administration of a calcium bolus (10 to 20 mL

of 10% calcium gluconate over 10 minutes) followed by a maintenance infusion of 1 to 2 mg/kg elemental calcium/hour. Calcium chloride contains three times more elemental calcium than calcium gluconate; one 10-mL ampule of 10% calcium chloride contains 272 mg (13.6 mEq) elemental calcium, whereas one 10-mL ampule of 10% calcium gluconate contains only 90 mg (4.6 mEq) elemental calcium. The serum calcium level typically normalizes in 6 to 12 hours with this regimen, at which time the maintenance rate can be decreased to 0.3 to 0.5 mg/kg/hour. In addition to monitoring calcium levels frequently during therapy, one should check Mg^{2+}, phosphorus, and K^+ levels and replete as necessary. Calcium should be administered cautiously to patients who are receiving digitalis preparations because digitalis toxicity may be potentiated. Once the serum calcium level is normal, oral therapy can be initiated.

  (2) **Oral therapy.** Calcium salts are available for oral administration (calcium carbonate, calcium gluconate). Each 1,250-mg tablet of calcium carbonate provides 500 mg of elemental calcium (25.4 mEq), and a 1,000-mg tablet of calcium gluconate has 90 mg (4.6 mEq) of elemental calcium. In chronic hypocalcemia, with serum calcium levels of 7.6 mg/dL (1.9 mmol/L) or higher, the daily administration of 1,000 to 2,000 mg of elemental calcium alone may suffice. When hypocalcemia is more severe, calcium salts should be supplemented with a vitamin D preparation. Daily therapy can be initiated with 50,000 IU of calciferol, 0.4 mg of dihydrotachysterol, or 0.25 to 0.50 μg of 1,25-dihydroxyvitamin D_3 orally. Subsequent therapy should be adjusted as necessary.

3. Hypercalcemia

  a. **Causes and diagnosis.** Causes of hypercalcemia include malignancy, hyperparathyroidism, hyperthyroidism, vitamin D intoxication, immobilization, long-term total parenteral nutrition, thiazide diuretics, and granulomatous disease. The finding of an elevated PTH level in the face of hypercalcemia supports the diagnosis of hyperparathyroidism. If the PTH level is normal or low, further evaluation is necessary to identify one of the previously cited diagnoses.

  b. **Clinical manifestations.** Mild hypercalcemia (calcium <12 mg/dL or <3 mmol/L) is generally asymptomatic. The hypercalcemia of hyperparathyroidism is associated infrequently with classic parathyroid bone disease and nephrolithiasis. Manifestations of severe hypercalcemia include altered mental status, diffuse weakness, dehydration, adynamic ileus, nausea, vomiting, and severe constipation. The cardiac effects of hypercalcemia include QT-interval shortening and arrhythmias.

  c. **Treatment of hypercalcemia** depends on the severity of the symptoms. Mild hypercalcemia (calcium <12 mg/dL or <3 mmol/L) can be managed conservatively by restricting calcium intake and treating the underlying disorder. Volume depletion should be corrected if present, and vitamin D, calcium supplements, and thiazide diuretics should be discontinued. The treatment of more severe hypercalcemia may require the following measures:

(1) NaCl 0.9% and loop diuretics may rapidly correct hypercalcemia. In the patient with normal cardiovascular and renal function, 0.9% NaCl (250 to 500 mL/hour) with furosemide (20 mg intravenously every 4 to 6 hours) can be administered initially. The rate of 0.9% NaCl infusion and the dose of furosemide should subsequently be adjusted to maintain a urine output of 200 to 300 mL/hour. Serum Mg^{2+}, phosphorus, and K^+ levels should be monitored and repleted as necessary. The inclusion of KCl (20 mmol) and $MgSO_4$ (8 to 16 mEq or 1 to 2 g) in each liter of fluid may prevent hypokalemia and hypomagnesemia. This treatment may promote the loss of as much as 2 g of calcium over 24 hours.

(2) Salmon calcitonin, in conjunction with adequate hydration, is useful for the treatment of hypercalcemia associated with malignancy and with primary hyperparathyroidism. Salmon calcitonin can be administered either subcutaneously or intramuscularly. Skin testing by subcutaneous injection of 1 IU is recommended before progressing to the initial dose of 4 IU/kg intravenously or subcutaneously every 12 hours. A hypocalcemic effect may be seen as early as 6 to 10 hours after administration. The dose may be doubled if unsuccessful after 48 hours of treatment. The maximum recommended dose is 8 IU/kg every 6 hours.

(3) Pamidronate disodium, in conjunction with adequate hydration, is useful for the treatment of hypercalcemia associated with malignancy. For moderate hypercalcemia (calcium 12 to 13.5 mg/dL or 3 to 3.38 mmol/L), 60 mg of pamidronate diluted in 1 L of 0.45% NaCl, 0.9% NaCl, or D5 W should be infused over 24 hours. For severe hypercalcemia, the dose of pamidronate is 90 mg. If hypercalcemia recurs, a repeat dose of pamidronate can be given after 7 days. The safety of pamidronate for use in patients with significant renal impairment is not established.

(4) Plicamycin (25 μg/kg, diluted in 1 L of 0.9% NaCl or D5 W, infused over 4 to 6 hours each day for 3 to 4 days) is useful for treatment of hypercalcemia associated with malignancy. The onset of action is between 1 and 2 days, with a duration of action of up to 1 week.

D. Phosphorus

1. Physiology. Extracellular fluid contains less than 1% of total body stores of phosphorus at a concentration of 2.5 to 4.5 mg/dL (0.81 to 1.45 mmol/L). Phosphorus balance is regulated by a number of hormones that also control calcium metabolism. As a consequence, derangements in concentrations of phosphorus and calcium frequently coexist. The average adult consumes 800 to 1,000 mg of phosphorus daily, which is predominantly renally excreted.

2. **Hypophosphatemia**
   a. **Causes**
      (1) **Decreased intestinal phosphate absorption** results from vitamin D deficiency, malabsorption, and the use of phosphate binders (e.g., aluminum-, magnesium-, calcium-, or iron-containing compounds).
      (2) **Renal phosphate loss** may occur with acidosis, alkalosis, diuretic therapy (particularly acetazolamide), during recovery from acute tubular necrosis, and during hyperglycemia as a result of osmotic diuresis.
      (3) **Phosphorus redistribution** from the extracellular to the intracellular compartment occurs principally with respiratory alkalosis and administration of nutrients such as glucose (particularly in the malnourished patient). This transient decrease in serum phosphorus is of no clinical significance unless there is a significant total body deficit. Significant hypophosphatemia may also occur in malnourished patients after the initiation of total parenteral nutrition (refeeding syndrome) as a result of the incorporation of phosphorus into rapidly dividing cells.
      (4) Hypophosphatemia may develop in **burn patients** as a result of excessive phosphaturia during fluid mobilization and incorporation of phosphorus into new tissues during wound healing.
   b. **Clinical manifestations**. Moderate hypophosphatemia (phosphorus 1 to 2.5 mg/dL or 0.32 to 0.81 mmol/L) is usually asymptomatic. Severe hypophosphatemia (phosphorus <1 mg/dL or 0.32 mmol/L) may result in respiratory muscle dysfunction, diffuse weakness, and flaccid paralysis.
   c. **Treatment.** A study of patients at Barnes-Jewish Hospital's surgical ICU (Saint Louis, MO) demonstrated that the use of an aggressive phosphorus repletion protocol based on a patient's admission weight (kg) and most recent phosphorus level (mg/dL) leads to more successful treatment of hypophosphatemia than physician-directed therapy (see Table 4-2). Adequate repletion of phosphorus is especially important in critically ill patients, who are more likely to experience adverse physiologic consequences from hypophosphatemia, including the inability to be weaned from the ventilator, organ dysfunction, and death. Phosphorus replacement should begin with intravenous therapy, especially for moderate (1 to 1.7 mg/dL) or severe (<1 mg/dL) hypophosphatemia (*J Am Coll Surg.* 2004;198:198). Risks of intravenous therapy include hyperphosphatemia, hypocalcemia, hypotension, hyperkalemia (with potassium phosphate), hypomagnesemia, hyperosmolality, metastatic calcification, and renal failure. Five to 7 days of intravenous repletion may be required before intracellular stores are replenished. Once the serum phosphorus level exceeds 2 mg/dL (0.65 mmol/L), oral therapy can be initiated with a sodium-potassium phosphate salt [e.g., Neutra-Phos, 250 to 500 mg (8 to 16 mmol phosphorus)

TABLE 4-2	Phosphorus Repletion Protocol		
Phosphorus Level	Weight 40–60 kg	Weight 61–80 kg	Weight 81–120 kg
1 mg/dL	30 mmol Phos IV	40 mmol Phos IV	50 mmol Phos IV
1–1.7 mg/dL	20 mmol Phos IV	30 mmol Phos IV	40 mmol Phos IV
1.8–2.2 mg/dL	10 mmol Phos IV	15 mmol Phos IV	20 mmol Phos IV

If the patient's potassium is <4, use potassium phosphorus.
If the patient's potassium is >4, use sodium phosphorus.
IV, intravenous; Phos, phosphorus.
Adapted with permission from Taylor BE, Huey WY, Buchman TG, et al. Effectiveness of a protocol based on patient weight and serum phosphorus levels in repleting hypophosphatemia in a surgical ICU. *J Am Coll Surg* 2004;198:198–204.

orally four times a day; each 250-mg tablet of Neutra-Phos contains 7 mmol each of K^+ and Na^+].

3. **Hyperphosphatemia**
   a. **Causes** include impaired renal excretion and transcellular shifts of phosphorus from the intracellular to the extracellular compartment (e.g., tissue trauma, tumor lysis, insulin deficiency, or acidosis). Hyperphosphatemia is also a common feature of postoperative hypoparathyroidism.
   b. **Clinical manifestations,** in the short term, include hypocalcemia and tetany. In contrast, soft tissue calcification and secondary hyperparathyroidism occur with chronicity.
   c. **Treatment** of hyperphosphatemia, in general, should eliminate the phosphorus source, remove phosphorus from the circulation, and correct any coexisting hypocalcemia. Dietary phosphorus should be restricted. Urinary phosphorus excretion can be increased by hydration (0.9% NaCl at 250 to 500 mL/hour) and diuresis (acetazolamide, 500 mg every 6 hours orally or intravenously). Phosphate binders (aluminum hydroxide, 30 to 120 mL orally every 6 hours) minimize intestinal phosphate absorption and can induce a negative balance of greater than 250 mg of phosphorus daily, even in the absence of dietary phosphorus. Hyperphosphatemia secondary to conditions that cause phosphorus redistribution (e.g., diabetic ketoacidosis) resolves with treatment of the underlying condition and requires no specific therapy. Dialysis can be used to correct hyperphosphatemia in extreme conditions.

E. **Magnesium**
   1. **Physiology.** Mg^{2+} (1.3 to 2.2 mEq/L or 0.65 to 1.10 mmol/L) is predominantly an intracellular cation. Renal excretion and retention play the major physiologic role in regulating body stores. Mg^{2+} is not under direct hormonal regulation.

2. **Hypomagnesemia**

   a. **Causes.** Hypomagnesemia on the basis of dietary insufficiency is rare. Common etiologies include excessive GI or renal Mg^{2+} loss. GI loss may result from diarrhea, malabsorption, vomiting, or biliary fistulas. Urinary loss occurs with marked diuresis, primary hyperaldosteronism, renal tubular dysfunction (e.g., renal tubular acidosis), chronic alcoholism, or as a drug side effect (e.g., loop diuretics, cyclosporine, amphotericin B, aminoglycosides, and cisplatin). Hypomagnesemia may also result from shifts of Mg^{2+} from the extracellular to the intracellular space, particularly in conjunction with acute myocardial infarction, alcohol withdrawal, or after receiving glucose-containing solutions. After parathyroidectomy for hyperparathyroidism, the redeposition of calcium and Mg^{2+} in bone may cause dramatic hypocalcemia and hypomagnesemia. Hypomagnesemia is usually accompanied by hypokalemia and hypophosphatemia and is frequently encountered in the trauma patient.

   b. **Clinical manifestations.** Symptoms of hypomagnesemia are predominantly neuromuscular and cardiovascular. With severe depletion, altered mental status, tremors, hyperreflexia, and tetany may be present. The cardiovascular effects of hypomagnesemia are similar to those of hypokalemia and include T-wave and QRS-complex broadening as well as prolongation of the PR and QT intervals. Ventricular arrhythmias most commonly occur in patients who receive digitalis preparations. We recommend maintaining a patient's magnesium at the upper limit of normal (2 to 2.5 mEq/L to prevent QT prolongation and arrhythmias.

   c. **Treatment**

      (1) **Parenteral therapy** is preferred for the treatment of severe hypomagnesemia (Mg^{2+} <1 mEq/L or 0.5 mmol/L) or in symptomatic patients. In cases of life-threatening arrhythmias, 1 to 2 g (8 to 16 mEq) of $MgSO_4$ can be administered over 5 minutes, followed by a continuous infusion of 1 to 2 g/hour for the next several hours. The infusion subsequently can be reduced to 0.5 to 1 g/hour for maintenance. The normal range of Mg^{2+} (1.3 to 2.2 mEq/L or 0.65 to 1.10 mmol/L) is probably below its physiologic optimum. Thus, except in cases of renal failure, vigorous correction of either severe or symptomatic hypomagnesemia is warranted. In less urgent situations, $MgSO_4$ infusion may begin at 1 to 2 g/hour for 3 to 6 hours, with the rate subsequently adjusted to 0.5 to 1 g/hour for maintenance. Mild hypomagnesemia (1.1 to 1.4 mEq/L or 0.5 to 0.7 mmol/L) in an asymptomatic patient can be treated initially with the parenteral administration of 50 to 100 mEq (6 to 12 g) of $MgSO_4$ daily until body stores are replenished. Treatment should be continued for 3 to 5 days, at which time the patient can be switched to an oral maintenance dose. Intravenous $MgSO_4$ remains the initial therapy of choice for torsades de pointes (polymorphologic ventricular

tachycardia). Furthermore, it is used to achieve hypermagnesemia that is therapeutic for eclampsia and pre-eclampsia.

    (2) Oral therapy. Magnesium oxide is the preferred oral agent. Each 400-mg tablet provides 241 mg (20 mEq) of Mg^{2+}. Other formulations include magnesium gluconate [each 500-mg tablet provides 27 mg (2.3 mEq) of Mg^{2+}] and magnesium chloride [each 535-mg tablet provides 64 mg (5.5 mEq) of Mg^{2+}]. Depending on the level of depletion, oral therapy should provide 20 to 80 mEq of Mg^{2+}/day in divided doses.

    (3) Prevention of hypomagnesemia in the hospitalized patient who is receiving prolonged parenteral nutritional therapy can be accomplished by providing 0.35 to 0.45 mEq/kg of Mg^{2+}/day [i.e., by adding 8 to 16 mEq (1 to 2 g) of $MgSO_4$ to each liter of intravenous fluids].

3. Serum Mg^{2+} levels should be monitored during therapy. The dose of Mg^{2+} should be reduced in patients with renal insufficiency.

4. Hypermagnesemia

    a. Causes. Hypermagnesemia occurs infrequently, is usually iatrogenic, and is seen most commonly in the setting of renal failure.

    b. Clinical manifestations. Mild hypermagnesemia (Mg^{2+} 5 to 6 mEq/L or 2.5 to 3 mmol/L) is generally asymptomatic. Severe hypermagnesemia (Mg^{2+} >8 mEq/L or 4 mmol/L) is associated with depression of deep tendon reflexes, paralysis of voluntary muscles, hypotension, sinus bradycardia, and prolongation of PR, QRS, and QT intervals.

    c. Treatment. Cessation of exogenous Mg^{2+} is necessary. Calcium gluconate 10% (10 to 20 mL over 5 to 10 minutes intravenously) is indicated in the presence of life-threatening symptoms (e.g., hyporeflexia, respiratory depression, or cardiac conduction disturbances) to antagonize the effects of Mg^{2+}. A 0.9% NaCl (250 to 500 mL/hour) infusion with loop diuretic (furosemide, 20 mg intravenously every 4 to 6 hours) in the patient with intact renal function promotes renal elimination. Dialysis is the definitive therapy in the presence of intractable symptomatic hypermagnesemia.

IV. PARENTERAL FLUID THERAPY. The composition of commonly used parenteral fluids is presented in Table 4-3.

    A. Crystalloids, in general, are solutions that contain sodium as the major osmotically active particle. Crystalloids are relatively inexpensive and are useful for volume expansion, maintenance infusion, and correction of electrolyte disturbances.

        1. Isotonic crystalloids (e.g., lactated Ringer's solution and 0.9% NaCl) distribute uniformly throughout the extracellular fluid compartment so that after 1 hour, only 25% of the total volume infused remains in the intravascular space. Lactated Ringer's solution is designed to mimic extracellular fluid and is considered a balanced salt solution. This solution provides a HCO_3^- precursor and is useful for replacing GI losses

TABLE 4-3	Composition of Common Parenteral Fluids[a]								
Solution	Volume[b]	Na+	K+	Ca2+	Mg2+	Cl-	HCO3 (as lactate)	Dextrose (g/L)	mOsm/L
Extracellular fluid	—	142	4	5	3	103	27	—	280–310
Lactated Ringer's	—	130	4	3	—	109	28	—	273
0.9% NaCl	—	154	—	—	—	154	—	—	308
0.45% NaCl	—	77	—	—	—	77	—	—	154
D5 W	—	—	—	—	—	—	—	50	252
D5/0.45% NaCl	—	77	—	—	—	77	—	50	406
D5LR	—	130	4	3	—	109	28	50	525
3% NaCl	—	513	—	—	—	513	—	—	1,026
7.5% NaCl	—	1,283	—	—	—	1,283	—	—	2,567

6% hetastarch	500	154	—	—	—	154	—	—	310
10% dextran-40	500	0/154[c]	—	—	—	0/154[c]	—	—	300
6% dextran-70	500	0/154[c]	—	—	—	0/154[c]	—	—	300
5% albumin	250,500	130–160	<2.5	—	—	130–160	—	—	330
25% albumin	20,50,100	130–160	<2.5	—	—	130–160	—	—	330
Plasma protein fraction	250,500	145				145			300

[a]Electrolyte concentrations in mmol/L.
[b]Available volumes (mL) of colloid solutions.
[c]Dextran solutions available in 5% dextrose (0 Na$^+$, 0 Cl) or 0.9% NaCl (154 mmol Na$^+$, 154 mmol Cl).
D5LR, 5% dextrose in lactated Ringer's solution; D5/0.45% NaCl, 5% dextrose per 0.45% NaCl; D5 W, 5% dextrose in water.

and extracellular fluid volume deficits. In general, lactated Ringer's solution and 0.9% NaCl can be used interchangeably. However, 0.9% NaCl is preferred in the presence of hyperkalemia, hypercalcemia, hyponatremia, hypochloremia, or metabolic alkalosis.

2. **Hypertonic saline solutions** alone and in combination with colloids, such as dextran, have generated interest as a resuscitation fluid for patients with shock or burns. These fluids are appealing because, relative to isotonic crystalloids, smaller quantities are required initially for resuscitation. A randomized, double-blinded study of a 250-mL dose of hypertonic saline (7.5% NaCl, 6% dextran-70) compared to placebo (0.9% NaCl) given to patients in hemorrhagic shock after sustaining blunt trauma showed that the patients receiving the hypertonic saline bolus had significant blunting of neutrophil activation and alteration of the pattern of monocyte activation and cytokine secretion with a only a transient increase in serum sodium that normalized within 24 hours. This immunomodulatory effect of hypertonic saline plus dextran may help to prevent widespread tissue damage and multiorgan dysfunction seen after traumatic injury (*Ann Surg.* 2006;243:47). However, another recent randomized controlled trial of patients with blunt trauma in hypovolemic shock that compared resuscitation with either lactated Ringer solution or 7.5% hypertonic saline and 6% dextran 70 demonstrated no significant difference in ARDS-free survival (*Arch Surg.* 2008;143(2):139). The possible side effects of hypertonic solutions include hypernatremia, hyperosmolality, hyperchloremia, hypokalemia, and central pontine demyelination with rapid infusion and should be administered with caution until more research becomes available.

B. **Hypotonic solutions** (D5 W, 0.45% NaCl) distribute throughout the total body water compartment, expanding the intravascular compartment by as little as 10% of the volume infused. For this reason, hypotonic solutions should not be used for volume expansion. They are used to replace free water deficits.

C. **Colloid solutions** contain high-molecular-weight substances that remain in the intravascular space. Early use of colloids in the resuscitation regimen may result in more prompt restoration of tissue perfusion and may lessen the total volume of fluid required for resuscitation. However, there are no situations in which colloids have unequivocally been shown to be superior to crystalloids for volume expansion. In fact, the SAFE (Saline versus Albumin Fluid Evaluation) study, which randomized 6,997 patients in the ICU to receive either 4% albumin or normal saline for fluid resuscitation, found no significant difference in outcomes, including mortality and organ failure, between the two groups (*N Engl J Med.* 2004;350:2247). Because colloid solutions are substantially more expensive than crystalloids, their routine use in hypovolemic shock is controversial. In addition, a post hoc study of ICU patients with traumatic brain injury revealed that patients who underwent fluid resuscitation with albumin compared to saline had significantly higher mortality rates (*N Engl J Med.* 2007;357:874). The use of colloids is indicated when crystalloids fail to sustain plasma volume because of low colloid osmotic pressure (e.g., increased protein loss from the vascular space, as in burns and peritonitis).

1. **Albumin preparations** ultimately distribute throughout the extracellular space, although the initial location of distribution is the vascular compartment. Preparations of 25% albumin (100 mL) and 5% albumin (500 mL) expand the intravascular volume by an equivalent amount (450 to 500 mL). Albumin 25% is indicated in the edematous patient to mobilize interstitial fluid into the intravascular space. The cost per liter of albumin is more than that of other colloid solutions and 30 times the cost of the intravascular volume-equivalent amount of crystalloid solutions; thus, albumin preparations should be used judiciously. They are not indicated in the patient with adequate colloid oncotic pressure (serum albumin >2.5 mg/dL, total protein >5 mg/dL), for augmenting serum albumin in chronic illness (cirrhosis or nephrotic syndrome), or as a nutritional source.

2. **Dextran** is a synthetic glucose polymer that undergoes predominantly renal elimination. In addition to its indications for volume expansion, dextran also is used for thromboembolism prophylaxis and promotion of peripheral perfusion. Dextran solutions expand the intravascular volume by an amount equal to the volume infused. Side effects include renal failure, osmotic diuresis, coagulopathy, and laboratory abnormalities (i.e., elevations in blood glucose and protein and interference with blood cross-matching). Preparations of 40- and 70-kD dextran are available (dextran-40 and dextran-70, respectively).

3. **Hydroxyethyl starch (hetastarch)** is a synthetic molecule resembling glycogen that is available as a 6% solution in 0.9% NaCl. Hetastarch, like 5% albumin, increases the intravascular volume by an amount equal to or greater than the volume infused. Hetastarch is less expensive than albumin and has a more favorable side effect profile than dextran formulations, making it an appealing colloid preparation. Hextend is a colloid that contains 6% hetastarch, balanced electrolytes, a lactate buffer, and physiologic levels of glucose. Relative to hetastarch in saline, Hextend seems to have a more beneficial coagulation profile, less antigenicity, and antioxidant properties.

    a. **Indications** include use as a plasma volume-expanding agent in shock from hemorrhage, trauma, sepsis, and burns. Urine output typically increases acutely secondary to osmotic diuresis and must not be misinterpreted as a sign of adequate peripheral perfusion in this setting.

    b. **Elimination** is hepatic and renal. Patients with renal impairment are particularly subject to initial volume overload and tissue accumulation of hetastarch with repeated administration. In these patients, initial volume resuscitation accomplished with hetastarch should be maintained with another plasma volume expander, such as albumin or crystalloid.

    c. **Laboratory abnormalities** include elevations in serum amylase to approximately twice normal without alteration in pancreatic function.

    d. Dosing of hetastarch 6% solution is 30 to 60 g (500 to 1,000 mL), with the total daily dose not exceeding 1.2 g/kg (20 mL/kg) or 90 g (1,500 mL). In hemorrhagic shock, hetastarch solution can be administered at a rate of 1.2 g/kg/hour (20 mL/kg/hour). Slower rates of administration generally are used in patients with burns or septic shock. In individuals with severe renal impairment (creatinine clearance <10 mL/minute), the usual dose of hetastarch can be administered initially, but subsequent doses should be reduced by 50% to 75%.

D. Principles of fluid management. A normal individual consumes an average of 2,000 to 2,500 mL of water daily. Daily water losses include approximately 1,000 to 1,500 mL in urine and 250 mL in stool. The minimum amount of urinary output that is required to excrete the catabolic end products of metabolism is approximately 800 mL. An additional 750 mL of insensible water loss occurs daily via the skin and respiratory tract. Insensible losses increase with hypermetabolism, fever, and hyperventilation.

    1. Maintenance. Maintenance fluids should be administered at a rate that is sufficient to maintain a urine output of 0.5 to 1 mL/kg/hour. Maintenance fluid requirements can be approximated on the basis of body weight as follows: 100 mL/kg/day for the first 10 kg, 50 mL/kg/day for the second 10 kg, and 20 mL/kg/day for each subsequent 10 kg. Maintenance fluids in general should contain Na^+ (1 to 2 mmol/kg/day) and K^+ [0.5 to 1 mmol/kg/day (e.g., D5/0.45% NaCl + 20 to 30 mmol K^+/L)].

    2. Preoperative management. Pre-existing volume and electrolyte abnormalities should be corrected before operation whenever possible. Consideration of duration and route of loss provides important information regarding the extent of fluid and electrolyte abnormalities.

    3. Intraoperative fluid management requires replacement of preoperative deficit as well as ongoing losses (Table 4-4). Intraoperative losses include maintenance fluids for the duration of the case, hemorrhage, and "third-space losses." The maintenance fluid requirement is calculated as detailed previously (see Section IV.D.1). Acute blood loss can be replaced with a volume of crystalloid that is three to four times the blood loss or with an equal volume of colloid or blood. Intraoperative insensible and third-space fluid losses depend on the size of the incision and the extent of tissue trauma and dissection and can be replaced with an appropriate volume of lactated Ringer's solution. Small incisions with minor tissue trauma (e.g., inguinal hernia repair) result in third-space losses of approximately 1 to 3 mL/kg/hour. Medium-sized incisions with moderate tissue trauma (e.g., uncomplicated sigmoidectomy) result in third-space losses of approximately 3 to 7 mL/kg/hour. Larger incisions and operations with extensive tissue trauma and dissection (e.g., pancreaticoduodenectomy) can result in third-space losses of approximately 9 to 11 mL/kg/hour or greater.

    4. Postoperative fluid management requires careful evaluation of the patient. Sequestration of extracellular fluid into the sites of injury or operative trauma can continue for 12 or more hours after operation. Urine output should be monitored closely and intravascular volume repleted to maintain a urine output of 0.5 to 1 mL/kg/hour. GI losses that exceed 250 mL/day from nasogastric or gastrostomy tube suction

TABLE 4-4	Estimation of Intraoperative Fluid Loss and Guide for Replacement
Preoperative deficit
Maintenance IVF × hr NPO, plus preexisting deficit related to disease state
Maintenance fluids
Maintenance IVF × duration of case
Third-space and insensible losses
1–3 mL/kg/hr for minor procedure (small incision)
3–7 mL/kg/hr for moderate procedure (medium incision)
9–11 mL/kg/hr for extensive procedure (large incision)
Blood loss
1 mL blood or colloid per 1 mL blood loss, or 3 mL crystalloid per 1 mL blood loss

IVF, intravenous fluids; NPO, nothing by mouth.

should be replaced with an equal volume of crystalloid. Mobilization of perioperative third-space fluid losses typically begins 2 to 3 days after operation. Anticipation of postoperative fluid shifts should prompt careful evaluation of the patient's volume status and, if needed, consideration of diuresis before the development of symptomatic hypervolemia.

V. ACID–BASE DISORDERS

A. **Diagnostic approach**

1. **General concepts**

a. **Acid–base homeostasis** represents equilibrium among the concentration of H^+, partial pressure of CO_2 (Pco_2), and HCO_3^-. Clinically, H^+ concentration is expressed as pH.

b. **Normal pH** is 7.35 to 7.45. **Acidemia** refers to pH of less than 7.35, and **alkalemia** refers to pH of greater than 7.45.

c. **Acidosis and alkalosis** describe processes that cause the accumulation of acid or alkali, respectively. The terms *acidosis* and *acidemia* and the terms *alkalosis* and *alkalemia* are often used interchangeably, but such usage is inaccurate. A patient, for example, may be acidemic while alkalosis is occurring.

d. **Laboratory studies** that are necessary for the initial evaluation of acid–base disturbances include arterial pH, arterial Pco_2 ($Paco_2$) (normal is 35 to 45 mm Hg), and serum electrolytes [HCO_3^-

TABLE 4-5	Expected Compensation for Simple Acid–Base Disorders		
Primary Disorder	Initial Change	Compensatory Response	Expected Compensation
Metabolic acidosis	HCO_3^- decrease	P_{CO_2} decrease	P_{CO_2} decrease $= 1.2 \times \Delta HCO_3^-$
Metabolic alkalosis	HCO_3^- increase	P_{CO_2} increase	P_{CO_2} increase $= 0.7 \times \Delta HCO_3^-$
Respiratory acidosis	P_{CO_2} increase	HCO_3^- increase	Acute: HCO_3^- increase $= 0.1 \times \Delta P_{CO_2}$ Chronic: HCO_3^- increase $= 0.35 \times \Delta P_{CO_2}$
Respiratory alkalosis	P_{CO_2} decrease	HCO_3^- decrease	Acute: HCO_3^- decrease $= 0.2 \times \Delta P_{CO_2}$ Chronic: HCO_3^- decrease $= 0.5 \times \Delta P_{CO_2}$

(normal is 22 to 31 mmol/L)]. Although base-excess or base-deficit calculations can be made, this information does not add substantially to the evaluation.

2. **Compensatory response to primary disorders.** Disorders that initially alter Pa_{CO_2} are termed *respiratory acidosis* or *alkalosis*. Alternatively, disorders that initially affect plasma HCO_3^- concentration are termed *metabolic acidosis* or *alkalosis*. Primary metabolic disorders stimulate respiratory responses that act to return the ratio of P_{CO_2} to HCO_3^- (and therefore the pH) toward normal. Similarly, primary respiratory disturbances elicit countervailing metabolic responses that also act to normalize pH. As a general rule, these compensatory responses do not normalize pH because to do so would remove the stimulus for compensation. By convention, these compensating changes are termed *secondary, respiratory,* or *metabolic* compensation for the primary disturbance. The amount of compensation to be expected from either a primary respiratory or metabolic disorder is presented in Table 4-5. Significant deviations from these expected values suggest the presence of a mixed acid–base disturbance.

B. **Primary metabolic disorders**

1. **Metabolic acidosis** results from the accumulation of nonvolatile acids, reduction in renal acid excretion, or loss of alkali. The most common causes of metabolic acidosis are listed in Table 4-6. Metabolic acidosis

TABLE 4-6	Causes of Metabolic Acidosis	
Increased anion gap	Renal tubular dysfunction
Increased acid production	Renal tubular acidosis
Ketoacidosis	Hypoaldosteronism
Diabetic	Potassium-sparing diuretics
Alcoholic	Loss of alkali
Starvation	Diarrhea
Lactic acidosis	Ureterosigmoidostomy
Toxic ingestion (salicylates, ethylene glycol, methanol)	Carbonic anhydrase inhibitors
Renal failure	Administration of HCl (ammonium chloride, cationic amino acids)
Normal anion gap (hyperchloremic)	

has few specific signs. The appropriate diagnosis depends on the clinical setting and laboratory tests.

a. The anion gap (AG; normal = 12 ± 2 mmol/L) represents the anions, other than Cl^- and HCO_3^-, which are necessary to counterbalance Na^+ electrically (all values are in mmol/L):

$$AG = Na^+ - [Cl^- + HCO_3^-]$$

It is useful diagnostically to classify metabolic acidosis into increased or normal AG metabolic acidosis.

(1) Increased AG metabolic acidosis (Table 4-6).

(2) Normal AG (hyperchloremic) metabolic acidosis (Table 4-6).

b. Treatment of metabolic acidosis must be directed primarily at the underlying cause of the acid–base disturbance. Bicarbonate therapy should be considered in patients with moderate-to-severe metabolic acidosis only after the primary cause has been addressed. The HCO_3^- deficit (mmol/L) can be estimated using the following equation:

$$HCO_3^- \text{ deficit} \left(\frac{mmol}{L} \right) = \text{body weight (kg)} \times 0.4$$

$$\times \left[\text{desired } HCO_3^- \left(\frac{mmol}{L} \right) - \text{measured } HCO_3^- \left(\frac{mmol}{L} \right) \right]$$

This equation serves to provide only a rough estimate of the deficit because the volume of HCO_3^- distribution and the rate of ongoing H^+ production are variable.

(1) **Rate of HCO_3^- replacement.** In nonurgent situations, the estimated HCO_3^- deficit can be repaired by administering a continuous intravenous infusion over 4 to 8 hours [a 50-mL ampule of 8.4% $NaHCO_3$ solution (provides 50 mmol HCO_3^-) can be added to 1 L of D5 W or 0.45% of NaCl]. In urgent situations, the entire deficit can be repaired by administering a bolus over several minutes. The goal of HCO_3^- therapy should be to raise the arterial blood pH to 7.20 or the HCO_3^- concentration to 10 mmol/L. One should not attempt to normalize pH with bicarbonate administration because the risks of bicarbonate therapy (e.g., hypernatremia, hypercapnia, cerebrospinal fluid acidosis, or overshoot alkalosis) are likely to be increased. Serial arterial blood gases and serum electrolytes should be obtained to assess the response to HCO_3^- therapy.

(2) **Lactic acidosis.** Correction of the underlying disorder is the primary therapy for lactic acidosis. Reversal of circulatory failure, hypoxemia, or sepsis reduces the rate of lactate production and enhances its removal. Because the use of $NaHCO_3$ in lactic acidosis is controversial, no definite recommendations can be made.

2. **Metabolic alkalosis (Table 4-7)**

a. **Causes**

(1) **Chloride-responsive metabolic alkalosis** in the surgical patient is typically associated with extracellular fluid volume deficits. The most common causes of metabolic alkalosis in the surgical patient include inadequate fluid resuscitation or diuretic therapy (e.g., contraction alkalosis), acid loss through GI secretions (e.g. nasogastric suctioning and vomiting), and the exogenous administration of HCO_3^- or HCO_3^- precursors (e.g. citrate in blood). Posthypercapnic metabolic alkalosis occurs after the rapid correction of chronic respiratory acidosis. Under normal circumstances, the excess in bicarbonate that is generated by any of these processes is excreted rapidly in the urine. Consequently, maintenance of metabolic alkalosis requires impairment of renal HCO_3^- excretion, most commonly due to volume and chloride depletion. Because replenishment of Cl^- corrects the metabolic alkalosis in these conditions, each is classified as Cl^--responsive metabolic alkalosis.

(2) **Chloride-unresponsive metabolic alkalosis** is encountered less frequently in surgical patients and usually results from mineralocorticoid excess. Hyperaldosteronism, marked hypokalemia, renal failure, renal tubular Cl^- wasting (Bartter syndrome), and chronic edematous states are associated with chloride-unresponsive metabolic alkalosis.

b. **Diagnosis.** Although the cause of metabolic alkalosis is usually apparent in the surgical patient, measurement of the urinary

TABLE 4-7	Causes of Metabolic Alkalosis
Associated with extracellular fluid volume (chloride) depletion
Vomiting or gastric drainage
Diuretic therapy
Posthypercapnic alkalosis
Associated with mineralocorticoid excess
Cushing syndrome
Primary aldosteronism
Bartter syndrome
Severe K⁺ depletion
Excessive alkali intake

chloride concentration may be useful for differentiating these disorders. A urine Cl^- concentration of less than 15 mmol/L suggests inadequate fluid resuscitation, ongoing GI loss from emesis or nasogastric suctioning, diuretic administration, or post-hypercapnia as the cause of the metabolic alkalosis. A urine Cl^- concentration of greater than 20 mmol/L suggests mineralocorticoid excess, alkali loading, concurrent diuretic administration, or the presence of severe hypokalemia.

- c. **Treatment principles** in metabolic alkalosis include identifying and removing underlying causes, discontinuing exogenous alkali, and repairing Cl^-, K^+, and volume deficits. Because metabolic alkalosis generally is well tolerated, rapid correction of this disorder usually is not necessary.
  - (1) **Initial therapy** should include the correction of volume deficits (with 0.9% NaCl) and hypokalemia. Patients with vomiting or nasogastric suctioning also may benefit from H_2-receptor antagonists or other acid–suppressing medications.
  - (2) **Edematous patients.** Chloride administration does not enhance HCO_3^- excretion because it does not correct the reduced effective arterial blood volume. Acetazolamide (5 mg/kg/day intravenously or orally) facilitates fluid mobilization while decreasing renal HCO_3^- reabsorption. However, tachyphylaxis may develop after 2 to 3 days.

(3) Severe alkalemia (HCO_3^- >40 mmol/L), especially in the presence of symptoms, may require more aggressive correction. The infusion of acidic solutions is occasionally indicated in the patient with severe refractory metabolic alkalosis and chloride loss, typically due to massive nasogastric drainage or complete prepyloric obstruction. Ammonium chloride (NH_4Cl) is hepatically converted to urea and HCl. The amount of NH_4Cl that is required can be estimated using the following equation:

$$NH_4Cl \text{ (mmol)} = 0.2 \times \text{weight (kg)} \times [103 - \text{serum } Cl^- \text{ (mmol)}].$$

NH_4Cl is prepared by adding 100 or 200 mmol (20 to 40 mL of the 26.75% NH_4Cl concentrate) to 500 to 1,000 mL of 0.9% NaCl. This solution should be administered at a rate that does not exceed 5 mL/minute. Approximately one half of the calculated volume of NH_4Cl should be administered, at which time the acid–base status and Cl^- concentration should be repeated to determine the necessity for further therapy. NH_4Cl is contraindicated in hepatic failure.

(4) HCl [0.1 N (normal), administered intravenously] corrects metabolic alkalosis more rapidly. The amount of H^+ to administer can be estimated using the following equation:

$$H^+ \text{ (mmol)} = 0.5 \times \text{weight (kg)} \times [103 - \text{serum } Cl^- \text{ (mmol/L)}].$$

To prepare 0.1 N HCl, mix 100 mmol of HCl in 1 L of sterile water. The calculated amount of 0.1 N HCl must be administered via a central venous catheter over 24 hours. The HCO_3^- concentration can be safely reduced by 8 to 12 mmol/L over 12 to 24 hours.

(5) Dialysis can be considered in the volume-overloaded patient with renal failure and intractable metabolic alkalosis.

C. **Primary respiratory disorders**

1. **Respiratory acidosis** occurs when alveolar ventilation is insufficient to excrete metabolically produced CO_2. Common causes in the surgical patient include respiratory center depression (e.g., drugs and organic disease), neuromuscular disorders, and cardiopulmonary arrest. Chronic respiratory acidosis may occur in pulmonary diseases, such as chronic emphysema and bronchitis. Chronic hypercapnia may also result from primary alveolar hypoventilation or alveolar hypoventilation related to extreme obesity (e.g., Pickwickian syndrome) or from thoracic skeletal abnormalities. The diagnosis of acute respiratory acidosis usually is evident from the clinical situation, especially if respiration is obviously depressed. Appropriate therapy is correction of the underlying disorder. In cases of acute respiratory acidosis, there is no indication for $NaHCO_3$ administration.

2. **Respiratory alkalosis** is the result of acute or chronic hyperventilation. The causes of respiratory alkalosis include acute hypoxia (e.g.,

TABLE 4-8	Common Causes of Mixed Acid–Base Disorders

Metabolic acidosis and respiratory acidosis

Cardiopulmonary arrest

Severe pulmonary edema

Salicylate and sedative overdose

Pulmonary disease with superimposed renal failure or sepsis

Metabolic acidosis and respiratory alkalosis

Salicylate overdose

Sepsis

Combined hepatic and renal insufficiency

Metabolic alkalosis and respiratory acidosis

Chronic pulmonary disease, with superimposed:
   Diuretic therapy
   Steroid therapy

Vomiting

Reduction in hypercapnia by mechanical ventilation

Metabolic alkalosis and respiratory alkalosis

Pregnancy with vomiting

Chronic liver disease treated with diuretic therapy

Cardiopulmonary arrest treated with bicarbonate therapy and mechanical ventilation

Metabolic acidosis and alkalosis

Vomiting superimposed on
   Renal failure
   Diabetic ketoacidosis
   Alcoholic ketoacidosis

pneumonia, pneumothorax, pulmonary edema, and bronchospasm), chronic hypoxia (e.g., cyanotic heart disease and anemia), and respiratory center stimulation (e.g., anxiety, fever, Gram-negative sepsis, salicylate intoxication, central nervous system disease, cirrhosis, and pregnancy). Excessive ventilation may also cause respiratory alkalosis in the mechanically ventilated patient. Depending on its severity and acuteness, hyperventilation may or may not be clinically apparent. Clinical findings are nonspecific. As in respiratory acidosis, the only effective treatment is correction of the underlying disorder.

D. **Mixed acid–base disorders.** When two or three primary acid–base disturbances occur simultaneously, a patient is said to have a mixed acid–base disorder. As summarized in Table 4-5, the respiratory or metabolic compensation for a simple primary disorder follows a predictable pattern. Significant deviation from these patterns suggests the presence of a mixed disorder. Table 4-8 lists some common causes of mixed acid–base disturbances. The diagnosis of mixed acid–base disorders depends principally on evaluation of the clinical setting and on interpretation of acid–base patterns. However, even normal acid–base patterns may conceal mixed disorders.

5 Hemostasis and Transfusion Therapy

Alejandro Bribriesco and Michael Avidan

There are two main goals of hemostasis: (1) **prevent bleeding from defects in vessel walls via the temporary formation of localized, stable clot** and (2) **repair of the injured vessel wall.**

I. **MECHANISMS OF HEMOSTASIS.** Hemostasis is centered on the creation and destruction of a fibrin-cross-linked platelet plug (thrombus). Thrombus formation is **limited to the area of vessel injury** and **is temporary** in nature. This involves a complex interplay of thrombotic, anticoagulant, and fibrinolytic processes that occur simultaneously. Injury, disease, medications, and scores of other factors can tip the homeostatic balance resulting in life-threatening hemorrhagic or thrombotic complications.

A. **Thrombus formation** occurs in response to endothelial damage that exposes collagen (subendothelial matrix) and tissue factor (TF) (smooth muscle) to circulating blood (*N Engl J Med.* 2008;359:938). Two critical and interdependent events occur simultaneously to create a stable, fibrin-cross-linked thrombus: (1) platelet plug formation and (2) blood coagulation.

1. **Platelet plug formation:** Exposed subendothelial collagen interacts with glycoprotein (GP) Ia/IIA and VI on platelets leading to tethering at an injured site. Platelet adhesion is reinforced by Von Willebrand factor (vWF) interaction with GP Ib/V/IX. Engaged GP receptors further activate platelets leading to release of vasoactive agents and expression of important adhesions molecules, such as GP IIb/IIIa involved in fibrin cross-linking of platelets.

2. **Blood coagulation** refers to the **generation of fibrin via thrombin** as the end-product of activation of serine proteases known as coagulation "factors." These include both enzymatic proteins and cofactors (e.g., factors V and VIII). As with platelet plug formation, blood coagulation is initiated by endothelial disruption with uncovering of TF, a membrane protein expressed on multiple cell types including vascular cells such as fibroblasts and medial smooth-muscle cells. Importantly, TF is the **sole initiator of thrombin generation** and therefore fibrin formation.

3. **Cell-based model of coagulation (*Thromb Haemost.* 2001;85:958):** Traditionally, the coagulation network was divided into intrinsic and extrinsic pathways (Fig. 5-1). Although useful for *in vitro* studies, this dichotomy does not reflect the *in vivo* environment. Recently a

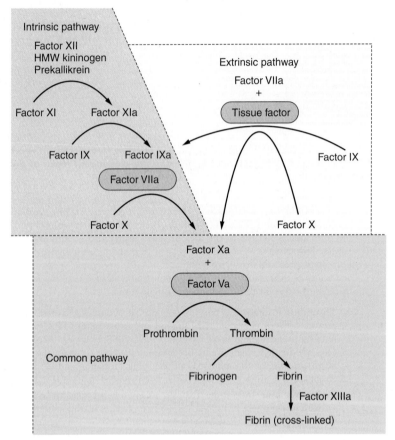

Figure 5-1. Blood coagulation cascade. Plasma zymogens are sequentially converted to active proteases (*arrows*). Nonenzymatic protein cofactors (*ovals*) are required at several stages of the cascade. Factors IX and X and prothrombin are activated on phospholipid surfaces. Thrombin cleaves fibrinogen, yielding fibrin monomers that polyme rize to form a clot. HMW, high molecular weight.

cell-based model of coagulation has developed that focuses on three critical steps (initiation, activation, propagation) with cellular TF as key.

  a. **Initiation:** Cells bearing TF are exposed to circulating factor VIIa creating a complex (extrinsic pathway) that activates both factor Xa and factor XIa (intrinsic pathway). This Xa–Va complex (prothrombinase complex) initiates thrombin activation as "the common pathway."

  b. **Amplification:** As noted above, vessel injury localizes and activates platelets at a site of vascular injury. In the amplification stage, thrombin fully activates platelet that allows accumulation of activated factors V, VIII, and XI on the platelet's phospholipid surface membrane.

   c. Propagation: Finally, the congregated factors assemble into the "Tenase" complex (VIIIa, IXa) and the prothrombinase complex that leads to large-scale production of thrombin **(thrombin burst).** Large amounts of thrombin are then available to (1) activate factors V, VIII, IX for further coagulation propagation (2) convert fibrinogen to fibrin, and (3) activate platelets via Par4 receptor, and (4) activate factor XIII that ultimately cross-links fibrin into a "mesh" that is required for stable platelet–platelet adhesion (thrombus). **Fibrinogen (factor I)** is important for thrombus strength and can compensate for low platelet levels.

B. Endogenous anticoagulants are important to restrict coagulation to the specific area of vascular injury and prevent pathologic thrombosis.

   1. The endothelium serves as a physical barrier sequestering subendothelial factors (TF, collagen) from platelets and circulating coagulation factors. Endothelial cells actively release antiplatelet factors [nitric oxide, prostacyclin (PGI_2)] as well as express surface enzymes that degrade ADP, a platelet-activating factor. Intact endothelial cells are also coated with thrombomodulin (see below) and heparin-like glycosaminoglycans that facilitate antithrombin (AT) activation.

   2. AT (previously known as antithrombin III) inhibits coagulation by binding several clotting factors (e.g., thrombin and factor Xa) and producing complexes that are cleared from the circulation. Heparin markedly accelerates AT-induced factor inhibition, increasing factor clearance, and leading to anticoagulation.

   3. The thrombomodulin–protein C–protein S system: Thrombomodulin, an endothelial membrane protein, binds with thrombin creating "anticoagulant thrombin" that accelerates the activation of protein C, a vitamin K-dependent proenzyme. Activated protein C inactivates factors Va and VIIIa in the presence of protein S.

   4. Other anticoagulant factors include TF pathway inhibitor (TFPI) that inactivates the TF/VIIa/Xa complex.

C. Fibrinolysis involves the dissolution and remodeling of thrombus (clot busting). Plasminogen is a plasma zymogen that is incorporated into a forming thrombus. Tissue plasminogen activator (tPA) converts plasminogen to its active form plasmin, breaks down clot, and allows for subsequent wound healing. Other plasminogen activators include urokinase and streptokinase. As with thrombus formation, fibrinolysis involves a complex interplay of positive and negative regulatory mechanisms. Negative feedback includes (1) α-2 antiplasmin in blood, (2) plasminogen activator inhibitor (PAI-1) from platelets and endothelial cells and (3) thrombin-activated fibrinolytic inhibitor (TAFI).

II. EVALUATION OF HEMOSTASIS. A detailed history and physical examination constitute the most important screening tools for hemostasis disorders in

TABLE 5-1 Preoperative Evaluation of Hemostasis, Bleeding Disorder, and Anemia

	History	Physical Exam	Drugs	Labs

Platelets	• Easy bruising
	• Frequent nosebleeds
	• Prolonged bleeding after:
	  • Minor injury
	  • Dental procedures
	  • Surgery
	  • Childbirth
		• Mucosal bleeding
		• Petechiae
		• Purpura
			• ASA
			• Clopidogrel
			• NSAIDs
				CBC with
				differential

Coagulation	• After unrecognized injury, **delayed** development of:
	  • Hematomas
	  • Hemarthrosis
	• Nutritional status (i.e., vitamin K)
	• Family history of males with bleeding disorder (i.e., hemophilia)
	• Atrial fibrillation, DVT/PE, or other conditions requiring anticoagulant therapy
		• Joint fullness, bruising
		• Hematomas
		• Broad/large scar formation
			• Warfarin
			• Heparin, LMWH
			• Herbs, supplements
				PT/INR
				PTT

Global	• Need for previous transfusions • Melena, hematochezia • Hematemesis • Hemoptysis • Family history of bleeding disorders	• Skin, conjunctival pallor • Tachycardia • Hypotension • Flow murmur		CBC Reticulocyte count Iron studies

Abbreviations: ASA, Aspirin; CBC, complete blood count; DVT, deep vein thrombosis; LMWH, low molecular weight heparin; NSAID, nonsteroidal anti-inflammatory drug; PE, pulmonary embolism; PT/INR, prothrombin time/international normalized ratio; PTT, partial thromboplastin time.

surgical patients (Table 5-1). A family history of bleeding or bleeding disorders should be elicited. Laboratory studies can further characterize or identify clinical suspicion. Although surgical patients can have hereditary disorders of hemostasis, acquired defects and medications affecting hemostasis are most common in this patient population. In cases of hereditary hemostasis disorders, it is often helpful to work with the patient's hematologist in perioperative management. Below, evaluation is divided into evaluation of platelets, coagulation, and global hemostasis.

A. **Evaluation of platelets**

1. **Laboratory evaluation**
   a. **Platelet count** (140,000 to 400,000/μL). Abnormalities in platelet number should be confirmed with a peripheral smear. Both thrombocytopenia and significant thrombocytosis require further investigation. It should be noted that the average life span of a normal platelet is **7 days.**
   b. **Platelet function.** No single test is adequate for screening platelet dysfunction due to limited sensitivity; therefore, the risk or severity of surgical bleeding cannot be reliably assessed. **Bleeding time** (2.5 to 9 minutes) measures the duration of bleeding to stop after a standardized superficial cut. Qualitative platelet disorders, von Willebrand disease (vWD), vasculitides, and connective tissue disorders prolong bleeding time.

2. **Platelet disorders**
   a. **Thrombocytopenia** is defined as a platelet count of less than 140,000/μL. If platelet function is normal, thrombocytopenia is infrequently the cause of bleeding unless counts are below 50,000/μL. Severe spontaneous bleeding occurs with platelet counts under 10,000/μL. Intramuscular injections, rectal examinations, suppositories, or enemas should be limited in patients with severe thrombocytopenia (<10,000/μL). Occult liver disease must be considered for thrombocytopenia of unknown etiology.
   b. **Drug-induced thrombocytopenia.** Many drugs can affect platelet production or cause increased platelet destruction thereby causing or exacerbating bleeding. Common drugs include antibiotics (trimethoprim–sulfamethoxazole, penicillins, rifampin), thiazide diuretics, and chemotherapeutic agents. Increased destruction of platelets is most commonly the result of an immune mechanism in which platelets are destroyed by complement activation by drug–antibody complexes. **All nonessential drugs should be discontinued until the cause of the thrombocytopenia is identified.** Drug-induced thrombocytopenia typically resolves within 7 to 10 days after cessation and clearance of the offending agent. Prednisone (1 mg/kg/day orally) may facilitate recovery of platelet counts.
   c. **Heparin-induced thrombocytopenia (HIT)** is a unique form of drug-induced thrombocytopenia in which two different forms have been recognized.

(1) **HIT type I** is a nonimmune, heparin-associated thrombo-cytopenia that typically begins within 4 days of initiation of heparin therapy. Platelet counts range between 100,000 and 140,000/μL. The incidence ranges from 5% to 30%. This form of HIT may not require cessation of heparin.

(2) **HIT type II** is a severe immune-mediated syndrome caused by heparin-dependent antiplatelet antibodies (anti-PF4-heparin complex) occurring 5 to 10 days after initial exposure to heparin but within hours after re-exposure. Platelet counts are often less than 100,000/μL or drop by more than 30% from baseline. In a minority of cases, thrombotic events ensue, including extensive arterial and venous thrombosis (*N Engl J Med.* 2006;355:809). If HIT is suspected, **all heparin products should be stopped immediately** until the diagnosis is refuted. Sources of heparin include flushes and heparin-coated catheters.

(a) **Lab tests:** HIT is a clinical diagnosis with laboratory find-ings. The enzyme-linked immunosorbent assay (ELISA, HIT panel) and serotonin release assay (SRA) may suggest the diagnosis if the associated clinical features are present. The ELISA is a sensitive test that is useful for screening but has low specificity. The SRA is the gold standard due to its high sensitivity and specificity and often used as a con-firmatory test. However, SRA is expensive and not widely available.

(b) **Treatment:** Because thrombotic complications can con-tinue even after the cessation of heparin, anticoagulation with nonheparin anticoagulants such a direct thrombin inhibitor (lepirudin or argatroban; see Section III.D.3) is recommended if there are no contraindications to anticoagulation. Platelet transfusion will exacerbate the process and is contraindicated. **If HIT is present, war-farin administration can potentiate a hypercoagulable state and has been associated with the development of venous limb gangrene.** Therefore, warfarin therapy should not be initiated until (1) platelet count >150K and (2) adequate alternative anticoagulant control have been achieved.

(3) **Dilutional thrombocytopenia** can occur with rapid blood product replacement for massive hemorrhage. No formula pre-dicts accurate platelet requirements in this setting (see section on "Massive Transfusion" for further discussion).

(4) **Other causes of thrombocytopenia** include disseminated intravascular coagulation (DIC), sepsis, immune thrombocy-topenic purpura (ITP), thrombotic thrombocytopenic pur-pura (TTP), hemolytic uremic syndrome (HUS), dialysis, and hematopoietic disorders.

3. **Thrombocytosis** is defined as a platelet count greater than 600,000/μL. Essential thrombocytosis is caused by myeloproliferative disease. Secondary thrombocytosis occurs with splenectomy, iron deficiency,

malignancy, or chronic inflammatory disease. Aspirin therapy (81 mg/day orally) is useful in prevention of thrombotic events in patients with myeloproliferative disorders and in decreasing fetal loss in pregnant women. Secondary thrombocytosis is generally not associated with an increased thrombotic risk and usually requires no specific therapy.

4. **Qualitative platelet dysfunction**
   a. **Acquired defects of platelets** are caused by uremia, liver disease, or cardiopulmonary bypass. Desmopressin acetate (DDAVP, 0.3 μg/kg intravenously 1 hour before operation) may limit bleeding from platelet dysfunction, particularly in uremic patients. Conjugated estrogens (0.6 mg/kg/day intravenously for 5 days) also can improve hemostatic function.
   b. **Hereditary defects** of platelet dysfunction (e.g., vWD, Bernard–Soulier syndrome, Glanzmann thrombasthenia, and storage pool defects) are less common and usually warrant consultation with a hematologist.

5. **Antiplatelet medications**
   a. **Aspirin** irreversibly acetylates cyclooxygenase, inhibiting platelet synthesis of thromboxane A2 and causing decreased platelet function. It is often used in the prevention and treatment of acute transient ischemic attacks, stroke, myocardial infarction, and coronary and vascular graft occlusion. Aspirin should be discontinued about 1 week before elective nonvascular operations to allow new, functional platelets to form.
   b. **Clopidogrel (Plavix)** is a thienopyridine that irreversibly inhibits platelet function by binding to the adenosine diphosphate (ADP) receptor that promotes aggregation and secretion. It is used to decrease thrombotic events in percutaneous coronary and vascular stenting and patients with unstable angina. Although the half-life of clopidogrel is 8 hours, the bleeding time remains prolonged over 3 to 7 days, demonstrating that complete recovery of platelet function takes 5 days. Therefore, patients should discontinue clopidogrel therapy 7 days prior to elective operations to decrease the risk of bleeding complications. Specifically, clopidogrel has become more prevalent with the increased use of coronary artery stents that require a full year of antiplatelet treatment for drug-eluting stents and at least 4 weeks with bare metal stents (*Chest.* 2008;133:776S). Discontinuation of clopidogrel within this time period carries a significant risk of stent thrombosis with resultant myocardial infarction. Continuation of aspirin, consultation with a cardiologist and consideration of preoperative "bridge" with GP IIb/IIIa inhibitors (see below) should be considered.
   c. **GP IIb/IIIa inhibitors include** abciximab (ReoPro), tirofiban (Aggrastat), and eptifibatide (Integrilin) and function by blocking platelet adhesion to fibrin. These agents are used in preventing coronary artery thrombosis after coronary angioplasty or in unstable angina. Although they have relatively short half-lives (0.5 to 2.5 hours), the bleeding time may remain elevated for longer

periods. It is recommended that surgery be delayed 12 hours after discontinuing abciximab and 4 hours after discontinuing tirofiban or eptifibatide. Zero-balance ultrafiltration may be beneficial in patients who need immediate surgical interventions (*Perfusion.* 2002;17:33).

d. Other medications: Dextran is used to reduce perioperative thrombotic events such as bypass graft occlusion because of its ability to decrease platelet aggregation and adhesion. **Nonsteroidal anti-inflammatory drugs (NSAIDS)** such as ketorolac (Toradol) inhibit cyclooxygenase, reversibly inhibiting platelet aggregation. **Hetastarch** can cause a transient decrease in platelet counts and should be used judiciously for perioperative colloid blood volume expansion

6. Platelet transfusions

   a. Indications. Platelet transfusions are used to control bleeding that is caused by thrombocytopenia or platelet dysfunction and to prevent spontaneous bleeding in situations of severe thrombocytopenia (<10,000/μL). In cases of bleeding or for minor surgical procedures, the transfusion threshold is often increased to a platelet count of less than 50,000/μL. For severe ongoing hemorrhage, before major operations and trauma, platelet counts greater than 100,000/μL should be the goal (*Ann Surg.* 2010;251:604). Preparations, volumes, and expected response are summarized in Table 5-2.

   b. Complications associated with platelet transfusions

   (1) Alloimmunization occurs in 50% to 75% of patients receiving repeated platelet transfusions and presents as a failure of the platelet count to increase significantly after a transfusion. In patients who need long-term platelet therapy, human leukocyte antigen-matched single-donor platelets slow the onset of alloimmunization.

   (2) Post-transfusion purpura is a rare complication of platelet transfusions seen in previously transfused individuals and multiparous women. It is usually caused by antibodies that develop in response to a specific platelet antigen Pl[A1] from the donor platelets. This condition presents with severe thrombocytopenia, purpura, and bleeding occurring 7 to 10 days after platelet transfusion. Although fatal bleeding can occur, the disease is typically self-limiting. Plasmapheresis or an infusion of intravenous immunoglobulin may be helpful.

B. Evaluation of coagulation

1. Laboratory evaluation

   a. Prothrombin time (PT) (11 to 14 seconds) is the clotting time measured after the addition of thromboplastin, phospholipids, and calcium to citrated plasma. This test assesses the extrinsic and common pathways and is most sensitive to factor VII deficiency. Test reagents vary in their responsiveness to warfarin-induced anticoagulation; therefore, the **international normalized ratio (INR)** is used to standardize PT reporting between laboratories.

TABLE 5-2	Blood Products			
Blood Product	Volume (mL)	Additional Factors	Expected Response	Common Use
PRBC 1 unit	200–250	Fibrinogen: 10–75 mg Clotting factors: none	Increase: 1 mg/dl Hgb 3% HCT	ABLA MTP Surgical blood loss
Platelets SDP (aphersis) RDP[b]	300–500 50 per unit	Fibrinogen: 2–4 mg/mL (360–900 mg) Clotting factors: equivalent of 200–250 mL of plasma (hemostatic level) "6 pack" of pooled RDP similar to SDP	Increase: 30–60 K/mm^3 Increase: 7–10 K/mm^3 per unit	Plt count <10K MTP Bleeding with known qualitative plt defect
FFP[a] 1 unit	180–300	Fibrinogen: 400 mg Clotting factors: 1 mL contains 1 active unit of each factor	Decrease: PT/INR PTT	Coagulopathy Warfarin overdose DIC
Cryo 10 pack		Fibrinogen: 1200–1500 Clotting factors: VIII, vWF, XII	Decrease: PT/INR PTT Increase: fibrinogen level	vWD DIC Hemophila A

[a]Note: Duration of FFP effect is approximately 6 hours. INR of FFP is 1.6 to 1.7.

[b]4–10 RDP units are pooled prior to transfusion.

Abbreviations: ABLA, acute blood loss anemia; Cryo, cryoprecipitate; FFP, fresh-frozen plasma; Hbg, hemoglobin; HCT, hematocrit; MTP, massive transfusion protocl; PRBC, packed red blood cells; plt, platelet; RDP, random donor platelets; SDP, single donor platelets.

b. **Partial thromboplastin time (PTT)** (26 to 36 seconds) is the clotting time for plasma that is pre-incubated in particulate material (causing contact activation) followed by the addition of phospholipid and calcium. Inhibitors or deficiencies of factors in the intrinsic or common pathways cause prolongation of the PTT. A prolonged PTT should be evaluated by a 50:50 mixture with normal plasma. Factor deficiencies are corrected by the addition of normal plasma, whereas PTT prolongation due to inhibitors remains abnormal.

c. **Activated clotting time (ACT)** assesses the clotting time of whole blood. A blood sample is added to a diatomate-containing tube, leading to activation of the intrinsic pathway. The ACT is used to follow coagulation in patients requiring high doses of heparin (i.e., vascular procedures, percutaneous coronary interventions, or cardiopulmonary bypass). Automated systems are available for intraoperative use, allowing accurate and rapid determinations of the state of anticoagulation. Normal ACT is less than 130 seconds, with therapeutic target values ranging from 400 to 480 seconds for cardiac bypass procedures and 250 to 350 seconds for noncardiac vascular procedures.

d. **Thrombin time (TT)** (11 to 18 seconds) is the clotting time for plasma after the addition of thrombin. Patients with a fibrinogen level of less than 100 mg/dL or with abnormal fibrinogen will have a prolonged TT. The presence of fibrin degradation products (FDPs) or heparin can also elevate the TT. Prolongation of the TT by heparin can be confirmed by the addition of protamine sulfate to the assay, resulting in normalization of the test.

e. **Factor assays.** Individual assays for specific coagulation factors can be useful in certain situations. Factor Xa activity may be used to assess the effect of low molecular weight heparin (LMWH). Factor VIII and IX levels are assessed in hemophiliacs prior to an operative procedure to guide transfusion of appropriate blood products. A fibrinogen level (150 to 360 mg/dL) can be measured directly by functional or immunologic quantitative assays. This level can be underestimated by the TT. FDP elevations (>8 μg/mL) occur in many disease states with increased fibrinogen turnover, including DIC, thromboembolic events, and during administration of fibrinolytic therapy. D-dimer levels reflect fibrinolysis and are useful in outpatient evaluations for pulmonary embolism (PE). The utility in surgical patients is less clear due to its nonspecific elevation in response to inflammation.

2. **Disorders of coagulation**

a. **Acquired factor deficiencies**

(1) **Vitamin K deficiency** leads to the production of inactive, noncarboxylated forms of **factors II (prothrombin), VII, IX, X, and proteins C and S.** The diagnosis should be considered in a patient with a prolonged PTT that corrects with a 50:50 mixture of normal plasma. Vitamin K deficiency can occur in patients without oral intake within 1 week, with biliary

obstruction, with malabsorption, and in those receiving antibiotics or warfarin.

(2) Liver dysfunction leads to complex alterations in coagulation through decreased synthesis of most clotting and anticlotting factors with the notable exceptions of factor VIII and vWF (from endothelium). Coagulopathy is worsened by uremic platelet dysfunction as well as thrombocytopenia from portal hypertension-associated hypersplenism. Spontaneous bleeding is infrequent, but coagulation defects should be corrected prior to invasive procedures. Fresh-frozen plasma (FFP) administration often improves the coagulopathy transiently. Any patient with liver disease should be thoroughly evaluated preoperatively including assessment of liver function (Childs-Pugh class; MELD score).

(3) Sepsis overstimulates the coagulation cascade reflected by decreased levels of anticoagulant factors such as protein C, protein S, and AT. This imbalance in hemostasis causes microvascular thrombi to form. These thrombi further amplify injury resulting in distal tissue ischemia and hypoxia. Therapy with activated protein C (drotrecogin alfa, Xigris) has been reported to decrease mortality in patients with severe sepsis as defined by an Acute Physiology and Chronic Health Evaluation (APACHE) II score greater than or equal to 25. However, higher rates of bleeding have been noted in patients receiving activated protein C compared to placebo (*N Engl J Med.* 2001;344:699). However, controversy exists regarding the use of activated protein C given the results of subsequent studies that question its efficacy and highlight the risks of bleeding (*N Engl J Med.* 2005;355:1332).

b. Hemophilia is an inherited factor deficiency of either factor VIII (hemophilia A) or factor IX (hemophilia B, Christmas disease). The diagnosis is suggested by patient history (Table 5-1) and an elevated PTT, normal PT, and normal bleeding time. Factor activity assays confirm the diagnosis and is an indicator of disease severity. Minor bleeding can often be controlled locally without the need for factor replacement therapy. DDAVP stimulates the release of vWF into the circulation, which increases factor VIII levels two- to sixfold. This may control minor bleeding in patients with mild disease. Major bleeding (e.g., during a surgical procedure) requires factor VIII replacement. Recombinant factor VIIa is FDA approved for the treatment of patients who have developed inhibitors to factor VIII or IX (see Section II.B.5.c). Cryoprecipitate contains factor VIII, vWF, and fibrinogen (Table 5-1) and can be used to treat patients with hemophilia A for control of bleeding. Purified factor IX is the treatment of choice for hemophilia B.

c. vWD is the **most common** inherited bleeding disorder with a prevalence as high as 1% of the general population. vWD is subcategorized (type 1 to 3) by the type of abnormality present in vWF.

DDAVP is effective to increase plasma vWF in type 1 disease but is ineffective for types 2 and 3. These disorders require replacement via blood products with high amounts of vWF and factor VIII, such as cryoprecipitate (Table 5-2).

d. **Other inherited factor deficiencies** account for fewer than 10% of severe factor deficiencies. Deficiencies of factor XII, HMWK, or prekallikrein do not cause bleeding and require no treatment.

e. **Inherited hypercoagulable disorders** place patients at risk for thrombosis (venous and/or arterial) and include deficiencies in body anticoagulants (AT, protein C, and protein S deficiencies), hyperhomocystinemia, and prothrombin gene mutations.

(1) **Activated protein C resistance (factor V Leiden)** is the most common hereditary coagulation disorder accounting for 40% to 50% of inherited hypercoagulable disorders. Factor V Leiden is caused by a genetic mutation in factor V that renders it resistant to breakdown by activated protein C leading to venous thrombosis. Routine preoperative screening in asymptomatic patients is unnecessary. Therapy for venous thrombosis consists of anticoagulation with heparin followed by warfarin therapy. The role of long-term warfarin anticoagulation for patients with a single thrombotic event is undefined.

(2) **AT deficiency** is an autosomal-dominant disorder (prevalence 1:500) that presents with recurrent venous and occasionally arterial thromboembolism, usually in the second decade of life. Assays for AT levels are typically decreased in the setting of acute thrombosis and also if the patient is receiving heparin. Patients with acute thromboembolism or previous history of thrombosis are typically anticoagulated. AT-deficient patients should have the AT level restored to more than 80% of normal activity with AT concentrate prior to operation or childbirth.

(3) **Protein C deficiency and protein S deficiency** are risk factors for venous thrombosis. In a state of protein C or S deficiency, factors Va and VIIIa are not adequately inactivated, thereby allowing unchecked coagulation. Besides the inherited type, protein C deficiency is encountered in patients with liver failure and in those who are receiving warfarin therapy. Symptomatic patients are treated with heparin [or low-molecular-weight heparin (LMWH)] anticoagulation followed by warfarin therapy. In individuals with diminished protein C activity, effective heparin anticoagulation must be confirmed before warfarin initiation because warfarin transiently lowers protein C levels further and potentially worsens the hypercoagulable state manifested as warfarin-induced skin necrosis (see below). Patients with protein C or S deficiency but with no history of thrombosis typically do not require prophylactic anticoagulation.

f. **Acquired hypercoagulable disorders**

(1) **Antiphospholipid antibodies** are immunoglobulins that are targeted against antigens composed in part of platelet and

endothelial cell phospholipids. Antiphospholipid antibody disorders may be detected by **lupus anticoagulant, anticardiolipin, or other antiphospholipid antibodies.** Patients with these antibodies are at risk for arterial and venous thrombosis, recurrent miscarriages, and thrombocytopenia.

g. **Other acquired hypercoagulable states** include malignancies, pregnancy or the use of estrogen therapy, intravascular hemolysis (e.g., hemolytic anemia or after cardiopulmonary bypass), and the localized propensity for thrombosis in arteries that have recently undergone endarterectomy, angioplasty, or placement of prosthetic vascular grafts.

3. **Anticoagulation medications**

a. **Principles and indications.** Anticoagulation is used to prevent and treat thrombosis and thromboembolic events. Before therapy is instituted, careful consideration must be given to the risk of thromboembolism and to anticoagulation-induced bleeding complications. Specific indications for anticoagulation therapy are discussed in detail in other chapters. Table 5-3 summarizes selected anticoagulant medications. Relative contraindications to anticoagulation therapy include recent surgical intervention, severe trauma, intracranial bleeding, and patients at risk of falling.

b. **Heparin**

(1) **Unfractionated heparin**

(a) **Administration.** Heparin is administered parenterally, either subcutaneously or intravenously. PTT should be measured before initiation of heparin, 6 hours after the initial bolus, and 6 hours after each change in dosing. Platelet counts should be measured daily until a maintenance dose of heparin is achieved and periodically thereafter to monitor for development of HIT.

(b) **Complications** that occur with heparin therapy include bleeding and HIT. If bleeding occurs, heparin should be discontinued, and immediate assessment of the PT, PTT, and complete blood count (CBC) should be undertaken. Gastrointestinal (GI) bleeding that occurs while a patient is therapeutically anticoagulated suggests an occult source and warrants further evaluation. HIT is an uncommon but potentially devastating complication of heparin therapy and must be recognized early (see Section II.A.2.c).

(c) **Heparin clearance** is rapid, occurring with a half-life of about 90 minutes. Reversal can be achieved more quickly with intravenous protamine sulfate. Each milligram of protamine sulfate reverses about 100 units of heparin. The PTT or ACT can be used to assess the adequacy of the reversal. Protamine should be used with caution because it can induce anaphylactoid reactions and other complications.

(2) **LMWH** preparations include enoxaparin, dalteparin, and tinzaparin. The anticoagulant effect of LMWH is **predominantly**

TABLE 5-3	Anticoagulant Medications					
Drug	Mechanism	Metabolism	Dose for DVT Prophylaxis	Dose for Therapeutic Anticoagulation	Therapeutic Target	Reversal Agent
Heparin	Potentiates antithrombin: IIa, Xa, IXa, XIa, XIIa inhibition	Hepatic, RES and 50% renal excretion	5000 U SC twice to thrice daily	Bolus = 80 u/kg Infusion = 18 u/kg/hr; adjust to target PTT	APTT = 60–80 s	Protamine: start with 25–50 mg
LMWH (e.g., Enoxaparin)	Potentiates antithrombin: Xa inhibition	Mainly renal excretion	40 mg SC once daily	1 mg/kg SC twice daily	Chromogenic anti-Xa assay: 0.6–1 anti-Xa U/mL	None
Fondaparinux	Potentiates antithrombin: Xa inhibition	Renal	2.5 mg SC once daily	5 or 7.5 or 10 mg SC once daily	Chromogenic anti-Xa assay	None
Rivaroxiban	Direct Xa inhibition	Likely liver	10 mg PO once daily		Chromogenic anti-Xa assay	None
Warfarin	Prevents carboxylation of X, IX, VII, II, protein C and S	Hepatic, marked genetic variability		2–10 mg PO daily; adjust to target INR.	INR = 2–4	Vitamin K: 1–10 mg PO or plasma; start with 2–4 units

Drug	Mechanism	Elimination	Dosing	Monitoring	Reversal
Lepirudin	Direct thrombin inhibition	Renal	Bolus = 0.4 mg/kg Infusion = 0.15 mg/kg/hr; adjust to target PTT	APTT = 60–80 (1.5–2.5 times control)	None
Bivalirudin	Direct thrombin inhibition	Proteolytic cleavage and renal (20%)	Bolus = 1 mg/kg Infusion = 0.2 mg/kg/hr; adjust to target PTT	APTT = 60–80 s	None
Desirudin	Direct thrombin inhibition	Renal	10–15 mg SC twice daily	Prolongs the APTT	None
Argatroban	Direct thrombin inhibition	Hepatic	Infusion = 2 mcg/kg/min; adjust to target PTT	APTT = 60–80 s; may prolong INR	None
Dabigatran etexilate	Direct thrombin inhibition	Renal (unchanged) and some conjugation with glucuronic acid	150 mg PO once daily	150 mg PO twice daily	None

due to factor Xa inhibition via potentiation of AT, and LMWH results in less thrombin inhibition than unfractionated heparin. The advantages of LMWH include a more predictable anticoagulant effect, less platelet interaction, and a longer half-life. Dosing is based on weight, and laboratory monitoring is not typically needed. LMWH may be used for longer-term therapy in patients with a contraindication to oral anticoagulant treatment (e.g., pregnant patients who cannot take warfarin). Because LMWH has a longer half-life and no effective antidote, it must be used with caution in surgical patients and in those in whom a bleeding risk has been substantiated.

c. **Direct thrombin inhibitors** are a class of compounds that bind to free and fibrin-bound thrombin. These agents inhibit thrombin activation of clotting factors, fibrin formation, and platelet aggregation.

(1) **Hirudin,** an anticoagulant originally derived from leeches, has been formulated as lepirudin and bivalirudin. **Lepirudin,** recombinant hirudin, binds irreversibly to thrombin, providing effective anticoagulation. The drug is approved in patients with HIT but may be considered in other severe clotting disorders. **Bivalirudin** is a truncated form of recombinant hirudin that targets only the active site of thrombin. Bivalirudin is FDA approved for HIT as well as for use during percutaneous coronary angioplasty and stenting.

(2) **Argatroban** is a synthetic thrombin inhibitor that is also approved for treatment of HIT.

d. **Warfarin** is an oral vitamin K antagonist that causes anticoagulation by inhibiting vitamin K-mediated carboxylation of factors II, VII, IX, and X as well as proteins C and S. The vitamin K-dependent factors decay with varying half-lives, so the full warfarin anticoagulant effect is not apparent for 5 to 7 days. When immediate anticoagulation is necessary, heparin or another agent must be used initially.

(1) **Administration.** Warfarin usually is initiated with a loading dose of 5 to 10 mg/day for 2 days, followed by dose adjustment based on daily INR results. The smaller dose is more likely to produce an INR of 2 to 3 with less excess anticoagulation and decreases the risk of a hypercoagulable state caused by precipitous drops in protein C levels during initiation of warfarin therapy (*Arch Int Med.* 1999;159:46). Elderly patients, those with hepatic insufficiency, and those who are receiving parenteral nutrition or broad-spectrum antibiotics, should be given lower initial doses of warfarin. A daily dose of warfarin needed to achieve therapeutic anticoagulation usually ranges from 2 to 15 mg/day. An INR of 2 to 3 is therapeutic for most indications, but patients with prosthetic heart valves should be maintained with an INR of 2.5 to 3.5. Once a stable INR is obtained on a stable warfarin dose, it can be monitored biweekly or monthly.

(2) **Complications.** The bleeding risk in patients who are treated with warfarin is estimated to be approximately 10% per year. The risk of bleeding correlates directly with the INR. Warfarin-induced

skin necrosis, caused by dermal venous thrombosis, occurs rarely when warfarin therapy is initiated in patients who are not already anticoagulated and is often associated with hypercoagulability caused by protein C deficiency. Warfarin can produce significant birth defects and fetal death and should not be used during pregnancy. Changes in medications and diet may affect warfarin or vitamin K levels and require more vigilant INR monitoring and dose adjustment.

(3) **Reversal of warfarin-induced anticoagulation** requires up to 1 week after discontinuation of therapy. Vitamin K administration can be used to reverse warfarin anticoagulation within 1 to 2 days, but the effect can last for up to 1 week longer. The appropriate vitamin K dose depends on the INR and the urgency with which correction must be accomplished. For patients with bleeding or extremely high INR levels (>10), 10 mg of vitamin K should be administered intravenously. Serial INR levels should be followed every 6 hours. In addition, FFP can be administered to patients with ongoing hemorrhage. Recombinant human factor VIIa (see below) has also been used (100 μg/kg) off label in cases of life-threatening bleeding.

e. **Indirect factor Xa inhibitors (Fondaparinux)** are small, synthetic, heparin-like molecules that enhance AT-mediated inhibition of factor Xa. Fondaparinux has been shown to be as effective in preventing DVT after hip and knee replacement. Monitoring of coagulation parameters is usually not necessary.

4. **Fibrinolytic therapy**
   a. Thrombolytic therapy is most often used for iliofemoral deep venous thrombosis (DVT), superior vena caval thrombosis, PE resulting in a hemodynamically unstable patient, acute thrombosis of peripheral, mesenteric, and coronary arteries, acute vascular graft occlusion, thrombosis of hemodialysis access grafts, and occlusion of venous catheters. Contraindications to fibrinolytic therapy are listed in Table 5-4. tPA (alteplase) or a recombinant analog (reteplase), as well as urokinase (Abbokinase), are used for lysis of catheter, venous, and peripheral arterial thrombi.

5. **Transfusion products for coagulopathy (Table 5-2)**
   a. **FFP** contains all the coagulation factors. However, factors V and VIII may not be stable through the thawing process and are not reliably recovered from FFP. Therefore, it can be used to correct coagulopathies that are due to deficiencies of any other coagulation factor and is particularly useful when multiple factor deficiencies exist (e.g., liver disease or massive transfusion). FFP effects are immediate and typically **last about 6 hours.** Factor VIII and IX deficiencies are best treated using specific factor concentrates.
   b. **Cryoprecipitate** is the cold-insoluble precipitate of fresh plasma and is rich in factor VIII and vWF as well as fibrinogen, fibronectin, and factor XIII. Cryoprecipitate may be used as second-line therapy in vWD or hemophilia but is most often used to correct fibrinogen deficiency in DIC or during massive transfusion.

TABLE 5-4	Contraindications to Fibrinolytic Therapy

Absolute Contraindications

Intolerable ischemia (for arterial thrombosis)

Active bleeding (not including menses)

Recent (<2 mo) stroke or neurosurgical procedure

Intracranial pathology such as neoplasm

Relative Contraindications

Recent (<10 d) major surgery, major trauma, parturition, or organ biopsy

Active peptic ulcer or recent gastrointestinal bleeding (within 2 wk)

Uncontrolled hypertension (blood pressure >180/110 mm Hg)

Recent cardiopulmonary resuscitation

Presence or high likelihood of left heart thrombus

Bacterial endocarditis

Coagulopathy or current use of warfarin

Pregnancy

Hemorrhagic diabetic retinopathy

c. **Recombinant human factor VIIa (rhFVIIa, NovoSeven)** is FDA approved for the treatment of hemophilia with inhibitors of factors VIII or XI. The recommended dose for this indication is 90 to 120 μg/kg, which can be repeated every 2 hours for 24 hours. However, the off-label use of rhFVIIa has exponentially grown as "rescue therapy" for patients with severe or dangerous bleeding that is not responsive to routine transfusion therapy. Although rhFVIIa used in blunt trauma was shown to reduce the overall blood transfusion requirement and reduce the incidence of multisystem organ failure and acute respiratory distress syndrome (*Crit Care.* 2006;10:R178; *J Trauma.* 2006;60:242), the safety of the drug is still in question. rhVIIa at pharmacologic doses may lead to unexpected thromboembolic events (stroke, MI, PE, DVT) due to its supraphysiologic activity and so NovoSeven should be used with caution (*J Am Coll Surg.* 2009;209:659). And point of fact, a recent meta-analysis of off-label rhVIIa use demonstrated an increased risk of arterial thrombosis **(including coronary artery thrombosis)** with a dose-dependent effect observed with doses >80 μg/kg (*N Engl J Med.* 2010;363:1791).

C. **Evaluation of global hemostasis**

1. **Laboratory tests:** Traditional *in vitro* tests such as PT/INR, PTT, and ACT are useful in the diagnosis and management of bleeding diathesis; however, abnormal values obtained in a test tube are not always indicative or representative of underlying hemostatic perturbation. Thromboelastrograph (TEG) evaluates hemostasis as a dynamic process where functional attributes such as kinetics of clot formation, growth, strength, and stability, are measured, thereby providing pertinent *in vivo* characterization of clot. This modality functions well in point of care situations such as during liver transplantation given the need for close monitoring and rapid evaluation of hemostasis and is currently being advocated as a tool for guiding and monitoring trauma resuscitation (*Ann Surg.* 2010;251:604) and cardiac surgery (*Anesth Analg.* 1999;88:312).

2. **Global disorders of hemostasis**

a. **DIC** has many inciting causes, including sepsis and extensive trauma or burns. The pathogenesis involves inappropriate generation of thrombin within the vasculature, leading to platelet activation, formation of fibrin thrombi, and increased fibrinolytic activity. DIC often presents with complications from microvascular thrombi that involve the vascular beds of the kidney, brain, lung, and skin. In some patients, the consumption of coagulation factors, particularly fibrinogen, and the activation of the fibrinolytic pathway can lead to bleeding. Laboratory findings in DIC include thrombocytopenia, hypofibrinogenemia, increased FDPs, and prolonged TT and PTT. Therapy begins with treatment of the underlying cause. Management of hemodynamics and oxygenation is critical. Correction of coagulopathy with platelet transfusions, FFP, and cryoprecipitate should be undertaken for bleeding complications but should not be given empirically given the potential risk of worsening inappropriate coagulation due to DIC.

III. ANEMIA

A. **Evaluation.** Anemia is defined as a hemoglobin level of less than 12 g/dL in women and less than 14 g/dL in men. A history and physical examination may determine the cause and acuity of anemia. Initial laboratory evaluation is usually a CBC, but a peripheral blood smear, reticulocyte count, and mean cell volume (MCV) may further help to identify the cause of the anemia. The blood smear is used to identify abnormalities in red blood cells (RBCs), white blood cells (WBCs), and platelets. The reticulocyte count assesses the bone marrow response to anemia. A normal or low reticulocyte count in the presence of anemia suggests an inadequate bone marrow response. The MCV differentiates different types of anemia.

B. **Anemias associated with RBC loss or increased RBC destruction**

1. **Bleeding** is the most frequently encountered cause of RBC loss. Most postoperative patients have an obvious etiology for blood loss; however,

sources of occult bleeding include the GI tract, uterus, urinary tract, and retroperitoneum. The hematocrit is not a reliable method to determine acute blood loss because the patient loses plasma in addition to RBCs.

2. **Sepsis.** Anemia is common is sepsis and is partially due to a decreased expression of the erythropoietin gene, but treatment with recombinant human erythropoietin has failed to demonstrate an increase in survival. Transfusions for a hematocrit level lower than 30% earlier in the stages of sepsis is associated with a decreased risk of mortality (*N Engl J Med.* 2001;345:1368).

C. **Hemolytic anemias**

1. **Acquired hemolytic anemias** are caused by autoimmune disorders, medications, or trauma. The direct Coombs test usually identifies autoimmune hemolytic anemia. Idiosyncratic drug-induced hemolytic anemia is rare but cefotetan-induced hemolysis is noteworthy because of its frequency and severity in surgical patients. Traumatic hemolytic anemias are often induced by malfunctioning prosthetic heart valves or vascular grafts.

2. **Hereditary hemolytic anemias** include the hemoglobinopathy of sickle cell disease, which is caused by abnormal hemoglobin that polymerizes under decreased oxygen tension. Dehydration and hypoxia must be avoided to prevent sickling, which is critical in patients who undergo general anesthesia. Other hereditary hemolytic anemias include RBC membrane abnormalities (e.g., hereditary spherocytosis) and RBC enzymopathies (e.g., glucose 6-phosphate dehydrogenase deficiency).

D. **Anemias associated with decreased RBC production**

1. **Iron-deficiency anemia** is most commonly caused by menstrual bleeding or occult GI blood loss. Sources of GI blood loss include gastritis, peptic ulcer disease, angiodysplasia, hemorrhoids, and colon adenocarcinoma. In men and postmenopausal women with iron-deficiency anemia, a complete GI evaluation for a potential source of blood loss is strongly recommended. Iron requirements for women increase during pregnancy owing to the transfer of iron to the fetus. Patients with a gastrectomy, achlorhydria, chronic diarrhea, or intestinal malabsorption may have diminished intestinal absorption of iron. The diagnosis is suggested by a hypochromic microcytic (MCV <80) anemia, low serum iron levels (<60 μg/dL), increased total iron-binding capacity (>360 μg/dL), and low serum ferritin levels (<14 ng/L). A trial of iron therapy typically establishes the diagnosis. Oral iron replacement (ferrous sulfate 325 mg orally three times a day) is usually sufficient treatment. Iron dextran also can be administered intramuscularly (100 mg/day) or as a single-dose intravenous preparation (1 to 2 g over 3 to 6 hours) in patients with malabsorption, poor compliance, or intolerance of oral preparations. IV administration of iron dextran must be closely monitored given the risk of severe anaphylactic reactions.

2. **Megaloblastic anemias (anemia with MCV >100)** are associated with a deficiency of cobalamin (vitamin B_{12}) or folic acid. Cobalamin, derived in the diet from meat and dairy products, is dependent on

intrinsic factor (IF) for absorption. IF is produced by gastric parietal cells, and the IF-cobalamin complex is absorbed in the terminal ileum. **Pernicious anemia** in which anti-IF antibodies occur places patients at risk. In addition, patients with gastrectomy, ileal resection or ileitis, intestinal parasites, or bacterial overgrowth can develop vitamin B_{12} deficiency. However, because only a small portion of the body's stores is used each day, vitamin B_{12} deficiency takes several years to manifest. In addition to anemia, vitamin B_{12} deficiency often causes a neuropathy (extremity paresthesias), weakness, ataxia, and poor coordination. In contrast to vitamin B_{12} deficiency, folic acid deficiency can develop within weeks from decreased intake (e.g., alcohol abuse), malabsorption, or increased use (e.g., pregnancy or hemolysis). Clinical suspicion, CBC and serum vitamin B_{12}, or folate levels establish the diagnosis. Therapy for vitamin B_{12} deficiency involves replacement with cyanocobalamin (1 mg/day intramuscularly for 7 days, then weekly for 2 months, then monthly). Folic acid is replenished (1 mg/day orally) until the deficiency is corrected. An incomplete response to therapy might indicate a coexisting iron deficiency, which occurs in one-third of patients with megaloblastic anemia.

3. **Other anemias** associated with decreased RBC production include anemia due to renal insufficiency, chronic disease, chemotherapy, and the thalassemias. Aplastic anemia is an acquired defect of bone marrow stem cells and is associated with pancytopenia. The majority of cases are idiopathic or autoimmune, but approximately 20% are drug related (e.g., gold, benzene, chemotherapeutics, anticonvulsants, sulfonamides, and chloramphenicol). Some are associated with an antecedent viral infection. A bone marrow biopsy helps to establish the diagnosis.

IV. **TRANSFUSION THERAPY.** The risks and benefits of transfusion therapy must be considered carefully in each situation. Informed consent should be obtained before blood products are administered. The indications for transfusion should be noted in the medical record. Before elective procedures that are likely to require blood transfusion, the options of autologous or directed blood donation should be discussed with the patient in time to allow for the collection process.

A. **Indications.** RBC transfusions are used to treat anemia and improve the oxygen-carrying capacity of the blood. A hemoglobin level of 7 to 8 g/dL is adequate for tissue oxygenation in most normovolemic patients. However, therapy must be individualized based on the clinical situation rather than a hemoglobin level. The patient's age, cardiovascular and pulmonary status, volume status, the type of transfusion (i.e., homologous vs. autologous), and the expectation of further blood loss should guide transfusion decisions. Of note, algorithm-guided approaches to transfusion that utilize laboratory and POC values (i.e., TEG) have been shown to be safe and decrease the number blood products transfused in cardiac surgery (*Br J Anesth.* 2004;92:178) and are being evaluated for trauma (*Ann Surg.* 2010;251: 604).

B. **Transfusions in critically ill patients.** Critically ill patients may be at increased risk for the immunosuppressive complications of transfusions and may benefit from a more restrictive transfusion protocol. This was demonstrated in the TRICC (Transfusion Requirements in Critical Care) trial, a randomized, controlled trial that showed significantly lower mortality rates with a restrictive transfusion strategy (transfusion for hemoglobin between 7 and 9 g/dl) (*N Engl J Med.* 1999;340:409). Patients with active cardiac ischemia or infarction may benefit from a higher hemoglobin level to improve oxygen delivery.

C. **Preparation.** Before administration, both donor blood and recipient blood are tested to decrease transfusion reactions. Blood typing tests the recipient's RBCs for antigens (A, B, and Rh) and screens the recipient's serum for the presence of antibodies to a panel of known RBC antigens. Each unit to be transfused is then cross-matched against the recipient's serum to check for preformed antibodies against antigens on the donor's RBCs. In an emergency situation, type O/Rh-negative blood that has been prescreened for reactive antibodies may be administered prior to blood typing and cross-matching. After blood typing, type-specific blood can be given. Certain populations of patients require specially prepared blood products. For example, patients who need chronic transfusion therapy and organ transplant should be administered leukocyte-depleted blood. Immunocompromised patients and those receiving blood from first-degree relatives should be given irradiated blood to prevent graft versus host disease (GVHD).

D. **Administration (Table 5-2).** Proper identification of the blood and patient is necessary to prevent transfusion errors. Packed RBCs should be administered through a standard filter (170 to 260 μm) and an 18-gauge or larger intravenous catheter. The rate of transfusion is determined by the clinical situation; typically, however, each unit of blood must be administered within 4 hours to prevent infection. Patients are monitored for adverse reactions during the first 5 to 10 minutes of the transfusion and frequently thereafter.

E. **Alternatives to homologous transfusion** exist and may provide advantages in safety and cost when used in elective procedures with a high likelihood of significant blood loss.

1. **Autologous predonation** is the preferred alternative for elective transfusions. Up to 20% of patients still require allogeneic transfusion, however, and transfusion reactions may still result from clerical errors in storage. Despite its intrinsic advantages, predonation is not cost-effective when the risk of transfusion is moderate or low.

2. **Isovolemic hemodilution** is a technique in which whole fresh blood is removed and crystalloid is simultaneously infused in the immediate preoperative period. The blood is stored at room temperature and reinfused after acute blood loss has ceased. Moderate hemodilution (hematocrit 32% to 33%) is as effective as autologous predonation in reducing the need for allogeneic transfusion and is much less costly.

3. **Intraoperative autotransfusion (Cell Saver)** in which blood from the operative field is returned to the patient can decrease allogeneic transfusion requirements. Equipment to separate and wash recovered

RBCs is required. Contraindications include neoplasm and enteric or purulent contamination.

4. **Erythropoietin** may be effective in decreasing allogeneic transfusion requirements when given preoperatively. Appropriate dose can be calculated based on anticipated transfusion requirements and is administered weekly over 2 to 4 weeks. Adjunctive use with autologous predonation has not consistently been shown to be effective. Chronic anemia, particularly anemia due to renal disease, is usually treated with erythropoietin (50 to 100 U/kg subcutaneously three times a week) rather than with transfusions. Erythropoietin should be used with caution in critically ill patients as it is associated with an increased risk of thrombotic events (*N Engl J Med.* 2007;357:965).

F. **Complications of transfusions**

1. **Infections.** Current methods of blood screening have greatly reduced the transmission rate of viral disease. Hepatitis B transmission is in the range of 1 in 205,000 units transfused. The risk of HIV or hepatitis C transmission is in the range of 1 in 2 million units transfused. Cytomegalovirus (CMV) transmission is a risk in CMV-negative immunocompromised patients and can be lowered by using either leukocyte-depleted or CMV-negative blood products. Bacteria and endotoxins can be infused with blood products, particularly in platelets that are stored at room temperature. Parasitic infections also can be transmitted, although rarely, with blood products.

2. **Transfusion reactions**

   a. **Allergic reactions** are the most common type of transfusion reactions and occur when the patient reacts to donated plasma proteins in the blood. Symptoms include itching or hives and can often be treated with antihistamines such as diphenhydramine (25 to 50 mg orally or intravenously). Prophylactic administration of diphenhydramine (Benadryl) and prednisone prior to a transfusion may be considered in patients with a previous history of allergic reaction. Rarely, severe reactions may involve bronchospasm or laryngospasm, which should prompt discontinuation of the infusion. Steroids and subcutaneous epinephrine may also be required.

   b. **Febrile nonhemolytic reactions** involve the development of a high fever during or within 24 hours of a transfusion. This reaction is mediated by the body's response to WBCs in donated blood. General malaise, chills, nausea, or headaches may accompany the fever. Because fever can be the first manifestation of a more serious transfusion reaction, the situation must be promptly evaluated. Patients with a previous history of a febrile reaction should receive leukoreduced blood products.

   c. **Acute immune hemolytic reactions** are the most serious transfusion reactions, in which patient antibodies react to transfused RBC antigens causing intravascular hemolysis. This typically occurs with ABO or Rh incompatibility. Symptoms include nausea, chills, anxiety, flushing, and chest or back pain. Anesthetized or comatose patients may show signs of excessive incisional bleeding or oozing from mucous membranes. The reaction may progress to shock or renal failure with hemoglobinuria. If a transfusion reaction is suspected, the infusion should be stopped immediately. Identities of the donor unit and recipient should be rechecked because clerical error is the most common cause. A repeat cross-match should be performed in addition to a CBC, coagulation studies, and serum bilirubin. Treatment includes maintenance of intravascular volume, hemodynamic support as needed, and preservation of renal function. Urine output should be maintained at greater than 100 mL/hour using volume resuscitation and possibly diuretics if resuscitation is attained. Alkalinization of the urine to a pH of greater than 7.5 by adding sodium bicarbonate to the intravenous fluids (two to three ampules of 7.5% sodium bicarbonate in 1,000 mL of D5W) helps to prevent precipitation of hemoglobin in the renal tubules.

   d. **Delayed hemolytic reactions** result from an anamnestic antibody response to antigens other than the ABO antigens to which the recipient has been previously exposed. Transfused blood cells may take days or weeks to hemolyze after transfusion. Typically there are few signs or symptoms other than a falling RBC count or elevated bilirubin. Specific treatment is rarely necessary, but severe cases should be treated like acute hemolytic reactions, with volume support and maintenance of urine output.

   e. **Transfusion-related acute lung injury (TRALI)** may be one of the most common causes of morbidity and mortality associated with transfusion. TRALI typically occurs within 1 to 2 hours of transfusion but can occur any time up to 6 hours later. Patients complain of shortness of breath and may have a fever. Support can vary from supplemental oxygen to intubation and ventilation. Although most cases resolve on their own, severe cases can be fatal.

   f. **GVHD** can occur after transfusion of immunocompetent T cells into immunocompromised recipients or human leukocyte antigen-identical family members. GVHD presents with a rash, elevated liver function tests and pancytopenia. It has an associated mortality of greater than 80%. Irradiation of donor blood from first-degree relatives of immunocompetent patients and all blood for immunocompromised patients prevents this complication.

3. **Volume overload after blood transfusion** can occur in patients with poor cardiac or renal function. Careful monitoring of the volume status and judicious use of diuretic therapy can reduce the risk of this complication.

4. **Massive transfusion,** usually defined as the transfusion of blood products that are greater in volume than a patient's normal blood volume in less than 24 hours, creates several risks not encountered with a lesser volume or rate of transfusion. **Coagulopathy** might arise as a result of platelet or coagulation factor depletion. This has led to the use of transfusion ratios in the trauma setting that involve the transfusion of platelets and FFP in concert with packed red blood cells (PRBCs). No definitive ratio has been established but ratios of 1:1 or 1:2 FFP:PRBC

are common. Blood products should be guided by the clinical situation and lab values (including TEG if available) rather than empirically based. **Hypothermia** can result from massive volume resuscitation with chilled blood products but can be prevented by using blood warmers. Hypothermia can lead to cardiac dysrhythmias and coagulopathy. **Citrate toxicity** can develop after massive transfusion in patients with hepatic dysfunction. Hypocalcemia can be treated with intravenous administration of 10% calcium gluconate. **Electrolyte abnormalities,** including acidosis and hyperkalemia, occur rarely after massive transfusions, especially in patients with preexisting hyperkalemia.

V. LOCAL HEMOSTATIC AGENTS. Local hemostatic agents can aid in the intraoperative control of bleeding from needle punctures, vascular suture lines, or areas of extensive tissue dissection. Anastomotic bleeding usually is best controlled with local pressure or a simple suture. Local hemostatic agents promote hemostasis by providing a matrix for thrombus formation.

A. **Gelatin sponge** (e.g., Gelfoam) can absorb many times its weight of whole blood by capillary action and provides a platform for coagulation. Gelfoam itself is not intrinsically hemostatic. It resorbs in 4 to 6 weeks without a significant inflammatory reaction.

B. **Oxidized cellulose** (e.g., Surgicel) is a knitted fabric of cellulose that allows clotting by absorbing blood and swelling into a scaffold. Its slow resorption can create a foreign body reaction.

C. **Collagen sponge** (e.g., Helistat) is produced from bovine tendon collagen and promotes platelet adhesion. It is slowly resorbed and creates a foreign body reaction similar to that of cellulose.

D. **Microfibrillar collagen** (e.g., Avitene and Hemotene) can be sprayed onto wounds and anastomoses for hemostasis, particularly in areas that are difficult to reach. It stimulates platelet adhesion and promotes thrombus formation. Because microfibrillar collagen can pass through autotransfusion device filters, it should be avoided during procedures that utilize the cell saver.

E. **Topical thrombin** can be applied to the various hemostatic agents or to dressings and placed onto bleeding sites to achieve a fibrin-rich hemostatic plug. Topical thrombin, usually of bovine origin, is supplied as a lyophilized powder and can be applied directly to dressings or dissolved in saline and sprayed onto the wound. Repeated use of bovine thrombin may result in formation of inhibitors to thrombin or factor V, which is not usually associated with a clinical bleeding disorder, although there may be dramatic alterations in the coagulation testing. Topical thrombin can be used effectively in anticoagulated patients.

F. **Gelatin matrices** (e.g., FloSeal) are often used in combination with topical thrombin intraoperatively. Typically, bovine thrombin (5,000 units) is sprayed onto the matrix, which is then applied to the site of bleeding.

G. **Fibrin sealants** (e.g., Tiseel and Evicel) are prepared by combining human thrombin and human fibrinogen. These components are separated prior to administration and are mixed during application to tissue via a dual-syringe system. An insoluble, cross-linked fibrin mesh is created with provides a matrix for thrombus formation.

6

Wound Healing and Care

Isaiah R. Turnbull, Thomas H. Tung, and John P. Kirby

Wound healing is the normal response to injury. Wound healing is divided into acute wound healing and chronic wound healing. *Acute wound healing* is the normal orderly process that occurs after an uncomplicated injury and requires minimal practitioner intervention. Chronic wound healing *does not* follow an orderly progression of healing and often necessitates a variety of interventions to facilitate closure.

ACUTE WOUND HEALING

I. **PHYSIOLOGY OF THE ACUTE WOUND.** Disruption of tissue integrity, whether surgical or traumatic, initiates a sequence of events directed at restoring the injured tissue to a normal state. Normal wound healing occurs in an orderly fashion and is a balance of repair and regeneration of tissue. Normal wound healing is affected by tissue type, the nature and extent of injury, and comorbid conditions. Wound healing is grouped into early, intermediate, and late stages.

A. **Early wound healing**

1. **Establishment of hemostasis.** Injury causes disruption of blood vessels with resulting hemorrhage. Severed blood vessels with smooth muscle in the vessel wall immediately constrict to minimize hemorrhage. Within minutes, the coagulation cascade is initiated and produces the end-product fibrin. The fibrin matrix binds and activates platelets, facilitating hemostasis. It also serves as the initial scaffold for wound healing. In later phases of wound healing, the fibrin matrix facilitates cell attachment and migration and serves as a reservoir for cytokines.

2. **Inflammatory phase** (days 1 to 4). The inflammatory phase is recognized at the skin level by the cardinal signs of *rubor* (redness), *calor* (heat), *tumor* (swelling), and *dolor* (pain). Injury immediately activates three plasma-based systems: the coagulation cascade, the complement cascade, and the kinin cascade. Proinflammatory factors attract leukocytes and facilitate their migration out of the intravascular space and into the wound. **Polymorphonuclear leukocytes (PMNs)** are the dominant inflammatory cells in the wound for the first 24 to 48 hours. They phagocytize bacteria, foreign material, and damaged tissue. They also release cytokines such as TNF-alpha and interleukin-1 that further stimulate the inflammatory response. The inflammatory phase progresses with the infiltration of circulating **monocytes** into the wound. Monocytes migrate into the extravascular space through capillaries and differentiate into **macrophages.** Macrophages are activated by the locally produced cytokines and are essential for normal healing

because of their important role in the coordination of the healing process. They phagocytize bacteria and damaged tissue, secrete enzymes for the degradation of tissue and extracellular matrix, and release cytokines for inflammatory cell recruitment and fibroblast proliferation. The inflammatory phase lasts a well-defined period of time in primarily closed wounds (approximately 4 days), but it continues indefinitely to the end-point of complete epithelialization in wounds that close by secondary or tertiary intention. Foreign material or bacteria can change a normal healing wound into one with chronic inflammation.

B. **Intermediate wound-healing** events involve mesenchymal cell migration and proliferation, angiogenesis, and epithelialization.

1. **Fibroblast migration** occurs 2 to 4 days after wounding. Chemotactic cytokines influence fibroblasts to migrate into the wound from undamaged tissue. Movement of cells occurs on the extracellular matrix, consisting of fibrin, fibronectin, and vitronectin.

2. While the wound is infiltrated by mesenchymal cells, **angiogenesis** takes place to restore the vasculature that has been disrupted by the wound.

3. **Epithelialization** restores the barrier between the wound and the external environment. Epithelialization of wounds occurs via the migration of epithelial cells from the edges of the wound and from remaining epidermal skin appendages. Migration of epithelial cells occurs at the rate of 1 mm/day in clean, open wounds. Primarily closed wounds have a contiguous epithelial layer at 24 to 48 hours.

C. **Late wound healing** involves the deposition of collagen and other matrix proteins and wound contraction. The primary function of the fibroblast at this stage becomes protein synthesis. Fibroblasts produce several proteins that are components of the extracellular matrix, including collagen, fibronectin, and proteoglycans. Glucocorticoids compromise wound healing by inhibiting protein production by fibroblasts.

1. **Collagen** is the main protein secreted by fibroblasts. It provides strength and structure and facilitates cell motility in the wound. Collagen is synthesized at an accelerated rate for 2 to 4 weeks, greatly contributing to the tensile strength of the wound. Oxygen, vitamin C, α-ketoglutarate, and iron are important cofactors for the cross-linkage of collagen fibers. If these are not present, wound healing may be poor.

2. **Wound contraction** is a decrease in the size of the wound without an increase in the number of tissue elements that are present. It involves movement of the wound edge toward the center of the wound through the action of myofibroblasts. It is differentiated from contracture, which is the pathologic and movement-limiting result of prolonged wound contraction across a joint primarily from scar formation. Wound contraction begins 4 to 5 days after wounding and continues for 12 to 15 days or longer if the wound remains open.

3. The final wound-healing event is **scar formation and remodeling.** It begins at approximately 21 days after wounding. At the outset of scar remodeling, collagen synthesis is downregulated, and the cellularity

of the wound decreases. During scar remodeling, collagen is broken down and replaced by new collagen that is denser and organized along the lines of stress. By 6 months, the wound reaches 80% of the bursting strength of unwounded tissue. It is important to note that a well-healed wound never achieves the strength of unwounded tissue. This process reaches a plateau at 12 to 18 months, but it may last indefinitely.

CHRONIC WOUND HEALING

I. **PHYSIOLOGY OF THE CHRONIC WOUND.** A chronic wound is a wound that fails to heal in a reasonable amount of time, given the wound's etiology, location, and tissue type. Prolonged or incomplete healing is caused by disruption of the normal process of acute wound healing. Most chronic wounds are slowed or arrested in the inflammatory or proliferative phases of healing and have increased levels of matrix metalloproteinases, which bind up or degrade the various cytokines and growth factors at the wound surface. Most often, there are definable causes of the failure of these wounds to heal. Treatment of these causes, along with maximal medical management of underlying medical problems, restores more normal healing processes. Treating a patient with a chronic wound involves identifying the type of wound, investigating the cause(s) of delayed healing, and improving the intrinsic (within the wound itself) and extrinsic (systemic) factors that lead to poor wound healing.

A. **Intrinsic or local factors** are abnormalities within the wound that prevent normal wound healing. These factors include (1) foreign body, (2) necrotic tissue, (3) repetitive trauma, (4) hypoxia/ischemia, (5) venous insufficiency, (6) infection, (7) growth factor deficit, (8) excessive matrix protein degradation, and (9) radiation. Factors that can be controlled by the surgeon include the blood supply to the wound; the temperature of the wound environment; the presence or absence of infection, hematoma, or seroma; the amount of local tissue trauma; and the technique used to close the wound.

B. **Extrinsic or systemic factors** also contribute to abnormal wound healing. Optimization of these factors is critical to healing a chronic wound: (1) diabetes mellitus, (2) steroids and antineoplastic drugs, (3) smoking, (4) collagen vascular disease, (5) repetitive trauma, and (6) chronic disease states in the kidney and liver.

II. **EVALUATION AND MANAGEMENT OF THE CHRONIC WOUND**

A. **Diagnosis.** Evaluation and management of a chronic wound must begin with a thorough history and physical examination.

1. **History.** One must establish whether the wound is new, recurrent, or chronic, how long it has been present, how it started, how quickly it developed, and whether it is improving or worsening. The patient must be questioned about existing comorbidities, with a focus on potential causes for immunosuppression (HIV,

steroids, chemotherapy), undiagnosed diabetes mellitus, peripheral vascular disease, coronary artery disease, rheumatologic disorders, and radiation exposure. Smoking and alcohol use should also be documented.

2. **Physical examination** should include the measured size and depth of the wound, and the tissues that are involved. The wound and the surrounding tissue should be evaluated for any signs of infection. The full extent of the wound should be defined including probing any undermined tissue flaps or drainage tracts with a sterile instrument. The surrounding tissue should also be evaluated for skin changes including maceration, hyperpigmentation, capillary refill, and pallor. For extremity wounds, a complete vascular assessment often requiring Doppler ultrasound of the arterial pulsations is a key component of the exam.

3. **Laboratory assessments** of serum electrolyte, hepatic transaminase, and bilirubin levels may aid with the diagnosis of diabetes and renal or hepatic dysfunction. A complete blood cell count may indicate infection with elevated white cell count or white cell abnormalities. Radiography can be performed to determine underlying bony pathology.

B. **Management** of the chronic wound must focus on optimization of host and local factors.

1. **Adequate nutrition** is necessary for appropriate wound healing. Sufficient calories, protein, vitamins, minerals, and water are necessary to aid in the healing. Patients who have severe malnutrition or whose gastrointestinal tract cannot be used should be placed on parenteral nutritional support.

2. **Underlying factors** that affect wound healing, such as chemotherapy, steroids, alcohol consumption, cigarette smoking, and blood glucose levels, must be modified as necessary to aid in the wound-healing process.

3. **Effective local wound care** is essential for the resolution of a chronic wound. Eradication of infection, aggressive debridement, and drainage of abscesses from the wound are important steps in local control.

4. **Antibiotics.** Systemic antibiotics should be administered to treat wounds that are actively infected with purulent discharge and or cellulitis. Topical antibiotics may be useful in slowly healing chronic wounds that are not actively infected but which have a quantitative bacterial count $>10^5$ CFU/mm^3 or which display secondary signs of infection such as friable granulation tissue, nonpurulent exudates, or abnormal foul odor (*Clin Infect Dis.* 2009;49:1541).

5. **Proper dressings** are an essential aspect of local care by helping to provide the appropriate environment for healing.

   a. Frequent damp-to-dry dressings are used when infection and drainage predominate. With the development of healthy granulation tissue, dressings should provide adequate protection and moisture to facilitate healing. Wounds with exudate should have this controlled by the dressing to protect the periwound from maceration.

b. Negative pressure dressings (NPD) provide subatmospheric pressure a local wound though a porous foam sponge sealed over the wound with a semipermeable adhesive barrier. Vacuum is applied by an external pump. NPD are particularly useful for wounds with soft tissue deficits and can also be used to facilitate closure of open sternal or abdominal wounds. NPD should not be placed directly over exposed bowel, blood vessels, or cortical bone. NPD are also contraindicated when there is active infection or necrotic tissue in the wound. They can be placed safely over exposed fascia or fascia substitutes such as biologic or nonbiologic hernia repair mesh.

6. Edema control is often necessary for wounds of the lower extremity due to venous insufficiency. Elevation and wrapping in an elastic bandage reduce edema and venous hypertension. Unna boot, Jobst compression garments, and pneumatic compression devices can also be used.

7. Surgical therapy may be necessary to aid in the healing of a chronic wound. Besides surgical débridement or skin grafting on a healthy bed of granulation tissue, revascularization procedures may be necessary to provide adequate blood flow to distal circulation that supplies a non-healing/or chronic wound.

III. SPECIAL CATEGORIES OF CHRONIC WOUNDS. Chronic wounds are a heterogeneous group. Chronic wounds associated with vascular disease, diabetes, pressure necrosis, and radiation therapy are frequently encountered, cause great disability within the population, and place a great burden on the healthcare system.

A. Diabetic foot ulcers

1. Differential diagnosis. The first step to treating any lower-extremity ulcer is to identify the cause of the wound. The three most common causes of lower-extremity ulcers are diabetes mellitus, venous stasis, and arterial insufficiency. Diabetic ulcers most frequently result from undetected/untreated trauma to the neuropathic foot. They are typically associated with very thick callus and most often occur on the patient's heels or on the plantar surface of the metatarsal heads. Venous stasis ulcers most often occur on the medial aspect of the patient's lower leg or ankle (gaiter distribution) and are associated with the chronic edema and hyperpigmentation seen with venous insufficiency. Arterial insufficiency ulcers tend to occur distally on the tips of the patient's toes, but they can also occur at or near the lateral malleolus. The surrounding skin is thin, shiny, and hairless; these individuals typically relate symptoms of claudication or rest pain. Peripheral pulses are diminished or absent. Unfortunately, lower extremity ulcers frequently result from a combination of these common etiologies, which must be considered when devising a treatment plan.

2. Pathogenesis of diabetic foot ulcers.

a. Peripheral neuropathy is believed to be the most significant contributor to the development of lower-extremity ulcers in diabetic patients through impaired detection of injury from poorly fitting shoes or trauma. Diabetic motor neuropathy is also associated with abnormal weightbearing. The motor neuropathy results in abnormalities such as hammertoes or hallux valgus, which shift weightbearing more proximally than normal on the metatarsal heads. Additionally, the dorsum of the toes at the posterior interphalangeal joints is often traumatized by ill-fitting shoes in patients with hammertoes.

b. Autonomic neuropathy leads to failure of sweating and inadequate lubrication of the skin. Dry skin leads to mechanical breakdown that initiates ulcer formation. Autonomic neuropathy also contributes to failure of autoregulation in the microcirculation; therefore, arterial blood will shunt past capillaries into the venous blood flow. This reduces the nutritive blood flow to the skin and predisposes to ulcer formation.

c. Ischemia contributes to the development and progression of lower-extremity ulcers. Patients with diabetic foot ulcers should also be evaluated for proximal arterial insufficiency that may be amenable to intervention, improving the chances of healing of the ulcer.

3. Evaluation and treatment

a. Examination. The quality of the peripheral circulation, the extent of the wound, and the degree of sensory loss as assessed with a 10-gauge monofilament skin tester should be recorded. Web spaces should be examined for evidence of mycotic infection, which may lead to fissuring of the skin and subsequent infection. Mal perforans ulcers occur on the plantar surface of the metatarsals and extend to the metatarsal head, leaving exposed cartilage. Evaluation of diabetic foot ulcers should include plain x-rays of the foot to evaluate for osteomyelitis.

b. Treatment. With appropriate treatment, 24% of diabetic found wounds will heal by 12 weeks, and 31% by 20 weeks (*Diabetes Care*. 1999;22:692). Critical to treatment of any diabetic foot wound is complete offloading of the ulcer with an appropriate diabetic shoe or other orthotic device.

(1) Clean wounds are treated with minimal debridement and damp gauze or hydrogel-based dressing changes. Hydrogel dressings may be more effective than damp gauze (*Cochrane Cochrane Database Syst Rev.* 2010;20:CD003556). Exudative wounds may benefit from alginate, hydrocolloid, or NPD that minimize contact of the wound base with wound exudate, which is hypothesized to inhibit wound healing. Close follow-up is essential.

(2) Infected wounds are diagnosed based on clinical signs of infection. Plain x-rays may show osteomyelitis or gas in the soft tissues. The progression of infection in diabetic patients can occur rapidly. Patients with a suspected infected diabetic foot ulcer should be admitted for inpatient wound care and broad-spectrum antibiotic therapy. Infected wounds require a thorough exploration with drainage of all abscess cavities and debridement of infected, necrotic, or devitalized tissues. The clean wound can then be managed with local wound care as described above.

(3) Antibiotic therapy. For infected wounds, initial antibiotic therapy should be broad spectrum directed at both Gram-positive and Gram-negative organisms. In the acute phase parenteral treatment is indicated. Wound cultures should be obtained prior to initiation of antibiosis. Duration of antibiosis depends on severity of infection. For mild infections limited to the soft tissue 1 to 2 weeks of therapy is sufficient; moderate or severe infections require 2 to 4 weeks of total antibiotic therapy. For osteomyelitis involving viable bone, 4 to 6 weeks of IV therapy may be indicated. Consultation with an infectious disease specialist is helpful in guiding therapy (*Plast Reconstr Surg.* 2006;117:212S).

(4) Prevention remains one of the most important elements in the management of the diabetic foot. Meticulous attention to hygiene and daily inspection for signs of tissue trauma prevent the progression of injury. Podiatric appliances or custom-made shoes are helpful in relieving pressure on weightbearing areas and should be prescribed for any patient who has had neuropathic ulceration.

B. **Leg ulcers**

1. **Arterial insufficiency ulcers** tend to occur distally on the tips of the patient's toes or near the lateral malleolus. The surrounding skin is thin, shiny, and hairless. Patients frequently complain of claudication or rest pain. Peripheral pulses are diminished or absent. When **arterial ulcers** are suspected, obtain vascular evaluation including a peripheral and central pulse exam and segmental limb pressures with calculation of ankle-brachial indices and toe-pressures. Neglected chronic arterial insufficiency can result in dry gangrene and mummification of the toes. Critical to treatment of these wounds is restoration of arterial inflow (see Chapter 19). After optimization of arterial inflow, devitalized tissue can be resected to facilitate healing. Arterial insufficiency wounds and dry gangrene must be carefully assessed for signs of infection. If infection is suspected, obtain wound cultures, débride infected tissue, and institute appropriate antibiosis.

2. **Venous stasis ulcers** are among the most common types of leg ulcers and typically occur on the medial leg in the supramedial malleolar location. A patient with a venous stasis ulcer typically has a history of ulceration and associated leg swelling or of deep venous thrombosis. See Chapter 20 for complete description of venous stasis ulcers and their treatment.

C. **Skin tears** are often seen in the elderly with skin that is markedly thinned and in the chronic steroid-using patient. The hypermobile skin, with its poor subcutaneous connections, is prone to rip under shearing forces, and patients often present with a flap of skin that is torn away from its wound bed. One should follow the principles outlined previously, with this exception: The skin flap should be trimmed of obvious necrotic portions, and the remaining flap should be secured in place over the wound bed only to the extent that it can be without tension. It is rare that such a wound should be sutured closed because the flap will most likely necrose under the tension of the swelling that occurs over the following 2 to 4 days. Topical management of the area that is intentionally left open is often easily achieved with a hydrogel dressing.

D. **Pressure ulcers**

1. **Pathophysiology.** Prolonged pressure applied to soft tissue over bony prominences, usually caused by paralysis or the immobility associated with severe illness, predictably leads to ischemic ulceration and tissue breakdown. Muscle tissue seems to be the most susceptible. The prevalence of pressure ulcers is 10% of all hospitalized patients, 28% of nursing home patients, and 39% of spinal cord injury patients (*JAMA.* 2006;296:974). Pressure ulcers increase mortality rates more than twofold, and are the cause of death in 8% of paraplegics (*Am J Surg.* 2004;188:9S). The particular area of breakdown depends on the patient's position of immobility, with ulcers most frequently developing in recumbent patients over the occiput, sacrum, greater trochanter, and heels. In immobile patients who sit for prolonged periods on improper surfaces without pressure relief, ulcers often develop under the ischial tuberosities. **Pressure ulcers are described by stages (Table 6-1).** Such wounds do not necessarily proceed through each one of these stages during formation but can present at the advanced stages. Likewise, as these wounds heal, they do not go backward through the stages despite their present depth (e.g., a nearly healed stage IV ulcer does not become a stage II ulcer but rather a healing stage IV ulcer, signifying that the tissues of the healing wound are abnormal). When

TABLE 6-1	National Pressure Ulcer Advisory Panel Classification Scheme

Stage	Description
I	Nonblanchable erythema of intact skin; wounds generally reversible at this stage with intervention
II	Partial-thickness skin loss involving epidermis or dermis; may present as an abrasion, blister, or shallow crater
III	Full-thickness skin loss involving damage or necrosis of subcutaneous tissue but not extending through underlying structures or fascia
IV	Full-thickness skin loss with damage to underlying support structures (i.e., fascia, tendon, or joint capsule)

a full-thickness injury to the skin has occurred, one cannot adequately stage the wound until the eschar is incised and the actual depth is determined. The examiner must also look for underlying bony breakdown, osteomyelitis, or an overall physiologic decline as the root cause of a "pressure" ulcer whose actual etiology may be multifactorial in nature, and any successful healing regimen must be equally multifactorial. The clinician must also consider whether such regimens are realistic and discuss assessments and care plans openly with the patient and family regarding realistic expectations and treatment goals.

2. **Prevention**
   a. Skin care. Skin should be kept well moisturized but protected from excessive contact with extraneous fluids. Take care during transfers to avoid friction and shear stress.
   b. Frequent repositioning. High-risk patients should be repositioned at a minimum every 2 hours, either while seated or in bed.
   c. Appropriate support surfaces. Adequate support surfaces redistribute pressure from the bony prominences that cause pressure ulcers. The appropriate surface is determined by the patient risk stratification using the Norton Scale (*Decubitus.* 1989;2:24.) and Braden Scale (*Nurs Clin North Am.* 1987;22:417). Static support surfaces: foam, air, gel, and water-overlay support surfaces are appropriate for low-risk patients. Dynamic support surfaces: these are support modalities that are powered and actively redistribute pressure. These include alternating and low air-loss mattresses. These surfaces are appropriate for high-risk patients.

3. **Treatment**
   a. Debridement. Eschar and necrotic tissue should be débrided. Sharp debridement of small wounds can be done at the bedside. Larger wounds require operative debridement. Once the bulk of eschar and devitalized tissue is removed, debridement can be continued with damp-to-dry gauze dressings or with enzymatic debridement with topical agents such as collagenase.
   b. Wound cleansing. The base of uninfected ulcers should be cleaned with saline irrigation or a commercially available wound cleanser at each dressing change. Antiseptic solutions such as hydrogen peroxide, povidone–iodine, or Dakin's solution should not be routinely used as they are toxic to tissues and impede healing. For actively infected wounds, a short course (3 to 5 days) of damp to dry dressing changes with ¼ strength Dakins' solution may facilitate local bacterial control. However, topical antiseptic solutions cannot take the place of appropriate debridement and systemic antibiotic therapy.
   c. Dressing. Dressings should be selected to ensure the wound base remains moist while keeping the surrounding skin dry. Damp-to-dry gauze and hydrocolloid dressings are appropriate. NPD are also useful for pressure ulcers and may facilitate closure as compared to traditional dressings (*Br J Nurs.* 2004;13:135). See section on negative pressure dressing for indications/contraindications to NPD.

    d. Infection and bacterial colonization. All open ulcers are colonized with bacteria. Surface colonization is best controlled with topical wound cleansing. Superficial colonization does not require antibiotic therapy. Evidence of active infection (purulence, surrounding cellulitis or foul odor) should prompt reexploration of the wound with debridement of any necrotic or infected tissue. Bacterial infection with greater than 10^5 organisms per gram of tissue can impair wound healing. Quantitative tissue cultures should be obtained from wounds that fail to heal. The underlying bone should be evaluated for osteomyelitis with appropriate imaging.

    e. Nutrition. Successful treatment of pressure ulcers requires adequate nutrition. Patients should be provided with 30 to 35 kcal/kg body weight and 1.25 to 1.5 g protein/kg body weight (*National Pressure Ulcer Advisory Panel Quick Reference Guide;* 2009). These estimates should be adjusted for factors such as recent weight changes, BMI, and renal failure or other comorbid conditions. Patient with non-healing pressure ulcers will benefit from a formal nutrition assessment by a dietician.

4. Surgical treatment. Most pressure ulcers heal spontaneously when pressure is relieved. *This remains the most important factor in their healing.* The healing process may require up to 6 months. Unless the patient was only temporarily immobilized, recurrences are common. Surgical management may include simple closure, split-thickness skin grafting, or musculocutaneous flap, but these measures should be reserved for well-motivated patients in whom a real reduction in risk factors for recurrence is possible. Urinary and fecal diversion reduce soiling and maceration of perineal and sacral wounds, which facilitates healing of these wounds.

E. Ionizing radiation. Although ionizing radiation is a useful mode of cancer therapy, it produces detrimental local effects on tissue in the field of radiation and impairs normal wound healing. Radiation injures target and surrounding cells by damaging DNA, decreasing proliferative capacity of cells, and decreasing perfusion through damage to the small blood vessels. The **timing of radiation therapy** as it relates to operative therapy has been an important aspect of oncologic care. The primary factors that determine the effects of preoperative radiation therapy on wound healing are the timing and the dose. These vary from tissue to tissue. Postoperative radiation therapy has no effect on healing if it is administered 1 week after wounding. The intentional (surgical) wounding of a previously irradiated area needs careful planning and consideration. Many of the cells in such an area have been permanently damaged; therefore, their proliferative capacity is decreased. In addition, the wound has decreased vascularity, which creates a relative state of hypoxemia. Furthermore, the dermis of such a wound is more susceptible to bacterial invasion. The combined factors place a previously irradiated area at extreme risk for abnormal wound healing if it is subjected to surgical intervention. It has long been realized for the foregoing reasons that **radiation-damaged skin and wounds heal poorly.** Local measures that must be undertaken with wounds affected by radiation follow the same principles of good wound care. These measures include infection control through aggressive débridement and systemic antibiotics, topical antibiotics to promote epithelialization, moist dressings, and lubrication of dry skin. Optimal nutritional status must also be emphasized.

PROPHYLACTIC SURGICAL WOUND CARE

I. **PREOPERATIVE PREPARATION.** Even though antibiotic prophylaxis and sterile surgical technique have gained widespread acceptance, surgical site infections (SSIs) remain a persistent problem occurring in 2 to 5% of operations and affecting 750,000 people annually in the United States (*Surg Infect.* 2006;7:S1). Clean surgical operations typically result in SSIs from Gram-positive aerobes representing pathogens in common skin flora (*Curr Infect Dis Rep.* 2004;6:426). Clean-contaminated, contaminated, or dirty operations usually result in polymicrobial infections with enteric Gram-negative and anaerobic bacteria along with skin flora pathogens. Antibiotic resistance is an increasing problem. The rate of *Staphylococcus aureus* resistance to methicillin, oxacillin, or nafcillin (MRSA) now approaches 60%, and the rate of *Klebsiella pneumoniae* resistance to cephalosporins is 50% (*Expert Rev Anti Infect Ther.* 2006;4:223).

A. **Patient factors.** Whereas some characteristics, such as age, cannot be altered, other patient factors can be optimized.

1. **Cigarette smoking** is a known risk factor for SSI (*J Am Coll Surg.* 2007;204:178) and a prospective, randomized trial demonstrated an 83% reduction in wound infections in the smoking cessation group compared to controls (*Lancet.* 2002;359:114). The Centers for Disease Control and Prevention (CDC) recommends smoking cessation at least 30 days prior to elective surgery.

2. The impact of **nutrition** on wound healing depends on the wound type. Wounds closed by primary intention often heal even in emaciated patients as long as there are no wound infections (*Annu Rev Nutr.* 2003;23:263). In contrast, wounds that heal by secondary intention are heavily dependent on the patient's nutritional status. Malnourished patients have increased rates of infection and delayed wound healing, and there is ample evidence that tailored preoperative nutritional repletion reduces these complications (*Plast Reconstr Surg.* 2006;117:42S).

B. **Operative factors**

1. **Chlorhexidine showers** the night before surgery reduce bacterial counts; however, no studies have demonstrated decreased SSI rates with preoperative showering (*Cochrane Database of Systematic Reviews* 2007: CD004985). Previous recommendations regarding showers as well as updates on other interventions as detailed in the following can be found on the CDC Web site.

2. **Shaving** is associated with an increased risk of SSIs. Meta-analysis of the available studies on hair removal demonstrate that **clipping** performed immediately before surgery was associated with significantly fewer infections as compared to shaving (*J Perioper Pract.* 2007;17:118).

3. **Prophylactic antibiotics** are indicated for some clean cases and most clean-contaminated cases. Antibiotics should be administered prior to the incision, with many regulatory groups recommending administration within 60 minutes (*Expert Rev Anti Infect Ther.* 2006;4:223). Most guidelines recommend postoperative discontinuation of prophylactic antibiotics within 24 hours (*Surg Clin North Am.* 2005;85:1115). Recently, large prospective, randomized trials have demonstrated no evidence to support the use of antibiotic prophylaxis in hernia surgery (*Ann Surg.* 2004;240:955; *J Am Coll Surg.* 2005;200:393).

II. PERIOPERATIVE

A. **Surgeon hand antisepsis** has traditionally been performed with a 5- to 10-minute scrub. Current guidelines include use of either (1) a traditional scrub with antimicrobial soap for 2 to 6 minutes or (2) use of alcohol-based surgical hand scrub following the manufacturer's recommendation for use. No difference in SSI is seen between these two techniques (*JAMA.* 2002;288:722).

B. **Surgical site antisepsis** starts with cleansing and removing visible debris, followed by a prep of the intended incision site to the periphery in concentric circles using a sterile instrument. Current practices include using 7.5% povidone–betadine foaming solution, 10% povidone–betadine paint, alcohol solutions, chlorhexidine/alcohol preparations, and alcohol-containing iodophor solutions. Chlorhexidine-based solutions may be superior to iodine-based solutions for clean-contaminated surgical cases (*N Engl J Med.* 2010;362:18).

C. **Active warming** to prevent intraoperative hypothermia has been demonstrated to reduce surgical infections in prospective, randomized trials (*N Engl J Med.* 1996;334:1209; *Lancet.* 2001;358:876). Current recommendations are (1) temperature monitoring for all cases (2) forced-air warmers for procedures expected to last greater than 30 minutes, and (3) warmed IV fluids for procedures expected to last greater than 1 hour (*JACS.* 2009;209:492).

D. **Tight glycemic control** is recommended in the perioperative period, although the mechanisms explaining the detrimental effect of hyperglycemia remain largely unknown. In 2001, Van den Berghe reported a randomized, prospective study of 1,548 surgical patients in which stringent glycemic control between 80 and 110 mg/dL resulted in 34% decreased mortality versus maintenance of 180 to 200 mg/dL (*N Engl J Med.* 2001;345:1359). In addition, continuous intravenous insulin infusion has been shown significantly to reduce the incidence of sternal wound infections when compared to sliding-scale insulin (*Ann Thoracic Surg.* 1999;67:352). The American Diabetes Association and the American Association of Clinical Endocrinologists recommend glycemic targets between 80 and 110 mg/dL for critically ill patients in the intensive care unit. For patients with noncritical illness, a prandial glucose of less than 110 mg/dL and a random glucose level of less than 180 mg/dL were recommended in the perioperative period (*Endocr Pract.* 2004;10(suppl 2):4).

E. **Other controllable factors** include the length of operation, gentle tissue handling, and supplemental oxygen to diminish SSIs.

WOUND CLOSURE AND CARE

I. TIMING OF WOUND HEALING

A. **Primary intention** occurs when the wound is closed by direct approximation of the wound margins or by placement of a graft or flap. Direct approximation of the edges of a wound provides the optimal treatment on the condition that the wound is clean, the closure can be done without undue tension, and the closure can occur in a timely fashion. Wounds that are less than 6 hours old are considered in the "golden period" and are less likely to develop into chronic wounds. At times, rearrangement of tissues is required to achieve tension-free closure. Directly approximated wounds typically heal as outlined earlier, provided that there is adequate perfusion of the tissues and no infection. Primary intention also describes the healing of wounds created in the operating room that are closed at the end of the operative period. Epithelialization of surgical incisions occurs within 24 hours of closure. CDC guidelines dictate that a sterile dressing should be left in place during this susceptible period to prevent bacterial contamination.

B. **Secondary intention,** or spontaneous healing, occurs when a wound is left open and is allowed to close by epithelialization and contraction. Contraction is a myofibroblast-mediated process that aids in wound closure by decreasing the circumference of the wound (myofibroblasts are modified fibroblasts that have smooth muscle cell-like contractile properties). This method is commonly used in the management of wounds that are treated beyond the initial 6-hour "golden period" or of contaminated infected wounds with a bacterial count of greater than 10^5/g of tissue. These wounds are characterized by prolonged inflammatory and proliferative phases of healing that continue until the wound has either completely epithelialized or been closed by other means.

C. **Tertiary intention, or delayed primary closure,** is a useful option for managing wounds that are too heavily contaminated for primary closure but appear clean and well vascularized after 4 to 5 days of open observation so that the cutaneous edges can be approximated at that time. During this period, the normally low arterial partial pressure of oxygen (PaO_2) at the wound surface rises and the inflammatory process in the wound bed leads to a minimized bacterial concentration, thus allowing a safer closure than could be achieved with primary closure and a more rapid closure than could be achieved with secondary wound healing.

II. WOUND CLOSURE MATERIALS AND TECHNIQUES

A. **Skin adhesives.** Topical adhesives (e.g., Dermabond and Indermil) can be used to maintain skin edge alignment in wounds that are clean, can be closed without tension, and are in areas not subject to motion or pressure. When applied to an incision that has been closed by subcuticular sutures, it can provide a waterproof and antimicrobial barrier that prevents ingress of bacteria (*Infect Control Hosp Epidemiol.* 2004;25:664). Infection rates with Dermabond are similar to those with traditional closure methods (*Neurosurgery.* 2005;56(suppl 1):147), with the advantages that there are no staples or sutures to remove and that patients may shower immediately.

B. **Steri-Strips.** Skin tapes are the least invasive way to close a superficial skin wound; however, because they provide no eversion of wound edges, the cosmetic result may be suboptimal. In addition, skin tapes tend to loosen if moistened by serum or blood and therefore are seldom appropriate for all but the most superficial skin wounds in areas of minimal or no tension. Their most frequent use is in support of a skin closure after suture or staple removal.

C. **Suture**

1. **Needles.** Curved needles are designed for use with needle holders, whereas straight (Keith) needles can be used with or without a holder. Two types are in common use: circular (tapered, noncutting) and triangular (cutting). Cutting needles are preferable for closure of tough tissue, such as skin, and noncutting needles are preferable for placing sutures in delicate tissues, such as blood vessels or intestine.

2. **Suture material.** Several characteristics differentiate the various suture materials. They include the following:

   a. **Absorbable versus nonabsorbable.** Among the absorbable materials, wide variability is found with regard to tensile strength, rate of absorption, and tissue reaction.

   b. **Monofilament versus braided.** Braided suture has better handling characteristics than monofilament suture, but the interstices between the braided strands that compose the suture are easily colonized by bacteria and thus pose an infection risk.

   c. **Natural versus synthetic.** Characteristics of commonly used suture materials are summarized in Tables 6-2 and 6-3.

3. **Staples** allow for quick closure. In areas of lower cosmetic sensitivity, such as the thick skin of the back or anterior abdominal wall, staples may produce cosmetic results approximating those of sutures. They are particularly useful for closure of scalp wounds.

D. **Skin suture technique**

1. **Basic surgical principles apply** closure without tension, elimination of dead space, aseptic technique, and (when closing skin) eversion of the skin margins. A dog-ear occurs when unequal bites are taken on opposing sides of a wound or incision, causing the tissue to bunch up as the end of the wound is approached. This can be prevented by carefully aligning the wound at the time of deep tissue closure (elimination of dead space) with interrupted absorbable sutures and by taking equal bites of tissue on both sides of the wound.

2. **Suture removal.** Suture scars occur when stitches are left in place too long, allowing epithelialization of the suture tracts. This complication can be minimized by timely suture removal. Facial sutures should be removed at days 3 to 5; elsewhere, days 7 to 10 are appropriate. These guidelines should be modified for the individual patient. Application of skin tapes after suture removal provides further support.

TABLE 6-2 Characteristics of Absorbable Suture Materials

Suture (Trade Name)	Manufacturing Process	Effective Strength (d)	Complete Absorption (d)	Absorption Profile			Application
				Tissue Reactivity	Handling		
Surgical gut	Collagen from sheep intestine submucosa	4–10	70	High	Poor		Used for quick-healing mucosa
Chromic gut	Catgut treated with chromic acid	10–14	90	Moderate	Poor		Used for quick-healing mucosa
Polyglycolic acid (Dexon)	Synthetic monofilament or braided	14–21	60–120	Minimal	Good		Subcutaneous sutures, mucosa, ligation of vessels
Polyglactic acid (Vicryl)	Synthetic braided, lubricated with polyglactin 370; undyed or purple	20–30	60–90	Minimal	Excellent		Subcuticular and subcutaneous sutures
Polydioxane (PDS)	Monofilament polyester	40–60	180	Minimal	Good		Used for extended support
Polyglyconate (Maxon)	Synthetic monofilament	40–60	180–210	Minimal	Excellent		More supple than polydioxane

TABLE 6-3	Characteristics of Nonabsorbable Suture Materials			
Suture (Trade Name)	Manufacturing Process	Tissue Reactivity	Handling	Application
Silk	Braided; derived from cocoon of silkworm larva	High	Excellent	Vessel ligation; high capillarity; should be avoided in areas prone to infection
Cotton	Braided	High	Excellent	Same as silk
Polyester	Braided terephthalate (Dacron), polyethylene (Mersilene), coated with Teflon (Tevdek), silicone (Ti-Cron), polybutilate (Ethibond)	Minimal	Good if uncoated; excellent if coated	Commonly used for fascia; uncoated sutures have excellent knot security; coated sutures require five throws for knot security
Nylon	Synthetic polyamide monofilament or braided (Nurolon, Surgilon)	Minimal	Good	Used for skin, fascia; requires five throws for knot security
Polypropylene (Prolene, Surgilene)	Plastic monofilament	Minimal	Good	High elasticity; commonly used for skin closure and vascular anastomoses; requires five throws
Polybutester (Novafil)	Plastic monofilament copolymer	Minimal	Good	Very high elasticity; used when tissue swelling is present
Steel	Alloy monofilament	None	Poor	Retention sutures, bone

III. OPEN WOUND CARE OPTIONS (SEE TABLE 6-4). This brief review is not meant to be comprehensive or an endorsement of any product or product category. It remains an area of intense research, clinical, and commercial interest in which availability and indications of both established and new products can be expected to change during the publication cycle of this manual. The clinician would do well to weigh each patient's response to treatment, the indications and risks of any particular product, and need for further treatment.

A. **Topical ointments.** Petroleum-based ointments that contain one or several antibiotics prevent adherence of dressings to the wound and, by maintaining moisture of the wound environment, accelerate epithelialization and healing of primarily approximated wounds.

B. **Impregnated gauze.** Gauze that is impregnated with petrolatum is used for the treatment of superficial, partial-thickness wounds to maintain moisture, prevent excessive loss of fluid, and, in the case of Xeroform, provide mild deodorizing. It can also be used as the first layer of the initial dressing on a primarily closed wound. The use of this type of gauze is contraindicated when infection of the wound is suspected and inhibition of wound drainage would lead to adverse consequences.

C. **Gauze packing.** The practice of packing an open wound with gauze prevents dead space, facilitates drainage, and provides varying degrees of débridement. The maximum amount of débridement is seen when the gauze is packed into the wound dry and removed after absorption and evaporation have taken place, leaving a dry wound with adherent gauze, which on removal extracts superficial layers of the wound bed (dry-to-dry dressing). This dressing is seldom indicated. Wounds that are in need of great amounts of débridement usually benefit most from sharp débridement in the operating room or at the bedside; dry-to-dry dressings are painful and violate the principle of maintaining a moist environment for the wounds. Moist-to-dry dressings provide a much gentler débridement, are less painful, and can include sterile normal saline or various additives. Dakin solution [in full (0.5% sodium hypochlorite), half, or quarter strength] can be used to pack infected open wounds for a brief period when antimicrobial action is desirable. Because of toxic effects upon keratinocytes, the use of Dakin solution is not indicated except in infected wounds for a short period (*Adv Skin Wound Care.* 2005;18:373). Improvement in the foul odor that often emanates from drained abscesses and other infected open wounds is an added benefit of using this additive.

D. **Hydrogels.** These water- or glycerin-based gels (e.g., IntraSite) can be used in shallow or deep, open wounds. The gel promotes healing by gently rehydrating necrotic tissue, facilitating its debridement, and absorbing exudate produced by the wounds, as well as maintaining a moist wound environment. A nonadherent, nonabsorbent secondary dressing is applied over the gel; dressings should be changed every 8 hours to 3 days, depending on the condition of the wound.

E. **Hydrocolloids.** These occlusive, adhesive wafers provide a moist and protective environment for shallow wounds with light exudate. They can remain in place for 3 to 5 days and can be used under compression dressings to treat venous stasis ulcers.

TABLE 6-4	Wound and Skin Care Products		
Product/Trade Name	Advantages	Limitations	Applications
Gauze			
Kerlix (roll gauze)	Débride mechanically	May disrupt viable tissue during change	Moderately/heavily exudating wounds
	Manages exudates by capillarity Permeable to gases	May cause bleeding on removal	Partial- and full-thickness chronic wounds (stages II, III, IV)
Gauze sponges	Fills dead space Conformable	May cause pain on removal Particulate matter may be left in wound	Acute wounds Secondary dressing
	Adaptable	Permeable to fluids and bacteria Limited thermal insulation May dehydrate wound bed (if allowed to dry) Damp to dry dressings contraindicated—wound ostomy Continence nurses (WOCN) Society Standards of Care, 1992	
Transparent Adhesive Dressings			
Tegaderm (3M)	Manages exudates by moisture vapor	Manage light exudates only	IV entry sites

(continued)

TABLE 6-4 Wound and Skin Care Products *(Continued)*

Product/Trade Name	Advantages	Limitations	Applications
Opsite (Smith & Nephew)	Impermeable to fluids and bacteria	May disrupt fragile skin	Minor burns or lacerations
	Permeable to gases	Application may be difficult	Reduces surface friction in high-risk areas (stage I)
	Visualization of wound		Lightly exudating partial-thickness chronic wounds (stage II)
	Conformable		Over eschar to promote autolytic débridement
	Low profile		Cover dressing
Hydrocolloids			
Restore Hydrocolloid (Hollister)	Forms moist gel in wound bed	Manages moderate exudates	Reduces surface friction in high-risk areas
DuoDerm (ConvaTec)	Impermeable to fluids and bacteria	Impermeable to gases	
Comfeel Ulcer Care Dressing (Coloplast)	Manages exudates by particle swelling	May traumatize fragile skin	Partial- and full-thickness wounds
Tegasorb (3M)	Thermal insulation good	Do not use over eschar or puncture wounds	Moderately exudating wounds
	Conformable	Use with extreme caution on diabetic ulcers	Venous stasis ulcers in conjunction with Unna boot
		Contraindicated in third-degree burns	

Wound Fillers			
AcryDerm strands	Wound filler	Not recommended in dry wounds or wounds with sinus tracts or tunnels	Absorbs moderate to minimal exudate
Absorbent Wound Dressing (AcryMed)	Absorbs exudate Forms moist wound bed		May be used in combination with other wound dressing to increase absorption or fill shallow areas
Hydrogels			
Amorphous	Forms moist wound bed	May dehydrate	Partial- and full-thickness chronic wound (stages II, III)
Restore Hydrogel (Hollister)	Conformable	Minimal absorption	
IntraSite Gel (Smith & Nephew)	Manages exudates by swelling	Requires secondary dressing	Partial- and full-thickness burns Diabetic ulcers Lightly exudating wounds
Enzymatic Débriding Agents			
Collagenase (Santyl, Smith & Nephew)	Liquefies necrotic tissue Contributes toward formation of granulation tissue and epithelialization of wounds	Conditions with pH higher or lower than 6–8 decrease enzyme activity	Débridement of chronic dermal ulcers and severely burned areas

(continued)

TABLE 6-4   Wound and Skin Care Products *(Continued)*

Product/Trade Name	Advantages	Limitations	Applications
Accuzyme (Healthpoint)	Does not attack healthy tissue or newly formed granulation tissue		
Absorbent dressings			
Bard Absorption Dressing (Bard Medical)	Manages exudates by osmotic action Cleans debris Reduces odor Maintains moist wound bed Permeable to gases Molds to wound contour Fills dead space Extends life of secondary dressing Daily dressing change Inexpensive	Permeable to fluids and bacteria May increase pH beyond physiologic levels May sting on application Requires secondary dressing	Heavily exudating wounds Full-thickness chronic wounds (stages III, IV) Malodorous wounds
Alginate			
Restore CalciCare (Hollister)	Forms moist gel in wound bed	Permeable to fluids and bacteria	Moderately/heavily exudating wounds

Sorbsan (Dow Hickman Pharmaceuticals)	Manages exudates by capillarity Permeable to gases	May produce burning sensation on application	Partial- and full-thickness wounds (stages III, IV)
Kaltostat (ConvaTec)	Molds to wound contour Fills dead space Irrigates easily from wound bed Reduces wound pain Fibers left in wound are absorbed May be used on clinically infected wounds Nonirritating	Requires irrigation before removal if allowed to dry out	Partial-thickness burns Skin donor sites
Solutions		
Normal saline (0.9%)	Noncytotoxic solution for wound care	Wound dehydrates if allowed to dry out If dressing saturated, may macerate periwound skin	Partial- and full-thickness wounds Dressing changes two to three times daily
Hydrogen peroxide	Chemical débridement of necrotic tissue when used as an irrigating solution	Cytotoxic to fibroblasts Has been documented to result in air embolus if instilled into wound cavities under pressure	Wound irrigation—use only half-strength and always rinse wound with normal saline

(continued)

TABLE 6-4 Wound and Skin Care Products *(Continued)*

Product/Trade Name	Advantages	Limitations	Applications
Povidone–iodine (Betadine)	FDA has not approved for use in wounds	Cytotoxic to fibroblasts until diluted to 1:1,000 May cause acidosis in burn patients Lasting systemic effects include cardiovascular toxicity, renal toxicity, hepatotoxicity, and neuropathy Impairs wound's ability to fight infection and increases potential for wound infection	None for wound care
Antibacterial Cream			
Silver sulfadiazine (Silvadene)	Broad-spectrum antibacterial (*S. aureus, E. coli, P. aeruginosa, P. mirabilis*, β-hemolytic streptococci)	Never approved by FDA for wound management Should not be used in presence of hepatic or renal impairment	Apply 1/8 in to clean, débrided wound daily or twice daily

Platelet-Derived Growth Factor

Becaplermin (Regranex, Ortho-McNeil Pharmaceuticals)	May promote wound healing in otherwise recalcitrant neuropathic ulcer Very few side effects	Dressing protocol may be confusing Wound must have adequate blood supply Wound must be free of infection No osteomyelitis Wound must be free of necrotic tissue Complex dosing	Calculate dose by multiplying length by width of wound in cm and divide by 4 Wound is irrigated with NS Apply precise amount of drug to wound, cover with NS dressing Leave in place for 12 hr Then irrigate wound with NS Pack wound with NS dressing Leave in place for 12 hr

FDA, Food and Drug Administration; *E. coli, Escherichia coli*; NS, normal saline; *P. aeruginosa, Pseudomonas aeruginosa*; *P. mirabilis, Proteus mirabilis*; *S. aureus, Staphylococcus aureus*; IV, intravenous.

Adapted with permission from Rolstad BS, Ovington LG, Harris A. Wound care product formulary. In: Bryand RA, ed. *Acute and Chronic Wounds: Nursing Management*, 2nd ed. St. Louis: Mosby; 2000.

F. **Alginates.** Complex carbohydrate dressings composed of glucuronic and mannuronic acid, derived from brown seaweed, are formed into ropes or pads that are highly absorbent (e.g., Kaltostat). Alginates are absorbable and are useful for the treatment of deep wounds with heavy exudate because they form a gel as they absorb wound drainage.

G. **Adhesive films.** These plastic membranes (e.g., Tegaderm) are self-adhering and waterproof, yet are permeable to oxygen and water vapor. They are appropriate for partial-thickness wounds, such as split-thickness skin graft donor sites or superficial abrasions. They can also be used as secondary dressings on wounds that are being treated with hydrocolloids or alginates.

H. **Collagen-containing products.** A number of collagen-containing products are available in powder, sheet, or fluid form. They are available as pure collagen, typically types 1 and 3, or combined with other materials such as calcium alginate (Fibracol). Some wounds respond better to collagen than to other dressing materials.

I. **Hydrofibers** represent a newer dressing category of strands; they are some of the most absorptive materials available for packing in a heavily draining wound.

J. **Growth factors.** Human recombinant platelet-derived growth factor (PDGF) is the only U.S. Food and Drug Administration-approved clinically available growth factor. Topically applied to a granulating wound, it promotes granulation tissue formation, angiogenesis, and epithelialization. A saline-moistened gauze dressing is applied daily at midday to help keep the wound bed moist. Although initial approval was for the treatment of diabetic plantar foot ulcers, the drug is often used on other wound types. Epidermal growth factor (EGF) is in clinical trials for the treatment of venous stasis ulcers.

K. **Skin substitutes.** There are many different types of biologically active materials and skin substitutes and a comprehensive review of their properties and use is beyond the scope of this chapter. The indication and usage of these products is guided by their biologic and material properties. Skin substitutes can be used to facilitate healing of chronic open wounds, to provide temporary or permanent wound coverage, and to bridge skin, soft tissue or fascial defects. The usage of individual products is guided by the manufacturer's recommendations and the nature of the wound.

1. **Xenograft products** (Permacol, EZ derm, Matriderm, Oasis) are derived from animal tissues and consist of a collagen and/or proteoglycan matrix designed to promote influx of fibroblasts.

2. **Allogeneic products** are acellular tissue substitutes derived from cadaveric sources (AlloDerm, Strattice, Graftjacket, GammaGraft) that can be used to provide wound coverage. Each of these products is differently processed and material properties guide usages including wound coverage and hernia repair.

3. **Bioengineered living tissues** are composites of a structural mesh and cultured keratinocytes. Cells can be derived from neonatal sources (Dermagraft, TransCyte, Apligraf, OrCel) or autologous skin (Epicel, Laserskin, Epidex, Hyalograft). These advanced products bring living, biologically active cells into the wound bed.

L. **Negative-pressure wound therapy.** Negative pressure created by vacuum-assisted closure devices (Wound VAC or Blue Sky or institutionally created dressings) appears to stimulate capillary ingrowth and the formation of granulation tissue in open wounds while keeping a relatively clean wound environment. VAC therapy is effective in the management of wounds as diverse as diabetic foot wounds, sacral ulcers, mediastinal dehiscence, perineum wounds, and wounds including prosthetic mesh (*Plast Reconstr Surg.* 2006;117:127S). Recently, VAC therapy has been reported to be successful in managing enterocutaneous fistulae (*J Wound Care.* 2003;12:343) and over areas with exposed bone (*Wounds.* 2005;17:137) or tendon (*J Burn Care Rehabil.* 2002;23:167). VAC therapy is contraindicated when there are exposed major blood vessels, untreated osteomyelitis, or cancer within the wound, and it is relatively contraindicated in anticoagulated patients.

M. **Hyperbaric oxygen.** Local hypoxia in wound tissue may contribute to delayed healing. Randomized clinical trials have demonstrated that hyperbaric oxygen treatment (HBOT) is successful in healing diabetic foot ulcers (*Diabetes Care.* 1987;19:81), preventing diabetic amputations (*Diabetes Care.* 1996;19:1338), and healing chronic ulcerations (*Plast Reconstr Surg.* 1996;93:829). Standard treatment protocols are based on appropriate debridement and wound care in conjunction with 90 minutes/day at 2 atmospheres of oxygen. The criteria for appropriate treatment are available on the Undersea and Hyperbaric Medical Society Web site, http://www.UHMS.org, and should be consulted for consideration to initiate treatment.

N. **Metallic silver-impregnated dressings.** The broad antimicrobial properties of silver have long been recognized. Silver-impregnated dressings are used extensively for burns, chronic leg ulcers, diabetic, and traumatic injuries. A variety of silver-based dressings are available with specific indications determined by the manufacturer.

IV. CARE OF WOUNDS IN THE EMERGENCY ROOM

A. **History and physical examination.** A careful history and physical examination of the whole patient should be performed, with attention to the time and mechanism of injury, initial treatments given, and prior or associated injuries. Medical, surgical, and immunization history and all known medication allergies should be documented. It is critically important that all injuries be identified, with appropriate prioritization of administered treatment plans. Careful neurologic and vascular examination should be performed distal to the site of injury and before administration of any anesthetics that could limit a later assessment.

B. **Anesthesia.** Lidocaine (Xylocaine) in concentrations from 0.5% to 2% is generally chosen for its rapidity of action (1 to 2 minutes). If longer duration is desired, bupivacaine (Marcaine) can be used; however, it may require up to 10 minutes to full onset. A 1:1 mixture of 1% lidocaine and 0.25% bupivacaine provides a rapid and reasonably long-acting local anesthetic to improve hemostasis and prolong the effect of the anesthetic. Mixtures containing epinephrine should not be used to treat wounds on distal extremities (nose, earlobes, fingers, toes, or penis) because the profound vasoconstriction may lead to ischemic tissue loss. Whenever local anesthetics are used, care should be taken to avoid intravascular injection by aspirating before infiltration. The maximum safe amount of anesthetic that can be administered to the patient should be calculated before starting treatment.

C. **Wound cleansing.** After adequate anesthesia is administered, the wound and surrounding skin should be cleansed in a gentle fashion. This is best accomplished with a standard wound-cleansing solution (e.g., Saf-Clens and Shur-Clens). It should be remembered that many standard scrub solutions are extremely toxic to all living cells; thus, they should never be used to wash the wound itself. A good rule to follow is that one should never place a solution in a wound that one would not place in one's eye. Wounds are best irrigated with saline or lactated Ringer's solution with pressures of 8 to 15 psi. An 18- or 19-gauge intravenous catheter or needle on a 35- to 60-mL syringe provides 8-psi irrigating pressure, which is adequate to irrigate most wounds. Battery-powered irrigation systems, available for portable use, deliver pressures of up to 15 psi and are easier to use when irrigating a wound with several liters of fluid. Abrasions should be scrubbed carefully with a gloved hand during cleansing to remove foreign material that might lead to traumatic skin tattooing.

D. **Wound hemostasis and exploration.** Direct pressure, elevation, and even the use of a blood pressure cuff as a tourniquet are effective means of limiting blood loss in the emergency setting. Electrocautery, suture ligation, or hemostat clamping of a bleeding site is best done by a practitioner who is familiar with the anatomy of the area because major nerves often lie adjacent to major arteries and any imprecision can lead to an iatrogenic injury worse than the initial trauma. Wounds should be explored carefully for foreign bodies and to determine the extent of injury. Multiplane x-ray views of the soft tissues of the wounded area can prove to be useful in locating radiopaque objects. If the wound contains difficult-to-locate or numerous foreign bodies, it can best be explored in the operating room.

E. **Débridement.** Traumatic breaks of the skin are often irregular, and the force of impact leaves a zone of surrounding skin and underlying tissue injury that is often best treated by judicious sharp débridement. All foreign material and devitalized tissue must be removed before wound closure is attempted. The goal of débridement is to obtain a clean wound with a bleeding skin margin that overlies healthy, viable tissue.

F. **Wound closure.** The decision to close a wound depends largely on the amount of contamination present and the amount of time that the wound has been open. Wounds that are older than 6 to 8 hours, puncture wounds, human bites, and wounds with gross infection should not be closed, with the possible exception of facial wounds, for in these the superior vascular supply can often overcome otherwise major contamination. At a microscopic level, wounds with greater than 10^5 bacteria/g of tissue are considered too heavily contaminated to close safely. Dog and cat bites should be allowed to heal by secondary intention, or they may be closed primarily over wicks only after thorough irrigation and débridement, with administration of appropriate antibiotics.

G. **Additional considerations for wounds in the emergency room**

1. **Tetanus prophylaxis.** Tetanus is a potentially fatal disorder that is characterized by uncontrolled spasms of the voluntary muscles. It is caused by the neurotoxin of the anaerobic bacterium *Clostridium tetani*. A tetanus-prone wound has one or more of the following characteristics: (1) more than 6 hours old; (2) deeper than 1 cm; (3) contaminated by soil, feces, or rust; (4) stellate configuration (burst-type injury with marked soft-tissue injury); (5) caused by missile, crush, burn, or frostbite; (6) contains devitalized or denervated tissue; and (7) caused by an animal or human bite. Recommendations for tetanus prophylaxis are summarized in Table 6-5.

2. **Antibiotics.** Antibiotic use does not allow closure of a wound that would otherwise be left open to heal secondarily, and it is not a substitute for good wound cleansing and débridement. Antibiotics should be chosen based on the indication (prophylactic or therapeutic), the location and age of the wound, and the mechanism of injury. In addition, one should consider the likely pathogen(s) that are most involved under the circumstances. Prophylactic antibiotics are indicated for immunocompromised patients and those with prosthetic heart valves or other permanently implanted prostheses. Prophylactic antibiotics should also be used when intestinal or genitourinary tract contamination is present, when an infection is likely to develop, or when an infection has potentially disastrous consequences (*Surg Clin North Am.*

TABLE 6-5	Summary of Immunization Practices Advisory Committee Recommendations for Tetanus Prophylaxis in Routine Wound Management			
Tetanus	Clean Minor Wounds		Tetanus-Prone Wounds	
Immunization	Td[a]	TIG[b]	Td	TIG
Unknown or less than three doses	Yes	No	Yes	Yes
Three doses or more	No (yes if >10 yr since last dose)	No	No (yes if >5 yr since last dose)	No

[a]Adsorbed tetanus and diphtheria toxoids, 0.5 mL intramuscularly. For children <7 yr, diphtheria-polio-tetanus is recommended.

[b]TIG (human), 250 units intramuscularly, given concurrently with the toxoid at separate sites. Heterologous antitoxin (equine) should not be given unless TIG is not available within 24 hr and only if the possibility of tetanus outweighs the danger of adverse reaction.

Td, tetanus-diphtheria toxoid (adult type); TIG, tetanus immune globulin.

Reprinted with permission from Centers for Disease Control and Prevention. Tetanus United States, 1987 and 1988. *MMWR.* 1990;39(3):37.

1997;77:3). For wounds that are likely to become infected, obtaining good wound cultures at the time of injury helps to better target the specific organism(s) that failed to respond to initial broad-spectrum antibiotic treatment.

3. **Furuncles and carbuncles.** Furuncles are small boils or abscesses caused by an infection of the hair follicle that extends into the subcutaneous tissue deep. Carbuncles are cutaneous infections of multiple hair follicles, characterized by the destruction of fibrous tissue septa. The usual causative organism is *S. aureus,* and the incidence and prevalence of skin abscesses has risen in parallel with the emergence of community-acquired MRSA (*Clin Infect Dis.* 2005;41:1373). Furuncles manifest as firm, tender, erythematous nodules. Predisposing factors include diabetes, corticosteroid use, impaired neutrophil function, or increased friction or perspiration as occurs in athletes or obese individuals. Whereas initial treatment can include oral antibiotics and warm compresses to promote drainage, if the furuncle exhibits fluctuance, an incision-and-drainage procedure is required. (1). Under local anesthesia and after site prep with chlorhexidine or an iodine-containing solution, the initial incision is made with a no. 11 scalpel with the blade oriented perpendicular to the skin and inserted into the area of maximum fluctuance. (2). A cruciform or elliptical incision will help to prevent premature epidermal closure with recurrent cavity formation. A hemostat or blunt finger dissection is used to probe and break up any loculations within the abscess cavity. (3). The cavity should be irrigated and packed with iodoform or plain gauze stripping, which will require regular packing change. The use of antibiotics after abscess drainage remains controversial and depends on appropriate clinical judgment. If antibiotics are administered and community-acquired MRSA is a possible cause of the infection, trimethoprim/sulfamethoxazole (TMP/SMX), doxycycline, clindamycin, or a third- or fourth-generation fluoroquinolone should be considered, and a 7-day course is generally sufficient (*Prim Care.* 2006;33:697). Oral, perirectal, or genital abscesses should be considered multibacterial, and agents such as amoxicillin–clavulanate or third- or fourth-generation fluoroquinolones should be used to cover Gram-positive, Gram-negative, and anaerobic organisms. Patients who are immunocompromised or diabetic may require intravenous antibiotic therapy. If oral or intravenous antibiotics are administered, a wound culture should be obtained from the abscess cavity prior to irrigation to determine whether the appropriate antibiotic has been selected. For all skin infections and drained abscesses, follow-up is extremely important.

H. **Bites.** The treatment of a bite wound beyond the basic treatment of copious irrigation and debridement is most dependent on the source of the bite.

1. **Human bites** typically occur during interpersonal conflict. Because the wound often seems relatively trivial, such as a small puncture wound or a laceration in a patient who is very upset or intoxicated, the patient may delay seeking treatment, which increases the likelihood

of the wound to become infected. A particularly troublesome bite is a small skin injury that is seen over the metacarpophalangeal joint of a patient who punched someone else in the mouth and sustained a tooth cut of the skin overlying the fisted knuckle. Such injuries often require operative joint irrigation and parenteral antibiotics. Unintentional bites of the lip or tongue sustained in a fall or during a seizure may also occasionally come to the attention of a surgeon. The oral flora of humans includes *Staphylococcus* and *Streptococcus* species, anaerobic bacteria, *Eikenella corrodens,* and anaerobic Gram-negative rods; antibiotic coverage should be directed initially toward these organisms.

2. **Mammalian animal bites.** Because infection is the most common complication of domestic animal bites, these bites should be considered contaminated and their immediate closure deferred. Infections that are caused by dog bites are usually polymicrobial, and pathogens include viridans streptococci, *Pasteurella multocida,* and *Bacteroides, Fusobacterium,* and *Capnocytophaga* species. Because these wounds are often larger open lacerations, only about 5% of dog bites become infected. The oral flora of the domestic cat is believed to be less complex, with *P. multocida* found in up to 60% of wounds caused by cat bites. Because these are smaller puncture wounds, up to 80% of these will become infected. Local laws require the confinement of animals to ensure that they do not manifest rabies. Rabies, a routinely fatal disease of the central nervous system, is caused by the rabies virus, which is a member of the rhabdovirus group and contains a single strand of RNA. Thanks in large part to an intensive immunization program, the incidence of rabies in the United States has been reduced greatly, to approximately five cases per year. Today, the major risk comes from wild animal bites. The recommendations for rabies prophylaxis and treatment are summarized in Table 6-6.

3. **Snake bites.** Ten percent of the snakes in the United States are venomous. Determining whether a venomous snake caused the bite is critical in the early management of bite injuries. Pit vipers usually leave two puncture wounds, whereas nonvenomous snakes generally leave a characteristic U-shaped bite wound. Poisonous snake venom contains many polypeptides that are damaging to human tissues, including phospholipase A, hyaluronidase, adenosine triphosphatase, 5-nucleotidase, and nicotinic acid dehydrogenase. The degree of envenomation and the time from injury determine the clinical manifestations. Immediate signs of envenomation include regional edema, erythema, and intense pain at the site of the bite. Systemic manifestations can ensue rapidly, especially with greater envenomation. The hematocrit and platelet count may fall, with concomitant elevation of the prothrombin time, partial thromboplastin time, and bleeding times. Without treatment, severe envenomation may lead to pulmonary edema, peripheral vascular collapse, direct cardiotoxicity, and acute renal failure. Coral snake venom is less toxic locally but can lead to profound neurologic sequelae. Early symptoms include nausea, euphoria, salivation, paresthesias, ptosis, and muscle weakness leading to respiratory arrest.

TABLE 6-6	Rabies Postexposure Prophylaxis Treatment Guide	
Species	**Condition of Animal**	**Treatment**[a]
Domestic cat or dog	Healthy and available for at least 10 d of observation	None; however, treatment should be initiated at the first sign of rabies[b]
	Suspected rabid[b]	Immediate
	Unknown	Contact public health department
Wild skunk, bat, fox, coyote, raccoon, or other carnivore	Regard as rabid; animal should be killed and tested as soon as possible	Immediate; however, discontinue if immunofluorescence test is negative

[a](1) Human rabies immune globulin, 20 IU/kg [if feasible, infiltrate half of dose around the wound(s), the rest intramuscularly in gluteal area] and (2) human diploid cell vaccine (HDCV), 1 mL intramuscularly in deltoid area (never in gluteal area) on days 0, 3, 7, 14, and 28. If the patient has previously been immunized, give booster HDCV only on days 0 and 3.
[b]Any animal suspected of being rabid should be killed and its brain studied with a rabies-specific fluorescent antibody.
Adapted with permission from Immunization Practices Advisory Committee. Rabies Prevention United States, 1991. *MMWR.* 1991;40(RR-3):1.

Treatment is most successful if administered promptly. Extremity wounds should be immobilized and a tourniquet applied proximal to the bite site to minimize the spread of the venom. Although small amounts of venom can be removed by suction through small incisions over the bite wound, a wider surgical excision of the bite removes even more, provided that it can be done in a timely fashion. Antivenom may help to neutralize the venom and should be administered intravenously as soon as possible after more severe bites or when systemic symptoms are noted. Current treatment includes CroFab, a Fab-segment–based product that lacks antigenic Fc antibody fragments. The antibody is produced by injecting sheep with one of four pit viper species indigenous to the United States: western diamondback rattlesnake, eastern diamondback rattlesnake, Mojave rattlesnake, and cottonmouth. The venoms of different species vary in composition and potency, but they are similar enough that CroFab can neutralize venom from many species, including those not included in the production process (*Am J Trop Med Hyg.* 1995;53:507). Indications for CroFab antivenom use are pit viper envenomation with worsening edema or any systemic symptom including coagulopathy. Relative contraindications include known hypersensitivity to CroFab, papain, or papaya (*Curr Opin Pediatr.* 2005;17:234). Shock is treated with circulatory support. Broad-spectrum antibiotics and tetanus prophylaxis are also indicated.

4. **Spider bites**
   a. The **black widow spider** *(Latrodectus mactans)* is found throughout the United States and prefers to inhabit dry, dark crevices. The female is distinguished by her shiny black body and a red hourglass mark on the abdomen. The actual bite may cause little pain, and victims often do not recall the event. The bite presents as a pale area surrounded by a red ring. The venom, a neurotoxin, causes muscular rigidity. Chest pain from muscular contraction follows upper-extremity bites, whereas lower-extremity bites may cause rigidity of the abdominal wall. Patients who present with abdominal wall rigidity, which might typically suggest an acute abdominal emergency, lack associated abdominal tenderness. Intense muscular spasms and pain are usually self-limiting and require no specific treatment. Severe cases may progress to respiratory arrest, which, along with shock, accounts for the observed mortality of approximately 5%. Therapy consists of respiratory and circulatory support, broad-spectrum antibiotics, narcotic analgesia, and muscle relaxants. Antivenin *(L. mactans)* is indicated for the very young or old and for patients with severe illness.
   b. The **brown recluse spider** *(Loxosceles reclusa)* is found throughout the central and southern United States, most often inhabiting dark, moist environments. It is 10 to 15 mm long, with a light tan to brown color, a flat body, and a violin-shaped band over the head and chest area of the back. Brown recluse venom is very locally toxic, containing hyaluronidase, and other elements that lead to coagulation necrosis of the area around the wound. Systemically, hemolysis with hemoglobinuria, hemolytic anemia, and renal failure may develop. Pain at the time of the bite is an inconsistent symptom; however, several hours after the bite, a characteristic lesion is seen, with a central zone of pale induration surrounded by an erythematous border. By this time, pain is severe. After approximately 1 week, a black eschar develops, which soon sloughs, leaving an ulcer that may continue to enlarge, with extensive necrosis of the underlying fat and subcutaneous tissues. Systemic illness most often occurs in children, with fever, malaise, nausea, and vomiting. Therapy is supportive, and mortality is rare. Many of these wounds will heal spontaneously. If necessary, excision of the wound should be deferred until the ulcer is well demarcated; broad-spectrum antibiotics are recommended.

7 Critical Care

Kendra D. Conzen and Laureen L. Hill

Patients are admitted to intensive care units (ICUs) because of either the presence or the risk of organ dysfunction. This chapter focuses on routine monitoring of the critically ill patient, the three most common reasons for surgical ICU admissions (respiratory, circulatory, and renal failure), and sepsis. It also addresses adjunctive topics, including sedation and analgesia, prophylaxis against stress-induced upper gastrointestinal (GI) hemorrhage, and the role of transfusion and glucose control in the care of the critically ill.

I. MONITORING OF THE CRITICALLY ILL PATIENT

A. Temperature monitoring. Critically ill patients are at increased risk for temperature alterations as a result of debilitation and predisposition to infection. All critically ill patients should have their core temperatures measured at least every 4 hours. While a rectal thermometer is the most accurate method of obtaining the core temperature, oral and bladder probes can reduce patient discomfort. Transcutaneous measurements are less reliable.

B. Electrocardiographic (ECG) monitoring. Continuous ECG monitoring with computerized dysrhythmia detection systems is standard in most ICUs. Continuous monitoring allows for rapid detection of dysrhythmias and assessment of heart rate and rhythm.

C. Arterial pressure monitoring

  1. Indirect arterial pressure measurement with a sphygmomanometer should be performed at least hourly or more often during titration of vasoactive drips.

  2. Direct arterial pressure measurement with intra-arterial catheters offers continuous measurement of arterial pressures and waveforms as well as easy, painless access for arterial blood gas (ABG) measurement. Arterial cannulation is warranted in patients with hemodynamic instability and in those who require frequent blood gas analysis. The most common site of insertion is the radial artery, which is chosen because of its accessibility and generally good collateral blood flow. If this is unavailable, alternatives include femoral and, less commonly, dorsalis pedis or axillary artery catheterization. These should be avoided in infants because occlusion may cause extremity ischemia and subsequent deformity. The extremity distal to the catheter should be assessed prior to insertion and frequently after insertion. The catheter should be removed immediately if there is evidence of distal ischemia. Rare infectious complications include local cellulitis and bacteremia, which may result from catheter colonization or contamination of the fluid-filled monitoring system.

D. **Central venous pressure (CVP) monitoring.** Central venous catheters provide access to measure CVP, CvO_2 and to administer vasoactive drugs and total parenteral nutrition. For techniques of catheter insertion, refer to Chapter 37.

E. **Pulmonary artery (PA) catheterization.** PA (also called *Swan-Ganz*) catheters are used to determine cardiac filling pressures, cardiac output (CO), PA pressures, systemic vascular resistance (SVR), and mixed venous oxygen saturation (SvO_2). They can be used in unstable patients with rapid changes in hemodynamic status to assess responses to treatment with fluid and cardioactive agents. It is important to note that the use of PA catheters has not been demonstrated to change mortality in prospective, randomized trials, in part due to error in interpretation and variation in management decisions.

1. **Continuous ECG and blood pressure monitoring and peripheral intravenous access** are required. An ECG must be checked prior to PA catheter placement to rule out left-bundle-branch block because PA catheter placement can induce transient right-bundle-branch block. If a patient with left-bundle-branch block needs a PA catheter, a transcutaneous pacemaker should be placed prior to PA catheter placement.

2. **Complications** associated with central venous access are described in Chapter 37. PA catheter **balloon rupture** exposes the patient to the risk of air and balloon fragment emboli. Balloon rupture should be suspected when air inflated into the balloon does not return; the diagnosis is confirmed if blood can be aspirated from the balloon port. If either of these occurs, the catheter should be removed immediately. **PA perforation** presents with hemoptysis, typically after balloon inflation. Management of this serious complication includes placement of the patient with his or her involved side in the dependent position and emergent thoracic surgical consultation. Atrial and ventricular **dysrhythmias** occur commonly during insertion of PA catheters and usually are self-limited.

3. **Esophageal Dopplers** (CardioQ, Deltex Medical) have been introduced as a less invasive alternative to PA catheters for goal-directed fluid therapy. Esophageal Dopplers measure descending aortic flow velocity over time, therefore SV is calculated by area under the velocity curve and a nomogram-based aortic diameter. Changes in SV with fluid can be used to titrate fluid administration. There has been no demonstration of improvement in outcomes associated with their use. Their potential risk is lower than with PA catheters; however, esophageal perforation can occur.

F. **Respiratory monitoring**

1. **Pulse oximetry** should be used in all critically ill patients. It provides quantitative, continuous assessment of arterial oxygen saturation (SaO_2). Probe malposition, motion, hypothermia, vasoconstriction, and hypotension may result in poor signal detection and unreliable measurements. Nail polish, dark skin, and elevated serum lipids falsely lower the SaO_2 measurement, whereas elevated carboxyhemoglobin

falsely raises the measurements. Methemoglobin results in a reading of 85%, regardless of oxygen saturation level.

2. **Capnography** provides quantitative, continuous assessment of expired CO_2 concentrations, and the gradient between arterial CO_2 partial pressure (Pa_{CO_2}) and end-tidal CO_2 ($ETCO_2$) measurements can be used to follow trends and the difference reflects the proportion of dead space ventilation. A rise in $ETCO_2$ can indicate a decrease in alveolar ventilation or an increase in CO_2 production, as seen with overfeeding, sepsis, fever, exercise, or acute increases in CO. A fall in $ETCO_2$ may indicate an increase in alveolar ventilation (when associated with a decrease in Pa_{CO_2}) or an increase in dead space (without a decreased Pa_{CO_2}), as seen with massive pulmonary embolism (PE) or air embolism, endotracheal tube (ET) or mainstem bronchus obstruction, ventilator circuit leak, or a sudden drop in CO.

II. **SEDATION AND ANALGESIA.** Altered mentation, which can span the spectrum from delirium to coma, is a common manifestation of acute illness. Delirium has independently been associated with increased ICU and in-hospital mortality (*Crit Care.* 2010;14:R210). Pain and emotional distress should be treated. Sedation allows critically ill patients to tolerate invasive supportive interventions such as intubation and mechanical ventilation. Titration of sedation is simplified by the use of an objective scoring system, such as the modified Ramsay scale (Table 7-1).

A. **Control of agitation.** The most frequently used agents are **benzodiazepines,** which are potent inducers of sedation, anxiolysis, and amnesia. The action of benzodiazepines appears to be mediated through γ-aminobutyric acid receptors, an inhibitory neurotransmitter. Effective doses of benzodiazepines may be higher in tolerant patients (e.g., those who have taken similar agents previously or who consume alcohol or smoke cigarettes regularly). Patients older than 50 years or those with preexisting

TABLE 7-1	Modified Ramsay Sedation Scale
Score	**Characteristics**
1	Anxious and agitated or restless, or both
2	Cooperative, oriented, and tranquil
3	Responds to commands only
4	Asleep, but responds to physical or auditory stimuli
5	Asleep, but responds sluggishly to physical or auditory stimuli
6	No response

cardiopulmonary, hepatic, or renal dysfunction are particularly susceptible to benzodiazepines and their metabolites. Initial doses should be reduced in these patients. Benzodiazepines have also been associated with higher rates of delirium (*Crit Care.* 2010;14:R38).

1. **Midazolam** has a short half-life (20 to 60 minutes) and a rapid onset (1 to 3 minutes) and offset of action. Although midazolam has a short half-life, when it is given as a continuous infusion for a prolonged period of time, metabolites accumulate, and patients may take a number of days to fully awaken.

2. **Lorazepam** has a longer half-life (10 to 20 hours) and a slower onset (10 to 20 minutes) of action. Unlike midazolam, lorazepam does not have active metabolites. However, similar to midazolam, the drug accumulates with prolonged use, and patients may remain sedated for a number of days after the agent is stopped. Lorazepam also precipitates in tubing over time due to the carrier vehicle used. Midazolam and lorazepam are acceptable alternatives for long-term sedation in the critically ill patient.

3. **Propofol** is a nonbenzodiazepine sedative-hypnotic that has an extremely short onset and offset of action and is usually delivered as a continuous infusion. It does not accumulate to the same degree as benzodiazepines and thus results in a shorter length of sedation after discontinuation. A major side effect of propofol is hypotension, especially in hypovolemic patients. Although it is more expensive than benzodiazepines, propofol is preferred for short-term sedation (<2 days) because of its rapid elimination. Prolonged use can cause hypertriglyceridemia and risk of pancreatitis or propofol infusion syndrome, evidenced by a metabolic acidosis.

4. **Dexmedetomidine** is a relatively selective α_2-adrenoreceptor agonist that may be helpful for short-term sedation of mechanically ventilated patients. Patients treated with this agent are more easily arousable than those sedated with either propofol or benzodiazepine infusions, experience less delirium, and have shorter ICU length of stay (*Intensive Care Med.* 2010;36:926; *Crit Care.* 2010;14:R38). Additionally, dexmedetomidine has analgesic and opiate-sparing properties. The main side effect is hypotension. Bradycardia has been observed in studies with loading doses and high maintenance doses. Dexmedetomidine is approved for use for a maximum of 24 hours, but has been safely administered for up to 5 days in clinical trials (*JAMA.* 2007;298:2644).

B. **Control of delirium**

1. **Antipsychotics: Haloperidol** is an antipsychotic medicine that can be used to treat delirium emergently. Major toxicities include hypotension, cardiac arrhythmias, prolongation of the QT interval, and extrapyramidal symptoms. Therefore, daily, scheduled dosing of atypical antipsychotics (e.g., olanzapine and quetiapine) may be preferable. ECGs should be checked daily in patients on long-term haloperidol.

C. **Control of pain.** Pain management is an important concern in the surgical ICU.

1. **Morphine** is administered as needed and for patient-controlled dosing because of its low cost and familiarity. Accumulation of active metabolites can occur in patients with renal impairment and its use should be avoided in those patients.

2. **Fentanyl** is the most commonly used opiate for continuous drips. It has a half-life of 30 to 60 minutes due to its rapid redistribution. Unlike morphine, fentanyl does not cause histamine release and is therefore less likely to cause hypotension.

3. **Hydromorphone** is a viable option for patients who are allergic to morphine or fentanyl. Hydromorphone has no active metabolites and can therefore be administered to patients with renal impairment.

4. **Meperidine** is used least frequently because of its side effects. Patients with renal or hepatic dysfunction are at risk for accumulation of normeperidine, a metabolite, which can cause neurotoxic side effects including seizures.

5. **Methadone** is a narcotic with a long half-life (8 to 59 hours) that can be used for pain management and to facilitate withdrawal from other narcotics. Substantial variability between individuals with regard to its pharmacokinetic properties mandates close monitoring of patients during initiation of treatment and conversion from other opioids.

6. **Thoracic or lumbar epidural catheters** are usually well tolerated, decrease the need for intravenous narcotics, and can substantially improve compliance with respiratory therapy. Significant risks include hypotension and intrathecal or intravascular catheter migration. Anticoagulation or active use of antiplatelet agents is relative contraindications due to risk for epidural hematoma and subsequent neurologic injury.

D. Regardless of which agents are used for sedation and analgesia, the presence of a **sedation protocol** decreases both length of stay in the ICU and the length of time a patient requires mechanical ventilation compared with physician-directed sedation.

E. For patients who require **long-term sedation and analgesia,** daily interruption of sedation to wakefulness produces decreased time on mechanical ventilation and shorter ICU stays, according to a prospective, randomized, controlled study (*N Engl J Med.* 2000;342:1477). However, this study did not include surgical patients, who have higher analgesia requirements than typical medical ICU patients. Therefore, the applicability of a "daily wake-up" to surgical ICU patients is less clear.

III. RESPIRATORY FAILURE

A. **Etiology.** Respiratory failure results from inadequate exchange of oxygen and/or carbon dioxide. Hypoxemia may be caused by ventilation/perfusion (V/Q) mismatch, hypoventilation, or impaired systemic delivery/extraction.

The extremes of V/Q mismatch are dead space ventilation (V/Q = ∞) and complete intrapulmonary shunt (V/Q = 0). Dead space ventilation refers to airflow within lung that does not equilibrate with blood gas content; this occurs in chronic obstructive pulmonary disease and PE. In contrast, intrapulmonary shunt results from perfusion of lung tissue that is poorly ventilated, such as in the setting of severe pulmonary edema, acute respiratory distress syndrome (ARDS), or pneumonia. Hypoventilatory hypoxemia may be caused by a failure of the mechanical ventilatory apparatus (e.g., neuromuscular disease, inspiratory muscle fatigue, and airway obstruction), which results in hypercapnia and hypoxemia. Although the etiology (possibly multifactorial) is important for longer-term treatment and prognosis, the early treatment of respiratory failure is similar regardless of the immediate cause.

B. **Diagnosis.** Signs or symptoms of respiratory impairment (e.g., tachypnea, dyspnea, or mental status changes) should prompt analysis of pulse oximetry and ABGs. Pulse oximetry monitoring results of less than 90% correspond to a partial arterial oxygen pressure (Pa_{O_2}) of less than 60 mm Hg, which seriously compromises tissue oxygenation. An acute rise in Pa_{CO_2} to greater than 50 mm Hg along with a pH of less than 7.35 (respiratory acidosis) implies a significant imbalance between carbon dioxide production and elimination (alveolar ventilation). **It is important to note that adequate oxygenation does not guarantee adequate ventilation.** A complete physical exam and portable chest x-ray are essential for figuring out the etiology of respiratory failure.

C. **Treatment**

1. **Oxygen therapy.** The objective of supplemental oxygen administration is to increase the relative concentration of oxygen in the alveoli. This is accomplished most commonly by delivering oxygen through a nasal cannula, simple face mask, or face mask with a reservoir (Table 7-2). The inspired oxygen concentration varies depending on the percentage of entrained air: The more air that is entrained (with an ambient oxygen concentration of 0.21), the lower the fraction of inspired oxygen ($F_{I_{O_2}}$). When the required $F_{I_{O_2}}$ is high (~0.60), a high–air-flow system with oxygen enrichment via a jet-mixing or Venturi apparatus is used, and the oxygen is delivered by a tight-fitting mask with a reservoir. Whenever possible, inspired oxygen should be humidified to prevent drying of the airways and respiratory secretions.

2. **Airway management.** Securing and maintaining a patent airway is the first priority in an unstable patient. The most common source of airway obstruction in a patient with an altered sensorium is the tongue. This is corrected easily by the chin-lift or jaw-thrust maneuver or by placing an oropharyngeal or nasopharyngeal airway. In a conscious patient, an oropharyngeal airway can cause retching and is usually poorly tolerated. If uncertainty exists about whether the airway is patent or protected from aspiration, ET intubation is indicated. In most cases, intubation is not urgent. **Unless the physician is skilled in the placement of an artificial airway, the appropriate maneuver is to give supplemental oxygen and to assist with bag-mask ventilation if necessary until someone with airway expertise arrives.**

TABLE 7-2	Oxygen Delivery Systems	
Type	**F$_{IO_2}$ Capability**	**Comments**
Nasal cannula	24%–48%	At flow rates of 1–8 L/min; true F$_{IO_2}$ uncertain and highly dependent on minute ventilation; simple, comfortable, and can be worn during eating or coughing
Simple face mask	35%–55%	At flow rates of 6–10 L/min
High-humidity mask	Variable from 28% to nearly 100%	Flow rates should be 2–3 times minute ventilation; levels >60% may require additional oxygen bleed-in; excellent humidification
Reservoir mask		
Nonrebreathing	90%–95%	At flow rates of 12–15 L/min; incorporates directional valves that reduce room air entrainment and rebreathing of expired air
Partial rebreathing	50%–80%	At flow rates of 8–10 L/min
Ventimask	Available at 24%, 28%, 31%, 35%, 40%, and 50%	Provides controlled F$_{IO_2}$; useful in chronic obstructive pulmonary disease patients to prevent depression of respiratory drive; poorly humidified gas at maximum F$_{IO_2}$

F$_{IO_2}$, fraction of inspired oxygen.

    a. Oral and nasal ET intubation. The oral route is usually the most expeditious. The nasal route can be used only when the patient is breathing spontaneously; significant skill is needed to direct the tip of the ET tube blindly past the vocal cords and into the trachea. Additionally, nasotracheal intubation poses a significant bleeding risk that can make subsequent airway management difficult. Once the tube is in the trachea, the adequacy of bilateral ventilation must be established using auscultation and a carbon dioxide indicator. A chest x-ray is used to document correct ET tube position.

    b. Noninvasive ventilation. Biphasic positive airway pressure (BiPAP) is a form of ventilation that is delivered by means of a tight-fitting mask (no ET tube), which allows independent control of positive inspiratory and expiratory pressures. It is most useful as a bridge to aid respiratory efforts in patients with mild-to-moderate respiratory insufficiency of short duration (e.g., asthma or COPD exacerbations or pulmonary edema) and frequently can prevent the need for intubation in patients with rapidly reversible respiratory failure. BiPAP may result in gastric distension, thereby increasing the risk of aspiration, particularly in the patient with altered sensorium.

c. **Tracheostomy** should be considered in the presence of severe maxillofacial injury to ensure an adequate airway or if prolonged intubation is anticipated. Timing of tracheostomy has been found to be significantly correlated with length of mechanical ventilation, as well as duration of ICU and hospital stay (*Crit Care Med.* 2005;33:2513). Tracheostomy provides a more secure airway, improves patient comfort and oral hygiene, increases patient mobility, and enhances secretion removal. **If a tracheostomy falls out before an adequate tract has formed, the patient should be reintubated orotracheally rather than subjected to a blind attempt to replace the tracheostomy.**

d. **Cricothyroidotomy** is useful in emergency situations when attempts to ventilate by bag-valve-mask and ET tube are unsuccessful. The technique is described in Chapter 37. Percutaneous cricothyroidotomy may also be performed if a kit is available and someone with expertise is present.

e. **Complications.** Immediate complications include passage of the ET tube into either the esophagus or the tissue surrounding the trachea. Either can lead to death if not promptly recognized. Of these, esophageal intubation is substantially more common. When an ET tube is placed in tissue surrounding the trachea (most common when attempting to replace a tracheostomy that has fallen out), it can lead to hemorrhage, pneumothorax, pneumomediastinum, subcutaneous emphysema, and injury to the recurrent laryngeal nerve. Delayed complications of ET intubation include hemorrhage, which results from erosion of the tube into a vessel (usually the brachiocephalic artery). Immediate orotracheal intubation, removal of the tracheostomy tube, insertion of the surgeon's finger into the tracheostomy site, and anterior compression of the brachiocephalic artery against the clavicle can be used treat the hemorrhage. ET tube cuff pressures should be monitored frequently and kept below capillary filling pressures (i.e., <25 mm Hg) to prevent tracheal ischemia, which, if untreated, can lead to tracheomalacia or tracheal stenosis.

3. **Mechanical ventilation** is indicated for the treatment of respiratory failure. The goal of treatment is to improve alveolar ventilation and oxygenation and to reduce the work of breathing, while other therapies are instituted to treat underlying disease processes.

a. **Modes of mechanical ventilation** can be divided into volume-control and pressure-control modes. The key to understanding the differences between these modes lies in the relationship between pressure and volume and the variable that is controlled. The goal of volume-control modes is to deliver a set tidal volume to the patient to ensure adequate alveolar ventilation; airway pressure varies depending on compliance (compliance equals the change in volume divided by the change in pressure ($C = \Delta V/\Delta P$). In contrast, the goal of pressure-limited modes is to deliver a set airway pressure; tidal volume varies depending on compliance.

(1) **Volume-control modes**

    (a) **Assist-control (A/C) ventilation** delivers a preset tidal volume at a set rate. As the machine senses each inspiratory effort by the patient, it delivers the set tidal volume. If the patient's respiratory rate is below the machine's set rate, ventilator-initiated breaths are delivered to make up the difference between the set rate and the patient's. A/C ventilation minimizes the work of breathing because the ventilator assists all breaths (hence, the term *full support*); however, for this reason, this mode is uncomfortable in the awake or minimally sedated patient if the patient's breaths are dyssynchronous with those delivered by the ventilator. Respiratory alkalosis from hyperventilation may develop in agitated patients.

    (b) **Intermittent mandatory ventilation (IMV),** like A/C ventilation, delivers a preset tidal volume at a set rate. IMV will assist spontaneous respiratory efforts through the use of pressure support in which a spontaneously initiated breath triggers fresh gas flow until the level of set pressure support is achieved.

(2) **Pressure-control modes**

    (a) **Pressure-support ventilation** delivers a preset inspiratory pressure but at no set rate. Constant inspiratory pressure continues until the inspiratory flow of gas falls below a predetermined level and the exhalation valve opens. Thus, tidal volumes are generated only when the patient is breathing spontaneously. This allows the patient to maintain control of inspiratory and expiratory time and thus tidal volume; as a result, this mode is the most comfortable for spontaneously breathing patients. The disadvantages of pressure-support ventilation are that (1) all ventilation depends on patient effort and (2) sudden increases in airway resistance decrease tidal volumes. Small amounts (5 to 8 cm H_2O) of pressure-support ventilation are used routinely to overcome the resistance to airflow caused by the ET tube and the inspiratory demand valves of the ventilator.

    (b) **Pressure-control ventilation** delivers a preset inspiratory pressure (as opposed to tidal volume) at a set rate. This mode is used in patients with poor (low) lung compliance who develop high inspiratory pressures when they are ventilated with the more traditional modes described previously. Thus, the advantage of this mode is that it allows the physician to set the airway pressure and thereby minimize barotrauma. The disadvantage is that the tidal volume varies depending on compliance. The sudden development of an increase in airway resistance (coughing, thick secretions, a kink in the ET tube, a Valsalva maneuver), for example, increases airway pressures and decreases tidal volumes to dangerously low levels.

For patients in whom conventional mechanical ventilation is failing to achieve adequate oxygenation, open lung ventilation may be considered. Open lung ventilation attempts to minimize shearing forces due to alveolar collapse by stenting alveoli open at end expiration. Criteria for using an alternative mode of ventilation include Fio_2 greater than 70%, SpO_2 less than or equal to 88%, PEEP greater than 15, and plateau pressures greater than 30.

  (3) **Airway pressure release ventilation (BiLevel)** is a style of ventilator support that allows a patient to breathe spontaneously at two levels of positive end-expiratory pressure (PEEP). The time at the lower PEEP level may be limited so that all breaths are taken at the upper PEEP level and the pressure is then released just long enough to allow the lung volume to decrease (airway pressure release). Alternatively, spontaneous breathing may occur at both levels. There is evidence to suggest that this improves patient comfort and synchrony with the ventilator.

  (4) **High-frequency oscillatory ventilation** (HFOV) uses substantially faster rates (180 to 300/minute) and smaller tidal volumes than conventional modes. The result is a relative decrease in diaphragmatic excursion, lung movement, and airway pressures. The physical mechanisms responsible for gas movement are complex and incompletely understood. Although HFOV has not been demonstrated to improve survival, it is associated with a trend toward decreased mortality in ARDS in a recent prospective, randomized trial (52% vs. 37%, $p = 0.102$) and represents a viable "rescue" therapy for those failing with conventional ventilation (*Am J Respir Crit Care Med.* 2002;166:801). HFOV may be considered when Fio_2 requirements exceed 70% and mean airway pressure is approaching 20 cm H_2O or higher or when there is a PEEP of greater than 15 cm H_2O in ARDS. Patients do not always need to be paralyzed to undergo HFOV, but they do need to be deeply sedated (Ramsay 5 to 6). Adjustable variables include oscillatory frequency (Hz), Fio_2, amplitude or power (tidal volume), and inspiratory time.

 b. **Ventilator management**

  (1) **Choice of ventilator mode.** Patient needs should be matched with the appropriate ventilator mode by considering each mode's advantages and disadvantages.

(2) F_{IO_2} should be adjusted to ensure adequate arterial oxygenation, which is a blood hemoglobin saturation of 92%. The lowest possible F_{IO_2} (ideally ≤ 0.40) should be used to achieve these levels of arterial saturation to prevent pulmonary oxygen toxicity.

(3) **Tidal volume.** There is no consensus on the optimal tidal volume for the postoperative patient who requires short-term mechanical ventilatory support. However, in ARDS, low tidal volumes are associated with improved survival. A multicenter, prospective, randomized trial demonstrated improved survival in patients who were ventilated with low tidal volumes (6 mL/kg ideal body weight) compared with high tidal volumes (12 mL/kg) (*N Engl J Med.* 2000;342:1301). As a result of this important study, the tidal volume should be adjusted to as low as 4 mL/kg ideal body weight as needed to maintain plateau pressures at less than 30 cm H_2O to minimize barotrauma but greater than 20 cm H_2O to minimize atelectasis.

(4) **Ventilatory rate.** Once the tidal volume has been determined, the rate is chosen (typically 8 to 16 breaths per minute) to provide adequate minute ventilation (the product of rate and tidal volume). The rate is adjusted to optimize arterial pH and $Paco_2$; an $ETCO_2$ monitor is useful in this regard.

(5) **Inspiratory–expiratory (I:E) ratio.** The normal I:E ratio is 1:2 to 1:3. Longer expiratory times allow patients with obstructive lung disease and decreased expiratory airflow to exhale fully and prevent stacking of breaths. In contrast, longer inspiratory times, which decrease peak airway pressures, are useful in patients with low pulmonary compliance. Inverse-ratio ventilation takes advantage of breath stacking, using I:E ratios from 1:1 to 4:1. Used only in patients with severe consolidating lung disease, inverse ratio ventilation is believed to improve gas exchange by progressive alveolar recruitment (mean airway pressures are higher, keeping a larger number of alveoli open for a greater percentage of the respiratory cycle). Inverse-ratio ventilation is used most commonly with pressure-control ventilation.

(6) **PEEP is intended to** increase functional residual capacity, increase lung compliance, and improve ventilation–perfusion matching by opening terminal airways and recruiting partially collapsed alveoli. PEEP of 5 cm H_2O is considered physiologic; higher levels are used when hypoxemia is moderate to severe. PEEP increases intrathoracic pressure and may decrease CO, reduces venous return to the heart, increases airway pressure, and alters pulmonary vascular resistance. PEEP levels of greater than 15 cm H_2O significantly increase the risk of barotrauma and spontaneous pneumothorax. Excess PEEP can also reduce lung compliance, decrease right ventricular (RV) filling, and increase RV afterload. PEEP applied to the spontaneously ventilating patient without inspiratory ventilatory support is called **continuous positive airway pressure (CPAP).**

(7) **Sedation and neuromuscular paralysis.** Sedation is often necessary in mechanically ventilated patients to control anxiety, allow the patient to rest, and synchronize breathing. However, a recent clinical trial demonstrated that patients who receive no sedation have more ventilator-free days and shorter ICU lengths of stay (*Lancet.* 2010;375:475). The need for paralysis is rare, except in patients with severe respiratory failure and decreased pulmonary compliance. If paralytics are necessary, they should be discontinued as soon as possible because long-term use is associated with paresis, which may last for weeks to months. Level of paralysis should routinely be assessed (e.g., with train-of-four neuromuscular testing).

(8) **Prone positioning** is one of several techniques that may have benefit as "rescue" strategies in patients with severe acute lung injury or ARDS. Patients are placed in a prone position for a scheduled period of time on a daily basis; theoretical benefits include recruitment of dorsal lung units, improved mechanics, decreased ventilation–perfusion mismatch, and increased secretion drainage (*JAMA.* 2005;294:2889). Although this therapy has been shown to benefit oxygenation, it has not been demonstrated to improve survival.

c. **Complications**

(1) **ET tube dislodgment and patient self-extubation** can produce a medical emergency characterized by life-threatening hypoxia and hypercarbia in those who are profoundly ill. For this reason, restraint of the patient's upper extremities is frequently required. If a patient does self-extubate, he or she should be closely observed because a surprising number of patients will be able to remain successfully extubated. If the patient shows any signs of respiratory distress, however, he or she should be immediately reintubated or placed on noninvasive ventilation, depending on the clinical scenario.

(2) **ET tube cuff leaks** should be suspected when there is an unexplained decrease in the returned expired volume associated with a fall in airway pressure. A cuff leak may indicate that the ET tube is at or partially above the vocal cords, and the tube may be advanced using a bronchoscope. A severe cuff leak should prompt change of the ET tube because there is increased risk of aspiration and decreased efficiency of ventilation.

(3) **Respiratory distress** may occur suddenly during mechanical ventilation due either to an acute change in the patient's status or to ventilator malfunction. The first priority is to disconnect the ventilator and switch to bag ventilation using 100% oxygen to ensure adequate ventilation and oxygenation. Increased airway pressures may indicate obstruction of the tube with secretions or a kink in the tube, bronchospasm, pneumothorax, inadequate patient sedation or migration of the ET tube into a mainstem bronchus. Check the ET tube for patency and suction; if there is a partial obstruction, use large-volume saline

lavage to clear the tube. If the obstruction is complete, remove the ET tube and reintubate the patient. Listen closely for any change in breath sounds consistent with a pneumothorax, new lung consolidation, or pleural fluid collection. A less common but important cause of respiratory distress is PE. **Check the ventilator's function** and, if it is normal, return the patient to the ventilator, making any needed changes in ventilator settings to ensure adequate ventilation and oxygenation. The results of an ABG and a chest x-ray are frequently helpful.

(4) **Barotrauma** from very high peak airway pressures ($\geq$50 cm H_2O) can lead to subcutaneous emphysema, pneumomediastinum, and pneumothorax. Whereas subcutaneous emphysema and pneumomediastinum usually are benign, a pneumothorax that develops while a patient is on positive-pressure ventilation is at high risk for tension pneumothorax and is usually treated emergently with tube thoracostomy.

(5) **Volutrauma is alveolar injury secondary to severe distention.**

(6) **Atelectrauma is alveolar damage caused by repetitive alveolar opening and closing in the setting of low surfactant or inadequate PEEP. In adults, this is most commonly associated with noncompliant alveoli in ARDS.**

(7) **Oxygen toxicity** refers to levels of intra-alveolar oxygen high enough to cause lung damage. The precise mechanism is not known, but it probably involves oxidation of cell membranes and generation of toxic oxygen radicals. An F_{IO_2} of 0.40 or less is considered safe even for long periods. Although experimental data demonstrate that microscopic damage to alveoli occurs after only a few hours of an F_{IO_2} of 1 in animals, convincing studies in human patients are impossible to perform due to ethical consideration. It appears prudent, however, to keep the F_{IO_2} at less than 0.60 whenever possible, often using higher levels of PEEP (8 to 12 cm H_2O) to help reduce the F_{IO_2}.

d. **Weaning off mechanical ventilation.** Although there are exceptions (e.g., immediate extubation of a healthy patient with normal lungs after general anesthesia), discontinuing mechanical ventilation may require weaning. In general, hemodynamic instability or high work of breathing (e.g., minute ventilation >15 L/minute) is contraindications to weaning. Reduction in the F_{IO_2} to 0.40 or less and of PEEP to 5 cm H_2O or less is accomplished first. The patient who has needed prolonged ventilatory support may require from several days to weeks to wean because of marginal respiratory muscle strength and the time required for the injured lungs to recover. The optimal strategy for weaning patients continues to be a topic of debate. The results of clinical trials indicate that the method of weaning from ventilator support is most likely of little consequence for patients who have been on mechanical ventilatory support for 2 weeks or less because the primary determinant of weaning success is simply resolution of the pathology that induced respiratory failure. At Washington University, patients are maintained on volume-control ventilation with daily CPAP trials to assess their suitability for extubation. The presence of a weaning protocol decreases patient time on the ventilator compared with physician-directed weaning.

IV. CIRCULATORY FAILURE: SHOCK

A. Shock is defined by global tissue hypoxia; it occurs when either the supply of or the ability to use oxygen is insufficient to meet metabolic demands. Shock can be recognized by evidence of end-organ dysfunction. If left uncorrected, shock leads to the death of cells, tissues, organs, and, ultimately, the patient. Understanding the **pathophysiology of shock** depends on an appreciation of the relationship of blood pressure [specifically, mean arterial pressure (MAP)] to CO and SVR: MAP is directly proportional to CO and SVR. Because CO is equal to stroke volume times heart rate, and stroke volume is proportional to preload, afterload, and myocardial contractility, MAP is usually proportional to heart rate, preload, afterload, and contractility. Compensatory changes in response to systemic hypotension include the release of catecholamines, aldosterone, renin, and cortisol, which act in concert to increase heart rate, preload, afterload, and contractility.

B. **Classification and recognition of shock** (Table 7-3). The morbidity and mortality of circulatory shock are related not only to the underlying cause

TABLE 7-3	Clinical Parameters in Shock					
Shock Classification	Skin	Jugular Venous Distention	Cardiac Output	Pulmonary Capillary Wedge Pressure	Systemic Vascular Resistance	Mixed Venous Oxygen Content
Hypovolemic	Cool, pale	↓	↓	↓	↑	↓
Cardiogenic	Cool, pale	↑	↓	↑	↑	↓
Septic						
Early	Warm, pink	↑↓	↑	↓	↓	↑
Late	Cool, pale	↓	↓	↓	↑	↑↓
Neurogenic	Warm, pink	↓	↓	↓	↓	↓

but also to the depth and duration of circulatory compromise. Early recognition and prompt intervention are therefore critical.

1. **Hypovolemic shock** results from loss of circulating blood volume (usually at least 20%) caused by acute hemorrhage, fluid depletion, or dehydration; these three are frequently distinguishable from one another by history. These patients typically are peripherally vasoconstricted, tachycardic, and have low jugular venous pressure.

2. **Distributive shock** is characterized by a hyperdynamic state consisting of tachycardia, vasodilation (with decreased cardiac filling pressures), decreased SVR, and increased CO; however, some patients present with hypodynamic septic shock and have decreased CO and hypoperfusion. Patients with hyperdynamic distributive shock feel warm. The most common causes of distributive shock include sepsis, the systemic inflammatory response syndrome (SIRS), neurogenic shock, adrenal insufficiency, and liver failure. **Neurogenic shock** results from interruption of the spinal cord at or above the thoracolumbar sympathetic nerve roots, which produces loss of sympathetic tone to the vascular system, causing vasodilation. The cardiovascular response is the same; patients are typically peripherally vasodilated (warm extremities) and tachycardic. Jugular venous pressure is usually low.

3. **Obstructive shock** results from etiologies that prevent adequate CO but are not intrinsically cardiac in origin. This type of shock may be caused by pulmonary embolus, tension pneumothorax, or cardiac tamponade. Jugular venous pressure is often elevated in these patients.

4. **Cardiogenic shock** results from inadequate CO due to intrinsic cardiac failure (e.g., acute myocardial infarction, valvular stenosis, regurgitation or rupture, ischemia, arrhythmia, cardiomyopathy, or acute ventricular septal defect). These patients typically are peripherally vasoconstricted and tachycardic. Their jugular venous pressure typically is elevated.

5. **Interventions common to all types of shock.** The goal of therapy is to ensure adequate delivery of oxygen to the peripheral tissues. Because oxygen delivery is proportional to the arithmetic product of Sao_2, hemoglobin concentration, and CO, each of these parameters should be optimized.

   a. **Sao_2.** It is necessary to administer supplemental oxygen, secure or provide an adequate airway, and check for adequate bilateral ventilation. A pulse oximetry (Sao_2) level that exceeds 92% should allow adequate delivery of oxygen at the periphery; however, levels should be maximized in the acute setting.

   b. **Hemoglobin concentration.** The hemoglobin concentration must be adequate to deliver oxygen to the tissues. One study indicated that for most critically ill patients, a transfusion trigger of 7 g/dL is appropriate, with the goal of keeping the hemoglobin concentration at 7 to 9 g/dL, except in patients with an ongoing myocardial infarction or severe ischemic cardiomyopathy (*N Engl J Med.* 1999;340:409). An important caveat is early goal-directed therapy in septic patients with SvO_2 less than 70 and hemoglobin less than 10 (*N Engl J Med.* 2001;345:1368).

c. **Cardiac output (CO).** The ECG tracing provides direct information about heart rate and several indirect clues about stroke volume. The atrial contraction provides approximately 15% to 25% of ordinary preload in normal patients and potentially up to 50% in patients with significant diastolic dysfunction, so the atrioventricular dyssynchrony observed in atrial fibrillation or third-degree atrioventricular block causes impairment of CO. This is clinically relevant for patients who have decreased ventricular compliance or decreased ejection fraction at baseline. Tachyarrhythmias decrease diastolic ventricular and coronary artery filling times. When it is severe (e.g., heart rate ~140 beats per minute), tachycardia predictably impairs preload, stroke volume, and CO. When treating tachycardia *per se,* it is imperative to distinguish between tachycardia as a compensatory response (e.g., sinus tachycardia secondary to hypovolemia) and tachycardia as a cause of shock (e.g., ventricular tachycardia). With the exception of the patient in pulmonary edema, *all* patients in circulatory shock should initially receive 10 to 20 mL/kg of a balanced salt solution, such as lactated Ringer's solution. The pace of volume infusion should reflect the depth of circulatory shock. To achieve rapid infusion rates, short, large-bore intravenous catheters (e.g., 14 or 16 gauge) in an peripheral vein are best. If this is not possible, an 8.5-French sheath inserted into a central vein is highly effective. **A multilumen central line is NOT an effective access for rapid volume resuscitation since resistance to flow is proportional to catheter length and inversely proportional to catheter lumen diameter raised to the 5th power.** The stopcocks should be removed from the venous lines to reduce flow resistance and deliver *warmed* fluids. Hypothermia is aggravated by rapid infusion of room temperature (i.e., 23 degrees centigrade) crystalloid and refrigerated blood, impairing the ability to unload oxygen from hemoglobin in the periphery and compromising all enzymatic processes, especially coagulation.

d. To assess the adequacy of resuscitation, peripheral pulses and urine output should be evaluated. Palpable pedal pulses or urine output that exceeds 1 mL/kg/ hour usually indicates a cardiac index of greater than 2 L/m^2/minute. These two simple techniques can be used to estimate cardiac performance in many patients. Patients who do not improve with initial resuscitative measures may require invasive hemodynamic monitoring. All patients in shock should be monitored with an indwelling bladder catheter. Metabolic acidosis, identified by an ABG determination and serum electrolytes, can reflect the depth of circulatory compromise and the adequacy of resuscitation; however, this is may not be true in patients with preexisting renal failure and baseline metabolic acidosis. Infusion of sodium bicarbonate should be reserved for patients with a pH of less than 7.15 because the sodium bicarbonate may actually worsen intracellular pH as the bicarbonate is converted to CO_2 at the tissue level, particularly if CO_2 elimination (i.e., effective ventilation) is impaired.

TABLE 7-4	Physiologic Changes in Hypovolemic Shock			
Blood loss (%)	<15	15–30	30–40	>40
Blood loss (mL)[a]	<750	750–1,500	1,500–2,000	>2,000
Heart rate (bpm)	NI	>100	>120	>140
Blood pressure	NI	SBP NI DBP ↑	SBP ↓ DBP ↓	SBP ↓↓ DBP ↓↓
Respiratory rate	NI	↑	↑↑	↑↑↑
Urine output	NI	↓	Oliguria	Anuria
Mental state	Minimal anxiety	Mild anxiety	Confusion	Lethargy

[a]Based on a 70-kg male patient.
bpm, beats per minute; DBP, diastolic blood pressure; NI, normal; SBP, systolic blood pressure.

6. **Specific therapy**
   a. **Hypovolemic shock.** Therapy focuses on control of ongoing volume loss and restoration of intravascular volume. External hemorrhage should be controlled by direct pressure. Internal hemorrhage may require further diagnostic tests and/or surgical intervention. The degree of volume deficit (Table 7-4) determines the type and volume of resuscitative fluid. Patients with blood losses of up to 20% of their circulating blood volume can be resuscitated using crystalloid solutions alone, typically lactated Ringer's solution. However, because salt solutions equilibrate with the interstitial space, volume replacement with these solutions alone requires three times the estimated volume deficit. Patients in whom diaphoresis, ashen facies, and hypotension develop have lost 30% or more of their blood volume and require urgent transfusion of blood. Individuals with severe dehydration often have profound metabolic and electrolyte abnormalities. Fluid administration should be modified once laboratory analysis of serum electrolytes is completed. With adequate volume resuscitation, vasoconstrictors and vasoactive agents can usually be avoided or discontinued.
   b. **Distributive shock**
      (1) **Septic shock (see Section V.C).**
      (2) **Critical illness-related corticosteroid insufficiency (CIRCI) can result from adrenal insufficiency or glucocorticoid resistance.** The diagnosis and treatment of adrenal insufficiency in septic shock are evolving and controversial. Per ACCM 2008

guidelines, adrenal insufficiency is best diagnosed by delta cortisol level < 9 ug/dL after a cosyntropin (synthetic ACTH, 250 ug) stimulation test or random total cortisol <10 ug/dL. There is a consensus that patients with primary adrenal insufficiency or those with septic shock refractory to fluid resuscitation and vasopressors should be treated with moderate dose hydrocortisone (50 mg IV every 6 hours) (*Crit Care Med.* 2008;36:1937). In many cases of CIRCI, dysfunction of the hypothalamic–pituitary axis is reversible and resolves with improvement in the underlying condition. Corticosteroids increase the risk of infection (*NEJM.* 2008;358:111).

(3) **SIRS** may result from noninfectious causes of inflammation (e.g., necrotizing pancreatitis, burns, and cardiopulmonary bypass). Treatment is supportive, with volume resuscitation, mechanical ventilation, and the administration of vasopressors as needed until the inflammatory process resolves.

c. **Obstructive shock.** Tension pneumo- or hemothoraces and pericardial tamponade require mechanical intervention. Tension pneumothorax is treated by needle decompression followed by tube thoracostomy. Hemothorax requires tube thoracostomy. Pericardial tamponade is treated by needle decompression, often with catheter placement for drainage. The treatment of PE varies based on the degree of hemodynamic compromise and must be individualized. Alternatives include systemic anticoagulation, thrombolysis, and surgical clot removal. Inferior vena cava (IVC) filters are used in patients who have a contraindication to systemic anticoagulation.

d. **Cardiogenic shock.** It is critical to distinguish shock caused by intrinsic myocardial dysfunction from extrinsic processes that interfere with venous return to the heart. Diagnosis may require echocardiography and cardiac catheterization. Management is directed toward maintaining adequate myocardial perfusion and CO with volume expansion and vasopressors, inotropes, or chronotropes (Table 7-5). Initial treatment is often guided by CVP measurements or, in severe cases, PA catheter data, while the precipitating cause of compromise is identified and treated. CVP is primarily useful for assessment of RV function and is not a reliable marker of volume status (*Chest.* 2008;134:172). Mechanical support with intra-aortic balloon counterpulsation may be necessary before and during recovery from definitive surgical treatment (see Chapter 30).

e. **Neurogenic shock.** As with septic shock, the initial intervention in neurogenic shock is volume infusion. A peripheral vasoconstrictor, such as phenylephrine or norepinephrine, is administered centrally to increase vascular tone if hypotension is refractory to volume infusion alone. Dopamine is useful in patients with neurogenic shock and bradycardia. Because patients with spinal shock tend to equilibrate body temperature with their environment, fluids and ambient room temperature must be kept warm.

TABLE 7-5   Vasoactive Drugs and Their Specific Actions

Class and Drug	Blood Pressure	Systemic Vascular Resistance	Cardiac Output	Heart Rate	Inotrope — Low Dose	Inotrope — High Dose	Renal Blood Flow	Coronary Blood Flow	Mvo₂
Alpha Only									
Phenylephrine	↑↑	↑↑↑↑	↓	↓	±	±	↓↓↓↓	± ↑↑	↑
Alpha and Beta									
Norepinephrine	↑↑↑	↑↑↑↑	↑↑↑	↑ ±	↑	↑	↓↓↓	↑↑	↑↑
Epinephrine	↑↑↑	↑↑↑↑	↑↑↑↑	↑↑↑	↑↑	↑↑↑	↓→± ↑	↑↑	↑↑↑
Dopamine	↑↑	↑↑	↑↑↑	↑↑	±	↑↑	↑↑↑	↑↑	↑↑
Beta Only									
Dobutamine	±	↓↓↓	↑↑↑↑	↑↑	↑↑↑	↑↑↑	±	↑↑↑	↑↑↑
Beta-Blocker									
Metoprolol	↓	→	↓↓	↓↓↓	↓↓	↓↓↓	±	↓↓	↓↓
Other									
Nitroglycerine	± ↓	↓↓	↑↓	± ↓	±	±	± ↓	→	↓↓
Hydralazine	↓↓	↓↓↓	↑↓	↑↑	±	±	± ↓	→	↓↓
Nitroprusside	↓↓↓	↓↓↓	↑↑↑	± ↑	±	±	↑↑	±	↓↓

Mvo₂, mixed venous oxygen saturation.

V. SEPSIS

A. **Definition.** Sepsis is defined as SIRS resulting from infection. There is a consensus clinical definition of SIRS: body temperature greater than 38°C or less than 36°C, heart rate greater than 90 beats/minute, respiratory rate greater than 20/minute or Pa_{CO_2} less than 32, and white blood cell (WBC) count greater than 12 or less than 4 or greater than 10% bands. Severe sepsis is multiple-organ dysfunction or hypoperfusion resulting from infection.

B. **Diagnosis**

1. **Appropriate cultures** should be obtained as part of the initial evaluation. Two or more blood cultures are recommended, one of which should be drawn percutaneously.

2. **Additional radiologic imaging and diagnostic procedures** should be performed as warranted.

C. **Treatment**

1. **Addressing the infection**
   a. **Antibiotic therapy**
      (1) **Broad-spectrum intravenous antibiotics** should be initiated within the first hour after obtaining appropriate cultures. Failure to do so results in significantly increased mortality from severe sepsis (*Chest.* 2000;118:146). The use of antifungal therapies and agents directed at highly resistant Gram-negative rods, methicillin-resistant *Staphylococcus aureus,* vancomycin-resistant enterococcus, and resistant pneumococcus should be guided by the clinical situation and local patterns of susceptibility.
         (a) The following increase a patient's risk for infection with resistant organisms:
            (i) Prior treatment with antibiotics during the hospitalization.
            (ii) Prolonged hospitalization.
            (iii) Presence of invasive devices.
      (2) For pneumonias, the initial broad-spectrum antibiotic coverage should be narrowed to focus on the causative organism(s) identified on culture. For intra-abdominal infections, therapies remain broadly directed at the range of intra-abdominal organisms.
   b. **Source control: drainage, debridement, or removal of the infectious source** as appropriate, through surgical or other means.

2. **Circulatory support**
   a. **Early goal-directed therapy** involves adjustments of cardiac preload, afterload, and contractility to balance oxygen delivery with oxygen demand before the patient even arrives in the ICU. A recent study demonstrated a hospital mortality of 30.5% for patients presenting in the emergency department with sepsis when treated with early goal-directed therapy compared with 46.5% for patients treated with standard therapy (*N Engl J Med.* 2001;345:1368).

    b. **In the first 6 hours,** the goals of resuscitation are as follows (*Crit Care Med.* 2008;36:296):

      (1) CVP 8 to 12 mm Hg.

      (2) MAP at least 65 mm Hg.

      (3) Urine output at least 0.5 mg/kg/hour.

      (4) Mixed SvO_2 at least 70%.

    c. **Vasoactive medications.** To maintain CO, heart rate usually is increased. Septic patients who fail to achieve rapid hemodynamic stability with fluids and small doses of vasoconstrictors often undergo insertion of a PA catheter to optimize cardiac performance. Because PA catheters have not been demonstrated to improve outcome in either high-risk surgical patients or ARDS patients, placing this form of invasive monitoring should not be automatic but should be decided on an individual basis. If a PA catheter is placed, higher filling pressures are typically needed (pulmonary capillary wedge pressure of 14 to 18 mm Hg) to optimize performance in the dilated, septic heart.

      (1) Dopamine and norepinephrine are both commonly used; however, phenylephrine is not beneficial in the setting of sepsis. A recent randomized controlled trial did not show a mortality difference between use of dopamine and norepinephrine, but dopamine was associated with a significantly higher rate of dysrhythmias (*NEJM.* 2010;362:779; *Shock.* 2010;33:375).

      (2) Circulatory concentrations of endogenous **vasopressin** increase initially, then decrease (*Crit Care Med.* 2003;31:1752), and they are lower in septic shock than in cardiogenic shock. Low-dose vasopressin increases MAP, SVR, and urine output in septic patients who are hyporesponsive to catecholamines. This may spare patients from high-dose catecholamine requirements, although its impact on survival is unclear.

  3. **Adjunctive treatments**

    a. **Activated protein C** has been demonstrated to reduce mortality in a large-scale prospective, randomized trial (*N Engl J Med.* 2001;344:699–709). Although this drug clearly improves survival in patients with severe sepsis and has a very short half-life, it is associated with an increase in serious bleeding and must be used with caution in patients in the immediate postoperative setting. Activated protein C can be started 12 hours after an operative procedure and should be held for approximately 1 hour before and after minor interventions such as central venous catheter placement. Of note, activated protein C is approved for use in patients with Acute Physiology and Chronic Health Evaluation (APACHE) II scores of greater than 25 and has not been documented to help patients with less severe forms of sepsis.

VI. UPPER GASTROINTESTINAL HEMORRHAGE PROPHYLAXIS. Patients in the ICU are at increased risk for stress-induced mucosal ulceration and resultant GI hemorrhage. Risk factors include head injury (Cushing ulcers); burns

(Curling ulcers); requirement for mechanical ventilation; previous history of peptic ulcer disease; use of nonsteroidal anti-inflammatory drugs or steroids; and the presence of shock, renal failure, portal hypertension, or coagulopathy. Strong data exist to support the use of drugs to maintain mucosal integrity in these patients at increased risk. In an evidence-based review of discordant meta-analyses, H_2-receptor antagonists (cimetidine, ranitidine, famotidine) were found to reduce significantly the incidence of clinically important GI bleeding in critically ill patients. Proton-pump inhibitors are useful in patients who bleed despite being on appropriate H_2-receptor antagonists.

VII. RENAL DYSFUNCTION

A. **Etiology and diagnosis.** Renal dysfunction commonly presents as progressive oliguria in the setting of increased renal function indices [blood urea nitrogen (BUN) and serum creatinine]. This can progress to renal failure and anuria (urine output <100 mL/day), which require renal replacement therapy (~5% of all ICU admissions). Renal insufficiency can also present as polyuria when decreased renal tubular function (fluid resorption) is not coupled with decreased glomerular filtration ("high-output" renal failure). Traditionally, the etiology of renal dysfunction has been divided into prerenal, intrarenal, and postrenal causes. A careful history and a review of the medical record are critical to making the correct diagnosis.

1. **Prerenal.** The glomerular and tubular function of the kidneys is normal, but clearance is limited as a result of decreased renal blood flow. This is the most common cause of renal insufficiency in the surgical ICU, and it is usually the result of inadequate volume resuscitation. The rise in the BUN typically is greater than that of the serum creatinine (BUN/creatinine ratio >20). The concentrating ability of the kidneys is normal, and thus the urine osmolality (>500 mOsm) and the fractional excretion of sodium (FE_{Na} <1) are normal.

   a. **Abdominal compartment syndrome** results from massive tissue (bowel) edema within the abdominal compartment or retroperitoneal hemorrhage, frequently although not exclusively as a complication of severe trauma and massive resuscitation. Increased intra-abdominal pressure decreases renal perfusion and retards renal venous and urinary outflow, inducing renal injury by a combination of pre-, intra-, and postrenal insults. Assessment of urinary bladder pressure via a Foley catheter serves as an indirect but accurate measure of intra-abdominal pressure (*J Trauma.* 1998;45:597). An acute increase in pressure greater than 25 cm H_2O demands intervention and typically surgical exploration (convert mm Hg to cm H_2O by multiplying mm Hg by 1.3).

2. **Intrarenal.** Tubular injury is most often caused by ischemia (i.e., prolonged prerenal state) or toxins. Nephrotoxins commonly encountered by ICU patients include aminoglycosides, intravenous radiocontrast agents, amphotericin, and chemotherapeutic drugs. Patients with pre-existing renal disease or diabetes are particularly susceptible. Intravenous

hydration before and during the administration of nephrotoxins should be used to decrease the incidence of renal insufficiency in patients at risk. The concentrating ability of the tubules is compromised, so the urine osmolality is low (<350 mOsm) and the FE_{Na} is greater than 1. Urinalysis and microscopic analysis of the urinary sediment may yield additional information about tubular pathology (e.g., presence of casts may indicate acute tubular necrosis).

    a. *N*-Acetylcysteine, an antioxidant, has been shown to prevent nephrotoxicity induced by intravenous dye in patients with preexisting renal dysfunction (*N Engl J Med.* 2000;343:180; *Am J Kidney Dis.* 2004;43:1).

    b. A prospective, single-center, randomized trial demonstrated that hydration with sodium bicarbonate is more effective than hydration with sodium chloride for prophylaxis of contrast-induced renal failure. The protocol was an infusion of 3 mL/kg/hour of 154 mEq/L of sodium bicarbonate in dextrose and water for the hour prior to contrast exposure, then 1 mL/kg/hour during the exposure and for 6 hours after (*JAMA.* 2004;291:2328).

  3. Postrenal. Bilateral obstruction of urinary flow can be caused by direct intraoperative injury or manipulation, prostatic hypertrophy, coagulated blood, or extrinsic compression (e.g., tumors). Urinary catheter malfunction must always be ruled out, typically by flushing the catheter with sterile saline. Ultrasound examination of the urinary system is used to rule out hydronephrosis.

B. Treatment

  1. Supportive measures. Initial therapy should be directed at minimizing ongoing renal injury by optimizing renal perfusion and discontinuing potentially nephrotoxic agents. Optimization of renal perfusion is usually accomplished by judicious volume resuscitation. If fluid resuscitation does not improve low urine output (<0.5 mL/kg/hour), measurement of pulmonary capillary wedge pressure or evaluation of cardiac function/filling with echocardiography can be used to guide fluid resuscitation and optimization of CO. Low-dose dopamine does not change progression to renal failure nor does it change mortality. **There is no role for "renal dose" dopamine in the ICU** (*Lancet.* 2000;356:2139). The doses or medications to be eliminated by the kidney should be adjusted for the degree of renal insufficiency. Refer to Chapter 4 for the treatment of the electrolyte (hyperkalemia) and acid–base disorders (metabolic acidosis) that accompany renal failure.

  2. Renal replacement therapy. Indications include complications of renal dysfunction that fail medical management, including hypervolemia, severe acidemia, refractory hyperkalemia, and uremia. Decisions about when and how to initiate renal replacement therapy are the subject of controversy and ongoing clinical trials.

    a. Intermittent. Because peritoneal dialysis is usually impractical in the surgical ICU, intermittent or continuous hemodialysis is the method of choice. Some hemodynamic impairment will ensue as a result of rapid, large shifts of fluid from the intravascular compartment through the dialysis filter. In healthy patients, this is usually well tolerated. However, hemodynamic deterioration (hypotension or dysrhythmias) can be induced in unstable patients due to decreased myocardial preload.

    b. Continuous venovenous hemodialysis (CVVHD) (*N Engl J Med.* 1997;336:1303) is used in patients with preexisting hemodynamic instability, usually in the setting of shock. CVVHD decreases the rate of fluid shifts and thus has less risk of hemodynamic compromise relative to HD. The disadvantage of this type of dialysis is that CVVHD requires constant systemic anticoagulation to prevent clotting of blood in the filter and continuous sophisticated nursing surveillance.

VIII. ANEMIA. It is not uncommon for patients in the ICU to receive multiple units of packed red blood cells during their critical illness. The prospective Transfusion Requirements in Critical Care (TRICC) trial reported that **transfusing all patients to a hemoglobin of 10 mg/dL either has no effect or may actually decrease survival in the critically ill** (*N Engl J Med.* 1999;340:409). Multiple meta-analyses and systematic reviews have found an increased association of transfusions with infection, transfusion-related acute lung injury (TRALI), hospital and ICU length of stay, and mortality. A restrictive transfusion strategy (transfusion for hemoglobin <7 mg/dL) is recommended in critically ill patients; except in those with acute coronary syndrome, severe hypoxemia, or active hemorrhage. A recent randomized controlled trial demonstrated that administration of recombinant erythropoietin did not reduce the rate of transfusion or reduce mortality in critically ill patients, but increased the risk of thrombotic events (*NEJM.* 2007;357:965).

IX. BLOOD GLUCOSE CONTROL. A recent study of 1,548 surgical patients randomly assigned to tight glucose control with intensive insulin therapy (blood glucose between 80 and 110 mg/dL) versus conventional control (blood glucose between 180 and 200 mg/dL and treatment only above 215 mg/dL) showed nearly a twofold decrease in mortality in the tight-glucose-control group. Intensive insulin therapy also reduced overall in-hospital mortality, bloodstream infections, acute renal failure, the median number of red cell transfusions, and critical illness polyneuropathy (*N Engl J Med.* 2001;345:1359). However, a follow-up study in medical patients did not demonstrate a benefit (*N Engl J Med.* 2006;354:449). Hypoglycemia remains a major risk of tight glucose control and has been associated with increased mortality. A goal blood sugar of less than 140 mg/dL seems safe and beneficial; further study will be required to determine the response of different patient populations to varying intensities of insulin therapy.

X. COMMONLY USED DRUGS. Table 7-6 lists commonly used ICU drugs and their doses.

TABLE 7-6 Drugs Commonly Used in the Intensive Care Unit

Drug	Dilution (Concentration)	Loading Dose	Initial Maintenance Dose	Comments
Diltiazem	125 mg/125 mL 0.9% NaCl or D5W (1 mg/mL)	0.25 mg/kg (followed by 0.35 mg/kg if needed)	5–10 mg/hr (max 15 mg/hr)	May cause hypotension
Dobutamine	250 mg/100 mL 0.9% NaCl (2,500 μg/mL)		2 μg/kg/min (max 20 μg/kg/min)	Selective inotropic (beta) effect; may cause tachycardia and arrhythmias
Dopamine	400 mg/250 mL 0.9% NaCl or D5W (1,600 μg/mL)		Dopa, 1–3 μg/kg/min; alpha, 3–10 μg/kg/min; beta, 10–20 μg/kg/min	Clinical response is dose and patient dependent; may cause arrhythmias and tachycardia
Epinephrine	5 mg/500 mL 0.9% NaCl or D5W, or 4 mg/100 mL 0.9% NaCl or D5W		0.01–0.05 μg/kg/min	Mixed alpha and beta effects; use central line; may cause tachycardia and hypotension
Esmolol	2.5 g/250 mL 0.9% NaCl or D5W (10 mg/mL)	500 μg/kg/min for 1 min (optional)	50 μg/kg/min (max 300 μg/kg/min)	Selective beta1-blocker; T1/2 9 min; not eliminated by hepatic or renal routes; may cause hypotension
Heparin	25,000 units/250 mL 0.45% NaCl (100 units/mL)	60 units/kg	14 units/kg/hr	Obtain PTT every 4–6 hr until PTT is 1.5–2 times control; may cause thrombocytopenia

Lidocaine	2 g/500 mL D5W (4 mg/mL)	1 mg/kg (can repeat two times if needed)	1–4 mg/min	Dose should be decreased in patients with hepatic failure, acute MI, CHF, or shock
Nitroglycerin	50 mg/250 mL D5W (200 µg/mL)		5–20 µg/min	Use cautiously in right-sided MI
Nitroprusside	50 mg/250 mL D5W (200 µg/mL)		0.25–0.50 µg/kg/min (max 10 µg/kg/min)	Signs of toxicity include metabolic acidosis, tremors, seizures, and coma; thiocyanate may accumulate in renal failure
Norepinephrine	8 mg/500 mL D5W (16 µg/mL)		0.2–1.3 µg/kg/min	Potent alpha effects; mainly beta1 effects at lower doses; use central line
Phenylephrine	10 mg/250 mL 0.9% NaCl or D5W (40 µg/mL)		10–100 µg/min	Pure alpha effects; use central line; may cause reflex bradycardia and decreased cardiac output
Vasopressin	20 units/100 mL NS (0.2 units/mL)		0.04 units/min	Do not titrate; higher doses may cause myocardial ischemia.

CHF, congestive heart failure; D5W, 5% dextrose in water; max, maximum; MI, myocardial infarction; PTT, partial thromboplastin time; T1/2, terminal half-life.

Esophagus

David M. Hoganson and Traves D. Crabtree

STRUCTURAL AND FUNCTIONAL DISORDERS OF THE ESOPHAGUS

I. **HIATAL HERNIA.** The distal esophagus normally is held in position by the *phrenoesophageal membrane,* a fusion of the endothoracic and abdominal transversalis fascia at the diaphragmatic hiatus. A hiatal hernia is present when a lax or defective phrenoesophageal membrane allows protrusion of the stomach up through the esophageal hiatus of the diaphragm.

A. **Epidemiology.** Hiatal hernia is the most common abnormality reported in upper gastrointestinal (GI) radiographic studies. An estimated 10% of the adult population in the United States has a hiatal hernia. The condition occurs most commonly in women in their fifth and sixth decades. Most hiatal hernias are asymptomatic; however, an estimated 5% of patients with a hiatal hernia have symptoms related to persistent gastroesophageal reflux (GER) disease.

B. The **type of hiatal hernia** is defined by the location of the gastroesophageal (GE) junction and the relationship of the stomach to the distal esophagus.

1. In **type I** or **sliding** hiatal hernia, the phrenoesophageal membrane is intact but lax, thereby allowing the distal esophagus and gastric cardia to herniate through the esophageal hiatus and placing the GE junction above the diaphragm. This is the most common type and is usually asymptomatic.

2. A **type II** or **paraesophageal** hiatal hernia occurs when a focal defect is present in the phrenoesophageal membrane, usually anterior and lateral to the esophagus, which allows a protrusion of peritoneum to herniate upward alongside the esophagus. The GE junction remains anchored within the abdomen, whereas the greater curvature of the stomach rolls up into the chest alongside the distal esophagus. Eventually, most of the stomach can herniate. Because the stomach is anchored at the pylorus and cardia, however, the body of the stomach undergoes a 180-degree organoaxial rotation, resulting in an upside-down intrathoracic stomach when it is herniated.

3. **Type III** represents a **combination** of types I and II. This type is more common than a pure type II and is characterized by herniation of both the greater curvature of the stomach and the GE junction into the chest.

4. A **type IV** hiatal hernia occurs when abdominal organs other than or in addition to the stomach herniate through the hiatus. Typically, these hernias are large and contain colon or spleen in addition to the stomach within the chest.

C. **Symptoms and complications** in patients with **sliding (type I)** hiatal hernias are related to GE reflux (GER; see Section II). **Paraesophageal and combined (types II, III, and IV) hernias** frequently produce postprandial pain or bloating, early satiety, breathlessness with meals, and mild dysphagia related to compression of the distal esophagus by the adjacent herniated stomach. The herniated gastric pouch is susceptible to volvulus, obstruction, and infarction and can develop ischemic longitudinal ulcers (termed *Cameron ulcers*) with frank or occult bleeding.

D. Diagnosis and evaluation

1. **Chest x-ray.** The finding of an air-fluid level in the posterior mediastinum on the lateral X-ray suggests the presence of a hiatal hernia. Differential diagnosis includes mediastinal cyst, abscess, or a dilated obstructed esophagus (as is seen in end-stage achalasia).

2. A **barium swallow** confirms the diagnosis and defines any coexisting esophageal abnormalities, including strictures or ulcers. It is the initial diagnostic study of choice. The positions of the GE junction and proximal stomach define the type of hiatal hernia.

3. **Esophagogastroduodenoscopy (EGD)** is indicated in patients with symptoms of reflux or dysphagia to determine the degree of esophagitis and whether a stricture, Barrett esophagus, or a coexisting abnormality is present. EGD also establishes the location of the GE junction in relation to the hiatus. A sliding hiatal hernia is present when greater than 2 cm of gastric mucosa is present between the diaphragmatic hiatus and the mucosal squamocolumnar junction.

4. **Esophageal manometry** to evaluate esophageal motility is essential in patients who are being considered for operative repair to rule out an esophageal motility disorder.

5. **CT scan** can be very useful for patients with large type III or type IV hernias to define the anatomy and guide preoperative planning.

E. Management

1. **Asymptomatic sliding hernias** require no treatment.

2. Patients with **sliding hernias** and **GER** with mild **esophagitis** should undergo an initial trial of medical management, consisting of H$_2$-blocking agents or proton pump inhibitors.

3. Patients who **fail** to obtain symptomatic relief with **medical therapy** or who have severe esophagitis should undergo esophageal testing to determine their suitability for an **antireflux procedure** (see Section II) **and hiatal hernia repair.** Additional indications for surgical evaluation are young patients who would require lifelong proton pump inhibitors, patients with ongoing regurgitation, patients with respiratory symptoms (cough, aspiration pneumonia) and Barrett esophagus.

4. Patients who do not experience reflux but have symptoms related to their hernia (chest pain, intermittent dysphagia, or esophageal obstruction) should undergo hiatal hernia repair.

5. All patients who are found to have a **type II, III, or IV hiatal hernia** and who are operative candidates should be **considered for**

repair. The management of asymptomatic paraesophageal hernias is a controversial issue. Some surgeons believe that all paraesophageal hernias should be corrected electively, irrespective of symptoms, to prevent the development of complications. However, recent data suggest that observation of the asymptomatic patient, especially for those older than 65 years, may be the safest course (*Ann Surg.* 2002;236:492). Operative repair, which can be performed using either an abdominal or thoracic approach, consists in reduction of the hernia, resection of the sac, and closure of the hiatal defect. In type III hiatal hernias, the esophagus frequently is shortened, and thus a thoracic approach may be preferred.

6. **Paraesophageal hiatal hernias** are associated with a 60% incidence of GER. Furthermore, the operative dissection may lead to postoperative GER in previously asymptomatic patients. Therefore, an antireflux procedure should be performed at the time of hiatal hernia repair. A recent prospective, randomized trial showed that the addition of a biologic mesh to reinforce the crural repair resulted in a decreased recurrence at 6 months (*Ann Surg.* 2006;244:481). Biologic meshes are decellularized human or porcine tissues (subintestinal mucosa or dermis) that are used as hernia repair mesh. Use of Prolene or PTFE prosthetic mesh can lead to erosion into the esophagus (*Surg Endosc.* 2009;23:1219). Thus, if mesh is utilized, biologic mesh is favored in the current era.

II. GASTROESOPHAGEAL REFLUX

A. **Prevalence.** GER is a normal event after a meal and during belching. Symptoms of heartburn and excessive regurgitation are relatively common in the United States, occurring in approximately 7% of the population on a daily basis and in 33% at least once a month. Often, these individuals have x-ray evidence of a hiatal hernia with a portion of the stomach above the diaphragm. Reflux and hiatal hernia are not always related, and each can occur independently.

B. **Pathophysiology** in GER relates to abnormal exposure of the distal esophagus to refluxed stomach contents. In 60% of patients, a mechanically defective lower esophageal sphincter (LES) is responsible for the GER. The sphincter function of the LES depends on the integrated mechanical effect of the sphincter's intramural pressure and the length of esophagus exposed to intra-abdominal positive pressure. Other etiologies of GER are inefficient esophageal clearance of refluxed material, fixed gastric outlet obstruction, functional delayed gastric emptying, increased gastric acid secretion, and inappropriate relaxation of the LES.

C. The classic **symptom** of GER is posturally aggravated substernal or epigastric burning pain that is readily relieved by antacids. Additional common symptoms include regurgitation or effortless emesis, dysphagia, and excessive flatulence. Atypical symptoms may mimic laryngeal, respiratory, cardiac, biliary, pancreatic, gastric, or duodenal disease.

D. Diagnosis and evaluation

1. **Contrast radiography (upper GI)** demonstrates spontaneous reflux in only approximately 40% of patients with GER. However, it documents the presence or absence of hiatal hernia; can demonstrate some complications of reflux, such as esophageal stricture and ulcers; and is an appropriate initial study. The study should include a full view of the esophagus as well as a complete evaluation of the stomach, pylorus, and duodenum.

2. **EGD** is indicated in patients with symptoms of GER to evaluate for esophagitis and the presence of Barrett changes. **Esophagitis** is a pathologic diagnosis, but an experienced endoscopist can readily distinguish the more advanced stages. Four general grades of esophagitis occur.
   a. **Grade I:** normal or reddened mucosa
   b. **Grade II:** superficial mucosal erosions and some ulcerations
   c. **Grade III:** extensive ulceration with multiple, circumferential erosions with luminal narrowing; possible edematous islands of squamous mucosa present, producing the so-called cobblestone esophagitis
   d. **Grade IV:** fibrotic peptic stricture, shortened esophagus, columnar-lined esophagus.

3. **Esophageal manometric testing** is appropriate in the patient with reflux symptoms once surgery is being considered. Manometry defines the location and function of the LES and helps to exclude achalasia, scleroderma, and diffuse esophageal spasm from the differential diagnosis. Characteristics of a manometrically abnormal LES are (1) a pressure of less than 6 mm Hg, (2) an overall length of less than 2 cm, and (3) an abdominal length of less than 1 cm. These values are abnormal, and a patient with one or more of these abnormal values has a 90% probability of having reflux. Manometry also assesses the adequacy of esophageal contractility and peristaltic wave progression as a guide to the best antireflux procedure for the patient.

4. **Esophageal pH testing** over a 24-hour period is regarded as the gold standard in the diagnosis of GER. It is now used mainly when the data from the remainder of the evaluation are equivocal and diagnosis of reflux is in doubt. Twenty-four-hour pH testing can be performed on an outpatient or ambulatory basis: The patient has an event button to record symptoms and keep a diary of body position, timing of meals, and other activities. This allows correlation of symptoms with simultaneous esophageal pH alterations. A **DeMeester score** is derived based on the frequency of reflux episodes and the time required for the esophagus to clear the acid. The occurrences of low pH episodes are compared with patient recorded symptoms to determine symptomatic correlation of the acid reflux (*J Am Coll Surg.* 2010;210:345). Refluxing volume can also be recorded even if it is normal pH to measure symptom correlation with volume reflux.

5. A **gastric emptying study** can be useful in evaluating patients with reflux and symptoms of gastroparesis. It may be especially pertinent in patients considered for redo surgery when there is suspicion of vagus

nerve injury. Patients with gastroparesis may benefit from a pyloric drainage procedure (i.e., pyloroplasty or pyloromyotomy) in addition to an antireflux procedure.

E. **Complications.** Approximately 20% of patients with GER have complications, including esophagitis, stricture, or Barrett esophagus. Other, less common complications include acute or chronic bleeding and aspiration.

F. **Treatment**

1. **Medical treatment** aims to reduce the duration and amount of esophageal exposure to gastric contents and to minimize the effects on the esophageal mucosa.

   a. Patients are instructed to remain upright after meals, avoid postural maneuvers (bending, straining) that aggravate reflux, and sleep with the head of the bed elevated 6 to 8 inches. Patients are also encouraged to not lie down to sleep within an hour of eating.

   b. **Dietary alterations** are aimed at maximizing LES pressure, minimizing intragastric pressure, and decreasing stomach acidity. Patients are instructed to avoid fatty foods, alcohol, caffeine, chocolate, peppermint, and smoking and to eat smaller, more frequent meals. Obese patients are instructed to lose weight, avoid tight-fitting garments, and begin a regular exercise program. In addition, anticholinergics, calcium channel blockers, nitrates, beta-blockers, theophylline, alpha-blockers, and nonsteroidal anti-inflammatory medications may exacerbate reflux and should be replaced with other preparations or reduced in dose if possible.

   c. **Pharmacologic therapy** is indicated in patients who do not improve with postural or dietary measures. The goal is to lower gastric acidity or enhance esophageal and gastric clearing while increasing the LES resting pressure.

      (1) **Antacids** neutralize stomach acidity and thus raise intragastric pH.

      (2) **H$_2$-receptor antagonists** lower gastric acidity by decreasing the amount of acid that the stomach produces.

      (3) **Proton-pump inhibitors** act by selective noncompetitive inhibition of the H$^+$/K$^+$ pump on the parietal cell and are the standard therapy for erosive and non-erosive esophagitis (*J Clin Gastroenterol.* 2007;41:131).

      (4) **Prokinetic agents,** such as metoclopramide (dopaminergic antagonist), can decrease GER by increasing the LES tone and accelerating esophageal and gastric clearance.

   d. **Transoral endoscopic suturing** to plicate the GE junction and endoscopic application of **radiofrequency energy** (Stretta procedure) to the lower esophagus are two novel endoluminal therapies that can be performed on an ambulatory basis and generally with the patient under light sedation. These therapies, approved by the Food and Drug Administration, have been evaluated in several small, non–placebo-controlled trials with limited posttreatment evaluation. Studies have demonstrated improved quality of life over baseline but no difference compared to laparoscopic fundoplication. Freedom from acid suppression medication is lower than with laparoscopic fundoplication surgery. These options remain experimental and controversial.

2. **Surgical treatment** should be considered in patients who have symptomatic reflux, have manometric evidence of a defective LES, and fail to achieve relief with maximal medical management. Alternatively, surgical therapy should be considered in symptomatic patients who have achieved relief with medical therapy but to whom the prospect of a lifetime of medicine is undesirable (i.e., because of cost, side effects, inconvenience, or compliance). Surgical treatment consists of either a transabdominal or a transthoracic antireflux operation to reconstruct a competent LES and a crural repair to maintain the reconstruction in the abdomen.

   a. A **laparoscopic, transabdominal approach** is preferred in most patients, although the transthoracic approach may be beneficial in some patients with a shortened esophagus. A shortened esophagus should be suspected when a stricture is present and in patients who have had a failed antireflux procedure. The transabdominal approach is recommended for patients with a coexisting abdominal disorder, a prior thoracotomy, or severe respiratory disorder.

      (1) **Nissen fundoplication** is the most commonly performed procedure for GER. It consists of a 360-degree fundic wrap via open or laparoscopic technique. Long-term results in several series of open procedures are excellent, with 10-year freedom from recurrence of greater than 90%. Short-term results of the laparoscopic approach are as good as the open-repair results for relief of GER symptoms, with concomitant shorter hospital stay, better respiratory function, and decreased pain postoperatively (*Br J Surg.* 2004;91:975). The complete fundoplication in this repair is very effective at preventing reflux but is associated with a slightly higher incidence of inability to vomit, gas bloating of the stomach, and dysphagia. During surgery, care must be taken to ensure that the wrap is short, loose, and placed appropriately around the distal esophagus to minimize the incidence of these complications.

      (2) The **Hill posterior gastropexy** aims to anchor the GE junction posteriorly to the median arcuate ligament and creates a partial or 180-degree imbrication of the stomach around the right side of the intra-abdominal esophagus. In the original description, Hill recommended using intraesophageal manometry during placement of the sutures to achieve a pressure of 50 mm Hg in the distal esophagus.

      (3) The **Toupet fundoplication** is a partial 270-degree posterior wrap, with the wrapped segment sutured to the crural margins and to the anterolateral esophageal wall. For patients in whom esophageal peristalsis is documented to be markedly abnormal or absent preoperatively, a partial wrap has often been used to lessen the potential for postoperative dysphagia.

   b. A **transthoracic approach** is a reasonable alternative in patients with esophageal shortening or stricture, coexistent motor disorder, obesity, coexistent pulmonary lesion, or prior antireflux repair.

   (1) Nissen fundoplication can be done via a transthoracic approach, with results similar to those obtained with a transabdominal approach.

   (2) The **Belsey Mark IV repair** consists of a 240-degree fundic wrap around 4 cm of distal esophagus. In cases of esophageal neuromotor dysfunction, it produces less dysphagia than may accompany a 360-degree (Nissen) wrap. Furthermore, the ability to belch is preserved, thereby avoiding the gas-bloat syndrome that may occur after a complete wrap. The Belsey wrap can be completed with an open thoracotomy or thoracoscopically (*Surg Endosc.* 2003;17:1212).

   (3) Collis gastroplasty is a technique used to lengthen a shortened esophagus. To minimize tension on the antireflux repair, a gastric tube is formed from the upper lesser curvature of the stomach in continuity with the distal esophagus. The antireflux repair then is constructed around the gastroplasty tube. A gastroplasty should be considered preoperatively in patients with esophageal shortening, such as those with gross ulcerative esophagitis or stricture, failed prior antireflux procedure, or total intrathoracic stomach (*Surg Clin N Am.* 2005;85:433). However, in many of these patients, the esophagus can be adequately mobilized to allow more than 3 cm of intra-abdominal esophagus and thereby avoid the need to lengthen the esophagus. Development of an angled endoscopic stapler has made laparoscopic Collis gastroplasty technically feasible.

III. FUNCTIONAL ESOPHAGEAL DISORDERS comprise a diverse group of disorders involving esophageal skeletal or smooth muscle.

A. Motor disorders of esophageal skeletal muscle result in defective swallowing and aspiration. Potential causes can be classified into five major subgroups: neurogenic, myogenic, structural, iatrogenic, and mechanical. Most causes of oropharyngeal dysphagia are not correctable surgically. However, when manometric studies demonstrate that pharyngeal contractions, although weak, are still reasonably well coordinated, cricopharyngeal myotomy can provide relief.

B. Motor disorders of esophageal smooth muscle and LES can be subdivided into primary dysmotilities and disorders that involve the esophagus secondarily and produce dysmotility.

   1. Primary dysmotility

   a. Achalasia is rare (1/100,000 population) but is the most common primary esophageal motility disorder. It typically presents between the ages of 35 and 45 years. Chagas disease, caused by *Trypanosoma cruzi* and seen primarily in South America, can mimic achalasia and produce similar esophageal pathology. Achalasia is a disease of unknown etiology, characterized by loss of effective esophageal body peristalsis and failure of the LES to relax with swallowing, resulting in esophageal dilatation. LES pressure is often (but not invariably) elevated. The characteristic pathology is alteration in the ganglia of Auerbach plexus.

(1) **Symptoms** include progressive dysphagia, noted by essentially all patients; regurgitation immediately after meals (>70%); odynophagia (30%); and aspiration, with resultant bronchitis and pneumonia (10%). Some patients experience chest pain due to esophageal spasms.

(2) The **diagnosis** is suggested by a chest x-ray, which often shows a fluid-filled, dilated esophagus, and absence of a gastric air bubble. A **barium esophagogram** demonstrates tapering ("bird's beak") of the distal esophagus and a dilated proximal esophagus. The bird's-beak deformity is not specific for achalasia and can be seen in any process that narrows the distal esophagus (e.g., benign strictures or carcinoma). **Esophageal manometry** is the definitive diagnostic test for achalasia. Characteristic manometric findings include the absence of peristalsis, mirror-image contractions, and limited or absent relaxation of the LES with swallowing. Endoscopy should be performed to rule out benign strictures or malignancy, so-called pseudoachalasia.

(3) **Medical treatment** is aimed at decreasing the LES tone and includes nitrates, calcium channel blockers, and endoscopic injection of botulinum toxin (blocks acetylcholine release from nerve terminals) in the area of the LES but this is only beneficial in about 10% of patients.

(4) **Surgical treatment with a modified Heller esophagomyotomy** has been shown to produce excellent results in 90% to 98% of patients, using open or laparoscopic techniques (*J Thorac Cardiovasc Surg.* 2010;140:962). Many esophageal surgeons favor extending the myotomy onto the stomach to avoid a common cause of failure, an incomplete myotomy due to inadequate mobilization of the esophagogastric junction. A concomitant antireflux procedure with the esophagomyotomy helps avoid late stricture due to GER disease caused by the incompetent LES combined with the inability of the aperistaltic esophagus to evacuate refluxed material. **Laparoscopic esophagomyotomy** combined with a posterior 270-degree Toupet fundoplication or anterior 180-degree Dor fundoplication to limit postoperative reflux is currently the primary surgical approach (*J Clin Gastroenterol.* 2008;42:603–609).

b. *Vigorous achalasia* is a term used to describe a variant of achalasia in which patients present with the clinical and manometric features of classic achalasia and diffuse esophageal spasm. These patients have spastic pain and severe dysphagia, likely because of residual disordered peristalsis ineffective in overcoming the nonrelaxed LES. Treatment is the same as for classic achalasia, except that consideration should be given to performing a longer esophagomyotomy (to the aortic arch). With relief of the obstruction caused by the nonrelaxing LES, the pain usually disappears.

  c. **Diffuse esophageal spasm** is characterized by loss of the normal peristaltic coordination of the esophageal smooth muscle. This results in simultaneous contraction of segments of the esophageal body.

   (1) The primary **symptom** is severe spastic pain, which can occur spontaneously and at night. In addition, dysphagia, regurgitation, and weight loss are common.

   (2) The **diagnosis** is confirmed with esophageal manometry, which usually demonstrates spontaneous activity, repetitive waves, and prolonged, high-amplitude contractions. Characteristic broad, multipeaked contractions with or without propagation are seen, and normal peristaltic contractions also may be present. Intravenous injection with the parasympathomimetic bethanechol (Urecholine) can provoke pain and abnormal contractions.

   (3) **Treatment** with calcium channel blockers and nitrates can reduce the amplitude of the esophageal contractions but usually is not beneficial. Surgical treatment consists of a long esophagomyotomy, extending from the stomach to the aortic arch, and often a concomitant antireflux procedure.

  d. **Nutcracker esophagus** refers to a condition characterized manometrically by prolonged, high-amplitude peristaltic waves associated with chest pain that may mimic cardiac symptoms. Treatment with calcium channel blockers and long-acting nitrates has been helpful. Esophagomyotomy is of uncertain benefit.

  e. **Hypertensive LES** is characterized by an elevated basal pressure of the LES. In contrast to achalasia, the LES relaxes normally and the peristalsis of the esophagus is normal. However, in up to half of these patients, there is a degree of hypertensive contraction of the esophagus. Reduced compliance of the LES may result in dysphagia symptoms. Medical management consists of calcium channel blockers and nitrates although a myotomy may be indicated for refractory symptoms.

2. **Secondary dysmotility** represents the esophageal response to inflammatory injury or systemic disorders, such as scleroderma, multiple sclerosis, or diabetic neuropathy. Inflammation can produce fibrosis, which can lead to loss of peristalsis and esophageal contractility. The most common cause of secondary dysfunction is the reflux of gastric contents into the esophagus.

  a. **Progressive systemic sclerosis,** or scleroderma, produces esophageal manifestations in 60% to 80% of patients, and often the esophagus is the earliest site of GI involvement. It is characterized by atrophy of the smooth muscle of the distal esophagus, deposition of collagen in connective tissue, and subintimal arteriolar fibrosis. Normal contractions are present in the striated muscle of the proximal esophagus.

  b. In a subset of patients with severe long-standing GER disease, erosive esophagitis and stricture formation occur as a result of the combination of an incompetent LES and poor esophageal emptying secondary to low-amplitude, disordered peristaltic contractions. Intensive medical treatment of the reflux is essential before operation. Most surgeons prefer a Collis gastroplasty and a Belsey antireflux procedure for these patients because of the presence of esophageal shortening and impaired peristalsis.

IV. **ESOPHAGEAL STRICTURES** are either benign or malignant, and the distinction is critical. **Benign strictures** are either congenital or acquired.

A. **Congenital webs** are the only true congenital esophageal strictures. They represent a failure of appropriate canalization of the esophagus during development and can occur at any level. An imperforate web must be distinguished from a tracheoesophageal fistula, although a perforate web may not produce symptoms until feedings become solid.

B. **Acquired strictures**

1. **Esophageal rings** or **webs** occur at all levels in relation to the etiology of the webbing process. An example is **Schatzki ring,** which occurs in the lower esophagus at the junction of the squamous and columnar epithelium. A hiatal hernia is always present, and the etiology is presumed to be GER. Esophagitis is rarely present. Treatment generally consists of medical management of reflux with periodic dilation for symptoms of dysphagia.

2. **Strictures** of the esophagus can result from any esophageal injury, including chronic reflux, previous perforation, infection, or inflammation.

C. **Symptoms** associated with a stricture consist of progressive dysphagia to solid food and usually begin when the esophageal lumen narrows beyond 12 mm.

D. **Evaluation and treatment** of a stricture begins with the categorical **exclusion of malignancy.** The diagnosis usually is based on a barium swallow. Esophagoscopy is essential to assess the location, length, size, and distensibility of the stricture and to obtain appropriate biopsies or brushings. Because a peptic stricture secondary to reflux always occurs at the squamocolumnar junction, biopsy of the esophageal mucosa below a high stricture should demonstrate columnar mucosa. If squamous mucosa is found, the presumptive diagnosis of a malignant obstruction should be made, although strictures due to Crohn's disease, previous lye ingestion, or monilial esophagitis are among alternative diagnoses. Most strictures are amenable to **dilation,** and this relieves the symptoms. Attention is then directed at correcting the underlying etiology. **Resection** can be required for recurrent or persistent strictures or if malignancy cannot be ruled out.

V. **ESOPHAGEAL DIVERTICULA** are acquired conditions of the esophagus found primarily in adults. They are divided into traction and pulsion diverticula based on the pathophysiology that induced their formation.

A. A **pharyngoesophageal (or Zenker) diverticulum** is a pulsion diverticulum. It is the most common type of symptomatic diverticulum. **Symptoms** include progressive cervical dysphagia, cough on assuming a recumbent position, and spontaneous regurgitation of undigested food, leading to episodes of choking and aspiration. A hypertensive upper esophageal sphincter (UES) or uncoordinated pharyngeal contraction and opening of the UES results in increased pharyngeal intraluminal pressure. Herniation of the mucosa and submucosa results in this false diverticulum (not all layers of pharyngeal tissue present in diverticulum). **Diagnosis** with a barium swallow should prompt surgical correction with cricopharyngeal myotomy and diverticulectomy or suspension. **Endoscopic approaches** (i.e., stapling to produce a myotomy) have been reported with low recurrence rates (*Mayo Clin Proc.* 2010;85:719), although transcervical myotomy and diverticulectomy remain the treatment of choice.

B. A **traction or midesophageal or parabronchial diverticulum** occurs in conjunction with mediastinal granulomatous disease often due to histoplasmosis or tuberculosis. Symptoms are rare, but when they are present, they mandate operative excision of the diverticulum and adjacent inflammatory mass. On rare occasions, these diverticula present with chronic cough from an esophagobronchial fistula.

C. An **epiphrenic or pulsion diverticulum** can be located at almost every level but typically occurs in the **distal 10 cm** of the thoracic esophagus. Many patients are asymptomatic at the time of diagnosis, and in those who are symptomatic, it is difficult to determine whether the complaints stem from the diverticulum or from the underlying esophageal disorder.

1. The **diagnosis** is made with a **contrast esophagogram;** however, endoscopic examination and esophageal function studies are essential in defining the underlying pathophysiology. In advanced disease, the diagnosis can be confused with achalasia owing to the dependency of the diverticulum and the lateral displacement and narrowing of the GE junction.

2. **Operative treatment** is recommended for patients with progressive or incapacitating symptoms associated with abnormal esophageal peristalsis. Surgery consists of diverticulectomy or diverticulopexy, along with an extramucosal esophagomyotomy. The myotomy extends from the neck of the diverticulum down to the stomach. When the diverticulum is associated with a hiatal hernia and reflux, a concomitant nonobstructive antireflux procedure (Belsey Mark IV) is recommended. Any associated mechanical obstruction also must be corrected.

TRAUMATIC INJURY TO THE ESOPHAGUS

I. ESOPHAGEAL PERFORATION

A. Overall, perforation is associated with a 20% mortality rate. The **etiologies** may be broadly divided into intra- and extraluminal categories.

1. **Intraluminal causes**

a. **Instrumentation injuries** represent 75% of esophageal perforations and may occur during endoscopy, dilation, sclerosis of esophageal varices, transesophageal echocardiography, and tube passage. The most common sites are the anatomic sites of narrowing of the esophagus (e.g., at the cricopharyngeus and GE junction).

      b. Foreign bodies can cause acute perforation, or more commonly follow an indolent course with late abscess formation in the mediastinum or development of empyema.

      c. Ingested caustic substances, such as alkali chemicals, can produce coagulation necrosis of the esophagus.

      d. Cancer of the esophagus may lead to perforation.

      e. Barotrauma induced by external compression (e.g., Heimlich maneuver), forceful vomiting (Boerhaave syndrome), seizures, childbirth, or lifting can produce esophageal perforation. Almost all of these injuries occur in the distal esophagus on the left side.

  2. Extraluminal causes

      a. Penetrating injuries to the esophagus can occur from stab wounds or, more commonly, gunshot wounds.

      b. Blunt trauma may produce an esophageal perforation related to a rapid increase in intraluminal pressure or compression of the esophagus between the sternum and the spine.

      c. Operative injury to the esophagus during an unrelated procedure occurs infrequently but has been reported in association with thyroid resection, anterior cervical spine operations, proximal gastric vagotomy, pneumonectomy, and laparoscopic fundoplication procedures.

B. Esophageal perforations initially manifest with **dysphagia, pain,** and **fever** and progress to **leukocytosis, tachycardia, respiratory distress,** and **shock** if the perforation is left untreated. Cervical perforations may present with neck stiffness and subcutaneous emphysema, and an intrathoracic perforation should be suspected in patients with chest pain, subcutaneous emphysema, dyspnea, and a pleural effusion (right pleural effusion in proximal perforations, left effusion in distal perforations). Patients with intra-abdominal perforations usually present with **peritonitis.**

C. The **diagnosis** of esophageal perforation is suggested by pneumomediastinum, pleural effusion, pneumothorax, atelectasis, and soft-tissue emphysema on **chest x-ray** or mediastinal air and fluid on **computed tomography (CT) scan.** Rapid evaluation with water-soluble or dilute **barium contrast esophagography** is mandatory, although contrast studies carry a 10% false-negative rate for esophageal perforations. Because esophagoscopy is used primarily as an adjunctive study and can miss sizable perforations, any discoloration or submucosal hematoma should be considered highly suspicious for perforation after trauma to the posterior mediastinum. Whenever an esophageal perforation is suspected, diagnosis and treatment must be prompt because morbidity and mortality increase in direct proportion to the delay.

D. Principles of management include (1) adequate **drainage** of the leak, (2) intravenous **antibiotics,** (3) aggressive fluid **resuscitation,** (4) adequate **nutrition,** (5) **relief** of any distal obstruction, (6) **diversion** of enteric contents past the leak, and (7) **restoration** of GI integrity. Initially, patients are kept on nothing-by-mouth status, a nasogastric tube is placed carefully in the esophagus or stomach, and they receive intravenous hydration and broad-spectrum antibiotics.

E. **Definitive management** generally requires operative repair, although a carefully selected group of nontoxic patients with a locally contained perforation may be observed. Patients with an intramural perforation after endoscopic procedures or dilation have a characteristic radiographic finding of a thin collection of contrast material parallel to the esophageal lumen without spillage into the mediastinum. Management with a nasogastric tube and antibiotics almost always is successful in these patients.

1. **Cervical and upper thoracic perforations** usually are treated by cervical drainage alone or in combination with esophageal repair.

2. **Thoracic perforations** should be closed primarily and buttressed with healthy tissue, and the mediastinum should be drained widely. Even when perforations are more than 24 hours old, primary mucosal closure usually is possible. When primary closure is not possible, options include wide drainage alone or in conjunction with resection, or with exclusion and diversion in cases of severe traumatic injury to the esophagus.

3. **Abdominal esophageal perforations** typically result in peritonitis and require an upper abdominal midline incision to correct.

4. **Perforations associated with intrinsic esophageal disease** (e.g., carcinoma, hiatal hernia, or achalasia) require addressing the perforation as described previously and surgically correcting the associated esophageal disease concomitantly.

II. **CAUSTIC INGESTION.** Liquid alkali solutions (e.g., **Drano** and **Liquid-Plumr**) are responsible for most of the serious caustic esophageal and gastric injuries, producing coagulation necrosis in both organs. Acid ingestion is more likely to cause isolated gastric injury.

A. **Initial management** is directed at hemodynamic stabilization and evaluation of the airway and extent of injury.

1. **Airway compromise** can occur from burns of the epiglottis or larynx and may require tracheostomy.

2. **Fluid** resuscitation and broad-spectrum **antibiotics** should be instituted.

3. **Vomiting should not be induced,** but patients should be placed on nothing-by-mouth status and given an oral suction device.

4. Steroids are of no proven benefit.

B. **Evaluation** with water-soluble **contrast esophagography** and gentle **esophagoscopy** should be done early to assess the severity and extent of injury and to rule out esophageal perforation or gastric necrosis.

C. **Management**

1. Without perforation, management is supportive, with acute symptoms generally resolving over several days.

2. **Perforation, unrelenting pain,** or **persistent acidosis** mandate surgical intervention. A transabdominal approach is recommended to allow evaluation of the patient's stomach and distal esophagus. If it is necrotic, the involved portion of the patient's stomach and esophagus must be resected, and a cervical esophagostomy must be performed.

A feeding jejunostomy is placed for nutrition, and reconstruction is performed 90 or more days later.

3. Late problems include the development of **strictures** and an increased risk of **esophageal carcinoma** (1,000 times that of the general population).

ESOPHAGEAL TUMORS

I. BENIGN ESOPHAGEAL NEOPLASMS are rare, although probably many remain undetected. The most common lesions are mesenchymal tumors such as GI stromal tumors and leiomyomas, followed by polyps. Less common lesions include hemangioma and granular cell myoblastoma.

  A. Clinical features depend primarily on the location of the tumor within the esophagus. **Intraluminal** tumors, such as polyps, cause esophageal obstruction, and patients present with dysphagia, vomiting, and aspiration. **Intramural** tumors, such as leiomyomas, usually are asymptomatic, but if they are large enough, they can produce dysphagia or chest pain.

  B. Diagnosis usually involves a combination of barium swallow, esophagoscopy, and perhaps CT scanning or magnetic resonance (MR) scan studies.

  C. Treatment of all symptomatic or enlarging tumors is **surgical removal.** Intraluminal tumors can be removed successfully via endoscopy, but if they are large and vascular, they should be resected via thoracotomy and esophagostomy. Intramural tumors usually can be enucleated from the esophageal muscular wall without entering the mucosa. This is done via a video-assisted thoracoscopic or open thoracotomy approach. Laparoscopic resection may be appropriate for distal lesions.

II. BARRETT ESOPHAGUS is defined as a metaplastic transformation of esophageal mucosa resulting from chronic GER. Histologically, the metaplastic epithelium must demonstrate **intestinal-type metaplasia** characterized by the presence of goblet cells. The columnar epithelium of Barrett esophagus may replace the normal squamous epithelium circumferentially, or it may be asymmetric and irregular.

  A. Prevalence. Barrett esophagus is diagnosed in approximately 2% of all patients undergoing esophagoscopy and in 10% to 15% of patients with esophagitis. Autopsy studies suggest that the actual prevalence is much higher because many patients are asymptomatic and remain undiagnosed. Most patients diagnosed with Barrett esophagus are middle-aged white men.

  B. The **symptoms** of Barrett esophagus arise from long-standing gastric reflux. Approximately 50% of patients with endoscopically proven Barrett have associated heartburn, 75% have dysphagia, and 25% have bleeding (*Ann Surg.* 1983;198:554).

  C. Diagnosis. Barrett esophagus may be suggested on x-ray by the presence of a hiatal hernia (associated with 80% of cases of Barrett esophagus) with esophagitis and an esophageal stricture. Confirmation of the diagnosis requires endoscopy and careful correlation between the endoscopic and histologic appearances.

D. Complications

1. **Esophageal ulceration and stricture** are more likely to occur in patients with Barrett esophagus than in those with GER alone. This probably reflects the more severe nature of the GER in patients with Barrett esophagus.

   a. **Barrett ulcers** are distinctly different from the common erosions seen in esophagitis in that they penetrate the metaplastic columnar epithelium in a manner similar to that seen in gastric ulcers. They occur in up to 50% of patients with Barrett esophagus and, like gastric ulcers, can cause pain, bleed, obstruct, penetrate, and perforate.

   b. **A benign stricture** occurs in 30% to 50% of patients with Barrett esophagus. The stricture is located at the squamocolumnar junction, which may be found proximal to the GE junction. Strictures secondary to Barrett esophagus are located in the middle or upper esophagus, unlike the routine peptic strictures that usually occur in the distal esophagus.

2. **Dysplasia.** The metaplastic columnar epithelium of Barrett esophagus is prone to development of dysplasia that can be detected only by biopsy. Dysplasia is categorized as low or high grade, with high grade being pathologically indistinguishable from carcinoma *in situ.*

3. **Malignant degeneration** from benign to dysplastic to malignant epithelium has been demonstrated in Barrett esophagus. Low-grade dysplasia is present in 5% to 10% of patients with Barrett esophagus and can progress to high-grade dysplasia and malignancy.

4. **Adenocarcinomas** that arise within the esophagus above the normal GE junction are characteristic of malignant degeneration in Barrett esophagus. The risk of development of adenocarcinoma in Barrett esophagus is 50 to 100 times that of the general population. In several long-term series, the incidence of malignant degeneration in Barrett esophagus was estimated at between 1 in 50 and 1 in 400 patient-years of follow-up.

E. Treatment

1. Uncomplicated Barrett esophagus in **asymptomatic** patients requires no specific therapy, but endoscopic surveillance and biopsy should be performed at least annually. Neither medical nor surgical treatment of reflux has been demonstrated to reverse the columnar metaplasia of Barrett esophagus. However, elimination of reflux with an **antireflux procedure** may halt progression of the disease, heal ulceration, and prevent stricture formation.

2. Uncomplicated Barrett esophagus in **symptomatic** patients should be treated using the same principles that apply to patients with GER without Barrett esophagus. In addition, symptomatic patients should have annual surveillance endoscopy with biopsy. After laparoscopic antireflux surgery, patients with Barrett esophagus have symptomatic relief and reduction in medication use equivalent to non-Barrett patients. Absence of progression to high-grade dysplasia or adenocarcinoma suggests that laparoscopic surgery is an effective approach for the management of patients with Barrett esophagus (*Am J Surg.* 2003;186:6).

3. **Barrett ulcers** usually heal with medical therapy. Frequently, 8 weeks of treatment with an H_2-receptor antagonist or proton-pump inhibitor are necessary to achieve complete healing. Recurrence of ulcers is common after discontinuation of therapy. Ulcers that fail to heal despite 4 months of medical therapy are an indication for rebiopsy and antireflux surgery.

4. **Strictures** associated with Barrett esophagus are managed successfully with periodic esophageal dilation combined with medical management. Recurrent or persistent strictures warrant an antireflux operation combined with intraoperative stricture dilation. After surgery, several dilations can be required to maintain patency during the healing phase. Rarely, undilatable strictures require resection.

5. **Dysplasia** on biopsy of Barrett esophagus indicates that the patient is at risk for the development of adenocarcinoma.

    a. **Low-grade dysplasia** requires frequent (every 3 to 6 months) surveillance esophagoscopy and biopsy. Medical therapy for GER is recommended in these patients, even when asymptomatic.

    b. **High-grade dysplasia** is pathologically indistinguishable from carcinoma *in situ* and is an indication for esophagectomy. Patients who undergo esophagectomy for high-grade dysplasia have up to a 73% incidence of having a focus of invasive carcinoma present in the resected esophagus. Cure rates of nearly 100% can be expected in patients whose cancer is limited to the mucosa and who undergo esophagectomy. However, because of the morbidity and mortality associated with esophagectomy, other methods of treatment are emerging, such as radiofrequency ablation. A recent randomized, multicenter trial demonstrated the success of radiofrequency ablation of low-grade dysplasia and high-grade dysplasia Barrett's at rates of 90.5% and 81.0% compared to medical management control group dysplasia ablation rates of 22.7% and 19.0%, respectively (*N Engl J Med.* 2009;360:2277).

6. **Adenocarcinoma** in patients with Barrett esophagus is an indication for esophagogastrectomy. Early detection offers the best opportunity to improve survival after resection, which overall is 20% at 5 years.

III. ESOPHAGEAL CARCINOMA

A. **Epidemiology.** Carcinoma of the esophagus represents 1% of all cancers in the United States and causes 1.8% of cancer deaths. The two principal histologies are adenocarcinoma and squamous cell carcinoma.

1. **Risk factors** for squamous cell esophageal cancer include African American race, alcohol and cigarette use, tylosis, achalasia, caustic esophageal injury, Plummer–Vinson syndrome, nutritional deficiencies, and ingestion of nitrosamines and fungal toxins. Geographic location also represents a risk factor, likely as a result of local dietary customs, with a high incidence noted in certain areas of China, Western Kenya, South Africa, Iran, France, and Japan.

2. **Risk factors** for adenocarcinoma of the esophagus include white race, GER, Barrett esophagus, obesity, and cigarette smoking.

B. Pathology

1. **Squamous cell carcinoma** was previously the most common type of esophageal carcinoma. It tends to be multicentric and most frequently involves the middle third of the esophagus.

2. **Adenocarcinoma** now constitutes the majority of malignant esophageal tumors and is the carcinoma with the greatest rate of increase in the United States. It is less likely to be multicentric, but it typically exhibits extensive proximal and distal submucosal invasion. Adenocarcinoma most commonly involves the distal esophagus.

3. **Less common malignant esophageal tumors** include small-cell carcinoma, melanoma, leiomyosarcoma, lymphoma, and esophageal involvement by metastatic cancer.

C. Most patients with early-stage disease are asymptomatic or may have symptoms of reflux. Patients with esophageal cancer may complain of **dysphagia, odynophagia, and weight loss.** Symptoms that are suggestive of unresectability include hoarseness, abdominal pain, persistent back or bone pain, hiccups, and respiratory symptoms (cough or aspiration pneumonia suggesting possible esophagorespiratory fistula). Approximately 50% of presenting patients have unresectable lesions or distant metastasis, which is largely responsible for the generally poor prognosis.

D. The **diagnosis** is suggested by a barium swallow and confirmed with esophagoscopy and biopsy or brush cytology.

E. **Staging.** A system for staging esophageal cancer allows assignment of patients to groups with similar prognosis, helps to determine if local or systemic therapy is needed, and allows comparison of response to different types of therapy. In recently updated staging (*Cancer.* 2010;116:3763), esophageal adenocarcinoma and squamous cell carcinoma are staged differently with squamous cell carcinoma having additional variable of anatomical location. (Table 8-1). Evaluation for lymph node and distant-organ metastatic disease is performed by combined positron emission tomographic and CT scanning. Endoscopic ultrasonography is more accurate than radiographic studies for determining the depth of wall invasion and the involvement of peritumoral lymph nodes. Upper esophageal and midesophageal lesions require bronchoscopy to evaluate the airway for involvement by tumor.

F. Treatment

1. **Surgical resection** remains a mainstay of curative treatment of patients with localized disease. It offers the best opportunity for cure and provides substantial palliation when cure is not possible. The overall 5-year survival rate is 19% to 32%, with higher rates for patients with lower stages of disease (*Ann Thorac Surg.* 2006;82:1073–1077).

   a. **Options for resection** include a standard transthoracic esophagectomy, a transhiatal esophagectomy, or an *en bloc* esophagectomy. Total esophagectomy with a cervical esophagogastric anastomosis and subtotal resection with a high intrathoracic anastomosis have become the most common resections and produce the best long-term functional results as well as the best chance for cure.

TABLE 8-1	TNM (Tumor, Node, Metastasis) Staging System for Esophageal Cancer

Definition of TNM

T: Primary Tumor

Tis	Carcinoma *in situ*/high-grade dysplasia
T1	Tumor invades the submucosa
T2	Tumor invades the muscularis propria
T3	Tumor invades adventitia
T4	Tumor invades adjacent structures
T4a Pleura, pericardium, diaphragm, or adjacent peritoneum	
T4b Other adjacent structures, e.g., aorta, cerebral body, trachea	

N: Regional Lymph Nodes

N0	No regional node metastasis
N1	1–2 regional lymph nodes
N2	3–6 regional lymph nodes
	N3 >6 regional lymph nodes

M: Distant Metastasis

M0	No distant metastasis
M1	Distant metastasis

G: Histologic Grade

GX: Grade cannot be assessed— stage grouping as G1
G1: Well differentiated
G2: Moderately differentiated
G3: Poorly differentiated
G4: Undifferentiated—stage grouping as G3 squamous

Adenocarcinoma Stage Grouping

Stage	T	N	M	G
0	Tis	0	0	1
IA	1	0	0	1–2
IB	1	0	0	3
	2	0	0	1–2
IIA	2	0	0	3
IIB	3	0	0	Any
	1–2	1	0	Any
IIIA	1–2	2	0	Any
	3	1	0	Any
	4a	0	0	Any
IIIB	3	2	0	Any
IIIC	4a	1–s2	0	Any
	4b	Any	0	Any
	Any	3	0	Any
IV	Any	Any	M1	Any

(continued)

TABLE 8-1	TNM (Tumor, Node, Metastasis) Staging System for Esophageal Cancer (Continued)

Squamous Cell Carcinoma Stage Grouping

Stage	T	N	M	G	Location
0	Tis	0	0	1	Any
IA	1	0	0	1	Any
IB	1	0	0	2–3	Any
IIA	2–3	0	0	1	Lower
IIB	2–3	0	0	1	Upper, middle
IIIA	2–3	0	0	2–3	Lower
IIIB	2–3	0	0	2–3	Upper, middle
IIIC	1–2	1	0	Any	Any
IV	1–2	2	0	Any	Any
	3	1	0	Any	Any
	4a	0	0	Any	Any
	3	2	0	Any	Any
	4a	1–2	0	Any	Any
	4b	Any	0	Any	Any
	Any	3	0	Any	Any
	Any	Any	1	Any	Any

Adapted from Rice TW, Rusch V, Ishwaran H, et al. Cancer of the esophagus and esophagogastric junction. *Cancer.* 2010;116:3763.

Esophagogastrectomy with anastomosis to the distal half of the esophagus is seldom used because troublesome postoperative reflux is common.

b. **Options for esophageal replacement** include the stomach, colon, and jejunum.

2. **Neoadjuvant therapy** with preoperative chemotherapy or chemoradiotherapy has been evaluated in a number of trials. Although it may enhance local control and resectability, the survival benefit is still debated. A recent prospective, randomized study demonstrated a survival advantage of trimodal neoadjuvant chemotherapy (cisplatin and fluorouracil) and radiation (50.4 Gy) followed by surgery versus surgery alone. Although the study only had 30 patients in the trimodal arm and 36 patients in the surgery alone arm, there was a 5-year survival advantage of 39% for trimodal therapy versus 16% for surgery alone (*J Clin Oncol.* 2008;26:1086).

3. **Radiotherapy** is used worldwide for attempted cure and palliation of patients with squamous cell esophageal cancer deemed unsuitable for resection. The 5-year survival rate is 5% to 10%. Palliation of dysphagia is successful temporarily in 80% of patients but rarely provides relief for longer than several months. Combination therapy involving radiation and concurrent administration of 5-fluorouracil with mitomycin C or cisplatin has been suggested to improve results and has replaced radiation alone in most protocols.

4. The goal of **palliative treatment** is the relief of obstruction and dysphagia.

  a. **Radiotherapy and chemotherapy** work best in patients with squamous cell carcinoma, particularly when it is located above the carina. Adenocarcinoma is less responsive to radiation, and the acute morbidity (nausea and vomiting) of external-beam irradiation of the epigastric area is substantial.

  b. **Esophageal bypass procedures** have been largely abandoned due to excessive complication rates.

  c. **Intraluminal prostheses** have been developed to intubate the esophagus and stent the obstruction. Self-expanding wire-mesh stents, often with a soft silicone (Silastic) coating, have been used with greater ease of insertion and satisfactory results. None of these prostheses allows normal swallowing, and in most cases no more than a pureed diet can be tolerated. Potential complications include perforation, erosion or migration of the stent, and obstruction of the tube by food or proximal tumor growth.

  d. **Endoscopic laser techniques** can restore an esophageal lumen successfully 90% of the time, with only a 4% to 5% perforation rate.

IV. COMPLICATIONS OF ESOPHAGEAL SURGERY. Esophageal surgery is fraught with potential complications, and consistently good results require meticulous attention to operative technique.

  A. **Postthoracotomy complications** can include atelectasis and respiratory insufficiency, pneumonia, wound infections, and persistent postoperative pain. Post-esophagectomy atrial fibrillation is particularly common at 17% (*J Thorac Cardiovasc Surg.* 2004;127:629).

  B. Complications related to an esophageal anastomosis consist primarily of leaks and strictures.

  1. Management of an **anastomotic leak** is based on the size of the leak, the location of the anastomosis, and the clinical status of the patient.

  a. A **cervical** anastomotic leak usually can be managed by opening the incision to allow drainage. Occasionally, the leak tracks below the thoracic inlet into the mediastinum, necessitating wider debridement and drainage. If a major leak occurs, esophagoscopy should be performed to rule out a significant ischemic injury to the stomach. If present, the anastomosis should be taken down and a cervical esophagostomy should be performed. The necrotic portion of the stomach should be resected, and the remaining stomach should be returned to the abdomen, with placement of a gastrostomy and feeding jejunostomy.

  b. **Intrathoracic** anastomotic leaks are associated with a high mortality rate. Small, well-drained leaks can be treated conservatively, but large or poorly drained leaks require operative exploration.

  2. **Strictures** usually are the result of a healed anastomotic leak, relative ischemia of the anastomosis, or recurrent cancer. Most can be dilated successfully.

C. **Complications of antireflux repairs** generally result from **preoperative** failure to recognize a confounding abnormality, such as poor gastric emptying or weak esophageal peristalsis, or **operative** miscalculations that result in too tight a fundoplication or excessive tension on the repair. Most of these complications require operative revision.

1. **Postoperative dysphagia** can result from a fundoplication that is too long or tight, a misplaced or slipped fundoplication that is positioned around the stomach rather than the distal esophagus, or a complete fundoplication in the setting of poor esophageal contractile function. It also can result from operative distortion of the GE junction, excessive narrowing of the diaphragmatic hiatus, or disruption of the crural closure and herniation of an intact repair into the chest.

2. **Persistent or recurrent reflux** after surgery suggests an inadequate or misplaced fundoplication, disruption of the fundoplication, or herniation of the repair into the chest.

3. **Breakdown of an antireflux repair** usually is recognized by a gradual recurrence of symptoms and can be confirmed by a contrast esophagram. Most commonly, disruption of a repair is due to inadequate mobilization of the cardia and excessive tension on the repair.

4. **Gas bloating** or gastric dilation secondary to swallowed air can occur if the fundoplication is too tight or if there is unrecognized gastric outlet obstruction or delayed gastric emptying.

Stomach

Fabian M. Johnston, J. Esteban Varela, and
William G. Hawkins

ANATOMY AND PHYSIOLOGY

The principal role of the stomach is to store and prepare ingested food for digestion and absorption through a variety of motor and secretory functions. The stomach can be divided into five regions based on external landmarks: the **cardia,** the region just distal to the gastroesophageal (GE) junction; the **fundus,** the portion of the stomach above and to the left of the GE junction; the **body,** or **corpus,** the largest portion of the stomach; the **antrum,** the distal 25% to 30% of the stomach, located between the incisura angularis and the pylorus; and the **pylorus,** a thickened ring of smooth muscle forming the distal boundary of the stomach. The arterial blood supply to the lesser curvature of the stomach is from the **left gastric** artery, a branch of the celiac axis, and the **right gastric** artery, a branch of the common hepatic artery. The greater curvature is supplied by the **short gastric** and **left gastroepiploic** arteries, branches of the splenic artery, and the **right gastroepiploic** artery, a branch of the gastroduodenal artery. Venous drainage of the stomach parallels arterial supply, with the left gastric (coronary) and right gastric veins draining into the portal vein, the left gastroepiploic vein draining into the splenic vein, and the right gastroepiploic draining into the superior mesenteric vein. The principal innervation to the stomach is derived from the right and left vagal trunks.

DISORDERS OF THE STOMACH

I. **PEPTIC ULCER DISEASE (PUD)** represents a spectrum of disease characterized by ulceration of the stomach or proximal duodenum due to an imbalance between acid secretion and mucosal defense mechanisms.

A. **Epidemiology.** In the United States, there are approximately 500,000 new cases of PUD each year, with an annual incidence of 1% to 2% and lifetime prevalence between 8% and 14%. Although there has been a steady decline in the incidence of PUD since the 1960s, ulcer-related mortality remains approximately 10,000 cases annually.

B. **Location.** The location of peptic ulcers can differ but generally duodenal ulcers are located at the antral–pylorus junction. Gastric ulcers usually fall within one of five categories (Modified Johnson Classification).

1. Type 1. Lesser curvature 60% to 70%, associated with low mucosal protection.

2. Type 2. Lesser curvature and duodenal 15%, associated with high acid secretion.

3. Type 3. Prepyloric 20%, associated with high acid secretion.

4. Type 4. Proximal stomach/cardia, associated with low mucosal protection.

5. Type 5. Anywhere in stomach, medication induced.

C. **Pathogenesis.** Four etiologic factors are responsible for the vast majority of PUD.

1. *Helicobacter pylori (H. pylori)* **infection** is associated with 90% to 95% of duodenal ulcers and 70% to 90% of gastric ulcers. Infection produces chronic antral gastritis, increased acid and gastrin secretion, and decreased mucosal resistance to acid.

2. **Nonsteroidal anti-inflammatory drug (NSAID)** use confers an eightfold increase in risk of duodenal ulcers and a 40-fold increase in risk of gastric ulcers due to suppression of prostaglandin production. Dose-dependent relationship, ulcers do not recur when NSAID discontinued.

3. **Cigarette smoking** (*J Clin Gastro.* 1997;25:1)

4. **Acid hypersecretion** occurs in the majority of patients with duodenal ulcers.

D. **Presentation** in uncomplicated ulcer disease is usually burning, gnawing intermittent epigastric pain that is relieved by food or antacid ingestion for duodenal ulcers but exacerbated by intake for gastric ulcers. Pain may be accompanied by nausea, vomiting, and mild weight loss. **Differential diagnosis** is broad and includes GE reflux disease, biliary colic and related biliary tract disease, inflammatory and neoplastic pancreatic disease, and gastric neoplasms. In later stages, ulcers may present with bleeding, perforation, and obstruction.

E. **Diagnosis** can be made by barium contrast radiography or upper gastrointestinal (GI) endoscopy. **Esophagogastroduodenoscopy (EGD)** is more sensitive and specific than contrast examination for PUD. In addition, EGD offers therapeutic options (ligation of bleeding vessels) and diagnostic options (biopsy for malignancy, antral biopsy for *H. pylori*). Once the diagnosis of PUD is confirmed, further testing should be carried out to determine its etiology.

1. *H. pylori* **infection** can be detected noninvasively by radiolabeled **urea breath test** or **serologic antibody testing.** Antral tissue obtained during endoscopy can be subjected to direct **histologic examination** or rapid urease testing using the **cod liver oil (CLO) test.**

2. **Fasting serum gastrin levels** should be obtained in patients who have no history of NSAID use and are *H. pylori*-negative or who have recurrent ulcers despite adequate treatment, multiple ulcers, ulcers in unusual locations (i.e., second/third portions of the duodenum and small bowel), or complicated PUD (hemorrhage, perforation, obstruction). Such atypical presentations suggest the possibility of **Zollinger–Ellison syndrome,** a rare entity causing PUD in 0.1% to 1% of patients.

3. **Endoscopic biopsy of gastric** ulcers is mandatory to exclude malignancy if symptoms or signs (weight loss, anemia, obstructions), or appearance of ulcer (associated mass, folds around ulcer) are present. Multiple biopsies are necessary to exclude malignancy.

F. **Treatment** of PUD has changed dramatically with the development of antisecretory drugs [histamine$_2$-receptor blockers and proton-pump inhibitors (PPIs)], and *H. pylori*-eradication regimens greatly diminishing the role of elective surgery for PUD. Equally important is lifestyle modification.

1. **Medical therapy**
   a. ***H. pylori* eradication** is the cornerstone of medical therapy for PUD. Regimens typically consist of an acid-reducing medication (PPI, H2 blocker, bismuth salicylates) combined with two antibiotics administered for 10 to 14 days (triple therapy). These regimens are 85% to 90% effective in eradicating *H. pylori*. Antisecretory therapy is then continued until ulcer healing is complete.
   b. **NSAID-associated PUD** is treated by discontinuing the offending medication and initiating antisecretory therapy. If the NSAID must be continued, PPIs are most effective for facilitating ulcer healing.
   c. **Smoking cessation** greatly facilitates ulcer healing, but compliance rates are low.
   d. **Follow-up endoscopy** to ensure healing is essential for gastric ulcers because up to 3% harbor malignancy.
2. **Surgical therapy** for uncomplicated PUD is exceedingly rare. Indications for elective operation for PUD include bleeding (acute/chronic), perforation, obstruction, failure of medical therapy (intractability), and inability to exclude malignancy.
   a. **Duodenal ulcers** are treated by one of three acid-reducing operations: (1) truncal vagotomy with pyloroplasty, (2) truncal vagotomy with antrectomy and Billroth I (gastroduodenostomy) or Billroth II (gastrojejunostomy) reconstruction, or (3) highly selective vagotomy (HSV). Truncal vagotomy with antrectomy yields maximal acid suppression with lowest ulcer recurrence rates (1% to 2%) but carries the highest postoperative morbidity (15% to 30%) and mortality (1% to 2%) rates. HSV has the lowest postoperative morbidity (3% to 8%) and mortality rates but is technically demanding to perform and has higher recurrence rates (5% to 15%).
   b. **Gastric ulcers** are typically treated with either wedge excision or antrectomy with inclusion of the ulcer, depending on ulcer location. Concurrent acid-reducing operation is reserved for acid hypersecreting patients (type II and III) or patients who are known to have refractory ulcer disease despite maximal medical management; this is rare today.

II. **COMPLICATED PEPTIC ULCER DISEASE** refers to PUD complicated by hemorrhage, perforation, or obstruction. These complications represent the most common indications for surgery in PUD. Although there has been a sharp decline in elective surgery for PUD, the rates of emergency surgery for complicated PUD have been stable over time.

A. **Hemorrhage** is the leading cause of death due to PUD, with associated 5% to 10% mortality. Evaluation and management begin with aggressive resuscitation and correction of any coagulopathy, followed by EGD. Although spontaneous cessation of bleeding occurs in 70% of patients, endoscopic therapy using thermal coagulation with or without epine-phrine is warranted in individuals who present with hemodynamic insta-bility, need for continuing transfusion, hematemesis or red stool, older than 60 years, and serious medical comorbidities, because these patients have a higher risk of recurrent bleeding. Endoscopic findings are impor-tant to note and can stratify the risk of rebleeding when noted. Risk of rebleeding increases with fresh or old clot, visible bleeding, visible vessel, or active bleeding in ascending order. **Indications for surgery** include repeated episodes of bleeding, continued hemodynamic instability, ongoing transfusion requirement of more than 4 to 6 units of packed red blood cells over 24 hours, and more than one unsuccessful endoscopic intervention.

1. **Bleeding duodenal ulcers** are usually located on the posterior duo-denal wall within 2 cm of the pylorus and typically erode into the gastroduodenal artery. Bleeding is controlled by duodenotomy and three-point ligation of the bleeding vessels. In hemodynamically sta-ble patients, consideration should be made for a concomitant acid-reducing procedure for those who have failed or are noncompliant with medical therapy. Postoperative *H. pylori* eradication is important to reduce the risk of recurrent bleeding.

2. **Bleeding gastric ulcers** present a diverse challenge because the patient's condition, comorbidities, and previous ulcer and medication history all play a role in surgical decision making. In unstable patients, biopsy followed by oversewing or wedge excision of the ulcer is gen-erally preferred. Stable patients are candidates for an acid reduction surgery such as antrectomy and vagotomy.

B. **Perforated peptic ulcer** typically presents with sudden onset of severe abdominal pain but may be less dramatic, particularly in hospitalized, eld-erly, and immunocompromised patients. The resulting peritonitis is often generalized but can be localized when the perforation is walled off by adja-cent viscera and structures. Examination reveals fever, tachycardia, and abdominal wall rigidity, and laboratory evaluation typically demonstrates leukocytosis. Abdominal X-ray reveals free subdiaphragmatic gas in 80% to 85% of cases. Aggressive fluid resuscitation and broad-spectrum antibi-otics followed by prompt operative repair are indicated in the vast majority of patients with perforated PUD. **Nonoperative treatment of perforated duodenal ulcer** can be considered in poor operative candidates in whom the perforation has been present for more than 24 hours, the pain is well localized, and there is no evidence of ongoing extravasation on upper GI water-soluble contrast studies (*Dig Surg.* 2010;27:161).

1. **Perforated duodenal ulcers** are best managed by simple omental patching and peritoneal debridement, followed by *H. pylori* eradica-tion. An acid-reducing procedure (preferably truncal vagotomy and pyloroplasty) should be added in stable patients who are known to be *H. pylori*-negative or have failed medical therapy.

2. **Perforated gastric ulcers** are best treated by simple wedge resection to eliminate the perforation and exclude malignancy. If wedge resection

of the ulcer cannot be performed due to its juxtapyloric location, multiple biopsies of the ulcer are taken and omental patching is performed.

C. **Gastric outlet obstruction** can occur as a chronic process due to fibrosis and scarring of the pylorus from chronic ulcer disease or as a consequence of acute inflammation superimposed on previous scarring of the gastric outlet. In general, gastric outlet obstruction secondary to PUD has become exceedingly rare with modern medical antisecretory therapy. Patients present with recurrent vomiting of poorly digested food, dehydration, and hypochloremic hypokalemic metabolic alkalosis. Management consists in correction of volume and electrolyte abnormalities, nasogastric suction, and intravenous antisecretory agents. EGD is necessary for evaluating the nature of the obstruction and for ruling out malignant etiology, and **endoscopic hydrostatic balloon dilation** can be performed at the same time. This is feasible in up to 85% of patients, but fewer than 40% have sustained improvement at 3 months (*Gastrointest Endosc.* 1996;43:98). **Indications for surgical therapy** include persistent obstruction after 7 days of nonoperative management and recurrent obstruction. Antrectomy to include the ulcer and truncal vagotomy is the ideal operation for most patients. In exceptional instances, truncal vagotomy with gastrojejunostomy may be preferred in those patients whose pyloroduodenal inflammation precludes safe management with Billroth I or II reconstructions.

III. **GASTRIC ADENOCARCINOMA** is the second most common cancer worldwide and the 10th most common malignancy in the United States. Its incidence has decreased dramatically over the last 60 years, perhaps secondary to improvements in refrigeration and diet. In addition, the anatomic pattern of gastric cancer is changing, with proximal or cardia cancers comprising a greater proportion of gastric cancers. Approximately one-third of gastric cancers are metastatic at presentation. The overall 5-year survival rate is 15%.

A. The **etiology** of gastric cancer is complex and multifactorial, involving a combination of genetic, environmental, and infectious risk factors. **Risk factors** for gastric cancer include male gender; family history; low socioeconomic status; polyposis syndromes; diets high in nitrates or salts, or pickled foods; adenomatous gastric polyps; previous gastric resection; Ménétrier disease; smoking; *H. pylori* infection; and chronic gastritis. Aspirin, fresh fruits and vegetables, selenium, and vitamin C may be protective against the development of gastric cancer.

B. **Classification.** Ninety-five percent of gastric cancers are adenocarcinomas arising from mucus-producing cells in the gastric mucosa. The **Lauren classification** system is most widely used and divides gastric cancers into two subtypes:

1. **Intestinal-type cancers** (30%) are glandular and arise from the gastric mucosa. Occurring more commonly in elderly men and in the distal stomach, they are associated with *H. pylori* and other environmental exposures that lead to chronic gastritis, intestinal metaplasia, and dysplasia. Hematogenous spread metastatic spread to distant organs is seen.

2. **Diffuse-type cancers** (70%) arise from the lamina propria and are associated with an invasive growth pattern with rapid submucosal spread. They occur more commonly in younger patients, females, and in the proximal stomach. Transmural and lymphatic spread with early metastases are more common, and diffuse-type cancers have worse overall prognosis.

C. **Presentation** of gastric cancer generally involves nonspecific signs and symptoms such as epigastric abdominal pain, unexplained weight loss, nausea, vomiting, anorexia, early satiety, and fatigue. Dysphagia is associated with proximal gastric cancers, whereas gastric outlet obstruction is more typical of distal cancers. Perforation and upper GI bleeding are the presenting manifestations in a minority of patients (1% to 4%) and generally portend advanced disease with poor prognosis. Classic physical findings in gastric cancer represent metastatic and incurable disease and include the following:

1. Enlarged supraclavicular nodes (Virchow's node).
2. Infiltration of the umbilicus (Sister Mary Joseph's node).
3. Fullness in the pelvic cul-de-sac (Blumer's shelf).
4. Enlarged ovaries on pelvic examination (Krukenberg's tumor).
5. Hepatosplenomegaly with ascites and jaundice.
6. Cachexia.

D. **Diagnosis** can be made by double-contrast upper GI barium contrast studies or by **EGD.** Endoscopy is generally the diagnostic method of choice because it permits direct visualization and multiple biopsies (≥7) of suspicious lesions. **Screening examination** by endoscopy or contrast studies is not cost-effective for the general US population, given the low incidence, but may be warranted in high-risk individuals, such as patients more than 20 years post-partial gastrectomy, patients with pernicious anemia or atrophic gastritis, immigrants from endemic areas (Russia, Asia), and patients with familial or hereditary gastric cancer. Mass screening in Japan, a country with a high incidence of gastric cancer, resulted in an increase in the detection of gastric cancer confined to mucosa and led to improvements in 5-year survival rates.

E. **Staging** is important in determining prognosis and appropriate treatment. The American Joint Committee on Cancer and International Union against Cancer (AJCC/UICC) jointly developed a staging system that is most widely used worldwide (Table 9-1). Once the diagnosis of gastric cancer is established, **computed tomography (CT) and endoscopic ultrasonography (EUS)** are the primary modalities employed for staging.

1. **CT scan of the abdomen and pelvis** is the best noninvasive modality for detecting metastatic disease in the form of malignant ascites or hematogenous spread to distant organs, most commonly the liver. Overall accuracy for tumor staging is 60% to 80% depending on the protocol used, but accuracy for determining nodal involvement is more limited and variable.

| TABLE 9-1 | TNM (Tumor, Node, Metastasis) Staging of Gastric Cancer |

T: Primary Tumor

T0	No evidence of primary tumor
Tis	Carcinoma *in situ*
T1	Invasion of lamina propria or submucosa
T2	Invasion of muscularis propria or subserosa
T3	Penetration of serosa
T4	Invasion of adjacent structures

N: Regional Lymph Nodes

N0	No regional node metastasis
N1	Involved perigastric nodes within 3 cm of tumor
N2	Involved perigastric nodes >3 cm from tumor edge or involvement of left gastric, splenic, celiac, or hepatic nodes

M: Distant Metastasis

M0	No distant metastases
M1	Distant metastases present

Stage Grouping			
Stage 0	Tis	N0	M0
Stage IA	T1	N0	M0
Stage IB	T1	N1	M0
	T2	N0	M0
Stage II	T1	N2	M0
	T2	N1	M0
	T3	N0	M0
Stage IIIA	T2	N2	M0
	T3	N1	M0
	T4	N0	M0
Stage IIIB	T3	N2	M0
	T4	N1	M0
Stage IV	T4	N2	M0
	Any T	Any N	Any M1

Adapted with permission from Fleming ID, Cooper JS, Henson DE, et al., eds. *AJCC Cancer Staging Manual,* 5th ed. Philadelphia: Lippincott Williams & Wilkins; 1998.

2. **EUS** adds to the preoperative evaluation of gastric cancer in several ways. It is superior to CT in delineating the depth of tumor invasion in the gastric wall and adjacent structures and identifying perigastric lymphadenopathy. EUS is the most accurate method available for T staging of gastric cancer, and accuracy for N staging approaches 70%. Addition of fine needle aspiration (FNA) of suspicious nodes increases accuracy even further and brings specificity to near 100%.

3. **Positron emission tomography (PET)/CT** combines the spatial resolution of CT with the contrast resolution of PET. It is most useful for its specificity in detecting nodal and distant metastatic disease not apparent on CT scan alone. Preliminary studies suggest that the use of PET/CT in staging patients with gastric cancer leads to upstaging in 6% and downstaging in 9% of patients.

4. **Laparoscopy** significantly enhances the accuracy of staging in patients with gastric cancer. Routine use of laparoscopy has been shown to detect small-volume peritoneal and liver metastases in 20% to 30% of patients believed to have locoregional disease, thereby avoiding unnecessary laparotomy in these patients (*J Gastro Liv Dis.* 2009;18:189; *J Minim Access Surg.* 2010;6:111). Although laparoscopic ultrasound enhances the accuracy of staging in other GI cancers, its role in gastric cancer awaits further study. Laparoscopy is not indicated in patients with T1 and T2 lesions, given the low incidence of metastases with these tumors (*J Am Coll Surg.* 2003;196:965).

F. **Treatment. Surgery** is the mainstay of curative therapy in the absence of disseminated disease.

1. **Extent of surgical resection** generally involves a wide resection to achieve negative margins with *en bloc* resection of lymph nodes and any structures involved by local invasion. In general, gross margins of 6 cm, confirmed to be negative intraoperatively with frozen section, are usually required to ensure microscopically negative margins on final histologic analysis.

    a. **Proximal tumors** of the stomach comprise up to half of all gastric cancers and can be resected by total gastrectomy or proximal subtotal gastrectomy. Total gastrectomy with Roux-en-Y esophagojejunostomy is generally the preferred option to avoid postoperative morbidity of reflux esophagitis and impaired gastric emptying associated with proximal subtotal gastrectomy. Tumors of the GE junction may require esophagogastrectomy with cervical or thoracic anastomosis.

    b. **Midbody tumors** comprise 15% to 30% of tumors and generally require total gastrectomy to achieve adequate margins.

    c. **Distal tumors** may be resected by distal subtotal gastrectomy or total gastrectomy with no difference in overall survival (*Ann Surg.* 1989;209:162; *Ann Surg.* 1994;220:176). However, nutritional status and quality of life are superior following subtotal gastrectomy, making it the preferred option when adequate margins can be obtained while maintaining an adequate gastric remnant (*Ann Surg.* 1997;226:613; *Ann Surg.* 2005;241:232).

    d. Early gastric cancers, defined as tumors confined to the mucosa, have limited propensity for lymph node metastasis and may be treated by limited gastric resections or **endoscopic mucosal resection.** Experience outside of Japan with early gastric cancers is limited.

    e. Laparoscopic gastric resections have been reported for the treatment of gastric cancer, with advantages of reduced pain, shorter hospitalization, and improved quality of life. Long-term outcome with respect to cancer recurrence awaits further study in a randomized, controlled fashion (*Ann R Coll Surg Engl.* 2010;92).

2. **Extent of lymphadenectomy** has long been a controversial issue in the surgical management of gastric cancer. Early retrospective Japanese studies showed improved survival with radical lymph node dissections. A standard (D1) lymphadenectomy entails removal of perigastric nodes, whereas an extended (D2) resection includes removal of nodes along the left gastric, hepatic, splenic, and celiac arteries. Although the results of major trials attempting to answer this question have yielded confounding results, it is generally agreed on that, at high-volume centers, D2 lymphadenectomies that preserve the distal pancreas and spleen can be performed without increased morbidity, and improves staging accuracy. D2 resection may yield a survival advantage in selected patients with stage II and III gastric cancers but available data are not convincing (*Am J Surg.* 2009;197:246; *Lancet Oncol.* 2010;11:439).

3. **Adjuvant therapy** for gastric cancer is important because the majority of patients with locoregional disease (all patients except those with T1–2N0M0 disease) are at high risk for local or systemic recurrence following curative surgery.

    a. Adjuvant combined modality therapy. Although adjuvant chemotherapy or radiation therapy alone has not shown much benefit in studies, recent trials have been able to demonstrate significant improvement in overall and disease-free survival rates in patients with resected gastric cancer treated postoperatively with 5-fluorouracil (5-FU)/leucovorin chemotherapy coupled with radiation therapy (*N Engl J Med.* 2001;345:725; *J Clin Oncol.* 2010;28:2430).

    b. Neoadjuvant chemotherapy for gastric cancer has the potential for improving patient tolerance, resectability rates (downstaging), and overall patient survival. A recently reported European trial demonstrated significant improvement in 5-year survival rates in patients with gastric cancer who were treated with six cycles of chemotherapy (three preoperatively and three postoperatively) compared to surgery alone (*N Engl J Med.* 2006;355:11). Chemotherapy regimen in this trial consisted of epirubicin, cisplatin, and 5-FU. Furthermore, preoperative chemotherapy improved curative resection rates.

4. **Palliative therapy** of gastric cancer is important due to overall low cure rates. Generally, patients with peritoneal disease, hepatic or nodal metastases, or other poor prognostic factors benefit most from endoscopic

palliation. Laparoscopic or open palliative surgical resection can be considered in patients with better prognosis and good performance status to prevent bleeding, obstruction, and perforation in patients with metastatic or otherwise unresectable cancer. Palliative surgical resections appear to provide superior relief of symptoms compared to surgical bypass. Palliative chemoradiation therapy also prolongs survival in patients and improves symptoms and quality of life when it can be administered safely.

IV. **PRIMARY GASTRIC LYMPHOMA (PGL)** accounts for fewer than 5% of gastric neoplasms. However, PGL comprises two thirds of all primary GI lymphomas because the stomach is the most commonly involved organ in extranodal lymphoma. PGLs are usually B-cell, non-Hodgkin lymphomas. Most PGLs occur in the distal stomach.

A. Patients typically present in their sixth decade with symptoms similar to those of gastric adenocarcinoma (epigastric pain, weight loss, anorexia, nausea, vomiting, and occult GI bleeding). Diagnosis is typically made using endoscopy, and staging to detect systemic disease is performed using CT of chest/abdomen/pelvis, bone marrow biopsy, and biopsy of enlarged peripheral lymph nodes.

B. Therapy of PGL has been advanced by the recognition that low-grade PGLs have features resembling mucosa-associated lymphoid tissue (MALT) and that the majority of low-grade MALT lymphomas are associated with *H. pylori* infection. Thus, **first-line therapy for low-grade MALT lymphomas is use of antibiotics directed at *H. pylori* eradication,** which leads to complete remission rates of 70% to 100%. Chemoradiation therapy is used as salvage therapy for failure of antibiotics. High-grade or non-MALT lymphomas are generally treated with chemoradiation therapy alone, with surgical resection reserved for those who fail chemoradiation or in emergency cases of hemorrhage or perforation.

V. **BENIGN GASTRIC TUMORS** account for fewer than 2% of all gastric tumors. They are usually located in the antrum or corpus. Presentation can be similar to that of peptic ulcer or adenocarcinoma, and diagnosis is made by EGD or contrast radiography.

A. **Gastric polyps** are classified by histologic findings. Endoscopic removal is appropriate if the polyp can be completely excised.

1. **Hyperplastic polyps** are regenerative rather than neoplastic and constitute 75% of gastric polyps. Risk of malignant transformation is minimal.

2. **Adenomatous polyps** are the second most common gastric polyp and are neoplastic in origin. The incidence of carcinoma within the polyp is proportional to its size, with polyps of greater than 2 cm having a 24% incidence of malignancy. Patients with familial adenomatous polyposis have a 50% incidence of gastroduodenal polyps and require endoscopic surveillance. Surgical resection with a 2- to 3-cm margin of

gastric wall can often be performed laparoscopically and is required if endoscopic excision is not possible.

VI. **GASTROINTESTINAL STROMAL TUMORS (GISTs)** comprise only 3% of all gastric malignancies and arise from mesenchymal components of the gastric wall. The median age at diagnosis is 60 years, with a slight male predominance. GISTs frequently display prominent extraluminal growth and can attain large sizes before becoming symptomatic.

   A. Presentation can be varied and includes asymptomatic masses found incidentally on physical exam or radiographic studies, vague abdominal pain and discomfort secondary to mass effect, and GI hemorrhage as a result of necrosis of overlying mucosa. Diagnosis is made by endoscopy and FNA biopsy. GISTs are graded according to tumor size and histologic frequency of mitoses. Staging is accomplished by CT of abdomen/pelvis and chest X-ray.

   B. **Treatment** is open or laparoscopic surgical resection with 2-cm margins of grossly normal gastric wall to ensure negative histologic margins. *En bloc* resection of any structures involved by local invasion should be attempted, although lymphadenectomy is not indicated because lymph node metastases are rare. Metastasis occurs by hematogenous route, and hepatic involvement is common, as is local recurrence after resection. GISTs are not radiosensitive or responsive to traditional chemotherapy. However, most GISTs express the **c-kit** receptor, a tyrosine kinase that acts as a growth factor receptor. **Imatinib mesylate (Gleevec™)** is a small-molecule inhibitor of the c-kit receptor that has become first-line therapy for metastatic or recurrent GIST. Approximately 60% of patients experience a partial response, and when maximal response is achieved, surgical therapy should be considered for patients in whom all gross disease can be removed.

VII. **GASTRIC CARCINOIDS** are rare neuroendocrine tumors accounting for less than 1% of all gastric neoplasms. Carcinoid tumors arise from enterochromaffin-like cells and can be secondary to hypergastrinemia associated with pernicious anemia or chronic atrophic gastritis. Tumors tend to be small, multiple, and asymptomatic, although larger solitary tumors may cause ulceration of overlying mucosa and symptoms similar to PUD. EGD with biopsy generally provides diagnosis. Treatment of large (>2 cm), solitary tumors is gastrectomy because these have the highest invasive potential. Treatment of smaller, multifocal tumors is less clear, with options ranging from observation, gastrectomy to include the tumors, and antrectomy without inclusion of tumors to reduce gastrin levels and induce tumor regression.

VIII. **POSTGASTRECTOMY SYNDROMES** are caused by changes in gastric emptying as a consequence of gastric operations. They may occur in up to 20% of patients who undergo gastric surgery, depending on the extent of resection, disruption of the vagus nerves, status of the pylorus, type of reconstruction, and presence of mechanical or functional obstruction. Clearly defining the syndrome that is present in a given patient is critical to developing a rational treatment plan (*World J Surg.* 2003;27:725). Most are treated nonoperatively and resolve with time.

A. **Nutritional disturbances** occur in 30% of patients after gastric surgery, either as a result of functional changes or postgastrectomy syndromes. Prolonged **iron, folate, vitamin B₁₂, calcium, and vitamin D deficiencies** can result in anemia, neuropathy, dementia, and osteomalacia. These can be prevented with supplementation.

B. **Dumping syndrome** is thought to result from the rapid emptying of a high-osmolar carbohydrate load into the small intestine. Gastric resection leads to the loss of reservoir capacity and the loss of pylorus function. Dumping syndrome is most common after Billroth II reconstruction.

1. **Early dumping** occurs within 30 minutes of eating and is characterized by nausea, epigastric distress, explosive diarrhea, and vasomotor symptoms (i.e., dizziness, palpitations, flushing, and diaphoresis). It is presumably caused by rapid fluid shifts in response to the hyperosmolar intestinal load from the stomach to the small intestine. The resultant food bolus causes a rapid shift of extracellular fluid into the bowel lumen.

2. **Late dumping** symptoms are primarily vasomotor and occur 1 to 4 hours after eating. The hormonal response to high simple carbohydrate loads results in hyperinsulinemia and reactive hypoglycemia. Symptoms are relieved by carbohydrate ingestion.

3. **Treatment** is primarily nonsurgical and results in improvement in nearly all patients over time. Meals should be smaller in volume but increased in frequency, liquids should be ingested 30 minutes after eating solids, and simple carbohydrates should be avoided. Use of the long-acting somatostatin analog octreotide results in significant improvement and persistent relief in 80% of patients when behavioral modifications fail (*Nat Rev Gastro Hepatol.* 2009;6:583). If reoperation is necessary, conversion to Roux-en-Y gastrojejunostomy or an isoperistaltic/antiperistaltic jejunal loop is usually successful.

C. **Alkaline reflux gastritis** is most commonly associated with Billroth II gastrojejunostomy and requires operative treatment more often than other postgastrectomy syndromes. It is characterized by the triad of constant (not postprandial) epigastric pain, nausea, and bilious emesis. Vomiting does not relieve the pain and is not associated with meals. Endoscopy reveals inflamed, beefy red, friable gastric mucosa, and can rule out recurrent ulcer as a cause of symptoms. Bile reflux into the stomach is occasionally seen. Enterogastric reflux can be confirmed by hydroxy iminodiacetic acid (HIDA) scan. Mechanical obstruction is absent, distinguishing alkaline reflux gastritis from loop syndromes. **Nonoperative therapy** consists of frequent meals, antacids, and cholestyramine to bind bile salts but is usually ineffective. **Surgery** to divert bile flow from the gastric mucosa is the only proven treatment. The creation of a long-limb (45-cm) Roux-en-Y gastrojejunostomy effectively eliminates alkaline reflux and is the preferred option for most patients (*Gastroenterol Clin North Am.* 1994;23:281).

D. **Roux stasis syndrome** may occur in up to 30% of patients after Roux-en-Y gastroenterostomy. It is characterized by chronic abdominal pain, nausea, and vomiting that is aggravated with eating. It results from functional obstruction due to disruption of the normal propagation of pacesetter potentials in the Roux limb from the proximal duodenum, as well as altered motility in the gastric remnant. Near-total gastrectomy to remove the atonic stomach can improve gastric emptying and is occasionally useful in patients with refractory Roux stasis. Use of an "uncut" Roux-en-Y reconstruction (*Am J Surg.* 2001;182:52) may preserve normal pacemaker propagation and prevent the development of the syndrome.

E. **Loop syndromes** result from mechanical obstruction of either the **afferent** or **efferent** limbs of the Billroth II gastrojejunostomy. The location and etiology of the obstruction are investigated by plain abdominal X-rays, CT scan, upper GI contrast studies, and endoscopy. Relief of the obstruction may require adhesiolysis, revision of the anastomosis, occasionally bowel resection, or conversion of Billroth II to Roux-en-Y gastrojejunostomy.

1. **Afferent loop syndrome** can be caused acutely by bowel kink, volvulus, or internal herniation, resulting in severe abdominal pain and nonbilious emesis within the first few weeks after surgery. Lack of bilious staining of nasogastric drainage in the immediate postoperative period suggests this complication. Examination may reveal a fluid-filled abdominal mass, and laboratory findings may include elevated bilirubin or amylase. **Duodenal stump blowout** results from progressive afferent limb dilation, leading to peritonitis, abscess, or fistula formation. In the urgent setting, jejunojejunostomy can effectively decompress the afferent limb. A more **chronic form** of afferent loop syndrome results from partial mechanical obstruction of the afferent limb. Patients present with postprandial right upper quadrant pain relieved by bilious emesis that is not mixed with recently ingested food. Stasis can lead to bacterial overgrowth and subsequent bile salt deconjugation in the obstructed loop, causing **blind loop syndrome** (steatorrhea and vitamin B_{12}, folate, and iron deficiency) by interfering with fat and vitamin B_{12} absorption.

2. **Efferent loop syndrome** results from intermittent obstruction of the efferent limb of the gastrojejunostomy. Patients complain of abdominal pain and bilious emesis months to years after surgery, similar to the situation with regard to a proximal small bowel obstruction.

F. **Postvagotomy diarrhea** has an incidence of 20% after truncal vagotomy and is thought to result from alterations in gastric emptying and vagal denervation of the small bowel and biliary tree. The diarrhea is typically watery and episodic. Treatment includes antidiarrheal medications (loperamide, diphenoxylate with atropine, cholestyramine) and decreasing excessive intake of fluids or foods that contain lactose. Symptoms usually improve with time, and surgery is rarely indicated.

IX. **SEVERE OBESITY** is a condition characterized by the pathologic accumulation of excess body fat. It is defined as a body mass index [BMI = weight (kg)/ height (m^2)] equal to or greater than 40, which generally correlates with an actual body weight 100 lb greater than ideal body weight.

A. **Epidemiology.** Obesity is a disease process that has reached epidemic proportions worldwide, with the highest prevalence in the United States, where 5% of the adult population is morbidly obese (*JAMA.* 2010;303:235). Obesity is also becoming increasingly prevalent in the pediatric population (*JAMA.* 2010;303:242).

B. The **etiology** of morbid obesity is poorly understood and thought to result from an imbalance in biologic, psychosocial, and environmental factors governing caloric intake and caloric expenditure. Risk factors for the development of morbid obesity include **genetic predisposition,** diet, and culture.

C. Most patients with morbid obesity present with one or more of a number of weight-related comorbidities. Patients with **central** obesity (android or "apple" fat distribution) are at higher risk for development of obesity-related complications than those with **peripheral** obesity (gynecoid or "pear" fat distribution). This is due to increased visceral fat distribution, producing increased intra-abdominal pressure and increasing fat metabolism (with subsequent hyperglycemia, hyperinsulinemia, and peripheral insulin resistance). Table 9-2 lists some of the medical complications associated with morbid obesity. In addition to the aforementioned comorbidities, obesity also increases mortality. One study showed an increase in mortality among morbidly obese individuals (*NEJM.* 2006;355:8).

D. **Treatment** of morbid obesity is of paramount importance because of the many medical sequelae associated with obesity, nearly all are reversible on resolution of the obese state.

1. **Lifestyle changes** in diet, exercise habits, and behavior modification are first-line therapy for all obese patients. In combination, such changes can achieve 8% to 10% weight loss over a 6-month period, but losses are sustained at 1 year in only 60% of patients. However, certain comorbidities, such as diabetes, benefit from as little as 3% weight loss, and lifestyle changes alone may be sufficient in patients with BMI less than 27.

2. **Pharmacotherapy** is second-tier therapy used in patients with BMI greater than 27 and in combination with lifestyle changes. Currently, sibutramine, an appetite suppressant, and orlistat, a lipase inhibitor that reduces lipid absorption, are the only approved drugs for weight loss treatment. Weight loss with these agents is 6% to 10% at 1 year, but relapse rates after discontinuation of the drugs are high.

3. **Bariatric surgery** is the most effective approach for achieving durable weight loss in the morbidly obese. Multiple studies have confirmed the superiority of surgery to nonsurgical approaches in achieving and maintaining weight reduction in the morbidly obese (*N Engl J Med.* 2004;351:2683; *Surg Obes Relat Disord.* 2010;6:347). A National Institutes of Health Consensus Development Conference on morbid

TABLE 9-2   Complications of Morbid Obesity

Cardiac
 Hypertension
 Coronary artery disease
 Heart failure
 Arrhythmias

Pulmonary
 Obesity hypoventilation syndrome
 Obstructive sleep apnea
 Respiratory insufficiency of
  obesity (pickwickian syndrome)
 Pulmonary embolism

Metabolic
 Type II diabetes
 Hyperlipidemia
 Hypercholesterolemia
 Nonalcoholic steatohepatitis

Musculoskeletal
 Degenerative joint disease
 Lumbar disc disease
 Osteoarthritis

Gastrointestinal
 Cholelithiasis
 Gastroesophageal reflux disease
 Hernias

Vascular
 Deep venous thrombosis
 Venous stasis ulceration

Infectious
 Fungal infections
 Necrotizing soft tissue infections

Genitourinary
 Nephrotic syndrome
 Stress urinary incontinence

Gynecologic
 Polycystic ovary syndrome

Neurologic/psychiatric
 Pseudotumor cerebri
 Depression
 Stroke
 Low self-esteem

Oncologic
 Cancers of uterus, breast, colon/
  rectum, and prostate

obesity established guidelines for the evaluation and treatment of morbidly obese patients with bariatric surgical procedures (*Ann Surg.* 2010;250:399).

  a. Indications. Patients who have failed intensive efforts at weight control using medical means are candidates for bariatric surgery if they have a BMI index greater than 40 or greater than 35 with weight-related comorbidities.

  b. Preoperative evaluation. A bariatric multidisciplinary team including primary care physicians, dietitians, physical therapists, anesthesiologists, nurses, and psychiatrists or psychologists evaluates a patient's weight history, dietary habits, motivation, social history, and comorbid medical conditions prior to surgery.

  c. Benefits of surgery are related to reversal of the disease processes associated with severe obesity. Hypertension completely resolves in 62% of patients and resolves or improves in 79%. Diabetes is completely resolved in 77% of patients and resolves or improves in 86%. Obstructive sleep apnea resolves or improves in 85% of patients and hyperlipidemia improves in 70% (*Lancet.*

2009;10:653; *NEJM.* 2007;357:741). The quality of life is mark-edly better. Most importantly, recent studies demonstrate reduced mortality rates in morbidly obese patients undergoing bariatric sur-gery compared to matched controls (*NEJM.* 2004;351:2683; *Ann Surg.* 2010;250:399).

E. **Bariatric surgical procedures** can generally be divided into two types: **restrictive procedures,** which limit the amount of food that can be ingested, and **malabsorptive procedures,** which limit the absorption of nutrients and calories from ingested food by bypassing predetermined lengths of small intestine. The four standard operations used to produce weight loss in the morbidly obese include adjustable gastric banding (AGB) and vertical banded gastroplasty (restrictive procedures), biliopancreatic diversion (BPD) with and without duodenal switch (DS) (malabsorp-tive procedures), and Roux-en-Y gastric bypass (RYGBP) (combination). Sleeve gastrectomy, the first component of a DS operation, increasingly is being performed alone as a restrictive procedure.

1. **Adjustable gastric banding (AGB)** involves open or laparoscopic placement of a silicone band with an inflatable balloon around the proximal stomach at the angle of His. The band is connected to a reservoir that is implanted over the rectus sheath. The patient under-goes serial adjustments to inflate the band and create a small proximal gastric pouch. Excess weight loss is approximately 50%. Perioperative mortality is exceedingly low (0.05%), and overall complication rate is near 11%. Most complications are related to band slippage, which presents with obstructive symptoms or problems with the port (kink-ing or leaking of access tubing). Band erosion can occur but is far less frequent than the aforementioned complications. Advantages include safety, adjustability, and reversibility, whereas disadvantages include need for frequent postoperative visits (*JAMA.* 2010;303:316/519).

2. **Roux-en-Y gastric bypass (RYGBP)** is the most popular bariatric sur-gical procedure performed in the United States. A 30-mL proximal gastric pouch is created by either transection or occlusion using a sta-pling device. A 1-cm-diameter anastomosis is then performed between the pouch and a Roux limb of small bowel. This results in a small reser-voir, a small passage for pouch emptying, and bypass of the distal stom-ach, duodenum, and proximal jejunum. The length of the Roux limb directly correlates with the degree of postoperative weight loss, with a 75-cm limb used for standard gastric bypasses and a 150-cm limb used for the superobese. Gastric bypass results in weight loss superior to that achieved with restrictive procedures, with mean excess weight loss of 70%. Perioperative mortality is 1%, and despite aggressive prophylaxis, **pulmonary embolism** (PE) remains the most common cause of death after bariatric surgery. Anastomotic leak at the gastrojejunostomy is another serious early complication, occurring in approximately 2% of cases. Unexplained **tachycardia** is often the only presenting sign of either complication in the perioperative period and warrants prompt investigation. Other early complications include wound infection (4% to 10%), gastric remnant dilation, and Roux limb obstruction. Late

complications include incisional hernia (15% to 25%), stomal stenosis (2% to 14%), marginal ulcer (2% to 10%), bowel obstruction (2%), and internal hernia (1%). Early or late **bowel obstruction** after RYGBP can be a life-threatening complication and generally requires prompt reoperation because of its association with internal hernia and potential for bowel strangulation. **CT scan with oral contrast** is the best diagnostic test to evaluate for leak or obstruction after RYGBP. Nutritional complications include folate, vitamin B_{12}, iron, and calcium deficiency. Dumping syndrome occurs in many patients and may reinforce dietary behavior modification to avoid sweets and high-calorie foods. Laparoscopic RYGBP is a technically challenging but safe procedure when performed by surgeons with advanced laparoscopic skills. Laparoscopic RYGBP produces equal excess weight loss and has similar mortality and leak rates as the open procedure. Its main advantages are reduced postoperative pain, reduced length of stay, and significantly reduced wound-related complications, such as wound infections, dehiscence, and incisional hernias (*NEJM.* 2009;361:445).

3. **Biliopancreatic diversion (BPD)** and **biliopancreatic diversion with duodenal switch (BPD-DS)** are two additional procedures for morbidly obese patients. BPD requires antrectomy with formation of a 200-cm alimentary channel and a 50- to 75-cm common channel. BPD-DS includes a sleeve gastrectomy, preservation of the pylorus, a 150-cm alimentary channel, and a 75- to 100-cm common channel. These procedures are done at select centers for the superobese and those who have failed to maintain weight loss following gastric bypass or restrictive procedures. Long-term outcomes indicate excess weight loss of 75% at 1 year, but nutritional deficiencies are more common than for RYGBP. Postoperative complications include anemia (30%), protein-calorie malnutrition (20%), dumping syndrome, and marginal ulceration (10%). These procedures are technically demanding and the applicability of these procedures to the obese population remains to be determined.

4. **Sleeve gastrectomy,** the first component of a DS operation, can be used alone as a purely restrictive procedure for the treatment of morbid obesity. It does not produce malabsorption and is technically easier to perform than BPD-DS or RYGBP. Preliminary reports have demonstrated 70% to 80% excess body weight loss at 1 year, but long-term outcomes and durability of this procedure remain unknown. It may be indicated as an initial procedure in the superobese population to induce enough weight loss to make BPD-DS or RYGBP technically more feasible (*Surg Obes Relat Disord.* 2010;6:1; *Ann Surg.* 2010;252:319).

10 Small Intestine

Susan C. Pitt and Steven R. Hunt

I. EMBRYOLOGY

A. **Origin.** The small intestine (SI) develops during the fourth week of fetal development. The duodenum arises from the foregut, while the jejunum and ileum derive from the midgut. The endoderm forms the absorptive epithelium and secretory glands. The remainder of the intestinal wall, including the muscularis and serosa, are created from the splanchnic mesoderm.

B. **Rotation.** During the fifth week of fetal development, the intestine herniates through the umbilicus and rotates 90 degrees around the axis of the vitelline duct and superior mesenteric artery (SMA). By the 10th week, the intestine returns to the abdominal cavity rotating an additional 180 degrees. This revolution positions the ligament of Treitz in the left upper quadrant and the cecum in the right upper quadrant. Cecal descent into the right lower quadrant later occurs at four months.

C. **Lumen formation.** Between the fourth and seventh weeks, the SI is lined by cuboidal cells. Rapid proliferation occasionally occludes the lumen, particularly in the duodenum, but patency is regained by the 10th week via apoptosis.

II. ANATOMY

A. **Gross anatomy.** The SI extends approximately 3 m from the pylorus to the ileocecal valve. The duodenum is only about 20 cm. The first portion or bulb is intraperitoneal, while the remaining second, third, and fourth portions are retroperitoneal. Biliary and pancreatic secretions enter the second portion of the duodenum at the ampulla of Vater. The jejunum and ileum are significantly longer and span approximately 100 and 150 cm, respectively. These segments of SI can be differentiated by examining the mesenteric blood supply. Jejunal arcades are larger, fewer in number, and have longer vessels between the arcades. The jejunum also has many circumferential mucosal folds called plicae circularis.

B. **Vascular supply.** The duodenum is supplied by the pancreaticoduodenal arteries that are branches of the gastroduodenal artery and SMA. The jejunum and ileum are supplied by the SMA. The superior mesenteric vein (SMV) runs parallel to the SMA, provides the venous drainage of the small bowel, and joins the splenic vein to form the portal vein.

C. **Lymphatic drainage.** The submucosal Peyer patches feed small lymphatics extending to the mesenteric lymph nodes. From there, drainage parallels the course of the named blood vessels and eventually accumulates at the subdiaphragmatic cisterna chyli before entering the thoracic duct.

D. Innervation. The vagus nerve supplies all abdominal parasympathetic fibers and plays an important role in regulating intestinal secretions and motility. These fibers cross mesenteric ganglia, particularly the celiac ganglion, and innervate the myenteric ganglion cells within the walls of the SI. Three sets of sympathetic nerves innervate the gut forming a plexus around the SMA. Sympathetic nerves modulate the intestinal blood supply, secretion, and motility as well as carry all pain signals from the intestine.

E. Anatomy of the intestinal wall is uniform from the duodenum to the ileocecal valve, consisting of four distinct tissue layers.

   1. The **mucosa** is composed of the epithelium, lamina propria, and muscularis mucosae.

      a. The **epithelium** has both villi and crypts. The *villi* are protrusions of the epithelial layer into the lumen that act to dramatically increase absorptive capacity, while the *crypts* contain pluripotent cells that give rise to absorptive enterocytes (over 95% of the epithelial layer). *Paneth cells* secrete lysozyme, tumor necrosis factor (TNF), and cryptdin that provide nonspecific immunity. *Goblet cells* secrete mucus. More than 10 different subpopulations of *enteroendocrine cells* exist that secrete a variety of hormones. Of note, the entire intestinal lining is replaced every 3 to 5 days.

      b. The **lamina propria** is a layer of loose connective tissue that contains Peyer patches – collections of lymphocytes that span the lamina propria and submucosa and provide mucosal immunity.

      c. The **muscularis mucosa** is a layer of muscle separating the mucosa from the submucosa.

   2. The **submucosa** is the strongest layer of the intestinal wall. Blood vessels and nerves run within this layer, including Meissner ganglion cells.

   3. The **muscularis propria** consists of a thicker, inner circular layer and an outer longitudinal layer of smooth muscle cells. The Auerbach (myenteric) ganglion cells are located between these smooth muscle layers.

   4. The **serosa** is a single layer of flat mesothelial cells composing the outermost layer of the small bowel. Serosa lines the extraluminal surface of the anterior duodenum and the entire jejunum and ileum.

F. Enterocyte histology. The absorptive capacity of enterocytes is due to the presence of microvilli and a glycocalyx coating outside the cell membrane. Digestive enzymes, such as disaccharidases, and Na-nutrient cotransporters are located in the apical membrane. Laterally, tight junctions prevent crossing of intraluminal contents across the epithelial layer. Intermediate junctions and desmosomes also help to maintain the barrier function of the intestinal epithelium. Na-K ATPases and passive nutrient transporters are found in the basal membrane.

III. PHYSIOLOGY of the SI involves a complex balance between absorption and secretion. The gut is also the largest endocrine organ in the human body.

A. **Absorption** is the principal function of the gastrointestinal (GI) tract.

1. **Water.** Under normal circumstances, approximately 7 to 10 L of fluid enter the SI each day, but only 1 L reaches the colon. Of this fluid, 2 L are derived from oral intake, 1 L from saliva, 2 L from gastric secretion, 2 L from pancreatic secretion, 1 L from bile, and 1 L from small-intestinal secretion. Alterations in small bowel permeability, tonicity of enteric substances, or rate of transit can result in diarrhea and large volume losses.

2. The majority of **electrolyte** absorption occurs in the SI. The most important electrolytes absorbed are sodium, chloride, and calcium. Sodium absorption occurs through passive diffusion, countertransport with hydrogen, and cotransport with chloride, glucose, and amino acids. Chloride is absorbed in exchange for bicarbonate, which accounts for the alkalinity of the luminal contents. Calcium is actively absorbed in the proximal SI by a process that is stimulated by vitamin D. Emesis, diarrhea, obstruction, and small-bowel ostomy effluent can result in impaired small-bowel electrolyte absorption.

3. **Bile salts** and **vitamin B_{12}-intrinsic factor** complexes are absorbed in the terminal ileum. Resection that leaves less than 100 cm of the ileum can result in bile acid deficiencies that limit absorption of the fat-soluble vitamins A, D, E, and K. Vitamin B_{12} deficiency can result in chronic megaloblastic anemia (pernicious anemia).

4. **Nutrients.** The absorption of carbohydrates, proteins, and fat is discussed in Chapter 2 and in the next section.

B. **Digestion.** Macronutrient digestion by salivary, gastric, biliary, and pancreatic secretions is covered in Chapter 2. This section discusses digestion at the level of the enterocyte.

1. **Brush border enzymes,** peptidases and disaccharidases, break down peptides and disaccharides into simple amino acids and monosaccharides.

2. **Active transport** via Na-K ATPases in the basolateral membrane of enterocytes keeps the intracellular Na concentration very low. This sodium gradient enables Na-nutrient cotransporters to move amino acids and monosaccharides into enterocytes.

3. **Passive transport.** After digestion by pancreatic lipases, triglycerides and fatty acids form micelles with bile salts. These micelles diffuse across the apical membrane and are reconstituted into chylomicrons, which subsequently enter submucosal lymphatics.

C. **Motility**

1. **Types of contractions.** *Circular muscle* contractions can temporarily segment the intestine for improved mixing of contents or they can propel food toward the colon if they progress caudad. When the *longitudinal muscle* contracts, sleeve contractions shorten the intestinal length helping to propel food forward.

2. **Neurohumoral effects.** Vagal cholinergic input and hormones such as motilin and cholecystokinin (CCK) stimulate contractions. Conversely, sympathetic neurons inhibit peristalsis.

3. During the **fasting state,** the migrating motor complex (MMC) performs the housekeeping function of clearing the lumen of debris. After a period of rest, random contractions of moderate strength are followed by several very strong contractions.

4. During the **fed state,** contractions occur more frequently and last longer, and multiple areas of the small bowel may contract at the same time. From each site of contraction, peristalsis proceeds caudally for a varying distance.

D. **Immunity.** Tight junctions between the enterocyte apical membranes provide a *barrier function* and prevent pathogens from crossing the epithelium. Mucosal plasma cells secrete immunoglobulin A (*IgA*), which binds intraluminal pathogens and targets them for destruction.

1. M cells are located in the epithelial layer over the Peyer patches. These cells facilitate direct antigen presentation to macrophages and lymphocytes thereby aiding acquired immunity to luminal pathogens.

2. T cells can be located within vacuoles of M cells and seem to have an immunosuppressive effect that may explain nonreactivity to ingested food.

E. **Endocrine** function is regulated by neural, hormonal (both autocrine and paracrine), and anatomic mechanisms.

1. **CCK** is produced by duodenal and jejunal I cells in response to intraluminal amino acids and fats. CCK causes gallbladder contraction, pancreatic enzyme secretion, and relaxation of the sphincter of Oddi.

2. **Enteroglucagon** from ileal and colonic L cells is released in response to intraluminal fat and bile acids and delays gastric emptying. Secretion can dramatically increase with inflammatory processes, such as Crohn's disease and celiac sprue.

3. **Gastric inhibitory peptide (GIP)** is secreted by duodenal and jejunal K cells in response to active transport of monosaccharides, long-chain fatty acids, and amino acids. GIP inhibits gastric acid and pepsinogen secretion and gastric emptying, but stimulates insulin release.

4. **Gastrin** is secreted in response to vagal stimulation and intraluminal peptides by duodenal G cells. Gastrin stimulates acid secretion by the gastric fundus and body and increases gastric mucosal blood flow.

5. **Motilin** is produced by duodenal and jejunal M cells in response to duodenal acid, vagal stimulation, and gastrin-releasing peptide. Motilin is involved in the MMC during the fasting state. Erythromycin is useful as a promotility agent due to its action as a motilin agonist.

6. **Secretin** is released by duodenal and jejunal S cells in response to acid, bile salts, and fatty acids in the duodenum. Secretin increases bicarbonate and water secretion from pancreatic ducts, and also inhibits gastric acid secretion and gastric motility.

7. **Somatostatin** broadly inhibits gut exocrine and endocrine function. Intestinal D cells and enteric neurons secrete somatostatin in response to intraluminal fat, protein, and acid.

8. **Vasoactive intestinal peptide (VIP)** is secreted throughout the SI in response to vagal stimulation. VIP increases mesenteric blood flow, intestinal motility, and pancreatic and intestinal secretions.

IV. SMALL-BOWEL OBSTRUCTION (SBO)

A. **Mechanical obstruction** of the SI can be partial, allowing some distal passage of gas or fluid, or complete, with total occlusion of the lumen. In a strangulated obstruction, the involved bowel has vascular compromise, which can ultimately lead to infarction and perforation of the intestinal wall. No clinical or laboratory values reliably differentiate simple from strangulated obstructions, although constant, as opposed to crampy, abdominal pain, fever, leukocytosis, and acidosis should raise the index of suspicion considerably. On the other hand, **ileus** implies failure of peristalsis without mechanical obstruction. Recent abdominal operations, electrolyte disturbances, trauma, peritonitis, systemic infections, bowel ischemia, and certain medications (i.e., narcotics) can all result in an ileus.

B. **Etiology**
   1. **Adhesions** are the *most common* cause of SBO in US adults and mostly result from previous abdominal operations or inflammatory processes, although isolated congenital adhesions or bands can occur as well. Intra-abdominal adhesions occur in more than 90% of patients following major abdominal surgery and account for about 60% to 70% of SBOs (*Ann R Coll Surg Engl.* 1990;72:60–63; *Eur J Surg.* 1997;163(suppl 577):5–9).
   2. **Incarcerated hernias** are the second most common cause of SBOs in industrialized nations and the most common cause of SBO worldwide. In children and patients without prior abdominal surgery, hernias are the most common cause of SBO in developed nations.
   3. **Intussusception** occurs when one portion of bowel (the intussusceptum) telescopes into another (the intussuscipiens). Tumors, polyps, enlarged mesenteric lymph nodes, or a Meckel's diverticulum may serve as lead points of the telescoped segment. As opposed to intussusception in children, an adult with intussusception should prompt workup for bowel pathology. Asymptomatic, transient intussusception is occasionally seen incidentally on an abdominal CT scan performed for other reasons.
   4. **Volvulus,** or the rotation of a segment of bowel around its vascular pedicle, is often caused by adhesions or congenital anomalies such as intestinal malrotation and more commonly occurs in the colon.
   5. **Strictures** secondary to ischemia, inflammation (Crohn's disease), radiation therapy, or prior surgery may also cause obstruction.
   6. **Gallstone ileus** occurs as a complication of cholecystitis. Fistulization between the biliary tree and the small bowel (cholecystoduodenal or choledochoduodenal fistula) allows one or more gallstones to travel distally and become lodged, typically at the ileocecal valve.

7. **External compression** from tumors, abscesses, hematomas, or other masses can cause functional SBO.

8. **Foreign bodies** typically pass without incident. Items presenting with obstruction may require operation if they cannot be retrieved endoscopically. Pathology due to swallowing foreign bodies is more common in institutionalized patients.

C. **Diagnosis** of SBO incorporates the full range of history, physical exam, and radiographic findings.

1. **Signs and symptoms.** Proximal SBOs present with early bilious **vomiting,** while distal obstructions present later, and emesis can be thicker and more feculent. Early in the disease course, **nausea** may be observed in the absence of vomiting. **Abdominal distention** typically increases the more distal the obstruction. **Abdominal pain** is poorly localized and often characterized as crampy and intermittent (i.e., colicky). **Obstipation,** complete absence of flatus and bowel movement, is observed once the distal bowel (beyond a complete obstruction) is evacuated. With a persistent obstruction, **hypovolemia** progresses due to impaired absorption, increased secretion ("third spacing"), and fluid losses from emesis. **Bloody bowel movements** suggest ischemia of the intestine or an alternative diagnosis.

2. **Physical examination.** Abnormal **vital signs** are generally indicative of hypovolemia (e.g., tachycardia and hypotension). **Abdominal exam** may reveal distension, prior surgical scars, and hernias. Palpation should make note of any masses. Peritoneal signs mandate prompt surgical evaluation and treatment due to the risk of bowel strangulation. Digital rectal examination may reveal the presence of an obstructing rectal tumor or impacted stool.

3. **Laboratory evaluation.** In the early stages of a SBO, laboratory values may be normal. As the process progresses, lab values commonly reflect dehydration demonstrating a contraction alkalosis (metabolic) with hypochloremia and hypokalemia. An elevated white blood cell (WBC) count, serum lactate level, and glucose, or an acidosis with a bicarbonate less than 20 may suggest strangulation (*Am Surg.* 2004;70:40; *Am J Surg.* 1994;167(6):575–578; *J Gastrointest Surg.* 2009;13(1):93–99).

4. **Radiologic evaluation**
   a. Characteristic findings of SBO on **abdominal plain films** are dilated loops of SI, air-fluid levels, and paucity of colorectal gas. These findings may be absent in early, proximal, and/or closed-loop obstructions. Gas within the bowel wall (pneumatosis intestinalis) or portal vein is suggestive of a strangulated obstruction and ischemia. Free intra-abdominal air indicates perforation of a hollow viscus. The findings of air in the biliary tree and a radiopaque gallstone in the right lower quadrant are pathognomonic of gallstone ileus. Paralytic ileus appears as gaseous distention uniformly distributed throughout the stomach, SI, and colon.
   b. **Contrast studies** (small-bowel follow-through [SBFT] or enteroclysis) can localize the site of obstruction and suggest an etiology. Barium

can be used if subtle mucosal lesions are suspected (i.e., lead point in a patient with recurring intussusceptions), but should be avoided in acute obstructions due to the risk of barium impaction. Water-soluble contrast agents are indicated as the initial contrast in most instances.

c. **Computed tomography (CT)** is an excellent imaging modality for diagnosing SBO. CT scans have the ability to localize and characterize the obstruction as well as provide information regarding the cause of the obstruction and the presence of other intra-abdominal pathology. Evidence suggests that CT scanning can improve the preoperative diagnosis of strangulation, with negative and positive predictive values greater than 90% (*J Gastrointest Surg.* 2005;9:690). In a recent study reviewing multiple preoperative clinical, laboratory, and radiologic findings at presentation, the most significant independent predictor of bowel strangulation in patients with SBO was the CT finding of reduced wall enhancement (sensitivity 56%, specificity 94%, likelihood ratio 9.3) (*J Gastrointest Surg.* 2009;13(1):93–99).

5. **Differential diagnosis**
   a. **Mesenteric vascular ischemia** can produce colicky abdominal pain, especially after meals. Acute occlusion often presents with marked leukocytosis and severe abdominal pain out of proportion to physical findings. Angiography confirms the diagnosis.
   b. **Colonic obstruction** can easily be confused with a distal SBO, especially if the ileocecal valve is incompetent. A water-soluble contrast enema can aid in diagnosis. The initial management and evaluation of large- and small-bowel obstructions are the same.
   c. **Paralytic ileus** is a common diagnosis in surgical patients. A thorough history, physical exam, and radiologic workup should differentiate ileus from obstruction. Narcotic and psychiatric medications, recent abdominal operations, and electrolyte abnormalities are common causes of ileus.
   d. As in paralytic ileus, radiography of primary **hypomotility** disorders reveals gas throughout the entire GI tract with particular distention of the small bowel. Treatment of these chronic diseases consists of prokinetic drugs and dietary manipulation.

D. **Treatment** of SBO is evolving and includes prevention at initial laparotomy.

1. **Prevention.** The highest risk of adhesive SBO occurs after ileal pouch-anal anastomosis, open colectomy, and open gynecologic surgeries (class I evidence). Intraoperative preventative principles, including meticulous hemostasis; avoiding tissue ischemia, excessive dissection and damage; and reducing residual foreign bodies, may be of benefit (class III evidence). Excluding acute appendicitis, laparoscopy results in fewer adhesions than open techniques (class I evidence). Available bioabsorbable antiadhesion barriers, such as hyaluronic acid/carboxymethyl-cellulose (Seprafilm®, Genzyme, Cambridge, MA), and icodextrin 4% solution (Adept®, Baxter Healthcare S.A.), have

been shown to reduce adhesions (class I evidence) (*Am J Surg.* [published online ahead of print September 1, 2010]). While randomized studies demonstrate that these barriers are beneficial in reducing the severity and number of adhesions after surgery, whether or not they reduce the incidence and severity of later SBOs is unclear. A multi-center trial of 1,701 patients comparing Seprafilm® to no treatment found no difference in the overall rate of SBO (12% for both). However, at a mean follow-up of 3.5 years, a very modest reduction in the risk of SBO *requiring operation* was observed (1.8% vs. 3.4%; $P < 0.05$) (*Dis Colon Rectum.* 2006;49(1):1–11).

2. **Nonstrangulated** obstructions can be treated nonoperatively if the patient is clinically stable. The cornerstone of treating any SBO is adequate fluid resuscitation to achieve a urine output of at least 0.5 mL/kg/hour. This resuscitation must meet maintenance fluid and electrolyte needs for a nothing-by-mouth (NPO) patient as well as replace prior and ongoing losses from nasogastric (NG) decompression. During any trial of nonoperative management, the patient must be observed closely and undergo serial abdominal examinations every 4 to 6 hours, preferably by the same person. If the patient deteriorates at any time (develops shock or peritonitis) or fails to improve within a few days, laparotomy is indicated. In patients with an SBO secondary to an incarcerated hernia, attempts to reduce the hernia can be made with mild sedation and manual pressure. If reduction is successful, the patient should be monitored carefully for evidence of bowel infarction or perforation. Severe initial tenderness or skin changes at the hernia site (erythema or ecchymosis) should increase the suspicion for strangulation. Inability to reduce the hernia requires urgent operation. Other situations that may warrant a trial of nonoperative therapy for a SBO include the early postoperative state, multiple prior SBOs, multiple previous abdominal operations with extensive adhesions or "frozen hostile abdomen," abdominal irradiation, Crohn's disease, and carcinomatosis.

3. **Strangulated** obstructions and the presence of peritonitis require prompt operative intervention. Mortality associated with gangrenous bowel approaches 30% if operation is delayed beyond 36 hours, but is closer to 10% when surgical interventions is prompt (*Am Surg.* 1988;54(9):565–569). Once again, fluid/electrolyte resuscitation with Foley catheter placement and NG tube decompression are crucial in the preoperative preparation of the patient.

4. **Fluid replacement** should begin with an isotonic solution. Serum electrolyte values, hourly urine output, and central venous pressure can be monitored to assess adequacy of resuscitation. Antibiotics should be given only as prophylaxis prior to surgery.

5. **Operative intervention** is generally performed via midline incision, though a standard groin incision can be used in the case of an incarcerated inguinal or femoral hernia. During the exploration and identification of the origin of obstruction, adhesiolysis is usually required and resection of gangrenous bowel may be necessary. The viability of

adjacent or compromised bowel must be determined, and a second-look operation within 24 to 48 hours should be planned if any doubt exists. If an obstructing lesion cannot be resected, an enteroenteric or enterocolonic anastomosis can bypass the area of obstruction. Placement of a gastrostomy tube for postoperative decompression should be considered in select cases, such as carcinomatosis or unresectable obstructing cancer.

E. **Prognosis.** The postoperative mortality from a nonstrangulating obstruction is very low. Obstructions associated with strangulated bowel carry a mortality of less than 10% if operation is performed shortly after presentation. Patients admitted to surgical services have been shown to have shorter hospital stays, earlier operative intervention, and reduced direct health-care costs when compared to patients admitted to a medical service (*Am Surg.* 2010;76(7):687–691). The same study also found that coronary artery disease and acute renal failure were associated with higher mortality.

V. **MECKEL'S DIVERTICULUM** is the most common congenital anomaly of the GI tract and occurs from failure of the vitelline or omphalomesenteric duct to obliterate by the sixth week of fetal development. A Meckel's lesion is a true diverticulum that contains all layers of the bowel wall and is located on the antimesenteric border of the ileum. Half of these lesions contain heterotopic mucosa, usually gastric (62%) or pancreatic (16%). The "*Rule of two's*" indicates that a 2% incidence; a 2:1 male:female ratio; patients usually present before 2 years of age; the location is about 2 feet from the ileocecal valve; and the base is typically 2 inches in width and often contains 2 types of mucosa.

A. **Presentation.** The vast majority of Meckel's diverticula are *asymptomatic.*

1. **Bleeding** is the most common presenting sign and tends to be episodic and painless. The source is typically from a peptic ulcer of the adjacent normal ileum caused by acid secretion from gastric mucosa within the diverticulum.

2. **Intestinal obstruction** from intussusception or an incarcerated hernia (Littré's hernia) is the second most common presentation. Obstruction can also occur due to volvulus of the small bowel around a fibrous band that connects the diverticulum to the anterior abdominal wall.

3. **Meckel's diverticulitis** occurs in 20% of symptomatic patients and is often mistaken for acute appendicitis. Intraluminal obstruction of the diverticulum leads to inflammation, edema, ischemia, necrosis, and perforation in a manner similar to appendicitis.

4. **Differential diagnosis** may include appendicitis, colonic diverticulitis, or Crohn's disease.

B. **Diagnosis.** In adults, the clinical diagnosis of a Meckel's diverticulum is extremely difficult except in the presence of bleeding. Preoperative diagnosis is made in under 10% of symptomatic patients (*J Am Coll Surg.* 2001;192:658–662).

1. **Radionuclide scans.** A *Meckel's scan* is based on the uptake of 99 m Tc-pertechnetate by ectopic gastric mucosa. In children, this test is the most accurate (90%) for diagnosing a Meckel's diverticulum, but is less accurate (46%) in adults because of the reduced prevalence of ectopic gastric mucosa within the diverticulum (*AJR.* 1996;166:567–573). The sensitivity and specificity of scintigraphy can be improved by pentagastrin and glucagon, or cimetidine. In the presence of bleeding, a tagged red blood cell scan can also be useful.

2. **Contrast studies.** SBFT and enteroclysis are diagnostic in up to 75% patients, but can be unreliable and variable between institutions.

3. **CT** and **sonography** are typically of little value because distinguishing between a diverticulum and intestinal loops can be very difficult.

C. Treatment

1. **Resection** is indicated in symptomatic patients. For patients who present with obstruction, simple diverticulectomy can be performed. Segmental small-bowel resections should be performed for acute diverticulitis, a wide-based diverticulum, volvulus with necrotic bowel, or bleeding.

2. **Incidental diverticulectomy** during surgery for other abdominal pathology is **not indicated.** Lifelong morbidity associated with the presence of a Meckel's diverticulum is extremely low.

VI. **SMALL-INTESTINAL BLEEDING** from small-bowel lesions is the most common cause of "obscure GI bleeding," which is defined as hemorrhage of unknown origin that persists or recurs after negative initial or primary endoscopic evaluation (colonoscopy and upper endoscopy). Obscure GI bleeding differs from "occult GI bleeding" in that occult bleeding refers to the initial presentation of a patient with a positive fecal occult blood test (FOBT) and/ or iron deficiency anemia (IDA), without visible fecal blood (*Gastroenterol.* 2000;118:201–221). Upper and lower GI bleedings are discussed in Chapters 9 and 12, respectively.

A. Diagnosis

1. **Enteroscopy**

   a. **Push enteroscopy** employs a 400-cm enteroscope to visualize well into the jejunum, but efficacy is highly dependent on the skill of the endoscopist. The ability to perform biopsy or therapeutic maneuvers is an advantage. Intraoperative use of the scope via a small enterotomy distal to the ligament of Treitz can sometimes further localize a bleeding source.

   b. **Extended small-bowel enteroscopy** depends on peristalsis to move the scope distally; thus, the procedure may require up to 8 hours for completion. Furthermore, therapeutic and biopsy capabilities are absent. When successful, as much as 70% of the SI can be visualized and may be more sensitive than conventional enteroclysis.

   c. **Capsule endoscopy** is a disposable "camera pill" that images the entire GI tract as it passes from mouth to anus. While data demonstrate that capsule endoscopy is superior to push enteroscopy and barium small-bowel imaging for diagnosing obscure GI bleeding (*Am J Gastroenterol.* 2005;100(11):2407–2418), its diagnostic yield is around 50% (*J Gastrointest Liver Dis.* 2010;19(2):141–145). Nevertheless, capsule endoscopy is the third test of choice for obscure GI bleeding after traditional upper and lower endoscopy.

d. **Double-balloon enteroscopy (DBE)** uses two inflatable balloons on the tip of an endoscope to relatively quickly negotiate the small bowel. The technique can be used antegrade or retrograde and allows therapeutic intervention. Although indications and clinical applications are evolving, DBE offers the promise that the SI may be fully accessible to endoscopic diagnosis and treatment in the same manner as the rest of the GI tract. In addition, endoscopic retrograde cholangiopancreatography (ERCP) can be performed in areas previously inaccessible due to surgery (i.e., post Roux-en-Y gastric bypass). DBE has a comparable diagnostic yield for obscure GI bleeding when compared to capsule endoscopy, though the latter is favored as the initial diagnostic test because of its noninvasive quality, tolerance, and ability to view the entire SI. Because of its therapeutic capabilities, DBE may be indicated in patients with a positive finding on capsule endoscopy or in patients with a normal capsule study and continued active bleeding (*Clin Gastroenterol Hepatol.* 2008;6(6):671–676).

2. **Imaging**
   a. A **tagged red blood cell** nuclear medicine scan is highly sensitive for the detection of GI bleeding, detecting rates of hemorrhage of 0.1 to 0.5 mL/minute. However, in the setting of SI bleeding, this test is of limited utility because of the lack of anatomic detail.
   b. **Angiography** has a better ability to localize small-bowel bleeding, although it is less sensitive than a nuclear medicine study (detects bleeding at 1 to 1.5 mL/min). The angiographer can also potentially therapeutically embolize the bleeding mesenteric vessel or leave a catheter in place to assist in intraoperative localization of the lesion. In addition, methylene blue can be selectively injected to stain the target segment of intestine immediately prior to or during surgery to aid in intraoperative localization.

B. Effective **surgical therapy** hinges on successful preoperative *localization* of the bleeding lesion. Unlike the remainder of the GI tract, the small bowel cannot be resected *en bloc* for intractable bleeding with a goal of long-term survival. Preoperative localization of the lesion for segmental resection is strongly advised because of the difficulty in identifying a source intraoperatively. The angiographic techniques described previously are invaluable in this regard. *Intraoperative enteroscopy* can be used to identify mucosal abnormalities in the majority of patients in whom upper endoscopy, colonoscopy, and push enteroscopy have failed to recognize as source of bleeding. However, the therapeutic efficacy in preventing recurrent hemorrhage has been reported to be less than 50% (*Am J Surg.* 1992;163(1):94–99).

VII. ENTERIC FISTULAS are a constant therapeutic challenge. A fistula is defined as a communication or tract between two epithelialized surfaces (e.g., bowel, skin, and bladder). Fistulas are categorized according to anatomy, output, and etiology.

A. **Anatomic considerations**

1. **External versus internal.** *External* fistulas are the most common and connect an internal organ system with the skin or atmosphere, for example, an enterocutaneous (ECF) or enteroatmospheric (EAF) fistula. *Internal* fistulas connect two hollow structures of the same or different organ systems. Examples include colovesicular and enteroenteric fistulas.

2. **Proximal versus distal.** *Proximal* fistulas are located in the stomach, duodenum, or jejunum and are usually associated with high outputs of 3 or more liters per day. Profound dehydration, malnutrition, and electrolyte disturbances are common with these fistulas. *Distal* fistulas arise in the ileum or colon and are associated with fewer complications than proximal fistulas, and they more often close with nonoperative treatment.

3. Anatomic, etiologic, and physiologic classifications are also used. Anatomical descriptions include the names of the organs involved such that a fistula between the small bowel and the colon is referred to as an enterocolonic fistula. These connections can be described based on the underlying etiology of the fistula as well (i.e., Crohn's, radiation-induced, postoperative, or cancer-based fistulae). Physiologic categorization of fistulas is centered on the *output* and is divided into *high* (>500 mL/day), *moderate* (200 to 500 mL/day), and *low* (<200 mL/day) output fistulas.

B. **Pathophysiology.** Fistula-associated complications may be life-threatening and require rapid intervention to avoid morbidity and mortality. The overall mortality for all enteric fistulas is 5% to 20%.

1. Loss of GI contents can lead to *hypovolemia* as well as *acid–base and electrolyte abnormalities.* High-output fistulas may release large volumes of fluid that cannot be adequately replaced by enteral means, leading to dehydration and intravascular volume depletion. Loss of large fluid volumes and associated electrolytes also results in metabolic derangements that correlate directly with the quantity of fistula output.

2. Malnutrition is caused by caloric intake insufficient to meet increased metabolic demands associated with fistula formation. In addition, substantial portions of the GI tract may be functionally excluded. The ensuing malabsorption leads to vitamin and mineral deficiency, as well as alterations in carbohydrate, fat, and protein metabolism.

C. **Etiology**

1. **Abdominal operations** are the leading cause of fistula formation. The risk is greatest for operations performed for inflammatory bowel disease, ischemia, malignancy, or extensive intestinal adhesions. Dissection may result in unrecognized enterotomies, devascularization, and

serosal disruption. Anastomotic disruption, leaks, and perianastomotic abscesses are also hazardous. Malnutrition and immunosuppression significantly increase the risk of fistula formation as well.

2. **Crohn's disease** of the small bowel is another common cause of ECFs or enteroenteric fistulas.

3. **Diverticular disease** results in fistula formation when localized abscesses drain into adjacent organs. Common examples include colovesical and colovaginal fistulas. Internal fistulas should be suspected in patients with diverticular disease who exhibit persistent or recurrent urinary tract infections or sepsis.

4. **Malignant** fistulas form when tumor perforates or invades adjacent structures. Healing does not occur if cancer is present, and resection is the only means of cure.

5. **Radiation enteritis** predisposes to fistula formation after operation, regardless of the temporal proximity of exposure.

6. **Trauma** (penetrating or blunt) to the abdomen or pelvis may also give rise to SB fistulas. Missed enteric injuries or those repaired in a contaminated field may be prone to leak and subsequent fistula formation. Unrecognized viscus rupture from blunt trauma that forms an abscess and drains into adjacent structures may have a similar result, seen most commonly with duodenum, colon, or pancreas injuries that infect the retroperitoneum.

7. **Other causes** of SB fistulas include a foreign body, vascular compromise, and various infectious diseases (amebiasis, tuberculosis, or actinomyces).

D. Diagnosis

1. **Imaging.** Anatomic definition via contrast radiography aids in determining prognosis and assists with the planning of operative repair. Fistulography is the best test that can be performed in mature fistula tracts (usually after 10 days) and typically provides good visualization of all tracts and sites of enteral communication (*Radiology.* 2002;224(1):9–23). Oral contrast studies, such as an upper GI with SBFT, can demonstrate contrast extravasation through the fistula, but are less sensitive than a fistulogram. SBFTs are valuable for assessing internal fistulas and sometimes distal obstructions. A contrast enema is the study of choice for rectal or colonic fistulas. In general, CT scanning is of limited value in assessing fistula anatomy, but should be used if an abscess or underlying malignancy is suspected.

2. **Endoscopy** can be useful to assess the bowel for underlying pathology, such as peptic ulceration, inflammatory bowel disease, or cancer. Fistula orifices themselves are, however, often difficult to identify by endoscopy.

E. Nonoperative treatment

1. **Spontaneous closure.** Approximately 40% of ECFs will close spontaneously typically after 4 to 6 weeks of sepsis-free, adequate nutritional support. A fistula with decreasing output and a healing wound should

be given additional time to close. Factors associated with increased rates of closure include low-output, long tract greater than 2 cm, small orifice less than 1 cm², a well-nourished state, and absence of abscess, sepsis, or active IBD. The difficult decision of how long to wait for spontaneous closure depends on individual circumstances and the complexity of the underlying illness. In a closed abdomen, waiting at least 3 to 6 months from the time of last laparotomy is advised before reoperating. For patients with enteroatmospheric fistulas, 6 to 12 months or longer may be needed before the underlying obliterative peritonitis subsides. Improved home intravenous (IV) therapy, parenteral nutrition, wound care, and somatostatin analogs have allowed longer periods of waiting for fistula closure to be possible. This time allows adhesions to attenuate and the patient to recover nutritional status and general health. If spontaneous healing does not appear likely, operative therapy is indicated after an appropriate waiting period.

2. **Fluid resuscitation and electrolyte correction.** The initial phase of ECF management focuses on hypovolemia correction followed by accurate measurement of ongoing fluid losses and prompt replacement. IV fluid administration is typically necessary because adequate enteral replacement of the increased fluid losses from the fistula is difficult. Electrolyte and acid–base status also must be followed closely. The composition of replacement fluids should be tailored to the type and the quantity of GI loses in order to meet the specific replacement demands (see Chapter 4, Table 4-1). In difficult cases, a basic metabolic profile can be measured on a sample of fistula output to direct fluid replacement.

3. **Sepsis control** is a mainstay of initial ECF treatment as sepsis remains the primary determinant of mortality from a fistula. Sepsis accompanies a large percentage of fistulas and is caused by undrained enteric leaks or abscesses. Furthermore, healing is impeded in the presence of sepsis.
   a. **Intra-abdominal abscess** presence should be excluded by a CT scan with PO and IV contrast in every patient presenting with a GI fistula. If found, percutaneous drainage should be performed.
   b. **IV antibiotics** directed against bowel flora are indicated when infection is present and used only when necessary. Reoperation for *source control* may be required to manage continuous bacterial seeding from the GI tract.
   c. **Infected wounds** are adequately opened and packed to allow complete drainage, debridement, and healing by secondary intention. Frequent dressing changes may be required.

4. **Nutritional support.** No level I evidence exists to support a nutritional route, although enteral feeding is widely preferred. Early, aggressive parenteral nutritional therapy has been shown to dramatically decreased mortality from fistulas (*Am J Surg.* 1964;108:157).
   a. **Complete bowel rest.** Initial NPO status reduces fistula drainage and simplifies the evaluation and stabilization of the patient. NG suction is beneficial only in the presence of distal obstruction.

    b. Enteral feeding is preferred as long as fistula output does not increase. Patients with low-output colonic or distal SI fistulas are often safely fed with standard enteral formulas. However, if the available bowel is short, elemental feeding may maximize absorption. In proximal fistula patients, feeding distal to the fistula is typically very effective (e.g., feeding jejunostomy tube in a gastric fistula). Direct feeding an intestinal fistula or fistuloclysis via a radiologically placed feeding catheter is another option.

    c. Parenteral nutrition can provide adequate nourishment when enteral feeding is not possible. Indications include intolerance to enteral nutrition, jejunal and ileal high-output fistulas, and proximal fistulas where distal enteral access is not possible. Complications of parenteral nutrition include biliary stasis, hepatic dysfunction, trace element (zinc, copper, chromium) and essential fatty acid deficiencies, and venous catheter-related difficulties.

  5. Control of fistula drainage. Fistula effluent is corrosive to the skin and must be controlled. For low-output fistulas, dressings can sometimes be used to simply absorb the effluent, but may impede healing and cause skin breakdown if prolonged contact occurs. Therefore, intubation of matured fistula tracts may be beneficial. For high-output fistulas, a suction or sump drainage system is preferable. Use of *somatostatin analogs* has revealed mixed results and has not been shown to increase the rate of fistula closure. Reports have demonstrated a reduction in fistula output (*Gut.* 2002;49(suppl IV):iv11–iv20; *Arch Surg.* 1992;127:97–99) and a decreased time to fistula closure (*Akt Chir.* 1994;29:96–99), but these results have not been uniformly replicated. Common practice also employs H_2-receptor antagonists or proton-pump inhibitors to reduce gastric and duodenal fistula output and provide stress ulceration prophylaxis though their efficacy in fistula management is unproven.

  6. Skin protection. Irritation and excoriation of the skin surrounding an ECF can be very painful, complicate wound management, and promote secondary infection. The skin surrounding a fistula should be examined and cleansed frequently as well as protected with a barrier device or powder. A vacuum-assisted wound closure device may help to control skin irritation and speed fistula closure (*World J Surg.* 2008;32:430–435). Early involvement of an enterostomal therapy nurse is critical in the management of fistula patients.

F. Operative treatment is indicated when a fistula fails to heal with non-operative management, or when sepsis cannot be controlled. Common conditions under which fistulas fail to close can be remembered with the aid of the mnemonic FRIEND: Foreign body, Radiation, Inflammation or Infection, Epithelialization, Neoplasm, or Distal obstruction. The goals of surgery are to eradicate the fistula tract and to restore the epithelial continuity of the associated organ systems.

  1. Gastric fistulas can arise from anastomotic breakdown or ulcer perforation. Most low-output gastric fistulas close spontaneously, such as occurs after removal of a gastrostomy tube. In cases where surgery is needed, primary repair or serosal patch placement is usually successful.

2. **Duodenal fistulas** typically close spontaneously with nonoperative management. When operative intervention is required, primary closure of small duodenal wall disruptions may be performed, but a duodenal stricture may result with primary closure of large defects. Defects that are in close proximity to the ampulla may also prevent primary closure. In these cases, duodenal wall integrity may be restored by a serosal patch using another segment of bowel. Alternatively, a Roux-en-Y duodenoenterostomy may be performed to divert duodenal output into the bowel.

3. **Small-bowel fistulas** typically require bowel resection and primary reanastomosis. In rare severe cases, a temporary diverting enterostomy may be necessary. For enteroenteric or other internal fistulas, openings that are in close proximity to the involved region can be resected *en bloc*.

4. **Large-bowel fistulas** are associated with high spontaneous closure rates. Fluid and electrolyte abnormalities are rare because outputs tend to be low. However, sepsis rates may be greater. If operative closure is required, a mechanical bowel preparation may be desired. Primary closure is rarely appropriate and resection with primary reanastomosis is preferred, but the choice depends on associated conditions, the nutritional status of the patient, and the location and complexity of the lesion. A proximal, diverting loop ileostomy should be considered if the anastomosis is suboptimal.

5. **Enteral feeding tubes** placed at the time of definitive repair may facilitate postoperative management.

VIII. **SHORT-BOWEL SYNDROME (SBS)** is a malabsorptive state and symptom complex that follows massive small-bowel resection. In adults, the normal length of the SI varies from 300 to 600 cm and correlates directly with body surface area. The length of combined jejunum and ileum that increases the risk for developing SBS in adults is less than 200 cm of functional bowel or less than 30% of the initial SI length with the presence of the terminal ileum. SBS may be seen with greater lengths of SI if an underlying disease, such as Crohn's or radiation enteritis, is present. Several factors determine the severity of SBS, including the extent of resection, the portion of the GI tract removed, the type of disease necessitating the resection, the presence of coexistent disease in the remaining bowel, and the adaptability of the remaining bowel. If an end enterostomy is performed, resection resulting in less than 100 cm of intact SI generally leads to SBS. If greater than one-third of the colon is in place, SBS may not develop until less than 75 cm or 1 mg/kg of SI remains. Children tend to develop SBS when only 30% or less of normal SI length for age is left, and infants may survive resection of up to 85% of their bowel because of enhanced adaptation and growth. Because the ileum has specialized absorptive function, complete resection is not well tolerated. On the contrary, the entire jejunum can usually be resected without serious adverse nutritional sequela.

A. **Etiology.** In children, the most common etiologies for SBS include necrotizing enterocolitis, congenital intestinal atresia, midgut volvulus, and gastroschisis. The leading causes of massive intestinal resection in adults and elderly patients are mesenteric ischemia, trauma, inflammatory bowel disease, strangulated hernia, SI or mesenteric neoplasms, volvulus, and portal vein thrombosis.

B. **Pathophysiology.** SBS is characterized by diarrhea, dehydration, electrolyte disturbances, steatorrhea, malnutrition, and weight loss.

1. **Adaptation.** The SI undergoes several adaptive changes in response to massive SI resection in an attempt to counteract the development of SBS. Structural adaptations, including greater bowel caliber, increased villus height, deeper crypts, and enhanced enterocyte proliferation and apoptosis, act to increase the absorptive surface area and nutrient transport of the bowel. Slower transit and increased nutrient absorption occurs through functional adaptations such as temporary hypergastrinemia, increased gastric acid secretion, slower gastric emptying (especially if colon present), substantially increased colonic absorption of water and electrolytes, and colonocyte degradation of carbohydrates into short-chain fatty acids (SCFA), which increases caloric uptake up to 50%. With resection of the jejunum, the distal SI has the greatest adaptive potential and can assume nearly all of the absorptive properties of the proximal gut.

2. **Fluid and electrolyte response.** Of the 7 to 10 L of fluid presented daily to the SI, only 1 to 2 L are delivered into the colon. Significant quantities of electrolytes are absorbed in this process. With SBS, this physiology is altered. Fortunately, the right colon can absorb a significant amount of the increased fluid it encounters with SBS.

3. **Malabsorption and malnutrition**

   a. **Gastric hypersecretion,** seen early in the postoperative period, can persist for prolonged periods. Increased acid load may injure distal bowel mucosa, leading to hypermotility and impaired absorption. The severity of hypersecretion correlates directly with the extent of bowel resection, and is generally more pronounced after jejunal than after ileal resection. Loss of an intestinal inhibitory hormone has been implicated.

   b. **Cholelithiasis.** Altered bilirubin metabolism after ileal resection increases the risk of gallstone formation secondary to a decreased bile salt pool causing a shift in the cholesterol saturation index. Terminal ileum resection, steatorrhea, and osmotic diarrhea lead to decreased uptake of bile salts. Chronic total parenteral nutrition (TPN) and resultant cholestasis also increase risk of cholelithiasis.

   c. **Hyperoxaluria and nephrolithiasis.** Hyperoxaluria results from excessive fatty acids in the colonic lumen binding intraluminal calcium. Unbound oxalate, which is normally made insoluble by luminal calcium binding and excreted in the feces, is then readily absorbed. The result is hyperoxaluria and calcium oxalate nephrolithiasis.

d. Diarrhea and steatorrhea. Rapid intestinal transit, hyperosmolar contents in the distal SI, disruption of the enterohepatic bile acid circulation, and bacterial overgrowth all promote steatorrhea and diarrhea. Fat absorption is severely impaired by ileal resection. Delivery of bile acids into the colon also produces a reactive, often severe watery diarrhea. Unabsorbed fats in the colon further inhibit absorption of water and electrolytes and stimulate secretion.

e. Bacterial overgrowth. Loss of the ileocecal valve permits reflux of colonic bacteria into the SI leading to bacterial overgrowth that impairs digestion and absorption of nutrients as the bacteria compete for nutrients with the enterocytes. Intestinal dysmotility further promotes bacterial colonization. Bacterial overgrowth and changes in the indigenous microbial population result in pH alteration and deconjugation of bile salts, with resultant malabsorption, fluid loss, and decreased vitamin B_{12} absorption. Infectious diarrhea (bacterial or viral) is a main cause of morbidity.

C. **Acute phase treatment.** The primary goal in the acute phase (initial 4 weeks) is to stabilize the metabolic, respiratory, and cardiovascular parameters related to the fluid shifts and sepsis that frequently accompany massive small-bowel resection. TPN, strict intake and output records, and close monitoring of serum electrolytes are critical in the early management of patients with SBS.

1. **Prolonged ileus** may result from deranged motility patterns and changes in intraluminal milieu. Parenteral nutrition should be provided until GI function resumes. If the ileus is unusually persistent, underlying mechanical obstruction or sepsis should be suspected and investigated.

2. **Gastric hypersecretion** requires H_2-receptor antagonists or proton-pump inhibitors to reduce the hypersecretory response and protect against peptic ulceration. Antacids take effect immediately and should be administered routinely in patients with SBS.

3. **Nutritional support** should be instituted early to maintain a positive nitrogen balance and to promote wound healing and adaptation of the remaining bowel. Enteral nutrition has a positive trophic effect on the bowel mucosa, stimulates the remaining intestine, and should be started as soon as possible, even if caloric goals are not met. Feeding tubes placed at laparotomy are often key. Initial feeds should be gradual, continuous low volume, low fat, and isosmotic. Isotonic salt-glucose solutions are useful.

D. **Maintenance phase treatment.** Maintenance therapy in SBS focuses on long-term nutritional goals, support of adaptation that takes place over the first 1 to 2 years, and addressing various clinical issues that arise.

1. **Nutritional support** with supplemental vitamins, trace elements and minerals (zinc, selenium, and iron), and essential fatty acids (linoleic acid) should be given parenterally until adequate enteral absorption is achieved. Absorption of the fat-soluble vitamins A, D, E, and K is especially prone to compromise. Vitamin B_{12} and calcium uptake are

also affected by altered fat absorption and should be supplemented. Potassium and magnesium losses should be closely monitored as well. Growth hormone and glutamine have been used with some success to treat inadequate adaptation and TPN dependence (*Ann Surg.* 2005;242:655–661). Nightly administration of chronic TPN can allow normal daily activity.

2. **Diarrhea** is often multifactorial in SBS, and dietary modifications can improve symptoms. H_2-receptor blockers reduce gastric acid production and secretory volume. Chelating resins like cholestyramine reduce intraluminal bile salts and resultant diarrhea but affect the systemic bile salt pool. Antisecretory medications, such as loperamide or somatostatin analogs, may be beneficial, although octreotide can inhibit the adaptation. Low-dose narcotics (diphenoxylate hydrochloride and atropine (Lomotil), codeine, or tincture of opium) are efficacious but addictive. Bacterial overgrowth should be evaluated by stool culture and antimicrobials, such as metronidazole or tetracycline, administered as needed.

3. **Late complications** are common and include nephrolithiasis, cholelithiasis, nutritional deficiencies (e.g., anemia, bone disease, and coagulopathy), liver dysfunction, TPN-related difficulties, and central venous catheter-related issues like thrombosis or sepsis. Anastomotic leaks, fistulas, strictures, and late bowel obstructions can also occur well beyond the early postoperative period and commonly require reoperation.

E. **Surgical therapy.** Various surgical procedures have been described for the management of SBS, but have not been widely adopted. The most commonly used intestinal lengthening procedures for patients with SBS are Serial Transverse Enteroplasty (STEP) and the Bianchi procedure that similarly have been shown to decrease TPN dependence, increase oral caloric intake, and reverse liver disease (*Ann Surg.* 2007;246(4):593–604). STEP is performed with a reusable GIA stapler that is applied to the bowel in sequence from opposite directions through small mesenteric windows creating a zig-zag like channel that lengthens the bowel. The Bianchi isolates the dual blood supply of the SI by separating the mesenteric borders, longitudinally divides the intestine, and creates an isoperistaltic end-to-end, handsewn anastomosis. Isolated small-bowel transplants or multivisceral transplantations (including the liver for patients with severe cholestatic cirrhosis from chronic TPN) are additional options for SBS. Prevention of complications and minimizing the extent of initial bowel resection that lead to SBS is extremely important.

IX. **CROHN'S DISEASE** is an idiopathic, chronic, granulomatous inflammatory disease that can affect any part of the GI tract from the mouth to the anus. This incurable, slowly progressive disease is characterized by episodes of exacerbation and remission. The incidence is 4/100,000, with a bimodal age distribution at 15 to 29 and 55 to 70 years old.

A. **Etiology.** The cause of Crohn's disease is unknown, but is believed to involve interplay between genetic and environmental factors. The genetic component is strong; Crohn's disease is 25 times more common among patients with a family history and has a concordance rate of 60% in monozygotic twins. Environmental aspects, such as smoking, also increase the risk of developing Crohn's disease. Pathogenesis likely relates to a defective mucosal barrier and/or dysregulated intestinal immunity that leads to a chronic inflammatory reaction within the intestinal wall.

B. **Bowel involvement.** The *terminal ileum* is the most common site of disease and is involved in 75% of cases. Three "patterns" of disease have been described.

   1. **Ileocolic** disease affects the terminal ileum (and in some cases the cecum) and is the most common form, affecting 40% of patients.

   2. **Small-bowel-only** disease (30% of patients) is confined to the more-proximal SI.

   3. **Colonic** disease (30% of patients) affects only the large intestine. Perianal involvement commonly coexists with more proximal forms, especially when the colon is affected. Anorectal disease confinement is rare (5%).

C. **Histology.** Grossly, diseased bowel is thickened, displays creeping fat and corkscrew vessels, and has a shortened fibrotic mesentery containing enlarged lymph nodes. Mucosal changes include pinpoint hemorrhages, aphthous ulcers, deep linear fissures, and *cobblestoning*. These findings commonly occur segmentally along the intestine rather than being contiguous causing *skip lesions*. Crohn's disease is characterized by fullthickness, *transmural inflammation* of the bowel wall that begins adjacent to the crypts and leads to the development of crypt abscesses, aphthous ulcers, and linear fissures. The transmural involvement can produce sinus tracts and fistulas between adjacent segments of bowel. *Granulomas* are also found in the bowel wall in 40% to 60% of patients and are detected in mesenteric lymph nodes in 25% of patients.

D. **Clinical presentation.** Crohn's disease has a highly variable presentation. Patient history is important in narrowing the differential diagnosis. Physical examination is performed with special attention to the abdominal and anorectal areas. No physical signs are pathognomonic for Crohn's disease, although the appearance of the perianal area may be highly suggestive. Laboratory evaluation is nonspecific.

   1. **Diarrhea** occurs in almost all patients and usually is not bloody unless the colon is involved. Patients with ileal disease may be bile salt deficient, resulting in steatorrhea. Mucosal inflammation with decreased absorption and increased secretion also results in diarrhea.

   2. **Abdominal pain** typically is intermittent, crampy, worse after meals, relieved by defecation, and poorly localized. A mass caused by thickened bowel, a phlegmon, or an abscess may be palpable.

   3. **Weight loss** occurs as a result of decreased oral intake, malabsorption, protein-losing enteropathy, and steatorrhea. Children with Crohn's disease develop vitamin and mineral deficiencies and growth retardation.

   4. **Constitutional symptoms** such as malaise and fever are common.

5. **Anorectal** disease is a common finding and may precede intestinal symptoms by several years. Such lesions include recurrent nonhealing anal fissures, large ulcers, complex anal fistulas, perianal abscesses, large, fleshy skin tags, and bluish skin discoloration. Perianal Crohn's disease is characterized by a multiplicity of lesions, lateral fissures, deep ulcers of the perianal skin and anal canal, and anal stricture.

6. **Extraintestinal manifestations** are numerous. The eyes may develop conjunctivitis, iritis, and uveitis. The skin may develop pyoderma gangrenosum, erythema nodosum multiforme, and aphthous stomatitis. Musculoskeletal manifestations include arthritis, ankylosing spondylitis, and hypertrophic osteoarthropathy. Finally, sclerosing cholangitis can lead to cirrhosis and liver failure.

E. **Imaging.** Radiological studies are indicated to help establish the diagnosis of Crohn's disease or to identify a complication that may require surgical intervention.

1. **Contrast radiography,** such as SBFT, enteroclysis (SBE), and water-soluble contrast enema, is valuable in the diagnosis of Crohn's disease and may reveal strictures or segments of ulcerated mucosa. SBE is considered the optimal investigation to exclude small-bowel disease in these patients, with a sensitivity of 93% and a specificity of 92% (*Eur Radiol.* 2000;10:1894–1898). However, in day-to-day practice, SBFT is simpler and may be preferred for its superiority in detecting mucosal disease, fistulas, or gastroduodenal involvement, but is operator dependent and not as good for strictures.

2. **Endoscopy** is most useful in diagnosis and for obtaining biopsy material in patients with terminal ileal and colonic disease. For patients with suspected Crohn's disease, ileocolonoscopy and biopsies from the terminal ileum as well as each colonic segment to look for microscopic evidence of disease are first-line procedures to establish the diagnosis. Similar to patients with ulcerative colitis, those with long-standing (>10 years) Crohn's colitis are at increased risk for adenocarcinoma, and surveillance colonoscopy for cancer is important. These patients also have an increased incidence of SI cancer.

3. **CT** with enteroclysis or enterography has improved significantly, leading to reports that it is complementary or even superior to barium studies for the detection of involved segments. CT is able to identify abscesses, focal inflammation, perforation, and wall thickening. Abscesses can be drained percutaneously under CT guidance.

4. **Magnetic resonance imaging (MRI)** is also useful for assessing the location, extent, and disease activity, particularly in specialized centers where MR has also undergone technical developments that may make it the method of choice complementary to ileocolonoscopy and biopsy. An added advantage of MRI is the ability to detect extramural complications including abscesses, fistulas, sacroiliitis, gallstones, and renal calculi. Magnetic resonance enteroclysis (**MRE**) has a reported sensitivity and specificity of 95% and 93%, respectively, for the primary diagnosis of Crohn's disease, but is more invasive than SBE (*Gut.* 2006;55:i1–i15).

F. **Complications.** Intestinal obstruction, stricture, fistula, perforation, intra-abdominal abscess, GI bleeding, and perirectal abscess and fistula can occur. Toxic colitis is a surgical emergency that can occur in these patients.

G. **Differential diagnosis.** Other inflammatory bowel diseases as well as common infectious abdominal conditions can mimic Crohn's disease.

1. **Ulcerative colitis.** Patients with Crohn's disease generally have less severe diarrhea, usually without gross blood. Perianal lesions, non-confluent skip lesions, transmural involvement, large mucosal ulcers and fissures, small-bowel involvement, *rectal sparing*, and the presence of granulomas all help to differentiate Crohn's disease from ulcerative colitis. Some patients who cannot be confidently diagnosed with either condition are labeled as having indeterminate colitis.

2. **Appendicitis.** Acute right-lower-quadrant abdominal pain due to Crohn's ileitis can mimic acute appendicitis.

3. **Infectious ileitis** presents with pain and bloody diarrhea. The diagnosis is made by stool culture.

4. **Other** diseases that present similarly to Crohn's disease include intestinal lymphoma, intestinal tuberculosis, ischemic enteritis, diverticulitis, severe gastroenteritis, pseudomembranous colitis, and irritable bowel syndrome.

H. **Treatment**

1. **Adequate nutrition** is essential both during and between disease flares, and enteral feeds should be continued whenever possible. A low-residue, high-protein, milk-free diet generally provides adequate nutrition. Vitamin and mineral supplementation may be necessary. Patients with severe or unresponsive disease should be given TPN and placed on total bowel rest.

2. **Medical management** is particularly important because Crohn's disease has no cure. Therefore, treatment seeks to palliate symptoms, correct nutritional disturbances, and reduce inflammation. Disease location, severity, and complications dictate therapeutic recommendations. Mild-to-moderate disease can be treated with oral aminosalicylates (sulfasalazine 3 to 6 g/day, or mesalamine 1 g four times/day). For ileal, colonic, or perianal disease, metronidazole, 500 mg three times/day, can be added. In patients with severe disease, steroid therapy should be initiated after active infection or abscess has been excluded. Prednisone, with initial daily doses of 40 to 60 mg orally, is a common outpatient treatment of acute flares; inpatients may receive hydrocortisone, 50 to 100 mg intravenously every 6 hours. Response to therapy should be evident within 7 days. Data show that infusions of infliximab (Remicade), a monoclonal antibody against (TNF), is effective for Crohn's flares and fistulas (*N Engl J Med.* 2004;350:876). Before receiving infliximab, no active source of infection should be present and purified protein derivative (PPD)-negative. Infliximab is particularly useful in poor surgical candidates who have failed medical management. After recovery from an acute flare, the medical regimen should be simplified

to prevent long-term complications. Steroids should be tapered as soon as possible to prevent side effects such as osteopenia, avascular necrosis, psychosis, and weight gain. The addition of immunomodulators, such as 6-mercaptopurine, may allow patients with refractory disease to taper off of prednisone.

3. **Surgical therapy** is indicated when medical therapy has failed to address acute complications of the disease, such as high-output fistulas, perforation, intra-abdominal abscess, severe colitis, bleeding, or obstruction from fibrotic strictures. Abdominal abscesses can usually be drained percutaneously with or without elective bowel resection later. Most Crohn's patients require operative treatment during their lifetime.

   a. At the time of operation, the most important principle is to correct the complication while *preserving bowel length* to prevent SBS. Resection to histologically negative margins does not significantly reduce the likelihood of disease recurrence; therefore, grossly normal margins of 2 cm are accepted. In the absence of free perforation, large abscesses, massively dilated bowel, severe malnutrition, or high-dose immunosuppression, primary anastomosis is safe. Stapling should be avoided in thick-walled bowel and a handsewn anastomosis is indicated. Recent series suggest that laparoscopic ileocolic resections are safe alternatives to open procedures, especially at the time of first operation (*Dis Colon Rectum.* 2003;46:1129). Issues that require special consideration beyond the scope of this chapter are duodenal disease, multiple skip lesions, and chronic fibrotic strictures in the setting of SBS.

   b. *Appendectomy.* Patients who are being explored for presumed acute appendicitis and are found to have Crohn's ileitis should have the appendix removed if the cecum is not inflamed. Conventional teaching has been that the terminal ileum should not be removed. This is controversial, however, given the low morbidity of ileocecal resection and the uncertainty of response to subsequent medical therapy.

   c. *Surgical complications* include anastomotic leaks, ECF fistulas, and sepsis related to intra-abdominal abscesses and wound infections.

I. **Prognosis.** Crohn's disease is a chronic, pan-intestinal disease that currently has no cure and requires chronic, lifelong treatment, with operation reserved for severe complications. Recently, however, specific "susceptibility genes" (e.g., *NOD2/CARD15*) have been identified in patients with Crohn's disease. Further study of the pathways involved may shed light on pathogenesis and lead to more effective medical treatments.

X. **NEOPLASMS** of the small bowel are uncommon and account for less than 2% of all GI cancers. Tumors of the SI present insidiously with vague, nonspecific symptoms, and, when benign, are often discovered incidentally. SI tumors can also be a lead point in an intussusception. The majority of malignant tumors eventually become symptomatic with weight loss, abdominal pain, obstruction, perforation, or hemorrhage.

A. **Benign tumors.** Benign small-bowel masses are more common than malignant.

1. **Leiomyoma** is the most common benign neoplasm of the SI and arises from mesenchymal cells. These tumors grow submucosally and project into the lumen of the small bowel. On a contrast studies, they appear as a smooth, eccentric filling defects with intact, normal-appearing mucosa. Histopathologic exam is needed to distinguish benign from malignant stromal tumors. Treatment consists of a segmental bowel resection.

2. **Adenomas** can occur sporadically as solitary lesions, or in association with familial adenomatous polyposis syndrome (Gardner variant). When symptomatic, these lesions can cause fluctuating pain secondary to intermittent obstruction, intussusception, or bleeding. Three types of SI adenomas exist: simple tubular, Brunner's gland, and villous adenomas. The duodenum is the most common site for all three types of adenomas. Tubular and Brunner's gland adenomas have a low malignant potential and can be treated with complete endoscopic polypectomy. Villous adenomas have significant malignant potential. If complete endoscopic resection is not possible, transduodenal excision with adequate margins is appropriate. Villous adenomas of the jejunum or ileum should be removed with a small-bowel resection.

3. **Hamartomas** arise in patients with Peutz–Jeghers syndrome, an autosomal-dominant, inherited syndrome of mucocutaneous melanotic pigmentation characterized by multiple GI polyps. Operative intervention is indicated only for symptoms. At surgery, all polyps larger than 1 cm should be resected. Because of an increased risk for *de novo* adenocarcinoma (arising separately from the hamartomas), patients need endoscopic screening.

4. **Other benign tumors** include **lipomas** that occur most often in the ileum and have no malignant potential. On CT, lipomas show fatty attenuation. **Hemangiomas** may be associated with Osler–Weber–Rendu disease and present with bleeding. Diagnosis can be made with enteroscopy, capsule endoscopy, or angiography. **Neurofibromas and fibromas** are less common tumors that can cause intussusception. **Endometriosis** can cause SI implants that appear as puckered, bluish-red, serosal-based nodules that can cause GI bleeding or obstruction.

B. **Malignant tumors**

1. **Adenocarcinoma** is the most common malignant small intestinal tumor. Forty percent occur in the duodenum, and their frequency decreases distally through the small bowel. Risk factors for the development of adenocarcinoma include villous adenomas, polyposis syndromes, Crohn's disease, and hereditary nonpolyposis colorectal cancer (HNPCC). Patients often remain asymptomatic for long periods of time and have distant metastases at diagnosis. The presenting symptoms depend on the location of the primary tumor. Periampullary tumors can present with painless jaundice, duodenal obstruction, or bleeding. More-distal tumors tend to present with abdominal pain and

weight loss from progressive obstruction. Contrast studies, CT, and endoscopy with or without ERCP can be used for diagnosis. *Treatment* consists of segmental small-bowel resection with excision of the adjacent lymph node-bearing mesentery. Any adherent structures should be resected *en bloc* if possible. Tumors of the terminal ileum should be resected along with the right colon. For carcinomas of the duodenum, a pancreaticoduodenectomy is usually required. In resections of duodenal adenocarcinomas, the 5-year survival rate is 56% for node-positive and 83% for node-negative disease, respectively (*Ann Surg Oncol.* 2004;11:380). Distal lesions tend to present at a later stage. Patients with metastatic disease at the time of diagnosis rarely survive past 6 months. 5-Fluorouracil–based chemotherapy regimens have been tried, but data on their efficacy are lacking.

2. **Gastrointestinal stromal tumors** (GISTs) arise from mesodermal-derived components of the SI and are equally distributed along the length of the intestine. These tumors grow extraluminally and cause symptoms late in their course. Because of their vascular nature, when these tumors outgrow their blood supply and necrose, they may hemorrhage into either the peritoneum or the lumen of the bowel. Mutations of **c-kit** (CD117; a tyrosine kinase responsible for neoplastic growth) allow diagnosis by immunohistochemistry. Curative *treatment* of GI stromal tumors is wide *en bloc* resection with tumor-free margins. Extensive lymph node resection is unnecessary because these tumors have a low potential for lymphatic spread. Traditional chemotherapy and radiation therapy are not effective in the treatment of metastatic GISTs. However, *imatinib mesylate (Gleevec)* is important in treatment and inhibits the overactive tyrosine receptor c-kit found on all GIST cells. Inhibition of this receptor has been shown to cause radiographic and histologic regression of metastatic lesions (*N Engl J Med.* 2001;344:1052). In the adjuvant setting following primary GIST resection, imatinib therapy improves recurrence-free survival (*Lancet.* 2009;373(9669):1097–1104. Sunitinib malate (Sutent) is the recommended option for second-line therapy of metastatic GIST that develop resistance to imatinib (*Lancet.* 2006;368:1329–1338). The role of resecting isolated pulmonary or hepatic lesions is unclear, but appears beneficial. Selected patients with metastatic GIST who have responsive disease or focal resistance (only one tumor has radiological evidence of growth) to tyrosine kinase inhibitor therapy appear to benefit from elective surgical resection (*Ann Surg.* 2007;245(3):347–352). Histologic grade and tumor size are the most important predictors of survival. After complete resection, the overall 5-year survival rate is 50%. In low-grade tumors [<10 mitotic figures/high power field (mf/hpf)], the survival rate is 60% to 80%, whereas in high-grade tumors (>10 mf/hpf), the survival rate is less than 20%. With local recurrence, the median length of survival is 9 to 12 months. With metastatic disease, the median length of survival is 20 months (*Br J Surg.* 2003;90:1178). However, imatinib mesylate treatment extends the 2-year survival rate to 78% for patients with metastatic disease (*Eur J Cancer.* 2004;40:689).

3. **Primary small-bowel lymphomas** are most common in the ileum because this area has the largest amount of gut-associated lymphoid tissue. Virtually all small-bowel lymphomas are non-Hodgkin, *B-cell lymphomas* that arise either *de novo* or in association with a preexisting systemic condition such as celiac disease, Crohn's disease, or immuno-suppression (iatrogenic, HIV, etc.). The presentation of these patients is highly variable. Imaging can help make a diagnosis, but operation is frequently required for histologic confirmation. Treatment of lymphoma localized to the SI involves wide resection of the affected segment of intestine and its associated mesentery. To stage the tumor accurately, the liver should be biopsied and the periaortic lymph nodes sampled. For widespread disease, resection of the affected intestine should be performed to prevent complications such as obstruction or bleeding. The role of adjuvant chemotherapy and radiotherapy remains controversial. The 5-year survival for patients with fully resected disease approaches 80%, but individuals with more advanced disease usually die within 1 year of surgery.

4. **Carcinoid tumors** arise from the Kulchitsky or enterochromaffin cells of the intestinal crypts. Most intestinal carcinoids occur within 2 feet of the ileocecal valve. Small-bowel carcinoid tumors tend to be much more aggressive than their appendiceal or rectal counterparts. Patients rarely manifest signs or symptoms of the tumor until late in the course, such as the local complications of GI obstruction, pain, or bleeding, or the systemic symptoms of the carcinoid syndrome. Metastases are rare in tumors smaller than 1 cm in size, while half of tumors between 1 and 2 cm metastasize, and almost all tumors larger than 2 cm spread.

   a. *Carcinoid syndrome* presence implies hepatic metastatic spread. Normally, hormones released by carcinoid tumors are metabolized by the liver and produce no symptoms. However, hepatic metastases drain into the systemic circulation and classic symptoms including *diarrhea* and transient *flushing* of the face, neck, and upper chest occur. Tachycardia, hypotension, bronchospasm, and even coma can also be observed. In long-standing carcinoid syndrome, patients develop right heart endocardial and valvular fibrosis. Classically, diagnosis of GI carcinoid tumors has been made by measuring a 24 hour urinary 5-hydroxyindoleacetic acid (5-HIAA), the breakdown product of serotonin that is secreted by the tumor. In patients with symptoms of the carcinoid syndrome, the sensitivity and specificity of this test nears 100%. Serum chromogranin A measurement is another commonly used test for diagnosis of GI carcinoids and has a similarly high sensitivity (80% to 100%), but is less specific than urine 5-HIAA levels (*Surg Oncol Clin N Am.* 2006;15:463–478).

   b. The **treatment** of carcinoid tumors is operative. The entire SI should be inspected because in 30% of cases synchronous lesions are present. Jejunal and ileal tumors should be treated with segmental resection including the adjacent mesentery. Small tumors (<1 cm) located in the third or fourth portions of the duodenum can be either locally excised or included in a segmental resection. For large duodenal tumors and periampullary tumors, a pancreaticoduodenectomy should be performed. In the presence of locally advanced disease with involvement of adjacent organs or peritoneum, aggressive resection should be undertaken to delay the occurrence of mesenteric desmoplastic reaction, hepatic metastases, and carcinoid syndrome. Solitary and accessible liver lesions should be resected. Adjuvant cytotoxic chemotherapy and radiotherapy are of little benefit. The somatostatin analog **octreotide** offers excellent palliation of carcinoid syndrome in patients with unresectable disease. Octreotide decreases the concentration of circulating serotonin and urinary 5-HIAA, and can relieve diarrhea and flushing in 90% of patients.

  c. Carcinoids are slow-growing tumors, and **prognosis** depends on the stage of the tumor. The overall 5-year survival rate is 60%. Patients with local disease that is completely resected have a normal life expectancy. For patients with resectable node-positive disease, the median length of survival is 15 years. The median length of survival drops to 5 years with unresectable intra-abdominal disease and is 3 years for those with hepatic metastases.

5. **Carcinomatosis** is diffuse studding of the peritoneal, mesenteric, and bowel surfaces by tumor nodules. Many tumors can cause peritoneal carcinomatosis, including cancer of the pancreas, stomach, ovaries, appendix, and colon. Carcinomatosis has an extremely poor prognosis, and surgical treatment is palliative, usually for obstruction. The only exception is pseudomyxoma peritonei, a low-grade malignancy, where patients may benefit from resection and intraperitoneal chemotherapy.

6. **Metastases** can spread to the small bowel and palliative resection may be appropriate if required for symptom relief. Several primary cancers are known to metastasize to the SI including melanoma, colorectal, gynecologic, breast, stomach, lung, prostate, and renal cancers among others. In patients who undergo laparotomy with or without small-bowel resection, complication rates are high (35%) and mortality significant (10%). Furthermore, median survival is poor (5 months), though patients with a history of colorectal cancer have been to shown to have better survival than patients other cancers. The extent of recurrent disease may be the primary factor that affects overall survival (*World J Surg Onc.* 2007;5:122). Cases should be considered individually and discussion made with patients over their poor prognosis. Palliative gastrostomy tubes to relieve obstruction with or without TPN may be appropriate in advanced cases where nonoperative management is chosen.

11 Acute Abdominal Pain and Appendicitis

William Symons and Alicia Kieninger

ACUTE ABDOMINAL PAIN

Acute abdomen is defined as the recent or sudden onset of severe abdominal pain. This can be new pain or an increase in chronic pain. Evaluation of the patient with acute abdominal pain requires a careful history and physical examination by a skilled physician in conjunction with selective diagnostic testing. Acute abdominal pain is the most common general surgical problem presenting to the emergency department. It has a vast **differential diagnosis,** including both intra- and extraperitoneal processes. The acute abdomen **does not always** signify the need for surgical intervention; however, surgical evaluation is warranted.

I. **PATHOPHYSIOLOGY.** This chapter focuses on intra-abdominal causes of abdominal pain. However, one must be cognizant of the fact that pathology on the surface of the abdomen (e.g., rectus sheath hematoma) or even outside the abdomen (e.g., testicular torsion) can present as abdominal pain. Abdominal pain arising from intra-abdominal pathophysiology originates in the peritoneum, which is a membrane comprising two layers. These layers, the visceral and parietal peritoneum, are developmentally distinct areas with separate nerve supplies.

A. Visceral pain

1. **Visceral peritoneum** is innervated bilaterally by the autonomic nervous system. The bilateral innervation causes visceral pain to be midline, vague, deep, dull, and poorly localized (e.g., vague periumbilical pain of the midgut).

2. Visceral pain is **triggered by inflammation, ischemia, and geometric changes** such as distention, traction, and pressure.

3. Visceral pain signifies **intra-abdominal disease** but not necessarily the need for surgical intervention.

4. **Embryologic origin** of the affected organ determines the location of visceral pain in the abdominal midline. **Foregut-derived structures** (stomach to the second portion of the duodenum, liver and biliary tract, pancreas, spleen) present with epigastric pain. **Midgut-derived structures** (second portion of the duodenum to the proximal two thirds of the transverse colon) present with periumbilical pain. **Hindgut-derived structures** (distal transverse colon to the anal verge) present with suprapubic pain.

B. Parietal pain

1. **Parietal peritoneum** is innervated unilaterally via the spinal somatic nerves that also supply the abdominal wall. Unilateral innervation causes parietal pain to localize to one or more abdominal quadrants (e.g., inflamed appendix producing parietal peritoneal irritation).

2. Parietal pain is **sharp, severe, and well localized.**

3. Parietal pain is **triggered by irritation of the parietal peritoneum** by an inflammatory process (e.g., chemical peritonitis from perforated peptic ulcer or bacterial peritonitis from acute appendicitis). It may also be triggered by mechanical stimulation, such as a surgical incision.

4. Parietal pain is **associated with physical examination findings of local or diffuse peritonitis** and frequently, but not always, signifies the need for surgical treatment.

C. **Referred pain** arises from a deep visceral structure but is superficial at the presenting site (Fig. 11-1).

1. It results from **central neural pathways** that are common to the somatic nerves and visceral organs.

2. Examples include **biliary tract pain** (referred to the right inferior scapular area) and **diaphragmatic irritation** from any source, such as subphrenic abscess (referred to the ipsilateral shoulder).

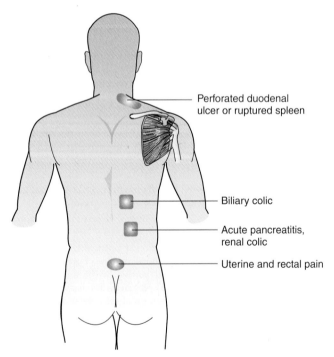

Figure 11-1. Frequent sites of referred pain and common causes.

II. EVALUATION of the acute abdomen remains heavily influenced by patient history and physical exam findings. Ancillary imaging and lab tests can help to complete the diagnosis and guide treatment decisions.

A. **History of present illness**

1. **Onset and duration of pain**

    a. **Sudden onset of pain** (within seconds) suggests perforation or rupture [e.g., perforated peptic ulcer or ruptured abdominal aortic aneurysm (AAA)]. Infarction, such as myocardial infarction or acute mesenteric occlusion, can also present with sudden onset of pain.

    b. **Rapidly accelerating pain** (within minutes) may result from several sources.

       (1) **Colic syndromes,** such as biliary colic, ureteral colic, and small-bowel obstruction.

       (2) **Inflammatory processes,** such as acute appendicitis, pancreatitis, and diverticulitis.

       (3) **Ischemic processes,** such as mesenteric ischemia, strangulated intestinal obstruction, and volvulus.

    c. **Gradual onset of pain** (over several hours) increasing in intensity may be caused by one of the following:

       (1) **Inflammatory conditions,** such as appendicitis and cholecystitis.

       (2) **Obstructive processes,** such as nonstrangulated bowel obstruction and urinary retention.

       (3) **Other mechanical processes,** such as ectopic pregnancy and penetrating or perforating tumors.

2. **Character of pain**

    a. **Colicky pain** waxes and wanes. It usually occurs **secondary to hyperperistalsis of smooth muscle** against a mechanical site of obstruction (e.g., small-bowel obstruction and renal stone). An important exception is **biliary colic,** in which pain tends to be constant, intense and lasts at least 30 minutes and up to several hours.

    b. **Pain that is sharp, severe, persistent, and steadily increases in intensity** over time suggests an infectious or inflammatory process (e.g., appendicitis).

3. **Location of pain**

    a. Pain caused by **inflammation of specific organs** may be localized [e.g., right upper quadrant (RUQ) pain caused by acute cholecystitis].

    b. Careful attention must be given to the **radiation of pain.** The pain of renal colic, for example, may begin in the patient's back or flank and radiate to the ipsilateral groin, whereas the pain of a ruptured aortic aneurysm or pancreatitis may radiate to the patient's back.

4. **Alleviating and aggravating factors**

    a. Patients with **diffuse peritonitis** describe worsening of pain with movement (i.e., parietal pain); the pain is ameliorated by lying still. This is in contrast to the patient with renal colic who is usually writhing in pain unable to sit still.

    b. Patients with **intestinal obstruction** have visceral pain and usually experience a transient relief from symptoms after vomiting.

(2) The presence of **occult blood in the stool specimen** may indicate GI bleeding from peptic ulcer disease.

f. **Pelvic examination** must be performed in all women of childbearing age who present with lower abdominal pain.

(1) **Cervical discharge** and overall appearance of the cervix should be noted.

(2) **Bimanual examination** should be performed to assess cervical motion tenderness, adnexal tenderness, and the presence of adnexal masses.

g. **Testicular and scrotal examination** is essential in all males who complain of abdominal pain.

(1) **Testicular torsion** produces a painful, swollen, and tender testicle that is retracted upward in the scrotum.

(2) **Epididymitis** may coexist with urinary tract infection (UTI). The epididymis is swollen and tender, and the vas deferens may also be inflamed.

E. **Laboratory evaluation**

1. A **complete blood count** with cell count differential is important in the assessment of surgical conditions and should be obtained in every patient with acute abdominal pain.

a. **White blood cell (WBC) count elevation** may indicate the presence of an infectious source.

b. **Left shift on the differential** to more immature forms is often helpful because this may indicate the presence of an inflammatory source even if the WBC count is normal.

c. **Hematocrit elevation** may be due to volume contraction from dehydration. Conversely, a **low hematocrit** may be due to occult blood loss.

2. An **electrolyte profile** may reveal clues to the patient's overall condition.

a. **Hypokalemic, hypochloremic, and metabolic alkalosis** may be seen in patients with prolonged vomiting and severe volume depletion. The hypokalemia reflects the potassium–hydrogen ion exchange occurring at the cellular level in an effort to correct the alkalosis.

b. **Low serum bicarbonate** or **metabolic acidosis** suggests general tissue hypoperfusion. This may indicate intestinal ischemia.

c. **Elevation of the blood urea nitrogen or creatinine** is also indicative of volume depletion.

3. **Liver enzyme levels** may be obtained in the appropriate clinical setting.

a. A **mild elevation of transaminases** (<2 times normal), **alkaline phosphatase, and total bilirubin** is sometimes seen in patients with acute cholecystitis.

b. A **moderate elevation of transaminases** (>3 times normal) in the patient with acute onset of RUQ pain is most likely due to a common bile duct (CBD) stone. Elevation of the transaminases often precedes the rise in total bilirubin and alkaline phosphatase in patients with acute biliary obstruction.

c. **Markedly elevated transaminases** (i.e., >1,000 IU/L) in the patient are more likely due to acute hepatitis or ischemia.

4. **Pancreatic enzymes** (amylase and lipase) should be measured if the diagnosis of pancreatitis is considered. It is important to note that the degree of enzyme elevation does not correlate with the severity of the pancreatitis.
   a. **Mild degrees of hyperamylasemia** may be seen in several situations, such as intestinal obstruction.
   b. **Elevation of lipase** is more specific for pancreatic parenchymal damage.

5. **Lactic acid level** may be obtained when considering intestinal ischemia.
   a. **Serum lactate** is an indicator of tissue hypoxia.
   b. Mild lactic acidosis may be seen in patients with arterial hypotension.
   c. Ongoing elevation of serum lactate despite resuscitation is indicative of progression of tissue ischemia (e.g., mesenteric ischemia or worsening sepsis).

6. **Urinalysis** is helpful in assessing urologic causes of abdominal pain.
   a. **Bacteriuria, pyuria, and a positive leukocyte esterase** usually suggest a UTI. Recurrent UTI in males is unusual and should always elicit an evaluation.
   b. **Hematuria** is seen in nephrolithiasis and renal and urothelial cancer.

7. β-Human chorionic gonadotropin must be obtained in any woman of child-bearing age. A positive urine result should be quantitated by serum levels.
   a. A **low level** (<4,000 mIU) is seen in ectopic pregnancy.
   b. **Levels above 4,000 mIU** indicate intrauterine pregnancy [i.e., one that should be seen on ultrasonography (US)].

F. **Radiologic evaluation** of the patient with abdominal pain is a key element in the workup. However, its use should be very selective to avoid unnecessary cost and possible morbidity associated with some modalities.

1. **Plain abdominal X-rays** often serve as the initial radiologic evaluation.
   a. The acute abdominal series consists of three X-rays: upright chest X-ray, and supine and upright abdominal X-rays.
   b. Free intraperitoneal air is best visualized on an **upright chest X-ray** with both hemidiaphragms exposed.
      (1) If the patient is unable to assume an upright position, a **left lateral decubitus X-ray** should be obtained.
      (2) Free air may not be detectable in up to 50% of cases of **perforated viscus** (*AJS*. 1983;146:830–836).
   c. The **bowel gas pattern** is assessed for dilation, air-fluid levels, and the presence of gas throughout the small and large intestine.
      (1) In **small-bowel obstruction,** one sees small-bowel dilation (valvulae conniventes) and **air-fluid levels** in the bowel proximal to the obstruction. There is a paucity of gas in the segment of bowel distal to the obstruction. The absence of air in

the rectum suggests complete obstruction (beware of the presence of colonic gas following rectal examination, or the colon that has not yet completely evacuated, despite the proximal obstruction).

   (2) A **sentinel loop** (i.e., a single, dilated loop of bowel) may be seen adjacent to an inflamed organ (as in pancreatitis) and is due to localized ileus.

   (3) The **"bent inner tube"** and **"omega"** signs are indicative of possible sigmoid and cecal volvulus, respectively.

d. Calcifications should be noted.

   (1) The vast majority of **urinary stones** (90%) contain calcium and are visible on plain X-rays, whereas only 15% of **gallstones** are calcified.

   (2) Calcifications in the region of the pancreas may indicate chronic pancreatitis.

   (3) Calcification in the wall of the aorta may suggest an AAA.

   (4) The most common calcifications seen in the abdomen are **"phleboliths"** (benign calcifications of the pelvic veins). Phleboliths can be distinguished from renal stones by their central lucency, which represents the lumen.

e. Intramural gas in the GI tract **(pneumatosis)** or gas in the biliary tree **(pneumobilia)** (in the absence of a surgical enteric anastomosis, or prior sphincterotomy) is suggestive of bowel ischemia. The **presence of gas** in the portal or mesenteric venous systems is an ominous finding when associated with intestinal ischemia and carries a mortality of >75%. However, portal venous gas can be associated with benign infectious processes that can be managed conservatively (*Arch Surg.* 2009;144(6):575–581).

2. Ultrasonography (US) may provide diagnostic information in some conditions. US is portable, relatively inexpensive, and free of radiation exposure. It is particularly useful in biliary tract disease and in evaluating ovarian pathology. US visibility is limited in settings of obesity, bowel gas, and subcutaneous air.

a. US can detect up to 95% of gallstones. Findings suggestive of **acute cholecystitis** include gallbladder wall thickening of greater than 3 mm, pericholecystic fluid, a stone impacted at the neck of the gallbladder, or a sonographic Murphy's sign. **Murphy's sign** is inspiratory arrest, while continuous pressure is maintained in the RUQ. Murphy's sign reflects the descent of an inflamed gallbladder with inspiration. When the inflamed gallbladder makes contact with the examiner's hand, the patient experiences pain, causing the inspiratory arrest. **Dilation of the CBD** (>8 mm, or larger in elderly patients) indicates biliary obstruction.

b. Pelvic or transvaginal US is particularly useful in women in whom ovarian pathology or an ectopic pregnancy is suspected.

c. Testicular US is adjunctive to physical exam in diagnosing testicular pathology (e.g., testicular torsion, epididymitis, and orchitis).

3. **Contrast studies,** although rarely indicated in the acute setting, may be helpful in some situations.
   a. **Contrast enema** is particularly useful in differentiating adynamic ileus from distal colonic obstruction.
   b. In most instances, a **water-soluble contrast agent** (e.g., Hypaque) should be used to avoid possible barium peritonitis in the event of bowel perforation.

4. **Computed tomographic (CT) scanning** may provide a thorough evaluation of the patient's abdomen and pelvis relatively quickly. Oral and intravenous contrast should be administered if not specifically contraindicated by allergy, renal insufficiency, or patient hemodynamic instability. CT scanning is the best radiographic study in the patient with unexplained abdominal pain. It is of particular benefit in certain situations, including the following:
   a. When **an accurate history cannot be obtained** (e.g., the patient is demented or obtunded or has an atypical history).
   b. When a patient has **abdominal pain and leukocytosis and examination findings are worrisome but not definitive for peritoneal irritation.**
   c. When a patient with a chronic illness (e.g., Crohn's disease) experiences **acute abdominal pain.**
   d. When **evaluating retroperitoneal structures** (e.g., suspected leaking AAA or nephrolithiasis).
   e. When evaluating patients with a history of **intra-abdominal malignancy.**
   f. Evaluation for acute mesenteric ischemia with **CT angiography.**
   g. Differentiating sources of pelvic and lower abdominal pain in women.

5. **Magnetic resonance imaging (MRI)** provides cross-sectional imaging while **avoiding ionizing radiation.**
   a. Image acquisition **takes longer** than for CT scan; patients must be able to lie on their backs for a prolonged period of time and cannot be claustrophobic.
   b. MRI has its greatest application in **pregnant women** with acute abdominal and pelvic pain (*AJR.* 2005;184:452; *J Magn Reson Imaging.* 2008;428–433).

6. **Radionuclide imaging studies** have few indications in the acute setting.
   a. **Biliary radiopharmaceuticals,** such as hepatic 2,6-dimethylaminodiacetic acid or di-diisopropyliminodiacetic acid, evaluate filling and emptying of the gallbladder. Nonfilling implies cystic duct obstruction and may indicate acute cholecystitis. This test is especially valuable in the diagnosis of acalculous cholecystitis and biliary dyskinesia.
   b. **Radioisotope-labeled red blood cell (RBC) or WBC scans** are sometimes helpful in localizing sites of bleeding or inflammation, respectively.

TABLE 11-1	Differential Diagnosis for Acute Abdominal Pain	
Upper abdominal		Perforated peptic ulcer Acute cholecystitis
Mid and lower abdominal		Acute appendicitis Acute diverticulitis Intestinal obstruction Mesenteric ischemia Ruptured AAA
Other	OB/GYN	PID Ectopic pregnancy Ruptured ovarian cyst
	Urologic	Nephrolithiasis Pyelonephritis/cystitis
	Nonsurgical	Acute MI Gastroenteritis Pneumonia DKA Acute pancreatitis Hepatitis

AAA, abdominal aortic aneurysm; DKA, diabetic ketoacidosis; MI, myocardial infarction; OB/GYN, obstetric/gynecologic; PID, pelvic inflammatory disease.

    c. Technetium-99m pertechnetate may be used to detect a Meckel diverticulum because this isotope is concentrated in the ectopic gastric mucosa that frequently lines the diverticulum. This diagnostic test is most frequently ordered in a child with lower GI bleeding.

  7. Invasive radiologic techniques may have a role in some situations, including angiographic diagnosis and therapeutic intervention for **mesenteric arterial occlusion and acute GI bleeding.**

III. DIFFERENTIAL DIAGNOSES. See Table 11-1.

APPENDICITIS

I. EPIDEMIOLOGY

  A. Appendectomy is the most common urgently performed surgical procedure.

  B. Lifetime risk of undergoing appendectomy is between 7% and 12%.

  C. The **maximal incidence** occurs in the second and third decades of life.

  D. The **male:female ratio** of approximately 2:1 gradually shifts after age 25 years toward a 1:1 ratio (*Am Fam Physician.* 1999;60(7):2027–2034).

II. PATHOPHYSIOLOGY

A. **Appendiceal obstruction** is the most common initiating event of appendicitis.

1. **Hyperplasia** of the submucosal lymphoid follicles of the appendix and appendiceal **fecalith** are the most common etiologies of obstruction (*Ann Surg.* 1985;202(1):80–82).

B. **Intraluminal pressure** of the obstructed appendiceal lumen increases secondary to continued mucosal secretion and bacterial overgrowth; the appendiceal wall thins, and lymphatic and venous obstruction occurs.

C. **Necrosis and perforation** develop when the arterial flow is compromised.

III. DIAGNOSIS.
The diagnosis of acute appendicitis is made by clinical evaluation. Although laboratory tests and imaging procedures can be helpful, they are of secondary importance.

A. Clinical presentation

1. **Classic presentation.** Appendicitis typically begins with progressive, persistent midabdominal discomfort caused by obstruction and distention of the appendix, stimulating the visceral afferent autonomic nerves (levels T8 to T10). Anorexia and a low-grade fever (<38.5°C) follow. As distention of the appendix increases, venous congestion stimulates intestinal peristalsis, causing a cramping sensation that is soon followed by nausea and vomiting. Symptoms include anorexia (90%), nausea and vomiting (70%), and diarrhea (10%). Once the inflammation extends transmurally to the parietal peritoneum, the somatic pain fibers are stimulated and the pain localizes to the right lower quadrant (RLQ). Peritoneal irritation is associated with pain on movement, mild fever, and tachycardia. One-fourth of patients present with localized pain and no visceral symptoms (*Br J Surg.* 2004;91(1):28–37). The onset of symptoms to time of presentation is usually less than 24 hours for acute appendicitis and averages several hours.

2. **Unusual presentations**
   a. When the appendix is **retrocecal or behind the ileum,** it may be separated from the anterior abdominal peritoneum, and abdominal localizing signs may be absent. Irritation of adjacent structures can cause diarrhea, urinary frequency, pyuria, or microscopic hematuria depending on location.
   b. When the appendix is **located in the pelvis,** it may simulate acute gastroenteritis, with diffuse pain, nausea, vomiting, and diarrhea.

B. Physical examination

1. The examination begins by **assessing the patient's abdomen** in areas other than the area of suspected tenderness. Location of the appendix is variable. However, the base is usually found at the level of the S1 vertebral body, lateral to the right midclavicular line at **McBurney's point** (two thirds of the distance from the umbilicus to the anterosuperior iliac spine).

2. **Rectal examination** is performed to evaluate the presence of localized tenderness or an inflammatory mass in the pararectal area. It is most useful for atypical presentations suggestive of a pelvic or retrocecal appendix.

3. In women, a **pelvic examination** is performed to assess for cervical motion tenderness and adnexal pain or masses.

4. A **palpable mass in the RLQ** is uncommon, but may suggest a periappendiceal abscess or phlegmon.

5. Specific physical examination findings for appendicitis include the following:

   a. The **obturator sign** reflects inflammation adjacent to the internal obturator muscle (as is sometimes seen in appendicitis). It may also be present within an obturator hernia. While the patient is supine with the knee and hip flexed, the hip is internally and externally rotated. The test is positive if the patient experiences hypogastric pain during this maneuver.

   b. The **iliopsoas sign** is seen when an adjacent inflammatory process irritates the iliopsoas muscle. It is classically observed in retrocecal appendicitis. The patient's thigh is usually already drawn into a flexed position for relief. The test is best performed with the patient lying on the left side. With the knee flexed, the thigh is hyperextended. The test is positive if the patient experiences pain on the right side with this maneuver.

   c. **Rovsing's sign** may also be seen in acute appendicitis. Indicative of an inflammatory process in the RLQ, Rovsing's sign is RLQ pain resulting from palpation in the left lower quadrant (LLQ).

C. **Differential diagnosis for RLQ abdominal pain is very broad**

1. **Gynecologic diseases must always be considered in the female patient with RLQ pain.**

   a. **PID** can present with symptoms and signs indistinguishable from those of acute appendicitis, but the two often can be differentiated on the basis of several factors. Cervical motion tenderness and milky vaginal discharge strengthen a diagnosis of PID. In patients with PID, the pain is usually bilateral, with intense guarding on abdominal and pelvic examinations. Transvaginal US can be used to visualize the ovaries and to identify tubo-ovarian abscesses.

   b. **Ectopic pregnancy** needs to be ruled out in all female patients of child-bearing age presenting with abdominal complaints. A positive pregnancy test should prompt US investigation.

   c. **Ovarian cysts** are best detected by transvaginal or transabdominal US.

   d. **Ovarian torsion produces** inflammation around the ischemic ovary that can often be palpated on bimanual pelvic examination. These patients can have a fever, leukocytosis, and RLQ pain consistent with appendicitis. A twisted viscus, however, differs in that it produces sudden, acute intense pain with simultaneous frequent and persistent emesis. Ovarian torsion may be confirmed by Doppler US.

2. Urologic diseases are also often confused with appendicitis

  a. Pyelonephritis causes high fevers, rigors, costovertebral pain, and tenderness. Diagnosis is confirmed by urinalysis with culture.

  b. Ureteral colic. Passage of renal stones causes flank pain radiating into the groin but little localized tenderness. Hematuria suggests the diagnosis, which is confirmed by intravenous pyelography or noncontrast CT. Abdominal plain films frequently show renal stones.

3. Other causes of RLQ tenderness

  a. Gastroenteritis is characterized by nausea and emesis before the onset of abdominal pain, along with generalized malaise, high fever, diarrhea, and poorly localized abdominal pain and tenderness. Although diarrhea is one of the cardinal signs of gastroenteritis, it can occur in patients with appendicitis. In addition, WBC count is often normal in patients with gastroenteritis.

  b. Meckel diverticulitis presents with symptoms and signs indistinguishable from those of appendicitis, but it characteristically occurs in infants.

  c. Peptic ulcer disease, diverticulitis, and cholecystitis can present clinical pictures similar to those of appendicitis.

  d. Mesenteric lymphadenitis usually occurs in patients younger than 20 years old and presents with middle, followed by RLQ, abdominal pain but without rebound tenderness or muscular rigidity. Nodal histology and cultures obtained at operation can identify etiology, most notably *Yersinia* and *Shigella* species and *Mycobacterium tuberculosis*. Mesenteric lymphadenitis is known to be associated with upper respiratory tract infections.

  e. Typhlitis, characterized by inflammation of the wall of the cecum or terminal ileum, is managed nonoperatively. It is most commonly seen in immunosuppressed patients undergoing chemotherapy for leukemia and in HIV-positive patients. It is difficult to distinguish preoperatively between typhlitis and appendicitis.

D. Laboratory evaluation. The following tests should be obtained preoperatively for patients with suspected appendicitis.

  1. Complete blood cell count. A leukocyte count of greater than 10,000 cells/μL, with polymorphonuclear cell predominance (>75%), carries a 77% sensitivity and 63% specificity for appendicitis (*Radiology.* 2004;230:472). The total number of WBCs and the proportion of immature forms increase if there is appendiceal perforation. In older adults, the leukocyte count and differential are normal more frequently than in younger adults. Pregnant women normally have an elevated WBC count that can reach 15,000 to 20,000 as their pregnancy progresses.

  2. Urinalysis is frequently abnormal in patients with appendicitis. Pyuria, albuminuria, and hematuria are common. Large quantities of bacteria suggest UTI as the cause of abdominal pain. A urinalysis showing more than 20 WBCs per high-power field or more than 30 RBCs per high-power field suggests UTI. Significant hematuria should prompt consideration of urolithiasis.

3. **Serum electrolytes, blood urea nitrogen, and serum creatinine** are obtained to identify and correct electrolyte abnormalities caused by dehydration secondary to vomiting or poor oral intake.

4. **A serum pregnancy test** must be performed on all ovulating women.

E. **Radiologic evaluation.** Diagnosis of appendicitis can usually be made without radiologic evaluation, particularly in young, thin males. In complex cases, however, the following can be helpful.

1. **X-rays** are rarely helpful in diagnosing appendicitis. An appendicolith can rarely be seen on plain films. However, suggestive radiologic findings include a distended cecum with adjacent small-bowel air-fluid levels, loss of the right psoas shadow, scoliosis to the right, and gas in the lumen of the appendix. A perforated appendix rarely causes pneumoperitoneum (*Can Assoc Radiol J.* 1988;39(4):254–256).

2. **Ultrasound** is most useful in women of child-bearing age and in children because this diagnostic modality avoids ionizing radiation. US also allows for evaluation of gynecologic pathology. Findings associated with acute appendicitis include an appendiceal diameter greater than 6 mm, lack of luminal compressibility, and presence of an appendicolith. An enlarged appendix seen on US has a sensitivity of 86% and specificity of 81% (*Radiology.* 2004;230:472). The sensitivity is better in thin patients. The perforated appendix is more difficult to diagnose and is characterized by loss of the echogenic submucosa and the presence of loculated periappendiceal or pelvic fluid collection. The quality and accuracy of US are highly operator dependent.

3. **CT scan,** originally recommended only in cases that were clinically complex or diagnostically uncertain, has emerged as the most commonly used radiographic diagnostic test. It is superior to US in diagnosing appendicitis, with a sensitivity of 94% and specificity of 95% (*Ann Intern Med.* 2004;141:537). CT findings of appendicitis include a distended, thick-walled appendix with inflammatory streaking of surrounding fat, a pericecal phlegmon or abscess, an appendicolith, or RLQ intra-abdominal free air that signals perforation. CT scan is particularly useful in distinguishing between periappendiceal abscesses and phlegmon.

4. **MRI** is an alternative when one needs cross-sectional imaging that avoids ionizing radiation. It is particularly useful in a pregnant patient whose appendix is not visualized on US (*Radiology.* 2006;238:891).

IV. TREATMENT

A. **Preoperative preparation.** Intravenous isotonic fluid replacement should be initiated to achieve a brisk urinary output and to correct electrolyte abnormalities. Nasogastric suction is helpful, especially in patients with peritonitis. Temperature elevations are treated with acetaminophen and a cooling blanket.

B. **Antibiotic therapy.** Antibiotic prophylaxis is generally effective in the prevention of postoperative infectious complications (wound infection, intra-abdominal abscess). Preoperative initiation is preferred. Coverage typically consists of a second-generation cephalosporin. In patients with acute nonperforated appendicitis, a single dose of antibiotics is adequate. Antibiotic therapy in perforated or gangrenous appendicitis should be continued for 3 to 5 days.

C. **Appendectomy.** With very few exceptions, the treatment of appendicitis is appendectomy. The decision to perform an open appendectomy via a transverse incision (e.g., Rockey-Davis and Fowler-Weir) or a laparoscopic appendectomy is surgeon preference.

1. **Laparoscopic appendectomy** is associated with marginally briefer postoperative lengths of stay, reduced postoperative pain, quicker return to full function, and lower risk of wound infection (*Surg Endosc.* 2006;20:495). However, these benefits have to balanced with the higher cost and longer operative time required for a laparoscopic appendectomy. Regardless of the technique, most patients undergoing routine appendectomy can be safely discharged from the hospital on the first postoperative day. Laparoscopic appendectomy is most useful when the diagnosis is uncertain or when the size of the patient would necessitate a large incision. Laparoscopy is useful in ovulating woman to evaluate for gynecologic pathology if the appendix is normal.

   a. **Patient positioning** during laparoscopic appendectomy is surgeon specific, but most surgeons place a Foley and tuck the left arm. Three ports are typically placed; a 10-mm port at the umbilicus, a 5-mm LLQ port, and a-5 mm supra pubic midline port. Some surgeons use a RUQ port instead of a LLQ port. The patient is then placed in Trendelenburg with the right side up so that gravity can assist in moving the small bowel out of the operating field.

   b. **The details of the procedure** will vary slightly according to surgeon preference. However, removal of the appendix begins by splaying out the mesoappendix. A window is made in the mesoappendix at the base of the appendix. The mesoappendix is divided using a vascular stapler or vascular sealing device. The appendix is then divided at its base using the endoscopic stapler. If a normal appearing appendix is identified upon entering the abdomen with the videoscope, another etiology of the acute abdomen such as a Meckel's diverticulitis, tubo-ovarian abscess, or Crohn's disease is sought. Some have advocated that there is no need to remove a normal appendix during a laparoscopic appendectomy (*Br J Surg.* 2001;88:251). However, most surgeons will remove the appendix if no other clear etiology of the abdominal pain is found.

2. **Open appendectomy** begins with a transverse incision lateral to the rectus at McBurney's point (one-third of the distance from the anterior superior iliac spine [ASIS] to the umbilicus). If a preoperative CT scan has been obtained, the location of the incision can be adjusted based on the location of the base of the appendix. The external and internal oblique and transversus abdominis muscle layers may be split in the direction of their fibers. After entering the peritoneal cavity, if purulent fluid is encountered it is sent for Gram stain and culture. Once the

cecum is identified, the anterior taenia can be followed to the base of the appendix. The appendix is gently delivered into the wound and any surrounding adhesions carefully disrupted. If the appendix is normal on inspection (5% to 20% of explorations), it is removed and appropriate alternative diagnoses are entertained.

D. **Drainage of periappendiceal abscess.** Management of appendiceal abscesses remains controversial. Patients with appendiceal abscesses who undergo immediate-appendectomy have a higher complication rate and longer hospital stay than patient who are treated nonoperatively (*Am Surg.* 2003;69:829). Patients who have a well-localized periappendiceal abscess can be treated with systemic antibiotics and considered for percutaneous US- or CT-guided catheter drainage, followed by elective appendectomy 6 to 12 weeks later (*Radiology.* 1987;163:23). This strategy is successful in more than 80% of patients. Many surgeons will argue that an interval appendectomy is not necessary (*Ann Surg.* 2007;246(5):741–748).

E. **Incidental appendectomy** is removal of the normal appendix at laparotomy for another condition. The appendix must be easily accessible through the present abdominal incision, and the patient must be clinically stable enough to tolerate the extra time needed to complete the procedure. Because most cases of appendicitis occur early in life, the benefit of incidental appendectomy decreases substantially once a person is older than 30 years. Crohn's disease involving the cecum, radiation treatment to the cecum, immunosuppression, and vascular grafts or other bioprosthesis are all contraindications for incidental appendectomy because of the increased risk of infectious complications or appendiceal stump leak.

V. APPENDICITIS IN PREGNANCY

A. The **incidence of appendicitis during pregnancy** is 1/1,500 pregnancies. Appendicitis is the most common nongynecologic surgical emergency during pregnancy (*Can Fam Physician.* 2004;50:355).

B. **The evaluation of a pregnant woman with appendicitis** can be quite confusing. Appendicitis must be suspected in any pregnant woman with abdominal pain.

1. Nausea and vomiting can be incorrectly attributed to the morning sickness that is common in the first trimester.

2. Tachycardia is a normal finding in pregnancy.

3. Fever a common finding in appendicitis is often not present in pregnancy.

4. Leukocytosis is common in pregnancy. A WBC of 12,000 cell/mL is a normal finding in pregnancy. However, a left shift is always abnormal and requires further investigation.

5. The most common location for pain in the pregnant woman is RLQ pain. It is frequently sited that the location of the appendix shifts during pregnancy due to displacement by the gravid uterus. However, when pregnant females at 19 to 26 weeks who underwent appendectomy were compared to nonpregnant females undergoing appendectomy, there

was no statistical difference in the location of the appendix (*Int J Gyn & OB.* 2003;81:3).

C. **Appendectomy during pregnancy** is indicated in a pregnant patient as soon as the diagnosis of appendicitis is suspected. A negative laparotomy carries a risk of fetal loss of up to 3%, but fetal demise rates reach 35% in the setting of perforation and diffuse peritonitis (*Southern Med J.* 1976;69:1161–1163). The choice to perform open versus laparoscopic appendectomy is still debated. Multiple retrospective studies have shown a laparoscopic approach to be as safe as open appendectomy. Some alteration in technique is required; insufflation pressure is set lower usually at 8 mm Hg and no higher than 12 mm Hg; the umbilical port is placed 6 cm above the uterine fundus. Prophylactic intraoperative tocolytic therapy has not been shown to be effective (*J Am Coll Surg.* 2007;205(1):37–42).

VI. APPENDICITIS IN CHILDREN

A. The **annual incidence of appendicitis in children** increases with age until a peak in the second decade of life (*Pediatr Emerg Care.* 1992;8:126–128). Appendicitis is the most common indication for emergent abdominal surgery in childhood. Delayed diagnosis is common, particularly in young children, and has been reported in as many as 57% of cases in children less than 6 years (*Ann Emerg Med.* 2000;36(1):39–51).

B. Appendicitis in young children can be a difficult diagnosis because of children's inability to articulate their symptoms and their increased rate of atypical presentation.

    1. **Physical exam findings** may be absent or unusual. As many as 50% of children lack of migration of pain to RLQ, 40% will not have anorexia and 52% will not have rebound tenderness (*Acad Emerg Med.* 2007;14(2):124–129). Although the classic signs of appendicitis (RLQ tenderness, guarding, and rebound tenderness) are noted less frequently, they may still be elicited and a complete exam should be performed.

    2. **Laboratory findings.** The WBC or the percentage of neutrophils is elevated in up to 96% of children with appendicitis (*Ann Emerg Med.* 2000;36(1):39–51). Pyuria may be noted in 7% to 25% of patients with appendicitis (*Ann Emerg Med.* 1991;20(1):45–50), although bacteria are not typically present in a clean catch specimen.

    3. **Imaging.** Despite increased utilization of CT and improved accuracy of imaging for acute appendicitis since the mid 1990s, substantially lower rates of negative appendectomy have not been achieved, and the perforation rate remains as high as 33% (*J Pediatr Surg.* 2004;39(6):886–890; discussion 886–890). In addition, the lifetime cancer mortality risk attributable to the radiation exposure from a single abdominal CT examination in a 1-year-old child is approximately one in 550. Currently, over 600,000 abdominal and head CT examinations are performed on children under 15 years of age per year. If these estimates are correct, approximately 500 individuals will ultimately die

from a cancer attributable to the radiation from CT scans (*Am J Roentgenol.* 2001;176:289–296). Given this increasing concern over ionizing radiation and its negative health effects, greater emphasis is being placed on US as the initial imaging modality of choice. The absence of nausea, lack of maximal tenderness in the RLQ, and absolute neutrophil count less than 6.7 had a negative predictive value of 98% for identifying children who could be safely observed or discharged without any imaging studies (*Pediatrics.* 2005;116(3):709–716).

VII. COMPLICATIONS OF ACUTE APPENDICITIS

A. **Perforation** is accompanied by severe pain and fever. It is unusual within the first 12 hours of appendicitis but is present in 50% of appendicitis patients younger than 10 years and older than 50 years. Acute consequences of perforation include fever, tachycardia, and generalized peritonitis. Treatment is appendectomy, peritoneal irrigation, and broad-spectrum intravenous antibiotics for 3 to 5 days, or until fever and leukocytosis resolve.

B. **Postoperative wound infection risk** can be decreased by appropriate intravenous antibiotics administered before skin incision. The incidence of wound infection increases from 3% in cases of nonperforated appendicitis to 4.7% in patients with a perforated or gangrenous appendix. Primary closure is not recommended in the setting of perforation (*Surgery.* 2000;127:136). Wound infections are managed by opening, draining, and packing the wound to allow healing by secondary intention. Intravenous antibiotics are indicated for associated cellulitis or systemic sepsis.

C. **Intra-abdominal and pelvic abscesses** occur most frequently with perforation of the appendix. Postoperative intra-abdominal and pelvic abscesses are best treated by percutaneous CT- or US-guided drainage. If the abscess is inaccessible or resistant to percutaneous drainage, operative drainage is indicated. Antibiotic therapy can mask but does not treat or prevent a significant abscess. Patients that continue to have fever and elevated white count beyond post-op day number 7 should have a CT to evaluate for abscess (*Cochrane Database Syst Rev.* 2005;20:CD001439).

D. **Other complications**

1. **Small-bowel obstruction** is four times more common after surgery in cases of perforated appendicitis than in uncomplicated appendicitis.

2. **Enterocutaneous fistulae** may result from a leak at the appendiceal stump closure. They occasionally require surgical closure, but most close spontaneously.

3. **Pylephlebitis** is septic portal vein thrombosis caused by *Escherichia coli* and presents with high fevers, jaundice, and eventually hepatic abscesses. CT scan demonstrates thrombus and gas in the portal vein. Prompt treatment (operative or percutaneous) of the primary infection is critical, along with broad-spectrum intravenous antibiotics.

12

Colon, Rectum, and Anus

Nicholas A. Hamilton and James W. Fleshman

COLORECTAL PHYSIOLOGY

I. NORMAL COLON FUNCTION

A. **Water absorption.** Normal ileal effluent totals 900 to 1,500 mL/day, with stool water loss typically less than 200 mL/day. The right colon maximally can absorb 6 L of fluid/day, and only when large-bowel absorption is less than 2 L/day does an increase in fecal water content result in diarrhea.

B. **Electrolyte transport.** Sodium and chloride absorption occur by active processes in exchange for potassium and bicarbonate in the right colon.

C. **Nutrition.** Although absorption of nutrients is minimal in the colon, mucosal utilization of short-chain fatty acids (SCFAs) produced by colonic bacteria can account for up to 540 kcal/day. Chronic absence of SCFAs such as butyrate and propionate results in "diversion colitis," a condition characterized by rectal bleeding and rare stricture formation. Subclinical diversion colitis occurs in almost all diverted patients and uniformly resolves following stomal closure.

D. **Motility patterns of the colon** allow for mixing and elimination of intestinal contents. Factors influencing motility include emotional state, amount of exercise and sleep, amount of colonic distention, and hormonal variations.

1. **Retrograde movements** occur mainly in the right colon. These contractions prolong the exposure of luminal contents to the mucosa and thereby increase the absorption of fluids and electrolytes.

2. **Segmental contractions,** the most commonly observed motility pattern, represent localized simultaneous contractions of the longitudinal and circular colonic musculature in short colonic segments.

3. **Mass movements** occur three to four times a day and are characterized by an antegrade, propulsive contractile wave involving a long segment of colon.

E. **Microflora.** One-third of the dry weight of feces is normally composed of bacteria. Anaerobic *Bacteroides* species are most prevalent (10^{11}/mL), whereas *Escherichia coli* has a titer of 10^9/mL. Bacteria produce much of the body's vitamin K. Endogenous colonic bacteria also suppress the emergence of pathogenic microorganisms. Antibiotic therapy can alter the endogenous microflora, resulting in changes in drug sensitivity (warfarin) or infectious colitides due to pathogenic microbial overgrowth (*Clostridium difficile* colitis).

F. **Colonic gas** (200 to 2,000 mL/day) is composed of (1) swallowed oxygen and nitrogen and (2) hydrogen, carbon dioxide, and methane produced during fermentation by colonic bacteria. Because hydrogen and methane are combustible gases that may explode when electrocautery is used for biopsy, adequate bowel cleansing is mandatory before using hot-snare techniques during colonoscopy.

II. DISORDERS OF COLONIC PHYSIOLOGY

A. **Constipation** is generally defined clinically **as one or fewer spontaneous bowel movements or stools per week,** though patients may use the term to describe a number of different defecatory symptoms.

1. **Etiologies** include medications (narcotics, anticholinergics, antidepressants, calcium channel blockers), hypothyroidism, hypercalcemia, dietary factors (low fluid or fiber intake), decreased exercise, neoplasia, and neurologic disorders (e.g., Parkinson disease and multiple sclerosis). Abnormalities of pelvic floor function (obstructed defecation), such as paradoxical puborectalis muscle function or intussusception of the rectum (internal or external rectal prolapse), may result in constipation, as may idiopathic delayed transit of feces through the colon (dysfunction of the intrinsic colonic nerves or colonic inertia).

2. **Evaluation.** Change in bowel habits is a common presentation of colorectal neoplasia. The initial evaluation of constipation should include digital rectal exam and colonoscopy. If this workup is negative and the patient fails to respond to a trial of fiber supplementation and increased fluid intake, the next step is a **colonic transit time study.** The patient is given a standard amount of fiber (12 g of psyllium per day) for a week prior to the test and continued throughout the study. On day 0, the patient ingests an enteric-coated capsule containing 24 radiopaque rings. Abdominal plain X-rays are obtained on days 3 and 5. Normal transit results in 80% of the rings in the left colon by day 3 and 80% of all the rings expelled by day 5. The persistence of rings throughout the colon on day 5 indicates colonic inertia. When the rings stall in the rectosigmoid region, functional anorectal obstruction (obstructed defecation) may be present. This may be evaluated with cine defecography, anorectal manometry, or both; the task is to look for nonrelaxation of the puborectalis muscle or internal intussusception of the rectum.

3. **Treatment** of colonic inertia initially includes increased water intake, laxatives (polyethylene glycol, 12 oz/day), fiber (psyllium 12 g/day), increased exercise, and avoidance of predisposing factors. In patients with long-standing, debilitating symptoms refractory to nonoperative measures, **total abdominal colectomy with ileorectal anastomosis** may prove curative. The risk of total intestinal inertia after surgery is significant, and the patient should understand this.

B. **Colonic pseudo-obstruction** (Ogilvie syndrome) is a profound colonic ileus without evidence of mechanical obstruction. It most commonly occurs in critically ill or institutionalized patients. Colonic obstruction or volvulus must be ruled out; Hypaque enema is often therapeutic as well as diagnostic. The initial management consists of nasogastric decompression, rectal tube placement, an aggressive enema regimen (e.g., cottonseed and docusate sodium enema), correction of metabolic disorders, and discontinuation of medications that decrease colonic motility (including narcotics). Neostigmine intravenous infusion (2 mg/hour) in a monitored setting has been shown to be useful in resistant cases (*N Engl J Med.* 1999;341:137). Rapid cecal dilation or a cecal diameter greater than 12 cm on plain abdominal X-rays requires prompt colonoscopic decompression. This is successful in 70% to 90% of cases, with a recurrence rate of 10% to 30% (recurrence is usually amenable to repeat colonoscopic decompression). Laparotomy is reserved for patients with peritonitis, at which time a total abdominal colectomy with end-ileostomy should be performed.

C. **Volvulus** is the twisting of an air-filled segment of bowel about its mesentery and accounts for nearly 10% of bowel obstruction in the United States.

  1. **Sigmoid volvulus** accounts for 80% to 90% of all volvulus and is most common in elderly or institutionalized patients and in patients with a variety of neurologic disorders. It is an acquired condition resulting from sigmoid redundancy with narrowing of the mesenteric pedicle.

    a. **Diagnosis** is suspected when there is abdominal pain, distention, cramping, and obstipation. **Plain films** often show a characteristic **inverted-U,** sausage-like shape of air-filled sigmoid pointing to the right upper quadrant. If the diagnosis is still in question and gangrene is not suspected, water-soluble **contrast enema** usually shows a **bird's-beak deformity** at the obstructed rectosigmoid junction.

    b. In the absence of peritoneal signs, **treatment** involves **sigmoidoscopy,** with the placement of a rectal tube beyond the point of obstruction. The recurrence rate after decompressive sigmoidoscopy approaches 40%; therefore, elective sigmoid colectomy should be performed in acceptable operative candidates. If peritonitis is present, the patient should undergo laparotomy and **Hartmann procedure** (sigmoid colectomy, end-descending colostomy, and defunctionalized rectal pouch). An alternative in the stable patient without significant fecal soilage of the peritoneal cavity is sigmoidectomy, on-table colonic lavage, and colorectal anastomosis with or without proximal fecal diversion (loop ileostomy).

  2. **Cecal volvulus** occurs in a younger population than does sigmoid volvulus, likely due to congenital failure of retroperitonealization of the cecum (in axial volvulus) or a very redundant pelvic cecum that flops into the left upper quadrant to kink the right colon (in bascule volvulus).

    a. **Diagnosis.** Presentation is similar to that of distal small-bowel obstruction, with nausea, vomiting, abdominal pain, and distention. Plain films show a **coffee bean-shaped,** air-filled cecum with the convex aspect extending into the left upper quadrant. A **Hypaque enema** may be performed, which shows a tapered (in axial volvulus) or linear cutoff (in bascule volvulus) of the ascending colon.

    b. **Management** involves urgent laparotomy and right hemicolectomy. Cecopexy has an unacceptably high rate of recurrent volvulus, and although cecectomy will prevent recurrence, it is technically more challenging than formal right hemicolectomy. Colonoscopic decompression **is not** an option.

3. **Transverse volvulus** is rare and has a clinical presentation similar to that of sigmoid volvulus. Diagnosis is made based on the results of plain films (which show a dilated right colon and an upright, U-shaped, dilated transverse colon) and contrast enema or computed tomography (CT). Endoscopic decompression has been reported, but operative resection is usually required.

D. **Diverticular disease**

1. **General considerations.** Colonic diverticula are **false diverticula** in which mucosa and submucosa protrude through the muscularis propria. Outpouchings occur along the mesenteric aspect of the antimesenteric taenia where arterioles penetrate the muscularis. The **sigmoid colon** is most commonly affected, perhaps owing to decreased luminal diameter and increased luminal pressure. Diverticula are associated with a low-fiber diet and are rare before age 30 years (<2%), but the **incidence increases with age** to a 75% prevalence after the age of 80 years.

2. **Complications**

a. **Infection (diverticulitis).** Microperforations can develop in long-standing diverticula, leading to fecal extravasation and subsequent peridiverticulitis. Diverticulitis develops in 10% to 25% of patients with diverticula (90% left-sided, 10% right-sided).

(1) **Presentation** is notable for left-lower-quadrant pain (which may radiate to the suprapubic area, left groin, or back), fever, altered bowel habit, and urinary urgency. Physical examination varies with severity of the disease, but the most common finding is localized left-lower-quadrant tenderness. The finding of a mass suggests an abscess or phlegmon.

(2) **Evaluation** by CT scan and complete blood count (CBC) is the standard of care. CT findings may include segmental colonic thickening, focal extraluminal gas, and abscess formation. Neither sigmoidoscopy nor contrast enema is recommended in the initial workup of diverticulitis because of the risk of perforation or barium or fecal peritonitis, respectively.

(3) **Treatment** is tailored to symptom severity.

(a) **Mild diverticulitis** can be treated on an outpatient basis with a clear liquid diet and broad-spectrum oral antibiotics for 10 days.

(b) **Severe diverticulitis** is treated with complete bowel rest, intravenous fluids, narcotic analgesics, and broad-spectrum parenteral antibiotics (e.g., ciprofloxacin and metronidazole). If symptoms improve within 48 hours, a clear liquid diet is resumed, and antibiotics are given orally when the fever and leukocytosis resolve. A high-fiber, low-residue diet is resumed after 1 week of pain-free tolerance of a liquid diet. Fiber supplements and stool softeners should be given to prevent constipation. A colonoscopy or water-soluble contrast study must be performed after 4 to

6 weeks to rule out colon cancer, inflammatory bowel disease (IBD), or ischemia as a cause of the segmental inflammatory mass.

(4) The lifetime likelihood of **recurrence** is 30% after the first episode and more than 50% after the second episode of diverticulitis. Young patients (<50 years) have the same risk of recurrent diverticulitis following an uncomplicated attack as their older counterparts (*Dis Colon Rectum.* 2006;49:1341). Resection of contained, nonfistulizing diverticulitis should be individualized according to patient lifestyle, tolerance of recurrent episodes and progression to complicated disease with stricture, fistula, or recurrent abscess.

(5) **Elective resection** for diverticulitis usually consists of a sigmoid colectomy. The proximal resection margin is through uninflamed, nonthickened bowel, but there is no need to resect all diverticula in the colon. The distal margin extends to normal, pliable rectum, even if this means dissection beyond the anterior peritoneal reflection. Recurrent diverticulitis after resection is most frequently related to inadequate distal margin of resection.

b. **Diverticular abscess** is usually identified on CT scan. A **percutaneous drain** should be placed under **radiologic guidance.** This avoids immediate operative drainage, allows time for the inflammatory phlegmon to be treated with intravenous antibiotics, and turns a two- or three-stage procedure into a one-stage procedure.

c. **Generalized peritonitis** is rare and results if diverticular perforation leads to widespread fecal contamination. In most cases, resection of the diseased segment is possible **(two-stage procedure),** and a Hartmann procedure is performed. The colostomy can then be reversed in the future. An alternative in the management of the stable patient undergoing urgent operation for acute diverticulitis without significant fecal contamination is sigmoidectomy, on-table colonic lavage (in the setting of a large fecal load), and colorectal anastomosis with or without proximal fecal diversion (loop ileostomy).

d. **Fistulization** secondary to diverticulitis may occur between the colon and other organs, including the bladder, vagina, small intestine, and skin. Diverticulitis is the most common etiology of colovesical fistulas. Colovaginal and colovesical fistulas usually occur in women who have previously undergone hysterectomy. Colocutaneous fistulas are uncommon and are usually easy to identify. Coloenteric fistulas are likewise uncommon and may be entirely asymptomatic or result in corrosive diarrhea.

(1) The presentation of **enterovesical fistula** includes frequent urinary tract infections and often is unsuspected until **fecaluria** or **pneumaturia** is noted. CT findings of air and solid material in a noninstrumented bladder confirm the diagnosis. Lower endoscopy, barium enema, intravenous pyelography, and cystoscopy often fail to demonstrate the fistula.

(2) A **colovaginal fistula** is usually suspected based on the passage of air per vagina. The fistula may be difficult to identify

on physical examination or the previously mentioned tests. The presence of methylene blue staining on a tampon inserted in the vagina following dye instillation in the rectum is diagnostic.

(3) **Definitive treatment.** Colonoscopy is performed after 6 weeks to rule out other possible etiologies, including cancer or IBD. Elective sigmoid resection is performed after preoperative placement of temporary ureteral catheters. Ureteral catheters can be very helpful in identifying the distal ureter in the inflammatory pericolonic mass, thereby shortening the operative time. Usually, the fistula tract can be broken using finger fracture, and the bladder defect can be repaired in a single layer. A Foley catheter is left in place for 7 to 10 days to allow this defect to heal. A colovaginal fistula is managed in a similar fashion. It may be helpful to interpose omentum between the colorectal anastomosis and the bladder or vaginal defect.

E. **Acquired vascular abnormalities and lower gastrointestinal (GI) bleeding** are more common in elderly patients than in younger individuals. Most cases of massive lower GI hemorrhage stop spontaneously, but surgery is required in 10% to 25% of cases.

1. **Etiologies** (with relative approximate incidence) of lower GI bleeding in industrialized nations include the following:

   a. **Diverticulosis (60%).** The media of the perforating artery adjacent to the colonic diverticulum may become attenuated and eventually erode. This arterial bleeding usually is bright red and is not associated with previous melena or chronic blood loss. Bleeding most commonly occurs from the left colon. Urgent resection of the affected colonic segment should be considered in patients with active ongoing bleeding (>6 units packed red blood cells (RBCs)/ 24 hours). Elective resection of the affected colonic segment should be performed in patients with recurrent bleeding or need for long-term anticoagulation or in those in whom excessive blood loss may be poorly tolerated.

   b. **IBD (13%).** Bleeding due to IBD tends to occur in a younger population; it is more commonly due to ulcerative colitis than Crohn's disease.

   c. **Benign anorectal disease (11%)** is discussed later in this chapter.

   d. **Neoplasia (10%)** of the colon and rectum rarely presents with massive blood loss, but rather with chronic microcytic anemia and possible syncope.

   e. Hemorrhage following **polypectomy** can occur up to 1 month postprocedure and has an incidence of 3% in some series.

   f. **Angiodysplasias (<5%)** are small arteriovenous malformations composed of small clusters of dilated vessels in the mucosa and submucosa. An acquired condition, they rarely occur before age 40 years and are more common in the right colon (80%). Diagnosis can be made by colonoscopy or angiographic features (delayed filling of a dilated venule).

2. **Massive lower GI bleeding** is defined as hemorrhage distal to the ligament of Treitz that requires more than **3 units of blood in 24 hours. Management** consists of simultaneously restoring intravascular volume and identifying the site of bleeding so that treatment may be instituted.

   a. **Resuscitation** is performed using a combination of isotonic crystalloid solutions and packed RBCs as needed, administered via short, large-bore peripheral intravenous catheters.

   b. **Diagnosing the site of bleeding** is more important initially than identifying the cause. Gastric lavage via a nasogastric tube must be performed to rule out an upper GI source of bleeding. Digital rectal exam can eliminate hemorrhoidal bleeding. The choice of localizing study depends on the estimate of bleeding rate.

      (1) **Nuclear scan** using technetium-99m sulfur colloid or tagged RBCs can identify bleeding sources with rates as low as 0.1 to 0.5 mL/minute. Tagged RBC scan can identify bleeding up to 24 hours after isotope injection, but they do not definitively identify the anatomic source of bleeding; hence, planning a segmental GI resection based on this study is not reliable. A rapidly positive scan indicates that angiography has a high likelihood of identifying the source.

      (2) **Mesenteric angiography** should be performed in the patient with a positive nuclear medicine bleeding scan to identify the anatomic source of bleeding. Angiography can localize bleeding exceeding 1 mL/minute and allows either therapeutic vasopressin infusion (0.2 unit/minute) or embolization, which together are successful in stopping the bleeding in 85% of cases. The advantage is that this can convert an emergent operation in an unstable patient with unprepared bowel to an elective one-stage procedure.

      (3) **Colonoscopy** frequently fails to identify the source of massive lower GI bleeds. With slower bleeding after the administration of an adequate bowel preparation over 2 hours, colonoscopy offers the therapeutic advantages of injecting vasoconstrictive agents (epinephrine) or vasodestructive agents (alcohol, morrhuate, sodium tetradecyl sulfate) or applying thermal therapy (laser photocoagulation, electrocoagulation, heater probe coagulation) to control bleeding.

      (4) In the rare **patients who continue to bleed with no source identified,** laparotomy should be considered. Intraoperative small-bowel enteroscopy may be performed if the source is not obvious at the time of exploration. If the source is still not identified, **total colectomy with ileorectal anastomosis or end-ileostomy** is performed. This is associated with an incidence of recurrent bleeding of less than 10%, but the mortality rate for patients who rebled is 20% to 40%.

3. **Ischemic colitis** results from many causes, including venous or arterial thrombosis, embolization, iatrogenic inferior mesenteric artery (IMA) ligation after abdominal aortic aneurysm repair, and from acquired

or autoimmune vasculopathies. It is **idiopathic** in the majority of patients. Patients are usually elderly and present with lower abdominal pain localizing to the left and melena or hematochezia. The rectum often is normal on proctoscopy owing to its dual vascular supply. Contrast enema may show **thumbprinting** that corresponds to submucosal hemorrhage and edema. Diagnosis depends on the appearance of the mucosa on colonoscopy. Although it may occur anywhere in the colon, disease is present most frequently at the watershed areas of the splenic flexure and sigmoid colon. In the presence of full-thickness necrosis or peritonitis, emergent resection with diversion is recommended. Patients without peritonitis or free air but with fever or an elevated white blood cell (WBC) count may be treated with bowel rest, close observation, and intravenous antibiotics. Up to 50% of patients develop focal colonic strictures eventually. These are treated with serial dilations or segmental resection once neoplasm is ruled out.

4. **Radiation proctocolitis** results from pelvic irradiation for uterine, cervical, bladder, prostate, or rectal cancers. Risk factors include a dose of greater than 6,000 cGy, vascular disease, diabetes mellitus, hypertension, prior low anterior resection, and advanced age. The early phase occurs within days to weeks; mucosal injury, edema, and ulceration develop, with associated nausea, vomiting, diarrhea, and tenesmus. The late phase occurs within weeks to years, is associated with tenesmus and hematochezia, and consists of arteriolitis and thrombosis, with subsequent bowel thickening and fibrosis. Ulceration with bleeding, stricture, and fistula formation may occur. Medical treatment may be successful in mild cases, with the use of stool softeners, steroid enemas, and topical 5-aminosalicylic acid products. If these measures fail, transanal application of formalin 4% to affected mucosa may be efficacious in patients with transfusion-dependent rectal bleeding. Patients with stricture or fistula require proctoscopy and biopsy to rule out locally recurrent disease or primary neoplasm. Strictures may be treated by endoscopic dilation but often recur. Surgical treatment consists of a diverting colostomy and is reserved for medical failures, recurrent strictures, and fistulas. Proctectomy is rarely required and is usually associated with unacceptable morbidity and mortality.

ANORECTAL PHYSIOLOGY

I. NORMAL ANORECTAL FUNCTION

A. The **rectum functions as a capacitance organ,** with a reservoir of 650 to 1,200 mL compared to an average daily stool output of 250 to 750 mL.

B. The **anal sphincter mechanism** allows defecation and maintains continence. The internal sphincter (involuntary) accounts for 80% of resting pressure, whereas the external sphincter (voluntary) accounts for 20% of resting pressure and 100% of squeeze pressure. The external anal sphincter contracts in response to sensed rectal contents and relaxes during defecation.

C. **Defecation** has four components: (1) mass movement of feces into the rectal vault; (2) rectal–anal inhibitory reflex, by which distal rectal distention causes involuntary relaxation of the internal sphincter; (3) voluntary relaxation of the external sphincter mechanism and puborectalis muscle; and (4) increased intra-abdominal pressure.

D. **Continence** requires normal capacitance, normal sensation at the anorectal transition zone, puborectalis function for solid stool, external sphincter function for fine control, and internal sphincter function for resting pressure.

II. **INCONTINENCE** is the inability to prevent elimination of rectal contents.

A. **Etiologies** include (1) **mechanical defects,** such as sphincter damage from obstetric trauma, fistulotomy, and scleroderma affecting the external sphincter; (2) **neurogenic defects,** including spinal cord injuries, pudendal nerve injury due to birth trauma or lifelong straining, and systemic neuropathies such as multiple sclerosis; and (3) **stool content-related causes,** such as diarrhea and radiation proctitis.

B. **Evaluation** includes visual and digital examination observing for gross tone or squeeze abnormalities. **Anal manometry** quantitatively measures parameters of anal function, including resting and squeeze pressure (normal mean >40 and >80 mm Hg, respectively), sphincter length (4 cm in men, 3 cm in women), and minimal sensory volume of the rectum. Pudendal nerve terminal motor latency **(PNTML)** testing and endoanal ultrasound provide neural and anatomic information.

C. **Treatment** depends on the type and severity of the defect. Neurogenic and minor mechanical anal sphincter defects are treated using dietary fiber to increase stool bulk and **biofeedback** to strengthen muscle and improve early sensation. Major defects require **anal sphincter reconstruction,** in which the anatomic sphincter defect is repaired. Artificial anal sphincters may be used in patients without a reconstructible native anal sphincter. Severe denervations of an intact anal sphincter may be managed with sacral nerve stimulation, artificial sphincters, or palliative diverting colostomy.

III. **OBSTRUCTED DEFECATION** (pelvic floor outlet obstruction) presents with symptoms of chronic constipation and straining with bowel movements. Problems may include **fecal impaction** and **stercoral ulcer** (mucosal ulceration due to pressure necrosis from impacted stool); both are treated with enemas, increased dietary fiber, and stool softeners. Attempts at surgical correction of any of the following conditions without addressing the underlying pathology are doomed to failure.

A. **Physiologic evaluation** includes (1) **defecography** to evaluate fixation of the posterior rectum to the sacrum and relaxation of the puborectalis and (2) **colonic transit study.**

B. **Anal stenosis** is a rare cause of obstructed defecation and presents with frequent thin stools and bloating. The most common etiologies include scarring after anorectal surgery (rare), chronic laxative abuse, radiation, recurrent anal ulcer, inflammation, and trauma. Initial treatment is anal dilation, although advanced cases are treated with advancement flaps of normal perianal skin.

C. **Nonrelaxation of puborectalis** results in straining and incomplete evacuation. Colonic transit time reveals outlet obstruction. Persistent puborectalis distortion is seen on defecography. Biofeedback is the treatment of choice.

D. **Descending perineum syndrome** occurs when chronic straining causes pudendal nerve stretch and subsequent neurogenic defect. **Rectocele** results from a weak, distorted rectovaginal septum that allows the anterior rectal wall to bulge into the vagina due to failure of the pelvic floor to relax during defecation.

IV. **ABNORMAL RECTAL FIXATION** leads to internal or external prolapse of the full thickness of the rectum.

A. **Internal intussusception (internal rectal prolapse)** causes outlet obstruction with mucus discharge, hematochezia, tenesmus, and constipation. Proctoscopy demonstrates a **solitary rectal ulcer** at the lead point of the internal prolapse. **Treatment** consists of increased bulk, stool softeners, and glycerin suppositories. **Indications for surgery** are chronic bleeding, impending incontinence, and lifestyle-changing symptoms. Surgical options are controversial. The most frequent procedure is transabdominal rectopexy (suture fixation of the rectum to the presacral fascia) and anterior resection of the sigmoid colon if constipation is prominent among the patient's complaints. Chronic ischemia of the solitary rectal ulcer causes entrapment of mucin-producing cells, eventually resulting in **colitis cystica profunda.** Treatment is low anterior resection and rectopexy.

B. **External rectal prolapse** is protrusion of full-thickness rectum through the anus. Symptoms include pain, bleeding, mucous discharge, and incontinence. Physical examination can distinguish rectal prolapse (concentric mucosal rings) from prolapsing internal hemorrhoids (deep radial grooves). **Risk factors** include increased age, female gender, institutionalization, antipsychotic medication, previous hysterectomy, and spinal cord injury. Evaluation includes **barium enema or colonoscopy** to rule out malignancy. In general, abdominal procedures trade higher operative morbidity with lower recurrence rates relative to perineal-only operations. Continence improves in almost all patients, regardless of procedure.

1. **Sigmoid resection and rectopexy** (Frykman–Goldberg procedure) shortens the redundant rectosigmoid colon with posterior sacral fixation. Prolapse recurs in less than 10% of patients following rectopexy with or without resection.

2. **Perineal proctectomy** (modified Altemeier procedure) is an alternative for patients with severe anal incontinence due to complete eversion and stretch of the anal canal. Recurrence rate is generally around 20%, although lower rates have been reported in retrospective, single-institution studies (*Dis Colon Rectum.* 2006;49:1052).

V. **HEMORRHOIDS** are vascular and connective tissue cushions that exist in three columns in the anal canal: right anterolateral, right posterolateral, and left

TABLE 12-1	Classification and Treatment of Symptomatic Internal Hemorrhoids	
Grade	**Description**	**Treatments**
I	Palpable, nonprolapsing enlarged venous cushions	Dietary fiber, stool softeners
II	Prolapse with straining and defecation, spontaneously reduce	Dietary fiber, stool softeners, elastic ligation
III	Protrude spontaneously or with straining, require manual reduction	Dietary fiber, stool softeners, elastic ligation, excisional hemorrhoidectomy, stapled hemorrhoidectomy
IV	Chronically prolapsed and cannot be reduced, often with dentate line released from internal position	Dietary fiber, stool softeners, excisional hemorrhoidectomy, stapled hemorrhoidectomy

lateral. **Internal hemorrhoids** are above the dentate line and thus covered with mucosa. These may bleed and prolapse, but they do not cause pain. **External hemorrhoids** are below the dentate line and covered with anoderm. These do not bleed but may thrombose, which causes pain and itching, and secondary scarring may lead to skin tag formation. Hard stools, prolonged straining, increased abdominal pressure, and prolonged lack of support to the pelvic floor all contribute to the abnormal enlargement of hemorrhoidal tissue. **Treatments** are based on grading and patient symptoms (Table 12-1); options include the following:

A. **Medical treatment** of first-degree and most second-degree hemorrhoids includes increased dietary fiber and water, stool softeners, and avoidance of straining during defecation. Refractory second- and third-degree hemorrhoids may be treated in the office by **elastic ligation.** The ligation must be 1 to 2 cm above the dentate line to avoid pain and infection. One quadrant is ligated every 2 weeks in the office, and the patient is warned that the necrotic hemorrhoid may slough in 7 to 10 days with bleeding occurring at that time. Patients on anticoagulation should have their anticoagulation stopped for a full 7 to 10 days after banding. Severe sepsis may occur after banding in immunocompromised patients or those who have had full-thickness rectal prolapse ligated by mistake. Patients present with severe pain, fever, and urinary retention within 12 hours of ligation. Patients with this life-threatening disorder should undergo examination under anesthesia, immediate removal of rubber bands, and debridement of any necrotic tissue, accompanied by broad-spectrum intravenous antibiotics.

B. **Excisional hemorrhoidectomy** is reserved for large third- and fourth-degree hemorrhoids, mixed internal and external hemorrhoids, and thrombosed, incarcerated hemorrhoids with impending gangrene. The procedure is performed with the patient in the **prone flexed position,** and the resulting elliptical defects are completely closed with chromic suture (Ferguson hemorrhoidectomy). Complications include a 10% to 50% incidence of urinary retention, bleeding, infection, sphincter injury, and anal stenosis from taking too much mucosa at the dentate line.

C. **Stapled hemorrhoidectomy** is an alternative to traditional excisional hemorrhoidectomy for large prolapsing, bleeding third-degree hemorrhoids with minimal external disease. This procedure is performed by a circumferential excision of redundant rectal mucosa approximately 5 cm superior to the dentate line using a specially designed circular stapler. (*Dis Colon Rectum.* 2004;47:1824). Stapled hemorrhoidectomy results in significantly less perioperative discomfort. There is significantly greater recurrence rate following stapled hemorrhoidectomy (*Cochrane Database Syst Rev.* 2006;4:5393).

D. **Acutely thrombosed external hemorrhoids** are treated by excision of the thrombosed vein outside the mucocutaneous junction, which can be done in the office or emergency room with the wound left open. If the thrombosis is more than 48 hours old, the patient is treated with nonsurgical management.

VI. **ANAL FISSURE** is a split in the anoderm. Ninety percent of anal fissures occur posteriorly and 10% occur anteriorly; location elsewhere should prompt exam under anesthesia and biopsy. Symptoms include tearing pain with defecation and severe anal spasm that lasts for hours afterward and blood (usually on the toilet paper). Manometry and digital rectal examination demonstrate increased sphincter tone and muscular hypertrophy in the distal one-third of the internal sphincter. An external skin tag or "sentinel pile" may also be present. Differential diagnosis includes Crohn's disease (fissure often in the lateral location), tuberculosis, anal cancer, abscess or fistula, cytomegalovirus, herpes simplex virus, chlamydia, and syphilis. **Ninety percent of patients heal with medical treatment** that includes increased fiber, sitz baths, and topical nifedipine ointment (0.2%) TID. If surgery is required, **lateral internal sphincterotomy** is 90% successful. Recurrence and minor incontinence occur in fewer than 10% of patients.

INFECTIONS

I. **COLITIS**

A. **Pseudomembranous colitis** is an acute diarrheal illness resulting from toxins produced by overgrowth of *Clostridia difficile* after antibiotic treatment (especially the use of clindamycin, ampicillin, or cephalosporins). Antibiotics already have been discontinued in one-fourth of cases, and symptoms can occur up to 6 weeks after even a single dose. **Diagnosis** is made by detection of **toxin A** in one of at least three stool samples or stool culture if toxin A is not found but symptoms are present. Proctoscopy demonstrates sloughing colonic mucosa or pseudomembranes, and CT often shows transmural colonic thickening. **Treatment** begins with stopping unnecessary antibiotics and starting oral or intravenous metronidazole. Oral (not intravenous) vancomycin is an alternative but more expensive therapy. For severe cases in patients unable to take oral medications, vancomycin enemas (500 mg in 250 mL saline) may be useful. Rarely, pseudomembranous colitis presents with severe peritoneal irritation and colonic distention with **toxic megacolon** or **perforation.** Emergency laparotomy with total colectomy and end-ileostomy is required.

B. **Amebic colitis** results from invasive infection by the protozoan *Entamoeba histolytica,* which is spread by the fecal-oral route. It is most commonly encountered in patients who have traveled abroad. The cecum usually is affected with small ulcers that may perforate or form an inflammatory mass or **ameboma. Diagnosis** is made by examining stool for ova and parasites, which is 90% sensitive in identifying the trophozoites. **Treatment** is oral metronidazole and iodoquinol. Surgical treatment is reserved for perforation or for ameboma refractory to treatment.

C. **Actinomycosis** is an abdominal infection that most commonly occurs around the cecum after appendectomy owing to the anaerobic Gram-positive *Actinomyces israelii.* An inflammatory mass often is present with sinuses to the skin that can drain **sulfur granules. Diagnosis** is confirmed by anaerobic culture (the organism may take up to 1 week to isolate), and **surgical drainage** combined with penicillin or tetracycline is required.

D. **Neutropenic enterocolitis** after chemotherapy occurs most commonly in the setting of acute myelogenous leukemia after cytosine arabinoside therapy. It is also seen frequently in patients undergoing chemotherapy for stage III or IV colon cancer. Patients present with abdominal pain, fever, bloody diarrhea, distention, and sepsis. The cecum often dilates, and there may be pneumatosis. **Initial treatment** includes bowel rest, total parenteral nutrition, granulocyte colony-stimulating factor (G-CSF), and broad-spectrum intravenous antibiotics. Laparotomy with total colectomy and ileostomy is required only if peritonitis develops.

E. **Cytomegalovirus colitis** presents with bloody diarrhea, fever, and weight loss. It affects 10% of patients with acquired immunodeficiency syndrome (AIDS) and is the most common cause for emergent abdominal surgery in patients with AIDS. Ganciclovir is the treatment of choice; emergent colectomy with ileostomy is reserved for toxic megacolon.

II. INFECTION OF THE ANORECTUM

A. **Anorectal abscess**

1. **Cryptoglandular abscess** results from infection of the anal glands in the crypts at the dentate line. The initial abscess occurs in the intersphincteric space. Infection then can spread (1) superficial to the external sphincter into the **perianal** space, (2) through the external sphincter into the **ischiorectal** space (which in turn may connect posteriorly via the deep postanal space, resulting in a horseshoe abscess), or (3) deep to the external sphincter into the **supralevator** space.

a. **Diagnosis** usually is obvious, with severe anal pain and a palpable, tender, fluctuant mass. An intersphincteric abscess yields only a painful bulge in the rectal wall and no external manifestations.

b. **Treatment** is surgical drainage, with the skin incision kept close to the anal verge to avoid the possible creation of a long fistula tract. Intersphincteric abscesses are drained by an internal sphincterotomy over the entire length of the abscess. Perianal and ischiorectal abscesses are drained through the perianal skin with a small mushroom-shaped catheter placed to keep the abscess unroofed. Antibiotic therapy is not necessary unless the patient (1) is immunocompromised, (2) is diabetic, (3) has extensive cellulitis, or (4) has valvular heart disease. Immunocompromised patients may present with anal pain without fluctuance because of the paucity of leukocytes. The painful indurated region must still be drained, and the underlying tissue must undergo biopsy and culture.

c. **Outcome from drainage alone** shows that 40% of patients develop a chronic fistula. We do not advocate fistulotomy at the initial operation because the internal opening may not be evident and a complicated fistulotomy may result in sphincter injury.

2. **Fistula-in-ano** represents the chronic stage of cryptoglandular abscess but also may be due to trauma, Crohn's disease, tuberculosis, cancer, or radiation.

a. Patients present with persistent fecopurulent **perianal drainage** from the external opening of the fistula. The location of the internal opening along the dentate line is approximated by using **Goodsall's rule:** fistulas with external openings anterior to a transverse plane through the anal canal penetrate toward the dentate line in a radial direction, whereas fistulas posterior to that plane curve so that the internal opening is in the posterior midline (see Fig. 12-1), and may involve the sphincters in one of four configurations (see Fig. 12-2).

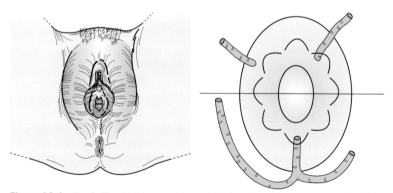

Figure 12-1. Goodsall's rule. The anterior–posterior location of the external opening of the fistula helps to identify the internal opening of the fistula.

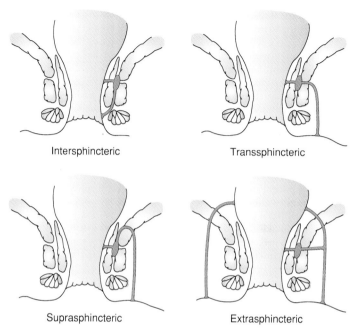

Interspincteric   Transsphincteric

Suprasphincteric   Extrasphincteric

Figure 12-2. The four main anatomic types of fistula. (From Mulholland MW, Lillemoe KD, Doherty GM, et al. *Greenfield's Surgery: Scientific Principles and Practice,* 4th ed. New York: Lippincott Williams and Wilkins, 2005, with permission.)

    b. Treatment depends on the level of the fistula and preexisting sphincter function. Placement of a soft, noncutting seton permits resolution of surrounding inflammation while preserving sphincter musculature. **Fistulotomy,** dividing the overlying internal sphincter, may be performed for intersphincteric fistulas, which necessitates incision to the anal verge without transversing any external sphincter (trans-sphincteric). **Fibrin glue injection** of the tract has a high failure rate but does not limit future options. A newer alternative is insertion of an **anal fistula plug** composed of lyophilized porcine submucosa to create a collagen scaffold to allow tract healing with variable results (*Dis Colon Rectum.* 2006;49:1817). Definitive treatment of a posterior midline fistula is fistulotomy, whereas anterior fistulas require sliding flap repairs if less invasive options fail.

B. Necrotizing anorectal infection (Fournier gangrene) can result in massive, life-threatening tissue destruction. Patients present with systemic toxicity and perianal pain. There may be crepitance and extensive necrosis under relatively normal skin. Synergistic flora (including clostridial and streptococcal species) of anorectal and urogenital origin may be involved. Immediate wide surgical debridement of all nonviable tissue and intravenous antibiotics are mandatory. Early treatment is critical, but mortality still approximates 50%.

C. **Pilonidal disease** occurs secondary to infection of a hair-containing sinus in the postsacral intergluteal fold 5 cm superior to the anus. Patients present with pain, swelling, and drainage when the sinuses become infected. The disease is most prevalent in men in the second and third decades of life. Symptoms are distinguished from perianal abscess by the lack of anal pain, the more superior location of the fluctuant mass, and the presence of midline cutaneous pits. Treatment is incision, drainage, and curettage, with allowance for secondary closure when the sinus is acutely inflamed. The disease tends to recur, however, and once the active inflammation has resolved, the sinus can be excised electively, with primary closure and a higher chance of cure.

D. **Hidradenitis suppurativa** is an infection of the apocrine sweat glands and mimics fistula-in-ano except that involvement is external to the anal verge. The treatment of choice is wide incision of the involved skin.

E. **Pruritus ani** is a common symptom of hemorrhoids, fissure, rectal prolapse, rectal polyp, anal warts and intraepithelial dysplasia of squamous or apocrine gland origin. Treatment is directed toward resolution of the underlying cause. Failure to find an underlying cause should prompt investigation of dietary factors (e.g., coffee and alcohol). Children should be evaluated for pinworms, which, if found, are treated with piperazine citrate.

F. **Condyloma acuminatum** is an anorectal and urogenital wart caused by infection with human papilloma virus. The disease is most commonly transmitted through anal intercourse and presents with visible perianal growth, often accompanied by pruritus, anal discharge, bleeding, and pain. Common treatments include topical trichloroacetic acid, Aldara (imiquimod), or excision with electrocoagulation under local anesthesia. Smoke generated by coagulation contains viable organisms and must be completely evacuated. Anal canal warts must be destroyed at the same time as external warts. Biopsies should be obtained looking for high-grade squamous intraepithelial lesions.

INFLAMMATORY BOWEL DISEASE

I. GENERAL CONSIDERATIONS

A. **Ulcerative colitis** is an inflammatory process of the colonic mucosa characterized by alterations in bowel function, most commonly bloody diarrhea with tenesmus. It has a male predominance. The disease **always involves the rectum** and extends continuously variable distances in the proximal colon. Patients often have abdominal pain, fever, and weight loss. As the duration of the inflammation increases, pathologic changes progress. Initially, mucosal ulcers and crypt abscesses are seen. Later, mucosal edema and pseudopolyps (islands of normal mucosa surrounded by deep ulcers) develop, and the end-stage pathologic changes show a flattened, dysplastic mucosa. The lumen is normal in diameter. Cancer must be considered in any colonic stricture in a patient with ulcerative colitis.

B. **Crohn's disease** is a transmural inflammatory process that can affect any area of the GI tract, from the mouth to the anus. It has a female predominance.

The disease has a segmental distribution, with **normal mucosa interspersed between areas of diseased bowel.** Common symptoms include diarrhea, abdominal pain, nausea and vomiting, weight loss, and fever. There can be signs of an abdominal mass or perianal fistulas on physical examination. The **terminal ileum** is involved in up to 45% of patients at presentation. Common pathologic changes include fissures, fistulas, transmural inflammation, and granulomas. Grossly, the mucosa shows aphthoid ulcers that often deepen over time and are associated with fat wrapping and bowel wall thickening. As the disease progresses, the bowel lumen narrows, and obstruction or perforation may result. Over time, the areas of stricture may develop dysplastic or even neoplastic changes.

C. **"Indeterminate colitis"** is a term used for cases in which the pathologic pattern does not fall clearly into one or the other of the aforementioned patterns (10% to 15% of patients with IBD). The indeterminacy can be due either to inadequate tissue biopsy or to a truly indeterminate form of disease.

D. **Extraintestinal manifestations** of IBD are common with ulcerative colitis and with Crohn's disease. Patients with either disease can develop dermatologic conditions such as erythema nodosum and pyoderma gangrenosum, ocular inflammatory diseases, and arthritis/synovitis. These typically correlate with the degree of colonic inflammation. Ulcerative colitis patients also can develop sclerosing cholangitis.

II. ULCERATIVE COLITIS

A. **Indications for surgery**

1. **Failure to respond to medical treatment.** Inability to wean from high-dose steroids after two successive tapers prompts evaluation for surgery.

2. The **risk of malignancy** is related to the extent and duration of the disease but not the intensity of the disease. Colitis-associated cancer usually infiltrates submucosally and has signet-ring histology. The risk increases by 1% per year after 10 years of disease. Colonoscopy is performed 7 to 10 years after the diagnosis and every 1 to 2 years thereafter, with random biopsies every 10 cm and directed biopsies of mass lesions. Resection is recommended for dysplasia or stricture.

3. **Severe bleeding** that does not respond adequately to medical therapy requires resection for control.

4. **Acute severe fulminant colitis** [white blood cell (WBC) count >16,000, fever, abdominal pain, distention] initially is treated with bowel rest, antibiotics, steroids, and avoidance of contrast enemas, antidiarrheals, and morphine. If the patient develops worsening sepsis or peritonitis, abdominal colectomy with end-ileostomy is performed.

B. **Surgical management** aims at removing the colorectal mucosa while maintaining bowel function as much as possible. Because the disease is localized to the rectum and colon, curative resection is possible. Sphincter-sparing procedures are preferred to preserve the functions of continence and defecation. However, they are associated with higher postoperative complication risk. Anal sphincter function is assessed with manometry to ensure normal function before contemplation of a sphincter-sparing procedure in a patient medically able to undergo the operation.

1. **Restorative proctocolectomy (ileal pouch–anal anastomosis, IPAA)** maintains enteral continuity through the anal sphincter mechanism and is the operation of choice in most patients. A total proctocolectomy is carried out to the anal transition zone. The rectum is transected, leaving the sphincters and levators intact. A distal ileal pouch is constructed over a distance of 15 cm in a J configuration, pulled through the sphincters, and stapled or sutured to the rectal cuff. Stapled anastomoses leaving a 2-cm cuff of anal canal mucosa technically are easier but require long-term surveillance of the residual mucosa. A diverting loop ileostomy is constructed, then reversed 3 months later after healing of the distal anastomosis. **Complications** include increased stool frequency (five to seven times daily), nocturnal soiling (20%), pouch fistula (<10%), and pouchitis (28%), an intermittent inflammatory process that typically responds to metronidazole. Pouch capacity increases over time; eventually, the patient needs to empty the pouch an average of four to five times daily. The pouch procedure can be performed laparoscopically.

2. **Total proctocolectomy with end-ileostomy** is performed in patients who have perioperative sphincter dysfunction or incontinence and in high-risk patients who would not tolerate potential postoperative complications. Most patients do well with a well-placed **Brooke ileostomy** that has a spigot configuration and empties into a bag appliance in an uncontrolled fashion. A **Kock pouch** or continent ileostomy does not empty spontaneously, does not require a permanent appliance, and requires cannulation six to eight times daily. These are more difficult to construct and prone to obstruction. This alternative is occasionally offered to patients who desire continence or who have severe skin allergies, which make ileostomy appliances problematic.

III. **CROHN'S DISEASE** is a chronic disease that is not surgically curable. Surgery should be performed only for complications of the acute disease, such as perforation, fistulas, and phlegmon or when chronic disease results in stricture formation. When a patient presents with a complication requiring surgery, all attempts should be made to prepare the patient so that a single operation will suffice and as much intestine as possible can be preserved. Preparations often include parenteral nutrition, antibiotics, anti-inflammatory medications, and percutaneous drainage of abscesses.

A. **Surgical management** of Crohn's disease is limited to resection of the diseased segment of intestine responsible for the complication. Resection is bounded by grossly normal margins; no attempt is made to obtain microscopically negative margins because outcome and recurrence are unaffected by this. If significant intra-abdominal infection or inflammation is encountered during surgery, a proximal ostomy is created to allow complete diversion of intestinal contents and resolution of the initial process. If no infection or inflammation is encountered, normal-appearing bowel can be primarily anastomosed. **Stricturoplasty** to preserve small-bowel length is favored by some groups, with single-institution retrospective reviews demonstrating comparable recurrence rates to resectional treatment (*J Am Coll Surg.* 2001;192:330).

B. **Small-intestinal Crohn's disease is covered in Chapter 10.**

C. **Colonic Crohn's disease** often requires operation after a shorter duration of symptoms than is typical for patients with either small-intestinal or ileocolic Crohn's disease. Perforation can occur without dilation of the colon secondary to thickening of the colonic wall. Surgical options include total abdominal colectomy with ileorectal anastomosis, total abdominal colectomy with an end-ileostomy, and maintenance of the rectum as a Hartmann pouch, or total proctocolectomy with permanent end-ileostomy. Rarely, colonic strictures can occur in an isolated segment, causing obstruction. The risk of colon cancer with Crohn's disease is 7% at 20 years; thus, any colonic stricture should be biopsied. Segmental resection is the treatment of choice for isolated segmental colonic Crohn's disease; stricturoplasty has no role in colonic strictures. All efforts should be directed to preserving the rectum in colonic Crohn's disease because restorative proctocolectomy is not an option.

D. **Rectal Crohn's disease** rarely occurs in isolation. Once the rectum has become so fibrotic that it loses its reservoir capacity, proctectomy should be considered. Precise **intersphincteric** dissection along the rectal wall beginning at the anal verge should minimize complications.

E. **Anal disease** occurs in 35% of patients with Crohn's disease, but only 2% present with disease confined exclusively to the perineum. Treatment of acute disease entails surgical drainage of perianal sepsis followed by medical therapy (steroids, bowel rest, antibiotics). Antitumor necrosis factor-α (TNF-α) antibody (infliximab) also has a role in acute and chronic perianal fistulas to reduce local disease activity and allow for subsequent surgical therapy. The ACCENT II (A Crohn's disease Clinical study Evaluating infliximab in a New long-term Treatment regimen) study was a landmark multicenter, double-blind, randomized trial of more than 300 patients with fistulizing Crohn's disease that demonstrated improved outcomes with anti-TNF-α therapy (*N Engl J Med.* 2004;350:876). Prolonged treatment with azathioprine is necessary to maintain remission. Ultimately, proctectomy or diversion may be the only way to return quality of life to the patient.

NEOPLASTIC DISEASE

I. The **etiology** of colorectal neoplasia has genetic and environmental components.

A. **Familial cancer syndromes** account for 10% to 15% of colorectal cancers (Table 12-2).

B. **Sporadic cancers** account for approximately 85% of colorectal neoplasia. First-degree relatives of patients with colorectal cancer have a three- to ninefold increase in the risk of developing the disease despite no identifiable inherited genetic mutation. Overwhelming evidence suggests that colorectal carcinomas develop from precursor adenomas and are associated with an

TABLE 12-2 Hereditary Colorectal Cancer (CRC) Syndromes

Syndrome	Percentage of Total RC Burden	Genetic Basis	Phenotype	Extracolonic Manifestations	Treatment	Notes
Familial adenomatous polyposis (FAP)	<1%	Mutations in tumor suppressor gene *APC* (5q21)	<100 adenomatous polyps; near 100% with CRC by age 40 yr	CHRPE, osteomas, epidermal cysts, periampullary neoplasms	TPC with end-ileostomy or IPAA or TAC with IRA and lifelong surveillance	Variants include Turcot (CNS tumors) and Gardener (desmoids) syndromes
Hereditary nonpolyposis colorectal cancer (HNPCC)	5%–7%	Defective mismatch repair: *MSH2* and *MLH1* (90%), *MSH6* (10%)	Few polyps, predominantly right-sided CRC, 80% lifetime risk of CRC	At risk for uterine, ovarian, small intestinal, pancreatic malignancies	Genetic counseling; consider prophylactic resections, including TAH/BSO	High microsatellite instability (MSI-H) tumors, better prognosis than sporadic CRC

			Mucocutaneous	Surveillance	
Peutz–Jeghers (PJS)	<1%	Loss of tumor suppressor gene *LKB1*/ STK11 (19p13)	Hamartomas throughout GI tract	Mucocutaneous pigmentation, risk for pancreatic cancer	Surveillance EGD and colonoscopy q3 yr; resect polyps >1.5 cm	Majority present with SBO due to intussuscepting polyp
Familial juvenile polyposis (FJP)	<1%	Mutated *SMAD4/DPC* (18q21)	Hamartomas throughout GI tract; >3 juvenile polyps; 15% with CRC by age 35 yr	Gastric, duodenal, and pancreatic neoplasms; pulmonary AVMs	Genetic counseling; consider prophylactic TAC with IRA for diffuse disease	Presents with rectal bleeding or diarrhea

AVM, arteriovenous malformation; CHRPE, congenital hypertrophy of retinal pigmented epithelium; CNS, central nervous system; EGD, esophagogastroduodenoscopy; GI, gastrointestinal; IPAA, ileal pouch–anal anastomosis; IRA, ileal–rectal anastomosis; TAC, total abdominal colectomy; TAH/BSO, total abdominal hysterectomy and bilateral salpingo-oophorectomy; TPC, total proctocolectomy.

increasing number of genetic mutations (the so-called **Vogel stein progression**). A single genetic mutation in the germline of a patient may cause an adenoma to develop. Further mutations in either tumor-suppressor genes or oncogenes are responsible for further development of the adenoma and eventually transformation to neoplasia. Genes implicated in this journey from normal epithelium to carcinoma include *K-ras, DCC,* and *p53.*

C. **Environmental factors** have also been proposed to play a significant role in the etiology of colorectal neoplasia. Dietary factors shown to increase cancer risk include a diet high in unsaturated animal fats and highly saturated vegetable oils. Increased fiber decreases cancer risk in those on a high-fat diet. Epidemiologic studies indicate that people from less-industrialized countries have a lower risk of colorectal cancer, likely due to dietary differences. This survival benefit disappears in people who immigrate to the United States.

II. **DETECTION.** **Surveillance** is the periodic complete examination of a patient with known increased risk. **Screening** is the limited examination of a population with the goal of detecting patients with increased risk.

A. **Screening** of the general population is recommended starting at **age 50** years by the American Cancer Society, the American College of Gastroenterology, and the American Society of Colon and Rectal Surgeons. Screening entails either dual-contrast barium enema with sigmoidoscopy or total colonoscopy, and these should be repeated every 10 years if normal or if the patient is not at high risk for colorectal neoplasia. Colonoscopy has a perforation risk of 0.1%, hemorrhage incidence of 0.3%, and mortality of 0.01%. It offers the advantages of obtaining a tissue diagnosis of any abnormality (potentially therapeutic) and greater sensitivity over barium enema. CT colonography is available for those patients unfit or unable to undergo endoscopic evaluation. Individuals over 40 should have yearly fecal occult blood testing.

B. **High-risk individuals** should be in a surveillance program. Previous cancer or polypectomy increases the risk of metachronous cancer by a factor of 2.7 to 7.7. Routine surveillance has been shown to reduce the incidence of metachronous cancer, although its influence on survival is unknown. High-risk patients are those with (1) ulcerative colitis of more than 10 years' duration, (2) Crohn's or ulcerative colitis with stricture, (3) a history or family history of polyps or cancer, or (4) a family history of adenomatous polyposis (FAP) or hereditary nonpolyposis colorectal cancer (HNPCC). Our surveillance algorithm calls for initial or perioperative colonoscopy followed by yearly examination until no lesions are detected, followed by examination every 3 years until no lesions are detected, and then examination every 5 years.

III. **POLYPS**

A. Nonadenomatous polyps

1. **Peutz–Jeghers syndrome** is an autosomal-dominant condition characterized by **hamartomatous polyps** of smooth muscle throughout

the GI tract and mucocutaneous pigmentation. Symptoms include bleeding or obstruction secondary to intussusception. Although hamartomas are benign, patients with Peutz–Jeghers syndrome are at increased risk for GI adenocarcinoma as well. Therefore, treatment of polyps greater than 1.5 cm in diameter is polypectomy. Surveillance colonoscopy and esophagogastroduodenoscopy (EGD) are recommended every 2 years, as well as periodic screening for breast, cervical, testicular, ovarian, and pancreatic cancer.

2. **Juvenile polyps** are cystic dilations of glandular structures in the lamina propria without malignant potential that may result in bleeding or obstruction. There are two peaks in incidence of isolated juvenile polyps: in infants and at age 25 years. They are the most common cause of GI bleeding in children and should be treated with polypectomy. **Multiple polyposis coli** (diffuse juvenile polyps) is an autosomal-dominant syndrome characterized by multiple juvenile polyps and increased risk for GI malignancy. These patients are considered for total abdominal colectomy or proctocolectomy with IPAA.

3. **Hyperplastic polyps** show epithelial dysmaturity and hyperplasia and are the most common colorectal neoplasm (10 times more common than adenomas). They have limited malignant potential and may serve as a marker for more aggressive diseases when >1 cm in size. We do not have strong data regarding long-term outcome. Most are less than 0.5 cm in diameter and rarely need treatment. However, those showing mixed adenoma/hyperplastic histology carry the same risks as adenomatous polyps.

B. **Adenomas** are benign neoplasms with unrestricted proliferation of glandular epithelium within the colonic mucosa but with no invasion of the basement membrane. The degree of differentiation decreases as a polyp becomes more like a cancer. *Severe atypia* refers to malignant cells in a polyp that have not invaded the muscularis mucosae (formerly known as *carcinoma in situ*). Adenomatous polyps fall into three broad categories, based on the percentage of villous composition:

1. **Tubular adenomas** are usually pedunculated and account for roughly 85% of adenomas. They have a 5% risk of containing malignant cells.

2. **Tubulovillous adenomas** account for 10% of adenomas. They have a 22% risk of containing cancer.

3. **Villous adenomas** are usually sessile and account for 5% of adenomas. Both size and induration of the polyp reflect cancer risk. For example, a 4-cm sessile villous adenoma has a 40% risk of cancer, whereas the same polyp with induration has a 90% risk.

C. **Treatment** consists of colonoscopic removal. Pedunculated polyps have a stalk and can be removed using the cautery snare. Semisessile and sessile polyps may require piecemeal extraction or endoscopic mucosal lift resection. The site of incomplete removal should be marked with 0.1 mL of India ink for possible later intraoperative or repeat colonoscopic identification. For sessile or large polyps (>3 cm) that cannot be removed endoscopically, surgical resection is required.

1. **The risk of metastatic cancer** in regional lymph nodes is 1% in a completely excised, pedunculated polyp in which cancer invades only the head of the polyp, unless there is lymphatic or vascular invasion. These cases may be treated with either colectomy or polypectomy with close follow-up. Invasion of the cancer down the stalk to the lower third requires colectomy.

2. **Sessile polyps** containing cancer require colectomy, even if completely excised, as the risk of local recurrence and lymph node metastasis is greater than 10% to 20%.

D. **Villous adenoma of the rectum** can present with watery diarrhea and hypokalemia. The risk of cancer in lesions greater than 4 cm with induration is 90%, and transrectal ultrasonography should be used to determine the depth of invasion before excision. Treatment of favorable lesions is by transanal, full-thickness local excision followed by closure of the defect with suture. The role of **transanal endoscopic microsurgery (TEM)** continues to evolve and has become an accepted approach to rectal villous adenomas. Accurate interpretation of the existing small series of patients with early rectal cancer undergoing TEM is difficult due to heterogeneous inclusion criteria, misstaging of rectal cancer, and varying surgeon experience. If the adenoma is large (>4 cm), circumferential, contains invasive cancer, or is located above the peritoneal reflection (generally 10 cm above the anal verge), a transabdominal proctectomy should be performed.

IV. COLON CANCER

A. The **incidence** of colorectal cancer in the United States has been stable since the 1950s, with 145,000 new cases (105,000 colon and 40,000 rectal) each year and 58,000 deaths each year. It is the third-most lethal cancer in men and women, with a slight female predominance in colon cancer and male predominance in rectal cancer. There is a 5% lifetime risk; 6% to 8% of cases occur before age 40 years, and the incidence increases steadily after age 50 years.

B. **Clinical presentation** of colon cancer depends on the location of the lesion. Many tumors are asymptomatic and discovered on routine screening colonoscopy. **Right-colon** lesions occasionally cause hematochezia, but more often bleeding is occult, causing anemia and fatigue. **Left-colon** lesions more often cause crampy abdominal pain, altered bowel habit, or hematochezia. In less than 10% of cases, left-colon cancer presents as large-bowel obstruction with inability to pass flatus or feces, abdominal pain, and distention. Approximately 50% of patients with other symptoms complain of weight loss, but weight loss is almost never the sole manifestation of a colorectal tumor. Rarely, colon cancer presents as perforation with focal or diffuse peritonitis or as a fistula with pneumaturia or feculent vaginal discharge. These symptoms may be difficult to distinguish from those of diverticulitis. Metastatic disease is usually asymptomatic but may present with jaundice, pruritus, and ascites or with cough and hemoptysis.

C. **Diagnosis and staging**

1. **Once the diagnosis is suspected based on history, physical examination, or screening tests,** every attempt should be made to obtain biopsy of the primary lesion and rule out synchronous cancer (3% to 5%). Colonoscopy to the cecum or flexible sigmoidoscopy and barium enema are acceptable. In patients presenting with obstructive symptoms, water-soluble contrast enema is performed to assess the degree and level of obstruction and to "clear" the colon proximal to the obstruction.

2. **Staging studies** to look for distant metastases include chest X-ray and abdominal CT scan. CT identifies liver metastases as well as adrenal, ovarian, pelvic, and lymph node metastases. Serum carcinoembryonic antigen (CEA) is a useful prognostic and surveillance tumor marker in colorectal cancer. CEA should be obtained preoperatively as part of the staging evaluation. Recently, positron emission tomography (PET)-CT has been shown to have greater sensitivity for detecting metastatic disease than CT alone. It is routinely performed prior to concurrent colectomy and liver resection for hepatic metastases.

D. **Surgical treatment**

1. **Bowel preparation.** Mechanical bowel preparation has been shown to be unnecessary in patients undergoing proximal colectomy (right, transverse, or splenic flexure). A modified mechanical prep may be used with Phospho Soda enemas to empty the rectum in patients undergoing left and sigmoid colectomy. A complete mechanical prep is currently recommended for patients undergoing restorative proctocolectomy but not abdominoperineal resection. All patients undergoing laparoscopic procedures may benefit from complete or modified prep to reduce stool volume and facilitate colonic manipulation. The choice of preparation varies by surgeon. All patients undergoing colectomy should receive preoperative intravenous antibiotics (typically cefoxitin or ciprofloxacin and metronidazole) within 1 hour of skin incision. We routinely administer prophylactic enoxaparin preoperatively to reduce the risk of deep venous thrombosis.

2. **Open operative technique** begins with a thorough exploration that includes palpation of the liver. After mobilization of the involved segment, the main segmental vessels are then ligated and divided, and *en bloc* resection of colon and any adherent structure is carried out. If curative resection is not possible, palliative resection should be attempted; if this cannot be done, bypass should be performed. For right-colon cancer, resection includes the distal 10 cm of terminal ileum to the transverse colon, taking the ileocolic, right colic, and right branch of the middle colic vessels. A transverse colon lesion is resected with either an extended right colectomy or a transverse colectomy, taking only the middle colic vessels. Left-colon lesions require dividing the IMA at its origin. If multiple carcinomas are present, or if a colon carcinoma with multiple neoplastic polyps is present, then a subtotal colectomy is performed. The specimen margin is inspected in the operating room to ensure at least a

2-cm margin (5 cm for poorly differentiated tumors). Pathologic evaluation should produce 12 lymph nodes in the mesenteric specimen.

3. **Laparoscopic colectomy** offers a shorter hospital stay and faster recovery for patients with colon cancer. Oncologically, it is guided by the same principles as open resection. The Clinical Outcomes of Surgical Therapy (COST) trial demonstrated noninferiority of the laparoscopic approach as compared to open surgery, with statistically similar times to tumor recurrence, wound implantation, and overall survival at 5 years (*Ann Surg.* 2007;246(4):655–662).

4. **Emergency operations** are undertaken without bowel preparation and have a higher incidence of wound infection. For obstruction, right colectomy still can be performed with primary anastomosis and no diversion. Options with a left-colon cancer include (1) resection with colostomy and either mucous fistula or Hartmann pouch, (2) resection with primary anastomosis, (3) resection with primary anastomosis and proximal diverting ileostomy, (4) subtotal colectomy and ileosigmoidostomy, and (5) colostomy with staged resection of the tumor in an unstable patient with markedly dilated colon. In all but the subtotal colectomy, the proximal colon must be evaluated in the postoperative period for synchronous cancer.

E. **Staging and prognosis.** The American Joint Committee on Cancer (AJCC) TNM staging identifies the depth of invasion of the tumor (T), regional lymph node status (N), and presence of distant metastases (M) (see Table 12-3). Stage I tumors do not involve the muscularis and have a 90% 5-year survival. Stage II tumors penetrate the muscularis and have a 60% to 80% 5-year survival. Stage III tumors involve lymph nodes and have a 60% 5-year survival. Stage IV tumors have distant metastases and a 5-year survival of 10% (see Table 12-4 for staging definitions). Unfavorable characteristics include poor differentiation, multiple lymph node involvement with tumor, mucinous or signet-ring pathology, venous or perineural invasion, bowel perforation, aneuploid nuclei, and elevated CEA.

F. **Adjuvant chemotherapy** remains a standard treatment of stage III and IV colon cancer or patients with stage II cancer in whom less than 12 lymph nodes have been harvested. Current therapy involves the combination of 5-fluorouracil/leucovorin with either irinotecan (FOLFIRI) or oxaliplatin (FOLFOX). The role of targeted therapy using vascular endothelial growth factor (VEGF) inhibitors (bevacizumab) or epidermal growth factor receptor (EGFR) inhibitors (cetuximab) in patients with k-ras mutations in the tumor may be beneficial. Patients with stage IIb tumors with poor prognostic factors may also benefit from adjuvant chemotherapy, although the risk-to-benefit ratio is not as great.

G. **Follow-up** is crucial in the first 2 years after surgery, when 90% of recurrences occur. Surveillance colonoscopy is recommended the first year after resection and then every 3 years until negative, at which time every 5 years is recommended. CEA should be checked every 3 months in the first year and every 6 months in the next 4 years, and rising levels should prompt a CT scan, a chest X-ray, and a PET scan to detect and stage recurrence. A yearly CT scan is recommended in patients with greater than stage I disease.

TABLE 12-3	TNM Categories for Colorectal Cancer
T	Local tumor spread
T0	No tumor
Tis	Tumor only involves mucosa and has not grown beyond muscularis mucosa
T1	Tumor extends into the submucosa
T2	Tumor extends into muscularis propria
T3	Tumor extends through muscularis propria but not beyond outermost layer of colon
T4	Tumor extends through other organs or structures or penetrates the visceral peritoneum
N	Nodal involvement
N0	No lymph node involvement
N1	Cancer cells in 1–3 nearby lymph nodes
N2	Cancer cells in 4 or more nearby lymph nodes
M	Distant spread
M0	No distant organ spread
M1	Spread to a distant organ or distant set of lymph nodes

V. RECTAL CANCER

A. The **pathophysiology** of rectal cancer differs from that of colon cancer because of several anatomic factors: (1) confinement of pelvis and sphincters, making wide excision impossible; (2) proximity to urogenital structures and nerves, resulting in high levels of impotency in men; (3) dual blood supply and lymphatic drainage; and (4) transanal accessibility. The rectum is defined by the NCI as within 12 cm above the anal verge on rigid proctoscopy.

B. Diagnosis and staging
   1. **Local aspects.** Digital rectal examination can give information on the size, fixation, ulceration, local invasion, and lymph node status. Rigid sigmoidoscopy and biopsy are crucial for precisely measuring the

TABLE 12-4	AJCC/Dukes Colorectal Cancer Staging	
AJCC	TNM	Dukes
0	Tis, N0, M0	—
I	T1–2, N0, M0	A
IIA	T3, N0, M0	B
IIB	T4, N0, M0	B
IIIA	T1–3, N1, M0	C
IIIB	T3–4, N1, M0	C
IIIC	Any T, N2, M0	C
IV	Any T, Any N, M1	—

distance to the anal verge and dentate line and for obtaining a tissue diagnosis. Flexible sigmoidoscopy cannot accurately assess the height of the tumor. **Transrectal ultrasonography** or **rectal protocol magnetic resonance imaging (MRI)** should be an integral part of staging rectal tumors.

2. **Regional aspects.** Pelvic CT, magnetic resonance (MR) scan, and transrectal ultrasound can yield information on the local extension of the tumor toward the bony pelvis and the proximity to the mesorectal envelope. Pelvic examination is necessary to assess the possible fixation of the tumor to adjacent genitourinary structures. Cystoscopy may be required in some men to evaluate extension into the prostate or bladder.

3. **Distant spread** is evaluated (as with colon cancer) with chest X-ray, abdominal CT, and serum CEA. PET scanning is frequently helpful in identifying recurrent disease or disease outside of the liver or lung.

C. **Surgical treatment goals** are to remove cancer with adequate margins, complete mesorectal package (total mesorectal excision, TME) and perform an anastomosis only if there is good blood supply, absence of tension, and normal anal sphincters. If any of these conditions cannot be met, the entire rectum must be removed and the patient left with a permanent colostomy.

1. **Bowel preparation** should be performed for planned restorative proctectomy or laparoscopic procedure. It is not necessary before abdominoperineal resection.

2. The **stoma sites on the abdominal wall should be marked** for possible colostomy on the left side, avoiding bony prominences, belt lines, and scars and staying medial to the rectus muscle at the summit of a fat

fold. The right lower quadrant should also be marked in the event that a temporary loop ileostomy is necessary. Stoma sites should be marked even if the surgeon is anticipating performing an anastomosis.

3. **Positioning and preparation.** If the patient has had previous pelvic surgery or the cancer is suspected to involve the bladder or ureter, ureteral stents should be placed after induction of anesthesia. The patient is placed in the dorsal lithotomy position, which gives access to the abdomen and perineum. A nasogastric tube, Foley catheter, and 34-French mushroom rectal catheter are placed, and the rectum is irrigated until clear with warm saline before instilling 100 mL of povidone–iodine (Betadine).

4. **Operative technique.** Operative goals include high ligation of the IMA at the aorta, careful attention to preserving gonadal vessels and the ureter, and transection of the colon at the descending/sigmoid junction with a purse-string suture around an end-to-end anastomosis stapler anvil in the remaining end of the proximal colon. Rectal dissection then proceeds posteriorly along the avascular presacral plane, laterally through the vascular lateral ligaments, and finally anteriorly, with preservation of the seminal vesicles or vagina. Dissection continues distally well beyond the tumor so that transection allows at least a 2-cm distal margin and a full removal of the rectal mesentery transected at a right angle at the level of the distal intestinal margin. The Dutch Rectal Cancer Trial demonstrated the value of this standardized surgical approach, **the TME,** reporting a local recurrence rate of only 2.4% at 2-year follow-up in patients receiving preoperative short-course radiation and TME (*N Engl J Med.* 2001;345:638).

5. **Surgical options** at this point depend on the height of the lesion, the condition of the sphincters, and the condition of the patient. An abdominoperineal resection is performed for tumors that cannot be resected with a 2-cm distal margin or if sphincter function is questionable. Low anterior resection using an intraluminal stapler is the operation of choice for tumors that can be resected with an adequate distal margin. A colonic J-pouch or coloplasty may also be constructed to recreate the reservoir function of the rectum. Generally, ultralow resections or those with marginal blood supply should be protected with a temporary diverting ileostomy. A hand-sewn coloanal anastomosis is required when the distal margin includes the anal transition zone.

6. **Complications**
   a. **Impotence** occurs in 50% of men and must be discussed preoperatively. The sites of nerve injury are the IMA origin, the presacral fascia, the lateral ligaments, and anteriorly at the level of the seminal vesicles. Prosthesis may be considered 1 year after surgery, once the pelvis is shown to be free of recurrence and the patient has had appropriate time to adapt to changes in body image.
   b. **Leakage** at the anastomosis occurs in up to 20% of patients, typically between postoperative days 4 and 7. Fever, elevated WBC count, increased or changed drain output, or abdominal pain during this period should prompt in-depth physical examination and CT scan evaluation. Intravenous antibiotics and bowel rest are usually

sufficient, but laparotomy and fecal diversion are necessary for large leaks. Patients at high risk for anastomotic leak and, therefore, candidates for diversion for loop ileostomy are those with low colorectal or coloanal anastomoses or recipients of neoadjuvant therapy.

c. **Massive presacral venous bleeding** can occur at the time of resection. This is controlled either with a pledget of abdominal wall muscle sutured to the sacrum or by packing the pelvis for 24 to 48 hours.

7. **Obstructive rectal cancer** requires emergent laparotomy on an unprepared bowel. The type of procedure depends on whether presurgical adjuvant therapy is considered. A decompressing transverse colostomy can be made through a small upper midline incision. This may be a blowhole type if the colon is massively dilated, or it may be a loop colostomy over a rod. If preoperative radiotherapy is not given, options include Hartmann resection, total colectomy with ileorectostomy, and low anterior resection protected by proximal diversion. Intraluminal stenting as a bridge to definitive therapy may preclude diversion.

D. **Adjuvant therapy** for rectal cancer should routinely be considered to reduce local recurrence and possibly improve overall survival.

E. **Neoadjuvant chemoradiation,** including chemotherapy with a 5-fluorouracil–based regimen, results in a modest survival benefit and decreased local recurrence over radiation therapy alone. It is generally reserved for patients with large, bulky tumors or evidence of nodal metastases (stage II/III, especially T4 lesions) in mid and low rectal tumors.

F. **Nonresectional therapy** is indicated in some early-stage cancers, patients with poor operative risk, and patients with widespread metastases. Options include transanal endoscopic microsurgical resection and endocavitary radiation in conjunction with external-beam radiation as the definitive treatment of favorable, but invasive rectal cancers.

G. If the patient has **incurable cancer** and a life expectancy of less than 6 months, external-beam radiation, with or without chemotherapy, combined with laser destruction or stenting the rectum can prevent obstruction. If the life expectancy exceeds 6 months, resectional therapy is attempted.

H. The major cause of **locally recurrent rectal cancer** is a positive margin on the pelvic side wall (radial margin). Recurrences tend to occur within 18 months and grow back into the lumen, presenting with pelvic pain, mass and rectal bleeding, or a rising CEA level. Diagnosis is confirmed by examination and biopsy as well as CT or PET scan. Treatment is not highly satisfactory, and there is a 10% to 20% palliation rate. If chemoradiation has not been given previously, it is given at this point using intensity-modulated radiation therapy (IMRT). Low anterior resection, abdominoperineal resection, or pelvic exenteration (resection of rectum and urinary bladder) is performed based on whether the sphincters and the genitourinary organs are involved in patients without distant disease.

VI. OTHER COLORECTAL TUMORS

A. **Lymphoma** is most often metastatic to the colorectum, but primary non-Hodgkin colonic lymphoma accounts for 10% of all GI lymphomas. The

GI tract is also a common site of non-Hodgkin lymphoma associated with human immunodeficiency virus. The most common presenting symptoms include abdominal pain, altered bowel habit, weight loss, and hematochezia. Biopsies are often not diagnostic because the lesion is submucosal. The workup is similar to that for colon cancer but should include a bone marrow biopsy and a thorough search for other adenopathy. Treatment is resection with postoperative chemotherapy. Intestinal bypass, biopsy, and postoperative chemotherapy should be considered for locally advanced tumors.

B. **Retrorectal tumors** usually present with postural pain and a posterior rectal mass on physical examination and CT scan (*Dis Colon Rectum.* 2005;48:1581).

   1. The **differential diagnosis** includes congenital, neurogenic, osseous, and inflammatory masses. Chordomas are the most common malignant retrorectal tumor; they typically are slow growing but difficult to resect for cure.

   2. **Diagnosis** is suspected based on CT scan and physical findings. Biopsy should not be performed. Formal resection should be undertaken.

C. Carcinoid tumor

   1. **Colonic carcinoids** account for 2% of GI carcinoids. Lesions less than 2 cm in diameter rarely metastasize, but 80% of lesions greater than 2 cm in diameter have local or distant metastases, with a median length of survival of less than 12 months. These lesions are treated with local excision if small and with formal resection if greater than 2 cm.

   2. **Rectal carcinoid** accounts for 15% of GI carcinoids. As with colonic carcinoids, lesions less than 1 cm in diameter have low malignant potential and are well treated with transanal or endoscopic resection. Rectal carcinoids greater than 2 cm in diameter are malignant in 90% of cases. Treatment of large rectal carcinoids is controversial, but low anterior resection or abdominoperineal resection is probably warranted.

VII. ANAL NEOPLASMS

A. Tumors of the anal margin

   1. **Squamous cell carcinoma** behaves like cutaneous squamous cell carcinoma, is well differentiated and keratinizing, and is treated with wide local excision and chemoradiation if large.

   2. **Basal cell carcinoma** is a rare, male-predominant cancer, and is treated with local excision.

   3. **High-grade squamous intraepithelial lesions** are becoming common in HIV-positive patients. Local excision or destruction of identified lesions during high-resolution anal mapping with 9% acetic acid can prevent progression to cancer.

B. Anal canal tumors

   1. **Epidermoid carcinoma** is nonkeratinizing and derives from the anal canal up to 6 to 12 mm above the dentate line.

      a. **Epidermoid cancer** usually presents with an indurated, bleeding mass. On examination, the inguinal lymph nodes should be examined specifically because spread below the dentate line passes to the inguinal nodes. Diagnosis is made by biopsy, and 30% to 40% are metastatic at the time of diagnosis.

b. **Treatment** involves chemoradiation according to the **Nigro protocol:** 3,000-cGy external-beam radiation, mitomycin C, and 5-fluorouracil. Surgical treatment is reserved for locally persistent or recurrent disease only. The procedure of choice is abdominoperineal resection; perineal wound complications are frequent.

2. **Adenocarcinoma** is usually an extension of a low rectal cancer but may arise from anal glands and has a poor prognosis.

3. **Melanoma** accounts for 1% to 3% of anal cancers and is more common in the fifth and sixth decades of life. Symptoms include bleeding, pain, and a mass, and the diagnosis is often confused with that of a thrombosed hemorrhoid. At the time of diagnosis, 38% of patients have metastases. Treatment is wide local excision, although the 5-year survival rate is less than 20%.

INTESTINAL STOMAS

A. **Ileostomy** creation and care was revolutionized with the description of the eversion technique by **Brooke** in 1952. Eversion eliminates the serositis reaction commonly observed from the proteolytic ileal effluent. Another advance has occurred with the widespread employment of trained nurse enterostomal therapists to educate and care for patients with ostomies.

1. **Physiology.** The small intestine adapts to ileostomy formation within 10 days postoperatively, with ileostomy output typically reaching a plateau between 200 and 700 mL/day. Because the effluent is highly caustic, it is crucial to maintain a stoma appliance that protects the surrounding skin and seals to the base of the ileostomy.

2. **Stoma construction** of either a loop ileostomy or end-ileostomy should include eversion of the functioning end to create a 2.5-cm spigot configuration. Stoma creation lateral to the rectus abdominis increases the risk of peristomal herniation. Precise apposition of mucosa and skin prevents serositis and obstruction. Preoperative marking of the planned stoma prevents improper placement near bony prominences, belt/pant lines, abdominal creases, and scars.

3. **Ileostomy care** requires special attention to avoid dehydration and obstruction. The patient is encouraged to drink plenty of fluids and to use antidiarrheal agents as needed to decrease output volume. Patients should be warned to avoid fibrous foods, such as whole vegetables and citrus fruits because these may form a bolus of indigestible solid matter that can obstruct the stoma. Irrigating the stoma with 50 mL of warm saline from a Foley catheter inserted beneath the fascia, in combination with intravenous fluids and nasogastric decompression, may relieve obstruction and dehydration. Alternatively, water-soluble contrast enema may be diagnostic as well as therapeutic.

4. **Reversal** of a loop ileostomy is relatively straightforward and rarely requires laparotomy. A side-to-side, functional end-to-end technique with a GIA stapler is utilized. Alternatively, the enterostomy is closed with sutures in two layers.

B. The **colostomy** construction technique depends on whether the goal is decompression or diversion. Ongoing surveillance of the remaining colon is necessary but often overlooked in patients with colostomies.

1. A **decompressing loop colostomy** vents the distal and proximal bowel limbs while maintaining continuity between the limbs.

2. **Diverting colostomies,** such as loop end-colostomy, are used following distal resection or perforation so that the distal limb is diverted from the fecal stream. All colostomies are matured in the operating room. If a stoma rod is used, it is removed 1 week after surgery.

3. **Complications** of colostomies include necrosis, stricture, and herniation. If necrosis (seen on endoscopy performed at bedside) does not extend below the fascia, it can be observed safely; otherwise, urgent revision is performed. **Parastomal hernias** are repaired only if they prevent application of a stomal appliance or cause small-bowel obstruction; these can be approached locally, although definitive treatment generally entails relocation of the stoma to a different site. Laparoscopic parastomal hernia repair has also been described.

4. **Hartmann reversal** is not a trivial procedure, with a reported morbidity rate of 20% to 30% (bleeding, anastomotic leak, abscess) and a mortality rate of 3%. Tagging the rectal stump with long, nonabsorbable sutures, mobilizing the splenic flexure during the initial resection and placing preoperative ureteral stents can facilitate reanastomosis. Placement of adhesion barriers at the time of initial exploratory laparotomy may reduce adhesions enough to allow laparoscopic colostomy closure.

13

Pancreas

Jonathan B. Mitchem and David C. Linehan

The pancreas is an entirely **retroperitoneal** structure. It is divided into four regions: the head/uncinate, neck, body, and tail. The head of the pancreas abuts the C loop of the duodenum and extends obliquely to the neck, anterior to the mesenteric vessels and portal vein. The neck then extends laterally into the body, which is generally accepted to begin at the left border of the superior mesenteric vein (SMV), lying posterior to the stomach and anterior to the splenic vessels. The pancreas then culminates in the tail that is associated with the splenic hilum anterior to the left adrenal gland. The pancreas receives its blood supply from both the celiac trunk and the superior mesenteric artery (SMA). The arterial supply of the pancreatic head is provided by the **inferior pancreaticoduodenal arteries** (from the SMA) and the superior pancreaticoduodenal arteries (from the gastroduodenal artery). The tail receives its arterial supply from branches of the splenic artery. Venous drainage is primarily by the pancreaticoduodenal veins, which drain into the portal vein. The pancreas has two ducts: the main pancreatic duct, called the **Duct of Wirsung,** which arises in the tail and traverses the length of the pancreas to terminate at the **papilla of Vater** within the wall of the duodenum; and the **Duct of Santorini,** which is much smaller and arises from the lower part of the head, terminating separately at the **lesser papilla.**

BENIGN PANCREATIC DISEASE

I. **ACUTE PANCREATITIS** is an inflammatory process of variable severity. Approximately 80% of cases of acute pancreatitis are self-limited and associated with mild transitory symptoms that do not cause fulminant morbidity or mortality. By contrast, 20% of patients develop a severe form of acute pancreatitis that is associated with a mortality rate as high as 40% (*Nat Clin Pract Gastroenterol Hepatol.* 2005;2:473). The exact mechanism by which various etiologic factors induce acute pancreatitis is unclear. However, most agree that the initial insult is **unregulated activation of trypsin within pancreatic acinar cells,** leading to autodigestion and an inflammatory cascade that may progress to SIRS (*Lancet.* 2008;371(9607):143–152).

   A. **Etiology.** The two most common causes of acute pancreatitis in the United States are **gallstones** and **alcoholism,** collectively accounting for nearly 80% of cases. Endoscopic retrograde cholangiopancreatography (ERCP) accounts for another 2% to 5% of cases. Other causes include the following:

   1. **Drugs** (1% to 2%):
      a. **Class I** (>20 reported cases, with at least 1 re-exposure case): azathioprine, steroids, sulfamethoxazole–trimethoprim, furosemide, opiates, valproic acid.
      b. **Class II** (10 to 20 reported cases with or without reexposure): hydrochlorothiazide, enalapril, octreotide, cisplatin, carbamazepine.
      c. **Class III** (<10 reported cases): statins.

2. **Metabolic:** hypercalcemia, hypertriglyceridemia (especially types I and V).

3. **Toxins:** scorpion bite, organophosphates.

4. **Infectious diseases** (mumps; orchitis; coxsackie virus B; Epstein–Barr virus; cytomegalovirus; rubella; hepatitis A, B, non-A, non-B; *Ascaris* species; *Mycoplasma pneumonia; Legionella sp.; Salmonella sp.*).

5. **Neoplasm:** intraductal papillary mucinous neoplasm of the pancreas (IPMN), pancreatic adenocarcinoma, etc.

6. **Trauma.**

7. **Autoimmune:** Sjogren syndrome, systemic lupus erythematosus (SLE), primary biliary cirrhosis (PBC), primary sclerosing cholangitis (PSC).

8. **Idiopathic.**

B. **Diagnosis**

1. Patients typically present with **epigastric pain,** often radiating to the back. Tenderness is usually limited to the upper abdomen but may manifest signs of diffuse peritonitis in more advanced cases. Occasionally, irritation from intraperitoneal pancreatic enzymes results in impressive peritoneal signs, simulating other causes of an acute abdomen. Nausea, vomiting, and low-grade fever are common, as are tachycardia and hypotension secondary to hypovolemia. Asymptomatic hypoxemia, renal failure, hypocalcemia, and hyperglycemia are evidence of severe systemic effects. Flank ecchymosis **(Gray-Turner sign)** or periumbilical ecchymosis **(Cullen sign)** is almost always manifestations of severe pancreatitis and have been associated with a 40% mortality rate. However, these signs are present in only 1% to 3% of cases and do not usually develop until 48 hours after the onset of symptoms.

2. **Laboratory studies**

   a. **Serum amylase** is the most useful test. Levels rise within a few hours of the onset of symptoms and may return to normal over the following 3 to 5 days. Persistent elevations of levels for longer than 10 days indicate complications, such as pseudocyst formation. Normal levels may indicate resolution of acute pancreatitis; however, there is no correlation between amylase level and etiology, prognosis, or severity. In addition, hyperamylasemia can be found in a variety of other clinical conditions including renal failure, intestinal obstruction, appendicitis, gynecologic disorders, sialoadenitis, and malignancy.

   b. **Serum lipase** generally is considered more sensitive for pancreatic disease (95%), and remains elevated for a longer period of time, which can be useful in patients with a delayed presentation.

   c. **Acute phase proteins** such as C-reactive protein (CRP), tumor necrosis factor-alpha (TNF-a), and interleukin-6 (IL-6) may be measured as a marker of severity.

   d. **Serum calcium** levels may fall as a result of complexing with fatty acids (saponification) produced by activated lipases.

   e. **Hepatic function panel** [aspartate aminotransferase (AST), alanine aminotransferase (ALT), bilirubin, alkaline phosphatase] should be checked to assess for concomitant biliary disease, or as an etiology of pancreatitis (gallstone disease) although normal values do not rule out biliary etiologies.

3. **Radiologic imaging** complements clinical history and exam because no single modality provides a perfect diagnostic index of severity.
   a. The specificity of **ultrasonography** (US) in pancreatitis can be greater than 95%, yet its sensitivity ranges between 62% and 95%, and both are highly user dependant. The pancreas is not visualized in up to 40% of patients due to overlying bowel gas and body habitus. The primary utility of US in acute pancreatitis is to evaluate for biliary etiology.
   b. **Computed tomography (CT)** is superior to US in evaluating the pancreas. The sensitivity and specificity of CT are 90% and 100%, respectively. Iodinated contrast enhancement is essential to detect the presence of pancreatic necrosis. CT may also be helpful in differentiating acute pancreatitis from conditions such as malignancy, small-bowel obstruction, or acute cholecystitis. CT findings include parenchymal enlargement and edema, necrosis, blurring of fat planes, peripancreatic fluid collections, bowel distention, and mesenteric edema. CT imaging may be useful in predicting the severity and course of disease using the modified CT severity index (CTSI, see below, *Am J Roent.* 2004;183:1261–1265). Every patient with a presumed diagnosis of acute pancreatitis does not require a CT scan. In general, patients who warrant further imaging include those in whom the diagnosis is not conclusive, any severely ill patient in whom necrosis is more likely (only after aggressive resuscitation so as to diminish risk of contrast-associated nephropathy), and any patient who exhibits a deterioration in clinical course or fails to improve after 4 days of medical management.
   c. **Magnetic resonance imaging (MRI)** is a useful substitute for CT scan in patients allergic to iodinated contrast or in acute renal failure with sensitivity 83% and specificity 91%. In addition, MRI/ MR cholangiopancreatography (MRCP) is better than CT at visualizing cholelithiasis, choledocholithiasis, and anomalies of the pancreatic and common bile ducts.

4. **ERCP** is not routinely indicated for the evaluation of patients during an attack of acute pancreatitis, and is a subject of some controversy. **Indications for ERCP** are as follows:
   a. **Preoperative evaluation** of patients with suspected traumatic pancreatitis to determine whether the pancreatic duct is disrupted.
   b. Patients with **jaundice, suspected biliary pancreatitis, and possible cholangitis** who are not clinically improving by 24 hours after admission should undergo endoscopic sphincterotomy and stone extraction. However, the literature is clear that early endoscopic intervention for gallstone pancreatitis does not beneficially influence morbidity or mortality (*Ann Surg.* 2008;247(2):250–257).
   c. **Patients older than age 40 years with no identifiable cause** to rule out occult common bile duct stones, pancreatic, or ampullary carcinoma or other causes of obstruction.

TABLE 13-1	Ranson Criteria

Admission

Age	>55 y
White blood cell count	>16,000/µL
Blood glucose	>200 mg/dL
Serum lactate dehydrogenase	>350 IU/L
Aspartate aminotransferase	>250 IU/L

Initial 48 hr

Hematocrit decrease	>10%
Blood urea nitrogen elevation	>5 mg/dL
Serum calcium	<8 mg/dL
Arterial Po_2	<60 mm Hg
Base deficit	>4 mEq/L
Estimated fluid sequestration	>6 L

Mortality	
Number of Ranson Signs	**Approximate Mortality (%)**
0–2	0
3–4	15
5–6	50
>6	70–90

    d. Patients younger than age 40 years who have had cholecystectomy or have experienced more than one attack of unexplained pancreatitis.

C. **Prognosis.** Because the associated mortality of fulminant acute pancreatitis approaches 40% and randomized studies have shown that early aggressive supportive care improves outcomes, attempts have been made to identify clinical parameters that predict patients at higher risk of developing severe outcomes.

    1. **Ranson criteria** (Table 13-1) constitute the most frequently utilized predictor of mortality associated with acute pancreatitis. The limitation of this assessment tool is that a score cannot be calculated until 48 hours after admission.

    2. **CTSI** is a prognostic scale based on CT findings, including peripancreatic fluid collections, fat inflammation, and extent of pancreatic necrosis was originally described by Balthazar et al. (*Radiology.* 1994;174:331–336) and then modified to a simpler model (*Am J Roent.* 2004;183:1261–1265). The usefulness of this criterion is limited to patients with normal renal function able to undergo contrast-enhanced CT, and by the fact that many patients with limited disease do not undergo CT imaging, potentially skewing study results (see Tables 13-2 and 13-3).

    3. The **Glasgow** scoring, like Ranson criteria, requires 48 hours to prognosticate patients and is based on clinical and laboratory values.

TABLE 13-2	CT Severity Grading Index (CTSI) Scoring Based on Imaging Characteristics

Scoring for Pancreatic Necrosis

0 Points	No pancreatic necrosis
2 Points	≤30% pancreatic necrosis
4 Points	>30% necrosis

Evaluation of Pancreatic Morphology, Not Including Necrosis

0 Points (grade A)	Normal pancreas
2 Points (grade B/C)	Focal or diffuse enlargement of the gland, including contour irregularities and inhomogeneous attenuation with or without peripancreatic inflammation
4 Points (grade D/E)	Pancreatic or peripancreatic fluid collection or peripancreatic fat necrosis
Additional 2 points	Extra pancreatic complications including one or more of the following: pleural effusion, ascites, vascular complications, parenchymal complications, or gastrointestinal tract involvement

4. The **Acute Physiology and Chronic Health Evaluation (APACHE) II** score was developed in 1985 for assessing critically ill patients and incorporates physiology, age, and chronic health. The major benefit of the APACHE II score is that it can be calculated at admission and updated daily to allow continual reassessment. However, the APACHE II score is somewhat cumbersome and difficult to calculate that limits its everyday use.

5. **Multiple Organ Dysfunction Score (MODS) and Sequential Organ Failure Assessment (SOFA)** have been shown to be important predictors of disease severity in critically ill patients and have been extended to patients with severe acute pancreatitis and are predictive of mortality and development of complications (*Br J Surg.* 2009; 96(2):137–150).

TABLE 13-3	Prognosis Based on CTSI Score	
Index	Predicted Morbidity	Predicted Mortality
0–3	8%	3%
4–6	35%	6%
7–10	92%	17%

D. Complications

1. **Necrotizing pancreatitis** occurs in about 10% to 20% of acute pancreatitis cases, and its presence correlates with prognosis (see CTSI above). It can be present at initial presentation or develop later in the clinical course. Necrosis is diagnosed on CT as failure to enhance with intravenous contrast.

2. **Infected pancreatic necrosis** occurs in 5% to 10% of cases and is associated with mortality as high as 80%, and is the cause of most late deaths (>14 days). Whether pancreatic necrosis visualized on CT scan is infected cannot be determined by imaging; however, some signs such as gas in the areas of necrosis can be suggestive. The gold standard for diagnosing infected pancreatic necrosis is fine needle aspiration (FNA), but this is rarely used in our practice, so infected pancreatic necrosis is more commonly a clinical diagnosis. Gram-negative organisms are more common than Gram-positive organisms (typically *Pseudomonas, Escherichia coli, Klebsiella, Proteus, Enterobacter*, and *Staphylococcus* species).

3. **Acute pseudocyst** (see Section V).

4. **Visceral pseudoaneurysm** is a rare complication in pancreatitis, but is most common among patients with necrotizing pancreatitis. Visceral pseudoaneurysm is believed to result from exposure of visceral arteries to the proteolytic pancreatic enzymes frequently extravasated during bouts of acute pancreatitis. The most common arteries involved are the splenic and left gastric arteries. Detection of pseudoaneurysms usually occurs 3 to 5 weeks following the onset of acute pancreatitis, but hemorrhage can occur at any time. A ruptured pseudoaneurysm can be a surgical emergency and often presents with signs and symptoms associated with upper gastrointestinal bleeding. Therapeutic angiography is the most appropriate first step in management as this can be both diagnostic and therapeutic (*Am J Surg*. 2005;190(3):489–495). For patients with lesions in the tail of the pancreas, distal pancreatectomy after stabilization may provide improved long-term hemorrhage control.

5. Because of the proximity of the splenic, superior mesenteric, and portal veins, **venous thrombosis** is not uncommon in patients with acute pancreatitis, and patients with severe disease are at higher risk. Although thromboses can be temporary, progression can lead to collateralization and gastroesophageal varices, but there is a low risk of bleeding (<10%) associated with venous thrombosis.

E. **Treatment.** Many predictors of poor outcome in acute pancreatitis are associated with end-organ dysfunction, and end-organ failure is highly associated with poorer outcomes. Therefore, the initial approach to managing acute pancreatitis focuses on supporting patients with aggressive fluid resuscitation and close monitoring.

1. **Supportive care**
   a. **Volume resuscitation** with isotonic fluids is crucial; urinary output is monitored with a Foley catheter targeting greater than 0.5 mL/kg/hr. If patients do not respond to initial resuscitation appropriately, central venous monitoring (CVP) may help direct further

resuscitation. During the course of resuscitation, patients should be maintained on continuous pulse oximetry as patients often require large volume fluid resuscitation and frequent monitoring of electrolytes, including **calcium,** is mandatory (at least every 6 to 8 hours initially).

b. **Gastric rest with nutritional support.** Nasogastric decompression is performed to decrease neurohormonal stimulation of pancreatic secretion. Acute pancreatitis is a hypercatabolic state, and nutritional support has been shown to have a significant impact on outcomes in critically ill patients. Enteral feeding is generally preferred to parenteral nutrition. Early enteral feeding in patients with severe acute pancreatitis is associated with lower rates of infection, surgical intervention, and length of stay (*BMJ.* 2004;328:1407). An ongoing randomized clinical trial (RCT) to investigate further the benefits of early versus normal initiation of enteral feeding is open in the Netherlands (*Trials.* 2011;12(1):73).

c. **Analgesics** are required for pain relief.

d. **Respiratory monitoring** and arterial blood gases should be done at least every 12 hours for the first 3 days in severe pancreatitis to assess oxygenation and acid–base status. Hypoxemia is extremely common, even in mild cases of acute pancreatitis given the volume of fluid resuscitation and the potential for development of sympathetic effusions. Pulmonary complications occur in up to 50% of patients.

e. **Antibiotics.** The routine use of antibiotic prophylaxis in acute pancreatitis, especially in mild-to-moderate cases, is not supported in the literature. Conflicting data exist regarding antibiotics in severe cases, as there are small prospective, randomized trials demonstrating significantly lower rates of septic complications in patients receiving antibiotics (*Ann Surg.* 2006;243:154) and subsequent data from a RCT that found differences in infection or surgical intervention (*Ann Surg.* 2007;245:674). A recent meta-analysis demonstrated no difference in mortality, infected necrosis or overall infections with antibiotic therapy; however, most data is anecdotal and a large multi-institutional RCT may be indicated to further evaluate this issue (*Cochrane Database Syst Rev.* 2010 May 12;(5):CD002941). When infection is confirmed or suspected, patients should be treated with broad-spectrum systemic antibiotics that cover Gram-negative bacteria and, depending on length of hospitalization, common hospital-acquired pathogens, including fungal organisms, as super infection can be seen commonly.

2. **Surgical treatment** must be entertained for the small percentage of patients who continue to deteriorate despite aggressive supportive therapy. Although there is no clear consensus of the indications for operative intervention, most surgeons advocate operative intervention in the setting of severe systemic illness refractory to medical management, diagnostic uncertainty, or life-threatening complications unable to be treated via endoscopic or angiographic means (intra-abdominal hemorrhage, visceral perforation, etc). The long-held belief that patients with infected pancreatic necrosis must undergo surgery has

become somewhat controversial, with some groups advocating an initial approach using percutaneous intervention and treating only those patients who fail to improve with surgical debridement (*NEJM.* 2010;362(16):1491–1502; *Br J Surg.* 2011;98(1):18–27). Additionally, patients with gallstone pancreatitis should undergo cholecystectomy as soon as medically feasible.

a. Wide debridement **(necrosectomy),** supplemented by either open packing or closed drainage, is the standard operative approach for managing infected necrotizing pancreatitis. At our institution, the preference is for wide debridement; drain placement and packing often with serial repeated debridement in the operating room. A positive correlation exists between repeated surgical interventions and morbidity, including fistula, gastric outlet obstruction, local bleeding, and incisional hernia. Marsupialization of the lesser sac allows rapid access to the pancreatic bed and can facilitate daily dressing changes (usually done in the intensive care unit).

b. **Pancreatic resection.** Because severe pancreatitis often leads to necrosis in large areas of the pancreas and peripancreatic fat, some have attempted to gain control of fulminant disease by resecting much or even the entire pancreas (partial or total pancreaticoduodenectomy, PD). Radical resection procedures place greater stress on already severely ill patients; PD or total pancreatectomy is associated with very high mortality and is not recommended in the acute setting.

c. **Gallstone-induced pancreatitis.** Ongoing choledocholithiasis is found in only 25% of biliary acute pancreatitis cases. Nonetheless, all patients with pancreatitis should be evaluated for the presence of gallstones because the etiology has specific therapeutic implications. Cholecystectomy should be carried out as soon as possible after recovery to prevent recurrent attacks of pancreatitis, as patients with biliary pancreatitis who do not undergo cholecystectomy have a 30% 6-week recurrence rate. During open or laparoscopic cholecystectomy, intraoperative cholangiography is recommended.

II. CHRONIC PANCREATITIS

A. **Etiology.** Alcohol (EtOH) abuse is the most common cause (70%); however, other etiologies include idiopathic, metabolic (hypercalcemia, hypertriglyceridemia, hypercholesterolemia, hyperparathyroidism), drugs, trauma, genetic (SPINK1, cystic fibrosis), and congenital abnormalities (sphincter of Oddi dysfunction or pancreas divisum). It also appears that tobacco abuse plays an important role in the development of chronic pancreatitis and particularly in patients with EtOH-related disease (*Arch Intern Med.* 2009;169:1035–1045). A history of recurrent acute pancreatitis (RAP) is present in some but not all patients with chronic pancreatitis.

B. **Pathophysiology.** Chronic pancreatitis is characterized by diffuse scarring and strictures in the pancreatic duct and commonly leads to endocrine or exocrine insufficiency, although substantial glandular destruction must occur before secretory function is lost. The islets of Langerhans have

agents or insulin therapy often is required. There is some propensity for hypoglycemic attacks, but diabetic ketoacidosis is rare.

c. **Narcotics** are often required for pain relief. In selected patients, tricyclic antidepressants and gabapentin may be effective.

d. **Abstinence** from alcohol results in improved pain control in approximately 50% of patients.

e. **Cholecystokinin antagonists and somatostatin analogs** have been considered for treatment of chronic pancreatitis, but have yet to show improvements in pain control.

f. **Tube thoracostomy or repeated paracentesis** may be required for pancreatic pleural effusions or pancreatic ascites. Approximately 40% to 65% of patients respond to nonsurgical management within 2 to 3 weeks.

2. **Endoscopic therapy.** Endoscopic sphincterotomy, stenting, stone retrieval, and lithotripsy have all been used with moderate success in the management of patients with ductal complications from chronic pancreatitis. There is no consensus on the usefulness of these interventions and further study is warranted. In addition to pancreatic-directed therapy, endoscopic celiac plexus block may improve symptoms in patients with severe pain. See Section V.A for the discussion of pancreatic pseudocysts.

3. **Surgical principles**

a. **Indications for surgery.** By far the most common indication is unremitting pain, but others include the inability to rule out neoplasm and management of complications (pseudocyst, aneurysm, and fistula).

b. **Choice of procedure.** The goals of surgical therapy are drainage and/or resection of the diseased pancreas to alleviate pain and complications associated with chronic pancreatitis. Procedures are classified as drainage, resectional, or a combination of both. Initially, drainage procedures were preferred due to the high morbidity and mortality associated with resection, as it is preferable for patients with low functioning glands to retain as much tissue as possible; however, drainage procedures are often only possible in patients with dilated ducts. As modern surgical techniques have developed, resection has become safer permitting the development of combination procedures (*Ann Surg.* 2010;251(1):18–32).

c. **Drainage only procedures** at our institution are uncommon because of poor relief of symptoms postoperatively.

(1) **Puestow** procedure includes a distal pancreatectomy with a distal pancreaticojejunostomy for drainage, with reported success in postoperative pain relief ranging between 61% and 90% (*Am J Surg.* 1987;153:207); success is strongly associated with a minimum duct size of 7 mm or greater, restricting this operation to a small number of patients (*Gastrointest Surg.* 1998;2:223). Because of poor results with the Puestow procedure, we more commonly use the Frey procedure (see below).

(2) **Longitudinal side-to-side pancreaticojejunostomy (Partington-Rochelle)** is a modification of the Puestow procedure,

eliminating the distal pancreatectomy portion. This procedure, as with the Puestow, can provide effective symptom relief, but achieves consistent success best in patients with large, dilated ducts.

d. Combined duct drainage-resection

(1) The Beger procedure is a duodenum-preserving resection of a portion of the pancreatic head. This operation preserves a small amount of pancreatic tissue within the C-loop of the duodenum and also in front of the portal vein. The pancreas is then transected at the pancreatic neck. Reconstruction requires two pancreaticojejunostomies. A Roux jejunal loop is anastomosed to both the proximal (duodenal) stump and the larger distal stump of the remaining pancreas. This procedure has shown excellent long-term results in altering the course of disease, controlling pain and safety (*Ann Surg.* 1999;230(4):512–519); however, since pancreatic neck transection is often impossible or unsafe, the Beger procedure is rarely performed at our institution.

(2) The Frey procedure is a modification of the Beger procedure consisting of a duodenum-sparing limited pancreatic head resection combined with a lateral pancreaticojejunostomy. In the Frey procedure, the pancreatic neck is not transected, but the pancreatic parenchyma is extensively cored out from the head to the extent of diseased segment distally. This is the most common procedure performed at our institution as postoperative morbidity has been shown to be lower in Frey patients than in those undergoing a pylorus-sparing Whipple procedure (19% vs. 53%). In addition, patient satisfaction indices were increased by 71% versus 43% in Whipple patients (*Ann Surg.* 1998;228:771).

e. Pancreatectomy

(1) PD (Whipple procedure) is indicated in cases in which the pancreatitis disproportionately involves the head of the pancreas, the pancreatic duct is of small diameter, or cancer cannot be ruled out in the head of the pancreas. For chronic pancreatitis, the pylorus-preserving technique is advocated. The use of vagotomy is controversial. For chronic pancreatitis, the Whipple has been shown to be inferior to both the Beger (*Int J Pancreatol.* 2000;27(2):131–142) and Frey (*Ann Surg.* 1998;228:771) procedures.

(2) Distal subtotal pancreatectomy is used for disease in the tail of the gland and in patients with previous ductal injury from blunt abdominal trauma with fracture of the pancreas and stenosis of the duct at the midbody level.

(3) Total pancreatectomy is performed only as a last resort in patients whose previous operations have failed and who appear to be capable of managing a pancreatic state. Some centers have combined this procedure with islet cell transplantation.

f. Celiac plexus block can be achieved surgically by either ganglionectomy or direct injection of sclerosing agents.

III. EXOCRINE PANCREATIC CANCER

A. **Incidence and epidemiology.** Pancreatic cancer is the fourth-leading cause of cancer-related mortality in the United States. Most patients have incurable disease at the time of diagnosis, and the overall 5-year survival is approximately 5%. The median age at diagnosis is 65 years (*Cancer Statistics.* 2010;60(5):277–300).

B. **Risk factors.** An increased risk of pancreatic cancer has been associated with smoking, alcoholism, family history, hereditary disorders [hereditary nonpolyposis colon cancer (HNPCC), von Hippel–Landau disease (VHL), Peutz–Jeghers syndrome, familial breast cancer (BRCA2), familial atypical multiple mole melanoma (FAMMM)], and chronic pancreatitis. Inherited pancreatic cancers represent approximately 5% to 10% of all diagnoses of the disease.

C. **Pathology.** Approximately 90% of pancreatic carcinoma is ductal adenocarcinoma. Seventy percent of pancreatic cancers occur at the head, 20% in the body, and 10% in the tail. Other periampullary tumors, such as carcinomas of the distal bile duct, duodenum, and ampulla of Vater, are less common and constitute approximately one-third of resectable periampullary cancers.

D. **Diagnosis.** The symptoms associated with pancreas cancer are almost always gradual in onset and are nonspecific.

1. **History and examination.** Patients complain of dull midepigastric pain, malaise, nausea, fatigue, and weight loss. Classically, the report of new-onset "painless jaundice" is believed to be pancreas cancer until proven otherwise. Pruritus may accompany obstructive jaundice. If obstructive jaundice is present, patients will also note darkening of the urine and "light-colored" stools. New-onset diabetes within the year prior to diagnosis is found in 15% of patients with pancreatic cancer, but the correlation is yet unclear. *Trousseau sign* (migratory thrombophlebitis) has been associated with pancreas cancer.

2. **Laboratory tests.**
   a. Elevated serum bilirubin.
   b. Elevated alkaline phosphatase.
   c. Prolonged obstruction may lead to mild increase in AST and ALT.
   d. **Tumor markers. CA19-9** is a useful marker to follow in patients with elevated levels prior to initiation of therapy; however, it is often low in patients with resectable disease and can be elevated in nonmalignant biliary obstructive disease. CA19-9 levels pretreatment may also have some role in prognosis (*Cancer.* 2009;115(12):2630–2639). Carcinoembryonic antigen (**CEA**) is a common tumor marker in a variety of gastrointestinal malignances but has been found to be elevated in only 40% to 50% of patients with pancreas cancer.

3. **Radiologic studies**
   a. **Plain films** of the abdomen are of little benefit. **Chest X-ray** is used to screen for pulmonary metastasis.
   b. Pancreatic cancer on **CT** appears as hypoattenuating indistinct mass that distorts the normal architecture of the gland, often paired with findings of a dilated pancreatic or biliary ductal system (the

so-called "double-duct" sign). If there is pancreatic ductal obstruction, it is also possible that the remainder of the gland will be atrophied. CT imaging should be a fine-cut, "pancreatic protocol CT" including 3-phases (arterial, venous, and portal venous) and thin slices (≤3 mm) to allow for assessment of the relationship of the mass to vascular structures as this is crucial to determine resectability. The use of CT to determine resectable versus borderline resectable disease is imperative as some advocate borderline resectable disease is a marker of worse biology and that these patients should undergo neoadjuvant therapy. The CT criteria used to define resectability were recently outlined in an expert consensus statement (*Ann Surg Oncol.* 2009;16(7):1727–1733):

(1) **Local resectable disease:** no distant metastases; no radiographic evidence of SMV and portal vein abutment, distortion, tumor thrombus, or venous encasement; clear fat planes around the celiac axis, hepatic artery, and SMA.

(2) **Borderline resectable:** no distant metastases; venous involvement of SMV/portal vein demonstrating tumor abutment with or without impingement and narrowing of the lumen, encasement of the SMV/portal vein but without encasement of the nearby arteries, or short segment venous occlusion resulting from either tumor thrombus or encasement but with adequate vessel to allow for safe resection and reconstruction; Gastroduodenal artery encasement up to the hepatic artery with either short segment encasement or direct abutment of the hepatic artery, without extension to the celiac axis; tumor abutment of the SMA not to exceed greater than 180° of the vessel circumference.

(3) **Unresectable:** Distant metastases; major venous thrombosis of the SMV or portal vein for several centimeters; encasement of SMA, celiac axis, or hepatic artery.

c. **Positron emission tomography (PET)** is limited to investigating for occult metastatic disease and has limited utility in primary diagnosis. A relatively high false-positive rate has been reported in pancreatitis when evaluating the pancreas for the diagnosis of cancer.

d. **Percutaneous (CT- or US-guided) needle biopsies** have a limited role, and are used only in unresectable patients who cannot undergo EUS-guided biopsy. If the patient has a pancreatic mass with disseminated lesions (e.g., liver lesions), these may be more accessible for tissue sampling.

e. **EUS** and **ERCP** play an important role in patients in which a mass is not seen on CT, obtaining tissue diagnosis when necessary (e.g., to determine candidacy for neoadjuvant therapy). Additionally, ERCP can be performed for drainage of biliary obstruction; however, this plays a minimal role in the treatment of patients with resectable disease as it is clear that preoperative stenting increases postoperative complications (*NEJM.* 2010;362(2):129–137). Preoperative stenting should only be undertaken in patients with an anticipated prolonged time to surgery (significant liver dysfunction, other medical comorbidities, neoadjuvant therapy).

    f. MRI and MRCP have improved over time and can provide information similar to that in conventional CT; however, MR technology is not the same across institutions, which results in differential quality in imaging.

    g. Staging laparoscopy historically has been undertaken to diagnose disease unable to visualize on CT. We recommend staging laparoscopy in patients with pancreatic adenocarcinoma (*Ann Surg.* 2002;235(1):1–7).

E. Treatment

  1. Resection

    a. PD (Whipple procedure) consists of *en bloc* resection of the head of the pancreas, distal common bile duct, duodenum, jejunum, and gastric antrum. Pylorus-sparing PD has been advocated by some, but there are no data demonstrating improved survival or lower morbidity (*Cochrane Database Syst Rev.* 2011;2:CD006053). Extended lymphadenectomy, including nodes from the celiac axis to the iliac bifurcation and nodes from the portal vein and SMA, has not been shown to affect survival but does increase morbidity (*Surg Oncol Clin North Am.* 2007;16:157). There has been a sharp decline in morbidity and mortality in specialized centers, with a 30-day mortality of less than 5%.

    b. Distal pancreatectomy. The procedure of choice for lesions of the body and tail of the pancreas is distal pancreatectomy. Distal pancreatectomy consists of resection of the pancreas, generally at the SMV laterally to include the spleen. Currently, distal pancreatectomy is undergoing considerable study. Some groups have published similar survival rates for open and laparoscopic resections (*J Am Coll Surg.* 2010;210(5):779–785), but only a trend toward lower postoperative stay, leading to considerable discussion regarding the appropriate method of approach. Additionally, we have recently described a technique that provides a more radical resection with improved R0 resection rates, the radical antegrade modular pancreatosplenectomy (RAMPS), when compared to traditional series (*J Am Coll Surg.* 2007;204(2):244–249), which is the procedure of choice for malignant tumors of the distal pancreas at our institution.

  2. Postoperative considerations. Delayed gastric emptying, pancreatic fistula, and wound infection are the three most common complications of PD. Up to 10% of patients require a nasogastric tube for longer than 10 days, but delayed gastric emptying almost always subsides with conservative treatment. The rate of pancreatic fistula has been demonstrated to be reduced to less than 2% by meticulous attention to the blood supply of the pancreaticoenteric duct-to-mucosa anastomosis (*J Am Coll Surg.* 2002;194:746). Most surgeons routinely place abdominal drains, although there no consensus has been reached regarding the utility and there may be potential harm that warrants further study. Distal pancreatectomy has a higher morbidity and leak rates than PD with an approximately 20% pancreatic leak rate in most series;

however, this is usually amenable to percutaneous treatment, and distal pancreatectomy has a similar mortality to PD.

3. **Radiotherapy and chemotherapy.**
   a. **Neoadjuvant therapy.** Some groups have shown an improvement in survival with neoadjuvant chemoradiation therapy (*J Clin Oncol.* 2008;26(21):3496–3502); however, this has yet to be validated in a RCT and is felt to be related to stage migration.
   b. **Adjuvant therapy.** There is a clear benefit to adjuvant therapy in pancreatic cancer (*J Gastrointest Surg.* 2008;12(4):657–661); however, the choice between chemoradiation and chemotherapy is less clear as there are conflicting studies (*Lancet.* 2001;358(9293):1576–1585; *Cancer.* 1987;59:2006–2010). The role of radiation therapy in pancreatic cancer and what role clinic-pathologic factors may play in selecting patients for radiation therapy has yet to be fully elucidated.

4. **Prognosis.** Surgical resection increases survival over patients with similar stage disease that do not undergo resection. Overall 5-year survival rates are approximately 20% for patients after resection. In patients with small tumors, negative resection margins, and no evidence of nodal metastases, the 5-year survival rate is as high as 40%. Median survival for unresectable locally advanced disease is 9 to 12 months, and for hepatic metastatic disease it is 3 to 6 months.

F. **Pseudotumors of the pancreas**

1. **Inflammatory and fibrosing conditions** of the pancreas such as chronic pancreatitis or mycobacterial infection may form dense, fibrotic masses, and segmental fibrosis that are difficult to differentiate from carcinoma preoperatively. Additionally, given the lethality of pancreatic cancer, lesions where malignancy cannot be ruled out should be resected.
   a. **Lymphoplasmacytic sclerosing pancreatitis** is often misdiagnosed as pancreatic cancer. Patients are typically young (30s to 50s) and may be associated with other autoimmune disorders (Sjogren's, ulcerative colitis, sclerosing cholangitis). When compared to patients with pancreatic cancer of all stages, these patients have increased levels of serum IgG4, which can aid in making this diagnosis (*Ann Surg Oncol.* 2008;15(4):1147–1154).

IV. CONGENITAL ABNORMALITIES

A. Failure of the ventral and dorsal pancreatic buds to fuse during the 6th week of development results in **pancreatic divisum.** In this condition, the normally minor duct of Santorini becomes the primary means of pancreatic drainage from the larger mass of pancreatic tissue. The condition is detected by either ERCP or MRCP, and the incidence is estimated to be as high 11% in autopsy studies, and there is the suggestion that this increases the risk of pancreatitis (*Gut.* 2011;Feb 15, epub ahead of print). Minor papilla endotherapy (MPE) may improve outcomes in patients with RAP, but has less of an effect on patients with chronic pancreatitis and often requires multiple interventions (*Gastrointest Endo.* 2008;68(4):667–673). Patients with severe symptomatic pancreas divisum may require surgical therapy.

B. Typical locations for **ectopic pancreatic tissues** include the stomach, duodenal or ileal wall, Meckel diverticulum, and umbilicus. Less common sites are the colon, appendix, gallbladder, omentum, and mesentery. Most ectopic pancreatic tissue is functional; islet tissue is most often present in the stomach and duodenum. Heterotopic pancreas may result in pyloric stenosis, disruption of peristalsis, peptic ulcers, or neoplasms.

C. Malrotation of the ventral primordium during the 5th week results in **annular pancreas:** a thin, flat band of normal pancreatic tissue surrounding the second part of the duodenum. The annular pancreas usually contains a duct that connects to the main pancreatic duct. Annular pancreas may cause duodenal obstruction and the treatment of choice is duodenoduodenostomy as opposed to resection for symptomatic patients.

V. CYSTIC DISEASES

A. **Pancreatic pseudocysts.** It is important to distinguish pseudocysts from tumors, cystic pancreatic neoplasms (CPN) and other fluid collections. An acute pancreatic fluid collection follows in approximately 25% of patients with acute pancreatitis. It is characterized by acute inflammation, cloudy fluid, a poorly defined cyst wall, and necrotic but sterile debris, and many resolve spontaneously. Pseudocysts differ from true cysts in that the have no epithelial lining. By definition, a fluid collection in the first 4 weeks is an *acute fluid collection;* after 4 weeks, it becomes an *acute pseudocyst.*

1. **Causes.** Pseudocysts develop after disruption of the pancreatic duct with or without proximal obstruction, usually occurring after an episode of acute pancreatitis. In children, most pseudocysts arise as a complication of blunt abdominal trauma.

2. **Diagnosis**
   a. **Clinical presentation.** The most common complaint is recurrent or persistent upper abdominal pain. Other symptoms include nausea, vomiting, early satiety, anorexia, weight loss, back pain, and jaundice. Physical examination may reveal upper abdominal tenderness, a mass. Occasionally, patients may present with rupture into the abdomen or fistula formation.
   b. **Laboratory tests**
      (1) **Amylase.** Serum concentrations are elevated in approximately one-half of cases.
      (2) **Liver function tests** occasionally are elevated and may be useful if biliary obstruction is suspected.
      (3) **Cystic fluid analysis** is discussed in Section V.B.2.
   c. **Radiologic studies**
      (1) **CT** is the radiographic study of choice for initial evaluation of pancreatic pseudocysts and is twice as sensitive as US in detection of pseudocysts. CT scan findings that determine prognosis include the following:
         (a) Pseudocysts **smaller than 4 cm** usually resolve spontaneously.
         (b) Pseudocysts with **wall calcifications** generally do not resolve.

      (c) Pseudocysts with **thick walls** are resistant to spontaneous resolution.

    (2) US detects approximately 85% of pseudocysts. Its use is limited by obesity and bowel gases, and is not able to delineate pancreatic and adjacent anatomy as well as CT, but it may be used in follow-up studies once a pseudocyst has been identified by CT scan.

    (3) MRI and MRCP can be useful to delineate ductal anatomy and are not associated with the risks of pancreatitis and infection with ERCP. MRCP is not as sensitive for small duct involvement as ERCP.

  d. ERCP allows for the determination of pancreatic duct anatomy and influences therapeutic intervention. Approximately one-half of pseudocysts have ductal abnormalities identified by ERCP, such as proximal obstruction, stricture, or communications with the pseudocyst. ERCP itself risks infection of a communicating pseudocyst.

3. Complications

  a. Infection is reported in 5% to 20% of pseudocysts and requires external drainage.

  b. Hemorrhage results from erosion into surrounding visceral vessels and occurs in approximately 7% of cases. The most common arteries are the splenic (45%), gastroduodenal (18%), and pancreaticoduodenal (18%) arteries. Immediate angiography has emerged as the initial treatment of choice.

  c. Obstruction. Compression can occur anywhere from the stomach to the colon. The arteriovenous system also can be subject to compression, including the vena caval and portal venous system. Hydronephrosis can result from obstruction of the ureters. Biliary obstruction can present as jaundice, cholangitis, and biliary cirrhosis.

  d. Rupture occurs in fewer than 3% of cases. Approximately one-half of patients can be treated nonsurgically, with total parenteral nutrition and symptomatic paracentesis or thoracentesis. Rupture is occasionally associated with severe abdominal pain and presents as a surgical emergency.

  e. Enteric fistula can occur spontaneously and usually results in resolution of the cyst.

4. Treatment depends on symptoms, age, pseudocyst size, and the presence of complications. **Pseudocysts smaller than 6 cm and present for less than 6 weeks have low complication rates.** The chance of spontaneous resolution after 6 weeks is low, and the risk of complications rises significantly after 6 weeks.

  a. Nonoperative. If the pseudocyst is new, asymptomatic, and without complications, the patient can be followed with serial CT scans or US to evaluate size and maturation.

  b. Percutaneous drainage can be considered for patients in whom the pseudocyst does not communicate with the pancreatic duct and for those who cannot tolerate surgery or endoscopy. External drainage is indicated when the pseudocyst is infected and without a mature wall. The results are variable, and the rate of complications (e.g., fistulas) may be high.

  c. **Excision,** including resection is only performed in unusual settings including bleeding, systemic sepsis, and concern for malignancy.

  d. **Internal drainage.** Cystoenteric drainage is the procedure of choice in uncomplicated pseudocysts requiring intervention. Drainage can be undertaken by either surgical or endoscopic means. Endoscopic cystogastrostomy or cystoduodenostomy has a 60% to 90% success rate, has been improved with improvements in EUS, and is the initial treatment of choice at our center. Endoscopic therapy also allows transsphincteric stenting in the case of duct-cyst communication. Characteristics that are relative contraindications to endoscopic drainage are high degree of necrotic debris and structural impediments (e.g., pseudoaneurysm). In the event drainage cannot be accomplished by endoscopic methods, surgical methods include Roux-en-Y cystojejunostomy, loop cystojejunostomy, cystogastrostomy, and cystoduodenostomy. A biopsy of the cyst wall should be obtained to rule out cystic neoplasm. At our institution, we favor the Roux-en-Y cystojejunostomy or cystogastrostomy in most patients.

B. **True pancreatic cysts**

  1. **Serous cystadenoma** are benign lesions and are usually asymptomatic. Symptoms correlate with size (>4 cm). They are more common in women, are most commonly located in the head of the pancreas, and account for 30% of all CPNs. Lesions are characterized by cuboidal epithelial cells, nonviscous fluid and low CEA and amylase on cyst fluid analysis. Asymptomatic serous cystadenomas should not be resected.

  2. **Mucinous cystic neoplasms (MCNs)** are considered premalignant lesions and account for approximately 50% of all CPNs. At presentation they are most likely to be asymptomatic, are twice as likely to present in women, and anatomically are more commonly located in the body or tail. The cystic lesions do not communicate with the pancreatic ductal system and are characterized by rests of ovarian stroma on pathologic analysis. A recent study showed invasive cancer in 17.5% of resected MCN, and this was associated with larger size (>4.0 cm) and advanced age (>55), indicating that noninvasive MCN are likely precursor lesions. Five-year survival was 100% for noninvasive MCN and 57% for patients with malignant lesions (*Ann Surg.* 2008;247(4):571–579). As there is a clear survival advantage for those patients who undergo resection prior to the development of invasive cancer, and it is felt that there is an adenoma-adenocarcinoma sequence, it is recommended that all patients with MCN undergo resection, although those with less risk of invasive cancer may undergo nonradical resection.

  3. **IPMNs** account for 25% of all CPNs and have a slight male predominance. They can be symptomatic and do communicate with the pancreatic ductal system. Characteristics of IPMN on ERCP include diffuse gland involvement, ductal dilation and thick, viscous fluid within the cyst. **IPMN are separated into three subgroups based on ductal involvement: main duct, side branch, and mixed;** and therapy is

different depending on subgroup. Main duct IPMN carries a malignant potential, up to 50% in some series (*Ann Surg.* 2004;239(6):788–799) and require resection. Given the risk of carcinoma associated with main duct involvement, it is recommended that mixed-type IPMN also be resected. Side branch IPMN represents a more controversial topic with evolving guidelines for resection, as 70% of patients with pure side branch IPMN had no invasive component in the same series (*Ann Surg.* 2004;239(6):788–799). Currently accepted criteria for resection of side-branch IPMN include symptomatic, size greater than 3 cm, and mural nodules. High cyst fluid CA19-9 has also been shown to be predictive of malignancy. Patients with IPMN requiring resection should undergo a standard oncologic resection (Whipple or distal pancreatectomy). Currently, there are mixed thoughts regarding the role of margin status and extending resection in IPMN, as this is a multifocal disease. The current recommendation is to extend resection based on invasive component or high-grade dysplasia only, and should be tailored to clinical situation (*World J Gastrointest Surg.* 2010;2(10):352–358). Additionally, there is no defined role for adjuvant therapy in cases of invasive cancer (*HPB(Oxford).* 2010;12(7):447–455), but this topic warrants further study.

4. **Other rare CPNs** (remaining 10%) include cystadenocarcinoma, acinar cell cystadenocarcinoma, cystic choriocarcinoma, cystic teratoma, and angiomatous neoplasms. All lesions with carcinoma noted on preoperative biopsy or with a concern for malignancy should undergo resection if tolerated.

14 Surgical Diseases of the Liver

Matthew R. Porembka and William C. Chapman

SURGICAL ANATOMY OF THE LIVER

I. **ANATOMIC NOMENCLATURE.** The standardized nomenclature for hepatic anatomy and resection is based on divisions delineated by the arterial and biliary anatomy (Figure 14-1; *HPB.* 2000;2:333).

A. **Internal anatomy: first division.** The liver is divided into two almost equally sized *hemilivers.* The plane between the hemilivers is the *midplane* of the liver that runs from the gallbladder fossa to the inferior vena cava (IVC) (Cantlie's line). Each hemiliver is usually supplied by one hepatic arterial branch, one bile duct, and one portal vein. A resection of a hemiliver is termed a *hepatectomy* or *hemihepatectomy* (e.g., right hepatectomy).

B. **Internal anatomy: second division.** Further divisions of the liver are based on the internal course of the hepatic artery and bile duct. These structures retain a high order of bilateral symmetry, whereas the portal vein does not. Its asymmetry results from retained portions from the fetal circulation. The liver is thus divided into four nearly equal **sections:** the right anterior and posterior sections and the left medial and lateral sections. A vessel supplying a section is a sectional vessel (e.g., the right anterior sectional artery).

C. **Internal anatomy: third division.** The liver is further subdivided into **segments** numbered I to VIII. These are the same as originally described by Couinaud. Resection of a segment is termed a *segmentectomy.*

II. OPERATIVE CONDUCT

A. **Open liver resection.** Optimal exposure for major liver resection can be achieved with a bilateral subcostal incision, with a midline extension to the xiphoid process as needed ("Mercedes Benz" **incision**). The ipsilateral vascular pedicles are isolated. The hepatic vein(s) draining the part of the liver to be resected are similarly isolated. During transection, maintenance of a low central venous pressure (<5 mm Hg) and placement of the patient in the Trendelenburg position reduce blood loss. A small amount of positive end-expiratory pressure (5 cm H_2O) is used to prevent air embolism. Vascular control can be augmented by intermittent occlusion of all hepatic inflow **(Pringle maneuver)** or total vascular exclusion. Postoperatively, frequent blood sugar measurements should be obtained. Monitoring and supplementation of phosphorous levels is important to support liver regeneration. Hyperbilirubinemia is unusual but may occur and persist for

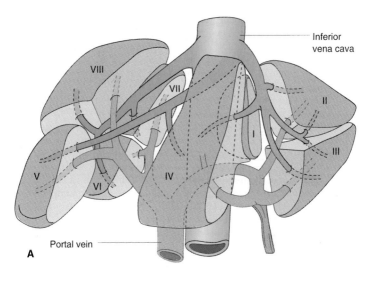

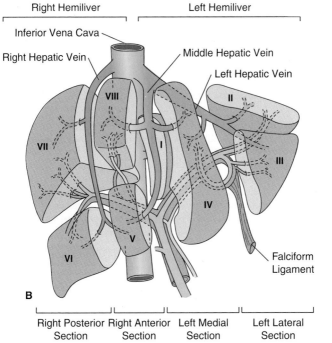

Figure 14-1. Anatomic divisions of the liver according to IHPBA/AHPBA-sanctioned terminology. Panel A depicts the segmental anatomy of the liver *in situ*. The first-order divisions (hemilivers), second-order divisions (sections), and third-order divisions (segments) are illustrated in Panel B. (From Greenfield's Surgery: Scientific Principles and Practice, LWW.)

days to weeks. Prolongation of the International Normalized Ratio (INR) may develop but usually is not severe; if necessary, fresh-frozen plasma is infused to keep the INR less than 2. Because of decreased clearance of hepatically metabolized drugs posthepatectomy, the dose of pain medications should be adjusted and monitored. The most common complication from liver resection is intra-abdominal abscess. Bile leaks from the cut surface of the liver or a damaged biliary duct may also occur. These manifest as a bile fistula or a *biloma,* a localized collection of bile. This can usually be managed by percutaneous drainage. Liver failure may result from insufficient residual functional hepatic parenchyma after extensive resections.

B. **Laparoscopic liver resection** has recently emerged as an option for hepatic resection. Types of minimally invasive resection can be classified as pure laparoscopic, hand-assisted, or hybrid procedures (which entail a combination of laparoscopic and open techniques). Although multiple case series have demonstrated similar mortality (0.3%) and morbidity (10.5%) for laparoscopic liver resection when compared to open procedures, no randomized controlled trial has compared both surgical approaches (*Ann Surg.* 2009;250(5):831–841). The learning curve is steep with these procedures with studies estimating 60 cases are required to develop proficiency (*Ann Surg.* 2009;250(5):772–782). Conversion to an open procedure occurs in about 4% of patients. Laparoscopic resection of malignant tumors (colorectal metastasis and hepatocellular carcinoma, HCC) has been demonstrated to be oncologically effective in carefully selected patients (*Ann Surg.* 2009;250(5):842–848; *Br J Surg.* 2009;96(9):1041–1048).

DISEASES OF THE LIVER

I. HEPATIC NEOPLASMS

A. Benign neoplasms of the liver

1. **Hemangioma is the most common benign liver tumor,** with the prevalence ranging from 3% to 20%. The majority are diagnosed in middle-aged women, and there is a female-to-male ratio of 5 to 6:1. The pathogenesis of hemangiomas is poorly understood. They are thought to represent hamartomatous outgrowths of endothelium rather than true neoplasms. Some of these tumors express estrogen receptors, and accelerated growth has been associated with high-estrogen states, such as puberty, pregnancy, and when oral contraceptives (OCPs) and androgens are used.

a. **Pathology.** Hemangiomas are usually less than 5 cm in diameter, but they can reach 20 cm or larger. Their blood supply is derived from the hepatic artery. Macroscopically, they are spherical, well circumscribed, soft, and easily compressible. Microscopically, the tumor consists of multiple large vascular channels lined by a single layer of endothelial cells supported by collagenous walls. Malignant degeneration does not occur, and spontaneous rupture is exceedingly rare.

b. Most hemangiomas are **asymptomatic** and are identified incidentally during imaging examinations for unrelated reasons. Patients with large lesions (>5 cm) occasionally complain of nonspecific abdominal symptoms such as upper abdominal fullness or vague abdominal pain. Intermittent symptoms may occur when there is necrosis, infarction, or thrombosis of the tumor. Life-threatening hemorrhage is extremely uncommon, even in large tumors, but can be precipitated by needle biopsy. **Kasabach–Merritt syndrome** is a rare consumptive coagulopathy resulting from sequestration of platelets and clotting factors in a giant hemangioma, and this is usually treated with urgent resection.

c. **Diagnosis.** Laboratory abnormalities are rare. Because of the possibility of severe hemorrhage from attempts at biopsy, diagnosis relies on imaging investigations. On ultrasound, hemangiomas appear as well-defined, lobulated, homogeneous, hyperechoic masses, although there may be hypoechoic regions representing hemorrhage, fibrosis, and/or calcification. Compressibility of the lesion is pathognomonic. Ultrasound is highly sensitive but not specific, with an estimated overall accuracy of 70% to 80%. Multiphasic (contrast) computed tomography (CT) scans reveal a low-density area with characteristic peripheral enhancement in the early phase. Subsequently, contrast enhancement progresses toward the center of the lesion until, in the delayed enhanced images, the tumor appears uniformly enhanced. The best imaging study is gadolinium-enhanced magnetic resonance imaging (MRI), with specificity and sensitivity approximately 90% and 95%, respectively. These tumors appear bright on T2-weighted images, with a similar pattern of enhancement as seen with multiphasic CT.

d. Most hemangiomas are treated safely with **observation.** Indications for intervention include symptoms, complications, and inability to exclude malignancy. In these select patients, the preferred treatment is surgical removal. Hemangiomas can usually be enucleated under vascular control (intermittent Pringle maneuver). Formal anatomic resection (e.g., right hepatectomy) is used when the tumor has largely replaced a distinct anatomic unit. Regression after low-dose radiation therapy or embolization in select cases has been described but should be reserved for large, unresectable lesions or for a patient unfit for surgery. In the very rare case of spontaneous hemorrhage, control with vascular embolization provides temporary help until a definitive operative approach can be safely implemented.

2. **Focal nodular hyperplasia (FNH)** is the second most common benign hepatic tumor, constituting about 8% of cases. The pathogenesis of FNH is a matter of debate. Currently, it is thought to represent a non-neoplastic, hyperplastic response to a congenital vascular malformation. FNH is found predominantly in women of child-bearing age, with a female-to-male ratio of 6 to 8:1. Although an association with OCPs has been suggested, the correlations are much lower than are those for hepatic adenomas (HAs).

a. **Pathology.** The lesions usually are solitary and small and often are located near the edge of the liver. Grossly, they are well circumscribed and lobulated but unencapsulated. Histologically, they are classically characterized by a dense, central stellate scar with septa radiating outward, thereby dividing the tumor into nodules. The parenchyma between the septa has the appearance of normal hepatic cords composed of hepatocytes, sinusoids, and Kupffer cells.

b. **Clinical manifestations** of FNH are rare. Epigastric or right-upper-quadrant pain with a palpable mass is present only in a small minority of patients. Spontaneous rupture with hemorrhage is extremely rare. Malignant degeneration has not been reported, but it is critical to distinguish FNH from the **fibrolamellar variant of HCC,** a malignant lesion that may have a similar central scar. It is important to note that the latter's scar is usually large and eccentric, with broad fibrous bands and calcifications.

c. **Diagnostic studies.** Although ultrasound is often the imaging study that first detects focal hepatic lesions, it does not discriminate FNH from other pathology well. FNH lesions have an echogenicity very similar to that of surrounding normal liver. However, distinguishing characteristics on multiphasic CT can be readily identified. In the late arterial phase, FNH has a bright homogeneous enhancement with a **hypodense central scar.** Delayed-phase images may show hyperattenuation of the central scar. Occasionally, the radiating septa may also be visualized. When MRI is employed, the central scar appears hyperintense on T2-weighted images, and when contrast is used, the enhancement pattern is similar to that seen on CT. Superparamagnetic iron oxide (SPIO) is an MR contrast agent that undergoes phagocytosis by the reticuloendothelial system (RES) (the Kupffer cells in the liver). On SPIO-enhanced T2-weighted images, FNH is hypointense but with a bright central scar. On hepatic scintigraphy with 99 m Tc-sulfur colloid, FNH has variable colloid uptake compared with the normal liver. However, intense colloid uptake (10% of cases, related to the number of Kupffer cells present) is a very specific finding for FNH. In combination, use of different imaging modalities, especially MRI, yields a precise diagnosis of FNH in 70% to 90% of cases. When the diagnosis remains in doubt, histologic examination is indicated.

d. **Treatment.** Elective resection is not indicated in asymptomatic patients when studies differentiate FNH from adenoma or malignant lesions. When the lesion is unresectable, it can be treated with transarterial embolization. OCPs should be stopped. There is no contraindication to pregnancy with this lesion, but close observation for tumor growth during pregnancy and the postpartum period is prudent.

3. **HA** is the benign proliferation of hepatocytes. It is not to be confused with the term "hepatoma," which refers to HCC. HA is found in young women and has a 10:1 female-to-male ratio. There is a strong association with all synthetic estrogen and progesterone preparations; however, the incidence has stabilized due to the decreased estrogen content found in OCPs. In addition, anabolic steroids may drive the growth of these lesions.

a. **Pathology.** Adenomas are usually solitary (70% to 80%), round, well-circumscribed lesions. Although they are unencapsulated, there is often a pseudocapsule formed by compression of normal surrounding tissue. Microscopically, they are made up of monotonous sheets of hepatocytes separated by dilated sinusoids. HA does not contain bile ductules, a key histologic finding distinguishing it from FNH where these are present.

b. HA is of clinical importance because of its tendency to **spontaneous rupture and hemorrhage.** The rate of rupture has been estimated between 25% and 35% with nearly 100% of all spontaneous ruptures occurring in lesions greater than 5 cm (*Ann Surg Oncol.* 2009;16(3):640–648). About one-third of patients with symptoms present with intraperitoneal bleeding, and others present with abdominal pain without rupture. More often, these lesions present with vague symptoms such as fullness or discomfort in the right upper quadrant or are detected incidentally. These lesions are potentially premalignant, with large or multiple tumors carrying a greater risk of malignant degeneration. Spontaneous rupture occurs more often in men, especially in steroid users. It may also occur during pregnancy due to rapid growth under the influence of estrogens.

c. **Diagnostic studies.** Ultrasonography can identify lesions but cannot differentiate an adenoma from a malignant lesion. Unlike FNH, HA frequently appears heterogeneous on CT due to intratumor hemorrhage, necrosis, and fat. On multiphasic CT, HA demonstrates **early enhancement,** often first in the periphery with centripetal progression. The relative lack of Kupffer cells in HA compared to FNH allows SPIO-enhanced MRI and scintigraphy with 99 m Tc-sulfur colloid to distinguish between these two entities.

d. Because of the risk of spontaneous rupture and malignant transformation, HA must be identified and treated promptly. Operative intervention after HA rupture is mandatory. Small (<5 cm), asymptomatic lesions occasionally regress with cessation of OCPs. Although radio frequency ablation (RFA) may be an option when there are multiple adenomas, resection of HA remains the standard therapy. **Indications** for operative intervention include the following:

(1) Patients with lesions that are 5 cm or greater in diameter.

(2) Tumors that do not shrink after discontinuation of OCPs.

(3) Patients who medically cannot stop OCP use with HA greater than 5 cm.

4. **Bile duct hamartomas** are the most common liver lesions seen at laparotomy. They are usually peripherally located and firm, smooth, and white in appearance. Typically, lesions are 1 to 5 mm in diameter, but they may be larger. Distinguishing them from miliary metastatic lesions (especially those from colorectal cancer or cholangiocarcinoma) may be difficult. Where there is uncertainty, biopsy should be performed.

B. **Malignant neoplasms of the liver** are either primary (such as HCC and cholangiocarcinoma) or secondary. The latter are far more common in Western countries.

1. **HCC, also known as hepatoma**

   a. **Demographics.** The annual incidence in the United States is approximately 2.4 per 100,000. The incidence is rising rapidly due in large part to the hepatitis C epidemic. There is a 2 to 3:1 male-to-female predominance. The incidence in African American men is almost twice that in white men. HCC is diagnosed mainly in the fifth and sixth decades.

   b. **Major risk factors** for cirrhosis in the United States include hepatitis C, alcohol abuse, autoimmune phenomena such as primary biliary cirrhosis and autoimmune hepatitis, and hereditary metabolic disorders. From 70% to 85% of HCC arises in the setting of cirrhosis. Malignant tumors of the liver occur in 4.5% of cirrhotic patients and in up to 10% when hemochromatosis is the inciting factor.

   c. **Pathology.** Gross patterns of HCC include the nodular type (aggregate of clusters of nodules), the massive type (single large mass), and the diffuse type (widespread fine nodular pattern). The right hemiliver is involved more frequently than the left. Microscopically, the formation of giant cells is a feature of HCC. HCC cells frequently invade venous branches (portal venous and hepatic venous), causing vascular dilation, which contributes to the nodular appearance of the liver.

   d. **Clinical manifestations.** Eighty percent of patients experience weight loss and weakness. Approximately 50% have abdominal pain that is dull, persistent, and occurs in the epigastrium or right upper quadrant. Acute severe abdominal pain infrequently has been associated with intraperitoneal hemorrhage due to rupture of a necrotic nodule or erosion of a blood vessel.

   e. **Diagnostic studies**

      (1) In cirrhotic patients, HCC may be associated with abnormal liver function tests due to hepatitis. Elevated **serum α-fetoprotein** (AFP) occurs in 75% of affected African patients but in only 30% of patients in the United States. AFP is also often elevated in chronic hepatitis and cirrhosis. A level greater than 200 ng/mL (normal <20 ng/mL) is suggestive of HCC, even in the cirrhotic patient.

      (2) **Radiologic studies**

         (a) **Ultrasonography** can be highly accurate in the detection of HCC, especially when coupled with concomitant AFP elevations.

         (b) **MR scan** can be useful in differentiating other small nodular masses from HCC. This is the most accurate imaging modality for distinguishing HCC from dysplastic or regenerative nodules in the cirrhotic patient.

         (c) **Multiphasic CT scan** with arterial and portal venous phase contrast imaging can distinguish among different types of liver masses. **HCC enhances in the arterial**

and not usually in the portal venous phase. Washout of contrast in the delayed (portal venous) phases of enhancement is an additional characteristic of HCC. Washout is defined as hypointensity of a nodule in the delayed phase compared with surrounding liver parenchyma. A mass in a cirrhotic liver that manifests arterial enhancement with washout has a sensitivity of about 80% with specificity of 95% to 100%.

(3) When required, laparoscopic or image-guided percutaneous biopsies may be used to obtain a tissue diagnosis. However, **a tissue diagnosis is *not* required before therapeutic intervention** (including surgical resection and liver transplantation) if other diagnostic modalities favor HCC as the diagnosis. Unresectable tumors likewise usually do not require biopsy to confirm the diagnosis because imaging and laboratory studies allow a definitive diagnosis in the majority of cases.

f. **Staging.** Several staging systems for HCC have been proposed. The most commonly used in the United States is the AJCC TNM (tumor, nodes, and metastases) classification. The individual TNM stages are grouped into overall stages: T1 to T4 with N0M0 correspond to stages I, II, IIIA, and IIIB, respectively, whereas N1M0 with any T stage is stage IIIC, and M1 disease is designated stage IV. Another commonly used system is the American Liver Tumor Study Group (ALTSG) staging system; this system uses a modified TNM staging system that provides T staging according to nodule size and number and is used as the basis for liver transplantation in patients with HCC. Other liver cancer staging systems like the Barcelona Clinic Liver Cancer (BCLC) system, the Cancer of the Liver Italian Program (CLIP) system, and the Okuda system expand on the TNM system by including tumor extent and assessment of liver function.

g. **Treatment**
(1) **Surgical resection** with anatomic resection is the treatment of choice for noncirrhotic patients who have HCC. However, this constitutes only 5% of HCC patients in the United States and up to 40% of those in Asian countries. A macroscopic margin of 1 cm generally is regarded as adequate. Overall 5-year survival rates for patients with HCC treated with resection is 40% to 50%, with recurrence rates of around 40% to 50%. The most important predictors of recurrence are microvascular invasion and multinodular tumors. Repeat hepatic resection for recurrence has been demonstrated to be safe and effective in selected lesions.

(2) **Orthotopic liver transplantation (OLT)** is theoretically the best treatment option for HCC because it removes the tumor together with the entire diseased liver, thus eliminating the risk of *de novo* or recurrent disease. Initial results of OLT for HCC were dismal. However, Mazzaferro and colleagues (*N Engl J Med.* 1996;334:693) demonstrated that when OLT is restricted to patients with a single tumor 5 cm or less or

patients with up to three tumors with the largest less than 3 cm in size (with no vascular invasion on imaging and absence of nodal and distant metastases), the 4-year actuarial survival rate was 75%, with recurrence-free survival of 83%. These so-called "Milan criteria" have subsequently been adopted by the United Network for Organ Sharing (UNOS). Recent reports (*Ann Surg.* 2008;248(4):617–625) suggest that even more-advanced stage III patients who are downstaged with pretransplant therapy have results similar to those with stages I and II HCC.

(3) **Local ablation** is the best treatment option for patients who have early-stage HCC and are not suitable for resection or OLT. In addition, these therapies may serve as bridges to OLT for those on the transplant waiting list. Indeed, downstaging tumors improve survival of HCC patients who subsequently undergo OLT. Today ablation is most frequently accomplished by physical ablation (radio frequency, microwave, or cryoablation) or with transarterial approaches. **RFA** has emerged as the procedure of choice in most centers. A needle electrode is placed into the tumor, destroying tissue by heating it to temperatures of 60°C to 100°C. RFA may be performed intraoperatively or percutaneously under imaging guidance. Extendable electrodes within the needle allow larger tumors to be ablated compared to ethanol injection, as well as allow the specific volume of tissue for ablation to be varied. **Transarterial chemoembolization (TACE)** involves selective intra-arterial administration of chemotherapeutic agents followed by embolization of the major tumor artery. HCC preferentially derives its blood supply from the hepatic artery rather than from a combination of the hepatic artery and portal vein as for normal hepatic parenchyma. TACE has a survival benefit for select patients with unresectable tumors, Child class A cirrhosis and tumors less than 5 cm. The procedure rarely may be complicated by hepatic failure due to infarction of adjacent normal liver. For this reason, it should not be used in decompensated (Child class C) cirrhosis.

(4) **Systemic chemotherapy and external beam radiation** have had poor results. Chemotherapy with conventional cytotoxic agents is ineffective and does not seem to modify the natural history of disease. Recent identification of signaling pathways in HCC has resulted in the development of drugs directed at specific therapeutic targets. One such drug is Sorafenib, a kinase inhibitor with antiangiogenic and antiproliferative properties that has shown modest efficacy in patients with advanced HCC. Toxicity may lead to decompensation of liver disease. Combining chemotherapy with surgical resection preoperatively or postoperatively has no benefit in terms of patient survival.

h. Without treatment, HCC has a very poor prognosis, with a median length of survival of 3 to 6 months after the diagnosis.

i. **Fibrolamellar hepatocellular carcinoma (FLC)** is a rare histologic variant of HCC. However, there is considerable evidence that FLC is distinct from HCC in its epidemiology, biology, and prognosis. Males and females are equally affected, commonly at a younger age (20 to 40 years old). It is uncommon for FLC to be associated with underlying liver disease such as cirrhosis. The histology of FLC strongly resembles that of focal nodular hyperplasia, but any etiologic association between them remains unproven. FLC appears as a hypoattenuated, well-defined, solitary mass on nonenhanced CT scan. On contrast-enhanced CT, the cellular portion enhances homogeneously; the central scar usually does not enhance, unlike the scar of FNH. FLC is best treated with complete surgical resection, which is possible in 80% of patients. Compared with standard HCC, FLC is associated with a better prognosis: Patients with resectable FLC have a greater 5-year survival rate (>70%) than noncirrhotic patients who have resectable nonfibrolamellar HCC. Late recurrence is common (more than two thirds of cases), and repeat resection of local disease should be considered (*Cancer.* 2006;106:1331). Liver transplantation is an option for unresectable but nonmetastatic lesions.

2. **Metastatic disease to the liver** represents the most common malignancy of the liver in the United States. The liver is a common site of metastasis from gastrointestinal (GI) cancers because it is the first organ drainage site of venous blood from the GI tract.

   a. **Colorectal cancer metastatic to the liver** is the prototype disease treated by partial hepatectomy. Approximately 50% of all patients with colorectal cancer develop metastases, and of these, about one-third have disease limited to the liver. Without treatment, hepatic metastasis has a dismal prognosis, with a median survival of 6 to 12 months. In contrast, numerous studies have shown that resection of hepatic metastases is associated with a 25% to 45% 5-year survival rate and a 20% 10-year survival rate. As a result, operative resection has been established as the most effective therapy for patients with isolated colorectal liver metastases.

      (1) **Staging.** The purpose of preoperative evaluation is to exclude the presence of extrahepatic disease and to identify all the metastatic lesions in the liver that require treatment. An abdominal/pelvic CT scan with oral and intravenous contrast is performed, along with chest X-ray. There should be a colonoscopy within the last 6 months to document absence of anastomotic recurrence or a metachronous colorectal cancer. Whole-body positron emission tomography (PET) after administration of ^{18}F-fluorodeoxyglucose (FDG) is valuable for the detection of occult metastases, both intra- and extrahepatic. On MRI, hepatic metastases appear as low-intensity lesions on T1-weighted images and intermediate intensity on T2-weighted images. MRI also provides greater visualization of vascular structures such as the hepatic veins and the IVC.

(2) **Partial hepatectomy.** The main objective in the resection of colorectal metastasis is removal of all disease with gross negative margins. Formal anatomic resection has not been demonstrated to improve survival (*Ann Surg Oncol.* 2009;16(2):379–384). Resection type should be based on the number and location of tumors, rather than on segmental anatomy. In the case of synchronous liver metastasis, the primary colonic tumor and the secondary liver tumor may be resected simultaneously or sequentially. Combined resection avoids a second laparotomy and reduces the overall complication rate without changing operative mortality. When the colorectal and liver resections are both extensive (e.g., extended hepatic lobectomy and low anterior resection), then a staged approach may be preferable. Factors predictive of poor prognosis after resection of hepatic colorectal metastases include node positivity of the primary tumor, multiple metastases, and size of the largest metastasis greater than 5 cm. An emphasis on the preservation of hepatic parenchyma may be of increasing importance in the setting of chemotherapy-associated steatohepatitis, and the growing number of patients undergoing repeated metastasectomy.

(3) **Postoperative follow-up** consists of serial physical examination, serum CEA level, and abdominal/pelvic CT scans every 3 to 4 months for the first 2 years, then every 6 months for the subsequent 3 years. Unfortunately, disease recurrence is common, but when cancer is isolated to the liver, repeat resection can provide additional survival benefit.

(4) For **unresectable hepatic colorectal metastases,** multidrug systemic chemotherapy (e.g., oxaliplatin plus infusional 5-fluorouracil/leucovorin, also known as FOLFOX) with or without bevacizumab, an anti-VEGF antibody, is offered to patients with adequate performance status. Hepatic arterial infusion (HAI) of the 5-fluorouracil derivative fluorodeoxyuridine (FUDR) has not been shown to offer better survival than systemic therapy, but may have greater response rates.

(5) **Local ablation** with RFA should be considered in patients unfit for operative resection or who have unresectable disease. In those patients with multiple scattered tumors, a combined approach of resection of the dominant or larger tumors with RFA of the remaining lesions may be feasible.

b. **Other liver metastases**

(1) **GI neuroendocrine tumors.** There are a number of reasons supporting resection of neuroendocrine hepatic metastases. These include their relatively long tumor doubling time, lack of effective chemotherapy, and the ability of metastasectomy to provide symptom palliation and long-term survival. For those patients with unresectable disease, hepatic artery embolization may provide symptom relief.

(2) There is limited experience with liver resection for **noncolorectal and nonneuroendocrine metastasis.** Liver resection may

provide the only chance for long-term survival. In a study at Memorial Sloan-Kettering Cancer Center of 96 patients with noncolorectal, nonneuroendocrine metastatic tumors of the liver, liver resection was associated with an overall actuarial survival of 37% at 5 years, with a median survival of 32 months (*Surgery.* 1997;121:625). The presence of liver metastasis from melanoma or cancer of the breast or stomach should be viewed as a marker of disseminated disease, and liver resection in these contexts is not recommended (*Annu Rev Med.* 2005;56:139).

II. **HEPATIC ABSCESS.** Liver abscesses may originate from bacterial, parasitic, or fungal pathogens. Bacterial abscesses predominate in the United States, whereas amebic (parasitic) abscesses are more common in younger age groups and in endemic areas.

A. **Pyogenic abscesses** in the liver occur secondary to other sources of bacterial sepsis. Up to 60% of cases arise from direct spread of bacteria from biliary infections such as empyema of the gallbladder or cholangitis. Ruptured appendicitis or diverticulitis is other potential sources for bacterial seeding to the liver.

1. **Pathogenesis.** For liver abscesses arising from an intra-abdominal infection, it is important to note that hematogenous seeding is *not* the usual pathway for the development of the abscess; rather, the mechanism of spread of infection to the liver is along channels within the peritoneal cavity. For unknown reasons, liver abscesses are usually found in the right lobe of the liver.

2. **Microbiology.** The bacteria cultured from pyogenic liver abscesses reflect the origin of the infectious process. Most commonly, **mixed species** are isolated, with one-third of cultures containing anaerobes. When the biliary tree is the source, enteric Gram-negative bacilli and enterococci are common isolates. When the abscess develops from hematogenous seeding, there is most likely a single organism responsible, such as *Staphylococcus aureus* or *Streptococcus milleri.* Fungal abscesses have been associated with patients who are recovering from chemotherapy. There should be suspicion of amebic abscesses in patients who are from or have recently traveled to an endemic area in the last 6 months.

3. **Fever and abdominal pain** are the most common symptoms, whereas nonspecific symptoms such as anorexia, weight loss, chills, and malaise may also be present.

4. **Laboratory findings** are usually nonspecific, such as leukocytosis and elevated serum alkaline phosphatase. A chest X-ray may demonstrate new elevation of the right hemidiaphragm, an infiltrate at the right lung base, or a right-sided pleural effusion. Definitive diagnosis is by CT scanning.

5. Treatment consists in identifying the infectious source as well as managing the liver abscess. **Pyogenic liver abscesses require drainage and systemic antibiotic therapy.** Drainage can be performed percutaneously in

most cases, but an operative procedure is recommended when there are multiple, large, loculated abscesses and in patients who otherwise require laparotomy for the underlying cause of the abscess. Drains are usually left in place until drainage becomes minimal, typically 7 days. Empirical antibiotic treatment should include coverage for bowel flora (e.g., metronidazole plus ciprofloxacin or monotherapy with piperacillin/tazobactam). Once identification has been made of the causative organism(s), antibiotic therapy should be modified to reflect their sensitivities. Aggressive antibiotic therapy should continue for at least 1 week beyond clinical recovery and resolution of the abscess on follow-up imaging.

B. **Amebic abscess** should be considered in *every* case of solitary hepatic abscess. Amebiasis is caused by the protozoan *Entamoeba histolytica*. This parasite exists in two forms: an infective cyst stage and a trophozoite stage, which is the form that causes invasive disease. Amebic liver abscess is the most common extraintestinal manifestation of amebiasis. Infection occurs by hematogenous spread from the gut via the portal venous system.

1. **Epidemiology.** Amebic liver abscesses are 7 to 10 times more frequent in adult men, despite an equal sex distribution of intestinal amebic disease. An abscess can develop after travel exposures of just 4 days.

2. Clinical symptoms are classically **persistent fever and right-upper-quadrant pain.** The presence of diarrhea (reflecting concurrent intestinal amebiasis) is more variable. Presentation usually occurs with 4 months after return from endemic areas. On examination, patients have hepatomegaly and point tenderness over the liver. Rupture of the abscess may cause peritonitis.

3. **Diagnosis.** Serologic tests for amebic infestation are positive in nearly 100% of affected patients. Ultrasound and CT are the most useful imaging modalities.

4. Treatment requires systemic **metronidazole** (750 mg orally three times a day, or 500 mg intravenously every 6 hours, for 7 to 10 days). Needle aspiration should be considered if there is no response to initial therapy or if there is doubt about the diagnosis. The material aspirated contains proteinaceous debris and an "anchovy paste" fluid of necrotic hepatocytes. After completion of the course of metronidazole, the patient should be treated with an intraluminal agent, even if stools are negative for amebae. Intraluminal agents include paromomycin, iodoquinol, and diloxanide furoate. Complications can include bacterial superinfection, erosion into surrounding structures, or free rupture into the peritoneal cavity. Although mortality is infrequent in uncomplicated cases, complicated cases may carry a considerable mortality (as high as 20%).

III. **HEPATIC CYSTS** can be divided into nonparasitic cysts and echinococcal cysts.

A. **Nonparasitic cysts** generally are benign. They can be solitary or multiple and often are identified incidentally on imaging for other symptoms.

1. Asymptomatic cysts require no treatment regardless of size. Large cysts may be symptomatic because of increased abdominal girth or compression of adjacent structures. Bleeding, infection, or obstructive jaundice can occur but are infrequent.

2. Symptomatic cysts can be unroofed operatively by either an open approach or, more recently, by laparoscopy. Infected cysts are treated in a similar manner to hepatic abscesses. If the cyst contains bile, communication with the biliary tree is assumed. It should be excised, enucleated, or drained, with closure of the biliary communication.

3. Polycystic kidney disease sometimes is accompanied by **polycystic liver disease,** which usually is asymptomatic. Symptoms generally are attributable to hepatomegaly from numerous cysts. Liver function is rarely impaired by the gross displacement of parenchyma by these massive cystic cavities. Symptomatic polycystic liver disease has been treated by drainage of the superficial cysts into the abdominal cavity and fenestration of deeper cysts into the superficial cyst cavities. Liver resection and retention of the least-cystic areas of hepatic parenchyma may be more effective. Neoplastic cystic lesions such as cystadenoma or cystadenocarcinoma rarely occur in the liver. These lesions are distinguished from simple cysts by the presence of a mass or septa. They are treated by resection or enucleation (in the case of cystadenoma) to completely remove cyst epithelium.

B. **Echinococcal cysts** are the most common hepatic cystic lesions in areas outside the United States. Approximately 80% of hydatid cysts are single and in the right liver. The most common presenting symptoms and signs are right-upper-quadrant abdominal pain and palpable hepatomegaly. Imaging by nuclear medicine scan, ultrasonography, CT scan, or MR scan can demonstrate the abnormality. The **cyst should not be aspirated** as an initial test because aspiration can cause spillage of the organisms and spread the disease throughout the abdominal compartment. A peripheral **eosinophilia** is often detected. Serologic tests include indirect hemagglutination and Casoni skin test, each of which is 85% sensitive. **Treatment** is primarily operative consisting of cyst aspiration, scolicidal treatment (hypertonic saline, 80% alcohol, or 0.5% cetrimide), and pericystectomy. Formal hepatectomy is rarely necessary except for large and/or multiple cysts. Postoperative therapy with mebendazole or albendazole has been advocated to prevent recurrence. Percutaneous treatment after antihelminthic treatment is increasingly utilized for treatment with acceptable results.

IV. **PORTAL HYPERTENSION (PH)** is defined as a chronic increase in portal pressure due to mechanical obstruction of the portal venous system. It is an almost unavoidable consequence of cirrhosis and is responsible for many of the lethal complications of chronic liver disease, including bleeding from gastroesophageal varices, ascites, and hepatic encephalopathy (HE).

A. The most common cause of PH in the United States is *intrahepatic* obstruction of portal venous flow from **cirrhosis** (most commonly due to alcohol and/or hepatitis C); intrahepatic portal venous obstruction can also be due to hepatic fibrosis from hemochromatosis, Wilson disease, and congenital fibrosis. *Prehepatic* portal venous obstruction due to congenital atresia or portal vein thrombosis is far less common. Posthepatic obstruction may occur at any level between the liver and the right heart. This includes thrombosis of the hepatic veins (Budd–Chiari syndrome), congenital IVC malformations (web, diaphragm), IVC thrombosis, and constrictive pericarditis.

B. **The clinical manifestations of liver disease with PH result from hepatic insufficiency and the mechanical effects of portal venous hypertension.**

1. **HE** is the spectrum of neuropsychiatric abnormalities in patients with advanced chronic liver disease. It results from portosystemic shunting of neurotoxins usually cleared by the liver. In addition to the usual signs of severe hepatic dysfunction (jaundice, ascites, spider telangiectasias, etc.), manifestations characteristic of encephalopathy include disrupted sleep–wake cycles (insomnia and hypersomnia), asterixis, and hyperreflexia. There are a number of conditions that can precipitate HE, including hypovolemia, hypoxia, GI bleeding, electrolyte and acid–base disorders, sedatives, hypoglycemia, and infection. An elevated ammonia level is the best-described neurotoxin associated with HE, but other agents not adequately cleared by the diseased liver have been implicated, such as γ-aminobutyric acid, mercaptans, and short-chain fatty acids. HE is a clinical diagnosis, and the utility of measuring ammonia levels remains controversial. Treatment is directed at the precipitating cause and reduction in ammoniagenic substrates using lactulose, with second-line therapy including oral antibiotics such as neomycin and rifaximin.

2. **Portosystemic shunting.** Increased blood flow through the portal vein leads to increased flow through collateral venous beds that bypass the liver, thereby connecting the portal circulation directly to the systemic circulation. The most clinically significant sites are those at the gastroesophageal junction connecting the left gastric vein (a part of the portal circulation) to the esophageal veins (systemic circulation). Other common collaterals develop when a recanalized umbilical vein collateralizes to the abdominal wall veins or a superior hemorrhoidal vein collateralizes to middle and inferior hemorrhoidal veins. Left-sided (**sinistral**) PH can be caused by isolated splenic vein thrombosis. This is most often caused by adjacent pancreatitis. Thrombosis results in increased pressure in the splenic vein at the distal end of the pancreas and the development of collaterals through the short gastric vessels and gastric mucosa back to the liver. This segmental area of PH typically causes gastric varices without esophageal varices.

3. The **mechanisms of ascites and edema** are salt and water retention by the kidneys, decreased plasma oncotic pressure, and increased lymphatic flow from increased portal venous hydrostatic pressure. Although the ascites can be massive, it is rarely life-threatening unless complications occur, such as erosion or incarceration of an umbilical hernia, respiratory compromise, and spontaneous bacterial peritonitis (SBP). The diagnosis of SBP is made by paracentesis and is likely when

ascitic fluid contains more than 250 polymorphonuclear leukocytes per microliter and if a single organism is cultured. The most common organisms are *Escherichia coli,* pneumococci, and streptococci. Frequently, however, it is not possible to obtain a positive culture, and so the diagnosis relies on ascitic fluid cell count and differential.

C. **Diagnosis.** Formal measurement of portal pressure by catheterization of the portal vein is seldom performed. Indirect evaluation by measurement of the hepatic wedge pressure after hepatic vein catheterization is considered the gold standard for diagnosis and monitoring PH. The hepatic venous pressure gradient (HVPG) is the difference between the wedged and free hepatic venous pressures. **PH is considered present when the HPVG is 8 mm Hg or greater.** Varices do not develop until the HVPG reaches 10 to 12 mm Hg. Reduction in the HVPG below 12 mm Hg is accepted as the therapeutic target for treating PH.

D. **Management of PH**

1. **Prophylaxis of variceal bleeding** includes both the prevention of variceal hemorrhage in patients who have never bled (primary prophylaxis) and preventing rebleeding in patients who have survived a bleeding episode (secondary prophylaxis). Every cirrhotic patient should be screened endoscopically for varices at time of diagnosis. Those without varices at this time should have endoscopy repeated after 2 to 3 years, whereas monitoring every 1 to 2 years is recommended when varices are present. **Propranolol** or nadolol therapy has been shown to markedly reduce risk of variceal bleeding, as well as slow the progression of small varices into larger ones. The dose should be titrated to the maximal tolerable dose and maintained indefinitely. For prevention of recurrent bleeding, endoscopic band ligation versus combination pharmacologic therapy (beta-blocker plus isosorbide mononitrate) have equivalent results. Transjugular intrahepatic portosystemic shunting **(TIPS)** has been shown to be superior to either endoscopic or pharmacologic therapies at reducing the rate of rebleeding. However, its use does not improve mortality, has been associated with a greater risk of encephalopathy, and is more costly than endoscopic procedures. Thus, it is limited to situations in which endoscopic therapy has failed or in patients who would not tolerate a rebleed such as those with Child class C cirrhosis (*Eur J Gastroenterol Hepatol.* 2006;18:1167).

2. **Management of active variceal hemorrhage.** Up to one-third of patients with hemorrhage from gastroesophageal varices die during the initial hospitalization for GI bleeding. All patients with known or suspected esophageal varices and active GI bleeding should be admitted immediately to an intensive care unit for resuscitation and monitoring. Endotracheal intubation to protect the airway, prevent aspiration, and facilitate the safe performance of endoscopy and other procedures is nearly always indicated. Vascular access via short, large-bore peripheral lines should be secured. Recombinant activated factor VII (rFVIIa) may be useful for correcting the prothrombin time in cirrhotics. Infection is a strong prognostic indicator in acute variceal hemorrhage, and use of antibiotics has been shown to reduce both the risk of rebleeding

and mortality. Once stabilized, the patient should have emergent upper endoscopy to document the source of hemorrhage. Because up to 50% of patients with known esophageal varices have upper GI hemorrhage from an alternative source, such as gastric or duodenal ulcer, a thorough endoscopy is required. Recommendations for specific therapy are (1) early administration of vasoactive drugs, even if active bleeding is only suspected, and (2) endoscopic band ligation after initial resuscitation.

a. The pharmacologic treatment of choice for active variceal bleeding in the United States is **octreotide** (intravenous bolus, then infusion for 5 days). It has been shown to be more effective for controlling bleeding than placebo or vasopressin, as well as have fewer side effects than vasopressin. Terlipressin is not available in the United States but is the only pharmacologic treatment associated with a reduction in mortality.

b. **Endoscopic therapy** is the definitive therapy for active variceal hemorrhage. Two forms of treatment are available: sclerotherapy and variceal band ligation (EBL). A meta-analysis found that EBL is superior to sclerotherapy in the initial control of bleeding and is associated with fewer adverse events and improved mortality (*Semin Liver Dis.* 1999;19:439). Emergent endoscopic therapy fails to control bleeding in 10% to 20% of patients. If a second attempt at endoscopic hemostasis fails, then more definitive therapy must be enacted immediately.

c. **Balloon tamponade** is useful as a temporary remedy for severe variceal bleeding while more definitive therapy is planned. The specially designed balloon catheters include the Sengstaken-Blakemore tube, the Minnesota tube, and the Linton-Nachlas tube. Each has a gastric balloon; the Sengstaken-Blakemore and Minnesota tubes also have an esophageal balloon. For safe and effective use of these devices, the balloons must be carefully placed according to the manufacturer's directions. The position of the gastric balloon in the stomach must always be confirmed radiographically before inflation because inflation of the larger gastric balloon in the esophagus can be disastrous. The pressure of the esophageal balloon must be maintained as directed by the manufacturer to avoid the complications of mucosal ulceration and necrosis. Balloon tamponade achieves bleeding control in 60% to 90% of cases, but should be used only when there is massive bleeding and for a short period of time (<24 hours) until definitive therapy is instituted.

d. **TIPS** can be used in the acute management of patients with variceal bleeding. It involves the intrahepatic placement of a stent between branches of the hepatic and portal venous circulation. Technical success rates approach 95%, with short-term success in controlling acute variceal hemorrhage observed in more than 80% of patients. The TIPS procedure can provide acute decompression of portal pressure and thus control refractory variceal bleeding. TIPS stenosis requires careful follow-up and revision procedures in a significant percentage of patients. Use of polytetrafluoroethylene (PTFE) stents rather than bare metal stents has dramatically decreased the rate of TIPS dysfunction, clinical relapses, and the need for interventions.

e. **Emergency portacaval shunt** generally is reserved for patients in whom other measures have failed and is almost never performed today. This operation carries significant in-hospital mortality and risk of HE, particularly because the patients undergoing the operation typically have failed other measures and have advanced liver disease. Only the technically simpler central portacaval shunts (end to side or side to side) should be used in the emergency setting because other shunts require more dissection and operative time.

3. **Management of ascites** must be gradual to avoid sudden changes in systemic volume status that can precipitate HE, renal failure, or death.

a. **Salt restriction** is the initial treatment. Sodium intake should be limited to 1,000 mg/day. Stricter limitations are unpalatable.

b. **Diuretic therapy** should be gradually applied in patients in whom ascites is not controlled by salt restriction. Weight loss should rarely be more than 500 g/day to avoid significant side effects. **Spironolactone** is the initial diuretic of choice at 25 mg orally twice per day. This dose may be increased to a maximum of 400 mg/day in divided doses. Furosemide (20 mg orally/day initially) may be added if spironolactone fails to initiate diuresis. Volume status must be monitored closely by daily weight check and frequent examinations during initial furosemide treatment.

c. **Paracentesis** is useful in the initial evaluation of ascites, when SBP is included in the differential diagnosis, and to provide acute decompression of tense ascites. Up to 10 L of ascites can be removed safely if the patient has peripheral edema, the fluid is removed over 30 to 90 minutes, and oral fluid restriction is instituted to avoid hyponatremia. Paracentesis can be used to provide acute relief of symptoms of tense ascites, including respiratory compromise, impending peritoneal rupture through an ulcerated umbilical hernia, or severe abdominal discomfort.

d. **TIPS** can be used for refractory ascites. Complete resolution of ascites has been reported in 57% to 74% of patients and partial response in another 9% to 22%.

e. A **peritoneovenous shunt,** which reinfuses ascites into the vascular space, is now rarely used for ascites refractory to medical therapy. The main complication of peritoneal venous shunting is disseminated intravascular coagulation, which can be fulminant after shunt placement and requires shunt occlusion. Shunts are **contraindicated** in patients with bacterial peritonitis, recent variceal hemorrhage, liver failure, advanced hepatorenal syndrome, or existing severe coagulopathy. The shunts tend to occlude with time and are used very rarely today.

4. **Control of HE** requires the limitation of dietary protein intake and the use of lactulose and oral antibiotics.

a. **Dietary changes** should be initiated first. Dietary protein should be eliminated while adequate nonprotein calories are administered. After clinical improvement, a 20-g/day protein diet may be administered, with increasing protein allowances of 10 g/day every 3 to 5 days if encephalopathy does not recur.

b. If the encephalopathy is not controlled by diet alone, oral agents can be added.

(1) **Lactulose** is a nonabsorbed synthetic disaccharide that produces an osmotic diarrhea, thus altering intestinal flora. The oral dosage is 15 to 45 mL two to four times a day. The dose then is adjusted to produce two to three soft stools daily. Alternatively, a lactulose enema can be prepared with 300 mL of lactulose and 700 mL of tap water administered two to four times a day.

(2) **Useful oral antibiotic preparations** include neomycin (1 g orally every 4 to 6 hours or 1% retention enema every 6 to 12 hours) and metronidazole (250 mg orally every 8 hours). The oral antibiotics are used as second-line agents to lactulose because, although they are equally effective, neomycin carries some risk of ototoxicity and nephrotoxicity, and metronidazole carries some risk of neurotoxicity.

Biliary Surgery

Marcus C.B. Tan and Steven M. Strasberg

I. CHOLELITHIASIS

A. The **incidence** of cholelithiasis increases with age. At the age of 60 years, approximately 25% of women and 12% of men in the United States have gallstones. In some countries (e.g., Sweden and Chile) and ethnic groups (e.g., Pima Indians), the incidence of gallstones may approach 50%.

B. **Pathogenesis and natural history.** Patients can be divided into three clinical stages: asymptomatic, symptomatic, and those with complications of cholelithiasis. There is generally a stepwise progression from stage to stage. Annually, only 1% to 2% of those with asymptomatic disease progress to the symptomatic stage. It is unusual (<0.5% per year) for an asymptomatic patient to develop complicated gallstone disease without first suffering symptoms.

1. **Cholesterol gallstones** (85% of stones, radiolucent) are associated with increasing age, obesity, female gender, and Western diet. The female-to-male ratio is 2:1, and the increased incidence among women is in part related to pregnancy and/or oral contraceptive use. Obesity is an independent risk factor, increasing the prevalence of cholesterol gallstones by a factor of 3. Western diet is closely related, and these stones are rare in vegetarians.

2. **Pigment gallstones** (15% of stones, radiopaque, two distinct types):
   a. **Black gallstones** are hard, spiculated, and brittle, and are composed of calcium bilirubinate, calcium phosphate, and calcium carbonate. Risk factors include hemolytic disorders, cirrhosis, and ileal resection.
   b. **Brown gallstones** are soft, associated with biliary stasis and infection (especially *Klebsiella* species), and are composed of bacterial cell bodies, calcium bilirubinate, and calcium palmitate.

C. **Asymptomatic gallstones**

1. **Diagnosis.** Asymptomatic gallstones are usually discovered on routine imaging studies or incidentally at laparotomy for unrelated problems. Common abdominal symptoms such as dyspepsia, bloating, eructation, or flatulence *without associated pain* are probably not caused by gallstones.

2. **Management.** There is no role for prophylactic cholecystectomy in most patients with asymptomatic gallstones, with a few exceptions.
   a. Patients with a **porcelain gallbladder** should undergo cholecystectomy due to a high risk of malignancy. Prophylactic cholecystectomy may be warranted in patients with asymptomatic gallstones who have other risk factors for gallbladder cancer as outlined in Section VI.C.1.

    b. Children with gallstones have a relative indication for cholecystectomy due to the general difficulty of declaring and interpreting symptoms in this population.

    c. In adult patients with **diabetes mellitus, spinal cord trauma,** and **sickle cell anemia,** prophylactic cholecystectomy is generally *not* indicated for *asymptomatic* or uncomplicated gallstone disease. Even after cholecystectomy, sickle cell patients may still develop bile duct stones.

    d. Management of **gallstones discovered at laparotomy** remains controversial because the literature is conflicting with regard to the incidence of biliary symptoms after surgery in patients in whom the gallbladder is not removed.

D. Symptomatic gallstones (biliary colic)

  1. Diagnosis largely depends on correlating symptoms with the presence of stones on imaging. Differential diagnosis includes acute cholecystitis, liver diseases, peptic ulcer disease, renal colic, gastroesophageal reflux, irritable bowel syndrome, and diseases based in the chest, including inferior wall myocardial ischemia/infarct or right-lower-lobe pneumonia. Appropriate testing is dictated by clinical suspicion of these entities.

    a. Symptoms. Biliary colic is the main symptom and is initiated by impaction of a gallstone in the outlet of the gallbladder, as characterized by the following:

      (1) Periodicity. The pain comes in distinct attacks lasting 30 minutes to several hours.

      (2) Location. The pain occurs in the epigastrium or right upper quadrant.

      (3) Severity. The pain is steady and intense and may cause the patient to restrict breathing. Frequently, it is so severe that immediate care is sought and narcotics are necessary for control.

      (4) Timing. The pain occurs within hours of eating a meal, often awakening the patient from sleep.

      (5) Other symptoms include back pain, left-upper-quadrant pain, nausea, and vomiting. These *usually* occur in addition to, rather than in place of, the pain as described.

    b. Physical signs include mild right-upper-quadrant tenderness, although there may be few abdominal findings during an attack. Jaundice is not caused by impaction of a stone in the cystic duct without inflammation. If jaundice is present, another cause should be sought.

    c. Diagnostic imaging. Ultrasound diagnosis is based on the presence of echogenic structures having posterior acoustic shadows. There is usually little or no associated gallbladder wall thickening or other evidence of cholecystitis. The bile ducts must be assessed for evidence of dilation or choledocholithiasis (gallstones in the common bile duct, CBD).

  2. Laparoscopic cholecystectomy (LC) is the appropriate treatment of the vast majority of patients with symptomatic gallstones (see Section I.F.1).

E. **Complications of cholelithiasis**

1. **Acute calculous cholecystitis** is initiated by obstruction of the cystic duct by an impacted gallstone. Persistence of stone impaction leads to inflammation of the gallbladder. Although the onset and character of the resulting pain resemble those of biliary colic, the pain is unremitting. Severe complications include empyema, gangrene, or contained or free gallbladder perforation. Abscess formation may develop in some cases.

   a. **Diagnosis** depends on the constellation of symptoms and signs and the demonstration of characteristic findings with diagnostic imaging.

      (1) The **symptoms** of acute cholecystitis are similar to but more severe and persistent than those of biliary colic. As the inflammatory process spreads to the parietal peritoneum, tenderness develops in the right upper quadrant or even more diffusely, and movement becomes painful. Systemic complaints such as anorexia, nausea, and vomiting are common. Fever may or may not be present. Elderly patients tend to have mild symptoms and may present only with reduced food intake. **Murphy's sign** (inspiratory arrest during deep palpation of the right upper quadrant) is characteristic of acute cholecystitis and is most informative when the acute inflammation has subsided and direct tenderness is absent. Mild jaundice may be present, but severe jaundice is rare and suggests the presence of CBD stones, cholangitis, or obstruction of the CBD caused by external compression from a stone impacted in an inflamed Hartmann's pouch **(Mirizzi syndrome).**

      (2) **Laboratory abnormalities** may include leukocytosis (typically 12,000 to 15,000 cells/μL), although often the white blood cell count is normal. Complications, such as gangrene, perforation, or cholangitis, are suggested by an extremely high white blood cell count (>20,000 cells/μL). Liver function tests (LFTs), including serum bilirubin, alkaline phosphatase, alanine transaminase (ALT), aspartate transaminase (AST), and serum amylase, also may be abnormal.

      (3) **Diagnostic imaging**

         (a) **Ultrasonography** is the most commonly used test for diagnosing acute cholecystitis and any associated cholelithiasis. Findings indicative of acute cholecystitis include gallbladder wall thickening, pericholecystic fluid, and a **sonographic Murphy sign** (tenderness over the gallbladder when compressed by the ultrasound probe). In one meta-analysis, the sensitivity and specificity of ultrasonography for diagnosing gallstones were 0.84 and 0.99, respectively. For the diagnosis of acute cholecystitis, the sensitivity was 0.88 and the specificity was 0.80 (*Arch Int Med.* 1994;154:2573).

         (b) **Radionuclide cholescintigraphy** can be useful as an adjunct in the diagnosis of acute cholecystitis; although its sensitivity and specificity for gallstones are lower than those for ultrasound. Scintigraphic scanning with hepatic 2,6-dimethyliminodiacetic acid (HIDA) enables visualization of the biliary system. The radionuclide is concentrated and secreted by the liver, allowing visualization of the bile ducts and the gallbladder normally within 30 minutes. Since the test depends on hepatic excretion of bile, it may not be useful in jaundiced patients. Nonfilling of the gallbladder after 4 hours is deemed evidence of acute cholecystitis. Administration of morphine may enhance the test by causing spasm of the sphincter of Oddi and thereby stimulating gallbladder filling.

(c) **Computed tomographic (CT) scanning** is now frequently performed to evaluate the patient with acute abdominal pain. CT can demonstrate gallstones, although it is less sensitive for these than ultrasonography. Other signs of acute cholecystitis on CT include gallbladder wall thickening, pericholecystic fluid, edema, and emphysematous cholecystitis (air in the gallbladder wall).

b. **Management**

(1) **Initial management** for patients with acute cholecystitis includes hospitalization, intravenous (IV) fluid resuscitation, and parenteral antibiotics (e.g., piperacillin/tazobactam). Separate coverage for enterococci is not necessary because they are rarely the solitary pathogen.

(2) The **Tokyo guidelines** (*J Hepatobiliary Pancreat Surg.* 2007; 14:91) provide further recommendations depending on the severity of acute cholecystitis (see Table 15-1). For mild acute

TABLE 15-1	Severity Grading for Acute Cholecystitis (According to the Tokyo Guidelines)
Grade	**Criteria**
Mild (grade 1)	Acute cholecystitis that does not meet the criteria for a more severe grade Mild gallbladder inflammation, no organ dysfunction
Moderate (grade 2)	The presence of one or more of the following: – Leucocytosis >18,000 cells per cubic millimeter – Palpable tender mass in the right upper quadrant – Duration >72 hr – Marked local inflammation including biliary peritonitis, pericholecystitis abscess, hepatic abscess, gangrenous cholecystitis, emphysematous cholecystitis
Severe (grade 3)	Presence of multiorgan dysfunction (e.g., hypotension, mental status changes, respiratory failure, and acute renal failure)

Miura F, Takada T, Kawarada Y, et al: Flowcharts from the diagnosis and treatment of acute cholangitis and cholecystitis: Tokyo Guidelines. Modified from *J Hepatobiliary Pancreat Surg.* 2007;14:78.

cholecystitis, early LC is recommended. For moderate acute cholecystitis, either early or delayed cholecystectomy may be performed. Early LC should be performed only by an experienced surgeon with conversion to open cholecystostomy if operative conditions make identification of critical structures difficult. In the small minority of patients with severe acute cholecystitis or with severe concomitant medical illness, **percutaneous cholecystostomy** can be performed. Drainage of the gallbladder in this manner almost always allows the episode of acute cholecystitis to resolve. Subsequently, the patient can undergo either cholecystectomy or percutaneous stone extraction and removal of the cholecystostomy tube. Such nonoperative stone removal as definitive treatment is reasonable in very elderly or debilitated patients who cannot tolerate general anesthetic.

(3) **Several prospective, randomized trials** have compared early versus delayed (6 weeks) LC for acute cholecystitis. Five recent meta-analyses of the existing literature showed no significant differences in early versus delayed procedures with regard to mortality, conversion rate, bile duct injury, and perioperative complications. However, these studies almost universally showed, in the early group, significantly fewer readmissions for interval complications (due to failure of conservative therapy in ~20% of patients) and a significantly reduced hospital length of stay (*Br J Surg.* 2010;97:141; *Cochrane Database Syst Rev.* 2006;4:CD005440; *Surg Endosc.* 2006;20:82; *Surg Today.* 2005;35:553; *Am J Gastroenterol.* 2004;99:147). Nonetheless, controversy still exists about the relationship between operation in the acute phase of inflammation and bile duct injury. A large registry series from Connecticut reported that when LC is performed for acute cholecystitis, the incidence of injury is three times higher (0.51%) than for elective LC and twice as high as for open cholecystectomy (*Arch Surg.* 1996;131:382).

2. **Choledocholithiasis** generally is due to gallstones that originate in the gallbladder and pass through the cystic duct into the common duct. In Western countries, stones rarely originate in the hepatic or common ducts, although these "primary" stones, usually brown pigment stones, are more prevalent in Asia.

a. **Diagnosis.** The most common manifestation of uncomplicated choledocholithiasis is **jaundice,** with bilirubin typically between 3 and 10 mg/dL. Biliary colic is common. The only finding on physical examination may be icterus. Ultrasonography usually demonstrates gallbladder stones and bile duct dilation. Because of obscuring gas in the duodenum, ductal stones are visible in only about 50% of cases. The diagnosis may be confirmed by endoscopic retrograde cholangiopancreatography (ERCP) or percutaneous transhepatic cholangiography (PTC), which can opacify the biliary tree and demonstrate the intraductal stones. Occasionally, the diagnosis of choledocholithiasis is confirmed by intraoperative cholangiography (IOC) at the time of cholecystectomy.

  b. Management depends on available expertise and clinical situation.

   (1) In patients with choledocholithiasis who also have cholelithiasis, standard management consists of LC and IOC, possibly followed by laparoscopic CBD exploration if stones are seen. Intraoperative measures to clear the CBD of stones include administration of IV glucagon, use of irrigation, blind passage of balloon catheters or stone baskets, or passage of these devices via choledochoscope. If the bile duct cannot be cleared of stones by laparoscopic exploration, open bile duct exploration or postoperative ERCP may be required, but this is uncommon.

   (2) In some cases, choledocholithiasis should be handled by ERCP or PTC. **ERCP with sphincterotomy and stone removal** is used in patients who are not surgical candidates or have had prior cholecystectomy. It is also used in patients who are jaundiced (these patients may have tumors as opposed to choledocholithiasis), including all patients with acute cholangitis. Patients with intrahepatic stones and those with many CBD stones are also usually treated with ERCP. ERCP with sphincterotomy carries a less than 1% risk of mortality and a 5% to 10% risk of morbidity, principally acute pancreatitis. An intraoperative cholangiogram should be performed at the time of surgery even when preoperative ERCP has been done because residual stones may be present in a small percentage of patients.

3. Biliary pancreatitis is caused by blockage of pancreatic secretions by passage of a gallstone into the common biliary-pancreatic channel. The greatest risk is carried by small (~2 mm) stones. Once the acute episode of pancreatitis has resolved, the gallbladder should be removed as expeditiously as possible to avoid recurrent pancreatitis. A longer delay may be justified in patients who have had severe pancreatitis and in whom local inflammation or systemic illness contraindicates surgery. An IOC should *always* be done at the time of the cholecystectomy to confirm that the bile duct is free of stones. In patients in whom cholecystectomy is contraindicated, endoscopic sphincterotomy (ES) may be protective against further attacks of pancreatitis.

4. Cholangitis is often caused by choledocholithiasis (see Section II.B).

5. Gallstone ileus (bowel obstruction caused by a gallstone) is an uncommon complication that results from a gallstone eroding through the wall of the gallbladder into the adjacent bowel (usually duodenum). Usually the stone migrates until it lodges in the narrowest portion of the small bowel, just proximal to the ileocecal valve. Patients present with symptoms of bowel obstruction and air in the biliary tree (from the cholecystenteric fistula). Treatment is exploratory laparotomy and removal of the obstructing gallstone by milking it back to an enterotomy made in healthy intestine. The entire bowel should be searched diligently for other stones, and cholecystectomy should be performed if the patient is stable and the inflammation is not too severe.

F. **Surgical management of symptomatic cholelithiasis and acute chole-cystitis**

1. **LC** has a low complication rate, and the patient's recovery and return-to-work times are excellent.

   a. **Indications.** Approximately 95% of patients with cholelithiasis are candidates for the laparoscopic approach. Contraindications include generalized peritonitis, cholangitis, concomitant diseases that prevent use of a general anesthetic, and the patient's refusal of open cholecystectomy should urgent conversion be required. Local inflammation in the triangle of Calot can prevent complete visualization of the appropriate structures and increases the risk of injury to the bile ducts or hepatic arteries.

   b. **Technique.** Because misidentification of the cystic duct is the commonest cause of biliary injury, the surgeon must use a technique to provide conclusive identification of the cystic duct and artery.

      (1) In the **Critical View of Safety Technique** pioneered at our institution, the triangle of Calot is dissected free of fat, fibrous, and areolar tissue. Importantly, the lower end of the gallbladder must be dissected off of the liver bed (*J Am Coll Surg.* 2010;211:132). A complete dissection demonstrates two and *only* two structures (the cystic duct and artery) entering the gallbladder, constituting the "critical view of safety."

      (2) **IOC** may be used as the sole method of ductal identification. In addition, an absolute indication is the need to confirm the ductal anatomy during LC whenever the critical view is not achieved. IOC is also indicated in patients with known choledocholithiasis, a history of jaundice, a history of pancreatitis, a large cystic duct and small gallstones, any abnormality in preoperative LFTs, or dilated biliary ducts on ultrasonography. **Laparoscopic ultrasound** as an alternative method for the detection of CBD stones is highly accurate and has decreased operative time and cost in experienced hands (*Surg Clin North Am.* 2000;80:1151).

   c. **Complications.** LC appears to be associated with a higher incidence (~2.5/1,000) of major bile duct injury than open cholecystectomy. The serious problems include both misidentification injuries and technical problems such as cautery-induced damage (*Surg Clin North Am.* 2010;90:787). In addition, there are also risks to other structures, including the hepatic artery and the bowel. Unretrieved gallstone spillage can be the source of infrequent but serious long-term complications such as abscess and fistula formation. Factors associated with an increased rate of conversion to an open procedure include emergent cholecystectomy, male sex, age greater than 60 years, obesity, gallbladder inflammation (acute cholecystitis), choledocholithiasis, and prior upper abdominal surgery.

2. **Open cholecystectomy** is performed in the minority of patients who have contraindications to LC, in patients who require conversion from

LC because of inability to complete the laparoscopic procedure, or when necessary in conjunction with a laparotomy for another operation (e.g., pancreaticoduodenectomy).

3. **Medical dissolution** of gallstones can sometimes be achieved with oral bile acid therapy, but given the proven effectiveness of LC, there is virtually no current application of medical dissolution. Development of gallstones after gastric bypass for morbid obesity is very common and may largely be prevented by bile acid therapy. The current optimal bile acid therapy for dissolution of gallstones is ursodeoxycholic acid (10 to 15 mg/kg/day).

II. ACALCULOUS CHOLECYSTITIS AND OTHER BILIARY TRACT INFLAMMATIONS

A. **Acalculous cholecystitis** typically occurs in severely ill hospitalized [i.e., intensive care unit (ICU)] patients, especially those with a history of hypotension. It is also associated with prolonged nothing-by-mouth (NPO) status and dependence on parenteral nutrition, with episodes of systemic sepsis, or during multiple-organ-system failure. Mortality rate is high, at around 30% (*Clin Gastroenterol Hepatol.* 2010;8:15).

1. A high index of suspicion is required to make the **diagnosis.**
   a. **Presentation** depends largely on the patient's concurrent medical conditions. Alert patients typically complain of right-upper-quadrant or diffuse upper abdominal pain and tenderness. However, many of these patients may not be alert, and therefore pain and tenderness are absent in up to 75% of patients. Unexplained deterioration in severely ill patients should lead to suspicion of this diagnosis.
   b. In sedated patients, **leukocytosis and abnormal LFTs,** although variable, may be the only indication of acalculous cholecystitis.
   c. Diagnostic **imaging** is essential for establishing the diagnosis because a false-positive result may lead to an unnecessary intervention in a critically ill patient.
      (1) **Ultrasonography** can be done at the bedside in the critically ill patient. Typical findings are similar to those of acute calculous cholecystitis. Limitations include overlying bowel gas, concomitant abdominal wounds or dressings, and the fact that gallbladder abnormalities are often seen in the ICU population (e.g., congestive heart failure may lead to gallbladder wall thickening), even in those patients not suspected of having acute cholecystitis.
      (2) **Hepatobiliary scintigraphy** (HIDA) can also be done at the bedside and has been demonstrated to be superior to ultrasonography in terms of sensitivity, specificity, and positive and negative predictive value (PPV and NPV) for the diagnosis of acute acalculous cholecystitis.
      (3) **CT scan** is as sensitive as ultrasonography for acalculous cholecystitis and has the advantage of providing more complete imaging of the abdominal cavity from the lung bases to the pelvis. However, CT requires transfer of the patient to the

radiology suite, which may be a prohibitive risk in the critically ill.

(4) In difficult cases, **percutaneous cholecystostomy** may be both diagnostic and therapeutic because an infected gallbladder can be decompressed and inciting stones extracted via the tube.

(5) **The choice of imaging** depends largely on the clinical picture, and a high index of suspicion is often necessary to make the diagnosis in sedated or unresponsive ICU patients. Because of its portability and low cost, ultrasound is almost universally the first test of choice, but if the diagnosis is in doubt, then scintigraphy can be added significantly to improve the diagnostic index. CT can be used to evaluate other potential sources of abdominal pathology, whereas percutaneous cholecystostomy may avoid a trip to the operating room for patients who are unable to tolerate surgery.

2. **Management** of acalculous cholecystitis must be tailored to the individual patient, but at the minimum involves systemic antibiotics, NPO status, and treatment of any comorbidities. Primary treatment involves decompression of the gallbladder, typically with a percutaneously placed tube. The definitive treatment is interval cholecystectomy.

B. **Acute cholangitis** is a potentially life-threatening bacterial infection of the biliary tree typically associated with partial or complete obstruction of the ductal system. Although acute cholangitis is often associated with cholelithiasis and choledocholithiasis, other causes of biliary tract obstruction and infection, including benign and malignant strictures of the bile ducts or at biliary-enteric anastomoses, parasites, and indwelling tubes or stents, also have a causative relationship. ERCP without concomitant stenting in the presence of a stricture may lead to cholangitis above the stricture. Therefore, patients should routinely be pretreated with antibiotics in case a stent cannot be placed.

1. **Diagnosis**

   a. Patients present with a spectrum of disease severity, ranging from subclinical illness to acute toxic cholangitis. Greater than 90% of patients with cholangitis present with fever. **Charcot's triad** (fever, jaundice, and right-upper-quadrant pain) remains the hallmark of this disease but is present in only 50% to 70% of patients. The advanced symptoms of **Reynold's pentad** (Charcot's triad with hemodynamic instability and mental status changes) are seen in less than 10% of patients, are more prevalent in the elderly, and suggest a more toxic or suppurative course of cholangitis (*J Hepatobiliary Pancreat Surg.* 2007;14:52).

   b. **Laboratory data** supportive of acute cholangitis include elevations of the white blood cell count and LFTs.

   c. Investigation of the biliary tree is mandatory to demonstrate and relieve the underlying etiology of the obstruction. Ultrasonography or CT scan may reveal gallstones and biliary dilatation, but **definitive diagnosis is made by ERCP or PTC.** These studies are both diagnostic and therapeutic because they demonstrate the level of

2. Extensive, diffuse stricture disease with end-stage cirrhosis is an indication for orthotopic **liver transplantation (OLT).** If the patient has undergone a previous decompressive operation, transplantation is technically more challenging but not contraindicated.

3. Because PSC is a risk factor for cholangiocarcinoma, **close surveillance** of patients is needed. The diagnosis is difficult because cholangiocarcinomas also masquerade as strictures. A dominant biliary stricture or elevated carbohydrate antigen 19-9 level should raise the suspicion of cholangiocarcinoma in a PSC patient and suggests the need for further evaluation.

D. **Prognosis.** Many patients have a course that progresses to cirrhosis and liver failure despite early palliative interventions. Liver transplantation likely improves survival and quality of life, and early referral for liver transplantation is indicated to decrease the risk of developing cholangiocarcinoma. Overall, the median length of survival from diagnosis to death or liver transplantation is 10 to 12 years.

E. **IgG4-associated cholangitis** (IAC) is a newly described entity that shares a number of clinical and radiologic features with PSC. However, in contrast to PSC, IAC mainly affects elderly men (typically older than 60 years), is not associated with IBD, and, most importantly, does respond to immunosuppressive treatment. IAC is considered a variant of IgG4-related systemic disease (*Digestion.* 2009;79:220).

V. **CHOLEDOCHAL CYSTS** are congenital dilations of the biliary tree that may occur in any bile duct but characteristically involve the common hepatic and CBDs. They are more frequently identified in women (3:1 ratio) and those of Asian descent. Sixty percent are diagnosed in patients under the age of 10 years. Diagnosis and treatment are essential because the cysts predispose to choledocholithiasis, cholangitis, portal hypertension, and cholangiocarcinoma, which develop in up to 30% of cysts and usually present in the fourth decade of life.

A. **An anatomic classification scheme** has identified five distinct types. Type I cysts are fusiform dilations of the CBD and are the most common (65% to 90%). Type II cysts are rare, isolated saccular diverticula of the CBD. Type III cysts, also termed *choledochoceles*, are localized dilations within the intraduodenal part of the CBD. Most lesions thought to be choledochoceles are in fact duodenal duplications. Type IV cysts are characterized by multiple cystic areas of the biliary tract, both inside and outside of the liver. Type V cysts are single or multiple lesions based only in the intrahepatic portion of the tract (Caroli disease).

B. **Diagnosis.** The classic triad of jaundice, a palpable abdominal mass, and right-upper-quadrant pain mimicking biliary colic is present only a minority of the time. Neonates frequently present with biliary obstruction, whereas older children suffer from jaundice and abdominal pain. Rarely, pancreatitis or duodenal obstruction can be caused by a choledochocele. Initial diagnosis is often made with ultrasonography and/or CT. Further evaluation of the cyst should be obtained with specific biliary imaging such as ERCP or MRCP.

C. **Treatment** is primarily surgical. Cyst excision with a Roux-en-Y hepatico-jejunostomy is the treatment of choice for types I and IV. Simple excision of the rare type II cyst has been performed. Local endoscopic cyst unroofing plus sphincteroplasty is usually effective for type III disease. Caroli disease can be treated with hemihepatectomy when it is confined to one side of the liver. More often, bilateral disease is present with associated liver damage and mandates OLT.

VI. TUMORS OF THE BILE DUCTS

A. **Benign tumors of the bile ducts,** usually adenomas, are rare and arise from the ductal glandular epithelium. They are characteristically polypoid and rarely are larger than 2 cm. Most are found adjacent to the ampulla, with the CBD being the next-most-common site. The malignant potential of these uncommon lesions is unclear.

1. Most patients present with **intermittent obstructive jaundice,** often accompanied by right-upper-quadrant pain. This presentation may be confused with choledocholithiasis.

2. **Treatment** should involve complete resection of the tumor with a margin of duct wall. High recurrence rates have been reported after simple curettage of the polyps. Lesions situated at the ampulla can usually be managed by transduodenal papillotomy or wide local excision.

B. **Cholangiocarcinoma** arises from the bile duct epithelium and can occur anywhere along the course of the biliary tree. Cholangiocarcinoma is an uncommon malignancy, with an incidence in the United States of approximately 0.85/100,000 population and representing about 2% of all cancers (approximately 5,000 new cases per year). Tumors tend to be locally invasive, and when they metastasize, they usually involve the liver and the peritoneum. They characteristically spread along the bile ducts microscopically for long distances beyond the palpable end of the tumor. The median age of onset is approximately 65 years. Predisposing conditions include male gender, PSC, choledochal cysts, intrahepatic stones, parasitic infestations such as *Opisthorchis* and *Clonorchis* species, and exposure to the radiocontrast agent Thorotrast (historical).

1. **Classification.** Cholangiocarcinoma has been classified according to anatomic location and growth pattern. The anatomic location classification includes three main types: intrahepatic (20%), extrahepatic upper duct (also called *hilar* or ***Klatskin tumor***, 40%), and extrahepatic lower duct (40%). Tumor morphology is also divided in three primary types: (1) a mass-forming (or MF) type that grows in a nodular fashion and projects into both the bile duct lumen and the surrounding tissues; (2) a periductal infiltrating (PI) type characterized by a cicatrizing growth pattern that infiltrates the walls of the bile ducts and grows both within them and along their exterior surfaces; and (3) an intraductal growing (IG) type that displays a polypoid or sessile pattern that forms intraductal excrescences of tumor that may grow along the inside of, but do not penetrate, the wall of the duct (also commonly

TABLE 15-2	Bismuth-Corlette Classification of Hilar Cholangiocarcinoma
Type I	Tumor remains below the confluence of the right and left hepatic ducts
Type II	Tumor involves the confluence of the right and left hepatic ducts
Type III	Tumor involves *either* the right *or* the left hepatic duct and extends to secondary radicals
Type IV	Tumor involves secondary radicals of *both* the right *and* left hepatic ducts

referred to as "papillary subtype"). The specific anatomic location and growth pattern of perihilar tumors are further described by the Bismuth-Corlette classification scheme as shown in Table 15-2.

2. **Staging** is currently based on the TNM (tumor, nodes, and metastases) system of the sixth edition of the American Joint Committee on Cancer (AJCC) guidelines. Intrahepatic malignancies are staged along with those of primary hepatic origin, whereas extrahepatic lesions have their own set of criteria (see Tables 15-3 and 15-4). Jarnagin and Blumgart developed a

TABLE 15-3	American Joint Committee on Cancer TNM (Tumor, Nodes, and Metastases) Staging for Extrahepatic Cholangiocarcinoma

Primary Tumor

TX	Primary tumor cannot be assessed
T0	No evidence of primary tumor
Tis	Carcinoma *in situ*
T1	Tumor confined to the bile duct histologically
T2	Tumor invades beyond the wall of the bile duct
T3	Tumor invades the liver, gallbladder, pancreas, and/or ipsilateral branches of the portal vein or hepatic artery
T4	Invades any of the following: main portal vein or bilateral branches, common hepatic artery, adjacent structures such as colon, stomach, duodenum, or abdominal wall

Regional Lymph Nodes

NX	Regional lymph nodes cannot be assessed
N0	No regional lymph node metastasis
N1	Regional lymph node metastasis

Distant Metastasis

MX	Distant metastasis cannot be assessed
M0	No distant metastasis
M1	Distant metastasis

TABLE 15-4	Staging of Extrahepatic Cholangiocarcinoma and Gallbladder Cancer		
Stage	TNM Status		
Stage 0	Tis	N0	M0
Stage IA	T1	N0	M0
Stage IB	T2	N0	M0
Stage IIA	T3	N0	M0
Stage IIB	T1–3	N1	M0
Stage III	T4	Any N	M0
Stage IV	Any T	Any N	M1

preoperative clinical T staging system for hilar cholangiocarcinoma (*Ann Surg.* 2001;234:507) that defines both radial and longitudinal tumor spread, which are critical determinants of resectability. It incorporates three factors based on preoperative imaging studies: (1) location and extent of ductal involvement, (2) presence or absence of portal vein invasion, and (3) presence or absence of hepatic lobar atrophy. This staging system has been shown to correlate well with resectability and survival (Table 15-5).

3. **Diagnosis**
   a. **Jaundice,** followed by weight loss and pain, is the most frequently encountered clinical feature at presentation.
   b. **Serum markers.** Numerous serum tumor markers are currently in use and/or being evaluated for their utility in the diagnosis of cholangiocarcinoma.
      (1) **Carbohydrate antigen 19-9 (CA19-9)** is a carbohydrate antigen that is traditionally associated with pancreatic cancer but is also the most commonly used marker in the diagnosis of cholangiocarcinoma. Sensitivity and specificity vary depending on the threshold used and on coexisting conditions such as inflammation and cholestasis. For example, two large studies encompassing over 300 patients each showed sensitivities and specificities of 73% to 76% and 63% to 74%, respectively, when a cutoff value of 37 U/mL was applied in a patient population without cholangitis. However, the specificity dropped to approximately 42% when patients with cholangitis were included (*Am J Gastroenterol.* 1999;64:1941; *Br J Cancer.* 1991;63:636). In two other studies of 55 and 74 patients with PSC, higher CA19-9 cutoffs of 180 and 100 U/mL yielded improved specificities of 98% and 91%, respectively, whereas

TABLE 15-5	American Joint Committee on Cancer TNM Staging for Gallbladder Cancer

Primary Tumor

TX	Primary tumor cannot be assessed
T0	No evidence of primary tumor
Tis	Carcinoma *in situ*
T1a	Tumor invades lamina propria
T1b	Tumor invades muscle layer
T2	Tumor invades perimuscular connective tissue; no extension beyond serosa or into liver
T3	Tumor perforates serosa and/or directly invades the liver and/or one other adjacent organ or structure, e.g., stomach, duodenum, colon, and extrahepatic bile ducts
T4	Tumor invades the main portal vein or hepatic artery or invades multiple extrahepatic organs or structures

Regional Lymph Nodes

NX	Regional lymph nodes cannot be assessed
N0	No regional lymph node metastasis
N1	Regional lymph node metastasis

Distant Metastasis

MX	Distant metastasis cannot be assessed
M0	No distant metastasis
M1	Distant metastasis

sensitivities were comparable to those of other series – 67% and 60%, respectively (*Gastrointest Endosc.* 2002;56:40; *Gastroenterology.* 1995;108:865). Thus, whereas a CA19-9 cutoff of around 40 U/mL is likely to be adequate in patients without any evidence of cholangitis or cholestasis, a higher value (probably in the 150 U/mL range) should be used for those patients with either of these concurrent conditions.

(2) **Carcinoembryonic antigen (CEA).** Although most commonly used for the diagnosis of colorectal cancer, CEA has also demonstrated some elevation in patients with malignancies of biliary origin.

c. **Diagnostic imaging**

(1) **MRCP** can be used for an all-purpose investigation of cholangiocarcinoma. It provides cholangiography, demonstrates the tumor and its relationship to key vessels, and detects intrahepatic metastases.

(2) **Ultrasonography** can demonstrate bile duct masses and dilation and provide rudimentary information on the extent of tumor involvement within the liver. Reports indicate that ultrasonography is more than 80% accurate in predicting portal vein involvement.

(3) **CT** may be helpful in delineating the mass and defining its relation to the liver, especially when MRI is contraindicated or cannot be tolerated.

(4) **Positron emission tomography (PET)** may be helpful in the diagnosis of cholangiocarcinoma; however, it is currently incompletely studied and not yet part of the standard diagnostic workup.

(5) **ERCP** is the most valuable diagnostic tool for cholangiography of lower duct tumors. Distal lesions may be indistinguishable from small pancreatic carcinomas on preoperative evaluation, and the distinction is often not made until final pathologic analysis. It is also valuable for upper duct tumors, but if obstruction is complete, the upper limit of the tumor cannot be delineated. Since the advent of MR cholangiography, ERCP is increasingly being used for preoperative **therapeutic decompression** of the biliary tree. Preoperative decompression of the biliary tree has the advantage of improving liver function prior to resection but has the risk of cholangitis and increased postoperative infection. It is not usually performed unless the bilirubin is greater than 10 mg/dL. When used, only the less-affected hemiliver should be decompressed so that it will hypertrophy while the undrained side (the side to be resected) atrophies. The side to be resected should be drained only if cholangitis is present. ERCP carries the potential added benefit of obtaining cellular material for **cytologic analysis,** either via ductal brushing, fine needle aspiration (FNA), or forceps biopsy. In an attempt to increase diagnostic yields, new molecular techniques have been applied to biopsy samples, including digital image analysis (DIA) and fluorescence *in situ* hybridization (FISH). These tests can detect genetic aneuploidy and chromosomal rearrangements as indicators of malignancy.

(6) **PTC** has been used when ERCP and MRI cannot precisely delineate the upper limit of a tumor. Under PTC guidance, FNA cytology can also provide a tissue diagnosis in many of patients. If a tumor is resectable, extensive efforts to obtain a tissue diagnosis before resection are inappropriate.

(7) **Endoscopic ultrasound (EUS)** with FNA represents an important development in the investigation of *lower* bile duct strictures and masses. It is useful as an alternative to ERCP for obtaining tissue to establish a cytologic diagnosis, especially if a primary pancreatic mass is suspected. A recent study demonstrated that EUS-FNA has a sensitivity, specificity, PPV, NPV, and accuracy of 86%, 100%, 100%, 57%, and 88%, respectively, for the diagnosis of extrahepatic cholangiocarcinoma (both hilar and distal CBD), and the test results positively changed the management of 84% of the study participants (*Clin Gastroenterol Hepatol.* 2004;2:209). The potential value of such a biopsy needs to be weighed against risks such as bleeding and potentially seeding the traversed peritoneal cavity with malignant cells (*Am J Gastroenterol.* 2004;99:45).

4. **Assessment of tumor resectability and treatment.** Resection remains the primary treatment of cholangiocarcinoma, although only 15% to 20% are resectable at presentation. Adjuvant radiation and chemotherapy have been attempted, but clinical trials are limited by the paucity of eligible patients.

   a. **Intrahepatic tumors** are best treated with hepatic resection. Resectability is assessed as for other types of intrahepatic tumors, with a goal of 1-cm tumor-free margins and retention of at least 30% of functioning liver mass. If resection of more than 60% of the hepatic parenchyma is required, preoperative portal vein embolization can be used to cause atrophy of the affected hemiliver and hypertrophy of the unaffected liver segments (future liver remnant).

   b. **Extrahepatic upper duct (hilar) tumors.** Because hilar lesions are generally not as easily biopsied, resection is often undertaken based on clinical assessment and radiographic demonstration of a mass lesion at the ductal bifurcation. With the rare exception of low-lying Bismuth I tumors in which a negative common hepatic duct margin may be obtained, resection of hilar tumors includes the bile duct bifurcation and the caudate lobe; ipsilateral hemihepatectomy is often required to obtain an R0 resection. Biliary reconstruction is performed as a Roux-en-Y hepaticojejunostomy. Pancreaticoduodenectomy may be necessary in some cases to obtain negative lower margins of the CBD. Vascular involvement is not an absolute contraindication to resection because portal venous resection and reconstruction may be possible. Contraindications to resection are as follows:

      (1) Bilateral intrahepatic ductal spread.
      (2) Extensive involvement of the main trunk of the portal vein.
      (3) Bilateral involvement of hepatic arterial and/or portal venous branches.
      (4) A combination of vascular involvement with evidence of contralateral ductal spread.
      (5) Lymph node involvement or distant spread.

      At select centers, patients with locally unresectable hilar cholangiocarcinoma are treated with neoadjuvant chemoradiation followed by OLT (*Transplant Proc.* 2009;41:4023).

   c. Some lesions situated in the **middle of the extrahepatic bile duct** may be approached with an excision of the supraduodenal extrahepatic bile duct, cholecystectomy, and portal lymphadenectomy. However, most malignant strictures in the mid-CBD are due to local invasion of a gallbladder cancer rather than cholangiocarcinoma.

   d. **Extrahepatic lower duct tumors.** The considerations are the same as for carcinoma of the head of the pancreas, although vascular involvement is much less common. In contrast to more-proximal tumors, approximately 80% of lower duct tumors are resectable by pancreaticoduodenectomy, and 5-year survival rates range from 17% to 39%. Tumors derived from the bile duct have a slightly better prognosis than those of pancreatic origin in the same region, probably reflecting a more favorable biologic behavior.

e. **Adjuvant therapy.** There is a lack of level 1 evidence supporting use of adjuvant therapy for resectable extrahepatic cholangiocarcinoma. Retrospective cohort studies comparing resection alone to resection plus adjuvant chemoradiation, and have suggested a slight survival advantage (*Am Surg.* 2001;67:839). The current NCCN guidelines recommend consideration of 5-FU or gemcitabine-based chemoradiation, especially in the setting of positive margins or lymph nodes.

5. **Palliation** for patients with unresectable disease involves surgical, radiologic, or endoscopic biliary decompression. When unresectability is demonstrated preoperatively or at staging laparoscopy, the first choice for biliary decompression is via endoscopic or percutaneous internal stenting. When encountered at laparotomy, internal biliary drainage is best achieved by choledochojejunostomy for lower duct lesions.

6. **Prognosis** is highly dependent on resectability of the tumor at presentation. Patients with resectable cholangiocarcinoma with microscopically negative margins and negative lymph nodes have a 5-year survival of approximately 35%, whereas median survival for patients with unresectable cholangiocarcinoma is only 3 to 6 months. An R0 resection is necessary for any chance of a cure because recurrence is almost universal within 5 years in patients with R1 resections. Other factors associated with increased survival include papillary phenotype, lower tumor grade, unaffected local lymph nodes, and a lack of vascular involvement.

C. **Gallbladder cancer** is the most common cancer of the biliary tract and the sixth-most-common cancer of the gastrointestinal (GI) tract, representing about 9,000 new cases per year in the United States. It is more aggressive than cholangiocarcinoma, has a poor prognosis, and accounts for approximately 6,000 deaths yearly. The incidence peaks at 70 to 75 years, with a 3:1 female-to-male ratio. There is a strong correlation with gallstones (95%). Histologically, nearly all gallbladder cancers are adenocarcinomas, and concomitant cholecystitis is frequently present. Tumors spread primarily by direct extension into liver segments IV and V adjacent to the gallbladder fossa, but also via lymphatics along the cystic duct to the CBD. Because of its generally late stage at presentation, only a small percentage of patients with a preoperative diagnosis of gallbladder cancer are resectable for potential cure.

1. **Risk factors**
   a. **The presence of gallstones** is the most common risk factor. Longer duration of cholelithiasis and larger stone size seem to further increase the risk, with reported cancer development odds ratios (ORs) of up to 10 for stones 3 cm or greater (*JAMA.* 1983;250:2323).
   b. **Polyps** 1.5 cm or greater in diameter have a 46% to 70% prevalence of cancer, whereas those in the 1- to 1.5-cm range have an 11% to 13% incidence. For polyps smaller than 1 cm, the risk of malignancy is <5%. Malignant polyps also tend to be sessile in nature and echopenic on ultrasound. Prophylactic cholecystectomy should be considered for polyps >1 cm in size or meeting morphologic criteria.

c. **Anomalous junction of the pancreatobiliary duct (AJPBD)** has been noted in approximately 10% of patients with gallbladder cancer, and up to 40% of patients with this anomaly develop a biliary tract malignancy. The anomaly represents a union of the pancreatic and biliary ducts outside of the duodenal wall, resulting in a long common channel. Subsequent reflux of pancreatic juice into the biliary system is thought to be the initiator of carcinogenesis.

d. **Porcelain gallbladder** is a condition characterized by calcification of the gallbladder wall. Although the overall incidence of carcinoma associated with porcelain gallbladder has been estimated at approximately 20%, studies have shown that gallbladders with diffuse intramural calcification rarely harbor cancer. Conversely, the selective mucosal calcification variant has been associated with malignancy in 7% to 42% of cases. Regardless, prophylactic cholecystectomy is generally recommended for any finding of gallbladder wall calcification on imaging studies.

e. **Other risk factors** include PSC, gallbladder infection with *E. coli* and/or *Salmonella* species, and exposure to certain industrial solvents and toxins.

2. **Diagnosis.** Approximately one-third of these tumors are diagnosed incidentally during cholecystectomy, and **cancer is found in 0.3% to 1%** of all cholecystectomy specimens. Symptoms of stage I and II gallbladder cancer are often directly caused by gallstones rather than the cancer, whereas stage III and IV cancers present with weight loss and symptoms typical of CBD obstruction. Suggestive ultrasound findings include thickening or irregularity of the gallbladder, a polypoid mass, or diffuse wall calcification indicative of porcelain gallbladder.

3. **Staging** is similar to that of cholangiocarcinoma, as shown in Tables 15-3 and 15-4. At present, there is insufficient data to determine the usefulness of FDG-PET.

4. **Treatment**
   a. **Mucosal disease** confined to the gallbladder wall (Tis and T1a tumors) is often identified after routine LC. Because the overall 5-year survival rate is as high as 80%, cholecystectomy alone with negative resection margins (including the cystic duct margin) is adequate therapy. Patients with a preoperative suspicion of gallbladder cancer should undergo open cholecystectomy because port site recurrences and late peritoneal metastases (associated with bile spillage) have been reported even with *in situ* disease.

   b. **Early disease** (T1b and T2 tumors) may be treated by radical cholecystectomy that includes the gallbladder, the gallbladder bed of the liver, as well as the hepatoduodenal ligament, periduodenal, peripancreatic, hepatic artery, and celiac lymph nodes.

   c. **Stage II or III disease** (invasion of adjacent organs or the presence of lymph node metastases) requires more radical resection. Depending on the extent of local invasion, extirpation may range from wedge resection of the liver adjacent to the gallbladder bed to resection of 75% of the liver. Dissection of the portal, paraduodenal, and hepatic artery lymph nodes should accompany the liver resection. Improvement in survival has been demonstrated after radical resection. Because of the aggressive nature of this malignancy, adjuvant chemoradiation is often recommended, but little proof of efficacy is available.

  d. Most gallbladder cancers have invaded adjacent organs, extend into the porta hepatis, or distantly metastasized before clinical diagnosis. **Extensive liver involvement or discontiguous metastases** preclude surgical resection. Jaundice may be palliated by percutaneous or endoscopically placed biliary stents. Duodenal obstruction can be surgically bypassed if present. Palliative chemotherapy (5-FU or gemcitabine-based) is recommended but has poor efficacy.

 5. Prognosis is stage dependent, and the respective 5-year survival rates are shown in Table 15-3. The median survival for stage IB cancers is less than 2 years, and for stage II lesions, it is less than 1 year. With stage II disease or higher, fewer than 20% of patients are alive at 2 years.

VII. BENIGN STRICTURES AND BILE DUCT INJURIES occur in association with a number of conditions, including pancreatitis, choledocholithiasis, Oriental cholangiohepatitis, PSC, prior hepatic transplantation, trauma, or iatrogenic injury after instrumentation or surgery. LC is the leading cause of iatrogenic bile duct injuries and subsequent benign strictures. Biliary malignancy may masquerade as a benign stricture. Attempts to differentiate between the two etiologies should be made prior to surgery because the patient may not be a candidate for a curative resection if an advanced stage of cancer is found.

 A. Risk factors for intraoperative bile duct injury have been divided into three categories: (1) patient-related factors, (2) procedure-related factors, and (3) surgeon/hospital-related factors (*J Hepatobiliary Pancreat Surg.* 2002;9:543).

  1. Patient-related factors
   a. Inflammation
    (1) Acute inflammation, such as that seen in acute cholecystitis, may cause the gallbladder, cystic duct, and CBD to appear as a single mass (*J Am Coll Surg.* 2000;191:661). This can lead to misidentification of the CBD as the cystic duct with subsequent clipping and transection.
    (2) Severe chronic inflammation and dense scarring may result from repeated bouts of cholecystitis and/or choledocholithiasis, effectively obliterating the triangle of Calot and leaving a shrunken, contracted gallbladder densely adherent to the common hepatic duct and/or right hepatic artery.
   b. Congenital anomalies including aberrant right hepatic ducts and aberrant course or insertion of the cyst duct can complicate LC and lead to CBD injury.
   c. Large, impacted gallstones may prevent proper retraction of the gallbladder and can obscure the anatomic relationships between the cystic duct and surrounding structures.

    d. Obesity can contribute to a difficult operation due to both intra-abdominal and extra-abdominal fat and loss of intra-abdominal domain during laparoscopy.

2. Procedure-related factors

    a. Operative technique likely represents the most important factor contributing to the risk of inadvertent bile duct injury.

    b. IOC can be extremely helpful in the avoidance of potentially devastating bile duct injury.

    c. Technical problems frequently arise secondary to other risk factors such as inflammation but may also occur even in the absence of a specific predisposing condition.

        (1) Inadvertent injury to a bile duct during the course of dissection most commonly results form the injudicious use of electrocautery, although sharp dissection and excessive traction on the gallbladder or adjacent structures may also contribute to this type of injury.

        (2) Failure to securely close the cystic duct may be due to a poorly placed or incompletely closed surgical clip, usually in the setting of a thickened fibrotic cystic duct or increased biliary pressure secondary to retained CBD stones. If there is any concern for incomplete closure, a **laparoscopic loop ligature** should be used.

        (3) Tenting injuries occur when the CBD or common hepatic duct is clipped after being elevated due to excessive traction on the gallbladder and cystic duct.

3. Surgeon/hospital-related factors

    a. The learning-curve effect may be due to a lack of sufficient operator experience with safe techniques for performing cholecystomy, either laparoscopically or open.

    b. Surgeon mindset, often characterized by a sense of infallibility even when faced with adversity, may result in biliary injury.

    c. Laparoscopic equipment must be regularly maintained in excellent working condition. Loss of insulation from electrocautery instruments may be particularly hazardous, and preventative systems should be employed.

4. The difficult cholecystectomy. In an attempt to preoperatively identify what factors might contribute to a "difficult cholecystectomy," 22,953 cases of LC performed in Switzerland were studied. Those factors associated with an increase in all intraoperative complications (not limited to only bile duct injury) included the presence of acute cholecystitis (OR = 1.86), male gender (OR = 1.18), patient age (OR = 1.12 per 10 years), increased body weight (OR = 1.34 for >90 kg vs. <60 kg), and surgeon experience (OR = 1.36 for 11 to 100 cases vs. >100 cases). Multivariate analysis also showed an increase in complications for each additional 30 minutes of operative time, with OR = 1.68 (*J Am Coll Surg.* 2006;203:723). Conversion to an open operation in the face of a difficult laparoscopic procedure should never be viewed as a surgical failure or complication but rather as a way to avoid potential injury to the patient.

B. **Classification.** A widely accepted classification scheme has been developed at this institution (*Surg Clin North Am.* 2010;90:787). Type A injuries are cystic duct leaks or leaks from small ducts in the liver bed. Type B and C injuries involve an aberrant right hepatic duct. Type B represents an occluded segment, whereas type C involves open drainage from the proximal draining duct not in continuity with the common duct. Type D injuries are *lateral* injuries to the extrahepatic bile ducts. Type E injuries (subtypes 1 to 5) are derived from the Bismuth classification and represent circumferential transections or occlusions at various levels of the CBD.

C. **Diagnosis**

1. **Presentation** depends on the type of injury. Approximately 25% of major bile duct injuries are recognized at the time of the initial procedure. Intraoperative signs of a major ductal injury include unexpected bile leakage, abnormal IOC, and delayed recognition of the anatomy after transection of important structures. If an injury is not recognized intraoperatively, the patient usually presents with symptoms within 1 week and almost always within 3 to 4 weeks after the initial procedure. Patients with a bile leak often present with right-upper-quadrant pain, fever, and sepsis secondary to biloma and may have bile drainage from a surgical incision. Patients with occlusion of the CBD without a bile leak present with jaundice. Occasionally, a delayed presentation of months or years is seen.

2. **Diagnostic imaging.** Axial imaging with CT scan or MRI is useful for detecting abdominal bile collections that require percutaneous drainage. MRCP with angiography is now often the initial imaging test of choice because of its ability to define the vascular as well as the biliary anatomy, as biliary injuries are frequently associated with vascular injuries. Ongoing bile leaks can also be diagnosed by HIDA scan. ERCP is also useful to demonstrate biliary anatomy, and therapeutic stent placement is often possible for ductal leaks. In the case of occlusion of the CBD, PTC can demonstrate the proximal biliary anatomy, define the proximal extent of the injury, and be used for therapeutic decompression of the biliary tree.

D. **Management** depends on the type and timing of the presentation.

1. If the injury is identified at the time of the initial procedure, the surgeon should proceed directly to open exploration and repair only if qualified and comfortable with complex techniques in hepatobiliary surgery or to control life-threatening hemorrhage. If the surgeon is not prepared to perform a definitive repair, a drain should be placed in the right upper quadrant and the patient immediately **referred to a specialist hepatobiliary center.**

2. **Immediate management.** Many of the simpler injuries can be successfully managed with ERCP and sphincterotomy, stenting, or both. Occlusive lesions require decompression of the proximal system via PTC. In general, if an injury requires operative repair and the patient is stable, the repair should be done within the first few days after the initial procedure while inflammation is at a minimum. If this is not

possible due to delayed diagnosis, longer-term temporization (at least 8 weeks) is required to allow the acute inflammation to resolve. In addition, if there is a concern about a vascular injury along with the bile duct injury, definitive repair should be delayed to more easily identify areas of ductal ischemia, which should not be incorporated in the repair.

3. Control of sepsis, percutaneous drainage, and adequate nutrition should be **optimized before definitive repair.**

4. **Operative repair,** when indicated, is best achieved by means of a Roux-en-Y hepaticojejunostomy, in which the bile duct is debrided back to viable tissue. All bile ducts must be accounted for, and an adequate blood supply must be apparent for each. A tension-free mucosa-to-mucosa anastomosis constructed with fine absorbable suture is desired. Excellent long-term outcomes have been described, with anastomotic stricture the most common, yet infrequent, complication (*Ann Surg.* 2009;249:426).

16 Spleen

Malcolm MacConmara and L. Michael Brunt

SPLENIC ANATOMY AND PHYSIOLOGY

I. SPLENIC ANATOMY

A. Macroscopic Anatomy. The spleen develops from mesoderm within the dorsal mesogastrium and following rotation of the gut becomes located in the **left upper quadrant of the abdomen** beneath the 9th to 11th ribs. It is approximately 12 cm long, 7 cm wide, and 4 cm thick and weighs 100 to 150 g. The costodiaphragmatic recess of the left pleural cavity extends as far as the inferior border of a normal spleen. It is **intimately related** to the splenic flexure of the colon, the greater curvature of the stomach, the left kidney, and the pancreatic tail. The tail of the pancreas extends laterally to within 1 cm of the splenic hilum in most patients and is in direct contact with the spleen in up to 30% of patients (Fig. 16-1).

Peritoneal reflections in the region surrounding the spleen form the fibrous suspensory "ligaments" through which most of the principal vascular structures course. These ligaments are splenocolic, splenorenal, gastrosplenic, and splenophrenic. Their division is one of the keys to splenectomy. The pancreas is partially invested in the leaves of the splenorenal ligament, just inferior to the contained splenic artery and its branches.

The **splenic artery** is a branch of the celiac trunk and follows a serpiginous path along the superior border of the pancreas. The terminal branching pattern into the spleen is most commonly distributive in which the main trunk arborizes into multiple arterial branches that enter the hilum broadly over its surface. Less commonly, the arterial supply has a magistral configuration, with one dominant splenic artery entering over a narrow and compact area (Fig. 16-2).

Accessory spleens occur in 10% to 20% of patients and are most commonly found at the splenic hilum, the gastrosplenic omentum, along the tail of the pancreas, and in the retroperitoneum posterior to the spleen. However, accessory splenic tissue can be found throughout the abdomen and pelvis (Fig. 16-3).

B. Microscopic Anatomy. The **spleen consists** of red pulp with interspersed areas of white pulp. The red pulp is highly vascular and is composed of large, branching, thin-walled sinuses, with intervening areas filled with phagocytic cells and blood cells, known as splenic cords. The white pulp has three components: periarteriolar lymphoid sheaths (T cells), lymphoid nodules (B cells), and the marginal zone.

II. SPLENIC FUNCTION.
The spleen has two major functions: (1) mechanical filtration of erythrocytes as part of the reticuloendothelial system and (2) a component of the immune system.

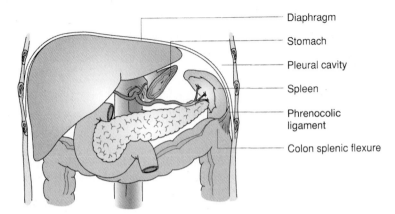

Diaphragm

Stomach

Pleural cavity

Spleen

Phrenocolic
ligament

Colon splenic flexure

Figure 16-1. Relationships of the spleen. Anatomic relation of the spleen to the liver, diaphragm, pancreas, colon, and kidney. The stomach is sectioned to illustrate the anatomic relation *in situ*. (Adapted from splenic disorders *Greenfields Surgery: Scientific Principles and Practice*. 4th ed., 2006.)

A. **Reticuloendothelial/Filtration System.** The spleen is highly vascular receiving 5% of the cardiac output. The red pulp serves as a mechanical filter for the removal of senescent erythrocytes (*culling*) and the remodeling of healthy red cells, including removal of nuclear remnants, denatured hemoglobin, and iron granules (*pitting*). A minor hematologic function of the spleen is to serve as a reservoir for platelets. In certain disease states (e.g., myelofibrosis), the adult spleen becomes a major site of extramedullary hematopoiesis.

B. **Immune System.** The white pulp is a nonspecific filter and removes blood-borne pathogens (e.g., bacteria and viruses) that are coated with complement. Encapsulated bacteria are also effectively removed from the circulation, likely via prolonged contact with macrophages in the splenic parenchymal cords. The spleen also participates in the specific immune responses. The white pulp architecture provides a platform for cytokine-regulated T

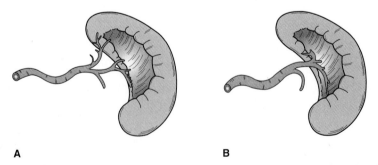

A   **B**

Figure 16-2. Variations in the splenic artery. The two most common variations of blood supply are illustrated: (**A**) Early branching characteristic of distributive and (**B**) magistral where the splenic artery branches close to the hilum of the spleen

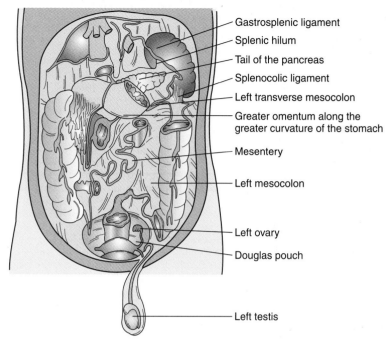

Gastrosplenic ligament
Splenic hilum
Tail of the pancreas
Splenocolic ligament
Left transverse mesocolon
Greater omentum along the greater curvature of the stomach
Mesentery
Left mesocolon
Left ovary
Douglas pouch
Left testis

Figure 16-3. Location of accessory spleens. Usual location of accessory spleens: *(1)* gastro-splenic ligament, *(2)* splenic hilum, *(3)* tail of the pancreas, *(4)* splenocolic ligament, *(5)* left transverse mesocolon, *(6)* greater omentum along the greater curvature of the stomach, *(7)* mesentery, *(8)* left mesocolon, *(9)* left ovary, *(10)* Douglas pouch, and *(11)* left testis.

and B cell interaction with antigen-presenting cells leading to specific cellular and antibody responses. The spleen also manufactures opsonins, namely, properdin, and tuftsin.

INDICATIONS FOR SPLENECTOMY

I. **GENERAL INDICATIONS.** The initial therapy for most hematologic disorders of the spleen is medical. In general, splenectomy is warranted only after the failure of medical therapy, as an adjunct to medical therapy, for diagnostic reasons, or in some cases as primary therapy for an underlying malignancy (see Table 16-1).

II. **SPECIFIC INDICATIONS**

A. **Hematologic splenic pathology**

1. **Thrombocytopenias**

   a. **Idiopathic (immune) thrombocytopenic purpura (ITP)** is the most common indication for elective splenectomy. It is an acquired

TABLE 16.1	**General Indications for Splenectomy**

1. **Cure or palliation of hematologic disease.** Idiopathic (immune) thrombocytopenic purpura and hemolytic anemias are the most common indications for splenectomy. Splenectomy may also be used to palliate other disease states (e.g., chronic lymphocytic leukemia, hairy cell leukemia, Felty syndrome), primarily via the control of cytopenias.

2. **Palliation of hypersplenism.** Patients with refractory cytopenias due to hypersplenism that require frequent transfusion or significantly limit the delivery of cytotoxic therapy may benefit from splenectomy.

3. **Relief from symptomatic splenomegaly.** Patients with a massively enlarged spleen can develop early satiety, abdominal pain, and weight loss from mass effect.

4. **Diagnosis of splenic pathology.** Solid mass lesions in the spleen can be an indication for splenectomy, particularly if a malignant diagnosis is suspected. Splenectomy may be used to establish a diagnosis of lymphoma in the absence of more easily accessible tissue but is no longer indicated for staging lymphomas.

5. **Control of splenic hemorrhage.** Although splenic injury is increasingly managed nonoperatively, splenectomy is the definitive treatment for patients with ongoing traumatic splenic hemorrhage. Splenic hemorrhage may also rarely occur spontaneously in disease states such as infectious mononucleosis.

disorder in which autoantibodies are produced against a platelet glycoprotein. The spleen is the major site for the production of antiplatelet antibodies and also serves as the principal site of platelet destruction (see Table 16-2).

(1) **Children** usually present with acute ITP, often associated with a recent viral syndrome. In 90% of cases, the disease spontaneously remits. Only refractory cases require splenectomy, and a waiting period of at least 12 months is recommended where possible (*Blood.* 1996;88:3–40). In younger children under 5 years where the risk of infection postsplenectomy is higher, temporizing therapies are especially important (*Br J Haematol.* 1999;105:871–875). Adolescent females have a disease course similar to that seen in adults (*Blood.* 2010;115:168–186).

(2) **Adults** typically present with a more chronic form of ITP that is much less likely to spontaneously remit. Asymptomatic patients with platelet counts greater than 50,000/mm^3 may simply be followed. Symptomatic patients or those with counts less than 30,000/mm^3 should be treated with oral glucocorticoids. More than 50% of patients respond to glu-

TABLE 16.2	Clinical Conditions that May Require Splenectomy	
	Common	**Uncommon**
Thrombocytopenias	Immune thrombocytopenic purpura	Thrombotic thrombocytopenic purpura
Anemias	Hereditary hemolytic anemias (hereditary spherocytosis) Autoimmune hemolytic anemias Congenital hemoglobinopathies (sickle cell anemia)	Thalassemias Hereditary elliptocytosis
Myeloproliferative and myelodysplastic disorders	—	Chronic myelogenous leukemia Polycythemia vera Myelofibrosis or myeloid metaplasia Essential thrombocytosis Myeloproliferative disorder not otherwise specified
Lymphoproliferative disorders	—	Chronic lymphocytic leukemia Hairy-cell leukemia Non-Hodgkin lymphoma (e.g., splenic marginal zone lymphoma) Hodgkin lymphoma
Neutropenias	—	Felty syndrome
Nonhematologic splenic disorders	Trauma Incidental splenectomy Vascular problems (splenic artery aneurysm, splenic vein thrombosis)	Splenic abscess Splenic cyst/pseudocyst Storage diseases

cocorticoids although many will not maintain normal counts after steroid discontinuation (*Am J Med.* 1995;98:436–442, *N Engl J Med.* 2003;349:831–836). In refractory cases, or in patients with bleeding, intravenous immunoglobulin (IVIG) is used, although the effects are transient (*Mayo Clin Proc.*

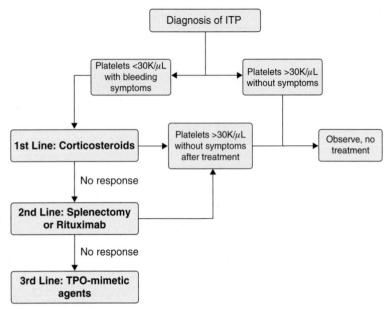

Figure 16-4. Treatment approach in ITP in adults. This diagram represents a simplified approach to the treatment of patients with ITP. A threshold platelet count of 30,000/μL for clinical decisions, rather than a range of platelet counts, is presented, but clinical symptoms and patients' concerns are more important for treatment decisions. (Adapted from George J, Leung LLP. Treatment and prognosis of immune (idiopathic) thrombocytopenic purpura in adults, *UpToDate*, 2011.)

2004;79:504–522). Newer second- line agents include rituximab (anti-CD20 monoclonal antibody) and thrombopoiesis-stimulating agents have demonstrated short-term effectiveness and may be used where splenectomy is refused (*Ann Intern Med.* 2007;146:25–33). Indications for splenectomy are failure to respond to medical therapy and intolerable side effects from steroid administration (Fig. 16-4). Indications for more urgent splenectomy in patients with ITP include need for other emergency surgery or a life-threatening bleed, including central nervous system hemorrhage. Most patients who respond to splenectomy do so within the first 10 postoperative days (*Am J Surg.* 2004;187:720–723).

(3) A systematic review of 135 case series spanning 58 years found a complete remission in two-thirds of patients. Either a complete or partial response was observed in 88% of patients. Complete response was defined as achievement of a platelet count of at least 100×10^9/L. A partial response included a platelet count response of at least 30×10^9/L. Variables associated with a response to splenectomy include younger age and response

to IVIG therapy. Mortality rates of 0.2% to 1% are similar to mortality due to medically treated severe ITP over 5 to 10 years (0.4% to 1.6%). Surgical complication rates range from 10% to 13% (*Blood.* 2004;104:2623–2634).

(4) Patients who fail splenectomy or relapse after an initial response should be investigated for **accessory splenic tissue.** A peripheral smear and magnetic resonance imaging or nuclear medicine studies with technetium (Tc)-99 m–labeled heat-damaged red cells are indicated. If accessory splenic tissue is found, re-exploration should be considered, although long-term response to removal of an accessory spleen is uncommon (*N Engl J Med.* 2002;346:995–1008). Rituximab has been of benefit to patients who fail to respond to splenectomy (*Am J Hematol.* 2005;78:275–280).

b. **Thrombotic thrombocytopenic purpura (TTP)** is characterized by the pentad of hemolytic anemia, consumptive thrombocytopenia, mental status changes, renal failure, and fever, although only hemolytic anemia and thrombocytopenia (without other obvious cause) are required to initiate therapy. Symptoms result from multiorgan microvascular thrombosis.

(1) **First-line therapy** for TTP is medical, with plasmapheresis. A randomized, controlled trial with 102 patients demonstrated significantly improved initial response (47% vs. 25%) and 6-month survival (78% vs. 63%) for plasmapheresis as compared with plasma infusion (*N Engl J Med.* 1991;325:393–397). Glucocorticoids, in addition to plasmapheresis, are prescribed in the rare case of relapse. Second-line medical treatment for relapsing or refractory cases includes rituximab, cyclosporin, and increased plasma exchange frequency.

(2) **Splenectomy** has limited indication in patients who do not respond to medical therapy or those with chronically relapsing disease and has shown benefit only when used in conjunction with plasmapheresis. Severe deficiency of ADAMTS-13, a von Willebrand factor-cleaving protein has been found in many TTP patients, and reports suggest splenectomy may restore ADAMTS-13 levels. A retrospective review of 33 patients found that those who were continuously dependent on plasmapheresis and underwent splenectomy had a postoperative relapse rate of 0.07 per patient-year. In those patients who were not continuously dependent on plasmapheresis, splenectomy reduced the relapse rate from 0.74 to 0.10 per patient-year (*Br J Haematol.* 2005;130:768–776).

2. **Anemias**

a. **Hemolytic anemias** constitute a group of disorders in which splenectomy is almost universally curative.

(1) **Hereditary spherocytosis** is an autosomal dominant disorder characterized by a defect in *spectrin*, a red blood cell (RBC) membrane protein. This defect results in small, spherical, relatively rigid erythrocytes that fail to deform adequately to

traverse the splenic microcirculation leading to sequestration and destruction in the splenic red pulp. In addition to anemia, patients may have jaundice from the hemolytic process and splenomegaly from RBC destruction in the spleen. Splenectomy is indicated in nearly all cases, but should be delayed to age 6 years in children to minimize the risk of overwhelming postsplenectomy sepsis. An exception is if the child is transfusion dependent. Prior to splenectomy, patients should have a right-upper-quadrant ultrasound, and if gallstones are present (usually pigment stones from hemolysis), a cholecystectomy can be performed concomitantly. The recently described technique of subtotal splenectomy (leaving a 10 cm^3 remnant) may reduce the risks of infection and sepsis (*Br J Haematol.* 2006;132:791–793).

(2) **Hereditary elliptocytosis** is an autosomal dominant disorder in which an intrinsic cytoskeletal defect causes the RBCs to be elliptical. Most patients have an asymptomatic and mild anemia that does not need specific treatment. Patients with symptomatic anemia should undergo splenectomy to prolong RBC survival.

b. **Acquired autoimmune hemolytic anemias** are characterized as either warm or cold, depending on the temperature at which they interact with antibody.

(1) **Warm autoimmune hemolytic anemia** results from splenic sequestration and destruction of RBCs coated with autoantibodies that interact optimally with their antigens at 37°C. Anti-immunoglobulin IgG antiserum causes agglutination of the patient's RBCs (positive direct Coombs test). Etiologies include chronic lymphocytic leukemia (CLL), non-Hodgkin lymphoma, collagen vascular disease, and drugs, although most cases are idiopathic. Primary treatment is directed against the underlying disease. If this is unsuccessful, therapy is corticosteroids. Nonresponders or patients requiring high steroid doses respond to splenectomy in 60% to 80% of cases (*Ann Surg.* 1998;228:568–578). Immunosuppressive and cytotoxic agents have a role in patients unable or unwilling to undergo splenectomy or in relapsed patients

(2) **Cold autoimmune hemolytic anemia** is characterized by fixation of C3 to IgM antibodies that bind RBCs with greater affinity at temperatures approaching 0°C and cause Raynaud-like symptoms combined with anemia. Hemolysis occurs either immediately by intravascular complement–mediated mechanisms or via removal of C3-coated RBCs by the spleen. Treatment is usually successful with use of increased protective clothing. Severe cases may benefit from treatment with low-dose alkylating agents, rituximab or interferon. Splenectomy has no therapeutic benefit.

c. **Congenital hemoglobinopathies**

1. **Sickle cell anemia** is due to the homozygous inheritance of the S variant of the hemoglobin β chain. The disease is usually

associated with autosplenectomy due to repeated vaso-occlusive crises, but splenectomy may be required for those patients with acute splenic sequestration crisis, evidence of hypersplenism, splenic abscess, and symptomatic splenomegaly.

2. **Thalassemias** are hereditary anemias caused by a defect in hemoglobin synthesis. β-Thalassemia major is primarily treated with iron chelation therapy, but splenectomy may be required to treat symptomatic splenomegaly or pain from splenic infarcts.

3. **Myeloproliferative and myelodysplastic disorders**
   a. **Chronic myelogenous leukemia (CML)** is a myelodysplastic disorder characterized by the *bcr-abl* fusion oncogene, known as the *Philadelphia chromosome.* This oncogene results in a constitutive activation of tyrosine kinase.
      (1) First-line therapy utilizes the tyrosine kinase inhibitor (TKI) imatinib mesylate (Gleevec). Alternative TKI treatments (*dasatinib* and *nilotinib*) are used in cases of intolerance or suboptimal response. Stem cell transplantation is used for cases of treatment failure in eligible patients (*Blood.* 2006;108:1809–1820)
      (2) A large prospectively randomized trial compared splenectomy plus chemotherapy or chemotherapy alone in the treatment of early phase of CML. Splenectomy had no effect on survival or disease progression, but it did increase the rate of thrombosis and vascular accidents (*Cancer.* 1984;54:333–338). Splenectomy is indicated only for palliation of symptomatic splenomegaly or hypersplenism that significantly limits therapy.
   b. **Polycythemia vera and essential thrombocytosis** are chronic diseases of uncontrolled RBC and platelet production, respectively. These diseases are treated medically, but splenectomy can be required to treat symptomatic splenomegaly or pain from splenic infarcts. Splenectomy can result in severe thrombocytosis, causing thrombosis or hemorrhage, which requires perioperative antiplatelet, anticoagulation, and myelosuppressive treatment.
   c. **Myelofibrosis and myeloid metaplasia** are incurable myeloproliferative disorders that usually present in patients older than 60 years. The condition is characterized by bone marrow fibrosis, leukoerythroblastosis, and extramedullary hematopoiesis, which can result in massive splenomegaly. Indications for splenectomy include symptomatic splenomegaly and transfusion-dependent anemias. Although the compressive symptoms are effectively palliated with splenectomy, the cytopenias frequently recur. In addition, these patients are at increased risk for postoperative hemorrhage and thrombotic complications after splenectomy.

4. **Lymphoproliferative disorders**
   a. **Chronic lymphocytic leukemia,** a B-cell leukemia, is the most common of the chronic leukemias and is characterized by the accumulation of mature but nonfunctional lymphocytes. Primary therapy is medical, with splenectomy reserved for those patients with symptomatic splenomegaly and severe hypersplenism.

b. The **non-Hodgkin lymphomas** are a diverse group of disorders with a wide range of clinical behaviors, ranging from indolent to highly aggressive. As with other malignant processes, splenectomy is indicated for palliation of hypersplenism and cytopenias or for diagnosis in patients with suspected persistent or recurrent disease after systemic therapy. Splenectomy plays an important role in the diagnosis and staging of patients with isolated splenic lymphoma (known as *malignant lymphoma with prominent splenic involvement*). In these cases, improved survival has been shown in patients undergoing splenectomy (*Cancer.* 1993;71:207–215).

c. Hodgkin lymphoma. Splenectomy has a limited role in the diagnosis and treatment of Hodgkin lymphoma due to refinements in imaging techniques and progress in the methods of treatment. Indications for surgery are similar to those for non-Hodgkin lymphoma.

d. Hairy cell leukemia is a rare disease of elderly men that is characterized by B lymphocytes with membrane ruffling. Splenectomy was previously regarded as the primary therapy for this disease, but improvements in systemic chemotherapy have reduced the role of splenectomy, which is now reserved for patients with massive splenomegaly or refractory disease.

5. Neutropenias

a. Felty syndrome is characterized by rheumatoid arthritis, splenomegaly, and neutropenia. The primary treatment is steroids, but refractory cases may require splenectomy to reverse the neutropenia. Patients with recurrent infections and significant anemia may benefit from splenectomy. Granulocytopenia is improved in approximately 80% of patients (*Arch Intern Med.* 1978;138:597–602). The clinical course of the arthritis is not affected.

B. Nonhematologic splenic disorders

1. Splenic cysts are uncommon and can be parasitic or nonparasitic. Most are located in the lower pole in a subcapsular position.

a. Parasitic cysts make up more than two-thirds of splenic cysts worldwide but are rare in the United States. The majority are hydatid cysts caused by *Echinococcus* species. They are typically asymptomatic but may rupture or cause symptoms due to splenomegaly. The primary treatment is splenectomy, with careful attention not to spill the cyst contents. The cyst may be aspirated and injected with hypertonic saline prior to mobilization if concern about rupture exists.

b. Nonparasitic cysts can be true cysts or pseudocysts, but this differentiation is difficult to make preoperatively.

(1) True cysts (or primary cysts) have an epithelial lining and are most often congenital. Other rare true cysts include epidermoid and dermoid cysts.

(2) Pseudocysts (or secondary cysts) lack an epithelial lining and make up more than two-thirds of nonparasitic cysts. They typically result from traumatic hematoma formation and subsequently resorb.

(3) **Treatment.** Splenic cysts are typically asymptomatic, but they may present with left upper abdominal or shoulder pain. Those smaller than 5 cm can be followed with ultrasonography and often resolve spontaneously. Larger cysts risk rupture and require cyst unroofing or splenectomy. Percutaneous aspiration is associated with infection and reaccumulation and is not indicated. Laparoscopic management of splenic cysts yields shorter hospital length of stay and fewer complications with no adverse effects (*Surg Endosc.* 2007;21:206–208).

2. **Splenic abscesses** are rare but potentially lethal if untreated. Approximately two-thirds are due to seeding from a distant bacteremic focus, most commonly endocarditis or urinary tract infection. Fever is present in nearly all cases, and abdominal discomfort and splenomegaly occur in one half of patients. Associated conditions include sickle cell anemia. Computed tomography (CT) scanning and ultrasonography are the best diagnostic modalities for splenic abscess. CT scanning typically shows an area of low homogeneous density with edges that do not intensify with intravenous contrast. Antibiotic therapy should be instituted immediately after blood cultures are obtained. More than 60% of identified infectious agents are aerobes, with one half being *Staphylococcus* and *Streptococcus* species. A minority of splenic abscesses involve fungal organisms, which can be cured with antifungal agents alone. Unilocular abscesses may be amenable to treatment by percutaneous drainage. Splenectomy, open or laparoscopic, in combination with postoperative antibiotics is the definitive therapy. Laparoscopic unroofing and open partial splenectomy are alternative spleen-preserving options.

C. **Other forms of splenic pathology**

1. **Trauma** to the adult spleen has historically been managed with laparotomy (most children have been successfully managed nonoperatively). With imaging advances, grading of this solid organ injury and conservative management in the stable adult patient have become standard therapy. The common grading system for splenic injury is listed in Table 16-3. Management depends on stability and age (adult vs. child) of the patient and associated injuries (Fig. 16-5).

2. **Incidental splenectomy** occurs when the spleen is injured iatrogenically during another abdominal operation. This can occur either by damage from a retractor in the left upper quadrant or from mobilization of the splenic flexure in colon resection. Capsular tears can often be treated with topical hemostatic agents or even with use of the argon beam coagulator, but if significant hemorrhage results and cannot be controlled expeditiously, splenectomy is indicated.

3. **Splenic artery aneurysm** is the most common visceral artery aneurysm and has a particular tendency to affect women, with increased incidence of rupture during pregnancy. Asymptomatic aneurysms less than 2 cm in size in patients in whom pregnancy is not anticipated can be followed closely with serial imaging. Operative management is

TABLE 16.3	American Association for the Surgery of Trauma Spleen Injury Scale (2008 Version)	
	Grade[a]	Injury description
I	Hematoma	Subcapsular, <10% surface area
	Laceration	Capsular tear, <1 cm parenchymal depth
II	Hematoma	Subcapsular, 10%–50% surface area; intraparenchymal, <5 cm in diameter
	Laceration	1–3 cm parenchymal depth that does not involve a trabecular vessel
III	Hematoma	Subcapsular, >50% surface area or expanding ruptured subcapsular or parenchymal hematoma
		Intraparenchymal hematoma >5 cm or expanding
	Laceration	3 cm parenchymal depth or involving trabecular vessels
IV	Laceration	Laceration involving segmental or hilar vessels producing major devascularization (>25% of spleen)
V	Laceration	Completely shattered spleen
	Vascular	Hilar vascular injury that devascularizes spleen

[a]Advance one grade for multiple injuries up to grade III.
With permission from Tinkoff G, Esposito TJ, Reed J, et al. American Association for the Surgery of Trauma Organ Injury Scale 1: spleen, liver and kidney. *J Trauma* 2008;207(5):646–655.

warranted for (1) larger (≥ 2 cm) or symptomatic aneurysms, (2) those in whom pregnancy is anticipated, and (3) pseudoaneurysms associated with inflammation. Endovascular management such as transcatheter embolization and laparoscopic excision has been used in selected patients. However, pain from splenic infarcts may occur as a result. For proximal and middle-third aneurysms, the aneurysms may simply be excluded by proximal and distal ligation, with the splenic blood supply then coming predominantly from the short gastric vessels. For distal-third aneurysms, resection with splenectomy is usually performed.

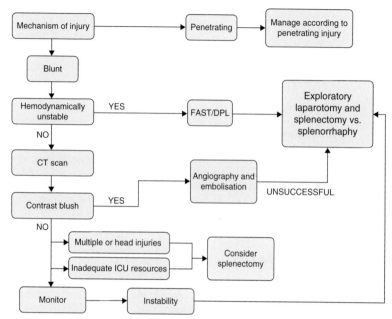

Figure 16-5. Treatment algorithm for splenic trauma. Algorithm for the diagnosis and management of traumatic splenic injury. (Adapted from Esposito TJ, Gamelli RL. Injury to the spleen. In: Feliciano DV, Mattox KL, Moore EE, eds: *Trauma*. 6th ed. Stamford, CT: Appleton & Lange.)

PREOPERATIVE CONSIDERATIONS IN SPLENECTOMY

I. VACCINATIONS

A. **Polyvalent pneumococcal vaccine (Pneumovax)** covers 85% to 90% of pneumococcal types and should be administered at least 2 to 3 weeks before splenectomy, or at least 14 days post-operatively, to all patients older than 2 years. The vaccine should be repeated every 5 to 7 years.

B. **Meningococcal vaccine** is a one-time vaccination for patients older than 2 years.

C. *Haemophilus influenzae* **type B** conjugate vaccine should be considered if the patient was not vaccinated in infancy.

II. CONSIDERATIONS FOR TRANSFUSION

A. **Patients with hematologic disease,** particularly those with autoimmune disorders, often have autoantibodies and are difficult to cross-match. Thus, blood should be typed and screened at least 24 hours prior to the scheduled operative time. Patients with splenomegaly should have 2 to 4 units of packed RBCs cross-matched and available for surgery.

B. **Patients with severe thrombocytopenia** (particularly those with counts <10,000/μL) should have platelets available for transfusion, but these should be withheld until the splenic artery is ligated so they will not be quickly consumed by the spleen. Most patients with thrombocytopenia from ITP can undergo splenectomy safely without platelet transfusion even in the setting of very low platelet counts.

III. PREOPERATIVE IMAGING

A. Either **ultrasound or CT** may be necessary in patients with malignancy or suspected splenomegaly to determine spleen size and to evaluate splenic hilar adenopathy that may complicate a laparoscopic approach. Imaging is not usually indicated in patients with ITP.

B. **Right-upper-quadrant ultrasound** is indicated preoperatively for those who are at high risk for developing gallstones (hemolytic anemias, sickle cell anemia) so that cholecystectomy may be performed concomitantly if indicated.

VI. OTHER CONSIDERATIONS

A. Perioperative stress-dose steroids treatment should be considered for patients receiving steroids pre-operatively and should be continued orally postoperatively and tapered gradually once a hematologic response to splenectomy has occurred.

B. Patients who are to undergo a laparoscopic splenectomy should be counseled preoperatively about the possibility of **conversion to open splenectomy or a hand-assisted approach** and should be prepared identically to those patients for whom an open procedure is planned.

OPERATIVE APPROACH

I. **LAPAROSCOPIC SPLENECTOMY** has become the preferred method for elective splenectomy for all but the most difficult or largest spleens. It is now increasingly used for selected patients with splenomegaly. **Contraindications** to laparoscopic splenectomy are presented in Table 16-4.

A. **Splenomegaly** increases the complexity of the laparoscopic approach because of the difficulty of manipulating the organ atraumatically and achieving adequate exposure of the ligaments and hilum. Large spleens are also more difficult to place in an entrapment bag using a strictly laparoscopic approach. Although the size limits for attempting laparoscopic or laparoscopic-assisted splenectomy are evolving, most moderately enlarged spleens (<1,000 g weight or 15 to 20 cm in length) can be removed in a minimally invasive fashion, often without a hand-port device. For spleens larger than 20 cm in longitudinal length or those that weigh between 1,000 and 3,000 g, the use of a hand port should be considered. The use of a hand port in this setting has been associated with reduced operative times, less blood loss, and lower rates of conversion to open operation (*Arch Surg.* 2006;141:755–761; discussion 61–62). In general, spleens

TABLE 16.4	Contraindications to Laparoscopic Splenectomy
Absolute contraindications	**Difficult cases**
Massive splenomegaly (>30 cm length)	Moderate splenomegaly (>20–25 cm)
Portal hypertension	Severe uncorrectable cytopenia
Splenic trauma, unstable patient	Splenic vein thrombosis
—	Splenic trauma, stable patient
—	Bulky hilar adenopathy
—	Morbid obesity

greater than 30 cm in craniocaudal length (and weighing >3,000 g) should be approached in an open fashion because of the reduced working space and increased difficulty in manipulating the spleen. A search for **accessory splenic tissue** should always be conducted, particularly if the patient has a hematologic indication for splenectomy.

B. **Outcomes of laparoscopic splenectomy.** Several large series of laparoscopic splenectomy have been published with excellent results. In a metaanalysis of 51 reports including 2,940 patients, laparoscopic splenectomy was associated with significantly fewer complications overall, primarily as a result of fewer wound and pulmonary complications.

II. **OPEN SPLENECTOMY.** The incision used is either an upper midline or a left subcostal incision. When significant splenomegaly is present, a midline incision is usually preferred. A drain is not routinely required unless it is suspected that the pancreatic tail may have been injured during the hilar dissection.

COMPLICATIONS OF SPLENECTOMY

I. INTRAOPERATIVE COMPLICATIONS

A. **Hemorrhage.** The most common intraoperative complication of splenectomy is hemorrhage, which can occur during the hilar dissection or from a capsular tear during retraction. The incidence of this complication is 2% to 3% during open splenectomy but is nearly 5% using the laparoscopic approach. Bleeding during laparoscopic splenectomy may necessitate conversion to a hand-assisted or open procedure.

B. Clinical evidence of **pancreatic injury** occurs in 0% to 6% of splenectomies, whether done open or laparoscopically. A retrospective review of one center's experience with laparoscopic splenectomy found pancreatic injury in 16% of patients; half of these were isolated instances of hyperamylasemia. If one suspects that the pancreatic parenchyma has been violated during laparoscopic splenectomy, a closed suction drain should be placed adjacent to the pancreas, and a drain amylase obtained prior to removal after the patient is eating a regular diet.

C. **Bowel injury**

1. **Colon.** Because of the close proximity of the splenic flexure to the lower pole of the spleen, it is possible to injure the colon during mobilization, but this complication is rare. Mechanical bowel preparation is not indicated pre-operatively.

2. **Stomach.** Gastric injuries can occur by direct trauma or can result from thermal injury during division of the short gastric vessels. Use of energy devices too close to the greater curvature of the stomach can result in a delayed gastric necrosis and perforation.

D. **Diaphragmatic injury** has been described during the mobilization of the superior pole, especially with perisplenitis, and is of no consequence if recognized and repaired. In laparoscopic splenectomies, it may be more difficult to recognize the injury given the pneumoperitoneum, but careful dissection of the splenophrenic ligament can minimize its occurrence. The pleural space should be evacuated under positive-pressure ventilation prior to closure to minimize the pneumothorax.

II. EARLY POSTOPERATIVE COMPLICATIONS

A. **Pulmonary complications** develop in nearly 10% of patients after open splenectomy, and these range from atelectasis to pneumonia and pleural effusion. Pulmonary complications are significantly less common with the laparoscopic approach.

B. **Subphrenic abscess** occurs in 2% to 3% of patients after open splenectomy but is uncommon after laparoscopic splenectomy (0.7%). Treatment usually consists of percutaneous drainage and the intravenous antibiotics.

C. **Wound problems** such as hematomas, seromas, and wound infections occur commonly (4% to 5%) after open splenectomy because of the underlying hematologic disorders. Wound complications after laparoscopic splenectomy are usually minor and occur less frequently (1.5%).

D. **Thrombocytosis and thrombotic complications** can occur after either open or laparoscopic splenectomy. The presumed causes of thrombosis after splenectomy may relate to the occurrence of thrombocytosis, alterations in platelet function, and a low-flow stasis phenomenon in the ligated splenic vein. As a result, splenomegaly is a major risk factor for splenic/portal vein thrombosis. Symptomatic portal vein thrombosis occurs more commonly than expected (8% to 10%) and can result in extensive mesenteric thrombosis if not recognized promptly and treated expeditiously. Symptoms of portal vein thrombosis may be subtle and include abdominal pain and low-grade fever. Massive splenomegaly and myelofibrosis are the two main risk factors for portal vein thrombosis.

E. **Ileus** can occur after open splenectomy, but a prolonged postoperative ileus should prompt the surgeon to search for concomitant problems such as a subphrenic abscess or portal vein thrombosis (*Surgery.* 2003;134:647–553; discussion 54–55).

III. LATE POSTOPERATIVE COMPLICATIONS

A. **Overwhelming postsplenectomy infection (OPSI)** is an uncommon complication of splenectomy that may occur at any point in an asplenic or hyposplenic patient's lifetime. The risk of overwhelming infection is very small with an estimated mortality of 0.73 per 1,000 patient years (*Ann Intern Med.* 1995;122:187–188). Patients present with nonspecific flu-like symptoms rapidly progressing to fulminant sepsis, consumptive coagulopathy, bacteremia, and ultimately death within 12 hours to 48 hours. Encapsulated bacteria, especially *Streptococcus pneumoniae, H. influenzae* type B, and *Neisseria meningitidis,* are the most commonly involved organisms. Successful treatment of OPSI requires early supportive care and high-dose third-generation cephalosporins. OPSI appears to have a higher incidence in children, particularly under the age of five. Daily prophylactic antibiotics have been recommended after operation in all children younger than 5 years and in immunocompromised patients because these patients are unlikely to produce adequate antibody in response to pneumococcal vaccination. All patients who have had splenectomy should be educated about the risk of OPSI, and the need for early physician consultation in the event that fever or other prodromal symptoms should occur.

B. **Splenosis** is the presence of disseminated intra-abdominal splenic tissue, which usually occurs after splenic rupture. Splenosis does not appear to be more common after laparoscopic splenectomy, but care should be taken during splenic morcellation to avoid bag rupture and spillage of splenic tissue.

17 Cerebrovascular Disease and Vascular Access

Abdulhameed Aziz and Gregorio A. Sicard

EXTRACRANIAL CEREBROVASCULAR DISEASE

Atherosclerotic occlusive disease of the extracranial carotid artery is a major risk factor for stroke, the primary cause of disability, and the third-most-common cause of death in the United States. More than 700,000 new strokes occur annually, with an estimated total cost of more than $40 billion. The initial mortality from stroke is approximately 30%. Of patients who survive the initial event, 10% recover almost completely, 30% recover with mild deficits, and 60% recover with significant deficits. Furthermore, 25% of survivors have stroke within 5 years. Carotid bifurcation disease is responsible for 25% to 35% of ipsilateral cerebrovascular events.

I. PRESENTATION

  A. The clinical presentation of patients with symptomatic occlusive disease is a **neurologic deficit.** However, many patients have an asymptomatic stenosis that is identified by a health-care provider based on auscultation of carotid bruits or screening Doppler study.
  B. **Lateralizing ischemic events** can result in aphasia (expressive or receptive), combined sensory and motor deficits, and various visual disturbances. Deficits such as these are usually associated with the anterior cerebral circulation [i.e., the internal carotid artery (ICA) and its branches].
    1. Transient ischemic attacks (TIAs) are transient hemispheric neurologic deficits that may last from several seconds to hours but fewer than 24 hours. TIAs that occur in rapid succession, interspersed with complete recovery but with progressively smaller intervals between attacks, are termed **crescendo TIAs** and carry a high risk of progression to a permanent neurologic deficit; emergent evaluation is mandatory.
    2. **Amaurosis fugax** (temporary monocular blindness), often described as a shade coming down over one eye, results from emboli lodging in the ophthalmic artery. Fundoscopic examination demonstrates Hollenhorst plaques.
    3. If the neurologic deficit persists beyond 24 hours, it is considered a **stroke.** In addition, some patients may present with a neurologic deficit that fluctuates, gradually worsening over a period of hours or days while the patient is under observation. This situation is considered a stroke in evolution and, like crescendo TIAs, needs prompt treatment.

C. Global ischemic events are manifested by symptoms such as vertigo, dizziness, perioral numbness, ataxia, or drop attacks. These are usually associated with interruption of posterior circulation supplying the brain stem (i.e., the vertebrobasilar system).

II. PATHOPHYSIOLOGY AND EPIDEMIOLOGY.
Ischemic events in patients with extracranial vascular disease can be the result of emboli or a low-flow state. Although it can cause clinical symptoms, disease of the vertebral arteries typically remains asymptomatic. On the other hand, even when it is asymptomatic, significant occlusive carotid arterial disease carries with it a doubling of baseline stroke risk. Once a significant carotid lesion results in an ipsilateral lateralizing cerebral event, the risk of stroke may be as high as 26% over 2 years.

III. DIAGNOSIS.
A careful neurologic examination is performed before obtaining any diagnostic studies. The presence of a carotid bruit warrants diagnostic evaluation. Imaging of the carotid arterial system attempts to classify the degree of stenosis, which is useful for determining prognosis. Because of methodologic differences in calculating the percentage of stenosis encountered in different studies, there is some disagreement about exact cutoff percentages. However, four levels of stenosis are typically described: mild (<50%), moderate (50% to 79%), severe (80% to 99%), and occluded (100%). A variety of noninvasive and invasive diagnostic studies are available.

A. **Color-flow duplex scanning** uses real-time B-mode ultrasound and color-enhanced pulsed Doppler flow measurements to determine the extent of the carotid stenosis. **This is the initial screening test for carotid disease.** The reliability of this study depends in large part on the abilities of the vascular technicians. When using an accredited vascular laboratory, treatment of most carotid lesions can be instituted based on ultrasound duplex scanning alone.

B. **Arteriography** remains the gold standard for the diagnosis of cerebrovascular disease. Unlike duplex scanning, however, arteriography is an invasive procedure with inherent risks, such as contrast allergy, renal toxicity, and stroke (2% to 4% of patients). Because of these risks and improvements in duplex ultrasonography, carotid arteriography is generally limited to patients with technically inadequate duplex ultrasonography, planning for carotid artery stenting (CAS), or for verification of carotid occlusion.

C. **Magnetic resonance angiography (MRA)** and **Computed tomographic angiography (CTA)** are reliable means of supplementary imaging but remain inferior to conventional angiography. Both have advantages of being noninvasive. Limitations of MRA include the appearance of lumen smaller than actual diameter, but with improvement after administration of gadolinium. CTA can be performed with excellent three-dimensional reconstructions but carries the risk of contrast-induced nephropathy. For patients with complete occlusion and contralateral high-grade occlusion, results of duplex ultrasound are often confirmed by CTA or angiography.

IV. MANAGEMENT

A. **Medical therapy.** It is important to make every effort to modify risk factors to prevent progression of carotid occlusive disease. Control of hypertension, cessation of smoking, management of lipid disorders, attainment of ideal body weight, and regular exercise should be undertaken. No drug therapy has been shown to reduce the risk of stroke in patients with asymptomatic carotid disease. Medical management in symptomatic patients is focused primarily on the use of antiplatelet agents, specifically aspirin. Aspirin is effective in reducing stroke and stroke-related deaths. In a meta-analysis of more than 8,000 patients, the risk of major vascular events was reduced by 22% in patients receiving aspirin (*Br Med J.* 1988;296:320). Low doses (81 mg/day) are as efficacious as higher doses (325 mg/day). Clopidogrel (Plavix) is a potent antiplatelet agent, but it has not been evaluated as part of medical therapy compared to carotid endarterectomy (CEA). Anticoagulation with heparin sodium is beneficial in patients who have cardiac emboli. In addition, heparin may be useful in preventing progression of thrombus in evolving nonhemorrhagic strokes. The major contraindication to heparinization is a recent hemorrhagic brain infarct; therefore, a CT scan of the brain should be obtained before heparin is given.

B. **Surgical/endovascular management** is the treatment of choice for extracranial cerebrovascular disease and has been documented to reduce stroke.

1. **Indications** for CEA have been extensively studied in both asymptomatic and symptomatic patients, comparing surgical treatment to best medical therapy. Two commonly cited studies include the Asymptomatic Carotid Atherosclerosis Study (ACAS) (*JAMA.* 1995;273:1421) and the North American Symptomatic Carotid Endarterectomy Trial (NASCET) (*NEJM.* 1991;325:445). In the ACAS trial, the ipsilateral 5-year stroke rate in asymptomatic patients with at least 60% stenosis was 5.1% in patients undergoing a CEA versus 11% receiving best medical therapy. For symptomatic patients with at least 70% stenosis in the NASCET trial, the 2-year ipsilateral stroke rate was 9% versus 26% in the CEA and best medical therapy groups, respectively. Based largely on these two definitive trials, current indications for CEA include the following:

   a. **Asymptomatic patients with greater than 70% stenosis.**

   b. **Symptomatic patients with greater than 50% stenosis.**

   c. **Symptomatic patients with greater than 50% stenosis** who have an **ulcerated lesion** or whose **symptoms persist** while they are on **aspirin** or other antiplatelet therapy.

   d. **Selected patients with stroke in evolution.** Surgery is performed to restore normal blood flow to allow recovery of ischemic brain tissue that is nonfunctional yet metabolically alive. Surgical candidates have mild-to-moderate neurologic defects and no evidence of hemorrhage on CT scan. The timing of surgery in these cases is controversial.

   e. **Selected patients with completed strokes.** Interventions in these patients are performed in the hope of reducing stroke recurrence, which is 7% to 8% per year with nonsurgical therapy. Candidates for surgery include patients with a mild deficit and (1) greater than 70% stenosis or (2) greater than 50% stenosis and an ulcerated plaque, and patients with a moderate deficit and a lesion greater than 70% with an occluded contralateral carotid artery. The timing of surgery in these cases is debatable; however, surgery traditionally has been delayed to reduce the risk of perioperative hemorrhagic stroke. A prudent approach is to wait 4 to 6 weeks postinfarction to minimize the risk of intracranial hemorrhage.

    f. Rarely, endarterectomy is performed on patients with **completely occluded carotid arteries.** Candidates for surgery include those who have:

       (1) Recent endarterectomy with immediate postoperative thrombosis.

       (2) Bruit disappears under observation while remaining asymptomatic.

       (3) Recent occlusion with fluctuating or progressive symptoms.

       (4) New internal carotid occlusion that can be operated on within 2 to 4 hours of the onset of symptoms.

2. **CEA** has been performed for more than 50 years and is the most commonly performed vascular operation. A beneficial outcome depends on meticulous technique. The use of such technique can keep the perioperative adverse event rate (stroke and death) below 3%.

    a. **Anesthesia** for CEA can be general endotracheal anesthesia, regional cervical block, or local anesthesia. The choice of anesthesia depends on a combination of patient factors and surgeon expertise. No single method of anesthesia has been demonstrated superior.

    b. During **exposure and mobilization** of the common carotid artery (CCA) and its branches, it is important to proceed with gentle dissection and minimal manipulation of the carotid bulb to prevent embolization from the atherosclerotic plaque.

    c. After **systemic heparinization** of the patient, the internal, external, and common carotid arteries are clamped, and a longitudinal arteriotomy is made from just proximal to the plaque in the CCA to just beyond the distal extent of the plaque in the ICA.

    d. Placement of tubing to **shunt** blood from the CCA around the operative field to the ICA during endarterectomy is a controversial practice. Adequate cerebral perfusion without shunting occurs in 85% to 90% of patients. Intraoperative neurologic assessment of the awake patient under local anesthesia can be as simple as having the patient squeeze a noise toy in the contralateral hand and answering a few simple questions after carotid occlusion. **Awake assessment** is the most sensitive and specific method of determining the need for shunt placement (*J Vasc Surg.* 2007;45:511). Patients who develop weakness or changes in mental status should be shunted. For patients under general anesthesia, an alternative method of cerebral perfusion is required, although some surgeons simply choose routinely to shunt these patients. Stump pressure and intraoperative electroencephalogram (EEG) monitoring are commonly used alternative methods for the determination of cerebral perfusion and subsequent need for shunting. Shunting can be performed safely without an increased risk of stroke (*Ann Vasc Surg.* 2006;20:482).

    e. The **plaque** is carefully separated from the media and removed. The CEA is closed using a running suture. A Cochrane review of patch angioplasty (venous or synthetic) shows that it is associated with a significantly reduced risk for perioperative ipsilateral arterial occlusion and decreased restenosis during long-term follow-up (*Cochrane Database Syst Rev.* 2009 Oct 7;(4) CD000160) Determining differences in the material for patch angioplasty requires further study.

f. Postoperative care

    (1) Immediately after endarterectomy, **neurologic function and blood pressure (BP) alterations** should be monitored. Hypertension and hypotension are common after endarterectomy and may cause neurologic complications. The extremes of BP should be treated with either sodium nitroprusside or phenylephrine (Neo-Synephrine) to keep the systolic BP between 140 and 160 mm Hg (slightly higher in chronically hypertensive patients). The wound should be examined for hematoma formation. Aspirin is resumed in the immediate postoperative period. Some advocate the use of dextran-40 (up to 20 mL/kg/day for up to 72 hours) as an additional antithrombotic agent, which can be started intraoperatively and continued into the early postoperative period.

    (2) Patient follow-up. A baseline duplex scan is obtained 3 months after the procedure and again at 12 months. Patients can then be followed yearly. Patients who can tolerate aspirin are given 325 mg/day.

g. Complications

    (1) Stroke rates must be low (3%) to make operative management of cerebrovascular disease reasonable, especially in asymptomatic patients.

    (2) Myocardial infarction (MI) remains the most common cause of death in the early postoperative period. As many as 25% of patients who undergo endarterectomy have severe, correctable coronary artery lesions. The timing of coronary intervention relative to CEA is under debate.

    (3) Cranial nerve injuries occur in 5% to 10% of patients who undergo CEA. The most commonly injured nerve is the marginal mandibular, followed by the recurrent laryngeal, superior laryngeal, and hypoglossal nerves.

    (4) Recurrent carotid stenosis has been reported to occur in 5% to 10% of cases, although symptoms are present in fewer than 3%. Two types of lesions have been characterized. Neointimal hyperplasia may occur early (within 2 to 3 years). Recurrent atherosclerosis also may cause restenosis (typically after 3 years at the bifurcation site). The presence of symptoms is an indication for treatment of a recurrent lesion. Frequently, these lesions do not lend themselves to endarterectomy and are best treated by CAS.

3. Carotid artery stenting

    a. The **indications** for CAS are the same as those for a CEA; however, this technique is under intense investigation. Several studies have been completed or are underway to examine the efficacy of CAS compared to CEA, particularly in high-risk patients. Outcomes have varied, especially as device technology and operator experience has improved. The CREST (Carotid Revascularization Endarterectomy v. Stenting Trial) randomly assigned patients with symptomatic or asymptomatic carotid stenosis to undergo carotid artery stenting or CEA. This trial showed the risk of stroke, MI, or death did not differ significantly in the group undergoing CAS and the group undergoing CEA. During the periprocedural period, there was a higher risk of stroke with stenting and a higher risk of MI with endarterectomy (*NEJM.* 2010;363:11–23).

(1) Because CEA is well tolerated and has a very low risk of complications, CAS is commonly reserved for **high-risk patients,** including patients with the following conditions:

(a) Severe cardiac disease.

(b) Severe chronic obstructive pulmonary disease (COPD).

(c) Severe renal insufficiency or end-stage renal disease (ESRD) requiring hemodialysis.

(d) Prior ipsilateral neck surgery.

(e) Prior neck radiation.

(f) Contralateral vocal cord paralysis.

(g) Surgically inaccessible lesion.

(2) **Relative contraindications** to CAS include the following:

(a) Severe tortuosity of common and ICA.

(b) Complex aortic arch anatomy (increasing difficulty as great vessels arise from ascending rather than transverse aortic arch).

(c) Severe calcification or extensive thrombus formation.

(d) Near-complete or complete occlusion.

b. CAS has evolved and is commonly performed in the following basic steps. Meticulous technique is critical for reducing the incidence of stroke. Special attention must be taken to avoid catheter and wire manipulation of the lesion prior to cerebral protection device deployment and to ensuring removal of all air bubbles within the angiography tubing.

c. Embolization of plaque debris has been shown to occur with almost any endovascular manipulation of a carotid artery lesion. Consequently, **embolic protection devices** have been developed that significantly reduce the risk of stroke during CAS. The typical device used today is a filter-like device that is advanced across the lesion and then opened in the distal ICA prior to angioplasty and stent deployment. Flow reversal is created after balloon occlusion of the external carotid artery (ECA) and CCA, thus eliminating the need to cross the lesion and possibly decreasing the risk of stroke.

d. Complications

(1) **Embolic stroke** is the most common complication of CAS. Risk factors include lack of a cerebral protection device, long or multiple lesions, and age older than 80 years. Thrombolysis may be a successful treatment option, especially if the source of emboli is an acute thrombus. When an embolus is composed of atheroma or chronic thrombus, however, mechanical removal of emboli may become necessary to restore flow.

(2) **Hemodynamic instability** may occur during manipulation and angioplasty of the carotid bifurcation. Bradycardia should be anticipated and treated with atropine prior to dilation of the carotid bifurcation. Postoperatively, as with CEA, patients should be monitored to avoid extremes of BP.

(3) **Restenosis** occurs in approximately 5% of patients at 12 to 24 months and is typically secondary to intimal hyperplasia. These lesions are often amenable to repeat angioplasty.

e. Follow-up using duplex ultrasound is important to identify patients with restenosis and is usually performed at baseline following CAS and then at 3, 6, and 12 months and every year thereafter. Significant elevation of peak systolic velocity from baseline should prompt further evaluation with angiography.

VASCULAR ACCESS FOR DIALYSIS

The success of hemodialysis depends on the rate of blood flow through the dialyzer. Flow rates of between 350 and 450 mL/minute are required to provide adequate dialysis within a reasonable time frame (3 to 4 hours). The dialysis access is a port or site in the body that provides the necessary blood flow for dialysis. The access should be easy to cannulate and last for years with minimal maintenance. The incidence of complications, such as infection, stenosis, pseudoaneurysm formation, thrombosis, and outflow deterioration, should also be low. To date, no vascular access fulfills all of these criteria.

I. INDICATIONS

A. **Temporary hemodialysis access** provided with short- or intermediate-term central venous access device (CVAD) is indicated when acute short-term dialysis is needed, as in (1) acute renal failure, (2) overdose or intoxication, (3) ESRD needing urgent hemodialysis without available mature access, (4) peritoneal dialysis patients with peritonitis, and (5) transplant recipients needing temporary hemodialysis during severe rejection episodes.

B. **Permanent hemodialysis access** is created using subcutaneous conduits having high blood flows when long-term hemodialysis is needed, as in (1) long-term treatment of chronic renal failure and (2) patients awaiting renal transplantation.

II. DIALYSIS ACCESS CATHETERS

A. **Nontunneled central venous catheters.** Short-term dialysis access includes percutaneous catheters in internal jugular, subclavian, or femoral veins. The **Quinton catheter** provides access for short-term hemodialysis in acute renal failure. Noncuffed, double-lumen catheters can be percutaneously inserted at the bedside and provide acceptable blood flow rates (250 mL/minute) for temporary hemodialysis – no more than 3 weeks for internal jugular or 5 days for femoral catheters due to considerations of infection and dislodgement.

B. Tunneled central venous silicone dialysis catheters. Tunneled catheters [e.g., **Tesio, Ash Split** (Bard Access Systems) and **Duraflow catheters** (AngioDynamics)] have cuffs that anchor them to the subcutaneous tissues. Tunneled, cuffed venous catheters should be placed preferentially in the right internal jugular vein because this site offers a more direct route to the cavoatrial junction and a lower risk of complications than other potential catheter insertion sites. Advantages of tunneled catheters include the ability to insert into a variety of sites, no maturation time requirement, no hemodynamic consequences, ease and cost of catheter placement and replacement, and a life span of the access of months to years. Disadvantages of tunneled, cuffed venous catheters include potential morbidity due to thrombosis, infection, risk of permanent central venous stenosis or occlusion, and lower blood flow rates than for atrioventricular grafts and fistulas.

C. Catheter complications

1. **Early dysfunction** usually occurs secondary to either malposition or intracatheter thrombosis. Almost all catheters inserted into a central vein develop a fibrin sleeve after insertion, resulting in **late dysfunction.** They are usually clinically silent until they obstruct the ports at the distal end of the catheter. They also serve as a nidus for infection.

2. **Central vein stenosis, thrombosis, or stricture.** Central vein stenosis arises from endothelial injury at the site of catheter–endothelial contact. Incidence increases with the use of nonsilicone catheters, with the use of a subclavian approach, and with a history of prior catheter-related infections. Removal of the CVAD may not improve the underlying problem and, by definition, sacrifices the access. Systemic anticoagulation remains the primary therapy.

III. ARTERIOVENOUS (AV) ACCESS NOMENCLATURE

A. Conduit. An **autogenous AV access** (also known as an **AV fistula,** a **native vein fistula,** and a **primary fistula**) is an access created by connecting a native vein to an adjacent artery. A **nonautogenous AV access** (also known as an **AV graft** or a **graft fistula**) uses grafts that are either synthetic or biologic. **Synthetic grafts** include expanded polytetrafluoroethylene (ePTFE, e.g., Gore-Tex or Impra) and polyester (e.g., Dacron) grafts. **Biologic grafts** include bovine heterografts, human umbilical veins, and cryopreserved allogeneic human vein grafts.

B. Configuration. A **direct access** often connects a native vein to an adjacent artery. An **indirect access** uses an autogenous or prosthetic material placed subcutaneously between the artery and vein. The course of the subcutaneous prosthesis may be **looped** (loop graft) or **straight** (straight graft).

IV. PREOPERATIVE EVALUATION

A. Timing. Ideally, any patient with renal insufficiency should be referred for surgical evaluation approximately 1 year before the anticipated need for dialysis. This point is reached when the creatinine clearance is less than

25 mL/minute or the serum creatinine rises above 4 mg/dL. This allows ample opportunity for appropriate access planning, and efforts can be instituted to ensure preservation of the native veins for later AV fistula creation.

B. **Preservation of access sites.** All ESRD patients should protect their forearm veins from venipuncture and intravenous catheters. Likewise, hospital staff should be instructed to avoid damaging these essential veins. The nondominant arm is preferred for initial access creation. Subclavian vein cannulation should be avoided at all costs because this may induce central venous stenosis, which could preclude later use of an entire arm.

C. **History.** A detailed assessment for the presence of peripheral vascular disease, diabetes mellitus, cardiopulmonary disease, and coagulation disorders best determines the type of vascular access needed for a particular patient. Any conditions that suggest stenosis or occlusion of the venous or arterial system should be elicited because these may limit options for dialysis access. These include prior central venous line; transvenous pacemaker; previous surgery; trauma; or radiation treatment to the chest, neck, or arm. Evidence of early cardiac dysfunction or volume overload indicates a patient at risk for congestive heart failure following fistula creation due to increased preload. Comorbid conditions that limit life expectancy, such as severe coronary artery disease or malignancy, may render a cuffed catheter the best option.

D. **Physical examination**

1. **Pulse examination.** The axillary, brachial, radial, and ulnar artery pulses are carefully palpated in both upper extremities, and, when indicated, the femoral, popliteal, and pedal arteries are palpated. Residual scars from previous central venous catheters or surgery should also be carefully assessed.

2. **Cardiovascular status.** Evaluation involves determining capillary refill, the presence of edema, unequal extremity size, and collateral veins on the chest wall. A tourniquet, gravity, and gentle percussion are used to distend the forearm and upper arm veins. Their patency and continuity can be addressed by palpation and detection of a fluid thrill.

3. **Segmental BP measurements.** Discrepancies between the two upper extremities should be noted.

4. **Allen test.** This is intended to assess the integrity of the palmar circulatory arches and allow assessment of the dominant blood supply to the hand.

E. **Duplex ultrasound scanning** can determine the diameter of the artery and the adequacy of the superficial and deep veins. For venous evaluation, tourniquets are placed on the patient's midforearm and upper arm. Details of the venous lumen, such as webs, sclerosis, and occlusion, can be visualized. Doppler venous studies may also identify suitable veins for AV fistula creation that are not readily visible on the surface anatomy, especially in heavier patients.

F. **Diagnostic imaging.** History or physical findings suggestive of central venous stenosis or previous complicated vascular access warrant further diagnostic imaging.

1. **Contrast venography** is the gold standard for determining the patency and adequacy of the superficial and deep venous systems, particularly the central veins.

2. **Conventional arteriography** also remains the gold standard for the evaluation of a suspected arterial inflow stenosis or occlusion. When in doubt as to the adequacy of the donor artery or the runoff, it is advisable to obtain an arteriogram that shows the entire arterial system from the origin of the subclavian artery to the distal branches. **MRA** can also be used for the same purpose and is particularly useful when severe contrast allergy, vascular disease, or poor renal function precludes arteriography.

G. **Laboratory studies.** Hyperkalemia and acidosis are the most common electrolyte abnormalities seen in ESRD patients. Therefore, preoperative testing should include evaluation of serum electrolytes and glucose to avoid possible procedural or anesthesia-related complications.

V. NATIVE VEIN AV FISTULAS

A. **Characteristics.** Native vein fistulas are created by connecting a vein to the adjacent artery, usually the radial or brachial artery. These are the safest and longest-lasting permanent means of vascular access, with the highest 5-year patency rates and minimum requirements for intervention. Disadvantages include a long maturation time of weeks to months to provide a flow state adequate to sustain dialysis. Revision of the outflow vein and hand exercises to increase flow to the extremity can accelerate fistula maturation. The patient's arterial and venous anatomy remains the most significant limitation because diseased vessels (e.g., due to diabetes or atherosclerosis) can hinder normal maturation or may preclude the creation of a fistula altogether. Of the ESRD population in the United States, approximately 30% have AV fistulas as their permanent dialysis access (*Kidney Int.* 2000;58:2178). The Kidney Disease Outcomes Quality Initiative (K/DOQI) guidelines recommend a 50% fistula placement rate for first-time access in ESRD patients.

B. **Location.** The Brescia–Cimino fistula at the wrist (creating an end-to-side anastomosis between the cephalic vein and radial artery) and the Gratz fistula at the elbow (i.e., anastomosing the cephalic vein to the brachial artery) are the two most commonly performed autogenous AV fistulas. Flow of arterial blood under pressure distends the outflow vein to produce the subcutaneous conduit. Peripheral sites should be used first, moving to more-central sites as the former sites fail.

C. **Construction.** Most procedures can be performed on an outpatient basis, using only conscious sedation administered intravenously and local anesthetics. The end of a superficial vein, usually the cephalic, is anastomosed to the side of the artery. A side-to-side anastomosis can result in venous hypertension and swelling in the distal extremity due to higher venous pressures. An end-to-end anastomosis performed in a radial artery fistula has the advantage of providing limited flow, thereby reducing a hypercirculatory state. The disadvantage is that the anastomosis is technically challenging and carries the risk of hand ischemia. This risk is particularly high in elderly and diabetic patients. The length (diameter) of the anastomosis dictates the blood flow in fistulas based on larger arteries (e.g., the brachial artery), making it an important determinant in the development of vascular steal symptoms in distal extremity.

VI. AV GRAFT

A. **Characteristics.** AV grafts consist of biologic or synthetic conduits that connect an artery and a vein and are tunneled under the skin and placed in a subcutaneous location. PTFE allows ingrowth of host tissue and formation of a pseudointimal lining, which resists infection and self-seals after needle puncture. The advantages of AV grafts over AV fistulas include (1) large surface area, (2) easy cannulation, (3) short maturation time, and (4) easy surgical handling. However, the long-term patency of AV grafts remains inferior to that of AV fistulas, despite a fourfold increase in salvage procedures. Synthetic grafts require 3 to 6 weeks before they can be used; this period allows sufficient time for the material to incorporate into the surrounding subcutaneous tissues and for the inflammation and edema to subside.

B. **Location.** AV grafts are typically placed between the brachial artery and the cephalic or brachial vein in the antecubital fossa and arranged in a loop configuration in the forearm. Upper-arm grafts can also be created between the brachial artery and basilic or axillary veins. When all upper-extremity sites are exhausted, attention is turned to the lower extremity, where loop grafts typically connect the superficial femoral artery and femoral or saphenous veins.

C. **Placement.** AV grafts are placed under local anesthesia with conscious sedation. Prophylactic antibiotics (e.g., second-generation cephalosporins) are commonly administered immediately prior to the surgery.

VII. COMPLICATIONS OF AV ACCESS

A. **Stenosis.** Pseudointimal hyperplasia within a synthetic graft or neointimal hyperplasia in a native AV fistula or outflow vein of a graft constitutes the most common cause of dysfunction. Approximately 85% of graft thromboses result from hemodynamically significant stenosis (*J Vasc Surg.* 1997;26:373). Arterial inflow lesions are less common but can lead to low flow as well as elevated recirculation, making it more difficult to distinguish them from outflow lesions. Elevated venous pressures, increased recirculation, or recurrent thrombosis necessitate a fistulogram and treatment of any underlying lesion(s) by angioplasty or surgical revision. Stenoses in long segments (>30% after angioplasty) or those that recur within a short interval require surgical intervention.

B. **Thrombosis.** Thrombosis occurring within a month of placement is often due to anatomic or technical factors, such as a narrow outflow vein, misplaced suture, or graft kinking. Early thrombosis of native vein fistulas often results in permanent loss of the access. Prolonged hypotension during and after dialysis occasionally precipitates thrombosis, as can trauma from needle puncture or excessive compression after needle removal following hemostasis.

By 24 months, 96% of grafts require thrombectomy, angioplasty, or surgical revision. Prosthetic AV shunt thrombosis can be managed by pharmacologic thrombolysis, mechanical maceration, or surgical thrombectomy, either separately or in combination. Fistulography at the time of treatment usually reveals the precipitating cause, allowing immediate intervention. Surgical thrombectomy should be followed by fistulography to detect stenosis not fully appreciable during standard balloon thrombectomy. The rate of secondary graft patency after intervention reaches only 65% at 1 year and 51% at 2 years (*Am J Kidney Dis.* 2000;36:68).

C. **Infection.** Infection and bacteremia in dialysis patients are usually caused by *Staphylococcus aureus*. The type of access constitutes the major risk factor for infection. AV fistula infections usually respond to a prolonged course (6 weeks) of antibiotic therapy. If septic embolization occurs, the fistula should be revised or taken down. AV graft infections occur in approximately 5% to 20% prosthetics placed and present a more challenging problem. Antibiotic treatment should cover Gram-positive organisms (including enterococci) as well as Gram-negative organisms (e.g., *Escherichia coli*). A superficial skin infection not involving the graft may respond to antibiotics alone. Focal graft infections can be salvaged with resection of the infected portion of the graft, but extensive infections and those that involve newly constructed, unincorporated grafts should be managed with complete excision. Evidence of bacteremia, pseudoaneurysm formation, or local hemorrhage should prompt graft removal, with placement of a new access at a different site.

D. **Pseudoaneurysm formation.** Pseudoaneurysms result from destruction of the vessel wall and replacement by biophysically inferior collagenous tissue, usually after repetitive puncture of the same vessel segment. A downstream stenosis predisposes to upstream aneurysm formation. Major complications include rupture, infection (which is promoted by intra-aneurysmal thrombus), and, rarely, antegrade or retrograde embolization. Prior to any intervention, imaging is indispensable for identification of thrombus and assessment of the venous anastomosis and outflow. Aneurysmal dilations of AV fistulae often can be treated by surgical correction, including partial or complete resection of the aneurysmal sac, repair of accompanying stenoses, and reconstruction of an adequate lumen. Aneurysm in an AV graft calls for replacement of the weakened graft segment.

E. **Arterial "steal" syndrome.** All AV accesses divert or "steal" blood from the distal circulation to a certain extent. A clinical syndrome resulting from this decrease in distal circulation occurs when the various local compensatory mechanisms fail; this syndrome is reported to occur in approximately 1% to 4% of patients with distal AV accesses (*Ann Vasc Surg.* 2000;14(2):138–144). The clinical presentations of arterial insufficiency in the tissues distal to the fistula may include ischemic pain, neuropathy, ulceration, and gangrene. Patients with diabetes, prior AV access, or atherosclerotic disease are at a higher risk. Patients with mild ischemia complain of subjective coldness and paresthesias without sensory or motor loss and can be managed expectantly with increasing exercise tolerance. Failure of these symptoms to improve may require surgical correction with banding or ligation. Severe ischemia requires immediate surgical intervention to avoid irreversible nerve injury.

F. **Venous hypertension.** Venous hypertension can be caused by the presence or development of outflow vein obstruction. It manifests as swelling, skin discoloration, and hyperpigmentation in the access limb. In chronic cases, ulceration and pain may develop. Management consists of correction of stenosis and disconnecting the veins that are responsible for retrograde flow and pressure transmission.

G. **Congestive heart failure.** Venous return to the heart, cardiac output, and myocardial work can significantly increase after AV fistula or graft placement, leading to cardiomegaly and congestive heart failure in some patients. Hypercirculation ensues if the outflow resistance is too low and the anastomosis is too wide. This problem is more common with ePTFE grafts and brachial artery fistulas. Correction involves narrowing the proximal shunt or graft with either a prosthetic band or suture ligature. Occasionally, a new access must be constructed using a smaller-diameter conduit or tapered prosthetic material.

VIII. VASCULAR ACCESS MONITORING

A. **Angiography** (fistulogram) remains the gold standard for the evaluation of access problems. However, the need for frequent evaluations and the invasive nature of angiography prevent it from being a practical option for routine surveillance.

B. **Doppler ultrasound** measures access flow and correlates with the presence and severity of stenoses detected by angiography. Blood flow below a critical level (350 mL/minute) or a reduction in flow over time (>15%) predicts the presence of stenosis and the development of thrombosis.

18 Thoracoabdominal Vascular Diseases

Enjae Jung, Jeffrey Jim, and Luis A. Sanchez

The vast majority of vascular diseases are secondary to atherosclerotic changes of the arterial wall, influenced to a degree by genetic predisposition and age. However, the evolution of the disease for most individuals can be modified by changes in environmental factors, particularly diet, smoking, and exercise. The arterial wall is comprised of the intimal, medial, and adventitial layers. Endothelium lines the intima. The media contains layers of smooth muscle cells and an extracellular matrix (ECM) of elastin, collagen, and proteoglycans. The adventitia is made of loose connective tissue and fibroblasts. An arterial aneurysm is a weakness of the arterial wall resulting in a permanent localized dilation greater than 50% of the normal vessel diameter. All three layers are dilated, but the majority of degeneration occurs in the media. Occlusive arterial disease, on the other hand, is caused by atherosclerotic change of the intima.

I. **ABDOMINAL AORTIC ANEURYSMS (AAAs)** are the most common type of arterial aneurysm, occurring in 3 to 9% of people older than 50 years of age in the Western world (*Br J Surg.* 1998;85:155). They are five times more common in men than in women and 3.5 times more common in whites than in African Americans. In the United States, ruptured AAAs are the 15th leading cause of death overall and the 10th leading cause of death in men older than 55 years, a rate that has held steady for the past two decades despite improvements in operative technique and perioperative management.

A. **Pathophysiology.** Ninety percent of AAAs are believed to be degenerative in origin, whereas 5% are inflammatory and the remainder are idiopathic (*J Vasc Surg.* 2003;38:584). AAAs are strongly associated with older age, smoking, white race, positive family history, hypertension (HTN), hyperlipidemia, and emphysema. Familial clustering of AAAs has been noted in 15% to 25% of patients undergoing aneurysm surgery. The risk of rupture correlates with wall tension in accordance with Laplace's law, such that the risk of aneurysm rupture increases exponentially with aneurysm diameter. Majority of AAAs are infrarenal; 25% involve the iliac arteries, and 2% involve the renal or other visceral arteries (*J Cardiovasc Surg.* 1991;32:636). Fourteen percent are associated with peripheral (e.g., femoral or popliteal) aneurysms (*J Vasc Surg.* 2000;31:863).

B. **Diagnosis**

1. **Clinical manifestations.** Seventy-five percent of AAAs are asymptomatic and are found incidentally. Aneurysm expansion or rupture may cause severe back, flank, or abdominal pain and varying degrees of

3. Complications from open AAA repair

   a. Arrhythmia, myocardial ischemia, or infarction may occur.

   b. Intraoperative hemorrhage can be reduced by clamping the aorta proximal to the aneurysm and the iliac arteries distally. Once the aneurysm is opened, retrograde bleeding from lumbar arteries must be controlled rapidly with transfixing ligatures. Blood should be salvaged in the operating room and autotransfused to the patient.

   c. Aortic unclamping is often associated with hypotension initially due to a sudden decrease in systemic vascular resistance, as well as release of previously sequestered vasodilatory metabolites back into the systemic circulation from the recently reperfused tissues. Thus, management of resuscitation, electrolytes, and pressors is critically important during this step.

   d. Renal insufficiency may be related to the use of intravenous contrast, inadequate hydration, hypotension, renal ischemic from a period of aortic clamping above the renal arteries, or embolization of the renal arteries.

   e. Lower-extremity ischemia may result from embolism or thrombosis, especially in emergency operations for which heparin might not be used. Embolism to the lower extremities can be prevented by minimizing manipulation of the aneurysm prior to clamping and by reperfusing the hypogastric arteries prior to reperfusion of external iliac arteries at the time of unclamping. Use of a Fogarty balloon catheter to remove distal emboli from lower-extremity vessels is indicated when leg ischemia is identified in the operating room.

   f. Microemboli arising from atherosclerotic debris can cause cutaneous ischemia (trash foot), which is usually treated expectantly as long as the major vessels are patent. Amputation may be required if significant necrosis results.

   g. Gastrointestinal complications consist of prolonged paralytic ileus, anorexia, periodic constipation, or diarrhea. This problem is diminished by using the left retroperitoneal approach. A more serious complication, ischemic colitis of the sigmoid colon, is related to ligation of the inferior mesenteric artery (IMA) in the absence of adequate collateral circulation. Symptoms include leukocytosis, significant fluid requirement in the first 8 to 12 hours postoperatively, fever, and peritoneal irritation. Diagnosis is confirmed by flexible sigmoidoscopy to 20 cm above the anal verge. Necrosis that is limited to the mucosa may be treated expectantly with intravenous antibiotics and bowel rest. Necrosis of the muscularis causes segmental strictures, which may require delayed segmental resection. Transmural necrosis requires immediate resection of necrotic colon and construction of an end colostomy.

   h. Paraplegia, a rare complication of infrarenal aneurysm surgery, may occur after repair of a ruptured AAA due to spinal cord ischemia. Supraceliac cross-clamping and prolonged hypotension increase the risk of paraplegia. Obliteration or embolization of important collateral flow to the spinal artery via the internal iliac arteries or an abnormally low origin of the accessory spinal artery (artery of Adamkiewicz) can result in paraplegia.

  i. **Sexual dysfunction** and retrograde ejaculation result from damage to the sympathetic plexus during dissection near the aortic bifurcation, especially around the proximal left common iliac artery.

E. **Endovascular management** of AAAs has dramatically decreased the acute morbidity of aneurysm surgery. It is important to note that the **indications** for endovascular treatment of AAA are no different than those for traditional open repair.

1. The most important **selection criterion** for endovascular treatment of an AAA is appropriate aortoiliac anatomy. Preoperative CT assessment includes the following factors:

   a. Length and diameter of nondilated and healthy infrarenal aorta (the neck). Commercially available devices allow treatment of a proximal neck between 10 and 15 mm long. The maximal aneurysm neck diameter that can be treated with standard devices is 32 mm.

   b. Angle between the neck and aneurysm. Significant angulation between the neck and adjacent aneurysm (≥60 degrees) makes proximal graft deployment technically difficult and is associated with a higher risk of treatment failure.

   c. Presence of intraluminal thrombus or significant calcification. Significant mural thrombus or atheroma in the proximal neck can prevent adequate sealing of an endograft and therefore represents a relative contraindication for endovascular treatment. Similarly, extensive calcification of the aortic neck also remains a relative contraindication.

   d. Shape of the aortic neck. The proximal neck segment geometry is also important in that a cone-shaped neck or reverse taper (i.e., widens more distally) may preclude adequate apposition of the endograft to the aortic wall.

   e. The most commonly used devices for endovascular repair are bifurcated endografts with limbs that extend into the bilateral iliac arteries. Iliac artery tortuosity, calcification, and luminal narrowing, in combination with the profile of the delivery system, are critical factors that play an important role in successful endograft delivery and deployment without complication.

   f. Patent aortic branches may influence the decision as to whether to proceed with endograft placement. A renal artery or large accessory renal artery arising from the proximal neck or the presence of a horseshoe kidney with multiple renal arteries is often a contraindication for endograft placement. Patent lumbar arteries arising from the aneurysm do not preclude endograft placement. A patent IMA associated with large mesenteric collaterals (e.g., meandering mesenteric artery) or a large patent IMA suggests abnormal mesenteric blood supply and risk of large-bowel ischemia with endograft coverage of the IMA orifice. Therefore, these vascular patterns are contraindications to endograft placement.

2. **Technique.** Endovascular devices are introduced retrograde through femoral arterial access. The most commonly utilized devices are

bifurcated and modular (consisting of two or more components) in design. Endografts typically have a full-length stent skeleton that maintains structural integrity and prevents graft kinking. Appropriate oversizing of stent grafts (by 10% to 15%) is based on preoperative assessment of arterial diameter to ensure adequate graft apposition to the aortic wall. If necessary, graft length can be tailored by means of overlapping extension segments in modular devices. The distal end of the iliac limbs is typically positioned proximal to the hypogastric orifices to maintain pelvic perfusion. Advanced endovascular (catheter and wire handling) skills are paramount to the success of endovascular aneurysm repair.

3. **Complications of endograft repairs of AAAs**

   a. Early complications include **branch occlusion, distal embolization, graft thrombosis, and arterial injury** (especially iliac artery avulsion at the iliac bifurcation in patients with small, calcified, diseased iliac arteries). These complications can often be corrected using endovascular techniques but may require emergent conversion to open repair.

   b. **Arterial dissection** may occur but this may not require additional treatment if the endograft spans the segment of dissection. Additional stents can be used to treat the dissected vessel if necessary.

   c. **Bowel ischemia** may occur postoperatively secondary to embolization or hypoperfusion, but this is rare compared to open surgical repair. **Renal dysfunction** may occur because of the nephrotoxicity of the contrast agent used for intraoperative angiography or because of direct injury due to embolization or renal artery occlusion.

   d. **Graft migration** occurs in 1% to 6% of patients, and is associated with challenging arterial anatomy and poor graft placement. This complication can typically be treated with secondary endovascular procedures.

   e. **Endoleak** is defined as failure to exclude the aneurysmal sac fully from arterial blood flow, potentially predisposing to rupture of the aneurysm sac (*J Endovasc Surg.* 1997;4:152). Management strategies for endoleaks discovered on follow-up imaging studies are evolving. For any endoleak that is associated with aneurysm sac enlargement, intervention is required. Endoleaks are usually corrected by endovascular means but may require conversion to open surgical repair.

      (1) In general, endoleaks from the proximal or distal attachment sites **(type I)** warrant intervention because they are frequently associated with increasing aneurysm sac size. Type I endoleaks may be sealed with angioplasty, or placement of a stent or endovascular graft component.

      (2) **Type II** endoleaks are due to collateral flow (IMA, lumbar arteries) and may be closely observed in the absence of aneurysm expansion. Type II endoleaks may be treated with embolization through collateral vessels (via the hypogastric artery for lumbar branch bleeding, via the superior mesenteric artery (SMA) for IMA bleeding) or directly through injection of the aneurysm sac via a translumbar approach, which is usually the most successful strategy.

(3) **Type III** endoleaks are caused by inadequate seal between graft components. They should be corrected as soon as they are diagnosed.

(4) **Type IV** endoleaks are due to porosity of the graft material. This is rare with newer generations of endografts.

4. **Results.** Relative to open surgical repair, endovascular treatment of AAA is associated with a reduction in perioperative morbidity, shorter duration of hospitalization (*J Vasc Surg.* 2003;37:262), and reduction in perioperative mortality (EVAR 1; *Lancet.* 2004;364:843–848; DREAM; *NEJM.* 2005;352:2398–2405). However, studies of long-term outcome comparing open versus endovascular repair have demonstrated similar rates of survival after 4 years (DREAM; *NEJM.* 2010;362:1881–1889; UK EVAR; *NEJM.* 2010;362:1863–1871). Close follow-up with CT scanning every 6 months initially and yearly after the first year is essential to maintaining long-term clinical success using this technique. Further advances in fenestrated and branched devices are allowing treatment of pararenal and other more complex AAAs.

II. THORACIC AORTIC ANEURYSMS (TAAs) are primarily a disease of the elderly. Ascending aortic aneurysms are most common (~60%) followed by aneurysms of the descending aorta (~35%) and of the transverse aortic arch (<10%). Most descending TAAs begin just distal to the orifice of left subclavian artery.

A. **Pathophysiology.** TAAs are divided into five main types: ascending, transverse, descending, thoracoabdominal, and traumatic. Ascending aortic aneurysms are usually caused by medial degeneration. Transverse, descending, and thoracoabdominal aortic aneurysms are related to atherosclerosis with HTN contributing to their expansion. Traumatic aneurysms are usually due to blunt injury to the chest.

B. **Diagnosis**

1. **Clinical manifestations** are usually absent; most nontraumatic TAAs are detected as incidental findings on chest imaging obtained for other purposes. A minority of patients may present with chest discomfort or pain that intensifies with aneurysm expansion or rupture, aortic valvular regurgitation, congestive heart failure, compression of adjacent structures (recurrent laryngeal nerve, left main-stem bronchus, esophagus, superior vena cava), erosion into adjacent structures (esophagus, lung, airway), or distal embolization.

2. **Radiologic evaluation. Chest x-ray** may reveal a widened mediastinum or an enlarged calcific aortic shadow. Traumatic aneurysms may be associated with skeletal fractures. **MR or CT imaging** with intravenous contrast provides precise estimation of the size and extent of aneurysms and facilitates surgical planning. **Echocardiography** may be useful in evaluating aneurysms involving the aortic arch. **Aortography** demonstrates the proximal and distal extent of the aneurysm and its relationship with aortic branch vessels arising from it.

C. **Surgical management** varies by type and location of the TAA. Repair of proximal arch aneurysms requires cardiopulmonary bypass and circulatory arrest. Preclotted woven polyethylene terephthalate (**Dacron**) is the graft of choice. Ascending and transverse arches are repaired through a median sternotomy incision. Descending and thoracoabdominal aneurysms are approached through a left posterolateral thoracotomy or thoracoabdominal incision. Intraoperative management of patients undergoing thoracotomy is facilitated by selective ventilation of the right lung using a double-lumen endobronchial tube. Cerebrospinal fluid drainage during and after surgery for descending and thoracoabdominal aneurysms can lower the incidence of postoperative paraplegia.

1. **Ascending aortic arch aneurysms**
   a. Size criteria for TAA repair are not as clearly defined as for infrarenal AAAs. **Indications** for surgical repair include symptomatic or rapidly expanding aneurysms, aneurysms greater than or equal to 6 cm in diameter, ascending (type A) aortic dissections, mycotic aneurysms, and asymptomatic aneurysms greater than or equal to 5.5 cm in diameter in patients with Marfan syndrome (*Coron Artery Dis.* 2002;13:85).
   b. **Operative management.** An aneurysm arising distal to the coronary ostia is replaced with an interposition graft. An aneurysm resulting in aortic valve incompetence is replaced with a composite valved conduit (**Bentall procedure**) or a supracoronary graft with separate aortic valve replacement. All ascending arch aneurysms due to Marfan syndrome or cystic medial necrosis are repaired with aortic valve replacement owing to the high incidence of valvular incompetence associated with aneurysmal dilation of the native aortic root. When a composite graft is used, the coronary arteries are anastomosed directly to the conduit.

2. **Transverse aortic arch aneurysms**
   a. **Indications** for repair include aneurysms greater than or equal to 6 cm in diameter, aortic arch dissections, and ascending arch aneurysms that extend into the transverse arch.
   b. **Operative management.** After opening the aorta under hypothermic circulatory arrest, the distal anastomosis is performed using a beveled graft, followed by anastomosis of a patch that incorporates the orifices of the brachiocephalic vessels to the superior aspect of the graft. The proximal anastomosis is constructed to the supracoronary aorta (if the aortic valve is not involved) or to a segment of the composite valved conduit interposed to complete the arch reconstruction. Involvement of the transverse arch and its branch vessels requires interposition grafting to the involved vessels.

3. **Descending thoracic aortic aneurysms**
   a. **Indications** for repair include asymptomatic aneurysms greater than or equal to 6 cm in diameter and any symptomatic aneurysms.
   b. **Operative management.** After the distal clamp is applied, a proximal clamp is placed just distal to the left subclavian artery or between

the left common carotid and left subclavian arteries. Selected intercostal branches are reattached to the aortic interposition graft. Left heart (atriofemoral) bypass is often used, both to protect the heart from overdistention and to provide distal blood flow while the aorta is clamped. Sodium nitroprusside may be given before cross-clamping to reduce proximal blood pressure, and cerebrospinal fluid drainage is used as an adjunct to decrease the incidence of postoperative paraplegia.

4. **Thoracoabdominal aneurysms**
   a. **Indications** for repair include aneurysms greater than or equal to 6 cm in diameter and any symptomatic aneurysms.
   b. **Operative management** consists of tube graft replacement along with anastomosis of the major visceral branches to the graft. Aneurysms involving the thoracic and proximal abdominal aortic segments may be approached through a left posterolateral thoracotomy extended to the umbilicus. Use of left heart (atriofemoral) bypass is a valuable adjunct, and drainage of cerebrospinal fluid may reduce the incidence of postoperative paraplegia. The thoracic aorta is clamped and opened to perform the proximal anastomosis, while visceral perfusion is maintained retrograde. The aorta is clamped distally opening the remaining aneurysm. The orifices of all major aortic branches are occluded with balloon catheters or vascular clamps. Temporary perfusion can be maintained to those branches during aneurysm repair by using balloon catheters connected to the atriofemoral bypass. The anastomoses of significant aortic branches to the graft are performed as a patch or with separate bypasses. The clamp is moved to the graft below the renal arteries to reperfuse all visceral vessels in a prograde fashion. The distal anastomosis is made either to the uninvolved aorta or to the iliac arteries.

5. **Traumatic aortic aneurysms**
   a. **Indications.** Urgent repair is indicated, except when precluded by more compelling life-threatening injuries or major central nervous system trauma.
   b. **Operative management.** These aneurysms may be repaired by primary aortorrhaphy, aneurysmectomy, and end-to-end reanastomosis or by interposition grafting. Endovascular techniques have also been reported.

D. Possible **complications** of thoracic aortic surgery include arrhythmia, myocardial infarction, intraoperative hemorrhage, stroke, aortic crossclamp shock, renal insufficiency, lower-extremity ischemia, microemboli, and disseminated intravascular coagulopathy. The incidence of paraplegia may be as high as 30% with some types of TAAs (*Ann Thorac Surg.* 2007;83:S856). This risk can be reduced by multimodal therapies used to minimize spinal cord ischemia: distal aortic perfusion, intercostal and lumbar artery reimplantation, pre- or intraoperative localization of spinal cord blood supply, hypothermia, cerebrospinal fluid drainage, and pharmacotherapy.

E. **Endovascular management of thoracic aortic aneurysm**

1. **Indications and technique.** Because of the considerable morbidity and mortality associated with surgical repair of descending thoracic aneurysms, the endovascular approach to aneurysm exclusion is particularly attractive. Treatment with endovascular stent graft placement requires specific anatomic criteria: adequate length (2 cm) and diameter (20 to 45 mm) of the proximal and distal aneurysm necks, absence of significant mural thrombus within the sealing zones, and aortic and iliofemoral anatomy amenable to device introduction. In situations in which the proximal neck length is too short, coverage of the left subclavian artery with placement of the graft over the origin of the left subclavian artery can be performed with or without an adjunctive left carotid-left subclavian transposition or bypass. Over the past decade, multiple devices have been developed for the use of treating descending TAAs.

2. **Results and complications.** Reported results for the use of endovascular devices are encouraging. Various studies have suggested low morbidity and mortality with high rates of aneurysm exclusion (*J Vasc Surg.* 2008;47:1094–1098; *J Vasc Surg.* 2006;43(suppl A):12A-19A; *J Vasc Surg.* 2008;47:247–257; *J Vasc Surg.* 2008;48:546–554). Fenestrated and branched grafts along with hybrid techniques using extraanatomic bypass procedures are being used to approach more complex aneurysm anatomy.

III. OTHER ARTERIAL ANEURYSMS

A. **Renal artery aneurysms** occur in approximately 0.1% of the general population and constitute approximately 1% of all aneurysms (*Semin Vasc Surg.* 2005;18:202).

1. **Pathophysiology.** These aneurysms can be either extrarenal (85%) or intrarenal (15%). Extrarenal renal artery aneurysms are subdivided into saccular (most common), fusiform, and dissecting. Saccular aneurysms classically occur near the bifurcation of the renal artery (*Semin Vasc Surg.* 1996;9:236). Fusiform aneurysms are poststenotic dilations associated with renal artery stenosis. Renal artery dissections are associated with renal artery fibroplasias. Intrarenal aneurysms may be congenital, traumatic, or related to collagen vascular disease.

2. **Diagnosis**

a. Most are asymptomatic and are found incidentally on imaging studies performed for other intra-abdominal pathology. Rupture and dissection may produce flank pain or hematuria (intrarenal aneurysms).

b. Physical examination commonly reveals **HTN and an abdominal bruit.** A palpable mass occurs in fewer than 10% of cases.

c. Laboratory tests may reveal anemia or hematuria.

d. Abdominal films may demonstrate **ring-shaped calcifications** in the renal hilum in patients with calcific saccular aneurysms. CT scan may reveal an incidental renal artery aneurysm. Arteriography confirms the diagnosis and details the anatomy of the renal branches.

3. **Operative management** is indicated for aneurysms greater than 2 cm, which rupture, are associated with dissection, or produce renal artery stenosis leading to HTN. Saccular aneurysms are repaired in women of childbearing age owing to an increased risk of rupture during pregnancy. Small aneurysms at the bifurcation can be treated with aneurysmectomy and reconstruction of the bifurcation. Aneurysmectomy with aortorenal or splenorenal bypass is advised for large aneurysms or stenotic lesions. Polar renal artery aneurysms can be excised with end-to-end arterial reanastomosis. *Ex vivo* renal artery reconstruction with renal autotransplantation is useful in patients with complex lesions that require microvascular techniques and for whom exposure *in situ* is inadequate. These procedures are time consuming, and adequate hypothermic protection from ischemic renal injury may be difficult with the kidney *in situ*. In general, operations requiring more than two branch artery reconstructions or anastomoses should be considered for *ex vivo* repair. Once repair is accomplished, the kidney can be transplanted orthotopically or heterotopically to the ipsilateral iliac fossa. Ruptured renal artery aneurysms are usually treated with nephrectomy as salvage of renal function is unlikely.

B. **Infected aneurysms** have risen in incidence with the increased prevalence of immunocompromised patients and invasive transarterial procedures.

1. **Pathophysiology.** Infected aneurysms can be divided in to four types: mycotic aneurysm, microbial arteritis with aneurysm, infection of preexisting aneurysm, and posttraumatic infected false aneurysm. *Staphylococcus aureus* is the most common pathogen, although *Salmonella* species (arteritis), *Streptococcus* species, and *Staphylococcus epidermidis* (preexisting aneurysms) also may occur. The risk of rupture for Gram-negative exceeds that for Gram-positive infections.

2. **Diagnosis**
   a. Clinical manifestations may be absent or include fever, tenderness, or sepsis. Physical examination may demonstrate a **tender, warm, palpable mass** in an infected peripheral aneurysm. Laboratory tests may reveal leukocytosis. Aerobic and anaerobic blood cultures should be obtained, but are positive in only 50% of patients.
   b. **MRI or CTA** can demonstrate an aneurysm and verify its rupture. **Angiography** delineates the characteristics of the aneurysm. Aneurysms that are saccular, multilobed, or eccentric with a narrow neck are more likely a result of infection.

C. Management
   a. **Preoperative.** Broad-spectrum antibiotics should be administered intravenously after aerobic and anaerobic blood cultures have been obtained.
   b. **Intraoperative.** Goals of surgery include (1) controlling hemorrhage; (2) obtaining arterial specimens for Gram's stain, aerobic and anaerobic cultures, and drug sensitivities; (3) resecting the aneurysm with wide debridement and drainage; and (4) reconstructing major arteries through uninfected tissue planes. Extra-anatomic bypass may be nec-

essary to avoid contamination of the graft. Inline reconstructions with antibiotic-impregnated grafts, cryopreserved homografts, or native veins are alternatives that can be used for arterial reconstructions depending on the location of the aneurysm and the extent of the infection.

   c. **Postoperative.** Adequate drainage of the aneurysm cavity and long-term antibiotic therapy for at least 6 weeks typically are required.

IV. **RENOVASCULAR DISEASE.** Stenosis or occlusion of the renal arteries may result in HTN, ischemic nephropathy, or both. **Renovascular HTN is the most common form of surgically correctable secondary HTN.** However, because of the predominance of primary HTN and difficulties in clinical diagnosis of renovascular HTN, its exact prevalence is difficult to assess.

   A. A high index of suspicion is necessary to distinguish patients with renovascular HTN from the majority of patients with primary HTN. There are several clinical features that may be used to identify patients with potential renovascular HTN (ACC/AHA practice guideline; 2005):

   1. The onset of **HTN** in a child/young adult or an adult older than the age of 55.

   2. **Accelerated, resistant, or malignant HTN.**

   3. HTN and unexplained impairment of renal function.

   4. HTN that is **refractory** to appropriate multidrug therapy.

   5. HTN in a patient with extensive coronary disease, cerebral vascular disease, or peripheral vascular disease.

   B. On **physical examination,** these patients may have an epigastric, subcostal, or flank bruit. However, majority of the patients have a normal physical exam. The finding of a unilateral small kidney on any imaging study is a possible indicator.

   C. Pathophysiology

   1. Renal arterial stenosis (RAS) is perceived by the ipsilateral kidney as a hypovolemic state, and activation of the **renin-angiotensin-aldosterone system** results in volume expansion due to angiotensin-II mediated sodium retention and severe HTN results from the combined effects of volume expansion and peripheral vasoconstriction. Even in the **absence of HTN,** a significant RAS may be present and may lead to renal failure.

      a. In **acute renal failure,** RAS should be considered in the differential diagnosis if the urinary sediment is unremarkable and there are no signs of acute tubular necrosis, glomerulonephritis, or interstitial nephritis. Acute ischemic nephropathy may occur within 2 weeks of starting an angiotensin-converting enzyme (ACE) inhibitor or other antihypertensive or diuretic.

      b. RAS may account for up to 20% of **unexplained chronic renal failure** in patients older than 50 years of age. The diagnosis is more likely in those with generalized atherosclerosis or uncontrolled HTN.

      c. Isolated unilateral RAS generally **do not** cause rise in serum creatinine.

2. **Atherosclerosis** accounts for nearly 90% of cases of renovascular HTN and usually affects the ostia and proximal 2 cm of the renal artery. Associated extrarenal atherosclerosis occurs in 15% to 20% of patients.

3. The second-most-common renovascular lesion is **fibromuscular dysplasia,** most commonly medial fibroplasia. These lesions are multifocal, have a characteristic **string-of-beads** appearance on angiography, and typically occur in young women.

D. **Diagnosis.** Testing for clinically significant renal artery disease must evaluate the **anatomic and physiologic changes.** Anatomic lesions of the renal arteries by themselves correlate poorly with physiologic effect. More important, they also correlate poorly with treatment response.

1. **Arteriography** remains the "gold standard" for the diagnosis of anatomic RAS. However, the usual risks of arteriography, especially the nephrotoxic effects of the contrast agent, are important caveats to consider.

2. In patients with a relative contraindication to arteriography, **duplex scanning** is useful for screening. However, this procedure is highly technician dependent.

3. **MR angiography** with gadolinium-based intravenous contrast is an excellent test for evaluating kidney and main renal artery morphology without the use of nephrotoxic agents.

4. Two commonly used tests to determine the functional significance of a renal artery lesion are **captopril renal scintigraphy** and **selective renal vein renin measurement.** These tests can be complicated to perform and interpret, especially in patients with bilateral disease or in those taking ACE inhibitors or beta-blockers.

E. **Management of fibromuscular disease**

1. RAS resulting from fibromuscular dysplasia rarely causes renal failure, and endovascular treatment of the lesions is frequently successful in treating the HTN.

2. **Endovascular techniques (balloon angioplasty) have a high success rate for the treatment of this arterial pathology.** For failure of endovascular treatment (see Section F.3), surgical therapy may be employed.

F. **Management of atherosclerotic disease** has a dual purpose: to control target organ damage from HTN and to avoid progressive ischemic renal failure. However, even with preoperative functional studies, response to therapy is difficult to predict because the HTN may be primarily essential and the renal failure due to hypertensive glomerulosclerosis.

1. **Medical therapy** with antihypertensive drugs is often successful in the management of patients with renovascular HTN and remains the cornerstone of treatment. A combination of beta-blockers and a calcium channel blocker, an ACE inhibitor, or an angiotensin II–receptor inhibitor is commonly used as first-line therapy.

2. **Surgical therapy**
   a. The recently published ASTRAL trial (*NEJM.* 2009;361:20) was a multicenter, randomized trial that compared medical management alone to medical management with endovascular revascularization. The investigators **did not** find a significant difference in rate of progression of renal impairment, blood pressure, or survival. However, they included patients with clinically insignificant lesions and excluded any patients whose doctors felt would benefit from revascularization. Until further clinical trials and guidelines can better identify those who might benefit from surgery, interventions should be offered only to those with severe disease who fail medical management. In patients undergoing aortic surgery for aneurysmal or occlusive disease with concomitant renal stenoses, consideration should also be given to renal revascularization.
   b. **Procedures**
      (1) **Aortorenal bypass** is the classic treatment of renal revascularization. The stenotic renal artery is isolated with a segment of infrarenal aorta, and bypass is accomplished using saphenous vein, autologous hypogastric artery (in children), or prosthetic graft.
      (2) **Renal endarterectomy** is another option and is often used for bilateral orificial lesions. Most commonly, a transverse arteriotomy is made over the orifices of both renal arteries.
      (3) **Alternative bypass procedures** are available for patients who are not good candidates for aortorenal bypass due to prior aortic surgery, the presence of severe aortic disease, or unfavorable anatomy. Grafts can be taken from the supraceliac aorta or the superior mesenteric, common hepatic, gastroduodenal, splenic, or iliac arteries. Results for these procedures are comparable to those for direct aortic reconstruction but with less morbidity and mortality.
      (4) **Nephrectomy** may be required in patients who have renal infarction, severe nephrosclerosis, severe renal atrophy, noncorrectable renal vascular lesions, failed revascularizations, or a normal contralateral kidney and who are high-risk surgical candidates.
   c. **Postoperative care**
      (1) **Immediately after operation,** patients should be kept well hydrated to maintain adequate urine output. Concern about the patency of the reconstruction may be addressed by a renal or duplex scan.
      (2) **Patient follow-up** should consist of routine blood pressure monitoring, a renal scan, and creatinine determination at 3 months, 12 months, and then yearly. Any recurrence of HTN or deterioration in renal function should prompt diagnostic imaging. Duplex scanning often serves as a useful surveillance test.
   d. **Complications** of surgery include persistent HTN, acute renal failure, renal artery restenosis, thrombosis, aneurysm formation, and distal embolization.

3. **Endovascular management of renal artery stenosis**
   a. **Indications** for angioplasty of RAS include failure of medical management of renovascular HTN in the absence of any clear indications for open aortic surgery. Balloon angioplasty is the treatment of choice for clinically significant fibromuscular dysplastic lesions. Angioplasty for atherosclerotic lesions has less favorable results but entails significantly less procedure-related morbidity than surgical bypass or endarterectomy. Surgical therapy may be preferred in cases of long-segment disease or occlusions or when atherosclerosis is severe and widespread (i.e., to avoid the risk of atheroembolic complications with intra-arterial instrumentation). Renal artery stents are routinely used for restenosis after previous angioplasty, treatment of procedural complications (e.g., dissection), and the treatment of atherosclerotic ostial lesions.
   b. **Technique.** Intravascular access to the renal artery may be obtained from the femoral, brachial, or axillary arteries (access from the upper extremity may be preferable in cases of caudally angled renal arteries). In patients at high risk for renal failure (e.g., type II diabetes and preexisting renal insufficiency), nephrotoxic contrast may be avoided and angiography can be performed using gadolinium or carbon dioxide (CO_2). Technical success for renal artery angioplasty is defined as a less than 30% residual stenosis and a pressure gradient across the lesion of less than 10 mm Hg.
   c. **Results.** Patients with fibromuscular dysplasia respond favorably to percutaneous transluminal angioplasty, with cure rates of greater than 50%. Patients with atherosclerotic disease respond less favorably in the long term, although immediate technical success is seen in almost all patients. Improvements in blood pressure are observed in approximately two thirds of patients; however, only 15% of patients with renal insufficiency demonstrate improved excretory renal function. In addition, up to 15% of patients exhibit decreased renal excretory function following intervention. Angiographic restenosis occurs in 15% to 20% of patients within 1 year of treatment, most commonly in small renal arteries (<4 mm). Based on these data, percutaneous angioplasty with stenting of atherosclerotic disease of the renal artery yields blood pressure, renal function, and anatomic results that are slightly inferior but comparable to contemporary surgical results. Percutaneous intervention is, however, associated with lower morbidity and mortality rates than open surgical procedures.

V. **MESENTERIC ISCHEMIA** can be a difficult diagnosis to make because most patients are asymptomatic until late in the disease process. Although considerable advances have been made in the perioperative care as well as the diagnosis and treatment of intestinal ischemia, mortality remains 60% to 80% (*Langenbecks Arch Surg.* 2008;393:163).

A. **Acute mesenteric ischemia (AMI)**

1. **Pathophysiology.** The most common cause of acute mesenteric ischemia (AMI) is embolization to the SMA, but other causes include

thrombosis of the SMA or portomesenteric venous thrombosis. Patients with AMI often have multiple **risk factors,** including significant cardiac disease (frequently atrial fibrillation) and severe atherosclerotic disease of nonmesenteric vessels, and may have a history consistent with chronic intestinal ischemia (CMI).

    a. Abdominal pain usually is sudden in onset and intermittent at first, progressing to continuous severe pain. It is often described as **pain out-of-proportion to exam.** These patients may also have bloody diarrhea before or after the onset of pain.

    b. Mesenteric venous thrombosis presents with varying manifestations, ranging from an asymptomatic state to catastrophic illness. Patients usually complain of prolonged, generalized abdominal pain that develops somewhat less rapidly than with acute mesenteric arterial occlusion. These patients may have occult gastrointestinal bleeding but no frank hemorrhage.

2. Diagnosis

    a. Angiography of the mesenteric circulation, including lateral views of the celiac axis and SMA, remains the "gold standard." However, most centers use **CT angiography** especially for the diagnosis of AMI.

    b. Other laboratory findings can include elevated white blood cell count with a left shift, persistent metabolic acidosis, and possibly lactic acidosis in more advanced cases, but are insensitive and nonspecific for the diagnosis of mesenteric ischemia (*Langenbeck's Arch of Surg.* 2011;396:3–11).

    c. Abdominal plain radiographs are of limited utility. After acute arterial occlusion, the abdominal plain x-ray appears relatively normal. After venous thrombosis, x-rays may show small-bowel wall thickening or air in the portal venous system.

3. Surgical therapy

    a. Patients with AMI frequently require intestinal resection; therefore, laparotomy with open revascularization is the preferred method of treatment.

        (1) Assessment of bowel viability at laparotomy is made based on the gross characteristics of the bowel. The bowel is likely viable if it appears pink and if arterial pulsations are present in the adjacent vascular arcades. A number of other techniques have been described, including the use of fluorescein dye, Doppler studies, and tissue oximetry, but these are not substitutes for experienced clinical judgment.

        (2) Second-look procedures are prudent when bowel viability is questionable. Whether to perform a second operation 24 to 48 hours after initial exploration is decided at the time of initial laparotomy, and that decision should not be changed even if the patient's condition improves. This approach is especially important in patients who have extensive bowel involvement and in whom resection of all questionable areas could result in short-bowel syndrome.

    b. For **venous occlusion,** surgical intervention rarely is helpful, although anecdotal reports suggest that portomesenteric venous thrombectomy may be beneficial. Similarly, the role of lytic therapy in the treatment of this disorder is unclear. It is imperative to begin systemic anticoagulation as soon as the diagnosis is made to limit progression of the thrombotic process. Frequently, the diagnosis is made at laparotomy. If the diagnosis is made before exploration, however, operation should be reserved until evidence of bowel infarction exists.

   c. Nonocclusive mesenteric ischemia (NOMI) is intestinal ischemia in the absence of thromboembolic occlusion. It occurs in patients with a low-cardiac-output state and chronic intestinal angina. Mortality associated with NOMI is high and treatment is directed toward improving circulatory support and increasing cardiac output.

4. Perioperative care usually requires maximal medical support; these patients frequently are hemodynamically unstable and develop multiple organ system failure. Admission to the intensive care unit, prolonged endotracheal intubation, parenteral nutrition, and broad-spectrum antibiotic therapy are typically required.

B. Chronic mesenteric ischemia (CMI)

1. Patients with CMI present with **intestinal angina,** which is pain related to eating, usually beginning within an hour after eating and abating within 4 hours (postprandial pain). Such patients experience significant weight loss related to the decreased intake secondary to recurrent pain (food fear). The diagnosis usually is made from obtaining a thorough history alone because physical finding are usually lacking.

2. Surgical therapy. Elective revascularization of the SMA and celiac artery using autologous or prosthetic grafts from the aorta or iliac arteries is the treatment of choice. Aortic endarterectomy is an alternative in patients with aortic and orificial disease. Advances in endovascular techniques have greatly expanded the use of percutaneous interventions for patients with CMI with excellent technical results.

3. Perioperative care. These patients often are malnourished. Some advocate parenteral nutrition for 1 to 2 weeks before surgery, which is continued postoperatively. Some patients develop a revascularization syndrome consisting of abdominal pain, tachycardia, leukocytosis, and intestinal edema. Concern about the adequacy of revascularization should prompt diagnostic imaging.

19 Peripheral Arterial Occlusive Disease

Jeremy Leidenfrost and Patrick J. Geraghty

The majority of occlusive disease is secondary to atherosclerotic change of the arterial intima. Major risk factors for developing atherosclerosis include cigarette smoking, diabetes, dyslipidemia, hypertension, and hyperhomocysteinemia. Some of these risk factors may be influenced to a degree by genetic predisposition. However, the evolution of the disease for most individuals can be modified by changes in environmental factors, particularly diet and exercise. Atherosclerotic disease is a systemic illness, and although symptomatic disease may predominate in one organ, subclinical disease, particularly of the coronary arteries, is generally present. In fact, 50% of the mortality associated with peripheral arterial reconstructions for atherosclerotic disease is cardiac in nature. Other, less common causes of occlusive disease include fibromuscular dysplasia, radiation-induced vascular injury, and the vasculitides (e.g., Takayasu arteritis and Buerger disease).

ACUTE ARTERIAL OCCLUSION OF THE EXTREMITY

Symptoms of acute arterial insufficiency occur abruptly. The presentation generally includes the **five Ps** of acute ischemia: **pain, pallor, pulselessness, paresthesias, and paralysis;** patients may also develop poikilothermy, the inability to thermoregulate. The level of occlusion may be localized by the absence of pulses and the level of coolness of the limb. If adequate collateral circulation is not present, irreversible changes may appear as early as 4 to 6 hours after onset. Therefore, priority must be given to restoration of blood flow within this time period. Once the occlusive process has begun, regardless of its cause, vasospasm and propagation of thrombus distal to the site of initial occlusion can contribute to further ischemia.

I. ETIOLOGY

A. The most common cause of acute arterial insufficiency is **embolization.**

1. **Cardiac sources** account for more than 70% of emboli and are usually the result of mural thrombi that develop due to cardiac aneurysms following myocardial infarction or arrhythmias such as atrial fibrillation. Other cardiac sources of emboli include valvular heart disease, prosthetic heart valves, bacterial endocarditis, and atrial myxoma.

2. **Arterial–arterial emboli** can result from ulcerated atheroma or aneurysms, although embolization from abdominal aortic aneurysms is distinctly rare. The *blue toe syndrome* occurs in patients with microemboli from unstable proximal arterial plaques and is characterized by intact pulses and painful ischemic lesions in the distal extremity. Atheroemboli

in the lower extremity secondary to plaque disruption by catheters can occur. The severely diseased distal aorta in some of these patients is evident on computed tomography (CT) scan and arteriography and has been termed *shaggy aorta*.

3. Venous–arterial emboli (paradoxical emboli) can result from an intracardiac shunt (e.g., patent foramen ovale) or intrapulmonary arteriovenous malformations (e.g., Osler–Weber–Rendu syndrome).

4. Occasionally, it is difficult to discern whether a person with advanced atherosclerotic disease has had an embolus or whether an already compromised vessel has undergone acute thrombosis. This is particularly true in patients without arrhythmias or prior myocardial infarction. The presence of contralateral pulses and the absence of a history of claudication may help in making this differentiation.

B. Direct arterial trauma is frequently obvious but may initially be occult. Arterial stenosis or occlusion occurs only after an intimal flap or arterial wall hematoma progresses sufficiently to cause symptoms. Arterial compromise can also occur in the setting of compression by joint dislocations (e.g., knee), bone fragments (e.g., tibial plateau fracture), or compartment syndrome.

C. Other causes of acute ischemia include arterial thrombosis, aortic dissection, venous outflow occlusion, and low-flow state.

II. DIAGNOSIS AND EVALUATION

A. If history and physical examination demonstrate clear evidence of embolization, **definitive therapy** should not be delayed. If there is a concern that the occlusive process may be thrombotic, however, **arteriography** may be indicated. Angiographically, embolic occlusions can be distinguished from thrombotic occlusions by their occurrence just distal to vascular bifurcations and by the concave shadow formed at the interface with the contrast. In select cases, thrombolysis may be a useful adjunct for defining underlying occlusive disease. In general, patients with acute ischemia unrelated to trauma should be considered to have coexistent cardiac disease. All patients should have an electrocardiogram and chest x-ray performed. After limb revascularization, a transesophageal echocardiogram can be useful in diagnosing a cardiac source.

B. Patients who present with penetrating **trauma,** long-bone fractures, or joint dislocations may have vascular injuries. In certain situations, duplex scan of the injured area can be useful in the diagnosis of intimal flap, pseudoaneurysm, or arterial or venous thrombi. Patients with penetrating injuries who display "hard" signs of arterial injury need urgent surgical intervention without preoperative angiography. **Hard signs** of arterial injury include the following:

1. Diminished or absent pulses distal to an injury

2. Ischemia distal to an injury

3. Visible arterial bleeding from a wound

4. A bruit at or distal to the site of injury

5. Large, expanding, or pulsatile hematomas

Soft signs of injury include the anatomic proximity of a wound to a major vessel, injury to an anatomically related nerve, unexplained hemorrhagic shock, or a moderately sized hematoma. In those with only soft signs, a careful documentation of pulses by **Doppler pressure** distal to the injury should be undertaken, along with comparison with the contralateral limb. A difference of greater than 10% to 20% suggests the need for arteriography or exploration.

III. MANAGEMENT

A. Once a diagnosis of acute arterial ischemia due to emboli or thrombi is made, **heparin** should be administered immediately. An intravenous bolus of 80 units/kg followed by an intravenous infusion of 18 units/kg/hour is usually satisfactory. Partial thromboplastin time (PTT) should be maintained between 60 and 80 seconds.

1. **Surgical therapy,** such as embolectomy, should be performed urgently in patients with an obvious embolus and acute ischemia. Embolectomy can be done under local anesthesia if the patient cannot tolerate general anesthesia. Once the artery is isolated, a Fogarty catheter is passed proximally and distally to extract the embolus and associated thrombus. In some cases, intraoperative thrombolysis may be necessary because distal vessels may be thrombosed beyond the reach of the Fogarty catheter. Distal patency can be proved with an intraoperative arteriogram, depending on the status of distal vessels and pulses after embolectomy. In the leg, if adequate distal perfusion is not established and an angiogram demonstrates distal thrombus, the distal popliteal artery and tibial arteries may be explored via angiographic or surgical approach. In conjunction with steerable guidewires, Fogarty catheters can be used to select the anterior tibial, posterior tibial, and peroneal arteries to retrieve distal thrombus. When angiographic approaches fail, popliteal artery cutdown can allow direct access to these vessels. The arteriotomy can be closed with a patch graft if there is arterial narrowing. Bypass grafting may also be required if significant preexisting arterial disease in the affected segment is discovered.

2. **Thrombolytic therapy** may be useful in patients with clearly viable extremities in whom thrombosis is the likely underlying cause of their acute ischemia. In general, the fresher the thrombus, the more successful thrombolysis can be. Thrombolysis and follow-up angiography frequently identify an underlying stenosis that may be treated by balloon angioplasty/stent or by surgical means.

a. Lytic agents are instilled through an intra-arterial catheter placed as close to the thrombus as possible. Current agents in use include alteplase, urokinase, and reteplase. These agents are also commonly used in conjunction with percutaneous mechanical thrombectomy for large clot burdens.

b. During thrombolysis, the patient is usually monitored in the **intensive care unit (ICU).** Thrombin time, fibrinogen level, fibrin degradation product level, PTT, and complete blood count are followed closely to limit the risk of hemorrhage. In general, the likelihood of serious hemorrhagic complications increases when fibrinogen levels drop below 100 mg/dL and the PTT rises above three to five times normal. Once the artery is open, the patient can be managed either with systemic anticoagulation or with surgical intervention (i.e., operative arterial reconstruction, balloon angioplasty).

3. Mechanical thrombectomy devices such as the AngioJet Thrombectomy system (Possis Medical, Minneapolis, MN) and the Trellis system (Bacchus Vascular, Santa Clara, CA) allow prompt debulking of acute thrombotic lesions, but are less effective at treating older adherent thrombus. These systems can be used with or without tPA. The Trellis system is designed for use with tPA which is contained between balloons and withdrawn after treatment to reduce systemic spread of lytic agent.

B. In the setting of **trauma,** operative exploration should be performed in any limb that is ischemic or if arteriography demonstrates a significant intimal flap or other pathology. In the presence of coexistent neurologic or orthopedic injuries, it is essential to reestablish arterial flow first, by direct repair, bypass grafting, or temporary shunting. At the conclusion of the orthopedic repair, the arterial repair should be reexamined to ensure that it has not been disrupted and has been correctly fashioned to the final bone length. In cases of joint dislocation, reduction of the dislocation should be accomplished first because this may alleviate the need for arterial reconstruction.

1. Intraoperatively it is essential to **obtain proximal and distal control** of the injured artery before exploring the hematoma or wound. When repairing an artery, an end-to-end anastomosis is preferable. A few centimeters of the artery can usually be mobilized proximally and distally to accomplish reapproximation. However, the uninjured leg or other potential vein harvest site should be prepared in case a conduit is required. It is preferable to use autologous tissue in this setting. In most stable patients, concomitant vein injuries are also repaired. A completion angiogram can help to document distal flow. This is especially important if significant spasm is present and distal pulses are not readily palpable.

2. In general, injuries to the subclavian, axillary, brachial, femoral, superficial femoral, profunda femoral, and popliteal arteries should be repaired. The radial or ulnar artery may be ligated if the other vessel is intact and functioning. Similarly, isolated injuries to the tibial arteries may be ligated if one or more of the tibial arteries remain intact.

IV. COMPLICATIONS

A. **Reperfusion injury** occurs after reestablishment of arterial flow to an ischemic tissue bed and may lead to further tissue death. It results from the formation of oxygen free radicals that directly damage the tissue and cause white blood cell accumulation and sequestration in the microcirculation.

This process prolongs the ischemic interval because it impairs adequate nutrient flow to the tissue, despite the restoration of axial blood flow. There is no proven therapy that limits reperfusion injury.

B. **Rhabdomyolysis** following reperfusion releases the by-products of ischemic muscle, including potassium, lactic acid, myoglobin, and creatinine phosphokinase. The electrolyte and pH changes that occur can trigger dangerous arrhythmias, and precipitation of myoglobin in the renal tubules can cause pigment nephropathy and ultimately acute renal failure. The likelihood that a patient will develop these complications relates to the duration of ischemia and the muscle mass at risk. **Aggressive hydration,** diuresis promotion with mannitol (25 g intravenously), and intravenous infusion of bicarbonate to alkalinize the urine are accepted methods of mitigating renal impairment secondary to rhabdomyolysis.

C. **Compartment syndrome** results when prolonged ischemia and delayed reperfusion cause cell membrane damage and leakage of fluid into the interstitium. The edema can result in extremely high intracompartmental pressures, particularly in the lower extremity. Additional muscle and nerve necrosis occurs when the intracompartmental pressures exceed capillary perfusion (generally >30 mm Hg). A four-compartment fasciotomy should be performed when there is concern about the possible development of leg compartment syndrome. **Fasciotomy should be routinely considered** in any patient with more than 6 hours of lower-extremity ischemia or in the presence of combined arterial and venous injuries.

D. Follow-up care is usually directed at treating the underlying cause of the obstruction. Patients with mural thrombi or arrhythmias require long-term anticoagulation. The in-hospital mortality rate associated with embolectomy is as high as 30%, mostly due to coexistent cardiac disease.

CHRONIC ARTERIAL OCCLUSIVE DISEASE OF THE EXTREMITY

The lower extremities are most frequently affected by chronic occlusive disease, although upper-extremity disease can occur. The principal early symptom of arterial occlusive disease is **claudication,** which is usually described as a cramping pain or heaviness in the affected extremity that occurs after physical exertion. Claudication is relieved by rest but recurs predictably with exercise. Lower-extremity occlusive disease may be subdivided into three anatomic sections on the basis of symptoms and treatment options. Aortoiliac occlusive disease, or "inflow disease," affects the infrarenal aorta and the common and external iliac arteries. Femoral–popliteal occlusive disease, or "outflow disease," affects the common femoral, superficial femoral, and popliteal arteries. Finally, tibial–peroneal disease, or "runoff disease," affects the vessels distal to the popliteal artery.

I. CLINICAL PRESENTATION

A. **Aortoiliac disease** presents with **symptoms of lower-extremity claudication,** usually of the **hip, thigh, or buttock.** It may coexist with femoral–popliteal disease, contributing to more distal symptoms as well. The symptoms usually develop gradually, although sudden worsening of symptoms suggests acute thrombosis of a diseased vessel. Patients ultimately develop incapacitating claudication but not rest pain unless distal disease is present as well. *Leriche syndrome* (sexual impotence, buttock and leg claudication, leg musculature atrophy, trophic changes of the feet, and leg pallor) is a constellation of symptoms that results from the gradual occlusion of the terminal aorta.

B. Patients with **femoral–popliteal** and **tibial–peroneal disease** present with claudication of the lower extremity, usually most prominent in the **calves.** More severe impairment of arterial flow can present as rest pain. **Rest pain** is a burning pain in the distal foot, usually worse at night or when the leg is elevated and often relieved by placing the leg in a dependent position. Examination findings of the chronically ischemic extremity include the following:

1. Decreased or absent distal pulses

2. Dependent rubor

3. Trophic changes that include thickening of the nails, loss of leg hair, shiny skin, and ulceration at the tips of the toes.

C. Symptomatic arterial occlusive disease of the **upper extremity** is relatively rare.

1. The proximal subclavian artery is most commonly affected by **atherosclerotic disease,** followed by axillary and brachial arteries. These patients typically present with arm claudication or finger–hand ischemia or necrosis. Occasionally, ulcerated plaques of the innominate or subclavian arteries can be a source of embolization to the hand.

2. Most patients with proximal subclavian lesions are completely asymptomatic. **Subclavian steal** can result when an occlusive subclavian artery lesion is located proximal to the origin of the vertebral artery. With exercise of the affected limb, the arm's demand for blood is supplied by retrograde flow in the ipsilateral vertebral artery, shunting blood from the posterior cerebral circulation and resulting in drop attacks, ataxia, sensory loss, or diplopia.

II. **DIAGNOSIS** of chronic arterial occlusive disease is concerned with determining the presence of **significant flow-limiting lesions** and distinguishing the disease from those that may mimic it, such as arthritis, gout, and neuromuscular disorders.

A. For patients presenting with **lower-extremity symptoms,** it is essential to examine the femoral and distal pulses at rest and after exercise. The absence of femoral pulses is indicative of aortoiliac disease, although some patients with aortoiliac disease have palpable pulses at rest that are lost after exercise. Bruits may also be appreciated over the lower abdomen or femoral vessels. It is also important to differentiate ulcers that arise from arterial insufficiency versus those generated by venous insufficiency and neuropathy.

1. Arterial insufficiency ulcers are usually painful and have an irregular appearance.

2. Neuropathic ulcers are painless and usually occur over bony prominences, particularly the plantar aspect of the metatarsophalangeal joints.

3. Venous stasis ulcers are located on the malleolar surface ("gaiter" distribution) and are dark and irregular in shape.

B. **Noninvasive testing** can quantify flow through larger vessels and tissue perfusion.

1. **Segmental arterial Doppler** readings with waveforms should be performed in all patients with suspected symptomatic arterial disease. The **ankle-brachial index (ABI)** (the ratio of the systolic blood pressure in the leg to that in the arm) allows one to quantify the degree of ischemia. In general, patients without vascular disease have an ABI of greater than 1, patients with claudication have an ABI of less than 0.8, and patients with rest pain and severe ischemia have an ABI of less than 0.4. Waveform changes help to localize the site of significant disease. Patients with history of claudication and normal resting waveforms require postexercise ABI measurements.

2. Transcutaneous measurement of **local tissue oxygenation** has been developed to attempt to quantify the physiologic derangements of ischemia. However, the usefulness of this test in the general vascular patient has not been validated.

C. **Digital subtraction arteriography** is the **gold standard** for evaluating the arterial tree before planned revascularization. Typical digital subtraction arteriography of the lower extremities includes images of the infrarenal aorta and the renal, iliac, femoral, tibial, and pedal vessels. Noninvasive angiography using imaging modalities such as magnetic resonance or CT has been gaining widespread use as the technology improves for both. **Magnetic resonance angiography (MRA)** is an excellent imaging modality for assessing PAD and is useful for selecting patients who are endoluminal candidates. However, MRA does have a tendency to overestimate the degree of stenosis and may be inaccurate in stented arteries. **CT angiography** produces high-resolution images of the vascular tree and gives other information about soft tissues that may be associated with PAD, such as aneurysms, popliteal entrapment, or cystic adventitial disease. However, diffuse calcifications may make interpretation of CT angiography images difficult. In addition, CT angiography does require iodinated contrast, which may adversely affect patients with renal insufficiency.

III. MANAGEMENT

A. With adequate control of risk factors, intermittent claudication follows a benign course in most patients. In patients presenting with claudication alone, 70% to 80% remain stable or improve and 10% to 20% worsen over the ensuing 5-year period. Only 5% to 10% of patients develop gangrene and are at risk for limb loss. Therefore, first-line treatment for patients with claudication should be medical therapy, with emphasis on risk factor modification. **Indications for surgical intervention include the following:**

1. **Limb salvage** is the goal of surgery in patients with ischemic rest pain or tissue loss (critical limb ischemia). These patients typically display multilevel occlusive disease. When significant aortoiliac disease and distal disease are jointly present in a patient with a threatened limb, however, an inflow (aortoiliac) procedure should be performed first.

2. **Prevention of further peripheral atheroembolization** from aortoiliac ulcerated plaques, even if there is little or no history of claudication, is an indication for exclusion and bypass or endarterectomy of the culprit lesion.

3. **Incapacitating claudication** that jeopardizes a patient's livelihood or severely influences his or her quality of life may be considered for revascularization after failure of risk factor modification and exercise therapy.

B. **Medical therapy** is available for those patients with symptoms who are not candidates for surgical intervention. However, no medical therapy is available to significantly reverse the changes of advanced atherosclerotic disease.

1. **Risk factor modification** is the most important intervention for reducing the impact of advanced atherosclerotic disease. Control of hypertension and serum glucose, cessation of smoking, management of lipid disorders, attainment of ideal body weight, and regular exercise should be the goals.

   a. **Lipid reduction** is imperative in patients with PAD because majority of the morbidity associated with PAD is related to cardiac events. On the basis of the Heart Protection Study involving statins, it is recommended to keep the low-density-lipoprotein level of patients with PAD less than a 100 mg/dL to help reduce the likelihood of morbidity associated with cardiac events (*J Vasc Surg.* 2007;45:645).

   b. **Antihypertensives** should be administered to normalize blood pressure. Medications such as beta-blockers or angiotensin-converting enzyme inhibitors have been shown in several studies to help reduce mortality-associated cardiovascular disease.

2. Because many of these patients have concomitant coronary artery or cerebrovascular disease, daily **aspirin** therapy (81 or 325 mg) is indicated to reduce the risk of myocardial infarction or stroke.

3. **Clopidogrel** is an **antiplatelet agent** that has been shown to reduce cardiac and cerebral events in patients with systemic atherosclerosis. Although rigorous proof of its utility following peripheral arterial interventions is lacking, clopidogrel is frequently prescribed following these procedures.

4. **Cilostazol** is a type III **phosphodiesterase inhibitor** and the newest agent available for treatment of claudication. Cilostazol inhibits platelet aggregation and causes vasodilation. Given at 50 mg or 100 mg twice daily, it increases walking distances when compared with placebo

and pentoxifylline. Early studies suggest that the drug is safe in most patients, although **its use is contraindicated in those with class III or IV heart failure** due to the toxicity of phosphodiesterase inhibitors in these patients.

C. **Preoperative care** of patients with PVD includes a complete arterial evaluation. In addition to angiographic evaluation of the symptomatic arterial tree, patients generally undergo screening for associated cardiac, renal, cerebrovascular, and pulmonary disease, so that any correctable lesions can be addressed. Myocardial complications account for the majority of early and late deaths; therefore, patients with questionable myocardial function may require more extensive cardiac evaluation. Screening for carotid disease should also be performed, including a history of stroke or transient ischemic attack and carotid auscultation.

D. **Open surgical therapy**

1. Aortoiliac occlusive disease

   a. Aortobifemoral grafting is the treatment of choice in low-risk patients with diffuse aortoiliac stenoses and occlusions. Aortobifemoral bypass may be performed through a transperitoneal or a retroperitoneal approach. Distal endarterectomy may be performed in conjunction with a bypass to improve outflow. Results are excellent, with reported patency rates of up to 95% at 5 years.

   b. Femorofemoral, ilioiliac, or iliofemoral bypasses are alternatives in high-risk patients with unilateral iliac disease. The patency rates are lower than those achieved with aortobifemoral grafts.

   c. Axillobifemoral bypass is an alternative for high-risk patients who need revascularization. This bypass avoids an intra-abdominal procedure and the need for cross-clamping the aorta. The patency rates are poorer than those achieved with aortobifemoral bypass.

   d. Aortoiliac endarterectomy may be considered for patients who have disease localized to the distal aorta and common iliac vessels, although its use is now uncommon. Advantages include the avoidance of prosthetic material and preservation of antegrade flow into the hypogastric arteries.

2. Femoral, popliteal, and tibial occlusive disease

   a. In patients with above-knee occlusion, an above-knee femoral–popliteal bypass may be constructed. In patients who have disease below the knee, a distal bypass may be performed to the below-knee popliteal, posterior tibial, anterior tibial, or peroneal arteries. If all tibial vessels are occluded, pedal vessels may serve as suitable outflow vessels. These grafts usually originate from the common femoral artery, although a more distal vessel may be used if the inflow into that vessel is unobstructed.

   b. The best results are obtained with the use of autologous vein as a conduit. The greater saphenous is the vein of choice, but the lesser saphenous vein or the arm veins provide suitable alternatives. These autologous grafts can be used either in situ or reversed. The advantages of the in situ bypass are that (1) the vein's nutrient supply is left intact and (2) the vein orientation allows for a better size match (the large end of the vein is sewn to the large common femoral artery, and the small end is sewn to the distal vessel). The advantage of the reversed-vein bypass is that endothelial trauma is minimized because valve lysis is not necessary.

c. When autologous vein is not available, polytetrafluoroethylene (PTFE) grafts and cryopreserved vein grafts can be used. Patency rates for PTFE above-knee grafts approach those achieved with venous conduit, but use of PTFE for more distal bypass procedures is associated with substantially lower patency and is reserved for patients with critical limb ischemia who lack venous conduit. An alternative technique when performing PTFE bypass is the use of a small cuff of vein (Miller cuff) or patch angioplasty (Taylor patch) at the distal anastomosis. These modifications are believed to improve prosthetic graft patency by improving compliance match at the distal anastomosis. Cryopreserved vein graft patency also fares poorly in comparison to native autologous conduit, but it may prove useful when bypass is required in an infected field.

d. Endarterectomy is most commonly used to address severe stenosis or occlusion of the common femoral and profunda femoris arteries.

e. Amputation is reserved for patients with gangrene or persistent painful ischemia not amenable to vascular reconstruction. These patients often have severe coexistent vascular and cardiovascular disease, and the survival rate for patients undergoing major amputations is approximately 50% at 3 years and 30% at 5 years.

   (1) The level of amputation is determined clinically. Important factors include the necessity of removing all the infected tissue and the adequacy of the blood supply to heal the amputation. A general principle is to preserve as much length of the extremity as safely possible, as this improves the patient's opportunity for rehabilitation. Revascularization before amputation may enable a more distal amputation to heal adequately.

   (2) Digital amputations are performed commonly in diabetic patients who develop osteomyelitis or severe foot infections.

   (3) Transmetatarsal amputations are usually performed when several toes are involved in the ischemic process or after previous single-digit amputations.

   (4) Syme amputation involves the removal of the entire foot and calcaneus while preserving the entire tibia. It is rarely appropriate for PVD.

   (5) Below-knee amputation (BKA) is the most common type of amputation performed for patients with severe occlusive disease.

   (6) Above-knee amputation (AKA) heals more easily than BKA and is useful in older patients who do not ambulate.

   (7) Hip disarticulation is rarely performed for PVD.

3. Upper-extremity occlusive disease

   a. For proximal subclavian disease, the choice of bypass procedure depends primarily on the patency of the ipsilateral common carotid artery.

b. If the ipsilateral common carotid artery is patent, carotid–subclavian bypass is performed through a supraclavicular approach using a prosthetic graft (vein grafts are to be avoided). Subclavian artery transposition to ipsilateral carotid artery is an excellent alternative if anatomically feasible.

c. If the ipsilateral carotid artery is occluded, subclavian–subclavian bypass may be performed. This is an extra-anatomic approach using a longer segment prosthetic graft, with reduced patency.

4. Intraoperative anticoagulation is employed during most vascular reconstructions. Generally, unfractionated heparin (100 to 150 units/kg) is administered intravenously shortly before cross-clamping and supplemented as necessary until the cross-clamps are removed. Anticoagulation can be monitored intraoperatively by following activated clotting time levels. The anticoagulant effect of heparin can be reversed with protamine administration.

E. Postoperative care

1. For open aortic procedures, early postoperative care is usually administered in the ICU, where frequent hemodynamic and hematologic measurements are performed. Assessment of distal pulses should be done intraoperatively, immediately after reconstruction and regularly thereafter. In uncomplicated cases, the patients are usually extubated on the day of surgery or on postoperative day 1. Patients are kept well hydrated for the first 2 postoperative days, after which third-space fluid begins to mobilize and diuresis ensues. Fluid management may be guided by central pressure monitoring. Antibiotics are continued for 24 hours postoperatively. A nasogastric tube is kept in place until return of bowel function. Patients are instructed not to sit with the hips flexed at greater than 60 degrees for the first 72 hours after graft placement, although ambulation as early as possible is encouraged.

2. For distal bypass grafts, **pulses should be assessed frequently.** Antibiotics are continued for 24 hours postoperatively or longer if infected ulcers warrant such treatment. Early ambulation is encouraged in patients without tissue necrosis. In patients who are unable to ambulate immediately, physical therapy can help to increase strength in the limb and prevent contracture. Sitting with the hips flexed to 90 degrees is discouraged in any patient with a femoral anastomosis. Patients should be instructed to elevate their legs while resting because this will mitigate the edema that develops in the revascularized extremity. Staples are left in place for 2 to 3 weeks because these patients frequently have delayed wound healing.

3. **Perioperative antithrombotic therapy** should include aspirin (81 to 325 mg/day) for all infrainguinal reconstructions. In patients sensitive to aspirin, clopidogrel (75 mg/day) may be substituted.

4. Postoperative oral anticoagulation has a more limited role. Owing in part to the increased risk of hemorrhage, anticoagulation with warfarin (international normalized ratio 2:3) is generally limited to grafts considered to be at a high risk for thrombosis.

5. Following major amputations, weight bearing is delayed for 4 to 6 weeks. Some advocate the use of compressive wraps to aid in the maturation of the stump. In all cases, early consultation with a physical therapist is recommended. Physical therapy is essential for maintaining strength in the limb, preventing contractures, and rehabilitating the patient once a prosthesis is fitted. In addition, as soon as the patient is ready, he or she should be fitted with a prosthetic limb and ambulation training should begin. Rehabilitation rates (ability to walk without assistance) for patients undergoing unilateral BKA or AKA are 60% and 30%, respectively. For those with bilateral amputations, rehabilitation rates drop to 40% for patients with bilateral BKA and 10% for patients with bilateral AKA.

6. **Long-term follow-up** for distal bypass grafts consists of serial evaluations of graft patency by clinical examination and duplex ultrasound. Less frequent follow-up is necessary for aortoiliac bypasses. Detection of severe stenosis predicts pending graft failure, and such grafts should be studied further by arteriography. Intervention to repair or revise stenosed grafts results in much higher long-term patency than repairing or replacing occluded grafts.

F. **Complications**

1. Early complications occur in approximately 5% to 10% of patients after aortic surgery and frequently relate to preoperative comorbid disease. Myocardial infarction, congestive heart failure, pulmonary insufficiency, and renal insufficiency are most common. Complications related directly to aortic reconstruction include hemorrhage, embolization or thrombosis of the distal arterial tree, microembolization, ischemic colitis, ureteral injuries, impotence, paraplegia, and wound infection. Late complications include anastomotic pseudoaneurysm or graft dilation, graft limb occlusion, aortoenteric erosion or fistula, and graft infections.

2. In distal revascularizations, most of the early complications are also related to comorbid conditions. Early graft thrombosis (within 30 days of surgery) most often results from technical errors, hypercoagulability, inadequate distal runoff, and postoperative hypotension. **Technical errors** are responsible for more than 50% of early graft failures and include graft kinks, retained valve leaflets, valvulotome trauma, intimal flaps, significant residual arteriovenous fistulas, and the use of poor quality conduit.

G. **Endovascular options**

1. Aortoiliac occlusive disease
   a. Indications. Balloon angioplasty and intravascular stent placement for aortoiliac occlusive lesions produce excellent results. These procedures are indicated for symptomatic stenotic or occlusive lesions. Short-segment stenoses (less than 3 cm in length) of the common and external iliac arteries display excellent long-term patency rates when treated with angioplasty alone, or with stent placement. Angioplasty failure (defined as residual stenosis of ≥30%, residual

mean translesional pressure gradient of ≥10 mm Hg, or flow-limiting dissection) is an indication for stent deployment.

b. Technique. Access for iliac artery angioplasty and stenting is generally via the femoral arterial approach. When the occlusive lesion is in the distal aorta or ostial common iliac artery, angioplasty should be performed using two balloons, one in each iliac artery and both partially projecting into the distal aorta ("kissing balloons"). The rationale for this technique is that lesions in proximity to the aortic bifurcation typically involve the distal aorta and both common iliac arteries. Unilateral balloon dilation may cause plaque shifting with compromise of the contralateral iliac artery lumen. Stenting may produce a more favorable result if postangioplasty dissection or lesion recoil is noted. Balloon-expandable and self-expanding stents are generally oversized 10% to 15% relative to the adjacent normal artery to ensure satisfactory stent apposition to the vessel wall. If stent deployment is required in proximity to the aortic bifurcation, "kissing stents" are utilized in a fashion similar to that described above.

c. Complications. Procedural complications of iliac angioplasty and stenting include bleeding, arterial dissection, vessel occlusion, arterial rupture, and distal embolization, which may result in the need for surgical intervention or amputation.

d. Results. Early balloon angioplasty failure can result from elastic recoil of atherosclerotic plaque or arterial wall dissection. These complications are potentially amenable to stent placement. Late failure is usually due to intimal hyperplasia or progressive atherosclerosis. Iliac artery balloon angioplasty 2-year patency rates between 60% and 70% have been reported. Reports of iliac artery stenting demonstrate 4-year patency rates as high as 85%. In general, the results of angioplasty and stenting are better for common iliac artery lesions than for external iliac artery lesions, and are better for short-segment disease than for long-segment disease.

2. Infrainguinal occlusive disease

a. Indications. Balloon angioplasty and stenting of infrainguinal occlusive lesions has been widely applied for the treatment of claudication and critical limb ischemia. Aggressive modification of risk factors, institution of antiplatelet and statin medications, and a trial of exercise therapy are recommended prior to intervention, particularly in the setting of claudication. The Trans-Atlantic Inter-Society Consensus (TASC) group has provided recommendations regarding the characteristics of femoropopliteal and infrapopliteal lesions that are best addressed by either endovascular or surgical therapy. See Table 19-1. Short, focal stenoses (TASC A) are felt to be amenable to endovascular therapy, whereas long-segment occlusions (TASC D) are best addressed by surgical bypass.

b. Technique. Arterial access for infrainguinal intervention is usually accomplished via retrograde contralateral femoral artery approach or ipsilateral antegrade femoral artery approach. The most frequent cause of treatment failure is the inability to negotiate across the stenosis or occlusion and into the distal outflow target vessel. In general,

TABLE 19-1	TASC Classification

TASC Classification	Lesion Characteristics
A	Single stenosis <10 cm Single occlusion <5 cm
B	Multiple lesions <5 cm Single or multiple lesions in the absence of continuous tibial vessels Single stenosis/occlusion <15 cm Heavily calcified occlusion <5 cm Single popliteal stenosis
C	Multiple stenoses/occlusions totaling >15 cm Recurrent stenoses/occlusions needing intervention after two prior interventions
D	Chronic total occlusions of CFA or SFA Chronic total occlusion of popliteal and proximal trifurcation vessels

CFA, common femoral artery; SFA, superficial femoral artery; TASC, The Trans-Atlantic Inter-Society Consensus.

once guidewire access to the distal target vessel has been established, technical success rates are excellent. Hydrophilic guidewires and catheters, occlusion crossing devices, lumen reentry devices, and specialized sheaths have been developed to facilitate this process.

c. **Complications.** Procedural complications of infrainguinal endovascular intervention include bleeding, arterial thrombosis, vessel perforation, flow-limiting dissection, arteriovenous fistula formation, and distal embolization. Severe complications may require surgical intervention or, rarely, amputation.

d. **Results.** Unfortunately, midterm and long-term outcomes data for endovascular intervention in the treatment of claudication and critical limb ischemia remain relatively scarce. For moderate severity lesions of the femoropopliteal distribution, the ABSOLUTE trial demonstrated that primary nitinol stenting may provide a patency advantage over plain balloon angioplasty, and that this may be sustained through 2 years of follow-up (*NEJM.* 2006;354:1879). Perhaps the most compelling data regarding endovascular versus surgical intervention have been derived from the Bypass versus Angioplasty in Severe Ischemia of the Leg (BASIL) trial from the United Kingdom (*J Vasc Surg.* 2010;51:52S). Although the initial results reported from the trial were widely interpreted as demonstrating equivalency between angioplasty and bypass surgery for this patient cohort, longer term follow-up has shown an advantage in both overall survival and amputation-free survival in those patients who underwent bypass surgery and survived beyond 2 years. Interestingly, the BASIL investigators noted that outcomes were worse for patients who underwent angioplasty followed by salvage bypass surgery, rather than a bypass-first approach. Good surgical candidates—in particular, those possessing good venous conduit—should be considered for surgical reconstruction. Endovascular intervention is the preferred approach for the medically compromised patient, particularly those lacking autologous venous conduit. Finally, hybrid open surgical/endovascular procedures are also utilized in the treatment of critical limb ischemia. Vascular surgeons who are skilled in both open surgical reconstruction and endovascular interventions will therefore tailor their therapeutic approach based on each patient's unique risk factors and arterial anatomy.

20 Venous Disease, Thromboembolism, and Lymphedema

Wande Pratt and Brian Rubin

VENOUS ANATOMY

Venous anatomy is divided into three compartments: the superficial, the perforating veins, and the deep compartment. In general, blood flows from superficial to deep through the perforating system. In the lower extremity, the major superficial veins are the *greater saphenous vein,* formed from the union of the dorsal vein of the great toe and the dorsal venous arch; the *lesser saphenous vein,* formed from the joining of the dorsal vein of the fifth toe and the dorsal venous arch; and the *posterior arch vein,* also called *Leonardo's vein,* beginning in the medial ankle and joining the greater saphenous vein below the knee. The deep veins in the leg are named according to their paired arteries. The deep veins of the calf typically are duplicated as venae comitantes with numerous communicating branches. The posterior tibial and peroneal veins also communicate with the soleal sinusoids. In the thigh, the deep venous system includes the superficial and deep femoral veins that join approximately 4 cm below the inguinal ligament. Perforating veins connect the superficial and deep systems through both direct and indirect mechanisms. Venous return from the lower extremities depends largely on compression of the deep veins by the muscles of the calf (gastrocnemius, soleus) during walking. Flow is unidirectional due to a series of one-way valves, which prevent reflux during this cycle of compression. Failure of these valves to close leads to pooling, stasis, and congestion of veins in the lower extremities, and subsequent distention of the superficial veins.

CHRONIC VENOUS INSUFFICIENCY

Chronic venous disease includes cosmetically undesirable telangiectasias, varicose veins, venous ulceration, and claudication. Advances in duplex scanning and minimally invasive surgical techniques such as subfascial endoscopic perforating vein surgery (SEPS) and thermal ablation techniques are used to tailor medical and surgical therapies, resulting in marked improvement in clinical outcomes and patient satisfaction.

I. PATHOPHYSIOLOGY

   A. **Etiology**

      1. Congenital (may present later in life).

      2. Primary (cause undetermined).

      3. Secondary (postthrombotic, posttraumatic, or other).

B. **Risk factors**
   1. Obesity.
   2. Tobacco use.
   3. Multiparity.
   4. Hormone therapy.
   5. Obstruction within a proximal segment (e.g., from adenopathy, arterial compression, or pregnancy).
   6. History of deep venous thrombosis (DVT). DVT accounts for most secondary cases and may be responsible for a significant number of other cases because many deep vein thrombi are asymptomatic.

C. **Reflux disease** from venous valvular incompetence accounts for most (>80%) chronic venous disease.
   1. Valve malfunction can be inherited or acquired through sclerosis or elongation of valve cusps.
   2. May also result from dilation of the valve annulus despite normal valve cusps.
   3. Varicose veins may represent superficial venous insufficiency in the presence of competent deep and perforator systems, or they may be a manifestation of perforator or deep disease.
   4. Valvular disease below the knee appears to be more critical in the pathophysiology of severe disease than the disease above the knee.
   5. The perforator veins are frequently implicated when venous ulcers exist, but any component of the venous system, either alone or in combination, may be incompetent.
   6. All of the above components need evaluation in the workup of chronic venous insufficiency (CVI) (*Am Surg.* 2010;76:125).

D. **Obstructive physiology** is a less common cause of venous pathology, with reflux often being present simultaneously.

II. DIFFERENTIAL DIAGNOSIS

A. **Arterial disease**
   1. Ulcers with discrete edges and pale bases; more painful than venous ulcers.
   2. Poor or absent pulses on exam.
   3. Dependent rubor.
   4. Pallor with elevation.
   5. Claudication.

B. **Lymphedema**
   1. Pitting edema without pigmentation and ulceration.
   2. Less responsive to elevation, usually requiring several days to improve.

C. **Squamous cell carcinoma**
D. **Trauma**

E. Arteriovenous malformation

F. Orthostatic edema

III. NOMENCLATURE

A. CEAP classification

1. Based on the conclusions of an international consensus committee.

2. Standardized nomenclature of chronic venous disease (*J Vasc Surg.* 2004;40:1248; *Eur J Vasc Endovasc Surg.* 1996;12:487).

3. CEAP: **C**linical signs, **E**tiology, **A**natomic distribution, and **P**athophysiology (Table 20-1).

4. Useful in defining clinical severity of disease and subsequent management strategies.

5. Assessing response to therapy over time with the system proves difficult.

B. Venous clinical severity score (VCSS)

1. Developed by the American Venous Forum in 2000, and revised in 2010; expands the existing system.

2. Ten clinical descriptors: pain, varicose veins, venous edema, skin pigmentation, inflammation, induration, number of active ulcers, duration of active ulceration, size of ulcer, and compressive therapy use.

3. Better assesses ongoing response to therapy.

4. The revised VCSS, in conjunction with the CEAP classification system, provides a standard clinical language to describe and compare management approaches to chronic venous disease (*J Vasc Surg.* 2010;52:1387).

IV. DIAGNOSIS

A. History

1. A history of any DVT or trauma.

2. Family history of varicose veins or CVI.

3. Complaint of lower-extremity edema, aching, skin irritation, or varicose veins. Leg pain is described as a dull ache, worsening at the end of the day, and often relieved with exercise or elevation.

4. In rare instances, individuals can experience acute, bursting pain with ambulation (*venous claudication*). Prolonged rest and leg elevation (20 minutes) are needed to obtain relief.

B. Physical examination

1. Ankle edema.

2. Subcutaneous fibrosis.

3. Hyperpigmentation (brownish discoloration secondary to hemosiderin deposition).

4. Lipodermatosclerosis.

5. Venous eczema.

TABLE 20-1	Classification of Chronic Lower-Extremity Venous Disease
Classification	**Definition**
C	Clinical classification C_0: No visible or palpable signs of venous disease C_1: Telangiectasias or reticular veins C_2: Varicose veins; distinguished from reticular veins by a diameter of 3 mm or more C_3: Edema C_4: Changes in skin and subcutaneous tissue secondary to CVD C_{4a}: Pigmentation or eczema C_{4b}: Lipodermatosclerosis or atrophie blanche C_5: Healed venous ulcer C_6: Active venous ulcer *S: Symptomatic (includes aching, pain, tightness, skin irritation, heaviness, muscle cramps, and other complaints attributable to venous dysfunction)* *A: Asymptomatic*
E	Etiologic classification E_c: Congenital E_p: Primary E_s: Secondary (i.e., postthrombotic) E_n: No venous cause identified
A	Anatomic distribution A_s: Superficial veins involved A_p: Perforator veins involved A_d: Deep veins involved A_n: No venous location identified
P	Pathophysiologic dysfunction P_r: Reflux P_o: Obstruction $P_{r,o}$: Reflux and obstruction P_n: No venous pathophysiology identified

CVD, chronic venous disease.

6. Dilation of subcutaneous veins, including telangiectasias (0.1 to 1 mm), reticular veins (1 to 4 mm), and varicose veins (>4 mm).

7. Ultimately, ulcers develop, typically proximal to the medial malleolus.

8. Any signs of infection should be noted.

9. Arterial pulses should be examined and are usually adequate.

C. **Noninvasive studies**
  1. **Duplex scanning**
     a. B-mode ultrasound imaging combined with Doppler frequency shift display.
     b. Used in assessing valvular incompetence and obstruction, presence of acute or chronic DVT.
     c. With the leg in a dependant position, cuffs are placed on the thigh, calf, and foot and inflated; then the cuffs are rapidly deflated in an attempt to create retrograde venous blood flow in segments of valvular incompetence.
     d. Competent valves generally take no more than 0.5 to 1 second to close.
     e. Detailed mapping of valve competence of each segment of the venous system is possible, including the common femoral, superficial femoral, greater saphenous, lesser saphenous, popliteal, posterior tibial, and perforator veins.
     f. Has a predictive value of 77% for diagnosing reflux leading to severe symptoms.
  2. **Descending phlebography** has a predictive value of 44%, previously considered the gold standard (*J Vasc Surg.* 1992;16:687). Descending phlebography is limited by its inability to study valves distal to a competent proximal valve.
  3. **Continuous wave Doppler**
     a. Easily performed in the office using a handheld probe.
     b. Helpful for screening for reflux at the saphenofemoral and saphenopopliteal junctions.
     c. Limited due to inability to quantitate reflux and to provide precise anatomic information.
  4. **Trendelenburg test**
     a. Largely replaced by the much more accurate duplex imaging studies.
     b. Patient's leg is elevated to drain venous blood. An elastic tourniquet is applied at the saphenofemoral junction, and the patient then stands.
     c. Rapid filling (<30 seconds) of the saphenous system from the deep system indicates perforator valve incompetence.
     d. When tourniquet is released, additional filling of the saphenous system occurs if the saphenofemoral valve is also incompetent.

V. NONSURGICAL TREATMENT

A. **Infected ulcers**
  1. Necessitate treatment of the infection first.
  2. *Staphylococcus aureus*, *Streptococcus pyogenes*, and *Pseudomonas* species are responsible for most infections.
  3. Usually treated with local wound care, wet-to-dry dressings, and oral antibiotics.
  4. Topical antiseptics should be avoided.
  5. Severe infections require intravenous antibiotics.

B. **Leg elevation** can temporarily decrease edema and should be instituted when swelling occurs. This should be done before a patient is fitted for stockings or boots.

C. **Compression therapy** is the primary treatment for CVI.

1. **Elastic compression stockings**
   a. Fitted to provide a compression gradient from 30 to 40 mm Hg, with the greatest compression at the ankle.
   b. Donned on arising from bed and removed at bedtime.
   c. Effective in healing ulcers, *but can take months* to obtain good results.
   d. Study of 113 patients treated with initial bed rest, local wound care, and elastic compression stockings demonstrated a 93% ulcer healing rate in a mean of 5.3 months (*Surgery.* 1991;109:575).
   e. Stockings do not correct the abnormal venous hemodynamics and must be worn after the ulcer has healed to prevent recurrence.
   f. Principal drawback is patient compliance.
   g. Recurrence for compliant patients in the same study was 16% at a mean follow-up of 30 months.

2. **Unna boots**
   a. Paste gauze compression dressings that contain zinc oxide, calamine, and glycerin.
   b. Used to help prevent further skin breakdown.
   c. Provide nonelastic compression therapy.
   d. Changed once or twice a week.

3. **Pneumatic compression devices**
   a. Provide dynamic sequential compression.
   b. Used primarily in the prevention of deep vein thrombi in hospitalized patients.
   c. Also used successfully to treat venous insufficiency.

D. **Topical medications**

1. Largely ineffective as a stand-alone therapy for venous stasis ulcers.

2. Topical therapy is directed at absorbing wound drainage and avoiding desiccation of the wound.

3. Antiseptics can be counterproductive. Hydrogen peroxide, povidone-iodine, acetic acid, and sodium hypochlorite are toxic to cultured fibroblasts and should be used for the shortest duration necessary to control ulcer infection.

VI. **SURGICAL THERAPY** is indicated for severe disease refractory to medical treatment and for patients who cannot comply with the lifelong regimen of compression therapy. Surgical therapy includes sclerotherapy, saphenous vein stripping, endovenous laser ablation of the saphenous vein, SEPS, and varicose vein stab avulsion.

A. **Preoperative evaluation.** All patients should undergo a thorough history and physical examination with special attention to symptoms of chronic venous disease, including aching pain, sense of heaviness in the legs, and fatigability with ambulation. Patients often describe their symptoms as worsening throughout the course of the day, particularly if they are required to stand for long periods. Diagnostic evaluation consists primarily of duplex imaging (including vein mapping, reflux studies, and assessment for DVT) in a reliable vascular laboratory. This allows for visualization of the affected venous segments and for determination of points of reflux. Valve closure time should be assessed, usually within the great saphenous vein, with times greater than 500 milliseconds considered abnormal.

B. Sclerotherapy

1. Effective in treating telangiectasias, reticular varicosities, and small varicose veins.

2. If saphenous reflux is present, it should be corrected first.

3. Contraindications include arterial occlusive disease, immobility, acute thrombophlebitis, and hypersensitivity to the drug.

4. **Sclerosing agents**
   a. 1% or 3% sodium tetradecyl sulfate.
   b. Sodium morrhuate (rarely used because of anaphylactic reactions).
   c. Hypertonic saline.
   d. Polidocanol (approved in March 2010, by the U.S. Food and Drug Administration).

5. Varices are marked while the patient is standing. A 25-gauge needle is used to inject 0.25 to 0.50 mL of sclerosant slowly into the lumen of larger veins. A 30-gauge needle is used for sclerosing reticular veins and telangiectasias in supine patients.

6. Compression stockings are applied at the end of the procedure and are worn for several days to 6 weeks. Patients should walk for 30 minutes after the procedure.

7. Complications include cutaneous necrosis, hyperpigmentation, telangiectatic matting (new, fine, red telangiectasias), thrombophlebitis, anaphylaxis, allergic reaction, visual disturbances, venous thromboembolism (VTE), and even death (*J Vasc Surg*. 2010;52:939; *Dermatol Surg*. 1995;21:19).

C. **Saphenous vein stripping,** once considered the gold standard for superficial venous surgery, has since been replaced by the use of minimally invasive techniques in many practices by the US surgeons treating CVI; however, the surgeons should be familiar with this technique. Stripping of the entire length of the saphenous vein is usually unnecessary. Typically, the vein is stripped from mid-calf or knee level to the saphenofemoral junction. If the entire vein is involved, one incision is made anterior to the medial malleolus and another just below the inguinal crease. A standard vein stripper is inserted into the vein lumen at one site and advanced through the lumen to the other site. High ligation of the vein is performed at the saphenofemoral junction, including all venous tributaries. Reconnection of the saphenous to the femoral system via multiple tributaries near the saphenofemoral junction is thought to be the major cause of recurrent varices. At the completion of the procedure, compressive bandages are applied to reduce hematoma formation, and compression stockings are worn for several weeks. Complications include ecchymosis, DVT, and saphenous nerve injury. Stripping only the thigh portion is probably the most important aspect of the procedure, and eliminates much of the risk to the saphenous nerve because this nerve is closely associated with the saphenous vein from the knee to the ankle. In addition, this preserves the portion of the vein below the knee to be used for arterial bypass if needed in the future (*Lancet.* 1996;348:210). Because the goal of stripping is to prevent reflux of the involved venous segment, removal of a limited portion of the saphenous system is now widely accepted. Ligation alone, however, is associated with high rates of recanalization and is therefore not adequate therapy.

D. **Endovenous ablation of the saphenous vein**
 1. This was shown to effectively treat saphenous reflux and associated varicose veins with less morbidity than saphenectomy (*J Vasc Surg.* 2003;38:207).
 2. A probe is inserted into the greater saphenous vein under ultrasound guidance. The probe emits either laser or radiofrequency energy, which coagulates and coapts the vein walls, causing complete obliteration of the lumen.
 3. Potential complications
    a. Skin burns.
    b. DVT.
    c. Pulmonary thromboembolism.
    d. Vein perforation and hematoma.
    e. Paresthesias.
    f. Phlebitis.
 4. Reported outcomes achieved with endovenous radiofrequency and laser obliteration are comparable to those resulting from saphenectomy (*Ann Vasc Surg.* 2010;24:360; *J Vasc Interv Radiol.* 2009;20:752; *J Vasc Surg.* 2008;47:151). Incomplete obliteration and recanalization occur in a small percentage of patients.
 5. A contraindication to endovenous obliteration is saphenous vein thrombosis.

E. **Subfascial Endoscopic Perforating Vein Surgery**
 1. This is associated with decreased morbidity and has gained recognition as an alternative treatment option.
 2. Performed by making small port incisions in unaffected skin in the calf and fascia of the posterior superficial compartment. Various types of endoscopes (laparoscopic, arthroplastic, or bronchoscopic) can be used for visualization. Carbon dioxide insufflation in the subfascial space may or may not be used. A balloon expander can expand the subfascial space to improve visualization. Typically, 3 to 14 perforators are identified and ligated.
 3. Most patients are discharged within 24 hours of surgery.

F. **Varicose vein stab avulsion**
 1. Preoperatively, the patient's varicose veins are carefully marked with indelible ink while the patient is standing. Some authors consider this to be the most important technical step.

2. Small incisions (2 to 3 mm) are made next to the markings. The vein is pulled out of the incision with a small vein hook, and the two arms of the vein are pulled taut and avulsed. This can be repeated many times to remove large clusters of veins. The small incisions can be closed with Steri-Strips. The patient's leg is covered with compression stockings for several days to weeks. This technique is often used in conjunction with saphenous stripping to provide optimal results. Alternatively, the greater saphenous vein can be removed by sequential avulsion instead of stripping.

VENOUS THROMBOEMBOLISM

I. **EPIDEMIOLOGY.** VTE, which includes DVT and pulmonary embolism (PE), is a common cause of death. The true incidence of DVT is difficult to determine because its clinical diagnosis can be inaccurate and often occurring in the setting of other critical illnesses. Venous thromboembolic disease represents a significant problem, with 250,000 hospitalizations for DVT/PE annually. Approximately 50% to 60% of DVT episodes are asymptomatic. Of those patients with DVTs, 30% will have a symptomatic PE with a mortality of 17.5% if untreated. DVT and PE occur in approximately 10% to 40% of general surgical patients without perioperative prophylaxis, and 40% to 60% following major orthopedic surgery (*Chest.* 2008;133:381S–453S).

II. **PATHOPHYSIOLOGY.** DVT starts as a platelet nidus, usually in the venous valves of the calf. The thrombogenic nature of the nidus activates the clotting cascade, leading to platelet and fibrin accumulation. The fibrinolytic system is subsequently activated, with thrombus growth if thrombogenesis predominates over thrombolysis. A thrombus can detach from the endothelium and migrate into the pulmonary system, becoming a PE; alternatively, it can also organize and grow into the endothelium, resulting in venous incompetency and phlebitis. Thrombi localized to the calf have less tendency to embolize than thrombi that extend to the thigh veins (*Am Rev Respir Dis.* 1990;141:1). Approximately 20% of cases of calf DVT propagate to the thigh, and 50% of cases of thigh or proximal DVT embolize.

III. **RISK FACTORS FOR VENOUS THROMBOEMBOLISM**

A. **Malignancy**
   1. Tumor cell activation of the clotting cascade can occur directly through interactions with factors VIIa, X, and tissue factor (TF).
   2. Indirect clotting activation can occur through stimulation of mononuclear cells to produce TF or factor X activators and stimulation of macrophages to produce TF activators.
   3. Reactive thrombocytosis can occur in patients, especially those with advanced disease of the lung, colon, stomach, or breast; it is caused by spontaneous clumping of platelets or increased levels of thrombopoietin, a glycoprotein regulating the maturation of megakaryocytes.

B. **Endothelial injury**

1. Adhesion of tumor cells to endothelium can lead to disruption of endothelial intracellular junctions and expose the highly thrombogenic subendothelial surface.

2. Chemotherapeutic drugs, such as bleomycin, carmustine, vincristine, and doxorubicin (Adriamycin), can also cause vascular endothelial cell damage.

C. **Venous stasis**

1. This is caused by immobility, venous obstruction, increased venous pressure, and increased blood viscosity.

2. Venous stasis promotes thrombus formation by reducing clearance of activated coagulation factors and by causing endothelial hypoxia, leading to reduced levels of surface-bound thrombomodulin and increased expression of TF.

3. Two very common causes of immobility leading to DVT formation are surgery and critical illness. Major chest surgery, abdominal/pelvic surgery, and lower-extremity surgery have all been associated with increased risk of DVT development. Similarly, a prolonged nonambulatory state, such as fracture of the hip, pelvis, or leg; multisystem trauma; neurologic injury; or other critical injury requiring bed rest can increase DVT risk.

D. **Oral contraceptives (OCPs) and estrogen hormone replacement therapy**

1. These have been linked to increased risk of venous thrombus formation. Many studies have found an odds ratio of 3 to 5 for risk of DVT in patients taking OCPs compared to non–OCP-using patients.

2. An increased risk is still found with patients using third-generation OCPs containing new progestins.

E. **Hypercoagulable states**

1. Primary hypercoagulable states are inherited conditions that can lead to abnormal endothelial cell thromboregulation.
   a. Decreased thrombomodulin-dependent activation of protein C (factor V Leiden mutation).
   b. Impaired heparin binding of antithrombin III.
   c. Downregulation of membrane-associated plasmin production.
   d. Increased serum prothrombin levels (G20210A prothrombin gene mutation).
   e. Decreased thrombogenic inhibitors (e.g., antithrombin III, protein C, protein S).

2. Secondary hypercoagulable states are states in which endothelial activation by cytokines leads to an inflammatory, thrombogenic vessel wall.
   a. Antiphospholipid syndrome.
   b. Venous trauma.
   c. Surgery.
   d. Hyperhomocysteinemia.

   e. Heparin-induced thrombopathy.
   f. Myeloproliferative syndromes.
   g. Cancer.
   h. Chemotherapy agents: cyclophosphamide, methotrexate, and 5-fluorouracil, cause a decrease in the plasma levels of proteins C and S.

IV. DIAGNOSIS

A. Initial evaluation

1. Approximately 75% of patients with suspected DVT or PE turn out not to have these conditions.
2. Assessment of risk factors (see Section III).
3. Clinical presentation
   a. Extremity pain.
   b. Increased circumference with respect to contralateral extremity.
   c. Dilation of superficial veins of the suspected extremity only.
   d. Calf pain on dorsiflexion of the ankle.
   e. Phlegmasia alba dolens represents a more severe manifestation of DVT in which the deep venous channels of the extremity are affected *while sparing collateral veins* and therefore maintaining some degree of venous return. Patients present with blanching of the extremity, edema, and discomfort.
   f. Phlegmasia cerulea dolens occurs with extension of thrombus into the collateral venous system, resulting in limb pain and swelling, accompanied by cyanosis, a sign of arterial ischemia.

B. Suspected DVT

1. Compression ultrasonography of the femoral, popliteal, and calf trifurcation veins is highly sensitive (>90%) in detecting thrombosis of the proximal veins (femoral and popliteal) but less sensitive (50%) in detecting calf vein thrombosis.
2. It represents the preferred diagnostic modality because it is less invasive than the reference standard of venography and is more sensitive than impedance plethysmography.
3. Approximately 2% of patients with initial normal ultrasound results have positive results on repeat tests performed 7 days later. Delayed detection rate is attributed to extension of calf vein thrombi or small, nonocclusive proximal vein thrombi.

C. Assessment of PE

1. **Contrast-enhanced spiral computed tomography (CT)** has sensitivity (70% to 90%) comparable to that of pulmonary angiography. Spiral CT is preferable to angiography (less invasive and less expensive).
2. Chest CT can be combined with CT angiography of pelvic and deep thigh veins to detect DVT as well as PE.
3. Patients with significant contrast allergy or renal insufficiency are not candidates for CT scanning.

4. Radionucleotide ventilation and perfusion lung imaging (V/Q scan) has been replaced by chest CT as the initial imaging test for suspected PE. V/Q scanning is used in situations in which CT is deemed not feasible. A V/Q scan result of "high probability" strongly suggests the presence of PE. However, more than 50% of patients have "intermediate probability" results. Because approximately 25% of these patients have PE, further evaluation or initiation of empiric treatment must be considered.

5. **Pulmonary angiography,** the reference test, is reserved for patients whose diagnosis is still uncertain.

V. PREVENTION AND TREATMENT OF VENOUS THROMBOEMBOLISM. For anticoagulation treatments following specific procedures, please see the recent guidelines published by the American College of Chest Physicians (*Chest.* 2008;133:381S).

A. **Low-dose unfractionated heparin (LDUH)**

1. This is given subcutaneously at 5,000 units 1 to 2 hours before surgery, and every 8 or 12 hours postoperatively (*N Engl J Med.* 1988;318:18).

2. LDUH reduces the risk of VTE by 50% to 70% (*N Engl J Med.* 1988;318:18) and does not require laboratory monitoring. Because of the potential for minor bleeding, it should not be used for patients undergoing cerebral, ocular, or spinal surgery.

B. **Graduated compression stockings**

1. These are effective in preventing DVT formation by reducing venous stasis.

2. In surgery patients, the use of graduated compression stockings appears to augment the protective benefit of low-dose heparin by nearly 75%. The combination of graduated compression stockings and LDUH is significantly more effective than LDUH alone, with DVT rates of 4% and 15%, respectively (*Cochrane Database Syst Rev.* 2000;1:CD001484; *Br J Surg.* 1985;72:7).

3. Graduated compression stockings are relatively inexpensive and should be considered for all high-risk patients, even when other forms of prophylaxis are used. Furthermore, the early use of either over-the-counter or custom-fit stockings following diagnosis of DVT results in a reduction in the incidence of postthrombotic syndromes (*Lancet.* 1997;349:759; *Ann Intern Med.* 2004;141:249).

C. **Intermittent pneumatic compression of the extremities**

1. Enhances blood flow in the deep veins, and increases blood fibrinolytic activity through upregulation of thrombomodulin, fibrinolysin, t-PA and endothelial nitric oxide synthase expression (*Acta Anaesthesiologica Scandinavica.* 2005;49:660).

2. For patients with significant bleeding risk with anticoagulation, pneumatic compression is an effective alternative.

3. Compression devices should not be placed on an extremity with known DVT.

4. In the case of known bilateral lower-extremity DVT, the compression devices can be placed on the upper extremity.

5. Pedal compression devices are also effective in patients whose body habitus does not allow conventionally sized devices to fit around the thighs or calves.

D. **Low–molecular-weight heparins (LMWHs)**

1. Several advantages over unfractionated heparin, with longer half-lives, a more predictable dose–response curve, a lower risk of heparin-induced thrombocytopenia (HIT), the possibility of ambulatory treatment at home and in laboratory animals, fewer bleeding complications with equivalent anticoagulation effects.

2. In large randomized trials of patients with DVT, outpatient treatment with a LMWH was as safe and effective as inpatient treatment with intravenous unfractionated heparin.

E. **Other medications** such as the direct thrombin inhibitors (DTIs) and fondaparinux represent a possible alternative to the unfractionated and LMWHs in the prevention of thromboembolic disease. The univalent DTI Argatroban as well as the bivalent DTIs (binding to both the active site and an additional accessory site on the thrombin molecule) lepirudin, bivalirudin, hirudin, and desirudin, administered by intravenous, intramuscular, or subcutaneous injection, offer an alternative to the heparins, particularly in situations in which heparin is contraindicated, such as HIT. These medications, however, are less suitable for long-term treatment (*N Engl J Med.* 2005;353:2827). Fondaparinux, the first synthetic pentasaccharide, blocks thrombin generation by accelerating the rate of factors IIa, VIIa, IXa, Xa, XIa, and XIIa inactivation by antithrombin. The agent possesses almost complete bioavailability after subcutaneous injection, with clearance by the kidneys in unaltered form (*Curr Opin Anaes.* 2006;19:52).

F. **Caval interruption with intracaval filters.** The American College of Chest Physicians recommends inferior vena cava (IVC) filter placement only in those patients with proven VTE with a contraindication for anticoagulation, a complication of anticoagulation, or recurrent VTE despite adequate anticoagulation. No randomized trials have examined the prophylactic use of IVC filters in any patient population. In fact, several meta-analyses found no difference in the rates of PE among patients with and without prophylactic IVC filters (*J Trauma.* 2000;49:140; *J Am Coll Surg.* 1999;189:314). Absolute and relative indications for caval interruption are listed in Table 20-2 (*Chest.* 2008;133:381S; *Am J Med.* 2007;120:S13; *Prog Cardiovasc Dis.* 2006;49:98; *J Am Coll Surg.* 2005;201:957; *Chest.* 2004;126:401S; *J Vasc Interv Radiol.* 2003;14:425; *Blood.* 2000;95:3669). Complications related to filter insertion occur in 4% to 11% of patients. The most common complications are related to thrombotic complications: insertion site thrombosis (2% to 28%); IVC thrombosis (3% to 11%); and recurrent DVT (6% to 35%). Other complications include filter migration, penetration of the IVC, filter fracture, vena caval obstruction, and guidewire entrapment. The specific types of

TABLE 20-2	Use of Inferior Vena Cava Filters

Absolute indications (*strongly* recommended according to evidence-based guidelines)
Proven VTE with contraindication for anticoagulation.
Proven VTE with complication of anticoagulation treatment.
Recurrent VTE despite anticoagulation treatment ("failure of anticoagulation").

Relative indications (*expanded* use; not guideline recommended)
Recurrent PE complicated by pulmonary hypertension.
Patients with DVT and limited cardiopulmonary reserve or chronic obstructive pulmonary disease.
Patients with large, free-floating ileofemoral thrombus.
Following thrombectomy, embolectomy, or thrombolysis of DVT.
High-risk trauma patients (head and spinal cord injury, pelvic or lower extremity fractures) with a contraindication for anticoagulation.
Patients with DVT who have cancer or burns, or are pregnant.

Contraindications for filter placement
Chronically thrombosed IVC.
Anatomical abnormalities preventing access to the IVC for filter placement.

VTE, venous thromboembolism; PE, pulmonary embolism; DVT, deep venous thrombosis; IVC, inferior vena cava.

retrievable and permanent filters are beyond the scope of this chapter, but the use of retrievable filters can reduce the incidence of thrombotic complications (*Am J Med.* 2007;120:S13).

G. The **choice of prophylaxis method** depends on the risk of VTE compared with the risk of anticoagulation. See Chapter 1 for a detailed description.

H. **Catheter-directed thrombolysis** of acute DVT with or without mechanical thrombectomy devices has been advocated to avoid sequelae of DVT. The goals are to restore venous flow, preserve venous valve function, and eliminate the possibility of thromboembolism. Technical success and early clinical benefit have been reported, but long-term data are unavailable. In patients with migration of DVT resulting in severe PE and hemodynamic instability, potentially life-saving thrombolytics should be considered (*Curr Opin Anaes.* 2006;19:52).

LYMPHEDEMA

I. PATHOPHYSIOLOGY

A. **Primary lymphedema** is the result of congenital aplasia, hypoplasia, or hyperplasia of lymphatic vessels and nodes that causes the accumulation of a protein-rich fluid in the interstitial space. Swelling of the patient's leg initially produces pitting edema, which progresses to a nonpitting form and may lead to dermal fibrosis and disfigurement.

1. Primary lymphedema is classified according to age at presentation.
   a. Congenital primary lymphedema (present at birth) represents 10% to 15% of all cases, which can be hereditary (Milroy disease) or nonhereditary.
   b. Praecox (early in life) or Meige disease represents 70% to 80% of cases.
      (1) It is seen in female patients 80% to 90% of the time.
      (2) It presents during the second and third decades of life, typically with localized swelling of the foot and ankle. Such swelling is worsened by prolonged standing.
      (3) A single lower extremity is affected in 70% of patients.
   c. Tarda (late in life) primary lymphedema, representing 10% to 15% of cases, is seen equally in men and women and presents after the third or fourth decade of life.

B. **Secondary lymphedema** results from impaired lymphatic drainage secondary to a known cause. Surgical or traumatic interruption of lymphatic vessels (often from an axillary or groin lymph node dissection), carcinoma, infection, venous thrombosis, and radiation are causes of secondary lymphedema. Secondary lymphedema in the context of filariasis, caused by the parasite *Wuchereria bancrofti*, represents the most common worldwide presentation of the disease.

II. DIAGNOSIS

A. **Clinical presentation**
   1. Symptoms
      a. Early lymphedema is characterized by unilateral or bilateral arm or pedal swelling that resolves overnight. With disease progression, the swelling increases and extends up the extremity, producing discomfort and thickened skin. With more advanced disease, swelling is not relieved overnight. Significant pain is unusual.
      b. Secondary lymphedema patients commonly present with repeated episodes of cellulitis secondary to high interstitial protein content.
   2. Physical examination
      a. Edema of the affected extremity is present.
      b. When a lower extremity is involved, the toes are often spared.
      c. With advanced disease, the extremity becomes tense, with nonpitting edema.
      d. Dermal fibrosis results in skin thickening, hair loss, and generalized keratosis.

B. **Imaging studies**
   1. **Lymphoscintigraphy** is the injection of radiolabeled (technetium-99m) colloid into the web space between the patient's second and third toes or fingers. The patient's limb is exercised periodically, and images are taken of the involved extremity and the whole body. Lymphedema is seen as an abnormal accumulation of tracer or as slow tracer clearance along with the presence of collaterals. For the diagnosis of lymphedema,

the study has a sensitivity and specificity of 92% and 100%, respectively (*J Vasc Surg.* 1989;9:683).

2. **CT and magnetic resonance (MR) scan** are able to exclude any mass obstructing the lymphatic system. MR scan has been able to differentiate lymphedema from chronic venous edema and lipedema (excessive subcutaneous fat and fluid).

3. **Lymphangiography** involves catheter placement and injection of radiopaque dye directly into lymphatic channels; it has largely been replaced by lymphoscintigraphy and CT. A decreased total number of lymphatic channels and structural abnormalities can be seen. Lymphangiography can demonstrate the site of a lymphatic leak in postsurgical or traumatic situations. Complications include lymphangitis and hypersensitivity reaction to the dye.

III. **DIFFERENTIAL DIAGNOSIS** includes all other causes of a swollen extremity.

A. **Trauma.**
B. **Infection.**
C. **Arterial disease.**
D. **CVI.**
E. **Lipedema.**
F. **Neoplasm.**
G. **Radiation effects.**
H. Systemic diseases, such as right ventricular failure, myxedema, nephrosis, nephritis, and protein deficiency. These causes must be excluded before invasive study.

IV. **TREATMENT**

A. **Medical management** is limited by the physiologic and anatomic nature of the disease. The use of diuretics to remove fluid is not effective because of the high interstitial protein concentration. Development of fibrosis and irreversible changes in the subcutaneous tissue further limit options. The objectives of conservative treatment are to control edema, maintain healthy skin, and avoid cellulitis and lymphangitis.

1. **Combination of physical therapies (CPT)** is the primary approach recommended in a consensus document by the International Society of Lymphology Executive Committee (*Lymphology.* 2009;42:51). CPT consists of a two-stage treatment program, beginning with skin care, followed by the application of compression bandages. Phase 1 involves gentle manual manipulation of tissues to direct lymph flow (manual lymph drainage), range of motion exercises, and multilayered compression bandage wrapping. Phase 2 conserves and optimizes results obtained in Phase 1; patients wear custom-made compression garments. In a study of 119 patients with 3-year follow-up, CPT reduced lymphedema by 63% (*Oncology.* 1997;11:99).

2. **Sequential pneumatic compression** has been shown to improve lymphedema. Several designs have been used with various degrees of

success. Elastic stockings or sleeves should be fitted and worn afterward to maintain results. Extremity elevation may also help.

3. **Skin care and good hygiene** are important. Topical hydrocortisone cream may be needed for eczema.

4. **Benzopyrones** (such as warfarin) have been effective in reducing lymphedema due to filariasis. Their action is believed to derive from enhanced macrophage activity and extralymphatic absorption of interstitial proteins.

5. **Cellulitis and lymphangitis** should be suspected when sudden onset of pain, swelling, or erythema of the leg occurs. Intravenous antibiotics should be initiated to cover staphylococci and β-hemolytic streptococci. Broad-spectrum penicillins, cephalosporins, or vancomycin usually are adequate. Limb elevation and immobilization should be initiated, and warm compresses can be used for symptomatic relief. Topical antifungal cream may be needed for chronic infections.

B. **Surgical options.** Surgical intervention is an alternative approach for patients whose lymphedema has been refractory to nonoperative therapies. Only 10% of patients with lymphedema are surgical candidates, and surgery is directed at reducing limb size. Indications for operation are related to function because cosmetic deformities persist postoperatively. Results are best when surgery is performed for severely impaired movement and recurrent cellulitis. Surgical therapies for lymphatic disease are not without consequence, and have largely been abandoned (*Cancer.* 2001;92:980).

1. **Total subcutaneous excision** is performed for extensive swelling and skin changes. Circumferential excision of the skin and subcutaneous tissue from the tibial tuberosity to the malleoli is performed. The defect is closed with a split- or full-thickness skin graft from the resected specimen or a split-thickness skin graft from an uninvolved site. Recurrent lymphedema and hyperpigmentation occur more frequently when split-thickness skin grafts are used.

2. Closure of disrupted lymphatic channels.

3. Omental transposition.

4. Lymphatic transposition includes direct (lymphovenous bypass, lymphatic grafting) and indirect (mesenteric bridge, omental flap) procedures. Lymphatic grafting is performed for upper-extremity or unilateral lower-extremity lymphedema. Good results have been reported in 80% of patients (*Plast Reconstr Surg.* 1990;85:64). A mesenteric bridge is formed by suturing a segment of mucosa-stripped ileum with intact blood supply to transected distal iliac or inguinal nodes. An omental flap placed in a swollen limb is believed to improve lymphatic drainage through spontaneous lympholymphatic anastomoses. Because of their complexity and associated complications, indirect procedures are not widely used.

5. Microsurgical lymphovenous anastomoses bypass the obstructed lymphatic system in patients with chronic lymphedema. With improved microvascular techniques, patency rates of 50% to 70% can be expected many months after surgery (*J Vasc Surg.* 1986;4:148).

Endocrine Surgery

Brian T. Bucher and Jeffrey F. Moley

THYROID

I. EMBRYOLOGY, ANATOMY, AND PHYSIOLOGY

A. **Embryology.** The thyroid gland develops from the endoderm of the primitive foregut and arises in the ventral pharynx in the region of the base of the tongue (later indicated by the foramen cecum). With further development, the thyroid descends into the neck anterior to the hyoid bone and laryngeal cartilages. Certain congenital anomalies such as ectopic thyroid tissue or thyroglossal duct cysts are directly related to this embryologic descent. The parafollicular cells, or C cells, are derived from the neural crest, migrate to the thyroid, and produce calcitonin.

B. **Anatomy.** The adult thyroid is a bilobar structure connected by an isthmus that lies anterior to the junction of the larynx and trachea. The blood supply to the thyroid arises from two pairs of main arteries: the superior thyroid artery (branch of the external carotid) and the inferior thyroid artery (branch of the thyrocervical trunk). The recurrent laryngeal nerve (RLN) usually courses 1 cm anterior or posterior to the inferior thyroid artery. Careful dissection around this artery is necessary to avoid injury to the RLN.

C. **Physiology.** The thyroid is stimulated to release thyroid hormone in response to thyroid-stimulating hormone (TSH) secreted from the anterior pituitary gland. TSH secretion is stimulated by thyrotropin-releasing hormone (TRH) from the hypothalamus. Thyroid hormone synthesis begins when dietary iodide is ingested, actively transported into the thyroid gland, and then oxidized by thyroid peroxidase into iodine. Iodination of tyrosine results in monoiodotyrosine (MIT) and diiodotyrosine (DIT). Iodine coupling of MIT and DIT results in the formation of triiodothyronine (T_3) and thyroxine (T_4), which are bound to thyroglobulin while in the thyroid. On release into plasma, 80% of T_3 and T_4 are bound to thyroxine-binding globulin (TBG). Only the unbound or "free" hormones are active (i.e., available to tissues) with T_3 being much more potent than T_4.

II. BIOCHEMICAL. **Evaluation of thyroid disorders** confirms clinically suspected abnormalities in thyroid function; however, test results must be interpreted in the context of clinical findings.

A. Measurement of TSH (0.3 to 5 mIU/L) is the most useful biochemical test in the diagnosis of thyroid illness. In most patients without pituitary disease, increased TSH signifies hypothyroidism, suppressed TSH suggests hyperthyroidism, and normal TSH reflects a euthyroid state.

B. Assessment of free T_4 (4.5 to 11.2 μg/dL) concentration supports identified abnormalities in TSH and provides an index of severity of thyroid dysfunction. Total T_4 (3 to 12 μg/dL) is affected by changes in hormone product or binding and does not directly reflect the small "free" or active T_4 fractions.

C. An indirect measurement of free T_4 can be obtained using the resin T_3 uptake (RT$_3$U). This assay measures unoccupied thyroid hormone-binding sites on TBG by allowing radiolabeled T_3 to compete for binding between TBG. The RT$_3$U is directly related to the FT$_4$ fraction and inversely related to the TBG-binding sites. The FT$_4$ index [FT$_4$I = total T_4 × RT$_3$U] (0.85 to 3.5) correlates more closely with the level of FT$_4$, eliminates ambiguity introduced by altered thyroglobulin levels, and is the preferred test for estimating FT$_4$.

D. Measurement of T_3 (80 to 200 ng/dL) is unreliable as a test for hypothyroidism. This test is useful in the occasional patient with suspected hyperthyroidism, suppressed TSH, and normal FT$_4$I (T_3 thyrotoxicosis).

E. Antithyroid microsomal antibodies are found in the serum of patients with autoimmune thyroiditis (Hashimoto thyroiditis). Anti-TSH receptor antibodies, which stimulate the TSH receptor, are detectable in more than 90% of patients with autoimmune hyperthyroidism (Graves' disease).

F. The American Thyroid Association has published evidence-based guidelines on the detection of thyroid dysfunction (*Arch Intern Med.* 2000;160(11):1573–1575). These guidelines recommend serum TSH as an initial screen test for thyroid dysfunction.

III. BENIGN THYROID DISORDERS

A. Hyperthyroidism reflects increased catabolism and excessive sympathetic activity caused by excess circulating thyroid hormones. Symptoms of hyperthyroidism include weight loss despite normal or increased appetite, heat intolerance, excessive perspiration, anxiety, irritability, palpitations, fatigue, muscle weakness, and oligomenorrhea. Signs of hyperthyroidism include goiter, sinus tachycardia or atrial fibrillation, tremor, hyperreflexia, fine or thinning hair, thyroid bruit, muscle wasting, and weakness, particularly of the proximal thigh musculature.

1. Autoimmune diffuse toxic goiter (Graves' disease) is the most common cause of hyperthyroidism and is caused by stimulating immunoglobulins directed against the TSH receptor. Diagnosis is made by history and physical exam, depressed TSH levels and detection of anti-TSH-R antibodies. Graves' disease may be treated with antithyroid drugs, ablation with radioactive iodine (RAI), or surgery.

   a. Ablation with RAI is the treatment of choice for most patients with Graves' disease. An initial dose given orally is 75% effective after 8 to 12 weeks. The initial dose is repeated in the 25% of patients with persistent thyrotoxicosis. Cure rates approach 90%, and hypothyroidism will eventually develop. Contraindications to radiotherapy include pregnant women, newborns, patients who refuse, and patients with low RAI uptake (<20%) in the thyroid. Treatment of children or young adults (<30 years) with RAI is controversial because of presumed long-term oncogenic risks.

C. FNA is the most accurate and cost-effective diagnostic modality for evaluating thyroid nodules. FNA can be performed at the bedside or under ultrasound guidance. The latter modality is preferred for small or difficult to palpate nodules. The cytologic results of FNA are divided into four categories:

1. Nondiagnostic cytology fails to meet the criteria for an adequate specimen. These patients should undergo repeat FNA under ultrasound guidance. Nodules that continue to yield nondiagnostic FNA specimens require either close observation or surgical excision.

2. Benign cytology requires no further diagnostic testing and can be clinically followed with serial ultrasounds for 6 to 18 months with gradually longer periods between ultrasounds if the lesion remains stable.

3. Cytology noting "follicular lesion of undetermined significance" or "atypia of undetermined significance" carries a 5% to 10% risk of malignancy. These patients should undergo repeat FNA (*CytoJournal.* 2008;5:6).

4. Intermediate or suspicious cytology is typically reported as "follicular" or "Hürthle cell" neoplasms. These lesions carry a 20% to 30% risk of malignancy (*Diagn Cytopathol.* 2008;36(6):425–437). Given the risk of malignancy, these lesions are typically treated with surgical excision (thyroid lobectomy). If the final pathology reveals thyroid cancer, no further treatment is necessary for small (<1 cm) low-risk tumors. For patients with large (>1 cm) or high-risk tumors, a completion thyroidectomy should be performed along with a lymph node dissection if clinically indicated (*Thyroid.* 2009;19(11):1167–1214).

5. Suspicious for malignancy and malignant are treated as thyroid cancer.

D. **Thyroid imaging**

1. Thyroid ultrasonography accurately determines gland volume, as well as the number and character of thyroid nodules (*Am J Med.* 1995;99:642). Features suggestive of malignancy on ultrasound include hypoechoic pattern, incomplete peripheral halo, irregular margins, and microcalcifications. Ultrasound is useful for guiding FNA biopsy and cyst aspiration. Cysts seen on ultrasound, especially those larger than 3 cm, are malignant in up to 14% of cases.

2. Technetium thyroid scanning can be useful in differentiating solitary functioning nodules from multinodular goiter or Graves' disease. Hypofunctioning areas (cyst, neoplasm, or suppressed tissue adjacent to autonomous nodules) are "cold," whereas areas of increased synthesis are "hot." Thyroid scans cannot differentiate benign from malignant lesions and therefore are not generally useful in the routine work-up of a thyroid nodule. Radioactive iodine scanning 4 to 24 hours after administration of oral iodine-131 (^{131}I) is useful for identifying metastatic differentiated thyroid tumors, confirming a diagnosis of Graves' disease, and predicting a response to ^{131}I radioablation.

3. CT scan and MR scan of the thyroid are costly and generally reserved for assessing substernal or retrosternal masses suspected to be goiters or for staging known malignancy.

E. In summary, thyroid lobectomy is indicated for (1) nodules with malignant or indeterminate aspiration cytology, (2) nodules in children, (3) nodules in patients with either a history of neck irradiation or a family history of thyroid cancer, and (4) symptomatic or cosmetically bothersome nodules.

V. THYROID NEOPLASMS

A. Differentiated (papillary and follicular) thyroid cancer is an indolent cancer (*N Engl J Med.* 1998;338:297). These tumors arise from thyroid follicular epithelial cells and are by far the most common thyroid cancer. Childhood exposure to radiation is the best documented etiologic factor. These cancers are rare in children and increase in frequency with age; the female-to-male ratio is approximately 2.5:1. The prognosis of thyroid cancer depends mostly on the patient's age as well as the extent and histologic subtype of the disease. In all, 85% to 90% of patients fall into a low-risk category with favorable prognosis. The American Thyroid Association Guidelines Taskforce has issued a management guideline for the work-up and treatment of differentiated thyroid cancers (*Thyroid.* 2009;19(11):1167–1214).

1. Papillary thyroid carcinoma (PTC) represents 85% of thyroid carcinomas. PTC is often multifocal and frequently metastasizes to cervical lymph nodes. Occult, clinically insignificant foci of microscopic PTC are found in 4% to 28% of autopsies or in thyroidectomy specimens for benign diseases. Despite its nonaggressive nature, PTC has metastasized to cervical lymph nodes in 20% to 50% of patient at the time of diagnosis. Therefore, preoperative neck ultrasound with subsequent FNA of suspicious nodes is recommended prior to surgical excision.

   a. Total thyroidectomy is recommended for the following conditions: tumors greater than 1 cm, presence of bilateral nodules, regional or metastatic disease, patients with a history of radiation therapy or first-degree relatives with PTC.

   b. Thyroid lobectomy is appropriate for patients with small (less than 1 cm), low risk, unifocal tumors without evidence of regional or metastatic disease.

   c. Lymph node dissection of the central neck compartment (level VI) and the lateral neck compartment (levels II, III, IV) should be performed in all patients with biopsy-proven lymph node metastases. Given 20% to 50% of patients with PTC have cervical lymph node metastases at the time of surgery, and neck ultrasound of the central compartment may miss occult metastasis, prophylactic central neck dissection (level VI) is recommended in high-risk patients (large tumors, bilateral tumors, radiation exposure).

   d. Radioablation of metastatic or residual cancer and residual thyroid tissue is performed with 75 to 100 mCi of ^{131}I at 4 weeks after total thyroidectomy while the patient is hypothyroid (i.e., TSH 30 μIU/mL on no replacement of T_4). Ablation may be repeated at higher doses if residual disease is detected on follow-up surveillance.

e. Lifelong long-term suppression of TSH therapy with thyroid hormone replacement decreases recurrences and may improve survival.

2. Follicular thyroid carcinoma (10% of thyroid carcinomas) is rare before age 30 years and has a slightly worse prognosis than PTC. Unlike PTC, follicular thyroid cancer has a propensity to spread hematogenously to bone, lung, or liver. Small (<1 cm), unilateral follicular carcinomas with limited invasion of the tumor capsule may be treated with thyroid lobectomy, whereas larger tumors (>1 cm), multicentric tumors, and tumors with more extensive capsular and vascular invasion or distant metastases are treated with total thyroidectomy. Radioablation is indicated after total thyroidectomy, followed by lifelong thyroid hormone suppression.

B. Medullary thyroid carcinoma (MTC) arises from the thyroid parafollicular C cells that derive from the neural crest and secrete calcitonin. MTC accounts for 5% to 10% of all thyroid cancers in the United States. MTC may occur sporadically (75% to 80%) or may be inherited, either alone or as a component of multiple endocrine neoplasia (MEN) type 2A or 2B (20% to 25%). Sporadic MTC usually is detected as a firm, palpable, unilateral nodule with or without involved cervical lymph nodes. Patients with hereditary MTC develop bilateral, multifocal tumors and often are diagnosed on the basis of family screening. MTC spreads early to cervical lymph nodes and may metastasize to liver, lungs, or bone. All patients with suspected or known MTC should be genetically tested for DNA mutations in the tyrosine kinase receptor *RET* proto-oncogene to exclude MEN 2A or MEN 2B syndromes. Similar to all thyroid malignancies, diagnosis is best made with an FNA of suspicious thyroid nodules. In addition, elevated basal serum calcitonin levels are elevated (>20 to 100 pg/mL). Neck ultrasound can identify regional metastases usually present prior to surgical resection. In addition, screening for a pheochromocytoma with serum or urine metanephrines/normetanephrines should be performed in all patients undergoing surgical resection of MTC. Total thyroidectomy alone is only indicated for patients with MEN 2 syndromes detected by genetic screening, who also have calcitonin levels less than 40 pg/mL. Otherwise, treatment of MTC is total thyroidectomy with removal of the lymph nodes in the central neck compartment (Level VI). A modified neck dissection is indicated for clinically involved ipsilateral cervical lymph nodes. There are no proven systemic chemotherapy options for MTC; however, clinical trials using multiple new agents are being carried out. The use of external beam radiation is controversial. The American Thyroid Association Guidelines Taskforce has issued a management guideline for the management of medullary thyroid cancer (*Thyroid* 2009;19(6):565–612).

C. Undifferentiated or anaplastic thyroid carcinoma (1% to 2% of thyroid carcinomas) carries an extremely poor prognosis, usually presents as a fixed, sometimes painful goiter, and usually occurs in patients older than 50 years. Invasion of local structures, with resultant dysphagia, respiratory compromise, or hoarseness due to RLN involvement can preclude curative resection. External irradiation or chemotherapy may provide limited palliation.

D. Primary malignant lymphoma of the thyroid often is associated with Hashimoto thyroiditis. Surgical resection is usually not indicated once a diagnosis is made.

VI. POSTOPERATIVE THYROID HORMONE REPLACEMENT is necessary after total or near total thyroidectomy or ablation with radioiodine. Oral levothyroxine is started before discharge at an average dose of 100 μg/day (0.8 μg/lb/ day). Adequacy of thyroid hormone replacement is assessed by measuring T_4 and TSH at 6 to 12 weeks after surgery. Adjustments to the dose should not be more frequent than monthly in the absence of symptoms and should be cautious (12.5 to 25 μg increments).

VII. MANAGEMENT OF COMPLICATIONS AFTER THYROIDECTOMY

A. Hemorrhage is a rare but serious complication of thyroidectomy that usually occurs within 6 hours of surgery. Management can require control of the airway by endotracheal intubation and, rarely, can require urgent opening of the incision and evacuation of hematoma with creation of a surgical airway before return to the operating room for wound irrigation and control of bleeding.

B. Transient hypocalcemia commonly occurs 24 to 48 hours after thyroidectomy. Patients are started on oral calcium carbonate (1 gram TID) for 2 weeks after total thyroidectomy. Intravenous replacement is achieved by mixing six ampules of 10% calcium gluconate (540 mg of elemental calcium) in 500 mL of 5% dextrose in water (D5W), for infusion at 1 mL/kg/hour. Permanent hypoparathyroidism is uncommon after total thyroidectomy. Normal parathyroid tissue removed or devascularized at the time of total thyroidectomy must be minced into 1×3-mm fragments and autotransplanted into individual muscle pockets in the sternocleidomastoid muscle to maximize the chances that the patient will not develop postoperative hypoparathyroidism (*Ann Surg.* 1996;223:472). Normal parathyroid tissue should never be discarded.

C. RLN injury is a devastating complication of thyroidectomy that should occur rarely (<1%). Unilateral RLN injury causes hoarseness, and bilateral injury compromises the airway, necessitating tracheostomy. Repeat neck exploration, thyroidectomy for extensive goiter or Graves' disease, and thyroidectomy for fixed, locally invasive cancers are procedures particularly prone to RLN injury. Intentional (as with locally invasive cancer) or inadvertent transection of the RLN can be repaired primarily or with a nerve graft, although the efficacy of these repairs is not known. Temporary RLN palsies can occur during thyroidectomy, and these usually resolve over a period of 1 to 6 weeks.

PARATHYROID

I. EMBRYOLOGY, ANATOMY, AND PHYSIOLOGY

A. **Embryology.** The inferior and superior parathyroid glands are derived from the endoderm of the third and fourth pharyngeal pouches, respectively. The inferior parathyroid glands are intimately associated with the thymus as it descends into the chest, which also develops from the third pharyngeal pouch. Therefore, ectopic parathyroid glands can be found anywhere along this tract as the thymus descends. The superior glands have a limited descent from the neck and are thus rarely found in ectopic locations.

B. Anatomy. Typically, the inferior glands are found inferior, lateral or posterior to the inferior pole of the thyroid, and anterior to the RLN. The superior glands are usually found at the posterior aspect of the thyroid lobe superior to the inferior thyroid artery, posterior to the RLN. Because the embryologic descent of the inferior parathyroid crosses that of the superior gland, they can rarely be found at the same level, above or below the crossing of the inferior thyroid artery and RLN.

C. Physiology. Serum calcium levels are maintained between 8.2 and 10.2 mg/dL by the interplay of parathyroid hormone (PTH), vitamin D, and calcitonin. Upon stimulation, chief cells of the parathyroid glands secrete PTH that (1) acts on the bones to stimulate the resorption of calcium and phosphate, (2) stimulates the kidneys to increase calcium resorption and inhibit phosphate resorption. Together these actions aim to increase the serum calcium concentrations and decrease the serum phosphate concentration. Vitamin D is absorbed through the small intestine and undergoes hydroxylation in the liver to $25(OH)D_3$. A second hydroxylation is performed in the kidney, under the control of PTH, to the active form of vitamin D, $1,25(OH)D_3$. Vitamin D stimulates bone and intestine calcium resorption to increase serum calcium levels. Calcitonin is synthesized by the parafollicular cells of the thyroid gland. Its actions antagonize those of PTH by inhibiting bone and kidney resorption of calcium. The net result is a decrease in serum calcium concentration.

II. BENIGN PARATHYROID DISORDERS

A. Primary Hyperparathyroidism (HPT)

1. Incidence. Primary HPT has an incidence of 0.25 to 1 per 1,000 population in the United States and is especially common in postmenopausal women. It most often occurs sporadically, but it can be inherited alone or as a component of familial endocrinopathies, including MEN types 1 and 2A.

2. Clinical findings. The more common clinical findings associated with HPT include nephrolithiasis, osteoporosis, hypertension, and emotional disturbances. In addition, patients can have very subtle symptoms such as muscle weakness, polyuria, anorexia, and nausea.

3. Laboratory assessment. The diagnosis of HPT is biochemical and requires demonstration of hypercalcemia (serum calcium 10.5 mg/dL) and an elevated PTH level. Patients with hypercalcemia and suspected HPT should have their serum calcium, phosphate, creatinine, and PTH measured. The assay of choice for PTH is the highly sensitive and specific intact PTH-level radioimmunoassay. Ionized calcium is a more sensitive test of physiologically active calcium. Hypercalcemia without an elevated PTH can be due to a variety of causes (especially malignancy, Paget disease, sarcoidosis, and milk-alkali syndrome) that must be excluded. Familial hypocalciuric hypercalcemia (FHH) commonly causes a mild hypercalcemia and elevated PTH, as seen in HPT. FHH is caused by loss-of-function mutations in the calcium-sensing

receptors expressed in the kidney and parathyroid gland. This leads to a loss of feedback inhibition of PTH secretion by the parathyroids and inadequate clearance of calcium in to the urine. FHH can generally be distinguished from HPT by a 24-hour measurement of urinary calcium. It can also be distinguished by measuring the renal calcium/creatinine clearance ratio. A ratio less than 0.01 suggests FHH; the ratios seen in HPT are generally much higher. Parathyroidectomy is ineffective for FHH.

4. Radiography. Parathyroid imaging has no role in the diagnosis of HPT, but does have a role in operative planning in patients diagnosed with HPT. Current practice makes use of several techniques to facilitate limited neck exploration to ensure a high success rate in the outpatient setting. These techniques include radio- and/or image-guided exploration (sestamibi or ultrasound guided), videoscopic exploration, and intraoperative intact PTH-level monitoring. The most frequently applied approach is preoperative sestamibi scanning, followed by direct excision of the identified gland and confirmation of cure by intraoperative PTH measurement. This intraoperative test requires the availability of a rapid assay of intact PTH, which confirms the success of the surgery immediately if the PTH level falls more than 50% at 10 minutes after the apparent source of PTH has been removed. If the preoperative localization scan is not informative, then a standard four-gland exploration is appropriate.

5. Parathyroidectomy

    a. Indications. Parathyroidectomy is indicated for all patients with symptomatic primary HPT. Nephrolithiasis, bone disease, and neuromuscular symptoms are improved more often than renal insufficiency, hypertension, and psychiatric symptoms. Parathyroidectomy for asymptomatic HPT is somewhat controversial. Recent guidelines by the AACE/AAES Taskforce on primary HPT recommend parathyroidectomy for the following patients: (1) those younger than 50 years of age; (2) those who cannot participate in appropriate follow-up; (3) those with a serum calcium level greater than 1 mg/dL above the normal range; (4) those with urinary calcium greater than 400 mg per 24 hours; (5) those with a 30% decrease in renal function; and (6) those with complications of primary HPT, including nephrocalcinosis, osteoporosis [T score <2.5 standard deviations (SD) at the lumbar spine, hip, or wrist], or a severe psychoneurologic disorder (*J Bone Miner Res.* 2002;17(suppl 2):N57).

    b. Neck exploration and parathyroidectomy for HPT result in normocalcemia in more than 95% of patients when performed by an experienced surgeon without any preoperative or intraoperative localization studies. A thorough, orderly search and identification of all four parathyroid glands are the cornerstones of the standard surgical management of HPT. In the current era, preoperative localization studies are used in conjunction with rapid intraoperative PTH measurement to enable "minimally invasive parathyroidectomy," which generally means directed unilateral neck exploration and/or local/monitored anesthesia care (MAC) anesthesia. Most often, a single adenomatous gland is found and resected; normal parathyroid glands should be left in place. Intraoperative measurement of PTH at 10 minutes demonstrating a 50% decrease and return to the normal level after resection of the adenoma is highly indicative of cure. In the event that an abnormally enlarged parathyroid or all four parathyroids cannot be found, a thorough exploration for ectopic or supernumerary glands should be performed. Ectopic superior glands may be found posterior and deep to the thyroid, in the tracheoesophageal groove, posterior to the inferior thyroid vessels, between the carotid artery and the esophagus. Undescended or incompletely descended glands may be found cranial to the superior thyroid pole, and excessive caudal migration may result in a gland residing in the middle mediastinum. Ectopic inferior glands are most likely found embedded in the thymus in the anterior mediastinum. Undescended inferior glands may be found in the superior neck between the carotid and the larynx. Occasionally, multiple parathyroid adenomas are found and should be removed, leaving at least one normal parathyroid behind. Four-gland parathyroid hyperplasia is rare, and its management is controversial. Acceptable options include total parathyroidectomy with parathyroid autotransplantation or 3.5-gland parathyroidectomy. The dictation of a clear, factual operative note detailing the identification and position of each parathyroid gland is essential as is pathologic verification of each parathyroid. This information is invaluable in the unlikely event of reoperation for persistent or recurrent HPT.

B. **Recurrent or Persistent Primary HPT**
1. **Diagnosis.** In all cases of postparathyroidectomy hypercalcemia, HPT must be reconfirmed biochemically, and 24-hour urinary calcium should be obtained to exclude FHH.
   a. **Imaging.** Preoperative localization is mandatory and includes careful review of the operative note from the initial surgery and concordant noninvasive studies. Approximately 70% to 80% of patients undergoing re-exploration after an initial failed operation have a missed gland that is accessible through a cervical incision. Reoperative parathyroid surgery carries a substantially higher risk of injury to the RLN and of hypocalcemia due to postoperative scarring and disruption of normal tissue planes. Preoperative localization should include ^{99m}Tc-sestamibi scintigraphy and ultrasound or CT scanning. These noninvasive studies are successful in localizing the missed gland in 25% to 75% of cases (*Radiology.* 1987;162:133). With combined use of CT scan, ultrasonography, and scintigraphy, at least one imaging study identifies the tumor in more than 75% of patients. For patients with discordant or negative noninvasive studies, invasive localization via venous sampling with rapid PTH can be used to identify adenomas.
   b. **Operative strategy.** The goal of re-exploration is to perform an orderly search based on the information gained from the initial operation and from localization studies.

(1) Missed parathyroid glands are found either in the usual position or in ectopic sites, as determined by the embryology of parathyroid development. Rarely, a parathyroid gland is intrathyroidal (especially in patients with multinodular goiter), and intraoperative thyroid ultrasound or thyroid lobectomy can be performed if an exhaustive search fails to identify the parathyroid adenoma. If four normal glands have been located, the adenoma is likely to represent a supernumerary (fifth) gland. Intraoperative ultrasound is an effective tool for localizing parathyroid glands in the neck.

(2) Mediastinal adenomas within the thymus are managed by resecting the cranial portion of the thymus by gentle traction on the thyrothymic ligament or by a complete transcervical thymectomy using a specialized substernal retractor (*Ann Surg.* 1991;214:555). Median sternotomy carries a higher morbidity and increased postoperative pain, and the possibility of these should be discussed with the patient preoperatively.

C. **Parathyroid Autotransplantation**

1. Indications for total parathyroidectomy and heterotopic parathyroid autotransplantation include HPT in patients with renal failure, in patients with four-gland parathyroid hyperplasia, and in patients undergoing neck re-exploration in which the adenoma is the only remaining parathyroid tissue. The site of parathyroid autotransplantation may be the sternocleidomastoid muscle or the brachioradialis muscle of the patient's nondominant forearm. Parathyroid grafting into the patient's forearm is advantageous if recurrent HPT is possible (e.g., MEN type 1 or 2A). If HPT recurs, localization is simplified, and the hyperplastic parathyroid tissue may be excised from the patient's forearm under local anesthesia.

2. Technique. Freshly removed parathyroid gland tissue is cut into fine pieces approximately 1 mm × 1 mm × 2 mm and placed in sterile iced saline. An incision is made in the patient's nondominant forearm, and separate intramuscular beds are created by spreading the fibers of the brachioradialis with a fine forceps. Approximately four to five pieces are placed in each site, and a total of approximately 100 mg of parathyroid tissue are transplanted. The beds are closed with a silk suture to mark the site of the transplanted tissue. Transplanted parathyroid tissue begins to function within 14 to 21 days of surgery.

3. Cryopreservation of parathyroid glands is performed in MEN patients and all patients who may become aparathyroid after repeat exploration. Cryopreservation may be performed by freezing approximately 200 mg of finely cut parathyroid tissue in vials containing 10% dimethyl sulfoxide, 10% autologous serum, and 80% Waymouth medium. Cryopreserved parathyroid tissue can be used for autotransplantation in patients who become aparathyroid or in patients with failure of the initial grafted parathyroid tissue. Viable cryopreservation and subsequent thawing must be performed in a Food and Drug Administration (FDA)-approved GMP (good medical practice) facility.

D. Postoperative Hypocalcemia

1. Transient hypocalcemia commonly occurs after total thyroidectomy or parathyroidectomy and requires treatment if it is severe (total serum calcium <7.5 mg/dL) or if the patient is symptomatic. Chvostek's sign (twitching of the facial muscles when the examiner percusses over the facial nerve anterior to the patient's ear) is a sign of relative hypocalcemia but is present in up to 15% of the normal population. This sign is not necessarily an indication for calcium replacement.

2. Patients with persistent hypocalcemia after total thyroidectomy or after parathyroid autotransplantation can require continued supplementation for 6 to 8 weeks postoperatively. Usually, patients are given calcium carbonate, 500 to 1,000 mg orally three times per day, and 1,25-dihydroxyvitamin D_3, 0.25 μg orally per day.

3. Hypocalcemic tetany is a medical emergency that is treated with rapid intravenous administration of 10% calcium gluconate or calcium chloride until the patient recovers. Specifically, one to two ampules (10 to 20 mL) of 10% calcium gluconate are given intravenously over 10 minutes, and the dose may be repeated every 15 to 20 minutes, as required. Subsequently, a continuous infusion of six ampules of calcium gluconate in 500 mL of 5% dextrose water is initiated at 50 mL per hour. Patients with severe hypocalcemia must also have correction of hypomagnesemia.

Hypercalcemia from secondary and tertiary HPT is treated initially with dietary phosphate restriction, phosphate binders, and vitamin D supplementation. Patients with medically unresponsive, symptomatic HPT (e.g., bone pain and osteopenia, ectopic calcification, or pruritus) may be surgically treated with total parathyroidectomy and heterotopic autotransplantation, or subtotal parathyroidectomy. Controversy exists as to what type of surgery is best and what postoperative level of parathyroid hormone is necessary to prevent adynamic bone disease after such procedures.

III. PARATHYROID CARCINOMA is rare and accounts for less than 1% of patients with HPT. Approximately 50% of these patients have a palpable neck mass, and serum calcium levels may exceed 15 mg/dL.

A. Diagnosis is made by the histologic finding of vascular or capsular invasion, lymph node or distant metastases, or gross invasion of local structures.

B. Surgical treatment is radical local excision of the tumor, surrounding soft tissue, lymph nodes, and ipsilateral thyroid lobe when the disease is recognized preoperatively or intraoperatively. Reoperation is indicated for local recurrence in an attempt to control malignant hypercalcemia.

C. Patients with parathyroid carcinoma and some patients with benign HPT may develop hyperparathyroid crisis. Symptoms of this acute, sometimes fatal illness include profound muscular weakness, nausea and vomiting, drowsiness, and confusion. Hypercalcemia (16 to 20 mg/dL) and azotemia are usually present. Ultimate treatment of "parathyroid crisis" is parathyroidectomy; however, hypercalcemia and volume and electrolyte abnormalities should be addressed first. Treatment is warranted for symptoms or a serum calcium level greater than 12 mg/dL. First-line therapy is infusion of 300 to 500 mL/hour of 0.9% sodium chloride (5 to 10 L/day intravenously) to restore intravascular volume and to promote renal excretion of calcium. After urinary output exceeds 100 mL/hour, furosemide (80 to 100 mg intravenously every 2 to 6 hours) may be given to promote further renal sodium and calcium excretion. Thiazide diuretics impair calcium excretion and should be avoided. Hypokalemia and hypomagnesemia are complications of forced saline diuresis and should be corrected. If diuresis alone is unsuccessful in lowering the serum calcium, other calcium-lowering agents may be used. These include the bisphosphonates pamidronate (60 to 90 mg in 1 L of 0.9% saline infused over 24 hours) and etidronate (7.5 mg/kg intravenously over 2 to 4 hours daily for 3 days); mithramycin [25 μg/kg intravenously over 4 to 6 hours daily for 3 to 4 days (malignant hypercalcemia only)]; and salmon calcitonin (initial dose, 4 IU/kg subcutaneously or intramuscularly every 12 hours, increasing as necessary to a maximum dose of 8 IU/kg subcutaneously or intramuscularly every 6 hours). Orthophosphate, gallium nitrate, and glucocorticoids also have calcium-lowering effects.

ENDOCRINE PANCREAS

I. EMBRYOLOGY, ANATOMY, AND PHYSIOLOGY

   A. Embryology. The pancreas originates from two diverticula in the foregut to develop the final adult form around the fifth and sixth weeks of gestation. The endocrine cells that form the pancreatic islets also originate from the foregut endoderm.

   B. Anatomy. In the adult, the pancreatic islets are scattered throughout the pancreas and are composed of four major cell types: A, B, D, PP cells. Beta cells occupy the center of the islets with the remainder of the cells scattered in the periphery.

   C. Physiology. Each of the various pancreatic endocrine cells produces different hormones with a variety of local and systemic actions

   1. A cells produce glucagon that is a polypeptide whose main function is to promote the conversion of hepatic glycogen to glucose and increase the systemic glucose levels.

   2. B cells produce insulin whose main function is to promote glucose transport into cells and therefore decrease systemic glucose levels.

   3. D cells produce somatostatin that functions to inhibit the release of other gastrointestinal hormones, gastric acid secretion, and small bowel electrolyte secretions.

   4. D_2 cells produce vasoactive interstitial peptide that serves as an enteric vasodilator.

   5. G cells produce gastrin whose actions increase the secretion of gastric acid and pepsinogen.

II. PANCREATIC ISLET CELL TUMORS are rare tumors that produce clinical syndromes related to the specific hormone secreted. Insulinomas are the most

common of these tumors, followed by gastrinoma, then the rarer VIPoma, glucagonoma, and somatostatinoma. Islet cell tumors are often occult, and their localization may be difficult, especially for small, multifocal, or extrapancreatic tumors. Islet cell tumors may occur sporadically or as a component of MEN type 1 or von Hippel–Lindau disease (nearly always multifocal) and may be benign or malignant, although prediction may be based on the hormone produced rather than the tumor size.

A. Insulinoma

1. **Clinical features.** Patients with insulinoma develop profound hypoglycemia during fasting or after exercise. The clinical picture includes the signs and symptoms of neuroglycopenia (anxiety, tremor, confusion, and obtundation) and the sympathetic response to hypoglycemia (hunger, sweating, and tachycardia). These bizarre complaints initially may be attributed to malingering or a psychosomatic etiology unless the association with fasting is recognized. Many patients eat excessively to avoid symptoms, causing significant weight gain. *Whipple's triad* refers to the clinical criteria for the diagnosis of insulinoma: (1) hypoglycemic symptoms during monitored fasting, (2) blood glucose levels less than 50 mg/dL, and (3) relief of symptoms after administration of intravenous glucose. Factitious hypoglycemia (excess exogenous insulin administration) and postprandial reactive hypoglycemia must be excluded.

2. **Diagnosis.** A supervised, in-hospital 72-hour fast is required to diagnose insulinoma. Patients are observed for hypoglycemic episodes and have 6-hour measurement of plasma glucose, insulin, proinsulin, and C peptide. The fast is terminated when symptoms of neuroglycopenia develop. Nearly all patients with insulinoma develop neuroglycopenic symptoms and have inappropriately elevated plasma insulin (>5 μU/mL) associated with hypoglycemia (glucose <50 mg/dL). Elevated levels of C peptide and proinsulin are usually present as well (*Curr Probl Surg.* 1994;31:79).

3. **Localization.** Insulinomas typically are small (<2 cm), solitary, benign tumors that may occur anywhere in the pancreas. Rarely, an insulinoma may develop in extrapancreatic rests of pancreatic tissue. Dynamic CT scanning at 5-mm intervals with oral and intravenous contrast is the initial localizing test for insulinoma, with success in 35% to 85% of cases. Endoscopic ultrasound is also effective but is operator dependent (*N Engl J Med.* 1992;326:1721). The effectiveness of indium-111 (¹¹¹In)-octreotide scintigraphy for localizing insulinoma (approximately 50%) is less than for other islet cell tumors because insulinomas typically have few somatostatin receptors. Selective arteriography with observation of a tumor "blush" is the best diagnostic study for the primary tumor and hepatic metastases. If a tumor is still not identified, regional localization to the head, body, or tail of the pancreas can be accomplished by portal venous sampling for insulin or by calcium angiography. Calcium angiography involves injection of calcium into selectively catheterized pancreatic arteries and measurement of plasma insulin through a catheter positioned in a hepatic vein.

4. Treatment of insulinoma is surgical in nearly all cases. Surgical management of insulinomas consists in localization of the tumor by careful inspection and palpation of the gland after mobilization of the duodenum and the inferior border of the pancreas. Use of intraoperative ultrasonography greatly facilitates identification of small tumors, especially those located in the pancreatic head or uncinate process. Most insulinomas can be enucleated from surrounding pancreas, although those in the body or tail may require resection. In general, blind pancreatectomy should not be performed when the tumor cannot be identified. Approximately 5% of insulinomas are malignant and 10% are multiple (usually in association with MEN type 1). Medical treatment of insulinoma with diazoxide, verapamil, or octreotide has limited effectiveness but may be used in preparation for surgery or for patients unfit for surgery.

B. Gastrinoma

1. Patients with gastrinoma and the Zollinger–Ellison syndrome (ZES) have severe peptic ulcer disease (PUD) due to gastrin-mediated gastric acid hypersecretion. Most patients present with epigastric pain, and 80% have active duodenal ulceration at the time of diagnosis. Diarrhea and weight loss are common (40% of patients). ZES is uncommon (0.1% to 1% of PUD cases), and most patients present with typical duodenal ulceration. Gastrinoma and ZES should be considered in any patient with (1) PUD refractory to treatment of *Helicobacter pylori* and conventional doses of H_2 blockers or omeprazole; (2) recurrent, multiple, or atypically located (e.g., distal duodenum or jejunum) peptic ulcers; (3) complications of PUD (i.e., bleeding, perforation, or obstruction); (4) PUD with significant diarrhea; and (5) PUD with HPT, nephrolithiasis, or familial endocrinopathy. All patients considered for elective surgery for PUD should have ZES excluded preoperatively.

2. Diagnosis of ZES requires demonstration of fasting hypergastrinemia and basal gastric acid hypersecretion. A fasting serum gastrin level of 100 pg/mL or greater and a basal gastric acid output (BAO) of 15 mEq/hour or more (>5 mEq/hour in patients with previous ulcer surgery) secure the diagnosis of ZES in nearly all cases. Fasting hypergastrinemia without elevated BAO is seen in atrophic gastritis, in renal failure, and in patients taking H_2-receptor antagonists or omeprazole. Fasting hypergastrinemia with elevated BAO is seen in retained gastric antrum syndrome, gastric outlet obstruction, and antral G-cell hyperplasia. A secretin stimulation test is used to distinguish ZES from these conditions. This test is performed by measuring fasting serum gastrin levels before and 2, 5, 10, and 15 minutes after the intravenous administration of secretin (2 units/kg). Eighty-five percent of patients with ZES have an increase in gastrin levels (>200 pg/mL over baseline) in response to a secretin stimulation test, whereas patients with other conditions do not. This test is most useful when ZES is suspected in patients who have had prior gastric surgery and in patients with moderately increased fasting gastrin levels (100 to 1,000 pg/mL).

3. Localization of gastrinoma should be performed in all patients considered for surgery. Approximately 80% of gastrinomas are located within the "gastrinoma triangle," which is an area contained by a triangle formed by the junction of the cystic and common bile ducts, junction of the 2nd and 3rd portion of the duodenum, and the junction of head and neck of the pancreas. Gastrinomas are often malignant, with spread to lymph nodes or liver occurring in up to 60% of cases. Approximately 20% of patients with ZES have familial MEN type 1; these patients often have multiple, concurrent islet cell tumors. Dynamic CT scanning, ^{111}In-octreotide scintigraphy, endoscopic ultrasound, and MR scan are useful noninvasive tests for localizing gastrinoma; however, preoperative localization is unsuccessful up to 50% of the time. Selective angiography with or without secretin injection of the gastroduodenal, superior mesenteric, and splenic arteries and measurement of hepatic vein gastrin can localize occult gastrinoma in up to 70% to 90% of cases.

4. In cases of ZES, the primary goal of medical treatment is acid suppression with reduction in basal acid output to less than 15 mEq/h. Medical treatment with proton pump inhibitors (PPIs) is highly effective at reducing basal acid output. These medications are indicated preoperatively in patients undergoing operation for cure and in patients with unresectable or metastatic gastrinoma. Omeprazole (60 mg/day) is initiated and titrated with a basal acid output less than 15 mEq/h. Other PPIs such as pantoprazole, lansoprazole, or esomeprazole have also been used to medically treat ZES.

5. Surgical management of ZES is indicated in all fit patients with nonmetastatic, sporadic gastrinoma. Goals of surgery include precise localization and curative resection of the tumor. Resection of primary gastrinoma alters the malignant progression of tumor and decreases hepatic metastases in patients with ZES. Intraoperative localization of gastrinomas is facilitated by extended duodenotomy and palpation, intraoperative ultrasonography, or endoscopic duodenal transillumination. Gastrinomas within the duodenum, pancreatic head, or uncinate process are treated by enucleation, whereas tumors in the body or tail of the pancreas can be removed by distal or subtotal pancreatectomy. Immediate cure rates are 40% to 90% for resections by experienced surgeons; however, half of patients initially cured according to biochemical tests experience recurrence within 5 years. Gastric acid hypersecretion is controllable with H_2 blockers or omeprazole in most patients with ZES, rendering gastrectomy unnecessary. If a gastrinoma cannot be localized intraoperatively, a parietal cell vagotomy may be performed. Surgical debulking of metastatic or unresectable primary gastrinoma facilitates medical treatment and prolongs life expectancy in select patients. Patients with ZES and MEN-1 most often cannot be cured surgically and usually are treated medically.

C. **Unusual Islet Cell Tumors**

1. VIPomas secrete vasoactive intestinal peptide and cause profuse secretory diarrhea (fasting stool output of >1 L/day), hypokalemia, and

either achlorhydria or hypochlorhydria (watery diarrhea, hypokalemia, and achlorhydria are the symptoms of Verner–Morrison syndrome). Hyperglycemia, hypercalcemia, and cutaneous flushing may be seen. Other, more common causes of diarrhea and malabsorption must be excluded. A diagnosis of VIPoma is established by the finding of elevated fasting serum vasoactive intestinal peptide levels (>190 pg/mL) and secretory diarrhea in association with an islet cell tumor. Octreotide (150 g subcutaneously every 8 hours) is highly effective as a means of controlling the diarrhea and correcting electrolyte abnormalities before resection. Most VIPomas occur in the distal pancreas and are amenable to distal pancreatectomy. Metastatic disease is commonly encountered (50%); nevertheless, surgical debulking is indicated to alleviate symptoms.

2. Glucagonomas secrete excess glucagon and result in type II diabetes, hypoaminoacidemia, anemia, weight loss, and a characteristic skin rash, necrolytic migratory erythema. Diagnosis is suggested by symptoms and by biopsy of the skin rash but is confirmed by elevated plasma glucagon levels (usually >1,000 pg/mL). Tumors are large and are readily seen on CT scan. Resection is indicated in fit patients after nutritional support, even if metastases are present.

3. Somatostatinomas are the rarest of the islet cell tumors and cause a syndrome of diabetes, steatorrhea, and cholelithiasis. These tumors are frequently located in the head of the pancreas and are often metastatic at the time of presentation.

4. Other rare islet cell tumors include pancreatic polypeptide-secreting, neurotensin-secreting, and adrenocorticotropic hormone (ACTH)-secreting tumors, as well as nonfunctioning islet cell tumors. These tumors usually are large and often are malignant. Treatment is surgical resection.

ADRENAL–PITUITARY AXIS

I. EMBRYOLOGY, ANATOMY, AND PHYSIOLOGY

A. **Embryology.** The adrenal cortex arises from the coelomic mesoderm around the fifth week of gestation. Steroidogenesis begins soon after and peaks during the third trimester. The adrenal medulla is populated by the neural crest cells originating from the neural ectoderm. The consequence of this migration is evident by the existence of paragangliomas (extra-adrenal pheochromocytomas) all along the paraspinal axis.

B. **Anatomy.** The adrenal glands are located in the retroperitoneum located superior to the kidney and lateral to the vena cava (right) and aorta (left). This relationship is important in determining the vascular supply to the adrenals. Each adrenal is supplied by three arteries: superior adrenal artery (arise from the inferior phrenic artery), middle adrenal artery (branch of the aorta), and inferior adrenal artery (branch of the renal artery). The right adrenal vein drains directly into the vena cava. The left adrenal vein drains into the left renal vein.

C. **Physiology.** The adrenal gland is histologically composed of four layers, each with their own biosynthetic products.

1. Adrenal Cortex

   a. Zona glomerulosa is responsible for mineralocorticoid production, of which aldosterone is the primary product. Aldosterone production is stimulated by angiotensin II and decreases in serum potassium levels. Aldosterone acts to increase circulating blood volume by increasing sodium and chloride reabsorption in the distal tubule of the kidney.

   b. Zona fasciculata produces the glucocorticoids of the adrenal glands, which cortisol is the primary product. Cortisol production is stimulated by the release of ACTH by the anterior pituitary. ACTH itself is stimulated by the release of corticotropin-releasing factor (CRF) by the hypothalamus. Glucocorticoids have extremely broad effects with the overall goal of inducing a catabolic state in the body in response to stress. Glucocorticoids increase blood glucose concentrations, stimulate lipolysis, enhance adrenergic stimulation of the cardiovascular system, and reduce the inflammatory response of the immune system.

   c. Zona reticularis produces the adrenal sex hormone androstenedione and DHEA. These hormones support the gonadal production of the same hormones.

2. The adrenal medulla produces catecholamines norepinephrine and epinephrine that act on peripheral alpha and beta adrenergic receptors. Alpha receptor stimulation produces peripheral vasoconstriction. Beta simulation of the myocardium via β_1 receptors increases heart rate and contractility. Stimulation of peripheral β_2 receptors causes relaxation of smooth muscles.

II. ADRENAL CORTEX

A. **Cushing Syndrome**

1. The clinical manifestations of Cushing syndrome include hypertension, edema, muscle weakness, glucose intolerance, osteoporosis, easy bruising, cutaneous striae, and truncal obesity (buffalo hump, moon facies). Women may develop acne, hirsutism, and amenorrhea as a result of adrenal androgen excess.

2. Pathophysiology of excess circulating glucocorticoids.

   a. Iatrogenic. The most common cause of Cushing syndrome is iatrogenic, namely, the administration of exogenous glucocorticoids or ACTH.

   b. Hypersecretion of ACTH from the anterior pituitary gland (Cushing disease) is the most common pathologic cause (65% to 70% of cases) of endogenous hypercortisolism. The adrenal glands respond normally to the elevated ACTH, and the result is bilateral adrenal hyperplasia. Excessive release of corticotropin-releasing factor by the hypothalamus is a rare cause of hypercortisolism.

c. Hypersecreting adrenal adenoma. Abnormal secretion of cortisol from a primary adrenal adenoma or carcinoma is the cause of hypercortisolism in 10% to 20% of cases. Primary adrenal neoplasms secrete corticosteroids independent of ACTH and usually result in suppressed plasma ACTH levels and atrophy of the adjacent and contralateral adrenocortical tissue.

d. Ectopic ACTH production. In approximately 15% of cases, Cushing syndrome is caused by ectopic secretion of ACTH or an ACTH-like substance from a small-cell bronchogenic carcinoma, carcinoid tumor, pancreatic carcinoma, thymic carcinoma, medullary thyroid cancer, or other neuroendocrine neoplasm. Patients with ectopic ACTH-secreting neoplasms can present primarily with hypokalemia, glucose intolerance, and hyperpigmentation but with few other chronic signs of Cushing syndrome.

3. Diagnosis of Cushing syndrome is biochemical. The goals are to first establish hypercortisolism and then identify the source.

a. Establishing the presence of hypercortisolism

(1) The best screening test for hypercortisolism is a 24-hour measurement of the urinary excretion of free cortisol. Urinary excretion of more than 100 μg/day of free cortisol in two independent collections is virtually diagnostic of Cushing syndrome. Measurement of plasma cortisol level alone is not a reliable method of diagnosing Cushing syndrome due to overlap of the levels in normal and abnormal patients.

(2) An overnight dexamethasone suppression test (dexamethasone, 1 mg orally at 11 PM and measurement of plasma cortisol at 8 AM) is used to confirm Cushing syndrome, especially in obese or depressed patients who may have marginally elevated urinary cortisol. Patients with true hypercortisolism have lost normal adrenal-pituitary feedback and usually fail to suppress the morning plasma cortisol level to less than 5 μg/dL.

b. Localization of the cause of hypercortisolism

(1) Determination of basal ACTH by immunoradiometric assay is the best method of determining the cause of hypercortisolism. Suppression of the absolute level of ACTH below 5 pg/mL is nearly diagnostic of adrenocortical neoplasms. ACTH levels in Cushing disease may range from the upper limits of normal (15 pg/mL to 500 pg/mL). The highest plasma levels of ACTH (1,000 pg/mL) have been observed in patients with ectopic ACTH syndrome.

(2) Standard high-dose dexamethasone suppression testing is used to distinguish a pituitary from an ectopic source of ACTH. Normal individuals and most patients with a pituitary ACTH-producing neoplasm respond to a high-dose dexamethasone suppression test (2 mg orally every 6 hours for 48 hours) with a reduction in urinary free cortisol and urinary 17-hydroxysteroids to less than 50% of basal values. Most patients with a primary adrenal tumor or an ectopic source of ACTH production fail to

suppress to this level. However, this test does not separate clearly pituitary and ectopic ACTH hypersecretion because 25% of patients with the ectopic ACTH syndrome also have suppressible tumors.

(3) Additional tests that may be useful include the metyrapone test (an inhibitor of the final step of cortisol synthesis) and the corticotropin-releasing factor infusion test. Patients with pituitary hypersecretion of ACTH respond to these tests with a compensatory rise in ACTH and urinary 17-hydroxysteroids, whereas patients with a suppressed hypothalamic-pituitary axis (primary adrenal tumor, ectopic ACTH syndrome) usually do not have a compensatory rise.

c. Imaging tests are useful for identifying lesions suspected on the basis of biochemical testing.

(1) Patients with ACTH-independent hypercortisolism require thin-section CT scan or MRI scan of the adrenal gland, both of which identify adrenal abnormalities with more than 95% sensitivity. Patients with ACTH-dependent hypercortisolism and either markedly elevated ACTH or a negative pituitary MRI scan should have CT scan of the chest to identify a tumor producing ectopic ACTH.

(2) Gadolinium-enhanced MRI scan of the sella turcica is the best imaging test for pituitary adenomas suspected of causing ACTH-dependent hypercortisolism.

(3) Bilateral inferior petrosal sinus sampling can delineate unclear cases of Cushing disease from other causes of hypercortisolism. Simultaneous bilateral petrosal sinus and peripheral blood samples are obtained before and after peripheral intravenous injection of 1 μg/kg of corticotropin-releasing hormone. A ratio of inferior petrosal sinus to peripheral plasma ACTH of 2 at basal or of 3 after corticotropin-releasing hormone administration is 100% sensitive and specific for pituitary adenoma.

4 Surgical treatment of Cushing syndrome involves removing the cause of cortisol excess (a primary adrenal lesion or pituitary or ectopic tumors secreting excessive ACTH).

a. Transsphenoidal resection of an ACTH-producing pituitary tumor is successful in 80% or more of cases of Cushing disease.

b. Treatment of ectopic ACTH syndrome involves resection of the primary lesion, if possible.

c. Primary adrenal causes of Cushing syndrome are treated by removal of the adrenal gland containing the tumor. All patients who undergo adrenalectomy for primary adrenal causes of Cushing syndrome require perioperative and postoperative glucocorticoid replacement because the pituitary-adrenal axis is suppressed.

B. Hyperaldosteronism

1. Primary hyperaldosteronism (Conn syndrome) is a syndrome of hypertension and hypokalemia caused by hypersecretion of the mineralocorticoid aldosterone.

a. Pathophysiology of hyperaldosteronism
   (1) An aldosterone-producing adrenal adenoma (APA) is the cause of primary aldosteronism in two thirds of cases and is one of the few surgically correctable causes of hypertension.
   (2) Idiopathic bilateral adrenal hyperplasia (IHA) causes 30% to 40% of cases of primary aldosteronism.
   (3) Adrenocortical carcinoma and autosomal dominant glucocorticoid-suppressible aldosteronism are rare causes of primary aldosteronism.

b. Diagnosis
   (1) Given the prevalence of essential hypertension, it is not cost-effective to screen all adults with hypertension for primary hyperaldosteronism. Adults who should be evaluated include those with new onset severe hypertension, those with absence of contributing factor, and those whose blood pressure is labile or poorly controlled with several antihypertensives.
   (2) Laboratory diagnosis of primary aldosteronism begins with the demonstration of hypokalemia (<3.5 mEq/L), inappropriate kaliuresis (>30 mEq/day), and elevated aldosterone (>15 ng/dL) with normal cortisol. The upright plasma renin activity (PRA) of less than 3 ng/mL/hour corroborates the diagnosis. A ratio of plasma aldosterone concentration (PAC) (ng/dL) to PRA (ng/mL/hour) of greater than 20 to 25 further suggests primary hyperaldosteronism. Confirmation of primary aldosteronism involves determination of serum potassium and PRA and a 24-hour urine collection for sodium, cortisol, and aldosterone after 5 days of a high-sodium diet. Patients with primary hyperaldosteronism do not demonstrate aldosterone suppressibility (>14 μg/24 hours) after salt loading. Before biochemical studies, all diuretics and antihypertensives are discontinued for 2 to 4 weeks, and a daily sodium intake of at least 100 mEq is provided.
   (3) Differentiation between adrenal adenoma and IHA is important because unilateral adenomas are treated by surgical excision, whereas bilateral hyperplasia is treated medically. Because suppression of the renin-angiotensin system is more complete in APA than in IHA, these two disorders can be distinguished imperfectly (with approximately 85% accuracy) by measuring plasma aldosterone and PRA after overnight recumbency and then after 4 hours of upright posture. Patients with IHA usually have an increase in PRA and aldosterone in response to upright posture, but patients with adenoma usually show continued suppression of PRA, and their level of aldosterone does not change or falls paradoxically. In practice, this test usually is not necessary because, after a biochemical diagnosis of primary hyperaldosteronism, sensitive imaging tests are used to localize the lesion or lesions.

c. Localization. High-resolution adrenal CT scan should be the initial step in localization of an adrenal tumor. CT scanning localizes an adrenal adenoma in 90% of cases overall, and the presence of a unilateral adenoma larger than 1 cm on CT scan and supportive biochemical evidence of an aldosteronoma are generally all that is needed to make the diagnosis of Conn syndrome. Uncertainty regarding APA versus IHA after biochemical testing and noninvasive localization may be definitively resolved by bilateral adrenal venous sampling for aldosterone and cortisol. Simultaneous adrenal vein blood samples for aldosterone and cortisol are taken. The ratio of aldosterone to cortisol is greater than 4:1 for a diagnosis of aldosteronoma and less than 4:1 for a diagnosis of IHA.

d. Treatment. Surgical removal of an APA through a posterior or laparoscopic approach results in immediate cure or substantial improvement in hypertension and hypokalemia in more than 90% of patients with Conn syndrome. The patient should be treated with spironolactone (200 to 400 mg/day) preoperatively for 2 to 3 weeks to control blood pressure and to correct hypokalemia. Patients with IHA should be treated medically with spironolactone (200 to 400 mg/day). A potassium-sparing diuretic, such as amiloride (5 to 20 mg/day), and calcium channel blockers have also been used. Surgical excision rarely cures bilateral hyperplasia.

2. Secondary aldosteronism is a physiologic response of the renin-angiotensin system to renal artery stenosis, cirrhosis, congestive heart failure, and normal pregnancy. In these conditions, the adrenal gland functions normally.

C. Acute adrenal insufficiency is an emergency and should be suspected in stressed patients with a history of either adrenal insufficiency or exogenous steroid use. Adrenocortical insufficiency is most often caused by acute withdrawal of chronic corticosteroid therapy but can result from autoimmune destruction of the adrenal cortex, adrenal hemorrhage (Waterhouse–Friderichsen syndrome), or, rarely, infiltration with metastatic carcinoma. The diagnosis and treatment of acute adrenal insufficiency in the treatment of patients in septic shock is very controversial. Two prospective randomized trials have shown different effects in the use of hydrocortisone in patients with septic shock (*N Engl J Med.* 2003;348:727; *N Engl J Med.* 2008;358:111–124).

1. Signs and symptoms include fever, nausea, vomiting, severe hypotension, and lethargy. Characteristic laboratory findings of adrenal insufficiency include hyponatremia, hyperkalemia, azotemia, and fasting or reactive hypoglycemia.

2. Diagnosis. A rapid ACTH stimulation test is used to test for adrenal insufficiency. Corticotropin (250 μg), synthetic ACTH, is administered intravenously, and plasma cortisol levels are measured on completion of the administration and then 30 and 60 minutes later. Normal peak cortisol response should exceed 20 μg/dL.

3. Treatment of adrenal crisis must be immediate, based on clinical suspicion, before laboratory confirmation is available. Intravenous volume replacement with normal or hypertonic saline and dextrose is essential, as is immediate intravenous steroid replacement therapy with 4 mg of

dexamethasone. Thereafter, 50 mg of hydrocortisone is administered intravenously every 8 hours and is tapered to standard replacement doses as the patient's condition stabilizes. Subsequent recognition and treatment of the underlying cause, particularly if it is infectious, usually resolves the crisis. Mineralocorticoid replacement is not required until intravenous fluids are discontinued and oral intake resumes.

4. **Prevention.** Patients who have known adrenal insufficiency or have received supraphysiologic doses of steroid for at least 1 week in the year preceding surgery should receive 100 mg of hydrocortisone the evening before and the morning of major surgery, followed by 100 mg of hydrocortisone every 8 hours during the first postoperative 24 hours.

III. ADRENAL MEDULLA: PHEOCHROMOCYTOMA

A. **Pathophysiology.** Pheochromocytomas are neoplasms derived from the chromaffin cells of the sympathoadrenal system that result in unregulated, episodic oversecretion of catecholamines.

B. **Clinical features.** Approximately 80% to 85% of pheochromocytomas in adults arise in the adrenal medulla, whereas 10% to 15% arise in the extra-adrenal chromaffin tissue, including the paravertebral ganglia, posterior mediastinum, organ of Zuckerkandl, and urinary bladder. Symptoms of pheochromocytoma are related to excess sympathetic stimulation from catecholamines and include paroxysms of pounding frontal headache, diaphoresis, palpitations, flushing, or anxiety. The most common sign is episodic or sustained hypertension, but pheochromocytoma accounts for only 0.1% to 0.2% of patients with sustained diastolic hypertension. Uncommonly, patients present with complications of prolonged uncontrolled hypertension (e.g., myocardial infarction, cerebrovascular accident, or renal disease). Pheochromocytomas can occur in association with several hereditary syndromes, including MEN types 2A and 2B and von Hippel–Lindau syndrome. Tumors that arise in familial settings frequently are bilateral.

C. The biochemical diagnosis of pheochromocytoma is made by demonstrating elevated plasma metanephrines or 24-hour urinary excretion of catecholamines and their metabolites (metanephrines, vanillylmandelic acid). If possible, antihypertensive medications (especially monoamine oxidase inhibitors) should be discontinued before the 24-hour urine collection, and creatinine excretion should be measured simultaneously to assess the adequacy of the sample.

D. Radiographic tests are used to demonstrate the presence of an adrenal mass.

1. CT scanning is the imaging test of choice and identifies 90% to 95% of pheochromocytomas larger than 1 cm. MR scan can also be useful because T2-weighted images have a characteristic high intensity in patients with pheochromocytoma and metastatic tumor compared with adenomas.

2. Scintigraphic scanning after the administration of ^{131}I-meta-iodobenzylguanidine (MIBG) provides a functional and anatomic test of hyperfunctioning chromaffin tissue. MIBG scanning is very specific for both intra- and extra-adrenal pheochromocytomas.

E. The treatment of benign and malignant pheochromocytomas is surgical excision.

   1. Preoperative preparation includes administration of an α-adrenergic blocker to control hypertension and to permit re-expansion of intra-vascular volume. Phenoxybenzamine, 10 mg orally twice a day, is initiated and increased to 20 to 40 mg orally twice a day until the desired effect or prohibitive side effects are encountered. Postural hypertension is expected and is the desired end point. β-Adrenergic blockade (e.g., propranolol) may be added if tachycardia or arrhyth-mias develop but only after complete α-adrenergic blockade. Patients with cardiopulmonary dysfunction may require a pulmonary artery (Swan–Ganz) catheter perioperatively, and all patients should be monitored in the surgical intensive care unit in the immediate post-operative period.

   2. The classic operative approach for familial pheochromocytomas is exploration of both adrenal glands, the preaortic and paravertebral areas, and the organ of Zuckerkandl through a midline or bilateral subcostal incision. In patients with MEN type 2A or 2B and a unilat-eral pheochromocytoma, it is acceptable to remove only the involved gland (*Ann Surg*. 1993;217:595). In patients with a sporadic, uni-lateral pheochromocytoma localized by preoperative imaging stud-ies, adrenalectomy may be performed by an anterior or posterior approach or (increasingly) by laparoscopic adrenalectomy. Intra-operative labile hypertension can occur during resection of pheo-chromocytoma. This can be prevented by minimal manipulation of the tumor but can be controlled most effectively with intravenous sodium nitroprusside (0.5 to 10 μg/kg/minute) or phentolamine (5 mg).

IV. **ADRENOCORTICAL CARCINOMA** is a rare but aggressive malignancy. Most patients with this cancer present with locally advanced disease.

   A. Syndromes of adrenal hormone overproduction may include rapidly pro-gressive hypercortisolism, hyperaldosteronism, or virilization. Large (>6 cm) adrenal masses that extend to nearby structures on CT scanning likely represent carcinoma.

   B. Complete surgical resection of locally confined tumor is the only chance for cure of adrenocortical carcinoma. Definitive diagnosis of adrenocorti-cal carcinoma requires operative and pathologic demonstration of nodal or distant metastases. Any adrenal neoplasm weighing more than 50 g should be considered malignant.

   C. Often, patients with adrenocortical carcinoma present with metastatic disease, most often involving the lung, lymph nodes, liver, or bone. Pal-liative surgical debulking of locally advanced or metastatic adrenocortical carcinoma may provide these patients with symptomatic relief from some slow-growing, hormone-producing cancers. Chemotherapy with mitotane may be somewhat effective. Overall, the prognosis for patients with adren-ocortical carcinoma is poor.

V. INCIDENTAL ADRENAL MASSES are detected in 0.6% to 1.5% of abdominal CT scans obtained for other reasons. Most incidentally discovered adrenal masses are benign, nonfunctioning cortical adenomas of no clinical significance. The AACE and AAES recommend all adrenal masses be evaluated with a 1-mg dexamethasone suppression test and a measurement of plasma-free metanephrines (*Endocr Pract.* 2009;15(suppl 1):1–20). Patients with coexisting hypertension should also be evaluated for primary aldosteronism. Surgery should be considered in all patients with clinically apparent functional adrenal cortical tumors and pheochromocytomas. Tumors greater than 6 cm should be surgically removed. Tumors less than 4 cm should be monitored clinically and radiologically in 3 to 6 months followed by annually for 2 years. Either open or laparoscopic adrenalectomy is acceptable. Laparoscopic adrenalectomy has been associated with shorter hospitalization and faster recovery. Its use is generally limited to malignant lesions less than 5 cm in diameter and benign-appearing lesions up to 8 to 10 cm in diameter.

CARCINOID TUMORS

I. Carcinoid tumors are classified according to their embryologic origin: foregut (bronchial, thymic, gastroduodenal, and pancreatic), midgut (jejunal, ileal, appendiceal, right colic), and hindgut (distal colic, rectal).

A. **Biochemical Diagnosis.** In general, the diagnosis of carcinoid rests on the finding of elevated circulating serotonin or urinary metabolites [5-hydroxyindoleacetic acid (5-HIAA)] and localizing studies. The best biochemical test is an elevated urinary 5-HIAA (normal, 2 to 8 mg/day).

B. **Radiography.** Rectal or jejunoileal tumors may be visualized by contrast studies, whereas bronchial carcinoids can be identified on chest X-rays, CT scans, or bronchoscopy. Abdominal or hepatic metastases are best identified by CT scanning, ultrasonography, or angiography. As with other neuroendocrine tumors, some carcinoids can be detected with metaiodobenzylguanidine (^{131}I-MIBG) scanning, and most are detectable by ^{111}In-octreotide scintigraphy.

II. SPECIFIC CARCINOID TUMORS

A. Carcinoid of the appendix is by far the most common carcinoid tumor and is found in up to 1 in 300 appendectomies. The risk of lymph node metastases and the prognosis of appendiceal carcinoids depend on the size: tumors less than 1 cm never metastasize, tumors 1 to 2 cm have a 1% risk of metastasis, and tumors larger than 2 cm have a 30% risk of metastasis (*World J Surg.* 1996;20:183). Extent of surgery for appendiceal carcinoid is based on size: simple appendectomy for tumors less than 1 cm, right hemicolectomy for tumors larger than 2 cm, and selective right hemicolectomy for tumors 1 to 2 cm. Prognosis for completely resected appendiceal carcinoid is favorable, with 5-year survival of 90% to 100%.

B. Small intestine carcinoid tumors usually present with vague abdominal symptoms that uncommonly lead to preoperative diagnosis. Most patients are operated on for intestinal obstruction, which is caused by a desmoplastic reaction in the mesentery around the tumor rather than by the tumor itself. Extended resection, including the mesentery and lymph nodes, is required, even for small tumors. Meticulous examination of the remaining bowel is mandatory because tumors are multicentric in 20% to 40% of cases, and synchronous adenocarcinomas are found in up to 10% of cases. An almost linear relationship exists between size of tumor and risk of nodal metastases, with a risk of up to 85% for tumors larger than 2 cm. Prognosis depends on the size and extent of disease; overall survival is 50% to 60%, which is substantially decreased if liver metastases are present. Small-bowel carcinoids have the highest propensity to metastasize to the liver and produce the carcinoid syndrome.

C. Rectal carcinoids are typically small, submucosal nodules that are often asymptomatic or produce one or more of the nonspecific symptoms of bleeding, constipation, and tenesmus. These tumors are hormonally inactive and almost never produce the carcinoid syndrome, even with spread to the liver. Treatment of small (<1 cm) rectal carcinoids is endoscopic removal. Transmural excision of tumors 1 to 2 cm can be done locally. Treatment of 2-cm and larger tumors or invasive tumors is controversial but may include anterior or abdominoperineal resection for fit patients without metastases.

D. Foregut carcinoids include gastroduodenal, bronchial, and thymic carcinoids. These are a heterogeneous group of tumors with variable prognosis. They do not release serotonin and may produce atypical symptoms (e.g., violaceous flushing of the skin) related to release of histamine. Gastroduodenal carcinoids may produce gastrin and cause ZES. Resection is advocated for localized disease.

III. THE CARCINOID SYNDROME occurs in less than 10% of patients with a carcinoid and develops when venous drainage from the tumor gains access to the systemic circulation, as with hepatic metastases. The classic syndrome consists of flushing, diarrhea, bronchospasm, and right-sided cardiac valvular fibrosis. Symptoms are paroxysmal and may be provoked by alcohol, cheese, chocolate, or red wine. Diagnosis is made by 24-hour measurement of urinary 5-HIAA or of whole-blood 5-hydroxytryptamine. Surgical cure usually is not possible with extensive abdominal or hepatic metastases; however, debulking of the tumor may alleviate symptoms and improve survival when it can be performed safely. Hepatic metastases also have been treated with chemoembolization using doxorubicin, 5-fluorouracil, and cisplatin. Carcinoid crisis with severe bronchospasm and hemodynamic collapse may occur perioperatively in patients with an undiagnosed carcinoid. Prompt recognition is crucial because administration of octreotide (100 μg intravenously) can be lifesaving.

HEREDITARY ENDOCRINE TUMOR SYNDROMES

I. MULTIPLE ENDOCRINE NEOPLASIA SYNDROMES

A. MEN-1 is an autosomal-dominant syndrome characterized by tumors of the parathyroid glands, pancreatic islet cells, and pituitary gland. Hyperparathyroidism occurs in virtually all patients. Clinical evidence of pancreatic islet cell and pituitary tumors develops in 50% and 25% of patients, respectively. Lipomas, thymic or bronchial carcinoid tumors, and tumors of the thyroid, adrenal cortex, and central nervous system (CNS) may also develop. The gene responsible for MEN-1, *MENIN*, is located on chromosome 11q13 and appears to act through transcription factors (*Science.* 1997;276:404). Genetic testing is available in many centers, but if it is not available, screening of family members should begin in their early teens, including yearly determinations of plasma calcium, glucose, gastrin, fasting insulin, vasoactive intestinal polypeptide, pancreatic polypeptide, prolactin, growth hormone, and β-human gonadotropin hormone.

1. Hyperparathyroidism. Because HPT is frequently the first detectable abnormality in patients with MEN-1, yearly calcium screening of asymptomatic kindred members is recommended. Patients with HPT and MEN-1 usually have generalized (four-gland) parathyroid enlargement. Surgery should consist of 3.5-gland parathyroidectomy or a total parathyroidectomy with autotransplantation of parathyroid tissue to the forearm. This method achieves cure in more than 90% of cases and results in hypoparathyroidism in less than 5%. Graft-dependent recurrent HPT, however, is seen in up to 50% of cases. It is managed by resecting a portion of the autografted material (*Ann Surg.* 1980;192:451).

2. Pituitary tumors occur in up to 40% of MEN-1 patients and most commonly are benign prolactin-producing adenomas. Growth-hormone, ACTH-producing, and nonfunctioning tumors are also seen. Patients may present with headache, diplopia, or symptoms referable to hormone overproduction. Bromocriptine inhibits prolactin production and may reduce tumor bulk and obviate the need for surgical intervention. Transsphenoidal hypophysectomy may be necessary if medical treatment fails.

3. Pancreatic islet cell tumors pose the most difficult clinical challenge and account for most of the morbidity and mortality of the syndrome. Gastrinomas (ZES) are most common, but vasoactive intestinal polypeptide-secreting tumors, insulinomas, glucagonomas, and somatostatinomas, are also encountered. The pancreas is usually diffusely involved, with islet cell hyperplasia and multifocal tumors. Tumors may be found in the proximal duodenum and peripancreatic areas (gastrinoma triangle), and these are virtually always malignant. The treatment goal is relief of symptoms related to excessive hormone production and cure or palliation of the malignant process. Patients frequently require medical and surgical therapy. Before surgical exploration, the patient should be evaluated for an adrenal tumor by measuring urinary excretion rates of glucocorticoids, mineralocorticoid, sex hormones, and plasma metanephrines.

II. **MULTIPLE ENDOCRINE NEOPLASIA TYPE 2 (MEN-2)** is characterized by MTC and includes MEN-2A, MEN-2B, and familial, non-MEN MTC [familial MTC (FMTC)]. These autosomal-dominant syndromes are caused by gain-of-function mutations in the *RET* proto-oncogene, which encodes a transmembrane tyrosine kinase receptor. Mutations in *RET* lead to constitutive activation (tyrosine phosphorylation) of the RET protein, which drives tumorigenesis. Genetic testing should be performed on all suspected individuals. Because MTC occurs universally in all MEN-2 variants, prophylactic thyroidectomy is indicated for all RET-mutation carriers. Current guidelines call for thyroidectomy in the first year of life for MEN-2B-mutation carriers and thyroidectomy before age 5 years in MEN-2A-mutation carriers (*J Clin Endocrinol Metab.* 2001;86:5658). Genetic counseling for parents of affected children is crucial prior to prophylactic surgery. In more than 50% of patients with MTC, the cancer recurs after primary surgical resection. Although reoperation is advocated for local recurrence, there is no accepted adjuvant regimen for effectively treating metastatic disease. Investigational therapies and clinical trials with targeted inhibitors of RET tyrosine kinase activity are being evaluated (*Surgery.* 2002;132:960).

A. **MEN-2A.** All patients with MEN-2A will develop MTC, whereas pheochromocytomas arise in approximately 40% to 50% of patients, and hyperplasia of the parathyroid glands arises in approximately 25% to 35%. Patients with MEN-2A also develop gastrointestinal manifestations, including abdominal pain, distention, and constipation as well as Hirschsprung's disease (*Ann Surg.* 2002;235:648). On genetic analysis, patients with MEN-2A and Hirschsprung's disease (MEN-2A-HD) share common mutations in either codon 609, 618, or 620 of exon 10 of the *RET* proto-oncogene. MTC generally occurs earlier than pheochromocytoma or hyperparathyroidism. Nonetheless, biochemical testing to exclude pheochromocytoma is mandatory in all MEN-2 and MTC patients prior to thyroidectomy.

B. **MEN-2B** is a variant of MEN-2 in which patients develop MTC and pheochromocytomas but not hyperparathyroidism. Patients also develop ganglioneuromatosis and a characteristic physical appearance, with hypergnathism of the midface, marfanoid body habitus, and multiple mucosal neuromas. MTC is particularly aggressive in these patients. MEN-2B patients also demonstrate multiple gastrointestinal symptoms and megacolon.

C. **FMTC** is characterized only by the hereditary development of MTC without other endocrinopathies. MTC is generally more indolent in these patients.

22 Trauma Surgery

Jennifer A. Leinicke and Douglas J.E. Schuerer

Injury is a leading cause of death and disability around the world. This chapter outlines an overall approach to trauma care, provides a framework for therapy, and highlights critical aspects of decision making and interventions. The Eastern Association for the Surgery of Trauma (EAST) Web site (http://www.east.org) provides evidence-based clinical guidelines and can be referred to for additional detail.

TRAUMA CARE

I. **PREHOSPITAL CARE.** Field professionals are responsible for performing the three major functions of prehospital care: (1) assessment of the injury scene, (2) stabilization and monitoring of injured patients, and (3) safe and rapid transportation of critically ill patients to the appropriate trauma center. The observations and interventions performed are important in guiding the resuscitation of an injured patient. The MVIT (*m*echanism, *v*ital signs, *i*njury inventory, *t*reatment) system of reporting is one method of communicating data to the trauma team in an efficient, fast, and organized manner.

A. The **mechanism of a trauma** partially determines the pattern and severity of injuries sustained in the event. For instance, motor vehicle collisions can cause direct contact between the driver's knees and the dashboard resulting in patellar fracture, posterior knee dislocation (with popliteal artery injury), femoral shaft fracture, and posterior rim fracture of the acetabulum. Also, feet-first falls from significant heights cause axial loading and a possible combination of calcaneal fracture, lower-extremity long-bone fracture, acetabular injury, and lumbar spine compression fracture.

B. **Vital signs,** including level of consciousness and voluntary movement, give insight into the clinical trajectory of the patient and are a key element in leveling trauma. Emergency medical service (EMS) providers typically measure and report these values, often in less than ideal conditions. Deterioration of vital signs *en route* to the trauma center suggests life-threatening injuries requiring immediate intervention.

C. The **injury inventory** consists of the description of injuries as observed by EMS personnel. Important prehospital observations include whether the patient was trapped in a vehicle, was crushed under a heavy object, or suffered significant exposure secondary to prolonged extrication. Such findings alert the trauma team to critical secondary injuries, including rhabdomyolysis, traumatic asphyxia, and hypothermia.

D. **Prehospital treatment** is aimed at stabilization of the injured patient and involves securing an airway, providing adequate ventilation, assessing and supporting circulation, and stabilizing the spine. EMS caregivers fulfill these goals through various therapies that include (but are not limited to) administration of oxygen and intravenous (IV) fluids, prevention of heat loss, and immobilization of the spine with a backboard and properly fitting hard cervical collar. All such interventions need to be taken into account during the initial evaluation, including immediate confirmation of any prehospital airway.

II. **INITIAL HOSPITAL CARE.** Trauma deaths have a **trimodal distribution:** (1) immediate death occurring at the time of injury due to devastating wounds; (2) early death occurring within the first few hours of injury due to major intracranial, thoracic, abdominal, pelvic, and extremity injuries; and (3) late death occurring days to weeks after the initial injury due to secondary complications (sepsis, acute respiratory distress syndrome, systemic inflammatory response syndrome, or multiple organ dysfunction and failure). Initial hospital care usually takes place in the emergency department and has two main components: the primary and secondary surveys.

A. **Primary survey.** The primary survey is a systematic, rapid evaluation of the injured patient following the **ABCDE algorithm** (*a*irway, *b*reathing, *c*irculation, *d*isability, *e*xposure). On completion of the survey, the patient should have an established airway with cervical spine control, adequate ventilation and oxygenation, proper IV access and control of hemorrhage, and an inventory of the patient's neurologic status and disability. Additionally, the patient should be completely exposed (all clothing removed) with environmental control. During the survey, a rudimentary history is obtained, if possible. This history follows the acronym **AMPLE** (*a*llergies, *m*edications, *p*ast medical history, *l*ast meal, *e*vents surrounding the injury).

1. **Airway.** Establishing a patent airway is the highest priority in the care of a trauma patient because, without one, irreversible brain damage from hypoxia can occur within minutes. The airway should always be secured under cervical spine control. The quickest way to evaluate airway patency is to engage the patient in conversation. A patient who is able to respond verbally has a patent airway. A patient who cannot respond verbally must be assumed to have an obstructed airway until proven otherwise. Every trauma patient initially should have oxygen administered (via nasal cannula or bag valve facemask) and an oxygen saturation monitor (i.e., pulse oximeter) placed. An oximeter device is helpful, but it is important to remember that its output readings can be misleading in certain clinical situations (e.g., patients with severe anemia, carbon monoxide poisoning, insufficient pulse pressure, hypothermia, or burns with inhalation injury).

   a. **Basic maneuvers to alleviate obstruction**

      (1) **Simple suctioning.** This removes obstructions caused by vomitus, phlegm, or other debris in the oropharynx.

      (2) **Jaw-thrust maneuver.** The tongue itself can occlude the airway. A jaw thrust can successfully displace the tongue anteriorly from the pharyngeal inlet, relieving the obstruction.

      (3) **Nasopharyngeal airway.** In the semiconscious patient, this can provide a conduit for ventilation, but it may result in emesis if it is used in fully conscious patients.

(4) **Oropharyngeal airway.** Mechanically displace the tongue anteriorly, securing airway patency. Because of the strong induction of the gag reflex and emesis, these devices should be used only in unconscious patients.

b. **Tracheal intubation** is indicated in any patient in whom concern for airway integrity exists (unconscious or semiconscious patients, patients with mechanical obstruction secondary to facial trauma or debris, combative and hypoxic patients). The emergent tracheal intubation of an uncooperative trauma patient is a high-risk undertaking. The most skilled operator available should secure the airway by the most expeditious means possible. The preferred method of intubation is via the orotracheal route using **rapid-sequence induction (RSI).** Nasotracheal intubation should be discouraged. Rapid-sequence intubation follows a systematic protocol to ensure successful provision of an airway. The patient is first **spontaneously ventilated with 100% oxygen.** During this time, a team member provides in-line cervical spine stabilization to prevent unintentional manipulation as the hard cervical collar is removed anteriorly. A separate team member provides anterior pressure on the cricoid cartilage (Sellick maneuver) to occlude the esophagus and prevent aspiration during intubation. There is increasing controversy as to the utility of cricoid pressure due to concerns about its efficacy and potential for obscuring the view of the vocal cords. Therefore, cricoid pressure should be removed if its use results in difficulty with securing the airway (*Resuscitation.* 2010;81(7):810–816). Following preoxygenation, a **short-acting sedative or hypnotic medication is administered** via a functioning IV line with a stopcock. The choice of medication depends on the clinical situation. In general, etomidate, 0.3 mg/kg intravenously, or a short-acting benzodiazepine, such as midazolam, 1 to 2.5 mg intravenously, is used because these medications tend to have minimal effects on the cardiovascular status of the patient. In addition, midazolam provides anterograde amnesia. Opiates, such as fentanyl citrate, 2 μg/kg intravenously, should be used only in patients who are adequately perfused because their mild cardiac depressant activity can cause unexpected cardiovascular decompensation in hypoxic, hypoperfused patients. Sodium thiopental, 2 to 5 mg/kg intravenously, is exclusively reserved for the well-perfused patient with a seemingly isolated head injury because it diminishes the transient elevation in intracranial pressure (ICP) associated with tracheal intubation. A **paralytic agent is administered immediately after the sedative.** Succinylcholine, 1 to 1.25 mg/kg intravenously, is the paralytic of choice because, as a depolarizing muscle relaxant, it has a rapid onset (fasciculations within seconds) and a short half-life (recovery within 1 to 2 minutes). Contraindications in the acute trauma setting are limited to patients with known pseudocholinesterase deficiency or previous spinal injury. Succinylcholine can be used safely in patients with acute burns or spinal trauma. Rocuronium, 0.60 to 0.85 mg/kg intravenously, is an alternative paralytic, but as a nondepolarizing relaxant, it has a slower onset (up to 90 seconds) and a longer half-life (recovery after 40 minutes) than succinylcholine. **After onset of paralysis, the endotracheal tube (the largest for patient size and airway) is inserted through the vocal cords under direct vision** with the assistance of a laryngoscope and with the balloon deflated. The tube position is usually around 21 cm from the incisors in women and 23 cm from the incisors in men. Proper positioning of the tube in the trachea should be confirmed by exhalation of carbon dioxide over several breaths (using a litmus paper device or capnometer). **Adequacy of ventilation** should be verified by bilateral auscultation in each axilla. A chest X-ray should be taken within the next few minutes and checked to ensure proper endotracheal tube position. Tracheal intubation should secure an airway within 90 to 120 seconds (about three attempts). If it is unsuccessful, an airway placed directly through the cricoid membrane is often necessary.

c. **Cricothyrotomy** is the method of choice for establishing a surgical airway in adults, for instances, in which orotracheal intubation is not possible (unsuccessful orotracheal attempts or massive facial trauma). The cricoid membrane is easily palpated between the cricoid cartilage and the larynx. Because it is both superficial and relatively avascular, it provides rapid, easy access to the trachea. A 1.5-cm transverse skin incision is made over the trachea, and a scalpel is used to poke a hole through the membrane. Care is taken to avoid exiting through the trachea posteriorly, injuring the esophagus. Next, the scalpel handle, a tracheal spreader, or a similar surgical instrument is used to expand the hole. Finally, a 6-mm endotracheal or tracheostomy tube is inserted into the trachea through the cricothyrotomy. Historically, a cricothyrotomy would eventually require revision to a tracheostomy to decrease the risk of tracheal stenosis, but this has been challenged, and many institutions now use the cricothyrotomy site as a tracheostomy site. Cricothyrotomy is contraindicated in children younger than 12 years of age because of the anatomic difficulty in performing the procedure and risk of stenosis. In this situation, percutaneous transtracheal ventilation is an alternative. Laryngeal mask airway (LMA) and Combitube are appropriate alternatives to cricothyrotomy when expertise is limited (EAST guidelines 2002).

d. **Percutaneous transtracheal ventilation** can provide a temporary airway until a formal surgical airway can be supplied, especially in young children in whom cricothyrotomy is not possible. A small cannula (usually a 14-gauge IV catheter) is placed through the cricoid membrane. The cannula is connected to oxygen tubing containing a precut side hole. Temporary occlusion of the side hole provides passage of oxygen into the lungs via the cannula. Exhalation occurs passively through the vocal cords. Through this means, alveolar oxygen concentrations can be maintained for up to 30 to 45 minutes.

B. **Breathing.** Once an airway is established, attention is directed at assessing the patient's breathing (i.e., the oxygenation and ventilation of the lungs).

A patent airway does not ensure adequate breathing because the trachea can be ventilated without successfully ventilating the alveoli. One hundred percent oxygen is administered through the secured airway. The chest is then examined, and important life-threatening abnormalities involving the thorax are identified and treated. The following are potentially fatal conditions that require immediate attention and treatment. (See Chapter 37 for a description of the **technique of tube thoracostomy.**)

1. Tension pneumothorax
   a. Diagnosis. Absence of breath sounds, hyperresonance, tracheal deviation away from the side of the abnormality, and associated hypotension due to decreased venous return.
   b. Treatment. Immediate decompressive therapy (a chest X-ray should not delay treatment) via placement of a 14-gauge IV catheter in the second intercostal space in the midclavicular line, immediately followed by tube thoracostomy.

2. Pneumothorax or hemothorax
   a. Diagnosis. Absent or decreased breath sounds without tracheal deviation usually indicate a simple pneumothorax or hemothorax on the affected side. A chest X-ray can usually confirm these conditions.
   b. Treatment. Tube thoracostomy (32 Fr. or larger for hemothorax), connected to an underwater seal-suction device adjusted to –20 cm water suction.

3. Flail chest
   a. Diagnosis. Paradoxical chest wall motion with spontaneous respirations (three or more contiguous ribs with two or more fractures per rib). Pulmonary contusion often accompanies such an injury. Chest X-ray often reveals the extent of fractures and underlying lung injury.
   b. Treatment. Adequate pain control (often with epidural analgesia), aggressive pulmonary toilet, and respiratory support. Many patients require early mechanical ventilatory support.

4. Open pneumothorax
   a. Diagnosis. A chest wound communicating with the pleural space that is greater than two thirds the diameter of the trachea will preferentially draw air into the thorax ("sucking chest wound").
   b. Treatment. Cover with a partially occlusive bandage secured on three sides (securing all four sides can result in a tension pneumothorax and should be avoided), preventing air from entering the thorax but allowing it to exit via the wound if necessary. Prompt tube thoracostomy should follow placement of the partially occlusive dressing.

5. Tracheobronchial disruption
   a. Diagnosis. Severe subcutaneous emphysema with respiratory comprise is suggestive; bronchoscopy is diagnostic.
   b. Treatment. Tube thoracostomy placed on the affected side will reveal a large air leak, and the collapsed lung may fail to re-expand. The patient is stabilized by intubation of the unaffected bronchus until operative repair can be performed (see Section V.D.2).

C. **Circulation.** The goal of this portion of the primary survey is to identify and treat the presence of shock. Initially, all active external hemorrhage is controlled with direct pressure, and obvious fractures are stabilized. The pulse and blood pressure (BP) are obtained. The skin perfusion is determined by noting skin temperature and evaluating capillary refill. Over time, end-organ perfusion during a trauma resuscitation is estimated using mental status and urine output as markers. Shock is defined as the inadequate delivery of oxygen and nutrients to tissue. The etiologies of shock can be divided into three broad categories: hypovolemic, cardiogenic, and distributive. The trauma team must be familiar with the manifestations and therapy of each category of shock because any of the three may be encountered in the injured patient.

1. **Hypovolemic shock** is the most common type of shock seen in trauma patients and occurs as a result of decreased intravascular volume, most commonly secondary to acute blood loss. It is divided into four classes (Table 22-1). In its severe form, it can manifest as a rapid pulse, decreased pulse pressure, diminished capillary refill, and cool, clammy skin. Therapy is restoration of the intravascular volume. Thus, the patient should have **two large-bore IV lines placed (14 or 16 gauge). The antecubital veins are the preferred sites.** Increasingly, intraosseous access is being used as a rapid way to gain access for both fluid resuscitation and medication administration for patients in whom peripheral IV access is difficult to obtain (*J Trauma.* 2009;66(6):1739–1741). If a peripheral IV catheter cannot be placed secondary to venous collapse, an 8.5-French cannula (Cordis catheter) may also be placed via the Seldinger technique into the **femoral vein.** The subclavian and

TABLE 22-1	Estimated Blood Loss by Initial Hemodynamic Variables			
	Class I	Class II	Class III	Class IV
Blood loss (mL)	Up to 750	750–1,500	1,500–2,000	>2,000
Blood loss (% blood volume)	Up to 15%	15%–30%	30%–40%	>40%
Pulse rate	<100	>100	>120	>140
Blood pressure (mm Hg)	Normal	Normal	Decreased	Decreased
Pulse pressure (mm Hg)	Normal or increased	Decreased	Decreased	Decreased
Urinary output (mL/hr)	>30	20–30	5–15	Negligible

internal jugular veins should be reserved for those patients in whom major venous intra-abdominal injury or pelvic fractures prevent effective use of a femoral approach. Short, wide IV catheters are used to maximize the flow of resuscitation fluids into the circulation (the rate of fluid flow is proportional to the cross-sectional area of a conduit and inversely proportional to the fourth power of its radius). A blood specimen should be simultaneously obtained for cross-matching and for any other pertinent labs. Resuscitation should consist of an **initial bolus of 2 L of crystalloid solution** (children should receive an initial bolus of 20 mL/kg). All fluids administered should be warmed to prevent hypothermia. If the patient remains hypotensive despite the initial fluid bolus, type O blood should be administered and an additional 2 L of fluid should be given. Premenopausal women should receive Rh- blood. Men and postmenopausal women can receive either Rh– or Rh+ blood. Once the patient is blood-typed, type-specific blood should be used. If massive transfusion is required [>10 units of packed red blood cell (PRBCs)], attempts should be made at maintaining a 1:1 ratio of PRBCs and fresh-frozen plasma (FFP). In the setting of penetrating torso injury involving a large blood vessel, less aggressive resuscitation (keeping BP around 90 mm Hg) until formal surgical control of the bleeding site is obtained has been shown to have some benefit in diminishing blood loss (*N Engl J Med.* 1994;331:1105). Resuscitative thoracotomy is sometimes indicated for severe cardiopulmonary collapse (see Section VI.A.1).

2. **Cardiogenic shock** occurs when the heart is unable to provide adequate cardiac output to perfuse the peripheral tissues. In the trauma setting, such shock can occur in one of two ways: (1) **extrinsic compression** of the heart leading to decreased venous return and cardiac output or (2) **myocardial injury** causing inadequate myocardial contraction and decreased cardiac output. Patients in cardiogenic shock secondary to extrinsic compression of the heart usually present with cool, pale skin, decreased BP, and distended jugular veins. They often respond transiently to an initial fluid bolus, but more definite therapy is always needed. Tension pneumothorax is the most common etiology. Cardiac tamponade is a less common cause. It usually occurs in the setting of a penetrating injury near the heart. Rapid diagnosis can be obtained with the use of ultrasound. Therapy consists of pericardial drainage and repair of the injury, usually a proximal great vessel or cardiac wound (see Sections V.D.5.a and V.D.6.a). Resuscitative thoracotomy may be required. Patients in cardiogenic shock secondary to myocardial injury can also present with cool skin, decreased BP, and distended jugular veins. Acute myocardial infarction can manifest in this way. Often, it is responsible for the traumatic event, but it can also occur as a result of the stress following an injury. Diagnosis of a myocardial infarction is via electrocardiogram (ECG) and troponin levels. Therapy should follow Advanced Cardiac Life Support guidelines, keeping in mind that anticoagulants may need to be avoided early until active bleeding related to the trauma has been excluded. Severe blunt cardiac injury (BCI) is another manifestation. It usually occurs in the

setting of high-speed motor vehicle crashes. An ECG and possibly an echocardiogram are essential. Therapy ranges from close monitoring with pharmacologic support in an intensive care unit (ICU) to operative repair (see Section V.D.6.b).

3. **Distributive shock** occurs as a result of an increase in venous capacitance leading to decreased venous return. Neurogenic shock secondary to acute quadriplegia or paraplegia is one type. Loss of peripheral sympathetic tone is responsible for the increased venous capacitance and decreased venous return. These patients present with warm skin, absent rectal tone, and inappropriate bradycardia. They often respond to an initial fluid bolus but often require pharmacologic support. Phenylephrine or norepinephrine can be used to restore peripheral vascular resistance. Chronotropic agents such as dopamine are sometimes used for bradycardic patients. Of note, the leading cause of shock in a trauma patient is hypovolemia, and thus neurogenic shock is usually a diagnosis of exclusion.

D. **Disability.** The goal of this phase of the primary survey is to identify and treat life-threatening neurologic injuries. Priority is given to evaluating level of consciousness and looking for lateralizing neurologic signs. The level of consciousness is quickly assessed using the **AVPU system** (ascertaining whether the patient is *a*wake, opens eyes to *v*oice, opens eyes to *p*ainful stimulus, or is *u*narousable). The pupils are examined, and their size, symmetry, and responsiveness to light are noted. Focal neurologic deficits are noted. Signs of significant neurologic impairment include inability to follow simple commands, asymmetry of pupils or their response to light, and gross asymmetry of limb movement to painful stimuli. Both intracranial and spinal injuries require urgent evaluation.

1. **Intracranial injuries.** Head injury remains a leading cause of trauma fatality in the United States. **Herniation (either uncal or cerebellar)** is often the final common pathway leading to death. Vigilance on the part of the trauma team can sometimes trigger interventions before such an event becomes irreversible. Measures used to prevent increases in ICP and herniation include head elevation to 30 to 45 degrees, sedation, and prevention of jugular venous outflow obstruction. Pharmacologic diuretic therapy is used to decrease ICP by reducing the volume of both the cerebrospinal fluid (CSF) and the brain. **Mannitol, 0.25 to 1 g/kg,** is the preferred agent, but hypertonic saline is also used. Sedation and therapeutic paralysis can acutely lower ICP, but they have the disadvantage of obscuring ongoing clinical neurologic examination. Although once advocated as an initial means of lowering ICP, hyperventilation is no longer recommended as a first-line therapy because of its adverse ischemic effects (it decreases ICP by causing intracranial vasoconstriction secondary to inducing hypocarbic alkalosis). It may be used in an acute setting with impending herniation until pharmacologic agents are available, and if it is used, the partial pressure of carbon dioxide (Pco_2) should be closely monitored and kept at a level of 30 to 35 mm Hg.

2. **Spinal cord injuries.** Acute injury to the spinal cord can result in neurogenic shock, which should be treated appropriately (see Section II.C.3).

In addition, spinal cord trauma produces debilitating neurologic loss of function. The appropriate acute management of such deficits remains controversial. Currently, the use of high dose corticosteroids is not routinely recommended due to increasing evidence that corticosteroids do not result in improved functional outcomes. Additionally, multiple trials have demonstrated an increase in mortality secondary to infection, specifically ventilator associated pneumonia, as well as increased hospital costs and length of stay [*Spine.* (Phila Pa 1976) 2009;34(20):2121–2124] (*J Trauma.* 2004;56(5):1076–1083).

3. **Neurosurgical consultation.** A neurosurgeon should be consulted immediately in all patients with severe neurologic injuries. Early radiologic evaluation of the central nervous system (CNS) to exclude evacuable intracranial mass lesions is also critical (see Section III.D.3).

E. **Exposure.** The last component of the primary survey is exposure with environmental control. Its purpose is to allow for complete visual inspection of the injured patient while preventing excessive heat loss. The patient is first completely disrobed, with clothing cut away so as not to disturb occult injuries. The patient then undergoes visual inspection, including logrolling to examine the back, splaying of the legs to examine the perineum, and elevation of the arms to inspect the axillae. The nude patient loses heat rapidly to the environment unless specific countermeasures are undertaken. The resuscitation room should be kept as warm as possible. Any cold backboard should be removed as quickly as possible and all soggy clothing should be taken off expeditiously. All resuscitation fluid should be warmed. Finally, the patient should be covered with warm blankets or a "hot air" heating blanket.

III. **COMPLETION OF THE PRIMARY SURVEY.** The completion of the primary survey should be followed by a brief assessment of the adequacy of the initial resuscitation efforts.

A. **Monitoring.** Appropriate monitoring is essential to determine the clinical trajectory of the injured patient. If not already in place, **ECG leads and a pulse oximeter** should be applied. A manual BP should be taken in all patients. An **automatic cuff** should be placed for subsequent serial BP measurements, although it should be kept in mind that such measurements can be inaccurate in a patient with a systolic BP less than 90 mm Hg. Finally, an **indwelling urinary catheter** should be placed. Before insertion of the catheter, however, the urethral meatus should be inspected and found free of blood (the labia and scrotum should not harbor a hematoma). In addition, all male patients require palpation of the prostate to ensure that it is in the normal position, not displaced superiorly ("high riding"). If any genitourinary structures are abnormal, a retrograde urethrogram is necessary. If it is normal, the catheter may be passed. If urethral injuries are present, immediate consultation with a urologist is required before attempting to pass the catheter.

B. **Laboratory values.** After placement of two IV catheters, blood should be sent for laboratory studies. The most important test to obtain is the cross-match. Other studies include blood chemistries, hematologic analysis, coagulation profile, blood gas with base deficit, toxicologic analysis (with ethanol level), urinalysis, and β-human chorionic gonadotropin level if the patient is a woman of child-bearing age. The hematocrit value is the most commonly misinterpreted measure because it is not immediately altered with acute hemorrhage. It should not, therefore, be considered to be an indicator of circulating blood volume in the trauma patient. Serial hematocrit values, however, may give an indication of ongoing blood loss.

C. **Adequacy of resuscitation.** The adequacy of resuscitation can best be determined by using urine output and blood pH. Resuscitation, therefore, should strive for a blood pH of 7.4 and a urinary output of 0.5 to 1 mL/kg/hour in adults (1 to 2 mL/kg/hour in children). Base deficit and lactic acid levels are also used as markers of adequate resuscitation and have been shown to have prognostic value.

D. **Radiographic investigations.** Essential radiographic investigations are ordered during this period. These tests can provide critical data regarding injuries sustained in a trauma, but their performance should not get in the way of ongoing physical examinations and interventions.

1. Plain radiography
   a. **Blunt trauma.** Patients who have sustained blunt trauma with major energy transfer require **chest and possibly pelvic radiographs.** If time permits and the patient is stable but unable to be clinically cleared, a formal three-view cervical spine series should be obtained if computed tomography (CT) is unavailable. The best screening exam to evaluate for cervical spine injuries is a CT extending from the occiput through T1 with coronal and sagittal reformats (see Section IV.C. for detailed description of cervical spine evaluation). If there is no evidence of spine or pelvic injury, an upright chest X-ray should be obtained because it provides crucial information with regard to hemothorax, pneumothorax, mediastinal widening, and subdiaphragmatic gas that sometimes cannot be gleaned from a supine film. Finally, plain radiographs should be obtained of any area of localized blunt trauma, especially if fractures are suspected on the basis of physical exam.
   b. **Penetrating trauma.** Patients who have sustained penetrating injuries require regional plane radiographs to localize foreign bodies and exclude perforation of gas-filled organs (e.g., intestines and lungs). When these films are being obtained, all entrance and exit sites should be identified with a radiopaque marker. This technique gives insight into the trajectory of the penetrating object and the potential organs injured.

2. **Trauma ultrasonography.** Many trauma centers now use **focused abdominal sonography for trauma (FAST)** as an initial radiographic screening evaluation for all trauma following the primary survey. As the name implies, it is a focused examination designed to identify free intraperitoneal fluid and/or pericardial fluid. An ultrasound machine is used to take multiple views of six standard areas on the torso: **(1) right paracolic gutter, (2) Morrison's pouch,**

(3) pericardium, (4) perisplenic region, (5) left paracolic gutter, and (6) suprapubic region. Free fluid in the abdomen and within the pericardium appears anechoic. FAST has many advantages: portable, rapid, inexpensive, accurate, noninvasive, and repeatable. Its disadvantages include operator variability as well as difficulty of use in morbidly obese patients or those with large amounts of subcutaneous air. It is most useful in evaluating patients with blunt abdominal trauma, especially those who are hypotensive. It may not be as useful in evaluating children or patients with penetrating trauma. It is important to note that if a FAST exam is negative, it does not exclude major intra-abdominal injury. Finally, some trauma centers use sonography to evaluate the thorax for traumatic effusions and pneumothoraces.

3. **CT.** The care of injured patients has been significantly changed by the use of CT scanning. Unnecessary laparotomy is associated with significant morbidity and cost. Because of CT, an increasing amount of both blunt and penetrating trauma has been safely managed nonoperatively. Triple-contrast CT (oral, IV, rectal) has been shown accurately to predict the need for laparotomy in patients with penetrating trauma, decreasing the incidence of unnecessary laparotomy. More recent evidence suggests that single-contrast CT scanning with a high-resolution, multislice scanner may obviate the need for oral and rectal contrast. In patients with an increased risk associated with radiation exposure (e.g., pregnant women and children), consideration should be given as to the risk of radiation exposure versus the potential benefit of any radiologic test ordered.

IV. **SECONDARY SURVEY.** The secondary survey follows the primary survey. It is a complete head-to-toe examination of the patient designed to inventory all injuries sustained in the trauma. Thoroughness is the key to finding all injuries, and a systematic approach is required. Only limited diagnostic evaluation is necessary for making decisions about subsequent interventions or evaluations. A review of important aspects of the secondary survey according to anatomic region follows. This review emphasizes only highlights and is not to be considered exhaustive.

A. **Head.** The patient should be evaluated for best motor and verbal responses to graded stimuli so that a **Glasgow Coma Score (GCS)** can be calculated. The GCS is highly reproducible and exhibits little interobserver variability. Severity of head trauma can be stratified according to the score obtained. Any patient with a GCS of 8 or below is considered to have severe neurologic depression and should be intubated to protect the airway. Inspection and palpation of the head are used to identify obvious lacerations and bony irregularities. All wounds require specific evaluation for evidence of depressed skull fractures or devitalized bone. Signs suggestive of basal skull fractures should be sought. These include periorbital hematomas ("raccoon eyes"), mastoid hematomas ("Battle's sign"), hemotympanum, and CSF rhinorrhea and otorrhea.

B. **The face** should be inspected for lacerations, hematomas, asymmetry, and deformities. The cranial nerves should be evaluated. The bones should be palpated in a systematic fashion to search for evidence of tenderness, crepitus, or bony discontinuity. In particular, the presence of a midfacial fracture should be sought by grasping the maxilla and attempting to move it. The nares should be examined for evidence of a septal hematoma. The oral cavity should be illuminated and inspected for evidence of mucosal violation (commonly seen in mandibular fractures). All dentures and/or displaced teeth should be removed to prevent airway occlusion. The conscious patient should be asked to bite down to determine whether abnormal dental occlusion is present (highly suggestive of a maxillary or mandibular fracture). The eyes should be examined for signs of orbital entrapment and the pupils reexamined. Finally, a nasogastric tube (contraindicated if there is a question of trauma to the midface) or orogastric tube (in patients who have midfacial fractures or are comatose) should be placed to decompress the stomach.

C. **The neck** should be inspected and palpated to exclude cervical spine, vascular, or aerodigestive tract injury.

1. **Cervical spine evaluation.** Assessing the status of the cervical spine is an important aspect of the secondary survey. Signs of cervical spine injury include midline cervical spine tenderness or vertebral step-off on palpation. Excluding the presence of a cervical injury can often be challenging. The proper algorithm is often dictated by the overall condition of the patient.

a. **Awake, unimpaired patient without complaint of midline neck tenderness.** In the awake, alert, oriented, cooperative, unimpaired, neurologically intact patient, the cervical spine should be palpated for signs of injury (e.g., midline cervical spine tenderness, and vertebral step-off). If the physical examination is normal, the patient may be allowed, under supervision, to move the neck through the full range of motion. If there is not any cervical spine pain during this movement, the likelihood of a cervical spine injury is very low, and the stabilizing cervical collar can be removed. Imaging of the cervical spine may not be necessary. If any cervical spine pain is elicited during this movement, the stabilizing cervical collar should remain in place, and a CT scan of the cervical spine extending from the occiput through T1 with coronal and sagittal reformats should be obtained. Plain radiographs do not provide any additional information and are not as sensitive as CT scanning, but in situations where CT is unavailable may be an acceptable substitute in patients at low risk of cervical spine injury.

b. **Awake, unimpaired patient with complaint of midline neck tenderness.** These patients should undergo a CT scan of the cervical spine extending from the occiput through T1 with coronal and sagittal reformats. If the CT is interpreted as normal, then the possibility of ligamentous injury should be entertained, and the patient should undergo MRI of the cervical spine. MRI should be performed within 48 hours when possible as nonspecific changes may occur after this time and make detection of ligamentous injury difficult. If these films are interpreted as normal, the likelihood of cervical spine injury is low, and the stabilizing cervical collar can be removed (a soft collar may be placed for comfort). The on call spine service (orthopedic or neurosurgery) should be consulted for any diagnosed injury.

c. **High-risk patients.** In patients who are awake, alert, and oriented but with multiple traumatic injuries or a high likelihood of cervical spine injury (pretest probability greater than 5%), a CT of the cervical spine should be obtained. Any suspicion for ligamentous injury should be followed immediately by MRI of the cervical spine. The on call spine service should be contacted for any injury.

d. **Unconscious or impaired patient.** In the unconscious or impaired patient, the cervical spine should be considered to be unstable until a reliable clinical examination can be performed because significant ligamentous instability can exist despite a normal CT scan. In patients with a short-term alteration of consciousness (e.g., chemically sedated or intoxicated), CT scan of the cervical spine should be obtained, and any suspicion of ligamentous injury followed up with an MRI. The stabilizing cervical collar should remain in place until the patient is fully awake and unimpaired. Patients with altered levels of consciousness of unknown duration (e.g., diffuse head injury patients) can be evaluated the same way. However, if the patient is unlikely to regain consciousness within 7 days, MRI should be obtained within 48 hours. If there is no evidence of injury on either the CT or MRI, a bedside upright lateral cervical spine film should be obtained, and the cervical collar can be removed if there is no evidence of misalignment. The film should be repeated with the collar off. If this again does not demonstrate misalignment, the cervical spine can be considered "cleared," although occult injury may still be present. If at any time in the above workup an injury is identified, a spine consult should be obtained. In the event that a patient who is likely to have altered consciousness for more than 7 days does not undergo MRI within 48 hours or injury, a spine consult should be obtained. The method used to clear the cervical spine is dependent on the consultant, but may include repeat plain films, CT, MRI, and/or flexion-extension studies under fluoroscopy (EAST guidelines 2009).

2. **Vascular/aerodigestive evaluation.** In addition to evaluating the cervical spine, the neck should be inspected for active hemorrhage and palpated for local tenderness, hematomas, and evidence of subcutaneous air. Wounds should be classified according to their depth and their location. A wound is considered superficial if it does not penetrate the platysma; it is considered deep if the platysma is penetrated. The neck is divided anatomically into three zones: **Zone I** covers the thoracic inlet (manubrium to cricoid cartilage), **zone II** encompasses the midneck (cricoid cartilage to angle of the mandible), and **zone III** spans the upper neck (angle of mandible to base of skull).

D. **Thorax.** Significant pulmonary, cardiac, or great-vessel injury may result from both penetrating and blunt trauma. In all cases, examination of the thorax includes inspection, palpation, percussion, and auscultation.

Particular attention should be directed at observing the position of the trachea, checking for symmetric excursion of the chest, palpating for fractures and subcutaneous emphysema, and auscultating the quality and location of breath sounds. Two points bear further comment. First, thoracic extra-anatomic air (subcutaneous air, pneumomediastinum, or pneumopericardium) is frequently noted on physical examination or chest radiography in trauma patients (*Surg Clin North Am.* 1996;76:725). Such a finding should alert the trauma team to four potential etiologies: (1) pulmonary parenchymal injury with occult pneumothorax (most common cause), (2) tracheobronchial injury, (3) esophageal perforation, and (4) cervicofacial trauma (usually self-limiting). Second, symmetric breath sounds are not a guarantee of adequate ventilation and oxygenation. End-tidal carbon dioxide, oxygen saturation, and arterial blood gas values must be monitored to ensure that breathing is intact.

E. **The abdomen** extends from the diaphragm to the pelvic floor, corresponding to the space **between the nipples and the inguinal creases** on the anterior aspect of the torso. When examining the abdomen during the secondary survey, the primary goal is to determine the presence of an intra-abdominal injury rather than to characterize its exact nature. Detecting those patients with occult injuries of the abdomen requiring operative intervention remains a diagnostic challenge. The mechanism of injury, however, often provides important clues.

1. **Penetrating trauma.** Stab wounds to the anterior abdomen can be divided into thirds: One third do not penetrate the peritoneal cavity, one third penetrate the peritoneal cavity but do not cause any significant intra-abdominal injury, and one third penetrate the peritoneal cavity and do cause significant intra-abdominal damage. As a result, the ability to exclude penetration of the peritoneal cavity in the patient with a stab wound to the abdomen has important therapeutic implications. In the stable patient without obvious signs of intra-abdominal injury (e.g., peritonitis), **local wound exploration** remains a viable screening option. It is a well-defined procedure that entails preparing and draping the area of the wound, infiltrating the wound with local anesthetic, and extending the wound as necessary to follow its track. If the track terminates without entering the anterior fascia, as occurs in approximately one half of the patients who undergo the procedure, the injury can be managed as a deep laceration. Otherwise, penetration of the peritoneum is assumed, and significant injury must be excluded by further diagnostic evaluation. Options include laparoscopy or celiotomy, CT, FAST, diagnostic peritoneal lavage (DPL), and admission with observation. Gunshot wounds within the surface markings of the abdomen have a high probability of causing a significant intra-abdominal injury and have therefore been taken to require immediate celiotomy, but this imperative has been challenged for those patients with stable hemodynamics and no peritoneal signs on physical examination. In a large retrospective study of patients with abdominal gunshot wounds, selective nonoperative management was reported to result in a significant decrease in the percentage of unnecessary laparotomies (*Ann Surg.* 2001;234:395). Current recommendations for nonoperative

management of penetrating trauma include the use of triple-contrast CT (accurately predicts the need for laparotomy) and serial examination. The majority of these patients can be discharged after 24 hours of observation (EAST guidelines 2007).

2. **Blunt trauma.** In the patient sustaining blunt abdominal trauma, physical signs of significant organ involvement are often lacking. As a result, a number of algorithms have been proposed to exclude the presence of serious intra-abdominal injury.

   a. **In the awake, unimpaired patient** without abdominal complaints, combining hospital admission and serial abdominal examinations is a cost-effective strategy for excluding serious abdominal injury as long as the patient is not scheduled to undergo an anesthetic that would interfere with observation. However, such patients are rare in the trauma setting.

   b. **Unstable patient with abdominal injury.** An unstable patient with injuries confined to the abdomen requires immediate celiotomy.

   c. **Unstable patient with multiple injuries.** If an unstable patient has multiple injuries and there is uncertainty about whether the abdomen is the source of shock, a FAST exam may be useful. If a patient is fairly stable and access to CT is readily available, head and abdomen/pelvis CT scans can be obtained. DPL may be useful in patients with head injuries requiring immediate operative therapy. In many large centers, a CT scan can be obtained as readily as the performance of a DPL.

   d. **Stable patient with multiple injuries.** If a stable patient has multiple injuries and the abdomen may harbor occult organ involvement that is not immediately life threatening, a CT evaluation is necessary. In addition to identifying the presence of intra-abdominal injury, CT scanning can provide information helpful for determining the probability that a celiotomy will be therapeutic. Laparoscopy has also been proposed as an adjunct in this situation.

F. **The pelvis** should be assessed for stability by palpating (not rocking) the iliac wings. Signs of fracture include scrotal hematoma, unequal leg length, and iliac wing hematomas. Careful inspection for lacerations (and possible open fracture) is undertaken.

G. **The back** should be inspected for wounds and hematomas, and the spine should be palpated for vertebral step-off or tenderness. If there are positive signs of spinal injury, CT scan should be obtained.

H. **The genitalia and perineum** should be inspected closely for blood, hematoma, and lacerations. In particular, signs of urethral injury should be sought (see Section III.A). A vaginal examination is needed to rule out open pelvic fractures and laceration. A rectal examination is mandatory to assess rectal tone and to look for the presence of gross blood in the rectum.

I. **The extremities** should be inspected and palpated to exclude the presence of soft tissue and orthopedic, vascular, or neurologic injury. Inspection should look for gross deformity of the limb, active bleeding, open wounds, expanding hematomas, and evidence of ischemia. Obvious dislocations or displaced fractures should be reduced as soon as possible. All wounds should be examined for continuity with joint spaces or bone fractures. The limb should be palpated for subcutaneous air, hematomas, and the presence and character of peripheral pulses. A thorough neurologic examination should be undertaken to determine the presence of peripheral nerve deficits. Radiographs of suspected fracture sites should be obtained, and ankle-brachial indices (ABIs) should be measured in the setting of possible vascular injury even if pulses are normal.

J. **General.** During the secondary survey (and throughout the initial evaluation of the injured patient), any rapid decompensation by the patient should initiate a return to the primary survey in an attempt to identify the cause. Finally, in any penetrating trauma, all entrance and exit wounds must be accounted for during the secondary survey to avoid missing injuries.

V. **DEFINITIVE HOSPITAL CARE.** With the completion of the primary and secondary surveys, definitive hospital care is undertaken. During this phase of care for the trauma patient, extensive diagnostic evaluations are completed and therapeutic interventions performed. In this section, important therapeutic principles are discussed according to the anatomic location of the injury.

A. **Head injuries**

1. **Lacerations.** Active bleeding from scalp wounds can result in significant blood loss. Initial therapy involves application of direct pressure and inspection of the wound to exclude bone involvement (i.e., depressed skull fracture). If significant bone injury has been excluded, the wound may be irrigated and debrided. A snug mass closure incorporating all the layers of the scalp will effectively control any hemorrhage and should be done as soon as possible (i.e., before CT evaluations).

2. **Intracranial lesions.** Traumatic intracranial lesions are diverse. They include extraparenchymal lesions, such as epidural hematomas, subdural hematomas, and subarachnoid hemorrhages, as well as intraparenchymal injuries, such as contusions and hematomas. CT is the diagnostic modality of choice. Acute therapy is focused on controlling ICP and maximizing cerebral perfusion pressure (CPP) to provide an adequate supply of glucose and oxygen to the injured tissue. CPP is defined as the difference between mean arterial pressure (MAP) and ICP (CPP = MAP − ICP). Maximization of CPP therefore involves manipulating both MAP and ICP, and this is achieved when the BP is adequate (MAP >70 to 80 mm Hg) and the ICP is normal (<10 to 15 mm Hg in adults). A CPP of more than 60 to 70 mm Hg is the goal.

   a. **MAP.** Maintaining an adequate MAP is very important in the patient with head trauma because hypotension is a major risk factor for poor outcome. Pharmacologic support may be used as necessary to maintain an adequate BP. Extreme hypertension should be avoided. Hypoxia is especially detrimental in traumatic head injuries, and all efforts to maintain adequate oxygenation should be made during trauma resuscitations.

   b. **ICP** is defined according to the modified Monro–Kellie hypothesis, which states that the intracranial contents are contained in a rigid sphere (skull). The three major constituents—brain, blood, and CSF—are distributed in a constant volume. An increase in the volume occupied by one constituent therefore must be accompanied by a decrease in the volume occupied by one of the remaining constituents or there will be a rise in pressure. In the trauma setting, early and rapid delineation of intracranial injuries by CT scan is important because it allows decisions regarding the need for ICP monitoring to be made early. Usually reserved for the ICU or operating room, ICP monitoring is usually accomplished via the placement of a **subarachnoid pressure monitor ("bolt").** An **intraventricular catheter** placed in the nondominant lateral ventricle can also be used. This placement has the advantage of providing a means of draining CSF when necessary.

3. For patients with severe traumatic brain injury (GCS less than or equal to 8) and no other contraindications (e.g., coagulopathy), prophylactic mild to moderate hypothermia (32 to 34 °C) has been shown to decrease mortality and increase the probability of good neurologic outcome. Hypothermia protocols should begin as early as possible (e.g., in the emergency department after CT scan) regardless of initial ICP or even before ICP is measured (*CJEM.* 2010;12(4):355–364). Patients with intracranial hemorrhage should be placed on seizure prophylaxis for 1 week. A neurosurgeon should be consulted early because emergent surgical intervention may be required.

B. Maxillofacial injuries

1. Lacerations. All lacerations of the face should be meticulously irrigated, debrided, and closed primarily with fine suture. Alignment of anatomic landmarks is essential. Given the highly vascular nature of the face, primary closure can be performed up to 24 hours after an injury (except a bite wound) as long as it is accompanied by adequate irrigation and debridement. Any deep laceration in the region of the parotid or lacrimal ducts should be examined for ductal involvement and consultation with the appropriate specialist undertaken.

2. Fractures. Patients with significant craniofacial soft-tissue injury or clinical signs of facial fractures require radiographic evaluation to determine bony integrity. Facial CT has supplanted most facial plain films other than the Panorex view (obtained for mandible fractures) and is often required in complex midface fractures to define fracture fragments in detail. Therapy is predicated on the type of fracture present.

a. Frontal sinus fractures. Nondisplaced anterior table fractures are treated with observation. Displaced anterior table fractures and posterior table fractures require operative intervention by a specialist.

b. Nasal fractures. Displaced fractures often need to be reduced operatively, with subsequent packing of the nasal cavity for stability. The presence of a septal hematoma requires immediate incision and drainage to prevent avascular necrosis and resultant saddle-nose deformity.

    c. **Maxillary fractures** are classified according to the LeFort system. These fractures often require complex open reduction and fixation by a surgical specialist.

    d. **Mandibular fractures.** Fractures of the mandible typically occur in areas of relative weakness, including the parasymphysial region, angle, and condyle. These injuries are often treated by maxillomandibular fixation, but such therapy requires a 4- to 6-week interval. Rigid fixation using plates is another option. Patients with open fractures should receive antibiotics covering mouth flora.

C. Neck injuries

1. **Penetrating neck wounds.** The diagnostic evaluation of penetrating neck trauma is evolving but has traditionally been determined by both the depth and location of the wound. Lacerations superficial to the platysma should be irrigated, debrided, and closed primarily. Lacerations longer than 7 cm should be evaluated and closed in the operating room to decrease the risk of infection. The traditional approach to wounds deep to the platysma is an evaluation based on the anatomic zone of the injury but is transitioning to a multislice CT angiography-based general approach.

    a. **Zone I injuries.** Thoracic inlet injuries commonly involve the great vessels. Routine four-vessel arteriography had been advocated by many surgeons because of the difficulty of clinical evaluation and operative exposure of this region. In two prospective studies (*Br J Surg.* 1993;80:1534; *World J Surg.* 1997;21:41), only 5% of zone I injuries required operation for vascular trauma. Furthermore, routine arteriography did not identify any clinically significant vascular injuries that did not already possess "hard" evidence of vascular trauma (severe active hemorrhage, shock unresponsive to volume expansion, absent ipsilateral upper extremity pulse, neurologic deficit) or "soft" evidence (bruit, widened mediastinum, hematoma, decreased upper-extremity pulse, shock responsive to volume expansion). In addition, patients who lacked clinical evidence of vascular trauma and were managed conservatively did not have any morbidity or mortality as a result of missed vascular injuries (*J Trauma.* 2000;48:208). Evaluation of the aerodigestive tract can also be approached selectively. Patients with clinical evidence of aerodigestive tract injury (hemoptysis, hoarseness, odynophagia, subcutaneous emphysema, or hematemesis) should undergo dual evaluation with bronchoscopy and meglumine diatrizoate (Gastrografin) or thin barium swallow. Esophagoscopy may be substituted for obtunded patients or patients otherwise unable to participate in a swallow study.

    b. **Zone II injuries.** Patients with evidence of obvious vascular or aerodigestive tract injury or patients with hemodynamic instability require immediate operative exploration. In stable patients without obvious injury, both selective operative management and mandatory operative exploration are equally justified and safe. CT angiography or duplex ultrasonography of the neck can be used in lieu of formal angiography in order to rule out arterial injury. Even without contrast administration, a CT of the soft tissues of the neck has been shown to rule out significant vascular injury if it demonstrates that the trajectory of penetration is well away from the vasculature. However, if the trajectory of penetration lies in close proximity to the vasculature, minor vascular injuries (e.g., intimal flaps) may be missed. Physical exam alone is inadequate to rule out injury to the aerodigestive tract. A CT of the soft tissues of the neck can be used to rule out significant aerodigestive tract injuries if the trajectory of penetration avoids the trachea and esophagus. However, if injury cannot be conclusively ruled out by CT, further workup must be undertaken. Esophageal injury may be evaluated by either contrast esophagram or esophagoscopy. The evaluation to exclude esophageal injury should be expeditious as a delay in esophageal repair greater than 24 hours significantly increases the risk of morbidity and mortality (EAST guidelines 2008). The trachea may be evaluated by bronchoscopy.

c. **Zone III injuries.** Upper neck injuries with clinical evidence of vascular involvement require prompt CT angiography owing to the difficulty of gaining exposure and control of vessels in this region. Embolization can be used for temporary or definitive management, except for the internal carotid artery. An injury without clinical evidence of vascular trauma may be managed selectively, with further evaluation by CT. Direct pharyngoscopy suffices to exclude aerodigestive trauma. In neck vascular injuries, endovascular stenting and/or embolization, especially in zones I and III, may be beneficial and should be considered if available.

d. **Operative therapy.** Regardless of the location of the cervical injury, common operative principles apply once surgical exploration is undertaken. Adequate exposure, including proximal and distal control of vascular structures, is essential. The most common approach is through an incision along the anterior border of the sternocleidomastoid muscle. A collar incision is reserved for repair of isolated aerodigestive injuries or for bilateral explorations (e.g., transcervical injuries). The track of the wound must be followed to its termination. Arterial injuries are repaired primarily if possible. Otherwise, prosthetic vascular grafts can be used. Veins can be ligated, except in the case of bilateral internal jugular injury. Tracheal and esophageal injuries should be repaired primarily using synthetic absorbable sutures. If these injuries occur in tandem, a well-vascularized flap of muscle or fascia should be interposed between the repairs to decrease the incidence of posttraumatic tracheoesophageal fistula. Unexpected laryngeal injuries should be evaluated with endoscopy. A drain may be placed if there is any suspicion of aerodigestive tract violation. This maneuver will allow for controlled cutaneous drainage of any leak, thereby preventing lethal mediastinitis. In the case of combined aerodigestive and vascular injuries, the aerodigestive repair should be drained to the contralateral neck to prevent breakdown of the vascular repair from gastrointestinal (GI) secretions should the aerodigestive repair leak.

2. **Blunt neck trauma.** Severe blunt neck trauma can result in significant laryngeal and vascular injuries. In the patient with a stable airway, CT is the best modality for evaluation of a suspected laryngeal injury because it can help to determine the need for operative intervention. Minor laryngeal injuries can be treated expectantly with airway protection, head-of-bed elevation, and possibly antibiotics. Major laryngeal injuries require operative exploration and repair. Blunt vascular trauma usually involves the internal or common carotid artery, but there may also be injury to the vertebral vessels without symptomatology. These injuries can be devastating because they often are not diagnosed until the onset of neurologic deficits. CT angiography is rapidly becoming the diagnostic test of choice over formal four-vessel arteriography, although nondiagnostic scans require formal angiography. Because the severity of the deficit and the time to diagnosis are strongly associated with outcome, a high index of suspicion is needed. An evaluation for vascular trauma should be performed in patients with any neurologic abnormality unexplained by a diagnosed injury, patients with epistaxis from an arterial source, and asymptomatic patients with injury patterns or mechanisms suggestive of a blunt carotid or vertebral artery injury (e.g., severe hyperextension or flexion with rotation of the neck; direct blow to the neck; significant anterior neck soft-tissue injury; cervical spine fracture; displaced midface fractures or mandibular fractures; basilar skull fracture involving the sphenoid, mastoid, petrous, or foramen lacerum; a GCS less than or equal to 8; or diffuse axonal injury diagnosed by CT). The current recommendation is for operative repair of surgically accessible lesions. Systemic anticoagulation (unless contraindicated) with heparin and/or antiplatelet therapy appears to improve neurologic outcome and is therefore recommended for surgically inaccessible lesions. Other anticoagulants are under evaluation for use in this setting (EAST guidelines 2007).

D. **Thoracic injuries.** Rapid diagnosis and treatment of thoracic injuries are often necessary to prevent devastating complications.

1. **Chest wall injuries.** Lacerations of the chest without pleural space involvement require simple irrigation, debridement, and closure. A chest wound communicating with the pleural space constitutes an open pneumothorax and should be treated accordingly (see Section II.B.4). Significant soft-tissue loss may occasionally be encountered and can be initially repaired with a biologic mesh. Complex myocutaneous flap or prosthetic closure, however, is often required for definitive treatment. Rib fractures are common, especially in blunt trauma. They are readily identified on chest X-ray. Any rib fracture can trigger a progression of pain, splinting, atelectasis, and hypoxemia. Preventing this cascade through the use of adequate analgesia and pulmonary toilet is essential. Parenteral narcotics are often required. In the case of multiple rib fractures, intercostal regional blockade using local anesthetics or epidural analgesia. Flail chest often results in significant respiratory compromise and must be treated aggressively (see Section II.B.3).

2. **Tracheobronchial injuries** often present with massive subcutaneous emphysema. Prompt diagnosis and initial stabilization are essential. The operative approach is dictated by the location of the injury. Upper tracheal injuries require a median sternotomy. Distal tracheal or right bronchial injuries are repaired via a right thoracotomy. Left bronchial injuries mandate a left thoracotomy. Penetrating injuries can be debrided and repaired primarily. Transections resulting from blunt injuries usually require debridement of the tracheobronchial segment with reanastomosis. Tracheal defects involving up to two rings can usually be repaired primarily through adequate mobilization. Complex bronchoplastic procedures or pulmonary resections are rarely required.

3. **Esophageal injuries** are most commonly encountered after penetrating trauma, and they can pose difficult diagnostic and therapeutic challenges. These injuries require prompt recognition because, as aforementioned, delay in diagnosis is often lethal. CT can be helpful for delineating the trajectory of the missile and possible esophageal injury. Esophagoscopy combined with meglumine diatrizoate (Gastrografin) swallow can detect virtually all injuries, but either modality is probably adequate for evaluating the thoracic esophagus (*J Trauma.* 2001;50:289). As in the case of tracheobronchial injuries, the operative approach is determined by the location of the injury. A right thoracotomy provides excellent exposure for most thoracic esophageal injuries, particularly those in the midesophagus. A left thoracotomy is recommended for distal esophageal injuries. Primary repair should be undertaken whenever possible and consists of closure using an absorbable synthetic suture. The repair can be buttressed with a vascularized flap (i.e., pleural or pericardial) or fundoplication (for distal injuries). Drain placement near (but not adjacent to) the repair is recommended. Treatment options in late-recognized esophageal injuries include esophageal repair and wide pleural drainage, diversion with injury exclusion, complex flap closure, and esophageal resection (reserved for the esophagus with underlying pathology). Morbidity and mortality are high in this situation.

4. **Pulmonary injuries.** All pulmonary injuries can potentially have an associated pneumothorax (simple or tension). Prompt diagnosis and treatment can be lifesaving (see Section II.B).

   a. **Pulmonary contusion** can be associated with both blunt and penetrating thoracic trauma. These lesions often have adequate perfusion but decreased ventilation. The consequent ventilation–perfusion mismatch results in severe hypoxemia. Diagnosis is often made by chest X-ray. Therapy consists of aggressive pulmonary toilet and respiratory support. Severe contusions often require intubation and mechanical ventilatory support. The management of such patients is extremely challenging because nonstandard modes of ventilation (e.g., pressure-controlled inverse-ratio or high-frequency oscillating ventilation) may be needed. Consultation with a critical care specialist is recommended.

   b. **Hemothorax** is typically diagnosed as opacification on chest X-ray, and it commonly arises from penetrating chest injuries. In the majority of cases, tube thoracostomy is sufficient therapy. A chest X-ray obtained after placement of the tube should be inspected for both tube placement and adequacy of drainage of the hemothorax. A persistent hemothorax with a properly placed thoracostomy tube should raise the possibility of persistent hemorrhage within the hemithorax. Operative intervention is often based on the amount of initial sanguinous drainage and ongoing hemorrhage from the tube. Guidelines vary according to institution and should be individualized to the clinical situation. In general, patients who drain *more than 1.5 L of blood at tube insertion or who have an ongoing blood loss greater than 200 mL/hour over 6 hours* should undergo operative thoracotomy for control of hemorrhage. Significant intrathoracic bleeding can result from pulmonary hilar or great-vessel injury (see Section V.D.5). Pulmonary parenchymal hemorrhage can often be controlled with pulmonary tractotomy and oversewing of bleeding intrapulmonary vasculature. Pulmonary resection (lobectomy or pneumonectomy) may be considered for intractable pulmonary hemorrhage (usually from a hilar injury). Morbidity and mortality after pneumonectomy in the trauma setting, however, are significant, and it should therefore be considered a last resort. Air embolism can develop in the setting of significant pulmonary parenchymal injury, especially in the patient on positive-pressure mechanical ventilation. It usually presents as sudden cardiovascular collapse, and therapy consists in placing the patient in steep Trendelenburg, aspirating air from the right ventricle, and providing cardiovascular support. Chest wall intrathoracic hemorrhage usually originates from an intercostal or internal mammary artery and is best treated by ligation. Evaluation for persistent hemothorax usually requires a CT scan and should be done before 5 days to ensure time for appropriate operative intervention.

5. Great-vessel injury

  a. Penetrating trauma. Thoracic great-vessel injury most commonly occurs secondary to penetrating trauma. These patients often present in profound shock with an associated hemothorax. Occasionally, they present with pericardial tamponade due to a proximal aortic or vena caval injury. Often, diagnostic investigations are not performed because immediate operative intervention is indicated (e.g., massive hemothorax and pericardial tamponade). In certain circumstances, however, diagnostic evaluation is possible and can be rather extensive. For example, the stable patient suffering from a transmediastinal gunshot injury requires evaluation of the thoracic great vessels, esophagus, trachea, and heart unless the trajectory of the missile clearly avoids these structures. CT angiography with three-dimensional reconstruction of the great vessels is the diagnostic modality of choice.

  b. Formal angiography is now generally limited to patients in whom an endovascular repair will be performed. The operative approach depends on the vessel involved. Median sternotomy is ideal for access to the proximal aorta, superior vena cava, right subclavian artery, and carotid artery. A left infraclavicular extension ("trap-door") to the median sternotomy provides exposure to the left sub-clavian artery, but a high left anterolateral thoracotomy is probably a better approach. Finally, rapid median sternotomy with either right or left infraclavicular extensions is most appropriate in the patient who has undergone resuscitative thoracotomy before arrival in the operating room. Whenever possible, primary repair should be performed for arterial and vena caval injuries. Prosthetic graft-ing may be necessary for complex reconstructions. Brachiocephalic and innominate venous injuries can be ligated. Endovascular approaches are increasingly used to repair these injuries.

c. **Blunt trauma** associated with rapid deceleration (e.g., motor vehi-cle crashes and falls) can result in thoracic great-vessel injury. The descending thoracic aorta just below the origin of the left subcla-vian artery is particularly prone to rupture from rapid deceleration because it is tethered by the ligamentum arteriosum. Often such a trauma results in complete transection of the aorta and immediate death from exsanguination. In some patients, however, only par-tial disruption of the aorta occurs, and there is tamponade of the hemorrhage. These patients can arrive at the trauma center alive. If their injury goes unrecognized, however, mortality is near uni-versal. All patients presenting with blunt trauma associated with rapid deceleration therefore must be screened with a chest X-ray. Those patients with positive findings on chest X-ray (widened mediastinum, obscured aortic knob, deviation of the left main-stem bronchus or nasogastric tube, and opacification of the aortop-ulmonary window) require further evaluation. A CT angiogram is then performed, and if it is interpreted as normal, the likelihood of a blunt aortic injury is near zero. Arteriographic evidence of an aor-tic injury mandates prompt operative intervention, depending on associated injuries. Transesophageal echocardiography is an alter-native diagnostic modality in patients who are unable to undergo helical CT or arteriography, but is not preferred because of its lim-ited views of the aortic arch. Endovascular repair is rapidly becom-ing the preferred operative intervention for blunt aortic injury and is associated with decreased postoperative mortality and ischemic spinal cord complications. However, there is minimal long-term outcomes data available on the durability of endovascular repair and associated late complications, such as endoleaks (*J Vasc Surg.* 2008;48(5):1345–1351). In addition, devices currently available may not be small enough for young trauma patients. A left anterolateral thoracotomy is the preferred open approach to this portion of the aorta. Often, a prosthetic interposition graft is inserted at the level of the injury, but primary repair can also be performed. Whether to use partial cardiopulmonary bypass as a circulatory adjunct or the "clamp-and-sew" technique remains controversial. Definitive studies demonstrating the superiority of one method or the other in terms of morbidity and mortality do not exist. However, sufficient pro-spective data do exist to recommend delaying operative repair in patients requiring other emergent interventions (e.g., laparotomy and craniotomy) for more immediately life-threatening injuries or in patients who are poor operative candidates due to age or comorbidities (*J Trauma.* 2000;48:1128). These patients require close pharmacologic control of their BP until surgical repair can be accomplished.

6. Cardiac injury

   a. **Penetrating trauma.** Cardiac injury is usually associated with penetrating anterior chest trauma between the midclavicular lines, but it can occur in the setting of penetrating trauma outside these anatomic landmarks. Pericardial tamponade should be suspected in the patient presenting in shock with distended neck veins and diminished heart sounds **(Beck triad).** Tension pneumothorax must be excluded, however, by auscultating the lung fields. In the hemodynamically stable patient with suspicion for an occult penetrating cardiac injury, echocardiography is the diagnostic modality of choice. Transesophageal examination is preferred. The presence of pericardial fluid warrants emergent operative exploration. Another diagnostic modality is immediate subxiphoid pericardial exploration, especially in the setting of multiple injuries requiring emergent interventions. This procedure is performed in the operating room under general anesthesia. The pericardium is exposed via a subxiphoid approach, and a 1-cm longitudinal incision is made along it. The presence of straw-colored fluid within the pericardium constitutes a negative examination. Blood within the pericardium mandates definitive exploration and cardiorrhaphy. In the hemodynamically unstable patient, resuscitative thoracotomy is often the means of diagnosis. The preferred operative approach to the repair of penetrating cardiac injuries is via median sternotomy. Atrial and ventricular cardiac wounds are repaired primarily using interrupted or running monofilament sutures. Skin staples may also be used (especially in the setting of resuscitative thoracotomy). A Foley may also be placed into the cardiac wound and the balloon inflated as a temporary measure until definitive management can be performed in the operating room. Care must be taken to avoid injury to coronary arteries during the repair. Wounds adjacent to major branches of the coronary circulation therefore require horizontal mattress sutures placed beneath the artery. Distal coronary artery branches may be ligated. Early consultation with a cardiothoracic surgeon is essential, especially in cases involving complex repairs or cardiopulmonary bypass.

   b. **Blunt trauma.** BCI should be suspected in all patients presenting with the appropriate mechanism of injury (e.g., motor vehicle crash with chest trauma) or in those manifesting an inappropriate cardiovascular response to the injury sustained. Presentations range from unexplained sinus tachycardia to cardiogenic shock with cardiovascular collapse. Cardiac enzymes have little to no *clinical* value in the diagnosis or treatment of BCI. ECG is the screening modality of choice. A normal ECG excludes significant BCI, whereas the presence of an ECG abnormality (i.e., arrhythmia, ST changes, ischemia, heart block, and unexplained sinus tachycardia) in the stable patient warrants further evaluation. In the unstable patient, a transthoracic echocardiogram should be performed to identify any dyskinetic/akinetic myocardium or valvular damage. If the transthoracic evaluation is suboptimal, a transesophageal study is mandatory (EAST guidelines 2010). Patients with frank myocardial or valvular rupture require emergent operative repair. Otherwise, supportive therapy with continuous monitoring and appropriate pharmacologic support (i.e., inotropes and vaso-pressors) in an ICU setting is warranted. Any arrhythmias are managed according to standard Advanced Cardiac Life Support protocols. Rarely, invasive mechanical cardiac support is neces-sary. Aneurysmal degeneration can be a long-term complication of BCI.

E. **Abdominal injuries.** The management of abdominal injuries must often be individualized to meet the needs of each patient, but certain guidelines apply. All patients undergoing laparotomy for trauma should be prepared and draped from the sternal notch to the knees anteriorly and from each posterior axillary line laterally to have access to the thorax if needed and to the saphenous vein for any potential vascular reconstruction.

1. **Diaphragmatic injuries** occur most commonly as a result of pen-etrating thoracic or abdominal trauma. Blunt trauma, however, can produce rupture secondary to rapid elevation of intra-abdominal pres-sure. Frequently, diagnosis is made during celiotomy, but injury can occasionally be recognized on radiographic studies (e.g., chest X-ray or CT). Therapy entails primary repair using permanent sutures in a horizontal mattress fashion. Immediate repair prevents the long-term complications associated with diaphragmatic hernias.

2. **Abdominal esophageal injuries** are managed much like thoracic esophageal wounds (see Section V.D.3). In addition to primary repair and drain placement, the fundus of the stomach can be used to but-tress the site via a 360-degree (Nissen) wrap. Exposure of this portion of the esophagus can be difficult. Often, the left lobe of the liver must be mobilized and the crus of the diaphragm partially divided. Finally, placement of a feeding tube should be considered to allow for enteral nutrition in the postoperative period.

3. **Gastric injuries.** Injuries to the stomach occur most often in the set-ting of penetrating trauma. Sanguinous drainage from a nasogastric (or orogastric) tube should raise the possibility of gastric injury. Diagnosis is usually made at laparotomy. Simple lacerations can be repaired in one layer using synthetic absorbable suture. Alternatively, a full-thickness closure can be reinforced with Lembert stitches. Massive devitalization may require formal resection with restoration of GI continuity via gas-troenterostomy. In such cases, vagotomy is helpful in reducing the risk of marginal ulcer.

4. **Hepatic injuries.** The use of CT in blunt trauma has increased the diagnosis of occult liver injuries, making the liver the most commonly injured abdominal solid organ.

   a. **Penetrating trauma.** The diagnosis of penetrating hepatic injury is usually made at exploratory laparotomy, although CT has been used to identify injuries. Hemorrhage in the setting of hepatic trauma can be massive, and familiarity with maneuvers to gain temporary and definitive control of such bleeding is essential.

      (1) **Initial hemostasis.** Rapid mobilization of the injured lobe with bimanual compression can often provide initial hemostasis. Perihepatic packing with laparotomy pads placed over the bleeding site and on the anterior and superior aspects of the liver to compress the wound is an extremely effective alternative. Temporary occlusion of the contents of the hepatoduodenal ligament (Pringle maneuver) with a vascular clamp decreases hepatic vascular inflow and is successful in controlling most intraparenchymal bleeding. It is often employed to allow further mobilization of the liver and exposure and repair of injuries. Occlusion times should not exceed 30 to 60 minutes because longer intervals of warm ischemia are poorly tolerated by the liver. Failure of the Pringle maneuver significantly to decrease bleeding suggests major hepatic venous involvement, including juxtahepatic and retrohepatic inferior vena cava injuries. Prompt recognition and temporary vascular control of such injuries via the placement of an atrial-caval shunt (Schrock shunt) can be lifesaving. Another option in this setting is total hepatic vascular isolation achieved by placing vascular clamps on the hepatoduodenal ligament (if not already done), the descending aorta at the level of the diaphragm, and the suprahepatic and suprarenal vena cava. Finally, bleeding from deeply penetrating injuries (e.g., transhepatic gunshot wounds) can sometimes be temporarily controlled through placement of an occluding intrahepatic balloon catheter.

      (2) **Definitive hemostasis** is attained via multiple techniques. Raw surface oozing can be controlled by electrocautery, argon beam coagulation, or parenchymal sutures [horizontal mattress stitches placed in a plane parallel to the injury using large absorbable (no. 2 chromic) sutures on a wide-sweep, blunt-tip needle]. Topical hemostatic agents are also useful (i.e., microcrystalline collagen, thrombin, and oxidized cellulose). Deeper wounds are usually managed by hepatotomy and with selective ligation of bleeding vessels. A finger-fracture technique is employed to separate overlying liver parenchyma within a wound until the injured vessel is identified, isolated, and controlled. Major venous injuries should be repaired primarily. Omental packing of open injuries can provide buttressing. Resectional debridement is limited to frankly devitalized tissue. Hepatic artery ligation is reserved for deep lobar arterial injuries where hepatotomy may result in significant blood loss.

Formal anatomic resection should be avoided because of its high associated morbidity and mortality. Finally, closed suction drains should be placed near the wound to help to identify and control biliary leaks.

(3) **Damage control** principles are frequently applied to complex hepatic injuries. Perihepatic packing with ICU admission and resuscitation, followed by return to the operating room in 24 to 48 hours, is common. Liberal use of this algorithm can decrease mortality.

b. **Blunt trauma.** The management of blunt hepatic trauma has undergone a dramatic change over the last decade, largely due to improvement in CT imaging. CT with IV contrast is the recommended diagnostic modality for evaluation of the stable patient suspected of having blunt hepatic trauma because it can reliably identify and characterize the degree of an injury. In the presence of hepatic trauma, therapy should be predicated on the hemodynamic status of the patient. The unstable patient requires operative exploration and control of hemorrhage as described (see Section V.E.4.a). The stable patient without an alternate indication for celiotomy should be admitted for close hemodynamic monitoring and serial hematocrit determinations. Operative intervention should be promptly undertaken for hemodynamic instability. Evidence of ongoing blood loss in the hemodynamically stable patient warrants angiographic evaluation and embolization of the bleeding source. Transfusions are administered as indicated. The frequency of follow-up CT evaluation of the lesion should be dictated by the clinical status of the patient. Resumption of normal activity should be based on evidence of healing of the injury. Stable patients therefore do not require strict bed rest. Complications of blunt hepatic trauma include biliary leak and abscess formation, both of which are readily amenable to endoscopic and percutaneous therapy. Delayed hemorrhage is rare, but pseudoaneurysm formation can occur with hemorrhage or hemobilia, requiring angiography and embolization. Nonoperative management is successful in the vast majority of blunt hepatic injuries and has even been reported in certain cases of penetrating hepatic wounds.

5. **Gallbladder injuries.** Injury to the gallbladder frequently coexists with hepatic, portal triad, and pancreaticoduodenal trauma. Treatment consists of cholecystectomy. The gallbladder also provides an effective means of assessing biliary tree integrity via cholangiography.

6. **Common bile duct injuries.** Penetrating trauma is most often responsible for common bile duct injuries. Like gallbladder injuries, they often occur in association with other right upper quadrant organ trauma. Most often, diagnosis is apparent at the time of laparotomy, but occult injuries can occur. Intraoperative cholangiography, therefore, is warranted when biliary involvement is suspected. Primary repair of the injured duct over a T tube is the preferred management, but Roux-en-Y choledochojejunostomy is sometimes required (i.e., when significant segmental loss

can be employed in an attempt to preserve immune function (requiring salvage of 40% of the splenic mass). Devitalized tissue should be debrided and the wound closed with absorbable horizontal mattress sutures (usually 2-0 chromic). Alternatively, the spleen can be wrapped in absorbable mesh. Partial resection is indicated for isolated superior or inferior pole injuries. In unstable patients or in patients in whom splenic salvage fails, splenectomy should be performed in an expeditious manner. Drainage of the splenic bed is not necessary unless pancreatic injury is suspected. All patients who undergo emergent splenectomy are at risk for overwhelming postsplenectomy sepsis infection. Although this complication is rare (maximum risk is 0.5% in prepubertal children), the mortality is up to 50%. Therefore, all patients undergoing emergent splenectomy require postoperative immunization against *Streptococcus pneumoniae, Haemophilus influenzae,* and *Neisseria meningitidis.* Some authors even recommend penicillin prophylaxis for children because they are at highest risk. Yearly viral influenza vaccines are also recommended for postsplenectomy patients.

b. **Blunt trauma.** Most blunt splenic injuries are initially treated with nonoperative observation. CT remains the diagnostic modality of choice. All hemodynamically stable patients without an alternate indication for laparotomy should undergo close observation with continuous monitoring of vital signs, initial bed rest, nasogastric decompression (unless contraindicated), and serial hematocrit determinations. Patients with CT evidence of a contrast "blush" or evidence of continuing blood loss who remain stable should undergo transfusion and selective angiographic embolization. Patients who are hemodynamically unstable or are failing nonoperative management (e.g., require continuing transfusion) should undergo operative exploration and therapy as described (see Section V.E.9.a). Most often, splenectomy is performed. CT reimaging should be performed as clinical status indicates, especially for high-grade injuries.

10. **Small-bowel injuries.** Given its large volume and anatomy (tethering at the duodenojejunal flexure), the small bowel is prone to both penetrating (e.g., gunshot) and blunt (e.g., lap belt) trauma. Diagnosis is made at laparotomy or via radiographic imaging (plain radiograph or CT). Treatment consists of primary repair or segmental resection with anastomosis. Mesenteric defects should be closed.

11. **Large-bowel injuries.** Colonic injuries typically occur secondary to penetrating trauma and are diagnosed at the time of laparotomy. A prospective multicenter study has demonstrated that the surgical management (primary repair vs. diversion) of penetrating colonic injuries did not affect the incidence of abdominal complications regardless of associated risk factors (*J Trauma.* 2001;50:765). The only independent risk factors for such complications were severe fecal contamination, large transfusion requirement (>4 units) in the first 24 hours, and single-agent antibiotic prophylaxis. *Primary repair, therefore, should be*

considered in all penetrating colonic injuries unless the patient experiences prolonged intraoperative hypotension.

12. **Rectal injuries.** Penetrating trauma is also responsible for most rectal injuries. They often occur in association with genitourinary or pelvic vascular trauma, and they can be diagnosed via proctoscopy, CT, or at laparotomy. Traditional management advocated rectal washout (debridement), diverting sigmoid colostomy creation, and presacral drain placement. However, a prospective, randomized trial showed that omission of presacral drains in the management of low-velocity penetrating rectal injuries did not increase infectious complications (*J Trauma.* 1998;45:656). Debridement (with primary repair of rectal wounds when possible) and diverting colostomy formation therefore seem sufficient management. The distal stump should be tagged with proline suture to facilitate identification at the time of reversal. Reversal can be undertaken after 6 weeks if barium enema reveals healing of the rectum and the patient is medically stable.

F. **Retroperitoneal vascular injuries.** Injuries to the major retroperitoneal vessels or their abdominal branches can be life threatening. These wounds usually present with frank intra-abdominal hemorrhage or retroperitoneal hematoma formation. Management is based on both mechanism of trauma and location of injury.

1. **Penetrating trauma.** The majority of retroperitoneal vascular injuries are the result of penetrating trauma. By definition, any hematoma formed by a penetrating mechanism is uncontained and requires prompt exploration.

   a. **Initial access and hemostasis.** At times, vascular injuries present with massive intra-abdominal bleeding, and familiarity with techniques to control such hemorrhage expeditiously and to obtain access to vessels efficiently can be lifesaving. Packing the site of injury with laparotomy pads is always a reliable temporizing option. Often, initial control requires occluding the supraceliac aorta at the level of the diaphragmatic hiatus using a vascular clamp, a T bar, or direct pressure. Division of the gastrohepatic ligament and mobilization of the stomach and esophagus can provide access to this section of the aorta. Occasionally, division of the diaphragmatic crus is necessary for more proximal control. Once the proximal aorta has been occluded, definitive identification and repair of vascular injuries require adequate exposure of the involved vessels. A left medial visceral rotation (Mattox maneuver) provides excellent access to the aorta, celiac axis, superior mesenteric artery (SMA), left renal artery, and iliac arteries. A right medial visceral rotation (Catell maneuver) readily exposes the vena cava (with a combined Kocher maneuver), right renal vessels, and iliac veins. The infrarenal aorta may also be approached via a transperitoneal incision at the base of the mesocolon.

   b. **Repair of vascular injuries.** Most aortic and iliac arterial injuries can be repaired directly by lateral arteriorrhaphy. On occasion, reconstruction with graft prosthesis or autologous venous graft is necessary for significant circumferential or segmental defects. If enteric contamination is extensive, extra-anatomic bypass with oversewing of the proximal stump is mandatory. Injuries to the celiac root or its branches (left gastric or splenic arteries) can often be ligated without adverse outcome, especially in young patients. Splenectomy must follow splenic artery ligation. Common hepatic artery injuries should be repaired when possible (via lateral arteriorrhaphy, resection and reanastomosis, or graft), but ligation can be tolerated at times. SMA defects must be repaired. Vena cava and iliac venous injuries are repaired by lateral venorrhaphy. Injuries to the superior mesenteric vein (SMV) and portal vein should undergo repair, but cases of successful outcome after ligation have been reported. Because of the risk of postoperative thrombosis leading to portal hypertension or superior mesenteric infarction, SMV and portal venous reconstructions must be closely followed, and anticoagulation is often administered. Finally, major renal arterial and venous injuries require primary repair, whereas partial nephrectomy is recommended for segmental vessel involvement. Endovascular treatment has an expanding role in the treatment of all vascular trauma and may be beneficial.

2. **Blunt trauma** can cause retroperitoneal vascular injury with resultant hematoma formation. Often, these hematomas are discovered at operative exploration, but they are sometimes seen on preoperative imaging. The character and location of the hematoma determine management.

   a. **Central abdominal hematomas (zone I).** All central abdominal hematomas caused by blunt trauma require operative exploration. Supramesocolic hematomas are usually due to injuries to the suprarenal aorta, celiac axis, proximal SMA, or proximal renal artery. They should be approached via a left medial visceral rotation. Inframesocolic hematomas are secondary to infrarenal aortic or inferior vena cava injuries and are best exposed by a transperitoneal incision at the base of the mesocolon. As with any vascular repair, proximal and distal control of the involved vessel should be obtained prior to exploration if possible.

   b. **Flank hematomas (zone II).** Flank hematomas are suggestive of renal artery, renal vein, or kidney parenchymal injury. Unless they are rapidly expanding, pulsatile, or ruptured, they should not be explored if they are discovered at the time of celiotomy. Radiographic evaluation of the ipsilateral kidney is necessary in this situation to assess its function, usually by means of CT imaging. Evidence of nonfunction should prompt arteriography of the renal artery because blunt abdominal trauma often causes intimal tears, with resulting thrombosis of the artery. If it is discovered within 6 hours of the injury, revascularization may be performed, although the success rate is only 20%. Otherwise, nonoperative management is preferred. Nephrectomy is sometimes indicated when laparotomy is performed for associated injuries in a stable patient. In this setting, removal of the nonfunctioning kidney will decrease long-term renal complications (e.g., urinoma, hypertension, and delayed bleeding). There is no proven benefit of obtaining proximal control of the renal vessels in terms of blood loss or renal salvage. Total or partial (to preserve renal mass) nephrectomy may be necessary for a shattered kidney.

    c. Pelvic hematomas. Central pelvic hematomas in the setting of blunt trauma are usually due to pelvic fractures. If they are discovered at celiotomy, they should not be explored unless iliac arterial injury is suspected (loss of ipsilateral groin pulse, rapidly expanding hematoma, or pulsatile hematoma) or rupture has occurred. Bleeding from pelvic fractures can be massive, and management should focus on nonoperative control. Unstable pelvic fractures in association with hypotension should undergo some form of external stabilization. In extreme circumstances, temporary control of hemorrhage can be achieved by wrapping a pelvic binder tightly around the pelvis. Formal external fixation should follow as soon as possible. It should also be considered in those patients with unstable pelvic fractures who require celiotomy or who are hemodynamically stable but have a need for continued resuscitation. Pelvic angiography with selective embolization is the preferred intervention for patients in whom major pelvic fractures are the suspected source of ongoing bleeding. It should also be considered in patients with major pelvic fractures when CT imaging reveals evidence of arterial extravasation in the pelvis or when bleeding in the pelvis cannot be controlled at laparotomy.

G. Genitourinary injuries. Injuries to the genitourinary tract are discussed in detail in Chapter 35. Three points, however, warrant discussion in the context of trauma. Urethral injuries complicate the placement of an indwelling catheter. Their diagnosis and management have been discussed (Section III.A). In blunt abdominal trauma, **gross hematuria *or* microscopic hematuria in the setting of hemodynamic instability** mandates urologic evaluation. The absence of hematuria, however, does not always exclude an injury to the urinary tract, especially in the setting of penetrating torso trauma. CT is the best imaging modality for demonstrating urologic injury in the trauma patient who does not require laparotomy for other reasons, and it provides information regarding kidney perfusion. Although once commonly used, excretory urography intravenous pyelogram (IVP) in the trauma patient is often unsatisfactory and is now rarely used. In patients with suspected bladder rupture, especially those with gross *hematuria or pelvic fluid on CT in the presence of pelvic fractures,* cystography should be performed. **CT cystography** has been demonstrated to be equivalent to conventional cystography in assessing bladder injury (EAST guidelines 2003).

H. Orthopedic injuries are discussed in detail in Chapter 34, but three important considerations bear mentioning.

    1. Blood loss. Fractures can produce large blood losses. A broken rib can be associated with a 125-mL blood loss, a forearm fracture with a 250-mL blood loss, a broken humerus with a 500-mL blood loss, a femur fracture with a 1,000-mL blood loss, and a complex pelvic fracture with a blood loss of 2,000 mL or more. Stabilization of fractures can minimize the amount of bleeding. Although the Medical Anti-Shock Trouser (MAST) (pneumatic antishock device) has been largely discredited as a device for raising BP, it may afford transient pneumatic stabilization to lower-extremity and pelvis fractures, thereby attenuating further blood loss while the patient is being prepared for more specific interventions (e.g., traction, fixation, or arteriography and embolization).

2. **Spinal fractures.** Fractures of the spine are multiple in 10% of cases. Complete radiographic evaluation of the spine is necessary, therefore, when a single fracture is discovered.

3. **Joint involvement.** Two joints overlie single-access arteries: the elbow and the knee. Fractures or dislocations of either of these joints increase the risk of ischemic complications of the involved distal limb. The integrity of the underlying artery therefore must be confirmed by duplex ultrasound or arteriography.

I. **Extremity injuries.** Extremity trauma can result in devastating injuries requiring the coordination of multiple specialists to perform complex reconstructions. The goal of management is limb preservation and restoration of function, and it should focus on ensuring vascular continuity, maintaining skeletal integrity, and providing adequate soft-tissue coverage.

1. **Penetrating trauma.** Penetrating-extremity trauma typically occurs in males younger than 40 years old. Multiple injuries can occur in association with such trauma, and a high index of suspicion is necessary for diagnosing and repairing them expeditiously.

2. **Vascular injuries.** A wounded extremity can tolerate approximately 6 hours of ischemia before the onset of irreversible loss of function. Quickly identifying and repairing vascular injuries, therefore, is essential in any extremity trauma. Immediate operative exploration is indicated for obvious (hard) signs of vascular involvement (pulse deficit, pulsatile bleeding, bruit, thrill, or expanding hematoma) in gunshot or stab wounds without associated skeletal injury. Arteriography should be employed for those patients with hard vascular signs in the setting of associated skeletal injury (fracture, dislocation) or shotgun trauma. Patients with possible (soft) signs of vascular injury (nerve deficit, nonexpanding hematoma, associated fracture, significant soft-tissue injury, history of bleeding or hypotension) require evaluation of vascular integrity. A useful algorithm is to check the ABI initially. If the ABI for the affected limb is greater than 0.9, no further radiographic evaluation is necessary. If it is less than 0.9, noninvasive Doppler ultrasonography, if technically feasible, should follow to exclude vascular injury. If ultrasonography is equivocal, arteriography is indicated; if it is positive, either operative exploration or arteriography can follow. Patients without hard or soft signs do not require arteriography to exclude vascular involvement. Occult vascular injuries can be managed nonoperatively, with subsequent repair as indicated, without an increase in morbidity. Arterial injuries should be repaired within 6 hours to maximize limb

salvage rates. The operative approach is similar to elective vascular procedures, and endovascular therapy may be feasible if available. Proximal and distal control of the involved vessel is essential. Primary repair using monofilament suture should be performed for limited arterial lacerations. For complex injuries (large segmental or circumferential defects), resection with reanastomosis, patch angioplasty, or interposition grafting is preferred. Whenever possible, autologous vein should be used instead of polytetrafluoroethylene (PTFE) for patching or grafting because of its higher patency rates. Ligation of single-artery forearm and calf injuries is possible in the presence of normal counterparts. Restoration of blood flow (via temporary shunt or formal repair) should precede any skeletal reconstruction in cases of combined injuries. Completion arteriography should be performed after any arterial repair. Venous injuries should undergo lateral venorrhaphy or resection with end-to-end reanastomosis if the patient is hemodynamically stable. Ligation with postoperative leg elevation and compression stocking placement (to reduce edema) is indicated in all other cases. Multiple compartment fasciotomies should be liberally used, especially after prolonged ischemia or in the presence of associated injuries.

3. **Skeletal injuries** are diagnosed with plain radiography. Restoration of skeletal integrity is attained by means of either internal or external fixation. Temporary vascular shunting should be performed before stabilization of an unstable fracture in the setting of combined injuries. External fixation is preferred in the presence of gross contamination or tissue loss (see Chapter 34 for further details).

4. **Soft-tissue injuries.** Definitive closure of large soft-tissue defects rarely occurs at the initial operation for extremity trauma. Complex wounds are often thoroughly irrigated and debrided, dressed, and reviewed daily in the operating room. Delayed closure is then undertaken and may require advanced soft-tissue flaps (pedicle or free). On rare occasions, a so-called mangled extremity may require primary amputation if there are severe soft-tissue defects, major bone injury, or unreconstructable peripheral nerve injury and loss of limb function.

5. **Blunt trauma.** Blunt extremity trauma can result in debilitating crush or near-avulsion injuries. Diagnosis and management are the same as in penetrating trauma, but limb salvage and preservation of function tend to be worse due to the extent of injury. These wounds often require the coordinated involvement of multiple specialists.

6. **Extremity compartment syndromes.** Compartment syndromes are common in distal extremity trauma. They typically occur in association with prolonged limb ischemia or external pressure, fractures, crush or vascular injuries (especially combined arterial and venous injuries), and burns. **Increased tissue pressure (>30 mm Hg)** within the inelastic fascial compartment leads to occlusion of capillary flow and ischemia. Signs and symptoms of compartment syndrome include **pain (especially on passive motion), pressure, paralysis, paresthesia, pulselessness, and pallor (the so-called six *P*s).** A high index of suspicion is necessary for early diagnosis because signs often occur

late in the process, especially the loss of pulses. Serial compartment pressure measurements should therefore be undertaken in any patient with risk factors. Fasciotomy of all involved compartments is necessary when pressures are 30 to 40 mm Hg (or lower if evidence of ischemia exists). Fasciotomy of all involved compartments should also be performed after repair of traumatic vascular injuries (particularly those presenting with ischemia), in extremities with combined vascular and orthopedic injuries, and in extremities at risk for massive edema or continued ischemia. In addition, fasciotomy should be performed if pressures cannot be obtained.

J. **Damage control surgery.** The concept of damage control is well accepted among trauma surgeons as a valuable adjunct in the surgical care of severely injured patients (*Surg Clin North Am.* 1997;77:753). The damage control philosophy centers on coordinating staged operative interventions with periods of aggressive resuscitation to salvage trauma patients sustaining major injuries. These patients are often at the limits of their physiologic reserve when they present to the operating room, and persistent operative effort results in exacerbation of their underlying **hypothermia, coagulopathy, and acidosis,** initiating a vicious cycle that culminates in death. In these situations, abrupt termination of the procedure after control of surgical hemorrhage and contamination, followed by ICU resuscitation and staged reconstruction, can be lifesaving. Although often discussed in the context of abdominal trauma, the practice of damage control can be applied to all organ systems. It is divided into three phases: initial exploration, secondary resuscitation, and definitive operation.

1. **Phase I (initial exploration).** The first phase in the damage control algorithm consists of performing an initial operative exploration to attain rapid control of active hemorrhage and contamination. The decision to revert to a damage control approach should occur early in the course of such an exploration. In the setting of abdominal trauma, the patient is prepared and draped as previously described (see Section V.E), and the abdomen is entered via a midline incision. Any clot or debris present on entering the abdomen is promptly removed. If exsanguinating hemorrhage is encountered, four-quadrant packing should be performed. The packing is then removed sequentially, and all surgical hemorrhage within a particular quadrant is controlled. Following control of bleeding, attention is directed at containment of any enteric spillage. Any violations of the GI tract should be treated with suture closure or segmental stapled resection. Anastomosis and stoma formation should be deferred until later definitive reconstruction, and any stapled ends of the bowel should be returned to the abdomen. External drains are placed to control any major pancreatic or biliary injuries. Laparotomy packs are then reinserted, especially in the presence of coagulopathic bleeding. Often, primary abdominal fascial closure is not possible secondary to edematous bowel or hemodynamic instability. Alternative methods of closing the abdomen include skin closure via towel clips or running suture, Bogota bag placement, prosthetic mesh insertion, abdominal wall zipper creation, or vacuum closure. Of

all these techniques, the vacuum closure is the most commonly used. It is fashioned by placing a nonadherent material (cassette drape) between the bowel and abdominal wall, with gauze and a suction device on top, which is then sealed with an adherent dressing. Closed suction drains covered with a sterile adhesive dressing eases wound care in the ICU. Throughout the initial operative exploration, communication among the surgeons, anesthesia team, and nursing staff is essential for optimal outcome.

2. **Phase II (secondary resuscitation).** The second phase in the damage control approach focuses on secondary resuscitation to correct hypothermia, coagulopathy, and acidosis. Following completion of the initial exploration, the critically ill patient is rapidly transferred to the ICU. Invasive monitoring and complete ventilatory support are often needed. Rewarming is initiated by elevating the room temperature, placing warming blankets, and heating ventilator circuits. All IV fluids, blood, and blood products are prewarmed. As body temperature normalizes, coagulopathy improves, but rapid infusion of clotting factors (FFP, cryoprecipitate, and platelets) is often still required. Development of "Massive Transfusion Protocols" has resulted in improved outcomes and decreased mortality following massive blood losses. Most protocols focus on delivering a minimum ratio of 2 units of FFP for every 3 units of PRBC and 1 unit of platelets for every 5 units of PRBC (*J Trauma*. 2008;65(3):527–534). Use of recombinant factor VIIa in this setting has been shown to decrease the need for blood transfusion. Circulating blood volume is restored with aggressive fluid and blood product resuscitation, improving end-organ perfusion and correcting acidosis. With these interventions, hemodynamic stability returns, urinary output increases, invasive monitoring parameters improve, and serum lactate levels and blood pH analysis improve. In the setting of abdominal trauma, a potentially lethal complication that can occur during this phase is abdominal compartment syndrome. It is a form of intra-abdominal vascular insufficiency secondary to increased intra-abdominal pressure. Presentation includes abdominal distention, low urinary output, ventilatory insufficiency in association with high peak inspiratory pressures, and low cardiac output secondary to decreased venous return (preload). Diagnosis is made via measurement of urinary bladder pressure (25 to 30 cm H_2O). When present, prompt operative reexploration is mandated to relieve the increased pressure. Vacuum or Bogota bag closure helps to prevent this complication. If surgical bleeding is found to be the cause of the intra-abdominal hypertension, it should be controlled and the abdomen closed. If severe edema of the intra-abdominal contents is the source of the compartment syndrome, the abdomen should be closed by using a vacuum closure to reduce intra-abdominal pressure. Following correction of the problem, phase II resuscitation is continued.

3. **Phase III (definitive operation).** The third phase of damage control consists of planned reexploration and definitive repair of injuries. This phase typically occurs 48 to 72 hours following the initial operation and after successful secondary resuscitation. In the setting of abdominal

trauma, all complex injuries are repaired, with precedence going to those involving the vasculature. Conservative principles should be applied. Risky GI anastomoses or complex GI reconstructions should be avoided. The abdomen should be closed primarily if possible. Otherwise, biologic mesh or simple skin closure and staged repair of the resulting ventral hernia should be performed. Even though the damage control approach allows for salvage of many severely injured patients, it is still associated with substantial morbidity and mortality. Outcome is often determined by providing excellent supportive care (ventilation, nutrition, appropriate antibiotics, and physical therapy with rehabilitation services).

VI. MISCELLANEOUS ASPECTS OF GENERAL TRAUMA CARE

A. **Resuscitative thoracotomy** is performed in a final attempt to salvage a certain subset of patients presenting in extremis to the emergency department. The goals are to control intrathoracic hemorrhage, relieve cardiac tamponade, cross-clamp the thoracic aorta, and restore cardiac output.

1. **Indications.** The indications for resuscitative thoracotomy have been refined over time. It should be used in the management of penetrating chest trauma associated with significant hemodynamic deterioration (systolic BP of <60 mm Hg) or cardiopulmonary arrest occurring within the emergency department or shortly before arrival. In addition, it can be used in certain cases of penetrating abdominal trauma fulfilling the same criteria.

2. **Technique.** Resuscitative thoracotomy is performed via an anterolateral left thoracotomy in the fifth or sixth intercostal space. The skin, subcutaneous tissues, and intercostal musculature are opened sharply. A Finochietto retractor is placed to spread the ribs and aid in exposure. First, the pericardium is identified and incised vertically anterior to the phrenic nerve. Any clot or debris is removed from around the heart. Specific cardiac injury is then sought, and repair is undertaken as previously described (see Section V.D.6.a). After cardiorrhaphy, air is evacuated from the heart by needle aspiration, and the adequacy of cardiac filling is assessed to determine intravascular volume status. In the absence of associated pulmonary vascular or great-vessel injury, vigorous volume resuscitation is undertaken. If peripheral vascular access is insufficient, direct infusion into the right atrial appendage can be performed. In severely hypovolemic patients, the descending thoracic aorta may be exposed and cross-clamped to maintain coronary and cerebral perfusion. The aorta should also be clamped if any intra-abdominal hemorrhage is suspected. During volume resuscitation, open cardiac massage is employed to provide adequate circulation. After restoration of adequate circulatory volume, the underlying cardiac rhythm is assessed, and internal cardioversion is used when appropriate. The patient should be transported to the operating room for definitive injury management and wound closure after a successful resuscitation.

3. **Complications of resuscitative thoracotomy** are many. They include lung injury while gaining access to the heart, transection of the phrenic nerve while performing pericardotomy, injury to the coronary vessels during cardiorrhaphy, and esophageal trauma while clamping the descending thoracic aorta. Therefore, care must be taken during each step of the procedure to avoid causing additional injuries. In addition, a member of the trauma team sustains a needle-stick or other sharp injury in roughly 10% of resuscitative thoracotomies performed in the emergency department. As this procedure is most commonly performed in a patient population at high risk of carrying blood-borne disease, the risk to the trauma team is not insubstantial and must be considered.

B. **Diagnostic peritoneal lavage (DPL).** Since the advent of FAST and rapid helical CT imaging, DPL is now rarely used in the evaluation of patients with suspected intra-abdominal injuries. It remains, however, a useful diagnostic modality in certain situations.

1. **Indications.** DPL is useful in excluding the presence of significant intra-abdominal organ injury in the presence of blunt trauma or a stab wound to the abdomen. It should be employed when less invasive techniques (e.g., serial abdominal examinations, CT, or FAST) are unavailable or if the patient develops unexplained hemodynamic instability while in the operating room for another injury. The only absolute contraindication to DPL is a planned celiotomy. Pelvic fracture, pregnancy, and prior abdominal surgery often mandate a change in indication and technique. All patients undergoing DPL require prior evacuation of the stomach via a gastric tube as well as drainage of the bladder by indwelling catheter.

2. **Technique.** Aspiration of 10 mL of gross blood or any enteric contents is considered a positive DPL. In addition, the microscopic presence of 100,000 red blood cells/μL or 500 white blood cells/μL in the setting of blunt abdominal trauma and the presence of 10,000 red blood cells/μL or 50 white blood cells/μL in the setting of penetrating abdominal trauma is considered a positive finding on DPL.

3. **Complications.** DPL can produce false-positive results due to bleeding near the incision or from pelvic fractures hemorrhaging into the anterior preperitoneal space of Retzius. False-negative findings can occur from improper placement of the catheter and infusion of fluid into the space of Retzius. Puncture of viscera is also possible, especially in the setting of pregnancy or adhesions from prior abdominal operations. An open technique is essential in such circumstances. Although it is associated with certain complications, DPL is a safe, simple, and reliable procedure for detecting intra-abdominal injuries with excellent sensitivity (95%).

C. **Deep venous thrombosis** with pulmonary embolus is the leading cause of preventable morbidity and mortality in trauma patients. Some form of prophylaxis is required in all such patients. When neural injuries (i.e., CNS or spinal cord injuries) are absent, subcutaneous low-molecular-weight heparin should be administered. When lower-extremity injuries do not preclude their use, sequential pneumatic compression devices are beneficial. Therapy combining compression devices with subcutaneous heparin is thought to be synergistic. Therapy should be initiated early because delay in the initiation of prophylaxis is associated with a threefold increase in venous thromboembolism (*J Trauma.* 2007;62:557). When the preceding techniques are contraindicated, serious consideration should be given to early placement of a vena cava filter. Although such a filter does not prevent thrombosis, it may decrease the risk of a deadly pulmonary embolus.

D. **Gastroduodenal ulceration.** Injured patients remain at risk for stress gastroduodenal ulceration and concomitant hemorrhage. Prophylaxis is therefore recommended. Enteral feeding remains the most effective method. Parenteral histamine-receptor blockers also prevent posttraumatic GI bleeding in ventilated or coagulopathic patients. Finally, newer IV proton-pump inhibitors may find a role in prophylaxis, but their expense may prove prohibitive.

E. **Rehabilitation in trauma care.** Rehabilitation is a crucial aspect of trauma care, and its planning should begin at the time of admission. Contractures and pressure sores can begin within hours of injury, and as a result, standardized prevention must be initiated promptly on the arrival of the patient on the ward. Regular turning of the patient, placement of air mattresses, and elevation of distal extremities (especially the heel) off the bed can decrease the formation of debilitating pressure sores. Specially designed orthotic splints, braces, and stockings prevent joint and scar contractures that can inhibit return of function. Finally, early physical and occupational therapy initiates the recovery process and prepares the patient for the often difficult rehabilitation to daily activity.

VII. **CONCLUSION.** A chapter of this nature is brief by necessity, but a comprehensive strategy for the care of patients who have been involved with traumatic events will clearly improve outcomes. This care should be coordinated by dedicated general surgeons with an interest or special training in trauma and should ideally use surgical specialty services staffed by individuals with trauma expertise. Although not all institutions will be able to have dedicated trauma-oriented surgeons on staff, the development of statewide trauma systems facilitates the care of patients by directing care of these patients toward those institutions with appropriate resources. For these statewide trauma systems to survive and for the hospitals within the systems to remain financially intact, there needs to be ongoing governmental financial support for the care of trauma victims. Trauma care now costs more than any other disease in the United States and requires comprehensive public health and governmental strategies for managing the complex issues surrounding it.

23 Transplantation

Elizabeth A. Fialkowski and Jeffrey A. Lowell

TRANSPLANT ORGAN PROCUREMENT

I. **DONOR SELECTION.** The greatest obstacle to transplantation is the lack of suitable donor organs. Live donation has provided an important solution, especially in kidney transplantation (live donors represented 49% of total donor pool in 2009) (https://www.unos.org). Less frequently, live donation is being utilized in liver, lung, and intestinal transplantation. The waiting list for organs grows each year; in the United States as of 2010 more than 108,000 people await a solid-organ transplant (http://www.unos.org).

II. **DECEASED DONORS** (formerly known as *brain-dead* or *cadaveric donors*). Strict criteria for establishing brain death include irreversible coma and the absence of brain stem reflexes (i.e., pupillary, corneal, vestibulo-ocular, and gag reflexes). Other useful diagnostic tests include blood flow scan, arteriography, and an apnea test. **Consent** is required, and the donor's medical history is reviewed. Ideally, the donor should have stable hemodynamics, although the use of vasopressors is common. A history of cardiopulmonary resuscitation (CPR) does not preclude donation, particularly with prompt resuscitation and recovery of vital signs. The criteria for donor organ use are not absolute; therefore, all patients meeting brain death criteria should be considered as potential donors. Contraindications for donation include the presence of a malignancy (with the exception of a primary brain tumor). **Exclusion criteria** for specific organs also exist. Potential kidney donors ideally have normal renal function before brain death. Underlying medical disease (e.g., diabetes and hypertension) or vascular disease time may preclude the use of a donor kidney. Kidney biopsy may assist in the decision to use donors with existing medical disease or advanced age. Selection of a donor liver takes into account donor size, ABO blood type, age, liver function studies, hospital course, hemodynamics, and prior medical and social history. "Expanded-criteria" liver and kidney donor (e.g., those not meeting traditional inclusion criteria) have been used with increasing success. **Hypothermic machine perfusion** assesses flow and resistance of donor kidneys. Its use in deceased donor kidneys, compared to static cold storage, may reduce the incidence of delayed graft function (defined as the need for hemodialysis in the first week posttransplant) and improve graft survival in the first year, based on data from a recent international randomized control trial (*N Engl J Med.* 2009;360(1):7).

III. **DONATION FOLLOWING CARDIAC DEATH (DCD)** refers to those potential organ donors who do not meet strict brain death criteria but who are considered to have nonrecoverable devastating neurologic insults. Life support is discontinued in the operating room, and organ procurement is initiated after a specified interval following cardiac asystole.

IV. **DECEASED-DONOR ORGAN RECOVERY.** The initial dissection identifies hepatic hilar structures, including the common bile duct, portal vein, hepatic artery, and any aberrant arterial blood supply, such as a left hepatic artery branch arising from the left gastric artery or a right hepatic artery from the superior mesenteric artery (SMA). After this dissection, the liver is flushed and cooled with University of Wisconsin (UW) preservation solution (a cold-storage solution containing a high concentration of potassium, lactobionate, hydroxyethyl starch, and other antioxidants) or HTK (histidine-tryptophan-ketoglutarate, a cold-storage solution containing amino acids, potassium, magnesium, calcium, and mannitol) via cannulae placed in the portal vein and the aorta proximal to the iliac artery bifurcation. A clamp is applied to the supraceliac aorta, and the abdominal viscera are flushed with either UW or HTK cold solution. The organs are packed with ice, while the solution infuses. The donor liver is removed with its diaphragmatic attachments, a cuff of aorta surrounding the celiac axis and the SMA, and a portion of the supra- and infrahepatic vena cava. The liver is packaged in UW or HTK solution and surrounded by iced saline during transportation. The remainder of the liver dissection is performed in the recipient's operating room under cold-storage conditions. The donor kidneys are removed *en bloc* and then separated. The ureters are dissected widely to minimize devascularization and are divided near the bladder. This technique minimizes risk of injury to the arteries and allows identification of multiple renal arteries. The pancreas may also be removed for transplantation, with the pancreas, duodenum, and spleen removed *en bloc*. The blood supply for the pancreas allograft comes from the donor splenic and superior mesenteric arteries, and outflow is via the portal vein. The small intestine mesentery below the pancreas is divided with a stapling device. With the advent of modern preservation solutions, donor livers can be preserved for up to 12 hours before revascularization (kidneys up to 24 hours), with a low incidence of allograft dysfunction. Ideally, cold ischemia time is minimized to less than 6 hours.

V. **HISTOCOMPATIBILITY**

A. **Cross-matching.** Antibodies to human leukocyte antigen (HLA) do not occur naturally but are produced upon exposure to foreign histocompatibility antigens that may occur after pregnancy, blood transfusions, or previous transplants. The traditional test used for detecting sensitization against donor histocompatibility antigens is termed a **cross-match** or **complement-dependent lymphocytotoxicity assay.** Several cross-match methods are available, each involving the addition of recipient serum, donor cells (T cells, B cells, or monocytes), and complement. If specific antidonor antibodies are present, antibody binding results in complement fixation and lysis of the donor lymphocytes. Flow cytometry can also be used, and permits the detection of noncytotoxic antibodies. Polymerase chain reaction (PCR) and enzyme-linked immunosorbent assay (ELISA) technology are being used increasingly for HLA typing, particularly for the major histocompatibility (MHC) class II HLA antigens. HLA matching is of practical clinical significance only in renal and pancreatic transplantation.

B. **Panel reactive antibodies (PRA).** The PRA assessment helps to predict the likelihood of a positive cross-match. It is determined by testing the potential recipient's serum against a panel of cells of various HLA specificities in a manner similar to the cross-match. The percentage of specificities in the panel with which the patient's sera react is the PRA. Most normal individuals do not have preformed anti-HLA antibodies and thus have a low PRA (0% to 5%). Patients who have been exposed to other HLAs or who have autoimmune diseases with antibodies recognizing HLAs may have a high PRA. These patients are more likely to have a positive cross-match.

IMMUNOSUPPRESSION

An increasing variety of immunosuppressive medications are available. The protocols outlined here are currently in use at Washington University and are intended only to serve as guidelines. Most protocols rely on the use of several drugs owing to the different mechanisms and synergies of these medications. In the first section below, a brief overview of the immunology involved in rejection will serve to introduce the roles of the various immunosuppressive medications.

I. IMMUNOLOGY OF REJECTION

A. **Immunologic response.** Organ procurement inevitably causes tissue injury and ischemia, leading to activation of interstitial immune cells (Dendritic cells, DCs) and release of reactive molecules called "Damage activated molecular pattern molecules (DAMPs)." Recipient endothelial, mesenchymal, and epithelial cells express surface and/or cytoplasmic receptors for these DAMPs. Presence of DAMPs induces cytokine and chemokine release, leading to an inflammatory response. The encounter between HLA on donor DCs and recipient T cells (via the T-cell receptor, TCR) is a key inciting event in cellular rejection, leading to activation and maturation of recipient T cells. These activated T cells secrete interleukin-2 (IL-2) and express IL-2 receptors, leading to division and proliferation.

B. **Immunosuppression. Corticosteroids** play the broadest role against rejection, targeting both the innate (e.g., DCs and DAMPs) and adaptive (e.g., T and B cells) responses, leading to inhibition of T cell proliferation. The initial encounter between donor DCs and recipient TCRs is blocked by the monoclonal antibody **OKT3.** Other antibodies target the signaling process that occurs with this encounter (e.g., **Alefacept**). Once the signaling events are underway, calcineurin inhibitors **(Cyclosporine, Tacrolimus)** block the early stages of T-cell activation. Autocrine stimulation of T-cells by IL-2 is blocked by monoclonal antibodies to the T-cell IL-2 receptor **(Daclizmab, Basiliximab).** Multiple signaling pathways are activated by IL-2 binding, including the MAP kinase, PI3 kinase, and JAK/STAT pathways, the last of which is blocked by a JAK3 inhibitor **CP-690 550,** currently in clinical trials. In addition to IL-2, the mammalian target of rapamycin (mTOR) molecule is a potent stimulus for T-cell division, and is targeted by **Sirolimus.** Later inhibitors of the cell cycle include **Azathioprine** (purine synthesis inhibitor) and **Mycophenolic** acid **(CellCept/ Myfortic** inhibits RNA synthesis).

II. IMMUNOSUPPRESSIVE MEDICATIONS

A. **Prednisone or methylprednisolone (Solu-Medrol).** Corticosteroids are part of most immunosuppressive regimens and are the first-line drug in the treatment of rejection. Steroids modify antigen processing and presentation, inhibit lymphocyte proliferation, and inhibit cytokine and prostaglandin production. After surgery, patients are placed on a steroid taper and maintained on a low dose of prednisone or eventually withdrawn from the drug altogether. Steroid avoidance and early steroid-withdrawal protocols have demonstrated good short-term results. Long-term results are unknown. Acute and chronic side effects of steroids include diabetes mellitus (DM) (10% of patients), infections, cataracts, hypertension, weight gain, and bone disease (osteoporosis, and joint deterioration with avascular necrosis).

B. **Tacrolimus (FK506, Prograf)** is a macrolide that has a mechanism of action similar to that of cyclosporine but is approximately 100 times more potent. Tacrolimus doses are adjusted to maintain 12-hour trough levels between 5 and 10 ng/mL [fluorescence polarization immunoassay (FPIA)]. The side effect profile is similar to that of cyclosporine but does not include hirsutism and gingival hyperplasia. Alopecia and posttransplant diabetes mellitus (PTDM) are more common with tacrolimus.

C. **Cyclosporine (Sandimmune, Neoral, Gengraf).** Cyclosporine is a small fungal cyclic compound, in a class of medications termed calcineurin inhibitors. These block T-cell activation, thus inhibiting T-lymphocyte proliferation, IL-2 production, IL-2 receptor expression, and interferon-γ release. Two-hour peaks and/or 12-hour troughs are monitored and adjusted based on time from transplant. Side effects include nephrotoxicity, hypertension, tremors, seizures, hyperkalemia, hyperuricemia, hypercholesterolemia, gingival hyperplasia, and hirsutism. Cyclosporine is metabolized by the liver. Common medications that may increase cyclosporine levels include diltiazem, verapamil, erythromycin, fluconazole, ketoconazole, tetracycline, metoclopramide, and cimetidine. Medications that decrease levels include intravenous trimethoprim/sulfamethoxazole, isoniazid, rifampin, phenytoin, phenobarbital, carbamazepine, and omeprazole.

D. **Sirolimus (Rapamune)** is an anti-T-cell agent that inhibits the mTOR molecule, blocking T-cell signal transduction. Side effects include thrombocytopenia, hyperlipidemia, oral ulcers, anemia, proteinuria, and impairment of wound healing.

E. **Mycophenolic acid (CellCept, Myfortic)** inhibits inosine monophosphate dehydrogenase (rate-limiting enzyme in guanine monophosphate synthesis,) inhibiting RNA synthesis. In so doing, this drug selectively inhibits T- and B-cell proliferation, cytotoxic T-cell generation, and antibody formation. It is used as an alternative to azathioprine, and is the antimetabolite of choice in most transplant programs. Major toxicities include gastrointestinal (GI) disturbances and increased cytomegalovirus (CMV) infection.

F. **Azathioprine (Imuran)** is an antimetabolite that is a thioguanine derivative of mercaptopurine. This purine analog alters the function or synthesis of DNA and RNA, inhibiting T- and B-lymphocyte proliferation. One of the major side effects is bone marrow suppression, manifested as leukopenia and thrombocytopenia. An important drug interaction occurs with allopurinol, which blocks the metabolism of azathioprine and increases the degree of bone marrow suppression.

G. **Polyclonal antithymocyte antibodies.** Polyclonal antibodies are immunologic products with antibodies to a wide variety of T-cell antigens, adhesion molecules, costimulatory molecules, cytokines, the T-cell receptor, and class I and II MHC molecules. These agents are used as induction therapy in the perioperative period or as rescue therapy following acute rejection. The most commonly used antithymocyte immunoglobulin in the United States is **Thymoglobulin.** Thymoglobulin, a rabbit-derived product, was shown to decrease the incidence of acute rejection in deceased donor renal transplants compared to use of an IL-2 receptor antagonist, basiliximab (*N Engl J Med.* 2006;355:1967). Common side effects include fever, leukopenia, and thrombocytopenia.

H. **Monoclonal antibodies. OKT3** is a murine monoclonal antibody that recognizes the T-cell receptor and blocks antigen recognition, hindering T-cell effector functions and potentiating T-cell lysis. OKT3 is usually administered to patients with steroid-resistant, severe rejection. Immediate side effects can include fever, chills, hypotension, respiratory distress, and pulmonary edema, all of which are secondary to the cytokine release syndrome. **Daclizumab (Zenapax)** and **basiliximab (Simulect)** are IL-2 receptor-specific monoclonal antibodies increasingly being used as induction therapy, which are begun immediately prior to transplantation and continued in the immediate postoperative period.

I. **Other immunomodulators** are under investigation and are at varying stages of development.

III. COMPLICATIONS OF IMMUNOSUPPRESSION

A. **Bacterial infections.** Pneumonia and urinary tract infections (UTIs) occur fairly commonly after transplantation. Infectious complications from opportunistic organisms are now uncommon because of appropriate prophylactic strategies.

B. **Viral infections.** The most common viral infections after transplantation include **CMV, Epstein–Barr virus (EBV), herpes simplex virus (HSV),** and **BK virus.** See Table 23-1 for a summary of prophylaxis and treatment for common viral and fungal infections.

   1. **CMV** infection can occur at any time but is most common 1 to 4 months posttransplant, in the absence of prophylaxis. CMV may infect the recipient's liver, lungs, or GI tract. Signs and symptoms include fever, chills, malaise, anorexia, nausea, vomiting, cough, abdominal pain, hypoxia, leukopenia, and elevation in liver transaminases. CMV peripheral blood PCR or serologic assays are the most common tools for diagnosis. CMV can be associated with significant morbidity and even mortality, but typically responds well to early diagnosis and treatment. There is also evidence that CMV contributes to allograft injury. Prophylaxis may be useful in any patient who receives a CMV-positive allograft because many of these patients develop a significant CMV

TABLE 23-1	Prophylaxis and Treatment of Infections in Immunosuppressed Patients

CMV
Prophylaxis
Ganciclovir, 1,000 mg PO TID (1 yr for D+/R−, 6 mo for D+R+, 3 mo for D−/R+,) *or*
Valganciclovir, 900 mg PO QD (reduce dose for renal insufficiency)
Treatment
Ganciclovir, 5 mg/kg IV q12 hr for 3 wk, *or*
Valganciclovir, 900 mg PO BID for minimum 3 wk and until virus cleared, in the absence of invasive disease
Consider unselected IgG, 500 mg/kg IV QID for 5 d for pneumonitis or colitis, *or*
Hyperimmune CMV IgG, 100 mg/kg IV QID for 5 doses for pneumonitis or colitis

Epstein–Barr virus
Prophylaxis
Acyclovir, 200 mg PO BID for life (D+/R−)
Treatment
Decrease immunosuppression
Ganciclovir, 5 mg/kg IV q12 hr for 3 wk
Chemotherapy for patients with lymphoproliferative disorders

Herpes simplex virus (HSV)
Prophylaxis
Acyclovir 200 mg PO BID for 3 mo [only D (donor)–/R (recipient)–; otherwise CMV treatment will also cover HSV]
For liver transplant patients, for 3–6 mo or until prednisone is <10 mg/d
Treatment
Decrease immunosuppression
Acyclovir, 5–10 mg IV q8 hr for 7–10 d

Candida
Prophylaxis of oral candidiasis
Nystatin, 5 mL (500,000 units) swish and swallow QID for 3 mo, *or*
Miconazole, troche suck and swallow QID for 3 mo, *or*
Fluconazole, 100 mg PO every week for 3 mo
Treatment of esophageal candidiasis
Fluconazole, 100 mg PO BID, *or*
Voriconazole, 200 mg PO BID

***Pneumocystis* pneumonia**
Prophylaxis
Trimethoprim/sulfamethoxazole, 1 single-strength tablet PO QD
Dapsone, 50 mg PO QD for sulfa allergy, *or*
Pentamidine, 300 mg per nebulizer every month for sulfa allergy and G6PD deficiency

BID, twice daily; CMV, cytomegalovirus; G6PD, glucose-6-phosphate dehydrogenase; IgG, immunoglobulin G; IV, intravenously; PO, orally; q12h, every 12 hr; QD, daily; QID, four times a day.

infection if left untreated. Treatment consists of decreasing immunosuppression and administering ganciclovir, which inhibits DNA synthesis. Valganciclovir, intravenous ganciclovir, and, to a lesser extent, oral ganciclovir dosing must be adjusted for renal dysfunction. The most common side effects of valganciclovir and ganciclovir are anemia, neutropenia, and thrombocytopenia.

2. **EBV** can infect B cells at any time after transplantation and may be associated with the development of a type of lymphoma, termed post-transplant lymphoproliferative disorder (PTLD), usually of monoclonal B-cell origin. Infiltration of the hematopoietic system, central nervous system (CNS), lungs, or other solid organs may occur. The patient usually presents with fever, chills, sweats, enlarged lymph nodes, and elevated uric acid. Diagnosis is made by physical examination; EBV serology; computed tomography (CT) scan of the head, chest, and abdomen (to evaluate lymph nodes or masses); and biopsy of potential sites or lesions. Treatment consists of reducing or withdrawing immunosuppression. Acyclovir prophylaxis for life may be considered in EBV donor$^+$/recipient$^-$ patients. In addition, **rituximab** (monoclonal antibody against the protein CD20 on the surface of B cells) with standard chemotherapy should be considered for resistant advanced disease or polyclonal tumors.

3. **HSV** causes characteristic ulcers on the oral mucosa, in the genital region, and in the esophagus. Renal transplant patients, if not on ganciclovir, are given prophylactic acyclovir. Active HSV infections are treated by decreasing the patient's immunosuppression and instituting acyclovir therapy. Side effects of acyclovir are rare but include nephrotoxicity, phlebitis, bone marrow suppression, and CNS toxicity.

4. **BK virus** is a member of the polyoma virus family. Approximately 90% of individuals are seropositive. BK viruria (detected by "decoy cell" shedding or PCR) develops in 30% of kidney transplant recipients and progresses to viremia in 15% of recipients within the first year. Persistent viremia leads to BK nephropathy, which occurs in up to 10% of kidney transplant recipients during the first year. There is no known effective treatment, though low-dose cidofovir (0.25 mg/kg intravenously every 2 weeks) has been tried. Until recently, early graft loss occurred in 50% of patients with BK nephropathy, and the other 50% were left with chronic allograft dysfunction. Recently, prospective monitoring and preemptive reduction in immunosuppression has been associated with prevention of nephropathy and better outcomes when nephropathy is diagnosed early.

C. **Fungal infections** can range from asymptomatic colonization to lethal invasive infections. Oral **candidiasis** can be prevented and treated with oral nystatin or fluconazole. Esophageal candidiasis can be treated with a short course of intravenous amphotericin B or fluconazole. Serious fungal infections are treated with intravenous amphotericin B, although use of less nephrotoxic agents such as caspofungin and anidulafungin is increasing.

D. **Other opportunistic infections.** *Pneumocystis jiroveci* (formerly *carinii*) *pneumonia* is a potentially lethal pneumonia that occurs in 5% to 10% of renal transplant patients receiving no prophylactic treatment. Patients typically present with fever, dyspnea, nonproductive cough, hypoxia, and pulmonary infiltrates. Diagnosis is made by bronchoalveolar lavage or lung biopsy. It can be prevented by low-dose trimethoprim/sulfamethoxazole, dapsone, or inhaled pentamidine. Treatment involves much higher doses of these agents, with a concomitant decrease in immunosuppression.

E. **Malignancies.** Cancers that occur at a higher frequency in transplant recipients include squamous cell carcinoma, basal cell carcinoma, Kaposi sarcoma, lymphomas, hepatobiliary carcinoma, and cervical carcinoma.

KIDNEY TRANSPLANTATION

I. **INDICATIONS.** **End-Stage Renal Disease (ESRD)** results when the functioning renal mass deteriorates to less than 10% to 20% of normal. **Indications** for renal transplantation include the presence of ESRD with an irreversible glomerular filtration rate (GFR) of less than 20 mL/minute. ESRD may affect multiple organ systems, resulting in altered fluid and electrolyte homeostasis, accumulation of metabolic waste products, anemia, hypertension, and metabolic bone disease. Excellent short- and long-term results can be achieved regardless of the cause of renal failure (Table 23-2). Renal failure secondary to DM is the most common disease process in the United States requiring renal transplantation, comprising as many as 25% of all cases.

TABLE 23-2	Causes of Renal Failure Requiring Transplantation
Type	Characteristics
Congenital	Aplasia, obstructive uropathy
Hereditary	Alport syndrome (hereditary nephritis), polycystic kidney disease, tuberous sclerosis
Neoplastic	Renal cell carcinoma, Wilms tumor
Progressive	Diabetic neuropathy, chronic pyelonephritis, Goodpasture syndrome (antiglomerular basement membrane disease), hypertension, chronic glomerulonephritis, lupus nephritis, nephrotic syndrome, obstructive uropathy, scleroderma, amyloidosis
Traumatic	Vascular occlusion, parenchymal destruction

II. CONTRAINDICATIONS

A. **Recent or metastatic malignancy.** In general, most transplantation centers require a significant (2- to 5-year) disease-free interval after the treatment of a malignant tumor. Exceptions include early-stage skin cancers and *in situ* cancers.

B. **Chronic infection.** The presence of any active, life-threatening infection precludes transplantation and the use of immunosuppressive therapy. If the infection can be treated either medically or surgically, the patient should be reconsidered for transplantation after therapy. Infection with the human immunodeficiency virus (HIV) is a contraindication to renal transplantation at most centers.

C. **Severe extrarenal disease** may preclude transplantation in certain circumstances, either because the patient is not an operative candidate or because the transplantation and associated immunosuppression may accelerate disease progression (i.e., chronic liver disease, chronic lung disease, and advanced uncorrectable heart disease). Severe peripheral vascular disease may also be a contraindication.

D. **Noncompliance.** Any patient with a history of repeated noncompliance with medical therapy should be considered high risk. A period of compliance before being placed on the waiting list is generally advised.

III. PREOPERATIVE WORKUP AND EVALUATION. Patients referred to a transplantation center are seen by a transplantation surgeon, nephrologist, social worker, and transplantation coordinator. Evaluation of a potential recipient is outlined in Table 23-3. The evaluation identifies coexisting problems or disease entities that must be addressed to improve the outcome of the transplantation. Family history is important because it may provide information about the patient's kidney disease and allows a discussion about potential living donors. When the evaluation is complete, the patient is presented at a multidisciplinary evaluation committee meeting, where a decision is made as to whether to accept the patient as a potential recipient. Allocation of a given organ to a specific patient is done using a computer-generated algorithm run by the United Network for Organ Sharing (UNOS) and is based on specific criteria, which are different for each organ [e.g., blood type, HLA matching, waiting time, prior sensitization (i.e., high PRA rating), and medical urgency for kidney allocation]. Once a patient is active on the waiting list, blood is sent monthly to the tissue-typing laboratory for cross-matching and to determine the PRA.

A. **Special considerations.** The lower urinary tract should be sterile, continent, and compliant before transplantation. In patients with a history of bladder dysfunction, DM, or recurrent UTIs, a voiding cystourethrogram may be obtained before transplantation. Transplant ureter implantation into the native bladder is preferred and usually can be achieved, even in small bladders and those that have been diverted previously.

B. **Pretransplantation native nephrectomy** has been avoided secondary to the anemia that develops following removal of endogenous erythropoietin production. It is only performed in patients with chronic renal parenchymal infection, infected renal calculi, heavy proteinuria, intractable hypertension,

TABLE 23-3	**Pretransplantation Evaluation of Renal Transplant Recipients**

Initial workup

History and physical examination

Laboratory analyses: complete blood count; partial thromboplastin time; prothrombin time; serum electrolytes; total protein, albumin, cholesterol, glucose, calcium, magnesium, and phosphorus; liver function tests; intact parathyroid hormone; prostate-specific antigen (men >40 yr); viral serologies (herpes simplex virus; Epstein–Barr virus; varicella-zoster virus; cytomegalovirus; hepatitis A, B, C; and human immunodeficiency virus); urinalysis and culture; purified protein derivative; panel reactive antibody; ABO and human leukocyte antigen typing; serum for frozen storage

Electrocardiography

Chest X-ray

Routine examinations

Dental

Stool guaiac (Hemoccult)

Pap smear

Mammogram (women >35 yr)

Ophthalmologic (diabetic patients)

Psychosocial
Secondary workup (based on preliminary finding)
Cardiac: exercise stress electrocardiography, dobutamine stress echocardiography, coronary angiography
Pulmonary: arterial blood gas, pulmonary function tests
Gastrointestinal tract: upper and lower endoscopy, right upper quadrant ultrasonography
Genitourinary: voiding cystourethrography, cystoscopy, retrograde ureterography

massive polycystic kidney disease with pain or bleeding, renal cystic disease that is suspicious for carcinoma, or infected reflux nephropathy. Erythropoietin renders pretransplantation nephrectomy more acceptable, especially in patients with intractable hypertension whose posttransplantation management can be difficult without nephrectomy.

C. **Living donors.** Living kidney donation has become an important part of renal transplant practice. Parent–child or sibling combinations are the most common, although biologically unrelated donors are increasingly being used. Advantages of living-donor transplantation include improved short- and long-term graft survival (1-year survival >95%), improved immediate allograft function, planned operative timing to allow for medical optimization (and, often, avoidance of dialysis), fewer rejection and infection episodes, and shorter hospital stays. Although expanded-criteria deceased donors (who tend to be older) have increased the donor pool, a living donor, if available, is preferred to a deceased donor. The primary goal in evaluating a potential living donor is to ensure the donor's well-being and safety. The donor must be in excellent health and must not have any illnesses, such as hypertension or diabetes, which may threaten his or her renal function in the future. The donor anatomy is evaluated with CT or magnetic resonance (MR) angiography. Donor kidneys are now commonly removed using laparoscopic or mininephrectomy techniques to minimize donor morbidity.

D. **Expanded-criteria donors (ECD).** These donors are usually over 60 years of age, or over 50 years of age with at least 2 of the following: hypertension, serum creatinine greater than 1.5 mg/dL, or death from a cerebrovascular accident. A recent retrospective study of more than 1,000 deceased donor renal transplants demonstrated higher rates of delayed graft function with ECD kidneys, but similar 5-year graft survival (*Transplantation*. 2010;89(1):88).

IV. **ABO INCOMPATIBLE TRANSPLANTATION.** Incompatibility due to blood type or HLA alloantibodies has historically been a barrier to living kidney donation. Since the 1980s, however, transplantation across this barrier has been accomplished – through ABO incompatible (ABOi) transplantation and paired exchange, which enables donors to be matched with compatible recipients.

A. **ABOi transplantation.** Isohemagglutinins are antibodies against blood group A and/or B. Production of these antibodies in a recipient leads to hyperacute rejection and graft loss. Using preoperative plasmapheresis to deplete these isohemagglutinins, as well as induction immunosuppression and pretransplant splenectomy, GP Alexander and colleagues in Belgium pioneered ABOi transplantation in the 1980s. Since this time, experience in Belgium, Japan, and the United States has included more than 1000 ABOi transplants, and long-term outcomes have been comparable to traditional living donor renal transplants (5-year graft survival approximately 79%). There remains a significant early risk of rejection in these transplants—approximately 10% to 30% develop acute antibody-mediated rejection (AAMR), and up to 10% have irreversible rejection within the first month. Isohemagglutinin levels inevitably return to baseline, and yet the majority of grafts survive this early high-risk period. These grafts undergo accommodation, whereby antidonor antibodies are present and yet there is no allograft injury. Animal models have suggested that upregulation of endothelial protective mechanisms may be involved in this process, but research is ongoing. Current protocols to optimize long-term ABOi graft survival include (1) preoperative plasmapheresis and immunoabsorption to reduce isohemagglutinin titers (goal ≤1:8), (2) induction with rituximab, and (3) immunosuppression regimens involving tacrolimus and mycophenolate (*Curr Opin Organ Transplant.* 2010;15:526).

B. **Paired exchange and chain donation.** A living kidney donor with an intended ABOi recipient, or living donor with no intended recipient (altruistic), can donate to an ABO compatible recipient through paired exchange and chain donation. This idea was started in New England in 2001, when UNOS created a network that matched appropriate living kidney donors to recipients, and led to the New England Program for Kidney Exchange in 2004. Complex computer algorithms now allow similar programs across the country, matching donor to recipient based on ABO blood type, HLA typing, and predicted cross-match results. The simplest example of a kidney-**paired exchange** occurs as a two-pair exchange – where Donor no. 1 is compatible with Recipient no. 2, and Donor no. 2 is compatible with Recipient no. 1. These matches can become more complicated with several pairs involved. **Chain donation** occurs when living donors are combined with deceased donor grafts to complete a set of compatible pairs. This includes nondirected or altruistic donors, who enable multiple recipients to undergo transplantation by their single gift. Extensive planning is required to coordinate these paired donations, and all centers must agree on the logistics in advance. Final cross-matches are conducted prior to surgery, and donor surgeons converse in the operating room prior to incision time. Ethical and legal concerns about donation across transplant centers led to an amendment of the National Organ Transplant Act (NOTA) in 2007, clarifying that interstate human organ paired donation is legal.

V. **PREOPERATIVE CONSIDERATIONS.** When a kidney becomes available, the recipient is admitted to the hospital, and the surgeon, nephrologist, and anesthesiologist perform a final preoperative evaluation. Routine laboratory studies and a final cross-match are performed. The need for preoperative dialysis depends on the patient's volume status and serum potassium. Generally, a patient with evidence of volume overload or serum potassium greater than 5.6 mEq/L (5.6 mmol/L) requires preoperative HD. Induction therapy with a polyclonal antibody preparation is given intraoperatively.

VI. **OPERATIVE CONSIDERATIONS**

A. **Technique.** In the operating room, a Foley catheter is inserted, and the patient's bladder is irrigated with antibiotic-containing solution. A central venous pressure (CVP) line is inserted, and a first-generation cephalosporin is administered. The transplant renal vein and artery typically are anastomosed to the external iliac vein and artery, respectively. A heparin bolus of 3,000 units is administered before clamping the iliac vessels. Before reperfusion of the kidney, mannitol (25 g) and furosemide (100 mg) are administered intravenously, and the patient's systolic blood pressure (BP) is maintained above 120 mm Hg, with a CVP of at least 10 mm Hg to ensure optimal perfusion of the transplanted kidney. The ureter can be anastomosed to either the recipient bladder or the ipsilateral ureter, although the bladder is preferred. Establishing an antireflux mechanism is essential for preventing posttransplantation reflux pyelonephritis. This is accomplished by performing an extravesical ureteroneocystostomy (Litch). A double-J ureteral stent is commonly used.

B. **Intraoperative fluid management.** The newly transplanted kidney is sensitive to volume contraction, and adequate perfusion is essential for immediate postoperative diuresis and acute tubular necrosis (ATN) prevention. Volume contraction should not occur, and volume status is constantly monitored by checking the patient's cardiac function, CVP, and BP. The initial posttransplantation urine outputs can vary dramatically based on many factors. It is imperative to know the patient's native urine volume to assess the contribution of the native and the transplanted kidney to posttransplantation urine output. Dopamine may be administered at a level of 2 to 5 μg/kg/minute intravenously to promote renal blood flow and support systemic BP.

VII. POSTOPERATIVE CONSIDERATIONS

A. **General care.** Many aspects of postoperative care are the same as those for any other general surgical patient. Early ambulation is encouraged, and the need for good pulmonary toilet and wound care is the same. The bladder catheter is left in place for 3 to 7 days.

B. **Intravenous fluid replacement.** In general, the patient should be kept euvolemic or mildly hypervolemic in the early posttransplantation period. Hourly urine output is replaced with one-half normal saline on a milliliter-for-milliliter basis because the sodium concentration of the urine from a newly transplanted kidney is 60 to 80 mEq/L (60 to 80 mmol/L). Insensible fluid losses during this period typically are 30 to 60 mL/hour and essentially are water losses that can be replaced by a solution of 5% dextrose in 0.45% normal saline at 30 mL/hour. Therefore, during the early posttransplantation period, the patient's intravenous fluid consists of one-half normal saline administered at a rate equal to the previous hour's urine output plus 30 mL of 5% dextrose in 0.45% normal saline. This formula requires the patient's volume status to be assessed repeatedly. If the posttransplantation urine output is low and the patient is thought to be hypovolemic (based on clinical and hemodynamic evaluation), isotonic saline boluses are given. Potassium chloride replacement usually is not required unless the urine output is very high, and even then it should be given with great care. Potassium chloride especially should be avoided in the oliguric posttransplantation patient.

C. **GI tract.** Gastritis and peptic ulcer disease occur secondary to steroid therapy in the transplantation patient. Therefore, patients are prophylactically treated with famotidine (20 mg/day orally or intravenously) or lansoprazole (30 mg/day orally).

D. **Renal allograft function or nonfunction.** If the patient's urine output is low in the early postoperative period (<50 mL/hour), volume status must be addressed first. If the patient is hypovolemic, 250 to 500 mL of isotonic saline should be given in bolus fashion and repeated once, if needed. If the patient is euvolemic, the bladder catheter should be irrigated to ensure patency. If clots are encountered, a larger catheter and/or continuous bladder irrigation may be needed. If the catheter is patent and the patient is euvolemic or hypervolemic, furosemide (100 to 200 mg intravenously for recipients of deceased-donor transplants, 20 to 40 mg intravenously for those with living-donor transplants) should be given. If diuresis follows these maneuvers, urine output is again replaced milliliter for milliliter with one-half normal saline. Early poor function of a transplanted kidney is most commonly due to reversible ATN. Immunologic and reperfusion injury also may play some role in the mechanism leading to ATN. Before the diagnosis of ATN can be made, however, noninvasive studies (renal Doppler ultrasonography or technetium-99 m renal scan) demonstrating vascular patency and good renal blood flow in the absence of hydronephrosis (renal ultrasonography) or urinary leak must be obtained. If flow is confirmed, dialysis can be continued until the transplanted kidney function recovers.

E. **Immunosuppression.** A variety of immunosuppressive protocols exist. The protocol in use at Washington University is discussed here and another is outlined in Table 23-5. Induction therapy with Thymoglobulin (1.5 mg/kg intravenously) is given intraoperatively and then daily during the first 2 posttransplantation days. Posttransplantation, patients receive tacrolimus (0.05 mg/kg orally twice a day to maintain trough 5 to 7 ng/mL), Myfortic (720 mg orally twice a day, reduced to 360 mg on day 5), and prednisone (1 mg/kg orally per day for days 1 to 3, 0.5 mg/kg orally per day for days 4 to 14, then 20 mg orally per day, decreasing by 2.5 to 5 mg each week to a goal of 5 mg/day by week 13). Methylprednisolone (7 mg/kg intravenously) is given in the operating room.

VIII. **REJECTION.** There are several different types of rejection. Some are preventable, whereas others can be treated with varying degrees of success.

A. **Hyperacute** rejection occurs when preformed anti-HLA antibodies bind the endothelium of the allograft and initiate a cascade of events culminating in vascular thrombosis and ischemic necrosis. Hyperacute rejection usually can be prevented by cross-matching donor lymphocytes with recipient serum. Hyperacute rejection usually occurs within minutes of cross-clamp release and is irreversible. Viability of the allograft can be assessed by intraoperative biopsy. The only therapeutic option is to remove the allograft immediately. This is extraordinarily uncommon in the modern era of cross-matching.

B. **Accelerated** rejection also appears to be antibody-mediated and usually occurs 12 to 72 hours after transplantation. The patient usually is anuric or oliguric and has fever and graft tenderness. Although treatment is not well defined, administration of an antilymphocyte preparation may salvage the graft. Accelerated rejection can lead to an immunologically mediated ATN from which good renal function recovery can occur.

C. **Acute** rejection is cell-mediated and involves T lymphocytes and soluble mediators called lymphokines. It happens in 10% to 40% of patients and typically occurs 1 to 6 weeks after transplantation. The development of a rising creatinine level should prompt the consideration of

TABLE 23-4	Treatment of Rejection
Corticosteroids	
Intravenous pulse, methylprednisolone	
7 mg/kg QD for 3 d	
Consider if rejection is early (<3 mo) or mild	
Oral pulse, prednisone	
3 mg/kg QD in 2–4 divided doses for 3–5 d	
After pulse, restart steroids at previous dose	
Use if patient is reliable and rejection is early or mild	
Tacrolimus	
Target 12-hr trough level 5–15 ng/mL	
Antilymphocyte preparations	
Thymoglobulin	
2–3 mg/kg IV for 3–4 d	
Myfortic	
720 mg PO BID	
Rapamycin	
4 mg PO QD, target level 8–20 ng/mL	
Plasmapheresis	
Consider for antibody-mediated rejection	

BID, twice a day; IV, intravenously; PO, orally, QD, daily.

rejection. Technetium-99m renal scan demonstrates decreased but persistent perfusion. Diagnosis is confirmed by percutaneous needle biopsy. There are two basic treatment modalities (Table 23-4): high-dose methylprednisolone and an antilymphocyte preparation. The latter generally is reserved for steroid-resistant rejection, although antilymphocyte therapy may be used as first-line therapy for moderate or severe rejections with arteritis. Maintenance immunosuppression may also be switched (i.e., from cyclosporine to tacrolimus). More than 90% of acute rejection episodes can be treated successfully.

D. **Chronic** rejection is a poorly understood phenomenon that can occur weeks to years after transplantation. Emerging evidence suggests that in addition to calcineurin toxicity, the humoral immune response is an important contributor. Detection of antidonor-specific antibodies, an elevated posttransplant PRA, or C4d staining on a biopsy is supportive of humoral or antibody-mediated rejection. Plasmapheresis, intravenous immunoglobulin, and rituximab have been used to treat antibody-mediated rejection.

IX. **SURGICAL COMPLICATIONS OF RENAL TRANSPLANTATION.** Wound seromas, hematomas, and infections are treated according to usual surgical principles. Other complications require special consideration.

A. **Lymphoceles** are lymph collections that occur because of lymphatic leaks in the retroperitoneum. They present one week to several weeks after transplantation and are best diagnosed by ultrasonography. Most are asymptomatic and are found incidentally. They may produce ureteral obstruction, deep venous thrombosis, leg swelling, or incontinence secondary to bladder compression. Most lymphoceles arise from leakage of lymph from the donor kidney. Treatment of symptomatic lymphoceles consists of percutaneous drainage. Open or laparoscopic internal drainage by marsupialization into the peritoneal cavity may be necessary because repeated percutaneous drainage is not advised and seldom leads to resolution of the lymphocele.

B. **Renal artery and vein thrombosis.** Arterial and venous thromboses most often occur in the first 1 to 3 days after transplantation. If the kidney had been functioning but a sudden cessation of urine output occurs, graft thrombosis should be suspected. A rapid rise in serum creatinine, graft swelling, and local pain ensues. If the allograft had not been functioning or if the native kidneys make a large amount of urine, there may be no signs of graft thrombosis. The transplanted kidney has no collateral circulation and has minimal tolerance for warm ischemia. The diagnosis is made by technetium-99m renal scan or Doppler ultrasonography. Unless the problem is diagnosed and repaired immediately, the graft will be lost and transplantation nephrectomy will be required.

C. **Urine leak.** The etiology is usually anastomotic leak or ureteral sloughing secondary to ureteral blood supply disruption. Urine leaks present with pain, rising creatinine, and possibly urine draining from the wound. Diagnosis is made by locating the fluid collection with ultrasonography and then aspirating the fluid and comparing its creatinine level to the serum creatinine level. A renal scan demonstrates radioisotope outside the urinary tract. Urine leaks are treated by placing a bladder catheter to reduce intravesical pressure and subsequent surgical exploration. If an anastomotic leak is found, the distal ureter can be resected and reimplanted. If the transplanted ureter is nonviable or if there is inadequate length, ureteroureterostomy over a double-J stent using the ipsilateral native ureter can be performed. The stent can be removed via cystoscopy several weeks later.

TABLE 23-5	Long-Term Maintenance Immunosuppression for Renal Transplantation
Myfortic	
720 mg PO BID	
Reduce to 360 mg PO BID when used with tacrolimus and for WBC <5,000/mm^3, diarrhea, first week posttransplant	
Prednisone	
1 mg/kg QD for days 1–3	
20 mg QD for days 4–14	
15 mg QD for week 3	
10 mg QD for week 4	
5 mg QD for week 5 and onward	
Tacrolimus	
5 mg PO BID, target level 5–7 ng/mL (FPIA)	
Levels >15 ng/mL are considered toxic	

BID, twice daily; FPIA fluorescence polarization immunoassay; PO, orally; WBC, white blood cell count; QD, daily.

X. **LONG-TERM FOLLOW-UP.** Immunosuppression (Table 23-5) and infection prophylaxis (Table 23-1) should be tapered with time. After the initial 3-month period, when acute rejection becomes less of a risk, tacrolimus and steroid doses are tapered. Chronic long-term immunosuppression can be maintained at lower levels than those required for induction. Rarely immunosuppression can be discontinued completely. Specific metabolic consequences of tacrolimus (including hypertension and nephrotoxicity) can be alleviated with dose reduction, but often specific therapy is needed. Dietary manipulation and gradual dose reduction are important to correct steroid-associated weight gain. Long-term complications of steroids can be minimized by using as low a dose of prednisone as possible. Antibiotic prophylaxis should be used before any surgical or dental procedure.

LIVER TRANSPLANTATION

I. **INDICATIONS FOR HEPATIC TRANSPLANTATION** include complications attributable to end-stage liver disease (ESLD). In the absence of other

TABLE 23-6	Most Common Indications for Orthotopic Liver Transplantation

Adults

Chronic hepatitis C	Primary biliary cirrhosis
Alcoholic liver disease	Primary sclerosing cholangitis
Chronic hepatitis B	Autoimmune hepatitis

Children

Extrahepatic biliary atresia	Primary hepatic tumors
α_1-Antitrypsin deficiency	Metabolic liver disease
Cystic fibrosis	

medical contraindications, virtually any disease resulting in ESLD is amenable to transplantation. The most common diseases for which orthotopic liver transplantation (OLT) is performed are listed in Table 23-6. Common indications for OLT in patients with ESLD include variceal hemorrhage, intractable ascites, encephalopathy, intractable pruritus, and poor synthetic function. Stage I or II hepatocellular carcinoma in a cirrhotic liver is an increasingly common indication for transplantation, within the Milan criteria (single lesions less than 5 cm or three lesions less than 3 cm). Improved long-term survival has been achieved in select patients undergoing transplantation for early-stage hilar cholangiocarcinoma, according to a protocol developed by the Mayo Clinic (*HPB* (Oxford) 2008;10(3):186). This protocol involves neoadjuvant chemotherapy, staging abdominal exploration, and subsequent transplantation.

II. **CONTRAINDICATIONS.** There are a few absolute contraindications to liver transplantation: multisystem organ failure, extrahepatic malignancy, poor cardiac or pulmonary reserve, refractory pulmonary artery hypertension, severe infection, and ongoing substance abuse. Renal insufficiency increases the morbidity of hepatic transplantation but is not a contraindication. Renal transplantation can be performed at the time of liver transplantation for patients with ESRD. Some degree of preoperative renal insufficiency is often reversible after successful liver transplantation.

III. **PULMONARY SYNDROMES IN LIVER DISEASE**

A. **Hepatopulmonary syndrome (HPS).** This syndrome has two defining characteristics: (1) intrapulmonary vasodilation in the presence of hepatic dysfunction or portal hypertension, with (2) a widened age-corrected alveolar-arterial oxygen gradient on room air (more than 15 to 20 mm Hg), with or without hypoxemia (PaO_2 less than 70 mm Hg). Increased pulmonary nitric oxide (NO) production in these patients leads to dilation of precapillary and postcapillary pulmonary vasculature, impairing oxygenation of venous blood. The mechanisms causing increased NO production, as well as the correlation between NO production and severity of liver disease, remain unclear. Ten to 20% of cirrhotic patients develop HPS, with increased mortality.

1. **Evaluation and diagnosis.** The most common complaint in patients with HPS is dyspnea, especially increased on standing (platypnea) because of increased blood shunting to lung bases where vasodilation predominates. Patients may have clubbing or cyanosis on physical exam. Chest X-ray may show interstitial changes in the lower lobes, and pulmonary function tests may demonstrate reduced diffusing capacity for carbon monoxide (DLCO)—but these findings are non-specific. The diagnosis is established by documenting both arterial gas exchange abnormalities and intrapulmonary vasodilation. While pulse oximetry may be used as a screening tool, arterial blood gas measurements are necessary because in less-advanced disease, a patient may not be hypoxemic (normal PaO_2 but widened PAO_2-PaO_2). The most sensitive test for pulmonary vasodilation is two-dimensional transthoracic echocardiography with agitated saline contrast. In normal patients, contrast bubbles are trapped in the pulmonary microvasculature and not seen in the left heart (except with intracardiac shunting). Visualization of bubbles in the left heart after three cycles is a positive test for HPS. In patients with intrinsic lung disease, radionuclide lung perfusion scanning using labeled macroaggregated albumin particles (99mTC MAA scan) is more specific for HPS. Labeled particles are usually trapped in the pulmonary microvasculature, but passage into the arterial circulation can be evaluated with imaging of the lung and brain. A shunt fraction of greater than 6% is diagnostic for HPS. High-resolution chest CT may also be used, but its role is still being defined.

2. **Treatment.** While medical therapies may transiently alleviate HPS (e.g., NO inhibition with methylene blue), transplantation is the only definitive therapy. Exception points are granted to patients with HPS to increase their Model for End-Stage Liver Disease MELD score (see section VI) and facilitate earlier OLT. A resting PaO_2 less than 60 to 65 mm Hg identifies patients who may meet exception criteria. Liver transplantation has been shown to improve and/or normalize gas exchange in more than 85% of patients, but changes in gas exchange are not immediate. Mortality after OLT is increased in patients with HPS. Severe preoperative hypoxemia (PaO_2 less than 50 mm Hg) and/or an MAA shunt fraction of at least 20% are predictive of postoperative mortality. This increased mortality is partially attributable to HPS-related postoperative complications including pulmonary hypertension, cerebral embolic hemorrhages, and prolonged ventilator requirement. Median survival of patients with HPS without OLT is approximately 5 months, versus 35 months with transplantation.

B. **Portopulmonary hypertension (POPH).** This syndrome is defined in the presence of portal hypertension, with a mean pulmonary artery pressure (PAP) of more than 25 mm Hg and a pulmonary capillary wedge pressure (PCWP) of less than 15 mm Hg. Additional criteria include an elevated transpulmonary gradient (mean PAP minus PCWP more than 10 mm Hg) and/or elevated pulmonary vascular resistance (more than 240 dyne sec/cm-5). The prevalence of POPH among cirrhotics being evaluated for transplantation is approximately 6%, and the presence of POPH does not correlate with severity of liver disease. The pathophysiology remains unclear, but is thought to be related to a hyperdynamic state in the setting of portal hypertension, with vascular shear forces and endothelial injury leading to the release of vasoactive substances and hypertension. Patients may have POPH with or without HPS. Symptoms relate to the degree of pulmonary hypertension, with dyspnea on exertion, fatigue, and peripheral edema. Transthoracic Doppler echocardiography is the best screening tool, demonstrating an elevated pulmonary artery systolic (PAS) pressure and right ventricular (RV) hypertrophy or dysfunction. An estimated PAS pressure of more than 40 mm Hg should prompt cardiac catheterization to differentiate intrinsic cardiopulmonary disease from POPH. Survival correlates with degree of RV dysfunction, and progression leads to cor pulmonale. Vasodilators (primarily intravenous prostacyclin) have been shown to improve PAP, but no agents have demonstrated prolonged survival. Outcomes of liver transplantation in patients with mild POPH (PAP less than 35 mm Hg) compare to patients without POPH, with similar postoperative risk. Moderate-to-severe POPH (PAP more than 50 mm Hg) is a contraindication to transplantation, with a perioperative mortality rate of approximately 40% and irreversible pulmonary hypertension.

IV. **HEPATORENAL SYNDROME.** Hepatorenal syndrome (HRS) is characterized by renal vasoconstriction in the setting of portal hypertension. The mechanisms leading to HRS are complex, and begin with splanchnic arterial vasodilation in response to increased portal vascular resistance. Despite increased cardiac output, flow is redirected to the splanchnic circulation with peripheral artery underfilling. In an effort to maintain peripheral BP, the renin-angiotensin-aldosterone system (RAAS) and sympathetic nervous system are activated, leading to vasoconstriction and sodium retention. Water retention follows, leading to accumulation of extracellular fluid as ascites and/or edema. Renal solute-free water excretion becomes impaired, primarily due to increased secretion of the antidiuretic hormone arginine vasopressin (AVP), leading to dilutional hyponatremia (serum sodium less than 130 mEq/L). Local renal vasodilators (e.g., prostaglandins) work to counteract renal vasoconstriction. With disease progression, however, local vasodilators lose the ability to maintain renal perfusion and renal failure ensues.

The incidence of HRS among cirrhotic patients with ascites is approximately 10%. These patients are classified according to severity into two types of HRS. Type one is defined by a doubling of the initial serum creatinine more than 2.5 mg/dL, or a 50% reduction in the initial creatinine clearance to less than 20 mL/min in less than 2 weeks. Type one HRS is acute and progresses rapidly. The median survival for these patients is 1 month, with 100% mortality at 12 weeks. Type two HRS is defined by a serum creatinine more than 1.5 mg/dL, without rapid progression to type one. Type two HRS patients typically have diuretic-refractory ascites. Survival is longer than in patients with type one HRS, but shorter than in patients without renal failure.

A. **Evaluation and diagnosis.** Sodium retention is the earliest functional abnormality in the spectrum of renal dysfunction in cirrhosis. Patients may present with ascites, dilutional hyponatremia, and/or low urinary sodium excretion (urine sodium less than 10 mEq/L). Renal dysfunction may progress to HRS without any identifiable precipitating factor, or may be related to an episode of spontaneous bacterial peritonitis (SBP), acute alcoholic hepatitis, or an operation. As many as one-third of patients with SBP develop type one HRS despite appropriate antibiotic treatment. Large volume paracentesis (more than 5 L) without albumin administration may also precipitate type one HRS. The diagnosis of HRS is based on a reduced GFR without other cause for renal failure. Major criteria for the diagnosis of HRS have been established by the International Ascites Club, including (1) low GFR (serum creatinine more than 1.5 mg/dL or 24-hour creatinine clearance less than 40 mL/min), (2) absence of shock, nephrotoxic drugs, fluid losses, or ongoing infection, (3) no sustained improvement in renal function following plasma expansion and diuretic withdrawal, and (4) proteinuria more than 500 mg/day and no ultrasonographic evidence of renal parenchymal disease or obstructive uropathy.

B. **Treatment.** Every patient with dilutional hyponatremia should be evaluated for OLT, as treating the underlying liver disease is the only definitive therapy. Fluid restriction to less than 1 L per day may slow the progression of dilutional hyponatremia. Antagonists to the V2 receptor of AVP are being investigated, and may improve solute-free water excretion. Once patients develop HRS, medical therapy aims to constrict the splanchnic circulation while expanding volume to improve renal perfusion. Use of the vasopressin analog terlipressin with albumin expansion has been associated with improved GFR and reduction in serum creatinine below 1.5 in patients with type one HRS. Transjugular intrahepatic portosystemic shunt (TIPS) and dialysis have been used as temporizing measures, but further studies are needed to define their role in HRS. Liver transplantation is the best treatment for patients with HRS. Priority is given to these patients, but unfortunately a significant number of patients with type one HRS die waiting for transplantation. The long-term outcomes for patients who receive a liver compare similarly to patients without HRS, with 85% survival at 1 year and 73% at 3 years.

V. **PREOPERATIVE EVALUATION.** Referrals to transplantation centers are made on an elective or urgent basis. The evaluation determines the need and urgency for OLT as well as its technical feasibility.

A. **Elective transplantation.** Under elective conditions, the potential candidate is presented to a multidisciplinary committee for evaluation. The patient's evaluation is based on history, physical examination, laboratory evaluation, results of endoscopic procedures, cardiac and pulmonary evaluation, and radiologic examination (Table 23-7). Active infection should be treated promptly, and transplantation should be postponed until the

TABLE 23-7	Pretransplantation Evaluation of Liver Transplant Recipients

Initial workup

History

Etiology of liver disease

Duration of liver disease

Complications of liver disease

Previous surgical procedures

Additional medical problems

Access to transplant center

Social support

Physical examination

Stigmata of chronic liver disease

Jaundice

Fluid retention

Nutritional status

Abdominal mass

Asterixis or encephalopathy

Growth and development (pediatric patients)

Laboratory analysis

ABO blood type; complete blood count; prothrombin time; partial thromboplastin time; serum electrolytes; urinary electrolytes; total protein, albumin, calcium, magnesium, and phosphorus; total and direct bilirubin; aspartate aminotransferase; alanine aminotransferase; alkaline phosphatase; γ-glutamyl transpeptidase; cholesterol serum ammonia; viral serologies (human immunodeficiency virus; hepatitis A, B, and C; cytomegalovirus; Epstein–Barr virus; and herpes simplex virus); urinalysis and culture; cell count; and culture of ascitic fluid and purified protein derivative

TABLE 23-7	Pretransplantation Evaluation of Liver Transplant Recipients *(Continued)*

Electrocardiogram

Chest X-ray

Arterial blood gas

Dobutamine stress echocardiography

Pulmonary function tests

Computed tomography or magnetic resonance imaging scan of the abdomen with liver volume

Esophagogastroduodenoscopy

Doppler ultrasonography

Psychosocial evaluation

Optional examinations

Computed tomography scan of chest and bone scan for patient with malignancy

Visceral angiogram

Cardiac catheterization

Endoscopic retrograde cholangiogram or percutaneous transhepatic cholangiography with brush biopsy for patients with sclerosing cholangitis (10% coincidence of cholangiocarcinoma in these patients)

Colonoscopy for patients with inflammatory bowel disease, sclerosing cholangitis, Hemoccult-positive stools, family history of colon cancer, previous history of colonic polyps

infection resolves. Patients with a recent history of alcohol or other substance abuse should be evaluated by a specialist prior to transplantation.

B. **Urgent transplantation.** Acceptable results with OLT can be achieved in select patients with fulminant liver failure. The pretransplantation evaluation is performed in a manner similar to that for the elective patient; however, timing, neurologic status, and hemodynamic stability may limit the number of tests obtained. A careful neurologic examination must be done in this setting, and the grade of coma should be determined. Patients in grade IV (unresponsive) coma have been shown in some studies to benefit from continuous perioperative monitoring of intracranial pressure (ICP) because untreated severe elevations in ICP can result in permanent brain injury and death. An attempt is made to keep cerebral perfusion pressure (mean arterial BP minus ICP) above 60 mm Hg. Low mean arterial BP is treated with vasopressors after volume resuscitation. Elevation in ICP is treated with hyperventilation, mannitol, and elevation of the head of the bed more than 45 degrees. ICP monitor placement may be complicated by severe coagulopathy and thrombocytopenia, which is common in these patients. Patients with acute hepatic failure may develop acute renal failure (ARF) as well, which can require hemofiltration or hemodialysis. Sepsis also is seen in acute hepatic failure and requires broad-spectrum antibiotics and antifungals. Pulmonary insufficiency is also common, and may require intubation, high-concentration oxygen, and positive end-expiratory pressure.

VI. ORGAN ALLOCATION. Livers are allocated based on the **MELD** scoring system. The MELD score is derived from the values for bilirubin, serum creatinine, and the international normalized ratio (INR) and ranges from 6 to 40 (http://www.unos.org). Livers are allocated to appropriate patients with the highest MELD scores. Special exception points may be granted, such as in cases of hepatocellular carcinoma, HPS or HRS. Children receive a Pediatric End-Stage Liver Disease (PELD) score.

VII. DONOR SELECTION. Selection of an appropriate donor liver takes into account donor size, ABO blood type, age, presence of infection, history of malignancy, liver function studies, hospital course, hemodynamic stability, and prior alcohol or drug use. Absolute contraindications to the use of a donor liver include the presence of extrahepatic malignancy and HIV. The use of expanded donor criteria allows transplantation of organs from older patients, patients with steatotic livers, and patients with hepatitis B or C.

VIII. HEPATIC TRANSPLANTATION PROCEDURE

   A. **Whole-organ liver transplantation.** Conceptually, OLT comprises three distinct sequential phases. The **first phase** involves the dissection and removal of the recipient's diseased liver. The **second phase,** known as the **anhepatic phase,** refers to the period starting with devascularization of the recipient's liver and ending with revascularization of the newly implanted liver. During the anhepatic phase, venovenous bypass (VVB) may be used. VVB shunts blood from the portal vein and infrahepatic inferior vena cava (IVC) to the axillary, subclavian, or jugular veins. Alternatively, many transplant surgeons will create a temporary portocaval shunt, which has the advantages of VVB with much less risk and cost. Maintenance of venous return from the kidneys and lower extremities results in a smoother hemodynamic course, allows time for a more deliberate approach to hemostasis, reduces visceral edema and splanchnic venous pooling, and lowers the incidence of postoperative renal dysfunction. The liver allograft is implanted by anastomosing first the suprahepatic vena cava and then the infrahepatic IVC. The portal vein anastomosis is performed, and blood flow to the liver is reestablished. Finally, the hepatic arterial anastomosis is performed. If the recipient hepatic artery is not suitable for anastomosis, a donor iliac arterial graft can be used as a conduit from the infra- or suprarenal aorta. The **third phase** includes biliary reconstruction and abdominal closure. Biliary continuity is established via a duct-to-duct anastomosis or a choledochojejunostomy. A duct-to-duct anastomosis is preferable, but may not be possible when there is a donor–recipient bile duct size discrepancy or a diseased recipient bile duct (e.g., with primary sclerosing cholangitis, biliary atresia, or secondary biliary cirrhosis). In a modification of the foregoing technique, the recipient's retrohepatic IVC is preserved, and the donor suprahepatic IVC is anastomosed to the confluence of the recipient's right, middle, and left hepatic veins. The donor infrahepatic IVC is then oversewn. The temporary end-to-side portacaval shunt is also created at the beginning of the hepatectomy.

B. **Reduced and split-liver transplantation** was developed to support the needs of pediatric patients awaiting appropriately sized transplants. Benefits include better size matching and using a single liver to provide grafts for multiple recipients. These benefits have translated to the adult population as well. The liver has a remarkable capacity for regeneration. It can be divided based on the anatomic segments of Couinaud into a left lateral section (segments 2 and 3), a left hemiliver graft (segments 2 to 4), or a right hemiliver graft (segments 5 to 8). The left lateral section is most commonly used in children. Comparison of the size of the donor and the recipient is used to determine the appropriate-sized graft. Yersiz and colleagues demonstrated that children receiving a left lateral section have similar survival outcomes and morbidity to pediatric recipients of similar live donor or whole-organ grafts (*Ann Surg.* 2003;238:496).

C. **Living-donor liver transplantation** has been developed as a result of the success of reduced liver transplantation. The left lateral section or left hepatic lobe is usually used as the donor graft for adult-to-child transplantation. Advantages similar to those observed with living related kidney donors have been observed, such as reduced ischemic time and the inherent benefits of an elective operation. Adult-to-adult living-donor liver transplantation necessitates the use of the larger right hemiliver. An amount of liver approximately equal to 0.1% of patient weight (e.g., 700 g for a 70-kg recipient) is required.

IX. POSTOPERATIVE CARE

A. **Hemodynamic.** Intravascular volume resuscitation usually is required in the immediate postoperative period secondary to third-space losses, increased body temperature, and vasodilatation. Adequate perfusion is assessed by left and right heart filling pressures, cardiac output, urine output, and the absence of metabolic acidosis. Hypertension is common and should be aggressively treated.

B. **Pulmonary.** Ventilatory support is required postoperatively until the patient is awake and alert, is able to follow commands and protect the airway, and is able to maintain adequate oxygenation and ventilation.

C. **Hepatic allograft function.** Monitoring of hepatic allograft function begins intraoperatively after revascularization. Signs of satisfactory graft function include hemodynamic stability and normalization of acid–base status, body temperature, coagulation studies, maintenance of glucose metabolism, and bile production. Reassessment of allograft function continues postoperatively, initially occurring every 12 hours. Satisfactory function is indicated by an improving coagulation profile, decreasing transaminase levels, normal blood glucose, hemodynamic stability, adequate urine output, bile production, and clearance of anesthesia. Early elevations of bilirubin and transaminase levels may be indicators of preservation injury. The peak levels of serum glutamic-oxaloacetic transaminase and serum glutamate-pyruvate transaminase usually are less than 2,000 units/L, and should decrease rapidly over the first 24 to 48 hours postoperatively. After the patient leaves the intensive care unit, liver function tests are obtained daily. If hepatic dysfunction becomes evident at any time, prompt evaluation must be undertaken and treatment must be initiated. It is important to correctly diagnose the cause of liver dysfunction because each cause has a unique treatment.

1. **Primary nonfunction and initial poor function.** The use of modern organ preservation solutions for organ preservation has decreased the incidence of primary nonfunction. For poorly understood reasons, however, 1% to 3% of transplanted livers fail immediately after the surgery. Primary nonfunction is characterized by hemodynamic instability, poor quantity and quality of bile, renal dysfunction, failure to regain consciousness, increasing coagulopathy, persistent hypothermia, and lactic acidosis in the face of patent vascular anastomosis (as demonstrated by Doppler ultrasonography). Without retransplantation, death ensues.

2. **Rejection.** Acute rejection is relatively common after liver transplantation, with 60% of recipients experiencing at least one cell-mediated or acute rejection episode. However, rejection is an extremely uncommon cause of graft loss. The most common causes of early graft loss include primary nonfunction and hepatic artery thrombosis.

3. **Technical complications.** A variety of technical problems can lead to liver allograft dysfunction, including hepatic artery stenosis or thrombosis, portal vein stenosis or thrombosis, biliary tract obstruction, bile duct leak, and hepatic vein or vena caval thrombosis. **Hepatic artery thrombosis** in the early posttransplantation period may lead to fever, hemodynamic instability, and rapid deterioration, with a marked elevation of the transaminases. An associated bile leak may be noted soon after liver transplantation due to the loss of the bile ducts' main vascular supply. Acute thrombosis may be treated by attempted thrombectomy. If this is unsuccessful, retransplantation is needed. Thrombosis long after liver transplantation may produce intra- and extrahepatic bile duct strictures and may be an indication for elective

retransplantation. Occasionally, hepatic artery thrombosis is completely asymptomatic.

   a. Portal vein stenosis or thrombosis is rare. When it occurs, the patient's condition may deteriorate rapidly, with profound hepatic dysfunction, massive ascites, renal failure, and hemodynamic instability. Although surgical thrombectomy may be successful, urgent retransplantation is often necessary. Late thrombosis may allow normal liver function but usually results in variceal bleeding and ascites.

   b. Bile duct obstruction is diagnosed by cholangiography. A single short bile duct stricture may be treated by either percutaneous or retrograde balloon dilation. A long stricture, ampullary dysfunction, or failed dilation necessitates revision of the biliary anastomosis. Fever and abdominal pain in the early posttransplantation period should raise the possibility of biliary anastomotic disruption, which requires urgent surgical revision.

 4. Recurrent infection and neoplasm. CMV can cause hepatic allograft dysfunction and usually occurs within 8 weeks of transplantation. Diagnosis is made by liver biopsy, with CMV inclusion bodies on light microscopy, or by peripheral blood PCR. Treatment consists of decreasing immunosuppression and administering ganciclovir (see Table 23-1).

   a. Viral hepatitis and malignancy (e.g., hepatoma, cholangiocarcinoma, and neuroendocrine tumors) can recur in the hepatic allograft but are uncommon in the early posttransplantation period. The clinical presentation includes elevated liver function tests, and diagnosis is made by liver biopsy. Imaging studies (e.g., CT scan and liver ultrasonography) are important in posttransplant surveillance for neoplasms. Patients transplanted for HCC should have regular surveillance with CT imaging and tumor markers.

   b. Hepatitis C virus (HCV) will recur in essentially all patients, but in most this is a mild hepatitis that does not lead to significant clinical sequelae. Occasionally, HCV recurrence is severe, and may lead to early recurrence of cirrhosis and liver failure. In general, retransplantation for early HCV recurrence is not performed. Various protocols for antiviral therapy for posttransplant HCV recurrence are under development.

   c. Hepatitis B virus (HBV) also recurs posttransplantation. Protocols are under investigation using different combinations of hepatitis B immune globulin (IG), hepatitis B vaccines, lamivudine, retroviral agents, and monoclonal antibodies. Strategies to prevent hepatitis B recurrence include the use of lamivudine before transplant to arrest viral replication, and posttransplant high-dose hepatitis B IG and lamivudine.

D. Electrolytes and glucose. The use of diuretics may result in hypokalemia, whereas cyclosporine or tacrolimus toxicity may cause hyperkalemia. Magnesium levels are maintained above 2 mg/dL (0.82 mmol/L) because the seizure threshold is lowered by the combination of hypomagnesemia and cyclosporine or tacrolimus. Calcium should be measured as free ionized calcium and kept above 4.4 mg/dL (1.1 mmol/L). Phosphorus levels should be maintained above 2.5 mg/dL (0.81 mmol/L) to avoid respiratory muscle weakness and altered oxygen hemoglobin dissociation. Glucose homeostasis is necessary because steroid administration may result in hyperglycemia, which is best managed with intravenous insulin because it is short acting and easily absorbed. Cyclosporine and tacrolimus are diabetogenic immunosuppressants and may alter glucose homeostasis. Hypoglycemia is a complication of liver failure, and in the presence of liver dysfunction, glucose administration may be necessary.

E. **GI tract.** H_2 blockade, proton-pump inhibition, and/or antacids are used to prevent stress ulcers. Endoscopy is performed liberally for any GI bleeding. Nystatin and GI tract decontamination solution containing gentamicin and polymyxin B are used in the perioperative period to prevent esophageal candidiasis and translocation of bacterial pathogens.

F. **Nutrition.** Patients who are severely malnourished should be placed on nutritional supplementation as soon fluid and electrolyte status has stabilized and graft function is deemed adequate. Patients with sufficient preoperative nutrition can be maintained on routine intravenous fluids until GI tract function returns (usually 3 to 5 days). Enteral nutrition is used as soon as the postoperative ileus resolves. Total parenteral nutrition (TPN) is indicated when the GI tract is nonfunctional.

G. **Infection surveillance.** The most common causes of bacterial infection after liver transplantation include line sepsis, UTIs, infected ascites, cholangitis, pneumonia, biliary anastomotic leak, and intra-abdominal abscess. Prophylactic antibiotics covering biliary pathogens are administered for the first 48 hours after liver transplantation. If a fever develops in the liver transplant recipient, a thorough examination should be performed. A chest X-ray and cultures of blood, urine, indwelling lines, and bile are necessary. A cholangiogram and Doppler ultrasonography of the liver can be performed to rule out perihepatic fluid collection and to evaluate hepatic vasculature.

H. **Posttransplantation immunosuppression.** The immunosuppressive agents used to prevent rejection include corticosteroids and tacrolimus. Myfortic may be added to reduce tacrolimus doses, which may be particularly useful in patients with renal disease or autoimmune liver disease.

X. **REJECTION.** Many liver transplant recipients experience at least one acute rejection episode, and it commonly occurs between days 4 and 21 postoperatively. Rejection is characterized by fever, increased ascites, decreased bile quality and quantity, and elevation of total white blood cell and eosinophil count, bilirubin, and transaminase levels. Rejection is diagnosed by percutaneous liver biopsy. In the early posttransplantation period, technical causes of hepatic dysfunction are ruled out by Doppler ultrasonography to ensure vascular patency, and cholangiography to rule out a bile duct obstruction or leak. Typical biopsy findings consistent with acute rejection include the triad of portal lymphocytes, endothelitis (subendothelial deposits of mononuclear cells), and bile duct infiltration and damage. The first-line treatment for acute rejection is a bolus of corticosteroids (methylprednisolone, 1 g intravenously). If the rejection responds appropriately, the patient undergoes steroid recycling.

PANCREAS AND ISLET TRANSPLANTATION

I. **INDICATIONS.** DM affects 7.8% of Americans and is the seventh-leading cause of death (as of 2007, www.diabetes.org). It is the leading cause of renal failure and blindness in adults. Other long-term complications caused by diabetes include myocardial infarction, stroke, amputation, and neuropathy. Invasive methods for maintaining euglycemia and preventing the long-term complications of DM include the use of autoregulating insulin pumps, pancreatic islet cell transplants, and whole-organ pancreatic transplantation.

Pancreas transplantation is commonly performed in the setting of kidney transplantation (either simultaneously or afterward) for diabetes complicated by ESRD. Pancreas-only transplants are also performed. Approximately 1,800 pancreas and islet transplants are performed per year in the United States.

II. **CONTRAINDICATIONS** to pancreas transplantation are the same as those for kidney transplantation, including disabilities secondary to DM (e.g., peripheral gangrene), intractable cardiac decompensation, and incapacitating peripheral neuropathy. Continued tobacco use also is considered a relatively strong contraindication.

III. **PREOPERATIVE WORKUP AND EVALUATION.** Workup of the potential pancreas transplantation patient is similar to that of the kidney recipient and identifies coexisting diseases, as outlined in Table 23-3. To allow identification of beneficial effects of pancreas transplantation on the complications of DM, a careful preoperative evaluation of the patient's neurologic and ophthalmologic status should be performed. Contraindications to pancreas donation include the presence of diabetes, pancreatitis, pancreatic trauma, or significant intra-abdominal contamination.

IV. **DECEASED-DONOR PANCREAS TRANSPLANTATION OPERATION**

A. Forms of pancreatic transplantation

1. **Simultaneous kidney–pancreas transplantation** may be considered in insulin-dependent diabetic patients who are dialysis dependent or imminent and have a creatinine clearance of less than 30 mL/minute. Some of the advantages of combined transplantation include the ability to monitor pancreas rejection by monitoring renal rejection, and exposure to only one set of donor antigens.

2. **Isolated pancreas transplantation.** The most widely accepted technique of pancreatic transplantation in the United States uses whole-organ pancreas with venous drainage into the systemic circulation and enteric exocrine drainage. Some centers advocate portal venous drainage. Under cold-storage conditions, the portal vein is isolated. If it is too short to allow for a tension-free anastomosis, an extension autograft is placed using donor iliac vein. The SMA and splenic artery then are reconstructed with a donor iliac artery Y-bifurcation autograft. Only

the second portion of the duodenum is retained with the pancreas. Then the portal vein is anastomosed to the iliac vein or the superior mesenteric vein, and the donor common iliac artery graft is anastomosed to the recipient's external iliac artery. The duodenal segment of the transplant is then opened, and a duodenojejunostomy is created. Alternatively, the duodenal segment can be anastomosed to the bladder. The pancreas transplant is placed in the right paracolic gutter, and if kidney transplantation is to be performed, it is done on the left side.

3. **Pancreatic islet cell transplantation** is still investigational and has not received widespread acceptance. Pancreatic islet cells are isolated and injected into the portal vein for engraftment in the liver. The major problems have been in obtaining enough islet cells to attain glucose homeostasis and failing to achieve long-term insulin independence. A large multicenter trial supported the proof of concept of islet transplantation (*N Engl J Med.* 2006;355:1318). Although 58% of patients were able to achieve insulin independence at some time during the trial, only 31% of those achieving insulin independence and 15% of those initially enrolled were insulin independent 1 year after transplantation.

B. **Exocrine drainage.** Most programs now use **enteric drainage,** which avoids the acidosis, volume depletion, and urologic complications associated with bladder drainage. Enteric drainage involves anastomosis of the duodenal segment to small bowel in a side-to-side fashion or via a Roux-en-Y limb. Disadvantages of enteric drainage include the inability to monitor exocrine secretions and a higher rate of technical failure.

V. POSTOPERATIVE MANAGEMENT AND MONITORING

A. **Immunosuppression** consists of quadruple therapy with antibody induction, tacrolimus, prednisone, and mycophenolate mofetil.

B. **Serum glucose** is followed during and after the transplantation. Intravenous insulin infusions are stopped within the first few hours after pancreas transplantation.

C. **Rejection** of the pancreas transplant is suggested by a rise in serum amylase or a fall in urinary amylase. Rejection of pancreas and kidney transplants usually occurs in parallel but may be discordant. The diagnosis of kidney rejection is suggested by a rise in creatinine, which is then confirmed by biopsy. Biopsy of the pancreas transplant is performed percutaneously or via cystoscopy. Rejection is treated with corticosteroids or antilymphocyte preparations.

D. **Graft-related complications.** Besides rejection, complications of pancreas transplantation include metabolic acidosis and dehydration. These are due to the loss of sodium and bicarbonate into the urine from the transplanted duodenum. Other common complications include pancreatitis, UTIs, urethritis, and anastomotic leak from the duodenocystostomy. Infections with CMV also may occur.

VI. EFFECT ON SECONDARY COMPLICATIONS OF DIABETES. The full effect of pancreatic transplantation on secondary complications of diabetes is unknown. Pancreatic transplantation may prevent the development of diabetic nephropathy in the transplanted kidney. It also may stabilize diabetic retinopathy and improve diabetic neuropathy.

INTESTINAL TRANSPLANTATION

Intestinal failure occurs when the functioning GI tract mucosal surface area has been reduced below the minimal amount necessary for adequate digestion and absorption of food. This may be caused by intestinal loss or intestinal disease (Table 23-8). The development of TPN has led to the possibility of long-term survival for infants and adults with intestinal failure. However, TPN has limitations and associated morbidity.

I. INDICATIONS. Adults and children who have documented intestinal failure without the potential for long-term survival on TPN are candidates for intestinal transplantation. **Intestinal failure** is said to occur when any child younger than 1 year requires more than 50% of his or her caloric needs from TPN after neonatal small-bowel resection or when a child older than 4 years requires more than 30% of calories from TPN. Older children and adults receiving more than 50% of their nutritional requirements from TPN for more than 1 year also should be considered for intestinal transplantation. Other considerations include elevated hepatic enzymes, multiple line infections, thrombosis of two of the central veins, and frequent episodes of dehydration.

II. DONOR INTESTINAL PROCUREMENT generally uses multiorgan recovery techniques. The liver, stomach, duodenum, pancreas, and small intestine are removed *en bloc* and separated under cold-storage conditions. Alternatively, the intestine may be recovered alone or with the liver.

TABLE 23-8	Causes of Intestinal Failure
Superior mesenteric artery thrombosis	Crohn's disease
Superior mesenteric artery embolization	Trauma
Necrotizing enterocolitis	Radiation
Volvulus	Malignancy (desmoid, polyposis)
Gastroschisis	Pseudoobstruction
Intestinal atresia	

III. **INTESTINAL TRANSPLANTATION OPERATION.** Patients who receive isolated intestinal allografts have vascular anastomoses created between the donor superior mesenteric vein and the recipient portal vein, and between the donor SMA and the recipient aorta. Vascular reconstruction for patients who receive combined liver–intestinal grafts parallels that for patients undergoing a standard OLT. Supra- and infrahepatic vena caval anastomoses are completed, and arterial inflow is accomplished after the portal vein anastomosis by using a patch of aorta that contains the SMA and celiac.

IV. **POSTOPERATIVE MANAGEMENT**

A. **Immunosuppression and infection prophylaxis.** Posttransplantation immunosuppressive protocols have varied greatly over the last decade, and a universally accepted standard protocol does not exist. Recent studies have demonstrated encouraging results with induction therapy (Thymoglobulin or Campath) followed by maintenance therapy with tacrolimus. Because the allograft ileum is more susceptible to rejection, ileoscopic biopsies through a temporary loop ileostomy are common. Watery diarrhea may be a sign of either rejection or superinfection. With the return of intestinal function, feedings are begun with an elemental diet and then advanced as tolerated. Viral and fungal infection prophylaxis includes ganciclovir, oral antibiotic bowel preparation, low-dose amphotericin B, and early removal of central lines.

B. **Potential complications.** Inherent risks with intestinal transplantation include up to 50% graft failure (rejection) at 3 years, although recent advances in immunosuppression and perioperative management have promising results (*Lancet.* 2003;361:1502). More than 1,900 intestinal transplants have been performed in the United States since 1990, with 180 transplants in 2009 (2 living donors, 178 deceased). For primary intestinal transplants, graft survival averages 78% at 1 year and 40% at 5 years (www.unos.org). Combined liver–intestine transplantation carries all the additional risks inherent in liver transplantation. Intestinal transplant recipients are at increased risk for the development of graft-versus-host disease and posttransplantation lymphoproliferative disease. Complications related to tacrolimus-based immunosuppression include DM, headaches, CNS neurotoxicity, peripheral neurotoxicity, and nephrotoxicity. As with any effective immunosuppressant, there is an increased risk of infection and malignancy.

ADDITIONAL REFERENCES

Abu-Elmagd KM. Intestinal transplantation for short bowel syndrome and gastrointestinal failure: current consensus, rewarding outcomes, and practical guidelines. *Gastroenterology.* 2006;130:S132–S137.

Everson GT, Trotter JF. *Liver Transplantation: Challenging Controversies and Topics.* Totowa, NJ: Humana Press; 2009.

McKay DB, Steinberg SM, eds. *Kidney Transplantation: A Guide to the Care of Kidney Transplant Recipients.* New York: Springer; 2010.

Norman DJ, Turka LA, eds. *Primer on Transplantation.* 2nd ed. Thorofare, NJ: American Society of Transplant Physicians; 2001.

Schiff ER, Sorrell, MF, Maddrey, WC. *Schiff's Diseases of the Liver,* 10th ed. Philadelphia: Lippincott Williams & Wilkins; 2007.

Schulak JA. What's new in general surgery: transplantation. *J Am Coll Surg.* 2005;200(3):409–417.

24 Burns

Derek Wakeman and Robert E. Southard

Burns are tissue injuries resulting from direct contact with flames, hot liquids, gases, surfaces, caustic chemicals, electricity, or radiation. Most commonly, the skin is injured, which compromises its function as a barrier to injury and infection and as a regulator of body temperature and fluid loss. More than 1.2 million persons in the United States sustain burns each year, of whom, 500,000 receive formal medical attention, more than 40,000 are hospitalized, and 4,000 die (www.ameriburn.org). Like trauma, mortality from burns occurs in a bimodal pattern: immediately after the injury or weeks later from sepsis and multiorgan failure. Recently, the focus on burn care as a subspecialty of surgery in dedicated patient care units has improved overall survival and quality of life. Finally, it should be emphasized that most burns are preventable and, thus, prevention strategies are of utmost importance.

ASSESSMENT AND MANAGEMENT OF BURN INJURIES

I. ASSESSMENT

  A. **Mechanism of injury.** Identify burn source, duration of exposure, time of injury, and environment. Burns sustained in a closed environment, such as a structure fire, often produce inhalation injury in addition to thermal trauma. Explosions can cause barometric injury to the eardrums and lungs and may also cause blunt trauma.

  B. **Associated injuries** can result from explosions, falls, or jumping during escape attempts.

  C. **Patient age** is a major determinant on outcome. Infants and elderly patients are at highest risk. Burns are a common form of child abuse and need to be considered in every child. Suggestive physical examination findings include stocking/glove injury patterns, lack of splash marks, and dorsally located contact burns of the hands (*Forensic Sci Int.* 2009;187:81). Elderly patients often have comorbid medical problems and decreased physiologic reserve.

  D. **State of health.** Preexisting medical problems should be noted, with particular attention paid to cardiac, pulmonary, renal, and gastrointestinal systems.

  E. **Prehospital treatment** is recorded, including care provided by the patient and by the emergency response team. Administered fluids are documented and subtracted from estimated fluid requirements for the first 24 hours of injury. Hypothermia is a significant complication, particularly during transport, and should be addressed both in the field and at the receiving facility. Common effective precautions include preheating patient-receiving areas and minimizing the use of wet dressings in the prehospital setting.

  F. **Primary survey** should follow the guidelines established by the American College of Surgeons' Advanced Trauma Life Support Course. Burned patients should be evaluated and treated as victims of multisystem trauma because there is significant morbidity associated from missed injuries secondary to an explosion, falls, etc.

1. **Airway** assessment and security are the foremost priority. Supraglottic tissue edema progresses over the first 12 hours and can obstruct the airway rapidly. The larynx protects subglottic tissue from direct thermal injury but not from injury due to inhaled toxic gases. Inhalation injury should be suspected if the patient was burned in an enclosed structure or explosion. Physical signs include hoarseness, stridor, facial burns, singed facial hair, expectoration of carbonaceous sputum, and presence of carbon in the oropharynx. The decision to intubate the trachea for airway protection should be made early and is preferable to cricothyroidotomy in the edematous and swollen neck. Awake intubation or intubation over a bronchoscope is the safest approach if there is any question about the ease or adequacy of airway exposure (*Curr Opin Anaesthesiol.* 2003;16:183).

2. **Breathing** is evaluated for effort, depth of respiration, and auscultation of breath sounds. Wheezing or rales suggest either inhalation injury or aspiration of gastric contents. Most severely burned patients develop early pulmonary insufficiency and respiratory failure. The etiology of this failure can be direct thermal injury to the upper airways or, more commonly, indirect acute lung injury secondary to activation of systemic inflammation. In addition, the decreased pulmonary compliance and chest wall rigidity of burn patients can lead to iatrogenic ventilator-induced lung injury. The use of lower tidal volumes, permissive hypercapnia, and the "open lung" approach to ventilation can significantly improve outcome (*N Engl J Med.* 2000;342:1301).

3. **Circulation.** Circulatory support in the form of **aggressive and prompt fluid resuscitation** is a cornerstone of early burn management. Burn injury causes a combination of hypovolemic and distributive shock characterized by the release of inflammatory mediators, dynamic fluid shifts from the intravascular compartment to the interstitium, and exudative and evaporative water loss from the burn injury. Full-thickness circumferential extremity or neck burns require escharotomy if circulation distal to the injury is impaired; however, escharotomies are rarely needed within the first 6 hours of injury.

4. **Exposure. Remove all clothing** to halt continued burn from melted synthetic compounds or chemicals and to assess the full extent of body surface involvement in the initial examination. Irrigate injuries with water or saline to remove harmful residues. **Remove jewelry** (particularly rings) to prevent injury resulting from increasing tissue edema.

G. **Burn-specific secondary survey**
   1. **Depth of burn** (Table 24-1)
      a. **First-degree burns** are limited to the epidermis. The skin is painful and red. There are no blisters. These burns should heal spontaneously in 3 to 4 days.
      b. **Second-degree burns,** which are subdivided into **superficial or deep partial-thickness burns,** are limited to the dermal layers of

TABLE 24-1 Treatment Algorithm for the Three Clinically Important Burn Depths[a]

Burn Depth[b]	Level of Injury	Clinical Features	Treatment	Usual Result
Superficial partial-thickness	Papillary dermis	Blisters Erythema Capillary refill Intact pain sensation	Tetanus prophylaxis Cleaning (e.g., with chlorhexidine gluconate) Topical agent (e.g., 1% silver sulfadiazine) Sterile gauze dressing[c] Physical therapy Splints as necessary	Epithelialization in 7–21 days Hypertrophic scar rare Return of full function
Deep partial-thickness	Reticular dermis	Blisters pale white or yellow color Absent pain sensation	As for superficial partial-thickness burns Early surgical excision and skin grafting an option	Epithelialization in 21–60 days in the absence of surgery Hypertrophic scar common Earlier return of function with surgical therapy
Full-thickness	Subcutaneous fat, fascia, muscle, or bone	Blisters may be absent Leathery, in classic, wrinkled appearance over bony prominences No capillary refill Thrombosed subcutaneous vessels may be visible Absent pain sensation	As for superficial partial-thickness burns Wound excision and grafting at earliest feasible time	Functional limitation more frequent Hypertrophic scar mainly at graft margins

[a]Epidermal (first-degree) burns present clinically with cutaneous erythema, pain, and tenderness; they resolve rapidly and generally require only symptomatic treatment.
[b]No clinically useful objective method of measuring burn depth exists; classification depends on clinical judgment.
[c]Sterile gauze dressings are frequently omitted on the face and neck.
Reprinted with permission from Monafo WW. Initial management of burns. *N Engl J Med.* 1996;335:1581.

the skin. **Superficial** partial-thickness burns involve the papillary dermis. They appear red, warm, edematous, and blistered, often with denuded, moist, mottled red or pink epithelium. The injured tissue is very painful, especially when exposed to air. Such burns frequently arise from brief contact with hot surfaces, liquids, flames, or chemicals. **Deep** second-degree burns involve the reticular dermis and thus can damage dermal appendages (e.g., nerves, sweat glands, or hair follicles). Hence, such burns can be less sensitive or hairs may be easily plucked out. Nonetheless, the only definitive method of differentiating superficial and deep partial-thickness burns is by length of time to heal. Superficial burns heal in less than 2 weeks; deep burns require at least 3 weeks. Furthermore, any partial-thickness burn can convert to full-thickness injury over time, especially if early fluid resuscitation is inadequate or infection ensues.

    c. **Full-thickness** (third- or fourth-degree) burns involve all layers of the skin and some subcutaneous tissue. In **third-degree** burns, all skin appendages and sensory fibers are destroyed. This results in an initially painless, insensate dry surface that may appear either white and leathery or charred and cracked. **Fourth-degree** burns also involve fascia, muscle, and bone. They often result from prolonged contact with thermal sources or high electrical current. All full-thickness burns are managed surgically, and immediate burn expertise should be sought.

H. **Percentage of body surface area (BSA) estimation.** The accurate and timely assessment of BSA is a critical aspect of the initial evaluation of burned patients. It will determine whether transfer to a specialized burn center is required as well as the magnitude of initial fluid resuscitation and nutritional requirements (*J Burn Care Res.* 2007;28:42).

    1. **Small areas:** The area of patient's hand (including palm and extended fingers) equals 1% of BSA (*Burns.* 2001;27:591).

    2. **Large areas:** "rule of nines": Regions of the body approximating 9% BSA or multiples thereof are shown in Table 24-2. Note that infants and babies have a proportionally greater percentage of BSA in the head and neck region and less in the lower extremities than adults (*Burns.* 2000;26:156).

TABLE 24-2	Rule-of-Nines Estimation of Percentage of Body Surface Area					
	Head and Neck	Trunk Anterior	Trunk Posterior	Extremity Upper	Extremity Lower	Genital
Adult	9	18	18	9	18	1
Infant	18	18	18	9	14	—

II. MANAGEMENT

A. Emergency room

1. **Resuscitation.** A surgical consultation is initiated for all patients with major injury.

   a. **Oxygen** should be provided to patients with all but the most minor injuries. A 100% oxygen high-humidity facemask for those with possible inhalation injury assists the patient's expectoration from dry airways and treats carbon monoxide poisoning.

   b. **Intravenous access.** All patients with burns of 15% or greater BSA require intravenous fluids. Two 16-gauge or larger peripheral venous catheters should be started immediately to provide circulatory volume support. Peripheral access in the upper extremities is preferred over central venous access because of the risk of catheter-related infection. An intravenous catheter may be placed through the burn if other sites are unavailable. Avoid lower-extremity catheters, if possible, to prevent phlebitic complications.

   c. **Fluid.** Improved survival in the era of modern burn care is largely attributable to early and aggressive volume resuscitation. Intravenous fluid in excess of maintenance fluids is administered to all patients with burns of 15% or greater BSA in adults (≥10% BSA in children) and generally follows established guidelines and formulas. Although several formulas have been described, most burn surgeons adhere to crystalloid-based formulations. In particular, fluid resuscitation based on the Consensus formula is widely used and has decreased the occurrence of burn-induced shock (*J Burn Care Res.* 2008;29:257).

      (1) **Consensus formula.** The estimated crystalloid requirement for the first 24 hours after injury is calculated on the basis of patient weight and BSA burn percentage. Lactated Ringer's solution volume in the first 24 hours = 2 to 4 mL × %BSA (second-, third-, and fourth-degree burns only) × body weight (kg). One-half of the calculated volume is given in the first 8 hours after injury, and the remaining volume is infused over the next 16 hours. Fluid resuscitation calculations are based on the time of injury, not the time when the patient is evaluated. Prehospital intravenous hydration is subtracted from the total volume estimate. It should be emphasized that formulas are only estimates, and more or less fluid may be required to maintain adequate tissue perfusion as measured by rate of urine output. Patients with inhalational injury, associated mechanical trauma, electrical injury, escharotomies, or delayed resuscitation require more fluid than that based on the formula alone. Furthermore, for children weighing 30 kg or less, 5% dextrose in one-quarter normal saline maintenance fluids should supplement the Parkland formula to compensate for ongoing evaporative losses. Patient body weight is determined early after the burn as a baseline measurement for fluid calculations and as a daily reference for fluid management.

    (2) Colloid-containing solutions should be held for intravenous therapy until after the first 12 to 24 hours postburn, at which time capillary leak diminishes. Although controversial, some burn specialists recommend starting colloid formulations after this initial period to decrease the required volume of fluid administered (*J Trauma.* 2005;58:1011). However, a recent study of 7,000 critically ill (nonburned) patients found that while colloid resuscitation resulted in less volume administered, it did not improve organ failure rates, ventilator days, or mortality (*N Engl J Med.* 2004;350:2247). Even more troubling, a Cochrane review found that the relative risk of death was 2.4 times higher in burned patients who received albumin than in those who were given only crystalloid fluids (*Cochrane Database Syst Rev.* 2002;4:CD001208).

  d. A **Foley catheter** is used to monitor hourly urine production as an index of adequate tissue perfusion. In the absence of underlying renal disease, a minimum urine production rate of 1 mL/kg/hr in children (weighing $\leq$30 kg) and 0.5 mL/kg/hr in adults is the guideline for adequate intravenous infusion.

  e. **Nasogastric tube** insertion with low suction is performed if patients are intubated or develop nausea, vomiting, and abdominal distention consistent with adynamic ileus. Virtually, all patients with burns of greater than 25% BSA will have ileus.

  f. **Escharotomy** may be necessary in full-thickness circumferential burns of the neck, torso, or extremities when increasing tissue edema impairs peripheral circulation or when chest involvement restricts respiratory efforts. Full-thickness incisions through (but no deeper than) the insensate burn eschar provide immediate relief (Fig. 24-1). Longitudinal escharotomies are performed on the lateral or medial aspects of the extremities and the anterior axillary lines of the chest (*World J Surg.* 2003;27:1323). Usually, they are done at the bedside and require no anesthesia. However, if the digits were burned so severely that desiccation results, midlateral escharotomies have minimal benefit. Escharotomies are rarely required within the first 6 hours after injury. Indications for escharotomy rest on clinical grounds. Traditionally, to aid in assessing peripheral circulation, the documentation of palpable peripheral pulse or the presence of a Doppler signal has been used. However, studies have indicated that correlation of intramuscular pressure with signs and symptoms of extremity compression, including Doppler pulse, is poor (*Am J Surg.* 1980;140:825). Infrared photoplethysmography has been a useful adjunct in assessing the need of escharotomies because photoplethysmography correlates well with blood flow and direct measurement of compartment pressure (*J Hand Surg.* 1984;9:314). Laser Doppler flowmetry has been shown to be predictive of the need for escharotomy and grafting in deep dermal upper extremity burns (*J Trauma.* 1997;43:35). Furthermore, laser Doppler imaging has been repeatedly shown to predict burn wound outcome and has been approved by the

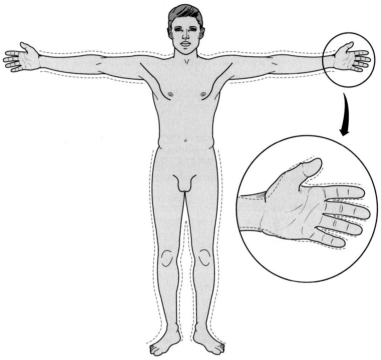

Figure 24-1. Placement of escharotomies. Midaxial escharotomies should be performed if vascular compromise occurs. Incisions should be performed through the dermis and subcutaneous tissue to allow maximal expansion of the underlying fascia.

Food and Drug Administration for assessing burn depth (*Burns.* 2008;34:761).

2. **Monitors.** Continuous pulse oximetry to measure oxygen saturation is useful. One caveat is that falsely elevated levels can be observed in carbon monoxide poisoning.

3. **Laboratory evaluation** includes a baseline complete blood cell count, type and crossmatch, electrolytes and renal panel, β-human chorionic gonadotropin (in women), arterial carboxyhemoglobin, arterial blood gas evaluation, and urinalysis. A toxicology screen and an alcohol level are obtained when suggested by history or mental status examination. A chest radiograph is obtained with the understanding that it rarely reflects early inhalation injury. Additional chest films should be obtained if endotracheal intubation or central catheter placement becomes necessary. An electrocardiogram is useful initially, particularly in elderly patients or those with electrical burns. Fluid and electrolyte fluxes during resuscitation and later mobilization of third-space edema can result in arrhythmias and interval electrocardiogram changes.

4. **Moist dressings** applied to partial-thickness burns provide pain relief from air exposure. Cool water applied to small partial-thickness burns can provide relief but must be avoided in patients with major burns (>25% BSA) and especially in infants, to avoid hypothermia. Cold water can also cause vasoconstriction and can extend the depth and surface area of injury.

5. **Analgesia** is given intravenously every 1 to 2 hours to manage pain but in small doses to guard against hypotension, oversedation, and respiratory depression.

6. Photographs or diagrams of the BSA involvement and thickness of burns are useful for documenting injuries. They also can facilitate communication between the various members of the team caring for the patient and serve medicolegal purposes in the case of assault or child abuse.

7. **Early irrigation** and debridement are performed using normal saline and sterile instruments to remove all loose epidermal skin layers, followed by the application of topical antimicrobial agents and sterile dressings. In general, it is safe to leave small blisters overlying superficial partial-thickness burns intact because they permit healing in a sterile environment and offer some protection to the underlying dermis. However, in larger and deeper partial-thickness burns, debridement of burn blisters should be done to relieve tension and purge inflammatory mediators. Nonviable tissue in the burn wound should be debrided early because the dead tissue provides a bacterial medium putting the patient at risk for both local and systemic infections. Early excision and grafting has been shown to benefit survival, blood loss, incidence of sepsis, and length of stay compared with serial debridement (*Burns.* 2006;32:145). If the burns resulted from liquid chemical exposure, they are irrigated continuously for 20 to 30 minutes. Dry chemicals are removed from the skin before irrigation to prevent them from dissolving into solution and causing further injury. Corneal burns of the eye require continuous irrigation for several hours and immediate ophthalmologic consultation.

8. **Topical antimicrobial agents** are the mainstay of local burn wound management. Prior to the use of topical antimicrobial agents, the most common organisms causing burn wound infections were *Staphylococcus aureus* and group A streptococci (*J Trauma.* 1982;22:11). Subsequent to the development of topical agents, gram-negative organisms, particularly *Pseudomonas aeruginosa,* and fungi are the most common causes of invasive burn wound sepsis (*J Burn Care Res.* 2011;32:324). Systemic antibiotics are not administered prophylactically but are reserved for documented infection. Bacterial proliferation may occur underneath the eschar at the viable–nonviable interface, resulting in subeschar suppuration and separation of the eschar. Microorganisms can invade the underlying tissue, producing invasive burn wound sepsis. The risk of invasive infection is higher in patients with multiorgan failure or burns greater than 30% BSA (*World J Surg.* 2004;22:135). When the identity of the specific organism is established, antibiotic

therapy is targeted to that organism. It may be useful on occasion to diagnose invasive infection. The technique requires a 500-mg biopsy of suspicious eschar and underlying unburned tissue. Wound infection is defined by more than 10^5 organisms per gram of tissue. Treatment requires infected eschar excision and appropriate topical/systemic antibiotic therapy.

a. **Silver sulfadiazine** (e.g., Silvadene): most commonly used agent. Advantages: broad spectrum (gram positive, most gram negative, some fungal), nonirritating, high patient acceptance, easy to use, fewest adverse side effects. It is formulated as a cream, which helps to minimize evaporative water and heat loss and thus diminishes caloric requirements. Disadvantages: some *Pseudomonas* resistance, poor eschar penetration, occasional transient leukopenia 3 to 5 days after use which is generally harmless and resolves regardless of cessation of treatment.

b. **Mafenide acetate** (Sulfamylon): advantages: broad spectrum, particularly against *Pseudomonas* and *Enterococcus* species, good eschar penetration. Disadvantages: painful, can cause allergic rash, readily absorbed systemically leading to metabolic acidosis via carbonic anhydrase inhibition. Therefore, its use is limited to small full-thickness burns.

c. **Polymyxin B sulfate** (Polysporin), neomycin, bacitracin: petroleum-based ointments. Advantages: painless, allow wound observation, tolerated well on facial burns, and do not discolor skin. Disadvantages: poor gram-negative coverage, poor eschar penetration. Mupirocin is an ointment with improved activity against methicillin-resistant *S. aureus* and gram-negative bacteria.

d. **Silver nitrate:** applied as a soak. Advantages: painless, complete antimicrobial coverage, useful for patients with sulfa allergy. Disadvantages: stains tissue gray to black making wound monitoring difficult. Also hypotonic and leaches electrolytes resulting in severe electrolyte abnormalities.

e. **Acticoat:** commercial dressing with impregnated silver ions. Advantages: easy application, excellent antimicrobial activity. Disadvantages: expensive, can only be left in place for 3 days.

f. **Dakin solution** (0.25% sodium hypochlorite): advantages: inexpensive, good antimicrobial activity. Disadvantages: cytotoxic (though less so at 0.025%) and can inhibit healing, must be changed frequently.

9. **Tetanus prophylaxis.** If last booster was administered greater than 5 years prior, tetanus toxoid 0.5 mL intramuscularly is given. If immunization status is unknown, 250 to 500 units of human tetanus immunoglobulin (Hyper-Tet) are given intramuscularly.

10. **Critical care issues with burns.** Issues include burn wound infection, pneumonia, sepsis, ileus, Curling's ulcer (gastroduodenal), acalculous cholecystitis, and superior mesenteric artery syndrome.

a. **Stress ulcer prophylaxis** (e.g., H_2 blockers or proton-pump inhibitors) should be provided for patients who have major burns and can receive nothing by mouth, especially those with coagulopathy (*Shock*. 1996;5:4).

    b. Deep venous thrombosis. Burn patients are at increased risk for deep venous thrombosis and should receive pharmacologic prophylaxis (*Burns.* 2004;30:591).

    c. Sepsis. In patients who survive the first 24 hours after injury, burn sepsis is the leading cause of mortality (*Burns.* 2006;32:545). The evidence-based recommendations of the Surviving Sepsis Campaign (*Crit Care Med.* 2008;36(1):296) include antibiotic therapy, source control, crystalloid resuscitation, vasopressor use, a hemoglobin transfusion trigger of 7 g/dL, an open-lung, low-tidal-volume ventilatory strategy, and maintenance of blood glucose less than 180 mg/dL.

B. Outpatient. Only minor first-degree or partial-thickness injuries should be considered for outpatient management. The decision to use outpatient management depends on many factors including patient reliability, opportunity for follow-up, and accessibility to health professionals. Surgical consultation is recommended at the time of initial evaluation in all but the most minor injuries.

    1. Dressings are often managed by the patient when the injury is easily accessible. Home health nursing is a useful adjunct when self-application is suboptimal or wounds are in early healing stages and require close follow-up. Silver sulfadiazine is often applied as a light coating, followed by sterile dressings once or twice daily.

    2. Antibiotics are not prescribed prophylactically. Their use is limited to documented wound infections.

    3. Follow-up usually occurs once or twice a week during the initial healing of partial-thickness burns and split-thickness skin grafts until epithelialization is complete. Thereafter, patients are followed at 1- to 3-month intervals to evaluate and treat scar hypertrophy (application of foam tape or Jobst garments), hyperpigmentation (avoidance of direct sunlight, use of sunscreen), dry skin (unscented lotion massage), and pruritus (antihistamines). Rehabilitation potential and therapy (physical, occupational, social, and psychological) are also evaluated.

C. Inpatient

    1. Transfer to a burn center should follow the guidelines of the American Burn Association (www.ameriburn.org). These criteria reflect multiple studies showing that age and BSA burn percentage remain the two most important prognostic factors.

        a. Partial-thickness burns greater than 10% BSA.

        b. Any full-thickness burn.

        c. Burns that involve the face, hands, feet, genitalia, perineum, or major joints.

        d. Any inhalation, chemical, or electrical injury (including lightning).

        e. Burn injury in patients with preexisting medical conditions that could complicate management, prolong recovery, or affect mortality.

        f. Burns in combination with significant associated mechanical trauma. Note, if the traumatic injury poses a greater threat to life, the patient should be stabilized at a trauma center before transfer to a burn unit.

g. Burned children in hospitals without qualified personnel or equipment for the care of children.

h. Patients requiring specialized rehabilitation, psychological support, or social services (including suspected neglect or child abuse).

2. Nutrition. Severe burns induce a hypermetabolic state proportional to the size of the burn up to 200% the normal metabolic rate. Early enteral feeding in burn patients helps to attenuate the catabolic response after burn injury and decrease the rate of infectious complications (*J Trauma*. 2003;54:755). The daily estimated metabolic requirement (EMR) in burn patients can be calculated from the Curreri formula: EMR = [25 kcal × body weight (kg)] + (40 kcal × %BSA). In children, formulas based on BSA are more appropriate. Protein losses in burn patients from both an increased oxidation rate and burn wound extravasation should be replaced by supplying 1.5 to 2 g/kg of protein/day (*Lancet*. 2004;363:1895). Therapeutic strategies should target prevention of body weight loss of more than 10% of the patient's baseline weight. Losses of more than 10% of lean body mass may lead to impaired immune function and delayed wound healing. Losses of more than 40% lead to imminent death (*Shock*. 1998;10:155).

a. Enteral feedings are the preferred route when tolerated and can be administered through an enteral feeding tube positioned in the duodenum. For severe burns, early feeding within the first 24 hours has been shown to improve a number of outcome measures including overall mortality (*Burns*. 1997;23(Suppl 1):519). Increasing feedings beyond the EMR is associated with the development of fatty liver (*Ann Surg*. 2002;235:152) and hyperglycemia (*J Trauma*. 2001;51:540), which have a negative influence on outcome in burned patients.

b. Total parenteral nutrition should be initiated after fluid resuscitation only if the patient is unable to tolerate enteral feeding.

c. Daily vitamin supplementation in adults should include 1.5 g of ascorbic acid, 500 mg of nicotinamide, 50 mg of riboflavin, 50 mg of thiamine, and 220 mg of zinc. Although results from high-dose antioxidant therapy are promising, further clinical trials are needed to define its role in burn patients (*J Burn Care Rehabil*. 2005;26:207).

d. Anabolic adjuncts, including growth hormone (*Ann Surg*. 2009 Sep 2, Epub), insulin-like growth factor, insulin, testosterone (*Crit Care Med*. 2001;29:1936), oxandrolone (*Pharmacotherapy* 2009;29:213), and propranolol (*N Engl J Med*. 2001;345:1223), have been shown to improve protein synthesis after severe injury. However, caution is advised as growth hormone therapy has been found to increase mortality in critically ill patients although patients with burns and sepsis were excluded from the study (*N Engl J Med*. 1999;341:785).

3. Wound care

a. Analgesia and **sedation** for dressing changes are necessary for major burns. Benzodiazepines can be used with or without ketamine for sedation. Ketamine can cause tachycardia, hypotension, and arrhythmias. Alternatively, in patients with a secure airway, intravenous propofol has the desired effects of ease of titration and quick onset/offset of action. Either of these sedative regimens in concert with narcotic analgesia is well tolerated.

b. Daily dressing changes. While the wounds are exposed, the surgeon can properly assess the continued demarcation and healing of the injury. Physical therapy with active range of motion is performed at this time, before reapplying splints and dressings.

c. Debridement of all nonviable tissue should take place using sterile technique and instruments when demarcation occurs. Partial-thickness eschar can be abraded lightly using wet gauze. Enzymatic treatments can be useful in dissolving eschar to develop granulation tissue for tissue grafting. All full-thickness eschar should be identified early, excised, and closed or covered before the development of wound colonization and infection.

d. Temporary dressings for massive burns with limited donor sites give stable coverage without painful dressing changes.

　　(1) Biologic dressings include allograft (cadaver skin) and xenograft (pig skin). These dressings provide the advantages of ease of acquisition and application while providing barrier protection and a biologic bed under which dermis can granulate. After several days, the allograft can be removed, and a meshed autograft may be replaced for definitive coverage. The use of cultured autologous epithelium (keratinocytes) has shown encouraging results, particularly for patients with massive burns (>80% BSA) and limited donor sites (*J Cell Mol Med.* 2005;9:592). However, this technology is currently limited by the time needed to grow the autograft (2 to 3 weeks) and the relatively lower take rate (50% to 75%).

　　(2) Synthetic dressings have become an attractive alternative for early wound coverage. Biobrane is a collagen-coated silicone membrane that prevents moisture loss, but, therefore, can trap infection. It is relatively painless and can be easily peeled from the wound after epithelialization. It is useful for superficial partial-thickness burns and skin graft donor sites. Trancyte is similar to Biobrane, but also has growth factors from cultured fibroblasts to theoretically aid wound healing. Integra consists of an epidermal analogue (silastic film) and a dermal analogue (collagen matrix), making it useful for full-thickness burns. Once adequate vascularization is seen through the silicone layer, the film is removed, and an ultrathin autograft is placed onto the artificial dermis, which allows more rapid reharvesting from the donor site (*J Burn Care Rehabil.* 2003;24:42).

4. Operative management

a. Early tangential excision of burn eschar to the level of bleeding capillaries should follow the resuscitation phase. Debate persists as to the optimal timing of burn wound excision (range is 1 to 10 days), although evidence exists demonstrating benefit from early excision

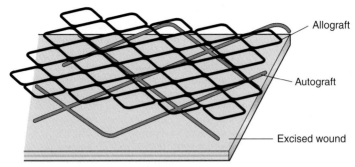

Figure 24-2. Combined skin graft to cover burn wounds too extensive for other methods. The widely meshed autograft would allow continued fluid fluxes during the more extended time required for epithelialization. A more narrowly meshed allograft placed superficial to the autograft can accelerate the process by providing temporary coverage while the autograft fills in.

(*Burns.* 2006;32:145). Excision can be performed using a knife for small surfaces and a power- or gas-driven dermatome for larger surfaces. For each trip to the operating theater, consider limiting burn excision to less than 20% BSA or 2 hours of operating time. Even within such limits, aggressive debridement frequently produces profound blood loss and hypothermia (*Crit Care Clin.* 1999;15:333).

b. Split-thickness skin grafts are harvested at a thickness of 0.012 to 0.015 in. (*Clin Dermatol.* 2005;23:332). For cosmetically sensitive areas, autografts are not meshed, or, if necessary, meshed at a narrow ratio (≤2:1). Grafts are secured with absorbable sutures or staples. For very large wounds, split-thickness skin grafts can be meshed up to 4:1 and may be overlaid with meshed allograft tissue (Fig. 24-2). However, cosmesis is poor, and graft take rates may be compromised. Nonadherent dressings and bolsters are applied to minimize shear forces on the fresh grafts. Splints or pins may be required to improve graft survival at joints and to prevent contracture. Ideal point positions are extensions in the neck, knee, elbow, wrist, and interphalangeal joints, 15-degree flexion at metacarpophalangeal joints, and abduction at the shoulder (*Clin Plast Surg.* 1992;19:721).

c. Vacuum-assisted closure devices have gained popularity as a means of securing skin grafts with improved take rates compared with standard bolster dressing (*Arch Surg.* 2002;137:930).

III. BURN MECHANISMS: SPECIAL CONSIDERATIONS

A. Inhalational. Thermal injury to the airway generally is limited to the oropharynx or glottis. The glottis generally protects the subglottic airway from heat, unless the patient has been exposed to superheated steam. Edema formation can compromise the patency of the upper airway, mandating early assessment and constant reevaluation of the airway. **Gases** containing substances that have undergone incomplete combustion (particularly aldehydes), toxic fumes (hydrogen cyanide), and carbon monoxide can cause tracheobronchitis, pneumonitis, and edema. Mortality may be increased by as much as 20% in these patients. **Carbon monoxide** exposure is suggested by a history of exposure in a confined space with symptoms of nausea, vomiting, headache, mental status changes, and cherry-red lips. Carbon monoxide binds to hemoglobin with an affinity 249 times greater than that of oxygen, resulting in extremely slow dissociation (250-minute half-life with room air) unless the patient is administered supplemental oxygen (40-minute half-life with 100% oxygen via nonrebreathing mask). The arterial **carboxyhemoglobin** level is obtained as a baseline. If it is elevated (>5% in nonsmokers or >10% in smokers), oxygen therapy should continue until normal levels are achieved. The increased ventilation–perfusion gradient and the reduction in peak airway flow in distal airways and alveoli can be evaluated using a xenon-133 ventilation–perfusion lung scan. **Management** of minor inhalation injury is by delivery of humidified oxygen. Major injuries require endotracheal intubation for airway protection, preferably with a large-bore tube (7.5 to 8 mm) to facilitate pulmonary toilet of viscous secretions. As discussed earlier, decreased pulmonary compliance is often seen after inhalation injury and can lead to iatrogenic ventilator-associated lung injury. Inhaled bronchodilators can be given to treat bronchospasm whereas nebulized heparin and N-acetylcysteine can limit cast formation. It should be mentioned that inadequate fluid resuscitation actually worsens pulmonary injury, likely due to concentration of neutrophils, whose reactive mediators cause lung injury. Prophylactic antibiotic usage is not indicated. Extubation is performed as soon as possible to prevent pneumonia because coughing clears pulmonary secretions more effectively than suctioning.

B. **Electrical**

1. **Factors influencing severity** include the voltage (high is >1,000 V), resistance, type of current, current pathway through the body, and duration of contact with an electrical source (*Annu Rev Biomed Eng.* 2000;2:477). Electrical current passes in a straight line between points of body contact with the source and the ground. When current passes through the heart or brain, cardiopulmonary arrest can result. In most cases, these injuries respond to resuscitation and usually do not cause permanent damage (*Ann Intern Med.* 2006;145:531). **Severity of injury frequently is underestimated** when only the entrance and exit wounds are considered.

   a. **Tissue resistance.** Heat and subsequent injury from thermal necrosis is directly proportional to resistance to current flow. Tissues that have a higher resistance to electricity, such as skin, bone, and fat, tend to increase in temperature and coagulate, causing deep thermal burns. Nerves and blood vessels have low resistance and readily conduct electricity (*Crit Care Clin.* 1999;15:319). In addition to direct tissue injury, thrombosis can occur with distal soft-tissue ischemia. Peripheral perfusion should be monitored closely because fasciotomy may become necessary to treat compartment syndrome. Fluid resuscitation requirements often are higher than calculated by published formulas.

b. Current

(1) Alternating current (household, power lines) can lead to repetitive, tetanic muscle contraction. In fact, when contact occurs between the palm and an electrical source, alternating current can cause a hand to grip the source of electricity (because of a stronger flexor than extensor tone) and lead to longer electrical exposure (*J Forensic Sci.* 1980;25:514). High-voltage injury, which is commonly seen in workers operating near power lines, can present with full-thickness, charred skin at the entrance and exit wounds, with full arrest, and with fractures sustained while current passed through the body or during a fall.

(2) Direct current emanates from batteries and lightning and causes a single muscle contraction, often throwing the person receiving the electrical shock away from the source of electricity. With a voltage of at least 100 million V and a current of 200,000 A, lightning kills 150 to 300 people in the United States every year. Injury can result from direct strikes or side flashes. Current can travel on the surface of the body rather than through it, producing a "splashed-on" pattern of skin burn.

2. Complications include **cardiopulmonary arrest** (more common with alternating current) (*Br Heart J.* 1987;57:279), **thrombosis, associated fractures** related to fall or severe muscle contraction (*Am J Surg.* 1977;134:95), **spinal cord injury** (*Neurology.* 2003;60:182), and **cataracts** (*J Burn Care Rehabil.* 1991;12:458). **Rhabdomyolysis** may occur and result in myoglobin release from injured cells of deep tissues. Precipitation of protein in the renal tubules can cause acute renal failure (*Burns.* 2004;30:680). Dark urine is the first clinical indication of myoglobinuria, and intravenous lactated Ringer's solution should be administered to maintain a urine output greater than 2 mL/kg/hr. Although somewhat controversial, concomitant administration of intravenous sodium bicarbonate and mannitol to solubilize hemochromogens can potentially minimize nephrotoxicity from myoglobinuria.

C. Chemical injury may result from contact with alkali, acid, or petroleum compounds. Removal of the offending agent is the cornerstone of treatment. Dry chemicals should be brushed off or aspirated into a closed suction container before irrigating with **copious** amounts of water for at least 20 to 30 minutes. Alkali burns penetrate more deeply than acid burns and require longer periods of irrigation. Irrigation has a threefold effect: it dilutes the chemicals already in contact with the skin, washes unreacted agent from the skin, and helps to correct the hygroscopic effects that some agents have on tissues (*ANZ J Surg.* 2003;73:45). Neutralizing the chemicals is not recommended because the resulting reaction generates heat, which can exacerbate the injury. All chemical injuries to the eye are potentially blinding and require copious irrigation with several liters of water and prompt referral to an ophthalmologist (*BMJ.* 2004;328:36). Tar can cause ongoing burns which can be quite deep if not removed promptly.

Treat them by cooling the tar with cold water followed by removing any remaining tar with adhesive remover.

D. **Cold injury**

1. **Hypothermia** is defined as a core body temperature less than 35°C. Mild hypothermia is classified as a core body temperature of 32°C to 35°C; moderate hypothermia is 30°C to 32°C; and severe hypothermia is less than 30°C (*CMAJ.* 2003;168:305). The elderly and children are particularly susceptible. Signs of hypothermia include reduced levels of consciousness, dysrhythmias, and skin that appears cold, gray, or cyanotic. Moderate to severe hypothermia is a medical emergency and necessitates maintenance of airway, breathing, and circulation. Core body temperature should be monitored by means of an esophageal or rectal probe. The heart becomes increasingly irritable at core temperatures below 34°C, and cardiac monitoring should be routine in all hypothermic patients (*Ann Emerg Med.* 1989;18:72). Asystole may occur below 28°C, and cardiopulmonary resuscitation should be started and maintained until the patient is rewarmed to at least 36°C. Rewarming can be passive or active. Passive rewarming involves using blankets to cover the body and head. The warming rate ranges between 0.5°C and 2°C per hour. Active external warming includes the use of heating blankets or a heated forced-air system, which can increase rewarming rates by 1°C per hour as compared with simple cotton blankets (*Ann Emerg Med.* 1996;27:479). Active internal rewarming can be started immediately in the case of severe hypothermia and includes the use of warmed intravenous fluids and oxygen, together warming at a rate of 1°C to 2°C per hour (*Resuscitation.* 1998;36:101). Although used rarely, active invasive rewarming methods can warm faster, at a rate 1°C to 4°C per hour. Examples of this approach include warmed peritoneal lavage, thoracostomy lavage, and bladder lavage. Extracorporeal rewarming of blood via a continuous venovenous bypass circuit or heated hemodialysis can rewarm at a rate of 1°C to 2°C every 5 minutes (*N Engl J Med.* 1997;337:1500).

2. **Frostbite** results from the formation of intracellular ice crystals and microvascular occlusion. Factors affecting severity are temperature, duration of exposure, and environmental conditions promoting rapid heat loss such as wind velocity, moisture, immobilization, and open wounds. The fingers, toes, and ears are most commonly injured, particularly when reduced tissue perfusion has resulted from other causes such as shock.

   a. **Classification**
      (1) **First-degree:** hyperemia and edema, without skin necrosis.
      (2) **Second-degree:** superficial vesicle formation containing clear or milky fluid surrounded by hyperemia, edema, and partial-thickness necrosis.
      (3) **Third-degree:** hemorrhagic bullae and full-thickness necrosis.
      (4) **Fourth-degree:** gangrene with full-thickness involvement of skin, muscle, and bone.

b. Treatment consists of rapid rewarming in a warm water bath between 40°C and 42°C until the tissue perfusion returns, which also may help to minimize tissue loss (*Surg Clin North Am.* 1991;71:345). Splinting and elevation of the frostbitten extremity may reduce edema and promote tissue perfusion. Because mechanical pressure or friction can injure the tissue further, massage and weightbearing are discouraged. Rewarming can be painful, and therefore intravenous analgesia should be provided. Any ruptured blisters should be debrided and covered with a topical antimicrobial and gauze. Tetanus prophylaxis is administered, and follow-up over several weeks is recommended to allow for demarcation of full-thickness injury. Escharotomy may be required for severe injury. Early amputation is not recommended because improvement in tissue viability can occur weeks after injury.

25 Skin and Soft-Tissue Tumors

Amber L. Traugott and Bruce L. Hall

DIAGNOSIS OF SKIN LESIONS AND SOFT-TISSUE MASSES

The surgical management of cutaneous oncology has dramatically changed over the last 100 years. As our understanding of tumor cell biology and immunology has improved through dedicated research, so has our ability to apply surgical efforts in a more directed fashion. When a patient presents to a surgeon with a lesion, a focused history and physical examination are crucial to derive the correct diagnosis. Biopsy to obtain a tissue sample followed by histologic examination remains the gold standard for the accurate diagnosis of cutaneous lesions. For large or deep soft-tissue tumors, radiologic evaluation often precedes biopsy.

I. **SKIN LESIONS**

    A. **History.** Pigmented lesions with a change in size, borders, and coloration are of concern for malignancy. In addition, the itching, bleeding, or ulceration should be assessed.

    B. **Physical examination.** The color, size, shape, borders, elevation, location, firmness, and surface characteristics should be noted for each skin lesion. If possible, photographs should also be taken. Uniformly colored, small, round, circumscribed lesions are more likely benign. Irregularly colored, larger, asymmetric lesions with indistinct borders and ulceration are worrisome for malignancy.

    C. **Biopsy.** A tissue diagnosis is needed for lesions that have worrisome features or *change* after a period of observation. Optimally, a full-thickness tissue is obtained via punch or excisional biopsy. Punch biopsy uses a cylindrical blade to remove a small core of skin: The sample should be obtained from the thickest portion of the lesion, avoiding areas of crusting, ulceration, or necrosis that may underestimate the thickness of the tumor. Excisional biopsy is the same as for soft-tissue masses, discussed in Section II.D. Use of non–full-thickness shave biopsy is generally discouraged because it may lead to inaccurate tumor thickness measurements; nevertheless, it does not appear to affect overall patient outcome (*Am J Surg.* 2005;190:913). A second consideration is that a shave biopsy site heals by secondary intention, giving an inferior cosmetic outcome.

II. **SOFT-TISSUE MASSES**

    A. **History.** Focused history includes location, duration, change in size, and presence of associated symptoms. An enlarging, painless mass is the most common presentation. There is frequently a perceived antecedent trauma. Pain is usually a late symptom. Lesions may be misdiagnosed as hematomas or strained muscle. Any symptom or perception of enlargement is concerning for malignancy.

B. **Physical examination.** Key features are size, anatomic relationships with surrounding structures, borders, and mobility. A neurovascular examination of the affected area should be performed.

C. **Radiologic evaluation**

1. **Magnetic resonance (MR) scan** is the best choice for imaging soft-tissue masses. It can be difficult to distinguish edematous normal tissue from tumor; T2-weighted images and gadolinium enhancement aid in this distinction.

2. **Computed tomography (CT)** is used to assess character and extent of larger, deeper tumors. Involvement of adjacent structures and surgical access to the tumor can be determined. CT-guided core-needle biopsy can be attempted for tumors with difficult surgical access. A CT scan of the chest is useful in patients with soft-tissue sarcomas (STSs) due to its specific pattern of metastasis. CT can also be helpful in evaluating the pelvis and retroperitoneum.

D. **Biopsy.** Ideally, the surgical oncologist who performs the definitive resection should perform the biopsy.

1. **Incisional biopsy** is the gold standard. A small incision should be made that can be excised at subsequent operation: It should be oriented parallel to the long axis of the extremity. Incisional biopsy rather than excisional biopsy should be performed for a mass greater than 3 cm (or >5 cm if it is consistent with a lipoma) in diameter. Drains should be avoided; meticulous hemostasis to prevent hemorrhage from spreading tumor is critical. If drains are needed, drain sites should be in line with the incision, to be excised at subsequent operation.

2. **Core-needle biopsy** provides a section of intact tissue for histologic analysis; it can provide the same information as an incisional biopsy if a good core of tissue is obtained. A very small incision allows easy entrance of the needle into the skin. Most indeterminate or negative results should be confirmed by incisional or excisional biopsy.

3. **Excisional biopsy** is performed for tumors that are probably benign or less than 3 cm in diameter. The usual approach is an elliptical incision around the tumor oriented parallel to the long axis of the limb and, when possible, along the skin lines of minimal tension. The tumor should be excised completely with a thin margin of normal tissue. Primary closure should be employed whenever possible.

4. **Fine-needle aspiration** (FNA) is the least invasive, but can be the least informative, method of tissue diagnosis. Multiple passes are made through a mass in various directions; the plunger is released before removing the needle from the mass. The specimen is then fixed and sent for cytopathologic evaluation. FNA usually cannot give the grade, but often it can determine the presence of malignancy and the

histologic type. Indeterminate results should be followed by further evaluation. FNA is the biopsy method of first choice in the head and neck.

BENIGN LESIONS

I. **SEBORRHEIC KERATOSES** are benign skin growths that originate in the epidermis. These lesions characteristically appear in older people as multiple, raised, irregularly rounded lesions with a verrucous, friable, waxy surface and variable pigmentation from yellowish to brownish black. Common locations include the face, neck, and trunk. If removal is desired, treatment may consist of excision or curettage followed by electrodesiccation, as well as topical agents, such as trichloroacetic acid, or cryotherapy with liquid nitrogen.

II. **ACTINIC KERATOSES** are caused by sun exposure and are found predominantly in elderly, fair-skinned patients. These lesions are small, usually multiple, flat-to-slightly elevated with a rough or scaly surface ranging from red to yellowish brown to black and are found in areas of chronic sun exposure. Unlike seborrheic keratoses, these lesions have malignant potential. Indeed, 15% to 20% of lesions become squamous cell carcinoma, although metastases are rare. Benign-appearing actinic keratoses may be observed. When indicated, treatment consists of topical application of 5-fluorouracil twice a day for 2 to 6 weeks.

III. **NEVI** Junctional nevus cells actually are located in the epidermis and at the dermal–epidermal junction. These nevi are small (<6 mm), well-circumscribed, light brown or black macules found on any area of the body. Nevi rarely develop in people older than 40 years, and any new lesion in someone older than 40 years should be considered a possible early melanoma.

IV. **EPIDERMAL INCLUSION CYSTS** are lined by epidermal cells containing lipid and keratinous material. Asymptomatic cysts may be removed for diagnosis, prevention of infection, or cosmesis. Excision of the cyst should include the entire cyst lining, preferably without interruption of the lining to prevent recurrence, and should include any skin tract or drainage site.

V. **NEUROFIBROMAS** are benign tumors that arise from Schwann cells and are seen most frequently in the setting of neurofibromatosis (von Recklinghausen disease). Neurofibromas are soft, pendulous, sometimes lobulated subcutaneous masses that vary widely in size. The overwhelming majority of these tumors do not require excision. These tumors are removed for symptoms of pain, an observed increase in size, or cosmetic reasons.

VI. **GANGLION CYSTS** are subcutaneous cysts attached to the joint capsule or tendon sheath of the hands and wrists; they are most commonly seen in young and middle-aged women. These lesions present as firm, round masses often seen on the dorsum of the wrist, but can also be found on the radial volar wrist, along the flexor tendon sheaths of the hand, or in the dorsum of the distal interphalangeal joint. After surgical excision, there is an extremely low recurrence rate. To prevent recurrence, the capsular attachment and a small portion of the joint capsule should be removed.

VII. **LIPOMAS** are benign tumors consisting of fat and are perhaps the most common human neoplasms. There is very little potential for malignancy; sarcomatous elements occur in less than 1% of cases. They are soft, fatty, subcutaneous masses and vary widely in size. Asymptomatic small tumors can be followed clinically, but symptomatic or rapidly growing tumors are of concern and should be removed. Large tumors (>5 cm) should be evaluated by core or incisional biopsy. Every effort should be made to excise lipomas cleanly at the first operation to prevent recurrence.

MALIGNANT LESIONS

I. **DERMATOFIBROSARCOMA PROTUBERANS (DFSP)** is a locally aggressive tumor that does not metastasize. Margins of 2 to 5 cm should be achieved if possible. Alternatively, Mohs micrographic surgery involves serial excisions of the tumor, with microscopic examination for areas of positive margins that have been mapped and are then re-excised, one section at a time, until a negative margin is reached. Although time consuming and expensive, this surgery has been advocated in the management of DFSP for improved tissue conservation, cosmetic advantages, and low recurrence rates (*Curr Opin Oncol.* 2006;18:341). DuBay et al. reviewed 62 patients treated for DFSP with wide local excision, Mohs surgery, or a combination approach. At a median follow-up of 4.4 years, there were no local or distant recurrences. Eighty-five percent of the lesions treated initially with Mohs surgery had histologically negative margins. This suggests that Mohs surgery can be effective and that negative margin resection should be achieved (*Cancer.* 2004;100:1008).

II. **DESMOID TUMORS** are nonmetastasizing but locally aggressive tumors that arise from connective tissue. Wide excision with a margin of normal tissue should be performed if possible, but limb function should be spared. Local recurrences are common, and re-excision is often required. Tamoxifen, nonsteroidal anti-inflammatory drugs (e.g., sulindac), or a combination have been used with only anecdotal success and may be attempted as an alternative to surgery. These drugs have been advocated in recurrent or unresectable cases as well. Recommendations regarding future pregnancies are conflicting and unclear. Patients with a desmoid tumor should undergo colonoscopy to exclude the diagnosis of familial adenomatous polyposis (*Fam Cancer.* 2006;5:275).

III. **MELANOMA.** The incidence of melanoma continues to rise at an epidemic rate (101.5% increase from 1970s to 1990s). Melanoma represents the fifth-most-common type of cancer (*CA Cancer J Clin.* 2006;56:106). The estimated direct costs of treatment of melanoma by Medicare alone were $249 million in 1996, with 51% of the costs for patients with stage III or IV melanoma. (*Arch Dermatol.* 2010;146:250).

A. **Lesions.** Most pigmented lesions are benign, but approximately one-third of all melanomas arise from pigmented nevi. It is essential to differentiate among benign, premalignant, and malignant lesions.

1. **Premalignant lesions**
   a. **Dysplastic nevi** have variegated color (tan to brown on a pink base); are large (5 to 12 mm); appear indistinct, with irregular edges; and have macular and papular components. There exists a familial association between dysplastic nevi and a high incidence of melanoma. Melanomas may develop *de novo* or from preexisting dysplastic nevi (*N Engl J Med.* 2003;349:2233).
   b. **Congenital nevi** are notable by their presence since birth and are commonly referred to as "birthmarks." They can be premalignant: There is an increased risk of melanoma developing from these lesions, particularly for nevi greater than 20 cm in diameter.

2. **Malignant lesions**
   a. **Superficial spreading melanoma** (SSM) is the most common form of melanoma (80%), with approximately one-half arising from a preexisting mole. The lesions usually are slow growing and brown, with small discrete nodules of differing colors. SSM tends to spread laterally but can be slightly elevated. SSM is found most commonly on the back in men and women and on the lower extremities of women.
   b. **Nodular melanoma** is the most aggressive form, rapidly becoming a palpable, elevated, firm nodule that may be dense black or reddish blue-black. A distinct convex nodular development indicates deep dermal invasion. Nodular melanomas arise from the epidermal–dermal junction and invade deeply into the dermis and subcutaneous tissue. Approximately 5% are amelanotic.
   c. **Lentigo maligna melanoma** usually is found on older patients as a large melanotic freckle on the temple or malar region known as **Hutchinson freckle.** It usually is slow growing but becomes large, often reaching 5 to 6 cm in diameter. Initially, it is flat, but it becomes raised and thicker, with discrete brown to black nodules and irregular edges.
   d. **Acral lentiginous melanoma** occurs on the palms, soles, and nail beds, occurs primarily in dark-skinned people, and metastasizes more frequently than do other melanomas, possibly related to later stage at presentation.
   e. **In-transit metastases** and **satellites** both signify a poor prognosis with a high risk of local recurrence and distant metastasis. In-transit metastases are lesions in the skin more than 2 cm from the primary lesion; they arise from tumor cells in intradermal lymphatics. Satellites are metastatic lesions in the skin within 2 cm of the primary tumor.

B. **History and risk factors.** A history for melanoma should include an assessment of risk factors and family history.

1. **Risk factors.** Each of the risk factors listed is considered to carry a more-than-threefold increase in risk for melanoma; the presence of three or more risk factors carries approximately 20 times the risk (*Curr Probl Surg.* 2006;43:781).

   a. Family or personal history of melanoma.

   b. Blond or red hair.

   c. Freckling of the upper back.

   d. Three or more blistering sunburns before age of 20 years.

   e. Presence of actinic keratosis.

   f. Blue, green, or gray eyes.

C. **Clinical features.** Early melanoma and dysplastic lesions can be recognized by the features highlighted in the mnemonic **ABCD:** *A*symmetry, *b*order irregularity, *c*olor variegation, and *d*iameter greater than 6 mm. Advanced lesions are more readily apparent and may be nodular or ulcerated.

D. **Staging and prognosis.** Tumor thickness is the most important factor in staging the tumor. Tumors less than 1 mm thick have 10-year survival of 92%, whereas 10-year survival for lesions more than 4 mm thick is 50% (*J Clin Oncol.* 2009;27:6199). Thickness is also correlated with the risk of regional node and distant metastasis (*J Clin Oncol.* 2001;19:3622). The Breslow thickness is a physical depth measurement of the primary tumor and is used to classify the tumor (see "T Classification" in Table 25-1). In contrast, the *Clark level* describes the *anatomic* level of invasion (Table 25-2). The Clark level was historically used as a staging criterion for melanoma; however, it is no longer used for this purpose as recent studies have shown it is not an independent prognostic factor. Mitotic rate of the primary melanoma has emerged as a better predictor of clinical outcomes in recent studies and has been incorporated into recent staging systems. The revised American Joint Committee on Cancer (AJCC) system of TNM (tumor, node, metastasis) classification for melanoma (Tables 25-1 and 25-3) is the standard classification system. This system was revised in 2009 to provide more accurate and precise information regarding patient prognosis (*J Clin Oncol* 2009;27:6199). Older age, male gender, satellitosis, ulceration, and location on the *b*ack, posterolateral *a*rm, *n*eck, or *s*calp (the BANS region) all carry a worse prognosis. The presence of regional node metastasis severely worsens prognosis (10-year survival, 20% to 60%). Distant metastases have a dismal prognosis (median survival, 2 to 11 months).

E. **Treatment**

1. **Surgery**

   a. **Wide local excision** is the primary treatment for most melanomas and premalignant lesions. Melanoma in situ (MIS) should be excised to clean margins. For all other malignant melanomas, the width of the surgical margin depends on the Breslow tumor thickness: Thin melanomas (Breslow thickness <1 mm) should have a margin of 1 cm; lesions thicker than 1 mm and all scalp lesions should have a margin of at least 2 cm. Several prospective, randomized trials

TABLE 25-1	American Joint Committee on Cancer TNM (Tumor, Node, Metastasis) Definitions of Melanoma	
T classification	—	—
Tis	Melanoma in situ	—
T1	≤1.0 mm	a. Without ulceration and mitosis <1/mm^2
	—	b. With ulceration or mitoses ≥1/mm^2
T2	1.01–2.0 mm	a. Without ulceration
	—	b. With ulceration
T3	2.01–4.0 mm	a. Without ulceration
	—	b. With ulceration
T4	>4.0 mm	a. Without ulceration
	—	b. With ulceration
Regional lymph nodes (N)	—	—
N1	One lymph node	a. Micrometastasis[a]
	—	b. Macrometastasis[b]
N2	2–3 lymph nodes	a. Micrometastasis[a]
	—	b. Macrometastasis[b]
	—	c. In-transit met(s)/satellite(s) without metastatic lymph node(s)
N3	≥4 metastatic lymph nodes, matted lymph nodes, or in-transit met(s)/satellite(s) with metastatic lymph node(s)	
Distant metastasis (M)	—	—
M1a	Distant skin, subcutaneous, or lymph node mets	Normal LDH
M1b	Lung mets	Normal LDH
M1c	All other visceral mets	Normal LDH
	Any distant mets	Elevated LDH

[a]Micrometastases are diagnosed after sentinel or completion lymphadenectomy (if performed).
[b]Macrometastases are defined as clinically detectable lymph node metastases confirmed by therapeutic lymphadenectomy or when any lymph node metastasis exhibits gross extracapsular extension.
LDH, lactic dehydrogenase; mets, metastases.
Modified from Balch CM, Gershenwald JE, Soong SJ, et al. Melanoma of the skin. In: Edge SE, Byrd DR, Carducci MA, et al., eds. *AJCC Cancer Staging Manual.* 7th ed. New York, NY: Springer; 2010: 325–44.

TABLE 25-2	Clark's Classification (Level of Invasion) of Melanoma
Level I	Lesions involving only the epidermis (in situ melanoma); not an invasive lesion
Level II	Invasion of the papillary dermis but does not reach the papillary–reticular dermal interface
Level III	Invasion fills and expands the papillary dermis but does not penetrate the reticular dermis
Level IV	Invasion into the reticular dermis but not into the subcutaneous tissue
Level V	Invasion through the reticular dermis into the subcutaneous tissue

have investigated margin requirements. A seminal trial addressed the efficacy of 2-cm versus 4-cm margins for Breslow thickness 1 to 4 mm (*Ann Surg.* 1993;218:262). There was no significant difference in the local recurrence rate, disease-free survival, or overall survival between the two groups at 10 years of follow-up (*Ann Surg Oncol.* 2001;8:101). These data suggest that a 2-cm margin is both safe and effective for primary melanomas between 1 and 4 mm, with a significant decrease in the need for skin grafting. In general, excisions should be closed primarily, with flaps or skin grafts reserved for large defects. Mohs micrographic surgery has been advocated for areas where wide and deep excisions are difficult, such as the face, or for MIS. Several single-institution series using Mohs techniques for facial lentigo maligna melanoma have shown highly variable recurrence rates ranging from 0% to 33% (*Int J Dermatol.* 2010;49:482).

b. **Elective lymph node dissection (ELND).** The term "elective" refers here to lymph node dissection done in the absence of clinically evident, palpable nodes (for palpable nodes, see Section 1.d of this part on therapeutic lymph node dissection). In the past, ELND was at times performed for the staging of patients presenting with localized melanoma. ELND provided an element of local control and reasonably accurate staging for patients with occult lymph node metastases (*Ann Surg.* 1991;214:491). Several large trials, such as the World Health Organization trial number 1, World Health Organization trial number 14, the Mayo Clinical Surgical Trial, and the Intergroup Melanoma Surgical Trial, investigated whether ELND provides benefit to patients, particularly regarding survival. The Intergroup Trial showed that ELND in patients with intermediate-thickness tumors (Breslow thickness 1 to 4 mm) improved survival, especially for patients under the age of 60 years.

Stage	Clinical Staging[a]			Pathologic Staging[b]		
0	Tis	N0	M0	Tis	N0	M0
IA	T1a	N0	M0	T1a	N0	M0
IB	T1b	N0	M0	T1b	N0	M0
	T2a	N0	M0	T2a	N0	M0
IIA	T2b	N0	M0	T2b	N0	M0
	T3a	N0	M0	T3a	N0	M0
IIB	T3b	N0	M0	T3b	N0	M0
	T4a	N0	M0	T4a	N0	M0
IIC	T4b	N0	M0	T4b	N0	M0
III[c]	Any T	≥N1	M0	—	—	—
IIIA	—	—	—	T1–4a	N1a	M0
—	—	—	—	T1–4a	N2a	M0
IIIB	—	—	—	T1–4b	N1a	M0
—	—	—	—	T1–4b	N2a	M0
—	—	—	—	T1–4a	N1b	M0
—	—	—	—	T1–4a	N2b	M0
—	—	—	—	T1–4a	N2c	M0
IIIC	—	—	—	T1–4b	N1b	M0
—	—	—	—	T1–4b	N2b	M0
—	—	—	—	T1–4b	N2c	M0
—	—	—	—	Any T	N3	M0
IV	Any T	Any N	M1	Any T	Any N	M1

[a]Clinical staging includes microstaging of the primary melanoma and clinical/radiologic evaluation for metastases. By convention, it should be used after complete excision of the primary melanoma with clinical assessment for regional and distant metastases.

[b]Pathologic staging includes microstaging of the primary melanoma and pathologic information about the regional lymph nodes after partial or complete lymphadenectomy, except for pathologic stage 0 or stage Ia patients, who do not need pathologic evaluation of their lymph nodes.

[c]There are no stage III subgroups for clinical staging.

Modified from Balch CM, Gershenwald JE, Soong SJ, et al. Melanoma of the skin. In: Edge SE, Byrd DR, Carducci MA, et al., eds. *AJCC Cancer Staging Manual*. 7th ed. New York, NY: Springer; 2010: 325–344.

ELND has not been conclusively shown to benefit other subgroups (*Ann Surg.* 1996;224:255). This remains a controversial issue.

c. **Sentinel lymph node biopsy (SLNB).** SLNB has greatly enhanced accurate staging of patients with melanoma. This technique is based on the documented pattern of lymphatic drainage of melanomas to a specific, initial lymph node, termed the *sentinel lymph node*, before further spread. The histology of the SLN is highly (although not perfectly) reflective of the rest of the nodal basin. If the SLN is negative for metastases, a more radical and morbid lymph node dissection can be avoided. This procedure requires expertise and a multidisciplinary approach involving radiology/nuclear medicine and pathology. The SLN can be accurately identified 96% of the time using radiolymphoscintigraphy and intraoperative dye injection and radioprobe guidance. SLNB appears to be most beneficial for intermediate-thickness melanomas (Breslow thickness 1 to 4 mm) (*Ann Surg.* 2001;233:250). Data from the Multicenter Sentinel Lymphadenectomy Trial (MSLT)-I, a prospective, randomized, multinational trial, support the role of SLN and immediate (vs. delayed) complete lymphadenectomy if the SLN is positive. In MSLT-I, 1,269 patients with intermediate-thickness melanomas (1.2 to 3.5 mm) were randomized to either wide excision only followed by observation (no SLNB) or to wide excision and SLNB. In the observation-only group, complete lymphadenectomy was performed only when there was clinical evidence of nodal recurrence (delayed), whereas the SLNB group underwent a complete (immediate) lymphadenectomy if nodal micrometastases were detected in any of the SLNs. The results from this landmark trial showed that the mean estimated 5-year disease-free survival rate was significantly higher in the SLNB group than in the observation-only group (78.3% vs. 73.1%, respectively; $p = 0.009$) (*N Engl J Med.* 2006;355:1307). Although 5-year melanoma-specific survival rates were similar in the two groups, the presence of metastatic disease within the SLN was found to be the most important prognostic factor predictive of overall survival. The 5-year survival rate was 72.3% in those patients with tumor-positive SLNs and 90.2% in those with tumor-negative SLNs. For thin melanomas (≤1 mm thickness), the incidence of positive SLN is 2 to 5% in retrospective series (*Surg Oncol Clin N Am.* 2007;16:35). Factors which were predictive of a positive SLN in patients with thin melanomas included Breslow thickness, Clark level, mitotic rate, and younger age (*Arch Surg.* 2008;143:892). Current practice guidelines issued by the National Comprehensive Cancer Network (NCCN) recommend that SLNB be considered for patients with high-risk stage IA melanoma and discussed and offered to patients with stage IB-IIC melanomas (*NCCN Clinical Practice Guidelines in Oncology—Melanoma.* 2010, v. 2).

d. **Therapeutic lymph node dissection** should be performed for involved axillary and superficial inguinal lymph nodes unless unresectable distant metastases are present. Ideally, therapeutic LND provides optimal locoregional control of disease and a chance of cure, with 5-year survival rates of 20% to 40% (*Ann Surg Oncol.* 1998;5:473). Surgical therapy of the inguinal region includes a superficial inguinal lymphadenectomy with inclusion of the deep pelvic region for either clinical evidence of disease (palpable pelvic nodes) or radiographic or intraoperative evidence of obvious lymph node involvement. Intraoperative pathologic analysis of clinically suspicious lymph nodes may be necessary to determine the presence of metastases and possibly the need for more extensive nodal dissection. The highest superficial inguinal node (Cloquet node) can also be analyzed by frozen section to help determine the need for deep dissection. Deep inguinal node dissection should be reserved for patients whose survival is thought to justify the potential morbidity of the procedure. Hughes et al. noted that patients who underwent a superficial and deep nodal dissection (*n* = 72) had a lower regional recurrence rate than those who underwent a superficial dissection only (*n* = 60), although there was no statistical difference in overall survival (*Br J Surg.* 2000;87:892). In some cases, nodal dissection does not benefit patients with advanced disease and should therefore be carefully considered.

e. **Resection of metastases.** The surgical options for patients with metastatic melanoma can be divided into two categories: Curative or palliative. Curative interventions for metastatic melanoma should carefully weigh the risks of the surgery against the potential benefits. Recent data on the surgical management of metastatic melanoma note that certain factors are associated with an improved overall survival: (1) ability to achieve a complete resection with negative margins, (2) the initial site of metastasis, (3) extent of metastatic disease (single or multiple sites), (4) disease-free interval after surgical removal of the primary melanoma, and (5) stage of initial disease (*Curr Opin Oncol.* 2004;16:155). Favorable sites for resection include the skin, subcutaneous tissue, lymph nodes, lung, and gastrointestinal (GI) tract. Skin and subcutaneous metastases demonstrated the best long-term results after resection, with a 20% to 30% 5-year survival and a median survival of 48 months. Unfavorable sites include metastases to the brain, adrenal, and liver (*Arch Surg.* 2004;139:961).

2. **Isolated limb perfusion (ILP)** is used for recurrent limb melanoma that is locally advanced and cannot be resected by simple surgical means. ILP delivers high-dose regional chemotherapy and establishes a hyperthermic environment to an extremity though its circulation has been isolated from the rest of the body. Melphalan is commonly used. A large, retrospective meta-analysis reported complete response rates for melphalan with mild hyperthermic ILP range from 40% to 82% (median 54%) (*Eur J Surg Oncol.* 2006;32:371). Adding tumor necrosis factor (TNF)-α to melphalan has been suggested to increase the complete response rate to 60% to 85%. Randomized, multicenter data collected through the American College of Surgeons Oncology Group (ACOSOG) comparing hyperthermic ILP with melphalan alone to

melphalan plus TNF suggested that addition of TNF did not significantly enhance short-term response rates in locally advanced extremity melanoma; however, addition of TNF was found significantly to increase the overall complication rate (*J Clin Oncol.* 2006;24:4196). Patients who are elderly or who have medical comorbidities or systemic metastases are generally not suitable for this therapy.

3. **Immunotherapy.** Endeavors in both animals and humans have established that the immune system can damage or destroy even very large established tumors (*N Engl J Med.* 1984;313:1485, *J Exp Med.* 2005;202:907). Complete and durable regression of stage IV melanoma has been reported using interleukin-2 (IL-2)–based immunotherapy alone (*J Clin Oncol.* 1999;17:2105). However, treatment using IL-2 in conjunction with vaccine therapy may be more effective. Patients with metastatic melanoma who received IL-2 therapy in conjunction with gp209–2M peptide vaccine had a response rate of 22.3%, compared with 12.8% in those treated with only IL-2 ($p = 0.01$) and 13.8% in those treated with IL-2 plus other vaccines ($p = 0.009$) (*Clin Cancer Res* 2008;14:5612). High-dose interferon also has been studied in several randomized clinical trials. A pooled analysis of these trials, in patients with resected stage IIb or stage III melanoma treated with high-dose interferon versus observation, showed a significant benefit for relapse-free survival [hazard ratio (HR) = 1.3 for observation, $p = 0.006$], but no benefit in overall survival (*Clin Cancer Res.* 2004;10:1670). A recent trial of pegylated interferon versus observation in patients with resected stage III melanoma similarly showed a significant improvement in 4-year relapse-free survival (45.6% vs. 38.9%, $p = 0.01$), but no benefit for overall survival. The choice to initiate interferon therapy should be made only after a discussion with the patient about the considerable adverse effects of the drug in the context of these limited benefits.

F. **Hereditary tumor syndromes.** Melanoma is familial in approximately 10% of cases, and in these cases, it is often associated with multiple atypical moles. **Familial atypical multiple-mole melanoma syndrome (FAMMM)** has also been called *dysplastic nevus syndrome, B-K syndrome,* and *large atypical nevus syndrome.* A National Institutes of Health Consensus Conference defined FAMMM using the following criteria: (1) the occurrence of malignant melanoma in one or more first- or second-degree relatives, (2) a large number of melanocytic nevi, usually more than 50, some of which are atypical and variable in size, and (3) melanocytic nevi that have certain histopathologic features, including architectural disorder with asymmetry, subepidermal fibroplasia, and lentiginous melanocytic hyperplasia with spindle or epithelial melanocyte nests. These lesions predominantly occur on the trunk but are also found on the buttocks, scalp, and lower extremities. The relative risk for developing melanoma when multiple atypical moles are present ranges from 5 to 11 based on multiple studies. The median age for melanoma diagnosis is 34. ***CDKN2,*** a cell cycle protein gene, has been found to contain germline mutations in some kindreds with familial melanoma (*Nat Genet.* 1994;8:15). Other malignancies have been related to mutations in the *CDKN2* gene, especially pancreatic cancer. There may be other genes contributing to FAMMM. **Screening** for FAMMM begins at around puberty and consists of yearly physical examinations, including a total-body skin examination. For patients who have a large number of moles, baseline photographs or computerized scanning are helpful. Patients should examine their skin regularly. Suspicious lesions should undergo biopsy. Sun exposure should be avoided. Regular ophthalmologic examinations should be performed due to the increased risk of ocular nevi and ocular melanoma.

OTHER MALIGNANT SKIN TUMORS

I. **BASAL CELL CARCINOMA** is the most common malignant neoplasm of the skin; it derives from the basal cells of the epidermis and adnexal structures. They are slow growing and rarely metastasize (<0.1%) but can be locally aggressive. Sun exposure is the most significant epidemiologic factor; consequently, this neoplasm is found most commonly on the skin of the head and neck (85%) in fair-skinned patients older than 40 years.

A. **Lesions.** It is particularly important to identify the morpheaform carcinoma because it is more aggressive, with a tendency toward deep infiltration and local recurrence. These carcinomas are flat, indurated lesions with a smooth, whitish, waxy surface and indistinct borders. The noduloulcerative form is the most common and is characterized by shiny, translucent nodules with a central umbilication that often becomes ulcerated, with pearly, rolled, telangiectatic edges.

B. **Treatment**

1. **Excisional biopsy** is adequate treatment for small tumors, with intraoperative frozen-section analysis (to confirm negative margins) and primary closure. Larger tumors may be diagnosed by incisional or punch biopsy followed by complete removal. A margin of 2 to 4 mm on all sides of visible tumor should be obtained, and positive margins on frozen-section analysis should be re-excised. Margins of dysplasia or actinic changes need not be re-excised because local recurrence generally does not occur in these cases. The patient should be warned about possible pigmentation persistence.

2. **Mohs micrographic surgery** may be useful for recurrent tumors or in situations in which tissue conservation is important.

3. **Curettage with electrodesiccation** can be performed for small superficial tumors, with little risk of recurrence.

4. **Liquid nitrogen** can be used for tumors less than 1 cm in diameter.

5. **Radiation therapy** can be used in certain situations for areas difficult to reconstruct, such as the eyelids. It also can be used for palliation in patients who have large tumors and who might refuse an extensive operation, especially the elderly. Although re-excision is indicated for recurrences or positive margins, radiation therapy can be used in individual circumstances.

II. **SQUAMOUS CELL CARCINOMA** is the second-most-common skin cancer in fair-skinned people and is the most common cancer in darkly pigmented people. As with the other skin malignancies, sunlight is the major etiology, with the greatest risk in elderly men who have a history of chronic sun exposure. The mean age of presentation is 68 years, and men predominate two to one. Squamous cell carcinoma can be found on any sun-exposed area, including mucous membranes. It also is known to develop from draining sinuses, radiation, chronic ulcers, and scars (particularly burn scars, in which case it is called a *Marjolin ulcer*).

A. **Lesions.** Squamous cell carcinoma presents as small, firm, erythematous plaques with a smooth or verrucous surface and indistinct margins with progression to raised, fixed, and ulcerated lesions. Ulceration tends to occur earlier in aggressive lesions. Most lesions are preceded by actinic keratosis, which results in a slow-growing, locally invasive lesion without metastases. If not preceded by actinic keratosis, the cancer tends to be more aggressive, with more rapid growth, invasion, and metastatic spread. Perineural invasion has a poorer prognosis and higher recurrence rate.

B. **Treatment** is similar to that for basal cell carcinoma. Tumor-free margins of 5 mm for tumors of less than 1 cm and tumor-free margins of 1 to 2 cm for tumors of more than 2 cm in diameter should be obtained. Curettage with electrodesiccation and laser vaporization has been used for small, superficial squamous carcinomas, but there is no way to assess margins of treatment. Solitary metastases should be resected if possible because there is a relatively high cure rate compared to other cancers.

SOFT-TISSUE SARCOMAS

Soft-tissue sarcomas represent a heterogeneous group of malignant tumors derived from mesodermal tissues. STS are rare, constituting approximately 1% of adult malignant neoplasms and causing 3,100 deaths annually; many general surgeons will see few of these tumors during their careers. Most of these tumors arise *de novo,* rarely from premalignant tumors. In a minority of cases, STSs are associated with cancer predisposition syndromes such as von Recklinghausen disease, Werner syndrome, or Li–Fraumeni syndrome. Lymphedema and radiation have been shown to be etiologic factors in certain rare sarcomas (*Am Surg.* 2006;72:665).

I. **LESIONS.** Sarcomas are classified by histologic cell type of origin and grade. The most common subtype is malignant fibrous histiocytoma (40%), followed by liposarcoma (25%). Patients typically present with an asymptomatic lump or mass that has grown to be visible or palpable. Retroperitoneal tumor can reach massive proportions before increased abdominal girth and vague symptoms bring it to the physician's attention. Tumors also may grow unnoticed to large sizes in the thigh or trunk.

II. **DIAGNOSIS.** Biopsy (usually core or incisional) is necessary for diagnosis. Care is needed to orient incisions to aid in the definitive operation. Even small, apparently benign lesions should be biopsied or excised. Adequate tissue must be provided to pathology for histologic assessment.

TABLE 25-4	American Joint Committee on Cancer Staging System for Soft-Tissue Sarcoma

Tumor grade (G) GX: Grade cannot be assessed G1: Well differentiated G2: Moderately differentiated G3: Poorly differentiated G4: Undifferentiated	**Stage IA** G1/GX, T1a, N0, M0 G1/GX, T1b, N0, M0 **Stage IB** G1/GX, T2a, N0, M0 G1/GX, T2b, N0, M0
Primary tumor (T) TX: Primary tumor cannot be assessed T0: No evidence of primary tumor T1: Tumor ≤ 5 cm in greatest dimension T1a: Superficial tumor[a] T1b: Deep tumor[a] T2: Tumor >5 cm in greatest dimension T2a: Superficial tumor[a] T2b: Deep tumor[a]	**Stage IIA** G2–3, T1a, N0, M0 G2–3, T1b, N0, M0 **Stage IIB** G2, T2a, N0, M0 G2, T2b, N0, M0 **Stage III** G3, T2a, N0, M0 G3, T2b, N0, M0
Regional lymph nodes (N) NX: Regional lymph nodes cannot be assessed N0: No regional lymph node metastasis N1: Regional lymph node metastasis	Any G, any T, N1, M0 **Stage IV** Any G, any T, any N, M1 —
Distant metastasis (M) MX: Distant metastasis cannot be assessed M0: No distant metastasis M1: Distant metastasis	— — — —

[a]Superficial tumor is located exclusively above the superficial fascia without invasion of the fascia; deep tumor either is located exclusively beneath the superficial fascia or superficial to the fascia with invasion of or through the fascia or is located superficial and beneath the fascia. Retroperitoneal, mediastinal, and pelvic sarcomas are classified as deep tumors.

Modified from Soft tissue sarcoma. In: Edge SE, Byrd DR, Carducci MA, et al., eds. *AJCC Cancer Staging Manual.* 7th ed. New York, NY: Springer: 2010; 291–298.

III. **STAGING AND PROGNOSIS (TABLE 25-4).** The AJCC staging system is based on tumor size, nodal status, histologic grade, and metastasis. Of these, size and grade are the most important.

   A. **Grade.** The grade of the tumor is the major prognostic factor. Grade is obtained from histopathologic analysis of biopsy tissue and is generally based on the mitotic index, nuclear morphology, and degree of anaplasia. However, interobserver variability is high, with some centers having different criteria: Rates of discordance even among expert pathologists of up to 40% have been observed.

   B. **Staging** for STS includes physical examination and CT or MR scan to assess the size and extent of tumor. Metastases most commonly are found in the lungs; CT scan of the lungs is a required study for grade II and III lesions. Abdominal CT scan is required for evaluation of retroperitoneal sarcomas. This study can assess for hepatic metastases, which are more common for this primary. Retroperitoneal and truncal STS have worse prognoses than extremity STS.

C. **Prognosis.** Almost 80% of metastases are to the lungs and occur within 2 to 3 years of diagnosis. If the pulmonary disease is resectable, 30% survival at 3 years can be expected. In addition, tumor size, grade, tumor rupture during surgery, margins after resection, and anatomic location all have an impact on various outcome measures such as local recurrence, overall survival, and tumor-free survival. Local recurrence should be resected aggressively, and long-term follow-up is required because late recurrences may occur.

IV. SURGICAL TREATMENT

A. **Resection.** Smaller, grade I tumors can be excised with a minimum 1-cm margin, usually without adjuvant radiation. Larger tumors may benefit from a larger margin or radiation to prevent recurrence. Grade II and III tumors, in general, require radiation therapy in addition to excision to avoid more radical surgery. Depending on the size and grade of tumor, compartment resection may be indicated.

B. **Limb-sparing resection** combined with radiation therapy offers survival equivalent to that achieved with amputation (*Ann Surg.* 1982;196:305). Limb-sparing procedures have a distinct psychological as well as functional advantage and are the procedures of choice for most tumors. The tumor should be removed with an envelope of normal tissue surrounding it, if possible. The resection should include the area of previous incision and biopsy and any drain sites. The resection field should be marked with clips to guide radiation therapy.

C. **Gastrointestinal stromal tumors (GISTs)** are sarcomatous tumors of the GI tract. These tumors are rare and most commonly arise from the stomach. GIST can present with acute or subacute GI bleeding, vague abdominal pain, a palpable abdominal mass, or as an incidental mass found on CT scan of the abdomen. These tumors are distinguished from other tumors of the GI tract by expression of c-*kit* (CD117). Surgical resection with microscopically negative margins is standard treatment. Imatinib mesylate (Gleevec), a tyrosine kinase inhibitor, has been approved to treat patients with unresectable or metastatic GIST. Patients with GIST that is resistant to imatinib may have a response to sunitinib, which has been approved as second-line treatment for these tumors.

D. **Retroperitoneal sarcomas** are considerably more difficult to treat because the tumors often involve vital structures. Operative intervention employs resection of as much tumor as possible with a wide margin. Organs associated with the tumor should be resected *en bloc* to completely remove the tumor. A recent large retrospective study demonstrated a 5-year recurrence rate of 48% for simple removal of involved tissues versus 28% for *en bloc* resection, with a non-significant trend towards improved overall survival with more aggressive surgery (*J Clin Oncol.* 2009;27:24). An initial tissue diagnosis is often obtained by core biopsy. Postoperative irradiation may be used in some cases but is associated with relatively high morbidity, often due to irradiation of normal intestines and other organs. Wide margins are often not achievable in the retroperitoneum and limit the effectiveness of surgery. For these reasons, preoperative irradiation therapy, with the tumor in place displacing normal organs, is increasingly favored. Studies are beginning to reveal recurrence and survival benefits. Some surgeons, however, remain concerned about irradiation making surgical dissection more difficult. For tumor recurrences, surgical resection is the therapy of choice. Gronchi et al. studied 167 consecutive patients who underwent operation for retroperitoneal STS; complete resection of all gross disease was achieved in 88% of patients. Overall survival at 10 years was 27%, and disease-free survival was 16%. The 10-year disease-free survival rate was 27% for patients who underwent resection for primary sarcomas compared with 5% for patients who underwent resection for recurrent retroperitoneal sarcoma (*Cancer.* 2004;100:2448). The data suggest that novel treatment approaches are needed for prevention of local, regional, and distant recurrences.

V. OTHER ADJUVANT THERAPY

A. **Interstitial perioperative radiation therapy (brachytherapy)** involves the use of catheters or implants placed at the time of surgery to provide radiation directly to the tumor bed. Afterloading involves loading of the radiation source through catheters postoperatively to deliver localized high-dose radiation to the tumor bed. Brachytherapy has at least two advantages: It requires a short course of in-hospital treatment rather than 5 to 6 weeks of outpatient external-beam radiation therapy, and it can provide dose control near sensitive areas, such as joints and blood vessels. There is evidence that it is effective at decreasing local recurrence for high-grade tumors when combined with surgery.

B. **Chemotherapy.** Several randomized, prospective trials have failed to show any improvement in survival with adjuvant chemotherapy for adult grade II or III sarcomas. The two drugs with the greatest efficacy are doxorubicin and ifosfamide; however, even these have, at best, a 40% to 60% response rate. Recent data from two institutional prospective sarcoma databases identified patients who underwent resection for high-grade extremity liposarcoma greater than 5 cm in size. Using contemporary cohort analysis, the authors concluded that doxorubicin is not associated with improved disease-specific survival, but that ifosfamide is associated with improved disease-specific survival (*Ann Surg.* 2004;240:697). Doxorubicin, ifosfamide, and dacarbazine are all used as single agents or in combination therapy. Gemcitabine–docetaxel combination therapy has also demonstrated improved progression-free survival and overall survival for metastatic STS (*J Clin Oncol.* 2007;25:2755).

C. **ILP** provides increased delivery of therapy (e.g., hyperthermic therapy and chemotherapy) to an extremity sarcoma while reducing systemic toxicity. There is some suggestion of decreased local recurrence with definite downstaging of the tumor, but there is no improvement in survival (*Ann Surg Oncol.* 2007;14:230).

VI. HEREDITARY TUMOR SYNDROMES: SARCOMAS. Soft-tissue sarcomas have been identified in several familial cancer syndromes, including Li–Fraumeni syndrome, hereditary retinoblastoma, and neurofibromatosis types 1 and 2. The prognosis is highly dependent on the tumor grade.

26 Hernia

Lora Melman and Brent D. Matthews

I. INGUINAL HERNIA

A. **Incidence. The true incidence and prevalence of inguinal hernia worldwide is unknown.** The etiology of inguinal hernia formation is a by-product of genetic, environmental, and metabolic factors, combined with individual patient factors that can vary over time such as activity level, immune status, infection(s), medications, personal habits (e.g., smoking), and change in body mass index (*Surg Clin North Am.* 2008;88:179–201). Laparoscopic studies have reported rates of contralateral defects as high as 22%, with 28% of these going on to become symptomatic during short-term follow-up. The male-to-female ratio is greater than 10:1. Lifetime prevalence is 25% in men and 2% in women. Two-thirds of inguinal hernias are indirect. Nearly two-thirds of recurrent hernias are direct. Approximately 10% of inguinal hernias will become incarcerated, and a portion of these may become strangulated. Recurrence rates after surgical repair are less than 1% in children and vary in adults according to the method of hernia repair.

B. **Terminology and anatomy**

1. **The inguinal canal** (Fig. 26-1) is a tunnel that traverses the layers of the abdominal wall musculature, bounded on the lateral deep aspect by an opening in the transversalis fascia/transversus abdominis muscle (internal inguinal ring), and travels along the fused edges of the transversus abdominis/internal oblique/inguinal ligament (iliopubic tract) posteriorly and layers of the external oblique musculature anteriorly, ending on the medial superficial aspect at an opening in the external oblique aponeurosis (external inguinal ring). The inguinal canal houses the spermatic cord (males) or the round ligament (females) and is subject to hernia formation due primarily to decreased mechanical integrity of the internal ring and/or transversalis fascia, allowing intra-abdominal contents to encroach into this space, forming a characteristic bulge.

2. **Direct hernias** occur as a result of weakness in the posterior wall of the inguinal canal, which is usually a result of attenuation of the transversalis fascia. The hernia sac protrudes through Hesselbach's triangle, which is the space bounded by the inferior epigastric artery, the lateral edge of the rectus sheath, and the inguinal ligament.

3. **Indirect hernias** pass through the internal inguinal ring lateral to Hesselbach's triangle and follow the spermatic cord in males and the round ligament in females. During dissection, an indirect hernia sac is typically found on the anteromedial aspect of the spermatic cord. Indirect hernias may become incarcerated at either the internal or external ring.

4. **In combined (pantaloon) hernias,** direct and indirect hernias coexist.

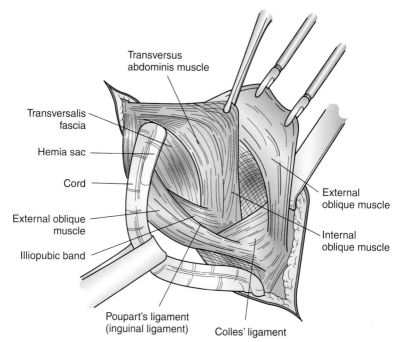

Figure 26-1. Anatomy of the right inguinal region.

5. A **sliding hernia** (usually indirect inguinal) denotes that a part of the wall of the hernia sac is formed by an intra-abdominal viscus (usually colon, sometimes bladder). In a **Richter hernia,** part (rather than the entire circumference) of the bowel wall is trapped. A **Littré hernia** is one that contains a Meckel's diverticulum. An **Amyand hernia** is one that contains the appendix.

6. **Incarcerated hernias** cannot be reduced into the abdominal cavity, whereas strangulated hernias have incarcerated contents with vascular compromise. Frequently, intense pain is caused by ischemia of the incarcerated segment.

C. Diagnosis

1. Clinical presentation

a. **Most inguinal hernias** present as an intermittent bulge that appears in the groin. In males, it may extend into the scrotal sac. Symptoms are usually related to exertion or long periods of standing. The patient may complain of unilateral discomfort without noting a mass. Often, a purposeful Valsalva maneuver can reproduce the symptoms and/or the presence of a bulge. In infants and children, a groin bulge is often noticed by caregivers during episodes of crying or defecation. Only in rare cases do patients present with bowel obstruction without the presence of a groin abnormality. All patients presenting with small bowel obstruction must be questioned carefully and examined for all types of hernia (i.e., inguinal, umbilical, incisional, etc.) as a possible etiology of obstruction.

   b. Physical examination. The main diagnostic maneuver for inguinal hernias is palpation of the inguinal region. The patient is best examined while standing and straining (cough or Valsalva). Hernias manifest as bulges with smooth, rounded surfaces that become more evident with straining. The hernia sac can also be examined more clearly by invaginating the hemiscrotum to introduce an index finger through the external inguinal ring. This may become uncomfortable for the patient and is unnecessary if an obvious bulge is present. It is often difficult, if not impossible, to determine whether the hernia is direct or indirect based solely on physical examination. Incarcerated inguinal hernias present with pain, abdominal distention, nausea, and vomiting due to intestinal obstruction.

2. **Radiographic evaluation.** X-ray studies are rarely indicated. Ultrasonography or computed tomographic (CT) scan may occasionally be used to diagnose an occult groin hernia, particularly in the obese patient. Plain abdominal radiographs may verify intestinal obstruction in cases of incarceration.

D. **Differential diagnosis.** Inguinal hernias should be distinguished from femoral hernias, which protrude below the inguinal ligament. Inguinal adenopathy, lipomas, dilation of the saphenous vein, epididymitis, testicular torsion, groin abscess, and vascular aneurysms/pseudoaneurysms all should be considered.

E. **Treatment**

1. **Preoperative evaluation and preparation.** Most patients with hernias should be treated surgically, although "watchful waiting" may be appropriate for individuals with asymptomatic hernias or for elderly patients with minimally symptomatic hernias (*JACS.* 2006;203:458–468). Associated conditions that lead to increased intra-abdominal pressure such as chronic cough, constipation, or bladder outlet obstruction should be evaluated and remedied to the extent possible before elective herniorrhaphy. In patients with symptoms of altered bowel habits (i.e., frequent straining/constipation), one may wish to assess the risk of underlying colorectal malignancy, depending on the age and family history of the patient. In cases of intestinal obstruction and possible strangulation, broad-spectrum antibiotics and nasogastric suction may be indicated. Correction of volume status and electrolyte abnormalities is important when there is associated small bowel obstruction.

2. **Reduction.** Temporary management includes manual reduction. In uncomplicated cases, the hernia reduces with palpation over the inguinal canal with the patient supine. If this does not occur, the physician applies gentle pressure over the hernia with the concavity of the palm of his or her hand and fingers. The palm of the physician's hand exerts a steady but gentle pressure and also maintains the direction to be followed: craniad and lateral for direct hernias, craniad and posterior for

femoral hernias. If the herniated viscera do not reduce, gentle traction over the mass with compression may allow bowel gas to leave the herniated segment, making the mass reducible. Sedation and Trendelenburg position may be required for reduction of an incarcerated hernia, but the difficulty of distinguishing between acute incarceration and strangulation should be noted, as the inguinal canal can become quite tender with or without ischemic contents. When an incarcerated hernia is reduced nonsurgically, the patient should be observed for the potential development of peritonitis caused by perforation or ischemic necrosis of a loop of strangulated bowel. Strong suspicion of strangulation (i.e., erythema over hernia site, pain out of proportion to examination, patient appears toxic, or persistent pain after reduction) is a surgical emergency; the patient should be expeditiously taken to the operating room to reduce the risk of death from intra-abdominal sepsis.

3. **Surgical treatment**
   a. **Choice of anesthetic.** Local anesthesia, which has several advantages over general or regional (spinal or epidural) anesthesia, is the preferred anesthetic for elective open repair for small- to moderate-sized hernias. Local anesthesia results in better postoperative analgesia, a shorter recovery room stay, and a negligible rate of postoperative urinary retention; it is the lowest-risk anesthetic for patients with underlying cardiopulmonary disorders. Commonly, a mixture of a short-acting agent (lidocaine 1%) and longer-acting agent (bupivacaine 0.25% to 0.50%) is used. The dose limits for local anesthesia are 4.5 mg/kg plain lidocaine or 7 mg/kg lidocaine with epinephrine and 2 mg/kg plain bupivacaine or 3 mg/kg bupivacaine with epinephrine. Use of local anesthesia for herniorrhaphy in our hospital is routinely supplemented by monitored anesthesia care and administration of intravenous midazolam and propofol. Virtually all patients who undergo hernia repair under local anesthesia can be managed as outpatients unless associated medical conditions or extenuating social circumstances necessitate overnight observation in the hospital. Laparoscopic hernia repair is almost always performed under general anesthesia to facilitate tolerance of pneumoperitoneum.
   b. **Treatment of the hernia sac.** For indirect hernias, the sac (peritonealized abdominal contents) is dissected from the spermatic cord and cremasteric fibers [Figure 26-1]. The sac can be ligated deep into the internal ring with an absorbable suture after reduction of herniated contents, or just invaginated back into the abdomen without ligation. Large, indirect sacs that extend into the scrotum should not be dissected beyond the pubic tubercle because of an increased risk of ischemic orchitis. Similarly, one should avoid translocating the testicle into the inguinal canal during hernia repair owing to the risk of ischemia or torsion. Cord lipomas are frequently encountered during repair and should be excised or reduced into the preperitoneal space to avoid future confusion with a recurrent hernia. Sliding hernia sacs can usually be managed by reducing the sac and attached viscera. Direct sacs are usually too broadly based for ligation and should not be opened. The redundant attenuated

tissue may be inverted and the inguinal floor reconstructed with a few interrupted sutures before placement of mesh.

c. **Primary tissue repairs** without mesh were the mainstay of hernia surgery for decades, prior to the development of synthetic meshes. While primary repair avoids placement of foreign prosthetic material, disadvantages of this approach include higher recurrence rates (5% to 10% for primary repairs and 15% to 30% for repair of recurrent hernias) due to tension on the repair and a slower return to unrestricted physical activity. Although the vast majority of hernias are now treated with a tension-free mesh repair, a primary tissue repair can be considered in contaminated wounds, in which placement of synthetic material is contraindicated. The principal features of the more commonly performed tissue repairs are the following:

(1) **Bassini repair.** The inferior arch of the transversalis fascia or conjoint tendon is approximated to the shelving portion of the inguinal ligament (iliopubic tract) with interrupted, nonabsorbable sutures. The Bassini repair has been used for simple, indirect hernias, including inguinal hernias in women.

(2) **McVay repair.** The transversalis fascia is sutured to the Cooper ligament medial to the femoral vein and the inguinal ligament at the level of, and lateral to, the femoral vein. This operation usually requires placement of a relaxing incision medially on the aponeuroses of the internal oblique muscle to avoid undue tension on the repair. The McVay repair closes the femoral space and therefore, unlike the Bassini repair, is effective for femoral hernias.

(3) **Shouldice repair.** In this repair, the transversalis fascia is incised (and partially excised if weakened) and reapproximated. The overlying tissues (the conjoint tendon, iliopubic tract, and inguinal ligament) are approximated in multiple, imbricated layers of running nonabsorbable suture. The experience of the Shouldice Clinic with this repair has been excellent, with recurrence rates of less than 1%, but higher recurrence rates have been reported in nonspecialized centers.

(a) **Open tension-free repairs.** The most common mesh inguinal hernia repairs performed today are the tension-free mesh hernioplasty (Lichtenstein repair) and the patch-and-plug technique. In the Lichtenstein repair, a piece of polypropylene mesh approximately 5 × 3 in. is used to reconstruct the inguinal floor (Fig. 26-2). The mesh is sutured to the fascia overlying the pubic tubercle inferiorly, the transversalis fascia and conjoint tendon medially, and the inguinal ligament laterally. The mesh is slit at the level of the internal ring, and the two limbs are crossed around the spermatic cord and then tacked to the inguinal ligament, effectively re-creating a new internal ring. This repair avoids the approximation of attenuated tissues under tension, and recurrence rates with this technique have been consistently 1% or less. Moreover, because the repair is

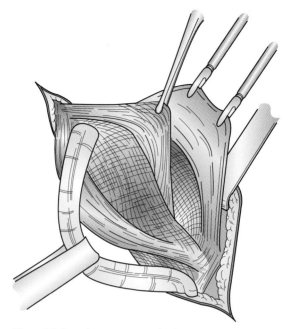

Figure 26-2. Lichtenstein tension-free hernia repair.

without tension, patients are allowed to return to unrestricted physical activity in 2 weeks or less. The mesh plug technique entails placement of a preformed plug of mesh in the hernia defect (e.g., internal ring) that is sutured to the rings of the fascial opening. An onlay piece of mesh is then placed over the inguinal floor, which may or may not be sutured to the fascia. Mesh plugs may be ideally suited for the repair of small, tight defects such as femoral hernias. Another technique involves the use of a bilayer mesh in which the posterior leaflet is placed in the preperitoneal space and the anterior leaflet is sutured to the same layers as that in the Lichtenstein repair.

(b) **Laparoscopic inguinal hernia repair.** The laparoscopic hernia repair is based on the technique of Stoppa, who used an open preperitoneal approach to reduce the hernia and placed a large piece of mesh to cover the entire inguinal floor and myopectineal orifice. Laparoscopic hernia repair is typically advocated in the elective setting; it is nonoptimal for patients presenting with signs and symptoms of incarceration or strangulation. Other contraindications to the laparoscopic approach include inability to tolerate general anesthesia and/or pneumoperitoneum, or the presence of a hernia with a significant scrotal component, which is more difficult to reduce laparoscopically. There are two approaches to laparoscopic repair of inguinal hernias:

(i) **Transabdominal preperitoneal (TAPP) repair.** In the TAPP technique, the peritoneal space is entered by conventional means at the umbilicus, the peritoneum overlying the inguinal floor is dissected away as a flap, the hernia is reduced, mesh is fixed over the internal ring opening in the preperitoneal space, and the peritoneum is reapproximated. The advantages of the TAPP approach are that a large working space is retained, familiar anatomic landmarks are visible, and the contralateral groin can be examined for an occult hernia.

(ii) **Totally extraperitoneal repair (TEP).** In the TEP technique, the preperitoneal space is developed with a dissecting balloon inserted between the posterior rectus sheath and the rectus abdominis and directed toward the pelvis inferior to the arcuate ligament (Fig. 26-3). The other ports are inserted into this preperitoneal space without ever entering the peritoneal cavity. The advantages of the TEP repair are that the peritoneum is not opened, which minimizes exposure of the mesh to the intra-abdominal viscera, thereby minimizing the risk of intestinal adhesions.

In either the TAPP or TEP technique, a large piece of mesh (6 × 4 in.) is placed over the inguinal floor and fixed superiorly to the posterior abdominal wall fascia on either side of the inferior epigastric vessels, medially to the Cooper ligament and the midline, and superolateral to the fascia above the internal ring. Staples/tacks must not be placed inferomedial to the internal ring or inferior to the iliopubic tract because of the risk of injury to the external iliac vessels (triangle of doom) and ilioinguinal, genitofemoral, lateral femoral cutaneous, and femoral nerves (triangle of pain). Studies comparing laparoscopic and open approaches to inguinal hernia repair have shown that laparoscopic repair is associated with less postoperative pain and faster recovery than open repair but that hospital costs have been higher for the laparoscopic technique. Operative times, complications, and recurrence rates (<3% for both laparoscopic and open repairs) have been similar. Recent randomized controlled trials, including the LEVEL trial of 660 patients randomized to Lichtenstein or TEP repair, concluded that laparoscopic repair was associated with earlier discharge from hospital, quicker return to normal activity and work, and significantly fewer postoperative complications than open

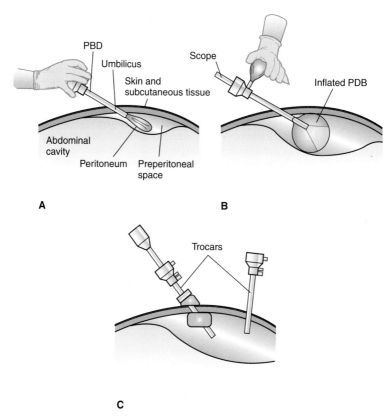

PBD
Umbilicus
Scope
Skin and
subcutaneous tissue
Inflated PDB
Abdominal
cavity
Peritoneum   Preperitoneal
space

A   **B**

Trocars

C

Figure 26-3. Laparoscopic total extraperitoneal approach with preperitoneal balloon dilation (PBD).

inguinal hernia repair. Operating times were significantly longer for laparoscopic repairs (p <0.001), but recurrence rate at mean follow-up of 49 months was similar (p = 0.64) (*Ann Surg.* 2010;251:819–824; *Int J Surg.* 2010;8:25–28). Another randomized trial comparing open and laparoscopic mesh inguinal hernia repairs at 14 Veterans Affairs (VA) institutions concluded that the open technique is superior to the laparoscopic technique for mesh repair of primary hernias due to decreased recurrence (4% vs. 10.1%) and complication rates (33.4% vs. 39%) (*N Engl J Med.* 2004;350:1819).

Special circumstances in which laparoscopic repair may also be favored include (1) recurrent hernias to avoid the scar tissue in the inguinal canal, (2) bilateral hernias, because both sides of the groin can be repaired with the same three small incisions used for the unilateral repair, (3) individuals with a unilateral hernia for whom a rapid recovery is critical (e.g., athletes and laborers), and (4) obese patients. Laparoscopic hernia repair is contraindicated in patients who have large scrotal hernias or who have undergone prior extensive lower abdominal or pelvic surgery.

d. **Complications.** Surgical complications include hematoma, infection, nerve injury (ilioinguinal, iliohypogastric, genital branch of the genitofemoral, lateral femoral cutaneous, femoral), vascular injury (femoral vessels, testicular artery, pampiniform venous plexus), vas deferens injury, ischemic orchitis, and testicular atrophy. Recurrence rates after tension-free mesh repairs for primary hernias are 1% to 2% or less.

e. **Recurrent inguinal hernias** are more difficult to repair because the scar makes dissection difficult and the disease process has continued. Recurrence within 1 year of initial repair suggests an inadequate initial attempt, such as overlooking an indirect hernia sac. Recurrence after 2 or more years suggests progression of the disease process that caused the initial hernia (e.g., increased intra-abdominal pressure, degeneration of tissues). Recurrences should be repaired because the defect usually is small with fixed edges that are prone to complications such as incarceration or strangulation. Repair can be done by an anterior approach through the old operative field or by a posterior (open preperitoneal or laparoscopic) approach. Prosthetic mesh is almost always used to reinforce attenuated tissues unless the operative field is contaminated.

F. **Prosthetic mesh in inguinal hernia repairs.** The choice of mesh for inguinal hernia repair is expanding rapidly as industries compete to produce the ideal prosthetic material that provides the right combination of strength to prevent recurrence and flexibility to minimize chronic postoperative pain and/or the sensation of feeling a foreign body. Examples of the three basic classes of synthetic meshes available to surgeons for use in inguinal hernia repair are summarized in Table 26-1. Recent randomized clinical trials demonstrate that lightweight polypropylene meshes for Lichtenstein hernia repair does not affect recurrence rates and offer improved aspects of postoperative pain and discomfort (*Hernia.* 2010;14:253–258). These results support the use of newer, lighter-weight mesh materials in inguinal hernia repair.

II. FEMORAL HERNIAS

A. **Incidence.** Femoral hernias constitute up to 2% to 4% of all groin hernias; 70% occur in women. Approximately 25% of femoral hernias become incarcerated or strangulated, and a similar number are missed or diagnosed late.

TABLE 26-1	Weight Classes of Mesh Used in Inguinal Hernia Repair		
Material	Marlex[a] (Heavyweight) Polypropylene	Prolene Soft[b] (Midweight) Polypropylene	Ultrapro[b] (Lightweight) Polypropylene, poliglecaprone
Weight (g/m^2)	95	45	28
Pore size (mm)	0.6	2.4	4
Burst strength (newtons)	1,218	590	576
Stiffness (newtons/cm)	59.1	49.1	43.2

[a]Davol, Inc., Cranston, RI.
[b]Ethicon, Inc., Somerville, NJ.
Adapted from Cobb WS, Burns JM, Peindl RD, et al. Textile analysis of heavy weight, mid-weight, and light weight polypropylene mesh in a porcine ventral hernia model. *J Surg Res.* 2006;136(1):1–7.

B. **Anatomy.** The abdominal viscera and peritoneum protrude through the femoral canal into the upper thigh. The boundaries of the femoral canal are the lacunar ligament medially, the femoral vein laterally, the iliopubic tract anteriorly, and the Cooper ligament posteriorly.

C. **Diagnosis**

1. **Clinical presentation**

   a. **Symptoms.** Patients may complain of an intermittent groin bulge or a groin mass that may be tender. Because femoral hernias have a high incidence of incarceration, small bowel obstruction may be the presenting feature in some patients. Elderly patients, in whom femoral hernias occur most commonly, may not complain of groin pain, even in the setting of incarceration. Therefore, an occult femoral hernia should be considered in the differential diagnosis of any patient with small-bowel obstruction, especially if there is no history of previous abdominal surgery.

   b. **Physical examination.** The characteristic finding is a small, rounded bulge that appears in the upper thigh just below the inguinal ligament. An incarcerated femoral hernia usually presents as a firm, tender mass. The differential diagnosis is the same as that for inguinal hernia.

   c. **Radiographic evaluation.** Radiographic studies are rarely indicated. Occasionally, a femoral hernia is found on a CT scan or gastrointestinal contrast study performed to evaluate a small bowel obstruction.

D. **Treatment.** The surgical approach can be inguinal, preperitoneal, or femoral.

1. **Inguinal approach.** A Cooper ligament repair (McVay) using the inguinal canal approach allows reduction of the hernia sac with visualization from above the inguinal ligament and closure of the femoral space. Occasionally, it may be necessary to divide the inguinal ligament to reduce the hernia. The repair can be performed with or without mesh.

2. **Preperitoneal approach.** A transverse suprainguinal incision permits access to the extraperitoneal spaces of Bogros and Retzius. The hernia is reduced from inside the femoral space, and the hernia defect is repaired preperitoneally, usually with mesh, but can be repaired primarily. This approach is especially useful for incarcerated or strangulated femoral hernias. Uncomplicated femoral hernias can also be repaired laparoscopically.

3. **Femoral approach.** A horizontal incision is made over the hernia, inferior and parallel to the inguinal ligament. After the hernia sac is dissected free, it can be resected or invaginated. The femoral canal is closed by placing interrupted stitches to approximate the Cooper ligament to the inguinal ligament or by using a plug of prosthetic material.

4. **Complications.** Complications are similar to those for inguinal hernia repair. The femoral vein may be especially susceptible to injury because it forms the lateral border of the femoral canal.

III. INTERNAL HERNIA

A. **Incidence.** Of patients who present with acute intestinal obstruction, less than 5% have an internal hernia. When internal hernias are complicated by intestinal volvulus, there is an 80% incidence of strangulation or gangrene.

B. **Etiology.** Internal hernias occur within the abdominal cavity owing to congenital or acquired causes. Congenital causes include abnormal intestinal rotation (paraduodenal hernias) and openings in the ileocecal mesentery (transmesenteric hernias). Other, less frequent types are pericecal hernias, hernias through the sigmoid mesocolon, and hernias through defects in the transverse mesocolon, gastrocolic ligament, gastrohepatic ligament, or greater omentum. Acquired causes include hernias through mesenteric defects created by bowel resections or ostomy formation. Internal hernia is also a common cause of small bowel obstruction after laparoscopic gastric bypass surgery, as the small bowel can herniate through a residual mesenteric defect. Adhesive bands from prior operations may also cause or contribute to mechanical obstruction.

C. **Diagnosis**

1. **Clinical presentation.** These hernias usually are diagnosed because an intestinal segment becomes incarcerated within the internal defect, resulting in small-bowel obstruction. Patients with congenital causes usually have not had prior abdominal surgery. The reported mortality in acute intestinal obstruction secondary to internal hernias is 10% to 16%. **Symptoms** usually are of intestinal obstruction without evidence of an external hernia. When there is intestinal obstruction or intestinal

strangulation, the diagnosis is based on clinical rather than on laboratory findings.

2. **Radiographic studies.** Plain abdominal films may show small-bowel obstruction. An abdominal CT scan can sometimes establish the diagnosis of an internal hernia preoperatively. Contrast studies may also sometimes be useful.

D. **Differential diagnosis** includes other causes of intestinal obstruction, such as adhesions, external hernia, malignancy, gallstone ileus, and intussusception.

E. **Surgical treatment.** The diagnosis of internal hernia is often made at laparotomy for small-bowel obstruction. Intestinal loops proximal to the obstruction are dilated, friable, and edematous above the obstruction and collapsed distal to it. Once the hernia is reduced, intestinal viability is assessed and nonviable intestine is removed. If a large percentage of bowel is of questionable viability, a limited bowel resection followed by a second-look laparotomy in 24 to 48 hours may preserve small-bowel length. The hernia defect should be closed primarily with nonabsorbable suture.

IV. ABDOMINAL WALL HERNIA

A. **Incidence and etiology**

1. **Incisional hernias** occur at sites of previous incisions at which there has been a division of abdominal wall fascia. Contributing factors include obesity, wound infection, malnutrition, smoking, and technical errors in wound closure. Hernias occur in up to 20% of patients undergoing abdominal operations and are most commonly seen with midline incisions. Most incisional hernias are now repaired with a mesh prosthetic via open or laparoscopic approach.

2. **Umbilical hernias** are congenital defects. They are more frequent in African Americans than in whites. Most newborn umbilical hernias close spontaneously by the second year of life. However, umbilical hernias are also common in adults. Patients with ascites have a high incidence of umbilical hernias. Small umbilical hernias can be present for years without causing symptoms and may even go unnoticed. Over time, however, these hernias can enlarge and become incarcerated, usually with preperitoneal fat or omentum. Umbilical hernias greater than 3 cm should be repaired with a prosthetic mesh.

3. **Epigastric hernias** are hernias of the linea alba above the umbilicus. They occur more frequently in athletically active young men. When small or in obese individuals, epigastric hernias may be hard to palpate, making the diagnosis difficult as well. Usually, they produce epigastric pain that may be falsely attributed to other abdominal diagnoses. The diagnosis is made by palpation of a subcutaneous epigastric mass; most such hernias occur within a few centimeters of the umbilicus and are associated with a small (1 to 2 cm) fascial defect.

4. **Spigelian hernias** protrude through the spigelian fascia, near the termination of the transversus abdominis muscle along the lateral edge

of the rectus abdominis near the junction of the linea semilunaris and linea semicircularis. Because the herniated visceral contents are intraparietal (between the abdominal wall muscles), these hernias can be difficult to diagnose and therefore are included in the differential diagnosis of obscure abdominal pain. Ultrasonography, CT scan, or laparoscopy can be useful confirmatory tools in patients with focal symptoms in the appropriate region.

5. The most **common type of lumbar hernia** is an incisional hernia from a previous retroperitoneal or flank incision. Lumbar hernias may also occur in two different triangles: the Petit triangle and the Grynfeltt triangle. Lower lumbar hernias of the Petit triangle are located in a weak area limited posteriorly by the latissimus dorsi, anteriorly by the external oblique muscle, and inferiorly by the iliac crest. Grynfeltt hernias are upper lumbar in location, below the lowest rib.

6. **Obturator hernias** are very rare hernias that occur predominantly in thin, older women and are difficult to diagnose. Patients classically present with bowel obstruction and focal tenderness on rectal examination. Pain along the medial aspect of the thigh with medial thigh rotation, known as the *Howship–Romberg sign,* results from obturator nerve compression and, when present, may aid in the clinical diagnosis of an obturator hernia.

B. **Treatment and operative management.** Small epigastric, umbilical, obturator, and spigelian hernias may be repaired primarily. Most incisional hernias as well as lumbar and obturator hernias require the use of a prosthetic mesh because of their size and high recurrence rates after primary repair.

1. **Open repairs.** The principles for ventral hernia repair include dissection and identification of all defects and repair with nonabsorbable sutures placed in healthy tissue. Most sizable incisional hernias are now repaired with some types of mesh prosthesis that should be anchored by nonabsorbable sutures placed in healthy fascial tissue several centimeters beyond the margins of the defect. The mesh should be durable and well tolerated by the patient, with a low risk for infection. A variety of mesh products are available for repair, including polypropylene, polytetrafluoroethylene ([PTFE], Gore-Tex), and a composite mesh of polypropylene and PTFE. Several newer composite mesh products (Table 26-2) with absorbable barriers coating polypropylene or polyester mesh are available to minimize tissue attachment to intraabdominal structures. One should try to avoid placing polypropylene mesh in direct contact with the intestine because of the risk of adhesion formation and fistulization.

2. **Laparoscopic repairs.** The laparoscopic approach is an increasingly used alternative method for repair of incisional hernias. The repair generally involves placement of a mesh prosthesis to cover the hernia defect. The contents of the hernia are reduced and the mesh is anchored in place with sutures and tacks with a minimum of 4 cm overlap past the edge of the hernia defect on all sides. A recent meta-analysis of 45 published series comparing open and laparoscopic ventral hernia repairs

TABLE 26-2	Commonly Used Biomaterials for Incisional Hernia Repair		
	Product Trade Name	Manufacturer	Components
Absorbable barrier composite meshes	Sepramesh	Genzyme Corp., Cambridge, MA	Polypropylene mesh on one side, absorbable sodium hyaluronate/ carboxymethylcellulose on the other side
	C-Qur	Atrium Medical, Hudson, NH	Lightweight polypropylene mesh (Prolite) coated with omega-3 fatty acid
	Paritex, Parientene	Sofradim Corp., Trevoux, France	Polyester mesh with bovine type I collagen coating covered with absorbable PEG/ glycerol layer
	Proceed	Ethicon, Inc., Somerville, NJ	Polypropylene mesh encapsulated with polydioxanone coated on one side with oxidized regenerated cellulose
Nonabsorbable, barrier composite mesh	Bard Composix	C.R. Bard, Inc., Murray Hill, NJ	Macroporous bilayer mesh; polypropylene and microporous PTFE
	Gore-Tex Dual Mesh	W.L. Gore & Associates, Flagstaff, AZ	PTFE with different architecture on the peritoneal (intra-abdominal) and parietal (abdominal wall) surfaces of the mesh
Bioremodelable materials (aka biologic meshes)	Surgisis	Cook Biotech, Inc., West Lafayette, IN	Acellular, extracellular matrix material derived from porcine small intestinal submucosa
	Alloderm	LifeCell Corp., Branchburg, NJ	Acellular dermal matrix harvested from cadaveric human dermis

(continued)

TABLE 26-2	Commonly Used Biomaterials for Incisional Hernia Repair *(Continued)*

Product Trade Name	Manufacturer	Components
Flex HD	Musculoskeletal Transplant Foundation, Edison, NJ	Acellular dermal matrix harvested from cadaveric human dermis
Strattice	LifeCell Corp., Branchburg, NJ	Acellular porcine dermal matrix
Permacol	Tissue Science Laboratories, Covington, NJ	Acellular, cross-linked porcine dermal matrix

PEG, polyethylene glycol; PTFE, polytetrafluoroethylene.

concluded that laparoscopic repair is associated with fewer wound-related (3.8% vs. 16.8%) and overall complications (22.7% vs. 41.7%) and has a lower rate of recurrence (4.3% vs. 12.1%) than open repairs (*Surg Endosc.* 2007;21:378–386). Contraindications to laparoscopic ventral hernia repair include inability to establish pneumoperitoneum safely, an acute abdomen with strangulated or infarcted bowel, loss of abdominal domain, or the presence of peritonitis.

C. **Prosthetic mesh in abdominal wall hernia repairs.** The recurrence rate for ventral incisional hernia repair is 31% to 54% when primarily repaired. The placement of prosthetic biomaterials in the retrorectus, preperitoneal space to repair ventral, incisional hernias as popularized by Rives, Stoppa, and Wantz has reduced the recurrence rate to between 4% and 24%. Long-term follow-up of a randomized controlled trial showed that the use of mesh results in a lower recurrence rate and less abdominal pain and does not result in more complications than primary repair (*Hernia.* 2006;10:236–242). Microporous PTFE remains a popular choice of mesh due to its adhesion-resistant properties for intra-abdominal placement. The microporous architecture and hydrophobicity of ePTFE prevent cellular penetration of intestine or abdominal viscera. There are also several absorbable barrier-coated meshes. Each product has its own characteristics, making it useful in various circumstances. This is summarized in Table 26-2. Currently, there is little outcomes data to support the use of one product over another. However, the use of mesh is superior to primary repair for incisional hernias.

27 Breast Diseases

Lauren Steward and Julie A. Margenthaler

ANATOMY

I. **THE BREAST.** Breast tissue is located between the subcutaneous fat and the fascia of the **pectoralis major** and **serratus anterior** muscles. It extends from the second/third rib to the inframammary fold. The lateral border is the anterior or midaxillary line and the medial border is the lateral edge of the sternum. Posterior to the breast and anterior to the pectoralis fascia is the *retromammary space*, which contains small lymphatics and vessels. Breast tissue can extend to the clavicle, into the axilla (axillary tail of Spence), to the latissimus dorsi, and to the top of the rectus muscle. Running through the breasts from the deep fascia to the skin are *suspensory ligaments* **(Cooper's ligaments);** involvement of these ligaments by cancer may cause skin dimpling.

A. **Vasculature.** The arterial supply is from the **internal thoracic artery (or internal mammary artery),** via perforating branches, and the **axillary artery,** via the long thoracic and thoracoacromial branches. Additional blood supply to the breast comes from branches of the second to fifth intercostals, subscapular, and thoracodorsal arteries. Venous drainage is mainly to the **axillary vein,** as well as the internal thoracic, lateral thoracic, and intercostals veins.

B. **Lymphatic drainage.** A superficial subareolar plexus (Sappey's plexus, which primarily drains the skin and some central portions of the breast) converges with a deep lymphatic plexus (which receives lymphatic drainage from the breast parenchyma) to form the perilobular and deep subcutaneous plexuses, which ultimately drain into the axillary and internal mammary lymph nodes.

C. **Innervation.** Lateral and anterior cutaneous branches of the second to sixth intercostals nerves innervate the breasts.

II. **THE AXILLA.** The borders of the axilla are defined as the **axillary vein** superiorly, **latissimus dorsi** laterally, and the **serratus anterior** muscle medially.

A. **Axillary lymph nodes** are classified according to their anatomic location relative to the **pectoralis minor** muscle.

1. **Level I** nodes. *Lateral* to the pectoralis minor muscle.

2. **Level II** nodes. *Posterior* to the pectoralis minor muscle.

3. **Level III** nodes. *Medial* to the pectoralis minor muscle and most accessible with division of the muscle.

4. **Rotter's** nodes. *Between* the pectoralis major and the minor muscles.

B. **Axillary nerves.** Three motor and several sensory nerves are located in the axilla. Preservation of all is preferred during an axillary lymph node dissection

(ALND); however, direct tumor invasion may require resection along with the specimen.

1. **Long thoracic nerve** travels from superiorly to inferiorly along the chest wall at the medial aspect of the axilla and innervates the serratus anterior muscle. Injury to this nerve causes a "winged" scapula in which the medial and inferior angle of the scapula abduct away from the chest wall with arm extension.

2. **Thoracodorsal nerve** courses along the posterior border of the axilla from superiorly to inferiorly on the subscapularis muscle and innervates the latissimus dorsi. Injury to this nerve causes weakness in arm abduction and external rotation.

3. **Medial pectoral nerve** travels from the posterior aspect of the pectoralis minor muscle around the lateral border of the pectoralis minor to the posterior aspect of the pectoralis major muscle. It innervates the lateral third of the pectoralis major; injury to this nerve results in atrophy of the lateral pectoralis major muscle.

4. **Intercostal brachial** sensory nerves: travel laterally in the axilla from the second intercostal space to the medial upper arm. Transection causes numbness in the posterior and medial surfaces of the upper arm.

CLINICAL ASSESSMENT

I. **HISTORY. Patients seek medical attention** most commonly for an abnormal mammogram, a breast mass, breast pain, nipple discharge, or skin changes. History should include the following:
- Duration of symptoms, change over time, associated pain or skin changes, relationship to pregnancy or the menstrual cycle, previous trauma.
- Date of last menstrual period and regularity of the menstrual cycle.
- Age of menarche.
- Number of pregnancies and age at first full-term pregnancy.
- Lactational history.
- Age at menopause or surgical menopause (i.e., oophorectomy).
- Previous history of breast biopsies or breast cancer.
- Mammogram history.
- Oral contraceptive and hormonal replacement therapy.
- Family history of breast and gynecologic cancer, including the age at diagnosis. This should include at least two generations as well as any associated cancers, such as ovary, colon, prostate, gastric, or pancreatic.

A. **Assessment of cancer risks**

1. Hormonal, environmental exposure and genetics are correlated to an increased risk for breast cancer. A family history of breast cancer in a first-degree relative is associated with a doubling of risk. If two first-degree relatives (e.g., a mother and a sister) have breast cancer, the risk is further elevated. *These familial effects are enhanced if the relative had either early-onset cancer or bilateral disease.* Breast-feeding may exert a protective effect against the development of breast cancer.

Overall, factors that increase a patient's risk by 1.5- to 4-fold include the following:

a. Increased estrogen or progesterone exposure due to early menarche (before 12 years of age) or late menopause (age >55 years).

b. Late age at first full-term pregnancy: women with a first birth after the age of 30 years have twice the risk of those with a first birth before the age of 18 years.

c. High body mass index after menopause.

d. Exposure to ionizing radiation.

2. BRCA1 and BRCA2 are breast cancer susceptibility genes associated with 80% of hereditary breast cancers but account for only 5% of all breast cancers. Women with BRCA1 mutations have an estimated risk of 85% for breast cancer by the age of 70 years, a 50% chance of developing a second primary breast cancer, and a 20% to 40% chance of developing ovarian cancer. BRCA2 mutations carry a slightly lower risk for breast and ovarian cancer and account for 4% to 6% of all male breast cancers. Screening for BRCA gene mutations should be reserved for women who have a strong family history of breast or ovarian cancer. The criteria for referral for genetic counseling, adopted from the National Comprehensive Cancer Network guidelines, are as follows:

a. Personal history of breast cancer diagnosed at age less than 40, less than 50 if of Ashkenazi Jewish ancestry, less than 50 with at least one first- or second-degree relative with breast cancer at age less than 50, and/or epithelial ovarian cancer at any age.

b. Personal history of epithelial ovarian cancer, diagnosed at any age, particularly if of Ashkenazi Jewish ancestry.

c. Personal history of male breast cancer, particularly if one first or second degree relative with breast cancer and/or epithelial ovarian cancer.

d. Relatives of individuals with a deleterious BRCA1 or BRCA2 mutation.

3. Previous breast biopsies. Some pathologic features are associated with increased cancer risk.

a. *No* increased risk is associated with adenosis, cysts, duct ectasia, or apocrine metaplasia.

b. There is a slightly increased risk with moderate or florid hyperplasia, papillomatosis, and complex fibroadenomas.

c. Atypical ductal hyperplasia (ADH) or atypical lobular hyperplasia (ALH) carries a four- to five-fold increased risk of developing cancer; the risk increases to 10-fold if there is a positive family history. Patients with increased risk should be counseled appropriately and should be followed with semiannual physical examinations and yearly mammograms.

4. Models for breast cancer risk. The original Gail model estimates the absolute risk (probability) that a woman in a program of annual screening will develop breast cancer over a defined age interval. The risk factors in this model include current age, age at menarche, age at first full-term pregnancy, previous breast biopsies, presence of ADH on earlier biopsy, and number of affected first-degree relatives. This model has been validated in white women, but may underestimate the risk of breast cancer in black women. It has not been validated in other populations. The National Surgical Adjuvant Breast and Bowel Project (NSABP) modified this model to project the absolute risk of developing only invasive breast cancer. This modified Gail model has been used to define eligibility criteria for entry into chemoprevention trials. The NSABP and the National Cancer Institute offer an interactive online risk assessment tool, which is available at http://www.cancer.gov/bcrisktool.

II. PHYSICAL EXAMINATION

A. **Inspect the breasts** with the patient both in the upright and supine positions. With the patient in the upright position, examine with the patient's arms relaxed and then raised, looking for shape asymmetry, deformity, and skin changes (erythema, edema, dimpling). With the patient in the supine position, examine the entire breast systematically with the patient's ipsilateral arm raised above and behind the head.

1. If a mass is found, determine its size, shape, texture, tenderness, location, fixation to skin or deep tissues, and relationship to the areola. Evaluate the nipples for retraction, discoloration, inversion, ulceration, and eczematous changes.

2. For nipple discharge, note its color and quality, where pressure elicits discharge, and whether it is from a single duct or associated with a mass.

B. **The axillary, supraclavicular, and infraclavicular lymph nodes** should be palpated with the patient in the upright position, with arms relaxed. The size, number, and fixation of nodes should be noted.

III. BREAST IMAGING

A. Screening for breast cancer. **Screening mammogram** lowers mortality from breast cancer. It is performed in the **asymptomatic** patient and consists of two standard views, mediolateral oblique (MLO) and craniocaudal (CC). The current recommendation from the National Cancer Institute and American College of Surgeons is **annual screening mammography for women aged 40 years and older.** Breast lesions on mammograms are classified according to the American College of Radiology by **BI-RADS (Breast Imaging Reporting and Database System)** scores:

- **0** = Needs further imaging; assessment incomplete.
- **1** = Normal; continue annual follow-up (risk of malignancy: 1/2,000).
- **2** = Benign lesion; no risk of malignancy; continue annual follow-up (risk of malignancy: 1/2,000).
- **3** = Probably benign lesion; needs 4 to 6 months follow-up (risk of malignancy: 1% to 2%).

- **4** = Suspicious for breast cancer; biopsy recommended (risk of malignancy: 25% to 50%).
- **5** = Highly suspicious for breast cancer; biopsy required (75% to 99% are malignant).
- **6** = Known biopsy-proven malignancy.

1. Malignant mammographic findings
   a. New or spiculated masses.
   b. Clustered microcalcifications in linear or branching array.
   c. Architectural distortion.

2. Benign mammographic findings
   a. **Radial scar.** Generally due to fibrocystic breast condition (FBC); associated with proliferative epithelium in the center of the fibrotic area in approximately one third of cases. Appearance often mimics malignancy; a biopsy is needed to rule out malignancy.
   b. **Fat necrosis.** Results from local trauma to the breast. It may resemble carcinoma on palpation and on mammography. The fat may liquefy instead of scarring, which results in a characteristic oil cyst. A biopsy may be needed to rule out malignancy.
   c. **Milk of calcium.** Associated with FBC; caused by calcified debris in the base of the acini. Characteristic microcalcifications appear discoid on CC view and sickle shaped on MLO view. These are benign and do not require biopsy.
   d. **Cysts** cannot be distinguished from solid masses by mammography; ultrasound is needed to make this distinction.

3. **Screening in high-risk patients:** For patients with *known BRCA mutations,* annual mammograms and semiannual physical examinations should **begin at the age of 25 to 30 years.** In patients with a *strong family history of breast cancer but undocumented genetic mutation,* annual mammograms and semiannual physical examinations should begin **10 years earlier than the age of the youngest affected relative and no later than the age of 40 years.**

4. **Magnetic resonance imaging (MRI)** is recommended for screening in *selected* **high-risk patients** with:
   a. A **lifetime risk of breast cancer greater than 20%** as defined by available risk assessment tools (e.g., BRCAPRO, Gail, Claus, and Tyrer-Cuskick models).
   b. BRCA mutations.
   c. A first-degree relative (parent, sibling, child) with a BRCA1 or BRCA2 mutation.
   d. History of radiation to the chest wall between the ages of 10 to 30 years (e.g., Hodgkin lymphoma patients).
   e. Li-Fraumeni, Cowden, or Bannayan–Riley–Ruvalcaba syndromes.

B. **Diagnostic imaging**

1. **Diagnostic mammograms** are performed in the symptomatic patient or to follow up on an abnormality noted on a screening mammogram. Additional views (spot-compression views or magnification views) may be used to further characterize any lesion. The false-negative and

false-positive rates are both approximately 10%. A normal mammogram in the presence of a palpable mass does ***not*** exclude malignancy and further workup should be performed with an ultrasound, MRI, and/or biopsy.

2. **Ultrasonography** is used to further characterize a lesion identified by physical examination or mammography. It can determine whether a lesion is solid or cystic and can define the size, contour, or internal texture of the lesion. Although not a useful screening modality by itself due to significant false-positive rates, when used as an adjunct with mammography, ultrasonography may improve diagnostic sensitivity of benign findings to greater than 90%, especially among younger patients for whom mammographic sensitivity is lower due to denser breast tissue. In the patients with a known cancer, ultrasound is sometimes used to detect additional suspicious lesions and/or to map the extent of disease.

3. **MRI** is useful as an adjunct to mammography to determine extent of disease, to detect multicentric disease in the dense breast, to assess the contralateral breast, to evaluate patients with axillary metastases and an unknown primary, and in patients in whom mammogram, ultrasound, and clinical findings are inconclusive. It is also useful for assessing chest wall involvement.

IV. BREAST BIOPSY

A. **Palpable masses**

1. Fine-needle aspiration biopsy (FNAB) is reliable and accurate, with sensitivity greater than 90%. FNAB can determine the presence of malignant cells and estrogen receptor (ER) and progesterone receptor (PR) status but does not give information on tumor grade or the presence of invasion. Nondiagnostic aspirates require an additional biopsy, either surgical or core needle biopsy (*Am J Surg.* 1997;174:372).

2. Core biopsy is preferred over FNAB. It can distinguish between invasive and noninvasive cancer and provides information on tumor grade as well as receptor status. For indeterminate specimens, a surgical biopsy is necessary.

3. Excisional biopsy should primarily be used when a core biopsy cannot be done. In general, this should be an infrequent diagnostic method. It is performed in the operating room; incisions should be planned so that they can be incorporated into a mastectomy incision should that subsequently be necessary. Masses should be excised as a single specimen and labeled to preserve three-dimensional orientations.

4. Incisional biopsy is indicated for the evaluation of a large breast mass suspicious for malignancy but for which a definitive diagnosis cannot be made by FNAB or core biopsy. For inflammatory breast cancer with skin involvement, an incisional biopsy can consist of a skin punch biopsy.

B. Nonpalpable lesions. Minimally invasive breast biopsy is the optimal initial tissue acquisition method and procedure of choice for obtaining a pathologic diagnosis of image-detected abnormalities. Correlation between pathology results and imaging findings is mandatory. Patients with histologically benign findings on percutaneous biopsy do not require open biopsy if imaging and pathological findings are concordant. Patients with high-risk lesions on image-guided biopsy (ADH, ALH, lobular carcinoma *in situ* (LCIS), radial scar) may have malignancy at the same site and should undergo a surgical biopsy.

  1. Stereotactic core biopsy is used for nonpalpable mammographically detected lesions, such as microcalcifications, which cannot be seen with ultrasonography. Tissue can be collected from several foci in disparate quadrants of the breast. Using a computer-driven stereotactic unit, two mammographic images are taken to triangulate the lesion in three-dimensional space. A computer determines the depth of the lesion and the alignment of the needle, which can be positioned within 1 mm of the intended target. Biopsies are taken, and postfire images are obtained of the breast and specimen. Contraindications include lesions close to the chest wall or in the axillary tail and thin breasts that may allow needle strikethrough. Superficial lesions and lesions directly beneath the nipple-areolar complex are also often not approachable with stereotactic techniques. Nondiagnostic and insufficient specimens should undergo needle-localized excisional biopsy (NLB, see later discussion), as should discordant pathologic findings on core needle stereotactic biopsy.

    a. Vacuum-assisted biopsy is generally used during stereotactic core biopsies and ultrasound-guided core biopsies. These devices employ large needles (9 to 14 gauge) to contiguously acquire tissue, which is pulled into the bore of the needle by vacuum suction. Multiple contiguous samples of tissue are collected while the probe remains in the breast. Volumes up to 1 mL can be collected during a single insertion. A metallic marking clip is usually placed through the probe after sampling is complete to allow for identification of the biopsy site if excisional biopsy or partial mastectomy were necessary. This is the preferred approach for lesions presenting with microcalcifications without a visible or palpable mass.

  2. Ultrasound-guided biopsy is the preferred method if a lesion can be visualized with ultrasound because it is generally easier to perform than a stereotactic core biopsy. Lesions with a cystic component are better visualized with ultrasound, and ultrasound-guided biopsy can be used to aspirate the cyst as well as to provide core biopsy specimens.

  3. NLB. A needle and hookwire are placed into the breast adjacent to the concerning lesion under mammographic guidance. The patient is then brought to the operating room for an excisional biopsy. Using localization mammograms as a map, the whole hookwire, breast lesion, and a rim of normal breast tissue are removed *en bloc*. The specimen is oriented, and a radiograph is performed to confirm the presence of the lesion within the specimen.

BENIGN BREAST CONDITIONS

I. **FIBROCYSTIC BREAST CHANGE (FBC)** encompasses several of the following pathologic features: stromal fibrosis, macro- and microcysts, apocrine metaplasia, hyperplasia, and adenosis (which may be sclerosing, blunt-duct, or florid).

A. FBC is common and may present as breast pain, a breast mass, nipple discharge, or abnormalities on mammography.

B. The patient presenting with a breast mass or thickening and suspected FBC should be reexamined in a short interval, preferably on day 10 of the menstrual cycle, when hormonal influence is lowest. Often, the mass will have diminished in size.

C. A persistent dominant mass must undergo further radiographic evaluation, biopsy, or both to exclude cancer.

II. **BREAST CYSTS** frequently present as tender masses or as smooth, mobile, well-defined masses on palpation. If tense with fluid, its texture may be firm, resembling a solid mass. Aspiration can determine the nature of the mass (solid vs. cystic) but is not routinely necessary. Cyst fluid color varies and can be clear, straw-colored, or even dark green.

A. Cysts discovered by mammography and confirmed as simple cysts by ultrasound are usually observed *if asymptomatic.*

B. *Symptomatic* simple cysts should be aspirated. If no palpable mass is present after drainage, the patient should be evaluated in 3 to 4 weeks. If the cyst recurs, does not resolve completely with aspiration, or yields bloody fluid with aspiration, then mammography or ultrasonography should be performed to exclude intracystic tumor. Nonbloody clear fluid does not need to be sent for cytology.

III. **FIBROADENOMA** is the most common discrete mass in women younger than 30 years of age. They typically present as smooth, firm, mobile masses. In approximately 20% of cases, multiple fibroadenomas may be present in the ipsilateral or contralateral breast.

A. They may enlarge during pregnancy and involute after menopause.

B. They have well-circumscribed borders on mammography and ultrasound.

C. They may be managed conservatively if clinical and radiographic appearance is consistent with a fibroadenoma and is less than 2 cm. If the mass is symptomatic, greater than 2 cm, or enlarges, it should be excised.

IV. **MASTALGIA.** Most women (70%) experience some form of breast pain or discomfort during their lifetime. The pain may be cyclic (worse before a menstrual cycle) or noncyclical, focal or diffuse. Benign disease is the etiology in the majority of cases. However, pain may be associated with cancer in up to 10% of patients. **Features that raise the suspicion of cancer are *noncyclic* pain in a focal area and pain associated with a mass or bloody nipple discharge.** *Once cancer has been excluded,* most patients can be managed successfully with symptomatic therapy and reassurance; a well-fitting supportive bra is an important first step in pain relief. In 15% of patients, the pain may be so disabling that it interferes with activities of daily living.

A. **Cyclic breast pain.** Often described as a heaviness or tenderness and is usually worse before a menstrual cycle. It may be maximal in the upper outer quadrant and radiate to the inner surface of the upper arm. It resolves spontaneously in 20% to 30% of women but tends to recur in 60%. Many patients experience symptomatic relief by reducing caffeine intake or by taking vitamin E, although there is no scientific evidence supporting this.

B. **Noncyclic breast pain.** Described as burning or stabbing and frequently occurs in the subareolar area or medial aspect of the breast. It responds poorly to treatment but tends to resolve spontaneously in 50% of women.

C. **Treatment of mastalgia**

   1. **Topical nonsteroidal anti-inflammatory drugs (NSAIDs)** (diclofenac gel) have been proven in a randomized, blinded, placebo-controlled study to have significant efficacy with minimal side effects and should be considered **first-line treatment** (*J Am Coll Surg.* 2003;196:525).

   2. **Tamoxifen** (an estrogen antagonist) has been shown to provide good pain relief in placebo-controlled trials with tolerable side effects (*Lancet.* 1986;1:287), although concerns over increased risks of endometrial cancer limit long-term use.

   3. **Danazol** (a derivative of testosterone) has been shown to be efficacious and has been used historically for severe breast pain (*Gynecol Endocrinol.* 1997;11:393), but significant side effects (hirsutism, voice changes, acne, amenorrhea, and abnormal liver enzymes levels) limit its use.

   4. **Bromocriptine** and **gonadorelin analogs** should be reserved for severe refractory mastalgia due to significant side effects.

   5. **Evening primrose oil** is often used but has been shown to have no benefit over placebo in clinical trials (*Am J Obstet Gynecol.* 2002;187:1389).

D. **Superficial thrombophlebitis** of the veins overlying the breast (**Mondor disease**) may present as breast pain. The thrombosed vein or "cord" may be palpated. NSAIDs and hot compresses can provide symptomatic relief. Antibiotics are not generally indicated.

E. **Breast pain in pregnancy and lactation** can occur from engorgement, clogged ducts, trauma to the areola and nipple from pumping or nursing, or any of the aforementioned sources. Clogged ducts are usually treated with warm compresses, soaks, and massage.

F. **Tietze syndrome or costochondritis** may be confused with breast pain. Patients are locally tender in the parasternal area. Treatment is with NSAIDs.

G. **Cervical radiculopathy** can also cause referred pain to the breast.

V. NIPPLE DISCHARGE

A. **Lactation** is the most common physiologic cause of nipple discharge and may continue for up to 2 years after cessation of breast-feeding. In parous nonlactating women, a small amount of milk may be expressed from multiple ducts. This requires no treatment.

B. **Galactorrhea** is milky discharge unrelated to breast-feeding. Physiologic galactorrhea is the continued production of milk after lactation has ceased and menses resumed and is often caused by continued mechanical stimulation of the nipples.

1. **Drug-related galactorrhea** is caused by medications that affect the hypothalamic–pituitary axis by depleting dopamine (tricyclic antidepressants, reserpine, methyldopa, cimetidine, and benzodiazepines), blocking the dopamine receptor (phenothiazine, metoclopramide, and haloperidol), or having an estrogenic effect (digitalis). Discharge is generally bilateral and nonbloody.

2. **Spontaneous galactorrhea** in a **nonlactating** patient may be due to a pituitary **prolactinoma.** Amenorrhea may be associated. The diagnosis is established by measuring the serum prolactin level and performing a computed tomography (CT) or MRI scan of the pituitary gland. Treatment is bromocriptine or resection of the prolactinoma.

C. **Pathologic nipple discharge** is either (1) bloody or (2) spontaneous, unilateral, and originates from a single duct. *Normal physiologic discharge* is usually nonbloody, from multiple ducts, can be a variety of colors (clear to yellow to green), and requires breast manipulation to produce.

1. **Pathologic discharge** is serous, serosanguineous, bloody, or watery. The presence of blood can be confirmed with a guaiac test.

2. Cytologic evaluation of the discharge is not generally useful.

3. **Malignancy is the underlying cause in 10% of patients.**

4. If physical examination and mammography are negative for an associated mass, the most likely etiologies are **benign intraductal papilloma, duct ectasia,** or **fibrocystic changes.** In lactating women, serosanguineous or bloody discharge can be associated with duct trauma, infection, or epithelial proliferation associated with breast enlargement.

5. A solitary **papilloma** with a fibrovascular core places the patient at marginally increased risk for the development of breast cancer. Patients with persistent spontaneous discharge from a single duct require a surgical microdochectomy, ductoscopy, or major duct excision.

   a. **Microdochectomy:** Excision of the involved duct and associated lobule. Immediately before surgery, the involved duct is cannulated, and radiopaque contrast is injected to obtain a **ductogram,** which identifies lesions as filling defects. The patient is then taken to the operating room, and the pathologic duct is identified and excised, along with the associated lobule.

   b. **Ductoscopy** utilizes a 1-mm rigid videoscope to perform an internal exploration of the major ducts of the breast. Once a ductal lesion is identified, this single associated duct with the lesion is excised.

   c. **Major duct excision** may be used for women with bloody nipple discharge from multiple ducts or in postmenopausal women with bloody nipple discharge. It is performed through a circumareolar incision, and all of the retroareolar ducts are transected and excised, along with a cone of tissue extending up to several centimeters posterior to the nipple.

VI. BREAST INFECTIONS

A. **Lactational mastitis** may occur either sporadically or in epidemics.

1. The most common causative organism is ***Staphylococcus aureus.***

2. It presents as a swollen, erythematous, and tender breast; purulent discharge from the nipple is *uncommon.*

3. In the early cellulitic phase, the treatment is antibiotics. The frequency of nursing or pumping should be *increased.* Approximately 25% progress to abscess formation.

4. **Breast abscesses** occur in the later stages and are often *not* fluctuant. The diagnosis is made by failure to improve on antibiotics, abscess cavity seen on ultrasound, or aspiration of pus. Treatment is cessation of nursing and surgical drainage.

B. **Nonpuerperal abscesses** result from duct ectasia with periductal mastitis, infected cysts, infected hematoma, or hematogenous spread from another source.

1. They usually are located in the peri/retroareolar area.

2. **Anaerobes** are the most common causative agent, although antibiotics should cover both **anaerobic and aerobic** organisms.

3. Treatment is surgical drainage.

4. **Unresolved or recurring infection requires biopsy to exclude cancer.** These patients often have a chronic relapsing course with multiple infections requiring surgical drainage.

5. Repeated infections can result in a chronically draining periareolar lesion or a mammary fistula lined with squamous epithelium. Treatment is excision of the central duct along with the fistula once the acute infection resolves. The fistula can recur even after surgery.

VII. GYNECOMASTIA is hypertrophy of breast tissue in men. It usually occurs secondary to an imbalance between the breast stimulatory effects of estrogen and the inhibitory effects of androgens. Possible etiologies include overproduction of estrogens, enhanced extraglandular conversion of estrogen precursors to estrogen, or decreased secretion of androgens from the testes.

A. **Pubertal** hypertrophy occurs in adolescent boys, is usually bilateral, and resolves spontaneously in 6 to 12 months.

B. **Senescent** gynecomastia is commonly seen after the age of 70 years, as testosterone levels decrease.

C. **Drugs** associated with this are similar to those that cause galactorrhea in women, for example, digoxin, spironolactone, methyldopa, cimetidine, tricyclic antidepressants, phenothiazine, reserpine, and marijuana. Drugs used for androgen blockade, such as luteinizing hormone releasing hormone analogues for the treatment of prostate cancer and 5-alpha reductase inhibitors for the management of benign prostatic hypertrophy, may also result in gynecomastia.

D. **Tumors** can cause gynecomastia secondary to excess secretion of estrogens: testicular teratomas and seminomas, bronchogenic carcinomas, adrenal tumors, and tumors of the pituitary and hypothalamus.

E. Gynecomastia may be a manifestation of **systemic diseases** such as hepatic cirrhosis, renal failure, hyperthyroidism, and malnutrition.

F. During the workup of gynecomastia, cancer should be excluded by mammography and subsequently by biopsy if a mass is found. The cause of gynecomastia should be identified and corrected if possible. If workup fails to reveal a medically treatable cause or if the enlargement fails to regress, excision of breast tissue via a periareolar incision can be performed.

MALIGNANCY OF THE BREAST

I. **EPIDEMIOLOGY.** Breast cancer is the **most common cancer in women,** with a lifetime risk of **one in eight women.** In 2010, approximately 209,000 new cases of invasive breast cancer and 54,000 new cases of noninvasive *in situ* carcinoma of the breast will be diagnosed (*Cancer Facts & Figures, American Cancer Society, 2010*). Approximately 40,000 women will die in 2010 due to breast cancer, making it the second-leading cause of cancer death in women (led by lung cancer).

II. **STAGING.** The management of breast cancer is guided by the extent of disease and the biologic features of the tumor. Treatment is multidisciplinary, involving surgeons, radiation oncologists, and medical oncologists. The disease is staged by the TNM (tumor, node, and metastasis) system (Tables 27-1 and 27-2). Workup should include the following (in addition to breast-specific imaging):
   • Complete blood cell count, complete metabolic panel, and chest x-ray.
   • A bone scan, if the alkaline phosphatase or calcium level is elevated.
   • CT scan of the liver if liver function panel is abnormal.
   • **Patients with clinical stage III** disease should undergo bone scan and CT scan of the chest/abdomen/pelvis due to a high probability of distant metastases.

III. **TUMOR BIOMARKERS AND PROGNOSTIC FACTORS** should be evaluated on all tumor specimens.

   Tumor size and **grade** are the most reliable pathologic predictors of outcome for patients **without axillary nodal involvement.** The **Nottingham score** combines histologic grade based on *glandular differentiation*, *mitotic count*, and *nuclear grade.* A higher grade is a *poor* prognostic factor.

   A. **Hormone receptors.** Expression of **ERs** and **PRs** should be evaluated by immunohistochemistry. Intense ER and PR staining is a *good* prognostic factor.

   B. **Her2/neu (ERB2):** *Her2/neu* is a member of the epidermal growth factor family and is involved in cell growth regulation. Overexpression due to gene amplification is seen in approximately 30% of patients with breast cancer. *Her2/neu* expression is measured by immunohistochemistry; and if

TABLE 27-1	American Joint Committee on Cancer TNM (Tumor, Node, Metastasis) Staging for Breast Cancer

Stage	Description
Tumor	
TX	Primary tumor not assessable
T0	No evidence of primary tumor
Tis	Carcinoma *in situ*
T1	Tumor ≤2 cm in greatest dimension
T1 mic	Microinvasion ≤0.1 cm in greatest dimension
T1a	Tumor >0.1 cm but not >0.5 cm
T1b	Tumor >0.5 cm but not >1 cm
T1c	Tumor >1 cm but not >2 cm
T2	Tumor >2 cm but <5 cm in greatest dimension
T3	Tumor >5 cm in greatest dimension
T4	Tumor of any size with direct extension into the chest wall or skin
T4a	Extension to chest wall (ribs, intercostals, or serratus anterior)
T4b	*Peau d'orange,* ulceration, or satellite skin nodules
T4c	T4a + T4b
T4d	Inflammatory breast cancer
Regional Lymph Nodes	
NX	Regional lymph nodes not assessable
N0	No regional lymph node involvement
N1	Metastasis to movable ipsilateral axillary lymph nodes
N2	Metastases to ipsilateral axillary lymph nodes fixed to one another or to other structures
N3	Metastases to ipsilateral internal mammary lymph node with or without axillary lymph node involvement, or in clinically apparent clavicular lymph node.
Distant Metastases	
MX	Presence of distant metastases not assessable
M0	No distant metastases
M1	Existent distant metastases (including ipsilateral supraclavicular nodes)

With permission from Fleming ID, Cooper JS, Henson DE, et al., eds. *AJCC Cancer Staging Manual,* 5th ed. Philadelphia, PA: Lippincott Williams & Wilkins; 1998.

equivocal by fluorescence *in situ* hybridization. Overexpression of *Her2/neu* is a *poor* prognostic factor, as it results in an increased rate of metastasis, decreased time to recurrence, and decreased overall survival. Patients with Her2/neu amplified tumors are treated with targeted monoclonal antibody therapies, such as trastuzumab (Herceptin) or lapatinib (Tykerb).

TABLE 27-2	American Joint Committee on Cancer Classification for Breast Cancer Based on TNM (Tumor, Node, Metastasis) Criteria		
Stage	Tumor	Nodes	Metastases
0	Tis	N0	M0
I	T1	N0	M0
IIA	T0, 1	N1	M0
	T2	N0	M0
IIB	T2	N1	M0
	T3	N0	M0
IIIA	T0, 1, 2	N2	M0
	T3	N1, 2	M0
IIIB	T4	Any N	M0
	Any T	N3	M0
IV	Any T	Any N	M1

With permission from Fleming ID, Cooper JS, Henson DE, et al., eds. *AJCC Cancer Staging Manual,* 5th ed. Philadelphia, PA: Lippincott Williams & Wilkins; 1998.

C. Other **negative markers** include those tumors that do not express any tumor biomarkers (**"triple negative"**), the presence of **lymphovascular invasion,** and other indicators of a high proliferative rate (>5% of cells in the **S phase;** >20% **Ki-67**).

IV. **NONINVASIVE (*in situ*) Breast Cancer.** Ductal carcinoma *in situ* (**DCIS**) or LCIS are lesions with malignant cells that have not penetrated the basement membrane of the mammary ducts or lobules, respectively.

A. **DCIS,** or intraductal carcinoma, is treated as a **malignancy** because DCIS has the potential to develop into invasive cancer.

- It is usually detected by mammography as clustered pleomorphic calcifications.
- Physical examination is normal in the majority of patients.
- It may advance in a segmental manner, with gaps between disease areas.
- It can be **multifocal** (two or more lesions >5 mm apart within the same index quadrant) or **multicentric** (in different quadrants).

1. Histology
   a. There are **five architectural subtypes:** papillary, micropapillary, solid, cribriform, and comedo. Specimens are also grouped as *comedo* versus *noncomedo.*

    b. The **high-grade subtype** is often associated with microinvasion, a higher proliferation rate, aneuploidy, gene amplification, and a higher local recurrence rate.

    c. ER and PR expression levels should be obtained if hormone therapy is being considered.

2. Treatment

    a. Surgical excision alone (via partial mastectomy) with **margins greater than 10 mm** is associated with a local recurrence rate of 14% at 12 years (*Am J Surg.* 2006;192:420). The addition of adjuvant radiation reduces the local recurrence rate to 2.5%. Approximately half of the recurrences present as invasive ductal carcinomas. **Surgical options** depend on the extent of disease, grade, margin status, multicentricity of disease, and patient age.

        (1) Partial mastectomy: For unicentric lesions. Needle localization is required to identify the area to be excised in most cases. Bracket needle localization (two or more wires to map out the extent of disease to be resected) for more extensive lesions is occasionally used.

        (2) Mastectomy: Total (simple) mastectomy with or without immediate reconstruction is recommended for patients with multicentric lesions, extensive involvement of the breast (disease extent relative to breast size), or persistently positive margins with partial mastectomy.

    b. Assessment of axillary lymph nodes: axillary dissection is not performed for pure DCIS.

        (1) Sentinel lymph node biopsy (**SLNB,** see later discussion) may be considered when there is a reasonable probability of finding invasive cancer on final pathologic examination (e.g., >4 cm, palpable, or high grade).

        (2) Some surgeons perform SLNB in all patients with DCIS undergoing mastectomy because SLNB cannot be performed postmastectomy if an occult invasive cancer is found. This is an area of ongoing controversy and research.

        (3) A positive sentinel node indicates invasive breast cancer and changes the stage of the disease; a **completion axillary dissection** is then indicated.

    c. Adjuvant therapy

        (1) For pure DCIS, there is no added benefit from systemic chemotherapy because the disease is confined to the ducts of the breast. However, in those patients with **ER-positive DCIS,** adjuvant **tamoxifen** can reduce the risk of breast cancer recurrence by 37% over 5 years and the risk of developing a new contralateral breast cancer (NSABP B-24 trial). However, there is no survival benefit. **Aromatase inhibitors** (e.g., **anastrozole, exemestane, letrozole**), which block the peripheral conversion of androgens into estrogens by inhibiting the enzyme aromatase but does not affect estrogen produced by the ovaries, are sometimes used as an alternative in postmenopausal patients.

TABLE 27-3	Van Nuys Scoring System[a]		
	Score		
	1	**2**	**3**
Size (mm)	d15	>15–40	>40
Margins (mm)	S10	<10 but >1	<1
Histology	Non–high grade without necrosis	Non–high grade with necrosis	High grade with or without necrosis

[a]A score of 13 points is given for each of the prognostic factors described, resulting in a total index score ranging from 3 to 9. Scores of 3 and 4 are considered low index values; scores of 5, 6, or 7 are considered intermediate; and scores of 8 or 9 are considered high.
Modified from Silverstein MJ, Lagios MD, Craig PH, et al. A prognostic index for ductal carcinoma *in situ* of the breast. *Cancer.* 1996;77:226–227.

(2) **Adjuvant radiation** should be given to patients with DCIS treated with partial mastectomy to **decrease the local recurrence rate** (NSABP B-17 trial). This is especially true for younger women with close margins or large tumors. However, there is no survival benefit. For older patients with smaller, widely excised DCIS of low or intermediate grade, the benefit of radiation therapy is less clear and adjuvant radiation may not be necessary.

d. **The Van Nuys Prognostic Index** (Table 27-3) is a numerical algorithm (based on lesion size, margin, tumor grade, presence of necrosis, and age) used to stratify patients with DCIS into three groups to determine which patient is at greatest risk of recurrence and would therefore benefit the most from a more aggressive treatment approach. The low-scoring group may be treated with partial mastectomy alone. The intermediate-scoring group has been shown to benefit from adjuvant radiation therapy, and the high-scoring group should undergo mastectomy because the risk of recurrence with partial mastectomy with or without radiation is high (*Adv Surg.* 2000;34:29).

B. **LCIS** is not considered a preinvasive lesion but rather an indicator for increased breast cancer risk of approximately 1% per year (~20% to 30% at 15 years) (*JNCCN* 2006;4:511) and is not treated as a breast cancer.

1. It may be multifocal and/or bilateral.

2. The cancer that develops may be invasive ductal or lobular and may occur in either breast.

3. LCIS has loss of **E-cadherin** (involved in cell–cell adhesion), which can be stained for on pathology slides to clarify cases that are borderline DCIS versus LCIS.

4. **Pleomorphic LCIS** is a particularly aggressive subtype of LCIS that is treated more like DCIS; it tends to have less favorable biological markers.

5. **Treatment options** are (1) lifelong close **surveillance,** (2) **bilateral total mastectomies** with immediate reconstruction for selected women with a strong family history after appropriate counseling, or (3) prophylaxis with **tamoxifen or raloxifene** (raloxifene has only been validated in the postmenopausal setting).

V. INVASIVE BREAST CANCER

A. **Histology** consists of five different subtypes: *infiltrating ductal* (75% to 80%), *infiltrating lobular* (5% to 10%), *medullary* (5% to 7%), *mucinous* (3%), and *tubular* (1% to 2%).

B. Surgical options for stage I and II breast cancer:

1. **Mastectomy** with or without reconstruction.

   a. **Radical mastectomy** involves total mastectomy, complete ALND (levels I, II, and III), removal of the pectoralis major and minor muscles, and removal of all overlying skin. This surgical approach is largely historical and is rarely, if ever, performed in modern practice.

   b. **Modified radical mastectomy** (MRM) involves total mastectomy and ALND. It is indicated for patients with clinically positive lymph nodes or a positive axillary node based on previous SLNB or FNAB.

   c. **Total (simple) mastectomy with SLNB** is for patients with a clinically negative axilla. A skin-sparing mastectomy (preserves skin envelope and inframammary ridge) may be performed with immediate reconstruction, resulting in improved cosmesis: the nipple-areolar complex, a rim of periareolar breast skin, and any previous excisional biopsy or partial mastectomy scars are excised.

   d. **Immediate reconstruction** at the time of mastectomy should be offered to eligible patients. Options include latissimus dorsi myocutaneous flaps, transverse rectus abdominis myocutaneous flaps, and inflatable tissue expanders followed by exchange for saline or silicone implants. Immediate reconstruction has been shown not to affect patient outcome adversely. The detection of recurrence is not delayed, and the onset of chemotherapy is not changed.

   e. **Follow-up after mastectomy:** physical examination every 3 to 6 months for 3 years, then every 6 to 12 months for the next 2 years, and then annually (*J Clin Oncol.* 2006;24:5091). Mammography of the contralateral breast should continue yearly. Regular gynecologic follow-up is recommended for all women (tamoxifen increases risk of endometrial cancer).

2. **Breast conservation therapy (BCT): partial mastectomy** and SLNB (or ALND; see later discussion) followed by breast irradiation.

   a. Several trials have demonstrated that BCT with adjuvant radiation therapy has similar survival and recurrence rates to those for MRM (*J Clin Oncol.* 1992;10:976).

b. **Contraindications for BCT:** not every patient is a candidate for BCT. Contraindications include patients who may be unreliable with follow-up or radiation therapy (may involve radiation treatment 5 days a week for 5 to 6 weeks); when the extent of disease prevents adequate negative margins; a high tumor-to-breast size ratio, which prevents adequate resection without major deformity; persistently positive margins on re-excision partial mastectomy; and inability to receive adjuvant radiation (e.g., prior radiation to the chest wall; first- and second-trimester pregnancy in which the delay of radiation to the postpartum state is inappropriate; collagen vascular diseases such as scleroderma).

c. For patients with large tumors who desire BCT, **neoadjuvant chemotherapy** or **neoadjuvant hormonal therapy** may be offered to attempt to reduce the size of the tumor to make BCT attempt possible.

d. **Partial mastectomy** incisions should be planned so that they can be incorporated into a mastectomy incision should that prove necessary. Incisions for partial mastectomy and either SLNB or ALND should be separate.

e. **Adjuvant radiotherapy** decreases the breast cancer recurrence rate from 30% to less than 7% at 5 years and is a required component of BCT.

f. **Follow-up after BCT.** Physical examinations are the same as those for mastectomy (see earlier discussion). A posttreatment mammogram of the treated breast is performed to establish a new baseline, no earlier than 6 months after completion of radiation therapy. Mammograms are then performed every 6 to 12 months after the new baseline mammogram until the surgical changes stabilize and then annually. Contralateral breast mammography remains on an annual basis. Regular gynecologic follow-up is recommended.

3. **Management of the axilla.** Approximately 30% of patients with clinically negative exams will have positive lymph nodes in an **ALND** specimen. The presence and number of lymph nodes involved affect staging and thus prognosis. However, complications are not infrequent (see later discussion). Thus, **SLNB** was developed to provide sampling of the lymph nodes without needing an ALND.

a. **SLNB** has been established as a standard of care for predicting axillary involvement in most patients with breast cancer. The procedure requires a multidisciplinary approach, including nuclear medicine, pathology, and radiology.

(1) It involves injection of blue dye (either **Lymphazurin or methylene blue**) in the operating room and/or **technetium-labeled sulfur colloid** (in the nuclear medicine department, radiology suite, or sometimes by the surgeon). The combination of blue dye and radioisotope provides higher node identification rates and increases the sensitivity of the procedure. The goal is to identify the primary draining lymph node(s) in the axillary nodal basin.

(2) A variety of injection techniques are used: **intraparenchymal** versus **intradermal** (intradermal methylene blue will cause skin necrosis at the injection site); **peritumoral** versus **periareolar.**

(3) The SLN is identified by its blue color, and/or by high activity detected by a handheld gamma probe, or by a blue lymphatic seen to enter a non-blue node. Palpable nodes are also sentinel nodes, even if not blue or radioactive.

(4) Twenty percent to 30% of the time more than one SLN is identified.

(5) Experienced surgeons (those who have performed at least 30 SLNBs, with ALND for confirmation) can identify the SLN in greater than 90% of patients, accurately predicting the patients' remaining axillary lymph node status in greater than 97% of cases.

(6) **If the SLN is positive for metastasis** (micrometastasis 0.2 mm or larger, *not isolated tumor cells*), **a standard completion ALND is the current recommendation.** A recent randomized trial compared the overall survival and axillary recurrence rates for patients with limited SLN metastatic disease who received breast conservation and systemic therapy and either had ALND versus no further axillary procedures (*JAMA.* 2011;305(6):569). There was no difference in the two groups, leading many to defer completion ALND for this subgroup of patients. All patients underwent lumpectomy, whole breast radiation, and systemic therapy; thus, the results cannot be generalized to all patients with a positive SLN.

(7) Serial sectioning and immunohistochemical staining of SLNB specimens may improve accuracy in detecting micrometastatic disease.

(8) Currently, **isolated tumor cells are considered N0** disease, and therapeutic decisions should *not* be based on finding these.

b. **ALND.** Patients with clinically positive lymph nodes should undergo ALND for local control. ALND involves the following:

(1) Removal of **level I** and **level II nodes** and, *if grossly involved,* possibly level III nodes. Motor and sensory nerves are preserved unless there is direct tumor involvement.

(2) An ALND should remove **10 or more nodes.** The number of nodes identified is often pathologist dependent.

(3) Patients with **4 or more positive lymph nodes** should undergo **adjuvant radiation to the axilla.** Selective patients with 1 to 3 positive nodes may also benefit from radiation therapy to the axilla.

(4) **Intraoperative complications:** potential injury to the axillary vessels and neuropathy secondary to injury to the motor nerves of the axilla (the long thoracic, thoracodorsal, and medial pectoral nerves).

(5) Most frequent **postoperative complications:** wound infections and seromas. Persistent seroma may be treated with repeated aspirations or reinsertion of a drain. Other complications include pain and numbness in the axilla and upper arm, impaired shoulder mobility, and **lymphedema.**

Lymphedema occurs in approximately 10% to 40% of women undergoing axillary dissection; radiation to the axilla increases the risk of this complication. The most effective therapy is early intervention with intense physiomassage; graded pneumatic compression devices and a professionally fitted compression sleeve can also provide relief and prevent worsening of lymphedema. Blood draws, blood pressure cuffs, and intravenous lines should be avoided in the affected arm, mainly to avoid infection in it. Infections of the hand or arm should be treated promptly and aggressively with antibiotics and arm elevation because infection can damage lymphatics further and cause irreversible lymphedema. Lymphedema itself increases the risk of developing **angiosarcoma.**

C. **Adjuvant systemic therapy** is given in appropriate patients after completion of surgery.

1. All node-positive patients should receive adjuvant chemotherapy.
   a. Regimens are guided by the tumor biomarkers. Typical regimens comprise four to eight cycles of a combination of cyclophosphamide and an anthracycline, followed by a taxane administered every 2 to 3 weeks.
   b. Patients with **ER-positive tumors** receive **adjuvant hormonal therapy** for 5 years. **Tamoxifen** is given to premenopausal women, and **aromatase inhibitors** are given to postmenopausal women (aromatase inhibitors are not used in premenopausal women because decreased feedback to the hypothalamus and pituitary increases gonadotropin secretion, stimulating the ovary to secrete more substrate).
   c. In postmenopausal women older than 70 years, chemotherapy is performed less frequently. In postmenopausal women with tumors with ER or PR positivity, tamoxifen or an aromatase inhibitor is frequently the sole adjuvant medical therapy.
   d. In patients with *Her2/neu*-**positive tumors,** polychemotherapy is combined with biological therapy targeting the *Her2/neu* protein: **trastuzumab** is a recombinant monoclonal antibody that binds to *Her2/neu* receptor to prevent cell proliferation. The NSABP trial B-31 and the North Central Cancer Treatment Group trial N9831 showed that adding trastuzumab to a chemotherapy regiment of doxorubicin, cyclophosphamide, and paclitaxel was associated with an increase in the disease-free survival by 12% and a 33% reduction in the risk of death at 3 years. It is usually administered intravenously monthly for 12 months. The most serious toxicity with the regiment was cardiac failure (*N Engl J Med.* 2005;353:1673).

2. **Node-negative patients** may have increased disease-free survival from adjuvant chemotherapy and/or hormonal therapy. An individualized approach is crucial and requires thorough discussion with the patient regarding the risks of recurrence without adjuvant therapy, the cost and toxicities treatment, and the expected benefit in risk reduction and survival.
   a. Up to 30% of node-negative women die of breast cancer within 10 years if treated with surgery alone.

    b. Node-negative patients who are at **high risk** and benefit the most from adjuvant chemotherapy include those with tumors greater than 1 cm, higher tumor grade, *Her2/neu* expression, aneuploidy, Ki-67 expression, increased percentage in S phase, lymphovascular invasion, and ER/PR-negative tumors.

    c. The NSABP B-20 trial and the International Breast Cancer Study Group trial IX showed that **polychemotherapy in combination with tamoxifen was superior to tamoxifen alone** in increasing disease-free and overall survival, especially in ER-negative patients, regardless of tumor size.

    d. The St. Gallen Consensus Panel in 1998 suggested that patients who have node-negative disease and whose tumors are 1 cm or less and ER-positive may be spared adjuvant chemotherapy but still may benefit from adjuvant endocrine therapy.

    e. The Web site http://www.adjuvantonline.com provides an online tool for physicians to use to calculate the added benefit of hormonal and chemotherapeutic therapies.

D. Adjuvant radiation

    1. Indications for adjuvant radiation to the chest wall and axilla **after mastectomy** include T3 and T4 tumors, attachment to the pectoral fascia, positive surgical margins, skin involvement, involved internal mammary nodes, inadequate or no axillary dissection, four or more positive lymph nodes, and residual tumor on the axillary vein. Presence of one to three positive axillary nodes is a relative indication.

    2. Randomized, prospective trials have shown a significantly decreased recurrence and improved survival in premenopausal women with these indications treated with chemotherapy and radiation therapy (*N Engl J Med.* 1997;337:949).

    3. Adjuvant whole-breast radiation **after BCT** decreases the breast cancer recurrence rate from 30% to less than 7% at 5 years.

    4. Complications. Radiation to the chest wall can cause skin changes. Infrequent complications include interstitial pneumonitis, spontaneous rib fracture, breast fibrosis, pericarditis, pleural effusion, and chest wall myositis. Radiation to the axilla can increase the incidence of lymphedema and axillary fibrosis. **Angiosarcoma** can occur as a late complication.

E. Locally advance breast cancer (LABC) comprises T3 or T4, N1 or greater, and M0 cancers **(stages IIIA and IIIB).**

    1. Staging in LABC. Because of the frequency of distant metastasis at the time of presentation, all patients should receive complete blood cell count, complete metabolic panel, bone scan, and CT scan of chest and abdomen before treatment.

    2. Noninflammatory LABC (chest wall or skin involvement, skin satellites, ulceration, fixed axillary nodes)

        a. Patients should receive **neoadjuvant chemotherapy** (often cyclophosphamide combined with an anthracycline and taxane), followed by surgery and radiation. The high response rates seen with this regimen for **stage IIIB** allow **MRM** to be carried out, with primary skin closure. Neoadjuvant chemotherapy also provides information regarding tumor response to treatment that may aid to guide further adjuvant therapy. Adjuvant radiation to the chest wall and regional nodes chemotherapy follow surgery; additional adjuvant chemotherapy is also necessary in select cases. SLNB may be used in selected patients with a clinically negative axilla.

b. Patients with **stage IIIA** disease receiving neoadjuvant chemotherapy who can be converted to **BCT** candidates have no difference in overall survival outcome.

c. Approximately 20% of patients with stage III disease present with distant metastases after appropriate staging has been performed.

3. Inflammatory LABC (T4d)

a. This is characterized by erythema, warmth, tenderness, and edema (*peau d'orange*).

b. It represents 1% to 6% of all breast cancers.

c. An underlying mass is present in 70% of cases. Associated axillary adenopathy occurs in 50% of cases.

d. It is often misdiagnosed initially as mastitis.

e. **Skin punch biopsy** confirms the diagnosis: in two third of cases, tumor emboli are seen in dermal lymphatics.

f. Approximately 30% of patients have distant metastasis at the time of diagnosis.

g. Inflammatory breast cancer requires **aggressive multimodal therapy** because median survival is approximately 2 years, with a 5-year survival of only 5%.

4. **Follow-up.** Because of higher risk for local and distant recurrence, patients should be examined every 3 months by all specialists involved in their care.

F. **Locoregional recurrence.** Patients with locoregional recurrence should have a **metastatic workup** to exclude visceral or bony disease and should be considered for systemic chemotherapy or hormonal therapy.

1. **Recurrence in the breast after BCT** requires total (simple) mastectomy. Provided margins are negative, survival is similar to that for patients who received mastectomy initially.

2. **Recurrence in the axilla** requires surgical resection followed by radiation to the axilla and systemic therapy.

3. **Recurrence in the chest wall after mastectomy** occurs in 4% to 5% of patients. One third of these patients have distant metastases at the time of recurrence, and greater than 50% will have distant disease within 2 years. Multimodal therapy is essential. For an isolated local recurrence, excision followed by radiotherapy results in excellent local control. Rarely, patients require radical chest resection with myocutaneous flap closure.

VI. CHEMOPREVENTION

A. The NSABP P-1 trial was the first large prospective, randomized chemopreventive trial to evaluate the efficacy of the estrogen antagonist **tamoxifen** to reduce breast cancer incidence in women at risk.

1. Women taking tamoxifen achieved an overall reduction in the risk of developing invasive breast carcinoma of 49% and a reduction in the risk of developing noninvasive breast cancer of 50%.

2. In subgroups of women with a history of **LCIS** and with a history of **ADH,** tamoxifen reduced the risk of developing invasive breast cancer by 65% and 86%, respectively.

B. The NSABP B-24 trial showed that tamoxifen provided a 37% overall risk reduction for all breast cancers (invasive and noninvasive) in women with **DCIS treated with lumpectomy and radiation.**

1. The **toxicities** of the drug include an increased risk of endometrial cancer, thrombotic vascular events, and cataract development. Women on tamoxifen also reported increased vasomotor symptoms (hot flashes) and vaginal discharge.

2. Tamoxifen also provided a significant reduction in hip fractures in women older than 50 years of age. There was no difference noted in the incidence of ischemic heart disease for women taking tamoxifen.

3. Tamoxifen has been approved by the Food and Drug Administration (FDA) for (1) the treatment of metastatic breast cancer, (2) adjuvant **treatment of breast cancer,** and (3) **chemoprevention of invasive or contralateral breast cancer in high-risk women.**

4. The **dosage** for chemoprevention is 20 mg/day for 5 years. It is estimated that chemoprevention could prevent as many as 500,000 invasive and 200,000 noninvasive breast cancers over 5 years in the United States alone.

5. The Study of Tamoxifen and Raloxifene (STAR) trial compared tamoxifen to **raloxifene** (a selective ER modulator). Raloxifene has not been approved by the FDA for chemoprevention, but was shown to provide equal risk reduction for the development of invasive breast cancers as tamoxifen. It was not as effective at reducing the risk of developing noninvasive breast cancer. Its side effect profile is somewhat different than that of tamoxifen, so it can be considered in patients with relative contraindications to tamoxifen.

SPECIAL CONSIDERATIONS

I. BREAST CONDITIONS DURING PREGNANCY

A. **Bloody nipple discharge** may occur in the second or third trimester. It results from epithelial proliferation under hormonal influences and usually resolves by 2 months postpartum. If it does not resolve by then, standard evaluation of pathologic nipple discharge should be performed.

B. **Breast masses** occurring during pregnancy include **galactoceles, lactating adenoma, simple cysts, breast infarcts, fibroadenomas, *and* carcinoma.** Fibroadenomas may grow during pregnancy due to hormonal stimulation.

1. Masses should be evaluated by ultrasound, and a core needle biopsy should be performed for any suspicious lesion.

2. Mammography can be performed with uterine shielding but is rarely helpful due to increased breast density.

3. If a breast lesion is diagnosed as malignant, the patient should be given the **same surgical treatment** options, stage for stage, as a nonpregnant woman, and the **treatment should not be delayed** because of the pregnancy.

C. **Breast cancer during pregnancy** may be difficult to diagnose due to the low level of suspicion and breast nodularity and density.

1. It occurs in approximately 1 in 5,000 gestations and accounts for almost 3% of all breast cancers.

2. **Workup is the same as in a nonpregnant woman.** The standard preoperative staging workup is performed. Laboratory values such as alkaline phosphatase may be elevated during pregnancy. For advanced-stage disease, MRI scan or ultrasound may be used in lieu of CT scan for staging. Excisional biopsy can be safely performed under local anesthesia if there is some contraindication to the preferred core needle biopsy.

3. **Therapeutic decisions** are influenced by the clinical cancer stage and the trimester of pregnancy and must be **individualized.** MRM has been the standard surgical modality for pregnant patients with breast cancer, but BCT can be offered to selected patients. The radiation component of BCT cannot be applied during pregnancy, and delaying radiation therapy is not ideal. For these reasons, BCT is usually not recommended to patients in their first or second trimester. For patients in the third trimester, radiation can begin after delivery. SLNB is starting to be used more frequently; the commonly used radioisotope is approved for use during pregnancy.

4. **Chemotherapy** may be given by the mid-second trimester.

II. **PAGET DISEASE OF THE NIPPLE** is characterized by eczematoid changes of the nipple, which may involve the surrounding areola.

A. Burning, pruritus, and hypersensitivity may be prominent symptoms.

B. Paget disease is almost always accompanied by an underlying malignancy, either invasive ductal carcinoma or DCIS.

C. Palpable masses are present in approximately 60% of patients.

D. Mammography should be performed to identify other areas of involvement. If clinical suspicion is high, a pathologic diagnosis should be obtained by wedge biopsy of the nipple and underlying breast tissue.

E. Treatment is mastectomy or BCT with excision of the nipple-areolar complex (sometimes called a central lumpectomy), followed by radiation therapy. The prognosis is related to tumor stage.

III. **BREAST CANCER IN MEN** accounts for less than 1% of male cancers and less than 1% of all breast cancers. BRCA2 mutations are associated with approximately 4% to 6% of these cancers.

   A. Patients generally present with a nontender hard mass. This contrasts with unilateral gynecomastia, which is usually firm, central, and tender.

   B. Mammography can be helpful in distinguishing gynecomastia from malignancy. Malignant lesions are more likely to be eccentric, with irregular margins, and are often associated with nipple retraction and microcalcifications. Biopsy of suspicious lesions is essential, and core needle biopsy is preferred.

   C. MRM was traditionally the surgical procedure of choice; however, SLNB has been shown to be effective in men. Thus, total (simple) mastectomy with SLNB is a valid option in men.

   D. Eighty-five percent of malignancies are infiltrating ductal carcinoma and are positive for ER.

   E. **Adjuvant hormonal, chemotherapy, and radiation treatment criteria are the same as in women.** Overall survival *per stage* is comparable to that observed in women, although men tend to present in later stages.

IV. **PHYLLODES TUMORS** account for 1% of breast neoplasms.

   A. They present as a large, smooth, lobulated mass and may be difficult to distinguish from fibroadenoma on physical exam.

   B. They can occur in women of any age, but most frequently between the ages of 35 and 55 years.

   C. Skin ulcerations may occur secondary to pressure of the underlying mass.

   D. FNAB cannot reliably diagnose these tumors; at least a core needle biopsy is needed. Histologically, stromal overgrowth is the essential characteristic for differentiating phyllodes tumors from fibroadenomas.

   E. Ninety percent are benign; 10% are malignant. The biologic behavior of malignant tumors is similar to that of **sarcomas.**

   F. **Treatment** is **wide local excision to tumor-free margins or total mastectomy.** Axillary assessment with either SLNB or ALND is **not** indicated unless nodes are clinically positive (which is rare).

   G. Currently, there is no role for adjuvant radiation; however, tumors greater than 5 cm in diameter and with evidence of stromal overgrowth may benefit from adjuvant chemotherapy with doxorubicin and ifosfamide (*Cancer.* 2000;89:1510).

   H. Patients should be followed with semiannual physical examinations and annual mammograms and chest radiographs.

28 Otolaryngology: Head and Neck Surgery

Sunitha M. Sequeira and Bruce H. Haughey

I. THE EAR

A. **Anatomy and physiology**

1. **External ear.** The auricle (pinna) is composed of elastic cartilage and channels sound waves to the external auditory canal, which is bone medially and cartilage laterally.

2. **Middle ear.** The middle ear is a mucosa-lined sinus in the temporal bone containing the ossicular chain. The tympanic membrane (TM) vibrates in response to sound waves, and transmits this mechanical energy via the ossicles (malleus, incus, and stapes) to the oval window of the cochlea. The difference in surface area between the TM and oval window, along with the lever action of the ossicles, results in a 22-fold amplification of sound energy. The eustachian tube (ET) connects the middle ear with the nasopharynx, allowing aeration of the middle ear, drainage of fluid, and protection from pharyngeal pathogens. It is opened by contraction of the tensor veli palatini muscle, during swallowing or yawning.

3. **Inner ear.** The end-organs of hearing and balance are surrounded by thick bone, the otic capsule. The cochlea is a snail-shaped structure containing the organ of Corti. The vestibular system consists of three semicircular canals, which sense angular acceleration, and the saccule and utricle, which sense linear acceleration, yielding a sense of spatial orientation and movement. The cochlea and vestibular system convert mechanical energy into neuroelectric inputs, which are transmitted to the pons via cranial nerve (CN) VIII, the **vestibulocochlear nerve.**

4. The **facial nerve** (CN VII) travels a complex path through the temporal bone, where it is vulnerable to trauma, and the middle ear. It innervates the facial musculature, stapedius muscle, and taste sensation for the anterior 2/3 of the tongue via the chorda tympani.

B. **Infectious/Inflammatory disorders**

1. **Otitis externa** ("swimmer's ear") is inflammation of the external auditory canal. Moisture and local trauma (e.g., q-tips) allow bacterial infection, causing severe ear pain, drainage, pruritus, canal swelling, and conductive hearing loss (CHL). It may progress to auricular swelling and facial cellulitis. Common pathogens include *pseudomonas aeruginosa* and fungus. Treatment includes topical antibiotic drops, antiseptic drying drops, and aural toilet.

    a. Persistent otitis externa in a diabetic or immunocompromised patient should raise concern for **necrotizing otitis externa** (malignant otitis externa), a potentially fatal skull base osteomyelitis that can spread intracranially. Patients have long-standing otalgia, otorrhea, and granulation tissue in the external auditory canal. Work-up includes computed tomography (CT) or magnetic resonance imaging (MRI) and radionuclide bone scans. Treatment is intravenous (IV) antibiotics and surgical debridement.

    b. A nonhealing, weepy erythematous ear canal lesion in an adult should undergo biopsy, for concern of squamous cell carcinoma (SCC).

2. Acute otitis media (AOM) is acute inflammation of the middle ear, usually of infectious etiology. Common in children, it presents with fevers, otalgia, irritability, decreased appetite, hearing loss, and a thickened, red, bulging TM. Typical pathogens are *Streptococcus pneumoniae, haemophilus influenzae,* and *Moraxella catarrhalis.* Risk factors include day-care attendance, cigarette smoke exposure, young age (immature immune system), male sex, winter months, and genetics. **ET dysfunction** significantly contributes to AOM—young children have immature, weak, and more horizontal ET cartilage, contributing to poor aeration of the middle ear and poor protection from pharyngeal pathogens. Breastfeeding is protective. Because spontaneous resolution often occurs, watchful waiting is preferred for children older than 2 years or nontoxic children older than 6 months (without severe otalgia or high fevers), to reduce antibiotic usage and resistance. Treatment (first line is amoxicillin) is indicated for symptoms longer than 48 to 72 hours or children younger than 6 months. For recurrent OM more frequent than three to four episodes in 6 months or four to six episodes in a year (recommendations vary), tympanostomy tube placement reduces the frequency of ear infections, facilitates diagnosis (as OM then manifests as ear drainage), and reduces the necessity for systemic antibiotics (by allowing topical treatment via ear drops). Adenoidectomy also reduces number of infections, and is performed if repeat ear tubes are needed.

3. Otitis media with effusion (OME), or **serous OM,** is fluid present in the middle ear without acute infection. It may result from resolving AOM or ET dysfunction. Patients present with hearing loss, aural fullness/pressure, and a dull, gray, or yellow TM with reduced mobility. OME usually resolves spontaneously. Tympanostomy tube placement is indicated for bilateral OME for greater than 3 months, unilateral OME for more than 6 months, and in children with hearing loss and concerns for speech/language delay. Adults with persistent unilateral OME should undergo evaluation of the nasopharynx for masses causing ET obstruction.

4. Complications from OM are uncommon and include TM perforation, tympanosclerosis, mastoiditis, facial nerve palsy, labyrinthitis, meningitis, intracranial abscess, sigmoid sinus thrombosis, and otitic hydrocephalus.

    a. Tympanosclerosis is hyalinization and calcium deposition onto the middle ear and TM, resulting in white plaques, in response to inflammation or trauma (e.g., tympanostomy tubes). It is usually asymptomatic but can cause ossicular fixation and hearing loss.

b. **Mastoiditis** is a clinical diagnosis, based on history of fevers, otalgia, postauricular tender swelling and a proptotic pinna. CT shows severity of infection, including subperiosteal abscess and intracranial complications. Mastoid fluid on CT without clinical correlation is not diagnostic of mastoiditis. Treatment is IV antibiotics; tympanostomy and/or mastoidectomy are indicated for no response or complications.

C. **Hearing loss** is classified as conductive, sensorineural, or mixed.

1. CHL is caused by pathology of the external auditory canal, TM, and middle ear, resulting in attenuation of sound energy delivered to the inner ear. In adults, the most common cause is impacted cerumen (wax). In kids, it is OM. Other causes include TM perforation, ossicular discontinuity or fixation, otosclerosis, and cholesteatoma.

2. **Sensorineural hearing loss** (SNHL) involves the cochlea or auditory neural pathway. The most common causes are presbycusis (age-related hearing loss), noise exposure, and hereditary. Other etiologies include viral or bacterial infections, ototoxicity (due to aminoglycosides, platinum-based chemotherapy, loop diuretics), vestibular schwannomas, temporal bone trauma, and autoimmune disease. Congenital SNHL occurs in 1 to 2 in 1,000 newborns, with approximately 50% from genetic etiology.

3. **Evaluation of hearing**

   a. **Tuning fork testing.** Bedside assessment of hearing is performed with a 512 Hz tuning fork. In the **Weber** test, the tuning fork is placed on patient's midline forehead or maxillary incisor teeth. Those with normal hearing perceive the sound as equal intensity in both ears. In CHL, sound is louder in the affected ear. In SNHL, sound is heard louder in the contralateral ear. In the **Rinne** test, the tuning fork is held lateral to the auricle (air conduction), and placed on the mastoid tip (bone conduction). In normal hearing, air conduction is perceived as louder; in CHL, bone conduction is louder.

   b. **Audiometry.** An audiogram tests air and bone conduction hearing to pure-tone sounds and speech sounds. Tympanometry measures ear canal volume, TM integrity and compliance, as well as the stapedial reflex (seventh/eighth CN reflex arc). SNHL is diagnosed as equal losses of bone and air conduction; CHL is loss of air conduction with normal bone conduction, resulting in an air-bone gap. In mixed hearing loss, there is an air-bone gap and a loss of bone conduction. Decreased word-discrimination scores out of proportion to pure-tone hearing loss suggest retrocochlear pathology (e.g., vestibular schwannoma). Reduced TM peak compliance on tympanometry is consistent with middle ear pathology (e.g., middle ear effusion).

   c. **Newborn screening.** Universal hearing screening leads to early detection of congenital hearing loss and early intervention to facilitate language development. Newborn hearing screens are performed with **otoacoustic emission** (OAE) testing, which detects sound waves generated by cochlear outer hair cells in response to sound. **Auditory brainstem response** (ABR) measures neural activity from the cochlea along the cochlear nerve (CN VIII) to the midbrain. Behavioral audiometry can be done when a child is approximately 9 months. In adults, ABR is useful for detection of vestibular schwannoma.

4. **Treatment of hearing loss**
   a. Most of hearing loss is treated with behavioral modification and hearing aids. Idiopathic sudden SNHL can be treated with high-dose systemic or intratympanic steroids.
   b. Profoundly deaf individuals who do not benefit from hearing aids are candidates for cochlear implant (CI), in which an electrode array is placed into the cochlea. A microphone worn near the ear receives and transmits acoustic signals to the implanted electrode, which then stimulates the cochlear nerve. Preimplant evaluation and postimplant rehabilitation are crucial factors in the effectiveness of the implant.
   c. CHL can often be treated successfully by restoring the sound conduction pathway. This may be done through repair of the TM (tympanoplasty), ossicular chain reconstruction, stapedectomy (for otosclerosis), or removal of cholesteatoma. Bone anchored hearing aids (BAHA) are implantable hearing aids that bypass the sound conduction pathway.

D. **A cholesteatoma** is a nonneoplastic epithelial-lined cyst containing keratinous debris that expands and causes bony erosion. Patients may present with hearing loss, otorrhea, otalgia, and a pearly-white mass in their middle ear or on their TM. It may also cause vertigo from perilymphatic fistula, facial paresis, and similar complications to OM. Treatment is surgical resection, with tympanoplasty and mastoidectomy. Cholesteatomas often recur.

1. *Primary-acquired* cholesteatoma results from ET dysfunction and negative pressure in the middle ear. A retraction pocket develops in the pars flaccida (the superior segment of the TM), collects squamous debris, and expands into the middle ear and mastoid.

2. *Secondary-acquired* cholesteatoma arises from a TM perforation with medial migration of squamous epithelium bordering the perforation.

3. *Congenital* cholesteatoma presents as a white mass in the anterosuperior quadrant with no prior history of otologic surgery, and an intact TM.

E. **Vestibular schwannoma** (acoustic neuroma) is a benign neoplasm of CN VIII arising in the internal auditory canal (IAC). They can be nonhereditary or associated with neurofibromatosis type 2. Symptoms include unilateral hearing loss, vertigo, imbalance, or facial paralysis due to facial nerve compression in the IAC. As they grow into the cerebropontine angle, they may cause additional CN deficits and headaches from elevated intracranial pressure. Work-up includes audiogram and MRI. ABR may be used to screen. Treatment is surgical excision via craniotomy. Many are slow growing and may be closely monitored, particularly in patients not suitable for surgery.

F. **Dizziness.** True **vertigo** originates from the inner ear, and is described as a sensation of spinning or moving. This must be distinguished from *nonotologic dizziness,* characterized by unsteadiness, lightheadedness, or syncope. Causes of this may be cardiovascular (orthostatic hypotension, vertebrobasilar insufficiency, cerebellar/brainstem infarction), metabolic (hypoglycemia, hypothyroidism, drug-induced), neurogenic (migraines, multiple sclerosis, neoplasm), or psychogenic. Diagnosis is primarily from history and physical exam (particularly provocation of nystagmus). Vestibular testing is complementary, and includes electronystagmography, caloric testing, rotational chair analysis, and dynamic posturography. Causes of vertigo are best organized by the chronology of symptoms:

1. **Seconds to minutes. Benign paroxysmal positional vertigo** (BPPV) is the most common cause of transient vertigo. It is precipitated by changes in head position and is caused by stimulation of the vestibular system by free-floating calcium carbonate crystals within the semicircular canals, usually in the posterior semicircular canal. It is diagnosed by the Dix–Hallpike maneuver. Canalith repositioning maneuvers (Epley technique) are immediately effective in 80% of patients with BPPV (*Otolaryngol Head Neck Surg.* 2006;135:529). Refractory cases may undergo semicircular canal plugging.

2. **Hours. Ménière disease** (endolymphatic hydrops) is characterized by episodic vertigo, hearing loss, tinnitus, and aural fullness. Treatment is salt restriction, diuretics, and vestibular suppressants. Intratympanic dexamethasone or gentamicin injection may be effective. Refractory cases can undergo endolymphatic sac surgery, labyrinthectomy, or vestibular nerve sectioning.

3. **Days. Viral labyrinthitis/viral neuronitis** (inflammation of the inner ear labyrinth or nerve, respectively) can cause days to even weeks of vertigo. Disequilibrium may persist for months. Treatment is supportive; vestibular rehabilitation can be helpful. Other causes include temporal bone trauma and vestibular schwannoma.

G. **Trauma**

1. An **auricular hematoma** presents as a tender, fluctuant subperichondrial swelling effacing the normal anatomy of the pinna. It can result in cartilage necrosis and a "cauliflower" ear deformity. Treatment is incision and drainage (I&D), with bolster placement to prevent reaccumulation.

2. **Foreign bodies** should be removed under binocular microscopy. If organic material is present, irrigation or topical drops should not be used, as this causes painful expansion of the material and difficult removal. Batteries (in the ear canal or upper aerodigestive tract) must be removed urgently, as leakage of contents can cause burns and later stenosis.

3. Traumatic **TM perforation** usually resolves spontaneously. Antibiotic drops may be prescribed prophylactically, and the patient should avoid

water entry into the ear canal. Chronic perforations may undergo surgical repair.

4. Temporal bone fracture results from high-velocity blunt trauma, often due to motor-vehicle accidents. Physical exam findings include Battle's sign (postauricular ecchymosis) and hemotympanum. Most fractures can be diagnosed by head CT, which is usually sufficient in an asymptomatic patient. High-resolution temporal bone CT is useful in the presence of facial weakness, cerebrospinal fluid (CSF) fistula, vascular injury, and for operative planning. Fractures are categorized as longitudinal (80%) or transverse (20%) with respect to the petrous apex. Transverse fractures are more likely to cause SNHL or facial nerve injury. Acute facial paralysis warrants surgical exploration and nerve decompression. Delayed facial weakness is likely secondary to nerve edema, and usually recovers spontaneously. CSF fistula/leak is a serious sequela of temporal bone fracture, and may present with middle ear effusion, clear rhinorrhea (drainage via ET), or clear otorrhea via a TM perforation. Most CSF leaks resolve spontaneously with conservative measures such as bed-rest and lumbar drain. Surgical repair is typically indicated for CSF leaks persistent for more than 1 week, as these are less likely to spontaneously close and are associated with risk of meningitis. In any case, patients should undergo formal audiometry 4 to 6 weeks after injury (allowing hemotympanum to clear) to assess hearing.

II. THE NOSE AND PARANASAL SINUSES

A. Anatomy and Physiology

1. The **nose** and **septum** are composed of bone superiorly and posteriorly, and cartilage anteriorly. The turbinates (superior, middle, inferior, and supreme) are mucosa-covered bony prominences from the lateral nasal cavity that humidify, warm, and filter inhaled air. The choanae open the nasal cavity into the nasopharynx. The nasopharynx contains the ET orifices bilaterally, and the adenoid pad centrally, which involute in late childhood. Superiorly, the olfactory nerve (CN I) penetrates the cribriform plate with receptors that sense smell. The nasal cavity is lined by ciliated mucosa rich in mucus glands, nerves, blood vessels, and inflammatory cells.

2. The **paranasal sinuses** are pneumatized cavities in the skull named for the bone in which they lie (frontal, sphenoid, ethmoid, maxillary). They reduce the weight of the skull, contribute to the resonance of voice, and cushion the cranial contents against trauma. They are lined with ciliated respiratory epithelium that directs clearance of mucus and inhaled particles into the nose, and then into the pharynx. Obstruction of the outlets of drainage, or ostia, can occur from anatomic abnormalities, inflammation, or masses, causing fluid accumulation and symptoms.

B. Congenital disorders

1. Congenital nasal masses include encephaloceles, dermoid cysts, and gliomas. They may present intranasally or extranasally as a midline

nose or lower forehead mass. MRI evaluates for intracranial extension. Treatment is surgical excision.

2. **Choanal atresia** is the persistence of the embryologic nasobuccal membrane, preventing communication between the nose and the nasopharynx. Bilateral choanal atresia presents with respiratory distress soon after birth, typically requiring intubation, as neonates are obligate nasal breathers. Diagnosis is confirmed by failure to pass a nasogastric tube. Unilateral choanal atresia often presents later in life. Choanal atresia is more commonly unilateral, associated with other anomalies, and in females. Choanal atresia is repaired surgically.

C. **Infectious/inflammatory disorders**

1. **Acute rhinosinusitis** arises from infectious, allergic, and drug-induced etiologies. Although most acute rhinosinusitis is viral, bacterial superinfection may occur, typically with *S. pneumoniae, H. influenzae, M. catarrhalis,* or *S. aureus.* Criteria for diagnosis include **two** of the following **major features:** facial pain/pressure, nasal discharge, nasal obstruction, anosmia or hyposmia, fevers (for acute sinusitis), and purulence in nasal cavity on exam; and **two minor criteria:** dental pain, halitosis, cough, ear discomfort, fatigue, and fevers (for chronic sinusitis). Treatment consists of saline nasal irrigations to improve mucociliary clearance, mucolytics to thin secretions, hydration, and antibiotics for bacterial sinusitis (first-line amoxicillin). Nasal topical steroids reduce symptom duration. Topical decongestion (e.g., oxymetalozone) aids in symptomatic relief; however, use *should not exceed three days,* as may result in rebound congestion, or *rhinitis medicamentosa.* Antihistamines dry mucous secretions, and therefore are not recommended unless allergy symptoms are present. Intraorbital or intracranial infectious complications may rarely occur.

2. **Chronic rhinosinusitis** is symptoms for more than 12 weeks with signs of inflammation on exam (nasal polyps, polypoid mucosal changes, or purulent drainage). Sinus CT may show mucosal thickening, sinus opacification, obstruction of the osteomeatal complex, and anatomic/bony abnormalities. Treatment typically includes combination of antibiotics, nasal saline irrigation, and topical nasal and/or oral steroids. Patients refractory to medical therapy benefit from **functional endoscopic sinus surgery (FESS)** (*Curr Opin Otolaryngol Head Neck Surg.* 2007;15:6). The objectives of FESS are to reestablish the patency of the sinus ostia, ventilate the sinuses, and selectively remove diseased mucosa or polyps.

3. **Fungal sinusitis**
   a. *Noninvasive fungal sinusitis,* caused by *Aspergillus* infection, includes mycetoma (fungus ball) and allergic fungal sinusitis. It is treated with steroids, saline irrigations, and FESS.
   b. *Acute invasive fungal sinusitis* is an aggressive, potentially fatal mucormycosis. Immunocompromised patients, particularly those with hematologic malignancies or diabetic ketoacidosis, are at risk. Management is IV antifungal therapy and surgical debridement of necrotic tissue.

D. **Nasal airway obstruction** has many causes, from rhinosinusitis to anatomic obstructions.

1. **Adenoid hypertrophy.** The adenoids are lymphoid tissue present in
the posterior nasopharynx that hypertrophy during childhood and then
atrophy with age. Adenoid hypertrophy can cause nasal obstruction,
snoring, sleep-disordered breathing, and recurrent OM. Adenoidectomy is often performed in conjunction with tonsillectomy.

2. **Nasal polyposis.** Nasal polyps are inflammatory, edematous, hyperplastic regions of nasal mucosa that often obstruct sinus drainage. The
etiology of nasal polyps is unknown, but they are commonly associated
with systemic diseases (cystic fibrosis, allergies, chronic rhinosinusitis, or Samter's triad: aspirin sensitivity, asthma, and nasal polyposis).
Nasal polyps are usually treated with nasal or systemic steroids and
surgical debulking.

3. **Nasal septal deviation** results from nasal trauma or differential
growth. The role of septal deviation in sinus disease is controversial
(*Otolaryngol Head Neck Surg.* 2005;133:190). Septal deviation can be
corrected (septoplasty) in conjunction with FESS if nasal obstruction
and sinus disease are present.

E. **Epistaxis** has many causes, including trauma, neoplasm, environmental
irritants, rhinitis, coagulopathies, and granulomatous diseases (e.g., Wegener's
disease and sarcoidosis). Unilateral recurrent epistaxis with nasal airway
obstruction should prompt evaluation for a mass. Most epistaxis is minor.
However, due to the significant vascularity of the nose, hemorrhage can
be life threatening. Address ABCs first (airway, breathing, circulation) and
treat underlying causes. The patient should pinch the cartilaginous nose
and lean forward to avoid swallowing blood; a vasoconstrictor such as oxymetalozone spray should be applied. Much of epistaxis resolves with these
measures. The most common site of bleeding is Kisselbach's plexus, on
the anterior caudal septum. Bleeding can be cauterized with silver nitrate
or electrocautery. The nose can also be packed using epistaxis balloons,
gauze, or absorbable hemostatic agents. Arterial embolization is reserved
for refractory cases. Preventative measures involve moisturization via nasal
saline spray, Vaseline application, and humidification of air.

F. **Neoplasms**

1. **Benign**

a. The most common benign lesion is the **inverted papilloma,** a
wart-like growth usually arising from the lateral nasal wall. It has a
10% incidence of malignant transformation into SCC. Wide local
excision is necessary to prevent recurrence.

b. **Juvenile nasopharyngeal angiofibromas** are vascular tumors
usually presenting in adolescent boys with nasal obstruction and
recurrent epistaxis. Treatment is surgical excision, with preoperative
embolization to reduce blood loss.

2. **Malignant**

a. **Nasopharyngeal SCC** is most common in Asia and Africa, where
it is often associated with the Epstein–Barr virus (EBV). Treatment

is chemotherapy and radiation, with surgical resection reserved for residual disease. Cervical metastasis is very common, in up to 80% at presentation.

b. Other sinonasal cancers include adenocarcinoma, adenoid cystic carcinoma, olfactory esthesioneuroblastoma, mucosal melanoma, and sinonasal undifferentiated carcinoma; other nasopharyngeal tumors include lymphoepithelioma and lymphoma.

G. **Trauma.** Maxillofacial fractures are usually due to blunt trauma. Operative repair is indicated for functional restoration and cosmesis.

1. **Nasal bone fractures** may result in cosmetic deformity and nasal airway obstruction. Epistaxis and airway management are the first priority. Closed reduction should be done 3 to 14 days after injury to allow improvement in swelling and avoidance of bony healing.

2. **Nasal septal hematoma** may occur with any nasal trauma. Blood collects between the septal mucoperichondrium and cartilage, which can cause cartilage ischemia, necrosis, and septal perforation. Large septal perforations can cause a "saddle nose" deformity. Treatment is I&D.

3. **Orbital blowout fractures** usually involve the medial and inferior orbit walls. Patients may have diplopia and hypesthesia of the cheek due to fracture along the infraorbital canal. Surgery is indicated for entrapment of the inferior rectus muscle causing restricted ocular movement, defects greater than 50%, or enophthalmos/hypophthalmos. Ophthalmologic evaluation for intraocular injury is also recommended.

4. **Le Fort fractures** involve the pterygoid plates (and other bones according to classification), mobilizing the maxilla from the skull base. Le Fort I fracture separates the maxillary alveolus from the upper maxilla via transverse fractures across the maxillary sinus and nasal septum. Le Fort II fracture creates a mobile pyramidal nasomaxillary segment by extending superiorly through the maxilla, across the orbital floor and nasal bones. Le Fort III fracture, or craniofacial disjunction, separates the entire midface from the cranium, extending through the zygoma and transversely through the orbits and nasal bones. The midface withstands the forces of mastication via the vertical and horizontal buttresses. Operative goals are to stabilize the buttresses, restore occlusion (dental relationship), and cosmesis.

III. ORAL CAVITY AND PHARYNX

A. **Anatomy and physiology**

1. **The oral cavity plays a crucial role in articulation and deglutition.** The oral cavity extends from the vermillion border of the lips anteriorly to the circumvallate papillae and junction of the hard and soft palate posteriorly. The pharynx is divided into the nasopharynx, oropharynx (which includes the lingual and palatine tonsils, and soft palate), and hypopharynx. Swallowing is a complex sensorimotor task involving soft palate elevation, elevation and retrusion of the tongue, laryngeal elevation, glottic closure, epiglottic retroflexion, and pharyngeal/esophageal peristalsis.

B. Congenital disorders

1. **Pierre–Robin sequence** is micrognathia, glossoptosis, and cleft palate, often resulting in significant airway obstruction and feeding difficulties. Airway obstruction can be treated with prone positioning, glossopexy, mandibular advancement, or tracheostomy.

2. **Cleft lip and palate.** Failure of the midface processes to fuse during embryogenesis results in clefts. Ideal management is by a multidisciplinary team, to address feeding, respiratory, hearing, cosmetic, speech, and psychosocial issues. Cleft palate causes abnormal insertion of the tensor veli palatini muscle, resulting in ET dysfunction, recurrent AOM, and OME. The otolaryngologist typically manages airway concerns, ear disease, velopharyngeal insufficiency, and sometimes cleft repair. Timing of repair is variable; cleft lips are often repaired after 10 weeks of age, and cleft palates by 1 year (to improve speech development).

C. Infectious/inflammatory disorders

1. **Ulcers** in the oral cavity are common and are usually related to viral infections, nutritional deficiencies, or glandular changes. Treatment is generally supportive. A variety of oral rinses are available that contain antifungal, antihistamine, antibiotic, steroid, and coating agents. Nonhealing ulcers should be biopsied for malignancy.

2. **Tonsillopharyngitis** is usually viral; bacterial infection (typically group A β-hemolytic streptococci) is seen in approximately 40% of children and 10% adults. Antibiotic treatment is reserved for rapid test (or culture) positive cases. Treatment is penicillin (β-hemolytic streptococci are generally not resistant) or clindamycin for penicillin-allergic patients. Current guidelines recommend tonsillectomy (+/– adenoidectomy), in children with seven to eight or more episodes per year, or five episodes per year for 2 years, or three episodes per year for 3 years. Tonsillectomy reduces frequency of episodes but may not eliminate tonsillopharyngitis.

3. **Peritonsillar abscess** (PTA) refers to purulence between the tonsil bed and capsule. It is characterized by fevers, severe throat pain, trismus, drooling, and a muffled "hot potato voice." Physical exam reveals a bulging, erythematous soft palate with uvular, and tonsillar deviation. Treatment is needle aspiration or I&D, and antibiotics.

4. **Retropharyngeal abscess** occurs primarily in children younger than 2 due to suppuration of retropharyngeal lymph nodes. Children present with irritability, fever, stiff neck, muffled speech, cervical lymphadenopathy, and posterior pharyngeal swelling. Contrast-enhanced CT delineates the extent of infection. Some patients may respond to IV antibiotics, otherwise oral intubation and transoral drainage is performed.

D. Neoplasms

1. **Benign**
   a. **Ameloblastoma** is a locally invasive tumor arising from odontogenic epithelium, most frequently occurring in the mandible. It often requires segmental mandibulectomy with reconstruction.

    b. Other neoplasms include papillomas and hemangiomas.

    c. Premalignant lesions include leukoplakia (white hyperkeratotic patches) and erythroplakia (velvet-red patches).

2. Malignant

    a. SCC is the most common neoplasm of the head and neck. Tobacco and alcohol abuse synergistically increase risk for SCC. Human papilloma virus (HPV; genotypes 16 and 18) infection is also a causative agent in a subset of SCC, particularly of the lingual and palatine tonsils, and is seen in younger patients, often without significant tobacco or alcohol use. SCC is also associated with chronic inflammation, chronic trauma (e.g., poorly-fitting dentures), betel-nut chewing, Plummer–Vinson syndrome, and sun exposure (for lip cancer). Work-up includes a thorough head-and-neck history and physical examination, contrast-enhanced CT, biopsy, and possibly positron emission tomography (PET) and MRI. Operative endoscopic biopsies are done to assess extent of the tumor, detect synchronous primaries, and provide tissue for pathologic analysis. Staging follows the TNM (primary Tumor, regional Nodal metastases, distant Metastasis) site-specific guidelines from the American Joint Committee on Cancer (AJCC). Treatment involves a multidisciplinary team consisting of head and neck surgeons, radiation oncologists, medical oncologists, pathologists, and speech/swallowing therapists. Treatment of SCC is complex and based on location, nodal involvement, local invasion, and metastasis. Early stage (I–II) cancers are usually treated with single modality therapy (surgery or radiation), and advanced stage (III–IV) with combined modalities (surgery and chemoradiation).

    b. Oral cavity and oropharyngeal SCC may present with a metastatic neck mass, nonhealing painful oral ulcers, otalgia, odynophagia, dysphagia, trismus, and/or dysphonia. Typical treatment is surgical resection of primary, and neck dissection for clinically palpable nodes or in cases where risk of metastasis exceeds 20%. Postoperative radiation is indicated for high-risk tumors: advanced T-stage, perineural invasion, close/positive margins, multiple malignant lymph nodes, and/or lymph node extracapsular extension. Chemotherapy may be added to radiation for extracapsular spread and positive margins. Lingual and palatine tonsil SCC associated with HPV infection is more responsive to therapy, with improved survival (*Laryngoscope.* 2010;120(9):1756–1772). Emerging approaches such as transoral laser microsurgery provide good oncologic and functional outcome. Primary chemoradiation may be used for large oropharyngeal cancers (in which resection would cause significant morbidity), with goal of protecting speech and swallowing function; however, chemoradiotherapy itself usually causes significant swallowing dysfunction.

    c. Other oral cavity and oropharyngeal cancers include minor salivary gland carcinomas, verrucous carcinoma, lymphoma, mucosal melanoma, and Kaposi's sarcoma.

E. **Obstructive sleep apnea (OSA)** is dysfunctional respiration during sleep due to upper airway obstruction. Symptoms of OSA in children often include behavioral, learning, and growth problems, whereas OSA in adults is usually manifest by excessive daytime sleepiness. Untreated OSA can lead to pulmonary hypertension and cor pulmonale. The most common cause of OSA in children is adenotonsillar hypertrophy, whereas in adults it is obesity. Overnight polysomnography is the gold standard for diagnosing OSA. Adenotonsillectomy is first-line treatment in children, improving polysomnography parameters and quality of life (*Laryngoscope.* 2007;117(10):1844–1854). In adults, OSA is usually successfully treated with continuous positive airway pressure (CPAP). Surgery (uvulopalatopharyngoplasty, tongue base reduction, maxillomandibular advancement, or tracheostomy) is reserved for refractory cases.

F. **Trauma**

1. **Mandible fractures** (MFs) occur most commonly at the angle and parasymphysis, as well as at the condylar neck. Fractures present with dental malocclusion, halitosis, and pain with crepitus while chewing or on manipulation. Panorex radiographs are usually sufficient to diagnose MF and visualize postreduction; however, high-resolution maxillofacial CT may be more sensitive. Imaging modality is usually influenced by surgeon preference. Minimally displaced fractures can be treated by closed reduction and external fixation (mandibulomaxillary fixation, or "wiring the jaw shut"), for 4 weeks. Open reduction and internal fixation with lag screws and/or plates are used for treating displaced or comminuted fractures. Fixation within 3 days has been shown to result in more favorable outcomes (*Laryngoscope.* 2005;115:769). Complications of MF include wound infection, malocclusion, nonunion, tooth loss, temporomandibular joint ankylosis, and paresthesias.

IV. THE SALIVARY GLANDS

A. **Anatomy and physiology**

1. There are three pairs of major salivary glands (parotid, submandibular, and sublingual) and many minor salivary glands in the mucosa of the oral cavity, oropharynx, and nasopharynx. These produce 1 to 1.5 L of saliva per day, which provides lubrication during mastication, inhibits bacterial growth, and contains digestive enzymes.

2. The largest salivary gland, the **parotid gland,** lies over the masseter muscle, and is the predominant producer of saliva during mastication, secreting serous saliva. The parotid duct (Stensen's duct) exits the buccal mucosa opposite the second maxillary molar. The facial nerve (CN VII) travels through the parotid gland, artificially dividing the gland into superficial and deep lobes. The **submandibular gland** is inferomedial to the mandible, and produces a mixture of mucinous and serous saliva. The submandibular duct (Wharton's duct) empties into the floor of the mouth just lateral to the lingual frenulum. The **sublingual gland** lies beneath the floor of the mouth mucosa, and secretes mucinous saliva.

B. **Inflammatory diseases**

1. **Acute sialadenitis** usually involves the parotid gland, presenting as a tender, indurated preauricular swelling, often with purulence expressible from Stensen's duct. It occurs from retrograde bacterial contamination from the oral cavity (usually *S. aureus* and oral anaerobes) due to stasis of inspissated saliva or stones. Postoperative, dehydrated, diabetic, and/or immunocompromised patients are particularly susceptible. Contrast-enhanced CT may be performed to evaluate for abscess or mass. Treatment is hydration, warm compresses, massage, antibiotics, and sialogogues (stimulants of saliva flow, such as lemon wedges).

2. **Sialolithiasis** (ductal calculi) most frequently affects the submandibular glands, causing transient swelling and pain when eating, and is diagnosed by palpation or radiography. Ductal stones are removed transorally using probing instruments, via open excision, or minimally invasively via sialoendoscopy. Symptomatic parenchymal calculi are treated with surgical removal of the gland.

3. **Chronic sialadenitis** is caused by stones or duct stenosis, and can result in gland hypertrophy and fibrosis. Those with significant pain can undergo resection of the gland.

4. **Viral infections** that can cause salivary gland inflammation include HIV (lymphoepithelial hyperplasia) and paramyxovirus (mumps, causing acute parotitis).

5. Noninfectious inflammatory systemic diseases such as Sjogren's disease and autoimmune disorders may cause bilateral parotid swelling due to lymphoid infiltration.

C. **Neoplasms.** Up to 80% of salivary gland neoplasms occur in the parotid gland, and of these 75% are benign. Half of submandibular neoplasms are malignant; the proportion of sublingual and minor salivary gland malignancies is even higher. The treatment of benign and malignant neoplasm is excision; however FNAB (US-guided if necessary) during the work-up is useful for surgical planning and patient counseling—to determine extent of resection, management of the facial nerve, and treatment of neck nodes. Other work-up includes CT and/or MRI. A history of skin cancer should be elicited, as scalp and facial skin cancer (e.g., SCC and melanoma) can metastasize to the parotid gland.

1. **Benign.** The most common neoplasm is **pleomorphic adenoma,** followed by **Warthin's tumor.** These tumors grow slowly, are painless, and usually occur in the parotid gland. Facial weakness is rare. Warthin's tumors may be bilateral and are associated with cigarette smoking. Treatment is excision with a cuff of normal parotid tissue, sometimes necessitating superficial parotidectomy, with facial nerve preservation. Both tumor types have a propensity for local recurrence.

2. **Malignancy** is suspected when pain, facial nerve paresis, fixation, and cervical lymphadenopathy are present. The most common malignancy is **mucoepidermoid carcinoma,** followed by **adenoid cystic carcinoma.** Other types include acinic cell carcinoma, adenocarcinoma, carcinoma ex-pleomorphic adenoma, and primary SCC. Treatment is

parotidectomy, with facial nerve sacrifice if involved in tumor, possible neck dissection, and possible adjuvant radiation therapy.

D. **Trauma.** Cheek lacerations can involve the parotid parenchyma, Stensen's duct, and branches of the facial nerve. Loss of facial function mandates exploration and epineural repair of the nerve if proximal (posterior) to a vertical line drawn at the lateral canthus. Injury to the parotid duct requires repair of the duct over a stent.

V. THE LARYNX

A. **Anatomy and physiology**

1. The larynx is divided into the **supraglottis** (which includes the epiglottis, arytenoid cartilages, false vocal cords/folds, and ventricles), the **glottis** (true vocal cords/folds), and **subglottis** (from the true vocal cords inferiorly to the cricoid cartilage). The thyroid and cricoid cartilages and the hyoid bone provide rigid support for the larynx.

2. The **superior laryngeal nerve** supplies sensory innervation to the supraglottic mucosa and motor innervation to the cricothyroid muscle. The **recurrent laryngeal nerve** provides sensory innervation to the remaining laryngeal mucosa and motor innervation to the intrinsic laryngeal muscles. Both are derived from the vagus nerve (CN X).

3. The larynx is a critical part of the aerodigestive tract for airway protection, deglutition, and phonation. Laryngeal elevation, glottic closure, and retroflexion of the epiglottis help to prevent aspiration during swallowing. Coughing occurs when the expiratory muscles contract to increase subglottic pressure against a closed glottis; the glottis then suddenly opens, resulting in a rapid outflow of air and expulsion of mucus from the airway.

4. Laryngeal or tracheobronchial obstruction results in **stridor.** Inspiratory stridor is usually from supraglottic obstruction. Biphasic stridor is caused by glottic or proximal tracheal obstruction. Expiratory stridor results from obstruction of the distal trachea or bronchi.

B. **Congenital disorders**

1. **Laryngomalacia** is the most common congenital disorder. Infants present with inspiratory stridor, typically exacerbated by feeding or crying. The etiology is likely neuromuscular hypotonia causing inspiratory supraglottic collapse. Awake flexible fiberoptic laryngoscopy demonstrates prolapse of the arytenoid mucosa into the airway on inspiration, shortened aryepiglottic folds, and often an omega-shaped epiglottis. Symptoms often worsen for the first 9 months of life and then improve, with 75% of patients asymptomatic by 18 months of age. Endoscopic supraglottoplasty is indicated for difficulty feeding and failure to thrive, apnea, cyanosis, or cardiopulmonary sequelae.

2. **Vocal cord paralysis** is the second most common laryngeal abnormality in the newborn, causing inspiratory or biphasic stridor (bilateral cord paralysis), aspiration, and weak cry. Etiologies include birth

trauma, neurologic disease (e.g., Arnold–Chiari malformation), and iatrogenic (e.g., patent ductus arterious ligation); it is often idiopathic. Diagnosis is made by awake flexible laryngoscopy. Work-up includes brain MRI and modified barium swallow (to evaluate for aspiration). Most noniatrogenic unilateral paralysis resolves spontaneously within the first year of life. Alternative feeding routes (nasogastric or gastrostomy tube) and speech therapy is utilized until then. Bilateral cord paralysis often requires tracheotomy.

3. **Subglottic stenosis** can cause inspiratory or biphasic stridor. Congenital stenosis is due to abnormally formed cricoid cartilage. Acquired stenosis is usually the sequelae of intubation. Mild stenosis often presents during upper respiratory infection (URI), resulting in croup-like symptoms. In less than 50% stenosis, patients often improve as they grow. Otherwise, surgical laryngotracheal reconstruction or cricotracheal resection may be necessary.

4. Other congenital laryngeal abnormalities include laryngeal atresia, webs, cysts, laryngeal clefts, and hemangiomas.

C. **Infectious/inflammatory disorders**

1. **Viral croup,** or viral laryngotracheitis, is glottic and subglottic inflammation usually from parainfluenza virus. It most frequently occurs in children younger than three, in the winter. Diagnosis is clinical—patients have a prodromal URI, followed by a barking cough, hoarseness, and inspiratory stridor. Lateral airway X-ray may show the "steeple sign" from subglottic edema. Treatment includes humidified air, glucocorticoids for moderate to severe croup, racemic epinephrine, and heliox. Recurrent croup should undergo rigid laryngoscopy and bronchoscopy after resolution to evaluate for underlying anatomic anomalies.

2. **Epiglottitis** is rare (due to *H. influenzae* type B vaccination), but a medical emergency. The presentation is acute (hours) with high fever, muffled voice, drooling, dyspnea, inspiratory stridor, and sitting upright. Treatment is urgent airway management and IV antibiotics.

3. **Acute laryngitis** is inflammation of the laryngeal mucosa and vocal cords resulting in hoarseness. Most cases occur in adults and are of viral origin. It is usually self-limited and treated by hydration and voice rest. Adult smokers with persistent hoarseness should undergo fiberoptic laryngoscopy to evaluate for lesions concerning for malignancy.

4. **Laryngopharyngeal reflux (LPR)** is characterized by hoarseness, cervical dysphagia, globus sensation, sore throat, cough, and chronic throat clearing, caused by retrograde movement of gastric contents. It is the most common cause of chronic laryngitis. In infants, it exacerbates laryngomalacia. Patients often do not have the heartburn/esophagitis associated with gastroesophageal reflux disease (GERD), and ancillary studies diagnostic of GERD may be inconclusive in LPR. Fiberoptic laryngoscopy primarily demonstrates laryngeal edema, but also can show erythema and thickening of the posterior glottic mucosa. Treatment is diet and behavioral modifications, as well as high-dose

proton-pump inhibitors (PPI). Treatment with twice-daily PPI for at least 3 months significantly improves symptoms and laryngeal appearance (*Otolaryngol Head Neck Surg.* 2008;139(3):414–420).

5. Other inflammatory lesions that affect the larynx include sulcus vocalis, contact ulcers, vocal cord nodules, granulomas, and smoker's laryngitis.

D. **Neuromuscular disorders**

1. **Vocal cord paralysis** occurs from recurrent laryngeal nerve injury, often due to surgery, neoplasm, or trauma to the neck or thorax. Recognized iatrogenic injuries should be repaired by primary epineural anastomosis or cable grafting. Patient with no history of surgery should undergo CT scan and/or MRI of the neck and chest. Unilateral paralysis may cause dysphonia and aspiration, depending on vocal cord position. Treatment consists of speech therapy and observation, as recovery often occurs over several months. Temporary vocal cord medialization via injection helps prevent aspiration and improve voice during nerve recovery, lasting up to 6 months. If significant problems persist, thyroplasty and laryngeal reinnervation are other surgical options. Bilateral paralysis can cause stridor from airway obstruction and is treated with arytenoidectomy, cordectomy, or tracheostomy.

2. **Chronic aspiration** is caused by loss of the protective functions of the larynx due to impaired motor activity or sensory loss. Aspiration can result in bronchopulmonary infection and airway obstruction. Patients may have coughing or choking during swallowing, or silent aspiration, which may present with sequelae such as fever and productive cough. Etiology includes cerebral compromise (stroke, brainstem neoplasm, traumatic brain injury), degenerative neurologic diseases (Parkinson disease, amyotrophic lateral sclerosis, multiple sclerosis), neuromuscular disorders (myasthenia gravis, muscular dystrophies), vagal or recurrent laryngeal nerve palsy, anatomic abnormalities (Zenker's diverticulum), and alteration of the larynx (cancer resection or radiation). Work-up includes chest X-ray and modified barium swallow study or functional endoscopic evaluation of swallowing (FEES) by speech therapy. Physical therapy with a speech therapist corrects many cases. Refractory cases may be treated with nasogastric or gastrostomy tube feedings or parenteral nutrition. Surgical treatments include tracheostomy, vocal cord medialization, and laryngectomy.

3. **Spasmodic dysphonia (laryngeal dystonia)** is laryngeal motion disorder with unclear pathophysiology. It is treated with botulinum toxin injections into the laryngeal musculature.

E. **Neoplasm**

1. **Benign**

   a. **Recurrent respiratory papillomatosis (RRP)** is the most common laryngeal neoplasm in children. Bulky papillomas, caused by HPV 6 and 11, arise on the larynx and tracheobronchial tree, causing hoarseness and airway obstruction. The mode of transmission is unclear, but thought to be vertical transmission during delivery from genital HPV infection. Treatment is repeated excision (with laser or microdebrider). Lesions usually recur. Malignant transformation to SCC can occur, but is rare.

2. **Malignant.** More than 90% of laryngeal malignancies are SCC (see Section III.D.2 for discussion of SCC). In the United States, glottic cancer is the most prevalent, followed by supraglottic cancer; subglottic cancer is rare. Presenting symptoms include dysphonia, odynophagia, dysphagia, otalgia, dyspnea, stridor, hemoptysis, and neck mass. Early stage (I or II) tumors are treated with surgery or primary radiotherapy. Advanced stage (III or IV) are treated with combination of surgery, radiotherapy, or chemoradiation. The oncologic gold standard is total laryngectomy. Organ-preservation treatments such as partial laryngectomy or primary chemoradiation offer good oncologic and functional outcomes, although the latter results in severe late toxicities in about 40%. Transoral laser microsurgery further reduces morbidity of partial laryngectomy compared with open partial procedures. Neck dissection is performed for supraglottic malignancies as rate of metastasis exceeds 20%. Glottic cancer has a low metastatic rate due to paucity of glottic lymphatics.

F. Trauma

1. Blunt or penetrating laryngeal trauma requires rapid airway assessment and management, often requiring intubation or awake tracheostomy. Work-up involves fiberoptic laryngoscopy, CT, and operative endoscopy. Laryngeal hematomas and small lacerations are managed conservatively with airway observation and humidified air. Displaced fractures and laryngeal instability require urgent tracheostomy followed by open reduction and internal fixation.

VI. THE NECK

A. Anatomy and physiology

1. The **anterior triangle** is defined by the body of the mandible superiorly, the anterior border of the sternocleidomastoid muscle laterally, and the midline anteriorly. It further divides into the submental, submandibular, carotid, and muscular spaces. The anterior triangle contains the carotid artery, internal jugular vein, nerves (CNs IX–XII and ansa cervicalis), larynx, trachea, pharynx, esophagus, submandibular, thyroid, and parathyroid glands, and strap muscles. The posterior triangle is bounded by the sternocleidomastoid muscle, the clavicle, and the trapezius muscle. It contains the spinal accessory nerve (CN XI), cervical and brachial plexuses, and thyrocervical trunk arising from the subclavian vessels.

2. The **cervical fascia** provides planes for passage of infection, hemorrhage, and surgical dissection. The superficial cervical fascia lies just beneath the skin. The deep cervical fascia has three layers: the superficial (or investing) layer, which is just deep to the platysma muscle and invests the sternocleidomastoid and trapezius muscles; the middle

(or visceral) layer, which envelops the thyroid gland, trachea, and esophagus; and the internal (or prevertebral) layer, which surrounds the deep neck musculature and cervical vertebrae.

3. The neck has an extensive **lymphatic system,** which is divided into six levels. Level I contains the submental and submandibular lymph nodes, level II through IV parallel the jugular vein, level V is the nodes of the posterior triangle, and level VI is the central compartment medial to the carotid artery. The retropharyngeal, suboccipital, and postauricular nodes are also distinct groups.

B. A **neck mass** is a common presenting complaint in which methodical work-up is important. History must focus on duration, progression, location, and associated symptoms (pain, URI symptoms, fevers, weight loss, dysphagia, voice changes, otalgia), past medical history, and social history (tobacco and alcohol use, travel history, animal exposures, sick contacts). Differential diagnosis is most strongly influenced by age. Neck masses in adults (particularly >40 years) are *presumed malignant until proven otherwise.* In contrast, neck masses in children are usually inflammatory; congenital etiology is less common and neoplasm is rare.

1. **Adult neck masses.** A neck mass that has not resolved after several weeks needs further evaluation. Eighty percent of adult neck masses are neo-plastic, most commonly metastatic SCC from an aerodigestive primary. A complete head and neck exam, with inspection of all mucosal and cutaneous sites, including indirect or fiberoptic laryngoscopy reveals a primary source in most cases. Work-up includes contrast-enhanced CT or MRI and, of paramount importance, fine needle aspiration biopsy (FNAB). PET is also important; however, because of low specificity, it should be ordered only once the patient is thoroughly evaluated by an experienced head and neck surgeon. If FNAB is negative, it should be repeated; ultrasound (US) guidance markedly improves yield. Unless lymphoma is suspected, core and excisional biopsies are avoided. Open/excisional biopsy of cervical metastatic SCC is not recommended since it is associated with increased risk of distant metastases and late locore-gional recurrence. If excisional biopsy is deemed necessary, for example, when lymphoma or other unusual diagnosis is found on FNA, intraop-erative frozen histologic analysis should be done and, if diagnostic of SCC, followed immediately by comprehensive neck dissection. Lym-phoma requires fresh tissue processing.

2. **Pediatric neck masses.** Children often have palpable hyperplastic lymph nodes; however, persistent masses larger than 2 cm should be investigated. Initial work-up is US, as this spares children radiation exposure, IV contrast, and sedation involved in CT and MRI. CT should be reserved for deep neck space infections, such as retropharyn-geal abscesses. Additional studies include WBC with differential and specific serologic tests for infectious etiologies.

C. **Congenital neck masses** are often cystic and may swell during a URI. The acute infection should be treated with antibiotics. I&D should be avoided, as it increases the difficulty of future excision (done when the inflammation has subsided). If necessary, needle aspiration may be performed for decompression. A cystic mass in adults should undergo FNAB as tonsillar SCC and papillary thyroid carcinoma can manifest as a cystic neck masses.

1. **Branchial cleft anomalies** comprise up to a third of congenital masses. The persistence of embryologic pharyngobranchial ducts can result in cysts, sinuses, or fistulae. The most common anomaly is of the second branchial cleft, which presents as a nontender, fluctuant mass anterior to the sternocleidomastoid muscle, with a deep tract that travels between the internal and external carotid arteries to the tonsillar fossa. Much less common are first branchial cleft anomalies, which present near the angle of the mandible or around the ear and may be associated with the facial nerve and ear canal. Third branchial cleft anomalies are rare; they present as a lower neck mass with tracts that end in the thyrohyoid membrane or pyriform sinus.

2. **Thyroglossal duct cysts** also make up a third of congenital neck masses. They arise from the failure of the thyroglossal duct to obliterate after the embryologic descent of the thyroid from the foramen cecum at the base of tongue to the low anterior neck. Patients present with a midline neck mass that moves vertically with swallowing and tongue protrusion, as the cyst tract is closely involved with the hyoid bone. Definitive treatment is the Sistrunk procedure, involving resection of the cyst, its tract, and the central portion of the hyoid bone, which reduces recurrence. Preoperative thyroid US ensures the cyst is not the sole functioning thyroid tissue. Transformation into papillary thyroid carcinoma may rarely occur.

3. A **hemangioma** presents as a reddish-bluish compressible mass in infancy that may have a bruit on auscultation, and increases in size with crying or straining. Cervical hemangiomas may be associated with subglottic, gastrointestinal, and spine vascular malformations. Hemangiomas typically grow rapidly during the first year of life, followed by slow involution at 18 to 24 months. Ninety percent resolve without need for treatment. Treatment is indicated for airway compromise, ulceration, dysphagia, thrombocytopenia, and cardiac failure. Recently, propranolol has been found to be an effective treatment (*N Engl J Med.* 2008;358(24):2649–2651; *Laryngoscope.* 2010;120(4):676–681). Steroids, laser therapy, and surgical resection are also other options.

4. **Lymphatic malformations** are soft, doughy, compressible lesions that may swell with URI. CT or MRI is done to evaluate extent. Treatment is indicated for cosmesis or symptomatic relief. Complete excision is difficult because of its infiltrative nature; debulking may be effective. Alternative treatments involve sclerotherapy.

5. Other congenital masses include laryngocele, dermoid cyst, teratoma, plunging ranula, and thymic cyst.

D. **Infectious/inflammatory disorders**

1. **Reactive lymphadenopathy** is commonly associated with viral URI, and is self-limited.

2. **Suppurative bacterial lymphadenitis** is common in children, usually from *S. aureus* or group A streptococcal infections. Treatment is IV antibiotics, with I&D for poor response.

3. **Acute mononucleosis,** caused by EBV infection, is a frequent etiology of cervical lymphadenopathy in young adults. It is associated with fevers, tonsillitis, and hepatosplenomegaly. Diagnosis is via monospot and/or EBV titers. Treatment is supportive.

4. **Deep neck space infections. Infections** can spread easily into potential spaces along the fascial planes of the neck. Etiology is most frequently dental infection, and also tonsillitis, trauma, or suppurative lymph nodes. Pathogens include streptococcal, staphylococcal, and oral anaerobic bacteria. Neck abscesses present with fevers, acute neck swelling, induration, redness, and tenderness. Dysphagia, odynophagia, and stridor/stertor may result from compression. Treatment is I&D and IV antibiotics. Ludwig's angina is cellulitis of the submandibular and submental spaces, causing retrusion of the tongue, a woody, firm floor of mouth, and potential for airway compromise. Treatment is airway control (intubation or tracheotomy) and IV antibiotics.

5. **Sialadenitis/sialolithiasis** (see Section IV.B).

6. Other infectious causes of lymphadenopathy include cat-scratch disease, atypical mycobacterial infection (subacute mass with violaceous overlying skin), and HIV (diffuse hyperplastic adenopathy).

7. Causes of noninfectious inflammatory lymphadenopathy include sarcoidosis, Kawasaki's disease, and Castleman syndrome. A low anterior midline mass may be thyroiditis.

E. Neoplasm

   1. **Benign**

      a. **Paragangliomas** are vascular tumors arising from paraganglionic cells of the autonomic nervous system. These are classified as jugulotympanic, vagal, sinonasal, laryngeal, and carotid body (most common) tumors. Catecholamine production, more commonly associated with multiple or familial presentation, is rare (3%). Treatment is surgical excision with preoperative embolization.

      b. Other benign tumors include lipomas, schwannomas, infiltrative fibromatosis, neurofibromas (associated with neurofibromatosis type I), and salivary gland neoplasms (see Section IV.C).

   2. **Malignant.** The most common malignant neck mass in adults is metastatic SCC, and in children, lymphoma. Location of the mass is suggestive of primary site, based on patterns of lymphatic drainage. Oral cavity cancers usually metastasize to the submandibular triangle. Lateral metastatic SCC at levels II and III typically arises from base of tongue, tonsil, or supraglottic larynx. Nasopharyngeal, scalp, and cutaneous tumors can metastasize to the posterior triangle. Central neck masses may be primary thyroid neoplasms. Papillary thyroid cancer can metastasize to any level of the neck. Masses in the supraclavicular fossa should elicit evaluation of the skin, trunk, lungs, and abdomen.

a. **SCC** of aerodigestive mucosa metastasizes to the neck at significant rates in oral cavity, nasopharynx, oropharynx, and supraglottic larynx primaries. (SCC is also discussed in Sections III and IV.) The neck is treated with lymphadenectomy, with possible adjuvant radiation and chemotherapy, often with combined modalities. Neck dissections are termed *therapeutic* for clinically palpable metastases or *elective* in the absence of clinical lymphadenopathy. *Radical* neck dissection includes resection of all lymph nodes, the sternocleidomastoid muscle, internal jugular vein, and spinal accessory nerve. *Modified radical* neck dissection reduces morbidity by sparing one or more of these structures. *Selective* neck dissection removes only nodal groups at greatest probability for containing metastases for a particular primary site.

(1) A special diagnostic dilemma is cervical SCC with unknown primary. In addition to the above work-up and treatment, patients should undergo operative panendoscopy with biopsies of the nasopharynx, and palatine and/or lingual tonsillectomy, as these are the usual sites of origin. Up to 40% of ipsilateral tonsil tissue harbors malignancy. PET/CT may also detect a primary source.

b. **Thyroid carcinoma.** Palpable thyroid nodules occur in 5% of women and 1% of men. Incidental diagnosis on imaging can approach 30%. Most patients are asymptomatic, but some may have dysphagia, difficulty breathing, and hoarseness. Up to 20% of nodules are carcinoma. Ninety percent of thyroid carcinomas are differentiated; 85% of these are papillary carcinoma, 10% follicular, and 3% Hurthle cell. Rare pathologies include lymphoma, metastatic lesions (e.g., melanoma), and anaplastic carcinoma. Initial work-up is TSH and US. Nodules larger than 1 cm, with suspicious US findings, or in high-risk patients, should undergo US-guided FNAB. Risk of malignancy is associated with older age, male sex, history of radiation exposure, and family history. Total thyroidectomy is indicated for FNAB diagnostic of malignancy, or in cases of suspected malignancy (suggestive FNAB or possibly high-risk patients). Lobectomy may be performed for indeterminate specimens (as incidence of malignancy is 20%), and low risk, small tumors. Tumor extent, completeness of resection, age, and metastases are important variables affecting prognosis. Up to 50% of patients with differentiated thyroid carcinoma have clinical cervical metastasis, particularly to the central compartment, although papillary carcinoma can metastasize to any level of the neck. For biopsy-positive lateral neck nodes, initial comprehensive *en-bloc* neck dissection is preferred to node-plucking. Postoperative radioactive iodine (in tumors able to take it up) is indicated for gross extrathyroidal extension, metastases, and large (>4 cm) tumors. Subsequent TSH suppression with levothyroxine reduces recurrence. Unresectable or anaplastic disease may undergo external beam radiation therapy. Chemotherapy is not routinely indicated.

    c. **Lymphoma.** The majority of head-and-neck lymphomas present in cervical lymph nodes, but also manifest in the tonsils, nasopharynx, paranasal sinuses, thyroid, and salivary glands. Up to 85% of Hodgkin's lymphoma presents as painless cervical lymphadenopathy, often with bulky, matted nodes. Patients are commonly pruritic, and may have "B symptoms" (fevers, night sweats, weight loss). Non-Hodgkin's lymphoma presents with similar symptoms, varying with subtype. Surgery aids in diagnosis and is not curative. FNAB provides cytologic material; tissue samples (obtained from core or excisional biopsy) are often required for architectural detail, flow cytometry, and immunophenotyping. Treatment is chemotherapy and radiation.

    d. **Adenocarcinoma** may be a primary salivary gland neoplasm or metastasis from the sinonasal airway, nasopharynx, salivary glands, and lungs.

F. **Trauma.** The neck is divided into three zones: zone I is the area inferior to the cricoid to 1 cm below the claviculomanubrial junction, zone II is between the cricoid and angle of mandible, and zone III is above the angle of mandible to the skull base.

    1. **Penetrating neck injuries** are wounds that violate the platysma. Zone II is most commonly involved. ABC's should be initially assessed, and ATLS protocol followed. Emergent surgical exploration is indicated for imminently life-threatening signs such as expanding hematoma, airway compromise, hemorrhage, and hemodynamic instability. In stable patients, mandatory versus selective neck exploration is controversial, as many explorations are negative. Management may be therefore directed by physical exam and adjunctive studies, with close observation for asymptomatic, hemodynamically stable patients (*J Oral Maxillofac Surg.* 2007;65(4):691–705). Signs such as bruits, crepitus, stridor, CN deficits, and hemoptysis support neck exploration. Vascular, laryngotracheal, and pharyngoesophageal injuries are evaluated by angiography (usually CT-angiography), water-soluble contrast esophagoscopy, and endoscopy. Hypopharyngeal injuries may be managed conservatively, with gastric decompression by nasogastric tube and IV antibiotics. Esophageal injuries close to the thorax can have considerable morbidity and mortality if gastric spillage occurs, and repair is recommended.

29 Plastic and Hand Surgery

Noopur Gangopadhyay and Thomas H. Tung

Plastic surgery has no defined anatomic territory and thus is a specialty built on principles and techniques rather than specific procedures. Plastic surgeons must optimize form and function in the setting of trauma, burns, congenital defects, postoncologic wounds, general reconstruction, and elective cosmetic improvements. Subspecialties include pediatrics, hand surgery, craniofacial surgery, peripheral nerve surgery, microsurgery, and aesthetic surgery. As the scope of plastic surgery is too broad to cover in one chapter, we discuss topics pertinent to the general surgeon that may be applied to a number of surgical situations.

BASIC TECHNIQUES AND PRINCIPLES

I. **THE RECONSTRUCTIVE LADDER.** When planning reconstruction, the simplest approach is often the best. The reconstructive ladder of soft-tissue coverage begins with consideration of the simplest approach (healing by secondary intention) and ends with the most complex (free tissue transfer), maximizing opportunities for success.

A. Healing by **secondary intention** is the simplest approach but is not always feasible. Absolute contraindications include exposed vessels, nerves, tendons, viscera, or bone. Relative contraindications include a large or poorly vascularized wound with a prolonged (>3 weeks) anticipated period of healing and undesirable aesthetic consequences.

B. **Primary closure** may provide the most aesthetically pleasing result, but excessive tension on the skin may cause displacement of neighboring structures (e.g., lower eyelid) or necrosis of the skin flaps.

C. **Skin grafting** is the most common method of large-wound closure. Skin grafts require a healthy, uninfected bed and protection from shear forces to survive. Wound surfaces such as bare tendon, desiccated bone or cartilage, radiation-damaged tissue, or infected wounds will not support skin graft survival. Exposed vessels, nerves, or viscera are relative contraindications for skin grafting.

D. **Local tissue transfers** of skin, fascia, and muscle may be used in regions with healthy tissue nearby. If the adjacent tissue cannot be adequately mobilized or the wound requires more bulk than is locally available, local flaps alone may not be adequate.

E. **Distant tissue transfers** were the mainstay of difficult wound closure until the advent of free tissue transfer in the 1970s. This involves transferring healthy tissue into the wound bed while leaving it attached to its native blood supply. The vascular pedicle is divided in a subsequent procedure.

Disadvantages of this technique include multiple operations, prolonged wound healing, immobilization for at least 3 weeks, and a limited choice of donor sites.

F. **Free tissue transfer** is the most technically demanding approach to wound closure but has several advantages, including single-stage wound closure, a relatively wide variety of flaps tailored to specific wound closure needs, and, in many cases, an acceptable aesthetic outcome.

G. **Negative-pressure wound therapy** has altered wound management by decreasing bacterial load and accelerating granulation. Wounds that previously would not have healed by secondary intention may now be treated adequately with vacuum-assisted closure. Furthermore, it may convert a wound that would otherwise need adjacent or free tissue transfer into a wound that needs only split-thickness skin grafting. Contraindications include the presence of malignancy, ischemic wounds, or inadequately débrided tissue beds.

II. TYPES OF GRAFTS

A. Skin grafts

1. **Split-thickness grafts** consist of epidermis and a variable thickness of dermis. Thinner grafts (<0.016 in.) have a higher rate of engraftment, whereas thicker grafts, with a greater amount of dermis, are more durable and aesthetically acceptable. Common donor sites are the thigh, buttock, and scalp.

2. **Full-thickness grafts** include epidermis and a full layer of dermis. Common donor sites include groin and postauricular and supraclavicular sites, but the hypothenar eminence and instep of the foot can also be used. The donor site is usually closed primarily. These grafts are generally used in areas for which a high priority is placed on the aesthetic result (e.g., face and hand). Thinner grafts have greater secondary contraction and do not grow commensurate with the individual. They have fewer adnexal cells and therefore have variable pigment, less hair, and less sebum, with a proclivity toward dryness and contractures. Full-thickness grafts, with more dermis and the requisite adnexal structures, exhibit less contraction and better cosmesis.

3. Grafts can be meshed in **expansion ratios** from 1.5:1 to 6:1. Meshing a graft allows coverage of a wider area using the same-size donor site and decreases the risk of seroma accumulating under the graft without a method of drainage. The interstices are covered within 1 week by advancing keratinocytes. However, because the entire area is not covered by dermis, meshed grafts are less durable, and the meshing pattern remains after healing, making them inappropriate for aesthetically important areas, such as the face.

4. **Graft healing.** Initial metabolism is supported by **imbibition** or diffusion of nutrients from the wound bed. Revascularization occurs between days 3 and 5 by ingrowth of recipient vessels into the graft (inosculation). Therefore, for a graft to take, the bed must be well vascularized and free of infection, and the site must be immobilized for a

minimum of 3 to 5 days. Prevention of shear forces is important during this period of inosculation. Although bare bone and tendon do not engraft, periosteum and peritenon can support skin grafts, especially if they are first left to form a layer of granulation tissue. Graft failures are most often the result of hematoma, seroma, or shear force prohibiting diffusion and vascular ingrowth.

B. **Tendon grafts** are used to replace or augment tendons. Preferred donor sites are palmaris longus and plantaris tendons.

C. **Bone grafts** are used for repair of bony defects. Iliac bone is used for donor cancellous bone, and ribs or outer table of cranium are used for donor cortical bone.

D. **Cartilage grafts** are used to restore the contour of the ear, nose, and eyelid. Preferred donor sites include costal cartilage, concha of ear, and nasal septum.

E. **Nerve grafts** are used to repair damaged nerves when primary repair is not feasible. Preferred donor sites include the sural nerve and lateral or medial antebrachial cutaneous nerves. Allogeneic nerve grafting has been described using a short course of immunosuppression (*Exp Neurol.* 2010;223(1):77–85).

F. **Dermal or dermal-fat grafts** are used for contour restoration. Preferred donor sites include back, buttock, and groin. The long-term survival of grafted fat is variable but is generally unreliable.

III. **TYPES OF FLAPS.** A flap is any tissue that is transferred to another site with an intact blood supply.

A. **Classification based on blood supply**

1. **Random cutaneous flaps** have a blood supply from the dermal and subdermal plexus without a single dominant artery. They generally have a limited length-to-width ratio (usually 3:1), although this varies by anatomic region (e.g., the face has a ratio of up to 5:1). These flaps are usually used locally to cover adjacent tissue defects but can be transferred to a distant site by use of a staged procedure. Depending on the size of the defect to be covered, moving a local tissue flap can create a donor defect, which may require skin grafting. All local flaps are comparatively easier to use with the loose skin of the elderly.

a. **Flaps that rotate** around a pivot point include rotation flaps (Fig. 29-1) and transposition flaps (Fig. 29-2). Planning for shortening of the effective length through the arc of rotation is important when designing these flaps. More complex rotation flaps include bilobed flaps (Fig. 29-3) and rhomboid flaps (Fig. 29-4).

b. **Advancement of skin** directly into a defect without rotation can be accomplished with a simple advancement, a V-Y advancement (Fig. 29-5), or a bipedicle advancement flap.

2. **Axial cutaneous flaps** contain a single dominant arteriovenous system. This results in a potentially greater length-to-width ratio.

a. **Peninsular flaps** are those in which the skin and vessels are moved together as a unit.

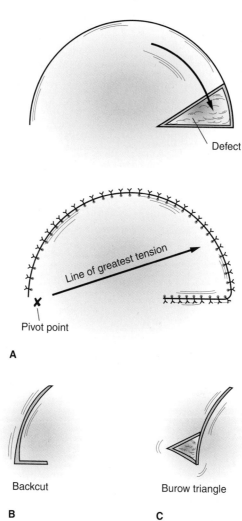

Defect

Line of greatest tension

Pivot point

A

Backcut

Burow triangle

B   **C**

Figure 29-1. Rotation flap. **A:** The edge of the flap is four to five times the length of the base of the defect triangle. **B, C:** A backcut or Burow triangle can be useful if the flap is under tension.

   b. Island flaps are those in which the skin is divided from all surrounding tissue but maintained on an isolated, intact vascular pedicle.
   c. Free flaps are those in which the vascular pedicle is isolated and divided. The flap and its pedicle are then moved to a new location and microsurgically anastomosed to vessels at the recipient site, allowing for long-distance transfer of tissue.

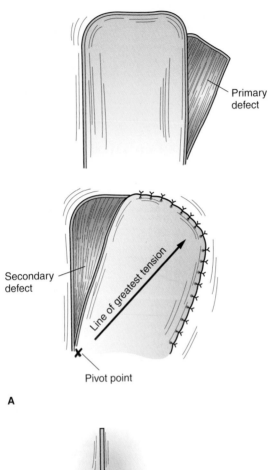

Figure 29-2. A: Transposition flap. The secondary defect is typically covered with a skin graft. **B:** A backcut may be added to reduce tension at the pivot point.

B. **Classification based on tissue type**

1. **Cutaneous flaps** include the skin and subcutaneous fat. These are generally random flaps because the axial blood supply is deep to the fat.

2. **Fasciocutaneous flaps** are axial flaps with a single dominant blood supply contained in the deep fascia along with the overlying fat and

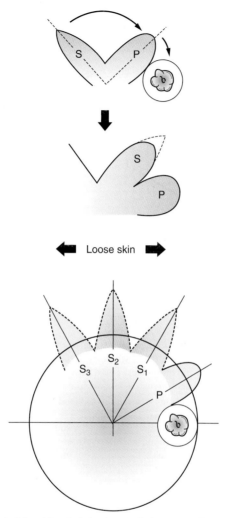

Figure 29-3. Bilobed flap. After the lesion is excised, the primary flap (P) is transposed into the initial defect, and the secondary flap (S) is moved to the site vacated by the primary flap. The bed of the secondary flap is then closed primarily. The primary flap is slightly narrower than the initial defect, whereas the secondary flap is half the width of the primary flap. To be effective, this must be planned in an area where loose skin surrounds the secondary flap site. Three choices for the secondary flap are shown (S_1, S_2, S_3).

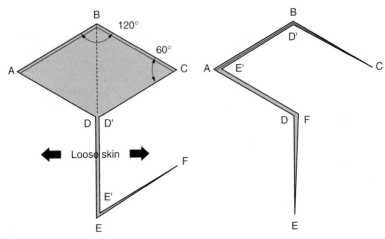

Figure 29-4. Rhomboid or Limberg flap. The rhomboid defect must have 60- and 120-degree angles so that the length of the short diagonal is the same as the length of the sides. The short diagonal is extended by its own length to point *E*. The line *EF* is parallel to *CD,* and they are equal in length. There are four possible Limberg flaps for any rhomboid defect; the flap should be planned in an area where loose skin is available to close the donor defect primarily.

    skin. A wide variety of fasciocutaneous flaps have been described, but those commonly used include radial forearm, anterolateral thigh, lateral arm, and groin flaps. These flaps are often utilized for coverage of mobile structures such as tendons.

3. **Muscle flaps** use the specific axial blood supply of a muscle to provide well-vascularized soft-tissue bulk. These flaps can often be transferred with the overlying skin as a myocutaneous flap. Alternatively, they may be transferred without the overlying skin to fill a cavity or may be covered with a skin graft. Considerations include the pattern of circulation,

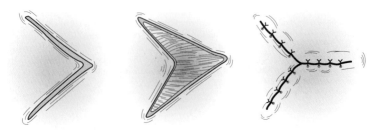

Figure 29-5. V-Y advancement. The skin to the sides of the V is advanced.

arc of rotation, donor-site contour, and donor-site functional defects. Commonly used muscle flaps include the latissimus dorsi, pectoralis major, rectus abdominis, gastrocnemius, soleus, gracilis, tensor fascia lata, trapezius, and gluteus maximus, but any muscle can potentially be transferred as a flap.

4. **A musculocutaneous flap** involves transfer of a muscle with the overlying skin and subcutaneous tissue. The skin is vascularized via myocutaneous or septocutaneous perforating vessels.

C. Specialized flaps

1. **Fascial flaps** are used when thin, well-vascularized coverage is needed (e.g., for coverage of ear cartilage or the dorsum of the hand or foot). The temporoparietal fascia flap is a classic example, but other fasciocutaneous flaps can be transferred without the overlying skin.

2. **Vascularized bone flaps** are designed to meet specific reconstructive needs, as dictated by loss of bony structure. Because they must be transferred to a specific location, they are generally transferred as free flaps. They may or may not include muscle and/or overlying skin. Commonly used bone flaps include free fibula, scapular spine, iliac (with overlying internal oblique muscle), and rib (with pectoralis major or intercostal muscle).

3. **Functional muscle** may be transferred with its accompanying dominant nerve. Common functional muscle transfers include transfer of gracilis for restoration of facial movement or latissimus for replacement of biceps function.

4. **Segmental muscle flaps** can be used when multiple sources provide blood supply to the muscle. A portion of the muscle is used as a flap, leaving behind a vascularized, innervated, functional muscle. This technique minimizes donor-site functional loss. Portions of the serratus anterior and gluteus maximus can be transferred as segmental flaps.

IV. **TISSUE EXPANSION** is a reconstructive technique that uses an inflatable silicone balloon to serially expand surrounding skin. This expansion adjacent to the wound provides donor tissue of similar color, texture, thickness, and sensation, with minimal scar formation and donor-site morbidity. The technique takes advantage of the skin's ability to accommodate a slowly enlarging mass beneath it by increasing its surface area. The idea is to create and develop donor tissue, harvest it, and leave the original donor site preserved.

A. **The advantages** include lower donor-site morbidity and the provision of donor tissue of similar quality to the recipient tissue. Tissue expansion is a simple and versatile technique that provides robust tissue.

B. **The disadvantages** are that it is a staged technique, there is a visible deformity during the period of expansion, it requires frequent visits for expansion, and there is a relatively high rate of complications, including infection and extrusion of the implant.

C. Technique

1. **Preoperative planning** involves assessing the defect size, locating matching tissue to be expanded, and deciding where final scars will be.

2. **Expander placement** is usually performed through an incision at the junction of the lesion and the area of proposed expansion. The length of the incision is controversial. Some authors propose one-third the length of the expander (it should be big enough to ensure full pocket creation). The filling port can be incorporated into the expander or placed in a separate pocket. In addition, the port may be externalized to minimize anxiety and pain during filling, especially in the pediatric population. Partially filling the expander on initial placement may reduce the duration of the expansion phase and reduce mechanical implant failure due to folding.

3. **The expansion phase** begins 2 to 3 weeks after expander placement. The expander is inflated weekly with saline, using sterile technique. The amount infused with each fill depends on patient comfort, skin tension, and blanching of overlying skin. A rough guide is 10% of expander volume per injection. The duration of the expansion phase can vary from 6 weeks to 3 months. Waiting 2 to 3 weeks after the desired volume is achieved allows the expanded skin to soften, decreasing the contraction at the time of flap transposition.

4. **Removal of expander** is straightforward. However, infection, exposure, or rupture may necessitate premature removal.

5. **The expanded tissue** is usually in the form of a random flap (rotation, advancement, or transposition). If more than one flap is necessary using expanded tissue, one must ensure that all flaps have adequate blood supply.

D. The **origin of the new tissue** is not completely understood. One potential source is new tissue created in response to the expansion process. Alternatively, tissue may derive from recruitment of adjacent tissues by stretching or creep and by stress relaxation. These possibilities are not mutually exclusive. Studies have shown that expansion gives rise to an increase in the thickness of the epidermis, a decrease in the thickness of the dermis, and atrophy of the underlying muscle and fat (*Plast Reconstr Surg.* 1994;93:1428–1432).

E. **Tissue expanders are indicated** for patients who cannot, or choose not to, tolerate the longer operative procedures or rehabilitation associated with more distant flaps. In areas where little suitable tissue is available (e.g., scalp), tissue expansion can be the aesthetically superior option. The patient must be motivated and understand the process. Common indications include burn alopecia, congenital nevi, male pattern baldness, and postmastectomy breast reconstruction.

F. **Relative contraindications** include malignancy or an open wound, active infection, and unwillingness to comply with multiple procedures. Similarly, tissue expanders cannot be placed under burned tissue, scar, skin graft, or a prior incision. In addition, tissue expanders are less effective in areas that will be irradiated because the skin in those areas thickens, scars, and contracts, minimizing the degree of expansion possible.

G. **Complications** include pain, seroma, hematoma (rates widely variable), infection (1% to 5%), exposure or extrusion (5% to 10%), and skin necrosis. Less common complications include striae, resorption of underlying bone, and neurapraxia.

ACUTE INJURIES

I. FACIAL TRAUMA

A. Examination. A facial trauma exam should assess soft tissue, nerve, and underlying bony injuries, with special attention to periorbital injuries. Note the location of lacerations, abrasions, and missing tissue that may indicate underlying facial nerve injuries or fractures. Gingival lacerations, malocclusion, and step-offs between the teeth may be a sign of a mandibular fractures. The examiner should query the five branches of the facial nerve (temporal, zygomatic, buccal, marginal mandibular, cervical) by having the patient raise the eyebrows, squeeze the eyelids shut, smile, and frown, noting any paresis or asymmetry. The facial skeleton should be palpated for bony step-offs indicating fractures. A brief ocular exam should include an assessment of gross vision, pupil reactivity, and intact extraocular movements. Examine the ears for lacerations as well as intact tympanic membranes. One should note gross deviations in the nose externally, and examine the nasal septum with an otoscope to assess for septal hematoma. Inspect the mouth for tongue or intraoral lacerations and avulsed teeth.

B. Imaging. A computed tomography (CT) scan with fine axial and coronal cuts through the facial bones is a fast, sensitive, and specific means of determining the location and orientation of facial fractures. A Panorex may be useful in the setting of isolated mandible fractures; however, many facial reconstructive surgeons want a more complete picture of the anatomy with a CT scan as a guide for the reconstructive plan, regardless of the diagnosis of a fracture on plain film.

C. Other work-up. Any patient with a mandible fracture should be examined for C-spine injuries. Mandible fractures are associated with a 10% incidence of C-spine fractures. Patients with bony orbital fractures should have an ophthalmology evaluation to rule out associated ocular injuries.

D. Soft-tissue repair. Facial lacerations should be copiously irrigated, and obviously devitalized tissue should be débrided. Local anesthesia may be used to block facial nerve branches prior to wound repair. The wound edges may be reapproximated using a few interrupted deep dermal 4-0 Vicryl or Monocryl sutures. A running superficial layer of 6-0 fast gut suture may be used to close the epidermis. If nonabsorbable sutures are used on the face, they should be removed within 5 days to prevent permanent suture marks.

    1. Eyelid lacerations should be referred to a facial reconstructive surgeon or ophthalmologist. Full-thickness lacerations of the ear and nose should be copiously irrigated, cartilage reapproximated with an absorbable monofilament suture [polydioxanone (PDS)], and skin closed in the usual manner. Full-thickness lip lacerations may be repaired using a three-layer closure. The orbicularis oris muscle should be reapproximated with 5-0 PDS, the mucosa repaired with 5-0 chromic, and the vermillion carefully aligned with 6-0 fast gut suture. Lacerations overlying fractures should be copiously irrigated and closed until definitive fracture fixation can be achieved.

E. **Fractures.** In the absence of airway compromise or ocular muscle entrapment, most facial and mandible fractures may be fixed electively within 1 to 2 weeks with good results and low incidence of infection. Patients with mandible fractures may be temporized until definitive fixation with a liquid diet, pain control, antibiotics covering intraoral flora (clindamycin), and good oral hygiene including Peridex (chlorhexidine) swish and spit three times per day. Indications for fracture reduction and fixation include alteration in dental occlusion with mandible and midface fractures, ocular muscle entrapment and inadequate eye support associated with orbital fractures, midface instability, and displaced fractures with obvious cosmetic implications. In light of these indications, not all facial fractures require operative intervention.

F. **Special situations**

1. Facial nerve injuries may be managed expectantly if they are medial to the lateral canthus because facial nerve branches, such as the buccal branch, are extensively arborized in these locations. Function will usually return without operative intervention, and it is exceedingly difficult to localize and repair nerve branches in this area. Facial nerve injuries should be referred to a facial plastic surgeon as soon as possible.

2. Eyelid lacerations situated in the medial aspect of the lid may be associated with injury to the lacrimal drainage system. These injuries should be evaluated by a facial plastic surgeon or ophthalmologist.

II. HAND TRAUMA

A. **Assessment** must be done using a systematic, efficient, and reproducible approach. Underestimating the extent of a hand injury or infection can lead to extended recovery or permanent loss of function.

1. **History.** The mechanism and timing of the injury, hand position at the time of injury, hand dominance, and patient occupation are all important to diagnosis and treatment.

2. **Examination**

a. **Inspect the position of the patient's hand,** paying attention to the resting position of the digits and any swelling or asymmetry as compared with the contralateral hand.

b. **Vascular assessment** requires observation of color, temperature, capillary refill, and the presence of pulses (palpable or Doppler) and an Allen test to verify the integrity of the palmar arches. Bleeding is controlled by application of direct pressure, not by blindly clamping tissue, because this often results in serious injury to surrounding structures. The use of tourniquets should be reserved for life-threatening exsanguinations only.

c. **Motor examination,** both active and passive, involves testing for integrity of the tendons.

(1) **Flexor digitorum profundus (FDP)** is tested by stabilizing the proximal interphalangeal (PIP) joint in extension and having the patient flex the distal interphalangeal (DIP) joint.

TABLE 29-1	Unambiguous Tests of Hand Nerve Function		
Test	**Radial Nerve**	**Median Nerve**	**Ulnar Nerve**
Sensory	Dorsum first web	Index fingertip	Little fingertip
Extrinsic motor	Extend wrist	FDP index	FDP small
Intrinsic motor	None	Abduct thumb perpendicular to palm	Cross long finger over index (interossei)

FDP, flexor digitorum profundus.

     (2) Flexor digitorum superficialis (FDS) is tested by stabilizing all other fingers in full extension and asking the patient to flex at the PIP joint.

     (3) Extensor tendons are tested by having the patient extend each finger individually. It should be noted that connections between neighboring tendons (juncturae tendinum) can mask a proximal laceration.

  d. Sensory testing includes gross examination of the ulnar, radial, and median nerves, which innervate the muscles in the hand and forearm (Table 29-1). It also involves careful examination of two-point discrimination on the palmar aspect of both the radial and ulnar sides of the digits and comparison with the uninjured hand. Normal two-point discrimination is 3 to 6 mm at the distal tip of the digit. The Strauch 10–10 test is also extremely useful in determining degrees of sensory loss. For this test, the patient rates his or her level of light touch sensation in an injured area on a scale of 1 to 10 as compared to the contralateral normal region, which is by definition a 10. This test should be used over multiple visits to chart the patient's subjective improvement with operative intervention or spontaneous reinnervation.

  e. Skeletal examination involves palpating for any tenderness, soft-tissue swelling, or deformity of the bones. Joint integrity is assessed by gently stressing the ligaments and noting any instability, crepitus, or pain. Any suspicion of fracture or dislocation requires radiographic examination.

3. Diagnostic radiology. Plain radiographs of the injured area, including the joint above and below if the physical examination warrants it, are indicated for almost all hand trauma and should be considered in cases of hand infections, particularly in penetrating trauma. Images should include true posteroanterior, lateral, and oblique views. If the injury involves the digits, separate laterals of the involved digits are indicated. The description of the fracture pattern should include the following: the bone(s) involved, open versus closed injury, simple versus comminuted, displaced versus nondisplaced, transverse versus oblique versus spiral, angulation or rotation of the distal fragment, and intra-articular versus extra-articular. Fractures in children involving the growth plate use the Salter–Harris classification.

B. Fractures

1. Principles of management

a. Reduction in displaced fractures can be attempted in the emergency room using local or regional anesthesia. However, early referral to a hand surgeon is essential for all hand fractures.

b. Postreduction radiographs should be done for all fractures after splinting or casting.

c. Splinting the fracture in a position that does not impair function during the healing phase is imperative. A splint made of plaster or fiberglass, appropriately padded and with the hand in the "intrinsic-plus" position, may be used for almost all hand injuries. The intrinsic-plus position places ligamentous structures in their longest position and minimizes stiffness should immobilization be required to treat the fracture. The interphalangeal (IP) joints are in full extension, the metacarpophalangeal (MCP) joints are at 60 to 90 degrees of flexion, and the wrist is at 20 to 30 degrees of extension. Individual digits can be splinted without involving the remainder of the patient's hand and wrist. A thumb spica splint is used for fractures that involve the thumb proximal to the IP joint. The MCP joint is placed in extension, the thumb abducted, and the wrist placed in 20 to 30 degrees of extension. Even if operative management of the fracture is planned, a reduction with splinting in the emergency room is still appropriate for patient comfort and to prevent stiffness.

d. Early motion is used whenever possible to minimize joint stiffness.

e. Operative intervention is considered if closed treatment does not obtain or maintain reduction in the fracture. Contaminated open fractures, associated soft-tissue injuries, malalignment (uncorrected rotated, angulated, or shortened deformities of the digit), and articular incongruity of greater than 1 mm are also indications for operative management.

2. Specific fractures

a. Phalangeal fractures require closed reduction and protective splinting for 4 to 6 weeks. Fractures of the distal phalanx may involve the nail bed apparatus or insertion of either the flexor or extensor mechanisms. Disruption of the extensor mechanism at the distal phalanx results in a mallet finger deformity and can be treated by splinting the DIP joint in extension. Other fractures of the distal phalanx can generally be treated with a protective splint. Stable middle and proximal phalanx fractures can be adequately treated by buddy-taping the injured finger to its neighbor. Certain fracture patterns are considered unstable and require operative fixation. As always, the goal of early motion is desirable.

b. Boxer's fracture is a common transverse fracture at the distal portion of the ring or small finger metacarpal, with volar angulation of the distal fragment. Volar angulation of the distal fragment of up to 45 degrees is acceptable in the fifth metacarpal because of its mobility, although this may cause prominence of the metacarpal head in the palm. Less angulation is accepted in the fourth metacarpal, and angulation greater than 15 degrees is unacceptable in the second and third metacarpals. Any rotation or scissoring of the finger must be corrected by reduction as well. It is unnecessary to immobilize the MCP joint, and protection with a volar splint brought to the middle palmar crease is used until the patient sees a hand surgeon. Buddy taping of the ring and small fingers may also be helpful.

   c. **Transverse metacarpal shaft fractures** are caused by axial loading and follow the same guidelines as neck fractures in terms of angulation. Oblique and spiral fractures result from torsional forces and are often best treated with operative fixation, protective splinting, and early range-of-motion exercises.

   d. **Bennett's fracture** is an intra-articular fracture at the base of the first metacarpal resulting from an axial load to the thumb. The distal fragment subluxes radially through the pull of the abductor pollicis longus and angulates volarly through the force of the adductor pollicis. The ulnar fragment of the base is held fixed by the volar beak ligament. Closed reduction and splinting often yield a reduction that is anatomic; however, the deforming forces usually move the fragments out of reduction, and these fractures are best treated with open reduction and fixation. Less common is the "baby Bennett's," or "reverse Bennett's," fracture of the fifth metacarpal base; it is similar to the Bennett's fracture, with the extensor carpi ulnaris representing the deforming force on the distal fragment.

   e. **Epiphyseal fractures in children** can lead to alterations in the growth of the involved bone. Treatment is similar to that for adults, although healing is often faster and immobilization is more acceptable because joint stiffness is less of a problem in children. Although reduction in the fracture is important, bone remodeling allows for angulation deformities of up to 20 or 30 degrees in the phalanges and metacarpals, provided it is in the anteroposterior plane. Rotatory deformity or radial or ulnar deviation should not be accepted because remodeling does not correct these deformities (*Emerg Med Clin North Am.* 2010;28:85–102).

   f. **Open fractures** require adequate irrigation, reduction, and fixation as necessary, with prophylactic antibiotic coverage.

C. **Dislocations and ligament injuries**

   1. **Principles of management**

     a. **Pre- and postreduction films** to confirm joint alignment and look for associated fractures.

     b. **Joint stability assessment** by stressing the periarticular structures and putting the joint through its range of motion. If instability is demonstrated, operative management should be considered. A stable joint is managed with protective splinting and early range-of-motion exercise.

     c. **Distal neurovascular assessment** before and after manipulation.

2. Specific dislocations

a. **DIP joint and thumb IP joint dislocations** are uncommon injuries treated with closed reduction followed by splinting for 3 weeks, along with early protective range-of-motion exercise, provided tendon function is normal.

b. **PIP joint injuries** are commonly known as "jammed fingers" and require careful assessment and follow-up to prevent long-term stiffness.

(1) **Dislocations may be dorsal or volar.** Volar dislocations may be difficult to reduce owing to interposition of the extensor apparatus. Volar dislocations may also result in disruption of the extensor tendon central slip and need close observation to watch for boutonnière deformity. Postreduction care consists of early hand therapy, or operative management if unstable or irreducible.

(2) **Volar plate injuries** are common and result from hyperextension of the PIP joint. The ligament can be strained, ruptured, or avulsed from the base of the middle phalanx with or without a bone fragment. If the injury is to soft tissue only or the avulsion represents less than 20% of the articular surface with a stable joint, treatment involves buddy-taping or extension block splinting with the joint in 30 degrees of extension and immediate range of motion. If the bone fragment represents 20% or more of the articular surface and there is associated instability, open reduction and internal fixation or volar plate arthroplasty are required.

c. **Finger MCP joint dislocations** are usually caused by forced hyperextension and are most often seen in the index and small fingers. The dislocation is usually dorsal and is usually reducible in the emergency room. If the volar plate is interposed in the joint, however, open reduction may be required. If the joint is stable after reduction, it should be splinted for protection and early motion started. Occasionally, the metacarpal head can be held volarly by the flexor tendons on one side and the intrinsic muscles on the other side such that longitudinal traction tightens the "noose" around the head and prevents reduction. Open reduction is required in these situations.

d. **Thumb MCP joint dislocations** are uncommon. The dislocation is usually dorsal and results from forced abduction. Closed reduction with a thumb spica splint and early range of motion is the usual treatment. The ulnar collateral ligament can be partially or completely torn and may avulse with a bone fragment from the proximal phalanx. If there is joint stability and congruity, the MCP joint is splinted for 4 weeks, leaving the IP joint free. If the joint is unstable or the proximal portion of the torn ulnar collateral ligament is displaced superficial to the adductor pollicis (Stener lesion), open reduction and internal fixation are required. **Of note, a stable lesion may be converted into an unstable (Stener) lesion by inexperienced examiners aggressively stressing the joint.**

e. **Carpometacarpal injuries** are usually dislocations with or without fractures. Ligamentous injuries are less common because the carpometacarpal articulation has less movement than do other joints. Dorsal dislocations with and without fractures result from a direct blow and are more common on the ulnar part of the hand. Closed reduction is frequently possible, but maintaining the reduction often requires percutaneous pinning of the joint.

D. Tendon injuries

1. **Flexor tendons** are frequently lacerated during everyday activities. Assessment and management of these injuries by a hand surgeon are critical to a satisfactory outcome.

   a. **The assessment** involves a careful history and examination; the examiner should look for a change in the resting tone of the digits (cascade) and assess the profundus and superficialis tendons independently. If flexion against resistance elicits pain, a partial laceration must be suspected. A careful neurovascular examination, including two-point discrimination, should be performed to evaluate for concomitant nerve or vessel injury.

   b. **Emergency room management** involves a thorough examination, then irrigation and closure of the wound, dorsal splinting with the patient's wrist in 20 to 30 degrees of flexion, the MCP joint at 90 degrees of flexion, and the IP joints in extension. Operative exploration and repair are appropriate for all lacerations through the tendon sheath because wrist and digit position at the time of injury can result in significant retraction with respect to skin laceration.

   c. **Anatomy: flexor tendon zones**

   (1) **Zone I:** at the DIP level, distal to the FDS insertion.

   (2) **Zone II:** from proximal A1 pulley (MCP joint) to FDS insertion.

   (3) **Zone III:** from distal transverse carpal ligament (carpal tunnel) to A1 pulley.

   (4) **Zone IV:** within the carpal tunnel.

   (5) **Zone V:** proximal to the carpal tunnel.

   d. **Technique of repair** involves a core, locking suture and an epitendinous repair. For tendon ruptures and lacerations within 1 cm of the FDP insertion, advancement and reinsertion of the tendon are used. A dorsal splint is applied, and a strict protected motion protocol directed by a hand therapist is started within 24 to 72 hours after repair and continues for 6 to 8 weeks.

2. **Extensor tendon injuries** result from lacerations and closed axial loading of the digits.

   a. **Zone I: over the DIP joint.** Mallet finger is a very common injury that results from forced flexion of the tip of the finger, with rupture of the terminal tendon from the distal phalanx. This leads to inability to extend the DIP. Mallet finger may be associated with an avulsion fracture or joint subluxation. These injuries are treated with splinting of the DIP joint in extension for 6 weeks. Operative management with reduction in the fracture and joint is only occasionally indicated. For open injuries, the tendon should be repaired and the joint pinned or splinted in extension for 6 weeks.

b. **Zone II: over the middle phalanx.** Lacerations in this zone should be repaired using a figure-of-eight or mattress technique. The DIP joint may be transfixed with a pin or splinted for 4 to 6 weeks.

c. **Zone III: over the PIP joint.** A complicated injury, since injury can occur to the central slip or lateral bands. A clue to central slip injury is the inability of the patient to initiate PIP extension from 90 degrees. If the patient is able to fully extend the PIP and DIP, at least one lateral band is intact. If untreated, these injuries can result in a boutonnière deformity (PIP flexion and DIP hyperextension). For open injuries, the tendon should be repaired and the joint transfixed with an oblique pin for 3 to 5 weeks. For tendon injuries associated with a fracture that is displaced, reduction and fixation of the fracture are advised. Protective splinting of the joint should be maintained for 6 weeks.

d. **Zone IV: over the proximal phalanx.** The lacerations are often partial because of the width of the tendon at this level. Splinting of the PIP joint in extension for 3 to 4 weeks is often sufficient for these injuries. Repair of the tendon is required if there is any extension lag of the IP joints.

e. **Zone V: over the MCP joint.** These injuries often occur as a result of a punching incident, particularly with a blow to the mouth. Contamination of the wound with oral flora can produce serious infection. Aggressive wound exploration must be undertaken to rule out joint space involvement because intra-articular infection can rapidly destroy cartilaginous surfaces. This often requires elongation of the laceration for adequate visualization and irrigation of the full extent of the wound. Only after the full extent of the wound has been evaluated and the wound aggressively cleansed can the tendon or tendons be repaired and the joint splinted in 20 to 30 degrees of flexion. The wrist is splinted in 30 degrees of extension. Dynamic splinting is useful to avoid adhesions and improve early motion.

f. **Zone VI: over the dorsum of the metacarpals and carpus.** Repair and splint as for zone V injuries.

g. **Zone VII: at the level of the extensor retinaculum.** Repair and splint as for zone V.

h. **Zone VIII: proximal to the extensor retinaculum.** Injury is often at the musculotendinous junction. Repair and splinting for 4 to 6 weeks are required.

E. **Amputation**

1. **Replantation or revascularization**

   a. **Indications** for replantation include amputation of the thumb, amputation of multiple digits, amputation at the metacarpal, wrist, or forearm level, and amputation at any level in a child. More controversial indications include amputation of the proximal arm and amputation of a single digit distal to the FDS insertion.

b. Contraindications for replantation include coexisting serious injuries or diseases that preclude a prolonged operative time, multiple levels of amputation, severe crush or degloving injury to the part, and prolonged ischemia time (12 hours for fingers and 6 hours for proximal limb amputations). Avulsion injury is a relative contraindication to replantation because of the extensive vascular and soft-tissue trauma.

c. Preparation for transfer involves a moist dressing on the stump and splinting for comfort. The amputated part should be wrapped in saline-moistened gauze and placed in a clear plastic bag on a mixture of ice and water. The part should never be placed directly on ice or immersed in saline. Radiographs of the stump and the amputated part are essential and can be done at the transferring facility, provided that this does not significantly delay transfer to the microsurgery center. Intravenous fluids, prophylactic antibiotics, and tetanus toxoid, when indicated, should be begun immediately to facilitate prompt transfer to the appropriate facility for replantation. The sequence of repair involves identification of neurovascular structures and tendons and preparation of the bone for fixation. After providing bony stability, the arteries are repaired, followed by repair of the tendons and then veins, nerves, and skin. The postoperative care involves careful monitoring of the splinted part (temperature, color, and turgor) and adequate intravenous hydration in a warm environment.

2. Revision amputation (nonreplantable amputation) management
   a. Principles
      (1) Complete assessment, including radiographs.
      (2) Antibiotics when bone is involved or soft tissues are crushed or contaminated.
      (3) Preservation of length.
      (4) Maintenance of sensation and motion.
      (5) Aesthetics.
      (6) Early motion.
   b. Fingertip injuries are optimally managed using primary closure without shortening. If this is not possible, lateral V-Y advancement or volar advancement flaps or skin grafts can be used to obtain closure. An alternative for small wounds (with no vital structures exposed) is closure by secondary intention.
   c. More proximal amputations involve shortening and contouring the bone, shortening the tendons, and identifying digital nerves and allowing them to be transposed away from the skin closure.
   d. A protective dressing that allows joint motion is recommended, with early referral to a hand therapist for range-of-motion exercises and later desensitization of the tip of the stump.

F. Infections

1. Management. Infections in the hand can progress rapidly via potential spaces and may risk the viability of tendons, bones, joints, and neurovascular structures by creating increased pressure from pus and edema in closed spaces.

a. **Surgical drainage** is required in most hand infections.

b. **Antibiotic coverage** should be directed against common skin flora such as *Staphylococcus aureus, Staphylococcus epidermidis,* and *Streptococcus* species.

c. **Gram stain and culture of wound.**

d. **Splinting and elevation of the hand.**

e. **Tetanus prophylaxis when appropriate.**

2. **Local infections**

a. **Paronychia** is a soft-tissue infection of the skin and soft tissue of the lateral nail fold; an **eponychial infection** may extend from this and involves the proximal nail fold. These localized infections often arise from self-inflicted trauma by nail biting or foreign-body penetration, such as a needle-stick. Treatment requires incision and drainage, with removal of the nail when the infection extends deep to the nail plate. Oral antibiotics are used if a cellulitis is present. **Chronic paronychia** is sometimes associated with underlying osteomyelitis or fungal organisms. Treatment may require marsupialization.

b. **Felon** is a localized infection involving the volar pulp of the digit and usually originates with a puncture wound, although a paronychial infection may spread volarly. Purulent fluid is usually under pressure in the fibrous septa of the tip of the digit. Management involves incision and drainage of the abscess (which can be between septa) and systemic antibiotics if there is an associated cellulitis. In general, the incision is located where the felon is "pointing"; however, it should be carefully planned to avoid sensitive scars and destabilization of the pulp of the finger. As with a paronychia, aggressive cleansing with soap and water after incision and drainage promotes drainage and avoids premature closing of the wound.

c. **Cellulitis** in the hand usually occurs secondary to a laceration, abrasion, or other soft-tissue injury. Management involves draining an abscess if present. The fluid should be sent for culture and sensitivity, and oral or intravenous antibiotics should be administered, depending on the severity. When associated with swelling of the digits and hand, splinting in the intrinsic-plus position and elevation prevent stiffness.

d. **After an animal bite,** the wound must be thoroughly irrigated to decrease the bacterial load and to remove any foreign body, such as a tooth. Bite wounds should be treated with oral antibiotics prophylactically and with intravenous antibiotics when an established infection is present. Although a greater percentage of cat bites become infected than do dog bites, the jaws of a dog are significantly more powerful and can inflict other injuries. The organisms most often involved from dog or cat bites include *Pasteurella multocida, S. aureus, Bacteroides* species, and *Streptococcus viridans.* Recommended oral antibiotics are amoxicillin–clavulanate or clindamycin with either ciprofloxacin or trimethoprim–sulfamethoxazole.

e. **Human bites** can involve particularly virulent organisms and frequently present in association with extensor tendon injuries or fractures sustained during physical altercations. An open wound, particularly if it overlies the dorsum of the hand with signs of infection or underlying soft-tissue or bony injuries, should prompt patient questioning about the source of the laceration. Typical organisms cultured from human bite wounds are *S. viridans, S. epidermidis,* and *S. aureus,* as well as anaerobic bacteria, such as *Eikenella corrodens* and *Bacteroides* species. Amoxicillin–clavulanate should be used prophylactically, and when signs of infection are present, treatment with ampicillin–sulbactam, cefoxitin, or clindamycin plus either ciprofloxacin or trimethoprim–sulfamethoxazole is recommended. Wound exploration should be carried out.

G. **Surgical emergencies**

1. **Compartment syndrome** is seen in the hand and forearm and results from increased pressure within an osseofascial space, leading to decreased perfusion pressure. If it is left untreated, muscle and nerve ischemia may progress to necrosis and fibrosis, causing Volkmann ischemic contracture.
   a. **Etiology.** Fractures that cause bleeding, crush and vascular injuries, circumferential burns, bleeding dyscrasias, reperfusion after ischemia, or tight dressings can lead to the syndrome.
   b. **Diagnosis** is based on a high index of suspicion, clinical examination, and symptoms of pain that are exacerbated with passive stretch of the compartment musculature, paresthesias, paralysis, or paresis of ischemic muscles. Pulselessness may occur and indicates a late finding (and is usually also a sign of irreversible damage) or the presence of major arterial occlusion rather than compartment syndrome. Measurement with a pressure monitor of a compartment pressure of greater than 30 mm Hg confirms diagnosis.
   c. **Treatment** of incipient compartment syndrome involves close observation and frequent examinations and should include removal of tight casts and dressings. Elevation of the extremity to, or slightly above, the level of the heart is recommended. Acute or suspected compartment syndrome requires urgent fasciotomies of the involved areas. Decompression within 6 hours of established compartment pressures is necessary to prevent irreversible muscle ischemia. Forearm fasciotomies involve volar, carpal tunnel, and dorsal compartments. Hand fasciotomies include dorsal incisions for interossei and adductor pollicis, thenar, and hypothenar compartments, as well as midaxial incisions of the digits (ulnar for the index, long, and ring fingers and radial for the thumb and small finger).

2. **Suppurative tenosynovitis** involves infection of the flexor tendon sheath, which is usually caused by a puncture wound to the volar aspect of the digit or palm.
   a. **Diagnosis: cardinal signs of Kanavel**
      (1) **Finger held in flexion.**
      (2) **Fusiform swelling of the finger.**

    (3) **Tenderness along the tendon sheath.**

    (4) **Pain on passive extension.**

  b. **Management** involves urgent incision and drainage in the operating room, with placement of an irrigating catheter in the sheath for continuous irrigation with saline. Irrigation is maintained for 24 to 48 hours. Intravenous antibiotics are administered. Frequent reassessment to verify resolution is critical to avoiding ischemic injury to the tendon secondary to the contained infection.

3. **Palmar abscess** is usually associated with a puncture wound. The fascia divides the palm into thenar, midpalmar, and hypothenar spaces; each involved space must be incised and drained. As with other infections, splinting, elevation, and intravenous antibiotics are required.

4. **Necrotizing infections** threaten both limb and life. The incidence of invasive group A streptococcal infection is on the rise (*N Engl J Med.* 1996;335:547) and can occur after surgery or trauma. Aggressive surgical débridement, high-dose penicillin, and supportive management are the mainstays of treatment. Additional therapy with gentamicin or clindamycin provides antibacterial synergy and blocks production of bacterial toxins. Immune globulin and hyperbaric oxygen are adjuvant therapies.

5. **High-pressure injection injuries** result from grease or paint injected at up to 10,000 lb/in^2. Although the external wounds are often small and unassuming, deep-tissue injury can be severe. Injury to the tissue is the result of both direct physical damage and chemical toxicity, and it leads to edema, thrombosis, and subsequent infection. Management involves urgent, thorough débridement, irrigation, decompression, systemic antibiotics, and splinting, with frequent reassessments and repeat débridement in 24 hours as required. When a digit has sustained significant injection, amputation may be required.

SPECIFIC PROBLEMS IN RECONSTRUCTIVE PLASTIC SURGERY

I. PERIPHERAL NERVE

A. **Clinical assessment** of neuropathy requires evaluation of both motor and sensory function as well as electrodiagnostic evaluation of nerve conduction and muscle innervation.

1. **Standard classification schemes** are available for classification of motor nerve function (Table 29-2). In addition, specific testing of moving or static two-point discrimination, vibration and pressure thresholds, or grip strength may be appropriate.

2. **Diagnostic studies** for quantification of nerve dysfunction include nerve conduction studies (NCSs) and electromyography (EMG). An NCS characterizes the conduction of large-diameter, myelinated nerves, and normal values may be present despite partial nerve injury. NCSs are useful in determining the degree of nerve dysfunction, the presence of segmental demyelination or axonal degeneration, the site

TABLE 29-2	Classification of Motor Function
Grade	Motor Function
M0	No contraction
M1	Perceptible contraction in proximal muscles
M2	Perceptible contraction in proximal and distal muscles
M3	All important muscles powerful enough to act against gravity
M4	Muscles act against strong resistance; some independent movement possible
M5	Normal strength and function

Adapted from SE Mackinnon, AL Dellon. *Surgery of the Peripheral Nerve.* New York: Thieme; 1988:118.

of injury, and whether the injury is unifocal, multifocal, or diffuse. EMG samples the action potentials from muscle fibers and can detect individual motor unit potentials, which may indicate early reinnervation and fibrillations, which represent denervation owing to axonal degeneration.

B. **Acute nerve injury** results from transection, crush, or compression and represents the loss of nerve function distal to the area of injury. Axons are myelinated by Schwann cells and organized into fascicles surrounded by the perineurium. The fascicles are bundled into nerves by the epineurium. The prognosis of injury to a peripheral nerve is dictated by which structures are disrupted. It is important to recognize in the acute setting that an injured nerve may be responsive to stimuli distally for 48 to 72 hours after transection. The severity of nerve injury has been organized into a grading scheme (Table 29-3). Operative repair is indicated for fourth-through sixth-degree injury.

1. **The technique of nerve repair** affects the eventual degree of recovery. Several basic concepts are used to optimize outcome.

   a. **Microsurgical technique** should be used, including magnification and microsurgical instruments and sutures. When conditions allow, a **primary repair** should be performed. The repair should be tension free.

   b. Positioning a limb or digit in extreme flexion or extension to facilitate an end-to-end repair is discouraged because of the joint and ligamentous problems that result. If a tension-free repair cannot be achieved in **neutral position,** transposing the nerve or placing an interposition nerve graft should be used.

TABLE 29-3	Classification of Nerve Injuries		
Sunderland[a]	Seddon[b]	Structure Injured	Prognosis
First degree	Neurapraxia	Schwann cell (demyelination)	Complete recovery within 12 wk
Second degree	Axonotmesis	Axon (Wallerian degeneration)	Complete recovery regeneration 1 mm/d
Third degree		Endoneurium	Incomplete recovery
Fourth degree		Perineurium	No recovery
Fifth degree	Neurotmesis	Epineurium	No recovery
Sixth degree		Mixed injury, neuroma incontinuity[c]	Unpredictable recovery

[a]Sunderland S. A classification of peripheral nerve injuries producing loss of function. *Brain.* 1951;74:491.
[b]Seddon HJ. Three types of nerve injury. *Brain.* 1943;66:237.
[c]Mackinnon SE. New direction in peripheral nerve surgery. *Ann Plast Surg.* 1989;22(3):257–273.

    c. An **epineural repair** is typically performed, but a grouped fascicular repair should be performed whenever the internal topography of the nerve is segregated into motor, sensory, or regional components.

    d. **Postoperative motor and sensory reeducation** will help to optimize outcome.

2. **Indications** for peripheral nerve repair include partial or complete transection or in-continuity conduction block. These represent fourth- to sixth-degree nerve injuries and can be difficult to distinguish from lesser grades of injury based on clinical examination alone. This is true because all grades of injury can lead to complete loss of function. Some guidelines for surgical intervention are listed in the following sections.

    a. **Nerves inadvertently divided** during operation are fifth-degree injuries and should be repaired immediately.

    b. **Closed-nerve injuries that localize near an anatomically restrictive site** (e.g., the ulnar nerve at the elbow or the common peroneal nerve at the knee) can result in neurologic deficit secondary to conduction block from edema and compression. If no recovery occurs within 3 weeks, management includes surgical decompression at that site. Iatrogenic nerve deficit from positioning during long operative procedures is managed similarly.

c. **Closed-nerve injury from blunt trauma or traction** is usually a first-, second-, or third-degree injury, and full recovery can be expected in most cases. Patients are closely followed for signs of recovery, including an advancing Tinel sign, indicating regenerating axons. Baseline NCS and EMG are obtained at 6 weeks. If there is no evidence of return of function at 3 months, repeat studies are obtained. If there is no improvement, the nerve is explored and repaired.

d. **Nerve deficit after sharp trauma** (e.g., a stab wound) usually is the result of partial or complete transection, and the nerve should be explored and repaired urgently.

e. **Loss of nerve function after gunshot or open blunt trauma** is usually the result of first- or second-degree injury, and recovery can be expected in most cases. These cases are usually treated as for closed injuries. If the nerve is visible or the wound is explored for other reasons (e.g., vascular repair), the nerve is explored. If the nerve is in continuity, it is managed as for a closed injury. If the nerve is not in continuity, it is usually best to tag the ends of the nerve for ease of identification and delay definitive repair until the zone of injury to the nerve is clearer (generally by 3 weeks).

f. **Nerve deficit from compartment syndrome** is treated by emergent fasciotomy. If decompressed early (within 6 hours), there is usually a rapid return of function.

g. **Decompression of injured nerves** (e.g., ulnar nerve transposition or carpal tunnel release) at sites distal to trauma can be useful to avoid retardation of nerve regeneration across these areas. Multiple sites of injury or compression can have additive effects, and for first-through third-degree injuries, decompression can improve outcome.

h. **Division of a sensory nerve** can lead to a painful neuroma as the regenerating axons grow into the surrounding soft tissue. If the resulting neural deficit results in loss of function or protective sensation, these nerves can be repaired. If not, the neuroma is excised and the cut end of the nerve is transposed proximally well away from the wound, preferably into a nearby muscular environment.

C. **Compression neuropathy** due to compression or repetitive trauma is a common clinical problem. Typically involved nerves include the median nerve at the wrist (carpal tunnel syndrome), the ulnar nerve at the elbow or wrist (cubital tunnel syndrome), the anterior or posterior interosseous nerves in the forearm, the brachial plexus at the thoracic outlet, the common peroneal nerve at the knee, and the posterior tibial nerve at the ankle (tarsal tunnel syndrome).

1. **Clinical assessment** of these conditions involves assessment of motor and sensory function, as well as provocative testing (reproducibility of symptoms with extrinsic nerve compression) and determination of whether the Tinel sign is present. EMG and NCS are appropriate if the clinical picture is unclear.

2. **Initial management** is usually physical therapy, behavior modification, and splinting to avoid repetitive compression. A period of at least 6 weeks of nonsurgical management without improvement is usually recommended before operation, although nerve compression at the cubital tunnel or thoracic outlet typically requires prolonged nonsurgical management. Operations generally involve **decompression** of the affected nerve or transposition to an unrestricted site.

II. SCALP, CALVARIAL, AND FOREHEAD RECONSTRUCTION

A. **Anatomy**

1. The **scalp** consists of five layers: skin, subcutaneous tissue, galea aponeurotica, loose areolar tissue, and pericranium.

2. **Five major paired vessels** provide the scalp with an ample collateral blood supply: the supraorbital, supratrochlear, superficial temporal, posterior auricular, and occipital arteries.

3. The **scalp receives sensory innervation** from the supraorbital and supratrochlear, branches of cranial nerve V1, the lesser occipital branch of C2 or C3, the greater auricular nerve, and the auriculotemporal branch of cranial nerve V3. The motor innervation to the frontalis derives from the frontal branch of the facial nerve.

B. **Scalp lacerations** are common concomitant sequelae of blunt trauma to the head. As such, there may be associated skull, cervical spine, or intracranial injuries. The rich blood supply to the scalp can produce significant blood loss, and hemostasis is important to prevent subgaleal hematoma. Radical débridement is seldom indicated, and primary repair is usually feasible. Repair of the galea generally helps to prevent hematoma formation.

C. **Partial-thickness scalp loss** from avulsion usually occurs at the subaponeurotic layer. Large avulsions may be skin grafted. One can expect 20% to 40% contraction of the skin graft over the first 6 to 8 months. After this has leveled off, the grafted area can be removed by serial excisions.

D. **Full-thickness scalp loss** can occur from trauma or tumor extirpation. The optimal treatment varies depending on the size of the defect.

1. **Small defects** (<3 cm) can often be closed primarily after undermining of flaps. Local flaps, either random or based on blood supply, can be raised. Scoring the galea in a grid pattern of perpendicular lines spaced 1 cm apart can allow for expansion of the flap. Rotation flaps should involve a margin of at least five times the length of the defect. Bipedicled flaps are well suited for coverage of the poles of the head (forehead, temporal areas, and nape of neck).

2. **Medium-sized defects** (3 to 10 cm) are usually covered with a scalp flap combined with skin grafting of the donor pericranium. Several specific flaps have been described for medium-sized defects, including the pinwheel flap, three-flap, and four-flap techniques described by Orticochea. All have been used with variable success.

3. **Large defects** (>10 cm) often require free tissue transfer. If the deficit is due to trauma, replant may be attempted. Because most of these

injuries are from industrial accidents involving avulsion, however, the injury to the arterial intima can extend far into the scalp. Latissimus dorsi or omental free flaps with split-thickness skin grafts are described for complete scalp loss.

E. **Calvarial defects** in the parietal or occipital regions require cranioplasty for protection. Temporal defects are somewhat protected by the temporalis muscle.

   1. **Alloplastic material** can be used to cover these defects, including titanium mesh, calcium hydroxyapatite, and methylmethacrylate. Polymethylmethacrylate (PMMA) is the most commonly employed because it is both durable and easy to use. However, it is exothermic on initial application and has reported infection rates of approximately 5% to 30%. Newer alloplastic materials are being developed to promote bony ingrowth and decrease the risk of infection. Some can be custom-made, based on three-dimensional reconstructions of computed tomographic scans.

   2. **Autogenous tissue** for cranioplasty includes split-rib grafts, split-table calvarial bone grafts, and bone paste. These are somewhat more difficult to use but have the advantage of a lower complication rate.

III. TRUNK

A. **Breast**

   1. **Postmastectomy breast reconstruction** offers restoration of an important symbol of femininity and sexual intimacy. Reconstruction of breast symmetry can lead to a significant improvement in body image and is an important part of cancer rehabilitation for many women (*J Natl Cancer Inst.* 2000;92:1422–1429).

      a. **The aims of reconstruction** are to create symmetric breast mounds and, if desired, a new nipple-areola complex. The aesthetic goal is defined by the patient and includes a symmetric appearance both clothed and unclothed. Extensive preoperative consultation is required to allow women to explore their options. It should be emphasized that each approach to breast reconstruction usually requires at least two procedures and that the reconstructed breast will never completely replicate the original. Reconstruction can be accomplished with or without the use of an implant, and most procedures can be performed either immediately at the time of the mastectomy or in a delayed fashion.

      b. **Reconstruction of the breast mound** is accomplished with an implant in approximately two thirds of cases (*Probl Gen Surg.* 1996;13:75). In most cases, enough skin is removed with the mastectomy that the desired size of the breast precludes closure of the wound without tension. When this is the case, a tissue expander is placed and serial expansions performed until the desired size is reached (usually after 6 weeks of expansion). At this time, the expander is replaced with a permanent implant filled with silicone gel or saline. The advantages of this approach to reconstruction are minimal additional operative time, fewer additional scars, and a shorter recovery period. The disadvantages include the risks of permanent implants (rupture, infection) and the inability to reproduce certain natural contours.

c. **Autologous tissue** can be used to recreate a breast mound in the form of pedicled (rectus abdominis, latissimus dorsi) or free (rectus abdominis, gluteus maximus) myocutaneous flaps. The advantages include a more natural appearance for some patients, permanent reconstruction without the potential for future procedures to replace a ruptured implant, and fewer complications with subsequent radiation therapy. Disadvantages include a relatively long procedure, additional scars, and potential donor-site morbidity.

d. **Reconstruction of the nipple-areola complex** is chosen by approximately 50% of patients undergoing breast reconstruction. Methods include local flaps or nipple-sharing grafts to reconstruct a nipple-like prominence. Split-thickness skin grafting or tattooing can be used to recreate an areola.

e. **Procedures on the contralateral breast to improve symmetry** may be performed concomitantly or subsequently and include modification of an inframammary fold, removal of dog ears, liposuction of flaps, or reduction mammoplasty or mastopexy of the contralateral side. Symmetry procedures are almost always covered by insurance.

2. **Reduction mammoplasty** is performed for women with a variety of physical complaints and aberrations in body image.

a. **Common symptoms** are listed as follows and are considered indications for reduction mammoplasty:

(1) **Personal embarrassment and psychosocial problems.**

(2) **Shoulder and back pain.**

(3) **Grooving of the soft tissue of the shoulders by bra straps.**

(4) **Chronic inframammary skin breakdown, rash, or infection (intertrigo).**

(5) **Inability to engage in vigorous exercise.**

(6) **Symptoms of brachial plexus compression (rare).**

b. A variety of procedures are designed to **reduce breast size.** All of them move the nipple-areola complex superiorly on the chest wall. The nipple-areola complex is maintained on a pedicled blood supply when possible, but in certain instances (e.g., pedicle length >15 cm or a patient who smokes), tenuous blood supply to the nipple-areola complex may require a full-thickness graft. There are always scars resulting from the movement of the nipple and resection of excess skin, and the configuration of these scars varies by the procedure chosen.

B. **Chest wall reconstruction**

1. **Before beginning chest wall reconstruction,** one must ensure complete resection of tumor and radiation-damaged or infected tissue.

2. **Dead space** in the chest allows for potential empyema and may be obliterated. This space is best filled with pedicled muscle (latissimus dorsi, pectoralis major, serratus anterior, or rectus abdominis) or omental flaps.

3. **Skeletal stabilization** is required if more than four rib segments or 5 cm of chest wall are missing. This can be achieved using autologous (rib, dermis, or fascial grafts or bulky muscle flaps) or prosthetic (Prolene mesh, Gore-Tex, Marlex-methylmethacrylate sandwich) material.

4. **Optimal soft-tissue coverage** usually requires pedicled myocutaneous flaps but can be achieved with pedicled muscle or omentum covered with split-thickness skin graft. Rarely, free tissue transfer is required.

5. **Median sternotomy dehiscence** owing to infection occurs in 1% to 2% of cardiac procedures. Predisposing factors include bilateral internal mammary artery harvest, diabetes mellitus, obesity, and multiple operations. Closure requires removal of wires and débridement of all infected tissue, including bone and cartilage. Closure of the resultant dead space is usually accomplished by advancing or rotating the pectoralis major and/or rectus abdominis muscles. The rectus abdominis muscle cannot be used as a rotational flap if the ipsilateral internal mammary artery has been harvested. Pedicled omental flaps are reserved as alternatives in case of initial failure.

C. Abdominal wall reconstruction

1. **Reconstruction of full-thickness abdominal wall defects** includes recreation of a fascial barrier and skin coverage. Restoration of a functional muscle layer is also helpful in maintaining abdominal wall functionality.

2. **Complete absence of all layers of the anterior abdominal wall** is usually the result of direct trauma or infection, with or without intra-abdominal catastrophe. The open abdomen can be temporized by skin grafts placed directly on bowel serosa, omentum, or absorbable mesh through which granulation tissue has formed. This allows for resolution of intra-abdominal edema and maturation of adhesions but usually results in a large ventral hernia.

3. **Primary closure of fascial defects** represents the best approach and can be assisted by sliding myofascial advancement flaps. Lateral release of the external oblique fascia, or "component separation," is ideal for midline musculofascial defects greater than 3 cm in size. Using bilateral relaxing incisions and release, a total of 10, 18, and 6 to 10 cm of advancement may be obtained in the upper, middle, and lower thirds of the abdomen, respectively (*Plast Recon Surg.* 1990;86:519). The anterior sheath of one or both rectus muscles can be divided and turned over to provide additional fascia for closure. Synthetic mesh may be used when fascial defects cannot be primarily closed. Allo-Derm, freeze-dried cadaveric dermis devoid of antigenic cells, also may be utilized for large fascial defects. AlloDerm may also be preferred when infection is a concern because it is revascularized and more resistant to infection. However, it stretches with time and therefore synthetic mesh is preferred especially for extensive defects. Myofascial flaps are required when the existing fascia is insufficient for closure after advancement and there is insufficient skin for primary closure. The most frequently used flaps are the tensor fascia lata, rectus femoris,

and vastus lateralis with overlying fascia. These flaps are usually not useful for closing more distant defects of the upper abdomen.

4. **Skin coverage** is accomplished with split-thickness skin grafts, the cutaneous portion of a myocutaneous flap, or local tissue rearrangement (e.g., bipedicled flap and V-Y advancement flap). Because skin grafts cannot survive directly on synthetic mesh, a muscle flap may be required to provide an adequate bed for skin grafting.

D. **Pressure sores**

1. The **etiology and staging criteria** are described in prior chapters.

2. **Principles of nonoperative management** of pressure sores include (1) relief of pressure by positioning changes and appropriate cushioning; (2) bedside débridement of devitalized tissue; (3) optimization of the wound environment with aggressive wound care; (4) avoidance of maceration, trauma, friction, or shearing forces; and (5) reversal of underlying conditions that may predispose to ulcer development as well as optimizing nutritional status. This type of aggressive nonoperative management is often optimally coordinated by specially trained wound care nurses.

3. **Operative management** with soft-tissue flap closure is only indicated for large, deep, or complicated ulcers and then only in patients who are able to care for their wounds. A high degree of cooperation from the patient and caregivers is essential because the recurrence of pressure sores at the same site or new sores at other sites after operation is high. This is especially true for individuals who have spinal cord injuries, whose rate of recurrence is 13% to 61% (*Am J Surg.* 2004;188:42–51). This is most likely the result of breakdown in the postoperative support and care systems in this population. Most surgeons, therefore, require demonstration of the patient's ability to care for wounds before embarking on operative closure. Flaps commonly used for closure of pressure ulcers around the pelvic girdle include gluteus maximus, tensor fascia lata, hamstring, or gracilis-based rotation or advancement flaps.

IV. **LOWER EXTREMITY.** Soft-tissue defects from trauma to the lower extremity are common. A multidisciplinary approach involving orthopedic, vascular, and plastic surgeons provides optimal care.

A. Lower-extremity injuries are first assessed according to **advanced trauma life support guidelines.** The general sequence of priorities is as follows:

1. The first priority is assessment for **concomitant life-threatening injuries and control of active bleeding.** Blood loss from open wounds is often underestimated, and patients must be adequately resuscitated.

2. The **neurovascular status** is determined. If a nerve deficit is progressive during observation in the emergency room, it is likely the result of ischemia from arterial injury or compartment syndrome.

3. **Bony continuity** is assessed by radiographs of all areas of suspected injury.

4. **Operative management** addresses bone stabilization followed by venous and arterial repair. Fasciotomies are indicated for compartment pressures greater than 30 mm Hg and by clinical suspicion from preoperative neurovascular examination. Fasciotomy must be performed within 6 hours to avoid ischemic contracture. Nonviable tissue is débrided, and an assessment is made about delayed or immediate soft-tissue coverage.

B. **Soft-tissue defects of the thigh** are usually closed by primary closure, skin grafts, or local flaps. The thick muscular layers ensure adequate local tissue for coverage of bone and vessels and adequate vascular supply to any fracture sites.

C. **Open tibial fractures** frequently involve degloving of the thin layer of soft tissue covering the anterior tibial surface. The distal tibia is a watershed zone, and fracture with loss of periosteum or soft tissue leads to increased rates of infection and nonunion.

1. Open tibial fractures are classified according to the scheme of **Gustilo** (Table 29-4).

2. **Gustilo types IIIb and IIIc** frequently require flap coverage of exposed bone.

a. The **proximal third** of the tibia or knee can often be covered by a pedicled hemigastrocnemius flap.

TABLE 29-4	Gustilo Open Fracture Classification
Classification	**Characteristics**
I	Clean wound <1 cm long
II	Laceration >1 cm long with extensive soft-tissue damage
III	Extensive soft-tissue laceration, damage, or loss; open segmental fracture; or traumatic amputation
IIIa	Adequate periosteal cover of the bone despite extensive soft-tissue damage; high-energy trauma with small wound or crushing component
IIIb	Extensive soft-tissue loss with periosteal stripping and bone exposure requiring soft tissue flap closure; usually associated with massive contamination
IIIc	Vascular injury requiring repair

Adapted from RB Gustilo, JT Anderson. Prevention of infection in the treatment of one thousand and twenty-five open fractures of long bones: retrospective and prospective analysis. *J Bone Joint Surg Am.* 1976;58A:453.

   b. The **middle third** of the tibia is often covered by a pedicled hemi-soleus flap.

   c. **Large defects of the distal third** of the tibia generally require coverage by free muscle transfer.

D. **Limb salvage reconstruction for neoplasm** differs from that for trauma in that large segments of bone, nerve, or vessels may require replacement. **Skeletal replacement** can be accomplished using an endoprosthesis, allogeneic bone transplant, or vascularized free bone (fibula) transfer.

E. **The foot** is divided into regions for purposes of soft-tissue defects caused by trauma or ischemic, diabetic, or infectious ulceration. Optimal coverage of the plantar surface provides a durable, sensate platform.

   1. **Small defects of the heel** can be covered using the non–weight-bearing skin of the midsole. Larger defects require free muscle transfer and split-thickness skin grafting.

   2. **The metatarsal heads** are often successfully covered using plantar V-Y advancement and fillet of toe flaps. Multiple fillet of toe flaps or free muscle transfer may be required for large defects.

   3. **For fitting of proper footwear,** coverage of the dorsum of the foot must be thin. If peritenon is present, the dorsum can usually be covered with a skin graft. Small areas of exposed tendon may granulate, but larger areas require thin fascial free flaps (temporoparietal, parascapular, or radial forearm) covered by skin grafts.

30 Cardiac Surgery

Anson M. Lee and Ralph J. Damiano Jr.

This chapter focuses on providing background and practical information regarding the treatment of adult patients undergoing common cardiac operations, particularly coronary artery bypass grafting (CABG) and valve repair or replacement. It also discusses the surgical treatment of heart failure and arrhythmia.

I. ANATOMY

A. **Coronary arteries.** The left and right coronary arteries arise from within the sinuses of Valsalva just distal to the right and left coronary cusps of the aortic valve.

1. The **left main coronary artery** travels posterior toward the pulmonary artery, then divides into its main branches, the **left anterior descending artery (LAD)** and the **left circumflex artery (LCx).** The LAD runs in the interventricular groove and arborizes into **septal** and **diagonal** branches. The LCx runs in the posterior atrioventricular (AV) groove and gives off **obtuse marginal** branches. In 10% to 15% of patients, the LCx gives off the **posterior descending artery (PDA),** termed a **left dominant coronary circulation.**

2. The **right coronary artery (RCA)** descends in the anterior AV groove, where, in **right dominant coronary circulation** (80% to 85% of cases), it gives off the PDA. In addition, the RCA gives off **acute marginal** branches.

B. **Coronary veins.** There are three principal venous channels for coronary venous drainage.

1. The **coronary sinus** is located in the posterior AV groove and receives venous drainage mainly from the left ventricular system. Its main tributaries are the great, middle, and small cardiac veins.

2. **Thebesian veins** are small venous channels that drain directly into the cardiac chambers.

3. The **anterior cardiac veins** drain the right coronary system, ultimately into the right atrium.

C. **Valves.** The valves of the heart are critical to its pump function. Their proper functioning is essential for the maintenance of pressure gradients and antegrade flow through the heart chambers.

1. **AV valves.** The function of the AV valves is to prevent atrial regurgitation during ventricular contraction. These valves are fibrous and continuous with the **annuli fibrosi** at the base of the heart. Furthermore, the leaflets are joined at their commissures and are further secured by **chordae tendineae,** which attach the free leaflets to the intraventricular papillary muscles.

   a. The **tricuspid valve** separates the right chambers and consists of a large anterior leaflet, a posterior leaflet, and a septal leaflet attached to the interventricular septum.

   b. The **mitral (bicuspid) valve** separates the left chambers and consists of a large anterior (aortic) leaflet and a posterior (mural) leaflet.

2. Semilunar valves. The **pulmonary** and **aortic** valves are essentially identical, except that the coronary arteries arise just distal to the aortic valve. The valves consist of three cusps, and each cusp comprises two lunulae. The lunulae extend from the commissure and meet at the midpoint, a thickening known as the **nodulus of Arantius.** During diastole, the three nodules coapt, forming a seal. Just distal to the valves are gentle dilations of the ascending aorta, known as **sinuses of Valsalva.** These structures play an important role in the maintenance of sustained laminar blood flow.

II. PHYSIOLOGY

A. **Electrophysiology.** Like all neuromuscular tissue, the myocardium depends on efficient and predictable electrical activation. The myocardium has specialized tissue responsible for the rapid and orderly dispersal of myocardial electrical activation. The myocardial cells communicate through **gap junctions.**

   1. The **sinoatrial (SA) node** is located at the junction of the anteromedial aspect of the superior vena cava and the right atrium. The **cardiac pacemaker** is determined by the cells that have the most frequent rate of spontaneous depolarization. In most instances, the pacemaker is at the SA node **(sinus rhythm),** which represents an area in the right atrium with the fastest **automaticity,** that is, spontaneous depolarization. In general, all myocardium demonstrates automaticity.

   2. The **AV node** is located in the interatrial septum, on the ventricular side of the orifice of the coronary sinus. It is designed to protect the ventricle from high atrial rates. In the event of SA node dysfunction, the AV node can assume a pacemaker role because this specialized tissue often has the next highest rate of spontaneous depolarization.

   3. The **bundle of His** originates in the AV node and descends through the membranous interventricular septum, just inferior to the septal cusp of the tricuspid valve. Also referred to as **Purkinje fibers,** it separates into the right and left branches at the junction of the membranous and muscular portions of the interventricular septum. In normal anatomy, this is the only electrical connection between the atria and the ventricles. The bundle of His functions to rapidly distribute the depolarization to the ventricular myocardium, starting with the ventricular septum; to the apex; then throughout the ventricle via the Purkinje fiber network.

B. **Mechanics.** The heart functions to convert electrical stimuli to chemical energy and eventually to mechanical energy. The mechanical forces are governed by the pressure, volume, and contractile state of the cardiac chambers. The determination of **rate, rhythm, preload, afterload,** and

contractility are critical to understanding effective cardiac mechanical function.

1. The **cardiac cycle** describes the relationship between the electrical status of myocardial membranes and the mechanical condition of the cardiac chambers. As the mitral valve opens, diastolic filling commences. Following atrial depolarization and contraction, the ventricle depolarizes and isovolumetric contraction begins [at **end-diastolic volume** (EDV)]. Once intraventricular pressure exceeds aortic pressure, the aortic valve opens and **ventricular ejection** occurs. As the aortic pressure overcomes ventricular pressure, the aortic valve closes. Isovolumetric relaxation commences until intraventricular pressure is lower than left atrial pressure, and the mitral valve opens.

2. **Preload** is defined as the EDV of the ventricle. It is practically measured by central venous pressure (CVP) or more accurately by **pulmonary capillary wedge pressure.**

3. **Afterload** is most widely defined as "resistance to ejection." It is more practically described as the **aortic pressure gradient** across the aortic valve.

4. **Starling's law** describes the relationship between EDV and contractility. As EDV is increased, ventricular contraction increases as the optimal sarcomere length is reached. However, once the optimal length is exceeded, contractility can decrease, as can be seen in pathologic states. This relationship is particularly important to optimize in right heart failure.

III. **PREOPERATIVE EVALUATION.** The preoperative evaluation of patients undergoing cardiac surgery is similar to the evaluation of patients undergoing any major operation. All patients should have a complete history and physical examination. Laboratory studies usually include a complete blood cell count; serum electrolytes, creatinine, and glucose levels; prothrombin (PT) and partial thromboplastin times (PTT); and urinalysis. An arterial blood gas measurement is indicated in patients with a history of chronic obstructive pulmonary disease, heavy tobacco abuse, or other pulmonary pathology. In general, 2 to 4 units of packed red blood cells should be available for use during the operation. For elective operations, this may be predonated autologous blood. A chest radiograph (posteroanterior and lateral) should be obtained to evaluate for calcification of the aorta and to examine for the presence of other intrathoracic pathology. In redo patients, a chest computed tomography (CT) scan is recommended to evaluate the proximity of the heart and aorta to the underside of the sternum. CT angiography also is helpful in determining the relationship of the previous bypass grafts to the sternum. The height and weight of the patient should be measured, and the body-surface area (in square meters) should be calculated.

A. Organ-specific evaluation

1. **Neurologic complications** after cardiac surgery can be devastating. Perioperative cerebrovascular accidents (CVA) occur in 4% of CABGs and up to 10% of triple valve cases (*Ann Thorac Surg.* 2003;75:472). CVA may result from aortic atherosclerotic or air emboli that are

loosened by cannulation, cross-clamping, or construction of proximal anastomoses. Postoperative arrhythmias such as atrial fibrillation (AF) are also a common cause of CVA following cardiac surgery. Underlying cerebrovascular disease in conjunction with alterations in cerebral blood flow patterns during cardiopulmonary bypass (CPB) may play a role in some patients. Patients with carotid bruits, known peripheral vascular disease, a history of transient ischemic attack, amaurosis fugax, or CVA should undergo noninvasive evaluation of the carotid arteries with Doppler ultrasonography before operation. Because of the strong association between carotid artery and left main coronary stenoses, patients with left main disease should undergo carotid Doppler examination preoperatively. In general, carotid stenoses greater than or equal to 80% are addressed by carotid endarterectomy or stenting before or in combination with the planned cardiac surgical procedure.

2. **Pulmonary disease,** particularly the obstructive form, occurs commonly in patients with cardiac pathology because cigarette smoking is a risk factor for both disease processes. A preoperative chest X-ray may demonstrate suspicious pulmonary pathology and can be used in combination with a preoperative arterial blood gas evaluation to identify patients who are at high risk for difficulty in being weaned from the ventilator postoperatively. Pulmonary function tests are indicated in high-risk patients. Smoking should be discontinued before operation, when possible.

3. **Peripheral vascular examination.** The presence and quality of arterial pulses in the radial, brachial, femoral, popliteal, dorsalis pedis, and posterior tibial arteries should be documented preoperatively as a baseline for comparison if postoperative arterial complications arise. Blood pressure (BP) should be measured in both arms to evaluate for subclavian artery stenosis. Significant subclavian artery stenosis may preclude the use of an internal thoracic (mammary) artery (ITA) as a conduit. A preoperative Allen test should also be performed to assess the palmar arch and the feasibility of using the radial artery for bypass conduit. For patients with varicosities of the saphenous veins or a history of vein stripping, preoperative vein mapping with ultrasonography can be done to assess the availability and quality of the saphenous vein conduit.

4. **Infection.** Operation should be delayed, if possible, in patients with systemic infection or sepsis and in those with cellulitis or soft-tissue infection at the site of planned incisions. Specific infections should be identified preoperatively and treated with appropriate antibiotic therapy. In patients who have fever or leukocytosis but require an immediate operation, cultures should be obtained from all potential sources (including central venous catheters), and broad-spectrum intravenous (IV) antibiotics should be administered preoperatively.

5. **Medications.** The cardiac surgery patient usually is taking a variety of preoperative medications. In general, nitrates and β-adrenergic blocking agents should be continued throughout the entire perioperative period (*Circulation.* 1991;84(5, Suppl):III236). Unless a specific contraindication exists, statins should be given to all patients because of their ability to reduce recurrent coronary artery disease (CAD) and

postoperative stroke rates (*Eur J Cardiothorac Surg.* 2006;30:300). If possible, antiplatelet agents (e.g., Plavix) are stopped before surgery to prevent hemorrhagic complications. Aspirin is continued in patients with acute coronary syndromes where the benefit of aspirin outweighs the risk of bleeding (*Eur J Cardiothorac Surg.* 2008;34:73). Digoxin and calcium channel blockers generally are discontinued at the time of operation and restarted only as needed in the postoperative period. For patients receiving heparin preoperatively for unstable angina, the heparin should not be discontinued before the operation because this may precipitate an acute coronary syndrome. For patients receiving warfarin preoperatively (including patients with mechanical valves), the warfarin should be discontinued several days before operation. Once the PT time [International Normalized Ratio (INR)] has normalized, anticoagulation can be accomplished using IV heparin.

B. **Cardiac testing**

1. The **electrocardiogram** (ECG) is an important tool diagnostic tool. It demonstrates the electrical activity of the cardiac cycle. Stress testing is used to detect CAD or to assess the functional significance of coronary lesions. The exercise ECG is used to evaluate patients who have symptoms suggestive of angina but no symptoms at rest. A positive test is the development of typical signs or symptoms of angina pectoris and/or ECG changes (ST-segment changes or T-wave inversion).

2. A **pulmonary artery catheter (Swan–Ganz)** is often used in the perioperative setting; it is placed prior to the start of a cardiac procedure. The PA catheter allows for measurement of intravascular and intracardiac pressures, cardiac output, and mixed-venous oxygen saturation (see Table 30-1).

3. The use of **echocardiography** is essential in modern practice. The real-time assessment of chamber size, wall thickness, ventricular function, and valve appearance and motion are possible. It also is an invaluable aid in assessing the presence of intracardiac air prior to weaning from CPB. With the addition of Doppler imaging, blood flow characteristics can be determined. Both transthoracic and transesophageal echocardiography are widely available. Transesophageal imaging is particularly helpful intraoperatively.

4. **Thallium imaging** is used to identify ischemic myocardium. The thallium in the blood is taken up by cardiac myocytes in proportion to the regional blood flow. Decreased perfusion to a region of the myocardium during exertion with subsequent reperfusion suggests reversible myocardial ischemia, whereas the lack of reperfusion suggests irreversibly scarred, infarcted myocardium. In patients who cannot exercise, thallium imaging can be performed after administration of the coronary vasodilator dipyridamole or adenosine.

5. **Coronary arteriography** is used to document the presence and location of coronary artery stenoses. Separate injections are made of the right and left main coronary arteries. In general, the atherosclerotic process involves the proximal portions of the major coronary arteries,

TABLE 30-1	Normal Hemodynamic Parameters	
Parameter	Normal Value	Unit
Central venous pressure	2–8	mm Hg
Right ventricular pressure (syst/diast)	15–30/2–8	mm Hg
Pulmonary artery pressure (syst/diast)	15–30/4–12	mm Hg
Pulmonary capillary wedge pressure	2–15	mm Hg
Left ventricular pressure (syst/diast)	100–140/3–12	mm Hg
Cardiac output	3.5–5.5	L/min
Cardiac index	2–4	L/min/m^2 BSA
Stroke volume index	1	mL/kg
Pulmonary vascular resistance	20–130	dynes · sec/cm^5
Systemic vascular resistance	700–1,600	dynes · sec/cm^5
Mixed-venous oxygen saturation	65–75	Percent

BSA, body-surface area; diast, diastolic; syst, systolic.

particularly at or just beyond branch points. A 75% decrease in cross-sectional area (50% decrease in luminal diameter) is considered a significant stenosis. Indications for coronary arteriography include suspected CAD (e.g., positive stress test), preparation for coronary revascularization, typical or atypical clinical presentations with normal or borderline stress testing when a definitive diagnosis of CAD is needed, and planned cardiac surgery (e.g., valve surgery) in patients with risk factors for CAD. Concomitant ventriculography can be used for assessing left ventricular function.

6. **CT angiography** is a relatively new technique for the detection of CAD. Its main application is for evaluating chest pain in patients with typical symptoms of angina pectoris but with low-to-intermediate risk factors for CAD, as it has a very high negative predictive value (99%) but a low positive predictive value (48%) for detecting CAD in these patients (*J Am Coll Cardiol.* 2005;52:1724).

IV. MECHANICAL CARDIOPULMONARY SUPPORT AND OFF-PUMP CABG

A. **CPB,** first introduced in 1954 by Gibbon, allowed for the development of modern cardiac surgery. It is intended as a support system during surgery and requires systemic anticoagulation.

1. A **venous reservoir** stores blood volume and allows for the escape of bubbles prior to infusion. A **membrane oxygenator** is used to perform the gas exchange function. A **heat exchanger** is necessary to maintain hypothermia when needed and to assist with patient rewarming. The **arterial pump** is usually a roller pump and requires frequent calibration to ensure accurate flows. The **cannulae** and pump tubing are constructed of Silastic or latex, which remain supple when cold. A **left atrial vent** can be used to remove any blood that enters the left-side circulation.

2. **Myocardial protection** strategies are critical to a good outcome. Hyperkalemic perfusate (warm or cold) based on blood or crystalloid may be infused into the aortic root and coronary ostia (antegrade) or via the coronary sinus (retrograde).

3. During CPB, the perfusionist, working with the surgeon, can effectively control perfusion rate, temperature, hematocrit, pulmonary venous pressure, and glucose and arterial oxygen levels.

4. CPB is generally considered safe, but side effects do exist. Most notably, **postperfusion syndrome** is characterized by a diffuse, whole-body inflammatory reaction that can lead to multisystem organ dysfunction. It is believed that most patients experience some form of inflammatory reaction following CPB, but only a fraction develop this syndrome. Other factors contributing to poor CPB tolerance are length of support (e.g., >4 hours) and patient age.

B. **Extracorporeal membrane oxygenation (ECMO)** is primarily used in infants with severe cardiopulmonary failure but can be used in adults. It is not a practical long-term therapeutic modality but rather an intermediate-term (days to weeks) artificial heart and lung support system. Most commonly, it is used to allow patients to recover from reversible myocardial dysfunction, adult respiratory distress syndrome, or pulmonary insufficiency of various etiologies.

C. **Off-pump coronary bypass** is an alternative method of doing CABG. In recent years, this method has been promoted by some as a way to decrease morbidity associated with the use of CPB. This technique of doing bypass grafting on the beating heart while supporting the myocardium with stabilizers has shown a decrease in morbidity by some groups (*J Thorac Cardiovasc Surg.* 2003;125:797; *BMJ.* 2006;332:1365). However, it is more technically challenging than on-pump techniques, and long-term outcomes were similar in a multicenter, randomized trial comparing on- and off-pump CABG in low-risk patients (*JAMA.* 2007;297:701). Long-term patency rates were also similar in a recent long-term follow-up study of two randomized control trials (*J Thorac Cardiovasc Surg.* 2009;137:295). A large VA-based, multicenter trial demonstrated worse patency and mortality at 1-year follow-up for patients undergoing off-pump CABG (*NEJM.*

2009;361:1827). Patients at high risk (e.g., those with severe atheromatous aortic plaque or renal failure or the elderly) may benefit, especially when done by surgeons experienced with this technique.

V. DISEASE STATES AND THEIR TREATMENT

A. **CAD** is the leading cause of death in adults in North America. Risk factors for CAD include cigarette smoking, hypertension, diabetes mellitus, hyperlipidemia, male gender, obesity, advanced age, rheumatoid arthritis, and a family history of CAD. The clinical presentation of CAD is determined by the distribution of the atherosclerotic lesions, the severity of stenosis, the level of myocardial oxygen demand, and the relative acuity or chronicity of the oxygen supply–demand mismatch. The three most common presentations for patients with CAD are angina pectoris, myocardial infarction (MI), and chronic ischemic cardiomyopathy.

1. **Angina pectoris** is a symptom complex resulting from reversible myocardial ischemia without cellular necrosis. Patients typically complain of retrosternal chest pain or pressure that often radiates to the left shoulder and down the left arm or into the neck. Angina occurs during times of increased myocardial oxygen demand (e.g., exercise) and resolves with rest or the administration of nitrates. Unstable angina refers to chest pain that occurs at rest or episodes of pain that are increasing in frequency, duration, or severity. Silent myocardial ischemia occurs when there is ECG evidence of myocardial ischemia in the absence of any angina or angina-equivalent symptoms.

2. **Acute MI** results when there is a critical decrease or interruption of myocardial oxygen supply with irreversible muscle injury and cell death. The patient typically presents with protracted and severe chest pain, at times associated with nausea, diaphoresis, or shortness of breath. There are accompanying increases in the troponin isozyme, creatine kinase-MB isozyme, or serum lactate dehydrogenase. ECG changes include ST-segment elevation, T-wave inversions, and the development of new Q waves. Early and late sequelae of acute MI can include atrial or ventricular arrhythmias, heart failure, rupture of the interventricular septum or ventricular free wall, dysfunction or rupture of the papillary muscle(s) and new mitral regurgitation (MR), and the development of a ventricular aneurysm.

   a. **Arrhythmias** are common during the first 24 hours after acute MI. In addition to potentially fatal ventricular arrhythmias, patients can develop supraventricular tachycardia, AF, atrial flutter, heart block of any degree, or junctional rhythms.

   b. **Congestive heart failure (CHF)** may result when a large portion (usually >25%) of the left ventricular myocardium is infarcted. Cardiogenic shock and death often occur with loss of more than 40% of the left ventricular myocardium. The extent to which the patient's activity is limited can be graded according to the **New York Heart Association (NYHA) classification:** class I, no symptoms; class II, symptoms with heavy exertion; class III, symptoms with mild exertion; class IV, symptoms at rest. There is additional discussion of CHF in Section D.

  c. Rupture of the interventricular septum occurs in approximately 2% of patients after MI (anterior wall in 60%, inferior wall in 40%) and leads to a **ventricular septal defect (VSD).** Septal perforation typically occurs when the myocardium is at its weakest, approximately 3 to 5 days after an acute MI, but it may develop 2 or more weeks later. An acute VSD is suggested by a new holosystolic murmur and an oxygen step-up from the right atrium to the pulmonary artery, as evaluated with a pulmonary artery catheter. This is determined by comparing the oxygen saturation of samples drawn simultaneously from the central venous port and the distal pulmonary artery port. A step-up of greater than 9% is generally held to be diagnostic of a left-to-right shunt. The diagnosis can be confirmed with echocardiography. More than 75% of patients survive the initial event and are candidates for urgent surgical repair of the VSD before they develop the sequelae of low-output syndrome (i.e., multiorgan system failure), which greatly increases the operative risk. An intra-aortic balloon pump (IABP) is indicated to support the failing circulation until surgical correction is possible. Ventricular free-wall rupture results in hemopericardium and cardiac tamponade, which often is fatal. For those patients who survive, emergent surgical repair is indicated.

  d. Acute MR is caused by papillary muscle dysfunction or rupture after an infarction that has extended into the region of the papillary muscles (usually the posteroinferior wall). The failing circulation should be supported with an IABP or temporary mechanical support, if necessary, until emergent operation can be performed.

  e. Ventricular aneurysm, a well-defined fibrous scar that replaces the normal myocardium, develops in 5% to 10% of individuals after acute MI. The majority of aneurysms develop at the anteroseptal aspect of the left ventricle after infarction in the distribution of the LAD coronary artery. Large dyskinetic left ventricular aneurysms can reduce the left ventricular ejection fraction (EF) substantially, resulting in signs and symptoms of CHF. These scars can also serve as the substrate for ischemic reentrant ventricular arrhythmias. In addition, the pooled blood that collects in the aneurysm can clot and shower emboli into the peripheral circulation.

3. Chronic ischemic cardiomyopathy can develop after several MIs. Diffuse myocardial injury results in diminishing ventricular function and, eventually, signs and symptoms of heart failure. This presentation is most common in patients with diffuse small-vessel disease (e.g., in patients with diabetes mellitus).

4. Coronary revascularization may be accomplished via percutaneous transluminal coronary angioplasty (PTCA) or CABG. Indications depend on the patient but generally include intractable symptoms and proximal coronary stenoses that place a significant portion of myocardium at risk.

  a. PTCA is often used for focal symmetric stenoses in proximal coronary vessels. It is generally contraindicated if there is significant left main coronary disease, three-vessel disease, or complex obstructive lesions (*N Engl J Med.* 2005;352:2174). PTCA is associated with restenosis, which may be reduced with the concomitant placement of **drug-eluting stents (DESs),** which inhibit neointimal hyperplasia. DESs have been associated with improved outcomes but have not eliminated the problem of restenosis or the need for reintervention (*J Am Coll Cardiol.* 2007;49:616).

b. CABG is indicated for patients with documented atherosclerotic CAD in several settings: (1) patients with unstable angina for whom maximal medical therapy has failed; (2) patients with severe chronic stable angina who have multivessel disease or left main or proximal LAD stenoses; (3) patients with severe, reversible left ventricular dysfunction (documented by stress thallium scan or dobutamine echocardiography); (4) patients who develop coronary occlusive complications during PTCA or other endovascular interventions; (5) patients who develop life-threatening complications after acute MI, including VSD, ventricular free-wall rupture, and acute MR; and (6) patients with diabetes mellitus and multivessel disease (*J Am Coll Cardiol.* 2004;44:1146).

c. Compared with balloon angioplasty alone, the need for repeat revascularization has dramatically decreased for patients in whom a stent was placed, from 50% of angioplasty patients to approximately 20% of stented patients at 1 year (*Lancet.* 2002;360:965). More recent studies have shown the reintervention rate to be lower, from 5% to 7% depending on the type of stent used (*J Am Coll Cardiol.* 2007;49:616). This decrease has been due to improved delivery systems and the development of DES. For patients with hemodynamic instability or refractory angina after failed angioplasty, IABP support or percutaneous CPB may be helpful before an emergent operation can be performed.

d. CABG results in initial elimination of angina in more than 90% of patients. Perioperative mortality ranges from 1% to 2% in low-risk patients to more than 10% to 15% in high-risk patients. Graft patency after CABG is related to the bypass conduit used and the outflow vessel. In one study, the left internal thoracic artery patency at 5 years was 98%, at 10 years it was 95%, and at 15 years it was 88%. The right ITA patency at 5 years was 96%, at 10 years it was 81%, and at 15 years it was 65%. The radial artery patency at 1 year was 96%, and at 4 years it was 89% (*Ann Thor Surg.* 2004;77:93). At 10 years, it was 83% (*J Thorac Cardiovasc Surg.* 2010;140:73). Reverse saphenous vein grafts have 10-year patency rates of approximately 80% to the LAD and 50% to the circumflex or RCA. Antiplatelet therapy using aspirin (81 to 325 mg/day) and Plavix beginning immediately after operation is recommended to increase the graft patency rate.

B. Valvular heart disease

1. Aortic valve

a. Aortic stenosis (AS). Left ventricular outflow obstruction can occur at the subvalvular, the supravalvular, or (most commonly) the valvular level. Aortic valvular stenosis is usually the result of senile degeneration and calcification of a normal or a congenitally bicuspid aortic valve. Less frequently, AS develops many years after an episode of acute rheumatic fever. AS places a pressure overload on the left ventricle. Adequate cardiac output is usually maintained until late in the course of AS, but at the expense of **left ventricular hypertrophy.** Physical signs include a systolic ejection murmur, diminished carotid pulses, and a sustained, forceful, nondisplaced apical impulse. Symptoms often develop when the valve area decreases to 1 cm^2 or less. **Angina pectoris** develops in approximately 35% of patients with severe AS and results from ventricular hypertrophy (e.g., increased myocardial oxygen demand and reduced coronary perfusion) and the high incidence of concomitant CAD. **Syncope** (15% incidence) probably results from fixed cardiac output and decreased cerebral perfusion during systemic vasodilatation. **CHF** is the presenting symptom in approximately one half of patients and usually manifests as dyspnea on exertion. The effect of aortic valve replacement (AVR) on patients with aortic valve stenosis is dramatic and well documented by several studies. For example, survival was 87% at 3 years in operated and 21% in unoperated patients in one study (*Circulation.* 1982;66:1105).

   b. **Aortic insufficiency (AI)** is usually the result of valve leaflet pathology from rheumatic heart disease (often associated with mitral valve disease) or myxomatous degeneration. AI also may result from other causes of leaflet dysfunction or aortic root dilation, including endocarditis, syphilis, connective tissue diseases (e.g., Marfan syndrome), inflammatory disease (e.g., ankylosing spondylitis), hypertension, and aortic dissection. Chronic AI results in volume overload of the left ventricle, causing chamber enlargement and wall thickening (although a relatively normal ratio of wall thickness to volume is usually maintained). Gradual myocardial decompensation often progresses either without symptoms or with subtle symptoms (e.g., weakness, fatigue, or dyspnea on exertion). Physical signs include a hyperdynamic circulation with markedly increased systemic arterial pulse pressure, known as **Corrigan's water-hammer pulse;** forceful and laterally displaced apical impulse; and a decrescendo diastolic murmur. Acute AI is not well tolerated because of the lack of compensatory chamber enlargement and thus often results in fulminant pulmonary edema, myocardial ischemia, and cardiovascular collapse.

   c. **AVR** is indicated for symptomatic patients with severe AS (defined as valve area <1 cm^2, or mean gradient >40 mm Hg or jet velocity >4 m/second). Surgery is also indicated in asymptomatic patients with severe AS undergoing CABG or other cardiac surgery and in patients with severe AS and left ventricular systolic dysfunction (i.e., EF <0.50). AVR may also be considered for (1) asymptomatic patients with severe AS and hypotension or symptoms with exercise, (2) patients who have a high likelihood of rapid progression (age, calcification, and CAD), (3) patients undergoing CABG who have mild-to-moderate AS with moderate-to-severe calcification of the valve, and (4) low-risk patients with extremely severe AS (valve area <0.6 cm^2 or gradient >60 mm Hg or jet velocity >5 m/second). Elderly patients (>80 years old) have had acceptable morbidity and mortality rates undergoing AVR, with greater than 50% 5-year survival (*Ann Thorac Surg.* 2007;83(5):1651).

For symptomatic patients with AI, indications for surgery include (1) severe AI, (2) chronic moderate to severe AI and left ventricular dysfunction (EF <0.5), and (3) patients with chronic severe AI who are undergoing other cardiac surgery. Patients without symptoms and normal left ventricular function but who have severe left ventricular dilatation (end diastolic dimension >75 mm) are also reasonable candidates (*J Am Coll Cardiol.* 2006;48:e1).

d. **Transcatheter aortic valve interventions** have received commercial approval for use in Europe and are undergoing multicentered randomized trials for approval in the United States. The Edwards Sapien valve is the closest to being approved in the United States. These valves can be implanted through a transfemoral or transapical approach without the use of CPB. Early results with both approaches have been reported in patients with high operative risk based on EuroSCORE calculations. In patients with risk of operative mortality averaging 27.6%, transapical implantation achieved 94% procedural success with 92%, 74%, and 71% 1-month, 6-month, and 1-year survival, respectively (*Eur J Cardiothorac Surg.* 2007;31:9). In the recently reported PARTNERS trial, there was a 20% absolute reduction in mortality at 1 year for transcatheter AVR in patients considered to be inoperable compared to maximal medical therapy (*NEJM.* 2010;363:1597).

2. **Mitral valve**
   a. **Mitral stenosis (MS)** is caused by rheumatic fever in most cases. Other, less common causes include collagen vascular diseases, amyloidosis, and congenital stenosis. MS places a pressure overload on the left atrium, with relative sparing of ventricular function. Left atrial dilation to more than 45 mm is associated with a high incidence of AF and subsequent thromboembolism. A transvalvular pressure gradient is present when the valve area is less than 2 cm^2, and critical MS occurs when the valve area is 1 cm^2 or less. Physical signs include an apical diastolic murmur, an opening snap, and a loud S_1. Symptoms usually develop late and reflect pulmonary congestion (e.g., dyspnea), reduced left ventricular preload (e.g., low–cardiac-output syndrome), or AF (e.g., thromboembolism).
   b. **MR** results from abnormalities of the leaflets (e.g., rheumatic disease, myxomatous degeneration, endocarditis), annulus (e.g., calcification, dilation usually due to a cardiomyopathy, or destruction), chordae tendineae (e.g., rupture from endocarditis or MI, fusion, or elongation), or ischemic papillary muscle dysfunction or rupture. The most common cause of MR in the United States is myxomatous degeneration. MR places a volume overload on the left ventricle and atrium, causing chamber enlargement and wall thickening, although a

relatively normal ratio of wall thickness to volume is usually maintained. Systolic unloading into the compliant left atrium allows enhanced emptying of the left ventricle during systole, with only slight increases in oxygen consumption. AF often develops due to left atrial dilation. Physical signs include a hyperdynamic circulation and a brisk, laterally displaced apical impulse; a holosystolic murmur; and a widely split S_2. Gradual myocardial decompensation often progresses in the absence of symptoms (e.g., dyspnea on exertion, fatigue). In acute MR, adaptation is not possible, and fulminant cardiac decompensation often ensues.

   c. **Repair of the mitral valve** is preferred over replacement whenever possible. Surgery is indicated in patients with moderate-to-severe MS, and symptoms or asymptomatic patients with severe pulmonary hypertension. Moderate MS is defined by a pressure gradient of 25 to 40 mm Hg across the valve or a valve area 1.0 to 1.5 cm², and severe MS is defined by a pressure gradient of >40 mm Hg or a valve area less than 1.0 cm² on echocardiography. Percutaneous mitral balloon valvuloplasty can be performed in selected patients. Surgery is indicated in symptomatic patients with acute or chronic severe MR with NYHA class II, III, or IV symptoms. Asymptomatic patients with chronic severe MR and mild-to-moderate left ventricular dysfunction (EF <0.6) are also candidates for surgery. MV repair is also indicated for asymptomatic patients with chronic severe MR when (1) there is evidence of LV dysfunction (EF <0.6 or end systolic diameter > 40 mm) or (2) the likelihood of successful repair is greater than 90% or (3) there is new onset of AF or (4) pulmonary hypertension (*J Am Coll Cardiol.* 2006;48:e1). Patients with AF and indications for MR repair/replacement should be considered for a Cox-Maze procedure at the time of surgery.

3. **Tricuspid valve**
   a. **Tricuspid insufficiency (TI)** most often results from a functional dilation of the valve annulus caused by pulmonary hypertension, which, in turn, may be caused by intrinsic mitral or aortic valve disease. Causes of primary TI include rheumatic heart disease, bacterial endocarditis (often in IV drug users), carcinoid tumors, Ebstein anomaly, and blunt trauma. Patients have a systolic murmur, a prominent jugular venous pulse, and a pulsatile liver. Mild-to-moderate TI usually is well tolerated.
   b. Significant **tricuspid regurgitation** may be repaired at the time of surgery for other cardiac anomalies. Intervention for isolated TI is uncommon. The majority of tricuspid valves can be repaired with annuloplasty techniques rather than replacement.

4. **Selection of a prosthetic valve** must be individualized for each patient. Despite many years of research, there still is no ideal prosthetic valve. The general considerations for selecting an appropriate prosthetic valve are summarized in Table 30-2.
   a. **Bioprostheses** are made from animal tissues, usually the porcine aortic valve or bovine pericardium. Examples include the Carpentier-Edwards, Hancock, St. Jude Biocor, and Edwards Perimount

TABLE 30-2	Selection of a Prosthetic Valve
Bioprosthetic valve	
Reoperation unlikely	
Age >60 y	
Previous thrombosed mechanical valve	
Limited life expectancy	
Anticoagulant-related complication or intolerance	
Unreliable anticoagulant risk	
Young women who wish to become pregnant	
Mechanical valve	
Reoperation likely	
Age <60 y	
Long life expectancy	
Small aortic annulus in a large patient	
Patient fear of reoperation	

stented valves and the St. Jude Toronto SPV, Sorin, and Medtronic Freestyle stentless valves. These prostheses are associated with a low rate of thromboembolism, even without long-term anticoagulation. However, they are less durable than mechanical valves. Their rate of deterioration depends on the patient's age and is relatively faster in younger patients and slower in the elderly. Overall, the mean time to failure is approximately 10 to 15 years. However, the bioprosthetic material life may be prolonged in newer valves due to modern preservation methods. In general, bioprostheses are the preferred valves for older patients (>60 years) or patients with a contraindication to anticoagulation (e.g., young women who desire future pregnancies).

b. **Mechanical valves** have excellent long-term durability, but the high rate of thromboembolic complications (0.5% to 3% per year) necessitates lifelong anticoagulation. All of these valves are manufactured from **pyrolytic carbon,** which was first discovered in 1966 and has the unique quality of thromboresistance. Examples include the St. Jude, Medtronic-Hall, Sorin, and MRCI (Medical Carbon Research Institute) valves. These valves typically are used in young patients who have a long life expectancy and can tolerate lifelong anticoagulation.

   c. **Allograft and autograft valves** are useful for replacement of the aortic valve, particularly in the setting of endocarditis (*J Heart Valve Dis.* 1994;3:377). These prostheses have reasonable durability and a low incidence of thromboembolism, but experience with them is limited by the supply of allografts and the relative difficulty of the autograft (Ross) procedure, in which a patient's pulmonic valve is used to replace the diseased aortic valve.

5. **Endocarditis.** The main indications for operation include hemodynamic instability, CHF, recurrent septic emboli, and persistent evidence of infection despite appropriate antibiotic therapy. Relative indications include severe acute mitral or aortic valvular insufficiency, heart block, intracardiac fistulas, fungal endocarditis, or infections with especially virulent organisms like oxacillin-resistant *Staphylococcus aureus.* The risk for reoperation for recurrent infective endocarditis is about 17% for IV drug users and 5% for non-IV drug users (*Ann Thorac Surg.* 2007;83:30). Antibiotic therapy alone may be sufficient for the first, uncomplicated episode of prosthetic valve endocarditis, but valve replacement is often required for the treatment of prosthetic valve endocarditis.

6. **Perivalvular leak** occurs when the implanted valve separates from the valve annulus. This may lead to clinically significant valvular regurgitation, which can be defined by echocardiography. Hemolytic anemia may be documented by an increased reticulocyte count, increased serum lactate dehydrogenase level, and increased urinary iron excretion. Replacement of the valve is indicated for perivalvular leak associated with symptoms, severe valvular regurgitation, or severe hemolysis.

7. **Thrombosis and thromboembolism.** Thrombus formation may occur on the surface of the artificial valve and lead to valve thrombosis or embolism. Embolic complications may include transient ischemic attack, stroke, or embolism other vital organs or the extremities. The use of appropriate anticoagulation with mechanical valves may reduce the risk of thromboembolism to the level (approximately 0.5% per year) associated with bioprosthetic valves (*Chest.* 2004;126:457S). The target INR for aortic valves is 2 to 3 and for mitral valves is 3 to 4.

8. **Hypertrophic obstructive cardiomyopathy (HOCM)** is characterized by asymmetric hypertrophy and fibrosis of the myocardium, causing obstruction of the outflow tract. The overall annual death rate of patients with HOCM is about 2% per year. In hypertrophic cardiomyopathy without obstruction of the outflow tract, the annual death rate is about 1% per year. Hypertrophic cardiomyopathy (with or without obstruction) is the most common cause of sudden cardiac death in young people. Medical therapy with β-blockade or calcium channel blockade is the preferred first-line treatment. Nifedipine, nitroglycerin,

angiotensin-converting enzyme inhibitors, and angiotensin II blockers are all generally contraindicated due to their vasodilatory properties, which can exacerbate the outflow tract obstruction. Surgical treatment of HOCM is myectomy, with a postoperative mortality of 1% or less (*Ann Thorac Surg.* 2000;69:1732). By convention, surgery is recommended for symptomatic patients who have failed medical therapy with a documented at-rest outflow tract gradient of at least 30 mm Hg. Long-term results have been excellent with symptomatic relief in over 80% of patients (*J Thor Cardiovasc Surg.* 1996;111:586). An alternate therapy is catheter-based septal alcohol ablation. Short-term results with success rates greater than 90% have been reported for catheter-based septal alcohol ablation (*Circulation.* 2005;112:293), but some long-term data have shown myomectomy to be superior to septal ablation (*Circ Heart Failure.* 2010;3:162). There is a much higher rate of pacemaker implantation with alcohol ablation. Generally, alcohol ablation is reserved for the elderly or patients considered high risk for surgery.

C. **AF** affects more than 2 million people in the United States, with approximately 160,000 new cases per year. It affects nearly 10% of individuals older than the age of 80 years. Morbidity includes patient discomfort, hemodynamic compromise, and thromboembolism.

1. Nonsurgical management of AF includes antiarrhythmic drugs, cardioversion, and catheter ablation. Although drugs can induce **chemical cardioversion,** the failure rate is high (50% at 2 years in some series) (*JAMA.* 2008;300:1784). In patients in AF, the use of chronic anticoagulation for stroke prevention has significant associated morbidity. Because the pulmonary veins have been shown to be the source of ectopic foci in many patients with paroxysmal AF (*Circulation.* 1999;100:1879), the use of catheter-based ablation and isolation of the pulmonary veins has gained popularity. Success rates have been improving, with the best centers achieving success rates of greater than 70% in patients with paroxysmal AF (*Heart Rhythm.* 2007;4:816). In patients with persistent or long-standing persistent AF, results have been worse.

2. The indications for the surgical ablation AF are (1) symptomatic AF in patients undergoing other cardiac procedures, (2) selected asymptomatic AF patients undergoing cardiac surgery in whom the ablation can be performed with minimal risk, and (3) standalone AF surgery should be considered for symptomatic AF patients who prefer a surgical approach, have failed one or more attempts at catheter ablation, or are not candidates for catheter ablation (*Heart Rhythm.* 2007;4:816). The **Cox-Maze procedure,** first performed in the late 1980s, was designed to eliminate multiple macroreentrant circuits in the atria that were felt to be responsible for fibrillation. Through a median sternotomy or right thoracotomy, a series of incisions on both atria, excision of the atrial appendages, and isolation of the pulmonary veins was performed. Long-term results have been outstanding, with a freedom from symptomatic AF of 97% at a median of 5.4 years and an operative mortality of less than 2% (*J Thorac Cardiovasc Surg.* 2003;126:1822). This

"cut and sew" procedure was difficult to perform, and consequently only a few groups adopted the operation. Recently, less invasive surgical procedures have been developed that have replaced the surgical incisions with linear lines of ablation. These ablation techniques have included cryosurgery, radiofrequency or microwave energy, and ultrasound. These new approaches have broadened procedural adoption and have had promising success rates (*Ann Surg.* 2006;244:583). If the entire Cox-Maze lesion set is performed, ablation-assisted procedures with appropriate ablation technology have had identical success rates to the original cut-and-sew procedure (*J Thorac Cardiovasc Surg.* 2007;133:389). Freedom from AF, off antiarrhythmic drugs approaches 80% at 1 year (*J Thorac Cardiovasc Surg.* 2008;135:870).

Other surgical approaches have included pulmonary vein isolation, with or without extended left atrial ablation lines, and with or without ganglionated plexi ablation. The advantage of these procedures has been that they can be performed with small incisions or thoracoscopically without the use of CPB (*J Thorac Cardiovasc Surg.* 2005;130:797). Results have been variable from center to center, but generally have been better with paroxysmal as opposed to long-standing persistent AF (*J Interv Card Electrophysiol.* 2007;20:89).

D. **Heart failure.** It is estimated that approximately 250,000 people suffer from advanced heart failure in the United States (*Curr Heart Fail Rep.* 2010;7:140). The management of heart failure involves medical and surgical care and both acute and chronic interventions. The surgical management of heart failure is discussed here.

1. The **IABP** is used as the first-line device to provide circulatory support in acute heart failure (*Ann Thorac Surg.* 1992;54:11).

   a. **Physiology.** The principal effect of the IABP is a reduction in left ventricular afterload. This occurs due to deflation of the balloon at the time of the opening of the aortic valve. The resulting effects include improved ventricular ejection and reduction in myocardial oxygen consumption. The IABP inflates during early diastole, increasing diastolic BP and thus also diastolic coronary artery blood flow.

   b. **Indications for the IABP** vary in relation to the timing of operation. In the preoperative period, the IABP is indicated for low-cardiac-output states and for unstable angina refractory to medical therapy (e.g., nitrates, heparin, and β-adrenergic blocking agents). Intraoperatively, the IABP is used to permit weaning from CPB when inotropic agents alone are not sufficient. In the postoperative period, the IABP is used primarily for low-cardiac-output states. The IABP can be used to support the circulation during periods of refractory arrhythmias and can also be used to provide support to the patient awaiting cardiac transplantation.

   c. **Insertion of the IABP** generally is accomplished percutaneously via the common femoral artery. Sheathless devices, because of their narrower diameter, may have decreased the incidence of lower-extremity ischemic complications. Correct placement should be confirmed by chest X-ray. The radiopaque tip of the balloon is positioned just below the aortic knob and just distal to the left subclavian artery. At operation, the IABP may be placed directly into the transverse aortic arch, with the balloon positioned down into the descending aorta. Before **removal of the IABP,** the platelet count, PT, and PTT should be normal. Manual pressure should be applied for 20 to 30 minutes after removal to achieve hemostasis and avoid the formation of a femoral artery pseudoaneurysm or arteriovenous fistula.

d. **Management** of the device after placement focuses on ensuring proper diastolic inflation and deflation. The ECG and the femoral (or aortic) pressure waveform are monitored continuously on a bedside console. The device may be triggered using either the ECG or the pressure tracing for every heartbeat (1:1) or less frequently (1:2, 1:3). Anticoagulation during IABP support is optional. If the balloon must be repositioned or removed, the device should be turned off first. IABP support is withdrawn gradually by decreasing the augmentation frequency from 1:1 to 1:3 in steps of several hours each.

e. **Complications of IABP** therapy include incorrect placement of the device, resulting in perforation of the aorta; injury to the femoral artery; and reduction in blood flow to the visceral or renal arteries. Ischemia of the lower extremity, evidenced by diminished peripheral pulses or other sequelae, may necessitate removal of the IABP or performance of an inflow arterial bypass procedure (e.g., femoral-to-femoral artery). Rupture of the balloon is an indication for immediate removal because blood may clot within the ruptured balloon, necessitating operative removal.

f. **Percutaneous Assist Devices** are devices that can be deployed via catheter-based approach and function as ventricular assist devices (VADs) without the need for open surgery. They are typically used only for short-term support, such as temporary support during high-risk percutaneous coronary interventions. Two examples of these are the TandemHeart and the Impella devices (*Expert Rev Cardiovasc Ther.* 2010;8:1247).

2. **Ventricular remodeling.** The progression of heart failure leads to dilation and structural changes in the ventricle by a process known as remodeling. Initially, these changes are compensatory, but eventually they result in pathologic states—including high wall stress, increased neurohormonal levels, and increased inflammatory mediators—that lead to CHF.

a. **Partial left ventriculectomy.** There are several techniques described to reduce the diameter of the left ventricle. In most series, after an initial improvement, heart failure parameters returned to their preoperative state. For the most part, these procedures have been abandoned in favor of assist devices and transplantation. A randomized control trial recently reported no difference between CABG alone and CABG with surgical ventricular remodeling in mortality and cardiac hospitalizations at 4 years (*N Engl J Med.* 2009;360:1705).

3. **Mitral valve surgery** has gained recent popularity for the therapy of CHF. MR secondary to heart failure and ventricular dilatation results from mitral annular dilatation and leaflet lengthening, leading to poor leaflet coaptation. The use of a mitral ring annuloplasty has been shown to be safe and effective for improving NYHA class, left ventricular EF, cardiac output, and left ventricular EDV (*J Thorac Cardiovasc Surg.* 2006;136:568). In fact, it has been estimated that up to 10% of patients undergoing heart transplant evaluation may benefit from mitral valve repair (*J Heart Valve Dis.* 2002;11:S26). However, the long-term results of mitral valve repair remain controversial (*J Heart Valve Dis.* 2000;9:364; *Circulation.* 2006;114:167). In cases in which papillary muscle dysfunction due to ischemia has changed valvular geometry dramatically, mitral valve replacement rather than repair may be more appropriate.

4. **Biventricular pacing** for cardiac resynchronization has emerged as a valid treatment modality for patients with heart failure and concomitant intraventricular conduction delay manifested by QRS complex greater than 120 ms. Absolute risk reduction in all cause mortality in two trials was about 10% at 1 year (*Cardiol Clin.* 2008;26:419). Cardiac resynchronization therapy is an important adjunct in this subset of patients with NYHA class III and IV heart failure.

5. **VADs** may be used to support the left side of the circulation (LVAD) or the right side of the circulation (RVAD). When both an LVAD and an RVAD are used, the combination is termed a **biventricular assist device (BiVAD).**

   a. The **physiologic effect** of a VAD is decompression of the left or right ventricle (or both) and restoration of cardiac output, resulting in decreased myocardial oxygen consumption. The goal of VAD therapy is either to permit recovery of myocardium that is not irreversibly injured (e.g., "stunned" myocardium) or to support the circulation in patients with a failing heart until a heart transplantation is possible. More recently, VAD therapy has been used in patients with end-stage CHF who are not candidates for transplantation.

   b. There are no formal **indications** for VAD implantation. Instead, VADS have been used in three separate broad categories. They are used for patients in which there is (1) an inability to separate from CPB despite inotropic and IABP support ("bridge to recovery"), (2) for intermediate-term cardiac support ("bridge to transplant"), and (3) for permanent replacement therapy ("destination therapy").

   c. **VAD subtypes.** Historically, there have been many different subtypes of VADs and a comprehensive review is beyond the scope of this text. Broadly, there are nonpulsatile devices, which include **centrifugal pumps** and **axial flow pumps,** and pulsatile devices, which include **external devices** and **long-term implantable devices.** No single type has been shown to be superior to the others, and device selection depends on surgeon familiarity and on practical advantages and disadvantages with each particular device.

      (1) **Centrifugal pumps** (BioMedicus Biopump and 3M Sarns Delphin) have been used most frequently as bridges to recovery in patients with postcardiotomy cardiogenic shock.

(2) **Axial flow pumps** (Jarvik 2000 Flowmaker, MicroMed DeBakey VAD, Thoratec HeartMate II) are small pumps, consume less power, and are completely implantable. These devices are designed for longer-term support (months to years). The devices have an impeller suspended by bearings and provide continuous flow. The speed of the pump and the adequacy of left ventricular preload determine output. All of these pumps have a cable that is externalized from the right lower quadrant of the abdomen that connects to the controller system. Many examples of these devices are undergoing clinical trials in the United States and some have Food and Drug Administration (FDA)-approved indications as bridge to transplant or destination therapy. Newer devices in development use magnetically suspended impellers to reduce friction and provide device longevity.

(3) **External pulsatile devices** (Abiomed BVS 5000, Abiomed AB5000, and Thoratec Intracorporeal Ventricular Assist Device) generally have the same indications as centrifugal pumps, although the duration of support may be somewhat longer. They consist of pneumatically driven compression sacs or chambers and mimic the native function of the heart. These devices can be used as a bridge to recovery in patients with acute fulminant myocarditis or MI. Typically these devices are implanted in a preperitoneal pocket.

(4) **Long-term implantable pulsatile devices** (WorldHeart Novacor and Thoratec HeartMate) are used primarily as bridges to transplantation in patients with chronic heart failure. They also are typically pneumatically driven devices with a compression chamber (see destination therapy in Section V.D.4.g below).

d. **Insertion** of VADs. In general, RVADs receive inflow from the right atrium and return outflow to the pulmonary artery using flexible cannulae or grafts. LVADs receive inflow from the left atrium or ventricle and return outflow to the ascending aorta.

e. **Management** of the VAD after placement focuses on maintaining proper function and adequate anticoagulation. The activated clotting time should be monitored frequently and maintained at approximately 200 seconds. Factors that affect **a low-flow-state status post-LVAD** include right ventricular dysfunction, pulmonary hypertension, hypovolemia, and tamponade. It is therefore critical that adequate ventilatory support be provided to correct hypoxemia and acidosis. Pulmonary vasodilators such as NO or inhaled prostacyclin are frequently used to lower pulmonary vascular resistance.

f. **Complications** of VAD therapy include excessive bleeding, thrombus formation, embolization, and hemolysis, which are most common with temporary support devices. Associated complications not related to the device specifically include respiratory failure (due to infection or fluid overload) and renal failure. For chronic devices, long-term complications include infections at the drive-line site, thromboembolism, and device failure.

g. **Destination therapy.** The recent Randomized Evaluation of Mechanical Assistance for the Treatment of Congestive Heart Failure (REMATCH) trial compared assist devices with best medical therapy and demonstrated an increased survival at 2 years (23% vs. 8%). In addition, there was a significant quality-of-life improvement (*N Engl J Med.* 2001;345:1435). The Thoratec HeartMate XVE Left Ventricular Assist System (LVAS) has been approved for destination therapy by the FDA for patients with chronic heart failure.

6. **Cardiac transplantation** can provide relief from symptoms in patients with end-stage cardiomyopathy who are functionally incapacitated despite optimal medical therapy and who are not candidates for any other cardiac corrective procedures. The first successful heart transplant occurred in 1967 in South Africa. There were 2,163 heart transplants performed in the United States in 2008, making this intervention an infrequently used but important modality in the management of heart failure. The 1-year survival following heart transplant is 88% for males and 77% females (American Heart Association Heart Disease and Stroke Statistics 2010 update).

a. **Accepted indications for heart transplant** include cardiomyopathy that is ischemic, idiopathic, postpartum, or chemotherapy induced. Patients are generally in class III or IV NYHA CHF, have a Heart Failure Survival Score of high risk (score derived from a predictive model based on clinical factors and peak oxygen consumption), and have a peak oxygen consumption of less than 14 mL/kg/minute after reaching an anaerobic threshold. Relative indications include instability in fluid balance or renal function despite best medical therapy, recurrent unstable angina not amenable to revascularization, and intractable ventricular arrhythmias.

b. **Relative contraindications to transplantation** include age older than 65 years, irreversible pulmonary hypertension (>4 Wood units), active infection, recent pulmonary embolus, renal dysfunction (serum creatinine >2.5 mg/dL or creatinine clearance <25 mL/minute), hepatic dysfunction (bilirubin >2.5 or alanine aminotransferase/aspartate aminotransferase >2× normal), active or recent malignancy, systemic disease such as amyloidosis, significant carotid or peripheral vascular disease, active or recent peptic ulcer disease, brittle diabetes mellitus, morbid obesity, mental illness, substance abuse, or psychosocial instability.

c. **Donor pool expansion.** Because of the shortage of acceptable donors, the use of an expanded donor pool has been advocated. Some centers have tolerated size mismatch, increased age (>55 years), malignancy, infection, or even donor bypass grafting for carefully selected high-risk recipients.

d. **Immunosuppressive therapy** generally includes a calcineurin inhibitor (cyclosporine or tacrolimus), steroids, and an antimetabolite (mycophenolate or mofetil). Recently, tacrolimus has replaced cyclosporine as the calcineurin inhibitor of choice. When rejection episodes occur, the majority can be reversed with bolus doses of IV steroids. When rejection episodes are resistant to increased steroid doses, the monoclonal antibody OKT3 or rabbit antithymocyte serum can be added to the treatment regimen. Immunosuppression is covered in more detail in Chapter 23.

  e. **Acute allograft rejection** is diagnosed by **endomyocardial biopsy.** Biopsy forceps are passed into the right ventricle percutaneously, using fluoroscopic or echocardiographic guidance, usually via the right internal jugular or femoral vein, and several biopsies are taken to document the presence and degree of rejection histologically. During the early postoperative period, biopsies are performed several times each month. After the first 6 months, the frequency of biopsies is decreased to one or two times per year. Whenever a patient develops evidence of a rejection episode, a biopsy is performed. Complications of endomyocardial biopsy are rare but include ventricular perforation, pneumothorax, injury to the tricuspid valve, transient ventricular or supraventricular arrhythmias, hematoma, and infection. **Coronary artery vasculopathy (CAV),** thought to represent **chronic vascular rejection,** occurs in a significant percentage of cardiac transplant recipients and is a major limitation on the long-term success of cardiac transplantation, being responsible for 30% of deaths in transplanted patients after 5 years (*J Heart Lung Transplant.* 2007;26:769). CAV is usually not amenable to conventional revascularization owing to small-vessel, nonfocal disease and often requires retransplantation. Routine echocardiography is also performed frequently to evaluate allograft function.

7. **Future therapy for heart failure**
  a. **Device therapy.** There has been a substantial improvement in devices over the last two decades. They have become smaller, more durable, and less prone to thrombotic complications. Continued advances in this area will likely expand the indications for these devices for long-term support (destination therapy).
  b. **Myocyte regeneration.** Several approaches, including those using embryonic stem cells, cardiomyocytes, cryopreserved fetal cardiomyocytes, skeletal myoblasts, bone marrow-derived mesenchymal cells, and dermal fibroblasts, are under investigation.
  c. **Xenotransplantation.** The primary difficulty in xenotransplantation is the management of rejection and cross-species infection. To date, such management has been unsuccessful, and the data do not yet justify clinical trials.

VI. **POSTOPERATIVE MANAGEMENT.** Postoperative care of the cardiac surgery patient is provided in three phases: in the intensive care unit (ICU), on the ward, and after discharge from the hospital.

  A. **Intensive care.** ICU care resources generally are required for 1 to 3 days after an operation requiring CPB.

  1. **Initial assessment.** Information on the patient's history, indications for operation, and technical details of the operation (e.g., coronary

arteries bypassed, conduits used, CPB time, and aortic cross-clamp time) should be related to the ICU staff by the surgeon. The anesthesiologist should relate information about the intraoperative course, including preoperative and intraoperative hemodynamic parameters (especially cardiac filling pressures) and current medications. A thorough physical examination should be performed, with attention to the cardiovascular system. A chest X-ray, ECG, complete blood count, basic metabolic panel, arterial blood gas, prothrombin and PTT, and magnesium level are usually obtained.

2. **Monitoring in the immediate postoperative period.** Continuous recordings are made of arterial, central venous, and occasionally pulmonary artery pressures (PAPs); the ECG; and arterial oxygen saturation using pulse oximetry. The pulmonary artery wedge pressure is measured from the Swan–Ganz catheter as indicated by the patient's status, and calculations are made of the cardiac output, cardiac index (cardiac output per unit of body-surface area), stroke volume, pulmonary vascular resistance, and systemic vascular resistance (by thermodilution technique). Normal values for these parameters are listed in Table 30-1. Immediate attention is necessary to determine the etiology and to correct deviations from normal values of any of these parameters. **Body temperature** is monitored continuously using a pulmonary artery thermistor or rectal thermometer. Because early postoperative hypothermia may increase afterload (systemic vascular resistance) and adversely affect blood clotting, hypothermia is treated aggressively (e.g., air-warming blankets). Warming is discontinued when the core temperature reaches 36°C. For patients with persistent fever, a search should be made for active infection and efforts made to decrease the patient's body temperature.

3. **Cardiovascular. Cardiac pump function** is assessed as described earlier. A cardiac index of 2 L/minute/m^2 is generally a minimum acceptable value. A mixed-venous oxygen saturation of less than 60% suggests inadequate peripheral tissue perfusion and increased peripheral oxygen extraction. Etiologies include reduced oxygen-carrying capacity (e.g., low hematocrit), reduced cardiac output, and increased oxygen consumption (e.g., shivering). Common causes of low cardiac output in the early postoperative period are hypovolemia, increased systemic vascular resistance due to persistent hypothermia or increased circulating catecholamines, and decreased contractility secondary to myocardial stunning or intrinsic myocardial dysfunction.

   a. **Preload** is increased by administering crystalloid solution (e.g., lactated Ringer's solution) or colloid solution (e.g., 6% hetastarch, 5% albumin) as needed to maintain the pulmonary arterial wedge pressure in the target range, as determined by the patient's diastolic compliance and systolic performance. Using blood products in a judicious manner is mandatory. At our institution, blood transfusion is indicated in patients with a hemoglobin below 8 g/dL.

   b. **Afterload reduction** in the volume-restored patient increases EF and cardiac output and decreases myocardial oxygen consumption.

The body temperature should be returned to the normal range, and hypertension should be controlled. In general, the mean arterial BP should be maintained near the preoperative level. For patients with valve replacement or aortic replacement, the systolic BP should be carefully controlled to prevent postoperative bleeding. Afterload is often initially titrated with parenteral infusions of sodium nitroprusside, nitroglycerin, or nicardipine, followed by a change to longer-acting parenteral or enteral agents once the patient's hemodynamic status has been stabilized.

c. **Contractility. Inotropic agents** are used only after ensuring an adequate preload and an appropriate afterload. Selection of a particular inotropic agent must be individualized based on the agent's specific effects on the heart rate, BP, cardiac output, systemic vascular resistance, and renal blood flow. All of these agents increase the work of the heart and increase myocardial oxygen consumption and thus should be used judiciously. Typically used agents include dobutamine (a beta-1 adrenergic agonist), milrinone (a phosphodiesterase inhibitor), and epinephrine (a nonspecific adrenergic agonist) at doses of 1 to 5 μg/kg/minute, 0.375 to 0.750 μg/kg/minute, and 0.01 to 0.1 μg/kg/minute, respectively. **Mechanical support** in the form of an IABP or a VAD can be considered if other measures are ineffective in restoring adequate ventricular ejection.

d. **Rate control.** The heart can be paced using temporary epicardial pacing electrodes (placed at the time of operation) at 80 to 100 beats/minute to increase the cardiac output. Pacing can be performed using only the atrial leads (atrial pacing, or AAI mode), only the ventricular leads (ventricular pacing, or VVI mode), or with both sets of leads (AV sequential pacing or atrial tracking with ventricular pacing). Optimal pacing always involves maintaining AV synchrony. VVI pacing should only be used in patients with atrial tachyarrhythmias. If epicardial pacing is not necessary, the epicardial pacemaker generator is set in a backup mode to provide ventricular pacing only in the event of marked bradycardia. The pacemaker output threshold (in milliamperes) should be set to approximately twice the minimum threshold required to capture.

e. **Arrhythmias,** including bradycardia from resolving hypothermia, heart block secondary to persistent cardioplegia effect, and supraventricular and ventricular tachyarrhythmias can be associated with reduced cardiac output and should be corrected. **Arrhythmias** occur in 40% to 60% of patients after cardiac surgical procedures and are more common in patients who receive inotropic support. Advanced cardiovascular life support guidelines should be followed.

(1) **Supraventricular arrhythmias** (AF, atrial flutter, atrial tachycardia) are most common and are associated with an increased risk of transient or permanent neurologic deficits (*J Card Surg.* 2005;20:425). Postoperative AF occurs in approximately 30% of patients and has a peak incidence on postoperative day 2 (*J Thorac Cardiovasc Surg.* 2011;141:559). To reduce the incidence of postoperative

arrhythmias, patients receiving β-adrenergic blocking agents and/or statins preoperatively should continue to be given these medications postoperatively. Patients with supraventricular arrhythmias and hemodynamic compromise should undergo immediate electrical cardioversion (with 50 to 100 joules). Because a frequent etiology is hypoxia or hypokalemia, the new onset of a supraventricular arrhythmia should be evaluated by measurement of the arterial oxygen saturation and the serum potassium. In many patients with hemodynamically stable arrhythmias, prompt correction of the partial pressure of oxygen (to >70 mm Hg) and the serum potassium level (to >4.5 mg/dL) may terminate the arrhythmia. For patients with **atrial flutter,** overdrive pacing may be used to terminate the arrhythmia. The patient's atrial temporary epicardial pacing wires are connected to a pacemaker generator, and either burst pacing (700 to 800 beats/minute for 3 to 4 seconds) or decremental pacing (stepwise decrease from 10% above the flutter rate to 180 beats/minute) is used. For patients who persist in AF for greater than an hour despite adequate rate control, consideration should be given for the initiation of rhythm control with amiodarone. A loading dose is given, orally if possible, and the patient is reassessed for a maintenance dose. For patients who persist in AF for greater than 8 hours despite amiodarone, anticoagulation should be considered to avoid the complication of stroke. IV heparin as a bridge to oral Coumadin with a goal INR of 2.0 to 3.0 should be started.

(2) **Ventricular arrhythmias** in the postoperative period are treated as they are in other patients. Ventricular arrhythmias other than premature ventricular contractions suggest underlying ischemic pathology. The drugs of choice for treatment have been lidocaine and amiodarone.

f. **Cardiac tamponade** is a potentially lethal cause of low cardiac output early after operation. Clinical features include narrowed pulse pressure, increased jugular venous distention, rising cardiac filling pressures, muffled heart sounds, pulsus paradoxus, widened mediastinal silhouette on chest radiograph, and decreased urine output. Definitive diagnosis is usually made by the equalization of diastolic heart pressures on Swan–Ganz catheter pressure recordings or transthoracic or transesophageal echocardiography.

g. **Perioperative MI** occurs in approximately 1% to 2% of patients and can be diagnosed by ECG changes, biochemical criteria (e.g., elevated troponin-I or creatine kinase-MB), or echocardiography. Long-term and acute survival may be adversely affected, especially if complications such as cardiogenic shock or ventricular arrhythmias develop.

h. **Postoperative hemorrhage** is relatively common after cardiac surgery and necessitates reexploration in up to 5% of patients. Hematologic parameters (complete blood count, PT, PTT) are measured on admission to the ICU and as needed. CPB requires heparinization, causes platelet dysfunction and destruction, and activates the fibrinolytic system. Initial focus is on adequate BP control, metabolic stability, maintenance of normothermia, and adequate reversal of heparin with protamine. For patients with significant postoperative bleeding (>200 mL/hour), consideration should be given to platelet transfusion to maintain the platelet count at greater than 100,000/μL and transfusion of fresh-frozen plasma if the INR is abnormal. Although definitive randomized studies have not been conducted, the use of recombinant factor VIIa in patients experiencing life-threatening, unresponsive bleeding has been effective in rare cases and should be considered in this situation (*Ann Thorac Surg.* 2007;83:707). Some surgeons advocate stripping the chest tubes every hour to prevent clotting. If clotting becomes apparent, sterile suction tubing can be used to evacuate blood clot. The formation of undrained clot in the mediastinum may result in cardiac tamponade. Indications for operative reexploration for bleeding include (1) prolonged bleeding (>200 mL/hour for 4 to 6 hours), (2) excessive bleeding (>1,000 mL), (3) a sudden increase in bleeding, and (4) cardiac tamponade. Pleural and mediastinal chest tubes generally are removed when the drainage is less than 200 mL in 8 hours.

4. **Pulmonary. Mechanical ventilation** is used in the initial postoperative period with typical settings: intermittent mandatory ventilation, 10 to 16 breaths/minute; inspired oxygen concentration, 100%; tidal volume, 10 to 15 mL/kg; and positive end-expiratory pressure, 5 cm H_2O. The patient can be extubated when (1) he or she is fully awake and has had a normal neurologic examination; (2) weaning parameters are satisfactory (e.g., respiratory rate <20 breaths/minute; minute ventilation <12 L/minute; negative inspiratory pressure >20 mm H_2O); (3) the arterial blood gas, with only continuous positive airway pressure, is satisfactory (pH approximately 7.40; CO_2 tension <45 mm Hg; oxygen tension >70 mm Hg); (4) there is little mediastinal bleeding (<100 mL/8 hours); and (5) there is hemodynamic stability. Most patients can be extubated shortly after operation. After extubation, oxygen is administered by high-humidity facemask with an initial inspired oxygen concentration of 0.4. The oxygen can be weaned, as tolerated, to keep the arterial oxygen saturation above 94%.

5. **Renal. Renal dysfunction** in the postoperative period can be due to decreased perfusion pressure during CPB or to inadequate perfusion of the kidneys in the postoperative period. Treatment of acute renal insufficiency in the postoperative period includes ensuring adequate hydration and avoiding nephrotoxic medications. Fluid and electrolyte balance is evaluated immediately after operation and hourly as needed. Early after operation, IV fluids are administered slowly (<30 mL/hour). A useful acute measure of a patient's intravascular volume status is the CVP, PAP, or pulmonary capillary wedge pressure. If these are not available and the patient is on the ward, the body weight, which is measured daily and compared to the preoperative

weight, can be used. Serum potassium levels are maintained at greater than 4.5 mg/dL to prevent atrial and ventricular arrhythmias, and concomitant repletion of magnesium is warranted (to >2 mg/dL). Metabolic acidosis can reflect a low-cardiac-output state.

6. **Neurologic. Neurologic examination** of the patient is performed on admission to the ICU and periodically as needed. Changes in the neurologic examination warrant immediate investigation. Shivering increases oxygen consumption and should be treated in the early postoperative period by warming the patient or by the administration of meperidine (50 to 100 mg intramuscularly or intravenously every 3 hours) or, for the ventilated patient, pancuronium (0.04 to 0.10 mg/kg intravenously) or vecuronium (0.08 to 0.10 mg/kg slow IV bolus, then 1 to 5 mg/hour IV continuous infusion). **Pain control** is accomplished using parenteral narcotics or nonsteroidal anti-inflammatory agents, or both, during the early postoperative period.

7. **Nutrition.** The patient is given nothing by mouth until after extubation. A clear liquid diet then is begun and is advanced to a regular diet as tolerated. Patients with prolonged ventilation should receive enteral feedings or if this is not possible, parenteral nutrition.

8. **Infection.** Infectious complications are uncommon after cardiac surgical procedures but may lead to substantial morbidity and mortality. Perioperative antibiotics should be started prior to surgery and administered for 24 hours. Prophylaxis with a second-generation cephalosporin has been associated with a fivefold decrease in wound infection rates compared to placebo in a meta-analysis (*J Thorac Cardiovasc Surg.* 1992;104:590). **Wound infection** occurs in 1% to 2% of sternotomy incisions and a higher proportion of saphenous vein harvest sites. Risk factors for deep sternal wound infection include diabetes mellitus, male gender, obesity, and, possibly, the use of bilateral ITAs during CABG procedures in patients older than 74 years (*Ann Thorac Surg.* 1998;65:1050). Serous drainage from the skin incision is worrisome and should be treated by application of a sterile dressing twice daily and the administration of IV or oral antibiotics. Purulent wound drainage, a sternal click, gross movement of the sternal edges, or substernal air on the chest X-ray may indicate a deep sternal infection. A CT scan of the chest can confirm this diagnosis. In general, deep sternal infections require operative débridement of devitalized sternal and substernal tissues, with cultures of the tissue; administration of broad-spectrum IV antibiotics; and vascularized muscle flap closure of the soft-tissue defect.

9. **Gastrointestinal. Gastrointestinal (GI) complications** are uncommon after cardiac surgical procedures. Stress gastritis can occur after CPB and is thought to be secondary to subclinical ischemia of the gut mucosa. Although overt GI hemorrhage is uncommon, when it does occur, it is associated with a high mortality. Patients should receive proton-pump inhibitor or H_2-receptor–antagonist therapy until a regular diet is begun. GI bleeding may arise from throughout the GI tract. Acute cholecystitis, usually acalculous, is associated with a high mortality.

B. **Ward.** Ward care focuses on convalescence, management of fluid balance, activity level, and diet.

1. **Fluid status.** The patient is weighed daily. Patients who were receiving diuretics preoperatively resume their regimen postoperatively. For patients who were not receiving diuretics preoperatively, oral diuretics are administered until the patient's weight falls to the preoperative value. For most patients, no restrictions are placed on the daily oral fluid intake.

2. **Activity.** The patient is encouraged to be out of bed to a chair and to ambulate as soon as possible after operation. Patients are instructed not to perform any heavy lifting (>10 lb) for a period of 4 weeks postoperatively.

3. **Diet.** A mild postoperative ileus may be present for several days after operation. A regular diet is begun as early as possible after operation. Some patients require a stool softener. Attention should be paid to maintaining a prudent diet that is low in salt and cholesterol.

C. **Postdischarge care.** Care after hospital discharge focuses on continued risk factor modification and surveillance for late complications. Common difficulties during the first 6 to 8 weeks after operation include decreased motivation, decreased appetite, depression, and insomnia. In general, these conditions are temporary, and the physician can provide reassurance.

1. **Physical rehabilitation** with a daily exercise program begins early after operation and continues after discharge from the hospital. Vigorous walking, with increasing distances and longer periods of activity, is the most useful form of exercise for most patients. Bicycling and swimming are acceptable alternatives after 6 to 8 weeks. Patients who were working before operation should return to work within 4 to 6 weeks after operation.

2. **Risk factor modification** may slow or possibly reverse the progression of atherosclerosis in bypass grafts after CABG.

   a. **Smoking** should be discontinued. Referral to organizations with smoking cessation programs should be made before operation, if possible.

   b. **Obesity.** Patients should reach an ideal body weight through planned exercise and dieting.

   c. **Hyperlipidemia** is a major risk factor for the development of graft atherosclerosis and should be treated aggressively, with diet modification and treatment with statins.

   d. **Hypertension** must be controlled.

   e. **Antiplatelet therapy** with aspirin and/or Plavix in patients who underwent coronary artery bypass should be initiated.

   f. **Postpericardiotomy (Dressler) syndrome** is a delayed pericardial inflammatory reaction characterized by fever, anterior chest pain, and pericardial friction rub, and it may lead to mediastinal fibrosis and premature graft occlusion. Treatment includes nonsteroidal anti-inflammatory drugs for 2 to 4 weeks or corticosteroids for refractory cases.

31 General Thoracic Surgery

Ankit Bharat and Bryan F. Meyers

Thoracic surgery encompasses the management of benign and malignant conditions of the esophagus, lung, pleura, and mediastinum. In this chapter, we focus on the systematic evaluation and treatment of the most common thoracic conditions. Disease processes of the esophagus, clearly within the realm of thoracic surgery, are discussed in a separate chapter.

I. **LUNG CANCER.** Lung cancer was a rare disease in the early 20th century. The incidence of lung cancer began to accelerate in the 1930s that mirrored the increased prevalence of cigarette smoking. Dr Alton Oschner was among the first to suggest the association between smoking and lung cancer. Cigarette smoking is the leading risk factor and smoking history influences risk stratification in the evaluation of a suspicious lesion. Currently, lung cancer is the second most common nonskin malignancy, following prostate in men and breast in women. Because of the high case fatality rate, lung cancer is responsible for a larger fraction of cancer deaths in both men and women (29% and 26%, respectively, *www.cancer.org*). An estimated 222,520 cases of lung cancer were diagnosed in 2010 and 157,300 patients died of the disease. Unfortunately, most newly diagnosed cases are not amenable to surgical resection and have poor prognosis. Lung cancer carries an overall 15% 5-year survival. In addition to smoking history, increasing age also increases the probability of lung cancer. Although trials conducted more than two decades ago to screen for lung cancer by either sputum cytology or chest X-ray imaging failed to show benefit, annual spiral computed tomography (CT) scanning can detect lung cancers that are curable (*N Engl J Med.* 2006;355:1822–1824). However, questions remain as to whether the test is sufficiently effective to justify screening people at high risk for lung cancer.

A. Radiographic presentation

1. **Solitary pulmonary nodule (SPN).** Because of the widespread application of CT technology, an estimated 200,000 SPNs are diagnosed each year. By conventional definition, these are circumscribed lung lesions in an asymptomatic individual. Lesions greater than 3 cm are called "masses."

2. **Radiographic imaging by CT** is used to both follow these lesions and predict outcome. The first step in the evaluation of an SPN is to evaluate any prior films. Factors favoring a benign lesion include absence of growth over a 2-year period, size of the lesion, and pattern of calcification. Calcifications that are diffuse, centrally located, "onion skinned"

(laminar), or popcornlike are generally benign. Eccentric or stippled calcifications may indicate malignancy. Lesion size greater than 2 cm, intravenous contrast enhancement, and irregular borders all predict malignancy.

3. **Positron emission tomography (PET) scanning** has demonstrated 95% sensitivity and 80% specificity in characterizing SPNs. PET imaging has a high negative predictive value for most lung cancers; however, bronchoalveolar carcinoma and carcinoid tumor can be negative by PET scan, and inflammatory and infectious processes can be falsely positive. The patient's overall risk factor profile must be considered. In the setting of low risk (e.g., young age, nonsmoker, and favorable features on CT), a negative PET scan has a high negative predictive value, but the same result in an elderly smoker is less reassuring, and further evaluation is warranted.

4. **Tissue biopsy** remains the gold standard for diagnosis. Tissue may be obtained by bronchoscopy in patients with central lung lesions or by CT-guided biopsy. This latter technique has 80% sensitivity for a malignant process and requires technical expertise. Surgical biopsy of SPN by either percutaneous radiographic needle biopsy or minimally invasive surgical techniques like video thoracoscopy and radial endobronchial ultrasound (EBUS) can provide a definitive diagnosis and definitive treatment.

B. **Pathology.** The two main classes of lung tumors are small-cell (oat cell) carcinoma and non-small-cell carcinoma.

1. **Small-cell carcinoma** accounts for approximately 20% of all lung cancers. It is highly malignant, usually occurs centrally near the hilum, occurs almost exclusively in smokers, and rarely is amenable to surgery because of wide dissemination by the time of diagnosis. These cancers initially respond to chemotherapy, but overall 5-year survival remains less than 10%.

2. **Non-small-cell carcinomas** account for 80% of all lung cancers and make up the vast majority of those treated by surgery. The three main subtypes are **adenocarcinoma** (30% to 50% of cases), **squamous cell** (20% to 35%), and **large cell** (4% to 15%). Most tumors are histologically heterogeneous, possibly indicating common origin. **Bronchioloalveolar carcinoma** is a variant of adenocarcinoma and is known for its ability to produce mucin and its multifocal nature. Over the last decade, it has been appreciated that carcinoid tumors (grade I), atypical carcinoid tumors (grade II), large-cell carcinoma, and small-cell tumors represent important subgroups of bronchogenic neuroendocrine carcinoma. This may explain the more aggressive behavior of large-cell carcinoma relative to other non-small-cell cancers.

C. **Symptomatic presentation** of lung cancer implies a worsening stage and is associated with an overall lower rate of survival.

1. **Bronchopulmonary features** include cough or a change in a previously stable smoker's cough, increased sputum production, dyspnea, and new wheezing. Minor hemoptysis causing blood-tinged sputum,

even as an isolated episode, should be investigated with flexible bronchoscopy, especially in patients with a history of smoking who are 40 years of age or older. Lung cancer may also present with postobstructive pneumonia.

2. **Extrapulmonary thoracic symptoms** include chest wall pain secondary to local tumor invasion, hoarseness from invasion of the left recurrent laryngeal nerve near the aorta and left main pulmonary artery, shortness of breath secondary to malignant pleural effusion or phrenic nerve invasion, and superior vena cava syndrome causing facial, neck, and upper-extremity swelling. A Pancoast tumor (superior sulcus tumor) can lead to brachial plexus invasion, as well as invasion of the cervical sympathetic ganglia, which causes an ipsilateral Horner syndrome (ptosis, miosis, and anhidrosis). Rarely, lung cancer can present as dysphagia secondary to compression or invasion of the esophagus by mediastinal nodes or by the primary tumor.

   The most frequent **sites of distant metastases** include the liver, bone, brain, adrenal glands, and the contralateral lung. Symptoms may include pathologic fractures and arthritis from bony involvement. Brain metastasis may cause headache, vision changes, or changes in mental status. Adrenal involvement infrequently presents with Addison disease. Lung cancer is the most common tumor causing adrenal dysfunction.

3. **Paraneoplastic syndromes** are frequent and occur secondary to the release of endocrine substances by tumor cells. They include Cushing syndrome (adrenocorticotropic hormone secretion in small-cell carcinoma), syndrome of inappropriate antidiuretic hormone (SIADH), hypercalcemia (parathyroid hormone-related protein secreted by squamous cell carcinomas), hypertrophic pulmonary osteoarthropathy (clubbing of the fingers, stiffness of joints, and periosteal thickening on X-ray), and various myopathies.

D. **Accurate clinical and pathologic staging is critical** in the management of patients with non-small-cell carcinoma because surgery is the primary mode of therapy for many stage I and II patients and selected stage III patients who have enough physiologic reserve to tolerate resection. It is critical to exclude metastatic disease prior to resection. The essential elements of staging include evaluation for lymph node involvement and evaluation for adrenal, brain, and bone metastasis. An anatomic staging system using the classification for tumor, nodal, and metastatic status was most recently modified in 2009 (AJCC 7th edition; Table 31-1).

1. **Chest CT to include the upper abdomen** provides useful information on location, size, and local involvement of tumor and also allows evaluation for liver and adrenal metastasis. CT scanning alone does not accurately determine the resectability of tumor adherent to vital structures. Patients with localized disease may require intraoperative staging to determine resectability. CT also can identify mediastinal lymphadenopathy. However, the sensitivity for identifying metastatic lymph nodes by CT is only 65% to 80% and the specificity is only 65%. With nodes larger than 1 cm, the sensitivity decreases but the specificity increases.

TABLE 31-1	American Joint Committee on Cancer Staging System of Lung Cancer

Tumor Status (T)

T1a	≤2 cm
T1b	>2–3 cm
	No invasion of visceral pleura or more proximal than lobar bronchus
T2a	>3–5 cm
T2b	>5–7 cm
	Involvement of bronchus ≥2 cm distal to the carina
	Invasion of visceral pleura
	Associated atelectasis or obstructive pneumonitis not involving entire lung
T3	>7 cm or tumor with any of the following characteristics:
	Invasion of chest wall, diaphragm, phrenic nerve
	Invasion of mediastinal pleura or parietal pericardium
	Associated atelectasis or obstructive pneumonitis of entire lung
	Tumor within main bronchus <2 cm from carina but does not involve carina
	Satellite nodules in the same lobe
T4	Tumor with any of the following characteristics:
	Mediastinal invasion
	Invasion of heart of great vessels
	Invasion of carina, trachea, esophagus, or recurrent laryngeal nerve
	Invasion of vertebral body
	Separate tumor nodules in a different but ipsilateral lobe

Nodal Involvement (N)

N0	None
N1	Hilar, interlobar, or peripheral lymph node zones
N2	Ipsilateral mediastinal lymph nodes, subcarinal, or aortopulmonary lymph nodes
N3	Contralateral mediastinal, hilar, or aortopulmonary lymph nodes; ipsilateral or contralateral scalene or supraclavicular lymph nodes

Distant Metastases (M)

M0	None
M1	Distant metastases present

| TABLE 31-1 | American Joint Committee on Cancer Staging System of Lung Cancer *(Continued)* |

Stage		5-y Survival
Ia	T1a/T1b N0 M0	50%–80%
Ib	T2a N0 M0	47%
IIa	T1a/T1b, N1 M0	36%
	T2a N1 M0	
	T2b N0 M0	
IIb	T2b N1 M0	26%
	T3 N0 M0	
IIIa	T1/ T2 N2M0	19%
	T3 N1/N2 M0	
	T4 N0/N1 M0	
IIIb	T4 N2 M0	7%
	Any T with N3 M0	
IV	Any T, any N, M1	2%

2. **PET imaging** is often used to stage patients with non-small-cell carcinoma, but its accuracy for detecting primary tumors and metastatic disease may be limited by the presence of inflammation and ongoing infection. In regions endemic for inflammatory processes such as tuberculosis and histoplasmosis, the usefulness of PET imaging for investigating mediastinal lymph nodes is limited. However, it can be useful for identifying occult distant metastatic disease to the liver, adrenals, and bone.

3. **Lymph node staging** of the mediastinum is done using either **EBUS**-guided fine needle aspiration or **mediastinoscopy.** The pretracheal, paratracheal, and subcarinal lymph nodes can be easily accessed by these techniques. With experience, the sensitivity and specificity of EBUS can approach that of mediastinoscopy. For sampling aortopulmonary nodes, either **Video-assisted thoracoscopic surgery (VATS)** or, less commonly, **anterior mediastinoscopy (chamberlain procedure)** is performed. Mediastinoscopy still remains the gold standard. Although invasive, it is safe, with less than a 1% complication rate. Routine use of these technique in the staging of patients with non–small-cell carcinoma should be favored, with the exception of select patients with clinical stage I lung cancer staged by CT and PET with no abnormal lymphadenopathy. These patients benefit little from lymph node staging (*J Thorac Cardiovasc Surg.* 2006;131:822–829). The timing of mediastinoscopy, whether at the time of thoracotomy or before a planned resection, is controversial and depends on the surgeon's preference and the availability of accurate pathologic evaluation of mediastinal lymph node frozen sections.

4. **CT or magnetic resonance (MR) imaging of the brain** to identify brain metastases is mandatory in the patient with neurologic symptoms but is controversial as a routine part of the work-up of symptomatic patients. Given the reported, albeit low, incidence of CNS metastasis in the setting of even small primary tumors, we advocate the routine use of brain imaging.

5. **Bone scan** is sometimes obtained in patients with specific symptoms of skeletal pain and selectively as part of the general preoperative metastatic work-up. The routine use of PET imaging in many centers has eliminated the routine use of this modality.

6. **Fiberoptic bronchoscopy** is important in diagnosing and assessing the extent of the endobronchial lesion. Although peripheral cancers rarely can be seen with bronchoscopy, preoperative bronchoscopy is important for excluding synchronous lung cancers (found in approximately 1% of patients) prior to resection. Bronchial washings with culture can be taken at the time of bronchoscopy in patients with significant secretions.

E. **Preoperative assessment of pulmonary** function and estimation of postoperative pulmonary assessment is the most critical factor in planning lung resection for cancer.

1. **Pulmonary function tests** and **arterial blood gas analysis** are the standard by which the risk of developing postoperative pulmonary failure is determined. In general, pulmonary resection is associated with a 1% to 2% mortality risk if preoperative FEV_1 (forced expiratory volume in 1 second) is greater than 1.5 L for lobectomy, greater than 2 L for pneumonectomy and is greater than 80% predicted. Predicted postoperative FEV_1 is less than 0.8L or less than 40% is associated with high mortality. **Diffusion capacity, quantitative ventilation–perfusion scan, and exercise testing** are indicated in patients with marginal function for accurate assessment of postoperative function. These tests allow the surgeon to estimate how much the planned target for resection contributes to the overall pulmonary function. Postoperative predicted FEV_1 postpneumonectomy = Preoperative FEV_1 × (1-fraction of total perfusion of the resected lung). Postoperative predicted FEV_1 postlobectomy = preoperative FEV_1 × (1-y/z), where y = functional or unobstructed segments to be resected and z = total number of functional segments. Preoperative diffusion capacity (DLCO) less than 80% is associated with two- or threefold increased risk of pulmonary complication and less than 60% with increased mortality. In general, an estimated postresection FEV_1 of 800 cc or greater suggests that the patient will tolerate a pneumonectomy. Preoperative hypercapnia (arterial carbon dioxide tension >45 mm Hg) may preclude resection.

2. **Evaluation of cardiac disease** is critical for minimizing perioperative complications. Patients with lung cancer are often at high risk for coronary disease because of extensive smoking histories. A detailed history and physical examination to elicit signs and symptoms of ischemia and a baseline electrocardiogram (ECG) are the initial steps. Any abnormal

findings should be aggressively pursued with stress tests or coronary catheterization.

3. **Smoking cessation** preoperatively for as little as 2 weeks can aid in the regeneration of the mucociliary function and pulmonary toilet and has been associated with fewer postoperative respiratory complications.

F. In summary, all patients should have a chest CT scan to evaluate the primary tumor and the mediastinum and to check for metastatic disease to the brain and adrenals. PET imaging or bone scan is useful to exclude bone metastasis. Lymph node staging with either EBUS or mediastinoscopy should be performed to exclude mediastinal lymph node metastasis prior to resection, except possibly in patients with clinical stage Ia disease. All patients should undergo a fiberoptic bronchoscopy by the surgeon before thoracotomy; this is usually done at the same setting as lymph node staging.

G. **Operative principles.** In the patient able to tolerate any resection, the minimal extent of resection is usually an anatomic lobectomy. Even in stage I disease, a limited resection, such as a wedge resection, results in a threefold higher incidence of local recurrence and a decreased overall and disease-free survival. Patients with limited pulmonary reserve may be treated by segmental or wedge resection. Most centers report operative mortality of less than 2% with lobectomy and 6% with pneumonectomy. Minimally invasive techniques for anatomic resection are becoming common and it is speculated that most resections will soon be performed via VATS.

H. **Five-year survival rates range** from 70% to 80% for stage Ia (T1N0) disease and 40% to 60% for stage Ib (T2aN0) disease. Stage I disease is generally treated with surgical resection alone. The presence of ipsilateral intrapulmonary lymph nodes decreases the overall survival to 36% for stage IIa (T1N1, T2aN1) disease and 26% for stage IIb (T2bN1) disease. Stage II cancers are also treated with surgical resection. However, adjuvant chemotherapy has been associated with improved 5-year survival and is now routinely recommended in patients with stage II or stage III disease. Adjuvant radiation therapy is considered in patients with close surgical margins or central N1 lymph node metastasis.

Certain patients with stage IIIa disease appear to benefit form surgical resection alone (T3N1M0). However, selected patients with mediastinal lymph node metastasis (N2 disease) may be candidates for surgical resection after neoadjuvant chemoradiation therapy. Patients with bulky, diffuse mediastinal lymphadenopathy are typically treated using definitive chemoradiation. The optimal regimen of chemotherapy, radiation, or a combination of both is being investigated in clinical trials. Stage IIIb tumors involve the contralateral mediastinal or hilar lymph nodes, the ipsilateral scalene or supraclavicular lymph nodes, extensive mediastinal invasion, intrapulmonary metastasis, or malignant pleural effusions. These tumors are considered unresectable. Stage IV tumors have distant metastases and are also considered unresectable. However, selected patients with node-negative lung cancer and a solitary brain metastasis have achieved long-term survival with combined resection.

II. **TUMORS OF THE PLEURA.** The most common tumor of the pleura is the rare but aggressive **mesothelioma.** Less common tumors include lipomas, angiomas, soft-tissue sarcomas, and fibrous histiocytomas.

A. **Malignant mesothelioma**

1. *Incidence:* Selikoff et al. first reported the link between asbestos and mesothelioma in 1968. It is estimated that asbestos exposure is associated with mesothelioma in 80% of the cases. Incidence of mesothelioma has been increasing since 1980 and about 2,500 to 3,000 cases occur each year in United States. Taking the latency period of 20 to 50 years from asbestos exposure, the peak incidence of mesotheliomas will be encountered by 2020.

2. *Epidemiology:* Mesothelioma is primarily a disease of men in the fifth through seventh decades of life. Patient presentation may be variable. Although benign mesothelioma variants are not associated with asbestos exposure and are asymptomatic, patients with the more common malignant form often report chest pain, malaise, cough, weakness, weight loss, and shortness of breath with pleural effusion. One-third of patients report paraneoplastic symptoms of osteoarthropathy, hypoglycemia, and fever.

3. *Diagnosis:* Tissue is necessary for definitive diagnosis. Cytology of pleural fluid has a 30% to 62% diagnostic yield. Needle biopsy of pleural is used in some centers and has a reported yield of 68%. However, thoracoscopy is the best modality with greater than 90% diagnostic yield. Further, it allows evaluation of pleural, pericardial, and diaphragmatic surfaces for staging. CT scan is useful in differentiating pleural from parenchymal disease. Malignant mesothelioma usually appears as markedly thickened, irregular, pleural-based mass, or thickened pleura with pleural effusion. Occasionally, only a pleural effusion is seen. Routine use of MRI is not recommended but it is superior to CT for identifying transdiaphragmatic extension of tumor into the abdomen or mediastinal invasion. PET scan is being increasingly used as it can identify distant metastatic disease that is missed by CT scan (*J Thorac Cardiovasc Surg.* 2003;126:11–15).

4. *Classification:* The most common and favorable subtype is epithelioid (50%), followed by sarcomatoid (15% to 20%), mixed, and desmoplastic. Careful distinction using histology and immunostaining is required between malignant mesothelioma, especially epithelioid type, and adenocarcinoma.

5. *Staging and treatment:* Three staging systems have been described: American Joint Commission against Cancer (AJCC), Brigham and Women's Hospital (BWH), and the Butchart. Median survival of patients with untreated malignant mesothelioma is 8 to 10 months. Smoking, male gender, advanced stage, and asbestos exposure are prognostic of worse survival. Epithelioid histotype has the most favorable survival. The treatment consists of a multimodal therapy comprising surgery, combination chemotherapy, and radiation. Surgical options include extrapleural pneumonectomy or pleurectomy/decortication.

Consensus is lacking on the choice of surgical procedure. However, for early stage cases, extrapleural pneumonectomy may offer the best chance of cure. The best reported 5-year survival following completion of the multimodal therapy in patients without nodal metastasis is 53% (*J Clin Oncol.* 2009;27:1413–1418).

III. **TUMORS OF THE MEDIASTINUM.** The location of a mass in relation to the heart helps the surgeon to form a differential diagnosis (Table 31-2). On the lateral chest X-ray, the mediastinum is divided into thirds, with the heart comprising the middle segment.

   A. **Epidemiology.** In all age groups, lymphoma is the most common mediastinal tumor. Neurogenic tumors are more likely in children. The likelihood of malignancy is greatest in the second to fourth decades of life. The presence of symptoms is more suggestive of a malignant lesion. Symptoms are often nonspecific and include dyspnea, cough, hoarseness, vague chest pain, and fever.

TABLE 31-2	Differential Diagnosis of Tumors Located in the Mediastinum	
Anterior	**Middle**	**Posterior**
Thymoma	Congenital cyst	Neurogenic
Germ cell	Lymphoma	Lymphoma
Teratoma	Primary cardiac	Mesenchymal
Seminoma	Neural crest	
Nonseminoma		
Lymphoma		
Parathyroid		
Lipoma		
Fibroma		
Lymphangioma		
Aberrant thyroid		

Modified from Young RM, Kernstine KH, Corson JD. Miscellaneous cardiopulmonary conditions. In: Corson JD, Williamson RCN, eds. *Surgery.* Philadelphia: Mosby; 2001.

B. **Evaluation.** Chest X-ray is often used as a screening tool and can lead to the diagnosis of a mass. This should be followed by a CT scan to further delineate the anatomy.

C. **Tumors.** Because of the prevalence of germ cell tumors, all anterior mediastinal masses should be evaluated with biochemical markers β-human chorionic gonadotropin (β-HCG) and α-fetoprotein (AFP).

1. **Teratomas** are usually benign and often contain ectodermal components such as hair, teeth, and bone. Elevation of both β-HCG and AFP is very rare, and it suggests a malignant teratoma. Treatment is surgical resection.

2. **Seminomas** do not present with an elevation in AFP, and fewer than 10% present with an elevation in β-HCG. Their treatment is primarily nonsurgical (radiation and chemotherapy), except in the case of localized disease.

3. **Nonseminomatous germ cell** tumors present with an elevation of both tumor markers. Again, the treatment is primarily nonsurgical, with the exception of obtaining tissue for diagnosis and resecting residual masses after definitive chemotherapy.

4. Tissue diagnosis is often crucial for the diagnosis and treatment of **lymphoma.** Treatment is primarily nonsurgical. Cervical lymph node biopsy, CT-guided biopsy, or mediastinoscopy with biopsy may be required. These lesions often present as irregular masses on CT scan.

5. Patients with paravertebral or posterior mediastinal masses should have their catecholamine levels measured to rule out **pheochromocytomas.**

IV. THYMUS GLAND

A. The physiologic role of thymus is still poorly understood. Tumors of thymus (thymomas) are composed of cytologically bland epithelial cells with a variable admixture of lymphocytes. Because these tumors are relatively rare, consensus on the classification and management of these tumors is lacking. Most behave as if benign, but the presence of invasion of its fibrous capsule defines malignancy. Whereas 15% of myasthenia gravis patients have a thymoma, approximately 50% of patients with a thymoma have some version of paraneoplastic syndromes, including myasthenia gravis, hypogammaglobulinemia, and red cell aplasia.

Although the role of the thymus gland in myasthenia gravis is poorly understood, it appears to be important in the generation of autoreactive antibodies directed against the acetylcholine receptor. Greater than 80% of cases demonstrate complete or partial response to thymectomy. Chances of improvement are increased if thymectomy is performed early in the course of disease (first signs of muscle weakness) or if the myasthenia is not associated with a thymoma.

B. **Preoperative preparation** of the patient with myasthenia gravis involves reduction in corticosteroid dose, if appropriate, and the weaning of anticholinesterases. Plasmapheresis can be performed preoperatively to aid in discontinuation of anticholinesterase agents. Muscle relaxants and atropine should be avoided during the anesthetic.

C. **Operative approach** for thymectomy for myasthenia in cases in the absence of a thymoma or a mass lesion is controversial. The options range from median sternotomy to a transcervical thymectomy. The transcervical approach involves a low-collar incision and is facilitated by using a table-mounted retractor to elevate the manubrium and expose the thymic tissue for resection. The transcervical approach has lower morbidity, but there are questions as to whether it is as efficacious as the transsternal approach. In bulky thymic disease, and for any tumors of the thymus, a median sternotomy approach is preferred to provide maximal exposure for complete resection.

V. PNEUMOTHORAX

A. Pneumothorax is the presence of air in the pleural cavity, leading to separation of the visceral and parietal pleura. This disruption of the potential space disrupts pulmonary mechanics, and, if left untreated, it may progress to tension physiology. In tension pneumothorax, cardiac compromise occurs and presents a true emergency. The etiology may be spontaneous, iatrogenic, or due to trauma. The etiology will determine the most appropriate short- and long-term management strategies.

B. **Physical examination** may demonstrate decreased breath sounds on the involved side if the lung is more than 25% collapsed. Hyperresonance on the affected side is possible. Common symptoms include dyspnea and chest pain. Careful examination for signs of tension pneumothorax (including deviation of the trachea to the opposite side, respiratory distress, and hypotension) must be performed. If there is no clinical evidence of tension pneumothorax, an upright chest X-ray will be required to establish the diagnosis. Smaller pneumothoraces may only be evident on expiration chest X-rays or CT scan. The clinical setting will influence their management.

C. **Management options** include observation, aspiration, chest tube placement with or without pleurodesis, and surgery. The etiology of the pneumothorax influences management strategy.

1. **Observation** is an option in a healthy, asymptomatic patient. This should only be reserved for small pneumothoraces. Generally speaking, if there is a lateral extension of pneumothorax on a plain radiograph, an intervention should be considered. Supplemental oxygen may help to reabsorb the pneumothorax by affecting the gradient of nitrogen in the body and in the pneumothorax.

2. **Aspiration** of the pneumothorax may be done using a small catheter attached to a three-way stopcock. This should be reserved for situations with low suspicion of an ongoing air leak.

3. **Percutaneous catheters** may be placed using Seldinger technique. Multiple commercial kits (like Cook's Thal-Quick) exist and allow for the catheter to be placed to a Heimlich valve or to suction. The catheters in

these kits are generally of small caliber, and their use is limited to situations of simple pneumothorax. Also, if there is any concern for lung adhesions, bedside percutaneous catheters should be avoided.

4. **Tube thoracostomy** remains the gold standard, especially for larger pneumothoraces, for persistent air leaks, when there is an expected need for pleurodesis, or for associated effusion.

   a. Chest tubes may be connected either to a Heimlich flutter valve, to a simple underwater-seal system, or to vacuum suction. The two most commonly used systems are the Pleurovac and Emerson systems. Both systems may be placed to a water seal (providing -3-cm to -5-cm H_2O suction) or to vacuum suction (typically -20 cm). Digital chest tube monitoring systems are also available now and can track the pleural pressure and air leak continuously.

   b. If the water-seal chamber bubbles with expiration or with coughing, this is evident that an air leak persists. In most cases, the tube stays in until the air leak stops.

5. **Bedside pleurodesis.** Sclerosing agents may be administered through the chest tube to induce fusion of the parietal and visceral pleural surfaces. Doxycycline, bleomycin, and talc have all been described.

   a. Bedside pleurodesis can be associated with an inflammatory pneumonitis in the lung on the treated side. In patients with limited pulmonary reserve, this may present as clinically significant hypoxia. Pleurodesis can be quite uncomfortable for the patient, and adequate analgesia is mandatory. Patient-controlled analgesic pump and bolus administration of ketorolac (if tolerated) are effective.

   b. **Doxycycline** is often used as the sclerosing agent for benign processes.

      (1) It is administered as 500 mg in 100 mL of normal saline. Doxycycline is extremely irritating to the pleural surfaces; therefore, 30 mL of 1% lidocaine can be administered via the chest tube before the doxycycline is given and used to flush the drug again. The total dose of lidocaine should not exceed the toxic dose, which is usually 5 mg/kg.

      (2) In patients with large air leaks, the chest tube should not be clamped, to prevent the development of a tension pneumothorax. Instead, the drainage kit should be elevated to maintain the effective water-seal pressure at -20 cm H_2O while keeping the sclerosant in the pleural space.

      (3) The patient (with assistance) is instructed to roll from supine to right lateral decubitus to left lateral decubitus every 15 minutes for 2 hours. Prone, Trendelenburg, and reverse Trendelenburg positions should also be part of the sequence if the patient is able to tolerate it.

      (4) The chest tube is unclamped and returned to suction after the procedure.

   c. **Talc** is a less painful sclerosing agent. Because of largely unfounded concern about introducing a potentially carcinogenic agent and permanent foreign body, it is generally limited to older patients with underlying malignant conditions (see Effusions, Section VII.A.4.a).

(1) Talc, 5 g in 180 mL of sterile saline split into 360-mL catheter syringes, is administered via the chest tube and then flushed with an additional 60 mL of saline. A handy aerosol is available for use in the operating room.

(2) The patient is instructed to change positions as described previously.

6. **Surgery** is performed using a video-assisted approach or by thoracotomy. Patients who have a persistent air leak secondary to a ruptured bleb but are otherwise well should be considered for surgery. By this point, patients have already undergone stabilization by chest tube placement (see Section V.D.3 for specific indications for surgery).

   a. Etiology

   (1) **Iatrogenic** pneumothoraces usually are the result of pleural injury during central venous access attempts, pacemaker placement, or transthoracic or transbronchial lung biopsy. Hence, a postprocedure chest X-ray is mandatory. Often the injury to the lung is small and self-limited. The extent of pneumothorax and associated injury should determine the need for invasive procedures. Observation or percutaneous placement of a chest tube may be appropriate in a patient who is not mechanically ventilated.

   (2) **Spontaneous** pneumothorax is typically caused by rupture of an apical bleb. Up to 80% of patients are tall, young adults, and men outnumber women by 6 to 1; it is more common in smokers than in nonsmokers. The typical patient presents with acute onset of shortness of breath and chest pain on the side of the collapsed lung. Patients older than 40 years usually have significant parenchymal disease, such as emphysema. These patients present with a ruptured bulla and often have a more dramatic presentation, including tachypnea, cyanosis, and hypoxia. There is a significant risk of recurrence, and pleurodesis or surgical intervention is considered after the first or second occurrence. Other etiologies of spontaneous pneumothorax include cystic fibrosis and, rarely, lung cancer.

   (3) **Indications for operation** for spontaneous pneumothorax include (1) recurrent ipsilateral pneumothoraces, (2) bilateral pneumothoraces, (3) persistent air leaks on chest tube suction (usually >5 days), and (4) first episodes occurring in patients with high-risk occupations (e.g., pilots and divers) or those who live at a great distance from medical care facilities. The risk of ipsilateral recurrence of a spontaneous pneumothorax is 50%, 62%, and 80% after the first, second, and third episodes, respectively.

Operative management consists of stapled wedge resection of blebs or bullae, usually found in the apex of the upper lobe or superior segment of the lower lobe. Pleural abrasion (pleurodesis) should be done to promote formation of adhesions between visceral and parietal pleurae. Video-assisted thoracoscopic techniques have allowed procedures to be less invasive in most cases. Using two or three small port incisions on the affected side, thoracoscopic stapling of the involved apical bulla and pleurodesis can be done. Alternatively, a transaxillary thoracotomy incision gives excellent exposure of the upper lung through a limited incision.

7. **Traumatic** pneumothoraces may be caused by either blunt or penetrating thoracic trauma and often result in lung contusion and multiple rib injury.

   a. **Evaluation and treatment** begin with the initial stabilization of airway and circulation. A chest X-ray should be obtained.

   b. **Prompt chest tube insertion** is performed to evacuate air and blood. In 80% of patients with penetrating trauma to the hemithorax, exploratory thoracotomy is unnecessary, and chest tube decompression with observation is sufficient. Indications for operation include immediate drainage of greater than 1,500 mL of blood after tube insertion or persistent bleeding of greater than 200 mL/hour. Patients with multiple injuries and proven pneumothoraces or significant chest injuries should have prophylactic chest tubes placed before general anesthesia because of the risk of tension pneumothorax with positive-pressure ventilation.

   c. **Pulmonary contusion** is associated with traumatic pneumothorax. The contusion usually is evident on the initial chest X-ray (as opposed to aspiration, in which several hours may elapse before an infiltrative pattern appears on serial radiographs), and it appears as a fluffy infiltrate that progresses in extent and density over 24 to 48 hours.

   d. The contusion may be associated with multiple rib fractures, leading to a **flail chest.** This occurs when several ribs are broken segmentally, allowing for a portion of the chest wall to be "floating" and to move paradoxically with breathing (inward on inspiration). The paradoxical movement and splinting secondary to pain and the associated pain lead to a reduction in vital capacity and to ineffective ventilation.

   e. All patients with suspected contusions and rib fractures should have aggressive pain control measures, including patient-controlled analgesia pumps, epidural catheters, and/or intercostal nerve blocks.

   f. **Intravenous fluid should be minimized** to the extent allowed by the patient's clinical status because of associated increased capillary endothelial permeability. Serial arterial blood gas measurements are important for close monitoring of respiratory status. Close monitoring and a high index of suspicion for respiratory decompensation are necessary. Intubation, positive-pressure ventilation, and even tracheostomy are sometimes necessary.

g. **A traumatic bronchopleural fistula** can occur after penetrating or blunt chest trauma. If mechanical ventilation is ineffective secondary to the large air leak, emergent thoracotomy and repair are usually necessary. On occasion, selective intubation of the uninvolved bronchus can provide short-term stability in the minutes before definitive operative treatment.

h. The unusual circumstance known as a **sucking chest wound** consists of a full-thickness hole in the chest wall greater than two thirds the diameter of the trachea. With inspiration, air flows through the wound because of the low resistance to flow and the lung collapses. This requires immediate coverage of the hole with an occlusive dressing and chest tube insertion to reexpand the lung. If tube thoracostomy cannot be immediately performed, coverage with an occlusive dressing taped on three sides functions as a one-way valve to prevent the accumulation of air within the chest, although tube thoracostomy should be performed as soon as possible.

VI. **HEMOPTYSIS** can originate from a number of causes, including infectious, malignant, and cardiac disorders (e.g., bronchitis or tuberculosis, bronchogenic carcinoma, and mitral stenosis, respectively).

A. **Massive hemoptysis** requires emergent thoracic surgical intervention, often with little time for formal studies before entering the operating room. The surgeon is called primarily for significant hemoptysis, which is defined by some as more than 600 mL of blood expelled over 48 hours or, more often, a volume of blood that is impairing gas exchange. Because the volume of the main airways is approximately 200 mL, even smaller amounts of blood can cause severe respiratory compromise. Prompt treatment is required to avoid life-threatening airway obstruction. As baseline lung function decreases, a lower volume and rate of hemoptysis is capable of severely compromising gas exchange.

1. A **brief focused history** can often elucidate the etiology of the bleed, such as a history of tuberculosis or aspergillosis. A recent chest X-ray may reveal the diagnosis in up to half of cases. Chest CT is rarely helpful in the acute setting and is thus unsafe and contraindicated in patients who are unstable. Smaller amounts of hemoptysis can be evaluated by radiologic examinations in conjunction with bronchoscopy.

2. **Bronchoscopy** is the mainstay of diagnosis and initial treatment of major episodes of hemoptysis. Although it may not eliminate later episodes of bleeding, it can allow for temporizing measures, such as placement of balloon-tipped catheters and topical or injected vasoconstrictors. In a setting of massive hemoptysis, the patient should be prepared for a rigid bronchoscopy, which is best performed in the operating room under general anesthesia. Asphyxiation is the primary cause of death in patients with massive hemoptysis. Rigid bronchoscopy allows for rapid and effective clearance of blood and clot from the airway, rapid identification of the bleeding side, and prompt protection of the remaining lung parenchyma (with cautery, by packing with epinephrine-soaked gauze, or by placement of a balloon-tipped catheter in the lobar orifice).

3. In cases in which the **etiology** and the precise bleeding source are not identified by bronchoscopy, ongoing bleeding requires protection of the contralateral lung. Selective ventilation, either with a double-lumen tube or by direct intubation of the contralateral mainstem bronchus, may be critical to avoid asphyxiation.

4. **After isolation of the bleeding site, angiographic embolization** of a bronchial arterial source may allow for lung salvage without the need for resection. The bronchial circulation is almost always the source of hemoptysis. Bleeding from the pulmonary circulation is seen only in patients with pulmonary hypertension.

5. **Definitive therapy** may require thoracotomy with lobar resection or, rarely, pneumonectomy. Infrequently, emergent surgical resection is necessary to control the hemoptysis. The etiology of the bleeding and the pulmonary reserve of the patient are important because many patients are not candidates for surgical resection.

VII. PLEURAL EFFUSION

A. Pleural effusion may result from a wide spectrum of benign, malignant, and inflammatory conditions. By history, it is often possible to deduce the etiology, but diagnosis often depends on the analysis of the pleural fluid. The presentation of symptoms depends on the underlying etiology, and treatment is based on the underlying disease process.

1. **Chest X-ray** is often the first diagnostic test. Depending on radiographic technique, an effusion may remain hidden. Although decubitus films are the most sensitive for detecting small, free-flowing effusions, the same volume may remain hidden in a standard antero-posterior film. A concave meniscus in the costophrenic angle on an upright chest X-ray suggests at least 250 mL of pleural fluid. CT scan and ultrasound can be particularly helpful if the fluid is not free flowing or if history suggests a more chronic organizing process such as empyema.

2. **Thoracentesis**
   a. The technique of thoracentesis is described in Chapter 37.
   b. The fluid should be sent for culture and Gram stain, biochemical analyses [pH, glucose, amylase, lactate dehydrogenase (LDH), and protein levels], and a differential cell count and cytology to rule out malignancy.
   c. In general, thin, yellowish, clear fluid is common with transudative effusions; cloudy and foul-smelling fluid usually signals infection or early empyema; bloody effusions often denote malignancy; milky white fluid suggests chylothorax; and pH less than 7.2 suggests bacterial infection or connective tissue disease.
   d. Larger volumes (several hundred milliliters) can often aid the cytopathologists in making a diagnosis. White blood cell count greater than $10,000/mm^3$ suggests pyogenic etiology. A predominance of lymphocytes is noted with tuberculosis. Glucose is decreased in infectious processes as well as in malignancy.

e. Pleural effusions are broadly categorized as either **transudative** (protein-poor fluid not involving primary pulmonary pathology) or **exudative** (resulting from increased vascular permeability as a result of diseased pleura or pleural lymphatics). Protein and LDH levels measured simultaneously in the pleural fluid and serum provide the diagnosis in nearly all settings.

f. Exudative pleural effusions satisfy at least one of the following criteria: (1) ratio of pleural fluid protein to serum protein greater than 0.5, (2) ratio of pleural fluid LDH to serum LDH greater than 0.6, or (3) pleural fluid LDH greater than two thirds the upper normal limit for serum.

3. **Transudative pleural effusion** can usually be considered a secondary diagnosis; therefore, therapy should be directed at the underlying problem (e.g., congestive heart failure, cirrhosis, or nephrotic syndrome). Therapeutic drainage is rarely indicated because fluid rapidly reaccumulates unless the underlying cause improves.

4. **Exudative pleural effusion** may be broadly classified based on whether its cause is benign or malignant.

   a. **Malignant** effusions are most often associated with cancers of the breast, lung, and ovary and with lymphoma. Diagnosis is often made by cytology, but in the event that this process is not diagnostic, pleural biopsy may be indicated. Given the overall poor prognosis in these patients, **therapy offered by the thoracic surgeon is generally palliative.**

      (1) **Drainage** of effusion to alleviate dyspnea and improve pulmonary mechanics by reexpanding the lung may be done with chest tube placement or indwelling pleurX catheters.

      (2) **Pleurodesis** with talc or doxycycline may prevent reaccumulation of the effusion.

   b. **Benign exudative effusions** are most often a result of pneumonia (parapneumonic). The process begins with a sterile parapneumonic exudative effusion and leads to a suppurative infection of the pleural space, empyema, if the effusion becomes infected. The initially free-flowing fluid becomes infected and begins to deposit fibrin and cellular debris (5 to 7 days). Eventually, this fluid becomes organized, and a thick, fibrous peel entraps the lung (10 to 14 days).

      (1) **Empyema.** Fifty percent of empyemas are complications of pneumonia; 25% are complications of esophageal, pulmonary, or mediastinal surgery; and 10% are extensions from subphrenic abscesses. Thoracentesis is diagnostic but is sufficient treatment in only the earliest cases.

      (2) The **clinical presentation** of empyema ranges from systemic sepsis requiring emergent care to chronic loculated effusion in a patient who complains of fatigue. Other symptoms include pleuritic chest pain, fever, cough, and dyspnea.

      (3) The **most common offending organisms** are Gram-positive cocci (*Staphylococcus aureus* and streptococci) and Gram-negative organisms (*Escherichia coli* and *Pseudomonas* and *Klebsiella* species). *Bacteroides* species are also common.

(4) Management includes control of the infection by appropriate antibiotics, drainage of the pleural space, and obliteration of the empyema space. Once the diagnosis is made, treatment should not be delayed. Specific management depends on the phase of the empyema, which depends on the character of the fluid. If the fluid does not layer on posteroanterior and lateral and decubitus chest X-ray, a CT scan should be done.

(a) Early or **exudative empyema** is usually adequately treated with simple tube drainage.

(b) Fibropurulent empyema may be amenable to tube drainage alone, but the fluid may be loculated. The loculations of empyema cavities are composed of fibrin.

(c) In advanced or **organizing empyema,** the fluid is thicker and a fibrous peel encases the lung. Thoracotomy may be necessary to free the entrapped lung.

(d) If a patient has a **persistent fluid collection with an adequately placed tube** as evidenced by chest CT, intrapleural fibrinolytic therapy may be indicated. Intrapleural streptokinase, 250,000 units, is divided into three doses, each in 60 mL of normal saline. A dose is administered and flushed with 30 mL of normal saline. The tube is clamped and the patient rolled as described for pleurodesis; then the tube is returned to suction. The procedure is repeated every 8 hours. Alternatively, 250,000 units can be administered daily for 3 days. The adequacy of treatment is determined by resolution of the fluid collection and complete reexpansion of the lung.

(e) A **postpneumonectomy empyema** is one of the most difficult complications to manage in thoracic surgery. Typically, there is a dehiscence of the bronchial stump and contamination of the pneumonectomy space with bronchial flora. The finding of air in the pneumonectomy space on chest X-ray is often diagnostic. The incidence of major bronchopleural fistula after pulmonary resection varies from 2% to 10% and has a high mortality (16% to 70%). Initial management includes thorough drainage (either open or closed) of the infected pleural space, antibiotics, and pulmonary toilet.

(f) Definitive surgical repair of the fistula may include primary closure of a long bronchial stump or closure of the fistula using vascularized muscle or omental flaps. The residual pleural cavity can be obliterated by a muscle transposition, thoracoplasty, or delayed Clagett procedure.

(i) Initially, a chest tube is inserted to evacuate the empyema. Great caution should be taken in inserting chest tubes into postpneumonectomy empyemas. A communicating bronchial stump–pleural fistula can contaminate the contralateral lung rapidly when decompression of the empyema is attempted. The patient should be positioned with the affected side down so that the remaining lung is not contaminated with empyema fluid. This procedure might best be handled in the operating room.

(ii) **After the patient is stabilized,** the next step usually is the creation of a **Clagett window thoracostomy** to provide a venue for daily packing and to maintain external drainage of the infected pleural space. This typically involves reopening the thoracotomy incision at its anterolateral end and resecting a short segment of two or three ribs to create generous access to the pleural space. The pleura is then treated with irrigation and débridement. After a suitable interval (weeks to months), the wound edges can be excised, and the pneumonectomy space is closed either primarily or with a muscle flap after it has been filled with 0.25% neomycin solution. Alternatively, the space can be filled with vascularized muscle flap.

VIII. CHRONIC OBSTRUCTIVE PULMONARY DISEASE (COPD), LUNG VOLUME REDUCTION, AND TRANSPLANTATION

A. The long-term consequences of smoking lead not only to lung cancer but also to **COPD.**

1. **Destruction of lung parenchyma** occurs in a nonuniform manner. As lung tissue loses its elastic recoil, the areas of destruction expand. This expansion of diseased areas, in combination with inflammation, leads to poor ventilation of relatively normal lung.

2. This leads to the **typical findings of hyperexpanded lungs** on chest X-ray: flattened diaphragms, widened intercostal spaces, and horizontal ribs. On pulmonary function testing, patients present with increased residual volumes and decreased FEV_1.

3. Despite maximal medical and surgical treatment, the **disease is progressive.** Surgical treatment is generally reserved for the symptomatic (dyspnea) patient who has failed maximal medical treatment, with the goal of improving symptoms.

4. The **goals of surgery** are to remove diseased areas of lung and allow improved function of the remaining lung tissue.

B. The mainstays of surgical treatment have been bullectomy, lung volume reduction, and transplantation. Prior to any surgical intervention, patients must be carefully selected. Smoking cessation for at least 6 months is mandatory, as is enrollment in a supervised pulmonary rehabilitation program.

1. **Bullectomy.** Patients with emphysema may have large bullous disease. Emphysematous bullae are giant air sacs and may become secondarily infected.

2. **Lung volume reduction** may be indicated in symptomatic patients who have predominantly apical disease, with FEV_1 greater than 20%

of predicted, and patients who may be too old for transplantation. However, several patients have undergone lung volume reduction prior to getting a lung transplant. Through a bilateral VATS approach or a sternotomy incision, one or both lungs have areas of heavily diseased lung resected. Patients with diffuse homogeneous emphysema are not candidates for this procedure.

3. Emphysema and α_1-antitrypsin deficiency have become the leading indications for lung transplantation. Other common indications include cystic fibrosis, pulmonary fibrosis, and pulmonary hypertension.

   a. Patients selected for lung transplantation generally are younger, have diffuse involvement of emphysema, and have FEV_1 less than 20%.

   b. Both single-lung and bilateral-lung transplantation have been performed for emphysema, although bilateral transplant patients have improved long-term survival.

   c. The only absolute indication for bilateral lung transplantation is cystic fibrosis because single-lung transplantation would leave a chronically infected native lung in an immunocompromised patient.

   d. Long-term, chronic allograft dysfunction in the form of bronchiolitis obliterans occurs in 50% of patients.

IX. ISSUES IN THE CARE OF THE THORACIC PATIENT

A. Postoperative care of the thoracic surgery patient focuses on three factors: control of incisional pain, maintenance of pulmonary function, and monitoring of cardiovascular status.

   1. The **thoracotomy incision is one of the most painful and debilitating** in surgery. Inadequate pain control contributes heavily to nearly all postoperative complications. Chest wall splinting contributes to atelectasis and poor pulmonary toilet. Pain increases sympathetic tone and myocardial oxygen demand, provoking arrhythmias and cardiac ischemic episodes. The routine use of epidural catheter anesthesia perioperatively and during the early recovery period has improved pain management significantly. Other effective analgesic maneuvers include intercostal blocks with long-acting local anesthetic before closure of the chest and intrapleural administration or local anesthetic via catheters placed at the time of thoracotomy.

   2. **Maintenance of good bronchial hygiene** is often the most difficult challenge facing the postthoracotomy patient. A lengthy smoking history, decreased ciliary function, chronic bronchitis, and significant postoperative pain all contribute to the ineffective clearance of pulmonary secretions. Even aggressive pulmonary toilet with incentive spirometry and chest physiotherapy delivered by the respiratory therapist, along with adequate analgesia, are insufficient on occasion. Diligent attention must be paid, including frequent physical examination and daily chest X-ray and arterial blood gas evaluation to detect any

changes in gas exchange. Atelectasis and mucus plugging can lead to ventilation–perfusion mismatch and ensuing respiratory failure. The clinician should make liberal use of nasotracheal suctioning, bedside flexible bronchoscopy, and mechanical ventilatory support if needed.

3. All physicians caring for the postthoracotomy patient should be familiar with chest tube placement, maintenance, and removal. The purpose of chest tube placement after thoracotomy and lung resection is to allow drainage of air and fluid from the pleural space and to ensure reexpansion of the remaining lung parenchyma.

    a. Chest-tube drainage is not used routinely with pneumonectomy unless bleeding or infection is present. Some surgeons place a chest tube on the operative side and remove it on postoperative day 1. Balanced pneumonectomy drainage systems have been advocated to balance the mediastinum during the first 24 to 48 hours. A chest tube in the patient with a pneumonectomy space should never be placed to conventional suction because of the risk of cardiac herniation and mediastinal shift.

    b. Chest tubes are removed after the air leak has resolved and fluid drainage decreased (usually <100 mL over 8 hours). Chest tubes usually are removed one at a time. The tube is removed swiftly and the site is simultaneously covered with an occlusive dressing. The technique of swift chest tube removal is critical to preventing air entry through the removal site.

4. Cardiovascular complications in the postoperative period are second in frequency only to pulmonary complications because the population that develops lung cancer is at high risk for heart disease. The three most common sources of cardiac morbidity are arrhythmias, myocardial infarctions, and congestive heart failure. A negative preoperative cardiac evaluation does not preclude the development of postoperative complications.

    a. Cardiac arrhythmias occur in up to 30% of patients undergoing pulmonary surgery. The most common arrhythmia is atrial fibrillation. The highest incidence occurs in elderly patients undergoing pneumonectomy or intrapericardial pulmonary artery ligation. All patients should have cardiac rhythm monitoring after thoracotomy for at least 72 hours.

    b. A number of trials have failed to reach consensus on optimal regimen for prophylaxis.

    c. Treatment of any rhythm disturbance begins with an assessment of the patient's hemodynamic status. Manifestations of these arrhythmias vary in acuity from hemodynamic collapse to palpitations. If the patient is hemodynamically unstable, the advanced cardiac life support protocol should be followed. After the patient has been examined and hemodynamic stability confirmed, an ECG, arterial blood gas sample, and serum electrolyte panel should be obtained. Frequently, supplementary oxygen and aggressive potassium and magnesium replenishment are the only treatment necessary. Premature ventricular contractions often are signs of myocardial ischemia.

They should be treated expediently with electrolyte correction, optimization of oxygenation, and evaluation for ischemia.

d. Chest pain associated with myocardial infarction often goes unnoticed by caretakers and patients due to thoracotomy incisional pain and narcotic administration.

e. Perioperative fluid management of thoracic surgery patients differs from that of patients after abdominal surgery. Pulmonary surgery does not induce large fluid shifts. In addition, collapse and reexpansion of lungs during surgery can lead to pulmonary edema. Pulmonary edema should be treated with aggressive diuresis. This is largely due to the limited pulmonary reserve, most graphically demonstrated in the pneumonectomy patient in whom 100% of the cardiac output perfuses the remaining lung. Judicious fluid management, including avoiding fluid overload and pulmonary edema, is critical in patients with limited pulmonary reserve. Discussions regarding intraoperative fluid management should be held with the anesthesiologist before surgery. Physicians may need to accept transiently decreased urine output and increased serum creatinine. Mild hypotension may be treated with intravenous α-agonists such as phenylephrine. Cardiac dysfunction may also be the source of postoperative oliguria, pulmonary edema, and hypotension and should always be considered in patients who are not responding normally. Echocardiography or placement of a Swan–Ganz catheter may guide treatment.

X. THORACOSCOPY

A. Diagnostic thoracoscopy

1. **VATS pleuroscopy** is performed in patients after thoracentesis and percutaneous pleural biopsy have failed to provide a diagnosis of suspected pleural disease. VATS frequently is used to diagnose malignancy in a solitary peripheral nodule. It is contraindicated in patients with extensive intrapleural adhesions or those who are unable to tolerate single-lung ventilation.

2. **VATS is approximately 95% accurate** for diagnosis of pleural disease.

B. Therapeutic thoracoscopy

1. **VATS is routinely performed** for a wide variety of thoracic procedures including lung biopsy/wedge resections, closure of leaking blebs, pleurodesis, sympathectomies, pericardiectomy, excision of mediastinal cysts, thymectomy, lobectomies, and bilobectomies. In fact, many centers are even performing VATS for pneumonectomies and esophagectomies. As this field continues to develop, there will be increasing trend toward the use of minimally invasive techniques in thoracic surgery. Robotics has also impacted thoracic surgery and lung resections are being performed at several centers with the robot.

   a. **Absolute contraindications** include extensive intrapleural adhesions or the inability to tolerate single-lung anesthesia.

  b. Relative contraindications include previous thoracotomy, tumor involvement of the hilar vessels, and previous chemotherapy or radiotherapy for lung or esophageal tumors.

2. The **patient is placed** in the lateral decubitus or semioblique position. Thoracoscopy requires selective intubation to allow collapse of the ipsilateral lung and to create a working space within the thorax (thus, insufflation gases are not needed). For most procedures, two to three incisions are required. The thoracoscope is placed through a port in the seventh or eighth intercostal space in the midaxillary line. Working ports for instruments generally are at the fourth or fifth intercostal space in the anterior axillary line and posteriorly near the border of the scapula. The endoscopic stapler, electrocautery, or laser can be used for resection. A chest tube is generally placed through one of the port sites.

3. **Complications** include hemorrhage, perforation of the diaphragm, air emboli, prolonged air leak, and tension pneumothorax.

4. **Postoperative thoracoscopy management**
  a. A chest X-ray is taken and checked for residual air or fluid.
  b. Chest tubes, if any, are removed when there is no air leak and the drainage decreases to satisfactory levels.
  c. Analgesia is provided by patient-controlled anesthesia or orally administered medication as needed.
  d. Diet is usually advanced by postoperative day 1.
  e. Physical activity is as tolerated with a chest tube. Depending on the procedure and diagnosis, patients can return to work in approximately 1 week.

32 Pediatric Surgery

Amy C. Fox and Patrick A. Dillon

Pediatric surgery is predicated on the fundamental fact that children differ from adults in anatomy, physiology, and their reaction to operative trauma, thereby making adjustments in care not merely matters of scale. Although some disease processes are managed similar to those in adults, this chapter addresses the more pediatric-specific surgical issues.

I. SPECIAL CONSIDERATIONS IN PRE- AND POSTOPERATIVE CARE

A. **Fluid, electrolytes, and nutrition**

1. **Fluid requirements.** Normal daily fluid requirements for children (Table 32-1) are higher than those of adults due to greater insensible losses. Infants have a high ratio of body surface area to volume and a limited ability to concentrate urine due to immature kidneys. Total body water is a higher percentage of body weight (75% in children vs. 60% in adults). Total blood volume in a full-term newborn measures approximately 85 mL/kg and decreases with age. Postoperative fluid replacement should be adjusted to support urine output between 1 and 2 mL/kg/hour.

2. **Electrolytes.** Maintenance fluids for children younger than 6 months old should include 10% dextrose in 0.25% saline with 20 mEq/L of potassium chloride. However, children older than 6 months old can be given 5% dextrose in 0.45% saline with 20 mEq/L of potassium chloride. Daily sodium requirements are 2 to 3 mEq/kg. Daily potassium requirements are 1 to 2 mEq/kg.

3. **Nutrition.** Normal daily caloric requirements per kilogram decrease as children age (Table 32-2). These estimated requirements must be increased to take into account altered metabolic states such as fevers, traumas, and burns.

   a. A newborn is expected to gain weight at about 15 to 30 g/day.

   b. Most infant formulas contain 20 kcal/oz. Caloric needs can be calculated by the following formula:

   Weight (kg) × 6 oz = Volume of formula needed to deliver 120 kcal/kg

   c. Carbohydrates should supply 50%, lipids 40%, and protein 10% of total calories in the diet.

B. **Preoperative preparation**

1. Nothing-by-mouth status (Table 32-3). Studies indicate that clear liquids ingested 2 hours before induction of anesthesia do not increase the risk of aspiration in children at normal risk of aspiration during anesthesia. In addition, children permitted fluids in a less restrictive fashion have a more comfortable preoperative experience in terms of thirst and hunger (*Cochrane Database Syst Rev.* 2009;(4):CD005285).

TABLE 32-1 Normal Fluid Requirements in Children

Weight (kg)	24-hr Fluid Requirements
<2 (premature)	150 mL/kg
1–10	100 mL/kg
11–20	1,000 mL + 50 mL/kg for each kg >10
>20	1,500 mL + 20 mL/kg for each kg >20

Weight (kg)	Hourly Fluid Requirements
0–10	4 mL/kg
10–20	2 mL/kg
>20	1 mL/kg

TABLE 32-2 Normal Daily Caloric Needs in Children

Age (y)	REE (kcal/kg/d)	Average (kcal/kg/d)
<36 wk	63	120
0–0.5	53	108
0.5–1	56	98
1–3	57	102
4–6	48	90
7–10	40	70
11–14	32	55
15–18	27	45

REE, resting energy expenditure.

TABLE 32-3 Nothing-by-Mouth Requirements in Children

Age	Clear Liquids	Solids/Formula/Breast Milk
<6 mo	2 hr	4 hr
>6 mo	2 hr	6 hr

2. Indications for preoperative antibiotic prophylaxis include patients with cardiac anomalies, ventriculoperitoneal shunts, and those with implanted prosthetic material.

C. Vascular access

1. Peripheral venous access can be obtained from the dorsal veins of the hand or foot, antecubital vein, saphenous vein, external jugular vein, or scalp veins.

2. Central venous access may be needed if peripheral access is exhausted or if drugs or nutrition need to be given centrally. Central veins can be accessed directly or via peripheral veins (i.e., peripherally inserted central catheter). Common sites for direct access are the subclavian, internal jugular, external jugular, and femoral veins.

3. Intraosseous (IO) access can be used in an emergency setting when attempts at obtaining vascular access have failed. A location 1 to 3 cm distal to the tibial tuberosity is recommended. The needle should be directed inferiorly during insertion. Alternatively, the femur may be reached by inserting the needle in a cephalad direction 3 cm proximal to the condyles. A bone marrow aspiration needle or a 16G to 19G butterfly needle is adequate. Contraindications to IO access include a fracture of the bone or previous IO catheter.

4. Arterial catheters are needed in some children. The potential sites for an arterial catheter include the umbilical, radial, femoral, posterior tibial, and temporal arteries. For the neonate, the umbilical artery can often be cannulated through the umbilical stump within the first 2 to 4 days of life.

II. ABDOMINAL PAIN IN CHILDREN

A. Abdominal pain is a common complaint in the pediatric age group with various etiologies (Table 32-4).

B. The differential diagnosis of abdominal pain must take the following into consideration: age, gender, duration of symptoms, circumstances at onset, and modifying factors.

C. The **history of present illness** is often difficult to obtain from a child; therefore, parents should be present to corroborate accurate information. While characteristics of the pain should be elicited, associated symptoms such as emesis (bilious, nonbilious, bloody), diarrhea, constipation, melena, hematochezia, or fever may be more likely to suggest surgical etiologies.

D. The **physical examination** is critical in determining how toxic a patient may be. A patient's ease and comfort are integral to a thorough and accurate physical exam.

1. Peritonitis may be elicited by various maneuvers such as palpation, percussion, manipulation of the hip, deep respiratory movements, or rectal examination.

2. Bimanual pelvic exam may be necessary in age-appropriate patients.

TABLE 32-4	Etiologies of Pediatric Abdominal Pain	
Very Common Causes	**Less Common Causes**	**Rare Causes**
Acute appendicitis	Intussusception	Henoch–Schönlein purpura
Viral infection	Lower lobe pneumonia	Nephrotic syndromes
Gastroenteritis	Intestinal obstruction	Pancreatitis
Constipation	Urinary tract obstruction	Hepatitis
Genitourinary tract infection	Inguinal hernia	Diabetic ketoacidosis
Trauma	Meckel diverticulum Cholecystitis Intra-abdominal mass	Lead poisoning Acute porphyria Herpes zoster Sickle cell anemia

III. NEONATAL SURGICAL PROBLEMS

A. **Congenital diaphragmatic hernia (CDH).** Incomplete diaphragm development at 8 weeks of gestation can result in herniation of abdominal organs into the chest which can prevent normal lung development. Posterolateral (Bochdalek) defects occur 85% of the time with over 90% of these occurring on the left side. CDH occurs in a 1:1 male-to-female ratio. CDH can be a lethal condition with mortality rates dependent on associated anomalies, the severity of pulmonary hypertension, and the degree of pulmonary hypoplasia. The less common Morgagni defect occurs in a parasternal anterior location and is usually associated with fewer pulmonary and systemic complications.

1. Diagnosis
   a. Signs and symptoms
      (1) Cardiorespiratory distress such as tachypnea, retractions, and cyanosis
      (2) Asymmetric chest
      (3) Reduced breath sounds on the affected side
      (4) Scaphoid abdomen
   b. Imaging
      (1) **Antenatal ultrasound and maternal–fetal magnetic resonance imaging (MRI)** are used to determine polyhydramnios and location of the fetal liver and give an estimation of fetal lung volumes.
      (2) Chest x-rays may demonstrate bowel in the thorax, a loss of the normal diaphragm contour, or mediastinal shift.

2. Management
   a. **Immediate postnatal care** includes supplemental oxygen or endotracheal intubation if the patient is in significant respiratory distress. Excessive bag-mask ventilation should be avoided as it can exacerbate gastrointestinal (GI) distension which further impedes lung ventilation. Decompression by orogastric or nasogastric intubation reduces distension of the stomach in the thoracic cavity.
      (1) Conventional ventilation
   b. Initial peak inspiratory pressures (PIP) less than 25 cm H_2O to minimize barotrauma.
   c. Maintain preductal oxygen saturation greater than 85% with minimal PIP.
   d. When stable, wean fraction of inspired oxygen (F_{IO_2}) for preductal oxygen saturation greater than 85%.
   e. In order to minimize PIP, arterial carbon dioxide tension of 45 to 60 mm Hg is acceptable.
   f. Maintain pH>7.2.
   g. Ventilator rates of 40 to 60 breaths per minute and 3 to 5 positive end-expiratory pressure (PEEP) are often required for adequate oxygenation and ventilation.
      (1) **High-frequency oscillating ventilation** is associated with decreased barotrauma and may be used if conventional ventilation fails.
      (2) **Inhaled agents—nitric oxide or epoprostenol and sildenafil—** may decrease the severity of pulmonary hypertension.
      (3) **Extracorporeal membrane oxygenation (ECMO)** is considered for patients with severe preductal hypoxemia or right-to-left shunting due to severe pulmonary hypertension. Patients with severe pulmonary hypoplasia may not be candidates for ECMO.
   h. **Operative intervention** is deferred until the patient has been stabilized.
      (1) A subcostal incision on the affected side allows the herniated abdominal contents to be reduced into the peritoneal cavity.
      (2) The diaphragmatic defect is repaired primarily or with a synthetic patch if the defect is large.
      (3) A laparoscopic or thoracoscopic approach may be utilized for repair in carefully selected patients.

B. **Tracheoesophageal malformations** are a spectrum of anomalies including esophageal atresia and tracheoesophageal fistula (TEF) separately or in combination (Fig. 32-1). There is a 1:1 male-to-female ratio. Over 50% of patients will have associated anomaly and 25% will have a VACTERL association (e.g., *v*ertebral defects, imperforate *a*nus, *c*ardiac defects, *t*racheo*e*sophageal malformations, *r*enal dysplasia, and *l*imb anomalies).

1. Diagnosis
   a. Signs and symptoms
      (1) Excessive drooling
      (2) Regurgitation of feedings
      (3) Choking, coughing, or cyanosis during feeding
      (4) **Resistance when passing a nasogastric tube**

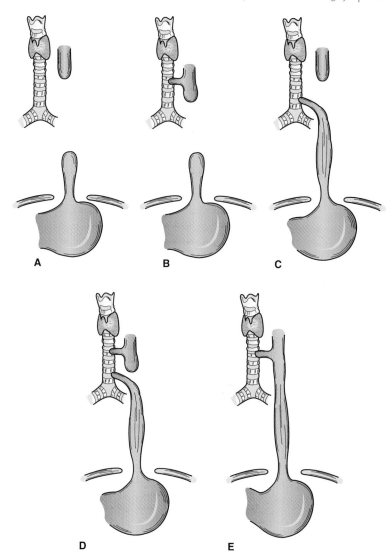

Figure 32-1. Variants of TEF. **A:** Atresia without fistula (5% to 7% of cases). **B:** Proximal fistula and distal pouch (<1% occurrence). **C:** Proximal pouch with distal fistula (85% to 90% of cases). **D:** Atresia with proximal and distal fistulas (<1% of cases). **E:** Fistula without atresia (H type) (2% to 6% occurrence).

b. Chest radiograph
  (1) Coiled orogastric tube in the esophageal pouch
  (2) Gas in the GI tract implies a distal TEF
  (3) Infiltrates suggestive of aspiration pneumonia

2. Management
  a. Preoperative management includes prevention of aspiration through elevation of the head of the bed 30 degrees and placing an orogastric or nasogastric tube into the proximal esophageal pouch for decompression. An ECHO should be obtained to evaluate the location of the aortic arch which helps determine the operative approach.
  b. Operative intervention is typically through a right extrapleural posterolateral thoracotomy. The fistula is ligated and the atresia is repaired in a one-stage procedure when possible. H type fistulas are often approached through a right transverse cervical incision.

C. Necrotizing enterocolitis (NEC) is an acute, fulminating inflammatory disease of the intestine associated with focal or diffuse ulceration and necrosis of the small bowel, colon, and rarely the stomach. While the cause is unknown, the pathogenesis is thought to be multifactorial involving an immature gut barrier defense and virulent bacteria. The incidence of NEC is 1 to 3 per 1,000 live births and is the most common GI emergency of neonates. It primarily affects premature infants and occurs in 10% of all babies born weighing less than 1,500 g.

  1. Diagnosis. A high index of suspicion is needed in making a diagnosis of NEC.
    a. Signs and symptoms
      (1) Patients may be lethargic, apneic, or have temperature instability.
      (2) Patients may have emesis, bilious nasogastric tube drainage, or high gastric residuals. The abdomen is often distended.
      (3) Bowel movements may be bloody.
      (4) Edema or erythema of the abdominal wall may indicate peritonitis, a localized response to inflamed bowel, or perforation of bowel. The skin may show pallor or mottling.
    b. Other adjunct studies
      (1) Laboratory studies may reveal a metabolic acidosis, thrombocytopenia, leukocytosis, or leukopenia.
      (2) Plain radiographs of the abdomen may reveal dilated loops of bowel, pneumatosis intestinalis, portal vein gas, or pneumoperitoneum. Contrast imaging is often avoided due to the risk of perforation.

  2. Management
    a. Nonoperative management
      (1) Patients are placed on bowel rest with nasogastric decompression and parenteral nutrition. Broad-spectrum antibiotics are initiated.
      (2) Serial abdominal examinations, plain radiographs, and laboratory studies help determine the progress of nonoperative management.

b. Operative management

    (1) Indications for operative treatment include pneumoperitoneum, bowel obstruction, intra-abdominal abscess, or sepsis unresponsive to treatment.

    (2) The two main surgical options are laparotomy or primary peritoneal drainage. A randomized controlled trial (RCT) suggests that the operation performed for perforated NEC does not alter mortality rates, dependence on parenteral nutrition 90 days after operation, or hospitalization duration (*N Engl J Med.* 2006;354(21):2225–2234).

c. Laparotomy includes resection of necrotic bowel and creation of stomas. If intestinal viability is questionable, re-exploration within 24 hours is essential.

d. Primary peritoneal drainage may be used as a temporizing measure in critically ill infants until they can tolerate a laparotomy or as a primary therapy.

D. Gastroschisis and omphalocele are congenital abdominal wall defects that differ in etiology and severity.

  1. Gastroschisis is an abdominal wall defect (usually <4 cm) that is believed to arise from an isolated vascular insult in the developing mesenchyme. It typically occurs to the right of the normal umbilical cord with abdominal organs herniating through the defect. In contrast to omphalocele, there is no membranous sac covering the eviscerated abdominal organs. The incidence of associated anomalies in gastroschisis is low, but approximately 10% may have an intestinal atresia.

  2. Omphalocele is an abdominal wall defect (usually >4 cm) of the umbilical ring in which the intestines protrude through the base of the umbilical cord and herniate into a sac. The high incidence (50%) of associated congenital anomalies (cardiac, chromosomal) often dictates the prognosis for infants with omphalocele.

  3. Diagnosis

    a. A **gastroschisis** defect is to the **right** of the umbilical cord with abdominal organs herniating through the defect. There is **no encompassing sac,** and the exposed bowel may develop a serositis.

    b. An **omphalocele** defect is at the **base** of the umbilical cord and can vary from a few centimeters to absence of most of the abdominal wall. A **sac** covers the herniated viscera. While rupture of the sac is infrequent, it can be distinguished from gastroschisis by the presence of residual sac in continuity with the umbilical cord and normal appearing bowel.

    c. Radiologic exams

      (1) Prenatal ultrasound may demonstrate either defect after 13 weeks of gestation.

      (2) A finding of omphalocele mandates a thorough search for other birth defects given the high incidence of related anomalies.

  4. Management

    a. Prenatal management. Serial ultrasounds may be necessary. If bowel dilation and mural thickening of the eviscerated bowel are detected, delivery at the time of lung maturity may be indicated. However, a systematic review found insufficient evidence to support induction of labor (*Br J Obstet Gynaecol.* 2009;116(5):626–636). Delivery should be planned at a tertiary care center with high-risk obstetrics and pediatric surgical expertise.

b. Postnatal management

    (1) Heat and fluid losses can be decreased by covering the exposed bowel in gastroschisis defects with moistened gauze and then wrapping the bowel with plastic wrap or placing the infant in a plastic bag to cover the lower body and defect. Fluids should be given as a bolus (20 mL/kg) to start resuscitation and then titrated to achieve a urine output of 1.5 to 2 mL/kg/hour.

    (2) The neonate can be positioned in a lateral position to prevent kinking of the mesentery and vascular compromise of the bowel.

c. Operative intervention

    (1) Viscera may be reduced primarily. If this is not possible, viscera are placed in a spring-loaded or self-made silo which is secured beneath the fascial edge. The silo and viscera can be reduced gradually over time (*J Pediatr Surg.* 2009;44(11):2126–2129).

    (2) The abdominal wall defect is then repaired in a primary fashion on an elective basis. Fewer complications may arise with this method of management compared to immediate reduction of viscera and primary closure (*J Pediatr Surg.* 2006;41(11):1830–1835).

    (3) The fascial defect can be extended in the midline for 1 to 2 cm if the bowel mesentery appears to be compressed by a narrow opening.

IV. ALIMENTARY TRACT OBSTRUCTION

A. Congenital causes of alimentary tract obstruction

    1. Intestinal malrotation results when the intestine fails to undergo its normal rotation and fixation during embryologic development. Symptoms most often present in the neonatal period but may present in adulthood. Malrotation places the intestine at greater risk for volvulus which is a surgical emergency.

    a. Diagnosis

        (1) Signs and symptoms

            (a) Bilious emesis in the newborn mandates evaluation for intestinal malrotation with volvulus.

            (b) The abdomen may be distended or tender. Patients may have hematemesis or hematochezia.

        (2) Radiologic studies

            (a) Plain radiographs commonly show a normal bowel gas pattern but may also show a "double-bubble" which is indicative of duodenal obstruction but is not diagnostic of volvulus.

            (b) An upper GI series is necessary to establish the diagnosis. Failure of the duodenum to cross to the right of the midline with a right-sided jejunum characterizes intestinal malrotation. Hallmark signs for volvulus include the "bird's beak" sign and a corkscrew appearance of the proximal small intestine.

b. Management. The operative intervention is a Ladd procedure. The bowel is eviscerated and rotated counterclockwise to correct the volvulus. Peritoneal (Ladd) bands are divided. The colon is positioned to the left and the small bowel to the right side of the abdomen. An appendectomy completes the procedure.

2. Intestinal atresia or stenosis usually results from an intrauterine vascular accident; however, duodenal atresia results from failure of recanalization of the duodenum.

a. Location. Distal ileum > proximal jejunum > duodenum > colon.

b. Diagnosis

(1) Prenatal ultrasound may show polyhydramnios or dilated bowel loops.

(2) Signs and symptoms

(a) Symptoms appear shortly after birth for atresia but may take weeks to months for stenosis or intestinal web.

(b) Patients may have bilious emesis or abdominal distension.

(c) Other symptoms include failure to pass meconium, failure to thrive, or poor feeding.

(3) Radiology

(a) A "double-bubble" sign is diagnostic of duodenal obstruction.

(b) Contrast enema may identify a distal intestinal atresia and can also identify obstruction secondary to meconium ileus or meconium plug syndrome.

c. Management

(1) Preoperative management includes nasogastric decompression and resuscitation with intravenous (IV) fluids. Antibiotics should be given preoperatively.

(2) Operative intervention

(a) Dependent on the site of atresia but a primary anastomosis is usually attempted for small bowel atresia and may require resection and/or tapering of the dilated proximal segment.

(b) Atresia involving the colon usually requires initial colostomy with delayed anastomosis.

(c) A duodenoduodenostomy or duodenojejunostomy is created to bypass the obstruction in duodenal atresia.

(d) Saline should be infused into the distal bowel to rule out synchronous intestinal atresias.

3. Hirschsprung disease is intestinal aganglionosis of the hindgut. The segment of aganglionosis can vary but over 80% of patients have a transition point in the rectosigmoid area. It can be familial or sporadic, and up to 7.8% of cases occur in patients for whom more than one family member is affected. Mutations in the *RET* protooncogene have been found in both familial and sporadic cases.

a. Diagnosis

(1) Signs and symptoms

(a) Neonates may present with abdominal distention, failure to pass meconium within the first 48 hours of life, infrequent defecation, or enterocolitis with sepsis.

(b) Older infants and children present with chronic constipation or failure to thrive.

(2) Radiology

(a) Plain radiographs show a pattern of distal bowel obstruction.

(b) Contrast enema usually demonstrates a transition zone between distal nondilated bowel and proximal dilated bowel; however, total colonic aganglionosis does not have a transition zone.

(3) Pathology is essential for making the diagnosis and requires a rectal biopsy. Full-thickness specimens are the ideal tissue samples to demonstrate the absence of ganglion cells. In neonates, rectal suction biopsy is often sufficient for diagnosis.

b. Management

(1) Preoperative management includes colonic decompression to prevent enterocolitis. Saline enemas may be used to evacuate impacted stool. A nasogastric tube should be placed if the child is vomiting.

(2) Operative goals are removal of aganglionic bowel and reconstruction of the intestinal tract by bringing innervated bowel down to the anus while maintaining normal sphincter function. There are multiple "primary pull-through" variations which achieve this goal such as the Swenson, Duhamel, Soave, laparoscopic endorectal pull-through (Georgeson), and transanal endorectal pull-through (Langer).

(a) Each of these operations has been modified to improve functional results and may be performed in the newborn period; however, surgery may be delayed to allow for increased weight gain or resolution of enterocolitis.

(b) Transanal endorectal pull-through is associated with fewer complications and fewer episodes of enterocolitis compared to transabdominal approaches without higher rates of incontinence (*J Pediatr Surg.* 2010;45(6):1213–1220).

(c) A diverting colostomy may be performed proximal to the aganglionic segment in patients who are unstable or who have massively dilated bowel.

4. Anorectal anomalies refer to various congenital defects (noted below) which can produce neonatal intestinal obstruction. The lesions may be classified as low, intermediate, or high depending on whether the atresia is below, at the level of, or above the puborectalis sling, respectively. These anomalies are associated with other congenital defects such as the VACTERL syndromes or cardiovascular defects.

- Males: Perineal fistula, rectourethral bulbar fistula, rectourethral prostatic fistula, rectovesical (bladder neck) fistula, imperforate anus without fistula, rectal atresia and stenosis.

- Females: Perineal fistula, vestibular fistula, imperforate anus with no fistula, rectal atresia and stenosis, persistent cloaca.
  a. Diagnosis
  (1) Physical examination may demonstrate various findings from no anus to perineal fistulas. Meconium on the perineum within 24 hours of birth may signify a perineal fistula (low defect).
  (2) Plain radiographs such as an obstructive series or an invertogram may be obtained. Sacral abnormalities may be identified. A contrast study may demonstrate a fistulous tract.
  b. Management
  (1) A perineal fistula (low defect) may be safely repaired without a colostomy. A high defect with probable rectourethral or rectovaginal fistula requires a colostomy and mucous fistula for initial management.
  (2) For the more complex anorectal anomalies, a three-step procedure is advocated with a diverting colostomy after birth, posterior sagittal anorectoplasty, and colostomy closure.

5. Meconium ileus is a neonatal intestinal obstruction caused by inspissated meconium that may occur in the setting of cystic fibrosis.
  a. Diagnosis
  (1) Prenatal ultrasound may demonstrate polyhydramnios.
  (2) Signs and symptoms may include abdominal distention, bilious emesis, failure to pass meconium within 24 to 48 hours of life, pneumoperitoneum, peritonitis, abdominal wall inflammation, hypovolemia, or sepsis.
  (3) Plain abdominal radiographs can show dilated loops of small bowel and a ground-glass appearance of air and meconium mixture. Given the thick meconium, air–fluid levels are often absent. Intra-abdominal calcifications suggest prenatal perforation and subsequent meconium peritonitis. Ascites or pneumoperitoneum also suggest perforation. However, up to 35% of infants with complicated meconium ileus show no radiographic abnormalities.
  (4) Water-soluble contrast enema can confirm the diagnosis by demonstrating a microcolon and inspissated meconium in the ileum.
  b. Management
  (1) Nonoperative management includes hydration with IV fluids and broad-spectrum antibiotics. A water-soluble contrast enema can be both diagnostic and therapeutic. This solution draws fluid into the bowel lumen and causes an osmotic diarrhea.
  (2) Operative intervention is indicated for complicated meconium ileus or when enema therapy fails.
      (a) An enterotomy is made followed by irrigation with 1% to 2% acetylcysteine solution. If gentle irrigation does not flush out the meconium, a 14-French ileostomy tube may be placed and routine irrigations are done beginning on postoperative day one.

        (b) If intestinal volvulus, atresia, perforation, or gangrene complicates the illness, the nonviable bowel is resected and an end ileostomy with mucus fistula is created. Routine irrigations are started. A primary anastomosis is delayed for 2 to 3 weeks later.

6. Meconium plug syndrome refers to altered colonic motility or viscous meconium believed to cause impaired stool transit and obstruction of the colonic lumen. Unlike meconium ileus, patients do not have cystic fibrosis. While diagnosis is similar to meconium ileus, operative intervention is rarely needed to relieve the obstruction. Suction biopsy is needed to rule out Hirschsprung disease. A sweat chloride test is needed to rule out cystic fibrosis.

7. Intestinal duplications are cystic or tubular structures lined by various types of normal GI mucosa. They are located dorsal to the true alimentary tract. They frequently share a common muscular wall and blood supply with the normal GI tract. In 20% of cases, enteric duplications communicate with the true GI tract. They are most commonly located in the ileum but may occur anywhere from the mouth to the anus.

  a. Diagnosis

    (1) Signs and symptoms are nonspecific and can include emesis, abdominal pain, abdominal distension, or an abdominal mass.

    (2) Abdominal ultrasound or GI contrast studies may show external compression or displacement of the normal alimentary tract. Technetium radioisotope scans may aid in diagnosis if the cyst contains gastric mucosa.

  b. Management involves resection of the duplication or internal drainage. Internal drainage may be indicated if the resection would require an extensive amount of bowel being removed. Internal drainage minimizes the risk of damage to the biliary system in the case of a duodenal duplication. When gastric mucosa is found in a cyst, it is stripped, and the cyst lumen is joined to the adjacent intestine.

B. Acquired causes of alimentary tract obstruction

1. Pyloric stenosis is the most common surgical cause of nonbilious vomiting in infants. It occurs in 1 of 400 live births. The male-to-female ratio is 4:1. It occurs generally in neonates who are 2 to 5 weeks of age. Patients often present with a hypochloremic hypokalemic metabolic alkalosis.

  a. Diagnosis

    (1) Signs and symptoms

      (a) Nonbilious, projective vomiting occurring 30 to 60 minutes after feeding is typical. Patients can also have formula intolerance which does not resolve with change of feeds.

      (b) Signs of dehydration include lethargy, the absence of tears, a sunken anterior fontanelle, dry mucous membranes, or decreased urine output.

      (c) The "olive" mass refers to a thickened pylorus which can be palpated to the right and superior to the umbilicus. It is approximately 2 cm in diameter, firm, and mobile.

(2) Radiologic studies

    (a) Abdominal ultrasonography notes a pyloric diameter greater than 14 mm, muscular thickness greater than 4 mm, and pyloric length greater than 16 mm. This is diagnostic of pyloric stenosis with approximately 99.5% sensitivity and 100% specificity (*Semin Pediatr Surg.* 2007;16(1):27–33).

    (b) An upper GI contrast study shows an enlarged stomach, poor gastric emptying, and an elongated, narrow pyloric channel or "string sign."

b. Management

    (1) Preoperative management involves aggressive fluid resuscitation which often requires a bolus (20 mL/kg) and then 5% dextrose in normal saline to achieve a urine output of 2 mL/kg/hour. Addition of potassium and changing to 5% dextrose in 0.45% normal saline occurs when urine output is adequate.

    (2) Operative intervention is indicated only after adequate resuscitation and correction of the metabolic alkalosis. A pyloromyotomy is division of the hypertrophied pyloric muscle, leaving the mucosa intact. This can be done through an open incision or laparoscopically. A double-blind RCT suggests that while both procedures are safe, laparoscopy results in decreased time to achieve full enteral feeds and a decreased postoperative length of stay over open pyloromyotomy without any additional complications (*Lancet.* 2009;373(9661):390–398).

    (3) Postoperative management. An electrolyte solution can typically be started by mouth 6 hours after pyloromyotomy. Over the next 12 hours, formula or pumped breast milk can be started and should reach goal within 24 hours. Parents should be advised that vomiting may occur postoperatively as a result of swelling at the pyloromyotomy, but this problem is self-limited. If the pyloric mucosa is perforated and repaired during surgery, nasogastric drainage is recommended for 24 hours.

2. Intussusception refers to an invagination of proximal intestine into adjacent distal bowel with resultant obstruction of the lumen (most common: ileocolic intussusception). A lead point of the intussusception is identified in only 5% of patients and is most commonly a Meckel diverticulum. This obstruction may compromise the arterial inflow and venous return. The highest incidence is at 5 to 10 months of age.

a. Diagnosis

    (1) A typical history is a previously healthy infant who presents with periods of abrupt crying and retraction of the legs up to the abdomen. Attacks usually subside over a few minutes but recur every 10 to 15 minutes. In 30% of cases, a recent viral gastroenteritis or upper respiratory infection may precede onset of symptoms.

    (2) Physical findings include a dark-red mucoid stool ("currant jelly" stool). Hyperperistaltic rushes may be heard during an episode. A sausage-shaped abdominal mass may be palpated or the tip of the intussusception may be felt on rectal examination.

    (3) Ultrasound can be used for screening in suspected cases of intussusception.

    (4) Barium or air-contrast enema confirms the diagnosis by demonstrating a "coiled spring" sign.

b. Management

  (1) Nonoperative management includes nasogastric drainage, IV fluid resuscitation, broad-spectrum antibiotics, and an early surgical consultation.

    (a) Pneumatic or hydrostatic reduction is attempted under radiographic guidance if no evidence of peritonitis exists and the patient is stable. This technique has a 90% success rate. The maximum safe intraluminal air pressure is 80 mm Hg for young infants and 110 to 120 mm Hg for older children. Recurrent intussusception in children less than 1 year old can be treated with repeated enema therapy.

    (b) Postreduction a patient should be observed for 24 hours. A liquid diet with advancement can be started once the child is alert. Recurrent intussusception occurs in 8% to 12% of patients.

  (2) Operative indications include failure of nonoperative reduction, peritonitis, sepsis, or shock. Recurrence after enema reduction in an older child is also an indication to operate as small bowel tumors which can serve as the lead point are more frequent in this age group.

    (a) During laparotomy, a transverse incision is made to deliver the bowel. Gentle retrograde pressure is applied to the telescoped portion of the intestine in an attempt at manual reduction. Proximal and distal segments should not be pulled apart because of the risk of bowel injury.

    (b) If manual reduction is not possible, resection of the involved segment and primary anastomosis should be done.

    (c) An incidental appendectomy should also be performed.

    (d) Recurrence of intussusception after operative treatment is approximately 1%.

3. Distal intestinal obstruction syndrome (DIOS), formerly known as *meconium ileus equivalent,* is caused by impaction of inspissated intestinal contents in older patients with cystic fibrosis. This problem occurs in 10% to 40% of patients with cystic fibrosis who are followed long term.

  a. Diagnosis requires a high index of suspicion in a child with cystic fibrosis who presents with chronic or recurrent abdominal pain and distention, vomiting, and constipation. An inciting cause such as abrupt cessation of pancreatic enzyme supplementation, dehydration, a dietary change, or exacerbation of respiratory symptoms is present.

    (1) Plain abdominal radiographs may show a ground-glass appearance of the intestine. Dilated small bowel with air–fluid levels is present.

    (2) Water-soluble contrast enemas demonstrate the inspissated intestinal contents.

b. Management

(1) Nonoperative management includes a water-soluble contrast enema to induce an osmotic diarrhea to flush the intestine and relieve the obstruction. GoLYTELY solution may be used in selective cases to relieve the obstruction from above.

(2) Operative management is indicated when enemas or conservative therapy are unsuccessful. It is also indicated when intussusception or volvulus complicates DIOS.

V. JAUNDICE IN CHILDREN

- This is a yellowing of the skin that reflects hyperbilirubinemia.
- In jaundiced infants, the total serum bilirubin usually exceeds 7 mg/dL.
- This elevated bilirubin may reflect a rise in either the **conjugated (direct)** or **unconjugated (indirect)** bilirubin, or both. This distinction is integral for establishing a differential diagnosis for jaundice.

A. Unconjugated hyperbilirubinemia occurs when bilirubin that has not been metabolized in the liver rises above normal serum values. Common causes include hemolytic disorders, breast-feeding, and physiologic jaundice of the newborn. More rare causes of unconjugated hyperbilirubinemia include indirect causes of increased enterohepatic circulation of bilirubin such as meconium ileus, Hirschsprung disease, and pyloric stenosis. Treatment typically involves phototherapy and correction of primary diseases.

B. Conjugated hyperbilirubinemia occurs when excess monoglucuronides and diglucuronides in the liver result in elevated levels of bilirubin in the serum. The most common causes include biliary obstruction, hepatitis (infectious, toxic, or metabolic etiology), or TORCH (*to*xoplasmosis, *r*ubella, *c*ytomegalovirus, and *h*erpes simplex virus) infections. Two surgical causes of conjugated hyperbilirubinemia include biliary atresia and choledochal cysts.

1. Biliary atresia is the most common cause of infantile jaundice that requires surgical correction. The etiology is unknown. The disease is characterized by progressive obliteration and sclerosis of the biliary tree. With age, obliteration of the extrahepatic bile ducts, proliferation of the intrahepatic bile ducts, and liver fibrosis progress at an unpredictable rate.

a. Diagnosis

(1) Signs and symptoms are often nonspecific such as jaundice, acholic stools, dark urine, and hepatomegaly.

(2) Percutaneous liver biopsy results range from classic biliary tree fibrosis to those unable to be differentiated from α1-antitrypsin deficiency or neonatal hepatitis.

(3) Technetium-99m iminodiacetic acid hepatobiliary imaging aids in differentiation between liver parenchymal disease and biliary obstructive disease. In biliary atresia, the liver readily takes up the tracer molecule, but no excretion into the extrahepatic biliary system or duodenum is seen.

(4) Ultrasonography notes shrunken extrahepatic ducts and a noncontractile or absent gallbladder.

b. Management

(1) Open liver biopsy and cholangiogram

    (a) The common bile duct is visualized by cholangiography in only 25% of patients with biliary atresia.

    (b) Cholangiography in the remaining 75% of patients demonstrates an atretic biliary tree.

(2) **Operative intervention**

    (a) The obliterated extrahepatic ducts are excised with subsequent hepaticojejunostomy in a **Kasai procedure.** When the distal common bile duct is patent, a choledochojejunostomy is constructed.

    (b) **Jaundice improves in two-thirds of patients after a Kasai procedure, but only one third will retain their liver after the first decade of life (*Eur J Pediatr.* 2010;169(4):395–402).**

    (c) **Liver transplantation** is the recommended option when liver failure occurs or the Kasai procedure fails.

2. **Choledochal cysts** are a spectrum of diseases characterized by cystic dilation of the extrahepatic and intrahepatic biliary tree. They are believed to be an embryologic malformation of the pancreaticobiliary system. Approximately 50% of children present within the first 10 years of life. There are five types:

- **Type I:** Fusiform cystic dilation of common bile duct (most common)
- **Type II: Diverticulum of the extrahepatic bile duct**
- **Type III: Choledochocele**
- **Type IV:** Cystic disease of the intra- or extrahepatic bile ducts
- **Type V:** Single or multiple intrahepatic ducts

a. Diagnosis

(1) **Signs and symptoms** include nonspecific findings such as jaundice, abdominal pain, abdominal mass, cholangitis, pancreatitis, portal hypertension, hepatic abscess, or cyst rupture.

(2) These cysts can be demonstrated on various radiologic tests such as ultrasonography, hepatobiliary scintigraphy, transhepatic cholangiography, magnetic resonance cholangiopancreatography, or endoscopic retrograde cholangiopancreatography.

b. Management

(1) The entire cyst is excised when possible. It is important to identify the pancreatic duct entrance into the biliary tree before excision.

(2) **Choledochojejunostomy**

(3) **Hepatic resection** if disease is intrahepatic and limited to a lobe or segment of the liver.

(4) **Liver transplantation** for diffuse intrahepatic disease.

VI. GROIN MASSES

A. Indirect inguinal hernias affect approximately 1% to 5% of children. Boys are affected more than girls, with an 8:1 ratio. Prematurity increases the incidence of inguinal hernia to between 7% and 30%. The incidence of bilateral hernias ranges from 10% to 40%. Bilateral hernias occur more frequently in premature infants and girls.

1. **Diagnosis** is made by a history and physical examination. A groin bulge is noted which extends toward the scrotum or vulva either by history or observation. This is sometimes reproduced only when the child laughs, cries, or stands. Boys may have a thickened spermatic cord.

2. **Management**

   a. Reducible hernias are repaired with high ligation of the sac through a low abdominal incision. The hernia sac is anterior and medial to the spermatic cord in boys and more difficult to locate among the muscle fibers running through the external ring in girls. The sac can contain small bowel, omentum, or ovary.

   b. Incarcerated hernias can often be reduced with gentle direct pressure on the hernia. Simultaneously applying caudal traction on the testicle in addition to direct pressure on the hernia may be necessary in some cases.

   c. Strangulated hernias require emergent operative repair. Even if a severely incarcerated/strangulated hernia is reduced, the child should be admitted and scheduled for urgent herniorrhaphy. If viability of sac contents is in question, the bowel must be examined before abdominal closure.

B. **Hydroceles** are fluid collections within the processus vaginalis that envelop the testicles. They occur in approximately 6% of full-term male newborns.

   1. **Communicating hydroceles** allow the free flow of peritoneal fluid down to the scrotum. The processus vaginalis is patent. This must be regarded as a hernia, with elective repair encouraged to prevent subsequent incarceration.

   2. **Noncommunicating hydroceles** confine the fluid to the scrotum. A portion of the processus vaginalis obliterates normally. This is usually a self-limiting process and resolves in 6 to 12 months.

VII. TUMORS AND NEOPLASMS

A. **Neuroblastoma** is a neoplasm of the sympathochromaffin system with an incidence of approximately 8 million cases per year. It is the most common extracranial tumor of childhood and accounts for 10% of all pediatric malignancies. The median age at diagnosis is 2 years, with 85% of the tumors being diagnosed before age 5 years.

   1. **Diagnosis.** Neuroblastoma is often an incidental finding on radiographic studies performed for other reasons. Patients may have an abdominal mass on exam. Rarely, children present with symptoms of fever, malaise, or abdominal pain. At the time of discovery, up to 75% of neuroblastomas are metastatic.

   2. **International Neuroblastoma Staging System**

      a. This system places patients in low-, intermediate-, or high-risk groups on the basis of age, surgical staging, and status of the **N-*myc* oncogene** as these factors significantly predict outcome.

      b. Children younger than 12 months at the time of diagnosis have a better prognosis for cure, whereas older patients are more likely to have disseminated disease and a poorer prognosis.

TABLE 32-5	International Neuroblastoma Staging System
Stage	**Characteristics**
1	Localized tumor confined to the area of origin; complete gross excision with or without microscopic residual disease; identifiable ipsilateral and contralateral lymph nodes negative microscopically
2A	Unilateral tumor with incomplete gross excision; identifiable ipsilateral and contralateral lymph nodes negative microscopically
2B	Unilateral tumor with complete or incomplete gross excision; with positive ipsilateral regional lymph nodes; identifiable contralateral lymph nodes negative microscopically
3	Tumor infiltrating across the midline with or without regional lymph node involvement; or unilateral tumor with contralateral regional lymph node involvement; or midline tumor with bilateral tumor involvement
4	Dissemination of tumor to distant lymph nodes, bone, bone marrow, liver, or other organs (except as defined in stage 4S)
4S	Localized primary tumor as defined for stage 1 or 2 with dissemination limited to liver, skin, or bone marrow

    c. The staging system incorporates **clinical, radiographic,** and **surgical** information to define the tumor stage (Table 32-5). While operative evaluation may be necessary for accurate staging, various tests are also used to stage patients: Plain radiographs of the chest and skull, bone scan, computed tomography (CT) scan, bone marrow aspirate, ^{131}I-meta-iodobenzylguanidine scan.

  3. Surgical treatment
    a. **Local disease** is treated through complete excision of the tumor with lymph node sampling.
    b. **Bulky** or **metastatic** disease is treated with chemotherapy and radiotherapy after undergoing tumor biopsy. If tumor shrinkage occurs with chemotherapy and radiation, delayed resection can take place.

B. Wilms tumor accounts for 6% of all malignancies in children and is the most common renal malignancy in children. Most children are diagnosed between 1 and 3 years of age with an annual incidence of approximately 5 to 7.8 per 1 million children younger than 15 years. The gender distribution is equal. Five percent of cases are bilateral.

  1. Diagnosis
    a. **History.** Patients typically present with vague symptoms of abdominal pain or fever; however, they may also have hematuria or a urinary tract infection.

Stage	Characteristics
1	Tumor confined to the kidney and completely removed by surgery
2	Tumor grew beyond the kidney (e.g., nearby fatty tissue or into blood vessels) but the kidney and affected tissue were completely removed surgically
3	Tumor is not completely removed. Tumor remaining after surgery is limited to the abdomen (e.g., abdominal lymph nodes, positive margin, peritoneal implants)
4	Tumor has spread through the bloodstream to other organs far away from the kidneys (e.g., lungs, liver, bone or distant lymph nodes)
5	Tumors are in both kidneys at the time of diagnosis

TABLE 32-6   Wilms Tumor Staging System

   b. **Physical examination.** A palpable flank mass is present in 85% of children. Wilms tumors are associated with other anomalies such as Beckwith–Wiedemann syndrome, hemihypertrophy, aniridia, and genitourinary anomalies.
   c. **Diagnostic studies.** Ultrasound can be helpful in determining tumor extension into the renal vein or vena cava. **Chest and abdominal CT** scans are necessary for staging (Table 32-6) to evaluate the contralateral kidney and to screen for pulmonary metastases. **Histologic examination** confirms the diagnosis.

2. **Management**
   a. **Surgery** and **chemotherapy** together result in a better than 90% chance of cure.
   b. **Surgical intervention** includes a radical nephrectomy with sampling of para-aortic lymph nodes. The hilar vessels are isolated and the contralateral kidney is also examined. If the Wilms tumor is found initially to be unresectable because of size or bilaterality, a second-look operation can be done after chemotherapy.
   c. **Chemotherapy.** Vincristine, doxorubicin, and dactinomycin are used, depending on the stage of the Wilms tumor.
   d. **Radiotherapy** is used for advanced stages of Wilms tumor.

C. **Hepatic tumors** make up fewer than 5% of all intra-abdominal malignancies. They are malignant in 70% of cases.
   • Hepatoblastoma
   • 39% of liver tumors
   • 90% occur before 3 years of age
   • 60% are diagnosed by 1 year of age
   • Hepatocellular carcinoma

- Presents in older children
- Approximately one-third of these patients have cirrhosis secondary to an inherited metabolic abnormality
  1. **Diagnosis.** Patients may present with abdominal pain or an enlarging abdominal mass. Serum alpha fetoprotein (AFP) may be elevated. CT or MR scan may demonstrate the lesion.
  2. **Management.** Surgical intervention typically includes primary tumor resection and lymph node sampling. Intraoperative histologic analysis of the liver margins is necessary to confirm complete removal of the tumor. Hepatoblastoma that is not initially resectable undergoes chemotherapy and re-exploration for curative resection.

D. **Teratomas** are composed of tissues from all germ layers (endoderm, ectoderm, and mesoderm). In neonates, sacrococcygeal teratomas are the most common. They are more common in girls (4:1). Complications of teratomas include hemorrhage and a high rate of recurrence if the coccyx is incompletely resected.

  1. **Diagnosis** can be made with prenatal ultrasound. CT scan can also be useful. A rectal exam must be completed.

  2. **Management**
     a. Antenatal diagnosis may necessitate delivery by cesarean section.
     b. Surgical intervention is typically during the first week of life.
        (1) A chevron-shaped buttock incision is made.
        (2) Resection of the tumor includes preservation of the rectal sphincter muscles, resection of the coccyx with the tumor, and early control of the mid-sacral vessels that supply the tumor.
        (3) Resection may require combined abdominal and perineal approaches for large intra-abdominal teratomas.
     c. Chemotherapy for malignant teratomas may shrink the tumor and allow for resection.

E. **Soft-tissue sarcomas** account for 6% of childhood malignancies. Greater than one half are rhabdomyosarcomas.

  1. **Diagnosis** is made with a CT or MR scan. However, **incisional biopsy** is usually required to determine the histologic type preoperatively.

  2. **Management**
     a. A multidisciplinary approach involving medical and radiation oncology is advised prior to starting therapy.
     b. Non-rhabdomyosarcomas require wide surgical excision.
     c. Rhabdomyosarcoma
        (1) Treatment is determined by the location of the tumor.
        (2) Complete resection of **head and neck tumors** is rarely possible, and they are usually managed with biopsy followed by chemotherapy.
        (3) **Trunk and retroperitoneal tumors** are treated with wide excision.
        (4) **Extremity tumors** are treated with wide excision, but resection of muscle groups and the use of radiotherapy or brachytherapy should also be considered.
        (5) A biopsy of the regional lymph nodes should be included in all procedures.

33 Neurosurgical Emergencies

Matthew R. Reynolds and Michael R. Chicoine

Neurosurgical emergencies involve a broad spectrum of illness, including traumatic injury to the brain and spine. Several nontraumatic settings also require emergent intervention. Among these are intracranial hemorrhage, elevated intracranial pressure (ICP), spinal cord compression, and infections.

NEUROSURGICAL TRAUMA

I. INTRACRANIAL TRAUMA

A. **Evaluation.** Initial management of head injury focuses on hemodynamic stabilization through establishment of an adequate airway, ventilation, and support of circulation, followed by the rapid diagnosis and treatment of intracranial injuries. The initial evaluation of patients with trauma has been discussed in detail previously (see Chapter 22) and will only briefly be discussed here with emphasis on the neurosurgical patient.

1. **Airway and ventilation.** Severe head injury frequently leads to failure of oxygenation, ventilation, and airway protection. Intubation in these cases is essential, and a low threshold for intubation in agitated patients requiring sedation must also be present. A rapid neurologic assessment performed before sedation and paralysis are induced is critical. When possible, cervical spine imaging and neurologic examination should be performed before intubation. Associated cervical spine injuries should always be assumed in the patient with a head injury until they are ruled out. Two-person in-line intubation is performed, with the second person securing the patient's neck with axial traction to avoid neck extension. Short-acting neuromuscular blocking agents are preferred in the acute setting. Nasal intubation can be performed in the absence of craniofacial injuries.

2. **Circulatory support** requires aggressive fluid resuscitation for treatment of arterial hypotension. In the absence of profuse scalp bleeding, however, intracranial hemorrhage is almost never the sole cause of systemic hypotension. Mental status examination should be performed after the mean arterial pressure (MAP) and cerebral perfusion pressure (CPP) (CPP = MAP − ICP) have normalized (e.g., CPP ≥60 mm Hg). In addition, the use of hypotonic fluids should be avoided in patients with head injuries because this could exacerbate cerebral edema.

B. **Neurologic evaluation**

1. **A rapid but systematic** neurologic examination is performed on the scene and is repeated frequently during transport and on initial presentation to the emergency room. Examination focuses on the three components of the **Glasgow Coma Scale** (GCS) (Table 33-1): Eye

TABLE 33-1   Glasgow Coma Scale[a]

Component	Points
Eye opening	—
Spontaneous	4
To voice	3
To stimulation	2
None	1
Motor response	—
To command	6
Localizes	5
Withdraws	4
Abnormal flexion	3
Extension	2
None	1
Verbal response	—
Oriented	5
Confused but comprehensible	4
Inappropriate or incoherent	3
Incomprehensible (no words)	2
None	1

[a]Glasgow Coma Score = Best eye opening + best motor response + best verbal response. If patient is intubated, the verbal score is omitted and an addendum of "T" is given to the best eye opening + best motor response score.

opening, verbal response, and motor response (*Lancet.* 1974;2:81). This score indicates injury severity and measures changes in the impairment of consciousness. Overall level of consciousness may be graded as normal (awake, alert, oriented, and conversant), somnolent (arousable to voice), lethargic (arousable to deep stimulation), or comatose (nonarousable to any stimulation). The cranial nerves (e.g., pupillary response, extraocular movements, facial symmetry, and tongue protrusion) should be examined. Unilateral pupillary dilatation may herald the onset of early brain herniation (see Section V.A.2). For this reason, the pupils of a head-injured patient should never be pharmacologically dilated in the acute setting. Strength and symmetry of the extremities should be noted, and sensory examination should be performed as thoroughly as the level of consciousness permits. Reflexes and sphincter tone should also be assessed. In the critically ill patient, examination is performed while the patient is off sedation and paralytic medications. Finally, the head-injured patient has a high incidence of associated injuries. Cervical spine evaluation is obligatory (see Sections IV.A.2 and IV.A.3) given the high incidence of injury to this region (~4% to 8%) in patients with traumatic brain injury (*J Neurosurg.* 2002;96 (3, Suppl):285).

2. **Systemic causes** of mental status impairment must be ruled out including metabolic (electrolyte or acid–base abnormalities, hypo- and hyperglycemia), toxic (drugs, uremia), hypothermic, or respiratory (hypoxia, hypercapnia) derangements. Seizures or cardiac arrest can also impair neurologic function.

C. **Radiographic evaluation** may begin with cervical spine plain radiographs, including anteroposterior, lateral, open-mouth (odontoid) views, and a lateral swimmer's view if needed (see Section IV.A.3.a). In many trauma centers, however, the rapidity and diagnostic accuracy of computed tomographic (CT) technology has supplanted X-ray imaging. A growing body of evidence demonstrates increased sensitivity of CT in detecting spine fractures in patients with blunt trauma compared to plain radiography (*J Trauma.* 2006;61:382). The initial emergency room evaluation should proceed rapidly to noncontrast head CT, and delay caused by evaluation of non–life-threatening injuries should be avoided until the patient's head is imaged. Centers without this capability should transfer the patient expeditiously to a facility with CT scanning and neurosurgical facilities. A normal CT scan without altered level of consciousness, neurologic deficit, or open injuries may allow the patient to be discharged to home with reliable supervision. Any exceptions may indicate a more severe injury with a higher risk of associated or delayed lesions and may require the patient to be admitted for observation.

D. **Seizures** should be controlled rapidly in patients with head injury. Intravenous lorazepam (Ativan) can be administered in 1 to 2 mg boluses and repeated until seizures are controlled. Airway protection must be available if significant doses of benzodiazepines are to be given. Phenytoin (Dilantin) should also be administered for seizures and is indicated for seizure prophylaxis in patients at high risk for early post-traumatic seizures

(GCS = 10 or less, intracranial hematoma, depressed skull fracture, cortical contusion visible on CT, penetrating or open injuries) for a duration of no more than 7 days if the patient remains seizure free (*N Engl J Med.* 1990;323:497). A loading dose of phenytoin or fosphenytoin (Cerebyx) in patients with poor intravenous (IV) access or status epilepticus may be given (15 to 20 mg/kg). Maintenance doses of phenytoin should then be started and drug levels followed to guide dosing. Alternatively, levetiracetam (Keppra) may be loaded orally, or intravenously, at 1,000 mg and then continued at 500 to 1,000 mg orally twice daily. The latter agent does not require serum drug level monitoring, has an acceptable side-effect profile, and is preferable in patients with hepatic disease. Levetiracetam appears to be as effective as phenytoin in the prevention of early post-traumatic seizures and may provide improved long-term outcomes in patients with severe traumatic brain injury (*Neurocrit Care.* 2010;12:165).

II. TYPES OF HEAD INJURY

A. **Focal (mass) lesions** are best diagnosed by CT scan of the head without contrast. Hemiparesis, unilateral pupillary dysfunction (the fixed and dilated pupil), or both can herald brainstem herniation from mass lesions, but these are imperfect localizing signs (*Neurosurgery.* 1994;34:840). Relative indications for surgical evacuation include neurologic symptoms referable to the mass lesion, midline shift greater than 5 to 10 mm, and elevated ICP that is refractory to medical management. Posterior fossa mass lesions can be particularly dangerous because brainstem herniation may have very few specific warning signs before death occurs (see Section V.A.2.b).

1. **Epidural hematomas (EDHs)** can cause rapid neurologic deterioration and usually require surgical evacuation if they cause significant mass effect (e.g., are greater than 1 cm in width) or clinical symptoms. Classically, EDH presents with a "lucid interval" after injury, which precedes rapid deterioration. This sign is inconsistent and nonspecific, however, and may also be seen with other forms of severe brain injury. EDH typically results from laceration of the middle meningeal artery due to fracture of the squamosal portion of the temporal bone. They appear on head CT scan as biconvex hyperdensities that typically respect the suture lines (Fig. 33-1, panels A and B). Location in the low-to-mid temporal lobe is particularly dangerous, given their propensity for midbrain compression and uncal herniation.

2. **Acute subdural hematomas (aSDH)** typically appear on head CT scan as hyperdense crescents as the blood spreads around the surface of the brain (Fig. 33-1, panel C). Often, aSDH results from high-speed acceleration or deceleration trauma and portend severe underlying intracranial injury. These injuries typically result from shearing/tearing forces applied to small bridging (emissary) veins that drain the underlying neural tissue into the dural sinuses. If surgical evacuation is indicated and delayed for more than 4 hours, these lesions have a high mortality (*J Neurosurg.* 1991;74:212, *N Engl J Med.* 1981;304:1511).

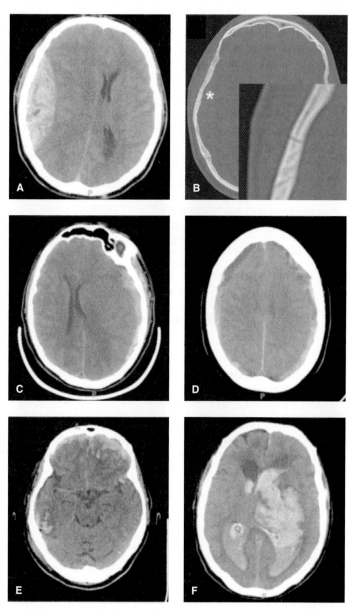

Figure 33-1. Noncontrast head CTs showing **(A)** large right-sided epidural hematoma with mass effect and midline shift, **(B)** bone windows from panel "A" demonstrating associated linear temporal bone fracture (*asterisk,* see inset), **(C)** left-sided acute subdural hematoma with significant midline shift, **(D)** bilateral mixed-density subdural hematomas with both acute (hyperdense) and chronic (hypodense) components, **(E)** bilateral frontal and right-sided temporal hemorrhagic contusions with surrounding edema (hypodense), and **(F)** large left-sided basal ganglia intraparenchymal hemorrhage (nontraumatic, likely related to hypertension) with intraventricular extension resulting in acute hydrocephalus.

3. **Chronic SDHs (cSDH)** can present, especially in the elderly and alcoholic population, days to weeks after the initial head injury. cSDH may cause focal neurologic deficits, mental status changes, metabolic abnormalities, and/or seizures. If necessary, a symptomatic cSDH can be treated with burr-hole drainage and subdural drain placement (*J Neurosurg.* 1986;65:183). Prophylactic anticonvulsants should be considered and steroids may be beneficial, though this remains unclear. Diagnosis is best made with a noncontrast head CT that typically shows a hypodense crescentic collection tracking between the dura and the brain (Fig. 33-1, panel D).

4. **Cerebral contusions** manifest on noncontrast head CT scan as small, punctuate hyperdensities that are commonly located in the basal frontal and temporal lobes (Fig. 33-1, panel E). These injuries may occur during blunt trauma to the head or with acceleration/deceleration injury. In many cases, damage occurs when the brain comes into contact with the sharp bony ridges on the interior skull base. Contusions may be observed in a "coup" pattern, whereby injury to the cerebral cortex occurs in the region immediately underlying the site of impact as the brain collides with the inert table of the skull. Alternatively, a "contrecoup" pattern occurs when the brain comes into contact with the opposite pole of the skull following the initial impact. Cerebral contusions may be appreciated in a significant proportion of patients with severe traumatic brain injury and have a tendency to progress in size and mass effect (*J Neurosurg.* 2010;112:1139).

5. **Intraparenchymal hemorrhage (IPH).** While also caused by hypertension, coagulopathy, hemorrhagic transformation of ischemic stroke or tumor, venous outflow obstruction, or a ruptured aneurysm or vascular malformation, IPH may be precipitated by trauma. These injuries manifest on noncontrast head CT as focal areas of hyperdensity, typically with hypodense surrounding areas of edema (Fig. 33-1, panel F). IPH can occur with high-energy traumatic mechanisms or in the setting of a low-to-moderate energy mechanism in a coagulopathic patient. Typically, laceration of larger cerebral vessels is the inciting event. Mechanical complications of mass effect may quickly progress to brain herniation in severe cases. Extension of bleeding into the ventricular system may result in **intraventricular hemorrhage** with increased risk of communicating or noncommunicating hydrocephalus due to impaired cerebrospinal fluid (CSF) reabsorption by the arachnoid granulations or a focal blockade of CSF flow, respectively.

B. **Nonfocal** sequelae of head injury include **cerebral edema** and **diffuse axonal injury (DAI).** Hallmarks of cerebral edema on head CT scan include obliteration of the basal cisterns and coronal sulci with loss of differentiation of the gray and white matter. In DAI, severe head injury and neurologic dysfunction can be associated with minimal changes on head CT scan (*J Neurosurg.* 1982;56:26). DAI represents the pathologic result of shearing forces on the brain. Often, small hemorrhages are seen in the corpus callosum, midbrain, or deep white matter.

C. **Open skull fractures** require operative irrigation, débridement of non-viable tissues, and dural closure. Evaluation of scalp lacerations should include attention to the integrity of the galeal layer and the underlying skull fractures. Prophylactic antibiotics may reduce the risk of infection. Surgical treatment of **depressed skull fractures** usually is required for depressions greater than the thickness of the skull table. Open, depressed skull fractures require elevation and débridement of depressed bony fragments as well as devitalized tissue, followed by a course of antibiotics. Fractures through the paranasal air **sinuses,** especially with associated pneumocephalus and dural tears, may require repair. The prophylactic use of broad-spectrum antibiotics to prevent meningitis in these cases is controversial.

D. **Basilar skull fractures** can be complicated by **CSF** leaks and are mostly managed nonoperatively. The use of prophylactic antibiotics is controversial in these cases. If drainage continues or recurs, a lumbar drain or surgical repair may be required because persistent leakage can lead to meningitis. Temporal bone fractures can be associated with damage to the seventh and eighth cranial nerves, the middle ear apparatus, or both.

E. **Missile injuries** require débridement, closure, and prophylactic antibiotics similar to those used for other open-head injuries. However, injuries from gunshot wounds present several associated problems. Shock waves can result in widespread destruction of brain tissue and vasculature. Operative management must address removal of accessible foreign bodies and bone fragments, evacuation of intracranial hematomas, débridement of entrance and exit wounds, and closure of dura and scalp. Overaggressive débridement near large vessels should be avoided to prevent further damage to vascular structures.

III. MANAGEMENT OF ELEVATED INTRACRANIAL PRESSURE

A. Monitoring

1. **Indications.** ICP monitoring is recommended if serial neurologic examinations cannot be used as a reliable indicator of progressive intracranial pathology. The current standard for ICP monitoring is in patients with an abnormal head CT scan and a GCS score less than 8. Alternatively, ICP monitoring should be performed in patients with a normal head CT scan and GCS score greater than 8 if two of the following three criteria are met: (i) Age greater than 40 years, (ii) unilateral or bilateral motor posturing, and (iii) systemic blood pressure less than 90 mm Hg on admission (*J Neurosurg.* 1982;56:650).

2. **ICP pressure monitors** are of several types. The **parenchymal bolt** consists of a fiberoptic or strain gauge catheter tip that measures ICP at the brain surface. **Intraventricular catheters** (ventriculostomy) are placed in the lateral ventricle with the tip at the foramen of Monro. These devices allow for drainage of CSF in the treatment of elevated ICP in addition to ICP monitoring. Newer monitors include those that measure ICP, cerebral temperature, and brain tissue oxygenation, and the utility of such devices is under investigation.

B. Treatment

1. **If elevated ICP** is suspected, such as with signs of herniation or acute neurologic deterioration, therapy should be empirically initiated until the ICP can be measured. If the patient is hemodynamically stable with adequate renal function, high-dose **mannitol** (0.5 to 1.0 g/kg IV bolus) is effective in acutely controlling elevated ICP. Fluid balance, serum electrolytes, and serum osmolarity should be carefully monitored, and a Foley catheter is placed to closely follow the osmotic diuresis. Mannitol is generally held if the serum osmolarity exceeds 320 mOsm/L. Hypotension should be avoided in these patients as data suggests that better outcomes occur with maintenance of CPP (MAP – ICP) of 60 mm Hg or greater (see Section III.C.1). A euvolemic, hyperosmolar situation is desirable; fluid replacement is usually necessary to avoid hypotension which may precipitate an ischemic episode that could worsen the underlying brain injury. Treatment is aimed at keeping ICP less than 20 mm Hg (*J Neurosurg.* 1991;75:S59). If elevated ICP is refractory to a single mannitol bolus, then standing high-dose mannitol therapy may be instituted at 0.5 to 1.0 g/kg IV every 6 hours.

2. **Hypertonic saline** is a useful adjunct to mannitol in the control of elevated ICP (*Crit Care Med.* 2003;31:1683). Hypertonic saline (23.4%), or "super salt," is effective for acutely reducing ICP in patients with severe traumatic brain injury (*J Trauma.* 2009;67:277). This agent may be preferable in hypovolemic patients, but requires central venous access for administration and frequent plasma sodium monitoring. Plasma sodium levels should not exceed 160 mmol/L. Hypertonic saline (23.4%, 30 to 60 mL IV every 6 hours) can be alternated with mannitol therapy in cases of refractory ICP.

3. Ventilatory support to maintain a mildly hypocapnic partial pressure of carbon dioxide (Pco_2) (~35 mm Hg) should be instituted, and **hyperventilation** (Pco_2 ~30 mm Hg) may be used in the acute setting for brief periods. Prolonged use of hyperventilation may worsen ischemia by compromising cerebral blood flow.

4. In addition to the initial treatment of elevated ICP (e.g., hyperosmolar therapy, mechanical ventilation), **simple measures** are taken, such as head elevation to 30 degrees (a neutral head position to enhance venous drainage), avoidance of circumferential taping around the patient's neck when securing the endotracheal tube, appropriate fitting of cervical spine collars if indicated, and adequate sedation before any stimulation. Elevated intrathoracic pressures (as with coughing, straining, or high positive end-expiratory pressure) can elevate ICP. Fever can also exacerbate ICP; aggressive treatment with antipyretics, cooling blankets, and intravascular cooling devices should be instituted to prevent hyperthermia.

5. **Sedation** can also be used to control ICP. Benzodiazepine or narcotic (e.g., fentanyl) infusions can be given and titrated to effect, with a goal of 3 on the Ramsay sedation scale (*Br Med J.* 1974;11:659). Intubation and mechanical ventilation usually are needed. Refractory elevation of ICP may require neuromuscular paralysis or even barbiturate coma with invasive hemodynamic monitoring.

6. **Surgical interventions** are directed primarily at removal of **mass lesions,** if present. In the absence of a mass lesion, uncontrollable ICP and a deteriorating neurologic examination may require **craniectomy,** with removal of a large bone flap to relieve pressure on the intracranial contents. Retrospective studies suggest that decompressive hemicraniectomy for uncontrolled intracranial hypertension may decrease mortality and improve outcomes in certain patients (*J Neurosurg.* 2006;104:469). Multicenter, prospective studies are underway to better evaluate the indications for surgical intervention in this difficult patient population (*Acta Neurochir Suppl.* 2006;96:17). Removal of CSF by **ventriculostomy** can reduce ICP; however, the small intracranial volume occupied by the CSF limits this effect.

C. **Considerations when managing elevated ICP**

1. **Cardiac considerations.** Adequate blood pressure should be maintained in the setting of elevated ICP, with care taken to avoid hypotension (systolic blood pressure <90 mm Hg), which has been associated with inferior outcome in severely head-injured patients (*Br J Neurosurg.* 1993;7:267). Maintenance of CPP greater than 60 mm Hg (or MAP >80 to 90 mm Hg) can be used as a treatment guideline (*Crit Care.* 2000;9(6):R670).

2. **Fluid and electrolytes.** Head-injured patients are at risk for development of either diabetes insipidus or the syndrome of inappropriate antidiuretic hormone (SIADH). Initially, the use of isotonic saline (with glucose and, if necessary, potassium) avoids exacerbating cerebral edema. Close monitoring of electrolytes is essential because alterations in sodium and water balance are common. **Diabetes insipidus** can develop rapidly and must be treated aggressively. Fluid hydration should match output. Often, the process is self-limiting, but persistent output of large amounts (>300 mL/hour) of urine with a low specific gravity (<1.005) may necessitate vasopressin treatment [desmopressin (DDAVP), 1 μg IV every 12 hours]. If SIADH with hyponatremia develops, treatment with restriction of free water intake usually is sufficient, although infusion of hypertonic (1.5% NaCl) saline may be necessary.

3. **Coagulopathy,** if present, should be corrected as expeditiously and safely as possible. For patients with an intracranial hemorrhage being treated with systemic anticoagulation for other medical morbidities (e.g., atrial fibrillation, deep venous thrombosis, pulmonary emboli), all anticoagulant agents should be discontinued. Blood products and other agents should be administered for a goal of international normalized ratio (INR) ≤1.4, prothrombin time (PTT) ≤40 seconds, and platelets ≥100,000. For patients on systemic antiplatelet agents (e.g., full-dose aspirin, clopidogrel [Plavix]), consideration should be given to platelet transfusion even in the setting of a normal platelet count. Recombinant factor VII may be given under circumstances of life-threatening intracranial hemorrhage with coagulopathy and the need for immediate normalization of coagulation parameters. Disseminated intravascular coagulopathy can also occur with severe head injury, such

as missile injuries, often developing several hours after the disruption of brain tissue. Coagulopathies should be aggressively treated with fresh-frozen plasma and vitamin K, especially if intracranial hemorrhage is present.

4. **Nutrition.** Nutritional demands are increased in head injury (*Neurosurg Clin North Am.* 1991;2:301). High-osmolarity tube feedings can reduce the risk of cerebral edema and provide adequate caloric intake. If tube feedings are not tolerated, parenteral nutrition may be necessary.

5. **Deep venous thrombosis prophylaxis.** Patients with severe head injury are at high risk for deep venous thrombosis and subsequent pulmonary embolism. Early use of intermittent pneumatic compression devices is highly recommended. Although efficacy remains controversial, recent studies suggest no increased risk of intracranial hemorrhage in head-injured patients who receive subcutaneous heparin (*J Trauma.* 2002;53:38) or enoxaparin (*Arch Surg.* 2002;137:701) within 72 hours of admission.

IV. **SPINAL TRAUMA. Evaluation** for spinal injury is indicated if focal pain, neurologic examination, or mechanism of injury warrants. Neurologic deficit involving the lower extremities after trauma may require evaluation of the entire spine to find an injury.

A. **Initial support**

1. As with all patients with trauma, attention should first focus on airway, breathing, and circulation (see Chapter 22 for initial evaluation of the patient with trauma). In the setting of known or suspected spinal cord injury, several additional points are worthy of mention. First, intubation should be performed early in patients demonstrating respiratory fatigue or otherwise requiring airway protection or ventilatory support. With cervical spine injury, fiberoptic intubation should be performed as this procedure requires less manipulation and reduces the risk of further neurologic injury. Second, in the paraplegic or quadriplegic patient who becomes hypotensive without an obvious source of internal or external hemorrhage, **neurogenic (or spinal) shock** should be considered. Hypotension associated with the loss of sympathetic tone seen in some high thoracic and cervical spine injuries does not respond to fluid challenge alone. Vasopressors (e.g., dopamine) reduce peripheral vasodilatation and improve cardiac output. Excessive fluid administration can worsen respiratory difficulty and spinal cord edema.

2. **Neurologic examination** includes a careful assessment of motor function, sensory function, and deep tendon reflexes. Multiple sensory modalities (light touch, pinprick, temperature sensation, and joint position sense) should be assessed, especially in the patient with an incomplete lesion. Useful landmarks for sensory dermatomes include the nipple (T4 level) and the umbilicus (T10 level). Sphincter tone as well as cremasteric and bulbocavernosus reflexes should be documented. Incomplete lesions are common and, as with sacral sparing of sensory function, carry prognostic significance (*Neurosurgery.* 1987;20:742).

3. **Radiographic evaluation**
   a. Standard radiographic evaluation of the cervical spine includes **anteroposterior, lateral, and open-mouth (odontoid)** views. A **swimmer's** view may be necessary to visualize C7 and the C7–T1 interspace, which is essential in the complete evaluation of the cervical spine. CT scanning with coronal and sagittal reconstructions is necessary if adequate plain films cannot be obtained and is replacing radiography as the standard of care in patients with blunt trauma (*J Trauma.* 2006;61:382). Of note, flexion/extension films remain the best means of surveying for fractures or subluxations that may suggest occult ligamentous instability that may not be visualized on CT. Anteroposterior and lateral views of the thoracic and lumbar spine are obtained as indicated or may be reconstructed from chest, abdominal, and pelvic CT if available. If a spinal fracture is found, the entire spine should be imaged because of the high rate of coincident injuries (*J Spinal Disord.* 1992;5:320).
   b. Other imaging modalities include **CT scans** to further evaluate known or suspected fractures. **Magnetic resonance imaging (MRI)** is sensitive for ligamentous injuries, intraspinal hemorrhage, and protruded intervertebral discs (*J Neurosurg.* 1993;79:341), which can cause deficit with or without bony abnormalities seen on plain films. Damage to the vertebral artery can occur with cervical injuries, especially if fracture through the foramen transversarium occurs. CT angiography, conventional digital subtraction angiography, or magnetic resonance angiography are pursued if neurologic damage is referable to vertebral artery injury.

B. **Instability.** Spinal instability must be suspected until ruled out. Ligamentous injury can occur in the absence of fracture, and instability can occur with normal plain films. Point tenderness, severe midline pain, or apprehension of neck movement also warrants careful assessment. In the minimally symptomatic, alert patient, cervical flexion/extension films can aid in the assessment of spinal stability. Flexion and extension must be done under the patient's own power, and motion should be stopped if pain or other symptoms arise. Limited flexion and extension motion on physical exam may significantly decrease the utility of flexion/extension radiography in detecting ligamentous instability (*J Trauma.* 2002;53:426). These patients should be left in a cervical collar and may require additional cross-sectional imaging to exclude occult injury.

C. **Treatment**
   1. **Methylprednisolone** is recommended only as an option in the treatment of spinal cord injury, given the increased risk of medical complications associated with its use (*Neurosurgery.* 2002;50:S63). Patients seen between 3 and 8 hours after injury may be treated with methylprednisolone, **30 mg/kg IV bolus** over 15 minutes, followed 45 minutes later by a **5.4 mg/kg/hour IV infusion** continued over the next 48 hours (*J Am Med Assoc.* 1997;277:1597). If steroids are administered within 3 hours of injury, IV infusion is given for only 24 hours. If patients are seen more than 8 hours after injury,

this protocol is not of proven benefit and is contraindicated. Steroids are also contraindicated in cases of penetrating spinal injury (*Neurosurgery.* 1997;41:576) and have been associated with increased postoperative complications after thoracolumbar spine stabilization (*J Trauma.* 2010;69:1479).

2. **Immobilization and reduction.** Suspected or known spine injuries require immobilization, initially with a rigid cervical collar and long backboard. Cervical spine subluxations and dislocations must be reduced under neurosurgical supervision. Fractures may be treated by external immobilization (e.g., halo external fixation) or by operative fusion, depending on the nature of the fracture and degree of instability. Thoracic and lumbar spine fractures are managed with operative stabilization or immobilization with an orthosis. Injuries with associated neurologic deficit, excessive displacement or angulation of the spinal column, or loss of vertebral body height are more likely to require operative stabilization. Before stabilization, patients are managed with bed rest and frequent log rolling. Although early surgical decompression and stabilization promote mobilization of the patient, the timing of surgery and the role of emergency surgery in the patient with acute neurologic deficit remain somewhat controversial (*Neurosurgery.* 1994;35:240).

3. **Cervical collar management.** If a patient with trauma has a normal level of alertness, no evidence of intoxication, no focal neurological deficit, no painful distracting injuries, no posterior midline cervical spine tenderness, and normal cervical spine range of motion, then no cervical spine imaging is required and cervical immobilization may be discontinued (*J Orthop Trauma.* 2010;24:100). If posterior cervical tenderness is present in the setting of negative cervical spine imaging, the collar may be cleared radiographically following adequate flexion/extension radiographs or a normal cervical spine MRI within 48 hours of the injury. If flexion/extension films are inadequate (e.g., due to pain and/or effort), the films may be repeated in 10 to 14 days while maintaining cervical spine precautions. In the obtunded patient with normal cervical spine imaging, the cervical collar may be cleared by normal flexion/extension radiographs taken under fluoroscopy, a normal cervical spine MRI taken within 48 hours of injury, or at the discretion of the treating physician (*Neurosurgery.* 2002;50 (3 Suppl):S36).

4. **Cervical spine injuries** are associated with the development of acute respiratory distress syndrome, hyponatremia, hypotension, bradyarrhythmias, ileus, and urinary retention. Patients with cervical spine injuries may require cardiorespiratory monitoring, isotonic fluid support, nasogastric decompression, urinary catheter placement, laxatives, and stool softeners to address these issues. Bladder and bowel dysfunction also are seen with lower spine injuries, although autonomic problems are rare in injuries below the upper thoracic spine.

5. **Penetrating injuries** to the neck and torso may result in fractures of the spine or penetration of the spinal canal.

6. **Venous thromboembolism risk** is significantly elevated in patients with spinal cord injury. Intermittent pneumatic compression devices with subcutaneous heparin or enoxaparin have been demonstrated to be equally safe in the acute management of spinal cord injury (*J Trauma.* 2003;54:1116).

V. OTHER EMERGENCIES

A. Nontraumatic intracranial hypertension and herniation syndromes

1. **Etiology.** Elevation of ICP may lead to compression of neurologic structures and irreversible neurologic damage. Nontraumatic causes include hemorrhagic and nonhemorrhagic mass lesions.

   a. Spontaneous **IPHs** may occur owing to hypertension, vascular malformations (arteriovenous malformations or aneurysms), tumor, angiopathy, vasculitis, or secondary hemorrhage into a large infarction.

   b. **Nonhemorrhagic lesions** include tumor, infection, and mass effect from edema after cerebral infarction.

2. Clinical **herniation syndromes** represent shift of the normal brain through or across regions within the skull secondary to increased ICP and/or mass effect. These syndromes are typically caused by a mass lesion and exist with presentations referable to the location of the lesion (Fig. 33-2).

   a. **Supratentorial** sites of herniation include uncal, central (transtentorial), and cingulate (subfalcine) herniation. **Uncal** herniation often results from temporal lobe mass lesions given the proximity of the temporal lobe to the midbrain. In this circumstance, the medial temporal lobe (uncus) is pushed over the tentorial incisura and exerts pressure on the midbrain. Unilateral pupillary dilatation may occur in the absence of a complete third cranial nerve palsy due to the compression of the parasympathetic fibers which travel on the exterior surface of the nerve (e.g., superficial to the motor fibers). Progressive lethargy (due to increased ICP), contralateral hemiparesis (due to compression of the cerebral peduncle/corticospinal tract), and contralateral visual deficits (due to compression of the posterior cerebral artery) also suggest uncal herniation. **Central (transtentorial)** herniation results from downward compression of brainstem structures through the tentorial incisura. Unresponsiveness, deep coma, and cranial nerve dysfunction are observed. Central herniation suggests a bilateral process or an interhemispheric lesion. **Cingulate (subfalcine)** herniation results from lesions causing a shift across the inferior aspect of the falx cerebri and can present with only lethargy or lower-extremity weakness (the latter from injury to the anterior cerebral arteries). Both falcine and uncal herniation can progress to a central transtentorial picture as further structures are compressed.

   b. **Infratentorial** herniation results from posterior fossa masses compressing the brainstem or from herniation of the cerebellar tonsils

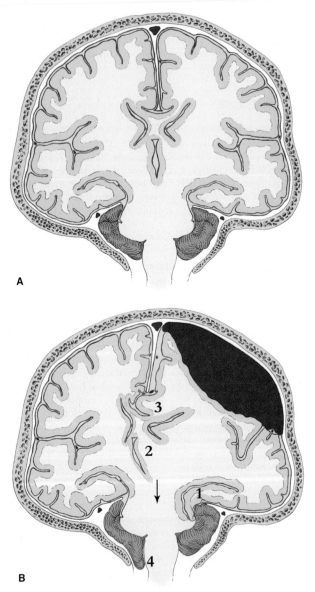

Figure 33-2. Brain herniation syndromes may be classified as supratentorial (above the tentorial notch) or infratentorial (below the tentorial notch). **(A)** Represents normal anatomy. **(B)** Shows herniation due to a mass lesion. Uncal *(1)*, transtentorial *(2)*, and subfalcine *(3)* are examples of supratentorial herniation. Tonsillar *(4)*, or downward cerebellar, herniation may be observed in the infratentorial compartment.

through the foramen magnum. Signs of infratentorial herniation include lower cranial nerve dysfunction and the rapid onset of respiratory or cardiac arrest with little warning.

3. **Treatment** of herniation requires control of ICP. The obtunded patient must have their airway controlled. Mannitol can be used, often with ICP monitoring (see Section III.A and III.B) to guide medical treatment. Mass lesions may need to be evacuated.

B. **Nonhemorrhagic lesions.** Diffuse cerebral edema also can produce ICP elevations that require treatment. **Metabolic derangements,** such as those seen in hepatic encephalopathy, can elevate the ICP. Edema can also develop secondary to large **infarctions** in the cerebral hemispheres, leading to delayed deterioration. Management of elevated ICP may be indicated in large cerebral infarctions, whether hemorrhagic or nonhemorrhagic.

1. **Brain tumors** rarely are surgical emergencies. Presenting symptoms include progressive headache, seizures, and localizing neurologic deficits. Uncommonly, acute neurologic deterioration is seen, usually suggestive of hemorrhage into the tumor. Evaluation and treatment are similar to those for any other acute intracranial mass lesion. High-dose **steroids** may have a potent effect on the brain edema associated with tumors. Urgent **surgical resection** of the mass lesion occasionally is required.

2. **Hydrocephalus** may result from various causes and can lead to rapid neurologic deterioration.

a. **Cerebellar tumors** or other mass lesions may cause fourth ventricle obstruction without preceding symptoms. Tuberculosis and bacterial meningitis also can cause hydrocephalus. Patients classically present with lethargy, headache, papilledema, sixth nerve palsy, or abnormalities of upward gaze ("setting-sun" sign). **Treatment** involves urgent placement of a catheter for external **ventricular drainage** (see Section III.A.2) to relieve the buildup of CSF.

b. **Shunt malfunction.** Internal ventricular drainage systems (shunts) require special attention. Malfunction can present with warning symptoms, such as headache or nausea, or with rapid deterioration of mental status, such as somnolence. Imaging, such as a head CT scan, can help in the diagnosis, but emergent operative revision may be indicated if mental status deterioration is present and shunt malfunction is suspected. A shunt series (plain films of the head, neck, chest, and abdomen) can visualize the entire course of the shunt and its connections, possibly leading to identification of a shunt tube fracture or stricture. Importantly, evaluation of shunt patency should always be performed under the guidance of a neurosurgeon given that as many as 33% of all shunt malfunctions will not have radiographic evidence of failure (e.g., large ventricles, grossly disconnected catheter) (*Pediatrics.* 1998;101:1031).

C. **Intracranial hemorrhage.** Spontaneous intracranial hemorrhage requires emergent intervention, and the sequelae of the associated mass effect also need to be addressed.

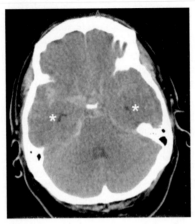

Figure 33-3. Noncontrast head CT depicting acute subarachnoid blood within the basal cisterns, bilateral sylvian fissures, and interhemispheric fissure. The anterior tips of the temporal horns may be visualized bilaterally (*asterisks*), representing early signs of hydrocephalus.

1. **Subarachnoid hemorrhage (SAH)** secondary to aneurysmal hemorrhage is a common neurosurgical emergency. The clinical **presentation** usually includes a history of severe sudden headache, nuchal rigidity, photophobia, lethargy, agitation, or a comatose state. Acute blood from a SAH appears hyperdense on a noncontrast head CT and is typically seen in the basal cisterns or sylvian fissure (Fig. 33-3). Lumbar puncture can make the diagnosis if the history is suggestive, even with a normal CT scan, but is not required when the scan is diagnostic. Treatments including surgical clipping and endovascular techniques aim to prevent rebleeding. Without intervention, rebleeding occurs in 50% of patients with a ruptured aneurysm in the first 6 months (*J Neurosurg.* 1985;62:321).

2. **Spontaneous intracranial hemorrhage** most commonly results from chronic hypertension, but other causes may include vascular malformations (e.g., aneurysm, arteriovenous malformation), arteriopathy (e.g., cerebral amyloid angiopathy, moyamoya disease), altered hemostasis, and hemorrhagic transformation of a tumor or infarct. While the optimal management of spontaneous supratentorial intracranial hemorrhage remains unclear, one large randomized trial suggests that early hematoma evacuation has no impact on outcome and mortality at 6 months as compared to initial conservative therapy (*Lancet.* 2005;356:387).

3. **Spontaneous intraventricular hemorrhage** may be an isolated event or result from extension of an IPH into the ventricular system. Patients are observed for the development of hydrocephalus, which may require external CSF drainage (ventriculostomy). In cases of unclear etiology, cerebral angiography may be helpful to delineate the cause.

4. **Pituitary apoplexy** occurs after hemorrhage into the pituitary gland, usually related to an underlying pituitary adenoma. Patients typically present with acute headache and visual symptoms, such as decreased acuity, visual field cut, ptosis, or diplopia, which result from compression of nearby cranial nerves. Life-threatening panhypopituitarism can occur. Treatment involves hormonal replacement, correction of any electrolyte abnormalities, and emergent CT or MRI scan to evaluate for hemorrhagic pituitary lesions. Emergent evacuation of hematoma may preserve vision.

D. Infections

1. **Cerebral abscesses** can result from hematogenous or local traumatic spread of a septic process. Infections may also involve the epidural or subdural spaces. Underlying abnormalities are common, such as an immunocompromised state or systemic arteriovenous shunting. Presenting symptoms include those of increased ICP, focal deficits, and seizures. An MRI or head CT scan with IV contrast shows an enhancing lesion. Early-stage cerebral abscess may respond to medical management alone. Abscesses larger than 3 cm, failure of medical management, and the need for tissue diagnosis are common indications for surgical drainage by open craniotomy or stereotactic drainage. Prolonged IV antibiotics are indicated.

2. **Spinal epidural abscesses** can become a surgical emergency. Severe neck or back pain in the setting of fever should raise concern. Although neurologic deficit may not occur initially, often progressive evidence of cord compression exists. MRI scan or myelography demonstrates the lesion. Surgical evacuation is most often necessary, although antibiotics alone can be attempted if neither neurologic compromise nor a large collection is present. Even with surgical drainage, an extended course of antibiotics is required. Disc space infection and spinal osteomyelitis can occur in association with, or separately from, spinal epidural abscesses. Antibiotic therapy usually is effective. An elevated erythrocyte sedimentation rate generally is present and falls with effective treatment.

E. Spinal cord compression

1. **Diagnosis.** Nontraumatic spinal cord compression can result from metastatic tumor or another adjacent mass lesion. Patients present initially with pain, followed by progressive or sudden neurologic symptoms. Lung, breast, and prostate are the most common sources of metastases (*Neurosurgery.* 1987;21:676). Examination usually reveals weakness, long-tract signs (spasticity, hyperactive reflexes, upgoing toes), or sphincter dysfunction. It is important to distinguish **myelopathy** from **radiculopathy.** The latter presents with pain, sensory changes, and weakness in a dermatomal pattern. Emergent MRI scan or myelography to demonstrate the presence and level of the lesion confirms diagnosis of cord compression. Imaging should extend to higher spinal levels if no lesion is found because, for example, a cervical lesion can present with only lower-extremity symptoms; alternatively, multilevel involvement can be present.

2. **Treatment** begins with **steroids** (dexamethasone, 10 mg intravenously, followed by 4 to 10 mg orally or intravenously every 6 hours; higher doses frequently are given for severe deficits). These are administered immediately if spinal cord compression is suspected. The neurosurgical priorities include **decompression** if a deficit is present and spinal **stabilization and fusion** if bony destruction is prominent (*Neurosurgery.* 1985;17:424). Vertebral corpectomy and reconstruction with internal fixation is often required because a simple laminectomy may not be helpful (*Lancet.* 2005;366(9486):643). Emergent **radiation therapy** to the area of compression may be preferable to surgical intervention in some cases.

Orthopedic Injuries

Kathleen E. McKeon and Michael J. Gardner

TREATMENT OF ORTHOPEDIC INJURIES

I. INITIAL ASSESSMENT

A. **Priorities of management. Assessment and management of ABCs** (*a*irway, *b*reathing, and *c*irculation) take precedence over extremity injuries. Multisystem-injured patients benefit from early aggressive treatment of extremity and pelvic trauma.

B. **History.** In addition to standard medical history, the mechanism of injury, especially the relative energy associated with the injury (e.g., low-energy fall vs. high-energy motor vehicle crash), is important to elucidate. An orthopedic history should also include preinjury functional level, especially previous occupation and ambulatory status.

C. Examination

1. An orthopedic examination includes inspection, palpation, range of motion, strength, stability, and body region–specific tests. Severe or multiple injuries can mask other injuries. Especially important in this setting is a complete primary evaluation where each joint and bone is inspected, and then a repeat secondary survey. **Inspect** the extremities for bruising, swelling, lacerations, abrasions, deformity, and asymmetry. Systematically **palpate** all extremities, noting tenderness, crepitus, and deformity of the underlying bone. In suspected cervical spine (C-spine) injury, maintain immobilization in a cervical collar until C-spine injury is ruled out radiographically and/or clinically. Logroll the patient to examine and palpate the spine.

2. **Assess extremity vascular status** by checking pulses, capillary refill, temperature, and color and comparing to the opposite side.

3. **Sensorimotor evaluation** (see Table 34-1). Muscle strength evaluation in the setting of acute spinal cord injury or peripheral nerve injury is critical, and serial exams are often required. A sensory examination includes light touch in dermatomal and peripheral nerve distributions. In upper-extremity or C-spine trauma, two-point discrimination of the fingers should be assessed. A normal peripheral nerve exam is often documented as "SILT (sensation intact to light touch) A/R/M/U and + EPL/APB/FDP2,5/IO" in the upper extremity and "SILT DP/SP/T and + TA/GS/EHL/FHL" in the lower extremity.

II. RADIOLOGIC EXAMINATION.
All trauma and unconscious patients should have screening chest x-ray, anteroposterior (AP) pelvis x-ray, and C-spine

TABLE 34-1	Peripheral Nerve Exam		
Nerve	Sensory	Motor	Muscle
Deep peroneal (DP)	Web space between great and second toe	Ankle and great toe dorsiflexion	Tibialis anterior (TA), Extensor hallucis longus (EHL)
Superficial peroneal (SP)	Lateral dorsum of foot	—	—
Tibial (T)	Plantar surface of foot	Ankle and great toe plantarflexion	Gastrocnemius and soleus (GS), flexor hallucis longus (FHL)
Axillary (A)	Lateral deltoid	Shoulder abduction	Deltoid
Radial (R)	Dorsal web space between thumb and index	Extension of thumb IP joint	Extensor pollicis longus (EPL)
Median (M)	Two-point discrimination of thumb, index, long	Abduct thumb perpendicular to palm, flex index DIP joint	Abductor pollicis brevis (APB), flexor digitorum profundus to index (FDP2)
Ulnar (U)	Two-point discrimination of ring, small	Spread fingers apart, flex small finger DIP joint	Interossei (IO), flexor digitorum profundus to small (FDP5)

IP, interphalangeal; DIP, distal interphalangeal.

radiographs or computed tomography (CT) scan. Although C-spine CT scans have replaced radiographs as an initial screening tool at many institutions, radiographs can be a useful adjunct. The overall alignment of the C-spine can be better appreciated on plain radiographs than on CT scan, so plain radiographs are mandatory if any injury is identified on the CT scan. Plain radiographs, especially flexion and extension views, are also mandatory if there is concern for any ligamentous injury. Lateral C-spine radiographs must visualize all cervical vertebrae to the C7–T1 junction.

Assessment of extremity fractures and dislocations should include a minimum of two views 90 degrees to each other (usually AP and lateral views) of the affected area and should include both the joint above and the joint below the injury. **Dislocations should be reduced as soon as possible,** without the benefit of radiographs if necessary, because they are often associated with neurovascular and soft-tissue compromise.

III. FRACTURES AND DISLOCATIONS

A. How to describe a fracture

1. Accurate descriptions of fractures and dislocations begin with the bone or joint involved. For fractures, the **anatomic region** refers usually to the proximal, middle, or distal portion of the bone. *Epiphyseal, metaphyseal,* and *diaphyseal* are commonly used descriptive terms of the fracture location. The **quality** of the fracture is described on the basis of its **orientation** and the **number of fracture fragments.** A fracture is **transverse** if it runs relatively perpendicular to the long axis of the bone and **oblique** if it is angled. **Spiral** fractures propagate around and along a long bone and are caused by a twisting injury. **Comminuted** fractures have, by definition, more than two fragments. **Intra-articular** fractures involve the joint surface.

2. **Alignment** always references the distal fragment relative to the proximal fragment. Key components are **angulation, translation, rotation,** and **shortening. Angulation** is angular deformity in the coronal or sagittal plane, **rotation** is deformity about the long axis of the bone, **translation** is nonangular coronal or sagittal displacement with decreased bony **apposition,** and **shortening** is loss of bone length though the fracture.

3. **Stable** fractures and dislocations are not likely to displace after reduction (the "setting" of a fracture or dislocation) and appropriate immobilization, whereas **unstable** fractures are either unable to be reduced or are likely to lose reduction despite adequate immobilization.

4. **Soft-tissue injury. Open** fractures are those with a disruption of the overlying skin and tissue such that the fracture communicates with the external environment. **Closed** fractures are those that do not communicate with the external environment. Abrasions or lacerations that do not communicate with the fracture site are considered closed, but should be carefully probed and examined before that determination is made. Fractures complicated by associated neurovascular, ligamentous, or muscular injury require prompt recognition and injury-specific treatment.

5. Joint **subluxation** refers to joint disruption and instability with decreased contact between joint surfaces. **Dislocation** refers to complete loss of contact between joint surfaces. Both are described by the position of the distal bone in relation to its proximal articulation.

B. **General management principles**

1. **Dislocation.** All dislocated joints, especially in the setting of **neu-rovascular compromise,** should be reduced **emergently,** even before initial radiographs are taken if possible. This can generally be accomplished via gentle longitudinal traction. Successful reduction reduces the risk and degree of soft-tissue injury (e.g., pressure necrosis) and neurovascular compromise. Postreduction radiographs are essential to confirm adequate reduction and to re-evaluate for associated fractures previously not visualized because of deformity associated with the dislocation. Persistently diminished or absent pulses may require arteriography and further evaluation.

2. **Fractures: Pediatric versus adult**
   a. **Management of pediatric fractures can be significantly different from the management of adult fractures. Children, especially those with open growth plates, have a greater potential for bony remodeling than adults,** and therefore a greater amount of malalignment is acceptable. In children, at least limited reduction of deformity is often necessary to decrease the risk of permanent deformity. Whereas in the adult, inability to achieve and obtain an acceptable reduction is a relative indication for surgical treatment. Fracture evaluation principles of history, physical exam, and radiographs are the same as in the adult. **Throughout this chapter, we will focus primarily on management of injuries in adult patients unless otherwise specified.**
   b. **Physeal plate injuries** ("growth plate") are common because this is the weakest part of the bone. The Salter–Harris classification categorizes these fractures into five types of increasing severity and likelihood of future growth disturbance (see Table 34-2 and Fig. 34-1).

TABLE 34-2	Salter–Harris Classification of Growth Plate Injuries
Type 1	Fracture through the growth plate without any metaphyseal or epiphyseal involvement
Type 2	Fracture through the growth plate is associated with a metaphyseal fracture
Type 3	Fracture through the growth plate is associated with an epiphyseal fracture
Type 4	Fracture through the metaphysis, across the growth plate, and exiting the epiphysis
Type 5	Severe crush injury to the growth plate

The Salter-Harris Classification of Growth Plate Injuries

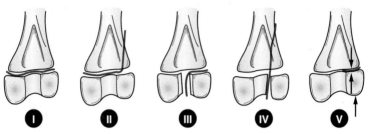

Figure 34-1. The five types of Salter–Harris growth plate injuries.

IV. SOFT-TISSUE INJURY

A. **Principles of management.** In general, isolated soft-tissue injuries, such as ligament sprains and muscle strains, are treated with *r*est, *i*ce, *c*ompression bandage, and *e*levation **(RICE therapy)** with or without immobilization.

1. **Skin lacerations/defects.** All devitalized tissue should be débrided. If the wound cannot be closed due to excessive tension, it should be covered with a moist saline dressing, and a delayed primary closure or skin grafting should be planned.

2. **Muscle**

   a. **Mechanism. Strains** of the **musculotendinous unit** are usually secondary to violent contraction or excessive stretch. Injury spans the range from stretch of the fibers to a complete tear with loss of function.

   b. **Physical examination. Swelling, tenderness, and pain with movement occur.** A defect may be palpable. RICE-type treatment of the muscle involved is adequate for most such injuries.

3. **Tendon.** Lacerated, ruptured, or avulsed tendons, especially those of the upper extremity, should be surgically repaired because such injuries result in loss of function. Examination reveals loss of motion or weakness. Open wounds with a tendon laceration are irrigated thoroughly, débrided, and closed primarily with early planned repair of the tendon in the operating room (OR). In grossly contaminated wounds, incision and débridement in the OR are needed. Splints are applied with the extremity in a functional position.

4. **Ligament.** Ligament **sprains** range from mild stretch to complete tear and are commonly sports related. Pain, localized tenderness, and joint instability may be present on examination. Radiographs may reveal joint incongruence. If the joint is clinically or radiographically unstable, treatment involves immobilization in a reduced position. If no evidence of instability is present, treatment based on the RICE principle is used, and early range of motion is encouraged.

V. SPECIFIC INJURIES BY ANATOMIC LOCATION

A. Shoulder

1. Fractures: Clavicle, proximal humerus, and scapula

   a. Clavicle fractures

   (1) **Typical mechanism.** A fall onto an outstretched hand or onto a shoulder.

   (2) **Typical physical signs.** A visible or palpable **deformity** is often present at the fracture site.

   (3) **Radiographic evaluation.** Two views of the clavicle and a chest x-ray to allow a comparison of clavicle length with the contralateral side.

   (4) **Typical management.** Most clavicle fractures heal with non-operative treatment and can be managed with a sling. Figure-of-eight splints offer no benefit over a sling, are usually poorly tolerated by patients, and therefore are usually not indicated. A severe deformity with tenting of the overlying skin is an indication for surgical intervention.

   b. Proximal humerus fractures

   (1) **Typical mechanism.** Commonly caused by a low-energy fall in the elderly.

   (2) **Typical physical signs.** Decreased range of motion, swelling, ecchymosis, and pain. The neurovascular exam is critical to rule out any associated injury to the brachial plexus.

   (3) **Radiographic evaluation.** Radiographic evaluation of the shoulder and proximal humerus should include three orthogonal views: An AP of the glenohumeral joint, scapular Y, and axillary. A dislocation can be missed if one relies solely on an AP and scapular Y-view, and an axillary view is mandatory.

   (4) **Typical management.** If nondisplaced and stable, can be treated with a sling and early, controlled mobilization. Significant comminution, especially of the greater and lesser tuberosities, and displacement place the humeral head at risk of avascular necrosis and are indications for surgical reduction and fixation, especially in the young. For such a fracture in the elderly, a primary shoulder arthroplasty (replacement) may be considered if stabile internal fixation cannot be achieved.

   (5) **When associated with dislocation.** Fracture dislocations of the shoulder are difficult to reduce closed. If there is an associated neurovascular compromise, these should be taken emergently to the OR for open reduction. Closed reduction, if performed, should be done cautiously to avoid neurovascular injury and to avoid displacement of an otherwise nondisplaced fracture.

   c. Scapula fractures

   (1) **Typical mechanism.** Scapula fractures are a marker of very high-energy chest trauma, usually involving a motor vehicle.

   (2) **Typical physical signs.** Tenderness to palpation over the scapula. Observe for signs of pneumothorax or other chest trauma with scapula fractures.

(3) **Usual radiographic evaluation.** Often first noted on chest CT in the evaluation of coexisting chest injuries. CT is the best way to evaluate for joint involvement.

(4) **Typical management.** Treatment in a sling unless intra-articular glenoid displacement necessitates surgical fixation.

2. **Dislocations**

a. **Shoulder dislocations (glenohumeral dislocation)**

(1) **Typical mechanism.** Anterior shoulder dislocations (most common, ~85%) occur with forced shoulder abduction or external rotation (or both). Less common posterior shoulder dislocations are associated with seizure and electrical shock.

(2) **Typical physical signs.** Shoulder dislocation presents with decreased and painful range of motion and the humeral head may be palpable anteriorly or posteriorly. A "sulcus sign," or indentation between the acromion and humeral head, is suggestive of dislocation. Whereas with fractures, a thorough neurovascular examination is critical and should be documented prior to and following any reductions.

(3) **Radiographic evaluation (see radiographic evaluation of proximal humerus fractures).** Posterior shoulder dislocations can be missed with traditional films if there is not an adequate axillary view. Evidence of glenoid rim fractures (Bankart lesion) or humeral head impaction fractures (Hill-Sachs lesion) associated with shoulder dislocations should be sought.

(4) **Typical management.** Reduction is performed under sedation with axial traction and bringing the arm up into full abduction above the head. Care should be taken with the elderly with any reduction because it is possible to fracture osteoporotic bone with minimal force. The arm is then immobilized in the position of greatest stability: Internal rotation for anterior dislocations and external rotation for posterior dislocations. Radiographs should be repeated to demonstrate reduction, and a postreduction neurovascular exam should be done. The redislocation rate is inversely proportional to patient's age and correlated with activity level and demand.

b. **Acromioclavicular (AC) dislocations ("a separated shoulder")**

(1) **Typical mechanism.** Fall directly onto the shoulder or a direct blow to the shoulder.

(2) **Typical physical signs.** Variable deformity and instability can be seen. Assess side-to-side asymmetry. Pain with shoulder motion and tenderness to palpation can be seen with sprains or dislocations of the AC joint.

(3) **Radiographic evaluation** (see proximal humerus and clavicle fracture sections). Stress views of the AC joint are taken holding 5- to 10-lb weights, comparing side to side for displacement; however, this can be quite uncomfortable and is not generally necessary.

(4) **Typical management.** AC joint dislocations can be treated with a sling and early motion in most cases. Significant displacement and deformity may require reduction and fixation, especially if the skin or soft tissue is tented or otherwise at risk.

c. **Sternoclavicular dislocations**

(1) **Typical mechanism.** Anterior dislocations can occur after a force is applied to the anterolateral shoulder. Posterior dislocations are usually secondary to a direct blow to the distal clavicle.

(2) **Typical physical signs.** Localized pain, swelling, and tenderness are seen. **Hoarseness, dyspnea, dysphagia, or engorged neck veins are red flags** for posterior sternoclavicular joint dislocations with neurovascular compromise and should prompt emergent evaluation and treatment.

(3) **Radiographic evaluation. Although often subtle, asymmetry can be seen on chest x-ray.** A CT scan may be indicated to evaluate the sternoclavicular joint to determine anterior or posterior displacement and to visualize adjacent neurovascular structures.

(4) **Typical management. Anterior sternoclavicular dislocation** can be treated with a sling or shoulder immobilizer, whereas **posterior dislocations** commonly require reduction because of potential neurovascular and airway compromise. This should be done in the OR under general anesthesia with general or thoracic surgery backup in case of injury to the lung or great vessels.

3. **Soft-tissue injury**

a. **Rotator cuff tears.** In the young, rotator cuff tears are caused by repetitive overuse (throwing in athletes) or by acute trauma. In the elderly, tears are commonly degenerative and chronic, but they can be acute. History reveals shoulder pain and weakness, especially with overhead activities, and decreased range of motion. In the young, treatment consists of open or arthroscopic tendon repair. In the elderly, function may not be as severely affected, and physical therapy for improved strength and motion may suffice.

b. **Pectoralis major rupture.** This is most often caused by heavy lifting. In addition to weakness and pain, there is often significant bruising, a palpable defect, and a visibly changed muscle contour. Initial treatment in the emergency room (ER) consists of sling immobilization. An open repair gives best results when performed early.

B. **Arm and elbow**

1. **Fractures**

a. **Humeral shaft fractures**

(1) **Typical mechanism.** Commonly caused by a fall onto an outstretched arm, especially in the elderly.

(2) **Typical physical signs.** Deformity of the upper arm, pain, ecchymosis. Evaluate closely for small lacerations that may represent open fractures. A careful neurovascular exam should

be performed. In mid-diaphyseal fractures, the radial nerve is especially vulnerable to injury because it is directly adjacent to the posterior humeral shaft in this region.

(3) **Radiographic evaluation.** Two orthogonal views of the humerus, including the shoulder and elbow joints.

(4) **Typical management.** Closed fractures are placed in a coaptation splint or Sarmiento brace. Secondary (following closed reduction) radial nerve palsy is considered an indication for surgical management to rule out incarceration of the nerve within the fracture. However, primary radial nerve dysfunction usually resolves spontaneously (over a period of months) and can be treated nonoperatively. Other indications for surgical fixation include open fractures, injuries to multiple extremities, concurrent injury below the elbow ("floating elbow"), or a body habitus that is not amenable to bracing.

b. **Distal humerus fractures**

(1) **Typical mechanism.** Fall onto an outstretched hand or directly onto the elbow. Supracondylar humerus fractures are the most common fracture seen in children, especially between the ages of 4 and 7 years.

(2) **Typical physical signs.** Swelling, pain, ecchymosis, and decreased elbow range of motion. In children, displaced supracondylar fractures are frequently associated with peripheral nerve injuries. Patients should undergo serial exams to rule out the development of compartment syndrome.

(3) **Radiographic evaluation.** Orthogonal views of the elbow should be taken. For supracondylar fractures in adults, stress views taken with gentle longitudinal traction can help to delineate the fracture pattern, especially in cases with significant comminution or deformity. A CT scan may be indicated for additional fracture characterization to aid in surgical planning. Nondisplaced elbow fractures in children may present only with a "sail sign" caused by the superior displacement of the anterior and posterior elbow fat pads by a joint effusion.

(4) **Typical management. Supracondylar fractures in children** can be treated in a splint acutely if they are nondisplaced but require percutaneous pinning and casting if they are displaced. Significant swelling and neurovascular embarrassment are indications for urgent reduction followed by close observation. In adults, displaced fracture, especially with intra-articular displacement, is an indication for open reduction with internal fixation.

c. **Radial head fractures**

(1) **Typical mechanism.** Fall onto an outstretched arm.

(2) **Typical physical signs.** These present with tenderness to palpation and pain with forearm rotation. An elbow effusion is present. Range of motion of the elbow is typically limited.

(3) **Radiographic evaluation.** Three views of the elbow joint, an AP, oblique, and a lateral, are obtained. These can present with

only subtle x-rays findings, and occasionally only an elbow effusion can be seen on plain x-ray. CT scans can be helpful in determining the size, location, and nature of a radial head fracture.

(4) **Typical management.** Radial head fractures with minimal involvement of the articular surface (<30%) can be treated nonoperatively with early range-of-motion exercises. Increasing head involvement is an indication for surgical management. Open reduction and internal fixation are performed when stable fixation is achievable (usually three or fewer fragments). In adults, radial head excision or replacement is performed if comminution precludes adequate repair.

d. Olecranon fractures

(1) **Typical mechanism.** Fall directly onto the elbow or a direct blow to the posterior elbow.

(2) **Typical physical signs.** A palpable defect may be present. If the entire triceps insertion is involved, the patient may not be able to actively extend the elbow.

(3) **Radiographic evaluation.** Three views of the elbow are obtained. The lateral view is typically the most useful in evaluating these fractures.

(4) **Typical management.** Nondisplaced **olecranon fractures** are treated with a posterior splint followed by early range of motion, but when they are displaced, surgical fixation is indicated.

2. Elbow dislocations (ulnohumeral)

a. Typical mechanism. Fall onto an outstretched hand.

b. Typical physical signs. Examination reveals pain, swelling, bruising, and deformity with loss of elbow flexion and extension and forearm supination and pronation. Posterior dislocations are most common but can also occur anteriorly, medially, or laterally. The dislocated segment can often be palpated. Whereas with other elbow injuries, a careful neurovascular exam should be performed.

c. Radiographic evaluation. AP and lateral radiographs of the elbow confirm the diagnosis and reveal the direction of dislocation and major associated fractures. Postreduction radiographs are essential to demonstrate concentric joint reduction and more reliably identify any associated fractures. Coronoid process and radial head fractures are frequently seen with elbow dislocations. A CT scan may aid in complex fracture dislocations.

d. Typical management. Initial treatment consists of prompt reduction (typically accomplished with axial traction and flexion) and assessment of stability by carefully extending the elbow after the reduction has been done. The joint should be splinted in a stable position, with arm flexed less than 90 degrees. Postreduction radiographs are taken, and postreduction neurovascular status is documented. Stable dislocations benefit from early, controlled motion, whereas unstable elbows may require surgical stabilization of fractures and/or ligament reconstruction.

3. Soft-tissue injury

    a. Biceps tendon rupture/avulsion is usually secondary to violent contracture or excessive stretch. Loss of power, pain with resisted elbow flexion, local swelling, and ecchymosis are seen, along with an abnormal muscle contour ("Popeye sign"), proximal retraction. Examine for side-to-side differences. Initial treatment is sling immobilization followed by early surgical repair or nonoperative management, depending on the patient's activity level.

C. Forearm, wrist, and hand

    1. Fractures

        a. Radius and ulna fractures (aka "both bone forearm fractures")

            (1) Typical mechanism. These are commonly caused by falls onto the elbow or outstretched arm and are common in both children and the elderly. A direct blow can cause a "night-stick fracture," a typically mid-shaft fracture of the ulna caused by a forceful blow to the arm positioned to protect the face, often with a bat or club during an assault.

            (2) Typical physical signs. Examination reveals deformity, pain, and focal tenderness. Variable amounts of swelling can be seen, and diaphyseal fractures can cause a compartment syndrome, so careful, serial examination may be needed (see Section VI.B). A Galeazzi fracture is a fracture of the distal half of the radius associated with disruption of the distal radioulnar joint; this joint must be tested for stability in all radius fractures. A distal fracture with spread of the hematoma into the carpal tunnel may present as an acute carpal tunnel syndrome with associated median nerve sensory and motor dysfunction. Note wrist swelling and ecchymosis, and test two-point discrimination of the fingers (normally <5 to 7 mm) and test motor strength of the thumb abductors.

            (3) Radiographic evaluation. AP and lateral radiographs that include the entire forearm including the elbow and wrist are the minimum required. Splinted postreduction films are obtained to confirm reduction.

            (4) Typical management. In children, most diaphyseal and wrist fractures can be managed with closed reduction and sugar-tong splinting. If an adequate reduction cannot be achieved in the ER, these are treated with closed reduction and pinning or with insertion of intramedullary thin flexible rods. In adults, shaft fractures that involve both bones are almost always treated with open reduction internal fixation (ORIF) after initial closed reduction and splinting is done in the ER to limit the stress on the surrounding soft tissues. Isolated radius and ulna fractures can be treated nonoperatively if they are minimally displaced. **Associated acute carpal tunnel syndrome is a surgical emergency.**

        b. Distal radius fractures

            (1) Typical mechanism. Fall on an outstretched hand.

    (2) **Typical physical signs.** Pain, deformity, swelling, ecchymosis, focal tenderness. Similarly to diaphyseal fractures, there can be an associated compartment syndrome or acute carpal tunnel syndrome, both of which are surgical emergencies.

    (3) **Radiographic evaluation.** Three views of the wrist with an AP, lateral, and oblique view. CT scans can be helpful in comminuted intra-articular fractures.

c. Scaphoid fractures

    (1) **Typical presentation.** A fall onto an outstretched hand with the wrist in radial deviation.

    (2) **Typical physical signs.** Local swelling, pain with wrist motion, and focal tenderness in the "anatomic snuffbox."

    (3) **Radiographic evaluation.** Three views of the wrist, an AP, lateral, and oblique as well as a scaphoid view taken with wrist in ulnar deviation. These fractures may not be visualized on plain x-rays at the time of injury.

    (4) **Typical management.** Nondisplaced scaphoid fractures are treated in a thumb spica splint. Suspected scaphoid fractures, with pain in the anatomic snuffbox but no fracture seen on x-ray, should be treated as nondisplaced fractures and immobilized in the ER. Fractures with greater than 1 mm of displacement are at risk of nonunion and avascular necrosis and benefit from internal fixation.

d. Metacarpal fractures

    (1) **Typical mechanism.** Crush injury or axial load onto a closed fist.

    (2) **Typical physical signs.** Swelling and bruising, often with flexion of the distal fragment causing the knuckle to be less prominent; the most common is the distal fifth metacarpal or so-called "boxer's fracture." Check for rotational deformity by observing for finger divergence with flexion of the metacarpal phalangeal joints and comparing with the contralateral side.

    (3) **Typical management.** Reduction and splinting in an ulnar gutter or volar slab splint with fingers in intrinsic plus position (see Section VII.A.2.c), re-examining for rotational malalignment. If unstable, significantly angulated, or rotationally malaligned, these may require closed reduction and pinning or ORIF.

e. Distal phalanx fractures

    (1) **Typical mechanism.** Crush injury.

    (2) **Typical physical signs.** These are typically associated with lacerations of the fingertip or nail-bed injuries.

    (3) **Radiographic evaluation.** Any patients with a laceration to the fingertip should have an AP and lateral of the finger to rule out any underlying fracture.

    (4) **Typical management.** While these are technically open fractures, they can be adequately irrigated and débrided in the ER

and do not require a formal I&D in the OR. If there is any question of a nail-bed injury, the nail should be removed. After irrigation and débridement, nail-bed lacerations should be repaired with 5-0 or 6-0 chromic gut. Lacerations in the skin can be repaired with 4-0 nylon. Preformed Alumafoam finger splints are used to immobilize the fracture.

2. Dislocations

a. Perilunate dislocations

(1) **Typical mechanism.** Lunate and perilunate dislocations usually occur after forced wrist hyperextension.

(2) **Typical physical signs. Perilunate dislocations** present with pain, limited wrist motion, tenderness, and possibly signs of median neuropathy caused by compression of the median nerve in the carpal tunnel by the displaced lunate. Observe closely for signs of acute carpal tunnel syndrome.

(3) **Radiographic evaluation.** AP and lateral views of involved joints are the minimum required. Perilunate dislocations can be subtle on plain x-ray, and a high index of suspicion is necessary. Oblique views aid in evaluating the position of displaced carpal bones. Scaphoid, capitate, and radial styloid fractures should be ruled out as associated injuries with lunate dislocations.

(4) **Typical management.** Perilunate dislocations are reduced using axial traction and hyperextension of the wrist while pressure is applied to the lunate. Avoid splinting the wrist in a flexed position because this increases risk of median nerve compression. After closed reduction in the ER, these usually require surgical treatment with stabilization of associated fractures and disrupted intercarpal ligaments.

3. Soft-tissue injury

a. Subungual hematomas are decompressed by burning a hole in the nail with electrocautery or with a large-bore needle after a digital block.

b. Nail-bed injuries require removal of the overlying nail with repair of the nail bed using absorbable suture and splinting open of the nail fold with sterile Vaseline-impregnated gauze or with the Betadine-soaked nail.

c. Tip amputations involving only soft tissue can often be allowed to heal by secondary intent or, if the area is greater than 1 cm^2, treated with local flaps. Exposed bone is resected back to a level that allows soft-tissue coverage.

D. Pelvic fractures

1. Disruptions of the pelvic ring

a. Typical mechanism. Pelvic ring injuries are typically of very high energy, as from a motor vehicle collision or a fall from tall heights.

b. Typical physical signs. Crepitus, pelvic instability, or pain with iliac wing compression or distraction should alert the examiner to possible pelvic ring injury. Inspect for soft-tissue injury including a degloving injury. Rectal and vaginal examinations are performed to check for blood, open communication with a fracture, or a high-riding prostate. Blood at the urethral meatus at time of catheterization is a sign of lower urogenital injury. Pelvic bleeding may result in a loss of 2 to 3 L of blood or more, and signs of hypovolemic shock must be monitored along with aggressive fluid replacement. High-energy pelvic fractures rarely occur in isolation, and significant associated injuries are likely. Palpate for spinal tenderness or step-offs, and treat all patients initially with spinal precautions. A thorough primary and secondary survey must be undertaken and documented.

c. **Radiographic evaluation.** An AP pelvis view is part of the standard trauma panel. The use of an abdominal–pelvic CT scan is becoming standard part of the trauma workup and is extremely useful in evaluating pelvic, sacral, and lumbar spine fractures. An L5 transverse process fracture suggests posterior pelvic ligamentous disruption. Once stabilized, pelvic ring fractures are further evaluated with pelvic inlet and outlet views. If genitourinary injury is suspected, a retrograde urethrogram and cystogram should be obtained. Other standard radiographs such as chest and C-spine films should be reviewed.

d. **Typical management.** The initial treatment consists of adherence to standard trauma ABCs. Maintenance of adequate intravascular volume and systolic blood pressure is essential in the hemodynamically unstable patient. In the persistently unstable patient, sources of bleeding other than the pelvis should be ruled out followed by emergent fixation of the pelvic ring in the emergency department, usually with a linen sheet tied around the pelvis or with a specialized pelvic binder to reduce pelvic volume until an anterior pelvic external fixation can be applied. Pelvic binders that remain in place for more than several hours must be often re-evaluated to rule out associated pressure necrosis of the skin. Because binders can cause increased patient discomfort and skin breakdown, they should be removed if patients remain hemodynamically stable or the fracture pattern does not allow decreased pelvic volume with lateral compression. Angiogram and embolization of bleeding pelvic vessels may precede or follow placement of provisional external fixation. If the patient is hemodynamically and otherwise stable, surgical intervention can be delayed to allow complete assessment of associated injuries and resuscitation of the patient. An open pelvic fracture has a very high morbidity, and a diverting colostomy should be considered. Patients are at high risk of developing a deep venous thrombosis (DVT) in association with these injuries, and appropriate prophylaxis should be initiated. Sacral fractures and sacroiliac joint disruptions can often be treated with percutaneous screws.

2. **Pubic rami fractures**
   a. **Typical mechanism.** Same level falls in an elderly patient.
   b. **Typical physical signs.** Groin pain, pain with weight bearing.

    c. **Usual radiographic evaluation.** An AP pelvis and inlet and outlet views are all used to evaluate the pubic rami. A CT is usually not required.

    d. **Typical management.** These patients are allowed to bear weight as tolerated, but frequently have significant pain with weight bearing initially. Intensive physical therapy is important to prevent these patients from becoming bedridden.

3. **Acetabular fractures**

    a. **Typical mechanism.** Usually the result of high-energy trauma such as an motor vehicle collision (MVC) or fall from height.

    b. **Typical physical signs.** Hip pain, pain with logroll. In cases with an associated hip dislocation, the limb may be shortened and externally rotated. A sciatic palsy is also possible with a posterior hip dislocation. Since these patients have usually been in a high-energy trauma, they may have several associated injuries and should have a carefully secondary exam.

    c. **Radiographic evaluation.** These fractures are usually identified on an AP pelvis taken as part of the initial trauma work-up. Judet (oblique) views of the pelvis and a CT scan with fine cuts through the acetabulum are also needed.

    d. **Typical management.** Skeletal traction may be indicated for fractures of the acetabulum, depending on the size and location of the fracture and an associated dislocation (see also Section V.F.2). Fractures involving the weight-bearing portion of the acetabulum are usually treated with surgical reduction and fixation.

E. **Hip and femur**

1. **Fractures of the hip and femur**

    a. **Hip fractures (femoral neck and intertrochanteric fractures)**

      (1) **Typical mechanism.** Commonly the result of low-energy falls or direct blows in the elderly, but in the young they are generally a result of more significant trauma. A stress fracture of the femoral neck typically presents as groin or medial thigh pain associated temporally with a recent increase in activity level or training.

      (2) **Typical physical signs.** Shortening of the limb may be seen in addition to pain with motion and the inability to bear weight. Rotational stability is typically lost with displaced hip fractures, with the leg falling into a shortened, externally rotated posture. A high index of suspicion must be maintained in the elderly after a low-energy fall presenting with complaints of groin or medial thigh pain (site of referred pain from the hip joint) because these may be the only signs of a nondisplaced hip fracture.

      (3) **Radiographic evaluation.** An AP pelvis view and hip films (AP and lateral views) are usually diagnostic. The femoral neck can easily be evaluated on a trauma pelvic CT if available. If history suggests a hip fracture in the elderly or a stress fracture in the young but no fracture is seen, magnetic resonance

imaging (MRI) or bone scan is indicated to rule out the occult fracture.

(4) **Typical management.** Displaced femoral neck fractures in the young require urgent anatomic reduction and internal fixation to reduce the **risk of avascular necrosis,** whereas stress fractures are treated with protected weight bearing. In the elderly, surgical treatment is generally the rule for hip fractures. Stable femoral neck fractures are usually treated with internal fixation (most commonly, percutaneous screws) and unstable femoral neck fractures with hip arthroplasty (hemi- or total hip arthroplasty). Peritrochanteric fractures are treated with various internal fixation methods, including the use of compression screw and plate or intramedullary nail. The utility of skin traction to increase patient comfort prior to surgery is controversial.

b. **Femoral shaft fractures**

(1) **Typical mechanism.** Usually high-energy injuries or gun shot wounds.

(2) **Typical physical signs.** Patients usually have gross deformity and instability. Even small lacerations that seem to be far away from the level of the fracture should be carefully evaluated to rule out open fractures.

(3) **Radiographic evaluation.** An AP and lateral of the femur, which include the high and knee joints, are usually the only x-rays required. Ipsilateral femoral neck fractures should be excluded.

(4) **Typical management.** Initial long-leg splinting and occasionally skeletal traction to increase comfort and stability while maintaining length and protecting the soft tissues (traction splints placed by emergency personnel should be promptly removed at the time of initial evaluation). Even closed femur fractures can be a source of significant blood loss, and appropriate blood replacement, especially in the multiply injured patient, is important. Most shaft fractures are treated with intramedullary nailing soon after the injury to allow early mobilization and decrease the risk of additional complications. In the unstable, multiply injured patient, external fixation may be the initial treatment of choice to minimize adverse systemic effects caused by the additional trauma of surgery. DVTs are common after pelvic and leg bone fractures, so prophylaxis (mechanical with or without chemical) is essential.

2. **Hip dislocations**

a. **Typical mechanism.** High-energy motor vehicle crash, often associated with acetabular fracture. In patients with previous hip replacement, dislocation is typically atraumatic, caused primarily by noncompliance with positioning precautions given after hip replacement.

b. **Typical physical signs.** Anterior dislocations typically leave the extremity abducted and externally rotated. Posterior dislocations cause greater shortening with an adducted and internally rotated posture. Sciatic nerve function should be assessed for palsy with posterior dislocations (the peroneal division is most commonly affected).

  c. Radiographic evaluation. Obtain appropriate pelvic films to evaluate for acetabular, femoral head, or hip fracture (see previous section) and to determine the direction of dislocation (requires adequate lateral view). In hip replacement, check for component positioning, loosening, or periprosthetic fractures.

  d. Typical management. In a native hip, once a hip dislocation is identified, **immediate closed reduction,** prior to an additional imaging, to reduce **risk of avascular necrosis** should be done. Most failed attempts at closed reduction are due to inadequate sedation and muscle relaxation, which are essential. Assessment of stability and postreduction neurologic exam are necessary. If stable once reduction is achieved, the leg is kept abducted with an abduction pillow. Skeletal traction is indicated when the hip remains unstable after a reduction is performed. Postreduction radiographs, including AP, lateral, and Judet views, are needed to confirm reduction and assess for associated fractures. Associated fractures are stabilized surgically. Patients with dislocated hip arthroplasties can usually be reduced closed, placed in an abduction brace, and discharged home.

F. Knee and tibia

  1. Fractures

    a. Supracondylar femur fractures

      (1) Typical mechanism. Can be low energy in the elderly, generally higher energy in younger patients.

      (2) Typical physical signs. Deformity and swelling about the knee. Evaluate carefully for any open wounds.

      (3) Radiographic evaluation. Four views of the knee (AP, lateral, and two obliques) help to identify fractures involving the knee. Traction views taken with gentle longitudinal traction for comminuted and displaced periarticular fractures may be necessary to understand the fracture pattern. A CT scan may be helpful for preoperative planning for complex intra-articular fractures.

      (4) Typical management. These fractures are initially reduced and splinted in the ER. Almost all these will require ORIF to restore anatomic alignment to the joint surface.

    b. Patellar fractures

      (1) Typical mechanism. Patella fractures are commonly caused by falling directly onto the knee or striking a dashboard.

      (2) Typical physical signs. Patella fractures often have a palpable defect and have an associated inability to perform a straight-leg raise.

      (3) Radiographic evaluation. Four views of the knee (AP, lateral, and two obliques) help to identify fractures involving the knee. A sunrise view can also be helpful in evaluating the patella.

(4) **Typical management.** Patella fractures with displacement, joint incongruity, or loss of active knee extension require reduction and surgical fixation. Nondisplaced fractures can be treated with a knee immobilizer and weight bearing as tolerated.

c. **Tibial plateau fractures**

(1) **Typical mechanism.** Motor vehicle collision, fall from a height, direct blow, and pedestrian versus car are all common.

(2) **Typical physical signs.** Large knee effusion, significant swelling in the lower leg, ecchymosis, and deformity. Tibial plateau fractures should be carefully monitored for compartment syndrome.

(3) **Radiographic evaluation.** Tibial shaft fractures require an AP and lateral of the tibia and views of the knee and ankle. A CT scan is usually required for preoperative planning.

(4) **Typical management.** Tibial plateau fractures are treated with splinting and early motion if they are nondisplaced and stable but require reduction and internal fixation for articular incongruity, significant displacement, deformity, or instability. Most plateau fractures associated with significant soft-tissue swelling or compartment syndrome are treated with a temporary, spanning external fixator across the knee followed by ORIF.

d. **Tibial shaft fractures**

(1) **Typical mechanism.** Motor vehicle collision, motorcycle collision, fall from height, and gun shot wound are all common mechanisms. Spiral fractures of the tibia are caused by twisting injury.

(2) **Typical physical signs.** Gross deformity and instability is usually present. The subcutaneous location of the tibia predisposes to open fractures. Observation and probing lacerations and skin defects for communication to underlying bone or fracture are necessary. Check nerve function and pulses and foot perfusion compared with the contralateral side. The patients should be carefully monitored to rule out compartment syndrome.

(3) **Radiographic evaluation.** AP and lateral x-rays of the tibia, including both the ankle and knee joints, are usually the only imaging required.

(4) **Typical management.** Stable tibial shaft fractures can be treated with casting; however, most are treated with intramedullary nailing to allow early weight bearing and motion. Open tibial shaft fractures often require multiple surgical débridements and soft-tissue coverage.

2. **Knee dislocations**

a. **Typical mechanism.** Knee dislocations are very high-energy injuries and require multiple ligamentous disruption to occur. In extremely obese persons, these can occur with a same level fall or even walking on uneven surfaces. These are very different from patella dislocations, which usually occur with a twisting force while in extension, often during sports, and usually reduce spontaneously.

  b. **Typical physical exam.** Knee dislocations present with deformity, shortening, ligamentous instability, and often signs of significant neurovascular compromise. Check side-to-side differences in pulse examination serially. Knee dislocations that have reduced spontaneously are easy to miss in the acute setting, and the knees should be examined for ligamentous instability in the setting of high-energy trauma.

  c. **Usual radiographic evaluation.** Look for associated fractures with knee dislocations with four views of the knee *after* reduction. Angiography or CT angiography is often performed with knee dislocations (see later comments). Obtain an MRI of the knee in the subacute setting to evaluate the associated ligamentous injuries.

  d. **Typical management.** Knee dislocations require immediate, emergent reduction. These should be reduced even before radiographs are taken if possible. The incidence of concomitant vascular injury is approximately 30%, and pedal pulse examination has a low sensitivity (79%) for detecting significant vascular injury. One should have a very low threshold for arteriography; and a vascular surgery consultation is mandatory in the presence of questionable pulses. If vascular repair is necessary, a spanning external fixator can be placed to stabilize the knee. After any vascular repair, prophylactic fasciotomy should be considered. Often, delayed ligamentous reconstruction is necessary to restore knee stability.

3. **Soft-tissue injuries**

  a. **Quadriceps and patellar tendon ruptures** are caused by violent contraction or excessive stretch. Palpable defects and a high-riding (with patella tendon rupture) or low-riding (with quadriceps rupture) patella on physical exam or lateral radiographs are hallmarks. Partial tears that do not affect the integrity of the extensor mechanism can be managed without surgery with protected motion. Injuries affecting the extensor mechanism require surgical repair.

  b. **Knee ligament disruption** is commonly seen with sports injuries involving a pivoting injury or a bending moment. A hemarthrosis is common. Physical exam demonstrates joint instability with testing. Common ligamentous injuries include anterior cruciate and medial collateral ligaments.

  c. **Meniscal tears** are more common than ligamentous injury and often occur in association with them. They present with a joint effusion, pain with deep flexion, and joint line tenderness. Rarely, a displaced segment can cause locking of the knee joint. Meniscal tears can be treated nonoperatively or, if symptoms persist, with arthroscopic débridement or repair.

G. **Distal tibia and ankle**

  1. **Fractures**
    a. **Pilon fractures**
      (1) **Typical mechanism.** Distal tibial intra-articular fractures (pilon fractures) are associated with an axial loading mechanism such as falls from a height or floor board injury from a motor vehicle accident.

(2) **Typical physical signs.** Deformity, instability, swelling, and ecchymosis about the ankle. Note soft-tissue injury, which is often significant with pilon injuries, including location of fracture blisters and whether the blisters are blood filled (marker of deeper injury).

(3) **Radiographic evaluation.** Obtain three views of the ankle (AP, lateral, and mortise). Foot films are used to evaluate for concomitant talus, calcaneus, or other foot fractures associated with high-energy pilon fractures. Traction views and a postreduction CT of pilon fractures help with fracture characterization and surgical planning.

(4) **Typical management.** Pilon fractures with significant shortening, comminution, or soft-tissue injury are best managed initially with closed reduction and placement of a spanning external fixator. External fixation is then maintained until the soft tissues can tolerate a formal open procedure. Soft-tissue management is critical in the presence of these injuries, especially pilon fractures.

b. **Ankle fractures**

(1) **Typical mechanism.** Ankle fractures are commonly caused by a twisting mechanism.

(2) **Typical physical signs.** Note deformity and instability of the lower leg and ankle joint. Perform and document a neurovascular exam. With ankle fractures, note the precise location of tenderness and swelling.

(3) **Radiographic evaluation.** Obtain three views of the ankle (AP, lateral, and mortise). With ankle fractures of questionable joint stability, obtain a stress mortise view by stabilizing the distal tibia and externally rotating the patient's foot and look for widening of greater than 2 mm of the medial joint space. Comparison views to the uninjured ankle can be helpful.

(4) **Typical management.** Stable, nondisplaced fractures of the ankle can be treated with immobilization and protected weight bearing. Unstable fractures (one with both medial and lateral injuries) and fractures with joint subluxation benefit from delayed open reduction and internal fixation once the swelling has decreased. All fractures should be reduced in the ER with postreduction radiographs demonstrating adequate joint and fracture reduction. If adequate joint reduction cannot be achieved or maintained, early surgical treatment (usually a spanning external fixator) is indicated to prevent further joint damage.

2. **Ankle dislocations**

a. **Typical mechanism.** Simple (not associated with fracture) ankle dislocations are uncommon. Fracture dislocations are caused by similar, but higher energy, mechanisms as those in other ankle fractures.

b. **Typical physical exam.** Look for deformity and pain with inability to bear weight. Dislocations are often associated with open fractures about the ankle. Document a neurovascular exam because significant soft-tissue injury and deformity place neurovascular structures at risk.

   c. **Usual radiographic examination.** Same as for ankle fractures.

   d. **Typical management.** These should be reduced emergently, even before radiographs are taken. Open injuries should be treated appropriately (see Section VI.C). Dislocations represent unstable injuries, and associated fractures are treated surgically. Whereas with pilon fractures, spanning external fixation may be an appropriate initial treatment.

3. Soft-tissue injuries

   a. **Ankle sprains** are commonly caused by inversion or eversion of the foot. Patients present with swelling, ecchymosis, and maximal tenderness along the injured ligaments medially or laterally. Radiographs are normal or reveal insignificant cortical avulsions. Initial treatment with rest, ice, and elevation is usually adequate, followed by physical therapy for proprioceptive training to reduce the risk of reinjury. Immobilization is generally not indicated.

   b. **A ruptured Achilles tendon** usually occurs during running, jumping, or vigorous activity, with sudden pain and difficulty in walking. Examination can reveal a palpable defect, weak plantar flexion, and (if a complete rupture) no passive ankle plantar flexion on squeezing the patient's calf (positive Thompson sign). Nonoperative treatment in a splint with the ankle plantar flexed is one treatment option, but is associated with higher rerupture rates than surgical repair.

H. Foot

1. Fractures

   a. **Calcaneus fractures**

     (1) Typical mechanism. Calcaneus fractures are the most common tarsal fracture and are usually the result of an axillary load such as a fall from height, often in a young laborer.

     (2) Typical physical signs. Calcaneal fractures are associated with considerable swelling and blister formation, heel widening, and significant tenderness and ecchymosis extending to the arch. Associated fractures are common and include those seen with an axial loading mechanism.

     (3) Radiographic evaluation. Obtain three views each of the ankle and the foot. A Harris view evaluates the calcaneal width and profiles the subtalar joint. A CT scan is usually obtained with displaced calcaneal fractures. Obtain lumbar spine films to evaluate for associated fracture.

     (4) Typical management. Calcaneal fractures should be placed in a well-padded splint and observed for compartment syndrome. Significant subtalar joint depression and comminution may require open reduction with internal fixation once soft-tissue swelling allows. Regardless of treatment, outcomes are often disappointing and result in significant disability.

b. Talus fractures

    (1) Typical mechanism. Talus fractures (the second most common) are also generally higher energy (motor vehicle collision or falls) and are usually caused by forced dorsiflexion (e.g., slamming on the brake at the time of impact).

    (2) Typical physical signs. Talus fractures can also present with significant swelling, and when they are associated with a dislocation of the tibiotalar joint and/or the subtalar joint, a significant deformity can be present. A careful neurologic exam should be performed and followed.

    (3) Radiographic evaluation. Obtain three views each of the ankle and the foot. CT scans are often helpful with talus fractures as well to evaluate the myriad of articular surfaces of the tibiotalar and subtalar joints, which are difficult to evaluate properly with plain radiographs.

    (4) Typical management. Talus fractures can be treated with cast immobilization if they are absolutely nondisplaced, but most talar neck fractures are treated with ORIF to decrease the risk of nonunion and avascular necrosis.

c. Metatarsal fractures

    (1) Typical mechanism. Metatarsal fractures can be seen with lower energy trauma. Stress fractures can occur in runners or others who have recently increased their distance or activity.

    (2) Typical physical signs. Stress fractures may present only with tenderness to palpation at the level of the injury.

    (3) Radiographic evaluation. Three views (AP, lateral, and oblique) of the foot. Metatarsal stress fractures, if suspected and not apparent on initial radiographs, may be seen on MRI or bone scan.

    (4) Typical management. Metatarsal fractures can generally be treated nonoperatively with splinting. First metatarsal fractures may be treated operatively if displaced. Transverse fractures of the proximal fifth metatarsal diaphysis (Jones fracture), due to being in a vascular watershed region, are prone to healing complications and require more aggressive treatment than other metatarsal fractures, including either strict non-weight bearing with cast immobilization or surgery. An avulsion of the base of the fifth metatarsal, the so-called "pseudo-Jones fracture," can be treated with early weight bearing.

d. Toe fractures. Toe injuries are best treated by "buddy taping" to the adjacent digit and giving the patient a hard-soled shoe for more comfortable ambulation. Distal phalanx fractures with nail-bed injuries or soft-tissue lacerations are treated the same as similar injuries in the fingers (see Section V.C.1.e).

e. Fractures in diabetic feet. Diabetics with peripheral neuropathy and injuries to the foot or ankle require special attention and care. Because of neuropathic changes, casts and splints must be well padded and adapted to any deformity of the foot. Typically, foot and ankle fractures in the diabetic require twice the normal period of immobilization. A hot, swollen foot in a diabetic patient should be examined radiographically for neuropathic fractures (the Charcot foot) and immobilized. This should be differentiated from cellulitis and infection with laboratory tests, although they can occur simultaneously.

2. **Dislocations**
   a. **Talar dislocations**
      (1) **Typical mechanism.** The level of energy is similar to that for calcaneal and talar fractures. Talar dislocation occurs with forced foot inversion.
      (2) **Typical physical signs.** With talar dislocations, there is often significant deformity. Dislocation of the talar body can commonly impinge on adjacent neurovascular structures and can be entrapped by tendons. Neurovascular compromise is possible and must be identified and treated emergently.
      (3) **Radiographic evaluation.** With a talus dislocation, obtain views of both the ankle and the foot. If it is associated with a fracture, perform imaging as noted previously.
      (4) **Typical management.** Talar dislocations are treated with emergent reduction to decrease the risk of avascular necrosis, neurovascular injury, and skin compromise. Soft-tissue interposition can prevent closed reduction, in which case open reduction is required. Associated fractures must be anatomically reduced and stabilized as described previously.
   b. **Lisfranc dislocations**
      (1) **Typical mechanism.** Lisfranc injuries are disruptions of the tarsal–metatarsal joints by either dislocation or fracture dislocation and are caused by a bending or twisting force through the mid-foot.
      (2) **Typical physical signs.** Lisfranc injuries are associated with significant swelling and mid-foot tenderness. Compartment syndrome of the foot may be present.
      (3) **Radiographic evaluation.** Lisfranc fractures are diagnosed radiographically by incongruity of the tarsometatarsal joints, most commonly between the medial base of the second metatarsal and the medial edge of the middle cuneiform, which are normally collinear. A CT scan may be useful if a significant fracture component is present.
      (4) **Typical management.** Lisfranc injuries are splinted, iced, and elevated in preparation for eventual operative reduction and fixation. An attempt at closed reduction should be made to help decrease soft-tissue swelling.

VI. OTHER ORTHOPEDIC CONDITIONS

A. **Orthopedic infections**
   1. **Septic arthritis.** Can occur in otherwise healthy persons, especially in children, but usually occurs in association with immunosuppression,

systemic infection, preexisting joint disease, previous joint surgery, or intravenous (IV) drug abuse. It is of special concern in patients with joint replacements.

a. **Examination** reveals tenderness, effusion, increased warmth, and **pain with passive motion.** Laboratory tests may demonstrate an elevated erythrocyte sedimentation rate (ESR), C-reactive protein (CRP), and/or white blood cell (WBC) count. Diagnosis is confirmed by needle aspiration and laboratory analysis of synovial fluid for cell count and differential, Gram stain, routine aerobic and anaerobic cultures, and crystal analysis. **Baseline radiographs** are obtained at the time of presentation (note that significant changes occur late, after 7 to 10 days).

b. **Treatment** with broad-spectrum IV antibiotics should be initiated **after** adequate joint fluid specimens are obtained. If septic arthritis is diagnosed, some means of joint lavage should be performed (serial aspirations, arthroscopic or open débridement) to prevent progressive cartilage degradation and further systemic illness.

2. **Osteomyelitis.** Childhood osteomyelitis most commonly results from hematogenous spread of bacteria to the metaphysis. Adult osteomyelitis typically occurs from direct inoculation via surgery, an open fracture, or chronic soft-tissue ulceration. Hematogenous spread may occur in cases of IV drug abuse, sickle cell disease, and immunosuppression.

a. **Physical examination** findings are similar to those in septic arthritis, if located about a joint, but may also reveal bony tenderness and drainage. Assess the soft tissues about the region. Examine for infective sources.

b. Appropriate **imaging studies** should always start with plain radiographs of the area. If typical changes are seen on plain x-ray, advanced imaging is usually not required. Of the advanced imaging modalities, MRI is the most useful in detecting occult osteomyelitis. Bone scans and tagged WBC scans are rarely useful unless the patient cannot undergo an MRI (*Semin Ultrasound CT MR.* 2010;31:100–106; *Int J Low Extrem Wounds.* 2010;9:24–30). Laboratory examination includes ESR, CRP, peripheral WBC count, and blood cultures.

c. **Treatment** typically involves 6-week-long course of empiric IV antibiotics (guided by cultures if available). Response to treatment is gauged clinically and with trends in the ESR and CRP. If response is inadequate, bone biopsy can be done to obtain further cultures for sensitivities. Débridement of the infected bone is sometimes required, especially in the presence of intramedullary or subperiosteal abscess. Associated septic arthritis is treated as outlined previously.

3. **Suppurative flexor tenosynovitis.** Patients present with tenderness along the flexor sheath, the finger held in a semiflexed position, and fusiform swelling of the entire finger (**Kanavel signs**). The patient will also have pain with palpation of the tendon in the palm and with wrist extension. Look for associated skin wounds (may appear quite innocuous). Immediate surgical decompression, irrigation, and débridement are indicated.

4. Abscess

    a. Hand. There are numerous potential spaces in the hand that can become infected. Surgical drainage is required, either in the ER or OR, depending on the extent of the abscess.

    b. Olecranon and prepatellar bursa can become infected and present with pain, redness, heat and fluctuance, often with a zone of cellulitis. Treatment is decompression and packing in the ER in addition to a course of oral antibiotics. A significant cellulitis may necessitate a brief course of IV antibiotics.

B. **Compartment syndrome** is characterized by an increase in tissue pressure within a closed osteofascial space sufficient to compromise microcirculation, leading to irreversible damage to tissues within that compartment, including death of muscle and nerves. The end result can be devastating, with a chronically wasted, contracted, paralytic extremity.

    1. Location. Although it occurs most frequently in the anterior, lateral, or posterior compartments of the leg or the volar or dorsal compartments of the forearm, it can also occur about the elbow or in the thigh, hand, or foot.

    2. Causes. Long-bone fracture, crush, or vascular injuries are common risk factors. Increased capillary permeability secondary to postischemic swelling, trauma, or burns may also contribute to compartment syndrome. Muscle hypertrophy, tight dressings, and pneumatic antishock garments (e.g., military antishock trousers) are less common causes.

    3. Examination

        a. On the basis of injury and physical findings, patients at risk for compartment syndrome should be identified early and examined frequently. The **five "P's"** are classically used to aide in diagnosis: The earliest and most important sign is pain out of proportion to the injury, particularly an increasing and disproportionate narcotic demand and unexpectedly poor response to appropriate pain medication, and **pain with passive motion** of involved muscles or tendons traversing the involved compartment. This sign alone is enough to diagnose compartment syndrome, and the patient should not be further observed for the development of any other signs. **Paresthesias** in the distribution of the peripheral nerves traversing the involved compartment occurs at an intermediate time. **Paralysis, pallor, and pulselessness** are late signs and likely indicate irreversible soft-tissue injury. If pulses are altered or absent, major arterial occlusion rather than compartment syndrome should be considered in the diagnosis.

        b. In the awake patient, compartment syndrome **is a clinical diagnosis.** However, when the clinical picture and physical examination are sufficiently uncertain or in the unresponsive patient, **compartment pressures** should be measured. Multiple measurements should be taken in different locations. Comparison to uninvolved compartments may be helpful. For pressures within 30 mm Hg of the diastolic blood pressure with equivocal clinical examination, fasciotomy is in order.

4. **Treatment.** Circumferential bandages, splints, or casts should be removed. Extremities should be elevated to above the level of the heart. Excessive elevation can be counterproductive. If the clinical picture deteriorates or physical examination worsens, then fasciotomy should be performed emergently.

C. **Open fractures and joints.** Lacerations or wounds near fractures or joints can communicate and should be carefully evaluated. If exposed bone is not evident, wounds should be probed to determine whether communication to fracture is present. Joints may be distended with sterile saline to check for extravasation from adjacent wounds, but this method is associated with poor sensitivity, and is not routinely used. Air in the joint on x-ray and fat droplets in blood from the wound also confirm communication with a joint or fracture, respectively.

1. **Treatment.** Assess wounds, remove any obvious gross contamination, apply moist saline or Betadine-soaked dressing, reduce the fracture or joint, and splint the extremity. Administer tetanus prophylaxis and IV antibiotics based on fracture severity. Type I and type II open fractures, defined as having a skin opening less than 1 cm for type I or less than 10 cm without gross contamination or significant bone stripping for type II, require a first-generation cephalosporin, usually cefazolin (Ancef). Vancomycin is used in patients with a penicillin allergy. With type III injuries (skin opening >10 cm, gross contamination, and/or significant soft-tissue stripping from bone), an aminoglycoside, usually gentamicin, should be added.

2. **Gunshot injuries**
   a. It is helpful to identify the **weapon caliber and type.** High-energy injuries (shotgun, rifle, or high-caliber (.357 or .44) handguns) with large associated soft-tissue wounds are treated like open fractures and require antibiotic prophylaxis and operative débridement. With lower energy injuries (most handguns, .22 rifles), antibiotic prophylaxis and débridement are generally not needed because less damage and contamination occur.
   b. **Physical exam.** Neurovascular status should be checked closely and followed. Deficits are usually due to concussive injury and not laceration, but developing deficits are a sign of compartment syndrome. Obtain radiographs to assess for bony involvement. If the wound is near a joint with concern for intra-articular involvement, aspirate to check for hemarthrosis.
   c. **Treatment.** Clean the skin, débride the wound edges, and irrigate thoroughly. Isolated soft-tissue injury is typically treated with local wound care with or without oral antibiotics. If a fracture is found, management of the bony injury is usually the same despite the mechanism.

3. **Traumatic amputation. A team approach is needed** to evaluate for possible reimplantation, and all necessary consultants should be contacted early.
   a. **Management. The proximal stump is cleaned,** and a compressive dressing is applied. Tourniquets are not used. Amputated parts are wrapped in moist gauze, placed in a bag, and cooled by placing on

ice (must avoid freezing damage). The amputated part can be sent to the OR before the patient for preparation. Reimplantation is most likely to be successful with a sharp amputation and not likely possible with crush injuries or other injuries with a wide zone of injury. Timing is of the essence, and a rapid and efficient evaluation is critical. Indication for reimplantation of fingers includes injury in a child, involvement of the thumb, multiple involved digits, and injury distal to the middle phalanx.

VII. PRACTICAL PROCEDURES

A. **Common splints and casts.** Splints and casts stabilize bones and joints and limit further soft-tissue injury and swelling and help to minimize pain. Splints are not circumferential and allow for more swelling than traditional casts but are less durable. Air splints are used only in the emergency setting because they increase pressure in the extremity and can compromise blood flow.

1. **Preparation and application.** Prefabricated splints and immobilizers can be used if available. Plaster splints consist of plaster and cast padding. The required length to include a joint above and below the injury is measured from the uninjured side. Any required reduction maneuvers are performed prior to splint application. Three to four layers of soft roll are applied against the skin, and extra padding is placed over bony prominences. A 10-layer-thick stack of plaster splint material is wetted in cold to lukewarm water and squeezed until damp. Hot water should be avoided because increased water temperature can lead to burns. The splint is applied over the soft-roll padding and wrapped lightly with an elastic bandage. The extremity is held in the appropriate position (any required molding to hold the reduction in place is done without making sharp indentations that can lead to skin breakdown) until the plaster is firm.

2. **Upper-extremity splints.** Removal of all of the patient's jewelry on the affected extremity is mandatory.

   a. **Commercial shoulder immobilizers, Velpeau dressing, and sling and swathe** are used for shoulder dislocations, humerus fractures, and some elbow fractures. A pad is placed in the axilla to prevent skin maceration.

   b. **Posterior and sugar-tong splints** are used in elbow, forearm, and wrist injuries. They are applied with the patient's elbow flexed to less than 90 degrees, the wrist in neutral to slight extension, and forearm in neutral rotation. Posterior splints consist of plaster along the posterior aspect of the arm, with a shorter "A-frame" piece on the lateral aspect across the elbow for added stability. Sugar-tong splints consist of one long strip of plaster that extends from the volar surface of the palm, down the volar forearm, around the posterior elbow, and along the dorsal surface of the forearm to the dorsal surface of the palm.

   c. **Thumb spica, ulnar/radial gutter, and volar/dorsal forearm splints** are used for forearm, hand, and wrist injuries. Finger injuries may be treated with prefabricated aluminum splint material.

For hand injuries, immobilization is performed with the patient's hand and wrist in a so-called **safe position or "intrinsic plus" position:** The wrist in 20 to 30 degrees of extension, the metacarpophalangeal joints in 70 to 80 degrees of flexion, and the interphalangeal joints extended.

3. **Lower extremity splints**
   a. **Thomas/Hare traction splints** are used by primary responders for femur fractures. Traction is applied by an ankle hitch, with counter traction across the ischial tuberosity. These should be replaced with an alternate form of immobilization as quickly as possible, because sloughing of the skin can occur around the ankle and groin.
   b. A **Jones dressing, consisting of bulky cotton padding underneath the plaster layers,** is used in acute knee, ankle, calcaneus, and tibial pilon fractures or any other foot or lower leg injury where a reduction is not needed in the ER and considerable swelling is expected. The injured extremity is wrapped with bulky Jones cotton, and then plaster splints can be applied to the posterior, medial, and lateral aspects as usual.
   c. **Short leg splints** are used in acute leg or foot trauma. They extend from below the knee to the toes and include posterior, medial, and lateral plaster slabs. Posterior slabs alone are inadequate. The ankle should be immobilized in the neutral position, with the foot as dorsiflexed as possible.

B. **Local anesthesia for fracture and joint reduction**
   1. **Digital nerve block.** The digital nerves of the fingers or toes can be blocked by infiltrating 2 to 5 mL of local anesthetic **without epinephrine** into the web spaces adjacent to the injured digit ensuring infiltration to the palmar or plantar skin. Ring blocks are needed for the thumb and great toes and involve circumferential subcutaneous infiltration about the digit.
   2. **Hematoma block** involves direct injection of lidocaine into a fracture site and is especially effective with fractures of the distal radius. Using sterile technique, a 21-gauge needle is inserted into the fracture site through the dorsal forearm. Aspiration of blood confirms the appropriate position of the needle in the fracture site. Approximately 8 to 10 mL of 1% of lidocaine without epinephrine is then infiltrated.
   3. **Intra-articular injection** is used to provide analgesia for reduction of intra-articular fractures and dislocations. Similar needle placement is used for joint aspirations. Under **sterile conditions,** the joint is entered with a needle with verification of placement by aspiration of blood (in the case of fracture) and the easy flow of the anesthetic from the syringe. The **ankle** may be entered anteriorly adjacent to either malleolus, and the **elbow** laterally in the triangle formed by the lateral epicondyle, radial head, and olecranon. Finally, the shoulder is entered either anteriorly 1 cm lateral to the coracoid process or posteriorly 2 cm distal and 2 cm medial to the posterolateral edge of the acromion aiming toward the coracoid.

Urologic Surgery

Samay Jain and Arnold Bullock

The discipline of **urologic surgery** encompasses the diagnosis and treatment of benign and malignant conditions of the genitourinary system including the kidneys, ureters, bladder, urethra, and the male external genitalia.

I. **HEMATURIA,** or blood in the urine, warrants a complete urologic work-up. Gross hematuria is visibly bloody urine, whereas microscopic hematuria is defined as *three or more red blood cells per high-power field* on microscopic evaluation of urinary sediment from two of three properly collected urinalysis (UA) specimens (*Am Fam Physician.* 2001;63:1145–1154).

   A. **Evaluation** consists of laboratory, radiologic, and urine studies.

   1. Urinalysis (macro- and microscopic), urine culture, and urine cytology should be obtained from a *freshly voided* specimen.

   2. A complete blood count, coagulation panel, and serum creatinine should be obtained.

   3. Radiographic imaging should be obtained to evaluate *both the renal parenchyma and the renal collecting system.* Cross-sectional imaging provides the most information with respect to total abdominal and pelvic anatomy. *Computed tomography* (CT) *urogram* is the preferred imaging modality; however, *magnetic resonance (MR) urogram* and *renal ultrasound with retrograde pyelograms* are adequate in appropriately selected patients (i.e., intravenous (IV) dye allergy, pregnancy).

   4. Cystoscopy is the *gold standard* for evaluating the lower urinary tract.

   5. If the etiology of the hematuria remains unclear, the patient should have a repeat UA, urine cytology, and blood pressure measurement at 6, 12, 24, and 36 months (*Urology.* 2001;57:604).

   B. Treatment of symptomatic gross hematuria

   1. Patients in **clot retention** require urologic consultation and bladder drainage with a large-caliber (larger than 22 French) three-way Foley catheter. The catheter should be manually irrigated and aspirated with normal saline or sterile water irrigant until the bladder is clot free. Continuous bladder irrigation (CBI) *should not be initiated* until the bladder is clot free.

   2. **Persistent gross hematuria from a lower urinary tract source (bladder, prostate, urethra)** requires operative management via *cystoscopy and fulguration* of the bleeding source. A *cystogram* is usually performed at the same time to rule out bladder perforation and/or vesicoureteral reflux (VUR).

   3. **Pharmaceutical options for lower tract bleeding**

      a. *Alum 1% and silver nitrate 1%* are astringents that act by protein precipitation over bleeding surfaces. They can be added to the CBI fluid and used to irrigate the bladder, given there is no bladder perforation or VUR.

b. ε-*Aminocaproic acid (Amicar)* is an inhibitor of plasmin that can be administered intravenously, orally, or intravesically with CBI. It is absolutely contraindicated in patients with upper tract bleeding or DIC and can be associated with thromboembolic complications.

4. Persistent hematuria from an upper urinary tract source (kidney, ureter) is usually from a hemorrhagic renal mass, angiomyolipoma, arterial–venous fistula or renal trauma. These patients require intervention by either urology or interventional radiology. Upper tract bleeding may need to be managed by angioembolization of the source of bleeding.

II. DISEASES OF THE KIDNEY

A. Renal masses can be categorized as cystic or solid masses.

1. Renal cysts occur in approximately 50% of persons older than 50 years and the vast majority are benign. Renal cysts can be diagnosed and evaluated with CT, MRI, or ultrasound. Cysts are graded according the *Bosniak* grading system which attempts to predict their malignant potential based on various radiographic criteria (*Urology.* 2005;66(3):484–488).

a. Bosniak I describes a benign simple cyst with a hairline thin wall that does not contain septa, calcifications, or solid components. Category I cysts have no risk of malignancy and do not require further imaging or follow-up.

b. Bosniak II includes cysts that contain a few hairline septa or minor wall calcification. Uniformly high attenuation lesions (high-density cysts) that do not enhance on contrast imaging are included in this group. Category II cysts have no risk of malignancy and do not require further imaging or follow-up.

c. Bosniak IIF is a subgroup of cysts that contain multiple *nonenhancing* hairline septa sometimes with nodular or thick calcifications. Approximately 5% to 20% of these lesions may be malignant, which can be determined by serial imaging.

d. Bosniak III describes indeterminate lesions with numerous, thick or irregular septa, in which measurable enhancement is present. Category III cysts have more than a 50% malignant potential and require surgical management.

e. Bosniak IV type cysts are clearly malignant and have all the features of Category III cysts in addition to soft-tissue components. Category IV cysts have more than a 90% malignancy potential and mandate surgical management.

2. Solid renal masses should be considered malignant until proven otherwise. The majority of renal masses are discovered incidentally. Approximately 13% to 27% of abdominal imaging will reveal a renal mass (*N Engl J Med.* 2010;362:624–634). The historical triad of flank pain, hematuria, and flank mass occurs less than 10% of the time. Most solid masses are **renal cell carcinoma** (85% to 90%); transitional cell cancer, oncocytoma (benign in most cases), sarcoma, lymphoma, and various metastatic tumors (lung, breast, gastrointestinal, prostate, pancreas, and melanoma) can also present as a renal mass.

   a. Evaluation of a renal mass requires radiographic characterization and assessment for metastatic disease.

      (1) CT scan and MRI are ideal studies to assess renal masses. All patients with a solid renal mass must have a noncontrast study followed by a contrast study to **assess for enhancement.** In patients with contraindications to IV contrast or gadolinium, ultrasonography can determine whether a mass is cystic or solid; Doppler ultrasonography is useful for evaluating the renal vein and vena cava.

      (2) Chest radiography is required to rule out metastasis. Bone scan is indicated in patients with an abnormal alkaline phosphates or bone-related complaints with known renal mass.

   b. The role of percutaneous **renal mass biopsy** has expanded in recent times with diagnostic accuracy approaching greater than 90% while maintaining a low complication rate (<5%) (*J Urol.* 2008;179(1):20–27).

   c. Staging of renal masses is described in **Table 35-1.**

  3. Paraneoplastic syndromes occur in 10% to 40% of renal cell carcinomas.

   a. Renin overproduction can present as hypertension.

   b. *Stauffer syndrome* is nonmetastatic hepatic dysfunction which resolves after tumor removal.

   c. Hypercalcemia is frequently caused by the production of parathyroid hormone–like protein (PTHrP) produced by the tumor.

   d. Erythrocytosis can result secondary to production of erythropoietin by the tumor.

B. Management of renal masses

  1. Benign cystic renal lesions require no intervention (see Section II.A.1).

  2. The management of solid renal masses depends on the tumor stage (*Eur Urol.* 2010;58:398–406).

   a. T1 lesions. Nephron-sparing surgery via partial nephrectomy.

   b. T2 lesions. Nephron-sparing surgery is preferred whenever possible; otherwise, radical nephrectomy is considered the standard of care.

   c. T3 and T4 lesions mandate radical nephrectomy.

  3. Metastatic renal cell carcinoma is resistant to radiation and chemotherapy. Targeted therapy with agents such as bevacizumab, sorafenib, and sunitinib as well as immunotherapy with interleukin-2 and IFN-α has shown survival benefit in select patients (*BMC Cancer.* 2009;9:34).

III. DISEASES OF T HE URETER

A. Ureteropelvic junction obstruction (UPJO)

  1. UPJO is often a **congenital anomaly** that results from a stenotic segment of ureter. Acquired lesions may include tortuous or kinked ureters as a result of VUR, benign tumors such as fibroepithelial polyps,

TABLE 35-1	AJCC 2010 TNM Staging for Renal Cell Carcinoma

Primary Tumor (T)

Tx	Primary tumor cannot be assessed
T0	No evidence of primary tumor
T1	Tumor 7 cm or less in greatest dimension, limited to kidney
T1a	Tumor 4 cm or less in greatest dimension, limited to kidney
T1b	Tumor greater than 4 cm but not larger than 7 cm and limited to kidney
T2	Tumor greater than 7 cm in greatest dimension and limited to kidney
T2a	Tumor greater than 7 cm but less than 10 cm and limited to kidney
T2b	Tumor greater than 10 cm and limited to kidney
T3	Tumor extends into the major veins or perinephric tissues but not into the ipsilateral adrenal or beyond Gerota fascia
T3a	Tumor grossly extends into the renal vein or its segmental branches or tumor invades perirenal and/or renal sinus fat but not beyond Gerota fascia
T3b	Tumor grossly extends into the vena cava below the diaphragm
T3c	Tumor grossly extends into the vena cava above the diaphragm or invades the wall of the IVC
T4	Tumor invades beyond Gerota fascia

Regional Lymph Nodes—Clinical Stage (N)

Nx	Regional lymph nodes cannot be assessed
N0	No regional lymph node metastasis
N1	Metastasis in regional node(s)

Distant Metastasis (M)

M0	No distant metastasis
M1	Distant metastasis

or scarring as a result of stone disease, ischemia, or previous surgical manipulation of the urinary system. The role of crossing vessels (present in one third of cases) has not been firmly established, although their presence may be associated with treatment failures.

2. **Presentation.** Although UPJO can be a congenital problem, patients may present at any age. Common symptoms are flank pain (which may be intermittent), hematuria, infection, and, rarely, hypertension.

3. **Radiographic studies** help to determine the **site** and **functional significance** of the obstruction. Diuretic renal scintigraphy is both a functional and anatomic study that can diagnose obstruction and give the relative functions of both kidneys. Ultrasound and retrograde pyelography may demonstrate hydronephrosis, but neither is diagnostic of functional obstruction.

4. **Treatment** (*Curr Urol Rep.* 2010;11:74–79)

   a. Observation is recommended for poor surgical candidates or patients who are completely asymptomatic with a known nonfunctioning kidney.

b. Endopyelotomy is a minimally invasive procedure where the obstructed ureter is incised via a ureteral catheter through a cystoscope; however, success rates are lower than pyeloplasty (53% to 94%).

c. Pyeloplasty is the gold standard for treatment which allows for concurrent removal of ureteral stones, if present. Although more invasive than endopyelotomy, success rates for pyeloplasty are consistently higher, with most series reporting success rates more than 90%. The trend for repair has shifted from open to laparoscopic and robotic-assisted with success rates being similar, but with less morbidity with respect to pain control and days of hospitalization.

B. Urolithiasis

1. Urolithiasis frequently presents as the acute onset of severe, intermittent flank pain often associated with nausea and vomiting. Although patients may present with microscopic or gross hematuria, 15% of patients may have no hematuria. Stone formation commonly occurs between the third and fifth decade and tend to have a male predominance.

2. Risk factors for stone formation are both environmental and patient-related. Relative hydration and diets that contain high animal protein or oxalate promote stone formation. Various medications including high doses of vitamins C and D, acetazolamide, triamterene, and indinavir (*Lancet.* 1997;349:1294) favor stone formation. Disease states including inflammatory bowel disease, type I renal tubular acidosis (RTA) or cystinuria, and hyperparathyroidism can increase patient risk for stones.

3. Types of calculi

   a. Calcium stones are radiopaque, make up the majority of all stones, and form in a wide range of pH. Risk factors for forming calcium-based stones include increased intestinal absorption, increased renal excretion, hyperparathyroidism, sarcoidosis, immobilization (causing calcium resorption from bone), and type I RTA.

   b. Uric acid stones (10% of stones) are radiolucent and form in acidic pH (<6.0); they can be associated with gout or Lesch–Nyhan disease.

   c. Cysteine stones (4% of stones) are radiopaque and form in acidic pH (<6.0). Risk factors include defective tubular resorption of cysteine that is inherited in an autosomal recessive manner.

   d. Magnesium ammonium phosphate or **struvite stones** (15% of stones) are radiopaque, form in alkaline urine, and are associated with urea-splitting organisms.

4. Evaluation of urolithiasis

   a. UA and urine culture should be performed.

   b. Serum electrolytes (including calcium and creatinine levels), uric acid, and parathyroid hormone levels are part of the standard work-up.

   c. Noncontrast CT scan has replaced IVP as the diagnostic study of choice in the acute setting to evaluate for stones (*Eur Radiol.* 2002;12(1):256–257).

    d. KUB (kidneys, ureters, bladder) is useful to monitor for stone passage of radiopaque stones and to assess whether the stone is amenable for extracorporeal shock

5. The clinician should determine if the patient's urolithiasis is most appropriately managed as an outpatient, inpatient, or with surgery. Patients with intractable pain, nausea, or emesis not adequately controlled by oral medication require **hospital admission** for hydration and analgesia. **Surgical intervention** is indicated in patients with as above findings but also including infection or signs of sepsis, obstructed solitary kidney, bilateral obstruction, large stone size, or azotemia.

    a. Medical expulsive therapy. Approximately 70% of stones smaller than 5 mm will pass spontaneously. Spontaneous stone passage can be aided with prescription of narcotic pain medication as well as daily alpha blocker therapy (tamsulosin) which has been shown to improve stone passage rates by up to 20%. Urine should be strained with each void and radio opaque stones can be tracked with KUB (*J Urol.* 1997;178:2418–2434).

    b. Surgical treatment. In the acute setting, patients meeting surgical criteria can be managed by ureteral stenting or percutaneous nephrostomy tube placement. With a negative urine culture and lack of stone progression, surgical options include extracorporeal shockwave lithotripsy, ureteroscopic stone extraction, and percutaneous nephrolithotomy.

IV. DISEASES OF THE URINARY BLADDER

  A. Acute bacterial cystitis is a common urologic problem which can present with suprapubic pain, dysuria, hesitancy, and frequency. Risk factors included recent bladder instrumentation, postmenopausal state, urinary retention, fistulae from GI tract, and female gender. Evaluation of patients requires **urine culture** with sensitivities. Males with a recurrent urinary tract infection (UTI) should have upper tract imaging (renal US), measurement of posturinary residual, and cystoscopy. Uncomplicated UTI (young women with no previous history of instrumentation and normal anatomy) should receive 3 days of empiric/culture-specific antibiotic treatment. Complicated UTI (male, previous manipulation, or abnormal anatomy) should receive 7 days of culture specific antibiotics and management of any underlying problem.

  B. Bladder cancer. Bladder cancer is found in up to 10% of patients with microscopic hematuria.

    1. Urothelial cell carcinoma (UCC) accounts for more than 90% of bladder tumors in the United States; squamous cell carcinoma and adenocarcinoma are less common. UCC has been linked to smoking, aniline dye, aromatic amine exposure, chronic phenacetin use, chronic indwelling Foley, chronic parasitic infection (*Schistosoma haematobium*), cyclophosphamide, radiation exposure.

    2. UCC is categorized as superficial or invasive. Staging is outlined in Table 35-2. Evaluation for UCC requires cystoscopy, voided urine

TABLE 35-2	AJCC 2010 TNM Staging for Urothelial Cell Carcinoma

Primary Tumor (T)

Tx	Primary tumor cannot be assessed
T0	No evidence of primary tumor
Ta	Noninvasive papillary carcinoma
Tis	Carcinoma *in situ;* "Flat Tumor"
T1	Tumor invades the subepithelial connective tissue
T2	Tumor invades the muscularis propria
pT2a	Tumor invades superficial muscularis propria
pT2b	Tumor invades deep muscularis propria
T3	Tumor invades perivesical tissue
pT3a	Microscopic invasion
pT3b	Macroscopic invasion
T4	Tumor invades any of the following: prostatic stroma, seminal vesicles, uterus, vagina, pelvic/abdominal wall

Regional Lymph Nodes—Clinical Stage (N)

Nx	Regional lymph nodes cannot be assessed
N0	No regional lymph node metastasis
N1	Single regional lymph node in the true pelvis
N2	Multiple regional lymph nodes in the true pelvis
N3	Lymph node metastasis to the common iliac lymph nodes

Distant Metastasis (M)

M0	No distant metastasis
M1	Distant metastasis

cytology, upper tract imaging via CT/MR urogram, or ultrasound with retrograde pyelography to rule out concurrent upper tract disease, although this is rare (1.8%; *Eur Urol.* 2008;54:303–331).

a. **Superficial tumors** (stages Tis, Ta, T1) are exophytic papillary lesions that do not invade the muscular bladder wall. These tumors can be treated and staged with transurethral resection (TUR). Instillation of mitomycin C within 24 hours of TUR has been shown to decrease recurrence by 12% (*Eur Urol.* 2008;54:303–314). Between 65% and 85% of superficial tumors recur; therefore, diligent follow-up is necessary. Recurrent tumors are treated with TUR and intravesical therapy (bacillus Calmette–Guérin or mitomycin C).

b. **Muscle-invasive UCC** (stage ≥T2) is treated with radical cystectomy and urinary diversion. Radical cystectomy involves radical cystoprostatectomy (removal of bladder, prostate, and possibly urethra) in the male and anterior exenteration (removal of bladder, urethra, uterus, cervix, and anterior wall of vagina) in the female. Appropriate metastatic evaluation for patients with invasive bladder cancer includes chest radiograph, CT urogram, bone scan, and liver function tests. Despite this aggressive management, only 50% of patients with invasive bladder cancer are rendered completely free of tumor because many have occult metastases at the time of surgery.

c. **Chemotherapy** is the treatment of choice for locally advanced or metastatic bladder cancer. Both neoadjuvant and adjuvant chemotherapy have been shown to benefit patients with advanced UCC ($\geq$T2) who also undergo surgery (*New Engl J Med.* 2003;349,9: 859–866; *Eur Urol.* 2009;55,2:348–358).

V. DISEASES OF THE PROSTATE

A. **Prostate cancer** is the most common noncutaneous malignancy in American men and the second leading cause of cancer death. Twenty percent of men with prostate cancer die of the disease. Prostate cancer rarely causes symptoms until it becomes locally advanced or metastatic. Risk factors for prostate cancer include being African American, advanced age, and family history (Table 35-3).

TABLE 35-3	AJCC 2010 TNM Staging for Prostate Carcinoma
Primary Tumor (T)	
Tx	Primary tumor cannot be assessed
T0	No evidence of primary tumor
T1	Clinically inapparent tumor neither palpable nor visible by imaging
T1a	Tumor incidental histologic finding in 5% or less of tissue resected
T1b	Tumor incidental histologic finding in more than 5% of tissue resected
T1c	Tumor identified by needle biopsy via screening (PSA, DRE)
T2	Tumor confined to the prostate
T2a	Tumor involves one-half of one lobe or less
T2b	Tumor involves more than one-half of one lobe, but not both lobes
T2c	Tumor involves both lobes
T3	Tumor extends through the prostatic capsule
T3a	Extracapsular extension
T3b	Seminal vesicle invasion
T4	Tumor is fixed or invades adjacent structures other than the SVs, such as external sphincter, rectum, bladder, levator muscles, and/or pelvic wall
Regional Lymph Nodes—Clinical Stage (N)	
Nx	Regional lymph nodes cannot be assessed
N0	No regional lymph node metastasis
N1	Metastasis in regional node(s)
Distant Metastasis (M)	
M0	No distant metastasis
M1	Distant metastasis
M1a	Nonregional lymph node(s)
M1b	Bone(s)
M1c	Other site(s) with or without bone disease

Modified from Prostate. In: Edge SE, Byrd DR, Carducci MA, et al., eds. *AJCC Cancer Staging Manual.* 7th ed. New York, NY: Springer; 2010:525–538.

1. Screening for prostate cancer includes digital rectal examination (DRE) and measurement of serum prostate-specific antigen (PSA).

   a. **Digital rectal exam.** DRE and PSA provide a better sensitivity for screening than either alone; therefore, DRE is an essential aspect of screening for prostate cancer (*J Urol.* 1994;151(5):1308–1309; *Nat Clin Pract Urol.* 2009;6(2):68–69). The normal prostate measures 3.5 cm wide at the base, 2.5 cm long, and 2.5 cm deep; it weighs approximately 20 g. The prostate should feel smooth and have the consistency of the contracted thenar eminence of the thumb.

   b. **PSA screening** remains controversial based on contradictory conclusions from two large, prospective randomized trials (*N Engl J Med.* 2009;360:1310–1319, 1320–1328). Current AUA guidelines recommend initial PSA screening at 40 years of age and then yearly screening at 50 years of age. Abnormal PSA results require detailed discussion with a urologist to determine the next best step in patient care (American Urological Association Clinical Guidelines 2008).

   c. Abnormalities in either the DRE (manifest as indurated nodules) or the PSA greater than 2.5 ng/mL should be evaluated by **trans-rectal ultrasound and needle biopsy of the prostate** (*National Comprehensive Cancer Network Clinical Practice Guidelines in Oncology* 2006, http://www.nccn.org).

2. Prostate cancer is diagnosed and graded by the **Gleason scoring system** (*J Urol.* 2010;183(2):433–440) This grading system relies on the overall architecture of the biopsy core and assigns a grade from 2 to 5 of the two most prominent architectural patterns to give a sum of 5 to 6 (low-grade disease), 7 (intermediate grade), or 8 to 10 (high grade).

3. Staging of prostate cancer is selectively completed.

   a. **Bone scan** should be obtained for patients with a life expectancy greater than 5 years and a PSA ≥20 ng/mL or Gleason 8 disease or T3-T4 disease or having symptomatic bone complaints.

   b. **CT/MRI of the abdomen and pelvis** should be obtained in patients with T3-T4 disease or if patients have a ≥20% probability of lymph node involvement based on current prostate cancer nomograms.

4. **Treatment options** for men with organ-confined prostate cancer include active surveillance (AS), radical prostatectomy (RP), and radiation therapy (RT, either external-beam or interstitial). These are stratified based on the aggressiveness of the cancer and the patient's life expectancy (NCCN Clinical Proactive Guidelines in Oncology, V.3.2010, www.nccn.org).

   a. **Very low risk** is classified as t1c, Gleason ≤6, PSA less than 6, fewer than three biopsy cores positive, ≤50% cancer in each core, PSA density less than 0.15 ng/mL/g.

   b. **Low risk** is classified as T1-T2, Gleason ≤6, PSA less than 10.

   c. **Intermediate risk** is classified t2b-T2c or Gleason 7 or PSA 10 to 20.

   d. **High risk** is classified as T3a or Gleason 8 to 10 or PSA more than 20.

    e. Treatment of **locally advanced disease** (t3b-T4) is tailored to the patient based on various factors and may consist of RT, RP, or androgen deprivation therapy.

    f. **Metastatic disease** is treated with androgen deprivation therapy.

Life Expectancy	Risk			
	Very Low	**Low**	**Intermediate**	**High**
<10 years	AS	AS	AS, RT, RP	RT, RP
≥10 years		AS, RT, RP	RT, RP	

5. **Prostatitis** is a diagnosis that spans a spectrum of disease entities. The classification and diagnostic criteria for the different forms of prostatitis recently have been changed in an effort to standardize diagnosis to improve research and clinical treatment. Prostatitis encompasses four clinical entities (*Am Fam Physician.* 2010;82(4):397–406).

    a. **Acute bacterial prostatitis (ABP)** presents with **signs and symptoms of urinary tract infection;** many patients have significant voiding complaints, fevers, and malaise. ABP requires prompt treatment with antibiotics. Urine should be cultured prior to initiating treatment. Most common organisms are *Escherichia coli, Klebsiella, Proteus* and *Pseudomonas,* and occasionally *Enterococcus.* Prostate exam will reveal tender, boggy enlarged prostate. Prostatic massage should not be performed as this could be potentially harmful. Empiric treatment should be started at the time of diagnosis and tailored to culture specific therapy when appropriate. Mildly to moderately ill-appearing patients are treated with a 6-week course of sulfamethoxazole (Bactrim) or ciprofloxacin. Severely ill-appearing or septic patients require hospital admission for IV antibiotics (ampicillin and gentamicin) until afebrile, before transitioning to oral medications listed above. If a patient does not improve on the prescribed antibiotic regimen, imaging of the prostate should be obtained by either a CT scan or transrectal ultrasound to rule out abscess.

    b. **Chronic bacterial prostatitis** is differentiated from other categories by the documented recurrent bacterial infection of expressed prostatic secretions, postprostatic massage urine, or semen. Treatment is with 4 to 6 weeks of antibiotics; fluoroquinolones have excellent prostatic penetration.

    c. **Chronic pelvic pain syndrome** is diagnosed in patients with continued pelvic pain but with no bacteria infection isolated from expressed prostatic secretions.

    d. **Asymptomatic prostatitis** is an incidental finding and usually does not require treatment.

B. **Benign prostatic hyperplasia (BPH)** is a histologic diagnosis and represents an increase in several epithelial and stromal elements of the prostate.

Men with BPH and benign prostatic enlargement on examination do not necessarily have lower urinary tract symptoms (LUTS).

1. **Evaluation.** Common signs and symptoms of BPH include hesitancy, decreased force of stream, frequency, urgency, postvoid dribbling, double voiding, incomplete bladder emptying, and nocturia. LUTS is a symptom complex of obstructive and irritative voiding problems. Bladder outlet obstruction is objective evidence of obstructive voiding problems and can include a demonstrated decrease in maximum urinary flow rate, increase postvoid residual urine, and cystoscopic findings of obstruction (American Urological Association Clinical Guidelines 2003).

2. Treatment
   a. **Watchful waiting** is best suited for patients without bothersome symptoms.
   b. **Medical therapy.** Men with **LUTS without BPH** are best treated by long-acting selective alpha blocker (tamsulosin, terazosin, doxazosin, alfuzosin). In patients with **LUTS and BPH,** the standard of care is combination therapy with an alpha blocker (i.e., tamsulosin) and a 5α reductase inhibitor (i.e., dutasteride or finasteride) based on the results of two large, prospective, randomized trials in which the risk of overall clinical progression of LUTS was lower with combination therapy than treatment with either drug alone (*N Engl J Med.* 2003;349:2387, *Eur Urol.* 2010;571):123–131).
   c. **Surgical therapy** is indicated in patients who have failed medical therapy or have severe symptoms of LUTS (complete urinary retention, bladder stones, persistent UTI, gross hematuria, renal failure). The gold standard is transurethral resection of the prostate, but transurethral laser ablation/vaporization offers similar functional results with less morbidity (*Eur Urol.* 2010;58(3):349–355).

VI. **URINARY RETENTION** may result from BPH, prostate cancer, or urethral stricture disease. Retention also can be associated with pelvic trauma, neurologic conditions, or various medications or the postoperative setting.

A. **Evaluation.** A history usually elicits the cause of retention. Patients with BPH who are treated with decongestants containing an α-agonist may develop urinary retention from increased smooth-muscle tone at the bladder neck and the prostate.

B. **Physical examination** reveals a distended lower abdomen. Prostatic enlargement is common on DRE. Serum electrolytes including creatinine level, UA, and urine culture should be obtained. Serum PSA concentration obtained during acute urinary retention often is spuriously elevated and is best measured at least 4 to 6 weeks after the acute event.

C. Treatment

   1. **Bladder decompression with a Foley catheter is the mainstay of treatment.** The proper technique of urethral catheter placement involves passing the catheter to the hub and inflating the balloon *only* after the return of urine.

2. **When a standard Foley catheter cannot be passed easily,** sterile 2% viscous lidocaine can be injected through the urethra. This anesthetizes and relaxes the sphincter, allowing gentle passage of a 16- to 22-French Coudé tip catheter. The catheter is passed gently with the tip directed upward. If the Coudé tip catheter does not pass easily, a urology consultation is required.

3. **Catheterization should not be attempted when a urethral injury is suspected.** Urethral stricture requires calibration and dilation or placement of a suprapubic tube by a urologist. Urinary clot retention usually requires bladder irrigation.

4. **Patients should be monitored for postobstructive diuresis, especially if the patient is azotemic.** This is a self-limited, physiologic response to a hypervolemic state. Occasionally, it can become a pathologic diuresis and may warrant hospital observation, with fluid and electrolyte replacement. Five-percent dextrose in 0.45% saline should be used for hydration. Urine output greater than 200 mL/hour for more than 2 hours should be replaced with 0.5 mL of IV 0.45% saline for each 1 mL of urine. Electrolytes should be checked every 6 hours initially and replaced as needed.

VII. DISEASES OF THE PENIS

A. **Priapism** is a persistent penile erection that continues hours beyond, or is unrelated to, sexual stimulation and typically only affects the corpora cavernosa. Priapism can be classified as nonischemic or ischemic.

1. **Non ischemic priapism** is a nonsexual erection caused by unregulated cavernous arterial flow usually brought about by perineal or genital trauma. A traumatic pudendal arterial fistula or cavernosal artery laceration may give rise to a high-flow state. Diagnosis is confirmed ultrasound demonstrating increased flow or by aspiration of bright-red, well-oxygenated blood. Blood gas analysis can be helpful in differentiating low-flow priapism from high-flow priapism. Treatment of nonischemic priapism *is not an emergency* as 60% of cases will resolve with observation. Selective arterial embolization of the ipsilateral branch of the pudendal artery embolization can be attempted after outpatient discussion of risks of the procedure [i.e., erectile dysfunction (ED)]. Surgical ligation of abnormal vessel(s) is reserved as a last resort as complications, such as ED, are higher with this approach.

2. **Ischemic priapism** is a nonsexual, persistent erection characterized by little or no cavernous blood flow. This is a **urologic emergency.** Symptoms include pain and tenderness. History should elicit various etiologies of priapism including: (i) Hematologic abnormalities, such as **sickle cell disease;** (ii) **drugs,** including antihypertensives (hydralazine, guanethidine, prazosin), anticoagulants, antidepressants, and psychotropic agents (especially trazodone), alcohol, marijuana, cocaine, and intracavernous injection of vasoactive substances (prostaglandin E_1, phentolamine, papaverine) used to treat ED; and (iii) **neoplasm (especially leukemia),** with venous occlusion, stasis, and emboli.

Physical examination reveals firm corpora and a flaccid glans. Stasis, thrombosis, fibrosis, and scarring of the corpora cavernosa eventually can result in ED if priapism is not treated promptly. Of note, phosphodiesterase type 5 (PDE5) inhibitors, which are used for the treatment of ED (see Section VII.B.4), are rarely associated with ischemic priapism.

  a. Treatment (American Urological Association Clinical Guidelines 2008)

    (1) First-line treatment involves corporal irrigation and aspiration of old blood from the corpora via a large bore needle (larger than 21 G).

    (2) Intracorporal injection of an α-**adrenergic agent** (phenylephrine, 250 to 500 μg/mL) is a useful adjunct to corporal irrigation. Doses should be administered every 2 to 5 minutes until detumescence is achieved. Patients should be monitored for hypertension and reflex bradycardia.

    (3) For patients with sickle cell disease, treatment involves aggressive hydration, supplemental oxygen, and blood transfusion if the hematocrit is low.

    (4) Surgical shunting should be considered only if multiple attempts at aspiration/irrigation and injection of a-adrenergic agents fail. Distal corpus cavernosum-to-glans penis (corpus spongiosum) shunting (**Winter or Al-Ghorab shunt**) is the initial surgical treatment. If distal shunting fails, then a more proximal **side-to-side cavernosospongiosal shunt (Quackel shunt) or cavernosaphenous shunt** may be necessary. Insertion of a malleable, temporary penile prosthesis can be used in cases where shunting has failed. The aim is to prevent corporal fibrosis to allow for elective revision of the prosthesis at a later date.

B. Erectile dysfunction is the inability to achieve or maintain an erection sufficient for satisfactory sexual performance. ED affects 52% of men aged 40 to 70 years according to the Massachusetts Male Aging Study; incidence increases with age, but the degree of mild ED remains fairly constant from age 40 to 70 years. Unfortunately, only 20% of men with ED discuss this condition with a health care provider. The overwhelming majority of men have an organic etiology of their ED.

  1. Initial evaluation entails a frank discussion of the complaint to define the true sexual disorder; one must differentiate ED from premature ejaculation, inability to climax, infertility, and loss of libido. Unlike men with organic ED, those with psychogenic ED have sudden onset and continue to have nocturnal erections. Loss of libido may signal hormonal disturbances. A complete history and physical examination is done to elicit possible underlying causes of ED, including heart disease, hypertension, diabetes, dyslipidemia, renal insufficiency, and endocrine disease (hypogonadism). Smokers have a twofold higher incidence of ED. Previous pelvic or penile surgery may be associated with ED.

2. **Attention should be paid to medications,** such as antihypertensives [central-acting agents (clonidine), α-adrenergic blocking agents (prazosin), β-blocking agents], antipsychotics, tricyclic antidepressants, and histamine (H_2) blockers, which may be associated with ED. Heavy use of alcohol and social drugs can also lead to ED.

3. **Physical examination** should focus on genital development and signs of endocrinologic or neurologic abnormalities.

   Appropriate laboratory testing includes serum chemistries, creatinine, CBC, UA, and a morning testosterone level. If the testosterone is abnormal, prolactin, FSH, and LH are obtained.

4. **Treatment.** The initial recommendation should be for lifestyle modification and management of the underlying disease. Smoking cessation, diet modification, and exercise have all been shown to improve erectile function and overall health. It is appropriate to counsel patients about available nonsurgical and surgical options for treatment and to encourage treatment until a satisfactory solution is found (AUA Clinical Guidelines 2009).

   a. **PDE-5 inhibitors (i.e., sildenafil)** are considered first-line therapy. PDE5 inhibitors inhibit the breakdown of cyclic guanosine monophosphate, allowing smooth-muscle relaxation in the corpus cavernosum. Side effects include headache, facial flushing, and dyspepsia. PDE5 inhibitors are contraindicated in patients who are taking nitrates because of a synergistic effect that results in hypotension. All are metabolized by the liver, so doses should be adjusted accordingly in liver failure patients.

   b. **Intracavernosal therapy.** Injection of vasoactive medications, such as alprostadil (prostaglandin E_1), directly into the corpus cavernosum is effective in 70% to 80% of patients. Side effects are pain with injection, hematoma or ecchymosis, and priapism. An **intraurethral alprostadil (MUSE)** suppository is also available and is effective in some men.

   c. **Vacuum erection device (VED).** For men who fail or are not candidates for medical therapy, a vacuum pump is efficacious, but many couples find it cumbersome and uncomfortable. Patients with difficulty in maintaining an erection due to cavernosal venous insufficiency may benefit from a constriction band.

   d. **Surgical options.** For patients who are refractory to noninvasive therapy, consideration may be given to a surgically placed penile implant. These devices have a high degree of success, and they are placed via small genital incisions. There are potential complications, such as infection (2%) and mechanical malfunction (2%).

VIII. DISEASES OF THE SCROTUM AND TESTICLES

Acute scrotal pathology can result in significant morbidity, testicular loss, and infertility. The diagnosis can be difficult to make and may require scrotal exploration.

A. **Testicular torsion** is the rotation of the testicle on its vascular pedicle that results in ischemia. This is a true urologic emergency which develops most often in the peripubertal (12 to 18 years old) age group, although it can occur at any age.

1. The **clinical picture** is one of acute onset of testicular pain and swelling, commonly associated with nausea and vomiting. Some patients give a history of a prior episode that spontaneously resolved (intermittent torsion). There usually is no history of voiding complaints, dysuria, fever, or exposure to sexually transmitted diseases. Risk factors include cryptorchidism (undescended testis) and "bell clapper" anatomy of the testicle, although this cannot be determined outside of scrotal exploration.

2. **Physical examination** reveals an extremely tender, swollen testicle high riding in the scrotum with a transverse lie. The cremasteric reflex (elicited by stroking the inner thigh) is absent on the affected side. In contrast to epididymitis, elevation of the scrotum does not provide relief of pain (Prehn sign) in torsion. Normal UA and the absence of leukocytosis help to rule out epididymitis. Testicular torsion is a clinical diagnosis, and, if enough suspicions exist, the patient needs to be explored without delay.

   a. **History.** Acute onset of testicular pain and swelling often associated with visceral complaints of abdominal pain and nausea and vomiting. LUTS and trauma are typically absent.

3. Testicular torsion is a **clinical diagnosis** and treatment should not be delayed to obtain imaging. However, if clinical diagnosis is equivocal or suspicion is low, color Doppler ultrasound can help to confirm or exclude the diagnosis with reported sensitivity and specificity greater than 95% (*Urology*. 2010;75(5):1170–1174).

4. **Treatment.** If testicular torsion is suspected based on history and physical exam, the patient should be taken for immediate scrotal exploration and bilateral orchiopexy. Manual detorsion of the testicle may be attempted in the emergency room, but bilateral orchiopexy is still indicated.

B. **Torsion of testicular appendage (appendix testis)** presents with symptoms similar to those of torsion of the testicle, usually in a prepubertal boy. The onset commonly is over 12 to 24 hours. Extreme tenderness over a palpable, nodular appendage, usually on the superior aspect of the testicle is frequently present. The "blue dot" sign may be present when the ischemic appendage can be seen through the scrotal skin (*Urology*. 1973;1(1):63–66). The testicle has a normal position, lies, and is freely mobile. The spermatic cord is nontender and there is usually a cremasteric reflex present. Similar to testicular torsion, torsion of an appendix testis is a clinical diagnosis. Imaging can be obtained if the clinical picture is unclear or for documentation. Unlike true testicular torsion, this is not an emergency. Treatment is **expectant** with anti-inflammatory agents; light physical activity and scrotal support can manage the symptoms until resolution over 7 to 14 days.

C. **Epididymitis** usually presents with a 1- to 2-day onset of unilateral testicular pain and swelling sometimes associated with dysuria, urethral discharge, or LUTS.

1. Typically, the **findings** include a painful, indurated epididymis, and pyuria. Urinalysis, urine culture, and CBC count are obtained. When clinically indicated, urethral swabs for gonococci and chlamydiae are sent for culture.

2. With **appropriate antibiotic coverage,** these patients can be managed as outpatients. Treatment is empiric with an oral fluoroquinolone for 3 to 4 weeks; antibiotics should be tailored based on culture results. Appropriate antibiotic therapy should be instituted for any diagnosed sexually transmitted disease. Nonsteroidal analgesics and scrotal elevation can reduce inflammation and provide symptomatic relief.

3. Moderate-to-severe cases of epididymitis may require hospital admission. Symptoms usually have been present for several days. Fever and leukocytosis are present. Broad-spectrum antibiotics and supportive measures of bed rest with scrotal elevation should be instituted. Ultrasonography can be useful to rule out abscess formation and assess testicular perfusion.

D. **Fournier gangrene** is a severe polymicrobial soft-tissue infection involving the genitals and perineum. Although the term *Fournier gangrene* usually is applied to men, necrotizing fasciitis of this area can occur in women. Prompt diagnosis and institution of treatment may be lifesaving. Roughly 19% of the patients have a genitourinary source (urethral stone, urethral stricture, and urethral fistulae), 21% have an colorectal source (ruptured appendicitis, colonic carcinoma, diverticulitis, perirectal abscesses, and/or fistulae), 24% have a dermatologic source, and nearly 36% have an unidentified source (*Br J Surg.* 2000;87:718). Diabetic, alcoholic, and other immunocompromised patients appear to be more susceptible. The clinical course is one of abrupt onset with pruritus, rapidly progressing to edema, erythema, and necrosis, often within a few hours. Fever, chills, and malaise are accompanying signs.

1. **Physical examination** reveals edema and erythema of the skin of the scrotum, phallus, and perineal area. This may progress rapidly to frank necrosis of the skin and subcutaneous tissues, with extension to the skin of the abdomen and back, reaching as high as the clavicles and down the thighs. Crepitus in the tissues suggests the presence of gas-forming organisms.

2. **Laboratory evaluation** should include a CBC, serum electrolytes, creatinine, arterial blood gas, coagulation parameters, UA, urine, and blood cultures. A KUB plain film may reveal subcutaneous gas. Cross-sectional imaging (CT scan) can be obtained to determine the source of infection, any undrained abscesses, and the subcutaneous gas, but should never delay definitive, operative treatment.

3. **The patient should be stabilized and prepared emergently for the operating room.** Broad-spectrum antibiotics that are active against both aerobic and anaerobic organisms should be started immediately. Aerobic and anaerobic wound cultures are usually polymicrobial.

4. **Wide débridement** is required, with aggressive postoperative support. The testicles are often spared because they have a blood supply discrete from the scrotum; orchiectomy is rarely indicated. Wound closure and

dermal coverage often is an extensive process, and recovery requires intense physical therapy and wound care. Despite improvements in critical care, antibiotics, and surgical technology, **mortality** ranges from 3% to 45% (*Br J Surg.* 2000;87:718).

E. **Nonacute scrotal masses**

1. **Hydroceles** generally are asymptomatic fluid collections around the testicle that **transilluminate.** Ultrasound evaluation is recommended to rule out serious underlying causes such as testicular malignancies. If hydroceles do enlarge and become symptomatic, they can be repaired by various transscrotal techniques. Hydroceles in infants may be associated with a patent processus vaginalis; parents give a history of intermittent scrotal swelling. These hydroceles usually resolve by 1 year of age. Those that persist or cause symptoms can be repaired by an inguinal approach.

2. **Spermatoceles** are benign cystic dilations involving the tail of the epididymis or proximal vas deferens.

3. **Varicoceles** are abnormal tortuosities and dilations of the testicular veins within the spermatic cord. On physical examination, they feel like a "bag of worms." A varicocele may diminish in size when the patient is supine. Because the left gonadal vein drains directly into the renal vein, varicoceles are much more common on the left side. Right-sided varicoceles may be associated with obstruction of the inferior vena cava. Varicoceles are the most common surgically correctable cause of male infertility; nevertheless, most men with varicoceles remain fertile. Varicocele repair results in improved semen quality in approximately 70% of patients. Surgical treatment of varicoceles is indicated for diminished testicular growth in adolescents, infertility, or significant symptoms. Any patient who presents with a **new-onset varicocele later in life warrants retroperitoneal imaging** to rule out a malignancy causing venous obstruction.

F. **Testicular tumors** are the most common solid tumors in 15- to 35-year-old men. The estimated lifetime risk for testicular malignancy is 1 in 500. Owing to improved multimodality therapy, overall 5-year survival for testis cancer is now 95%. Risk factors associated with testicular tumors include cryptorchidism, HIV infection, and gonadal dysgenesis with Y chromosome (Table 35-4).

1. **The typical clinical finding is a painless testicular mass,** although one third of patients may present with pain. Pulmonary or gastrointestinal complaints or an abdominal mass may reflect advanced disease. Scrotal sonography is mandatory; seminomas appear as a hypoechoic lesion, and nonseminomatous tumors appear inhomogeneous. α-Fetoprotein, β-human chorionic gonadotropin, and lactic acid dehydrogenase are serum tumor markers that help to identify the tumor type and completely stage the tumor. The markers are used to monitor the effectiveness of therapy and to screen for recurrence.

2. **Staging of testicular tumors** is outlined in Table 35-5. All patients with testicular carcinoma should have cross-sectional imaging of the retroperitoneum and pelvis as well as a chest X-ray to assess for distant disease.

TABLE 35-4 AJCC 2010 TNM Staging for Testes Carcinoma

Primary Tumor (T)

pTx	Primary tumor cannot be assessed
pT0	No evidence of primary tumor
pTis	Intratubular germ cell neoplasia
pT1	Tumor limited to testis and epididymis without vascular/lymphatic invasion; tumor may invade the tunica albuginea but not the tunica vaginalis
pT2	Tumor limited to testis and epididymis with vascular/lymphatic invasion, or tumor extending through into the tunica vaginalis
pT3	Tumor invades the spermatic cord with or without vascular/lymphatic invasion
pT4	Tumor invades the scrotum with or without vascular/lymphatic invasion

Regional Lymph Nodes—Clinical Stage (N)

Nx	Regional lymph nodes cannot be assessed
N0	No regional lymph node metastasis
N1	Metastasis with a lymph node mass 2 cm or less in greatest dimension, or multiple nodes, none greater than 2 cm in greatest dimension
N2	Lymph node mass >2 cm but <5 cm or multiple nodes with one mass >2 cm, but none >5 cm
N3	Lymph node mass >5 cm in greatest dimension

Distant Metastasis (M)

M0	No distant metastasis
M1	Distant metastasis
M1a	Nonregional nodal or pulmonary metastasis
M1b	Distant metastasis other than to nonregional nodes and lung

Serum Tumor Markers (S)

S0	Marker study levels within normal limits
S1	LDH <1.5× normal and hCG <5,000 and AFP <1,000
S2	LDH 1.5 to 10× normal or hCG 5–50,000 or AFP 1,000–10,000
S3	LDH > 10× normal or hCG >50,000, or AFP >10,000
Sx	Marker studies not available or not performed

Modified from Testis. In: Edge SE, Byrd DR, Carducci MA, et al., eds. *AJCC Cancer Staging Manual.* 7th ed. New York, NY:Springer; 2010:539–543.

3. **Initial therapy** for all testicular tumors is radical inguinal orchiectomy. The type of tumor and the stage of the disease determine further therapy.

   a. **Seminomas** constitute 60% to 65% of germ-cell tumors. Low-stage seminomas are treated with adjuvant RT to the retroperitoneum. Advanced disease is usually treated with a platinum-based chemotherapy regimen.

   b. **Nonseminomatous tumors** include the histologic types of embryonal carcinoma, teratoma, choriocarcinoma, and yolk sac elements, alone or in combination. Nonseminomatous tumors are more likely

TABLE 35-5	AAST Organ Injury Severity Scale	
Grade	**Type**	**Description**
I	Contusion	Microscopic or gross hematuria, urological studies normal
	Hematoma	Subcapsular, not expanding with no parenchymal laceration
II	Hematoma	Not expanding perirenal hematoma confined to renal retroperitoneum
	Laceration	<1.0 cm parenchymal depth of renal cortex with no urinary extravasation
III	Laceration	>1.0 cm parenchymal depth of renal cortex with no collecting system rupture or urinary extravasation
IV	Laceration	Parenchymal laceration extending through renal cortex, medulla, and collecting system
	Vascular	Main renal artery or vein injury with contained hemorrhage
V	Laceration	Completely shattered kidney
	Vascular	Avulsion of renal hilum

to present with advanced disease. Patients with clinically negative retroperitoneal nodes with normal tumor markers are treated with retroperitoneal lymph node dissection, prophylactic chemotherapy, or close observation. Patients with high-stage disease with elevated markers receive platinum-based chemotherapy followed by retroperitoneal node dissection if there is residual disease.

IX. **GENITOURINARY TRAUMA** is relatively uncommon and associated with only 10% of all traumas. Injuries should be identified during the secondary survey after life-threatening injuries have been addressed and initial resuscitation has been undertaken.

A. **Renal trauma**

1. The kidneys are the most commonly injured urologic organ occurring in 1.2% to 3.3% of all traumatic injuries. Over 80% are blunt in nature and anywhere from 4% to 10% are penetrating (*Br J Urol.* 2004;93(7):937–954). The grading system for renal injuries is shown in Table 35-5.

2. **Microscopic hematuria** (>three RBCs per high-power field) or gross hematuria is present in more than 95% of patients with a renal injury. A voided specimen is best for UA, but if the patient cannot void or is unconscious and no blood is at the meatus, a well-lubricated urethral catheter should gently be passed.

3. All patients with **gross hematuria and blunt trauma** should be evaluated with a CT scan using IV contrast. If the patient is stable, 10-minute-delayed imaging is helpful to evaluate for collecting system injuries. Patients with microscopic hematuria and shock (systolic blood pressure <90 mm Hg) should be imaged with a CT scan after they are stabilized. Patients with microscopic hematuria, no shock, and no evidence of significant deceleration or renal injury do not need radiographic evaluation of their urinary system (*J Urol.* 1989;141:1095).

4. The **degree of hematuria** does not correlate with the severity of the injury (*Br J Urol.* 2004;93(7):937–954), and any patient with a suspected renal injury due to rapid deceleration requires radiographic evaluation. Disruption of the ureteropelvic junction should be considered in children with deceleration or hyperextension injuries.

5. Most **blunt renal injuries** can be managed conservatively; fewer than 10% of blunt renal injuries require surgery or procedural intervention. Ongoing hemorrhage can be managed with selective renal artery angioembolization.

6. **Penetrating renal trauma** with microscopic hematuria (>three RBCs per high-power field) or gross hematuria requires radiographic assessment with CT scan. Preferably, this is done before exploration to evaluate the injured kidney and to confirm function of the contralateral kidney. A normal contralateral kidney may influence the surgeon's decision (repair vs. nephrectomy) on management of the injured kidney. Intraoperative palpation of a contralateral kidney may be misleading.

7. **Absolute indications for intraoperative renal exploration** include hemodynamic instability, persistent and life-threatening hemorrhage from renal injury, expanding or pulsatile perirenal mass, or renal pedicle avulsion. Selective exploration can be advocated in patients with a perirenal hematoma secondary to penetrating trauma and instability precluding evaluation with cross-sectional imaging.

B. **Ureteral injuries** account for approximately 3% of all urologic traumas and are most often associated with **penetrating trauma and multiple associated injuries** (*Br J Urol.* 2004;94(3):277–289). A high index of suspicion often is necessary to make the diagnosis, and many ureteral injuries have a delayed presentation. The absence of gross or microscopic hematuria has been documented in 30% of patients.

1. **Radiographic findings** include extravasation and, more commonly, delayed function; proximal dilation; and deviation of the ureter. A CT may demonstrate medial extravasation; delayed images are necessary to assess ureteral patency.

2. **Adequately visualizing the ureter during laparotomy** is important for diagnosing ureteral injury; IV or intraureteral injection of indigo carmine or methylene blue may help to assess the integrity of the urothelium.

3. For purposes of determining the **type of repair,** the ureter is divided into thirds:

   a. Injuries to the distal one third of the ureter are best managed by **ureteral reimplantation.** Additional length to provide a tension-free anastomosis may be gained by using a Psoas hitch and, if necessary, a Boari bladder flap.

   b. Injuries of the middle or upper third of the ureter are best managed by **ureteroureterostomy.** An omental wrap may be used to protect the repair. Stents and drains are recommended for all ureteral repairs.

C. Bladder injuries present in 2% of all blunt trauma and 6% of all pelvic fractures (*Br J Urol.* 2004;94(1):27–32).

1. Ninety-five percent of bladder injuries present with **gross hematuria** (*Urol Clin North Am.* 2006;33:676). CT cystogram should be obtained in any patient with gross hematuria and pelvic fracture. Relative indications for a cystogram include gross hematuria without a pelvic fracture, microscopic hematuria with pelvic fracture, or isolated microscopic hematuria.

2. **CT cystogram** is the most sensitive imaging modality for bladder injury. The bladder should be filled retrograde by gravity via an indwelling Foley catheter with 350 mL of dilute (3% to 5%) contrast. Postdrainage films are not necessary; merely clamping the Foley to allow bladder filling with excreted contrast does not constitute an adequate study.

3. **Treatment**
   a. All patients with penetrating trauma to the bladder and **intraperitoneal extravasation** of contrast require **surgical exploration and repair** of the bladder (*Urol Clin North Am.* 2006;33:67).
   b. Patients with blunt trauma and **extraperitoneal extravasation** of contrast can be managed nonoperatively with **catheter drainage** for 10 days. A cystogram should be performed prior to catheter removal. Greater than 85% will have healed by the 10th day from injury. Surgical repair is indicated if the bladder does not heal over the catheter after 3 weeks, or if concomitant vaginal or rectal injury, or bladder neck injury/avulsion, or in patients undergoing pelvic fracture plating.

D. Urethral injuries occur in 5% of patients with pelvic fractures and should be suspected when blood is at the meatus or the mechanism of injury is such that urethral injury might have occurred. Physical examination in patients with urethral injury may reveal penile and scrotal edema and ecchymosis. Rectal examination can reveal a high-riding prostate or boggy hematoma in the expected position of the prostate. If a urethral injury is suspected, a **retrograde urethrogram** must be performed prior to Foley catheter placement.

1. **Posterior urethral injuries** involve the prostatic and membranous urethra to the level of the urogenital diaphragm. These injuries are caused mainly by blunt trauma, and management is dependent on the degree of injury. Partial disruption of the urethra is best managed with urethral catheterization when possible. Complete disruption requires suprapubic catheter placement in the acute setting with attempt at endoscopic primary realignment within 72 hours. After realignment, primary repair is performed in the delayed setting (3 to 6 months from injury). Unstable patients require suprapubic tube placement and realignment when stable. Primary surgical repair of a posterior urethral injury is not recommended

in the acute setting as it is complicated by higher rates of impotence, incontinence, and stricture (*Urol Clin North Am.* 2006;33:87).

2. **Anterior urethral injuries** include injuries to the bulbous and penile urethra distal to the urogenital diaphragm. Straddle injuries and penetrating trauma are the most common causes of these types of injuries. Injuries contained by Buck fascia often have a characteristic "sleeve of penis" pattern, whereas urethral or penile injuries in which Buck fascia is disrupted are contained by the Colles fascia and have a "butterfly" appearance on the perineum. These injuries are best managed with urethral catheterization and delayed surgical repair (3 months after injury).

E. **Penile trauma**

1. **Penile fracture** occurs when excessive bending force is applied to the erect penis resulting in a tear of the tunica albuginea. Patients describe an auditory "pop" heard during intercourse followed by rapid detumescence and swelling of the penis/scrotum. Inability to void or blood at the meatus indicates concomitant urethral injury, seen in 15% to 20% of penile fractures. Physical exam demonstrated edema and ecchymosis/hematoma confined to penis if Buck fascia is intact or in butterfly pattern in perineum if hematoma is contained within Colle fascia. Imaging is generally **not indicated,** unless urethral injury is suspected. Hematuria, inability to void, or blood at the meatus are all indications for **urethrography/urethroscopy.** Immediate/early surgical exploration with repair is the standard of care and is associated with better outcomes than delayed repair (>36 hours).

2. **Minor penile lacerations and contusions** can be managed in the emergency room.

3. **Serious blunt or penetrating trauma** with injury to the corpus cavernosum requires surgical exploration, débridement, and repair of the corporal injury. A retrograde urethrogram or flexible cystoscopy is necessary to rule out urethral injury. Broad-spectrum antibiotics should be given, particularly in human bite injuries.

F. **Testicular injury** may occur as a result of blunt or penetrating trauma. History and physical examination are the keys to diagnosis of testicular rupture. The presentation is marked by acute and severe pain, often with associated nausea and vomiting. Physical examination may reveal a hematoma or ecchymosis of overlying skin. All penetrating scrotal gunshot wounds deep to the dartos fascia require surgical exploration. **Ultrasonography** can help to diagnose testicular injury associated with blunt trauma with a 100% sensitivity and a specificity of 93.5% (*J Urol.* 2006;175:175). The orchiectomy rate is less than 10% for ruptured testicles explored within 72 hours after injury. Repair consists of hematoma evacuation, débridement of the necrotic tubules, and closure of the tunica albuginea (*Br J Urol.* 2004;94(4):507–515).

G. **Scrotal avulsion and skin loss** are most often a result of motor vehicle accidents. Because of the redundancy and vascularity of scrotal skin, various options are available for local flaps and coverage of the testicles. Wounds should be copiously irrigated and débrided; clean wounds may be closed in layers, whereas grossly contaminated wounds should be cleaned and packed with sterile gauze dressings.

36 Obstetric and Gynecologic Surgery

Lindsay M. Kuroki and Premal H. Thaker

OBSTETRIC AND GYNECOLOGIC DISORDERS

I. **VAGINAL BLEEDING.** A thorough history including pattern and intensity of bleeding, date of last menstrual period, and physical examination is sufficient to determine the etiology. A pregnancy test must be performed in all women of reproductive age. Hemoglobin (Hgb) and hematocrit (Hct) should be drawn to determine whether the abnormal bleeding is chronic or heavy. An endometrial biopsy should be performed in all postmenopausal women with bleeding to rule out endometrial carcinoma.

A. **Obstetric etiologies.** Bleeding during pregnancy has different etiologies depending on the trimester. Differential diagnosis of first trimester bleeding includes spontaneous abortions (SABs), postcoital bleeding, ectopic pregnancy (see Section IIA), lower genital tract lesions/lacerations, and expulsion of a molar pregnancy. Third trimester bleeding occurs in 4% to 5% of pregnancy and most commonly is caused by placenta previa, abruption, vasa previa, preterm labor, and lower genital tract lesions/lacerations. Overall, 30% to 40% of all pregnancies are associated with vaginal bleeding and approximately half of these result in SABs.

1. **Terminology**
   a. **Threatened abortion:** any vaginal bleeding during the first half of pregnancy without cervical dilation or expulsion of products of contraception (POCs); cervix closed.
   b. **Missed abortion:** fetal death before 20 weeks' gestation with retention of POCs; cervix closed.
   c. **Inevitable abortion:** cervical dilation with or without ruptured membranes.
   d. **Incomplete abortion:** partial passage of POCs; cervix open.
   e. **Complete abortion:** expulsion of all POCs from the uterine cavity; cervix closed.

2. **Presentation and clinical features.** Classically, patients present with vaginal bleeding and crampy, midline, lower abdominal pain. Bleeding from the urethra or rectum, and cervical/vaginal lacerations, should be excluded. Passage of tissue may represent a complete or incomplete abortion.

3. **Physical examination.** Vital signs are within normal ranges unless extensive vaginal bleeding or septic abortion occurs with resultant

tachycardia and hypotension. Septic abortions can cause elevated temperatures, marked suprapubic tenderness, or purulent discharge through the cervical os.

4. **Laboratory investigation**
   a. **Hgb and Hct.** Plasma volume expansion in pregnancy may result in a lower mean Hgb during the second trimester. With acute blood loss, the Hgb/Hct can be normal until compensatory mechanisms restore normal plasma volume.
   b. **White blood cell (WBC) count with differential** is useful to evaluate febrile morbidity. Septic abortion is associated with a left shift and an elevated WBC count.
   c. **Blood type and screen** are essential to identify Rh-negative patients at risk for isoimmunization. Any woman with pregnancy-related vaginal bleeding who is Rh negative should be given Rho immunoglobulin (RhoGAM) if she has not received it within the last 12 weeks (see Section I.A.6.g).
   d. **Quantitative β subunit of human chorionic gonadotropin (hCG).** The sensitivity of a pregnancy test (urine or serum) can vary depending on the type of test performed (i.e., latex agglutination, enzyme-linked immunosorbent assays, radioimmunoassay). A urine pregnancy test gives a rapid qualitative result, although the sensitivity is variable. Serum pregnancy tests are more sensitive and yield a quantitative level of hCG that assists in evaluating the status of a pregnancy. Serial serum hCG values along with ultrasonography can help to distinguish an early, viable intrauterine pregnancy (IUP) from an abnormal pregnancy. In most normal IUPs near 6 weeks' gestation, hCG increases by at least 66% every 48 hours (ACOG Practice Bulletin 94. *Obstet Gynecol.* 2008;111:1479). Patients with stable clinical examinations can be followed with serial hCG values until they reach the sonographic threshold values at which an IUP can be visualized (see Section I.A.5).
   e. **Progesterone levels** are prognostic, independent of hCG levels. Values less than 5 ng/mL have 100% specificity in confirming an abnormal pregnancy. Levels more than 20 ng/mL are usually associated with a normal IUP.

5. **Imaging studies.** Ultrasonography may be useful in demonstrating a viable pregnancy. Vaginal probe ultrasonography should demonstrate an intrauterine gestational sac (if it exists) at hCG levels more than 1,500 to 2,000 mIU/mL versus an abdominal ultrasonography, where the threshold is more than 6,000 mIU/mL. Cardiac activity can be seen at 10,000 mIU/mL.

6. **Treatment**
   a. **Threatened abortion.** Patients with a pregnancy that is viable or of indeterminate viability who present with vaginal bleeding and a closed internal cervical os are followed expectantly with a repeat ultrasound in 7 days, repeat hCG in 48 hours, or both.

b. Missed abortion. Patients may be followed expectantly or undergo surgical or medical therapy. Expectant management should include weekly coagulation studies [i.e., complete blood cell (CBC) count, prothrombin time, partial thromboplastin time, fibrinogen, and fibrin degradation products] because of the risk of disseminated intravascular coagulopathy (DIC). Patients should bring any tissue passed to the hospital for pathologic verification. If POCs have not passed within 3 weeks, evacuation should be scheduled.

c. Inevitable abortion. Patients occasionally are followed expectantly with monitoring for infection but typically undergo uterine evacuation (see Section I.6.f). If fever develops, intravenous (IV) antibiotics with polymicrobial coverage are administered, followed by evacuation. These patients require admission and careful monitoring of coagulation factors because they are at risk of DIC.

d. Incomplete abortion. Uterine evacuation is indicated. If POCs are not recovered, an ectopic pregnancy should be ruled out.

e. Complete abortion. Only short-term observation is necessary, given that all POCs are expelled, the cervix is closed, and bleeding and cramping are minimal.

f. Evacuation of the uterus. Suction curettage is done safely in the first trimester and can be performed in the emergency department if significant cervical dilation exists. A stable patient with a first trimester missed abortion can undergo dilation and curettage (D&C) as an outpatient. In the second trimester, a dilation and evacuation or medical induction of labor under gynecologic consultation is performed. After curettage, prophylactic antibiotics [doxycycline 100 mg orally (PO) two times a day for 7 days], ergot alkaloids (methylergonovine maleate 0.2 mg PO three times a day for 2 to 3 days) for uterine contraction, and antiprostaglandins (ibuprofen 600 mg PO every 6 hours as needed for pain) commonly are prescribed. If heavy vaginal bleeding, abdominal pain, or fever occurs after evacuation, investigation for retained POCs, uterine perforation, and endometritis is warranted.

g. RhoGAM is given to any pregnant patient with vaginal bleeding who is Rh negative with a negative antibody screen. The recommended dose of RhoGAM for first trimester events is 50 μg intramuscularly (IM); anytime thereafter, 300 μg IM is sufficient [ACOG Practice Bulletin 4. *Obstet Gynecol.* 1999;93(5):771–774].

h. Pathology. Any tissue passed or obtained from uterine evacuation must be evaluated for chorionic villi. If villi are not identified, further investigation is necessary to exclude ectopic pregnancy or incomplete abortion. Hydatidiform mole should also be excluded on final pathology.

B. Nonobstetric etiologies of vaginal bleeding (Table 36-1).

TABLE 36-1 Nonobstetric Causes of Vaginal Bleeding

Differential Diagnosis	Laboratory Data	Signs and Symptoms	Treatment
Menses	CBC count, urine hCG	Cyclic bleeding every 21–35 days	Iron therapy if indicated
Dysfunctional uterine bleeding	CBC count, urine hCG, endometrial biopsy if >35 y, duration >6 mo	Non-cyclic bleeding; may have associated dysmenorrhea, fatigue, or dizziness	Hormonal therapy if patient is hemodynamically stable; if unstable, transfuse as needed, IV estrogen or high-dose OCPs
Infection: gonorrhea/*Chlamydia* cervicitis	Cervical culture, wet prep	Purulent vaginal discharge, possible spotting	Ceftriaxone, 125 mg IM × 1; azithromycin, 1 g PO × 1
Trichomonas vaginitis	Wet prep	Yellow-green frothy vaginal discharge, possible spotting	Metronidazole, 500 mg PO bid × 7 days or 2 g PO × 1 (if pregnant, defer until second trimester)
Sexual trauma	Rape kit	Vaginal bleeding and/or discharge	Emergency contraception, prophylactic treatment for STDs; if laceration, pack vagina, possible surgical repair
Malignancy	Endometrial biopsy, Papanicolaou test smear, cervical biopsy	Postmenopausal, postcoital, or intermenstrual bleeding	Refer to gynecologic oncologist

bid, twice daily; CBC, complete blood cell; hCG, human chorionic gonadotropin; OCPs, oral contraceptive pills; STDs, sexually transmitted diseases; IM, intramuscular; IV, intravenous; PO, oral.

II. **ABDOMINAL PAIN.** The differential diagnosis for nongynecologic etiologies includes appendicitis, gastroenteritis, irritable bowel, ischemic bowel, cholecystitis, ureteral colic, and urinary tract infection. Pregnancy should be excluded in all reproductive age women.

A. **Ectopic pregnancy** occurs when the blastocyst implants outside the uterine cavity; 97% of pregnancies occur in a fallopian tube (tubal pregnancy).

1. **Presentation and clinical features.** More than 90% of patients with tubal pregnancies have abdominal or pelvic pain, although some may be asymptomatic. Early unruptured ectopic pregnancies often present with amenorrhea, vaginal spotting, and colicky, vague lower abdominal pain, whereas, patients with a ruptured ectopic pregnancy may report severe pain, syncope, and dizziness. Pleuritic chest pain and shoulder pain from diaphragmatic irritation by blood can also occur. A ruptured ectopic pregnancy is a true surgical emergency, as it can quickly result in rapid hemorrhage, shock, and even death.

2. **Physical examination.** Vital signs vary greatly, from normal blood pressure and pulse to hypotension and tachycardia due to cardiovascular collapse secondary to hemorrhage. Although patients with unruptured ectopic pregnancy may demonstrate only mild tenderness, peritoneal signs (e.g., tenderness, rigidity, guarding, rebound) can also be present. Pelvic masses sometimes are palpable, but lack of one does not exclude ectopic pregnancy. The uterus may appear small for presumed gestational date.

3. **Laboratory investigation**
   a. **CBC count**. Hgb/Hct may indicate the degree of hemorrhage, except in acute blood loss. The WBC typically is normal/slightly elevated and does not demonstrate increased percentage of immature neutrophils.
   b. **Blood type and screen** should be obtained to identify Rh-negative patients and, if appropriate, order cross-match blood on hold for possible transfusion (see Section I.A.6.g).
   c. **hCG.** Although ectopic pregnancy can occur with any quantitative serum hCG value, these data can be useful for ultrasound interpretation. Serial hCG values that do not increase appropriately are suspicious for an ectopic pregnancy (see Section I.A.4.d).
   d. **Progesterone** values rarely aid in the diagnosis of ectopic pregnancy (see Section I.A.4.e).

4. **Imaging studies.** Ultrasonography is most useful in excluding an ectopic pregnancy by demonstrating an intrauterine gestational sac or fetus. Stable patients with an hCG less than 1,500 mIU/mL should be followed with serial hCG titers. An hCG more than 2,500 mIU/mL and absence of a gestational sac in the uterus indicate either a nonviable intrauterine or an ectopic pregnancy. Ultrasound findings consistent with ectopic pregnancy include a uterus without a well-formed gestational sac—although a pseudosac (intrauterine fluid collection) may be present—free intraperitoneal fluid, and sometimes an adnexal mass representing a tubal pregnancy.

5. **Diagnostic studies**
   a. **Culdocentesis** is useful for detecting hemoperitoneum, although it is used infrequently because sonographic evaluation for free intra-peritoneal fluid often is sufficient. A culdocentesis is performed by passing a needle aseptically into the posterior vaginal fornix. Aspiration of clear yellow fluid is normal; no fluid is nondiagnostic. Aspiration of clotting blood is likely from an intravascular source and nondiagnostic, whereas nonclotting blood with an Hct above 15% is consistent with hemoperitoneum.
   b. **D&C** can be performed to differentiate between an ectopic pregnancy and incomplete abortion after excluding a normal early IUP. Curettage products that float in saline are suggestive of chorionic villi. If villi are not identified, laparoscopy to exclude ectopic pregnancy is indicated.

6. **Treatment**
   a. **Surgical therapy.** Comparing systemic methotrexate with tube-sparing laparoscopic surgery in hemodynamically stable patients, randomized trials have consistently shown no difference in over-all tubal preservation, tubal patencies, repeat ectopic pregnancies, or future pregnancies. The mainstay of surgical management for ectopic pregnancy is a conservative approach that preserves the tubes.
      (1) **Laparoscopy** is preferred for diagnosis and treatment of tubal pregnancy; however, laparotomy is indicated if the patient is hemodynamically unstable.
      (2) **Conservative surgical therapy** is recommended in patients who wish to preserve reproductive potential. **Linear salpingostomy** in the antimesosalpinx portion of the tube performed with fine-tip electrocautery is preferable when the ectopic pregnancy is unruptured and located in the ampulla of the tube. After removal of the pregnancy from the tube, the base is irrigated and hemostasis is achieved with cautery. The tube is left to heal by secondary intention. **Segmental resection** often is performed when the tube is ruptured and the ectopic pregnancy is in the isthmic portion of the tube.
      (3) **Nonconservative surgical therapy** includes **salpingectomy** (removal of tube) for tubal rupture or severe hemorrhage and **cornual resection** for interstitial pregnancies. Pregnancy rates after salpingectomy have been shown to be equivalent to those following linear salpingostomy, although the incidence of recurrent ectopic pregnancy may be slightly higher with salpingostomy.
      (4) **Follow-up.** Patients treated with conservative surgical management or after rupture or spillage of trophoblastic tissue have a 5% incidence of persistent, viable trophoblastic tissue. Weekly quantitative hCG values should be followed until negative. If the levels plateau or increase, reevaluation is indicated.

b. **Medical therapy** with methotrexate, a folic acid antagonist, can be used in compliant outpatients who are hemodynamically stable. Success depends on treatment regimen, gestational age, and hCG levels. Candidates for treatment with methotrexate include gestational sac less than 3.5 cm in diameter, an intact tube, no fetal heart motion, no evidence of hemoperitoneum, and no history of hepatic, renal or hematologic dysfunction. Baseline laboratory tests, which include hCG, Rh factor, CBC count, hepatic enzymes, and serum creatinine, should be obtained. The most common adverse effects of therapy are bloating and flatulence, followed by stomatitis, hair loss, and anemia. A transient rise in hepatic enzymes may be observed. Repeat quantitative hCG levels should be drawn on days 4 and 7. If hCG levels fail to decline less than 15% between days 4 and 7, a second dose of methotrexate should be administered and a new day 1 assigned. Quantitative hCG values are followed until negative. Approximately 20% of patients have an inappropriate fall in hCG levels and require surgical intervention. *Separation pain* refers to the increase in abdominopelvic discomfort that is commonly experienced by patients undergoing treatment and is thought to be caused by tubal stretching during resolution of the pregnancy. Patients are counseled to rest and take oral analgesics but cautioned to seek immediate reevaluation to rule out rupture if pain does not resolve within 1 hour. While undergoing treatment, patients should avoid alcohol and folic acid because these may interfere with methotrexate; refrain from intercourse, as this may increase the risk of rupture (ACOG Practice Bulletin 94. *Obstet Gynecol.* 2008;111:1479).

B. **Pelvic inflammatory disease (PID)** is a polymicrobial infection of the upper genital tract. The majority of cases occur in sexually active 15- to 30-year-old women. It rarely occurs in nonmenstruating women and during pregnancy. Factors promoting progression of infection from the lower to upper genital tract include events that cause breakdown of the cervical mucus barrier, such as douching, intrauterine device insertion, hysteroscopy, D&C, endometrial biopsy, and hysterosalpingography. Risk factors include a history of sexually transmitted diseases (STDs) or PID, multiple sexual partners, and age younger than 25 years. Causative pathogens are primarily *Neisseria gonorrhoeae* and *Chlamydia trachomatis*, although other vaginal flora microorganisms (e.g., anaerobes, *Gardnerella vaginalis*, *Haemophilus influenzae*, enteric gram-negative rods, *Streptococcus agalactiae*), as well as cytomegalovirus (CMV), *Mycoplasma hominis*, *Ureaplasma urealyticum*, and *Mycoplasma genitalium*, have been associated with PID.

1. **Presentation and clinical features.** Patients with PID typically have lower abdominal and pelvic pain, which may be constant, dull, sharp, or crampy. PID is aggravated by movement and often occurs around or during menses. Other signs/symptoms include purulent vaginal discharge (75%), abnormal vaginal bleeding (<50%), fever (<33%), dyspareunia, and dysuria. Nausea and vomiting with associated ileus may occur but are usually late symptoms.

2. **Physical examination** reveals lower abdominal tenderness, including peritoneal signs of rebound and guarding, adnexal tenderness with or without fullness or palpable mass, mucopurulent vaginal discharge, and cervical motion tenderness. Cervical motion tenderness is not pathognomonic of PID, because it is a nonspecific sign of peritoneal irritation that can be elicited in any patient with peritonitis from any cause.

3. **Laboratory investigation.** Pregnancy must be excluded. Leukocytosis and an elevated erythrocyte sedimentation rate (ESR) suggest a severe infection. Evaluation of a saline mount of vaginal secretions under high magnification usually reveals numerous WBCs. If none are present and the discharge appears normal, PID is unlikely. A cervical swab for DNA probe analysis of *N. gonorrhoeae* and *C. trachomatis* should be obtained, although bloody samples may give false-negative results. Alternatively, a voided urine assay (URI probe) may be used. Women with PID should also be screened for other STDs including HIV and hepatitis B and for rapid plasma reagin (RPR).

4. **Imaging studies.** Ultrasonography is used to detect tubo-ovarian abscess (TOA) if a mass is palpable on examination or if no improvement is noted after 48 hours of antibiotics. Abdominal plain films, magnetic resonance imaging (MRI), or computed tomography (CT) scan may also be used to investigate other etiologies of a patient's pain if the diagnosis is uncertain.

5. **Diagnostic studies**
   a. The Centers for Disease Control and Prevention (CDC) issued guidelines for the diagnosis of acute PID that are intended to serve as clinical criteria for initiating treatment. **Minimum criteria** include lower abdominal tenderness, adnexal tenderness, and cervical motion tenderness. **Additional criteria** include abnormal cervical/vaginal discharge, temperature more than 101°F (38.3°C), elevated ESR, elevated C-reactive protein level, and documented infection with *N. gonorrhoeae* or *C. trachomatis*. **Definitive criteria** include histopathologic evidence of endometritis on endometrial biopsy, transvaginal ultrasonography showing fluid-filled tubes or TOA, and laparoscopic abnormalities consistent with PID.
   b. **Culdocentesis** seldom is necessary to make the diagnosis of PID. However, aspiration of purulent material confirms an infectious process (see Section II.A.5.a).
   c. **Laparoscopy** revealing erythema and edema of the fallopian tubes and purulent material confirms the diagnosis and provides the opportunity to collect direct cultures of infected organs. However, laparoscopy should not be considered a routine means of establishing a diagnosis.

6. **Treatment** of PID depends on the severity of the infection.
   a. **Inpatient therapy** is indicated for patients with nausea and vomiting, possible surgical emergencies, pregnancy, suspicion for TOA, immunodeficiency, failed outpatient therapy, or for patients in whom preservation of reproductive potential is important. According to 2007 CDC guidelines, inpatient parenteral treatment

regimens include cefotetan 2 g IV every 12 hours or cefoxitin 2 g IV every 6 hours and doxycycline 100 mg PO/IV every 12 hours. Oral doxycycline is preferred because of pain with IV administration. Alternative regimens include (1) clindamycin 900 mg IV every 8 hours and gentamicin 2 mg/kg IV load followed by 1.5 mg/kg IV every 8 hours and (2) ampicillin/sulbactam 3 g IV every 6 hours and doxycycline 100 mg PO/IV every 12 hours. Inpatient treatment is continued until the patient is afebrile for 48 hours and has decreased pain on pelvic examination. Patients then are transitioned to PO doxycycline ± metronidazole for a total of 14 days. Those with discrete pelvic fluid collections and TOAs may be candidates for ultrasound-guided vaginal aspiration and pelvic drain placement by interventional radiologists; concurrent antibiotics should be administered.

   b. Outpatient therapy. Clinical outcomes among women treated with PO therapy are similar to those treated with IV therapy. Oral regimens include (1) one dose of ceftriaxone 250 mg IM, plus doxycycline 100 mg PO twice daily ± metronidazole 500 mg PO twice daily for 14 days; (2) cefoxitin 2 g IM and probenacid 1 g PO administered concurrently in a single dose plus doxycycline ± metronidazole; or (3) third-generation cephalosporin (e.g., cefotaxime) plus doxycycline ± metronidazole. Patients should follow-up within 48 to 72 hours to ensure improvement.

   c. Surgery should be considered for patients with symptomatic pelvic masses, or ruptured TOAs, who do not clinically improve after 48 hours of IV antibiotics.

C. Corpus luteal cysts develop from mature follicles in the ovary. Intrafollicular bleeding can occur 2 to 4 days after ovulation creating a hemorrhagic cyst. Corpus luteal cysts usually are 4 cm or more in diameter but can be more than 12 cm. Diagnosis can be difficult in pregnancy because a cyst may be confused with an ectopic pregnancy.

   1. Presentation and clinical features. Patients can be asymptomatic or may present with unilateral, dull lower abdominal/pelvic pain. If the cyst has ruptured, the patient may complain of sudden onset of severe pain.

   2. Physical examination reveals adnexal enlargement, tenderness, or both with or without peritoneal irritation if the cyst has ruptured. It is important to ensure hemodynamic stability because some patients can bleed significantly from a hemorrhagic cyst.

   3. Laboratory investigation. A CBC count and hCG should always be obtained. Ultrasonography can aid in visualizing a cyst or free fluid in the pelvis, indicative of recent cyst rupture. Culdocentesis may be performed to search for blood in the cul-de-sac in cases of suspected cyst rupture.

   4. Treatment usually is conservative, allowing for spontaneous resolution. Oral contraceptive pills (OCPs) can be used to suppress ovulation and future cyst formation. Nonsteroidal anti-inflammatory drugs

(NSAIDs) or short courses of narcotics are commonly prescribed for pain control. Surgical treatment with laparoscopic cystectomy is rarely indicated unless significant ongoing intraperitoneal hemorrhage is present.

D. Adnexal torsion accounts for an estimated 3% of gynecologic surgical emergencies. Torsion occurs when the ovary, tube, or both structures twist on the infundibulopelvic ligament. Incomplete torsion results in occlusion of the venous and lymphatic channels, causing cyanotic and edematous adnexa. Complete torsion interrupts the arterial supply with subsequent ischemia and necrosis of the adnexa. Torsion occurs most commonly in the reproductive age group, more frequently on the right side, and typically with large ovaries or benign ovarian masses (50% to 60%). Concurrent pregnancy is present in 15% of cases.

1. **Presentation and clinical features.** History and physical examination are critical, as adnexal torsion is primarily a clinical diagnosis. Patients with torsion present with acute, severe, sharp, intermittent, unilateral lower abdominal or pelvic pain and nausea. Intermittent torsion may present with periodic pain for days to weeks from twisting and untwisting of the adnexa. The pain often is related to a sudden change in position.

2. **Physical examination** can reveal tachycardia or bradycardia (from vagal stimulation) and fever if there is necrosis. Unilateral abdominal tenderness or a tender adnexal mass often is found on pelvic examination. Peritoneal signs may be present as the ovary undergoes necrosis.

3. **Diagnostic studies.** Ultrasonography may visualize an adnexal mass. Doppler ultrasonography has moderate sensitivity and specificity in diagnosing torsion. Blood flow around the adnexa is reassuring but does not exclude torsion, which is mainly a clinical diagnosis. Visualization by laparoscopy confirms the diagnosis.

4. **Treatment** involves immediate surgical intervention. If only partial torsion or no evidence of tissue necrosis exists and the patient desires future fertility, preservation of adnexa with untwisting and transfixation of the ovarian pedicle is possible. Cyst resection and exclusion of underlying malignancy (rare) should be performed. If necrosis of the adnexa is present or the ovary is felt to be nonviable, a salpingo-oophorectomy should be performed.

E. Fibroids or leiomyomas are benign tumors of uterine smooth muscle that vary in size from less than 1 cm to more than 20 cm.

1. **Presentation and clinical features.** Although most fibroids are asymptomatic, one-third of patients have dysmenorrhea or abnormal menstrual bleeding, including menorrhagia (heavy menses) or metrorrhagia (intermenstrual bleeding). Symptoms can also result from pressure on the bladder or rectum. Fibroid degeneration may cause fever and acute pain that is self-limited and usually responsive to NSAIDs.

2. **Physical examination** may reveal an enlarged, irregular uterus.

3. **Diagnostic studies.** Ultrasonography confirms uterine size and the presence of myomas. In patients older than 35 years with abnormal bleeding, an endometrial biopsy should be performed to rule out endometrial pathology, including hyperplasia and carcinoma.

4. **Treatment** is determined by symptoms and the patient's desire for future fertility. Prostaglandin synthetase inhibitors (e.g., ibuprofen or naproxen sodium) are useful for pain control; hormonal therapy (e.g., OCPs and medroxyprogesterone acetate) can be used to regulate bleeding; and gonadotropin-releasing hormone agonists (e.g., Lupron) can also be used to shrink fibroids. Uterine artery embolization by interventional radiology (IR) is another alternative in which the uterine arteries are embolized using polyvinyl alcohol particles of trisacryl gelatin microspheres with or without metal coils causing uterine leiomyoma devascularization and involution. Surgery (myomectomy or hysterectomy) is reserved for patients who have failed medical management and no longer desire future fertility (ACOG Practice Bulletin 96. *Obstet Gynecol.* 2008;112:387).

F. **Dysmenorrhea** is painful lower abdominal cramping that occurs just before and during menses. It affects 40% of women of reproductive age and is often accompanied by other symptoms including diaphoresis, tachycardia, headache, nausea, vomiting, and diarrhea.

1. The **etiology** of dysmenorrhea is thought to be related to increased prostaglandin levels.

2. **Treatment** includes prostaglandin synthetase inhibitors (e.g., ibuprofen or naproxen sodium) beginning before the onset of menses or OCPs to suppress ovulation.

G. **Adnexal masses** are often found incidentally either on pelvic examination or in the operating room. In the United States, women have a 5% to 10% lifetime risk of undergoing surgery for a suspected ovarian neoplasm, with 13% to 21% of these cases resulting in a diagnosis of malignancy. To guide surgeons in their management, criteria have been developed that aid in assessing the malignant potential of adnexal masses (ACOG Practice Bulletin 83. *Obstet Gynecol.* 2007;110:201).

1. **Presentation and clinical features.** Most adnexal masses are asymptomatic unless they are associated with torsion or are large enough to compress surrounding structures. Less than 2% of adnexal masses are malignant, although up to 34% may be malignant in postmenopausal women.

2. **Physical examination** may reveal adnexal fullness or a discrete mass. Attention should be paid to the size, number (unilateral vs. bilateral), mobility, texture (solid, cystic, nodular), and presence of ascites.

3. **Diagnostic studies.** Ultrasonography can reveal the size and characteristics of adnexal masses (i.e., complex, simple, nodular, septations, papillary excrescences, etc.) as well as the assessing free fluid in the pelvis. A CT scan is less useful for visualizing the pelvis.

4. **Treatment.** A large (>10 cm) adnexal mass warrants surgical exploration. Smaller masses in premenopausal women may be observed for 6 to 8 weeks unless certain factors make it likely to be malignant. Patients undergoing expectant management should be counseled on the warning signs of torsion. If the mass grows or persists on repeat ultrasonography, surgery is indicated. Controversy exists regarding the management of small, asymptomatic adnexal masses in postmenopausal women. Small, unilocular cysts may be observed for some time, although most physicians have a lower threshold for surgery in these patients because the risk of malignancy increases with increasing age. Laparoscopy has been shown to be as effective and safe as laparotomy for the removal of masses of size less than 10 cm, with decreased morbidity and shorter hospital stay. Fixed and solid masses or those associated with ascites require laparotomy and a gynecologic oncologist on standby. Benign adnexal masses frequently encountered include cystic teratomas (dermoid cysts), endometriomas, and serous and mucinous cystadenomas. Dermoids and serous cystadenomas are frequently bilateral and necessitate a close inspection of the contralateral ovary. Mucinous cystadenomas can be associated with pseudomyxoma peritonei and therefore warrant evaluation of the appendix because appendiceal mucoceles and carcinomas can also result in pseudomyxoma. Other benign, solid ovarian tumors include Brenner tumors, fibromas, and thecomas.

III. **NONOBSTETRIC SURGERY IN THE PREGNANT PATIENT.** Common indications for surgery in the pregnant patient are appendicitis, adnexal mass, and cholecystitis. It is preferable to treat pregnant patients conservatively and, if safely possible, defer surgery to the postpartum period. However, delay of an indicated surgical procedure can be devastating. If nonemergent surgery is required, it is safest to proceed in the second trimester. Surgery in the first trimester carries a risk of fetal loss and malformation because organogenesis occurs, whereas surgery in the third trimester carries a risk of inducing preterm labor.

A. **Preoperative considerations.** Pregnant patients are at increased risk for aspiration because of upward displacement of the stomach and the inhibitory effects of progesterone on gastrointestinal motility. A nonparticulate antacid should be given shortly before induction of anesthesia. In the second half of pregnancy, patients should be placed in the left lateral position to decrease vena caval and aortic compression. If the fetus is of viable gestational age, continuous fetal monitoring should be employed; otherwise, heart tones should be documented pre and postoperatively. Patients between 24 and 34 weeks' gestation should be given a course of antenatal glucocorticoids (betamethasone or dexamethasone) more than 48 hours prior to surgery to promote fetal lung maturity should preterm delivery occur.

B. **Laparoscopy in pregnancy.** The second trimester is the optimal time to safely perform laparoscopy in pregnancy because the uterus is not large enough to obstruct visualization, allowing for minimal uterine manipulation. Current practice techniques are based on the Society of American Gastrointestinal Endoscopic Surgeons (SAGES) Guidelines of Laparoscopic Surgery During Pregnancy (*Surg Endosc.* 1998;12:189). To highlight, trocar placement is best accomplished by an open Hasson technique, with the additional trocars inserted under direct visualization. Carbon dioxide pneumoperitoneum at 12 to 15 mm Hg appears safe and is unlikely to result in fetal hypoxia or acidosis. Any cervical or uterine manipulator should be avoided in pregnant patients, as it can cause artificial rupture of membranes, preterm labor, or injury to fetus. Overall, laparoscopic surgical procedures may result in decreased morbidity and mortality, a reduced cost with shorter hospitalizations, and a decreased risk of thromboembolic disease compared with laparotomy.

C. **Anesthetic** selection is based on the maternal condition and the planned surgical procedure. For general anesthesia, all patients should be intubated using cricoid pressure to minimize the risk of aspiration. Anesthetic inhalation agents and narcotic analgesia are commonly used. Regional anesthesia may be complicated by hypotension, which is potentially poorly tolerated by patient and fetus.

D. **Postoperatively,** fetal-uterine monitoring and tocolytic agents are used depending on gestational age and degree of maternal symptoms. Document fetal well-being.

IV. TRAUMA IN PREGNANCY

A. **Presentation and clinical features.** Trauma is the leading cause of morbidity and mortality in the United States in women younger than 40 years and complicates approximately 1 in 12 pregnancies. After initial interventions are aimed at stabilizing the mother according to advanced cardiac trauma life support protocols and assessing the extent of injury, fetal well-being should be established by calculating gestational age, monitoring fetal heart tones, determining viability, and administering antenatal glucocorticoids if appropriate for fetal lung maturity.

B. **Types of abdominal trauma**

1. **Penetrating trauma** places the uterus and fetus at great risk during the later stages of pregnancy. Evaluation and treatment are similar to those in the nonpregnant patient; surgical exploration is usually necessary. Amniocentesis to establish fetal lung maturity or to detect bacteria or blood may be helpful if time permits.

2. **Blunt trauma** in pregnancy is associated most often with motor vehicle accidents. Despite the concern for abdominal seat-belt injuries, restrained pregnant patients fare better than those who are unrestrained. Intrauterine or retroplacental hemorrhage must be considered because 20% of the cardiac output in pregnancy is delivered to the uteroplacental unit.

3. **Abruptio placentae** occurs in 1% to 5% of minor and 40% to 50% of major blunt traumas. Focal uterine tenderness, vaginal bleeding, hypertonic contractions, and fetal compromise frequently occur. DIC may

occur in almost one-third of abruptions. Work-up includes a DIC panel including coagulation factors, fibrinogen, as well as a Kleihauer–Betke screen to assess for fetal-maternal hemorrhage in Rh-negative patients.

  a. **Management of abruptio placentae** depends on fetal age, degree of placental separation, and estimated blood loss determined by ultrasonography. At viability, continuous fetal heart monitoring is performed and the mode of delivery is dictated by both fetal and maternal cardiovascular stability. The immediate maternal and fetal threat must be weighed against the morbidity associated with prematurity, with the threshold for delivery decreasing with increasing gestational age.

C. **Special considerations of trauma in pregnancy**

  1. **Fetal-uterine monitoring** is effective in determining fetal distress, abruptio placentae, and preterm labor caused by trauma for pregnancies of more than 20 weeks. Doppler auscultation of fetal heart tones is sufficient for previable pregnancies (>12 weeks' gestation).

  2. **Ultrasonography** is an effective tool for establishing gestational age, fetal viability, placental characteristics, and placental location.

  3. In **positioning** the pregnant patient, avoid placing her supine to optimize venous return. During cardiopulmonary resuscitation, a 15-degree wedge into the left lateral decubitus position should be used if possible.

  4. **Tetanus prophylaxis** in a pregnant patient should be administered in the same manner and for the same indications as in the nonpregnant patient.

  5. **Peritoneal lavage,** usually by the open, above-the-fundus technique, can be used to detect intraperitoneal hemorrhage while avoiding the uterus, which is localized by examination and ultrasonography [ACOG Practice Bulletin 251. *Obstet Gynecol.* 1999;92(3):394–397].

  6. **Radiation** in the form of diagnostic studies places the fetus at potential risk for SAB (first several weeks of pregnancy), teratogenesis (weeks 3 to 12), and growth retardation (>12 weeks' gestational age). These effects and secondary childhood cancers are unlikely at doses of more than 10 rads (chest x-ray film, <1 rad; CT scan of abdomen and pelvis, 5 to 8 rads). Uterine shielding should be used when possible. Studies should be ordered judiciously, but imaging deemed important for evaluation should not be omitted (ACOG Committee Opinion 299. *Obstet Gynecol.* 2004;104:647).

  7. **Perimortem or postmortem cesarean delivery** should be accomplished within 10 minutes of maternal cardiopulmonary arrest to optimize neonatal prognosis and maternal response to resuscitation.

  8. **Isoimmunization** must be considered in the Rh-negative patient, and RhoGAM should be administered when fetal maternal hemorrhage is suspected (see Section I.A.6.g).

  9. All **blood products** should be screened and negative for CMV.

  10. **Prophylactic cephalosporins** are safe in all trimesters of pregnancy.

V. GYNECOLOGIC MALIGNANCIES. The female genital tract accounts for more than 83,750 new cases of invasive carcinoma annually in the United States, resulting in approximately 27,710 deaths in 2010 (*CA Cancer J Clin.* 2010;60:260–267). Mortality can be reduced by earlier detection. Five-year survival rates after proper treatment of cancers diagnosed at stage I (confined to primary organ) approach 90%, but fall to 30% to 50% when diagnosed at advanced stages. A brief overview of vulvar, cervical, endometrial, and ovarian cancers is presented with emphasis on diagnosis and initial management. A complete discussion of gynecologic malignancies including less common cancers (vaginal, fallopian tube, and gestational trophoblastic disease) is beyond the scope of this manual. Patients should be referred to a gynecologic oncologist for comprehensive management.

A. **Vulvar carcinoma** is primarily a disease of postmenopausal women, and the average age at diagnosis is 68 years. The etiology has been linked to human papillomavirus (HPV) infection in younger patients and is associated with chronic vulvar conditions including dystrophies, lichen sclerosis, and condylomata. Squamous cell histology predominates (90%), followed by melanoma and adenocarcinoma.

1. **Presentation and clinical features.** Vulvar cancer often presents as a hyper- or hypopigmented lesion. It may be ulcerated, pruritic, painful, or asymptomatic and may have been treated with a variety of antibiotics and ointments before diagnosis.

2. **Diagnosis.** Accurate diagnosis requires biopsy and histopathologic evaluation of suspicious areas.

3. **Treatment** of vulvar cancer depends on the stage. Surgery ranging from local excision to radical vulvectomy with bilateral inguinal lymph node dissection generally is the primary treatment. Local, groin, and pelvic adjuvant radiation is administered depending on the pathologic findings. Basal cell carcinoma requires only a wide local excision.

4. **Prognosis** depends on stage (Table 36-2). A landmark paper by Homesley et al. showed that the extent of nodal disease and tumor diameter are independent predictors of survival. Patients with stage I tumors have a 5-year survival of 90% or better, whereas those with positive lymph nodes have a 5-year survival of approximately 50% to 60%, depending on the number and location of positive lymph nodes (*Am J Obstet Gynecol.* 1991;164:997). Improved 5-year survival rates for intermediate- and high-risk patients may be attributed to advancements in adjuvant chemoradiation therapy as well as diagnosing younger patients with less advanced disease (*Gynecol Oncol.* 2007;106:521).

B. **Cervical carcinoma.** Although detection of preinvasive disease has increased, the incidence of invasive cervical cancer has dramatically decreased in the United States because of widespread screening by cervical cytology (Papanicolaou smears). However, cervical cancer remains the leading cause of cancer-related deaths among women in developing countries (National Cervical Cancer Coalition Web site, http://www.ncccc-online.org/). In the United States, approximately 12,200 new cases and

TABLE 36-2	Vulvar Cancer Staging	
TNM	**FIGO**	**Definition**
T1	I	Tumor confined to the vulva
T1a	IA	Lesions ≤2 cm in size with stromal invasion ≤1 mm
T1b	IB	Lesions >2 cm in size or with stromal invasion >1 mm
T2	II	Tumor of any size, extending to adjacent perineal structures (lower one-third urethra, lower one-third vagina, anus) with negative nodes
T3	III	Tumor of any size with or without extension to adjacent perineal structures (lower one-third urethra, lower one-third vagina, anus) with positive inguinofemoral lymph nodes
T3a	IIIA(i) IIIA(ii)	With 1 lymph node metastasis (≥5 mm) 1–2 lymph node metastasis(es) (<5 mm)
T3b	IIIB(i) IIIB(ii)	With ≥2 lymph node metastasis (≥5 mm) ≥3 lymph node metastasis(es) (<5 mm)
T3c	IIIC	With positive lymph nodes with extracapsular spread
T4	IVA(i) IVA(ii)	Invades two-third upper urethral, two-third upper vagina, bladder/rectal mucosa, or fixed to pelvic bone, or Fixed or ulcerated inguinofemoral lymph nodes
M1	IVB	Distant metastasis including pelvic nodes

FIGO, International Federation of Gynecology and Obstetrics; TNM, tumor, node, metastasis.

4,210 deaths occur annually. The goal of evaluating abnormal Papanicolaou smears with colposcopy-guided biopsies for appropriate patients is to diagnose and treat preinvasive disease (*JAMA.* 2001;285:1500). Risk factors for cervical cancer include a history of STDs, HIV infection, multiple sexual partners, early age of first intercourse, lower socioeconomic status, smoking, and HPV infection. Because the majority of squamous cell cancers of the cervix contain high-risk HPV DNA, especially from HPV 16 and 18, HPV vaccines (Gardasil and Cervarix) have been developed and are recommended for females aged 9 to 26 and 10 to 25 years, respectively, although the impact in eradicating cancer will take several decades.

1. **Presentation and clinical features.** Patients may be asymptomatic or present with irregular or postcoital vaginal bleeding or a foul-smelling/watery discharge. Advanced stages may present with leg pain (sciatic nerve involvement), flank pain (ureteral obstruction), renal failure, or rectal bleeding.

2. **Diagnosis** is by biopsy via speculum examination of a visible or palpable lesion. Staging remains clinical and is based on a thorough bimanual and rectovaginal examination, cystoscopy, and proctoscopy. Appropriate adjuvant radiographs include chest radiogram, IV pyelogram, and barium enema. Positron emission tomographic scan is a useful diagnostic modality for assessing distant disease activity. Stage, which is never changed by intraoperative findings, remains the most important prognostic factor, with 5-year survival rates of 88% for stage I disease and 38% for stage III disease, respectively (Table 36-3).

3. **Treatment** depends on stage and lymph node status.
    a. **Microinvasive disease** [stage IA1, depth of invasion less than 3 mm, diameter less than 7 mm, negative lymph vascular space invasion (LVSI)] can be treated with cervical conization alone or with extrafascial hysterectomy. Reproductive age patients desiring fertility with stages IA1 with LVSI, IA2, or IB1 (preferably with a cervical lesion <2 cm and no extracervical disease) may be offered a radical vaginal or abdominal trachelectomy with a lymph node dissection and cerclage placement (*Gynecol Oncol.* 2010;117:350). Lesions with greater depth of invasion, multifocal disease, or upper-vaginal involvement (stages IA2 to IB1) require a radical hysterectomy (removing the parametria and upper vagina) and a complete pelvic and sometimes para-aortic lymphadenectomy. Although radical hysterectomy is only appropriate for a subset of patients, radiotherapy is applicable to any patient with early-stage cervical cancer. The most common complication after radical hysterectomy is bladder dysfunction. Ureteral fistulas, infection, hemorrhage, and lymphocyst formation are less common.
    b. **Radiotherapy** is the appropriate treatment for advanced-stage disease. Combined surgery and radiotherapy for advanced stages does not improve survival but dramatically increases the rate of treatment-related complications such as ureteral and bowel obstruction, strictures, and fistula formation. The nature of radiation is based on stage, lesion size, and lymph node status. Both external beam (teletherapy) and intracavitary (brachytherapy) radiation are used in various combinations. Complications from radiotherapy depend on dose, volume, and tissue tolerance. Acute complications include transient nausea and diarrhea. Early complications including skin ulceration, cystitis, and proctitis occur within the first 6 months after treatment. Late complications (>6 months after treatment) may include bowel obstruction secondary to strictures, fistulas, hemorrhagic cystitis, and chronic proctosigmoiditis. Recent studies indicate that adding cisplatin to radiation decreases the risk of dying from cervical cancer by 30% to 50% over radiation alone (*Lancet.* 2001;358:781).

TABLE 36-3		Cervical Cancer Staging
TNM	**FIGO**	**Definition**
T1	I	Cervical carcinoma confined to the cervix (disregard extension to the corpus).
T1a	IA	Preclinical invasive carcinoma, diagnosed by microscopy only. Deepest invasions ≤5 mm and largest extension ≥7 mm
T1a1	IA1	Microscopic stromal invasion ≤3 mm in depth and extension ≤7 mm
T1a2	IA2	Tumor with stromal invasion between 3 and 5 mm in depth and extension <7 mm
T1b	IB	Clinically visible tumor confined to the cervix but larger than IA2
T1b1	IB1	Clinical lesions ≤4 cm in size
T1b2	IB2	Clinical lesions >4 cm in size
T2	II	Invades beyond the cervix but not to the pelvic side wall or the lower one-third of the vagina
T2a	IIA	Tumor without parametrial involvement
T2a1	IIA1	Tumor ≤4 cm
T2a2	IIA2	Tumor >4 cm
T2b	IIB	Tumor with parametrial involvement
T3	III	Extends to the pelvic side wall and/or involves the lower one-third of the vagina and/or causes hydronephrosis or nonfunctioning kidney
T3a	IIIA	Invades lower one-third of the vagina with no extension to the pelvic side wall
T3b	IIIB	Extends to the pelvic side wall and/or causes hydronephrosis or a nonfunctioning kidney
T4	IVA	Invades mucosa of the bladder/rectum and/or extends beyond the true pelvis
M1	IVB	Distant metastasis

FIGO, International Federation of Gynecology and Obstetrics; TNM, tumor, node, metastasis.

    c. Patients with **pelvic recurrence** after radical hysterectomy are often treated with radiation. Those with isolated central recurrence may be candidates for pelvic exenteration. Five-year survival ranges from 20% to 62% after exenteration, with an operative mortality of 10%. Response to chemotherapy alone in recurrent cervical cancer is poor.

  4. Uncontrolled vaginal bleeding from cervical cancer occasionally is encountered in the emergency department. In most cases, bleeding can be stabilized with tight vaginal packing after which a transurethral Foley catheter should be placed. Acetone-soaked gauze is the most effective packing for vessel sclerosis and control of hemorrhage from necrotic tumor. Emergent radiotherapy or IR embolization may be necessary.

C. Endometrial carcinoma. Endometrial carcinoma is the most common gynecologic malignancy in the United States. An estimated 43,470 new cases will be diagnosed in 2010, with approximately 90% being adenocarcinomas arising from the lining of the uterus. Risk factors for endometrial cancer include Caucasian race, obesity, early menarche, late menopause, nulliparity, tamoxifen therapy, estrogen replacement therapy, infertility, hereditary nonpolyposis colon cancer (HNPCC), and factors leading to unopposed estrogen exposure. Hysterectomy with bilateral salpingo-oophorectomy effectively reduces endometrial and ovarian cancer risk in women with HNPCC and should be offered after completion of childbearing or at time of colectomy. Complex atypical endometrial hyperplasia, a precursor lesion, progresses to carcinoma in 29% of cases if left untreated. Only 1% to 3% of cases of hyperplasia without atypia progress to carcinoma. Hyperplasia can be treated conservatively with progestins and close observation with follow-up endometrial biopsy. Extrafascial hysterectomy is suggested for persistent hyperplasia in patients who have completed their childbearing. Pregnancy and OCP use appear to be protective.

  1. Presentation and clinical features. The most common symptom is abnormal vaginal bleeding, often in a postmenopausal patient. Approximately three-fourths of patients present with stage I disease. Endometrial sampling should be considered mandatory in all postmenopausal women. Although endometrial carcinoma is rare in women younger than 35 years, patients in this age group who have persistent noncyclic vaginal bleeding, are nonresponsive to medical management, or are morbidly obese should undergo endometrial assessment (ACOG Practice Bulletin 65. *Obstet Gynecol.* 2005;106:413).

  2. Physical examination should include an evaluation for obesity, hirsutism, and other signs of hyperestrogenism. The uterus may be enlarged or of normal size.

  3. Diagnosis is by transcervical aspiration (e.g., Pipelle), which usually is performed as an office procedure, or by hysteroscopy/D&C, which is performed in the operating room. Ultrasonography may assist in diagnosing an intrauterine abnormality.

  4. Treatment generally consists of a laparoscopic or open-staging procedure including pelvic washings, extrafascial total hysterectomy,

TABLE 36-4	Endometrial Cancer Staging	
TNM	**FIGO**	**Definition**
T1	I	Tumor confined to the corpus uteri
T1a	IA	Invades one-half or less of the myometrium
T1b	IB	Invades more than one-half of the myometrium
T2	II	Invades cervical stroma but does not extend beyond the uterus
T3	III	Local and/or regional spread as specified
T3a	IIIA	Involves the serosa and/or adnexa
T3b	IIIB	Vaginal and/or parametrial involvement
N1	IIIC IIIC1 IIIC2	Metastasis to the pelvic and/or para-aortic lymph nodes Positive pelvic nodes Positive para-aortic lymph nodes with or without positive pelvic lymph nodes
T4	IVA	Invades the bladder and/or bowel mucosa
M1	IVB	Distant metastasis including intra-abdominal and/or inguinal lymph nodes

FIGO, International Federation of Gynecology and Obstetrics; TNM, tumor, node, metastasis.

bilateral salpingo-oophorectomy, and sometimes omentectomy. Pelvic and para-aortic lymphadenectomy is considered both diagnostic and therapeutic and should be performed in patients who have a tumor of more than 2 cm, deep myometrial invasion, tumor grade of 2 or 3, or suspicious lymph nodes. Intraoperative evaluation of the uterus should be performed by bivalving the uterus and obtaining a frozen section as needed. Adjuvant radiotherapy and/or chemotherapy are used postoperatively in patients with poor prognostic factors who are at high risk for recurrence. Hormonal therapy can also be used.

5. **Prognosis** generally is favorable, with 5-year survival of more than 90% for patients with surgical stage I tumors (Table 36-4). Prognosis depends on the tumor grade, depth of myometrial invasion, adnexal involvement, pelvic cytology, LVSI, and lymph node spread. Rare histologies, such as clear-cell or papillary serous cancers and sarcomas arising from the wall of the uterus, do not share the overall good prognosis

of early-stage adenocarcinomas. African American women have mortality rates nearly twice that of Caucasian women.

D. **Ovarian carcinoma** is the deadliest of all the gynecologic malignancies. There will be approximately 21,880 new cases diagnosed in 2010. More than two-thirds of patients in whom epithelial ovarian cancer is diagnosed eventually die from this disease (13,850 per year in the United States) (*CA Cancer J Clin.* 2010;60:260–267). Besides tumors arising from the ovarian coelomic epithelium, which are the most common, germ cell (often in younger patients) and stromal primary tumors can occur. Two-thirds of epithelial ovarian cancers are diagnosed at advanced stages with extraovarian metastasis. Incidence increases steadily with advancing age to a total lifetime incidence of 1 in 68. Risk factors include nulliparity, late menopause, early menarche, use of infertility drugs, and personal or family history of breast or ovarian cancer. Genetic cancer syndromes including *BRCA1* or *BRCA2* mutations and HNPCC have also been associated with an increased risk of ovarian cancer, and prophylactic removal of ovaries and fallopian tubes decreases the risk of gynecologic cancer in these patients. Use of OCPs, pregnancy, and tubal ligation appear to be protective.

1. **Presentation and clinical features.** Women with early-stage disease are generally asymptomatic. In advanced stages, patients may present with vague abdominal pain or pressure, nausea, early satiety, weight loss, or swelling.

2. **Diagnosis** of ovarian cancer at early stages has proved to be clinically difficult (Table 36-5). No cost-effective screening test has proven to be reliable in detecting stage I disease (confined to the ovaries). Bimanual examination remains the most effective means of screening, followed by surgery for histologic diagnosis. Ultrasonography of the pelvis (preferably transvaginal) and CT scans are effective adjuncts. CA 125 antigen is not effective for mass screening but serves as an effective tumor marker in patients with initial elevations once diagnosis has been established and treatment is initiated.

3. **Treatment** is primarily aggressive surgical debulking for all patients with a good performance status. Complete staging includes pelvic washings on entering the peritoneum, total abdominal hysterectomy, bilateral salpingo-oophorectomy, omentectomy, pelvic and para-aortic lymph node dissection, and peritoneal biopsies. Optimal cytoreduction (residual disease <1 cm) improves response to adjuvant chemotherapy and overall survival. In young women with early-stage disease, fertility-sparing surgery can often be performed with removal of the uterus and contralateral ovary after childbearing age is completed. However, complete staging at initial surgery is still necessary. Patients with disease outside the ovary are treated with 6 cycles of paclitaxel and platinum–based chemotherapy either IV or intraperitoneally. The inclusion of bevacizumab (a humanized monoclonal antibody against vascular endothelial growth factor-A) to primary chemotherapy in ovarian cancer is being evaluated in a phase III trial.

TABLE 36.5		Ovarian Cancer Staging
TNM	**FIGO**	**Definition**
T1	I	Tumor limited to one or both ovaries
T1a	IA	Limited to one ovary; capsule intact, no tumor on ovarian surface, no malignant cells in ascites or peritoneal washings
T1b	IB	Limited to both ovaries; capsule intact, no tumor on ovarian surface, no malignant cells in ascites or peritoneal washings
T1c	IC	Limited to one or both ovaries with any of the following: capsule ruptured, tumor on ovarian surface, malignant cells in ascites, or peritoneal washings
T2	II	Tumor involves one or both ovaries with pelvic extension
T2a	IIA	Extension and/or implants on uterus and/or tubes; no malignant cells in ascites or peritoneal washings
T2b	IIB	Extension to other pelvic tissues; no malignant cells in ascites or peritoneal washings
T2c	IIC	Pelvic extension with malignant cells in ascites or peritoneal washings
T3	III	Tumor involves one or both ovaries with microscopically confirmed peritoneal metastasis outside the pelvis and/or regional lymph node metastasis
T3a	IIIA	Microscopic peritoneal metastasis beyond the pelvis
T3b	IIIB	Macroscopic peritoneal metastasis beyond the pelvis ≤2 cm
T3c	IIIC	Peritoneal metastasis beyond the pelvis >2 cm and/or regional lymph node involvement
M1	IV	Distant metastasis (excludes peritoneal metastasis)

FIGO, International Federation of Gynecology and Obstetrics; TNM, tumor, node, metastasis.

4. **Prognosis** correlates directly with stage and residual disease after debulking. Median survival depends on optimal cytoreduction at initial laparotomy. Median survival for optimally debulked advanced-stage tumors is nearly 80% at 1 year; the 5-year relative survival rate for all stages is 46% (*CA Cancer J Clin.* 2010;60:260–267).

37 Common Surgical Procedures

Kathryn J. Rowland and Bradley D. Freeman

This chapter reviews concepts, indications, and technical aspects of procedures commonly performed in hospitalized surgical patients, focusing on central venous catheterization, thoracic and peritoneal drainage procedures, airway access, and laparoscopy.

Basic rules govern the successful performance of surgical procedures: (1) Necessary equipment, supplies, lighting, and assistance should be available before starting the procedure; (2) the patient should be positioned to optimize exposure; (3) patient comfort must be ensured, and appropriate analgesia and sedation must be provided so that the patient can cooperate with and tolerate the procedure; and (4) sterile technique should be practiced when appropriate. Adherence to standards regarding consent, time-out, and documentation should be followed, as always.

I. **CENTRAL VENOUS CATHETERIZATION.** Central venous catheterization is commonly used in surgical patients both for diagnosis [central venous pressure (CVP) determination or pulmonary artery catheter for hemodynamic monitoring] and treatment [fluid infusion, administration of vasoactive agents, or mechanical device (e.g., pacemaker or inferior vena cava filter insertion)]. Several approaches to access the central venous system exist, each with advantages and disadvantages. Before placement of a central venous access device (CVAD), the patient should be evaluated for the presence of an indwelling central venous device, such as a transvenous pacemaker, and for signs of central venous obstruction, such as distended collateral veins about the shoulder and neck. **Contraindication:** Venous thrombosis is an absolute contraindication to catheter placement at the affected site. Relative contraindications include coagulopathy [international normalized ratio (INR) >2 or partial prothrombin time (PTT) >2 times control] refractory to correction and thrombocytopenia (platelet count <50,000/μL). For an elective procedure, the INR should be corrected to less than 1.5, PTT to less than 1.5 times control, and platelet count to greater than 50,000/μL.

A. **Types of catheters.** Catheters are classified on the basis of number of lumens, lifespan (short, intermediate, long-term), site of insertion (subclavian, internal jugular, femoral, peripheral), subcutaneous tunneling, anti-infective features (Dacron or silver-impregnated cuff, and/ or antibiotic-impregnated catheters), and tip structure (valved, non-valved). Prior to insertion, one should carefully consider the indications for placement, the expected duration of treatment, and the number of lumens necessary to achieve the treatment goals. Multilumen catheters are associated with slightly higher rates of infection than single-lumen catheters, and the choice of catheters should minimize the number of lumens while allowing for optimal patient care (*Crit Care Med.* 2003;31:2385).

1. **Short-term (nontunneled) CVADs.** The advantages of single-lumen and multilumen nontunneled catheters include low cost, bedside placement and removal, and ease of exchange of damaged catheters. A variety of products are available based upon the clinical need for administration of multiple drugs **(triple-lumen catheter)**, the rapid administration of fluids (multiaccess catheter [**MAC**]; Arrow International, Teleflex Medical, Research Triangle Park, NC), hemodialysis or pheresis (**Hemo-Cath;** MedComp, Harleysville, PA; or **Quinton Permcath;** Covidien, Mansfield, MA), or to allow for hemodialysis or pheresis with an additional lumen available for fluid or drug administration (**Mahurkar; Covidien** or **Trialysis;** Bard Access Systems, Murray Hill, NJ).

2. **Intermediate-term, peripherally inserted CVADs.** Peripherally inserted central catheters **(PICCs)** are composed of Silastic or polyurethane and can be kept in place for several days to several months for inpatient or outpatient therapy. These catheters are commonly used for home total parenteral nutrition (TPN) or intravenous antibiotic administration. PICCs can be inserted using local anesthetic at the bedside via cephalic, basilic, or median cubital veins. Proper position should be radiographically documented with a chest radiograph. These catheters have low risk of insertion-related complications, such as pneumothorax, and infection. Disadvantages of PICCs result from their small diameter and length (40 to 60 cm) and include low flow rates, problems with withdrawal occlusion, and risk for thrombophlebitis (*J Vasc Interv Radiol.* 2000;11:1309). Power injectable PICCs allow for more rapid flow rates of fluids and are compatible with the power injectors used for radiocontrast studies. Careful consideration is necessary prior to insertion in renal patients as PICCs can injure the upper-extremity veins, thus limiting suitability for future arteriovenous hemodialysis access.

3. **Intermediate-term, nontunneled CVADS.** These catheters contain a silver-impregnated gelatin cuff (Vitacuff; Vitaphore Corporation, San Carlos, CA), which is designed to be positioned subcutaneously and to serve as a barrier to migration of bacteria from the skin. The gelatin dissolves within a short time, facilitating removal. The **Hohn catheter** (Bard Access Systems, Murray Hill, NJ) is the prototypical CVAD of this type, and it may remain in place for several months.

4. **Long-term, tunneled CVADS.** Tunneled catheters enable indefinite venous access for prolonged nutritional support, chemotherapy, antibiotics, hemodialysis, or blood draws. The subcutaneous portion of the catheter contains a Dacron cuff that functions to induce scar formation, anchoring the catheter in place, and preventing bacterial migration from skin. Most tunneled catheters are manufactured using silicone, which is more flexible and durable than other materials. Examples include the **Hickman** and **Broviac**

catheters (Bard Access Systems, Murray Hill, NJ). The **Groshong catheter** (Bard Access Systems, Murray Hill, NJ) differs by the presence of a slit valve at the tip, which seals it from the bloodstream. Unlike other catheters, which require daily or weekly heparinized saline injections, Groshong catheters are flushed with normal saline with decreased flushing frequency and thus they are well suited for patients with history of heparin allergy or heparin-induced thrombocytopenia.

5. **Implanted venous ports.** Ports are used primarily for chronic therapy (>6 months) for which only intermittent access is needed. Common indications include chemotherapy and frequent hospitalizations (e.g., patients with sickle cell disease or cystic fibrosis). Access is commonly obtained via the internal jugular or subclavian veins, and a reservoir is placed in a subcutaneous pocket created in the infraclavicular fossa. Most models contain a silicone or polyurethane catheter connected to a metal or plastic reservoir with a dense silicone septum for percutaneous needle access. Models vary in height and presence of a dual or single chamber. Advantages of ports over other CVADs include a lower incidence of infection and less maintenance (monthly heparin flushes when not in use). Plastic ports are magnetic resonance scan compatible and are as durable as ports with reservoirs constructed of metal. Power injectable ports compatible with the power injectors used for radiocontrast studies are available. Port access requires skin puncture with a special noncoring (Huber) needle to prevent deterioration of the septum.

B. **Internal jugular approach**

1. **Indications.** The internal jugular vein is easily and rapidly accessible in most patients. Advantages of this site include decreased risk of pneumothorax compared with the subclavian approach and ready compressibility of the vessels in case of bleeding. For the unsedated or ambulatory patient, this may be an uncomfortable site and may hinder his or her neck movement. Maintaining a sterile dressing on the insertion site can be difficult, especially in the presence of a tracheostomy. This is a commonly used site of central venous access for the placement of tunneled catheters and ports where the catheter's exit site is on the chest.

2. **Technique.** Imaging devices (such as ultrasonography) are being increasingly used to delineate the vascular anatomy and enhance the safety of vascular access procedures (*Curr Opin Crit Care.* 2008;14:415; *Crit Care Med.* 2007;35:S186). Ultrasound guidance has been shown to increase both the overall success rate and first attempt success rate at internal jugular central venous cannulation on meta-analysis (*BMJ.* 2003;327:361). If available, such devices should be used, particularly in patients in whom anatomic landmarks are obscure. The pulse of the common carotid artery is palpated at the medial border of the sternocleidomastoid (SCM) muscle at midneck. The internal jugular vein is located lateral to the common carotid artery and courses slightly anterior to the artery as it joins the

subclavian vein (Fig. 37-1). The physician stands at the head of the bed. The patient is placed in the Trendelenburg position at an angle of 10 to 15 degrees, with his or her head flat on the bed and turned away from the side of the procedure. The skin is prepared with a chlorhexidine-based antiseptic solution, which has been shown to be superior to providine–iodine solutions in the prevention of catheter colonization (*Infect Control Hosp Epidemiol.* 2008;29:847). Sterile drapes are applied. One percent lidocaine is infiltrated subcutaneously over the belly and lateral border of the SCM. Two equally effective approaches to the internal jugular vein are described: the central and posterior approaches. For the central approach, a 21-gauge "seeker" needle is introduced approximately 1 cm lateral to the carotid pulse into the belly of the SCM. At a 45-degree angle, the needle is slowly advanced toward the ipsilateral nipple. For the posterior approach, the seeker needle is introduced at the lateral edge of the SCM and directed toward the sternal notch at a 45-degree angle. Constant negative pressure is exerted on the syringe, and entry into the vein is confirmed by the return of venous blood. Pulsatile, bright red blood suggests arterial access and mandates removal of the needle and direct manual pressure to the site for 10 minutes. The vein should be entered within 5 to 7 cm with both approaches. If the vein is not entered, the needle should be withdrawn and redirected for another attempt. Redirection of the needle should be inserted just below the surface of the skin because of the potential of the needle tip to lacerate adjacent vessels if redirected within the subcutaneous tissues. Under ultrasound guidance, the carotid artery (noncompressible, pulsatile) and internal jugular vein (compressible, nonpulsatile) are visualized and the vein is punctured under direct ultrasound guidance. Following venous access with the seeker needle, a 14-gauge needle is then introduced just inferior to the seeker needle and is advanced along the same path until venous blood is aspirated. The **Seldinger technique** is employed, whereby a flexible guidewire is passed into the vein through the 14-gauge needle, and the needle is removed over the wire. It is important to maintain control of the guidewire at all times. In cases of low flow, venous placement can be confirmed at this point by ultrasound visualization of the wire within the internal jugular vein. A nick is then made in the skin at the puncture site with a no. 11 blade to allow passage of the dilator. The dilator is threaded over the wire and creates a tract for the passage of the less rigid central venous catheter. The dilator is removed with the guidewire in place and the catheter is introduced over the wire and advanced to 15 to 20 cm so that its tip is at the junction of the superior vena cava (SVC) and the right atrium. The guidewire is then removed. In patients with difficult anatomy or indwelling devices (vena cava filters, pacemakers), fluoroscopy should be used to guide placement. Aspiration of blood from all ports and subsequent flushing with saline confirm that the catheter is positioned in the vein and that all of its ports are functional. The catheter is then secured to the patient's neck at a minimum of two sites, and a sterile dressing is applied. A chest radiograph is obtained to confirm the location of the catheter tip and to rule out the presence of a pneumothorax.

3. **Complications**

a. **Pneumothorax.** All percutaneously placed neck catheters carry a risk of pneumothorax. Every attempt at placement of a central venous catheter, successful or unsuccessful, should be followed by an erect chest radiograph before the catheter is used or catheter placement is attempted at another site. Presence of a small pneumothorax may be observed with serial chest radiographs. Unstable hemodynamics, worsening respiratory status, or expanding pneumothorax mandates tube thoracostomy placement (see Section II.B for procedure details).

b. **Carotid artery injury.** Carotid artery puncture complicates internal jugular cannulation in as many as 10% of cases, representing 80% to 90% of all insertion-related complications. Inadvertent carotid artery puncture is usually tolerated in the noncoagulopathic patient and treated by direct pressure over the carotid artery. If the carotid artery is punctured, no further attempts at central venous access should be made on either side of the patient's neck and the patient must be observed for the development of a neck hematoma and resultant airway compromise. Although carotid artery puncture is usually benign, it can be life threatening when it results in inadvertent intra-arterial cannulation, stroke, hemothorax, or carotid artery–internal jugular vein fistula. In the hemodynamically unstable or poorly oxygenating patient, it is not always possible to distinguish venous blood from arterial blood by appearance. This can lead to inadvertent cannulation of the carotid artery. If the dilator or catheter is 7 French (F) or smaller, it can usually be removed and direct pressure held over the carotid puncture site without further detrimental sequelae. Catheters larger than 7F should be removed in a setting in which operative repair of the arteriotomy can be performed.

c. **Guidewire-related complications.** Advancement of the guidewire into the right atrium or ventricle can cause arrhythmia, which usually resolves once the wire is withdrawn. Central venous catheter insertion in patients with indwelling devices (such as vena cava filters or pacemakers) must be performed under fluoroscopic guidance to minimize the possibility of entanglement of the guidewire with these structures.

d. **Venous stenosis.** Venous stenosis can occur at the site where the catheter enters the vein, which can lead to thrombosis of the vessel. Because the upper extremities and neck have extensive collateralization, stenosis or thrombosis is usually well tolerated.

e. **Other.** Air embolus, perforation of the right atrium or ventricle with resultant hemopericardium and cardiac tamponade, and injury to the trachea, esophagus, thoracic duct, vagus nerve, phrenic nerve, or brachial plexus can all complicate the placement of central venous catheters.

C. **Subclavian vein approach**

1. **Indications.** The subclavian approach to the central venous system is generally most comfortable for the patient and easiest to maintain. The Centers for Disease Control and Prevention (CDC) published guidelines in 2002 that recommend subclavian access as the preferred site in patients at risk for CVAD infection (*MMWR Recomm Rep.* 2002;51:1). A prospective observational study found that catheter-related bloodstream infection (CRBSI) incidence was lowest in subclavian access, higher in jugular access, and highest in femoral access and recommended that sites for CVAD placement be considered in that order (*Crit Care.* 2005;9:R631). In the presence of an open wound, tracheostomy, and tumors of the head and neck, CVAD should be placed in the subclavian position to minimize infection risk.

2. **Technique.** The subclavian vein courses posterior to the clavicle, where it joins the internal jugular vein and the contralateral veins to form the SVC (Fig. 37-1). The subclavian artery and the apical pleura lie just posterior to the subclavian vein. The patient is placed in the Trendelenburg position with a rolled towel between the scapulas, which allows the shoulders to fall posteriorly. The skin is prepared with a chlorhexidine-based antiseptic solution, draped, and

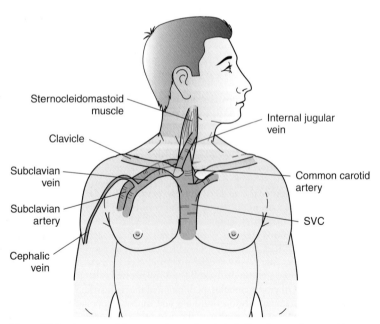

Figure 37-1. Anatomy of the upper chest and neck, including the vasculature and important landmarks. SVC, superior vena cava.

1% lidocaine is infiltrated subcutaneously in the infraclavicular space near the middle and lateral third of the clavicle. The infusion of lidocaine is carried into the deep soft tissue and to the periosteum of the clavicle. A 14-gauge needle is introduced at the middle third of the clavicle in the deltopectoral groove. The needle is kept deep to the clavicle and parallel to the plane of the floor and is slowly advanced toward the sternal notch. Constant negative pressure is applied to the syringe. Once the needle enters the subclavian vein, the guidewire, the dilator, and the catheter are introduced by the **Seldinger technique.** As with the other approaches, all catheter ports are aspirated and flushed to ensure that they are functional. A chest radiograph is obtained to confirm the location of the catheter tip and to evaluate for pneumothorax.

3. **Complications.** The complications of subclavian venous catheterization include those described in the previous section. Puncture of the subclavian artery can be troublesome because the clavicle prevents the application of direct pressure to achieve homeostasis. Therefore, this approach should be avoided in the patient with uncorrectable coagulopathy. If the artery is punctured, the patient should be placed on hemodynamic monitoring for the next 30 to 45 minutes to ensure that bleeding is not ongoing. Inadvertent cannulation of the subclavian artery with the dilator or catheter is a potentially fatal complication. The dilator or catheter should be left in place and angiography performed. Removal of the catheter should be done in the operating room so that open arteriotomy repair may be performed if necessary. Left-sided subclavian catheter placement poses the risk of injury to the thoracic duct, brachiocephalic vein, and SVC with the needle or dilator. Attention must be paid to the final position of the catheter tip when placed on the left side to avoid abutting the SVC wall, which poses the immediate or delayed risk of SVC perforation.

D. **Femoral vein approach**

1. **Indications.** The femoral vein is the easiest site for obtaining central access and is therefore the preferred approach for central venous access during trauma or cardiopulmonary resuscitation. This approach does not interfere with the other procedures of cardiopulmonary resuscitation. It should be remembered that a femoral vein catheter does not actually reach the central circulation and may not be ideal for the administration of vasoactive drugs. The femoral approach is also favored during trauma resuscitation except when there is an injury to the inferior vena cava. The femoral vein catheter inhibits patient mobility, and the groin is a difficult area in which to maintain sterility. Therefore, it should not be used in elective situations, except when upper-extremity and neck sites are not available. This may be the only site available in patients with upper-body burns. Catheters placed at any site during a medical emergency (including cardiopulmonary or trauma resuscitation) when sterile technique cannot be assured should be replaced within 48 hours of insertion to minimize the risk of CRBSI.

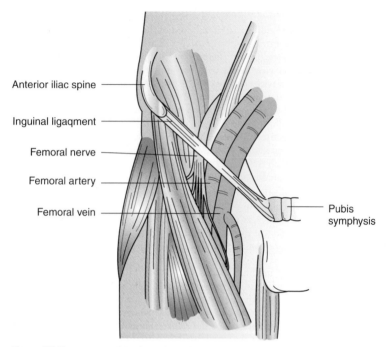

Figure 37-2. Anatomy of the femoral vessels.

2. **Technique.** The femoral artery crosses the inguinal ligament approximately midway between the anterosuperior iliac spine and the pubic tubercle. The femoral vein runs medial to the artery as they cross the inguinal ligament (Fig. 37-2). The skin is prepared with a chlorhexadine-based antiseptic solution, draped, and 1% lidocaine is infiltrated in the subcutaneous tissue medial to the femoral artery and inferior to the inguinal ligament. The pulse of the femoral artery is palpated below the inguinal ligament, and a 14-gauge needle is introduced medial to the pulse at a 30-degree angle. It is directed cephalad with constant negative pressure until the vein is entered. Once the needle enters the femoral vein, the guidewire, the dilator, and ultimately the catheter are inserted using the **Seldinger technique.** When a femoral pulse cannot be palpated, as in cardiopulmonary arrest, the position of the femoral artery can be estimated to be at the midpoint between the anterosuperior iliac spine and the pubic tubercle, with the vein lying 1 to 2 cm medial to this point. Once the catheter is successfully placed, all three ports are aspirated and flushed to ensure that they are functional.

3. **Complications.** Injury to the common femoral artery or its branches during cannulation of the femoral vein can result in an inguinal or

retroperitoneal hematoma, a pseudoaneurysm, or an arteriovenous fistula. The femoral nerve can also be damaged. Injury to the inguinal lymphatic system can result in a lymphocele. The possibility of injuring peritoneal structures also exists, particularly if an inguinal hernia is present. Errant passages of the guidewire and the rigid dilator run the risk of perforating the pelvic venous complex and causing retroperitoneal hemorrhage. Late complications include infection and femoral vein thrombosis.

E. **Catheter maintenance.** Proper care of access sites and devices is crucial to their long-term function. CVADs require sterile dressing changes at least weekly. Our institution uses sterile, occlusive, transparent dressings; however, this has not been shown superior to the use of sterile, gauze dressings secured with tape (*Cochrane Database Syst Rev.* 2003;(4):CD003827). More frequent dressing changes may be needed for those patients who are immunocompromised. Chlorhexidine gluconate–impregnated sponges (BioPatch; Ethicon Inc, Somerville, NJ) applied to the skin at the site of catheter insertion beneath an occlusive dressing have been shown to reduce CRBSIs (*JAMA.* 2009;301(12):1231–1241). Application of topical antibiotic beneath an occlusive dressing may provide a moist culture medium for bacterial growth and should be avoided. Catheter lumens should be flushed on a regular basis to prevent thrombosis. Heparin has been shown to be superior to saline for decreasing thrombotic occlusions of central venous catheters (*JPEN J Parenter Enteral Nutr.* 2010;34:444) (see Section I.G. for further details).

F. **CRBSIs** occur with a prevalence ranging from 3% to 7% and has a mortality rate of up to 20% (*Infect Control Hosp Epidemiol.* 2000;21:375). CRBSIs prolong intensive care unit stays, increase total hospital days, and have an attributable cost of nearly $12,000 per incidence (*Crit Care Med.* 2006; 34:2084). Catheter colonization—or bacterial growth from the catheter tip—occurs in 20% of central venous catheters.

1. **Epidemiology.** CRBSIs are generally caused by coagulase-negative staphylococci (37%), followed by gram-negative bacilli (14%), enterococci (13.5%), coagulase-positive *Staphylococcus aureus* (12.6%), and *Candida albicans* (5%) (*Am J Infect Control.* 1999;27:520). Treatment of these organisms has become increasingly difficult now that 60% of *S. aureus* isolates and 90% of coagulase-negative *Staphylococcus* isolates are resistant to oxacillin. The percentage of enterococcal isolates resistant to vancomycin has also increased, from 0.5% in 1989 to 28.5% in 2003 (*Am J Infect Control.* 2004;32:470). The majority of catheter infections are monomicrobial.

2. **Pathogenesis.** Infection occurs by two routes. First, endogenous skin flora at the insertion site migrate along the external surface of the catheter and colonize the intravascular tip. Second, pathogens from contamination at the hub colonize the internal surface of the catheter and are washed into the bloodstream when the catheter is infused. Occasionally, catheters may become hematogenously seeded from another focus of infection. Rarely, infusate contamination or break in sterile technique leads to CRBSI.

3. **Definitions and diagnosis.** Catheter colonization is defined as greater than 15 colony-forming units of microorganisms on semiquantitative culture. The definition of CRBSI requires bacteremia or fungemia in a patient with CVAD and meeting of the following criteria: (1) clinical signs of infection (fever, chills, tachycardia, hypotension, leukocytosis), (2) no identifiable source for bloodstream infection other than the CVAD, and (3) isolation of the same organism from semiquantitative culture of the catheter and from the blood (drawn from a peripheral vein taken within 48 hours of each other) (*Clin Infect Dis.* 2009;49:1). Diagnosis of CRBSI with coagulase-negative staphylococci requires two positive blood cultures or a positive catheter culture.

4. **Presentation and treatment.** Catheter infections may manifest with local, regional, or systemic signs. Treatment is based upon consideration of multiple factors, including severity of infection, causative organism, type of catheter, and remaining options for vascular access.
    a. **Local and regional catheter-related infections** (*Clin Infect Dis.* 2009;49:1). Local exit-site infections may present with pain, erythema, induration, or drainage. In general, short-term (nontunneled) CVADs should be removed if an exit-site infection is present. For long-term (tunneled) CVADs, an uncomplicated exit-site infection (without purulent drainage, in the absence of systemic signs, and with negative blood cultures) can be treated with topical antibiotics, systemic antibiotics for skin flora, and more frequent dressing changes and care. Catheter removal is required if systemic antibiotic therapy fails. Tunnel infection or port abscess, purulent drainage, or systemic manifestations (leukocytosis, positive blood culture) require catheter removal, incision and drainage, and systemic antibiotics.
    b. **Bacteremia** (*Clin Infect Dis.* 2009;49:1). Bacteremia is the most severe manifestation of a catheter-related infection and often presents with fever and leukocytosis. In the setting of bacteremia, indwelling catheters generally should be removed and the patient should be treated with a course of systemic antibiotics. Empiric antibiotic treatment while awaiting culture results should consist of coverage against gram-positive cocci, including methicillin-resistant staphylococci. For lower-extremity CVADs, coverage against gram-negative bacilli and *Candida* should be included as well. In select patients with limited vascular access and other potential sources for infection, salvage of the catheter can be attempted with broad-spectrum antibiotics and antibiotic lock therapy for 10 to 14 days. Persistent bacteremia after 72 hours necessitates catheter removal. The presence of fungemia requires immediate removal of the catheter, with initiation of antifungal treatment. Rewiring of the existing catheter should not be performed in the setting of CRBSI.

5. **Risk factors.** The risk for infection varies with the catheter insertion site, with the femoral vein associated with a much higher infection rate than subclavian vein access (19.8% vs. 4.5%) (*JAMA.* 2001;286:700).

Jugular venous catheterization carries an intermediate risk of infection. The likelihood of infection directly correlates with length of time a catheter has been in position. PICCs in intensive care unit patients have been demonstrated to have similar rates of CRBSI as that of non-tunneled CVADs but have longer time to the development of infection (*Am J Infect Control.* 2010;38:149).

6. **Prevention.** The largest impact in reducing CRBSIs has been achieved via inexpensive interventions and educational initiatives on basic infection control practices. When instituted together, hand hygiene, chlorhexidine-based skin preparation, maximal barrier precautions, avoidance of the femoral vein for insertion, and daily review of the necessity for and removal of all unnecessary central venous catheters have been demonstrated to result in an up to 66% reduction in CRBSI (*N Engl J Med.* 2006;355:2725).

   a. **Antimicrobial-impregnated catheters.** Antimicrobial-coated catheters, ionic silver cuffs, and antibiotic-impregnated hubs have been developed in efforts to reduce CRBSI. In a multicenter, randomized, double-blind, controlled trial, second-generation chlorhexidine-silver sulfadiazine (CHSS)–impregnated CVADs reduced microbial colonization compared to uncoated catheters (*Ann Intern Med.* 2005; 143:570). A subsequent meta-analysis found that rifampin/minocycline–impregnated CVADs reduced the rate of microbial colonization and CRBSI (*J Antimicrob Chemother.* 2007;59:359). Not all studies have supported a decreased rate of CRBSIs with antimicrobial-impregnated catheters over that achieved with educational initiatives and infection prevention bundles of care alone (*Crit Care Med.* 2009;37(2):702). The emergence of resistant organisms resulting from the use of antimicrobial-impregnated catheters remains a potentially important concern. The current data are inconclusive; however, many support the use of antimicrobial-impregnated catheters, especially in high-risk patients.

   b. **Routine (elective) catheter replacement.** Routine catheter replacement (either changing position to a new site or rewiring an existing catheter after an arbitrary length of time) has not been demonstrated to decrease the incidence of catheter-related infections. Thus, CVADs should be left in place until discontinuation is clinically indicated.

G. **Thrombosis** (*J Natl Compr Cancer Netw.* 2006;4:889). Difficulty in aspirating blood or infusing fluid from a previously functional catheter may be indicative of partial or complete catheter blockage. Blockage may be due to kinking of the catheter, occlusion of the catheter tip on a vessel wall, or luminal thrombosis. The spectrum of thrombotic complications ranges from fibrin sleeve formation around the catheter to mural or occlusive thrombus. Although only 3% to 5% of central venous catheters develop clinically significant thromboses, ultrasonography with color Doppler imaging has been found to detect venous thrombosis in 33% to 67% of patients when the indwelling time of the CVAD was greater than 1 week.

A negative Doppler ultrasonography in a symptomatic patient should be followed by venographic assessment because thrombi in the central upper venous system (SVC, brachiocephalic, and subclavian veins) are better detected by venography.

1. **Intervention** (*Lancet.* 2009;374:159). Inspection of the catheter and repositioning of the patient to exclude mechanical obstruction should first be performed. Empiric thrombolytic intervention with alteplase (2 mL of 2 mg/2 mL alteplase administered into the catheter lumen and allowed to dwell for at least 30 minutes) is generally an effective and safe means of restoring CVAD function and blood flow without resorting to catheter replacement. If this procedure fails or if the patient is symptomatic, imaging with Doppler ultrasonography or venography should be performed. In the presence of a venous thrombosis, the catheter should be removed and systemic anticoagulation should be initiated.

H. **Catheter removal.** Catheters should be removed as soon as they are no longer clinically indicated, given the increased risk of CRBSIs with increased catheter duration (*Surg Infect.* 2010;11(6):529). Proper internal jugular or subclavian catheter removal requires placement of the patient in Trendelenberg positioning (head down). To prevent an air embolus, the patient is instructed to perform the Valsalva maneuver; taking a deep breath in, holding the breath, and bearing down (to create a high intrathoracic pressure) during removal. The catheter tip should always be inspected to verify that it is intact. Manual pressure is applied for 5 minutes while the patient breathes normally (or longer for patients with coagulopathy or for removal of larger-bore catheters). Once hemostasis is obtained, an occlusive dressing is applied. In the absence of clinical suspicion for CRBSI, the catheter tip should not be routinely cultured (*Clin Infect Dis.* 2009;49:1).

II. THORACIC DRAINAGE PROCEDURES

A. Thoracentesis

1. **Indications.** Thoracentesis can provide both diagnostic and therapeutic benefit for patients with pleural effusions. Pleural effusions are categorized as transudative or exudative. Transudative effusions are associated with conditions of increased hydrostatic pressure or decreased colloid osmotic pressure such as volume overload, congestive heart failure, or cirrhosis. Exudative effusions are associated with conditions resulting in inflammation such as infection or cancer. This differentiation is based on gross, microscopic, and biochemical characteristics. Diagnostic thoracentesis is indicated for an effusion of unknown etiology. Pleural fluid lactate dehydrogenase (LDH), protein, pH, glucose, amylase, lipid, Gram stain, culture, and cytology should be performed. A pleural fluid–serum LDH ratio greater than 0.6 and a fluid–serum protein ratio greater than 0.5 indicate an exudative effusion, whereas a fluid–serum LDH ratio less than 0.6 and a fluid–serum protein ratio

less than 0.5 indicate a transudative effusion. Therapeutic thoracentesis is indicated to relieve respiratory compromise resulting from large pleural effusions. For recurrent pleural effusions, when repeated therapeutic thoracentesis is needed, chest tube drainage and pleurosclerosis should be considered.

2. **Technique.** Erect and lateral decubitus chest radiographs or equivalent imaging studies (such as computed tomographic scan) should be obtained to assess the size and location of the effusion as well as whether the effusion is free flowing or loculated. For free-flowing effusions, the patient is seated upright and slightly forward. The thorax should be entered posteriorly, 4 to 6 cm lateral to the spinal column and one to two interspaces below the cessation of tactile fremitus and where percussion is dull. Loculated effusions can be localized by ultrasonography, and the site for thoracentesis is marked on the skin. The site is prepared with chlorhexadine and draped with sterile towels. One percent lidocaine is infiltrated into the subcutaneous tissue covering the rib below the interspace to be entered. The infiltration is carried deep to the periosteum of the rib. Next, with negative pressure placed on the syringe, the needle is advanced slowly over the top of the rib to avoid injury to the neurovascular bundle, which lies just inferior to the rib. The needle is advanced until pleural fluid is returned and is then withdrawn a fraction to allow for injection of lidocaine to anesthetize the pleura. Lidocaine is then infiltrated into the intercostal muscles as the needle is withdrawn. Most thoracentesis kits contain a long, 14-gauge needle inserted into a plastic catheter with an attached syringe and stopcock. The needle–catheter apparatus is introduced at the level of the rib below the interspace to be entered. With negative pressure applied to the syringe, the needle is slowly advanced over the top of the rib and into the pleural cavity until fluid is returned. Aspiration of air bubbles indicates puncture of the lung parenchyma; the needle should be promptly removed under negative pressure. Once the needle is in the pleural space, the catheter is advanced over the needle toward the diaphragm. Special attention is taken not to advance the needle as the catheter is being directed into the pleural space. A drainage bag is attached to the stopcock to remove the pleural fluid. The amount of fluid removed depends on the indication for the thoracentesis. A diagnostic thoracentesis requires 20 to 30 mL of fluid for the appropriate tests; a therapeutic thoracentesis can drain 1 to 2 L of fluid at one time. Care should be taken when draining large volumes of effusions, as fluid shifts can occur and cause hemodynamic instability. A chest radiograph should be obtained after the procedure to evaluate for pneumothorax and resolution of the effusion.

3. **Complications.** Pneumothorax is the most common complication of thoracentesis. Small pneumotharaces (i.e., <10%) are generally well tolerated and can be followed with serial radiographs every 6 hours. Tube thoracotomy (see Section II.B) is indicated for large pneumothoraces. Reexpansion pulmonary edema can occur in situations when a large amount of fluid is removed. Hemothorax, empyema, injury

to the neurovascular bundle, laceration of the lung parenchyma, and subcutaneous hematoma are other potential complications.

B. Tube thoracostomy

1. **Indications and contraindications.** Tube thoracostomy is indicated for a pneumothorax, hemothorax, recurrent pleural effusion, chylothorax, and empyema. In an emergent situation such as a tension pneumothorax, a needle thoracostomy using a 14-or 16-gauge needle inserted in the second intercostal space, midclavicular line, can allow for air decompression while awaiting tube thoracostomy.

2. **Tubes.** The size of the thoracostomy tube needed depends on the material to be drained. Generally, a 32F to 36F tube is used for the evacuation of a hemothorax or pleural effusion. In a pneumothorax, a 24F to 28F tube is used. Alternatively, a percutaneous small-bore (18F) chest tube (Thal-Quick; Cook Medical, Bloomington, IN) can be placed by the Seldinger technique.

3. **Anatomy.** Understanding of thoracic anatomy is needed to prevent injuries to the lung parenchyma, diaphragm, intercostal neurovascular bundles, and mediastinum during chest tube placement. Adhesions of the lung to the chest wall may be present and complicate insertion and advancement of the thoracostomy tube. During normal respiration, the diaphragm can rise to the level of the fourth intercostal space; insertion of the chest tube lower than the sixth interspace is discouraged. The tube should be passed over the top of the rib to avoid injury to the intercostal neurovascular bundle, which runs in a groove on the inferior aspect of each rib.

4. **Technique.** The patient is placed in the lateral position with the site of insertion (affected side) up, and the head of the bed inclined 10 to 15 degrees. The patient's arm on the affected side is extended forward or above the head. With the skin prepared and draped, 1% lidocaine is infiltrated over the fifth or sixth rib in the middle or anterior axillary line into the subcutaneous tissue covering the rib below the interspace to be entered, carried deep to the periosteum of the rib. With negative pressure placed on the syringe, the needle is advanced slowly over the top of the rib until a rush of air or fluid is returned. The needle is then withdrawn a fraction to allow for injection of lidocaine to anesthetize the pleura. As the needle is withdrawn, lidocaine is infiltrated into the intercostal muscles. A 2- to 3-cm transverse incision is then made through the skin and subcutaneous tissue. A curved clamp is used bluntly to dissect an oblique tract to the rib (Fig. 37-3A). With careful spreading, the clamp is advanced over the top of the rib. The parietal pleura is punctured with the clamp, and an efflux of air or fluid is usually encountered. A finger is introduced into the tract to ensure passage into the pleural space and to lyse any adhesions at the point of entry (Fig. 37-3B), ensuring that there is no lung adherent to the thoracic wall. With the clamp as a guide, the thoracostomy tube is introduced into the pleural space (Fig. 37-3C); the tube is directed posteriorly or basally for a dependent effusion and apically for a pneumothorax. A

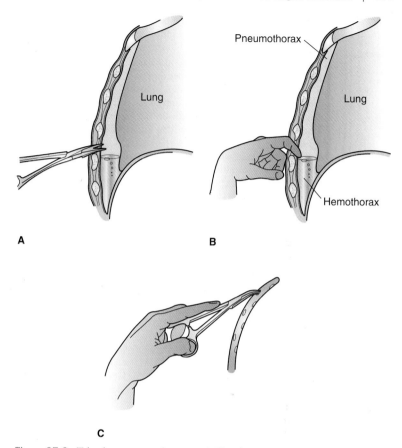

Figure 37-3. Tube thoracostomy placement. A: Pleural space entered by blunt spreading of the clamp over the top of the adjacent rib. B: A finger is introduced to ensure position within the pleural space and to lyse adhesions. C: The thoracostomy tube is placed into the tunnel and directed with the help of a Kelly clamp. The tube is directed posterior and caudal for an effusion or hemothorax and cephalad for a pneumothorax.

clamp placed at the free end of the thoracostomy tube prevents drainage from the chest until the tube can be connected to a closed suction or water-seal system. The thoracostomy tube is advanced until the last hole of the tube is clearly inside the thoracic cavity. When the tube is positioned properly and functioning adequately, it is secured to the skin with two heavy silk sutures and covered with an occlusive dressing to prevent air leaks. A U-stitch around the tube is commonly placed for use as a purse-string suture to close the tract once the tube is removed. A chest radiograph is obtained after the procedure to assess for lung reexpansion and tube position. Under certain circumstances, such as the presence of loculated pleural effusions or prior thoracic surgery, radiographic guidance is required for tube placement.

5. **Complications.** Placement of a thoracostomy tube in the inferior aspect of the chest may result in inadvertent injury to adjacent abdominal organs (such as the spleen, liver). Failure to guide the tube into the pleural space can result in dissection of the extrapleural plane. Extrapleural tube diagnosis can be difficult, but anteroposterior and lateral chest radiographs should reveal a lung that has failed to reexpand and suggest a chest tube placed outside the thorax. The tube should be removed and placed within the thoracic cavity to reexpand the lung. Parenchymal, hilar injuries, or cardiac injuries can occur with overzealous advancement of the tube or dissection of pleural adhesions. Other complications include subcutaneous emphysema, reexpansion pulmonary edema, phrenic nerve injury, esophageal perforation, contralateral pneumothorax, and neurovascular bundle injury. Late infectious complications include empyema, infection along the thoracostomy tube tract, and abscess; following strict sterile technique during tube placement may minimize these complications.

III. PERITONEAL DRAINAGE PROCEDURES

A. **Paracentesis**

1. **Indications.** Paracentesis is a useful diagnostic and therapeutic tool. Diagnostic paracentesis is most commonly indicated in the surgical patient to determine the presence of infection in ascites. Accordingly, ascites should be submitted for cell count, Gram stain, microscopy, and culture. A therapeutic paracentesis is indicated for patients with respiratory compromise or discomfort caused by tense ascites and in patients with ascites refractory to medical management. Relative contraindications include previous abdominal surgery, pregnancy, and coagulopathy.

2. **Technique.** Patients should be in a supine position. The bladder should be empty. Level of the ascites can be determined by locating the transition from dullness to tympany with percussion. Depending on the height of the ascites, a midline or lateral approach can be used. Care must be taken with the midline approach because the air-filled bowel tends to float on top of the ascites. Ultrasound guidance can help in identification of ascites, obtainment of successful ascitic fluid, and avoidance of injury to the bowel (*Am J Emerg Med.* 2005;23:363). The skin at the site of entry should be prepared and draped. One percent lidocaine is infiltrated subcutaneously and is carried to the level of the peritoneum. For the midline approach, a needle is introduced at a point midway between the umbilicus and the pubis symphyses. For the lateral approach, the point of entry can be in the right or left lower quadrant in the area bounded by the lateral border of the rectus abdominis muscle, the line between the umbilicus and the anterior iliac spine, and the line between the anterior iliac spine and the pubis

symphysis. A simple diagnostic tap can be achieved by inserting a 22-gauge needle into the peritoneal cavity and aspirating 20 to 30 mL of fluid. Constant negative pressure should be applied to the syringe, and care should be taken not to advance the needle beyond the point where ascites is encountered. For a therapeutic paracentesis, a 14-gauge needle fitted with a catheter allows for efficient drainage of larger volumes of ascites. With either the midline or the lateral approach, once ascites is returned, the catheter is advanced over the needle and directed toward the pelvis. A drainage bag is attached to the catheter to collect and measure the fluid removed.

3. **Complications.** Injuries to the bowel or bladder can occur with paracentesis. Emptying the bladder prior to the procedure, avoiding the insertion of the needle near surgical scars, and maintaining control of the needle once inside the peritoneum help to minimize these injuries. Intraperitoneal hemorrhage from injury to a mesenteric vessel can occur. Laceration of the inferior epigastric vessels can lead to a hematoma of the rectus sheath or the abdominal wall. In patients with large, recurrent ascites, a persistent leakage of ascites from the site of entry can result. Peritonitis or abdominal wall abscesses can also result. Removal of a large amount of ascites can result in fluid shifts and hemodynamic instability.

IV. EMERGENCY AIRWAY ACCESS

A. **Endotracheal (ET) intubation**

1. **Indications.** Establishment of a secure airway is the first priority in the management of an acutely ill patient. A thorough description of this topic is beyond the scope of this text. A brief overview of the salient aspects of this technique is provided.

2. **Technique.** Preoxygenation with a bag-valve-mask apparatus and 100% oxygen, suction, adequate sedation, muscle relaxation, an appropriately sized ET tube, and a functional laryngoscope are required. Two types of laryngeal scope blades are available: a straight blade (Miller) and a curved blade (Macintosh). The straight blade may provide better visualization in children, and the curved blade may be better for patients with short, thick necks. The physician should be comfortable using either blade. With the physician at the patient's head, the head is positioned so that the pharyngeal and laryngeal axes are in alignment (Fig. 37-4A). The patient's head and neck are fully extended into the "sniffing" position. With the nondominant hand, the physician opens the patient's mouth with the thumb and the index finger on the patient's lower and upper teeth, respectively. The oropharynx is inspected, and foreign bodies or secretions are removed. The blade of the laryngoscope is introduced and used to sweep the patient's tongue to the side. The blade is then advanced with gentle traction upward and toward the patient's feet. Once the epiglottis is visualized, the tip of the blade is positioned in the vallecula. Great care must be taken not to use the handle as a lever against the patient's teeth and lips,

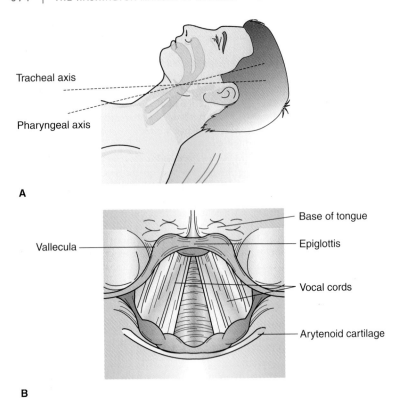

Figure 37-4. Orotracheal intubation. **A:** Fully extending the patient's head into the "sniffing" position aligns the pharyngeal and laryngeal axes. This allows for the best visualization of the airway. **B:** View of the larynx and airway during oral intubation of the trachea.

as this can result in damage and chipping of the teeth. The glottic opening and vocal cords should come into view (Fig. 37-4B). If not, gently increasing the upward and caudal traction or having an assistant place external pressure on the cricoid and thyroid cartilage can be helpful. If the glottic opening still cannot be visualized, the blade should be removed and the patient oxygenated and repositioned prior to additional attempts. Once the glottic opening is adequately visualized, the ET tube is advanced under direct vision until the cuff passes through the vocal cords. The cuff is inserted roughly 2 cm past the vocal cords, and the patient's incisors should rest between the 19- and 23-cm markings on the tube. The stylet and the laryngoscope are carefully removed while maintaining control and position of the ET tube. The cuff is inflated, and proper position is confirmed by auscultating bilateral breath sounds and determining end-tidal carbon dioxide. Once position is confirmed, the ET tube is secured to the patient. An anteroposterior chest radiograph is obtained to confirm position. Ideally, the tip of the ET tube should be 2 to 4 cm above the carina.

3. **Complications.** Chipped teeth, emesis and aspiration, vocal cord injury, laryngospasm, and soft-tissue injury to the oropharynx can all complicate ET intubation.

B. **Cricothyroidotomy**

1. **Indications.** Cricothyroidotomy is indicated when attempts at establishing translaryngeal intubation fail.

2. **Technique.** Most cricothyroidotomies are done in emergent situations. An understanding of the anatomy in the region of the trachea is necessary to minimize complications. The thyroid cartilage is easily identified in the midline of the neck (Fig. 37-5). The cricoid, the only complete cartilaginous ring, is the first ring inferior to the thyroid cartilage. The cricothyroid membrane joins these two cartilages and is an avascular membrane. Inferior to the cricoid and straddling the trachea is the isthmus of the thyroid gland. The thyroid lobes lie lateral to the trachea, and the superior poles can extend to the level of the thyroid cartilage. The area should be prepared, draped, and anesthetized with 1% lidocaine. A vertical skin incision is made. The cricoid cartilage is identified and held firmly and circumferentially in the physician's nondominant hand until the end of the procedure. With a no. 11 or 15 blade, a small, 3- to 5-cm transverse incision is made over the cricothyroid membrane. The incision

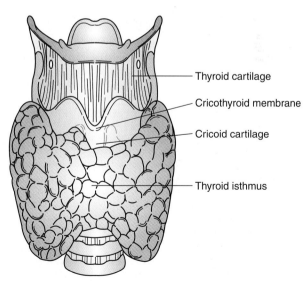

Thyroid cartilage

Cricothyroid membrane

Cricoid cartilage

Thyroid isthmus

Figure 37-5. Anatomy of the larynx.

is carried deep until the airway is entered through the cricothyroid membrane. The index finger of the physician's nondominant hand can be used to identify landmarks as the dissection proceeds should the field become obscured. The tract is widened using a clamp, a tracheal dilator, or the end of the scalpel handle. The tracheostomy tube is inserted along its curve into the trachea and the cuff is inflated. An ET tube can be used if a tracheostomy tube is not immediately available. Proper position should be confirmed with end-tidal capnography.

3. **Complications.** Creation of a false passage when inserting the tracheostomy tube is the most common complication. This should become evident by the absence of breath sounds, lack of end-tidal carbon dioxide, and the development of subcutaneous emphysema. Pneumothorax can also occur. Injury to surrounding structures, such as the thyroid, parathyroids, esophagus, anterior jugular veins, and recurrent laryngeal nerves, can occur in situations of urgency. Subglottic stenosis and granuloma formation are potential long-term complications.

C. **Percutaneous tracheostomy**

1. **Indications.** Percutaneous tracheostomy (PT) has become increasingly popular for the establishment of a nonemergent airway. The advantages of PT over surgical tracheostomy (ST) are primarily related to reduced tissue trauma and the ease of bedside performance, which avoids transportation of critically ill patients to the operating room. Several studies support the cost-effectiveness of this approach (*Crit Care Med.* 2001;29:926). Contraindications include unstable cervical spine, inability to identify anatomic landmarks, refractory coagulopathy, and difficult oropharyngeal anatomy such that reestablishing a translaryngeal airway would be difficult in the event of airway loss. PT should only be performed electively.

2. **Technique.** PT should be performed under bronchoscopic guidance. The patient should be adequately sedated and positioned in a moderate degree of neck extension. An initial 1.5-cm skin incision over the first tracheal ring is made and blunt dissection is performed down to the level of the pretracheal fascia, using a mosquito hemostat. The existing endotracheal tube is withdrawn into the subglottic position, permitting a needle to be introduced between the first and second or second and third tracheal rings midline. A guidewire is inserted through the needle and the needle is then removed, leaving the guidewire in place. Progressive dilation of the tracheal stoma is achieved using beveled plastic dilators over the guidewire (Seldinger technique). Once the stoma has been adequately dilated, the tracheostomy tube is introduced into the trachea over the guidewire, using a dilator as an obturator. The tracheostomy is then secured to the skin, using heavy, nonabsorbable, monofilament suture.

3. **Complications.** There are no significant differences in the rate of intraprocedural complications between PT and ST (*Crit Care.* 2006;10:R55). Postoperative complications include accidental decannulation, bleeding, and stoma infection and may be reduced with PT as compared to ST (*Crit Care Resusc.* 2009;11:244). The complications

associated with cricothyroidotomy, including creation of a false passage, pneumothorax, injury to surrounding structures, and long-term subglottic stenosis and granuloma formation, can also occur with PT.

V. LAPAROSCOPY. An overview of general laparoscopic principles is provided. Readers are referred elsewhere in this manual for information pertaining to specific disease processes.

A. **Advantages.** Laparoscopic procedures may result in less patient discomfort, shorter hospitalizations, and more rapid convalescence than with open techniques.

B. **Contraindications**

1. **Absolute contraindications** include the inability to tolerate general anesthesia and uncorrectable coagulopathy.

2. **Relative contraindications**

a. **Prior abdominal surgery** may require alternative port locations to avoid intra-abdominal adhesions. Laparoscopic adhesiolysis may be necessary to improve exposure.

b. **Peritonitis** may limit access secondary to adhesions.

c. **First- and third-trimester pregnancy.** Laparoscopy is more safely undertaken in the second trimester for conditions that require urgent surgical management (i.e., cannot be safely delayed until after delivery).

d. **Severe cardiopulmonary disease** may be exacerbated by hypercarbia that occurs secondary to insufflation of carbon dioxide as well as changes in pulmonary and cardiovascular mechanics during periods of increased intra-abdominal pressure. These effects can be minimized using lower intra-abdominal pressures (8 mm Hg) in conjunction with abdominal wall lift devices.

e. **Massive abdominal distention** may result in an increased risk of iatrogenic bowel injury.

C. **Access and pneumoperitoneum.** A working space is created in the patient's abdomen by insufflating carbon dioxide after access is obtained either by a closed or open technique. While both techniques have been shown to be safe, some studies suggest a lower complication rate with open direct insertion (*Surg Laparosc Endosc Percutan Tech.* 2005;15:80). Optical access trocars have been advocated in the morbidly obese population (*Surg Innov.* 2008;15:126).

1. **Closed technique.** A Veress needle is placed most commonly at the umbilicus through a small skin-stab incision. Two serial clicks are heard as the needle penetrates the fascia and peritoneum, respectively. The surgeon aspirates the needle with a 10-mL syringe partially filled with saline to look for blood or enteric contents. The surgeon injects 3 to 5 mL of saline through the needle. If any resistance is met, the syringe is most likely in the abdominal muscle or omentum and should be repositioned. If no resistance is met, the surgeon aspirates the syringe again and removes the plunger. Observing the saline pass freely into

the abdomen with gravity (drop test) confirms proper intra-abdominal placement. The abdominal cavity is insufflated via an automatic pressure-limited insufflator to 10 to 15 mm Hg. The initial intra-abdominal pressure should be less than 10 mm Hg. As the abdomen expands, pneumoperitoneum is confirmed by percussion. After insufflation, the abdominal wall is stabilized manually, the Veress needle is removed, and the initial trocar and port are inserted blindly in a direction away from critical abdominal structures.

- a. **Elevated pressure** with low flow (1 L/minute) on insufflation usually indicates placement of the Veress needle into a closed space (e.g., pre- or retroperitoneal, within the omentum).
  - (1) First, the port's insufflation valve should be confirmed to be open.
  - (2) If so, the Veress needle is removed and reinserted with a subsequent drop test.
  - (3) If the **needle position is in doubt,** an open insertion technique should be used.
- b. **Return of blood, cloudy or bilious fluid, or enteric contents** after Veress needle placement mandates needle repositioning and inspection of the violated abdominal organ.

2. **Open insertion** of the initial port is by a direct cut down through the abdominal fascia. A Hasson (wedge-shaped) port is placed under direct vision and secured to the abdominal fascia with stay sutures.

3. **Complications**
   - a. **Gas embolism is life threatening.** With right ventricular outflow obstruction, expired end-tidal carbon dioxide falls, with concomitant hypotension and a "mill-wheel" heart murmur.
     - (1) Insufflation is stopped and the pneumoperitoneum is released.
     - (2) The patient should be placed in a steep Trendelenburg position with the right side up to float the gas bubble up toward the right ventricular apex and away from the right ventricular outflow tract.
     - (3) Air from the right ventricle is aspirated through a central venous catheter.
   - b. **Brisk bleeding** after trocar insertion warrants emergent conversion to open laparotomy. The trocar should not be removed until proximal and distal control of the injured vessel is achieved.

4. **Alternatives to carbon dioxide pneumoperitoneum** have been advocated because of the potentially deleterious effects of hypercapnea. Alternative pneumoperitoneum gases such as nitrous oxide, helium, and argon have been evaluated experimentally. Increased intra-abdominal pressure can occur with any insufflation gas (e.g., compression of the vena cava with decreased venous return to the heart, resultant hypotension, decreased renal blood flow, and diminished urinary output). External abdominal wall lift devices are available to create a working space without pneumoperitoneum.

D. **Port placement.** The location of ports has been standardized for most procedures, and several general rules for port placement have been established. All additional ports should be placed under direct video visualization.

Before inserting the port, the surgeon indents the abdominal wall manually and identifies the location with the video camera. Transilluminating the abdominal wall identifies significant vessels to avoid. The skin and peritoneum are anesthetized locally. The surgeon makes a small stab incision with a no. 11 blade. The trocar is introduced in a direct line with the planned surgical target to minimize torque intraoperatively. The tip of the trocar should be visualized as it passes through the peritoneum.

1. The **camera port** should be behind and between the surgeon's two operative ports to maintain proper orientation.

2. **Working ports** are placed lateral to the viewing port, with the operative field ahead. All ports should be at least 8 cm apart to avoid the interference of instruments with one another. Ports should be approximately 15 cm from the operative field for the site to be reached comfortably by standard 30-cm instruments and to maintain a 1:1 ratio of hand–instrument tip movement.

E. **Exiting the abdomen.** The surgeon should survey the abdomen at the conclusion of the procedure to detect any visceral injury or hemorrhage. The operative site is irrigated, and hemostasis is obtained. Inspection of the peritoneal side of all port sites as the trocars are removed allows verification of hemostasis. Port-site fascial incisions that are larger than 5 mm should be closed with permanent or long-term absorbable suture to avoid the risk of incisional herniation. This can be done through the port-site incision or under video guidance with a fascial closure device (also known as a "suture passer"), which is particularly helpful in obese patients.

F. **Converting to open surgery.** A laparoscopic case may need to be converted to an open case for a number of reasons.

1. **Elective conversion**
   a. **Surgeon experience** is critical. The surgeon's threshold for conversion should be low while gaining experience.
   b. **Failure to progress** is the most common reason to convert. This can be secondary to adhesions, inflammatory changes, poor exposure, or altered or aberrant anatomy. In cases of unclear anatomy, avoiding injuries should take precedence over avoiding laparotomy.
   c. The surgeon may discover **a disease not appropriate for minimally** invasive methods (e.g., gallbladder cancer or colon cancer invading adjacent organs).
   d. **Technical problems or instrument malfunction** may occasionally require conversion. The surgeon must check that all equipment is in working order before starting the operation.

2. **Emergent conversion** should be performed in the event of severe bleeding or complex bowel injuries if repair is beyond the skill level of the surgeon.

G. **Postoperative management** for most laparoscopic procedures is similar to that for open procedures, although laparoscopic surgery is associated with less postoperative pain and shorter hospital length of stay and recuperation time.

38 Common Postoperative Surgical Emergencies

Elizabeth T. Robertson and Christopher D. Anderson

This chapter explores the common syndromes facing postoperative patients and initial stages of management. Many of these syndromes have different etiologies depending on postoperative day. The topics include altered mental status, oliguria, hypotension, tachycardia, nausea/vomiting, shortness of breath, and chest pain.

I. **ALTERED MENTAL STATUS/COMBATIVE PATIENT.** The physiologic changes from surgical stress can alone affect neurologic function. In addition, after major surgery, patients are placed in unfamiliar surroundings, are woken throughout the night, and are administered novel, powerful medications. All of these must be taken into account and a differential should be generated before the reflexive administration of sedatives or antipsychotics.

A. The patient in **postoperative day 0** is recovering from general anesthesia, whose effects can last up to 48 hours. At the postoperative check, approximately 4 hours after completion of the surgery, mental status should be evaluated.

1. The patient will likely be drowsy but should be arousable to voice or light touch. If he or she is not, narcotics are likely to blame. If his or her respiratory rate is depressed, stimulate the patient and encourage deep breathing. If the patient is obtunded in the early postoperative period, consider naloxone injection and continuous infusion. An arterial blood gas (ABG) can be obtained to determine if the patient needs ventilator assistance to recover from carbon dioxide narcosis. Intensive care monitoring may be required.

2. If the patient responds to stimulation with combativeness, he or she is usually calmed with reorientation. The amnestics administered during general anesthesia can cause a patient to repeatedly lose orientation. In addition, many anesthetic agents agonize the γ-aminobutyric acid receptors, causing disinhibition. If the patient is not easily reoriented by health care workers, a close friend or family member can be more effective.

B. In **postoperative days 2 and 3,** consideration should be given to alcohol withdrawal. Further discussion is available in Chapter 1 Section III.A.4.

C. **Elderly patients** have less neurologic reserve and are the largest population to suffer from mental status changes. Their other organ systems are also delicate, often requiring intensive care unit (ICU) admissions and resultant ICU delirium. The effects of sedative and pain medications can be quite prolonged in this population and additional administration should only be done with careful consideration.

D. **Sudden mental status changes** in a previously stable patient should be emergently worked up for medical causes. If the patient is completely unresponsive, begin the basic life support (BLS) algorithm. Evaluate for breathing and a pulse and call a code. If the patient is obtunded, but protecting his or her airway, further medical evaluation can commence.

1. Obtain a full set of vital signs. Hypoxia can result in mental status suppression and also agitation. If the patient was complaining of an antecedent headache, hypoxia should be high on the differential. Hypotension and arrhythmias can also cause mental status changes.

2. A fingerstick for blood glucose should be done. With the advent of intensive glucose control, more hypoglycemic events have been noted (*JAMA.* 2008;300:933). Any newly obtunded patient should have a rapid bedside glucose measurement.

3. Consideration should be given to inadvertent or unknown extra administration of narcotic agents. A dose of 0.04 mg of naloxone is a reasonable trial dose.

4. A stat head computed tomographic (CT) scan is reasonable to evaluate for intracranial hemorrhage.

5. A complete blood cell count, basic metabolic profile, ABG, and current type and screen should be obtained to evaluate for hemorrhage, early signs of infection, and electrolyte disturbances as well as preparing for blood resuscitation should that be necessary. An electrocardiogram and serial troponins should be obtained to evaluate for arrhythmias and myocardial infarction (MI).

II. **OLIGURIA.** Low urine output in the postoperative period has several different causes that can be organized by postoperative day. One must consider the operative procedure and the definition of oliguria. Oliguria in a post–renal transplant patient is very different from that in a patient with oliguria after a Whipple procedure. In addition, patient characteristics can change the approach. For example, a patient with chronic kidney disease who is lasix dependent cannot tolerate multiple liters of fluid without close monitoring of his or her pulmonary status.

A. On postoperative day 0, the patient is few hours out from the operating room and has endured a serious trauma. The patient is being actively resuscitated and oliguria is likely due to hypovolemia. Total body fluid is increased, but most of the fluid is being third-spaced from the extensive capillary leak secondary to the systemic inflammatory response. Fluid bolus administration is the usual remedy. A true bolus given in the ICU is 1 L of crystalloid administered on a pressure bag through a large-bore catheter. Transient increases in the central venous pressure and mean arterial pressure can be demonstrated in a hypovolemic patient.

1. Hemorrhage is an important cause of hypovolemia on postoperative day 0. If you have given 1 or 2 L of fluid (or 10 to 20 mL/kg in a

pediatric patient), it is reasonable to check the hemoglobin level. If the hemoglobin level is low, consideration can be given to transfusion and/or return to the operating room for exploration.

2. Mechanical causes of oliguria should also be considered. If the patient has an indwelling Foley catheter, careful examination should be done to evaluate for kinking or inadvertent clamping. The Foley catheter can be flushed to determine if it is clogged. If the patient does not have an indwelling urinary catheter, serious consideration should be given to placing one. This will not only decompress a distended nonfunctional bladder but will also allow for close serial monitoring of urine output to avoid renal compromise.

3. After pelvic surgery ureteral injury can cause oliguria, often along with hematuria. This is most common in a reoperative field. Serum creatinine level can increase due to intraperitoneal urine resorption. Intraperitoneal drain fluid can be evaluated for the creatinine level. CT scan with delayed images can demonstrate ureteral anatomy, but there is often hesitation to administer intravenous dye in patients with an elevated creatinine level. A retrograde ureteropyelogram can provide similar information.

4. An unusual cause of oliguria in the early postoperative period is cardiac insufficiency. Patients who have preexisting congestive heart failure should undergo intensive monitoring with consideration given to a central catheter, CardioQ, or even Swan-Ganz catheter. If a patient with no known cardiac dysfunction is not responding to fluid challenges and has worsening respiratory function, it is reasonable to check troponins, take electrocardiograms (EKGs), and perform cardiac echocardiography to evaluate ventricular volume status.

B. During postoperative days 1 and 2, new-onset oliguria is less likely to be due to fluid sequestration. Fluid mobilization usually occurs by postoperative day 3. Other causes of oliguria should be considered.

1. Ileus and small bowel obstruction can lead to fluid sequestration inside the bowel, as gastrointestinal secretions are not propelled to the colon for usual reabsorption. In addition, distended bowel becomes edematous and pulls fluid from the intravascular space. These patients require nasogastric (NG) tube decompression and volume resuscitation but for slightly different reasons than in the very early postoperative patient.

2. In the first few postoperative days, patients are administered a multitude of agents to manage infection risk, pain, and postoperative nausea. Some of these agents can be nephrotoxic, and a careful evaluation of a patient's medication list can reveal the offending agent.

3. Delayed hemorrhage should be considered, especially if anticoagulation for a patient's preexisting condition has been restarted. Operative site bleeding is less likely than immediately postoperatively, but the risk of gastrointestinal bleeding begins to increase in this stressed population. Hemoccult evaluation of stools and gastroccult evaluation of gastric secretions are reasonable.

C. In postoperative days 3 to 10, one should consider ileus recurrence with fluid sequestration as well as oliguria as an early sign of severe sepsis.

III. **POSTOPERATIVE HYPOTENSION** should immediately raise concerns of postoperative bleeding. There are more mundane causes, but this should always be considered. If hypotension is not quickly resolved, transfer the patient to a higher level of care.

A. First, ensure that the blood pressure reading is accurate. Get a manual blood pressure reading to confirm the noninvasive cuff blood pressure. Be sure to get a full set of vitals as well. If the patient is tachycardic and febrile, you can move quickly along the severe sepsis pathway.

B. Severe hypovolemia can cause hypotension and is usually accompanied by tachycardia. The notable exception to this is the patient on β-blocker, in whom tachycardia is blunted. Oliguria accompanies hypotension in this situation, and the management of hypovolemic shock is covered in Section II.A.

C. Anesthetics and analgesics are also common causes of postoperative hypotension. These drugs vasodilate the patient, and hypotension can be managed with volume administration.

D. After restarting home medications, patients can develop unexpected hypotension. With further investigation, you often discover that the patients do not adhere to their home medication prescriptions and this is the first day they have ever taken all of their antihypertensives together.

IV. **TACHYCARDIA** can be found in most of the other syndrome presentations discussed here. Anyone who is under stress from hypotension, pain, or shortness of breath will likely develop a sinus tachycardia. Tachycardia can be divided into mild (<120) and severe (>130) and management depends on rhythm determination.

A. Mild sinus tachycardia is often due to postoperative pain, atelectasis, and hypovolemia. This patient should have these issues managed and be observed until the tachycardia resolves.

B. Severe sinus tachycardia needs to be proven on an EKG. It can be difficult to identify a supraventricular tachycardia when the heart rate is 150. If it is truly sinus, the patient has potentially suffered a pulmonary embolus (PE) or is in stage 2 shock. These patients need a monitored bed and aggressive work-up with a PE protocol CT scan, blood cultures, chemistry, and hematology laboratory values. Consider invasive monitoring with a central catheter and an arterial catheter.

C. Severe nonsinus tachycardia is managed according to Advanced cardiac life support (ACLS) protocol. These patients should also be managed in a monitored setting. The stress of surgical recovery can induce atrial fibrillation with rapid ventricular response in a patient who has never experienced it before.

V. **NAUSEA AND VOMITING** attributable to anesthesia can affect up to 30% of patients (*Anesthesiology.* 1992;77:162). During postoperative days 0 and 1, aggressive management with antiemetics can be employed. Multimodal therapy with ondansetron, phenergan, compazine, scopolamine, and even decadron can be required. Propofol also has excellent antiemetic effects but should be administered only in a monitored setting by a sedation provider.

A. Patients who have undergone antireflux operations should be aggressively managed with antiemetics before symptoms arise. Any sign of nausea should prompt medication administration. There should be a low threshold to place an NG tube. Even one episode of retching can cause an esophageal wrap to slip.

B. Patients who have undergone extensive intra-abdominal procedures and are more than 24 hours out from anesthesia should be evaluated before administration of antiemetics. Up to 20% of these patients will suffer an ileus requiring nasogastric decompression (*Dis Colon Rectum.* 2000;43:61). Administration of antiemetics will not resolve the symptom long term, and the ileus can progress to a severe state. If the patient is nauseated, distended, burping, and has not passed flatus, you should consider placing an NG tube.

C. A patient with an NG tube in place who complains of nausea should have the NG tube manipulated until functioning properly. This often requires an experienced clinician to coax the tube into doing its job. This may even require replacement of a larger-bore NG tube.

VI. **SHORTNESS OF BREATH** is often thought of as being a primary respiratory problem, but it can be a symptom of systemic illness.

A. **Volume overload** is a common cause of shortness of breath beyond the immediate postoperative period. Patients sequester fluid during and immediately after surgery and mobilization usually begins on postoperative day 2. If the patient is significantly volume expanded and crackles are heard on auscultation, intravenous lasix administration can rapidly relieve symptoms. Chest radiograph will demonstrate volume overload, but even an emergent radiograph in the ICU can take up to 30 minutes.

B. **Reactive airways** are common in postoperative smokers and asthmatic patients. The local trauma of an endotracheal tube can induce bronchospasm (*Anesth Analg.* 1995;80:276). Work of breathing is increased and expiratory wheezes are auscultated. If the patient is able to use an inhaler, this is preferred, but if the patient is tachypneic, nebulized β-agonists and anticholinergics are appropriate.

C. **PE** can cause shortness of breath, but tachycardia or pleuritic chest pain is more common. PE protocol CT scan will definitively diagnose PE, but a patient who is short of breath should not be sent to the scanner alone. If the patient is in extremis, consider intubation before obtaining the radiologic study.

D. **Pneumonia** can cause shortness of breath and is accompanied by fever, elevated white blood cell count, and productive cough. Chest radiograph provides diagnosis, and sputum culture can guide antibiotic therapy.

E. Shortness of breath can also be a result of MI, intra-abdominal complication, systemic sepsis, and fever.

VII. CHEST PAIN. The work-up for chest pain in the postoperative period mirrors the work-up in an emergency department, with the added consideration of incisional pain. Chest pain work-up begins with a close questioning of the patient on the type of pain, which narrows the differential significantly. A substantial heaviness is very different from pain inferior to the xiphoid in a patient with a high midline incision. After a complete history is taken, most chest pain complaints warrant a new set of vital signs, laboratory evaluation, and a chest radiograph.

A. **Myocardial infarction.** Consider serial troponins and EKGs in any patient complaining of chest pain. In our practice, we often "rule out" a high-risk patient with three serial troponins in postoperative day 0. This evaluates a patient for intraoperative ischemia, which is actually rare. Postoperative MIs classically occur on postoperative day 2 and any new development of chest pain should prompt a full work-up for MI.

B. The complete work-up of MI includes serial troponins and EKGs as well as a current set of electrolytes and hemoglobin levels. If your index of suspicion is high, apply oxygen to the patient and administer morphine to manage the pain. Place the patient on telemetry monitoring. Aspirin administration can be lifesaving and nitroglycerin should be considered if the blood pressure could tolerate it. β-Blocker has also been shown to benefit patients with an MI (*Am J Cardiology.* 1999;84:76). If the troponin levels are elevated or the EKG demonstrates new ST depressions, an emergent cardiology consultation should be obtained. Even if the patient is not a candidate for cardiac catheterization, they will assist with follow-up for the post–MI patient.

C. PE is a very common postoperative occurrence, and autopsy studies demonstrate that it is more common than clinicians appreciate (*Chest.* 1995;108:978). Chest pain with a sensation of shortness of breath and low oxygen saturations should raise the possibility of PE. Work-up should begin with a chest radiograph and consideration should be given to a PE protocol CT scan. If a patient has marginal renal function a ventilation-perfusion (VQ) scan is a reasonable option.

D. Other causes of postoperative chest pain include pleural effusion and musculoskeletal pain from intraoperative positioning or referred incisional pain. These can be differentiated with a plain chest radiograph and physical examination.

Index

Note: Page locators followed by f and t indicates figure and table respectively.